# Classic Erotica

# CLASSIC EROTICA

Wordsworth Editions

In loving memory of
MICHAEL TRAYLER
the founder of Wordsworth Editions

2

Readers who are interested in other titles from
Wordsworth Editions are invited to visit our website at
www.wordsworth-editions.com

For our latest list and a full mail-order service, contact
Bibliophile Books, 5 Thomas Road, London E14 7BN
tel: +44 (0)20 7515 9222  fax: +44 (0)20 7538 4115
e-mail: orders@bibliophilebooks.com

First published in 2007 by Wordsworth Editions Limited
8B East Street, Ware, Hertfordshire SG12 9HJ

ISBN 10:  1 84022 271 9
ISBN 13:  978 1 84022 271 5

Typeset in Great Britain by Antony Gray
Printed and bound by Clays Ltd, St Ives plc

# The Romance of Lust

## WILLIAM POTTER
## & FRIENDS

# Chapter One

There were three of us – Mary, Eliza, and myself. I was approaching fifteen, Mary was about a year younger, and Eliza between twelve and thirteen years of age. Mamma treated us all as children, and was blind to the fact that I was no longer what I had been. Although not tall for my age, nor outwardly presenting a manly appearance, my passions were awakening, and the distinctive feature of my sex, although in repose it looked magnificent enough, was very sufficiently developed when under the influence of feminine excitement.

As yet, I had absolutely no knowledge of the uses of the different organs of sex. My sisters and I all slept in the same room. They together in one bed, I alone in another. When no one was present, we had often mutually examined the different formations of our sexes.

We had discovered that mutual handlings gave a certain amount of pleasing sensation; and, latterly, my elder sister had discovered that the hooding and unhooding of my doodle, as she called it, instantly caused it to swell up and stiffen as hard as a piece of wood. My feeling her little pinky slit gave rise in her to nice sensations, but on the slightest attempt to insert even my finger, the pain was too great. We had made so little progress in these *attouchements* that not the slightest inkling of what could be done in that way dawned upon us. I had begun to develop a slight growth of moss-like curls round the root of my cock; and then, to our surprise, Mary began to show a similar tendency. As yet, Eliza was as bald as her hand, but both were prettily formed, with wonderfully-full and fat mounts of Venus. We were perfectly innocent of guile and quite habituated to let each other look at all our naked bodies without the slightest hesitation; and when playing in the garden, if one wanted to relieve the pressure on the bladder, we all squatted down together, and crossed waters, each trying who could piddle fastest. Notwithstanding these symptoms of passion when excited, in a state of calm I might have passed for a boy of ten or eleven.

My father had left us but moderately provided for, and mamma, wishing to live comfortably, preferred giving me lessons along with my sisters at home to sending me to school; but her health beginning to fail, she inserted an advertisement in *The Times* for a governess. Out of a large number of applicants, a young lady, of the name of Evelyn, was selected. Some ten days afterwards she arrived, and became one of the family.

We did not see much of her the first evening, but after breakfast the following morning, mamma accompanied her to what was considered our schoolroom, and said, 'Now, my dears, I place you under Miss Evelyn's care;

you must obey her in all things; she will teach you your lessons, as I am unable to do so any longer.' Then, turning to our new governess, 'I fear you will find them somewhat spoiled, and unruly; but there is a horse, and Susan will make you excellent birch rods whenever you require them. If you spare their bottoms when they deserve whipping, you will seriously offend me.' As mamma said this, I observed Miss Evelyn's eyes appear to dilate with a sort of joy, and I felt certain that, severely as mamma had often whipped us, if we should now deserve it, Miss Evelyn would administer it much more severely. She looked amiability itself, and was truly beautiful in face and person, twenty-two years of age, full and finely formed, and dressed always with the most studied neatness. She was, in truth, a seductive creature. She made an instantaneous impression on my senses. There was, however, somewhat of a sternness of expression, and a dignity of carriage, which caused us at once to fear and respect her. Of course, at first, all went smoothly enough, and seeing that mamma treated me precisely as she did my sisters, I came to be regarded as quite a child by Miss Evelyn. She found that she had to sleep in the same room with my sisters and myself. I fancied that on the first night Miss Evelyn did not approve of this arrangement, but gradually became familiarised with it, and seemed to think no more about it.

When bedtime came, we all kissed mamma and retired early, as usual. Miss Evelyn followed some hours later. When she came in, she carefully locked the door, then looked at me to see if I was asleep. Why, I know not, but I was instinctively prompted to feign sleep. I did so successfully, notwithstanding the passing of the candle before my eyes. So she at once commenced undressing. When her back was turned, I opened my eyes, and greedily devoured her naked charms as they were gradually exhibited before me. The moment she turned round, I was again as if asleep. I have said that my passions had begun to develop themselves, but as yet I did not understand their force or direction. I well remember this first night, when a fine ripe woman gradually removed every particle of dress within a couple of yards of me – the effect of each succeeding charm, from her lovely and beautifully formed bubbies to the taking off her shoes and stockings from her well-formed legs and small feet and ankles, caused my prick to swell and stiffen to a painful extent. When all but her chemise was removed, she stooped to pick up her petticoats that she had allowed to fall to her feet, and in lifting them, raised also her chemise, and exposed to my view a most glorious bottom – dazzlingly white and shining like satin. As the light was full upon it, and she was still in a stooping position, I could see that below her slit she was well covered with dark hair. Turning round, to put her petticoats on a chair, and to take up her nightgown, she slipped her chemise from her arm, and letting it fall to the ground while she lifted the nightgown over her head, I had for some seconds a view of her beautiful belly, thickly covered with dark curly hair over the mount of Venus. So voluptuous was the sight, I almost shuddered, so intense was my excitement. She now sat down on the bed to take off her shoes and stockings. Oh! what beautiful thighs, legs, ankles, and feet she had!

I am now advanced in life, and have had many handsome and well-formed women, but I never saw limbs more voluptuously formed.

In a few minutes the light was extinguished, and a rushing rill flowed into the night-vase; very different from the gentle tricklings from myself and sisters as we often squatted down opposite each other and crossed water, laughing at the different sources from which they flowed. My sisters often envied me the power of directing the spurt where I pleased, so little were we from dreaming of the real intent of that projecting little instrument.

I heard the charming creature get into bed, and shortly breathe hard. As for me, I could not sleep. I lay awake the greater part of the night, afraid to be restless, lest I should disturb Miss Evelyn and give her reason to think I had been observant of her undressing. When at last I dozed off, it was but to dream of all the charms I had seen.

About a month passed thus. Every night Miss Evelyn became more and more at her ease, and confident of my mere childishness, often gave me glorious and lengthened glimpses of her beautifully developed charms: although it was only about every other night that I could enjoy them, for, as they always produced sleeplessness afterwards, the following night nature assured her rights, and I usually slept profoundly when I would infinitely have preferred continued gazing on the charms of my lovely governess. But, doubtless, those exhausting sleeps helped to throw her off her guard, and gave me better opportunities than I should otherwise have had. Once or twice she used the nightware before putting on her nightgown, and I could see the rosy-lipped opening embosomed in exquisite dark curls, pouring out its full measure of water; showing a fine force of nature, and driving me wild with excitement. Yet it is singular that I never once thought of applying to my fingers for relief from the painful stiffness that nearly burst my prick asunder.

Whether mamma had observed my very frequent projection of my trousers, or began to think it better I should not sleep in the same room as Miss Evelyn, I cannot say, but she had my bed removed into her own. However, I was so thoroughly treated as a mere boy by everyone in the house, that Miss Evelyn seemed to forget my sex; and there was at all times a freedom of carriage and an *abandon* in her attitudes that she certainly would not have indulged in if she had felt any restraint from considering herself in the presence of a youth of the age of puberty.

In cold weather I used to sit on a low stool by the fire – Miss Evelyn was seated in front, I had my lesson-book on my knee, and she herself would place her beautiful feet on the high school fender, with her work in her lap, while she heard my sisters repeat their lesson, totally unconscious that for half an hour at a time she was exposing her beautiful legs and thighs to my ardent gaze; for sitting much below her, and bending my head as if intent on my lesson, my eyes were below her raised petticoats. Her close and tight-fitting white stockings displayed her well-formed legs, for while confined to the house during our morning lessons she did not wear drawers; so that in the position she sat in, with her knees higher than her feet on the already high fender, and her legs somewhat apart to underswell of both thighs, and the lower part of her fine large bottom, with the pinky slit quite visible, nestled in a rich profusion of dark curls, were fully exposed to my view. The light from the fire glancing under her raised petticoats tinged the whole with a glow, and set me equally in a blaze of desire until I was almost ready to faint. I could have rushed headlong under her petticoats, and kissed and fondled that delicious opening and all its surroundings. Oh, how little she thought of the passion she was raising. Oh! dear Miss Evelyn, how I did love you from the dainty kid slipper and tight glossy silk stocking, up to the glorious swell of the beautiful bubbies, that were so fully exposed to me nearly every night, and the lovely lips of all that I longed lovingly to embrace.

Thus day after day passed away, and Miss Evelyn became to me a goddess, a creature whom, in my heart of hearts, I literally worshipped. When she left the schoolroom, and I was alone, I kissed that part of the fender her feet had pressed, and the seat on which she sat, and even the air an inch above, imagination placing there her lovely cunt. I craved for something beyond this without knowing exactly what I wanted; for, as yet, I really was utterly ignorant of anything appertaining to the conjunction of the sexes.

One day I had gone up to my sisters' bedroom where the governess slept, that I might throw myself on her bed, and in imagination embrace her beautiful body. I heard someone approaching, and knowing that I had no business there, I hid myself under the bed. The next moment Miss Evelyn herself entered, and locked the door. It was about an hour before dinner. Taking off her dress, and hanging it on the wardrobe, she drew out a piece of furniture, which had been bought for her, the use of which had often puzzled me; she took off the lid, poured water into its basin, and placed a sponge near it. She then took off her gown, drew her petticoat and chemise up to her waist and fastened them there, straddled across it, and seated herself upon it.

I thus had the intoxicating delight of gazing on all her beautiful charms, for when she tucked up her clothes, she stood before her glass, presenting to my devouring glance her glorious white bottom in all its fullness, turning to approach the bidet, she equally exposed her lower belly and beautiful mount, with all its wealth of hair. While straddling over the bidet before she sat down, the whole of her pinky-lipped cunt broke on my enraptured sight. Never shall I forget the wild excitement of the moment. It was almost too much for my excited senses; fortunately, when seated, the immediate cause of my almost madness vanished. She sponged herself well between the thighs for about five minutes. She then raised herself off the bidet, and for a moment again displayed the pouting lips of her cunt – then stood fronting me for two or three minutes while she removed, with the rinsed sponge, the trickling drops of water which still gathered on the rich bush of curls around her quim. Thus her belly, mount and thighs, whose massy-fleshed and most voluptuous shape were more fully seen by me than they had heretofore been, and it may easily be conceived into what a state such a deliberate view threw me.

Oh, Miss Evelyn, dear, delicious Miss Evelyn! what would you have thought had you known that I was gazing on all your angelic charms, and that my eager eyes had been straining themselves to penetrate the richness of those charming pouting lips which lay so snugly in that rich mass of dark curling hair. Oh! how I did long to kiss them; for at that time I had no other idea of embracing and still less of penetrating them.

When her ablutions were completed, she sat down and drew off her stockings, displaying her beautiful white calves and charming little feet. I believe it was this first admiration of the really exquisitely formed legs, ankles and feet, which were extraordinarily perfect in make, that first awakened my passion for those objects, which have since always exercised a peculiar charm over me. She was also so particularly neat in her shoes – little dark ones – that were *bijoux* to look at, I often took them up and kissed them, when left in the room. Then her silk stockings, always drawn up tight and fitting like a glove, set off to the greatest advantage the remarkable fine shape of her legs.

Putting on silk for cotton stockings, she took down a low-bodiced dress, finished her toilet, and left the room. I crawled out from under the bed, washed my face and hands in the water of her bidet, and even drank same in my excitement.

Some six weeks had now elapsed since the arrival of Miss Evelyn. The passion that had seized me for her had so far kept me most obedient to her slightest command, or even wish, and, from the same cause, attentive to my lessons, when not distracted by the circumstances already detailed. My example had also had the effect of keeping my sisters much in the same groove, but it was impossible this could last – it was not nature. As long as all went smoothly, Miss Evelyn seemed to be all amiability. We fancied we could do as we liked, and we grew more careless.

Miss Evelyn became more reserved, and cautioned us at first, and then threatened us with the rod. We did not think she would make use of it. Mary grew impertinent, and one afternoon turned sulky over her lessons, and set our teacher at defiance. Miss Evelyn, who had been growing more and more angry, had her rise from her seat. She obeyed with an impudent leer. Seizing her by the arm, Miss Evelyn dragged the struggling girl to the horse. My sister was strong and fought hard, using both teeth and nails, but it was to no purpose. The anger of our governess was fully roused, and raising her in her arms, she carried her forcibly to the horse, placed her on it, held her firmly with one hand while she put the noose round her with the other, which, when drawn, secured her body; other nooses secured each ankle to rings in the floor, keeping her legs apart by the projection of the horse, and also forcing the knees to bend a little, by which the most complete exposure of the bottom, and, in fact, of all her private parts too, was obtained.

Miss Evelyn then left her, and went to mamma for a rod. In a few minutes she returned, evidently flushed with passion, and proceeded to tie Mary's petticoats well up to her waist, leaving her bottom and her pinky slit quite bare and exposed directly before my eyes. It was quite two months since I had seen her private parts, and I was well surprised to observe the lips more pouting and swelled out, as well as the symptoms of a mossy covering of the mount much more developed. Indeed, it was in itself more exciting than I had expected, for my thoughts had so long dwelt only on the riper beauties of Miss Evelyn that I had quite ceased to have any toying with Mary.

This full view of all her private parts reawakened former sensations and strengthened them. Miss Evelyn first removed her own scarf, laying bare her plump ivory shoulders, and showing the upper halves of her beautiful bubbies, which were heaving with the excitement of her anger. She bared her fine right arm, and grasping the rod, stepped back and raised her arm; her eyes glistened in a peculiar way. She was indeed beautiful to see.

I shall never forget that moment – it was but a moment. The rod whistled through the air and fell with a cruel cut on poor Mary's plump little bottom. The flesh quivered again, and Mary, who had resolved not to cry, flushed in her face, and bit the damask with which the horse was covered.

Again the arm was raised, and again, with a sharp whistle, it fell on the palpitating buttocks below it. Still her stubborn temper bore her up, and although we saw how she winced, not a sound escaped from her lips. Drawing back a step, Miss Evelyn again raised her hand and arm, and this time her aim was so true that the longer points of the rod doubled between the buttocks and concentrated themselves between the lips of Mary's privates. So agonising was the pain that she screamed out dreadfully. Again the rod fell precisely on the same spot.

'Oh! oh! oh! Dear, dear Miss Evelyn. I will never, no, never, do so again.'

Her shrieks were of no avail. Cut succeeded cut, yell succeeded yell – until the rod was worn to a stump, and poor Mary's bottom was one mass of weals and red as raw beef. It was fearful to see, and yet such is our nature that to see it was, at the same time, exciting. I could not keep my eyes from her pouting quim, the swelling lips of which, under the severity of the punishment it was undergoing, not only seemed to thicken, but actually opened and shut, and evidently throbbed with agony. But all this was highly exciting for me to witness. I then and there resolved to have a closer inspection at a more convenient opportunity, which did not fail me in the end.

Meanwhile, her spirit was completely cowed, or rather, crushed. Indeed, we were all fully frightened, and now knew what we had to expect, if we did not behave ourselves. There was now no fear of any manifestation of temper, and we felt we must indeed obey implicitly whatever our governess chose to order. We instinctively learned to fear her.

A very few days after this memorable whipping, some visitors arrived – a gentleman and lady. The gentleman was an old friend of mamma's, who had lately married, and mamma had asked them to visit her on their wedding tour and spend a short time with us.

The gentleman was a fine-looking man, tall and powerfully built; the lady rather delicate looking, but well shaped, with good breasts and shoulders, small waist and spreading haunches, well-formed arms, small hands and feet, and very brilliant eyes.

I think it was about three days after their arrival that one afternoon I went into the spare room, which was occupied by these visitors; while there, I heard them coming upstairs. The lady entered first, and I had just time to slip into a closet and draw the door to; it was not quite closed, but nearly so. In a minute the gentleman followed, and gently shutting the door, locked it. Mrs Benson smiled, and said: 'Well, my love, you are a sad teaser; you let me have no rest. Surely, you had enough last night and this morning without wanting it again so soon?'

'Indeed, I had not,' he said, 'I never can have enough of your delicious person. So come, we must not be long about it, or our absence will be observed.'

He seized her round the waist, and drew her lips to his, and gave her a long, long kiss; squeezing her to him, and moving himself against her. Then seating himself, he pulled her on his knee, and thrust his hands up her petticoats, their mouths being glued together for some time.

'We must be quick, dear,' she murmured.

He got up, and lifted her on the edge of the bed, threw her back, and taking her legs under his arms, exposed everything to my view. She had not so much hair on her mount of Venus as Miss Evelyn, but her slit showed more pouting lips, and appeared more open. Judge of my excitement when I saw Mr Benson unbutton his trousers and pull out an immense cock. Oh, dear, how large it looked; it almost frightened me. With his fingers he placed the head between the lips of Mrs Benson's sheath, and then letting go his hold, and placing both arms so as to support her legs, he pushed it all right into her to the hilt at once. I was thunderstruck that Mrs Benson did not shriek with agony, it did seem such a large thing to thrust right into her belly. However, far from screaming with pain, she appeared to enjoy it. Her eyes glistened, her face flushed, and she smiled most graciously on Mr B. The two appeared very happy. His large cock slipped in and out quite smoothly, and his hands pressed the large glossy buttocks and pulled them to him at each home thrust. This lasted nearly five minutes, when all at once Mr B. stopped short, and then followed one or two convulsive shoves – he grinning in a very absurd way at her. He remained quiet for a few minutes, and then drew out his cock, all soft, with slimy drops falling from it to the carpet. Taking a towel, he wiped up the carpet, and wrapping it round his cock, went to the basin and washed it.

Mrs Benson lay for a few minutes longer all exposed, her quim more open than before, and I could see a white slime oozing from it.

You can hardly imagine the wild excitement this scene occasioned me. First, the grand mystery was at once explained to me, and my ignorant longings now knew to what they tended. After giving me plenty of time to realise all the beauties of her private parts, she slipped down on the floor, adjusted her petticoats, and smoothed the disordered counterpane, and then went to the glass to arrange her hair. This done, she quietly unlocked the door, and Mr Benson went out. The door was then relocked, and Mrs B. went to the basin, emptied and filled it, then raised up her petticoats, and bathed the parts between her legs with a sponge, and then rubbed all dry with a towel; all this time exposing everything to my ardent gaze. But, horror of horrors! she after this came straight to the closet where I lay hid – opened the door, and gave a slight scream on discovering me there. I blushed up to the ears, and tried to stammer out an excuse. She stared at me at first in silent amazement; but at last said: 'How came you here, sir, tell me?'

'I was here when you came up; I wanted my football, which was in this closet, and when I heard you coming, I hid myself, I don't know why.'

For some minutes she seemed to consider and examine me attentively. She then said: 'Can you be discreet?'

'Oh, yes, ma'am.'

'You will never tell anyone what you have seen?'

'No, ma'am.'

'Well, keep this promise, and I shall try what I can do to reward you. Now, go downstairs.'

I went to the schoolroom, but I was greatly agitated, I scarcely knew what I was doing. The scene I had witnessed had complete possession of my thoughts. In years but a boy, the mystery now practically explained to me had awakened all the passions of a man. Instead of studying my lessons, my thoughts wandered to Mrs B., thrown back on the bed with her fine legs and thighs fully exposed; above all, the sight of the pinky gash, with its fleecy hair at the bottom of her belly, which I had seen for some minutes all open and oozing out the slimy juice that followed the amorous encounter they had been indulging in. It seemed so much more developed than Miss Evelyn's. I felt sure that Miss Evelyn could never take in such a thick long thing as Mr B. had thrust into his wife, and yet it appeared to go in so easily, and moved about so smoothly, and so evidently to the satisfaction and utmost delight of both, as was proved by their ardent embracings, fond murmurs, and voluptuous movements, especially just before they both ceased together all movement whatever.

Then I thought, how delicious it would be to treat Miss Evelyn in the same way, and to revel with my stiff-standing prick in her delicious quim, which in my mind's eye I saw before me as I had viewed it on her rising from the bidet, when I lay hid under the bed. Then I thought of my sister Mary's smaller, although very attractive little quim, and I resolved, as that was the easiest to get hold of, to initiate her in all the newly discovered mysteries. I fully determined that my own first lesson, as well as hers, should be taken on her little fat chubby cunt. Then the recollection of its pouting and throbbing lips under the fearful flagellation she had undergone, began to excite me, and made my cock stand stiff and throb again. All the weeks of excitement I had now constantly been under had produced a wonderful effect on my pego, which had become considerably more developed when in a state of erection. As you may suppose, with such distracting thoughts, I did not get on with my lessons. Miss Evelyn, for some reason or other, was out of humour that morning, and more than once spoke crossly to me for my evident inattention. At length she called me to her, and finding that I had scarcely done anything, she said: 'Now, Charles, I give you ten minutes longer to finish that sum, if not done in that time I shall whip you; you are exhibiting the mere spirit of idleness. I do not know what has come over you, but if persisted in, you shall certainly be punished.'

The idea of the beautiful Miss Evelyn whipping my bare bottom did not tend to calm my excitement, on the contrary, it turned my lewd thoughts upon the beauties of her person, which I had so often furtively gazed upon.

It was close upon four o'clock, at which hour we always broke up for a run in the garden for an hour, and during this period I had resolved to begin instructing Mary in the secret mysteries I had so lately been a witness to. But fate had ordered it otherwise, and I was to receive my first practical lesson and be initiated on the person of a riper and more beautiful woman; but of this hereafter. At four o'clock I had done nothing with my task – Miss Evelyn looked grave: 'Mary and Eliza, you may go out, Charles will remain here.'

My sisters, simply imagining that I was kept in to finish my lessons, ran into the garden. Miss Evelyn turned the key in the door, opened a cupboard, and withdrew a birch rod neatly tied up with blue ribbons. Now my blood coursed through my veins, and my fingers trembled so that I could hardly hold my pencil.

'Put down your slate, Charles, and come to me.'

I obeyed, and stood before my beautiful governess, with a strange commixture of fear and desire.

'Unfasten your braces, and pull down your trousers.'

I commenced doing this, though but very slowly. Angry at my delay her delicate fingers speedily accomplished the work. My trousers fell to my feet.

'Place yourself across my knees.'

Tremblingly, with the same commixture of feeling, I obeyed. Her silk dress was drawn up to prevent its being creased – my naked flesh pressed against her snowy white petticoats. A delicate perfume of violet and vervain assailed my nerves. As I felt her soft and delicate fingers drawing up my shirt, and passing over my bare posteriors, while the warmth of her pulpy form beneath me penetrated my flesh, nature exerted her power, and my prick began to swell out to a most painful extent. I had but little time, however, to notice this before a rapid succession of the most cruel cuts lacerated my bottom.

'Oh, dear! Oh, dear! Oh, dear! Oh, Miss Evelyn. I will do the sum if you will only forgive me. Oh, oh, oh, etc.'

Holding me firmly with her left arm, Miss Evelyn used the rod most unmercifully. At first, the pain was excruciating, and I roared out as loud as I could, but gradually the pain ceased to be so acute, and was succeeded by the most delicious tickling sensation. My struggles at first had been so violent as greatly to disorder Miss Evelyn's petticoats, and to raise them up so as to expose to my delighted eyes her beautifully formed silk clad legs up to the knees, and even an inch or two of naked thigh above.

This, together with the intense tickling irritation communicated to my bottom, as well as to the friction of my cock against the person of Miss Evelyn in my struggles, rendered me almost delirious, and I tossed and pushed myself about on her knees in a state of perfect frenzy as the blows continued to be showered down upon my poor bottom. At last the rod was worn to a stump, and I was pushed off her knees. As I rose before her, with my cheeks streaming with tears, my shirt was jutting out considerably in front in an unmistakeable and most prominent manner, and my prick was at the same time throbbing beneath it with convulsive jerks, which I could by no means restrain.

Miss Evelyn glared at the projection in marked astonishment, and her open eyes were fixed upon it as I stood rubbing my bottom and crying, without attempting to move or button up my trousers. She continued for a minute or two to stare at the object of attraction, flushing scarlet up to the forehead, and then she suddenly seemed to recollect herself, drew a heavy breath, and rapidly left the room. She did not return until after my sisters came back from the garden, and seemed still confused, and avoided fixing her eye upon me.

In two days afterwards, all disagreeable marks of this very severe whipping had disappeared. On the following day we were invited to pass the afternoon at the grange, a beautiful place about two miles from us. The afternoon was fine and warm; we walked there, and arrived about four o'clock. Mr and Mrs Robinson were in the drawing-room, but at once desired us to go in the garden and amuse ourselves with their three daughters, whom we would find there. We went at once, and found them amusing themselves on a swing. Sophia, the eldest, about nineteen, was swinging a sister about two years younger, a very fine, fully developed young woman. Indeed, all three sisters were finer women and more beautiful than the average of young ladies.

Another sister, Agnes, was not seated, but standing on the board between the ropes. Sophia was making both mount as high as possible. They were laughing loudly, when we found them, at the exposure each made – one i n advancing, the other retiring. Agnes's light dress of muslin and single petticoat, as she retired and the wind came up from behind, was bulged out in front, and exposed her limbs up to her belly, so that one could see that her mount was already well furnished. The other, in advancing, threw her legs up, and exposed all the underside of her thighs and a part of her bottom, and you could just discern that there was dark hair between the lower thighs and bottom.

As they considered me but a child, I was no check to their mirth and sport. On the contrary, they gave me a long rope to pull down the swing when at its highest, and I sat down on the grass in front for greater convenience. The fine limbs and hairy quims exposed freely before me from moment to moment excited my passions. None of them wore more than one petticoat, and they had no drawers, so that when they mounted to the highest point from me, I had the fullest possible view of all. My cock soon rose to a painful extent, which I really believe was noticed and enjoyed by them. I observed, too, that I was an object of attention to Miss Evelyn, who shortly seated herself in the swing, and allowed me to swing her with the end of the rope. I even fancied that she threw up her legs more than was at all necessary; at all events, she naturally, with the strong feelings I had towards her, excited me more than all the rest.

We all were as merry as could be, and we passed a delightful evening until eight o'clock, when it began to rain. As it continued, and became very heavy, Mr Robinson ordered out the closed carriage to take us home. It was a brougham, only seated for two. Mary took Eliza on her knee, Miss Evelyn took me upon hers. I know not how it happened, but her lovely arm soon passed round my body as if to hold me on her knee, and her hand fell, apparently by accident, exactly on my cock – the touch was electric. In an instant, my member stood stiff and strong beneath her hand. Still Miss Evelyn, who must have felt the movement going on beneath her fingers, did not remove her hand, but rather seemed to press more upon it. In my boyish ignorance, I imagined she was not aware of what was happening. The motion and jolting of the carriage over rough road caused her hand to rub up and down upon my erected and throbbing member. I was almost beside myself, and to conceal my condition I feigned sleep. I let my head fall on Miss Evelyn's shoulder and neck – she allowed this.

Whether she thought I had really fallen asleep I know not, but I was quite sensible that her fingers pressed my swollen and throbbing cock, and I fancied she was measuring its size.

The tight grasp she managed to gain, and the continued jolting of the carriage, brought me up at last to such a pitch state that a greater jolt than usual, repeated two or three times in succession, each followed by a firmer pressure of her charming fingers, caused me such an excess of excitement that I actually swooned away with the most delicious sensation I had ever experienced in my life. I was some time before I knew where I was, or what I

was about, and was only made conscious of our arrival at home by Miss
Evelyn shaking me to rouse me up. I stumbled up, but though partially
stupefied, I fancied Miss Evelyn's eyes shone with a brilliancy I had never
before observed, and that there was a bright hectic flush on her cheek. She
refused to go into the parlour, but hurried to bed on pretence of a headache.

When I retired to bed, and took off my shirt, I found it all sticky and wet
in front.

It was thus I paid down my first tribute to Venus. I thought long over this
evident approach to familiarity on the part of Miss Evelyn, and went to sleep
with a lively hope of a more private interview with her, when I trusted that
her evident passion would initiate me in the pleasures to be derived from her
beauteous body.

But again fate intervened, and another, not less beautiful, more experienced,
and more inclined for the sport, was to be my charming mistress in love's
revels.

Two days after this, Mr Benson was unexpectedly called away on pressing
affairs, which he feared might detain him three weeks. He left Mrs B. with
us. As he had to be driven about nine miles to the town where the coach
passed, mamma took the opportunity of going to the town with him. Mrs B.
complained of not being equal to the fatigue, and mamma told Miss Evelyn
she would like her company, and as the two girls wanted new shoes, they
could go also; I was to remain at home, and mamma desired me to be quiet
and attentive to Mrs Benson, and keep her company. This arrangement was
made when we were at breakfast. On leaving the room I was followed by
Mrs Benson, who, observing no one, said to me, with a peculiar look: 'I shall
want you to hold my skeins, Charlie, so don't go out of the way, but be ready
for me as soon as they are gone.'

She then went up to her bedroom, where Mr B. immediately joined her,
no doubt to re-enact the scene I had already witnessed from the closet on a
previous day. They were fully half an hour occupied together. At length, all
was ready, and off they went, leaving me to a fate I had little dreamt of.

Mrs B. proposed we should go up to the drawing-room which looked out
to the garden, and was nowhere overlooked. I followed her, and could not
help admiring her fine figure as she preceded me in going upstairs. Although
pale in complexion, she was well made, and very elegant in her carriage, and
sat down on a low easy-chair, throwing herself completely back, and crossing
one leg over the other, apparently without being aware that she carried her
petticoats up with the action, and exhibited the beautiful underleg up to the
garter.

I had never forgotten the day, when secreted in the closet, I had seen
them completely exposed, and how charming they were. Her present
negligent attitude, although far from the same exposure I speak of, was still,
with the former recollection running in my head, enough to set my whole
blood on fire. I have before remarked what a power beautiful and well-

stockinged legs, and ankles and small feet, had upon my nervous system, and so it was now. As I gazed upon her handsome legs, ankles, and feet, I felt my prick swell and throb in a manner that could not fail to be perceptible to Mrs B, especially as her head lay on a level with that part of my person as I stood before her.

Although she continued knitting, I could see that her eyes were directed to that part of my person, and fixed upon the increasing distention of my trousers. In a few minutes she gave me a skein of worsted to hold, and desired me to kneel in front of her, so as to bring my hands down to the level of the low chair on which she was seated.

I knelt close to the footstool on which her foot rested; it was raised up, and a very slight movement brought it against my person, at first rather below where my throbbing prick was distending my trousers. As she commenced to wind her ball, she gradually pushed her foot further forward, until the toe actually touched the knob of my cock, and occasionally moved it right and left, exciting me beyond measure.

I flushed up to the very ears, and trembled so violently that I thought I should have dropped the skein.

'My dear boy, what is the matter with you, that you blush and tremble so, are you unwell?'

I could not answer, but blushed more than ever. The skein at length was finished.

'Charles,' she said, 'get up, and come here.'

I rose and stood by her side.

'What have you got in your trousers that is moving?'

And here her busy fingers commenced unbuttoning them. Released from confinement, out started my prick – stiff as iron, and as large as that of a youth of eighteen. Indeed, I was better hung than one boy selected out of five hundred of that age. Mrs B., who had pretended to be perfectly astonished, exclaimed: 'Good gracious, what a pego! Why Charles, my darling, you are a man not a boy. What a size to be sure!' and she gently handled it. 'Is it often in this state?'

'Yes, ma'am.'

'For how long?'

'Ever since Miss Evelyn came.'

'And pray, sir, what has Miss Evelyn's coming had to do with it?'

'I – I – I – I –'

'Come now, Charles, be candid with me; what is it you mean where you say Miss Evelyn has caused you to be in such a state, have you shown her this, and has she handled it?'

'Oh! dear no; never, never!'

'Is it her face, her bosom, or her legs that have captivated you?'

'It was her feet and ankles, ma'am, with her beautiful legs, which she sometimes exhibited without knowing.'

'And do all ladies' legs and ankles produce this effect upon you?'

'Oh, yes, ma'am, if they are neat and pretty!'

'And what makes you so excited now?'

'It was the sight of your beautiful legs just now, and the recollection of what I saw the other day, ma'am,' I stammered out, blushing more than ever.

While this conversation was going on, her soft hand grasped my distended prick, and had commenced slowly slipping the loose skin over the swollen head, and allowing it to slip back again.

'I suppose, Charles, after what you saw in the closet, you know what this is meant to do.'

I muttered out an indistinct reply that I did, and I hung down my blushing face.

'You have never put it into a lady, have you?'

'Oh! dear no, ma'am.'

'Would you like to do so?'

I did not answer, but sheepishly held down my head.

'Did you see what I had in the same place, when you were in the closet?'

I muttered, 'Yes, ma'am.'

'Would it afford you any pleasure to see it again?'

'Oh, yes; so much!'

Mrs B. rose, went to the window, drew down the blind, then gently turned the key in the door. Returning to the chair, and drawing well up her dress, petticoats and chemise, she exposed all her person up to the middle of her belly; and sat down stretching herself backwards, and opening her thighs well.

'Well, my dear boy, look at it if you wish.'

I was no longer shy. Nature prompted me to an act of gallantry that gratified the lady immensely. Falling on my knees, I glued my lips to the delicious spot, pushed my tongue in as far as I could, and sucked it. It was quite spunky; I had no doubt but that Mr B. had fucked her two or three times just before leaving. This, however, made no difference to me. The attack was as unexpected as it was delightful to the lady. She placed both hands on my head and pressed my face against her throbbing cunt. She was evidently hotly excited, not only by what I was then doing, but by the scene, the conversation, and the handling of my prick, which she had been indulging in. She wriggled her bottom nervously below me, I continued greedily to lick her moist and juicy cunt.

'Oh! oh! dear Charles, what exquisite delight you are giving me. Oh! oh!'

And she pressed my face more fully into the gaping sheath, and thrusting her bottom up at the same time, spent right into my mouth, over my cheeks, chin, and neck. Her thighs closed convulsively round my head, and for some moments she remained still. I continued to lick away, and swallowed the delicious spunk that still flowed from her. At last she spoke again: 'Oh! you darling Charles, I love you for ever; but get up, it is now my turn to give you a taste of the exquisite pleasure you have given me.'

I raised myself, and she drew me to her, and gave me a long kiss, licking her own sperm from off my lips and cheek; and desiring me to thrust my tongue into her mouth, she sucked it deliciously, while her soft hand and gentle fingers had again sought, found, and caressed my stiff-standing prick. She then desired me to lay myself on the floor, with three pillows to raise my head, and lifting up all her petticoats, and striding across me, with her back to my face, she knelt down, then stooping forward, she took my standing prick in her mouth, and at the same time lowering her buttocks, brought her beautiful cunt right over and down upon my mouth, the pillows exactly supporting my head at the proper level, to command a thorough enjoyment of the whole, which now I had completely before my eyes.

In the former sucking my own position hid everything from view beyond the rich mass of hair adorning her splendid mount of Venus, which I found to be much more abundant than it had appeared to me when I had seen it from the closet. When I applied my lips to the delicious gap, I found that she had the most beautiful silky light curls running up to and around her charming pink bottom-hole, and losing themselves in the chink between the buttocks. I applied myself furiously to the delicious gash, and sucked and thrust my tongue in alternately. I could see by the nervous twitching of her buttocks, and the bearing down of her whole bottom on my face, how much she was enjoying it. I, too, was in an ecstasy of delight. One hand gently frigged the lower portion of my prick, while the other played with my balls, and her beautiful mouth, lips, and tongue sucked, pressed, and tickled the head of my excited prick. The more furiously I sucked her cunt, the more her lips compressed the head of my pego, and her tongue sought to enter the urethra, giving me almost overpowering delight. Such reciprocal efforts soon brought on the ecstatic crisis. I cried out: 'Oh, lady! oh, dear lady! let me go; I am dying!'

She knew well enough what was coming, but she had her own way, and at the instant that she again poured down upon my mouth and face a plenteous discharge, her own rosy mouth received a torrent of my sperm.

For some minutes we lay mutually breathless and exhausted. Then Mrs B. rose, shook down her clothes, assisted me to rise, and taking me in her arms, and pressing me lovingly to her bosom, told me I was a dear charming fellow, and had enraptured her beyond measure. She then embraced me fondly, kissing my mouth and eyes, and desiring me to give her my tongue, sucked it so sweetly.

'Now, fasten up your trousers, my darling boy.'

When I had done so, the blind was drawn up, and the door unlocked.

We sat down, I by her side with one arm round her lovely neck, and the other clasped in her hand.

'I am sure I can depend upon your prudence, my dear Charles, to keep all this a profound secret from everyone. Your mamma thinks you a child, and will suspect nothing. I shall take an opportunity of suggesting that you shall sleep in the small room adjoining my bedroom, and with which there is a door of communication. When everyone is gone to bed, I shall open the door, and you shall come and sleep with me, and I will let you enjoy me as you saw Mr B. do the other day. Will you like that?'

'Oh! above all things, oh, yes. But you must also allow me to kiss that delicious spot again that has just given me such pleasure. Will you not, ma'am?'

'Oh, yes, my darling boy, whenever we can do so safely, and unobserved; but I must impress upon you never to seem very familiar with me before anyone, or to take the slightest liberty unless I invite you to do so. Anything of the sort would certainly draw attention, and lead to our detection, and at once put an end to what I mean shall be a delightful connection for you as well as myself.'

I, of course, promised the most perfect obedience to her very prudent directions. The ice was broken, and we allowed no ceremony to stand between us. I grew again very excited, and would fain have proceeded at once to try again to fuck her as well as suck her, but she was inexorable, and told me I should only spoil the pleasure we should afterwards have in bed. The day passed like an hour in her charming society.

The carriage brought mamma and party to dinner. Mamma hoped I had behaved well, and been attentive to Mrs B. in her absence. She answered nothing could be better, and that I was quite a model youth – so gentle and so obedient.

My mother found that she had caught cold, and had febrile symptoms after dinner. Mrs B. persuaded her to retire to bed, and accompanied her. When in her room, she apparently noticed, for the first time, my little bed. She took the opportunity of suggesting that it would be much better to remove it to the small room, so as to leave my mother in perfect quiet, which my coming to bed might disturb.

This was said in such an innocent natural manner, that no suspicion was excited on the part of mamma or anybody else. Mamma only making the objection that my early rising might by my noise disturb Mrs B. in the next room.

'Oh, no; I am not so easily disturbed, besides he has been so well behaved all day, that I am sure, if I tell him to be quiet in the morning, he will not fail to do so.'

So it was settled, and my bed was at once removed to the little room.

I know not what Miss Evelyn thought of this; at any rate, she made no remark, and I went to bed early. It will easily be conceived that I did not go to sleep. The hours struck one after the other, and no appearance of my amiable instructress. The remembrance of all her charms was ever present to my mind's eye, and I longed once more to dart my tongue into her moist and juicy cunt, as well as to try the new method that was to initiate me into the real secrets of Venus.

The long delay of her coming put me in a perfect fever. I tossed and tumbled in bed; my prick throbbed almost to bursting. Fortunately, I had never frigged myself, and that resource never occurred to me, or I might have rendered myself quite incapable of enjoying the raptures my beautiful benefactress towards entranced me with. At last I heard voices and footsteps on the stairs. Mrs B. bid Miss Evelyn good-night, and the next minute her door was opened, closed again, and the key turned in the lock. I had taken the precaution to do so with my door. I heard her use the night-vase, and then she opened my door, at once coming up to my bedside. Seeing me wide awake and quite flushed, she kissed me, and whispered: 'Have you not been to sleep, Charles?'

'No, ma'am,' I answered, in the same subdued tone, 'I could not sleep.'

'Why, my dear boy?'

'Because I was going to sleep with you.'

Her lips pressed mine, and her soft hand, thrust under the clothes, sought for and caressed my stiff-standing prick – it was as hard as iron.

'Poor boy, I am afraid you have been suffering. How long has it been in this state?'

'All the evening, ma'am, and I did think you were such a long time in coming.'

'Well, Charles, I could not come sooner without causing suspicion – I thought Miss Evelyn was suspicious, so I pretended to have no desire to go to bed; and even when she showed evident symptoms of drowsiness after her long ride, I rallied her upon it, and begged her to sit up with me yet a little; until at last she could hold out no longer, and begged me to let her retire. I grumblingly complied, and she is thrown completely off any scent on our account, as she could never suppose I was as impatient as you to come here. I shall undress as fast as possible, and then do my best to relieve you of this painful stiffness. Get up, shut this door, and come to my bed. My room has an inner baize door, and we shall there be certain of not being overheard.'

I instantly complied, and she commenced undressing. Every detail of her charming toilet was devoured by my greedy eyes. Her smooth, glossy, and abundant hair, arranged in braids, was neatly fastened in under a coquettish lace cap with pretty blue ribbons. Her *chemise de nuit* of the finest, almost transparent cambric was edged with fine openwork. She looked divine. The drawers of the commode contained scent bags of that peculiar odour which is generally found to perfume the persons of the most seductive women. In another moment she was in bed, clasping me in her arms.

'Now, Charles, you must be a good boy, and make no noise, and allow me to teach you your first love lesson, see I will lay myself down on my back, thus – do you place yourself on your knees between my out-spread thighs – there, that is a darling – now let me lay hold of your dear instrument. Now lay yourself down on me.'

I placed myself on her beautiful smooth and white belly and pressed against the hair of her mount. With her long taper fingers she guided my prick – I trembled in every limb and almost felt sick with excitement – but when I felt the delicious sensation caused by the insertion of my skinned pintle between the smooth warm oily folds of the lady's cunt, I gave but one shove which carried me up so that I swooned away on her belly and milk-white bosom.

When I came to myself I still lay on her belly, enfolded in her lovely arms, my prick sheathed up to the cods in her delicious cunt, which was throbbing in the most ecstatic way and pressing and closing with every fold on my prick – which had hardly lost any of its pristine stiffness; as my eyes began to discern her features, an exquisite smile played upon my darling companion's lips.

'You sad rogue,' she whispered, 'you have given me a baby; what have you been doing to make you spend so soon, and in such a quantity. Did you like it?'

'Oh, dearest madam, I have been in heaven – surely no joy can be greater than you have given me.'

'But you do not know as yet everything that is to be done, and to how much greater an extent the pleasure may be enhanced by mutual efforts; move your instrument gently in and out – there, that is delicious, but not so fast. Good, is it not nice!'

And she moved in unison with me, meeting each slow thrust down by an equal movement upwards, and squeezing my prick in the most delicious manner internally, as she retired again to meet succeeding thrusts in the same way.

Oh! it was ecstatic – my prick, swollen to its utmost size, seemed to fill her exquisite vagina, which although capable of easily accommodating the larger prick of Mr B., appeared to be sufficiently contracted to embrace tightly with its smooth and slippery folds my stiff throbbing prick. So we continued, I shoving myself into her, and she upheaving her beautiful bottom to meet me. My hands removed everywhere, and my mouth sucked her lips and tongue, or wandered over her pulpy breasts sucking their tiny nipples. It was a long bout indeed, prolonged by Mrs Benson's instructions, and she enjoyed it thoroughly, encouraged me by every endearing epithet, and by the most voluptuous manoeuvres. I was quite beside myself. The consciousness that I was thrusting my most private part into that part of a lady's person which is regarded with such sacred delicacy caused me to experience the most enraptured pleasure. Maddened by the intensity of my feeling I at length quickened my pace. My charming companion did the same, and we together yielded down a most copious and delicious discharge.

Although I retained sufficient rigidity to keep him in his place, Mrs B. would not allow any further connection with her, and she made me withdraw, and bade me go to sleep like a good boy, and she would give me a further lesson in the morning.

Finding that she was determined on this point, and that she disposed herself to slumber, I felt I was obliged to follow her example, and at last fell fast asleep. It might be about five in the morning, quite light at that time of year, when I awoke, and instead of finding myself, as usual, in my own little bed – I found my arms round the person of a charming woman, whose large plump smooth bottom lay in my lap, pressing against my belly and thigh. I found my prick already in a rampant state, and it at once began throbbing and forcing its way between the delicious cheeks of her immense bottom, seeking the delightful sheath it had so enjoyed the previous part of the night. Whether Mrs B. was asleep or not, I do not know, but am inclined to think she really was so, from the muttered mistake she made in waking. She was probably dreaming, for she mechanically raised her thighs. I pressed my prick stoutly forward against her luxurious body, knowing that the entrance to the temple of pleasure which had so entranced me the night before lay in that direction. I found more difficulties than I expected, but at length began to penetrate, although the orifice appeared much tighter than on the previous evening. Excited by the difficulties of entrance, I clasped the lady firmly round the waist and pushed forcibly and steadily forward. I felt the folds give way to the iron stiffness of my prick, and one-half of it was fairly embedded in my extremely tight sheath. I put down my hand to press my prick a little downwards to facilitate the further entrance; you may imagine my astonishment when on so doing I found myself in the lady's bottom-hole, instead of her cunt. This at once explained the difficulty of entrance. I was about to withdraw and place it in the proper orifice when a convulsive pressure of the sphincter caused me such exquisite satisfaction by the pressure of the folds on the more sensitive upper half of my prick, which was so delicious, and so much tighter, and more exciting than my previous experience of the cunt that I could not resist the temptation of carrying the experiment to the end. Therefore, thrusting my two fingers into her cunt, I pressed my belly forwards with all my might, and sheathed my prick in her bottom-hole to its full extent. Mrs B. at this awoke, and exclaimed, 'Good Heavens! Fred, you hurt me cruelly. I wish you would be content with my cunt, I shall be unable to walk tomorrow. You know it always has that effect. It is downright cruel of you – but since you are in, stay quiet a little, and then continue to frig me with your fingers, as you know that eventually gives me great pleasure.'

She calls me Fred, what can she mean? I was, however, too agreeably situated to speculate on anything, but as I was now buried within her bottom-hole, I lay quiet for a few minutes as she had requested; and as her complaints subsided, and I felt a slight reciprocating movement, I, too, moved within her, working at the same time my two fingers in her cunt. By this time she was wide awake, and became conscious of who was her bed-fellow.

'What are you about, Charles?' she exclaimed, 'do you know where you are?'

'I did not know I was doing anything wrong.'

'Doing wrong, indeed! My, a lady's bottom-hole was never intended for a pego. How came you to put it in there?'

'I cannot tell; I did not do it on purpose. I thought I was going into the same delightful place I was in last night.'

All this time I was moving my prick in and out of one aperture, and my fingers were working away in the other. The tightness of the sheath round my prick was delicious beyond anything I could conceive, and I think, from the way the lady conducted herself, she liked it as much as I did. At any rate, she permitted me to go on until I had a delicious discharge; and she herself spent all over my hand.

When the bout was over, she jumped out of bed, went to the basin, and with a sponge purified herself. After which, she said: 'My dear boy, you had better come and wash yourself, too; and take care not to make a mistake of this kind again, as it is sometimes attended with disagreeable consequences.'

It was now perfect sunny daylight, and my enchanting mistress looked so lovely in her almost transparent cambric nightshift that I was emboldened to ask her to let me see her perfectly naked in all her glorious beauty of form. She gratified me at once; but, laughingly, pulled off my nightshirt, and said: 'I, too, must have the pleasure not only of contemplating your promising youthful charms, but of embracing your dear form disencumbered of all the superfluities of dress.'

We clasped each other in a most enrapturing embrace, and then my lovely and engaging companion allowed me to turn her in every direction so as to see, admire, and devour every charm of her exquisitely formed body. Oh! she was indeed beautiful – shoulders broad, bosom, or rather upper neck, flat, not showing any projection of the collar bone; bubbies firm, well separated and round, with most exquisite rosy nipples not much developed; a perfect waist, small naturally, with charming swelling hips, and an immense bottom – it was almost out of proportion, large, but oh, how beautiful. Then her belly, undulating so excitingly, and swelling out, the lowest part into a very fine and prominent mons Veneris, covered with a thick crop of silky and curly light hair; then the entrance to the grotto of Venus had such delicious pouting lips, rosy, but with hair still thick on each side, which is often not the case even with women who have a sufficient tuft above, how beautiful where it exists as it did in this charming and perfect woman, continuing in beautiful little curls not only down to but around her lovely pinky and puckered little bottom-hole, the delights of which I had already, in this infancy of my love education, tasted and enjoyed. Her two alabaster thighs, worthily supporting by their large well-rounded fleshy forms, the exquisite perfections of the upper body, I have already described. How beautiful, elegant, and elongated her legs were, rising from well-turned ankles and most tiny beautiful feet. Her skin was white as milk, and dazzlingly fair and smooth. To my young eyes she was a perfect goddess of beauty. Even now, in advanced life, I can remember nothing that, as a whole surpassed her, although I have met many with points unsurpassingly beautiful – some carry it in the bosom, some in the general carriage, some in the mount of Venus and bottom combined, for these two are generally prominent together, and some in legs and thighs; but this divine creature, without having the appearance of it when dressed, was, when stripped, perfect in all her parts as well as beautiful in face – caressing and voluptuous by nature, and lending herself, with the most enchanting graces to instruct me in all the mysteries of love, and let me say, of *lust* also.

We caressed each other with such mutual satisfaction that nature soon drove us to a closer and more active union of the bodies. Fondly embracing one another, we approached the bed, and being equally excited threw our-selves upon it, and, in the exquisite contact of our naked flesh, enjoyed a long, long bout of love, in which my most charming companion exhibited all the resources of amorous enjoyment. Never shall I forget the luxury of that embrace. She checked my natural tendency to rush at once to a completion. I think we must have enjoyed the raptures of that embrace fully half an hour before bringing on the grand finale, in which my active companion showed the extraordinary suppleness of her delicious body by throwing her legs over my back, pushing my bottom forward with her heels, and raising and sinking her bottom in unison with each thrust of my terribly stiff prick, which seemed to swell and become thicker and harder than ever. In retiring from each thrust, her cunt seemed to close upon my prick with the force of a pair of pincers. We both came to the ecstatic moment at the same time, and both actually screamed with delight; my ardent mistress in her fury of excitement actually bit my shoulder and drew blood; but I felt it not – I was in the seventh heaven of delight, and lay for long almost insensible on her beauteous body, clasped in her loving arms.

On coming to our senses: 'Oh, my beloved boy,' she said, 'never, never, have I experienced such pleasure. You are a perfect angel. I only fear I shall come to love you too much.'

We turned on our sides without dislodging the dear instrument of our enjoyment, and my lovely friend prattled on and delighted me with her toying, embracing, and gaiety. My prick had once more swelled up, and I wished to quietly enjoy a fuck in the luxurious position in which we lay; but my lovely friend said: 'That must not be, my dear Charles, I must consider your health. You have already done more than your age warrants, and you must rise and go to your bed to recover, by a sound sleep, your strength.'

'But feel how strong I am,' and I gave a forcible thrust into her glowing and well-moistened sheath. But, though she certainly was greatly excited, she suddenly turned round and unseated me, and drew away from me, refusing to take it again. As she was quite naked, the movements of her beauteous form were most graceful and enchanting, and one leg being thrown backwards left her lovely cunt full in view, and actually gaping open before me. Seized with the strongest desire to suck and kiss it, as I had done the night before, I begged that at least she would grant me that last favour, as it could not in any way do me harm. To this she readily consented, and lay down on her back, opening her glorious thighs, and with a pillow under her bottom so as to raise up her cunt into a better position for me to gamahuche her, as she called it. Before letting me begin, she said: 'My dear Charles, do you see that little projection at the upper part of my quim, that is my clitoris, and is the site of the most exquisite sensation; you see it is rather hard, even now, but you will find as you titillate it with your tongue or suck it, that it will become harder and more projecting, so apply your lips there.'

I did as my lovely mistress desired, and soon found it stiff and standing up nearly an inch into my mouth.

The convulsive twitches of her buttocks, the pressure forward of her hand on my head, all proved the exquisite felicity my lovely friend was enjoying. I slipped my hand under my chin – the position was awkward, but I managed to thrust my thumb into her cunt. My forefinger was somewhat in the way – but finding it exactly opposite the rosy hole of her bottom, and all being very moist there, I pushed it forward and it easily entered. I could not move my hand very actively, but I continued to gently draw my finger and thumb a little back together, and then thrust forward again. It seemed to add immensely to the pleasure I was giving her; her whole body quivered with excessive excitement. My head was pressed so firmly against her cunt that I had difficulty in breathing, but I managed to keep up the action of tongue and fingers until I brought on the exquisite crisis – her buttocks rose, her hand pressed hard on my head and her two powerful and fleshy thighs closed on my cheeks on each side and fixed me as if in a vice, while she poured down into my mouth and all over my chin, neck, and hand a perfect rush of sperm, and then lay in convulsive movements of enjoyment, hardly knowing what she was doing. As she held me so fast in every way, I continued to lick up the delicious discharge, and continued at the same time to pass my tongue over her clitoris. This, by producing a new excitement, brought her senses round. So relaxing her hold of me with her thighs she said: 'Oh, my darling Charles, come up to my arms that I may kiss you for the exquisite delight you have given me.' I did so, but took care, in drawing myself up, to engroove my stiff-standing prick in the well-moistened open cunt that lay raised on a pillow so conveniently in the way.

'Oh, you sad traitor,' cried my sweet companion. 'No, I cannot, I must not allow it,' but I held her tight round the waist, and her position was too favourable for me to be easily unhorsed.

'Ah! you must not, my dear boy. If you will not consider yourself, con-sider me. I shall be quite exhausted.' I shut her mouth with my kisses and tongue, and soon the active movements I was making within her charming vagina exercised their usual influence on her lubricity, so as to make her as eager for the fray as myself.

'Stop, my dear Charles, and you shall have it in a new position, which will give you as much more pleasure as it will me.'

'You are not going to cheat me, are you?'

'Oh, no! my darling, I am now as much on fire as you are – withdraw.'

I obeyed, half in fear. My fair mistress turned herself round, and getting on her hands and knees, presented to my ardent gaze her magnificent bottom. I thought she meant me to once more put it into the rosy little orifice, and said so.

'Oh! no,' she replied, 'not there'; but putting her hand under her belly, and projecting it backwards between her thighs, she said: 'Give it me and I will guide it into the proper place.'

Before doing so I stooped forward and pushing my face between the glorious cheeks on her bottom, sought and found the lovely little orifice, kissed it, and thrust my tongue in.

'Oh! don't Charles, dear, you tickle me so,' then flinching, and squeezing her buttocks together, I had nothing for it but to put my prick in her hand. She immediately guided it to and engulfed it in her burning cunt up to the very hair. I found I apparently got in fully an inch further this way – the position also gave my beautiful instructress more power of pressure on my prick – then her glorious buttocks, heaving under my movements, and exposed in all their immensity, was most exciting and beautiful. I seized her below the waist with a hand upon each hip, pressing her magnificent back-side against me each time that I thrust forward. Oh! it was indeed glorious to see. I was beside myself, and furious with the excitement the view of all these charms produced upon me. My charming mistress seemed equally to enjoy it, as was evinced by the splendid movements of her body; till at last overcome by the grand finale, she sank forward on her belly, and I followed on her back, without losing the position of my throbbing prick within her. We both lay for some time incapable of movement, but the internal squeezing and convulsive pressure of her cunt on my softened, but still enlarged prick, were exquisite beyond imagining. At last she begged me to relieve her. Getting out of bed, she sighed deeply, kissed me tenderly, and said, 'My dear Charles, we must not be so extravagant in future, it will destroy us both – come, let me see you to your bed.' The sight of my lovely mistress standing naked in all the glory of her beauty and perfection of form began to have its usual effect upon my prick, which showed symptoms of raising his head again; she gave it a pat, stooped down, and for a moment plunged its head into her beautiful mouth, then seizing my nightshirt, she threw it over my head and conducted me to my own bed, put me in, tucked me up, and tenderly kissing me, left the room, first unlocking my door and then locking the door of communication between the two rooms. Thus passed the first glorious night of my initiation into all the rites of Venus, and at the hands of a lovely, fresh and beautiful woman, who had only been married long enough to make her a perfect adept in the art. Never, oh never!

have I passed such a night. Many and many a fine woman, perfect too in the art of fucking, have I enjoyed, but the novelty and the charm, the variety and the superiority of the teacher, all combined to make this night the *ne plus ultra* of erotic pleasure.

It need not be said that, exhausted by the numerous encounters I had had in love's battlefield, I fell into a deep and sound sleep, until aroused by being rudely shaked up. I opened my eyes in astonishment. It was my sister Mary. She threw her arms round my neck, and kissing me, said: 'You lazy boy, do you know they are *all* down at breakfast, and you still asleep. What has come over you?'

'Oh!' I said, 'I got frightened with a horrible dream, and lay awake so long afterwards that when I did sleep, I overslept myself.'

'Well, get up at once,' and pulling the clothes quite off me, she laid bare my whole private parts, with my cock, as usual in youth on waking, at full stand.

'Oh! Charlie,' said Mary, fixing her eyes upon it in astonishment at its thickness and length. 'How your doodle has grown,' and she laid hold of it. 'Why it is as hard as wood, and see how red its head is.' Without her knowing why, it evidently had its natural effect on her senses, and she flushed as she squeezed it.

'Ah! my dear Mary, I have learnt a great secret about that thing, which I will tell you the first time we can be quite alone and secure from interruption. Just now there is no time, but before you go downstairs, let me see how your poor little fanny is.'

We had been used to these infantile expressions when in our ignorance and innocence we had mutual examinations of the difference of our sexes, and my sister was still as ignorant and innocent as ever. So when I said that I had not seen it since it was so ill-treated in the terrible whipping she had received from Miss Evelyn, she at once pulled up all her petticoats for me to look at it.

'Lie back for a moment on the bed.'

She complied. I was delighted. The prominence her mons Veneris had assumed, the increased growth of moss-like little curls, and the pouting lips of her tiny slit – all was most promising and charming. I stooped and kissed it, licking her little prominent clitoris with my tongue; it instantly hardened, and she gave a convulsive twitch of her loins.

'Oh! Charlie, how nice that is! What is it you are doing? Oh, how nice! Oh, pray go on.'

But I stopped, and said: 'Not at present, my darling sister, but when we can get away together I will do that and something much better, all connected with the great secret I have got to tell you. So run downstairs, and tell them why I had overslept myself, but not a word to anyone about what I have told you. I will be down in a trice.'

She went away, saying: 'Oh, Charlie, dear, what you did just now was so nice, and has made me feel so queer; do find an early opportunity of telling me all about it.'

Very few minutes sufficed to finish my toilet and bring me to the breakfast table.

'Why, Charlie,' broke out my mother, 'what is this horrid dream?'

'I can hardly tell you, my dear mother, it was so confused; but I was threatened to be murdered by horrid-looking men, and at last taken to high rocks and thrown down. The agony and fright awoke me, screaming, and all over perspiration. I could not sleep for hours after, even though I hid my head under the clothes.'

'Poor child,' said Mrs Benson, who was quietly eating her breakfast. 'What a fright you must have had.'

'Yes, ma'am, and at the same time, as I awoke with a scream, I was afraid I might have disturbed you, for all at once I remembered I was no longer in mamma's room, but next door to you. I hope I did not awake you?'

'Oh, no, my dear boy; I never heard you, or I should have got up to see what was the matter.'

So it passed off, and no further observation was made about it, but I once caught Mrs Benson's eye, and the expression and a slight nod was a sign of approval of my story. After breakfast we went as usual to the schoolroom. I thought Miss Evelyn was kinder in her manner to me than usual. She made me stand close to her when saying my lessons, occasionally letting her left arm fall round my neck, while she pointed to my book with the finger of the right, and there was always a certain pressure before raising her arm again. These little caresses were frequently repeated, as if she were wishing either to accustom me or herself to a habit of it, so as, doubtless, gradually to increase them to something more definite. I could not help feeling what a different effect these endearments would have had twenty-four hours earlier; but now, momentarily satisfied passions, and the new love that had seized me for Mrs B., prevented at first the inevitable cockstand that would otherwise have been produced by these approaches of Miss Evelyn. Not that I had given up all desire to possess her. On the contrary, my last night's instruction only made me more anxious to have Miss Evelyn too. Therefore, I by no means repulsed her present caresses, but looked up innocently in her face, and smiled affectionately. In the afternoon she was more expansive, and drew me to her by her arm round my waist, and pressed me gently to her person, saying how well I was attending to my lessons, and how sorry she was to have been obliged to punish me so severely the week before.

'You will be a good boy in future, will you not, dear Charlie?'

'Oh, yes; as long as you are so kind to me. I love you so much, and you are so beautiful when you speak so kindly to me.'

'Oh, you little flatterer.'

And she drew me to her lips and gave me a sweet kiss, which I returned with eagerness. I felt my prick had raised itself up to its full extent as these caresses were exchanged, and as Miss Evelyn held me tight pressed against her thigh, she must have felt it throbbing against her. That she did so, I have no doubt, as her face flushed, and she said: 'There, now, that will do, go to your seat.'

I obeyed; she rose in an agitated manner, left the room, and was absent for a quarter of an hour. I had no doubt but that she was overcome by her feelings, and I thought to myself she will manage to have me some of these days. I could afford to leave it to her own discretion, as my charming mistress of last night was there to keep me in exercise and cool the effervescence of passion under which I should otherwise have laboured. Nothing particular occurred during the day; Mrs B. was apparently indifferent about me, and never sought to approach or be in any way familiar; I studied her looks and followed her example. Mamma sent me early to bed, as she feared I had not had sleep enough the previous night by reason of my bad dream, and hoped I should have no more of the kind. This time my beautiful mistress found me sound asleep when she came to bed. She did not awake me until she had completed her night toilet, and was all ready to receive me in her arms. I sprung up, and in an instant, without a word being said, had her on her back, and was into her delicious cunt as far as I could drive my stiff-standing prick. My energy and fury seemed to please and stimulate the lady, for she replied to every eager thrust with as eager a spring forward. In such haste matters were very speedily brought to a crisis – with mutual sighs, and 'oh's' and 'ah's,' we sank exhausted, and lay for a very short time, when charming Mrs B. said: 'Why, Charles, you are quite wild to me; what a hurry you have been in, but it was very nice, and I forgive you, but you must be more rational in future.'

'Oh, my beloved mistress, how can I help it; you are so beautiful, and so good to me; I quite adore and love every part of your charming body. I know I was too impetuous, but I must make it up by kissing and fondling the dear source of all my joys.'

She did not resist, but let me do as I liked. Pushing myself down the bed, I applied my lips and tongue to her lovely cunt, all wet with our mutual discharge, which was so sweet to the taste that I first began licking between the lips, and then applied myself to her excited clitoris, and with my finger and thumb working as on the previous morning I threw her into an ecstasy of delight, until again she had a delicious discharge. Then creeping up, I thrust my prick into her well-moistened and velvety cunt – as you may imagine it was rampant as ever after my mouth contact with the exquisite quim I had been sucking.

'Stop, Charles, darling, I will show you another position, where you can lie easily with your dear delightful prick up to the hilt in the sheath you have so charmingly excited. Here, lie down by my right side – on your side.'

She lay down on her back, and throwing her right leg over my hips, told me to bend my knees forward and open my legs, or rather lift up my right leg. She placed her left thigh between my thighs, then slightly twisting her bottom up towards me brought the lips of her cunt directly before my prick, which she seized with her delicate fingers, and guided safely into Venus's grotto. I gave one or two shoves, and she a leave or two, to house him comfortably.

'And now,' she said, 'we will take it reasonably in this way; we can go on, or stay occasionally; embrace, cuddle, or talk, just as we please. Are you quite comfortable?'

'Oh! deliciously so!' I replied, as my hand wandered all over her beautiful belly and bubbies, and then my mouth sucked the last.

'There, darling, that will do for the moment; I want to have some talk with you. First, let me thank you for your very discreet behaviour this day, it quite justifies the confidence I had in you. Your story of the dream was capital and just suited the purpose. I hope, my dear Charlie, that under my auspices you will become a model lover – your aptitude has been already proved in several ways. First and best, with all the appearance of a boy, you are quite a man, and even superior to many. You have already shown great discretion and ready wit, and there is no reason to fear that you will become a general favourite with our sex, who soon find out who is discreet and who otherwise – discretion is the trump card of success with us. Alas! few of your sex understand this. Let me impress one lesson on you, my dear Charles. You and I cannot continue long on our present footing. My husband will return and carry me away, and although circumstances will throw us at intervals into each other's arms – for you may be sure you will be always welcome to me – yet my very absence will force you to seek other outlets to the passions I have awakened and taught their power. I have one piece of advice to give you as to your conduct to newer lovers – for have them you must, my dear Charles, however much you may fancy yourself now attached to me; with these, let them all for some time imagine that each possesses you for the first time. First of all, it doubles their satisfaction, and so increases your pleasure. Your early discretion causes me to think that you will see all the advantages of this conduct. I may add that if they suppose you have had previous instruction, they, if they are women, will never rest until they have drawn from you the secret of your first instructress. You might, of course, tell some tale of a "cock and a bull," but in searching for the truth and cross questioning you when you are least aware of it, they will lead you into contradictions, and the truth will at last be ferreted out. Now this would be unjust to me, who have risked a good deal to give you the delightful instructions of last night, and, as I hope, of many more. So you see, my dear Charles, in all early cases you must enact the part of an ignoramus *seeking* for instruction, with vague ideas of how to set about it. I hope, while I am near you,' she added, 'no such occasion will arise, but I feel certain, with your passions and your power, dear, darling fellow – push away – I! – I! – I feel for cer–certain they will ar–arise.'

Thus ended the very wise and excellent advice this charming woman was giving me. Do not imagine that I did not pay great attention, and, indeed, her very reasonable maxims became the guide of my after-life, and I owe to them a success with women rarely otherwise obtained. Her sensible remarks had been drawn out to such a length, that my prick had so far rebelled that he had throbbed inside of her delicious cunt so forcibly as to produce a happy movement of her body that interrupted and cut short her words.

'Charlie, my darling, pass your middle finger down and rub it on my clitoris, and then suck the nipple of my bubby next you, and work away with your glorious prick.'

I did as desired. She seconded me with an art quite peculiar to herself, and at last we both died away in that love's death which is so overpowering and so delicious. The glorious position we were in rendered it almost impossible to lose ground, spend as often as you please; but if my prick had been one that would have shrunk to nothing, the wonderful power of retaining it within her possessed by my delicious mistress would have prevented the possibility of exit.

In after-nights I have often fallen sound asleep with it entirely engulfed within her, and awoke hours afterwards to find her extraordinary power of retention had held him firm, notwithstanding his having shrunk up to a mere piece of doughy flesh. In this instance, after recovering our senses, I still retained my place, and we recommenced our conversation; my lovely instructress giving me many and most useful hints for my after-life. I have often since dwelt on the wisdom of all she so charmingly taught me, and wondered how so young a woman could have so thorough a knowledge of her sex and the world. I suppose love is a great master and inspired her on this occasion. I may here remark that for forty years afterwards this charming woman and I remained the fastest of friends after being the most ardent of lovers. She was the depository of all my erotic extravagancies, and never showed any jealousy, but really enjoyed the recital of my wildest love combats with others.

Alas! death at last took her from me, and I lost the mainstay of my existence. Forgive this digression, but I am writing long after these events, and sorrows will have their vent. Woe is me!

To return to present joys. We continued talking and toying, until I was again anxious to commence love's combat. My prudent mistress wished me to finish for the time, and to sleep and refresh ourselves for renewed efforts; but youth and strength nerved me for the fight, and being securely fixed, I held her as in a vice, with my thighs around only one of hers that could have allowed her to escape. Passing my finger down on her stiffened clitoris I so excited her that she had no wish but to bring matters to a crisis.

'Stop, my dear,' she said, 'and we will renew our pleasure in another attitude.'

So withdrawing her leg off my loins, she turned on her side, so as to present her glorious buttocks before me, and pressed them into my belly and against my thighs, which seemed to introduce my prick even further than he was within before. Besides, in all these positions, where a woman presents her splendid backside to you, it is always more exciting and has a greater hold of you than any other way. We did both most thoroughly enjoy this splendid fuck, and without withdrawing, both fell into the sweetest imaginable slumber. This was one of those occasions in which, having fallen asleep engulfed, I awoke some five hours later, to find my prick still lightly held within the velvety folds of one of the most delicious cunts ever created for the felicity of man, or of, I may say, woman either. You may easily imagine how soon my prick swelled to his wonted size on finding himself still in such charming quarters. I let him lie quite still, barring the involuntary throbs he could not avoid making, and bending my body away from my lovely mistress, I admired her breadth of shoulders, the beauty of her upper arm, the exquisite *chute* of her loins, the swell of her hips, and the glorious projection and rotundity of her immense buttocks. I slowly and gently pushed in and out her juicy sheath, until, awakened by the exquisite sensations of my slow movements, all her lubricity was excited, and we ended one of our most delicious encounters, finishing, as usual, with a death-like exhaustion. She declared I had done enough for one night, and jumping out of bed, compelled me to betake myself to my own room, where, I must confess, I very shortly slept as sound as could be, without at the same time oversleeping myself.

Thus passed several successive nights, until the full of the moon, when one day Mrs B. complained of headache and feeling unwell. I was very much alarmed, but she took occasion to tell me it was quite natural, and she would explain to me how it was so at night. I was obliged to be content with this. At night, she came and sat on my bed, and told me all the mysteries of the case. How women, not with child, had these bleedings monthly, which, so far from being hurtful, were a relief to the system, and that they happened at the full or the new moon, generally at the former. Further, that all connection with men must cease at such a time. I was in despair, for my prick was stiff enough to burst. However, my kind and darling mistress, to relieve me from the pain of such distention, took my prick in her mouth, and performed a new manoeuvre. Wetting her middle finger with her saliva, she thrust it up my bottom-hole, and worked in union with the suction of the knob, and the frigging of the root of my prick with the other hand. I had a most exquisite and copious discharge, the pleasure being greatly enhanced by the action of the finger up my fundament. My charming mistress swallowed all I could give her, and did not cease sucking until the last drop had exuded from my throbbing prick.

I was obliged to be satisfied with this, and my mistress informed me I could have no more enjoyment for four or five days; which, to my then impatience, was like condemning me to as many ages of hope deferred. I observed, while she was kissing me, that her breath had a peculiar odour, and I asked her what she had been eating.

'Why do you ask, my dear boy?'

'Because of the difference of your breath, generally so sweet and fragrant.'

She smiled and said it was all from the same cause she had just been explaining to me, and was very generally so with women at that period. I mention this because it was the means of my discovering that Miss Evelyn was exactly in the same state. She had continued her endearing caresses without proceeding much further than I have already described, excepting more frequently kissing me. She now always did so on first entering the schoolroom, and also when we were dismissed. I suppose to prevent an observation or inference, she had adopted the same habit with my sisters. On this day, having drawn me with her arm round my waist close to her, when she kissed me I felt the very same odour of breath that I had observed in Mrs Benson. She too was languid that day and complained of headache. I also observed a dark line under her eyes, and on afterwards observing Mrs B., saw precisely the same – so I became convinced they were unwell from the same cause. Mrs B. had told me that most women were so at the full of the moon – which was then the case.

The next day my mother proposed to drive to town, and probably knowing the state of the case, asked Mrs B. and Miss Evelyn to accompany her, as she thought the airing would be beneficial. They at once accepted – my younger sister cried out, 'Oh, mamma, let me go with you also.' Mary interposed, and thought she had the best right – but Lizzie said she had spoken first. I managed to give Mary a wink and a shake of the head, which she instantly comprehended, so gracefully giving way, although with apparent reluctance, it was arranged that Eliza should accompany the ladies. I now felt my opportunity was at hand to initiate my darling sister into the delightful mysteries that I had just been myself instructed in.

At eleven o'clock the carriage drove up, and we stood looking after them until they were lost to sight. Then returning into the parlour, Mary threw her arms round my neck, and kissing me, said: 'Oh! I am glad, Charlie, you winked to me, for now you know we can do as we like, and you can tell me all about this secret, and you must kiss my little fanny as you did before, it was so nice. I have thought of nothing else, but how to have it done again.'

'Well, my darling, I shall do all that, and more, but we cannot do so here. I tell you what we will do – we will pretend to go for a long walk in the country, but instead of that, we will pass through the shrubbery into the orchard and hazelwood, and so gain the little remote summerhouse, of which I have secured the key; there we shall be safe from all observation.'

This little summerhouse was at some distance from the house, and in a lonely corner of the orchard, raised on an artificial mount, so that its windows should command a lovely view beyond the walls of the grounds. It was about ten feet square – was beautifully sheltered, and the ladies in summer took their work there, and occupied it for hours every fine day; so it was furnished with tables and chairs, and on one side a long couch without a back. It had already entered into my idea that this was the spot I should contrive to get to with Mary – little thinking how chance would throw so glorious an opportunity in my way so soon. It was always kept locked to prevent it being used by the servants, gardeners, or others. I knew where the key was kept, and secured it when the ladies were dressing for their drive – so after staying sufficiently long to prevent any suspicion, and saying then we were going for a long walk in the country, so as to prevent them seeking for us at the summerhouse if any visitors should chance to call, we sallied out, but re-entered the grounds where we could not be observed, and speedily gained the spot we had in view – entered and locked the door. Then I drew down the blinds, threw off my coat and waistcoat, and told Mary to take off her shawl and bonnet, and outer gown.

'But why all this, Charlie, dear?'

'First, my darling – all those are in the way of kissing and toying with your charming little fanny, and next, I don't want anything to appear tumbled when we go back.'

This was enough, and she did everything as I desired, indeed, more, for she took off her petticoat and little corset, saying she would be cooler thus. So, following her example, I took off my trousers, saying she would be better able to see and play with my doodle. When these preliminaries were accomplished, I drew her on my knees – first pulling up her shift and my own shirt, so that our naked flesh should be in contact. Seeing that her chemise fell off from her bosom, I first felt her little bubbies, which were beginning to develop themselves, and had the tiniest little pink nipples that even my lips could hardly get hold of. She had pulled up my shirt to look again at the great change that had occurred to my prick – of course, our preliminaries had already excited it to a stiff-standing position.

'Oh, Charlie, what a size it is to be sure, and how nice to pull this skin over its head; look how it runs back again. Oh! how funny!'

It was time to stop this, or she would have soon made me discharge.

'Well, then, what is the great secret, and what has it to do with your doodle and my fanny?'

'I will tell you, but you must never say a word to a soul – not even to Eliza, she is too young yet.'

'Well, go on.'

'I was one day seeking something in the closet in Mrs Benson's room, when I heard them coming, and had only the time to slip into the closet. They entered, locked the door, and Mr B. laid her on the bed, and lifted up all her petticoats so that I saw her fanny quite surrounded with hairs, as yours will be by and by. Mr B. stooped down, and applied his tongue as I did to you the other morning.'

'Oh, yes; and it was so nice, Charlie!'

'That is exactly what Mrs B. said when he had done. Then he pulled out his doodle, such a size, much bigger than mine, and whipped it into her fanny. I was quite frightened, and thought he must have killed her. But no, it went in quite easy; and she hugged and kissed him while he pushed it up and down for some time, till they both stopped all at once. He then drew it out, hanging down all wet, and asked if it had not given her great pleasure. "Delightful," she said. "I have now got used to it, but you know you hurt me, and made me so sore the first time you did it." After this they left the room, and I got away without being discovered. But I found out what our two things were made for, we will do as they did, so lie down on the couch whilst I kneel at the end, and begin in the way I kissed it the other morning.'

'Oh, Charlie, if it is all like that, I shall be so pleased with it.'

Down she squatted, drawing up her chemise. My hand wondered all over her charming belly and mount. Then kneeling down, and putting her legs over my shoulders and my hands under her thighs and bottoms, I applied my tongue at once to her little clitoris, which I found was already stiff, and showing its head at the upper part of her pinky slit. The action of my agile tongue produced an instantaneous effect – her loins and thighs heaved up her bottom to press her little pouting cunt against my face. Mechanically she put her hand on my head, and muttered terms of endearment.

'Oh, darling Charlie, how delicious! Oh! do go on! it is so nice, etc.'

I wanted no stimulant, but licked away until, with shortened breath; and greater heavings of her body, she began to stammer: 'Oh! oh! I feel so queer – ah, stop; I am going to faint – I, I, I, can't – can't bear it any longer – oh! – oh!' Her limbs relaxed, and she died away in her first discharge, which was very glutinous and nice, but only scanty in quantity. I let her quiet until she came to; then looking in her face, and smiling, I asked her how she liked it.

'Oh! I was in heaven, dear Charlie, but I thought it was killing me – it was almost too much to bear – nothing could be more delicious.'

'Oh, yes!' I replied, 'there is something more delicious still, but, I must kiss you in this way again before we try the other; the more moist the inside is the easier I shall get in.'

'But, Charlie, you don't mean to say you will ever get in your doodle, now that it has grown so big.'

'Well, we will try, and if it hurts you too much we can stop.'

So I began again to gamahuche her; this time it took a longer effort to produce the ultimate result; but apparently with still greater effect, and a more copious discharge. Her little cunt being now relaxed, and well moistened with her own discharge and my saliva, and well inclined to receive my prick, I spat upon it and lubricated it from head to root. Then rising from my knees, I stretched myself over Mary's belly, and gently directing my prick, and rubbing it up and down first between the lips, and exciting her clitoris by the same action, I gently and gradually inserted its head between the lips of her charming little cunt. There was less difficulty than might have been expected, the gamahuching and double spending had relaxed the muscles, and her passions being excited also acted on her organs of generation; at all events, I got in the head, and about two inches of its length without her murmuring anything beyond: 'How big it feels – it seems to stretch me so.'

All this was exciting me dreadfully, and it was only by the greatest effort that I did not thrust rudely forward. I now felt I was pushing against some obstacle, I thrust hard and hurt her. She cried out, begged me to stop. I was so near the finale that I felt I must go on. So, plunging forward, I rushed at the impediment, and made her cry out most lustily. Probably another push would have decided my position, but nature could hold out no longer, and I yielded down my erotic tribute to her virginal charms, without having actually deflowered her. So far, perhaps, it was fortunate, because I poured into her a torrent of sperm which was not only balm to her partially wounded hymen, but so relaxed and lubricated the interior of her cunt as greatly to facilitate my after-efforts.

I lay quiet still for some time, and the gradual swelling out and throbbing of my prick reawakened her young passions. She said: 'Charlie, my dear, you said that it would prove delicious in the end, and I can feel it is becoming so. I have no more pain, and you shall go on just as you like.'

As my prick stiffened at her endearing words and involuntary pressures, and as I had it completely under control, since I had taken the edge off its immediate appetite by the last discharge, I held it literally well in hand; and as I had lost no ground by withdrawing, I started with the advantage of possession. First I slipped my hand down between our two bellies and began frigging her clitoris, which immediately excited her passions to the highest pitch.

'Oh! Charlie, dear, now push it all in – I do so long for it – and I don't care how it hurts me.'

I had been giving short thrusts more to stimulate her passions than to alleviate my own; and as she was totally unaware of what was going to happen, she widened her thighs and heaved up her bottom, expanding her vagina in the act. I gathered my strength together, and as my cock was standing as stiff as iron, I suddenly drove it forward, and felt that I broke through something, and gained two inches more insertion at least. The effect on my poor sister was most painful, she shrieked out lustily; strove hard to unsheath me, wriggled her body in all directions to effect this; but I was too securely engulfed for that, and all her struggles only enabled me the more easily to sheathe him up to the very hairs. So excited was I by her tears and screams, that I was no sooner there than a torrent of sperm burst from me, and I lay like a corpse on her body, but perfectly maintaining the ground I possessed. This death-like quiet lasted some minutes, and, to a certain extent, assuaged the violence of the pain I put poor Mary to. Doubtless, also, the balmy nature of the ample quantity of sperm I had shot up to her womb helped to soothe her suffering. At all events, when we were both able again to converse, she unbraided me with the agony I had caused her, and wished me to get off her at once; but retaining the advantageous possession of her very tight and delicious sheath, I told her all was now over, and we might look forward to nothing but enrapturing pleasure.

Some minutes had elapsed in these remonstrances on one side and coaxings on the other, when I suddenly felt her charming little cunt actually throb upon and give an involuntary squeeze to my prick, which was still throbbing within her. He was far too ready to stand at any time, still more when engulfed in the exquisite young cunt he had just initiated into love's mysteries – *bref*, he stood stiff as ever, and Mary, at first with a shudder of fright, then with all the energy of awakened passion, began to move her body under me. I held off from any interference, feeling certain that if the desire came naturally to her it would doubly enhance my own pleasure. My foresight did not fail me. Mary's passions became fully aroused, and when so, the trifling soreness passed out of mind, and we actually had a most delicious fuck, in which my prick appeared as if in a vice, and Mary wriggled her backside almost as well as the more artistic movements of Mrs Benson. All things must come to an end, but this did so amid screams of delight on both sides. This single bout began and finished the education of my darling sister. She hugged and fondled me afterwards, declaring I was quite right in telling her pleasure followed pain; for nothing could exceed the enrapturing nature of the sensation my prick had produced. She thought now that it was not a bit too big, but just made to give the utmost satisfaction. We remained locked in each other's arms, my prick still engulfed in its tight and exciting sheath. We fondled and prattled, until it became again in a state of violent erection, equally stimulating her tight little cunt, so that we were forced to recommence our love encounter. I found that my dear little sister possessed naturally the power of throbbing on or nipping a prick, which the French call *casse-noisette*. It is a great gift and adds immensely to the man's pleasure, and I should think to the woman's too. In my sister's case it began from the very first complete insertion of my prick and the years that I afterwards continued to fuck her added nothing to this delicious accomplishment, except in the variety of positions in which it could be exercised.

The dear girl was in ecstasies at the pleasure she had received, and at the pain which seemed to be past. Oh! she was so sweetly caressing that I could not withdraw from her, and we fondled and toyed until again my cock rose to his first vigour, and she nothing loath, began her new and naturally taught gift of bottom upheavings and cunt pressures until again we sank exhausted in the death-like ending of love's battles. On recovering our senses, I was obliged to withdraw and relieve my sister of the dead weight of my body on her person.

It has always struck me as extraordinary how the most delicate women will support a heavy man on their persons, not only without flinching, but even with ease and pleasure – but so it is. On rising and withdrawing, we were both alarmed to see that my prick was all bloody, and that blood and semen were oozing from her cunt. We had no idea this would be the case, and at first I was as frightened as she was. A moment's reflection showed me that it was only the natural result of forcing my way in, and that the pleasure since enjoyed proved it to be of no consequence. I soon convinced and calmed my sister on the point – fortunately the sofa covering was red, and applying my handkerchief, I wiped up all the semen mixture, and, in fact, no marks remained; the same handkerchief wiped all results from Mary's dear little cunt, and as her shift had been kept well up, fortunately no stains appeared upon that.

We now ate some luncheon and drank some wine that we had prudently brought with us. We then began playing and romping together – she wanting always to get hold of my prick, and I to pull her about in every way. It was gloriously warm weather, so I proposed we should off with everything. In a trice we were as naked as we were born, and flew into each other's arms in a frenzy of delight, then we had a mutual thorough inspection. My darling sister gave every promise of becoming a magnificent woman – her shoulders were already wide – her arms well shaped, although still thin – her waist small – the swell of the hips already well developed – as to her bottom, it stuck out well and hard behind, quite charming to see, and giving promise of very ample dimensions hereafter. I made her kneel on the low couch, with her head well up and her thighs open; kneeling behind, I gamahuched her until she spent; then rising, shoved my prick into her cunt, in her then position, and had a downright good poke, which she, too, found was a way that gave her extra excitement. We passed thus some hours in mutual delights. I taught her the side fuck which had so charmed me with my delightful instructress, and I found dear Mary even an apter scholar than myself had proved. The afternoon advancing, we dressed, and eradicating all signs of what we had been doing, returned to the house, mutually promising to keep thoroughly secret all that had passed and agreeing that no sign of unusual familiarity should escape us. I strongly advised Mary to get some warm water and bathe her cunt well, for, as may be supposed, I had taken the opportunity of teaching her the true erotic language as applied to the organs of generation of both sexes, and the name of the connection itself, 'fucking'.

Thus delightfully ended the first lesson in love taught to my sister, and such was my first triumph over a maidenhead, double enhanced by the idea of the close ties of parentage between us. In after-life, I have always found the nearer we are related, the more this idea of incest stimulates our passions and stiffens our pricks, so that if even we be in the wane of life, fresh vigour is imparted by reason of the very fact of our evasion of conventional laws.

We had both returned to the drawing-room for more than an hour before the arrival of the ladies. Dear Mary complained of feeling sore and stiff in every limb. I had advised her to lie down on the sofa and try to sleep. I did the same, and happily we both dozed off, and never awoke until the loud rat-tat of arrival at the house door roused us up. I told Mary to hide all appearance of pain, and only to say, as an excuse for going early to bed, that we had gone further afield than we at first intended, and that she was very tired. We were both sent early to bed, for I was still treated as quite a boy, and I was sound asleep when my charming Mrs B. woke me up by her warm caresses. I could well have spared them that night, but when did one of my years not respond to the endearments of the woman he loved, and who yielded all to him? She sucked me dry as usual, and I slept soundly till morning.

The next three days passed without anything to record. Mary did not allow her real soreness to appear, but went through her sufferings heroically, for she told me afterwards she felt very severe pains all over; doubtless her whole nervous system had been overexcited, and this was the natural reaction; it was so far fortunate that not a shadow of a chance of our having fresh connection occurred, so she had time perfectly to recover from the ill effects of her first initiation into the erotic raptures. I continued to have the relief each night of the charming mouth of my loved and beautiful instructress. At last, the abominable *menses*, as she called them, were past and gone. For a full twenty-four hours after, she would not allow me to reassume all the privileges she had previously granted, and admit me to share her bed. She told me this was necessary to prevent any recurrence, and also that in some cases a virulent white discharge occasionally followed for some hours, sufficiently acrid to affect my local health, and that, she added, was now 'too precious' in her estimation 'to risk in any way'. I thought it hard at the time, but it was only another proof of the thoughtful wisdom of this estimable woman. At last, I was again in full possession of her charming person. Oh! how we did revel in all the luxuries and lubricity; almost every night my enchanting friend found some new position to vary and enhance our erotic raptures. In one of these, laying me down flat on my back, then straddling over me, she sank on her knees, and with body erect, lifted up or rather bent back my stiff-standing prick until it was fairly below her open cunt, then guiding it exactly to the proper entrance, she sank her body slowly down upon it until fully engulfed, hair crushing hair, then as slowly rose again, drew off until all but the nut was uncovered, then once more sank down. In this position we could both see the whole process. At length, becoming too excited, she sank on my bosom, then one arm and hand pressed her splendid buttocks down on my throbbing prick after every elevation of her mag-nificent backside while my other hand, doubling round behind her, intro-duced the middle finger up her charming bottom-hole, and worked in and out in unison with both our heaving movements, until stopped by the grand crisis, when death-like languor overcame us both almost at the same moment. I must not forget to mention that from time to time I paid a visit to the small and rosy orifice that lay so near to the more legitimate altar of Venus. It was a variety of enjoyment that my lovely mistress acknowledged to me she at times felt much inclined to enjoy, but only after having the front path of pleasure well fucked and lubricated with sperm, which alone caused the other mucous membrane to feel inclined that way.

I will here insert a characteristic letter from my loved mistress to her intimate and bosom school friend, with the reply thereto. It was several years before they were shown to me, and some time after I had possessed *both* the charming writers, for we all three became fast friends; indeed, I may call myself or rather my prick, the pivot on which their friendship turned, yet there never was the shade of jealousy on either part, but in these remarks I am anticipating what I may, perhaps, be hereafter tempted to describe more fully. I give these letters now, because they immediately refer to the events I am at present relating. They show the secret working of my loved mistress's mind, and the voluptuous nature of her temperament, and the satisfaction that my delicious initiation had given. Her affectionate and flattering remarks, relating to myself, are greater than I deserved. The following is the first letter addressed to her friend –

*Mrs Benson to the Hon. Mrs Egerton*

Dear Carry – I am about to keep my promise, and give you an account of our honeymoon. You, my dear, must be equally faithful, and reply as frankly as I am now about to write to you.

Two giddier girls than you and I never entered the bonds of matrimony, or more earnestly longed for the sights connected with it. Well, after the usual breakfast, we left by rail for Leamington, where we were to pass our first night. We had a *coupé* to ourselves; and beyond seating me on his knee, and kissing me, Fred behaved with much decency and propriety. We arrived and dined. The hour between tea and bedtime was sufficiently tedious, as both of us were naturally much preoccupied. My husband wrote a letter to mamma, telling her of our safe arrival, and of his intense happiness. After which he asked me if I would go to bed, in the most matter-of-fact way imaginable. I murmured an affirmative, scarcely knowing what to say. He rang for a candle, and told me he would follow shortly. It seemed like a dream to me. The maid showed me to a room containing a large four-post bedstead, heavily hung with curtains, and provided with old-fashioned furniture.

I seated myself on the edge of the bed and began to meditate. I sat thus, for, I daresay, ten minutes, and then commenced undressing, I had put on my nightgown, and removed everything but my stockings, when I heard footsteps approach the door. I opened, and my husband entered, closed it, and turned the key. Oh! Carry, I did feel so funny. I was undressed in a bedroom with a man, and that man had a right to my person. He seated himself in an armchair, and drew me on his knee. Nothing but my thin nightgown separated my bottom from his bare knee, for he had quite undressed in an adjoining room and had nothing on but his shirt under his dressing-gown, which flew open as he sat down. He drew my lips to his, and kissing me, thrust his tongue between them, while his hand first caressed and squeezed my bosom, which, you know, is pretty full and well developed; it then wandered down upon my thigh, pressed and felt the fleshy form. Little by little he approached my belly, and for a moment pressed my mount. These preliminaries are at all times exciting, but now they made me almost ill, so great was my confusion. Seeing this, he drew up my nightgown, and placed his hand, first on my naked thigh, then he felt my mount, and you know, Carry dear, what a forest I have got there. He seemed delighted with it. His fingers played with the silky curls, drawing them out to their full length, so long that it appeared to surprise him, and his eyes sparkled, and his face showed much excitement.

'Open your thighs, dearest,' he whispered.

I obeyed mechanically, and his middle finger forced itself between the lips of my cunt, and commenced rubbing my clitoris. You know, by experience, what an excitable one it is and to what a size it develops itself when excited. Again Fred seemed delighted with his discovery.

'Does that please you, my darling?'

'Yes,' I faltered out.

He thrust his finger up my cunt, then rose up, threw off his dressing-gown, took me in his arms, and lifted me on the bed, placing a pillow under my head. Then letting my legs fall over the sides, he knelt on the floor, and separating my thighs with his arms, stooped and kissed my quim. He did more, he sucked and then licked with his tongue my already excited clitoris. It set me on fire, and I could not avoid showing it by the convulsive twitchings of my loins and buttocks.

'Do you like that, my love?'

'Oh! yes; so much! – so very much!'

I was nearly mad with the excitement he was putting me into. He again stood up, and lifting my legs, his hands pressed them again and again.

'What delicious legs,' he exclaimed.

I could see his shirt bulging out. He leant forward, and with his arms under my legs, lifted them well up, and I felt a stiff thick thing pressing against my cunt. His left hand opened the lips, his right hand guided it between them, and a cruel push lodged its great head completely within. Neither you, or I, Carry, were strictly virgins, our fingers and other means had opened our vaginas to a certain extent. We had played too many tricks together to have left our maidenheads quite intact, so that the passage was less difficult than it might have been. Nevertheless, it had never been penetrated by the male organ, and that of my husband was of the largest. I experienced, therefore, a great deal of pain, and cried out: 'Oh, my dear Fred, you hurt me dreadfully, what are you doing?'

'Doing, my darling! why, I am getting into you. Have a little patience, and I will make you mad with pleasure.'

Another determined thrust sent him halfway, and then with another, still more violent, he lodged himself up to the hilt within. I screamed with real pain, and struggled to free myself.

'Good heavens, sir, you are killing me; I will not endure such treatment.'

He heeded me not, but holding me fast by the thighs commenced shoving in and out furiously. A sensitive woman never receives an insertion of this kind with impunity. The friction began to excite feelings that first deadened the pain of entrance, and then began to awaken the delicious sensations of lubricity. The enjoyment I began to experience was delicious, and I could not refrain from heaving up to meet his thrusts.

'That is right, my angel; was I not correct in saying it would soon turn from pain to pleasure? Do you not enjoy it now?'

'Yes; but you make me feel so funny. I don't know what – it – is.'

His increased and rapid movement filled me with delight. I bounded up and down in response to his thrusts, and felt so queer when, all of a sudden, he gasped for breath, stopped, and I felt a greater and stiffer swelling of his instrument, and then a gush of hot liquid dashed against my womb, which continued running for some seconds. This, Carry, was my first experience of what a man can do for us.

Withdrawing his huge affair – for he since admits he is larger than most men – letting go my thighs – he pressed down upon me, and tenderly embraced me, and said that I had behaved admirably; in future there would be no more pain, and from what he had already experienced he felt sure I was made for the fullest enjoyment that husband and wife could indulge in. After a little fondling, he rose, drew off my stockings, and helped me into bed, immediately following me. On throwing back the clothes to enter the bed, he said he must kiss the dear little hairy thing that had given him such pleasure. He kissed and toyed with it, admiring the profusion of hair on my mount, the whiteness and beauty of my belly, and then, baring my breasts, admired, kissed, and sucked them. All this not only excited me, but I could see very well it had again caused his affair to stick out. Seeing that I was timidly glancing at it, he seized my hand, and made me lay hold of it, showed me how the skin covered and uncovered its head; then becoming rampageous, he got on my belly and between my thighs, and again introduced his cock to where it had already given such pleasure. He still rather hurt me, and made me smart for a little while, but as the interior was well lubricated by his former discharge, the penetration was easily accomplished. When up to the hilt, and the two hairs were closely joined, he paused and said: 'We will take it less impatiently this time, that my darling Bessie may enter into all the joys of fucking, for that is what we call it, my dear; so I shall go slowly to work until my darling's passions awake and urgently call for more rapid movements.'

He did so, and gradually produced the most lascivious excitement in my whole body. I writhed beneath him in the utmost ecstasy, threw my arms round his body, and hugged him to me.

'Oh! you are an angel,' he cried, 'and made for enjoyment. Throw your legs also over my back – there, that is it – and now I will hasten my movements, and we will die away together.'

Oh, the delight he gave me was inexpressibly delicious; his rapid and eager thrusts were as eagerly met by the upheaving of my bottom to reciprocate them. The grand crisis seized us simultaneously, and we sank momentarily exhausted in each other's arms, leaving the dear exciter of such joys soaking within. My dear husband was so pleased, he kissed and fondled me in the sweetest manner, telling me that never woman before had yielded him such intense pleasure, that nature had prompted me to as much enjoyment as if I had been already married a month.

We were locked closely in the warmest embrace; his tenderness and fondling began to have its effect on my passions, and involuntarily I made some internal convulsive twitchings.

'I feel you, my darling, calling on my instrument for renewed efforts; he will soon respond.'

And, in fact, I felt it swelling and swelling so deliciously that I could not help continuing the interior pressures, although feeling confusedly ashamed of the notice my husband took of it.

'Don't be afraid, my sweetest love, but give way to whatever your passions dictate, and thus you will best please me, and give to yourself double enjoyment. I mean to initiate you into every secret that the rites of Venus possess, and wish that my loved wife should become a devoted votary, and I will do my best that she may revel in all the luxuries of perfect coition.'

We completed this course with even greater *abandon* than before, and I began to enjoy his embraces beyond anything our imaginations used to suggest. This time he withdrew and lay down by my side, and taking me within both his arms, continued his charming endearments. I never slept that night; I was in a fever of restless excitement. My husband fucked me five times before he dozed off. Towards morning I tossed and tumbled, and could not sleep. Daylight soon came, my restlessness had shaken all the bedclothes off, except a part of the sheet, and turning towards my husband, I perceived that the sheet stuck up over the lower part of his body. Curiosity seized me – I looked at him, and saw he was evidently sleeping So gently removing the sheet, I beheld the dear instrument of all my last night's joys as well as pains. You know how we used to long to see a man's cock when we were at school, and how, when we did sometimes see a boy's limp thing hanging down, we used to wonder what change would come over it, and how. Well, here was an opportunity of examining, at my ease, the wonderful curiosity that had so puzzled us. The last edge of the sheet passing over it touched its ruby head; it throbbed and pulsated to the view. I was afraid this had awakened Fred, but no, he slept as sound as ever. So I gently raised myself on my bottom, and gazed on the dear object I had so longed to see and feel. There it stood up like a pillar, rather bending towards his belly: and what surprised me much was to see a dark strongly wrinkled bag at its roots, with apparently two large balls inside; the hair on its roots spread in dark mass up to his navel, and beautifully bright and curling it was. I approached my lips, and made the action of kissing, without touching it. Whether it felt my warm breath, I know not, but it actually throbbed a response. What a great big thing it was, equally long as it was thick. I did not think I could encircle it with my hand; I longed to try, but was afraid I should waken Fred, and what would he think of me, I blushed at the very idea; but my passions became excited, and too strong to resist the temptation. So first lying gently down again, I very quietly dropped my arm over him and touched his cock, it throbbed at the touch, but Fred slept on. So raising myself again, I very gently laid hold of it. It was as much as I could grasp below the head, but was beyond my grasp at the root; I found it took three of my hands to measure its length from the root to the nut, which stood out in all its redness above. I was almost breathless with excitement, and lost some of my caution. Stooping down, I gently kissed the ruby head, when, before I knew where I was, it was pushed up into my mouth, and my husband's voice said: 'Oh, you dear darling creature! how kind of you to waken me so luxuriously!'

I was horrified at being discovered; and blushing up to the eyes, I hid my face in his bosom.

'Do not be ashamed, my angel, it is now as much yours as mine, and have you not as much right to see, kiss, and handle it? come, don't be ashamed.'

However, I could not face him, and when he tried to raise my head I turned my back. He seized me round the waist, and, before I knew where I was, passed a hand between my thighs, and guided his huge cock to the lips of my cunt, and was in me, I thought further than ever, in a moment. It is true the previous toying with his instrument had terribly excited me, and I had felt that my cunt had become very moist, but I had no idea that anything could be accomplished in that position. I was most delightfully undeceived, for not only did it feel tighter in it, but transferring his fingers from guiding his prick, he touched and played with my clitoris, and produced such excessive lubricity that I went off and spent with a scream of delight before he was ready; but continuing with finger and cock to ravish me inside and out, he soon brought me again to such a pitch of lewdness that I was quite ready to spend with him when the grand crisis arrived. Nothing could exceed the pleasure; my internal pressures, he declared, were the most exquisite he had ever experienced. My clitoris, too, he declared was quite unique. You remember how it used to stick out when excited as far as the first thumb joint, and how, when sometimes I played the husband on your belly, you declared that it actually entered between the lips of our cunt, rubbed against your smaller development, and gave you great pleasure, as indeed it gave me. My husband has often examined and sucked it, and admires it beyond measure. At present he did not withdraw, declaring that I held him so tight he did not think he could pull it out if he tried. In fact, it was involuntary on my part, and I could not help clinging to his dear instrument for the life of me.

Oh, how he fondled and embraced me, making me partially turn my body so that he might kiss and tongue me, and then suck my bubbies; his busy finger all the time tickling and frigging my clitoris. I soon felt his cock swelling so deliciously within me, and he shortly recommenced his rapturous pushings in and out. We made a long, long bout of it, and I am sure that I spent twice before joining him at the last moment, when he died away in a shout of joy that I feared must have been heard by the servants in the house, who long before this had been on the move. After this we lay soaking and enjoying it for more than half an hour, when my husband declared he felt as if a wolf was at his stomach, and that he must have some breakfast. He got up and quickly dressed, desiring me to lie still, and he would bring me some breakfast in bed, and that, while it was getting ready, he would order some warm water to bathe myself with. I felt his delicacy, and loved him for it. The water came, I was much refreshed after using it, and got into bed again, but I felt awfully stiff and done up all that and next day.

My darling husband waited on me himself at breakfast, stimulating me to eat freely as a means of restoring my lost strength; which he very soon put to the test again, for he fucked me three times during the day, and each time he gave me greater pleasure than before. He was just as active at night. And the whole three weeks we stayed at Leamington, he never fucked me less than four times a night, declaring that I had become most perfect in the exercise.

We then came here, our old friend, Mrs Roberts, having kindly insisted upon our paying her a long visit. Fred has been called away suddenly and will not return for a month. I am sure you will pity me, as you know my temperament is too hot to keep chaste so long. You remember Charlie Roberts; you would consider him a child, but he is not so. One afternoon Fred followed me into my bedroom, as was usual, and gamahuched and fucked me on the edge of the bed. I was about to leave the room after he was gone, when on opening a closet, in which my dresses were hung, who should I discover but this same Charlie. I was in a fix.

There was no doubt the lad had seen everything. I spoke kindly to him, and he promised secrecy. In order to ensure it, I determined to have his maidenhead. A few days afterwards my husband left me, and the girls with their mamma and the governess went to town with him, leaving Charlie to keep me company. I went upstairs with him to the drawing-room, and seating myself in a low chair, crossed my legs carelessly, exposing them, and letting the garter and part of the bare skin of one thigh be visible. The effect was what I expected. I saw Charlie's eyes fixed on the exposure, he blushed scarlet, and I could distinctly see his cock swell out under his trousers. In a little while I had unbuttoned them, and, oh, Carry, would you imagine it, I found he had the cock of a man. I could scarcely believe my eyes. He is not quite fifteen, and yet he is almost as large as Fred. Here was a godsend, indeed! I drew up my petticoats, and the gallant little fellow instantly fell on his knees, kissed and sucked my cunt. To reward him, I placed him on his back on the couch, and got on the top of him. I took his pego into my mouth, and pressed my cunt against his face, we devoured each other with our luxurious caresses until we both spent copiously. Nothing was lost, we both greedily swallowed all we could get.

At home he is looked upon as still a child, and I had little difficulty in arranging for him to sleep in a little dressing-room adjoining my bed-room, with which there is a door of communication. He was sent early to bed, but when I came I found him still awake, expecting me, and I had the delicious treat of initiating him into the pleasures of fucking. If you ever wish to enjoy *par excellence* this pleasure, get hold of a vigorous boy who has never had a woman. My good fortune threw into my hands a wonderfully provided youth, whose aptitude, as well as size and powers, it would be very difficult to match. I had already given him several lessons in the enrapturing art when we fell asleep, and now I must mention a little episode, which it would not do to omit.

In the morning I was dreaming of Fred, when I became conscious that something was entering me. I was in that half-dreaming state when it is difficult to be quite certain what is happening, but gradually I became aware that although there was no doubt I was being entered, it was not in the usual way. My husband had frequently of late pushed his prick up my bottom-hole, and as he told me that all husbands did so, I could make no objections. I, therefore, at first took it for granted that Fred, finding my naked bottom in his lap, could not resist the temptation of entering it. I, therefore, humoured him, and so moved my bottom as to facilitate his complete entrance, and began to feel myself the excitement it occasioned, but as I became wider awake, I gradually called to mind that Fred had left me, and that Charlie was my bedfellow. The audacity of the young rogue paralysed me but his delicious movements had become too nice for me to think of dislodging him. He insisted that he was quite unconscious of his mistake, and that he believed himself buried in the delicious grotto of the night before. It probably was so, for so perfect an ignoramus as he is, although ever so apt a scholar in Venus's rites, he could hardly have imagined there could be any entrance in the smaller orifice. I let him go on, and with his well hung cock in my bottom, and two or three fingers in my cunt, he fucked and frigged me most deliciously, until we both spent in an agony of pleasure. If, Carry, you have not tried this route I strongly recommend you to do so without delay, but you must be well fucked in the first instance, to stimulate a desire in those parts, and your lover must be up to the art of frigging you at the same time, or you can pass your hand under your belly, and rub your clitoris, which was the plan I adopted with Charlie, until I taught him the art of rubbing the clitoris properly. As there is always more excitement when this is done by a male, it is better to have them when one can, but, *faute de mieux* – one can do it oneself with much additional lascivious satisfaction.

To give you an instance of the precocious aptitude of this dear little fellow, I mounted upon him one morning, keeping my body erect, that we might see the delicious instrument in its action of being engulfed and then withdrawn, a most exciting pose which I recommend you to try, if your husband has not already taught it to you.

At last, overcome by the lascivious movements, I sank on his bosom. He pressed my bottom down with one hand, and with the other embracing the nearer buttock, introduced his middle finger up the rosy orifice of my bottom, and frigged me in unison with our ups and downs of fucking, giving me the most delicious additional sensations.

What do you think of that for a *tyro*? His discretion, too, is extraordinary. The first night after I sent him to his own bed, he overslept himself. I had not thought of that, and had not looked into his little room before descending to breakfast. His sister was sent to call him. He at once excused himself by saying he had had a bad dream; she came down and told us. In a few minutes he followed, and in the most natural way possible, told a tale of fright, declared he had awoke screaming and afterwards had been so frightened that he could not sleep, and turning to me in the most natural way, hoped his scream had not disturbed me. He never came near me, or appeared in any way attracted by me – a discretion worthy of a man of the world. Oh! my dear Carry, I shall make a great deal of this boy. We have had several delicious nights since, and he improves wonderfully. Splendidly as my husband fucks, Charlie already beats him. He is quite as often ready, indeed, oftener, and it is I that hold him back, but there is something still so charmingly infantine in his way of caressing me, and then the lascivious idea he is all my own, and that I initiated him in love's mysteries, adds an inexpressible charm to our lascivious encounters. I feel that I shall almost regret my husband's return, as it will force me to give up this delicious indulgence. Not the slightest shadow of suspicion of our doings is excited in the family, thanks to the very guarded and admirable conduct of Charlie, which is above all praise.

Write to me soon, my dear Carry, and be sure you are as candid as this long, long letter is to you, for the life of me I could not make it shorter. I only hope you will give me one as long, and have as much delicious intelligence for me. I know you too well to suppose that you have not found means as I have done, to try what other men are made of, although you can scarcely have had such wonderful luck as mine. Write then, and write without reserve. Our mutual affection is too sincere to any concealment whatever between two such loving and lewd lascivious friends.

Ever your affectionate friend,

E. BENSON

Such was the long letter my adored mistress wrote at the time to her school companion. It will be seen that their attachment had led to something more than the usual fingerings and caressings of school girls, indeed, had led them on to the lewdest and most lascivious indulgences that two girls could practise in common, and had first excited their passions and given them the delicious power of pleasing coition they were both so perfect in, for, as I before said, about two years after this time, I was the possessor of both and many and many an orgy we three had together, without the shadow of jealousy on any side. It will be seen that Mrs Egerton, in her reply, even looks forward to the delicious indulgence, which in the end was happily effected and long continued. The following is her reply –

*The Hon. Mrs Egerton to Mrs Benson*

How can I ever sufficiently thank my darling Lizzie for her delicious letter. I have devoured its delightful details a dozen times already. I keep it in my bosom, and renew the pleasure of its perusal at every spare moment. *Too long*? Oh! with such a charming power of description, why did you not cover fifty more pages. Never in my life have I enjoyed such an exquisite description of those dear lascivious encounters. How delighted I am at your good fortune in meeting with such a miracle of a boy as that dear Charlie Roberts. Why, he has every quality of a man, united to the charm of extreme youth. What a splendid man he will become, the very perfection of a lover, and already possessing so lewd and lascivious a lubricity. Oh! how I envy you his possession. What luck for him too, to have fallen into the hands of so delicious a teacher as my beloved Lizzie is. Am I not myself her pupil, and were you not my own delicious instructress in all that one of our sex could teach each the other.

You will remember a long-standing engagement entered into, between us made, when we were both so lewd and so longing for the real knowledge of man, and how we pledged ourselves that if either got possession of a lover, we should manage after a while to share him between us. Your description of Charlie Roberts has brought this pledge most vividly to my recollection. I am sure my dear Lizzie will not be angry or jealous when I avow that I long to participate with her in the possession of that darling boy; and if my Lizzie is as of old, I feel certain she will rather indulge and cultivate this propensity than otherwise. Think how easy it will be for us both to arrange the meeting of all three together, because I wish to possess him *in common*, certain that it will increase the lascivious pleasure of coition. No one will suspect us when we drive out, two women with one man. It will naturally be supposed that one fears the other, and so there will be no danger. See, here I am at once anticipating future scenes, but it is all owing to the extremely exciting and lascivious details you have so vividly given me.

I have no such delicious scenes to depict as those you have so delightfully described to me. My honeymoon passed off in a much more commonplace way than yours. Our marriage, which was performed within a day of your own, went off as such events do. My husband was loving, without being very warm. I felt very much as you describe on going to bed the first night, but the discretion or delicacy of my husband, which I could well have pardoned him for dispensing with, left me time not only to get into bed, but kept me waiting there some time. He entered like yours in his dressing-gown, but immediately put out the light and found his way into bed, as best he could. He crept to my side and embraced me tenderly enough, and began to fondle and kiss me, telling me how dearly he loved me, etc., but for some time he avoided any indecent liberties. I suppose he thought it necessary to gain my confidence and quiet any alarm I might be in. He might have saved himself the trouble, for in reality I was longing for and at the same time somewhat dreading an attack on my maiden charms. At last, little by little, he approached the object of delight, and eventually begging me not to be alarmed, he mounted upon me and effected the object of his desires. He did not hurt me much, not nearly as much as I expected, nor so much as you seem to have suffered. I deemed it politic to affect more suffering than he really inflicted. Towards the end I had slight scintillations of pleasure, but not worth mentioning; it is true my husband is not so well-armed as yours and Charlie appear to be, and he is also much colder in his passions; for instance, he did not attempt to fuck me again, although I would have been gratified if he had done so; perhaps he thought he was being considerate towards me, but, merely embracing me in his arms, he talked himself and me to sleep.

In the morning he again fucked me, this time giving me something like pleasure, but I was altogether disappointed with my night's experience. It was not such as you or I, my dear Lizzie, had pictured to ourselves, in our anticipations of the marriage night. My husband since has never exceeded twice a night, but he has become more exciting, and has generally made me spend twice to his once, first exciting my passions by feeling all my private parts, and frigging my clitoris, so that I generally have lubricated the passage by my own discharge before he attempts to make an entrance. I find he likes this, and so far it pleases me, because only one discharge would leave me in a state of excitement unbearable. He has never attempted any of those lewder and more lascivious methods, of which you have had such delicious experience. Altogether, I cannot but say I am disappointed. My husband is loving, and very anxious that I should improve my mind in every way. You know I was rather more proficient than usual at school in Italian. My husband speaks it fluently, and as we mean to spend a winter at Rome, was anxious that I should have further instruction. He asked me if my school teacher was a good one, but I did not encourage that idea. You may remember our former master was a Count Fortunio, so handsome and so enterprising that you and I had both formed the plan of having him, and had already put over some of the preliminaries when, unfortunately, he was caught with that impudent Miss Peace, with whom, doubtless, he had accomplished everything. Of course, he was instantly changed for another, and we saw no more of him, to the sad disappointment of our then libidinous hopes. My husband proposed advertising for a master, when I had the happy instinct to tell him that schoolmistresses generally applied to Rolandi of Berner's Street, for language masters, and that, if he would write or call he would be sure to get every information. That evening, after dinner, as we sat dozing over the fire in the library – very imperfectly lighted – my husband informed me that he had seen Rolandi, who had most strongly recommended a very gentlemanly man, moving in good society, namely, the Count Fortunio. I started in amazement; fortunately, owing to the half-light we were in, my surprise and confusion were unnoticed by my husband. He said that he had been referred to one or two gentlemen of standing as to the Count's character, that he called upon them, and felt satisfied that I could not be in better hands. You may imagine what an effect this information had upon me. All night long I could think of nothing else. What seemed most difficult to me was the hiding from my husband our previous knowledge of each other. I feared the Count would at once recognise me and claim acquaintance, which was what I most wished to avoid; to you, from whom I have no secrets, I may own it immediately occurred to me that this would be an opportunity (for which I had in heart been longing) of obtaining the services of a lover I could trust. How to manage it I knew not, but chance, that favourer of all wrongdoers, stood me in good stead.

My husband had intended to be present to receive the Count. Fortunately, a letter arrived in the morning requiring his instant attendance in the City about the sale of some stock, of which he was trustee. He begged me to see the Count, and arranged as to hours of attendance, etc., the more frequently the better. I felt my embarrassment was at an end; the next thing was to avoid letting the servants, those domestic spies on our conduct, see the first meeting. There was a small room off our drawing-room that had no door but the opening into the drawing-room; this was fitted up as a sort of boudoir writing-room, and my husband had pointed it out as a convenient place for me to take my lessons in.

Here, therefore, I posted myself, and awaited the hour of arrival, to which he was punctual. He was announced and I told the servants to show him in. I sat purposely with my back to the entrance, apparently engaged in writing, as if I did not know he had approached, until I heard the door of the drawing-room shut. I then rose, turned, and smilingly held out my hand. He started with surprise, but immediately and gallantly kissed the hand held out to him.

'I hope you are not disappointed in finding who is going to be your pupil.'

'Oh, no, certainly not; I did not know you under your married name; but I am so happy to renew an acquaintance which at one time had such charming promise.'

'Stop, signor, I am now married, and it is necessary to be very cautious. I do not wish to deny that I am much pleased to renew acquaintance with you, but it must be with great reserve. Sit down by my side, and be reasonable.'

'Reasonable! and by the side of one whom I so much loved, and from whom I had such hope. Oh! dear Mrs Egerton, you are surely not going to treat me as a mere master. You would render me miserable if you did so. How can I help admiring one whom I so fondly loved, and with whom I hoped for such happiness long ago.'

Here, having possession of my hand, his other arm was passed round my waist, and he drew me to his lips, and I must own, I reciprocated the ardent kiss he gave me. You remember how handsome he is, and how soft and loving was the expression of his eyes. Well, my dear, to cut matters short, I was so excited that I hardly observed that he had passed his hand up to my petticoats, until I found he had got it on my mount. My passions being excited, and knowing that my husband could not return, and also that he had given strict orders that I was not to be disturbed in my Italian lessons, I gave way unreservedly to the excitement the Count raised. Before I well knew where I was, he was on his knees in front of the low chair on which I was seated. He had thrown up my petticoats, and I felt a long and extremely hard prick rush up my cunt, and begin the most lively action. In fact, he carried me (not unwillingly I must avow) by storm, and made haste to secure the fortress at once, so that I had a very quick fuck, that did not assuage the fire he had raised within me. He has since apologised for his haste, saying that he wished to secure possession of me before I could think of resistance, so as to ensure more facilities of connection hereafter. We had no lesson in language that day, but another bout of love, in which he did his utmost, and with perfect success, to give me the most delicious enjoyment.

In fact, my dear Lizzie, I may say it was the first fuck that thoroughly realised *my*, or rather our, anticipations of the act. We arranged the line of conduct necessary to be followed so as neither to compromise me or him either. In a short time we had again a delicious fuck. Seated, with out-stretched legs, on a chair, he got me to straddle over him, and sink down on his stiff upstanding prick. I have tried this position kneeling, with my husband on his back; but it does not equal the chair fuck. One has so much better a spring from one's feet than from one's knees, besides, the man is brought more face to face, and there is more facility for mutual embracings; but both ways have their charm. I had repeatedly observed that the Count apparently lost his place, and on recovering it, partially penetrated the smaller orifice, which you so picturesquely describe. I thought it accident, and as it hurt, I always put him back, and joked him on his awkwardness. But after I read your dear delightful letter, I became convinced that he had a wish to penetrate there, without the courage to tell me so.

I must confess to you, that our stolen embraces at home had become too unsatisfactory, and the Count had arranged for a private house to be at our disposal. Of an afternoon I drove out shopping, called at Swan and Edgar's in Regent Street, leaving the carriage at the door, walked upstairs, made some trifling purchase, paid for and left it until I should call in an hour; then descending by another staircase, left by the Piccadilly entrance, and taking a cab, joined my expectant lover, where he was waiting for me. There stripping perfectly naked, we enjoyed each other most lasciviously, and practised every act of lubricity. When satiated with our efforts, a second cab conducted me to St James's passage, in Jermyn Street, from whence I gained on foot Swan and Edgar's in Piccadilly, received my parcel, and rejoined my carriage. Thus no suspicions were excited, either in the household or otherwise.

We have met thrice since your dear delicious letter fired my imagination, and I have seized the occasion to taste the sweets of the neighbouring altar to Venus's legitimate one. After the Count had fucked me twice I turned my back as if wishing it in a way we often enjoyed it, but took care to place my bottom in such a position that the smaller orifice was nearest to his standing prick. Whether he saw my drift I know not, but finding with his finger how conveniently it lay, he plunged boldly forward, and half sheathed himself at the first push. I started with the sudden pain, and should have disengaged myself at once, notwithstanding that I purposely placed myself to receive his prick in my bottom-hole, but with his arms round my waist I was perfectly powerless, and another thrust sent him up to the hilt, but really hurting me most sensitively; I begged him to desist and withdraw, but he said: 'I will remain quite quiet for a time, and you will see that your pain will diminish, and then you will like it.'

I could not help myself, and sure enough he was right. Shortly I felt no pain; slipping one hand down, he began to frig my clitoris, and in a little time, finding by the involuntary movements of my loins that my passions were excited, he began to move very slightly and slowly. I soon found a strange excitement seize me, which increased to such a degree that I almost fainted, when my nature gave down its divinest essence. We have since repeated the new experience, but I quite agree with you in thinking that we must be well fucked first.

The Count is a master of his weapon, which, neither quite so long as you describe your husband's nor nearly so thick at the point, is very much so at the root, and as stiff and hard as iron. I assure you, the wild excess of passion he drives me into is indescribable. You shall experience the delight of his fucking, for, with you and me, there must be no difficulty, diversion, nor jealousy. Nay, I shall try to seduce your husband, with a view to cover our delinquencies. I would offer you mine, but, truly, he is not worth having to a woman who can find better, as my dear Lizzie so charmingly does. We have managed matters so prudently that my husband has taken a great fancy to the Count, and he dines frequently at our house.

We have often talked of you. I told him of your marriage, and of a probability of your eventually settling in London. I marked the sparkle of his eyes at the news, but was silent as to your letter and adventures. It is better we should manage the affair between us when you are here.

So you see, after all, I have not come off so badly, although, I must say, tamely in comparison with the delicious adventures of my dear and charming Lizzie. I think, when we meet, we shall be able to get up parties of the most delightful kind. I even hope we may induce the Count to join you and Charlie in a *partie carrée*; what fun and pleasure we should have, and then the delight of exchanging lovers at each bout. Oh! the very idea has set me on fire; fortunately, I am expecting my lover at every moment. I will close my letter with this lascivious picture, and in hopes of someday realising it with my loved Lizzie,

Whose most affectionate and attached friend,

I shall ever remain,

CARRY EGERTON

Such were these two charming letters, and I may immediately mention now that the lascivious picture dear Carry drew of a *partie carrée* – we four the actors – was afterwards realised to the utmost extent of every salacious enjoyment that the most experienced lubricity could suggest.

The Count and I often sandwiched them between us, which they declared to be the *ne plus ultra* of pleasure, while the upper operator gamahuched the unoccupied quim. Nay, these giddy delicious creatures were not satisfied until they had induced us to alternate the joys of coition with each other; but that was rarely the case. These enchanting women were so exquisitely seductive that, while we had them at our disposal, we sought no other source of delight. But I am digressing, and talking of events that occurred long after the period which I am more particularly describing.

The three weeks' absence of Mr Benson terminated, alas, far too soon; in fact, time flew so quick that it hardly appeared three days when a letter arrived announcing his return for the next day. My heart was ready to burst, but I managed to make no show or mention when Mrs B. told the news at breakfast. Mrs B. observed that I turned pale, but no one else remarked anything. We contrived to meet for a short time in the middle of the day, and she embraced me tenderly, with tears in her eyes, and looking so loving that my passions became overexcited, and hers too. Notwithstanding, the imprudence of the risk, we there and then had a most delightful and salacious fuck; and at night this charming woman allowed me full liberty to do anything I liked; and as often as nature would support us we revelled in a sea of lubricity. How often I cannot say, although my loved mistress declared that I had spent ten times. I am certain she did oftener than that, for neither closed an eye, nor ceased from the most loving embraces. She exerted all the wonderful powers of seduction for which she was so distinguished. Never mortal man could have passed a more intoxicating night of pleasure. We heard movements in the house before we parted with mutual tears coursing down our cheeks.

It was with difficulty I tore myself from her; indeed, I could not have done so if she had not herself risen, and tenderly embracing me, told me to have courage and hope, for, somehow or other, we should manage an occasional interview. Particularly cautioning me to be perfectly on my guard when her husband came, she said it would be better if I kept out of the way until after the first interview was over, as it might be too much for me to see him embrace her. I did as she desired. No one noticed me in the confusion of his arrival.

Mamma had insisted upon my returning to my bed in her room, as she was sure Mr Benson would require the dressing-room. Mrs B., from policy, objected, saying that there was no occasion, that I had been so quiet she had never once been concious of my being there, etc., but mamma had her own way, and I really believe very much to the satisfaction of Mrs B. herself; for I doubt, if Mr B. had been aware of my close proximity, whether he would altogether have liked it. Nevertheless, he so completely treated me as little more than a child that I am quite sure he had no suspicion of my having occupied his place so continuously during his absence.

Mr and Mrs B. retired shortly after his arrival, doubtless to plunge into all the joys of venery after his long absence, and his wife's supposed privation of them. The idea of that being the case did not so much annoy me as I expected; on the contrary, imagination portrayed them in all the agonies of delight, and actually excited me extremely. All at once, the idea struck me that I might be purposely hid in the closet, behold all their delicious encounters, and when he had left his wife to put herself to rights, and the key was turned upon him, I might then in my turn, fly into my enchanting mistress's arms, and revel in all the joys her well moistened and juicy cunt could give. I determined to propose this to dear Mrs Benson the first moment I could get her apart from all observation.

I was a little *distrait* in the schoolroom that day, but an appeal from Miss Evelyn recalled me to my senses. She asked me what I could be thinking of; I held down my head and blushed. Already an adept in dissimulation, I faltered out that it was of herself and of her endearing caresses the day before, which had made me feel so queer all over. In fact, the previous day she had hugged me rather close to her, and kissed me more lovingly than usual, which really had, at the time, inflamed my desires, and given me great hope of matters coming to a more satisfactory termination with her. She patted my cheek, and kissed me again, saying I was a naughty boy to have any such thoughts, and I must not indulge in them, or she would not love me any more. But there was a sparkle in her eye, and a flush on her cheek, which showed me she was anything but displeased.

At our usual break-up at four o'clock, I went to the parlour to see if, by chance, I could get a secret word with Mrs B., but found that she and her husband had again retired. I knew what that meant; it set me too on fire, and I flew to the garden where my sisters had gone to play. I gave Mary a hint, which she readily understood, and proposed a game of hide and seek. To prevent Eliza interrupting us, I took up a stone, which I furtively dropped again, and proposed that Eliza should guess first, in which hand I had got it, and if she guessed wrong she was to be the seeker. Of course, she guessed wrong. So we bound up her eyes, and she was to stand behind a tree and count one hundred before she attempted to look for or seek us. We made a detour, and as fast as we could run reached the summerhouse, which, as all the ladies were in the house occupied, I knew to be untenanted. We entered and locked the door, in an instant I had Mary down on her back on the sofa, my head between her thighs, and my tongue in her cunt, and then on her clitoris. She was as eager for it as myself. A week had passed since the happy day of giving up her maidenhead to me. She had thoroughly got over all the pains and inconveniences of that day, and was as ready for a renewal of what could only be joys now as I was. She spent in my mouth almost as soon as I began to gamahuche her clitoris. Waiting an instant to lick up and swallow the soft and delicious young discharge, I rose, pulled out my bursting prick, and engulfed it in her well-moistened sheath with one rapturous shove up to the hilt, positively taking away her breath by the energy of the attack. I was almost as rapid in coming to a conclusion as she had been. Nevertheless, she died away a second time, the moment she felt the warm gush of my raging discharge. We lay some minutes rapt in the lascivious lap of lubricity. But in our young and unbroken energies, nature soon reasserted her power. I must give my sister the palm. It was the internal pressures of the inner folds of her deliciously tight cunt that first awakened my vigour. Somewhat more slowly we began another love encounter, which speedily became much more rapid and energetic, ending as usual in an ecstasy of delight, and closing with actual cries of intense pleasure.

It was well we had completed our second course, for we heard the footsteps of Eliza, who, after in vain searching for us near to where we had left her, had at last sought us in the summerhouse. I had just time to arrange my trousers and unlock the door when she arrived and burst in upon us. She said it was unfair to go so far away, but we only laughed, and proposed that Mary should now seek us. We were standing outside below the mound, tying on the handkerchief, when Miss Evelyn was seen approaching. She came up and noticed the flush still on Mary's cheeks, but we at once told her that we had been playing at hide and seek, and had had a good run, and that it was now Mary's turn to be the seeker. However, Miss Evelyn said she thought we had had enough exercise for the time, and that it would be better to walk gently about to get cool, as it only wanted a few minutes of the hour for renewing our lessons, so we all demurely returned to the house. A reflection struck me that it would be necessary to initiate my sister Eliza in our secrets, and although she might be too young for the complete insertion of my increasingly large cock, I might gamahuche her while fucking Mary, and give her intense pleasure. In this way we could retire without difficulty to spots where we should be quite in safety, and even when such was not the case, we could employ Eliza as a watch, to give us early notice of anyone approaching. It will be seen that this idea was afterwards most successfully carried out to the immense increase of my pleasure.

It was a lovely summer evening. After dinner Mr B., who, doubtless, had no longer any amorous longing, after having twice retired during the day, challenged Miss Evelyn to a game at chess, of which she was a great proficient. Mamma, Mrs B., and the two girls stepped out into the flower garden, to enjoy the beauty of the evening. Fortunately mamma fancied she felt chilly, and shortly went back again, taking the two girls with her, and setting Mary down to the piano. I seized the happy moment, and drew Mrs B. to a seat, far removed beyond the hearing of any listeners but in sight of the windows. There I unfolded to her the plan I had proposed to myself; she smiled at my precocious ingenuity, but added it would not be safe to leave the closet door open, even partially, as by chance Mr B. might open it, and that would never do; but she might lock me in – or rather I might do so from the inside.

'Ahh! but then I want to see it all – it is so exciting to see Mr B. working into that divine body of yours.'

She laughed heartily at my remark, and said I was a lewd lascivious young rascal – adding: 'But are you not jealous to see another in possession of me?'

I admitted that that was my first impression, but on thinking over it, I had become convinced I should like her and enjoy her all the more lasciviously if I were a witness to their love contests, but I must be able to see them.

'Well! can you not bore a couple of holes an inch and a half apart, below the middle panel and cut a narrow slit from hole to hole? I will take care to place myself in a proper position, and do my best to gratify your premature lubricity. My darling boy, you progress wonderfully, and make me proud of my pupil.'

Seeing she took it thus kindly, I said: 'Do tell me, my beloved mistress, how often he has fucked you today?'

'Will it please you really, my dear Charlie, to know that?'

'Oh! yes, so much.'

'Well, then, six times in the morning, and four before dinner. He was bursting with desire, and could not hold. He spent twice before giving me time to come once, but then you know, my dear Charlie, how actively you had been employing your time all the previous night, you sad rogue that you are.'

'Did you enjoy it much, my dear Mrs B.?'

'Why, if I must tell you, you little curiosity box, I did; you know how powerfully my husband is hung, and loving him as I do, it is impossible to undergo his powerful and lascivious embraces without feeling all one's libidinous passions stirred up within me, but even while in his possession, my dear boy, I thought of your young charms, and the fierce delights we had enjoyed together last night. My husband little imagined it was of you, not him, that I was thinking and stimulating myself to wild upheavings of voluptuous movements, while he was revelling in all the lubricity of his own passions, and fucking me to my heart's content.'

'Oh! how delicious! my angelic mistress,' I cried, 'the pleasure of your vivid description almost makes me faint with desire – oh! that I could possess you at once.'

'You must not think of that, my dear darling boy, we must manage it tomorrow; I shall go into the house at once, and occupy your mother's attention; do you get a gimlet and chisel, slip up at once to my bedroom, and prepare a peephole for tomorrow; be careful to put it low down, below the projection of the middle panel of the door in which the lock is placed, and take care to remove the pieces of wood you take out. I shall put the key inside of the door. Your sisters always take two hours at the piano after your midday meal, our luncheon is served at the same time. Mr B. is sure to require my attendance in my room after that, but I shall detain him by some excuse till I observe that you have disappeared, and after giving you sufficient time, we shall follow, and you shall have the extraordinary satisfaction you require; but above all remember – not a movement to betray yourself until my husband leaves and I have locked the door behind him.' So saying, she pressed her lovely hand on my stiffly excited member, rose and joined mamma. I lost no time in following her advice, and happily executed all I wanted, and returned unconcernedly to the drawing-room, without my absence having occasioned any remark. Next day I got safely to my hiding-room, and had comfortably stowed myself away in such a position that the opening I had made was on a level with my eyes, before they arrived. She, dear creature, anticipating my vista, had merely slipped on a dress, without a corset, and told her husband that he was so insatiate that she was obliged to be ready at a moment's notice to satisfy his inordinate passion, so she had only to take off her gown to be at her ease. 'Most admirable, my darling wife, but drop off everything, and let me contemplate, at my ease, all the beauties of your exquisite body.'

No sooner said than done, and my lovely mistress stood in all the glory of her magnificent and beautiful naked form. He kissed and fondled her from head to foot, laid her on the bed and gamahuched her till she squealed again with pleasure. Then pulling out his magnificent prick, he plunged it into her delicious cunt at a single bound, evidently giving her the most exquisite delight, as was evidenced by the instantaneous clasping of him with her arms and legs, and the rapid wriggling of her backside. They soon ran a first course, but Mr B. remained engulfed in the closely fitting sheath of his salacious wife. She evidently exerted herself more than usual both for her own pleasure as well as to give satisfaction to me, for once when she turned her head in my direction I caught her eyes, and she smiled, giving a still more vigorous heave than usual, and showing me all her cunt at full stretch with the noble prick in it. I was ready to burst. At last their bout was over for the present; Mr B. withdrew his prick, all slimy from its sheath, pendant, but still full of size.

Most extraordinary! I would have given a good deal to have dared to rush out, put it in my mouth and suck it dry, I can hardly describe how strongly this desire took possession of me. It was the first promptings of a passion I have since often indulged in, where I have met with companions with whom I could join in orgies of both sexes. Mrs B. professed to be dead beaten by the constant and frequent renewals of these interviews in addition to night work and lay perfectly still, while he performed his ablutions and readjusted his habiliments.

'Fasten the door after me,' said he, as he ardently pressed her form in his arms and kissed her. She had continued stretched on the bed, exactly facing me, with legs widely extended, so as to show me the whole of her lovely cunt, which I could see still panted under its late excitement. My charming mistress told me it was palpitating not for what had passed, but for what it was waiting for. She rose at last and closed the door, turning the key upon her husband. She then approached the bidet to purify herself, but I bounded from the closet, seized her in my arms, dashed her back on the bed and immediately glued my lips to her glowing and foaming cunt, with all the froth and spending of her husband oozing out. I greedily devoured it, and raised her to such a frenzy of lewdness that she dragged me up and cried, frantically – 'For God's sake, fuck me – fuck me!'

Of course my cock was bursting to do so; with one shove he was sheathed to the cods; my loved mistress spent with that alone, so highly was she excited, not only by the preparations, but as she herself acknowledged to me, by the idea of the instantaneous infidelity to her husband, at the moment after he had just fucked her – such is the wild imagination of women when they give way to every libidinous thought. It would have been exactly the same if some equally fortunate lover had been awaiting my retiring from the field. The idea of success in deception is a passion with them, and they would almost sacrifice anything to obtain it. Before I could arrive at the grand crisis, she was again ready, and we died away in an agony of blissful lubricity – she held me, as usual, so tight that I never thought of withdrawing from the folds of her delicious cunt, but lay still enjoying the never-ceasing compressions of its velvety folds, which sometimes really had almost the force of a vice. I was rapidly ready for a second bout, which, like the first, ended in ecstatic joys, beyond the power of description. My charming mistress thought I ought now to desist, but pleading my forty hours' fast (for, of course, she knew nothing of my fucking Mary), I begged her to allow me to run one more course.

'Then, my darling Charlie, you must let me turn on my side, for I am so heated with your weight and my husband's that I must have some relief, but there is no occasion for you to withdraw, leave me to manage it.'

With an art quite her own, she accomplished her object, her splendid buttocks' pressing before my eyes against my belly fired me immediately. My cock swelled and stood firm as ever. Then passing an arm round her body, I used my fingers on her excited and stiffly projecting clitoris. We had a much longer and more voluptuous fuck than before; nothing could exceed the delicious movements of my divine mistress; she twisted her body so that I could suck one of her bubbies, while I fucked and frigged her; she spent with such a scream of delight that I am sure she must have been heard in the house, had it not been for the inner baize door to the room. She continued throbbing so deliciously on my prick that I began to flatter myself I should obtain a fourth favour, but she suddenly bolted out of my arms and out of bed. Turning round, and taking my whole prick into her mouth, and giving it a voluptuous suck, she said: 'No, my loved boy, we must be prudent if we mean to have a repetition of these most exquisite interviews. You have given me most ecstatic pleasure, and by moderation, and running no risk in too long indulgence of our passions, we may safely manage to enjoy similar interviews every day. Get into the dressing-room, remain there until I leave my room and pass your door. After I have seen that no one is near, I will cough twice, wait a minute longer, then quietly leave and descend by the back stairs.'

All was happily effected, and for the week longer they remained with us, I found means to repeat the charming lesson every day, without raising suspicion in anyone's mind.

At last this admirable woman departed. It was with difficulty I could bear the scene, but I gulped down my feelings as best I could. She had become a universal favourite, and all regretted her leaving, so that my distress was not noticed in the general regret. It was more than two years before fortune favoured me in again meeting with this charming woman. And then we saw very much of each other, both alone and with other congenial spirits, of which, perhaps, I may hereafter write a detail; but at present I have got events to relate that followed fast on her departure.

I have said that Miss Evelyn had been gradually growing more familiar in her manner of partially caressing me. She drew me closer to her, almost invariably placing her arm round my waist, frequently kissing and pressing me against her firm and well-formed bosom. This had frequently an evident effect on my lower person, even while I was kept less excitable by the constant relief my passions were obtaining in the arms of my adored Mrs B. Now I no longer had that vent, for the little relief I could get at rare intervals from my sister Mary was as nothing, after the constant exercise I had been provided with for a whole month. Ever since I had practised that little deception on Miss Evelyn by attributing to her embraces the evident distraction I was in on the day of Mr Benson's return, she had increased her pressures of my person, and could not but feel my stiff prick throbbing against her thigh, while she closely pressed my body against it with her arm. I often noted the increased sparkle of her eyes and changes of colour on her face when she kissed me, and I put up my hand and caressed her cheek. At times she would push me suddenly away, and beg me to resume my seat; frequently she would quit the room in an agitated manner, till this led me to suppose that an internal conflict was going on, and that passion urged one course, reason another. Remembering the sage advice given to me by my loved and beautiful mistress, Mrs B., I resolved to play the part of an innocent ignoramus, and let her own passions develop and produce the result I so longed for. I doubt if I could have held out but for the relief I found in dear Mary's embraces, who, each time we could manage to meet, became more and more attractive, and more capable of giving and receiving pleasure. We had some difficulty in keeping Eliza blind to our doings. At last Mary agreed to initiate her into gamahuching, and to tell her I did so to her when we shut ourselves up together, and that if she would keep the secret, I would do the same to her; but that it was necessary that one should keep watch while the other amused herself with me, for fear Miss Evelyn should chance to come. Mary proceeded to gamahuche her, which delighted Eliza beyond measure; indeed, although a year and a half younger, she speedily showed a development of passion superior to Mary. At first I only gamahuched her, letting her play with my prick as I did so, but not attempting to instruct her in the art of insertion into her charming little quim, which already showed symptoms of a hairy growth on her well-formed and very prominent mount. When I had done enough in this way, Mary, who had previously been fucked by me, returned, and Eliza took up the watch, while I appeased in Mary's deliciously tight cunt the thirst that gamahuching Eliza had raised.

It was thus I could more coolly await the gradual approximation that Miss Evelyn's evident passion for me was bringing about. That she struggled against it was evident, but passion was gaining the advantage, as was shown by her nervous tremblings and sudden clutches, drawing me up to her parched lips, and sometimes pushing me away with a shudder that shook her frame and paled her lovely checks. I fancied that nature had been too much for her on these occasions, and that in reality the sudden clutching was the approach of love's crisis, and that when she shuddered and suddenly repulsed me, she was discharging. It was evident this could not continue. At last the happy day for which I so longed arrived. Mamma was going to go to the town, and taking my two sisters with her, to get something or other for them. She invited Miss Evelyn to accompany her, but the latter declined, on the excuse of an alleged headache. In truth, the violent nature of the conflict going on between her passions and her prudence had visibly affected her health; she had become pale and anxious-looking, and my mother was somewhat uneasy about her. She told her not to occupy herself too much with my lessons that day, and only give me work for an hour in the morning and an hour in the afternoon, and begged her to take a quiet stroll in the garden, and rest as much as possible.

On leaving us, she cautioned me to be as gentle and obedient as possible, as Miss Evelyn was poorly and out of spirits. Mamma and the girls departed. Miss Evelyn, almost as pale as death, and quite visibly trembling, falteringly begged me to go to our schoolroom and study the lesson she had given me the previous evening, saying she would join me shortly. I went, but no lesson could I do that day. The evident agitation and apparent illness of Miss Evelyn distressed if not alarmed me; I was still too inexperienced in her mind. It was a phase of woman's nature which I had as yet no knowledge of. I had merely a vague kind of idea that it all tended to the ultimate gratification of my libidinous hopes, and I only held off to a certain extent in obedience to the counsel my loved Mrs Benson had so wisely impressed upon me, and was waiting in lively hopes of the result I so ardently wished for.

At last Miss Evelyn joined me, her eyes were swollen and red as if she had been weeping; my own filled with tears when I saw her, and I approached, hesitatingly, and said: 'Oh, my dear governess, I am so grieved to see you look so poorly. Oh, do nothing today, and I promise to work twice as hard tomorrow.'

At the moment I really felt quite distressed at the sad expression of her features. For an instant she smiled languidly, then, by some compulsion of feeling, she seized me in both arms and drawing me to her bosom, covered me with kisses; her eyes became almost perfectly brilliant.

'Oh, you dear, dear, darling boy, I love you beyond expression. Kiss, oh, kiss me! my darling! and comfort me, because I love you all too well.'

Then, again, there was a change, she seemed to fear she had said too much, and turned away her head and tears started to her eyes, but her arms did not relax the embrace in which she held me. I was deeply moved at her evident agitation. I thought she was really ill, and suffering greatly; so I threw my arms round her neck, kissing her tenderly, and weeping myself, tried to comfort her in my inexperienced way, sobbing out: 'Oh, dear, dear Miss Evelyn, do be comforted, I so dearly love you that it makes my heart bleed to see you so unhappy. Oh, let me see you smile, and do try not to cry so. Why are you so unhappy and low spirited? Oh, that I could do anything to make you happy?' And redoubling my endearments, she again turned her lovely face to me. Again there was the unnatural fire in her eyes, and a hectic glow flushed her cheek.

'You darling angel of a boy; it is *you* that makes me so unhappy.'

I started back in surprise.

'*I* make *you* unhappy! Oh! Miss Evelyn, how can that be, when I adore the very ground you stand on, and love (*sobbing*) – love (*sob*) – love you more than anything in the world.'

She seized my head in her two hands, glued her lips to mine, gave me a long, long kiss of love; then, pressing me to her bosom: 'Oh, say that again, my loved, my darling boy; it is the love I feel for you that is breaking my heart, but I can resist it no longer. Will my Charlie love his Evelyn always as he does now?'

'Oh, how could I do otherwise? I have worshipped you from the first moment of your arrival, and have had no other idea. What can I do to prove it – try, oh, try me. I have never breathed a syllable of my love for you, even to yourself, let alone other people.'

Her eyes, sparkling with passion, were searching the depths of mine, as if to fathom my thoughts. I, too, began to feel my amorous passions excited by her warm embraces and kisses. She held me tight to her body, and could not help feeling the hard substance that jutted out against her.

'I believe you, my Charlie, and will trust you with my life – with more, with my honour! I can no longer resist my fate. But, oh! Charlie, love me always, for I run a fearful risk in loving you as I do.'

She again drew me to her lips, my hands clasped her neck in a close embrace. Her hands wandered – pressed upon my throbbing prick. With trembling and hasty fingers she unbuttoned, or rather tore open, my trousers, and her soft fingers clasped my naked instrument.

'Oh, I shall die, dear Miss Evelyn; what must I do to make you happy?'

My apparent ignorance could not but please her. She sank back on the long low chair on which she was seated, apparently accidentally drawing up her petticoats with her hand in falling back. I threw myself on my knees, and pushing her petticoats further up disclosed the rich, dark, curly beauty of her mount. She covered her burning face with her hand, while, pressing my head forward, I began pressing her beauteous cunt, sucking it without daring to lick her clitoris. She tried to push me away – 'No! no! I must not.'

But I suppose my proceedings fired her passions still more, for she was quite moist and juicy, and I have no doubt had already had one discharge while embracing me so warmly. She suddenly said: 'Come then, my loved boy, and I will be all in all to you.'

Drawing me up – nothing loath – I was soon extended on her belly, with my stiff-standing cock pressing against her cunt. I had still the prudence not to show any knowledge of the act. I sighed deeply: 'Oh! my loved Miss Evelyn, do help me, I know not what to do.'

Her hand glided down between us, she guided my glowing instrument between the longing lips of her delicious cunt. I pushed, and buried the head and two inches of its body at the first thrust. The second brought it against an unexpected obstacle, for it never had struck me that Miss Evelyn was a virgin. I pushed hard at it.

'Oh, Charlie, love, be gentle, you are hurting me very much.'

Knowing that the best way would be to excite her by short shoves, without at first trying to go further, I did so, and she began to feel all the raging desires that so formidable a prick as mine must excite, when moving between the soft velvety folds of her tight and juicy quim. I held myself in, and continued my proceedings until the convulsive movements of her loins, and the increased pressure of the folds of her cunt, showed me that the crisis was approaching, and she was about to spend. She hugged me close in her arms, and at the moment of spending involuntarily heaved up her bottom. This was the very moment I was with difficulty waiting for. I retired a little and plunged forward with irresistible force. I burst my way through every barrier, up to the very roots of my prick. The attack was as painful as unexpected. Miss Evelyn gave a shriek of agony and swooned away. I at once improved the opportunity, and thrusting in and out with the utmost vigour, broke down every obstacle, and enlarged the opening by side movements as much as possible, while she was insensible to the pain. I then died away myself in an agony of delight. I lay soaking within the delicious sheath until her convulsive shudders and short sobs showed that my now fully deflowered mistress was recovering her senses. The thought of the unexpected victory I had won had already begun to make my cock stand again, although it was still comparatively soft. I could feel an involuntary pressure on it, as she came to a full consciousness of our position. She threw her arms round my neck, gave me a most impassioned kiss, and then sobbed and cried as if her heart would break.

It is a curious idiosyncrasy of my nature to be most libidinously excited by a woman's tears, and although I really suffered to see her in such grief, it stiffened my prick to its utmost dimensions. I tried to comfort her with words, but she sobbed, sobbed on. I suddenly thought that a renewal of action might bring about a revulsion of feeling, and began vigorous movements. She sighed deeply, but I could tell by the nervous twitchings of her loins that her passions were being excited. They soon decided the contest. She threw her arms round my waist, and pressed me to her, devouring my mouth with her kisses. Nature prompted her movements, and in a very few minutes we both poured down a plenteous offering on Venus's altar. She shook and trembled as she felt the warm gush within her, and squeezed me with all her might to her bosom. We lay in a trance for some ten minutes, my charming governess fainting with love, and giving my delighted prick the most luscious pressure, which speedily fired him to new efforts. Miss Evelyn herself was most amorously excited, and we again dashed on love's delicious path – to end, as usual, in the death-like swoon of satiated passion. When we came to our senses, my loved mistress, embracing me tenderly, and throwing her eyes up to heaven, said: 'Oh, my dear darling boy, you made me suffer horribly at first, but I have been in heaven since. Oh, how I love and adore you. But we must rise, my Charlie, we may be discovered. We have, in fact, run great risk, as the door has not been fastened.'

I rose, and withdrew my prick from her reeking quim, which seemed by its close pressure to let me go with regret. I found it was all bloody.

'Stop, Charles, let me wipe it with my handkerchief, lest it stain your shirt.'

She did so, and folding it up and placing it in her bosom, said: 'I shall keep this precious relic as a memorial of the sacrifice I have made to you, my loved boy. Ah! Charlie, you cannot yet understand the value of that sacrifice and the risk of ruin I have run for your sake. I love you as I never loved anyone before, or can ever love again. My honour and happiness are now in your hands, and it is on your discretion they rest. Be careful never to exhibit any liberty of conduct towards me or to mention to anyone what has occurred.'

It may readily be imagined I gave her every assurance on that head, and told her I loved her too dearly, and was too grateful for the ecstatic happiness she had taught me how to enjoy, for any chance of betrayal to take place through my indiscretion. She embraced me tenderly, told me to go straight to the garden, that she must seek some repose after all that had happened, and we should meet again at midday meal.

I did as desired, full of sweet thoughts at the exquisite delights she had afforded me, and already longing for the afternoon school hour to renew the enrapturing union of our souls and bodies. Miss Evelyn did not come down to her luncheon, but had something sent up to her room. However, she joined me in the schoolroom at two o'clock, as usual. She was very pale, but embraced me tenderly, and was very endearing. Of course, I immediately became excited, and very enterprising, but she gently repulsed me, and requested that I would leave her quiet that day, as she felt not only exhausted, but in pain, and would be all the better for perfect repose. I begged hard to be allowed some slight favours, if not all, but she was inexorable. Finding that I could neither do any lessons nor be quiet, she said: 'Then we must go into the garden, I think the fresh air and a gentle walk will do me good.'

It instantly occurred to me that if I could draw her away to the summer-house, I should have a better chance of succeeding in again enjoying her delicious embraces. Accordingly, when she went up to her room to put on her bonnet and shawl, I possessed myself of the key, to be prepared for any chance of success.

We walked about the flower garden for a time, Miss Evelyn taking my arm, and most lovingly conversing with me. She walked somewhat stiffly. We sat down for a rest, shortly she felt the heat of the sun too great, so I proposed a walk in the shaded shrubbery. I kept prattling on, so as not to let her see how far I was leading her away, she appeared surprised that we had got so far, when we came in sight of the summerhouse.

'Oh! Charlie, my dear, I am afraid it will fatigue me too much to walk all the way back without rest and we have not the key.'

'Sometimes it is left in the door, I will run and see.' Off I bounded, slipped the key in the lock, and ran back to say it was there, she followed me in, and sank on the long backless sofa, which had already served me so often. I begged her to extend herself at length. I placed pillows for her head, and drew a chair for myself near her. She did not appear to have any suspicion of any act on my part, but lay down on her side. She took my hand in hers, and we began a conversation, very interesting, in as much as it was how we should regulate our conduct, so as not to raise any suspicion of our amorous connection, and also of how we should manage to meet from time to time.

'You, dear boy,' she said, 'I cannot now live without the comfort of your embraces, but you must remember, in my dependent position, discovery would be my ruin. I rely on your silence and discretion, and if I am as dear to you as you, my adored Charlie, are to me, I may safely trust to you.' I threw my arms round her neck, and told her I loved her all too dearly, and longed too much to return to her endearing and delicious embraces, for her to have any fear of my committing either her or myself. She fondly embraced and kissed me. I became fired with passion. My hand wandered, her position only enabled her to make a feeble resistance, I reached her beauteously covered mount, she murmured supplications to be left alone, and held her thighs close together. She was not aware of my knowledge of the parts, so inserting my finger into the upper part of the lips, I reached her clitoris, and began rubbing in and out, purposely, in an awkward way, but taking care to hit the right point.

'Charlie, my Charlie, you must not do that – I – I cannot bear it.'

At the same time she threw her arm round my neck and drew me to her lips, which glued themselves to mine. I felt her thighs yield and open. I immediately improved the occasion, and began frigging her with my middle finger up her quim. Her passions became inflamed.

'Come then, my darling boy, to my arms, I cannot resist you longer.'

In an instant I was unbuttoned and had my trousers down, and was between her legs almost before she had concluded her sentence. The excitement of my caresses had moistened her juicy cunt, and the head of my prick entered without any difficulty. In my ardour I was about to rush on with a vigorous shove, when she implored me to be more gentle, as she still smarted from our morning encounter. Moderating my movements, and gently insinuating my stiff instrument, I gradually made my way up to its utmost limits, and hardly occasioned even a grimace of pain. Here I stopped, leaving it sheathed up to the root, and making it throb from instant to instant. Then seeking my loved Miss Evelyn's mouth, our lips and tongues met. Her arms round my waist became tighter in their embrace. The delicious folds of her luscious juicy quim began to throb and press on my excited member. Allowing her to become thoroughly excited, I waited until she actually quite unexpectedly yielded down her nature, and spent profusely, to the exquisite pleasure of my saturated organ. I still held all off, to give her time after the delight of that spend, which was probably the first of unalloyed ecstatic pleasure she enjoyed; for as I was an inactive participator, there was nothing to cause any action on the still-raw edges of her broken maidenhead. Her internal pressures were most exquisite. Our embraces with tongues and lips were like the billing and cooing of doves, and very rapidly brought her again to a raging point of desire. I then began with slow and gentle movements, drawing my prick slowly nearly all the way out, and then as slowly driving it up to the hilt. Her previous very copious discharge had so oiled the delicious folds of her cunt, that no pain was felt, only the intense pleasure. At last it became overpowering; her arms were thrown round my waist, and her legs were involuntary cast over my hips. Nature prompted her to the most delicious movements of her bottom; she met my forward thrusts, and responded to them in the most libidinous manner.

'Go on, go on, dear Charlie – faster! – faster!'

I wanted no spur. Fast and furious grew our movements, until at last, with a mutual cry of delight, we sank in each other's arms in the blissful ecstasy of the most complete enjoyment. It was several minutes before we regained our senses, and both our organs of generation were pulsating, the one within the other, in all the luxury of satiated passion. With her beauteous legs still thrown over mine, she moved her arms to my neck, kissed me voluptuously, and mingled the sweetest accents of gratification with the most endearing caresses and flatteries. I lay, as it were, in the Paphian bower of bliss, in a state of exquisite sensations quite impossible to describe. It seemed even a greater pleasure than the more active state of delight we had been to. I could have lain so for hours, but for that excitable prick of mine, whose sensibilities were far too rapidly set in motion by the luscious pressures of that most delightful cunt in which it lay engulfed. It had gradually resumed its pristine firmness, and was now at full stand, throbbing impatiently for further combats. I began to move. Miss Evelyn said: 'Oh, my Charlie, you must cease, my dear boy; we must not only be prudent, but consider your youth and health. Do, oh! do! my dear boy. Oh! – pray cease.'

Her words were cut short by the increasing passion that the vigorous movements of my prick occasioned to her whole system. She could resist no longer, but with arms and legs closely embracing me, and devouring me with kisses, she threw herself into the fight, and with body and soul so seconded me that we died away in screams of delight, and sank quite insensible in each other's arms.

It was many minutes before we recovered speech. I still lay entirely embedded in her most exquisite cunt, and would have liked to have continued in her delicious embrace. But Miss Evelyn so imploringly beseeched me to cease for this time, and pointed out how necessary prudency was, if we ever wished to meet again, that I felt compelled to raise myself from her body. But, in doing so, I slid off downwards, and before she could prevent me, I glued my lips to the open pouters below me, and greedily devoured all her delicious discharge, and did not desist until I had so licked her clitoris as to make her spend most copiously again. At first she had tried to resist, saying: 'Charlie, what on earth are you at? You must not, my dear boy, it is dreadful.'

But, as I roused her passions, her hand, instead of trying to draw away my head, held it firm and pushed it well against her throbbing and delicious quim, her thighs closed against the sides of my head, and she almost swooned away with the ecstasy of her discharge. I greedily swallowed it and rising completely, took her in my arms, and placing her on her bottom, sweetly kissed her.

'Oh, what a charming creature you are, my beloved Miss Evelyn, I adore you from the sole of your feet to the crown of your head.'

'But you, my beloved Charlie, have more than justified my imprudence. You have given me a joy which I could never have dreamt of. I am yours, body and soul; do with me as you like. I, too, adore the very ground you tread on.'

We continued exchanging the sweetest vows of affection, until, seeing my prick rising to its usual stiffness, she said: 'Oh, my darling, you must put this away; it would be most imprudent to continue any longer. Now, let me button it up.'

First stooping and kissing it, she put it into my trousers with some difficulty, buttoned me up, and we strolled towards the house.

Our conversation turned on our chance of fresh encounters. She begged I would not think of attempting anything of the kind next day, and she would try and arrange for the day after, although my sisters were terribly in the way.

I suggested she should keep me in as when she flogged me, nay, indeed, she should flog me in reality if she liked.

She laughed at my idea, but said something might be done in that way as a blind. So I said: 'I will neglect my lesson on purpose to furnish an excuse.'

'We shall see, we shall see. Meanwhile, remember to be very prudent.'

We reached the house; she retired to her room until mamma returned. Very kind inquiries were made, she said she had suffered severely from headache, but, on the whole, felt better and hoped that a good night's rest would put her all to rights We all retired early, both mamma and the girls were tired with their drive and shopping. I had resumed my bed in the little dressing-room, and went to sleep with thoughts of my delicious day's doings, to dream of re-enacting them with every amorous excess that the utmost lubricity could suggest.

The next day Miss Evelyn began to resume her former looks – the struggle was at an end. She was very gentle in her manner, and seemed even more affectionate than usual to my sisters, who, fancying she was not very well, were attentive, rather trying to anticipate her wishes than following them. There was rather a greater appearance of reserve than previously in her manner to me, but when I went up to her to repeat my lessons, there was a warmer clasping of my waist and a suppressed manner that showed she was restraining her desire to press me to her bosom. Her face slightly flushed, and she turned her beautiful eyes upon me with such an endearing expression of affection that I could have thrown myself into her arms but for the check upon my ardour which her own reserve imposed upon me.

Nothing more took place between us that day. At our usual hour of recreation, from four till five, Miss Evelyn retired to her room to repose after the efforts of restraint that she had put upon herself all day, and left us to ourselves. I need not say an immediate resort to the summerhouse followed. There, first deliciously fucking Mary, and then gamahuching Eliza, with the addition of gently introducing, at the same time, a finger a short distance up her quim, I finished off with another voluptuous fuck with Mary. I thus was enabled to bear the bridle Miss Evelyn put upon the indulgence of my appetite in her person, and was apparently more reasonable than in reality. She again, on the second day, failed to give me the opportunity I so longed for. Thinking she might hesitate, from fear of discovery, and the fact of having no apparently reasonable excuse of being alone with me, I determined to play the idler next day in the afternoon. On being called up, I had done nothing. Miss Evelyn looked grave, but blushed deeply at the same time.

'What do you mean, Charlie, by this idleness? Go, do your lesson, or I shall be obliged to punish you.'

She took me by the arm, and gently pressed it as she told me to resume my seat. At four o'clock, of course, my lesson was as far as before from being done.

'Mary and Eliza, you can go into the garden. Charles will remain until he finishes his lesson, or is punished for his idleness.'

They left and Miss Evelyn locked the door after them. Then we flew into each other's arms, and indulged in the most endearing caresses for a very few seconds. I had been in a state of most violent erection for some time, so that my hand was up her petticoats immediately. I gently pushed her back on her low long easy-chair, and kneeling in front, first thrust my head between her thighs, and taking a glance at her beautifully haired cunt, already all moist and juicy, showing that she was as ready as myself, I gamahuched her until she spent in my mouth, and sucked the delicious liquid most greedily. There was something peculiarly sweet in her spend, and my tongue sought the innermost lining of her delicious quim as far as its limited length would admit, that I might not lose a drop of her exquisite nectar, worthy indeed of the gods. The excitement I occasioned her was almost too much for her to bear, she drew me up, saying: 'Oh! Charlie, my angel of a boy, come, oh, come to my arms.' I raised myself up, threw myself into her arms, and in a moment I was engulfed up to the cods in her exquisite and throbbing cunt; she closed upon me with arms and legs, we were both too violently excited to pause for any of the more voluptuous movements of less violent desires, but rushed on in passion's wildest ecstasy, both far too eager to think of any restraint, and with the utmost vigour on both our parts, we ran our first course with great rapidity. My adored Miss Evelyn had quite got over every feeling of pain, and could not but be delighted with the heat and vigour of my attack. We both died away together, at the ecstatic moment pouring down a mutual flood of spunk to cool the inflamed members that had the instant before been in such tumultuous action. Darling Miss Evelyn hugged me close to her bosom, and threw her beautiful eyes, screaming with passion, up to the ceiling, as if to thank heaven for the joys she had felt. Our lips then met and glued themselves together in one long, long kiss of love, which quickly lighted up our lust; she was as eager as myself, and we had another vigorous encounter, ending in all the agonies of delight, as before. Then after a longer interval of the most endearing caresses and fond accents of murmured love, we ran our third course, with more abandon, lengthening out our exquisite sensations by slower and quicker movements and pauses between – in which my beautiful governess began to develop an art in which she shortly became even superior to the more experienced Mrs Benson, who had so charmingly initiated me into love's mysteries.

There was a peculiarly charming and endearing softness in the manner of Miss Evelyn which was most winning and most exquisitely attractive. It was evidenced even in her mode of handling my prick; without grasping it, her hand appeared to pass over it hardly touching it, but in so exciting a manner that after any number of encounters, she could raise it by her fairy touch in a moment. Our third encounter lasted quite half an hour, and when we sank in the death-like luxury of discharge, our whole souls seemed to exude with the exquisite distillation of our seed. We had long before regained our senses. I was still engulfed in her delicious cunt, but she begged me to relieve her of my weight. We rose, she shook her petticoats down, and assisted me to arrange my trousers. I then sat down and took her on my knee. Our lips met in a mutual warm kiss of gratified passion. She thanked me for the joys of paradise I had given her – and for my discretion in procuring an excuse for our meeting. She acknowledged that she had been as impatient as myself, but was obliged to take every precaution against raising the slightest suspicion in the house.

'You must always remember, my darling boy, that for me discovery would be my ruin for ever. I risk everything to possess you, my beloved boy, I would care little for discovery, if it would not also separate us for ever. That idea, my adored Charlie, is insupportable, I can no longer exist without you.' Here she threw her arms round my neck, and burst into tears.

I have already described the effect of tears on my unruly member, which, while I was consoling and vowing eternal attachment to my loved mistress, burst from its bonds and stood out in all its glory. I took her soft and beautiful little hand, and laid it on it. She grasped it tightly, and looking at it, while smiling through her tears, said: 'My Charlie, what a great big thing it is. I wonder how it could ever get into me without killing me.'

'You shall soon see that,' said I, and changing places, I laid her down, lifted her petticoats and was into her in a moment. She begged me to proceed slowly, and to lengthen out our pleasures as much as possible. We had a most glorious and truly delicious fuck; my lovely and charming mistress giving me most ecstatic pleasure by the exquisite pressures of the internal folds of her delicious and lascivious cunt.

We lay enraptured for long after we had spent, and then resumed our sitting position, and arranged everything in order, as the time for the return of my sisters from their hour of recreation was close at hand.

Our conversation naturally turned upon how we should arrange for our next meeting. Miss Evelyn insisted that we must not think of meeting more than once in three or four days, as otherwise we might raise suspicions fatal to our meeting at all. However reasonable this was, I raised an outcry against such a tantalising delay, and begged hard for a shorter period between our intervals.

'It cannot be, my darling boy, remember discovery would separate us for ever. By prudence, we may long continue these delicious meetings.'

I suddenly suggested that as I slept alone in the little room, which, when the spare room was unoccupied, was far away from everyone, she might steal along at night, when all were asleep, and thus I could enjoy the whole of her exquisite charms, without hindrance. She did not reply, but I could see her eye sparkled, and her cheek flushed as if already in imagination she was revelling untrammelled in all the luxury of voluptuousness such a plan opened out. However, she did not at once accept, but kissing me fondly, called me her dear and ingenious boy, and said she would think over my suggestion. We resumed our lessons on my sisters' return. Miss Evelyn was again four days before she gave me another opportunity of an amorous meeting. It was only my purposed insubordination that obtained me this interview. We again indulged in all the luxuries of carnal enjoyment, as far as could be done, incommoded as we both were by dress and locality. Reverting more strongly than ever to my plan of meeting in my lonely room, I begged so hard that at last she promised to come the night of the following day. I was obliged to put up with this, although I would fain have had her come that very night, but as her passions were evidently gaining stronger possession of her, and she was becoming more loving, and more voluptuous than ever, I felt certain she would not disappoint me on the next night.

The delicious idea of revelling in charms I had so often furtively gazed on, kept me away from my sisters next day. Under a plea of headache I went early to bed, and took up some oil, to oil the hinges and lock of the door, to be prepared for my loved mistress. I lay long awake, and was almost in despair of her coming, when I heard the clock strike twelve. All at once I became aware she was at my bedside. She had entered the room with so gentle a step that, though on the watch for her, I did not hear her even when she opened the door, shut, and locked it. She had come in her dark-grey cloak, and when at my bedside this was dropped on the floor, she stood in nothing but a very fine and thin chemise. She flung herself in my arms, as I rose to embrace her, and we instantly sank closely clasped in each other's arms. I was far too sharply set to practise any preliminaries. I turned her on her back, and was into her in a moment, with one vigorous thrust, which almost took away her breath, and gave her intense delight. I was too quick for her, however, as I spent in two or three shoves into that delight-giving cunt. But as this hardly allayed the fires of my too ardent desires, the convulsive internal movements of her unsatisfied orbit quickly restored my scarcely reduced member to a renewed vigour. Miss Evelyn being greatly excited by the unsatisfying nature of my first bout, was extremely warm, and throwing her arms and legs around my body, we again rushed headlong into all the fury of fucking, and as my previous spendings had somewhat reduced the power of immediate discharge, I was able to suit my movements exactly to those of my most active companion, and we sank together in all the voluptuousness of satisfied desires, lying long locked in each other's arms, before we were again in a state to renew our combats in love's delicious domain. We spent the interval in whispered vows and fond endearments and embracings of each other's naked charms, both of us admiringly passing our hands over every part of our bodies.

Miss Evelyn at last concentrated all her attention on my well-developed member, which she most endearingly embraced and fondled tenderly, very quickly putting him into an ungovernable state of erection. I was lying on my back, and she partially raised herself to kiss my formidable weapon; so gently putting her upon me, I told her it was her turn to do the work. She laughed, but at once mounted upon me, and bringing her delicious cunt right over my prick, and guiding it to the entrance of love's grotto, she gently sank down upon it and engulfed it until the two hairs pressed against each other. A few slow up-and-down movements followed, until, becoming too libidinous for such temporising delays, she sank on my belly, and began to show most wonderful activity of loins and bottom. I seconded her to the utmost, and finding she was so excited, I slipped my hand round behind and introduced my middle finger in the rosy and very tight orifice of her glorious backside. I continued to move in and out in unison with her up-and-down heavings. It seemed to spur her on to more vigorous actions, and in the midst of short gaspings and suppressed sighs, she sank almost senseless on my bosom. I, too, had quickened my action, and shot into her gaping womb a torrent of boiling sperm.

We lay entranced in the raptures of satiated desire for a long time. At last she came to her senses, and fondly kissing me, turned off, and we lay side by side closely embraced.

'Oh! my beloved Charlie, what exquisite delight you have given me; you are the most delicious and loving creature that ever could be created. You kill me with pleasure, but what was that you were doing to my bottom? What put such an idea into your head?'

'I don't know,' I replied. 'I put my arm round to feel the beautiful globes of your bottom, and found in grasping one that my finger was against a hole, all wet with our previous encounters, and pressing it, I found that my finger slipped in; you gave it such a delicious pressure when in, that the idea entered into my head that, as it resembled the delicious pressure your enchanting other orifice gives my shaft when embracing you, this orifice would like a similar movement in it to that which my shaft exercised in your quim. So I pressed on, and it seemed to add to your excitement, if I may judge by the extraordinary convulsive pressures you gave my finger when you died away in all the agony of our final rapture. Tell me, my beloved Miss Evelyn, did it add to your pleasure as much as I fancied?'

'Well, my darling Charlie, I must own it did, very much to my surprise; it seemed to make the final pleasure almost too exciting to bear, and I can only account it a happy accident leading to an increase to pleasure I already thought beyond the power of nature to surpass. Naughty boy, I feel your great instrument at full stretch again, but you must moderate yourself, my darling, we have done enough for tonight. No, no, no! I am not going to let him in again.'

Passing her hand down, she turned away its head from the charming entrance of her cunt, and began handling and feeling it in apparent admiration of its length, thickness, and stiffness. Her gentle touch did anything but allay the passion that was rising to fever heat; so sucking one of her bubbies, while I pressed her to me with one arm under her, and embracing her on the other side, I passed my hand between our moist and warm bodies, reached her charming clitoris, already stiff with the excitement of handling my prick. My titillations soon decided her passions, and gently prompting her with the arm under her body, I turned her once more on the top of me. She murmured an objection, but offered no resistance; on the contrary, she herself guided my throbbing and eager prick into the voluptuous sheath that was longing to engulf it. Our movements this time were less hurried and more voluptuous. For some time she kept her body upright, rising and falling from her knees. I put my finger to her clitoris, and added to the ecstatic pleasure she was so salaciously enjoying. She soon found she must come to more rapid and vigorous movements, and lying down on my belly, embraced and kissed me. Toying with our tongues, I put an arm round her waist, and held her tight, while her glorious buttocks and most supple loins kept up the most delicious thrust and pressures on my thoroughly engulfed weapon. I again stimulated her to the highest pitch of excited desires by introducing my finger behind, and we both came to the grand crisis in a tumultuous state of enraptured agony, unable to do ought, but from moment to moment convulsively throb in and on our engulfed members. We must have lain thus languidly and deliciously enjoying all the raptures of the most complete and voluptuous gratification of our passions for fully thirty minutes before we recovered complete consciousness. Miss Evelyn was first to remember where she was. She sprang up, embraced me tenderly, and said she must leave me at once, she was afraid she had already stayed imprudently long. In fact, it was near five o'clock in the morning. I rose from the bed to fling my arms round her lovely body, to fondle and embrace her exquisite bubbies. With difficulty she tore herself from my arms. I accompanied her to the door, and with a mutual and loving kiss we parted, I to return and rapidly sink into the sweetest slumber, after such a delicious night of most voluptuous fucking.

She came again three times in the next six nights; each time we renewed our mutual joys, with ever increasing voluptuous indulgencies. On coming to me for the fifth time, she said: 'Dear Charlie, I have only come to kiss you, and say I cannot stop.'

'Cannot stop!' I cried, 'and why not, beloved Miss Evelyn?'

'I am not well, but cannot explain more.'

I had sprung out of bed, and clasped her in my arms, then passing a hand down to her beauteous and well-covered mons Veneris, I found that she was tied up there in cloth. I immediately remembered how my loved Mrs Benson had been exactly in the same way. I then also remarked the peculiar odour of breath, but pretending ignorance, I begged to know what had happened to my darling little grotto.

'I cannot tell you more, my dear boy, but it will keep me away from you for four or five nights.'

'But why should that be the case; cannot you let me enter that delicious cave of delight only once?'

'No, no, impossible! my dear Charlie, absolutely impossible! It would do me very great harm, and you too. Let us be quiet in that way, and I shall be the sooner well again to come and embrace you as before.'

'Oh! but darling, how can I support five nights' absence, I shall go mad with desire and burst – feel how he grows, and is longing for his loved companion.'

Her soft and gentle hand caressed it. I thought to succeed by a *coup de main*, but she was too quick for me.

'No, Charles, I am serious, and you must not try to force me, or I shall never come near you again.'

I saw she was in earnest, and flung myself on the bed in a pet.

'Come, my darling Charlie, be reasonable, and I will do my best to give you some satisfaction. Lay yourself on your back – so. I will kneel on the floor at right angles to you, because you must not attempt to touch me down there. That is a dear boy.'

So taking my prick in her soft hand, she gently moved it up and down; then, suddenly stopping, took it into her mouth, sucking as much as she could get in, and titillating the knob with her tongue, while one hand frigged at the root of my prick and the other gently handled my two crisped-up cods. She prolonged the pleasure by occasional pauses, and at last, on finding the electric-like sensations coming, she hastened her movement, and I poured a torrent of sperm into her mouth. She continued her delicious sucking until not a drop more was left for her to swallow. This was the first time she ever gamahuched me, but it was not the last by scores of times. Ever after we improved upon the model, and added other endearments. When not under her courses, we mutually gamahuched each other, and she was the first to repeat upon me, with the intensest gratification, the delicious introduction of a finger behind while gamahuching me. At present, when she had thus taken the edge off my carnal appetite, she lovingly embraced me, and left me to my lovely slumbers. Of course, the four days' grace, saving two more passing visits 'to keep me cool', as she said, turned all to the advantage of my sisters, whom I fucked and frigged to their utmost gratification and delight.

I thus passed about four months, Miss Evelyn becoming a perfect adept in love's delicious mysteries; but, although I had attempted to enjoy the orifice of the lower temple of Venus, my member was too large, and gave too much pain, to completely succeed, so that I became the faithful worshipper at the more legitimate altar of love. My sisters were gradually developing their forms. Mary particularly so. The hair on her quim had increased to a most charming, curling profusion. Her hips spread out, and her bottom, hard and prominent, promised to be very large. Eliza, too, began to show increased bubbies, and an enlarged and mossy mons Veneris.

We were approaching summer, and near the full of the moon, Mary had complained of feeling very low-spirited, and very much inclined to cry. I tried to comfort her, and thought success would best attend my efforts if I fucked her. So enticing her down into the garden, we entered the summer-house, and I at once proceeded to action. She was rather unwilling, she could not say why, but had an instinctive reluctance. She yielded, however, to my entreaties, and I fucked her without apparently exciting her in the usual way. I consequently withdrew as soon as I had run the first course, and at once discovered what ailed poor Mary. My member was covered with blood. For the first time, her courses had come upon her. She was greatly alarmed, but I told her I had heard it was quite natural to young women when they reached a certain age, that she had better tell mamma at once, who would instruct her what to do. I carefully wiped my reddened member, and then retired to my room to purify myself. That very night, on Miss Evelyn coming to me, I found she was exactly in the same state. She gave me my usual relief with her soft hand and caressing lips, and then left me for five nights.

I now found myself reduced to my dear little sister Eliza. Up to this time I had never actually fucked her, and her maidenhead was still intact. She was now approaching fourteen, and the down on her charming little cunt was becoming more decided; her bubbies too, under the erotic excitement of my *attouchements* and gamahuching, had assumed a decided prominence. My finger had somewhat rendered the opening of her little pinky slit more easy of access. So I resolved to complete her carnal education and fuck her thoroughly. The opportunity was perfect; both Miss Evelyn and Mary retired to their rooms to lie down at our usual hour's recreation, Eliza and I at once hied to the summerhouse, and locked ourselves in. I immediately laid her down on the long couch, and gamahuched her until she spent in my mouth, and then continued until she was again almost mad with desire. I then told her I should initiate her into a new mystery, more delicious than any she had yet experienced, but that the first initiation was always painful.

'Oh! what is it, my dear Charlie, everything you do is so nice, I know I shall like it – what is it?'

'Then you must know, dear Eliza, that this little cunt of yours is made for the express purpose of having a prick put into it; only, as mine is so large, and you are still so small and so young, I was afraid it would give you too much pain to do it sooner; but now, I think, I may get it in, if I do it gently.'

'Oh, Charlie, dear, put it in at once, I have often felt I should like it so; but, as you never attempted to do it, I thought it was a mere fancy of mine. Have you ever put it inside Mary's quim?'

'Often; nay, always, my darling.'

'Does she like it?'

'She adores it.'

'Then put it into me directly, Charlie.'

I wanted nothing better, and told her that in order thoroughly to enjoy it, she must strip. In a minute she dropped off everything, while I took off my trousers – coat and waistcoat having been laid aside already. I had brought a towel to lay on the couch below her bottom, to prevent any telltale stains. Laying her down on her back, with her bottom close to the end, her legs gathered up, and her two feet resting on the sofa, with her knees falling outwards (in the very best position for my intended operation), I put a pillow on the floor, on which I knelt, thus bringing my cock a little above her quim to give me a good purchase. I then first gamahuched her well again, until she spent and cried out: 'Oh, put it in, my dear Charlie, I do feel to want it so!'

She was already well moistened by her previous discharges, and by my licking the lips of her cunt, and covering them with saliva, with which I also, at the same time, wetted my prick itself. I then made the point approach the charming pouting and longing lips of her sweet little cunt, and rubbing it first up and down between the lips, proceeded to insert its knob between them. Thanks to the precautions taken, and the excitement I had raised by my previous caresses with tongue and prick, the immediate entrance was effected with greater ease than might have been expected. No sooner was it in about an inch beyond the knob than the passion of excitement I had raised so stimulated the natural lubricity of Eliza's nature that she heaved up her buttocks energetically, letting her knees drop quite down sideways, thus favouring to the utmost my forward thrust made at the moment, so that my prick was sheathed in an instant more than half his length, and but for the obstacle of her maidenhead, which he then met with, would have been entirely engulfed. As it was, it gave her a very sharp pang of pain, which made her shrink back, and utter an: 'Oh! Charlie!'

'Do not fear, I will be gentle, keep still a moment and then you will find the pain pass away, and great pleasure follow.'

So we lay still for a time, until I felt those involuntary internal pressures, the true precursors and infallible indication of rising desires; so commencing a slow and continuous in-and-out movement, I shortly produced such an excess of pleasure in her delicious orbit, that her movements became almost furious, nature alone prompting her to second me with as much art as if she had already been long instructed in the delicious movements so calculated to add to the libidinous delights of true enjoyment.

But Eliza was a rare example of a truly salacious and voluptuous nature, and proved herself in that way far in advance of Mary; although she was of a very warm temperament, Eliza's passions were far more excitable, and in the end she became one of the most voluptuous fuckers possible, abandoning herself to all the wildest raptures that the most erotic nature could suggest. Of this, hereafter. At present I had worked her up to the utmost pitch of excited desire; she was in the very act of discharging, and as I withdrew for a final thrust and she heaved up her buttocks in an agony of pleasure, I felt it was now or never, and striking home with all my force, I burst with irresistible strength through every obstacle and tore my way inwards until sheathed to my very cods. Poor Eliza! at the very moment she thought herself in the seventh heaven of delight, she experienced the most excruciating agony. She gave a piercing cry and fainted away; her arms fell senseless from my body – her legs would have also fallen, but twining my arms round them, I continued for several successive thrusts to penetrate fully and easily into every recess, for I myself was wound up to a fearful state of excitement. I died away in an excess of joy, sending a torrent of balmy sperm to soften and mitigate the pain of her terribly torn quim. Finding that Eliza could not regain consciousness, I rose somewhat in alarm, and was horrified to see the quantity of blood that followed my withdrawal. It was fortunate my forethought of the towel, as it had not only saved the sofa, but helped to stanch her swollen and bleeding quim, and to wipe the blood from her thighs and bottom. I had effected all this before the dear girl showed the least symptoms of animation. She first sighed, then shivered, and at last opened her eyes, and looked confusedly at me, and asked: 'What has happened to me, Charlie?'

Then observing how she was lying naked, she recovered her complete consciousness of all the circumstances of the case.

'Oh! Charlie, now I know; I thought you had killed me; Charlie, oh! it was so frightfully painful. How could you hurt me so, and just as I thought it was the most heavenly pleasure I had ever experienced in all my life.'

'My darling, it is all over now, and it will never hurt again, and we shall both of us have greater pleasure than ever, but not just now; it has been greater pain to you than I thought it would be, and for the present we must not attempt any more.' I helped her to rise, but she felt very faint, and I had great difficulty in getting her dressed. She was shocked to see the bloody state of the towel. I told her to put my handkerchief between her thighs, and partly up her slit, to prevent any marks of blood staining her shift. I then laid her down on the sofa, while I ran to get some water from the fountain in the garden. I took a glass and the towel with me. I returned with the water, which greatly refreshed Eliza. I begged her to lie still as long as she could stay. However, when she attempted to walk, she found herself very much incommoded with the smarting pain. I was terribly afraid lest this would be observed when we got to the house, so I suggested she should purposely fall down when in sight of anyone, and say she could not move because she had hurt her knee by the fall.

This stratagem succeeded admirably. We were seen approaching by Miss Evelyn, my mother, and Mary. Dear Eliza acted her part admirably, was seen to fall heavily, and screamed. They all rushed out, we lifted her carefully on her legs, and supported her to the house, she complaining of the pain in the knee and ankle. My mother insisted on her going to bed at once, and having embrocations and hot towels applied. Eliza let them do as they liked, and eventually was left to quiet repose, which soon relieved the painful sensations she had undergone. Next day she complained of great stiffness, and walked lame, but thought the hot applications had prevented the swelling, so thus happily passed off all observations of suspicion of the real circumstances of the case. It was not until the third day after that I attempted to make an entrance. Of course, I excited her first to the utmost by a long continued gamahuching. She then let me, but with fear and trembling, introduce my bursting member into the delicate folds of her cunt. As I was very gentle in my movements, the pain was scarcely felt, and when once well sheathed, and the first thrusts given slowly and luxuriously, the whole lubricity of her nature was soon awakened, and by the time I was ready to spend she was as ready to second me, and we died away in a mutual flood of delighted ecstasy. She held me close, and would not let me withdraw.

'No, Charlie, it took some trouble to get it in, let it stop where it is so deliciously engulfed,' and at once, anticipating her natural desires, she began the most exquisite pressures upon me, which very shortly brought us both up to the point of demanding more active measures. However, I rather restrained her, and told her we must retard our movements to increase our pleasures, because mere quick repetitions would only exhaust her, without yielding the true ecstasies of enjoyment. I, therefore, taught her the pleasures of the slow movements, and I worked her up to spending point, without giving way myself. The dear little creature clung to me with the most close and endearing embraces, as if she should force a complete amalgamation of our two bodies, and died away in the sweetest bliss of contented desire, with such a heavenly expression of ecstasy on her face as made me devour it with kisses. I had great difficulty in restraining myself from precipitately following her example; her delicious movements at the moment of spending, and the close pressures on my prick, were so exciting that resisting them was quite a triumph of control. I succeeded, and lay quite quiet, embalmed in the delicious suction of those exquisite folds of her charming little cunt, which exercised the most delightful pressures as well as suction on my enraptured priest. I left it entirely to her to lie as we were as long as she pleased, or to again begin the dear, delightful friction that should once more make us dash on passion's furious course, to end as usual in the ever delicious ecstasies of the final crisis.

This last bout had been a double one for my sister; she all but swooned away with the rapture my spending in unison with her produced. She declared it was a death of the most delicious ecstasy, which it was perfectly impossible to describe. She clung to me, kissing me in the most endearing manner, and telling me how happy I had at last made her by completing the insertion of my prick in her cunt. It was worth the suffering of twenty times as much agony to arrive at so exquisite a result as every fuck I now gave her conferred upon her. We adjourned to the flower garden, that we might be seen playing together, and not excite suspicion by our constant dis-appearance, now that we were only two together. Of course, Mary knew what we were at and probably guessed that I had completed the initiation of Eliza. She smiled, and gave me a significant pressure of the hand, when we met again in the schoolroom to resume our lessons. For two days more, I enjoyed Eliza all to myself; at each new fuck, she became more and more perfect in conferring as well as receiving pleasure.

On the third day, Miss Evelyn whispered, 'tonight', as she gave me a stolen pressure of the hand. She came, and we indulged in every whim of our fancy. I had further the delicious pleasure of gazing on all her naked beauties, as it was daylight before we parted; I had gamahuched her twice, and fucked her five times. She gave me credit for a long fast, and allowed so much indulgence on that account, but told me I must in future be more moderate, for her sake, if not for my own. She allowed three nights to pass before again coming to me. I cannot say I regretted it, because now that Eliza was initiated, as well as Mary, we indulged in the most delightful orgies of fucking and gamahuching at the same time. At first, we used to fuck with one laid on her back to be fucked, while the other backed on her knees over the face of the one being fucked, and was gamahuched by her, while I introduced my finger into the rosy orifice of the bottom before me. But we found the most voluptuous way was for one to lie down on her back, and the other on hands and knees over her. She thus brought her mouth over the cunt of the one lying down, and presented her bottom to me, who knelt behind her. The one below guided my prick into the cunt above her face; she had thus all the satisfaction of seeing our action, while with one hand she tickled my cods, and the other felt my bottom-hole, and inserted a finger. Meanwhile, she was gamahuched and bottom-frigged at the same time by the one I was fucking, and we used all three to die away in agonies of enraptured delight, to recommence with a change of places between the two girls. Sometimes I tried to introduce my prick into the rosy little orifice of Mary's backside, but, although the finger-frigging gave her much additional pleasure while her cunt was operated upon by my virile member, she as yet could not support the insertion of my large prick. I had not even attempted little Lizzie, but one day, when Miss Evelyn and Mary were again under menstruation, and I had dear Lizzie all to myself, she was seized with such an irresistible desire to ease herself, that she had only time to get behind a bush and squat down. I remained waiting for her, when she called to me, to ask if I had any paper. I advanced to give her some. She was in a half-standing position, with her clothes held up to her waist. While giving the paper, my eyes accidentally fell upon what she had voided. I was struck with its extra-ordinary thickness. I made no observation at the time, but it raised an idea that preoccupied me much. I had often thought over the pleasure that fucking Mrs Benson's bum-hole had given me, hence I had tried to initiate both Miss Evelyn and Mary in that delightful route of pleasure, but, as before stated, had been unable to succeed with them from the great develop-ment of my weapon. Thinking that if they could not bear the insertion, there could be no possibility of success with my younger and less developed sister, I had never attempted with Lizzie more than the insertion of one finger. It is true, with her it seemed to produce more excitement than either upon Miss Evelyn or Mary. The sight of the extraordinary dimensions of the matter she had voided now suggested the idea that if her apparently very small and rosy-lipped bottom-hole could allow so large a mass to come out, with gentle efforts my scarcely larger machine might be inserted. I de-termined to try the initiation into that route of delight the very next day. Remembering that dear Mrs Benson always made it a rule that she should be first well fucked and gamahuched, and the prick well moistened, I began by exciting dear Lizzie to the utmost. I first fucked her, and made her spend twice to my once; then gamahuched her until she implored me to shove my prick into her. I had managed to introduce my two forefingers at once into her bottom, and had frigged her while sucking her cunt, without apparently giving any pain; on the contrary, from her movements I fancied she felt greater excitement. I took care to enlarge, as much as possible, or rather to stretch her bottom-hole as open as I could with my two fingers. It was at the moment of her greatest excitement, when she was pressing me to fuck her at once, that I said: 'My dearest sister, there is still another mystery of sensual voluptuousness that you have as yet not experienced or been initiated into, and I am about to instruct you in it.'

'Oh, what is it? dear Charlie; but do anything you like, and as quick as possible.'

'Well, then dear, it is this sweet little orifice in your bottom that I am going to introduce my prick into. It may give you some little pain the first time, but by gentleness of movement, and halting from time to time when it hurts too much, we shall get him completely inserted, and then it will be an immense pleasure to both of us.'

'Dear, dear Charlie, do as you like, your darling prick can only give me the greatest delight; I am dying to have him into me, I don't care where, as long as I get the dear creature into me. I suppose I must be on my hands and knees.'

Upon which she turned with great agility, and presented the two hard and already promising globes of her charming backside. I lost no time in first thrusting my prick up to the hilt in her cunt, to moisten it. It made her shudder again with excess of lust, and she exercised such a pressure upon it that I had some difficulty in withdrawing it. It was so snug and nice therein that it was a great temptation to run a course in her cunt at once, but having the other object in view, and knowing that I wanted all its stiffness to succeed, I did summon up courage enough to withdraw; then applying the very plenteous saliva in my mouth that gamahuching her had stimulated, I added it to the already moistened prick, and applyied some to her bum-hole. Introducing a well-wetted finger, I put the knob of my formidable prick to the small and smiling orifice that lay before me. The disproportion struck me as so great that I dreaded success would be much too painful for her, but remembering the dimensions of what had come out of it, I boldly proceeded with the operation. I got in over the knob without making her flinch, but, as I proceeded to push gently forward, and had got in about two inches, she cried: 'Stop a little, Charlie, it feels so queer – I can't bear it in further.'

I stopped where I was, but slipping a hand under her, I applied my finger to her clitoris, holding her bottom tight against me with the other hand round her waist, so as not to lose ground. My agile finger soon worked her passions up, and I felt her bottom give convulsive twitches on my prick. I allowed her to become still more excited, and then gently pushing forward found I was slowly, and almost imperceptibly, gaining ground. My prick was then inserted about two-thirds of its length, when, thrusting rather too sharply, she again cried out, and, but for the arm that held her fast round the waist, would have unseated me.

'Oh, Charlie, dear, do stop; it seems to choke me, and makes me feel so queer, that I thought I was going to faint.'

'I shall lie quite still, now, dear Lizzie. It is quite in' – this was a little bit of deception to calm her fears – 'and when the pain of insertion passes, which will be the case in a minute, we shall have nothing but pleasure.'

So I kept my prick just where he was, but redoubled my frigging her clitoris, and very soon brought her up to spending point, resolved that I would not attempt complete insertion until I felt she was in the raptures of sensual discharge. This quickly came upon her, and it was the delicious movement of her own buttocks that sheathed my prick to the hilt without an effort on my part, and so far from giving her pain, made her positively scream with the intense voluptuousness of her sensation in spending. She could not speak for many minutes, but continued the exquisite pressures of the sphincter muscle on my enraptured prick. But for my determination not to give way, and rather to wait for another bout that would completely initiate dear Lizzie in all the luxury and abandon of this delicious mode, I must have at once vigorously finished my own course. My restraint was well rewarded. The first words my beloved sister uttered were those of almost delirious joy at the extraordinary delight I had given her. Never, never, had any fuck so enraptured her. She turned up her lovely face to me, and tears of sensuality and voluptuousness filled her eyes.

I had hardly begun my titillations on her still excited clitoris, which, by the way, had lately considerably developed itself, when she was as eager for another bout as I was. I held sufficient restraint on myself to practise every salacious movement, that I might give Lizzie such exquisite pleasure as should induce her on future occasions to grant me the use of her charming bottom-hole whenever I should desire. I worked her up to the utmost pitch of the most salacious excitement, and at the moment when she spent, in an agony of shrieking ecstasy, I poured a perfect flood of spunk right up into her entrails. We both sank forward, but without unseating me, quite over-powered by the intensity of our delight. When we came to our senses, I rose from off her. On withdrawing my prick, I found a few traces of blood, but of no moment. I wiped my prick on my handkerchief, and also wiped between the cheeks of dear Lizzie's bottom, for fear any tell-tale marks should be made on her linen. I then helped her up, and she threw her arms round my neck, and sweetly kissing me, thanked me for a new lesson in love, which had overwhelmed her with delight.

Thus ended the first lesson that Lizzie ever received by that route of pleasure, and I may incidentally state that she was peculiarly constituted for giving and receiving the most exquisite pleasure in that way. She afterwards developed into a magnificent woman, with one of the naturally largest and finest backsides I almost ever met with; and she came to love backward fucking to the utmost extent. In after-days, when married, she told me that her husband was a *muff*, who had no idea of enjoying a woman but in one way. She had often deceived him, and slipped it into her bottom-hole without his ever having any suspicion of the sort of pleasure he had given her.

Three months passed with the rapidity of a dream, while we indulged in these scenes of delicious lubricity and voluptuousness, without ever attracting any observation within the house and, more curious, without Miss Evelyn either discovering or suspecting anything between my sisters and myself – thanks to my natural powers and the unfailing resources of youth. Both she and my sisters thought they each gave me as much as I could get through, and, therefore, neither ever imagined I could seek carnal delights in other arms. So it was but now there happened one or two events which had a considerable effect on the after-tenor of our loves.

A neighbour, a very nice good-looking man, about thirty-five years of age, a gentleman farmer, very well off, had for some time past always waited for us at the church door on Sundays, apparently for a chat with mamma, Miss Evelyn, and us. He treated and evidently considered us as mere children, nor did he appear to fix particular attention to anyone.

One Monday, my mother received a note from him, to beg she would grant him a short interview on the following day, as he wished for her advice on a subject of much interest to him. Mamma's reply begged him to come at eleven o'clock, when she would be happy to see him.

He came, and was particularly neatly dressed. My mother had been very agitated all the morning, and looked flushed and nervous as the hour drew near; I really believe the old lady fancied it was for an idle avowal to herself that he was coming. Be that however as it may, the object of his visit turned out to be a proposal to Miss Evelyn, with an offer of marriage. He was ready to make such settlements upon her as could not but be satisfactory. He told my mother that before speaking to Miss Evelyn, whom be had loved from her first appearance in the parish, and whose quiet, modest character had daily made a deeper impression, he thought it only his duty to first break the subject to her, and to ask her permission for an interview with Miss Evelyn, and next, if he was acceptable to her, for leave to visit at our house, while courting his wished-for wife. He further stated that be had never ventured to hint the state of his feelings to Miss Evelyn, and prayed my mother to be the kind intermediary in opening the subject to her, and to beg as a favour that she would grant him an interview to state his case in person on the following day, so that he might learn his fate from her own lips. My mother, although probably inwardly a little disappointed, had the interest of Miss Evelyn too much at heart not to take up the matter warmly, and urged, with all the volubility elderly ladies can so well exercise, whenever the marriage of a younger friend is in question, all the benefit that would accrue to her from so advantageous a proposal. Miss Evelyn was really taken quite by surprise, and stammered out some vague expressions of wishing for time to consider.

'Stuff and nonsense, my dear, remember your dependent position, and the advantages this match holds out to you. You must not think or talk of delay. He will be here tomorrow, and I hope his eloquence will soon decide the question in his favour.'

Poor Miss Evelyn burst into tears and said it was so sudden and she was so ill-prepared to take any decision. She would, however, think over it very seriously and in the morning be better able to give an answer. My mother seeing that she was much agitated by what she had told her, very kindly said: 'Give the children a holiday this afternoon, and I advise you to keep your own room, and write to your widowed mother, to tell her of the offer, and to ask her advice how you should act.'

We thus had many hours to ourselves. I had heard all that had passed, and felt a sad pressure at my heart, when I began to realise that the proposal of Mr Vincent would, if accepted, lead to our separation, and deprive me of my loved Miss Evelyn. The idea made me very sad, and I showed no alacrity in taking advantage of our extra hours of recreation with my sisters, until Mary began to rally me about my melancholy, and asked what I meant by it. I at once said: 'Don't you see, if Miss Evelyn marries Mr Vincent we shall get another governess, and can we ever expect to get one who is so kind and excellent a teacher, and who troubles us so little at our *games*.'

'Ah! that is very true, and we should be horribly annoyed if we were watched and interrupted. However, more reason that we should make the most of the present moment, so come along, Charlie, and let us have some real good fucking. We have plenty of time, mamma is not very well. No one will come near us, and there is nothing to hinder our having a jolly time of it, all three stark naked together, so come along.'

Her words had already changed the current of my ideas; before she ceased speaking my prick responded, which her quick eye immediately observed, and patting it with her hand, she said: 'Ah! my dear little dummy, I am glad to see you are of my opinion, so come along.'

Away we went, and a most glorious afternoon of orgies we spent.

Miss Evelyn came to me at night and threw herself into my arms, in an agony of sobs and tears, and pressing me to her throbbing bosom, she sobbed out: 'Oh! my dear Charlie, I love you so dearly, you have become as necessary to me as life itself. I cannot bear the thought of parting from you, my loved one. You, whom I have initiated into all the delights of mutual love. Oh! the thought of parting is bitter, and breaks my heart. Oh! love me, my own darling boy, and press me to your heart.'

I did more, for, as I have before stated, a woman's tears have a never-failing effect on the erective nerves of my machine. It was but the commencement of a night of most luxurious enjoyment. Miss Evelyn put no restraint either on herself or me, but indulged in every act of lubricity and voluptuousness that her salacious passions could suggest, as if she already felt that these delicious nights of *abandon* and voluptuousness were drawing to a close. In fact, when eventually she left me in the morning, and I thought over all she had said, it became evident to me that she had already made up her mind to accept the very advantageous offer made to her. The instinctive intelligence of woman had at once shown to her that such an opportunity was not to be lost for the sake of a mere boy, whom circumstances must naturally soon remove far away from her. At the same time, doubtless, the idea that I was all her own making, for she never had any suspicion of my previous initiation, held a charm over her, to say nothing of the powerful weapon she had so unexpectedly found by her side, and which had so great an influence over her passions. We spent a most luxurious night, and hardly closed our eyes, notwithstanding my afternoon's debauch; such is the power and resources of nature, in a well-constituted youth of fifteen and upwards, that Miss Evelyn had rather to force our embraces, than to stimulate by any artificial excitement my ever-ready prick. I won from her a promise to come next night, and let me know what fate was in store for us.

Next day Mr Vincent was true to his appointment. Mamma received him with Miss Evelyn by her side, and after the usual compliments, rose and apologised for leaving them, as she had household duties to attend to. Miss Evelyn informed me afterwards that Mr Vincent, on my mother leaving the room, rose from his seat, and approaching her, said, in the most frank, gentlemanly manner: 'You are aware, my dear Miss Evelyn, of the object of my visit, and I augur from your kind condescension in giving me this interview that my suit is not disagreeable to you.'

Then taking her passive hand, and pressing it to his heart, he continued: 'I have loved you, Miss Evelyn, from the first moment of my seeing you. I feel that my future happiness hangs on your lips, for without your love, my life would now be a blank. I am here today to offer you my hand and fortune. If I have not yet your heart, I seek to be allowed to cultivate your society, that I may try to win it.'

Then seeing that she was greatly agitated, he begged her to be seated (for she had risen when he approached and took her hand), he led her to a sofa, and seated himself by her side. He pressed for an answer. She said: 'You must be fully aware, Mr Vincent, that your generous offer has taken me greatly by surprise. I feel most grateful to you for it, but must implore you to allow me to pause, until at least I have heard from my mother, to whom I will communicate the noble offer you have made to me, a poor governess, who cannot but feel grateful to you for condescending to think of her in such a way.'

'Ah! say not so, my dear Miss Evelyn, and believe me, it is no sudden impulse that has driven me to your feet, but ardent love, and real admiration of your great beauty and admirable conduct, ever since you entered this family.'

The dear creature smiled through her tears upon me when she recounted those terms of affection that Mr Vincent poured out to her.

To be brief – before they parted he won from her that his frequent meetings at church, and elsewhere, had gained him something more than esteem, but hopeless of ever becoming his wife, she had done her utmost to suppress warmer feelings. Oh! woman, thy name is deception! So she sent him away the happiest man in existence. He rode over every day afterwards, and was with Miss Evelyn from four to five; indeed, he was often the cause of our having half an hour's longer recreation. He also frequently dined with us. Miss Evelyn's mother naturally jumped at the offer, and most delightedly gave her consent.

When Mr Vincent heard of this, be became very urgent in claiming an early day for making him the *happiest of men*. Miss Evelyn wanted a delay of six weeks, but this raised such an outcry on his part, seconded by my mother, that at last she was driven from six weeks to a month, and then to a fortnight from that date; so all became extremely busy in getting ready marriage dresses, etc. The marriage was to take place from our house, and my mother insisted that she should provide the marriage breakfast. Mrs Evelyn was invited to our house for a week at the time of the marriage, to keep my mother company. My two sisters and a young sister of Mr Vincent's were to be the bridesmaids, and a young man, courting Miss Vincent, to be bride-groom's man. So all was thus arranged, and eventually came off most happily. When Mrs Evelyn arrived she occupied the spare room, where charming Mrs Benson had so deliciously initiated me in all the pleasures of sensuality and passion.

To return to the day when Mr Vincent had his first interview, and declared his love and admiration, and ended with the offer of marriage. Before going away, he rang for mamma, thanked her for all her kindness to him, informed her how happy Miss Evelyn had made him in granting permission to prosecute his suit for her hand, etc. Then begging the favour of a chaste kiss, he left, all radiant with hope.

The interview had naturally been very trying for Miss Evelyn. She was so evidently nervously agitated that my mother begged her to go to her room, and lie down to repose herself. After so much agitation she must be quite unfit for any schoolwork, and she herself would hear our lessons that morning, and give us an afternoon's holiday in honour of the happy event that had occurred.

We thus, my sisters and I, were thrown again into another prolonged opportunity of fully enjoying ourselves, but, notwithstanding the wonder-fully regenerative power that nature had gifted me with, I felt that if I wanted to enjoy again my dear Miss Evelyn, who had promised to be with me that night, I must not only restrain myself from such excess as we had indulged in the previous day, but also manage to get some sleep, of which I had scarcely tasted the night before; so I contented myself with first gamahuching and then fucking each sister. Afterwards I gamahuched them again, and made them each spend five times, so as to satisfy them without exhausting myself, and then finishing off with a delicious fuck in Lizzie's bottom-hole, while each gamahuched the other. This quite satisfied them, and they allowed me to steal up to my room to sleep, Mary promising to call me in time for tea. I slept the sleep of the just for some three hours, and came to tea perfectly ready for anything that could happen that night. It was well it was so, for now that there could not be any long lapse of time before we must part, Miss Evelyn became a very glutton for pleasure, and every art and position was made use of to stimulate and lengthen out our joys. She came every night, even up to the very night before the marriage, although in the last three nights before the event came off, her mother, Mrs Evelyn, slept in the spare bedroom with which my room communicated. Nevertheless, we met and carried on our amorous sports with bated breath and suppressed sighs.

We had of late often tried in our moments of greatest excitement to introduce my prick into her delicious tight little bottom-hole. Once, by a sudden manoeuvre, I managed to get in at the moment she was spending, and actually made an entrance as far as about two inches beyond the nut, and I think I should have fully succeeded at that time if my own excitement had not made me spend too soon. This oiled the way, and my prick, having already fucked several times, becoming too limp, the squeeze of her bottom actually forced him out, as if she were voiding herself naturally. I fancied that, at the moment, but for my too excited passion, she would have rather I had completely initiated her. However, the night preceding her marriage, I at last succeeded. We had fucked in every varied way. She was on her knees, with her head on the pillow, and I on my knees, behind her; this was a favourite way of hers, as she declared I got further in, nay, seemed to touch her heart and fill her whole body; besides the frigging her clitoris and the action of my finger in her bottom-hole added greatly to the raptures this position gave her. She had been already well fucked, and we had mutually gamahuched each other, so her whole system was in a most excited and well-moistened state. Taking care to put two fingers at once into her bottom-hole, I worked them so as to stretch it as much as possible, while exciting her with my prick in her cunt, and a finger on her clitoris. Just as she was going into the raptures of spending, I dropped from my mouth a quantity of saliva on to her bottom-hole, and as she was pushing her buttocks back to me, I suddenly withdrew my prick and with one vigorous thrust, I housed him half his length in her delicious bum-hole. She almost cried out aloud at the suddenness of the attack, and would have flinched away but for the grasp of both my hands upon her hips; a more vigorous shove sent me up to the hilt against her beautiful buttocks. She whispered: 'For heaven's sake, dear Charles, do stop a moment, I can't bear it, and must cry out if you do not be quiet for a time at least.'

As I was safely fixed, it exactly suited me to remain still, for had I gone on, a push or two would have made me spend. Now fairly engulfed, I wished not only fully to enjoy it myself but, if possible, make her enjoy it too. So remaining quite still, as far as regarded my prick, I stole one hand down to her clitoris, and began to excite that; the other I ran up to her bubbies, and played with the nipples, a thing which I had found out excited her almost as much as playing with her clitoris. Her passions were soon reawakened, and the involuntary twistings of her loins and pressures of her sphincter convinced me that, in a very short time, I should work her up to the utmost; and so it was, and immensely she enjoyed both her own spend and mine, when she felt my hot spunk shooting up into her very entrails. We sank gently on our sides after this bout, but without unsheathing me; and here embracing, kissing and tongueing each other when she turned her head, and sometimes sucking the nearest nipple to me, we soon were in a state to renew our delicious combat. A second course was run in the delightful callipygian recesses of Venus's second temple of lubricity. This was our last bout, for, alas, it was getting the hour when the house would be all astir. My lovely mistress embraced me most tenderly and acknowledged that I had at last taught her a new pleasure. She wept as she tore herself from my arms, and I wept too when she left me, as I thought I had now lost her for ever as a mistress, and what a charming one she had been to me!

Morning came, and with it bridesmaids, bridegroom and best man. To church we all went, my sisters perfectly enchanted with the idea of being bridesmaids, and beautifully arrayed in new dresses. They were also still more delighted with some handsome jewellery presented by Mr Vincent. In their eyes, he became the handsomest and finest man they had ever seen. The breakfast went off as usual, and when the bride, who had changed her bridal dress for a neat travelling one, came down, pretty near all were in tears on taking leave of her. She pressed me tenderly to her bosom, and whispered: 'Courage, Charlie, dear.'

It was almost too much for me, but I managed to restrain any extreme demonstration of my grief. The carriage door was shut, and off they rattled to spend the honeymoon at Leamington. The friends assembled remained until the evening, and after the sensations of the day, and the fatigues of the previous night, I was glad to get to bed. I cried myself to sleep, thinking that another at that moment was revelling in all the delights of amorous enjoyment of those charms that had been so long in my sole possession.

Thus ended one of the most delightful episodes of my life, and although I, at some rare intervals, from time to time found an opportunity of enjoying my loved mistress, they were flying fucks, very delicious, but very unsatisfactory.

This was the first great incident that had the effect of changing the tenor of our existence for some time, but I will reserve the details of our after-adventures for the second part of these reminiscences of my early experiences.

# Chapter 2

The house was scarcely itself even the day after the marriage. Mrs Evelyn was still with us, and did not leave until the following day. She and my mother spent most of the day in the summerhouse, so that our pastimes therein were interrupted. Mary complained of severe headache, which, in fact, was the premonitory symptom of her courses, which declared themselves violently in the evening. I had arranged with my sisters to steal up to their room when all were asleep, as now that we had lost our governess, they had it all to themselves. I went, of course, but found only Eliza capable of entering into our sensual enjoyments. I made her come to me in Miss Evelyn's bed, and while fucking her, was thinking all the time of my darling governess; and even when I was fucking her, I could only remember the complete insertion of my prick into Miss Evelyn's bum-hole the very night before her marriage, and wondered whether or not her husband had discovered her loss of maidenhead. And yet, I fancied woman's natural cunning would easily deceive him, as millions before him have been deceived. Coupling Mary's attack and Miss Evelyn's choice of the marriage day on the full moon, I could not help imagining that she intended to help her deception by the advent of her menstruation. It will be seen hereafter how far I was correct in my conjecture. I passed a delicious night in the arms of my charming Lizzie, and only stole away just in time not to be observed by the early-rising servants. Mrs Evelyn departed the next day. My mother, feeling poorly, desired Lizzie to sleep with her, so perforce I had to pass a very quiet night, but which the agitation and excessive venery of the last week rendered very acceptable.

Another week passed without anything particular beyond Mary being able to join Lizzie and me in our orgies. The doctor had recommended my mother to go for a few weeks to the seaside, and she resolved that we should all go for six weeks before engaging a new governess. So we left town for a charming little retired village on the west Welsh coast. It was but a small place, with one street, and some straggling houses here and there, but with a beautiful stretch of sand ending in abrupt rocks. Our lodgings were but small; a sitting-room and bedroom above a shop, and two rooms over that. I slept in the small back room off the sitting-room, my mother had the front upper room, and my two sisters were in the room beside her, with only a thin partition between them. We found ourselves obliged to seek for some outside place to enjoy the erotic pleasures that had now become necessary to us. Very few visitors ever came near the retired little village. In our explorations, we found that at the far end of the sands, there were some nice retired spots behind the rocks, which soon became the scenes of our sensual enjoyments. The place was more than a mile from the village, and we could see if anyone was coming towards us for the whole distance; but still as we might forget how fast time flies, we prudently established either one or the other of my sisters as a sentinel, to give us warning if anyone was approaching. So I took them in turn, laid them down, had a mutual gamahuche, and then a fuck; after which the previous watcher took the place of the one just fucked, and the same process was followed in her case. We had done this for three days, and were congratulating ourselves upon having found out so safe a place to indulge all our propensities in. We always spent the mornings with mamma, who kept us so far to our lessons, but after the midday meal, which mamma also made her dinner hour, she retired for a siesta. We went out for a long walk, and something better. I have said we fully enjoyed the first three days without any apparent chance of discovery. On the fourth, while Lizzie was on the watch in front, and Mary and I after a delicious gamahuche had just died away in all the ecstasies of a prolonged fuck up to the moment of discharge, and I was saying to her: 'Did not that feel delicious, and was it not up to the hilt?'

'I should think so, with such a rammer as that up her cunt,' said a strange voice close to us.

You may easily suppose how we started with surprise.

'Oh, don't do that, I did not mean to spoil sport,' said the same voice.

It was a very gentlemanly man, with a soft quiet voice, and charming amiable expression of countenance, who stood smiling upon us close to our side, with his breeches open, and his standing pego in his hand. So great was our surprise that we never thought of the state we were in. Mary lay with legs spread out, and belly exposed, and cunt gaping open; and I with my breeches down, and my great big cock pendant, it is true, but hardly diminished in thickness.

The stranger said again: 'I am not here to spoil sport, on the contrary, to aid you in every way. I observed you accidentally two days ago. I am here, a stranger, like yourselves. I know you to be brother and sisters, and admire you all the more for being above the usual prejudices of that relationship. But you must be aware that as I know all about you, the best way is to let me be a participator in your sport. Then you not only shut my mouth, but it will be the means of vastly adding to all your pleasures, as well as giving me the most intense satisfaction. Now, for instance, your elder sister there, who was about to replace the younger on the watch, will be all the more satisfied, if I fuck her first. Don't be alarmed, my dear,' said he, as he observed a sudden move of Mary, who all at once recollected how exposed her whole person was. 'I shall do nothing without your full consent, but I am quite sure your brother, who takes you each in turn, will rather be pleased than otherwise, to see you in my arms, or I much mistake his character.'

I could not help, internally, thinking how exactly be had hit off my very thought, for I had just been calculating, in my own mind, how much better it would be for us to make him a participator with us, rather than an enemy by a refusal. So I at once averred that as it had turned out, it was likely to add greatly to all our pleasure, and I begged Mary to let him have his way. The natural reluctance of woman to appear too easy of access made her simulate a refusal, but as she still lay on her back, I leant over her. Opening her legs, I begged him to kneel between and help himself. He gallantly, on kneeling, first stooped forward, and gave a good lick-up of all her cunt's spunk-covered lips, and then proceeded to gamahuche her, which quickly made her as anxious for his prick as he was to fuck her. As soon as they were fairly at it, I whistled, and beckoned to Lizzie to come up. You may easily imagine her surprise to see Mary in the arms of a strange man; but as the sight had had its usual effect on my sensitive organ, and as it was standing, almost ready to burst, I made her kneel opposite to them, and introduced my prick into her cunt from behind, so that we could both see the delicious fuck going on before us. It redoubled our excitement, and all four of us spent together in cries of rapture. After this bout we sat down to make further acquaintance, which, you may suppose, was not difficult, after such an introduction. Our new friend gave us some hints very useful for future proceedings, meanwhile he was feeling young Lizzie's cunt with one hand, and my prick with the other, very nicely and gently frigging it. He brought me to full stand very quickly, and then made me lie on my back, while he proceeded to admire and praise the extraordinary development. He declared it was the greatest for one of my age he had ever met with, and his experience was very extensive. When it was at full stand, he stooped forward, and in the most delicious manner, sucked my prick. It was more exciting than when either of my sisters, Miss Evelyn, or Mrs Benson had gamahuched me. He also inserted a finger in my bottom-hole, and eventually made me spend in his mouth, which he greedily swallowed, nor did he cease sucking until every drop was drawn out of me. This had, of course, excited him, and he said: 'Now, I must have the young one in her turn.'

Lizzie, nothing loath, lay down on the grass at once, I conducted his prick into her cunt, and frigged his bottom-hole, while their bout lasted. His prick was one of the middlings, not very long, nor very thick, but of a uniform size throughout, without any large projection of the nut, like mine. He advised us to stop for that day, and to walk towards the village with him, and then when in full sight, but far beyond hearing, we could sit down and concert measures for future pleasures of the most delicious lubricity.

'I see,' he said, 'that we shall just hit it. I shall greatly add to your pleasures, and you to mine; you have something yet to learn, and I am the very person to instruct you in even higher delights than any of you have yet enjoyed.'

We followed him as desired, and, seated on a sand hillock, we held a long conversation, and arranged everything for future indulgencies. We agreed

to meet at the rocks next day at our usual hour, he undertaking to be there
ahead of us, to see that no lurking stranger should have hidden himself, as he
had done that day. He would think over the matter in the meantime, and
contrive some way of meeting where we could be fully at ease, and strip
ourselves naked, so as to enjoy a complete orgy of the most salacious
lubricity. He showed us where he was lodged, a small inn a little way out of
the village with its front to the road. Behind the stables, there was attached
to it a small cottage, consisting of a bedroom above, with a dressing-room,
or small bedroom if necessary, over the passage; the door opened upon the
coast, and there was no other communication with the inn than by going
round past the stable yard to the front door. The servant of the inn came
round in the morning, and laid his modest breakfast of tea, eggs and toast,
and when he was done, cleared away and made his bed, etc. He took his
dinner in the inn parlour at the hour the landlord and family dined. Nothing
overlooked his windows, and he was sufficiently away from the village not to
be easily observed, still less so from the inn. On approaching his lodgings
from the sands, he was almost as safe from observation as if he had lived in a
lonely house far distant from any other. I am thus particular in describing his
lodgings, as the advantages of the situation afterwards induced us to turn them
to profitable use. Our friend's name was MacCallum, James MacCallum, an
offshoot of the great Scotch clan of that name, then in about his thirtieth year,
fond of sporting, particularly fishing. His room was surrounded with the
necessary implements, and he much frequented Wales, from its advantage of
possessing so many good trout streams. He it was who gave me a taste for the
piscatory art, and I afterwards accompanied him on many a fishing excursion,
which often led to new and singular erotic adventures, of which I may,
perhaps, hereafter recount a few. His ordinary residence was London, and
our present acquaintance led to some most intimate relations of true erotic
extravagance, of which more anon.

Meanwhile, we met at the rocks on the next day, a Saturday. We found
Mr MacCallum at his post, and all being secure, proceeded to action. It was
Mary's turn to take the first watch. Our friend constituted himself master of
the ceremonies. He desired me to take off my breeches, and Lizzie to take
off her gown and ease her corset, for as yet she wore no stays; then telling me
to lie down on my back, he made Lizzie kneel at my head, with her bottom
to me, and then to press back so as to bring her charming little cunt over
my mouth, her under-petticoat and chemise being well canted over her
shoulders. I thus had complete command of her clitoris with my tongue, and
she could sink her buttocks quite down on my face, so that I could shove my
tongue well up her cunt, and lick up all her spendings when she discharged;
and at the same time, while embracing the charming plump hard buttocks
with one hand, the other was left free to frig her bum-hole, and stimulate her
passions up to the utmost. I have already told you how naturally she
had taken to posterior pleasures. While thus engaged, Mr MacCallum

proceeded to gamahuche my prick in the most delicious manner, for he had an art in this delightful accomplishment that far exceeded that of the many by whom I have been gamahuched – of course, he added the *postillon*, as the French say, by frigging my bottom-hole at the same time. He made me most voluptuously discharge in his mouth at the very instant dear Lizzie was pouring into mine her delicious spendings. We lay enraptured for some time before we could stir.

Then rising, I wished to return the compliment Mr M. had paid my prick, by sucking his. But this he declined, saying: 'I shall teach you all a new pleasure before we part, and my powers are not quite so active as your youth enables you to be, so for the moment we will indulge in close observation and sweet caresses of our members until by gentle titillations I get you two more prepared for the amorous contest – '

He gamahuched Lizzie while handling my prick, and a very short period elapsed before he had us both in such a state of excitement that we were ready for anything he chose to direct. This time he also required me to lie down on my back, but he placed Lizzie on the top of me, and guided my prick himself into her delicious tight little notch. When fully inserted, which was completely accomplished before she quite lay down upon me, he desired us to go slowly to work. For a short time, with his face close to my cods, he watched the in and out movement of my prick, inserting a finger into both Lizzie's bottom and mine. Then rising, he said: 'Stop a little, my dears, but don't withdraw. I am about to give your sister a lesson in the double action of most delicious pleasure.'

Then spitting on his prick, and applying a quantity of saliva to the rosy orifice of her bottom, he proceeded to insert his prick – little thinking how fond she was of taking pleasure in this route, and how often she had already enjoyed it. He took every precaution not to hurt her, and to be as gentle as possible, telling her to push out her bottom, and to strain as if she wanted to void something, which he told her would facilitate his entrance, and give her less pain. You may imagine how secretly pleased Lizzie was; she did all he desired – and with great gentleness he succeeded in sheathing his prick up to the close junction of his belly against her buttocks.

'Capital, my dear, you have borne it admirably. I see you will make an apt scholar; now you will have nothing but the most ecstatic raptures from the action of two pricks at once. Now, Charles, it is for you to work, and for your most charming sister to continue only the exquisite pressures she is already at this moment so rapturously conferring on our excited members.'

We thus commenced the first lesson we ever had in the double fuck. Dear Lizzie was almost mad with the agonising sensations of rapturous pleasure the double thrusting produced upon her erotic nerves. I, too, felt the rubbing of Mr M.'s prick so closely upon mine, for the slight membrane dividing the bottom passage from the vagina, by the powerful stretching of the two members between which it was sandwiched, became so thin a division that it really appeared as if there was nothing between our pricks. Such ecstatic excitement brought matters to a speedy conclusion. Lizzie screamed so loudly with her excess of pleasure that it somewhat alarmed Mary, who came running up to see what was the matter. Her surprise was great at the sight she beheld, but we were far too deliciously wrapt in the lap of most salacious luxury and lubricity to be sensible to any interruption. As for Lizzie she was in convulsions of ecstasy, which ended in quite a hysteric attack which rather alarmed us, and made us withdraw from the exquisite sheaths in which we had been engulfed with such rapture. It was some time before dear Lizzie recovered her senses, and then she burst into tears, declaring she had never before known what pleasure meant, and she had been in the seventh heaven of delight, that she could wish for no better death than to die in such agony of pleasure. She then threw herself into Mr M.'s arms, and kissing him with the utmost fervour, said: 'Oh, you dear man, how I love you for teaching me such a delicious way of loving; you shall have me whenever and wherever you please. I shall love you as much as I do my darling brother Charlie.'

She then turned to me and warmly embraced me too. Then, putting on her gown, she proceeded to take up the watch, while Mary remained to be likewise initiated in the luxury of the double fuck. She somewhat dreaded the experiment, but having witnessed the ecstasies of pleasure it had thrown Lizzie into, she was not unwilling to try if it could be accomplished with Mr MacCallum's somewhat less massive member. He put us through the same preliminary manoeuvres of backing Mary on her knees over my mouth, and while he sucked my prick, he feasted his eyes at the same time on Mary's really finely developed buttocks, giving him promise of great after-pleasure. He even begged me to leave her bottom-hole to his finger so that he frigged the bum-hole of the sister while he sucked the prick of the brother, a combination which afforded him the most racy delight Mary was greatly excited, and spent most copiously in my mouth, while I quickly followed suit in the mouth of Mr M, who did not allow a drop to be wasted. When we had reposed ourselves sufficiently, his lascivious touches and caresses and praises of our parts soon sufficiently re-excited us to let him see if we might again proceed to action. As before, I lay down on my back, and Mary, straddling across me, had my prick guided into her longing cunt by the hand of Mr M. When I was fairly engulfed in her hot and throbbing cunt, she began her exquisite *casse-noisette* pressures, which talent she possessed in the greatest perfection; then she bent down to me and I clasped her in my arms and glued my lips to hers in a loving kiss and tongue embrace. Her bottom presented itself in all its beauty to our worthy master of the ceremonies, who, delighted with its more fully blown beauties than that of the younger sister, paid first due homage to it by fondly kissing it, and thrusting his tongue up the rosy orifice, titillating her excessively, then wetting his prick he applied it to the tender rosebud-like dimple at first without success, Mary telling him she did not think he could possibly succeed.

'Patience and perseverance, my dear girl,' said he, 'will enable me to get into a mouse; we must try another way; it is that great huge monster of a prick in your cunt that is so blocking up the route as to close almost entirely the way to the more secret temple of salacious delights. Withdraw for a moment.'

I did so; upon which he plunged in an instant up to the hilt in her cunt and gave a few shoves to excite her and throw her off her guard, for he told us afterwards, the first difficulty was all owing to Mary's involuntary opposition, by squeezing in her bottom-hole, instead of pushing it out. When he thought he had sufficiently excited her, and made her suppose he was going to continue regularly fucking her, he suddenly withdrew the two fingers he had in her bum-hole, by a jerk substituted his prick, and before Mary was aware, had sheathed it more than halfway into her bottom. She gave a half scream, but his hold of her hips, and my close embrace of her waist, for I all along knew what he was at, prevented her from flinching and throwing him out, which was her first impulse. He said: 'I will keep still, and any unpleasant feeling will go off in a moment.'

He stopped for two or three minutes, which I occupied in first rubbing the end of my prick on Mary's clitoris, which was a well-developed one, and when by her nervous movements I found her passions were being roused, I slipped it into her tightened cunt without much difficulty. Mr M. took the opportunity of finding me penetrating to glide in on his point of attack up to his utmost limit. Mary gasped again, and declared it was choking her. However, by a little more patience, and then by very gentle movements, we gradually worked her up to the utmost state of excitement, and she, as well as both of us, went off in a delirium of enraptured felicity. She lay panting and throbbing between us for nearly a quarter of an hour.

I was already in a state for renewed efforts, but Mr M. rose, and withdrew his reeking prick from the tight recess in which it had enjoyed such ecstasies, and told us we must be content with that day's work, expressly as he had a plan in his head for the next day, that would require us to have all our erotic powers at command. Then, as before, we approached the village, so as to be seen, but not overheard, so that our going away to more distant places should create no suspicion. Mr M. then informed us that we could come to his cottage the next afternoon, instead of the rocks; we should be able to undress ourselves in the buff, and have a perfect orgy of salacious delights. We heartily approved of this plan, and after an amusing conversation, we parted to meet the next day on the sands, but in the contrary directions to the rocks, for the purpose of afterwards approaching his cottage from the least observable site.

After dinner the next day we started at our usual hour apparently for our ordinary promenade, but after leaving the village, and allowing most of the people to be safely stowed away in church for the afternoon service, we turned on our steps and made for Mr M.'s door. He saw us coming, and was ready to admit us, without knocking. We immediately adjourned to the bedroom upstairs, and lost no time in all of us stripping stark naked. After some preliminary admiration of the two girls, whose forms were certainly cast in beauty's mould, we lay down in bed. I and Lizzie mutually gamahuched each other, with the usual accompaniments in the charming orifices of our bottoms. Mr MacCallum and Mary, for he had taken a great fancy to her and her splendid bottom, followed our example, After we had a happy and most delicious spend, and then mutual embraces and kisses, we put the girls into all conceivable poses, until we were once more ready to go on with something more serious than gamahuching. Mr M., as usual, acted as master of the ceremonies, and ordered Mary to lie down on her back, then Lizzie reversed upon her, so that she could gamahuche Mary's cunt, and tickle her bum-hole, while Mary was to frig Lizzie's clitoris with one hand, and play with my cods with the other, Mr M. himself guided my prick into the delicious bottom-hole of Lizzie, and when we were all fixed, and he had frigged my bum-hole with two fingers, he said: 'Now I am going to initiate you, Charlie, into the delight of being alike operator and receiver.'

So saying, he moistened his tool and spit in my bum-hole, and proceeded very gently to introduce his prick therein. I have described his cock as not very thick at the point, consequently the first part introduced itself very easily, but when the pillar pushed its way in, and began to stretch the parts, it produced a curious sickening feeling, very like as if I had received a kick on the bottom, so I was obliged to ask him to halt a little. He was too experienced in the art not to fully understand my feelings, and knew well it would go off in a minute or two, if I was left quiet. So pausing until I told him he might now try to get in further, he drew back a little and applying more spittle to the shaft, gently and firmly, and slowly guided his prick up to the hilt, or as far as his belly and my buttocks would allow. Again pausing a little, until feeling by the throbbing of my prick, which produced the same pressure on my bum-hole, that I was warming to the work, he began slow movements of thrusts in and out, which, together with the hot and voluptuous pressures and movements of my own little partner excited both by Mary's finger and my prick, began to fire my passions, and we soon grew very fierce in our movements. Nothing I could ever have imagined equalled the extraordinary and delicious ecstasy that the double actions produced upon my erotic nerves. I gasped, I shuddered with the agony of intense pleasure, and at the moment when the grand and rapturous finale approached, I actually brayed exactly like a donkey, which, in after cooler moments, amused all of us. The action of pleasure had come upon all at once, and we sank in an inert mass on those below us. How poor Mary endured it astonished us, but the scene had so excited her that she said it never occurred to her, and she felt nothing.

We eventually rose, and after a necessary purification, partook of wine and cake, which Mr MacCallum, with great foresight, had provided. After that he would not allow us to fuck for some time; and we had a regular romp all about the room, which we enjoyed very much, and nothing was heard but slaps on our bottoms, and the wildest rollicking laughter – until our two cocks, by their stiff-standing, showed that we were again ready to enter on new combats. This time Lizzie lay down, Mary gamahuched her. Mr M. got into her bum-hole, and I proceeded to attempt to do the same to him, but all to no purpose. I was too heavy hung for his bottom-hole, a very small one for a man. He had every wish to accommodate me, but do what I would, I could not overcome the physical difficulties. So reversing our positions, I lay on my back, Mary straddled over me, took my prick into her cunt and, stooping down, presented her anus so that M. succeeded more easily than the day before in getting into her burn-hole. Lizzie standing up with a leg on each side of Mary's and my body, brought her quim up to M.'s mouth, and he luxuriously gamahuched her, while his finger acted postilion in her bottom. The erotic storm raged with great fury for a long time, and then, growing more fast and furious, brought us all standing in ecstasies of the most salacious enjoyment, for us to sink once more into the annihilation of satiated desire. We lay long wrapped in close embrace. Recovering our senses in long-drawn sighs, we again refreshed ourselves with wine and cake, and as our passions were not so quickly reawakened as those of our more excitable companions, we proceeded to gamahuche them, without their exercising a like skill upon our pricks. We then had another romp, and replacing Mary below and Lizzie above, I, this time, fucked her cunt, at her request, as she said it must not be altogether neglected. M., as previously, took me behind, and as there was a greater facility, so there was greater enjoyment, and as our previous exertions had taken off the sharper appetite, we were enabled to draw out our pleasure to a much greater length, until at last we died away in all the agony of such a glorious conjunction of parts. We had one more delicious general fuck before we parted. Lizzie was again fucked by me, and buggered by Mr M., which she declared she preferred to any other combination, my prick so deliciously gorging her tight little cunt, and making M.'s prick, from the pressure of my larger weapon in the cunt, feel as tight in her bottom as my prick did, when nothing but Mary's finger was in her cunt. We ran our course with even greater luxury and lasciviousness than before. Lizzie actually was hysterical with the force of her enjoyment, and we all sank sideways off poor Mary, and lay long locked in each other's arms. This, for that day, ended our most delightful orgy. We purified ourselves, and then dressed. We parted with many sweet embraces, and promises of renewing the delightful scenes we had just gone through, and, in fact, we often and often repeated them, varying from time to time with a visit to the rocks, lest we should draw observation upon us by constantly going to the cottage.

Our six weeks came to an end so rapidly that we could hardly believe the time had already passed. Mamma one morning informed us we were to leave on the day after the next. You may suppose our disappointment, but there was no help for it. We met that day at the rocks, we were melancholy at the thought of parting with our charming friend, whom we now really loved. We were not nearly so fiery as usual, but resolved to have one thorough good orgy the next day at the cottage, as a farewell benefit to us all. We met, as agreed on, and put in force every art to augment our pleasures, and every contrivance to excite anew our powers to the utmost. Both M. and I must have spent six to seven times, but the girls being more easily excited in their finer organs of coition, went off in ecstasies some nine or ten times; until fairly exhausted, we had, from want of power, to give up the game, dress and part. We hoped to meet again. The girls wept at parting with our delightful friend, to whom we owed so many delicious orgies. We exchanged addresses, and he promised to come on a fishing excursion to our neighbourhood, where he hoped we should find means of renewing the lascivious sports we had already so much enjoyed. We tore ourselves away from him at last. It will be seen in the sequel, that unforeseen events carried me to London, or rather away from home, before we could meet again; and it was in London, at his own chambers, where we again renewed our charming intercourse, and practised every art of venery.

We returned home, and mamma again advertised for a governess, and stated that she required one of not less than thirty years of age, and with much experience in teaching. Numerous responses were made to the advertisement; but one lady desired to see mamma and her pupils before accepting the place, at the same time forwarding very satisfactory testimonials. Mamma was rather struck with the style of letter, and the unusual demand of previous acquaintance before entering into final arrangements. So she wrote to Miss Frankland, begging her to come and spend three days with us, and if her visit should prove as agreeable to both as her letter had done to mamma, she had no doubt matters might be arranged to their mutual satisfaction. Accordingly, at the expected hour, Miss Frankland arrived. She was, to our then thinking, an elderly lady, rather above thirty years of age than under, of tall and commanding figure, somewhat large, but no superfluous fat, broad shouldered, and wide hipped, with bosoms well separated, but not too prominent. Her hair was coal black, and her eyes equally so, but with the most determined expression, rendered more so by very thick eyebrows, which met in the middle. She showed also a well-marked downy moustache, and the small curly hairs below her head, at the back of her neck, literally lost themselves beneath her high-necked dress. She always wore long sleeves, and never showed bare arms. I afterwards found the reason of this was that her arms were so black with thick hair that she was ashamed to let them be seen, although, in reality, beautifully formed and plump. Her mouth was large; it showed animal passion, but at the same time determined firmness of character. You could not call her handsome, but there was altogether an appearance of face, expression, and person that might well be styled a fine woman. As for us, at the period of first seeing her, we only marked the determined character of her countenance, and at once dreaded her becoming our governess, as we felt we should not only have one who would master us, but who would also be severe in every way. Youth is often a better physiognomist than it is credited with. It will be seen in the sequel whether we had judged correctly or not. Suffice it to say that her three days' visit ended in her being perfectly satisfied with the offered position, and mamma being equally satisfied with her. We did not know at the time, but afterwards found out, that she had made it a *sine qua non* that she should have *carte blanche* as to the use of the rod. She had observed to mamma that she thought we had been too leniently treated by our late governess, and it would be necessary to exert severe discipline, which, in her own experience, she had always found most efficacious. My mother, who had during the last two months found us rather headstrong and wilful, quite chimed in with her idea, and gave every authority to do quite as she liked, either with her girls or her son.

Terms being so arranged, Miss Frankland required a week to make all her arrangements before definitely taking up her new residence. My mother, thinking we should be well kept in on the arrival of Miss Frankland, left us in uninterrupted liberty until then; you may be sure we improved the occasion, and did our best to make up for the loss of our inestimable and amiable friend, Mr MacCallum. Not only did we make use of the summerhouse by day, but every night I stole up to my loved sisters' room, where we tried to emulate the luxurious scenes of lubricity we had lately been so deliciously indulging in at the seaside in Wales. Of course, the week passed far too quickly, and on the appointed day my mother drove into the town to bring Miss Frankland home, on the arrival of the coach. My two sisters accompanied her, as something or other was always wanted for the girls; and as Miss Frankland and her luggage would quite fill the carriage on their return, I was left by myself at home, a most fortunate circumstance, as it turned out.

I was somewhat annoyed at being left alone. But how true it is that 'man proposes and God disposes'. Had I gone with them I should have missed a most delicious and unexpected treat. I had strolled to the summerhouse in a sort of despair at the lost opportunity of again fucking my sisters before the arrival of the dreaded governess. I was listlessly gazing out of the window when I suddenly became aware of a lady waving her hand to me from a gig coming down the road which our summerhouse commanded. In an instant I recognised Mrs Vincent. To run down the hillock, unbolt the private door, and welcome her to our house, was the work of a moment. I begged her to get out and walk to the house through the grounds, her servant could drive round to the stables and wait there. She did so at once. I gave her no explanation of all being absent until I had her safe in the summerhouse. Without a word I seized her round the waist, and pressing her back on the couch, quickly unbuttoned my trousers, and pulling up her petticoats, was pushing my stiff prick against her belly before she was almost aware of my intentions.

'My dear Charlie,' she cried, 'what are you at? We shall be discovered, and it will be my ruin.'

'Oh, no, my ever loved Mrs Vincent; they are all away to town, and we have nothing to fear.'

She loved me too well to make further resistance; on the contrary, seconding me with all her accustomed art, we both quickly sank in all the voluptuous raptures of satisfied desire. I would not quit my position, but kissing her rapturously, I shoved my tongue into her mouth, and stopped her remonstrances. The excitement of meeting her after a two months' separation stimulated my passions to the utmost, and with hardly bated breath I began a fresh career, but with more moderation and greater pains to make her a perfect participant in the raptures I myself was receiving. She thoroughly enjoyed it, and being relieved from any fear of surprise, after my informing her of the absence of all the family, she gave way to all the force of her ardent amorous propensities, enjoyed our delicious fuck thoroughly, and spent at the same time as myself with screams of satiated passion. After this I withdrew. She kissed me most tenderly, and said I was as bad and wild a boy as ever, that she loved me too tenderly ever to refuse me anything I desired, and begged me to sit by her side and talk of old times.

'No,' I said, 'on the contrary, tell me all about yourself; I have not seen you since your marriage day, and I want to know how the after-part went off. I was in dread lest our embracings should have left traces that would make your husband suspect you were not all he had anticipated.'

'You are a strange boy, my dear Charlie, and more of a man in every way than many ten years older than yourself. Who would have thought such ideas would have been running through so young a head. Well, my darling boy, I was somewhat uneasy on that very point myself, and, indeed, had fixed the marriage day when I expected I should be unwell on the very night, but in that I was disappointed; nothing came, and I was driven to act in the best way I could. I kept my legs close together. I got my hand down to that part of my person, and kept squeezing my affair as close as possible. I pressed hard with my fingers on his weapon as he forced an entrance, and all at once gave way with a scream of apparent pain, as he gave an extra thrust, and let him penetrate at once. An inexperienced husband takes much on credit and imagination, I quite satisfied him that he was the first possessor of my person; but, oh! my beloved Charlie, I found I was really already in the family way, and you, my dear fellow, are the father of the baby now within my womb.'

'What? I! I! the father of your baby? Oh, dear, darling Mrs Vincent; oh, say that again.'

'It is indeed true, my dear Charlie; and the knowledge that I first possessed you, and you me, reconciles me to giving my husband a child that is not his.'

'My child! my child!' I cried, and I danced round in a paroxysm of delight at the idea of being a father. It seemed at once to elevate me to manhood, and puffed me up with pride. I rushed upon dear Mrs V., embraced her most warmly, and pushing her back on the sofa, said: 'I must see how the little angel looks in his cell.'

I turned up her petticoats, and exposed all her beauteous belly, already by its swelling showing there was more there than ever went into her mouth. Her cunt too had become more prominent. I stooped, kissed her lovely quim, gave it a good suck, then gamahuched her till she cried out for my prick to fuck her, and a most exquisite and rapturous fuck we had. The thought that I was baptising my own babe with my sperm stimulated my lubricity, and we ran a course of the most libidinous delights until we dissolved away in the most voluptuous death-like exhaustion of satisfied desires.

'Charlie, my darling, you must get up; remember you may injure the dear little creature by too great an excess, so pray rise.'

I rose at once, but only to embrace her most tenderly. She complained of feeling somewhat faint, and said we must now go to the house to get some wine. We put ourselves in order, and all radiant at the thoughts of paternity, I strutted along as proud as a peacock, and thinking no small beer of myself. I hardly knew whether I stood on my head or my heels, and was quite extravagant in my conduct. Dear Mrs V. was obliged seriously to caution me before I could come to a proper reserved behaviour in presence of the servants. She rested about half an hour, and was about to order the gig up to the door, but I implored her to send it round to the road below the summerhouse, as I should all the longer have the pleasure of being with her. She smiled, and again gave me a pat on the cheek, as much as to say, 'I understand you, you rogue,' but did as I suggested. So we proceeded through the grounds, and were at the summerhouse some time before the gig could be harnessed and come round to the road below. I did not wait for that, but embracing darling Mrs V., wanted to push her down on the sofa.

'No, no, dear Charlie, that will tumble my dress too much, and we shall have no time to put it in order; stop, I will kneel on the low couch, and you will stand behind, I can guide you from below, and you know I always thought you got further in and gave me more pleasure that way than any other.'

She knelt down, and I canted her clothes right over her shoulders, and exhibited her fine buttocks, which, now she was in the family way, had widened out, and were fatter and rounder than ever. First gluttonously kissing them, I brought my prick right against them. Mrs Vincent projected her hand behind, seized and guided him into her glowing and longing cunt, and he plunged at one bound up to the hilt.

'Gently, Charlie dear,' she cried, 'remember our dear baby is there, and you must not be too violent.'

This at once reduced me to moderation. I had a hand on each hip, and as I slowly glided in, I pressed her splendid buttocks backwards to meet me. I kept my body upright so as to enjoy the lovely sight of the movement of her bottom.

'Put your arm round and feel my clitoris, Charlie, dear.'

I did so for a minute, and then whispered: 'It is such delight to gaze on your splendid bum in action, so pray apply your own finger to your clitoris, and let me enjoy the lovely sight.'

'Very well, darling.'

And I could feel her frigging away most furiously. This enabled me to introduce first one and then two fingers into her most delicious bottom-hole. When I found she was in the greatest state of excitement, I suddenly shifted my prick, and substituted it for my fingers. In her surprise and excitement, she had no time to resist, and I glided in, not too rapidly, quite up as far as I could go. She flinched a little, and called me a bad fellow, but I held her hips too tight to allow of her unseating me, even if she had wished. I begged she would let me go on, for I had never forgotten the delight of doing it this way the night before her marriage. She made no reply, but I could feel redoubled action with her finger on her clitoris; and the muscular twitchings of her loins and sphincter soon convinced me that nothing would please her better than finishing our course where I was – and most delicious it proved. We should have died away in loud cries of agonised delight but for the necessity of prudence, for doubtless the gig was then awaiting but a few yards off. My darling mistress seemed unwilling to let me withdraw; she held my prick in such close and firm embrace, throbbing on it from moment to moment, and so exciting him that she shortly felt he was again stiffening inside of her. She rose on her legs, and by that action unsheathed me. Then, turning round, she threw her arms about my neck, and most tenderly embraced me, thanking me for having given her such exquisite proofs of love.

'But I must go, my dear Charlie, and I hope we shall have occasionally some other delicious opportunity of enjoying such raptures again. Say everything kind to your mother and the girls, and tell them I shall come ever again shortly and see them all.'

I saw her into her gig, and watched her until a turn in the road hid her from my sight. I returned to the summerhouse, and kissed the spot she had last pressed with her lovely body. My soul was filled with love of her, and pride that I was man enough to put a babe into her belly. I strutted about the room, and if anyone could have seen me I should doubtless have appeared ridiculous. Mamma, our new governess, and the girls returned to tea. I told them of Mrs Vincent's visit, and her regret at finding them absent, also of her promise to drive over again on an early day. My mother hoped I had been attentive to her. I said I had, as well as I could, and had got some wine and biscuits as she complained of not feeling very well; she thought the jolting road had tired her.

It may well be supposed that after the impression our new governess had made upon us, we were very attentive for some time. Indeed, her system of teaching was really excellent; she was far superior, in that respect, to our former governess. She had a method of interesting you in what she was teaching, and for quite two months we paid such great attention, and made such really extraordinary progress, that she could not help praising us highly to mamma while we were in the room. This was bad policy, because, with the natural thoughtlessness of youth, we fancied ourselves so clever that we became less attentive. This was patiently borne with for some time, probably in consequence of our previous good behaviour. But at last Lizzie was somewhat impudent when blamed rather harshly by Miss Frankland.

'Oh! it has come to that, has it? We shall see.'

She continued our lessons until four o'clock as usual, and then desired Lizzie to remain where she was; she dismissed Mary and me, locked the door on poor Lizzie, and went away, doubtless for a rod. She soon returned, and locking herself in, most severely whipped poor Lizzie's bottom. She sent her out when it was finished, and Lizzie joined us, weeping bitterly from the pain she was suffering. We laid her on the couch, and turned her petticoats over her head to cool her bottom, which she declared felt as if burning hot coals were spread over it. I kissed the dear red buttocks that were all covered with weals and looked like raw beef, but no blood had been drawn. We fanned her with our handkerchiefs, which she said was a delightful relief. In a very few minutes she began to wriggle her bottom in a state of excitement, and cried out: 'Dear Charlie, do shove your prick into my cunt, it has begun to long for a fuck.'

I wanted nothing but this to instantly act, for the sight of her bare bum had already made my cock stand as stiff as iron. She raised herself on her hands and knees, presenting the back entrance to her cunt, and telling me it was there she must have it instantly. I plunged up to the hilt in a moment, for she was as juicy and moist as if she had spent, which it is more than probable was the case. Very few powerful thrusts on my part, seconded by energetic action on hers, and she spent again with a scream of delight, and with a pressure on my cock that almost hurt it. She hardly paused a moment before she cried out: 'Shove on, dear Charlie, push it in further if you can, I am burning with desire.'

She wriggled her backside in every way in the most lascivious and delicious manner, and when she felt the crisis approaching, by the increased swelling and hardness of my prick as well as the peculiar electric effect at the moment, she met my flood of sperm with so copious a discharge that it literally spurted out and deluged my cods and thighs. She held me tight, and would not allow me to withdraw until I had myself spent four times and she seven at least. We then rose, her nerves calmed by the repeated doses of hot boiling sperm shot into her interior. She declared that never in all her fucking had she felt such insatiable desire, or more ravishing delight in satisfying it, that she would undergo a dozen such floggings to have the same rapturous enjoyment.

'I am sure,' she said, 'it was all the effect of the rod, I never felt anything like it before.'

Mary all this time had been but a spectator, and a pleased one to see the erotic fury of her sister and my powerful efforts to allay it. It is true we had both had a delicious fuck during the time poor Lizzie was catching it on her backside, and I had just gamahuched her deliciously afterwards as Lizzie came in in such pain.

Miss Frankland had retired to her room, and looked still flushed and somewhat wild looking when she joined us after the usual hour's recreation. As may well be supposed, we were all as attentive as possible. There was one circumstance that evidently pleased Miss Frankland immensely. When Lizzie, in her turn, went up to repeat her lesson, she suddenly threw her arms round Miss Frankland's neck, and with tears running over her cheeks, sobbed out: 'Dear Miss Frankland, pray forgive me, and let me kiss you, for I love you dearly.'

There was a bright sparkle of delight in Miss Frankland's eyes. She clasped Lizzie round the waist, and drew her to her lips in a long sweet kiss of love, which seemed as if it would never end. We observed Miss Frankland's colour rise. She at last put Lizzie away, and said she was a dear amiable girl, whom she could not help loving.

'Go to your seat, you are too agitated, my dear, to say your lesson just now; so send Mary up.'

Lizzie came back to her seat, but I could not help fancying I saw a complete expression of erotic desire on her countenance. When afterwards we were alone together, she told us that when the governess kissed her, she felt Miss F.'s tongue glide into her mouth, and 'tip her the velvet' in a most delicious and exciting manner, and she believed that if they had been alone they must have given each other mutual embraces of a warmer description. This led me to think that Miss Frankland was herself rendered lecherous by the action of even wielding the rod. Lizzie during the whole of the next week did nothing but rave of the excessive excitement that her whipping had put her into, and the extreme felicity she felt in having her salacious lechery satisfied. We were not able to meet every day, for frequently Miss Frankland accompanied us, and joined in the youthful sports we then gave way to. Lizzie continuing to harp on the extraordinary enjoyment the whipping had procured her, after it was over, fired the imagination of Mary, until she was wound up to a pitch of actually longing to be whipped. In such a case it was easy to incur the penalty; she had but wilfully to neglect her studies, and she was sure to get it. This she accordingly did, and it resulted as before. When released, she rushed to the summerhouse, and without any preliminaries, called upon me to fuck her directly; and a very similar scene followed to that which had occurred when dear Lizzie was whipped. Mary did not, however, give way to the uncontrollable desire to throw herself into Miss Frankland's arms as Lizzie had done. Miss F., as usual, retired to her room after the punishment was over, and was late in coming down, with the same flushed face and excited eye. I became convinced that she herself was salaciously excited by the act, and I began to fancy that with such passions, if I could but excite her in any way, it might be worth my while. When once these lecherous ideas were raised in my imagination, desire soon painted her with every charm of beauty, and I became excessively lewd and anxious to possess her. The more I looked at and scanned the really beauteous proportions of her finely developed form, the more my determination to have her took root, and grew strong within me.

About this time Miss Frankland, who had become a great favourite with mamma, obtained permission to take possession of the spare bedroom, with an understanding that she was to cede it to any visitor who might come. Of course, this circumstance made my desire to get into her good graces doubly strong, inasmuch as the opportunity of sleeping with her afterwards could be so easily effected. I determined to watch her when retiring to bed, and try to get a view of her naked form. For this purpose I removed the stopping of moistened bread I had put in the hole I made to see Mr Benson fucking his wife. I lay awake, until she came to bed. I saw her undress, but only caught sight of her naked bubbies, over her chemise. As I have said, they were not large, but widely separated, with a fine flat neck up to the throat. I mean that she showed no collar bone, which is a great beauty in woman. She had evidently been quite naked, and had used the bidet, but the extent of the slit in the door did not allow me to command the part of the room where she had used it. I remedied this defect next day, and the following night was rewarded with a most glorious sight. You may well suppose that I did not let sleep overcome me, but was at my post as soon as ever I heard her enter her room. I was on my knees in a moment, at my peephole, and saw her deliberately undress to her chemise. She then arranged all her magnificent head of hair, brushing it out as far and further than her arms would extend; and after well brushing and combing it, she plaited and rolled it up, in a great big rouleau behind, then washing her hands, she drew out the bidet, poured water into it, and then divested herself of her shift. She was standing in front of the dressing-table, with two candles shining on her, so that when she lifted her shift over her head, I had a well-lighted full view of her wonderfully covered belly. She was all over hair; it was as black as coal, and shone as if polished in all its beautiful curls. I am now an old man, but never have I seen the equal to that dear woman in a hairy belly. It was quite up to her navel, and several inches down the inside of her thighs, besides running thickly in the chinks of her bottom, and with two bunches where the beautiful back dimple is usually situated, as thick, and even thicker than

ordinary women have in on their mounts. In addition to this, there was a
beautiful little line of curls that ran up her belly, as far as between her
bubbies, to say nothing of the very hairy thighs, legs, and arms. I never saw a
more deliciously hairy woman, and she was all that such excessive growth of
hair denoted – passionate and lecherous to a degree, when once she had
confidence in her companion, to let her feelings have vent. Of course, I am
now describing my after-experience; at the moment I was only dazzled by
the extraordinary richness and quantity of that exquisite ornament – hair –
not only in splendid quantity on the head, but in a profusion such as I had
never then and have not since witnessed. I was struck dumb with astonishment and admiration. She laved her hairy cunt, and all the adjacent parts,
then wiped herself dry, put on her nightgown, extinguished her light, and,
of course, got into bed. So did I but only to toss and tumble, and at last,
in troubled sleep, to dream of that most gloriously covered cunt, and to
imagine myself revelling therein. So great was my excitement that I had the
first wet dream I ever experienced. It is needless to say, it was under the
dreaming idea that I was enjoying to the utmost that wonder cunt.

I was quite exhausted by morning with such a restless night, and was not
only very *distrait*, but was really so fatigued that I could not attend to my
lessons. Of course Miss Frankland noticed this, and being unaware of the
cause, attributed it to wilful idleness and bravado of her authority. She spoke
very gravely and seriously to me, and told me if I did not improve my
conduct by next day it would be her painful duty to punish me with severity.

'I expect to see you exhibit very different conduct tomorrow, otherwise
you will drive me to do that which I would much rather not.'

It rained hard that afternoon, and we had to amuse ourselves within
doors. On retiring for the night, I determined to watch again for Miss
Frankland, but my want of rest the previous night overpowered me, and I
fell fast asleep until far in the night. I rose and crept to my peep-hole, but all
was dark. I could hear Miss Frankland breathing heavily. The thought at
once struck me that I might safely steal up to my sisters' room, as they were
now alone, since Miss F. had the previous night removed to the spare
bedroom, where she was now fast asleep. So softly opening my door, and
leaving it ajar, I crept along the passage, gained my sisters' room, and gently
awakening them, jumped in between them, to their great joy and satisfaction. We immediately began with a gamahuche, I taking Mary's cunt,
while Lizzie crossed her legs over her head, and was gamahuched by Mary,
whose finger was at the same time acting postilion to her charming bottom-
hole, while I had the exquisite prospect before me of their operations. As
soon as ever Mary spent I made Lizzie lie down on her back, with her
head towards the bottom of the bed, Mary knelt over her in the opposite
direction, presenting her very full backside, which was daily developing
larger proportions. I plunged into her cunt, plugging her little rosy bum-
hole at the same time with my middle finger, while Lizzie did as much for

me, at the same time rubbing Mary's clitoris with the fleshy end of the thumb, while Mary, at the same time she herself was fucked and frigged in two places, was employed in gamahuching Lizzie, and frigging her bottom-hole with two fingers, Lizzie declaring that one finger felt as nothing. We lengthened out our delicious proceedings until excess of excitement compelled us to give way to all the fury of our feelings, and we managed to spend all together with such rapturous and lascivious delight as rendered us quite powerless for some time. We then had a delicious cuddle, the girls having each one hand on my prick and the other on my buttocks. When we had once more worked ourselves up to fucking heat, we reversed the previous position, and I fucked Lizzie. Mary was gamahuched and bottom-fingered by Lizzie, while she employed herself with Lizzie's clitoris and my bum-hole. Lizzie was far hotter and more salacious than any of us, and spent copiously on my delighted prick, which enjoyed excessively the warm bath of glutinous liquid that was poured down upon it. I gave a few slow-drawn thrusts in and out, to moisten well its whole shaft, and removing my two fingers from her delicious bottom-hole, and wetting it with my saliva, I withdrew my prick from the reeking sheath of her cunt, and to her great delight slowly housed it in her longing and exquisitely delicious bottom-hole, keeping it quiet there for some time, so as not to spend before Lizzie was ready. I enjoyed the delicious throbbing of her body, which at last becoming too exciting, I stooped over her, passed a hand under her belly, replaced Mary's fingers, rubbing her clitoris while Mary frigged her cunt with two fingers thrust into it. We thus quickly brought matters to an end, and died off in all the ecstasies of satiated lust. As daylight was beginning to dawn, I tore myself from their loving embraces, gained my room in safety, and slept the sleep of the just until late in the morning.

My orgy with my sisters had so far satisfied my animal passions that I rather began to dread the severity I knew Miss Frankland would use if I came under her hand. This made me so far attentive next day as to satisfy her; and as it was a fine afternoon she came out to walk in the garden, while we innocently amused ourselves. That evening I kept awake, and again enjoyed the superb display of Miss Frankland's wonderfully hairy cunt, all the lower part of her body was as black as a chimney sweeper's. The sight awakened every lustful feeling within me. I felt I must possess her, and determined to brave the severest infliction she could give me with the rod. I somehow, instinctively, arrived at the conclusion that this extraordinary profusion of hair could only grow where nature had implanted the hottest animal passions, and had but to greatly excite them to turn their lust to my advantage. I determined that tomorrow I should bring things to a crisis, and that I might be equal to every effort I went to my bed, and did not attempt to steal up to my sisters' room. Next day nothing could be made of me in the morning; Miss Frankland sternly warned me that if such conduct was pursued after dinner nothing should save my skin from a severe scourging.

However, my mind was made up, and I went in 'for the whole hog', as our vulgar Yankee cousins say. I was more idle and insubordinate than ever. Miss F. looked thunder; at four o'clock she ordered me to stay, and the girls to go. She then locked the door, took out from the desk a formidable rod, and told me to approach her. I did so – really half in fear, for she could look dreadfully fierce and determined, as was the case when I came up to her side.

'Now, Charles,' she said, 'your conduct, for two or three days past, has been such as I cannot put up with. Your mother has given me full power to punish any of you severely, if I think you deserve it; you are getting to be of an age that I hoped you would have so acted as to give me no cause of offence, but I am sorry to see my hopes are disappointed. I am now about to punish you; submit to it quietly, or it will be all the worse for you. Unbutton and put down your trousers.'

I felt I must submit, but when brought to this point I really so much dreaded her that there was not the slightest erection in poor cockey.

While I was undoing my trousers, I observed that Miss Frankland had quite lifted up her outer frock, and had sat down, evidently intending to flog me across her knee. Both being ready, she told me to put the footstool by her side and kneel upon it, then desiring me to bend forward over her knees she put one hand over my body to hold me down; then uncovering my bottom, and taking the rod, which was by her side, she raised her arm and gave me a fearful cut, which made me not only flinch, but cry out most lustily. Blow followed blow, causing at first great agony, that made me cry again in good earnest; then the very continuance of the blows seemed to deaden the parts until I hardly felt them. This was succeeded by a titilation and lascivious excitement which speedily brought my prick out in the fullest vigour. I then began to push it against Miss Frankland's thigh, and to wriggle myself nearly off her knees. Seemingly to prevent this, she passed her left arm quite round my body, bringing her hand under my belly, and, apparently by accident, against my prick, which she grasped, and I could feel her hand pass both up and down it as if she was measuring its length and thickness, continuing all the time to shower down blow after blow on my devoted backside. As she held a firm grasp on my prick, I pretended to be evading the blows, while in reality I was thrusting it in and out of her hand with the utmost energy and excitement, which speedily brought on the delightful crisis, and with a cry of rapture I gave down a copious discharge into her hand, and sank almost senseless on her lap. I pretended complete loss of consciousness, which she believing, she gently felt, and even frigged a little, my prick, pressing me the while close to her body, and then I felt a shudder run through her whole frame. I have no doubt she was in a paroxysm of lust, and had spent. I gave her time to recover a little, and then pretending to come to my senses, but in a confused state of ideas, said: 'Oh, what has happened? I have been in heaven!'

Then raising myself, and apparently only just recognising Miss Frankland, I threw my arms round her neck, and exclaimed: 'Dear Miss Frankland, do flog me again if it will produce again such ecstasies as I never before experienced.'

Her face was flushed, her eye shone with all the fire of libidinous passion. My prick had hardly lost its stiffness when I spent, and was now projecting out firmer than ever.

'Why, Charles, I thought you a mere boy, while you are quite a man with such a thing as this.'

'Oh!' I cried, 'do continue to hold it, you give me such pleasure!'

'Has anyone else ever held it in this way?'

'No, I never felt anything like it before.'

'But don't you know what this is meant to do?'

'Oh, yes, it is what I piddle from.'

She laughed, and asked if it was often in its present state of stiffness.

'Every morning when I awake it is so, and it hurts me very much until I piddle.'

'And has no one ever taught you any other use of it?'

'No, what use can it be of?'

'You dear innocent boy, if I could trust you, I would teach you a secret that this dear thing would greatly enjoy. But can I trust you?'

'Oh, certainly, dear Miss Frankland, I know what you mean now, to repeat the delicious sensations you gave me a few minutes ago. Oh, do, do! do it again, it was far too nice for me ever to tell anybody, as long as you will do it for me.'

'Well, Charles, I will trust you. Do you know that women are differently formed from you?'

'Yes, I used to sleep in mamma's room, and I have often been surprised to see that she piddled from a long hole, and has not got a doodle like I have to piddle from.'

'My dear innocent Charlie, that long hole was made to take in this dear fellow here that is throbbing almost to bursting in my hand, and if you promise me faithfully never to tell anyone, I will teach you how it is done.'

You may be sure my protestations of secrecy were most earnest.

'Look here then, my dear boy, and see what I have got between my legs.'

She laid herself back on the long chair, drew up her petticoats, and exhibited to my charmed gaze the wondrous wealth of hair she possessed. Opening her legs, I saw the wide-spread rosy lips showing themselves in beautiful contrast to the coal-black hair that grew in the greatest profusion all round the lower lips, and extended also some five or six inches down the side of each thigh. But what at the moment most astonished me, and drew all my attention, was to see a deep red clitoris standing out from the upper part of her cunt quite stiff, and as long and as thick as the middle finger of a man. I very nearly betrayed myself at the sight, but, fortunately, was able to keep up the character of apparent ignorance I had hitherto shown, and said: 'You, also, have got a little doodle to piddle with?'

She laughed, and said: 'It is very different from yours. Give me yours here, that I may kiss it.'

She fondled it for a second or two, and then could not resist the impulse to take it into her mouth and suck it.

'Oh, what pleasure! I shall die!'

'Not yet, dear boy; kneel down there, and I shall instruct you in the real secret of pleasure.'

But, before she could do anything, I threw my head down crying out: 'I must give this pretty little fellow a taste of the pleasure you have just given mine.'

And in an instant I had the delicious thing up to the root in my mouth, sucking furiously at it. Her twistings, and the up-and-down action of her loins, showed how rapturously I was exciting her; in fact, I brought on the crisis, when she pressed my head down hard upon it, and closed her thighs on each side of my head, as she poured over my chin and breast a perfect torrent of sperm. A minute after she seized my arms, and drew me up on her belly, then slipping her hand down between us, she seized my prick and guided him, nothing loath, into her burning hot and foaming cunt. She placed her hands on my buttocks, and pressing me right up to the hilt, began a movement, which she told me how to second, that in a very short time brought down an exquisite spend from me. The idea that she was giving me the first lesson in love, and of being the first possessor of my person, seemed to excite her lust to the utmost, and she immediately followed my discharge with another, so copious that it spurted all over my thighs. Her force of pressure on my prick in her agonies of enjoyment was so great as nearly to hurt me. I never knew anyone but her with such strength of pressure of cunt on the prick. She has often actually brought tears into my eyes, so powerful was her grip that it made me really feel as if in a vice. She lay back with closed eyes and panting bosom in a rapturous trance of lascivious lubricity, her throbbing cunt holding me tightly pressed between its palpitating folds in the most delicious imprisonment, and from time to time grasping my prick with a pressure that very shortly restored it to its fullest vigour and stiffness. She was as hot as fire and responded immediately to the renewed life she found stirring within me. She gave way to her salacious lust with, if anything, a more passionate excess than the first time. My superb weapon seemed to stir up within her a force of lubricity that nothing could seem to satisfy. Her hands clutched my buttocks convulsively, and seemed to wish to force my whole body into her wildly excited cunt. With such vigour was the action carried on that the grand crisis soon arrived, most rapturous to both, and almost maddening to Miss Frankland. The heavings of her body and gaspings for breath were quite hysterical, while, with one of those real vice-like pressures, I felt as if she were nipping my prick in two. It was not a mere throbbing pressure, but a long continued convulsive squeeze, as if her cunt had been seized like the jaws of the mouth with lockjaw, and could not open. It was nearly ten minutes before she recovered her senses. She seized my head between her hands, kissed me most lovingly, declared I was the dearest creature that ever lived, that she had never before had anyone who had so satisfied her, and filled her with inexpressible rapture, etc. This fondling had again brought up my prick to full stand. Miss Frankland said: 'Dear Charlie, we must be prudent, as the time is drawing near for your sisters' return.'

But there was no stopping, the exquisite pleasure of her splendid interior cunt pressures was irresistible. My movements speedily determined matters in my favour. Miss Frankland's temperament was far too warm not to quickly set her passions to the highest fucking heat; and again we had a most exquisite fuck, lengthened out more luxuriously by the more urgent fires of desire having been moderated by the three previous discharges. With more abandon we both sank in the death-like ecstasies of the delicious melting away in all the luxury of contented and voluptuous discharges. Miss Frankland lay for some short time luxuriously closing in my delighted prick, but raising her body, she said: 'Charles, we must cease for the present.'

And, pushing me away, I was forced to withdraw; but her dear cunt seemed as reluctant as myself, and held my prick so tight that I had to pull hard to draw it out, and, at last, he left with a noise like drawing a cork from a well-corked bottle. Before I rose, or she could hinder me, I threw myself down and glued my lips to her reeking cunt, and greedily licked up the foaming sperm that had surged out of her well-gorged quim. She with difficulty drew away her body, but as I rose she clasped me to her bosom and kissed me most fervently, and licked her own sperm off my richly covered lips. Begging me to button up, and putting herself to rights, she desired me to sit down by her side. She wiped my mouth with her handkerchief, arranged my disordered necktie, collar, and hair. We then embraced most tenderly, and she thanked me for the immense gratification I had given her; she praised my parts as being of extraordinary development and more satisfying than any she had yet had any experience of. This was the second time she referred to other experiences. I took no notice of this all the time, as if I was supposed to be too ignorant or innocent to think any harm of it, but I determined in some excess of passion to get her to give me a recital of some of her previous experiences.

Before my sisters came in, she said: 'I shall try and arrange some means for our meeting unobserved tomorrow. Meanwhile, you must sit as if you had been severely punished, and I shall assert that you had done everything to resist my authority, for which I had punished you further by not allowing you to leave the schoolroom.'

I said not a word to Miss F. about the ease of meeting by merely opening the door of communication between our rooms. I was afraid to make her suspicious of a former use of it. But I determined, when she came to bed, to rap at the door and beg her to open it, and I had no doubt she would be as delighted as myself to find with what facility she could indulge to the utmost every libidinous passion which her lascivious nature could suggest. My sisters returned, and appeared disappointed that I had not been able to join them, as they had anticipated a glorious fuck or two each, after the whipping had excited me as it did them. They told me afterwards they had been obliged to content themselves with a double mutual gamahuche, but it did not make up for my absence.

While they were all engaged after tea, I slipped up to Miss Frankland's room to see that the key was in the lock of the door between our two rooms. I opened it, oiled the hinges, and locked it again from her side. I also, with a view to sometimes slipping up to my sisters' room, oiled my own and their doors, hinges, and locks, as now that the ice was broken with Miss Frankland, it would be necessary to be doubly careful not to excite suspicion of my visits to my sisters. Having finished everything to my satisfaction, I joined them in the drawing-room, and while my sisters were playing duets on the piano to mamma, I challenged Miss Frankland to a game of chess. She, of course, was a far superior player to me, but our legs meeting under the chess table, her little charming foot sought mine, rested on it, and pressed it from time to time. This distraction of her ideas enabled me to win two games successively. My mother sent the girls to bed, and told me to follow their example, but as I did not wish to lie long waiting for Miss Frankland's appearance in her bedroom, I pleaded for relaxation in the hour of retiring, to enable Miss Frankland to regain her chance of beating me, at the same time pressing her foot as a sign to her to second my request. She took the hint, though she had no idea of the object. Mamma came near us to look over our game. This induced Miss Frankland to play with more caution and thought, and she won three games in succession, making her the final winner. Mamma now said I must go to bed, as it was very late for me. She still treated me as a child. I, however, had gained my object in obtaining nearly two hours' delay in going to bed, so that I had not long to wait before I heard Miss Frankland enter her room. I determined to let her finish her toilet before I called her attention to me. I watched through my peep-hole, and could now calmly and leisurely see all the beauties of her well-developed form, and the rich wealth of hair she possessed. She went through all her ablutions as usual. I observed she also used a syringe to thoroughly purify the inside of her glorious cunt. When she had dried herself, and was about to pull on her chemise, I rapped on the door of communication, and in a loud whisper called her attention to me.

'Are you there, Charlie?'

'Yes, pray unlock the door and open it, that I may come to you.'

She actually had not yet discovered that the door, locked and bolted on her side, communicated with my bedroom, but her delight at the discovery was greater than her surprise. I flew into her arms, and was hugged to her bosom, and covered with kisses. But as my prick was in a bursting state of erection, I drew her to the bed, upon which we both threw ourselves, she on her back, and I above, and in an instant I was engulfed up to the cods in her glorious and glowing cunt, and we ran an eager course of rapturous thrustings, until nature could stand no more, and we sank in all the delights of a most delicious mutual spend. I lay soaking in bliss for some time, and after fondling each other, Miss Frankland said: 'Get up, dear Charlie, and let us get into bed.'

For we had been in too great haste to do otherwise than tumble on the top to it. My charming bedfellow also rose for a necessary purpose, which I had interrupted when I knocked at the door. She sat down on the *pot de chambre*, and a mighty rush of water followed. I cried: 'Oh, do let me see you piddle from your beautiful fanny.'

I still kept up my character of innocence, and used none but infantine words in reference to our organs of generation.

She laughed, but pulled up her shift, and raised her thighs above the pot, so advancing the light, I had the delicious sight of her wide-stretched cunt, pouring out a stream of piddle with great force. Her position brought out all the beauties of the vast widespread mass of black curly hair that thickly covered all the lower part of her magnificent quim, ran down each thigh, up between her buttocks, and opening out on her back, had two bunches just below the two beautiful dimples that were so charmingly developed below her waist. There was as much hair there as most women have on their mons Veneris. Her whole body had fine straight silky hair on it, very thick on the shoulders, arms and legs, with a beautiful creamy skin showing below. She was the hairiest woman I ever saw, which, doubtless, arose from or was the cause of her extraordinary lustful and luxurious temperament. The sight I was indulging in brought out my pego in full bloom; as we both rose she saw it sticking out under my shirt.

'Off with all that, and let me gaze on your charming young perfections.'

I did as she desired, begged her to do the same, and there she stood, in all the glory of her superb form. We encircled each other's naked bodies, and then turned each other round to gaze on all the exciting charms displayed to each other.

'Come, my darling boy, and let me kiss and fondle you all over.'

She laid me on my back, reversed herself above me, and taking my prick in her mouth, after first feeling it most gently, and praising its large proportions, again declaring it was the finest she had ever seen, she began to gamahuche me with a skill such as I had never before experienced, and gave me the most exquisite and most luxurious delight. For my part, seeing her wonderful clitoris, stiff standing out of the bright red lips of her luscious cunt, I took it bodily into my mouth, sucked it, and rolled my tongue about it, to the evident delight of my salacious companion. Her buttocks rose and fell, and the lips of her cunt immediately before my eyes opened, or closely

pressed the lips together, showing the delicious nature of her enjoyment. I
felt her put her hand to my bottom and insert her finger, and begin frigging
me there. I let her see how it pleased me. She stopped a moment, to beg me
to do the same to her, anticipating my earnest desire to do so. I lost no time
in following her example. The parts adjacent were well lubricated by our
previous indulgence, and first inserting two fingers into her deliciously juicy
cunt to moisten them, I slipped one of them into her charming bottom-hole,
and finding great ease of space, slipped the second in as well. My other hand
and arm embraced and caressed her magnificent backside, which rose and
fell on my face with unwearied speed, as my finger frigged her bottom-hole
in unison with her movements, and my mouth more closely sucked her
stiffly excited clitoris.

Her whole body became convulsed with erotic movements showing what
force of lubricity our mutual embracings were most rapturously exciting. I,
too, grew wild with desire, and was equally energetic in my movements, and
would have thrust my prick down her throat but for her hand, which
grasped the lower part of the shaft. The rapturous crisis came at last and laid
us prostrate with soul-killing ecstasies. We each retained the dear object of
our mutual caresses within our lips and our fingers remained within the
delightful recesses that had so much contributed to the excessive raptures
we had enjoyed. We lay for some time in this sweet languid enjoyment.
Miss Frankland then rose off me, saying: 'My darling boy, we must now get
into bed.'

We did so, quite naked as we were, closely embracing, and covering each
other with kisses and caresses, murmuring soft terms of endearment, and in
whispered accents told of the ecstatic joys each had given the other. Our
hands wandered over every charm. Miss Frankland had an art of gently
passing her fingers over my prick that had the instant effect of raising him
into the fullest vigour. It was the most exquisite method of feeling my cock I
ever experienced. She seemed scarcely to touch it, but drew her fingers
along its length, from foot to head, with a delicacy of touch I have never
found equalled by any other woman. The effect was magical, and invariable,
no matter how many times I might have fucked her before. With her hot
temperament, and excessive lubricity, it was almost a necessary art. She was
one of those libidinous natures that could well employ several men at once.
At my happy age, she found ready to her hand one who could respond to
her every desire in every way, so happily does nature second youth and
health that she never found me wanting, when called on. There was no
excess of lubricity we did not afterwards practise. We satisfied our passions
in every way in which they could be indulged, nor did we hesitate at
anything which imagination could fancy would stimulate them. She was
surprised at my aptitude, and rejoiced and congratulated herself on having
found so powerful and charming a satisfier of her libidinous nature. How
delighted she was to think she was the first to cull the sweets of my

innocence, and how happy to find so apt a scholar, who in one sweet lesson became a master of the art.

The more I gained experience of the charming sex, the more I appreciated the wisdom of the counsels of my really first and ever-loved mistress, dear, charming, lovely Mrs Benson. How truly she had foretold that all who might hereafter think that they were giving me the first lesson in love would doubly, trebly, a hundredfold enjoy the sweet intercourse from such self-deception. Here was my fiery Miss Frankland, who had had considerable experience in the amatory world, pluming herself upon instructing an innocent youth in all the mysteries of the passions for the first time. It evidently added immensely to her excitement. Indeed, in our after-conversation, she avowed that as it was the first time she had ever taken the maidenhead of a youth, so it had been the greatest degree of excitement she had ever experienced. I might fancy her delight at finding, combined with such a satisfaction, a wonderfully well-hung youth, and who proved so apt, and so equal to every luxurious whim that the most erotic lust could suggest. But I digress.

At present, her magic touch had brought me up to bursting point, she threw a leg over me, and raising her body, said she would help herself this time. Guiding my prick to the wanton lips that were longing for him, she sank slowly down on the stiff pole on which she was so delightedly impaling herself, until our hairs were crushed beneath her weight, and nothing more could be engulfed. She again rose, until the edge of the nut showed itself at the mouth of her cunt, and then as slowly sheathed it again. She continued this exquisite movement for some time, to our delicious mutual enjoyment, then falling down on my belly, and telling me to pass my arm round her bottom and finger her as before, she glued herself to my lips, our tongues interlaced, and shot in and out of our luxurious mouths; our movement grew fast and furious, until we sank again in all the luxury of the last grand crisis. It was the very act of voluptuous rapture, and we lay lost to every sense but that of erotic ecstasy and satisfied lust. When we recovered our senses, she lay down by my side, cuddling me most closely, and toying and prattling, until she thought we had paused long enough. She slid her hand down to my prick, and very quickly, by her delicious and delicate handling of it, renewed its full vigour. Throwing her right leg over me, while lying on her back, she heaved up her body into a position half-turned to my belly, I lying on my side; she then bid me embrace her other thigh between mine, then guiding cockey to the entrance, she gave a push backwards, to meet my forward thrust, when it was instantly sheathed to the hilt.

'Now, my darling boy, in this way we can lengthen out our pleasures as long as we please; you can make me spend oftener than yourself, which will satisfy my very lustful nature, and not overexhaust your young powers.'

Giving one or two delicious side wriggles to her bottom, and nestling her backside close to my belly, she told me to pass my left arm under her waist, that I might embrace her left bubby and finger its nipple, a proceeding which she told me was as exciting as playing with her clitoris – then turning her head, our tongues interlaced; she put my right hand down to her stiff-projecting clitoris, which I continued to frig just as I might have done to a boy's cock. Keeping up a slow in-and-out movement with my prick, excited by so many points of lascivious friction, she spent most copiously before I was prepared to join her. Her head sank back in the ecstasy of her discharge, drawing away from me, and leaving my mouth free. I instantly dropped it upon her other firm and elastic bubby at which I sucked away, pushing my prick as far as possible into her cunt, and leaving it there, without movement, to enjoy the rapture-giving pressures of her delicious cunt, slowly passing my hand up and down her still sufficiently indured clitoris. She lay for some time in the luxurious enjoyment of the position, then once more sucking my lips, she thanked me over and over again for the pleasure I had given her, heightened as it was by knowing that it had not exhausted me. I began to move slowly in and out, keeping up my movements at the other points of excitement. She was ready on the instant to second me, and as she meant this time that we should spend together she left nothing to desire. Her movements were of the most exciting and stimulating description, and we were not long before the ecstatic moment arrived, and we sank in the lap of luxury, pouring forth streams of ecstatic bliss. We lay close-locked in the most delicious embrace, only conscious of unutterable joy. It was some time before we could venture to break this exquisite trance of enjoyment. It was followed by the sweetest toyings and prattlings, until again my delighted prick, stimulated by the internal pressures of the luxurious sheath in which it had remained engulfed, again awoke her scarce-slumbering passions to dash on pleasure's heavenly course. Again she spent before me with, if anything, increased rapture, and, after a pause, renewing her lascivious movements in response to my own, we sank in a perfect death-like swoon of thoroughly satiated lust, and gradually and imperceptibly fell into the deepest slumber for many hours, locked as we were in each other's arms. Her wonderfully retentive power of cunt held my happy prick a willing prisoner through our long sleep. I awoke first, to find it standing stiff within the charmed circle which, even in her sleep, was deliciously grasping it with its nervous folds. I passed my hand down to her clitoris, and began fucking her. She heaved her bottom up and down, and murmured some incoherent words, being evidently still under the influence of sleep, and probably dreaming of some former events, for in her half-expressed murmurings, I could make out something: 'Henry – my only – ever loved one – meet again – oh! how ineffable – how exquisitely delicious. Do push it in – more faster – beloved of my soul.'

She clasped me with a hug, as if she would make but one body of us both, and spent with a scream of agonised delight, pouring down and spurting out a perfect torrent of boiling spunk all over my cods and thighs.

'Dearest, beloved Henry, it is too much,' she uttered, and fainted away.

I lay quite still, and determined not to speak until she should come to herself. It was evident her dreams had brought back some former loved and happy man and no doubt the fact of my being in possession, in full fuck, had made her believe in the reality of her sleeping thoughts. She was quite a quarter of an hour before recovering her senses; daylight had broken, and she looked round in a sort of alarm, and exclaimed: 'Where am I?'

Then her eye catching my face: 'Oh! my darling Charlie, it is you! I have been dreaming of being far away, and, I suppose, the fact of your dear weapon throbbing within me made me think of former events. Well, the dream had its pleasures, if only in a dream.'

'It was no dream, my dear Miss Frankland, or at least, only partially so, as far as regarded your loved Henry – for that was the name you applied to me, and most deliciously did you embrace me under the idea, and die away in an excess of pleasure I quite envied; but you alarmed me by really fainting afterwards. I am so pleased to have turned a mere vision of the night into ecstatic reality, and I am not at all jealous of your former lover, because had you not had any, you would, probably, never have loved me. Oh, no! I should never be jealous of you, my dear mistress. I would even like to see you in all the ecstasies of passion, in the arms of another, provided that I should share in your delights.'

She listened in all astonishment, acknowledged that she had imagined herself in the arms of one she had greatly loved, and had thought the whole affair was a dream, and was not conscious of its absolute reality as to her being fucked.

'Well, I must have mine now, feel how it is bursting for relief.'

'Yes, yes, the dear fellow, push him away, my Charlie, and you will see, I shall enjoy the real Charlie quite as much as the dreamt-of Henry – of whom I shall someday speak to you. You are worthy of him and of me – and I fear I shall love you as I do him, far too dearly.'

Then lending herself to the work we were at, she did, indeed, exert all her lascivious power, and we enjoyed such a fuck as seldom falls to mortals here below. We lay prostrate and panting with satisfied lust, until, prompted by the urgency of natural wants, we were both obliged to rise and relieve ourselves. My darling mistress then used her bidet and told me to lave my parts in the basin, as it was not only cool and refreshing, but also reinvigorating. After which, as it was now broad daylight, she allowed me to pose her, and turn her in every position, that I might admire and handle every part of her superb form. Her bottom was larger and harder than any I had yet seen, and, indeed, excepting one, of which, dear reader you will presently hear something, it was about the finest in form and size of any I ever met with. Of course, this handling was not effected without producing erotic excitement in both parties. Miss Frankland had occupied herself as much with me as I had done with her, and her beautifully large clitoris was showing its head in full stand from among the vast mass of bushy curls surrounding it. I proposed we should have a mutual suck on the floor, with her bottom to the light, that I might have a full view of all her glorious parts. She humoured my fancy, and pulling a couple of pillows off the bed to prop up my head, she stepped across my body, and kneeling down, took my prick in her mouth, and brought her splendid backside and lascivious cunt down to my face. I first glued my lips to the open cunt, thrust my chin in, and then my tongue, as far as I could reach, licking the luscious moisture which our previous handlings had excited; it was as sweet and delicious as cream. This stimulated her very much, and she closed the sides of her cunt upon my tongue so closely as to give it a good squeeze. I never saw a woman but her, who had such a wonderful power in that way. My nose actually felt it was reciprocating the pressures of the cunt, so I changed the venue, and slipped my tongue into her bottom-hole, evidently to her excessive delight. But things were approaching a crisis, and she cried to me to take her clitoris in my mouth, and substitute fingers in both the other orifices. This I quickly did, while she sucked and postilioned me, handling the root of my prick and my buttocks with the delicious gentle titillations in which she had such skill, until, in an excess of joy, we both poured a tribute of sperm into each other's mouths, and both greedily swallowed it. After this, we got into bed again, to have one loving cuddle before parting. Of course, it ended in raising such a storm of desire as only a fuck could allay; she said: 'My loved Charlie, this must really be the last.'

I told her it had so excited me to see her splendid bum before my eyes, when we were on the floor, that I should like to kneel behind and put it in that way. I really meant into her cunt, but she thought I meant her bottom-hole, and said: 'Well, you are a strange boy, what on earth made you think you could put that great big thing of yours into my bottom-hole; but, to tell you the truth, after being well fucked, I rather like it that way, so you shall try, but you must be gentle in getting in.'

I said, 'I did not know I could do it that way with my prick. I meant to put it into your cunt from behind, but now, from what you say, I should like to try what the other is like.'

You see, I was keeping up my apparent ignorance. She turned on her face, and keeping her head on the pillow, drew up her knees to her belly and exposed, to the greatest advantage, her glorious backside. I knelt behind, but previous to beginning, I glued my lips to the delicious orifice, and shoved my tongue in as far as I could, and deliciously excited her. Then approaching my stiff-standing prick, and thrusting it into her cunt up to the roots two or three times, so as to lubricate it thoroughly, I withdrew and placed it before the smaller temple of lust; then, by a gentle uniform pressure, I gradually and almost imperceptibly glided in to the utmost extent. She pushed her bottom out, and, I could feel, was straining as if to void something, which is the real method to accelerate the entrance of a prick in that enchanting channel with the least difficulty and pain. We then commenced a slow movement – she wanted me to stoop forward and place my arm round her body, and frig her clitoris, but I begged her to do it herself, and allow me the luxury of looking on the delightful wriggling of her superb backside, and also the sight of my own prick surging in and then withdrawing. She humoured me, and we had a most exquisite fuck. Her bottom-hole had hardly so tight a pressure as she could exercise with her cunt, but, nevertheless, it held me in very firmly, and had a peculiar heat which was most exciting. We both died off together, she so completely overcome with ecstatic delight that her body sank flat on the bed, drawing me with her, without unsheathing my weapon. We lay for a short period, she convulsively shuddering from time to time with the intense degree of excitement this delicious route had produced upon her. At last, she begged me to rise and relieve her. As we must now separate, I rose. She assisted me in my ablutions, put on my nightshirt, conducted me to my bed, fondly kissed and thanked me for the exquisite night of every species of delight I had conferred upon her, promising a repetition the following night. She left me and locked the door of communication, but previously unlocked mine, in case I should oversleep myself.

Thus ended the first delightful night I ever passed with that most charming and deliciously lascivious woman – the first of many scores that followed, but in none of which were her raptures more intense, if as much. She ever after dwelt on the night when she had been the happy means of initiating me into all.love's mysteries. She never knew of my previous experiences, and always plumed and prided herself on being my first instructress.

The next day I was somewhat somnolent, of which you may be sure Miss Frankland took no notice. She retired to her own room, when we went for our recreation. My sisters scolded me for not coming to them the previous night, but I told them that Miss F. had continued to move about her room for so long a time, that I had fallen fast asleep, and even then had not had enough; they might have observed how sleepy I had been all day. However, to satisfy them, I gamahuched them both, and fucked them both while each was giving the other a second gamahuche, so that then each spent three times to my twice. I thus kept in my forces for the renewed delights I anticipated at night. I went to bed early and slept soundly at once, having no anxiety about keeping awake, feeling certain that Miss F. would awaken me as soon as she was ready to take me to her arms. She came, and we passed another most delicious night of every salacious and libidinous enjoyment. A third night followed, which differed only in the lascivious proposition of Miss Frankland to deflower my bottom-hole, with her wonderfully pro-minent and elongated clitoris, little dreaming that there, too, she had been anticipated by our loved and charming friend MacCallum. She had, how-ever, all the imaginary pleasure of first possession. As you may well suppose, I did not attempt in any way to enlighten her ignorance thereon. We had gamahuched each other, I had fucked her twice in the cunt, and once in her bottom-hole, when the fancy seized her to bugger me with her clitoris. Of course, I made no objection; on the contrary, sucking it up to a proper stiffness, I placed myself on my hands and knees in the most favourable position to satisfy her erotic fancy. She first slipped her tongue into my bottom-hole, then spat upon her clitoris, and then anointed my aperture with the delicious slime of her well-fucked cunt, and then, with the utmost ease, pushed the dear thing up to its utmost limits. I humoured her in every way, wriggling my bottom sideways, which she declared was a vast improvement on her back and forward movements. She passed her arm round my belly and, with that exquisitely delightful touch on my prick for which she was so distinguished, she excited me to the utmost, making my *sphincter ani* respond to the throbbings of my exquisitely delighted prick, and equally exciting her lascivious passions with the idea of first possession of that narrow abode of voluptuousness. She could feel, by the electric excitement of my prick, how near I was to spending, and quickening the action of hand and clitoris, we both died away together in all the raptures that such an extra-exciting conjunction could produce.

Several nights thus passed in the indulgence of every form of the most lascivious enjoyment. We used to amuse our periodic moments of relaxation in trying who could suggest any new position or varied manner of effecting the delicious junction of our bodies. On one occasion, referring to the state of excitement her flogging had thrown me into, I asked her, as if I did not know the fact very well already, if the application of the rod on the bottom of a woman, or the mere act of being flogged, at all excited her sex. She told me both acted with great force on her erotic nerves. She thought, from experience, that being whipped caused the greatest excitement and produced the greatest longing to be fucked.

'Then,' said I, 'do you think it had erotically excited my sisters?'

'Certainly, especially your sister Eliza. I do not know whether you noticed her sudden impulse to embrace and kiss me, after her return to schoolwork the day I flogged her; that was a stray erotic impulse, and had we been alone, I could not have avoided responding to it in a way that would have delighted her, and initiated her into some of the delicious mysteries of venery. Nay, I think, but for my happy discovery of your great and delightful merits, I should have sought for and found an opportunity of being alone with that dear girl, for you must know we can lasciviously embrace our own sex with immense mutual pleasure which, although not equal to that which this noble fellow' – taking hold of my prick – 'inspires, is not without its merit and even, as a little variety from time to time, is very enticing.'

'Then, I suppose, you still have some hankerings after the virgin charms of dear Lizzie?'

'I have, and what is more, I believe both Mary's and her passions have already developed themselves. I have sometimes fancied I heard suppressed sighs and gentle movements going on in their beds, and I shrewdly suspect they were practising masturbation on each other. I did not interfere, and after what has passed between you and me, I will tell you that I had a little plan in my head to let them proceed to such lengths that, when I chose to make the discovery, they would be at my mercy. I then could initiate them in every lascivious and voluptuous delight that woman can have with woman. The happy discovery of your excellences, and the perfect facility my change of room has given for meeting without the slightest chance of discovery, has, for the present, driven that idea out of my head. I am, however, indebted to it for the change of room, as I asked for it solely to leave the two girls the utmost liberty to indulge in their voluptuous mutual enjoyment, certain that it would increase and give them every desire for the further instruction I could impart to them.'

'I suppose you would have fucked them with this dear stiff little thing?' said I.

'Oh, yes, you darling, but you have so excited me talking about it, that you must fuck me directly.'

We indulged in a most exciting fuck, and when recovered from the confusion of ideas the delightful crisis always produces, we resumed our conversation on the interesting subject of my sisters. I observed that she had not lately flogged them again.

'All your fault; I am now so satisfied with you that I no longer seek for relief to pent-up desires in that way.'

'Tell me, dear Miss Frankland, did flogging my sisters excite you much?'

'It did, even to spending; but the fear of proceeding further with them at that time rendered me ferocious. The very severity I used was, as it were, in revenge for stopping short of other salacious embraces, but if once I had gone so far as to make them partakers of my lubricity, I should never have flogged them again so severely; only to such a gentle extent as would raise their passions to an uncomfortable pitch, rendering them slaves to my burning lust. Even now I have, from time to time, a desire to do so, especially with dear Eliza. I think she has far more of venereal lust in her nature than Mary. You would not object, dear Charlie?'

'Not in the least, if you will only give me the voluptuous satisfaction of hearing all the details from your lips afterwards; it would stimulate us both to additional raptures, and spur our desires to renewed combats.'

'I don't think it wants much to do that; your glorious prick is as hard as iron.'

'It was the lascivious idea of your enjoying Lizzie that made it get up, but I must fuck you again, or it will burst.'

'I, too, my dear boy, am inflamed at the idea; put it in behind this time; I have a great letch in that way at this moment.'

I did as I was directed, and so great was the agony of delight when we died away, that she sank on the bed dragging me after her, and we lay almost insensible, soaking in bliss for quite half an hour. We did not again renew our conversation that night, but I determined to push her forward to carry out her idea, and also to give Lizzie a hint to second her wishes in every way, without giving Miss Frankland any idea of what had passed between Lizzie and me, and being equally reserved as to my nightly connection with Miss Frankland.

The following night, we passed again in all the amatory delights we could imagine. After our deep midnight sleep, which always took place locked in each other's arms, and poor cockey held firm as if in a vice, I awoke her first, and found my prick stiff-standing in her cunt, which was involuntarily pressing it in the delicious interior folds. I began moving gently, until she was so excited as to wake up too. Then she joined me in all the raptures of a delicious and voluptuous fresh morning fuck. We then rose to satisfy natural wants, and cool our excited nerves by a copious ablution. As we were returning to bed, I observed that Miss Frankland took something out of her wardrobe wrapped up in a handkerchief, and placed it under her pillow with a certain air of mystery. I said nothing. After purifying ourselves we always indulged in a voluptuous gamahuche; after which Miss Frankland generally asked, as a favour, that I should finish off *in culo*. I loved her delicious bottom-hole too dearly ever to refuse. She placed herself as usual on her knees, thighs well drawn up, and head down, so as to make the most of her glorious backside. After I had followed the usual preamble of thrusting in and out of her luscious and juicy cunt, so as to lubricate my prick well, I then introduced it, always with the slow and gradual pressure, until it was sheathed to the hilt, when we generally paused some minutes to reciprocate mutual throbs and pressures. In this lascivious pause, I saw her hand steal under the pillow, draw out the handkerchief and put it under her belly. I shortly found a considerable substance entering her cunt, and making my quarters still more tight and narrow. I began to move, and found the substance in the other entrance keeping time to my movements. I had a tight hold of her projecting clitoris, which I had frigged up to a stiff-standing point. I slipped my hand down and found she was dildoing herself with what proved to be a very handsome dildo, in not very formidable proportions.

'That's right, my darling,' I cried, 'why did you not do it openly, you ought to know that my greatest wish is for you to enjoy these salacious meetings in every possible voluptuous manner; frig on then, my beloved, and be sure that if it adds to your delight, it adds to mine.'

'Thank you, my darling Charlie, shove away, I am in the seventh heaven of delight in having as good as two pricks working in me at once.'

She would have explained more, but her words were cut short by the ecstasies the double fuck produced, and she spent copiously before me, on finding which I held back, and was rewarded by making her spend eventually, with the utmost excess of delight, twice to my once. By this time it was broad daylight, and too late in the morning to enter into any conversation on the new partner in our amatory combats, which was reserved for the next meeting.

This did not occur so soon as we expected, for that day Miss Frankland's flowers declared themselves. It was a fortunate thing for me that she had them at the period of the new moon, and as Mary had them at the full, it enabled me to dedicate a night or two to my beloved sisters, who considered I had been neglecting them of late. I said I had not felt very well, and that I began to think that our excessive fucking was becoming too much for me. They must remember I was one to two, and I felt if I continued to over-exert myself, I should break down and fail altogether.

'That would never do, dear Charlie, and it is very true, you do twice our work and more, because we don't pour down such a torrent as you do when we spend, you must take care of yourself, we will not be so exacting in future, but cool ourselves first by a mutual gamahuche between Lizzie and me.'

I thus arranged a certain amount of cessation of fucking in that quarter, that I might dedicate the more to the far more exciting powers of the delicious and salacious Miss Frankland.

I had always remained in my own bed until I heard her heavy breathing, denoting that she slept, before I dared to leave my own room to go to my sisters. The desire of racking me off, as dear charming Mrs Benson used to call it, might have seized her, and my absence would have discovered all. However, she had, no doubt, considered that it would be all to her advantage that I should be left perfectly quiet to recruit my system, after the heavy drain on my amatory resources which she had kept up for the previous fortnight. She never sought in any way to excite me until a day and a night after the cessation of her menses. She told me it was much better to have done with it entirely at once, rather than, by erotic excitement, keep up the discharge for a week or more.

'And it is not, my dear Charlie, from any want of randy lust on my part, for, especially at first, there is an extreme desire to be well laboured by the biggest prick one could find in existence; the natural irritation of the parts seem to be increased by the way in which the sensual system is affected in that quarter. Former experience has taught me that it is much better to bear this, than by seeking for erotic excitement to keep up the natural discharge for twice as long as it would otherwise endure. Besides which, there would have been a danger of affecting your dear health. Sometimes conjunctions, at such a period, produce a urethral irritation very prejudicial to a man, and such as might deprive me of the delight of your embraces for some weeks. So you see, my own beloved boy, that in every way it is prudent to avoid any amorous excitement at such a period, however hard nature may press for venereal relief. Some women hazard all this, and for a momentary gratification, run risks perfectly unwarrantable, not only for themselves, but above all for their lovers. I, too, my darling, have had my day of imprudence.

Knowing the result, I should be both cruel and stupidly insensate to let you run the risk of what already occurred.'

As she recounted those sage counsels, I could not but remember my loved Mrs Benson, whose advice had been of such service to me, and here was another loved mistress instructing me in further matters connected with the sex. It certainly was a stroke of great good fortune for me to have met, at so early an age, two such admirable women, not only most amorous and lascivious, but instructing me in the real knowledge of their sex, and the world, at the very time that they were indulging my every lascivious desire, as well as their own. Mistresses of their art, no mystery in love's catalogue of excitements, and of means of gratifying the same, was unknown to them. But they knew, too, how to inculcate wisdom for future conduct. I owe every amatory success of my after-life to the admirable teachings of these two charming and estimable women.

The next night, after we had sacrificed sufficiently often to Venus, to enable us more calmly to resume the delightful discussion on the various ways of pampering and exciting the passions, I turned the conversation on flogging. To take you, dear reader, into my confidence, I was seized with an uncontrollable letch to flog the superb bottom of my loved mistress. I had often seen it palpitating under the vigorous attacks of my stiff-standing pego, while belabouring either of the delicious entrances to the temples of lust. I had often given her glorious bottom good sound slaps of the hand, but I longed to apply to it in earnest a good birch rod, see it flush to a raw meat hue, and then to shove my prick with the utmost force into either or both of the delicious orifices. I thought the best way of arriving at this desired object was to refer to her own description of a less severe flogging exciting the passions with pain. She had also admitted that it excited her equally to be flogger or floggee, so I proposed that she should exercise a gentle discipline on my bottom, to try its efficacy. She jumped at the idea, but there was no rod in her room, perforce the ceremony was put off until the next night. On that occasion, she advised me first to indulge in every excess of lubricity, and when nature should begin to flag, then the real efficacy of the rod would be experienced. She aided me with the utmost skill in every act of most voluptuous and luxurious venery. We mutually poured down six tributes to our blessed Mother Venus, with very little cessation, for we both wished to feel somewhat exhausted before trying the effects of the birching system. We lay quiet for a short time, and then dear Miss Frankland began exciting me, but only in an ordinary way. My prick had already been too well satiated with the previous encounters to respond at once to the calls made on it.

'Ah,' said she, in her sweetest way, 'I see we want the rod here. Prepare yourself, sir, and take care to make no resistance, or it will be the worse for your bottom.'

Following her cue, I began to implore pity, to promise I would behave better in a short time, etc., etc. But she was inexorable, and ordered me to lie across her knees. Then, taking me round the waist, she gave a smart cut or two, really sharp, that made me for the moment wince.

'Take care, sir, you are resisting, and you know your punishment will be severe if you so continue.'

'Forgive me, mistress dear, and I will never do so again.'

'We shall see.'

Cut three, sharp, though not so severe. I did not finch.

'Ah! that is something like a good boy, now we shall have no difficulty.'

She began a series of less and less severe blows, until it ended in a gentle irritable titillation, which very shortly began to show its effects by the stiffness of my pego – fiercely shoving against the naked thigh of my loved castigator, who, passing a hand round my body, laid hold of it, delighted to find how efficacious her proceedings had been. Pretending to be quite exhausted, she sank back on the bed, and said she could do no more. I sprang upon her, and we had two more *coups* without withdrawing, with the greatest excess of voluptuousness. It was now my turn, and as she let me slip out of her delicious cunt, I took that up as a cause of dissatisfaction.

'What! you naughty girl,' I cried, 'is that the way you treat your master, bundling him out of his room in that manner; here, give me the rod, I must make your bottom pay for your ill conduct – here, kneel on this footstool, and lay your body over my thighs, no resistance, or it will be the worse for you.'

'Oh! pray, sir, do forgive me this time,' and she knelt at my side, and pretended to cry. I forced her down, and she presented her glorious back-side, in all its splendour of rotundity and size, before my delighted gaze. I seized her round the waist, and first gloated my sight with all the full and lascivious charms, not only displayed, but in my power, and I armed with a splendid rod. I gave her two or three sharp cuts, which made her beauteous buttocks wriggle, but called forth no remonstrances; but as I continued, in all the rage of lust the exercise excited, to flog away most severely, she begged me to be somewhat more gentle. But I flogged on with increased vigour, until she began to writhe under the severity of the punishment I was inflicting. She struggled fiercely, at last, to be free, but she was completely in my power, and I did not spare her until I saw that, changing from severe pain, her feelings were turning to a storm of lechery and lust. She became frantic with excitement, and screamed out: 'Cease, darling Charlie, and fuck me directly. I am dying for it.'

I threw down the rod, jumped on the bed, and drew up her loins, so that she was placed in a kneeling position, she herself seized my bursting prick, and carried it to the lips of her cunt, where he instantly engulfed himself to the hilt. Her movements became lascivious beyond expression, and were urged with a vigour, which brought down in a very short time a torrent of sperm from both of us. We were too much excited to stop short, and almost without a pause, a second course was run still more voluptuously. She was not even then satisfied, but making me lie on my back, she reversed herself upon me, and we commenced a mutual gamahuche. I succeeded in making her spend again, and she was able to bring my pego up to standing point.

'Now, Charlie, dear, we must finish off behind.'

So getting again on her hands and knees, she guided my willing prick to the narrower abode of felicity. After first steeping it for a moment in the moisture of her foaming and reeking cunt, I thrust it into her bottom-hole. I seized hold of her clitoris, she had her dildo all ready, and working it herself with one hand, we ran a last course of most lustful and lecherous enjoyment, which ended in such killing raptures that we both sank all but insensible on the bed. Exhausted as we were by the wild excesses we had indulged in, we fell, without moving or regaining our senses, into a deep and profound slumber, until almost too late in the morning, so that I had to regain my room the moment we awoke, without attempting any further amorous toyings. Thus ended my first experiences as a flogger. The sensation was so new, and the temptation to lay on with a vengeance was so great, that I had gone beyond all reasonable bounds in inflicting such a severe punishment on the glorious bum of my beloved Miss Frankland. I must, however, do her the justice to say that she comprehended and excused the feelings under which I acted, only begging me, on any future occasion, not to let them carry me away so far as they had done on this. We several times renewed this bum flogging, but with more moderate inflictions – sufficient to excite highly without actually punishing the patient, whichever of us it might be.

We often after this made flogging the theme of our discussions. I gradually led on to the idea she had expressed of Lizzie's evidently amorous disposition. She still affirmed that such was her conviction. I then suggested that it would be worth her while to try and gratify it, as well for Lizzie's sake as for the satisfaction of her own letch in that way.

'I suppose you could easily find a pretext if you desired to do so?'

'Yes, easily enough, the idea excites me, and I shall indulge it.'

I do not remember what the pretext was, but Lizzie was kept in next afternoon at four o'clock – Mary and I proceeded to the summerhouse. I knew we should not be interrupted by Lizzie, and that I need not hold in for her satisfaction. So I gave Mary all the benefit of our being alone, and we had four most exquisite and refined indulgencies in every attitude admitted of by the legitimate entrance to love's temple. For, as yet, I had never been able to gain an entrance to the narrower orifice, which was too small for my formidable weapon to penetrate. It is odd how easily Lizzie accommodated me in her delicious bottom-hole, while Mary, older and more womanly in form, was as yet unable to make room for me in that strait path of bliss. When night came, I was all curiosity to know how my dear mistress had carried on matters with Lizzie. She told me that Lizzie had been somewhat nervous at first, but she had spoken kindly to her and told her how her amiable and loving conduct after her first whipping had won her affection. She did not mean to be so severe as on the former occasion, but that discipline must be kept up.

'So come, my dear girl, drop off your frock, as I shall mine, that the bundle of clothes may be out of the way, as well as to avoid their being creased.'

Seeing that Lizzie still trembled a little after she had dropped her gown, she took her in her arms, and kissing her lovingly, desired her not to be afraid – she would not punish her much.

'Lift up all your things, my dear, and let me see if any marks of the former punishment remain.'

Lizzie had a very prominent and very promising bottom. Miss Frankland felt it all over, and admired loudly its form and firmness, declaring it was quite beautiful to look at, and how womanly it was growing.

'Turn round, and let me see if you are as womanly in front. Upon my word, a well-formed mount with a charming mossy covering.'

Her hand wandering over her form excited Lizzie, whose face flushed and eyes glistened with rising desires. Miss Frankland herself became moved, but proceeded at once to lay her across her lap, and began with gentle switches, just sufficiently sharp to attract the blood in that direction, which, of course, acted with double force on all the already excited erotic organs. Lizzie began to wriggle her bum in all the lasciviousness of lust under the excited gaze of Miss Frankland, who, seeing how matters were going on in her favour, increased the force of her blows, but only sufficiently to excite her patient still more lecherously – until driven to an excess of lust, she cried out: 'Oh, my loved Miss Frankland, I am dying with pleasure, do embrace and caress me.'

Miss Frankland lifted her up, and drew her to her bosom and lips, and, while sucking her tongue, slipped her hand down and found Lizzie's quim wet with her flowing spunk, and her little clitoris stiff with the erotic passion that was consuming her. She frigged her until she spent again, while their tongues were in each other's mouth. As Lizzie spent, Miss F. shoved a finger up her cunt, which, of course, met with no resistance, but as Lizzie possessed in perfection the art of nipping, she was sufficiently tight to leave a doubt of anything but finger-fucking.

'Ah, you little puss, you have been playing with this before now, tell me the truth?'

'I will tell you everything, if you will only play with me again. Ever since you flogged Mary and myself, we have both been so often burning down there, and have found out that feeling it, and pushing fingers in, was so nice, although at first we often hurt ourselves. But you do it so much better than Mary – oh, do, do it again, dear Miss Frankland!'

'I shall do it much better, my darling, with what I have got down there – look here!'

And, lifting up her petticoat and chemise, she exposed, to the absolute astonishment of Lizzie, her extraordinary mass of hair, and her fiery red clitoris glowing and sticking out of its black mass of curls.

'How beautiful!' cried Lizzie. 'I declare, you have got a doodle, for which I have been so longing; I must kiss it.'

Stooping down, she took it in her mouth, and sucked it.

'Stop, dear Lizzie, we shall both enjoy it.'

Taking the cushion from the chair, she lay down on her back on the floor, telling Lizzie to turn her face the other way, and to kneel down across her body, so that both their mouths could adapt themselves to each other's quim.

Lizzie told me afterwards that she took care to show no previous knowledge, but to let Miss Frankland initiate her apparently into all the ceremonies of gamahuching.

Miss Frankland glued her lips to dear Lizzie's charming quim, while Lizzie took her extraordinary clitoris into her mouth. After a few ardent caresses Miss Frankland pushed a finger up Lizzie's bottom-hole, then paused an instant to tell Lizzie not only to follow her example in that respect, but use her other hand in her quim while sucking her clitoris. Then, both adapting themselves as prescribed, they gamahuched on, until both could no longer move from the excessive raptures produced by their profuse discharge. After this first bout Lizzie became curious to see all the wonderful hair-covered organ and limbs of Miss Frankland, who gratified her to the utmost extent of her wishes. Nor did she leave this inspection entirely to Lizzie, but reciprocated it. Undoing her dress above, she uncovered the charming budding beauties of Lizzie's bubbies, and began sucking the nipples. Their mutual caresses and handlings very quickly refired these hot and lecherous women. After a little renewed gamahuching, until both were wild with excitement, Miss Frankland proposed to put her clitoris into Lizzie's quim; told her to kneel down and kneeling behind her, she sheathed it with ease in the hot and juicy folds of Lizzie's beautiful cunt. Passing her hand under Lizzie's belly, she frigged her clitoris until again nature gave down her delicious tribute, and they sank in all the voluptuous languor that follows. A third time they renewed their salacious and lascivious raptures, then resumed their dresses, so as to be ready to receive us. Miss Frankland begged Lizzie to keep her counsel and not reveal, even to Mary, what had passed. But Lizzie urged Miss F. to admit Mary into the new mysteries she had just herself been taught, and said she could assure her that Mary had a far more beautiful body than hers, and would like it quite as well as she did.

'Well, my dear, I shall think of it, and find an occasion to flog her, as I have done you.'

'Oh, that will be jolly!' cried Lizzie. 'She will like it just as much as I do; it is so nice, you must flog me every day, dear Miss Frankland. I loved you from the first, I adore you now.'

They embraced most lovingly, but our return put an end for the present to any further conversation.

These details were accompanied and interrupted by two or three delicious and most voluptuous fucks, without once withdrawing my burning prick from her equally heated and throbbing cunt – for her description of these proceedings was most exciting. When she had finished, I withdrew, that we might gamahuche each other, and lick up all the delicious spunk in which her juicy cunt abounded. Then we renewed our combats, sacrificing to holy Mother Venus in both orifices. Then we slept as only easy-conscienced people like ourselves could sleep. Like giants refreshed by slumber, we renewed our devotions on every altar before separating in the morning.

Two days later, Mary was initiated by Miss Frankland in a like manner to Lizzie, while Lizzie and I made the most of our time in the summerhouse. Excited by her naïve description of her scene with Miss Frankland, we indulged in every salacious device that we could cram into the hour's absence, which, by the way, we lengthened out by more than a quarter of an hour, for which Miss Frankland thanked me at night. Her scene with Mary had been one of even greater lubricity, in consequence of Mary at once lending herself to everything, and acknowledging that she knew from Lizzie what she had to expect. Besides, Mary's more developed form and something about her greatly excited Miss F., and she was quite amorous upon her. She had done so much in the way of spending, that after I had gamahuched and fucked her two entrances three times, she required the stimulus of the rod to bring her up to the highest point of lascivious lubricity. And, to tell the truth, afterwards I required and received it myself. Thus our voluptuous passions acted one on the other, and we passed an exhausting night in every excess and refinement of venery, in which Miss Frankland's dildoes, for she had two, of different sizes, played no small part in both our persons.

Now that the ice was broken, I easily persuaded Miss F. to have occasion-ally first one, and then the other, of my sisters to sleep with her, alleging that an occasional early night's rest would recruit my powers, and that when she dismissed her bedfellow in the morning, I could finish her off in force; she could thus initiate them in mutual floggings, and in the use of dildo. Of course, I need not say that my ultimate object was to succeed in our making it a general orgy. In this indeed it ended, but not exactly as I had intended – though that mattered not, as long as the desired object was attained. I had the delightful opportunity, too, of watching, through my peep-hole, many of the delicious scenes of lubricity enacted. When driven to the fiercest excess of passion, I used to withdraw, steal up to the unoccupied sister, and vent my raging lust in every indulgence with her.

This had been carried on for about a fortnight, one or other of the girls sleeping every other night with Miss Frankland. Lizzie, it appeared, had often professed to long to see a real cock, and had managed to worm out of Miss F. that she had enjoyment of mine. The little hussey importuned Miss F. to let her see me fucking her, saying that she could easily hide behind the curtains, and I would never know. Miss F., whose passions were at the utmost tension of desire, consented, and placing Lizzie where she could see without being seen, opened my door, but found an empty bed. She at first suspected that I had gone to one of the female servants, but thought she would make sure to see if Mary was not the object. So she stole softly upstairs, and found us in the act of enjoying a double gamahuche, which, as it was in the early morning light, she could see without difficulty. She had the kindness to let us enjoy it to the end, and then dragging me off, said: 'Oh! Charles! this is dreadful! Why could you not be content with me? – have I ever refused you? Do you know this would be the ruin of all of us if ever it should become known? You are too young to know the dreadful consequences of discovery.'

Here she burst out in a torrent of tears – it was evident from real fear of the sad results that might ensue, and not from any feeling of jealousy. I threw myself into her arms, and as she had herself acknowledged our intimacy, I had less difficulty in alluding to it. I caressed and fondled her, and told her there was no fear of discovery – less now than ever – as we would be all interested alike in keeping our secret; she would cover my intimacy with my sisters, and they would cover my intimacy with her. All at once she said: 'How long has this been going on? – tell me truly.'

I had long prepared myself for such a question, and at once replied that, after the description of the libidinous scenes that had taken place between her and them, and her exquisite account of their young charms, I got so lecherous upon them that I had sought Mary out while she was engaged with Lizzie, and Lizzie when Mary was with her; they were both too much delighted to refuse me anything, and we had now enjoyed each other about a dozen times. I had previously told my sisters to support any story I might recount to Miss F. Lizzie had stolen up after she found Miss Frankland had passed through my room, and now both confirmed the tale told. We surrounded Miss Frankland, caressing her in every way. My pego got terribly excited. Drawing up my nightshirt, I said: 'Let this dear fellow make peace between us, and become equally dear to all I know, my loved mistress, that my sisters are longing to see him exercised on your glorious person, and buried in your delicious hairy cunt, so let me offer up sacrifice to its juicy charms. Lizzie has just said you sought me for the purpose – see, the dear clitoris is raising its head – let Mary lie down under you to suck your clitoris, and see my prick close above her eyes in vigorous action filling your exquisite cunt. You can gamahuche her and Lizzie can look on behind, witness the glorious sight, and act postilion to my bottom-hole.'

'Well, my beloved children, the die is cast, it is no use crying after spilt milk, so let us make the best of it. I never could resist the eloquent look of this loved and long thick thing, that was made for giving poor woman all she could crave for.'

So arranging our relative positions as I had prescribed, we ran a course of the most luxurious and salacious enjoyment imaginable. Lizzie, who had taken possession of one of the dildoes, manipulated herself, while watching every voluptuous movement of our bodies, and we all managed to spend most rapturously together. We could not afford to do more at that moment, as time was creeping on, and the household would soon be astir. Miss Frankland regained with me my room, her own door being locked, and kissing me tenderly, said I was a bad boy, but she supposed it must eventually have come to this, so it was well it was sooner than later.

Thus passed our first general orgy, which was the precursor of many much more luxuriously and salaciously libidinous, and which I shall more minutely describe as events progress.

Miss Frankland would not allow us to have a general orgy the next night. She was now aware of our summerhouse doings – only of late begun, as she supposed – for my story had been too plausibly off-hand not to deceive her. She had felt convinced, by all that occurred on our first fucking, that she had had the delightful pleasure of taking my maidenhead. She was quite satisfied on that count. But she now suspected that what I had just begun, I should be too glad to repeat. She accompanied us to the garden in our recreation hour, so that nothing erotic took place. We sat down all together after a little running about, and Miss F. opened to us a rule of conduct we must in future pursue. She said: 'However delightful it would be for you all, as well as for myself, to meet every night, it would in the first instance become a dangerous habit (dangerous because of engendering carelessness in the necessary precautions against discovery) and next, and above all, it would be the destruction of our loved and darling Charlie. He could not possibly long continue such excessive venery as three loved objects at once would constantly require of him.'

Seeing my inclination to interrupt her, and declare that I felt quite equal to it, she stopped me, and told us I was too young to know what such excessive indulgence would lead to; that we must trust to her experience and be guided by her, and we should all find the advantage of it. Three times a week was the utmost she could allow, when we should be all together. The other nights she would take care that I committed no excess. Such were the sage counsels of this admirable woman, and such in future became the programme of our proceedings. I rebelled and kicked against what I thought at the time too great a restriction, but eventually I became convinced that greater pleasure followed the enforced delays. Of course I slept with Miss Frankland on what might be called our off nights, but she soon established a custom of restraining my spendings to twice a night, allowing me to excite and make her spend as often as I pleased. I was difficult to manage at first, but eventually settled down in great regularity to the rules she dictated, and, indeed, enforced. I soon found out the wisdom of her proceeding, for often afterwards, my lagging efforts required the spur of the rod to be applied in earnest for the completion of our orgies.

The second night after the discovery of my intercourse with my sisters was the first of meeting all four together, in Miss Frankland's room. We had been sent, as usual, early to bed, and Miss F. had privately recommended us to go quietly to sleep as soon as possible, and not to be under any anxiety.

She herself would go for the girls, after all the household had retired. As for me, it was the plan I had always adopted, as it enabled me to reap the greater amount of enjoyment, and its longer continuance, by the rest I had previously secured. Winter had passed away, and summer had come round again. It was a lovely, warm, moonlight night. As soon as we were all assembled, stripping to the buff was the order of the night; then followed charming embraces and mutual posings, so as each should admire the beauties of all. Hands wandered everywhere over every charm, chiefly concentrating on the wonderful and finely developed form of the fascinating Frankland, whose richness of coal-black hair was so deliciously exciting. It soon became necessary to calm the first effervescence of our passions, which we always did by a general gamahuche. Miss Frankland, who had taken an extraordinary letch for Mary, paired off with her, while Lizzie and I accommodated each other. Miss Frankland, who had provided herself with a store of dildoes, furnished us all with one, differing in size, according to the intention of their application. As Mary's bottom-hole as yet could only accommodate a moderate size, Miss F. kept the smallest for her particular use, the others were indiscriminately used. Thus armed, we proceeded to enter on all the voluptuous excesses of gamahuching in every form, lengthening out our pleasures as much and as long as possible, that we might pass the whole night in the most libidinous raptures. When the ecstatic moment overtook us, our mouths had to cease their operations to give vent to the expressions of the rapturous nature of our feelings. We lay panting for some time before being able to rise and resume our mutual caresses. Now that we had taken off the edge of our lustful appetite, we prepared more calmly for further and more voluptuous combinations. The upper coverings of the bed were entirely removed, so that it presented nearly a square field of combat for love's encounters, admirably adapted for its purpose. We held a council as to our next movements, and finally decided to begin as follows: Mary to lie down on her back, Lizzie reversed above her, Miss Frankland was to indulge in her letch for Lizzie, which was that of fucking her bottom-hole with her extraordinary clitoris, while I was to fuck Miss Frankland's cunt, and postilion her smaller orifice with two fingers, Lizzy was to postilion Mary with her finger, while gamahuching her, Mary to apply the smaller dildo to my bottom-hole, and frig Lizzie's cunt with a larger one. It was also agreed we should run two courses in this voluptuous group, varying only in the substitution of my prick in Miss Frankland's bottom-hole, instead of her cunt, in which was to be placed one of the dildoes. We were none of us to press matters to a speedy termination, but to make the most of the exquisite conjunction of our parts. We enjoyed a most salacious and voluptuous fuck, and so managed matters as all should spend together in perfect raptures of lubricity and lust. Notwithstanding the pleasure of the final discharge, we managed, as previously agreed, to hold our mutual positions, our parts palpitating with repeated throbbings on or in the delicious quarters with which they were conjoined. These soon reawakened our passions, which we as yet had done but little to calm, and when sufficiently heated, the slight change agreed upon was effected. I plunged up to the hilt in the glorious and hairy bottom-hole of the divine Frankland, who gave almost a scream of delight as she felt my huge pego rushing up into her burning entrails. We had to pause some minutes to allow her excitement to subside to a certain extent, or she would have discharged after two or three thrusts of my potent weapon. We then proceeded more leisurely, and after drawing out our enjoyment in the most salacious and voluptuous manner, the ecstatic moment seized us all together, with such an excess of wild enjoyment that with screams of almost agonised delight, we poured into or upon each other whole torrents of hot boiling sperm, and sank almost insensible into a confused heap of naked forms. We were a long time in recovering our senses. Then disentangling ourselves, we rose and laved our parts in cold water, not only to purify ourselves, but as a stimulant to further exertions in all the wildest excesses of lubricity that any of us could fancy. But we always managed so as to make Miss F. think that she was the author of any new salacious idea or suggestion. In fact she nearly was so in every case, for her experience in every letch, and its gratification in every form of libidinous refinement, was great. We owed to her many new and delicious combinations in our salacious orgies. After partaking of wine and cake, which Miss F. had taken care to secure, we indulged in some delicious romping and pulling about of the rich curls and hairy coverings of nearly all Miss Frankland's superb form. The girls above all admired the magnitude, hardness, and beauty of her truly magnificent buttocks, and what with one now and then sucking her bubbies, and at other times toying with her already standing clitoris, we soon brought her to such a state of excitement that, seizing hold of Mary, she got her on the table and gamahuched her, while Lizzie, creeping under, sucked her clitoris, and I pushed my prick from behind into her cunt. We brought on a delicious spend, and the glorious creature died away in excess of pleasure along with Mary, while I had not yet arrived at the climax. So I contented myself with making my prick throb to her delicious squeezings, until the fatigue of the position required us to break up the pose. She was so far calmed that she could now propose and discuss after-proceedings, and what our next form of enjoyment should be. As Mary had had an extra spend with Miss Frankland, Lizzie was now placed on her knees, with her head well down. I thrust my prick into her longing cunt. Miss Frankland standing up, strode across Lizzie's body in front of me, here I introduced first a smaller dildo up her bottom-hole and then a larger one up her cunt, both up to the cod pieces. She then pushed forward her belly and put her stiff-standing clitoris into my mouth, and placed her two hands on my head. I then passed one hand under her open legs, and seizing both dildoes in one hand, proceeded to work them up and down both holes at once, in unison with my suction of her clitoris, and my fucking movements in Lizzie's cunt, who at the same time was frigging her own clitoris with her fingers. Mary, armed with two dildoes, applied one to my bottom-hole, while she fucked herself with the other. In this way, we ran a most exciting and delicious course. Miss F., in the ecstatic moments, seemed as if she would have pressed my head into her belly. She was so charmed with the voluptuous delights this pose had given that she cried out we must not change until another course was run. Lizzie said she must change from front to back, and begged Mary to hand her a dildo with which she might frig herself. The women were ready directly, but my pego was longer in answering the call, so Miss Frankland told Mary to apply the birch rod skilfully. This she did with great art, working the dildo, which was still in her cunt while so occupied. The effect was almost electrical, and my glorious rampant prick filled dear Lizzie's delicious and longing bottom-hole to her utmost delight. Miss F. begged Mary to give her a gentle stimulus with the rod. Nothing could better have pleased Mary, for she admitted afterwards she had long had the greatest letch to flog that glorious and immense backside. With such stimulants as these, this course proved one of the most salacious and voluptuous we had yet had. The ecstatic ending was accompanied with screams of delight, as we died away in the death-like swoon of rapturous and satiated desires. We rose again to purify and refresh ourselves, and for some time after lay closely embraced on the bed. As Mary had not yet had my prick in her cunt, Miss F. proposed that I should fuck her, that Lizzie should kneel close behind us, she could fuck Lizzie's bottom-hole with her clitoris, and work one dildo up my bottom, while she worked a second in her own. No sooner said than done. Lizzie's head was shoved almost below Mary's belly, so as to bring Miss F. close enough to me to operate as she desired, and we ran another delicious course with such extreme pleasure that all sank sideways down on the bed and dropped into a sound slumber. We did not awaken until so late that we only had time to lave ourselves in cold water, finish off with a general gamahuche, and then regain our separate rooms. On this last occasion, Miss Frankland said she must gamahuche me, as she delighted to break her fast on cream. The joke amused the two girls amazingly.

It was about this time Mrs Vincent gave birth to a fine boy. I have not spoken of her since our first interview after her marriage in the summer-house, when all had gone into the town to bring out Miss Frankland. We had only had two stolen interviews since that time, which I have not mentioned, because they were too hasty and with too little comfort to have been thoroughly enjoyed; then she became too heavy with child to afford me any further opportunity. Mamma wrote a congratulating letter to Mr Vincent, wishing him joy of the advent of a son and heir, little dreaming that her own son was the father thereof. This brought a visit from Mr Vincent, to beg that mamma would kindly become godmother to the little fellow. My mother at once assented, and asked who the godfathers were. He said an uncle, from whom they had expectations, had consented to be one, but he was at a loss to know whom to ask as second.

'Why not ask Charlie, he was always very fond of your wife as his governess, and he, too, has an uncle from whom we hope someday to receive something handsome.'

'That is a very good idea of yours, Mrs Roberts, and if you will kindly send for Charles, I shall put it to him. If he consents, it saves me all further trouble.'

I was sent for, and, you may be sure, accepted immediately, thanking Mr Vincent for the honour he did me, and hoping that Mrs Vincent would be equally agreeable that I should be godfather, although so young.

'Leave that to me, my dear wife is so much attached to me that my wish is her law, so do not make yourself uneasy on that head.'

It may well be supposed I was not at all uneasy, but quite certain that it was the very thing Mrs V. would have proposed if she had not been withheld by prudence. We heard afterwards from Mr V. that she had simulated objections on account of my youth, but the very first moment she could say a word to me in private, it was to tell me what delight it had given her that her husband should have fulfilled in the matter the very wish nearest and dearest to her heart.

The ceremony eventually came off as had been proposed, but it was at very rare intervals that I could find an opportunity of renewing our old combats in the field of Venus. Meanwhile I had no reason to regret this, as far as indulgence of my erotic passions went, because, for nearly two years, that is until I had passed my eighteenth birthday, I continued to enjoy uninterrupted bliss in the arms of the luxurious and fascinating Miss Frankland, or in orgies with her and my sisters, which culminated in every excess of venery capable of being enjoyed by three women and one youth. In fact, we all indulged rather too freely, if I may judge from the fact that, at least to Miss Frankland and myself, the rod had almost become a necessity, and occasionally even my sisters admitted it gave them a fillip. Under the able tutorship of Miss Frankland, we became the most perfect adepts in every voluptuous indulgence of lubricity. But I must also give her the credit of never neglecting our education. Indeed, I may say it gained by the intimate union of our bodies. For that estimable woman impressed upon us that to keep her friendship and confidence we must do justice to her teaching. I have already said her system of instruction was very superior to anything we had previously known, and now that she had won our unbounded love and affection, there was nothing we were not ready to do in school to second her efforts for our mutual improvement. She had very superior attainments – spoke French and German like a native, had sufficient knowledge of Latin and Greek to ground me well in them, and her knowledge of music was very superior. I have hardly ever heard anyone with a more charming touch on the piano. In the two years that followed our first orgy, we made really astonishing progress. We all spoke French very fairly, had a pretty good knowledge of German, especially Mary, who really spoke it well; as for myself I was well up in French, fairly so in German, and with a very good groundwork of Latin and Greek.

It was about this time that an event happened which completely changed the order of my life. My mother had hinted that I had some expectations from an uncle. These were very vague. He was my father's brother, but they had never agreed, and we were almost strangers to each other. He died, and one day we were all surprised, not to say delighted, to hear from his executor, a Mr Nixon, a rich merchant in London, that my uncle had left my mother four hundred pounds a year, as long as she did not marry again. At her death, the said annuity was to be divided between my two sisters, independent of any coverture. The residue and bulk of the property was settled on me, under trust to Mr Nixon until I was of age, with a request that I should be brought up to the law and entered as a barrister in the Inner Temple. Further, a sum of five hundred pounds was allowed for a new outfit, in every way becoming to all of us. Mr Nixon announced, that in a fortnight, he would take the opportunity of being in our neighbourhood to come over and make the necessary arrangements consequent upon the altered state of affairs. He added that the residue of the property would yield about one thousand pounds a year, and that, therefore, my education must be looked to more closely than it probably had been. Here was, indeed, a change. My father had left the house and grounds, and something like six hundred pounds a year in the funds, entirely to my mother as long as she remained a widow, or until her death. Afterwards one hundred and fifty pounds per annum to each of my sisters, and the house and residue to me – a moderate income requiring other efforts to make it comfortable to one's upbringing. Here I was now the heir eventually to something like fifteen hundred pounds a year, two country houses, and a very fair house besides, attached to my uncle's house. You may easily imagine the joy of the whole family when from a somewhat pinched economy, we found ourselves in easy circumstances, with at once quite double our previous income. We indulged in somewhat wild dreams of what all this might produce; but mamma brought us to our senses by informing us that until I was of age Mr Nixon would entirely control our destinies, and that it was more than probable he would insist upon sending me to a public school. This news dashed all our hopes to pieces with a vengeance, because it was precisely on our greater freedom that we had been counting, and now there was every probability our delightful intercourse and delicious orgies would come to an abrupt termination. We exchanged sad and crestfallen looks on hearing this from mamma, and met in a very disconsolate humour that night in Miss Frankland's room; but that charming and estimable woman cheered us up with the hope that if a temporary separation did occur, it would only lead to our safer and more perfect reunion hereafter.

'And, to tell you the truth,' she said, 'my dear Charlie, we have been of late too much for you, and your health and constitution will benefit by a forced inactivity, for I have observed some symptoms about you lately that prove we three have taxed you too hard. I have no doubt I shall be retained as governess to your sisters, and leave me alone to keep them to a point that will not disappoint you when we meet again, which must always occur at intervals of not longer than six months.'

To our loving minds six months seemed an age. At the same time Miss F.'s remarks had, to a certain extent, reassured us, and although we could not enter into our orgy with the usual fury and letch, nevertheless we managed to pass a night sufficiently rapturous in the enjoyment of our libidinous passions, which many would have thought excessive.

In due course Mr Nixon made his appearance. He was a pleasant-looking elderly gentleman, and a complete man of the world. Finding that I had been educated entirely at home under governesses, he fancied I must be a milk-and-watery ignorant youth, and had already hinted as much to mamma – who, having told me, put me on my mettle. Mr Nixon sent for me into the parlour alone, and began an agreeable conversation apparently leading to nothing, probably with a view not to render me nervous and timid, gradually turning the conversation upon educational subjects. He was agreeably surprised to find the progress I had made, not only in historical and geographical subjects, but in languages, and above all was surprised at my knowledge of Latin and Greek. He was particular in asking if some clergyman had not lent his aid to the governess. After dinner, during which he paid great attention to Miss Frankland, he warmly complimented her on her system of teaching and its extraordinary success. At the same time he observed that, as his dear old friend had desired that his nephew should become a barrister, it would be necessary he should be sent to some clergyman taking a few boys, and then to King's College, London, before entering a barrister's chambers. Miss Frankland at once admitted the justice of the remark, and hoped that Charles would not shame her teaching.

'Quite the contrary, I assure you, Miss Frankland. I have been struck with the admirable groundwork you have established, and especially the advantages you have given him of the knowledge of modern languages. I am so much pleased that I intend to beg of Mrs Roberts to keep you as the able governess of the girls, until they are so much older as to require a little knowledge of the world, which a metropolitan ladies' school is sure to impart.'

All this was said with a certain deference of manner to Miss Frankland, that I felt certain the old gentleman was greatly struck with her person, as well as her system of teaching. But of this it is probable my readers will learn more hereafter.

My mother, hearing of the intention of sending me to some clergyman, immediately suggested that her own brother-in-law, the Revd Mr Brownlow, rector of Leeds, in Kent, a retired village close to the castle of that name, would be a suitable person. He was a gentleman who had taken honours at Cambridge, and was in the habit of receiving one, two or even three young gentlemen, but never more, to prepare them for the universities. At that moment, she knew by a letter from her sister that he had a vacancy. His name, she said, stood high as an instructor, as Mr Nixon would find on inquiry; and as Charles had never been away from home, it would be a great satisfaction to her to know that he was under the care of her own sister. Mr Nixon said he perfectly agreed to her suggestion, provided, as to which he had no doubt, his inquiries justified his sending me there. He left us with a promise of an early decision, and, indeed, before the week had passed we received his full concurrence to my mother's suggestion. So my aunt was written to, and it being the period of the holidays, Mr and Mrs Brownlow were asked to come over and spend a week, and then I could return with them to Kent. We had not seen aunt or uncle since we were little children, and only remembered her as a very tall immense person. The distance had prevented personal intercourse, and we only knew of them by interchanges of hams, Canterbury brawn, and oysters at Christmas time. As they replied by return of post, saying they would be with us in two or three days following their letter, you may be sure Miss Frankland and all of us made the most of what was to be the last of our mutual orgies for the time. No restrictions were put upon us, and every night was dedicated to the god of lust and voluptuousness.

At last the fatal day arrived. My mother and the two girls went into the town to fetch uncle and aunt out, leaving Miss Frankland and me to our studies. You may well suppose it was the prosody of love and not that of grammar that occupied us. There was a tenderness of manner, and a loving kindness and fondling, which I had not before observed in Miss Frankland, and which I should have thought alien to her character. Embracing me tenderly, and pressing me lovingly to her bosom, she burst into a flood of tears, and sobbed as if her heart would break, as her head sank on my shoulder. I tried to comfort her in the best way I could, and as my kind reader knows, a woman's tears always had a most potent effect on my prick, I placed it in her hand, she hysterically laughed amidst her crying, but instantly sank her head down to the loved object, embraced, sucked, and frigged it until I poured a flood of boiling sperm into her mouth, which she greedily swallowed, and continued sucking until not a drop was left. Then rising once more to caress and embrace me, she said: 'Yes, my own beloved boy, that was indeed a means to stop my tears, I not only adore it, but have come to love you, my darling, more than I ever loved anything in my life – you are my own scholar, bodily and mentally. I shall miss you greatly, and I bitterly regret our parting; but we shall meet again, although never with such freedom and ease as we have done. You will spend your holidays at home, and we shall make the most of them. I can feel the dear object already to be made the most of again, and so it shall, dear fellow, so come to its own nest.'

These last fond words were addressed to my prick, which, already rampant again, was claiming attention. We went at it, hammer and tongs. Recruited at luncheon, we renewed the raptures of lubricity as that estimable woman alone knew how to indulge them. We were the less reasonable, as it had been decided by us the night before that I was to find out the habits of the coming couple, before I should venture on leaving my room to slip up to theirs, and thus I had a night of relaxation before me.

At five o'clock the carriage drove up, and uncle and aunt were welcomed to our house. My uncle was a tall, portly, unctuous-looking clergyman, quite a gentleman in his manners, and with a very agreeable voice. My aunt, who was some fifteen years my uncle's junior, was very tall for her sex, a fine portly figure, broad shouldered, large bubbies well apart, a small waist for her size, immense hips and evidently buttocks to more than match. She was very stout, but stood firm upon her pins, and walked with great elasticity of step, showing there was a good deal in her, or rather she could take a good deal out of anybody. She had a profusion of fair hair, with thick eyebrows, that promised abundance elsewhere. Her eyes were of a deep blue that could look very far into you. She had a very pleasing expression, a small mouth, and very white teeth. Her complexion was exceedingly fair, her arms immense, but beautifully formed, hands and feet small, fat and plump. She looked thirty-five, but was nearly forty, and was altogether a most desirable woman to look at, on a large scale. She embraced me tenderly, which I did not fail to return, and complimented me and the whole family on our late good fortune. The first introduction was altogether most agreeable, and I already began to imagine I might not be so badly off after all.

We were allowed to sit up rather later than usual, and as my aunt was fatigued with her day and night's journey, they were glad to follow our example almost immediately. I had only just time to get undressed, when I heard them enter the room which Miss Frankland had vacated the previous day. This had previously been arranged, and she now slept in my sisters' room, as formerly, until we should depart. I quickly blew out my light, for fear they should observe it shining through the chinks I had made. Kneeling down, I began to watch the proceedings. The first thing my aunt did was to squat on the pot just opposite my peep-hole, and as she held up her dress well, I could see that she had a most prominent mons Veneris, thickly covered with very fair ringlets. Her power of piss was something wonderful, it was like a cataract in force and quantity, and at once made my mutinous prick stand at the mighty rush of waters that could be so plainly heard. As she rose, and before she dropped her dress, I saw her splendid proportions of limb, the like of which had never before met my eyes. Alas! it was but a passing glimpse. However, I determined to watch on, hoping to see a further display in the course of undressing. She took off all her upper clothes, until nothing but her stays and chemise remained. I could now mark the real grandeur of her proportions. The stays kept in the waist, and allowed the splendour of her hips and buttocks to stand out in all their glory. Never in my life have I seen a finer backside than my aunt had got. I am now speaking from a vast amount of after-inspection and adoration, but in its covered magnificence in which I at this moment viewed it, it appeared the finest backside I have ever met with, and was in fact the one I alluded to some time back, when I observed that Miss Frankland's was the finest but one I ever saw. It is true, her stoutness added greatly to its prominence, but though stout, even very stout, it was not a stoutness you could call fat. For in after-intimacy, which became of the very closest and most voluptuous nature, I was never able to pinch her in any muscular part. She had the hardest, as well as the biggest, backside I ever met with. I am quite sure that when she was standing upright, a child might have stood on the immense projections of her buttocks. Her thighs were positively monstrous in their mighty proportions, as hard as iron, exquisitely moulded, and of a fairness and smoothness that rivalled ivory, which, in another respect, they much resembled, namely, in feeling cold to the touch. Her legs were worthy of the glorious frame they supported, and finished off with a pair of charming, clean run ankles, and very small feet for her size. As her chemise was short sleeved, the grand magnificence and beauty of form of her splendid arms and neck, where the bubbies came out in all their perfection and brilliancy of skin, were fully displayed. As may be supposed, not a bone was to be traced in her upper neck, but all was dazzling in colour and flesh, which is such a beauty in woman. When a woman shows her gaunt collar bones, it is a proof of bad breeding, and a common nature. Aunt's truly grand bubbies rose magnificently over her bodice, which I thought at the time was their support, but this glorious woman required nothing of the sort, for when perfectly stripped, her bubbies stood out firm and projecting in all their grandeur, and they were of the largest, worthy of all her other fully developed charms. Her belly alone was somewhat too prominent, when standing up, but as she never had had children, it did not at all hang flabbily, and ended in one of the most prominent and largely developed montis Veneris I have ever met with, profusely covered with the fairest of curls, which did not prevent her lovely creamy skin from shining through them. She was well provided with hair on that part, but after the extraordinary hairy covering that Miss Frankland possessed, and with which I had so often toyed, all other women appeared as nothing in that way. My aunt, after donning a nightrobe, sat down to her toilet, and proceeded to let down her massive bunch of tresses. Here, she was, indeed, richly gifted, her hair was all her own, in the utmost profusion, and, tall as she was, fell much below her buttocks, and was so thick that she could let it spread over both back and front, and completely cover her nakedness. Titian must have had such another magnificent head of hair for one of his models, for it exactly resembled, except in being somewhat of a fairer hue, his celebrated Magdalen, in the Pitti Palace, at Florence, where she is represented covered only with the rich profusion of her ringlets. Such was my aunt, and often and often afterwards has she indulged all my fancies, by showing herself off in every voluptuous attitude with this, the greatest ornament of woman, flowing in the utmost profusion over her glorious and mighty charms. Meanwhile, the doctor had undressed, but it may well be supposed perfectly unnoticed by me. I had better game in view. He, too, had donned a *robe de chambre*, and sat down by his wife to have a chat over the occurrences of the day. Of course, their conversation very naturally turned upon myself. They began by congratulating themselves that the good fortune of the family was partly reflected on them, by the circumstances of my being put under the doctor's care. The lady remarked how doubly fortunate it was, as the little scandal that had happened had, for some time, prevented their having any pupils at all. The doctor said: 'Never mind that, my love, this little fellow will soon be the decoy duck for others; he seems a nice, gentle lad, but I shall seek to have some talk with him tomorrow, and see what he is made of; boys, under women's instructions, are generally mere milk-sops.'

'I don't think you will find it so in this case,' added my aunt. 'I am not a bad judge of character, and I feel certain that Miss Frankland is too stern and firm of purpose not to have bent any boy's will to her bidding; I fear, on the contrary, she has, if anything, been too severe with him, for my sister told me that she had full power to wield the rod, but, after one or two severe bouts, she completely mastered them, and that their progress was really very great, and most satisfactory, as Mr Nixon, Charles's guardian, who had examined him, had reported most favourably thereon. But he appears to be insignificant, and undersized, thin as a whipping post, pale, and somewhat sickly-looking, he appears much younger than he is, and seems hardly fitted for what you and I would delight in. Eh! dear doctor?'

I did not understand at this time what her allusion meant, but it was followed by the doctor stooping forwards, kissing her, and, I have no doubt, tongueing her too. He first thrust a hand below her beauteous bubbies, and then pulling up her chemise, began foraging between her legs. She put down her hair brush; and laid hold of his cock, but quickly said: 'Don't excite me, my dear, you see this poor fellow can do nothing without a rod, and we have none here, so be quiet and go to bed, that is a good boy.'

Obeying her, he rose, threw off his robe, put on a nightcap, and tumbled into bed, and was sound asleep before his magnificent spouse had finished her toilet. When it was concluded, she took off her stays, and drew her chemise over her head, I doubt if it could have fallen over her enormous buttocks. She then walked across the room in my direction, stark naked as nature made her, and strikingly magnificent in the firmness of her tread, and the glorious uprightness of her truly superb grandeur of form. I was positively awestruck. I could imagine her to be Juno in all her glory before

Jupiter, and well he might be tempted to stray to the forbidden path of love, if Juno had such a backside as the enormous and glorious one my aunt possessed. She again squatted down, naked as she was, and poured out another torrent into the pot. I felt overpowered at the sight, and staggered back to my bed, and for the first time in my life felt constrained to rack off by self-pollution the excesses of lust the gazing on such superhuman beauties had engendered. I could hardly refrain from shouting out to relieve my till then suppressed excitement, especially when nature gave way, and there spurted forth a jet of sperm, actually from the bed against the door towards which I had pointed my prick while wildly frigging it, and in imagination shoving it into aunt – anywhere; for if ever the saying that 'there was plenty of good fucking about all these parts' was applicable to anyone, it was supremely so in my glorious aunt's case. Anyone might shove his prick against any part of her body, and spend at once from excess of lust, at her very beauty and splendour of form and exquisite colour and fineness of skin. Never, never have I met her equal. Her power of fuck, too, was on a par with the immensity of size, and of a quality to please the most fastidious, or the most lustful. Such were the first experiences that I had of my aunt's person, and as my narrative extends, the reader will become more intimate with her person and proceedings. I sank to sleep, to dream of possessing her in every way, rivalling Jupiter with Juno, and Mars with Venus, mere visions of the night, but which were in after-days converted into sweet realisations of the most voluptuous and rapturous nature.

The next day, at our hour of recreation, Miss Frankland walked out with us, and seeking a retired part of the grounds, while the girls amused themselves, I recounted to Miss F. all I had seen and heard. She at once came to the conclusion that I was destined to fall into the arms of my aunt.

'I am so far pleased, my dear Charlie, that it will be into those of an extraordinary fine woman; you must, after your present experiences with me, have had someone to go to, and certainly you could not have a finer. There will, evidently, be every facility, for I read those hints, which have puzzled you, as intimating anything but reserve, once you are admitted into the inner arcana of their lives, or I am much mistaken. There is one point I must strongly caution you about, and your general prudence and great good sense will make you appreciate its importance. Your aunt is evidently much experienced in erotic pleasures. If at once she found in you the extraordinary adept you are, she would never cease tormenting you until she discovered who had been your instructress. Now it must be evident to you that if she thought you and I were intimate in that way, she might draw evil inferences with regard to your sisters, or if not going so far as to think we had equally corrupted them, it is probable enough she might seek to remove me from their society. So you see, my darling boy, though it may be very difficult to do, you must, for all our sakes, determine to appear quite innocent and ignorant of everything connected with indulgence in amorous passions. You must not let yourself appear excited, but leave her to take all the initiatory steps, and I much mistake if she will not be extremely ready to do so, but all the more so if she finds you apparently innocent. However much you now know of love's proceedings, you must keep a guarded check upon your feelings, so as not to let your knowledge become apparent in the smallest degree. She will, eventually, be twice as well pleased if she fancies she has had your first fruits. Before you leave, I shall give you some short hints as to how to conduct yourself.'

All this time I was getting rampageous, so begging her to stoop forward upon a stump, I tilted up her petticoats and fucked her from behind, frigging her delicious clitoris, and making her spend at the same time as myself. It was a hasty fly, but very sweet nevertheless, for we were both conscious that it was necessary to make the most of the short time I had yet to remain at home. I mentioned my aunt's remark about having no rod at hand, and it was agreed that Miss Frankland should put one on an upper shelf of her wardrobe, and accidentally leave the key in the door. As this wardrobe remained in the room uncle and aunt were sleeping in, woman's curiosity was sure to induce an examination of it. This answered a double purpose, for Miss F. so arranged things that some excellent books full of little bits of paper inserted here and there, at highly moral or religious passages, led both uncle and aunt to have a very high idea of her moral character – for these were works that apparently could only be for her own private reading.

The rod was placed, and the bait laid next day. Meanwhile, that afternoon, the doctor called me aside, and put me through a conversational sort of examination. I was studiously modest, but being very fairly grounded by the admirable system of teaching pursued by Miss Frankland, I not only satisfied him, but he took occasion to compliment Miss Frankland very highly for the admirable groundwork she had laid. I fancied also, as he continued in conversation with her, that he grew more kindly and unctuous, as if the spirit of lust was infusing itself in his veins, as he continued to converse with and gaze on that most engaging and lust-creating creature.

That night I watched, as before, their preparations for sleep, and heard their conversation. This time the doctor was profuse in his praise of me, but aunt thought I was timid and lifeless; there seemed no spirit about me, as there ought to be, she added, at his age, but this education by females makes girls of boys. I thought to myself, I guess, I shall very soon undeceive you on that point, my dear aunt. The doctor went quietly to bed; aunt stripped and used the bidet, giving me a most exciting and voluptuous view of all her full-blown charms. No sooner was her light out, and she in bed, than I slipped out and crept up to my sisters' room, where three randy cunts were impatiently awaiting my advent with an equally randy and inflamed pego. We indulged in every complicated combination of lust and lubricity, and never ceased until daylight forced my unwilling retreat. Before leaving, as the rod was to be put in the wardrobe, and the key left in the door, it was arranged that the next night the girls, and Miss F., too, if she could, were to endeavour to sleep soundly before I came. For if our stratagem succeeded, I should remain to see the result, which would probably occupy more than an hour or two. I would awaken them by applying Moses' rod to their water courses, as doubtless I would be in a rampageous state, if our expectations of the doctor's and aunt's tendencies that way were realised.

I kept myself awake until aunt and uncle came to bed, and then I immediately placed myself *en vedette*. At first no notice was taken of the key being in the lock. Aunt continued her operations, and uncle became somewhat more tentative than usual, when aunt, finding by placing her hand on his prick that it was mere useless desire, rose and scolded him. He grew more emboldened, and followed her up, wishing to feel her splendid cunt. It so happened she had drawn back as far as the wardrobe itself, until the key actually hurt her back.

'Ah what have we here?' she cried, and then turning round, said that as the key had been left in the lock, there could be no harm in looking in. Her husband became as curious as she. Of course, the first things they saw were the prearranged books. They were seized upon with avidity probably with the expectation of finding something smutty, but to their surprise, and especially that of the doctor, it was quite the reverse.

'Well, I should never have thought this; do you know, my dear, I had begun to suspect that, under a demure exterior, there was lurking an enormous deal of animal passion in that Miss Frankland, but if so, these works prove that it is under complete regulation. More's the pity, for she is made for the real enjoyment of the passions.'

'Oh you have been speculating in that quarter, have you, you old lecher?'

'Well, my dear, you know we have both liberty to stray now and then, and you, yourself, have not a little availed yourself on our mutual understanding.'

'Now, doctor, you are too bad; do I not quite overlook all your weakness for the younger members of your own sex, and do I not lend myself to your fantasies in that way, when chance deprives you of any opportunity of pederasty?'

'Well, well, my love, I was not upbraiding you, you are too dear and too kind to me to permit of anything beyond a joking allusion; but what have we here? A birch rod! by all that is holy.'

Reaching up to the high shelf, he drew down the rod. At first they suspected Miss Frankland operating on herself, but the perfectly untouched state of the rod proved that it was there in reserve only, and had not yet been used.

'What a lucky chance,' cried my aunt. 'I shall now be able to birch you into something like a fit state to fuck me – and you shall birch me afterwards, if it will only produce a second fuck, back or front, whichever you like.'

'You are an angel, my darling wife, and I shall try to content both orifices; it is an abominable shame that, with such a gloriously made magnificent woman as God has given me in your noble form, I should ever require any other stimulant than a glance at your exquisitely exciting proportions; but I suppose it is age that weakens our sensibilities.'

'You are right, my dear John, for I, who used to think your dear old cock was enough for me, find I require the excitement of younger ones to give me the real excess of pleasure my constitution demands; it would be a shame if I did not humour all your little caprices, when you so readily throw opportunities in my way. I only wish this nephew of mine had been more worthy of us, we should have made him a glorious *bonne bouche* between us, equally to his satisfaction as to ours.'

'Well, my dear, the air of Kent, and more manly treatment, may yet develop his somewhat stinted growth, and under your tuition, he may yet prove not so bad an object as you seem to think, at all events, he may serve as a *pisaller*, until a better turns up; but you must proceed with caution, for he seems as modest as a maid.'

'My dear John, your modest ones always make the best, when once broken in. I only wish his physique had been more to my liking, but we shall see, we shall see; meanwhile let us both strip to the buff, and proceed to make the most of this happy discovery of the rod – the very thing we most wanted and wished for.'

Aunt rapidly twisted up her magnificent tresses, and as rapidly stripped to the skin; the doctor likewise. I assure you he was a well-made, muscular, portly, handsome man, with a large well-filled pair of cods. His pego still hung down his head, but had a certain amount of size, doubtless stimulated by the exciting nature of their conversation and reminiscences. His skin and his cock were beautifully white, and the ban of his prick of a tempting scarlet. I felt at the moment that, if I dared, I would have bolted into the room, and sucked it into such a stiffness as would have instantly satisfied the insatiable cunt of my glorious aunt. This was a delight to be left for a future day, when I allowed the doctor all the credit and pleasure of persuading me to do that which I was burning with desire to do. But I digress. No sooner were both fully prepared than my aunt, in a stern voice, ordered the doctor to approach.

'Come here, sir, I must whip you, you have not done your duty as you ought lately, and you are a very naughty boy.'

The doctor, putting on the air of a schoolboy, begged to be excused this time, but his inexorable mistress was not to be moved, and seizing him by the arm, pulled him over her broad and massive thighs, and with one arm round his waist, seized his cock in her hand, and began whacking away at his backside in such real earnest and, apparently, with all the force of her powerful arm, that I began to think the doctor must cry out in earnest. But he took it all without a murmur, only wriggling his fat and smooth buttocks about in a way that rather inferred satisfaction than suffering. Presently my aunt, who, doubtless, knew by the grip of his prick that matters had arrived at the point her own passions had most at heart, lifted him up, and said: 'Now I must put you in pickle, but as your great red buttocks are too large to be pickled, I shall pickle your prick instead. So come here, sir, and let me put this rampant fellow into my pickle tub, where, I promise, the salt brine will soon bring down his pride.'

I suppose this was the sort of childish yet lascivious talk which pleased them both, for uncle, who had risen, and who now presented a much finer weapon than I had given him credit for, pretended to fear this further punishment, and begged and entreated to be let off – he had been punished enough, etc., etc. Aunt, however, leading him by the prick to the bed, threw herself on the edge, and lying back, drew up her enormous thighs almost to her belly, and showed to my gloating gaze her tremendous salmon-coloured gash, all covered with spunk, for the operation had made her spend profusely. I never saw so large a cunt, nor such an extensive triangle as lay on the side of each lip between it and the commencement of the buttocks, beautifully covered with the fairest curls.

'There, sir, is your place of punishment, stoop and kiss it before I imprison your indecent cock within it.'

The doctor, nothing loath, stooped and gamahuched her so well that her mighty backside wriggled beneath his head, and made everything in the room jingle; her hand pressed his head until I thought it would have been pushed in altogether. At last, she spent with a shout of delight. He hastily gobbled it all up, and rising, without more ado, thrust his stiff-standing weapon up to the hilt, I might almost say cods and all, in her longing and magnificent cunt. Here, he soaked for some minutes, and I could see by the convulsive movements of her backside how much aunt was enjoying it. They soon became bent on more active movements, for throwing her splendid legs over his back, she began an up-and-down movement, much more active than I could in any way have given her credit for. They went at it in real earnest for a longer time than I expected, but when the mighty crisis came, it was with an energy, and passionate struggles worthy of the strength and substance of the two love wrestlers. I could see her cunt all foam again around the roots of the increased size of uncle's very respectable prick, and then they lay in apparent apathy for full twenty minutes, but one could see by the convulsive throbs of their whole bodies what delicious transports of rapture they were enjoying. Uncle was the first to rise, but only to stoop and greedily to lick up all the foaming spunk which the wide-spread entrance to her glorious cunt exhibited. This being done, she, too, rose, and throwing her arms round the doctor's neck, drew his mouth to hers, and seemed to suck his slimy lips, and gain for herself as much as she could of the delicious spunk the doctor had been revelling in. This lasted some minutes. Then my aunt turned him down on the bed, and took a long suck at his prick, now hanging limp, but still of a goodly thickness. Then she thanked him for the great satisfaction he had given her, and declared it was almost as good as the first days of their union. Then after toying and cuddling on the bed for a time, she said they must now proceed to a little further castigation, on her bottom this time, as he had promised to give her a double dose.

'Yes, my love, but you know you promised I should take my choice of which temple I should make my sacrifice at.'

'My own John, you know, that after being once well fucked, the hinder hole is my preference, that is understood.'

They accordingly rose, and uncle, furnishing himself with the rod, desired aunt to kneel on the edge of the bed, and present her magnificent backside projecting out fair for his birching. This she immediately did, and being directly before my eyes, I had a full front view of her gloriously large wide-open cunt, and all the pinky brown *aureola* around her charming bottom-hole, over which the little fair ringlets showed in great beauty. I need not say that my own John Thomas was in all the pride and panoply of prickdom, and ready to burst with excitement. My uncle took the rod in hand as soon as aunt was in position, and placing himself on one side, while his left hand passed under her belly to frig her clitoris, he had his right hand free to inflict any amount of whipping. And, I must say, neither one nor the other spared the rod; they laid it on right soundly, but drew forth no word or sign of complaint. My aunt soon began to wriggle her stupendous backside, in a way to show how very exciting the birching was to her. Her exquisitely creamy white skin began to see the scarlet of the blood rushing to the surface under the infliction received. The redder it became so did the evident palpitating movement of her two resplendent orbs increase, until uncle, too, showed how the glorious sight was stimulating his less easily excited system, by the stiffening and uprising of his pego. Aunt's hand slipped down to it, and being well acquainted with its habits, pronounced it to be as equally ready as herself. Turning her body lengthways, but still on her knees, the doctor scrambled up behind her, and first stooping, licked up the foam on her cunt, for she had already spent once; and then, rolling his tongue about the beautiful indentation leading to her delicious bottom-hole, he thrust it in as far as he could there. Then rising on his knees, he first plunged his jolly good prick into her cunt for two or three shoves, and then drawing it out well lubricated, presented its point to her exquisite bottom-hole, and plunged it up to the hilt at a single thrust. Aunt gave a cry and shudder of delight as she felt it penetrate to her very entrails. The doctor, satisfied for the moment, lay soaking in the exquisite pressure that aunt's sphincter and was applying to his happy prick. He looked down upon her glorious buttocks, handling them with evident pleasure. I saw aunt's hand steal down to her cunt, and could observe that she was actively frigging her clitoris. She shortly cried out to uncle not to be so idle, but to commence the delicious movements she expected from him.

He did – they did; and such a scene of excitement it was to see so magnificent a woman with such a mighty backside in all the agonies of enjoyment that I could hold out no longer, but seizing my bursting prick in my hand, two or three rapid movements up and down, and tight graspings of the shaft, brought on the ecstatic rapture of so lascivious a spend that I actually fainted and fell heavily on the floor. It was fortunate that aunt and uncle were so hotly engaged that an earthquake might have shook the house without their being conscious of it. So as I only fell from my knees, it never disturbed one moment of their pleasure. I must have been some minutes without consciousness, for when I came to my senses, and was able to resume my inspection, I found their crisis was past, but that uncle still lay soaking in the narrow cell he so delightfully occupied. He was gazing with evident pleasure on the still palpitating buttocks of the divine backside immediately below him. Neither was in any hurry, but they dwelt for a considerable space of time in this repose of lubricity. At last, his cock, reduced in bulk, slipped out of its close quarters. Then, rising, and helping aunt out of bed, they warmly embraced each other, kissed and tongued, and aunt thanked him for a most rapturous fuck. Aunt then sat down on her bidet, and uncle used the wash basin. After purifying themselves, and aunt showing all the extraordinary fine development of her glorious form, they put on their nightdresses, blew out the lights and tumbled into bed.

I immediately hastened to gain my sisters' room, with my cock standing stiffer than ever. I entered gently – they were all asleep. My two sisters lay reversed, with their heads between each pair of thighs; they had evidently fallen asleep after a mutual gamahuche in the very attitude in which they had spent. Miss Frankland had apparently waited for me, but feeling drowsy, had thrust her very fine hairy backside right out of bed, ready to attract my attention the moment I should come. So gently approaching, and bringing the light to bear on the beautiful sight, I spit upon and lubricated the end of my prick, and very gently introduced him into her ever delicious cunt. I managed fully to engulf it before applying my finger to her bottom-hole, and my other hand to her clitoris. She had already in her sleep involuntarily squeezed me with her usual force. Then, suddenly applying all my energies, I began an active movement, which instantly awoke her. She was as ready for the sport as I was, and in a very few minutes we ran a most rapturous course of intense delight, and spent with an energy which proved the strength of the excitement I had been under. As I was standing by the bedside, and she lying on it with her fine bottom projecting beyond the edge, it was not a position to remain long in; besides, I was still dressed. So, withdrawing, I undressed myself. My sisters had slept through all this, so first preparing everything for an excessive orgy, by getting out dildoes and birch rods, we awoke the two darlings, who, rising, stripped to the buff. The three dear creatures were all curiosity to know what had kept me so long – more than two hours and a half, and what had been done.

I recounted all the proceedings, except in so far as they had talked of initiating me, for neither Miss Frankland nor I wished my sisters to be acquainted with that matter. They laughed heartily, and little Lizzie said she must act aunt, first flog me and be fucked; then be flogged by me, and have my darling prick up her bottom-hole to follow. We laughed and humoured her, and that scene came off with considerable *éclat*. Miss Frankland fucking Mary, for whom she had a great letch, in the cunt first, and in the bottom, after my example on Lizzie, in the second place. Lizzie and I then laved our parts and prepared for fresh encounters, and we then began a more regular course of the most lascivious lubricity, in which dildoes and rods played conspicuous parts, both becoming necessary under the excessive indulgencies of these last few nights. I stole to my room long after daylight, and slept soundly for an hour or two. You may be sure our lessons were of the lightest in these few days that were left us, and I was allowed to doze off during school hours.

Miss Frankland again walked with me alone in the garden, to give me, as she thought, last lessons in the way I should act with aunt, who she now felt more certain than ever would very soon attack and carry my person when she reached home and had the place and time all to herself. I listened with apparently great attention; as the reader knows, I was already an adept in the art she wished to indoctrinate – thanks to the admirable advice of my ever charming real first instructress, the lovely Mrs Benson. But I could not help thinking how completely these two admirable women had the same wisdom and knowledge of the world with which they were so anxious that I, too, should become conversant.

The next night, the doctor and aunt went quietly to bed, the doctor declaring that his previous night's doings would prevent any more that night. So I only had one more gaze at all aunt's magnificent beauties, which had a never-failing effect on my excitable weapon, and which she sent away when her light was put out in a perfectly fit state for the work that awaited him in my sisters' room. I came upon them sooner than expected, and found the three rolled into one body, two gamahuching each other, and Miss Frankland's clitoris in Mary's bum-hole. For a wonder they did not hear me as I gently opened the door, and I patiently waited till the lascivious crisis brought down a delicious spend from them all. When clapping my hands applaudingly, I cried: 'Bravo! bravo! encore!'

I was so far glad, for to confess the truth the pace was telling, and I began to require more and more of the rod. However, we had but this and the next night at our disposal, and the knowledge that we must soon cease our delicious orgies nerved us all to increased efforts.

Again our passions raged furiously, and broke out in spurts of foaming sperm. Every desire our lascivious lubricity could suggest was carried out to increase our pleasures or renew our exhausted resources, until time warned us again to separate.

The next day there was no school time – it was spent in packing and preparing for departure. My poor mother took it much to heart – she was a most affectionate creature, as innocent as a babe. I often wondered where we three got all the natural wantonness of our characters, for mamma had nothing of it. I suppose it must have come from our grandparents, as aunt had it in the fullest degree, and was almost the equal of the adorable Miss Frankland, who only excelled her in having Greek blood in her veins, which, doubtless, accounted for the extreme heat of her lubricity. Someday I will recount the chief events of her romantic story, which she herself, in after-time, fully related to me. The day was a sad one for us all, even sadder than the next, the actual day of departure. As often happens, the anticipation of evils is greater than the reality when they come.

That night, my aunt and the doctor had another whipping bout, but this time she only succeeded in getting a single course out of the doctor. As before when all was over, I slipped away to pass the last delicious night with the dear creatures, with whom I had now carried on the most rapturous orgies for more than two years past. My sisters were rapidly developing into remarkably handsome, fine young women, especially Mary, who, having the advantage of a year and a half over Lizzie, was naturally more filled out and formed, although Lizzie promised in the end to be, and in fact became, the finer woman, and had also by far the hotter temperament of the two. We passed the night in the most refined orgies, interspersed with tears of regret at our parting, and soft endearments leading to perfect furies of lubricity, until I was nearly fainting with exhaustion. We tore ourselves asunder with difficulty, and the three angelic creatures held their door open, and with streaming eyes watched my receding form; twice, on looking back, I could not help returning again and again to throw myself into their arms for a last loving embrace; but like all things human, it came to an end, and I reached my bed and sobbed myself to sleep.

It is needless to dwell on our parting next day. My mother accompanied us to the town where we were to take a coach. It drove up. My poor mother could hardly utter her blessing and farewell, and I saw the tears coursing down her venerable cheeks as she waved her handkerchief before the coach turned the corner that shut us from her view. Of course my heart was full, whose could be otherwise when quitting home for the first time. My aunt put her arm round my waist, and laid my head on her ample bosom, and comforted me as well as she could; but a full heart must vent itself. Fortunately, we had the inside all to ourselves. My aunt was very tender, and so was the doctor. I soon sobbed myself to sleep; even in the bitter grief of the moment, I had some slight comfort in the idea of pressing those glorious orbs. My aunt frequently kissed me, and I returned it with full pouting lips, which I fancied rather pleased her. I slept until the coach stopped for supper, ate heartily, and, as may be supposed after my late week of hard work, soon again slept like a top.

I did not awake until it was broad daylight, and, like all heavy sleepers, was awake and sensible of what was going on before opening my eyes. I became conscious that a hand was gently pressing and apparently taking the size of my standing pego, which the pressure of water on my bladder had occasioned to be in an erection of the hardest. I lay quite still, continuing to breathe heavily, but unable to prevent sundry throbbings of my pego, occasioned by the soft hand of my aunt, who was gently following its form from the outside of my trousers. It appeared she had only just commenced her manipulations, not having previously observed the bulging out of its large dimensions under my trousers. She pressed her knee against that of the doctor opposite, who I presume, was dozing off, and in a whisper I heard her draw his attention to my extraordinary development.

'Feel it, my dear, but very gently, so as not to waken him, it is the largest prick I have ever felt, and altogether beats the late Captain of Grenadiers you used to be so jealous of.'

The doctor did feel, and I think aunt would have unbuttoned my trousers, had not the coach suddenly pulled up at the inn we were to breakfast at. So perforce they shook me up. I acted the suddenly awakened sleeper very well. As soon as we were out of the coach, I whispered to the doctor: 'If you please, uncle, I want to piddle very bad.'

'Come here, my dear boy.'

And taking me behind some wagons in the innyard, where we would not be seen, he said: 'Here, we can both piss down this grating.'

And, forsooth, to encourage me, pulled out his own standing pego. I saw what he wanted, and out with my own in all its length and strength.

'Good heavens, Charles, what an immense cock you have got – does it often stand like that?'

'Yes, uncle, every morning it hurts me so until I piddle – it gets worse and worse, and bigger and bigger – it was not half so big a year ago. I don't know what to do to cure myself of this hardness, which is very painful.'

'Ah, well, I must speak to your aunt, perhaps she can help you. Have you ever spoken to anybody else about it?'

'Oh, dear no! I should have been quite ashamed; but when I saw you also had the same hardness, I was very glad to ask your advice, dear uncle.'

'Quite right. Always consult me about that part of your body, whatever you may feel.'

We breakfasted, and I could see, on regaining the coach, that uncle and aunt had a satisfactory exchange of words on the subject. We got to the rectory in Kent in time for dinner, at which I was the object of great and devoted attention of both, especially of my aunt.

Our previous long journey made an early retreat to bed a necessity for all of us. They both conducted me with much *empressement* to my bedroom, a very comfortable one, having a communication at one end with a corridor, and, on the right-hand side entering, another door communicating with my uncle's dressing- and bathroom, and these opening into their bedroom, which had a similar dressing-room on the other side fitted up with wardrobes for female gear, and dedicated to my aunt's sole use. I was left to a quiet night's rest, which I most thoroughly enjoyed, and slept profoundly until late in the morning. I was awakened by my uncle drawing all the clothes off me. Of course, I was rampant, as usual. He gazed for a moment or two without speaking at my enormous cock at full stand. He then said it was nine o'clock, and breakfast was ready, that he had not liked to disturb me sooner, as I was in so sound a slumber, but now it was time for me to get up.

'I see,' he added, 'that your doodle, as you call it, has got the hardness you spoke of yesterday.'

Then he laid hold of it, and gently squeezed it – it filled his grasp. He evidently enjoyed the pleasure of handling it, but contented himself with saying that my aunt must see to giving me some remedy the next day, when she should come and inspect it in the morning, so as to see how hard it was, and how it hurt me.

I replied that it would be very kind of aunt, but what would she think of my showing my doodle to her; mamma had told me, when I slept in her room, always to piddle in a corner, and never let anyone see it.

He laughed at my apparent simplicity, and said: 'Your mamma was quite right as to people in general, but it is quite a different thing with your aunt, whose close relationship authorises her doing what she can to relieve her dear nephew, in whom we both take such an interest; besides, I suppose your mamma never saw it in this size and hardness?'

He was gently handling it all the time of our conversation.

'Oh, no! mamma never saw it but at night, when it was quite shrunk up, and that is nearly a year ago, when I used to sleep in her room; it is since then it has grown so large and hurts so much, and throbs so violently as it is doing now in your hand. It makes me feel so queer, dear uncle, and I shall be so much obliged to dear auntie if she will but give me a remedy to relieve the pain I suffer.'

He laughed again, and said: 'I shall speak to your aunt, and we shall see we shall see; but get up now, we shall find your aunt waiting for us. So make haste and dress; come downstairs, you will find us in the dining-room.'

He left me, and I could hear him laughing to himself, as he walked along the corridor, doubtless at my apparent innocent simplicity. I saw at once that I should be called upon to show myself a man next day; but I already felt the advantage of the advice both my admirable mistresses had given me, as to making all new conquests believe that they had my first fruits. I determined to adhere to the game I was playing, and I foresaw that the pleasure of supporting such a thing would greatly enhance the delight aunt would naturally take in being fucked by my really monstrous cock.

I was soon down to breakfast, and was most warmly embraced by my gloriously beautiful aunt, who, in a graceful dishabille, looked more charming than ever. She hugged me for more than a minute in her arms, and devoured me with kisses. I have no doubt the doctor had recounted our interview, and by the sparkle of her eye, and the flush on her face, as she so closely embraced me, she showed that already her passions were excited, and she was longing for the hour in which she could indulge them. However, all that day, they were kept under restraint. The doctor had some parish business to attend to, and aunt leaving me for an hour after breakfast, while she attended to some necessary household affairs, afterwards took me an over the house and grounds, and then we had a walk through the village. The house was one of those snug rectory houses situated in their own grounds which abound in England, but few have so glorious a prospect as was seen from the front of the house. Leeds, in Kent, is situated on the ridge of hills running east and west, and commanding views over the rich and beautiful weald of Kent. The rectory faced the south, and the ground falling rapidly beyond the garden left a splendid landscape in full view. Although close to the village and the church, both were planted out by a thick belt of evergreen trees, which extended to north and east, sheltering the house and grounds from every adverse wind. The house itself was very commodious, but unassuming. The south front had a large projecting half-circle, with three windows in it, and a window on each side of the half-circle; this formed the drawing-room below and my uncle's bedroom, and two dressing-rooms above. To the right, looking at the house, there was a wing with an open-arched passage leading to a greenhouse and vinery, while above ran a suite of three rooms, each with one good-sized window overlooking the garden. These were the three rooms kept for the same number of young gentlemen who might be taken in for preparation for the University – a number the doctor never exceeded. Of these rooms I was at present the only occupant. They were built so as to be shut off from all the rest of the house by a door on the landing, leading into the corridor, from which a door communicated with the doctor's dressing-room, and with each of the three rooms. At the end was a water-closet for general use. I have already mentioned the first of these rooms had a second door of communication with the doctor's dressing-room, and this was appropriated to me. Below these rooms, but looking north, and communicating with the village by a covered way and having a playground into which it looked, was the schoolroom, taking up about half the space of the rooms above. Beyond the covered way to the village was a quiet garden square, into which the doctor's study looked. This study was separated by a passage from the schoolroom, and had double baize doors both on the house and schoolroom sides. It was in fact the doctor's sanctum sanctorum, of which more will be told in the sequel. In this manner, the schoolroom part of the house was quite shut off from the rest, and was nowhere overlooked.

To return to the habitable part. The west front contained a small library, opening from the drawing-room, and beyond a comfortable dining-room, communicating with the kitchen and offices, which overlooked the court-yard of the entrance to the house, above these were the domestics' bed-rooms, etc. The entrance was from the north into a handsome entrance-hall, with a good broad staircase leading to the upper landing, which, turning westward, led to three extra bedrooms above the library and dining-room. It was thus a very convenient house and well-adapted for a clergyman adding scholastic duties to his other ministrations. I forgot to say that the first bedroom, in the west wing, had a door of communication with my aunt's dressing-room, which I afterwards found had often served for amorous propensities by making it the bedroom of some favoured lover. The grounds were charmingly laid out with a profusion of flowers. There was a perfectly shaded walk in the east shrubbery, leading from the greenhouse down to a most charming summerhouse overlooking the very finest prospect, and perfectly secure from all observation. It was furnished very appropriately for amorous purposes, the couches being low, broad, and with patent spring-cushions. In the sequel, it was the scene of many a bout of lubricity.

My aunt took me through all that I have described. When we arrived at the summerhouse, I could see that it was with difficulty she restrained her great desire to possess me; I would most willingly have rushed into her longing arms, and fucked her to her heart's content, but prudence withheld. I had undertaken to act a part, and must go through with it. No doubt aunt was withheld by a similar motive. She and the doctor had resolved that nothing to alarm my modesty – heaven save the mark! – was to be attempted till the next morning. So with a deep sigh she led me away from the summerhouse into the village, where we met the doctor, and returned to luncheon. After luncheon, the doctor took me for a walk again through the picturesque village along the ridge of hills, to enjoy the beautiful views of Leeds Castle, the doctor giving me very many interesting historical details connected with it. After a most pleasant and lengthened walk, we returned in time to dress for dinner. I found that one of the rules of the house was that no matter, whether alone or with company, the doctor invariably insisted on regular evening costume at dinnertime. This has many advantages. In the first place, it gives at least half an hour's occupation, an object in itself worth something to persons living in the country, and then it gives a *cachet* or rather *chic* to your dinner party, however small it may be, and is in itself a certain amount of restraint on excessive exuberance of spirits, and thus may be considered as a disciplinary element of education, tending to keep up that reserve and self-restraint characteristic of Englishmen.

Beyond a marked attention to me in every way, our dinner and evening passed without anything worthy of record. I was evidently high in their favour, probably for the reason that both began to have great hopes that I would serve their purpose in every way. We retired early to rest, and I thus obtained three nights of uninterrupted rest, recruiting me after all the excesses I had indulged in before quitting home. It was so far fortunate, that I was thus ready to satisfy the strong passions of my aunt, who was insatiable when once her lust was let loose. I awoke earlier than on the previous morning, and shortly afterwards, hearing a movement in the doctor's dressing-room, I feigned sleep. It was as I expected, the doctor coming to me in company with my aunt. They approached my bedside. I had laid myself on my back purposely to allow the thin summer-covering to be lifted up and bulged out by my stiff-standing pego. I heard the doctor whisper to aunt, to draw her attention to it. She gently slipped her hand under the clothes, and grasped it in her soft fat fingers, upon which it throbbed so violently that I thought it politic to waken at once. My aunt was not at all put out, but held it still in her hand with a gentle pressure. She said: 'My dear nephew, your uncle has brought me to see if I cannot relieve the extreme hardness and pain you feel in this immense thing of yours. Let me see it.'

She now threw off the coverlet, and brought to light my large prick in all the glory of the stiffest stand.

'My word! what a monster!' she cried.

Her eyes sparkled, and her face flushed as the sight met her full gaze. The doctor approached, and also handled it with evident delight.

'My dear, will you be able to put it into your natural warm bath? It is so very large!'

'Oh! I have not the slightest doubt but that I shall be able to soothe and deliver it of all pain – poor fellow, how it throbs! Does it hurt much, dear Charles?'

'Oh, yes; your hand seems to make it even harder than before, but, at the same time makes me feel so very queer, as if I were going to faint. Do relieve me, dear auntie, the doctor says you can if you like.'

'I will do so, certainly, my dear boy; but the method is a great secret, known only to your uncle and myself; and you must assure me you will never mention it to anyone, or tell how I cured you. It is only my strong affection for you that makes me anxious to do anything I can to relieve you. Do you promise to be discreet?'

'My dear aunt, you may be sure I shall be too much obliged to you ever to think of revealing your great kindness. Do, pray, do it at once; I feel so queer, and I am bursting with pain.'

'Well, then, make room for me beside you, and I shall lie down; the doctor will cover us up, and I shall soon reduce the stiffness.'

She got into bed, lay down on her back, pulled the sheet over us, laying bare her splendid belly, and, at the same time, opening her magnificent limbs and desiring me to get upon her, telling me she had a sheath in her body, which, when my hard doodle was put within, would soon relieve it of its stiffness. I got awkwardly upon her. She seized my standing prick, and placing its knob between the already very moist lips, told me to push it in as far as it would go. It glided into its delicious sheath up to the cod piece in a moment.

'Oh, heavens!' I cried, 'how nice! Dear, dear, auntie, what shall I do now, I feel as if I were going to die.'

My apparent innocence seemed to add to her pleasure. She threw the sheet that covered us on one side, and with arms and legs clasped round my body, begged me to move my bottom up and down, so as to make my doodle go in and out. I followed her directions, and she seconded me with rare art, squeezing my instrument with wonderful pressures as I withdrew and she retired, to meet again the up-and-down shock with the most lascivious delight. I felt the hand of the doctor embracing my testicles and gently pressing them. I became aware that the crisis was approaching, and shoved home with a cry of rapture, but remembering my part, I exclaimed: 'Oh, I am dying, dear aunt; oh! oh! stop! stop! I – can't – can't – bear it.' I sank away, but could hear aunt murmuring: 'Dear, darling, delicious boy, I never had such a glorious prick in me, or a better fuck before. I fear the dear child has fainted from the excess of pleasure, and the newness of the sensation, but his glorious prick still throbs deliciously within me – only feel its root, doctor, how stiff it is.'

I felt the doctor grasping it, making it throb violently as he did so.

'The dear boy is as stiff as ever. You will get another fuck out of him the moment he comes to himself. I am glad of that, for it is delightful to see you at it, especially with so splendid a prick operating upon you – it is the greatest treat you have ever given me in that way.'

'I don't wonder at that, my dear, for I never met with such a fine prick in my life before, and little thought my nephew could have had such a splendid one in his trousers when we first saw him. Oh, I am lewder than ever, and am spen–spen–spending. Oh! – oh!'

And she poured down another copious hot flow on my enraptured prick. I let her revel in the ecstasies of her second lascivious discharge until I found that her libidinous passions were again excited, and longing for more active operations. I pretended not to know where I was, and began a faltering: 'Oh, where am I? What has happened? I have been in paradise!'

Lifting up my head, I apparently recognised aunt in surprise: 'Oh, dear; how came I here? Oh, remember, auntie, you promised to relieve my hardness, and it seemed so nice, but I feel it is harder than ever; you will try and relieve me again, won't you, dear auntie?'

'Certainly, my dear nephew, you must do as you did at first, move in and out, and I shall second you; and perhaps we shall succeed this time better than before.'

Of course, I was less *gauche*, and she more energetic. I felt the doctor insert a moistened finger up my fundament, and move it in unison with our thrusts. Aunt cried out to me to go on faster and faster, and we soon came to the grand crisis, dying away together in sobs and sighs of delighted enjoyment. I again sank on her noble panting bosom, really overcome with the rapture-giving delights of that most delicious cunt. On lifting my love-humid eyes to the face of my aunt, she seized my head in both hands, and drew my lips to her in a long, long kiss of satisfied lust, and thrust her tongue into my mouth, which I immediately sucked. She then begged me to give her mine. After tongueing together for a minute or two, she asked if my doodle was in less pain, and if its hardness was reduced.

'A little, dear auntie, but I feel it is getting hard again – you must try once more, if you please – oh! it is so nice!'

And my prick throbbed up and stiffened to prove the truth of my words. But the doctor here interrupted us by saying that he must have his own stiffness reduced, at the same time presenting his really fine prick at full stand before our faces.

'You must get up, my dear boy, and your aunt will allay your new hardness in another way, in which she will be able to relieve both our hardnesses together.'

Reluctantly I rose, withdrawing my reeking prick at more than half stand. Looking down as I rose on the truly large and magnificent foaming gash from which I had just withdrawn, I cried: 'Oh, dear aunt, what a wonderful sight it is; I must kiss it for the efforts it has made to relieve me.'

I threw my head down upon it, kissed it, licked its wide open lips all foaming with fuck as they were, thrusting my tongue in as far as it would go. This evidently gave aunt great delight. But the doctor drew me off, told me to lie down on my back, and made aunt straddle over me. She took hold of my now completely standing prick, bent it back, and directing it aright, sank upon it until her ample bush of hair lay crushed on mine. She rose up and down two or three times in a slow delicious movement, and then bending forward, glued her lips to mine while I threw my arms round her glorious body.

I could feel the doctor getting up between my legs on his knees, and then felt his prick was rubbing against the lips of the cunt fully distended round my large pego, doubtless for the purpose of lubricating it before thrusting it into aunt's magnificent backside. I felt the rubbing of his prick against mine through the thin partition, as he glided slowly up into her entrails. We then began our joint movements, but aunt beat us both, and spent twice before joining in our final finish, which was ushered in by loud cries of delight from all three as the death-like ecstasy seized us, and we sank in that half unconscious state of supreme bliss. It was some time before any of us spoke a word. The doctor rose first, and withdrawing his prick from the delicious orifice in which it had been engulfed, showed by the way it hung down its pendant head that aunt had at all events allayed its stiffness. He desired aunt to rise also, but I felt by her throbbing cunt, and the pressure she put on my prick as she rose from it, so that it came out with a loud flop, that she would fain once more have done me the service of allaying any stiffness that might re-arise. However, it was much limper than before, although still of a goodly thickness. When she got on her legs, she stooped forward, kissed it, took it in her mouth, and most lovingly sucked it, saying how delighted she would be to relieve me whenever it was troublesome. They begged me to get up and dress, and we should meet at breakfast. They then withdrew, to complete their own toilets. I lay for some minutes in the dreamy delight of thinking over the delicious event that had just taken place, and amused at the last remark of my aunt, which seemed to infer that she thought I was innocent of the real meaning of the performances that had just taken place. I determined to act as if it were so.

We met at breakfast, aunt kissed me most lovingly. I thanked her for her great kindness in relieving me from pain in so delicious a manner, and told her I could not help loving her more than I had ever loved anyone before, and said I hoped she would kindly relieve me every morning, for I always suffered at that time from the painful hardness, though I should never be sorry for that, as long as she would so kindly allay it. I put my hands quite in a childish way on each cheek, and held up my mouth for a kiss, which was given to me in the lewdest way. She called me her dear boy, and told me that she would always help me as she had done that morning, as long as she found I was discreet, and never told how she did so. You may be sure that my promises were most earnestly reiterated. So we kissed again, and sat down to an excellent breakfast with sharpened appetites from our early exercise, and did full justice to the viands set before us. The doctor gave me a book of history, and desired me to read for a couple of hours, and said that at luncheon we would talk over the subject of my reading. I studied attentively for the time prescribed, and then aunt came to ask me to walk in the grounds with her. Insensibly or not, she led me to the summerhouse, and sat down on a low ottoman. I sat down beside her. She drew me to her, kissed me, and clasped me to her bosom, murmuring terms of endearment, and pressing me to her glorious bubbies. Of course, my unruly member fired up at once. To prevent her imagining it was lasciviousness that prompted me, I said: 'Oh, my dear aunt, I do so want to piddle; my doodle at once gets as hard as wood if I at all restrain the inclination to do so, just feel how stiff it has become; will you let me go and piddle?'

'My dear boy, I will go with you, and unbutton your trousers for you.'

We went among the trees. Her busy fingers undid my trousers, and helped to bring forward my lordly cock in its glory. Fortunately, I did want to piddle, and aunt held it up as I did so, her eyes sparkling with lust as she handled it, and her face flushed with her excited passions. She remarked what an astonishing size it was, gently rubbing it up and down. Of course, it became more rampant than ever. Throwing my arms round her stooping neck, I asked her if she could not again relieve the excessive hardness and pain it was in.

'To be sure, my dear boy. Come here again into the summerhouse, where we cannot be observed.'

We entered. She put a cushion on the floor for my knees, threw herself on her back, and lifted all her petticoats well over her belly, exposing her very hairy cunt, and its splendid pinky gash, already moist from her excitement. I threw myself on my knees, and stooping down, said: 'I must kiss the dear reliever of my pains.'

I kissed and tongued, until my aunt begged me to raise my body, and come upon her, that she might quickly put me out of pain. I rose, and slipped my stiff member up to the hilt in her longing cunt, almost taking away her breath by the suddenness and completeness of the insertion. Her legs and arms were round me in a moment, and at it we went hammer and tongs, until we quickly spent with cries of delight, and sank in momentary oblivion, soon to recover our full sensations, and dash again on passion's furious course, this time aunt pouring down her hot boiling discharge before me, and again when she felt the torrent of my sperm shooting up to the top of her womb. Our final crisis was even more ecstatic than the first time, and we lay longer in the soft languor of the after-sensations. The excessively voluptuous nature of her inward pressures soon re-illuminated all my libidinous desires, and refired my prick with renewed force. We soaked for a short time, each indulging in the delicious inward throbbings, until our lust could stand no longer such mere preliminary work, and stimulated anew, we rushed with freshened passions into the fray. The fiery nature of my lustful aunt paid down two tributes to Priapus to my one. This time our sensations were so ecstatic in spending that we really lost all consciousness, and lay for long locked in the closest embrace. I could feel that we were both becoming re-excited, but my aunt begged me to rise, saying that was enough for the present, the stiffness was allayed, and my weight was too much for her to endure longer. I rose, but again buried my face in the wide gash of that glorious cunt, and before rising completely, I licked up the delicious foam, and even ventured to give, as it were, an accidental lick to her little knob of a clitoris, for she was not much distinguished in that way; she shivered with excitement, when I touched it, and even pressed my head down upon it, when she felt the pleasurable pressure.

'My dear boy, what exquisite delight you give me! Continue for a little to keep moving your tongue on that hard projection.'

I did so. Her splendid backside wriggled below in the fullest enjoyment. She rapidly came to the ecstatic ending, nearly thrusting my whole face into her vast orbit, and spurting out a very torrent of sperm, all over my face and neck. She seized me by the shoulders to draw me up, that she might kiss me. My prick had regained its full vigour, and could not fail to slip in of itself into that most lascivious and gaping cunt when it reached the entrance. My aunt started at such an unexpected result, but was too much gratified to hesitate for an instant. Throwing legs and arms around me, her supple loins were in immediate action. I myself was equally in a state of wild lubricity, so that our course was even more rapid than at first, and we both spent and sank together in the delicious after-languor as soon as the ecstatic joy of the first rush of the exquisite discharge was over. My aunt, who could not but be most highly gratified, still kept up the appearance of relieving me, she desired me to rise, and said we must go, as luncheon time was at hand.

'But, my darling nephew, you must yourself endeavour to keep down your hardness, and not allow it to become stiff so often – you will injure me with your violence.'

'Oh, my darling aunt, you give me relief with such exquisite pleasure that my doodle seems to harden only for the purpose of your relieving it – see bow it is again bulging out of my trousers,' for she had buttoned it up. She put her hand upon it, and squeezed it, but said, with a deep sigh: 'Come along, come along, or I do not know what might happen.'

She drew me away, but by the manner in which she squeezed my arm, I could feel she was herself still greatly excited. Her prudence alone enabled her to resist further indulgence, as she seemed to think I was still unaware of the real nature of our proceedings. We found the doctor waiting for us at the luncheon table. He guessed by the flushed face of my aunt the nature of our late employment, and asked if I had been again troubled with my unnatural hardness.

'Yes, poor fellow,' said my aunt, 'it appears that whenever he wants to piddle, and cannot do so at once, it troubles him in that way, and I have had some difficulty in allaying it. I succeeded at last, but I have told my dear nephew that he must endeavour himself to restrain it in the daytime, as it is not always in my power to relieve him.'

'Quite right, my love; my dear Charles, you must endeavour to follow the wishes of your aunt.'

Of course I promised, and with such a look of innocence that I could see they exchanged smiles at it. We sat down to luncheon. Afterwards the doctor, seating himself by my side, began a conversation on the historical subject I had been studying. Our conversation became really very interesting. The doctor was a man of great erudition, and of varied knowledge, and had a manner, special to himself, of making almost any subject most interesting. Hours flew by, and it was only when aunt entered about five o'clock, to take a cup of tea, as was her wont, that we were aware how time had flown. The doctor praised my knowledge of history, and the pertinency of the questions I had put to him, in a manner highly flattering to me, and I could see that I had risen much in his estimation, quite apart from any erotic influences. He proposed a constitutional walk before dinner, and much interested me by his instructive conversation during it. Our dinner was most agreeable. In the drawing-room aunt, a most admirable performer on the piano, enchanted us with her skill and taste. The doctor challenged me to a game at chess. He was, of course, far superior to me, but he praised my style of play, saying I should become a great proficient with time and practice. We retired, as usual, about half-past ten, the doctor seeing me to my room, and promising to bring aunt in the morning to see if I was still troubled with that painful hardness. I thanked him warmly, but with much simplicity, as if quite unaware of the real nature of the application of the remedy. He left me to my repose. The quiet nights of sound sleep made my day efforts pass off without any exhaustion, and I felt my erotic powers increasing in force.

I slept soundly – and so long that I was only awakened by the caressing hand of my aunt on my stiff-standing pego. She had gently lifted off all the coverings, and I lay quite exposed to eye and touch.

'Oh, my darling aunt! how kind of you to come this early to relieve that troublesome thing.'

I held out my arms. She stooped down to kiss me. I clasped her to my bosom. Our lips met, and our tongues darted fiery lust into our bodies. She threw herself down by my side, I was on to her in a moment. The doctor took hold of my pego, and guided it into the delicious orbit of his wife. Dear aunt begged me to do as I did yesterday, if I wanted relief. Our action became fast and furious. Her legs and arms wound round me in loving pressures. Her active backside wriggled in delight. The doctor had introduced first one finger, and then two, into my fundament, and added greatly to the fury of my lust, so that I spent in an agony of pleasure, as quickly as the fiery lust of my aunt produced her hot and plentiful discharge. I sank on her charming bosom, panting with the force and fury of our coition, but as with all very fast fucking, my virile member hardly flinched from his first vigour, and a very few of aunt's exquisitely delicious internal pressures sufficed to bring him up to the fullest stiffness. We were about to plunge again with renewed ardour into all love's wildest excitement, but the doctor insisted upon our first changing places, that he, too, might have his hardness allayed. Our change of position was instantly accomplished, and dear aunt, after impaling herself on my upright member, sank on my bosom and was clasped in my longing arms. The doctor scrambled up behind her, and lost no time in sheathing himself in her fine and beautiful bottom-hole, and then we ran a double course of delight, dear aunt taking the lead as usual, and deluging us with her hot and delicious discharges before we were ready to pour into her a double dose of delight, which again made her spend with fury and cries of rapturous enjoyment, in which we both joined before we all sank in love's exquisite inanimation. On recovering ourselves the doctor withdrew, but I was already as stiff as before. Aunt began a most effective and delicious movement above me, which soon brought on another grand finale, and we died away in mutual delight. I could feel that the doctor was gently handling my cods, both during and after our last combat. When, by our mutual throbbings, he saw that we were about to become fit to enter on another career, he begged his wife to rise from off me. But the idea of losing her and her extra pressures made my prick immediately resume an erect position, so that when she rose from off it, it was shown in a completely standing state.

'What! again, Charles?' said the doctor. 'Your member is sadly unruly. My dear, you must again try to allay it, but put yourself this time on your knees, and we shall see if that position be better adapted for the purpose of relieving this immense object.'

He was gently and admiringly handling it all the time. His wife was quite aware of his object, and, indeed, so was I. Our last bout had helped to restiffen his prick, and although not yet quite rampant, it was evident that when my bottom was in full view, and so placed as to be got at with facility, it would be quite as stiff as necessary. When his wife had knelt down, and by lowering her head had exposed all the wondrous grandeur of the most superb backside that ever met my eyes, my prick bounded with joy. The doctor still grasping it, and feeling it throb so wildly, saw that his game was sure. He pointed out all the beauty of aunt's second orbit of love, and told me it was in that he had allayed his own hardness, and as the other orifice had not succeeded in quieting me, he recommended my entering within the narrow path of ecstasy. I professed no surprise, but seemed to take it quite as a matter of course in the simplest innocence of manner. Uncle continued to handle my tool as I mounted on my knees behind aunt. Guiding the almost bursting weapon into the delicious cunt in the first place, to be lubricated there, and then telling me to withdraw it, he directed it to the smaller orifice, and desired me to push gently and smoothly in. It glided in slowly up to the meeting of my belly against the enormous buttocks of that sublime backside. There I paused for a minute or two within the throbbing sheath. Aunt had pushed her bottom well out, and by the action of apparently voiding, had faciliated the entrance. She winced once or twice, but on the whole, as she told me afterwards, took in my enormous tool with less difficulty than she expected. After a few slow movements, during with I caressed and devoured with admiration the glorious orbs beneath my dearest gaze, uncle desired me to lean forward and embrace my aunt's splendid bosom. As soon as I did this, and began slowly to thrust in and out of the delicious sheath in which I was so rapturously engulfed, I felt uncle's hands wandering over my buttocks, followed by the introduction of two fingers into my anus. My throbbings on them showed how much he pleased me. He asked if it added to the pleasure I was enjoying.

'Oh, yes, dear uncle, immensely.'

'Then,' said he, 'as I, too, am suffering from hardness, I shall try to allay it in your bottom, as you are doing in my wife's; don't be afraid; if I hurt you I shall stop.'

'Do just as you like, dear uncle, both you and aunt are so kind as to do all you can to relieve my pain, and I should be very ungrateful if I did not do all in my power to relieve you.'

'You are a darling boy, and I shall love you dearly.'

He knelt behind me, and spitting on his cock, presented it at my bum-hole, and pressing gently forward, soon sheathed it to the utmost depth. He did not hurt me at all, as I was too much used to being dildoed there to have felt any difficulty of approach, but I deemed it politic to beg him to be gentle from time to time, as if it were a virgin vale he was entering. He fancied as much, and that was just as good. When once he was fully within, after a few throbs, which were felt most deliciously on his delighted prick, we proceeded to more active work. Aunt, in the meantime, by more pressure on my prick, and by frigging her own clitoris, which I was quite aware she was doing, had spent profusely; and, as the case with all the mucous membranes of the body which sympathise with the cunt's discharge, her bottom-hole became quite moist and deliciously heated. The doctor and I then went at it with fiery force, and soon gave down nature's tribute, and mutually poured a flood of sperm up the entrails we were respectively belabouring.

We lay for some time after in all the luxury of soaking in the delicious apertures. I fell to nothing, and reluctantly withdrew until I again became rampant, and keeping myself more erect, with a hand on either immense hip, I devoured with greedy eyes all the glories beneath my gaze. Fired by such a truly magnificent sight as these huge buttocks were when in an entire state of wriggle, I again spent with cries of agonised delight, and in all the ecstasy of fully satiated lust, sank almost insensible on the broad and beautiful back of my aunt, who herself had spent several times, squealing like a rabbit, and eventually falling flat on her belly, overcome with exhausted lust, drawing me with her still held a willing prisoner in her glorious and exquisite bottom-hole. We lay entranced for some time, until the doctor, who, during our last bout, had purified himself, told us we must now get up. With difficulty I tore myself from out of that delicious sheath, and rose with my cock at last pendant. The doctor congratulated me on the success of the last move. His wife lay still panting with all the delight of satisfied desire, and we had to help her up. She threw herself into my arms, and hugged me close to her heaving bosom, kissed me tenderly, and hoped she had relieved me of all pain. I was her own darling boy, and she would always be truly happy in relieving me of that inconvenience whenever it troubled me. I was internally amused at their continuing to keep up this idea, but I humoured them, and appeared the most innocent simpleton, notwithstanding all that had occurred. The day passed much as the previous one. After two hours' reading, aunt again proposed a walk, which, of course, ended at the summer-house, where again a pressure of water brought on the painful hardness, which aunt succeeded in allaying after four most exquisite bouts of love, varied by a thoroughly good double gamahuche between the last two acts. Aunt must have spent at least ten times, and appeared thoroughly contented, but continued to attribute it to her gratification at having relieved me of my painful hardness. Again I passed hours in instructive conversation with my learned uncle, and after a similar evening to the last, we retired at our usual hour.

Next morning I was awakened by uncle alone, who told me that my aunt was somewhat poorly, and could not come, adding: 'I am sorry it is so, for this little fellow is as hard as usual.'

'Oh, I am so sorry dear aunt is poorly, both on her account and my own. What shall I do, dear uncle? It is so hard and painful.'

'Well, my dear boy, I must try to allay it myself. I love you too dearly to leave you in this state. I am not so good at allaying this painful attack as your aunt, but as you know you were successfully relieved in her bottom, and I in yours, yesterday, we shall try today if I can accommodate this huge fellow, of which I have some doubts. Take off your nightshirt as I do mine, it will be more expedient.'

In an instant we were both stark naked. We threw ourselves into one another's arms and lovingly kissed each other. Our tongues met in a delicious sucking – our hands took each a prick, and we had a most exciting and loving embrace. The doctor then took my prick in his mouth, sucked it a little, and well lubricated it with his saliva, spitting on the lower part of the shaft and rubbing it round with his finger. He then knelt, and presenting a really beautifully rounded bottom of the fairest hue, he pushed it out, showing a light brown corrugated bum-hole, most tempting to look at. He desired me to wet it with my saliva. I stooped and applied my mouth and tongue to the appetising morsel, and thrust my tongue in as far as it would go (to his evident delight), leaving it well moistened. I then brought my prick to the entrance; he shoved his backside well out, and acted as if he desired to void himself. A firm but slow pressure quickly engulfed the knob. The doctor desired me to rest a moment, and drop some spittle on the shaft. Again it was firmly pushed forward, and gradually it won its way up, the belly against the buttocks, without much flinching on the doctor's part. After resting a while, he desired me to bend forward and feel his cock while I should move backwards and forwards in the sheath until I was relieved. I had a most delicious fuck. The doctor's bottom-hole was quite hot internally. His pressures with the sphincter were exquisitely delicious, and he had acquired the charming side-wriggle so exquisite in quim fucking. Of course this was an old letch of his, which his position as schoolmaster had given him so many opportunities of indulging in, and the still greater pleasure of initiating others in it. At this very moment he was delighted with his delusion about me in that respect. Of course I never undeceived him, and he had all the extra delight of the idea. My younger and hotter passions had made me spend before he could; so after indulging me in a delicious soak after the ecstasy of the discharge, he drew my attention to the rigidity of his own member, which, he said, I must now allow him to allay in turn.

'Of course, my dear uncle, I am too sensible of your great kindness in relieving me to hesitate about giving you the same relief.'

I now withdrew. He rose for a mutual loving embrace, and then I stooped and taking his fine milk-white prick with its lovely vermilion knob into my mouth, most deliciously sucked it, making my tongue tickle the entrance to the urethra, to his infinite delight. He murmured out soft terms of endearment; then getting exceedingly lewd, he begged me to kneel down as he had done. He then kissed and gamahuched my bottom-hole, making my prick stand and throb again with delight. Then spitting on his prick he quickly sheathed it in my glowing backside. After pausing to enjoy the exquisite pleasure of complete insertion, he stooped, and passing a hand round my belly laid hold of my stiff-standing prick with one hand, while he gently pressed the bollocks with the other. We then proceeded to active measures. He soon made me spend, which I did with loud cries of delight, giving him the most exquisite pleasure by the pressures the act of spending made me exercise on his pleased prick. He soon resumed his thrusts, and eventually we both spent together in the most ecstatic joy. I sank forward on the bed, dragging the doctor with me still embedded in the rapture-giving aperture of my backside. We lay long in all the enchantment of delight. At last he withdrew completely reduced, but was surprised to see me still in a rampant state. When I got up he took my prick in his hand, praised its noble proportions, and again stooping, took it in his mouth, frigging the lower shaft with one hand; he then introduced two fingers into my bottom-hole, continued his suction and movement on my prick in unison with the working of his fingers up my bum-hole, and in this manner quickly produced a delicious discharge in his mouth. I had placed my hands mechanically on his head, and I nearly choked him as I thrust my prick half-way down his throat as I spent. He greedily swallowed every drop, and then rising, embraced me lovingly, telling me I had given him the greatest treat in the world, and he loved me dearly. After this he invited me into his dressing-room, and we both entered the bath together and mutually laved each other. Then we dressed and joined aunt at breakfast. She had not the least air *d'une malade*, but with a sly smile hoped the doctor had proved as efficient as herself.

'Oh, yes, my dear aunt, and I am so much obliged to both of you for your solicitude in relieving the pain I suffer in the morning, but it seems to me that it more frequently and more severely attacks me than ever. I only hope I shall not tire out your kindness by such frequent appeals to your aid.'

'Oh, my darling nephew, do not imagine anything of the sort. We are but too happy to be of any service to you.'

This was accompanied with a knowing smile cast at each other, caused by my apparent uncommon simplicity, but which they were evidently glad to see. We sat down and enjoyed a capital breakfast.

The day passed quite as the two preceding ones. Aunt asked me to walk with her, and as before ended by leading me to the summerhouse, where, after relieving my distress symptoms, as she called them, three times, and finding that the relief was still inefficacious, she proposed to try if by adopting my uncle's position she could not be more successful. So kneeling on the low ottoman, and throwing her clothes over her back, she exposed all the glories of that most splendid backside, and dazzled my sight with its huge magnificence and ivory-like surface, perfectly milk-white, the pureness of which was equally perceptible through the rich light curly hair that spread bush-like between her legs and, wandering beautifully upwards between the cheeks of the enormous orbs, stole round the charming corrugated aperture that I was about to penetrate, the rosy circle of which appeared all too small to admit my very large virile member. I threw myself on my knees, and first licking out the wide open lips of her wondrously fine cunt, and taking care to pay my respects to the small knob of her indurated clitoris, I transferred all my attention to the smaller and most charming orifice. After kissing it most lovingly, I thrust my tongue in as far as it would go, and rolled it about to her infinite delight, while with my left hand below I kept pressing and frigging at her excited clitoris. She wriggled her glorious backside in all the agonies of the delicious excitement until she spent most profusely, actually hurting my tongue with the tightness of the squeeze her sphincter muscle gave as she poured down her plentiful discharge over my chin and neck.

In her grand excitement, and wild with the fury of her lust, she cried out: 'Oh! fuck me, my darling, and shove your glorious prick into my bottom-hole. Oh! fuck – fuck – fuck me directly!'

Inwardly delighted at this natural outbreak of her passions, naming matters by their more appropriate terms, I replied by acts, without any words at the moment. It may well be imagined I was myself in the most rampant fury of desire. So bringing my raging prick up to her magnificently large cunt, all foaming as it was with her recent discharge, I plunged with a furious bound up to the codpiece at once. She met my forward lunge with a backward push and a cry of delighted satisfaction. I moved a few times in and out, so that my prick was white with the foam of her delicious cunt. Then suddenly withdrawing I presented it at the entrance of the more secret temple of Venus, and more gently pushed it home, she helping me with outthrust buttocks and outward straining of the entrance, so that I most charmingly glided slowly into the glowing furnace that was awaiting with such lascivious desire to engulf and devour my longed-for prick. For, as I have before observed, my dear aunt was gluttonous of a bottom-fuck, after being so fucked in cunt as I had already served her. It was so deliciously tight and hot that I lay in the exquisite rapture of complete insertion for some minutes. I had seen my aunt's arm move in a manner to convince me she was frigging her own clitoris, in fact, the movement of her hand frigging herself was felt by my codpiece. I let her continue, until finding by the involuntary wriggling of her bottom that she was about again to spend, I aided her with my prick, and had hardly made many moves before she poured down another tribute of lust, with a squeal of delight, and with such pressure on my prick as nearly drove him at once to a similar discharge. I did my best, and succeeded in not following suit. My aunt was insatiable, and I was glad to let her spend as often as possible, and I so managed matters that she spent again before joining me in the final crisis, which seized us together, and we died away in joyous cries of thoroughly, though but momentarily, satisfied desire. I sank on that magnificent back, as the languor that follows the ecstatic moment overtook me, but it was only for a short time. The exquisite internal pressures that my amorous and glorious aunt was exercising on my delighted prick were too exciting not rapidly to produce a reaction; none the less rapidly for being in such a delicious retreat as the pleasure-giving aperture of that gloriously exciting backside. I was lying down on her broad back, so passing one hand round to her large but firm bubby, I took its nipple between my fingers. The other hand sought the knob of her still stiff clitoris. I excited both while making a very gentle move with my hardly fully standing prick. I felt at once how this gratified her; indeed, she often afterwards assured me that such frigging, with the movement of the softened prick gently working within her, was most exciting, and almost better than when it was in full force. I soon made her spend again. Another of her delights was to have a stiff prick shove away into her the instant after she had spent, when she herself was at the moment incapable of further action. She in after-days proved that her greatest pleasure was to have a fresh-standing prick near, to take the place of one that had made her spend, and had spent itself, and have it thrust into her with all the vigour and lust the sight of the previous fucking had inspired and fired it with. At this moment, as I had not spent, it was the exact counterpart her libidinous imagination could have desired. I fucked and frigged on until we both gave down in cries of joy our united tribute to Venus. We both sank this time down on the couch in utter forgetfulness of all but the ecstatic bliss with which we were overcome. We long lay soaking in all the delightful sensations my adorable aunt's convulsive clutchings of my prick with her delicious close pressures excited. At last she begged me to withdraw, although she could feel me now restiffening under the delights of that exquisite interior. I would fain have recommenced.

'You must not, my dear boy, it is more than nature can support, and I must consider your youth; you have delighted me even beyond previous delights – rise then my love, and let me embrace, thank, and love you as I shall always do.'

I rose, and we threw ourselves into each other's arms, lovingly kissing and tongueing each other. Aunt then buttoned me up, first kissing and taking a mouthful of my prick for a moment between her lips, and then putting him away, calling him 'my pretty doodle'. I seized the expression, and said: 'Dear aunt, you called it my prick just now, and begged me to fuck you, and to shove it well into your cunt. Are these the real names for my doodle and your fanny, and what does 'fuck' mean, my darling aunt? Do tell me, dear auntie? and teach me the language I ought to use when you are so kindly relieving me of the pains of my now so frequent hardness. I don't know whether you have observed it, dear auntie, but I never enter this summer-house with you, but it becomes painfully hard at once; to be sure, you give me such exquisite pleasure in relieving me that I could wish to have constant hardnesses as long as you were near to calm them. Is this natural, dear aunt, or a disease? Pray tell me, and teach me all the endearing terms you so lavish upon me while I am reducing my hardnesses.'

My apparent simplicity evidently pleased her. She probably thought, too, that as I must sooner or later really thoroughly understand the nature of our intercourse, it would be much better she should, as it were, make a confidant of me, and attach me more securely to herself. She begged me to be seated and she fully explained everything to me. Of course I was even better acquainted than herself with all she communicated, but I confirmed the idea she evidently entertained of her being my first instructress by various naïve remarks on all she was telling me. Of course I proved an apt scholar, and by my close-put questions brought out all her own knowledge, and left nothing for me to learn. At the end, I said: 'Do all women have such a delightful sheath – cunt I mean – between their legs as you have, dear aunt?'

'Yes, my darling; but you must never stray to others; you will find none so fond of you, or I may add, without vanity, so capable of satisfying this dear fellow; but come, I see it will be dangerous to allow him to stay here longer.'

She rose, but I quickly unbuttoned and produced my prick in an almost grander state than ever. I begged of her to let me have one more 'fuck' now that I knew what it all really meant. I put it into her hand. Her own previous descriptive lesson had aroused her lasciviousness. She fondly grasped it, and stooping down, kissed it, saying she could not resist its eloquent look. Throwing herself back on the couch, with her clothes up, her feet on the edge, and her legs apart, her glorious cunt lay open in its moist magnificence. I threw myself on my knees and gamahuched her until she spent: and now, knowing her greatest letch, I instantly brought my bursting prick up to her foaming cunt, plunged in and began a furious movement, accompanying it with all the most endearing bawdy phrases she had just, as she thought, taught me.

'Oh, my most gloriously cunted aunt, do I fuck you? Wriggle your arse faster – that's it! Do you feel my prick up to the hilt in your delicious cunt? Oh! what pleasure you do give me!'

She replied as broadly. Passing her hand down she pressed my cods, and asked if thus squeezing my bollocks added to my pleasure.

'Oh, yes, my love, your cunt, your arse, your bubbies, are all delicious. Oh, I never before knew there could be such additional pleasure to our fucking as using these endearing words produces.'

We were both so excited by the bawdy terms we so profusely used that we went off in the utmost excess of ecstasy, and died away thoroughly satiated with our libidinous and most lasciviously delicious fuck. It was time to finish. So sliding off her, I again buried my face in her delicious gaping and foaming cunt, my mouth, lips, nose, and cheeks were covered with sperm; she drew me to her lips and licked it all off. Then repairing our disordered dress we returned to the house, and found the doctor impatiently awaiting us. Our flushed and excited faces at once showed that we had been indulging in the greatest excess. He joked aunt upon her skill in allaying such frequent attacks as I now appeared subject to.

Aunt informed him that she had inadvertently in her lust made use of expressions which had betrayed so much to me that she had found it necessary to leave me nothing more to learn, and I was now fully aware of the true nature of our connection; after luncheon he himself might further enlighten me, for she was certain that complete confidence would be the best policy to pursue; it must come about, sooner or later, and it was far better it should come from him than that I should learn it elsewhere. He said she was quite right, and that he would further instruct me after luncheon, so we set to work on the viands before us, to which I did ample justice.

I was thus, as they supposed, newly initiated in the mysteries of the coition of the sexes. I shall reserve further details of our more intimate and expansive experiences for the third chapter of this true romance of lust, which continues the account of my early experiences.

## Chapter Three

After the luncheon which closed the last chapter, a churchwarden occupied uncle for about an hour. When he had left, uncle proposed a walk in the garden. I could see at once what this was meant to lead to, as he almost immediately turned in the direction of the summerhouse. When we got there he sat down on the couch, and begged me to sit beside him.

He opened the subject at once by saying: 'My dear Charlie, I am very much pleased that your aunt has opened your eyes to the real nature of our actions with you, which your simple innocence had imagined to be a mere kindly relief to the overgorged vessels of your virile member. Accident might have made you acquainted with this through some less interested channel, and you might have innocently betrayed your future position. I believe you to possess a large fund of good sense and discretion, and the advice I shall give you as to the conduct to pursue in future will not only be received with confidence as meant for your future good, but listened to attentively and acted upon. The world, my dear boy, and by that I mean society in general, condemns the practices we have lately been indulging in with you. Their narrow prejudices ignore the fact that nature alone prompts to these delightful acts, and that the great god of nature gifted us with the powers necessary for their performance. But, as the world has chosen to brand them with its censure, men of prudence, like myself, whilst apparently conforming outwardly to such stupid prejudices, know how in secret fully to enjoy them. I am blessed in your darling aunt with a wife who fully understands and humours my desires. She is rarely splendid in the glorious beauties of her body, and in temperament hot as the most erotic of our sex could desire. Even in your ignorance you must have felt the wonderful power of conferring carnal ecstatic pleasure she possesses, and have heard how, in the energy of her passion, she allows her lust to betray her into the use of grossly bawdy terms – but which, as they have enlightened you when best prepared to receive such knowledge, is rather fortunate than otherwise. I speak thus frankly to you, my dear boy, because I have found you of a rare facility in giving and receiving erotic pleasures, and of a temperament worthy of the descent from the same stock as your aunt. You are worthy of each other, and formed to enjoy to the utmost each other's carnal delights, and I bless my happy star that has brought you both under my own roof. Henceforth there must be no secrets between us. It was at my earnest wish that your aunt relieved you, and, of course, I had my own object in view. In the first place I require some extra excitement to be able myself to indulge in these delightful combats in love's domain. You and your aunt's copulations were to me more exciting than you can imagine. You will have observed, too, what is the real quarter to which, when excited, I pay my devoirs. Glorious as is the backside of your incomparable aunt, your young charms, virgin in that respect, excited me still more. I began by gentle touches, and then tried the insertion of my finger, when I saw you were far too busy operating within the orbit of your lustful and lusty aunt to observe or even feel what I was doing. I found a facility about your bottom as perfect for enjoyment as your truly magnificent prick or cock was fitted for operating in its way. It was then I suggested to your aunt to mount upon you, and afterwards made you aware that your aunt possessed another aperture which could equally well allay what you then looked upon as a source of pain. My object was to lead you to the same point. Your innocent docility lent itself with easy simplicity to all my desires. I saw that you entered readily into your aunt's glorious bum-hole, and allowed me to work with two fingers in your own. Finding that it rather gave you pleasure than otherwise, I proposed to abate my own stiffness in your bottom. Your affectionate docility enabled me to obtain unfailing ecstasy. Your after-fucking of me, while I was in my wife's bottom, conferred the utmost erotic bliss upon me, as you have experienced when operating and being operated upon. These are the moments of a felicity your stupid prejudiced worldlings know nothing of; and these are the pleasures which, now that we have initiated you into all their secret mysteries, we will enjoy to the utmost. To the true votaries of these love orgies, grossness of language is a stimulant to passion. Fuck – frig – bugger – cunt – prick – bollocks – bubbies – arsehole – are all sacred words only to be pronounced when in the exercise of love's mysteries. At all other times a guarded decency of word, act and gesture is imperative, as enhancing the delight of an unbridled vocabulary in the voluptuousness of raging lust. I shall from time to time inculcate sage precepts on this point – enough for the present. Let us now indulge in mutual embraces.'

So ending, he took me in his arms and glued his lips to mine. Our tongues met. Both our hands wandered, his to my prick, which immediately responded to the touch, while my hand was placed on his prick, which was only at half-cock. I rapidly unbuttoned him and brought it forth, then stooping I took it in my mouth, sucked it and fingered the root with my hand. Then passing my other hand below, I sought to penetrate with my finger into the interior of his fundament. He rose to a standing position to enable me to enter his anus more easily. His prick quickly standing fiercely showed how much I excited him. I ceased not until he was in an agony of pleasure – forcing my head down on his prick until it entered almost completely into my mouth, and shooting his sperm right down my throat. I continued to suck and frig him until I produced somewhat of a restiffening of his prick. He begged me to rise, that he might take mine in his mouth, desiring me at the same time to take off my trousers and lie down on the couch. I did so. He knelt at my side, and first handling and examining it with loudly expressed admiration of my noble weapon, he took its head in his mouth, and then with his hand on its lower shaft, and finger up my fundament, brought on a similar crisis as that I had produced on himself. He just as greedily swallowed all. I had allowed my hand to fall down by the side of the couch, where it encountered his prick, which had resumed its pristine vigour.

'Come my dear uncle,' said I, 'and let us put it into its favourite corner.'

I rose, and kneeling, turned my backside full in his face. He stooped, caressed, kissed and tongued the rosy orifice. With the plentiful saliva with which the operation of sucking my prick had filled his mouth, he moistened my bum-hole and his own prick, and then easily glided up to the hilt within my delighted backside. Resting for a while in all the ecstasies of insertion, which I heightened by my internal pressures, he seized my prick which had stood again at once at the pleasing sensation occasioned by the introduction of his prick in my bottom. Thus frigging my prick and fucking my arse, with occasional pauses to lengthen out our pleasures, he at last brought matters to a most exquisite termination, and we died away in cries of joy as we poured forth a mutual torrent of sperm. Uncle continued soaking in all the blissful after-sensations, which I did everything in my power to enhance by the delight-giving pressures of my sphincter muscle. When he withdrew and rose to his legs, he helped me up, and drew me to his bosom, and we had a long kiss of gratified desire, tongueing each other the while, and handling our bollocks with mutual gratification. My uncle was profuse in his praises of my docility and aptitude, declaring that his pederastic enjoyment of my person excelled all he had ever experienced in his long practice of the habit, and my delicious sideways wriggle was superior to the very fine bum-fucking his adorable wife had the art of giving him: then there was the further excitement of handling the very finest prick he had ever met with.

'It is no flattery to you, my dear Charles,' he said, 'but mere justice to its superb dimensions and admirable power.'

Here he stopped, and sucked anew its reeking head, getting a few more drops out. We then purified ourselves – a basin with water was kept in a small cupboard purposely for such occasion, for I afterwards learned the place had been the scene of innumerable contests of the same kind with aunt and other boys. Having readjusted our disordered habiliments, we left the grounds, and took a long quiet walk in the fields, the good doctor inculcating admirable advice in me, whom he considered an innocent tyro in love's ways. Nevertheless, all he taught me only strengthened my high opinion of the wisdom of dear Mrs Benson, and the adorable Frankland, whose opinion of what was likely to happen to me at the rectory had been so quickly realised. We returned in time to dress for dinner. The evening passed as the previous ones. I was conducted to my room, and left alone to recruit my forces by a quiet night's rest. I may here incidentally mention that it was a rule of uncle and aunt, very rarely departed from, to send their favourites to their lonely couches as a means of restoring their powers, and reinvigorating them for daylight encounters – both the dear creatures loving to have the fullest daylight on all the charms of their participants in pleasure, at the same time yielding an equally undisguised inspection of their own. This was their principle reason, but they also considered it advisable as a restorative, and a useful precaution not to overstrain the energies of the youths they both so much enjoyed. My late experiences at home had already taught me the advantage and utility of a quiet night's rest after frequent contests in the fields of Venus and Juno.

I slept on this occasion with a deep and continuous slumber, until I was awakened by my uncle, who came to summon me to the arms of his wife, who, in the splendour of her full-blown charms, awaited me in her own bed, naked as the day she was born. Her arms outstretched, she invited me to the full enjoyment of her glorious person. The doctor drew my nightshirt over my head, and in a moment I was locked in the close embrace of that superb creature. We were both too hot to wait for further preliminaries, but went at it in furious haste, and rapidly paid our first tribute to the god of love. The doctor had acted postilion to both of us, with a finger up each anus. The exquisite pressures of my aunt's cunt reinvigorated me almost without a pause, and we proceeded at once to run a second course. Uncle got three fingers into her divine bottom-hole, as her legs were thrown over my waist, and her immense buttocks well thrown up enabled him to have full play between the cheeks of her backside. This double operation made the dear lascivious creature spend again in a very few movements, and giving her hardly time to finish her discharge, I fucked on with double force, and with prick as hard as wood, as fast I could work. This furious onset, which was the most exciting thing she knew of, rapidly caused a third discharge. To prevent my own prick from spending too quickly, I held somewhat back; then again we went at it fast and furious, and the dear lustful creature, with cries of joy, spent again with me, and fainted from excess of pleasure; but her glorious cunt continued to throb on my delighted prick, as if it would nip it off by the roots. I never met with so lusciously large a cunt, or one with a greater power of pressure. She could quite hold even an exhausted prick a complete prisoner in these most delicious and velvety folds. Great as was the power of Miss Frankland's cunt in that way, aunt beat her.

I may here mention an occurrence that took place some time after this period. It was during a rare opportunity from an accidental absence of the doctor, when I was sleeping with my gloriously beautiful aunt. I had fucked her to her heart's content before we slept, and again on waking, in full daylight, after which we rose to relieve our natural wants. I laid myself down on the floor, that I might completely see my dear aunt piddle from her splendid cunt. It was a glorious sight, which instantly fired my passions and was at once followed by a fuck on the floor, my aunt's enormous backside being quite cushion enough, and we enjoyed the novelty of the thing amazingly. She was loud in her praises of my indefatigable prick, which, with is vigour and superb dimensions, was beyond all she had ever seen or felt, and just fitted her large and luscious cunt, which had never before been so well filled. This remark reminded me of a desire I had long had to have a thorough investigation of that immense and splendid object. I expressed a wish to that effect.

'My darling boy, anything you like, you could not have a better opportunity, my legs point to the window, so you have the fullest sight – look, feel, frig, fuck, or bugger, all is at your free disposition – only give me a pillow from the bed, as the floor is too hard for me to continue so long as you are likely to be.'

I jumped up and gave her two pillows. Then laying her limbs wide open, with knees bent, the magnificence of that luscious cunt lay in all is grandeur before me. I have before described what a large, but splendidly proportioned woman she was – small feet, and clear-run ankles, large, but admirably turned calves, very small knees, above which rose the very finest and fleshiest of thighs, worthy supporters of what I have already described as the largest and finest backside my eyes ever lighted on. Immense hips, and wonderfully and naturally small waist, above which were her superb, large, fine and firm bubbies, that stood out, when naked, as hard and firm as those of the youngest of women; a charming neck and well-poised head with most pleasing and beautiful features crowned the whole. Her arms were superb, and equal in proportion to her other grand and splendid limbs. The flesh was of the most delicious creamy white, without a spot or a blemish. The hair of the head was plentiful in the extreme, and so long and thick that when undone it fell all around her and below her superb buttocks, so that she could shake it out all round and completely hide her nakedness. Often and often has she allowed me to pose her in every way, and shake it out all over her, and well she might, for no matter how often I might have fucked her previously, it was sure to produce at least three more encounters, one of which was always in her backside, a most favourite way with her and which she declared was by far the most pleasurable provided the other aperture had been previously well fucked. With such a taste, of course, her greatest pleasure was to have two pricks in her at once, the *ne plus ultra* of erotic satisfaction. To return to the inspection I was about to describe, it was really the first at my full disposition, for although I had often gamahuched, felt and seen the beautiful object, it was when my passions were excited, and when the gratification of lust alone prompted me, a state of mind opposed to close observation of natural beauties. Now, repeated tributes to the god of lust had cooled my ardour for the moment, and left me to the perfect enjoyment of the sight before me, with the temper to inspect its full-blown beauties in the minutest way. I have said before that my aunt had one of the broadest, most prominent, and most beautiful mounts of Venus that I ever saw. It was thickly covered with beautiful silky fair curls, which did not hinder you from seeing her exquisite skin below. The sweep round, to pass between her thighs, was bold and graceful. In the middle was a well-defined semicircular depression, from whence the large, thick and beautifully pouting lips of her cunt, which in her present position lay partially open, commenced. You could just see where the clitoris lay snug. I have already observed that this was not largely developed, nor were the inner labia of her cunt at all projecting, indeed, they were not visible, unless her legs, with bent knees, were stretched apart, as at present. On each side of these luscious pouting lips, and the long immense pinky gash, was a triangle of considerable space, such, in fact, as is only to be seen in a woman of the splendidly large proportions of my aunt; this was covered as much as her mount with fair silky curls, which ran down to her beautiful corrugated and rosy bottom-hole. Nothing could be finer or more beautiful than the sight, as she thus lay fully exposing every part in the broadest daylight. After handling and admiring all, I laid the lips well back and apart, and there they kept open. Nothing could be more charming than the interior of that most enchanting cunt; of an exquisite salmon-pink in colour, nothing was out of order. The clitoris, which bulged out in excitement from my touches of all the parts around, lay first in the upper partition of the pouting lips; then below came, slightly open, a charming entrance to the urethra, larger than usual, to allow the mighty rush of waters to pour from it when piddling; below this was the opening of the vagina, which I parted with my fingers, and could see even to the corrugated sides of that exquisite pleasure-giving sheath; then followed some sinuosity of pinky flesh, whose duty it was to stretch to allow the largest prick to penetrate. Half an inch beyond was the rosy orifice of her bottom. Such was the exquisite scene before my delighted eyes. I proceeded with my internal examination. Thrusting in three fingers of each hand, I forced open by literal pressure the lips, until I could see to a depth of four or five inches. It was a most beautiful sight. The sheath appeared to have ribs running round it about half an inch apart, and I could see they were the means of causing the exquisite pressures her cunt could so ecstatically exercise. Indeed, excited by my *attouchements*, I could see them contracting and relaxing. It was, doubtless, these ribs that seemed to exercise a sort of peristaltic motion on the prick, when reposing at full stand in that glorious cunt. I was able so widely to open this splendid vagina that I thought I would try to get my hand altogether in. Projecting my fingers forward, with the first and fourth drawn under the middle ones and the thumb between, I pushed them forward, and as the whole cunt was reeking with my last discharge, and was well lubricated, I glided on; there was a little difficulty at the knuckles, but I exerted a slight, gentle pressure, and in all went. Aunt winced a little, and asked what I was doing. I told her.

'It is all in, my darling?'

'Yes, auntie.'

She closed upon it, and squeezed it quite hard.

'Oh, how nice!' she exclaimed, 'push it further in.'

I advanced, and could feel the end of her womb, which appeared like three points to fingers and the thumb drawn together, and looked at endways is something like what it felt – of course, without the nails. Aunt asked me if I could double my fist where it was. I had no difficulty, as the part yielded to the greater bulk. Aunt cried out: 'My darling boy, that is delicious; push it further in.'

I did so, and began working within her, backwards and forwards. She wriggled her splendid backside in ecstasy, and before I had made a dozen movements, poured down upon my hand and arm a torrent of almost boiling liquid, and went off with a cry of enjoyment. Her arms and legs relaxed, and she lay quite still in the utmost after-enjoyment, but with a pressure on my arm and fist quite wonderful. Knowing how she liked the movement to be continued at such a moment, I worked in and out slowly. She soon recovered, seconded my movements and again went off in all the fury of lust, accompanied with shouts of excitement, urging faster movements, and in all the fury of her most libidinous nature spending again most profusely. All this had now brought me into as furious a state as herself. I wanted to withdraw and substitute my prick, not only from the state of excitement I was in, but also to experience the effects of such a well-stretched cunt upon my lesser-sized weapon. But so tight did my aunt hold my imprisoned hand that I could not withdraw. I begged her to let it go, as I wanted to fuck her instantly, but she prayed me to give her one more taste of my exquisite manoeuvres, it was a joy beyond anything she had ever before experienced, so she begged her darling boy to comply. On I went as she desired, and a more exciting picture of furious lust never met my sight. I helped her final discharge by thrusting two fingers in her bum-hole. Never shall I forget the grip she gave my arm and fingers when she spent. It was positively painful, and showed the enormous force of passionate lust. She went off in such a fury of excitement that I thought she had fainted outright. But her pressures continued all the time. It was long before she recovered her senses, and my arm was aching and my prick bursting. At last she exclaimed: 'Oh! where am I? I have been in paradise.'

'Dear aunt,' I cried, 'do let me out. I am bursting to fuck you, and I can't get my arm out if you don't relax your grip of my wrist.'

'I can't help it, my dear boy, it is involuntary, put your other hand on my mount, and pull steadily, but not with a jerk.'

I did so, and really it required considerable force to withdraw it, notwithstanding I had previously unclenched my hand. I jumped immediately upon her, and at one bound plunged into that vast cavity, up to the cods. It immediately closed upon me, and tight as she usually held me, she really appeared to do so this time tighter than ever, so wonderfully gifted was the longest, highest, and most luscious cunt I ever fucked. You may easily imagine the rapid ending of such raging lust. I spent with cries more like the braying of a donkey than any other sound, and then lay like one dead on that glorious belly, with head reposing between the firm and splendid bubbies, my aunt clasping me to her bosom, panting with all it had just granted. We lay long in ecstatic trance of the delicious after-sensations. Our mutual internal throbbings gradually re-excited our passions. With renewed ardour I quickly made my lascivious and libidinous aunt spend again on my delighted prick, which kept ramming at her during the swoon-like pause which spending produced; she had taught me this was exquisite delight to her. She soon resumed the full swing of her lust, but suddenly stopping, said: 'Charlie, my darling, withdraw, and shove it in behind.'

She quickly turned round, with great agility, prompted by the excess of her desires. I was behind her in an instant, and as my prick was reeking with the fuck she had just so plentifully bedewed it with, and the divine lower orifice had also received its tricklings, I had no difficulty in pushing firmly but not too forcibly right up to the meeting of her stupendous buttocks and my belly. She sighed deeply with delight, when she felt me fully embedded, and began the delicious side-wriggle, while I remained for some minutes quiet, that I might enjoy the superb beauty of those mighty orbs, in all their play of passion. Aunt grew furious with lust. Her hand was actively frigging both clitoris and cunt. She called out to me to shove on; two or three thrusts on my part, and the dear, lecherous creature again poured down her nature. I paused to restrain my own discharge, but made my prick throb within its most exquisite sheath, which never ceased responding most deliciously. It was but for a minute or two for then my own fierce passion drove me to very energetic action. My delighted aunt seconded my move-ments, fast and furious grew our sport, until, with cries of the wildest lust, we both spent deliciously together. I sank on her glorious bottom and back, embracing her superb bubbies with both hands until her exquisite pressures again renewed my forces and drove me on to another delightful career in which again the hot lust of my aunt drew down from her several discharges to my one. At last we sank both together, in all the joys of fully satiated desire. Again I lay for some time on that broad and beauteous back, until aunt said I must withdraw, as she had a great natural want. I instantly withdrew; out he came with a loud plop, followed immediately by a tremendous succession of farts. Aunt professed to be quite horrified, but I only burst into a loud fit of laughter and told the dear creature to fart, piss or shit, whenever she felt inclined, I should only love her the better. She said she must at once do the latter, and was running off to the water closet as soon as she could hurry on some clothes. But I drew out the chamber, and begged her to sit down there at once. It would give me pleasure and excite me as well. She was too hard pressed to hesitate, so sitting down, she had a 'hell of a let-fly', as a military friend of mine used to say. I stooped over her back, caressed her bubbies and when she turned up her delighted face, our lips were glued together in a loving kiss, while my nose sniffed the really delicious odour that came from her. When she had done, she begged me to hand her a towel to wipe herself.

'No, no, my darling aunt, nothing of the sort; stoop down forward on to your knees, and I will lick the delicious orifice clean with my tongue.'

She laughed, kissed me, and told me I was a darling boy, just after her own heart, but hardly expected I had already acquired the tastes of my uncle, the rector, whose letch lay in that practice. She let herself down on her knees as her sublime arse raised itself from the pot, and stooping her head low down, presented her immense buttocks before me, with the chink between well stretched open. I moved the pot on one side, threw myself on hands and knees, and eagerly kissing the exquisite orifice, greedily licked it clean; thrusting my tongue well within, I rolled it about, to the great delight of dear aunt, whose passions were instantly aroused, and her divine backside began to wriggle. I shoved my thumb up her cunt, and frigged until she spent. Meanwhile my own unruly member had become distended to his full size, and was throbbing with desire. So raising my body erect, I brought him again to the rosy orifice I had just been tongueing, and to my aunt's infinite delight, again housed him as far as he could go, and again began active operations, which I continued until aunt's lasciviousness again made her spend. I paused a little after this, or otherwise I should have gone off myself. Stooping over the glorious bottom, I replaced her hand with my own, and began frigging her clitoris, till her passions, again excited, made her begin ecstatic movements, in which I joined until the grand crisis seized us both together, ushered in with cries of joy. We spent, and sank down sideways on the floor in quite a death swoon of ecstatic and satisfied lust. Here we lay quite exhausted for some time. At last aunt let me out, and begged me to rise.

'I must purify you, my darling boy, as you did me.'

And seizing my limp prick in her mouth she sucked it clean, until she began to feel symptoms of the resurrection of the flesh. She hastily rose, and said: 'No, Charlie, you have done far too much tonight. I must see you to your bed, that you may get at least a couple of hours sleep.'

She took up my nightshirt, threw it over me, led me to my bedroom, tenderly embraced me, and thanked me for such a night of pleasure as she had never in all her life enjoyed the equal. Then locking me in, she retired to her own bed. It may well be supposed that after such exertions, I slept the sleep of the just for many hours. My aunt had frequently come to look at me, but seeing me in so sound a slumber, would not have me disturbed – a politic proceeding, as it resulted in a fuller indulgence in the summerhouse that day than would have happened if my powers had not been restored by refreshing sleep.

This kind of life had been going on for nearly three weeks. The doctor became less easy to move. One morning I had fucked my aunt twice; the doctor's prick at the end of the second had stiffened to about half-stand. I took it into my mouth, which, with handling his bollocks and postilioning his bottom-hole, brought him up to the full standard. He proposed to bugger aunt while I did the same kind office to himself. A caprice seized me, and I proposed, on the contrary, that we should both fuck aunt's capacious cunt at once. Aunt, for form's sake, cried out against it, but the idea tickled the fancy of my uncle, who would not only enjoy all the beauties of my aunt's glorious backside in motion, but could postilion her as well. So I lay down on my back, aunt straddled me, and presented her splendid bum to the attack of her excited husband. He first thrust his prick up to the hilt in her luscious and well-bedewed cunt; when well lubricated, he withdrew, to allow me to take my place in full possession; then bringing his stiff-standing prick against the root of mine, pressing it well down, he gently shoved forward, and gradually sheathed himself within the well-stretched and capacious orbit of my aunt, who winced a little in pretended pain, but who, by the grip she immediately gave to the double fuck within her, showed how much gratified she was. After a pause of enjoyment, I gave the signal for exact joint movements, both pulling out gently, and sliding slowly in again. Two or three thrusts, aided by the doctor's finger in her bottom-hole, sufficed to make dear lecherous aunt spend profusely. We increased our speed but still not fast, which quickly re-awakened all aunt's lust. Before we ourselves were ready, the dear lascivious creature again poured down her nature, boiling hot, on our delighted pricks. This produced such excitement upon us that we could no longer restrain our own desire to come to the ecstatic conclusion. Our movements became more rapid. We each felt the electric-like sensation of the approaching crisis. Aunt doubly felt the influence of our increasing speed and hardness, and was as ready as ourselves to pour down the tribute to the goddess of love or lust, holy Mother Venus. The novelty, the pressure, and the excess of pleasure declared itself in the loud cries of the last crisis, as we all died away in the enrapturing sensations produced by the intense satisfaction our desires had experienced. We lay long, wrapped in the after-ecstasy; aunt's delicious internal movements began again. The doctor's prick had shrunk to a merry piece of inanimate dough, and he withdrew, begging us at the same time to change our position, and let him enjoy seeing me attack my aunt in the rear. This inflamed me at once. Aunt rolled from off me, I took my place behind, and we ran a most delicious course, rendered much more excitable to me by the introduction of uncle's two fingers up my fundament, which kept time with my action in the delicious aperture of my aunt's most superb and glorious backside, the movements of which beneath my delighted gaze had not been the least stimulating part of the enjoyment. The crisis was most ecstatic, and I sank exhausted on her broad buttocks and beautiful back, to clasp her lovingly in my arms and sob out bawdy terms of the warmest endearment. The doctor, who had very much enjoyed the sight, but who pointed out the sadly downcast state of his prick, which had been in no wise excited by the scene, said to his wife: 'My darling, we must have recourse to the grand remedy. It will also initiate dear Charlie into a new mystery of love, of which he can have no idea.'

I guessed at once what he meant, but professing extreme ignorance, I begged him to tell me what it was. Aunt rose and said: 'My darling, your uncle requires his blood to be excited by flogging his buttocks with a birch rod.'

'How odd,' said I, 'I never felt anything but the severest pain when I was flogged, and I took precious good care not to deserve it again. How then can it excite?'

'You shall see, my dear.'

She opened her wardrobe and produced a formidable rod of fine fresh-cut birch twigs. The doctor begged me to lie down on my back, he got over me, and we commenced sucking each other's pricks. Mine stood at once, as the doctor, in addition to sucking, thrust a couple of fingers up my bottom-hole, and frigged away as fast as he sucked. The doctor's buttocks were left at the mercy of aunt, who flogged away at them with no gentle hand. I spent before the doctor could quite get his prick to standing point, but the copious torrent I poured into his mouth, and his after-suction on my prick, in addition to the red raw state of his buttocks, at last brought him up to full stand. He wanted to put it into me when ready, but aunt said that as flogger she had herself become greatly excited, and must have it herself.

'While this dear prick,' throwing herself on it, and sucking it, 'shall fuck me at the same time.'

I was quite ready, and she straddled across me, and guided my now longing prick into her luscious cunt. She soon stopped, and we tongued each other while the doctor was mounting to the assault on her delicious bottom-hole. As soon as he was housed, we began another charming course, in which aunt, as usual, spent frequently before our less lecherous natures were ready to join in one general and exquisite discharge. We went off in furies of delighted lust, and then sank exhausted in the delicious after-sensation. We long lay in the sweet inanition and luxury of satiated lust. At last, we disconnected ourselves, rose, and laved each other with cold water, more as a restorative than as a purification. Aunt and I had two bouts after – one in front and one behind. The doctor would not allow a fresh application of the birch, as he said it would only produce so great an exhaustion as would require days to restore. I retired after this, but ever afterwards the doctor was regularly birched before he could even copulate once. Sometimes he required to flog my aunt's glorious bum to excite his fading powers, declaring that it was almost as exciting as being flogged. He even gave it me gently, although I hardly ever required it, but I professed my surprise at its efficacy.

The holidays were at an end, but I was as yet the only boarder. There were, however, some twenty or thirty youths from the neighbourhood, who were day scholars at the doctor's school. Among these the doctor had his pick in the flogging way, but he never allowed them to know anything of our other proceedings, or to imagine that the birching which took place was otherwise than as a punishment for faults or inattention. However, I was generally the chosen companion of these whippings, in which I acted as horse, or holder of the boy to be flogged. Of course, I took good care to expose as much as possible their lovely cocks, as well as their plump bottoms, and as this excited me as well as the doctor, it often ended, after the culprit was dismissed, in my flogging the doctor, followed by a mutual rack off in each other's bottoms.

There was one fine, plump, girlish-looking youth named Dale, who was here for the first half. He had not as yet been brought up for punishment, although the doctor had confided to me the letch he had taken to flog his fine fat bottom. One day, Master Dale brought a sealed note from his widowed mother, who lived about a mile from the village, in a charming *cottage orné*. The doctor read the note. By chance I was looking at him, and saw a smile of joy light up his features.

'Come here, Master Dale,' said he, in a mild and gentle voice, 'your mother tells me that you have behaved in a most shameful manner to your pretty young cousin, who is residing with your mamma.'

Master Dale blushed scarlet, for he was not aware until now that anyone had been a witness to the scene that had taken place between him and his pretty cousin.

This was what had passed. The cousin, a lovely girl of fifteen, was in a secluded spot in the garden, near an arbour, the preceding afternoon. She was bending down, tying up a flower close to the ground, which made her stoop to such a degree that she could only reach it with ease by having her legs wide apart. Her back was towards the walk by which young Dale was advancing. As he approached unheard by her, he could not fail to see peeping out between the stretched open expanse of snowy drawers the inner part of her well-rounded globes of dimpled ivory. Her shift had somehow worked upwards, and revealed all the charms of her delicate young bum and plump white thighs. The sight inflamed the youth beyond measure. He crept up noiselessly quite close to her, and, stooping down until his head was below the level of her raised petticoat, he feasted his eyes for some time with the lovely prospect before him, her little virgin rosebud slit, its pink and pouting lips, plump little mount already delicately shaded with a curly foliage that promised soon to be much more dense, together with the swell of her lovely young thighs and calves. All this was quite unsuspected by the object of his admiration, who was absorbed in her garden operations. At length, however, the excited youth could not resist the temptation of applying his soft warm hand to the parts he was admiring, which made Miss scream slightly, thinking it was some insect up her petticoats, and exclaim: 'Oh, dear! oh, dear!'

But turning her head round, she discovered the delinquent.

'Forgive me, Ellen dear, but really you exposed so very pretty a sight while stooping that upon my word I could not help it.'

Now girls are curious as well as boys, perhaps more so; and if the truth must be told, Miss had for some time past longed for an opportunity to become better acquainted with things in general, and, therefore, thought here was a chance not to be thrown away. So, after some little show of resistance on her part, for decency's sake, it was agreed between them that he should have a good look at *hers*, if he would afterwards show her *his*. Miss Ellen had never seen a male 'diddle', as she and her young playfellows called it, not even that of a boy, and she was all excitement and expectation to feel with her own hand the 'funny thing', for so a communicative servant-maid had described it, who at the same time had fully explained the theory of its use, which made Miss long to obtain some practical knowledge also. So to the arbour they both adjourned. Miss Ellen first lay back upon the seat, while the young rogue unfastened her drawers, and pulling them down, feasted his eyes with a full view of her virgin charms as long as he pleased, for Miss Ellen was a lecherous little maid, who really felt a precocious pleasure in being thus exposed to the close observation and admiration of one of the opposite sex, although for form's sake she covered her blushing face with her delicate little hands. He touched *it*, pressed *it*, rubbed *it* with his finger. Her thighs trembled and opened. Taught by nature, he imprinted a burning kiss on the lovely little quim before him. She sighed, and mechanically put her hand on his head and pressed it closer to her naked skin. Guided by his feelings, he indulged in movements of his lips and pressures which speedily excited the amorous little maid to such an extent as to make her give down with a deep and trembling sigh the first tribute of her virgin cunt. Feeling the warm liquid oozing from the pouting orifice on his closely pressed lips, he could not help tasting it with his tongue. This reawakened very quickly the sensibilities of the lecherous little thing, and awoke her to the desire to practise a like pleasure with his cock. So reminding him of his promise, she made him stand up before her, while she undid his trousers with her fairy fingers, all trembling with excitement, and drew out his stiff affair, which already gave promise of a very respectable future, now swollen to a size it had never before known. Delighted at the sight of so bewitching a plaything, she made him lie down as she had done, and kneeling beside him, with cheeks glowing with excitement, she closely examined every part of the rampant little member. Strange to say, no hand, hardly even its owner's, had as yet invaded its virgin precincts, and it had not yet had its ruby head fully uncovered, although he was upwards of fifteen. The delight caused by the touch of her warm hand pressing and encircling his stiffened cock was most exquisite. She was not long, however, before she became curious to see what could possibly be underneath the skin that covered its rounded head. In her toying, she sought to draw the skin back over the head, but a slight cry of pain from him caused her to stop. Yet when, be she young or be she old, is a woman's curiosity to be baulked? She had managed to draw it back a short way, and now it suddenly occurred to her that by the help of a little moisture her object might be accomplished without hurting the dear fellow. By an impulse of passion she stooped and took the rosy head into her delicious little mouth, closing her coral lips around it, and lubricating it with her tongue, to the intense gratification of the youth, who involuntarily wriggled his body about voluptuously, and could not help raising it up to her mouth This movement, combined with the pressure of the lips, perfectly succeeded, without further pain, in completely unhooding the charming little cock she was so deliciously embracing in the soft folds of her lips. She lifted up her head to see the result. The tight foreskin had closed below the nut, and left the now fiery red head bursting with excitement, and visibly throbbing with intensity of passion. Her joy and delight at this full revelation of the 'funny thing', as she continued to call it, now knew no bounds. She drove him nearly frantic with her ardent caresses – she again drew the covering over the vermilion head, and still finding that it did not easily return again, she thrust her head down upon it, and with lips, mouth and tongue began again her attempt to unhood it. Poor Dale was brought up to the wildest state of excitement, his hands involuntarily pressed down her head, his body rose to meet it, and at that ravishing instant the grand crisis seized him, and, with a cry of delight, he shot forth his first tribute to Venus within the delicious mouth in which he was enclosed. The ecstatic gush poured down the throat of the dear girl, and she gulped it all down by the mere effort to avoid choking. Poor Dale's hands fell down insensibly from her head, which she instantly withdrew to gaze on the youth. To her great surprise she beheld the so lately rampant weapon drooping its head and withdrawing within its shell, while some few drops of a milky-white creamy-like liquid were slowly oozing from the small orifice of its head. While she gazed it reduced itself to a mere shadow of its former state, and the foreskin slowly covered again the so lately fiery and bursting head. She was lost in wonder, and was about to express her surprise at the strangeness of the whole affair, but they now became aware that footsteps were approaching. Fortunately for them, as they thought, the noise of the gravel underfoot was distinguishable at such a distance that they had time to arrange their clothes, and when Dale's mother appeared at the arbour, she found them, on entering, quietly seated and talking together; and, thanks to the youth's discharge in his cousin's sweet mouth, without any tell-tale flushings of his face. Little did they suspect she had already seen all.

This then was Master Dale's misconduct, and this it was that had been fully and minutely detailed in the note sent by this mother to the doctor, with a request that he should punish him well in whatever way he should think proper. The note further begged to know the terms for his becoming a boarder with the doctor, as she could no longer have him residing in her house with her orphan niece, whose guardian she was. You may easily imagine the double delight of the doctor. Another boarder, a point of some consequence to him after a previous scandal which, although hushed up, had deprived him of house pupils; and now with two, he foresaw a quick return to his full number; and then his delight at having to flog young Dale, and the erotic pleasure of drawing from him the exciting description of their young love and voluptuous actions.

'Now Master Dale,' said the doctor, 'you and I have an account to settle, follow me.'

And without a word further he led him into his private room, where, as was generally understood in the school, he birched the worst offenders. Arrived in the room alone with the young culprit, he locked the door, and taking a large cutting birch rod from a closet, sat down on a sofa. He called the youth to him and told him to unbutton and let down his trousers, and tuck up his shirt well under his waistcoat. This being done, the doctor said: 'Now, Master Dale, we shall see if this birch will cool your itching for feeling your pretty cousin's private parts.'

Poor Dale had never yet been punished more severely than by the hand of his mamma, and certainly trembled at the sight of the formidable birch rod threatening his now bare bottom; yet, notwithstanding his fears, the allusion to the pretty private parts of his cousin so fired his imagination that his cock instantly stiffened and stood out, to the infinite delight of the doctor, who augured therefrom a future further felicity. Keeping him standing close beside him and enjoying the sight of his youthful charms so deliciously exposed immediately before his eyes, he proceeded: 'So, Master Dale, you have, it seems, been gratifying yourself with looking and feeling between the legs and thighs of a pretty young girl of fifteen, your cousin, is she not?'

'Yes, sir,' sobbed out the youth.

The doctors gaze was fixed upon the stiff and rampant member of the youth, watching the throbbings produced by every allusion to the luscious scene of the day before.

'Now, come, tell me all about it,' said he, putting his arm round the sobbing boy's waist, and making him stand still closer beside him. 'Was she such a very pretty girl?'

Another throb of the rampant member.

'Yes, sir.'

'And you saw all her legs, thighs, plump little bottom, rosy pouting little slit' – (*throb – throb – throb*) – 'moist with the dew of excitement and amorous play eh?'

The little machine seemed ready to burst at the thought of it.

'And did it have the same effect as I see it now has on *this*? Dear me, how naughty it is.'

And here the lecherous doctor took the rampant little cock in his hand and pressed it.

'And what did she do to this; did she touch it so?' squeezing it gently.

'Yes, sir,' stammered out the youth, who was getting greatly excited.

'And so?' said the doctor, passing his hand gently and caressingly up and down the stiffened and throbbing little cock.

'Yes, sir.'

'And so, too, I'll be bound,' pushing back the foreskin off the head, and as quickly replacing it, several times.

'Ye–es. Oh! sir; oh! oh!'

The boy's feelings, as the doctor swiftly frigged his cock, began to be exquisite. The doctor could not resist the temptation of bringing things to a crisis. Clasping the youth tightly with one arm, he continued his toying with the plaything in a quick exciting manner, apparently without reflecting upon what he was about, uttering at intervals: 'Dear me,' and, 'How naughty it was of you; but how pretty she must have been to tempt you to do so, was she not?'

The lovely youth was now in paradise. In the exquisite sensations of pleasure he felt he was losing all consciousness, when the doctor suddenly stopped short and said: 'This is indeed a pretty piece of business, seducing your young cousin; you must be cured of such doings in future by means of a good flogging with an excellent birch rod, and on this your saucy bottom.'

Here he let fall the arm that had clasped the boy's waist, and let his hand wander over the plump, hard and lovely orbs. The doctor now took up the rod which he had previously dropped to occupy his hand with the charming young prick he had just been so deliciously frigging. Shaking the rod angrily at the now trembling youth, he exclaimed, in a fierce voice: 'Now, you young rascal, down, down on your knees, and beg to be flogged.'

The poor boy was forced, trembling, to obey. This over, the doctor commanded the delinquent to lie down across the sofa. Reluctantly he complied and straddled across it with his snow-white plump backside fully bared to view, and a fair mark to the threatening rod. He looked like a young Adonis displaying his beauties to a satyr. The doctor was greatly excited at the lovely prospect, and gloated his eyes on the beautiful display, and, then and there, there sprang up a determination fully to enjoy the ravishing of these virgin charms before many weeks were over. Lifting the rod on high, he cried out: 'Now, you young villain, I'll teach you to look up young ladies petticoats again, I warrant.'

Clasping him tight round the waist, the doctor caused the rod to descend smartly on the lovely hillocks of the boy's charming backside.

'There! there!' cried the doctor at each blow.

'Oh! sir, oh! Do pray forgive me!' screamed the beautiful youth, as he felt the stinging strokes descend on his hitherto virgin posteriors.

'Oh sir. Oh! sir. I'll never do so any more. Oh! sir. I won't indeed. Oh! pray, sir, have mercy.'

The doctor, whose erotic passions were fully aroused, was deaf to all his entreaties, and kept on flogging harder and harder, and faster and faster while the poor boy's bottom bounded and tossed upon the sofa; but he was kept in a firm position by the strong arm of the doctor, who, to hold him the faster, had laid hold of the stiff cock still at full stand.

'No, no,' said he, 'you shall not escape my cuts, I assure you,' cutting at the lovely delicate buttocks with all his might.

'Oh! oh! sir; mercy, mercy; I can't bear it.'

'You must bear it, you young rascal, you shall have no mercy until I have made your bottom bleed for your crime.'

The poor youth, from the pain he was suffering, bounded up and down on the sofa as he felt the stinging blows descend upon his bottom. This action caused his standing cock to rub up and down in the warm hand of the doctor, who seemed to have accidentally laid hold of it. The effect was such that the poor youth hardly knew whether he felt most pleasure or pain, for while his posteriors were of a burning heat, the warmth flew to the opposite part, which was so deliciously clasped in the doctor's caressing hand. He ground his teeth with pleasure and pain, he ceased to cry out, but sobbed and moaned with the excess of indefinable feelings. The doctor never ceased lecturing him, dwelling continually on the beauties of his lovely young cousin and the scene in the arbour. He thought but of her, of her lovely pink little slit so sweetly shaded with soft downy short curls; how she had so charmingly caressed his cock, until he felt a heave and a shudder, another, a sensation as if he was going to expire, a short cry, a catching of his breath. Wildly and vigorously he thrust his member down on the doctor's warm hand, he shut his eyes, he felt not the rod, although the doctor redoubled the strokes with all the force of his arm, and drew blood at every cut. A bound, a convulsive start, and he felt as if his lifeblood were coming from him – out it spurted in large drops on the sofa and on the doctor's hand. The youth had with difficulty shed another tribute to Venus. For a moment or two he felt as if in paradise, but a sharp cut from the rod quickly aroused him. He was soon fully alive again to its tortures.

'Why, you young rascal, what is this you have been doing on my best sofa, eh, sir?' said the doctor.

Another sharp stroke demanded a reply.

'I, sir. Oh! sir; indeed I – that is – indeed, I don't know.'

'No lies or evasions here, sir, for they will not avail you. Your bottom shall pay for this nastiness. Why, what is it? What can it be? I never saw the like of this in my life, I declare,' and he examined it with his eyeglass, saying more to the same effect.

Poor Master Dale was, we know, quite in the dark as to what it could be, or how it came there.

'Has this ever occurred to you before,' asked the doctor.

'Yes, sir, yesterday, when my cousin was caressing it in her mouth,' replied the frightened youth, 'but I really don't know how it happened, and did not mean any harm.'

'Oh, indeed! said the doctor, 'your mother did not mention that. Did she see you?'

'No, sir, it happened just as she was coming through the shrubbery, and was all over before she reached the arbour.'

'And so your cousin took it into her mouth; why did she do that?'

'She was curious to see what was under the skin of its head, and finding it would not go back without hurting me, she put it into her mouth to wet it and make it go back easier, which it did for the first time; she pulled it forward again, and again put it into her mouth to push the skin back with her lips, when I felt funny all over, and something came out of me into her mouth.'

'Indeed! Well, you must tell me all about that another time. This flogging will be enough for the present, but I shall punish you for your nastiness some other time. Put up your trousers; in a day or two I shall want you in this room to pay for your dirty conduct.'

The poor boy retired, sobbing hysterically.

The second day after this the doctor sent for Master Dale, who, in the meantime, had occupied the bedroom next to mine. The doctor was in his private room in his dressing-gown, long and flowing, so that for the moment it concealed the fact that he had nothing but his shirt on below it. He received Master Dale somewhat sternly, saying: 'Now, sir, for your punishment for your last nasty misconduct.'

'Oh, sir,' said the frightened and trembling youth, 'I really could not help it,' and he began to cry. 'Oh! pray, sir, don't flog me so hard again.'

'The more trouble that you give me, the harder will be the flogging. Now take off your jacket and waistcoat.'

The youth did so.

'Now come close to me.'

The doctor then lowered down Dale's trousers, and raising his shirt, contemplated with great pleasure the pretty belly of the lovely boy, and then turning him round, under pretence of seeing if the weals of the last flogging were still visible, he gazed on his white firm backside and swelling thighs, examining the marks still left from the previous punishment. He then turned him round, and inspected the pretty little cock, which, under the mortal fear he was in, hung down its head in a limp and pitiable state.

'And so this is the little offender,' said he, applying his hand to it, and squeezing and pressing it gently. 'What a naughty little thing it is!'

The youth could not avoid showing the pleasure these lascivious caresses gave him, and smiled.

'Oh, don't smile, sir, this is no laughing matter. Look at the marks of the mess you made on my sofa,' pointing to it. 'I can't have my furniture spoiled in this manner, so if your little cock is to be naughty again, I must flog you upon my knees, but first come here; take off these trousers, which hanging about the legs are only in the way there. Now sit down on my knee, and tell me all about this naughty little thing.'

He drew aside his robe, so that the boy's bare bottom came in naked contact with his brawny naked thighs, and the youth could feel the doctor's prick swelling up, although that part was still covered by his shirt. The doctor, taking hold of the youth's now standing prick, asked if it had ever behaved so badly before the scene with his pretty young cousin.

'No sir, never. I never thought of it until I got sight of her bare bottom and other parts by accident.'

The doctor continued his toyings, caressing the young balls, and feeling all over the plump and firm backside.

'Why, he is going to be naughty again!' said the doctor, as the youth's prick throbbed under his exciting touches. 'I must flog your bottom for all this, for it is very naughty and improper. Why, you seem to take a pleasure in it.'

'Oh, sir, I never felt anything so delightful,' said Master Dale.

'The more reason I should punish you; but remember, you bad boy, if you are to do that dirty thing again, you must do it on my knee, and not on the sofa.'

The doctor then took the birch in hand, and with his arm round the boy's waist, drew him to him, but before laying him across his knee, he slipped the boy's shirt over his head, leaving him stark naked in all the glorious fairness of skin and beauty of form. The doctor's eyes gloated over the charming sight, and becoming too excited to pause longer, he drew up his own shirt, displaying his fine pego at full stretch. He bent the boy's warm body over his brawny thighs, and with his arm pressed his glowing form against his own rampant pego – Dale's young stiffened cock rubbing against the naked thigh he lay on. The doctor now raised the rod, and said: 'Now, sir, for your punishment. I must flog this round, hard, little bottom, till it reddens again.'

Whack, whack, went the birch rod, but with much less force than on the previous occasion, but still sufficiently stinging to cause the youth to move up and down, rubbing his cock against the doctor's thighs, and causing him such ecstasies as hardly to allow him to feel the blows. His warm soft flesh, too, rubbing against the doctor's large, stiff tool, soon put them both in a delirium of delight. The doctor then changed his position, and drew the boy more over his belly, so that his great prick could get between the boy's thighs, rubbing under his balls in the trough between the buttocks, while the boy's cock rubbed against the doctor's belly.

'Now,' said the doctor, 'I have got you fast, and must teach you not to play such naughty tricks in future.'

Whack, whack, again went the rod, causing the most delicious movements of the boy's backside upon the doctor's excited prick, and not less upon his own, which was rubbing against the doctor's belly, giving fresh pleasure at each repetition of the blow. But neither of them had spent yet. The boy's bottom was now red with a glowing heat, and his cock was in a state of intense excitement, and the doctor's tool was as stiff and randy as possible. The doctor now ceased his flogging, and squeezing the boy tight against his person, said: 'Well, you have not done that naughty thing today – the flogging has done you good.'

The lovely boy looked up and smiled. He had felt the doctor's large prick working away between his thighs, and pressing against the cleft of his buttocks. As the doctor relaxed his hold, the boy turned half round, thus releasing it from its confinement. Looking down, he beheld the large stiff monster embedded in a forest of dark curly hair, presenting a startling contrast to his own small member, which was as yet hardly fledged with a silky down around it.

'Ah!' said the doctor, who observed the flush of excitement the sight of his superior prick gave the boy, 'what a shame it is of you to compel me to flog you in this manner, without my trousers. I must give you a lecture – so sit on my knee, thus,' placing him so that his lovely bottom should press against the huge prick. Taking the boy's cock in his hand, he said: 'How stiff it is.'

'Yes, sir, I can't help it.'

'Well, you must not play such naughty tricks. I can't allow it. You are too young yet.'

The doctor worked the skin of the sweet boy's cock up and down.

'Was that the way your pretty cousin played with it?'

'Yes, sir, and then she took it in her mouth.'

'And did you like to have it done to you, you bad boy?'

'Oh! yes, sir, it is such pleasure.'

'Does it really give you so much pleasure?'

'Yes indeed, it was most delicious.'

'Dear me, I must try if it would do so to me, take hold of my cock and rub it up and down, as she did, that I may know how it feels.'

The dear boy had already longed to do so, but had been afraid to say so. He now seized with avidity the noble prick, so stiffly standing beside him. He could hardly grasp it in his hand, and worked the skin up and down in the most delicious manner. The doctor was in ecstasies.

'Oh, you naughty boy, to teach your master such bad things.'

'Is it not very nice, sir?' said the charming youth, as the doctor's buttocks responded to every stroke of his hand.

'Well, it is, indeed, very nice, I could not have believed it; but if ever I catch you at it again, you may be sure I shall flog you.'

And the doctor responded to every rub upon his prick with another rub upon the boy's cock, until almost at the same moment a most delicious mutual spend was the result of their lascivious toyings.

'Now,' said the doctor, 'put on your clothes, and remember you must avoid such naughty tricks in future, or your bottom will pay for it.'

The doctor made me aware of this, and arranged for a meeting of us three, under the pretence of inattention which I was to simulate and draw young Dale into some fault that would require punishment. It was also arranged that I was to initiate him still more into the secret pleasures of mutual satisfaction, so as to prepare him for still greater gratification to the lecherous doctor, who liked nothing better than teaching the young idea how to shoot.'

Accordingly, after passing a delicious night with my lovely and glorious aunt and the doctor, in which we practised every delightful method of enjoyment, and in which the doctor stimulated himself by recalling and describing the exciting interview with the innocent youth, I left them, and entered young Dale's room. He had insensibly kicked off all the clothes, and lay on his back exposed, with his promising young cock at full stand, throbbing from time to time; and by the involuntary movements of his body, and the smile on his face, he was evidently realising, in his sleep, the scene he had enacted with his pretty young cousin. He was quite charming to look at; his young and throbbing prick was deliciously fair, and you could see the blue veins coursing through it; the top was only partially uncovered, the point of the head showing its vermilion tip in fine contrast to the creamy white and crossed blue veins of the stiffened shaft. His balls were as yet not fully developed, but such as they were, they formed a closely drawn up little bag crimped and wrinkled, and felt as hard as stones. I gently handled them, which made him heave his bottom in evident ecstasy. It was all so beautiful and enticing, and I could not resist stooping down, and taking the delicious morsel in my mouth. Pressing the glorious head with my lips, I thrust, to his infinite delight, the foreskin back; his buttocks instinctively rose to meet my voluptuous and lascivious proceeding. He awoke on the instant, but in that dreamy state that made him think he was only realising the previous dream. His hands embraced my head, and pressed it down closer on the delicious prick which already touched the back of my mouth. He cried out in an ecstasy of delight.

'Oh, my darling Ellen, what a joy you are giving me. Oh! oh! it is greater than I can bear.'

I felt by the electric stiffening of his young cock that the crisis was close at hand. I tickled his tightened balls with my hand, and pressed a finger hard against his bottom-hole, but without entering more than the depth of the nail, at the very instant that he poured his young tribute into my longing mouth. I immediately swallowed the greater portion, lubricating the still throbbing shaft with a part. For some minutes he lay on his back, with closed eyes, in all the after-enjoyment, heightened by the continued suction of his still throbbing prick, which I kept up for a short time. At last he opened his eyes. It was broad daylight, and when I lifted my head, his eyes seemed almost to start out of their sockets in a sort of incredulous surprise, at finding it was not his dear young Ellen, but me, his school companion. For a minute or two he was speechless with consternation, until taking hold of his fast receding little cock, I asked if I had not given him quite as much pleasure as his darling Ellen had previously done.

'Is it you? and Ellen! how do you know anything about my cousin?'

'Your cousin, is she? I did not know that, but when I came in, you were dreaming of her, and muttering in your sleep of the delight she gave you by sucking your prick; so I thought I would give you the true pleasure of the thing, and thus realise your dream; besides, I myself not only love to suck a prick, but also to have my own sucked, and I could neither resist the opportunity, nor fail to be delighted that you should already have practical knowledge of its enjoyment – did I not give you the greatest pleasure?'

'Oh, yes; it was most delicious, and then I thought it was my pretty cousin, even after I awoke, which made it doubly delightful, for I had no idea it would be so nice with another boy.'

'Why not? see this charming little fellow is already raising itself up again at the mere thought; look how its head is showing its ruby face, and how it throbs. Ah! I must suck it again – it is so delicious.'

I threw myself upon it, and devoured it at once, rapidly moving my head up and down, and titillating the orifice of the urethra with my tongue. I quickly drove him half mad with excitement. My mouth was full of saliva. I slobbered some out on my fingers, and lubricated all about the aperture of his charming backside, and then, as he became still more furious in the upward lunges of his bottom, and downward pressures of his hands on my head, I thrust my middle finger up his fundament, and worked away, frigging it in unison with the movements of my mouth. I drove him half frantic with pleasure, the ecstasy again seized him, and with a cry of agonised delight, and a convulsive shudder, he poured a still more copious draught of love's essence into my mouth, which, as before, I greedily swallowed. He lay panting in ecstatic joy for a much longer period than before, with convulsive upward thrusts of his still half-stiffened prick within my mouth, which still continued its pressures and suctions to his infinite delight. At last I rose. He held out his arms. I precipitated myself into them; our lips met in sweet embrace. I thrust my tongue into his mouth, and solicited him to do the same, and we had some delicious tongueing, nature having at once achieved his love education. We were closely entwined in a loving embrace. I had become terribly excited notwithstanding the hard work I had undergone during the night, and my prick stood stiff as iron pressing against his belly. Suddenly the thought occurred to him that he ought to gratify me in like manner as I had done him. He proposed it, and begged me to turn from off him, and lie on my back. I immediately complied, and pulling up my shirt, displayed my immense splitter in all its glory.

'Good heavens!' he cried, 'what an enormous cock! Why, it is bigger than the doctor's.'

'Oh! you have seen the doctor's, have you?'

He blushed, and acknowledged it. I drew from him an account of their proceedings, which I already knew, but I was at the same time delighted to have surprised the acknowledgement from him, in his wonder at seeing my large proportions. I made him show me all he had done to the doctor, and the doctor to him, as all this was paving the way for future proceedings with the doctor – in fact, the innocent youth was already playing into our hands. His admiration and handling of my prick was meanwhile exciting me up to

the greatest pitch. As I had continued questioning him regarding his proceedings with the doctor, he could only play with my prick in his hands.
Now that matters were getting too warm for further discussion, he stooped
down, but could only get the head and a small portion of the upper part of
the shaft into his mouth. His lips closed beneath the gland in the most
exquisite manner. I begged him to grasp the lower part of the shaft with one
hand, and to thrust a finger of the other up my bottom-hole, which I had
already lubricated by spitting on my fingers and conveying the saliva in the
desired direction. He obeyed with the docility of an apt apprentice – and
thus working in unison, quickly brought on the ecstatic crisis. I seized his
head in my hands, and, at the final discharge, thrust it down on my delighted
prick, as I poured out a perfect torrent of sperm, nearly choking the poor
youth with the length of prick I thrust into his mouth. He was obliged to
withdraw for an instant to take breath, but I was pleased to see that he
instantly resumed his delicious sucking of my prick, which he continued to
do until it gradually shrank up to very diminished proportions. I then drew
him upon me, and we had another sweet embrace of lips and tongues, and
then, side by side, we held a long converse on erotic matters. He told me
all the tale of his affair with his cousin, and although I was already well
acquainted with it, I was glad to draw all the particulars from his own mouth.
I had seen the note his mother wrote to the doctor. The minuteness and
undisguised description she had therein given struck me as very strange, and
I suspected that she herself must be a lewd and lecherous person to have
done more than merely hint at the affair, indeed actually to have dwelt,
doubtless in erotic delight, on such details. So I pumped him as to what sort
of woman his mamma was. His description showed that she was a fine, full-
grown woman, old, in his opinion, but in reality in the prime of life, between
thirty-five and forty. He had not scanned her proportions with any erotic
thought and did not seem to attach the idea of the woman to her – only that
of the mother. But I drew out of him that she was broad in the shoulders, full
in the bosom, with a small waist, small feet and small hands, a very fine head
of hair and fine eyes – evidently a desirable woman. Already I had set my
imagination in play, and began to hope I might someday work my way into
her favour. It will be found how well I succeeded, as these true memories will
describe when I arrive at the period of my success with her. For the present,
I had advanced the erotic education of the dear youth considerably, and thus
prepared him for further initiation at the hands of the doctor and his
glorious and magnificent *cara sposa*, who had already determined to enjoy his
first fruits in cunny land. We had a similar enjoyment, carried somewhat
further the next morning, in which we practised more fully the frigging of
the bottom, and discussed the pleasure it produced. I was gradually leading
him on. That morning I purposely arranged that we should be late in
entering the schoolroom. The doctor sternly reprimanded us, and told us
we must attend him in his private room after twelve o'clock. Poor Dale

turned pale as he heard this, dreading the punishment to come of which his experience was so recent and so severe.

At twelve we, apparently ruefully, entered the doctor's *sanctum sanctorum*. He had preceded us by some few minutes, and had already donned his long dressing-gown, by which I was certain that he had at the same time doffed his pantaloons.

'Now then, boys, you must prepare for your punishment, I cannot allow this evidently wilful inattention. Off with your clothes except your shirts and stockings.'

We hesitatingly stripped; poor Harry Dale weeping at the thought of the dreaded punishment. I deemed it prudest also to draw a long face. The doctor spread a towel over his sofa, saying we had such naughty cocks that we were constantly dirtying his sofa. He then desired us to kneel on it with our heads down, and our tails well up. He then rolled up our shirts, and tucked them in above the small of our backs, in doing which he indulged in various lascivious touchings, which excited us as well as himself, and all our three cocks were at full stand. Harry Dale turned his head to gaze at mine, and could not resist putting his hand upon it, and gently pressing its large stiff shaft. Young Dale's smaller, but very beautiful member, which was daily developing itself in a striking manner, also excited me, and I reciprocated his caresses.

'This will never do,' said the doctor, 'I must flog this evil spirit out of you.'

He threw off his dressing-gown – to be more at his ease he said – and taking rod in hand, applied it gently in turns to each of our projecting bottoms. It was not for punishment but for excitement that he operated upon us. He quickly threw our bottoms all in a glow, and our ex–citement became intense, and we wriggled our bums in evident delight. This was the point the doctor wished to attain, that he might arrive at his desired object, which was the possession of young Dale's bottom-hole.

'Stop, stop, my dear boys, I see you are at your naughty tricks again, but there must be no spending yet; get up. We must all strip to the buff, and I shall show you how they used to flog me when I was at school. Stand up, Charles.'

I did so, and the doctor for an instant handled, in evident delight, my huge stiff-standing pego, drawing young Dale's attention to its much larger dimensions than his own.

'Now, lean half forward on the sofa Dale, put your arms round his waist, and stow away this charming rampant little fellow between the cheeks of Charles's buttocks. Charles, do you spit on your hand, and moisten between the cheeks, and then press with your hand his throbbing young prick against the cleft.'

I did as directed. Young Dale felt so deliciously sheathed that he thrust his cock well forward.

'Now,' said the doctor, 'you are properly horsed, as we used to say, and now for a little more flogging of these fine hard, rosy mounts,' and he lasciviously caressed them before applying the rod.

Whack – whack – whack – fell the strokes, sufficiently sharply to make Master Dale wince and wriggle his bottom to and fro. Quickly the exciting pleasure overcame all pain, and his lust rising, he thrust furiously in the artificial channel he was operating in. I now shortened the grasp of my hand on his shaft, and pressing it somewhat upwards, raising my buttocks at the same time, I directed it so fairly upon the aperture that at the next push it entered fully two inches within; then again favouring his return stroke, he completely sheathed himself up to the meeting of his belly against my buttocks. I gave him a pressure which had an instant effect, and he began to thrust fast and furiously, evidently enjoying it to the utmost. I let him feel the full enjoyment of his new quarters, only telling him to lay hold of my cock and frig me; and then I cried out to the doctor: 'Flog him well, sir, he has thrust his cock into my bottom-hole.'

This was the very thing the doctor most wished for. So he continued his flogging only to such an extent as to still more inflame the lust of the now lecherously excited boy, who shortly brought on the final crisis and died away in delight as he shot his first tribute within the divine temple of Priapus. At the moment of the crisis coming on, the doctor had ceased his flogging and wetting two fingers gradually introduced them into the bottom-hole of young Dale, and frigged him in unison with his movements into me, so that the ecstasy was almost more than the poor boy could bear. He lay almost inanimate on my back, but his still throbbing half-standing cock responded to the inward pressures I was exercising upon it. The doctor had ceased his flogging to admit and caress the well-formed posterior of the charming boy. Becoming greatly excited, he drew him off me, and closely embraced him, but professing at the same time to be greatly shocked; his prick, meanwhile, gloriously stiff, pressed hard against young Dale's belly. The doctor then relaxing his hold, young Dale gazed, with pleased enjoyment, at the size and stiffness of the doctor's cock, and, by an impulse of passion, took it in hand, knelt before him, put it into his mouth and sucked it lasciviously. The doctor placed his hands on Dale's head, and pressed it down for a minute or two, and then begged the dear youth to rise, as he did not yet wish to spend – thanking him for the exquisite pleasure he had given him.

'Now,' said he, 'it is your turn to flog, so Charlie, you must be horsed upon me, and Harry Dale shall take a first lesson in the art of flogging upon your posteriors.'

The pose was arranged as before. My formidable weapon was placed between the cheeks of the doctor's fine fat backside. His hand pressed my cock as I had done to Dale's. Dale took the rod in hand, and at the very first cut made me wince, for the young rogue laid on with a will. The doctor had applied a good quantity of saliva to the end of my prick, and thrusting out his buttocks, he quickly guided it into the longing orifice, in which I vigorously sheathed myself to the utmost extent. I seized his cock and squeezed it gently, but he begged me not to make him spend but to enjoy myself to the utmost, crying out at the same time to young Dale: 'Flog him well, Harry, for he has thrust his great tool up my bottom-hole; it is wonderful how it ever could get in.'

Indeed so little could young Dale believe in the possibility of such a thing that he stopped flogging to assure himself of the fact, by both touch and sight. I drew my prick out and in, that he might be perfectly satisfied of the truth, and the doctor wriggled his backside to and fro to show what pleasure it gave him. Of course, all this was preliminary to the grand attack he meant afterwards to make on the virgin aperture in young Dale's bottom. After Harry had assured himself of the fact, he pitched into my poor bottom with redoubled vigour, which, though it greatly excited me at the moment, made my poor bum smart for days afterwards. I quickly sent a torrent of sperm far into the entrails of the doctor to his great delight, but he tenaciously avoided spending lest his powers should fail to overcome the natural obstacle of a virgin bottom-hole, especially in one so young as Dale. Consequently, after retaining me for some few moments in the delightful pressures of the internal folds, he allowed me to withdraw, all reeking with my own sperm. It was now the doctor's turn to be flogged by me, while he was horsed on Harry's loins. As Harry had already found out what pleasure a bottom-hole gave to the plugger of it, and had also seen how the doctor seemed to enjoy, and so easily engulfed, the much larger weapon I possessed, be had no idea there could be any pain accompanying it, and consequently he lent himself entirely to every direction that was given him. He placed himself in the easiest position, stuck his bottom well out, stretching wide the channel between the orbs, and exposing a charming little rosy aperture most tempting to the sight; indeed, the doctor instantly knelt to pay his devotions to it, devouring it with kisses, and thrusting his lecherous tongue within its tight little folds, taking the opportunity thoroughly to lubricate it with his spittle. This preliminary, followed by a little frigging with his middle finger, which produced nothing but pleasurable sensations in the dear youth, completely captivated him. The doctor wisely informed him that the first attack was sure to be somewhat painful, but that if he felt it so, he was not to draw away his body, but simply to complain, and the doctor would instantly remain quiet without withdrawing, and he would then find that the strange sensation would rapidly pass off, and allow a further progress, which would be again arrested if the pain was renewed. In this way he would eventually find that the pleasure would become indescribably delicious, as he had seen how both Charlie and himself had enjoyed it. Poor Dale assured the doctor he might proceed at once, and he would be perfectly docile. So the doctor first asking me to suck his cock a little to moisten it well, put the charming youth in the best position, telling him to strain as if he wished to void himself, then applying his well-lubricated pego to the rosy orifice, by gentle pressure, he succeeded,

with hardly a twinge of pain to the dear boy, in housing the head and about
two inches of the shaft within the delicious receptacle. Here the pain became
so great that young Dale would have withdrawn himself away from the
doctor had the latter not taken the precaution to seize him by the two hips,
and hold him as if in a vice, but without attempting a further insertion then.

'Keep still, my dear boy, and I will not move, and you will find in a minute
or two that the strange sensation will pass away.'

Turning his head to me, he said: 'Charlie, gently frig the dear boy.'

I immediately did so, which rapidly had the effect of exciting him up to a
pitch that made him forget all pain, and he even thrust his bottom further
back, and as I had taken the opportunity of the pause to drop some more
spittle on the lower shaft, a further gentle pressure forced it in almost up to
the hilt. Here, again, young Dale cried out to stop, it was so painful.

The doctor paused again. I continued caressing his now inflamed and
stiffened prick. His convulsive twitches, caused by my lascivious caresses,
were followed by involuntary wrigglings, which of themselves completed
the entire insertion of the doctor's excited prick. He still continued quiet,
allowing the passions of the youth to become still more excited. Then
gradually and gently withdrawing, and as gently again thrusting within, he
went on until the youth's movements betrayed the raging lust that possessed
him – then the doctor increased his pace. I frigged on fast and furious, and in
a few minutes they both died away in wild excess of the most ecstatic joy. As
to Dale, his gaspings and wild cries of delight proved that the final joys were
almost too great for him to bear. The doctor had drooped his head upon his
chest, and closed his eyes, in all the gratification of having ravished the first
fruits of this charming youth's beauteous bottom, and I could see by his
momentary convulsive thrusts, and the pressures of his hands on Dale's hips
to draw the bottom more completely against his belly, as well as by the
broken sighs that heaved his bosom, how exquisitely he was enjoying his
triumph. Gradually his cock reduced its dimensions, but even when quite
down and soft, it left the tight sheath it was in with a 'plop' showing how well
and close those delicious folds had embraced it. The doctor would not allow
young Dale to rise until he had embraced and kissed the lovely bottom that
had just yielded him such intense satisfaction. Then, drawing the youth to
his bosom, he embraced him most tenderly, and thanked him for the heroic
manner in which he had borne the attack, and told him he would never
suffer so much in after-attacks as he had done in this first taking of the
virginity of his bottom-hole.

It was thus this dear youth was initiated into our mysteries, and hence-
forward he became an apt disciple, and by being introduced into our interior
circle, added much to the variety and enjoyment of our orgies. For, as may
well be supposed, my glorious and most lecherous aunt thoroughly enjoyed
the taking of his first tribute in the legitimate temple of holy Mother Venus.
I was present on the occasion, which was supposed to be unknown to the

doctor. The first *coup* was on her belly, the sight of which and her truly magnificent cunt wildly excited Dale, and his cock stood stiffer and really bigger than ever. It was quite surprising how rapidly it developed when once he got thoroughly into hardness. He fucked aunt twice, spending as rapidly as she herself, lecherous as she was at all times. I acted postilion to them both. I stopped further combats until I too could enter the field. So aunt mounted upon him, and falling forward lent her divine backside to all my fantasies. Twice we ran a course without changing. Then aunt herself claimed my big prick for the contentment of her randy cunt. We quickly changed positions. I, on my back, received dear aunt's delicious cunt on my stiff-and-hard-as-wood standing pego. She straddled over me, and sank her luscious orbit down upon me until our two hairs were crushed between us. Here, by rising and falling, she had another delicious discharge before bending down to be embraced by my loving arms. She then presented her most glorious bottom to the wonder and admiration of dear Harry, who had been caressing and kissing it, and at the critical moment had thrust a frigging finger in, and turning his head in front had greatly increased the pleasure of my loved and lecherous aunt by sucking the large nipple of her wondrously fine bubby. When once she was fairly down on my belly, Harry scrambled up behind, and quickly inserted his already fine but still comparatively small prick, which, of course, found ready entrance where my splitter had previously opened and greased the way; but he gave a cry, almost of pain, or at least of surprise, an finding the sudden grip which my aunt, with her wonderful power of pressure, instantly gave him. At it we went, fast and furious, until again the grand crisis overtook my lascivious aunt, who spent deliciously. We boys both paused a second or two to allow her to enjoy her discharge to the utmost; then recommencing with increased vigour and speed, we soon both discharged at one and the same time our freights into the delighted vessels that were conferring such exquisite enjoyment upon us. Aunt, too, did not fail to join us at the ecstatic moment. We lay for many minutes panting in all the after-sensations of the most exquisite joys humanity can revel in. We kept it up for several hours, aunt sucking young Dale's toothsome prick while I gamahuched and postilioned her to her infinite satisfaction. In this way, and with repeated changes from one receptacle to the other, but always both occupied at once, we at last gained a reprieve, and retired to well deserved repose. The doctor, who had kept out of the way on this our first bout with my glorious aunt, afterwards apparently surprised us together, and, after giving us and receiving a pretty sharp flogging, he joined in all the ecstasies of our orgies. He especially delighted in being into my bottom while I fucked his wife, and he himself had the double pleasure of having young Dale's fast growing pego into his bottom at the same time. It was some time longer before I succeeded in completely sheathing my huge prick in the delicious bottom-hole of the dear youth, but at last I succeeded to the utmost extent of my wishes, and although I continued to hurt him for some weeks after the first attack, he could at last entertain me with perfect ease, and we were thus enabled to play successively into each other's bottoms, and every one of us enjoyed the exquisite delight of fucking and being fucked at the same time.

As we grew more lasciviously intimate, I often turned the conversation on his mother and cousin. At last I told him, I thought from his description that his mother would be a good fuck, and that if ever I had the opportunity, I might cover his attack on his cousin by fucking his mother; only we must lead her to believe that she took my virginity. The idea pleased him. He began to think his mother must be a desirable woman for me, as I was so largely hung; and then the opportunity that I would give him to enjoy his longing for his cousin was an inducement to second my views to the utmost. Towards the close of the half-year his birthday occurred, and his mother could not do less than have him home for the day. She felt that her niece would be in greater security when Harry begged she would allow him to bring with him the doctor's nephew – myself, to wit – telling her that we had become very close friends as well as schoolfellows. I had previously told him I should play the complete innocent, but should take care some time or the other during the day to put myself in such a position that his mother should get a glimpse of my prick, so that if not immediately successful, I might pave the way for future success. His birthday fell on a Saturday. We were only asked to spend the day, with the intention of returning in the evening. Accordingly, on the happy day we made our appearance after breakfast. I have before said that his mother lived in a very pretty *cottage orné*, about a mile and a half from the parsonage. We were most kindly received by her. She first lovingly embraced her son, wishing him many happy returns of the day, declaring that he was much improved, etc. She then turned to me, and gracefully and kindly bade me welcome. The niece was a charming girl, just budding into womanhood. She blushed greatly in welcoming her cousin, and bashfully did the same to me. We spent the earlier hours in conversation; the mother having much to ask and to hear from her son, from whom she had never before been separated. I had thus time to scan her well. She was a fine, broad built, well-standing-up woman, with broad shoulders, and hips that gave promise of good form beneath. Without being beautiful, her face was a well-formed oval, with really fine eyes, to which her son's description had hardly done justice. It appeared to me that a good deal of suppressed passion lurked in their expression, and I already began to think she would be a real *bonne bouche* if once we could come to close quarters. After luncheon we strolled in the garden. The leaves had already fallen, but the afternoon was bright and warm for the end of November. I told young Dale to keep close to his mother, and not show any wish to stray away with his cousin – feeling certain that if she became anxious about their movements I should have no chance to play off my little game. All went as I could wish; we threw his mother off her guard, and she then began to show closer attention to me. I acted the ingenuous and innocent youth to perfection, but at the same time, in thinking of her charms, I let my prick get up to half-stand, so as to show its large proportions under my trousers. I very soon perceived that it had struck her notice, and her attention became concentrated upon me. She questioned me a good deal, and especially sought to find out if *peculiar* intimacy existed between her son and me. I played the innocent, and professed that the utmost intimacy existed; but when she tried to find out if it had gone to what she really meant, I gave such an innocent character to our intimacy that she was quite convinced of my thorough ignorance of all erotic tendencies, and she became more endearing in her manner of addressing me.

Harry and I had previously agreed that after I addressed to him some particular frivolous remark, he should seize the first occasion near a shrubbery to go on more ahead, and alarm his mamma by turning round a corner. Our stratagem succeeded. She immediately hastened to follow them. As soon as she had turned the corner I drew out my tool, now at full stand, and placed myself so that when she returned she should see it fully developed, while I would take care not apparently to see her, but be intent upon piddling. To the utmost of my wish it fell out. She had told her son to stop and returned to join me. My eyes being turned downwards did not let her become aware that I was watching for her, but I could see the bottom of her petticoats as she turned the corner, and also that she came to a sudden stop, which must have been at the moment she caught sight of the noble proportions before her. I took care to pass my hand once or twice backwards or forwards while pissing and then shook my prick deliberately, and exposed the whole length and breadth of it for a minute or two before buttoning it up, during which I could see she stood perfectly still, rooted to where she had first stopped. After I had buttoned up, I stooped down, apparently to tie my shoe, but in fact to give time for it to be supposed I had not seen her previous approach. So when I rose up she was already at my side. There was a flush on her cheek and a fire in her eye that showed the bait was swallowed. My role was to play the perfect innocent, and appear quite unconscious of her having seen me.

She took my arm, and I could feel that her hand trembled. She led me along, hastily at first, until we joined her son and niece. After that she became uncommonly endearing in her manner to me, making such remarks as she thought would show her that I was not so innocent as I looked, if my replies had jumped with her expectations. But I was in reality too experienced not to pay her off in kind, and ended in making her believe that she had a perfect virgin to deal with. We walked on; she was evidently much preoccupied, becoming at times quite silent for a minute or two, and then, gently pressing my arm, she would make some endearingly flattering remark, at which I would look lovingly but innocently up to her face to thank her for her kind opinion. On these occasions her eyes sparkled in a peculiar manner, and her colour went and came. After a while, her hand left my arm and rested on the opposite shoulder, in a half embrace, which became warmer and warmer, her conversation became more affectionate. She was profuse in her congratulations that her son had found so charming a schoolfellow; and here she halted, and turning half in front of me, said that she felt that she could love me as if I were indeed her own dear son; and, stooping slightly, she sought a kiss of maternal affection. I threw my arms round her neck, and our lips met in a long and loving kiss – very warm on her side, but a simple though affectionate kiss on mine.

'Oh!' I said, 'how happy I shall be to call you my mamma, it is so good of you to allow me to do so and I will love you as if you were she. This half-year has been the first time in my life that I ever was separated from my mother – and, although my dear aunt is as kind as possible to me, still I can't call her mamma. My guardian won't allow me to go home for the Christmas holidays, but now I shall have a dear, kind new mamma to make me happy.' Here I again raised my lips for an embrace, which was given with even more than the previous warmth. Her arm had fallen to my waist, and she pressed me with energy to her bosom, which I could feel was unexpectedly firm, and even hard. I had great difficulty in keeping my unruly member down, that she might think I took her warm embraces as nothing more than affectionate friendship. I succeeded, however, and this, of course, more than ever convinced her of my entire ignorance of carnal desires. As I closely embraced her, and glued my lips to hers, she became greatly agitated, trembled visibly, sighed convulsively, and then pushed me from her, and seemed suddenly to recover herself, seized my arm, and hurried on after her son. For, as may well be supposed she had purposely loitered behind to allow them to get out of sight, before she indulged her uncontrollable desire to embrace me. She spoke not a word until we came in sight of them, apparently sauntering along, innocently enough.

But Harry afterwards told me that having seen how his mother had halted to gaze at my prick, which he knew beforehand I meant she should see, he had watched us through the shrubbery, and afterwards had noticed her warmth of manner to me, and the loitering of her walk. He had turned a corner some distance ahead of us, and was out of sight when his mother stopped to embrace me, as described above. He guessed she would be in no hurry to follow him. So rapidly advancing with his cousin, he got some way before us, and choosing a place where he could see us through the bushes when we did follow, he sat down on a garden seat, and drew his cousin on his lap, asking her if she did not regret their hasty separation after their last delicious interview, and telling her his mother had seen them, which was the cause of his being sent as a boarder to the doctor. She was much surprised to hear this, as her aunt had never breathed a word of it to her; and she had been greatly distressed at his being sent away from home. Of course his hands were not idle; but first, unbuttoning his trousers, he put his cock, now much increased in size, into her hand. She at once observed how much larger it had become, and began to caress it. He meanwhile was busy frigging her little clitoris. He found that she was already quite moist, and he had hardly frigged her a minute, when, with a sigh and an 'Oh! how much more pleasure you give me than my aunt does,' she spent profusely, grasping his prick with painful tenacity. Her breath was taken away for some minutes. When she recovered a little, and was gazing lovingly with half-closed eyes upon him, he at once recurred to her unexpected confession.

'When does my mother do this to you?'

'Ever since you were sent away; your mother took me to sleep with her, as she said she felt so lonely after you left. For some time she used to embrace me very lovingly, and hold me close pressed to her bosom. As I always went to bed before her, I was generally sound asleep when she joined me. I used at first to wonder how when I awoke in the early morning my chemise was drawn up close to my neck, and your mother's was in the same state, and our two naked bodies closely united by the embracing arms of your mother. I even one morning found that my hand was held by hers against that part which you are now feeling so nicely. She had fallen asleep in this position, but I could feel that she was as moist there as you have just made me. I could not help feeling it was very nice and, gently removing her hand, I began to feel all over her in that part and, do you know Harry, she is all covered with such thick and curly hair there. In groping about, I felt the lips pouting and thick, and on trying I found I could get my fingers in. I pushed on and I had got up to the knuckles when I felt a convulsive pressure upon them, and her body was projected towards me with a heave of her bottom, then drawn back, and pushed forward again, while her arms pressed me closer to her, and she commenced some loving expressions in her sleep. I felt something grow hard against my thumb – it was just what you have been feeling – "Oh! go on," she cried.'

'I renewed my tickling operations again, and I made her spend,' Harry continued. 'As she came to her senses, I gamahuched her; I thrust my tongue up her sweet little cunt, and licked up all the delicious spendings. As I rose, with prick erect and standing stiff out of my trousers, she seized it in her mouth, and, with very little sucking, made me spend to excess, and the dear girl swallowed it with all the luxury of the utmost voluptuousness. We had no time for more at that moment, as I caught sight of mamma's dress through the trees. I buttoned up hastily, and we strolled along, as if nothing had happened. It was in our after-walk, when we had allayed mamma's suspicion, that my dear Ellen continued her confessions.

'The stiff thing pressing against her thumb was mamma's clitoris, which, by her account, is wonderfully developed. She, knowing from her former experience with me that it was the point of most exquisite enjoyment, turned her finger upon it, and began awkwardly playing with it. It was at this moment that the greater excitement awoke mamma, who finding to her surprise what Ellen was doing, seized her hand, and pressing and rubbing it with more art against her clitoris, continued its action with exclamations of delight, declaring that Ellen was her dear precious loved girl, and then with a positive cry of delight, spent profusely over Ellen's hand. After panting for some time in perfect bliss, she turned and took Ellen in her arms, kissing her most warmly, and thrusting her tongue into Ellen's mouth, and then demanding hers in return. After much embracing, mamma asked her how she came to do what she found her doing when she awoke. Ellen described how she found her hand held against it, and their two naked bodies pressed against each other – that she was surprised at this, and wondered how it came so; that on moving her hand she felt mamma give a throb down there, and a push of her body forward, which made her finger slip easily in; this still more surprised her, as she had tried often if her fingers could get into her own, but it hurt her so much that she had given it up as impossible; and now she had found one where all her fingers, up to the knuckles, slipped in quite easily; the inside movements, and the heavings of her aunt's body, showed that it gave her pleasure. In continuing her movements she had felt something hard at the upper part pressing against the side of her hand; she withdrew her fingers to feel this strange thing, and in doing so awoke her aunt.'

' "And you know the rest, dear auntie. I was so glad that I had given you so much pleasure," was what Ellen told Harry she had said.

' "Dear, dear girl!" auntie replied, "I shall love you more dearly than ever; yes, and you, too, shall have the utmost pleasure. I have long wished to initiate you into the secrets of womanhood, but thought you too young to be able to keep secret such intimacy as we may indulge in. Often in your sleep, with your lovely naked charms exposed to me and pressed against my own lascivious person, have I enjoyed you and even made use of your own hand all unconscious in sleep, to excite me to a still greater pitch; last night I had enjoyed you to the utmost, kissing your lovely budding and hidden charms, and must have unconsciously dropped off to sleep with my hand still pressing yours against my secret charm. But now I must initiate you into the same joys, even in a more exquisite way."

'Upon this she begged me to throw off my chemise, while she did the same. We stood up to do this, and your mother took the opportunity to pose me in every way, admiring and kissing me all over. I did the same to her, and I can assure you, dear Harry, your mother is far better made than I am, both in the bosom and the bottom, and with such firm thighs and legs, and her affair is so well developed and pouting, and with such silky curls all around it. I can feel you passing your fingers through the curls of mine; but though it has more than it had when last you felt and caressed it, it is nothing to dear auntie's. When she had much excited me, and was evidently herself greatly so, she desired me to lie across the bed on my back, and to draw my knees up so as to let my feet rest on the edge. She then placed a footstool in front, and kneeling upon it, after first feeling and caressing me down there, she glued her lips to it, and after sucking a while began to play with her tongue upon what you have been so deliciously rubbing. She licked me most exquisitely, and soon made me die away in ecstasy of delight. She sucked it for some time after, while I lay in a languid state of joy. When at last she rose, she threw herself on the bed, and our two naked bodies became closely united in the most loving embrace. Her lips were wet with the moisture that had escaped from me, its peculiar aromatic odour *m'enivrait* and I could not help licking the creamy juice from off her lips.

' "Oh, my beloved aunt," I cried, "you have given me the joy of paradise, I must try and do as much for you:"

' "My darling Ellen, you will make me positively adore you. I now only regret that I had not sooner taken you into my confidence, as I at once perceive I might have done so in perfect safety. Yes, my darling you shall indeed try, and I shall instruct you as we advance how to obtain the greatest amount of pleasure from our libidinous and lascivious enjoyments; delights that are without risk, and from which we shall have no anxieties as to fatal results, which are the consequence of connection with the opposite sex, who only make use of us for their own sensual enjoyment, and abandon us at the very moment they ought to console and cherish us the most."

'Dear aunt, again embracing me tenderly, threw herself in the same position I had previously lain in. I knelt on the cushion as she had done. But before proceeding to do as she had done to me, I could not help pausing to gaze with delight on her natural charms. Oh! dear Harry, you cannot imagine the beauty of that part of your mamma. Her stomach is of the purest white, smooth and firm, round and beautiful. Below a crease commences a large plumped-out swelling seen through the fair and thick silky curls that so much adorn it, then grandly rounded sinks down between her thighs, and the beautifully pouting lips rise richly tempting through the thickest of hair, that goes far beyond between the large rounded orbs that project behind. At the upper part of the lips, where they form a deep indented half circle, I could distinguish a stiff projecting object, as long and thicker than my thumb. I now know that this is the centre of exquisite joy. Your mother has since taught me to call it her clitoris, and says that although seldom so strongly developed as in her case, it exists in every woman and becomes stiff and excited as the final crisis of joy approaches. I glued my lips around this charming object, and sucked it, and played with my tongue around its point. Your mother, in an ecstasy of delight, wriggled her bottom below me, and with both hands pressing my head down on the excited point, gave utterance to the most loving and sensual expressions. She begged me to pass the flat of my hand under my chin, and introduce my thumb within the lips below where I was sucking, and move it backwards and forwards as much as I could. I did so, and immediately found that it added greatly to your mother's delight. Faster and faster grew her movements, until, with a cry of delight, a firm pressure of my hand against her affair, and still firmer pressure on my thumb, she suddenly ceased all movement, her hands relaxed their hold of my head, the stiffness left her clitoris, and beyond convulsive graspings of the interior of her affair upon my thumb, she lay for some time inanimate. At last she recovered her senses, she seized me under the arms, and drew me upon her belly, her hands pressed my bottom down close upon her person, until I found that my affair was nestled in the rich profusion of curls that so finely adorned hers. She thrust her tongue into my mouth, and sucked off all the rich creamy substance that had flowed from her in such abundance. She blessed the happy chance that had led her to give me her confidence; told me that for long she had only enjoyed the unsatisfactory delight of lonely self-gratification, and said that now we should revel in mutual delight of every sensual indulgence that woman can have with woman. We lay for some time enjoying such delicious communings, until compelled to rise by the lateness of the hour. We have since practised every method of enjoyment given to two of the same sex. Your mother has often introduced her stiff excited clitoris within the lips of my affair as far as it would go, but I have always longed, my dear Harry, for you to penetrate still further with that larger and longer thing you have got, although what I have seen today of its increased size has made me greatly fear it can never get in.'

Thus ended her ingenuous description. Harry, of course, promised that he would never hurt her, that those parts were made to yield, that, doubtless, his mother's large clitoris had hurt her at first, but had given her great pleasure afterwards.

Yes, that was so, and it was that that gave her courage, and if they could only get the opportunity she would allow him to do anything he pleased.

It may well be supposed this account of Ellen's intercourse with her aunt fired my imagination and made me resolve to have her. Indeed, I began to conceive that there would be no occasion for me to make any effort, that all would be done by dear mamma herself. We had returned to the house after this agitated walk. Mamma was evidently greatly preoccupied, but at length she appeared to have come to a final determination, for she told Ellen to go up to her room, and begged us two boys, as she called us, to go out and amuse ourselves for an hour. It was during this interval that Harry narrated his interesting conversation with his cousin. Her lively description had set his imagination on fire, and he now declared his regret that it was not to be he who would enjoy his lasciviously sensual mother. Neither of us had any doubt but that she would now find an opportunity of enjoying me. If we had, our doubts were solved on re-entering the house. Mamma first, for form's sake, kissing her son, and then far more warmly kissing me, informed us that she had written to the doctor that we had been such good boys that she would feel greatly obliged if he would allow her son to remain with her until Monday, and also leave his nephew to keep him company and prevent any of his former misbehaviour which, she was happy to say, he appeared to have forgotten, but still it would be better he should have the safeguard of so intelligent and discreet a friend as she was glad to see he had found in the doctor's nephew. My uncle, without knowing exactly what to make of this note, had consented. Hence her joy in being able to communicate the pleasing intelligence – doubly so to me, as I immediately anticipated the downfall of my assumed virginity. Dear mamma was all radiant with joy, and conveyed me at once to where she intended I should sleep. I marked that it was in an out-of-the-way room, easy of access, but not likely to be interfered with by passers-by.

'And here, my dear son – for you know in future you are always to call me mamma – I hope you will find yourself comfortable, and that you will not be alarmed because you are in an out-of-the-way part of the house, but in case you should, before I go to bed, I shall come to see that you are comfortably asleep.'

Here she kissed and embraced me warmly. I repaid her most affectionately, but apparently in all innocence. She sighed, as I thought with regret that she could not at that moment go further, and then led me away.

The afternoon, the dinner, and the evening passed away without anything worthy of remark, except that mamma was frequently absent and preoccupied. She sat by me on the sofa while Ellen played to us; her hand sought mine, and frequently squeezed it affectionately. Harry sat by Ellen, which enabled me often to raise my head and pout my lips for a kiss in a boyish way. It was never refused. She dwelt on my mouth sensuously with half-opened lips, but apparently afraid to tip me the velvet of her tongue. She frequently gave a shudder and trembled, and was evidently greatly excited. In the course of the afternoon, Harry and I had had an opportunity of exchanging ideas. I told him I was certain his mother would come to me that night, and he might be sure if she did that she would remain till daylight. I advised him to watch her, and when he saw her leave her bedroom to come to me, then he could slip into his cousin's room, and effect his purpose, but to be sure to retire at the first sign of dawn. I said that if at that time his mother wanted to leave me, I would keep her another quarter of an hour to enable him to put matters to rights with his cousin, and regain his own room. I advised him also to put a towel under his cousin's bottom, as he was sure to make her bleed, and he must take it away in the morning to prevent any traces of what he had done being perceived by his mother, and to tell Ellen to feign deep sleep on his mother's return, and to appear quite unconscious in the morning of her aunt having been absent. A little before ten o'clock mamma thought it time for her children, as she called us, to go to bed. Her son and niece both kissed her, and I, too, claimed a kiss of my new mamma. It was taken and returned in quite a passionate way, her lips seemed loath to leave mine, and her arms encircled me in a very loving embrace.

'Dear mamma,' I said, 'I shall love you ever dearly.'

'My darling boy, I already love you as if you were indeed my son.

She sent the others to their bedrooms, but escorted me herself to mine. I could see that she trembled greatly, and was evidently glad to put down the candlestick. She turned down the bedclothes for me, hoped I would sleep well, and, with considerable agitation, again embraced me most passionately. I could feel that her tongue would fain have thrust itself between my lips. I had great difficulty in restraining myself, but somehow I managed to do so. She at last left me, saying she would give a look in to see that I was comfortable before she herself went to bed. I told her it was very kind of her, but that there was no necessity for her doing so, as I always went to sleep like a top the moment I lay down.

'I am glad of that, my dear child, but nevertheless I will look in, lest the strange bed should prevent your sleeping.'

And again she hugged me passionately against her firm and well-formed bosom, kissing me with a long, long kiss. Quitting me with a deep sigh, at last she said good-night, and shut the door, apparently going away. But I fancied that she stopped short, and that I could hear her gently stealing back, probably in the hope of seeing me undress, and of catching a view of my huge pego. So I determined she should have her curiosity indulged. I hurried off my clothes, and before putting on one of Harry's nightshirts, which had been laid on the bed for me, I took up the chamber pot, and turned to front the keyhole, stark naked, and cock in hand. It was at half-cock, but when I had piddled I made it throb and raise its head, and gave it a rub or two, and a shake very deliberately, so that she might be still more bent on possessing it. I took up the nightshirt, and turning to the light, was very awkward in getting it on, so as to give time for a good sight of my prick at full stand against my belly. I then blew out the light, and tumbled into bed very quickly. I listened attentively, and could hear a deep half-suppressed sigh, and then footsteps stealing quietly away. I lay awake cogitating as to how I should receive her, whether to feign profound sleep, and so let her take all the initiative, or whether to pretend that the novelty of the bed, and thinking over her affectionate kindness to me had kept me awake. I decided upon pretending to be sound asleep, chiefly that I might see how she would carry out her designs, and also as allowing me to play the surprised one.

In little more than half an hour after all had retired to rest I saw the glimmer of light through the keyhole. I had studied a pose that would facilitate matters. I lay on my back, the clothes partially thrown off my breast, and the hand next to the side on which she must approach, placed above my head. Of course my cock was at full stand and as I had thrown off the heavy counterpane, it easily lifted up and bulged out the sheet and light blanket. I closed my eyes, and breathed heavily. The door was gently opened, and she entered. She turned to close it, and I gave a peep through a half-opened eye, and saw that she had only on a loose *robe de chambre*, which was thrown open in turning, so that I could see there was nothing but her shift below. I even caught sight of her beautiful bosom, which at once caused my prick to throb almost to bursting, so that when she came to my side, it stood up most manfully. She paused, evidently intent on the sight. She then held the light towards me, and spoke in an undertone, asking me if I was awake. Of course I only breathed the heavier, and lay with my mouth half open, as if in the very deepest first slumber. She then turned her attention to the bulging-out substance, and ventured to touch it gently; then, growing bolder, she still more gently grasped it from above the clothes, and then turned the light on my face, but I gave not a sign. She then put the candle down, and, taking a chair, sat down close to the bed. Here she again spoke to me in a subdued tone. Finding no cessation of the deep breathing, she gently insinuated her hand below the already favourably turned-down bedclothes, and with great care slipped it down to my prick, which she grasped softly. I could now feel her whole body tremble, her breath came fast and short. She passed her hand gently up from the root to the head, its size evidently greatly exciting her. When she grasped the head, it gave a powerful throb. She eased her hand, and, I felt certain, turned to see if it had disturbed me. But I slept on profoundly. She seemed to gain more confidence, for both hands were now applied, and it was evident she had assumed a kneeling posture, the better to favour her designs. I could feel her pass one hand over the other, until she found the head was still partially above the third grasp. I heard her give an involuntary exclamation of surprise at its size. Her curiosity growing by what it fed on, she now commenced with the utmost caution gently to remove the bedclothes, that she might see, as well as feel. When this was accomplished, she rose and brought the light, again passed it before my eyes, and then moved it down towards my prick. Being sure she was now far too deeply engaged to turn her eyes towards mine, I half opened them, and beheld her bending close over the great object of attraction. I heard her exclaim half aloud: 'How wonderful! I never could have imagined such a thing, and in such an innocent boy, too. Oh! I must possess – yes – I must possess it.'

Here she grasped it more forcibly than before. Then, rising, she put the candle on the pot stand, which she removed to the foot of the bed. Then taking my prick in both hands, she gently rubbed it up and down, and even stooped and fondly kissed the nut. It throbbed more violently than ever at this, and I thought it time to start, and appear to awake. She instantly quitted her hold of it, and stood up, but was too agitated to think of covering me. I opened my eyes in apparent great surprise, but recognising mamma, I said: 'Oh! is that you, dear mamma? I was dreaming such a nice dream about you. Oh, do kiss me,' purposely not seeming to notice that my person was all naked.

She stooped and kissed me tenderly, saying: 'My dear, darling boy. I came to see if you were comfortable, and found you lying uncovered, and with this extraordinary thing sticking up.'

She had seized it with her left hand, as she stooped to kiss me. On the instant, I determined to play off the same game that had succeeded so well with my aunt.

'My dear mamma, I should not have dared to speak to you about *that*, but it does give me much pain by becoming so hard that it throbs, as you may feel, at the least touch. I don't know what to do; and it makes me feel so queer too, especially at the gentle pressures you have just given it; dear mamma, can you tell me how I can cure it, and I will love you so dearly.'

Here she stooped and kissed me very luxuriously, actually thrusting her tongue into my mouth. I sucked it, and told her how sweet it was. But my prick becoming perfectly outrageous, I implored her to tell me what I could do to relieve it. She looked at me long and intently, blushing and turning pale by turns.

'Yes, my dear boy, I could relieve you, but it is a secret that I hardly dare confide in one so young.'

'Oh! you may trust me, my dear mamma, you know I am becoming a young man, and men must know how to keep secrets, or they would be despised, besides, so dear and loving a mamma as you are to me would doubly make me keep secret anything you confide to me on those terms.'

'I will trust you, my darling boy, but you will at once see by what I shall do, how completely I sacrifice myself to do you good.'

Upon this, she threw off her robe, and sprang into bed by my side.

'Oh! how nice of you, dear mamma,' said I, as I took her in my arms, and kissed her lovingly. 'Feel, mamma, how much harder it is, so tell me at once how I am to relieve it.'

'Well, my dear child, we women are made to relieve such stiffnesses as this; we possess a sheath to put it in, and then it gradually softens.'

'Oh! where – where – dearest mamma, do tell me?'

She took my hand and put it down on her cunt, already quite wet with the excitement she had been in.

'There, feel that, do you not find an opening?'

'Oh, yes, but how am I to get in there – won't it hurt you?'

'I will show you.'

She turned on her back, opened her legs, and desired me to mount on her belly, with my legs between hers, then guiding my rampant pego, and rubbing its great head up and down the lips to moisten it, she told me to push gently downwards, for it was so large that I would otherwise hurt her. Playing the novice to perfection, I awkwardly but gently soon thrust it in, up to the codpiece. She uttered an 'Oh! oh!' when it was fairly hilted; then throwing her legs over my loins, and her arms round my waist, she begged me to move my bottom backwards and forwards, always thrusting it in as far as I could. Three or four pushes finished me off, in the great excitement I was under. She, too, died away with a great convulsive sigh. I took care to cry out: 'Oh! my dear mamma – oh! stop. I am dying – I – I – am dy–dy–ing.'

Her convulsive internal pressures were delicious, and quickly roused my prick up again. She also had come to, and had glued her lips to mine – giving her own, and then asking in return for my tongue to suck.

'Oh! what heavenly joys, my dear mamma, you did, indeed, reduce its hardness, but just feel – it has got hard again, you must reduce it once more.'

'My beloved boy, I shall always be ready to do so, but it must be the most sacred secret between us, or I should never be able to do it again.'

You may well suppose my protestations were of the strongest. At it we went again, and again, and again. Mamma declared that I was a most apt scholar. Four times did I pour into her foaming and fiery cunt torrents of sperm. At last she insisted upon my withdrawing, saying it would injure my health to indulge any more. So I withdrew, and we embraced each other most lovingly. I now expressed a wish to see the wonderful place that had given me the ecstasies of paradise. She lent herself with admirable grace and ease to my boyish curiosity, and even threw off her shift, making me do the same, that she too might admire the undisguised beauties of my form. There was no pretence in the great admiration I expressed for her really superb form, but I expressed it in a naïve and innocent way, that made her laugh heartily, and confirmed her idea that she was not only the first naked woman I had seen, but that she was the first I ever knew, or who had taught me what sensual pleasure meant, and great was her delight in thinking she had taken my virginity, and been the first to initiate me in love's delightful mysteries. Of course, I did everything I could in order to carry on the deception she was so much pleased with, and I may add this was the last time I ever did so, for daily becoming more of a man, I took *things* by the forelock at once, and rarely failed to succeed. We got up, and she turned herself round in every way for me to see the rare beauties of her person – herself explaining to me where she was well made – bosom, buttocks, belly so white and smooth, without a wrinkle, although she had had a son. She was, indeed, one of those rare cases where nothing remains to tell of such an event. Her bosom, without being so large as aunt's, was gloriously white and firm, with such pink nipples, larger than in a maid, but sticking out hard and inviting a suck. Then her cunt – for she laid herself on her back, opened her legs, and allowed me the closest inspection. I have already alluded to her clitoris, as described by Ellen to Harry; it was charmingly developed, about half the length of Miss Frankland's, and not so thick. As I felt her cunt and introduced my fingers to hold it open, she got excited, and Master Clitoris raised his head, and came out of his corner in full stand. I professed great surprise to find she had a little doodle of her own. I purposely used the boyish expression. I began to play with it.

'Oh!' I said, 'I must kiss it.'

I did so, and began to suck it. She got dreadfully lewd, and seizing upon my now-again-standing prick, drew me upon her, and introduced once more my master weapon. With greater slowness until the final crisis drew near, we had another delicious fuck. She was a woman of very warm passions, and the long pent-up seclusion she had kept herself in with regard to our sex being once broken, now that the flood-gates were opened, there was no resisting the torrent of her lascivious passions. Twice again did we fuck without withdrawing. Then, after hugging and thanking me for the ecstasies I threw her into, she rose for a natural purpose, and advised me to do the same, and we would then both lave ourselves with cold water to restore our nerves. She laved me and I her. She then insisted on my lying down on my back, while she admired what she called the masterpiece of Nature. From seeing and feeling, she soon came to sucking. Up he got in a moment. Playing the ignoramus, I asked if it was not possible that we could both enjoy that pleasure at once.

'Oh, yes, my dear boy. I am so delighted to find that this pleases you! Lie on your back, I shall get over you in the reverse way, and while I suck this enormous jewel, whose head I can hardly get into my mouth, you shall do as you like with my notch.'

'Is that what you call it, dear mamma?'

'That is one name, and it has many others, but you men generally call it cunt, as we call yours prick, it is just as well you should know their ordinary names, as children only call them fanny and doodle.'

'Prick and cunt – oh! I shan't forget, so let me have that beautiful cunt to suck.'

We had a mutual gamahuche, and both greedily swallowed the double result, and continued our caresses of both parts, until they were again in full vigour, and inspired with a desire for more solid enjoyments.

'My darling boy, you are so apt and excellent a scholar that I must show you there are several ways of allaying the stiffness of this dear fellow, who seems as desirous as ever to have his hardness taken out of him. I shall show you how my husband liked best to enjoy me.'

She scrambled up on her knees, and presented her very fine bottom, told me to kneel behind and give her my prick in her hand, which she thrust out backwards between her thighs. I did so. She told me it would appear to get further in this way, and, in fact, it did. After it was all in until thighs and buttocks met, she told me to admire, praise, and handle the splendid cheeks of her bottom, and said that such praise greatly excited her. Of course I did so, admiring not only their size and fairness, but also the beautiful curly silk meshes that ran between the cheeks, covered her beautifully pink bottom-hole, charmingly puckered as it was, and ran up to the flat of her back. After I had so excited her, she begged me to lean forward, and to handle one bubby while I should play with her clitoris with the other hand. I did all this tolerably well, but with somewhat of awkwardness. She said I would soon be perfect. We ran again two courses before she fell forward, dragging me down without withdrawing, and then turning on our sides, still intertwined, we fell off into a deep slumber, and did not awaken till daylight. Mamma jumped out of bed, unseating me by the act. She was alarmed lest the hour should be late enough for the household to be up. I tried hard to persuade her to reduce once more the hardness which had again seized me as she might see and feel for herself.

'No, my dear boy, we must not be imprudent, my niece may have awakened and grown anxious at my absence, and she may rise to seek me; so goodbye, my darling, go to sleep again.'

She embraced me tenderly, but I could not prevail upon her to go further, although she promised to seek an opportunity during the day, and to give me as much as I liked the next night. She left me, and I pondered over the lucky chance that had put so desirable and fine a woman into my arms, and also congratulated myself on the stratagem by which I had fully convinced her that she was my first insructress in the art of love, a circumstance ever dear to the ardent imagination of the darling sex. I easily fell asleep again, wondering how Harry in the meantime had got on with his cousin. My dear mamma would not allow me to be disturbed. She entered my room once or twice, and found me sleeping soundly.

At last she again entered, just as I had satisfied a natural want for which I had risen. To rush to her, to embrace her tenderly, to fasten the door, and compel her, not much against her will, to come towards the bed, to beg her to lie on her belly on the bedside, to cant her petticoats up, to kneel and gamahuche her cunt from behind until she begged me to rise and fuck her, was but the work of a minute or two. And then my stiff-standing pego, aided by the mouthful of thick saliva occasioned by the gamahuche, was directed at her cunt, and driven home as far as the buttocks of her fine backside would allow. My prick being fairly sheathed, I paused for a moment to handle and praise the beauty of her posterior orbs. Then, stooping, I nibbled at her bubbies with one hand, and frigged her clitoris with the other. Sharp set, with my long rest and refreshing sleep, I rapidly ran a first course, but not quicker than the lascivious nature of dear mamma, who joined me in a copious discharge with the most ecstatic joy, and the most delicious inward pressures. For she was a perfect and most accomplished actor in the combats of love, and in her own way was worthy of my glorious aunt and my loved Miss Frankland, and as thoroughly accomplished as they in all the abandon of lust and lubricity, although at the moment I had only proved things in an ordinary way. Her exquisite internal suctions almost prevented the slightest relaxation in my delighted pego, and after a minute or two of indulgence in the after joy, I began again almost before dear mamma had recovered her senses, when she tried to tear herself away. But before she knew where she was I had succeeded in again firing her ardent and lascivious nature, and she became as eager for a second course as myself. This was naturally longer than the first fiery one. I raised myself upright on my knees, contemplated with the utmost delight the uncommon active play of her loins, and the exquisite side-wriggling of her very fine backside. I loudly praised her delicious manoeuvres, and seconded them to the utmost, until getting more and more excited, fast and furious grew our movements. I bent down to second her by frigging her clitoris, and the final crisis seized us both with its agony of joy, and I sank almost insensible on her back. We lay for a short time lost to everything, until mamma, remembering the risk we ran of discovery, begged me to withdraw, and let her go away. She rose and threw herself into my arms, glueing her lips to mine with a most loving kiss. Then stooping, she gave my now pendant prick a most delicious suck, making her tongue play into and around the mouth of the urethra. This was so delicious that the delighted member instantly showed its appreciation of the pleasure by starting up in full swing. Mamma gave it a pat, and said he was a most charming and delicious boy, who did not know how to behave himself. Again she kissed me, and tore herself away, but I could easily see the regret was as great on her side as mine. She told me her son had been as lazy as I was, and said that breakfast was waiting for us both. I quickly finished my toilet and found them all at the breakfast table.

Ellen blushed deeply when she saw me. A glance from Harry assured me he had succeeded, and that Ellen not only knew what I had been about, but also that I knew what she had been doing. Hence her high colour when she saw me. I smiled, and nodded to her knowingly, and as she had observed the intelligent glance that passed between Harry and me, it did not tend to put her at her ease.

Mamma, of course, knew nothing of what had passed in her bed while she was with me, and was all affectionate attention to the whole party, but with a marked tendency to pay me more particular attention. Our breakfast was late, so we had to hurry ourselves for church. Mamma drove Ellen in a small pony phæton, while Harry and I took a short cut across the fields.

Harry told me how he had watched his mother and had quietly approached my door, and as the bed was exactly opposite the keyhole, had seen and enjoyed her proceedings, especially as he knew that I only pretended sleep.

'By Jove,' he said, 'what a fine woman mother is! I could not tear myself away, and remained until you both went at it again, stark naked. My mother's beautiful hairy cunt, fine bubbies and backside, nearly drove me mad with desire. I could have violated her if she had been alone. And, then, her energy in fucking was superb. I could hold out no longer, but rushed to dear Ellen's side. She was asleep. I took her in my arms, and awoke her by feeling her delicious young cunt. She opened her eyes, and thinking it was mamma she turned round to repay the compliment, and started on having hold of my pego.'

' "Why! Harry dear, how came you here? We shall be caught by mamma."

' "Oh, no, my love, mamma is better engaged, and has slipped away to Charlie's room to get done to her what I am going to do to you."

'She was too much alarmed to believe me, and I was obliged to bring her to your door. I first peeped, and saw you were still at it. Mamma's legs and alms thrown around you allowed me to see your great big thing rushing in and out, and driving home with immense vigour. I whispered to Ellen to peep. While she did so, stooping, I sat down on the floor and gamahuched her. She spent almost immediately, and was so excited that it quite filled my mouth. I rose on my legs, and bringing my prick against her cunt, made an entrance as far as over the nut, but was myself so excited with all I was doing, and all I had previously seen, that I went off in an agony of delight and with a suppressed cry, which must have been heard by you and mamma if you had not been so busily engaged. Ellen had been so excited and so intent on the to her new scene enacting before her eyes, that she had never ceased gazing on it, and left me to do whatever I pleased, but my cry alarmed her, especially as in my last forward push I had sent her head with some noise against the door. She rose, and so unseated me from the slight hold I had got of her cunt. She turned round to embrace me most excitedly, and whispered that we must go elsewhere. I took her round the waist, and we quickly regained mamma's bed. The light enabled me to find a towel. I told Ellen it was to prevent any moisture betraying our acts. She was far too excited and wishful for the article to make the slightest resistance, or even pretence of refusal. I begged her to throw off her shift, as she had seen both Charlie and mamma were quite naked. She at once complied, being now as eager for the fray as myself. I, too, threw off my nightshirt. For a moment we embraced each other's naked bodies. My cock was as stiff as iron. She lewdly laid hold of it, while I handled her charming young cunt. I helped her on to the bed and she at once lay down on her back, and threw open her legs as she had seen mamma do. I stopped and gave her cunt, all oozing with her own and my spunk, a warm kiss, and with a lick or two on her budding clitoris, I fired her even to greater excess than she had yet been in.

' "Oh, come to my arms, my dear Harry, and let us do as they were so delightedly doing."

'She had noted with what rapture mamma was enjoying you, and she had noted, too, what a much larger cock yours was than mine; so she had naturally reasoned that if one so big gave her aunt so much delight, my smaller one could not possibly hurt her, hence her eagerness to have me at once. I did not baulk her, but throwing myself between herwide-spread thighs, I soon brought the point of my prick to the longing lips of her little virgin cunt. I rubbed it up and down in between the pouting and self-opened lips, partly to moisten it, and partly still more to excite her lust. I then gently pressed it forward, and introduced just its head, and drawing it in and out, made her beg me to go further. I did so, slowly, until I found there was an impediment. I knew that I must burst through this and that it would hurt her, so I continued withdrawing and re-entering without going further until she became so voraciously lewd as to throw her legs around my loins and heave her bottom up to meet my thrusts. I seized the fortunate moment and with one downright violent thrust burst through every barrier and buried my prick in her up to the very hilt. The attack and its result was so unexpected by Ellen that when she felt the knife-like thrust of agony she gave a shriek of pain, and made an immediate effort to throw me off. I was too firmly seated for any other result of her struggles than the still more complete rupture of her maidenhead, which my forward thrust had partially effected. I lay for some time quite tranquil, and when her immediate pain wore off I commenced a gentle in and out movement, which, without exactly exciting her, produced a pleasing sensation. I then went on faster and faster until the crisis came upon me, and I shot into her a torrent of boiling sperm that by its balmy nature mollified the previous smarting; so that when I had recovered from the delicious ecstasies of my first success, and my prick gradually resumed its former vigour, I found by the somewhat increased pressure upon it that her passions were re-awakening. Three times did I fuck her before I withdrew, the last one appeared to give her more pleasure, but still she complained of a smarting pain as I passed over and over the shattered hymen. I advised her to rise and lave herself as a relief, and to wash away the stains of blood from her thighs. The towel was a fortunate thought on your part, but, in fact, I had followed in all my movements the sage counsels you had given me from the experience you had had in taking the virginities of Mrs Vincent and your two sisters, or I should otherwise probably have bungled the matter, although my experience with your magnificent aunt has naturally put me up to all the art of fucking. I had some difficulty in persuading Ellen to let me put it in again, as she declared she had endured perfect agony when I broke through her maidenhead. However, I gamahuched her well, got her passions up, moistened the shaft well, and was very gentle in entering and in my first movements. I spent without making her do so. But the well-greased sheath now allowing more easy movements, she gave down her nature with considerable pleasure as I spent the second time. Still there was fear and restraint – fear lest mamma might come back – so I thought it advisable to retire to my own room, being quite certain that now the road is open her lascivious nature will not be long in enabling her to enjoy the sport to the utmost. By the way, she could not help wondering how mamma could take in your immense pego; why, she said, it was as thick as her wrist and much longer than her hand, and yet it seemed to slip into mamma with ease and pleasure, "while yours, dear Harry, which is not thicker than my two forefingers, and hardly much longer, has given me such pain." I assured her it was only for the first night, and that if she would bathe it with warm water two or three times during the day, and put up a little glycerine as far as where it hurt, which her finger could easily reach, she would find that tomorrow night there would no longer be any pain felt, and she would enjoy it as much as she had seen mamma do. With this advice I left her to her repose, and gained my own room unobserved.'

After this we concerted together as to what we should say to the doctor, who was sure to question us. Mrs Dale's cottage was not in our parish, but she had driven over to our church, partly to throw off all suspicion from the doctor's mind, and also to thank him for allowing us to stay with her. We, therefore, knew that we should have to go to the rectory and stay for luncheon. We agreed that we should not on this occasion take the doctor into our confidence, but that we should tell him we had purposely been very quiet and discreet, so as to throw Harry's mother off her guard. That Ellen slept with her, so that it became doubly necessary to gain her confidence. This being arranged before we reached church, we entered. After service we all adjourned to the rectory. The doctor escorted Mrs Dale, Harry, Ellen, and I my aunt. Aunt, pressing my arm, asked me if I had had Mrs D., as she seemed a fine woman worth having.

'Oh, dear no. I have had no opportunity, even if she would have consented. I have been playing the ingenuous youth to help Harry with his cousin. I thought we had somewhat thrown her off her guard, but she was still jealous and watched him closely. Ellen slept with her, which rendered things more difficult for Harry. She has closely examined me as to the sort of intimacy existing between us. I threw such an air of candour and innocence over my replies that she was quite delighted Harry had met with such a companion. I fully expect she will break out in praises of my *modest* and discreet conduct.'

Indeed, so it turned out, and Mrs Dale did it with such an air of candour that aunt was quite convinced nothing as yet had occurred between us. While the ladies discussed the dresses and bonnets of all who had appeared in church, uncle took Harry and me for a walk in the garden until luncheon was ready. Here he began, as aunt had done, to question us as to our proceedings, and the reason for Mrs D. asking permission for us to stay. The same replies that had satisfied aunt satisfied him that nothing as yet had taken place beyond my gaining the confidence of Mrs D.

'My dear Charlie,' said uncle, 'you have only now to manage somehow or other to let her see your great big cock without apparently your being aware of it, and I will warrant, from my knowledge of woman's nature, that she will find a way to have you – only mind you play the innocent, and be very awkward, and let her appear to teach you, which will give double pleasure and prevent any questioning as to how you have gained your instruction, if she thought you instructed.'

I smiled inwardly at these sage directions, and thought how completely all persons knowing in the ways of the world gave the same advice. But little did uncle then think that I had acted up to the very letter what he was advising for my future conduct. We re-entered the house on the luncheon-bell ringing. Mrs Dale complimented the doctor on the advance her son had made both in manners and instruction, and quite naturally congratulated herself on his finding so very modest and gentlemanly a companion in the doctor's nephew – myself to wit.

Returning home, Ellen begged she might be allowed to walk, doubtless calculating on having Harry for a companion. But mamma, while agreeing to her request, was still sufficiently on her guard to take Harry in the phæton, and leave me to escort Ellen. Here was a chance! Ellen blushed, but took my arm as we left the rectory. Uncle gave me a knowing look, and a glance at Ellen, as we parted, as much as to say, I guess what will happen. We walked away steadily enough until the first hedge hid us. I stopped, and embraced Ellen tenderly, saying how glad I was to be able to congratulate her on the happy chance her aunt had given her by coming to me for the night. She was a good deal confused at thinking that I should know how she passed the night. I rallied her upon this, told her that no secret existed between Harry and me, and that, in fact, if I had not lent myself to the game, she would not have had the opportunity for the great pleasure she must have had in Harry's arms. I knew she had not had much, but I wished to draw her on, and to make her open out as to her feelings, being determined to make the most of any confidence on her part. She replied that, indeed, she had done nothing but suffer, and would not have allowed Harry to do what he did if she had known the pain it would give her; she had been deceived by seeing how much aunt had seemed to enjoy what was so greatly superior in size to what Harry had. I smiled at her allusion to the size of my pego, and knowing that her curiosity must be creating in her a desire to see it, I told her it was well for her, in the first instance, to have had the smaller weapon to penetrate her, and that now she would never again suffer, even by the introduction of so large a one as mine.

'Oh, but when I think of the immense size of yours, I could never dare to allow you to try, although aunt did seem to enjoy it, when you pushed it in with such force.'

'My dear Ellen, it was the size alone that tempted mamma; if I had not been larger than Harry, I doubt if ever she would have come to me last night.'

'But how could she dare to do so?'

'Curiosity to enjoy an unusually large cock, my dear.'

'Did you know she was coming?'

'Yes, and no. I saw that her passions were excited, when I had once *accidentally* allowed her to see my large proportions.'

'Yes, Harry told me what you were about, but I hardly expected aunt would have dared to come to you – how did it happen?'

'Well, if you will promise *never* to let your aunt know that I have told, I shall tell you. She came and found me *apparently* asleep, first felt me, and seeing I did not awake, carefully uncovered me, looked at, handled and kissed it, upon which, as my cock was nearly bursting, and I could stand it no longer, I awoke, and innocently complained of the stiffness I suffered from in that part, and begged her to tell me if there was any means of relieving it. She told me there was but it was a great secret she hardly dared trust me with – and even if she could do so, she was afraid of a great long thing like *that*, three of her hands long below the head! but that if I promised secrecy, she would try. Then she lay down and taught me how to put it in, and I know you afterwards enjoyed the sight of our being in full action, quite naked – did you not enjoy it, dear Ellen?'

'Well, dear Charlie, it was very exciting, and made me feel queer all over; but is it really three hands and a head long?'

I was delighted at the question, as it showed me she was ready for what I intended should be done. Curiosity once excited was sure to go to the utmost length, if it had the opportunity. I had purposely been hurrying on to gain a dense copse through which our path lay, and I knew there was a snug glade where we would be in perfect security. It was the dinner hour of the peasantry, and no one else was likely to come that way. Just as we entered the copse, she had put her last question. I told her I would show her, if she would step a few yards beyond the footpath. She objected, for form's sake saying: 'What would Harry say?'

'There is no occasion for him to know anything about it, but even if he did, has he not himself shown you mamma and me in full enjoyment of her sweet charms; but, unless you tell him you may be sure I never shall, it will not take a minute, and as we have already walked very fast, we have plenty of time, and our absence will not be observed.'

With professed reluctance she allowed me to lead her where I wished. Having arrived at the favourable spot, I sat down on a gentle slope, and begged her to sit down beside me. As you may well suppose, my prick was rampant, and almost bursting open my trousers, so that as soon as I un-buttoned, out it flew in all its splendour. She gave a half scream of surprise as she gazed upon its large proportions, and declared it looked larger than when she had seen it with aunt. Her face flushed, and her eyes sparkled as she gazed, but she seemed half frightened to touch it. I took her hand and placed it on it. She immediately grasped it convulsively, but sighed deeply. I had lain back on the grass that it might stand out boldly before her and I told her to try if it was not three hands and a head long. She immediately passed one hand over the other from the root, and said it was really monstrous, and she wondered how aunt could have got it into her.

'Oh, my darling, I hope someday you will find that you can take it all in with the utmost delight, but I should not think of trying until you have had some more practice with Harry.'

Meanwhile she was handling it with great excitement, and while saving she was sure I could never succeed with her, she was evidently longing to be able to take it in. I saw I must work her up more so I said: 'Dear Ellen, you know what pleasure it gave you and Harry to play with each other with your mouths, it is now your turn to let me see your dear little thing – and then you must lie over me reversed, so that we may enjoy ourselves with tongues and mouths.'

She let me at once pull up her petticoats, but said she feared that even for that she was still too sore from Harry's work last night. I asked if she had bathed it in warm water and put glycerine up.

'Oh, yes.'

At first it smarted, but before going to church, she had done it three times, and no longer felt any pain, but still was afraid of my finger going up. I was introducing it at the moment. It passed in its full length without hurting her.

'Now, pull up your petticoats well, and lie down on me, while I do the same with this charming little cunt; my tongue can only give it the utmost pleasure.'

She herself was now so much excited that she was ready enough to comply with my desires. She got upon me, her petticoats well canted over her back. She glued her lips to my prick, and sucked and frigged it with an energy that proved how highly her passions were fired. Her cunt was already in a foam of spendings, which I first licked up. Then sucking her tiny clitoris, stiffly projecting slightly out, I thrust my middle finger up her cunt, and by the wriggling of her backside, saw how much she enjoyed it. Introducing a second finger to moisten it, I withdrew both, and, turning my hand sideways, made each finger enter a separate aperture. She was already nearly in the grand crisis; it came upon her before I was ready. She poured a greater discharge into my mouth than I thought the young thing could have spent. It took her breath away, and she released her suction of my prick for a minute. But on my begging her to continue sucking, she did so with increased energy, and I poured out a torrent of sperm that shot down her throat and nearly choked her, but the dear girl never let go for all that, and sucked away until not only was there not a drop left, but by her delicious titillations she had brought my prick up to its utmost vigour again. I, too, had reawakened her passions. She wanted to renew the sport in this way again, but I begged her to allow me to rub the head of my prick up and down between the well-moistened lips of her cunt, and then to spend with the point, or at most the head, within it. She asked if she could trust me to stop if it hurt her.

'Of course, my darling,' I said, 'nothing shall be done, or rather everything shall cease the moment you tell me to stop.'

Half afraid, yet wishing to try, she changed her position to a kneeling one. I canted her petticoats well over her back, and first kissing and handling her hard and plump buttocks, which promised a future perfection, I stooped and again licked her charming pouting cunt with all its budding fair young curls. Then applying my surcharged mouthful of saliva to my already well-moistened prick, I lubricated it completely from point to root, and then applied it to the half-opened lips. Rubbing it up and down here, and over the clitoris, I excited her to the greatest pitch.

'Oh! Charlie dear,' she cried, 'try if its head will go in now, and I will try to bear it.'

I was only too glad of the permission, and very rapidly got it in over the nut, but it was very tight. I drew it half out again, and then, on repeating this five or six times, found I was imperceptibly gaining ground.

'Oh! dear Charles, it is delicious! Try on, gently.'

I did so, and had got rather more than half-way in when she went off in an agony of delight, deliciously pouring her warm liquid over my enchanted prick, giving, at the same time, such a push backwards, which, meeting a firm, though gentle forward movement on my part, joined with the natural relaxation following her discharge, drove me up to the hilt in the very tightest little cunt it has ever been my good fortune to sheath myself in. I seemed to fill every cranny, and to have stretched every part to its utmost distention. My aunt with her great cunt had a power of pressure that seemed almost to nip off your prick, Miss Frankland, too was great in that way. But this was more like a very well made first-rate kid glove, two sizes too small for your fingers, yet giving way without bursting, and fitting every irregularity of the nail or finger; just so her little cunt fitted my prick exactly like a glove, and it was truly most ecstatic. A gentle withdrawing, and then as gentle resheathing, so excited me that I shot a torrent of sperm up into her very womb. She gave quite a cry of ecstasy, and I could feel the tight sheath exercising a running movement along the whole length of my prick, and still more tightly closing all round it – if that were possible. It was so exquisitely delicious that both of us were almost instantly in readiness for another course.

She asked if I was all in.

'Oh, yes, my dear, do you think you could have taken any more?'

'Oh, no, it appears to fill me to bursting, and to be up to my very heart. I could not have supported more, but could hardly believe I had it all, as I did not think it possible, and was afraid there was more to come.'

'Did it give you any pleasure?'

'Oh, yes; and does so still – push on, dear Charlie, and don't spare me, it is heavenly.'

She wriggled and heaved her backside. I seized her by each hip and favoured her side movements by, as it were, drawing her off and on; faster and faster we moved, until at last the crisis seized us both together. Her head sank with a deep sigh, or rather cry of ecstasy. She would have fallen forward on her belly, but that my grip of her hips held her bottom close up to my belly, with my prick thrust into the innermost end of her cunt, until I felt the three points of the opening of her womb, like the nailless ends of three fingers grasping, as it were, the very point of my prick, and opening them-selves to receive the whole discharge of my sperm within its innermost recesses. Nothing could be more delicious, and as I held her fast, I was myself in a state of perfect ecstasy. At last addressing some endearing expressions, and getting no reply, I found that the dear girl had quite fainted away, and was insensible in every respect except in the continued convulsive throbs of her delicious tight cunt. However, finding that she did not recover her senses, I gently withdrew my still stiff prick. Very little sperm followed the withdrawal. I wiped her cunt dry with my handkerchief, and was glad to see there were no blood stains. I laid her gently down on her back, ran to a little stream, and taking two handfuls of water, came back, threw some on the still throbbing cunt, and sprinkled her face with the drops that still adhered to my palms. This had the desired effect; she opened her eyes, raised herself on her bottom, and threw her arms round my neck as I knelt by her side. Telling me I had made her taste of the joys of heaven, she kissed me, and then burst into a hysterical flood of tears. I comforted her as best I could and asked why she wept.

'I don't know, dear Charles, but the last time made me feel both sick and faint just after you had given me such ecstasy as I never dreamt was possible. I believe I then fainted, and even now, I don't know why but I feel quite hysterical.'

I kissed her tenderly, begged her to rise and come to the spring, where she could drink, and said if she squatted down on her feet I would bathe and cool her dear little cunt, which would probably put all to rights. She did so, and was quickly quite restored to herself again. She said she supposed it was my enormous size.

'But it did not hurt me, dear Charles, it only gave me too much pleasure; but you will do it to me another time whenever we have any opportunity, will you not, dear Charlie?'

I assured her I should always be too glad to do so, but that we must neither let her aunt nor Harry know of our proceedings. This being arranged, and she having quite recovered from the pallor her fainting fit had caused, we resumed our course homeward, and so hurried on that Harry, who had come to meet us, found us getting over the stile of the last field, and was even disappointed that we had got so far, for we were now in sight of the cottage. He had hoped to find us much further back, and that I might have favoured his having a go at his cousin before reaching home. Ellen squeezed my arm. I said it was just as well as it was, for any imprudence might have awakened his mother's suspicions, and prevented a night of pleasure, which would be far better than any uncomfortable field affair.

When we arrived at home, mamma thought that Ellen looked fatigued, and advised her to go and lie down on her bed, and take an hour's siesta. She told us boys we had better do the same, as she had some private matters to attend to. Harry and I saw immediately what was meant, and we betook ourselves to our respective rooms, I to expect mamma, who did not fail to come, and Harry to watch her, and then make the most of the opportunity with his cousin. I quickly undressed, and when mamma came I found she had divested herself of stays and undergarments; so when she undid her gown, and let fall her shift, she stood in all the naked glory of her beautiful form. I flew to embrace her most lovingly. Both our hands wandered and being both in full heat, we were at it in a moment fast and furious. I drove on, admirably seconded by dear mamma, and we quickly both gave down at the same instant a most delicious libation on the altar of Venus, and then died away in all the after-enjoyment. We lay for nearly a quarter of an hour soaking in the delicious bliss of satisfied desire. Mamma, on coming to her senses, kissed me most tenderly, and declared she had never believed it possible that she could have had such exquisite delight.

'But then, my dear Charles, I never dreamt that any man, let alone a boy like you, could be so magnificently hung. Oh, it is also such joy to me to think I have first taught you the real joys of coition, and tasted the first sweets of that most glorious weapon. My dear Charlie, I must contemplate its beauties in this full light; withdraw the dear fellow and turn on your back.'

I did so. She rose, and turning in the reverse position, brought her lovely foaming cunt right down on my mouth. I sucked up all the delicious foam oozing from the aperture. Then drawing into my mouth her half-stiffened clitoris, which was then pendant like a little boy's cock, I soon sucked it into its utmost rigidity, frigging her rich pouting cunt with two fingers, the while. She, on her part, was not idle, first playing with my prick, covering and uncovering its head, which soon made it stand up in all of its glory. She was profuse and loud in its praises. Then getting too excited for mere admiration, she took it in her mouth and sucked it, and manipulated it with one hand, fingering my codpiece with the other. I then found her fingers were feeling and tickling my bottom-hole. She took her mouth from off my prick, and paused a moment; then again applied her finger to my fundament, and made it gently penetrate as far as it would go. The previous pause had evidently been for the purpose of moistening her finger with her saliva that it might slip in easily. I was delighted to find that she had come to this, but pretending ignorance, I stopped my proceedings to ask her what she was doing to my bottom, which could give me such exquisite delight.

'It is my finger, my dear Charles; my late husband was always delighted with my doing this, and used also to add greatly to my pleasure by doing the same to me.'

'Shall I do so to you, dear mamma?'

'Oh, yes, my darling boy; moisten your finger first and then do it in my bottom-hole, as you have been doing it in my cunt.'

'But I think I can do both at the same time, they are so close together.'

'You are a delightful darling; do so, and it will be double pleasure to me.'

So I immediately commenced to postilion her to her and my extreme gratification. We soon spent with the utmost delight, and both swallowed all we could get, continuing our suctions until the passions of both were again excited. I now declared I must fuck her again in the kneeling position, in which she had before given me such exquisite pleasure. As she drew a little higher up, I flung my arms round her fine backside, and glued my lips to her bottom-hole, and thrust my tongue in and out.

'Oh, Charles, dear, what are you doing? Oh! how delightful.'

And she wriggled her backside over my mouth in a most voluptuous and lascivious way.

'Oh, rise my darling, and fuck me; you have made me so very lewd.'

I drew myself up on my knees behind her, and was into her with a wild ferocity that made her cry out with joy as she felt the mighty instrument rush within her. I stooped and frigged her clitoris at her desire, but wishing to contemplate the glorious movement of her backside, I begged her to frig herself that I might be able to do so. Seizing hold of her hips, I drew her splendid bottom off and on my stiff and glowing prick with such immense delight to her that she went off and spent profusely, the hot stream bathing my delighted prick. But having already fucked Ellen so shortly before, and having spent twice at the present time, I remained for a while quiet, with mamma's exquisite cunt deliciously throbbing round it to the infinite enjoyment of my cock. I stooped and nibbled with my fingers at one of her nipples. I played with and frigged her very fine clitoris, which was soon in stiff-standing excitement again. Being cool myself, I soon worked her up into the wildest state of excitement by my frigging and the throbbings of my prick, aided with occasional long slowly drawn-out movements, and then as slowly regaining ground until within the last three inches, when it was thrust vigorously forward, and kept there for her convulsive pressures on it. I kept this up until she was almost wild with lust, and cried out for more vigorous movements. I did not immediately comply, but continued my exciting proceedings until she bit the pillow in the madness of her lust. Then I drove on fast and furious, amid cries of delight and ecstasy on her part, until the grand crisis overtook us both at the same instant in a perfect fury and agony of delight. I had previously left the frigging to her, and had seized her hips and enjoyed the glorious sight of the furious contortions of her bottom under the excessive lubricity of her wildly excited lasciviousness. She died away in such excess of ecstasy that she would have fallen on her belly but for the grip I had upon her hips, and the pressure with which I drew back her glorious bottom against my belly. I threw back my head in the agony of delight, and brayed like a donkey as I had done once before when fucking the luscious Frankland, and felt the three pointed entrance to her womb close upon and nibble at the point of my prick so delightfully, just as dear Ellen's had done in the wood. As I came to my senses I spoke to dear mamma, and found that she too had fainted away, and was quite insensible to everything but the convulsive inner movements of her delicious cunt. I withdrew and laid her gently down on her side; bringing a tumbler of water, a sponge and towel, I opened her splendid thighs and sponged and bathed her cunt, which showed but little trace of the torrent of sperm I had just poured into it. I then sprinkled her face, and she came to with a deep sigh. Her first utterance was to bless me for the joy I had given her, which was in fact too much, and then she burst into tears and became quite hysterical. I thought it odd that I should have produced the same effect upon her more accustomed and more developed organs as I had done on dear Ellen. I comforted her in my boyish way, and asked how it was that the effect should have been different from anything she had previously experienced with me.

'Ah! my dear boy,' she said, with a deep sigh, 'you have caused me such extreme sensations that I fear you must have got me with child; you seemed to penetrate my very womb, and to excite me far beyond anything I ever previously remember.'

'My loved mamma, can I possibly get a child?'

'Get a child, indeed!' she replied. 'Yes, a dozen, with such a great monster of a cock that so excites us poor women.'

I embraced her most tenderly, and said I was so happy to think I should be the father of a child of hers.

'Alas! my dear boy, it may be joy to you, but what a sorrow it will be to me if such should be the case; think how I should lose position in the world if it should be known, and even if by going abroad I could hide my shame from the public, still what shifts and contrivances I should be put to to ensure secrecy; but never mind, my darling, I would run twice such risk to enjoy your person, and secure your affection; you must ever cherish and love me, my Charlie, for I risk good name and fame for you; but now I must be gone, or we shall be sought for; try and sleep a little, my dear boy, for I am sure you need it after your exertions, and remember you must gain strength to renew them this night.'

She kissed me lovingly, rose, put on her things and left me to repose. But I could not help thinking of what she had said about fearing that that peculiar fuck in which she had fainted portended fructification. If so, I thought dear Ellen will probably be in the same predicament, for the result was precisely the same with her. I may here observe that mamma's fears became certainties, both in her case and Ellen's. Eventually they both left the country together, when staying would have brought on discovery. And, curiously enough, they were both delivered of daughters on the same day. Of both I was the happy father, although Harry had the credit of Ellen's child, but she herself always asserted to me that it was the delicious fuck in the wood that did the mischief. And from the peculiar effect produced on both mothers on that day, I never had any doubt of the real paternity; besides, the child grew up my very image. Mamma's daughter was superbly developed when she became a young woman. She had even a larger clitoris than Miss Frankland, with which she absolutely deflowered her sister-cousin at the age of fourteen. I may also incidentally observe that at the age of fifteen I had both their maidenheads, as far as the male sex was concerned. And Harry and I often fucked them together in every way; and my darling daughter with her long and large clitoris has often fucked my bottom, while I was doing the same to her sister, with Harry below fucking her whom he believed to be his daughter. But this belongs to my later experience and has nothing to do with the present period of my life, though, perhaps, I may be tempted hereafter to enter into all the details of my middle age and later experiences.

Dear reader, pardon me this digression. To resume, I slept soundly for an hour, then rose, and strolled in the garden with Harry, who related to me how he had taken advantage of mamma's occupation to steal into Ellen's room. She had been much afraid, the sly pussy, to allow him to enter again, but when once he got within and she found it did not hurt her, but on the contrary made her extremely lewd, they had two splendid fucks. Then stealing along to my door to peep as to how we were getting on, we so excited them again that he had another from behind, while she stooped and peeped all the time, for it was when I was fucking mamma from behind, on my knees, and they concluded it would be our last for the present. When they had brought matters to a finish they separated, and mamma had found Ellen fast asleep.

'But, by Jove, Charlie,' said Harry, 'how splendidly mother fucks. I quite envied you, and I shall never rest until I get into her myself; how gloriously she wriggles her backside, and how lusciously she enjoys fucking; to be sure such a mighty prick as yours is enough to stir up every passion; it astonished, and I think made Ellen more lewd, although she is sure she could never take in such a monster.'

I smiled at thinking how easily the very youngest of the fair sex deceives us, but I took care not to let Harry know my opinion.

We re-entered for dinner, and spent a pleasant evening, which was the forerunner to the delights of the night. Mamma came as soon as she thought Ellen fast asleep, which Ellen took very good care should soon be the case. In a moment, she was quite naked, and clasped to my equally naked body. I had been expecting her, and thinking over the delights of our last fuck, so that I was rampant before her arrival. She was equally eager for the fray, and at it we went hammer and tongs, and soon brought the first bout to a close, in mutual 'ah's!' and 'oh's!' of delight. We soaked for some time in the delicious enjoyment. Then mamma scolded both herself and me for our precipitation, saying that we threw away all the luxury and abandon of fucking when we went at it in such haste; it was in that way mere animal instinct, and wanted all the lascivious delight of lubricity and skill in fucking. She said, now that the edge was taken off our appetites, we must begin again with a mutual gama-huche. She rose first to piddle, and allowed me to see the rush of water from her delicious cunt. Then lighting two more candles, she placed two at the foot of the bed, and two at the head, by which we should both have the advantage of seeing all we were caressing. Then I lay down on my back, and she mounted on me, in reverse, thus bringing her bottom down over my face. I thrust my tongue up her cunt, and licked up the delicious spunk oozing down from the inside. Her piddle had washed all away from the pouting lips. Then taking her charming clitoris in my mouth, I sucked it up to its greatest stiffness. I had thrust three fingers into her cunt, and when I found she had thrust hers into my bottom, I transferred them all into her beautiful pink bum-hole. They were very greasy from my sperm coming down upon them when in her cunt, and as she favoured their entrance by pushing out her bottom, all three slipped in, without, apparently, her thinking it was more than one. I was delighted to see how easily it stretched out, for this gave me great ground to hope that I should be able to manage to get my large pego within, which I was fully resolved upon doing, but it required a little artfulness to do so without raising her suspicions that it was no new road to me. She brought matters to a conclusion much as before, and when re-excited, mamma proposed to teach me a new way, which was by her mounting on me, and staking herself on my standing pego. Like others before her, she did not stoop down upon me until she had made herself spend where she was, while I saved myself for further fucking.

When she died off, she sank on my bosom. I clasped her waist with one arm, sucked the bubby nearest my mouth, and reaching round my other arm, I brought my hand over her bottom to the delightful orifice, first moistening my finger with her spending which was oozing out between the lips of her cunt and my standing prick. I thrust my finger into her bottom-hole, and worked it in and out, to her infinite satisfaction. She cried out in the excess of her lewdness: 'Oh! my dear boy, that is just as my dear husband used to do, and it gave me great pleasure, but not near so much as you do, for your dear prick is twice as large as his was, and fills me with an excess of pleasure which was never approached with him.'

All this led up to a superb and lascivious fuck, in which we both died away in mutual ecstasy, with cries of voluptuousness, and then lay soaking in delight until her weight forced me to beg her to turn on her side. We then had a long sweet chat of love. Turning the talk on her suspicions of my having got her with child at the morning prayers, I remarked that she had had only one child by her husband, and as he had lived many years after Harry's birth and, from what she said, she had continued to be enjoyed by him, it was, therefore, not probable she would now be in the family-way.

'That appears probable, my dear boy, but then he took precautions not to get any more children.'

'But what precautions could he take, and how did he do so?'

'You are a curious boy, but I shall tell you. He used to continue long at it, making me spend two or three times before he did, and then when he felt it coming he used to withdraw, and his prick being all moist, he would slip it into my bottom, and spend there as soon as ever he got the head of it inside.'

'And did that give you any pleasure, mamma?'

'He had excited me, and made me spend several times before he did so; beyond slight irritation I did not feel much pleasure, as he was generally so near the crisis that he could scarce do more than get its head in before off he went.'

'Did he ever get it in altogether – and then did it give you pleasure?'

'Sometimes he did when he had drawn it out of my cunt too soon; in such cases he used to pause until by rubbing my clitoris he got me into a renewed state of lewdness, and then the pleasure was peculiar and great.'

'Oh, my dear, mamma, you must let me too fuck you in that way, and then you know we shall get no children.'

'My darling Charlie, it is impossible that this great big thing could ever get into that orifice; my late husband's was not half your size, and he had great difficulty unless I had already spent three or four times and relaxed all those parts. I should not dare to let you attempt it.'

'Oh, yes my darling mamma, you will let me just get its point in and spend there. I should so like to try. We will fuck two or three times first, and then after the third time I shall frig you till you spend first; and so I shall be ready just to put in the point for you to try how it feels.'

'But, my dear boy, the least throb on my part will push it out, unless it is in over the nut, and only look what a size it is. I can hardly grasp it, and although it is so velvety it is quite hard. Oh, the dear fellow, let me kiss it, and then do you fuck me again, my darling.'

She bent her body, gave me a delicious suck, then throwing herself on her back and opening her beautiful thighs, invited me to mount her. Before doing so I also bent and sucked her charming and well-developed clitoris, until she squealed again with pleasure, and begged me to put it into her. I threw myself on her belly, and with one vigorous shove drove my rampant prick up to the hilt, making her all shake again. She was so hotly wound up that she spent with the single shove, and poured a flood of hot liquid over my delighted prick. I, too, would have gone off in two more thrusts had she not thrown her arms and legs around me, and slipping her hands over my buttocks, held me tight pressed against the pouting and greedy lips of her salacious cunt as if she would shove in bollocks, buttocks and all, if it were possible. So keeping it tightly thrust in up to the lowest hair, which lay all crushed between us, I let her indulge in all the delight of perfect conjunction, responding to her delicious throbbing cunt with powerful throbs of my own highly excited prick. For more than a quarter of an hour did she lie panting and convulsively sobbing in the perfect ecstasy of enjoyment. At last she drew my mouth down to hers, and thrust her sweet tongue into my mouth; I sucked it, and her hands relaxing the pressure of my buttocks against her cunt, I began a slow in and out movement that soon renewed her utmost lubricity. Most actively and divinely did she second me with an art quite her own. Fast and furious grew our movements, until, like all things human, they came to an end in a death-like agony of delight, in which my very soul seemed to take flight, and we lay all unconscious for I don't know how long, enjoying all those exquisite after-delights which a prick soaking in the cunt of a beautiful and lewd woman so enchantingly confers. When we recovered, we rolled over sideways, and still intertwined and conjoined in the sweet priapic bonds, we lay billing and cooing with all those soft loving murmurings and bitings so befitting such moments. At last, both were again ready and longing for the fight. I proposed the delicious kneeling position. She saw at once my object, and said I was a little traitor, who wanted to surprise her bottom-hole.

'But, my darling boy, it is really impossible.'

I embraced, flattered, cajoled, and implored her until at last she promised that if I would engage on honour not to go further, she would try and support the entrance of my prick as far as over the nut, but that I must really withdraw it if it was too painful for her. So these preliminaries being arranged, she got into position. First stooping to lick out her delicious cunt, and give a suck or two at her charming clitoris, I brought my eager prick to the pouting and longing lips of her delicious cunt, and after two or three rubs, thrust it in with a rush that made my belly smack against her glorious backside. We then lay quiet, throbbing mutually in the luxury of voluptuousness. I passed a hand under her belly, and frigging her clitoris quickly, made her come in an ecstasy of delight. I only gave her time for one or two throbs of my prick, and knowing that nothing so much delights a lecherous woman as quick movements almost immediately after spending I commenced a rapid series of thrusts, shoving my prick well up to the hilt every time, and talking grossly all the while, such as: 'Does not that shove make you quiver? There you have it to the bollocks in your lascivious and delicious cunt,' etc.

She grew madly lewd, called me her own dear delightful fucker.

'Yes, yes; I feel it is up to the root. I have it well in, my dear boy. Your dear, great big prick, it kills me – kills – kills me – with – joy. Oh! oh! oh!'

She squealed again with all the lewdness of the most delicious spend. She had hardly gone off, and was yet in all the throes of delight when I, too, feeling I could hold out no longer, suddenly withdrew the reeking shaft, and bringing it to bear against the corrugated and beautiful orifice of her bottom, attempted to introduce it. Notwithstanding the fury of my excitement, I was sufficiently gentle to push in without force, and sheathed it over the nut without difficulty or drawing a murmur from dear mamma, who fulfilled her promise, and did her utmost to help me by pushing out her big bum, and offering no resistance with her sphincter muscles. I was so highly wound up that even if I had not promised to be content with the insertion of the head, I could not have gone on further, as the access seized me with such killing sweetness that I melted away, shooting a torrent of sperm far up into her entrails, and then losing all power of even the slightest further thrust. I suppose it was the long holding back to let mamma spend two or three times that had wrought me up to such a high pitch of nervous excitement that when I spent I seemed to lose all power of further advance. This was the first time I ever felt this momentary impuissance, but it was by no means the last; it generally follows the holding back of your spending powers in the fuck that leads to it. The delicious throbbings of dear mamma's luscious cunt, which were repeated in her arse, soon reawakened my momentarily dormant powers. My prick had gone down more than usual, so that it was only a soft half-stiffness that ensued, but enough to enable me to give it a forward movement, and it slipped almost imperceptibly in quite as far as it could go before dear mamma had recovered from the ecstasy of her last discharge. As she came to, I continued convulsively catching my breath, as if I were still in that exquisite sensation of half consciousness. I felt her pass her hand between her thighs, and heard her murmur: 'Why, I declare he is up to the hilt!'

Her gentle touch on my cods, which she took in her hand and fondly caressed, made my prick stiffen sensibly. She felt this, and caressed them more until she made it stand as stiff as ever, still embedded to the utmost in that delicious bottom, which by its increased throbbings, seemed rather to welcome the stranger than repulse him. I pretended now to recover my full consciousness, and cried out: 'Oh, where am I? I have never known such heavenly joy.'

She raised her face up from the pillow: 'Why, you naughty boy, you have actually gone in up to the hilt; ah, you have broken your promise; but I forgive you, only don't move yet.'

I assured her I did not know how it got there, as I had spent and lost consciousness as soon as ever his head was within.

Here I throbbed, and was met by as delicious a pressure. I passed my hand round her belly, and found her clitoris stiff and excited. I rubbed with the fingers of the other hand at one of her hard projecting nipples. She soon grew madly lewd, and began a side-wriggle on my rampant prick. I lay still, determined to let her passions demand movement of my part. I had not to wait long. She begged me to try a gentle movement; I obeyed, and slowly withdrew but a short way, and as slowly returned. Soon her lubricity got beyond all bounds. She begged me to draw out further and somewhat quicker – then quicker and quicker, until we both were in an excess of furious lust, which knew no bounds. We rushed on to the final crisis with mutual cries of agonised delight; indeed, mamma squealed so loud that I afterwards thought she must have been heard. Her pleasure was of the wildest, and when I poured a flood of sperm up her entrails at the very moment she herself was spending, we both fell forward and fainted away. I was too much lost in ecstatic joy myself to observe this, but lay long a tightly held prisoner engulfed in that most exquisite joy-giving aperture. At last I became aware that mamma had really fainted. So drawing my prick out with somewhat of a good pull, for he was most tightly held, and came out with a flop, I rose and brought some water to mamma. I sprinkled her face, and she opened her eyes, which beamed the intensest love upon me. Her lips murmured something, I put the tumbler to her mouth, she drank with avidity. Then looking at me again with the most loving expression, she said: 'My darling boy, you will kill me with delight. Never – oh, never – have I known such joy. It was too much for me, and I fear I am also injuring you. We must be more moderate in future. Help me up, for I must rise. Your last *coup* requires me to absent myself for a few minutes.'

She rose, threw her robe over her shoulders, and left the room to go to the water closet. I hoped that she would not go into her own room and discover how matters were going on there. Fortunately she was afraid of awakening Ellen and so prevent our continuing bedfellows for the rest of the night. She returned. I had purified myself in the meantime, and now acted as her *femme de chambre*, and laved all the parts.

'My dear boy, we must not do this again for some time, do you know I have passed blood, and was very sore when relieving myself.'

We got again into bed. She would not allow of any further fuckings, but tenderly embracing me, and putting my head on her bosom, she soon fell asleep. She awoke me at dawn with kissing me and feeling my stiff-standing pego. She laid herself on her back, and we had two most delicious fucks without withdrawing. I knew that if I did withdraw she would take herself off. Nevertheless, she took most kindly to the second, as it would be our last until we had another opportunity of meeting. She exerted all her wonderful skill and her movements were of astounding agility. She twined herself round me almost serpent-like. Our mouths and tongues were equally engaged, and the final crisis was beyond description exquisite. I tried hard for a third course, but we had already prolonged our sports to so dangerous an hour, for we could hear them opening the lower window shutters, that she gave me a sweet kiss of thanks and tore herself away. I lay thinking over the joys of that ecstatic night, and then rose and dressed quickly, as we were to breakfast and then walk home, where we were expected at nine o'clock. However, after breakfast, mamma drew me into her sanctum, a house store-room, to give me some directions.

Of course, no sooner was she there, than pushing her towards the table, I canted up her petticoats over her back and gave her a good fuck, getting in from behind. She yielded with a good grace, notwithstanding her protestations that it was not for that she had come, as if it had been for anything else! Oh! woman, woman! how thou seekest to deceive, even when gaining the very object thou hast in view.

Harry told me they had peeped in and seen what we were at but he was not so ready as me, and had not been able to go and do likewise.

We loitered all too long, and did not get back to school until after ten o'clock. The doctor sternly ordered us to attend him in his sanctum at twelve o'clock. We knew what that meant – a good flogging, and then the doctor enjoying the account of our successes. At twelve o'clock we entered the doctor's room, and he followed us immediately after. He scolded us sternly for being late, and said he meant to flog us both well for our idleness and, he had no doubt, debauchery. We knew immediately that he meant to lay on. From time to time he was fond of really seriously flogging someone and we now saw that such was his present intention, although we also knew it would end in an orgy, after we had excited him sufficiently by recounting the details of the fucking which he no doubt felt certain had taken place. He made us all strip, and choosing to take Harry first he made me the horse to flog him on. When all was ready, he began by some real sharp cuts on Harry's backside, and then commenced his remarks.

'So, young gentleman, you have been seducing your cousin, have you?' –
whack – whack – whack – 'And then making that the excuse for neglecting
your school.' Whack, whack, whack. 'I thought I had formerly whipped out
all idea about fucking your cousin.' Whack, whack, whack.

Poor Harry writhed in real pain.

'Oh, sir, I'll never do it again without your leave.'

'My leave indeed!' Whack, whack, whack.

The doctor now laid on for some time most unmercifully until the
revolution of pain turned to lubricity, and Harry's cock began to stand,
rapping fiercely at my bottom as he writhed under the sharp infliction of the
rod. Upon seeing the expected effect, the doctor relaxed his severity, and
changing the rod to his other hand, afterwards only tickled the bottom to
keep up the excitement. Taking hold of the standing prick, he said: 'So this is
the article that has been doing all the mischief.'

He frigged it a little, stooped and gave it a suck.

'Ah, yes, I find it still tastes of cunt, and smells the true odour of it; so you
have been at it this morning again. Let me hear how it happened.'

Here Harry was let go. The doctor seated himself, Harry stood before
him, while the doctor in delight, handled his stiff-standing pego.

'Now, let me hear.

'Well, sir, when Charlie occupied mamma –'

'Oh, that is it, is it?' cried the doctor, 'we shall have all that out of him, by
and by; go on.'

'I slipped into Ellen. She made some difficulty for fear mamma should
catch us; but I took her and showed her through the keyhole, how she was
having Charlie into her. Ellen was astonished at Charlie's immense size, and
seeing how easily and delightedly mamma accommodated him, she thought
that my smaller size could not hurt her, and she let me do it. But I made her
scream and bleed when I got in far enough to reach her maidenhead. She
tried to shake me off, but I was too firmly seated for that, and I fucked her
then, and again before I withdrew. I laved her cunt and applied some
glycerine, and this morning did it again without hurting her any more. And
she liked it so much that afterwards she would kiss and suck it, and made me
spend in her mouth, and then got me up again for a final go.'

'Upon my honour, a very pretty affair,' cried the doctor. 'Now suck my
prick, as she sucked yours.'

This Harry did, till the doctor was rampant. He then made him cease, but
ordered me to mount on Harry's back. I knew I should catch it sharp, as the
doctor was just excited enough to wish to be more so. And preciously he
gave it me – interpolating questions as to how I had accomplished my
wicked ends. I told him it was his own advice to me to let her see my prick,
which I did, and the bait took. Whack – whack – whack.

'And did you act this innocent sin?'

'Oh, yes! do spare me, sir, and don't lay on so hard.'

Whack – whack – whack

'Spare you, indeed! and how did she fuck?'

'Oh, most splendidly, sir.'

Whack – whack – whack.

'How often did you do it?'

'I hardly know, sir; we were at it all night, and again this morning.'

'Did she suck your prick?'

'Oh, yes, sir.'

Whack – whack – whack.

'What did she think of it?'

'She said it was the finest she had ever seen, and that I must keep it for her only.'

'Well, that will do; now suck my prick, as she did yours.'

He was soon excited up to the top of his bent. He made Harry take the rod, and belabour his backside, and I had to stoop over the table, while he fucked and frigged me, repeating all the time the account we had given him of our fucking. After he spent, he dismissed us, having gained his object.

\* \* \*

Shortly before our Christmas holidays commenced, dear Mrs Dale informed me, while I was sleeping with her one Saturday night, that she found from the stoppage of certain things, she was in the family-way by this sad rogue of a fellow, taking my large though at the time soft and inert instrument into her caressing hand.

'Oh, my darling mamma, is it so indeed?'

My prick rose to bursting point at the very idea, and in an instant I was on her, and we ran a most delicious course, in which both died away in rapturous insensibility. Being thus cooled, mamma began to discuss the probabilities, and what ought to be done, if it should turn out as she feared. She explained to me that as yet she could not speak with certainty, but remembering the fainting on the first night, and the cessation of her monthlies, the nature of which she explained to me, little dreaming that I was perfectly *au fait* with the whole matter, she had every reason to dread that her fears where too well founded. This would make it necessary for her to go abroad, when she would be so far advanced as to be likely to draw observation. But she said it would not do to distress ourselves about that until we were more certain of the event. However, the very idea nerved me to renewed efforts, and again, and again, we rushed into all the ecstasies of passion in every form and way; especially did I gamahuche and suck up her precious balm, and in like manner she, too, sucked me until exhausted nature laid us both in the lap of Morpheus. We renewed our delightful pastimes when morning light awoke us after our refreshing slumbers. Several times during the Sunday we adjourned to mamma's bedroom for the same purpose, and again had a glorious night of it before separating on the

Monday morning. The following Sunday, after another Saturday night of
bliss, we all went over to church, which heavy rain had prevented on the
previous week, and after service went to the rectory for luncheon. Here, in
course of conversation, Mrs Dale mentioned that business would require her
presence in London for some days, and that she proposed starting on
the following Thursday, which was the day after our breaking up for the
holidays. She said also that she would take her son with her to London. The
doctor here observed that he, too, must go to London, to see a gentleman
who had some idea of sending his son to the rectory, and if Mrs Dale could
defer the departure until Saturday, it would be very agreeable to him to be
her companion on the journey. This was readily acceded to, and my dear
aunt, who guessed to what this tended, and who had herself taken a great
fancy to Ellen, and longed to embrace her young charms and gamahuche
her, chimed in with a proposal that as the dear girl would thus be left quite
alone, she would be most happy if she would accept her invitation to occupy
the bedroom that opened out of her own room during Mrs Dale's absence.
The latter, who little dreamt of my connection with her dear niece, and
thought that the protection of my aunt would be a safeguard to her, jumped
at the invitation, and expressed her gratification and thanks for so kind a
consideration on my aunt's part. I have not alluded to Harry all this time, but
of course, whenever his mother and I were occupied in amorous alliance, he
was equally engaged in the same delicious pastime with Ellen. And, I may
add, that once or twice I had seized a favourable opportunity of gratifying
the little lecherous creature with what she called a feast of my noble prick.
She, of course, was delighted at my aunt's proposition as she at once foresaw
how she would have me all to herself for more than a week. A single glance
from her explained all this; and when, on leaving, she found an opportunity
of taking my hand, her pressure of it was most eloquent. So all parties were
delighted, for Harry, when we got together alone said – 'By Jove, Charlie, I
am so jolly glad; I'll bet you anything I'll fuck my mother before I come
back. You know how I long to be in the delicious cunt that bore me; the
moment I heard she meant to take me with her, my cock stood ready to
burst.'

My uncle, too, who also longed to fuck Mrs Dale, had his intentions in
that direction favoured by the arrangement concluded. The following night,
when I was in bed with aunt and him, in the interval of a charming little
orgy, and after he had fucked me while I was in aunt's bottom and for the
moment could do no more, the conversation turned on the coming journey.
He expressed the pleasure he felt at the opportunity it gave him of indulging
in a long desired object. The lecherous old fellow also alluded to a future
opportunity it would give him of enjoying the younger charms of the niece.

'Of course, you and my dear wife between you will break her in to allow of
any action on my part; and, by the way, my dear, I would suggest that you
should surprise Charlie in the act, and tear them asunder in pretended rage –

that Charlie should seize you, and say he would make you by force a participator in the act, on the pretence of shutting you up for finding fault: you must break from his arms, and fly to your own bed, he must catch you as you try to enter it, and push his great big cock into you, on which you must cry for help, and call upon Ellen to come to your succour; she will come, but I do not judge her right if she will not rather assist Charlie, by holding you, than otherwise. You must afterwards appear much offended; but it may be safely left to the influence of Charlie's great prick to reconcile you to the incest, then relaxing, as if gained over by it, you can join in their sports.'

Thus this admirable man, with his great knowledge of the world and sex, gave us excellent advice, which, as I shall state in the sequel, we followed pretty exactly. Meanwhile aunt, excited by expectation, had taken my prick in her mouth, and sucked it into firmness, then mounting upon me, she began such an exciting action, wriggling her magnificent backside, that it fired my uncle anew. Finding his prick stood sufficiently stiff, he knelt between my legs, and greatly to the satisfaction of my darling aunt, gave her the double pleasure of two pricks fucking her at the same time, one before and the other behind.

My guardian had desired that I should continue with my uncle during the holidays, and I was to leave him altogether at the end of the next half. I did not know his object at the time, but I found that he himself went down to my mother, and stayed for a fortnight, paying great attention to Miss Frankland. He announced his wish that my sisters should go to a first-rate finishing school in London in the summer, and seeing Miss Frankland look somewhat disappointed, he sought an interview with her, and laid himself and his fortune at her feet; expressing a wish that if she accepted him, their marriage should take place on her separation from her pupils. This was too good an offer to be refused, and after the usual grimace of being perfectly unprepared for such a proposal, and desiring to have a day or two to consider it, she accepted the offer. I at once anticipated immense gratification from this connection. I should naturally, when in London, have every opportunity of enjoying that adorable creature, and it will be seen in the fourth chapter of these memoirs, to what delicious orgies this connection led. You may be sure that my loved mistress, the adorable Benson, and the no less lascivious Egerton, welcomed so glorious a creature as Miss Frankland, at that time become Mrs Nixon, and how the Count's eyes glistened when he beheld her in all the majesty of her superb and hairy form; how the two women gamahuched her splendid clitoris, and how the Count and I strove which should most fully satisfy her lascivious and lustful passions. But all this will be seen in its proper place in the sequel.

Meanwhile the day arrived for the departure of uncle and Mrs Dale, with Harry. As the coach passed through our village, Mrs Dale drove over bringing Ellen with her, to leave her at the rectory, as arranged. All the proprieties were duly observed. They departed, Harry going outside, with only the doctor and Mrs Dale in the interior. I squeezed my uncle's hand, and gave him a knowing look, which he returned, with a meaning wink – and off they went. When we returned to the house, my aunt took Ellen up to the room adjoining her own, with which there was a door of communication which, I have before observed, had been made use of by my uncle on more than one occasion. When they came downstairs, with kind consideration, for she could see by the protrusion in my trousers the state I was in, aunt said: 'My dear, I have some household duties to arrange, so you must excuse me; meanwhile Charlie will show you our grounds, and amuse you for an hour or two. When luncheon is ready I shall order the large bell to be rung for you.'

Ellen had not yet removed her bonnet, and taking up her shawl, we sallied out. You may be sure we lost no time in reaching the summerhouse, already known to you as arranged for and dedicated to the service of Venus. A fire was always kept laid, which I immediately lighted, but as it was a bright sunny day, and the place looked south, it was not at all cold. While I was occupied at the fire, Ellen threw off her bonnet and shawl, and undid her belt – she wore no stays. I seized her in my arms, and gently laid her on the couch – her petticoats were freely canted up, showing her beautiful belly and now more fully fledged cunt. I stooped and gamahuched her at once. She was so excited that in two minutes she sighed deeply, pressed my head down to the lips of her cunt, and gave down her sweet and balmy sperm. I myself was already so rampant that not waiting to lick it up, I brought my huge pego to the charming orifice, and plunged in one effort up to the hilt, quite taking away her breath. But she recovered herself in an instant, and with all the energy of her younger lubricity, quickly brought us both to the grand final ecstasy, in which soul and body seem to die away in a joy too great for poor humanity to bear. We remained locked in each other's embrace, and lost to all around for some time. On our coming to our senses I rose, and said we must go to work more lasciviously the next time. The fire having burnt up, and the room being small, it was already of a pleasant temperature. So begging Ellen to strip, I threw off my own clothes, and we quickly stood in all the beauty of nature, admiring each other. Some delicious preliminaries preceded our next encounter which we procrastinated over till passion could no longer be restrained, and again we died away in all the raptures of satisfied lust, and sank once more into the soft languor of the after-enjoyment. Next we had a mutual gamahuche, and then a final fuck for the present, as it was time to dress and be ready when called to luncheon. As soon as our toilets were finished, I took her on my knee, and told her how I should steal along to her bedroom at night, so that she must not lock her door. I told her also that we must be as quiet as possible, as aunt slept in the next room. She was delighted with the prospect of having me all to herself for the whole night, naïvely telling me that I gave her so much more pleasure than Harry did, that I seemed to fill her whole body with a joy almost too intense, and now that she was to have me every night, she hoped her aunt would stay away for a month. Here the dear creature threw her arms round my neck, and kissing me, thrust her sweet little tongue into my mouth. You may be sure I reciprocated, and putting a hand up her petticoats, and a finger up her charming little cunt, was just about to turn her on the sofa, when my aunt opened the door, and stopped further proceedings. She pretended not to see Ellen's confusion, hoped I had amused her, and told us to return to the house, as luncheon was ready. We, of course, obeyed. With sharpened appetites, produced by our late warm exercise, we indulged in a plenteous meal, aunt taking care to ply me with champagne, in which, as may well be imagined, she had her object. She afterwards ordered me to my room, to do the daily task the doctor had set for me, and which, as she said, she was to see to the doing of – giving me a sly wink.

'Ellen, my dear,' she added, 'you must keep up your practice at the piano daily, for an hour and a half at least.'

She thus separated us. I went to my room, lay down, and fell fast asleep, but in about half an hour, was awakened by the warm embrace of my glorious and wantonly lustful aunt. She stooped down, and taking my limp prick in her mouth, rapidly sucked it into its accustomed firmness. As soon as that was accomplished, she begged me to rise and undress. She herself had come only in a loose morning dressing-gown, which she instantly threw off, and jumped on my bed, where she lay stark naked, in all the splendid development of her superb form. I was naked in a jiffy, but knowing she would want some extensive fucking, I threw myself upon her cunt, and gamahuched her until she spent twice before I mounted upon her, and introduced my large tool into her longing cunt. Here, also, I played with her, and did not spend myself until she had twice given down her own contribution. This encounter was on her belly, with her magnificent legs twisted above my loins for a fulcrum to her splendid action, for few women could equal her in the delicious wriggle of her glorious backside. After we had soaked for some time in all the ecstasies of the after-languor, I withdrew, to place her on her hands and knees for the next bout, but took advantage of her position to gamahuche her again into spending twice before I withdrew my insidious tongue. Then turning round, and gazing in rapture on that most noble and massive bottom, which, as I have before remarked, I never saw equalled by any woman, I stooped, and closely embraced and kissed its divine orifice, tickling her into wild excitement by thrusting my tongue therein, so much so that she begged me to fuck her at once. I mounted behind, her hand passed under her belly and guided me into her throbbing hot and longing cunt. I gave one violent lunge, and sent my prick at the first thrust up to the hilt. This so excited the dear creature that in one or two delicious wriggles on my stationary prick, and with a pressure that seemed as if it would nip it off, she spent profusely, squealing all the time like a rabbit. I was very glad to give her so many discharges, without myself being forced to

spend, for I wished to be able to do my duty by Ellen at night. Aunt lay for
several minutes panting and throbbing on my prick most deliciously, until I
could no longer bear to be inactive, although the pleasure of looking down
on the glorious and palpitating orbs below me had given me the greatest
satisfaction. But now, stooping down upon her, I passed one hand under to
excite her clitoris, and with the other took hold of one of her beautiful large
and hard bubbies and began manipulating its nipple – a proceeding most
powerfully exciting to dear auntie. It awoke all her lust and the dear
lascivious creature again spent before I was ready to follow suit. The pause
that followed allowed my excitement to subside a little, and enabled me to
hold out until her lust recovered its wonted energy. She again, with her
pressures and movements, soon compelled me to more rapid action, but this
time I determined to enjoy the exquisite delights of her delicious bottom-
hole. So when she became very hot, I suddenly withdrew, and, happily
hitting at once on the delicious orifice, plunged at the first thrust up to the
cods, taking dear aunt's breath away, but she instantly recovered, and as she
loved sodomy to her heart's core, I could not have done anything better
suited to her libidinous passions. It was glorious to see the energy with which
she met and responded to my thrusts, her superb buttocks working with
surprising energy, and giving me, at each stroke, when I buried my prick to
the hilt, the most exciting pressures. Both being so lustfully excited, matters
were not long in coming to the final ecstasy. I felt as if my whole soul was
poured into her when, with loud cries of the liveliest enjoyment, I spent with
fury, in the very heart of her entrails. She was perfectly overcome with
delight, and sank senseless on her belly, dragging me down with her, for the
grip of her sphincter was too strong to let anything out that was within. We
both became insensible to everything but the delicious death-like languor of
the after-enjoyment. We lay long in this trance of joy, and when dear auntie
came to her senses, she begged me to rise, as she must go downstairs. I did
so, and when she rose from the bed, she took me in her loving arms, and
kissing me tenderly, thanked me for the enormous pleasure I had given her,
and said no one in the world was my equal, and that I ought to thank her
much that she allowed anyone else to participate in my exquisite power of
fuck. She gathered up her gown, and left me to dress. I soon was downstairs,
and found Ellen, who looked as if she expected me to find an opportunity to
fuck her at once. But after the encounters I had already had, both with her
and with aunt, though I had kept myself from excess with the latter, I felt no
inclination to press matters again to a conclusion, especially seeing that I
intended passing the night with her So assuring her we should be likely to be
caught if imprudent and so lose all chance of nightwork, she was satisfied to
be quiet and reasonable. Aunt coming in, we spent the afternoon in pleasant
conversation, and a walk together in the garden. After dinner I fell sound
asleep on the sofa. The two women, each with the same object, left me to my
deep repose, and only awoke me when it was time for all to retire. Thus

refreshed, I was all ready for the night's work before me. I allowed half an hour to elapse, that all the house might be in their bedrooms, and then, with merely a loose dressing-gown on, I stole along to dear Ellen's room, opened the door and entered. She was already in bed, impatient for my arrival; she had left both lights burning and there was a cheerful blaze from a good fire. I dropped my robe, and was in an instant stark naked and in her longing arms. Under our mutual impatience, our first was a rapid course. Then followed a long enjoyment of the after-languor, and then a more prolonged and rapturous embrace. After soaking in bliss for some time, we rose, and I posed her before the fire, gazing delightedly on all her young charms. The hair on her cunt had become much more developed than before, her bosom too was filled out, even her hips and bottom seemed enlarged, doubtless owing to the fucking she had had since I first knew her, which had naturally hastened her ripening into womanhood. I grew very excited by this inspection of her increasing charms, and determined to have a fuck on the rug before the fire. In order to enjoy it the more, I drew forward a cheval glass, projected it forward, and lying down, directed her to move it until I was satisfied I could see all the play of her bottom in the position I meant to fuck her. So lying down on my back, I made her stride across my head and settle down on her knees, and bringing forward her delicious little cunt over my mouth, I gamahuched her until she had twice given down her balmy essence. Then she shifted her position lower down, until just above my prick, which by this time was rampant with desire. I guided its point to the rosy-lipped orbit, and bringing her own weight to bear upon it, she sank, delightfully impaled upon the upright stake. I made her rise and fall a few times, that I might enjoy the sight of its entrance and exit. Then gently drawing her down upon me, I folded one arm round her slender waist, and turning my head, found that the cheval glass, inclined forward, reflected as it were from above her beautiful bottom and back, and of course her cunt stretched to the utmost with my huge prick, and above it the sweet little corrugated pink aperture of her bottom. With my free arm I embraced one hip, and bringing my hand round, moistened it with the plenteous spunk of her cunt, and insinuated a finger into the smaller abode of bliss. Her excitement grew furious, and knew no bounds. The action of her backside was glorious to see reflected in its active risings and fallings. I let her do all the work, which enabled me to hold back my own, until she approached a second discharge, when the heat of her cunt seemed to fire me with additional powers, and the action of both our backsides became fast and furious, and soon brought down the ecstatic discharge, which instantly laid us low, panting with all the wild passions we had just allayed. We lay long locked in each other's arms in the ecstasy of blissful enjoyment. Then rising, we embraced tenderly, and retook us to bed. I would have excited her and myself to another effort, but she begged off, saying that she felt quite exhausted and overcome with the day and night's work we had already enjoyed. Indeed, I did not wonder at it, for I had made her spend seven or eight times more than myself. Nor did I regret her resolution, as I knew the morning would bring my aunt into the field, and then the two would try my powers to the utmost.

We slept profoundly, and morning was already advanced before we awoke. From a displaced chair I saw that aunt had been in to look at us, so I knew she was on the watch. I threw the clothes off dear Ellen that I might gaze on all her young charms. The want of covering awoke her. She lovingly looked up at me, and throwing her arms round my neck as I bent over her, drew my head down to hers, and impressed a loving kiss on my lips. Our tongues interlaced – a hand slipped down and encircled my rampant and throbbing prick. I turned, and placing my knees between her legs, was about to penetrate love's bower when the door leading to my aunt's room flew open. My aunt entered, gave a scream of surprise – well acted – and cried out: 'Good gracious! What do I see? Who would have thought it – '

And, apparently to save Ellen, she rushed forward, seized me by the arm, and with a certain degree of cooperation my part, drew me out of bed, saying: 'I am horrified beyond measure. How dare you commit such a sin and crime as to seduce a young girl under my care? Cover yourself up, sir, directly, and go to your own room.'

I boldly declared I would do no such thing; on the contrary, as she had spoiled my sport with Ellen, I was determined she should pay for it herself.

'How dare you talk to me, you dreadful boy?'

'Not dreadful at all, dear aunt, look at this poor dumb thing and see how he longs to be into you.'

Upon this I seized her in my arms as if to throw her on the bed. She made a pretended struggle, during which she gave a tender squeeze to my rampant prick. Then, breaking from me, she fled to her own room, pretending to endeavour to shut the door in my face but taking care to give way and hasten towards her bed. I caught hold of her as she bent forward as if to get into it, and canting up her chemise, the only article of dress she wore, I was into her longing and luscious cunt from behind up to the hilt in one thrust. She gave a subdued scream, and called to Ellen to come and prevent me from violating her. Ellen came, but wisely would only look on while I worked away manfully.

'Ellen, why don't you pull him away – he is ravishing me – and oh, horror! – committing incest.'

She pretended to struggle greatly, but cleverly did so to her own profit, by wriggling her backside so as to send me further up into her cunt.

'Oh, Ellen, Ellen, do help me.'

'Ah, no,' said Ellen, 'I shall let him do it, and then you cannot tell upon me.'

My aunt seemed greatly distressed at this, and actually managed to shed tears, then buried her face in the bed as if in despair, but all the time most actively seconding me. As the crisis drew near, she raised her head, and said:

'Heaven pardon me, this mere simple schoolboy is exciting me to such pleasure as I never before felt.'

She then gave way to all her lubricity, and we brought matters to a crisis in the utmost ecstasy of enjoyment. Aunt's head sank on the bed, while the rapturous inward pressures of her cunt soon began to raise my prick to its pristine vigour. She felt its throbs and responded to them, but no doubt thinking that an immediate repetition would betray our previous intimacy, she turned her face and body suddenly round, and completely unseated me, my prick coming out with a plop. She began again to weep (women can do so at pleasure) and to scold me for the dreadful crime I had committed; to do so to her was incest – here followed sob upon sob. I threw my arms round her neck, and kissing her tears away, laid all the blame on that rampant fellow – taking her hand and placing it on my still stiff prick. She drew her hand away quickly, but not before she had given it a gentle squeeze. She told me I was a dreadful boy, and that I must go away and leave her and Ellen to think over what could be done in such an awful dilemma.

Here Ellen came forward, and tenderly kissing her begged her not to send me away.

'I do so love him, dear madam, and I do so long to have him now – it was so exciting to see him having you, that I shall die if you don't let me have him now.'

'Dreadful! dreadful!' said aunt. 'Why, I thought I was just in time to save you.'

'Oh, no, he had slept with me all night, and has often had me before, but he was not the first who had me, so there was no violation nor seduction.'

'Then you must have seduced him, you wicked minx, for a more innocent boy never was known.'

Poor Ellen, confounded at the accusation, repelled it as untrue, and said she knew well enough who seduced me.

Aunt for the moment felt this as a home thrust, for be it remembered, she fancied she had had my maidenhead.

'What do you mean by that? I insist upon you speaking out.'

Ellen gave way and said it was Mrs Dale who first had me. 'She had accidentally seen how powerfully Charlie was armed, and then could not resist teaching him how to use his weapon. I saw them doing it, and hence I longed for it myself. Look, dear madam, what a noble one it is. I am sure, if you had known of it, you could not yourself have resisted having it; try it, try it once more, and I am sure you will forgive us, and share our joys.'

I seconded this good advice. Aunt seemed to be afraid of me, and jumped into bed. While she was on her hands and knees I also jumped up, and catching her round the waist, held her fast until I could also kneel behind her and bring my prick into play. With all her apparent attempt at resistance everything was done in such a way as to facilitate rather than prevent matters going forward. Of course I was in her in a moment, and then remained quiet for a few minutes to let her enjoy her inward pressures for which she was so famous. She had buried her head in the pillow, crying out: 'It is dreadful! – it is dreadful!'

Ellen came and leant over the bed embracing her, and telling her not to resist, but to take it in freely, and then she was sure it would give her the utmost pleasure.

'It is that which horrifies me, my dear, I never felt anything so exquisite in my life before; but then think of the sin – with my own nephew! it is quite an incestuous connection.'

'What does that matter, dear aunt? for I shall call you aunt too, you are so loveable and so beautiful. Oh, it was such a pleasure to see him doing it to you and you are so gloriously fine a woman, I longed to be a man to have you.'

She had embraced aunt's splendid bubbies, than which nothing could more please her, and now she begged to be allowed to suck one. Aunt gave way, and was delighted. She slipped the hand next to Ellen down to her charming cunt – Ellen opened her legs – Aunt's fingers began frigging her.

'Ah, my dear, how I loved to embrace my own sex at your age, our tongues acted instead of men, and I could still delight in a fine fresh one like this, it would almost reconcile me to what this bad wicked boy is doing.'

'Oh, that would be charming! – do let us do it at once. Charlie can withdraw for a moment while I get under you, and while you lick me I can excite you and see the glorious work above me.'

'You tempt me much, my dear girl, but what would your aunt say if she knew?'

'But she never will know,' said Ellen, who was all the time arranging herself on the bed.

Aunt moved aside to allow Ellen to get under her; Ellen begged aunt to throw off her chemise that both their bodies might be in close contact. Aunt was longing to do so, yet made some grimaces about it. She at length complied, and striding across Ellen, threw herself with avidity on the delicious young cunt below, and began to gamahuche her *à mort*. I instantly resumed my position. Ellen guided my prick into aunt's burning cunt, then frigged aunt's clitoris, and worked a finger in my fundament, while aunt was so delightfully gamahuching her. We all rapidly came to the grand finale, with an excess of lubricity rarely equalled. We were all somewhat exhausted by this bout, and, as it was getting late, we rose. Aunt pretended to forgive my violating her for the pleasure I afterwards afforded her. She embraced Ellen tenderly, and said she had so enjoyed her person she hoped to renew such a delight. Then taking hold of my prick she kissed it and sucked it until it stood upright, and said: 'I don't wonder, my dear, at your having it when once you had seen it, and I envy Mrs Dale the pleasure of having first enjoyed such a monstrous thing. If I had known he was so wondrously provided, I doubt if I could have resisted the temptation to teach him how to make use of it myself – my only wonder is how such a little thing as you have got could ever take it in.'

Ellen laughed, and said that her cousin Harry had opened the way, or she doubted if ever she could have admitted it, but I was so gentle while getting in, and when once in, it filled up every crevice so deliciously, that she should grieve much if she were refused access to it in future.

'So, dear aunt, I hope you will let him do it to us both. I can do to you what you have just done to me, because before we had him and Harry, aunt and I used to amuse ourselves in that way. Aunt is immense in that particular, she could put it a little way into me, and gave me great pleasure, and she said that I sucked it better than either her late husband or any of half a dozen schoolfellows who used to amuse each other; so, dear aunt, you must let me do it to you while Charlie is in me, and then you will do it to me while he is in you. Only fancy how nice it will be.'

'Oh, you dear little coaxer, you are enough to seduce an angel.'

So all was arranged that Ellen should come from her room and I from mine, and we should meet in aunt's bed at night. We did so meet, and a most glorious eight days we spent. I showed aunt that I could get into Ellen's bottom-hole, and thereby gave her immense pleasure, and with more reason the same result would occur with her. She gave an apparently reluctant consent, and, that done, there was no bridle to the utmost lubricity that the most wanton lust could devise. Aunt took immensely to Ellen, and gamahuched her *à mort*, while the other repaid her in kind. I did not regret this for it relieved me from too excessive work. Thus we passed a most delightful eight days before the absent ones joined us. Both uncle and Harry had succeeded in their desires. From each I had the fullest details, but as their stories would in some particulars repeat themselves, I shall relate the events in a connected narrative.

Uncle and Mrs Dale had the inside of the coach to themselves, Harry riding outside. Uncle began by praising Harry; and then reverting to the time he was first sent to the rectory, and the note Mrs Dale sent with him; he asked, not without a knowing smile, if the intimacy she had formerly feared had been at all renewed, because he had observed that Harry appeared worn and pale on his return on the Mondays, and was dull and stupid that day. Mrs Dale seemed somewhat alarmed at hearing of this, probably she began to think that something might have occurred between the cousins while she was busied with me; uncle observed her uneasiness, and, guessing the cause, said: 'My dear Mrs Dale, if anything has taken place, and anything comes of it, I am a man of the world, and you may rely upon my assistance and discretion to take such steps as may tend to keep it from the knowledge of the world.'

She thanked him, and said she would be glad to accept his aid if any unfortunate event should have happened – but she hoped not.

Uncle saw that her fears were excited, so he held on to the subject, so at last she avowed that she feared there might have occurred some passages between the two cousins, for she had foolishly trusted that all thought of that had gone out of their heads, and she might not have taken such precautions as she ought to have done.

'Well, my dear madame, my services are at your disposal in case of any necessity, I am not in reality straitlaced, although, in my position, I am obliged to appear so. I feel certain that my experience would be able to suggest the best way of hushing up the scandal if such should be likely to occur.'

Mrs Dale was profuse in thanks, and the doctor became warmer in his discourse, saying that for such a woman as herself, whom he had long admired and coveted, he would do anything.

'For, my dear madam, though I am in the church, something of the old Adam still adheres to me, and the sight and touch of one who has so charmed me as you have done makes a young man of me again.'

Here his arm glided round her charming little waist. He drew her to him, and with some coyness and words of refusal, she yielded her lips to his embrace. His other hand, lifting up her petticoats, sought to feel her beauteous cunt. Again resistance of hand and tongue, but a yielding for all that, and the doctor soon got possession of her lovely cunt. Finding her large and fine clitoris in a state of stiffness, he knew that her passions were excited. So opening her legs, he got between them down on his knees, and as he had previously unbuttoned his trousers in readiness and the fresh cunt stimulating his powers, he pulled out his prick fully erected, and quickly established himself up to the hilt within, the lady up to the last declaring she could not allow him, but wriggling her bottom to perfection as soon as she felt the doctor's very fine prick working within her. She then hugged and seconded him, kissing and tongueing to his heart's desire. They soon brought things to the ecstatic conclusion, to the great satisfaction of both parties.

Of course, after this there was no difficulty in arranging for a comfortable meeting in London. Indeed, it was resolved that they should lodge in the same house and have contiguous apartments. On their arrival in town they put up at one of those large lodging houses in Norfolk Street, Strand, and were fortunate in finding the first-floor bedrooms vacant. The house was a double one, or rather two houses opening into each other. The doctor's bedroom was in the front, and a former door of communication with the back room was locked on one side and bolted on the other. Mrs Dale took the back room, from whence opened a small room with a bed in it, where Harry was lodged. The doctor had thus easy access when the lady chose to withdraw the bolt on her side. After consultation it was thought more advisable that she should go into the doctor's room, so that Harry might not by any possibility hear any love exclamations that might happen to escape them in the excess of their amorous amusements. Of course, the doctor, who knew all about Harry's great desire to fuck his mother, and that he meant to do so by one way or another in London, communicated his intention of having Mrs Dale into sleep with him that night, and, therefore, begged Harry to defer his attempt until after the first night, and then the doctor would aid him in his efforts.

The wily doctor fully intended, after Harry had perfectly succeeded, to become the future companion of their incestuous intercourse. Harry's bed-room door had one of those old-fashioned brass locks that were screwed on to the inside of the door, with a brass covering for the bolt at the side – not morticed as is now usual. Mrs Dale locked her son in after he retired to bed. Harry noticed the circumstance and smiled to think how easily he could foil her but as he had promised the doctor to make no attempt on his mother that night, he went to bed and slept soundly. Next day he provided himself with a turn-screw and a small phial of sweet oil. When mamma was busy at cards, he slipped upstairs and easily unscrewed the brass receiver of the bolt; he oiled the screws and worked them in and out until they went freely and then screwed the covering on again, and felt secure of entering mamma's room whenever he pleased. It had been combined between the doctor and him that by means of gamahuching and frigging, mamma should be put into a state of great excitement without allowing her to be satisfied, so that her passions might be in favour of being fucked, no matter by what prick. For this purpose the doctor was to keep her with him till dawn. At night Harry watched through the keyhole, and when he saw his mother pass into the doctor's room, he at once unscrewed the covering, shot back the bolt, and screwed the cover on again. He was thus all ready for any event, and if his mother was astonished at his entrance, he could say he found the door open, and she must have forgotten to lock it. Thus prepared he went to bed and slept soundly. He was awake before seven o'clock, and gently opening the door a little, he could see by the opposite open door, and the light in the doctor's room, that mamma had not yet left him. He drew on his woollen socks, and sitting where the light flashed through the keyhole, awaited his mamma's return, which occurred very shortly after. The shutting off the light by closing the door of communication told him that she had returned to her own room. He heard her sit down on the pot, and the force of the flow of water proved how healthy she was. He heard her rustle into bed. Then throwing off his dressing-gown and socks he opened the door and approached his mother's bed. Being awake, she instantly saw him in the half-daylight that came from the shuttered window.

'Harry! What on earth brings you here, and how did you open the door?'

'I heard you moving, dear mamma, I could not sleep for the cold. I got up and tried the door, it was not locked, you must have omitted to turn the bolt, but I should have rapped and called to you, if it had not been open. I want you to let me get warm in your nice warm bed, and you will cuddle your poor Harry – will you not, dear mamma?'

'If you will be quiet, and speak lower, for the doctor may hear you; you may come in, and if you turn your back, I will warm you.'

Harry lost no time in lying down by her side, and being really very cold, and even shivering, he was glad enough to do as she bid him, and turn his back, and cuddle his bottom into his mother's belly. She said: 'Poor boy, he is indeed cold, now go to sleep in mamma's arms.'

Of course, he had no such intentions. Speedily getting warm, he turned his face to mamma, and whispered, in the same tone as she used: 'Oh, how I love my beautiful mamma.'

Pressing his belly against hers, he let her feel his prick standing against her mons Veneris.

'Harry! What do you mean by embracing me in that way – don't you know I am your mother, sir?'

He had seized with one hand her beautiful firm bubbies, and was evidently in full amorous excitement, as she could feel by the stiff pego pushing against her mount of Venus.

'My darling mamma, if you knew how much I love you and how I have longed to embrace your beautiful body.'

'Go along, you impudent boy, do you not know it would be sinful to indulge in such sentiments with your mother? – leave me directly.'

'Oh, no, mamma, I can't indeed, my own mamma. I mean to possess you; what harm can there be in returning to whence I came?'

Here he transferred his hand from her bubby to her splendid mons Veneris, and showed what his words meant. She pretended to be very angry, and endeavoured to push him away, but he held her round the waist with his other arm too well

'Desist this instant, or I shall cry out.'

She really appeared very angry but, nevertheless, did not exceed a whisper during all the colloquy before or after. Harry now thought of his best argument.

'Why do you attempt to repulse me in this way, dear mamma? Why should you not let me enjoy your person as much as you like Charlie to do it?'

She gave a start at this home thrust.

'What do you say, you naughty boy? and where did you hear such a falsehood as that? is that one of your friend Charlie's inventions, after all the kindness I have shown him?'

'My darling mamma, Charlie never opened his lips to me on the subject. I speak from what I saw with my own eyes.'

'What do you mean? Tell me directly.'

'Well, my loved mamma, do you remember the first Saturday night that Charlie and I slept at home? After retiring to my room, I was obliged to go downstairs to the water closet, where I went in my stockings, and without a light, not to disturb you. I was coming up again, when a sudden flash of light shone out in the upper passage. Mounting the stairs, and when my head was on a level with the upper floor, I saw you going towards Charlie's room. I went into my own, but left the door open to see when you would return; finding you did not come back, I crept softly along the passage, until I came to the turning that led to Charlie's room. The light shone through the keyhole. I quietly approached. You know the bed exactly faces the door – and there, my darling mamma, I saw you initiate Charlie into what was to him a previously unknown pleasure. Oh! my beloved mother, the sight of your naked charms, of the delicious way in which you were giving him his first lesson in love, maddened me with desire. I was almost tempted to come in upon you and violate you, if you would not consent. It was in that state that I remembered that Ellen was asleep in your bed. I ran there, and throwing off the little I had on, I lay down beside her, and began feeling her private parts. She awoke and said: ' "Dear aunt, do you wish me to do the same to you?"

'Her hand passed down to my erect member, she gave a cry of astonishment. I whispered it was only me.

' "Oh! you must leave me directly. Aunt can only have gone to the water closet, and will be back directly."

'She was not to be pacified until I convinced her that there was no chance of your speedy return, so I was obliged to bring her along to Charles's door; we saw you quite naked, rising and falling on the enormous weapon that Charles has. I never before saw it erect and could scarcely believe my eyes; nor was it less wonderful the way in which you so charmingly took it in. It greatly excited Ellen, as well as me. We returned to your room – the fire still burned. I laid her down on the rug before it, and took her maidenhead. She had seen how Charlie's monstrous affair went easily into you, and felt how much less mine was, so she never dreamt of it hurting her, and she let me get fairly within the lips; then, while making her spend, I suddenly thrust it through all impediments, and the affair was done; she gave a scream, as it hurt her, but I had shut the door and none of you heard it. I let her sleep after this, and did not do it again till morning. The next night we again watched your delicious proceeding. Ellen was less sore, and we repeated your example several times. She continues to this day to wonder at the enormous size of Charlie's tool, and is surprised at your taking it in so easily. But, oh, my mother, how my passions have been excited by your glorious charms. What is Ellen compared with you? She did very well to relieve my agony of desire to possess you, when I knew you were better occupied, and that I could not do so – but that is all. It is you, and you alone, my beloved mother, whom I adore, and I wildly long to possess this dear and magnificent cunt beneath my hand.'

Mrs Dale was perfectly flabbergasted at this recital.

'You abominable boy, how dared you to follow me, and be a spy upon your mother; and to make it known to Ellen, too; doubtless you have been boasting of it, and telling others.'

'No, indeed, mamma, Ellen and I were on oath that we would never reveal to any mortal the delicious sight we had seen – so you see, darling mamma, that you can fully trust your own boy. Oh, do let me do it; feel how my poor thing throbs.'

Here I must give you Harry's own account of what took place.

'I took her hand with very little resistance, and I could feel her fingers gently clasped my prick, before she withdrew her hand.

' "But no – it cannot be – it would be incest."

'She twisted her body round, so that her magnificent bottom came against my belly. As she turned, I slipped my hand down, and laid hold of her shift, so that in turning it left her bottom bare, and sticking out against me. I lost not an instant, and before she had quite settled down, I brought my stiff-standing pego against her delicious cunt from behind, and as it was reeking from her previous spendings produced by the rector's gamahuching, I plunged it at one shove as far as her buttocks against my belly would allow, at the same time dropping my hand from her waist to her cunt, so that when she sprang forward, as if to turn me out, I met her clitoris, it was quite stiff, showing her to be really in a state of amorous excitement. This attack on the clitoris made her as quickly move back, which double movement thoroughly engulfed me. I lost no time in proceeding to the most active movements in and out. This was too much for her, she could not resist entering into the encounter with all the force of her passions, and we ran a very rapid course, ending in the most ecstatic delight, and with sighs of joy we lay clasped together in all the delicious after-languor. I could feel by her exquisite internal pressures that her lust was not yet alleviated, and this nerved me to fresh efforts. After a feigned resistance, dear mamma passed her hand behind her, and putting it on my buttocks, assisted in sending me further in at each home thrust. We were longer this bout, and enjoyed it more. After the usual indulgence in the after-joy, she turned, and embracing me tenderly said: ' "Oh, my dear child, this is very wrong, but very delicious. You must be very discreet, my dear Harry, for if it were known it would disgrace us both for ever."

' "My sweet mamma, do not fear; have you ever seen anything like indiscretion in the last six weeks, although I was madly longing for you? Oh, kiss me, my beloved mother."

'The sweetest of kisses followed, our tongues met, her hand wandered; already she found my pego standing.

' "My darling I must kiss it, it is so much more developed than I could have expected, and as hard as iron."

' "Not as large as Charlie's, mamma."

' "That is true, my dear; but it is the stiffness, and not the size, that gives the real pleasure. Of course, when both are combined, as with Charlie, they are irresistible."

'Meanwhile I was feeling her cunt: her clitoris, which you know is largely developed, stood stiff.

' "Mamma, darling, what a size this is. Ellen told me you could put it into her."

' "Oh! the bad girl, to tell tales out of school."

' "Never mind, mamma, I must suck it while you play with mine."

'I turned on my back with my heels up – mamma lay down upon my belly reversed. I sucked her clitty while frigging her cunt, and she sucked my prick until we both spent, and each licked or sucked all the balmy sperm that issued from the other. We continued our caresses until my prick showed its readiness for another encounter. Mamma took me on her belly this time, and as soon as I was engulfed, threw her legs over my loins, and, by the most lascivious actions, contributed to our enjoyment. Her glorious bottom heaved in unison with mine, our tongues were interlaced, and at last with sweet murmurs of delight, we died away in each other's arms in the most luxurious ecstasy of thoroughly gratified desire. We lay long insensible of all around, throbbing in pressures of lascivious delight, which would have soon led to another love bout, but that mamma whispered it would be imprudent to continue, for the sun was up, and breakfast time had arrived. I withdrew from the sweet cunt with great regret, and in slipping out of bed brought my mouth down to it, and gave it a loving kiss and suck, played with the magnificent covering of bushy ringlets, and then tore myself away with difficulty. Thus ended my first possession of my adored and glorious mother, which was followed by night upon night of the most lascivious enjoyment. I returned to my room, and was dressed and downstairs before her. The doctor took an opportunity to inform me that she had excused herself from joining him the next night on the pretence of not feeling well, but in reality it was to have me all to herself for the whole night; and a most delicious night it was. She displayed and exercised her libidinous passions to the utmost. Never before had I such a treat. It was, perhaps, the closeness of the relationship that added to the excitement, but it appeared to me that she beat even the doctor's splendid wife. Oh, she was so loving, too. The way she fondled me in her arms and caressed me was irresistible. I can't tell how often we did it – we were at it all night. The next night, under pretence of fearing to exhaust me, she forced me to retire to my room after two fucks, and locked me in. I had previously been informed by the doctor that he had bespoken her for that night, and begged me to fuck her first, that the pleasure of gamahuching her might be enhanced. I, therefore, did not do more than make a feigned resistance to her when she told me I must go to my own bed. She said she would let me have one embrace before she rose in the morning but that one was converted into two exquisite spends. The next night the doctor wished to repose, as he purposed surprising me in the morning. I laid myself out for this, and when mamma was asleep I rose as if to piddle. I unbolted the door and shook up the doctor, and then returned to bed. I had agreed with him to make more noise than usual in the final ecstasy; he was to wait long enough to allow of the after-enjoyment, as if he was taking time to clothe himself a little, and was then to come in with a light. My mother still slept. It was about four o'clock in the morning. I began feeling her glorious buttocks, and, sliding under the clothes, turned her legs apart – she insensibly slipped upon her back, I took her charming clitoris between my lips, and soon sucked it into stiffness. The excitement awoke her – she had dreamed I was fucking her – and so was hot and randy. She drew me upon her bosom, threw the clothes off, and her glorious limbs clasped my loins – her two hands pressed on my buttocks, as if to drive me further home, and we ran a most delicious course, I feigned to be even still more excited than I really was, and almost brayed at the ecstatic moment of ejaculation. Mamma herself was too far gone in delight to notice the loudness of my braying. She lay panting and throbbing on my prick, almost in a state of insensibility to aught else beside. Her eyes were closed, so that she did not observe the entrance of the light carried by the doctor. It was not until he was standing by the bedside, and made all exclamation of surprise, that she was aware of his presence.

'She gave a scream – though not very loud – and covered her eyes with her hand. I scrambled off her. The doctor, with great politeness, begged her pardon for his intrusion, but hearing what appeared to him an unearthly noise, he had feared she was taken ill.

'Here the usual resource of woman – tears – fell plentifully from mamma. The doctor most affectionately begged her to calm herself.

' "My dear madam," said he. "I do not in any way blame you for this. I am a man of the world, and I know that incest is practised to a far greater extent than is at all imagined, and to prove that it in no way offends me, I may at once tell you that it was my own mother who initiated me into these delightful mysteries. I see that this dear boy looks terribly frightened at my being a witness to the delight he must have had; but to put him at his ease, we may as well inform him that we, too, have indulged in that delicious game. I may add that this is not the first time I have joined in orgies with more than one man or woman, and nothing gives me more pleasure than to embrace one reeking from the arms of another, especially if I have been a witness to the previous encounter. See, my dear madam, how this dear instrument stands stiff in proof of what I say, and to ensure my silence dear Harry must not object to my enjoying you after and before him."

'So saying he dropped off his trousers and jumped into bed. He was met with feeble remonstrances from my mother at doing it before her son: but I assured her that I rather preferred to see her at work, as she knew, than otherwise, especially as she evidently enjoyed it so much. So the doctor forthwith mounted her. There could be no doubt that she enjoyed it equally with him. My cock stood at the sight. I put it into her hand, and she squeezed it lovingly – then stooping I sucked one nipple, and you know how this excites her, and dipped a hand behind the doctor, and after gently tickling his bollocks, acted postilion to his bottom-hole. They ran a most exciting course and died away in mutual raptures. No sooner did he turn off than I jumped up into his place, and in one moment was up to the cods in that overflowing cunt. Mamma feebly expostulated, but the doctor begged her to let him have the pleasure of witnessing the vigour of the youth. I knew that at heart mamma was delighted, for all women especially enjoy having a fresh prick into them immediately after a previous one has been withdrawn.'

This is quite true – witness my own dear Benson in our early days; her greatest delight was to have me the instant B. retired, and she avowed that nothing could give her greater pleasure. I knew a lady in after-life whom I and three others used to have together, and no sooner was one off than another was on and sometimes two at once. She used to tell us how she deceived her husband. When in Florence she had eight lovers, and she had had them all on the same night without any of them knowing of the others. She managed it in this way. She made them come two at ten o'clock, two at half-past ten, two at eleven, and two a half-past eleven. They were put in four different rooms with convenient sofas. She ran to No. 1 in a merely loose robe, which was instantly thrown off. She was a magnificently made creature, the sight of whose charms would inflame anyone. She rapidly got two goes from the first without withdrawing. Then saying that her husband would be seeking her if she did not leave him, she rang for her German valet, who used to fuck her himself, and who afterwards confirmed her story to me, who showed the gentleman out of the room. Off she ran to No. 2, told him she had only got away by letting her husband have a go, and that he thought she had only gone to the water closet so he must do it once and leave her. Of course the cunt full of fuck only excited him the more, and he very soon racked off to her great satisfaction, and was dismissed, leaving the rooms vacant for the two at eleven. As there was not five minutes to spare she ran to the third room, where another lover was waiting. The same pretence was made as to the last, but as he was largely hung, she got two *coups* from him and then packed him off, and in the same way ran to the others, always with the same story, getting two *coups* out of three running, who were the best fuckers, and waiting with the last until he could do no more.

The same lady told me that once while living at Dieppe her husband ran over to England for a few days. During his absence she had four young men to supper every night, and made them all fuck her on the sofa squabs laid on the floor, accommodating one in her bottom at the same time. During the day her landlord, a married man, used to come in and rack her off besides. At one time she was left alone at Mannheim, where she made acquaintance with an officer, who introduced a second, and a third, until she knew eight in all. She had the whole lot once to supper, and they all fucked her three times each. She was a wonderfully fine woman, and could take no end of fucking. Her father had initiated her at twelve years of age. She was of Greek origin, and actually was hairy and menstruated at that early age. But all women are rakes in their hearts, and numbers never encumber them.

During Harry's encounter with his mother, the doctor stood beside them, and handled Harry's bollocks and acted postilion to him. Mamma took to it most kindly. The sight again inflamed the doctor, the incestuous idea enhancing the excitement. As Harry withdrew, he begged Mrs Dale to get on her hands and knees and let him put it in from behind. He would rather have gone in behind but did not think she was as yet quite prepared to allow that. He only said that the movement below his eyes of such a fine bottom as hers added to the excitement. He further proposed that she should kneel over Harry's body reversed, so that she might gamahuche him, and he frig her beautiful clitoris.

'You mean to kill me between you,' she said, but all the same complied. She sucked Harry's prick and he spent in her mouth; she swallowed his sperm with great gusto, spending herself at the same moment in advance of the doctor. Harry kept frigging her clitoris with one hand, while the other was frigging the doctor's bottom-hole. It was a long bout, she made Harry spend twice in her mouth, while she spent thrice to the doctor's once, all dying away together in the final fuck. They lay long lost to everything, and when they recovered, they separated and retired to their own rooms.

The ice being thus broken, the remaining days were passed in the most refined lasciviousness. The doctor had his way with her bottom, and asked her leave to have Harry's after Harry had had his mother's bottom-hole, while the doctor was fucking her, and had fucked the doctor upon another occasion, the doctor crying out – 'Hi, hi, hi!' as if it hurt him, and he was losing his maidenhead. He professed immense satisfaction, when she let him have Harry, declaring that he could not tell whether having her both ways, having Harry, or being had himself, was the greatest pleasure. Mamma declared that to have both apertures filled at the same moment was the most delicious. It was then the doctor said he would try. So fucking mamma in a kneeling position he presented his great backside to Harry and was well fucked. It was after this complete initiation that they returned home, and after such proceedings, the transition to a general entry into our orgies was easily arranged. As they were to arrive to a late dinner, it was resolved that Mrs Dale should stay the night, and we would see what that would bring forth. They arrived accordingly. Mrs Dale went to Ellen's room, taking Ellen with her to help her at her toilet. There ensued an explanation between them. Mrs Dale felt that there must be an explicit avowal on both sides. She admitted to Ellen that Harry had come to her bed, and only succeeded in his horrible purpose by telling her how he and Ellen had seen her operations with Charlie, and had followed her example.

'And now, my dear Ellen, as there must be no secrets between us, tell me if you and Charlie have got together.'

'Well, yes, we have. You know I had seen how immense he was, and yet with what pleasure you took him in. So curiosity made me give way one day that we were in the summerhouse, and he slept with me afterwards.'

'Does the doctor's wife suspect?'

'Oh, yes, she knows all about it. I forgot to bolt the door one night; in the morning Charlie made too much noise. She came in, merely in her chemise, ran up and pulled him off me, without imagining she ran any risk herself. Charlie seized her in his arms, and swore he would do as much to her, to prevent her telling. She was horrified, and fled to her own room, but had not time to shut him out; he forced the door open, she ran to her bed, intending to ring for the servant, he caught her as she had one knee up on the bed, and was into her from behind before she could accomplish her purpose. She cried out to me, to come and pull him away. I went, but told her Charlie was right, as it would prevent her splitting upon us. I rather think that Charlie's large proportions gave her much pleasure for she soon ceased to struggle, indeed she had her back to him, and his strong arms round her waist prevented her using her hands. She cried much afterwards, and talked about the greatness of the crime. She had then got into bed. Charlie followed, to coax and console her, and, of course, got into her again. I thought she enjoyed the second, for her bottom heaved to meet him. She afterwards accused him of the crime of seducing a young lady, her guest, but I stopped that, by avowing that my cousin had had me previously. Then she accused me of seducing Charlie, and here, I must implore your pardon, for I let out inadvertently that you had initiated him, for I had seen you having him.'

'Oh, you bad girl, how could you be so cruel and imprudent?'

'Well, dear aunt, there is no great harm done. Charlie's aunt was soon quite appeased and regularly joined us after this. She is as fond, if not fonder, of gamahuching me as you used to be; she has grown greedy for Charlie's immense cock, envies your having had the first of him, and says that if she had known of his wonderful proportions, she could not have resisted initiating him herself. She hopes that, through my means, she will become more intimate with you. I have told her of your beautiful clitoris. She dotes on the gamahuche, and vows that she will never be happy till she has done it to you.'

This explanation was a great relief to the widow, who knew she was all right with the doctor, and now foresaw that it would be all right with his wife also and they would have complete freedom to indulge in the wildest lubricity. So having dressed, they descended to dinner. The doctor had explained all their London doings to his wife, so that after dinner the three ladies exchanged confidence. Aunt was so eager to see and suck Mrs Dale's large clitoris that they adjourned to aunt's bedroom, where the doctor discovered them in the midst of their operations. Mrs Dale was stretched on her back, with extended thighs, while aunt, with her head pressed by Mrs Dale's hands down on her cunt, was sucking at the splendid clitoris, and working some fingers in and out of her cunt. They were too intent on their pleasure to notice his entrance. Aunt's petticoats were above her hips, as she knelt. The old boy's cock stood, he advanced, knelt down, got between her legs, and fucked her as she was, begging her to continue her lascivious operations on Mrs Dale. When he had finished, he congratulated both ladies on the intimate friendship established between them and said it was the dearest wish of his heart. He assured Mrs Dale that his wife was the best woman in the world, and never grudged him a little variety.

'So I have acknowledged my infidelity with you, and it appears my nephew has been taking my place, in my absence. She tells me you instructed Charlie, and that he is monstrous when in erection, as big again as me, or as a certain Grenadier Captain, once a favourite of my wife's. I am curious to see it. She tells me also that he has been sleeping with your charming niece Ellen, who, I must confess, has raised in me a great desire to possess her. Now, my dear madam, if you will consent to invite Charlie to sleep with you and Ellen, I could come in, after you have each had a turn or two out of Charlie, and take Ellen, while you would have Charlie all to yourself. My wife won't object, and I hope you will give your consent.'

'Well, my dear doctor, after what has occurred between us, I can refuse you nothing, but I think dear Harry should have some comfort. I suppose, my dear madam, that the doctor has told you of my son surprising and violating me. Your husband reconciled me to his caresses, and I can assure you that without the enormous size of Charlie, he has a charming way that may please any woman. From what the doctor says, you are free from prejudices, why should you be left out in the cold, while we are all enjoying ourselves, why should you not go to his bedroom, and see what he is made of. I, his mother, can strongly recommend him to your favour.'

So it was arranged.

During the evening, Mrs Dale whispered to me to come to them after the domestics had gone to bed. I went and fucked them both three times, twice in front and once behind, the one who was being fucked always gamahuching the other. When I began to tail off, Mrs Dale arose, unbolted the door of communication with uncle's room, and invited him to Ellen's arms, who was very glad to have a little further experience of another man's prick. Uncle gallantly gamahuched her before fucking her, then begged to see my wonderful prick, pretended to be perfectly astonished at its monstrous dimensions, and wondered how Ellen's little cunt could ever have taken it in. It was a tight fit certainly, but the dear creature liked it none the worse for that. Before fucking Ellen, he begged Mrs Dale to let him guide my large prick into her. After enjoying our first movements, and being excited into sufficient consistency, he proceeded to fuck dear Ellen; even he had some difficulty in entering, notwithstanding the libations I had previously poured into her, but being once fairly hilted, he declared it was one of the tightest little cunts it had ever been his good fortune to fuck. After this, we proceeded each our way, and with a longer interval, brought matters to the exquisite conclusion, panting and throbbing for some time afterwards.

The doctor now retired, and we arranged ourselves for repose. We were awakened in the morning by the entrance of aunt and Harry. He flew to his mamma's arms, who lay down on Ellen to gamahuche her while Harry was fucking her. Aunt and I coupled in the old-fashioned way. Uncle entered while we were in full operation, and seeing the tempting backside of Harry, scrambled up behind and fucked his bottom. After we had done, aunt pretended to be shocked at his attack on a boy's bottom – a woman's was a different thing.

'Well, then, my dear, get upon Charlie the next time, and I shall fuck your truly magnificent bottom!'

And he drew Mrs Dale's attention to the glorious proportions, not only of aunt's bottom, but of her body, and all her limbs.

'Oh, it is indeed glorious,' said she. 'I must, my dear madam, gamahuche you. I have not forgotten the exquisite pleasure you gave me in that way.'

'Willingly,' cried my aunt, 'provided you give me your clitoris to occupy me.'

'Certainly, that will suit me admirably; but you must lie upon me, that I may have the pleasure of gazing on that magnificent bottom, and caressing the immense rotundities of your buttocks.'

Oh, it was a glorious sight to see these two wanton lascivious women in the full enjoyment of each other. It set us all on fire, and the moment they had done I slaked the fire within me in the capacious but tight cunt of my aunt, while uncle fucked her bottom-hole. Mrs Dale lay under Ellen, while Harry fucked Ellen from behind, and Ellen gamahuched her aunt, who herself guided her son's prick into Ellen's cunt, and tickled her clitoris, at the same time acting postilion to her son's bottom-hole.

Oh! it was a splendid bout – we were all so excited and it was also the first meeting of us all in one orgy. We all died away in a perfect heaven of ecstasy, and lay long in the after-enjoyment. Our previous night's work made this the last for the time, and we all separated to seek some welcome repose before breakfast time.

Mrs Dale remained our visitor for three days, during which we met in the doctor's bedroom every night, and renewed our delicious orgies. Mrs Dale carried off her son and niece, and I promised to come over to her cottage on the following Saturday, when Harry and I took turn and turn about with the two dear creatures, sometimes fucking one between us, two at once. When the school resumed its work, Mrs Dale and Ellen always dined at the rectory on Sunday and slept there, when we made a general orgy in the old style.

This continued until our midsummer holidays, when I was to leave the rectory for King's College. Mrs Dale's and Ellen's pregnancies, daily becoming nearer to the period of parturition, were getting more difficult to conceal. We had long discussions with uncle as to what was best to be done. It was at last arranged that they should leave the cottage as if for a tour on the continent, but in reality should only go to Paris, and take apartments in the house of a good *accoucheuse* in the environs, and remain quiet there till the period of delivery. It was not necessary for them to go before we broke up, and the doctor and Harry and I could accompany them; after I had seen my guardian on my return to London, I had no doubt of getting his leave, and the necessary means to visit the continent up to the middle of October, when the classes would begin. It all fell out as arranged. Nothing of either pregnancy was visible, thanks to the full robes worn.

We accomplished our journey and found a capital *accoucheuse* in a beautiful neighbourhood. Harry, uncle and aunt remained with Mrs Dale and Ellen, while I returned to London. I saw my guardian, who, after putting me through an examination, expressed himself much pleased with my progress, said the visit to the continent would expand my mind, and that he would furnish me with the means. He recommended that I should visit my mother first for a fortnight, and announced that at about the end of that time the girls would come up to London to enter a first-rate finishing school. He further told me he and Miss Frankland were to be married at the same time, my sisters were to be bridesmaids and I could be present at the marriage before going abroad. All this being arranged, I ran down home. My mother was delighted to see me, and thought me grown and much improved. It is needless to say how glad my sisters and Miss Frankland were to see me. They had had no fucking except by tongue or dildo, so you may imagine the fury with which they set upon me the first two or three nights We resumed all our lascivious operations of former days. My sisters had developed into splendid women, the youngest still the most libidinous. Dear Miss Frankland, on my congratulating her on her intended marriage, lovingly told me that it was the prospect of being near me that had reconciled her to it. We spent a most delicious fortnight, which passed like a day.

I found an opportunity of fucking my old governess, Mrs Vincent that was. My son was a fine little fellow, toddling about and talking already. His mother loved me as much as ever, and was become a finer developed woman, more amorous and lecherous than she used to be. She said no one could be kinder or more loving than her husband, and she had never been unfaithful to him but with me, whom, as her own formation, she must always love, and would never refuse me anything I asked when it could be safely done. At the sole opportunity I had, I fucked her three times without withdrawing, and finished with a bottom-fuck. I may here mention that a little girl followed nine months from that period, which she always assured me was mine.

My mother, the girls, and Miss Frankland all came up with me to London. The marriage went off with *éclat*. My guardian made very handsome presents to my sisters, and gave me a gold watch, chain and seals, together with a handsome cheque for my travelling expenses. He and his bride, whom I fucked just before she went to church, departed for Scotland, to return by the English lakes, for their honeymoon trip. A few days afterwards, having had two or three nights excellent fucking with my sisters, mamma and I conducted them to their school, and left them with tearful *adieux*. My mother was to remain in town for a week until uncle and aunt's return, when she intended to accompany her sister to the rectory and remain there until I returned from the continent. I was quickly again in Paris. We took rooms near the two darlings, where uncle and aunt remained for the week they had yet to stay. We took mamma and Ellen several times to the play, and they slept with us every night. Uncle and aunt left at the end of the week, but we kept on the apartments for the dear women to come to us, fucking them as much as we could. It seemed as if pregnancy stimulated their lubricity, for we could hardly satisfy them. We had at least always to take them on hands and knees, although neither of them ever showed much in front – their babes lying just between – but, by Jove, their hips expanded splendidly. Dear mamma measured a yard across, and her backside projected almost as much as my aunt's. She loved to be fucked in her bottom-hole to the last. We actually had them both up to the night before the day they were each confined. Nothing could be more favourable than their time. As I formerly stated, each had a little daughter.

On the ninth day afterwards they were both able to rise, but as it would have been very prejudicial to renew our intercourse before another three weeks had elapsed, Harry and I went off for a walking excursion in Switzerland, which we traversed in all directions, with continual delight at the glorious scenery. We did not touch a single woman. When very sharp set we fucked each other, but very little even of that, so that we renovated our constitutions and returned in robust health, ready to do justice to the charms of the two darlings who impatiently awaited our return.

It is needless to repeat the description of the delicious fucking with which they welcomed us. They appeared more lovely than ever, especially Ellen, who had developed into womanhood. We made arrangements to leave the two darling children in the hands of a healthy wet nurse, and set out on an expedition down the Loire to Tours, Bordeaux and the Pyrenees, returning at the end of September via Montpellier, Nîmes, Avignon and Lyons.

The two babes were in excellent health. Arrangements were made for their remaining with their foster mother for a year, and we all returned to London together.

We had three nights' delicious fucking before they returned to the country, and promises were made that they would come to town from time to time to renew our orgies My mother and aunt came up to see me settled in my lodgings, which were taken in Norfolk Street, and I was entered at King's College.

I passed a delicious night with aunt before she left; and ran down with my mother to see her safe home. On my return I found my guardian had returned. I called to pay my respects to his wife. I found her alone, and we managed her first piece of adultery, which, as you may suppose, was not the last. But as this third chapter is already a long one, I shall close it here.

The fourth will introduce us to London, and renew the delicious intercourse with Mrs Benson, as well as with my guardian's wife, and our dear friend MacCallum, as well as many other friends.

## Chapter Four

I concluded my last chapter by saying that I had taken lodgings in Norfolk Street, Strand, for the convenience of being near King's College. It was at the house of a Mrs Nichols, a tall, powerfully built, masculine, but also kind and motherly-looking widow of fifty-two who was an attentive and bustling landlady, looking herself to the better cooking and having a plain cook, who was also a general servant, to help her downstairs and two nieces to do the waiting and attendance on her lodgers upstairs. The younger was there alone when I entered the lodgings; her elder sister had had what they called a 'misfortune', and was then in the country until she could be unburthened of it. She was expected back in about six weeks. Meanwhile, as the winter was not the season, I was the only lodger, and the younger had only me to attend to; her name was Jane; she was but a little thing, but very well made, good bubbies and bottom, which I soon discovered were firm and hard, projecting fully on both sides. She was fairly good looking, but with a singularly innocent manner of freedom about her that made me imagine she had as yet had no chance of a 'misfortune'. In a week we became intimate, and after often praising her pretty face and figure, I snatched a kiss now and then, which at first she resented with an attractive yet innocent sort of sauciness. It was in her struggles on these occasions that I became aware of her firm and hard bosom and bottom.

Up to this time, my flirtations were without ulterior object, but the reality of the attractions of these hidden charms raised my lustful passions. I gradually increased my flatteries and caresses, squeezed her bubbies when I sometimes drew her on my knee and was kissing her, and, as at first she resisted my drawing her to my knee, took occasion to lay hold of her buttocks, which I found more developed than I could have supposed. Gradually her resistance to these little liberties ceased and she would quietly sit on my knee and return the kisses I gave. Her dress was a little open in front, so from feeling her bubbies outside, I gradually got to feeling their naked beauties inside. I now thought I could attempt greater familiarities, so one day when I had her seated on my knee with one arm round her waist, I pressed her to my lips, and while so engaged, whipped my free arm up her petticoats, and before she had become aware of the movement, had got my hand upon her mount, a very nicely haired one. She started up to a standing position, but as I held her close clasped round the waist she could not get away, and her new position enabled me the easier to get my hand between her thighs and thus to feel her charming pouting little cunt. I began attempting to frig her clitoris, but stooping she drew her cunt away, and looking at me with a droll innocent expression of alarm, and with a perfect unconsciousness of the import of her words, cried – 'Oh! take care what you are at. You don't know how a lodger this last summer suffered for seizing me in that way and hurting me very much. I screamed out, aunt came up, and, do you know, he had £50 to pay for his impudence.'

I could not but smile at the extraordinary innocence of the girl.

'But I do not hurt you, dear Jane,' said I, 'and don't mean to do so.'

'That was what he said, but he went on in a most horrible way, and not only hurt me very much, but made me bleed.'

'It would not be with his hand, you see I only gently press this soft hairy little thing. I am sure that doesn't hurt you.'

'Oh, no! if that was all I should not mind it, it was when he pushed me on the sofa, and pressed upon me, that he hurt me terribly, and you must take care what you are about, or you too will have to pay £50.'

There was a curious air of innocence in all this; it was evident to me the fellow had got into her, and broken her hymen with violence, and then her screams had prevented his finishing his work. Her manner convinced me that she was really not aware of the consequences, or rather had not as yet really had her sexual passions aroused.

'Well, my dear Jane, I neither intend to hurt you or make myself liable to pay £50, but you will not refuse me the pleasure of feeling this nice little hairy nest; you see how gentle I am.'

'Well, if you will do me no more hurt than that, I shan't refuse you, because you are a nice kind young gentleman, and very different from the other rough fellow, who never chattered with me and made me laugh as you do – but you must not push your fingers up there, it was something he pushed up there that hurt me so.'

I withdrew my finger, and as, at my request, she had opened her thighs a little, I felt and caressed her very nice little cunt, and with a finger pressed externally above her clitoris, I could see that she flushed and shivered on feeling me there. However, I did no more than gently press and feel all her hairy mount and fat pouting cunt; she said I must let her go, or her aunt would be coming up.

The first step was now gained. Gradually I progressed further and further; felt her charming bare arse as she stood before me, got her to let me see the beautiful curls she had got on her cunt, then came to kissing it, until at last she opened her thighs and let me tongue it, to her most exquisite delight. I made her spend for the first time in her life, and soon she came to me for it. I had gradually introduced a finger up her cunt while licking her clitoris and exciting her so much that she was unconscious of my doing it; then two fingers, and after she had spent deliciously, I made them perform an imitation of a throb, which made her jump and ask what I was doing. I asked if she did not feel that my fingers were inside her sweet fanny.

'You don't say so. It was there I was so hurt.'

'But I do not hurt you, dear Jane?'

'Oh, dear no, it makes me feel queer, but it is very nice.'

'Well, now you know that I have two fingers inside, I will use my tongue again against your charming little clitoris, and work the fingers in and out.'

I did so, and she soon spent in an agony of delight, pressing my head down hard on her cunt, and crying – 'Oh! oh! it is too great a pleasure!' and then dying off, half insensible. Another time I repeated this she told me not to forget to use my fingers. Having made her spend twice I took her on my knee, and told her that I possessed an instrument that would give her far more pleasure than tongue or finger.

'Indeed?' said she, 'where is it? I should so like to see it.'

'You won't tell.'

'Oh, no!'

So I pulled out my stiff-standing prick, and made her stare in amazement. She had really never seen a prick, although it was evidently a prick that had deflowered her, for with my fingers I had explored her cunt and found no hymen there. I put her hand upon it and she involuntarily grasped it firmly.

'This enormous thing could never get into my body; look, it is thicker than all your fingers put together, and only two fingers feel so tight.'

'Yes, darling, but this dear little thing stretches, and was made to receive this big thing.'

I was exciting her clitoris with my finger and she grew evidently lasciviously inclined; so I said, 'Just let me try, and if it hurts you I will stop; you know I am always gentle with you.'

'So you are, my dear fellow, but take care not to hurt me.'

She lay down on the bed, as I desired, with feet up and knees laid open. I spat on my prick and wetted the knob and upper shaft well, then bringing it to her cunt, well moistened by my saliva in gamahuching her, I held open the lips with the fingers of my left hand, and half buried its knob before getting to the real entrance.

'Don't flinch, dearest, I shall not hurt,' and I got it well over the knob, and buried it one inch further.

'Stop!' she cried, 'it seems as if it would burst me open, it so stretches me.'

'But it does not hurt you, dearest?' I had immediately stopped before asking the question.

'No not exactly, but I feel as if something was in my throat.'

'Rest a little, and that will go off.' I slipped a finger down on her clitoris, and as I frigged it she grew more and more excited, giving delicious cunt pressures on my prick as it gradually made its way by the gentle pushing I continued to make without other movements. It was more than half in when she spent; this not only lubricated the interior, but the inner muscles relaxing, a gentle shove forward housed it to the hilt, and then I lay quiet until she recovered from the half fainting state her last discharge had produced; soon the increased pressures of the inner folds showed that her passions were awakening afresh. She opened her eyes and, looking lovingly, said I had given her great pleasure, but she felt as if something enormous was stretching her inside to the utmost. Had I got it all in?

'Yes, dearest, and now it will be able to give you greater pleasure than before.' I began a slow withdrawal and return, frigging her clitoris at the same time, for I was standing between her legs. She soon grew wild with excitement, nature prompting her, her arse rose and fell almost as well as if she was mistress of the art. The novel combination of prick and finger quickly brought on the ecstatic crisis. I, too, was wild with lust, and we spent together, ending in an annihilation of all our senses by the extreme ecstasy of the final overpowering crisis. We lay panting for some time in all the after-joys. Dear Jane begged me to give her some water, as she felt quite faint. I withdrew, still almost in a standing state, got her some water, helped her up, seated her on the sofa and kissed her lovingly as I thanked her for the exquisite joy she had given me. She threw her arms round my neck, and with tears in her eyes told me I had taught her the joys of heaven, and she should always love me, and I must always love her, for now she could not live without me. I kissed and dried her eyes, and told her we should in future enjoy it even more when she got accustomed to it.

'Let me see the dear thing that gave me such pleasure.'

I pulled it out, but it was no longer at the stand; and this surprised her. I explained the necessity of its being so, but said she would quickly see it rise and swell to the former size if she continued to handle it so nicely. It rose almost before I could say as much. She fondled it, and even stooped and kissed its ruby head. We should quickly have got to another bout of fucking if the ringing of the call bell had not brought us to a sense of its imprudence; so after arranging her hair and dress, she hastily descended with some of the breakfast things.

Of course, so good a beginning led to constant renewals and Jane quickly became extremely amorous, and under my instruction a first-rate fucker.

As all my dear friends were not in London, I was fortunate in having such a *bonne bouche* to comfort me. My sisters passed every Sunday with me, and both got some good fucking out of me in every way, without raising any suspicions in the house.

A month after I had taken up my residence at Mrs Nichols's, Jane's sister returned. She was a much finer woman than Jane, broad shouldered with a wide-spread bosom, which, in after-days, I found had not suffered by her 'misfortune' – but then she had not given suck. Her hips were widely projected, and she was grand and magnificent in her arse. Naturally of a very hot temperament, when once she had tasted the magnificent weapon I was possessed of, she grew most lasciviously lustful, and was one of the best fuckers I ever met with. Her power of nip almost equalled my beloved aunt's. Jane was fair, Ann was dark with black locks and black hairy cunt – a very long cunt, with a small tight hole in it, and above it a wide-spread projecting mount, splendidly furnished with hair. Her clitoris was hard and thick, but with little projection. She also became madly fond of arse-fucking and particularly liked me to spend therein. This was partly to prevent any consequences leading to a second 'misfortune'.

On her first arrival Jane was much afraid she would discover our connection and we took every precaution, although I, in my heart, wished this might occur, for as she occasionally waited on me, I grew lecherous upon one whose charms, even covered, excited me greatly. I always flattered and praised her magnificence of figure whenever she came alone to me, but as Jane generally was running in and out, I did not attempt further action. One morning I overheard Mrs Nichols tell Jane to put on her bonnet and go to Oxford Street on some errand; I knew thus that Ann would attend on me, and there would be no chance of interruption from Jane, so I determined to come at once to the point. We had become on friendly, chatty terms, and when she had laid breakfast I asked her to help me on with my coat, which done, I thanked her and with one arm round her waist drew her to me and kissed her. 'Hallo!' said she, 'that is something new,' but did not attempt to withdraw, so giving her another kiss, I told her what a glorious woman she was, and how she excited me – just see. I held one of her hands, and before she was aware, placed it on my huge prick that bulged out of my trousers as if it would burst its way through. She could not help squeezing it, while she cried: 'Goodness, gracious! what an enormous thing you have got!'

Her face flushed and her eyes sparkled with the fire of lust that stirred her whole soul. She tried to grasp it.

'Stop,' said I, 'and I will put it in its natural state into your hand.'

So I pulled it out and she seized it at once, and most lasciviously gazed upon it, pressing it gently. She evidently was growing lewder and lewder, so I at once proposed to fuck her, and thinking it best to be frank, and put her at her ease, I told her that I knew she had had a 'misfortune', but if she would let me fuck her I should be on honour to withdraw before spending, and thus avoid all chance of putting her belly up.

She had become so randy that she felt, as she afterwards told me, she could not refuse so splendid a prick of a size she had often dreamt of, and longed for.

'Can I trust you?' said she.

'Safely, my dear.'

'Then you may have me – let me embrace that dear object.'

Stooping, she kissed it most voluptuously, shivering at the same time in the ecstasy of a spend produced by the mere sight and touch. She gave one or two 'oh's', and drawing me to the bed by my prick, threw herself back, pulling her petticoats up at the same time. Then I beheld her splendid cunt in all its magnificence of size and hairiness. I sank on my knees and glued my lips to the oozing entrance, for she was one who spent most profusely, her cunt had the true delicious odour, and her spunk was thick and glutinous for a woman. I tongued her clitoris, driving her voluptuously wild. So she cried: 'Oh! do put that glorious prick into me, but remember your promise.'

I brought it up to that wide-spread, large-lipped and immense cunt. I fully expected that, big as I was, I should slip in over head and shoulders with the greatest ease. So you may imagine my surprise to find the tightest and smallest of entrances to the inner vagina I almost ever met with; it was really with greater difficulty I effected an entrance than I had with her little sister, whose cunt presented no such voluptuous grandeur. It was as tight a fit as Ellen's was to me on our first coition. Tight as it was, it gave her nothing but the most exquisite pleasure; she was thoroughly up to her work, and was really one of the most voluptuous and lascivious fuckers I have ever met with, excellent as my experience has been. I made her, with fucking and frigging, spend six times before I suddenly withdrew my prick, and pressing its shaft against her wet lips, and my own belly, spent deliciously outside. Shortly after it rose again, and this time after making her spend as often as before, for she was most voluptuously lustful, when I withdrew, she suddenly got from under me, and seizing its shaft with one hand, stooped and took its knob between her lips, and quickly made me pour a flood of sperm into her mouth, which she eagerly swallowed and sucked on to my great delight.

We should have had a third bout but for the necessity of her going down to her aunt.

I breakfasted, then rang to take away. Again we had a delicious fuck, and a third when she came to make the bed and empty the slops. This third time I begged her to kneel on the sofa, and let me see her gloriously grand arse, and when I had to retire I would show her a way that would continue both our pleasure. So after fucking her from behind, and making her spend far oftener than me, I withdrew, and pushing it up between the lips over the clitoris, with my hand round her waist, I pressed it tightly against her cunt and clitoris, and continuing to wriggle my arse, made her spend again as I poured a flood all up over her belly. She declared it was almost as good as if inside.

After this very shortly I proposed to push its nose into her bottom-hole, and spend just within.

She was reluctant at first, but she ended in not only liking the point there, but deliciously enjoying my whole prick within, and eventually it was always the receptacle of a first discharge induced by fucking, and a second fuck was completely carried on in that more secret altar of lust. She became a first-rate *enculeuse*.

It soon happened that both sisters knew of the other enjoying me, and it ended in their slipping down from their attic, where both slept in the same bed, to my room, and we had most delicious fucking and double gamahuching.

Ann was by far the finer and the more lascivious fuck, but little Jane had a certain charm of youth and also of freshness, which got her a fair share of my favours.

We carried this on for several weeks until use made us careless and noisy.

The aunt, when no lodgers occupied the room, slept overhead, and, probably being sleepless one morning, when it was early daylight, heard our voices, came down and surprised me in the very act of fucking Ann and gamahuching Jane, who stood above her and presented her cunt to my lecherous tongue. A loud exclamation from their aunt roused us up at once.

'Get to bed, you dreadful hussies.'

They fled without a moment's hesitation.

Mrs Nichols then began to remonstrate with me on the infamy of my conduct. I approached the door apparently to get my shirt, for I was stark naked, but in fact to shut and lock my door, and then to turn on Mrs Nichols, who apparently had quite forgotten she had only her short shift on, which not only allowed the full display of very fine, firm and ample bubbies but, not falling below the middle of her thighs, showed remarkably well-made legs and small knees, with the swelling of immense thighs just indicated.

My stiff-standing prick in full vigour, and if anything, still more stimulated by the unexpected beauties shown by Mrs Nichols, I turned upon her and seizing her round the waist from behind, pushed her forward, and before she could recover herself I had hauled up her 'cutty sark', seen a most magnificent arse and was into her cunt – not without somewhat painful violence – before she could recover from the surprise of the attack.

She screamed out murder, but there was no one who could hear but the girls, and they knew better than to interrupt me. I kept fucking away in spite of her cries and, passing an arm round her body, with my finger I got to her clitoris, which sprang out into considerable proportions. My big prick and the frigging of her clitoris produced their natural result. In spite of herself she grew full of lust. I felt her cunt pressures, and knew how her passions were rising. Speedily, in place of resisting, she began to cry, 'Oh, oh,' and breathe hard, and then most gloriously wriggled her splendid arse, and as I spent she too was taken in the delicious ecstasy of the final crisis. She lay throbbing on my delighted prick until it stood as stiff as before. I began a slow movement, she made no resistance, except crying out, 'Oh! dear, oh! dear,' as if in spite of regrets, she could not help enjoying it; indeed, at last she said: 'Oh! what a man you are, Mr Roberts; it is very wrong of you to do this, but I cannot resist enjoying it myself. It is years since I did such a thing, but as you have done it, it makes me wish you should do it again. Let us change position.'

'Very well, but you must throw off this tiresome chemise, or I won't withdraw.'

As her lust was so excited, she made no objection, so withdrawing, I stood up; she drew her shift over her head, and displayed a far more splendid form, with an exquisitely fair and dimpled skin, than I could have thought possible.

'My dear Mrs Nichols, what a fine and perfect form you have got, let me embrace you in my arms.'

She was nothing loath, flattered by my praise. She laid hold of my cock with one hand, and closely clasped me with the other arm, while I threw an arm and hand round on her truly magnificent arse, and with my other hand pressed on a wonderful pair of bubbies as hard and firm as any maid of eighteen. Our mouths met in a loving kiss, our tongues exchanged endearments. She said: 'You have made me very wicked, let me have this enormous and dear fellow again.'

I said I must first gaze on all her beauties, especially on her gorgeous and enormous bottom. She turned herself round in every way, delighted to find that I so ardently admired her.

She then lay down on her back, and spread wide her legs, and called to me to mount and put it in.

'First I must kiss this beautiful cunt, and suck this superb clitoris.'

Her mount was covered with closely curled brown silky locks; her cunt was large with grand thick lips and well-haired sides. Her clitoris stood out quite three inches, red and stiff. I took it in my mouth, sucked it, and frigged her cunt with two fingers, which went in with the greatest ease, but were nipped tightly the moment the entrance was gained, and I frigged and sucked until she spent madly with absolute screams of delight. I continued to suck and excite her, which quickly made her cry out: 'Oh, darling boy, come and shove your glorious prick into my longing cunt.'

I sprang up and buried him until our two hairs were crushed between us. She held me tight for a minute without moving, then went off like a wild Bacchante, and uttered voluptuous bawdy expressions.

'Shove your delicious prick further and harder. Oh, you are killing me with delight.'

She was a perfect mistress of the art, gave me exquisite pleasure, and, I may add, proved afterwards a woman of infinite variety, and became one of my most devoted admirers. Our intrigue continued for years, while her age, as is the case with good wine, only appeared to improve her. Her husband was not a bad fucker, but having only a small prick, had never stimulated her lust as my big splitter had done.

We had on this first occasion three other good fucks, which she seemed to enjoy more and more.

As I had previously fucked the girls pretty well, my prick at last refused to rise and perform. We had to stop fucking, but I gamahuched her once more after again posing her, and admiring her really wonderfully well-made and well-preserved body. She had a good suck at my cock, without bringing him up again.

At last we separated, but not before she made a promise that she would sleep with me that night, and a glorious night we had. I had the more difficult task of reconciling her to my having her nieces. I used to have them one night, and sleep with her the next.

Ann, as I have said, was one of the lewdest and most lascivious women I had ever known. I had told them of the beauty of their aunt's whole person, and of her wonderful clitoris, and how she liked me to gamahuche it. This awakened the tribadic passions of Ann to gamahuche her aunt.

I, at last, persuaded her to let Ann join us, and both were afterwards extremely glad I had done so, for both were thorough tribades, and lasciviously enjoyed each other, while being fucked by me in turns. Mrs Nichols too, once she got used to arse-fucking, delighted in it, and we had the wildest orgies together.

Meanwhile, my very dear friend MacCallum had returned to town. He lived in the outskirts, but had taken a small set of chambers at Lyon's Inn, a sitting-room and bedroom, where he had a complete library of bawdy books and pictures to excite to new efforts passions palled with excess. It was here I took my sisters, and every Sunday we four, stripped to the buff, indulged in every excess the wildest lust could prompt.

At Christmas, uncle, aunt, the Dales and Ellen all came to town, and taking the same rooms with others that uncle and Mrs Dale and her son had formerly down in Norfolk Street, we had the most glorious orgies.

I confessed that I had debauched my sisters during the weary months I had been left alone with them, and advised their initiation into our society. Uncle greedily snatched at the idea, so did aunt and Harry Dale, but his mother and Ellen rather discouraged it. However, the majority had it, and aunt went to the school, and took them away for the holidays. I had instructed them to keep up the idea of a late initiation by me, and how much they liked it when done, carefully avoiding the least reference to former freedoms.

They afforded a very effective aid to the wild variety of our orgies. Uncle especially affected them, and was never tired of fucking, sucking or gama-huching their splendid charms. Aunt, whose lech was for fresh young women, was unbounded in her admiration and tribadic use of their bodies.

I made a confident of Harry Dale about our reunions at MacCallum's, and, with the latter's leave, introduced him to our orgies in the Inn.

MacCallum took greatly to the fine tight arse of young Dale. He also wished to have Ellen introduced. I took occasion to break the matter to her, and in the end she made a delicious addition to those private orgies. In March, Mrs Benson, Mrs Egerton, and husbands came up to town.

I had written to the Benson, and got a note from her the moment she arrived. I called immediately, and finding her alone, her husband having gone to the city, was received with delight. After flying into each other's arms, nature was too fierce for any amorous preliminaries. A sofa received our ardent bodies, and before one could think, legs were opened, cunt invaded, and a most rapid fuck, too rapid for luxury, was run off. Then while recovering from our first delirium of pleasure, we had time for a few words of mutual praise and admiration of improvements in both; but it was not until I had fucked her four times, and made her spend at least twice as often, that we found time to enter into close converse upon past events.

I had known by letter of the intrigue with the Count, Mrs Egerton, and herself, and now heard, from her own mouth, more exciting details. She told me how Mrs Egerton was eager to possess my unusually great prick, adding: 'By the way, she must be alone at this hour. Come along, we may have some fun today.'

I had not seen Mrs Egerton for many years, in fact, not since long before I had last fucked Mrs Benson. We went. Her reception was all I could wish.

Mrs Benson told us to lose no time, but to run off at least an introductory embrace when the field was so clear. Mrs Egerton made no objection; the Benson acted mistress of the ceremonies, pulled out my prick and lifted the Egerton's petticoats, turning both sides to view, and making the Egerton handle and admire the nobleness of my prick; then telling her to kneel and present her fat arse to my lustful gaze, she guided my longing prick into her really delicious cunt; and a most excellent fuck we had, which, as Mrs Benson said, would put us at our ease in an interview she had planned for next day, in which the Count was to join us, and telling me I should have to show my mettle to rival the Count.

We met next day at a quiet house in Percy Street, Tottenham Court Road. The ladies had gone to the Soho Bazaar, leaving their carriage in Soho Square, going out by another entrance in a back street, and driving up in a cab to us in Percy Street.

At an evening call I had made, to be introduced to Mr Egerton, I had met and been introduced to the Count. We had walked home as far as his apartments, in Berners Street, and arranged to meet in Percy Street, before the arrival of our beautiful and dear friends. Thus we were impatiently awaiting their coming when they arrived.

It is needless to say no sooner had they entered and the mere embrace and kiss of welcome been given, than they retired to another room, opening into the one where we were, to take off all encumbrances to the wildest lust, while we, too, disencumbered ourselves of all our clothes. We were quicker than they were, and the Count was in the act of handling and admiring the grandeur of my prick when the two beautiful creatures entered in nature's only robe, and well might we exclaim: 'Woman, when unadorned is adorned the most,' for two more beautiful women or more perfectly lovely in shape could hardly be seen. Women, too, as voluptuous and lascivious in their passions as any of their sex could be, and it was now our delight to enjoy and satisfy their ardent lust by fucking them in every way, as well as for the first time giving them the joy of having two real pricks in them at once. The charming Benson, as my original initiator in love's mysteries, claimed my first embrace, the Count fucking Mrs Egerton. We were so placed that each could see the other, and thus enjoy the excitement of the scene. The dear creatures spent thrice to our once.

Then the Egerton claimed me while the Count refilled the cunt I had just quitted.

Again we made them spend thrice to our once. They preferred these preliminary encounters to the more lascivious excesses we were about to enter upon as exciting and preparing their passion for more voluptuous embraces.

Both the dear creatures loved a prick *in culo* from time to time, but as yet they had not had the opportunity of having a prick in each aperture at once.

The Egerton, to whom my prick was as yet a novelty, said she must have it in her cunt while the Count planted his lesser but very fine prick in her arse.

The Count's prick was quite as long, or nearly so, as mine, and even thicker close to the roots, but tapered up to a small pointed knob, so that for the *enculage* he had greater facility than my huge-knobbed affair, whose head was as thick as any part of it. This difference of formation made the dear creatures both prefer my prick in front while the Count attacked them in the rear. They generally each got two, with me below and the Count above. But, although it was at first somewhat painful when my huge prick took the rearward side with the Count in front, they soon got accustomed to it, although invariably beginning, after our preliminary fucking, with the Count first *in culo*.

The Egerton, as I said before, made her first trial of two pricks fucking her at once, by having me below her. I lay down on my back, she straddled over me, the Benson claimed the place of conductress to the instruments of pleasure; first giving a suck to my prick, she guided it into the delicious cunt of her friend, who sank down upon my stiff-standing pego, deliciously impaling herself thereon, and went off in a voluptuous discharge on feeling its huge head engulfed to the utmost; she rose and fell upon it in an upright position, until she had spent a second time, and had brought up her passion to the wildest rage of lust, then falling into my longing arms, she called out to the Count to shove his prick at once into her arse.

The Benson had, meanwhile, sucked and moistened the Count's fine prick, making him as eager as the Egerton to be into her beautiful arsehole. The Benson conducted it to the divine entrance of that rapture-giving receptacle, which he entered at first with little difficulty, but as the thickening of his prick by its further entrance began to stretch the tender folds between our two pricks, the Egerton cried out for a momentary pause, as it was producing the strange sensation that one prick alone produces in the earlier stage of sodomitic embraces.

The Benson came to her aid by desiring the Count to withdraw about half the distance he had gained and having whipped up some warm soapsuds she well wetted his lower shaft and then he more easily recovered lost ground, and gained a complete lodgement within the tremendously stretched affair, for as I have said, the lower part of his shaft was thicker than I could grasp.

The Egerton felt as if the two apertures were about to be torn into one, and cried out for a few minutes' cessation.

We both lay still, beyond the involuntary throbbing of our pricks, pressed as they were against each other, for the at-all-times-thin membrane dividing cunt from arsehole was now stretched to the fineness of gold leaf, and to our sensations did not appear to exist at all.

These double throbbings soon stirred up all the wild lubricity of the Egerton's nature, first showing itself in the responsive inward pressures of the delicate widely stretched folds of both receptacles; then, increasing in fiery lust, she cried out for us to begin gently our first movements. We drew in and out in unison together, at first slowly, but the Egerton finding that we were producing the most excessive delight to her double-gorged receptacles, cried out: 'Oh! oh! It is heavenly; fuck faster, you angelic fuckers. Oh! faster, faster. Oh! oh! it is too much.'

She spent in such an agony of ecstasy as to faint clean away.

We were not aware of this, not having ourselves spent as we had only paused to let her enjoy her most heavenly discharge to the utmost. Then, first with throbs, and then with in and outward movements, we soon recovered her from her trance of excessive joy. Her passions were more violently stirred than before. She wriggled her arse convulsively sideways, she raved in the grossest bawdy terms, and so excited us that we all three came to the final crisis in wild cries of the grossest lust, and died away in an agony of bliss, so overpowering that we lay, almost insensible, soaking in the sacred vases in which were compressed our well-satisfied pricks. Meanwhile the Benson, wildly excited by the scene enacted below her eyes, sought relief by kneeling beyond my head, for we always fucked on the floor with mattresses spread widely around; she then backed her splendid arse over my head, and brought her cunt to my mouth, and I gamahuched her continuously until my own delicious spending annihilated all power of movement for the time being.

The Egerton, in the agony of her pleasure at the moment of the last spend, had fastened her teeth on the glorious arse of the Benson before her, and bit so hard as actually to draw blood and make the Benson spring forward with a sudden start and cry. But we were all too lost in the ecstatic joys even to hear the cry of pain she uttered.

At last the Egerton gave signs of returning life. The Benson had risen and was eager for her turn, but Mrs Egerton implored that she might have once again a taste of these more than heavenly joys while both pricks were still engulfed within her and thus avoid the pain of entrance.

This was so reasonable that the Benson yielded with a good grace.

The Count, to indemnify her, begged her to stride over our two bodies, so as to bring her delicious cunt to his mouth, which, as he was kneeling, was just at the proper level; so he gamahuched, and embracing her splendid arse, postilioned her at the same time; thus we were a chain of delight.

This bout was drawn out to great length.

The Egerton must have spent half a dozen times, and when we both at last jammed our pricks up in the ferocity of lust, making all three give down life's essence in an almost killing ecstasy, she really fainted quite away, and so alarmed us that we withdrew to use such remedies as were at hand to bring her to; even then she was quite hysterical. We laid her in the bed; she was relieved by a copious flood of tears, which she assured us were those of joy at the exquisite and overpowering delights we had conferred upon her. She begged us now to gratify the Benson with the same ecstatic joys we had bestowed upon her, and she would be a quiet and delighted spectator of our doings.

It was now my own loved Mrs Benson's turn to experience the inexpressible delights of the double junction. From her love of my splendid splitter, of which she had taken the first sweets, and which had been initiated in her deliciously adulterous cunt into the divine mysteries of love, and the still more sacred and secret joys of the second altar dedicated to the worship of unutterably sensual Priapean raptures; from this circumstance and the constant use of the rear receptacle practised by her husband, whose prick was a very fine one, the initiation into the *double jouissance* was less nervously effected than with the less used arsehole of the more delicate Egerton, but at the same time two such pricks operating at once made her wince a little before we were fairly engulfed to the cods, the banging together of which in their close proximity added greatly to the stimulating of our lust.

The sweet Benson lent herself most readily to the work, and seconded us by her art in wriggling her arse and the delicious cunt and sphincter pressures; enjoying herself at once and more rapidly than the Egerton, she got four delicious discharges before our somewhat more sluggish senses would allow us to come to the grand final crisis, which seemed to stimulate the divine Benson to a point of raving lust, which showed itself in cries of the grossest bawdy; shouting to us to shove our pricks in further and faster, calling us all the loudest blackguard names she could put her tongue to – absolutely roaring as the final discharge seized her in the very same instant that we poured floods of sperm into both interiors, she then sank, annihilated by the excess of the voluptuous delights conferred upon her, but lay throbbing and pulsating in all the after-joys of the utmost venereal satisfaction. We lay long in this delicious inanition of such voluptuous excesses.

The darling Benson exercised her delicious 'nippers' in both orifices, which soon had their expected effect, and shortly the flesh gave symptoms of its 'resurrection' to mundane joys, after having passed through the heavenly delights of Paradise, truly rising from the most delicious graves in which they were lying so exquisitely buried. Like her lovely predecessor she was eager for more, and if it were possible our second course was superior to the first, at all events it was longer drawn out, for the previous draughts on our slackening appendages made the further delivery an effort requiring longer pumping, and thus swelled the amount of pleasure by lengthening the process before arriving at the grand final crisis.

The Benson, much more ungovernable in her passion than we were, must have spent six or seven times in our last effort, and died away in, if anything, greater abandon than in our first course, and eventually sank, completely overcome by the entire satisfaction of her raging lust for the time being. We, too, both wanted a respite, so we all rose.

The two dear creatures when once on their legs found instant necessity to evacuate their rear receptacles of the double cargo taken in, and disappeared for a few minutes.

We all purified ourselves and well laved everything with ice cold water to reanimate them the sooner. We then sat down to a stimulating refreshment, in which we all drank at least a bottle of champagne apiece, in the midst of delightful and exciting bawdy wit and obscene stories, in which our darling *fouteuses* showed a witty proficiency.

In half an hour we began to take up our positions. It was my turn to take them in the rear, but both begged off for that day. The pause for refreshment had given time to make them feel sore after the great stretching they had undergone for the first time, so my turn was delayed for three days, that being the usual delay in their orgies to prevent suspicion by too frequent absences, but not excluding any opportunity that might occur for a rack-off in the meantime. So we only each fucked them once and closed our exquisite orgy for that day; parting with every expression of fully satisfied desires, and the warmest kisses and embraces.

The Count and I walked to his apartments to refresh ourselves there with hot tumblers of toddy; whisky being a great favourite of his, and, in his opinion, the best restorative after our exhausting efforts with the two insatiable creatures.

He congratulated himself on my accession to these orgies, as being a great relief to the burden he had had in satisfying both in both ways when all alone with them.

However, the Count was all indefatigable and an unwearied fucker, but two such insatiable cunts often had tried his powers to the utmost; he had found whisky toddy a remedy at once efficacious and agreeable. I myself with my private excesses at home was glad to know so pleasant a restorative. The Count and I became the most intimate and attached friends; through him I perfected myself in Italian, and not many years after this, passed some happy months with him in Italy after he had been amnestied, returned to his country and recovered part of his once large property, but of that hereafter.

I called next day on my adored Benson, who had developed into a glorious woman, more lovely and lustful than ever.

We had but a moment to ourselves, and could not use it for amatory purposes, but as we both had much to relate we agreed to meet at our house in Percy Street the next day.

This house was taken furnished for love purposes only, and merely an old woman was kept to take care of and arrange matters when we were gone; it was held in the Count's name but paid for by the two fair users of it They had latchkeys each, and the place was kept ready for everyday use.

The dear libidinous Benson avowed that she used it for other lovers unknown to the Count or the Egerton; paying the old woman liberally, she had all her own way.

We met there the next day, rushing into each other's arms; after assisting each other in the undressing, we had three exquisite fucks, during which the delighted Benson spent seven times; then we had a long and uninterrupted talk over old times, and my after-doings. I told her all, and how the Vincent, my elder sister, Miss Frankland, my aunt, and Mrs Dale had all thought me an innocent, receiving his first lesson in their delicious cunts, and how true and wise had been her sage counsels. She listened in wonder and delight, drew from me descriptive pictures of our conjunctions and thrice interrupted my narrative to have a delicious fuck to calm the excitement raised by the lascivious descriptions of my acts with all those most glorious women. I told her also of my intrigue at my lodgings with the two sisters and their aunt.

My description of the latter set her off in raging lust, and produced another most excellent fuck. But afterwards she told me I must find other quarters in some place where Mrs Egerton and she, or either of them, could call and receive comfort without observation.

I told her I was inscribed for chambers in the Inner Temple, which I had reason to believe I should get in a week or two. This much pleased her, and it will be seen that I succeeded in getting just such a set as exactly suited the great object in view, approachable without being under the observation of others, commodious and agreeable, where all that the dear Benson wished to be added to our set were brought together, and the wildest orgies of the most insatiable lust were carried on.

My description of my aunt, of Mrs Dale, and especially of Miss Frankland, now Mrs Nixon, excited all the tribadic passions for which the dear Benson was so famous.

Her clitoris, which was formerly prominent, was more so now, and she dearly loved to gamahuche her own sex. In that way she took a great fancy to my sisters, especially Eliza, who had all the same instincts very decidely pronounced. So we had the prospect of the most consummate orgies in near view, and most gloriously in the end we realised our wildest expectations.

In men we were more restricted; the Count would only consent to have Harry Dale and my uncle in any orgy of which he formed part. He was nervously timid about his sodomistic tendencies being known to many, and only yielded on account of the relationship and the close ties bewteen myself and Harry Dale, who eventually shared my chambers; we lived together, so perforce he was obliged to put up with his presence.

He soon came to delight in having Harry's prick in his bottom when fucking others at our orgies. It will thus be seen that the Count's timid exclusiveness shut out from these family orgies my dear and esteemed friend and master James MacCallum. However, in a certain sense, it was an advantage, as we had at least the pick of the young ones, in my two sisters and Ellen, who wanted very little persuasion to join our Lyon's Inn orgies. And our excellent friend had some of his own set, both male and female, to meet us, either with one, two or all, for we could not always manage to have the whole of the dear creatures together. *En revanche*, dear MacCallum had several youthful Ganymedes, whose tight young bottom-holes were a great solace when cunts were altogether absent. We thus had two distinct and separate sets of orgies, which had all the natural effect of novelty, and by exciting comparison, made us turn from one to the other with renewed passions and power of enjoyment.

As my sisters could only come on Sundays, that was our exclusive day, and we made an entire day of it, but I, in the end, persuaded Ann to join our orgies with MacCallum, and she proved a first-rate addition in every way.

I have already stated that she was of a most libidinous temperament, and developed into one of the most lascivious and lustful of women one could possibly find, and as she had rare beauties and splendour of form, she was made to raise the most raging lust in man or woman, for she, too, was as fond of tribadic indulgences as my aunt or the delicious Frankland. Her position as a servant prevented our introducing her to Ellen or my sisters. As a matter of worldly prudency it was best not to trust her with the knowledge of their complying with all our lustful demands on their charming persons.

The Count, myself, and our two charming lovers met on the appointed day to renew our delicious orgies. After both of us had fucked each dear creature came the *double jouissance*.

We took the adorable Benson first, that the scene of our erotic sports might stir the lust of the darling Egerton to a greater heat. It was my turn to lay my offering on the secret altar of Priapus, while the Count filled her cunt with delight.

As I have before said, the arsehole of the Benson was much more used that that of the Egerton, whose husband never dreamt of such a horror, as she would call it. Mr Benson, on the contrary, delighted in it, and seldom passed a night without paying his devoirs to that delicious aperture. So, although it was but the second time she had indulged in the *double jouissance*, yet her lust enabled her to take in with greater ease my big prick in her arsehole, with the Count's fine prick in front, than when our parts were reversed. She revelled in the wild fury of raging lust created by the glorious ecstasy of having a prick in each aperture, screamed with wild cries of heavenly joy, spent furiously and eventually died away in an overpowering and indescribable felicity. She soon recovered her senses and begged for another bout before withdrawing. Of course there was immediate compliance and another more soul-killing encounter was run off with the usual death-like termination.

I had continuously gamahuched the Egerton who straddled over the two bodies below her, and brought her delicious cunt to my mouth, while my arms encircled her beautifully formed and cream-coloured buttocks, at the same time acting postilion with two fingers to increase her lustful gratification.

We purified ourselves after this, and drank some champagne, then standing stiff at the prospect of now possessing the lovely body of the Egerton, we took up the same position as before, the Count under, in cunt, the Egerton above, with her deliciously fair arse exposed to my embraces first, and my big prick afterwards.

The adored Benson gave it a suck first, and well wetting the knob, guided it to the narrow entrance of love's secret bower. Its head was soon housed, and although still creating strange feelings, the previous day's attack had made the entrance more facile.

With little halting we drove on to the first delicious discharge. The second bout was all divine pleasure, and ever after the delicious Egerton enjoyed it completely.

These delicious orgies with these two lovely women were indulged in on every third day.

I became a favourite with both their husbands, thanks to a kind of sheepish innocence that I had the power of putting on.

At the same time as my education had been well attended to and as I myself was fond of study, attentive to my college instruction, and anxious for a knowledge of foreign languages, I had become fairly proficient in German and Spanish, and well read in French and Italian. The latter was perfected by the Count's friendship, as we were much together and spoke nothing else. Perhaps it was this which led to a greater friendship for me on the part of Mr Egerton, who was an excellent Italian scholar. His wife's intrigue with the Count had also perfected her, so that when we all four dined together Italian was the only language spoken among us.

The dear Benson, too, was a perfect mistress of the Count's tongue, as well she might be, having it so often in her mouth; and as it is a soft language that lends itself to love and lust, it became ours in all our orgies.

The delicious Frankland, now Mrs Nixon, returned to town with the spring. By that time I was established in my chambers in the Inner Temple, and had them simply furnished, but with every accessory for love's combats, in couples or in the wildest orgies. The adorable Benson inaugurated and dedicated them to the service of holy mother Venus and her son Cupid, as well as the more lustful Eros.

The Egerton and the Count afterwards came to consecrate them to the worship of Priapus, and we had a most delicious orgy on that sacred celebration.

It was on this occasion that those two wild lustful creatures insisted on seeing the Count and me in conjunction together. The Benson guided me into the Count's bottom, while he was in the bottom of the Egerton, and the Egerton conducted the Count into my bottom while I was luxuriating in the delicious arsehole of my adored Benson. It satisfied a longing desire on their parts to see man with man, and did not displease either the Count or myself, who, in our secret hearts, had each wished to possess the other.

The Count was a powerful and very hairy man, and had an especially very full hairy arsehole, which to me was wildly exciting.

In that I differed from my dear friend MacCallum, who loved bare-arsed youths with no hair there, telling me that coarse hairy arsed men rather disgusted him, and although in his wide sodomitic experience he had had such, it was with a certain repugnance that went against the grain.

In that I differed from him entirely, the hairier and the coarser a man's arsehole was the more it excited me. In that respect the Count was exactly to my taste. He was very hairy all up the chink of his arse, and had a very coarse skin and an almost black arsehole; so deep a brown it was, the very sight of it always drove me mad with lust.

He as much loved me from another cause. His great letch was to frig a fine prick while buggering the possessor, hence, as he had never met with so fine a one as mine, he was insatiably fond of being into me and frigging me at the same time.

We thus had two points of private attraction, that made us become the closest of friends, but we did not let any of our dear female participants know of the mutual joys of which they were not participants.

The superb Frankland, now my guardian's wife, also came alone to my chambers, and we had a renewal of all our wildest experiences. She told me it was such a comfort to her, for although her husband, Mr Nixon, was very loving, and did all he could, still it was nothing but exciting her to long for others, especially for my own huge prick, of which she never knew but that she had been the first initiator of it into love's delicious recess in either sacred grove.

So fresh and eager as she was for the fray, you may easily imagine the wild excess we indulged in, sucking, gamahuching, fucking and buggering. I cannot tell how often in every way her exciting and glorious body carried me away to an excess beyond anything I could have thought myself capable of.

When fairly exhausted, and we could uninterruptedly talk over all that had occurred since I had left my mother's house, she heard in full detail, for the first time, all my adventures.

I had given her, at the time of her marriage, a hint of how matters had gone, yet without any details, which now she was voracious to hear. I told her of my aunt's and uncle's apparent seduction of me, nor did I hide our goings-on with young Dale, and my after-possession of Ellen and his mother, who was the last to believe herself my seducer, for as I told the delicious Frankland (I can never bear to call her Nixon), I had followed her sage advice, and up to the Dale had played off the innocent game with perfect success; but now that I was a man I threw all that overboard.

'Indeed,' said she, 'and who have you been throwing it overboard with.'

I laughed at her ready taking of me up, and then went on to a full confession of all my intrigues.

She did not like my having taken up with the two servants, the nieces of my late landlady, thinking it derogatory in one endowed with a prick that any lady would be too glad to possess, but she was very much struck with my description of the superb body and wonderful lubricity of the Nichols.

It excited her much, especially when I told her that she had given me the idea of her near approach in body and wantonness to herself. It will be seen hereafter to what a closer alliance with the Nichols this led. Pressed by her enquiries, I acknowledged my intrigue with the Benson, the Egerton and the Count. This evidently excited her lust, as I could see by the wild sparkle of her eye. It led to an immediate and delicious fuck, and when we had recovered from its ecstatic finish, to closer and more searching enquiry as to how I got into such intimacy; but I had expected this somewhat jealous scrutiny, and was quite prepared for it. I led her to believe they had been here nearly all the winter. I told her my mother had desired me to call and see the Bensons as friends of hers. I had done so. The Bensons quickly observed how largely I was furnished, very soon gave me encouragement, of which I did not want much after the late intercourse I had had with herself, aunt, and Mrs Dale. Thus matters came quickly to their natural conclusion. She was perfectly astonished at my powerful weapon, and as she and her dearest friend already shared lovers, I was quickly introduced to her friend Mrs Egerton, and they had me together, and let me into the secret of their intrigue with the Count, which was followed by my initiation into their orgies.

My praises of these two ladies, and my saying how glorious it would be for her to make a fifth, and my description of the exquisite body and the tribadic tendencies of Mrs Benson, fired her wild imagination, and woke up all her tribadic lusts, and it ended in her begging me to give a luncheon at my chambers to the Benson and the Egerton, that she might be introduced to them, more especially as they really moved in a society somewhat higher than Mr Nixon's connections, although, in point of wealth, the Nixons were far superior.

The little luncheon came off most agreeably. The ladies all took to each other most warmly; seeing which, I boldly broke the ice, and telling the Benson and the Egerton that dear Mrs Nixon had initiated me in love's mysteries, as had both of them, the wisest thing we could do would be to throw away all restraint and have a jollification all round. To set them at their ease – for there was a momentary hesitation – I pulled out my prick at full stand, and said: 'There's a prick worthy of all your exquisite cunts, and one, too, that has enjoyed them all, and been enjoyed by every one of you. So throw away all hesitation and let him enjoy you all again. Who is to have him first?'

They laughed, and all approached and handled it, interchanging their opinions upon its being the very finest one that any of them had ever seen.

'Ah, now,' said I, 'that is just the thing, you are at once put at ease, then let us do it with ease; strip is the word, and let us have it luxuriously.'

They laughed, kissed each other, and said the dear fellow must have his way, and all at once proceeded to undress.

The glorious and wonderfully hairy body of the Frankland perfectly astonished them, and raised their tribadic passions to fever heat, especially the Benson, who threw herself on that glorious form in an ecstasy of delight, more especially as, the Frankland's passions being excited, her long red clitoris stood out from the dense black mass of hair which covered not only her belly and mount, but all down and around her cunt. Nothing would satisfy the Benson but an immediate mutual gamahuche, for, with true tribadic instinct, these two beautiful and libidinous women divined their mutual letch for that particular lascivious inclination, and at once proceeded, one on top of the other, to gamahuche each other wildly. The Egerton and myself seized the opportunity of having a delicious fuck together, which we brought to a conclusion before the others had satisfied their immediate desires.

The Frankland, who at first was under, was now above, and as she knelt and pushed out her stupendous arse to bring her cunt over the Benson's mouth, the sight of its hairy arsehole roused my desire to fuck it, and my cock responded instantly, so kneeling behind her, I introduced it to the well-known receptacle, and to her infinite additional delight, sodomised her to perfection. This was another means of putting them all at ease, and I fucked and buggered them all until neither handling nor suction could get my prick to raise his head again.

You may easily imagine after this how delighted they were to make the glorious Frankland a participator in our orgies with the Count. Nor shall I forget the wild gaze of surprise and lust when the Count first beheld the splendid and hairy form of the glorious Frankland when she entered the room in all the dazzling splendour of her perfect nakedness. These two natures were made for each other, both salacious in the extreme, both vigorous in body and untiring in the most libidinous excesses of the wildest lust, both hairy to a degree – perhaps showing the meaning of that vast display all over both their bodies. They were instantly attracted to each other, flew into the closest of embraces, and sinking on the floor where they met, two strokes were racked off before they came to a state of more moderation, amenable to our general operations. It had been all the same an exciting scene to us.

The Benson was madly stimulated by the sight of the Frankland's superb body; her long red clitoris, not satisfied with the double rack-off with the Count, appeared only to be more excited, and stirred the whole soul of the adorable Benson. She threw herself in reverse upon the Frankland before she had time to raise herself, seized with her mouth the wonderful clitoris, called upon me to fuck her from behind, and then, with fingers up arsehole and cunt, worked furiously. The dear Frankland responded on the fine clitoris of the Benson, and postilioned me at the same time. We ran off two bouts in this delicious position, and then with more regulated passions rose to form more general combinations.

The Count had fucked the Egerton while we were engaged above the divine Frankland. Our first pose was suggested by the Egerton, who had been as yet less fucked than any. She had been also greatly taken with the glories of the Frankland's superb body, and especially struck with her extraordinary clitoris, and had taken the curious letch of wishing to have it in her bottom-hole while riding St George on my big prick. We all laughed at her odd choice, but agreed at once, especially the Frankland, whose greatest letch was to fuck very fair young women with her long and capable clitoris. A fairer creature than the lovely Egerton could not be found. The Frankland admitted that in her inmost heart she had longed thus to have the Egerton from the moment she had first seen her, and her delight and surprise at finding the dear Egerton had equally desired to possess her, fired her fierce lust with increased desire. I lay down, the Egerton straddled over, and feeling the delight of my huge prick when completely embedded, she spent profusely with only two rebounds. Then sinking on my belly she presented her lovely arse to the lascivious embraces of the salacious Frankland, whose first act was to stoop, embrace, kiss, and tongue the beautiful little pinky aperture, wetting it with her saliva, she brought her fine long clitoris, stiff as a prick, and plunged within. The letch that both had taken for the same indulgence lent enchantment to the act, and their wild imaginations created an excess of joy that the smaller size of the Frankland's clitoris, in comparison with the dimensions of our longer pricks, might not have led one to suppose possible.

Twice we indulged in this excess, the women going off half a dozen times to my once.

I had aided the Frankland by using a double dildo, which at once filled both apertures This excellent instrument was an invention of the Frankland, which she had suggested to a Parisian dildo maker, and she had had it made in two or three sizes. It became very useful in our orgies, as from disparity of numbers an odd couple were left out, when the *double jouissance* was in operation, and then the two outsiders, with tongues and dildoes, could gamahuche with great satisfaction.

During our tribadic junction, with the Egerton fucked by the Frankland in the arse, the Count had first fucked and then sodomised the Benson to their mutual satisfaction. We all rose, purified, and refreshed ourselves with wine and biscuits while discussing what our next move should be. The Count had not yet had the Frankland *in culo*, and suggested, as it was her introductory meeting, that the greater honours should be conferred on her on this happy occasion, so I was to fuck her while he enjoyed her in the rear quarters. The Egerton and the Benson should use double dildoes on each other, or in any other way amuse themselves.

This was a most exquisite encounter, and with such unutterable enjoyment that we hardly paused between the first and second, and it was not until we had deluged thrice both interiors that we withdrew. The delighted Frankland had never ceased spending, but so vigorous a nature could easily have taken twice as much; but the other dear creatures had now to be conciliated.

The Count next took the Benson in cunt while I blocked the rear aperture, and the Frankland once more enculed the Egerton, who dildoed herself in cunt at the same time; all of us ran two courses. We then rose, purified, and refreshed. When our pricks were ready it was the Egerton who took me in front and the Count behind, and the Benson, who had grown lewd on the Frankland's clitoris, was sodomised by her and dildoed by herself. The Egerton still suffered a little in the double stretching, so that we ran but one exquisite bout, enabling us, whose powers began to fail, to be re-excited and to finish with the *double jouissance* in the glorious body of the Frankland.

We carried this on until the midsummer holidays, when, at their desire, I introduced the Benson, Egerton, Frankland and the Count to my uncle, aunt, Mrs Dale, Ellen and Harry, and we had some glorious orgies in my chambers.

The splendour of my aunt's arse captivated the Frankland and the Count. The latter soon got into young Dale's arse, which he did one day when arriving for the very purpose half an hour before the appointed time for all to meet. I was present, and was so excited at the sight that I seized upon the Count's arse and delightedly astonished him by giving the double enjoyment.

It was after this, as Harry remained to live with me, that he was introduced to our general orgies, and thus we occupied all the dear creatures at once, and most voluptuous and lascivious meetings we all enjoyed, the Count occasionally giving us a private visit.

Meanwhile Ellen had been put to the same finishing school where my sisters already were, with permission to go out with them on the Sundays, when we always had a delicious orgy at our dear friend MacCallum's. He, like the Count, had taken a peculiar fancy for the tight young arsehole of Harry Dale, without altogether deserting the women, especially my sister Eliza, whose delight in rear sports was supreme, and she never would be fucked but when she had a prick in each aperture, preferring mine in her cunt with either Dale or MacCallum operating in the rear.

Knowing the hours when I could not be interrupted by any of my lady friends, I did not neglect the superb Nichols, but had her and Ann to come together for an hour and a half, from half-past nine to eleven a.m., and most delicious fucking I had with both. I had equally initiated them into the mysteries of rear delights, and both took it with great gusto. Upon finding this I gradually descanted on the exquisite delights of the *double jouissance* with two male pricks, filling with ecstasies indescribable the two apertures at once.

When once I had excited their desires on this point, I mentioned my dear friend James MacCallum, as one in whom we could all confide, and with some little hesitation obtained their consent to introduce him. I had already mentioned the matter to him; told him he might think the Nichols too old, but she was gloriously superb in body, and so extraordinarily well preserved that her body was twenty years younger than her face and her lust and fucking powers were far superior to a woman of twenty-five. Besides, I hinted that he might persuade Ann, and perhaps her sister Jane, to join our Lyon's Inn revels.

We met by appointment on a given morning. I advised MacCallum to come sooner, and when the women came, under the pretence of his not being able to join us that morning, I would get them stripped, and when all was ready he should appear in buff, and so break any *mauvaise honte* they might have at first undressing before him.

He was wonderfully struck with the superb body of the Nichols, and, as the stranger, we gave him his choice. He clasped her in his nervous arms, devoured her with kisses, and incontinently laying her down on the mattressed floor, proceeded to fuck her in the good old English fashion, with legs and arms around her body. Ann and I gazed for a little on the splendid action of her aunt's arse, and the evident way in which she milked the teat as it withdrew each time he heaved his arse to re-enter with exciting vigour. We could hold no longer and each ran a course of ecstatic delight ending in all the frenzy of lust to die inanimate the next instant.

Our charming partners had spent repeatedly during our encounter. They wanted an immediate renewal, but MacCallum suggested a change of partners and of position, that is to say, fucking them on their knees with their splendidly developed buttocks turned up but taking them in the cunt.

This change was rapidly effected. We placed ourselves in such a position that each could see all the action of the other. It was a splendid fuck, and as our edge was taken off we drew it out a considerable length, giving the dear recipients the opportunity of spending four or five times to our once.

After recovering from the soaking after-joys of this delicious encounter, we had some champagne and some smutty talk, as well as outspoken praise of their splendid power of fuck; feeling their cunts and they our pricks till renovated and renewed, we arranged for further action. As it was their introductory lesson in the double enjoyment, the splendid Nichols had, of course, first choice. She chose me for cunt, and to his intense delight, our dear friend for the rear attack. Ann was to straddle over her aunt and me, and be gamahuched both in cunt and arsehole by our friend. We had no difficulty in hilting ourselves to the cods in both apertures, but so excited was the Nichols that with the mere throbbings of our pricks on completely housing ourselves, she spent, squealing like a rabbit. We gave her time fully to enjoy it, and then commenced a slow, regulated movement, which quickly drove the Nichols into a state of killing agony of delight, screaming with excess of ecstasy. Again we paused to allow of the utmost enjoyment, but renewed when her delicious cunt and arse pressures announced a return of craving appetite. These pauses enabled us to bring on seven overpouring discharges on her part, until she was quite exhausted, especially when we both came together in an excess of joy that ended in perfect inanition, on recovering from which we relieved the Nichols of the double cargo within her.

She had already almost strangled me with her embraces in the unutterable joys I had procured her. Rolling off on her side she drew MacCallum also to her, to embrace him for the intense gratification he had afforded her. We again refreshed the inward man, after a purification and laving with cold water as a restorative. Then Ann took up her position in her turn, for she, too, wished to try the novel experiment with the smaller prick in her arsehole.

The Nichols felt exhausted for the moment so lay on the sofa and enjoyed the sight of our three persons in all the delirium of raging lust and sodomy. The experiment enchanted Ann as it had overpoweringly enchanted her aunt. She, too, spent seven or eight times before joining us in our soul-killing discharge. The Nichols had lain still for about two thirds of the time this bout continued; she then rose to straddle across Ann and me, and was about to present her magnificently large cunt to be gamahuched by MacCallum, but he begged her to turn her bottom to him and heave it well up, while resting her hands on Ann's shoulders. He then could first contemplate and handle her huge superb buttocks, then transferring his hands to her clitoris and cunt, he licked and tongued the grand aperture of her arse – rough, brown, and corrugated, just my taste.

We had a most glorious bout, ending in all the ecstatic joys of spending and after-delights. Ann was as greatly gratified with the *double jouissance* as her aunt had been before. We again laved and refreshed, and closed this most delicious orgy with MacCallum first in the Nichols' cunt, with my big and doted-on prick in her arse, which, now she was used to it, pleased her more than ever.

In the same order we double-fucked Ann, although she expressed her greater gratification of MacCallum in her arse and my splitter in her cunt. Again we gamahuched them both, but as time would not allow of our resurrection, then they left us.

My guardian, at his marriage, had bought a house in Portland Place, but the lease of its then tenant only expired on the 30th March the following spring, and before being occupied it had to be entirely repainted and decorated, so that July was nearly at an end before they could comfortably take up their residence in it. Meanwhile they had apartments at a hotel near Hyde Park Corner.

When once they were completely housed, which was not the case until the middle of August, my guardian desired his wife to send the carriage for the girls every Sunday morning. Hearing that Ellen was their intimate friend, she became included in the invitation. This put an end to our Sunday orgies in our friend MacCallum's chambers, much to our mutual regret.

As far as Harry and I were concerned the ever thoughtful and delicious Frankland came to our aid. Pretending that the girls must need walking exercise, she always after luncheon proposed they should walk down to their brother's chambers in the Temple, take him and Harry as their further companions up to Kensington Gardens or the Zoo, and bring all back to dinner.

My guardian always took a siesta on Sundays after luncheon, for being too old to fuck his wife every night, Saturday night, or rather Sunday morning, when he had nothing in the way of business to trouble him, was dedicated to two or three hours of extra dalliance with his adored wife. She told me he was very amorous upon her, could not do much fucking, indeed, she thought his efforts that way were even more than he ought to do at his age, but he was never tired of gamahuching her and posing her in every attitude when stark naked; of course she lent herself to every wish of the old man, and had, after great persuasion, which only her love and attachment to him could have made her yield to, allowed him the honours of her beautiful arsehole. This requiring, as he said, an extra firmness of prick, she further did him the extra favour of toying with and sucking his prick up to the utmost stiffness. So she had made him absolutely adore her, and she could turn him round her little finger. Her word and will was law, so she could do as she liked.

She told me on several occasions that she thought he was exerting his erotic powers to too great an extent, and that she did all she could to moderate his excitement, but all to no purpose; he was infatuated with the glorious charms of her body, or what is called *cunt-struck*, perhaps the strongest passion that can seize on man and dangerous for a man of advanced years. Well, his Sunday afternoon's siesta was long, and left the Frankland at liberty to come to my rooms with my sisters, where strip was the word, and fucking in every variety followed.

I soon found we must have other help; the pace I was going at was beginning to tell, so with the consent of the darling Frankland I made a confidant of the Count, and asked him to join our Sunday's orgy. You may imagine with what joy he accepted, for apart from his delight in seeing me in incestuous connection with my sisters, their young charms, especially Eliza's, had great attraction for him, as had the Frankland, so similar in lust and temperament. We had thus most delicious orgies every Sunday afternoon, until the end of October of the following year, when my sisters had finished their schooling and I, too, had left college, entered at the Middle Temple, and had been for three months in a conveyancer's office, reading up previous to being called to the bar.

It was then that Mr Nixon's health gave symptoms of serious disturbance, and his doctor recommended him to pass the winter in a warmer climate. His wife suggested the advantage travelling would be both to the girls and myself; she had only to express the wish to have us all together, and we were warmly invited to join them.

We passed through Switzerland, Milan and Florence to Rome, where we took up our residence for four months.

The Egertons and Bensons happily spent the same winter in Rome.

My rooms were in an adjoining palace to where Mr and Mrs Nixon and my sisters resided, there not being accommodation for me. I thus had a charming entresol of five rooms all to myself; one of which looked on and over the Tiber, and was in no way overlooked. To this room we constantly resorted for orgies.

The Egerton had passed some winters in Rome, and she had two or three clerical lovers, and these had introduced two others to the Benson on her former visits, and all had been accustomed to general orgies. You may imagine the delight of these priestly debauchees when they found themselves introduced to our circle of three fresh cunts, and such splendid ones, and all without any mock-modest prejudices but up to every excess of lubricity. So to five women we thus had six men, and eventually a very handsome young priest, debauched by the others, joined our party, and we carried on the wildest and most extravagant orgies of every excess the most raging lust could devise. We made chains of pricks in arseholes, the women between with dildoes strapped round their waists which each shoved into the arsehole of the man before her, while his prick was into the arsehole of the woman in his front.

These holy fathers had immense resources in the way of infinite variety, stimulating to excesses of debauchery that very soon brought the rod into requisition.

We all from time to time enjoyed the double coition, the women invariably so at every meeting.

These holy fathers had all very fine pricks, but none so large as mine, and many of them loved to have my prick in their arses when opportunity offered. In such delights the winter passed rapidly away.

In the spring Mr Nixon's health seemed very precarious, and we moved to Naples, where from necessity our extreme indulgence in venereal excesses was much curtailed.

In May we returned to England, but poor Mr Nixon was evidently fucked out. The Frankland told me that the more his health failed the more lewd he seemed to grow. His passion for gamahuching her cunt had increased, and even his prick seemed to gather new vigour as life ebbed away, for hardly a night passed without his fucking her; at night he took her in the cunt, and at morning, in full daylight, kneeling and feeling her splendid arse, he took her in the rear aperture. He and she too felt it was killing him, but his infatuation was overpowering, and he declared if it did kill him he could not die a happier death. In fact a month after we returned he had an apoplectic fit actually when his prick was spending in her arsehole. He lived but a month afterwards. He left all his property to his wife absolutely, with legacies of £2,500 to each of my sisters, and £1,000 to me.

This sad event cast a gloom for some time over all our pleasures.

The Frankland took my sisters to reside with her, but all went down to spend the first three months of mourning quietly with my mother. She, too, took ill when we were with her, and died before the three months were up. This drew me down to home, now mine, and the dear Frankland continued to stay with us for two months longer, and then left for London. We three orphans remained for all that winter in our old home, settling a variety of things.

My sisters now with their succession to some £600 apiece, the £1,000 left them by our uncle, and the £2,500 by Mr Nixon, and the £400 which I promised them as a marriage present, and with their great beauty of form and face, for both had grown into remarkably fine young women, became very eligible matches.

Many country families sought us out after the first three months of our mourning, and several offers were made to the girls. They were both somewhat fastidious after the life they had led, but eventually both were married. Mary to a very nice fellow, who proved, as she told me, a first-rate fucker. He got her with child, and they had a son, a fine boy, in the tenth month of their marriage. She was very happy, now and then coming to see me, and getting a jolly good fuck from my renovated prick, for now that he was lying fallow, my somewhat exhausted system was getting quite recruited.

Alas! poor Mary lost her husband by cholera in the second year of their marriage. He had a handsome estate, and left her well off, and sole guardian to his son, who grew up a very fine fellow, and when at puberty became the solace of his widowed mother, who had initiated him into all love's mysteries.

Eliza was not quite so fortunate as her sister in her husband; he was a good sort of man who, one would have thought, would just have suited the hot temperament of Eliza, well and powerfully built, and with an air of being a man of erotic passions; but he turned out to be of a languid unimpassioned nature, who could not imagine any other manner than simply mounting on a woman's belly and fucking her once a night, and with no conception of using either preliminaries or aids to her passions. So that he left poor Eliza only in a state of excitement instead of giving any satisfaction to her lascivious nature. She did, eventually, work him up to good-night and good-morning, but for her full satisfaction she used to seek elsewhere, and even to content herself with the embraces of a manservant, who, if not good looking, proved to have a splendid and powerful prick, and nearly daily gave her comfort. She also occasionally came to me, when she had both apertures well exercised, and left me much comforted.

She never had any children, and so managed her intrigues as never to be found out.

I returned to London in the spring, and was called to the bar.

I went the western circuit for odd assizes, and then abandoned the bar as a profession.

Harry Dale, with more perseverance, as well as greater necessity for exertion, continued in the profession, was duly called to the bar, and eventually became a rising and successful barrister, and at this period of our old age is now a distinguished judge.

But to return to our earlier days.

Harry and I carried on our intrigue with the Nichols and Ann, aided by our dear friend MacCallum. Also from time to time with the Benson, Egerton and Count, to which gatherings generally the darling Frankland brought her exquisite charms to intoxicate us with pleasure.

This delightful reunion was sadly affected by the loss of the Count, who received an amnesty – I think I before have said he was a political exile – returned to his own country, and we never again had his delightful aid in our sadly shortened orgies.

The Count and I met in a future year at his old castle on the hills of Pied, of which I shall have much more to say on a later occasion.

It was a sad loss, especially for the Egerton, who dearly loved the Count. He had been her first lover, indeed, her initiator in the real mysteries of Venus. It will be remembered that her husband was one of those old insensible natures that think it is only necessary hastily to 'piss their tallow', as Falstaff says, as quickly as they can, and leave a poor woman just sufficiently excited to be madly anxious for a thorough good fucking. It is these insensate cold-blooded husbands who raise, without satisfying, their wife's erotic passions, and drive them perforce to seek salacious comfort in other arms.

Oh! how many women if only fucked with some regard to their own naturally lewd feeling, would have never committed adultery or made a scandal. Many are the women who have told me, with tears in their eyes, of the cold insensible conduct of their husbands, who, never fucking them but when their sluggish natures feel the want, then turning upon them without the slightest preparatory handling or embracing, mount, shove it in, give a few in-and-out movements, spend, and then withdraw, just as they have done enough to excite their poor wives' passions without satisfying them, and thus leaving them a prey to inordinate longing that forces them to seek relief of the passions the selfish brutes of husbands have only raised without allaying.

I remember an intrigue I had with an Italian countess. Her husband, a tall and very capable man, was an extreme bigot, who thought it deadly sin to indulge in any caresses or carnal excitement, or even for his wife to expose any naked flesh to raise concupiscent ideas, so she had to have her night-gown closed up to her throat, with long sleeves and skirts and in the centre a slit through which he performed his duty when in want of relief to himself.

He never kissed or embraced her body at any time, but lay like a log by her side, with his back turned to her. When his own passions prompted him to fuck, which was very seldom, he was naturally quite ready and rapidly finished his *coup*. He used to turn to her, wake her up with a shake and cry out, 'Marietta, porgemi il vaso generativo' (Marietta, reach me the generative vase), upon which she stretched herself on her back; he got on her without lifting her petticoats or feeling her cunt, but opening the slit, pointed his prick to her cunt, thrust it up to the hilt, and being himself in want of spermatic relief, in a very few strokes spent, just staying in long enough to 'piss all his tallow', and then withdrew, turning his back again to sleep, leaving his wife just sufficiently excited to have enjoyed it but madly longing for the further satisfaction he did not afford. She said he was quite capable, too, of giving satisfaction if his bigotry had allowed him. We used to fuck at a tremendous rate, and I always commenced with a 'Marietta, Marietta, porgemi il vaso generativo,' and then proceeded to fuck and laugh like mad.

Of course, irritated as her hot passions were by her booby of a husband, she resorted, not only to me, but to whomsoever she could get to satisfy the cravings of her irritated cunt.

The Bensons and Egertons again left in the autumn for Rome.

The Frankland, not yet out of her year's widowhood, did not go much into society, and we saw much more of her than before. She came at least three times a week to my chambers, when Harry and I gave her the comfort she so much required; first each fucking her singly twice over, and then three double-pleasure fucks, with change about in the apertures; finishing off with a mouth fuck from one or the other, and a double gamahuche.

About once a week the amorous and delicious-fucking Nichols with Ann would come of a morning, when we managed to send both away satisfied for the day.

When winter drove our friend MacCallum home from his fishing, we renewed some excellent orgies at his chambers, where Ann, and afterwards Jane, occasionally came. By the way, Jane's arse had developed in an extra-ordinary manner, and became one of the most exciting delights of our orgies at MacCallum's. He also now joined in our morning encounters with the Nichols and her niece.

At Christmas time the Frankland, Harry, and I all went down by invitation to the rectory, where uncle welcomed with great delight the glorious and exciting Frankland. Mrs Dale and Ellen joined our party. Dear aunt positively devoured me with her caresses, and before I was shown up to my room, had drawn me into her little room downstairs, had a suck at my prick, leant her body on the table, stuck out her immense arse, and had me into her cunt for a rapid rack-off; but this only excited me to renewed efforts, for the touch and sight of her splendid buttocks instantly produced a stiffness which she herself at once took advantage of, drawing my prick out of her cunt and guiding it into the inviting entrance to the secret altar of Juno and of Venus Callipyge. Both courses were run off at a gallop, and were a momentary allaying of the insatiable salacity of my most lewd and lascivious aunt. She next conducted the Frankland (I can never call her Nixon) into her bedroom, under pretence of showing her to it. She no sooner had her there than up went her petticoats, and aunt glued her lips to the wonderful clitoris of the divine Frankland, and using fingers up both apertures, made the Frankland quickly give down her first offering to the obscene god.

As soon as aunt's tribadic rage to possess the Frankland was thus abated for the moment, she allowed Mrs Nixon to remove bonnet and shawl, but then as quickly demanded and obtained a double gamahuche, the Frankland the more readily consenting as she knew aunt had taken the keen edge off my lecherous appetite, and she would revel in the thick raging sperm I had shot into both orifices. These preliminaries settled, we were able to be much more tranquil all the afternoon.

The Dale and Ellen came to dinner; I slipped into their room when all were dressing for dinner, and had a delicious rack-off in both their lecherous and longing cunts. Uncle had equally enjoyed the tight favourite arsehole of Harry Dale, he having conducted him to the well-known summerhouse for that purpose as soon as we arrived.

We could all thus peaceably enjoy the good things set before us, and during our wine after dinner exchange accounts of all events that had passed since last we met, and they were varied, for Mr Nixon's death and legacies to my sisters and myself were subjects of congratulation, while the death of my mother was, on the contrary, one of condolence and sympathy.

By ten o'clock we all broke up, but with the whispered request to all to repair to aunt's bedroom half an hour after the household had retired. We were all too interested in the delicious orgy there to take place to fail. Blazing fires in both that and the adjoining room had been kept up all the afternoon; plenty of lights were burning so as to illuminate all sides at once. We all met in mere night wrappers, and as soon as we were assembled and the word 'off' given, they were thrown aside, and we all stood in nature's lovely nakedness. Aunt, in her eager and lascivious inspirations, flung herself on my naked body, drew me to the bed, and had me into her longing and delicious cunt at once, and with legs and arms thrown round me, was instantly pressing furiously forward, notwithstanding the remonstrance of my uncle, who wished to arrange a general plan of operations so as to include all at once. Aunt's voluptuous eagerness produced a rapid discharge on her part. Seeing this, while she was in the momentary ecstasy of spending he was able to drag me from her arms, fortunately before I had weakened my powers by spending for a fourth time that day. Aunt, too, was now in a condition to listen to reason, and bring her ideas of our after-combinations into play.

As we had brought the Count with us for a week's stay, we were just four cocks to four hens; so we could couple in the first instance on an exact equality, it being necessary by previous good fucking to bring the women's passions up to a boiling heat of lust to make them enter into our greater excesses with all the wild energy of the most salacious lubricity. Aunt had taken a great fancy to the Count when up at midsummer.

Uncle was most lecherous on the glorious Frankland. I took most readily to the luscious and lascivious Dale, who was equally eager to repossess the prick which she firmly believed she had initiated into all the joys of cunt, and a most delicious fuck we had, she spending furiously and frequently to my once.

Harry was equally pleased to pair off with his loved cousin, whose maidenhead he had undoubtedly taken.

The women would gladly have had each fucker run a second course without drawing. But both aunt and uncle opposed this, as both more exhausting and less variety. So aunt chose me, uncle took the exciting young cunt of Ellen, Harry turned on to his mother's cunt, from whence he had originally come into the world, and the Count got the glorious Frankland, of whom he was never tired. This course was more prolonged by the men than the first, with the object of somewhat allaying the insatiable lust of the women by making them spend infinitely oftener than their fuckers.

We so managed matters that we all came together or nearly so, and the women followed suit at the last final crisis, which was ushered in with wild cries of lust, and then a sudden overpowering silence fell on all as they lay panting in all the after-joys that follow the ecstatic discharge of life's essence.

We rose for a general embrace of our naked bodies, then a romp, and a mutual slapping of arses and seizing of pricks and cunts, a very exciting game, which soon brought evidences of renewed vigour in all except poor uncle, who required a longer pause and an extra excitement before he could indulge in a third encounter.

The Count took the delicious arsehole of the Frankland, who begged for me as her fucker. Aunt got Mrs Dale under for a double gamahuche, while Harry crammed his prick up aunt's arse. Uncle enjoyed a delicious gamahuche with Ellen, who sucked his limp prick all the time without any success.

This was a delicious bout for us all, and ended in heavenly raptures.

Our second double couplings began with myself in my aunt's cunt, which incest stimulated uncle to a stand, and he took to his wife's arse while her nephew incestuously fucked her cunt. The Count took to the delicious and most exciting tight cunt of the Dale, while her son shoved his prick into his mother's arse, to her unspeakable satisfaction. Ellen and the Frankland amused themselves with tribadic extravagances.

This bout was long drawn out, and afforded inexpressible ecstasies to all concerned. And after the wild cries and most bawdy oaths that instantly preceded the final ecstasy, the dead silence and long after-enjoyments were drawn out to a greater length than before. After which we all rose and purified, and then took refreshment of wine and cake, while discussing our next arrangement of couples.

Uncle had, fortunately for him, managed not to spend in the last bout; he, therefore, was still capable of entering an arsehole, and he chose the delicious arse of the Frankland to receive this final offering, for after that he was done for that night. I was below engulfed in the exquisite cunt of the Frankland. The Count fucked Ellen while Harry was into her behind. Aunt and Mrs Dale mutually gamahuched and dildoed each other. This, too, was a long-drawn-out affair and ended in perfectly convulsive ecstasies and cries of the wildest sensuality that our most salacious passions could prompt.

I then took my aunt's arse while the lecherous Dale was underneath gamahuching and dildoing her, and by putting the Dale close to the edge of the bed, the Count stood between her legs, which were thrown over his shoulders, and thus he fucked her, having taken a letch to fuck her cunt, which was an exquisite one for fucking – her power of nip being nearly equal to the Frankland, and only beaten by aunt's extraordinary power in that way. We thus formed a group of four enchained in love's wildest sports together.

The Frankland was gamahuched by uncle while having Harry's prick in her arse, Ellen acting postilion to Harry's arse while frigging herself with a dildo.

The closing bout of the night was the Count into aunt's arse, my prick into the Frankland's arse, Harry enjoying an old-fashioned fuck with his mother, and Ellen under aunt to dildo and be gamahuched and dildoed by aunt. We drew this bout out to an interminable length, and lay for nearly half an hour in the annihilation of the delicious after-joys. At last we rose, purified, and then restoring our exhausted frames with champagne, embraced and sought well-earned sleep in our separate chambers.

I slept the sleep of the just, and awoke late to find aunt sucking my stiff-standing prick at the very instant it was filling her mouth with a deluge of creamy spunk. She sucked on to get all out, and in doing so brought him up to scratch again, so jumping out of my low bed I made her kneel on it, stick out her enormous arse, and licked her reeking cunt until I could stand it no longer. Then bringing my huge prick I plunged in a single vigorous thrust up to the very top of her cunt, and made her squeal and spend with that alone. Pausing to let her enjoy it, I recommenced and ran a delicious course in that most exquisite cunt, and would have done so a second time, after a pause of ecstasy, if Harry Dale had not rushed into the room to say that all were impatiently awaiting me to sit down to breakfast. Aunt just stayed to give a final suck to my prick, and then vanished. I hastened to wash and dress, having sent Harry off to beg they would not wait for me.

On joining them the sly jokes they cut at my apparent laziness proved that they knew of the cause of detention. I looked at dear aunt, and at once saw by the air of gratification on her dear plump face that she herself had been boasting of her exploit, for it was all her own doing.

Being Sunday, we all went decorously to church. The doctor gave us a very unctuous sermon on the goodness of virtue and chastity. It was a really fine sermon, and delivered with an unction that forbade the possibility of supposing that the preacher could practicce in reality the very reverse of his doctrine. It much pleased some of the country gentlemen, and one or two with their wives waited for the doctor leaving the church, to compliment him on his eloquence and admirable teaching. The flattered doctor ended by inviting two rather distant residents to luncheon at the rectory, so that we formed a numerous party, all on our best behaviour. It was quite edifying to hear the pious and virtuous remarks of the admirable Frankland, and the no less virtuous and correct Dale. It gained them the *entrée* into the exclusive set of both these high country families, and eventually led to an excellent marriage for the dear little Ellen. So much for the success of dissimulation. Vice playing the part of virtue, and succeeding to perfection. So goes the world. One thing is certain, that on this occasion it enforced chastity, in one sense at least, that we had no opportunity of practising vice that afternoon. The charming Frankland-Nixon made a great impression on the wives as well as the husbands; it was well known that she was a very wealthy widow, and they may have had some design of securing her for a son or nephew, or at least having the chance at it. She thanked them with that grace and charming ease of manner which so distinguished her and made her so captivating, excusing herself from visiting, during the first year of her widowhood, anywhere but among family friends, and as her late husband was Charles Roberts's and his sisters' guardian, she considered his family as almost her own. They hoped to have the pleasure of seeing her some future day.

The whole visit passed off very pleasantly, and left us only an hour for a stroll in the garden and time to dress for dinner. It will be recollected that the doctor was a great exacter of full evening dress at dinner, as tending to keep up proper appearances.

We met at the accustomed hour at night in aunt's room, in the full dress of Adam and Eve before they munched the apple.

This night was dedicated chiefly to sacrifices to Venus Apostrophia, for the doctor commenced by having the Count while he was fucking his wife, and when able to get his fine old cock in for another go, would only again have it in my arse, while I was doing the same to aunt's glorious immensity with the Count below fucking her.

That was the end of poor uncle's powers for that night, but he gamahuched all the women at the finish of their encounters with us three men. We gave them all the *double jouissance*, while those unoccupied carried on their own little game with tongue or dildo.

It was again a night of most exquisite enjoyment.

The following and remaining nights of our visit brought into requisition the rod before uncle could get his dear old prick to stand, and I myself tailed off on the next Sunday night, the last of our visit, so that uncle, seeing what he called the laziness of my prick, seized the rod and gave me as sound a flogging as ever he had done in my schoolboy days. The fact was that he had been longing to renew on my arse his letch for giving a really severe whipping. He had already by dint of the same punishment fucked the arses of the Count and the divine Frankland, and was now so excited anew that his prick stood as stiff as ever it did; and my red excoriated arse excited and renewed his very fine prick; but first I insisted upon moving to aunt's arse, who at that moment was having a last fuck from the Count, and this incestuous group closed our orgies on this occasion, for we left for town the next day.

After breakfast in the morning I slipped into the Dale's room, and had a parting fuck both with her and Ellen. Harry came in while we were at work, Ellen under the Dale gamahuching her, and I above administering a rear adieu. Harry stopped us for a moment until he could withdraw Ellen and take her place, that he might have a parting fuck with his loved mother, who thus had the two pricks she most loved in the world into her together. We drew our pleasure out to the utmost length our lust would allow of and spent in the most ecstatic joy that poor human nature could support.

Aunt had gone to the Count's bedroom at the very time we were meeting in Mrs Dale's. Notwithstanding which, her insatiable cunt made her draw me into her sanctum downstairs for a final fuck at the last moment of our parting.

Harry Dale staying behind to pass a week at home with his mother, the adorable Frankland, the Count and I returned to town together. On the journey up we agreed to dine at Very's in Regent Street, and have a comparatively quiet night all together at my chambers, which we did, luxuriating in having the glorious naked body of the delicious Frankland between us. After we had each bedewed both her front and rear orifices with our life's balmy essence, we slept soundly till morning, when we renewed our double offerings on those glorious and delicious altars, then breakfasted.

This was the last occasion but one of our having the Count, whose time for departure to his own country was drawing near.

He left that day on a visit to a family in Scotland, whose son and heir was really the fruit of his loins.

On his return some fortnight later we again passed a night with our exquisite friend the Frankland, and being both fresh from the country, we administered so many delicious *coups* to both apertures as quite contented her salacious love of prick. We parted next day with our loved friend the Count, but not for the last time, as I shall relate in its proper place a delightful visit we paid to him in his old ancestral castle, and a *recontre* we had with him and his sister in Turin.

I saw my loved Frankland to her home and left town myself the same afternoon for my home in the country, to arrange for various repairs and alterations required on the property.

I took my dear friend MacCallum with me. We spent a pleasant ten days, varied with a visit first from one of my sisters and then from the other, for two nights each, and jolly nights we spent fucking in every way.

Mary's belly was up, but she declared it only made fucking more delicious than ever to her, still more with the *double jouissance*, in which she preferred the smaller prick of MacCallum to mine in her arse.

When Eliza came she stayed a third night, and taxed our powers to the utmost; she was such a glutton for fuck on this occasion, declaring that her husband's want of power, as well as tact, left her more lewd after his fucking her than she was before, so that she had been forced by the excess of unsatisfied lust produced by her husband to have recourse to the fine prick of her footman, a powerful young fellow, otherwise very plain, and not likely to inspire jealousy in any husband, but with whom she rarely could do more than get a rack-off in a hurry, which was far from satisfaction sufficient for her hot passions. It was this that made her revel with such insatiable desire in the possession of our almost untiring pricks. Differing from Mary in her love of rear-fucking, it was my big prick she loved best to have in her arse, while MacCallum's lesser shaft satisfied her less exacting cunt She was certainly one of the lewdest creatures ever made, wildly lascivious and full of variety. She had the most engaging ways with her, and could raise a prick from the dead. She was a worthy pupil of the Frankland, and had all the love and longing for prick, and cunt too, that our deliciously insatiable aunt was so famous for. She grew older, becoming one of the most desirable women, and I never tired of fucking her in both orifices whenever the opportunity presented itself.

I returned to town just in time to have a parting orgy with the Count and the Frankland in my chambers, which I before said was a night of the wildest orgies.

MacCallum was called to the country by the illness of some of his family, and was absent for six months, so I was left with Harry to have occasional orgies together with the Frankland three times a week, and with the Nichols and Ann or Jane once a week by way of variety, but as they only came for a morning visit, these were not exhausting encounters, so that we lay comparatively fallow till the return of the Benson and the Egerton, when they and the lovely Frankland taxed us to the utmost twice or thrice a week.

Thus time progressed. The Frankland had been a widow for nearly two years when she proposed to travel for two or three years without returning in the interval to England. She wished me to accompany her, and made a most surprising and unexpected proposition to me.

She said, 'Charlie, my own darling, I love you more dearly than ever. It is true I am considerably older than you, but you are now twenty-five years of age, and therefore a full-grown man. I wish to endow you with all my great wealth, and I offer you my hand in marriage. Do not suppose I want to monopolise this dear prick.' (We were in bed naked, and had just concluded a most exquisite fuck.) 'No, with our love of variety we will still seek it out, but as husband and wife we can do so with perfect ease and safety; whereas if not married and travelling together we should be compromised at every city we stopped at. What say you, my darling Charlie?' Here she threw herself on my bosom, with loving eyes upraised to mine.

'Say, beloved of my soul! Why, look how the very idea has raised my prick to instant life. If anything in the world could delight me more than another it is your generous, noble offer. To dedicate my life to the woman I love more than any other is a joy greater than I can express. I thank you from my soul, adorable creature as you are. Oh! come to my arms as my future wife and let us revel in the glorious idea.'

Such was the way in which the happiness was conferred on me which endured for long years, although, alas, my widowed heart now all hopelessly laments that most lovable of women and best of wives. Oh, what happiness it was as long as I possessed her.

Florence Frankland and I were married a few days after this by special license.

The Benson and the Egerton were present and Harry Dale was my best man. We adjourned to her house, now ours, to breakfast. They also stayed to dinner and slept at our house, that we might celebrate our marriage with a parting orgy, for we announced to our friends that in marrying, so far from renouncing our orgies, we meant our union to promote ever varying ones, and that on our return we would renew the exquisite ones we had so often enjoyed with them.

Harry and I did all we could on that happy occasion to satisfy three of the finest women in the world, whose delicious power of fucking was never surpassed and rarely equalled.

Oh! we had such a delicious night. As to the women, their amorous gamahuching of each other was ever renewed, and was most exciting to see.

After breakfast that morning they stopped to see us off, and threw old slippers after us for luck.

We posted down to aunt's for a day and a night on our way to the continent.

They were, of course, delighted with my marriage as bringing great wealth into the family; indeed, my darling presented aunt with a cheque for £1000.

Mrs Dale and Ellen came over, and we had another delicious night's orgy, in which all exerted themselves to the utmost.

We parted from dear aunt and uncle, Mrs Dale and Ellen, after luncheon, and posted down to Dover; there we slept at Birmingham's Hotel, where we had our real first night's fucking all to ourselves and enjoyed every endearment that two lovers could devise.

We crossed to Calais next day.

The sea was smooth at first, but we found it after passing the Foreland very rough. My dear wife suffered severely; fortunately I myself never felt better, and was thus able to devote every attention to the dear sufferer. She was left even after we landed with nausea and a severe headache, so that night at Devaux's Hotel we slept each in one of the separate beds in the same room, as is usual in French hotels, and indeed in continental hotels in general.

My darling wife was far from feeling well next morning, but fancied that posting on to Abbeville would rather tend to recovery than otherwise. We accomplished this easily between breakfast and dinner, found a very comfortable hotel with very fair cooking and excellent wines. My wife enjoyed her dinner, and felt something like herself after it. We slept together by bringing the two beds side by side, but only took a single fuck before sleeping, and next morning a double one.

We spent the day at Abbeville, wandering through its quaint streets and seeing its fine unfinished cathedral. The following day we posted to Amiens, visiting its very beautiful cathedral, and then went on to Beauvais, passed next day there, and on the following day posted up to Paris and drove to Meurice's Hotel in the rue de Rivoli.

We had previously written for a set of rooms *au premier*, overlooking the Tuileries Gardens, with orders to have dinner ready at a given hour. We arrived just in time to change our travelling costume and to sit down to a luxurious dinner. Here, as we had ordered, our bedroom contained a proper large bed for both to sleep in. This hotel being much used by the English was furnished with French taste but English comfort.

The dilatory manner of our journey, the agreeable breaks we had made at different interesting towns, had quite restored my beloved wife to all her accustomed health, energy and lubricity. The comfort of the bed, the stimulating cheer, and the excellent wine also nerved me to meet her utmost lasciviousness, and we had a night such ss we used to have when I first had her in my mother's spare bedroom.

We recalled those happy days, and revelled in a lascivious act of the hottest lust. My adored wife excelled herself, and I myself was fully up to the mark; we fucked ourselves to sleep, with prick left soaking in her deliciously tightest of cunts, so that on awaking in full daylight I found my cock stiff standing in her cunt, which was giving it most delicious pressures, quite involuntarily, for the darling was not yet awake. I roused her by gentle movements, and the frigging of her long delicious clitoris, so that she awoke to joys of which we never tired. On this occasion natural wants compelled a temporary withdrawal to relieve our distended bladders. We found that it was already past ten o'clock, so she smacked my bare bottom and sent me off to my dressing-room, that both might get ready for breakfast, for which our appetites were already craving. I slipped on a dressing-gown, went into our sitting-room, rang for a waiter, and ordered breakfast to be got ready immediately, so that by the time we were dressed it was on the table all smoking hot, and we sat down and did full justice to it.

We spent several days in visiting the wonders of Paris.

I had heard of a famous bawd residing at No. 60, rue Richelieu, and another, Madame Leriche, in the rue de Marc, where they had rooms, from which, through cleverly arranged peep holes, any operation in the next room could be distinctly seen.

Madame Leriche's girls were instructed to get the finest men they could see in the street, to bring them in, and there to pretend to be so struck with their beauty that they would not be content without having them quite naked, stripping themselves at the same time. When quite naked they caressed their pricks, waltzed round the room, taking care to stop exactly opposite each hidden opening, and there caress, handle and show the standing prick to any looker-on, eventually fucking in such a position as all peepers could fully see and enjoy.

The fun of the thing was the perfect unconsciousness of the men as to the purpose of all these gyrations. They took it proudly as a homage to their virility, and the power of their charms over their new conquest, and were doubly lustful in consequence, little imagining it was all a well-acted scene, got up for an exhibition to please others, and show all their virile gifts. Sometimes both man and girl were very attractive, and I used to fuck my loved Florence while in the act of peeping.

The place where we sat to see was a small narrow room, with just space for a couch on one side and two chairs at the end, next to each peep-hole. Three other similar narrow rooms looked into the same operating room.

One day we had an exciting fuck from the exhibition of a very fine man fucking his girl with a splendid prick. We were kneeling on the couch with my prick soaking in the quietude of the after-joy. We heard a scuffling with suppressed bawdy exclamations on the other side of the thin partition next to us. We, too, had made use of bawdiness. I had whispered to Florence how deliciously tight her hairy cunt was, and how splendidly her enormous arse moved below my eyes as I fucked her.

We now discovered that the couple next to us had overheard us, for we could just hear her ask if her arse's movement and size pleased him as much as their neighbour's seemed to have done.

'Oh, yes, my angel, you wriggle your immense arse to perfection, and your cunt is almost too tight.'

'Then fuck on with your splendid prick as hard as our neighbours were at it.' A happy thought seized me. I put my finger to my lip to give the hint to Florence, slipped out into the passage and peeped through the keyhole, which commanded the whole of the narrow room. I beheld a handsome man fucking a superbly stout woman, kneeling with her head down low, but towards the door. Her arse uncovered and held aloft was a remarkably fine one, wriggling indeed to perfection.

I slipped back, described it to my dear wife, and suggested our speaking to them through the partition as soon as they were done, to avow that we had heard all their goings-on as they had ours, and to propose that we should form a *partie carrée*.

Florence jumped at the idea, just as their sighs and the shaking of their couch against the partition announced the grand final crisis.

We allowed them some minutes for the after-satisfaction; we then heard the lady beg him to do it again as she felt his cock was stiffening within her cunt.

'No wonder,' said he, 'when your delicious tight cunt is giving me such exquisite pressures.'

We thought this a happy moment, as they were both in a state of lasciviousness; so tapping at the partition, and raising my voice just sufficient to be clearly heard, I said: 'You have been following our example, and seem as lustful as we are, suppose we join parties and exchange partners. I am sure you must be two desirable persons, and you will find us worth knowing. It will be a novelty exciting to all, and will lead or not, as it may be, to a further acquaintance or just a momentary caprice. What say you?'

A pause and a whisper was followed by: 'Eh! bien, nous acceptons.'

'Come to us, for I am half undressed,' cried the gentleman.

We rose and went in unto them, even in a biblical sense. My slight peep had given me an idea of two handsome persons, but a full view proved them to be eminently so. He was still up to the hilt from behind. She lifted her head to look at us on entering, but left her splendid arse exposed, and did not for the moment alter her position. We handled and pressed it. The gentleman feeling my wife's arse cried out to his dearie: 'Here's an arse equal to yours.'

Meanwhile, as I stood by her side feeling hers, she slipped her hand into my flap, and in answer to his exclamation, said: 'There's a prick bigger than yours. Oh, I see we shall all be delighted.'

She rose and pulled out my standing prick to show it to her husband, for like us they turned out to be a most salacious couple of married people.

My wife laid hold of the husband's prick, and declared it to be a very fine one, and a delicious variety which was always charming.

I proposed, as the room and couch could only accommodate one couple, that I should take his wife into our room, and leave mine with him, and as the two couches were close to the partition between, we could excite each other by our mutual sighs and bawdy exclamations. This was at once agreed to.

We all of us stripped to the buff; my new companion was magnificently made – very much of my aunt's figure, with a splendid arse, although not so enormously developed as dear aunt's. Her cunt was delicious, a grand mons Veneris, sweetly haired with silky curls; her pouting cunt had the true odour, and was very tight, and her pressures and action left nothing to desire.

I gamahuched her first – her clitoris was well defined and stiff. Her bubbies were superb, and stood firmly apart, face charming with lovely and lovable blue eyes, full of the sparkle of lust; lips red and moist, inviting a tongue.

We indulged in delicious preliminaries; she had a good look at my prick, declared she had thought her husband's could not be beaten, but admitted mine was longer and larger. She sucked its head. Then lying back on the couch she begged me to mount on her belly, as she liked to commence in that pose. I mounted upon her, got my prick gradually up to the crushing of the two hairs, and then alternately tongueing her sweet mouth or sucking a nipple of her lovely bosom, ran a most delicious course, making her spend thrice to my once.

Our other equally occupied couple had evidently got a course ahead of us, and were changing into the position in which we had first fucked our wives.

We, too, followed in the same attitude, and really the fine arse of my *fouteuse*, her naturally small waist, seen to perfection in this position, and her noble shoulders beyond could hardly be excelled, and were most inviting and inciting. I plunged with one fierce thrust up her reeking cunt, and by the very violence of my attack made her spend on finding it up to the cods, giving me at the same time a cunt pressure almost equal to my loved wife's.

She was so delightful a fucker that I fucked her thrice more before drawing out of that exquisite receptacle.

On comparing notes afterwards I learnt that my wife's fucker had done just as much, and though not so cunt-satisfying a prick as mine, the variety and novelty gave it an extra charm that more than made up for any diminution of size.

We were thus all mutually delighted with our change of partners. An acquaintance begun so delightfully led to a warm friendship and a constant interchange of these most agreeable refinements, including every variety of the gamahuche and *la double jouissance* to all parties.

We all went together to witness some rear-operations between two men, for which the old bawd's house, No. 60, rue de Rivoli, was quietly known to be the rendezvous. I made a first visit alone to see if it would be worth our while and had an interview with the old bawd, a bold masculine woman of a certain age, who must have been very desirable in her younger years, for even now many who frequented her house finished off in her fully developed charms. Her habit being, as I was told, to come in to the man after one of the girls had left him to purify herself, and herself to lave his prick from mere love and excitement of handling a prick, and from long practice she had an art of doing it in a way to raise another perpendicular, which led to its being allayed in the full-blown charms of the bawd herself.

I was shown into her sanctum, and there I told her that I knew she could arrange an exhibition of sodomy; I said that I only wanted to see the operation, as it appeared to me impossible, and I should like the two fellows to be well hung and good looking, if such she could procure.

'I have the very thing for you under my hand if you can wait a quarter of an hour.'

As that exactly suited my purpose I said I would.

She rose, rang the bell, and when a tap came to the door, went out and gave some orders. When she came back she said to me, 'I have some very fine girls, all entirely without prejudices, would you like to have one up? I have them of all ages, from twelve to twenty-five; and also one or two handsome boys to have in company with them, to excite the slower powers of elderly men or those who like such additions.'

I thanked her, but told her my only object at present was to see an actual scene of sodomy. So to occupy me she opened a small cupboard, and took out some bawdy books, admirably illustrated. The examination of these was exciting; her experienced eye detected the effect in the distention of my trousers, the extent of which seemed so to astonish her that she laid her hand upon it, gave an exclamation of surprise at its size, and saying she must see so noble a prick, unbuttoned my trousers, and pulled it out. She handled it charmingly and looked so lewd that I don't know what might have happened, for I had already slipped a hand up to an enormous big and hard arse, when a tap came to the door, and a voice announced simply that all was ready. This at once recalled me to myself, although the bawd would willingly have made me before adjourning to the other room.

She said, 'What a pity not to let me have this magnificent prick into me. I wish the fellows had not come so soon, I am certain I could have got it if we had not been interrupted, and I can tell you you would have found me as good a fuck yet as the finest young woman you could meet with.'

I laughed, and to quiet her, said, 'We may have that another time, for you are a very fine and desirable woman.' With this placebo she rose and accompanied me to the room where the two men awaited us. They were two tall, good-looking young men, evidently *garçons de cafés*, a class much addicted to this letch, and acting as paid minions to those wanting them.

They naturally concluded that such was my object. They were already stripped, and both their very fair pricks were nearly at full stand. They each turned themselves round, and asked which arse I wished to operate on, and which prick was to operate upon me.

The old bawd, whose interest it was to induce me to have them, handled their pricks with great gusto, and pointing out the firmness and attractiveness of their arses, bid me feel how hard they were, as well as the stiffness of their pricks and the rough crispness of their bollocks.

I felt them, and would gladly have had them both, but I knew they had an infamous habit of *chantage*, that is of denouncing to their gang any well-to-do man they got within their meshes: go where he would in Europe, he was sure to be waited on and money screwed out of him by threatening to denounce his practices; so shaking my head and refusing to let the old bawd pull out my prick, which might then have become too unruly, I firmly told her she knew I only came there to see what the operation was like, and had no idea of having my own person handled by them.

A mutual glance of disappointment was exchanged between the bawd and the men, but they put themselves at my disposal, and asked which was to be the recipient and which the operator. I pointed out the largest prick as the operator. They drew a sofa into the best light, and one knelt on it, presenting a very tempting arsehole to his fellow minion; after moistening it and spitting on it, the old bawd, with apparent relish, guided the prick of the other to the aperture, and it glided with all ease into the well-accustomed receptacle.

I was seated by their side with my eyes on a level and close to the point of junction. A very exciting scene, for he went up to his cods, and fucked right earnestly while the recipient wriggled his arse to perfection, and seemed really to enjoy it. They spent with cries of joy in great delight, it excited me very much, and the observant old bawd could see my prick bounding within the confinement of my trousers.

Hoping to overcome my reluctance to take part in the programme, she stimulated them to change places, and the recipient became the operator, and the other the recipient. I was awfully lewd, but resisted even that; after they had done I gave them a Napoleon apiece in excess of the price paid to the bawd, left them to dress, and retired with the bawd to make other arrangements.

On shutting the door and entering the corridor I perceived at once some doors opening upon small rooms adjoining the operating room; on my attempting to open one the bawd seized my arm in great alarm, and said: 'You must not go in there.'

I smiled and said, 'Oh, I understand, come along.'

When once more in her sanctum I said, 'I see you have had peepers watching the operations, so it is well I resisted any complicity in the action, but the discovery that you have the peep-holes already simplifies my object. I have come here to report upon the effect of this scene of sodomy. A friend who dares not do as much requires such a stimulant to enable him to fuck a woman he much desires to have, and who is my mistress. Now it so happens I want very much to fuck his mistress, and we have made a compact that if this scene is likely to excite him, we are to come to your peep-holes, and while he is thus enabled to fuck my woman I shall fuck his. I am thus explicit that you may know our real object. I suppose that by now the witnesses to our operations today have left, so let me see the rooms that I may judge how far they will suit and which will most favour our object.'

The old bawd complied directly, but still longing to have my big prick into her, she pulled her petticoats up to her navel and, showing an enormous mons Veneris, thickly haired, and turning round a still finer arse, said would I not like to assuage my excited prick in one or other of her really splendid attractions?

I said not at present, thank you. And tightening my trousers over it, showed her that it had quite drooped its head, and was no longer in the humour.

She undertook to raise it very quickly, but I politely declined, on the play of want of time thoroughly to enjoy so splendid a woman.

With a sigh of disappointment, for the size of my prick had evidently raised her lewdness to fiery zest, she led the way. Two or three of the peeping rooms were too small for four, but one was arranged for a *partie carrée*. I made an arrangement for the second day from then, and requested, if possible, to have four buggers together, to do it in various positions, and once at least in a chain of three pricks into the arses before them at the same time; I paid in advance half of the high price we were to pay, and fixed the hour of one o'clock in the afternoon, in order to have plenty of daylight to see and thoroughly enjoy all the excitement.

I left but allowed the old bawd just on going away to take out my prick and give it a suck by way of allaying a little the great desire she had for it. She doubtless expected to raise such a heat as would compel my passions to satisfy her, but I had now sufficient command of it to keep it down.

Our grand scene of sodomistic encounters took place as arranged; the De Grandvits, as our new friends were called, and ourselves, with a basket containing two bottles of champagne, biscuits and glasses, betook ourselves to No. 60, and were installed in the chosen chamber some five minutes before the arrival of the sodomites. We saw them undress, slap each other's arses, and feel each other's pricks to get them in fighting order.

The old bawd was there and lent an effective helping hand where wanted. They all declared it would much assist their operations if she would strip and let them see her flitting round and aiding in their efforts.

She knew herself to be much more attractive in body than face, and complied directly, and really added much to the excitement of the scene.

They began by coupling in threes, so that one after the other held the delicious position of middle man – be fucked and fucking. The spare fourth fucking the old bawd, much to her gratification and ours.

The first outsider was now placed in the middle, and the previous recipient became his attacker in the rear, while the previous rear-fucker became the recipient of the outsider. The late middle man, instead of fucking the bawd, buggered her to her apparent satisfaction.

This was just what I wanted, for we had not as yet, in our *parties carrées* with the De Grandvits, indulged even in bottom-fucking the women, but this, as we afterwards found, was equally indulged in in private by them as well as ourselves. Now we enjoyed the sight of the old bawd wriggling in delight with loudly uttered exclamations of pleasure at having her bottom well fucked, for it was the largest prick of the four and a very fine one that was into her arse.

We had already racked off in the cunts of each other's wives at the first display.

'Let us try that,' whispered my wife to De Grandvit, 'it appears to give the old woman vast delight.'

It was what De Grandvit had been longing for in his inward soul. At the proposition of my adored wife his cock sprang into its utmost stiffness. She knelt on a chair before a peep-hole. De Grandvit brought his fine prick, which he had moistened with his spittle, up to her delicious hairy arsehole and with very little effort housed it to the hilt.

At the whispered wish of my darling Florence he did not press to a rapid conclusion, but drew the fuck out to a most exciting length, and to an ecstatic ending in which they had great difficulty in suppressing exclamations of the delight afforded.

I had followed the lead given; the delicious big arsed De Grandvit had, like her husband, a long previous wish to be so fucked, and from practice of that divine coition had no difficulty in taking in with vast pleasure my bigger prick.

We both ran two exquisite courses in their delicious arseholes, and then separated that all might see the grand finale of the four sodomites each in the arse before him, and the fourth front man into the immense and magnificent arse of the old bawd. This ended their exhibition.

I should add that all in turn had either fucked or buggered the old bawd to her infinite gratification both in person and purse, for she claimed after-wards – and received – a good additional *douceur* for the extra sight of her own fine body, naked and in double action.

When they were dressed she got out the liqueur bottle and gave them all a dram and a biscuit. We, too, partook of our champagne and biscuits while discussing the charms of the scenes just witnessed.

My darling wife chimed in with the remark of how much more the middle man had seemed to enjoy it than the two outsiders.

I added a remark that I had heard that such a position was the *ne plus ultra* of delight.

'Then why should we not try it?' said the glorious De Grandvit.

'I quite agree with you,' said the husband. 'Who shall begin?'

I thought, as the idea of trying it was first suggested by his wife, she ought to have her own idea first realised in her magnificent person. I would fuck her while he went into her arse.

This was immediately adopted. I lay down on my back, the delicious De Grandvit mounted on me, rose and fell, and spent before she stooped on my belly and presented her splendid arse to her impatient husband, who for some minutes knelt prick in hand behind her. With gentle care and well-moistened prick he got housed at last in his wife's delicious arsehole, and then slowly at first, but more energetically afterwards, we ran a most exquisite course.

As no one was now in the adjoining chamber, no restraint was put upon our lascivious exclamations. The De Grandvit was in such a delirium of ecstasy that she screamed again and died away in absolute annihilation of all sense but that of the utmost satisfied lust.

My darling wife had straddled across us and been gamahuched deliciously by De Grandvit while *enculant* his wife.

We next changed the venue; he fucked my wife while I plunged into her glorious arse; the De Grandvit, straddled across the others, was gamahuched by me as her husband had gamahuched my wife. This course, too, was run in an ecstasy of enjoyment to all concerned, and ended our orgy on that occasion. We arranged our dresses, finished our champagne, called up the old bawd, satisfied her demands, and thanked her for the exciting scene she had procured us. On asking her, she admitted that the other peeping rooms had been occupied by couples, and that one elderly gentleman had had two of her page boys to operate and be operated upon while the scene before him excited him to the necessary extent to take a part in it himself. He had just left, having stayed to listen to our proceedings and had told her the two gentlemen had in consequence of the scene witnessed initiated the women into the *double jouissance*, and the excitement of listening and hearing had enabled him once more to get into the handsomest boy, and have the other in him.

She hinted that we ought to come again, and have the boys in, for she said the gentlemen, that is ourselves, would find an immense additional pleasure in letting the boys penetrate their bottoms while they were into their ladies in both apertures.

We laughed, and said we should consider her offer, but for the present we were fucked out.

We did not forget the bawd's proposal of having a boy to fuck us while *enculant* the dear women. A hint to my darling wife brought this out at our next meeting. After the dear creatures had both enjoyed the *double jouissance*, my wife said to Madame De Grandvit: 'We are really quite selfish, here are our two loved husbands giving us the unutterable joys of the double junction, and yet not enjoying it themselves. You remember how the old woman at No. 60 spoke of the raptures the addition of her boys would give to the bottoms of our husbands while they were administering the double coition to us. Why should they not try the same on themselves, and give us the delight of seeing them in all the ecstasies their double embrace confers upon us? We know how they delight in being postilioned, which shows how much they would like the real thing if they dared avow it. It is for us to break down the barriers of prejudice and false shame. Here, Charlie, let me dedicate your bottom to the lust of our dear friend De Grandvit.'

My beloved wife was at the moment handling the prick of De Grandvit, and its full-standing stiffness showed he was ready to face any difficulty.

I pretended a fear of its size being too great to allow of entrance into that narrow path of bliss without great pain to the recipient.

'You can never know that till you try,' cried my darling wife.

In all this she was only acting a part prompted by myself, for I was most anxious not only to have De Grandvit into my own arse, but was longing to be into his great, coarse, hairy, corrugated deep-brown arsehole. In this I differed greatly from our dear friend MacCallum, who loved the delicate unfledged arseholes of youths, while to me it was necessary to be the very reverse of the fair sex, whose arseholes in general are of a delicate pink with puckered-up charming little orifices, which, of course, have their charm; but when with men to me it was twice as exciting to find them like my dear friend the Count's, quite contrary to those of the fair sex. Dark-brown, roughly corrugated, and coarse hairs all round them were the arseholes that raised all my lust, and made sodomy a delicious contrast to merely fucking the arseholes of women; such an arsehole as I most loved to fuck was Monsieur De Grandvit's.

I had suggested to my wife to tempt him with mine for the sole object of getting into his. He bit at the bait, so I shoved my prick into his wife's arse, my wife conducted his prick into my delighted bottom. I made some affected grimaces, but of course took him in with the greatest ease. My darling wife acted postilion to him, and frigged his wife with her other hand, so we ran a delicious course of the wildest lust.

As we had already served out our wives too many fucks, one trial was sufficient for the moment. De Grandvit was in ecstasies at the delight I afforded him, especially as he appeared to be revenging the affront I gave to him by being into his wife *in culo*.

My adored wife, with her happy art of handling and exciting a prick, none the less willingly that she was getting it up to go into her own hungry and delicious arsehole, soon brought De Grandvit to the necessary stiffness.

I wanted no other stimulant than the expected satisfaction of a letch I had long had to be into his fine, rough, hairy arsehole. As soon as he was fairly hilted in my adored wife's splendid bottom, his better half took my prick in hand, put it into her mouth to suck and moisten it, and then guided it into that narrow abode of bliss I so longed to possess. It really was the first time De Grandvit's arsehole had ever been penetrated by a prick, although he had long wished for such an experience; there was therefore some real grimacing, for mine was not a prick of the ordinary dimensions, that might penetrate any arsehole, but a prick of the biggest, so I was obliged to be very gentle and make frequent halts.

My darling wife was obliged to exert all her delicious means of keeping his fine prick in her arse at full stand by cunt pressures and her delicate handling of his bollocks; at last I was fully engulfed, and pausing until all strange feelings had subsided, a gentle movement and my darling wife's admirable seconding enabled us to end the course in the wildest ecstasies of the most delicious delight, and to sink on the broad back of my splendid wife, completely annihilated by the most exquisite joys of satiated lust.

Once this delicious practice had been indulged in, you may be sure it did not end with a single experience, but was thereafter the *bonne bouche* or finish of all our after-orgies.

My beloved wife, whose eye for a capable man was infallible, had observed a genteel, tall, good-looking young German waiter in the hotel, who looked superior to his place. He turned out to be the son of a wealthy hotel proprietor at Frankfurt, who had sent his son to Meurice's in a sort of apprenticeship, to learn how a large Parisian hotel was managed. In such a situation they receive no wages and have even in general to pay a premium for the privilege – this practice, which is general with German innkeepers, accounts for the number of genteel-looking waiters that are met with in the large hotels of great capitals, and who are found to be of superior education and information when spoken to in a friendly and familiar manner.

This was eminently the case with our friend Carl. My wife had taken rather a fancy to him, not at first erotic, and she observed that after she had talked to him familiarly he had begun to be very deferential to her and with a certain manner that she, with the instinct of a woman, saw at once arose from amorous admiration. Casting her eye downwards she detected the effect produced in his trousers whenever she was kindly civil to him. She increased her familiar conversation, which evidently allayed any fear he might have had, and she could soon see by the increased bulging out of his trousers, not only that he was growing more lewd upon her, but that he was evidently very well furnished.

She learnt that he was the son of a wealthy father, well educated, only now placed in the position of a servant in order to know, by obeying, how to command, and also to gain the experience which large and well-frequented hotels alone could teach how best to conduct his own hotel hereafter.

She told me all about it, and thought he might be moulded to our purposes. Even if not she had taken a caprice to him so that in any case it would be a gratification to her to possess him.

So I lent myself to aid her by purposely absenting myself either at breakfast or luncheon, under pretext of going to take one or the other with bachelor friends.

As Carl was told off to especially attend upon us, and no other servant ever came near unless rung for, my wife had easy opportunity and, with her practised skill in seduction, had him into her on the second day.

He proved an admirable stallion; grew passionately lewd on the splendid person of my wife, and became in fact cunt-struck upon her, probably the strongest bond that can entangle a man. It becomes an infatuation that makes him the slave of the cunt that has attracted him. There are few men of hot temperament who have not experienced this over-mastering infatuation, and they know that even supposing the object becomes perfectly unworthy, unfaithful, abusive, and indulges every vice openly before them, they may wince, they may thoroughly despise her, but the chain holds them fast in adamantine bonds, which neither the persuasion of friends nor their own knowledge of the perfect unworthiness of the object can tear asunder.

Such became the fate of Carl, and my wife moulded him, with all her wily skill, to our lascivious purposes. When he was once under her enchantment, I made a run over to England on some urgent matters – purposely leaving the field open – and my wife completed her conquest, had him in every way, postilioned him, and wormed out of him that at college he had indulged in sodomitical practices with young students like himself; but knowing how prejudicial it would be to him in his profession, he had weaned himself from the habit with men, but dearly loved the *enculage* with women, and doubly adored my wife when he found her extraordinary and exquisite talent in that way. She also, after much apparent hesitation, in answer to his eager and continual questioning, admitted that her husband was much addicted to worshipping her bottom, and had taught her its divine use. She ever cautioned him against any imprudence on my return, for she said she had her suspicions that I had a letch for men, and if I discovered their liaison, would be apt to avenge myself that way.

'Oh, if he would still allow me to possess your enchanting person he might make what use he pleased of me.'

This was the point aimed at from the beginning. My wife wrote to me, and we arranged that I should announce my return for a certain morning, and that she should have Carl to sleep with her the previous night.

I arrived in the middle of the night, walked into the room, found him in bed, played the angry husband, swore I must have revenge, and that as he had cuckolded me I must avenge the affront by being into his person.

He objected, for form's sake, but said he would yield to anything if I would not drive him away from the adorable madame.

'That will depend upon the manner in which you satisfy my desires.'

'Oh, do what you like, dear sir, if only you will allow me to love madame.'

'We shall see, we shall see; let me look at your prick. Oh, a good size, even when down. Let me see it at full stand.'

My wife here interfered, and said Carl was so good that she was sure he would prove a satisfaction to me. She took his prick in hand, and with her art of handling a prick, had it at full stand in a minute and asked me if she could possibly have refused so handsome a prick as that. And, indeed, it was a very fine one.

Carl was a very fair young man, with a most beautiful and satiny skin. His prick was exquisitely white, and the blue veins showed themselves coursing through in a most tempting way – it was seven and a half inches long, by quite six in circumference, was thick up to the vermilion nut, although gently diminishing from the root, the glans being smaller than the shaft close up to it; a hollow, like that which you sometimes see in the neck of a bottle, ran all round the edge of the nut, and thus made it a head to the shaft. My wife declared that its shape gave her great pleasure in both orifices. It certainly was a very attractive prick, and now that it was at full stand I made him lie on his back on the bed, took it in my mouth, sucked and frigged it until he spent in an agony of delight

I then made him turn over on his belly, that I might admire his ivory-like buttocks, which I caressed and kissed in every way. My wife slipping her hand under his belly soon recovered the stiffness of his prick. I now desired him to kneel that I might be into his bottom.

His exquisitely white buttocks, marble-like in polish, hardness, and coldness to the touch, were most attractive to women as well as to me.

While thus kneeling with head low, and the chink between the buttocks well spread open, his exquisite small, pink, corrugated arsehole with almost invisible fair, short ringlets around it was truly lovely and exciting.

As a rule, I like to fuck a rough, hairy-arsed man, but I can all the same appreciate the delight in such an exquisite arsehole as Carl possessed. To me also it had the attraction of its first possession. When it was thus first fully displayed to my delighted eye, I flung myself on my knees, kissed and tongued the exquisite and delicious orifice, and speedily got furiously lewd upon it; and rarely have I fucked an arse more deliciously incentive to sodomy.

'Oh, poor fellow,' cried my wife, 'you must let this fine object' (his prick) 'be housed in me first, and then he will less feel the introduction of your large instrument.'

I immediately consented, on which he cried out in delight: 'Oh, do what you like with me, as long as your adorable lady will permit me to possess her.'

'Well,' said I, 'see, her cunt is reeking with your spunk, so I will first bathe my prick therein, to make it go easier into your arse.'

We took up kneeling positions. He filled the delighted cunt of my wife, and presented his really beautiful arse to my raging lust. I humoured the entrance a little, but once within over the nut, I plunged recklessly forward, somewhat too roughly, for it made him wince, and he would have escaped from me if he had not been doubly imprisoned. The pause I gave him after being fully engulfed calmed the strange sensation, and we gradually increased our movements until both died away in excessive delight, especially to him, for it was his first experience of *la double jouissance*, and it gave him such exquisite enjoyment that he begged me not to withdraw, but to run a second course. My darling wife thinking it would increase his lewdness if she changed his prick from her cunt to the more divine orifice, withdrew it and placed it in the grove sacred to the secret rites of Priapus.

He enjoyed the ecstasies of paradise on this last occasion, and we all fell on the bed completely overcome by the soul-killing joys of the discharge, and lay soaking in all the after-pleasure for some time, until my darling wife begged us to relieve her of our overpowering weight. We rose and purified ourselves, and then I posed him standing up, admiring the really fine proportions and beauty of his handsome fair form. I sucked his prick until it stood, and then told him he must give me the pleasures of the middle, which he was so highly praising as the utmost exquisite enjoyment he had ever experienced.

My darling wife was delighted. She got on her knees. I entered her delicious cunt in the first bout, and I quickly housed Carl's prick in my arse.

We ran an exquisite course, and then a second with only a change of my prick to Florence's arse instead of cunt. Carl was after this obliged to leave us, as the morning was getting on

I sent him away the happiest of men by telling him as long as he placed his arse at my disposal, he should have my wife always at the same time.

Thus we had secured another fine prick to our general orgies. We told the Grandvits of our fortunate *trouvaille*.

Monsieur made some difficulty about his being a servant, and the fear of discovery of our orgies through his indiscretion; but hearing that he was much superior to a servant he consented to his introduction.

After they had seen and admired him, they expressed their extreme satisfaction at the result of his joining us – for both Madame and Grandvit loved to have him into all their orifices. We could now fuck both women at once, and the double pleasure could be given to either sex without there being any outsider.

Every third night they slept in our hotel, and that night we never ceased conjunctions in every variety, with pauses for refreshment, purification, pleasant bawdy talk, fun and frolic.

For a month longer this delicious existence lasted, and then it was time for us to proceed southward. We parted from the Grandvits with much regret, but promised to return in the spring and visit them at their country house. I may here add that we did so, and enjoyed our visit to the utmost; and, in the second year of our absence, they accompanied us into Germany, where at last we left dear Carl. He had begged us to let him go as my valet with us to Italy.

His intended stay in Paris was within a month of its termination; he wrote to his father that the opportunity of travelling through Italy under the offer we had made was too advantageous to be lost. His father consented, and thus for eighteen months he was our constant companion and participator in all our lascivious conjunctions.

Carl accompanied us to London on our first return home, and resided with us for three months. I told the Benson and the Egerton of our good fortune in discovering him, and the exquisite addition to our party of us and the De Grandvits he had been.

They were instantly alive to the delight of possessing him.

I had continued the occupation of my chambers in the Temple, in which Harry Dale still resided; it was there we erected our altar to the Apostrophian Venus, and held our orgies.

Carl delighted our old friends, who were never tired of having him one way or another, while Harry or I administered to the *double jouissance*.

A new prick to a woman is like a fresh cunt to a man, and for the time gives additional zest to the lust which rages in us. So it was with the darling Benson and the lovely Egerton. They revelled in the possession of Carl. They knew they could only have him but a short time, and they made the most of him.

My beloved wife, with that kindly consideration for everyone which distinguished her, quite abandoned Carl to these two dear insatiable cunts, and contented herself with presiding over our orgies, dictating new and exciting poses to our two friends, leaving Carl and me to their embraces, and consoling herself with a fuck now and then from Harry Dale, when we two were simply fucking each his dame. She told them, 'I can have Carl and Charlie whenever I like at home, so must leave them to you for the three months that Carl can only give us.'

We met thrice a week. My wife used to drive to the dear creatures and take them up, the husbands being much gratified at the affection shown by my wife to them, and never having the slightest suspicion of the object my wife had in taking them out. As to our own servants they knew the chambers belonged to their master, and they knew we lunched there, but they never imagined their mistress would take ladies to share in their master's embraces. So that we carried on our intrigue in perfect safety and impunity.

It was a sad day when we left with Carl, who never again returned to England. Our darling companions had become much attached to him, and parted with close embraces, and with bitter tears bade him adieu.

We parted from him at Frankfurt, where his father, retiring to a country life, left him proprietor of a capital hotel, to which in after-years we often resorted when going to and from the German spas, and always stayed some days to renew the orgies we all so loved. His love for my adored wife's cunt endured for ten or twelve years, when an advantageous marriage softened it, perhaps more through the jealousy of his wife who, suspecting, caused us to desist from using his hotel. He had shortly got a family of a boy and two girls growing up, which completely ended our acquaintance.

To return to the time of our conducting him to Frankfurt with the Grandvits, they afterwards accompanied us on a tour of Switzerland, but left us at Sion, when we turned our steps across the Simplon to Italy.

We were invited by our friend the Count to visit him for a month at his old castle in the hills of San Giovanni, overlooking all the ground of Bonaparte's earlier battles in his first Italian campaign.

We followed the right bank of Lake Maggiore to Arona and Allessandria, and thence by Acqui gained the castle of the Count on the hill above. It was situated in the midst of glorious scenery. From the summit of a hill near the glorious line of the Alps could be seen Monte Rosa, Mont Blanc, Mont Cenis, Monte Giovi, and thence round the Apennines, while the Gap leading to Savona gave a view of the sea, the southern suburb of Genoa, and the line of coast leading to Spezia.

It was a glorious view, and we often directed our steps to the summit from whence it was seen, during our month's stay with our loved and delightful host.

His old castle was partially ruinous, but quite habitable. However, his father had built a comfortable house in the garden, at the base of the rock.

The castle crowned a perfect perpendicular detached mass of rock, round one side of which rushed a mountain torrent, and the approach was a very steep zigzag with now ruinous defences, a very steep and difficult ascent. It is true from a low entranced cave at the foot a secret stair led up from the garden, of which I shall have more to say in relating some incidents of the Count's earlier history, as confessed to us in our close and intimate intercourse.

We were warmly welcomed by our dear friend, who, leading us to our rooms, had a rack-off of his waste steam in the ever delicious cunt of my loved wife, who, it will be recollected, had a great penchant for the Count when she used to prefer him at our Percy Street orgies. When the Count retired, I plunged my excited prick into the balmy bath he had prepared for me in my wife's cunt, fucking her fast and furiously the instant he retired, a change she loved above all things; this calmed us for the moment, and enabled us to wait for night.

We had expected to find a young sister of the Count's with him but at our orgy at night he told us that since his return home he had had this sister, and that in fact at that moment she was staying with an *accoucheuse* at Turin, and he expected to hear of her delivery by every post. We congratulated him on finding so delicious a bit of incest to his hand on his return to his country.

'Ah!' said he, 'it is much more delicious than you think.'

'Indeed, how is that?'

'She is my own daughter as well as sister.'

'What a delicious idea!' cried I, 'what a cockstand, and what a fuck it must have been to you! But you must have had your own mother to bring about such a delicious result. Do let us hear all about it, my dear Count, it will excite us all to renewed efforts, as incest always does.'

This conversation occurred during a long pause we had made in our first night's orgy when quietly seated after purification, restoring our powers with champagne and some slight refreshments prepared by our host for the occasion. We had already had three hours of the most delicious fucking in every possible combination, being all, especially the Count, fresh and in excellent order for a thorough excess. So we all were glad of a respite, and listened to the exciting story of the Count's delicious double incest. As we did not hear all at that sitting, I will finish an account of our doings, and then give a connected narrative or sketch of that strange intrigue, and some other of his earlier escapades, merely adding that his account of his affair with his mother set us all off in such an excitement of lust, followed by such an excess of fucking in bouts of *double jouissance*, in which not only my adored and most lascivious wife came in for her full share, but both the Count and myself enjoyed the double bliss in our turn. We carried on to such an excess that we were quite knocked up, and were so overpowered with sleep the next evening that by common consent we quietly went to bed, and deferred till morning any fresh deeds in the fields of love and lust.

We found this so refreshing to our powers of fucking that we regularly adopted the system of lying fallow the earlier portion of every other night.

We passed a most agreeable time with walks and rides through the lovely scenery and explorations of the old castles. The Count himself had two, but the one immediately above his house was by far the most interesting and was the original seat of his ancestors, wild robber barons of their day; and many a black deed was reported in the traditions of the peasantry around.

The castle, although in a valley between the hills, stood on a high perpendicular isolated rock some hundred and fifty feet above its base; it was crowned with a very high building to make up for want of space at the foundation, and had besides a very lofty and bold round tower, rising high enough above the sides of the valley to serve as a lookout beyond them. The habitable part was reached from the main gate by a steep stair and at one of the landings was a trap door opening upon a profoundly deep shaft; tradition said that this was a trap for personal enemies, who, on pretence of reconciliation, were invited to the castle; on thir passing over the trap it opened, and they were precipitated to the bottom. It was the common tradition of the peasantry that wheels with scythes attached chopped them to pieces at the bottom.

It is a curious fact that tradition may preserve a truth where least expected. Our friend the Count for six months lay hidden in the secret recesses of this old castle at the time a price was set on his head for treason. This led him to all sorts of explorations, in which he had discovered many hiding places. Knowing of this tradition about the cutting up of bodies at the bottom of this deep shaft, he got his two younger brothers to let him down by a long cord, and really found the remains of machinery and wheels with rusty blades attached. After he had finally escaped, a more regular search was made, and it was discovered that a communication with the torrent on a former higher level had let the water pass underneath the castle, and turn a water wheel which cut up the bodies and made them float away by the outlet. Human skulls and bones were found, singularly verifying the truth of tradition.

At the time the Count was a fugitive hiding therein, the old apartments were used as a granary to store the rent in kind of his father's tenantry. As there were suspicions of his having taken refuge there, the place had been two or three times ransacked by the police without their discovering him – thanks to the ingenious hiding places he had discovered. But for this very reason every precaution had to be taken, and no beds or bedding, plates, knives, chairs or tables were there; he slept on the corn, spread three feet thick on the floor, or sat on it when tired. His mother, with provisions under her petticoats, would saunter in the garden, and, when unobserved, slip into the low cavern and ascend by the secret stairs, and seated on the corn by his side, would wait until he had done, to take everything away, and leave not a trace of anyone being provisioned up there.

These details are explanatory of what follows.

The Count had been one of the Royal Guard for two years at Turin, and being a handsome young fellow, had as much fucking at command as he could wish for. When shut up for months in his asylum the passions that had been kept under by constant gratification began to torment him; from the loopholes of the castle he could see the peasant women working on the mountainside, and in stooping showing their legs even up to the bare skin, and this used to drive him mad with desire. He did not frig himself, but at night stole down to the garden, secured a large pumpkin or two, took them up to his retreat, cut small holes in their sides, and then thrust his stiff-standing prick into them, forcing the hole to the size of his prick, and then working the pumpkin with both hands till he spent deliciously; he used to get six or seven fucks in these artificial cunts, then throw away the finished one on the torrent side of the castle. This gave him some relief, but his lust grew fiercer every day, and on one occasion became uncontrollable.

His mother, who had married at fifteen, was now a fine ripe woman in her thirty-sixth year. One day, after setting down the things she had brought up, she lifted her outer gown that she might not show she had been sitting on corn; the Count was already seated much below her body on the low corn. His mother accidentally on this occasion drew up all her clothes, showing the whole of her fine arse, and in stooping backwards to seat herself all her fine hairy and gaping cunt was visible to his lower sight. This was too much for the Count; in a moment his prick sprang to the fiercest stand and he instantly unbuttoned his trousers; his mother finding she had brought her bare arse on to the corn, leant over on the side opposite to her son to tuck her petticoats under her, but the Count seized her round the waist with one arm and, with his body pressed on her already bent body, forced her quite down on her side and was into her cunt up to the hilt; he thrust it up so fiercely as not only to make her shriek with surprise, but also with pain. She struggled to be free, but was held down with all the energy of his ferocious lust. Very few thrusts in and out were required to bring down the first rush of his sperm and this lubricated her cunt; his prick never yielded but stood as stiff as ever, and with hardly an instant's pause he recommenced a more delicious action than the previous one. His mother was much distressed in mind at the first horror of the incest, but being a ripe woman of hot lubricity, could not feel a fine prick deliciously belabouring her cunt without having her lust excited in spite of herself. As all pain of the unprepared forcing of her cunt had passed away, and the plentiful rush of her son's spunk lubricated all the passage, she soon could not control her passions, and seconded him with an art which left nothing to desire. His long deprivation fired him to unusual efforts, and he fucked her five times before he withdrew.

When she sat up she said, 'Oh! Ferdinand, what have you done! How could you do so? Violate your own mother. It is dreadful.'

The poor Count, seeing her much distressed, burst into tears, threw his arms round her neck, and weeping told her he could not help it.

She patted his head, and said. 'Poor fellow, poor fellow.'

On this he lifted his head to kiss her. She, too, wept, and they mingled tears and caresses together; this almost instantly restored his prick to its pristine stiffness. He bent his mother back on the corn, and although she resisted a little, and said it was too dreadful his wanting to commit such a sin again, she opened her legs when he got over her, and did not prevent his pulling up her petticoats. In no time he was again into her this time well-moistened and really longing cunt, for her passions were now become lascivious.

Thrice more did he fuck her, each time more deliciously than before, and in all seconded by the most splendid action of his mother's arse, and the most exciting pressures of the inner folds of her really delicious cunt.

At last she left him, but after so delightful a commencement every day saw a renewal of these delicious encounters.

His mother proved an adept in every resource of lust. Being a splendidly made woman, and salacious in the extreme when once she had given way to her lubricity, she indulged in every whim of lust. She always, after a few days' fucking, came very lightly dressed, with no stays or other encumbrances, so that they used to strip and fuck at ease in every way. The Count assured us that much as he had since enjoyed some of the finest women, never had one given greater pleasure than his delicious, lewd and salacious mother; doubtless the fact of it being incest added to the usual gratification given by a ripe, well-made, luscious-cunted woman.

After the first week of their delicious encounters, his mother said to him, 'My dear Ferdinand, we are very imprudent, you may get me with child if we do not adopt precautions. Your father does not wish to have any more children, and takes care not to get them.'

'How does he prevent it, my dear mamma?'

'Well, dearest, he goes slowly to work, and while he has it in me rubs his finger on the point where you are now feeling' (he was gently rubbing up her clitoris, a well-developed one) 'until he has made me enjoy it several times, and when he finds he is about to discharge he suddenly withdraws it, and pushes the head of it into my bottom and spends there. You must do the same, but you must not put all this long thick fellow in. Oh! come to my arms my son, you have excited me until I must have it immediately.'

Upon which the Count mounted and fucked so deliciously that with arms and legs round his body and loins, devil a bit would she allow him to withdraw, but spent with him most ecstatically, and quickly called for more, so that it was not until the third time of his being about to spend, that throwing her fine legs high in the air, and bringing her arse with a heave well up, and taking his prick out with her hand, she guided it to the delicious smaller orifice, and as all was reeking with the previous discharge, slipped it in, not the head only, but the whole shaft. She cried out, 'Not so far, not so far,' but as he began shoving in and out she quickly got excited, and wriggled her arse with all her accustomed skill, and spent deliciously again as he shot his spunk right up into her incenstuous entrails.

He passed a hand between their bodies to press a finger on her clitoris; this made her cunt throb, which was felt by his prick, and quickly sent him up upon another delicious enjoyment of the tight recess of obscene lust, and a second most exquisite and luscious course was run, equally to his mother's as to his satisfaction. Then he withdrew to relieve her body of the weight she had so long sustained, they mutually embraced their naked bodies, and sweetly conversed on the exquisite joys they had just participated in. His mother declared his father gave her nothing like the lascivious joys she received from his dear son. They toyed and kissed until handling his prick with skill, she got two more delicious fucks, one in each receptacle, and they parted for the day.

By the second month she discovered that what she dreaded had happened. Her son had got her with child; she wept when she com–municated this unfortunate result, but the Count, like me, always stood fiercely at a woman's tears. Several splendid fucks followed, all in the cunt – the mischief was done, and precautions were no longer necessary.

His mother abandoned herself to him with a greater excess of lust than she had ever yet done, and fucked with an excellence, vigour and energy that drew from him eight discharges in a wonderfully short time. The fact of his having put a baby into her appeared to stimulate both their passions. She declared she never in her life had enjoyed fucking more. They used the grossest bawdy terms in their intercourse, as if it was one barrier more broken down between them, and made their incestuous love more exciting and a greater destruction of all natural ties between them.

Before parting they consulted about how best to fix the parentage on her husband.

He was a man of fifty-five and therefore past the ardour of passion – taking even his fucking coolly – and for this reason more difficult to hood-wink. She knew that he awoke with a cockstand, although that did not always lead to a fuck. Upon this they founded their hopes, and at last arranged she should drug his coffee, and when he was still asleep in the morning she should handle his prick, get him up, turn her bum, put it into her cunt, work him gently, make him spend which would awake him, hold him in, pretend she herself was in the acme of delight, but on coming to her senses, upbraid him with having spent inside.

This all happened as planned; he did awake on spending, but his wife exerted such unusually delicious pressures upon his delighted prick, that he got so excited as to fuck her again, and she took care he should spend inside a second time; she pretended to be carried away by passion as much as he was. But she remonstrated afterwards upon the imprudence of what he had done, especially in having so excited her that she could not help spending at the instant he did, which made it more dangerous. She did not know how it was, but she had never before seemed to receive such pleasure from him as he had given her that morning.

'Well, my darling, it is a curious coincidence, but you never seemed to me more delicious or more lasciviously excellent in your fucking than you did just now. As it is but once let us take more care in future, and hope nothing will come of this little and delightful imprudence.'

But of course there did, as the Count related to us, and seven months after this morning fucking his mother gave birth to a daughter. 'I had already been in exile for five months when this event came off; I had letters from my mother after she got about and for some years afterwards, telling me that my sister was a beautiful child and growing up the *image of her father*, underlining those words for me to put the true construction on them. Poor darling mamma, she died four years ago, and my father followed her two years later. I never saw either of them again.

'Before I escaped from Italy I had passed five months in the constant possession of my beloved mother. As her pregnancy advanced her salacious avidity for my embraces seemed to increase. She was insatiable, but with such variety of charm and art that I never failed to answer to her call. Every refinement and excess of the wildest and grossest lust was practised by us.

'My father possessed a small collection of the grossest bawdy books; my adored and salacious mother purloined from time to time the lewdest and we read and excited ourselves in the realisation of the wildest and grossest scenes therein depicted.

'My mother was an instance of a woman getting once out of bounds and then stopping short of no excess, and became boundlessly corrupt. There was no horror we two could possibly commit that we did not indulge in.

'My father, when once the pregnancy was undoubted, was less reticent of his fucks. My mother at my request used to stimulate him to fuck her just before coming up to me, so that I used to shove my prick into the paternal sperm, sometimes in her cunt, and sometimes in her arse, and eventually used to lick it up before fucking her either way. The incest of her son upon the immediate fuck of her husband was, she said, the most stimulating to her excessive lust of anything I could possibly do.

'My father was obliged to go to Turin for ten days; it was the time of new moon, when nights were dark. My mother used to put on a dark cloak and come up to me; we lay down on her cloak, and, stark naked, gave ourselves up to the wildest lust until dawn, when mother slipped away to the house and left me well inclined to sleep until she returned with my food.

'Oh! it was a happy time, its combinations of solitude and incest, combined with my lusty youth, for I was only nineteen years old at that time, made me be constantly at her call, and she never went away before her excessive lust had been satisfied for the moment. Had circumstances permitted her to stay with me longer than she usually did, she would have got more frequent fucks out of me; at night, when she could come, she got ten and sometimes eleven discharges from me, and probably herself spent twice as often. I was indefatigable.

'In all her after-letters to me she constantly avowed grief that she had lost her most loved son; that she was in*con*solable, punning on the *con* in the word, which is French for "cunt".

'Various allusions of that sort were in all her loving letters. Often and often when I have been slack in fucking a woman, and my prick not answering when called on, I have had only to conjure up some of these scenes with my mother for my cock to spring to the stand instantly, to the immense satisfaction of my momentary *fouteuse*, and it is so yet; a thought of her reanimates it at once.'

Here my adored wife slipped her hand under his dressing gown, and found his prick standing fiercely, she seized it, and pretending to be his mother, cried out: 'Come, oh, come! my beloved Ferdinand, into your own loving mother's arms.'

She fell back on the couch, he got between her legs, kneeling on the floor, having thrown off his robe, exhibiting his fine hairy arse – one of those I so dearly loved. The sight fired my salacious prick, so kneeling behind, I guided it into his arsehole, and while he fucked my adored wife, I sodomised his superb arse. We ran two delicious courses, then my wife took me in her cunt, while the Count buggered his supposed mother, for that stimulating idea was kept up. A second fuck followed in the same pose, with both her apertures filled to satiety.

This concluded that delicious orgy; we had a half-night's rest the following night, as usual, to recruit, that we might better enjoy a perfect excess on the subsequent night.

It was in this way we kept up our powers, and only near the end of our visit had we any occasion to apply the birch, and that to no great excess.

It was in the middle of the second night that the Count continued his recital of the result of the intrigue with his mother. His sister-child, for she was both, was born in his first year's exile. Beyond his mother's description of her, that she was growing up a beautiful girl, the image of her father, meaning her son, the Count, he had no other intelligence of her. She had just turned eleven when her mother died; for two years after that sad event she kept house for her father. He then dying, the second brother took possession of the property. As the state had deprived him of all civil rights, the property was given up to the brother. On his return, after being amnestied, the Count had to go to law with his brother to get back his property. His sister-

daughter, who had been unhappy with her brother's wife, gladly left them to
keep house with the Count. She was then in her seventeenth year, splendidly
developed in bosom and bottom with lovely and lustful deep-brown eyes,
the very image of her father, although she only knew him as her brother.
The recollection of the fierce joys he had had with his own and her mother,
drove him wild with lust to possess the incestuous fruit of that intrigue. He
used of an evening after dinner to have her sit on his knee while he related
his adventures abroad, intermingled with kissing and toying. He praised
her splendid bubbies and felt them; he said he could not believe that her
immense prominence behind was real unless he felt the bare skin. With little
resistance this was permitted once, then indulged in, until from less to more
he got to feeling and frigging her cunt, while he put his own standing prick
into her caressing hand. There could be but one end of this. He took her
maidenhead, and then she crept into his bed every night. He initiated her
into every excess of venery, and ended by getting her with child. It was
concealed as long as possible, and then, on pretence of a visit to a friend in
Turin, to see some fêtes, he conducted her to an *accoucheuse*, and left her
there until her parturition was over.

I may here mention that just five weeks after that event came off we met
them in Turin, on our way home from Venice. She was a beautiful girl. The
Count introduced us as old friends, with whom everything could be done in
common.

We stopped a fortnight, and initiated her into all the mysteries and
extravagances of the wildest lust, and she proved so apt a scholar that she
almost equalled in action and enjoyment the greater experience of my
beloved wife.

The Count had taken apartments in Turin for the winter, and finding his
sister-daughter so facile a pupil he intended getting up a *partie carrée* to
continue these delightful orgies. His child was a lovely fruit of double incest,
and gave promise of being a lovely woman. Her mount was charmingly
plump, and the pouting lips of her delicious little cunt were already lust-
exciting. The Count hoped he would be able to fuck her when old enough
and promised me a participation when the time came.

I may here add he had her always to bed with him and her sister-mother
every morning, and in the bath with him.

She grew up admirably developed. From between seven and eight years
old he gamahuched her delighted cunt; at eight began rubbing his prick on
her clitoris, and by nine had gradually stretched it that he could enter nearly
his whole length, and spend there.

We long knew each other, and he always said he was practising the
lesson my adored wife Florence had instructed him in, when relating to us
the incidents of her earlier days, and of her gradual violation by her own
father.

I shall defer this story that I may at once describe the after-fate of this beautiful child, whom I and my wife often enjoyed between us when she was entrusted to us by her father.

After a visit to us in England he left her to perfect her English for six months with us. We certainly perfected her erotic education while she perfected herself in English by her own ready talent for language, for although only in her sixteenth year, she spoke five languages perfectly, besides all the local dialects of Italy, which differ greatly from each other. Her stay with us was much prolonged, for at the time she was about to leave us she proved to be with child by me. In due course of time she was safely delivered of a daughter.

Her father, who came over to take her home after the advent, ceded the dear little object of my connection with her mother to my wife's prayers. We had no children of our own, and she would adopt her. The Count, who in his heart was delighted at the proposition, left her with us. He afterwards had a son by this beautiful and charming daughter and granddaughter of his at one and the same time.

It is now long years ago, and that son legally adopted is now Count in succession after his father's death.

We paid many visits during these years to each other during which the Count related to us some of the episodes in his life, which I give in his own words.

'You ask me to relate my first experiences. My earliest initiation into the secret mysteries of love's recess was rather a curious one, and one which ended very disagreeably for the fair nun who sought to teach me the gentle art of love.

'You must know that after Bonaparte's first conquest of Northern Italy, when he had turned the Alps by the Savona depression and, by the battles of Montenotte and others in that neighbourhood, gained the interior plains and carried all before him, Piedmont was annexed, and after the then French fashion, all church property was seized. Monks and nuns were turned loose in the world, with a promise of small pensions which never were paid. A nun of a convent in our neighbourhood was one thus thrown on the world. To sustain life she opened a little school for boys and girls of tender age. The neighbouring gentry, willing to assist a worthy creature reduced to poverty by no fault of her own, sent their children to her for primary instruction; my mother had taken a great fancy to Sister Bridget, as she was called, and I was sent to her school. I had just entered into my twelfth year, but was a fine grown boy for my age, and I can remember that my prick when standing in the morning had already shown proofs of fair development, which gave promise of its future prominence. I think I was the biggest boy in the school, all the others being two or three years my junior. I was in perfect ignorance as to the relation between the different sexes. The nun seemed to have taken a fancy to me, she used to embrace me with her arms, and kiss me with very pouting lips, and I could feel that she seemed to suck in my breath. She made me stand very close to her in repeating my lessons so that her arms or elbows, apparently by accident, were always pressed against the spot where my, at first insensible, prick lay hid. Without knowing how it came about, these sort of accidental pressures at last excited it to stand, which she, no doubt on the watch, was delighted to perceive. Seeing how she could now excite it to the point she wished to arrive at, she said aloud one day – "Fernandino, you must stay to repeat that lesson after the school rises. You want a little extra instruction which I cannot give you while occupied with all the class." I thought this a kindness on her part, but her object was very different. When all had gone and we were left alone, she desired me to come nearer, the elbow played its usual game, my cock stood, she pressed harder against it, then cried out, "Dear me! what is that hard thing in your trousers? let me see." She unbuttoned them, put in her soft hand, and drew out my prick. "How curious that is. Is it always so?" "No, not always." "Well, how comes it so now?" "I don't know, but sometimes in moving to show me my lesson your elbow touches it, and it gets into that state." All this time she was handling my prick in the gentlest and most exciting manner, indeed she very quickly produced the spasmodic joys of heaven thus brought down to mortal man, of course with only the nervous result. This was all that was attempted the first time; she told me to button up, saying that it was a very bad thing to encourage that habit, and I must be prudent and not let others know of its being improperly hard and stiff.

'This sort of thing continued for a day or two. Finding I had said nothing about it to anyone, she proceeded to effect her grand object. I was kept in as before. She excited me as usual, and soon had it out stiff-standing. "Now," said she, "I will initiate you into love's mysteries. I see you are discreet and can be trusted; lie down on your back on this school form." I did so. She lifted my shirt, my trousers were already down on my legs, she felt the shaft and appendages, then kneeling by my side she sucked it deliciously until it felt as if it would burst. She then rose and straddled over the low form and my body, pulled her petticoats up to her navel, and to my great surprise showed an immense thick mass of hair, covering the whole of her lower belly. Guiding my prick to the entrance of her cunt, she gradually engulfed the little object by letting her body descend upon it. I felt a certain smarting of pain in her first movements, and my prick partially softened, but quickly regained all its stiffness by the pleasure she gave me by her up and down movements on it. I went off as before in a paroxysm of choking delight; she, too, spent, for I was conscious of a stream of warm liquid flowing on my cock. She tightly held me where I was, and by cunt pressures quickly brought it up to full stiffness again, and a second delightful paroxysm followed.

'After this I fairly shrank to nothing, and dropped out. On rising I saw that there was a wetness streaked with blood all over my cock and cods; the sight of blood frightened me, and, boylike, I began to cry; she wiped it all off, and skinned back my prick to wipe under it but here the raw surface made it painful, and even drew a show of blood; previously my foreskin had been attached to the projecting edge of the nut, her action of sinking on it had torn it off and forced it down on the shaft, doubtless this is the maidenhead of a boy, and hence the first smarting pain and the slight loss of blood that followed. She tried to detain me that she might get some warm water, which she told me would put it all to rights. I was too frightened, and ran off home crying all the way, and like a stupid lubberly boy, sought my mother and told her all that Sister Bridget had done and showed how sore she had made my cock. My mother, enraged, ran at once to the school, where in a back room Sister Bridget resided. She berated her well, and in her anger let it all out, so that the poor woman lost all her scholars, and was reduced to perfect poverty. However, a young Count in the neighbourhood, who had been long trying to have her, now persuaded her to accept his protection; she had the wisdom to make him settle indefeasibly a pension upon her, so as to be safe from future abandonment. I, of course, soon regretted the stupidity of my conduct. As soon as cured of the slight soreness of my cock, my imagination recurred to the pleasure her handling and sucking had given me, and the delicious paroxysms she had produced, but, alas! all too late. However, now I was awakened to the true use of a prick, and our women servants and the peasant girls in the neighbourhood, who knew of my affair with the nun, gave me encouragement, and I fucked them right and left, in the fields, under the bushes, in stables or lofts, and carried on this for a year; but at last I was discovered by my father, and sent off to college at Savona. Colleges in Italy have schools attached for younger students, like your King's College, in London.

'Here I found a youngster but six months older than me, the son of a friend of my family. I told him the story of my affair with the nun. We used to get leave to go to the water closet from different masters, so as not to be supposed to go together by design. From feeling our cocks and frigging ourselves until we spent, which we both now could do, my friend suggested that I should put it into his bottom, which a young usher in his first school had taught him to do. He was a plump, good-looking lad, with wonderfully large buttocks, and with an arsehole which from the usher's practice, whose cock was full grown, was so widened and sunk in that it really looked more like a vulva than an arsehole. By this time my cock was nearly as large as it is now; notwithstanding it entered up to the hilt without difficulty, and I used to fuck him most deliciously. It is a curious fact that he liked to be the recipient, and to be frigged by me at the same time. Although he got into my arsehole a few times it was merely from curiosity; his letch was to be fucked and frigged. While at college together this quite satisfied us, and we never sought the dangerous intercourse of the strumpets of the town, and so avoided the horrible diseases that so many of our fellow students suffered from, many for all their lives after. For years this agreeable intercourse lasted, and was only cut short by my exile.

'Meanwhile, on my return home for the vacation, I had not forgotten

Sister Bridget, and longed intensely to renew my acquaintance with her. I easily discovered her abode and contrived a meeting one day; she scowled at me, and turned off in another direction. But I found out she had a favourite walk in a lonely direction. I hid myself until she approached too near to get away, seized her hand, implored her to forgive the folly of a mere boy, who had ever regretted his ignorant stupidity, but who was now a man, and longed to prove his devotion to her. Here I had unbuttoned my trousers with the other hand, and pulled out a very fair prick, at full stand.

' "There!" cried I, "see how the recollection of the paradise I lost grieves him to the heart, let the poor dumb creature plead for me."

'I placed the hand I held upon it and she grasped it tightly: "O! Fernandino, I always loved you, and but for your indiscretion should have had you all to myself for months." I threw my arms round her neck, our mouths met in a loving kiss, her tongue darted fire into my soul. I drew her, a willing participator, into some side bushes. She sank on the ground, her legs fell apart; I lifted her petticoats, her rich fleece and palpitating cunt were irresistible, I flung myself upon her, gamahuched her until she spent twice, and then fucked her three times before I withdrew. I would willingly have continued the delicious junction, but that she implored me for prudence's sake to rise. We parted, but not before arranging for other meetings, which took place in the woods and barns, wherever most convenient. Her protector going for a week to Turin during one of my vacations, I was admitted to her room at night by climbing the roof of an outhouse, and then stark naked we indulged in every excess. She was hot and lewd to the utmost, a splendidly made women, with an insatiable cunt when once our sports began. She was, as I before mentioned, most hairy, had a well-developed clitoris, and fucked with as much pleasure in the rear attack as in her tight delicious throbbing cunt. She loved above all things to gamahuche a prick, sucked it most charmingly, but with greater art licked around the hollow below the nut, and down the under side of the prick, with an occasional lick of the bollocks, all in so exciting a manner that no matter how often I had fucked her, she was sure to get another and another. This charming intrigue continued until I went to Turin.

'During my connection with Sister Bridget I learnt the whole history of her convent life. She was forced to take the veil by her family, much against her will, for she even then felt the prickly sensation of desire, making her cunt throb at the idea of coition with the male sex. She quickly found a friend with similar desires, but more experience, who first taught her all the art of tribadism, and then confessed to having connection with the youngest father confessor. This priest came once a week to confess the nuns, to hear of their liaison, and to inflict what penalty he liked. He told her he would flog her, and then punish her where she sinned, which, in fact, meant putting his prick into her cunt when in a kneeling position. This sort of thing was done to see if she took it in with gusto, and when it was found that was the case, their hour of confession was a scene of every excess, stark naked, for neither wore aught but the frock of monk or nun. This delicious indulgence lasted until the dissolution of the convent, and you know the rest.'

Another recital of the Count much amused us. The Count was admitted at seventeen into the Royal Guard, where each private was born a gentleman, and held the rank of sub-lieutenant in the army. Here he had many intrigues, and took the maidenhead of a charming and beautifully made girl, who was being brought up for the stage as an opera dancer, for which she showed early capacity. She proved a great success when brought forward. She dearly loved our friend, and was supposed to be faithful to him, although she had developed excessive wantonness and lubricity under his able tuition. His flight and exile separated them.

Years afterwards he met a lovely, magnificent, fully developed woman, splendidly attired, walking in the Regent's Park. He did not recognise her, but was looking at her with longing eyes, when suddenly she seized him by the arm, and exclaimed in the patois of Piedmont, 'Ces tu si, Buzaron?' (Is that thou thyself, Buzaron?) This latter word is a familiar expression of carnal affection which literally means 'big bugger'.

Their intercourse became of the warmest , even though she was now a first-rate *danseuse*, very highly paid. The Count had been the first to have her and she really loved him, and in London stuck faithfully to him, for love alone, for she never would accept even the smallest present. She, of course, had plenty of splendid offers from noblemen, but as long as the Count would have her she was faithful to him. When, which a knowing woman's tact senses, she saw a falling off, she released him, and, although never refusing her person to him, took to others as well. She was a very lovely bird, and used to relate the erotic experiences of her previous years. Many of these were most amusing, but one in especial showed the ardent nature of her temperament. She had accepted, when dancing at Genoa, an eligible offer from the Lisbon Opera proprietors, and had to take passage on an Italian brig; she was the only passenger, and her berth was in the same open cabin as that of the captain and mate. On the second day out the captain showed signs of wishing to have her. She was already longing for a fuck, to which she had been daily habituated on shore, so she lent herself most willingly to his desires, then to those of the mate; eventually she served all the ship's company, without any jealousy of captain or mate; for the system in those days made captain and crew all equally interested in the success of the voyage from the terms of their agreement.

The captain, mate and carpenter were owners of the vessel. The crew of a boatswain and four picked men received food, mostly dried fish, but no wages. They were entitled to a certain share of the profits of the voyage, and thus were interested in its success, and on very different terms of intimacy with the captain than ordinary sailors would be.

The voyage lasted six weeks, and during all that time she had every man in the ship into her every day, and from fair front-fucking had eventually satisfied them in both apertures, and often had had one in each orifice, and sucked a third to spending point, which she deliciously swallowed; she had even taken the *prémices* of the little twelve-year-old cabin boy, and she declared that she never enjoyed so complete a satisfaction of her excessive lascivious lust as in that happy voyage of six week's duration.

The Count, who had split his sides with laughter as she recounted this extraordinary indulgence in every enjoyment of lust, related in the amusing patois of Piedmont, told us that notwithstanding such excessive indulgence in both orifices, and by pricks, many of which were of immense dimensions, not the slightest appearance of such ample stretching could be detected on the closest examination, and that in either orifice she could almost nip your prick off. She had one of those exceptional constitutions and splendid forms that no excess injures, and which is ready for any number of pricks, able to reduce them all to inanition while remaining as ready as ever to recommence the utmost excess of lust as soon as another set presented themselves.

As a sequel to the Count's confessions, I shall here give my adored wife's account of her early life in the form of a narrative, for when it was told to me it was interrupted by various lustful encounters produced by the lascivious and exciting nature of her revelations.

She was the daughter of a Greek mother, married to a high clergyman of the Church of England, a man of great erudition, who had taken the highest honours at Oxford. When fellow of his college he was tutor to a great nobleman's son and had travelled for years with him, hence his wide acquaintance with the languages of modern Europe. In Greece he had fallen over head and ears in love with her mother, had tried to seduce her, and, failing that, married her. He was a man of most lustful propensities; her mother was of a beauty most attractive and exiting to such a man, having lustrous and most lustful eyes, an extraordinary wealth of hair, which when undone reached to her heels, thick and meeting eyebrows and a well-defined moustache, all enough to drive a sensualist like her father mad. So failing all other means to have her, he married her, and, as far as she could afterwards learn from him, she was in all voluptuously lewd, carnal acquirements, everything the wildest imagination of lust could desire. It was from her mother she inherited all that deliciously haired body, and from both parents her intensely lascivious passions. She lost her mother just as she had attained her eighth year. During her mother's life she had generally crept into their bed in the mornings to have a cuddle, and had often been a witness to the fucking of her mother by her father, and had, at other times, played with his prick until it stood, and even made him spend with her toyings. She owned to a sensual gratification in this, but at that early age without any idea of the possibility of its being put into her. She always accompanied papa to his bath, and he invariably dried her and finished by kissing her mount and her cunt, and without tongueing it.

After her mother's death he always had her to sleep the whole night with him, and when she was in her ninth year had commenced gamahuching her clitoris, which even at that early age he declared gave promise of exceeding in projection the fine one with which her mother had been provided.

In this manner he soon awakened all the latent lubricity of her nature. Afraid to force an entrance at that early age, after exciting both her and himself, he used to rub his great prick between the lips of her cunt, and against her clitoris, until worked up to spending point, when he transferred his prick to her mouth, and spent therein, he having taught her to practise that voluptuous and delicious method.

It was naturally impossible to stop short *dans un tel beau chemin*, and it ended by his first getting the knob of his prick into her small tight slit and spending there, then gradually forcing his way further and further in, until she, driven mad by such excitement, felt the utmost desire to have it into the deepest recess of her longing cunt, and begged him to shove it in harder and further.

With such a spur to his passions, unable to control himself, he burst through all obstacles, and completely deflowered her, giving her greater agony than she expected, which was subsequently completely alleviated and converted into the most exquisite sensations. Once he had fairly fucked her, he continued to do so constantly until she reached puberty – which declared itself by the coming-on of her monthly courses even before she was twelve years of age. Already an extensive moss-bed of sable silky short curls adorned her mount and body.

At this period her father told her he must take precautions against getting her with child; at first he drew out and spent in her mouth, which she dearly loved, but becoming lewd on her bottom-hole, which he constantly fingered, he declared it was too much derangement of position to get it into her mouth, and suggested merely driving the knob into the arsehole, and spending therein, which he could do by merely heaving up her arsehole as high as her cunt had been, and so entering without any change of position on his or her part. Of course it soon came from the knob only to the utmost length of his prick in her arse, and gradually she came so to like it that often the entire encounter of three or four *coups* was delivered in her arsehole to her infinite satisfaction; and thus her father enjoyed the first fruits of every aperture in her body.

He it was that instructed her so deeply in classic literature as well as modern languages, but always choosing such lewd works to carry out her education as Meursius and Suetonius in Latin, Athenæus with his supper conversations in Greek, especially drawing her attention to his chapter on boy love, Boccaccio and Casti in Italian, the uncastrated editions, the adventures of Casanova, and the hundreds of French bawdy books, with the most exciting illustrations of all these works and many others besides. The lecture on them always led to a good fucking in one aperture or the other, practising the particular description that excited their lewdness

He so depraved her mind that she soon longed for other experiences than all he could give, and she cast about for an *aide-du-con*. This she first found in their young and handsome footman, who proved not only discreet, but completely up to his work, and uncommonly well furnished. They occupied in every voluptuous excess the hours papa had to attend to the extensive and rich parish of which he was the rector.

I must tell the rest in her own words; she said: 'Continued immunity in our excesses led to excessive incautiousness, and caused the discovery of our intrigue by my father, who appeared shocked and distressed at the discovery, but he was quickly reconciled, as it ended in his having the youth himself and introducing him into our incestuous orgies, in which he both fucked and was fucked by my father when they were not giving me the exquisite delight of having both together. And for five or six years I had but these two charming satisfiers of my lust.

'At this period a beautiful youth of fourteen, the son of a younger brother of my father, and, consequently, my first cousin, came to live with us. He was an orphan, left by his mother under the guardianship of my father. I was some three years his senior and he took to me as an elder sister, was very loving in that character only, and used to embrace and kiss me most affectionately. I, for my own part, soon began to have other feelings

'On his first arrival, in grief at the loss of his only surviving parent, he feared to go to bed alone, so I used to accompany him, and help to undress him. He was all innocence; his mother, up to her recent death, had done the same, so he had no *mauvaise honte*, and I helped off his shirt and helped on his nightgown, and even witnessed his diddling before he got into bed, when I tucked him in and kissed him before leaving.

'Of course with my then complete knowledge and practice of every art of lust, I could not but look for and discover all his secret charms, then always in a state of repose, but promising a future development. I grew lewd upon him one morning, after an orgy with papa and the footman, who had not altogether satisfied me. I was tempted to go along to my cousin Henry, to waken and cuddle him, knowing that he would probably awaken with a cockstand, as usual with youths, and even men.

I slipped along, and at once saw what I expected, for he was only partially covered with the sheet and the prominence of his prick was unmistakable. I gently removed the sheet, and was delighted to see that his instrument, insignificant enough when down, was of a very respectable volume when erect, and quite capable of giving any woman perfect satisfaction from its excessive hardness. I gently took it in my hand to feel it, it throbbed at the touch, and felt like a piece of wood in hardness, with a velvet covering.

'I got into his bed by his side without awakening him, taking care to pull up my chemise so as to let him feel the contact of my bare skin. I pulled the sheet over us, took him in my arms, and woke him with a kiss.

'He was surprised and delighted at finding me by his side, but as yet had no idea but that of cuddling and caressing me. In throwing my arms around him I had taken care to pull his nightgown up to his loins, so that his naked body pressed against mine as we embraced.

'In apparent surprise I cried out, "What is that pressing so hard against my body," at the same time moving my hand and laying hold of it. It throbbed violently to the touch. I threw the sheet off to see what it could be.

' "Dear me," said I, "how is this? What a change! it was not like that when I put you to bed last night. How has it become in this strange state?"

' "It is so, dear cousin, when I want to pee in the morning, and goes down afterwards."

' "Then jump up and pee, and I want to do the same."

'He took the pot and piddled. I took another and piddled, standing with legs wide apart, and holding the chamber pot partly between and partly under my thighs, so that he could perfectly see the whole of my cunt, and the flow of water from it.

'He stared with astonishment; it was really the first time he had any knowledge that women were differently formed down there than he was.

' "How funny," cried he, "you piddle from a chink, and have no doodle. I should like to see it nearer."

'I told him I would lie down on my back on the bed, and he could look as much as he pleased, but he must never tell anybody what he would see, because it was a great secret.

'He promised, of course. I lay down on my back, having first thrown off my chemise, stretched wide my legs and told him he would see better if he knelt between my legs, some slight distance from the object to be seen.

'He got up and began a close examination, admiring the immense quantity of hair I had already got, opened the lips, caressed what he called the little doodle, my clitoris, which was rampant with lewdness. I told him to feel inside with his middle finger; he pushed it up and I nipped it, to his astonishment, so that he could hardly withdraw it. Nature, unknown to him, acted her part; his cock, which had gone down after piddling, stood stiffer than ever. I laid hold of it, and said: ' "How comes this, Henry? You can't want to piddle again."

' "No, no, but I feel queer all over, I don't know why, and it seems to have raised my doodle as you see."

' "If you will keep it secret I will show how it comes about."

'He promised that he would never, never, tell anything I should teach him. So I said: ' "Come to my arms, lie down on my belly, and I will teach you. There, that is it."

'His cock beat fiercely against my cunt. I passed my hand down, guided it between my pouting lips, then placing my hands on his buttocks pressed down and forced his charming shaft up to the hairs of my longing cunt, foaming with my father's and footman's sperm, so that he slipped in with the greatest ease; but no sooner was he hilted than one of my exquisite cunt-pressures made him cry out with unexpected pleasure, while I spent with the delicious conviction that I was enjoying the first fruits of a beautiful youth. I told him how to move in and out, nature did the rest the moment he knew what to do. A very few thrusts brought down his first tribute on the altar in the exquisite recess of Venus, the voluptuous goddess of love. I joined in the delicious discharge.

'Once having experienced the joys of coition the dear boy fucked me five times before I could get him to withdraw, and it was only the fear of discovery that induced him at last to get off me. We had a delicious cuddle, and I promised to come every morning I could do so with safety. Impressing upon him the absolute necessity of secrecy and caution, if he wished to have any repetition of the delightful lesson I had given him, I returned to my room, gratified beyond measure in having taken a maiden tribute. Women who have the luck of such good fortune alone know the exquisite delight of initiating a virgin prick into love's mysteries and our longing cunts.

'We carried on this delicious intercourse for months before it was discovered, but use begets want of caution, and my father at last discovered it. Poor Henry thought himself happily excused by allowing my wanton parent to take possession of his bottom while fucking me. My warm embraces enabling him to support the great and curious pain and pleasure attending a first penetratian of that delicious narrow aperture dedicated to the obscene god. It ended in his complete initiation into our orgies with the footman. His addition to the orgy enabling more complex and lustful combinations than two men and a woman alone could indulge in.

'My father, who lived quite up to his income, died and left me with a very small capital at his death, which happened after the coming of age of my cousin Henry, to whom I had become violently attached. Indeed, it was my first love, and had all the devotion and ardour of that passion. He had a small independence, and we lived together for two years after my father's death, secretly sleeping together.

'The interference of relatives who, without suspecting our real sensual intercourse, preached upon what the world would say, etc., induced me to undertake a governesship, for which the great instruction I had received from my papa more than fully qualified me. I saw the reasonableness of this, and also thought it was more likely to strengthen Henry's love than otherwise. But the parting was a great trial. He had grown a fine man, with a superb prick although far inferior to this monster,' laying hold of mine at the moment standing-stiff and wanting but her touch to make me bend her back and fuck her off hand, so exciting had been her recital.

She resumed after the episode, by saying her system of teaching was eminently successful. From time to time she was comforted by interviews with her loved Henry, besides satisfying the lust of both the father and sons of the families she lived with, teaching and taking the maidenheads of several youths, but in none receiving the gratification her loved Henry had given her, until, as she flatteringly said, she had the good fortune to enter our family and find such a jewel as I possessed.

She had occasionally found girls of such a warm temperament that she was induced to initiate them into the art of gamahuchery. It was in this character of instructress that she had first taken the rod to the bottoms of her pupils, and it was seeing the erotic effect produced on them as recipients that first gave her the letch of being herself birched. After this she had had a vast variety of youths, fathers of families, and old worn-out patients, whom she birched into action.

From one situation to another she had arrived at ours; since which time I knew all her doings.

The Count's son and my daughter meanwhile grew up to puberty. We watched their progress with great interest. They were both initiated in all love's delicious mysteries by their respective parents.

My lovely little Florentia, for we christened her in my adored wife's name Italianised, which became familiarly Entee, was a great comfort to us. From childhood she always came to cuddle us in bed before we rose. She was so beautifully made that we used to strip her naked and kiss her whole body, which always gained my dear wife an extra fuck, especially after she reached her tenth year, when her form was rapidly developing into puberty. Being from infancy familiar and accustomed to be always stripped by us, she had no shyness; indeed she became so exciting that often I grew rampant and fucked my dear wife while she was present. She grew to like to see us do it, and used to play with my big cock, and bring him up to the scratch. It ended as it was sure to end, in my gradually toying with her from one excitement to another, until she was completely fucked in her thirteenth year.

Ten years after that epoch, I lost my beloved wife, and would have been quite inconsolable but for the sympathising endearments of this darling child, who became so necessary to my existence that twelve months after my adored wife's decease I married her. She was a perfect Italian beauty, and no one supposed she was other than an orphan adopted by my late wife.

Now, in my old age, she is the comfort of my life and the mother of my beautiful son, whom we have named Charley Nixon, in memory of both my first adored wife and my guardian, through whom he will inherit great wealth. The dear little fellow is now eighteen years of age, handsome, well grown, and very well furnished, although not so monstrous in that way as his father. His dear mother has initiated him in every delight, and he has all the fire of lust that his old father had before him. He often comes to us at night, indeed, it is the only thing that enables me from time to time to get a cockstand and a fuck at his mother. To see them in all the agonies of lust, fucking furiously before my delighted eyes, so excites me now and then, but, alas, it has come to be a gratification few and far between. But occasionally to suck up his young sperm after the excitement of their love combat produces a stiffness for my beautiful wife to mount upon me and then have our charming son to put his prick into her bottom for this, too, is necessary to my failing vigour, and the contact of his vigorous young prick against the thin filmy substance separating us feels as nothing. I am long in spending, and his delighted mother gets two and sometime three delicious discharges in her arse before my lazy prick deluges her cunt with my incestuous sperm.

We are thus a happy family, bound by the strong ties of double incestuous lust. It is necessary to have these loved objects to fall back upon, for alas! all the earlier partakers of my prick are now dead and gone. Aunt and uncle, the Dales, the Nichols, my beloved Benson and her friends the Egertons.

I have already mentioned the Count's death, and both my sisters have left me alone, and I should have been a dreary and solitary old man but for my beloved wife and son, who solace me and replace the void in my heart I should otherwise have so sadly felt.

I shall here end this long tale of my erotic life.

A curious event has happened lately, the divorce of a Mr Cavendish from his wife for adultery with the young Count de la Rochefoucault. The details brought before the court were of the most scandalous nature, especially the letters exchanged between them when the Count had to go to Rome, where he was attaché to the French Embassy. When the husband's counsel handed up the letter with the sworn notary's translation, he remarked that he thought they were too horribly scandalous to be read in court. The judge scanned a few of them and, addressing the counsel, said: 'I am perfectly of your opinion, my learned brother. I shall take them home and make a point of them in my address to the jury.'

It will be seen that they were of such a nature that doubtless the old judge, who was no other than my dear old chum Harry Dale, gave his wife two or three extra fucks on the strength of the lust produced by those exciting and extraordinary lascivious letters from a young man of only twenty-one years of age, showing quite as early an initiation into all the luxury of the utmost depravity as any of my own details of my early experiences with my darling old aunt.

Some of the letters are a string of imaginary events as to how far they could carry their imaginations. The Count constantly alludes to the inferiority of his descriptions to those given in her replies. Alas! as he possesses those exciting replies of the lady, they cannot be got at, but from his descriptions, and the remarks on certain gross familiarities, it's evident she was gifted with as lascivious and lustful a temperament as either my aunt or the divine Frankland.

A chance threw these interesting letters into my possession, and I can assure the reader they are the veritable sworn translations of the letters found in Mrs Cavendish's davenport when it was broken open by her husband, and produced at the trial. The Count had evidently dreaded such an event, and it will be seen he constantly implores her to destroy his letters as soon as read. But, with the infatuation of her sex, she kept them to furnish the sole evidence by which she lost her place in society and became a lost woman. It is added that she was a woman of forty-five, and the mother of several children, but it is these randy voluptuous matrons who have the most attractions for a young man who feels flattered and is proud of, as he thinks, conquering a woman in a good position in society. It is evident enough that she was no tyro in every depravity of lust, and probably had passed through many hands before he gained her. He appears to have been really cunt-sruck, which, as I have before observed, is one of the strongest infatuations that a man can have.

# Addenda: Letters produced in the Divorce Case of Cavendish v. Cavendish and Rochefoucault

I tried last night, my angel, to write you a half sheet, but it was as much as I could do to read your letter a second time, and it was only by making a great effort that I was able to write a few lines. However, this morning I will try and continue, in order to reward you, not for that one which you have deprived me of from pique, but for those bewitching ones which I have lately received.

I have just received your letter 17, begun August 3rd, 11 o'clock at night, and bless you for the idea of addressing it to Pal. B., it is infinitely preferable, and there is no fear of any risk ['indiscretion' in original] either now or later.

I am delighted when I think of the pleasure you derived from what I sent you the other day. I only decided upon it in fear and trembling. I do not understand what you mean by letter direct to Albano. If you do not send it per Embassy bag I should not have it here till Monday; you would have done much better to have put it in the parcel. All last night I slept very badly, no doubt in consequence of a presentiment I had that I should not receive a half sheet, and that you were annoyed at my going to Albano, and I thought of a mass of things as disagreeable as they are painful. Of your birthday, for instance, the 1st of October, which will be an opportunity for your husband to make you a present in return for the set of studs which you gave him on his birthday, when you, no doubt, will give him something.

As to your brown cloak which your husband gave you, etc., etc., I request that on your birthday when he makes you his usual present, whatever it may be, you accept it and say, 'I thank you,' and, without even looking at it, put it upon the table, immediately speak of something else, and when he has left the room, put it away out of sight without ever speaking of it again, or appearing to know what has become of it.

I have just been interrupted for an hour and a half by Monsieur de Fiennes – very agreeable is it not? You must forgive me if I am unable to write to you at length; what I have said to you above is for the future, but the past is over since he has those studs. I forbid you to give him something in future, unless you cannot possibly do otherwise; and, in that case, you must give cigarettes or anything which does not last. I will see what is to be done about your shawl, was it not your husband who gave it to you? Thanks, my treasure, to walk so far from him; it is so good of you to give up to me that walk, which I hate when you take it with him.

Ah! new projects again, but let us hope these will be the last, how I pity you. You were so well you told me two days ago, and now you are already obligated to take some powder – it is your husband's system. Nice health you seem to have; you have good reason for believing that the regimen you have hitherto followed is a good one, it succeeds so well! Poor darling, I can comprehend how uncomfortable these frequent agitations must make you. I suffer from them so often myself.

I will make you some drawings later. I have not the time today. Those uncertainties of your mother are terrible. Oh, yes, I am in despair at that departure, particularly before my lot is decided, and knowing, as I do, that you are unhappy. But, my child, do not fear to let it be known in every direction that you cannot endure your husband, and that you have taken a disgust to him. Do not hesitate to give the true reasons when you refuse to do anything, simply, 'Yes, or No, the hand, but with . . . it is not necessary. I can dispense with it, nothing of that sort is necessary.' And then, when that has produced the desired effect, add, 'We can only live under the same roof upon those conditions, for sooner would I go away altogether than that it should be otherwise.' Speak in this manner; it won't answer very well at first perhaps; but he will soon get accustomed to it. 'How do you do?' in the morning, and 'Good-night,' at night. Then gradually get into the way of saying 'Mr C.' when talking of, or speaking to him. You may be told it is not the custom. Answer you don't care, it is not the custom to be such an idiot as he is. Ah, you are too sad, poor child, all that is charming, and all our superstitions. Moreover, one must think of what has been, not of what will be, and compare it with what is. The progress is very delightful and consoling.

Do not be unhappy about my horse, he did not go very well, and then I do not care about driving in a carriage when you are on foot.

I have made two drawings, one prettier than the other, and I have had a copious emission.

Mrs S. has made no tentative overtures towards me. She is often that way inclined, and with everybody. Be calm then; but, after all, you are perfectly so, only you pretend to be otherwise. God bless you for speaking so often of your pretty rose-coloured silk stockings. I like them so much, and adore you for wearing them, although it is not the custom, above all in the daytime. Doubtless it is very coquettish, pretty and wondrously exciting. Even only to think of them gives me an erection. And that rice powder! how divine you must look. It is to be hoped that the powder in your hair will not give ideas to your husband and embolden him – take care. Thanks for thinking so often of me, my idolised angel. Adieu, my good, my best treasure, I love and embrace you tenderly. I will have my revenge, for I, too, had prepared a half sheet, but will not send it till tomorrow.

*Rome, Saturday, for Sundays's Post – August 6th, 1859, 2 o'clock*

I wish to give you a little surprise, my own dear little darling, in sending you this letter, which you will receive with a half sheet upon which you had not reckoned on Tuesday morning, so as to supply the place of Sunday's post. It was to give you this little surprise, and in no way of retaliation, that I did not send a half sheet in my letter of this morning. It was very unkind of you not to send yours upon the pretext that I was at Albano, but you will have been ashamed of it since. Besides, even supposing that I had been there, I should not have committed any indiscretion with your envelopes, which are so excellent, and, if one had felt inclined to do so, your letter was sufficient to make me indifferent to it. I suspect you of not having prepared what is necessary. I shall be sure to see if it be so; tomorrow's letter ought to contain two.

I continue your letter 17, and I perceive with rapture that you have had a thick cream-like emission of enjoyment. How delicious it would have been in my tea. How I should like to send you some like it also. It is a good thing that my letter to the little girl was successful. Will you tell Madame de Delmar that I am sorry to hear that she is suffering, particularly as her ordinarily detestable dispositon only becomes more thick and execrable. Suppress this latter part if you think it better.

Ah! you think that Madame Salvi has played her cards well, and in what way, I ask? You are too bad, too implacable. I do not like that in you. I have told you that your suspicions wounded me, and I think you can believe me when I tell you that I have completely changed my conduct in that respect. Besides, what can I possibly do. I am very uncomfortable here. The Abdol don't want me; besides, the Duke has given me to understand that I ought occasionally to go and see his wife, and the Borgh bother me with all their children.

Thanks, my good angel, for the letter Des Pierre. If it be decided that you leave, I shall go for a few days to Civita – sad and mournful consolation. Why do you tell me that you will go barefooted when I go to see you. I am quite of your opinion that your feet are only too delicious. The costume rather disgusted me than otherwise, without, however, producing any effect upon me. Tomorrow I shall pay the Duchess de Grano a visit, and since it seems to put you out, shall not return again to Albano.

Heaven knows that the pleasure is not great, and that I care very little for it. The other day I did not even find it any cooler there. The Duchess of St Albans leaves on the 20th for Schwalback and England on account of the apprehensions about war – another subject of uneasiness for me – such is life. I can go and live with the Duchess de Grano and Salvi. No one would say anything about the one, and not much about the other, whatever you yourself might say, but that annoys me exceedingly, and disgusts me, and I dare not do so with you. You might, however, have been my ambassadress, see what it is to be so seductive, so graceful, so pretty, so kind and gentle. Just fancy, dearest, that I have not answered Madame Rudiger. I must really do so today. She is a person one must be careful with.

I have always this phrase before my eyes. 'I prepared a divine half sheet yesterday evening, but dare not send it!' Very agreeable, and very kind of you! well, I do not complain. They have been so heavenly during the last three days, and mine are so shameful. How nice it is for me to think that I should have sufficient influence over you to get you to sit perfectly naked at my table. Long ago might you have had that influence over me, and even have enforced requirements more depraved, and more degrading than that if you had wished it, and with what rapture! Adieu, my angel what a happiness to give you this trifling pleasure.

\* \* \*

When I shall have undressed my adorable little mistress it will be nine o'clock, she will be mad with desire, delirious from passion and rapturous exactions [exigencies], her maddening look exciting me in the highest degree will arouse all the strength I possess, and enable me to exhaust her so completely that she herself will attain the height of happiness; the greater the refinement and delicacy of my caresses the greater will be your happiness, the more languishing will your eyes become, the more will your pretty mouth unclose itself, the more will your tongue become agitated, the more will your bosoms, firm and soft as velvet, become distended, and their nipples grow large, red, and appetising; then will your arms grow weaker and then will your angelic legs open themselves in a voluptuous manner, and then seeing ourselves reflected on all sides in the mirrors, shall I take you in my arms in order to excite you [*branler*, frig] with my hand, whilst your little rosy fingers will similarly excite me with vigour, and I shall suck your divine nipples with passion. When the agitation of your little legs, of your lovely little bottom [*derrière*], of your head, and those murmurs of pleasure [*rugissements*] prove to me that you are at the point of emission, I shall stop and carry you to a piece of furniture made to sustain your head, your back, your bottom, and your legs, and having near your cunt [*con*] an opening sufficiently wide to allow my body to pass erect between your legs; then shall I fuck [*enfiler*] you with frenzy with my enormous and long member, which will penetrate to the mouth of your womb; being squeezed by your pretty legs, which will bring me closer to you, I shall wriggle [*remuerai*] my strong pretty member, which you love, with more vigour than ever; my private parts [*organes males*, testicles] will touch your little bottom, and this contact will provoke such an abundant flow of the essence of love in your little cunt that I shall be as if I were in a bath.

How I fear to leave off there! But we shall see. Do not write to me by the night post, it is useless! It is true that when I am near you in a carriage I have difficulty in remaining quiet. Oh, no, you do not alarm me by your insatiability, mine is much greater than yours, there is not the slightest comparison to be drawn between us in a physical point of view, but as far as our moral nature and heart are concerned we can rival each other, and I am very happy on that account.

1:40 p.m. I was most annoyingly interrupted by the luncheon bell, and afterwards I played a game of Fourreau (a game all the fashion at Verteuil), and here I am again. I have just refused to accompany my father and mother in a drive in the neighbourhood, so that I shall be able to write to you more at length, unless, indeed, I write to Fallenay.

*   *   *

You tell me that you like the little costume, but that is all you say, and you give me no details as to the colours, the length and shape. I will believe my treasure, my jewel, that your bosoms will be white, swollen and soft as velvet, and it is very nice of you to tell me that my hands will have difficulty in holding them and putting their ruby tips to my mouth.

You are quite right in saying that you will develop my virility, it is you who have made my member what it is now. I repeat, on my word of honour, perhaps you will not like to hear these details, but, nevertheless, I shall say it, you are the first woman in the world who has stimulated that essence which flows from my prick [*queue*], which your kisses have rendered so pretty, and it is you who have plucked the flower of my virginity. Never have I had [*baisé*] any other woman, and whatever may be the misfortunes to which I may be destined, it will always be an immense and ineffable happiness to me to think that I have given and lost it through the luscious draughts you offer [*par tes délices*]. It is, and it will be, perhaps, the greatest blessing, and the only consolation of my life. But before God it is a great one, and my enjoyment has not been such as one can expect to find in this world. I do not believe that he who had the madness to rob you of yours was as pure as myself, and as for voluptuous pleasures, if there be any greater than that which I know, I promise you never to learn or seek it, although I don't require this at your hands. I do not wish to have any other woman spoken of, they all disgust me, even to look at them. You know it, and you know that there is nothing, absolutely nothing, in you to disgust me, but all that belongs to you maddens me, and I love and adore all; it has become a madness, and you know it; for when you are kind you give at least the idea by letter of that which you would not do if you had the slightest doubt.

You know that I have sucked you between the legs at those delicious moments when you made water, or when you had your monthly courses, and that my happiness will be complete when you will allow me, and when circumstances will allow you, to let me lick [*passer la langue*] at that ineffable moment when your little love of a jewel of a bottom has just relieved itself. In you everything appears different and pure, the purity which reigns in your every feature, the excess of refinement which exists in your whole body, your hands, your feet, your legs, your cunt, your bottom, the hairs of your private parts, all is appetising, and I know that the same purity exists in all my own desires for you. As much as the odour of women is repugnant to me in general, the more do I like it in you. I beg of you to preserve that intoxicating perfume; but you are too clean, you wash yourself too much. I have often told you so in vain. When you will be quite my own, I shall forbid you to do so too often, at most once a day, my tongue and my saliva shall do the rest.

If it is necessary let the doctor cauterise you [*toucher*], that is to say with his instrument, and mind he does not fall in love with you; I bet he has never before seen anything so seducing, so pretty, or so perfect. It is to be hoped that the irritation does not proceed from the size of my member.

You did quite right to go to the play, and I regret sincerely to have spoilt the pleasure you had in going, it shall not happen again.

As to the place George had, that is perfectly indifferent to me.

Ah! you think that the portrait was done afterwards. You are not sure of it, but it is a matter of no moment, my much loved one. I shall not be the less happy to have the photograph if you are good enough to give it to me, not too much in miniature. I shall be very grateful for it.

If I said that Galitzan was clever, I was wrong; he has lost his mother, I shall be more kind to him. He is a person one can depend upon; his letters are silly productions. Those Russians have always the imagination easily excited.

Yes, my father has always the same answer. Thanks for your obliging offer of gloves, my mother must settle about it.

\*     \*     \*

I shall still have lavished the following caresses upon you, angel of my delight, were I a little calmer. I had a dream, such as it was, about it last night, and only remember it just now by way of explanation of my mad excitement of this morning. I saw you as I was asleep, you were by my side frigging me with your fingers of love, and you heard me say to you, 'I see you there.' You are as lovely as Venus, your lusciousness and lasciviousness are at their very height, your body is completely perfumed with your urine, in which I forced you to bath yourself for my enjoyment, so that I might lick you. You have painted the most seductive parts of your person. Your shoulders are white, your rosy bosoms reveal themselves through a rose-coloured gauze, trimmed with bows of the same hue. Your thighs, as well as your navel and your heavenly bottom, are revealed through a heavenly gauze, your legs are clad in rose-coloured stockings. The sperm flows; but how much I needed it! This is true, for my testicles were swollen in an alarming manner.

\*     \*     \*

Oh, my child, my pretty little mistress, if you only knew how much I suffer from the excessive heat, and the privation in which I live! Without exaggeration, my testicles are enormous. My member is as large, straight and stiff as my arm. I am mad from desire for you. I had the unhappy idea of going to bed again. My mind was full of a dream I had had, of which you were, of course, the subject. Then I thought of the caresses which you would have been obliged to submit to, and at last, in consequence of your yesterday's half sheet, so pretty at the beginning and at the end, but yet quite beside the question, and found myself engaged in the act of rubbing myself with frenzy, and of stroking myself and of frigging my prick [*la pine*] until I was exhausted, before I could discharge the merest drop; that was too much for me, and now I desire you like a mad man. If a delicious half sheet does not arrive by the Embassy bag, I know not what will become of me. I have had an emission. I am saved. I shall feel myself so relieved. You have forbidden my going with other women. You are determined that I shall not have a discharge with anyone but yourself, and that I have fucked [*baisé*] no one but you. Oh! how I must love you.

It is two o'clock in the morning, I have violated and well worked you, kissed, frigged, licked and sucked you, obliged you to yield to my desires, the most debauched, the most shamelessly degrading during the whole of the afternoon. All the afternoon, too, I have got you to suck my member and my testicles. I have made you pass your tongue between my toes and under my arms. I have compelled you to paint your body, to drink my urine. I was almost on the point of getting you fucked and licked by a pretty Lorette, perfectly naked, between your legs, and to make you piss into her cunt in order to make the depravation more debased than ever. I have had discharges from jealously. I have discharged at least forty times; and when, after having left you to go to my club, I returned home, and finding you fast asleep from exhaustion, I awakened you and insisted upon your frigging me with your rosy fingers, all the while licking my several parts. You implore me. You are wearied, but I am intractable. You must do it in order to excite you as much as I am myself excited. I suck your breast with frenzy. The sucking that I have given your bosoms, and the fear you have lest I should fetch a young girl to violate you with her breasts in your cunt, filling your womb with her milk, excite your senses, and then you hear a voice whose sound alone so pleasingly tickles your womb, saying to you, 'My pretty mistress, I implore you to abandon your [?] to me. I will love you so fondly. I will be too kind and gentle, I am so handsome, I will do all you can possibly wish. I know so well how to have and suck a woman, my member is enormous, it is beautiful, rose-coloured, large, long, hard and vigorous. Yield yourself to me.'

Tell me if you like this one.

\*       \*       \*

When you are ready you will call me so that I may come and say my daily 'How do you do?' You will begin by taking my prick out of my trousers, then half opening your gown, you will lift up your pretty chemise with one hand, and will pass your other arm, soft as satin, round my neck. I shall embrace you tenderly, then I shall lick your snow-white shoulders, your bosoms, which seem to be bursting from the imprisonment of your rose-coloured stays embroidered with lace. I shall lick between your legs, over your divine little bottom, your nymph-like thighs being at the bottom of my knees; then you will place your angelic little feet, with your stockings on, one after the other in my mouth. After this you will send me into the dining-room, in order to get rid of the servants, and, by this time, filled with an amorous and impassioned languor, each of your movements breathing forth the frenzy and voluptuousness of passion, you will come and join me. There will be only one chair, and the table will be laid for only one person. We shall each of us have only one hand free, I the right, and you the left; then you will sit upon my left leg, which you have found the means to make naked; you will have unfastened your gown in such a way that it will hang down behind, and your right hand will caress and stroke my enormous prick, which you will have taken between your legs without putting it into your angelic cunt, whilst my left arm will wind itself round your lovely waist in order to bring you still nearer to me.

After breakfast, which will have lasted till half-past twelve, and which will have given you strength, we will go into the little rose-coloured boudoir. I shall place myself in a low narrow chair, and as I shall be very much excited by your enchanting looks, my enormous member will come out of its own accord from its prison, and you will sit astraddle upon me, introducing, with the greatest difficulty, my pretty and vigorous prick into your pretty girl-like cunt, when wriggling about from sheer enjoyment you will stop your movements every time I tell you I am on the point of discharging, so as to increase my desires and my transports of happiness. Then in half an hour's time you will get up and place yourself upon the sofa, whilst I, at your desire, shall slip off all my clothes; then you will get up from the sofa and take off your dressing-gown, only keeping on what you have underneath. In my turn I will stretch myself on the sofa, getting every moment more delirious with passion, for your dress, betraying the delicious outlines of your figure, without revealing them entirely, will render me almost beside myself, and will make my prick so long and so stiff that you will hardly be able to sit on its point without being fucked, in spite of its size, which will force from you sighs and murmurs of rapture. At last, when once seated, fucked by my manly and powerful prick, you will throw yourself backwards. I should lean my enraptured legs against your bosoms, in order that you might lick my feet, while you would pass your amorous and divine legs, softer, whiter, and more rose-tinted every day, over the whole breadth of my chest, placing your tiny goddess-like feet in my mouth. As our desires would augment at every moment, you would allow me, would even ask me to take off your garters, your pretty stockings, and your slippers, in order to procure me the luxury of licking every part of your body there, and of realising in the most perfect manner the intense enjoyment arising from the contact of the most delicate, the most womanlike, the most voluptuous member of your body. My hands would frig your little love of a member, my manly prick would kiss your celestial womb, and my thighs would caress your delicious bottom. When I have worked you in this way for hours, ceasing every moment you were on the point of emission, I should, as I withdrew my member, let you at last discharge, and then an immense stream of love would flow into my mouth, which suddenly and as if by enchantment would find itself in the place of my member while your bosoms would be covered with that white essence of which you are the only source in my eyes (I had never known it before Homburg), and which would escape from my amorous member.

Every day after dinner, reclining voluptuously on a couch, you would snatch a few moments of repose while I was taking off all my clothes. When I had finished, and when I, filled with love, had shown myself to your contemplation, you would give up to me your place upon the sofa, and assuming the most seductive, the most coquettish, and the most graceful attitudes, would come and play with my member, whose vigour would arise solely from the sight of your pretty costume, which, I am convinced, would render you more delicious than the most graceful fairy. You would love me so deeply that I should cease to have any power of will, you would have exhausted me, sucking me completely dry, nothing would remain in my prick, which would be more full of desire, more enormous, and stiffer at every moment. My languishing eyes, gentle as love itself, surrounded by large dark blue circles caused by your look, your tongue, your bosom, your cunt, your member, your heavenly little bottom, your legs, your fingers, and your angelic little feet would tell you how complete was my happiness, my intoxication, my ecstasy, and my faint, exhausted but happy voice would give you the same assurance, would murmur with rapture in your ears – 'Oh how I love you, my lady love, my divine little virgin, caress me yet once more, again, still again, it is a dream. Thank you, oh, thank you and yet again. Oh I am in heaven, do not pause, I implore you, suck me harder than ever; lick me well; oh! what rapture; ask me what you will, it shall be yours. You are my mistress, no other but you in the whole world can transport me in this way. Frig me with your knees. Oh! oh! oh! I am going to discharge,' and my half-opened mouth would prove to you my enjoyment, and the thirst I had for the bliss you could confer.

Then, more full of passion than ever woman lover had ever been, and enraptured as you listened to my voice, so completely beneath your sway, listening only to your own love, you would raise your little coquettish petticoat, and pressing your dear little loves of calves more closely together, for you would be on your knees, resting upon my little blue veins, you would frig me in this manner, with greater vigour than ever, sitting down every now and then upon your fine little heels, in order the better to release my beautiful prick, perfectly straight and rudely swollen and inflamed with passionate desires, from between your divine thighs, as soft as satin, and as white as snow, to better introduce the wet tips of your lovely and velvet-like bosoms into the seductive little hole of my member, whilst my knees raised slightly behind would gently caress your bottom, so as to give you some little satisfaction in your turn; and at last, unable any longer to retard the moment of emission, you would bend forward, resting upon both your hands, to increase my desire, and keeping yourself back a little distance from me, while your petticoats would now cover my head, and act almost like an electrical conductor upon me, you would intoxicate me with the perfume exhaled from your legs, from your member, from your cunt, from your bottom, and lastly, you would slake my thirst and complete the celestial transport by pissing, with eager rapture, between my burning lips some of that woman's nectar which you would alone possess, and which, emanating from you alone in the world, is worthy of the gods. It would be half-past eight.

You cannot form any idea of my excitement at this moment. I hope you will like this, and will answer me prettily. Am I sufficiently in love? And do you believe there will be another woman in the whole world beside yourself for whom I shall have any desire? Oh, how wild is the longing that I have for you at this moment; and this nectar I have spoken of, from whom else could I care for it, could I endure it even, whilst from you what mad delight! Tell me, do you believe this? You know it perfectly well, I am sure; these are not mere words. Tell me that you will piss into my mouth again when I ask you. I am now going to try to sleep, but what chance of doing so with this love that consumes me. I must await your pretty letter of tomorrow morning, for it is that alone which will excite the flow and stream.

\* \* \*

At half-past eight you would like to conform to the usages of this room of mirrors, and as your desires have become greatly inflamed by my own state, and by the soft and unusual temperament of our bodies, you would ask me to undress you, in order that, being completely naked, I might the more easily overwhelm you with my most passionate caresses. I should then strip you of everything, except that in order that your feet might not come into immediate contact with the looking glasses upon which we should be walking, I would slip on your feet a pair of tiny little slippers, with little silk soles, at a distance they would hardly be visible.

Someone is coming. Adieu till tomorrow.

And larger and stouter than those of my little darling, and so indifferently shod with shoes. (Their boots are pretty.)

Adieu, my angel, I finish this so as to be enabled to add a few lines to the picture – it is late. I love you with all my soul, with love, respect and adoration. Nothing yet has been heard about de L. R. It is very bad weather, and my father is still no better.

\* \* \*

I would take you for a drive either in a pretty barouche or in a phæton, your toilette would be beautiful but simple. I would only insist upon your wearing a veil, for my love and happiness would render me somewhat egoistical with regard to others. We should not be serious all the time of our drive, for at every instant I should steal a kiss, and your feet would be resting on mine.

We should return home about half-past five to dress for dinner. You would change everything, and without paying any attention to what our servants might think I should put on a loose pair of trousers, prettier than those I had worn this morning, but, like them, opening in the front. As for you, my own love, I should insist upon your dressing yourself as a ravishingly pretty little *danseuse*, with some little difference, however, in my favour. Your hair would be in curls, falling all round your head, upon your beautiful naked shoulders. You would crown them with a pretty garland of flowers, such as I like for Aimée. You should wear a light-coloured muslin dress, very low and very short, up to the knees, your arms bare, and the skirts exceedingly full (the body of which would be transparent, and refine and reveal the divine shape of your angelic bosoms), your legs, perfectly naked, would be visible amongst a mass of folds of muslin, and would be covered by little openwork stockings of rose-coloured silk, fastened at the instep by bows, like the dress, and on your tiny virgin feet you would have little satin shoes, without soles. To pass into the dining-room, so as to avoid catching cold, and also prevent the servants revelling in the sight of my treasure, you would envelop yourself from head to foot in a long veil. During dinner I would try to remain tolerably quiet so that you might eat and strengthen yourself for the evening, which would be a fatiguing one. Our servants would have directions not to enter until we rang; during each course you would open your veil, and turning towards me (for you would be on my right hand), you would place your pretty legs across mine; immediately my manly prick, which your love would render daily more and more delicious, would display its vivacity, and you would caress it with your lovely satin-like calves, your chair enabling you to do this, being tolerably large, with only one arm on the right, while mine would be much lower, that would not fatigue you much, and this is what you would say to me, 'Am I not bewitching and delicious? Do you not think me voluptuous? and regard me as your mistress, holding you under my entire subjection? I am very happy to please you this way.' And I should answer, 'Yes, I am your slave; you give me the greatest enjoyment that can be had; there is not a woman in the world who possesses the attractions you have; you make me do anything, you are the queen of voluptuousness, of enjoyment. No one knows how to make love as you do.' At last, at the dessert, you would glide gently upon my lap, allowing your petticoats to flow behind. I should suck your bosoms, for as the servants would be getting their own dinners, I should have thrown your veil quite off, and you would then appear enveloped in all your many charms. Then I should give you your dessert, which would consist of a biscuit moistened with that white essence which you alone in the whole world have known and know how to produce in me, and for my reward you would allow me to make my wine for dessert. I would then place my wine-glass between your legs, opened voluptuously wide, and you would let that delicious urine flow into it. The intoxication that this fragrant liquor would produce would be the signal for my most passionate caresses.

You would begin by placing yourself astride me, and I should thrust with the greatest difficulty my virile member between your legs. In this position we should leave the dining-room, I carrying you along by the stiffness of my member, while every step I took would make you wild with excess of enjoyment. We should go into a pretty boudoir, the floor of which would be completely covered with looking glasses, filled with furniture intended by shape and softness to augment the voluptuousness of our embraces. No costume whatever would be put on in this room. Nudity alone would have a right to remain there. There would be pieces of furniture to excite the senses and whereon to recline, others enabling us to suck each of our members, to lick, to frig, to kiss, to enjoy, to complete our performance, to discharge, to fuck, in one word, to supplement and promote the extremest refinements of the most celestial and most perfect of all enjoyments.

*                *                *

The continuation on some future occasion. My fear of exciting you will depend somewhat upon my letter of this evening or tomorrow, and particularly upon the frank and sincere reply for which I ask you for the day after tomorrow.

Send me back the beginning.

You cannot have the faintest idea of my dread when one of these sheets is on its way.

Why do you trouble yourself to pay so much attention to style and writing – that takes time. I never read mine over, and that is so much time gained.

### English translation of the letter written
### by the Count almost entirely in cypher

Here is the response of my heart, my beloved adored one.

Thou shall have it as soon as I shall dare to send it to you.

Thou shalt belong to me entirely one day, perhaps in eighteen months, and then here is the existence which you shall have the grief to be compelled to lead.

In the apartment which I depicted to you the other day, and with the toilette that I require of my beloved lady, my lady mistress is to render herself every day between eleven o'clock and noon.

She will find there her loving husband, all fresh and in every respect desirable [*gentil*], clothed in a dressing-gown of very light texture.

From noon until three o'clock this is the programme.

At noon thou wilt stretch thyself on thy easy-chair, thou wilt loosen a little thy girdle and open thy pretty dressing-gown. I on my bent knees at your side shall lick you with my tongue, while my arm shall encircle thy divine waist and thy two naked arms shall encircle my neck; afterwards softly widening thy virgin legs thou will cast aside all that which hides from the eyes, and you will place me between those divine legs.

Successively I shall lick with voluptuousness thy neck, thy shoulders, under thy arms, thy breasts. I shall suck with force those chaste little bosoms, which by their swelling would desire to escape from the pretty little rose-coloured stays; then passing to thy intoxicating cunt, I should suck it with such an amount of frenzy that thou wouldst discharge for the first time in my mouth.

This done it will have so much excited me that, taking thy place, it will become your turn to mount between my legs, and licking all my chest thou wilt finish by frigging with passion my prick, which will become longer and straighter than ever.

As soon as thou shalt feel the enjoyment coming thou wilt cease, in order to lick the parts adjoining. At one o'clock thou wilt want to make water, then my mouth adhering between thy legs, thou wilt allow me to swallow all, then lying down again on thy little belly, I shall lick with fury thy bottom so voluptuous, and thy delicious legs. Afterwards it will be thy turn to continue thy caresses upon me.

At two o'clock, both of us elevated in a supreme degree, lifting up thy little chemise in front we shall do the business, that is to say, that surrounding me with vigour with thy legs, thou wilt make efforts in order to fuck thyself [*enfiler*], but my member will be to such a degree enormous that we shall have all the trouble in the world (the delights corresponding to the efforts). At last, once entered, thou wilt procure, by my movements and my pauses, such enjoyments that I shall hear you uttering the softest murmurs of thy voice, and so that thou wilt wriggle thyself on my ravished prick which will still further augment thy transports.

Thou wilt enjoy thyself thus three times. At the third time I shall suck thy breasts with such passion that thy eyes depicting a heavenly languor and a divine abandonment, thou wilt empty out upon me thy delirium-causing seminal fluid.

That will last until half-past two o'clock, then we shall sleep together thus until three o'clock and at three o'clock thou wilt go to dress thyself in order to go out or to receive visit.

Behold, the following part shall come to you if the commencement pleases you.

Mem. The commission herein is returnable in Paris, 24th June, 1866.

# A Weekend Visit

ANONYMOUS

# *Chapter One*

One morning, when I came down to breakfast, I found the following letter on my plate –

*The Nunnery, Wednesday*

DEAR JACK – What are you doing with yourself? Have come here for a few days, but find the place most terribly dull, only mother and Alice being here. Can't you come down for a long weekend and amuse three lonely females? I am writing at mother's suggestion. Do come.

Yours ever

MAUD

The invitation was very welcome. I *was* at a loose end that week, and London in July is not the pleasantest of places. Moreover The Nunnery was a charming house to visit. So promptly I wired grateful acceptance, adding that I would arrive that same afternoon by teatime.

Now allow me to introduce my reader to my *dramatis personae* and to the scene.

'Mother' was my old friend, Mrs Helen Bell; we were children together, and I was present at her wedding and godfather to her only child, Maud, my correspondent. Helen was scarcely seventeen when she married. Maud was born the following year, and was now twenty-two; Mrs Bell was therefore not yet forty, and was frequently taken for Maud's elder sister. She now was in her prime, a splendidly shaped woman, rather tall, slightly inclining towards *embonpoint* but very graceful in her movements, and very attractive. Her husband had died three years ago, and had left her a pretty place and ample means; her re-marriage had been confidently predicted but so far she had shown no desire to re-enter the wedded state.

She lived quietly and was the Lady Bountiful of the neighbourhood. She was wonderfully free of prejudices and particularly tolerant of the frailties of her own sex.

Maud, her daughter, was also a widow, her husband having died just a year ago, leaving her well provided for so long as she did not marry again and lived 'a chaste and proper life', to quote from his will. I was her trustee as well as her godfather, and it devolved on me to see that the conditions of the will were conformed to. But she was of a particularly ardent temperament – as also was her mother – and her involuntary cry of dismay when she heard her husband's will read warned me that there would be trouble unless I took care.

She was a beautiful girl, having inherited her mother's good looks together with her father's height – in fact she was unusually tall. She possessed a most voluptuous figure and loved to display it. Unlike her mother (who was a brunette) Maud was a charming blonde with a mass of golden hair and blue eyes, which fairly captivated me when after some years' absence from England I returned home just in time for her wedding, and I found myself horribly envious of the good fellow whom she married and who thus obtained the fullest rights over her charms. On his death my duties as her trustee constantly brought us into close relations, and it was impossible for me not to note how her enforced celibacy was distressing her, while she could not but be aware of my passion for her. One day when I was nearly mad with desire after her and she had been unusually confidential, I ventured to suggest that so long as the trustee was satisfied in his capacity as such, he in his capacity as godfather and dear friend might afford her the relief she so ardently craved. She delightedly conferred on me the further appointment of lover, and as opportunities presented themselves she received in my arms the solace that her ardent feminine temperament required from time to time, the happy gratification of which tended to heighten and ripen her attractions as well as to maintain her in perfect health.

'Alice' was Mrs Bell's companion, practically her adopted daughter. Her mother was a schoolmate and dear friend of Mrs Bell and on her death the latter took charge of Alice (who was totally unprovided for) and had her educated properly. When Maud married, Mrs Bell brought Alice home as her companion. She was a charming little maiden of that almost indescribable English type that necessitates the use of adjectives such as 'sweet', 'cuddlesome', 'dainty', 'scrumptious', etc., a universal favourite and one of the accepted belles of the neighbourhood; and although she had only just turned eighteen she had received more than one good offer of marriage, all of which she had refused. Mrs Bell used to say half in fun and half in earnest that Alice was in love with me and that no one else would ever get her. I cannot say that I reciprocated the affection, but I will confess that I began to think Alice was a flower the plucking of which would be a treat for a god.

She absolutely worshipped Mrs Bell, and whatever her own private opinions and ideas might be she was ready to conform to the slightest wish Mrs Bell might express – a characteristic that will be found greatly to affect the events that I am about to relate.

Mrs Bell's residence, The Nunnery, was a comfortable old-fashioned house that stood in its own grounds some four miles from a country town. There were really two buildings, the house itself, and the wing that contained the domestic offices and the servants' rooms. The house had a ground floor and first floor; a sort of one-storeyed passage gave the servants access – so that at night the family and visitors were quite separated from the domestics, a feature that also will be found to affect my narrative. Mrs Bell's bedroom occupied the whole of one end and looked out over the grounds, and communicated with Alice's bedroom and the room generally allotted to visitors by curtained doors.

# Chapter One

As I journeyed down I wondered whether Maud's invitation meant anything of special significance. I knew that she had told her mother of our relations, and that Mrs Bell in her broad-minded way did not object (in view of the terms of the will and knowing her daughter's erotic temperament) so long as no scandal arose. But to allow Maud and me to have each other under her own roof seemed to me too improbable to be expected.

Maud met me at the station. She was driving herself in a waggonette without a groom. My light baggage was soon put inside – I took my place beside her and we started off for The Nunnery.

When clear of the town the road began a long and somewhat steep ascent. Maud made the horse walk, then turning to me said: 'Now, Jack, I want to talk to you seriously.'

'Good Heavens! what have I done now!' I exclaimed.

Maud laughed. 'It is not what you have done but what you are required to do that I want to talk about,' she replied. 'Now Jack, be a good boy and promise you'll do as we all want – all of us mind!'

'Of course I will if I can!' I rejoined gallantly. 'What is it? – anything very serious or very difficult?'

Maud shook with laughter. 'Jack, you're too funny! Yes, it is very serious and it may be difficult! I'm going to call a spade a spade as it will be the easiest and quickest way! Jack, we all – all, mind you, including Alice – want you to . . . have us! There!'

'What!' I exclaimed, staring at her in absolute surprise.

'It's quite true, Jack dear!' Maud replied, colouring faintly, 'that's what we want you to do. Now listen!

'I've been wanting you badly, my lover! – Oh, so badly – and I told mother that either you must come to me or I must go to you! She didn't like your having me under her own roof. I didn't want to go up to town. A sudden idea struck me. As you know, Jack, mother is still a young woman – I get my hot temperament from her, and I know how she hates her lonely bed! And she loves you, Jack! So I slipped my arm round her, and whispered coaxingly: "Look here, mummy, let us get Jack down and . . . share him!" She blushed like a schoolgirl. "Mummy," I again whispered – "you know you want . . . something . . . very badly, just as badly as I do!" – she quivered responsively – "Won't you let me get it for you?" – again she blushed deeply – "Come, mummy darling, share Jack with me!" And I kissed her and kept whispering to her, till she murmured, "Very well, my darling – it's sweet of you! If Jack is willing it shall be as you wish!" There, sir, what do you say?'

'I'm lost in astonishment!' I stammered – and so I was. 'Maud,' I added presently, 'you're not playing a trick on me, are you?'

'I'm telling you God's truth, Jack,' she replied, speaking now quite seriously and looking me straight in the eyes. 'You won't say no to mother, will you Jack?'

'Of course not, dear!' I replied as I placed my hand on hers – 'I place myself absolutely at your disposal and hers in all honour and loyalty, and will not spare myself in your service!'

Maud looked lovingly at me and I saw her eyes were dewy. Presently she said softly, 'Thank you for what you have said, my own true lover. I am proud and happy to think that you will at my request do to mother what you have so often done so sweetly to me!' Then after a pause she added in a lighter vein, 'And you'll find your virtue brings its own reward, Jack! – for mother is a lovely woman, sir!'

I laughed. 'But what about little Alice!' I asked.

'Oh! we managed to square her without much difficulty!' Maud replied, smiling at the recollection. 'You know Jack, that Alice will do anything if mother wishes her to do it. We got her quietly the same afternoon, and told her that we both were getting very anxious about her because we could see that her stinted natural desires were beginning to affect her health and looks. She was awfully staggered. Then mother drew her on her lap and took her in her arms, kissed her tenderly and said lovingly: "My darling, my second daughter, the one man in the world we believe you love is coming down here for a few days – your Jack!" Alice blushed deeply. "If you will consent to let him put you right, Maud and I will keep you company and let him have us also, so that we can be together in my room where we can look after you! Will you consent, darling?" Poor Alice didn't know what to say – she was dreadfully taken aback! "Say yes, darling," whispered mother lovingly.

'Slowly came the answer: "If you wish it, auntie, yes!"

'Between us we hugged and kissed and soothed her, and now she's all right about it though very timid! Jack, you're going to be a lucky man!'

'Going to be!' I exclaimed, looking tenderly at her as my hand slid on to her lap and amorously pressed the region of love. 'Am I not so already, seeing that I have the run of this treasure!' – and again my hand rested over the organ of her sex. 'And as if that was not enough luck for any man, you are going to put me in possession of the finest woman and the prettiest girl in this part of the county! Maud darling, how can I ever thank you sufficiently?'

Maud laughed wickedly. 'Just keep a little bit in hand for me, darling,' she replied – 'we are going to work you very hard, but don't forget my brokerage!'

I laughed. 'If there should be only one drop left in me and you want it, darling, you shall have it! Now tell me, how do you propose to work this job? – have you made out a list of hours and appointments for me as they do for stallions or am I to sit on the landing till some door opens and I am beckoned in?'

Maud laughed amusedly. 'You must arrange all that with mother after tea,' she said – 'she wants a talk with you and I have arranged to take Alice off, so as to leave you together. *Entre nous*, Jack, I think her idea is that we shall always meet in her bedroom as soon as the house is quiet, attired only in our nighties, and there and then decide on the evening's programme.' As she spoke we drove through the gates. 'There she is . . . see, she has got Alice by the hand so as to make her meet you and get it over . . . how Alice is blushing!'

'We're delighted to see you, Jack dear!' said Mrs Bell as we alighted. 'We were so glad to get your wire saying you would come!' And she kissed me affectionately, somewhat to Maud's surprise, for this was an unusual proceeding.

'You don't know how glad I was to get out of town, Helen!' I replied as I returned her salute. 'How are you, Alice? – why, you're not looking quite yourself!' I added as I took her little hands in mine and drew her towards me – 'I really must look after you!' I continued, as for the first time I kissed her virgin cheeks, now covered with blushes at what she evidently thought was a reference to the trouble alleged by Mrs Bell and Maud. They regarded her affectionately, but I could see they had difficulty in smothering a smile at my audacity and its effect on Alice.

'Show Jack to his room, Maud,' said Mrs Bell as she passed her arm lovingly round the still blushing Alice – 'tea will be ready in five minutes and I expect you will want it!'

'Jack! how could you!' exclaimed Maud, choking with laughter when we reached the security of my room – 'poor Alice! how a certain part of her must have tingled!'

'I couldn't help it!' I replied, as I joined in her silent mirth, 'it was a sudden inspiration, and I think a happy one!'

'Very!' she gurgled – then pressed herself amorously against me looking tenderly into my eyes. I divined her desire and whispered softly, 'Finger or tongue, darling?'

'Finger!' she murmured – 'no time for the other just now, but I must have something quickly!' Promptly I dropped into an easy-chair and took her on my knees, and as my hand stole up under her clothes and travelled along her delicious legs she threw her arms round my neck, pressed her lips on mine, and parted her thighs to assist my hand which just then was searching for the slit in her drawers – which it soon found; then my eager fingers rested on the already moist lips of Maud's cunt, now throbbing and pouting with sexual excitement. Hugging me tightly to her, Maud now began to wriggle on my knees in the most divine way as she felt my finger penetrate her cunt in delicious agitation and then craftily attack her excited clitoris. 'Oh! Jack! . . . oh! . . . d–a–r–l–i–n–g!!' she gasped brokenly in blissful ecstasy – then straining me to her she ejaculated, 'I'm coming!! . . . I'm coming!!! . . . oh! finish me!!' Promptly my finger played on her clitoris. I felt an indescribable quiver pass through her – and then she inundated my happy finger with a profuse emission as her head dropped on my shoulder in her ecstatic rapture.

I allowed her to rest undisturbed by any movement on my part till she recovered from her half-swoon. As she came to herself, Maud drew a long breath, slowly raised her head – then looking lovingly at me with still humid eyes she passionately kissed me, murmuring. 'Oh! darling! that was good!' and slowly rose from off my knees. Suddenly she stooped and whispered in my ear, 'Shall I do anything to you, Jack?' at the same time placing her hand gently on the fly of my trousers. I shivered with delight at her touch and nearly yielded to temptation, but retained sufficient self-control to deny myself the sweet pleasure she was offering to me.

'No, dearie!' I said, 'I'd like it awfully, but I must reserve myself for tonight and you three!'

'Oh, you good boy!' she whispered – then after kissing me again she said in her usual voice, 'Now I'll leave you and will join you presently at tea; I can now get on well till tonight! Oh, Jack! I do hope you'll have me first!' then disappeared.

I found Mrs Bell and Alice already at the tea-table. Alice again blushed on seeing me, and I fancied that Mrs Bell looked somewhat enquiringly at me. 'Where's Maud?' she asked.

'I expected to find her here,' I replied – 'she went on to her room after showing me to mine; here she comes!'

We chatted gaily. I gave them the latest news from London and they detailed the county gossip to me, for I knew many of the families. And so tea passed, and when we rose I was glad to note that Alice's shyness and restraint had disappeared.

True to her undertaking, Maud drew Alice's arm through hers and led her off into the garden, while I chatted with Mrs Bell and followed her into her own particular boudoir. As I closed the door she came towards me with open arms and love in her beautiful eyes, drew me to her and kissed me sweetly, whispering, 'Jack! it is good of you to come to the help of us poor women – but what can you think of us to ask it!'

I returned her kiss lovingly, then passed my arm round her waist and led her to a settee for two, into which we settled ourselves in delightfully close contact. 'There is only one thing I can think, Mrs Bell,' I replied softly as I looked into her eyes – 'you, Maud and Alice are simply angels.'

She laughed and blushed prettily, then whispered, 'You called me Helen when you arrived – I want to continue to be Helen to you now that we are going to be so . . . so . . . intimate!' I drew her to me and tenderly kissed her, and for a moment she rested silent in my embrace.

Presently she freed herself. 'I want to talk with you, Jack – you and I have to arrange matters! Maud has told me that you will . . . play! Now have you anything to suggest?'

'I'd rather leave myself in your hands, Helen darling,' I said, noting delightedly her pleasure at my form of address. 'I'm sure that you and Maud have discussed matters and that you have some scheme cut and dry. And there is sweet little Alice, who is differently placed from you two – I'm sure you can arrange for her initiation better than I possibly can! But tell me,

Helen, is Alice really willing to . . . to . . . surrender her maiden treasure to me? – it seems incredible!'

'She really is willing, Jack,' Mrs Bell replied; 'you have her heart and her love, Jack, and she is quite willing to let you have her body, her maidenhead! And Jack, may I say that I also love you, dear, and willingly give myself to you!' And drawing me to her she kissed me passionately.

I was very touched. 'I haven't words to say what I feel, Helen darling,' I whispered in her ear – 'but may I have a chance tonight to show you how I appreciate your wonderful kindness and love!'

She blushed prettily. 'This is what I want to talk about and to arrange with you, Jack dear,' she replied softly. 'May I tell you our ideas?'

'Please do!' I answered, and drew her against me so that she could whisper – for I recognised she could whisper what she could not say in the usual way. And to indicate my recognition of the sweet intimacy into which she had now admitted me, my disengaged hand stole towards her corsage and lovingly wandered over her voluptuous bust.

Mrs Bell began. 'You know, Jack, that all the servants sleep in the domestic wing, leaving us alone in the house. They cannot see the lights in my room and they know that I sometimes read for hours after I retire – because I am alone!' she added with a blush and smile. 'By half-past ten the house is quite quiet. My idea is that instead of your visitin' us in our own rooms in turn and perhaps attracting attention by the lights, we all should meet in my bedroom, clad only in our nighties, and that you should work your sweet will on us in the presence of each other. There will then be no jealousies – things will more or less be done on the spur of the moment – and the feeling that each one is assisting the others and contributing by her presence to the piquancy of the proceedings will add zest to our pleasures. How does it strike you? – I see a smile on your lips!'

'I think your idea a most charming one,' I replied, looking fondly at her and amorously playing with the swell of her bosom – 'may I confess that I know from personal experience how much the pleasure of . . . having a woman . . . is enhanced by the presence of another girl. But our case is so exceptional that I could not refrain from a smile as its peculiarities struck me!'

'In what way?' she asked, somewhat anxiously I thought.

'You will let me use plain words and not beat about the bush?' I enquired.

'Certainly, Jack,' she replied with a self-conscious smile and blush.

'Well, Helen, you and Maud are mother and daughter – not many daughters are . . . fucked . . . in the sight of their mothers, and fewer mothers still allow their daughters to watch them being fucked! Are you sure you and Maud won't mind? I shall insist on your being stark naked!'

'Quite sure!' Helen replied stoutly – but she coloured violently. I kissed her tenderly.

'It will be awfully delicious!' I said delightedly, and I felt a responsive quiver run through her.

I continued. 'Now we come to Alice. To speak plainly, she has to be ravished by me, eh Helen?'

'That's really what it amounts to, Jack,' she replied slowly, blushing deeply.

'Will she agree to be violated in public, so to speak – would she not prefer the privacy of her own room and to lose her maidenhead alone with me?'

'I don't think so, Jack,' Helen replied, looking soberly at me; 'she is very young and very timid and nervous, and really both Maud and I thought that she seemed relieved when we told her that we would be present to look after her while she was being ravished!'

'Then, Helen, I think your idea is really splendid and am ready to fall in with it. I would like to make just one suggestion – some one of us should be appointed each evening to direct the proceedings and to say what is to be done, and the others are to give implicit obedience. Deal the cards round every evening when we meet in your room, and whoever gets the ace of spades is to be the queen or king of that evening.'

'Oh, Jack! what a lovely idea!' she exclaimed delightedly – 'we can make a regular revel of every meeting then!'

I kissed her. 'I have seen the game played, Helen, and I'm sure you all will love it! One question more – do we meet this evening?'

She blushed. 'We thought we might do so, Jack, if you were willing and not too tired after your long journey!'

'The prospect of seeing you in all your naked beauty, Helen, and of making you die of ecstasy in my arms would be enough to banish all fatigue did it exist, which it does not. So we will meet!' She kissed me rapturously.

'Is Alice to be . . . sacrificed . . . this evening, or do you propose that she should be saved for tomorrow, and be educated a little by the help of object lessons furnished by you and Maud tonight? What do you think, Helen?'

'We thought we would leave that to you, Jack,' she replied, – 'we considered that you ought to have the right to choose.'

I drew her closely to me. 'Then we'll keep Alice for tomorrow night, darling, and I'll devote myself to you and Maud tonight. But we will make Alice show herself to us naked tonight – and as our loving pranks are sure to excite her virgin self, I must claim the privilege of affording her the relief she will crave. Now Helen dear, just one point more; will you mind if I have Maud first, and then you?'

'Of course not, Jack,' Helen replied with a smile – 'I think you ought to, especially if she wishes it.'

'I'm sure she will, for she is so terribly mad with desire!' I said. 'The sight of you in my arms, quivering with ecstasy, will probably drive her wild! Besides this, Helen, it will be better for Alice to have you with her when she sees . . . fucking . . . for the first time!' (Helen kissed me rapturously).

'I'll do Maud as soon as I can arrange it – then we'll play for a bit with Alice and utilise her naked charms to excite us – and then, my darling, you and I will have a long sweet fuck!' (Again Helen kissed me rapturously.)

'I'll then dissolve the meeting – but I'll slip back to you, and we'll have a sweet time by ourselves! Now, one final kiss, and we'll join the others. Get Maud away and tell her what we have arranged – I'll entertain Alice; perhaps you'll also tell her that she is to be reserved as tomorrow night's *bonne bouche* – she then will be more at her ease tonight, and we'll use her to excite us. Now, Helen darling!' and after a long passionate kiss, lips on lips, we strolled into the garden. As arranged, Helen soon disappeared with Maud, leaving me with Alice, who at first was very shy and timid – but when she found that I did not touch on the topic of her sacrifice she soon regained her usual easy and charming demeanour. In due course came dinner, then cards and music – and so bedtime was comfortably and happily reached.

## *Chapter Two*

Carefully and ceremoniously we wished each other good night while the servants were removing the cakes and glasses and closing the house. When I was undressed and ready for the fray I glanced at the clock and to my disgust found it was only ten minutes past the hour and that I had twenty horrid minutes to wait. It could not be helped. I got into a comfortable chair and recalled the dinner table with the three ladies in their dainty evening attire – how my eyes dwelt on what they were kind enough to display in the way of bosom – how my prick throbbed at the thought that very soon I should see those bosoms unveiled and bare. Then my thoughts wandered to the surrounding bedrooms and their occupants – I could imagine Maud dragging off her garments in her excitement and surveying herself naked in the mirror preparatory to slipping on her only robe – I could picture Mrs Bell's agitation as she carefully prepared herself for the fucking for which she so longed – and I could almost see Alice as she nervously undressed herself to appear before me clad in her nightie only. At dinner she chattered away so freely and delightfully and seemed so much at her ease save for a certain suppressed excitement that I felt certain she had been told that her ordeal had been postponed to the following night and that she therefore was to play the part chiefly of spectator and maid of honour.

At last the clock in the hall chimed the half-hour; promptly I rose, turned out my lights and noiselessly slipped out on to the landing; a thin line of light indicated Mrs Bell's room and that the door was ajar. Into it I went.

Mrs Bell *et* Alice were there, sitting together, Mrs Bell's arm round Alice's waist. They had only their nighties on, the most dainty and provoking garments I ever saw. As I approached them they both rose. Helen opened her arms to me and clasping me to her she said, 'Welcome here, Jack!' and kissed me; then pushing me towards the blushing Alice she said, 'Now

Alice!' – whereupon the sweet girl threw her arms round me and held up her face to be kissed. I took her in my arms and, pressing her closely to me, I showered hot kisses on her lips till she gasped for breath, when I released her and she took refuge alongside of Mrs Bell again.

Just then Maud appeared, wearing the most ravishing nightie I had ever seen – for it was semi-transparent. She kissed us all in turn, then looked inquiringly at her mother.

'Jack dear, we want you to direct the proceedings tonight rather than choose someone by the fall of a card – then we shall learn the game better and how to play it!' said Mrs Bell, looking at me and slightly colouring – 'We'll all promise to do whatever you wish and in the way you wish. Will you be so kind?'

'Why, of course, Helen!' I answered, concealing my joy – for was not I now master of the situation?

'And if you don't mind, Jack, will you be content with Maud and me only tonight, and let Alice see for herself how the game is played; then tomorrow we will put her at your disposal!' added Mrs Bell, passing her arm round Alice's waist protectingly as the blushing girl nestled closely against her.

'Why, certainly, Helen dear!' I replied with a smile to Alice; 'but I suppose that Alice is willing to take her part in everything else that we may play at?'

Mrs Bell turned to Alice. 'What do you say, dear?' she asked lovingly.

Alice hesitated for a moment, then colouring deeply replied in a low voice 'Yes, auntie, if you wish it.'

'There's your answer, Jack!' said Mrs Bell with a smile. 'Now, my lord, your handmaidens await your commands!'

'Alice dear, come and sit on my knees,' I said. Hesitatingly Alice left her aunt's sheltering arm and gently placed herself on my knees, sitting so that she faced Maud and her mother. I slipped my left arm round her to hold her in position and lovingly kissed her. It was a delicious sensation to feel her soft weight in my thighs and to note the little tremors that pulsated through her, for she now was fairly quivering with excitement.

'Helen, will you now show yourself to us?' I said – 'Maud dear please strip your mother stark naked, and then come here to look at her with us!'

'Oh! Jack! no, no!' protested Helen, flushing furiously. But Maud delightedly seized her. 'Stand up, mummy!' she cried as she set to work to unbutton Mrs Bell's nightie. Slowly and reluctantly Helen complied; quickly Maud pulled the nightie off her and threw it on the bed – and Mrs Bell stood naked in front of us, one arm and hand in front of her breasts while with the other hand she covered her cunt.

I felt Alice thrill. I glanced at her – she was rosy red, but her eyes were riveted on her aunt's naked figure. Maud remained by her mother as if expecting further orders – I could see that she was quivering with suppressed excitement.

'Maud, pull your mother's hands away and clasp them together at the back of her head – and then come here!' I commanded.

'No, Jack! no!' pleaded Helen, who evidently was reluctant to expose her cunt to our gaze. But Maud slipped behind her, gripped her wrists in her strong young arms and pulling them backwards she placed them in the desired position, and quickly joined Alice and me, standing behind my chair, her eyes glittering with something very like lust.

In silence we three gazed at Helen – the broken breathing of the two girls betraying their suppressed excitement. Helen naked was certainly a thrilling spectacle – her flushed face, her glorious figure, her wonderful breasts heaving in her agitation, her splendidly round thighs and legs, her grandly swelling hips and haunches, and the bewitching forest of close curling silky hair that clustered over and concealed her cunt.

'Jack! isn't she glorious!' whispered Maud in glowing admiration. I nodded. 'Make mother turn slowly round, Jack, so that we can see her from all points and in profile!' whispered Maud again breathlessly. A quick flush told me that Helen had heard her daughter's suggestion. 'Please, Helen!' I said gently – 'very slowly, please!' Reluctantly Helen complied, affording us the most charming succession of views of her magnificent naked self. When she was in full profile I made her stand still – the sight of her in this position was simply wonderful, the sweep and spring of her back and bottom, the curve of her belly, her proud upstanding breasts with their saucy nipples, and the glorious bush of hairs – it simply fascinated us and I could feel my prick beginning to stiffen and began to wonder if Alice noticed it. After gazing our fill I made Helen continue her revolving – but stopped her again to revel in the view of her splendid buttocks and haunches and her plump thighs. Then starting her again I allowed her to complete the round, and again she faced us, now visibly trembling with apprehension and shame.

'Go and kiss her, girls!' I whispered. Up sprang Alice – simultaneously she and Maud seized Mrs Bell and smothered her with their ardent kisses. It was a sweet sight to watch – but time was valuable and so I joined the group and rescuing Helen from the excited girls I installed her on my knees, naked as she was, showering burning kisses on her quivering lips, while my hands sought her glorious breasts and squeezed them.

'Now Maud, its your turn!' I said; 'strip dear and show us your naked beauties. Help her to take off her nightie, Alice!'

In a trice Maud stood naked before her mother and me, a lovely vision of voluptuous slenderness. To me the sight was familiar, but to her mother and to Alice it was a revelation which struck them dumb with admiration. Helen's broken breathing told me how much the sight of her daughter's naked loveliness was affecting her, while Alice simply thrilled with undisguised pleasure, her eyes dwelling almost wonderingly on the glorious wealth of golden fluffy hair that grew on Maud's mount of Venus and sheltered her cunt. We made Maud turn herself slowly round, just as her mother had done, revelling in the spectacle of her bewitching slenderness; and when she again faced us, her cheeks suffused with blushes, I stealthily watched Helen's eyes as they wandered over her daughter's voluptuously naked body, her delicious breasts and her golden-haired cunt.

'Haven't you seen her like this before?' I whispered in her ear. Helen blushed. 'No!' she replied softly – 'Maud was quite a little thing when I last undressed her – now, well Jack, I'm beginning to wish I was a man, for her sake!' – and she laughed wickedly, while Alice who was standing just behind us, leaning on the back of our chair, broke into a ripple of amused girlish mirthful laughter,

'Then you can appreciate what my sensations are, dear!' I said as I amorously played with her breasts.

'I can guess them, Jack, by the mutinous movements of something I am sitting on!' Helen replied as she moved herself provokingly on my knees, smiling significantly at me.

It was only too true! The sight of her glorious nakedness, so quickly followed by the display of Maud's voluptuous charms, the inflammatory influence of our close contact and the excitement arising from my handling of her breasts (her cunt I did not dare to touch at the moment) all set me on fire. My prick was like a rod of iron. It was full time to have Maud.

I glanced over my shoulder at Alice. She was still intently gazing at Maud, and evidently very excited by her naked beauty. Her eyes were gleaming, her lips partly open, while her bosom throbbed and heaved. She evidently was dominated by intense curiosity which for the time being overpowered her maidenly reserve and training, and some subtle instinct (probably sexual) told her that a crisis was approaching.

'Helen!' I whispered loudly enough for Maud and Alice to hear, 'I must have Maud! Do you mind?' Maud blushed prettily, but Alice became crimson as she glanced quickly at me.

'Do, Jack!' Helen replied, kissing me ardently – then she rose so as to set me free. 'Come, Alice,' she added, reseating herself and pointing to her lap, on which Alice instantly installed herself, quivering with suppressed eagerness. Helen kissed her affectionately and whispered something in her ear that I could not catch but which made Alice colour still more furiously.

In an instant I was naked, my prick standing stiff and rampant in magnificent erection. Maud's eyes glistened joyfully at the sight, but Alice shrank back, startled, in Helen's arms, exclaiming 'Oh! oh! auntie!' her eyes widely dilating with surprise and alarm.

'Come here, Jack,' said Helen quietly, as she passed her hands caressingly and re-assuringly over Alice. I slipped an arm round Maud, and the pair of us went up together to Helen's chair and stood in front of and close to her and the still startled Alice. 'Now look again, dear!' said Helen softly as she pointed to my prick. Timidly Alice did so, blushing a rosy red, her astonished eyes travelling from the threatening rubicund head along the shaft to its root in my forest of hairs, under which my dangling balls were clearly visible, the sight of which evidently filled her with wonder and amazement. With silent curiosity we watched Alice as she gazed on the masculine organ which was so shortly to be lodged in her virgin cunt, and we wondered as to what thoughts were flashing through her mind at the sight of the instrument of her approaching violation.

Presently Alice drew a deep breath and hid her face against Helen's shoulder, a tremulous wriggle passing through her as she did so. Our eyes met Helen's in an amused smile. Had Alice's sexual excitement at the sight of my prick proved too much for her? Had she spent? But the very idea that Alice's maiden cunt was quivering in ecstasy set Maud and me on fire. 'Come, darling!' I exclaimed – and quickly I led her to Helen's bed, which was covered with a plum-coloured counterpane well calculated to set off our nudity – and on it Maud hastily extended herself on her back.

'Quick, Alice! wait a moment, Jack!' cried Helen, as she hurriedly rose, and slipping an arm round the flushed, trembling and wildly excited girl she brought Alice to the bedside. Maud's legs were now widely parted to accommodate me, and her golden-haired cunt was in full view, its pouting coral lips being clearly visible through the cluster of fluffy golden curls. 'Look, dear!' whispered Helen to Alice, indicating Maud's cunt with her finger – 'isn't it lovely!' Alice's eyes gleamed as they glanced from Maud's cunt to my impatient prick, intently watching our every movement. 'Go on, Jack!' said Helen softly. Quickly I placed myself in position between Maud's legs, and let myself down on to her breasts; and as her arms closed lovingly round me, I brought my prick to bear against the lips of her throbbing excited cunt and gently forced it in. 'Look, Alice, look!' whispered Helen excitedly, Alice's eyes dilating with astonishment as she saw how easily Maud's cunt engulfed my prick. Soon it was buried in Maud till our hairs intermingled.

'Oh! Jack . . . darling!' Maud murmured ecstatically with half-closed eyes, as after showering burning kisses on her sweet lips I began to fuck her. Instantly she threw her legs across my loins and strained me against her breasts with her strong young arms.

'Watch them, darling!' whispered Helen eagerly, her voice betraying her own agitation at the sight. But the injunction was unnecessary. Alice's eyes were riveted on our quivering, wriggling, heaving naked bodies, and not a single movement passed unnoticed.

Soon mutual ecstasy began to steal over us. Wilder and fiercer became my down-thrustings, madder and more frenzied became Maud's wriggles and plunges under me. Then the blissful climax was reached – an indescribable convulsion swept through both of us – 'Ah! . . . Ah!! . . . A-h-h-h!!! . . . ' ejaculated Maud brokenly as she felt herself inundated with the boiling torrent that I frantically shot from me as I spent rapturously into her. For a moment or two we lay rigid, locked in the closest and sweetest of embraces –

then we collapsed into temporary forgetfulness of everything but the heavenly bliss we had tasted in each other's arms, the echoes of which were still thrilling through us. Alice had witnessed a fuck.

When I had recovered myself and remembered my surroundings I looked cautiously round for Helen and Alice. I found they had returned to the chair. Helen, still naked, was seated in it, and Alice, still in her nightie, was on her lap, but she had coiled herself up and had twisted herself round so as to be lying face to face with Helen, tightly clasped bosom against bosom in her arms. Her attitude had somehow pulled her nightie tightly across her bottom, and revealed so delicious an outline that I involuntarily quivered with pleasure. This quiver aroused Maud, who dreamily opened her eyes; as they met mine a smile of heavenly satisfaction irradiated her countenance – her lips met mine and we exchanged long passionate kisses expressive of our gratitude for the divine raptures we had communicated to each other.

'Look at your mother and Alice!' I whispered softly. Maud looked and broke into a merry laugh, which made Helen and Alice start up almost guiltily; and as we slowly slipped out of each other's embrace and rose from Helen's bed, they came to meet us, blushing self-consciously.

Maud rushed into her mother's arms murmuring, 'Oh, mummy darling!' while Helen responded, 'Oh, Maud dear! oh, you happy girl!' as they kissed each other passionately.

I held out my arms silently to Alice, who timidly slipped into my embrace and let me kiss her lips. 'Darling, did we please you?' I whispered with a twinkle in my eye. She blushed crimson, averted her eyes, but remained silent; whereupon I added, 'Never mind, dear, you'll tell me better tomorrow night!' whereupon she quivered nervously.

Then to my utter surprise she raised herself on tiptoe, turned her blushing face to me and whispered very softly in a voice full of emotion, 'Kiss me again, Jack, and promise to be kind to me tomorrow when my time comes!'

'My darling!' I exclaimed, strangely moved – and again clasping her to me I kissed her passionately over and over again.

Helen's voice interrupted us. 'Jack, you can get to your room through that door; it's open tonight; Alice dear, come with us!' The three women disappeared into Helen's bathroom, and acting on her hint I slipped into my room and indulged in a most welcome ablution and purification of my organ; then feeling greatly refreshed by the operation I, still naked, returned to Helen's room just as she, also naked, came in alone from her bathroom.

Having the room to ourselves we rushed into each other's arms and kissed each other tenderly; the feel of her flesh against mine was simply exquisite, and I thrilled to think that before long she would be locked in my arms in the closest of embraces.

'Jack! it was just wonderful!' she murmured; 'Maud says it was the best . . . fuck . . . she ever had!'

'And what did Alice think of it, Helen?' I asked eagerly.

She laughed. 'Alice is absolutely staggered, Jack! In her wildest and wickedest moments she never imagined anything approaching what she has now seen; the sight of you and Maud in each other's arms excited her terribly – and when the wonderful finale was reached, I took her away and made her sit on my lap in the fashion you saw, for I am sure that otherwise she would have used her hands to get relief for her feelings! I was very bad myself!' she added with a self-conscious blush.

'Did you spend, Helen?' I asked mischievously.

'No, no, Jack!' she responded smilingly, 'but I was hard put to it to control myself!'

'Do you think Alice spent?' I asked somewhat anxiously.

'No, Jack, I know she didn't, but she admitted to Maud in the bathroom just now that she very nearly did!'

'Where is she now?' I enquired.

'In my bathroom with Maud,' Helen replied. 'I thought it as well to leave the two girls together and I expect Alice is plying Maud with questions! I think you will have the sweetest of pupils tomorrow night, Jack dear!' she added with a smile – 'I am looking forward to it with very pleasurable expectations.'

'When the girls join us, Helen, we'll make Alice show us herself naked,' I said; 'we'll play with her and tease her and excite her again and then I'll satisfy her desires and cravings in a way she will think is just heavenly. By that time I shall be ready to fuck you, my darling' (she kissed me rapturously), 'a good, long and slow fuck!' (another passionate kiss). 'After that we'll dissolve the meeting – but I'll slip back to you through that door; it won't be midnight, so we can have a long sweet time together by ourselves in your bed and in each other's arms' (more passionate kisses). 'Here they come!'

As we disengaged ourselves from our sweet embrace Maud and Alice with arms interlaced emerged from Helen's bathroom, Maud looking radiant, while Alice's face simply beamed with happiness; for she had now witnessed an act of fucking, and her maiden dread had been chased away by the sight of our rapturous transports. Also she had the pleasurable knowledge that she would presently be watching Helen in my arms; and so when Maud sank into an easy-chair Alice settled herself down comfortably on Maud's lap and smiled brightly at us.

But her happy complacency was about to be rudely disturbed. I had drawn Helen again on to my knees and was playing with her glorious breasts while she exchanged a laughing badinage with Maud which greatly amused Alice. Presently my right hand slipped down over Helen's stomach, and after gently tickling her navel it descended towards her cunt, which up to now I had not touched. Hastily she stopped me. 'No, Jack, you mustn't!' she exclaimed somewhat shamefacedly, 'you mustn't touch me there – I'm too excited – I should go off!'

Maud and Alice shook with silent laughter, then Maud said mischievously,

'Hurry up, Jack, or you'll lose the train,' which provoked further laughter in which Helen and I joined.

'I've got at least twenty minutes yet, Maud,' I replied, 'I'm not built on the revolver principle, I can't keep on firing – I've got to load my gun again and must not hurry the process or I will not be able to do your mother justice!'

'Twenty minutes!' exclaimed Maud dolefully – 'what shall we do all that time?'

'Let me see,' I replied. 'I am director tonight! I think that we cannot fill up the time better than by putting Alice through some of her paces; come, Alice dear, slip out of your nightie and show us yourself naked, to begin with!'

The happy smile fled from Alice's face and a look of dismay succeeded it as she cried, 'Oh, no, Jack, please no!'

'An excellent idea, Jack,' cried Maud delightedly – 'come Alice, let me undress you!' – and she commenced to unbutton Alice's nightie.

'No, no, don't, Maud!' cried Alice, resisting stoutly, but Helen rushed to Maud's assistance. Between them they got the nightie off Alice, then each seized a wrist and gently forced her to stand in front of me stark naked

Delightedly did my eyes rove over Alice's shrinking naked body. Helen held her firmly by one wrist, Maud by the other; her arms were thus forced away from her sides and so allowed her lovely outlines the fullest display – and as her hands were captive she could not hide her most private parts from my eager gaze. Her skin was like milk. She had the loveliest little breasts I ever saw, so sweetly full and ripe, and so deliciously saucy with the little pink nipples pointing outwards; while the exquisitely subtle curves of her figure as it swept inwards to her waist and then swelled outwards over her hips and on to her legs were dreams of beauty. Her thighs were gloriously plump and round, and melted into the daintiest of calves with slender ankles and tiny arched feet. Her beautifully rounded belly was surmounted with a large and deep navel and sloped gently down to its junction with her thighs, her hill of Venus being unusually large and prominent and fleshy, and covered with a delicious tangle of closely curling silky hair, through which the delicate pink lips of her cunt were visible. She was just the daintiest, sweetest, prettiest little maiden one could imagine – and her delicious young freshness crowned everything

I sat still, simply enraptured. Before me stood a wonderful trio: Helen and Maud, tall, splendidly voluptuous, stark naked, holding between them Alice in her dainty nakedness, her face suffused with deep blushes which surged down to her dear little breasts, as half-laughingly and half-nervously she begged to be let loose.

'Bring her here to me,' I said at last, separating my legs widely – an act that seemed really to alarm Alice and compelled Helen and Maud to use gentle force; and soon the naked struggling girl stood between my thighs held firmly there by Helen and Maud, now deeply interested in the proceedings.

'Don't touch me, Jack! please don't!' begged Alice, now quite frightened and trembling violently with flushed face and cast-down eyes. I placed my hands just behind her hips, noting delightedly how she squirmed when I touched her, while the sight of her palpitating bosom and heaving breasts began to re-animate my prick

'Alice dear,' I said softly, 'you're behaving very naughtily, and you are breaking your promise to do anything I wish as long as you are let off doing one special thing tonight. Do you think we would hurt you, dear? On the contrary, we're going to give you the sweetest time you've ever had, and prepare you for tomorrow! Now, darling, take courage! Come and kiss me, and smile again!'

I pressed her coaxingly towards me as I spoke; for a brief moment Alice stood irresolute – then she raised her eyes, looked lovingly at me, smiled trustingly, and yielding to the gentle pressure of my hands she allowed herself to be drawn forward till she was resting against me. Then she held up her lips to me to be kissed. 'My darling!' I whispered passionately, clasping her in my arms; and pressing her warm soft body against mine, I kissed her over and over again.

'Now you can let go of her hands, Helen, for Alice has become a good girl again!' I said with a smile as I arranged Alice on my knees, retaining her in that position with my left arm and keeping my right in readiness to feel her naked person – the sweet warmth and pressure of her bottom on my prick beginning to infuse fresh life to my somewhat limp organ. Helen meanwhile had settled herself again in her chair and faced me; she took Maud on her lap and then began to play with Maud's lovely breasts and generally to feel her, all the time looking significantly at me.

I took the hint and said to Alice, 'Look at those two, dear, it's a pretty game, isn't it!' Alice coloured vividly, then laughed uneasily, but watched Helen and Maud attentively.

Helen then exclaimed, 'Don't you know this game, Jack? – it's only "Follow my Leader"! I'm leader – whatever I do to Maud you are to do to Alice!'

'Oh! auntie!' exclaimed Alice, considerably startled at the idea. She turned and looked at me inquiringly. I smiled encouragingly and asked, 'Shall we play, dear?' Her colour rose, she hesitated, then whispered, 'Yes, if you wish it, Jack!' – then laughed gaily as if amused by her audacity.

Helen commenced by kissing Maud on her lips; I did the same to Alice. Helen next placed her hand just below Maud's breasts and felt her all over her stomach, roving backwards and forwards at her sweet will and some-times going perilously near Maud's cunt. I followed suit, revelling in the feel of Alice's firm, soft and springy flesh and sweet skin, smiling mischievously at her as she winced when my hand neared her cunt. Helen then devoted her attention to Maud's hips, haunches, buttocks and thighs, her hand dwelling lovingly on the plumper and fleshier parts, which she gently squeezed and caressed, visiting them again and again. Delightedly I did the same to Alice, who now began to show signs of agitation; and when I followed Helen's l ead and forced my hand between Alice's plump thighs (so closely pressed together) and began to luxuriate in her rich, juicy, smooth flesh (my hand travelling dangerously near to her cunt), she ejaculated confusedly, 'Oh, Jack! . . . Oh, Jack!' – then laughed nervously at her own discomfiture.

Helen here refreshed herself by kissing Maud, a proceeding I was not slow to follow with Alice and which she appreciated. 'Shall we go on, Jack?' then asked Helen.

'Shall we, Alice?' I queried with a smile.

'I'm quite willing, Jack,' she replied with a blush, then added laughingly, 'only auntie is getting very daring!'

'I'll pay you out, my beauty!' retorted Helen as she joined in the laugh. 'Now Maud!' – and she began to tickle Maud's navel, making her wriggle prettily with the titillation.

I applied my finger to Alice's navel. 'Oh! Jack dear!' she exclaimed with heightening colour and increasing agitation as she began squirming and writhing and twisting herself about, joining nevertheless in Helen's triumphant laughter.

'Now we'll try something else!' said Helen mischievously – and to Alice's dismay she gently attacked Maud's breasts, keeping her eyes on Alice. Delightedly I followed suit, and before Alice could interpose her free hand my eager hand had flown up to her bosom and had captured her left breast.

'Don't, Jack!' cried Alice, flushing furiously as she seized my hand and endeavoured to drag it away from its tempting prey, nevertheless laughing (though somewhat uneasily) at her complete discomfiture – but she found me too strong for her; and when I whispered gently, 'You must submit, dear – this is part of your preparation for tomorrow,' she loyally though reluctantly accepted the position and surrendered her sweet twin globes to my tender mercies, her agitated breathing and restless movements indicating her perturbation and emotion at my hand's invasion of her maiden breasts.

Helen and Maud had suspended their game – that is to say, Maud was still on her mother's lap with her mother's arm round her, and Helen's right hand was still playing with her daughter's beautiful breasts; but they evidently found it much more interesting and exciting to watch Alice's first experience with kind but inquisitive male fingers. The shock of feeling a man's hand on her maiden breasts had to a certain extent died away, and Alice was now lying resting on me, her right arm clasping me round my neck, her left hanging by her side, the hand tightly gripping the chair rail – the distant expression in her eyes as they idly fell on objects without seeming to see them indicating her intense absorption in the sensations of the moment as she felt her virgin breasts stroked, caressed and squeezed by my eager though gentle hands. For me it was a delicious occupation. Alice's little bubbies were so firm and yet so springy and fleshy and above all so virginal that my fingers absolutely revelled in their feel; and for some considerable time I could not bring myself to relinquish them.

At last, with a strong effort I tore my hand away, and sliding it down to her navel I brought Alice back to a consciousness of her surroundings and whereabouts by gently tickling that sensitive part of her. As her eyes resumed their duties they met those of Helen and Maud, beaming sympathy and signalling encouragement, and she smiled gratefully at them as she roused herself, murmuring, 'Oh, Jack dear, don't!' At this juncture Helen caught my eye, then slowly ran her hand from Maud's breasts over her stomach and down to her cunt, where her fingers began gently to pull and play with the lovely tangle of fluffy golden hair that clustered there. Alice became scarlet. It had never occurred to her that her cunt was to be felt, and when my hand followed Helen's lead and slipped downwards over her belly she clutched my wrist wildly, threw one thigh closely over the other so as to defend the approach, and exclaimed agitatedly, 'No, no, darling! – no, Jack dear! – you mustn't touch me there!' – then kissed me frenziedly as if to dissuade me.

I let my hand remain in her grip and said quietly and soothingly, 'You must play the game, dear! – besides that, what did I tell you just now?' She looked questioningly and imploringly at me with eyes full of dismay. I drew her to me and kissed her lovingly, whispering, 'Cannot you trust yourself to me, darling?'

For reply she nestled her soft cheek against mine, and then murmured, 'Jack! must you do it?'

'Yes, Alice dear!' I replied softly – 'and tomorrow you will thank me for insisting!' For a moment she hesitated – then without a word she released my wrist and slowly and reluctantly unlocked her thighs. 'May I, darling?' I asked gently.

'Yes, dear!' she replied softly and tremulously, then pressed her cheek still more closely against mine till our lips nearly rested on each other – she tightened her clasp round my neck as if to nerve her for the ordeal, while her eyes sought Helen's and rested appealingly on her as if asking for her sympathy and guidance.

I decided that this time I would invade Alice's maiden cunt by the valley formed by her closely pressed thighs, at the head of which I should find her hill of Venus, its unusual size and prominence being intensified by her sitting position – which made the tangle of curly silky hairs stand out like a bush. Accordingly I did so; to Alice's surprise I dropped my hand lightly on her thighs, about halfway down them, then moved it upwards between their soft smooth surfaces till it arrived at her shrubbery, when (following Helen's lead) I played amorously with her hairs, now pulling them gently, now twining them round my fingers, now softly brushing them – a proceeding that seemed to excite Alice judging from the way in which she agitated her bottom on my knees. After a little of this toying I proceeded with forefinger and thumb to explore the region covered by her hairs, pressing and squeezing its deliciously soft springy flesh, but carefully avoiding the tender sensitive opening – till Alice's involuntary wrigglings and squirmings and the increasing agitation of her bosom told me that she had arrived at the condition of erotic sexual excitement that I desired. Then I gently applied my forefinger to the lips of Alice's tender maiden cunt.

'Oh! Jack!' she cried, drawing herself back hurriedly as if to escape from my finger, which however not only retained but improved its position, and now began to move along the delicate slit – creating the most exquisite tickling sensations, which Alice evidently enjoyed. She clutched me tighter than ever round my neck, she quivered voluptuously, she brought her lips to bear upon mine and began to kiss me ardently – and when my finger inserted itself into the virgin recesses of her cunt and commenced to agitate itself seductively, Alice fairly lost control of herself and surrendered herself unrestrainedly to the gratification of her sexual desires and her newly born erotic lust.

I glanced triumphantly at Helen – but to my astonishment she was busily engaged with Maud. Her hand was buried well between Maud's thighs, and her finger was evidently hard at work in her daughter's cunt, for Maud was wriggling and quivering and jerking herself about in extreme lascivious frenzy – and it was clear that the ecstatic crisis was at hand. The piquant spectacle of Helen frigging Maud – of a mother frigging her daughter – was too much for me. I redoubled my ministrations to Alice and set to work deliberately to make her spend. Helen and Maud were by now far too excitedly absorbed in their own voluptuous sensations to pay any attention to us.

'Jack! oh! darling!' gasped Alice almost incoherently as, wriggling violently, she jerked herself madly forward as if to encourage my finger to more furious exertion in her cunt.

'Oh! mummy! Oh, mummy dear! . . . keep on! . . . keep on!' ejaculated Maud wildly in her near delirium.

Seeing that Alice was now on the verge of erotic collapse, I attacked her virgin clitoris and furiously tickled it. 'Ha! . . . Ha! . . . Ha!!! . . . ' she gasped – then with an indescribable spasmodic paroxysm she spent voluptuously, bedewing my finger with her creamy virgin essence.

Almost simultaneously Maud went off with a half-strangled cry of 'Ah! . . . Mummy darling!' clinging frantically to Helen as the spasms of her sexual rapture vibrated through her and quenched the fires of her lust.

Maud was the first to come to herself, which she did very soon; she kissed her mother gratefully and they both came across to me to welcome Alice back 'from the angels'; she being still unconscious, I cautiously drew my finger out of her cunt, and with the air of the victor I exhibited it to them, wet, glistening and sticky with Alice's maiden spend, the display provoking them to silent laughter. Just then Alice moved herself uneasily, then drew a long breath and dreamily opened her eyes; as they met Helen's the recollection of her whereabouts and of what she had been doing flashed on her. She blushed violently, sprang to her feet, and buried her face in her hands, murmuring shamedly, 'Oh, auntie! auntie!' Helen took her affectionately in her arms, and said, 'There is nothing to be ashamed of, darling – we've not come to scold but to congratulate you on your début!' Overjoyed Alice kissed her gratefully, embraced Maud, then threw herself into my arms (I had then risen) murmuring, 'Oh, darling! darling!'

But my prick had been so irritated and inflamed by the movements of her soft warm bottom on it that it stood rampant and stiff and stark. 'Oh, look at poor Jack!' cried Maud as she pointed to it – 'and poor mother too, who has not yet had anything; wait half a minute for us, Jack. Come, Alice!' and the two girls rushed off into Helen's bathroom. Hurriedly Helen and I performed our ablutions, mad for each other; then I placed her on her bed, put a hard cushion under her bottom and separated her thighs, and sat by her impatiently waiting for the girls' reappearance, the while feasting my eyes on Helen's beautiful cunt now so gloriously displayed, while Helen gently stroked my raging prick.

Very soon the girls hurried in, beaming with pleasurable excitement and anticipation. 'Now Jack, into mother!' cried Maud. I needed no encouragement. In a trice I was on the bed and between Helen's legs, and was just about to plunge my prick into her cunt when Alice innocently intervened. 'Please Jack, may I feel it?' she asked. In spite of ourselves, we all laughed.

'Yes, dear!' I replied, 'you may feel me and you may put me into Helen!' The touch of her soft maiden hand nearly made my tool burst with pleasure. 'Now, Alice dear!' I cried as I let myself down on to Helen. Holding my prick in her dainty fingers Alice cleverly guided its head into Helen's throbbing and expectant cunt, and delightedly watched it as it disappeared inch by inch, Helen all the time whinnying with the rapture of again feeling a male organ lodged in her. But we were both too ardent and excited to take our pleasure slowly, as we had intended. As soon as Helen found me well up her cunt and felt my arms close firmly round her till her breasts flattened against me, she began to agitate herself under me wildly, wriggling and writhing, jerking herself about, moving her legs restlessly, sometimes stretching them, at other times twisting them round me. To prolong her blissful transports I lay on her as motionless and as rigid as I possibly could, leaving her to really fuck herself, in the hope that her furious movements would provoke her into spending quickly – and so it happened, for soon she strained me passionately to her and jogging herself upwards violently she spent rapturously, ejaculating brokenly, 'Oh, my darling! . . . my dar . . . ling . . . ' with such voluptuous quivers and tremors that she nearly set me spending also. I was however able to resist the sweet temptation, and when her spasms of pleasure ceased to thrill through her I began to fuck her delightfully slowly; but another cyclone of sexual passion and lust swept through Helen, and again she began to riot under me in furious plungings and curvettings, her head rolling from side to side in the vehemence of her desires. I could not any longer control myself. I let myself go and rammed fiercely into her. Fiercely Helen responded by jerking herself madly upwards as if to meet my down-thrusts. Then ensued a veritable cyclone of heaves from her and fierce ramming thrusts from me in the wildest fury – then the ecstatic crisis overtook me, and frantically I spent into Helen, she receiving my boiling tribute with the most voluptuous and rapturous transports of bliss as she herself yielded to nature and spent madly in thrills of delight.

For some little while we lay lost to the world, tightly clasped in each other's arms – then slowly we came to; our lips met in tender kisses and then I slowly drew my prick out of Helen's cunt and rose. Maud and Alice at once fell on her and kissed her passionately – then Maud whispered something in her mother's ear and promptly Helen rose and with a loving glance at me she disappeared with the two girls. I slipped into my room and quickly performed a most necessary and welcome ablution; then I put on my night attire as a hint to Maud and Alice that the seance was closed.

Before long they all returned and following my lead they put on their nighties . . . then Helen said, 'Now my dears, it is time for bed. Good-night, Jack dear! Oh, how good you have been to all of us!' and tenderly she kissed me.

'Good night, Jack! and thank you so much!' said Maud archly as she kissed me.

Alice said nothing, but when our lips met in a passionate kiss she breathed, 'Oh, my darling!'

Then we retired to our separate rooms.

## *Chapter Three*

In about fifteen minutes Helen noiselessly opened my door and said softly, 'Jack!' and promptly I went into her room, once more naked. She was still in her nightie; I begged her to take it off, and again she stood before me in all her glorious nudity. I pointed to her bed, and soon we lay on it side by side, my left arm round her while my right hand after playing a little with her lovely breasts wandered down to her cunt.

Presently I took hold of her hand and gently conducted it to my prick, which still lay limp and inert. With a loving smile she began to play with it, sometimes stroking it, sometimes caressing it, feeling my balls and pulling my hairs, evidently delighted in her occupation. Needless to say it was not long before my organ began to show signs of returning life, and soon it was in fair erection again.

'Why Jack! You're ready again!' she whispered admiringly as she continued to play and fondle it.

'Yes, darling! thanks to you!' I murmured with a kiss of gratitude – 'and you?'

Helen blushed prettily, then wriggled lasciviously as my finger slipped into the warm and moist interior of her cunt – no answer was necessary as her eyes proclaimed her readiness.

My prick now was in full erection. I whispered to Helen, 'Put it into you, darling!' She looked uncomprehendingly at me. I whispered again, 'Straddle across me, dear . . . that's right, now take hold of my prick and put it into your cunt yourself . . . now sink down on it, and let yourself take it all in . . . slowly darling, that's the way . . . now lie on me!'

In surprise and wondering astonishment, Helen obeyed, hesitatingly at first – but when she began to impale herself on my rampant prick she comprehended the sweet manoeuvre and lent herself almost too energetically to it; but soon she had my prick stiffly lodged up her cunt, then she lowered herself gently on to me murmuring, 'Oh, Jack! how delicious! how heavenly!' as with a few voluptuous wriggles she settled herself luxuriously on me, her eyes sparkling with delight as my arms closed round her and imprisoned her. As for me I was in the seventh heaven of bliss as I lay under Helen, clasping her luscious and palpitating naked body in my arms with my prick engulfed in her moist, warm and throbbing cunt. Her full large breasts lay sweetly on my chest, our eyes looked straight into each other's, her ripe lips rested on mine and our breaths mingled as we exchanged long passionate and burning kisses in our mutual rapture. And so we lay silent for a while, absorbed in the exquisite sensations of the moment.

'Am I to do anything, Jack?' Helen presently whispered.

'Not just now, darling,' I replied softly – 'just keep as you are and rest yourself on me, lie limply, dear, and let me enjoy your delicious weight on me. We'll have a sweet talk, all the time tasting each other, then when we can no longer wait you'll have to . . . fuck me – and yourself on me – you'll have to do all the work this time!'

'Oh, Jack!' Helen murmured delightedly, her eyes sparkling again with pleasurable anticipation – and involuntarily she began to agitate herself voluptuously on me. Quickly I passed my hands along her back to her bottom and gripping her gloriously plump fleshy buttocks I checked her movements, whispering, 'Steady, Helen darling! lie still, dear – or you'll set us both off! – let us prolong this delicious agony, and when we let ourselves go our pleasure will be all the greater.'

'Oh, Jack! I couldn't help it!' Helen murmured faintly, then she suddenly caught her breath, her eyes half-closed and an indescribable tremor quivered through her. She had provoked herself into spending. I patted her bottom tenderly. Then she raised her humid eyes to mine, and kissed me rapturously as she whispered, 'Oh, Jack, that was lovely! Now I will lie quiet and be a good girl!' And again she voluptuously settled herself on me.

I transferred my hands from her bottom to her breasts and fondly caressed

Helen's delicious bubbies as they rested sweetly on me, and again we lay silent for a while.

Presently she whispered in my ear, 'Jack, are you going to . . . to ravish Alice this evening?'

'I think so, darling!' I replied, 'provided of course that she is willing to let me have her! Has she said anything to you?'

'No,' Helen answered, 'but I'm sure she wishes you to . . . fuck her, dear! The sight of first Maud and then me in your arms excited her terribly – you should have heard her questions when we were in the bathroom – I think she would have liked to have been ravished there and then!'

'Then she shall be deflowered this evening!' I said – 'the very idea of holding her tight in my arms while I force my prick into her maiden cunt is enough to . . . make me spend now!' Helen kissed me passionately, and began to jog herself gently on me.

'Steady, darling!' I whispered warningly as I soothed her. 'Alice has a largish cunt, has she not?'

'Yes,' Helen replied with an arch smile, 'Alice has quite a large cunt – as large as mine!' she added with a conscious blush and an involuntary wriggle. 'You'll hurt her very little, I fancy, Jack, and it will be sweet to see her in your arms, especially when she feels herself inundated for the first time with warm love-juice!' and her eyes glistened as she amorously kissed me. Then she whispered in sudden agitation, 'Jack! I must. . . ! – may I, darling?'

I nodded with a loving smile and folded my arms again round Helen so as to hold her firmly against me. Again she whispered, this time flushing deeply, 'Darling, promise to lie quite still, and let me do . . . everything!' and again I nodded smilingly.

Voluptuously Helen arranged herself on me, kissed me tenderly, laid her cheek against mine and gripping me tightly she began to jog herself up and down on my prick, agitating herself on me in the most delicious way and making me fairly thrill with delight. At first she moved herself slowly and rhythmically – but before long the increasing flutters of her bosom, clasped so tightly against me, and her broken breathing indicated her rapidly growing lust; soon she was wriggling furiously on me, her bottom heaving and tossing wildly as she worked herself up and down on my stiff and rampant prick with riotously rapid movements. Soon the blissful crisis overtook her – a convulsive quiver thrilled through her, and with a half-strangled inarticulate cry Helen spent rapturously and collapsed, her whole body pulsating as the spasms of pleasure shot through her.

True to my promise I lay absolutely rigid and motionless – but I had to exercise all my powers of self-control to prevent myself from joining her in spending – and as she lay quiet on me I gradually regained complete hold over myself again. Then I whispered in her ear, 'Go on again, darling!' Helen instantly roused herself from her semi-swoon, and soon she was again raging wildly on me, wriggling furiously and ramming herself down on my prick in the wildest erotic excitement. Then for the second time she spent blissfully, quivering voluptuously in my arms in the throes of her ecstasy. Again I allowed her to lie quiet till she could collect herself – and then I whispered, 'Now, darling, we'll finish together!' As if stimulated by the knowledge that her excited cunt was now about to receive the blissful injection, Helen clasped me more tightly than ever to her, kissed me passionately and set to work to fuck me (I really cannot describe her movements more truly). It did not take her long to break down my defence – and I was a willing victim. With long furious strokes of her wildly agitated bottom she worked herself up and down on my now raging prick – then when my involuntary and uncontrollable quivers told her that she had overcome my stubborn resistance she agitated herself madly on me in a hurricane of wild heavings and wrigglings and squirmings, in which I joined with frenzied up-thrustings – till, no longer able to refrain, I shot a torrent of boiling love-juice into Helen just as she for the third time yielded to nature and spent in exquisite transports of rapture. Oh, God! how I spent into her – and how ecstatically Helen received the deluge of hot semen that I poured frantically into her. Then we both collapsed, and lay motionless, clinging exhaustedly to each other.

How long we thus lay I do not know. I came to first. Helen was lying on me limp and nerveless, her head resting on my shoulder – she had fainted under the violence of her spending and the intensity of her spasms of pleasure. Gently and caressingly I passed my hands over her naked person, squeezing her breasts and endeavouring to bring her to herself, all the while whispering fond words of love in her ear. Presently Helen moved uneasily, then drew a long breath or rather a deep sigh of utter satisfaction, and slowly raised her head half-unconsciously with a glazed look. As her humid eyes opened they met mine and flashed instant recognition. A wonderful smile indicative of the intensest satisfaction and happiness irradiated her face – 'Jack! my darling!' she murmured rapturously as she pressed her lips to mine and showered kisses on me till we both gasped for breath. Then slowly and reluctantly she drew herself off my now limp and dejected prick, rose, and tottered to her bathroom. Promptly I slipped into my room and indulged in a welcome and necessary ablution, then returned to Helen's room just as she herself reappeared. She ran straight into my welcoming arms. I led her to a chair and installed her on my knees, and in soft murmurs and with loving kisses we testified to each other the pleasure we had mutually tasted.

'Now my darling, good-night!' I said finally and drew Helen tenderly to me.

'Good-night, my darling, darling Jack!' she murmured as our lips sought each other – 'Oh! how happy you have made me!' and passionately she kissed me, then rose and led me to my door, as she had to lock it after me. 'Sleep well, my darling!' she added archly – 'do not forget that tomorrow night you have to violate Alice!' I laughed, gave her a final kiss and thus we parted.

And so ended our first evening at The Nunnery.

We all met at breakfast next morning, the ladies looking radiant; Helen and Maud's faces wore a look of happy satisfaction, while Alice was a veritable blush-rose. After the usual bright meal Helen disappeared to her boudoir to write letters, and Maud adjourned to her bedroom for mysteries in millinery connected with a visit she was about to pay. Alice confessed to having no plans; to me she seemed nervous and preoccupied, her thoughts no doubt reverting constantly to her coming ordeal. Since I arrived and had been told of the wonderful and almost incredible thing she was willing to do, I was most anxious to get her by herself for a little so that I might let her understand how I appreciated it – but no opportunity had been vouchsafed; and so I decided to monopolise her all the morning, for I felt morally certain that she then would be all the happier when she was made over to me that evening in Helen's room – and to that end I suggested that I should take her on the river till lunchtime. Delightedly she accepted the proposition, and soon we were in the boat and off, she in the stern seat with the tiller ropes and I on the rowing thwart, in easy chatting distance of her.

She had on a walking dress – and what between the lowness of her seat and the shortness of her dress, more of her shapely legs and slender ankles cased in dainty stockings were visible to my delighted eyes than she quite approved of; and she strove by sundry tugs and readjustments to lessen the exhibition – but without success. I watched her in amused silence – and when she resigned herself to the inevitable and resumed her usual pose on the stern cushions with slightly heightened colour, conscious that my eyes were admiringly dwelling on her pretty extremities, I frankly laughed out loud and said chaffingly, 'Well, you are a funny girl, Alice – why are you so unkind this morning in the matter of showing yourself to me, when you were so sweet and kind last night, and are going to be so again tonight!'

Alice coloured deeply, then laughed in pretty confusion and said, 'Places and surroundings have to be considered, Jack, my dear – I am quite sure that you would not like me here now just as I was last night!'

'Wouldn't I!' I rejoined ardently – 'when we get to that little sheltered backwater on the left, I'll row in, so as to give you an opportunity of changing your attire!'

'You're very considerate – and I'm much obliged to you, Jack,' she replied, laughing merrily and apparently quite at her ease with me – 'but I'm afraid you must deny yourself the . . . may I say, pleasure!' she added archly.

'Well, I suppose lovely woman must have her way! At all events we'll go in just the same,' I replied with mock resignation. 'Steer in, dear, and take us right to the end, in the thick of the trees.' – and soon we found ourselves in a delicious nook and in absolute privacy. I tied the boat to a convenient root so that we could not drift, then I squeezed myself into the stern seat by Alice's side (she sweetly making room for me) and slipped my left arm round her waist.

'This is very romantic!' I remarked softly as I drew her to me – 'will not the poetry of the spot tempt you to become a wood nymph?'

Alice laughed gaily and shook her head. 'I never went in for theatricals, Jack,' she rejoined.

'I'm not asking you to do so now, dear,' I replied – 'theatricals mean dressing up, my suggestion implied the very contrary!'

She laughed merrily, then nestling close to me she whispered gently, blushing divinely, 'In less than twelve hours you'll see what you wish, Jack, won't that do, dear?'

I clasped her tightly to me and made her shift herself on to my lap, then I kissed her passionately. 'My darling!' I whispered, 'I was only teasing you! . . . And are you really going to be so sweet and kind to me tonight as to give me your . . . maiden self!'

Alice smiled tenderly and gently nodded her head, her eyes looking lovingly into mine. I kissed her sweetly and gratefully and for a moment or two our emotions enforced silence.

Presently I whispered, 'Tell me, darling, do you really wish this? Are you really willing to . . . lose your virginity, your maidenhead?'

A vivid blush suffused her cheeks – for a few moments she was silent and I could feel how she was trembling; then she murmured with deep emotion, 'Had anyone else . . . been suggested, I would have said indignantly, No! . . . No! . . . No! . . . but to you, Jack, I say, Yes! . . . Yes! . . . Yes! . . . '

I was too moved to speak . . . I could only kiss her sweet lips over and over again – and she could read in my eyes my emotion. Helen's chaffing remark that no one but myself would ever win Alice flashed through my brain – and an overwhelming desire to reward in the one and only right way Alice's love and trust, as evidenced by the wonderful sacrifice of her virginity that she was willing to make, surged through me.

I held her to me more closely than ever, and looking straight into her loving eyes I said softly, 'Darling, you rebuke me! You are willing to surrender to me a girl's most precious treasure, and to give it to me freely and without regard to your future happiness. Will you let me do what I can to ensure that happiness to you? Alice, my darling, will you become my wife?'

She gazed at me in absolute wonder, her eyes widely open in startled surprise; it was clear that she could not believe her ears. I smiled tenderly at her and whispered, 'Would you like to hear it again? Alice darling, will you become my dear little wife?'

The look of startled surprise vanished – in its place came a simply wonderful smile – she caught her breath – her eyes filled with happy tears which however could not put out the love-light that was in them – her lips parted, and she murmured brokenly, 'Oh! Jack! . . . Jack!' as she clung lovingly to me.

I bent down and kissed her tenderly on her quivering lips, and said gently, 'That means "Yes" . . . Oh! my darling! . . . my darling!' And for a while we remained silent, our eyes looking into each other's and brimming over with love.

Presently Alice whispered with a curious smile, half-anxious and half-roguish, 'Jack! what about tonight, darling?'

I laughed, she also after a moment's hesitation. 'We had better let the arrangement stand good, darling,' I replied, 'we must think of Helen and Maud, for were it not for them we should not now be . . . sweethearts!' (she kissed me delightedly). 'We must not disappoint them. I don't think we will tell them anything until after . . . after.' Alice blushed vividly and kissed me sweetly, 'after you have tasted Love's raptures in my arms. You're happier now about it, eh darling?'

'I'm yours now entirely and absolutely, Jack,' Alice murmured gently, her eyes full of love – 'I'm your happy sweetheart now – I'll gladly be your mistress tonight, and your little wifie as soon as ever you like. So do just what you like with me and to me!' and she smiled lovingly and trustingly.

I kissed her gratefully, and a sweet idea came into my brain; and with a mischievous smile I said, 'I'm going to take you at your word, darling!' – and slipped my right hand under her clothes, arresting its movement upwards when it got to her dainty knees.

'Oh, Jack!' she exclaimed as she started up hurriedly and strove to defend herself, at the same time laughing merrily at her discomfiture and the way I had turned her words against herself. I looked smilingly at her but kept my hand where it was on her knees.

'What do you wish to do, darling?' she whispered in pretty confusion.

'I want to call on a maiden who has just become engaged, and to offer her my congratulations,' I replied with mock gravity – 'I know she is at home and so with your leave I'll go on.'

Alice laughed merrily and gently reparted her thighs as my hand passed along them, as if to facilitate its approach to her cunt, all the while looking at me with eyes full of love. Delightedly my hand travelled over her luscious thighs clad in dainty drawers, till it reached the tender junction – then slipping through the opening it arrived at its destination. 'Oh, darling!' breathed Alice, squirming deliciously as she felt my fingers on her maiden cunt – and as I pulled and played with her silky hairs and stroked and caressed her exquisitely springy and juicy flesh she threw her arms round my neck and pressing her lips on mine she kissed me passionately, agitating herself charmingly all the time. Soon my finger gently made its way between the lips of her cunt and into the warm throbbing moist interior, where it inquisitively explored its sweet recesses, dwelling significantly on the weblike hymeneal membrane that I was that same evening to break through, and then as she was now beginning to wriggle in earnest I challenged her excited clitoris and set to work to frig Alice. 'Oh, Jack! . . . darling!' she panted rapturously as she jogged herself to meet my finger, gently at first and then more and more wildly and rapidly till in a storm of uncontrollable jerks and squirmings and wriggles the ecstatic crisis overtook her and she inundated my happy finger with her virginal love-juice.

Alice had kept her lips pressed on mine throughout, deliciously punctuating with ardent kisses her transports while being felt and frigged. When the last spasms of pleasure had died away, she gave me one long clinging, burning kiss and, looking gratefully at me with her still humid eyes, she murmured rapturously, 'Oh, Jack! it was just heavenly!'

'Nicer than last night, dear!' I asked quizzingly.

'Oh! yes, yes!' she replied in tones of the deepest conviction that set me off in a laugh in which she soon joined. 'Last night I was too timid and nervous, and so awfully surprised by everything I saw, and so excited also, that I could not let myself go as I did just now!' she added colouring prettily.

'Then you'll let yourself go tonight, darling!' I whispered significantly. She blushed like a peony, looked tenderly at me, and with a loving smile she nodded her head assuringly. 'Now it is time for us to start home – one final kiss, darling!' I said feelingly. 'We're going to be very happy, love, for we are wise enough to recognise that a bedroom has joys as well as a drawing-room. Now, my sweet . . . !' and lovingly we kissed each other. Then we resumed our proper places in the boat and soon were out in the river again, this time homeward bound, talking sweet nothings in supreme happiness.

Presently Alice with a little hesitation said somewhat seriously, 'Please promise me one thing, Jack! – when we are married please keep on being kind and good to Auntie Helen and to Maud – I shall be so very miserable if I should be the cause of their being left without the sexual satisfaction they so ardently desire and need. You will promise this, Jack darling?'

I was very touched by her devotion. 'I promise willingly, dear,' I replied earnestly – then with a mischievous smile I added, 'We'll have our bedrooms arranged like those in The Nunnery, darling – we will always put up Auntie Helen and Maud in the rooms that communicate with ours, so that they can slip in quietly – and we'll have regular orgies when they come up, eh, darling!'

Alice beamed on me, then laughed merrily, exclaiming, 'Oh, Jack! it will be fun!'

As we neared the house Helen came down to meet us. 'I've been wondering what became of you two!' she exclaimed – 'Now come along, lunch is ready – we must feed you up, Alice darling, and you also, Jack,' she added laughingly, and slipping her arm round Alice she led her towards the house. I fastened the boat and tidied up generally and then followed them.

## Chapter Five

After lunch the ladies retired, frankly admitting that they were going to 'rest' so as better to fit themselves for the excitements of the evening. I announced my intention of walking to the neighbouring little town to try and do some shopping; but they all so vigorously protested against my taking an eight-mile walk and knocking myself up that at Helen's pressing request I consented to be driven in.

The object of my visit was to try to obtain two pairs of strong leather wristlets, softly padded and fitted with brass Ds so that they could be strapped together or each arm secured singly. I was fortunate enough to find the very thing at the saddler's; he stitched the Ds on while I waited and I bore them off in triumph. My readers will come across them presently.

I was back at The Nunnery by teatime, after which Maud took Alice off for a short walk, while Helen and I strolled in the gardens. She was delightfully full of the pleasures she had tasted in my arms on the previous night – 'Jack! I'm another woman today!' she exclaimed rapturously, adding with a merry smile, 'I didn't know I wanted it so badly!' She went on to tell me that she had kept Alice with her all that afternoon as she feared that the girl's natural apprehension of the ordeal of being ravished might make her nervous and perhaps hysterical when the moment arrived were she allowed to think about it too much previously – but, she said, 'While Alice does seem a little to dread the . . . operation itself, she really seems to be almost looking forward to surrendering her maidenhead to you. I'm sure she loves you, Jack!'

'Dear little thing!' I replied with feeling – 'the thought of having to ravish her this evening excites me terribly!'

Half-past ten again was a very long time in coming, but at last the clock chimed the half-hour and promptly I entered Helen's room, where I found Maud and Alice, the latter really looking nervous and agitated, although she greeted me with a sweet smile. We kissed each other all round, and then Helen placed Alice in my arms with a significant smile that made the blushing girl grow still more rosy as I fondly kissed her again, and then passed my arm round her waist so as to keep her with me.

'Now let us begin!' I said briskly. 'Helen, may we move that long dress box with the padded top into the middle of the room?' Quickly she and Maud effected the change, then looked enquiringly at me. 'Thanks, dears!' I said – 'now Helen, lie down on your back, naked, with your legs widely apart, and let me have a good study of your cunt!'

'Oh, Jack!' she exclaimed, colouring vividly as she looked pleadingly at me – but I only laughed at her and pointed to the box; whereupon Helen reluctantly took off her nightie and placed herself on her back in the position desired. Quickly I knelt between her knees with Maud and Alice on either side of me, their eyes gleaming with excitement, and together we delightedly inspected Helen's superb cunt – gazing admiring on the thickly clustering growth of hairs on Venus's Hill and the delicate salmon-pink of its lips, poor Helen all the while blushing like a schoolgirl. Then with gentle fingers I drew the lips apart and disclosed Helen's clitoris (evidently much excited), the quivering folds of pink tender flesh and the delicious passage in which I had already been twice voluptuously lodged.

At last I removed my hands, and leaning forward I ardently kissed Helen on her cunt – she squirming prettily – and rose. 'Don't move yet dear,' I said; 'now Maud, strip yourself naked and lie on your mother face upwards – let your legs hang down outside hers, so that we can compare both cunts.'

'Oh, Jack!' both mother and daughter cried aghast as they looked ashamedly at each other; but I was obdurate. Alice was now rosy red, but her eyes glittered with eager anticipation, and she smiled delightedly at me as our eyes met; she undoubtedly was enjoying herself.

Reluctantly Maud complied. When she had stripped herself naked I made her straddle across Helen, then gently lowered her backwards till she lay flat on her mother, who passed her arms round her daughter and maintained her in the desired position. Their cunts now were displayed one just above the other, a charming spectacle.

'Now, Alice dear, strip yourself naked also!' I said gently to her. Much surprised and somewhat disconcerted Alice slowly complied, and shame-facedly stood naked before me; after a delightful but hasty glance at her lovely timid shrinking naked figure, I made her kneel between Helen's parted legs and sit on her heels. Then I myself knelt behind her, passed my arms round her and gently seized her breasts with my chin resting on her right shoulder, so that we could together feast our eyes on the piquant sight – the cunts of mother and daughter.

In admiring silence we gazed our fill, Alice's trembles testifying to her suppressed excitement: 'Aren't they sweet!' I whispered. Alice nodded eagerly, too excited to speak, her eyes shining with something akin to lust. After a little further silent contemplation I whispered again, 'Open Maud's cunt, dear, so that we can see what the inside is like!' Joyously Alice complied, and with her pretty little fingers she pulled widely apart the delicate lips of Maud's cunt and revealed the lovely interior, salmon-tinted and juicy, surmounted by a projecting and angry-looking clitoris, which seemed to attract Alice's eyes.

'Now open Auntie Helen's, dear,' I whispered. Quickly Alice lowered her hands, and placing the tips of her fingers on either side of Helen's well-defined and pouting slit she held Helen's cunt open for my inspection. 'Do you see any family likeness, dear?' I asked with a smile.

Alice laughed silently – 'Of course!' she said softly, 'they're exactly like each other. Only auntie's is so much bigger and. . . and. . . looser!' she added with a mischievous smile which made me fondle and squeeze her dear little breasts more actively than before. Then of her own accord Alice began to stroke and play with the glorious pair of cunts in front of her, devoting a hand to each – while Helen and Maud wriggled and squirmed deliciously, uttering involuntarily little cries of pleasure as Alice's gentle fingers wandered caressingly over their sensitive and ticklish cunts – her eyes dancing with delight.

'I think they have had enough, dear!' I said presently, and Alice and I rose and assisted Helen and Maud to their feet.

'Now, Jack, Alice must let us examine her virgin cunt before you alter it for ever!' cried Maud excitedly.

'Oh, no, Maud! Oh, no, Jack, please!' Alice pleaded, blushing vividly.

'I'd also like to study it, dear!' I said, 'and this will be our last chance. So lie down, darling!'

Shamefacedly and with burning blushes Alice slowly complied; delightedly Helen and Maud forced her legs widely apart and kneeling together between them they proceeded to examine Alice's maiden treasure, while behind them I also knelt, my head between theirs, my arms round them both, my hands each occupied with a breast. After minutely inspecting Alice's full and prominent *mons Veneris* and gently playing with the hair that grew so prettily on it, they tenderly pulled the delicate close-fitting lips apart and excitedly gazed at the virgin interior, the web-like membrane that defended the stronghold of Alice's virginity receiving their closest and most interested attention. 'There's your job, Jack!' exclaimed Maud wickedly, as she pointed to it – on hearing which poor Alice shivered involuntarily but most prettily.

At last they rose. 'Darling! it's very sweet!' murmured Helen in Alice's ear as she fondly kissed her and began to help her to rise. Meanwhile I had attracted Maud's attention, and by protruding the tip of my tongue between my lips I made her understand my intentions. She nodded delightedly and quickly got behind Alice and caught hold of her breasts and so prevented her from getting up, while I said gently, 'Lie still, dear, we want you a little longer!' – and knelt down on her right motioning to Helen to place herself similarly on Alice's left.

'Oh! Jack! what are you going to do to me?' Alice cried, half-alarmed by these mysterious preparations.

'Something very sweet, darling!' cried Maud – 'don't be frightened, just lie still.'

In an undertone I directed Helen to hold Alice's left leg firmly while I imprisoned her right leg between my right arm and my side – then bending down I placed my lips on Alice's tender cunt and lovingly kissed it.

In spite of Maud's reassuring words Alice had been watching my every movement intently; she saw my head bend forward and down – then she felt my lips touch her cunt and imprint on it a kiss that sent a quiver through her. Startled by the sensations now aroused she cried, 'Oh, Jack! don't!' and tried to close her legs and rise but we were too strong for her and forced her to remain as she was. Again I kissed her sweet cunt – again she quivered violently and struggled to get free, crying, 'Don't, Jack! please don't!' Her face was now like a peony and she was thrilling in every limb – my kisses on her maiden cunt had evidently set her on fire and her lustful desires had passed beyond her control. Just then I imprinted a burning kiss on her clitoris itself, pressing my lips down on her soft springing flesh as I did so. 'Ah!' Alice ejaculated sharply, agitating herself divinely as her lust began to dominate her. Then I lightly ran the tip of my tongue along her tender slit and began to lick the lips of her cunt.

'Oh! . . . Oh! . . . ' Alice gasped in a strange half-strangled voice, closing her eyes in ecstasy – no longer resisting but yielding to her now imperious erotic desires. Helen, to whom this sweet pastime was an absolutely new revelation, was a study – with eager gleaming eyes, dilated nostrils, and slightly parted lips. She watched Alice with the keenest interest, Alice now being in the throes of the wildest erotic frenzy, wriggling, quivering deliciously, thrilling with rapture as my loving tongue tickled and licked her now inflamed cunt. I ceased for a moment, to feast my eyes on her and to exchange significant smiles with Maud and Helen – then I whispered to the latter, 'Help me to hold Alice's cunt open so that I can get my tongue inside!' at the same time placing my left hand alongside of Alice's slit. Quickly comprehending my wishes Helen placed her fingers opposite to mine, and together we pulled Alice's cunt widely open – then after an admiring glance at its pinky juicy luscious interior now evidently throbbing in intense sexual excitement I inserted my tongue deeply into it and began to agitate it subtly with uncontrollable desire! Wildly she tossed and jerked herself upwards as if to meet the thrusts of my tongue, her head rolling from side to side in her blissful transports and her breasts dancing with the palpitations of her heaving bosom, while she ejaculated brokenly incoherent exclamations in the fury of her erotic rage. I saw it was time to bring on the ecstatic crisis, and so my tongue attacked her throbbing and excited clitoris, sucking and tickling it passionately. 'Ha! . . . ha! . . . ha! . . . ' she cried chokingly in a paroxysm of rapture, then she spent frantically in exquisite bliss and delicious spasmodic quivering as my still devoted tongue absorbed the sweet maiden love-juice of her hot discharge as it revelled in its delicious environment between the lips of her cunt.

When I found that the spasms of pleasure were ceasing to thrill through Alice I withdrew my tongue and lips from her cunt and rose. As I did so Helen gave a gasp of astonishment and pointed to my mouth with an expression of horror, for my moustache was plentifully bedewed with Alice's spendings. I chuckled contentedly at her and disappeared into my room where I quickly put myself in order again and then rejoined them. Alice had just come to herself; Helen and Maud were kneeling either side of her and kissing her fondly as they stroked her breasts as if to stimulate her. I heard Maud say softly, 'Didn't I tell you, dear, that you were going to taste something very delicious? – oh! you are a lucky girl!'

Just then Alice caught sight of me – she sprang up, threw herself into my arms, flung hers round my neck and kissed me passionately over and over again, murmuring, 'Oh, darling! . . . darling!' till she had to cease for want of breath. Then Maud took her off for a necessary toilet, leaving me with Helen.

By now I was in a furious state of erection – it was absolutely necessary for me to get some relief from somebody. I seized Helen and whispered fiercely, 'Will Alice be ready to be ravished when she comes back or must she be allowed to wait a bit?'

'Better let her wait a little, dear,' she answered, looking sympathisingly at me – and I could see that she also was very erotically excited and was longing for relief.

'Then either you or Maud will have to take me on, dear!' I replied. 'I must have one of you – feel!' and I conducted her hand to my raging prick.

'Oh! poor thing!' she exclaimed, adding with a smile, 'either Maud or I will be delighted to have it inserted into us, dear. Who shall it be?'

'You, darling, if I dare choose!' I answered, 'but we had better get Alice to deal the cards and settle that way. Here she comes!' and as I spoke Alice and Maud appeared, Alice absolutely radiant with delight.

I tore off my night kit and pointed to my prick in tremendous erection. 'Alice darling, please deal the cards to Helen and Maud and settle who is to have the honour – whoever gets the ace of spades must be the one to relieve me!'

Excitedly Alice shuffled and cut the cards, then dealt them face upwards to Maud and Helen; after a few rounds the ace of spades fell before Helen. A look of delight flashed over her face as she looked delightedly at me.

'Come, darling!' I said. She wanted no pressing, but quickly slipped on the bed and placed herself in position. In a moment I was on her – in another I had buried my prick in her expectant cunt. Then clasping her tightly against me I rammed fiercely into her; she ably seconded my furious movements, and soon we both spent ecstatically, she quivering rapturously as she felt herself inundated by my boiling discharge. A rapid but most delicious fuck.

'Quick, Jack! let me up!' Helen whispered. Hastily but reluctantly I rose off her and set her free, laughing as she rushed off to her bathroom followed by Maud.

'May I come with you, Jack?' whispered Alice timidly. 'Yes, of course, dear, come along!' I replied looking fondly at her, then slipping my arm round her waist I led her into my room and put the door to. 'Oh, Jack! do let me do you, dear!' she begged excitedly, her eyes beaming merrily – and without waiting for a reply she set to work, and in the sweetest and most delicious fashion she sponged and bathed my prick, the touch of her gentle little hands thrilling through me and reviving me wonderfully.

When she had finished I took her little hands in mine and thanked her with a kiss – then said softly, 'Now, dear, in about a quarter of an hour I propose to take you and . . . violate you sweetly! May I do so?'

Alice looked me straight in the eyes lovingly and trustfully, then replied gently, 'Yes, darling!' then held up her lips to be kissed.

'You are quite sure, sweetheart?' I asked searchingly but with a tender smile.

'Quite sure, Jack!' she replied blushing prettily as she again met my eyes squarely and bravely, 'take me, and . . . fuck me, darling!' she whispered and hid her face on my shoulder in bashful confusion. I clasped her closely against me and sought her lips with mine, and kissed her passionately over and over again till she gasped for breath.

'Now let us go back,' I said and we returned together to Helen's room which we found empty.

'Oh! I'm so glad we're first back,' Alice exclaimed delightedly – 'they won't know that I've been with you, Jack. Don't tell them, dear!' she added merrily, smiling her thanks as I gave the required promise. Just then Helen and Maud appeared. Helen ran up to me, threw herself into my arms and kissed me, saying laughingly, 'Jack dear, it was just heavenly!'

'Darling, of course it was,' I replied, 'for you fuck like an angel!' – at which interchange of compliments Alice and Maud laughed heartily, Helen soon joining them.

'Come to me, Alice dear,' said Helen as she seated herself in her favourite chair, 'you and I are entitled to a rest!' – and quickly Alice settled herself in Helen's lap and, greatly daring, gently played with her auntie's breasts.

'I suppose that means that you and I are not entitled at present to rest, eh dear?' I said to Maud meaningly – 'come and discuss the situation' – and seating myself I drew her on my knees and gently toyed with her cunt.

'Well, Jack,' she said presently, 'what are we to do?'

'I'm afraid your choice is limited to finger or tongue, dear,' I replied with a significant smile.

'And a very sweet option too!' Maud answered cheerily. 'Jack, I'd like to be sucked, a long slow suck!' And she looked at me invitingly. We rose, and I arranged her on Helen's box face upwards with her legs nicely apart – Helen and Alice kneeling one on each side of her the better to watch the proceedings, Alice being particularly keen to witness what she herself had just tasted so deliciously.

After a little sweet toying with Maud's cunt, I stooped down and kissed it ardently, my lips travelling right along the coral slit and making Maud quiver voluptuously – while Helen and Alice intuitively commenced to play with her breasts. Then I ran my tongue slowly along the lovely opening, touching it very lightly, and evidently giving Maud exquisite pleasure – for she began to wriggle delightfully, half jogging herself up as if to meet my tongue, whereupon I stiffened it and forced the tip well into her orifice, then stabbed and darted and thrust downwards strongly, first slowly and then more rapidly as I noticed her agitation increase. Again I ran my tongue along her slit, this time with more of a licking action, reverting to the orifice every now and then, till I had worked her up to a frenzy of unsatisfied longing lust without touching her clitoris. Maud's movements now became tumultuous, even lascivious and wanton in their wrigglings and writhings, their twistings and contortions; she was evidently on the point of spending and longing to spend, but yet delaying the culmination of her pleasure in order to prolong the blissful agony of the struggle against herself. Being desirous of humouring her desires I continued my alternate lickings and thrustings, avoiding touching her clitoris – but soon it was patent to me that Maud was losing her powers of self-control, then promptly I attacked her clitoris, sometimes simply licking and tickling it, sometimes taking it gently between my lips and sucking it. Maud now seemed to go mad. Alice told me afterwards that she was an extraordinary sight in her erotic fury. She plunged, curvetted, wriggled and tossed herself about so wildly that I had the greatest difficulty in keeping my mouth planted on her cunt! Suddenly her body stiffened, her breasts became tense, an indescribable spasm convulsed her – and with a delirously strangled 'Ah–h!' she spent rapturously, her whole body thrilling voluptuously as the spasms of pleasure quivered through her, while she distilled her love-juice so plentifully that my tongue, lips and moustache were all spattered with the feminine essence of Love.

Again Helen's shocked eyes met mine as I raised my head from her daughter's cunt, and again I chuckled contentedly at her as I went off to my room, leaving Maud in her charge till she came to. I was more than jubilant – I had now done my duty to both Helen and Maud, and now I was about to enjoy the exquisite pleasure of depriving Alice of her virginity.

So I hurried back as quickly as I could. Maud had recovered and had got up, and was on her way to the bathroom when I appeared. She stopped, threw her arms round me fondly and kissed me passionately over and over again – then said roguishly, 'Jack, your tongue is really almost as good as . . . your prick!' then vanished, followed by Alice and our merry laughter.

'Now I suppose you will take Alice, Jack!' said Helen eagerly. I nodded. 'Then I'll get everything ready for her,' she rejoined, with a meaning smile as she produced the towels that she had provided to protect her bed quilt from the tell-tale stains that Alice's defloration was sure to cause. She glanced at my prick. 'You are hardly ready yet, Jack! – we'll have to work you up, sir!' she added smilingly. 'Let me make a start,' and seating me at her side she commenced to play with my limp and flaccid penis. The touch of her hand was heavenly, and soon I began to feel my forces revive.

Maud and Alice now reappeared, and when the latter caught sight of the bed so obviously prepared for her and saw Helen getting me ready, her courage seemed suddenly to leave her; she nervously exclaimed, 'Oh! I can't! . . . I can't do it!' and tried to run away into her room.

But Maud caught her and held her gently but firmly, and said with an encouraging smile, 'Nonsense dear! here, mother, will you take Alice and give me Jack, and I'll have him ready in two twos in a way that you do not know! Come along, Jack!'

I guessed her intention and laughed, then made way for Alice – who was quickly folded in Helen's arms and soon soothed and caressed till she had recovered from her sudden timidity. I think however that the sight of Maud and me had more to do with her reviving interest. Maud had made me lie on my back on Helen's dress box – with a gentle thumb and forefinger she had raised my limp prick and with the other hand she had gently captured my balls – and she was just beginning sweetly to lick the latter and tickle the former with her kind tongue, to the unbounded astonishment of both Helen and Alice, the latter evidently forgetting her nervousness in the excitement caused by Maud's proceedings. 'See, mother,' exclaimed Maud presently, 'Jack is coming along finely! – I'll have him ready for you, Alice, in a minute!' and with eyes dancing with delight she resumed her delicious ministrations and soon my prick was standing stiff and rampant and ready to ravish Alice.

'Come dear!' said Helen to Alice as soon as she saw I was ready; then she and Maud led the still reluctant and nervous girl to the bed, and having made her lie down they drew her legs apart and generally arranged her to receive me. Then each kissed her tenderly, whispering something that I did not catch but which brought the blushes again to Alice's cheeks. 'Now, Jack!' said Helen invitingly, 'she's ready for you!' and she pointed to Alice's maiden cunt, lying so deliciously and temptingly open to attack.

I hurried to the bed, stooped over Alice, and whispered, 'Give me your last maiden kiss, darling!' and fairly sucked the life out of her mouth; then quickly I slipped on to the bed, got between Alice's legs, and lowering myself gently on to her I brought the head of my prick to bear on her little cunt – then shoving firmly but gently I succeeded in getting it into her a little way before my progress was blocked; tightening my clasp of her I shoved harder and harder, but without breaking through her maiden defences, and evidently hurting her, for she cried, 'Oh, Jack!' as if in pain, at the same time wriggling uncomfortably and apprehensively. Collecting myself, I lunged strongly downwards, something seemed to give way, and my prick seemed to glide into a sheath of delicious warmth and exquisite softness – while a smothered shriek from Alice proclaimed to Helen and Maud that she had lost her maidenhead. Taking every care not to hurt her needlessly I drove my prick deeper and deeper up her virgin sheath till I was fully buried in her, our hairs intermingling, then my mouth sought hers, and passionately I kissed her quivering lips, receiving from her her first kiss as a woman.

Oh! my sensations of triumph. I was possessing Alice, I had captured her maidenhead, and she was now lying quivering and trembling, closely locked in my arms with my prick buried in her – and now I was about to give her the sweetest of lessons. Delightedly I set to work to fuck her in earnest, going slowly and gently at first for I was afraid of hurting her – but when I noted that her nervousness and pain were turning deliciously to wondering rapture and heavenly ecstasy as I agitated myself on her, holding her tightly clasped against me, I began to move more and more freely. Soon Alice herself began to respond – I could feel her bosom commencing to heave and palpitate, her breathing became broken and agitated, and then she commenced to move herself under me in the most deliciously provocative manner, which fairly set me going. Quicker and quicker I rammed into her – wilder and more tumultuous became our movements. Then came the climax, and deliriously I spent into Alice, deluging her virgin interior with my boiling tribute which she received with wondering rapture and indescribable bliss, while she simultaneously surrendered herself to the dictates of her newly born lust and spent in the most exquisite transports of delight.

We lay locked tightly in each other's arms, motionless save for the involuntary quivers occasioned by lingering spasms of pleasure. Gladly would I have continued to remain so, but Helen begged me to get off Alice so as to set her free to be carried off to the bathroom and looked after. And after inprinting a passionate kiss on her unconscious lips I reluctantly rose and hurried off to my room.

When I returned I found Maud waiting for me. In reply to my eager enquiries she told me with an assuring smile that Alice was 'quite all right and very happy now that the ordeal had been passed' – that I had hurt her very little indeed, but not unnaturally her cunt was sore and should be left for the present untouched till tomorrow evening when I would find Alice only too ready to be fucked again.

While we were talking, Helen and Alice returned. I took Alice in my arms and after some tender kisses I told Helen and Maud of our arrangements for the future and (at Alice's request) of her wish that we all should continue to live as we then were doing and enjoy each other all round. Their surprise and delight I will not attempt to describe. Suffice it to say that after mutual congratulations and compliments Helen insisted on the seance being closed, so that we all might get the benefit of a long night's rest so as to enjoy the following evening thoroughly – for, as she said with an arch smile, 'We women will all be equal and ready for anything and everything whenever wanted!' And then after tender good-nights all round we retired to our respective rooms.

# Chapter Six

At breakfast next morning I was delighted to see all three ladies appear as radiant as ever, Alice especially. She was looking more charming and attractive than I had ever seen her; her nervo-erotic excitement had been sweetly allayed, she had now no ordeal to dread, and she had the proud satisfaction of feeling that she now stood level with Maud and Helen in matters sexual, and could do whatever they did – and this combination of happy circumstances made her eyes sparkle and imparted to her a pretty vivacity that was simply bewitching and made me look forward to enjoying her in the coming evening. There was no doubt that all three had been badly in need of sexual satisfaction and were revelling in the pleasures they had tasted naked in my arms – and I doubt whether a happier trio could have been found in the country.

But the morning post brought a damper in the form of a letter to Maud from the friends she was looking forward to visit. It begged her to come to them at once – not later at all events than the following day – so that she might join in sundry frivolities that had been hastily organised.

'I must go!' she wailed half-mournfully – 'for I haven't any excuse except that I want to stay here and be fucked by Jack, and I can't possibly give that as a reason for not going!' she added with a quizzical smile. 'Oh! isn't it unfortunate!' she exclaimed.

'Cheer up, dear!' I cried as I laughed at her really comical despair – 'Don't forget that I now have to make weekends to see my sweetheart, who says that you and Helen may borrow me! So it is not as bad as it might be.'

Maud brightened up at once. 'Thanks for reminding me, Jack!' she answered smilingly – then turning to Alice she said, 'and thanks to you, darling, for as kind and unselfish a thing as ever one girl did for another!' and going over to Alice she kissed her gratefully and lovingly. 'Jack!' she exclaimed, 'you must plan a regular orgy for tonight, one that will keep me going for a week!' and she laughed happily.

'All right!' I replied, joining in her gaiety – 'let us adjourn to the garden out of earshot, and see what brilliant ideas we can raise!' and we all trooped off merrily and, settling ourselves under the trees, set to work to think hard.

I broke the silence after a little time by asking, 'Has anyone anything to suggest?' They all shook their heads with a self-conscious laugh. 'Then let me put my idea before you, such as it is!' I added, smiling at the eagerness with which they all leant forward to listen, their eyes fixed expectantly on me.

I proceeded. 'When I was in Budapest I saw a game played by three girls and a man; its name translated into English was The Victim and her

Torturers. One of the girls was chosen by lot to be the Victim, the others then became the Torturers, the man being the Chief Torturer and the others were to obey him implicitly. All four stripped themselves naked – the Victim was then tied down securely on a bed, and for a certain specified time the others did just what they liked to her, their object being to make her spend as often as possible by teasing and provoking and exciting her, no pain-causing play being allowed. Every now and then some two of the Torturers seemed to find the game too exciting – then they would mutually satisfy each other's lustful desires while the third looked on and let the Victim have a bit of a rest in which to pull herself together a little.

'How would this game suit us for tonight? We are three women and one man. As Maud wants as much as she can get tonight, we might make her Victim and give her a good hour's doing – during which we Torturers can also enjoy ourselves as our natures may demand. Or I shall be Victim. The Victim, I ought to have explained, is considered to have the best of the fun. Or each of you can have a twenty minutes' turn, drawing cards to settle the order!'

Helen, Maud and Alice looked interrogatively at each other, then broke into hearty laughter. 'A most excellent idea, Jack dear!' exclaimed Helen – 'what do you say, girls?' Maud and Alice nodded delightedly. 'Carried unanimously!' declared Helen – adding with an affectionate glance at me, 'with our best thanks to Jack!'

'Now I had better leave you to settle among yourselves which of the three alternatives is to be the order of the evening – I'd rather that you decided this without me. So I'll stroll to the river and back,' and I rose.

'One moment, Jack !' cried Alice excitedly – 'we want to know if the Victim will be . . . fucked!' she asked with pretty blushes.

We all laughed merrily.

'The girl I saw as Victim was fucked twice, dear, in the hour – once by the Chief Torturer and once by me – they saw how the game excited me and they kindly made me free of the girl! It was a piquant sensation to fuck a tied-down girl, and she seemed to approve of it also!'

'Ah!' Alice exclaimed, her eyes sparkling. Then I moved off, and they fell to work eagerly to discuss and arrange the evening's programme.

In a remarkably short time I heard them calling me and I rejoined them. 'We've settled everything, Jack!' said Helen – 'we'll each have a twenty-minute turn, Maud first, Alice next and I last; you're to be Chief Torturer and boss of the show and we others will do as you may direct.'

'Capital!' I exclaimed laughingly, 'we'll have a great time!' whereon they all burst into hearty laughter.

'Now, mother, come along and help me to pack!' cried Maud as she hooked her arm into Helen's – 'Alice, we leave Jack in your charge!' and off they went to the house, laughing merrily.

'What shall we do, dear?' I asked of Alice, 'another row?'

'Oh, yes please, Jack!' she exclaimed delightedly and soon we were off in the boat, she steering and I rowing. As we neared the backwater I began to wonder whether she would take us in – and sure enough with a self-conscious smile she steered the boat in. I made fast as on the previous morning and then seated myself by her on the stern cushions.

'Why have you brought us in here, dear?' I asked softly as I slipped my left arm round her waist and drew her to me.

She yielded herself sweetly to my pressure, then whispered with a blush, 'To thank you, darling, for what you did so sweetly to me last night!' and with love in her eyes she kissed me tenderly.

'But it is I who should thank you, Alice dear!' I replied softly, 'For you let me take from you for ever your most precious possession, your maidenhead!'

Alice shook her head and looked tenderly at me. 'If you only knew how bad I've often been, dear, and how wonderful I'm feeling now, you would understand my gratitude!'

I kissed her lovingly. 'Let it be so, dear!' I replied softly, 'and let me show you tonight how I appreciate the privilege of fucking you!' She blushed and laughed merrily.

'Did I hurt you much, darling?' I whispered.

'Very little – you were so gentle with me, Jack!' she said softly – 'I am a little sore – but I don't intend to let it rob me of tonight's pleasures!' and she laughed gaily.

'May I judge for myself?' I whispered mischievously. Alice blushed and nodded, and slightly shifted herself so as to facilitate the movements of my eager hand which already had found its way under her clothes and was travelling along between her thighs. Soon it passed through the opening of her drawers and reached her cunt, she flinching deliciously as she felt my finger touch her cunt gently and caressingly.

'It is a bit swollen, dear,' I whispered as I tenderly played with her hairs. Alice nodded, smiling happily and evidently enjoying having her cunt felt by me. After a little more toying with her hairs and her delicious flesh I gently forced my finger into her down to where her maiden barrier used to be; she winced in spite of herself as my finger touched the sore spot, but to my delight she allowed me gently to soothe the inflamed flesh, whispering, 'Oh, Jack, that's nice!' as my finger entered the sheath-like passage now open for life, and penetrated deeper and deeper into her – the feel of her moist juicy folds of flesh being exquisitely delicious.

'Don't you think that your cunt will be all the better for a little of your own lubricant, dear, your very own manufacture?' I asked with a significant smile. For a moment Alice looked puzzled, then suddenly blushed prettily and nodded delightedly. Lovingly I set to work to frig her, agitating my finger inside her cunt – at first slowly then more and more rapidly as she wriggled and quivered with pleasure – till she spent voluptuously, inundating my finger with her sweet essence of love, which I proceeded to distribute all over her inflamed flesh to her evident satisfaction. Then, withdrawing my hand, I helped to adjust her disordered dress and soon we were back on the river, both delighted by the little episode.

On the way home Alice told me with a roguish smile that they all were so eager to taste the sensation of being fucked while fastened down that they had unanimously adopted the twenty-minute-turn suggestion. Then she exclaimed archly, 'Jack, tell me some special way to excite Auntie Helen and Maud when they are tied down!'

I laughed, and replied, 'Get your cook to give you half a dozen long and finely pointed feathers, and tickle their cunts, dear!'

She clapped her little hands together in delight at the idea, exclaiming with sparkling eyes, 'Oh, Jack! how lovely! how I'll make them wriggle tonight!' evidently overlooking the fact that any specially brilliant idea of hers would be adopted by the others when her turn to be tied down came; but the anticipation of witnessing the struggles of the three ladies in turn when the feather was applied to their respective cunts was so tempting that I refrained from warning her of the probable consequences of her enterprise.

## *Chapter Seven*

The day passed away uneventfully, and at half-past ten we all met in Helen's room, the three ladies in visible but suppressed excitement. 'We won't waste time,' I said briskly, 'so everyone naked please!' and in a trice I again had the pleasure of viewing their naked charms. Then I produced the wristlets and straps, the sight of which produced much laughter; and quickly under my directions Helen and Alice fastened them on Maud's wrists and ankles.

I made her lie down face upwards on her mother's bed and secured her wrists to the opposite bedposts by the straps; then to her surprise and consternation and to Alice's undisguised delight I directed Helen and Alice to pull Maud's legs widely apart and strap her ankles to the corner posts, so that she lay spreadeagled, exposing all her most secret charms to us and utterly unable to prevent us from doing what we liked to her. In silence we gloated over the provoking spectacle – then turning to Helen and Alice I said, 'Now dears, Maud is at your absolute disposal for fifteen minutes – then I shall want her to myself! Now, go ahead!'

With a cry of joy Alice threw herself on Maud's prostrate and helpless self and excitedly showered kisses on her lips and cheeks and eyes, then turning herself slightly she seized hold of Maud's breasts and after kissing the pretty coral nipples she took them between her lips and sucked each breast in turn, all the while squeezing and handling them – Maud lying helpless in shame-faced confusion, the colour coming and going on her cheeks, and a nervous

smile passing over her face when her eyes met ours. I glanced at Helen –
her eyes were riveted on her daughter's naked body and glittered with a
peculiar light, and as I stealthily watched her I noticed how she was
shivering. It certainly was not from cold, and recollecting how she was
fascinated and excited on the first evening when her daughter stood before
her naked for the first time and how she from that moment seemed never
tired of looking at Maud's naked beauties, I guessed that unknown to
herself a lusting desire after her daughter had sprung up in her. Seeing that
Alice and Maud were absorbed with each other, Alice in the hitherto
untasted pleasure of playing with another girl's naked charms, Maud with
the also hitherto untasted sensations of having her most private parts
invaded and handled by feminine fingers, I drew Helen out of earshot and
whispered to her, 'You look as if you want to have, Maud, eh! dear?' She
coloured vividly and nodded vehemently with a self-conscious smile, too
embarrassed to speak. 'Why don't you, then?' I continued. Helen stared at
me in surprise. 'Get on Maud, grip her tightly, and rub your cunt against
hers sweetly.'

'Oh, Jack, really?' Helen stammered in growing excitement, her bosom
heaving with her agitation. I nodded with a reassuring smile, adding, 'Try
it, dear! – lots of women solace themselves in this way when they cannot
get what they really want!' She looked incredulously at me. I smiled
encouragingly; then her eyes wandered to Maud, who was lying motionless
save for an occasional quiver – Alice had deserted her sweet breasts and was
now busily engaged with her cunt, which she was kissing and stroking
and examining, the procedure evidently giving Maud the most exquisite
pleasure judging from her half-closed eyes and her beatific expression – a
most voluptuous sight, which apparently swept away Helen's hesitation.
She turned to me and murmured almost inaudibly, 'I long to do it, Jack, but
she wouldn't like it!'

I took her trembling hands, that betrayed her lust, and whispered
coaxingly, 'Maud has got to put up with anything that any of us wish to do
to her during her twenty-minute turn, dear – when she guesses what you
contemplate she probably will protest, but as soon as she feels your cunt on
hers she will love you more than ever! Try her, dear!'

Helen hesitated, looked hungrily and longingly at Maud and then at me,
then back at Maud.

At that juncture Alice exclaimed, 'I'm only keeping on till you come,
auntie!'

Helen shivered again, her eyes now glittering wildly with lust and desire,
then with an effort she muttered huskily, 'Jack! I must . . . have her!' and
moved towards the bed.

'Come along, auntie! I've got Maud nicely excited, and you can now finish
her off in any way you like!' exclaimed Alice merrily; and after imprinting a
farewell kiss on Maud's cunt she rose as if to make way for Helen, while

Maud languidly opened her eyes and dreamily smiled a welcome to her mother; but when she saw Helen scramble on to the bed and place herself between her widely parted legs in an attitude that could only indicate one intention and noted the lust that was glittering in Helen's eyes she became alarmed, and cried, 'No, no, mother, no, no!' as she desperately tried to break loose – while Alice flushed as red as a peony, her colour surging right down to her breasts as she intently watched Helen with eyes widely open with startled surprise. Helen paused a moment as if gloating over the naked beauties of her daughter, then she let herself down gently on Maud who again cried, 'No, no, mother, no!' as she felt her mother's weight come on her and her mother's arms close firmly round her as Helen arranged herself on Maud – first breast against breast, then cunt on cunt – then having her daughter at her mercy she began to move herself on her lasciviously, just as if she was lying impaled on a man.

Hardly had she commenced to agitate herself on Maud than the latter exclaimed in an indescribable tone of astonished delight, 'Oh! . . . oh! . . . oh! . . . Mummy . . . dar . . . ling!' which sent Alice's blushes surging again all over her bosom as she glanced shamefacedly at me. I crossed over to her and slipped my arms round her, noting as she nestled against me how she was quivering with erotic excitement. Helen had evidently set her daughter's lust on fire, for Maud now was wildly agitating and tossing herself about under her mother and heaving herself furiously up as if to press her cunt more closely against her mother's as she passionately kissed Helen. Suddenly she wriggled violently, then spent in delicious thrills and quiverings – Alice's gentle but subtle toyings had so inflamed her that it needed but little to finish her. Recognising what had happened, Helen suspended her movements and rested lovingly on Maud whom she set to work to kiss ardently, evidently enjoying the thrills and spasms that convulsed her daughter as she spent. Soon Maud began to respond to her mother's provocations and agitated herself under Helen in the most abandoned and lascivious way, which set Helen off in a fresh frenzy of uncontrollable lust. With wildly heaving buttocks and tempestuous wrigglings of her hips and bottom Helen pressed her cunt more closely than ever against her daughter's, rubbing her clitoris against Maud's till Maud again spent rapturously. Suddenly Helen's body stiffened and grew rigid – then an indescribable convulsion swept violently through her, and with incoherent ejaculations and gasps she spent madly on Maud's cunt – then collapsed and lay inert on her daughter, motionless save for the voluptuous thrills that quivered through her with each spasm of spending. And so mother and daughter lay in a delirium of ecstasy, their cunts pressed against each other, utterly absorbed in the sensations of the moment and the divine pleasure that for the first time in their lives they had mutually given to each other.

In delighted silence Alice and I watched this voluptuous episode, and when the delirious climax had passed Alice turned to me and huskily whispered, 'Jack! Oh, Jack!' and looked pleadingly into my eyes. I saw what she wanted; I drew her closer against me and slipped my hand down to her throbbing and excited cunt. She was so madly worked up that it only required one or two quick but gentle movements of my finger to make her spend ecstatically, and her thrills of rapture as she stood upright supported by me nearly set me off; but with a strong effort I controlled myself, for in a minute or two I had to fuck Maud. So I bade her run away and freshen herself and to bring the feathers with her when she returned; then being curious to see how Helen and Maud would regard each other when they came to themselves, now that their fit of lust had been satiated, I watched them closely.

Very soon, with a long-drawn breath of intense satisfaction Maud dreamily opened her eyes – she seemed hardly conscious; but when she found herself unable to move hand or foot and recognised that her mother was lying on her, the happenings of the evening instantly flashed through her brain and sent the hot colour surging over her cheeks and bosom at the consciousness that she had just been ravished by her mother; and when her eyes caught mine she coloured more furiously than ever, but smiled gratefully as I noiselessly clapped my hands together with a congratulatory smile. Then she turned her face towards Helen and a look of intense love came over her as she regarded her still unconscious mother. She brought her lips to bear on Helen's cheek and kissed her lovingly, whispering, 'Mummy! Mummy! . . . Mummy darling! . . . ' Then with a deep sigh Helen came to herself; she quickly realised the position and flushed scarlet as she half-timidly sought Maud's still humid eyes; but when she read in them her daughter's happy satisfaction she kissed Maud passionately and murmured in evident relief, 'Oh, my darling! I couldn't help it! . . . you looked so sweet! . . . and you were so luscious!' and after another long clinging kiss she slipped off Maud.

Alice had just rejoined me, and as Helen rose to her feet our eyes inquisitively sought her cunt and that of Maud. They were a curious sight; both mother and daughter must have spent profusely as their hairs were sticky and plastered down by their joint spendings. Noticing the direction of our looks Helen glanced at Maud's cunt and then at her own, and horrified at what she saw she exclaimed in charming confusion, 'Oh, Alice, do see to Maud!' and rushed off to her bathroom followed by our hearty laughter, in which Maud merrily joined with pretty blushes when we told her the cause.

Helen soon returned and joined me. 'Well?' I asked mischievously. She blushed and replied softly, 'Jack, it was just lovely, just wonderful! – I couldn't have believed it! Maud was simply luscious!' I laughed. 'Make Alice do me presently, Jack! – I'd love to feel her on me!' I nodded laughingly – then glancing at the clock I exclaimed, 'Only seven minutes more for Maud! – she must now be really tortured for four minutes, and then she is to be brutally outraged in your presence. Now set to work and give her a severe tickling!' and I handed a feather to each.

'No, no, Jack!' cried Maud, flushing painfully and tugging at her fastenings – 'No, no, don't tickle me! I can't stand it!' – but Helen and Alice joyously arranged themselves one on either side of her and with a smile of anticipated enjoyment they began to touch her lightly with their feathers – first in her armpits, then under her chin, then all round and over her lovely breasts, Helen taking one and Alice the other – Maud all the time struggling and squirming in the most provocative way as she begged them to desist. From her breasts they passed to her navel, then on to the lines of her groin, and finally along the soft and sensitive insides of her thighs, Maud now plunging wildly and evidently suffering real torture from the subtle titill-ation she was being made to undergo. Then after a short pause and a significant glance at each other they applied their feathers to Maud's cunt.

'Ha! . . . Ha! . . . Don't! – in mercy's name, stop!' Maud almost shrieked, writhing frantically and straining at her fastenings. Half-alarmed at the effect of their action Helen and Alice stopped and looked at me as if for instructions. I glanced at the clock – there was rather more than one minute left. I felt positive that Maud could endure the sweet agony for that time and that it would make the ensuing fuck all the more delicious to her – so I determined that she should go on being tortured and I signalled to them to recommence – and to prevent the house from being alarmed I held my handkerchief firmly over Maud's mouth so as to stifle her cries. Promptly Helen and Alice complied, their eyes gleaming with lustful enjoyment at the sight of Maud's naked body quivering in agony; applying their feathers again to her cunt they tickled her delicately but cunningly all along its sensitive lips and when these poutingly opened involuntarily under the stress of the titillation and disclosed the coral flesh of her interior, Alice delightedly plunged her feather into the tempting gap while Helen amused herself by tickling Maud's clitoris, now distinctly visible in angry excitement. Maud by now was nearly frantic – twisting, wriggling, squirming and screwing herself madly in vain attempts to escape from the torturing feathers – and in spite of my handkerchief the shrieks and cries were distinctly audible to us. It was evident that the limit of her powers of endurance was being reached and that she was on the point of hysterics, so I signalled to Helen and Alice to stop; just as I did so she cried frenziedly, 'Fuck me, Jack! Oh, fuck me!' In a moment I was on her, with two strokes I buried my prick in her raging volcano of a cunt and began to fuck her. Hardly had I started than she spent deliriously. I suspended my movements for a few moments during which I kissed her ardently – then with renewed lust and unsatisfied desire I again began to fuck her, the sensation of holding her naked, struggling but helpless body in my arms and the knowledge that she was tied down and at my mercy imparting a most extraordinary piquancy to the operation. Furiously I rammed into her, deliriously she responded to my fierce down-thrusts by jerking herself madly upwards! Then the heavenly climax overtook us simultaneously – and just as she for the second time spent rapturously I shot my boiling tribute frantically into her, she receiving it with the most exquisite quiverings and thrills.

As soon as Helen saw that the ecstatic crisis had come and gone, she and Alice unstrapped Maud; and as soon as I slipped off her they carried her off, while I retired to my room for the necessary ablutions. But to my surprise Helen came in before I had commenced. 'Alice is looking after Maud, so I have come to attend to you, dear!' she said archly, and sweetly she sponged and freshened my exhausted prick, finally kissing it lovingly.

I asked her if she thought that Alice would be equal to twenty minutes' torturing such as we had administered to Maud, also whether Alice's cunt was fit to receive me again. To the latter enquiry she gave a decided affirmative and added that Alice was eagerly looking forward to be fucked, but she agreed with me that we had better reduce the term of Alice's torture to fifteen minutes. I asked with a smile if either she or Maud proposed to fuck Alice, so that I might arrange accordingly – she replied that she would not as she must reserve herself for her approaching turn, but she would not be surprised if Maud was tempted, only Maud was very exhausted by her struggles while being tickled, and, she added with a self-conscious smile and blush, 'I am almost sure she intends to have me when my turn comes!' So we settled that Alice should be thoroughly well felt by her and Maud, then I was to suck her, then we should tickle her cunt and finally I should fuck her.

When we returned to Helen's room we found Maud busy attaching the straps to Alice's slender wrists and ankles, and soon she and Helen had Alice securely fastened to the four bedposts. I noted with amusement that they pulled Alice's legs much wider apart than I would have done, in fact so widely did they separate them that the lips of her cunt were slightly open. She looked perfectly delicious in her helpless nudity, her pretty cunt being exhibited to perfection – and as Helen and Maud gazed silently at her I could see that their erotic desires were being rekindled. Suddenly they threw themselves on Alice and showered kisses on her – then they proceeded to feel her all over, their hands visiting caressingly her most private parts, after which they squeezed her dainty breasts and kissed her cunt, laughing delightedly as she wriggled and flinched under their provocative touchings.

'Come, mummy, let us see the result of Jack's work last night!' cried Maud merrily – and with gentle fingers they opened Alice's cunt and eagerly inspected its interior, noting with amusing animation the changes caused by her violation. Presently Helen gently inserted her finger into the newly opened passage, watching Alice carefully as she did so, laughing when in spite of herself Alice winced when the sore spot was touched; but she confirmed her opinion that Alice was fit to be fucked, thereby receiving from Alice a smile of satisfaction. Then they glanced at me as if awaiting instructions.

'Now Alice, you're going to be sucked!' I said with a meaning smile, to which she responded, evidently not objecting to this sweet form of torture. Turning to Helen and Maud I directed them to play with and suck Alice's breasts while I attended to her cunt; and with charming eagerness they addressed themselves to the exquisite morsels of Alice's flesh and blood allotted to them, preluding their operations with ardent and salacious kisses and then proceeding to feel and stroke Alice's dainty bubbies, now holding them up by their little pink nipples, then imprisoning them between both hands and gently squeezing them – Alice betraying her rising excitement by her quick flushes and nervous laughs.

Presently Maud pressed between her hands the breast she was torturing so sweetly so as to make the delicate nipple stand up – and then she lovingly took it between her lips. 'Oh, Maud!' ejaculated Alice squirming voluptuously. Helen promptly followed suit, her action eliciting another irrepressible cry from Alice, now rosy red at the sight of her breasts in the mouths of Helen and Maud and the caressingly tickling sensations imparted to her by the play of their warm tongues on her sensitive nipples. I considered it was about time I joined in the play, so lowering my head I placed my lips on Alice's cunt and fondly imprinted lascivious kisses all along her tender slit. 'Ah Jack!' she cried, as she instantly commenced to wriggle divinely; and when I ran the tip of my tongue gently along her cunt's lips and delicately licked and tickled them, she began to agitate herself voluptuously, twisting herself as much as her fastenings would permit and wildly thrusting her cunt upwards to meet my tongue. Presently I noticed that its lips began to open as if involuntarily; as they did so I forced my tongue between them, thrusting, darting and stabbing downwards as deeply as I could into the almost virginal interior and creating in her all but ungovernable erotic fury, under the influence of which she writhed and tossed herself about in the most lascivious fashion. It was clear that she was quickly approaching the blissful crisis – so withdrawing my tongue from her sweet orifice I seized her clitoris between my lips and sucked it fiercely while my tongue cunningly tickled it. This finished Alice off – with an indescribable wriggle she spent in delirious bliss and collapsed in rapturous delight, punctuating the spasms of her ecstasy with the most voluptuous quivers and thrills, then lay inert and exhausted, with turned-up and half-closed eyes. But very soon she opened them again, and murmured faintly, 'Oh, please kiss me!' Instantly Helen and Maud threw themselves on her and showered loving kisses on her helpless cheeks till they restored her to life again; then they tenderly sponged and washed her cunt and gently got her ready for her next torture, while I removed from my lips and moustache the traces and remains of her spend.

When I returned, I found Alice was herself again and keenly curious to know what now was going to be done to her. In response to the enquiry in her eyes I leant down and told her we now proposed to tickle her cunt – did she think she could stand it? She trembled nervously then said, 'I'll try – only stop me from screaming!'

'Then we'll gag you, dear!' I said, and carefully I twisted a large hand-kerchief over her mouth. 'Now, darling,' – and I signalled to Helen and Maud to commence to torture Alice.

It was just as well that I had gagged her, for at the first touch of the feathers on her sensitive cunt the muscles of her arms and legs violently contracted as she involuntarily tried to escape from, or at all events to dodge the tickling tips – then, when this natural movement was frustrated by the straps, she shrieked in spite of herself as the feathers continued to play on and between the lips of her cunt, then struggled and wriggled frantically. A delighted smile now appeared on the faces of Helen and Maud at the sight of the delightful agony that Alice was suffering and joyously they continued their delicious occupation of tickling her cunt. Alice now was an exquisite spectacle – in her desperate efforts she twisted and contorted her lovely naked body into the most enticing attitudes, while the sound of her stifled hysterical screams was like music to us, and although it was only a few minutes since I had fucked Maud, my prick became rampant and stiff, as if eager to renew acquaintance with Alice's cunt. It was evident that the subtle titillation was trying Alice severely, but so delightful was the sight of her struggles and wriggles that I allowed Helen and Maud to continue the sweet torture, till Alice hysterically begged me to stop it – which I then reluctantly did.

As I removed the gag from her mouth she gasped, 'Oh, Jack! it was awful!'

'But you liked it, dear!' I said with a smile.

'Well, yes!' she admitted with a constrained laugh, 'But it is too exciting for me! – please don't torture me any more!' she begged prettily.

'Very well, dear!' I replied, 'but then you must end my torture!' and I pointed to my rampant prick. Alice blushed, smiled, and then nodded lovingly to me – and promptly I slipped between her legs and bringing my prick to bear on her excited cunt I gently forced it in – using every precaution not to hurt her – till it was completely buried in her warm, throbbing and fleshy sheath.

'Ah!' she murmured rapturously as she felt herself possessed again by me, but this time without pain. I clasped her closely to me till her breasts were flattened against my chest – and then I set to work to make Alice taste the pleasure of being fucked.

She was terribly excited both by the tickling her cunt had received and by her eagerness again to experience the exquisite raptures she had enjoyed in my arms the previous night in spite of the pain of her violation; and as I commenced to move myself on her slowly but sweetly I could feel how she was straining at her fastenings in order to accommodate herself to the sensations of the moment; then as I proceeded to fuck her she murmured ecstatically, 'Oh! . . . oh! . . . my darling! . . . how . . . heaven–ly!' as she closed her eyes in rapture and wriggled and quivered under me voluptuously as she felt my prick working up and down in her cunt. Soon the blissful ecstasy began to overwhelm us both – Alice agitated herself under me in a perfectly wonderful way as I rammed furiously into her; then her body suddenly stiffened, an indescribable thrill quivered through her as she rapturously spent – at the same moment I shot into her frantically my boiling tribute of love – and then we both collapsed in delicious transports, oblivious of everything but our voluptuous sensations – Alice enraptured by the exquisite pleasure that she was now fully able to taste, and I overjoyed at again having fucked her deliciously dainty self.

We soon came to ourselves. Meanwhile Helen and Maud had set Alice at liberty; and so after a long passionate kiss I slipped out of her and retired to my room, accompanied by Maud, Helen taking charge of Alice. Sweetly Maud attended to me, then somewhat eagerly she asked what I proposed to do to her mother, confessing with a blush that she was longing to enjoy her.

'Certainly do, dear!' I replied, delighted at the prospect of again seeing the mother and daughter relieving their lust by means of each other, naked. Joyfully Maud kissed me, and we hurried back as Helen and Alice had returned and were awaiting us.

Alice evidently was full of elation at her newly acquired sexual freedom; and eager to enjoy her privileges she caught hold of Helen and drew her to the bed, at the same time calling to Maud to help her to fasten Helen down to the four corner-posts. With great glee Maud complied, and very soon Helen lay extended on her back with her limbs strapped to the four posts and a hard pillow under her bottom, absolutely at our mercy.

'Now, Maud, you may have your mother to yourself for the next five minutes,' I said; a vivid blush surged over Helen as she heard her fate and glanced half-shamefacedly at her daughter, who, however, smiled lasciviously at her with the assured air of a conqueror. Alice ranged herself alongside of me, slipped her arm round me and with her unoccupied hand gently played with my balls.

Maud bent down and kissed her mother first on her lips and then salaciously on each breast and finally on her cunt; then seating herself alongside Helen she gently ran her delicate forefinger along the lips of her mother's cunt. 'Oh, Maud, don't!' cried Helen, shifting herself uneasily and squirming deliciously under the licentiously free touches of her daughter's finger – but Maud continued deliberately to irritate her mother's cunt till she had worked Helen into an almost uncontrollable degree of erotic excitement, making her plunge and wriggle and twist herself in the most voluptuous manner. It was a charming sight to watch the daughter's delicately slender forefinger at work on her mother's sexual organ, half-hidden in the luxuriant growth of hair that crowned Helen's cunt, driving her slowly to the very verge of spending but forbidding her the blessed relief, and making her tug wildly at her fastenings in her semi-delirium – till no longer able to endure the maddening desire to spend, Helen cried agonisedly, 'Oh, Maud, do finish me!'

With a gratified smile Maud leisurely mounted on the bed and placed herself between Helen's widely parted legs, and with eyes glistening with lust she arranged herself on her mother so that their breasts and cunts rested on each other – then fiercely seizing Helen's helpless body she set to work to rub her cunt against her mother's. 'Ah! darling!' exclaimed Helen in ecstatic delight, as with half-closed eyes she surrendered herself to be fucked by her daughter, jogging herself spasmodically upwards so as to press her cunt more closely against Maud's. Soon their movements became furiously tempestuous, especially Maud's, who plunged and rammed and curvetted herself on her mother's fastened-down body in her efforts to bring on the madly desired crisis. Suddenly she cried, 'I'm coming!!' and with a hurricane of down-thrustings she spent deliciously on her mother's cunt just as Helen with an irrepressible ejaculation of 'Ah! – Ah!' yielded to nature and collapsed, spending ecstatically in her daughter's arms.

As soon as her paroxysms of pleasure had died away Maud kissed her mother lovingly, rose off her and rushed to the bathroom, shielding with her hands her cunt from our inquisitive eyes; but Helen, being tied down, had to remain as she was with her cunt fully exposed, all glistening and sticky from her daughter's spending. With charming confusion and shamefaced blushes she endured our amused scrutiny – then catching Alice's eyes she murmured, 'Please, dear!' whereupon Alice prettily proceeded to remove all traces of the double spend; and by the time Maud returned Helen was ready to be submitted to Alice's caprices.

'What now, Jack?' she asked hesitatingly.

I pointed to Alice. 'You've to satisfy her lust now, dear – go ahead, Alice!' – and installing myself comfortably in an armchair I drew Maud on my knees so that together we might watch Helen under Alice's hands.

For a moment Alice stood undecided, her eyes wandering over Helen's helpless and naked self; then she set to work to play with Helen's beautiful breasts, which she stroked and squeezed and caressed, finally sucking each in turn, keeping her eyes fixed on Helen's tell-tale face as if to assess the result of her toying. What she concluded evidently encouraged her, for with a wicked smile she armed herself with a finely pointed feather and placed herself by Helen's side in a position from which she could command Helen's cunt.

'No, no, Alice! don't tickle me!' cried Helen hastily as she nervously tugged at her fastenings, laughing nevertheless at her predicament. Alice, however, only smiled mockingly at her and proceeded to apply the feather to Helen's cunt, passing the tip lightly but searchingly along its sensitive lips that were still excited from the friction induced by Maud's cunt. 'Don't, Alice!' again cried Helen, squirming charmingly – but seeing that she was doomed to undergo the sweetly subtle torture she nerved herself to endure it, clenching her teeth and firmly closing her lips so as not to cry out.

Then followed a lovely spectacle. Having had her own cunt severely tickled, Alice had learnt where the most sensitive and susceptible spots were and also the most telling way in which to apply the feather to them. Availing herself of this knowledge she so skilfully tickled Helen's cunt that in a very short space of time she had Helen struggling and writhing in the most frantic contortions, straining at her fastenings so frenziedly that the bedposts began to creak – her closed eyes and clenched lips and her heaving breasts and palpitating bosom heightening the provocative effect of her naked tossing and agitated self. But although she heroically refrained from screaming it was evident that she was fast reaching the limits of her powers of endurance; and the gaping of her cunt dumbly indicated the excitement erotically raging there. I succeeded in catching Alice's eye and signalled to her to stop, which she instantly did – and not unwillingly, for her flushed face and glittering eyes betrayed the lustful concupiscence that now possessed her and which she was longing to satisfy by means of Helen's naked helpless body. She dropped the feather and impulsively threw herself on Helen, and was proceeding to work herself on her as she had seen Maud do, when Helen gasped brokenly, 'Wait . . . a moment . . . darling! . . . ' Although she now was absolutely trembling with unsatisfied lust Alice sweetly and sympathisingly suspended her movements; she clasped Helen tightly to her, her breasts resting on Helen's, and showered ardent and salacious kisses on Helen's flushed cheeks and quivering lips till Helen had sufficiently collected her disordered faculties – when she opened her eyes and smiling amorously at Alice murmured, 'Now, darling!'

Alice needed no encouraging. Gripping Helen tightly she furiously rubbed her cunt against her aunt's, her deliciously youthful figure and her frenzied and uncontrollable but exquisitely graceful movements forming a wonderful contrast to Helen's matured but voluptuous body, so rigidly and relentlessly strapped down into practical passivity. So new was Alice to the art of fucking that in place of prolonging the exquisite pleasure and slowly bringing on the sweet climax she concentrated all her energies on procuring the satisfaction of her erotic lust. Wildly she rubbed her cunt against Helen's till the ecstatic crisis overwhelmed them both – then simultaneously they spent, Alice with a rapturous cry of, 'Auntie! . . . oh! auntie! . . . ' accompanied by the most voluptuous thrills of carnal delight, while Helen ejaculated deliriously, 'Oh! . . . Oh! . . . Alice! . . . dar–ling!! . . . ' as she lasciviously quivered in her amorous transports.

In silence and spellbound, Maud and I had watched Helen and Alice, but the sight was too much for Maud; and when Alice set to work to fuck Helen, Maud whispered hoarsely to me, 'Jack! . . . Jack! . . . ,' and agitated herself on my knees in such a way that her desire was unmistakable. Instantly my hand sought her cunt – there was no time for any sweet preliminaries, my finger went straight to her throbbing clitoris and so adroitly did I frig her that just as Helen and Alice were surrendering themselves to their lust and began to spend, Maud also distilled her sweet love-juice with an ecstatic discharge all over my hand.

I let the three women rest undisturbed till the throes of their spending had ceased; then, when Alice slipped off Helen after passionately kissing her, Maud seized her and dragged her to me, exclaiming, 'Show us your cunt, dear!'

Bashfully Alice stood still as we delightedly inspected her sexual organ, all smeared with the love-juice that had proceeded from herself as well as from Helen.

I showed her my hand – 'This is Maud's!' I said with a wicked smile; wiping it gently on her hairs I added; 'Now your cunt carries the sweet essence of all three of you, darling!' – to her blushing confusion, which Maud terminated by dragging her off to the bathroom.

Helen was still in her semi-swoon, looking most fetching in her exhausted nudity; quietly I armed myself with sponge and towel and gently set to work to clean her cunt. This roused her from her torpor – she slowly opened her eyes, but when she recognised me and what I was doing to her she started into full life and hotly blushing exclaimed, 'Jack! . . . Oh, darling, that is not for you to do!'

Suspending my work for the moment I replied, smiling significantly, 'My darling Helen, as I am about to be the next occupant of this sweet abode of love, may I not put it in order for myself?'

She smiled tenderly at me and raised her face as if inviting a kiss; and as I bent downwards she whispered softly, 'Darling, may I suggest my next torturing?' I nodded with an encouraging smile. Helen blushed deeply, then murmured bashfully, 'Do you mind . . . sucking me? I have never had it done to me yet, and I would like to try it!'

'Certainly, dear!' I replied, delighted at her request, then added, 'and after that?'

She blushed again, then replied softly, 'Fuck me, darling!' Enraptured, I kissed her passionately in token of compliance; then I set to work again, and thoroughly sponged and purified her sweet cunt inside as well as outside – and by the time Maud and Alice reappeared Helen was herself again and eagerly anticipating the new experience she was about to taste.

When the two girls returned I placed them on the other side of Helen – they guessed from my position what I was going to do to her and with expectant smiles they quickly took their places. Then lowering my head I brought my lips to bear on Helen's eager cunt and kissed it sweetly, first in the very centre of her clitoris – each kiss making her shiver with pleasure. Next I began to pass my tongue backwards and forwards along her slit, licking it delicately but provokingly. 'Oh, Jack! . . . Oh! . . . Oh!' Helen exclaimed agitating her bottom and hips voluptuously while a smile of beatitude crept over her face. Seeing that she was now revelling in the erotic sensations aroused by my tongue I continued to lick and tongue-tickle her till her cunt began to gape and pout amorously, when I darted my tongue into her orifice as deeply as I could and tickled the deliciously warm soft interior. This set Helen raging with erotic lust. 'Oh! . . . Oh! . . . Jack! . . . My . . . dar . . . ling!' she gasped brokenly as she violently wriggled in lascivious transports as I tickled the most sensitive part of herself with my tongue and then took it gently but firmly between my lips while I passionately sucked it. This finished Helen. Her struggling body suddenly stiffened, a violent convulsion swept through her, and with an incoherent, half-strangled cry she spent rapturously with the most lascivious quivers and thrills.

As I reluctantly raised my head from Helen's cunt the two girls noiselessly clapped their hands gleefully, evidently delighted by what they had witnessed; and as Helen was still absorbed in her ecstatic oblivion they accompanied me to my room, watching with much amusement the removal from my lips and moustache of the traces of Helen's spend.

'What next, Jack?' they eagerly asked.

'The usual finale, dears,' I replied smiling, 'only I am going to pull the straps so tight that Helen won't be able to move at all, and so will lie like a log while she is being fucked! When I give you the signal just tighten the straps as much as ever you can, even if she cries out!'

Helen had come to herself when we rejoined her, and welcomed us with her usual kind smile; the girls at once kissed her warmly, and eagerly enquired how she liked being sucked. Helen blushingly confessed that she had found it just heavenly. 'As good as . . . what you are about to receive, mother dear?' asked Maud teasingly.

Helen laughed. 'Do not forget, dear, that I have tried it only once, while the other – well, I know and love!' she replied evasively.

'Well Helen,' I intervened, 'I was going to fuck you – would you prefer to be sucked again?'

She blushed, hesitated, then said gently, 'The old way, Jack, please; I like to be in your arms, dear, and to feel myself possessed by you, and to . . . spend in response to you!'

'Then fucked you shall be, darling!' I replied as I kissed her tenderly – 'shall I do it now?'

'Give me a minute or two, please Jack!' she pleaded, then turning to the girls she said softly, 'Dears, will you try to work me up.'

'I know a better way for both of us,' I said – and straddling across Helen I seated myself on her chest, placed my prick between her breasts, and with my hands I pressed the latter together, round and over it, at the same time lasciviously squeezing them as I gently logged my prick backwards and forwards between them, revelling in the delicious contact of Helen's full and soft breasts against my now excited organ – its stiffness together with the provoking friction seeming to communicate to Helen some of its ardour, for in spite of her shamefaced confusion at the sight of her breasts being put to such a use her bosom soon began to heave and palpitate and her colour to come and go. I nodded to the excited girls, and they immediately set to work to pull the straps as tight as ever they could, laughing merrily at Helen's dismay and protests when she found herself practically unable to move at all. 'Now, darling!' I said – and working myself backwards over her stomach I slipped into position between her legs, threw myself on her helpless and rigidly extended body, and with one powerful stroke I drove my prick up to its roots in Helen's longing cunt as I took her in my arms and began slowly to fuck her.

'Ah! . . . Jack!' she breathed blissfully. My sensations were extraordinarily piquant. Although Helen lay motionless under me I could feel that she was involuntarily struggling desperately against her fastenings by her muscular contractions and broken breathing and the agitated movements of her only free part, her head, which she rolled and tossed so restlessly and unceasingly that I had the greatest difficulty in catching her lips to kiss them – while her up-turned eyes, clenched teeth and half-closed lips indicated that her inability to indulge herself in the relief afforded by even slight wriggles was concentrating the whole of her erotic lust and lascivious cravings in the battlefield itself, her terribly excited cunt. The tension was evidently getting too much for Helen, so I set to work to fuck her hard, plunging and ramming myself into her quicker and quicker and more and more wildly till the blissful climax arrived – then madly I deluged the recesses of her thirsting cunt with a torrent of boiling love-juice which Helen received with incoherent ejaculations of rapture as she herself spent ecstatically in transports of lascivious delight.

Leaving Helen to lie in happy oblivion I slipped off her, and with the aid of the girls I freed her from her fastenings. Just as this was achieved she came to, and dreamily rolled off her bed; Maud at once took charge of her while Alice accompanied me into my room and again sweetly bathed and dried my exhausted prick – then suddenly stooped down and kissed it lovingly, blushing hotly as she did so. It was the first time she had let herself go, and I augured so favourably of her action that I ventured to whisper as I kissed her, 'Before long, dear, you must let me teach you how to suck it as well as kiss it!' – in response to which she looked lovingly at me and nodded her head with a tender smile of promise!

We re-entered Helen's room simultaneously with herself and Maud. Helen threw herself into my arms and kissed me lovingly, seemingly over-joyed by her experiences. We chatted together for a little, and then after affectionate good-nights we all sought our respective rooms, well pleased with ourselves and each other.

# Chapter Eight

After breakfast next morning Maud started on her visit, Alice and I accompanying her to the station to see her off – and as it was a fine morning we decided to walk back. While *en route* a telegraph lad on his bicycle overtook us, and recognising Alice he pulled up and handed her a telegram addressed to me; it was from my solicitors, and it asked me if I could attend at their office at noon on the next day but one to meet the vendors of a property I was desirous of buying. I showed it to Alice and explained that I practically had no option but to attend, and I wired back agreeing to do so; she was very downcast at so unexpectedly sudden a termination of my visit, but when I told her that I could return within three or four days if Helen could again receive me, she cheered up.

But on reaching home we were startled to find Helen in her boudoir wrapped up in a shawl and sitting by a low wood fire. She told us that when she was dressing that morning she was afraid she had caught a cold – 'I certainly have been exposing myself to the air a good deal since you came down, Jack!' she said laughingly – and since morning it had become worse, and she was trying to stop it.

I told her that I had been recalled to town and must go up on the following morning, but that I could be back within three or four days if I might then resume my visit.

'Of course, Jack dear!' she replied warmly, 'surely you know that we will be only too delighted to put you up again and as often as you like!'

'May I take it that I shall be put up both in the house and in my hostesses?' I asked audaciously.

'You may, Jack!' Helen replied with emphasis, as she and Alice broke into merry laughter at my witticism – then more quietly she added, 'I mustn't put you up me tonight, darling, for with this cold on me it would be very inadvisable, but I do not know why Alice should not be your hostess tonight, for she has now qualified herself!' and she smiled affectionately and meaningly at Alice, who with sparkling eyes threw herself on Helen and kissed her gratefully, exclaiming, 'Oh, auntie, it is sweet of you! You don't know how I've been longing to have Jack all to myself for a while!' And so it was settled that I should that night visit Alice in her room.

In spite of her protests, Alice and I kept Helen company all the afternoon and evening, during which I managed to find an opportunity of asking Alice to put on her daintiest underwear when she dressed for dinner and also to let me undress her when bedtime came – to both of which requests she gave a blushing promise.

In due course bedtime did come – Helen kissed us both lovingly and then said somewhat pointedly to Alice, 'A sweet time to you, my darling, please be very careful and run no risks!' With a self-conscious blush Alice faithfully promised; then we retired to our respective rooms, and when half-past ten chimed I slipped noiselessly into Alice's bedroom, attired only in my dressing gown, and was rapturously welcomed by her. True to her promise she had not begun to undress; and when I took her in my arms in all her pretty finery, the thought that I was about to take off her dainty garments one by one till she stood naked before me made me thrill with lascivious emotion.

As may be well supposed I had never been in Alice's bedroom, nor had I ever caught a glimpse of its interior. It was a veritable little nest, furnished simply but in exquisite taste, and curiously in keeping with its sweet occupant. On the walls hung some beautiful watercolour paintings and scattered all over the mantel, dressing-table, the top of the chest of drawers, etc., were her girlish treasures, knick-knacks, framed photos and the hundred and one trifles girls love to accumulate. But in my present frame of mind two articles attracted me – first, Alice's bed, a pretty single bedstead of white enamelled wood covered with a dark bedspread, and next, an unusually large cheval-glass that stood across a corner; on the first Alice would lie quivering in my arms as I fucked her, while the second would reflect our naked figures as our hands wandered audaciously over each other.

She seated me in a low easy-chair, placed herself on my knees, then threw her arms round my neck and kissed me passionately, murmuring, 'Oh, my darling! it is nice to have you here all to myself, and to feel we can do just whatever we like!'

'And what are you going to like, dear?' I asked as I returned her kiss.

'Something naughty, darling!' she replied, blushing prettily, 'I feel . . . wicked tonight!' she added, laughing gaily.

Clearly my presence in her room and the prospect of having her clothes taken off her by me had inflamed Alice's imagination; and promptly I resolved that I would take the opportunity to initiate her into some of the finer mysteries of the art of fucking.

'We won't waste any time, darling!' I said softly, 'I'm not going to leave you until you have drawn out of me every drop of my love-juice – so you'll have every opportunity of being . . . naughty!' Alice hugged me to her in huge delight at this announcement, and kissed me passionately; then, obedient to my unspoken suggestion, she rose and with an indescribably subtle gesture she intimated that she stood at my disposal.

I also rose, and throwing off my dressing gown I exhibited myself to her stark naked save for my shoes and stockings. She blushed prettily at the sight, her eyes dwelling fondly on my prick which was beginning to show signs of interesting itself in the proceedings. I slipped my arm round her waist and drew her to the cheval-glass saying, 'Let us see how we look!'

'Oh, Jack!' Alice exclaimed – half-shocked at the contrast of my naked self with her fully dressed self so faithfully reflected in the glass – then laughed merrily as she watched my hand wander amorously over her bosom and also her hand as it gently took hold of my prick and caressed it.

'Now, darling, let me undress you!' I said tenderly to her – 'you'll have to show me how to get your dress off you, but the rest I can manage myself!' Alice laughed somewhat constrainedly, then under her whispered directions I removed all her jewellery and ornaments, unfastened and took off her dress, unbuttoned and slipped off her bodice, and untied and pulled off her petticoat, she yielding herself to me but blushing furiously as her attire became scantier and scantier, till she stood in her corset, under which the fringe of her chemise hung provokingly nearly down to her knees and revealed her pretty and slender calves cased in black silk stockings and dainty shoes. I feasted my eyes on her charming dishabille, making her turn herself so that I could view her sideways as well as before and behind, she colouring delightfully at witnessing my admiration – then I resumed my delightful occupation by unlacing and removing her corset after first inspecting her sweet little breasts as they nestled in its pouches. Then I made her draw her arms through the shoulder straps of her chemise and let it fall to her feet; I dealt with her practically transparent vest in the same way – and then Alice stood before me naked to her waist and wearing only the daintiest of deliciously frilly drawers, black silk stockings and shoes.

'Now see how you look, dear!' I said, and led her again to the glass.

'Oh, Jack!' she cried, laughing shamefacedly, 'I'm positively indecent!' and her blushes redoubled.

'I'm going to make you look more indecent still, darling!' I said with a meaning smile, 'Please get out that large black hat with the dark feather and put it on.'

'Oh, Jack! what an idea!' she exclaimed in fits of laughter, but nevertheless sweetly complying she put on the hat.

'Now, darling, stand again in front of the glass and watch yourself as I take down your drawers; then step out of them!'

Now, red as a rose and trembling with erotic excitement, Alice placed herself in front of the mirror – I knelt behind her, undid the tape fastening of her drawers but kept them in position with my hand – then watching her intently in the mirror I suddenly pulled them down to her feet.

'Oh, Jack!' she cried as her eyes caught sight of herself naked to the knees, and involuntarily she shielded her cunt with both hands.

'Raise your feet one at a time, darling!' I whispered; obediently she did so. I threw her drawers on to a chair, rose, and standing behind her and looking over her shoulder I grasped her slender wrists and drew her hands apart and backwards, revealing the sweet triangular patch of hairs that my soul so loved. 'There darling,' I whispered, 'now you do look both indecent and naughty!' Alice blushed beautifully as she surveyed her naked self in the glass, smiling at her bizarre nudity with something suspiciously skin to admiration of herself, 'Isn't it a pity that you can't fuck yourself, darling!' I asked with a teasing smile.

Alice turned to me with eyes bubbling over with merriment at my suggestion, and nodded vigorously her assent, then broke into hearty laughter at the idea.

'Well, darling, that's impossible – but come to bed and I'll teach you how to fuck yourself on me!' and I led her gently away and stripped her absolutely naked by removing her hat, stockings and shoes. Then I placed myself on my back on her bed, with her pillows beneath my bottom.

Alice looked at me with undisguised astonishment. 'Come, darling, straddle across me and put me into yourself!' I said invitingly. At once she comprehended the arrangement, and with pretty blushes she followed my whispered directions; and while I supported her with my arms, she with her dainty hands lovingly seized my prick and inserted it into her cunt – and when she had sunk down on it until it was buried inside her I lowered her gently till she lay on me and cradled her in my encircling arms, when I whispered amorously, 'Now, my darling, the game is in your own hands. I shall simply lie still and leave you to fuck yourself slow or fast as your fancy may dictate!' and kissed her lovingly.

Alice's eyes sparkled with delighted anticipation as I explained her duties to her. She passed her arms round my neck as if to anchor herself on me, kissed my lips ardently as she murmured, 'Oh, darling, it is just heavenly!' – then looking me straight in the eyes and smiling lasciviously she commenced very gently to agitate herself on my prick, pressing her mount of Venus so strongly down against my groin that our hairs intermingled. She continued this delicious agitation for a little, then her eyes began to flicker and her breathing to be broken – while her bosom heaved and palpitated excitedly against my chest. Soon her movements became more tempestuous; her bottom began to waggle and jog itself up and down more and more fiercely as her sexual concupiscence grew hotter and hotter. She now was in the throes of lust; she pressed her cheek against mine, clutched me more closely round my neck and worked herself furiously up and down on my prick – then spent deliciously with voluptuous thrills and quivers.

True to my undertaking I lay like a log under Alice, holding her plunging body firmly and closely against mine and encouraging her with salacious kisses – but when she collapsed after spending and lay limp and inert on me, I slipped my hands on to her glorious bottom and set to work to stimulate her to fresh exertions by caressing and fondling her rich and plump flesh. Presently with a sigh of deep content Alice raised her head from off my shoulder, and with humid eyes she looked tenderly at me as she imprinted a long sweet kiss on my lips. 'Go on again, dear!' I whispered stimulatingly. Instantly Alice's eyes brightened and her limpness disappeared.

'Oh, Jack. May I?' she exclaimed excitedly. I nodded encouragingly. 'Oh, darling!' she ejaculated rapturously as she kissed me passionately – then tightening her grip round my neck she recommenced to work herself voluptuously up and down on my prick.

This time I left Alice to maintain her balance and position on me without the help of my encircling arms; and while she fucked herself blissfully I gently encouraged her by stroking and tickling her breasts as they rested sweetly on my chest, squeezing them amorously when I noticed that the ecstatic climax was overtaking Alice. Soon she again spent rapturously, kissing me passionately as the spasms of pleasure thrilled through her – then with hardly a pause she set to work to fuck herself more furiously than ever, plunging and raging riotously on me with wild frenzied down-thrustings of her tossing and agitated bottom. My powers of self-control succumbed under her fierce assault; deserting her breasts I threw my arms round her, gripped her tightly to me, jerked myself madly upwards – then shot my hot discharge into Alice just as she for the third time spent in delicious transports, flooding my happy prick with her sweet essence of love.

As soon as the spasms of pleasure ceased to thrill through her Alice slipped off my prick, and whispering, 'Lie still, darling, till I return!' she disappeared, mindful of Helen's parting admonitions. Meanwhile, I lay peacefully on Alice's dainty bed, thrilling at the recollection of the exquisite pleasure I had just been privileged to taste with her in my arms, and endeavouring to decide what next I should do to her; but before I could come to any decision Alice returned armed with basin, sponge and towel, and deliciously bathed and refreshed my now flaccid prick – then lay herself down by my side, encircled by my arm.

'Well, dear?' I said interrogatively as I smiled lovingly at her.

Alice blushed prettily. 'Darling, it was just heavenly!' she replied softly, then whispered, 'Jack, I went off three times!'

I laughed, then replied, 'I know you were very . . . naughty in the way you were wriggling on me, dear. Have you any naughtiness left?' Alice nodded roguishly, then broke into merry laughter. 'And what particular naughtiness are you now yearning after, dear?'

Alice hesitated for a moment, then whispered bashfully, 'Darling, may I watch your . . . thing grow from what it now is to the big stiff thing it is when you . . . put it into me?'

'Certainly you may, dear!' I replied smiling approvingly – 'and if you like to use your hands and lips you can greatly expedite the resurrection!'

Alice raised herself on her elbow and looking radiantly at me exclaimed, 'Darling, I'd love to do so – and at the same time have a real good look at your . . . thing for we've been too . . . busy up to now!' – and she laughed wickedly.

'You're evidently going to be very naughty again, dear, but I suppose I must put up with it! Now let me arrange ourselves for your special benefit!' – And shifting my position I placed myself so as to lie on my back across Alice's bed, then carefully guiding her I made her straddle across me and lie face downwards on my stomach, reversed in *soixante-neuf* style, so that her cunt hung just above my face while she had right before her eyes my penis and balls, and free hands with which to manipulate them.

'There, darling! I think that is about right!' I said – 'for while you are satisfying your natural curiosity and . . . amusing yourself, you are giving me something to look at and perhaps to kiss if you sufficiently excite me!'

'Oh, Jack! you are clever – this is just lovely!' Alice exclaimed delightedly as she voluptuously wriggled herself on my stomach till she had settled herself comfortably on me – then I felt her soft but intensely exciting fingers gently seize my penis and balls.

As I thrilled with pleasure at the contact of Alice's hands with my genital organs, I accidentally turned my head in the direction of her toilet table, and to my great delight I saw ourselves reflected in the glass, visible to me but not to her. Meanwhile Alice, thinking herself unobserved, threw off all constraint and set to work openly to indulge her curiosity. I could see the sparkle in her eyes as with rapt excitement she examined my penis and balls, handling them with wonderful gentleness as she pulled my hairs and drew back the loose skin off the rubicund head and caressed my balls, and generally investigated thoroughly every feature of my sexual equipment.

Presently I felt a premonitory shiver run through her, and I could see by the reflection of her tell-tale face in the glass that some fancy or caprice was tempting her, but that she had not yet surrendered herself to it. Alice was evidently hotly debating something in her mind – whether to do it or not – for her colour came and went and her bosom rose and fell in pretty agitation as she played with my private parts.

Intuitively I guessed that the idea of sucking me had suddenly suggested itself to her – and with the object of seeing whether it was so, as well as to encourage her into doing it, I softly kissed her cunt, then watched her intently in the glass. She shivered violently, blushed hotly, raised my penis towards her lips – then as she lowered her face to meet it she checked herself as if in doubt. Again I kissed her cunt – again another quiver followed by a strangely yearning look at my penis, which now began to swell and assert itself as it rested between her gentle fingers. I tried the effect of a third kiss, and to my huge delight I saw Alice lower her lips to my penis, and felt her lovingly kiss its sensitive head – then after regarding it fondly she kissed it over and over again. With each kiss my penis grew stiffer and thicker and angrier-looking, till it stood erect and rampant; Alice had not only witnessed its resurrection but had brought about the miracle, and a smile of gratified triumph played on her face as she regarded her handiwork.

Now she had to be induced to suck me. Following the same tactics of suggestion I began to lick and tickle her cunt with my tongue. Alice quivered voluptuously and half-closed her eyes for a moment in bliss – then to my surprise she kissed my balls ardently as they lay in the palm of her hand and after a little hesitation commenced to apply her tongue to them, the exquisite sensation together with the provocative sight sending me wild with delight. She now was fairly wriggling on me with lust – I thrust my tongue into her cunt as deeply as I could with a darting, stabbing action. Alice now raised her mouth from my balls, her face aflame, her eyes simply blazing with lust; then slowly she guided my prick into her mouth and began to suck it ardently while her tongue played lasciviously on and round its now excited head.

My sensations were just heavenly – and the sweet knowledge that I was engaged in taking the maidenhead of Alice's mouth only heightened my ecstasy. My hands had been playing alternately with her delicious bottom and her breasts – but now I flung them round her dainty waist; and clasping her firmly so as to control her plunging wriggles I set to work to suck her into spending. Every now and again I caught a glimpse of her face as reflected in the glass. Alice seemed as if she was in a delirium – her eyes were almost closed, her right hand held my balls and her left hand clasped my penis – she had nearly half of my prick in her mouth, and instinctively she was working her lips up and down on it as if to pump up my love-juice, driving me mad with pleasure. Knowing she must be on the verge of spending, I fiercely attacked her clitoris, and seizing it with my lips I tickled it with my tongue. A violent convulsion swept through her – then Alice spent rapturously, suspending her suction of my prick while the spasms of pleasure thrilled through her, but retaining it in her mouth. I felt myself going. 'Stop, darling! . . . I'm coming! . . . ' I cried as I struggled to drag my prick out of her mouth – but Alice kept it imprisoned and tightly held between her lips and teeth, then resumed her suction in so delicious a manner as to break down all my powers of control; and no longer able to restrain myself I jerked myself upwards violently and spent frantically in Alice's mouth, shooting my hot essence down her throat, jet after jet, in my ecstatic bliss; but as I did so, in spite of my delirious rapture I turned to see how Alice bore the sudden flooding of her mouth with my love-juice. To my surprise and intense relief she absorbed my deluge without flinching, swallowing each jet as it shot into her mouth and keeping her lips tightly closed round my prick till the last drop had oozed out and it had begun to shrink – when she drew it out of her mouth and with an amused expression watched it shrivel up and dwindle away to a third of its size. Then without a word she rose off me and disappeared, leaving me in a state of confusion and apprehension that can easily be imagined. But whether I had offended her or not, I had to purify myself; and having done so I awaited events.

In a few minutes Alice returned rosy red but smiling happily. I took her in my arms murmuring, 'Oh, darling!'

She kissed me warmly and whispered, 'Did I do it all right, Jack?'

Relieved beyond measure I kissed her passionately, then whispered back, 'Darling, you sucked me like an angel!' – which set her off into silent but merry laughter; and then we lay down together again, Alice this time placing herself on me with her cunt resting on my prick and her arms round my neck.

'Why did you call out to me to stop, Jack?' she asked presently, with a half-smile on her lips – 'didn't you want to . . . finish?'

'I didn't know whether you would be willing to let me . . . finish in your mouth, darling,' I replied – 'and so I tried to make you stop before it was too late – but you wouldn't and I had to let myself go. Were you expecting it?'

'Yes!' she whispered with a blush and a smile – then continued, 'you may remember that just before you . . . violated me!' (here she tenderly kissed me) 'Maud sucked you till you got stiff! Well, when I was helping her to pack yesterday I asked her about it and she told me how to do it and that you would . . . finish in my mouth and that I was to swallow what came from you! So I was looking out for it – but I didn't expect such a lot!' she added roguishly – 'it was hard work to get it all down!'

I kissed her lovingly. 'And you didn't mind, dear?'

'Not after the first swallow!' Alice replied laughing and blushing prettily.

'And you'll do it again?' I asked with a tentative smile.

'Whenever you like and as often as you like, darling!' Alice replied tenderly as she sweetly kissed me. I gratefully hugged her, and we lay silent for a moment, our lips pressed against each other.

'And what else did you learn from Maud, dear?' I asked with some interest.

'Oh, lots of things, Jack!' Alice replied, laughing merrily. 'We talked a lot and she told me a lot! Jack, when she comes back, we are going to have a night together in her room, and she is going to teach me some . . . tricks!' – and again she laughed merrily.

'I wish I could be there to see you!' I murmured regretfully, 'you two will make a perfectly lovely pair – and to watch you experimenting on each other stark naked would be a treat for a king! You and Maud haven't yet fucked each other, have you?'

'No, not yet!' replied Alice, colouring slightly, 'no one has fucked me except you, darling; but I fucked auntie last night!' she added with evident satisfaction.

'And you no doubt will be doing so again before long!' I added with a meaning smile, whereupon Alice kissed me. 'But don't practise too much with her, dear, for Maud will have been chaste for a fortnight and will take a lot of satisfying, and to have your charming self at her disposal will excite her more than ever. Mind you write and tell me all that you do with her and also with your aunt!' I added, and with pretty blushes Alice nodded a promise.

Meanwhile her sweet hand had not been idle but had busied itself by playing with my prick and endeavouring to restore it to life – and it now was beginning to show signs of returning animation. 'Jack, you're coming again!' Alice whispered delightedly as she redoubled her delicate attentions.

'And how will you take it this time, dear?' I whispered.

She hesitated for a moment, then whispered back, 'Under you darling, just like the very first time!' – and slipping out of my arms she bent herself forward, lowered her head, took my prick into her sweet mouth and began to tongue it divinely, while she stroked and caressed my balls with her gentle little fingers. Promptly my prick responded to her invitation and became stiff and rampant – but so delicious was the sensation communicated by her soft lips and warm tongue that I let her continue to suck me till fear of a catastrophe impelled me to stop her.

Almost regretfully Alice released my prick from its sweet imprisonment in her mouth, and after a final kiss of its now excited and throbbing head she resumed her original attitude at my side and whispered, 'Darling, was that all right?'

'Simply heavenly, dear!' I replied as I kissed her gratefully – 'now turn over on your back and receive the reward of your sweet kindness!'

With sparkling eyes Alice quickly complied, then separated her legs widely, exhibiting her exquisite cunt in the most inviting way. Without delay I slipped on to her, and taking her luscious body in my arms I slowly and voluptuously pushed my prick into her longing cunt till it was completely buried in her and our hairs intermingled – Alice quivering with rapture as she felt her cunt being thus deliciously invaded. 'Twist your legs round me, dear!' I whispered. Instantly comprehending Alice threw her legs across my loins and gripped me tightly to her as if trying to force my prick still deeper into her, at the same time hugging me closer against her breasts with her arms.

Our mouths sought each other, and as our lips met in passionate kisses I began slowly to fuck Alice. The moment she felt my prick moving in her cunt she gripped me more tightly than ever with her legs and then commenced to wriggle under me in the divinest fashion, arousing in me the most voluptuous sensations of lust sweetly being satisfied. Never in all my life had I been in such close contact with a girl as I then was with Alice. I was absolutely locked up between her arms and legs and tightly pressed against her soft warm luscious flesh, while with fierce desire I clutched her to me till her delicious breasts were flattened against me and I could feel every pulsation of her quivering self as Love's sweet frenzy by degrees overwhelmed us both – till no longer able to restrain myself I spent deliriously into Alice just as she for the second time flooded my excited prick with her warm love-juice.

But our lust was not yet satisfied – we were mad to enjoy each other again – and my prick remained stiff and rampant in Alice's cunt. So, after a brief pause during which our lips were sweetly engaged with each other, we recommenced our now lascivious pastime. This time our pleasure was deliciously prolonged as our carnal rage had been gratified, and we could devote ourselves to voluptuous copulation as connoisseurs and revel in the exquisite raptures attending the satisfaction of our lust, as little by little we approached the heavenly climax. How many times Alice spent I cannot even guess – she seemed to pass from one blissful ecstasy to another, her half-closed eyes and slightly parted lips, her incoherent ejaculations and voluptuously involuntary movements as she wriggled beneath me testifying to the rapturous transports she was tasting as I slowly fucked her. But before long it became evident that Alice was getting exhausted – and by now I also was furious to dissolve myself in ecstasies in her delicious interior. So I whispered to her, 'Now, darling, let us finish together!' She opened her eyes languorously with a smile of ineffable pleasure, kissed me lovingly, then set to work to second my now vigorous rammings and thrustings. Soon we were fucking each other madly with the most unbridled lascivious fury.

Suddenly Alice gasped, 'Now, darling! . . . now!' at the same time wriggling hysterically under me. Promptly I let myself go, and just as I felt her warm essence bedew the head of my prick again, I spent convulsively into her with a rapture I have seldom tasted, shooting into her every drop of love-juice that I could discharge.

Under the excess of our rapturous pleasure we both lost consciousness. I, at all events, was in a state of oblivion till the chiming of a clock aroused me. It was 2 a.m! I still lay on Alice, locked up between her arms and legs – my prick was still lodged up her cunt – and she was still clasped closely to me and apparently sleeping happily. I was loath to disturb her, but it was imperative that we should separate and retire quietly for the rest of the night. So reluctantly I roused Alice with loving kisses; she opened her eyes in bewilderment – and when the position of affairs dawned on her she flushed rosy red, then whispered shamefacedly and hurriedly, 'Oh, do let me get up, darling!' at the same time hastily releasing me from my sweet imprisonment between her arms and legs. Gently I slipped out of her embrace and set her free in turn; then hurriedly we assumed our night gear and after a tender 'Good-night', accompanied by many kisses, I noiselessly slipped out of Alice's room and regained my chamber.

Next morning I was delighted to see Helen appear at breakfast, apparently all right again, though a little pulled down. She had been into Alice's room, and in the absence of the latter she gently chided me for allowing Alice to indulge her newly acquired sexual privileges to a possibly injurious extent. Just then, however, Alice appeared, radiant, a vision of happy satisfied girlishness which effectively dispelled Helen's anxieties; and she then proceeded to chaff us both in her usual kindly way – till Alice seized her and with eager insistence made Helen promise with pretty blushes that on the first night of my return she would place herself at my disposal for the whole night.

In due course the hour of my departure arrived, and after a tender farewell and many kisses I tore myself away from the hospitable mansion where I had passed as delicious a weekend as ever has been vouchsafed to mortal man.

# Venus in India

---

## 'CAPTAIN CHARLES DEVREAUX'

# CHAPTER ONE

## *A Call to Arms*

The war in Afghanistan appeared to be coming to a close when I received sudden orders to proceed, at once, from England to join the first battalion of my regiment, which was then serving there. I had just been promoted captain and had been married about eighteen months. It pained me more than I care to express to part with my wife and baby girl, but it was agreed that it would be better for all of us if their coming to India were deferred until it was certain where my regiment would be quartered on its return to the fertile plains of Hindustan from the stones and rocks of barren Afghanistan. Besides, it was very hot, being the height of the hot weather, when only those who were absolutely forced to do so went to India, and it was a time of year particularly unsuitable for a delicate woman and a babe to travel in so burning a climate. It was also not quite certain whether my wife would join me in India, as I had the promise of a staff appointment at home, but before I could enter upon that I had of necessity to join my own battalion, because it was at the seat of war. But it was annoying to have to go, all the same, as it was clear that the war was over, and that I should be much too late to participate in any of its rewards or glories, though it was quite possible I might come in for much of the hardship and inconvenience of the sojourn, for a wild, and not to say rough and inhospitable country is Afghanistan; besides which it was quite possible that an Afghan knife would put an end to me, or that I might fall a victim to a common murder instead of dying a glorious death on the battlefield.

Altogether my prospects seemed by no means of a rosy colour, but there was nothing for it but to submit and go, which I did with the best grace possible but with a very heavy heart.

I will spare the readers the sad details of parting with my wife. I made no promise of fidelity, the idea seemed never to occur to her or to myself of there being any need for it, for although I had always been of that temperament so dear to Venus, and had enjoyed the pleasure of love with great good fortune before I married, yet I had, as I thought, quite steadied down into a proper married man, whose desires never wandered outside his own bed; for my passionate and loving spouse was ever ready to respond to my ardent caresses with caresses as ardent; and her charms, in their youthful beauty and freshness, had not only not palled upon me, but seemed to grow more and more powerfully attractive the more I revelled in their possession. For my dearest wife, gentle reader, was the life of passion; she was not one of those who coldly submit to their husbands caresses because it is their duty to do so, a duty, however, not to be done with pleasure or joyfully, but more as a species of penance! No! With her it was not, 'Ah! no, let me sleep tonight, dear. I did it twice last night, and I really don't think you can want it again. You should be more chaste, and not try me as if I were your toy and plaything. No! Take your hand away! Do leave my nightdress alone! I declare it is quite indecent the way you are behaving!' and so forth, until, worn out with her husband's persistence, she thinks the shortest way after all will be to let him have his way, and so grudgingly allows her cold cunt to be uncovered, unwillingly opens her ungracious thighs, and lies a passionless log, insensible to her husband's endeavours to strike a spark of pleasure from her icy charms. Ah! no! With my sweet Louie it was far different; caress replied to caress, embrace to embrace. Each sweet sacrifice became sweeter than the one before, because she fully appreciated all the joy and delight of it! It is almost impossible to have too much of such a woman, and Louie seemed to think it quite impossible to have too much of me. It was, 'Once more, my darling! Just one little more! I am sure it will do you good! and I should like it!' and it would be strange if the manly charm which filled her loving hand were not once more raised in response to her caresses, ready once again to carry rapturous delight to the deepest, richest depths of the trembling voluptuous charm for the special benefit of which it was formed, a charm which was indeed the very temple of love.

Having ascertained from the adjutant general, that my destination was Cherat, a small camping ground, as I heard, on top of a range of mountains forming the southern limit of the valley of the Peshawar, and having received railroad warrants, via Allahabad, for the temporary station of Jhelum, and dak warrants from that spot to Cherat itself, I made my preparations for the long journey which still lay before me; amongst the necessaries for mind and body I purchased were some French novels which included that masterpiece of drawing-room erotic literature *Mademoiselle de Maupin* by Théophile Gautier.

The route from Bombay via Allahabad to Peshawar runs almost entirely through a country as flat as a table. Only once on this journey, about which I fear I may become tedious, did the tempter accost me, and then so clumsily as quite to frustrate his well-meant intentions. I had to make a few hours' stay in Allahabad and to pass that away pleasantly I wandered about, examining the tombs of the kings and princes who reigned in past times over the banks of the Ganges and the Jumna, and in seeing such sights as I could find to amuse and interest me. As I was returning to my hotel a native accosted me in very good English.

'Like to have woman, sahib? I got one very pretty little half-caste in my house, if master like to come and see!'

Oh! dear *Mademoiselle de Maupin*!

I felt no desire to see the pretty little half-caste! I put this self-abnegation down to virtue, and actually laughed, in my folly, at the idea that there existed, or could exist, a woman in India who could raise even a ghost of desire in me!

The station beyond Jhelum is reached, I having but one mighty river to pass before I leave the bounds of India proper and tread the outskirts of central Asia, in the valley of the Peshawar. But it took some two or three days and nights of continuous travel in a dak *gharry* [carriage], before I reached Attock. The dak *gharry* is a fairly comfortable mode of conveyance, but one becomes tired of the eternal horizontal position in which it accomodates the weary traveller. Crossing the Indus in a boat rowed over a frightful torrent with the roar of the waters breaking on the rocks below, was a very exciting experience, especially as it happened at night, and the dark gloom added a magnifying effect to the roar of the suspected danger. Another dak *gharry* waited, into which I got, lay down and went to sleep, not to waken until I reached Nowshera.

Ah! *Mademoiselle de Maupin*! What a lovely girl! Who can she be? She must, I fancy, be the daughter of the colonel commanding here, out for her morning walk, and perhaps, judging from the keen expectant glance shot in at me through the half-open sliding door of the *gharry*, expecting somebody, perhaps her fiancé; perhaps that is why she looked so eager and yet so disappointed!

Oh, dear reader! just as I opened my eyes I saw, through the half-open door, this perfect figure of feminine beauty! A girl clothed in close-fitting grey-coloured dress with a Teria hat archly sloped on her lovely and well-shaped head! That beautiful face! How perfect the oval of it! What glorious, yet rather stern eyes! What a delicately formed nose! Truly she must have aristocratic blood in her veins to be so daintily formed! What a rosebud of a mouth! What cherry lips! God! Jupiter! Venus! What a form! See those exquisite rounded shoulders, those full and beautiful arms, the shape of each so plainly visible so close does her dress fit her; and how pure, how virgin-like is that undulating bosom! See how proudly each swelling breast fills out her modest, but still desire-provoking, bodice! Ah! The little shell-like ears, fitting so close to the head. How I would like to have the privilege of gently pressing those tiny lobes! What a lovely creature she looks! How refined! How pure! How virginal.

And all these impressions flashed through my mind from a glimpse, a very vivid glimpse it is true, and she seemed so absolutely and completely removed from ordinary mankind that I never dreamt I should ever see her cunt; according to plan I was going to change horses at Nowshera and proceed immediately to Cherat.

But on arriving at the post office, which was also the place for changing horses, the postmaster, a civil-spoken Baboo, told me that he could give me horses only as far as Publi, a village about halfway between Nowshera and

Peshawar, and that from that place I must make the best of my way to
Cherat, for there was no road along which dak *gharrys* could be driven, and
my good Baboo added that the said interval between Publi and Cherat was
dangerous for travellers, there being many lawless robbers about. Moreover,
he added, the distance was a good fifteen miles. He advised me to put up at
the public bungalow at Nowshera until the brigade major could put me in
the way of completing my journey.

   This information was a great surprise and a great damper to me! How on
earth was I to get up to Cherat with my baggage if there was no road? How
could I do fifteen miles under such circumstances? To think I had come so
many thousands of miles, since I had left England, to be balked by a
miserable little fifteen. However, for the present there seemed nothing to be
done but to take the excellent Baboo's advice, put up at the public bungalow
and see the brigade major.

   The public bungalow stood in its own compound, a little distance from the
high road, and to get to it I had to drive back part of the road I had travelled.
I dismissed my driver, and called for the *khansama* [house-steward], who
informed me that the bungalow was full, and that there was no room for me!
Here was a pretty state of affairs! but whilst I was speaking to the *khansama*, a
pleasant-looking young officer, lifting the *chick* [bamboo blind] which hung
over the entrance to his room, came out on to the verandah, and told me that
he had heard what I was saying that he was only waiting for a *gharry* to
proceed on his journey down country, and that my coming was as opportune
for him as his going would be for me. He had, he said, sent at once to secure
my dak *gharry*, and if he could get it, he would give up his room to me but
anyhow, I should, if I did not dislike the idea, share his room which contained
two bedsteads. Needless to say I was delighted to accept his kind offer, and I
soon had my goods inside the room, and was enjoying that most essential and
refreshing thing in India, a nice cool bath. My new friend had taken upon
himself to order breakfast for me, and when I had completed my ablutions and
toilet, we sat down together. Officers meeting in this manner very quickly
become like old friends. My new acquaintance told me all about himself,
where he had been, where he was going to, and I reciprocated. Needless to say
the war, which was now practically over, formed the great topic of our general
conversation. Getting more intimate, we of course fell, as young men do – or
old, too, for the matter of that – to discussing love and women, and my young
friend told me that the entire British Army was just simply raging for women!
That none were to be got in Afghanistan, and that, taking it as a general rule,
neither officers nor men had had a woman for at least two years.

   'George!' he cried, as he laughed, 'the Peshawar polls are reaping a rich
harvest! As fast as a regiment arrives from Afghanistan, the whole boiling lot
rush off to the bazaars, and you can see the Tommy Atkinses waiting outside
the knocking shops, holding their pricks in their hands and roaring out to
those having women to look sharp!'

This was of course an exaggeration, but not to so great an extent as my gentle reader may suppose.

We had just finished our cheroots after breakfast, when the young officer's servant drove up in the same dak *gharry* which had brought me from Attock, and in a few minutes my cheerful host was shaking hands with me.

'There's somebody in there,' said he, pointing to the next room, 'to whom I must say goodbye, and then I'm off.'

He was not long absent, again shook my hand, and in another minute a sea of dust hid him and the *gharry* from my sight.

I felt quite lonely and sad when he was gone, for, although the bungalow was full, I was left in a small portion of it walled off from the rest, so that I didn't see any of its other occupants – though I might occasionally hear them. I had forgotten to ask who my next door neighbour was, and indeed I did not much care as I was so bothered, wondering how I should get up to Cherat. It was now nearly ten o'clock, the sun was pouring sheets of killing rays of light on the parched plain in which Nowshera is situated, and the hot wind was beginning to blow, parching one up, and making lips and eyes quite sore as well as dry. I did not know what to do with myself. It was much too hot to think of going to the brigade major's, so I got another cheroot, and taking my delightful *Mademoiselle de Maupin* out of my bag, I went and sat behind a pillar on the verandah, to shelter myself from the full force of the blast and try to read; but even this most charming damsel failed to charm, and I sank back in my chair and smoked listlessly whilst my eyes wandered over the range of lofty mountains which I could just distinguish quivering through hot, yellow-looking air. I did not know at the time that I was looking at Cherat and had I had any prescience of what was waiting for me there, I should certainly have gazed upon those hills with far greater interest than I did.

Reader dear, do you know what it is to feel that somebody is looking at you, though you may not be able to see him, to be aware for a fact that somebody is looking at you? I am extremely susceptible to this influence. Whilst sitting thus idly looking at the most distant thing my eyes could find to rest upon, I began to feel that someone was near, and looking intently at me. At first I resisted the temptation to look around to see who it was. I felt so irritable, that I resented, as an insult, the looking at me which I felt certain was going on; but at last this strange sensation added to my unrest and I half turned my head to see whether it was reality or feverish fancy.

My surprise was unbounded when I saw the same lovely face which I had caught a glimpse of that morning peering at me from behind the slightly opened *chick* of the room next to mine. I was so startled that instead of taking a good look at the lady I instantly gazed on the hills again, as if turning my head to look in her direction had been a breach of good manners on my part; but I felt she was still keeping her eyes fixed on me, and it amazed me that anyone in the position which I imagined she held (for I was firmly convinced that I was right as to my surmise that my unknown beauty was a lady, and a colonel's daughter) should be guilty of such bad manners as to stare at a perfect stranger in this manner. I turned my head once more, and this time I looked at this lovely but strange girl a little more fixedly. Her eyes, large, lustrous, most beautiful, seemed to pierce mine, as though trying to read my thoughts. For a moment I fancied she must be a little off her head, but just then, apparently satisfied with her reconnaissance, the fair creature disappeared from sight. From that moment my curiosity was greatly aroused. Who was she? Was she alone? Or was she with the unknown colonel in that room? Why was she staring at me so hard? By Jove! There she was at it again! I could stand it no longer. I jumped up and went into my own room and called the *khansama*.

'*Khansama*, who is in the room next to mine?' and I pointed to the door which communicated with the room the lady was in, which was closed.

'A memsahib, sahib.'

A memsahib! Now I had been in India before, this was my second tour of service in the country, and I knew that a memsahib meant a married lady. I was surprised, for had anyone asked me, I should have said that this lovely girl had never known a man, had never been had, and never would be had, unless she met the man of men who pleased her. It was extraordinary how this idea had taken root in my mind.

'Is the sahib with her?'

'No, sahib!'

'Where is he?'

'I don't know, sahib.'

'When did the memsahib come here, *khansama*?'

'A week or ten days ago, sahib!'

It was plain I could get no information from this man, only one more question and I was done.

'Is the memsahib quite alone, *khansama*?'

'Yes, sahib: she has no one with her, not even an *ayah* [maid].'

Well! this is wonderful! How often did my young friend who had only gone away this morning, know her? You, gentle reader, with experience, no doubt have your suspicions that all was not right, but for the life of me I could not shake off the firm notion that this woman was not only a lady, but one exceptionally pure and highly connected.

I went back to my seat on the verandah, waiting to be looked at again, and I did not wait long. A slight rustle caught my ear. I looked around and there was my lovely girl showing more of herself. She still looked with the same eager gaze without the sign of a smile on her face. She appeared to be in her petticoats only, and her legs and feet, such lovely, tiny, beautiful feet, and such exquisitely turned ankles, were bare; she had not even a pair of slippers on. A light shawl covered her shoulders and bosom, but did not hide either her full, well-shaped, white arms, her taper waist or her splendid and broad hips. These naked feet and legs inspired me with a sudden flow of desire, in spite of the fact that her lovely face and its wonderful calm yet severe expression had hitherto driven all such thoughts from my mind.

Giacomo Casanova, who certainly is a perfect authority on all that concerns women, declares that curiosity is the foundation on which desire is built, that, but for that, a man would be perfectly contented with one woman, since in the main all women are alike; yet from mere curiosity a man is impelled to approach a woman, and to wish for her possession. Something akin to this certainly influenced me. A devouring curiosity took possession of me. This exquisite girl's face inspired me to know how she could possibly be all alone here at Nowshera, in a public bungalow, and her lovely naked feet and legs made me wonder whether her knees and thighs corresponded with them in perfect beauty, and my imagination painted in my mind a voluptuous motte and delicious cunt, shaded by dark locks corresponding to the colour of the lovely eyebrows, which arched over those expressive orbs. I rose from my chair and moved towards her. She instantly withdrew and as instantly again opened the *chick*. For the first time I saw a smile wreathe her face. What a wonderfully different expression that smile gave it! Two lovely dimples appeared in her rounded cheeks, her rosy lips parted and displayed two rows of small perfectly even teeth, and those eyes which had looked so stern and almost forbidding, now looked all tenderness and softness.

'You must find it very hot out there on the verandah!' said she, in a low, musical voice, but with a rather vulgar, common accent which at first grated on my ear, 'and I know you are all alone! Won't you come into my room and sit down and chat? You will if you are a good fellow!'

'Thank you!' said I, smiling and bowing as I threw away my cheroot and entered whilst she held the *chick* so as to make room for me to pass. I caught the *chick* in my hand but she still kept her arm raised, and extended; her shawl fell a little off her bosom which was almost entirely bare, and I saw not only two most exquisitely round, full and polished globes of ivory, but even the rosy coral marble which adorned the peak of one of them. I could see that she caught the direction of my glance, but she was in no hurry to lower her arm, and I judged, and rightly, that this liberal display of her charms was by no means unintentional.

'I have got two chairs in here,' said she, laughing such a sweet-sounding laugh, 'but we can sit together on my bed, if you don't mind!'

'I shall be delighted,' said I, 'if sitting without a back to support you won't tire you!'

'Oh!' said she, in the most innocent manner, 'you just put your arm round my waist, and then I won't feel tired.'

Had it not been for the extraordinary innocent tone with which she said this, I think I should at once have lain her back and got on top of her, but a new idea stuck me: could she be quite sane? And would not such an action be the very height of blackguardism?

However, I sat down, as she bade me do, and I slipped my left arm around her slender waist and gave her a little hug towards me.

'Ah!' she said, 'that's right! Hold me tight! I love being held tight!'

I found that she had no stays on at all. There was nothing between my hand and her smooth skin but a petticoat and a chemise, both of very light muslin. She felt so awfully nice! There's something so thrilling in feeling the warm, palpitating body of a lovely woman in one's arms; it was only natural that not only did my blood run more quickly, but I began to feel what the French call the 'pricking of the flesh'. There she was, this really beautiful creature, half naked and palpitating, her cheeks glowing with health, though paler than one is accustomed to seeing in our more temperate Europe, her lovely shining shoulders and bosom almost perfectly naked, and so exquisite! The nearer I got my eyes to the skin the better did I see how fine was its texture. The bloom of youth was on it. There were no ugly hollows to show where the flesh had receded and the bones projected. Her beautiful breasts were round, plump and firm looking. I longed to take possession of those lovely bubbies! To press them in my hand, to devour them and their rosy tips with my mouth! Her petticoats fell between her slightly parted thighs and showed their roundness and beautiful form perfectly as though to provoke my desire the more, desire she must have known was burning me, for she could feel the palpitating of my agitated heart even if a glance of her eyes in another and lower direction did not betray to her the effect her touch and her beauty had on me. She held out one and then the other of her fairy feet, so white and perfect, as though to display them to my eager eyes. The soft and delicious perfume which only emanates from a woman in her youth, stole in fragrant clouds over my face, and her abundant wavy hair fell like silk against my cheek. Was she mad? That was the tormenting thought which would spring up between my hand and the glowing charms it longed to seize!

For some few moments we sat in silence. Then I felt her hand creep up under my white jacket and toy with the buttons to which my braces were fastened behind. She undid one side of my braces and as she did so said, 'I saw you this morning! You were in a dak *gharry* and I just caught a glimpse of you.'

Her hand began to work at the other button. What the deuce was she up to?

'Oh yes!' I said, looking into her twinkling eyes and returning the starry glances which shot from them, 'and I saw you too! I had been fast asleep, and just as I opened my eyes my sight fell upon you and I – '

She had unbuttoned my braces behind, and now stole her hand round and laid it, back up, on the top of my thigh.

'And you what?' said she, gently sliding her extended fingers down over the inside of my thigh: she was within a nail's breadth of the side of my prick which was now standing furiously!

'Oh!' I exclaimed, 'I thought I had never seen such a lovely face and figure in the world!'

The fingertips actually touched Johnnie! She slightly pressed them against him, and looking at me again with the sweetest smile, said: 'Did you really! Well! I'm glad you did, for do you know what I thought, when I saw you lying inside the *gharry*?'

'No, dear!'

'Well! I thought that I would not mind if I had been travelling with such a fine looking, handsome young man!'

Then after a short pause she continued: 'So you think me well made?' and she glanced down proudly on her swelling breast.

'Indeed I do!' I exclaimed, quite unable to restrain myself any longer. 'I don't know when I ever saw such a lovely bosom as this, and such tempting, luscious bubbies!' and I slipped my hand into her bosom and seized a glowing globe and as I pressed it gently and squeezed the hard little nipple between my fingers, I kissed the loving upturned mouth which was presented to me.

'Ah!' she cried, 'who gave you leave to do that? Well! Exchange is no robbery and I will have something nice of yours to feel for myself, too!'

Her nimble fingers had my trousers unbuttoned, my braces undone in front too, and with a whisk of her hand she had my shirt out, and with it my burning, maddened prick, of which she took immediate and instant possession.

'Ah!' she cried. 'Ah! oh! what a beauty! How handsome! bell-topped! and so big! Isn't he just about stiff! He's like a bar of iron! and what fine big balls you've got! My beautiful man! Oh! How I would like to empty them for you! Oh! you'll have me now! Won't you? Do! Do! oh I feel that I could come so nicely if you only would!'

Would I have her? Why! Gods in Heaven! how could a mortal man brimful of health, strength, youth and energy like myself, receive such an appeal to his ears and senses, and not comply, even if the fair petitioner were not half nor quarter as beautiful as this lascivious and exquisite creature, whose hands were manipulating the most tenderly sensitive parts which man possesses. For all reply I gently pulled her on her back; she still kept a firm but voluptuous hold on her possessions as I turned up her petticoat and chemise. Gliding my burning hand over the smooth surface of her ivory thigh, I uncovered, I think, the most luscious cunt I have ever seen or felt in my life! Never had my hand reposed on so voluptuous and full a motte! Never had my finger probed a charm so full of life and so soft outside, so smooth and velvety inside, as it did now. That this most perfect cunt, and the domain around and above it, were in my possession! I was eager to get between her lovely thighs, to snatch my almost painfully strained prick from her hands and bury it up to its balls, and further, in this melting charm, but she stopped me. With her face and bosom flushed, her eyes dancing in her head, and a voice choked with the greatest excitement she cried: 'Let us put on our skins first!'

I was standing before her, my prick at an angle of at least seventy degrees, my balls and groins aching, for the most vigorous action had set in and my reservoirs had already been filled to the utmost they could hold. I felt I must either have this beautiful wild girl or burst!

'What do you mean?' I gasped.

'I'll show you! See!'

And in a moment she had, as it were, jumped out of her clothes, and stood, all naked and glowing, and radiant with a beauty fed by all that is voluptuous and erotic, before me.

In a moment – or perhaps a little longer, for I had boots and socks as well as coat, shirt and trousers to take off, but at all events, in a brace of shakes – I was as naked as she! I can shut my eyes now and there before me see this exquisitely formed creature, surely quite the equal of the beautiful Mademoiselle de Maupin, standing in all her radiant nudity before me. That form so purely perfect, so inimitably graceful, those matchless limbs! That bosom with its hills of living snow topped with rosy fire and that more than voluptuous motte, a perfect 'hill of Venus' clothed with the richest dark bushes of curly hair, sloping rapidly down, like a triangle standing on its point, until its two sides, folding in, formed the deep soft-looking inside line which proclaimed the very perfection of a goddess-like cunt. The only thing which slightly marred this perfect galaxy of beauty was the occurrence of some slight wrinkles which, like fine lines, crossed the otherwise perfect plain of her fair belly, that exquisite belly with its dimpling navel!

Gods! I rushed at this lovely creature, and in another moment I was on top of her, between her wide-opened thighs and resting on her beautiful bosom. How elastic did her beautiful bubbies feel against my chest and how soft, how inexpressibly delicious, did her cunt feel, as inch by inch I buried Johnnie in it, until my motte jammed against hers and my balls hung, or rather squeezed, against her lovely white bottom and I could get in no further. And what a woman to have! Every movement of mine brought forth an ex- clamation of delight from her! To hear her you would have imagined it was the very first time her senses had been powerfully excited from their very foundation! Her hands were never still, they promenaded over me, from the back of my head to the intimate limits of my body to which they could reach. She was simply perfect in the art of giving and receiving pleasure. Every transport of mine was returned with interest. Every mad thrust met with a corresponding buck which had the effect of taking my prick in to its extreme root! And she seemed to do nothing but come or spend! I had heard of a woman 'coming' thirteen or fourteen times during one fuck, but this woman seemed to do nothing else from beginning to end. But it was not until I had arrived at the exciting, furious, ardent, almost violent, short digs, that I knew to what an intense degree my Venus enjoyed pleasure! I thought she was in a fit! She almost screamed! She gurgled in her throat! She half crushed me in her arms, and putting her feet on my behind, she pressed me to her motte, at the end, with a power I should never have thought she possessed. Oh! the relief! the exquisite delight of that spend on my part! I inundated her, and she felt the spouting torrents of my love darting in hot quick jets and striking against the deep-set part of her almost maddened cunt! She seized my mouth with hers, and shot her tongue into it as far as she could, touching my throat, whilst her whole body from head to heel literally quivered with the tremendous excitement she was in! Never in my life had I such a fuck! Oh! why is there no better word to express what is really heaven upon earth?

The tempest past, we lay in one another's arms, tenderly gazing into one another's eyes. We were too breathless to speak at first. I could feel her belly heaving against mine, and her throbbing cunnie clasped my prick as though it were another hand, whilst her motte leaped and bounded! As I looked into that angelic face, and drank in the intense beauty of it, I believed this to be no abandoned woman but rather Venus herself whom I held thus clasped in my arms, and whose tender and voluptuous thighs encircled mine! I could have wished that she had held her peace and let me dream that I was the much desired Adonis, and she my persistent, longing Venus, and that I had at length complied with her amorous wishes and found the heaven in her arms of which, before I entered her matchless cunt, I had no notion! But my airy fancies were dispelled by her saying: 'You are a good poke and no mistake! Oh! You know how to fuck! No fellow ever fucks like that without he has been taught!'

'Yes!' I said, pressing her in my arms and kissing the ruby lips which had just spoken so coarsely, albeit truly and pointedly. 'I have been well trained! I had good lessons in my boyhood, and I have always tried to practise them as often as possible!'

'Ah!' she said, 'I thought so! You do the heel and toe better than any man I've ever had, and I've had, I dare say, many more men than you've had women!'

Frank and how!

'What do you mean by heel and toe, my pet?'

'Oh! Don't you know? You do it at any rate! and splendidly! Heel and toe is to begin each stroke at the very beginning and end it at the very end. Just give me one long stroke now!' I did so. I withdrew until my prick was all but out of her panting cunnie, and then gently but firmly drove it home, as far and as deep as I could, and then I rested again on her belly.

'There,' she cried, 'that's it! You almost pull it out, but not quite, and never stop short in your thrusts, but send your prick home, with a sharp rap of your balls against my bottom! That's what's good!'

And she appeared to smack her lips involuntarily.

At length I withdrew and my fairest nymph at once commenced a most minute examination of that part of me and its appendages which had pleased her so much. Everything was, according to her, absolutely perfect, and if I were to believe her there had not passed under her observation so noble and handsome a prick, and such beautiful well-balanced balls as I had. That she was the mistress of my balls especially pleased her! She said they were so big! She was sure they must be full of spend, and she intended, she told me, to empty them before she would consent to my leaving Nowshera!

This first sacrifice simply whetted our appetites, and still more inflamed with the minute examination of one another's charms, we fell to again, and writhed in the delicious agonies of another amorous combat! It was about two o'clock before I left her, and we had not been at any time more than ten minutes 'out of action'. The more I had of this exquisite creature, the more I longed to have her. I was fresh, young, strong, vigorous, and it was nearly two months (a long time for me) since I had last indulged in the delights of Cyprian pleasures. No wonder my Venus was pleased with me, and called my performance a perfect feast.

They say that love destroys appetite for food. Perhaps it does when it is love unrequited, but I give you my word, dear reader, that I was ravenous for my tiffin after my morning's work. I was really glad to get something to eat. What with the heat of the combat we had been through and the parching effect of the terrible hot winds blowing, I was dried up, as far as my mouth was concerned, though far from being so as regards the proceeds of my balls. I never felt so fit for woman as I did that day, and I never probably have had so much fucking with so little loss of physical force. Doubtless my steady married life with its regular hours, regular meals and regular, never excessive, sacrifices on the altar of Venus had much to do with the steady power I felt so strong in me, but over and above that was the fact of my new lady love being extraordinarily beautiful and voluptuously lascivious, and the erotic excitement raised in me, was, of course, great in proportion to the cause which gave birth to it. In spite of my hunger for food, I would certainly have remained with her on that most congenial of beds and have revelled on in her joyous arms and filled her with more of the quintessence of my manly vigour, but she told me she always slept in the afternoon, was hungry herself, and wanted my force to be expended between her lovely thighs that night for the solace of her liveliest of cunts!

Whilst the *khansama* was laying the table, I saw a note addressed to me leaning against the wall, on the mantelpiece (for in northern India the winters are sharp enough to render a fire not only pleasant but sometimes quite necessary), and taking it and opening it, wondering who the writer could be as I was perfectly unknown in this part of the world, I found it to be from my young officer friend who had quit Nowshera that morning. It ran thus:

DEAR DEVEREAUX – In the room next to yours is one of the loveliest of women and best of pokes! *Verbum sap.*!
Yours,                                                                                   J. C.

PS – Don't offer her any rupees or you will offend her mortally, but if you are inclined to have her, and I think you will be on seeing her, just tell her so and you won't have to ask twice.

Ah! Dear young chap, now I understand why you were so reticent this morning and did not like to tell me that I had a lady for my next-door neighbour! Well! Poor girl! I am afraid that you must be put down as one of the 'irregulars', although it is a shame to think ill of one who has given me the first few hours of real delight since I left home!

These thoughts naturally brought my beloved little wife into my recollection and I was somewhat staggered to feel I should so completely have forgotten her and my marital vows! But I was altogether too full of desire. Desire only just whetted and crying for more! More! I was in fact half mad with what some call lust and others love and, wife or no wife, nothing short of death would, or should, prevent my fucking that heavenly girl again and again until I really could not raise a stand. I longed for evening. I burnt for night. I ate my tiffin like a ravenous tiger, hungry for food, but thirsting for the sweet savour of the blood of a victim I knew to be within easy reach. Tiffin put away, I lit a cheroot, and began wandering round and round my room, glancing impatiently at the door which closed the communication between it and that of my supposedly now sleeping Venus, and like a Wellington I wished and prayed – not for night and Blücher but for night and her awakening! Suddenly it struck me as very funny that were some catastrophe to separate this girl and me, neither of us would be able to say who the other was! We had not exchanged names. My young friend the officer who signed his initials J. C. had not told me. I did not even know his name though he knew mine, probably from seeing it painted on my baggage. Of a surety, this lovely Venus must have a history, and I resolved to try and get her to give me her version of it, from which no doubt I could make out what was true and what was invention – for that she would tell me the exact truth I hardly expected. Oh! when would she awake?

Should I go and peep and see? By Jupiter, I would –

Throwing away the fresh cheroot I had lighted, I crept, in my stockinged feet, to her *chick*, and pulled it slightly open, and there on the bed, fast asleep, I saw my lovely enslaver. She had simply put on a petticoat and was lying on her back with her hands clasped under her shapely head, her arms bent in a charming position, opened out, showing the little growth of hair under the armpit, hair the same in tint, but not so rich in colour, as that magnificent bush I had moistened so liberally, aided by her own offerings, this morning; her bosom, with its two priceless breasts, so beautifully placed, so round, polished and firm, indeed her entire body down to her slender waist, was altogether nude! One knee, that next to me, was bent, the small graceful foot planted on the bedclothes, each gem of a toe straight and separated from its neighbour in a way that would have charmed the most fastidious sculptor that ever lived, whilst the other leg, bare from the groin downwards, was extended at full length, the lovely foot which terminated it resting against the edge of the bed, so that her thighs, those lovely voluptuous and maddening thighs, were parted! Gods! could I remain outside while so much beauty was freely displayed and I could feast my burning eyes upon it whilst its lovely owner slept?.

I went gently and noiselessly in, and passing round to the other side of the bed, so that my shadow might not fall on that exquisite form and hide the light, already softened by the *chick*, from it, I gazed in silent rapture on the beautiful girl who had made me enjoy the bliss of the Mohammedan's heaven in her voluptuous embraces that forenoon. How lovely was her sleep! Who, looking on that face so pure in all its lines, so innocent in all its expressions, could imagine that in that soul there burned the fire of an unquenchable Cytherian furnace. Who, looking on those matchless breasts, could imagine that lovers innumerable had pressed them with lascivious hand or lip, and been supported by them when they trembled in the agonies and the delight of having her? The fair broad plane of her belly was still hidden by the upper portion of her petticoats, but the fine lines, which I had noticed when she 'put on her skin', had told me the tale that perhaps more than once it had been the breeding place of little beings, who, cast in such a beauteous mould, must needs be as beautiful as their lovely mother! Who, gazing in the girlish face and looking at those virginal breasts which seemed as if they had never been disturbed by pent-up milk and whose rosebud-like nipples seemed never to have been sucked by the cherry lips of babies, could connect such charms with the pains, the cares and duties of maternity? No! surely, like the fair houris of Mohammed's paradise, she must have been created for the fulfilment of the pleasure only, not for the consequences of the kiss of love! But the wrinkles told a different tale, and I should like to examine them more closely. It would be easy to do if only they were exposed; all that I had to do was to lift, gently so as not to disturb her sleep, that part of her petticoat which still hid her there, and lay the garment back upon her waist.

With a hand trembling with excitement, I did so! Lo! my nymph was almost as naked as she was born! God of gods! What a blaze of exciting beauty! I had uncovered the sweet belly to look at the wrinkles, but my eye was captured before it lifted its gaze so high! As the bird is caught in the snare surrounding the luscious bait exposed to it, so were my eyes entangled in the meshes of that glorious forest-like bush growing on that voluptuous motte and shading a cunt the like of which for freshness, beauty and all that excites desire could not have existed in anybody but the great Mother of Love, Venus herself. It seemed to me impossible that this beauteous portal to the realms of bliss could have been invaded by so many worshippers as her speech of the morning had led me to believe. It looked far from having been hard used. What grand full lips it had. How sweetly it was placed. How pretty did the fine, dark hairs which crossed it look against the whiteness of the skin, whose infoldings formed that deep enticing line. What a perfect forest overshadowed it, and how divine were the slopes of that glorious hill, the perfect little mountain, which led down the sweet descent to the deep vale between her thighs, and ended in that glowing grotto in which love delighted to hide his blushing head and shed the hot tears of his exulting joy.

But what is that? What is that little ruby tip I see beginning to protrude, near the upper meeting of those exquisite lips which open slightly showing the pearly mouth! She moves. See! I think she must be dreaming! She slightly closes the bent leg towards that one outstretched! It is her most sensitive clitoris, as I live! See! It grows more and more! and by the gods! it actually moves in little jerks, just like an excited prick standing stiff and mad at the thoughts of hot desire!

I gazed at the tranquil face of the sleeping beauty; her lips moved and her mouth opened slightly showing the pearly teeth! Her bosom seemed to expand, her breasts to swell: they rose and fell more rapidly than they had been doing before this evident dream of love, fulfilled or about to be, invaded the soft heart of this perfect priestess of Venus! Ah! her bubbies do move! Their rosebuds swell out, they stand, each like an eager sentinel perched on the snowy tip of his own mountain, watching for the loving foe who is to invade this dreaming girl in a soft and sharp and hot encounter.

Again those thighs close on one another. Heavens! again they open to show the domain of love, excited, moving, leaping, actually leaping! That glittering ruby clitoris is evidently striving to feel the manly prick of which my charmer dreams. Why not turn the dream into a sweet and luscious reality?

I do not hesitate. I swiftly strip and in a moment I am as naked as I had been that morning, but I would like to see whether, as when I raped my cousin Emily, my second love, I could actually get into this sleeping girl before she woke to find me in her glowing cunt.

So I gently got over the thigh next to me and, with knees between hers, supported myself upon my hands, one on each side of her, while, stretching out my legs backward, I kept my eyes fixed on the sweet and burning cunnie I intended to invade. I lowered my body until I brought the head and point of my agitated and jerking prick exactly opposite its lower half, and then I manoeuvred it in!

Gods! The voluptuousness of that moment! I could see myself penetrating that seat of love and luxury! I could feel the cap fall back from the tingling head of my prick and fold behind its broad purple shoulders! For a moment I glanced at her face to see if she had perceived the gallant theft I was making of her secret jewel! No! She was asleep, but in the excitement of an erotic dream! Little by little I pressed in further and further, only withdrawing to give her more pleasure. I am nearly all in – her thick and lofty bush hides the last inch or so of my prick from my eyes, our hairs commingle, my balls nudge her and she wakes with a start!

In a moment her eyes met mine with that keen, almost wild glance, which had so impressed me when I saw her out of the *gharry*, but in a moment they changed and beamed with pleasure and affectionate caresses.

'Ah! Is it you?' she cried. 'I was dreaming of you! You darling man to wake me so sweetly!'

Some burning kisses, some close, close hugs, some little exclamations of delight, and then breast to breast, belly to belly, mouth to mouth, we play for the ninth or tenth time, I really don't know which, that same excited tune which had sounded all that morning so melodiously to our ravished senses. Heel and toe, as she called it, and other delicious movements mingled every part, then hot, quick, thrilling short digs and the torrents of two volcanoes of love burst forth simultaneously and mingled their lava floods in the hot recesses buried below the sylvan slopes of the hill of Venus.

The *ghurry* or gong, on which the non-commissioned officers of the guard sound the hour of the day in India, rang five o'clock. We had been in intense action nearly a whole hour, and my charming beauty was for the fifteenth time examining what she called my 'wonderful' prick and balls – wonderful, because the first showed no symptoms of fatigue, and the second no sign of exhaustion or depletion.

'I don't believe this can be a proper prick at all!' said she feeling it, pressing it, and kissing its impudent-looking head, first on one side and then on the other.

'Why?' I asked laughing.

'Because its always stiff as a poker – always standing!'

'That is because it admires your delicious cunt so much, my darling, and it is always in a hurry to get back into it after it has been taken out!'

'Well! I never saw one like it before! All other men that I have had always grew soft and limp after the second go if not the first – and generally took a good deal of coaxing to get to stand again, unless one gave them lots of time! But yours! I never, never, met one like it! It will give me a lot of trouble, I can see, to take all the starch out of it!'

'Oh! but I can assure you, my most lovely girl, that with ordinary women I am just as you describe the men you have known. I can assure you it must be your extraordinary beauty which has such a powerful effect upon me! Come!' I continued, opening my arms and thighs, 'Come and lie on top of me and let me kiss you to death!'

Enraptured by the lavish, but not unmerited, praise of her beauty, she threw herself, with a cry of delight, on top of me, and my prick found a sweet resting place between our respective bellies. She took and gave me the sweetest kisses, murmuring little words of love and passion like a cat purring, until I was just going to propose that she should put her thighs outside mine, and let me have her *à la* St George, when a sudden idea seemed to strike her. She raised herself on her hand and asked me: 'I say! Have you reported your arrival to the station staff officer?'

What an idea! Fancy talking of such commonplace things just as I was about to propose the most delicious thing a woman can have from a man, the very poetry of life and love! I could not but think of Mrs Shandy asking her husband, when he was in the middle of that operation which resulted in Tristram nine months later, whether he had wound up the clock.

'My dear girl!' I cried. 'Bother the station staff officer and all his reports. Come! I am hungry for another sweet go! I want this cunt!' and I slipped my hand under her belly and between her thighs, and my middle finger into her palpitating cunnie.

'No!' she said, forcefully pushing my invading hand away. 'No! Not one more fuck until you have gone and reported yourself! Ah! you don't know the regulations, I see! But I do! I have not been in India all these years without learning what they are, and Major Searle, the brigade major here, is a perfect beast and devil! You may depend upon it, he knows you are here, and he would be only too delighted to get a chance of sitting on you, and he will be able to do so if you don't report yourself before dark. Remember you got here early this morning!'

I tried to convince her that I did not care a fig for Major Searle and all the Bengal regulations to boot! I said I was on duty, the post of honour being between her lovely thighs and my Johnnie anxious to go his rounds of her darling cunnie, and I did not think I could properly quit my duty in her body to go and perform another which would do quite well enough tomorrow, by which time, in all probability, Johnnie would have come off guard and would require a rest from his labours! But it was of no use; she declared I did not know my man, she told me a great deal more, from which it was very plain that something unpleasant had occurred between herself and Major Searle, and that it really did matter very much, to herself if not to me, that I should report my arrival, and do so at once.

Never did man more unwillingly do anything than I did, when, in obedience to my lovely tyrant's commands, I dressed and walked out to find the house of the brigade major. I know other men will not believe me or give me credit when I say that I felt as if I had not had one single fuck since I left England. That my balls and groin ached and I had all the sensations of a man who is soon about to have the fuck he has most looked forward to, for which he has lived chastely and kept himself in reserve in order to enjoy more that for which he burns, I can only state as a fact, and let others believe or not as they like. Certain it is, that there are times when either from length of abstinance, or the way in which a woman affects him, a man exhibits far greater power in the fields of Venus than at other times. Let me imitate Théophile Gautier, and request my readers, male and female, to remember that special time, when the former had that splendid night, and the latter had the active, big, strong lover, the best of all she ever had as far as fucking goes.

In this state I walked over to the bungalow which was pointed out to me as that of the brigade major. I was so far fortunate that I met him just as he was going out for a walk before dinner with his smooth English terrier.

'May I ask whether you are Major Searle, the brigade major, sir?'

'Yes, I am!'

'I should have come earlier to report my arrival, sir, but I have travelled so far in dak *gharries* that I have been lying down all day, and it was so very hot when I got up that I have deferred my coming to report myself until now.'

'And who may you be, sir?'

'I am Captain Charles Devereaux, of the First East Folk Regiment of Infantry, and I am on my way to Cherat to join my battalion on promotion.'

'Oh! indeed! How do you do, Captain Devereaux! I am sorry that I did not know you at first! Will you come in or are you inclined for a little stroll? Will you come over to the mess of the 130th and let me introduce you to the officers? I am afraid you won't get to Cherat quite so soon as you may wish; every blessed machine with wheels has been ordered for a week to come, so that if I were offered *lakhs* [thousands] of rupees I could not get you a conveyance here – besides which the road from Publi to Shakkote, at the foot of the hill, is rutted and bad for anything heavier than an *ekka* [one-horse native carriage], and you would have to go up the hill to Cherat either on foot or on horseback when you got there.'

The whole manner of the man changed when he found I was an officer, and what was more a captain, i.e. just one grade below himself in rank. Had I been a subaltern, he might have kept up a higher degree of *hauteur*.

At first I thought my new acquaintance rather an agreeable man. He spoke affably and pleasantly. He asked me about my voyage, my stay in Bombay and journey up country. He spoke about the war which would practically come to an end when the Khandahar expedition had blown Ayub Khan and the conquerors of the ill-fated Marwand to the four winds of Heaven; then he returned to the subject of Nowshera, the dak bungalow and its inmates. He spoke of my well-known (as far as her most secret charms were concerned but otherwise perfectly unknown) mistress and commenced a series of very subtle questions, which, from their very guardedness, showed me that there was one person, and one circumstance, which he was approaching like a cunning cat stalking a sparrow, taking every cover as a guard as he crept up to it. I remembered the evident repugnance my new love had shown when speaking of Major Searle, and I fenced his questions until at last he asked me openly: 'Have you seen a woman, a rather lady-like person, in the bungalow?'

'I have seen one lady,' I replied, 'but there may be more than that for all I know in the house; I have not been over it, so I cannot tell if the one I have seen is the person you refer to.'

'Well!' said he, 'let me warn you that the woman I refer to is the wife or a non-commissioned officer – she is very pretty, and, I regret to say, about the most abandoned woman in India, if not in the whole world. She must be suffering from nymphomania, for she cannot see a man without she asks him to have her, and as she is really lovely to look at it is quite on the cards that if she asks a young man, fresh out from England like you, he might accept the proposition, and think that he had fallen in with a very good thing indeed – but – pardon me – let me finish – the penalty for adultery with a European woman in India is two years' imprisonment and a fine of two thousand rupees, and expulsion from India of the woman herself. Already the woman I speak of has rendered herself liable to expulsion hundreds of times; no one has as yet informed against her, but her conduct at Peshawar has been so scandalous and indecent that proceedings will most likely be taken against her. A strict watch – of which she is not aware – is being kept on her, and some unfortunate fellow, say yourself, for you are young and no doubt do not dislike the ladies – ha! ha! ha! – might find himself a victim of her lust, for lust it is and nothing else.'

'Well! Major Searle,' I replied, 'I am a married man and so I hope less liable to temptation from the path of duty than the unfortunate bachelor. Many thanks, however, for your timely warning, for of course I know that, married or single, a man may become the victim of his passions, especially when taken off his guard by a pretty woman!'

'Ah! You speak truly!' he replied, 'and I can tell you that this wretched creature is as lovely as a houri, and as lustful as the most able whore in Babylon.'

I had not lived so long a life in the worship of Venus without having seen a good deal of the hidden springs of men's minds, and I came to the conclusion that this tirade of friend Major Searle's was not altogether spoken on the side of virtue, or caution, but that it was a kind of warning, 'Don't you touch that woman, she is my preserve, and no one hunts in the forest between her thighs but myself!'

Our arrival at the mess brought the conversation to a close. Like most messes of regiments which have been some time in India, this one was composed of a nice set of generally hospitable officers, all more or less languid from a long residence in a hot and unhealthy climate. They were also too much accustomed to seeing new faces, through the men going to or returning from Afghanistan, to be very greatly interested in me, but they were cordial and kind, made me drink a couple of pegs, asked me to dinner the next night, which happened to be their guest night, and begged me to consider myself an honorary member of their mess so long as I should remain in Nowshera.

I would willingly have excused myself from accepting their kind invitation to dinner, because I was so infatuated with my charming girl in the dak bungalow that the thought of being out of reach of her brilliant charms was purgatory to me, and my senses, but Major Searle was there, and his eyes were on me, and I felt that if my surmises as to the relations between himself and my lovely woman were correct, I had better ward off any suspicion on his part by cordially accepting the invitation, which I accordingly did with all the warmth I could muster. This seemed to relieve the major, for he turned and chatted with another officer. They asked Searle whether he would come and meet me at dinner, but he said he had some work to do tomorrow evening, but if he could find time he would gladly come and rattle the balls about at a game of billiards later in the evening.

After waiting a decent time I said I would go and have a look about whilst daylight lasted, and Searle proposed to accompany me. The man bored and bothered me and I wished him in hell, for my ideas about him began to become very jealous. I thought it extremely likely that he had fucked my charmer, indeed I was certain he had, but I could not suffer him to continue to do so whilst I was in Nowshera. I meant to keep her delicious cunt for myself; she had offered it to me, and I was its present master and entitled to remain so! I knew of the law and of the fine of which he had spoken, and they did not frighten me (as like all Draconian laws, it was seldom it was put in force), but I could not hide from myself that a jealous man, especially one who was something of a brute, would be able to interfere very sadly with such a liaison as I had now on hand, and make it very uncomfortable for the woman too. I had the sense, however, to try and keep my feelings under control and be as agreeable as possible. Our walk was a very simple and short one, for it was straight from the mess to the dak bungalow, whither Searle, as if unconsciously, led the way. I offered him a peg but he declined, as he said the liquor in the bungalow was vile, which was true, and they had no ice. Neither had the mess, then. Ice was unknown beyond Jhelum. But the mess had the simple means, so easily used whilst the hot, dry winds last, of cooling liquids by placing bottles in baskets of wet straw, in a position where the wind blows upon them. The rapid evaporation soon causes the temperature of the bottles to fall very low, and ice is not wanted. I did not know or had forgotten this, but I very soon had it put into practice by the *khansama*, and that very night and every day following I had cool drinks.

We sat on the verandah until it was dark. The gallant major never referred to my connection, whose brilliant and piercing eyes I felt darting their rays at us from behind the *chick*, and whose ears I was sure were drinking in every word. Then Searle went, only referring to his important conversation with the warning words: 'Don't forget what I told you!'

'All right, major. Many thanks. Good-night.'

When it was certain that he was gone, my lady glided on to the verandah and occupied the chair that Searle had sat in.

'What has that brute been telling you about me?' she asked, her voice quivering with passion.

I gave her an exact account of all that had passed between us, and when I told her, though in much softened language, about the way he had spoken of her, she rose to her feet and walked up and down the verandah in a towering rage – like an infuriated tiger.

'The black-livered blackguard!' she exclaimed. 'Oh! truly a nice man to preach continence and virtue! I should like to know who drove his wife to the hills to become the real whore she is! Yes! she is a whore if you like! She asks money from her men! It's five hundred rupees a night to have her, it is! I never yet asked a man for a pice, and I would not take one, or a million, as payment! If I do fuck, I fuck for pleasure, and because I like my lover! But I hate a cad! and if ever there was a cad in this world, it is Major Searle,' and she spat on the floor in token of her disgust for him!

I used all my arts of gentle persuasion to try and calm her down, and at length succeeded. She told me that Searle had never had her with her permission.

I propose, but not just at present, to take you, my patient readers, into my confidence, and tell you what were the adventures of her amorous life, but before doing so I must explain how the abhorred attentions of Major Searle were put a complete end to and how Lizzie Wilson rid herself of a man who had been her plague for some years.

I had hired a native servant as my factotum when I stayed in Lahore *en route* for my destination at Cherat; a capable man he was, and one who had an eye to business, for whether he was married or not I do not know, but he brought a very fine young native woman with him and, as the reader will hear, her talents were not thrown away at Cherat – although for myself I had far finer game to follow than was afforded by Mrs Soubratie's brown skin and somewhat mellow charms. Though no more than twenty she had gone the way of almost all Indian women and her bosom had begun to flow so that her bubbies, otherwise fine and plump, hung in a despondent manner. Such defects, however, are so common that they are little heeded by the British officers or soldiers, who whet their appetite on the fine, juicy cunt, rather than on other personal graces of the dame who affords them pleasure.

Soubratie, hearing I was going to mess, got out my nice, new, clean, white mess clothes, and himself gorgeously adorned and armed with a lantern, saw me safely across the compound, ankle deep in dust, to the mess of the regiment, there to partake of the generous hospitality of the glorious 130th. Is it any use to describe the ante-room, with its swinging punkahs, chairs, tables and pictures, carpets, books, newspapers, trophies of the chase, etc., etc. Shall I tell how the staff and self-important adjutant welcomed me in a proper and decent style; how the colonel seemed to inspect me; how the other officers, whom I had not yet met, greeted me with a polite 'glad to see you' from their lips, and 'I wonder what the devil kind of a fellow you are' glance from their eyes. Most regiments are alike; when you have seen one you have seen all. The English officer is undoubtedly a fearful 'stick' and of all weary humdrum lives, mess life is the most dreary. Along with the air of *ennui* and lassitude, however, there is a wicked, devil-may-care current, which forms the pith of an officer's life, and I knew well that when a good dinner had been eaten, a good share of fairly good wine drunk, and cigars and pegs had become the evening fare, I should hear a great deal more than I was likely to at the dinner table, where propriety and stiffness more or less ruled the roost. Accordingly, I was now regaled with old stories of the war, tales of savagery and cowardly cruelty on the part of the Afghans, with an occasional growl at the generals and authorities who, it seemed, must have been incompetent to a degree or far more significant results would have accrued from the valour of the British troops. I knew how to discount all this, and listened with interest, more or less affected, to my new friends' views.

But the 'cloth off the table' brought a subject which is always congenial to the fore. Woman, lovely woman, began to be discussed. My young acquaintance J. C.'s statement as to the complete absence of women from Tommy Atkins' quarters in Afghanistan and the consequent immense demand for cunts on his return to civilisation and comfort was immediately confirmed. In those days (it has been very recently altered) the regulations obliged a certain number of native girls to be especially engaged for the services of each regiment, and these ladies of the camp accompanied their regiment wherever it marched in India, just as much a part and parcel of it as the colonel, adjutant and quartermaster. But Tommy likes variety as well as other people, and in every place where there is a bazaar or shops there are establishments for ladies of pleasure and these latter earn a good many four-anna bits which should by rights find their way into the pockets of the proper regimental whores. The recent influx of troops into Peshawar from Afghanistan had created an enormous demand for cunts, and Nowshera, Attock, even Rawalpindi, Umballa and other places had been denuded of 'polls' who gathered like birds of carrion where the carcass lay. This was a great grievance for the officers of the gallant 130th, who were almost as badly off for women as they had been when they been at Lellabad and at Lundi Kotal, at which latter place a Gurkha soldier who had got a bad case of clap from some native woman was universally spoken of as the 'Lucky Gurkha!' Not because of the clap, *bien entendre*, but because, though he suffered afterwards, he had managed to secure for himself a pleasure so uncommon, under the circumstances, that it seemed like water a thousand miles distant to a traveller lost in the great Sahara!

Once the subject of love and women was started rolling the tongues of those who had been most reticent during dinner were set wagging, and I found a most entertaining host in the fat, pudgy, double-chinned major, who seemed to take a fancy to me. He proposed that we should adjourn outside where the band of the regiment was performing some operatic airs and lively dance music, and there we sat, in those voluptuous Madras long armchairs, enjoying whatever coolness there was in the air, the sounds of the suggestive music and the brilliancy of the myriad bright stars which glittered overhead, literally like 'diamonds in the sky'.

'Searle, our brigade major, said he would come later this evening,' said the major, 'but I rather think he won't.'

'Why?' I asked.

'Because he is cunt-struck with a very pretty little woman in the dak bungalow.'

This I guessed was a shot to me.

'Indeed! Well! I hope he will succeed and get his greens! Poor chap!'

'Oh! Do you! Well! We were all saying that it was a damned shame, because we had made up our minds that you were surely in her good graces yourself, and we thought it mean of Searle to try and cut in whilst you were out! ha! ha! ha!'

'Oh! I said quietly, 'but I am a married man, major, and have just left my wife, and do not go in for that sort of thing! So, as far as I am concerned, Major Searle is welcome to the lady if he can persuade her to grant him her favours.'

'Well! But Searle is a married man himself, Devereaux!'

'Oh! I dare say! I don't mean to imply that a married man is impervious to the charms of other women because he is married. I am not straitlaced, and I dare say should be quite as liable as anybody else to have a woman who was not my wife, but you know I have not been married long enough to be tired of my wife, and I have not been long enough away from her to feel any inclination to commit adultery yet!'

'Well! Searle is married – but he's a brute! Yet I somehow pity the poor devil too! I don't know how it is, but he and his wife, a devilish fine woman, a perfect Venus in her way, don't get on altogether well; in fact she has left him!'

'Oh! my! do you say so?'

'Yes! Now mind you, Devereaux, you must not give me as your authority, but I can tell you that he treated that poor woman like hell, half killing her with a blow from the side of his hairbrush; devilish nearly smashed her skull, you know, and after that she left him, and went and set up on her own account at Ramsket.'

I am sure my dear readers are amused at my assuming the air of a thoroughly moral young husband still contented with the breasts of his spouse, as Solomon, I think it is, tells us we ought to be, but of course I was not going to amuse my new friend, or indeed any others, with tales which somehow spread so wonderfully quickly, and in rapidly widening circles, until they reach the ears of those we would least wish to hear them. Really and truly, my heart and conscience pricked me when this conversation brought to mind my beloved little Louie, and I thought of her in her lovely bed, perhaps weeping in sad silence as she prayed for the safety, welfare and quick return home of one whom she loved so dearly, who made her joyous by day and gave her rapturous fun at night, her husband, and the darling father of her angel baby girl. But alas! the spirit is willing and the flesh weak, as I have remarked before, and the weakness of the flesh exceeds the strength of the spirit all too often.

But the conversation was bearing directly on a subject which was becoming interesting to me since I had seen Searle and heard Lizzie's indignant remark that his wife was a regular whore, whose price for her charms was, however, uncommonly high. I did not mind what my fat major said about Searle's designs on Lizzie that evening, because Lizzie would have to have been a most unaccountably stupid deceiver if she had merely expressed abhorrence of him to blind me! No, I felt certain the abhorrence was real and true, and I had no fear that I should find that she had afforded him a retreat, either hospitable or the reverse, in her sweet cunt when I got home to her again.

'How do you mean "set up on her own account", major?' said I.

'Oh! hum! well! look here, bend your head a little nearer to me! I don't want to talk too loudly! Well! she is – that is, any fellow almost, who cares to give her a cool five hundred rupees, can have her.'

'What!' said I in well-affected incredulous tones, 'you want to persuade me that an officer's wife, a lady like Mrs Searle must be, has actually done such a monstrous, not to say such an idiotic thing, as not only to leave her husband, a thing I cannot understand, but to set up as a whore, and in such a place as Ramsket? Surely, major, you are mistaken! Remember! we are told to believe nothing we hear and only half of what we see!'

'I know! I know!' said he, still as calmly as if he were Moses laying down the law, 'but look here, Devereaux, you won't tell me I am a liar if I say the proof of the pudding is in the eating, and that my proof of what I say is that I, Jack Stone, have had Mrs Searle, and paid for my game! Yes, sir! Rupees five hundred did Jack Stone pay Mrs Searle for a night in Mrs Searle's bed.'

'Goodness, and you have actually – '

'I have actually fucked her, sir! and fucked her well! and a damned fine poke she is too, I can tell you, and well worth the five hundred she asks for the fun. Such a damned fine poke is she that Jack Stone, who is not a rich man but must lay up for a rainy day, has put three times five hundred rupees away in the bank of Simla, and means to lodge them some day soon in the bank of Ramsket, of which the banker and sole proprietress is Mrs Searle, the bank itself being her goloptious cunt, between her goloptious thighs. Did you mark that, young man!'

'And does Searle know this?' I asked, still incredulous.

'What? that I have had his wife?'

'No, not that you in particular have had her, but that she is had by other men, and for money paid down on the nail.'

'Know it! of course he does! It's her way of paying him off for his brutal conduct to her, to drive him nuts by writing and telling him how nicely she is dragging his name through the mud.'

'Then why does he not divorce her?' I cried indignantly, for I felt that it was monstrous for a wife, no matter what her grievance might be, to behave in such an outrageous manner.

'Ah! – but sink your voice a little lower, Devereaux, not that all this is not perfectly well known by our fellows, but about the divorce. Well, you see, if what I have heard is true, a divorce is the last thing Searle can get, or would care to ask for, no matter how much he might wish it could be managed.

'Certain little things would come out at the trial, and he might find himself not only minus a wife whom he hates, but also minus his liberty and what remains of his honour, and I don't think anyone would care to become a convict, even to rid himself of his wife!'

'What little things?' asked I, quite bitten with curiosity.

'Oh! Searle was a long time in Persia before he married, and he got the Persian taste for boys! Sodomy, you know!' And the modest major sank his voice to a whisper. 'Sodomy! he tried to get Mrs Searle to acquire a taste for it herself, but she, like a proper woman, indignantly refused to comply. It might have stopped there, but one night Searle, full of zeal and brandy, actually ravished his poor wife's – hem – hem – hem, well! – bum! and from that day she hated him – quite naturally, I think! Then, of course, she gave him the nag, nag, rough side of her tongue, until he nearly killed her, as I told you, in his passion. Then she went and set up at Ramsket.'

'But,' said I, horrified to hear such a disgusting story, so loathsome on either side, 'how is it she can demand such enormous sums for what I expect equally good returns can be got almost anywhere in India!'

'Oh! but you don't know. First of all, Mrs Searle is in society – she is, I suppose, the most beautiful woman in India, if not in all Asia!'

'In society!'

'Yes! bless you! you don't understand. Now come! You, who have seen the world at home! Have you not heard how Mrs So and So is suspected of poking, and yet you have met her every night at the best houses? Have you not seen common or fast women, who dare to do what your own wife or sister dare not, and nobody says more than that they are fast? Do you suppose you know what women actually do poke, and those who only get the credit for it? It is just the same with Mrs Searle. She lives in a pretty little bungalow, some three miles deep in the hills of Ramsket; she calls it Honey-suckle Lodge, but the funny fellows call it Cunnie Fuckle Lodge. Ha! ha! ha! and she has named the hill it is on Mount Venus; she stays there all the hot weather; in the cold weather she goes to Lucknow or Mteerut or Agra or Benares or wherever she likes. No fellow has her without an introduction. The Viceroy is damned spoony on her, and that is sufficient to keep the fashionable people quiet. People suspect, people know, but people pretend to think it impossible that the quiet lady, living in a little bungalow, away from all the world, minding her garden and her flowers, is anything but a poor, persecuted wife whose husband is a brute!'

'Oh! that is it! So to have her you must get an introduction?'

'Yes! Without that you might as well cry for the moon!'

'And how is it to be managed?' I asked out of simple curiosity, for I had no notion of having Mrs Searle, but I was interested in this curious story of which I did not know how much to believe or how much to discredit.

'Ha! ha! ha! Devereaux! I fancy you are beginning to think whether you can find five hundred rupees for yourself, eh?'

'Not a bit!' said I indignantly, 'I have no idea of such a thing, but simply asked out of curiosity!'

'Well!' said the pudgy little major, puffing his cheroot hard as it had nearly gone out, 'no harm to tell you, anyhow! You can get an introduction

from any man who has had her! I could give you one for instance. See! This
is how I had her. I had heard of Mrs Searle and had, like everybody else,
heard funny reports about her, which, like I see you do now, I only half
believed. Well! I did not then know she lived at Ramsket, but chance made
me pitch upon that place to spend three weeks leave in during the hot
weather of '75. The Viceroy and his staff were spending the time there also,
and everybody was wondering why he chose Ramsket instead of Naini Tal.
There is reason in everything and Mrs Searle was his reason, no doubt.
However, without being too long winded, I met Lord Henry Broadford, the
Assistant Military Secretary, you know. Broadford was at school with me,
and is a damned good fellow. One day, soon after I went to Ramsket, I was
standing talking to Broadford, when the finest, handsomest woman I had
ever seen walked by, and Broadford took off his hat and smiled, and she
bowed. She looked full at me as I took off my hat and, by George, sir! she
made my heart thump in my bosom, she was so lovely. When she was out of
earshot I said, "Harry, who is your friend? By God, she is a clinker and no
mistake!"

' "Don't you know," says he, "why that is the famous Mrs Searle."

' "Is it," says I. Then I asked him if he knew whether it was true she poked,
as people said.

'Broadford looked at me and grinned and said: "Would you like to know
for certain, Stone?"

'And I said, "Yes."

' "Well," says he, "the most certain way is to poke her yourself, for you
might not believe me if I told you that I was in bed with her up to five o'clock
this morning!"

' "I don't believe you, you beggar!" said I, "you are laughing at me."

' "All right!" says he, "have you five hundred rupees to lose on a bet?"

' "Well!" I hesitated; five hundred is a large sum and the subject was not
worth it.

'Seeing me hesitate, he said, "Well, would you give five hundred rupees to
have Mrs Searle yourself, Jack?"

' "Yes," said I, plump as could be.

' "Then come along with me," said Broadford.

'Well, we went to my hotel, and there Broadford made me write a
cheque, and get five one-hundred-rupee notes from the native banker, new
and crisp, in exchange. Then he made me write a letter addressed to Mrs
Searle, in which I asked her might I come and take dinner with her on such
and such a day? naming the day. I was more than half afraid the fellow was
humbugging me, but he pulled out a case from his pocket, and showed me a
lovely photo in it of a stark-naked lady, cunt and all complete, and, says he,
"Mrs Searle gives one of these to each of her lovers, and she gave me this this
morning; see, her name, date and the number of times I had her last night!"
Well, I looked at the photo, and sure enough there was no mistaking it was

the lady I had just seen, besides which I remembered having seen photos of her taken in the plains.

'By God! sir! the sight of such lovely charms settled my hash. I told Broadford that he would have to bear the brunt if anything went wrong. He swore all would be right, and after I had signed my name to the note to Mrs Searle, he added his initials and "WTBF?"

' "What does that mean?" I asked.

' " 'Will there be fuck?' of course!" Well, this done, I put the five good crisp notes in the letter, and we went to the post office, registered it, and then I began to think I had been made a fool of. But it was all right. The day afterwards I got a registered letter. It was from Mrs Searle. In it were my five notes. She said she was very sorry but that she did not think she could have the pleasure of my company at dinner for another ten days, would I write again in about a week's time, if that would suit me, and she would be sure not to disappoint me. I rushed off, found Broadford, and nearly had a fit of apoplexy from excitement. By his advice I waited some eight days, then sent another letter, and again enclosed the notes, and I added after my own signature, WTBF? Next came a letter by hand. It said, "My dear Jack", this time. It invited me to dine the next evening at eight and ended with "Matilda Searle. TWBF."

'And did you go?'

'Oh! What a question! Of course I did. By God, sir! I was simply bursting. Even now I can hardly tell my story with any degree of quiet! Well, I went; I was received by her in an awfully pretty little drawing room, most beautifully furnished and bristling with knick-knacks, mirrors, pictures and everything that can make a room handsome and elegant. The floor was covered with carpet into which one's feet sank as one walked on it. Mrs Searle was sitting reading when I arrived, and as soon as the bearer had gone out of the room she came and took my hand, shook it, and then kissed me! I was so excited; I felt such a sense of false shame, that at first I was like a stuck pig! But she quickly put me at my ease, sat on the sofa, made me sit next to her, jammed her knee against mine and, whilst asking me where, how and when I had known Lord Henry Broadford, showed off her splendid shoulders and magnificent bosom. I had been awfully randy on my way there, I had been randy all the days I had been waiting for her, but I was so knocked over by the elegance I saw on my first arrival that I declare, if the truth were told, I felt inclined to run away. But little by little, as I got to see the woman I was going to have, as I began to hear her talk as if we were quite old chums, and at her touch – the contact of her hand on mine, to say nothing of the kisses which from time to time she gave me – I began to pluck up courage. So by way of showing her I was no fool but expected something, I offered to put my hand on her bosom, and take hold of one of her glorious bubbies, of which I saw nearly half over her dress. But she laughed and said it was not time for that yet, that when we had dined, and I had had my smoke, we would go to bed, where I should find her all I could wish for, and where I should have the fullest liberty, so long as I did not exceed the bounds which every honest man observed who had a woman. Well! I kissed her and begged her pardon. I had a rosebud in my buttonhole, and she took it out and said, "See, I place your rose where you shall be!" and she put it between her bubbies and said, "there it is, a rose among the lilies, but that is all of you I can allow at present to be there." Well, sir! we had a splendid dinner. In spite of my impatience I did justice to a rattling good feed, and afterwards she made me smoke a cigar, and when it was nearly done she said she would go and undress, and that when I heard a little bell ring, I was to go to her bedroom which she had already pointed out to me. Soon I heard the bell and I went. Oh! I was delighted! By God, sir! I have had many fine women, but I never saw one who was a patch on Mrs Searle when undressed. She had on a quite transparent kind of nightgown, which covered her from neck to heels. It had no sleeves, and her arms were something splendid. Her bubbies looked more enticing covered with this transparent stuff, than when I saw them bare. Her nipples looked like strawberries, red and luscious. I would have been able to see her cunt, but all the whole of the way, from her chin to her feet, there was a broad rose-coloured ribbon, which fell exactly over it, so that I could only see the fringe of hair on either side where it passed over her bush. I declare, Devereaux, I cannot describe the night I had with her, for it would drive you wild and you would be trying to slip into that woman at the dak bungalow, and it would never do, you being, as you say, a married man, but I never – never – never had such a glorious fucking in my life. It is true I was five years younger than I am now, and as I keep a pretty little piece of brown meat, and have my regular greens twice a week, I might not be able to do as good a turn now, as I did then, but I had that woman eight solid times, sir, seven times before I went to sleep, and once in the morning. She said herself that she did not expect it of me at first sight, as she said I was too fat, and fat men were bad pokes as a rule. When I went away after breakfast she gave me a case like the one Broadford had shown me, and told me not to open it until I got home, and she told me she relied on me not to show it to anyone, unless I thought them a fit fellow for her to have. I'll show it to you now! Ha! Bearer! *Kitmutgar! koi, hai!* and the excited major shouted to the servants, one of whom came. By his orders the major's bearer brought a little writing dispatch-box, and from this he took a small case, some six inches by four in size, and then, giving me a nudge, he walked to the ante-room of the mess, which was deserted, and showed me a very well-executed photo of a perfectly naked woman. On the back of the photo was written: *From M. Searle to Jack Stone – 15 June 1875 – 8.*

'Now!' said the major, 'any time you would like to have that woman, you drop me a line and I will give you the necessary introduction.'

I thanked him heartily, but I must say I did not feel tempted to give five hundred rupees for the favours of any woman, just then, and mentally I made comparisons between my Lizzie and Mrs Searle which were not favourable to the latter, though, according to the photo, she was certainly a fine woman.

Then, after smoking another cigar, and drinking a couple more pegs and talking Mrs Searle and fuck generally, I left to go home, and I looked forward to returning to Lizzie and getting rid of some of the hot blood which was running in a desperately excited manner through my throbbing veins, for the little major's conversation had been the reverse of cooling.

It was very nearly midnight when I reached the bungalow and there was not a light in the place. The stars had shown in the road fairly well, but the verandah and rooms, on my side at least, were pitch dark. I imagined that Lizzie must have grown tired of waiting up for me and taken the opportunity of getting a good sleep before I came home, since it was highly likely that, after a good mess dinner and quantities of generous wine, I would be rather lively and keen and put her into that condition too.

Full of this idea, and determined if possible to give her a surprise sweet-awakening by getting into her whilst she slept, I stole on tiptoe towards my room, to undress there and then join her in her 'naked bed'. But as I crossed the verandah something white gleamed on one side and, on looking, I saw it was Lizzie, sitting in my easy chair, apparently, from her position, asleep. I stole up behind her and bending over her I kissed her soft cheek, at the same time stealing my hand into her glorious bosom, and caressing her warm, swelling, elastic bubbies, which always gave me such delight to feel. Oh! What nice things good bubbies are to feel!

'Ah! is that you, Charlie, dear! I must have been half asleep,' she said.

'Yes! darling!' I said softly, still pressing the delightful globes in my hand, one after the other, and kissing the sweet mouth turned up towards me.

Lizzie seemed to enjoy my caresses, for she merely returned my kisses and patted my face lightly with her hand. I found that although she was still dressed, her clothes were loose on her, and that I could pass my hand between the band and her waist, and her beautiful skin felt so soft, so satiny, so smooth, it delighted me as though I had never felt it before. From her bosom I descended until I reached the pretty plain of her lovely belly and here I let my roving hand wander from side to side as it gradually crept lower and lower until it reached the upper fringe of the glorious bush which so splendidly adorned her dome-like motte, and then I threaded my way through this pathless forest until I reached the spot where the infold formed the precious and voluptuous deep line of her delicious cunt. I passed my middle finger in the groove, just tipping the awakened and slippery little clitoris, until I reached the entrance to the rich depths I sought for.

Lizzie said nothing; my left hand, which was over the bosom, felt the breast rise a little more tumultuously, and my arm bore a slightly increased strain as she leaned her head back upon it, but that was all. It was so dreamy, so exquisite, that I stood in that position, caressing the warm moist cunt, kissing the cherry lips with little caresses of mine, as if I were a dove billing its mate.

Suddenly a change seemed to come over me. I was no longer in India; it was no longer Lizzie whose charms I was master of, but my own beloved little beautiful wife. I remembered how, on the third night of our blissful and heavenly honeymoon, she had preceded me to bed; how it was the month of July, and the night was warm and balmy, the scent of the blossoming lime trees filling the air with its sweet aroma. I had given my Louie ten minutes to undress and perform those necessary little acts to make her comfortable for the night, which no young married woman likes to do in the presence of her husband, and then I had gone up to follow her into the bed, my beautiful heaven, in which I expected to find her, a luscious feast for my still ardent and excited and quite uncloyed desire. But when I went to the room she was still dressed. She was seated at the open window, reclining back into her chair. There were no candles. The stars were shining brightly but softly; the heavy masses of foliage on the trees loomed dark against the skies, and there was silence outside, except the occasional rustling of the leaves as the amorous zephyrs kissed the heads of the trees they loved, and the poetry of the moment filled me with a degree of tenderness and love I had not experienced in a similar manner since Louie and I had been made one at God's holy altar. Like Lizzie, she had only half turned to accept my kisses, with a little question as to whether it was me – as though it could be anyone else! – as I had glided my happy hand into her so lately virgin bosom, and caressed the swelling globes which it had so delighted me on my wedding night to find did exist in truth and reality, beautiful, round, firm, polished, elastic and rose-crowned; for Louie had been so jealous of those exquisite beauties, that even when I had seen her dressed for the evening, in her low-necked gown, not one line of the lovely hemispheres did she show, and I had to imagine beauties to exist where my fancy painted them; and I had prayed I might find she really had sweet bubbies; for alas! how often is man deceived in his expectations as to the physique of his beloved bride. Neither of us spoke; we were too happy; and over her beautiful bosom my wanton hand had descended, until, finding her waistband loosened, it had explored the sweet pastures of silvery belly and crossed the rough surface of the mount of Venus; as my finger pressed in Cupid's furrow, the lovely little clitoris, ever on the watch, had sprung up to salute it with a moist and eager kiss; a thrill, which I could feel, passed over my Louie's form, and as she felt the strong middle finger bury itself in the hot depths of her velvety cunt, she had pressed my face to her burning cheeks, and murmured, 'My man! Oh! my beloved man!'

Full of overflowing sentiment, which this entrancing quiet and this voluptuous scene of love and passion had inspired me with, I quite forgot where I was, and whom I was caressing. I kissed Lizzie rapturously and I murmured in a voice which must have quivered with deep emotion, 'Oh! my darling! my own, own, darling.'

Lizzie started. She disengaged my hands and, standing up, she exclaimed in a voice which sounded strange to me, so different was it from her ordinary tone, 'Charlie! Charlie! Don't speak to me like that! Don't! there's a good fellow!'

'Oh! Lizzie! what have I done?' I said in alarm.

'Oh! you must not speak to me like that! You know you don't love me, Charlie dear. You don't love me like you do your wife, and if you did it would only make me unhappy. Oh! Charlie! the one thing which would take away the only pleasure I have in life, would be to know that some man really and truly loved me. I could not leave my husband and live with him, and I must have a man as often as I can. You don't understand. When a woman has led the life I have she can't steady down unless some illness puts an end to all feeling of desire in her. She must go on as she is till death, or at least till decay of all her bodily powers. Confess now, it was not Lizzie Wilson you were speaking to but your wife!'

'Well, Lizzie, dearest!' I said, quite thunderstruck with her vehemence and her outcry against love, 'I won't tell you a lie. I did for the moment forget where I was. It was this way – but sit down darling – and I will tell you truly.' She did so, and still standing over her, and again possessing myself of the sweet charms between her thighs, to which she admitted me full rights as a true friend but not as an earnest and passionate lover, I told her about the scene of which I have given my readers a faint notion, as regards the delicious commingling of the adoration of the heart and the worship of the senses.

When I had finished Lizzie heaved a prodigious sigh and said: 'Charlie! Take my advice and don't be too long sending home for that true wife of yours! She will keep you from harm out here, and it is not right, it would be a cruel shame to condemn her to pass the life of a nun whilst you are amusing yourself in India, fucking to your heart's content women who do not deserve such delight. For, mark my words, you are not the kind of man to go without women, nor will you find a station where there are not women, pretty and fine, who will not leave you alone – they will be as eager to have you as you will be to have them. Yes! believe me, if ever a man was formed to strike a woman's fancy it is you. Send for your wife, for otherwise some mischief will be brewed, and you may be made to repent that you left her at home.'

These words, spoken with great earnestness, struck me very forcibly. It seemed also so like Satan rebuking sin that I could hardly help feeling amused. After a pause of a second or two, during which I gently stroked the sweet cunt under my hand, I said: 'All right, Lizzie! I believe you are quite right! I will send for my wife as soon as you advise, but come in, there's a darling, and let us enjoy the fleeting hour. It seems like ages since I last had my prick in this sweetest, softest, juiciest little cunt of yours!'

To this she replied, 'Searle has been here tonight.'

My goodness! All my blood ran cold. I felt now as if my Louie, in answer to my prayer to come to bed, so that I might enjoy her loveliness, told me, 'Too late, my dear, So and So has just been fucking me and I'm not inclined for any more!'

'Searle!' I exclaimed, snatching my hand away from under her clothes. 'Searle! Oh! Lizzie! and did you let him have you?'

'I did not say that he had me, Charlie, so you need not get into a fit of jealousy, you silly boy! No! If there is one man in the world to whom I would forever say no, it is Searle; but he was here all the same.'

I breathed. Somehow Lizzie had grown dear to me, she had been so nice, such a splendid fuck, and so tender towards me in spite of her disclaimer of love.

'What did he want, Lizzie?'

'What you say you do now, Charlie! But oh! we had such a row! I declare it has given me quite a headache! Oh! Searle! you . . . cursed beast!'

'And what did he do or say Lizzie! Tell me!'

'Well, you had hardly got across the road before Searle, who had apparently been watching for you to go, sneaked on to the verandah around the corner, and asked if I had got his note. Now I had received a note from him which I had kept to myself, and which I had not shown you, dear, for I did not want to make you jealous; a fine production it is, too, and a very useful one for me, I can tell you. I think he must have been either drunk or mad when he wrote it, for he could not have written a more damning piece of evidence against himself if he had tried to do it in his sober senses. Oh! Mrs Searle would give a cartful of her rupees to have it, for she could then get the divorce she longs for. Plenty of good fellows are ready to marry her if she could get divorced, and I know she has often said she would be glad to give up her present life; but Searle knows this, and his only revenge against her is to behave so prudently as not to give her any chance. If ever he has a woman it is so on the sly that no one knows it. Well, he has written down in black and white that he has had me – and since Mrs Searle left him, too. Let's light a candle and I'll show you the letter!'

Full of curiosity and rather astonished to find how the truth comes out, for I had certainly understood Lizzie to say that Searle had never had her, nor ever should have her by her permission, I went for my candle and lit it. Lizzie then took the precious letter out of her pocket and gave it to me to read.

It commenced with prayers and entreaties to let him come and have her whilst I was at mess. It said that he knew well that I did nothing all day and night but fuck her, that by this time she must be tired of me and at least that a little of her accustomed change of diet would be agreeable. From prayers, it went to using threats. Her husband's regiment was at Peshawar, now with a newly appointed colonel who was death on adultery and fornication, and he had given out that the first time he found any of it going on amongst the married women of his regiment, he would set the penal laws on the subject in force and that he (Searle) had plenty of evidence which would put me (Devereaux), into prison and send her out of the country branded as an unchaste woman, a whore and an adulteress, and that unless she admitted him to her embraces he would help the colonel to make good his word. Then came more prayers and more earnest entreaties – then offers of a thousand rupees (twice what his own wife charged) – jewellery, anything, if she would but consent, and then in a postscript, he boasted that he had already fucked her, at Agra, on an occasion when, stunned by a fall from an overthrown *gharry*, she had been carried into his bungalow, and seeing who she was, and determined not to lose the precious opportunity, he had raped her in her unconscious state, and enjoyed the 'wealth of her voluptuous cunt' – he actually used these last words.

'The intense blackguard,' I exclaimed, moved to great wrath by the reading of this precious epistle.

'You may say so, Charlie! But now hear what the brute did. At first he asked had I got his letter. I said yes. Then he asked me in a wheedling tone would I consent and let him have me. I said not for all the thousand rupees in India, that he was too loathsome a brute for me to touch with the end of a barge-pole, let alone take in my arms. Then he began to threaten me with our new colonel, saying that I could not get away from here now unless he, Searle, gave me an order for a *gharry*, that everything like a cart with wheels was engaged for the next ten days, and that long before that time was over the regiment would be on the march from Peshawar to Muttra, and that the colonel, finding me here instead of at Muttra, where he had ordered me to go, would be furious, and he, Searle, would take the opportunity then of telling him why I stopped at Nowshera, namely, to have three separate officers who stayed here, two on their way down country, and one on his way to join his battalion at Cherat, and he would tell who these officers were, and it would go hard on them, each of them would lose two thousand rupees or get two years' imprisonment, and "then they will have good reason to curse you for being a damned little bitch, for why should you condemn them to these fines and punishment when by letting me have you for an hour or two you can prevent any harm arising, and I will keep my word if you don't . . . " and he got more and more angry.

'I told him I would see him damned before I would let him touch me, and I dared him to report me, or you or the others, and I reminded him of what he had said in his letter, and how completely I would cover myself, and you, and others by it, and I advised him to go away quietly or I would call the *khansama*. That put him in as complete a passion as ever I saw a man. He rushed at me and swore he would have me. I put myself like a shot behind a chair. He stopped for a moment, unbuttoned his trousers, pulled out his prick, which was in a furious state, and then rushed at me again. I shouted for the *khansama*, but Searle did not mind. He seized me around the waist, and lifted me off the floor, and ran with me into my room, dashing the *chick* down as he lunged into it. But I was not going to be ravished without making the best defence I could. I got my ten nails well into his cheeks, and scrawned them down as hard as I could. I could see and feel the blood spurting. Searle yelled and cursed, swore and called me the most awful, dreadful names. I gave him as good a clawing as I could, but he got me down on the bed, pulled my petticoats up to his face, and lay on top of me with all his weight, trying to get his knees between mine. But I kept my thighs locked hard; although he pounded with his knees on my thighs, and nearly choked me with his hand on my throat, he could not get between them. I could feel the tip of his prick banging against my motte like a bar of iron, but he never once got it nearer my cunt than that. At last, finding that he could not manage to make me open my legs to him that way, he began to put his hand between my thighs, and to pinch me most frightfully. Oh! he gave me dreadful pinches. I am sure I am all black and blue, but his weight was off me now, I was able to scream; and I yelled. I called out murder! murder! help! help! as loud as I could, and at the same time I tried to get hold of his balls, so as to crush them if I could, but he managed to keep them out of my reach, whilst he pinched, scratched and beat my thighs as though he would tear them to pieces. But before my fast failing strength left me, help came. Two young civilians came in today from Peshawar, whilst you were dressing for the mess, and got a room on the other side of the bungalow. They at last heard my screams, and came running to see what was the matter. When Searle saw them he ordered them out of the room, saying that I was his wife, and that he had a right to treat me as he liked; but I tried to get out of his clutches, and I implored the young men to save me, and I said that Searle was not my husband and was trying to rape me. The young men then ordered him off my bed, and as he did not obey, one of them pulled him off. Then Searle went for him, for he was blind mad with rage and passion, but the young man was pretty cool, and he gave Searle a most dreadful blow in the face with his fist – oh! I was so delighted to hear it – it made him stagger and the blood spurt from his nose. But Searle seemed really like a lunatic. He rushed again at the young man, and hit him several nasty blows, so that the second one came to his friend's assistance. I urged the two on and Searle got a thrashing, I can tell you! Still he would not quit. By this time the *khansama*, the principal coolies, your servant Soubratie and everyone belonging to the bungalow had come. I could not help continuing to scream. Everybody went for Searle, and at last he was turned out of the house yelling and fighting like a wild beast. Some soldiers came running off the road, and at first, seeing who Searle was, wanted to help him, but the young men told them what he had done, and apparently they don't love Searle at the barracks, for these men joined in beating him, and upon my word I began to get frightened. I thought they would kill him between them all. Oh! the row was tremendous. Presently down came the picket from the barracks; the soldiers seeing them ran away. Searle was lying on the ground, a crowd around him; some men had torches alight, and the *khansama* had got a lantern, and you never saw such a group as they formed. The young men who had helped to save me from being ravished explained the whole matter to the NCO of the picket, and as Searle's trousers were open, and his prick showing, though no longer stiff and standing, he understood the whole thing. Searle, though hardly able to breathe, wanted them to take the young men prisoner, but the NCO begged them to go away, and persuaded him to let himself be carried home, for he could not walk. Oh! Charlie! it made me so sick and ill! I don't know how I have been able to tell you so much – my head is splitting, and I feel all pounded to death by that brute.'

I leave my readers to appreciate the state of anger and disgust toward Searle which this vivid narrative of poor Lizzie's produced. Oh! I had come home hoping for such a sweet night of delightful fucking, but it was plain that that was out of the question, and indeed, all desire, other than for vengeance on Searle, had gone out of my head. Lizzie looked very ill, when I came to examine her by the light of the candle, and I begged her to go to bed.

'Yes, dear!' she said. 'It is the best place for me, but oh! Charlie dear! I am afraid I cannot have you tonight! Poor boy! I am sure you came home expecting to have some grand fucking, and I am so grieved to disappoint you, but I feel too sick!'

'You poor darling girl!' I cried. 'I had hoped, as you say, to have some more delicious fucks with you tonight, but of course it cannot come off now. Come to bed and let me help you to undress.'

She did as I asked her. I undressed her and was shocked to find the state she was in. Her throat was bruised a little but her poor thighs were one mass of contusions, all scored by the fingernails of the monster who had attacked her. I kissed them, 'to make them well', and poor Lizzie smiled faintly and kissed me, and then lay down and begged me to leave her alone. But hardly had she put her head on the pillow than she called out that she was going to be sick.

'Oh! Charlie! Help me to my bathroom!'

But I ran and got her a *chillumchee* [brass basin] and brought it to her, and she, poor creature, was deadly sick. I held her burning forehead in my hands and did all I could to comfort her, and to assist, and at last, completely exhausted, she sank back and her whole appearance alarmed me. When I came home she was fairly cool, but now she was the colour of a penny, and her skin was hot, parched and burning. I guessed she had a fever and the suddenness of the attack alarmed me. All that night I tended her, keeping her well covered up to induce perspiration, and from time to time gave her water to drink for which she moaned. Nobody who has not watched a sickbed under circumstances somewhat similar can tell how tedious, how weary, such a watch is, especially when, as in my case, the watcher is ignorant of what he ought to do, and has to go by instinct, as it were. At length, just as the morning began to break, Lizzie seemed to fall into a sound sleep. Her breathing was more regular and easy, her colour was more natural, and – blessed be heaven – her skin was again cool and moist. It was evident that the strength of the attack had passed.

Satisfied that Lizzie was really in a healthful sleep, I got myself a cool peg, and then going back to the bedside I sat down in my chair, leaned my head against her pillow and fell into a sound sleep myself. How long I slept I do not know but I was at length awakened by Soubratie, who touched me and murmured that sickening: 'Sa–hib! S–a–a–hib!' in my ear with which your native servant always rouses you.

'What is it?' said I, raising my heavy head.

'Major Stone, sahib! Outside on verandah! Wanting see master!' replied Soubratie who spoke English like a native.

'Major Stone! Oh! yes! all right! Tell him I will be with him in a moment, Soubratie.'

'Yes, sahib!'

I felt desperately tired and not in a pleasant humour at having my much needed rest broken. However, after a yawn or two, and an anxious glance at poor Lizzie, who seemed to have quite regained her ordinary appearance and to be having a really sound and refreshing sleep, I tightened the strings of my pyjamas, and went on to the verandah, where I heard the footsteps of my friend the major as he moved about somewhat impatiently. Seeing me come from Lizzie's room in sleeping costume, he put up his hands in mock deprecation and said, *sotte voce*: 'Oh! Oh–h–h! Captain Devereaux! Oh–h–h!' and he put on such a comical look I could not help smiling.

'Not so fast, major, please! Appearances may be against me, but I think I can give a satisfactory explanation. The lady who lives in that room was most dreadfully ill last night and I, out of pure charity, have been nursing her!'

'In your nightshirt and pyjamas, exactly! I expect she required a little cordial administered by an enema, only in front instead of behind, and required your services and elixir! Oh! Devereaux! it won't do, my boy, but Jack Stone is not the man to preach; still he would like his friends to be frank with him, so, Devereaux, you may as well tell the truth and confess that, full of my description of Mrs Searle, and the splendid night I had between her plump white thighs, you came home and spent, I hope, as good a night with the fair lady in there! Confess now!'

'Quite wrong, major, I can assure you! I plead guilty to having been much moved and stirred by your voluptuous narrative, and as human nature is frail, I dare say might have spent such a night as you believe, only that the lady was, as I said, fearfully ill, and all owing to that blackguardly brute Searle, too!'

'Ah!' said the major, 'that is just what I have come to enquire about. Look here, Devereaux, there is a devil of a row on. Searle was brought home last night between seven and eight o'clock, whilst we were at mess, with five or six ribs broken, his right leg broken above the ankle, his nose smashed flat, his front teeth driven down his throat, and battered, cut and bruised all over. In fact, the doctor hardly expects him to pull through, he is so fearfully weak, and so completely smashed to bits. The corporal of the picket reports that hearing a disturbance going on in the dak bungalow, he doubled his men down and caught sight of two men of the 130th running away, and hearing loud voices in the bungalow compound, he found a crowd of natives and two civilians, Europeans, standing round the brigade major, who was lying on the ground, all doubled up, and from what he could gather there was a woman at the bottom of it, but he could give no clear account of what had happened, or how it had happened, or anything. Well, the colonel is, of course, much put about. We none of us love Searle, who is a sulky brute, if a good officer, but a brigade major can't be half killed without a row being made about it, so he has sent me to try and find out all about it and as I guessed you would very likely have heard something, I came first to you.'

I then gave the gallant major a succinct account of the whole business, as told me by Lizzie. I had to undergo some unmerciful chaffing from Stone about her, and found it impossible to hide from him the truth about my relations with her. But he promised to be mum, and, as he said, there was no need for my name to be mentioned at all in the business, at all events at present, and perhaps not at all, as I was not at the bungalow when Searle was there but at the mess, luckily for me!

Armed with his news, and quite interested how it was that Lizzie should have had such violent ill usage, and should have passed through such a terrible scene, he returned to make his report to his colonel, and about four o'clock he sent me a note, or chit as it is called in India, to say that the colonel had agreed to hush the whole matter up, and simply report Major Searle on the sick list, and him – Jack Stone – acting station staff officer. He went on by saying that the sooner the parties were out of Nowshera the better, and he advised me to prepare Lizzie for a start; he would order a dak *gharry* for her as soon as one could be got, and a couple of *ekkas* for me, the *ekka* being the only wheeled vehicle which could run on such a road as there was from Publi to Shakkote.

Meanwhile, after Stone had gone, I returned to my post beside poor Lizzie. I watched her for a short time and presently she woke; seeing me still there, and neither shaven nor dressed, she rightly concluded that I had not been to bed all night.

'Oh! Charlie! how kind! how good of you! How can I ever repay you!'

'By getting well as quick as you can, my Lizzie. And then – '

'Ah! Won't I just! If I was kind before I will be doubly kind now! But I am all right! I had a bad go of fever last night, and my poor legs are stiff and sore, but I am well! If I only had some quinine, now would be the time to take it, just to keep off a second attack of fever.'

I had purchased a bottle of this invaluable powder at Bombay, and I ran and got it, and gave her the quantity she said would be right, in a glass of water.

'There,' she said, having made a wry face as the bitter dose ran down her throat, 'now something to eat, for I feel faint for want of food and I am hungry. You see I was bad, my Charlie, but I think it was more fright than anything else.'

I had, when I left her to go and get my peg that morning and before I went to sleep, called Soubratie and ordered him to prepare and have ready whenever it might be called for, some strong beef tea, and this I had brought, hot and refreshing, to Lizzie, who was really moved at this additional proof of my care and devotion to her.

'Oh! Charlie! If all men were only like you!' she exclaimed, and the soft tears of gratitude rolled down her lovely cheeks. I kissed them off and she put my hand on one of her swelling breasts, saying: 'There! my Charlie! I would let you have me this morning if I could, but I feel too weak for that. I dare say when I have had another good sleep I shall be better, and then darling, we will fuck, won't we!'

I laughed and said we would and put her hand, in my turn, on my bunch of charms, and showed her how greatly fatigue and watching had reduced the strength and vigour of what the most ardent battles between her shapely thighs had failed to subdue. Poor Lizzie! She looked so disappointed! But as her little hand toyed with my limp prick and played with my relaxed balls, fresh life came, and to her joy she succeeded in raising a perfect standard, to be planted as soon as possible in the keeping of her fort. But both of us were wearied and tired out, and I told her she should go to sleep, and that I would go to my own bed and sleep too, for I was dead tired, and with more sweet kisses and caresses she turned on her side and was soon asleep. I then left her and going to my own room threw myself on my much needed couch, in the cool breeze of the swinging punkah, and was soon sound asleep.

Whilst Lizzie and I are thus *hors de combat*, it will, I think, be a good time to tell my dear readers her early history, and I will endeavour to keep her words as nearly as possible. So, gentle readers, imagine that Lizzie and I are either seated on the verandah, after our dinner, or are in or rather on the bed together, whilst she tells her artless tale, certain portions of which she and I illustrated by very suggestive action when either her memory added fuel to the amorous passion which made her blood boil or my wanton fancy stirred all the man in me.

'Well, Charlie, I was born and bred in Canterbury. My earliest recollections are all associated with that dear old place, and for the first thirteen years of my life I never left it. My mother is the only parent I can remember. My mother was a dressmaker by trade and custom was good. She never seemed in want of money, whether she had work or not; on the other hand, though we had an honest plenty in our house, there were no luxuries, nothing for mere show, except perhaps in one of the rooms kept for ladies to try their dresses on, where she had some little knick-knacks for appearance's sake. As a child I used to think that a splendid room, and wonder if anyone else had as fine things as my mother had! So you must understand we had a sunny, warm house, good food, good plain clothes, good beds, in fact, everything which was required for real comfort, but nothing superfluous.

'My mother kept no servant, that is, no one actually lived in the house as such; an old charwoman came every morning and did what scrubbing and cleaning was required. My mother and I did light dusting, made our beds, etc., and cooked our simple meals. Until I was twelve years old I went to school, and as I was pretty quick, I learnt perhaps more there than girls usually do. And there, too, I formed acquaintances among the other girls, and as our conversations were not always about lessons and sums, apples or lollipops, I gathered some information about the relations of the sexes, about lovers and their ways, which I did not repeat to my mother. However, what I did learn in this way in no respect had any effect upon me or my morals. I knew I had a little cunnie, and that I should have babies one of these days, and that I should have regular monthly illnesses. I believed that I should marry, and when I did, I believed that my husband would put his 'thing' into my 'little thing' and that in time I should have a child, as I saw all married women do, but although girls used to talk about these matters, there was never any reference to the vast delight to be found in fucking. We were all too young to know more than something vague and undefined. But before I was thirteen my mother withdrew me from school, no only because I was growing very tall for my age, but because my bosom began to form, and two lovely little doves of breasts to push out on either side of my chest. With what pride and pleasure did I see them grow. Even my mother, when she bathed me regularly every Saturday in a tub before I went to bed, remarked on them, and said to me one day, "Lizzie, you will have a perfect bosom. I don't remember ever seeing prettier or better placed breasts, or any which looked to be so quick growing." And I would notice her eye give a quick look down at my cunnie, and I guessed she was looking to see if my hair there was beginning to sprout. But my bubbies were a good bit grown before any came. However, the hair and my menses came almost together. First there was a profusion of little black-looking points all over what you call my motte, Charlie, and hairs grew from them very rapidly, so quickly indeed that by the day I was thirteen I had quite a nice bush which I could twine round my finger. My cunnie, too, underwent a marked change. It seemed to grow fatter and become more formed. I can hardly explain, but I am sure you must have noticed similar changes in your prick and balls when your bush began to grow. You may say, then, that as far as outward appearances were concerned, I was quite a woman at thirteen and I had a fair amount of flesh on my bones, a lovely bosom, a nice waist, fine swelling hips, good thighs and very pretty feet and ankles. I was too well formed altogether for short dresses, and my mother made me some long ones, in which I used to admire myself in the tall glass in the trying-on room. Still although I certainly did admire myself, it never entered my head to court the admiration of men. I had not, as yet, felt the least spark of desire, and if, as I dare say she did, my mother watched to see any signs of coquetry or flirting in me, she saw none, for there were none to be seen. However, I was much nearer the realisation of the hidden stores of pleasure I had within me, than either she or I was aware of.

At the back of our house was a longish bit of garden, say something like fifty or sixty feet long, by thirty or forty feet wide. This garden was my mother's pride, for she raised early potatoes, and all kinds of vegetables in it for our use, besides plenty of pretty and sweet flowers, so that we always had nice vegetables for dinner, and nosegays for our table and mantelpiece. At the end of the garden was a lane on the side of which was a row of stables where the officers of the cavalry used to keep their private horses. I used to be very fond of leaning against our little wicket to see those beautiful horses, all bridled and saddled, being taken to their masters for exercise. Sometimes the officers themselves came to have a look at the stables, but they paid no attention to me, so I was quite accustomed to looking on without being spoken to. About August, however, when I was a little more than three months older than thirteen, some stables, which had been empty, were taken by an officer who had three beautiful horses. I was curious to see who this officer was, for he was new, and so one evening I was watching for him, hoping he would come, when I saw a tall, slight, but a fine and very handsome young officer in undress uniform, stable jacket, breeches, long boots and spurs, and his gold-laced cap well on one side and far back on his head, come walking at a smart pace down the lane, smacking his boot every now and then with his riding whip and looking right and left, as if he were taking everything in and that everything was new to him.

He looked at me, too, and gave me a good stare, and then he saw the stable beside me, muttered something to himself, looked at me again, and with a little mock salute with his whip he turned into the stable. Then I knew that that was the new officer. There was something about him which took my fancy at once. He seemed so different from the others I had seen. They had always looked so heavy and black about the face, and altogether as if nothing was worth noticing on either side of them; whilst my new officer was so trim and jaunty, so pretty and nice looking, and he had actually smiled at me, and shown me that he had seen me. I felt quite a flutter when he made his little mock salute, and half drew back from the gate I was leaning on, but I did not go away. I wanted to see him again, so I stayed. Presently out he came, talking to the groom, then the groom went back into the stable. The young officer looked up the lane and down the lane whilst he pulled on his gloves, then, seeing me, he came playfully towards me, made me a little bow, smiled, and saying, "Good evening, Polly. A nice evening this," he turned and walked rapidly away. A new flutter again came into my bosom. I know I looked wistfully after him, and was delighted when, turning his head, he looked back at me from a little distance, and again waved his whip at me. Poor little fool that I was! I had fallen in love and I did not know it! But so it was!

'Well, evening after evening this young officer and I met this way. Nothing more than what I have described passed between us. If an evening came and he did not appear, I used to feel so grieved. I missed him dreadfully. I found out that his name was the Honourable Charles Vincent, and that he was a captain in the Hussars. I heard the grooms speak and that was how I knew; besides, all his horses had a big C. V. worked in white letters on their clothing,.

'Did I tell you that at the end of our garden, in the corner and next the road, was a little old shed without any door? No? Well, there was and I had planted honeysuckle and clematis and a climbing rose against it and as a schoolgirl used to love to learn my lessons there, when it was fine, warm weather. The honeysuckle and rose and other climbing plants had grown very well, and the dirty old shed was transformed by them into quite an elegant bower.

'One evening my handsome officer did not come as usual. I was vexed and sorry, for I did love seeing him, and he always seemed to look for me. I heard his groom talking to the men in the next stable, saying he wondered the captain did not come, that the bay mare was sick and he had told his master of it. So I knew my hero was coming. I went into my bower and sat down and listened and peeped through the chink into the lane. Soon the grooms all went away but one, and that was Captain Vincent's. At last he seemed to be altogether out of patience, and I heard him swear and talk to himself, saying he would be damned if he would stay any longer; he would go and get his glass, and then he would come back. So he locked the stable and put the key into his pocket and went off.

'Well, I waited and waited! At last I heard the footstep I knew so well, and with a heart beating as if I had really expected and ardently wished for a lover, I went out and stood as usual at the gate. The sun was setting and all the lane was in shadow. Captain Vincent came walking quickly, saw me, smiled as usual, saying, "Good evening, Polly!", and tried the door of his stable. Finding it locked he kicked at it, so, as I knew there was no one in there, I called out, "Sir, the groom waited for you, and after a while said that he must get his glass, but that he would come back."

' "Oh! did he, Polly? Thank you, my dear!" and then coming near me he went on, "How long ago was it that the groom went?"

' "Oh!" said I, guessing, for the time had seemed dreadfully long to me while waiting, "about three quarters of an hour, I should say, sir."

' "Three quarters of an hour," the captain exclaimed, looking at his watch, "well, then he should be along soon now, I should think. And how are you, Polly? I see you here every day. What a pretty hand! What a lovely girl you are, Polly! I declare I must marry you! Will you marry me, Polly, if I ask you?"

'Well, of course I was a little fool, but I could not help being pleased beyond measure at his admiration, though it was quite plain to me that his question about marriage was only a joke.

' "Oh! sir!" said I, "don't be making fun of me! You know I cannot marry you, sir!"

' "Well," said he, "at any rate you could give me a kiss, child, could you not, Polly?"

'I felt my face burning. It was just what I was longing for. Oh! I cannot tell you how I had longed to be taken notice of by him. I looked around carefully, and seeing no one in sight, I said: "If you are quick, sir, because someone might see and then there would be talk."

'The words were hardly out of my mouth before the gallant and eager captain had his lips to mine, and gave me such a kiss as I had never had before in my life, a kiss which seemed to go right through my body down to my very feet!

' "Polly!" said he, in a low voice, "could I come into your summerhouse after I have seen my horses and chat with you a little while?"

'I knew there might be a little chance of mother seeing him, so I said quickly and with a palpitating heart, "Yes sir! I'll go in now, and wait, and you can come in when your are ready, but please don't stand there talking to me – for fear – you know!"

' "I understand," said he, his eyes blazing as they looked into mine, and he turned away and walked a little down the lane, in the direction the groom had gone. I went into the 'summerhouse', as he called it, and stood watching at the chink. Oh! how my heart beat! Would he kiss me again! How I wished the groom would come, for if I stayed out too long my mother might call for me to come in. At last the groom came and the captain and he had some little talk, but no quarrel. I think I prevented that, for I am sure Captain Vincent was angry when he found his man had not waited for him, but now he was certainly glad. He did not stay long in the stable. He and the groom came out together, and walked away down the lane. Oh! what a pang I felt! Was he not coming then? How cruel! how cruel! I could not help it, I sat down and began to cry and sob, and all of a sudden there was my lover, inside the little house. He had come back as quick as he could, and had only walked the groom out of the lane to get rid of him. I sprang up as he came in, and he saw I had been crying, and he sat down and pulled me on his knee, and with one arm around my waist and his right hand on my bosom, he gave me, oh! hundreds of kisses! He seemed quite excited, and I was simply beside myself with happiness and joy.

' "Oh! Polly!" he said, "do you know I've been longing to kiss you ever since I first saw you; you are the very prettiest, loveliest girl I ever saw."

'I could only smile. It was rather dark now in the little house, but I could see him clearly enough. He kissed my face all over, and my neck too, and his hand closed over the bubbie it was nearest. I liked it too much to tell him to take it off, but I knew he ought not to have done that. All the time he was kissing me he called me his pet, his little dove, his lovely little darling, and so forth, and I stroked his hair and gave him sweet kisses too.

'At last he said, "How old are you, Polly?"

' "My name is not Polly, sir! It's Lizzie!"

' "Well! How old are you, Lizzie? Sixteen? Seventeen?"

' "Sixteen! Seventeen!" I replied. "No, sir! I am thirteen!"

' "Why Poll – that is Lizzie, you must be more than thirteen! Who ever saw so fine a girl as you only thirteen?"

' "Well, sir," I said laughing, "I really am only thirteen!"

'He looked at me; he put his hand on my other bubbie and gave it a delightful squeeze, as if feeling it, and then he replaced his hand on its old place on the first bubbie.

' "Then," said he, "I expect this, these rather, are only padding!"

' "What?" said I.

' "Why! these bub – these – what do you call them? Your bosom, Poll – that is, Lizzie!"

' "Indeed, sir;" said I indignantly, "there is no padding about me. I do not require padding! Not I, indeed!"

' "Oh!" said he, laughing, "but, Poll – that is, Lizzie! – I wish I could remember your name, my pet! No girl of thirteen has such fine, well-developed bubbies as these!" and he pressed them again and again. "They are much too fine for a girl of thirteen! You must be older than you think!"

' "No indeed, sir! I know I am only thirteen!"

' "Well! Then I don't believe these are real! They must be padding, Poll – that is, Lizzie!"

'I was vexed. Why should he be so persistent? Why should he believe that my breasts were not good flesh and blood but only padding? So I said, "If you think I am only made up, sir, please don't feel them any more!"

' "But," said he, "Polly – Lizzie, I don't say that they are not real, the fact is, I don't know what to think. There is a mistake somewhere, but don't be angry, my pet! Come – kiss!"

'Those delicious kisses! Those delightful pressures of his hands!

' "Lizzie, let me put my hand inside your dress!"

'And so saying he began to pull at the front of my bodice which was fastened by hooks and eyes. They bothered him and he grew so dreadfully impatient that I, who was quite as anxious that he should be certain that I was not padded as he was to feel my bubbies that he found so nice through my clothes, at last pushed his too eager hands away and undid the obstinate front which opposed him.

' "There!" said I laughing, "you can get your hand in now, but there is still a petticoat inside to unbutton."

'But the petticoat gave him little trouble, and as if he were snatching for a prize which would escape him if he was not very quick, he thrust his strong but gentle hand between my shift and stays, and closed it over the firm little globe he found there.

' "Oh!" he exclaimed, making a kind of sipping noise with his lips as if he were taking something hot to drink, "Oh! Lizzie! Polly! Lizzie! what a splendid little bubbie, and what a smooth little nipple! Let me feel the other one now!"

'And he reversed his hand and pushed it on to my right breast, which he went mad over like he had the other. The effect on him was wonderful. I cannot describe my sensations to you, Charlie, because you, being a man, cannot understand what a girl feels when her breasts are so nicely handled by a man as mine were then, but a kind of all-overish feeling came over me. I felt that I wanted to put my arms around my lover and clasp him to me! It felt that there was something more that I wanted from him; a something which I could only get by pressing my body to him as close, close, as possible, but in the position I was, with his arm raised up and his hand pushing at my bosom, I could not think of folding him in my embrace. All I could do, I did. I put my arm round his neck and pulled his face down to mine, and kissed his mouth with a passionate energy which put him into a still greater ferment. "Undo your collar, Lizzie! Oh! I must see and must kiss those splendid little gems of bubbies."

'Oh! how his voice thrilled through me! I felt as if I trembled all over and his voice trembled also. It was passion, desire, love which had seized both of us. One knew its meaning well! – the other – myself – was still in a state of ignorance very soon to be cleared away.

'I did not hesitate to obey him. I undid my collar, and he, pulling my dress wide open and off my shoulders and bosom, poured a torrent of kisses on my swelling breasts and I – oh! – I leant back, supported by his strong arm, and gave myself and my thrilling bubbies to him to do with as he liked. It was beyond description. How his mouth flew from mount to mount. How his lips climbed each hill, and his teeth seized each little ticklesome nipple in its turn, and his hot breath descended into the valley between my breasts, and swept down over my body until my waistband stopped its further progress. But oh, whilst his lips were so busy, his right hand, in my lap, pressing between my thighs, was producing ravages in another part of my body. I felt inclined at first to resist, not because I did not like it, but because I felt a feeling of shame rise in me, almost stronger than the intense sensation of pleasure his moving fingers gave me.

' "Ah!" said I.

' "What, darling!" How he said that one word, 'darling', as if his soul breathed it from his heart of hearts.

' "Oh! don't put your hand there, sir!"

' "Oh! yes! yes! yes! oh! my delicious Polly Lizzie. What is your name? I must! Oh! Lizzie, I shall not be happy now until I have had you! You know what that means, don't you, darling? Say you will let me have you? Won't you?"

'Well, I didn't know exactly, but I began to guess that love, marriage and the "putting of his big thing into my little thing", as the girls said talking of husbands and wives, were all very intimately connected and the pleasure the proximity of his fingers caused in my melting little cunnie made me think that the "putting" must be something heavenly – and I was right!

'I don't know whether I said "yes" or "no" to his question but he acted as if I had said "yes" anyhow! For he suddenly put his hand under my dress, and before I could say "Scissors!" he had it as high as it could go between my thighs, at the same time pressing me to him and kissing my mouth. My drawers, that came up to the waist in front, offered a slight obstacle, but his eager and nimble fingers found their way in! Oh! the delicious sensation of those fingers as they caressed my cunnie! and the ravishing feel of the one which he pushed in deep between its glad lips. I no longer attempted to prevent his doing what he liked. It was much too delicious. I opened my thighs a little more, and whilst he sucked my mouth with long burning kisses that finger went in and out, every movement giving me more and more exquisite pleasure until at last a throb, a thrill! a kind of jump seemed to pass through cunt, motte, belly and all of me, and my lover exclaimed, "Ah! ah! oh! Lizzie, darling! I have made you spend!"

'Then for a moment he took his hand from between my thighs and I felt him doing something to himself. In a voice shaking with emotion and excitement he said, "Where is your hand, Lizzie? Give me your hand!"

'He took it and put it on what felt like a great big thick stick, thicker than a broom handle, and hot and awfully hard, except for the outside, which felt like velvet, and which was loose and moveable. It was so big that I could hardly get my fingers round it. The very feel of it, however, made my brain whirl round. "What is this?" I gasped.

' "It is me! Lizzie! it's me. It is my – my – my prick! Don't you know, darling, darling, Lizzie – that is what fits in here!" He had his finger moving in my cunnie again, setting me wilder still. "Let me put it in, darling Lizzie! It would kill me if you said no!"

' "Oh!" I gasped, for I could hardly speak, "you can't do it, sir! It is much, much too big!" and as I spoke I felt the curious, soft and elastic head which crowned his powerful weapon.

'For a reply my lover put me off his knee on to the seat, jumped up, undid his braces, pulled down his trousers, pulled up his shirt and I had an astonished glimpse of what looked like an enormous white bar, with a red tip, growing out of a perfect forest of black hair.

'Before I could either speak or resist, my impatient Charles, as he made me call him, pulled up my dress, petticoats and all, and pulled me on his knees, so that I had one leg on either side, then, whilst he drew the lower part of my body towards him, he made me lean back. I had to bend my knees to do so, and stand on the tips of my toes, whilst he was seated on the very edge of the seat. Oh! what a shock of delicious pleasure I received and how astonished I was when I felt that he had pulled me right onto what he called his prick, and that with a little kind of pop it had gone right into my cunt.

'Except for quickly, over and over again, "my darling! my darling!" he said nothing, and as for me I was too much in heaven to think of speaking. To support myself, however, I had to put my arms around his neck, and I hung back so as to give myself to him as nature taught me to do.

'Charles did not make any attempt to take my maidenhead then. He wished to allure me by giving me nothing but pleasure, and oh! he succeeded! He pushed his big prick in until my maidenhead prevented further ingress and then he pulled it back until it was almost out, and each time he did so I felt my cunt open and its lips slip over his vast head. Again I felt that exquisite spasm, and Charlie cried out that he had made me "spend" again, but soon he got powerfully agitated, his movements grew quicker and quicker, his thrusts more energetic, until all of a sudden he crushed me to his bosom, keeping his prick in my cunt, as deep as he could, and I felt that he was pouring something in hot, quick jets into me! It made me "spend" again, and then I felt something hot running all down my thighs, inside my drawers, and that all my bush and that part of me was inundated with something which had come from him. I felt almost inclined to faint with the inexpressible pleasure I felt, when all of a sudden I heard, "Lizzie! Liz–z–zie!"

' "Who is that calling you?" said Charles, quickly putting me off him and pushing my clothes down whilst at the same time he jumped up, tucked away that thrilling thing of this, which he had called his prick, and arranged his clothes as best he could.

' "Oh!" I cried, feeling dreadfully guilty and frightened, "It's mother!"

' "Well," said Charlie, giving me a hurried kiss, "don't be frightened; fasten your dress – call out that you are coming!"

' "I'm coming, mother!" I cried.

' "Come then, child!" was the answer as my mother went indoors.

'My lover peered through the tangled honeysuckle which hung over the hole I called my "window" and saw her go in. Then he took me in his arms and hugged and kissed me, and taking my left hand he put it on his huge, stiff prick, which was standing inside his drawers all up his belly, under the front buttons of his trousers, and put his right hand between my thighs, and pressing my throbbing cunnie, he kissed me again and again, and begged me to meet him the next evening at the same time, but to be careful not to let my mother notice anything strange in my behaviour and appearance. I promised, gave his delightful prick one more tender squeeze, and ran happy, but still nervous, to the house.

'After I had gone up to undress for the night I made a minute examination of my naked self. So I was a beautiful girl, was I? I had better bubbies than most other girls and my little cunt was a perfect gem! If only Charles could come to me in bed! How perfect it would be! He would do to me all night long what he had done to me in the summerhouse! But he was coming again next evening! I would try and get to sleep as fast as I could and dream of him.

'But sleep would not come. I was too excited. I found myself putting my finger into my cunnie as deep as I could, and pushing it in and out, as Charlie did his, but his finger was so much bigger than mine, it had given me more pleasure, and as for his prick, oh! was it possible so huge a thing could by any possible means all fit into my cunt? I could not believe it and yet he had told me it could. Why did it not all go in then this evening? Perhaps it was because he was so hurried! It might require more time. It was ever so long before I did sleep, and then, alas, I was disappointed! I did not dream of my lover or anything else.

'Well, the next day did seem long! But I took the greatest pains to seem quite myself, though I felt I had undergone a tremendous change. I did not feel like the little girl who only looked for her admired young officer to be happy at the bare sight of him. I now expected, wanted, desired much more! And I got it! For, although when he came and found me seated in the little house, he at first did nothing more than kiss me, and feel my bubbies and cunnie through my dress, because as he said my mother was so near it would be dangerous if I were in such a state of undress that I could not run out at once when she called, and meet and divert her from the summerhouse, yet, little by little, he grew more and more excited; he did not, indeed, open the bosom of my dress, but he put his hand under my petticoats, and caught hold of my cunnie and set it mad with his caressing fingers, and I, in my turn, felt his iron-stiff prick, until at last he said, "I think, Lizzie, we must have just one poke," and he asked me would I like to get his "man" out. Oh! would I not! I at once commenced unbuttoning his trousers and I got my hand in and pulled away his shirt and oh! the delight of getting that splendid big, hot thing in my grasp! and Charlie, delighted too, told me to be careful but to feel his balls, telling me how to get at them and I did! The darlings! How nice they felt! Like two fine eggs in a bag of velvet! and then he pulled down his drawers and again took me on his knees, and I had the same delight of feeling his prick just popping its big hard head in and out of my cunnie and of spending, and the quick thrusts and his almost groans of pleasure, and the hot quick jets of spend he poured into and all over my excited cunt! This time we were not interrupted by my mother, and whilst he held me, still with his prick in me, he asked me, "Lizzie, will you come and sleep with me? It would be so grand to be both in our skins in a nice warm bed! and then I could have you properly. I can't do it here. All of my prick ought to go inside you, but I cannot get half nor a quarter of it in."

' "Oh! I should like it, but how can I ever sleep with you, my dear Charlie?"

' "Oh! you must come away with me, of course! Tomorrow! Meet me here and I will take you to Dover. We will spend a week there! Well, will you come, Lizzie?"

'It seemed impossible. The idea of running away from home was so new to me and at first I could hardly bear the thought of it, but Charlie easily persuaded me; but what his persuasive voice said in words his still more

persuasive prick said in eloquent silence to my eager little cunt! Oh! my cunt
was on Charlie's side.

'I said I would do whatever he liked, and just what he told me. So, still
keeping me in this delicious position, on him, he told me to get what few
things I required, and to bring them during the next day, when I could best
do so unobserved by my mother, and put them in the summerhouse, and to
be sure to have my best dress and best hat and to bring all I had best, because
I should travel as his wife, and I must look very nice indeed as his wife
should. Then he said he would not come for me before nine o'clock, and I
must manage to be quite ready. He wanted to know whether I should find it
difficult to get out of the house so late, as, if so, we must make another plan.
But I knew I could do it easily, and I did so long, long for the time to come. I
assured him I would be quite ready, and as nicely dressed as he could wish
for – my mother being a dressmaker and I being a good "model", she always
had me well dressed, saying I was her walking advertisement.

'So, after a night of almost complete sleeplessness and what seemed an
eternity of waiting, the fated hour came. I carried out Charlie's instructions.
I took, bit by bit, the things I required, and hid them in the summerhouse,
and when Charlie came he found me dressed and ready. I had changed my
clothes and left those I usually wore every day on the seat, where my mother
found them a few hours later. I was in such a ferment of mind and body that
I have a most indistinct recollection of how we left the little summerhouse. I
left it a virgin, not quite a chaste one it is true, and when I came back I was
one no more! Heigh oh!

'Well, I remember things more distinctly from the time Charlie put me
into a first-class carriage, and followed me when he had seen my port-
manteaus into the baggage van. There was only one other occupant, an old
gentleman, who had evidently travelled from London. He took off his
spectacles to look at me, and seemed so satisfied that I was worth looking at
that he hardly once took his eyes off me until we reached Dover. It irritated
me more than I can tell, being so stared at, but it amused Charlie immensely
and he gave me sly little nudges from time to time and whispered in my ear
that I had made a new conquest.

'However, I kept quiet, though I would have loved to say something pert
to the old gentleman. The fact was that my nerves were strung to such a
pitch of excitement that I often wonder my brain was not turned. We went
to the Ship Hotel, which, of course you know, is close to the pier at Dover,
and Charlie took a private sitting room and a double-bedded sleeping room,
and put himself down in the visitors' book as Captain Charles Vincent and
me as his wife, with the Honourable before our names.

'I felt very nervous indeed. Everyone seemed to look very hard at me. In
my heart I said to myself, "They know." But at last we went upstairs to our
sitting room. There Charlie took me in his arms and gave me, as he said, all
the kisses and fond caresses and passionate embraces he would have given

me in the train had not the horrid old gentleman been there. He took off my hat and cloak and went back a few steps to admire me, as he said, and when he had looked me over for a moment he ran up and again clasped me in his arms, saying, 'Oh! Lizzie! I have never seen you so well dressed before. You look as perfect a lady as could be, and only thirteen, my darling. This swelling bosom, these lovely bubbies and those splendid hips don't belong to a child of thirteen, but to one of nineteen or twenty; and your beautiful, really beautiful face, though delightfully young looking, is by no means that of a child!' and he kissed and petted and fondled me, and put his naughty, delightful hand between my thighs, and I began to lose all the nervousness I had, and leaned against him with a heart brimful of love and affection; and desire made me throb all over.

'Charlie insisted on our having some supper, and we had a bottle of champagne. I did not feel in the least hungry and I told him so, but he said he was certain I had eaten nothing all day. He confessed it had been the same with him, and unless we ate and drank we should have no strength to support us during the night. "If you think you are going to get a wink of sleep before four o'clock, and perhaps at all tonight, you are vastly mistaken my Lizzie darling," and his eyes poured forth volumes of dazzling light into mine.

'Before we had our supper brought Charlie had given me two rings; I have them both now. Here they are where he first put them. A wedding ring and a keeper with pearls, diamonds and rubies. This was my mock marriage and real honeymoon. I was afterwards really married with the same ring and that marriage was followed by a mock honeymoon. It was well he did this, for we were waited on by a handsome and pert maid, and several times I noticed her eyes fixed on my hands as if to see whether I carried the outward and respectable mark of matrimony. I wonder how many similar rings Charlie had given to other girls? He was a great ravisher of maidens. A great hand at seduction in all its phases – a perfect hunter after women – and I was only one of a great number who had passed from virginity to womanhood through the gates of his arms, for, like my last Charlie, my first Charlie began cunt-hunting very young and being, like you, handsome, well furnished with the necessary weapons and rich, he scored far more successes than failures. He always said I was the gem of all he had had, and that he found me by accident. Certainly he had no trouble with me, for like a ripe peach, I fell the moment his fingers touched me.

'Well! after supper the maid wanted to know whether she should assist me to undress when I went to bed, and Charlie answered for me, saying that I was obliged but I should not require her services that night, and he added that we were not to be disturbed in the morning, as we had come a long journey, and would probably sleep it out. The girl, I could see, struggled to suppress a smile. I was too plainly very recently married, if married at all, and I think she saw well enough that our night would not be passed in sleep! I know I blushed! I could not help it. As she left the room I caught her running her eye over Charlie, and unless I am mistaken, she thought she would willingly change places with me, and take her chances of getting any sleep in Charlie's bed.

'And now I am very near the end of the life of my poor little maiden-head which died before I was fourteen. Few perish quite so early, but I am afraid, at least in that class of life in which I was born, few survive fifteen or sixteen. There are too many opportunities for such girls to get rid of these little pests! – I had just found that I had one only to see or rather to feel it disappear forever.

'Charlie, as soon as the maid was gone, begged me to go to bed! Now it is strange but true, and I think it is natural, that eager as I was to be had, delighted at the idea of being in bed with him, knowing the pleasure I had already had from his sweet prick, even so the 'bed' rather alarmed me. I would willingly have put it off, but Charlie begged and besought me not to delay his happiness and mine too, and feeling a little like a real virgin bride, no doubt, I suffered him to lead me to our room. "Now darling! darling!" cried Charlie, "I must go and take half a dozen whiffs of a cigar and see who is in the house, so as to find out if there is anyone I had better keep you hidden from. I won't be long. You unfasten your clothes but don't take them off. I will be your maid tonight – and – your man too!"

' "Oh! Charlie! don't be long! Don't leave me all by myself!"

' "No one will come and eat you, my pet! Besides," said he smiling, "you may like to find yourself alone for a few minutes."

'I understood I did require it very much, and I said no more to detain him. I saw the necessary article, and in my mind I thanked my Charlie for his kind thought. It seemed so delicate of him, too, and I felt my heart bound towards him.

'Before I followed his instructions and loosened my clothes. I peeped out of the window. Then suddenly remembering what I had to do, I let the blind fall from my hands and set to work unhooking my dress, and unbuttoning and loosening the strings, and whilst I was doing this my Charlie came in, with quick, eager steps, catching me in his arms, putting one of his thighs between mine and exclaiming, "All right, my Lizzie! There's no one here that knows me or whom I know. Now! my pet! let me undress you! We will put our skins on and have a lovely – oh, a lovely night in that heavenly bed."

'Oh! he was quicker at taking off my clothes than my experience in the summerhouse at home would have made me believe possible. In a brace of shakes he had me naked, all but my chemise, stockings and boots. I thought he would leave me my chemise, but you will see! To take off my boots and stockings, he made me sit down on a chair, and his naughty hands kept on pushing up my chemise, to be out of his way, higher up my thighs than was at all required, and somehow my cunnie would come (as he said) in his way. It was lovely! He tickled me so, he made me laugh – he excited me so, that to pay him out I put my now naked foot between his thighs. At once he took it, and put the sole of it on to his beautiful stiff prick and a thrill like electricity shot all through me. My touch made him hurry up too. Both stockings were off now, and I was going to rise off the chair, but he pushed me back and said he must see my shoulders and bubbies bare! In a moment he had my chemise off my shoulders, so that it lay round my middle; all above it was perfectly naked. With a cry of delight he fell with his mouth on my bosom, kissing, biting, nibbling, whilst he pressed between my thighs and stroked them beneath my chemise with his hands. Then, suddenly rising, he caught me in his arms, pulled me straight up, and, my chemise falling to the floor, he lifted me up, kicked it away, and put me down in front of him as naked as I was born.

'"Oh! Charlie!" I exclaimed, "how could you! Let me have my chemise!" and I put my hands, naturally, over my motte and cunnie, for I felt shame glowing all over me, to be so dreadfully naked in the presence of a man!

'"Oh! my lovely, my beautiful Lizzie! I cannot let you cover up that lovely form and those exquisite charms! Look, girl! Here! Come! Look at yourself in this glass, and say whether you ever saw anything prettier in your life!' And he half pushed, half carried me, a most unwilling victim at that moment, before the long glass in the door of the wardrobe.

'Oh! I can hardly tell you what an impression my own reflection made on me! The moment before I felt as if I were crimson all over, from shame at being completely naked in the presence of Charlie, but now I was so struck with what I saw before me that all feelings of shame vanished and were replaced by a flood of pleasure. I had never seen myself, as a whole, naked in the glass, for I had no such mirror in my own little bedroom at home, and it never struck me to strip myself and see what I was like, when clothed in nothing but my naked charms, with the assistance of the cheval glass in mother's trying-on room. Besides all the surroundings were in favour of my seeing myself to the highest advantage now. The wallpaper of the room was dark, and reflected light badly, so that my figure in the mirror stood out against a dark background and showed up with dazzling whiteness. I could not but admire myself. Mother had often said I was a well-made girl, but she never expatiated much on my figure or my charms. Here I had them all before me, and I was amazed and delighted at the revelation! You, Charlie, have seen me naked and know what I am like now. Well! I was nearly as rounded in form and full in figure and shape of my limbs as now. What perhaps struck me first, most of all, was what a nice unblemished skin I had. Next, how lovely my shoulders and bosom were, how slender my waist, and how beautifully my hips gradually expanded until they were wider than my chest. My pretty little bubbies, well separated, each looking a little away from the other, each perfectly round where it sprang from my bosom, and both tapering in lovely curves until they came to two rosebuds points, next caught my delighted eyes. I had never seen them look so lovely as they did now, as they gleamed and shone, apparently whiter than the body from which they grew, as the light flashed upon them. My belly was smooth, broad and dimpled in the centre with a sweet little navel, like a perfect plain of snow which appeared the more dazzling from the thick growth of hair which curled in dark rich brown locks on the triangle of my motte, gradually growing thinner and less close as it tapered to that point which, receding between my rounded thighs, divided at the spot where my pretty, demure little cunnie commenced to form. I could not see the whole of my cunnie when I stood upright, for it turned in between my thighs too quickly, so to say, as if it felt that it should hide itself until love demanded it to be displayed by the action of opening my legs. My thighs, knees, calves, ankles and feet next came in for their share of inspection, and by the time I had looked myself over from head to toe, I came to the conclusion that Charlie was right, and that a lover should be permitted to gaze with enraptured eyes on charms of no common class of beauty. Don't think me vain, but I have been too often told that I am beautiful to believe that every man who has seen me naked is and has been a liar.

'Well, whilst I was thus intoxicating myself with my own reflection Charlie was not idle. He had completely stripped himself, and came eagerly up, as naked as myself. He put his arm round my neck, and stood beside me, adding his masculine beauty to the picture I saw in the glass before me.

' "Now, Lizzie! is not that a perfect picture? Don't we make a real handsome couple?"

'I could only respond by putting my arm around his waist and pressing him to my side. His warm body sent a thrill through me, as I felt it in this delicious close contact, and I saw a little ruby and shining point suddenly protrude between the upper lips of my excitable little cunt. Oh! Charlie looked splendid! I took my eyes off myself to gaze at him in wonder and admiration. He looked so powerful, yet so lithe. His shoulders were as broad as mine were narrow, and his hips as narrow as mine were broad. His deep and manly chest contrasted with my more graceful but completely feminine bosom. His arms, long and muscular, seemed perfect models in marble, and every movement on his part showed the firm muscles move under the skin beneath which there was little of that soft fat or flesh which made my limbs and body so pliant and smooth. But naturally, it was his long, stiff, straight, grand-looking prick and the big rough bunch which formed his handsome balls underneath, in their velvety wrinkled bag, which chiefly attracted my burning eyes, for there it was, that truly stalwart prick, pointing up at my face! It seemed a formidable weapon indeed, so strong, so conquering, so irresistible. Its head, of a more or less rosy colour with a suspicion of violet at the edges, was half uncovered, and its almost impudent look amused me as it seemed to scan me with its slit-like little eye on its top. I could see that this splendid weapon was broader and thicker at its base, where it sprang from the forest of hair which clothed my lover's motte, and slightly tapered until it reached its head, where it suddenly widened again only to taper quickly off to a rounded blunt point, where its "eye" was. Charlie took my hands, put one under his balls and the other on his prick and made me feel and press them for a moment. I almost fainted with the thrilling emotion this feeling of him sent through me, and clasping me to him, he pressed himself against me so that his mighty spear-like weapon was closed in between his belly and mine. I could feel its point high above my navel, and I remember wondering whether, supposing he could get it in, I should feel it up inside me as far as that! At the same time I felt certain that to get so huge a volume as that into my tight little cunt would be impossible. I was convinced of that.

'After a few more thrilling caresses on the part of each of us Charlie said, "Now, Lizzie!" and lifting me up in his great strong arms, he carried me like a baby to the other side of the bed where he laid me down on my back, pulling the sheets down. Oh! I was inclined to have him! My whole body panted for him! My bubbies seemed to be swelling as if they would burst and the little red nipples on them were as hard as peas and tickling me! As for my cunt, it was raging! Such a throbbing as went on in it I had never felt before, not even when he had half fucked me at Canterbury. I expected him between my thighs, which I opened for him, but instead of taking his place there at once, my irritating lover commenced kissing me on the mouth, cheeks, eyes, ears, throat and all of that part, whilst his hand wandered over my bosom from bubbie to bubbie, which he tenderly felt and pressed. He did not seem to be in half the hurry I was. If his intentions were to drive me half frantic with desire, to raise up all that was lascivious in my senses, he certainly succeeded to perfection! But really he was right. I always think a good preliminary engagement of hands and lips makes a fuck much more delicious than when one comes to close quarters without any at all. Charlie's lips descended from my lips to my bosom. He laid his head between my breasts and turning it from side to side kissed each bubbie as his lips encountered its warm, rounded side, and whilst so doing his naughty hand crept, crept, crept over my belly, down my groin, down my thighs, up again, all round my motte, then skimmed my bush with its fingertips, then just touched, but no more, the line of my cunnie, until I could hardly endure the almost agonising pleasure he caused me! Then suddenly he took a firm bite of one breast, and in went his strong finger, right up to the knuckle, with a bang against my cunt, and this he repeated, biting, but not hurting, my other bubbie; then, with repeated kisses, his mouth roved over my belly, down one groin, down that thigh, up the other, just like his hand had done, until suddenly he brought it up right to my quivering cunnie, which he almost burnt with his kisses! I could feel his tongue darting at my agitated, excited clitoris, and at last, unable to bear it any longer, I almost screamed to him to leave off that, and give me what I craved for. He turned a dreamy look at me, then suddenly seemed to wake up, as it were.

' "Oh! I nearly forgot!" said he as he ran to the mantelpiece and brought from it what looked like a pot of pomatum. "This is cold cream, my Lizzie! As you have never had all me inside you yet, and your delicious little cunt it as tight as can be, some of this will help us both! Hold the pot, darling, and let me anoint your cunnie Queen of my Prick!"

'He took fingerful after fingerful of the cream, and put so much of its cool substance inside my cunt I thought he meant me to have it all. It was so sweet and cool and pleasant, I liked it for its own sake as much as for the sake of feeling his finger push it as far in as it could.

' "Now," said he, "anoint my prick King of your Sweet Cunt, my Lizzie!' and he turned that awful mad-looking weapon towards me. I took it, close to the root, with my left hand, and with my right I anointed its head; as I stroked the cream down, its hood slipped right off, and gathered behind its spreading shoulders, and here Charlie made me put a great lot of the cream. Then with both hands I, by his directions, put all that remained in the pot on the shaft of his prick, until it shone as though dipped in oil! Oh! the feeling of that prick! I am sure you remember the excitement you must have felt the first time you had a good, free and complete "feel" of a girl, Charlie? Well! think of what I experienced, for that grand prick, those glorious balls, were all mine, to press and caress in perfect freedom for the first time.

'Charlie made me wipe my hands on his curly hair and then, with a triumphant, "Now Lizzie, open your thighs! Now, for heaven and bliss and all that is delicious!" he pushed me on to my back, and was between my willingly opened arms and thighs before I could wink! He made me introduce himself into my cunnie, then he put one hand under my head and the other under my hips and with a slight pressure forced, or, rather, easily slid, his weapon in as far as it had ever gone before. At first, as if careful not to raise any doubts in my mind, he contented himself with toying in and out, as he had done at Canterbury, giving me delicious pleasure, but suddenly he gave a thrust which stopped my breath, and he kept up such a fearful pressure that it began to hurt me not a little but a good deal, I can tell you.

' "Oh! Charlie!" I cried out, "Don't, darling, you are hurting me dreadfully."

'He said nothing, but gave me a kiss; then laid his cheek to mine, and gathered me more firmly than ever in his arms, and again seemed to burst violently into my insides!

'I almost screamed but Charlie would not listen to my entreaties! Again and again did he batter, and at last, with a sickening sensation of rending and tearing, I felt that the obstacle, whatever it was, had gone before his dreadful prick, and that each stroke, each thrust, was carrying it deeper and deeper into my insides! I really feared he had burst my poor little cunnie, and that I should die, in consequence; but, before I could express myself in words, I felt that every atom of that awful prick was buried in me, for I could feel Charlie's balls against me distinctly, and as for our bellies, they were completely pressed together, as well as our mottes! Then Charlie relaxed that tremendous grip on me, and raising his face looked eagerly into mine, and smiled and kissed me and said, "Ah! Lizzie, darling! I hope I did not hurt you very much. You had such a dreadfully tough little maidenhead, and your little cunt is a tight one – so much the better! for you will have the more pleasure! Do I hurt you now, darling?" and he kissed me tenderly.

' "Not now! but oh, Charlie! you don't know how much you did hurt me! I hope you have not done me any harm!"

' "Not a bit," said he laughing. "I am glad it does not hurt you! But now for pleasure, my Lizzie! You lie quite still and let me fuck you quietly and you will see whether you won't forget any pain I gave you."

'Then commenced those splendid, exciting, thrilling, long strokes. Even that very first time I felt great pleasure from them, and afterwards, when all soreness had completely disappeared, every time was like plunging into a new world! My cunt was like a violin, and Charlie's prick like the bow, and every stroke raised the most ravishing melody on the senses that could be experienced or imagined! Oh! I am sure he was right when he said that never was there a girl so plainly brought into the world for fucking and fucking only, as myself! I adore it! I can't live without it! And at times I cannot imagine how any man or woman can pass a day without having it at least once or twice.

'That was how I lost my maidenhead before I knew I had one! Ah! That week at Dover will always be remembered by me as the most exquisite in my life. Charlie was never done! He was so kind too! He took me for long drives, showed me the castle, took me out boating; we laid perfect fairy plans for our future. I was to be his own pet love! I was to live in a sweet little house in London, to have my own carriage and servants and all that I could want, and I should be his darling mistress, almost his wife. Not once did I remember my poor mother, or my duty to her as a child. I declare it seems most terribly selfish – but oh! I was ravished with my lover, and the whole world seemed centred in him! And yet when the test of that cunt-burning love came to be applied, you will see how it stood.

'Yes! Yes! It was an exquisite dream! Such a dream as I have often wished to have again but never in my happiest moments since have been able to approach!

'Well, it was all settled. Charlie's leave would be up now that our six days' honeymoon was spent. We were to have one more blissful night in one another's arms, and oh! how I had learned to love being well fucked! How I had come to appreciate its ravishing joys, its indescribable delights!

'We were, I say, to have one more night at Dover, and then Charlie was to take me to London, leave me in a hotel for a day, get more leave, and come and hunt up a nice little house for me, etc., etc., as he had planned, and I was to be his kept mistress. The idea of returning to Canterbury to my mother had completely faded from my mind. From her arms I had been snatched away to quite another and perfectly different life, and like the brilliant fly, I could no longer think of resuming my life as a grub. The thing was impossible, so impossible that I never gave it a single thought.

'But – ah! there are a good many "buts" in the world, which like stones in the road are apt to upset the steadiest and most courageous – but, the last evening of our stay in the Ship Hotel a note was brought to me, just as I was going to take off my things. Charlie and I had been for a long drive over to the camp at Shorncliffe. A glance at the writing showed me it was from my mother! I dropped on to a chair and Charlie, seeing me look as if I should faint, ran up in alarm.

' "What is it, my darling? Who is this from?"

' "Oh! Charlie," I ejaculated, "it is from my mother!"

' "The devil! What does she want? What business is it of hers, I should like to know, to come interfering?" cried poor Charlie, who forgot that she had every possible business to do so.

' "What does she say?" he went on impatiently, for I had not the courage to open the note but held it in my shaking hand. "Here, girl! give it to me! Let me see what the old – h'm – old lady says. Lizzie, your mother says she is on the pier and asks you to come out for a moment to see her, or she will come in and see you here! You had better go, darling! It would not do to have her kick up a row in here. Will you go with her if she asks you, Lizzie? Tell me! God damn and blast it all! What an unfortunate thing! Lizzie, Lizzie! You must not leave me! I cannot live without you! I must have you! Do you hear?"

'I was drowned in tears and my bosom was torn with sobs. I love Charlie! Oh! I did! What girl would not love a lover who had adored, worshipped and fucked her as Charlie had me? But on the other hand, I loved my mother too. How dearly I did not know until now. The two affections, the old and the new, wrestled within me. I was at the parting of the ways, and if it had been possible I would have liked to have walked on both of the roads.

' "Oh! Charlie!" I cried, as I threw myself in his arms, "I cannot say! I cannot say! Perhaps mother will tell me that after what I have done she won't have me home again!"

' "And then!" cried poor Charlie eagerly.

' "And then, of course, I would come with you, Charlie."

' "That means if your mother – confound her! – says come home, Lizzie, you will leave me?"

' "Can't I go home with her if she will have me and come to you another time, Charlie dearest?" said I.

' "Well," he cried, "now let us get rid of this uncertainty, Lizzie! Though it rests with you, I fancy! If you had any pluck at all you would send her word that you could not see her!"

' "Then she would come in here, Charlie. You don't know my mother! She is very kind, but if she says she will do a thing, she does it!"

' "By Jove! Yes! I forgot! She would come in here and then there would be a devil of a row! Run! Lizzie! run, and keep her out like a good girl!"

'I dried my eyes, went quickly downstairs, out of the hotel and on to the pier, along which I walked, straining my eyes in the fast gathering darkness to see where my mother could be. At last I saw a figure standing just in front of the recess, and I recognised my mother and flew to her. She received me with open arms, folding me tightly to her bosom, and there we both stood clasped together, and both sobbing as if our hearts would break.

'Charlie, I can't go into the details of that sad meeting. You must spare me and let me only say that my mother did not say one word of upbraiding or scolding; she told me that she had nearly died of fear and sorrow when she found me gone and keeping her wits about her she spread no report, asked nobody about me, but putting two and two together came to the conclusion that if I had gone with anybody it would probably have been an officer of the Hussars. Then she found out that Captain Vincent had his stables behind our house and that he had gone on leave from the very day I had disappeared and accidentally she saw his name and that of his wife in the Dover papers, as being at the Ship. She had found out that he was not married, had come straight to Dover, on a chance had sent the note, hoping that the Honourable Mrs Vincent might be myself, as indeed it was! She said that whatever mischief had been done had been done, and that the only thing to do was not to make it worse by raising a scandal. She told me to go back to Charlie, to stay with him for the night, to manage to return home after dark to Canterbury, where she would meet me and have a cab ready outside the station. Our reserved and quiet way of living had prevented our neighbours noticing my absence, and unless some future event happened nobody need know anything about it.

'All my dreams of a little house in London came to an end. I loved my Charlie, it is true, but it was cunt love more than that of the heart, and my mother easily prevailed on me to give him up.

'Charlie, poor fellow, was overjoyed when he saw me return. He fancied I was coming back for good, and his disappointment was intense and bitter when he knew that I had firmly resolved to return to my own home, and not to go to London with him! but presently when the first bitter draught was swallowed, he said that of all wonderfully wise women he had ever heard of, my mother beat all in getting me back to him for the night.

'Ah! well! I had a quiet and not altogether unhappy life with my mother until I was fifteen. The Hussars had left Canterbury and though I naturally often thought of Charlie, I was rather indignant that he never apparently once tried to see me again. He told me afterwards that he had done all he could think of to get letters to me. Perhaps my mother intercepted them. I never got any of them. I hate the next episode in my life. One day I met a sergeant, dressed in the old and beloved Hussar uniform. I got talking to him, and from talking to walking, and from walking to lovemaking, and from lovemaking to fucking! I could not help it! I wanted a man most dreadfully, and all my cunt's old fire came back at the sight of the Hussar uniform. Of course, I acted deceitfully, and kept all from my mother, who had hoped by trusting me fully to prevent all such action on my part. My new lover was only on furlough. He had not been gone long before I found I was, this time, let in for a baby. My distraction nearly killed me, and all the more because I feared to tell my mother. But time told her. My figure lost its elegant shape and I had to confess – the awful, awful pain of that confession. But true to herself, my mother lost none of her wits. She found out my second seducer, went and saw him, found him to be the master tailor of the regiment, told him what an excellent dressmaker I was, proposed marriage, held out the promise of a fair dowry, her savings for many years – poor mother! – and I was married to Sergeant Thomas Wilson in time to save the legitimacy of my baby. But we did not live happily.

'One day when my husband was out, Charlie came to see me. Oh! I was glad to see him. We had a long explanation and it all ended in his having me on my husband's bed! I was fucked again – joyful thought – by the darling man who had taught me what a sweet thing it was! But hardly had Charlie gone than in came Tom. Going from room to room he saw his own bed tumbled, and then he grinned! He accused me of having had Charlie whom he had met, and of whom he had heard, goodness knows how, and there and then he made me an offer which I accepted. It was that to bring him custom, I should let myself be – admired. He would hear nothing, see nothing, know nothing! I was too unhappy with him not to jump at an offer which would give me back Charlie! All that had to be done was that a suit of clothes should be ordered from time to time, and Charlie ordered at least a dozen. More and more officers followed his example and soon my husband had them all, every one, from colonel to junior lieutenant, on his books, and I had them all as my lovers. I had several children. I only know the father of one for certain, and that was my husband. I think the second was Charlie's, but I am not sure. None lived. That is my story, a sad mixture of happiness and misery, folly on my side and wisdom on my mother's.'

I could not but wonder how it could be that such a sweet countenance could be the seat of a temple in which Venus reigned, not only to the exclusion of all other gods and goddesses, but with more than ordinary power. I must leave my gentle readers to form their own opinions of this lovely wanton, but that there was much good in her I became convinced the more I knew her. At all events it is not for me to throw the stone of condemnation at her. To enjoy a woman and then run her down is not my style. Lizzie must have had a yearning for a purer and a better life, for she was constantly urging me to send for my beloved Louie, warning me that if I did not I should most certainly constantly wander from the path of virtue, and also saying that it was not fair to any woman, especially one who loved her husband, in every sense of that expansive word, to leave her to pine alone. Well, it was my hope that either I should rejoin my Louie in England, or that she should come out to me in India, but the fates were against us.

During the remainder of my stay in Nowshera, I enjoyed my tender Lizzie in all tranquillity and my tender girl readers may be sure that every opportunity was taken, and none lost, of procuring both for her and for myself the most complete pleasure which our active senses could expect. Her poor thighs were still marked by the violence of the brute Searle when I last saw them, but the sweet, sweet cunt between them lost neither beauty nor attraction on that account. To this day I look back upon that week of ardent fucking with regretful delight. I have never yet succeeded in regretting having sinned against heaven and my dearest wife in having broken the seventh commandment with Lizzie. 'Stolen waters are sweet,' saith Solomon, and I, Charles Devereaux, say to that, 'Amen, Amen, verily that is true.'

Our new station staff officer, my good friend Major Stone, got a dak *gharry* for Lizzie and two *ekkas* for me, and we started off on our respective routes on the same day; Lizzie started in the morning and I in the evening, she making for India proper, and I for Shakkote, at the foot of the hills on which Cherat is situated. It was not without a pang on each side that we parted, and we exchanged locks of hair, pulled from our respective bushes. I have hers still and never look at its now somewhat faded curl but that the delicious days and nights I spent in her fair arms at Nowshera come back to my memory with a force that, if she only knew it, adds to the happiness I feel every time I recall the joys I experienced so keenly between her delightful and voluptuous thighs; and my Louie does not lose, I can assure you, by my having been unfaithful with Lizzie!

I took Soubratie with me, leaving 'Mrs Soubratie' to look after my luggage for which her husband was to return when he had seen me safe as far as Shakkote. I heard that she proved the delight of the gallant officers at Nowshera during her husband's absence, and that she brought a big bag full of rupees with her to Cherat, where her charms enabled her to add a good many more to the stock earned by her active and diligent cunt.

Of my journey, of my arrival at Cherat and of the two lovely maidens I found there, who as yet had not known a man, but to whom it was my most happy privilege to communicate the thrilling sensations of soft desire and voluptuous sentiment, I must tell my readers in the chapters which follow.

## CHAPTER TWO

## *A Position of Trust*

I never in my life journeyed in such an uncomfortable conveyance as an *ekka*, and I only hope that none of my fair readers may be subjected to such aches and pains as I had to suffer. But what is an *ekka*? some of my fair readers may ask. I will tell you. It is a two-wheeled conveyance much used in northern India. It has no springs. It has a platform of but three square feet on which you sit as best you can. It is drawn by a small pony. The shafts generally rise so the platform on which you sit generally slopes back. The driver sits on the shafts, and if, as is very likely, he is highly odoriferous, you get the benefit of his evil smell. But that is not all about the *ekka*. It has its good points. It can go almost anywhere. It is light and strong. Many and many a time I have seen one carrying half a dozen natives, who can squat with ease where one European cannot find half room enough for himself. It is a cheap conveyance, and it is generally a most gorgeous one to behold, for from every one of its four corners there rises a pillar of white carved with all the cunning of the Indian carpenter's art. Over this is a dome, generally surmounted by some brass ornament, and the entire *ekka* is painted in the most brilliant colours and ornamented with quaint patterns cut out of brass and hung with little tinkling bells and, in fact, presents the sort of barbaric appearance which pleases the native eye and fancy so much.

Amongst the European soldiers and their wives the *ekka* is known as a Jingling Johnnie, a name which perfectly describes the noise it makes when in motion, for it does nothing but jingle, thus adding to the civilised ear as much torment as its uncomfortable shape and motion do to other parts of his anatomy. Altogether it is not the kind of carriage which I can recommend as forming one of the comforts of Indian travel.

Added to the great discomfort the *ekka* afforded were several others. First the road had been cut to pieces by the thousands of men and carts of all descriptions, including artillery, light and heavy, which for the last two or three years had been constantly pouring along it, over all the road, to and from Afghanistan. It was consequently inches deep in dust as fine as flour. This dust rose during the day and did not settle for hours; it formed a perfect fog which choked the driver, dried up his mouth and filled his eyes and ears, besides covering me from head to foot. Again, how many camels died on the march? I believe they numbered tens, even twenties of thousands. Judging from the stench which hardly without break filled the air between the outskirts of Nowshera and Publi, there must have been a fair proportion of those deceased camels all along the road. As fast as possible the carcasses were either burnt or buried, but enough were left above ground to sicken even the strongest stomach.

I fell fast asleep and did not wake until the *ekka* stopped and I found myself in a little grove of trees close to which was the last military outpost with its guard of native infantry; here I was told I had to dismount as I was at Shakkote.

Towering high above me and looking perfectly unclimbable was a lofty range of mountains whose torn sides testified to the violence with which the rain dashed upon them in its hurry to reach the lower level. Cherat, I was told, was on the very summit, and was some four and half thousand feet above where I stood; that is higher than Snowdon, the highest mountain I had yet ascended, and these mountains seemed twice as steep. A couple of ponies stood at the door of the shanty, one had a saddle on, the other not. I asked whose ponies these were, and hearing that they had been sent down to meet an officer expected with baggage, I asked no more questions, but at once claimed my right to them, which fortunately was not contested. Mounted on my pony and directing Soubratie to be quick to strap my portmanteau as best he could on the other animal, I told the *syce* or groom who was in charge of my beast to proceed, and show me the way, which the half-naked savage did.

At last, after a perilous ascent, my pony staggering with immense fatigue and the fearful strain the terrible climb had cost him, we reached the top. The pony's trot soon died down into a quiet walk along a very good, well-made path, some five or six feet broad, which followed the edge of the valley, across which I saw facing me a pretty cottage, and good heavens! quite a sweet-looking English lassie, walking with a child, evidently taking her early-morning walk. I therefore encouraged my pony to put on his best paces, and almost as soon as I had caught sight of her, the unknown girl seemed to see me too, for she stopped in her walk and stood looking towards me. I soon got within twenty or thirty yards of her, for the path rounded the end of the valley, at the head of which was the cottage.

The first view I had of her close up, showed me that she was a really pretty girl – not exactly beautiful in the sense that Lizzie Wilson was, but more like my own beloved Louie, sweet, feminine, pretty in every sense. Her cheeks, rounded with health, were coloured like the rose, showing that the climate of Cherat certainly agreed with her. Her skin was perfectly clear; and her lips, those dear lips which were in days yet to come to be so often joined to mine in passionate ecstasy, were of the brightest red, that red that only belongs on the lips of the young, and which my experience has shown me is a sign of a nature tender, passionate and voluptuous. Her throat was beautifully formed, round and full, and her figure was that of a maiden passing from the stage of girlhood to that of womanhood. I could see that although her bosom was not yet fully developed, it was already adorned with two charming little mounds;

it was certainly not a pair of empty stays which formed the slight hemispheres on either side, but good, sound, solid flesh. Her waist, though not so tapering as Lizzie's, was sweetly small, and her hips had that generous breadth which announces a fine, beautifully shaped belly, fit couch for any man to repose upon! Repose! Can a man be said to repose when he lies between the thighs of his darling, and fucks her with movements so full of sweetness, of joy, of ardent rapture for both him and her? I know not! – but no matter – my maiden showed two well-shaped little feet and ankles beneath her petticoat, as she stood watching my approach, and a smile began making her eyes alive with a kind expression of welcome, and two bewitching dimples began to form which gave her lovely face the appearance of great sweetness, just such a look as might well take any man by storm who saw it for the first time.

I took off my hat and bowed, and asked this charming girl, 'Can you kindly tell me where I should go to find Colonel Selwyn?'

'Papa is at the orderly room, but he will be home soon. This is our house. I suppose you are Captain Devereaux?'

'Yes! I have only just arrived. I have been travelling all night and I am afraid I am more than dirty, and you must kindly excuse me for venturing to come near you in such a condition. You see I did not know which way to go, but left it to my pony and he brought me to you.'

'Well! Won't you let the *syce* take him, and come in and meet my mother and have a cup of tea? Papa won't be long, I am sure.'

'I am very much obliged to you Miss Selwyn, but I really feel much too grimy and dirty to present myself for the first time to Mrs Selwyn! It would make a bad impression I am sure and I should be sorry for that, for it might perhaps have the effect of her taking a dislike to a man who, since he has seen Miss Selwyn, would wish to be on good terms with her father and mother!'

'Don't talk rubbish!' said this downright little maiden, blushing and looking as pleased as punch. 'My mother will, I am sure, make every allowance, and I am sure you must want a cup of tea or a peg, which perhaps you would prefer. Do come in!'

At this moment a lady, somewhat taller than Miss Selwyn, accompanied by another girl, much the same height as her sister, came to the door of the bungalow, evidently attracted by the voices they heard.

'Oh! mama!' cried my friendly maiden, 'here is Captain Devereaux, just arrived. I have asked him to come in and see you, and have a cup of tea or a peg, but he says he wants to see papa first, and is much too – too – well! dirty! Do make him come in!'

'Hush! Fanny! you let your tongue run away with you too fast! I am glad to see you, Captain Devereaux. I suppose you have had a terrible time at Nowshera during the last week. We heard you were there and could not move on account of the troops returning from the war wanting all the *ekkas* and carts.'

I made my excuse, saying that I considered it my first duty to report myself to the colonel, and that then, after I had made my toilet, I would do myself the honour of calling.

Fanny looked at me with reproachful eyes, as much as to say, 'You might as well have done what I wanted.' The other girl looked at me out of her great lustrous eyes, her mouth smiling slightly, while Mrs Selwyn gave me directions how to find my way to the orderly room, viz., by going back a part of the way I had come until I found a road leading to the barracks in which all the regimental offices were situated, about a mile from where we stood. Making my bow, and thanking Mrs Selwyn, giving the now pouting Fanny a bright look, as full of thanks as my dust-filled eyes would permit me, and taking another long look at the daughter whose name I had not yet learnt, I handed over my pony to the *syce* and walked along in the direction I had been told to go.

Before turning the corner I looked back. Fanny was alone, still standing in front of the house, looking after me. Her attitude was one of wistfulness. Somehow I felt she had been snubbed, and I was sorry for her, but glad to find my lines would be cast amongst people who, at first sight, seemed to be so lady-like and nice as Mrs Selwyn and her two daughters. These thoughts rather interfered with my admiration of the wild and savage beauty of the scenery I was passing through. Presently, turning a jutting shoulder of the cliff wall, I saw, perched on a slight eminence above me, a long, low wooden structure of large proportions, having an extensive red-tiled roof. Seeing a group of soldiers in their khaki, or mud-coloured, uniforms standing at the door I guessed this was the building housing the regimental offices, and passing through the group, I entered what seemed to be one vast hall with wooden pillars supporting its roof. The first person I saw proved to be the paymaster; hearing my name, he welcomed me warmly enough and showed me whereabouts I should find Colonel Selwyn, whose office was at the far end of the building. Thither I proceeded. The colonel was seated at his table dispensing justice. Around him stood officers in uniform, some red, some khaki, some blue, who had to bring up men. I scanned their faces. I knew none of them, and not being in uniform myself, and moreover covered with dust and dirt, I dare say I did not present a very favourable appearance. I waited until the last unhappy 'Tommy' was weighed off and then, advancing to the table, reported myself as Captain Devereaux, just arrived to join the battalion. Colonel Selwyn looked at me with interest for a moment, whilst the hitherto glum and stern-looking faces of the surrounding officers broke into smiles of welcome.

'Ah!' said the colonel, rising, 'glad to see you, Devereaux! I heard you were stuck at Nowshera. You came at an unlucky time when all the conveyances were engaged. I am afraid you had a wretched time of it down there!'

He shook me warmly by the hand, and introduced me to various officers, who did the same, and then, recommending me to go and get a peg before anything else, he asked the others to show me the way to the mess, saying he must himself hurry off home.

I accompanied my new brothers-in-arms, who led the way chatting and laughing and making many enquiries of me, until we reached the miserable shanty, called by courtesy 'the mess'.

I will not go in for a description of each and every officer. Suffice it to say that they were a very fair sample of the officers who form a proportion of every regiment in Her Majesty's Service. The seniors as usual proved to be selfish and greedy. The captains verged on the same state, but the subalterns were, as usual, gay devil-may-care, generous and ever ready to share their pittance with a brother in distress.

First thing I learnt was that, as water was very scarce, it was doubtful if I should get a wash that day; everyone was on an allowance, and my coming was not provided for. The next, that unless I had a *chokidar* [native watchman] neither my property nor my throat would be safe, since it was impossible to keep robbers out of the camp at night.

All this was a strange and by no means welcome contrast to the life I had been so lately leading at Nowshera, where I had the soft and delicious cunt of a perfect Venus to revel in. But as almost always is the case, my lines eventually turned out to be not cast in altogether so bad a mould as first appearances led me to expect.

In a few days I had found a nice little mud bungalow which would hold me. It is true it swarmed with the most formidable-looking and really dangerous centipedes, but I never got bitten by any, so that they only helped to keep me in a pleasant state of excitement, and I killed many of them. What made up for a great deal of the discomfort at Cherat was the delicious, cool and bracing air. I felt invigorated and strengthened by it. I enjoyed to the fullest inhaling it; and the savage grandeur of the scenery added enjoyment to breathing the pure mountain breezes which played upon it.

Soubratie had returned to Nowshera for his wife and my baggage, and it was nearly a fortnight before he returned. It was so difficult getting a cart, he said, he had to stay until Stone could get one for him, but I suspect that the profit arising from Mrs Soubratie's facile charms amongst the officers at Nowshera had much to do with his extra-long delay. I had not mentioned Mrs Soubratie to anybody and indeed hardly thought of her, but I got a most unmerciful chaffing about her the first night of her arrival. A married man! Just from his wife's arms! To engage a woman! It was in vain I endeavoured to defend myself, until I said that, as far as I was concerned, any fellow might have her, that it was my belief she would not be coy! At first my comrades would not believe me, but when they realised that such was indeed the case, their joy was unbounded. Like elsewhere, all the regiment's whores had deserted when the cry for 'cunt' went over the land from Peshawar on the arrival of the troops from Afghanistan and for several months neither officers nor men had enjoyed the sweet solace of a good luscious fuck at Cherat unless, as was the case in a few instances, he happened to be married and his wife was with him.

Mrs Soubratie was allowed no rest. That night she went from tent to tent, from hut to hut, and by morning a dozen officers had once more tasted of that meat of which, until exhausted nature can take no more, man never tires.

There was at this time in Cherat several officers of other corps or regiments in charge of details who had been sent up from Peshawar to recruit their health in our cool and salubrious air. With these gentlemen my story has nothing to do, except that perhaps I should do Mrs Soubratie the justice to tell my gentle readers that her active and much-sought-after cunt drew the coin it loved from their balls, and the coin she liked from their willingly opened purses. But there were two officers of the army medical department whom I must mention more particularly, because the action of one of them unconsciously pushed and almost forced me into that road which ended in pretty Fanny Selwyn's delicious little cunt, whence it branched off into that equally sweet one between her sister Amy's plump white thighs.

The two doctors were Surgeon Major Jardine and Surgeon Lavie. The former was a huge, coarse Scotchman, of low birth and low mind. Coarse in appearance and conversation, he was equally coarse in manners and soul, and I was amazed, after some months had elapsed, to find that he had not only thought of Fanny as a prospective wife, but had actually proposed to her.

He kept good natured and that is about all I can say for him. He was by no means handsome, though he was certainly very big; and in the eyes of some women huge proportions and the appearance of a Hercules strangely out-weigh beauty of countenance and elegance of figure. Such women should be cows and consort with bulls.

Lavie was very different. He was a gentleman by birth and education. In mind he was as refined as Jardine was coarse. In manner he was decidedly reserved and shy, not given to much self-assertion, an interested listener and one who, when he did open his lips, spoke to the point. I used to take most pleasant walks with him, and soon he and I became real friends. In fact, Lavie was the quite unconscious instrument by which the road leading to the sweet little cunts of Fanny and Amy Selwyn was made, levelled and smoothed for me and along which I travelled almost unconsciously until I innocently arrived whither I was being conveyed.

It must not be supposed that I delayed making my first formal call on Mrs Selwyn and her fair daughters. Indeed I went to see them the second day of my arrival at Cherat, when I had at last succeeded in having a bath and a shave, neither of which feats I had been able to accomplish the day of my arrival.

The colonel was at home also and I saw the entire family. I was charmed with Mrs Selwyn, who was an enchanting woman, still beautiful though, alas! rapidly nearing the grave. She was tall and must always have been slender, and judging from the remains of her now faded charms she must, when young, have been more than ordinarily lovely. Her face had suffered far less ravagement than her person, and she still had most beautiful features and glorious eyes, but her poor bosom, alas! had entirely lost its billowy form, and I can hardly find the words to describe the condition of her body. Curious to say, though she knew she was delicate, and her husband had only too good reason to know it also, neither one seemed to have the remotest idea that her ever increasing emaciation must end in an early death; early, for Mrs Selwyn was not much more than forty years of age. Lavie, when I questioned him about her, would shake his head and say it was of no use hinting anything to the colonel, and that the only time he had ventured to do more than hint, the colonel had got quite angry and told him he was much too inexperienced a doctor to presume to give an opinion, and that all her life Mrs Selwyn had been as she then was, and he was sure she would outlive them all.

Naturally the conversation I had with this family, which was to prove so interesting in every sense to me, when I first called, rambled over a great space, for they knew from my darling Louie's letters, which had reached Cherat before I had, that I must be either married or engaged. I confessed to the former condition, which Mrs Selwyn declared she was delighted to hear. I thought, all the same, that as she had daughters rapidly growing up, she would have been better pleased had she found I had a heart still to be disposed of. Of one matter I was pleased to find that both she and the colonel were entirely ignorant, viz., that there was such a person in the world as Lizzie Wilson. They had, of course, heard that the brigade major at Nowshera had met with some kind of severe accident and was to be sent home as soon as he could be safely moved, and they questioned me about that accident, as it happened, as they knew, during my stay at Nowshera. I told them all I was disposed to allow I might know, stating that the story I heard was that Major Searle, having made himself obnoxious to the soldiers at Nowshera, had been waylaid and badly beaten by some of them.

'Ah!' said the colonel, 'that accounts for the extraordinary reticence on the part of the commanding officer down there! I could get no details of any kind from him, by either heliograph or letter – of course he does not like to publish the fact that his men have been guilty of so gross a breach of discipline as to beat an officer!'

'Fanny! Amy! dears, now run away to your lessons,' said Mrs Selwyn. 'My girls have no governess, Captain Devereaux, the poor things have to learn as best they can. India is a bad country for young children, but I could not leave them at home. We have not money enough to keep two establishments.'

I could see by Fanny's face that she quite understood why she was being sent out of the room, viz., that her mother wished to speak 'secrets', and although, as I afterwards found, she was not always ready to obey an unwelcome order without more or less remonstrance, she on this occasion rose and led the way, followed by Amy and the younger children.

When the room was left to the Colonel and Mrs Selwyn and myself, Mrs Selwyn said: 'Whilst you were at Nowshera, Captain Devereaux, did you hear any strange reports about Mrs Searle?'

'Well!' said I hesitatingly, as though not quite willing to enter on any details of scandal, 'I did, but I must say I do not entirely believe what I heard!'

'Then you have heard that she is separated from her husband?'

'Yes!'

'Did you hear anything else?'

'I heard that she was still in India, living at Ramsket, I think it was.'

'Ah! Well, she is as bad a woman as ever drew breath! A disgrace to her sex! I think it scandalous that the government should not force her to leave India! If there is a law which could be brought to bear! But the Viceroy – ' and she made an expressive stop.

'Oh my dear!' interposed the colonel, 'you forget to say that if Mrs Searle is no better than she should be, it is on her husband the chief blame should fall!'

'Oh! I know! I know!' exclaimed Mrs Selwyn warmly and with much excitement, 'Oh! Captain Devereaux! I wonder whether you heard what led to the separation?'

'I can't say I did,' said I, telling a most tremendous lie, of course, but curious to see how Mrs Selwyn would reveal to me, as I could see she was dying to do, that Searle had compelled his wife to commit sodomy.

'Well, read the first chapter of Romans and especially that verse alluding to the conduct of certain men towards men! I cannot be more explicit, Captain Devereaux, and as it is my face feels as though it were burning!' and indeed her ordinarily pallid features were crimson, whether with shame or anger I could not well determine.

'I understand perfectly, Mrs Selwyn,' said I, 'and if Mrs Searle has disgraced her husband's name, I think it is hardly more than he can have deserved!'

'But she has disgraced her own, too, Captain Devereaux! Fancy what the natives must think when they see a lady – for she is a lady by birth and education and all – sell her charms to anyone who can afford to pay five hundred rupees for the possession of them – there is only one name for such a woman, and it is not prostitute, but one more vigorous and of course Saxon.'

I soon became a welcome guest at the colonel's house. The family was what we would call 'homely'.

During our married life Louie and I had lived very quietly. It was in bed that we lived a stormy life if anywhere! Fanny Selwyn, though not to be compared in character with my Louie, did in many ways remind me of her so that I found a charm at the colonel's house which made an invitation to tea always agreeable. On one of those early occasions on which I dined with them, our conversation fell on the advantages of education, and Fanny said, with an accent of great yearning, 'I know I do so wish I had a governess! I shall never be able to teach myself from books without help, and as for teaching a child anything more than their multiplication table and abc, it is the blind leading the blind.'

'What is your special difficulty, Miss Selwyn?' asked I.

'Oh! everything! But perhaps anything harder than arithmetic beyond the rule of three!'

After dinner I asked her to show me what sums they were she found so difficult, and after a little pressure she brought one of simple fractions. I showed her how simple it was, did one after another for her, and finally pressed her to try her hand at one herself. She did, and though being afraid to express her ignorance, as she said, to her infinite delight she got the right answer. One would have thought I was a perfect god to see the delight of Fanny at what she said was all my doing, and I was so pleased at having been able to give her so much real and innocent pleasure, that the spirit moved me to propose that, as I had so much leisure, I could not do better than come for an hour or so every morning to assist at the lessons if Colonel and Mrs Selwyn had no objection. Mrs Selwyn jumped at the offer, but the colonel hung back a little. Whether this was because he might have thought of Fanny's growing bubbies and consequent approach to an age when desire, easily raised by close and constant communication with a young and lively male, might seize upon her youthful cunnie, even though the young man was married, or rather because he fancied I was generously rushing in on a task of which I should soon grow uneasy and repent having undertaken, I don't know. But I at any rate stuck to my offer and it was accepted.

At first I had a tremendous amount of chaffing to undergo from my brother officers, who could not understand my motives; some hardly hid their suspicions that I aimed at seducing Fanny and Amy, others looked upon me as a lunatic who did not know how to appreciate the charms of perfect idleness, but I did not mind.

But as for Fanny! She afterwards told me that in those Cherat days she looked upon me as the most wonderful man in the whole world, for I knew everything. Poor little Fanny. The truth was she knew nothing, and my acquirements in the educational line were to her prodigious. It was not marvellous, therefore, that I obtained over her a degree of power which although hardly perceptible to her, existed like the steel hand in the velvet glove. My word of praise or commendation made her joyously happy, a tear would spring in her eyes if I forgot myself and hinted that she really should have done better. It was an association of real and true happiness, undisturbed by the flames of passion but full of affection on either side the communion, as it were, of beloved brother and dear sister.

The effect on me was very 'purifying'. Little by little I thought more of Fanny and Amy and less of Lizzie Wilson, more of the extraction of the square and cube root than of the matchless cunt of that superbly beautiful Venus; although at times one or the other of my charming pupils, leaning over my shoulder, may have had her rosy cheek, blooming with health and youth, touching mine, her fresh sweet breath mingling with mine, and a rising breast making itself felt against my shoulder, yet, as though fast asleep, my prick remained perfectly quiescent, for his master never once thought of the two blooming little cunts to which he could even then have easily found a way had he been inclined to take advantage of the dear girls' ignorance and inexperience.

Soon the most complete trust was reposed in me by Colonel and Mrs Selwyn, and after hearing 'lessons' I often was permitted to take the girls for a ramble down the wild and beautiful Chapin Gaant, or wherever our fancy led us to stray.

One evening Drs Jardine and Lavie were invited with myself to dinner at the colonel's. Jardine, at that time, as I afterwards learned, was looking forward to asking for Fanny's hand in marriage. I certainly had no idea of it, judging from his demeanour and Fanny's apparent indifference to him that evening as on other occasions. As usual, towards the close of the party, she had come and sat beside me and chatted in her ordinary lively manner. Her mind was fast opening up and receiving new ideas, and a month's tuition had had a great effect upon her. I little knew that Jardine was watching all this with jealous eyes, but on our way home he said: 'You seemed to be all there, Devereaux, this evening.'

'How do you mean, doctor?' said I.

'Why, the little girl seemed to have neither eyes not ears for anybody but yourself. And you seemed to have her hands comfortably squeezed between your own. Ha! Ha! Ha!' and he gave one of those disagreeable guttural laughs which I so much disliked.

'Look here, Jardine!' said I, rather nettled, 'I can assure you I don't like the way you speak. Miss Selwyn is nothing to me but an amiable little girl to whom I give some lessons which amuse me and I hope instruct her. She is quick and clever and very intent to learn, and it is only natural that she should like to talk about her work to me, when her whole heart is set upon learning.'

'Ah! if you don't teach her any other lessons besides, my boy! What had you to do squeezing her hands, eh?'

'I deny it!' answered I hotly, 'your eyes must have deceived you!'

'Well!' he said, 'perhaps so! But at any rate, Devereaux, you should remember you have a wife of your own and should remember you should not take up too much of the young ladies' attention but leave some chance to us poor bachelors.'

I did not reply. I felt angry and vexed that my innocent attentions should be found fault with by a man who professed to see nothing desirable in a woman above her pelvis.

We were now approaching a row of huts in which lived a number of married women of other regiments who had been sent up from Peshawar out of harm's way until their husband's regiments had got back from Afghanistan. Mrs Selwyn, woman-like, had insisted on these married quarters being securely guarded by sentries, whose duties were not only to prevent any 'unauthorised person' from visiting them, but to prevent any woman leaving her hut after dark. This was a source of great irritation to all concerned. The officers wanted the women to fuck, and the women would have been only too glad to be fucked; they had had great times at Peshawar, where they scarcely went a day or a night without experiencing that delight of delights, and where they harvested bags of rupees from their innumerable and ever changing adorers, but here at Cherat they were, as it were, in a nunnery, and they pined for the longed-for prick, and the accompanying rupees.

It was a very dark night, and a kind of drizzle was falling, a most unusual thing. The first sentry, challenged and being answered, allowed us to pass. As we went along the front of the low enclosures before each hut, Jardine said, in a fairly loud voice, 'To think of all these lovely women here, and not a chance of having one of them! I believe they are all bursting with randiness, and would give rupees, instead of asking for them, to be well fucked!'

'Right you are, sir!' came a feminine voice in decidedly Irish tones. 'Right you are, and shall I come with your honour now?'

'By George! Yes! Come along! but we shall have to pass another sentry. Here! Put on my cloak and cap. There! that'll do famously! Now, Lavie! Devereaux! Let the girl walk between you and I'll go in front.' Saying this Jardine put his cap on what I could see was the head of a fine and buxom young woman, though it was too dark to see her features. She buttoned his cloak around her, and without any more ado we four proceeded. Lavie and I carried on a conversation with Jardine in order to deceive the alert sentry we had yet to pass, and soon we had our lass safe from all danger of immediate discovery.

'Now to my hut!' said Jardine, 'you are my property for tonight and this is the way to my hut!'

'Faith, sir!' said she, laughing, 'I'm thinking of taking ye all! I could do it aisy, one after another, and indeed all ye cud do to me tonight wud hardly make up for three months total abstinence. I've not had a man all that time, and I did not become a married woman for that anyways!' With a laugh we condoled with her, and she continued: 'Oh! it's aisy it wud be for any of us to come up to you gentlemen any and ivery night when there's no moon, but you see there's some so jealous and catankerous! There's women down there,' pointing down towards the 'married quarters', 'who would love to come out on the prowl for officers, but who hate it falling to anyone but themselves! Only for that and the reports suchlike make, there would be half a dozen of us in yer honour's beds ivery night!'

'Well! we are wasting time,' said Jardine impatiently. 'Devereaux, you won't have much chance tonight, so you had better go home and fuck Mrs Soubratie, if you want a woman.'

'Thanks,' said I dryly, 'but I don't think I want any woman. All the same I wish you every pleasure. Good-night,' and off I went.

Was it virtue? What was it?

Lavie told me next day that Jardine kept Mrs O'Toole until two o'clock, and then passed her on to him, and that so ravenous was she that he was completely *hors de combat* by four, and that but for the distance of my bungalow from the 'married quarters', and the near approach of daybreak, I would have had a visit from the lively woman. I was glad she had not come, for I knew, when put face to face with a nice fresh cunt, I should not have hesitated to fuck it, and Mrs Selwyn would have heard of it, as she did of Jardine and Lavie. This was not the only visit Mrs O'Toole paid the doctors, and they kept it a deep secret from the other officers, but the secret oozed out somehow and Mrs O'Toole was one of the very first women sent down to the plains when Cherat was gradually denuded of all the officers and men of my regiment.

Early in October a telegram came from Peshawar which sent a thrill of joy through the hearts of the Tommies at Cherat, and made the officers feel happy too, but which somewhat displeased Mrs Soubratie. It ran thus, 'Twelve plump fresh, young whores will leave Peshawar for Cherat today.' This was the telegram from the *kotwal* [police-officer] at Peshawar to our regimental *kotwal*. The moment Colonel Selwyn heard of it he telegraphed back, 'Keep the women until I have inspected them.' He did not tell Mrs Selwyn of the nature of his duty, but he told her he had been called for by the general at Peshawar to go down and see him on important business, and he lost no time about it. I only heard of his intended visit to Peshawar after the colonel had actually departed and it made me uneasy. The house was very much exposed, being at the head of the Chapin Gaant, and the robbers had been particularly active lately. It is true the Selwyns had a *chokidar*, which is the way English people in India purchase immunity from the robbers, the *chokidars* being always selected from those tribes or villages in the vicinity which furnish the greatest number of robbers, but there had been many instances lately of theft and in some cases of violence and bloodshed at night, so that my faith in *chokidar*dom was rather shaken. The nights, too, were brilliantly lit by the moon, of which the splendour can hardly be imagined by those who have never seen that luminary in the East.

I knew that from her delicate state of health, Mrs Selwyn could hardly give the colonel much pleasure of nights, if indeed he could ever fuck her at all, and I also knew, from certain little stories the colonel told me in private, that he was as fond of a good juicy cunt as any man. I guessed, therefore, that the news of the twelve plump, fresh young whores of the telegram had brought upon him a flood of desire and that he had gone to Peshawar not only to inspect them but also to try them, and fuck them, and see whether they came up to the description given of them. My suspicions were well founded, for when I went to Peshawar myself, some two months later, the *khansama* at the public bungalow told me that Colonel Selwyn sahib was the finest man he had ever seen, and that he always had four women every night; and Jumali, one of the twelve, told her colleagues that the colonel had at Peshawar fucked her every night during his stay, and took three others, turn by turn. Poor colonel! He had the biggest balls of any man I ever saw, and no wonder if at times his bottled-up emotions burst forth! I believe myself that the sentries guarding the 'married quarters' at Cherat were put there by Mrs Selwyn more as a preventative against the colonel than against the other officers; at any rate, this visit to Peshawar had very nearly fatal consequences for some of the colonel's own family.

The first night I could hardly sleep from ill-defined dread of what might be going on at the far end of the camp, a mile away from me, where the Selwyn house was, and towards morning I rose, whilst the lovely landscape was lighted by the moon only, and walked rapidly until I reached the colonel's house. Everything seemed all right. The *chokidar* was at his post, giving from time to time that horrid cough which they all give, a kind of sentry's 'all's well'. The next two nights succeeding I took the same walk with the same result. But the next night (at the very time the colonel must have been between the dusky thighs of the last but one of the twelve fresh young whores whom he had gone to inspect), I was just turning the corner where the path joined that from which I had first seen pretty Fanny Selwyn, when I heard a sound which made me shiver with apprehension! I thought I could distinguish my name being called upon. I set feet to ground with all my force, and ran as I had never run before! A few minutes brought me to the house, and during those few minutes the fearful shrieks never ceased. It was for me that someone, some girl was calling and – Oh! God! – the shrieks were suddenly stifled just as I got to the verandah! There, on the ground, with his throat cut from ear to ear, his head thrown back and a horrible yawning gap, from which a stream or river of blood was still gushing, separating his chin from his chest, lay the luckless *chokidar*, whose cough had given me such comfort when I heard it on the preceding nights. I trod in his slippery gore before I perceived it but I had no time to lose. The window of what I knew to be Fanny's bedroom was wide open. It was a high lattice window, opening like a door, and the sill of it was no more than two and a half or three feet from the ground. I sprang through it at a bound, and there before me I saw a tawny Afghan struggling between a pair of quivering thighs, completely naked and uncovered, and those thighs and feet and legs I knew to be Fanny's.

For a moment I stood paralysed with horror. The position of the accursed Afghan was exactly that of a man who in fucking a woman has completed the exquisite short digs and is pressing his prick way home while pouring out his burning spunk! His struggles were exactly those of a man under such circumstances, and his whole weight seemed to be resting on the quivering form of the prostrate girl. I could not see her face, but her poor left hand lying motionless and palm upwards told me that she was insensible, if not dead. It was only a moment I stood thus. Then, with a stifled cry of rage and despair, I rushed at the sacrilegious brute who was thus defiling the temple reared for beings altogether superior to such as him; he had not heard me jump in at the window for the floor was *chaman* [extremely hard lime and mortar] and my shoes had India rubber soles, being, in fact, my lawn-tennis shoes. I seized him by the collar of his coat, and gave one wrench, pulling up so suddenly that he had no time to let go his hold of poor Fanny, but dropped her as soon as he recovered from his surprise. The lifeless manner in which the unfortunate girl fell back with a thud on the bed, her head almost disappearing on the other side of it, gave me a further terrible shock. I was convinced she was dead. But the rotten material of which the burly brute's coat was made, gave with a shrill-sounding tear, and a cloud of stinking dust rushed forth from it as though from the explosion of a musket. Without attempting to attack me in return, and with a stifled cry of alarm, the fiend made for the window. Before he reached it, however, I had hold of his coat again, but could not manage to get close to him, he was so quick, and I could only make a grab at his shoulder as he fled. Again the rotten cloth gave way, this time, however, not quite so quickly, but too quickly to enable me to grasp the man himself. As the garment almost fell off, his blade or long glittering knife fell to the floor; wrenching himself away, the filthy brigand bounded out of the window, dashed across the path and appeared to hurl himself head-foremost down the steep side of the valley. I could hear him crashing and tearing through the bushes, for all was silent as death. Satisfied that not only was the brute gone, but that there were no others hiding near at hand, I turned with a heart full of sickening fear and dread to the bed across which the lifeless form of the unfortunate Fanny was stretched. The verandah outside somewhat darkened the room even in the daytime, but the powerful light of the moon reflected from the ground and the rocky slopes still managed to illuminate the bedchamber, and the small oil lamp, which generally burns all night in every person's room in India, added its feeble rays to show me what looked like the desolation of death!

Fanny's foot just touched the ground. Her pretty legs with such beautiful and slender ankles, the calves round, graceful and well developed, were wide apart, as were her full and really splendid thighs, white as snow and polished as marble.

I could not but see the darling little cunt, for it was looking straight at me, and the light of the little lamp shone full on it showing me that the bush, which topped the rounded, sloping motte above it, was thickest in the centre, and not very rich or abundant. I shivered when I saw that sweet, sweet, cunt, that holy land all smeared with blood, and a thick drop oozing from its lowest point of entrance. My God! My God! She had then been raped, outraged, ravaged! And by a blasted, cursed and never-too-much-damned, stinking, filthy, lousy Afghan. The incredible insolence which could have animated a native, in time of peace and within our own borders, to commit such a crime, astounded me, but I had no time to indulge in thoughts or rather to dwell upon them, for these thoughts rushed through my brain like lightning. I bent over the poor lifeless girl and raised her head. Her eyes were closed, her face looked so pure, so peaceful and though the colour had fled from her cheeks I thought I had never seen Fanny Selwyn look so beautiful. Her lips, slightly parted, showed the rows of pearls which formed her teeth, small, beautiful and perfectly regular. She felt warm. Of course she would be warm, for if life had indeed departed, she could not have been dead five minutes, so rapidly had events passed – though it has, as usual, taken me many words to describe them. Her lovely sylph-like form felt warm to my touch. Oh! how elegant were its lines! How pure, fine and spotless was that satiny skin! How beautiful were those swelling, rising breasts – not yet full grown, but giving promise of one day being more exquisitely beautiful, even, than they were now – the snowy breasts of a nymph of sixteen summers. The little coral beads which surmounted them seemed to me to have more colour in them than they would have shown had death really taken possession of this elegant form. I put my hand on her heart! Oh! thanks be to God, she was not dead! Her heart was beating and firmly too. In an ecstasy of delight, I kissed those mute lips, and could not resist closing my hand, as I was accustomed to do when kissing lovely girls, over the sweet little bubbie near her heart. It was lovely! so firm! so hard! so sweetly filling to the hand. It was an unwarranted liberty, but I could not resist the temptation! But suddenly I thought about the base effects of the deeds of the monster who had ravished her virginity. My eyes glanced again down over the lovely, smooth, dimpled belly, over the delightfully but only slightly forested slopes on the rising hill of Venus, till they travelled along the deep line of her soft little cunt. What if within those so lately virgin portals were lodged the accursed spawn of a loathsome Afghan! What if, as might be the case if she lived, that lovely little belly were to swell to become the source, the mould of a child to be looked upon with horror and dismay! Oh! what should I do! Suddenly the idea struck me to endeavour to prevent such a terrible catastrophe by opening the beauteous gates of the temple and trying to encourage the beastly slime to flow out. No sooner thought of than done. I did not hesitate! I passed my trembling middle finger into that soft little cunt, until my knuckles prevented further ingress. To my inexpressible joy I discovered that Fanny had not been ravished. The close little maiden-head was distinctly there, unbroken, unscathed! I felt it well to make quite sure, and then, withdrawing my finger from the hot depths, delighted to find by its moisture that the aperture was still alive, I once more looked to see if I could discover the source of the blood, if blood it was which covered that lovely cunt. I could not imagine what it could be from, and fearing that perhaps the frightful and agonised shrieks I had heard might have arisen from the torture of some dreadful internal wound, caused by the violence of the ruffian who had assailed her, I parted the hair of her dear little bush to see whether there could be a wound hidden by it, and feeble though the light was by which I worked, it was too easy, alas! (for I love a fine, thick, curly forest to adorn the sacred mount of Venus!) to see every particle of skin under it, and there was not so much as a scratch. On moving about my foot suddenly trod on something soft and flabby: I picked up the object it had encountered and found it to be a cloth covered with blood, and I had hardly to glance at it to recognise the source of all my alarm. Poor Fanny, in fact, had her menses, and the blood I saw was the harmless result. I almost laughed with joy and amusement. But whatever might be the cause of the blood, there could be no doubt that the girl, in such a serious faint, must be in a bad way, and I began to get alarmed on that account. I had laid her in a more commodious position, hoping she would come to quickly, as I had generally seen women do who had fainted, but she lay so dreadfully motionless. Her moving breasts alone told my eye that she was alive. They rose and fell but through a very small space. Poor, dear little breasts! I caressed them. I pressed them. I gently pinched the little rosebuds. But Fanny's eyes remained hard closed. I passed my hand all over her, over her smooth sides, over her dimpled belly, over the precious motte, down her lovely and beautiful thighs. I even slipped my finger again into her luscious cunt, hoping to awaken her from her torpor, and though I pressed the velvet lips together, and could feel the active little clitoris swelling under my titillations, Fanny felt it not. At last I spied a tumbler on the table, and I sprinkled her face and undulating bosom with the cold water. She moved! Cold had done what warm caresses had failed to do – she opened her glorious eyes, gazed wildly at me for a moment and then shrieked with fear and dreadful alarm. I clasped her in my arms and tenderly pressed her to me, she struggling violently all the while.

'Fanny! Fanny! Miss Selwyn! Fanny dearest,' I cried in imploring and soothing accents, 'it is I! Captain Devereaux! Don't be frightened, there is no one to hurt you now! I hunted that fellow and he has run for his life!'

My voice calmed her somewhat. The poor girl turned her face to my bosom and clutched me wildly, whilst she burst into an agony of weeping and cried aloud like a child. Her convulsive sobs and almost hysterical movements forced her hard little breasts against me, and I could feel them distinctly, although I had my coat and waistcoat on and she was naked. I caressed her, tried to soothe her and she clung all the closer to me. I felt I was a brute, but her nudity, the warmth of her body, her clasped arms, and above all the sympathetic sensations her bubbies caused all over my bosom, made my prick stand with tremendous force. I had no idea of profiting from my situation, but I could not help feeling the delicious excitement of the moment. All the time I kept trying to prevail on Fanny to subdue her emotion of terror. I spoke, I know, in the fondest manner. I was much moved myself, and I found myself calling her My darling! My tender beloved little pet! and similar endearing epithets. Fanny at last seemed to cock her ears and listen. Her sobs grew less violent. She left off crying aloud and turned her face up to mine and I kissed the cherry lips and tried to dry the flowing tears on her cheeks with my mouth. Oh! she liked that!

'Oh! dear Captain Devereaux, you have saved me! How can I ever thank you?'

'By being good now, dear Fanny! By trying to recover your courage and tell me how that brutal Afghan got into your room?'

'Was he an Afghan? I could not see well! I was asleep and suddenly I felt a hand between my thigh . . . – on me – somewhere – and when I opened my eyes I saw two natives – '

'Two!' I exclaimed.

'Yes! Two! I am sure of it! There were two; one had his big face close to me – the one who had his hand on me – on me – somewhere! The other had a knife in his hand and was grinning! I could see his teeth! Then I shrieked and tried to jump out of bed, but the man whose hand was – who had his hand on – who had his hand on – who – '

'Yes! darling!' I said, seeing she was embarrassed, 'the man who was attacking you.'

'Yes! He put his hand on my chest and held me down. I hit him in the face, and must have hurt his eye, for he cried out and put his hand to it, and I jumped up, escaped for a moment and began to call out as loud as I could. He reached round for me and caught me, and I felt him tear my nightgown, and he dashed me down on the bed and fell upon me with all his might and seized my throat with his two hands, and I suppose I fainted then, for I remember nothing else. Oh! how did you come here, dear, dear, dear Captain Devereaux?'

All this time the gentle, frightened girl had her arms round me. She did not appear aware that, except for the upper parts of her arms, she was as naked as the day she was born. In fact, although able to talk now, it was plain to me that she had not yet fully realised her exact position. She clung to me with the grasp of the drowning; and this was what was so charming, and yet so dear, as it was like the embrace of a girl who feels the lively and moving prick giving her rapture beyond compare.

'I had been nervous ever since your father went to Peshawar, Miss Selwyn, and every night I have patrolled to satisfy myself that you were safe. I heard your shrieks and that is how I happened to arrive just in the nick of time.'

Fanny raised her head and looked at me with eyes from which love and gratitude both darted most speaking rays.

'Kiss me!' she cried, with passion plainly thrilling through her, 'you are a good fellow!'

I did not wait to be asked twice. I passed my thirsty lips to hers in one long, deep draught, but whilst doing so a question struck me. What had become of the second Afghan? Had this thought not occurred to me, I really don't know what might have happened. I was rapidly losing control over my passions; Fanny was in a glow of more than loving gratitude; a very little pressing and I felt sure she would welcome me between her thighs, and in spite of her 'illness' I should have there and then swept away the charming maidenhead I had discovered to be safe and secure. A standing prick has no conscience, saith the proverb, and as to that, mine was worse than standing! It was in a terrible state of agonised extension and fighting to crack the outer skin!

But that second Afghan!

'Fanny! Did you not say you saw two men? One with a knife?'

'Yes! I certainly did!'

'Where is the second?'

'I don't know! I suppose he must have run away when he saw you.'

'But where to? Your door is shut! There is only one window and I am certain that he could not have got out of that. That man is in the house somewhere.'

It being plain that the second Afghan was not in the room, I insisted on searching the house. It struck me as odd that no one seemed to have been roused by Fanny's shrieks, and yet I had heard them a hundred yards off when I was outside the house. Cursing my folly in delaying when each moment might be precious, and for thinking of how sweet it would be to fuck Fanny, when perhaps Amy might be lying ravished or murdered, I sprang to the door, though poor Fanny did all she could to try and hold me back. She was alarmed at the idea of seeking danger and was frightened for me, but I persisted.

Between her door and her sister's was a passage. But I must first say I had picked up the knife my Afghan had dropped. This I held sword-like in my hand. I opened Amy's bedroom door suddenly and quickly, and there I saw another sight which made me sick with horror. The Afghan was apparently buggering Amy. Apparently? Alas! no! He was actually doing it! And like the other ruffian whom I had so fortunately caught just in time to prevent any real damage being done to the suffering Fanny, this devil's spawn was so intent on his rich enjoyment that he did not at first notice my entry. All took place so rapidly that I cannot attempt to imitate time in my very true history. I dashed at the villain who withdrew his glistening black prick from poor Amy's bottom so suddenly that it made a 'pop' like a cork coming out of a bottle. He reared himself upright, seized a long knife from off the bed, where he had placed it ready for use before he had begun buggering the poor girl, and with a shout of triumphant defiance and the expression of a fiend courting further victory, he rushed at me crying in terms of abuse common to gentle Hindu and savage Afghan alike that he had defiled both my sister's cunt and my mother's cunt, then, passing from the general to the particular, 'I have fucked and buggered your sister – I will now bugger you too!'

In my rage I roared in reply, 'I'll be buggered if you do!' quite an unnecessary piece of bad language on my part. I now found what a mistake I had made in not holding my knife dagger-wise instead of as a sword, for before I could make any attempt to stab my huge antagonist he had his knife twice in me, once in my left shoulder and once in my breast. He was trying to stab me down to the heart through the shoulder, and had I not sprung back, his second stab would have succeeded. As it was he cut me terribly all down the left breast. I, however, caught my knife well into his left side and turned hard. Fanny, screaming at the top of her voice, had fled the moment she saw this second devil, and all the time the combat lasted I could hear the hills and rocky caverns resounding with her shrill shrieks, for she had gone to the open window and was literally hysterical. Meanwhile the burly and really immense Afghan was getting the better of me. He was far more accustomed to using the dagger than I was, who had never fought with one in my life. He stabbed me many times, but fortunately, chiefly in the left arm, though I caught some fearful rips in the chest like the first one. I began to fight at random, for I felt bewildered by his extraordinary activity and lightning-like blows which I had to ward off as best I could or avoid by jumping from side to side like a cat, but at last a lucky and desperate stab from me laid the red brute lifeless at my feet. I had struck him an upward blow in the stomach, and the keen knife, having penetrated his clothes and outer flesh, had passed, as through a pat of butter, up to the hilt into his body and transfixed his heart. He lay on the floor a moment writhing and trampling with his feet, and then he gave a dreadful gasp or two and died! To the last his fierce eyes seemed to bore deadly hatred into mine, and I could not help shuddering, even in victory, at the terrible escape I had had.

At first I was overcome with faintness and fatigue. I could hear Fanny yelling but could not go to her assistance. I sat on the bed next to the motionless Amy and panted; I did not feel my wounds much, but they made me sick. Poor Amy was lying on her face, which I could not see. She was stark naked. Her arms were tied behind her back, her elbows being made to meet. Bandages, also fastened behind, passed apparently over her face and confined her rich flowing locks at the back of her head. I had not time, nor spirit, to fall to admiring her lovely form, but to this day I see those rich full hips and those beautiful hemispheres, between which was that back entrance so lately defiled by the beastly Afghan's black prick. At last, somewhat recovered, I began with hands trembling with fatigue and excitement to try and undo the bandages. They were knotted too tightly, however, and I had to use the knife I held to cut them, and wherever I touched her the blood streamed from me on to her fair white skin, until she looked as if she were weltering in her own gore; but at last I suceeded, and got the arms free, and the bandage off her face, then putting my hands under her, I turned her on her back. In so doing I unconsciously grasped two full and firm bubbies which adorned her bosom far more richly than Fanny's did hers, for, though some eighteen months younger than her sister, Amy was more 'grown up' in body than Fanny. I was in an agony to know if the Afghan's brutal boast was true. Had he fucked as well as he had undoubtedly buggered the unfortunate girl? Hardly noticing then the fact that the bush which curled all over the plump and well-shaped motte under my eyes was far thicker and more grown than on Fanny's, I slipped an enquiring finger into the palpitating and sweet little cunt, feeling sick at heart with dread and apprehension! Oh! joy! she had not been fucked. Her dear little maidenhead was intact. Buggered she had been, but not ravished.

Full of this good and important discovery, I ran to Fanny, whose voice was hoarse, and implored her to go to her sister's assistance. Already I could hear voices of men running up the steep path which led from the bazaar in the valley on the other side of the house, and fearing lest, in their zeal to help, a number might break in and discover the two girls naked as they were, I implored Fanny to put on her petticoats and to go and cover Amy. But Fanny had quite lost all self-possession. She indeed went to Amy's room, but on seeing her naked, bleeding and apparently dead, and the gory carcass of the slain Afghan lying on the floor in a lake of blood, she rushed out again, screaming and crying like one demented.

I ran to the door in time to prevent the *kotwal* from letting any of his men climb in through the window, and I begged him to set guards round the house, to remain where he was, and to send at once for Dr Lavie and the picket of the regiment. Satisfied that my orders were being carried out, and that though bursting with curiosity neither *kotwal* nor *peons* would try to get inside the house, I went to Fanny who was crouched in one corner of the room, and endeavoured to assuage her fears, telling her that Amy was only in a faint, and that it was my blood and not hers which covered her body. The poor girl had received so many shocks to her nerves that at first it was almost impossible to rouse her to her senses, or make her understand that her sister must be attended to. I called her attention to the chattering and hubbub outside, and I really was anxious to get her out of the room, for I could hear the remarks made to each newcomer and the ughs! and ohs! with which each one saluted the dead body of the murdered and unfortunate *chokidar*.

I wished this piece of news not to get to Fanny's ears yet awhile, and at last I persuaded her to go and look after Amy. I threw a dark blanket over the bloody corpse of the abominable Afghan, and Fanny, with visible shudders, picked her way over the blood-spattered floor. She did not seem to appreciate that she was, to all intents and purposes, naked. The Afghan had not, as the one in Amy's case had done, torn her nightdress completely off her. He had rent it from top to bottom in front, and Fanny still had her sleeves on her arms, short sleeves which permitted her arms to be almost entirely seen.

Perhaps feeling the fluttering remnants of her nightdress made her think that she was covered, but as a matter of fact I saw (and as I saw I admired, and as I admired I desired) the whole of her body in front, and she looked bewitching, with her eyes wildly glancing about and her sweet little bubbies rising and falling rapidly as her bosom expanded and contracted with her quick breathing. Her pretty motte, pushing out a little into a perfect cushion, rapidly narrowed to the point where the plump little gem of a cunt showed its deep and tempting line. Her bush was not thick enough to permit me yet to see that line which is visible when a naked girl stands upright and is not conscious that she is displaying her secret charm of charms to an admiring man, and when she sat down beside her completely naked sister I could compare cunts, and fancy which one would give me the greater pleasure to fuck.

Goodness! what strange thoughts do get in a man's mind at inopportune moments! I was perfectly conscious that what I had to do was to relieve Amy, and further search the house, and yet there I was debating those two lovely girls' cunts in my mind, and comparing their bubbies, their forms and their thighs.

I got Fanny the water and bade her sprinkle Amy, and I begged her again to be quick and put something on, for, 'You are perfectly naked, my dear girl!'

'Oh! What does it matter? What does it matter?' she said, bursting into tears again. 'I feel as if I should die!'

'But look, Fanny darling, you must not give in so! Remember, you are a lady and a soldier's daughter, and be brave! That's right, dry your tears. I have sent for Dr Lavie and expect him here. But quick and bring Amy around. She breathes all right,' I added, laying my two hands on her lovely bubbies. 'Sprinkle her well! That's right! She will soon be all right! Then cover her up in bed and get in with her. You have not been half so badly used as she has!'

'How?' asked Fanny, in a voice of surprise.

'She was gagged by that ruffian,' I said, pointing to the dead Afghan under the blanket, 'and he had tied her arms behind her, and I don't know what else he may have done.'

Fanny had been long enough in India to have learnt all about the theory of fucking, even if she had not been old enough before leaving England to know it in that happy land.

She burst out, 'Oh! poor, poor, Amy! Oh! Captain Devereaux, what shall we do? What shall we do?'

I understood her cry.

'Don't be alarmed, dearest Fanny. I don't think the ruffian did any wicked deed that will leave bad results. But I am sure Amy must have fought, and perhaps got badly bruised and hurt.'

I could not tell her that I had actually seen the Afghan's prick in Amy's bottom up to his beastly balls, and Fanny had run away too soon to have seen it herself, and she knew nothing of sodomy at that time. I persuaded her to be brave whilst I went and visited the rooms, saying that I felt sure no other

Afghans were in the house, but I would first make sure. Before going, however, I called in the *kotwal*, and posted some of his men in the passage, shutting Amy's door so that no curious eye could see the naked girls.

The first room I visited was the colonel's bedroom. There was Mrs Selwyn apparently fast asleep. I tried in vain to rouse her. I opened her eyes and the immensely distended pupils told me the reason for her torpor. Opium! Drugged! There had been premeditation, and there must be a traitor, or a traitress, in the house.

I next went to what was called the nursery. There Mabel, a fine girl about twelve or thirteen, slept with the younger children, and an *ayah* ought to have been there also. But there was no *ayah*!

Mabel was awake, crying and sobbing. She gave a little shriek as I came into the room, but the moment she saw me, she sprang out of bed in such a hurry and in such disorder that although there was but the feeble little light, burnt as I have said by everybody at night, I not only saw her sweet little cunt to perfection, but could see that already a downy growth was shading the motte, which promised to be beautiful when the season for collecting the ripe fruit from the garden of Venus duly arrived. Mentally I ejaculated to myself, 'I seem to be destined to see all the fuckable Selwyn cunts tonight.' For Mabel could certainly have taken me then, young as she was. I knew the measure of a cunt which would admit my prick by this time. However, let me proceed.

Mabel, delighted to see me and not, as she feared, an ogre or a robber, flew into my arms and hurt my left one and my chest wounds so much that I could not refrain from calling out. She started back and roared when she saw her nightdress all covered with blood. I had great difficulty in pacifying her, but got her back into bed, where I kissed her and begged her to stay quiet. I told her how the robbers had come, and I had killed one, after being wounded myself, and that everybody was safe and sound, and that I would tell her more in the morning. She was a biddable girl and really was very quiet, lying down and promising to be good. I examined the two other children and found them in the same state of stupor as Mrs Selwyn. Evidently they had been drugged and the whole thing was a plot. The *ayah*'s absence assured me of this. Had she run away to give the alarm, help would have come long before, but the *kotwal* had told me that it was Fanny's unearthly screams that had aroused the bazaar. It seemed plain to me that the mission of those two Afghans had been to rape, perhaps to bugger also, Fanny, Amy and Mabel, and that Mrs Selwyn and the two younger children had been drugged to prevent their adding any outcry in case of a squalling match on the part of poor Fanny and her sisters whilst they were being raped, etc. The man I had killed had done his work better than the fool who took Fanny, for he had commenced by gagging Amy, who could not utter a sound, even whilst she was being buggered, poor child! Had she not been gagged, I would have heard her when I was trying to bring Fanny around and perhaps poor Amy might have been spared. I went back to Amy's room, but dreadfully sick, ill and in pain. She expressed her gratitude more by her eyes than by her voice and she put up her sweet face so imploringly to be kissed that I bent down, though it hurt me to do so, and gave her some warm kisses on her trembling lips. Then bidding Fanny to remain where she was, in bed with Amy, I went to see whether there was any sign of Lavie and the picket.

I had not to wait long. But during the interval the *kotwal* told me that three of the colonel's house servants were lying dead in the go-downs of the outhouses, viz., the cook, the bearer and the sweeper, and that the *chuprassy* [office-messenger] could not live long, having been repeatedly stabbed, and two children had their throats cut. It was a fearful massacre and I could hardly believe that two men could have done it. There must have been more, but I only saw two and no one lived to tell the entire story of this ferocious attack.

Soon the regular beat of drilled and disciplined men was heard as the picket came as quick as they could up the steep ascent from the bazaar, and jolly little Crean, the wild sprig from the Green Isle, and Lavie both appeared. In as few words as possible I put them in possession of the facts. Lavie instantly sent off for his stomach pump, which he had not brought, not expecting he would require that implement. Crean set his sentries and scoured the bushes and rocks but found nothing new. The bodies of the slain were put in one outhouse by themselves, and as soon as Lavie said the young ladies could bear it, the party entered their room and carried off the huge carcass of the dead Afghan. He was an enormous man, and I shuddered for poor Amy's bottom when I saw the immense size of his now dead, limp and hideous prick! No wonder it fitted tight and made a 'pop' when he had suddenly pulled it out of her unhappy behind! I had determined not to tell Lavie what I had seen that prick doing, but left him to suppose that I had arrived just in time to prevent a rape.

Then, and not till then, did I let him see the state I was in.

Dear reader, have you ever been wounded? If you have, you will remember how sickening it was when the skilful surgeon dressed your wounds. Mine were not dangerous, except one where the knife had just penetrated inside my ribs, but they grew necessarily painful as they got uncovered and the clothes were pulled, no matter how gently, away from them. Lavie insisted on my going to bed in Fanny's room. He said I must remain perfectly quiet and drink nothing but water (for I was dying of thirst and longed for a peg), for fear of inflammation setting in. Luckily, I had lost so much blood that unless I did something foolish there was little fear of my getting into a bad state from inflammation; still, it was wisest to take every precaution.

The state I was in, I wondered how my prick could have stood so exorbitantly stiff such a short time since, whilst I was toying with Fanny's cunt, trying to bring her to, for now it felt as if it would never stand again! I felt so deadly weak. The excitement was over and the reaction had set in. I blamed myself, for I thought that had I had my wits about me I would have left Fanny's cunt alone and visited the other rooms first, and then in all probability poor Amy would never have been buggered. I wondered, did she know she had been? Or did a merciful heaven render her insensible before the brutal Afghan defiled her bottom with his beastly prick? I hoped the latter. I wondered at Fanny; I thought she would have been more heroic, but I made due allowance for her, and oh! she did look so lovely, and so did Amy, when they were both naked! And what a charming little cunt Mabel had too! And so on, and so on, until I fell into a kind of delirious sleep from which I did not awake for several days.

I remember that awakening very vividly. It was bright daylight. The window was open, as well as the door of the room, and the sweet cool air blew gently in upon me in the most refreshing manner, sometimes mingled with loud laughter which came rolling up the hillside from the busy bazaar. The twelve fine young whores had arrived, and I dare say I heard the happy laughter of some of the Tommies waiting anxiously for their turn for a jolly good fuck. I heard of this event from my young friend Crean, who told me later that Jumali was really an A1 poke, and a splendid and very pretty woman. In fact, Jumali was the favourite of all those useful and graceful women. It was she who, I afterwards heard at Peshawar, had always commenced the night with the colonel to be followed by three or four of the other fresh and plump ones. Ah! that 'inspection' cost the colonel dear, and might have cost him more than it did. Poor Amy! Poor Amy!

Well, then, I woke up, and at first wondered where I could be, but my arm in a sling, and a feeling of painful stiffness all over me, quickly recalled my wandering memory. There was someone in my room. I could hear him or her gently stirring on the chair, but I could not see who it was. I called out in a weak voice, 'Is anyone there?'

'Oh! Captain Devereaux! Are you all right then? Do you know me?' cried the sprightly Fanny, who came swiftly and smiling to my bedside, looking as fresh as a rose and as neat as usual, for Fanny was a very tidy girl at all times.

'Know you!' I cried in surprise, 'of course I know you, Fanny dear!'

'Mama! Mama! Papa! Come, Captain Devereaux is not silly now. Come! Come!' she cried, running out of the bedroom.

Mrs Selwyn soon came as fast as her weakness would permit her, for the deadly narcotic which had been administered to her had made her exceedingly ill, and this was the first day she had left her bed since the events which I have, I fear, so feebly described, took place. At first she could not speak from emotion. The tears rose to her eyes and sought along the lashes a place to roll forth, which at last they did. She took my unbound hand in both of hers and pressed it, and at length finding her voice, said, with much emotion and very slowly, 'Oh! Captain Devereaux! Captain Devereaux! What do we not owe you?'

'Nothing at all, dear Mrs Selwyn.'

'Nothing! Oh no! We owe you everything, the lives and honour of our girls! We can never repay you!' and without another word she bent down and kissed me, letting her tears fall upon my cheeks.

I could not but feel moved. Fanny stood by looking on with a mixture of amusement and apprehension on her face. Very comical. She was evidently amused at her mother kissing me, but why she should be apprehensive I could not tell. At all events she said nervously, 'He does not call me Louie now, mama!'

'Why! Did I call you that?' said I.

'Oh yes! You seemed to think I was your wife! You would insist that I should come to bed! You said you wanted me very badly, and I do not know what other rubbish.'

'Well! Fanny! That shows that Captain Devereaux loves his wife and that his only thoughts were on her when he was delirious!'

'Was I delirious?' I asked in amazement.

'I should think you were,' said Fanny, bursting into almost uncontrollable laughter. 'The things you said to me! You would have it I was your wife!'

'Ah, me!' said Mrs Selwyn. 'I never saw your wife, Captain Devereaux, but I never in my life wished a man not to be a married man as I wish you were not!'

'Because then he would marry me!' laughed Fanny.

There was a little awkward pause which I ended by saying, 'And I should have got a good and very lovely wife in that case, Fanny!'

Fanny blushed and looked more than pleased. Her eyes assumed that look which at times gave them the appearance of speaking love and affection.

'Ah now!' said I, laughing, 'if I were only a Mohammedan and you another, Fanny, I could marry you now! But you see we have the misfortune to be Christians.'

'Worse luck,' said Fanny with a sigh.

'Well! said Mrs Selwyn, 'I can only say that if it could be a pleasure to a mother to give her daughter to a man, it would have indeed been a pleasure to me to give Fanny to you, Captain Devereaux, for you have deserved her.'

'And who can tell,' said Fanny, innocently and quite unconscious of the sense of her words, 'but he may have me yet!'

'Come, Fanny! Captain Devereaux's beef tea. I can see he is tired. We have been talking too much to him and Dr Lavie will be furious with us if he finds it out.'

The colonel here entered the room. He looked the picture of misery and woe. His conscience smote him. He knew that the young man lying prostrate and unable to move before him on his daughter's bed was in that condition owing to his lust. Poor man! He knew that a number of innocent persons had gone to their doom for the same cause, and that his wife and one daughter were still ill from effects springing from the same cause. I took his grieved appearance to be simply that of sympathy, but as he wrung my hand, he said quietly to me, 'Devereaux, I owe all to you and you owe all to me!'

'How, colonel?'

'I owe you the honour and lives of my girls – and – I ought never to have gone to Peshawar!' and he drew his hand across his eyes and groaned heavily.

Presently he added, 'Lavie tells me it will be some little time before you are strong enough to resume your duties, and that he would like to see you in your own quarters which are nearer to him, but he allows that you will be better in a house where you can be nursed and looked after, so you will remain here till you are quite well and strong again.'

'Thanks very much, colonel. I hope, however, I shall soon be all right. How is Amy?' I added, 'I have not seen her.'

'She is still in bed, poor girl!' said the colonel. 'The attack made on her had a very curious and I am sorry to say a serious effect. She has had a recurrence of an ailment which attacked her as a baby.'

'There! Never mind,' said Mrs Selwyn, 'never mind what is the matter with Amy. Captain Devereaux will be contented with knowing she has received a shock – not to be wondered at – and is still very low and depressed. Come, Fanny! get Captain Devereaux his tiffin!' and mother and daughter both left the room.

'It is a most singular thing,' said the colonel, looking carefully out of the door before he spoke, 'but poor Amy as a baby had a relaxed sphincter and – you understand? And it has come on again. Lavie says it is most unusual, but hopes to get her all right again so long as she is not allowed to pass anything but liquid. You understand?'

I felt inclined to burst with laughter, only I was so weak, and I remembered that my amusement arose from poor Amy's having been buggered.

'But, colonel, what could have brought it on now?'

'Lavie says shock, only shock.'

My goodness! I had noticed the peculiarity in the colonel before, viz., a determination not to see, or want of power, perhaps, to see, things as they were. He knew as well as, perhaps better than, I did, how addicted Afghans are to sodomy. Another man would have at once suspected this relaxation of the sphincter in poor Amy to be due to her having been buggered, but, like the ostrich, the colonel buried his head in the sand of obstinacy, and refused to see what was apparent. He did not wish to think a daughter of his could be buggered, therefore she had not been buggered. That is all.

Lavie, too, questioned me very closely as to what I saw the Afghan do when I caught him with Amy.

'Now, Lavie,' said I, 'I don't know what you expect to hear, but let me tell you this, the light in her room was very dim, I could not see very well. The moment I saw him, he seemed to see me, and we were hard at it trying to kill one another immediately!'

'You could tell me more, Devereaux, I am certain. I see I must tell you what I fear happened. Poor Amy has the sphincter of her – her – anus ruptured – at least, I say it is ruptured. Jardine says it is only unnaturally distended. If it is ruptured, an operation will be necessary. If Jardine is right none may be wanted. I should feel myself on safe ground if I knew for a certainty that she was buggered, for then the state of her anus would be explained. The colonel says, however, that as a child Amy always had a weak sphincter; even so, some violence must have brought it on so badly again.'

'Lavie, you are a gentleman, and I can trust you, but don't let it go any further, don't even tell Jardine, for it may be one of the unhappiest things that can happen to poor Amy to have the truth known. She was buggered and completely buggered too! The blasted Afghan's prick was buried in her arse as deep as his balls and he roared at me that he had buggered her and would bugger me too!'

'I thought so,' said Lavie, gravely. 'I knew I was right. I am certain it is rupture and not abnormal distention of the sphincter. But I am afraid, Devereaux, that the mischief has been done. Nobody, of course, knows for certain, but everybody in the whole camp believes that Amy was buggered, and the men are ready to kill every Afghan that comes in. Most unfortunately, the lessons you have been giving to the girls come in so handy for a joke, too. It was young Crean who started it when Jardine said he was not sure but that Amy had been buggered. Says Crean, "Then she is BA, Buggered Amy! Oh! ho! Now we can chaff Devereaux and congratulate him on one of his pupils having taken her degree." '

When I was well enough an official enquiry was held and, briefly, these were the facts which were elicited.

The soldiers were, on arrival at Cherat, warned that if they ever went shooting on the mountainsides, they must always be in parties of five or six. If fewer in number, they might be attacked; if greater, it might alarm the natives. But the whores had deserted, and the only fucking the men could get as such was at the danger of their own lives and those of the obliging women they could from time to time find herding goats and cattle. It appeared that two parties of six men each, making a total of twelve, met accidentally at a lonely place in the glen, in which were two fine young Afghan lassies in charge of some cattle. The offer of a rupee from each man made the maidens joyful and they willingly earned twelve rupees each, for each man had each girl turn about. The girls returned delighted to their village and the Tommies came back to camp much relieved.

The promise had been given of more rupees for more fucking, but alas, the promise never could be fulfilled. Somehow or other the tribesmen found it out. The inevitable consequence for the poor unfortunate girls was that their noses had been cut off and, thus mutilated, they had been paraded before the assembled men, women and children; then they had been slowly burned to death. Moreover – these poor girls having been considered to have been virgins – a desperate vengeance was to be taken on the English at Cherat. It was a pity that Mrs Selwyn should have engaged her *ayah* at Peshawar, where she had gone to meet her husband on his return from the war. This *ayah* had Afghan blood in her veins and Mrs Selwyn made a mortal enemy of her by boxing her ears for some impertinence or slackness of duty.

This happened just about the time when the irate tribesmen were looking out for English virgins to rape. Fanny, Amy and Mabel were the only fuckable girls in Cherat, and the *ayah*, knowing what was happening, plotted with the tribesmen to give these poor innocents into their hands at the first opportunity. When Colonel Selwyn went to inspect the whores, the consequences were what I have endeavoured to narrate. It goes without saying that that the *ayah* disappeared and was never heard of again. But for the fortunate circumstance of my having that extreme feeling of uneasiness, all three girls would certainly have been raped, buggered and perhaps killed too; as it was, only poor Amy was buggered.

It is curious how events hang one upon another. The flight of the *ayah* necessitated the hiring of another, and Mrs Selwyn engaged, on the recommendation of a lady of Peshawar, a woman whom I felt certain she never would have entertained had she seen her first, for Sugdaya was the most lovely native woman I ever saw. Mrs Selwyn knew that owing to her own weak health and consequent inability to give the colonel those satisfying nights of really succulent fucking which keep married men chaste and quiet, a man of his passionate temperament must feel desire at times press him immensely. To admit so tempting a piece of flesh as Sugdaya into her house was therefore rash to a degree, but once done it was impossible to undo. Sugdaya was modest in demeanour and assiduously avoided the colonel, devoting herself to her duty to Mrs Selwyn and the Misses *baba* [term of affectionate respect for the children of the family], and in fact becoming Mrs Selwyn's right hand.

CHAPTER THREE

## *Captain Devereaux Bows to the Inevitable*

At last came the longed-for orders. We were to start to march in December to Rawalpindi, there take the train – the line having been opened as far as that now – and then proceed to one of the nicest stations in Bengal – Fackabad.

If I had time I should like to describe this march in detail, for marching in India is truly delightful, but I can only tell of two incidents of which the first affected relations between Colonel Selwyn and myself, and the second raised me to Heaven only to plunge me down into Hell. Let me explain.

The first night of the march we encamped at Shakkote at the foot of the hill. Lavie and I, who were inseparable, went for a stroll and did not get back to camp until after dark. Going to my tent I met Soubratie outside who made me a mysterious sign and told me in a whisper that the colonel sahib was asleep on my bed.

Out of curiosity and wondering why he should have chosen my bed instead of his own, I gently and in spite of Soubratie went and peeped. My camp lantern was dimly burning, turned down as low as possible where it stood on the ground, but there was light enough for me to see that a man was on my bed between the thighs of a woman and fucking her deliciously. I could not see their faces, but I could see their bottoms and such an enormous pair of balls hanging and quite hiding any part of the cunt which might otherwise, perhaps, have been seen when the prick to which they belonged was drawn out of it as far as could be before the next home thrust, that had not Soubratie told me it was the colonel, I should have guessed it was he. I could not resist it. I went straight in as though I had expected nothing. The poor colonel looked up, blurted something, and I roared with laughter!

'I really beg your pardon, colonel! I did not know you were here! Never mind, I won't say a word and I won't disturb you.' And before he could say anything I left the tent.

By and by out he came. I made as if I didn't wish to see him, but taking me by the arm he said, 'Devereaux, Devereaux, I must offer you a thousand apologies! For God's sake don't tell anybody! My dear boy, if your wife were as delicate as mine, you would understand how impossible I find it to go without a woman. Don't betray me, Devereaux! Don't! It would kill Mrs Selwyn! I can't help it but she would not understand. Oh! boy, speak!'

'Of course I won't tell, colonel. But why on earth do you look at Mrs Soubratie when you have such a lovely *ayah* in Sugdaya?'

'Because, my boy, take my advice, if you ever fuck a woman who is not your wife, don't let her be one of your own household. Now! if you would like to fuck Sugdaya yourself, you are welcome. Would you?'

'My dear colonel, I am really very greatly obliged, very greatly indeed, but I think I lost too much blood up the hill there to feel the want of a woman again before my wife joins me.'

'Well! If you do – you know – Sugdaya or any other – remember,' said the colonel.

I am sure he did not intend to include Fanny or Amy in the 'any other'.

On the third day of our march we arrived at Nowshera. How my heart beat at seeing the familiar dak bungalow, once the very temple of Venus, in which I had officiated as her high priest, and had offered so many sacrifices to her with joy and thanksgiving in her favoured shrine between the fair

Lizzie Wilson's voluptuous and beautiful thighs. I was tired with the march – not that the distance we had taken was at all excessive but I had not yet recovered my strength after the tremendous blood-letting at Cherat. Lavie had marched with me. The colonel and his family, attended by Jardine, had gone ahead, and sat on the very verandah where the struggle between Lizzie and Searle had taken place. They looked at us as we marched by with the regiment to the camp ground behind the bungalow, between it and the Kabul river. Amy and Mrs Selwyn had each been brought in a *dhooli* or palanquin, and Jardine and the colonel kept Fanny company.

In the evening after I had strolled to the banks of the river, from visiting which I had been withheld on my first stay by the superior attractions of Lizzie's delightful cunt, I got back to my tent where I found Soubratie mounting guard again, and he told me with a grin that the colonel sahib was there speaking to his woman in master's tent. I went and peeped in very quietly and had the felicity of seeing the colonel without his coat or trousers on, lying beside Mrs Soubratie, whose fine, fat brown cunt he was manipulating with his hand while she was grasping those balls so remarkable for their colossal size. Evidently the interested pair were making ready for a second assault and soon I saw this accomplished. The colonel, evidently, enjoyed himself very much and judging from the little feminine ripple of laughter which from time to time issued from Mrs Soubratie, she likewise profited by the nice titillation which her admirer's very full-sized prick was occasioning her. Soon came the vigorous short digs and then the final hard squeeze home, which told me in eloquent silence that the colonel was inundating the shrine with the oil of his manhood; then, withdrawing his prick from its hot retreat, he lay down panting for a few minutes and after a little while got up and commenced dressing his nether limbs. Had I seen this good performance some weeks earlier before I had been so disabled by my wounds I should have been driven nearly frantic and have had my own prick in such a state of alarming stiffness and fury, that I should probably have waited to see the colonel safe out of the tent, and then gone in myself and in spite of Mrs Soubratie's big hands, which always spoiled any idea of fucking her that came into my mind at Cherat, where I had at the time no other available cunt, I should have gone in and had a round or two with her then and there, and worked off the extra effervescence of my feelings. But now! Oh! It was sickening to me! Not a stir came in my prick. Not a ghost of a stand. Not even a ripple.

But ah! during the next day, during the next evening, a delightful and most cheerful change in this respect came over me! If any medical man should happen to read this exact narrative of my feelings and history he may be able to account for it, but I cannot, at least I cannot give scientific reasons, which no doubt he can and will to any enquiring soul. Well, the next morning I got a nice little note from Fanny:

DEAR CAPTAIN DEVEREAUX – Mamma wants to know why you are making yourself such a stranger. We have caught hardly even a glimpse of you for a long time now. Will you come and dine with us tonight? It will be an early dinner, at six, because we have to get up early tomorrow morning for the march. Do come!

Yours always affectionately,

FANNY SELWYN

I sent back a little note accepting, feeling a strange beating of my heart, for Fanny had grown much too dear to me and the reader knows why I did not cultivate her love more ardently than I did.

Meanwhile honest Jack Stone had been to see me and told me that the unfortunate Searle had died of cholera on his way to Bombay.

Stone was dreadfully anxious that I should not add fuel to the flames as regards reports about Mrs Searle and her establishment at Honeysuckle Lodge and the reason for this became apparent to me some years later, when I met him and a lady whom he introduced to me at Brighton as Mrs Stone. This lady's features struck me as being somehow familiar to me, and on racking my brains I remembered they were extremely like those of the naked lady in the photograph he had shown me on that eventful night when Searle had tried to ravish Lizzie Wilson. The gallant Jack had made Mrs Searle an honest woman again in the sight of the world, and had gained an equally honest right for himself to fuck her whenever he liked without having to pay five hundred rupees for that grand pleasure. She seemed a fine voluptuous creature with decidedly large, well-formed bubbies, and I dare say old Jack had many goloptious nights between her goloptious thighs, fucking her goloptious cunt, as he had expressed it.

It was not without still further heart stirrings that I found the Selwyns occupying my old room in the bungalow as their sitting room and using what had been Lizzie Wilson's room as a bedroom for the girls and children. The door which communicated between the two rooms was open, and there, as I sat beside Fanny at dinner, I saw the very bedstead on which I had so often fucked the beautiful Lizzie with rapture indescribable. As I looked at it and revolved past scenes in my mind, Fanny caught the direction of my eyes.

'That is my bed,' said she innocently.

'Is it?' I replied mechanically.

Oh! What had come over me that the sight of that bedstead did not make my prick rage? I am sure I was dull and stupid at dinner. The colonel, however, was in high glee and I knew why.

The poor man had at last outwitted his careful wife and obtained the much-longed-for fuckable cunt. So he was beaming and overflowing with anecdote. I let him talk and behaved as a respectful listener, only occasionally replying to some question Fanny put from time to time, hoping to bring on one of our old free and unconstrained conversations. The way she stuck to me all that evening touched me. Instead of being offended at my obstinate silence she came and sat next to me on the verandah, where I smoked cheroot after cheroot, listening to the colonel's continual chatter until at last Mrs Selwyn, with a warning that it was growing late, carried him off to bed, leaving me with Fanny alone.

'What is the matter with you, dear Captain Devereaux?' at last she said, laying her gentle little hand on mine. 'You have hardly spoken one word to me since you came. I am afraid the march is too much for you and you feel done up.'

'Well! Fanny, I do but I don't know that it is exactly the march. I can't quite tell you what it is, but I have never been myself since that fierce night of the Afghan.'

'Ah! Mama says she is sure that has something to do with you being so gloomy. Why should you be? If I had killed an Afghan under such circumstances I should be so proud there would be no holding me.'

'Ah! Fanny dear, before that night I was a man. I had power, force, strength, but ever since I have felt that I have none left – no power – do you understand?'

'Power? What do you mean by power?'

'That which makes a man acceptable to his wife, dear!'

'Oh!'

Did Fanny understand? I fancied she did; after a little silence she said, 'Do you know I had such a funny – such a nice dream about you last night! I dreamt it three times – but I am afraid – that is, I don't believe it can ever come true for all that.'

'What was it?'

'I dreamt that you came whilst I was asleep in that room and woke me just like the Afghan did – only more gently – you woke me in the same manner as he did and you asked me to let you warm yourself in my arms and you did plead so very earnestly that I said you might and then – '

'And then?' said I eagerly.

'Well! I don't quite know how to tell you! However, you got into bed and right on to me and folded me to you so tight – Oh! so tight! and – I don't know what you did exactly – but Oh! – it was so delightful and you were so happy – but I awoke – all of a sudden – and you were not there. I positively cried for – Oh, Captain Devereaux – you know we all love you!'

If this was not straight talk I don't know what it was but the effect on me was magical. In a moment my weakness seemed to leave me and my long dead and useless prick sprang up in all pristine might and stood as it had stood for Lizzie Wilson. The whole atmosphere seemed redolent of fucking; desire as strong as ever assailed me. Fanny's bosom, I could see, was rising and falling rapidly. It seemed to me that she was then and there offering herself to me if I would but have her. Her hand tightened on mine and I gently drew it forward intending to lay it on my now rigid prick and to show her that I understood and was quite ready if she was so willing. A standing prick, dear reader, has no conscience! All my fine resolutions not to take advantage of Fanny had flown to the four winds of heaven! I could remember nothing but the sweet vision I had had of her dear little cunt, spoiled as its beauty was by the unclean blood of the menses but tempting all the same. Whether she actually felt my prick or not I did not then know for at that moment Mabel came quickly out of the bedroom and said, 'Fanny, mama says you must not stay up any longer and that you are to come to bed.'

Without even saying good-night but with a firm squeeze of her hand on mine Fanny jumped up and ran.

Excited as I was with the tumult of joy and passionate desire in my heart and the stream of luxurious wine, I jumped up too and, taking Mabel round the waist, I kissed her again and again, pressing her two nice young little bubbies as I did so to her vast delight.

'What a regular woman you are growing, Mabel! What a fine bosom you have! What perfect little bubbies! I suppose you have plenty of hair here,' and I slipped my hand down to her motte and pressed my itching finger between the thighs to her little cunt.

'Oh! Captain Devereaux!' she exclaimed in a low tone. 'You bad naughty man!' but she made no defence; I sat down and pulled her to my knee and had my hand under her petticoats like a shot and my finger buried in her little warm and virgin cunt before she knew what I was up to!

'Mabel! Mabel! You are a woman!' I exclaimed, quite beside myself with excitement. 'Don't you think you want a husband?'

'Yes,' she whispered, hotly returning my burning kisses. 'I often feel I should like a man.'

God only knows what I should have done, but I think I might say that Mabel's maidenhead would have been done for there and then had it not been for Fanny's voice ringing angrily out of the room, 'Mabel. Come to bed!'

With a last feel of the sweet little cunt which alas! I had not had time to make spend and with a last kiss, fully returned by the gratified girl who at only twelve was precocious indeed, I let Mabel go, whispering to her 'not to tell' and rejoicing over my fully regained power and 'standing'. I went home to my tent and quickly undressed and viewed with delight that fine stalwart Johnnie who had so often stood to me so well in my encounters with the lovely foe.

I had ravishing dreams. I fucked I don't know how many of my former lady loves but neither Fanny nor Amy came in for their share. In the morning I woke and found not only my dear old prick to my joy and delight standing as full as in days of yore but also unmistakable signs of a most prolific wet dream – a sure sign that my balls had recovered their power of secreting the essence of man.

As I went to fall in with my company I met the regimental postman who handed me a letter which I saw at a glance was from my beloved Louie. I had a conviction that there would be bad news in it. Bad news! Oh! what had I become when I deemed it bad news to hear that she was starting by the next mail to come to join me in India! And further that she had waited until now to announce that we had another baby to expect – the fruits of our too prolific fucking – about March next. She had not been sure and did not like to mention it until she was certain; the usual signs did not show themselves; but now she was certain that a baby was really in existence and had run nearly six months of its natural life! Then – if she did come – and Louie was a woman of her word – I should have before me a time when I should not have that intense pleasure in fucking her which I had when her womb was free from lading.

She said from my letters my spirits seemed increasingly low, that she was getting more and more alarmed and that *conte que conte* she would come and join me; she did not know where but she would find out in Bombay on landing. Next mail here! she must be in the Red Sea now! Or perhaps in the Indian Ocean and she would get to Fackabad almost as soon as we would! Oh! Fanny! Fanny! How could I have you now? Gods! To think that the day had come when I did not want the woman who at one time had persuaded my soul and my senses that I should never care for another; the woman whose darling cunt alone made my prick stand and had taken the shine out of all others! I was, I tell you, dear readers, torn with contending emotions. It was too late to stop Louie. She was as surely on her way as I had felt Mabel's dear little cunt! I should never fuck it now! No! nor Fanny's either. And just as I had at last made up my mind that I could no longer, without dishonour to myself or either of these charming girls, stay the craving which we all three felt.

No wonder Lavie who soon joined me on the dusty road found me glum and cast down.

'Look here, Devereaux!' said he. 'I know well what it is. You are just killing yourself with the foolish fancy that your prick will never stand again! Now listen to me! Be wise and give up such absurd ideas! You will find the old gentleman lift himself up again some day soon if you will leave him alone and let him wear off his sulks; but if your mind dwells on it you may render yourself permanently impotent, for the mind has great power over the senses. I'll just tell you a little story of myself as an illustration. It happened at Woolwich three years ago; I had been on duty at the Herbert Hospital and a brother officer came walking home with me in the evening, a fellow I was very fond of. It was about nine o'clock and on passing the artillery barracks I saw a very nice-looking girl, evidently a poll, standing on the pavement. I wished her good-night and asked her if she was expecting anybody. "Yes dear," she said, "I was expecting you."

' "Oh!" said I, "then come along and I'll go home with you. Where do you live?"

' "In Wood Street," said she.

' "That is not your street, Lavie," said my friend, "and it is mine, so you had better let me see the young lady home and go to your lodging yourself."

' "Not I," I replied laughing. "I want a poke and I am going to fuck this girl – am I not, my dear?"

' "Of course," said she, "you asked me first and I'll come with you but if your friend likes I'll go to him or he can come to me when you are done."

' "Buttered buns!" said my friend laughing. "No, thank you. Tomorrow night, however, if you will meet me at the road to the cemetery at eight I will take you home and we will have it out then."

' "All right," said she.

'Well, we walked on and soon were at Wood Street and, just as the girl turned in at her gate and I was following her, my friend called out to her, "You had far better have come with me for Lavie is good for nothing and you'll get no change out of his balls tonight." The girl laughed and so did I.

'Well, we went upstairs to her bedroom and undressed and she was as fine and nicely made a little poll as you ever saw: good bubbies, nice skin, good arms and legs, and a fine black bush hiding a soft fat little cunt! But by Jove! I could not get a stand! The words of my friend kept ringing in my ears and I kept thinking to myself my God! fancy if it comes true! – and true it did come, simply because I doubted my own power. The poor girl was very much put about. Everything she could think of was tried – but in vain – to make my brute of a prick stand. I wanted to pay her and leave her, for I was miserable, but she like a little darling would not let me go. "You try and sleep," said she, "I won't touch you any more and I dare say your prick will be all right by morning and we can fuck then." I thought I never would sleep but at last I dozed off and, I suppose in an hour's time, woke up and found I had a glorious stand. The girl was fast asleep with her back towards me. Without wakening her I got one of my legs between hers, working myself round and along her until I had the right direction, and when she woke I had my prick buried in her cunt up to my balls. Well, she would not have it that way but insisted on my doing Adam and Eve and I never enjoyed a night's fucking more. I had her seven or eight times and when I went away after she had given me some breakfast she asked me if she had not done right to not let me go? She said she knew it was only nervous depression and the effect of fancy and that she had more than once had experience with it and so was not surprised when she was disappointed. So you see, Devereaux, how I, who had no such cause as you have to be weak, lost my power from simple imagination. Don't you indulge in fears any more.'

I thanked Lavie heartily for his sympathy and then told him how I had quite unexpectedly recovered; how I had had a wet dream and how delighted I had been. He was glad to hear what I had told him as he had begun to get alarmed for me but he evidently was curious to know why I was so very despondent. So I told him it arose from my having received a letter from my wife announcing her speedy arrival in India with a six months' baby in her belly and I said I was alarmed for her safety. Lavie was quite taken in and the rest of our conversation turned on the folly of pregnant women undertaking long and tedious journeys; the terrors of the hot weather; infant mortality in India and so forth, but my mind lamented the lost chance of dear Fanny's cunt just as it seemed so well within my reach.

On arrival at Akhtora I went direct to the Selwyn tent and found Mrs Selwyn and the colonel sitting in the shade of it, for the sun was burning hot although the air was so cool, it being in the middle of the delicious cool weather of northern India. Fanny who was sitting by her mother's side blushed. Oh! she blushed a beet-red blush which fortunately her mother did not see. Mabel standing in the tent door leaning against the door-pole grinned at me and turned red too for a moment and knowing that she had a dark background she gave me a perfect contour of her rising bosom, swelling out her fine little bubbies as much as she could and showing her legs too by occasionally putting her foot up against the opposite door-pole as high as she could reach. She had extremely good legs and very pretty feet and ankles. Jardine and Amy were sitting at the far corner of the tent. The colonel soon went off to see the camp and I then told Mrs Selwyn about Louie's letter.

Both she and Fanny called out in surprise at the sudden determination Louie had taken and looked at one another. Poor Fanny turned as white as death. So white that I thought she was going to faint. Mrs Selwyn saw it but fortunately did not put it down to the real cause.

'Fanny! Fanny! God bless the child! Did you ever see a mortal turn so white in a second?'

Fanny's faintness, however, only lasted a second. With that wonderful determination which I afterwards found to be so strong a feature of her character, she pulled herself together again and said it was nothing.

'Nothing!' exclaimed her mother. 'I'll tell you what it is, you are over-doing yourself. This march and the long rides are wearing you out, You must ride in the *dhoolie* like Amy and me.'

'Oh! Mother!' cried Fanny. 'I assure you it is really nothing! I really am as strong as a horse and quite fit to bear – ' but here she paused as if seeking for a word.

'A husband and get children!' cried the impudent Mabel.

'Mabel!' cried Mrs Selwyn, 'how dare you! How dare you say such things and before Captain Devereaux, too! Go into the tent, miss, and don't presume to come out until I let you! I'll give you a whipping, miss! Go in I tell you!'

Mabel looked at me and as she turned to obey, laughing, acted as though she had a baby in her arms which she was giving suck to. Her mother did not see it but I did and was amused as well as a little, a very little, shocked, of course.

'It is all this horrible India!' cried Mrs Selwyn to me. 'Fanny, dear, is not that your papa coming back? Get up and see, that's a dear girl.'

'Yes,' continued Mrs Selwyn, 'it is wonderful how precocious children become in India, both in mind and body. Now look at that naughty Mabel. She is not much more than twelve years old and as you see I still keep her in short frocks to let her remember that she is not grown up yet. But, dear Captain Devereaux, I can tell you that Mabel is grown up and could marry tomorrow and get children as fast as could be. You would be surprised if you were to see her in her bath. Of course, you are a married man so I can speak to you about such things; if you were a bachelor I could not. So I can tell you that Mabel has breasts like a woman, thighs like a woman and hair – hem! ahem! what was I saying? Oh! yes, she is fully developed.'

I could hardly help laughing at the slip she had so nearly made when she mentioned 'hair', but I refrained for the thought of hair around that pretty little cunt, which I had now both seen and felt, entered my mind and I sighed to think that probably my prick would never gain entrance there, nor indeed, to that darling one for which my whole body craved, that between lovely Fanny's thighs.

'Well, Mrs Selwyn,' I said, 'the only thing for it is to do as I say. Try and not notice anything which is not too openly said and done in the way of sexual precociousness and try to lead the youthful mind into another channel. I promise you I will try and do my best to second you.'

'Ah! my dear, Captain Devereaux, how kind you are!' And the good lady let some tears run down her cheeks. Positively I felt an awful beast. For I had not at all intended to lead the girls themselves into any other channel than that which would the most speedily bring my prick slick into their charming cunts.

Oh! Lizzie Wilson! Lizzie Wilson! What a pity it was I ever had you. But for that I should have been overjoyed at my Louie's coming to me; but alas! Lizzie's delightful cunt had brought back all that old burning love of change which had made me a cunt-hunter before I was married.

I must leave my sympathising readers to realise the contending passions which tore me. There were now dancing before me two sweet, sweet cunts – Louie's and Fanny's; Mabel's did not count. I had the most intense desire to taste Fanny's. I felt so sure it would be superb to fuck the girl on account of her passionate temperament. I had the liveliest recollection of my Louie's and the more I recalled it to mind the more I loved the thought of it and the stiffer it made my prick to stand.

I had fully expected on arrival at Fackabad to have found Louie there or a letter announcing her arrival at Bombay, whereas what I did find was a letter written in the greatest despondency saying that upon application to the agents of the P & O she was told that there would be no room for her until the third steamer after the one she had intended coming by. Sure that she was coming, I behaved accordingly and kept as much out of Fanny's way as I could without being downright rude. Even Mrs Selwyn complained of my making myself such a stranger. The colonel did not mind because Mrs Soubratie satisfied his every want regularly, I having taken a bungalow just at the back of the Selwyns so making it very handy for the poor colonel when he felt cunt-hungry, which was very often. But Fanny was awfully offended with me. There was no deceiving her. She knew quite well what it meant and that I was simply sacrificing her happiness to the exigencies of the case. Yet at times, when I was unavoidably thrown into her society more closely than at others, I could not so well preserve the gravity of my demeanour as to prevent her seeing that I admired her and what a real pleasure it was for me to be with her. Once indeed she said to me, 'Captain Devereaux, once upon a time I thought you the wisest man I ever knew.'

'And what do you think me now, Miss Selwyn?'

'A fool!' said she with emphasis. Jumping up, she walked away with her head in the air and in the most disdainful manner.

After that I thought that the sooner Louie came the better. If once a woman despises a man it is a poor chance he has of ever having her.

But it seemed to me that there would never be a chance of poor Louie's coming. By some extraordinary error on somebody's part she missed the steamer and then came a catastrophe which caused a silence of two mails and indeed nearly ended her life. I think what I felt most was Fanny Selwyn's apparent nonchalance when she heard that Louie's life was in great danger. At one time she would have found it difficult to avoid expressing openly her joy at such a catastrophe, for if Louie died she would (she was sure of it) marry me, but now she coldly hoped that poor Mrs Devereaux might recover. The accident which so nearly put an end to poor Louie very nearly put an end to my offspring also. Our little baby girl, playing at the top of the stairs, very nearly tumbled down them. Louie who was watching her sprang to help her and in doing so tripped and not only fell but precipitated herself and the baby down the whole flight. Fortunately the child was not seriously injured but poor Louie, being in the family way, was terribly hurt. The result was a premature confinement and the delivery of a dead boy and a hovering between life and death for some weeks. My anxiety was fearful. Poor Mrs Selwyn did all she could to comfort me. All the family, even Mabel (who had developed into a very naughty girl, forever talking *double entendre* since I had tickled her cunnie at Nowshera), showed their sympathy with me, except Fanny, who openly said that I did not deserve a good wife and so God was taking mine from me. I can tell you that there was much more hate than love between us at that time. Fortunately it was, however, only skin deep. Fanny and I were both deceiving ourselves. She imagined that she detested me as much as she had loved me before and I tried to think that after all she was by no means as desirable as I had at first thought and that if I had the chance now I would not fuck her.

So days and days rolled by. There was an assumed truce between us and things might have gone on so until Fanny and I should have been separated in the natural course of events – but all was in the hands of Venus who smiled at our puny efforts to guide our own course. The time for the sacrifice had arrived; the veil of Fanny's maidenhead was doomed to destruction and in the shrine of her virgin cunt was to be set up that prick which had once been the god of her ardent devotion. Yes, Fanny Selwyn with joy opened her thighs to me and I will now tell you how it all came about.

Fackabad is a large station. A European and a native regiment are always quartered there with a battery of artillery and a squadron of native cavalry; there were plenty of civilians too so that we had some very good society in the place. In this way it was very different from Cherat where there were no civilians and only our regiment and the details of others. At Fackabad we had a judge, a deputy commissioner, a civil doctor, a civil engineer and a number of other civilians, besides a Roman Catholic priest, a Church of England padre and a Presbyterian minister. In addition to these male exhorters, who lived pure and simple and blameless lives, we had a number of very charming youthful ladies known as the Zenana Mission, one of the fair female missionaries being so beautifully furnished with charms both of face and person that she raised desire far more carnal than spiritual in the minds of those mundane inhabitants of the cantonment who like myself worshipped the Creator in his creatures.

Lawn tennis, polo and cricket occupied the quiet ones and all were attractive pursuits on the beautiful evenings when the cool shade made exercise delightful and even necessary, for it can be very cool from the end of November to the beginning of March in the northern part of India; we soldiers had plenty of parades, with drills both morning and evening, except on Thursdays and Sundays, days always devoted to rest and ease in that country. If we had been idle at Cherat we made up for it now at Fackabad and there were not a few who welcomed the coming hot weather – hot winds, hot nights, hot days – for the sake of the nominal parades and the minimum amount of work, for man is by nature an idle animal when his pleasures are not concerned.

Hence my patient readers can readily understand that as the houses of the cantonment spread over a very considerable space and our work lay in very different directions, I really saw very little of my once constant companions. We saw one another at mess in the evenings and would say a few words to one another but I was never much addicted to staying longer than to smoke a cigarette after dinner; I was only too glad to go home and to take off my uniform and, clad in loose clothes, to sit in my long armchair and smoke and read at my ease rather than stay late after mess. Besides I was sore at heart. I was in great anxiety about poor Louie after her accident and I could not but recognise that so far as Fanny Selwyn was concerned the course of true love not only did not run at all smooth but that to all appearances the frail bark in which I had sailed down that current had got stranded if not altogether wrecked. I felt defeated and defeated through my own fears and I felt somewhat degraded in her eyes – in the eyes of a girl who had almost invited me to fuck her. I felt that she despised me and my want of that courage which is so valued by the girl full of desire and passion. But instead of trying to regain my lost footing in her esteem I had quite come to the conclusion that I must give up all idea of Fanny, that the enterprise I was once so naturally embarked upon had been providentially nipped in the bud and that to endeavour again to embark upon it would be to tempt providence to pour down the vials of its wrath upon my foolish head; but I was unhappy all the same; I did not like it.

Venus, behind her ambrosial clouds, naked, loving, beautiful, smiled as she read my heart.

I might have kept up my acquaintance more vigorously with the Selwyns but for Mabel. That little girl, ever since I had tickled her cunnie at Now-shera, evidently looked forward to being fucked by me very soon and she was more than daring whenever I visited her family. She plagued me beyond bearing. Her delight was, by word, look or gesture, to make my prick stand, no matter whether her mother was standing beside us, and my embarrass-ment was simply enormous. Pretending to consider herself a mere child, she would in spite of her mother's too feeble chidings seat herself on my lap and hiding her hand under her feel for and clutch my infernal fool of a prick, which would stand furiously for her though I wished it cut off at such moments. If I happened to be spending an evening at her father's house and to be engaged in a game of chess with one of the two girls, Mabel would find an opportunity to slip unnoticed under the table, crawl to my knees and with her nimble fingers unbutton my trousers and, putting in her little exciting hand, take possession of all she found there. I should have laughed at it only I was terrified lest this very forward play might be discovered. I had to sit tight up against the table and do my best to seem unconcerned whilst Mabel's moving hand was precious nearly making me spend! – a catastrophe I am thankful to say she never quite succeeded in bringing about. I took every chance to beg and implore her to be more careful of herself and me but her reply would be to toss up her short frocks and treat me to a complete exposure of her lovely thighs, downy motte and sweet young cunt, which she would insist on my feeling and which I was too weak to resist doing. It was the torture of Tantalus I was called upon to endure and the consequence was as much absence as I could keep from the colonel's house and the feeling on Fanny's side that my object was to avoid her. I could not tell Fanny the truth for she would have been madder than ever to hear that I had felt Mabel's cunt for the first time immediately after she had told me of the wonderful and delicious dream she had had of my fucking her at Nowshera.

The month of March had arrived; the sun was daily gaining power which before the end of the month would be tremendous. This is the season when fruit is most abundant in northern India and I daily feasted on figs, peaches, grapes and even strawberries. The letters I had lately received had been of a more cheerful character and you know what it is to be relieved of such killing anxieties.

One morning at the beginning of March I came home from parade and whilst I was drinking my tea and eating my *chotah-hazry* of fruit and bread and butter the postman came and handed me a letter addressed to me by the darling Louie herself. It brought a joy not to be expressed in words. Ah! but if every cloud has its silver lining so does every rose have its thorn. For though her doctor assured her that no permanent injury had been done to her he had told her that on no account must she go to a hot climate and on doubly no account was she to sleep with her husband if he came home for, though so sweetly, so gloriously, so entrancingly genial, fucking was the last thing she should do for at least two long years to come! Else he would not be responsible for her complete cure and immunity from danger. He even warned her that fucking might result, if too soon indulged in, in pain and anything but pleasure, and he said that as I was 'providentially' in India it was well to allow me to remain where I was out of the way of doing her any harm.

Poor Louie. She told me that the tears were rolling down her cheeks as she wrote the sentence of the banishment of my prick from her longing – really longing – cunt. 'It is only for a short season, though two years seems a long time to young people like us, my beloved darling husband Charlie! Still just fancy what grief and utter desolation would be ours if our coming together too soon resulted in what the doctor threatens – the complete death of all that lovely love which made our marriage-bed so supremely delightful to both of us! Oh! I love my Charlie and I desire the staff of his manhood – that splendid 'prick' as you have taught me to call it – too much, too well, to like to think of endangering all the happiness and delight I can give him and all the rapture and heaven he can give me. No! I will stay at home and be a nun and who can tell but that when the time comes I may not be, as it were, a new bride for my darling husband to enjoy, without that fearful shyness which to some degree marred the joy I experienced when he first entered the virgin territory of which he and he alone is Lord and Master!'

I was joyful. I was so full of the thought of my Louie that the thought never struck me that part of my joy might arise from the fact that she could no longer stand in my path towards a certain delightful little cunt. That cunt was between Fanny Selwyn's thighs. I say I did not think consciously of Fanny but as my story will now tell I had no Louie to raise a warning finger and say, 'Not into that cunt but into mine only must your prick glide, Charlie!'

I saw Lavie come down the verandah towards me.

'Ah! Lavie, good-morning! How are you old chap? Sit down!'

'No, thank you, Devereaux,' said he with a half-sigh.

'Why what is the matter with you, Lavie? You sigh like a calf kicked away by its mother. Has Jumali or any other frail one given you the clap?'

For some minutes he remained as he was, then, slowly raising his head, he looked at me with the queerest expression and said, 'Devereaux, I can trust you. You swear you won't tell a soul if I tell you what it is?'

'Of course,' I replied wondering what on earth it could be.

'Well,' said he speaking extremely slow, 'I love Fanny Selwyn!'

'Good God!' cried I, roaring with laughter, 'is that all? But man alive! if you are in love it should make you frisky and not as gloomy as a sick cat!'

'Ah! but she does not love me,' he groaned.

'How do you know?'

'Oh! I know it only too well!'

'But, my dear fellow, can you tell me why you know it so well? Perhaps I may be able to give you some comfort if you will treat me as your mental physician and tell me the truth and nothing but the truth.'

Lavie groaned, leant his elbows on the table, hid his face in his hands and at last he said, evidently with an effort. 'Last Sunday evening she would not walk with me to church – '

I roared with laughter! It was so superb! A young lady does not walk to church with a gentleman who admires her and thereby proves that she does not love him!

Well I heard the whole of his story, which was that up at Cherat he had been very much struck with Fanny Selwyn and in secret he had been fanning the spark of love within him which had at last burst into flame. He had indeed never shown Fanny any marked attention but as she never seemed to avoid him and always spoke kindly and politely to him he imagined she accepted his quiet way of showing his admiration and that in due course she would give him to understand that she quite understood and that she was quite ready to marry him. But on that unlucky Sunday evening he was sitting on his verandah without his coat on, expecting he would see Fanny and her sisters pass on their way to church and if he called out they would wait as they had done on previous occasions until he had got his coat on, for it was very hot and he did not wish to put that garment on a moment sooner than was absolutely necessary. But Oh! grief! dismay! horror! Fanny would not wait and not only did she not wait but when he hurried out after her he saw her and her sisters running – yes, actually running – away. It killed this poor heart! His hopes were violently dashed to the ground! There was nothing in life worth living for now it was plain that Fanny did not love him.

I listened with ever-increasing amazement. Hitherto I had looked upon Lavie as a particularly sensible fellow, but the story he told me and his reasoning were absolutely childish and proved him, when in love at all events, to be an egregious ass and fool. I, however, liked him a deal too much not to feel sorry for him and I set to work to comfort him and succeeded in doing so by telling him that, accepting his story as absolutely true, it only proved that Fanny Selwyn amused herself by giving him a chase after her. I admitted that she was a fine enough girl for any man to take some little trouble in trying to run after and I wondered that she had not been snapped up – young as she was, not quite seventeen – a year ago.

But do what I would I could not screw Lavie's courage up to going at once to see her (she lived only just across the road within seventy yards of my bungalow), declare himself and find out what her real feelings were towards him. He flunked it. I told him in vain that faint heart never yet won fair lady. All I could persuade him to do was to go and see Colonel and Mrs Selwyn and see whether they would countenance his suit. To this at last he assented and went off leaving me more than astonished at his pusillanimity. For Lavie was a man of strong passions, an ardent fucker; he had a reputation with Jumali and her companions of being one of the very best pokes in all Fackabad and I should have thought that where his prick led the heart his courage would have followed. For it was evident to me that he was much more cunt-struck with Fanny Selwyn than smitten with what we mean by the honourable term love.

Whilst I was still thinking over this astounding announcement of his and inwardly congratulating myself on my being free of any form of responsibility towards Fanny, he returned, his face wearing the appearance of satisfaction. He had seen the colonel and his wife and they had been very kind. They said they could not urge Fanny to marry him but they had no objection to his doing so himself. That their girls should choose for themselves and if Fanny chose to be his wife they would not say no. But when I asked him had he there and then asked to see Fanny he said he had not – another day would do! Gods alive! I did my best to make him go at once but it was of no use. He was satisfied to a certain degree and would live on what hopes he had extracted from the permission he had been granted. I said to myself that Fanny would not thank her papa and mama! Well! I knew Fanny better than he. None the less I hoped against hope that she would take him.

Why? Why? Ah! a smile comes; the more I looked back on the past, the more did I think it impossible that I could have even a chance in Fanny's heart. She had deliberately called me a fool. She had in a hundred little acid feminine ways shown me that she despised me and I believed that she would be more than delighted to say something sharply cutting if I ever showed that I sought her love once more. When a girl offers herself, take her, for she won't be likely to ask you again, my dear male friends! Moreover, although my faith in Lavie had been rudely shaken by his asinine ideas of conduct, I thought he would make Fanny a good husband. He was essentially a gentleman, he had a good profession at his back and I knew he would fuck her to her heart's content, and when a woman is well fucked she is always contented and happy.

I have known so many instances of girls marrying against their wills, going from the altar to the nuptial couch perfect victims, yet becoming quite happy women simply and solely because their husbands turned out to be first-class fuckers This is absolute gospel and my gentle readers may believe it.

I was sitting reading Louie's delightful, loving, passionate letter for the fiftieth time, my prick standing deliciously all up my belly under the buttons of my trousers as it thought of the dear cunt it had so often fucked and spent in, when I was suddenly astonished at seeing Mrs Selwyn and Fanny walking into my room unannounced. It was very hot and I was surprised at seeing Mrs Selwyn, who was so delicate, expose herself too much to the sun.

'Oh Mrs Selwyn! What on earth has made you come over here in this blazing sun? If you wanted me why did you not send word for me? Here sit down under the punkah! Here is a chair! There now! Tell me what I can do for you and you know I will do it.'

Mrs Selwyn looked at Fanny and smiled. Fanny looked at me with the queerest expression of half-fun, half-earnestness in her glorious violet eyes. She looked extremely pretty. She had not lost any of the fresh colour she had brought down in her face from Cherat. Clad in a thin muslin dress, her bosom was that of a glorious nymph. Its two little mountains, evidently much grown since I had seen them bare and uncovered some months before, were swelling out in the most voluptuously tempting manner on either side. Her well-rounded and healthfully shaped thighs were equally well shown off by the soft folds of her dress and her lovely little feet and ankles, crossed in front of her, ended a fine pair of well developed legs which I did not wonder Lavie would like to open and take his pleasure between. Fanny seemed to me altogether more beautiful this day than I had ever seen her before. But I looked upon her as never to be mine and so schooled was I in this thought that, much as I admired her, my prick grew none the stiffer and was standing simply and solely for the sweet cunt between my Louie's thighs, thousands of miles away.

'Now, Mrs Selwyn, please tell me to what I owe this unexpected and pleasant visit?'

Mrs Selwyn looked at Fanny and smiled. Fanny returned the look and did not smile; on the contrary, she looked rather put out.

'Well! Captain Devereaux, I, that is Fanny and I, have a crow to pluck with you. What made you send Dr Lavie on a wooing errand to my house?'

'I never sent him at all, Mrs Selwyn.'

'Then he told me an untruth for he certainly told Colonel Selwyn and me that you had sent him to ask permission to pay his addresses to Fanny.'

'Well,' I said, 'there is just this much truth in that assertion, Mrs Selwyn, and I will tell you just what took place between Lavie and me this morning. I was sitting on the verandah outside here when he came looking the picture of misery and woe. For some time he would not tell me what was the matter with him but he sat and held his head in his hands and sighed and groaned in the most dismal manner. At last he said that he loved Miss Selwyn.'

Both Mrs Selwyn and Fanny here burst out with merry laughter, Fanny's being sweet, silvery and hearty. There was no unkind ring to it but it was evident that she was greatly amused.

'Yes! and then!'

I said that was no reason to be so miserable and he said, 'But she wouldn't walk to church with me last Sunday evening.'

'The fool!' cried Fanny, again going off into another merry peal.

'That is what I thought, too. I had a long talk with him and asked him did Miss Selwyn know of his feelings towards her? He said he expected she did. I asked him had he spoken to her? He said no. Well, I said, if you have not done that yet you had better do so as soon as possible and not go imagining all kinds of things. But he seemed to be frightened at the idea. At last I suggested that at least he might see you, Mrs Selwyn, and the colonel and see if you approved of his proposal. The fact was I did not know what to do with him. He acted on my hint and went and apparently received a satisfactory reply for he seemed much relieved when he came back to me.

For a moment or two neither of the two ladies spoke. Fanny looked at me half-reproachfully; Mrs Selwyn was evidently cogitating something. My prick, no longer interested in Fanny's cunt and the current of its thoughts recalled from Louie's sweet secret charms, had begun to drop a bit and I waited to hear the next thing.

'Well! Neither Colonel Selwyn nor I would object to Dr Lavie. He is a nice fellow, a thorough gentleman, and no one could have been more attentive or kinder than he was to poor Amy when she was ill after the attack of those horrid Afghans at Cherat, but then both Colonel Selwyn and I think it only right and fair to let Fanny choose for herself. We cannot bring ourselves to advise her at all. Anybody may come forward as a suitor so long as he is a gentleman and has sufficient means to keep a wife, so far as we parents are concerned. So Fanny must speak for herself in this matter.'

I looked enquiringly at Fanny who coloured a little and then turned pale whilst the movements of her lovely breasts showed that some thoughts, perhaps not pleasant ones, were agitating her. 'All I can say at present,' said she speaking slowly and deliberately, 'is that I find he is not the man I can marry!' She laid some little stress on the word marry.

'Perhaps,' said I, 'when you consider Dr Lavie you may grow to think him eligible, Miss Fanny.'

'I don't think so,' said she, 'I like Dr Lavie well enough as a friend but I do not feel as though I could ever love him and I could never have a man unless I loved him.'

'Well, give him a chance,' said I. 'Hear what he has to say and perhaps when you examine him from the point of view he desires you may see more in him than you do now.'

'I suppose,' said she a little sharply, 'you would be delighted to see me take him, Captain Devereaux.'

'I would if I were sure you would be happy with him, Miss Selwyn, but not otherwise. Lavie is a great friend of mine and I know him to be a real good fellow. I think he is a little off his head just now but when I look at you I am not surprised. Is not Fanny looking really very pretty, Mrs Selwyn?'

Both mother and daughter looked as pleased as could be at this compliment, but it was not said merely to please for Fanny did really look uncommonly lovely and I had spoken the words quite unaffectedly and spontaneously.

'I have often wondered,' I continued 'that Fanny has not been snapped up long ago! Such a pretty girl, a girl so nice, so desirable in every way, should by this time have had a great number of adorers and several offers of marriage. I cannot make out where the men's eyes are.'

'Oh, Fanny can tell you, if she likes,' responded the mother, 'that she has had two or three offers. There was one gentleman in particular who was very much in earnest – a Dr Jardine – who on the march down proposed to her.'

'Dr Jardine!' I exclaimed.

'Yes! He asked Fanny but she said no and then he asked the colonel and me to try to persuade her to take him but we told him we objected to such a course and if Fanny said no it meant no as far as we were concerned.'

'I am glad Fanny did not say yes,' I replied.

'Why?'

'Because Dr Jardine might be a clever doctor but he is a bad man and quite unsuitable for Fanny in every way. At least that is my opinion.'

'I think so too,' said Mrs Selwyn decisively. 'Still if Fanny had said yes we should not have declined though we might have been grieved she should wish for such a man as Dr Jardine.'

'What made you marry, Captain Devereaux?' suddenly cried Fanny.

'My dear child! What a question to ask!' exclaimed Mrs Selwyn.

'I married,' said I laughing, 'because I had at last found the girl I fancied; the girl, in fact, who seemed to me to be altogether superior to any I had seen in my life and the one I fell really and truly in love with.'

'And I suppose,' said Fanny, trying to seem cheerful, 'that you have never seen anyone since whom you would have married had you not met your wife first?'

The question was too plain to me and for the life of me I could not resist giving the answer which I knew she wanted but which the tone of her voice told me she did not expect.

'I can easily and truly answer your question, Miss Selwyn. It is true I am not easily pleased but I have seen one lady since I married whom I should have asked to marry me had I not already been married,' and my eyes told Fanny who that lady was.

The colour again mounted in profusion to her lovely face, her eyes glistened and shone with satisfaction; she looked at me from head to foot and her entire appearance told me, 'Had you asked me I would have said yes and the sooner the better!'

Poor Lavie. I saw now only too well that he was right and whomever it was that Fanny loved it was not him. A secret satisfaction filled my soul and a flood of voluptuous desire came over me as I again ran my eyes over Fanny's graceful form and charming appearance and my slumbering prick once more swelled and swelled until I thought it would burst the buttons and spring out to frighten the mother and daughter.

I saw Fanny and her mother halfway home and the way Fanny pressed the moist palm of her hand in mine sent a thrill through both of us and I could see that she had quite made up her mind to have me at the earliest opportunity. By God! How my balls and groin did ache all that day.

# CHAPTER FOUR

## *Forbidden Fruit*

It was in the middle of March; the sun was simply blazing through the day; the crows and fowls, all birds in fact, went about in the shade with their beaks wide open and wings lifted from their bodies, so much did they feel the blasting heat at this time. I was seated in my long armchair dressed only in the thinnest of jerseys without sleeves and the lightest of pyjamas – in fact as naked as I could well be, for the clothes I had on hid only the colour of my skin and even that very imperfectly. The punkah slowly swinging from side to side poured down a breeze of cooling air upon me and wafted away the smoke of my cheroot. It was midday and frightfully hot; I could hear the leaves of the trees crackling under the sun's rays; suddenly to my intense astonishment Mrs Selwyn and Fanny rushed rather than walked into my room.

Mrs Selwyn seemed half-demented; Fanny looked as if she had been crying and seemed fearfully annoyed. Both looked reproachfully at me. I jumped up, apologised for my state of dishabille (for I had not even slippers on and was in my bare feet) and got them chairs under the punkah. But before she attempted to sit down Mrs Selwyn cried, 'Captain Devereaux you must, you really must, insist on Dr Lavie ceasing to annoy us any more! He is killing me! He is mad! I am certain he is not right in his mind! He is killing Fanny too! Oh!' and down she flopped into her chair.

I looked at Fanny but said nothing. Mrs Selwyn then told me that Lavie had taken to calling at all hours, even at night when everyone had gone to bed, and that he moaned and raved and wept. That Colonel Selwyn had spoken to him kindly, harshly, every way; had ordered him never to come again and so forth; but it had no effect and they were at their wits' ends because they feared if they took any other – that is forcible – means to keep him out of the house it would only create a scandal and that people were dying with laughter over Lavie's miserable courtship as it was.

Whilst she was telling me this and I was wondering what I could do, in came Lavie, his eyes glaring, his face pale, his lips hard set. He went straight up to Mrs Selwyn and asked her to go into another room which I had and which was empty.

I begged him to sit down where he was but he smiled inanely at me and said he would not keep Mrs Selwyn two seconds and she weakly rose and followed him. Fanny drew her chair near mine and begged me to do what I could.

'Oh, dear dear, Captain Devereaux, do rid us of this monster!' was her cry. I took her hand and assured her that I would; that I had a plan and that was to get him sent to some other station. I knew the PMO very well indeed and I would represent the case to him. Poor Fanny was delighted. She gave me one of those looks which meant 'kiss me!' I hesitated a moment but at last I could resist no longer. Jumping up I seized the willing girl round the waist lifted her to her feet, and pressing her to me, I kissed her red, red mouth over and over again.

'Oh, my darling Fanny!' I exclaimed in a low tone quivering with passion that communicated itself to her. 'How I do blame myself for having countenanced that idiot's making love to you!'

'Oh! Charlie, Charlie,' she cried pressing her swelling bosom to mine, letting me pull her to me until our bodies seemed to form one and not denying me the thigh I took between my own thighs nor the motte, the sweet delicious motte, against which I thrust myself. 'I know now that you love me as I love you! Oh! my darling darling! I forgive you! But oh! if it were not for that I would hate you.'

'And do you really and truly love me, Fanny? Oh my sweetest own girl. You must be all mine! Every bit of you, heart, soul, body, all!'

'Oh! I do I do!' cried the excited girl in an ecstasy of passion. 'Oh! can you not feel that I do?'

'With your heart, my own love?' and I pressed a delicious and firm round hard elastic bubbie in my hand.

'Yes! Yes!'

'On your soul?' and I glided a hand swiftly between her thighs and pressed the equally elastic and soft motte and delicious cunt with my fingers. For a moment Fanny drew her hips back but on my again pressing her motte and throbbing cunt with my hand, she closed her thighs on it, giving me such a kiss as I had never yet had from her. That was her answer. Gods! Gods! I took my hand away. I put my arms round her yielding waist. My prick, furious, mad, raging to get at her, made a perfect tent pole and stood out from my pyjamas. But for the pyjamas it would have risen at a bound to an angle much too acute with my body to have enabled me to do what I did, but the pyjamas held it's head somewhat down and I pressed the mighty weapon against Fanny's quivering motte with all my force whilst I kissed her and felt her tumultuous bubbies, which she was pressing against my bosom as though she was trying to flatten them against it. Feeling my urgent thrusting and putting down her hand, she said, 'Oh! what is that pressing against me?'

'It is me, my darling,' I whispered, in a voice hardly audible or articulate from the excess of passionate emotions, 'it is me! There take me in your dear hand and take possession of the treasure which is yours henceforth and yours only.' (Poor Louie! Had she heard those words spoken in a moment of blinding passion . . . !)

'Oh! my darling, my darling!' exclaimed Fanny, absolutely beside herself with ecstasy. 'My darling, my darling!' and her little hand nervously and excitedly kept clasping my burning prick as if she hardly knew what to say or do but in delight inexpressible.

'Yes! Yes! Darling Fanny! This is for you. For it must be admitted to this abode! To the temple of love!' I again had my hand excitedly caressing her now maddened cunt, between thighs more than willingly opened to admit it!

Fanny could not stand this caressing. She let go of my prick and tried, clothed as she was to impale herself on it. It slipped beneath her motte. She felt it do so. She pulled up her dress a little and suddenly opening her thighs she closed them equally suddenly on my prick which felt just as though it had been in her cunt! Gods! Gods! I think I should have burst – only nature came to my relief and I poured forth a torrent of hot burning spend! This recalled me to my senses.

Gently pushing Fanny away, I begged her to seat herself whilst I went and changed into trousers. The intelligent and excited girl saw the necessity as she looked at me in the quite transparent pyjamas flooded with spend and extended in front by my enraged prick, whose colouring and shape were as clear as if seen in crystal water. But instead of sitting down she came and peeped at me from behind the purdah as I took off my pyjamas and fed her eyes on the galaxy I showed her with pleasure indescribable. She saw the mighty prick, its ponderous well-shaped balls and the forest out of which they grew. She knew that they were now all hers and as she gazed she tried to quiet the throbbing of her hot little cunt by putting her hand between her lovely thighs. But before I had finished putting these treasures away from sight some stir made her drop the purdah and flee to a chair and when I came out in shirt, trousers, socks and shoes she was seated in it. She looked for her new possessions and with burning eyes asked me where they had gone. For all answer I took her willing little hand and laid it on my prick which was buttoned back against my belly. Once more did the excited, 'My darling! my darling!' resound, but in whispered tones; then feeling frightened lest our disordered minds might betray themselves to Mrs Selwyn, who was still talking to Lavie but might at any moment come into our room, I got a book of views and opened it so as to look as if Fanny and I had been examining it during their absence.

'You made the wet come in me as well as yourself, my darling! my darling!' whispered Fanny.

'Did I? Well! my sweetest, next time such wet comes it must not be outside of us but inside you! Inside here! Do you understand?'

For an answer Fanny kissed me, whilst she pressed the hand I had slipped between those thighs which if ever opened for a man would first be opened to admit me!

Whilst thus engaged in deliciously feeling one another and talking the language not the less eloquent because it was dumb, Mrs Selwyn came almost staggering into the room. She was evidently overcome with emotion and was far too excited herself to notice any appearance of heat in either Fanny or myself. She managed to reach the chair to drop into it but for a moment or two could not speak a word. Fanny and I, both in alarm, were at her side at once and waited for Mrs Selwyn to speak.

'Oh! Captain Devereaux!' she whispered and then paused for breath for she was panting with agitation. 'Go in! go in to that – that – mad-man and for goodness' sake, for God's sake, I implore you to calm him and tell him he must not persecute me in this manner. He talks of cutting his throat if I do not give him Fanny!'

'I will settle him, Mrs Selwyn,' said I as quietly as I could. 'I will go in now. Fanny, look after your mother, there's a good creature,' and so saying I made her eyes speak volumes. They said to me, 'Get rid of Lavie and then we will fuck, my Charlie!'

I went into the next room and there I found the miserable lover who had that very morning been talking whilst I had been acting! That very morning! Why it was not yet five minutes since I had had my prick not in Fanny's darling little cunt indeed but between her thighs and had spent a perfect flood and had shown her my prick and balls naked and had had her hand caressing my prick and herself calling me 'darling' and telling me I had made her spend as she had made me! I must say I felt a considerable amount of contempt for Lavie and wondered where all that good sense had gone for which I had once given him so much credit. Poor devil! The fact was he was quite out of his mind and his lunacy had taken the form of a passion for Fanny Selwyn, but no one knew or suspected the facts at that time. No wonder it was no use my speaking to him or advising him to desist from following Fanny for a while at least. He moaned and groaned and wept and behaved in the most extraordinary manner. At last I persuaded him to go home, promising I would see him again the next day, but when he had gone and when I had ascertained that Fanny and Mrs Selwyn had gone too, I put on my helmet and went myself to Dr Bridges our PMO and put the whole case to him and begged him to get Lavie removed to some other station. Bridges hemmed and hawed at first but at last he said that he had noticed that Lavie was not doing his work as well as he used to and he would see him and come to a conclusion in a day or two. I had to be content with that; it was something.

That afternoon I got a little note from Fanny saying that mama had desired her to write and ask me to dine with them unless I had a prior engagement. That was the propriety part but in the corner written very small and hurriedly was, 'Do come, my darling!' I sent reply that I should have much pleasure in accepting the invitation and I went.

As I suspected it was for the sake of a council of war that I was wanted and I told Colonel and Mrs Selwyn that I had seen old Bridges and both thought it was an excellent move. The poor colonel was especially anxious to get rid of Lavie, for that fellow used to come in by whichever door of my bungalow happened to suit him at any time of the day he wanted to see me, and as he used to come some nine or ten times a day the colonel was twice nearly caught in one of my spare rooms fucking Mrs Soubratie and for a week or more he had been entirely without his accustomed greens as he never knew when Lavie might perhaps find him partaking of them between Mrs Soubratie's brown thighs. The colonel also naturally wanted to put an end to the courtship, which was ridiculous and scandalous, so he determined to see Bridges himself and insist on Lavie's being sent away.

After dinner we all walked up and down the fine avenue in the cool evening air, under a sky lit up by a myriad of lovely stars. We talked of nothing but Lavie until Mrs Selwyn, getting tired, took the colonel in, leaving Fanny, Amy, Mabel and me walking together. Amy got rid of Mabel and I would have been as glad as Fanny if we could equally have got rid of Amy too. Our conversation naturally turned on love and matrimony and Amy said, 'Well! I only hope nobody will ever ask me to marry them. I will surely say no!'

'Why?' said I laughing.

'Oh! Fancy going to bed with a man! I should die of shame!'

'Your mother goes to bed every night with your father, Amy, and she does not die of shame.'

'Oh, that's different!'

'I don't see it.'

'Well! anyhow I should die of shame. Would not you, Fanny?'

Fanny hesitated. She had hold of my hand and gently squeezing it she said, 'I think that would depend upon whether I loved the man or not.'

'Exactly,' said I. 'I know my wife was rather ashamed the first night I came to sleep with her but long before morning she laughed at her foolish fears!'

'Oh! Do tell us all about it!' cried Amy, who seemed to have an eagerness to know how such a change could come over my wife in such a short time.

'Well!' I said, 'I will tell you willingly but mind you if I do I shall have to touch on subjects it is not usual to speak of to young virgins.'

'Never mind,' said Amy, 'it is dark and you will not be able to see our blushes.'

I was delighted at the prospect of being able to inflame still more if possible the already highly raised passions of Fanny, whose little hand trembled in mine, and I commenced, 'Well! I will not tell you all about the marriage ceremony because, I dare say, you are familiar with the open-daylight mysteries of marriage. It is of the secret side of matrimony, of the nuptial couch, of which I speak and I warn you once I begin I can't leave off. So if I say anything which sounds shocking you will have to hear it in silence. Do you care for me to go on?'

'Yes!' cried both girls and glancing at Amy I saw her press her hand for a moment between her thighs, for dark as it was it was not too dark for me to see that much. I was satisfied. It was evident that her little cunnie was tickling and I was determined that it should tickle her a good deal more before I was done. Not that I had any designs on Amy's cunt; I aimed at Fanny's rather.

'Well! my bride and I went to Brighton to spend the first night or so of our honeymoon. All the way in the train we had to appear calm, to speak to one another as naturally as could be, but I could see that Louie was not quite the same as she had been before that day. Had we been going to Brighton unmarried and not as we were, bride and bridegroom, I am sure she would have talked and laughed in a free and open manner whereas now some thought which I could easily guess at was oppressing her. That thought was of course that her whole life was going to change now that I had rights over her body which I had never had before and that surely in a very few hours' time I should be exercising them. She told me afterwards she had often longed for that time but now it had come she felt nervous.'

'No wonder,' said Amy again, pressing her cunnie with a trembling hand. I saw the movement quick as it was and made my prick more comfortable under the buttons of my trousers, an act which Fanny saw and which she responded to by a hard squeeze of my hand.

'Ah! no wonder! as you say Amy. And yet if our courtships were more natural and less conventional than they are, there would be none of this unnatural restraint. Why I loved my Louie as I had never loved a girl before. There was not a part of her I did not ardently desire to kiss, to devour! The very ground she stood on, the chairs she sat in, were all sacred to me! In fact, I loved her! I had fancied I loved others before but I now knew for the first time what love was. Ah! it is not all a matter of the heart alone but of the body also. I wonder if either of you two girls has any notion of what passion is? When all one's being is stirred up by the thought of the presence of the beloved, of the desired one! I suppose, in fact, I know that girls do experience much physical excitement when the passion comes on but in a man the change from quiescence to storm and fury is enormously marked. Yet in our cold way of making love, which is the conventional way, it would appear to be proper to forget all ideas of knowledge of difference of sex or even the meaning of marriage. A lover may speak of his mistress's beautiful face, her beautiful figure or her beautiful hips or her beautiful legs or thighs but never under any circumstances of that most exquisite and beautiful charm of charms which, made for him and for him alone, lies between those beautiful thighs.'

'Oh! Captain Devereaux! For shame!' cried out Amy.

'Do be quiet!' exclaimed Fanny. 'Captain Devereaux is quite right, Amy, and you know it.'

Amy laughed and seemed uneasy and remained silent.

'Well! I was thinking all the way down to Brighton of all those charming charms which were now mine and which I was literally burning to possess myself of, but ever and anon would come the thought how might I do it? How was I to dare to lay a hand on my Louie which must startle her modesty, however much her thoughts may have run on the consummation of our marriage? Such thoughts in her I considered not at all unlikely, for modest and virtuous as my Louie was I knew from her general demeanour that, although innocent, she could not be ignorant.

'Afterwards Louie told me that similar conflicts had been plaguing her. She longed for my marital embraces on the nuptial couch with great ardour but she dreaded the first steps. Oh! she longed to give herself to me she said but she feared that in so doing I might lose something of that valued respect for her which I had constantly shown. She feared to be immodest. How could she give me her naked charms without doing that which from her babyhood she had learnt to look upon as immodest to a degree? No wonder we felt an unnatural degree of restraint, a kind of fear of one another, for although when passion drives hard two lovers can be absolutely and unashamedly naked to one another, without such passion that nakedness which ought to be so glorious and so divine may be degraded to indecency and nastiness.'

'I cannot imagine it ever being anything else!' exclaimed Amy, vigorously caressing herself between her thighs. 'However – '

'Amy I wish to goodness you would be quiet and let Captain Devereaux tell his story!' cried Fanny petulantly. For some time she had been walking with her own hand constantly on her thrilling little cunt, quite indifferent whether I noticed it or not. I pretended not to do so, however.

'Well!' I resumed, 'at last we arrived at Brighton. Having eaten our dinner we tried to appear calm to one another. Louie ventured to sit on my knees with her arms round my neck but was careful not to press her bosom against mine. Having exhausted every available topic of conversation and, I admit, having behaved like a pair of fools, so terribly afraid were we of one another, I ventured to hint that it was time to go to bed. "Oh!" said Louie (hiding her hot and blushing face in my neck), "not yet, Charlie darling! It is not half-past ten! I never go to bed so early!" Then for the first time did I pluck up a little courage. I kissed her over her lips and I whispered, "This is our wedding night, my darling, darling Louie."

'She darted at me one quick little look, then cast down her eyes, gave me a kiss and whispered, "Well don't come up too soon, there's a good fellow. Oh! Charlie! I wish it was tomorrow!" she jumped up and ran out of the room.

'Thus having ventured to hint at what was to follow on this our wedding night I felt inspired with some degree of courage and with courage came desire in floods far greater than I had yet experienced with Louie. I literally burned to have her! How long would it be before I might go up? There was a clock on the mantelpiece and it seemed to take an hour to mark one minute. At the end of ten minutes I could stand it no longer. I was in real pain – for you must know if passion means pleasure it means pain too until it is indulged.'

Here Fanny looked at me and pressed my hand. Ye gods! I wished Amy anywhere else but where she was. My voice trembled as I resumed.

'On going upstairs to our bedroom I saw Louie's pretty little boots outside the door. I hailed this as a good omen. I picked them up and kissed them and then, giving a little warning knock but without waiting to be told to come in, I turned the handle and entered. Louie was in her nightdress, just getting into bed. She gave a little cry, "Oh! you have come sooner than I expected!" and she huddled herself under the clothes showing only the upper part of her face. Oh! once she was in bed I seemed to shake off my most unnatural cowardice. I closed the door and running over to her I turned the clothes off her face and neck and I put one arm round her shoulders and rained the most burning and ardent kisses on her sweet lips; at the same time I slipped my hand into her bosom and for the first time took possession of the two most beautiful globes which adorned it. Louie did not draw back. She in no way tried to prevent my caressing her there. I was more than tempted to let my hand stray much lower and to seek for the temple of love of which the closely barred door is to be found at the foot of the forested hill sacred to the goddess of love!'

'Gracious!' cried Amy. 'Where and what is that?'

'As if you did not know, Amy!' exclaimed Fanny indignantly.

'You will soon hear, Amy,' said I. 'Well! I did not do so. Louie had both her arms around me and held me tight but I should have liked to have undone the front of her nightdress altogether and to have kissed the beautiful breasts I had found there, but poor Louie, who would have liked me to have done that too, was still a prey to the struggles of her dying modesty. At last I slipped my hand under her armpit and tickled her. With a loud shriek she let me go but she did not cover herself up any more. She lay looking at me with really longing eyes whilst I rapidly undressed. I put my watch on the table. I managed to get off my clothes and put on my nightshirt without offending modesty very much and I was just going round to the other side of the bed to get in when Louie told me I had not wound my watch and that she had not wound hers either. "Oh!" I cried, "let them run down, my Louie, never mind now!" "No!" said she, "Charlie darling, don't let us begin our married life by leaving undone anything which we ought to do." Oh bother! To please her I wound up both watches with a hand trembling with excitement and then jumped into bed.'

'Did you not blow out the candle?' asked Amy.

'Amy! if you interrupt any more,' cried Fanny angrily, 'I will ask Captain Devereaux not to let you know what happened next.'

'No, I did not blow out the candle, Amy; Louie said something about it but I pretended not to hear. I jumped into bed and put my arms around her and I hugged her to me. For just a moment she resisted a little stiffly but the next moment she yielded; she hid her face, which was all on fire, in my neck and whilst I kissed her frantically I put down my hand and gently drew up the veil which interposed itself between me and those glorious charms which could not much longer be kept from me or remain virgin. With as much delicacy as possible I passed my trembling hand over the smooth surface of her exquisite thighs until I reached the "bush with frizzled hair implicit", as Milton says.'

'Captain Devereaux!' shrieked Amy.

'And finding the sweet entrance to the temple I caressed it with an ardour which Louie could feel pouring in burning flames from my fingers. All she did or said was to hug me closer and murmur, "Oh! Charlie! Oh! Charlie." Finding her so quiet I – '

'What?' cried both girls in suffocating tones.

'I begged her to make place for me and let me worship her with my body as I had promised to do in my marriage vows. Gently she turned on her back and putting one knee first and then the other between hers I gently, but in the greatest excitement, lowered myself on to her beautiful body and then awoke every hidden source of pleasure and passion in her as I made the High Priest enter the Holy of Holies. Oh! dear girls, the rapture of that moment! To feel that I was really and truly joined to her and that the same throb which pulsated in and through her equally pulsated in and through me! It was a glimpse of heaven! It was love! Love in its very highest fulfilment. Louie gave herself to me without further restraint – all fear was gone, all ill-placed modesty was banished – and before morning light had come to take the place of that still yielded by the nearly burnt-out candles, my Louie lay perfectly naked – and not red with shame – in my equally perfectly naked embrace. There was not a part of our bodies which we hadn't mutually caressed and gazed upon and eaten up with kisses ardent and plentiful! Our sacrifices were without number! We kept no count! but the entire night was spent in revels which the angels, sexless and passionless, must have envied had they the means of realising, even in imagination, what they were like!'

Neither Fanny nor Amy had done more than breathe during the last part of this recital and their steps had grown so short that we hardly moved over the ground. It was evident to me that what constrained them was the fact that each of them was trying to control the powerful throbbing of her little cunt by squeezing her thighs together tightly. We were near the front of the bungalow and Amy, without a word but with her hand still pressed between her thighs, suddenly darted into the house. Fanny remained with me. I took and put her hand on my burning and terribly stiff prick whilst I at the same time kissed her and caressed her delicious cunt.

'Come! Oh! come! quickly,' said she.

I felt her draw me towards the lawn on one side of the house where some thick shrubs grew. I guessed her intention. Arrived at the edge of the grove I unbuttoned my trousers and taking her hand slipped it in. Fanny eagerly seized the tremendous weapon she felt but alas my shirt was still in the way and so excited was she that all she could do was to exclaim, 'My darling My darling!' as her little hand nervously clutched and grasped my burning prick in alternate tightening and loosening of her fingers. Not expecting Amy to return since I suspected she had gone in to solace her little cunt with the help of a finger or a plantain or anything which could imitate the 'high priest' I had spoken of, I stood and enjoyed to the fullest Fanny's excitement and the pleasure her hand gave me; yet, whilst so standing, I suddenly and luckily saw Amy coming. I whispered to Fanny, 'Take care! Here is Amy!'

'Ho! ho! There you are!' she cried, 'kissing I do declare.'

'No,' said Fanny in muffled tones, 'I have sprained my ankle!'

'Yes!' said I immediately, glad and delighted to find Fanny so quick witted as to invent a reason on the spur of the moment for my not turning round. I had my prick sticking right out of my trousers, covered still by my shirt indeed (which had interfered with poor Fanny's endeavours to feel it naked in her hand), but it would have been instantly seen by Amy if Fanny had not leant against me, as it were for support, whilst I did my best to put back my most unruly and raging member.

'Yes,' I repeated, 'poor Fanny somehow turned her ankle and I am afraid it is hurting her very much, poor girl!' Then addressing Fanny I said, 'If you will let me apply my grandmother's remedy I am sure I can relieve the pain even if I cannot take it away altogether but the sooner you let me do so the more certain the result.'

Fanny gave a kind of groan as she said, 'Oh! do whatever you like and quickly for it is hurting me so!'

I knelt on one hand keeping myself close to Fanny's petticoat whilst with rapid fingers I managed to fasten a couple of the more important buttons so as to keep my beast of a prick a tight prisoner. Then taking hold of her right ankle with my left hand I pretended to press it with my other hand but the temptation to do more was too strong and Fanny felt with delight my wicked delicious hand rapidly find her well-turned and beautiful leg and press her calf most voluptuously and amorously as it got higher and higher. She bent a little more over me, resting her hands on my shoulders, and gave a little groan from time to time.

'It will be better soon I think,' said I as my hand reached her smooth, warm, polished and plump thigh. Fanny had really beautiful legs and thighs. My prick bounded and throbbed.

'Yes! I think it will!' gasped Fanny, 'if you continue as you are doing now.'

Amy stood by looking on and sympathising but quite unable to see what I was doing.

I rapidly moved my hand up that glorious virgin thigh, pressing it and feeling it delightedly as I mounted, until I arrived at the spot between the delicious columns of ivory. I turned my hand back down and gently seizing the two soft full lips of her plump little cunt I pressed them together by alternate squeezes, so as to tickle and excite the clitoris, until Fanny could hardly stand still. Then slipping my big middle finger in up to the knuckles and using my other finger as a fulcrum against her swelling and bushy motte, I imitated what my prick would have done had it had a fair chance, until, almost expiring with pleasure, Fanny deluged my exciting and lascivious hand with a perfect torrent of hot spend which ran down my wrist and arm. I caressed the sweet responsive cunt with my most voluptuous touches and then, hardly able to keep a steady face, I asked her, 'Well, how does it feel now, Fanny?'

'It is all right! Oh! thanks – that was nice! Now the pain is quite gone.'

'Did what he did really do you any good?' asked Amy wonderingly.

'Of course it did, you silly girl!' cried Fanny, 'or I shouldn't have said so!'

'Well! That is wonderful!' said Amy, 'I'll tell mama!'

'Don't do anything of the sort,' exclaimed Fanny, 'you would only frighten her, I dare say. It was nothing but a sprain. Anyway I'm all right now.'

'Mama told me to tell you to come in,' said Amy.

'Oh bother!' cried Fanny, 'Amy, there's a good girl, go and ask her to let me stay on a little longer.'

Amy was not inclined to do so and much to Fanny's and my dissatisfaction we had to go in. Before we did enter the house, however, Fanny managed to throw both her arms round my neck and give me two most ardent kisses without being seen by Amy. Gods! how my balls and groin did nearly split with aching.

After I got home I had the inevitable visit from poor Lavie. What a terrible plague he was! I did my best as usual to try to reconcile him to his fate and I strongly urged him to do as much fucking as he could.

He said he had been doing this regularly and irregularly every night but could not work off his passion for Fanny and I resolved to do my best to get him removed before going to bed. I wrote to Dr Bridges and I told him that I feared that Miss Selwyn was not safe; that Lavie prowled about all night round her house and that he had a perfect lust for her which might induce him to attempt to rape her. I really believed this, for Lavie was like one mad for Fanny. He had begun a habit of muttering to himself and I had over-heard a semi-threat to fuck Fanny whether she liked it or not. Calling Soubratie from his slumbers I told him to take the letter first thing in the morning to Dr Bridges – and the results will be seen in the events of that never-to-be-forgotten day, the seventeenth of March, the very next day, the day on which Fanny Selwyn attained the double dignity of seventeen years of age and womanhood, the day I at last took her most charming maiden-head, fucking her both to her and my heart's content and relieving her sweet cunt and my balls and groin of the load which had oppressed them since we had declared our mutual passion.

I knew the seventeenth was Fanny's birthday but I had no idea I should be invited to assist at keeping the feast. However, after breakfast I had two very agreeable visits. As usual I was very much undressed, having nothing on me but my short-sleeved jersey and pyjamas, for it was much too hot and there was far too blazing a sun outside for me to expect visitors. The first who came to see me was old Bridges our PMO, who seemed very anxious about

Lavie. He said he had lately noticed a considerable alteration in him, a laxity in the way he carried out his duties which he could not account for until he heard of his unfortunate love affair. He now wanted to know about the subject of my last letter because it was of a very serious nature and if I did think there was any danger he would telegraph to Simla for permission to send Lavie to Benares where he understood there was room for another doctor. I easily satisfied Bridges on this head.

During our conversation I had noticed his eyes constantly directed at the still-blue-and-red-looking scars on my left arm caused by the knife of the brutal Afghan who had buggered poor Amy, and after he had finished speaking about Lavie, the good doctor went in for a complete history of the scars. I showed him the rose-looking ones on my chest and Bridges exclaimed that I ought to consider myself the chosen of Providence for I had had the most extraordinary escape he had ever heard of. Of course, I did not tell him about poor Amy's catastrophe but he had heard the rumour that she had been buggered. I lied to him. I told him the rumour was false and I was glad to be able to do so (although I had to tell a lie) because I knew that Bridges would talk and would look upon anyone who persisted in believing in the buggery as a slanderer whom he must at once put down.

Hardly had he gone and I resumed my book and cheroot than in ran Mabel in real hot haste. She sprang into my arms and gave me a number of hearty kisses and then, looking over her shoulder to be sure that no one had come yet, she pulled at the strings of my pyjamas and before I knew what she was up to had my prick in her hands as stiff as a poker. As I have said before I should never at any time object to so great a pleasure as having my prick and balls handled by a very pretty girl, whom I knew to be fuckable, but Mabel was so frightfully daring I guessed she had not come alone and asked her. To my horror she said that her mama with Fanny and Amy were on their way over and she had run ahead to peep at her pet if she could manage it before they came into the house. As she spoke I heard Mrs Selwyn's voice and the footsteps of the three coming along the veranda. Hastily pushing Mabel to one side I ran to my bathroom where I at once splashed myself with water as though I had been bathing my face and neck and then fastening my towel around my waist so that it would hang down in front and hide the evidence of my terribly excited prick, I came into the sitting room and, as if quite surprised, greeted the ladies and begged them to excuse my dishabille.

My open jersey showed the really terrible-looking scars that Mrs Selwyn and Amy had not seen since the bandages had been taken off. With little cries of horror and sympathy, which did me good to hear, all three inspected them and Mrs Selwyn laid her finger on one on my chest and asked was it still tender. I said not. There and then my darling Fanny – pretending to feel one – took as much of my left breast as she could gather in her hand and gave me a tender little squeeze as I would have done to one of her own sweet pretty bubbies had I had the chance. Amy exclaimed at the thick hair between my breasts and I made her blush by saying softly to her and Fanny: 'Ah! Amy you are as beautiful as can be!' You've Jacob's beauty in your face and Esau's where it should be! Whereas I am Esau all over!'

'For shame!' said Amy.

Fanny only smiled and reddened and I knew she longed to let me see that she, too, had Esau's beauty covering the mount above her lovely cunt.

Well, the visitors, having talked the whole story of the attack on their house at Cherat over again, now declared the object of their visit, which was to invite me to dinner that evening. They were not going to ask anyone else, but Mrs Selwyn said she had looked upon me so much at one time as quite one of the family, that she hoped I would let myself be prevailed upon to come and see them very much more frequently than I had recently done. Fanny looked at me with imploring eyes, full of passion and desire, and she looked so lovely, so delicious, so voluptuously tempting, that I could not have declined, even had my old virtuous intentions returned again. Ah! no! Those virtuous intentions had altogether died away and my prick stood upon them, stiff and erect and swollen with pride, as a perfect conqueror naturally feels when he has overcome his foe. I therefore accepted, with every manifestation of real and unmistakable pleasure and as I escorted Fanny out of the house, following her mother and sisters, I took the opportunity of letting her judge the sincerity and strength of my passion by the relative force and intense stiffness of my prick. But for the friendly towel I might have made an exhibition of myself, that is sure, and I felt thankful to Mabel after all, though at first I was vexed at the insane liberties she had taken with me under such dangerous circumstances.

Now, dearest reader, I hope you are as interested in Fanny's sweet, thrilling little cunt as I was. As interested in hearing about the fucking of it as I would be. Girls, darlings, who may read these dear but naughty pages, I hope your delectable little cunnies are moistening and tickling with sympathy, and, Oh! ye, my male readers, may those pricks, which I trust are stiffly standing, have sweet cunts in which to cool their ardour not far off!

Fanny, seventeen years old, was this day promoted to the dignity of *décolletage* and when she welcomed me that evening I found her as proud as a peacock, in all the glory not of extended tail but of a very lovely exposed bosom. The two darling little breasts were indeed more hidden than I could approve of, but I could see some small portion of their smooth and polished globes and my delighted eye gazed on the sweet path between them which, followed lower, would end in her exquisite little cunt. Alas! the presence of her father, mother, sisters and little brother Harry, prevented me taking my privileges as her lover and once more feeling those beautiful bubbies, but I gave my eyes such a feasting that I found it necessary to be very careful how I moved for fear of displacing my terrible prick, which had, as usual, become unmanageable. I sat next to Fanny at dinner and whenever occasion offered gently pressed her thigh, a compliment she returned as often as she could.

At length Mrs Selwyn proposed that we should all go in and play a round game of cards but, once it was set going, Fanny and I very quickly managed to lose all our cards. We then pretended to watch the game very eagerly; in reality I had one of her legs on my knee with her foot hanging between my calves, where I pressed it. I whispered to her to come out, but she seemed afraid to attract attention and did not stir. We were near the corner of the table, which was a long rectangular one.

Everybody else was deep in the game going on. I became desperate. We were losing an opportunity which might not recur that evening. I unbuttoned my trousers and getting my prick out, free from my shirt, I took Fanny's hand and put it on it. She gave a perfect jump! Her hand tightened on the subject of her delightful thoughts and wishes and her bosom rose and fell to such a degree that, together with her intense colour, made me fear she would burst! But in a moment or two she got up and said she would go out for a moment, it was so hot.

'Do, darling,' said her mother, 'I dare say Captain Devereaux will go with you.'

Fanny went at once and I, rising quickly and turning my back on the company, walked with rapid strides after her, my prick completely out and pointing like a bow-sprit at the ceiling. Oh! that walk across the room! How I dreaded anyone calling me back. But Venus, dear Venus, protected her servants and I joined Fanny on the verandah safe and unsuspected. Neither of us spoke a word to the other; our feelings were too intense and hers altogether too agitated.

Quietly and swiftly we made for the friendly shrubs, of which I have spoken before. Arrived on the grass between them, I put my cracking prick again into Fanny's trembling hand, whilst I rapidly undid my braces and unbuttoned the rest of my trousers; for though poor Fanny tried her utmost to manage this, she was in such a state of nervous excitement that her strength seemed to fail her. However, all strength did not fail me. I soon had the pleasure of putting my heavy and painfully swollen balls into Fanny's curious and eager hands and she, with the instinct of pleasure and extreme tenderness, felt and touched them as though the slightest rough handling would surely destroy such delicate jewels. All this was delicious to me, but I was all the same in a desperate hurry to get our first fuck over for fear of interruption. I rolled my shirt up, so as to leave as much as possible of my belly naked and then pushing my trousers a little down off my hips, I took the sweet and eagerly longing Fanny round the waist and laid the willing girl on the ground. Not one single attempt at playing false modesty did the dearest girl make. She allowed me to lift the front of her dress well up and lay it carefully back upon her, so as to crease it as little as possible and next to do the same with her petticoats and, last of all, to take up her chemise so as to leave her lovely, sweet, dimpled belly as naked as mine; for Fanny, as I had discovered the evening before, wore no drawers and from her waist to her knees she was quite and sweetly naked. Dim as was the light, there was enough to show me her beautiful thighs, shining white, and the dark triangle of her bush; yea, even the soft line of her delightful little cunt was apparent! I gave it one burning kiss, which made the excited Fanny jump, and then, without further delay, I took my position between her thighs, put my left hand under her head to give it support, to raise it above the rather harsh and rough grass beneath it, pressed my lips to hers and adjusted the point of my eager prick against the soft portals of her equally excited cunt!

Glory! glory! I am in!

As he entered that beautiful temple of heat and passion, my prick doffed his headdress and did not stay his progress till pulled up by the virgin veil of Fanny's maidenhead! Whispering to her to 'Raise your hips a little, my darling, to let me put my hand under you,' I drew back for a strong forward thrust. I had not time to spare her. Fanny did not require to be educated up to that point which makes the rending in twain of the maidenhead a less timorous thing for the sweet victim. She wanted all my prick in and showed it by the firm way she pushed up against me and the frank manner with which she gave me her delicious little cunt. I made the thrust. For one hardly appreciable little space of time the doomed maidenhead resisted. There was a little check, a sudden yielding, accompanied by a slight tremor of Fanny's form and a very, very little cry, and I was in the Holy of Holies. God! but I acted as I always have done. I remembered that, whatever my pleasure might be, my chief object in fucking a girl must be to give her pleasure. So it was when by rapid movements backwards and forwards, by thrilling sweeps of my burning prick, commencing at the very outside of her cunt and only ending with the feeling of resistance to further progress, I finally succeeded in being buried up to my balls and motte in the cunt of the exquisite and passionate girl, who helped me all she could! I felt as if I had never taken a maidenhead before, as if this was my first conquest of a maiden's cunt! – delightful love which can make even old pleasure appear new! Long before I came to the thrilling and maddening short digs, I had Fanny hardly able to keep from crying out aloud with the hitherto unknown rapture of being fucked! Of an ardent and generous temperament she 'came' frequently and always with a thrilling tremor which shook her from head to foot and she spent abundantly and copiously. As long as possible I kept back my offering, for once in Fanny, I did not care who came. Not that it was so in reality, but my blood was up, my prick was up and nothing now should interfere with the bliss I found I enjoyed. So that I made the first fuck of Fanny last as long as I could. But alas, how short! how much too short is even the longest fuck a man can make! I could not restrain the lava torrents very long and amidst a chorus or rather a duet of sighs, voluptuous groans and little cries and at the rushing end of the maddening short digs, at last came that burst of spend which makes a man drive in his prick as though he would send it through his lovely comrade and press his motte to hers as though to flatten it forever.

Certainly Fanny was well anointed with the holy oil that first time. I had only spent once, or rather twice, since I had fucked Lizzie Wilson. The first time was when I had the wet dream at Nowshera and the last time was when I had sham fucked Fanny yesterday in my bungalow and I was boiling over. But all things come to an end and after enjoying for awhile the leaps of Fanny's motte and the compressions of her lovely little cunt, I withdrew my still iron-stiff prick and wiped the sweet girl between the thighs with my handkerchief. Fanny lay still on the ground, her eyes turned up to the stars and her thighs open in the most voluptuous attitude, whilst I rapidly restored the disorder of my attire. She seemed like one in an ecstasy. At length I roused her and assisted her to rise to her feet. For a moment she seemed hardly able to stand without support and then she threw her lovely arms around me, and pressing me to her, she gave me a shower of kisses which I returned with interest.

'Oh, my darling!' she cried, 'at last you have loved me as I have so longed, longed to be loved! But oh! I am all wet down my legs!'

Of course. Her overfilled cunt was overflowing and that reminded me that I must take care of Fanny. Kneeling down and telling her to let me do what I liked, I passed my hand up her thighs and introducing two fingers as far as they would go into her hot, soft little cunt I used them like glove stretchers and succeeded in bringing another flow of imprisoned spend down my hand and wrist and so relieved Fanny of what might otherwise have proved a dangerous burden. She asked me why I did that.

'I will tell you another time, darling. But come, let me wipe you once more and then we will take a turn of the avenue and see whether anyone is coming out.'

Fanny submitted to the further wiping with a voluptuous surrender of herself, which was exquisitely delicious to me. Oh what a jewel she was, if I could but wear her properly! What an immense pleasure did I see before me in training this ardently voluptuous girl to enjoy in its fullness the pleasure she could give! She loved me, I knew, and she loved my prick even more; but it should, if possible, be my care to make her adore my prick without loving me the less.

We walked slowly together, arm in arm, for we feared any more lover-like attitude lest eyes might see what none must even suspect. Twice we walked up and down before the house and looked in to see whether any move suggested an exit of anybody, but as far as we could see all were busily engaged. Then Fanny did one of those bold things which made me respect her so much. She went in, spoke to her mother and asked when someone would be coming out and was told to go and enjoy the walk with me as the game was not likely to end very soon. She came to me all radiant and joyful.

'Come, darling Charlie!'

I knew what she meant. We hurried to our temporary nuptial couch between the shrubs. Here Fanny performed my toilet and I performed hers and when we were, both of us, as naked as could possibly be without actually taking off our clothes we joined in another one of those particularly rap-turous fucks which neither man nor woman forgets all the days of their lives. Oh! dear readers, my pen fails me when I try to write down the burning reminiscences of those burning moments, but all my soul, my heart and my life seemed to be centred in Fanny and the seat and acme of pleasure to be in her cunt, between her beautiful thighs!

'Oh! Fanny!' I said, as we walked up and down, 'to have you properly we should both be in a comfortable bed and naked as we were born! How can we manage it? Can I come to you, darling? Could I not come in by the far bathroom door, across your room and into your bed?'

'Oh, no! It is impossible,' she replied. 'Amy sleeps in my room and my bed creaks – and – but, leave it to me, darling Charlie, and I will find a way! In the meanwhile let us enjoy one another as much as we can, as we have done. Oh! Charlie! I never, never, never could have enough of you, or as much of you as I should like!'

The remainder of the evening passed quietly and I went home about eleven o'clock. Arrived there I carefully spread my handkerchief to dry, for it had on it the precious bloom, mixed with our offerings, of the sacrifice of Fanny's maidenhead.

Before going to bed I, as usual, sat in my chair and tried to view calmly all the immense happiness I had attained. But I was still in quite a state of excitement. I had indeed fucked Fanny twice, but here were my balls aching. Was it really so impossible to get at her in her house? Should I risk going over presently and having a try? I knew I could make her hear me from the verandah, for I could whisper her name through the lattice of her window. I must fuck her again and very soon! I was rapidly coming to the conclusion that I could not really wait any longer, but must go to look for Fanny, when to my great surprise and intense joy – as well, however, as alarm – in came Fanny herself.

'Oh! Fanny darling, how did you come here?'

'I walked over, of course,' said she. 'Oh! my own love! Oh, my own darling Charlie, I could not sleep after I went to bed. I lay and tossed about. I longed for you, my darling! my darling! and at last I made up my mind that no matter what would happen, I would risk all and come to you – and now, see! I am come to give myself, wholly and entirely to you! Naked as I am by nature, I give myself to you all naked, there!' she exclaimed, as she tossed aside the grey cloak and the nightdress she was clothed in and took her feet out of her slippers, 'there! see! do you like me so, Charlie? Am I pretty enough to please you, my own, own darling?'

Was she pretty enough? There standing before me, lit up by the light of the reading lamp, shining white against the darkness beyond, stood a perfect nymph. A perfect incarnation of youth and freshness and beauty!

Fanny had one of those fresh, clean-looking skins, so desirable in women. Her arms were full, round and beautifully shaped. Her shoulders sloped exquisitely and her bosom, like that of a young nymph, was adorned with a pair of well-separated, boldly self-sustained breasts, so often seen in sculpture and yet really so rare in nature. The little coral nipples showed clear and red, a lovely brilliant red, like that of her lips, and each sweet bubbie looked a little away from the other. Her form was the perfection of elegance, that of a really well-made girl, and her ivory belly, dimpled by a lovely navel, was a couch fit for Jupiter himself. Below that fairest belly was the swelling mount of Venus and with pleasure I saw that her bush was considerably grown, as indeed were her breasts, since I had last looked on them at Cherat. But below that mount, receding between her really beautiful thighs, was that most tempting deep line, which formed a cunt to be desired by the gods themselves! A cunt all mine now! A cunt no man had ever caressed or fucked before. I had done so today! A cunt which longed for me and which was brought over by Fanny for me to fuck, to love now! A cunt which I had indeed tasted, but had not yet fully savoured, but of which the first rapid, incomplete taste had made me eager to devour more and more!

Fanny had, as I have said before, really beautiful thighs. Indeed her arms, legs and feet were among her strongest points and could be models for any artist. They struck me as particularly beautiful in the light in which I now saw them and the sweetness, the glowing sweetness of really healthy youth shone from them, much enhanced near the groin by the dark curls of her fairly grown, dark brown bush. The more I gazed at all these exquisite charms, the stiffer did my prick grow and the more did I realise what a prize I had so fortunately obtained. Fanny, as though conscious of the power her beauty had over me, stood smiling, with lips slightly parted, as though waiting for that burst of praise, admiration and passion to which she felt she was entitled. Had she been conscious of not being well made, of her skin not being really pleasant to look upon, she would never have given herself, all naked, in this manner to me, for women's modesty too often is the quality under which they hide their blemishes. I have never yet fucked a really pretty and well-made woman who, from the first, objected to appearing naked before me. On the contrary the better the forms were the easier did the fair and beautiful owners of them find it to exhibit them to me without disguise.

'Oh! Fanny! you are lovely. My darling girl, you are the very perfection of beauty! Come, let me eat you up!'

Fanny's eyes blazed with pleasure, happiness and passion! She came with a little cry of joy and threw herself on to me as I reclined in my long chair. My prick opposed her belly and she pushed it to one side to enable her to lie on me and press me in her energetic arms, whilst she rained hot, burning, happy kisses in my equally responsive mouth. All the while she was murmuring little passionate love sentences into my ears and she moved her breasts from side to side over my bosom, so that I could feel the hard little coral nipples scoring it, as it were, and the firm elastic bubbies passing like waves across it. I gently pressed her lovely haunches in my two hands and tried to reach her warm little cunt from behind, but she laughingly kept it from me. She lay along my left thigh and side, with her arm round my neck, her left hand moving up and down my excited prick, occasionally grasping and feeling my balls most tenderly, whilst she said in tones of greatest excitement and the deepest feeling, 'Oh, Charlie! Charlie! You don't know how I love and adore you, my own darling. I though I knew what love was, but I did not. There was a time when I thought I never could give myself to you, unless I was sure that I could call myself your wife and make you marry me. But now! now! I feel that I do not want to marry you. What I should like to be would be your own beloved concubine. Yes! to have you I would willingly be a servant in your house and wait upon your wife if I might, from time to time, sleep with you and have you as I had you this evening on the grass! I wish concubines were allowed now. They had them in the old days – why should not a man have more than one wife now? Why should he not have concubines, too? Let me speak. When I went to bed I felt so happy. I had had you – twice! Think of that! Twice had this darling thing of yours been buried deep in me. Twice had I felt it pour the splashing essence of my Charlie into me! Oh! I could feel it so well, so distinctly, and each time it seemed to kill me with pleasure. The more I thought of it and remembered all you did, the more did I long to have it again, the more did I want to feel these' (she gently handled my balls) 'pressed against me, for they told me when my Charlie was all inside me! And I remembered what you offered to do, to come to me and have me in my own bed, how you said you could so easily come to me, by the far bathroom door and I was almost sorry I had said no, for after all we might have gone into the next room and lain on the floor and there would have been no creaking bed to waken Amy. I tried to sleep, I could not – my – I don't know what you call it, Charlie, but in Hindustani it is called *choot* – '

'Cunt, darling!'

'Cunt? Is that the English name for it? A nice soft name. I won't forget it. Cunt! Well, my cunt troubled me terribly and called for this – what do you call it, Charlie, dearest?'

'Prick, darling!'

'Prick? What a funny name! Prick! well, never mind. My cunt then called for its darling prick and at last I could not stay in my bed any longer. I jumped up. I went and looked at Amy. She was fast asleep. I went and looked into the nursery. Sugdaya was asleep on the floor. I listened at papa and mama's room and could hear them both snoring. So I took my grey cloak and slippers and ran out of the house, by the bathroom door, and here I am with my own Charlie. Are you glad, darling? Are you glad that Fanny has come and is in your arms now?'

'Oh! my Fanny! My Fanny! How could I be anything but glad, darling, darling girl. Yet I feel a little nervous on your account, Fanny, if you should happen to be missed! What a row there would be if you were found here! Now if I were found in your room, it would not be half so bad, because no one could say that you had invited me there, but it would be different if you were found in my house!'

'Oh! I am not at all afraid of that, Charlie! I feel sure in my heart that no one will miss me or find me out.'

'But, darling, Lavie is such a night bird, he often comes much later than this to see me and – by Jove! I hear him coming now!'

Fanny started up into a sitting posture. She still had my prick in her hand and we both listened for a moment. The footsteps came rapidly towards the door. We could hear them crushing the gravel on the avenue and it was plain that in another moment Lavie could be in the room. I recognised his footsteps and knew it was he. Fanny was about to jump up but I held her tight. The footsteps paused beside the door then paused a little longer then passed on! Lavie appeared to me to hesitate and it was clear to me that he was changing his mind and that, as he so often did, he would go first and walk around the Selwyns' house and then return to bore me. The moment he had commenced his walk again I told Fanny to pick up her chemise, cloak and slippers and run into my bedroom and lie down and cover herself with the cloak; if possible, I would stop Lavie and send him home.

Fanny darted with her goods into the bedroom and I went out on to the verandah. My fright was so real and sincere that my prick had at once lost all its stiffness and hung with very abashed head whilst I again tied the strings of my pyjamas. I got its hood on to its poor shrivelled head again and set off to catch Lavie, but when I got round the corner of the verandah he was nowhere to be seen or heard.

Uneasy, I hurried back to my sitting room, meaning to visit Fanny and see that no light entered my bedroom in case Lavie happened to return that way, for each of my rooms had four doors by which it could be entered on all four sides, as is common in Indian houses where every provision is made for the most thorough circulation of air, and as I entered my sitting room I met Lavie coming out of my bedroom.

I am sure my anxious and generous-minded readers will not accuse me of cowardice when I confess that my hair stood on end with fright when I saw the unhappy doctor coming out of the room where I believed Fanny to be lying naked on my bed! In any case, I trust they will give me credit for not losing my presence of mind under great peril. It was not for myself I feared. Fanny! Had Lavie seen her? Then goodbye to her reputation and future happiness. One glance at his absent-minded, moody face, told me that that misfortune, or rather piece of evil fortune, had not taken place. I steadied my face as much as I could, for I was indeed intensely agitated, and said, 'Why, Lavie! where have you come from? I thought I heard your footsteps outside and went to call you in, but I could not see you. I fancied I was a victim of imagination.'

'I did pass your door. I meant to come in but changed my mind and went on. Then I thought I must come in and tell you what I think. So I came in by the other side of the house.'

'Well, sit down old fellow. What do you want to tell me?'

'No, Devereaux! I will not sit down! I will never sit down in your house again.'

'Goodness! Why not?'

'Look here, Devereaux!' said he in most menacing tones, 'I believed you were my friend. I told you that I loved Fanny Selwyn and you promised to help me to get her. But it is my belief, I am sure of it, that instead of speaking up for me you said and did everything to make the Selwyns and Fanny in particular think me a fool and a bad match! You can't deny it!'

Now in reality, nothing could be more untrue and unjust than this stupid accusation. I had, at first, done all I could to help Lavie with Fanny. Lavie's words offended me. Nevertheless, I am sure I should have forgiven him, if I had not already fucked Fanny. Instead, I seized the opportunity of banishing him from my house forever, and all the more eagerly because I knew that my naked darling was waiting for me on my bed, in the next room.

'Lavie!' I exclaimed in determined tones, 'if this is what you have come to tell me, let me show you the door. Do you see it, sir? Out you go and never come into my house again! I consider you the most ungrateful wretch I ever had to deal with!'

Lavie glared at me, hesitated, then slowly walked to the door, where he once more paused and, turning, said, 'Yes! I will go! I will never call you friend again! You won't succeed in keeping Fanny Selwyn from me for as sure as God is in heaven I will fuck that girl!!'

I thought it prudent not to answer him. He glared again at me for a moment and then slowly walked down the avenue, out to the road, and departed in the darkness.

I stood watching him for a moment or so and was just going to close the door when I saw a light approaching. Cursing in my heart whoever was coming to interrupt my solitude on such an evening, I waited to see who it was. It was Dr Bridges' *chuprassy* with a note:

DEAR CAPTAIN DEVEREAUX – Make your mind easy about Doctor Lavie. I have permission by telegraph from Simla to send him to Benares and he shall go tomorrow.

Yours very truly,

J. BRIDGES

'Thank Dr Bridges and give him my regards!' I told the *chuprassy*, who, with a lordly salute, turned and departed. I shut the door and bolted it, took my lamp and swiftly went into my bedroom.

Fanny was lying on my bed covered with the grey cloak. She raised herself on her elbow, holding the cloak ready to cover herself with in case of need, but displaying to my delighted eyes almost all the glories of her lovely nudity. I saw her bosom to perfection and her body, foreshortened, offered itself to my eyes in a position new to me in her. Oh! how I can see even now the delicious bush of her motte making a sharp-pointed triangle towards her thighs, for she had them close shut and was leaning on her left elbow. My prick had been about dead from the alarm it had received, but at this exquisite sight it raised itself again in all its glory; running to Fanny, I clasped her in my arms and told her all was safe so far, Lavie had gone, and I gave her Bridges' note to read. Fanny was delighted. She threw her arms around me and called me all the loving names she could think of. Then casting her cloak completely off her on to the floor, she opened her arms and parted her knees and with eyes darting the most voluptuous desire and in a voice thrilling with passion, she said, 'Oh! Charlie, darling, don't let us lose any more time!'

Although the scenes I had gone through were enough to make me forget everything, yet the delicious pleasure I expected to take between those lovely thighs I kept before me constantly. Foreseeing that I should, now that I had once fucked Fanny, fuck her many times, I had prepared that indispensable *savoir* sponge which should render innocuous those otherwise pleasant but dangerous streams of spend which would naturally gush from me and inundate the shrine of love. I did not expect Fanny in my house indeed, but I had the sponge in a little glass wide-necked bottle, with a weak solution of phenyl and water, ready to be carried in my pocket for use in her house, where I hoped next to have the joy of fucking her. This I now got and placed handy on the floor. Then I stripped. I stood completely naked before her. She gave a cry of joy and admiration and put forth both her hands to grasp my big, swollen and immensely strong prick and the potent balls beneath it; with delicious rapture, I felt her lissome fingers twining round the objects which by touch alone filled her with still more delightfully voluptuous and deliciously lascivious longings.

'Oh! let me kiss it! let me kiss it, Charlie!' she cried and smiling I brought the head of my excited prick to her ruby lips. With unmistakable rapture she pressed her mouth to the rounded tip and her tongue to the little orifice in it. I took my part: bending over her, I parted her willingly opened thighs with my hands and covering her glowing little cunt with my mouth, I shot my tongue as deep into it as I could. Fanny, who had never been so caressed before, uttered a little cry of pleasure. I could feel her hands, both hands, grasp my prick with renewed force and ardour and, as though to repay the compliment she felt I was paying her cunt with my tongue, she took the head of my prick right into her mouth, passing her tongue all over it and making me thrill through and through with the rapturous sensation!

But such caresses serve only to excite to madness almost. Turning to her I caught her arms and pushed her on her back. I took the sponge and squeezing the superabundant moisture out of it, I pressed it into her little cunt, her tight little cunt, and getting between her thighs, I quickly followed it with my prick and then, mouth to mouth, bosom to bosom, belly to belly, we had our first really luscious, fully voluptuous, deliciously delightful and rapturous fuck.

Fanny, voluptuous by nature, was truly formed for fucking. Not even Lizzie Wilson could have better or more fully evinced the pleasure, the rapture she felt, than did Fanny. Although she had never been taught the refinements of fucking, she seemed, instinctively, to drop into them and nothing could have been more graciously superb than the way in which she gave a firm little buck each time she felt my balls come against her. Had I not known that it was I who had taken her maiden-head that very day, I should have concluded that Fanny had often been fucked before that night, but my heart was easy on that score. With some girls it seems natural, others can be taught, but most require to be trained.

When the hot, quick, rapturous short digs came, Fanny almost lost her senses, so much was all that was sensuous in her touched. Her voice rattled, or rather gurgled in her throat, her eyes opened their widest and seemed more gloriously beautiful than ever. In her agonies of pleasure she nipped my shoulder with her teeth, whilst I thrust my tongue into her ear and she met my torrents of hot spend with foaming floods of her own.

Then came that exquisite period when, as though exhausted, we relaxed our grasp on one another and lay quite still, her bosom heaving under mine, making me feel the full elasticity of her lovely bubbies, her belly rising and sinking, her motte leaping and giving mine little blows, whilst her cunt squeezed my prick with a force which made me fully conscious of how powerfully pleasure had affected her.

Then came all those sweet, sweet little expressions of love, devotion, passion, those kisses over such parts of the body as we could reach, and then finally the withdrawal from one another's arms and the immediate and satisfactory inspection of those charms which had been the chief extremes of our mutual pleasure.

'Oh! Charlie! How grand! How big. Who ever would have thought so small a thing as I have could take in such a lovely monster?'

'Ah! darling Fanny! But your sweetest little cunt is really very tight! But not too tight all the same.'

'Oh no! It can take it, Charlie! But why did you put the sponge in?'

I was glad to explain. I gently drew it out by the thin silken thread I had fastened to it; the outer end of the thread was tied to a little crossbar of silver to prevent the sponge being entirely sucked up into her cunt by the backward and forward strokes of my prick, and I showed her the great quantities of spend which I had poured into her and I explained to her the formation of her womb and how, in order to avoid a possible baby, the mouth of the womb should be prevented from being watered by the prolific produce of my balls and that, still further to deaden the vitality of that spend, I had used phenyl.

She quite understood me as I explained and kissed me again and again, thanking me for the great care I took of her and saying that she had never thought of any danger. I told her I had written to Cawnpore for a powerful enema and sent a receipt to be made up which would be more effective and pleasant than the phenyl, as it would have rose-water as one of its ingredients and would have a more pleasant aroma; and then I proposed that she should get up and let me wash her pretty cunt, so that I might pay it again the homage of my kisses. To this she joyfully assented. I got a basin of water and a towel and bathed her hot little cunt. She enjoyed the freshness of the water and when I had dried her bush and cunt and thighs she insisted on washing my prick in her turn, laughing and happy.

'Now!' said I, 'my darling, lie across the bed and put one leg over each of my shoulders. That's right!'

I hid my face between her thighs, my mouth on her sweet, sweet cunt and my upstretched hands grasping each a polished globe of her bosom. Fanny lay still for half a minute, while I searched the depths of that voluptuous little cunt with my tongue and pressed my nose on to her excited little clitoris, but at last she snatched those charms away from me and said, 'Oh! at least let us lie so that I can do the same to you as you do to me, my Charlie!'

Delighted to find her so ready to play every air on the sonata of voluptuousness, I stretched her on the bed and took my position over her, leaning on my elbows, embracing each of her thighs with an arm and again searching her cunt with my tongue, whilst my chin tickled her clitoris and I gave my prick to her mobile lips and sweeping tongue and my balls to her agitated and excited fingers! And then once more placing the sponge of safety within the rosy portals of the temple, I reversed my position and again thrilled the deliciously lascivious and voluptuous girl with my impassioned fucking.

And so the night wore away. We laid no plans for the future. Here in the happiness of one another we never thought how we were going to manage to meet and fuck without fear of detection. We were just like a bride and bridegroom and this, the first night of our marriage.

Towards four o'clock Fanny, thoroughly exhausted from the strain on her nerves and senses, sank off to sleep in my arms after the last ablution and I must have fallen asleep too. Suddenly I felt a hand on my nose, gently pressing my nostrils, and opening my eyes I saw Sugdaya!

'Hush, sahib!' she said, 'Miss Fanny *baba* must come home now, before the day breaks!'

'How did you know she was here, Sugdaya?'

'Oh!' she said, laughing softly, 'I have known a long time that Miss Fanny *baba* meant to be fucked by master. I kept my eyes open and I saw you in the shrubs last evening. I saw you go twice and I saw everything! Miss Fanny *baba* did not tell me, but I said to myself, when the honey does not come to the bear, the bear goes to the honey. I went to see if Miss Fanny *baba* was in her bed at midnight and I found it empty. I came over here and have been watching your pretty pranks through that door and now you must wake her up, sahib, and let her go with me!'

'Wait a moment Sugdaya,' said I, gently withdrawing my arm from under Fanny's neck and getting out of bed. 'Come into the next room.'

Sugdaya followed me. I unlocked my dispatch-box and took a roll of twenty-five rupees out and laid them on the table. Then taking Sugdaya's right hand I put it on my balls. She smiled and gently grasped them, with a voluptuous folding of her hand and fingers which made me know that she was not at all unwilling to feel them on her own account and knew why I had put them into her hand. Then slipping my right hand under and between the folds of her robe, I found her cunt and covering it with my palm, I dictated to her and she repeated: 'May my cunt wither and burn and shrivel if I betray the girl against whose bottom these balls have pressed. May Vishnu, Ram, Sita and Lakshmi curse me if I break my oath.'

Sugdaya laughed on the completion of this very necessary ceremony and said, 'Oh! sahib! no oath was required to bind me not to betray Missy *baba* or you! I am more than glad Miss Fanny *baba* has had the pleasure of being fucked. No girl needed it more. She will eat and drink and sleep all the better for it and I know that the sahib will not proclaim his conquest in the byways but hold his tongue!'

'You may be sure of that, Sugdaya!' said I, kissing her, 'and when Miss Fanny *baba* goes away from Fackabad, will you let me fuck this nice cunt of yours?'

'Before then if the sahib wishes!' laughed Sugdaya.

I had been caressing her well-formed, elastic, prominent and perfectly smooth motte, for Sugdaya like all Indian women either plucked out or shaved off every vestige of hair from that region. She had, in her turn, been caressing and feeling, with hands evidently not strange to the act, my prick, which was in that vigorous condition women love to find.

'Now, sahib!' said Sugdaya, pressing her swelling breasts against my chest, 'there is time for one more. Come! wake Miss Fanny *baba* as a lover should rouse his beloved!'

Nothing loth, I accompanied her to my bedroom, quite ready to do as Sugdaya had suggested, but Fanny, tired out with the long and exciting night's arduous and always ardent combats, was lying on her side, fast asleep, with one hand between her knees. She looked so lovely as she lay slightly curled up and her dear little face looked the picture of sweet innocence.

Sugdaya read my thoughts, for she said, 'Her cunt is asleep, sahib, but when I waken it up you will see another expression on her face!'

Looking round for something she evidently wanted, Sugdaya saw some peacock feathers, and selecting one which suited she approached Fanny and deftly commenced drawing the soft feather along the line of her cunt, which, gathered up as she was, I could hardly see anything at all of. At first there seemed to be no effect, but Sugdaya, with the utmost patience, continued those soft caressings with the feather and Fanny presently murmured something in her sleep and turned a little more over forwards as though she felt too tired for any more fucking and deprecated the invitation. I glanced at Sugdaya who smiled and seemed in no way discouraged. She withdrew the feather and passed it several times over my prick, up and down, before she recommenced operating on Fanny. Whether the feather conveyed any subtle influence with it from my prick or whether, what seemed more likely, the continued soft rubbings of the down along her soft cunt lips caused a sweet excitement within, Fanny murmured again and, slowly turning on her back, opened her lovely thighs a little, so that the rays of the lamp distinctly lit up the whole of those domains of which, in the name of love and Venus, I had taken possession. Sugdaya reversed the feather and with the quill stroked Fanny's bush, occasionally touching the tip of her lovely cunt also. Presently out peeped the little ruby point, glittering with generous moisture, and the slight tremor of her motte, with the almost imperceptible, but still marked, parting of the rounded lips of her cunt, told us that desire had laid his wanton hand on the charm which we wished to arouse from its state of torpor. Still Fanny remained fast asleep. Her bosom rose and fell more rapidly. Her lips moved and her eyelids quivered. A smile wreathed her lovely mouth and she parted her lips as though to speak, but, except for those of her delicious little cunt, all her senses were still locked in the embrace of sleep. The sweet girl's thighs opened wider and wider and her feet separated. She drew up her knees. It was evident, from her quick breathing and the rapid quiverings of her motte, that voluptuousness had fastened itself on her. Sugdaya gave me a nod and I, very gently and with as much quiet as possible, got between my darling's knees. Bending forward I rested on both knees, as I had done with Lizzie Wilson, and Sugdaya, seizing my prick, directed it so as to strike the doors of the temple at that very spot where they opened with the least pressure. I glided in, still keeping my belly from touching that of Fanny, and it was not till my balls touched her that she awoke.

'It is true, then! Not a dream!' she exclaimed. 'Oh, my Charlie! I forgot for a moment that you were my real lover and I thought that I was only dreaming my Nowshera dream again! I was afraid to open my eyes till I felt your dear balls against me!'

I stopped her further speech with my ardent kisses and Sugdaya, who had discreetly moved a little to one side, out of reach of Fanny's eyes, witnessed the voluptuous combat, which judging by the vigorous way she crossed her thighs and the occasional passing of her hand between them must have moved her very much. What a grand, grand poke that was! I enjoyed it more than any I had hitherto had and when I withdrew my proud and delighted prick from the overflowing cunt of my darling, she exclaimed, 'That is the best one we have had yet, Charlie!'

Sugdaya came forward. Fanny seemed no way put out by her presence and I afterwards found out that for months Sugdaya had been inculcating the joys of love in all three girls and that she had urged Fanny in particular to do all she could to seduce me. It accounted for the extraordinarily bold conduct of Mabel who, before Sugdaya entered the Selwyn house, had, like her sisters, been very modest and reserved. It accounted too, to a great degree, for the free conduct, if I may so call it, of Fanny in telling me of her dream when at Nowshera, for when I first knew the Selwyns there were not three purer-minded girls in all India than these three young maidens and I certainly did no more than foster the plant of desire when I saw it was growing.

It was still dark when the two girls left my bungalow; having seen them depart in safety, I returned to my room, put out my lamp and lay down, certain of a grand sleep, for there would be no parade that morning and I need not get up early. I remembered that in our last fuck I had not used the all-important sponge, but it gave me no cause for alarm, it being a well-attested fact that the last few spends of a man who has fucked all night are not at all prolific.

CHAPTER FIVE

## *Sibling Rivalry*

The colonel continued fucking Mrs Soubratie very comfortably in my house, where, in the spare room next to my bedroom, I had a special bedstead for him and his dusky concubine. So papa and daughter got their greens regularly and all went on as tranquilly and as happily as could be. But alas! a terrible crisis overhung this happy family.

I have spoken of Mrs Selwyn's delicate health. About July she began to fade rapidly. The close, hot atmosphere of the rains, with its accompanying relaxing effect, pulled her down, hand over hand. To the terrible grief of her husband and children she breathed her last. That night, by the most extraordinary good fortune, Fanny was not with me. The only night that she had not come over for weeks. Thus did Venus watch over the safety of her tender adorers.

I will pass over that sad time, during which I was for a period deprived of my Fanny's company, but it did not last long and once more we were united.

But the poor colonel, I grieve to say, took to driving away his cares, as so many do, by the aid of the bottle. For some weeks he did not even come over to fuck Mrs Soubratie. The loss of his wife brought to his memory those many years of sweetest happiness he had had with her and he used to speak to me of the grief it gave him to think that he should have committed adultery, and with a native woman too, during Mrs Selwyn's last year of life. This stung his conscience. But I knew that a man with such balls as he had could not long remain a monk and little by little I cheered him up until desire returned and he once more made Mrs Soubratie happy and drew upon that storehouse of happiness between her luscious thighs.

Of Mabel's pranks I have hardly time to speak. She used to implore me to fuck her. She would use every possible inducement, but I was too fond of Fanny to wish to give her a rival, especially as her affectionate passion for me seemed to increase with our intercourse. I had what I loved, a charming girl, all mine, to be my companion by day and by night. Mabel could make my prick stand indeed and I would willingly, gladly, have fucked her but for Fanny. Little by little Fanny was taking Louie's place in my heart and she wisely hid all signs of jealousy of Louie, if indeed she felt any. We both lived in the present hour; it was so happy, so congenial and neither of us looked ahead. If we regretted anything, it was having lost so many months and weeks and days when we might have enjoyed one another as we did now, but if such thoughts entered our minds they simply served to make us all the more determined to lose no more time.

About the time that the colonel recommenced fucking the (to him) delightful cunt of Mrs Soubratie another death at Fackabad caused a change in our world. 'Brigadier' Colonel Wilson suddenly left this world for the next and Colonel Selwyn was appointed to the vacant post. This was a capital stroke of luck for me, for Major Mortimer, the station staff officer, son-in-law to Colonel Wilson, had to go home to attend to his late father-in-law's property and look after his wife's interests and I was, on Colonel Selwyn's recommendation, appointed acting staff officer. But for my darling Fanny's sweet cunt I do not think I should have got this appointment, not that the colonel thought me in the least unfit for the office, but Fanny turned his thoughts to me and gently but persistently urged that I was the one who should get the post, though, by rights, some other officer who had been longer in India than I should have had it. But you see, dear reader, that the sweet delights I gave Fanny, through her charming little cunt, made her very solicitous about me and *amor vicit omnia* in this instance. So my soldier readers, if you want to get good appointments through your colonel, fuck his daughter well, as I fucked my darling Fanny. Really and truly, all joking apart, this appointment was very pleasant. I had no longer to command my company. I had nothing to do with my regiment as an officer of it in the way of duty. I had therefore no morning parades, no drills, nothing to lug me out of bed at ungodly hours in the morning. I only attended general parades when the colonel did. I had a good deal of signing my name to letters, etc., prepared by my clerks, but as everything was in good order the work was light. The emolument of my office did not matter much, as I had no need of money, having plenty of my own; but for all that the extra rupees were not by any means a nuisance to receive. Darling Fanny profited by my not having to go to parade. Some mornings when we had slept later than usual it had happened that she had had to run home without her daybreak fuck; now she always had one and sometimes two and she was just as ardent and eager for them as ever my sweet Louie had been. Oh! I was really very happy and contented.

But, although no real harm was done, yet a circumstance occurred which might have brought all this happiness to a disastrous end.

Colonel Selwyn's command comprised all the army, not only at Fackabad but also several other stations where there were detachments of troops. Amongst these was Rampur some seventy miles off and to be reached only by dak *gharry*. One evening early in October, that is just a year after I had seen my darling's cunt for the first time and since Amy had been buggered, the colonel electrified Fanny and rather astonished me, who had no notion of his intentions, by saying that he thought he would go in a couple of days' time and commence his inspection of the troops at Rampur and that he would take Fanny with him.

'Oh, papa! but I would much rather not go!' cried poor Fanny, looking at me with an aggrieved and startled face, 'could you not take Amy?'

The colonel, who had not yet drunk enough brandy and soda to be befuddled, looked rather angrily at Fanny. 'No! I said you were to accompany me, Fanny! And I shall not take Amy, I don't like to be dictated to by my daughters!'

'I did not mean to dictate, papa,' urged poor Fanny, who struggled visibly to restrain an outburst of temper, 'but I should really be obliged if you would let me remain here and if you would take Amy or Mabel instead. Come, there's a dear, good, kind papa. Do.'

Now the colonel was a weak man and therefore obstinate. He was offended at Fanny's outburst and he had got into a sudden rage. He looked black as thunder and roared at Fanny, 'Miss Fanny! I have said that you will go with me! Let me hear no more about it!'

He turned his eyes to me and for a moment I wondered had he any suspicions as to the very intimate terms Fanny and I were on? Yet how could he have discovered them so suddenly? I was mistaken, however.

'Miss Selwyn,' said I, seeing Fanny ready to cry with vexation. 'Do you know I rather envy you? I hear that Rampur is a very pretty place and that the road there takes you through some very lovely scenery, though it is all plains. I only wish the colonel would take me too, as his staff officer.'

'Well, Devereaux, so I would, but for that confounded new order which requires special application to be made for permission to take a staff officer with one when on these irregular inspections. I am afraid you must wait a little longer. But I will take Fanny.'

There was living in the compound next to mine the Protestant padre of Fackabad, one Mr Corbett, a married man with a very amiable and young and not too straitlaced wife. These people were great friends of the Selwyns and Mrs Corbett, who knew I was fond of Fanny, often teased me about her. I had even 'confessed' to her that I admired Fanny so much that had there been no Mrs Devereaux, I should have been very much inclined to ask

Fanny to become that lady. But long practice had made me a consummate actor and Mrs Corbett, without thinking me a saint, never suspected that the cunt she knew I must fuck (she was a woman of the world), whilst Louie's was not available, lay between Fanny's thighs of snow. No, she fancied that I relieved my necessities between some brown thighs and more than hinted that Sugdaya owned them. I rather encouraged the idea and if ever I had cause to mention Sugdaya, I spoke of her with that apparent consciousness that made Mrs Corbett more certain than ever that I did fuck Sugdaya regularly. So we were both contented.

It was with the Corbetts that Colonel Selwyn arranged to leave his children during his absence with Fanny at Rampur. Their house was large enough to accommodate them easily and no country in the world makes such temporary movements more easy to perform than India. All that was required was that a few bedsteads should be carried over and the thing was done.

The last night had to be a very short one for Fanny and me. Her father intended starting at four in the morning and Fanny had to leave me at half-past two. She was ravenous. In the few hours she still had to enjoy my prick she lost not a moment and the interludes between act and act only lasted just as long as it took the pretty hands to operate the resurrection of my prick, a thing extremely easily performed, I am glad to say. I may tell my fair readers here that as a little boy, when I first began to understand why I had a little prick and girls had little cunts, I had marvelled at the story of Hercules and wondered how taking fifty maidenheads and putting fifty virgins in the family way in one night could be considered a 'labour'. Well, I had had no practical experience then, but later I learnt from women of all classes whom I fucked, that I was more abundantly blessed than any man they had ever met in having an unconquerable prick and a pair of balls which never ran completely dry. I do not mention this to boast, but only to say how thankful I am that such has been my lot. So poor Fanny left me with her sweet cunt throbbing with pleasure and a heart grieved to think that it would be perhaps nearly a fortnight before it would throb again from being well fucked by me.

For my part I was as grieved as Fanny. I loved that girl. She was a second edition of Louie. I never could have enough of her, by day or night. I was certain that her absence would be as grievous to me as my separation from Louie was. It took me a long time to feel desire again after I had left Louie, as the readers of my first chapter will remember, and I felt very nearly the same now that Fanny was gone. There was this difference, however: when I left my Louie I had an idea it might be years before I should again know the glorious pleasure of fucking her and fucking her meant in my mind, then, fucking at all. I really and truly thought that I had done with women, i.e., all other women than my Louie. My readers may remember the soft influence of Mademoiselle de Maupin and the realisation of that beauteous power in the person of the lovely and delicious and really lascivious Lizzie Wilson. Her cunt proved its power and the far distant one, between poor Louie's thighs, no longer tyrannised over my (till then) moral prick and modest balls. Well then, I did look forward this time to some more luscious fucking, at no very remote day, for Fanny's dearest little cunt would surely again be mine within a fortnight to caress, to kiss, to fuck to my heart's content. Still it was a grievous annoyance to lose it, even for that short time.

The day passed wearily, far more so than I anticipated it would. My thoughts were all with Fanny. I knew she went away grieving and all my sympathies were with her. I went to bed early, hoping to get some sleep and so pass away as many hours in an unconscious state as possible.

I don't know how long I had been thus sleeping, when I woke, feeling my nose gently pinched, and there was Sugdaya!

The first idea that came into my mind was that Sugdaya, mindful of my little speech to her on the first night that I fucked Fanny, had taken advantage of my words literally, and that Fanny having left Fackabad, though only temporarily, she had come to be fucked herself. The dear reader will remember that I had proposed to Sugdaya to fuck her whenever Fanny went away (I meant for good) and now I imagined that Sugdaya wanted to take my words literally.

'Well, Sugdaya, what is it?'

'Sahib! Miss Fanny *baba* wants me to ask you to come over to her. She is in bed and wants master!'

'Good God! Has there been an accident, Sugdaya? What made the colonel come back? I hope no one is hurt! How is Miss Fanny *baba*?'

'There has been no accident, sahib!' said Sugdaya laughing, 'no one has been hurt. Miss Fanny *baba* is quite well but her cunt is hungry for this,' and she took possession of my prick. I did not repel her. I never repel a pretty woman when she takes hold of me there.

'I'll come at once, Sugdaya! But tell me, why did the colonel come back?'

'He has only come back for the night, sahib!' said Sugdaya, sitting on the edge of the bed and gently moving her hand, in the most delicious manner, up and down my prick. I lay on my back and let her. It was so pleasant and I wanted to hear particulars. 'They got as far as Dharra, that is the first stage, you know, sahib! – Ah! What a handsome grand prick you have, sahib – no wonder Miss Fanny *baba* loves it! And grand balls too! Some day you know, sahib, you must fuck me, you know you promised!'

'So I will, surely, Sugdaya. But take care. Don't make me spend.'

'No, sahib,' said poor Sugdaya with a sigh, 'Miss Fanny *baba*'s cunt must make it do that! I'll play with your balls only,' and she began those caresses with the fingertips which are so exquisitely delicious.

'All right, Sugdaya. That is very nice. Now tell me, what did they do at Dharra?'

'Oh! sahib! There were no fresh horses ready. The colonel sahib wanted to go on with those which had come with him from Fackabad, but the *gharry* man would not. Then they found it would not be possible for them to leave

Dharra that day and the colonel sahib waited and when the horses were rested came back slowly to Fackabad. He and Miss Fanny *baba* will try again tomorrow morning – now! Come, sahib. Poor Miss Fanny *baba* wants you badly.'

I jumped up, fastened my pyjamas, felt Sugdaya's nice little brown cunt and bubbies, kissed her, sham fucked her a little and saw plainly that I had only to say, 'I'll fuck you instead, Sugdaya,' and she would gladly have taken Fanny's place; but although all this sporting was dangerous, I had no idea of being unfaithful to Fanny and, with steps as noiseless and swift as possible, Sugdaya and I went hand in hand over to the colonel's bungalow.

Before Sugdaya let me in by the bathroom door she said, in a low tone, 'Don't speak to Miss Fanny *baba*, sahib. The colonel sahib is not sleeping well and he might hear you. For that reason, too, Miss Fanny *baba* has only a small light in her room. Just go in – get right into bed with her and fuck her quietly and nicely.'

This was the very first time I had ever been in the colonel's bungalow to fuck Fanny in her own bed. I had fucked her in the compound and, on one or two occasions which I have not mentioned, I had fucked her in the drawing room, taking her on my knees, but I had never fucked her in her own bed and the idea seemed delicious to me. Though no longer a virgin herself, her bed was a virgin and it seemed to me it would be like taking her maidenhead a second time. I went into her room then, palpitating with desire and with my prick as vigorous as if the long week or ten days had passed during which I had expected to be a widower.

The room was all but pitch dark. There was a light indeed but so covered that not even its miserable feeble rays could fall on the bed which I dimly saw and on which I could just discern the figure of a girl, who looked naked. I could not distinguish any features, only a general form, but Fanny's bush struck me as looking much darker in this darkness than usual. Sugdaya led me still by the hand and when at the bedside whispered in low tones: 'Don't make any noise, sahib. I will go and lie at the colonel sahib's door.'

And she left me and glided out into the pitch darkness of the other room.

Delighted to be with Fanny again, so much sooner than expected, I gently got into her bed, fearing to make it creak, but it was firm – now at any rate – for it made no sound. A gentle but nervously hurried hand took possession of my prick whilst I drew honey from the warm lips and pressed the lively bubbies I found one after the other. I longed to speak, but the first attempt I made was met with a warning 'hush!' from her, whilst a gentle little pull at my burning prick told me that the darling girl wanted to draw it, in silence, to the equally burning little cunt, of which the soft lips were already moistened in anticipation of the delight it expected. Carefully, making no creak occur from the bedstead, I gently turned over on to the dear girl, whom I could feel panting with hot desire, and taking my place between her exquisite thighs I drew my quivering prick against that throbbing and excited cunt, enraptured at the idea that I was now at last fucking her in her own bed. Fanny kissed me as though in an ecstasy, my prick glided in, doffing his cap as he did so, and then – to my extreme surprise – was met with a complete denial of further ingress.

At first I imagined that Fanny was practising on me. I had taught her how to imitate a virgin bride – that by straightening her legs stiffly, raising her belly as high as possible and withdrawing her cunt from the invading prick, as well as by taking a slightly crooked position sideways, she could make it difficult for her husband, when she had one, to get into her. But on putting my hand to feel how her thighs were placed, I found her knees well bent. I could not detect any wilful upraising of the belly, nor any refusal of her darling cunt. I tried again. No go. There was a real obstruction. What could it be from? I tried again. There was the same result. I began to feel hot with shame and wondered could my prick possibly be failing me. Oh no! It was as stiff as when I first had Fanny. As stiff as it always had been when between the delicious thighs of a girl! I quietly and suddenly slipped off Fanny and put an enquiring finger up her cunt. I imagined that she might have manufactured a *savoir* sponge – for Sugdaya had not asked me to bring mine and I had forgotten to do so – and that this was causing the obstruction. Fanny let me feel her without making the least objection and I felt – a maidenhead! Oh! There was no doubt about it. In a moment the idea flashed upon me that it was not Fanny, but Mabel. I strained my eyes, but could not make out the face so close to me but yet so hidden in the darkness.

'It is not Fanny!' I said in my lowest tones. 'Is it you – Mabel?'

My question was answered by a peal of loud, merry laughter which, considering that I still believed the colonel to be in the house and just across the drawing room, astonished me for two reasons – first, it was not Fanny's laughter nor Mabel's – but Amy's – and secondly it was so noisy!

Sugdaya came running in. When she saw me with my finger in Amy's cunt, which she easily saw by the lamp she carried, and my look of astonishment and Amy writhing in uncontrollable laughter, she joined in and rolled about in excessive merriment!

'Ah! sahib! sahib! What a lucky man you are that all the Misses *baba* think that there is only one sahib that can fuck and that one Captain Devereaux, sahib. Well, Miss Amy *baba*. Did he fuck you nicely?'

'No,' cried Amy, 'he can't do it.'

'Can't do it,' cried I in anger, for I felt I had been most cruelly deceived. 'Can't do it, Miss Amy. I'll show you that I can do it and well, too.'

And so saying, I again plumped on top of her, inserted my indignant prick and, stretching Amy in such a manner that she could not possibly escape me, I forced my excited weapon as hard as I could against the rash maidenhead which had by the voice of its owner sneered at me.

'Oh–h–h! Captain Dev–er–eaux! O–h–hh! for God's Sake! Oh! You are killing me – you – are – killing me! Ah–hh–h! Oh! Oh! Oh! Oh! –'

It was a rough job. Amy's maidenhead was thrice as strong as Fanny's and much more unyielding than the majority of those it has been my excellent good fortune to take. And I did not feel tender-minded towards her. I am afraid I was more rough than I should have been – but oh! had she not deceived me and robbed her sister? So without mercy I went way up, until that really sweet little cunt was filled and stretched to the uttermost and my balls rattled against her bottom, just at the exact spot where the Afghan's had first had that pre-eminent happiness.

But Amy, though she said I hurt her dreadfully forcing my prick in so roughly, was by nature voluptuous like Fanny. Her, 'Ah! Now that's nice. Ah! Do that again. Oh, my! Oh, Captain Devereaux! How you tickle!' told me that and, my temper having been satisfied by my first burst of anger, I fucked her as sweetly as I could and was rewarded by her spending copiously and ravishingly, at the exact moment that I inundated her cunt with the first boiling torrent which had ever been poured by man into it.

Sugdaya stood by holding the lamp and watching with keen and voluptuous interest the real combat between my prick and Amy's cunt and when she perceived by the cessation of my movements and the way in which Amy was holding her breath, that I was inundating the shrine, she gave vent to the prolonged 'oh–h–h – ' as though she envied the girl who was getting such delight.

'Now! Miss Amy *baba*! Now! You have been well fucked,' she cried.

'Yes. I suppose I have,' said Amy, in a kind of dreamy manner, usual with her when her thoughts were much occupied; then waking up as if from a trance, she clasped me tight and gave me kiss after kiss.

'Ah! that is all very well, Amy,' I said, 'but I have a bone to pick with Sugdaya and you. A very nice pair you are. Do you know what you have done?'

'Yes, dear,' said Amy, laughing and closing her legs over me for I had commenced to withdraw my prick from her strongly palpitating cunt. 'I do. I laid a very neat trap and caught a very splendid bird and I have him now in my cage.'

'It's all very well, Amy. You have won this round – but oh!' and I felt my voice quiver with the anguish I really felt, 'you do not know what you have done! Here! Let me go.'

'No, indeed,' said Amy, folding me tighter and tighter and forcing her cunt about my prick, which had been half pulled out of it. 'No! I won't let you go. You are my property now, Captain Devereaux, I have fairly caught you! To think of letting you go yet! Oh dear no! You will have to fuck me now as often as you have fucked Fanny. And as she has had you ever since last March, you will have to pay me a good deal of attention before I shall be even with Fanny.'

'Oh, Amy!' I cried, bitterly, for I assure you, dear reader, much as I love fucking and well worth fucking as Amy was and still is, I felt that I had been betrayed, and though done in perfect innocence, doing what I now had done would come nigh to breaking Fanny's heart. Now I loved Fanny. I was passionately devoted to her and not for all the cunts in the world did I feel inclined to outrage her by fucking her sister before her own sweet cunt could be said to have ceased throbbing from the very recent fucking it had had from my prick. I did not desire Amy. The stand I had, when I got into bed with her, was not for her cunt, nice as it was, but for Fanny's. 'Oh! Amy! I'll tell you what you have done! You have broken poor Fanny's heart.'

'Pooh! Ha ha ha,' laughed Amy. 'What do I care? Broken her heart indeed. Oh! Poor Fanny! Much I pity her! What more right has she to you, I should like to know, than I have, or Mabel. She is not your wife. But to hear her talk and to hear you too, Captain Devereaux, one would think there was no Louie in the world. I tell you I have every bit as much right to you as Fanny has, and mind, if you refuse to fuck me, you will never fuck her again, I can tell you!!!'

This thrust I felt was no empty one. Amy had once said she could not imagine herself going to bed with a man and that for herself to be stark-naked in the presence of a stark-naked man would be something too horrible to contemplate. Here she was, however, stark-naked in my stark-naked arms and the will to fuck was all on her side, not mine. It was plain all her former ideas had become completely changed; and her whole tone and manner was that of a strong-minded woman who knew what she was about and that she could compel, if she could not gain her ends by any more gentle means. Unfortunately it lay in her power to put an end to the delicious liaison between Fanny and me. I lay quietly in her arms, thinking how I could escape this terrible dilemma.

'How do you know that I fuck Fanny, Amy?'

'How do I know? Now, Captain Devereaux! Do you take me for a complete fool? Do you think that Fanny could leave this room, with me sleeping in it, night after night, without my knowing it sooner or later? Do you think I cannot put two and two together as well as yourself? Why! I have known it these five months at least. I taxed Fanny with it and she could not deny it and she told me herself too, about how you fucked her twice that evening of her birthday, when she and you left us playing cards. Well! I didn't care! I thought her a fool for her pains, but by degrees I began to think it must be nice – as Sugdaya has always told me it was – to be fucked and the moment I heard that Fanny was to go to Rampur with papa, I laid a plan with Sugdaya to catch you! Ah! now, my boy! You wanted me to go to Rampur but here I am. You wanted Fanny's cunt, did you? Now you are in mine and I think mine must be every bit as nice as Fanny's. I have better and bigger breasts, too, and more hair than she has and I don't think you have any reason to complain of Fanny either.'

I saw it was no use trying to urge a higher tone with Amy. It was no use talking to her of love. Fucking was all she could see in my intimacy with Fanny, nothing nobler.

'So you see, my dear Captain Devereaux, you will now have two wives in India and one at home; perhaps three wives in India, because Mabel, I know, wants to be fucked too, and you will have to do it.'

'I will not!' I cried passionately and angrily.

'Oh! dear, yes, you will. The thing is in a nutshell. Do you really love Fanny? Are you really so fond of her as you say?'

'Oh, Amy! You don't know how fond.'

'Very well! Then I suppose you would be awfully sorry if anything happened to prevent you fucking her again.'

'Don't speak of it!'

'Oh! but I will. I have only some night to pretend to be ill, call papa and let him see Fanny's bed empty and Sugdaya not to be found in the house and I think Fanny will never see your prick again, Captain Devereaux.'

I groaned.

'What an ass a man is!' cried Amy, half angrily, half laughingly. 'I should like to know who has such a grand chance of having three pretty girls all to himself, all ladies of his harem. And the idea shocks him. Now! Captain Devereaux – and do be careful what you say. Is it a bargain? Do you promise to fuck Mabel and me whenever we like? For if you don't you may say goodbye to Fanny.'

Now I had had a good deal of experience with girls and women and have often been helped into a nice little cunt by the owner of another, but I never was treated in this way before. The idea that if I did not fuck Amy and Mabel I should lose Fanny was paradoxical! I felt a child in Amy's arms and that I had learned my lesson wrong. I thought I should lose Fanny if I fucked her sisters, not if I did not do so. It seemed it was all wrong. Yet a little reflection told me that the laws of ordinary life did not obtain in this instance and that to keep possession of Fanny's dearest cunt, I must fuck those of her sisters also!

'I think you very hard-hearted, Amy. I see I have nothing better to do than surrender; when the Devil drives, needs must.'

'Thank you for the compliment,' laughed Amy. 'Well, the devil in this instance flatters herself that she has a very nice cunt and desires her slave to amuse her for the rest of this night!'

All this conversation having taken place in English was unintelligible to Sugdaya, who looked on with surprised and perplexed eyes, but when Amy told her what the result of the conversation had been, that nor only had I consented to go on fucking her, but that I would fuck Mabel, too, she was delighted and said: 'Oh! sahib! Now I am very glad indeed. Won't Miss Mabel *baba* be glad to hear it too!'

I begged her to go over to my bungalow and bring my enema and *savoir* sponge and I asked Amy to get up and let me assist her in washing her cunt, which required it badly. Sugdaya left and Amy rose. Of course, the sheet was a sea of blood. Amy was rather frightened when she saw it, but I comforted her by saying that no girl who has really lost her maidenhood, ever did so without losing a lot of blood. Whether the tone of my voice was more gentle than it had been, or whether my comforting words struck a chord of gratitude in her heart, I don't know, but she put her arms around my waist and lifted her face up and kissed me affectionately.

'Ah, Captain Devereaux, now let us be really good friends; we need not quarrel because we fuck, need we?'

The absurdity of such a question struck me with all its force and I could not help laughing heartily. I looked at Amy. Naked as she was, I could see all her form and person perfectly and she was really a splendid girl. Her hair, both of her head and bush, was darker in colour than Fanny's and very much more abundant. Her arms, thighs and legs were full as white and as well formed, her waist was more slender and her hips were wider than those of her sister; and her bubbies, beautiful, round, full and coral tipped, were fully one-third larger. Her hands and feet were small and well shaped and as her face was very pretty, with a fine oval form and with large, dark, lustrous eyes, she was altogether very desirable and a fine addition to my 'harem'. My angry feelings and the regret I so sincerely felt for having been made to be unfaithful to Fanny began to die away at the sight of all these beauties and Amy received caresses from my hands and kisses from my lips which made her as proud as could be, for she rightly judged that had her beauty not been very real, she would hardly have got off so soon for her cruel treatment of me.

'Come!' said she. 'Come, Captain Devereaux. Help me to wash myself and let Sugdaya find us fucking when she comes back.'

The ablution was quickly performed. Amy had never seen my prick and balls before, nor indeed those of any man, though she had had a very big one up her bottom once! She therefore delayed a little while washing me and thoroughly enjoyed the sight and feel of those treasures.

Sugdaya returned just in time to see me getting home well for the first time and consequently was an excited spectator of the first good-will fuck I gave Amy. Like the voluptuous-minded creature she was, she greatly added to my pleasure by manipulating my balls, which she took possession of between my thighs from behind. Amy seemed frantic with pleasure. Every stroke I gave her threw her into ecstasies. I think Mrs Selwyn must have had a voluptuous nature and I know that the colonel dearly loved fucking. Certainly Fanny and Amy had inherited their parents disposition towards sensuousness and it was my extreme good fortune to have been the first to inspire their loving cunts with desire and make them throb and overflow with pleasure.

Once more, good friends, Amy and I passed the rest of that night in the most delicious manner possible. Long before the hour, four o'clock, at which she had to leave to go to the Corbetts' bungalow, whence she had come, we had become very confidential and I had managed to extract a promise from her that she would not insist upon my fucking Mabel yet awhile. I pleaded hard. I said that poor Fanny might forgive me having fucked her, Amy, but that it would be almost too much to expect her to accept that two more cunts were to share my prick with hers. But Amy was determined that nothing should be done outside the strict bargain and she only agreed to this arrangement on the understanding that I was to fuck her every night until Fanny returned. I willingly acquiesced. It was agreed that I should meet her where we then were, every night at ten o'clock, for the Corbetts being early people and going to bed at nine regularly, Amy could easily keep that appointed hour. Sugdaya was sorry for Mabel, but at least I had promised to fuck her in due course; she only hoped I would not delay too long.

We left the Selwyns' bungalow together. I had nothing on but my thin jersey, pyjamas and light slippers. Sugdaya and Amy walked as far as the entrance to my compound with me and we exchanged caresses and kisses, hot and strong on either side; Amy, in happy good-natured contempt for the proprieties, even requested me to stroke Sugdaya's nice brown cunt before kissing her for the last time! With my fingers still throbbing from this exquisite contact with two such blooming cunts, I walked rapidly up my avenue, not thinking of anything but what I now considered my extreme good luck, for I had had a really delicious night between Amy's fair thighs and had enjoyed so much undeniable pleasure both from her cunt and from her curiously improper mind that, for the present at all events, my sorrow on Fanny's account was considerably deadened.

All this part of my history is still painful for me to remember. I do not deny the sweetness of Amy's really delicious little cunt. It was of the very finest sort and I had very real pleasure fucking it. It had the advantage of being a new one for me. It had been deflowered by me. It belonged to as pretty a girl as there was in India. It was extremely sensitive to pleasure and a perfect fountain under my vigorous treatment of it, but . . . alas for the buts – Oh! how much more delightful to me it would have been had I not been so entrapped into it. I could now understand what a woman feels like who has been fucked against her will and without her consent. Over and above these latter feelings was the absolute certainty of the pain – the mental and heartfelt agony Fanny would surely experience – when she came to hear that, within twenty-four hours of my being between her thighs, I had passed between those of her sister, and that subsequently, night after night, I had fucked Amy.

Amy certainly gave me no rest. I don't think she realised it was possible to exhaust a man. Feeling herself always ready to be fucked, she regarded the stand of a prick as quite voluntary on the part of the lover. Thanks to the splendid constitution I had been born with and the powers which, from what women have told me, I fancy very few men are endowed with, I was quite 'able' for Amy and never disappointed her a single time. In fact, I believe she would have been the first to say, 'I've had enough', had we continued this night-after-night fucking. She was quite prepared to share me with Fanny and wished, really wished, me to fuck Mabel too.

She knows differently now. She is married now and has discovered that there are men and men. In her last letter to me, received not a week ago, she spoke very penitently of the way she treated me at Fackabad and says she had no idea of what a treasure she had in me. It is very nice to be told this now but I did not enjoy being used by her as a complete tool at Fackabad.

The colonel wrote only once from Rampur and Fanny not at all. I was glad and sorry not to have had a letter from her. She told me, when she came back, that she was burning to write, but feared her father's asking questions and perhaps seeing her letter; she said if once she began to write, she could not have kept her pen from speaking the sort of passionate words she was so accustomed to use when we were in our skins together.

So she thought it best not to write except one short little note.

On the morning of the day we expected them back from Rampur, just as I was putting on my pyjamas and jersey and looking at the naked Amy, who had so cruelly robbed me of my peace of mind and Fanny of her full possession in future of my prick and balls, Amy said, 'Oh! by the by, Captain Devereaux, I've something for you here.'

'What is it, Amy?'

'Oh, a letter from Fanny.'

And she put her hand under her pillow and drew forth a little note she had put there overnight and had 'forgotten' to give me earlier.

'Oh! Amy, why did you not give me this before?'

'I forgot.'

'You know I love Fanny. It is cruel of you, Amy!'

'Pooh! What do I care! Lord what a rage Fanny will be in when she hears the news.'

'It will break her heart.'

'Fiddle-de-dee! She will roar and cry and call me names and you too, Captain Devereaux! Oh! she will tear your eyes out!'

'I will tell her the truth, Amy, and then if she can forgive me I shall be happy – but – will she?'

'Of course, she will. Bless you, I know Fanny better than you do, Captain Devereaux. She will try it on. Yes, she will try it on. She will rave and storm and threaten, but if you treat her cooly and let her know that it of no use crying over spilt milk, but there is more milk for her if she chooses to take it, she will quiet down fast enough. Fanny is not quite such a fool as not to know that half a loaf is better than no bread. But she is greedy. She never offered to share you with me and now she must. It serves her right. And I am rather glad you don't like fucking me, because it serves you right too!'

'But Amy, I do like fucking you! As far as mere fucking goes you are quite as god as Fanny!'

'Thank you for nothing! Mere fucking! You won't persuade me you see anything more in Fanny than a nice little cunt! I don't believe it. No! no! Captain Devereaux. You are sore because you have to fuck me whether you like it or not. If it weren't for that you would not be sorry to have both me and Fanny, aye and Mabel too, and Sugdaya and every other woman in Fackabad also!'

It was no use trying to make Amy sensible that although cunts may be equally delicious from a physical point of view and all girls equally young, nice and beautiful, yet love distinguishes one above all others and makes one the most delicious of all. I left her in disgust, mad with myself because I could not master my prick and because I could not help confessing that she was a perfect and exquisite poke.

On going back to my bungalow I read the precious note from Fanny. It was full of love and happiness at the prospect of being once more in my arms. Poor, dear girl! She appeared not to have the least qualm about Amy or anyone else occupying my thoughts during her absence. So far from imagining that I should take advantage of her being at Rampur and endeavour to get into Amy or Mabel, she said that she hoped on her return to hear that I had not forgotten that they were her sisters and to find that I had, for her sake, been kind to them and been to visit them at Mrs Corbett's, where she imagined they must have been very lonely without her and papa.

This note gave me the greatest possible pain. What would Fanny say when she discovered the truth? It would nearly kill her! She trusted me so completely. She did not dream of a rival and she could have no notion that she would find a most formidable rival and oppressor in Amy, her own sister. What a deep and designing game Amy had played! And how patiently had she waited until she could put her scheme into action. Herein I saw Sugdaya's hand. No one but a native, or one governed by a native, could have possessed their souls and senses in such a state of entire patience as Amy had done. For she was everything but cool and composed while I fucked her. She was such flame and fury that it was impossible to suppose that she did not enjoy to the fullest the glorious pleasures my prick and balls procured her. She must consequently have endured the most real pains of unsatisfied desire and, like the Spartan boy, have suffered the agonies of having her living flesh gnawed at whilst she smiled in apparent calmness on all. I dare say it was the recollection of these poignant sufferings which made all her words and actions towards me so cruel and spiteful. However, she had been well fucked and perhaps, when I had smoothed down Fanny and calmed the storm which threatened a catastrophe, we might so manage as at all events to render Amy amiable. For if Fanny, as I fully expected she would, declared she would no longer be fucked by me, I determined I would not fuck Amy any more and as Amy liked being well fucked so much, so very much, she might discover that any ill advised attempt to drive a man might result in a revolt whereby her newly acquired kingdom over my prick might be lost.

Full of these turbulent thoughts, I lay down, but could not sleep. Hour after hour passed away. Full daylight came and brought with it, one by one, the numerous signs of life – the birds, insects, animals and men. But I heeded them little; all my thoughts were concentrated on 'What will Fanny say?' and 'How shall I ever recover my position in her love and admiration?' The devil take Amy and damn Sugdaya for her infamous plotting and scheming!

A good swear relieves a man when the cause for irritation is passed and gone, but alas! no amount of cursing will soften the expected pains of approaching doom – else mine would have obviated the misery I expected, for I swore enough to blow all misery to the winds, had the misery been upon me and not still in the offing.

Fanny and the colonel were not expected to arrive until seven in the evening and Amy and the children were not to leave the Corbetts until a little before that hour. I passed that most wretched day in writing a letter to Fanny trying to explain what had happened in such a way as not to inculpate Amy any more than necessary, but yet to exculpate myself.

Needless to say all my efforts were in vain and each letter I wrote seemed worse than the last and all were destroyed by me. Oh! dear readers, may you never, not one of you, have reason to suffer such torture as I endured. It would not have been so bad had I deliberately with malice aforethought been unfaithful to Fanny. But to have been so trapped and betrayed into doing what I really had not meant to do, was a cause of the greatest mental anguish to me. Suppose I told Fanny the exact truth, was it likely she would believe me? Would she not also say and with a great show of justice, that I need not have gone on fucking Amy?

Ah! she had no prick and balls to drive her as I had. It would be difficult to understand, too, that in order to keep Amy in good humour, I had to go on fucking her; and yet I felt I really had no better card to play. I could not help it if I found fucking Amy truly delicious. I dare say a girl who is raped, rather enjoys the sensation, although in her heart she may feel the deadliest enmity against the man who rapes her, because it is done without her consent. I really could not prevent my prick standing and stiffly raging when it was near Amy's cunt. A prick is like a gun. The enemy can take it and use it against its proper owner. It shoots just as straight and as hard for the one as for the other and has no will in the matter at all. All that my prick saw in Fanny was a delicious and sweet cunt between her thighs; it saw exactly the same thing between the thighs of Amy – and its one desire was to get into that one which was nearest. This is certainly not the case with most cunts. It was in Lizzie Wilson's, but hers was by no means the one to give the rule. Look at Amy. Amy wanted to be fucked. Well, she had plenty of friends who would have been delighted to have fucked her, but she never hinted her desire to one of them. Look at Mabel. If anything she was worse and hotter than Amy. The reader will see in time what she did. My prick was always ready for Mabel's cunt and, but for the most determined opposition, it would have got into it. Oh! let a woman understand this: 'A standing prick has no conscience!'

Everything comes to an end and that horrible day came to an end too, but not until I had at last written a little note to Fanny in which I begged her not to come over to see me for a very particular reason which I could tell her as soon as I could find an opportunity on the morrow. This note I took with me to Amy at the Corbetts and we went out into the garden together, Amy refusing to let Mabel accompany us.

'Well you do look bad, Captain Devereaux. Are you so awfully afraid of Fanny then? You are as white as a ghost.'

'I am not afraid of Fanny, Amy. Nothing she could say to me could be half so painful as what my conscience tells me. But the fact is I could not sleep a wink when I got home this morning.'

'Ha! ha! ha! ha!' laughed Amy, as merrily and cheerfully as if I had told her something more than ordinarily pleasant and delightful. 'Oh! I do like to hear that! What a fool you are, Captain Devereaux! I wonder you don't put more value on yourself. Now if I were you, I should say to Fanny, if she is at all cross, "Look here Fanny! You can take me or leave me – it is all one to me. I can't fuck any the more because I have two cunts instead of one to fuck. Only Amy will get all the more if you leave me.'

'That would be adding insult to injury, Amy.'

'Well! what of it? Is it not the truth?'

'You don't consider the pain such speaking would give poor Fanny.'

'Pain! And pray did she consider what pain I suffered from her not even asking me would I like to be fucked by you when she was. Sisters should share. I only ask for my share. I don't want to take you altogether away from Fanny, but I must be fucked as well as she.'

'Well, I should not be surprised if it all came to an end now.'

'Why?'

'Because I expect when Fanny hears the news she will go into one of her dreadful states of excitement and do or say something rash before your father; and if he hears of what has happened he will certainly take steps to prevent any more of my fucking of his daughters. He could, for instance, as easily get me sent to another station as I could get Lavie sent to Benares. Nobody need know why, but you and Fanny would have to find another beau, if fucking is all either of you wish for.'

This speech made Amy thoughtful. She had entirely lost sight of the possible effects a too brilliant triumph over Fanny might have.

'That is worth thinking about, Captain Devereaux.'

'It is, Amy, in all solemn earnest. Now will you do me a favour?'

'What is it?'

'Will you give this note to Fanny for me?'

'What have you said in it?'

'All I have said is to ask her not come over to me tonight.'

'Have you told her what has happened?'

'No!'

Amy walked on in silence evidently thinking what she should do. I imagine she had intended to crow vigorously over Fanny, but my warning had made her begin to reconsider this. As we walked we approached the stable and Amy, who had been twisting my note to Fanny between her fingers suddenly looked up.

'Oh! Here we are at the stable,' said she.

'Yes,' said I, reading her thoughts, 'but Amy dear I really could not do it now!'

'What nonsense!' she cried reddening. 'I never asked you either – but now, for saying that, you shall!'

'I really can't, Amy.'

'Bosh! come Captain Devereaux, I wish to be fucked now, this instant. It may be my last chance, if so much depends upon Fanny, as you seem to think. I will not throw away a chance. Come into the stable at once and do what you are bid.'

'I will go into the stable, Amy, but you will see I speak nothing but the truth when I tell you that I am not able to fuck you now.'

I went in.

'Now,' said Amy, 'explain yourself.'

'Here is the best explanation possible,' said I undoing my braces and letting down my trousers. 'Look and see if you can get that into your cunt, Amy.'

Amy raised my shirt and saw me in a state she had never considered possible. My prick hung dead and nerveless, my balls were loose in an elongated and relaxed bag, everything denoted the most marked fatigue.

'You are foxing!' cried Amy angrily, stamping her foot. 'Make it stiff, at once! Do you hear me! Ah! Do Captain Devereaux!' she continued in an imploring tone of voice. 'Don't be so unkind to me.'

I heard her with a mixture of amusement and pain.

I was amused at her thinking I was my prick's master and able to make it stand or not, at my pleasure; and pained that I was really unable to comply with her wishes and fuck her, for I felt if I could gratify her now she would be in better humour and be more inclined to spare Fanny and so soften down the announcement of her triumph.

'Amy dear, I would if I could. But the want of sleep and the painful anxiety about Fanny that I have been under all day have killed me; but try if you can make it stiff yourself! I really am not fooling. I should very much like to fuck you, if I could. Here let us lie down in this grass and while you see what you can do with your hands, I will feel your nice, soft cunt.'

We lay down and Amy cuddled up to me, looking at times into my face with a keen gaze as if to see whether I was deceiving her or not, whilst she handled my prick and my balls in the most voluptuously exciting manner possible. It was of no use whatever. I was in a state of mental and bodily prostration and my prick remained as limp as ever, though my balls gradually drew up into a tighter bunch than they had been in before Amy's gentle fingers titillated them.

After about ten minutes of these mutual caresses I withdrew my hand, wet with her frequent spendings, from between Amy's lovely thighs and said: 'I am afraid we must give up the idea of it, Amy. My prick is too dead. Too tired.'

'Too obstinate and too abominably selfish, you mean,' said Amy in great anger. 'Take that for the sulky beast you are,' and with these words addressed to my prick she suddenly gave it a stinging slap with her hand not only hurting it considerably, but making my poor balls throb with pain.

'Oh, Amy! Oh, my! You have hurt me.'

Now if a woman has a tender place in her heart for anything in this world it is for a man's prick and balls. Let my readers think for a second and nearly all must recollect instances where women of their acquaintances have heard with apparent indifference of men being mutilated in any other particular but have shown the very greatest sympathy and have shuddered when they have been told of the mutilation of prick or balls, or both. Amy was no exception.

'Oh! Captain Devereaux! I really did not mean to hurt it so much. Oh, poor thing, poor thing.' She hung over me, as I had turned on to my face, for I had some extremely sharp pains in my groin and a dull heavy pain at the lower part of my belly. I felt Amy's hand groping along my right groin and at first I resisted a little, but a sharp bit of grass happening to run into my prick, I made a sudden move, which enabled her to get at that which she wished to caress and soothe. Suddenly, to my astonishment, for I had no sensation to tell me the fact, she cried out: 'Oh, Captain Devereaux! It's stiff. It's stiff. It's standing beautifully.'

The pain I had endured had been sharp enough, but it passed like a sudden twinge of toothache. Amy's exclamation seemed to drive it away and I could now feel that I had indeed a glorious stand. I felt so grateful to Amy that I turned and caught her in my arms and kissed her before I pushed her on her back and got between those beautiful rounded, snowy thighs, which she uncovered for me with immense haste as though she feared the stiffness of my prick might go as suddenly as it had come. It was a lovely fuck! A completely glorious fuck! and at the end, whilst I was still lying with my motte hard pressed to hers, which leaped and jumped, and whilst I was still enjoying the throbbing and squeezing and twitching of her deliciously excited and melting little cunt, I could not help saying: 'Oh, Amy, try and win Fanny over and we will have many another like this.'

The episode did me considerable good. It gave me more hope towards Fanny, for I left Amy in a much more amiable mood than that in which I had found her and my limp prick and the idea of what might happen should Colonel Selwyn discover that I had fucked Fanny were things both new to her that I was sure were going to do their work on her mind. Fanny would be angry, grieved and more or less destroyed by hearing the news, but bad as that would be it would be so much worse if accompanied by the stinging and triumphant insults which I felt certain Amy, in true sisterly fashion, had prepared for her.

Since I had become station staff officer, I had been relieved of the necessity of dining at the mess of my regiment, so that I used my freedom in this respect pretty largely and seldom dined there two nights running. The truth is, I dislike mess dinners more than I can express and I do not think anybody can like them as a continuance. This night, however, I was glad to go and sit at dinner with my brother officers, for their chat helped me to pass away some of those purgatorial hours between my last fucking of Amy and the time when I was to meet Fanny.

On my way home I looked in at the colonel's bungalow. I knew I had better take the bull by the horns and I rather expected to find Fanny ill or unable to see me. But no, there the sweet girl was, glad and happy – she was all too evidently still unaware of my terrible infidelity. It was clear, too, that Amy had not given her my note, for poor Fanny took the opportunity of whispering to me that she was quite well and that she had a lot to tell me when she came over. Amy was a perfect study. She acted her part to perfection. She was just exactly the same Amy she had been, to all appearances, before Fanny went to Rampur and before there had been any question of my fucking her. I warn Amy's husband, should he read these pages, that he might as well not attempt to keep her under watch and guard. If Amy ever takes a fancy for some young fellow, she will have her way with him and that right under her husband's nose and he won't know it. Her manner to me was astounding. Since the moment she had got me in the trap between her thighs, she had been so unlike the old Amy, that the sudden assumption of a driving, domineering, hard-hearted, wilful woman's manner had stunned me, as much as her extraordinary behaviour. She had had me quite under a spell in consequence. She had jumped upon and crushed me by the suddenness of the blow. But tonight she had so completely resumed her old manner, appearance and tone it was hard to believe we had fucked something like fifty different times during the past week. Alas! My prick which had refused to stand that afternoon for her until she had beaten it, did what it had never done in the old days before Fanny went to Rampur (those old days, which though only separated from these new times by a week, seemed so long, long ago) for it stood stiffly the moment Amy came near me. In the old days that irrepressible organ would have remained quiescent until Fanny's approach would have aroused it to assume its grand proportions, but tonight it grew stiff the moment it perceived the nearness of Amy's cunt.

I went home then, knowing that the storm had yet to burst, for I imagined that when she and Amy retired for the night, Amy would surely tell Fanny all and the first effect of her grief and indignation would be to make her take a vow never to see me again.

But instead of going to bed I sat up. My head buzzed with fatigue and excitement, but tired as I was, I knew that if I did go to bed I should not sleep. Whilst I was thus seated in a half-dreamy and truly painful state of mind, I got a shock which woke me to life and action in a moment, for I heard the swift, light steps of Fanny coming down the verandah. Before I could rise she burst into my room, as if life, or all that was worth having, depended upon the swiftness of her movements. On seeing me she stopped dead. A glance at her face told me she was in possession of the news. Poor Fanny! Ah! Gentle reader! Tell me, do you know anything in this world so hideously painful, so agonising to the mind and heart, as the discovery that the person in whom your confidence is placed, in whom all your love and devotion, heart and soul, are invested, is false, a traitor! Fanny had never loved before she loved me. With the wholeheartedness of youth she had given herself to me – heart, soul, body – unreservedly and she trusted in me as in her God.

For a moment she stood looking at me, her lovely eyes expressing all the pain she felt but at the same time a kind of hesitancy to believe what she now knew was real and not a dreadful dream. Her lips were parted as though to speak, but no words came. Her bosom heaved tumultuously and her lovely firm breasts seemed as though the struggle going on within her would make them burst their points through the bodice. I had seen Fanny in a passion many times, but never in such a state as she now appeared in. Her look fascinated me. She seemed to be trying to read my inmost soul through my eyes and I remained dumb.

'Oh! Charlie!' she cried, all of a sudden, 'tell me it is not true! Oh, why did you do it? Oh! I never thought that my Charlie would be so – so – so – cruel to me!' She bent her lovely head and commenced to sob and weep violently without noise.

This was awful. I had never been so tried in all my life before. I jumped up and approaching her sat by her side, not daring to lay a hand upon the girl whom I felt I did not dare to touch with my polluted fingers.

For fully five minutes we stayed thus, until Fanny, raising her face, all wet with tears and once more flushed, turned her streaming eyes upon me and staggering forward fell into my arms. I caught her in them. I kissed that face all lovely still though quivering with the devouring pain she felt and Fanny let me do so, let me press her to my bosom, let me draw her towards my chair and let me take her into my lap, where I held her tenderly lying against me, whilst she still wept and sobbed.

Suddenly she rose into a more upright position and looking at me, said, 'Why don't you speak to me? You are crying too! What are you crying for?'

'Because, Fanny darling, I can't help it! I can't see you, the girl I love, in such dreadful grief and not feel sorry.'

'I am a fool for coming,' she said. 'Let me go! I'll never, never, never, speak to you again!'

'Stay!' I cried, holding her. 'Stay, Fanny! You have heard only one side of the story. It is only fair to me to hear mine. I swear to you that I never had the remotest idea of being unfaithful to you and that it was not until I was actually in Amy's cunt that I knew it was not you whom I was fucking.'

Fanny loved me. That is the only explanation of the patience with which she heard me. In her heart, that heart so dreadfully wounded, she wished to find the palliation of my sin. Had her pride only been wounded, she would never, or could never have forgiven me, but love covers a multitude of sins and Fanny heard my story, not only with patience, but with eagerness.

With passions as strong as mine, with a cunt as susceptible to pleasure as my prick, she could understand me when I said that the first fuck with Amy over, I found it impossible to tear myself away from a cunt so fascinating, so blooming as that between Amy's thighs; and as I proceeded and told my story, in such a way as to make it more than evident that, much as I appreciated her sister's cunt, I did not love Amy, whereas my whole soul was bound up in her, she at last threw her arms round my neck and kissed me and then wept again, but without that violence, which was all the more dreadful because subdued, which marked the first outbreak of her passion.

For hours we sat thus talking. Fanny quite understood her position. She loved me too much to be able to carry out her passionately expressed threat never to speak to me again, yet it was but too evident that she must consent to share me with Amy at once and with Mabel later on. She herself remembered what she had said about concubines and, with a sorrowful smile, she congratulated me on having now three really pretty ladies in my harem. As she grew more cheerful, so did I, and venturing at last on an act, I undid the lace of her bodice and uncovered her lovely breasts, which I once again devoured with my lips, in a manner so full of passion that the poor girl all but fainted from excess of emotion. Snatching the lovely bubbies from my eager lips, she put her mouth to mine and beginning with the top button of my trousers she undid them all, one by one, until, reaching the last, she inserted her little hand and, pulling up my shirt, took possession of my stiff and impudent prick, which looked her boldly and unblushingly in the face.

'Yes,' she cried, 'it is not my Charlie, but you who are the traitor. Oh! you villian!'

Hard words, but Oh! what soft caresses. I am afraid my prick, like Galileo, paid no attention to her speech, but was too hungry for that dear little cunt which he had been the first to open. Happy reconciliation. Fanny in a few moments more stood in her naked beauty before me and in another moment had all but forgotten the agonies of the recent hours in the convulsions of the delirious pleasure I presented.

Sugdaya awoke us. That lovely traitress was delighted to find us naked in bed together. Fanny would have quarrelled with her, but she had listened to me and had swallowed Sugdaya with her other inevitable griefs and our last luscious fuck took place under the eye of that lovely native girl and born procuress, who was to be so useful to me in finding me sweet cunts, besides her own, during the next three or four years.

Now, reader, did you think for any moment that things could have turned out so? Did not our beloved goddess Venus stand on my side? I saw her divine and beneficent hand in every turn of our amatory survey and never had she a more ardent priest than me. For I did my utmost never to lose a chance of making her holy altars between the thighs of my lovely 'concubines' smoke with the incense of my offerings.

Oh! those exquisite nights! Those revels when like a god of olden times I sported with my naked nymphs, passing from between the arms of one to between the thighs of the other, the change from one cunt to the second giving me fresh life and greater strength! There was certainly an increase of voluptuous pleasure and delight, but alas! the purity and depth of love which had existed between Fanny and me suffered. We never again were, or could be, what we had been to one another.

And now it remains but for me to show you how, at last, I filled up the cup of Mabel's joy by fucking her and then I will close the history of my association with those three beautiful and delicious Selwyn cunts.

Neither Fanny nor Amy seemed to be in the least degree anxious that I should fuck Mabel. This was natural enough so far as Fanny was concerned, but Amy, as my dear reader may remember, had made it a *sine qua non* that Mabel was to have her share of my prick and balls. Experience, however, began to teach her that a whole loaf is better than half of one, and a half-loaf is better than a third of one. So I never heard any more from her of the obligations I was under to fuck Mabel. But it was impossible to prevent Mabel's knowing of my nightly visits to her father's bungalow, and what went on there in consequence, and I have little doubt she often witnessed scenes of joy, in which she burned to play her part, from behind the purdah. Besides, I am certain that Sugdaya, who felt no scruples, incited her to claim her share and this is how she got it.

# *Mabel has Her Way with Me*

One lovely day in December (this is in the delightful cold weather) I was preparing to go out to pay some visits when I saw Mrs Soubratie hurrying up from the servants' house. I guessed that the colonel must have come over for a moment to get a morning fuck and, as I wanted to see him, I thought I would wait until he had taken his pleasure and then I would do so. Although it was an understood thing between us that he was at liberty to fuck Mrs Soubratie whenever he liked in my house, yet as a rule we did not meet on those occasions, so that unless I actually saw him between her thighs, or saw Mrs Soubratie pass my door, I rarely knew the exact moment these pleasant meetings were taking place.

I waited therefore, seated in my chair. I had not been sitting more than a minute when Mabel appeared, bursting with laughter which she was finding it hard to contain. Coming on tiptoe to me she whispered: 'Oh! Captain Devereaux! Come here! Come here.'

I rose. She took my hand and leading me into my bedroom she took me to the door in which was a window, covered with a thin muslin blind, which looked into the room and on to the bed in which the colonel always fucked Mrs Soubratie. There, of course, I saw, as did Mabel, the colonel about halfway through a nice, fat fuck, and Mabel, delighted beyond description, feasted her eyes on her father's splendid prick passing, in measured cadence, up and down and in and out of the brown cunt of Mrs Soubratie. The sight was too voluptuous, especially as Mabel was there, not to affect me greatly and I unbuttoned my trousers and put my now burning prick into Mabel's palm. At the same time I intruded my hand past her petticoats and caressed the little cunt, now well covered with curly locks, which immediately responded to my caresses with such an overflow that it surprised me. Still affected powerfully by seeing her father's glistening member disappearing and reappearing as he fucked Mrs Soubratie in his stolid fashion, and his balls, those huge balls, bouncing as they swung backwards and forwards, Mabel quietly moved her hand up and down my prick, until a sudden thrill of pleasure round its collar warned me that if she continued so doing I should spend; all the more also, because of sympathy, the colonel being now at the vigorous short digs. I therefore kept her hand quiet until, the colonel having finished and Mrs Soubratie having made her salaam and left the room, the show had come to an end.

'Well, Mabel!' said I, when the colonel had walked off with that jaunty side step he always adopted after a good fuck, 'you came in the very nick of time to see that!'

'Yes!' said she, looking at my prick and gently feeling my balls, which she had foraged for and got out. 'Sugdaya told me I should see something, if I came over here now. I thought she meant this,' she continued looking up at me with a smile, 'but I fancy she must have meant that I should see papa with Mrs Soubratie.'

'She may have meant both, Mabel dear! But take care, child! You will make me spend if you move your hand like that!'

'Oh! What fun that would be! Let me? Do, Captain Devereaux! I should so like to see it.'

'Well!' said I, shivering with pleasure, 'all right, dear, but let me take off my trousers first or they will be spoilt.'

I saw that the time had come. This was Mabel's hour and I shut my bedroom door and bolted it.

'Now, Mabel! Take off your frock and stays and stockings and we will go to bed together.'

'Oh no!!'

'Oh yes!'

'Oh, how delightful! Oh, you good, good, good Captain Devereaux!!' she cried in an ecstasy of joy. 'But let us go regularly to bed and take off all our clothes.'

'Very well!' said I, laughing, and in another couple of minutes we were both as naked as we were born.

Mabel was very pretty. Like Fanny and Amy, she had a very nice, pure, even white skin. Her limbs still required a little more flesh to give them the roundness that is so desirable, but her little bubbies were really charming and the plump motte had quite as much hair on it as Fanny's and her nudity charmed me; my nakedness pleased her immensely; though she had often enough handled my prick and balls, she said this was the first time she had ever really seen them.

Now, it is chilly enough in the cold weather to make one's skin rather want clothing, so I picked up Mabel, laid her on the bed and, getting in myself, pulled the bedclothes well up to our chins and there we lay cuddled together. Mabel had again got hold of my prick, which she was working in such a way that I knew I would spend immediately if she did not leave off.

'Wait! Mabel, you will really make me spend all over you.'

'I shall like that,' she cried. 'I should like to see what a man's spend is like.'

'Very well,' said I, laughing, 'then see.'

I threw down the bedclothes and almost at the same moment let fly a torrent of spend which I could restrain no longer. Mabel shrieked, for the first jet struck her full in the face, the second under the chin, the third splashed against her bubbies and the remaining jets I directed to her belly and finally to her bush, taking care so to hold her hand as to give her the benefit of every drop.

'Oh! That was nice!' cried Mabel. 'What a lot. How creamy it is. Like hollandaise, only thicker; but you must have quite emptied your balls.'

'Oh no. There's lots in them, Mabel, and when, in a minute or so, I fuck you, they will go on making more for you.'

I wiped the lovely streaming body of my bedfellow as I spoke and, expecting to find a rather obstinate maidenhead, I thought it wise to begin with her as soon as possible, so that by the time I next spent, she would have had a good fuck.

Judge of my surprise, on taking my position between her open thighs, to meet with absolutely no resistance! There was not only not the ghost of a maidenhead, but it was evident to me that the cunt I was in had been most thoroughly well opened. If Mabel had already been fucked, who had done it? I made no remark, however, for I was too much amused and delighted with her expressions of delight and pleasure. Like Fanny and Amy, her cunt was a perfect fountain, easily made to play by the movements of my prick within it, and Mabel made me laugh with her continuous, 'There I go again!' But when I came to the short digs and in my turn inundated her lovely little cunt with a sea of spend, Mabel clutched me with all her force to her convulsed and quivering body and exclaimed, 'Oh! how much better a real prick is than a cucumber!'

The cat was out of the bag! A cucumber!

The first fuck over, Mabel told me amidst rapid kisses and never-ending caresses that Sugdaya had taught her how pleasant a sensation could be produced by a three-quarter-ripe banana, with its peel half removed. From a small banana she had progressed to one of larger size, always to the detriment of her maidenhead, until one day, seeing a very nice smooth cucumber, the straightness and size of which struck her as being peculiarly adapted for her experiments, she picked it, went indoors and finished off with a vegetable what, but for that, would have been decided by my prick of flesh!

Mabel was a lascivious little girl, a grand poke. Like Lizzie Wilson her mission in life is to fuck. The dear reader will not be surprised to hear that she has joined that select number of fair women who, nominally 'kept' by wealthy lovers, take delight in relieving the pains of numerous adorers, and enjoy along the winding paths of intrigue the voluptuous pleasures to be gathered, like flowers, along their shaded ways. If Mabel's present ties were legitimate she would be the Duchess of —. To her was the glory of having been the first to give palpable proof of the ecstasies of fucking to no less a personage than one of the royal princes.

Neither Fanny nor Amy showed any ill will towards Mabel on account of our mutual participation in the sacrifice, and up to the last night of their stay in Fackabad these amiable girls were poked by me, sometimes in company, sometimes singly, unless 'illness' prevented.

In March of the following year, just twelve months after I had taken Fanny's maidenhead, the girls went home to England, the colonel having retired from the service.

Our parting was extremely painful. We made exchanges of locks of hair from our respective bushes and so eager were the girls for mementoes of mine that it was months before my prick grew out of a forest as thick, or rather as long, as it was when first I pressed it against that of Lizzie Wilson at Nowshera.

# The Autobiography of a Flea

STANILAS DE RHODES

## Chapter One

Born I was – but how, when, or where I cannot say; so I must leave the reader to accept the assertion *per se*, and believe it if he will. One thing is equally certain, the fact of my birth is not one atom less veracious than the reality of these memoirs, and if the intelligent student of these pages wonders how it came to pass that one in my walk – or perhaps, I should have said jump – of life, became possessed of the learning, observation and power of committing to memory the whole of the wonderful facts and disclosures I am about to relate, I can only remind him that there are intelligences little suspected by the vulgar, and laws in Nature the very existence of which have not yet been detected by the advanced among the scientific world.

I have heard it somewhere remarked that my province was to get my living by blood sucking. I am not the lowest by any means of that universal fraternity, and if I sustain a precarious existence upon the bodies of those with whom I come in contact, my own experience proves that I do so in a marked and peculiar manner, with a warning of my employment which is seldom given by those in other grades of my profession. But I submit that I have other and nobler aims than the mere sustaining of my being by the contributions of the unwary. I have been conscious of this original defect, and, with a soul far above the vulgar instincts of my race, I jumped by degrees to heights of mental perception and erudition which placed me for ever upon a pinnacle of insect-grandeur.

It is this attainment to learning which I shall evoke in describing the scenes of which I have been a witness – nay, even a partaker. I shall not stop to explain by what means I am possessed of human powers of thinking and observing, but, in my lucubrations, leave you simply to perceive that I possess them and wonder accordingly.

You will thus perceive that I am not a common flea; indeed, when it is borne in mind the company in which I have been accustomed to mingle, the familiarity with which I have been suffered to treat persons the most exalted, and the opportunities I have possessed to make the most of my acquaintances, the reader will no doubt agree with me that I am in very truth a most wonderful and exalted insect.

My earliest recollections lead me back to a period when I found myself within a church. There was a rolling of rich music and a slow monotonous chanting which then filled me with surprise and admiration, but I have long since learnt the true importance of such influences, and the attitudes of the worshippers are now taken by me for the outward semblance of inward emotions which are very generally non-existent. Be this as it may, I was engaged upon professional business connected with the plump white leg of a young lady of some sixteen years of age, the taste of whose delicious blood I well remember, and the flavour of whose –

But I am digressing.

Soon after I had commenced in a quiet and friendly way my little attentions, the young girl in common with the rest of the congregation rose to depart, and I, as a matter of course, determined to accompany her.

I am very sharp of sight as well as of hearing, and that is how I saw a young gentleman slip a small folded piece of white paper into the young lady's pretty gloved hand, as she passed through the crowded porch. I had noticed the name Bella neatly worked upon the soft silk stocking which had at first attracted me, and I now saw the same word appeared alone upon the outside of the billet-doux. She was with her aunt, a tall, stately dame, with whom I did not care to get upon terms of intimacy.

Bella was a beauty – just sixteen – a perfect figure, and although so young, her soft bosom was already budding into those proportions which delight the other sex. Her face was charming in its frankness; her breath sweet as the perfumes of Arabia, and, as I always said, her skin as soft as velvet. Bella was evidently well aware of her good looks, and carried her head as proudly and as coquettishly as a queen. That she inspired admiration was not difficult to see by the wistful and longing glances which the young men – and sometimes also those of more mature years – cast upon her. There was a general hush of conversation outside the building, and a turning of glances generally towards the pretty Bella, which told more plainly than words that she was the admired one of all eyes and the desired one of all hearts – at any rate among the male sex.

Paying, however, very little attention to what was evidently a matter of everyday occurrence, the young lady walked sharply homewards with her aunt, and after arrival at the neat and genteel residence, went quickly to her room. I will not say I followed, but I 'went with her', and beheld the gentle girl raise one dainty leg across the other and remove the tiniest of tight and elegant kid boots.

I jumped upon the carpet and proceeded with my examinations. The left boot followed, and, without removing her plump calf from off the other, Bella sat looking at the folded piece of paper which I had seen the young fellow deposit secretly in her hand.

Closely watching everything, I noted the swelling thighs, which spread upwards above her tightly fitting garters until they were lost in the darkness and closed together at a point where her beautiful belly met them in her stooping position; they almost obliterated a thin and peach-like slit, which just showed its rounded lips between them in the shade.

Presently Bella dropped her note, and being open, I took the liberty to read it. *I will be in the old spot at eight o'clock tonight*, were the only words which the paper contained, but they appeared to have a special interest for Bella, who remained cogitating for some time in the same thoughtful mood.

My curiosity had been aroused, and my desire to know more of the interesting young being which whom chance had so promiscuously brought me in pleasing contact prompted me to remain quietly ensconced in a snug though somewhat moist hiding place, and it was not until near upon the hour named that I once more emerged in order to watch the progress of events.

Bella had dressed herself with scrupulous care, and now prepared to betake herself to the garden which surrounded the country house in which she dwelt.

I went with her.

Arriving at the end of a long and shady avenue the young girl seated herself upon a rustic bench, and there awaited the coming of the person she was to meet.

It was not many minutes before the young man whom I had seen in communication with my fair little friend in the morning presented himself.

A conversation ensued which, if I might judge by the abstraction of the pair from aught besides themselves, had unusual interest for both.

It was evening, and the twilight had already commenced: the air was warm and genial, and the young pair sat closely entwined upon the bench, lost to all but their own happiness.

'You don't know how I love you, Bella,' whispered the youth, tenderly sealing his protestation with a kiss upon the pouting lips of his companion.

'Yes I do,' replied the girl, naïvely, 'are you not always telling me? I shall get tired of hearing it soon.'

Bella fidgeted her pretty little foot and looked thoughtful.

'When are you going to explain and show me all those funny things you told me about?' asked she, giving a quick glance up, and then as rapidly bending her eyes upon the gravel walk.

'Now,' answered the youth. 'Now, dear Bella, while we have the chance to be alone and free from interruption. You know, Bella, we are no longer children?'

Bella nodded her head.

'Well, there are things which are not known to children, and which are necessary for lovers not only to know, but also to practise.'

'Dear me,' said the girl, seriously.

'Yes,' continued her companion, 'there are secrets which render lovers happy, and which make the enjoyment of loving and of being loved.'

'Lord!' exclaimed Bella, 'how sentimental you have grown, Charlie; I remember the time when you declared sentiment was "all humbug".'

'So I thought it was, till I loved you,' replied the youth.

'Nonsense,' continued Bella, 'but go on, Charlie, and tell me what you promised.'

'I can't tell you without showing you as well,' replied Charlie; 'the knowledge can only be learnt by experience.'

'Oh, go on then and show me,' cried the girl, in whose bright eyes and glowing cheeks I thought I could detect a very conscious knowledge of the kind of instruction about to be imparted.

There was something catching in her impatience. The youth yielded to it, and covering her beautiful young form with his own, glued his mouth to hers and kissed it rapturously.

Bella made no resistance; she even aided and returned her lover's caresses.

Meanwhile, the evening advanced: the trees lay in the gathering darkness, spreading their lofty tops to screen the waning light from the young lovers.

Presently Charlie slid on one side; he made a slight movement, and then without any opposition he passed his hand under and up the petticoats of the pretty Bella. Not satisfied with the charms which he found within the compass of the glistening silk stockings, he essayed to press on still further, and his wandering fingers now touched the soft and quivering flesh of her young thighs.

Bella's breath came hard and fast, as she felt the indelicate attack which was being made upon her charms. So far, however, from resisting, she evidently enjoyed the exciting dalliance.

'Touch it,' whispered Bella, 'you may.'

Charlie needed no further invitation: indeed he was already preparing to advance without one and instantly comprehending the permission, drove his fingers forward. The fair girl opened her thighs as he did so, and the next instant his hand covered the delicate pink lips of her pretty slit.

For the next ten minutes the pair remained almost motionless, their lips joined and their breathing alone marking the sensations which were overpowering them with the intoxication of wantonness. Charlie felt a delicate object, which stiffened beneath his nimble fingers, and assumed a prominence of which he had no experience.

Presently Bella closed her eyes, and throwing back her head, shuddered slightly, while her frame became supple and languid, and she suffered her head to rest upon the arm of her lover.

'Oh, Charlie,' she murmured, 'what is it you do? What delightful sensations you give me.'

Meanwhile, the youth was not idle, but having fairly explored all he could in the constrained position in which he found himself, he rose, and sensible of the need of assuaging the raging passion which his actions had fanned, he besought his fair companion to let him guide her hand to a dear object, which he assured her was capable of giving her far greater pleasure that his fingers had done.

Nothing loth, Bella's grasp was the next moment upon a new and delicious substance, and either giving way to the curiosity she simulated, or really carried away by her newly-roused desires, nothing would do, but she must bring out and into the light the standing affair of her friend.

Those of my readers who have been placed in a similar position will readily understand the warmth of the grasp and the surprise of the look which greeted the first appearance in public of the new acquisition.

Bella beheld a man's member for the first time in her life, in the full plenitude of its power, and although it was not, I could plainly see, by any means a formidable one, yet its white shaft and redcapped head, from which the soft skin retreated as she pressed it, gained her quick inclination to learn more.

Charlie was equally moved; his eyes shone and his hand continued to rove all over the sweet young treasure of which he had taken possession.

Meanwhile, the toyings of the little white hand upon the youthful member with which it was in contact had produced effects common under such circumstances to all of so healthy and vigorous a constitution as that of the owner of this particular affair.

Enraptured with the soft pressures, the gentle and delicious squeezings, the artless way in which the young lady pulled back the folds from the rampant nut and disclosed the ruby crest, purple with desire, and the tip, ended by the tiny orifice, now awaiting its opportunity to send forth its slippery offering, the youth grew wild with lust, and Bella, participating in sensations new and strange, but which carried her away in a whirlwind of passionate excitement, panted for she knew not what of rapturous relief.

With her beautiful eyes half-closed, her dewy lips parted, and her skin warm and glowing with the unwonted impulse stealing over her, she lay, the delicious victim of whosoever had the instant chance to reap her favours and pluck her delicate young rose.

Charlie, youth though he was, was not so blind as to lose so fair an opportunity; besides, his now rampant passions carried him forward despite the dictates of prudence which he otherwise might have heard.

He felt the throbbing and well-moistened centre quivering beneath his fingers, he beheld the beautiful girl lying inviting him to the amorous sport, he watched the tender breathings which caused the young breast to rise and fall, he recognised the strong sensual emotions which animated the glowing form of his youthful companion.

The full, soft and swelling legs of the girl were now exposed to his sensuous gaze.

Gently raising the intervening drapery, Charlie still further disclosed the secret charms of his lovely companion until, with eyes of flame, he saw the plump limbs terminate in the full hips and white palpitating belly.

Then also his ardent gaze fell upon the centre spot of attraction – on the small pink slit which lay half-hidden at the foot of the swelling mount of Venus, as yet hardly shaded by the softest down.

The titillation which he had administered and the caresses which he had bestowed upon the coveted object had induced a flow of the native moisture which such excitement tends to provoke, and Bella lay with her peachlike slit well bedewed with Nature's best and sweetest lubricant.

Charlie saw his chance. Gently disengaging her hand from its grasp upon his member, he threw himself frantically upon the recumbent figure of the girl.

His left arm wound itself round her slender waist, his hot breath was on her cheek, his lips pressed hers in one long, passionate and hurried kiss. His right hand, now free, sought to bring together those parts of both which are the active instruments of sensual pleasure, and with eager efforts he sought to complete conjunction.

Bella now felt for the first time in her life the magic touch of a man's machine between the tips of her rosy orifice.

No sooner had she perceived the warm contact which was occasioned by the stiffened head of Charlie's member, than she shuddered perceptibly, and already anticipating the delights of venery, gave down an abundance of proof of her susceptible nature.

Charlie was enraptured at his happiness, and eagerly strove to perfect his enjoyment.

But Nature, which had operated so powerfully in the development of Bella's sensual passions, left yet something to be accomplished, ere the opening of so early a rosebud could be easily effected.

She was very young, immature, certainly so in the sense of those monthly visitations which are supposed to mark the commencement of puberty; and Bella's parts, replete as they were with perfection and freshness, were as yet hardly prepared for the accommodation of even so moderate a champion as that which, with round intruding head, now sought to enter in and effect a lodgement.

In vain Charlie pushed and exerted himself to press into the delicate parts of the lovely girl his excited member.

The pink folds and the tiny orifice withstood all his attempts to penetrate the mystic grotto. In vain the pretty Bella, now roused into a fury of excitement and half-mad with the titillation she had already undergone, seconded by all the means in her power the audacious attempts of her young lover.

The membrane was strong and resisted bravely until, with a desperate purpose to win the goal or burst everything, the youth drew back for a moment, and then desperately plunging forward, succeeded in piercing the obstruction and thrusting the head and shoulders of his stiffened affair into the belly of the yielding girl.

Bella gave a little scream as she felt the forcible inroad upon her secret charms, but the delicious contact gave her courage to bear the smart in hopes of the relief which appeared to be coming.

Meanwhile, Charlie pushed again and again, and proud of the victory which he had already won, not only stood his ground, but at each thrust advanced some small way further upon his road.

It has been said, *ce n'est que le premier coup qui coûte*, but it may be fairly argued that it is at the same time perfectly possible that *quelquefois il coûte trop*, as the reader may be inclined to infer with me in the present case.

Neither of our lovers, however, had, strange to say, a thought on the subject, but fully occupied with the delicious sensations which had over-powered them, united to give effect to those ardent movements which both could feel would end in ecstasy.

As for Bella, with her whole body quivering with delicious impatience, and her full red lips giving vent to the short excursive exclamations which announced the extreme gratification, she gave herself up body and soul to the delights of coition. Her muscular compressions upon the weapon which had now effectually gained her, the firm embrace in which she held the writhing lad, the delicate and moistened, glove-like sheath, all tended to excite Charlie to madness. He felt himself in her body to the roots of his machine, until the two globes which tightened beneath the foaming champion of his manhood, pressed upon the firm cheeks of her white bottom. He could go no further and his sole employment was to enjoy – to reap to the full the delicious harvest of his exertions.

But Bella, insatiable in her passion, no sooner found the wished-for junction completed than, relishing the keen pleasure which the stiff and warm member was giving her, she became too excited to know or care quite what was happening, and in her frenzied excitement, quickly overtaken again by the maddening spasms of completed lust, pressed downwards upon the object of her pleasure, threw up her arms in passionate rapture and then, sinking back in the arms of her lover, with low groans of ecstatic agony and little cries of surprise and delight, gave down a copious emission, which finding a reluctant escape below, inundated Charlie's balls.

No sooner did the youth witness the delivering enjoyment he was the means of bestowing upon the beautiful Bella and become sensible of the flood which she had poured down in such profusion upon his person, than he was also seized with lustful fury. A raging torrent of desire seemed to rush through his veins and furiously he plunged his instrument to the hilt in her delicious belly; then, drawing back, he extracted the smoking member almost to the head. He pressed and bore all before him. He felt a teasing, maddening feeling creeping upon him; he tightened his grasp upon the young mistress, and at the same instant that another cry of rapturous enjoyment issued from her heaving breast, he found himself gasping upon her bosom, and pouring into her grateful womb a rich tickling jet of youthful vigour.

A low moan of salacious gratification escaped the parted lips of Bella, as she felt the jerking gushes of seminal fluid which came from the excited member within her; at the same moment the lustful frenzy of emission forced from Charlie a sharp and thrilling cry as he lay with upturned eyes in the last act of the sensuous drama.

That cry was the signal for an interruption which was as sudden as it was unexpected. From out of the bordering shrubs there stole the sombre figure of a man; it came and stood before the youthful lovers.

Horror froze the blood of both.

Slipping from his late warm and luscious retreat and essaying as best he could to stand upright, Charlie recoiled from the apparition as from some dreadful serpent.

As for the gentle Bella, no sooner did she catch sight of the intruder than, covering her face with her hands, she shrank back upon the seat which had been the silent witness of her pleasures and, too frightened to utter a sound, waited with what presence of mind she could assume to face the brewing storm.

Nor was she kept long in suspense.

Quickly advancing towards the guilty couple the newcomer seized the lad by the arm while with a stern gesture of authority he ordered him to repair the disorder of his dress.

'Impudent boy,' he hissed between his teeth, 'what is it that you have done? To what lengths have your mad and savage passions hurried you? How will you face the rage of your justly offended father? How appease his angry resentment when in the exercise of my bounden duty, I apprise him of the mischief wrought by the hand of his only son?'

As the speaker ceased, still holding Charlie by the wrist, he came forth into the moonlight and disclosed the figure of a man of some forty-five years of age, short, stout and somewhat corpulent. His face, decidedly handsome, was rendered still more attractive by a pair of brilliant eyes, which, black as jet, threw around fierce glances of passionate resentment. He was habited in a clerical dress, the sombre shades and quite unobtrusive neatness of which drew out only more prominently his remarkably muscular proportions and striking physiognomy.

Charlie appeared, as well indeed he might, covered with confusion, and it was to his infinite and selfish relief that the stern intruder turned to the young partner of his libidinous enjoyment.

'For you, miserable girl, I can only express the utmost horror and my most righteous indignation. Forgetful alike of the precepts of the holy mother church, careless of your honour, you have allowed this wicked and presumptuous boy to pluck the forbidden fruit! What now remains for you? Scorned by your friends and driven from your uncle's house, you will herd with the beasts of the field, and exiled as by Nebuchadnezzar of old, shunned as contamination by your species, you will be glad to gather a miserable sustenance in the highways. Oh, daughter of sin, child given up to lust and unto Satan. I say unto thee – '

The stranger had proceeded thus far in his abjuration of the unfortunate girl, when Bella, rising from her crouching attitude, threw herself at his feet, and joined her tears and prayers for forgiveness to those of her young lover.

'Say no more,' at length continued the stern priest; 'say no more. Confessions are of no avail, and humiliations do but add to your offence. My mind misgives me as to my duty in this sad affair, but if I obeyed the dictates of my present inclinations I should go straight to your natural guardians and acquaint them immediately with the infamous nature of my chance discovery.'

'Oh, in pity, have mercy upon me,' pleaded Bella, whose tears now coursed down her pretty cheeks, so lately aglow with wanton pleasure.

'Spare us, father, spare us both. We will do anything in our power to make atonement. Six masses and several paters shall be performed on our account and at our cost. The pilgrimage to the shrine of St Eugulphus, of which you spoke to me the other day, shall now surely be undertaken. I am willing to do anything, sacrifice anything, if you will spare this dear Bella.'

The priest waved his hand for silence. Then he spoke, while accents of pity mingled with his naturally stern and resolute manner.

'Enough,' said he, 'I must have time. I must invoke assistance from the Blessed Virgin, who knew no sin, but who, without the carnal delights of mortal copulation, brought forth the babe of babes in the manger of Bethlehem. Come to me tomorrow in the sacristy, Bella. There in the precincts, I will unfold to you the divine will concerning your transgression. At two o'clock I will expect you. As for you, rash youth, I shall reserve my judgement, and all action, until the following day, when at the same hour I shall likewise expect you.'

A thousand thanks were being poured out by the united throats of the penitents, when the father warned them both to part. The evening had long ago closed in, and the dews of night were stealing upwards.

'Meanwhile, good-night and peace; your secret is safe with me, until we meet again,' he spoke and disappeared.

## Chapter Two

Curiosity to learn the sequel of an adventure in which I already felt so much interest, as well as a tender solicitude for the gentle and amiable Bella, constrained me to keep in her vicinity, and I, therefore, took care not to annoy her with any very decided attentions on my part, or to raise resistance by an ill-timed attack at a moment when it was necessary to the success of my design to remain within range of that young lady's operations.

I shall not attempt to tell of the miserable period passed by my young protégée in the interval which elapsed between the shocking discovery made by the holy father confessor, and the hour assigned by him for the interview in the sacristy which was to decide the fate of the unfortunate Bella.

With trembling steps and downcast eyes the frightened girl presented herself at the porch and knocked.

The door was opened and the father appeared upon the threshold.

At a sign Bella entered and stood before the stately presence of the holy man.

An embarrassing silence of some seconds followed. Father Ambrose was the first to break the spell.

'You have done right, my daughter, to come to me so punctually; the ready obedience of the penitent is the first sign of the spirit within which obtains the divine forgiveness.'

At these gracious words Bella took courage, and already a load seemed to fall from her heart.

Father Ambrose continued, seating himself at the same time upon the long-cushioned seat which covered a huge oak chest: 'I have thought much, and prayed much on your account, my daughter. For some time there appeared no way in which I could absolve my conscience otherwise than to go to your natural protector and lay before him the dreadful secret of which I have become the unhappy possessor.'

Here he paused, and Bella, who knew well the severe character of her uncle, on whom she was entirely dependent, trembled at his words.

Taking her hand in his, and gently drawing the girl to the same seat, so that she found herself kneeling before him while his right hand pressed her rounded shoulder, he went on.

'But I am wounded to think of the dreadful results which would follow such a disclosure, and I have asked for assistance from the Blessed Virgin in my trouble. She has pointed out a way which, while it also serves the ends of our holy church, likely prevents the consequences of your offence from being known to your uncle. The first necessity which this course imposes is, however, implicit obedience.'

Bella, only too rejoiced to hear of a way out of her trouble, readily promised the most blind obedience to the command of her spiritual father.

The young girl was kneeling at his feet. Father Ambrose bent his large head over her drooping figure. A warm tint lit his cheeks, a strange fire danced in his fierce eyes; his hands trembled slightly, as they rested upon the shoulders of his penitent, but his composure was otherwise unruffled. Doubtless his spirit was troubled at the conflict going on within him between the duty he had to fulfil and the tortuous path by which he hoped to avoid the awful exposure.

The holy father then began a long lecture upon the virtue of obedience and absolute submission to the guidance of the minister of the holy church.

Bella reiterated her assurances of entire patience and obedience in all things.

Meanwhile, it was evident to me that the priest was a victim to some confined, but rebellious spirit which rose within him, and at times almost broke out into complete possession in the flashing eyes and hot passionate lips.

Father Ambrose gently drew the beautiful penitent nearer and nearer, until her fair arms rested upon his knees and her face, bent downwards in holy resignation, sank almost upon her hands.

'And now, my child,' continued the holy man, 'it is time that I should tell you the means vouschsafed to me by the Blessed Virgin by which alone I am absolved from exposing your offence. There are ministering spirits who have confided to them the relief of those passions and those exigencies which the servants of the church are forbidden openly to avow, but which, who can doubt, they have need to satisfy. These chosen few are mainly selected from among those who have already trodden the path of fleshly indulgence; to them is confided the solemn and holy duty of assuaging the earthly desires of our religious community in the strictest secrecy. To you,' whispered the father, his voice trembling with emotion, and his large hands passing by an easy transition from the shoulders of his penitent to her slender waist – 'To you, who have once already tasted the supreme pleasure of copulation, it is given to assume this holy office. Not only will your sin be thus effaced and pardoned, but it will be permitted you to taste legitimately those ecstatic delights, those overpowering sensations of rapturous enjoyment, which in the arms of her faithful servants you are at all times sure to find. You will swim in a sea of sensual pleasure, without incurring the penalties of illicit love. Your absolution will follow each occasion of your yielding your sweet body to the gratification of the church, through her ministers, and you will be rewarded and sustained in the pious work by witnessing – nay, Bella, by sharing fully – those intense and fervent emotions the delicious enjoyment of your beautiful person must provoke.'

Bella listened to this insidious proposal with mingled feelings of surprise and pleasure.

The wild and lewd impulses of her warm nature were at once awakened by the picture now presented to her fervid imagination – how could she hesitate?

The pious priest drew her yielding form towards him, and printed a long hot kiss upon her rosy lips.

'Holy Mother,' murmured Bella, whose sexual instincts were each moment becoming more fully roused. 'This is too much for me to bear – I long – I wonder – I know not what!'

'Sweet innocent, it will be for me to instruct you. In my person you will find your best and fittest preceptor in those exercises you will henceforth have to fulfil.'

Father Ambrose slightly shifted his position. It was then that Bella noticed for the first time the heated look of sensuality which now almost frightened her.

It was now also that she became aware of the enormous protuberance at the front of the holy father's silk cassock.

The excited priest hardly cared any longer to conceal either his condition or his designs.

Catching the beautiful child in his arms he kissed her long and passionately. He pressed her sweet body to his burly person, and rudely threw himself forward into closer contact with her graceful form.

At length the consuming lust with which he was burning carried him beyond all bounds, and partly releasing Bella from the constraint of his ardent embrace, he opened the front of his cassock, and exposed, without a blush, to the astonished eyes of his young penitent, a member the gigantic proportions of which, no less than its stiffness and rigidity, completely confounded her.

It is impossible to describe the sensations produced upon the gentle Bella by the sudden display of this formidable instrument.

Her eyes was instantly riveted upon it, while the father, noticing her astonishment, but detecting rightly that there was nothing mingled with it of alarm or apprehension, coolly placed it into her hands. It was then that Bella became wildly excited with the muscular contact of this tremendous thing.

Only having seen the very moderate proportions displayed by Charlie, she found her lewdest sensations quickly awakened by so remarkable a phenomenon, and clasping the huge object as well as she could in her soft little hands, she sank down beside it in an ecstasy of sensual delight.

'Holy Mother, this is already heaven!' murmured Bella. 'Oh! father, who would have believed I could have been selected for such pleasure!'

This was too much for Father Ambrose. He was delighted at the lubricity of his fair penitent, and the success of his infamous trick (for he had planned the whole, and had been instrumental in bringing the two young lovers together and affording them an opportunity of indulging their warm temperaments, unknown to all save himself, as, hidden close by, with flaming eyes, he watched the amatory combat).

Hastily rising, he caught up the light figure of the young Bella, and placing her upon the cushioned seat on which he had lately been sitting, he threw up her plump legs and separating to the utmost her willing thighs, he beheld for an instant the delicious pinky slit which appeared at the bottom of her white belly. Then, without a word, he plunged his face towards it, and thrusting his lecherous tongue up the moist sheath as far as he could, he sucked it so deliciously that Bella, in a shuddering ecstasy of passion, her young body writhing in spasmodic contortions of pleasure, gave down a plentiful emission, which the holy man swallowed like a custard.

For a few moments there was calm.

Bella lay on her back, her arms extended on either side, and her head thrown back in an attitude of delicious exhaustion, succeeding the wild emotions so lately occasioned by the lewd proceedings of the reverend father.

Her bosom yet palpitated with the violence of her transports and her beautiful eyes remained half-closed in languid repose.

Father Ambrose was one of the few who, under circumstances such as the present, was able to keep the instincts of passion under command. Long habits of patience in the attainment of his object, a general doggedness of manner and the conventional caution of his order, had not been lost upon his fiery nature, and although by nature unfitted for his holy calling, and a prey to desires as violent as they were irregular, he had taught himself to school his passions even to mortification.

It is time to lift the veil from the real character of this man. I do so with respect, but the truth must be told.

Father Ambrose was the living personification of lust. His mind was in reality devoted to its pursuit, and his grossly animal instincts, his ardent and vigorous constitution, no less than his hard unbending nature, made him resemble in body, as in mind, the satyr of old.

But Bella only knew him as the holy father who had not only pardoned her offence, but who had opened to her the path by which she might, as she supposed, legitimately enjoy those pleasures which had already acted so strongly on her young imagination.

The bold priest, singularly charmed, not only at the success of his stratagem which had given into his hands so luscious a victim, but also at the extraordinary sensuality of her constitution, and the evident delight with which she lent herself to his desires, now set himself leisurely to reap the fruits of his trickery, and revel to the utmost in the enjoyment which the possession of all the delicate charms of Bella could procure to appease his frightful lust.

She was his at last, and as he rose from her quivering body, his lips yet reeking with the plentiful evidence of her participation in his pleasures, his member became yet more fearfully hard and swollen, and the dull red head shone with the bursting strain of blood and muscle beneath.

No sooner did the young Bella find herself released from the attack of her confessor upon the sensitive part of her person already described, and raised her head from the recumbent position into which it had fallen, than her eyes fell for the second time upon the big truncheon which the father kept impudently exposed.

Bella noted the long and thick white shaft, and the curling mass of black hair out of which it rose, stiffly inclining upwards; and protruding from its end was the egg-shaped head, skinned and ruddy, and seeming to invite the contact of her hand.

Bella beheld this thickened muscular mass of stiffened flesh, and unable to resist the inclination, flew once more to seize it in her grasp.

She squeezed it – she pressed it – she drew back the folding skin and watched the broad nut as it inclined towards her. She saw with wonder the small slit-like hole at its extremity and taking it in both her hands, she held it throbbing close to her face.

'Oh! father, what a beautiful thing,' exclaimed Bella, 'what an immense one, too. Oh! Please, dear Father Ambrose, do tell me what I must do to relieve you of those feelings which you say give our holy ministers of religion so much pain and uneasiness.'

Father Ambrose was almost too excited to reply, but taking her hand in his, he showed the innocent girl how to move her white fingers up and down upon the shoulders of his huge affair.

His pleasure was intense, and that of Bella was hardly less.

She continued to rub his limb with her soft palms and, looking up innocently to his face, asked softly – 'if that gave him pleasure, and was nice', and whether she might go on, as she was doing.

Meanwhile, the reverend father felt his big penis grow harder and even stiffer under the exciting titillations of the young girl.

'Stay a moment; if you continue to rub it so I shall spend,' softly said he. 'It will be better to defer it a little.'

'Spend, my father,' asked Bella, eagerly, 'what is that?'

'Oh, sweet girl, charming alike in your beauty and your innocence; how divinely you fulfil your divine mission,' exclaimed Ambrose, delighted to outrage and debase the evident inexperience of his young penitent. 'To spend is to complete the act whereby the full pleasure of venery is enjoyed, and then a rich quantity of thick white fluid escapes from the thing you now hold in your hand, and rushing forth, gives equal pleasure to him who ejects it and to the person who, in some manner or other, receives it.'

Bella remembered Charlie and his ecstasy, and knew immediately what was meant.

'Would this outpouring give you relief, my father?'

'Undoubtedly, my daughter; it is that fervent relief I have in view when I offer you the opportunity of taking from me the blissful sacrifice of one of the humblest servants of the church.'

'How delicious,' murmured Bella; 'by my means this rich stream is to flow, and all for me the holy man proposes this end of his pleasure – how happy I am to be able to give him so much pleasure.'

As she half-pondered, half-uttered these thoughts she bent her head down; a faint, but exquisitely sensual perfume rose from the object of her adoration. She pressed her moist lips upon its top, she covered the little slitlike hole with her lovely mouth, and imprinted upon the glowing member a fervent kiss.

'What is this fluid called?' asked Bella, once more raising her pretty face.

'It has various names,' replied the holy man, 'according to the status of the person employing them; but between you and me, my daughter, we shall call it spunk.'

'Spunk!' repeated Bella, innocently, making the erotic word fall from her sweet lips with an unction which was natural under the circumstances.

'Yes, my daughter, spunk is the word I wish you to understand it by, and you shall presently have a plentiful bedewal of the precious essence.'

'How must I receive it?' enquired Bella, thinking of Charlie, and the tremendous difference relatively between his instrument and the gigantic and swollen penis in her presence now.

'There are various ways, all of which you will have to learn, but at present we have only slight accommodation for the principal act of reverential venery, of that permitted copulation of which I have already spoken. We must, therefore, supply another and easier method, and instead of my discharging the essence called spunk into your body, where the extreme tightness of that little slit of yours would doubtless cause it to flow very abundantly, we will commence by the friction of your obedient fingers, until the time when I feel the approach of those spasms which accompany the emission. You shall then, at a signal from me, place as much as you can of the head of this affair between your lips, and there suffer me to disgorge the trickling spunk, until the last drop being expended I shall retire satisfied, at least for the time.'

Bella, whose zealous instincts led her to enjoy the description which her confessor offered, and who was quite as eager as himself for the completion of this outrageous programme, readily expressed her willingness to comply.

Ambrose once more placed his large penis in Bella's fair hands.

Excited alike by the sight and touch of so remarkable an object, which both her hands now grasped with delight, the girl set herself to work to tickle, rub and press the huge and stiff affair in a way which gave the licentious priest the keenest enjoyment.

Not content with the friction of her delicate fingers, Bella, uttering words of devotion and satisfaction, now placed the foaming head upon her rosy lips and allowed it to slip in as far as it could, hoping by her touches, no less than by the gliding movements of her tongue, to provoke the delicious ejaculation of which she was in want.

This was almost beyond the anticipation of the holy priest, who had hardly supposed he should find so ready a disciple in the irregular attack he proposed; and his feelings being roused to the utmost by the delicious titillation he was now experiencing, he prepared himself to flood the young girl's mouth and throat with the full stream of his powerful discharge.

Ambrose began to feel he could not last longer without letting fly his roe, and thereby ending his pleasure.

He was one of those extraordinary men, the abundance of whose seminal ejaculation is far beyond that of ordinary beings. Not only had he the singular gift of repeatedly performing the veneral act with but very short respite, but the quantity with which he ended his pleasure was as tremendous as it was unusual. The superfluity seemed to come from him in proportion as his animal passions were aroused, and as his libidinous desires were intense and large, so also were the outpourings which relieved them.

It was under these circumstances that the gentle Bella undertook to release the pent-up torrents of this man's lust. It was her sweet mouth which was to be the recipient of those thick slippery volumes of which she had had as yet no experience, and, all ignorant as she was of the effect of the relief she was so anxious to administer, the beautiful maid desired the consummation of her labour and the overflow of that spunk of which the good father had told her.

Harder and hotter grew the rampant member as Bella's exciting lips pressed its large head and her tongue played around the little opening. Her two white hands alternately bore back the soft skin from its shoulders and tickled the lower extremity.

Twice Ambrose, unable to bear the delicious contact without spending, drew back the tip from her rosy lips.

At length Bella, impatient of delay, and apparently bent on perfecting her task, pressed forward with more energy than ever upon the stiff shaft.

Instantly there was a stiffening of the limbs of the good priest. His legs spread wide on either side of his penitent. His hand grasped convulsively at the cushions, his body was thrust forward and straightened out.

'Oh, holy Christ! I am going to spend!' he exclaimed, as with parted lips and glazing eyes he looked his last upon his innocent victim. Then he shivered perceptibly, and with low moans and short, hysteric cries, his penis, in obedience to the provocation of the young lady, began to jet forth its volumes of thick and glutinous fluid.

Bella, sensible of the gushes which now came slopping, jet after jet, into her mouth and ran in streams down her throat, hearing the cries of her companion and perceiving with ready intuition that he was enjoying to the utmost the effect she had brought about, continued her rubbings and compression until gorged with the slimy discharge, and half-choked by its abundance, she was compelled to let go of this human syringe, which continued to spout out its gushes in her face.

'Holy Mother!' exclaimed Bella, whose lips and face were reeking with the father's spunk. 'Holy Mother! What pleasure I have had – and you, my father, have I not given the precious relief you coveted?'

Father Ambrose, too agitated to reply, raised the gentle girl in his arms, and pressing her streaming mouth to his, sucked humid kisses of gratitude and pleasure.

A quarter of an hour passed in tranquil repose uninterrupted by any signs of disturbance from without.

The door was fast, and the holy father had well chosen his time.

Meanwhile Bella, whose desires had been fearfully excited by the scene we have attempted to describe, had conceived an extravagant longing to have the same operation performed upon her with the rigid member of Ambrose that she had suffered with the moderately proportioned weapon of Charlie. Throwing her arms round the burly neck of her confessor, she whispered low words of invitation, watching, as she did so, their effect on the already stiffening instrument between his legs.

'You told me that the tightness of this little slit,' and here Bella placed his large hand upon it with a gentle pressure, 'would make you discharge abundantly of the spunk you possess. What would I not give, my father, to feel it poured into my body from the top of this red thing?'

It was evident how much the beauty of the young Bella, no less than the innocence and *naïveté* of her character, inflamed the sensual nature of the priest. The knowledge of his triumph – of her utter helplessness in his hands – of her delicacy and refinement – all conspired to work to the extreme the lecherous desires of his fierce and wanton instincts. She was his. His to enjoy as he wished – his to break to every caprice of his horrid lust, and to bend to the indulgence of the most outrageous and unbridled sensuality.

'Ay, by heaven! it is too much,' exclaimed Ambrose, whose lust, already rekindling, now rose violently into activity at this solicitation. 'Sweet girl, you don't know what you ask; the disproportion is terrible, and you would suffer much in the attempt.'

'I would suffer all,' replied Bella, 'so that I could feel that fierce thing in my belly, and taste the gushes of its spunk up in me to the quick.'

'Holy Mother of God! It is too much – you shall have it, Bella, you shall know the full measure of this stiffened machine, and, sweet girl, you shall wallow in an ocean of warm spunk.'

'Oh, my father, what heavenly bliss!'

'Strip, Bella, remove everything that can interfere with our movements, which I promise you will be violent enough.'

Thus ordered, Bella was soon divested of her clothing, and finding her confessor appeared charmed at the display of her beauty, and that his member swelled and lengthened in proportion as she exhibited her nudity, she parted with the last vestige of drapery, and stood as naked as she was born.

Father Ambrose was astonished at the charms which now faced him. The full hips, the budding breasts, the skin as white as snow and soft as satin, the rounded buttocks and swelling thighs, the flat white belly and lovely mount covered only with the thinnest down; and above all the charming pinky slit which now showed itself at the bottom of the mount, now hid timorously away between the plump thighs. With a snort of rampant lust he fell upon his victim.

Ambrose clasped her in his arms. He pressed her soft and glowing form to his burly front. He covered her with his salacious kisses, and giving his lewd tongue full licence, promised the young girl all the joys of paradise by the introduction of his big machine within her slit and belly.

Bella met him with a little cry of ecstasy, and as the excited ravisher bore her backwards to the couch, already felt the broad and glowing head of his gigantic penis pressing against the warm moist lips of her tender virgin orifice.

And now the holy man, finding delight in the contact of his penis with the warm lips of Bella's slit, began pushing it in between with all his energy until the big nut was covered with the moisture which the sensitive little sheath exuded.

Bella's passions were at fever height. The efforts of Father Ambrose to lodge the head of his member within the moist lips of her little slit, so far from deterring her, spurred her to madness until, with another faint cry, she fell prostrate and gushed down the slippery tribute of her lascivious temperament.

This was exactly what the bold priest wanted, and as the sweet warm emission bedewed his fiercely distended penis, he drove resolutely in, and at one bound sheathed half its ponderous length in the beautiful child.

No sooner did Bella feel the stiff entry of the terrible member within her tender body, than she lost all the little control of herself she had, and setting aside all thought of the pain she was enduring, she wound her legs about his loins, and entreated her huge assailant not to spare her.

'My sweet and delicious child,' whispered the salacious priest, 'my arms are round you, my weapon is already half-way up your tight belly. The joys of paradise will be yours presently.'

'Oh, I know it; I feel it, do not draw back, give me the delicious thing as far as you can.'

'There, then, I push, I press, but I am far too largely made to enter you easily. I shall burst you, possibly; but it is now too late. I must have you – or die.'

Bella's parts relaxed a little, and Ambrose pushed in another inch. His throbbing member lay skinned and soaking, pushed half-way into the girl's belly. His pleasure was most intense, and the head of his instrument was compressed deliciously by Bella's slit.

'Go on, dear father, I am waiting for the spunk you promised me.'

It little needed this stimulant to induce the confessor to an exercise of his tremendous powers of copulation. He pushed frantically forward; he plunged his hot penis still further and further at each effort, and then with one huge stroke buried himself to the balls in Bella's tight little person.

It was then that the furious plunge of the brutal priest became more than his sweet victim, sustained as she had been by her own advanced desires, could endure.

With a faint shriek of physical anguish, Bella felt that her ravisher had burst through all the resistance which her youth had opposed to the entry of his member, and the torture of the forcible insertion of such a mass bore down the prurient sensations with which she had commenced to support the attack.

Ambrose cried aloud in rapture, he looked down upon the fair thing his serpent had stung. He gloated over the victim now impaled with the full rigour of his huge rammer. He felt the maddening contact with inexpressible delight. He saw her quivering with the anguish of his forcible entry. His brutal nature was fully aroused. Come what might he would enjoy to his utmost, so he wound his arms about the beautiful girl and treated her to the full measure of his burly member.

'My beauty! you are indeed exciting, you must also enjoy. I will give you the spunk I spoke of, but I must first work up my nature by this luscious titillation. Kiss me, Bella, then you shall have it, and while the hot spunk leaves me and enters your young parts, you shall be sensible of the throbbing joys I also am experiencing. Press, Bella, let me push, so, my child, now it enters again. Oh! Oh!'

Ambrose raised himself a moment, and noted the immense shaft round which the pretty slit of Bella was now intensely stretched.

Firmly embedded in her luscious sheath, and keenly relishing the exceeding tightness of the warm folds of youthful flesh which encased him, he pushed on, unmindful of the pain his tormenting member was producing, and only anxious to secure as much enjoyment to himself as he could. He was not a man to be deterred by any false notions of pity in such a case, and now pressed himself inwards to his utmost, while his hot lips sucked delicious kisses from the open and quivering lips of the poor Bella.

For some minutes nothing now was heard but the jerking blows with which the lascivious priest continued his enjoyment, and the cluck, cluck of his huge penis, as it alternately entered and retreated in the belly of the beautiful penitent.

It was not to be supposed that such a man as Ambrose was ignorant of the tremendous powers of enjoyment his member could rouse within one of the opposite sex, and that its size and disgorging capabilities were of such a nature as to enlist the most powerful emotions in the young girl in whom he was operating.

Indeed Nature was asserting herself in the person of the young Bella. The agony of the stretching was fast being swallowed up in the intense sensations of pleasure produced by the vigorous weapon of the holy man, and it was not long before the low moans and sobs of the pretty child became mingled with murmurs, half-choked in the depth of her feelings, expressive of delight.

'Oh, my father! Oh, my dear, generous father! Now, now push. Oh! push. I can bear – I wish for it. I am in heaven! The blessed instrument is so hot in its head. Oh! my heart. Oh! my – oh! Holy Mother, what is this I feel?'

Ambrose saw the effect he was producing. His own pleasure advanced apace. He drove steadily in and out, treating Bella to the long hard shaft of his member up to the crisp hair which covered his big balls, at each forward thrust.

At length Bella broke down, and treated the electrified and ravished man with a warm emission which ran all over his stiff affair.

It is impossible to describe the lustful frenzy which now took possession of the young and charming Bella. She clung with desperate tenacity to the burly figure of the priest, who bestowed upon the heaving and voluptuous body the full force and vigour of his manly thrust. She held him in her tight and slippery sheath to his balls.

But in her ecstasy Bella never lost sight of the promised perfection of the enjoyment. The holy man was to spend his spunk in her as Charlie had done, and the thought added fuel to her lustful fire.

When, therefore, Father Ambrose, throwing his arms close round her taper waist, drove up his stallion penis to the very hairs of Bella's slit and, sobbing, whispered that the 'spunk' was coming at last, the excited girl, straightway opening her legs to the utmost, with positive shrieks of pleasure let him send his pent-up fluid in showers into her very vitals.

Thus he lay for full two minutes, while at each hot and forcible injection of the slippery semen, Bella gave plentiful evidence, by her writhings and cries, of the ecstasy the powerful discharge was producing.

## *Chapter Three*

I do not think I ever felt my unfortunate infirmity in the matter of a natural inability to blush more acutely than on the present occasion. For even a flea might have blushed at the wanton sight which thrust itself upon his vision on the occasion I have herein recorded. So young, so apparently innocent a girl, and yet so lewd, so lascivious in her inclinations and desires. A person of infinite freshness and beauty – a mind of flaming sensuality fanned by the accidental course of events into an active volcano of lust.

Well might I have exclaimed with the poet of old: 'O Moses!' or with the more practical descendant of the Patriarch: 'Holy Moses!'

It is needless to speak of the change which Bella's whole being underwent after such experiences as these I have related. They were manifest and apparent in her carriage and demeanour.

What became of her youthful lover I never knew nor cared to enquire, but I am led to believe that holy Father Ambrose was not insensible to those irregular tastes which are so largely ascribed in his order, and that the youth was led by easy stages to lend himself, no less than his young mistress, to gratification of the insensate desires of the priest.

But to return to my own observations so far as they extended to the fair Bella.

Although a flea cannot blush, we can observe and I have taken upon me to commit to pen and ink all those amatory passages in my experience which I think may interest the seeker after truth. We can write, at least this flea can, or else these pages would not now be before the reader, and this is enough.

It was several days before Bella found an opportunity of again visiting her clerical admirer, but at length the chance came, and, as might be expected, she quickly availed herself of it.

She had found means to apprise Ambrose of her intention of visiting him, and that astute individual was accordingly ready to receive his pretty guest as before.

Bella no sooner found herself alone with her seducer than she threw herself into his arms, and pressing his huge carcass to her little form, lavished upon him the most tender caresses.

Ambrose was not slow in returning to the full the warmth of her embrace, and thus it happened that the pair found themselves hotly engaged in the exchange of burning kisses, and reclining face to face upon the well-cushioned seat before alluded to.

But Bella was not likely now to be contented with kisses only; she desired more solid fare, which she knew from experience the father could give her.

Ambrose, on his part, was no less excited. His blood flowed quickly, his dark eye flamed with unconcealed lust, and his protuberant dress displayed only too plainly the disorder of his senses.

Bella perceived his condition – neither his inflamed looks, nor the evident erection, which he took no trouble to conceal, escaped her – and she sought to add to his desires, if possible, not to diminish them.

Soon, however, Ambrose showed her that he required no further incentive, for he deliberately produced his fiercely distended weapon in a state the bare sight of which drove Bella frantic with desire. At any other time Ambrose would have been more prudent of his pleasures than thus early to have proceeded to work with the delicious little conquest. On this occasion, however, his senses ran riot with him, and he was unable to check the overwhelming desire to revel at once and as soon as possible in the juvenile charms thus offered him.

He was already upon her body. His great bulk covered her figure most powerfully and completely. His distended member bore hardly against Bella's stomach, and her clothes were already raised to her waist.

With a trembling hand Ambrose seized the centre chink of his wishes – eagerly he brought the hot and crimson tip towards its moist and opening lips. He pushed, he strove to penetrate – he succeeded: the immense machine slowly but surely entered – already the head and shoulders had disappeared. A few steady, deliberate thrusts completed the conjunction, and Bella had received the whole length of Ambrose's huge, excited member in her body.

The ravisher lay panting upon her bosom in complete possession of her inmost charms.

Bella, into whose little belly the vigorous mass was thus crammed, felt most powerfully the effects of the throbbing and hot intruder.

Meanwhile, Ambrose began to thrust up and down. Bella threw her white arms around his neck, and twined her pretty silk-clad legs all wantonly about his loins.

'How delicious,' murmured Bella, kissing rapturously his thick lips, 'Push up me – push up me harder. Oh, how it forces me open – how large it is! How hot – how – oh my – oh!'

And down came a shower from Bella's storehouse, in response to the strong thrusts received, while her head fell back and her mouth opened in the spasms of coition.

The priest restrained himself; he paused an instant; the throbbing of his long member sufficiently announced his condition; he wished to prolong his pleasure to the utmost.

Bella squeezed the terrible shaft in her innermost person, and felt it grow harder and even stiffer while its purple head pressed up to her young womb.

Almost immediately afterwards her unwieldy lover, unable to prolong his pleasure, succumbed to the intensest of keen and all-pervading sensation with his glutinous fluid.

'Oh, it is coming from you,' cried the excited girl. 'I feel it in gushes. Oh! give it me – more – more – pour it into me – push harder; do not spare me! Oh, another gush! Push – tear me if you like – but let me have all your spunk.'

I have before spoken of the immense quantity Father Ambrose possessed the power of discharging, and he now surpassed himself. He had been bottled up for nearly a week, and Bella now received such a tremendous stream of his nature that his discharge more resembled the action of a syringe than the outpouring from the genitals of a man.

At last Ambrose dismounted, and Bella, on standing once more upon her feet, felt a clinging slippery stream trickling down her plump thighs.

Hardly had the father withdrawn than the door leading into the church opened, and, behold, two other priests presented themselves within its portal. Concealment was, of course, impossible.

'Ambrose,' exclaimed the elder of the two, a man apparently between thirty and forty years old, 'this is against our rules and privileges, which enact that all such sport shall be had in common.'

'Take it then,' growled the person addressed. 'It is not too late – I was going to tell you of what I had got, only – '

'Only the delicious temptation of this young moss-rose was too much for you, my friend!' exclaimed the other, seizing, as he spoke, upon the astonished Bella, and forcing his large hand up her clothes to her soft thighs. 'I saw it all through the keyhole,' whispered the brute in her ear. 'You need not be frightened, we shall only treat you the same, my dear.'

Bella remembered the conditions of her admittance to the solace of the church, and supposed this was only a part of her new duties. She therefore rested unresistingly in the arms of the newcomer.

Meanwhile, his companion had passed his strong arm around Bella's waist, and covered her delicate cheek with kisses.

Ambrose looked stupid and confounded.

The young lady thus found herself between two fires, to say nothing of the smouldering passion of her original possessor. In vain she looked from one to the other for some respite, some means of extrication from her predicament.

For, be it known, that although she fully resigned herself to the position into which the cunning of Father Ambrose had consigned her, a bodily feeling of weakness and fear of the new assailants nearly overcame her.

Bella read nothing but lust and raging desire in the looks of the new-comers, while the non-resistance of Ambrose disarmed all thought of defence on her own part.

The two men had now got her between them, and while the first speaker had pushed his hand as far as her rosy slit, the other lost no time in possessing himself of the well-rounded cheeks of her plump buttocks.

Between them Bella was powerless to resist.

'Stay a moment,' at length suggested Ambrose. 'If you are in earnest to enjoy her, at least do so without tearing her clothes to pieces, as you both seem inclined to do. Strip, Bella,' continued he, 'we must all share you, it seems; so prepare to become the willing instrument of our united pleasures. Our convent contains others no less exigent than myself, and your office will be no sinecure, so you had better remember always the privileges you are called upon to fulfil, and be ready to relieve these holy men of the fiery desires which you well know how to assuage.'

Thus directed there was no alternative.

Bella stood naked before the three vigorous priests.

Murmurs of delight burst from all when Bella stood timidly forth in her beauty.

No sooner did the spokesman of the newcomers, who was evidently the senior of the three, perceive the beautiful nudity now presented to his passionate glances than, without hesitation, he opened his dress, and giving liberty to a large and long member, caught the beautiful girl in his arms, bore her back to the couch, and then, spreading open her pretty thighs, he planted himself between them and, hastily bringing the head of his raging champion to the soft orifice, thrust forward and at one bound buried himself to his balls.

Bella gave a little cry of ecstasy, as she felt the stiff insertion of this new and powerful weapon.

To the man in full possession of the beautiful girl the contact was ecstasy, and the feeling with which he found himself completely buried in her body to the hilt of his rampant penis was one of indefinable emotion. He had no idea he should so readily penetrate her parts, but he had omitted to take into account the flood of semen which she had already received.

The Superior, however, gave her no time for reflection, but commenced to run his course so energetically that his long and powerful strokes produced their fullest effects upon her warm temperament, and almost immediately caused her to give down her sweet emission.

This was too much for the wanton ecclesiastic. Already firmly embedded in the tight and glove-like sheath, he no sooner felt the hot effusion than he uttered a long growl, and discharged furiously.

Bella relished the spouting torrent of the strong man's lust, and throwing out her legs, received him to his utmost length in her belly, allowing him there to vent his passion in the jetting streams of his fiery nature.

Bella's lewdest feelings were roused by this second and determined attack upon her person, and her excitable nature received with exquisite delight the rich libations the two stalwart champions had poured out. But prurient as she was, the young lady found herself much exhausted by this continued strain upon her bodily powers, and it was therefore with some dismay that she perceived the second of the intruders preparing to take advantage of the retirement of the Superior.

But what was Bella's astonishment to discover the gigantic proportions of the priest who now presented himself. Already his dress was in disorder and before him stood stiffly erected a member before which even the vigorous Ambrose was forced to cede.

Out of a curling fringe of red hair sprang the white column of flesh, capped by the shining dull red head, the tight and closely shut orifice of which looked as if it was obliged to be careful and to prevent a premature overflow of its juices. Two huge and hairy balls hung closely below, and completed the picture, at sight of which Bella's blood began once more to boil, and her youthful spirit to expand with longing for the disproportionate combat.

'Oh! my father, how shall I ever get that great thing into my poor little person?' asked Bella, in dismay. 'How shall I be able to endure it, when it does go in! I fear it will hurt me dreadfully!'

'I will be very careful, my daughter. I will go slowly. You are well prepared now by the juices of the holy men who have had the good fortune to precede me.'

Bella fingered the gigantic penis.

The priest was ugly in the extreme. He was short and stout, but built with shoulders broad enough for a Hercules.

Bella had caught a sort of lewd madness; his ugliness only served further to rouse her sensual desires; her hands could not meet round his member. She continued, however, to hold it, to press it and unconsciously to bestow upon it caresses which increased its rigidity and advanced the pleasure. It stood like a bar of iron in her soft hands.

Another moment and the third assailant was upon her, and Bella, almost equally excited, strove to impale herself upon the terrible weapon.

For some minutes the feat seemed impossible, well lubricated as she was by the previous overflowings she had received.

At length a furious lunge drove in the enormous head. Bella uttered a cry of real anguish; another, and another lunge: the brutal wretch, blind to all but his own gratification, continued to penetrate.

Bella cried out in her agony, and wildly strove to detach herself from her fierce assailant.

Another thrust, another cry from his victim, and the priest had penetrated her to the quick.

Bella had fainted.

The two observers of this monstrous act of debauchery seemed at first inclined to interfere, but it seemed as if they experienced a cruel pleasure in witnessing the conflict, and certainly their lewd movements, and the interest they evidently took in observing the minutest details, argued their satisfaction.

I draw a veil over the scene of lust which followed, over the writhings of the savage as – securely in possession of the person of the young and beautiful girl – he slowly spun out his enjoyment, until his gross and fervid discharge put an end to his ecstasies, and allowed an interval in which to restore the poor girl to life.

The stalwart father had discharged twice before he drew out his long and reeking member, and the volume of spunk which followed was such as to fall pattering in a pool upon the wooden floor.

At length, sufficiently recovered to move, the young Bella was permitted to perform those ablutions which the streaming condition of her delicate parts rendered necessary.

## *Chapter Four*

Several bottles of wine, of old and rare vintage, were now produced, and under their potent influence, Bella slowly recovered her strength.

Within an hour the three priests, finding that she was sufficiently restored to entertain their lascivious advances, once more began to show signs of a desire for a further enjoyment of her person.

Excited no less by the generous wine than by the sight and touch of her lewd companions, the girl now commenced to pull from their cassocks the members of the three priests, whose enjoyment of the scene was clearly manifested by their absence of restraint.

In less than a minute Bella had all three of their long and stiff affairs in full view. She kissed and toyed with them, sniffing the faint fragrance which arose from them, and fingering the blushing shafts with all the eagerness of an accomplished Cyprian.

'Let us fuck,' piously ejaculated the Superior, whose prick was at that moment at Bella's lips.

'Amen,' chanted Ambrose.

The third ecclesiastic was silent, but his huge penis menaced the skies.

Bella mused as to which she would choose as her first assailant in this new round. She selected Ambrose.

Meanwhile, the doors being secured, the three priests deliberately stripped themselves, and thus presented to the brilliant gaze of the youthful Bella three vigorous champions in the prime of life, each armed with a stalwart weapon, which stood once more firmly in their fronts and wagged about threateningly as they moved.

'Oh, fie! What monsters!' exclaimed the young lady, whose shame, however, did not prevent her handling alternately these redoubtable engines.

They sat her upon the edge of the table and one by one they sucked her young parts, rolling their hot tongues round and round in the moist red slit in which all had so recently appeased their lust. Bella lent herself to this with joy, and opened to the utmost her plump legs to gratify them.

'I propose she shall suck us one after the other,' exclaimed the Superior.

'Certainly,' assented Father Clement, the man of the red hair and huge erection. 'But not to finish so. I want her once more in the belly.'

'No; certainly not, Clement,' said the Superior. 'You have well nigh split her in two as it is; you must finish down her throat or not at all.'

Bella had no intention of again submitting to an attack from Clement, so she cut short the discussion by seizing on the fat member and putting as much of it as she could into her pretty mouth.

Up and down the blue nut the girl worked her soft moist lips, every now and then pausing to receive as much of it as possible within her mouth. Her fair hands passed around the long, large shaft, and clutched it in a tremendous embrace as she watched the monstrous penis swell harder with the intensity of the sensations imparted by her delicious touches.

In less than five minutes Clement began to utter sounds more like the howlings of a wild beast than the exclamations of the human lungs, and spent in volumes down her gullet.

Bella drew down the skin along the long shaft, and encouraged the flood to end.

Clement's spendings were as thick and hot as they were plentiful, and squirt after squirt of spunk flew into the girl's mouth.

Bella swallowed it all.

'There is a new experience I must now instruct you in, my daughter,' said the Superior, as Bella now applied her soft lips to his own burning member. 'You will find it productive of more pain than pleasure at first, but the ways of Venus are difficult, and only to be learnt and enjoyed by degrees.'

'I shall submit myself to all, my father,' replied the girl; 'I know my duty now better, and that I am one of those favoured ones selected to relieve the desires of the good fathers.'

'Certainly, my daughter, and you will feel the bliss of heaven in advance while obeying our slightest wishes, and indulging all our inclinations, however strange and irregular they may be.'

With that he took the girl in his strong arms, and bore her once more to the couch, where he placed her on her face, thus exposing her naked and beautiful posterior to the whole company. Next, placing himself between the thighs of his victim, he pointed the tip of his stiff member at the small orifice between Bella's plump buttocks and, pushing forward his well-lubricated weapon by slow degrees, began to penetrate her in this novel and unnatural manner.

'Oh – my! ' cried Bella, 'you are in the wrong place – it hurts. Pray – oh! Pray – ah! Have mercy. Oh! pray spare me! Holy Mother! I die!'

This last exclamation was caused by a final and vigorous thrust on the part of the Superior, which sent his stallion member up to the hairs that covered the lower portion of his belly and left Bella in no doubt that he was up her body to the balls. Passing his strong arm around her hips, he pressed close to her back; his stout belly rubbed against her buttocks, and his stiff member was kept thrust into her rectum as far as it would go. The pulsations of pleasure were evident throughout its swollen length, and Bella, biting her lips, awaited the movements of the man which she well knew he was about to commence in order to finish his enjoyment.

The other two priests looked on with envious lust, slowly frigging their big members the while.

As for the Superior, maddened by the tightness of this new and delicious sheath, he laboured at her round buttocks until, with a final lunge, he filled her bowels with his hot discharge. Then drawing his instrument, still erect and smoking, from her body, declared that he had opened up a new route to pleasure, and recommended Ambrose to avail himself of it.

Ambrose, whose feelings during this time may be better imagined than described, was now rampant with desire. The sight of his confrères enjoying themselves gradually produced a state of erotic excitement within him that it became necessary to quench as soon as possible.

'Agreed,' he cried. 'I will enter by the Temple of Sodom, and you, meanwhile, shall fill with your sturdy sentinel the Halls of Venus.'

'Say rather "of legitimate enjoyment",' rejoiced the Superior with a grin. 'Be it as you say; I should well like another taste of so tight a belly.'

Bella still lay upon her belly upon the couch, her rounded posterior fully exposed, more dead than alive from the brutal attack which she had just suffered. Not a drop of the semen which had been injected into her so plentifully escaped from the dark recess, but below her slit still ran with the combined emission of the priests. Ambrose seized her.

Placed across the thighs of the Superior, Bella now found his still vigorous member knocking against the lips of her pink slit; slowly she guided it in, as she lowered herself upon it. Presently it all entered – she had it to the roots.

But now the vigorous Superior, passing his arms around her waist, drew her down upon him, and sinking backwards brought her large and exquisite buttocks before the angry weapon of Ambrose, who straightway bore directly at the already well-moistened aperture between their hillocks.

A thousand difficulties presented themselves to be overcome, but at length the lecherous Ambrose felt himself buried in the entrails of his tender victim.

Slowly he drew his member up and down the slippery channel. He spun out his pleasure and enjoyed the vigorous bounds with which the Superior was treating the fair Bella in front.

Presently, with a deep sigh, the Superior reached his climax, and Bella felt him rapidly filling her slit with spunk. She could not resist the impetus, and her own overflowings mingled with those of her assailant.

Ambrose, however, had husbanded his resources, and now held the pretty girl in front of him, firmly impaled upon his huge affair.

In this position Clement could not resist the opportunity, but watching his chance while the Superior was wiping his person, he drove himself in front of Bella, and almost immediately succeeded in penetrating her belly, now liberally bedewed with their slippery leavings.

Enormous though it was, Bella found means to receive the red-haired monster which now stretched her delicate body with its entire length, and for the next few minutes nothing was heard but the sighs and lustful moans of the combatants.

Presently their motions grew harder; Bella expected every moment would be her last. The huge member of Ambrose was up her posterior passage to his balls, while the gigantic truncheon of Clement made all froth again within her belly.

The child was supported between the two, her feet fairly off the ground, and subject to the blows, first in front and then behind, with which the priests worked their excited engines in their respective channels.

Just as Bella thought she would lose consciousness, she became aware by the heavy breathing and the tremendous stiffness of the brute in front that his discharge was coming and the next moment she felt the hot injection flow from the gigantic prick in strong and viscid jets.

'Ah! I spend,' cried Clement, and with that he squirted a copious flood up little Bella, to her infinite delight.

'Mine's coming too,' shrieked Ambrose, driving home his vigorous member, and pouring a hot jet of his spunk into Bella's bowels at the same time.

Thus the two continued disgorging the prolific contents of their bodies into that of the gentle girl, while she experienced the double flood, and swam in a deluge of delights.

Anyone would have supposed that a flea of average intelligence only would have had enough of such disgusting exhibitions as I have thought it my duty to disclose; but a certain feeling of friendship as well as sympathy for the young Bella impelled me still to remain in her company.

The event justified my anticipations, and as will hereafter appear, determined my future movements.

*        *        *

Three days only elapsed ere the young lady met the three priests by appointment in the same place.

On this occasion, Bella had taken extra care in regard to her toilet, and the result was that she now appeared more enchanting than ever, in the prettiest of silk dresses, the tightest of kid boots, and the tiniest of lovely and well-fitting gloves.

The three men were in raptures, and Bella was received in so warm a manner that already her young blood mounted hot in her face with desire.

The door was promptly secured, and then down went the nether garments of the reverend fathers, and Bella, amid the mingled caresses and lascivious touches of the trio, beheld their members baldy exposed and already menacing her.

The Superior was the first who advanced with the intention of enjoying her. Boldly placing himself in front of her little form, he bore roughly against her, and taking her in his arms, covered her mouth and face with hot kisses.

Bella's excitement equalled his.

By their desire, Bella denuded herself of her drawers and petticoats, and retaining only her exquisite dress, silk stockings and pretty kid boots, offered herself to their admiration and lascivious touches.

A moment later and the father, sinking deliciously upon her reclining figure, had pushed himself to the hairs in her young charms, and remained soaking in the tight conjunction with evident gratification.

Pushing, squeezing, and rubbing against her, the Superior commenced delicious movements, which had the effect of raising both his partner's susceptibilities and his own. His prick, in its increased size and hardness, bore evidence of this.

'Push! Oh! Push me harder,' murmured Bella.

Meanwhile, Ambrose and Clement whose desires could ill brook the delay, sought to engage some portion of the girl's attention.

Clement put his huge member into her soft white hand and Ambrose, nothing daunted, mounting on the couch, brought the tip of his bulky affair to her delicate lips.

After a few moments, the Superior withdrew from his luscious position.

Bella rose upon the edge of the couch. Before her were the three men, each had his member exposed and erect before him, and the enormous head of Clement's engine turned back almost against his fat belly.

Bella's dress was raised to her waist, her legs and thighs were in full view, and between them the luscious, pinky slit, now reddened and excited by the too abrupt insertion and withdrawal of the Superior's prick.

'Stay a moment,' he observed; 'let us proceed with order in our pleasures. This beautiful child is to satisfy all three, therefore it will be necessary both to regulate our enjoyments, and also to enable her to support the attacks to which she will be liable. For myself I do not care whether I come first or second, but as Ambrose spends like an ass and will probably make all smoke again in the regions he penetrates, I propose to pass first. Certainly Clement must be content with the second or third place, or his enormous member would not only split the girl, but what is of far more consequence, spoil our pleasure.'

'I was third last time,' exclaimed Clement. 'I see no reason why I should always be last. I claim the second place.'

'Good, so let it be then,' cried the Superior. 'You, Ambrose, will have a slippery nest for your share.'

'Not I,' rejoined that determined ecclesiastic; 'if you go first, and that monster Clement has her second, and before me, I shall attack "by the breech" and pour my offering in another direction.'

'Do with me as you will,' cried Bella, 'I will try and bear all. But, oh, my fathers, make haste and begin.'

Once more the Superior drove in his stalwart weapon. Bella met the stiff insertion with delight. She hugged him, she bore down against him, and received his jets of emission with ecstatic outbursts of her own.

Clement now presented himself. His monstrous affair was already between the plump legs of the young Bella. The disproportion was terrible, but the priest was as strong and lewd as he was largely made, and after sundry violent and ineffectual efforts, he got in and commenced to ram the whole of his asinine member into her belly.

It is impossible to relate how the terrible proportions of this man roused the lascivious imaginations of Bella, or with what a frenzy of passion she found herself deliciously crammed and stretched by the huge genitals of Father Clement.

After a struggle of full ten minutes, Bella received the throbbing mass up to the big balls, which pressed her bottom below.

Bella threw out both her pretty legs, and allowed the brute to revel at his leisure in her charms.

Clement showed no anxiety to cut short his luscious enjoyment, and it was a quarter of an hour before two violent discharges put an end to his pleasure.

Bella received them with deep sighs of delight, and gave down a copious emission of her own upon the thick inpourings of the lustful father.

Clement had hardly withdrawn his monstrous affair from the belly of the young Bella, than, reeking from the arms of her huge lover, she fell into those of Ambrose.

True to his expressed intention, it is now her beautiful buttocks he attacks, and seeks with fierce energy to insert the throbbing head of his instrument within the tender folds of her posterior's aperture.

In vain he seeks to gain a lodgement. The broad head of his weapon is repulsed at each assault, as with brutal lust he tries hard to force himself inwards.

But Ambrose is not to be so easily defeated; he essays again, and at length a determined effort lodges the head within the delicate opening.

Now is his time – a vigorous lunge drives in a couple of inches more and with a single bound the lascivious priest then buries himself to the balls.

Bella's beautiful buttocks had a decided attraction for the lustful priest. He was agitated to an extraordinary degree, as he bore forward in his fierce efforts. He pressed his long and thick member inwards with ecstasy, regardless of the pain the stretching was causing her, as long as he could feel the delicious constrictions of her delicate young parts.

Bella utters a dreadful cry. She is impaled upon the stiff member of the brutal ravisher. She feels his throbbing flesh in her vitals and endeavours, with frantic efforts, to escape.

But Ambrose, passing his strong arms round her slender waist, restrains her, while he follows each movement made by her, and retains himself in her quivering body by a continued inwards strain.

Thus struggling, step by step, the girl crossed the apartment, having the fierce Ambrose firmly embedded in her posterior passage.

Meanwhile, this lewd spectacle was not without its effect upon the beholders. A shout of laughter issued from their throats, and both applauded the vigour of their companion, whose visage, inflamed and working, bore ample testimony to his pleasurable emotions.

But the sight also quickly aroused their desires, and both showed by the state of their members that they were as yet by no means satisfied.

Bella having by this time arrived close to the Superior, the latter caught her in his arms, and Ambrose, taking advantage of this timely check, commenced to push his member about in her bowels, while the intense heat of her body afforded him the liveliest pleasure.

By the position in which the three were now placed, the Superior found his mouth on a level with Bella's natural charms, and instantly gluing his lips thereto, he sucked her moistened slit.

But the excitement thus occasioned required more solid enjoyment, and drawing the pretty girl across his knees as he sat upon his seat, he let loose his bursting member and quickly drove it into her soft belly.

Thus Bella was between two fires, and the fierce thrusts of Father Ambrose upon her plump buttocks were now supplemented by the fervid efforts of the Superior in the other direction. Both revelled in a sea of sensual delights, both bathed themselves to the full in the delicious sensations they experienced, while their victim, perforated before and behind by their swelling members, had to sustain as she could their excited members.

But a further trial awaited the young Bella, for no sooner did the vigorous Clement witness the close conjunction of his companions, than, inflamed with envy, and stung by the violence of his passions, he mounted the seat behind the Superior, and taking possession of poor Bella's head, presented his flaming weapon against her rosy lips, then forcing the tip, with the narrow aperture already exuding anticipatory drops, into her pretty mouth, he made her rub the long, hard shaft in her hand.

Meanwhile, Ambrose found the insertion of the Superior's member in front quickly bring on his proceedings, while the latter, equally excited by the back action of his comrade, speedily began to feel the approach of the spasms preceding and accompanying the final act of emission.

Clement was the first to let fly, and he sent his glutinous discharge in showers down the throat of little Bella.

Ambrose followed, and falling on her back shot a torrent of spunk up her bowels, while the Superior at the same moment loaded her womb with his contributions.

Thus surrounded, Bella received the united discharge of the three vigorous priests.

## *Chapter Five*

Three days after the events detailed in the preceding pages, Bella made her appearance in her uncle's drawing-room, as rosy and as charming as ever.

My movements in the meantime had been erratic, for my appetite was by no means small, and new features always possessed a certain piquancy for me which prevented too protracted a residence in one locality.

It was thus I found means to overhear a conversation which not a little astonished me; but which, as it bears directly upon the events I am describing, I do not hesitate to disclose.

It was thus I became acquainted with the real depth and subtlety of the character of Father Ambrose.

I am not going to reproduce this discourse here as I heard it from my vantage-ground; it will be sufficient, if I explain the principal ideas it conveyed and relate the application.

It was clear that Ambrose was annoyed and discomforted at the abrupt participation of his confrères in the enjoyment of his latest acquisition, and he concocted a daring and devilish scheme to frustrate their interference, while at the same time appearing himself to be entirely innocent of the business.

In short, with this view, Ambrose went direct to Bella's uncle, and related how he had discovered his niece and her young lover in Cupid's alliance, and how there was no doubt she had received and reciprocated the last tokens of his passion.

In so doing the wily priest had an ulterior object in view. He well knew the character of the man with whom he had to deal. He knew also that sufficient of his own real life was not entirely hidden from the uncle.

In fact, the pair pretty well understood one another. Ambrose had strong passions, and was amatory to an extraordinary extent. So was Bella's uncle.

The latter had confessed as much to Ambrose, and in the course of his confession, had given evidence of such irregular desires as to raise no difficulties in making him a ready participator in the plans which the other had originated.

Mr Verbouc's eyes had long been cast in secret upon his niece. He had confessed it. Ambrose brought him suddenly a piece of news which opened his eyes to the fact that she had begun to entertain sentiments of the same sort for others of his sex.

The character of Ambrose occurred immediately to him. He was his spiritual confessor, he asked his advice.

The holy man gave him to understand that his chance had come, and that it would be to their mutual advantage to share the prize between them.

This proposition touched a chord in the character of Verbouc of which Ambrose was already not entirely ignorant. If any fact lent greater enjoyment to his sensuality, or gave more poignancy to his indulgences, it was to witness another in the act to complete carnal copulation, and then afterwards to complete his own gratification by a second penetration and emission upon the body of the same victim.

Thus the compact was soon made; an opportunity was found; the necessary privacy secured, for Bella's aunt was an invalid and confined to her room; and then Ambrose prepared Bella for the event about to take place.

After a short preliminary discourse, in which he cautioned her not to say a word of their previous intimacy, and informed her that her relative had somehow discovered her intrigue, he led her round gradually to the fact which he had all along had in view. He even told her of the passion her uncle had conceived for her, and declared, in plain terms, that the surest way to avoid his heavy resentment was to prove obedient to all he might require of her.

Mr Verbouc was a man of hale and vigorous build, and of about fifty years of age. As her uncle he had always inspired Bella with the greatest respect, in which was mingled not a little awe of his presence and authority. He had treated her since the death of his brother, if not with affection, at least not unkindly, though with a reserve which was natural to his character.

Bella had evidently no reason to hope for any clemency on this occasion, or to expect any escape from her indignant relative.

I pass over the first quarter of an hour, the tears of Bella, and the embarrassment with which she found herself at once the recipient of her uncle's too tender embraces and of the censure she so well deserved.

The interesting comedy proceeded little by little, until Mr Verbouc, taking his pretty niece between his knees, audaciously unfolded the design he had formed of enjoying her himself.

'There must be no silly resistance, Bella,' continued her uncle; 'I will have no hesitation, no affectation of modesty. It is sufficient that this good father has sanctified the operation, and I must therefore possess and enjoy your body as your imprudent young companion has already done with your consent.'

Bella was utterly confounded. Although sensual, as we have already seen, to an extent not often found in girls of such tender age, she had been brought up in those strict and conventional views which assorted with the severe and repelling character of her relative. All her horror of such a crime at once rose before her. Not even the presence and alleged sanction of Father Ambrose could lessen the distrust with which she viewed the horrible proposal now deliberately made to her.

Bella trembled with surprise and terror at the nature of the crime contemplated. This new position shocked her. The change from the reserved and severe uncle, whose wrath she had always deprecated and feared, and whose precepts she had long accustomed herself to receive with reverence, to the ardent admirer, thirsting for possession of those favours which she had so recently bestowed upon another, struck her dumb with amazement and disgust.

Meanwhile Mr Verbouc, who was evidently not disposed to allow time for reflection, and whose disorder was plainly visible in more ways than one, took his young niece in his arms, and despite her reluctance, covered her face and neck with forbidden and passionate kisses.

Ambrose, to whom the girl turned in this exigency afforded her no solace, but on the contrary smiling grimly at the other's emotion, encouraged him by secret glances to carry to the last extremity his pleasures and his lubricity.

Resistance, under such trying circumstances, was difficult.

Bella was young and comparatively powerless in the strong grip of her relative. Lashed to frenzy by the contact and obscene touches in which he now indulged himself, Mr Verbouc sought with redoubled energy to possess himself of the person of his niece. Already his nervous fingers pressed the beautiful satin of her thighs. Another determined push, and in spite of the close pressure which Bella continued to exert in her defence, the lewd hand covered the rosy lips, and the trembling fingers divided the close and moistened chink of modesty's stronghold.

Up to this point Ambrose had remained a quiet observer of this exciting conflict; now, however, he also advanced, and passing his powerful left arm round the young girl's slender waist, seized both her small hands in his right, and having thus pinned her, left her an easy prey to the lascivious approaches of her relative.

'For mercy's sake,' moaned Bella, panting with her exertions, 'Let me go; it is too horrible – you are monstrous cruel! I am lost!'

'Nay, my pretty niece, not lost,' replied her uncle, 'only awakened to those pleasures which Venus had in store for her votaries, and which love reserves for those who are bold enough to seize upon them and enjoy them, while they may.'

'I have been horribly deceived,' cried Bella, little softened by this ingenious explanation. 'I see it all. Oh! shame. I cannot let you, I cannot let you, I cannot. Oh, no! I cannot. Holy Mother! Let me go, uncle. Oh! oh!'

'Be quiet, Bella; you must indeed submit; I will enjoy you by force, if you do not allow me to do so otherwise. There, open these pretty legs, let me feel these exquisite calves, these soft luscious thighs; let me put my hand upon this heaving little belly – nay, hold still, little fool. You are mine at last. Oh, how I have longed for this, Bella!'

Bella, however, still kept up a certain resistance, which only served to whet the unnatural appetite of her assailant, while Ambrose held her firmly in his clutches.

'Oh, the beautiful bottom!' exclaimed Verbouc, as he slipped his intruding hand beneath the velvet thighs of poor Bella, and felt the rounded globes of her charming *derrière*. 'Ah! the glorious bottom. All is mine now. All shall be fêted in good time.'

'Let me go,' cried Bella. 'Oh! oh!'

These last exclamations were wrung from the pretty girl, as between them the two men forced her backwards upon the couch which stood conveniently within reach.

As she fell, she reclined upon the stout body of Ambrose, while Mr Verbouc, who had now raised her clothes, and lewdly exposed the silk-clad legs and exquisite proportions of his niece, drew back for a moment to enjoy at his ease the indecent exhibition which he had forcibly provided for his own amusement.

'Uncle, are you mad?' cried Bella, once more, as with wriggling limbs, she vainly strove to conceal the luscious nudity now fully exposed. 'Pray, let me go.'

'Yes, Bella, I am mad – mad with passion for you – mad with lust to possess you, to enjoy you, to satiate myself upon your body. Resistance is useless; I will have my will and revel in those pretty charms, in that tight and exquisite little sheath.'

Thus saying, Mr Verbouc prepared himself for the final act of incestuous drama. He unfastened his nether garments, and discarding all considerations of modesty, wantonly allowed his niece to behold in full view the plump and rubicund proportions of his excited member, which, erect and glowing, now menaced her directly in front.

A moment later and Verbouc threw himself upon his prey, firmly held down by the recumbent priest; then applying his rampant weapon point blank to the tender orifice he essayed to complete the conjunction by inserting its large and long proportions in the body of his niece.

But the continued writhing of Bella's young form, the disgust and horror which had seized upon her, and the almost immature dimensions of her parts, effectually prevented him from gaining so easy a victory as he desired.

Never had I longed so ardently to contribute to the discomfiture of a champion as on the present occasion and, moved by the complaints of the gentle Bella, with the body of a flea and the soul of a wasp, I hopped at one bound to the rescue.

To dig my proboscis into the sensitive covering of the scrotum of Mr Verbouc was the work of a second. It had the desired effect. A sharp and tingling sensation of pain made him pause. The interval was fatal, and the next moment the thighs and stomach of the young Bella were covered with the wasted superfluity of her incestuous relative's vigour.

Curses – not loud, but deep – followed this unexpected contretemps. The would-be ravisher withdrew from his vantage-ground, and unable to continue the conflict, reluctantly put up the discomfited weapon.

No sooner had Mr Verbouc released his niece from this trying position than Father Ambrose commenced to manifest the violence of his own excitement, produced by his passive observance of the foregoing erotic scene. While still retaining his powerful grasp on Bella, and thus gratifying his sense of touch, the appearance of his dress in front plainly denoted the state of affairs as regarded his readiness to take advantage of the occasion. His redoubtable weapon, seemingly disdaining the confinement of his garments, protruded itself into view, the big round head already skinned and throbbing with eagerness for enjoyment.

'Ay!' exclaimed the other, as his lewd glance fell upon the distended weapon of his confessor, 'here is a champion who will brook no defeat, I warrant,' and deliberately taking it in his hand, he manipulated the huge shaft with evident satisfaction.

'What a monster! How strong it is – how stiff it stands!'

Father Ambrose rose, his crimson face betrayed the intensity of his desire; placing the frightened Bella in a more propitious attitude, he brought the broad red knob to the moistened aperture, and proceeded to force it inwards with a desperate effort.

Pain, agitation and longing coursed each other through the nervous system of the young victim of lust.

Although the present was not the first occasion on which the reverend father had stormed the moss-covered outworks, yet the fact of her uncle's presence, the indelicacy of the whole scene, and the innate conviction, now first dawning upon her, of the trickery and selfishness of the holy man, combined to repel within her those extreme sensations of pleasure which had before so powerfully manifested themselves.

But the proceedings of Ambrose left Bella no time for reflection, for feeling the delicate sheath press glove-like around his large weapon, he hastened to complete the conjunction, and with a few vigorous and skilful bounds, plunged himself to the balls in her body.

Then followed a rapid interval of fierce enjoyment – of rapid thrusts and pressures, firm and close, until a low, gurgling cry from Bella announced that Nature had asserted herself, and that she had arrived at that exquisite crisis in love's combat, when spasms of unspeakable pleasure pass rapidly, voluptuously through the nerves, and with head thrown back, lips parted, and fingers convulsively working, the whole body rigid with the absorbing effort, the nymph gives down her youthful essence to meet the coming gushes from her lover.

Bella's writhing form, upturned eyes and clutching hands sufficiently bespoke her condition without the ecstatic moan which broke laboriously from her quivering lips.

The whole bulk of the potent shaft, now well lubricated, worked deliciously within her young parts. The excitement of Ambrose increased each instant, and his instrument, hard as iron, threatened with each plunge to discharge its reeking essence.

'Oh, I can do no more; I feel my spunk is nearly coming. Verbouc, you must fuck her. She is delicious. Her belly clips me like a glove. Oh! Oh! Ah!'

Stronger, closer thrusts – a vigorous bound – a sinking of the strong man upon the slight figure of the girl – a harsh, low gasp – and Bella, with ineffable delight, felt the hot injection spouting from her ravisher and pouring in volumes, thick and slippery, far within her tender parts.

Ambrose reluctantly withdrew his smoking prick, and left displayed the glistening parts of the young girl, from which trickled a thick mass of his spending.

'Good,' exclaimed Verbouc, on whom the scene had had a powerfully exciting effect. 'It is now my turn, good Father Ambrose! You have enjoyed my niece under my eyes; that is as I wished, and she has been well ravished. She has also partaken of the pleasure with you, my anticipations are realised; she can receive, she can enjoy; one can satiate oneself with her, and in her body; good – I am going to begin. My opportunity has come at last, she cannot escape me now. I am going to satisfy my long cherished desire. I am going to appease this insatiable lust for my brother's child. See this member, how he raises his red head; it is my desire for you, Bella; feel, my sweet niece, how hard your dear uncle's balls are – they are filled for you. It is you who have made this thing so stiff and long and swollen – it is you who are destined to bring it relief. Skin it back, Bella! So, my child – let me guide your pretty hand. Oh! no nonsense – no blushes – no modesty – no reluctance – do you see its length? You must take it all into that hot little slit that dear Father Ambrose has just so well filled. Do you observe my big globes beneath, Bella darling? They are loaded with the spunk I am going to discharge for your pleasure and my own. Yes, Bella, into the belly of my brother's child.'

The idea of the horrid incest he contemplated evidently added fuel to his excitement, and produced within him a superabundant sensation of lustful impatience, which exhibited itself no less in his inflamed countenance than in the stiffened and erected shaft which now menaced Bella's moistened parts.

Mr Verbouc took his measures securely. There was indeed, as he said, no escape for poor Bella. He mounted upon her body, he opened her legs. Ambrose held her firmly against his belly as he reclined. The ravisher saw his chance, the way was clear, the white thighs already parted, the red and glistening lips of the pretty young cunt confronted him. He could wait no longer; parting the lips and pointing aright the dull red head of his weapon to the pouting slit, he now drove forward, and at one bound, with a yell of sensual pleasure, buried himself to his utmost length in his niece's belly.

'Oh, Lord: I'm in her at last,' screamed Verbouc. 'Oh! ah! What pleasure – how nice she is – how tight. Oh!'

Good Father Ambrose held her fast.

Bella gave a violent start, and a little scream of pain and terror, as she felt the entry of her uncle's swollen member, while, firmly embedded in the warm person of his victim, he commenced a quick and furious career of selfish pleasure. It was the lamb in the clutches of the wolf, the dove in the talons of the eagle – merciless, regardless of her own feelings, the brute bore all before him, until, too soon for his own hot lust, with a scream of agonised enjoyment, he discharged, and shot into his niece a plentiful torrent of his incestuous fluid.

Again and again the two wretches enjoyed their young victim. Their hot lust, stimulated by the prospect of each other's pleasures, drove them to madness.

Ambrose essayed to attack her in the buttocks, but Verbouc, who doubtless had his own reasons for the prohibition, forbade the violation, and the priest, no ways abashed, lowered the knob of his big tool, and drove it up furiously into her little slit from behind. Verbouc knelt below and watched the act, and at its conclusion sucked, with evident delight, the streaming lips of his young niece's well-filled cunt.

That night I accompanied Bella to her couch, for though my nerves had received a dreadful shock, my appetite had suffered no diminution, and it was lucky, perhaps, that my young protégée was not possessed of so irritable a skin as to resent to any great extent my endeavours to satisfy my natural cravings.

Sleep had succeeded the repast with which I had regaled myself, and I had found a deliciously warm and secure retreat amid the soft and tender moss which covered the mount of the fair Bella when, at about midnight, a violent disturbance roughly roused me from my dignified repose.

A rude and powerful grasp was upon the young girl, and a heavy form pressed vigorously upon her little figure. A stifled cry came from her frightened lips, and amid vain struggles on her part to escape and more successful efforts to prevent that undesirable consummation on the part of her assailant, I recognised the voice and person of Mr Verbouc.

The surprise had been complete; vain was all the feeble resistance that his niece could offer, as with feverish haste, and dreadfully excited by the soft contact of her velvet limbs, the incestuous uncle fiercely possessed himself of her most secret charms, and strong in his hideous lust, drove his rampant weapon into her young body.

Then followed a struggle in which both played a distinct part.

The ravisher, fired equally by the difficulties of his conquest, as well as by the exquisite sensations he was enjoying, buried his stiff member in the luscious sheath, and sought by his fervid thrusts to ease his lust in a copious discharge, while Bella, whose prudent temperament was not proof against so strong and lascivious an attack, strove in vain to resist the violent efforts of Nature, which, roused by the exciting friction, threatened to turn traitor, until at length with quiverings limbs and gasping breath, she surrendered and gave down the sweet outpourings of her inmost soul upon the swollen shaft which so deliciously throbbed within her.

Mr Verbouc was fully aware of his advantage and changing his tactics, like a prudent general, he took care not to expend all his own climax and provoked a fresh advance on the part of his gentle combatant.

Mr Verbouc had no great difficulty in the matter, and the conflict appeared to excite him to fury. The bed trembled and shook, the whole room vibrated with the tremulous energy of his lascivious attack, the two bodies heaved, rolled and plunged in an undistinguishable mass.

Lust, hot and impatient, reigned paramount on both sides. He lunged – he strove – he pushed – he thrust – he drew back until the broad red head of his swollen penis lay between the rosy lips of Bella's hot parts. He drove forward until the crisp black hairs of his belly mingled with the soft mossy down which covered the plump mount of his niece, until, with a quivering sob, she expressed at once her pain and her pleasure.

Once more the victory was his, and as his vigorous member sheathed itself to the hilt in her soft person, a low, tender, wailing cry bespoke her ecstasy as once more the keen spasm of pleasure broke over her nervous system; and then, with a groan of brutal triumph, he shot a hot stream of trickling fluid into the furthest recesses of her womb.

Endowed with the frenzy of newly awakened desire, and still unsatisfied with the possession of so fair a flower, the brutal Verbouc next turned his half-fainting niece upon her face, and contemplated at his ease her lovely buttocks. His object became evident as, procuring some of the spendings with which her little slit was now loaded, he anointed her anus, pushing his forefinger therein as far as it would go.

His passions were again at fever point. His prick menaced her plump bottom, and turning upon her recumbent body, he placed the shining knob to the tight little aperture, and endeavoured to ram it in. In this, after a time, he succeeded, and Bella received in her rectum the entire length of her uncle's yard. The tightness of her anus afforded him the most poignant pleasure, and he continued to work slowly up and down for at least a quarter of an hour, at the end of which time his prick became hard as iron and she felt him squirting hot floods of spunk into her bowels.

It was daylight before Mr Verbouc released his niece from the lustful embraces in which he had satiated his passion and slunk weakly away to his own cold couch; worn and jaded, Bella sank into a deep slumber of exhaustion, from which she did not awake until a late hour.

When next Bella emerged from her chamber, it was with a sense of change in herself which she neither cared nor sought to analyse. Passion had asserted itself in her character; strong sexual emotions had been awakened, and had also been gratified. Refinement of indulgence had generated lust, and lust had rendered easy the road to unrestrained and even unnatural gratification.

Bella, young, childlike, and so lately innocent, had suddenly become a woman of violent passions and unrestrained lust.

## *Chapter Six*

I shall not trouble the reader with the conditions under which one day I found myself snugly concealed upon the person of good Father Clement, or pause here to explain how it was I was present when that worthy ecclesiastic received and confessed a very charming and stylish young lady of some twenty years of age.

I soon discovered from their subsequent conversation that the lady was not of titled rank, though closely connected, but married to one of the wealthiest landed proprietors in the neighbourhood. Names are of no importance here. I, therefore, suppress that of this fair penitent.

After the confessor had ended his benediction, and had concluded the ceremony by which he became the repository of the lady's choicest secrets, he led her, nothing loath, from the body of the church into the same small sacristy where Bella had received her lesson in sanctified copulation.

The door was bolted, no time was lost, the lady dropped her robe, the stalwart confessor opened his cassock, disclosing his enormous weapon, the ruby head of which now stood distended and threatening in the air. The lady no sooner perceived this apparition, than she seized upon it with the air of one to whom it was by no means a new object of delight.

Her dainty hand stroked gently the upright pillar of hard muscle and her eyes devoured its long and swollen proportions.

'You shall do it to me from behind,' remarked the lady, '*en levrette*, but you must be very careful; you are so fearfully large.'

Father Clement's eye glistened under his large head of red hair, and his big weapon gave a spasmodic throb that would have lifted a chair.

In another second the young lady had placed herself on her knees upon the seat, and Clement, coming close behind her, lifted up her fine white linen, and exposed a plump and well-rounded bottom beneath which, half-hidden by the swelling thighs, were just visible the red lips of a delicious slit, luxuriantly shaded with the ample growth of rich brown hair which curled about it.

Clement wanted no further incitement; spitting on the knob of his great member, he pushed its warm head in between the moist lips, and then with many heaves, and much exertion, he strove to make it enter to the balls.

He went in – and in – and in, until it seemed as though the fair recipient could not possibly stow away any more without danger to her vitals. Meanwhile, her face betrayed the extraordinary emotion the gigantic ram was occasioning her.

Presently Father Clement stopped. He was in up to his balls. His red crispy hair pressed the plump cheeks of the lady's bottom. She had received the entire length of his yard in her body. Then began an encounter which fairly shook the bench and all the furniture in the room.

Passing his arms around the fair form in his clutches, the sensual priest pressed himself inwards at every thrust, only withdrawing one half his length the better to force it home, and the lady quivered again with the exquisite sensations so vigorous a stretching was affording her. Then her eyes closed, her head fell forward, and she poured down upon the invader a warm gush of Nature's essence.

Meanwhile, Father Clement worked away in the hot sheath, each moment only serving to render his thick weapon harder and stronger until it resembled nothing so much as a bar of solid iron.

But all things have an end, and so had the enjoyment of the good priest, for having pushed and strove and pressed and battered with his furious yard until he too could hold back no longer, he felt himself upon the point of discharging his metal, and thus bringing matters to a climax.

It came at last, as with a sharp cry of ecstasy he sank forward upon the body of the lady, his member buried to the roots in her belly and pouring a prolific flood of spunk into her very womb. Presently all was over, the last spasm had passed, the last reeking drop had issued, and Clement lay still as death.

The reader must not imagine that good Father Clement was satisfied with the single coup which he had just delivered with such excellent effect; or that the lady, whose wanton sympathies had been so powerfully assuaged, desired to abstain from all further dalliance. On the contrary, this act of copulation had only roused the dormant faculties of sensuality in both, and again they now sought to allay the burning flame of lust.

The lady fell on her back; her burly ravisher threw himself upon her, and driving in his battering ram until their hairs met, he spent again and filled her womb with a viscid torrent.

Still unsatisfied, the wanton pair continued their exciting pastime.

This time Clement lay upon his back, and the lady lasciviously toying with his huge genitals, took the thick red head of his penis between her rosy lips, and after stimulating him to the utmost tension by her maddening touches greedily induced a discharge of his prolific fluid, which, thick and warm, now spouted into her pretty mouth and down her throat.

Then the lady, whose wantonness at least equalled that of her confessor, stood across his muscular form, and after having secured another determined and enormous erection, lowered herself upon the throbbing shaft, impaling her beautiful figure upon the mass of flesh and muscle until nought was left to view save the big balls which hung close below the stiffened weapon. Thus she pumped from Clement a fourth discharge, and reeking in the excessive outpouring of the seminal fluid, as well as fatigued with the unusual duration of the pastime, she disappeared to contemplate at leisure the monstrous proportions and unusual capabilities of her gigantic confessor.

## *Chapter Seven*

Bella had a female friend, a young lady a few months older than herself, the daughter of a wealthy gentleman who lived very near Mr Verbouc. Julia was, however, of a less voluptuous and ardent disposition and, Bella soon found, was not ripe enough to comprehend the sentiments of passion nor understand the strong instincts which provoke to enjoyment.

Julia was slightly taller than her young friend, slightly less plump, but was formed to delight the eye and ravish the heart of an artist with her faultless shape and exquisite features.

A flea cannot well be supposed to describe personal beauty, even in those on whom he feeds. All I know is that Julia was a luscious treat to me, and would one day also be so to someone of the opposite sex, for she was made to raise the desires of the most callous, and to charm by her graceful manners and ever pleasing shape the most fastidious votaries of Venus.

Julia's father possessed, as we have said, ample means; her mother was a weak simpleton, who busied herself very little about her daughter, or, indeed, anything beyond the religious duties in the exercise of which she spent a great part of her time, or the visitations of the old *dévotes* of the neighbourhood, who encouraged her predilections.

Monsieur Delmont was comparatively young. He was robust, he was fond of life, and as his pious better half was far too much occupied to afford him those matrimonial solaces which the poor man had a right to expect, he went elsewhere.

Monsieur Delmont had a mistress – a young and pretty woman, who I concluded was, in her turn, indisposed after the fashion of such people to be content only with her wealthy protector.

Monsieur Delmont by no means confined his attentions even to his mistress; his habits were erratic, and his tastes decidedly amatory.

Under these circumstances it was not wonderful that his eye should have fallen upon the budding and beautiful figure of his daughter's friend, Bella. Already he had found opportunities to press the pretty gloved hand, to kiss – of course in a properly paternal manner – the white brow and even to place his trembling hand – quite by accident – upon the plump thighs.

In fact, Bella, wiser far and more experienced than most girls of her tender age, saw that he was only awaiting an opportunity to push matters to extremities.

This was just what Bella would have liked, but she was too closely watched, and the new and disgraceful connection upon which she was only just entering occupied all her thoughts.

Father Ambrose, however, was fully alive to the necessity of caution, and the good man let no opportunity pass by, while the young lady was in his confessional, of making direct and pertinent enquiries as to her conduct with others and theirs with his penitent. It was thus Bella came to confess to her spiritual guide the feelings engendered within herself by the amatory proceedings of Monsieur Delmont.

Father Ambrose gave her some good advice, and immediately set Bella to work to suck his penis.

This delicious episode over, and the traces of enjoyment removed, the worthy man set out, with his usual astuteness, to turn the fact he had just acquired to his advantage.

Nor was it long before his sensual and vicious brain conceived a plot which in criminality and audacity I, as a humble insect, have never known equalled.

Of course, he had at once determined that the young Julia should eventually be his – that was only natural – but to accomplish this end and amuse himself at the same time with the passion which Monsieur Delmont evidently entertained for Bella, was a double consummation which he saw his way to by a most unscrupulous and hideous plan, which the reader will understand as we proceed.

The first thing to be done was to warm the imagination of the fair Julia, and develop in her the latent fires of lust.

This noble task the good priest left to Bella who, duly instructed, had easily promised compliance.

Since the ice had been broken in her own case, Bella, to say the truth, desired nothing better than to make Julia equally culpable as herself. So Bella set to work to corrupt her young friend. How she succeeded, we shall presently see.

It was only a few days after the initiation of the young Bella into the delights of crime in the shape of incest, which we have already related, but the girl had had no further experience, Mr Verbouc having been called away from home. At length, however, he returned, and for the second time Bella found herself alone and serene with her uncle and Father Ambrose.

The evening was cold, but a pleasant warmth was imparted to the luxurious apartment by a stove, while the soft and elastic sofa and ottomans with which the room was furnished gave an air of listless repose. In the brilliant light of a deliciously perfumed lamp, the two men appeared like the luxurious votaries of Bacchus and Venus, as they reclined only lightly clad, and fresh from a sumptuous repast.

As for Bella, she surpassed herself in beauty. Habited in a charming négligé, she half-disclosed and half-concealed those budding sweets of which she might well be proud.

The lovely rounded arms, the soft, silk-clad legs, the heaving bosom, whence peeped two white, exquisitely formed and strawberry-tipped *pommettes*, the well-turned ankle, and the tiny foot, cased in its close-fitting little shoe: these and other beauties lent their several attractions to make up a delicate and delicious whole, with which the pampered deities might have intoxicated themselves, and in which two lustful mortals now prepared to revel.

It needed little, however, to excite further the infamous and irregular desires of the two men, who now, eyes red with lust, regarded at their ease the luxurious treat in store for them.

Secure from all interruption, both sought in lascivious *attouchements* to gratify the craving of their imaginations to handle what they saw.

Unable to restrain his eagerness, the sensual uncle stretched out his hand, and drawing his beautiful niece close to him, allowed his fingers to wander between her legs. As for the priest, he seized on her soft bosom, and buried his face in its young freshness.

Neither allowed any considerations of modesty to interfere in their enjoyment, and the members of the two strong men were fully exposed and standing excitingly erect, the red heads shining with the tension of blood and muscle below.

'Oh, how you touch me,' murmured Bella, opening involuntarily her white thighs to the trembling hand of her uncle, while Ambrose almost stifled her with his gross lips as he sucked delicious kisses from her ruby mouth.

Presently her delighted hand pressed within its warm palm the stiffened member of the vigorous priest.

'There, my sweet girl, is it not large? And does it not burn to spout its juices into you? Oh, my child, how you excite me. Your hand, your little hand! Ugh! I am dying to thrust this into your soft belly! Kiss me, Bella! Verbouc, see how your niece excites me.'

'Holy Mother, what a prick! See, what a nut it has, Bella. How it shines, what a long white shaft, and how it curves upwards, like a serpent bent on stinging its victim. Already a drop gathers on its tip, look, Bella.'

'Oh, how hard it is! How it throbs! How it thrusts forward! I can scarce hold it, you kill me with such kisses, you suck my life away.'

Mr Verbouc made a forward movement, and at the same moment again disclosed his weapon, erect and ruby red, the head uncapped and moist.

Bella's eyes glistened at the prospect.

'We must regulate our pleasures, Bella,' said her uncle. 'We must endeavour, as much as possible, to prolong our ecstasies. Ambrose is rampant with lust; what a splendid animal he is, what a member, he is furnished like a jackass. Ah, my niece, my child, that will stretch your little slit, it will thrust itself right up to your vitals, and after a long course it will discharge a torrent of spunk for your pleasure.'

'What joy,' murmured Bella; 'I long to have it up me to the waist.'

'Yes, oh yes; do not hasten too soon the delicious end; let us all work for that.'

She would have replied, but the red bulb of Mr Verbouc's stiffened affair at that moment entered her mouth.

With the utmost avidity Bella received the stiff and throbbing thing between her coral lips, and allowed as much of the head and shoulders as could accommodate themselves to enter. She licked it round with her tongue; she even tried to force the tip into the red opening at the apex. She was excited beyond herself. Her cheeks flushed, her breath came and went with spasmodic eagerness. Her hand still grasped the member of the salacious priest. Her tight young cunt throbbed with the pleasures of anticipation.

She would have continued to tickle, rub and generally excite the swollen tool of the lecherous Ambrose, but that worthy man signed to her to stop.

'Stay a moment, Bella,' sighed he, 'you will make the spunk come so.'

Bella released her hold of the big white shaft and lay back so that her uncle could work leisurely in and out of her mouth. Her eyes greedily rested upon the huge proportions of Ambrose all the while.

Never had Bella tasted a prick with so much delight, as she now did the very respectable weapon of her uncle. She, therefore, worked her lips upon it with the utmost relish, sucking greedily the moisture which from time to time exuded from the tip. Mr Verbouc was in raptures with her willing services.

The priest now knelt down, and pushing his shaven head between the knees of Mr Verbouc, as he stood before his niece, he opened the girl's plump thighs and, parting the pink lips of her delicate slit with his fingers, thrust in his tongue and covered her young and excited parts with his thick lips.

Bella shivered with pleasure: her uncle grew stiffer, and pushed hard and viciously at her beautiful mouth. The girl placed a hand on his balls, and gently squeezed them. She skinned back the hot shaft and sucked it with evident delight.

'Let it come,' said Bella, rejecting for a moment the glistening nut in order to express herself and take breath. 'Let it come, uncle, I should like to taste it so much.'

'So you shall, my darling, but not yet, we must not be too quick.'

'Oh! How he sucks me, how his tongue licks me! I am on fire; he is killing me.'

'Aha, Bella, you feel nothing but pleasure now, you are reconciled to the joys of our incestuous connection.'

'Indeed I am, my dear uncle, give me your prick again in my mouth.'

'Not yet, Bella, my love.'

'Do not keep me too long. You are maddening me. Father! Father! Oh, he is coming to me, he is preparing to fuck me. Holy Mother! What a prick! Oh, mercy! He will split me.'

Meanwhile Ambrose, driven to fury by the delicious employment he had been engaged in, became too excited to remain longer as he was, and taking the opportunity of Mr Verbouc's temporary withdrawal, he rose and pushed the beautiful girl back upon the soft lounge.

Verbouc seized upon the formidable penis of the holy father and, giving it one or two preliminary shakes, pushing back the soft skin which circled the egg-shaped head and directing the broad flaming head to the pink slit, urged him to drive it up vigorously into her belly as she lay before him.

The moistened condition of the child's parts assisted the insertion of the head and shoulders, and the priest's weapon was quickly engulfed. Vigorous thrusts succeeded, and with fierce lust in his face and little mercy for the youth of his victim, Ambrose fucked with a will. Her excitement obliterated all sense of pain and stretching wide her pretty legs she allowed him to wallow as completely as he desired in the possession of her beauty.

A loud moan of rapture escaped from Bella's parted lips, as she felt the huge weapon, hard as iron, pressing up her womb, and stretching her with its great bulk.

Mr Verbouc lost nothing of the salacious sight, but standing close to the excited couple, he placed his own hardly less vigorous member in his niece's convulsive grasp.

Ambrose no sooner felt himself securely lodged in the beautiful body beneath him that he curbed his eagerness, and calling to his aid the wonderful power of self-control which he possessed in so extraordinary a measure, he passed his trembling hands before the hips of the girl, and pulling apart his dress exposed his hairy belly, with which at each deep thrust he rubbed her soft *motte*.

Now, indeed, the priest commenced his course in earnest. With strong and regular thrusts he buried himself in the tender form beneath him. He pressed hotly forward; Bella threw her white arms around his brawny neck. His balls beat upon her plump bottom, his tool was up her to the hairs, which, black and crisp, plentifully covered his big belly.

'She has it now! Look, Verbouc, at your niece. See, how she relishes the administrations of the church. Ah, what pressures! How she nips me in her tight, naked little cunt.'

'Oh, my dear, dear. Oh! good father, fuck on, I am spending; push, push it in. Kill me with it, if you like, but keep moving. So! Oh! Heavens. Ah! Ah! How big it is; how you enter me!'

The lounge fairly worked again, and cracked beneath his rapid strokes.

'Oh, God!' cried Bella, 'he's killing me – it's really too much – I die – I am spending,' and with a half-shriek, the girl went off and flooded the thick member which was so deliciously forging her – a second time.

The long prick grew hotter and harder. The knob swelled also, and the whole tremendous affair seemed ready to burst with luxury. The young Bella moaned incoherent words, in which the word fuck was alone audible.

Ambrose, now fully prime, and feeling his great affair nipped in the young parts of the girl, could hold out no longer, and catching hold of Bella's bottom with both hands, he pressed inwards the whole tremendous length and discharged, shooting the thick jets of his fluid, one after another, deep into his playfellow.

A roar like that of a wild beast escaped him, as he felt the hot spunk spout from him.

'Oh! it comes; you are flooding me. I feel it. Oh! delicious!'

Relentlessly the priest's prick bore hard up into Bella's body, and its swollen head continued to inject its pearly seed right into her young womb.

'Oh, what a quantity you have given me,' remarked Bella, as she staggered to her feet and beheld the thick, hot fluid running in all directions down her legs. 'How white and slippery it is.'

This was exactly the condition of affairs which her uncle most craved, and he therefore proceeded leisurely to avail himself of it. He regarded her beautiful silk stockings all drabbled; he pushed his fingers between the red lips of her young cunt and rubbed the exuding semen all over her hairless belly and thighs.

Placing his niece conveniently before him, Mr Verbouc exposed once more his stiff and hairy champion, and roused by the exceptional circumstances he so much delighted in, he contemplated with eager zeal the tender parts of the young Bella, all covered as they were with the discharge of the priest, and still exuding thick and copious gouts of his prolific fluid.

Bella, at his desire, opened her legs to her utmost. Her uncle eagerly pushed his naked person between her plump young thighs.

'Hold still, my dear niece. My prick is not so thick, nor so long as Father Ambrose's, but I know well how to fuck, and you shall try whether your uncle's spunk is not as thick and pungent as any ecclesiastic's. See, how stiff I am.'

'Ah! how you make me long,' said Bella. 'I can see your dear thing waiting for its turn; how red it looks. Push me, uncle, dear, I am ready again, and good Father Ambrose has plentifully oiled the way for you.'

The hard and red-headed member touched the parted lips, all slippery as they were already, the apex readily entered, the big shaft quickly followed, and with a few steady thrusts, behold this exemplary relative buried to the balls in his niece's belly, and lolling luxuriantly in the reeking evidence of her previous unholy enjoyment of Father Ambrose.

'My darling uncle,' exclaimed the girl, 'remember whom you fuck. It is no stranger, it is your brother's child – your own niece. Fuck me then, uncle, give me all your strong prick – fuck! Ah, fuck, fuck, till your incestuous stuff pours into me. Ah, ah! Oh!' and overpowered with the salacious ideas she conjured up, Bella gave way to the most unbridled sensuality, to the great delight of her uncle.

The strong man, content in the gratification of his favourite lechery, dealt his rapid and powerful strokes. Swimming as was the condition of his fair opponent's slit, it was nevertheless so naturally small and tight that he found himself clipped in the most delicious way by the narrow opening, and his pleasure rapidly advanced.

Verbouc rose and fell upon the delicious body of his young niece; he drove fiercely inwards at every bound, and Bella clung to him with the tenacity of yet unsated lust. His prick grew hard and hot.

The titillation soon became almost insupportable. Bella herself enjoyed the incestuous encounter to the utmost. At last, with a sob, Mr Verbouc fell forward spending upon his niece, while the hot fluid spouted from him and again inundated her womb. Bella also reached the climax and, while she felt and welcomed the powerful injection, gave down as equally ardent proof of her enjoyment.

The act being thus completed, Bella was permitted to make the necessary ablutions, and then, after a revivifying glass of wine all round, the three sat down and concerted a devilish plot for the defilement and enjoyment of the beautiful Julia Delmont.

Bella avowed that Mr Delmont was certainly amorous of her, and evidently only wanted an opportunity to push matters on towards his object.

Father Ambrose confessed that his member stood straight out at the bare mention of the fair girl's name. He confessed her, and he now laughingly acknowledged that he could not keep his hands off himself during the ceremony; her breath caused him agonies of sensual longing, it was perfume itself.

Mr Verbouc declared himself equally anxious to revel in those tender sweets of which the description made him wild with lust, but how to carry the plot into execution was the question.

'If I ravished her without preparation, I should burst her parts,' exclaimed Father Ambrose, displaying once more his rubicund machine, smoking yet with the unremoved evidence of his last enjoyment.

'I could not have her first. I need the excitement of a previous copulation,' objected Mr Verbouc.

'I should like to see the girl well ravished,' said Bella. 'I should watch the operation with delight and when Father Ambrose has rammed his big thing into her, you, uncle, could be giving me yours to compensate me for the gift we were making in favour of the pretty Julia.'

'Yes, that would be doubly delicious.'

'What is to be done,' exclaimed Bella. 'Holy Mother! how stiff your thing is again, dear Father Ambrose.'

'An idea occurs to me which gives me a violent erection only to think of; put in practice it would be the acme of lust, and consequently of pleasure.'

'Let us hear,' exclaimed both at once.

'Wait a moment,' said the holy man, suffering Bella lightly to skin down the purple head of his tool and tickle the moist orifice with the tip of her tongue. 'Now, listen to me,' said Ambrose. 'Mr Delmont is amorous of Bella there. We are amorous of his daughter, and our child here, who is now sucking my weapon, would like the tender Julia to have it thrust up to her vitals, just by way of giving her wicked salacious little self an extra dose of pleasure. So far we are all agreed. Now give me your attention, and for the moment, Bella, let go my tool. This is my plan. I know the little Julia is not insensible to her animal instincts – in fact, the little devil already feels the pricking of the flesh. A little persuasion and a little mystification would do the rest. Julia will consent to have relief from those gentle pangs of carnal appetite. Bella must encourage the idea. Meanwhile, Bella can lead the dear Mr Delmont further on. She may allow him to declare himself, if he will; in fact this is necessary to the success of the plot; I must then be called in; I will suggest that Mr Verbouc is a man above all vulgar prejudices, and that for a certain sum to be agreed upon he will surrender his beautiful virgin niece to his impassioned embraces.'

'I hardly know about that,' commenced Bella.

'I don't see the object,' interposed Mr Verbouc. 'We shall be no nearer the attainment of our aim.'

'Wait a moment,' continued the holy man. 'We are all agreed so far – now, Bella shall be sold to Mr Delmont; he shall be allowed to take his fill of her beautiful charms in secrecy, she shall not see him, nor he her – at least, not her countenance, which shall remain concealed. He will be introduced to an agreeable chamber, he will behold the body, utterly nude, of a lovely young girl, he will know it is his victim, and he will enjoy her.'

'Me!' interrupted Bella, 'why all this mystery?'

Father Ambrose smiled a sickly smile.

'You will see, Bella – be patient. We want to enjoy Julia Delmont. Mr Delmont wants to enjoy you. We can only accomplish our purpose by preventing any scandal at the same time. Mr Delmont must be silenced, or we may suffer for our violation of his child. Now my design is that the lascivious Mr Delmont shall violate 'his own daughter' in lieu of Bella, and that having thus opened the way for us, we shall avail ourselves of the fact to satisfy our lust also. If Mr Delmont falls into the trap, we can either allow him the knowledge of his incest and reward him with the real enjoyment of our sweet Bella, in return for the person of his daughter, or otherwise act as circumstances may dictate.'

'Oh! I am nearly spending,' cried Mr Verbouc; 'my weapon is bursting! What a trick! What a delicious sight.'

Both men rose – Bella was enveloped in their embraces – two hard and large weapons pressed against her soft figure. They led her to the couch.

Ambrose fell upon his back; Bella mounted upon his body, took his stallion penis in her fair hand, and pushed it into her slit.

Mr Verbouc looked on.

Bella lowered herself down, until the huge weapon was wholly lodged. Then she lay down on the burly father and commenced an undulating, delicious series of movements.

Mr Verbouc saw her beautiful bottom rising and falling – parting and closing with each successive thrust.

Ambrose was in to the hilt, that was evident, his big balls hung closely underneath, and the fat lips of her budding parts came down to them each time she let herself fall upon him.

The sight proved too much for him. The virtuous uncle mounted the couch, directed his long and swollen penis to the posteriors of the fair Bella, and with little difficulty succeeded in housing its extreme length in her bowels.

His niece's bottom was broad and soft as velvet, and the skin white as alabaster. Verbouc, however, did not care to stop for contemplation. His member was in, and he felt the tight compression of the muscle at the little entrance acting upon it like nothing else in the world. The two pricks rubbed together with only a thin membrane between.

Bella felt the maddening effect of this double *jouissance*. Terrific grew the excitement, until at length the very rapture of the struggle brought its own relief and floods of spunk inundated the fair Bella.

After this, Ambrose discharged twice in Bella's mouth, where her uncle also emitted his incestuous fluid, and this finale closed the entertainment.

The way in which Bella performed this operation was such as to call forth the warmest encomiums from her companions.

Seating herself upon the edge of a chair, she received them standing in front of her, so that their stiff weapons were nearly on a level with her coral lips. Then taking the velvet gland entirely into her mouth, she employed her fair hands to rub, tickle and excite the shaft and its appendages. Thus the full nervous power of her playfellow was employed and with his bursting penis at full stretch, he enjoyed the luscious titillation, until Bella's indelicate touches proved too much, and amid sighs of ecstatic emotion, her mouth and gullet were suddenly flooded with a spouting stream of spunk.

The little glutton swallowed all; she would have done the same for a dozen, had she had the chance.

# Chapter Eight

Bella continued to afford me the most delicious of pastures. Her young limbs never missed the crimson draughts which I imbibed, or felt to any grave inconvenience the tiny punctures which I was forced most reluctantly to make to obtain my living. I determined, therefore, to remain with her – although of late her conduct had become, to say the very least, somewhat questionable and slightly irregular.

One thing I remarked for certain, and that was that she had lost all feelings of delicacy and maidenly reserve, and lived only for the delights of sensual gratification.

I was soon satisfied that my young lady had lost nothing of the lesson she had received of her share in the conspiracy in course of preparation. How she played her part I now propose to relate.

It was not long before Bella found herself within the mansion of Mr Delmont, and, as luck would have it, or shall we say rather as that worthy man himself had expressly designed it, in the company of the amatory proprietor.

Mr Delmont saw his chance, and, like a clever general, instantly pressed on to the assault. He found his fair companion either wholly innocent of his intention, or else wonderfully willing to encourage his advances.

Already Mr Delmont had his arm around Bella's waist, while apparently quite by accident, her soft right hand pressed beneath his nervous palm, lay upon his manly thigh.

What Bella felt beneath showed plainly enough the violence of his emotion. A throb passed quickly through the hard object which lay concealed, and Bella was not without the sympathetic spasm that told of sensuous pleasure.

Gently the amorous Mr D drew the girl towards him, and hugged her yielding form. He printed suddenly a hot kiss on her cheek, and whispered flattering words to absorb her attention from his proceedings. He essayed more; he gently moved Bella's hand about the hard object, until the young lady perceived that his excitement was likely to become too rapid.

Throughout Bella firmly adhered to her role: she was coy innocence itself.

Mr D, encouraged by the non-resistance of his young friend, proceeded to other and still more decided steps. His wanton hand roved along the edge of Bella's light dress, and pressed her yielding calf. Then, suddenly, with a warm and simultaneous kiss on her red lips, he quickly passed his trembling fingers underneath and touched her plump thigh.

Bella recoiled. At any other time she would have gladly flung herself upon her back, and bade him do his worst; but she remembered her lesson, and went on with her part to perfection.

'Oh! how rude you are,' cried the young lady, 'what a naughty thing – I cannot let you do that. Uncle says nobody must be allowed to touch that – at any rate not without first – ' Bella hesitated, stopped, and looked silly.

Mr Delmont was curious as well as amatory.

'Without first what, Bella?'

'Oh, I must not tell you. I ought to have said nothing about it; only you, by doing such a rude thing, made me forget.'

'Forget what?'

'Something that my uncle has often told me,' answered Bella simply.

'What is it? Tell me.'

'I dare not – besides, I do not understand what he means.'

'I will explain it, if you tell me what it was he said.'

'You promise not to tell?'

'Certainly.'

'Well, then, he says I must never let anyone put his hands there, and that whoever wants to do so, must pay well for it.'

'Does he really say that?'

'Yes, indeed he does; he says that I am able to bring him a good round sum in that way, and that there are plenty of rich gentlemen who would pay for that which you want to do to me, and he says he is not so stupid as to lose such a chance.'

'Really, Bella, your uncle is a strict man of business. I did not think he was that kind of man.'

'Oh, yes, but he is,' cried Bella. 'He is very fond of money, you know, in secret; and I know scarcely what he means, but he sometimes says he shall sell my maidenhead.'

'Is it possible?' thought Mr Delmont. 'What a man he must be, what a wonderful eye to business he must have,' he said aloud.

In fact, the more Mr D thought about it, the more convinced he became of the truth of Bella's ingenious explanation. She was to be bought. He would buy her; better far that way than to run the risk of discovery and punishment by resorting to a secret liaison.

Before, however, he could do more than revolve these sage reflections in his own mind, an interruption occurred in the arrival of his own daughter Julia, and very reluctantly he had to release his companion and arrange himself with an eye to propriety.

Bella made a rapid excuse and went home, leaving the event to take its chance.

The route taken by my fair young lady lay through several meadows and along a cart-track which emerged into the great highway very near her uncle's residence.

The time was afternoon, and the day was unusually fine. The lane had several sudden turnings, and as Bella pursued her way, she amused herself watching the cattle in the neighbouring pastures.

Presently the lane became bordered with trees, the long straight line of trunks dividing the roadway from the footpath. Across the nearest meadow she saw several men at work tilling the ground, and at a little distance, a group of women had ceased for a moment from their labour of weeding to exchange some items of gossip.

On the opposite side of the lane was a hedge, and looking through this Bella saw a sight which fairly startled her. Within the meadow were two animals, a horse and a mare. The former had evidently been occupied in chasing the latter about the ground, and had at last pinned his companion in a corner not far from where she stood.

But what startled and surprised Bella most was the wonderful erectioned excitement of a long and grizzly member which hung below the belly of the stallion, and ever and anon sprang up with an impatient jerk against his body.

The mare had evidently remarked it too, for she now stood perfectly quiet with her back towards the horse.

The latter was too pressed by his amorous instincts to dally long beside her, and to the young lady's wonder she beheld the great creature mount up behind the mare and attempt to push his tool into her.

Bella watched with breathless interest, and saw the long swollen member of the horse at length hit the mark and disappear entirely in the hinder parts of the mare.

To say that her sensual feelings were roused would be but to express the natural result of so salacious an exhibition. She was more than roused; her libidinous instincts were 'fired'. She clasped her hands and gazed with interest on the lewd encounter; and when, after a rapid and furious course, the animal withdrew his dripping penis, Bella brooded upon it with an insane longing to seize it for herself, and handle the great pendant thing for her own gratification.

In this excited frame of mind, she found that some sort of action was necessary to relieve her from the powerful influence which oppressed her. Making a strong effort, Bella turned her head, and but a moment later, taking half a dozen steps forward, came straight upon a sight which certainly had no tendency to allay her excitement.

Right in her path stood a rustic youth of some eighteen years; his handsome but somewhat stupid features were turned towards the meadow where the amorous steeds were disporting themselves. A gap in the back which bordered the roadway afforded him an excellent view, in the contemplation of which he was evidently as much interested as Bella had been.

But what claimed the attention of the girl was the state of the lad's clothing, and the appearance of a tremendous member, ruddy and well developed, which, barefaced and fully exposed, unblushingly raised its fiery crest full in his front.

There was no mistaking the effect the sight in the meadow had produced, for the lad had already unbuttoned his nether garments of coarse material, and had his nervous grasp upon a weapon of which a Carmelite might have been proud. With eager eyes he devoured the scene being enacted before him in the meadow, while his right hand skinned the standing column and worked it vigorously up and down, utterly unconscious that so congenial a spirit was witnessing his proceedings.

A start and the exclamation which involuntarily broke from Bella caused him at once to look round, and there in full view before him stood the beautiful girl to whom his nudity and his lewd erection were at the same moment completely exposed.

'Oh, my goodness!' exclaimed Bella, as soon as she could find words, 'what a dreadful sight! What a wicked boy! Why, what are you doing with that long red thing?'

The boy, abashed, attempted awkwardly to replace in his breeches the object which had provoked the observations, but his evident confusion and the stiffness of the thing itself rendered the operation very difficult, not to say tedious.

Bella came kindly to the rescue. 'What is that? Let me help you – how came it out? How large and stiff it is, what a length it is! My word! what a tremendously big one you've got, you naughty boy – !'

Suiting the action to the word, the young lady laid her delicate white hand upon the standing penis of the boy, but squeezing it in her soft warm grasp only, of course, made it the more unlikely to re-enter its retreat.

Meanwhile the lad, gradually recovering his stolid presence of mind, and beholding how fair and apparently innocent was his new acquaintance, ceased to betray any desire to assist her in the laudable endeavours to conceal the stiff and offending member. Indeed, it became impossible, even if he had desired it; for no sooner had her grasp closed upon it, than it acquired even larger proportions, while the distended and purple head shone like a ripe plum.

'What a naughty boy!' observed Bella. 'Whatever shall I do,' she continued, looking archly into the handsome face of the rustic.

'Ah, how nice that is,' sighed the lad – 'who could have thought that you were so near me, when I felt so bad, and it first began to throb and swell so just now.'

'This is very, very wicked,' remarked the young lady, tightening her grasp, and feeling the rankling flames of lust rising higher and higher within her; 'this is dreadfully wrong and naughty; you know it is, you bad boy.'

'Did you see what those horses were doing in the meadow?' asked the boy, looking wonderingly at Bella, whose beauty seemed to dawn upon his dull mind as the sun steals over a showery landscape.

'Yes, I did,' replied the girl, innocently. 'What were they doing it for – what did it mean?'

'It means fucking,' responded the youth, with a lewd grin. 'He wanted the mare, and mare wanted the stallion, and so they came together and fucked.'

'Lord, how curious!' exclaimed Bella, looking with the most childish simplicity from the great thing in her hands to the boy's countenance.

'Yes, it was droll, wasn't it? And, my goodness, what a tool he'd got, miss, hadn't he?'

'Immense,' murmured Bella, thinking partly all the time of the thing she was skinning slowly backwards and forwards in her own hand.

'Oh, how you tickle me,' sighed her companion, 'what a beauty you are, how deliciously you rub it. Please, go on, miss, I want to spend.'

'Do you, indeed,' whispered Bella, 'shall I make you spend?'

Bella saw the stiffened object reddening with the gentle titillation she was giving it until the plump top looked almost ready to burst. The prurient idea of watching the effect of continued friction took violent possession of her.

She applied herself with redoubled energy to the lewd task.

'Oh, please, yes – go on; it is near coming. Oh! oh! How nice you do it; hold tight – go faster – skin it well down. Now, again. Oh! my goodness. Oh!'

The long hard tool grew hotter and stiffer, as the little hands flew upon it.

'Ah! ugh! – It's coming! – Ugh! Hoo!' exclaimed the rustic lad in broken accents, while his knees quivered, his body straightened, his head rolled back and, amid contortions and stifled cries, his large and powerful penis squirted forth a rapid stream of thick fluid over the dear little hands which, eager to bathe themselves in the warm and slippery flood, now lovingly embraced the big shaft and coaxed from it the fast outpouring seminal shower.

Bella, surprised and delighted, pumped out every drop – she would have sucked it, had she dared – and then, drawing out her cambric handkerchief, she wiped the thick and pearly mess from her hands.

Then the youth, abashed and stupid, put up the expiring member, and regarded his companion with a mingled air of curiosity and wonder.

'Where do you live?' at last he found words to enquire.

'Not very far from here,' replied Bella; 'but you must not try to follow me, or to find out, you know; if you do,' continued the young lady, 'it will be the worse for you, for I shall never do that again, and you would be punished.'

'Why don't we fuck like the stallion,' suggested the youth whose ardour, only half-appeased, began again to warm up.

'Someday, perhaps; not now, for I am in a hurry. I am late; I must go at once.'

'Let me put my hand up your clothes? Say, when you will come again?'

'Not now,' said Bella, withdrawing herself gradually, 'but we will meet again.'

She cherished a lively recollection of the stalwart affair in his breeches.

'Tell me,' continued she, 'have you ever fucked?'

'No, but I should like to . . . Don't you believe me? Well, then – yes, I have.'

'How shocking,' exclaimed the young lady.

'Father would like to fuck you,' said he, without hesitation, taking no notice of her movement to depart.

'Your father! Dreadful. How do you know that?'

'Because father and I fuck the girls together. His tool is much bigger than mine.'

'You say so. But do you really mean that your parent and you do such dreadful things in company?'

'Yes, when we get the chance. You should see him fuck. Oh! by gum!' and he grinned idiotically.

'You don't seem a clever boy,' said Bella.

'Father's not so clever as me,' replied the lad, widening his grin, and showing his prick, again half-stiff. 'I know how to fuck now, though I only had it once. You should see me fuck.'

And Bella saw the big tool pointing and throbbing.

'Whom did you do it with then? You naughty boy.'

'A girl of fourteen. Father and I both fucked her.'

'Which of you did it first?' demanded Bella.

'I did, and father caught me. So then he wanted his go, and made me hold her. You should see him fuck, by gum!'

A few minutes more Bella was again on her way and reached her house without further adventures.

## *Chapter Nine*

When Bella related the result of her interview with Mr Delmont that evening, a low chuckle of delight escaped the lips of her two co-conspirators. She said nothing, however, of the young rustic she had encountered by the way. With that part of the day's performances she considered it quite unnecessary to trouble either the astute Father Ambrose, or her no less sagacious relative.

The plot was evidently about to thicken. The seed so discreetly sown would certainly fructify, and as Ambrose thought of the delicious treat which would certainly someday be his in the person of the beautiful young Julia Delmont, his spirits rose, and his animal passions fed by anticipation on the tender dainties hereafter to be his, until the result became visible in the huge distension of his member and the excitement which his whole manner betrayed.

Nor was Mr Verbouc less touched. Sensual to the last degree, he promised himself a luscious repast on the newly opened charms of his neighbour's daughter, and the thought of the treat to come acted equally on his nervous temperament.

There were yet some details to arrange. It was clear that the simple Mr Delmont would come to feel his way as to the truth of Bella's assertions respecting her uncle's willingness to sell her maidenhead.

Father Ambrose, whose knowledge of the man had led him to suggest the idea to Bella, knew well with whom he was dealing – indeed, which of those that had the privilege to count him their confessor did not exhibit their inmost nature to their holy man in the sacred right of confession ?

Father Ambrose was discreet, he faithfully observed the silence enjoined by his religion, but he made no scruple to use the facts he thus acquired for his own ends – and what those were the reader by this time knows as well as I did.

Thus the plot was arranged. Upon a certain day to be agreed upon, Bella was to invite her friend Julia to pass the day with her at her uncle's house, and Mr Delmont, it was intended, should be instructed to come and fetch her home. After a certain interval of flirtation between him and the innocent Bella, all being explained to him and previously arranged, she was to withdraw, and under the pretext that it was absolutely necessary that some such precaution should be taken in order to avoid the possibility of scandal, she was to be presented to him in a convenient chamber recumbent upon a lounge, where her beautiful body and charms were to be at his disposal, while her head remained concealed behind a carefully closed curtain. Thus, Mr Delmont, eager for the tender encounter, could snatch the jewel he coveted from the lovely victim, while she – ignorant of who her assailant might be – could never thereafter accuse him of the outrage or feel shame in his presence.

Mr Delmont was to have all this explained to him, and his acquiescence was considered certain; only one reservation was intended. No one was to tell him that his own daughter was to be substituted in Bella's place. He would only know that when all was over.

Meanwhile, Julia was to be gradually prepared in secret for what was to take place, no mention, of course, being made of the final catastrophe, or the real participator in it. But here Father Ambrose felt himself at home, and by means of well-directed enquiries, and a great deal of unnecessary explanation in the confessional, he soon brought the young girl to the knowledge of things of which she had never previously dreamed; all which Bella took care to explain and confirm.

All these matters had been finally disposed of in conference, and the consideration of the subject had produced by anticipation so violent an effect upon the two men that they were now in train to enjoy their present good fortune in the possession of the fair young Bella with an amount of ardour they had never surpassed.

My young lady on her side, was nothing loth to lend herself to their fantasies, and as she now sat or lay back on the soft lounge with a stiff standing member in either hand, her own emotions rose proportionately, until she longed for the vigorous embraces she knew were about to follow.

Father Ambrose, as usual, was the first. He turned her round, placed her on her belly, and directing her to extend her plump white buttocks as far back as possible, he stood for a moment contemplating the delicious prospect and the small and delicate slit which was just visible below. His weapon, redoubtable and well provided with Nature's essence, rose fiercely and menaced either entry into love's delightful shades.

Mr Verbouc, as before, disposed himself to witness the disproportionate assault, with the evident intention of enjoying his favourite role afterwards.

Father Ambrose regarded, with a lecherous expression, the white and rounded promontories straight in front of him. The clerical tendencies of his education were exciting him to commit an infidelity to the goddess, but the knowledge of what was expected of him by his friend and patron restrained him for the time.

'Delays are dangerous,' said he, 'my balls are very full; the dear child must have their contents, and you, my friend, must delight yourself with the abundant lubrication with which I shall provide you.'

Ambrose, on this occasion at least, spoke nothing but the truth. His huge weapon, surmounted by the dull purple head, the broad proportions of which resembled the glowing ripeness of some fruit, stood stiffly up towards his navel, and his immense testicles, hard and round, appeared surcharged with the venomous liquor they were aching to discharge. A thick, opaque drop – an *avant-courier* of that gush which was to follow – stood on the blunt apex of his penis, as, bursting with lechery, the satyr approached his prey.

Hastily bending down the stiff shaft, Ambrose put the big nut between the lips of Bella's tender slit and, all anointed as it was, commenced to push it up her.

'Oh, how hard! How large you are!' cried Bella; 'you hurt me; it is going in too far. Oh! stop!'

As well might have Bella appealed to the wind. A rapid succession of thrusts, a few pauses at intervals, more efforts, and Bella was impaled.

'Ah,' exclaimed the ravisher, turning in triumph to his colleague, while his eyes sparkled and his lewd mouth watered with the pleasure he was having. 'Ah, this is luscious, indeed; how tight she is, and yet she has it all. I am up here to my balls.'

Mr Verbouc took a careful survey. Ambrose was right. Nothing but his two huge balls remained visible of his genitals, and they were pressing close up between Bella's legs.

Meanwhile, Bella felt the heat of the invader in her belly. She was sensible of the skinning and uncovering of the huge head within her, and instantly, her lewdest emotions overtaking her, with a faint cry, she spent profusely.

Mr Verbouc was delighted.

'Push! push!' said he, 'she likes it now, give it her all – push!'

Ambrose needed no such incentive, seizing Bella round the hips, he buried himself in her at each bound. The pleasure rose upon him fast; he drew back his smoking penis, all except the nut, and then lunging forward, he emitted a low groan and squirted a perfect deluge of hot fluid into Bella's delicate body.

The girl felt the warm and trickling stuff shooting violently up her, and once more gave down her tribute. The great gushes which now came slopping into her vitals from the powerful stores of Father Ambrose, whose singular gift in this particular I have before explained, caused Bella the liveliest sensations, and she experienced the keenest pleasure during his discharge.

Scarcely had Ambrose withdrawn, than Mr Verbouc took possession of his niece, and commenced a slow and delicious enjoyment of her most secret charms. After an interval of fully twenty minutes, during which time the salacious uncle revelled in pleasure to his heart's content, he completed his gratification in a copious discharge, which Bella received with throbs of delight, such as no other than a thoroughly prurient mind could relish.

'I wonder,' said Mr Verbouc, after he had regained his breath and refreshed himself with a large draught of rich wine, 'I wonder how it is this dear child inspires me with such overwhelming rapture. In her arms I forget myself and all the world. The intoxication of the moment carries me with it, and I enjoy I know not what of ecstasy.'

The observation, or reflection, call it what you will, of the uncle, was partly addressed to the good father, and, no doubt, was partially the result of interior workings of the spirits which involuntarily rose to the surface and formed themselves into words.

'I could tell you, I think,' said Ambrose sententiously, 'only perhaps you would not follow my reasoning.'

'Explain, by all means,' replied Mr Verbouc. 'I am all attention, and I should of all things like to hear your reason.'

'My reason, or rather, I should say, my reasons,' observed Father Ambrose, 'are manifest when you are in possession of my hypothesis.'

Then, taking a pinch of snuff, a habit which the good man usually indulged before delivering himself of any weighty reflections, he continued: 'Sensual pleasure must always be proportional to the adaptability of the circumstances which are intended to produce it. And this is paradoxical, because the more we advance in sensuality, and the more voluptuous our tastes grow, the greater becomes the necessity that these circumstances should be themselves at variance. Do not mis–understand me; I will try to render myself more clear. Why does a man commit a rape when he is surrounded by women willing to afford him the use of their bodies? Simply because he is not content to be in accord with the opposite party to his enjoyment, and it is her very unwillingness which constitutes his pleasure. No doubt there are instances in which a man of brutal mind, and seeking only his own sensual relief, where it is not possible to find a willing object to his gratification, forces a woman, or a child, to his will, with no other object than the immediate relief of those instincts which madden him; but search the record of such crimes, and you will find that by far the greater number are the result of deliberate design, planned and executed in the face of obvious and even lawful means of gratification. The opposition to his proposed enjoyment serves to whet his lewd appetite, and the introduction of the feature of crime and violence add a zest to the matter which obtains a firm hold upon his mind. It is wrong, it is disallowed, therefore it is worth seeking, it becomes delicious. Again, what is the reason that a man of vigorous build, and capable of gratifying a fully developed woman, prefers a mere child of fourteen? I answer, because that very disparity affords him delight, gratifies the imagination, and constitutes that exact adaptability of circumstances of which I speak. In effect it is, of course, the imagination which is at work. The law of contrast is constant in this as in all else. The distinction merely of the sexes is not of itself sufficient to the educated voluptuary – there are needed further and special contrasts to perfect the idea he has conceived. The variations are infinite, but still the same law is traceable in all. Tall men prefer short women, fair men dark women, strong men select weak and tender women, and these women are fondest of vigorous and robust partners. Cupid's darts are tipped with incompatibilities and feathered with the wildest incongruities; none but the inferior animals, the brutes themselves, will copulate indiscriminately with the opposite sex, and even these have their preferences and desires, as irregular as those of mankind. Who has not seen the unnatural conduct of a couple of street dogs, or laughed at the awkward efforts of some old cow who, driven to market with the common herd, vents her sensual instincts by mounting upon the back of her nearest neighbour? Thus I respond to your invitation, and thus I give you my reasons for your preference for your niece, for the sweet but forbidden playmate, whose delicious limbs I am now moulding.'

As Father Ambrose concluded, he looked for an instant upon the fair girl, and his great weapon rose to its utmost dimensions.

'Come, my forbidden fruit,' said he, 'let me pluck you, let me revel in you to my heart's content. This is my pleasure – my ecstasy – my delirious enjoyment. I will swamp you in spunk, I will possess you in spite of the dictates of society – you are mine, come!'

Bella looked upon the ruddy and stiffened member of her confessor, she noted his excited gaze fixed upon her young body. She knew his intention, and prepared herself to gratify him.

Already had he frequently entered her tender belly and thrust the full length of that majestic penis into her small and sensible parts. Pain at the distension had now given way to pleasure, and the young and elastic flesh opened to receive the column of gristle, with only just enough of uneasiness to make her careful in its reception.

The good man looked for a moment upon the tempting prospect before him, then, advancing, he divided the rosy lips of Bella's slit and pushed in the smooth gland of his great weapon: Bella received it with a shudder of mingled emotion.

Ambrose continued to penetrate until, after a few fierce thrusts, he buried his length in her tight young body, and she had him to the balls.

Then followed a series of pushes, of vigorous writhings on one part, and of spasmodic sobs and stifled cries upon the other. If the pleasures of the holy man were intense, those of his youthful playmate were equally ecstatic, and his stiff affair was already well lubricated with her discharge when, with a groan of intense feeling, he once more reached his consummation, and Bella felt a flood of spendings burn violently into her vitals.

'Ah, how you have inundated me, both of you,' said Bella, noticing as she spoke a large pool which covered her legs, and lay upon the sofa-cover between her thighs.

Before either could reply to the observation, a succession of cries made themselves heard in the quiet chamber and, becoming weaker and weaker as they continued, at once arrested the attention of all present.

And here I should acquaint my reader with one or two particulars which hitherto, in my crawling capacity, I have not thought it necessary to mention. The fact is that fleas, although no doubt agile members of society, cannot be everywhere at once, though no doubt they can and do make up for this drawback by the exercise of an agility rarely equalled by others of the insect tribe.

I ought to have explained, like any human storywriter, though, perhaps, with less circumlocution and more veracity, that Bella's aunt, Mrs Verbouc , to whom my readers were very cursorily presented in the opening chapter of my history, occupied a chamber to herself in a wing of the mansion, where she spent much of her time, like Madame Delmont, in devotional exercises, and, with a happy disregard of mundane affairs, usually left all the domestic management of the house to her niece.

Mr Verbouc had already reached the stage of indifference to the blandishments of his better half, and but seldom now visited her chamber or disturbed her repose for purposes of exercising his marital rights.

Mrs Verbouc , however, was still young – only thirty-two summers had as yet passed over that pious and devout head; Mrs Verbouc was handsome, and the lady had also brought her husband the additional advantage of a considerable fortune.

Mrs Verbouc , in spite of her piety, sometimes languished for the more solid comforts of her husband's embraces, and relished with a keen delight the exercise of his rights on his occasional visits to her couch.

On this occasion, Mrs Verbouc had retired at her usual early hour, and the present digression is necessary to explain what follows. While this amiable lady, therefore, is engaged in those duties of the toilet which even fleas dare not profane, let us talk of another and no less important personage whose conduct it will be necessary also to investigate.

Now it happened that Father Clement, whose exploits in the lists of the amorous goddess we have already had occasion to chronicle, rankled under the fact of the young Bella's withdrawal from the Society of the Sacristy and, knowing well who she was and where she was to be found, had for some days prowled about the residence of Mr Verbouc to try and regain possession of that delicious prize of which it will be remembered the cunning of Ambrose had deprived his confrères.

In this attempt Clement was aided by the Superior, who also bitterly lamented his loss, without, however, suspecting the part that Father Ambrose had played. On this particular evening Clement had posted himself near the house, and seeing an opportunity, set himself closely to watch a certain window which he made sure was that of the fair Bella.

How vain, indeed, are human calculations! While the forlorn Clement, robbed of his pleasures, was relentlessly watching one chamber, the object of his desires was bathed in salacious enjoyment between her two vigorous lovers in another.

Meanwhile, the night advanced, and Clement, finding all quiet, contrived to raise himself to the level of the window. A faint light was burning in the room by which the anxious *curé* could detect a lady reposing by herself in the full enjoyment of sound slumber.

Nothing doubting of his ability to win Bella to his desires, could he only gain her ear, and mindful of the bliss he had already enjoyed while revelling in her beauties, the audacious scoundrel furtively opened the window and entered the sleeping-chamber. Well wrapped in the flowing frock of a monk, and disguised in its ample cowl, he stole across to the bed, while his gigantic member, already awake to the pleasures he promised himself, stood fiercely up against his hirsute belly.

Mrs Verbouc , roused from a pleasant dream and never doubting but that it was her faithful spouse who thus so warmly pressed her, turned lovingly towards the intruder, and, nothing loath, opened her willing thighs to his vigorous attack.

Clement on his side, equally sure that the young Bella was in his arms and, moreover, not unwilling to admit his caresses, pushed matters to a crisis; mounting in hot haste between the lady's legs, he brought his huge penis opposite the lips of a well-moistened slit, and fully aware of the difficulties he expected to encounter in so young a girl, thrust violently inwards.

There was a movement, another plunge downwards of his big bottom, a gasp on the part of the lady, and slowly but surely the gigantic mass of hard flesh went in, until it was fairly housed. Then, as it passed in for the first time, Mrs Verbouc detected the extraordinary difference. This penis was at least double the size of her husband's – doubt was succeeded by certainty. In the dim light she raised her head; above was visible, close to hers, the excited visage of the ferocious Clement.

Instantly there was a struggle, a violent outcry and a vain attempt to disengage herself from her strong assailant.

But come what might, Clement was in full possession and enjoyment of her person. He never paused, but, on the contrary, deaf to her cries, he broke in to his utmost length, and strove, with feverish haste, to complete his horrid triumph. Blind with rage and lust he was insensible to the fact of the opening of the door and to the blows which rained upon his hinder parts; with set teeth and the subdued roar of a bull, he reached his crisis and poured a torrent of semen into the unwilling womb of his victim.

Then he awoke to his position, and fearing the results of his detestable outrage, he rose in all haste, and withdrawing his foaming weapon, slipped from the bed upon the side opposite his assailant. Dodging as well as he could the cuts which Mr Verbouc aimed at him and keeping the hood of his frock over his features to avoid detection, he rushed toward the window by which he had entered; then taking a headlong leap he made good his escape in the darkness, followed by the imprecations of the infuriated husband.

We have already stated in a former chapter that Mrs Verbouc was an invalid – that is, she fancied herself to be one – and to a person of weak nerves and retiring habits my reader may picture for himself what was likely to be the effect of undergoing so indelicate an outrage. The enormous proportions of the man, his strength, his fury almost killed her, and she lay without consciousness on the couch which had witnessed her violation.

Mr Verbouc was not naturally endowed with astonishing attributes of personal courage and when he beheld the assailant of his wife rise satisfied from the pursuit he allowed Clement to retreat in peace.

Meanwhile, Father Ambrose and Bella, following at a respectful distance from the outraged husband, witnessed from the half-opened door the unfolding of the strange scene.

As soon as the ravisher rose, Bella and Ambrose both instantly recognised him; indeed, the former had had, as the reader knows already, good reason to remember the huge lolling member which dangled dripping between his legs.

Mutually interested in maintaining silence, a look exchanged between them was sufficient to indicate the necessity for reserve, and they withdrew before any movement on the part of the outraged woman betrayed their proximity.

It was several days before poor Mrs Verbouc was well enough to leave her bed. The shock to her nerves had been dreadful, and nothing but the kind and conciliatory manner of her husband enabled her to hold up at all.

Mr Verbouc had his own reasons for letting the matter pass, and he allowed no considerations beyond expediency to weigh with him.

On the day after the catastrophe I have recorded above, Mr Verbouc received a visit from his dear friend and neighbour Mr Delmont, and after being closeted together for over an hour, the two parted with beaming smiles and the most extravagant compliments. The one had sold his niece, and the other believed he had purchased that precious jewel: a maidenhead.

When Bella's uncle made the announcement that evening that the bargain had been struck, and the affair duly arranged, there was great rejoicing among the conspirators.

Father Ambrose immediately took possession of the maidenhead, and driving in to the girl the whole length of his member, proceeded, as he explained it, to keep the place warm, while Mr Verbouc, reserving himself, as usual, until his confrère had done, afterwards attacked the same mossy fort, as he facetiously expressed it, just to oil the passage for his friend.

Then the whole of the details were finally arranged, and the party broke up, confident in the success of their stratagem.

## *Chapter Ten*

Ever since the meeting in the green lane with the rustic whose simplicity had so much interested her, Bella had dwelt upon the expressions he had used, and the extraordinary disclosure of his parent's complicity in his sensuality. It was clear that his mind was simple almost to idiocy, and from his remark: 'Father's not so clever as me,' she assumed that the complaint was congenital, and wondered if the father really possessed the same, or – as declared by the boy – even greater proportions in his organs of generation.

I plainly saw, by her habit of thinking partly aloud, that Bella did not reckon much of her uncle's opinion, or stand any longer in fear of Father Ambrose. She was doubtless resolved to follow her own course, whatever it might be, and I was not, therefore, at all astonished when I found her wending her way the following day at about the same hour in the direction of the meadows.

In a field hard by the spot where she had beheld the sexual encounter between the horse and his mate, Bella discovered the lad engaged in some simple agricultural operation, and with him was another person, a tall and remarkably dark man of about forty-five years of age.

Almost as soon as she saw them, the lad observed the young lady, and running towards her, after apparently a word of explanation to his companion, he showed his delight by a broad grin.

'That's father,' said he, pointing over his shoulder, 'come and frig him.'

'For shame, you naughty boy,' said Bella, much more inclined to laugh than to be angry. 'How dare you use such language?'

## Chapter Ten

'What did you come for?' asked the boy. 'Did you come for fucking?'

By this time they had reached the man, who stuck his spade into the ground, and began to grin at the girl in very much the same fashion as his son.

He was strong and well built, and by his manner Bella could see the boy had told him the particulars of their first meeting.

'Look at father, ain't he a randy one?' remarked the youth. 'Ah! You should see him fuck!'

There was no attempt at disguise; the two evidently understood each other and grinned more than ever. He seemed to accept it as a huge compliment, but he cast his eyes upon the delicate young lady, the like of whom he had probably never met before, and it was impossible to mistake the look of sensuous longing which shone in his large black eyes.

Bella began to wish she had never come.

'I should like to show you father's big doodle,' said the lad, and suiting the action to word, he commenced to unbutton the trousers of his respectable parent.

Bella covered her eyes, and made a movement in retreat. Instantly the son stepped behind her. Her refuge in the lane was thus cut off.

'I should like to fuck you,' exclaimed the father, in a hoarse voice. 'Tim would like to fuck you as well, so you must not go away yet. Stop and be fucked!'

Bella was really frightened.

'I cannot,' she said; 'indeed you must let me go. You must not hold me like that: you must not drag me along; let me go. Where are you taking me?'

There was a small building in the corner of the field, and they were now at the door. Another second and the pair had pushed her inside and shut the door, lowering a large wooden bar across it after them as they entered.

Bella looked round and saw that the place was clean and half-filled with hay in trusses. She saw that resistance would be useless. It would be best to be quiet, and perhaps, after all, the strange pair would not hurt her. She noticed, however, that the trousers of both stuck out in front, and doubted but that their ideas were in harmony with their excitement.

'I want you to see father's cock; by gum! you ought to see his cods, too.'

Once more the lad began unbuttoning his father's breeches. Down went the flap and out stuck his shirt with something under it which caused it to bunch up in a curious manner.

'Oh, do hold still, father,' whispered the son; 'let the lady see your doodle.'

With that he raised the shirt, and exposed in Bella's face a fiercely erected member with a broad plum-like nut, very red and thick, but not of unusual length. It had a considerable bend upwards, and the head, which was divided down the middle by the tightness of the frenum, bent still further back towards his hairy belly. The shaft was immensely thick, rather flat and hugely swollen.

The girl felt her blood tingle as she looked upon it. The nut was as large as an egg – plump, and quite purple. It emitted a strong smell. The lad made her approach, and pressed her white, lady-like little hand upon it.

'Didn't I tell you it was bigger than mine?' continued the boy. 'Look here; mine is not nearly as thick as father's.'

Bella turned. The boy had his trousers opened and his formidable penis in full view. He was right – it could not compare with his father's for size.

The older of the two now caught her round the waist. Tim also essayed to cling to her, and to get his hand under her clothes. Between them she swayed to and fro. A sudden push cast her upon the hay. Then up went her skirts. Bella's dress was light and wide, she wore no drawers. No sooner did the two catch sight of her plump, white legs than they snorted again, and both threw themselves on her together. A struggle now ensued. The father, much heavier and stronger than the boy, got the advantage. His breeches were about his heels; his big, fat prick was out and wagged within three inches of her navel. Bella opened her legs, she longed for a taste of it. She put down her hand. It was hot as fire, and as hard as a bar of iron. Mistaking her intention, the man rudely withdrew her arm, and roughly helping himself, put the tip of his penis to the pink lips. Bella opened her young parts all in her power, and with several forcible lunges the peasant got about halfway in. Here his excitement overcame him. He discharged violently, getting right up as he did so; a stream of very thick fluid spouted into her and as the big nut lay against her womb, he sent a quantity of his semen into it.

'Eh, you are killing me!' cried the girl, half-smothered, 'what is all that you are pouring into me?'

'That's the spunk; that's what that is,' remarked Tim, as he bent down and watched the operation delightedly. 'Didn't I tell you he was a good 'un to fuck.'

Bella thought the man would now get off, and allow her to rise, but she was mistaken; the large member which was now crammed into her only seemed to grow more rigidly stiff, and to stretch her worse than ever.

Presently the peasant began to work himself up and down, pushing cruelly into Bella's young parts at each descent. His enjoyment appeared to be extreme. The discharge which had already taken place caused his truncheon to slip in and out without difficulty, and made the soft region foam with the rapid movement.

Bella gradually became dreadfully excited. Her mouth opened, her legs went up and her hands were convulsively clenched on either side. She now favoured every effort and delighted to feel the fierce plunges with which the sensual fellow buried his reeking weapon in her young belly.

For a quarter of an hour the conflict raged on both sides. Bella had discharged frequently, and was on the point of giving down a warm emission, when a furious spouting of semen rushed from the man's member and inundated the young lady's parts.

The fellow then rose, and withdrawing his dripping prick, from which the last drops of his plentiful ejection were still exuding, he stood moodily contemplating the panting figure he had released. Still threatening stood his huge rammer in front of him, yet smoking from the warm sheath, Tim, with true filial care, proceeded to wipe it tenderly and return it, pendant and swollen with its late excitement, within his father's shirt and breeches.

This done, the lad began to cast sheep's eyes on Bella, who still remained, slowly recovering herself, upon the hay. Looking and feeling, Tim, who met with no resistance, commenced to push his fingers about in the region of the young lady's private parts.

The father now came forward, and taking his son's weapon in his grasp, began to frig it up and down. It was already stiffly erected, and presented a formidable mass of flesh and muscle in Bella's face.

'Goodness me! I hope you are not going to put that into me,' murmured Bella.

'I am, though,' answered the lad, with one of his silly grins. 'Father frigs me, and I like it, and now I mean to fuck you.'

The father guided the splitter towards the girl's thighs. Her slit, already swimming in the spendings which the peasant had thrown into it, quickly received the ruby nut. Tim pushed it in, and stooping over her, shoved in the long shaft, until his hairs rubbed Bella's white skin.

'Oh, it's dreadfully long,' cried she; 'you are shockingly big, you naughty boy. Don't be so violent. Oh you kill me! How you push. Oh! you can't get in any further; pray be gentle; there, it's quite up me. I can feel it up to my waist. Oh, Tim, you horrid, bad boy!'

'Give it to her,' muttered the father, who was feeling the lad's balls, and tickling all round between his legs all the time. 'She'll take it, Tim. Ain't she a beauty? What a tight little cunt she's got, ain't she, boy?'

'Ugh, don't talk, father, I can't fuck.'

For some minutes there was silence, save for the noise of the two heaving, struggling bodies in the hay. After a while the boy stopped. His prick, though hard as iron and stiff as wax, had not apparently spent a drop. Presently, Tim pulled it right out, all smacking and glistening with moistures.

'I can't spend,' said he, mournfully.

'It's the frigging,' explained the father. 'I frig him so often that he misses it now.

Bella lay panting and all exposed.

The man now applied his hand to Tim's cock, and began vigorously rubbing it up and down. The girl expected every moment he would spend in her face.

After a while passed in thus further exciting his son, the father suddenly applied the burning nut to Bella's slit, and as it passed up, a perfect deluge of sperm issued from it and flooded her interior. Tim set himself to work to writhe and struggle, and ended by biting her in the arm.

When his discharge had quite terminated, and the last throb had passed through the boy's huge rammer, he slowly drew it out and let the girl rise.

They had no intention, however, of letting her go, for after undoing the door, the boy looked cautiously round, and then replacing the wooden bar, turned to Bella.

'What fun, wasn't it,' he remarked. 'I told you father was good at it, didn't I?'

'Yes, you did, indeed, but you must let me go now; do, there's a good boy.'

A grin was the only response.

Bella looked towards the man, and what was her terror to see him in a state of nudity, all save his shirt and boots, and with an erection that threatened another and even fiercer assault upon her charms.

His member was literally livid with the tension and stuck up against his hairy belly. The head had swollen enormously with the previous irritation, and from its tip a glistening drop hung pendant.

'You'll let me fuck you again?' enquired the man, as he caught the young lady by the waist and put her hand on his tool.

'I'll try,' murmured Bella, and seeing there was no help for it, she suggested his sitting on the hay, while straddling across his knees, she tried to insert the mass of gristly flesh.

After a few heaves and pushes it went in, and a second course, no less violent than the first, commenced. A full quarter of an hour elapsed. It was now apparently the elder who could not be brought to the point of emission.

'How tiresome they are,' thought Bella.

'Frig it, my dear,' said the man, withdrawing from her body his member, even harder than before.

Bella clasped it with both her small hands and worked it up and down. After a little of this excitement she stopped, and perceiving a small spurt of semen exude from the urethra, she quickly placed herself upon the huge pommel, and had hardly housed it before a flood of spunk rushed into her.

Bella rose and fell, thus pumping him, till all was finished, after which they let her go.

\*　　　\*　　　\*

At length the day arrived, the eventful morning broke, when the beautiful Julia Delmont was to lose that coveted treasure which is so eagerly sought after on the one hand, and often so thoughtlessly thrown away upon the other. It was still early when Bella heard her foot upon the stairs, and the two friends were no sooner united than a thousand pleasant subjects of prattle found their way into their talk, until Julia began to see that there was something which Bella was keeping back. In fact, her loquacity was simply a mask for the concealment of some piece of news which she was somewhat reluctant to break to her companion.

'I know you have something to tell me, Bella; there is something I have not heard yet which you have to tell me; what is it, darling?'

'Can't you guess,' she said, with a wicked smile playing round the dimpling corners of her rosy lips.

'Is it anything about Father Ambrose?' asked Julia. 'Oh! I feel so dreadful and awkward when I see him now, and yet he told me there was no harm in what he did.'

'No more there was, depend upon it; but what did he do?'

'Oh, more than ever. He told me such things, and then he put his arm round my waist, and kissed me, till he almost took my breath away.'

'And then,' suggested Bella.

'How can I tell you, dearest! Oh, he said and did a thousand things, until I thought I was going out of my senses.'

'Tell me some of them at least.'

'Well, you know that, after he had kissed me so hard, he put his fingers down my dress, and then he played with my foot and my stocking, and then he slipped his hand up higher, until I thought I was going to faint.'

'Oh! you little wanton, I feel sure you liked his proceedings all the while.'

'Of course I did. How could I do otherwise? He made me feel as I had never felt in my life before.'

'Come, Julia, that was not all – he did not stop there, you know.'

'Oh no; of course he did not, but I cannot tell you his next proceeding.'

'Away with such childishness,' cried Bella, pretending to be piqued at her friend's reticence. 'Why not avow all to me?'

'If I must, I suppose there is no help for it, but it seemed so shocking, being all so new to me, and yet not wrong. After he had made me feel as if I was dying of a delicious shivering sensation, which his fingers produced, he suddenly took my hand in his and placed it upon something he had which felt like a child's arm. He bid me clasp it tightly. I did as he directed me, and then looking down, I beheld a great red thing, all white skin and blue veins, with a funny, round purple top, like a plum. Well, I saw that this thing grew out from between his legs, and that it was covered below with a great mass of curly black hair.'

Julia hesitated. 'Go on,' said Bella.

'Well, he kept my hand upon it, making me rub it over and over, it was so large, and stiff, and hot!'

'No doubt it was, under the excitement of such a little beauty.'

'Then he took my other hand and placed both together on his hairy thing. I felt so frightened when I saw how his eyes glared and his breathing grew hard and quick. He reassured me. He called me his dear child and, rising, bade me fondle the stiff thing in my bosom. It stuck out close to my face.'

'Is that all?' asked Bella, persuasively.

'No, no, indeed it is not, but I feel so ashamed. Shall I go on? Is it right that I should divulge these things? Well then, after I had held this monster in my bosom a little time, during which it throbbed and pressed me with a warm delightful pressure, he asked me to kiss it. I complied at once. A warm sensuous smell arose from it, as I pressed my lips upon it. At his request I continued kissing it. He bade me open my lips and rub the top between them. A moisture came at once upon my tongue, and on an instant a thick gush of warm fluid ran into my mouth, and spurted over my face and hands. I was still playing with it when the noise of a door opening at the other end of the church obliged the good father to put away what I had hold of – 'for,' he said, 'it is not for the common people to know what you know, or to do what I permit you to do'. His manner was so kind and obliging, and he made me think I was quite different from all the other girls. But tell me, Bella, dearest, what is the mysterious news you have to tell me? I am dying to know.'

'Answer me first whether or not the good Ambrose told you of joys – of pleasures derived from the object you trifled with, and whether he pointed out any means by which such delights could be indulged without sin?'

'Of course he did – he said that in certain cases such indulgence became a merit.'

'As in marriage, for instance, I suppose.'

'He said nothing about that, except that marriage often brought much misery, and that even marriage vows might, under certain circumstances, be broken advantageously.'

Bella smiled. She recollected having heard somewhat the same strain of reasoning from the same sensual lips.

'Under what circumstances did he mean then that these joys were permitted?'

'Only when the mind was firmly set upon a good motive, beyond the actual indulgence itself, and that, he says, can only be when some young girl, selected from others for the qualities of her mind, is dedicated to the relief of the servants of religion.'

'I see,' said Bella, 'go on.'

'Then he said how good I was, and how meritorious it would be for me to exercise the privilege he endowed me with, and devote myself to the sensuous relief of himself and others whose vows prevented them from either marrying or otherwise gratifying the feeling which Nature has implanted in all men alike. But tell me, Bella, you have some news for me – I know you have.'

'Well, then, if I must – I must, I suppose. Know then, that good Father Ambrose has arranged that it will be best for you to be initiated at once, and he has provided for it here today.'

'Oh, me! You don't say so! I shall be so ashamed, so dreadfully shy.'

'Oh, no, my dear, all that has been thought of. Only so good and considerate a man as our dear confessor could have so perfectly arranged everything as he has done. It is designed that the dear man shall be able to enjoy all the beauties your witching little self can afford him, while, to make a long matter short, he will neither see your face, nor you his.'

'You don't say so! In the dark, then, I suppose?'

'By no means; that would be to forgo all the pleasures of sight, and he would lose the rich treat of looking upon those delicious charms the dear man has set his heart upon possessing.'

'How you make me blush, Bella – but how, then, is it to be?'

'It will be quite light,' explained Bella, with the air of a mother to her child. 'It will be in a nice little chamber we have; you will be laid upon a convenient couch, and your head will be passed through and concealed by a curtain which so fills a doorway leading to an inner apartment that only your body, all naked to the view, will be exposed to your ardent assailant.'

'Oh, for shame! Naked, too!'

'Oh, Julia my dear, tender Julia,' murmured Bella, as a shudder of keen ecstatic feeling rushed through her, 'what delights will be yours; how you will awake to the delicious joys of immortals and find, now that you have approached that period called puberty, the solaces which I know you already stand in need of.'

'Oh, don't Bella, pray, don't say that.'

'And when at length,' continued her companion, whose imagination had already led her into a reverie to which outward impressions were quite impervious, 'when at length the struggle is over, the spasms arrive, and that great throbbing thing shoots out its viscid stream of maddening delight, oh! then she will join that rush of ecstasy, and give down her virgin exchange.'

'What are you murmuring about?'

Bella roused herself.

'I was thinking,' she said, dreamily, 'of all the joys of which you are about to partake.'

'Oh, don't,' Julia exclaimed, 'you make me blush, when you say such dreadful things.'

Then followed a further conversation, in which many small matters had their place, and while it was in progress I found an opportunity to overhear another dialogue, quite as interesting to me, but of which I shall only furnish the summary for my readers.

It took place in the library, and occurred between Mr Delmont and Mr Verbouc. They had evidently understood each other on the main points at issue, which incredible as they may appear, were the surrender of Bella's person to Mr Delmont in consideration of a certain round sum to be then and there paid down, and afterwards its investment for the benefit of 'his dear niece', by the indulgent Mr Verbouc.

Knave and sensualist as the man was, he could not quite bring himself to the perpetration of so nefarious a transaction without some small sop to stay the conscience of even so unscrupulous a being as himself.

'Yes,' said the good and yielding uncle, 'the interests of my niece are paramount, my dear sir. A marriage is not unlikely hereafter, but the small indulgence you demand is, I think, well compensated for between us, as men of the world, you understand, purely as men of the world, by a sum sufficient to reward her for the loss of so fragile a possession.'

Here he laughed, principally because his matter-of-fact and dull-witted guest failed to understand him.

Thus it was settled, and there remained only the preliminaries to arrange. Mr Delmont was charmed, ravished out of his somewhat heavy and stolid indifference, when he was informed that the bargain was forthwith to be executed, and that he was to take possession of that delicious virginity he had so longed to destroy.

Meanwhile, the good, dear, generous Father Ambrose had been some time in the house and had prepared the chamber where the sacrifice was to take place.

Here after a sumptuous breakfast, Mr Delmont found himself with only a door between him and the victim of his lust. Who that victim was, he had not the remotest idea. He only thought of Bella.

The next moment he had turned the lock and entered the chamber, the gentle warmth of which refreshed and stimulated the sensual instincts about to be called into play.

Ye gods! What a sight burst upon his enraptured vision. Straight before him, reclining upon a couch, and utterly nude, was the body of a young girl. A glance sufficed to demonstrate the fact that it was beautiful, but it would have taken several minutes to go over in detail and discover all the separate merits of each delicious limb and member. The well-rounded limbs, child-like in their plump proportions; the delicate bosom just ripening into two of the choicest and whitest little hills of soft flesh; the roseate buds which tipped their summits; the blue veins which coursed and meandered here and there and showed through the pearly surface like little rivulets of sanguine fluid only to enhance the more dazzling whiteness of the skin. And then, oh! then, the central spot of man's desire, the rosy close-shut lips where Nature loves to revel, whence she springs and whither she returns – *la source* – it was there visible in its almost infantine perfection.

All indeed was there except – the head. That all-important member was conspicuous by its absence, and yet the gentle undulations of the fair maiden plainly evidenced that she suffered no inconvenience by its non-appearance.

Mr Delmont exhibited no astonishment at this phenomenon. He had been prepared for it, and also enjoined to maintain the strictest silence. He therefore busied himself to observe and delight himself with such charms as were prepared for his enjoyment.

Meanwhile, no sooner had he recovered from his surprise and emotion at the first view of so much naked beauty, than he found certain evidences of its effects upon those sensuous organs which so readily respond in men of his temperament to emotions calculated to produce them.

His member, hard and swollen, now stood out in his breeches and threatened to burst from its confinement. He, therefore, liberated it, and allowed a strong and gigantic weapon to spring into the light and rear its red head in the presence of its prey.

Reader, I am only a flea. I have but limited powers of perception, and I fail in ability to describe the gentle gradations and soft creeping touches by which this enraptured ravisher approached his conquest. Revelling in his security, Mr Delmont ran his eyes and his hands over all. His fingers opened the delicate slit, over which as yet only a soft down had made its appearance, while the girl, feeling the intruder in her precincts, wriggled and twisted to avoid, with the coyness natural under the circumstances, his wanton touches.

But now he draws her to him; his hot lips press the soft belly – the tender and sensitive nipples of her young breasts. With eager hand he firmly seizes her swelling hip, and pulling her towards him, opens her white legs and plants himself between.

Reader, I have already remarked I am only a flea. Yet fleas have feelings, and what mine were I will not attempt to describe when I beheld that excited member brought close to the pouting lips of Julia's moist slit. I closed my eyes; the sexual instincts of the male flea rose within me, and I longed – yes! how ardently I longed to be in Mr Delmont's place.

Meanwhile, steadily and sternly he proceeded in his work of demolition. With a sudden bound he essayed to penetrate the virgin parts of the young Julia. He failed – he tried again, and once more his baffled engine flew up and lay panting on the heaving belly of his victim.

During this trying period Julia must certainly have spoilt the plot by an outcry more or less violent but for a precaution adopted by that sage demoraliser and priest, Father Ambrose.

Julia had been drugged.

Once more Mr Delmont returned to the charge. He pushes, he forces forward, he stamps his feet upon the floor, he rages and he foams, and oh, God! the soft elastic barrier gives way and he goes in – in with a feeling of ecstatic triumph; in, until the pleasure of the tight and moist compression forces from his sealed lips a groan of pleasure. In, until his weapon, buried to the hair which covers his belly, lies throbbing and swelling yet harder and longer in its glove-like sheath.

Then followed a struggle no flea can describe – sighs of blissful and ravishing sensations escape his open slobbering lips, he pushes, he bends forward, his eyes turn up, his mouth opens, and, unable to prevent the rapid completion of his lustful pleasures, the strong man gasps out his soul and with it a torrent of seminal fluid which, thrown well forward, squirts into the womb of his own child.

All this time Ambrose had been a hidden spectator of the lustful drama, and Bella had operated on the other side of the curtain to prevent any approach to utterance on the part of her young visitor.

This precaution was, however, unnecessary; for Julia, sufficiently recovered from the effects of the narcotic to feel the smart, had fainted.

# Chapter Eleven

No sooner was the struggle over, and the victor, risen from the quivering body of the girl, beginning to recover himself from the ecstasy into which so delicious an encounter had thrown him, than suddenly the curtain was slid on one side, and Bella herself appeared in the opening.

If a cannon-shot had suddenly passed close to the astonished Mr Delmont, it could not have occasioned him one half the consternation which he felt as, hardly believing his own eyes, he stood, open-mouthed, alternately regarding the prostrate body of his victim and the apparition of her he supposed he had so recently enjoyed.

Bella, whose charming *négligé* set off to perfection her young beauties, affected to appear equally stupefied, but apparently recovering herself, she drew back a step, with a well-acted expression of alarm.

'What – what is all this?' enquired Mr Delmont, whose agitation had prevented him from remembering that he had not as yet even readjusted his clothes, and that a very important instrument in the gratification of his late sensual impulse hung, still swollen and slippery, fully exposed between his legs.

'Heavens! that I should have made such a dreadful mistake,' cried Bella, giving furtive glances at this inviting exhibition.

'Tell me, for pity's sake, what mistake, and who then, is this?' exclaimed the trembling ravisher pointing, as he spoke, to the recumbent nudity before him.

'Oh, come – come away,' cried Bella, hastily moving towards the door, closely followed by Mr Delmont, all anxiety for an explanation of the mystery.

Bella led the way into an adjoining boudoir, and closing the door firmly, she threw herself upon a luxuriously disposed couch, so as to exhibit freely her beauties, while she pretended to be too overwhelmed with her horror to notice the indelicacy of her pose.

'Oh! what have I done! what have I done!' she sobbed, hiding her face in her hands in apparent anguish.

A horrible suspicion flashed across the mind of her companion; he gasped out, half-choking with emotion: 'Speak – who is that – who?'

'It was not my fault – I could not know that it was you they had brought here for me, and – and – not knowing better – I substituted Julia.'

Mr Delmont staggered back – a confused sense of something dreadful broke upon him – a distress obstructed his vision, and then gradually he awoke to the full sense of the reality. Before, however, he could utter a word,

Bella, well instructed as to the direction his ideas would take, hastened to prevent him time to think.

'Hush! she knows nothing of it – it has been a mistake, a dreadful mistake, and nothing more. If you are disappointed, it has been my fault – not yours; you know I never thought for a moment it was to have been you. I think,' she added, with a pretty pout, and a significant side-glance at the still protruding member, 'it was very unkind of them not to have told me it was to have been you.'

Mr Delmont saw the beautiful girl before him; he could not but admit to himself that, whatever pleasures might have been his in the involuntary incest in which he had been a party, they had, nevertheless, failed of his original intention, and lost him something for which he had paid so dearly.

'Oh, if they should find out what I have done,' murmured Bella, changing a little her position, and exposing a portion of one leg above the knee.

Mr Delmont's eyes glittered. In spite of himself, as his calmness returned his animal passions were asserting themselves.

'If they should find me out,' again sighed Bella, and with that she half-rose and threw her beautiful arms round the neck of the deluded parent.

Mr Delmont pressed her in a close embrace.

'Oh, my goodness, what is this?' whispered Bella, whose little hand had seized the slimy weapon of her companion, and was now engaged in squeezing and moulding it in her warm grasp.

The wretched man felt all her touches, all her charms, and, once more rampant with lust, sought no better fate than to revel in her young virginity.

'If I must yield,' said Bella, 'be gentle with me; oh! how you touch me! Oh! take away your hand. Oh! heavens! What do you do?'

Bella had only time to catch a glimpse of his red-headed member, stiffer and more swollen than ever, and the next moment he was upon her.

Bella made no resistance and, fired by her loveliness, Mr Delmont quickly found the exact spot, and taking advantage of her inviting position, pushed with fury his already lubricated penis into her young and tender parts.

Bella groaned.

Further and further inwards went his hot dart, until their bellies met together, and he was up her body to his balls.

Then commenced a rapid and delicious encounter, in which Bella did her part to perfection, and roused by this new instrument of pleasure, went off in a torrent of delight. Mr Delmont quickly followed her example, and shot into Bella a copious flood of his prolific sperm.

For several moments both lay without motion, bathed in the exudation of their mutual raptures, and panting with their efforts, until a slight noise made itself heard, and before either had attempted to withdraw, or change from the very unequivocal position they occupied, the door of the boudoir opened, and three persons made their appearance almost simultaneously.

These were Father Ambrose, Mr Verbouc and the gentle Julia Delmont.

The two men appeared bearing between them the half-conscious figure of the young girl, whose head, languidly falling on one side, lay on the shoulders of the robust priest, while Verbouc, no less favoured by his proximity, supported her slender form by her nervous arm, and gazed in her face with a look of unsatisfied lust, such as only a devil incarnate could have equalled. Both men were in a state of hardly decent dishabille, and the unfortunate little Julia was as naked as when, scarcely a quarter of an hour before, she had been violently ravished by her own father.

'Hush!' whispered Bella, putting her hand upon the lips of her amorous companion, 'for God's sake, do not incriminate yourself. They cannot know who has done it; better suffer all than confess such a dreadful fact. They are merciless – beware how you thwart them.'

Mr Delmont instantly saw the truth of Bella's prediction.

'See, thou man of lust,' exclaimed the pious Ambrose, 'behold the state in which we found this dear child,' and placing his big hand upon the beautiful unfledged *motte* of the young Julia, he wantonly exhibited his fingers, reeking with the paternal discharge, to the others.

'Horrible,' observed Verbouc, 'and if she should be found with child!'

'Abominable,' cried Father Ambrose. 'We must, of course, prevent that.'

Delmont groaned.

Meanwhile, Ambrose and his companion led their beautiful young victim into the apartment, and commenced to cover her with those preliminary touches and lascivious pawings which precede unbridled indulgence in luxurious possession. Julia, half-awake from the effects of the sedative they had given her, and wholly confounded by the proceedings of the virtuous pair, appeared barely conscious of the presence of her parent, while that worthy, held in position by the white arms of Bella, still lay soaking on her soft white belly.

'The spunk running down her legs,' exclaimed Verbouc, eagerly inserting his hand between Julia's thighs; 'how shocking!'

'It has even reached her pretty little feet,' observed Ambrose, raising one of her rounded legs under pretence of making an examination of the delicate kid boot, upon which he had truly observed more than one gout of seminal fluid, while, with a glance of fire, he eagerly explored the rosy chink thus exposed to view.

Delmont groaned again.

'Oh, good Lord, what a beauty!' cried Verbouc, smacking the rounded buttocks. 'Ambrose, proceed to prevent any consequences from so unusual a circumstance. Nothing less than a second emission from another vigorous man can render such a thing positively safe.'

'Yes, she must have it – that is certain,' muttered Ambrose, whose state during all this time may be better imagined than described.

His cassock stuck out in front – his whole manner betrayed his violent emotions. Ambrose lifted his frock, and gave liberty to his enormous member, the ruby and inflamed head of which seemed to menace the skies.

Julia, horribly frightened, made a feeble movement to escape. Verbouc, delighted, held her in full view.

Julia beheld for the second time, the fiercely erected member of her confessor, and knowing his intention from the previous initiation she had passed through, half-fainted with trembling fear.

Ambrose, as if to outrage the feelings of both, father and daughter, exposed fully his huge genitals and wagged his gigantic penis in their faces.

Delmont, overcome with terror, and finding himself in the hands of the two conspirators, held his breath and cowered by the side of Bella, who, delighted beyond measure by the success of the scheme, kept counselling him to remain neutral and let them have their will.

Verbouc, who had been fingering the moistened parts of the little Julia, now yielded her to the furious lust of his friend, and prepared himself for his favourite pastime of watching her violation.

The priest, beside himself with lubricity, divested himself of his nether garments and, his member standing grimly all the while, proceeded to the delicious task which awaited him. 'She is mine at last,' he murmured, and seizing his prey, he passed his arms around her and lifted her from the ground. Bearing the trembling Julia to an adjoining sofa, he threw himself upon her naked body and endeavoured with all his might to accomplish his enjoyment. His monstrous weapon, hard as iron, battered at the little pink slit which, although already lubricated with the semen she had received from Mr Delmont, was no easy sheath for the gigantic penis which threatened her.

Ambrose continued his efforts. Mr Delmont could only see a heaving mass of black silk, as the robust figure of the priest writhed upon the form of his little daughter. Too experienced to be long held in check, however, Ambrose felt himself gaining ground, and too much master of himself to allow the pleasure to overtake him too soon, he now bore down all opposition, and a loud shriek from Julia announced the penetration of the huge rammer.

Cry succeeded cry, until Ambrose, at length firmly buried in the belly of the young girl, felt he could go no further, and commenced those delicious pumping movements which were to end at the same moment his pleasure and the torture of his victim.

Meanwhile Verbouc, whose lustful emotions had been intensely excited by the scene between Mr Delmont and Julia, and subsequently by that between the foolish man and his niece, now rushed towards Bella, and releasing her from the relaxing embrace of his unfortunate friend, at once opened her legs, regarded for a moment her reeking orifice, and then at one bound buried himself in an agony of pleasure in her belly, well anointed by the abundance of spunk which had been already discharged there. The two couples now performed their delicious copulation in silence, save for the groans which came from the half-murdered Julia, the stentorian breathing of the fierce Ambrose, and now the grunts and sobs of Mr Verbouc. Faster and more delicious grew the race. Ambrose, having forced his gigantic penis up to the curling mass of black hair which covered its root into the tight slit of the young girl, became perfectly livid with lust. He pushed, he drove, he tore her open with the force of a bull; and had not Nature at length asserted herself in his favour by bringing his ecstasy to a climax, he must have succumbed to his excitement in an attack which would probably have for ever prevented a repetition of such a scene.

A loud cry came from Ambrose. Verbouc well knew its import, he was discharging. His friend's rapture served to quicken his own. A howl of passionate lust arose within the chamber as the two monsters loaded their victims with their seminal outpourings. Not once, but three times did the priest shoot his prolific essence into the very womb of the tender girl before he assuaged his raging fever of desire.

As it was, to say that Ambrose simply discharged would give but a faint idea of the fact. He positively spurted his semen into the little Julia in thick and powerful jets, uttering all the while groans of ecstasy as each hot and slippery injection rushed along his huge urethra and flew in torrents into the stretched receptacle. It was some minutes ere all was over, and the brutal priest arose from his torn and bleeding victim.

At the same time Mr Verbouc left exposed the opened thighs and besmeared slit of his niece, who lying still in the dreamy trance which follows the fierce delight, took no heed of the thick exuding drops which formed a white pool upon the floor between her well-stockinged legs.

'Ah, how delicious,' exclaimed Verbouc; 'you see, there is pleasure after all in the path of duty, Delmont, is there not?' turning to that dumbfounded individual. 'If Father Ambrose and myself had not mixed our humble offerings with that prolific essence of which you seem to have made such good use, there is no knowing what mischief might have ensued. Oh, yes, nothing like doing the thing which is right, eh, Delmont?'

'I don't know. I feel ill; I am in a kind of dream, yet I am not insensible of sensations which cause me renewed delight. I cannot doubt your friendship – your secrecy. I have much enjoyed, I am still excited, I know not what I want! – Say something, my friends.'

Father Ambrose approached, and laying his big hand on the shoulder of the poor man, he encouraged him with a few whispered words of comfort.

As a flea I am not at liberty to mention what these were, but their effect was to dissipate in a great measure the cloud of horror which oppressed Mr Delmont. He sat down and gradually grew more calm.

Julia also had now recovered, and seated on either side of the burly priest, the two young girls ere long felt comparatively at ease. The holy father spoke to them like a father and he drew Mr Delmont from his reserve, and that worthy, having copiously refreshed himself with a considerable libation of rich wine, began to evince evident pleasure in the society in which he found himself.

Soon the invigorating effects of the wine began to tell upon Mr Delmont. He cast wistful and envious glances towards his daughter. His excitement was evident, and showed itself in the bulging of his garments.

Ambrose perceived his desire and encouraged it. He led him to Julia, who, still naked, had no means of concealing her charms. The parent looked on all with an eye in which lust predominated. A second time would not be so very much more sinful, he thought.

Ambrose nodded his encouragement. Bella unbuttoned his nether garment, and taking his stiff prick in her hand, squeezed it softly.

Mr Delmont understood the position, and the next moment was upon his child. Bella guided the incestuous member to the soft red lips; a few pushes and the half-maddened father was fully entered in the belly of his pretty child.

The struggle that followed was intensified by the circumstances of his horrible connection. After a fierce and rapid course, Mr Delmont discharged and his daughter received in the utmost recesses of her young womb the guilty spendings of her unnatural parent.

Father Ambrose, whose sensual character thoroughly predominated, owned one other weakness, and that was preaching; he would preach by the hour together, not so much on religious subjects as on others much more mundane, and certainly not usually sanctioned by Holy Mother Church.

On this occasion he delivered a discourse which I found it impossible to follow, and went to sleep in Bella's armpit until he had done.

How far in the future this consummation might have been, I know not, but the gentle Bella, having obtained a hold of his great lolling affair in her little white hand, so pressed and tickled it that the good man was feign to pause by reason of the sensation she produced.

Mr Verbouc also, who, it will be remembered, coveted nothing so much as a buttered bun, knew only too well how splendidly buttered were the delicious little parts of the newly-converted Julia. The presence of the father also – worse than helpless to prevent the utmost enjoyment of his child by these two libidinous men – served to whet his appetite, while Bella, who felt the slime oozing from her warm slit, was also conscious of certain longings which her previous encounters had not appeased.

Verbouc commenced again to visit with his lascivious touches the sweet and childish charms of Julia, impudently moulding her round buttocks and slipping his fingers between their rounded hillocks.

Father Ambrose, not less active, had got his arm round Bella's waist, and putting her half-nude form close to him, he sucked licentious kisses from her pretty lips.

As the two men continued these toyings, their desires proportionately advanced until their weapons, red and inflamed by previous enjoyments, stood firmly in the air, and stiffly menaced the young creatures in their power.

Ambrose, whose lust never wanted much incentive, quickly possessed himself of Bella, who, nothing loth, let him press her down upon the sofa which had witnessed already two encounters, and still further exciting his skinned and flaming pogo, the daring girl let it enter between her white thighs, and favouring the disproportionate attack as much as she could, she received its whole terrible build in her moistened slit.

This sight so worked upon the feelings of Mr Delmont, that he evidently needed small encouragement to attempt a second *coup* when the priest had done.

Mr Verbouc, who had for some time been throwing lascivious glances towards Mr Delmont's young daughter, now found himself once more in a condition to enjoy. He reflected that the repeated violation she had already experienced at the hands of her father and the priest had fitted her for the part he loved to play, and he knew, both by touch and sight, that her parts were sufficiently oiled by the violent discharges she had received to gratify his dearest whim.

Verbouc gave a glance towards the priest, who was now engaged in the delicious enjoyment of his niece, and then closing upon the beautiful Julia to take his turn, he succeeded in reversing her upon the couch and with considerable effort thrust his stout member to the balls into her delicate body.

This new and intensified enjoyment brought Verbouc to the verge of madness; he pressed himself into the tight and glove-like slit of the young girl, and throbbed all over with delight.

'Oh, she is heaven itself!' he murmured, pressing in his big member to the balls, which were gathered up tightly below. 'Good Lord, what tightness – what slippery pleasure – ugh!' and another determined thrust made poor Julia groan again.

Meanwhile Father Ambrose, with eyes half-shut, lips parted, and nostrils dilated, was battering the beautiful parts of the young Bella, whose sensual gratification became evident in her sobs of pleasure.

'Oh! my goodness! You are – you are too big – enormous! Your great thing. Oh! it's up to my waist. Oh, oh! it's too much; not so hard – dear father – how you push! – you will kill me. Ah! gently – go slower – I feel your great balls at my bottom.'

'Stop a moment,' cried Ambrose, whose pleasure had become insupportable, and whose spunk was nearly provoked to rush out of him. 'Let us pause. Shall I change with you, my friend? The idea is lovely.'

'No, oh, no! I cannot move, I can only go on – this dear child is perfect enjoyment.'

'Be still, Bella, dear child or you will make me spend. Don't squeeze my weapon so rapturously.'

'I cannot help it – you kill me with pleasure. Oh! go on, but gently. Oh, not so hard! Don't push so fiercely. Heavens! he's going to spend. His eyes close, his lips open. My God! you kill me – you slit me up with that big thing. Ah! Oh! Come then! Spend, dear – Father – Ambrose. Give me the burning spunk. Oh! push now harder – harder – kill me, if you like.'

Bella threw her white arms round his brawny neck, opened wide her soft and beautiful thighs, and took in his huge instrument, until his hairy belly rubbed on her downy mount.

Ambrose felt himself about to go off in rapturous emission right into the body of the girl under him.

'Push – push now!' cried Bella, regardless of all modesty, and giving down her own discharge in spasms of pleasure. 'Push – push – drive it up me. Oh, yes, like that. Ah, God, what a size! What a length – you slit me, brute that you are. Oh, oh! oh! You are off – I feel it. Oh, God what spunk! Oh, what gushes!'

Ambrose discharged furiously, like the stallion that he was, thrusting with all his might into the warm belly below.

He then reluctantly withdrew, and Bella, released from his clutches, turned to regard the other pair. Her uncle was administering a shower of short thrusts at her little friend, and it was evident a climax must soon be put to his enjoyment.

Meanwhile, Julia, whose recent violation and subsequent hard treatment by the brutal Ambrose had sadly hurt and enfeebled her, had not the slightest pleasure, but lay an unresisting and inert mass in the arms of her ravisher.

When, therefore, after a few more pushes, Verbouc fell forward in a voluptuous discharge, she was only aware that something warm and wet was being rapidly injected into her, without experiencing any other sensations than languor and fatigue.

Another pause followed this third outrage, during which Mr Delmont subsided into a corner and appeared to be dozing. A thousand pleasantries now took place. Ambrose, while reclining upon the couch, made Bella stride over him, and applying his lips to her reeking slit, luxuriated in kisses and touches of the most lascivious and depraved nature.

Mr Verbouc, not to be behindhand with his companion, played off several equally libidinous inventions upon the innocent Julia.

The two then laid her flat upon the couch, and felt over all her beauties, lingering with admiration upon her yet unfledged *motte*, and the red lips of her young cunt.

After a time the desires of both were seconded by the outward and visible signs of two standing members, eager again for a taste of pleasures so ecstatic and select.

A new programme was now, however, to be inaugurated. Ambrose was the first to propose it. 'We have had enough of their cunts,' said he, coarsely, turning to Verbouc, who had passed over to Bella, and was playing with her nipples. 'Let us try what their bottoms are made of. This lovely little creature would be a treat for the Pope himself, and ought to have buttocks of velvet and a *derrière* fit for an emperor to spend into.'

The idea was instantly seized upon, and the victims secured. It was abominable, it was monstrous, it was apparently impossible when viewed in all its disproportionate character. The enormous member of the priest was presented to the small aperture of Julia's posterior – that of Verbouc threatened his niece in the same direction. A quarter of an hour was consumed in the preliminaries, and after a frightful scene of lust and lechery, the two girls received in their bowels the burning jets of their impious discharges.

At length a calm succeeded to the violent emotions which had over-whelmed the actors in this monstrous scene.

Attention was at length directed to Mr Delmont.

That worthy, as I have before remarked, was quietly ensconced in a corner, apparently overcome with sleep, or wine, or possibly both.

'How quiet he is,' observed Verbouc.

'An evil conscience is a sad companion,' remarked Father Ambrose, whose attentions were directed to the ablution of his lolling instrument.

'Come, my friend – it is your turn now, here is a treat for you,' continued Verbouc, exhibiting for the edification of all the most secret parts of the almost insensible Julia; 'come and enjoy this. – Why, what is the matter with the man? Good heavens, why – how – what is this?'

Verbouc recoiled a step.

Father Ambrose leant over the form of the wretched Delmont – he felt his heart.

'He is dead,' he said, quietly – and so it was.

## Chapter Twelve

Sudden death is so common an event, especially among persons whose previous history has led to the supposition of the existence of some organic deterioration, that surprise easily gives place to ordinary expressions of condolence, and this again to a state of resignation at a result by no means to be wondered at.

The transition may be thus expressed: 'Who would have thought it?'

'Is it possible?'

'I always had my suspicions.'

'Poor fellow!'

'Nobody ought to be surprised!'

This interesting formula was duly gone through when poor Mr Delmont paid the debt to Nature, as the phrase goes.

A fortnight after that unfortunate gentleman had departed this life, his friends were all convinced they had long ago detected symptoms which must sooner or later prove fatal; they rather prided themselves on their sagacity, reverently admitting the inscrutability of Providence.

As for me, I went about much as usual, except that for a change I fancied Julia's legs had a more piquant flavour than Bella's and I accordingly bled them regularly for my repast matutinal and nocturnal.

What could be more natural than that Julia should pass much of her time with her dear friend Bella, and what more likely than that the sensual Father Ambrose and his patron, the lecherous relative of my dear Bella, should seek to repeat their experiences upon the young and docile girl!

That they did so, I knew full well, for my nights were most uneasy and uncomfortable, always liable to interruption from the incursions of long hairy tools among the pleasant groves wherein I had temporarily located myself; intruders which frequently nearly drowned me in a thick and frightfully glutinous torrent of animal semen.

In short, the young and impressionable Julia was easily and completely broken up, and Ambrose and his friend revelled to their heart's content in her complete possession.

They had gained their ends, what mattered the sacrifice to them?

Meanwhile other and very different ideas were occupying the mind of Bella, whom I had abandoned, and feeling, at length, a degree of nausea from too frequent indulgence in my new diet, I resolved to vacate the stockings of the pretty Julia and return – *revenir à mon mouton*, as I might say – to the sweet and succulent pastures of the prurient Bella.

I did so, and *voici le resultat!*

One evening Bella retired to rest rather later than usual. Father Ambrose was absent upon a mission to a distant parish, and her dear and indulgent uncle was laid up with a sharp attack of gout, to which he had lately become more subject. The girl had already arranged her hair for the night. She had also denuded herself of her upper garments and was in the act of putting her *chemise de nuit* over her head, in the process of which she inadvertently allowed her petticoats to fall and display before the glass her beautiful proportions and exquisitely soft and transparent skin.

So much beauty might have fired an anchorite, but alas! there was no such ascetic there present to be inflamed. As for me, she only nearly broke my longest feeler and twisted my right jumper, as she whirled the warm garment in the air above her head.

One present there was, however, whom Bella had not counted upon, but upon whom, it is needless to say, nothing was lost.

And now I must explain that ever since the crafty Father Clement had been denied Bella's charms, he had sworn a very unclerical and beastly oath to renew the attempt to surprise and capture the pretty fortress he had once already stormed and ravished. The remembrance of his happiness brought tears into his sensual little eyes, and a certain distension sympathetically imparted itself to his enormous member.

Clement in fact had sworn a fearful oath to fuck Bella in a natural state, in her own unvarnished words, and I, flea though I be, heard and understood their import.

The night was dark; the rain fell – Ambrose was absent. Verbouc was ill and helpless – Bella would be alone – all this was perfectly well known to Clement, and accordingly he made the attempt. Improved by his recent experience in his geography of the neighbourhood, he went straight to the window of Bella's chamber, and finding it, as he expected, unfastened and open, he coolly entered and crept beneath the bed. From this position Clement beheld with throbbing veins the toilette of the beautiful Bella until the moment when she commenced to throw off her chemise, as I have already explained. In so doing Clement saw the nudity of the girl in full view, and snorted internally like a bull. From his recumbent position he had no difficulty in viewing the whole of her body from the waist down, and as she faced from him, his eyes glistened as he saw the lovely twin globes of her bottom opening and shutting as the graceful girl twisted her lithe figure in the act of passing the chemise over her head.

Clement could restrain himself no longer; his desires rose to boiling point, and softly but swiftly gliding from his concealment, he arose behind her and without an instant's loss of time clasped her naked body in his arms, placing as he did so, one of his fat hands over her rosy mouth.

Bella's first instinct was to scream, but that feminine resource was denied her. Her next was to faint, and this she probably would have done but for one circumstance. This was the fact that, as the audacious intruder held her close to him, a certain something, hard, long and warm, very sensibly pressed inwards between her smooth buttocks and lay throbbing in their separation and up along her back. At this critical moment Bella's eyes encountered their image reflected in the opposite toilet-glass, and she recognised, over her shoulder, the inflamed and ugly visage, crowned by the shock circle of red hair, of the sensual priest.

Bella understood the situation in the twinkling of an eye. It was nearly a week since she had received the embraces of either Ambrose or her uncle, and this fact had no doubt something to do with the conclusion she formed on this trying occasion. What she had been on the point of doing in reality, the lewd girl now only simulated.

She allowed herself to recline gently back upon the stout figure of Clement, and that happy individual, believing she was really fainting, at once withdrew his hand from her mouth and supported her in his arms.

The unresisting position of so much loveliness excited Clement almost to madness. She was nearly naked, and he ran his hands over her polished skin. His immense weapon, already stiff and distended with impatience, now palpitated with passion, as he held the beautiful girl in his close embrace.

Clement tremblingly drew her face to his, and imprinted a long and voluptuous kiss upon her sweet lips.

Bella shuddered and opened her eyes.

Clement renewed his caresses.

The young girl sighed.

'Oh!' she exclaimed, softly, 'how dare you come here? Pray, pray leave me at once – it is shameful.'

Clement grinned. He was always ugly – now he looked positively hideous in his strong lust.

'So it is,' said he, 'shameful to treat such a pretty girl like this; but then, it's so delicious, my darling.'

Bella sobbed.

More kisses, and a roving of hands over the naked girl. A great uncouth hand settled over the downy mount, and a daring finger, separating the dewy lips, entered the warm slit and touched the sensitive clitoris.

Bella closed her eyes, and repeated the sigh. That sensitive little organ instantly commenced to develop itself. It was by no means diminutive in the case of my young friend, and under the lascivious fingering of the ugly Clement, it arose, stiffened and stuck out, until it almost parted the lips of its own accord.

Bella was fired – desire beamed in her eyes; she had caught the infection, and stealing a glance at her seducer, she noticed the terrible look of rampant lust which spread itself over his face as he toyed with her secret young charms.

The girl trembled with agitation; an earnest longing for the pleasure of coition took absolute possession of her, and unable longer to control her desires, she quickly insinuated her right hand behind her, and grasped, but could not span, the huge weapon which drove against her bottom.

Their eyes met – lust raged in those of both. Bella smiled, Clement repeated his sensual kiss, and insinuated his lolling tongue within her mouth. The girl was not slow to second his lecherous embraces, and allowed him full liberty of action, both as to his roving hands and active kisses. Gradually he pressed her towards a chair, and Bella, sinking upon it, awaited impatiently the next overtures of the priest.

Clement stood exactly in front of her. His cassock of black silk, which reached to his heels, bulged out in front, while his cheeks, fiery red with the violence of his desires, were only rivalled by the smoking lips, as he breathed excitedly in the ecstasy of anticipation.

He saw that he had nothing to fear and everything to enjoy.

'This is too much,' murmured Bella, 'go away.'

'Oh! impossible now I have had the trouble of getting here.'

'But you may be discovered, and I should be ruined.'

'Not likely – you know we are quite alone and not at all likely to be disturbed. Besides, you are so delicious, my child, so fresh, so young and beautiful – there, don't withdraw your leg. I was only putting my hand on your soft thigh. In fact, I want to fuck you, my darling.'

Bella saw the huge projection give a flip up.

'How nasty you are! – What words you use.'

'Do I, my little pet, my angel,' said Clement, again seizing on the sensitive clitoris, which he moulded between his finger and thumb; 'they are all prompted by the pleasure of feeling this pouting little cunt that is slyly trying to evade my touches.'

'For shame!' exclaimed Bella, laughing in spite of herself.

Clement came close and stooped over her, as she sat; he took her pretty face between his fat hands. As he did so, Bella was conscious that his cassock, already bulging out with the force of the desires communicated to his truncheon, was within a few inches of her bosom.

She could detect the throbs with which the black silk garment gradually rose and fell. The inclination was irresistible; she put her delicate little hand under the priest's vestment, and lifting up sufficient of it, felt a great hairy mass, which contained two balls as large as fowl's eggs.

'Oh, my goodness, how enormous!' whispered the young girl.

'All full of the beautiful thick spunk,' sighed Clement, playing with the two pretty breasts which were so close to him.

Bella shifted her ground, and once more grasped with both hands the strong and stiffened body of an enormous penis.

'How dreadful, what a monster!' exclaimed the lewd girl. 'It is a big one, indeed; what a size you are!'

'Yes, isn't that a cock?' observed Clement, pushing forward and holding up his cassock the better to bring the gigantic affair into view.

Bella could not resist the temptation, but raising still higher the man's garment, released his penis entirely, and exposed it at full stretch.

Fleas are bad measurers of size and space, and I forbear to give any exact dimensions of the weapon upon which the young lady now cast her eyes. It was gigantic, however, in its proportions. It had a large and dull red head, which stood shining and naked at the end of a long gristly shaft. The hole at the tip, usually so small, was, in this instance, a considerable slit, and was moist with the seminal humidity which gathered there. Along the whole shaft coursed the swollen blue veins, and behind all was a matted profusion of red bristling hair. Two huge testicles hung below.

'Good heavens! Oh, Holy Mother!' murmured Bella, shutting her eyes and giving it a slight squeeze.

The broad, red head, distended and purple with the effect of the exquisite tickling of the girl, was now totally uncapped, and stood stiffly up from the folds of loose skin, which Bella pressed back upon the great white shaft. Bella toyed delightedly with this acquisition, and pressed still further back the velvety skin beneath her hand.

Clement sighed.

'Oh, you delicious child,' he said gazing at her with sparkling eyes; 'I must fuck you at once, or I shall throw it all over you.'

'No, no you must not waste any of it,' exclaimed Bella; 'how pressed you must be to want to come so soon.'

'I cannot help it – pray, remain quiet a moment or I shall spend.'

'What a big thing – how much can you do?'

Clement stopped and whispered something into the girl's ear, which I could not catch.

'Oh, how delicious, but it is incredible.'

'No, it is true, only give me the chance. Come, I am longing to prove it to you, pretty one – see this! I must fuck you!'

He shook the monstrous penis, as he stood in front of her. Then, bending it down, he suddenly let it go. It sprang up, and as it did so, the skin went back of its own accord, and the big red nut came out with the opened urethra exuding a drop of semen.

It was close below Bella's face. She was sensible of a faint, sensuous odour, which came up from it and increased the disorder of her senses. She continued to finger and play with it.

'Stop, I entreat you, my darling, or you will waste it in the air.'

Bella remained quiet a few seconds. Her warm hand still clasped as much as she could of Clement's prick. He amused himself meanwhile in moulding her young breasts, and in working his fingers up and down in her moist cunt. The play made her wild. Her clitoris grew hot and prominent; her breathing became hard and her pretty face flushed with longing.

Harder and harder grew the nut, it shone like a ripe plum. Bella's was crimson with desire; she furtively regarded the ugly man's naked and hairy belly – his brawny thighs, thickly covered also with hair like an ape. His great cock, each moment more swollen, menaced the skies, and caused her indescribable emotions.

Excited beyond measure, she wound her white arms around the stout figure of the great brute and covered him with rapturous kisses. His very ugliness increased her libidinous sensations.

'No, you must not waste it, I cannot let you waste it,' and then, pausing for a second, she moaned with a peculiar articulation of pleasure and, lowering her fair head, opened her rosy mouth and instantly received as much of the lascivious morsel as she could cram into it.

'Oh! how nice; how you tickle – what – what pleasure you give me.'

'I will not let you waste it. I will swallow every drop,' whispered Bella, raising her mouth for a moment from the glistening nut.

Then again sinking her face forward, she pressed her pouting lips upon the big tip, and parting them gently and delicately, received the orifice of the wide urethra between them.

'Oh, Holy Mother!' exclaimed Clement, 'this is heaven! How I shall spend! Good Lord! how you tickle and suck.'

Bella applied her pointed tongue to the orifice and licked it all round.

'How nice it tastes; you have already let out a drop or two.'

'I cannot continue, I know I cannot,' murmured the priest, pushing forward and tickling with his finger at the same time the swollen clitoris that Bella put within his reach. Then she took the head of the great cock again between her lips, but she could not make the whole of the nut enter her mouth, it was so monstrously large.

Tickling and sucking – passing back in slow delicious movements the skin which surrounded the red and sensitive ridge of his tremendous thing, Bella now evidently invited the result she knew could not long be delayed.

'Ah, Holy Mother! I am almost coming; I feel – I – Oh! oh! now suck. You've got it.'

Clement lifted his arm in the air, his head fell back, his legs straddled wide apart, his hands worked convulsively, his eyes turned up, and Bella felt a strong spasm pass through the monstrous cock. The next moment she was almost knocked backwards by a forcible gush of semen which rushed spouting in a continuous stream from his genitals and flew in torrents down her gullet.

In spite of all her wishes and endeavours, the greedy girl could not avoid a stream issuing from the corners of her mouth as Clement, beside himself with pleasure, kept pushing forward in sharp jerks, each one of which sent a fresh jet of spunk down her throat. Bella followed all his movements, and held fast hold of the streaming weapon until all was done.

'How much did you say?' muttered she, 'one tea-cupful – there were two.'

'You beautiful darling,' exclaimed Clement, when at last he found breath. 'What divine pleasure you have given me. Now it is my turn, and you must let me examine all I love in those little parts of yours.'

'Ah, how nice it was; I am nearly choked,' cried Bella. 'How slippery it was, and, oh, goodness, what a lot!'

'Yes. I promised you plenty, my pretty one, and you so excited me that I know you must have received a good dose of it. It ran in streams.'

'Yes, indeed it did.'

'Now I am going to suck your pretty cunt, and fuck you deliciously afterwards.'

Suiting the action to the word, the sensual priest threw himself between Bella's milk white thighs, and thrusting his face forward, plunged his tongue between the lips of the pinky slit. Then rolling it around the stiffened clitoris, he commenced a titillation so exquisite that the girl could hardly restrain her cries.

'Oh, my goodness. Oh, you suck my life out. Oh! I am – I am going off. I spend!' and, with a sudden forward movement towards his active tongue, Bella emitted most copiously upon his face, and Clement received all he could catch in his mouth with the delight of an epicure.

At length the priest arose; his big weapon, which had scarcely softened, had now resumed its virile tension, and stuck out from him in a terrible erection. He positively snorted with lust as he regarded the beautiful and willing girl.

'Now I must fuck you,' said he, as he thrust her towards the bed. 'Now I must have you, and give you a taste of this cock in your little belly. Oh, what a mess there'll be!'

Hastily throwing off his cassock and nether garments, he compelled the sweet girl likewise to denude herself of her chemise, and then the great brute, his big body all covered with hair and brown as a mulatto, took the lily form of the beautiful Bella in his muscular arms and tossed her lightly on the bed. Clement regarded for a moment her extended figure as, palpitating with mingled desire and terror, she awaited the terrible onslaught; then he looked complacently upon his tremendous penis, erect with lust, and hastily mounting, threw himself upon her and drew the bedclothes over him.

Bella, half-smothered beneath the great hairy brute, felt his stiff cock interposed between their bellies. Passing down her hand, she touched it again.

'Good heavens! what a size, it will never go into me.'

'Yes, yes – we will get it in, all of it, up to the balls, only you must help or I shall probably hurt you.'

Bella was saved the trouble of a reply, for the next moment an eager tongue was in her mouth and almost choking her.

Then she became aware that the priest had raised himself slightly, and that the hot head of his gigantic cock was pressing inwards between the moist lips of her little rosy slit.

I cannot go through the gradations of that preliminary conjuncture. It was full ten minutes in the accomplishment, but in the end ungainly Clement lay buried to the balls in the pretty body of the girl, while with her soft legs raised and thrown over his brawny back, she received his lascivious caresses. Thus planted, he gloated over his victim and commenced those lustful movements which would result in his ridding himself of more scalding fluid.

At least ten inches of stiff nervous muscle lay soaking and throbbing in the little girl's belly, while a mass of coarse hair pressed the battered and delicate mount of poor Bella.

'Oh, my! Oh! my, how you hurt,' moaned she. 'My God! you are splitting me up.'

Clement moved.

'I can't bear it – you are too big, indeed. Oh! take it out. Ah, what thrusts.'

Clement pushed mercilessly two or three times. 'Wait a second, my little devil, until I smother you with my spunk. Oh, how tight you are. How you seem to suck my cock – There, it's in now, you have it all.'

'Oh, mercy.'

Clement thrust hard and rapidly – push followed push – he squirmed and writhed on the soft figure of the girl. His lust rose hot and furious. His huge penis was strained to bursting in the intensity of his pleasure and the tickling, maddening delight of the moment.

'Ah, now I am fucking you at last.'

'Fuck me,' murmured Bella, opening still wider her pretty legs, as the intensity of the sensations gained upon her. 'Oh, fuck me hard – harder,' and with a deep moan of rapture she deluged her brutal ravisher with a copious discharge, pushing upwards at the same moment to meet a dreadful lunge. Bella's legs were jerked up and down, while Clement thrust himself between, and forced his long, hot member in and out in luscious movements. Soft sighs, mingled with kissings from the set lips of the lusty intruder, occasional moans of rapture and the rapid vibrations of the bedstead all bespoke the excitement of the scene.

Clement needed no invitation. The emission of his fair companion had supplied him with the moistening medium he desired, and he took advantage of it to commence a rapid series of in-and-out movements, which caused Bella as much pleasure as pain.

The girl seconded him with all her power. Gorged to repletion, she heaved and quivered beneath his sturdy strokes. Her breath came in sobs, her eyes closed in the fierce pleasure of an almost constant spasm of emission. The buttocks of her ugly lover opened and shut, as he strained himself at every lunge into the body of the pretty child.

After a long course he paused a moment.

'I can't hold any longer, I'm going to spend. Take my spunk, Bella, you will have floods of it, pretty one.'

Bella knew it – every vein in his monstrous cock was swollen to its utmost tension. It was insupportably big. It resembled nothing so much as the gigantic member of an ass.

Clement began to move again – the saliva ran from his mouth. With an ecstatic sensation, Bella awaited the coming seminal shower.

Clement gave one or two short, deep thrusts, then groaned and lay still, only quivering slightly all over.

Then a tremendous spout of semen issued from his prick and deluged the womb of the young girl. The big brute buried his head in the pillows and forced himself in with his feet against the bedstead end.

'Oh, the spunk,' screamed Bella. 'I feel it. What streams, Oh, give it me. Holy Mother! What pleasure it is!'

'There, there, take that,' cried the priest, as once more, at the first rush of semen into her, he pushed wildly up her belly, sending at each thrust a further warm squirt into her.

'There, there. Oh, what pleasure!'

Whatever had been Bella's anticipations, she had had no idea of the immense quantity this stalwart man could discharge. He pumped it out in thick masses, and splashed it into her very womb.

'Oh, I am spending again,' and Bella sank, half-fainting, beneath the strong man, while his burning fluid continued still to dart from him in viscid jets.

Five times more that night Bella received the glutinous contents of Clement's big balls, and had not daylight warned them it was time to part, he would have recommenced.

When the astute Clement cleared the house, and hastened, as the day broke, to his humble quarter, he was forced to admit he had had his belly full of pleasure, even as Bella had had her belly full of spunk. As for that young lady, it was lucky for her that her two protectors were incapacitated, or they must have discovered in the painful and swollen condition of her young parts that an interloper had been trespassing on their preserves.

Youth is elastic – everyone says so. Bella was young and very elastic. If you had seen Clement's immense machine you would have said so. Her natural elasticity enabled her not only to sustain the introduction of this battering-ram, but also in about a couple of days to feel none the worse for it.

Three days after this interesting episode Father Ambrose returned. One of his first cares was to seek Bella. He found her, and invited her to follow him to a boudoir.

'See,' cried he producing his tool, inflamed and standing at attention, 'I have had no amusement for a week; my cock is bursting, Bella, dear.'

Two minutes later her head was reclining on the table of the apartment, while, with her clothes thrown completely over her head, and her swelling posteriors fully exposed, the salacious priest regarded her round buttocks and slapped them vigorously with his long member. Another minute and he had pushed his instrument into her from behind, until his black frizzly hair pressed against her bottom. Only a few thrusts brought from him a gush of spunk, and he sent a shower up to her waist.

The good father was too much excited by long abstinence to lose his rigidity, and drawing down his stalwart tool, he presented it, all slippery and smoking, at the tight little entrance between those delicious buttocks. Bella favoured him, and well anointed as he was, he slipped in, and gave her another tremendous dose from his prolific testicles. Bella felt the fervent discharge, and welcomed the hot spunk as he discharged it up her bowels. Then he turned her over on the table, and sucked her clitoris for a quarter of an hour, making her discharge twice in his mouth, at the end of which time he employed her in the natural way.

Then Bella went to her chamber and purified herself, and, after a slight rest, put on her walking dress and went out.

That evening Mr Verbouc was reported worse, the attack had reached regions which caused serious anxiety to his medical attendant. Bella wished her uncle a good-night and retired.

Julia had installed herself in Bella's room for the night, and the two young friends, by this time well enlightened as to the nature and properties of the male sex, lay exchanging ideas and experiences.

'I thought I was killed,' said Julia, 'when father Ambrose pushed that great ugly thing of his up my poor little belly, and when he finished I thought he was in a fit, and could not understand what that slippery warm stuff could be which kept splashing into me, but, oh . . . !'

'Then, my dear, you commenced to feel the friction on that sensitive little thing of yours, and Father Ambrose's hot spunk spurted all over it.'

'Yes, that it did. I am always smothered, Bella, when he does it.'

'Hush! What was that?'

Both the girls sat up and listened. Bella, better accustomed to the peculiarities of her chamber than Julia could be, turned her attention to the window. As she did so, the shutter gradually opened, and there appeared a man's head. Julia saw the apparition, and was just about to scream, when Bella motioned her to keep silence.

'Hush! Don't be alarmed,' whispered Bella, 'he won't eat us, only it's too bad of him to disturb one in this cruel fashion.'

'What does he want?' asked Julia, half-hiding her pretty head under the clothes, but keeping a bright eye all the time upon the intruder.

All this time the man was preparing to enter, and having sufficiently opened the shutter, he squeezed his large figure through the opening, and alighting in the middle of the floor, disclosed the bulky form and ugly sensual features of Father Clement.

'Holy Mother! A priest,' exclaimed Bella's young visitor, 'and a fat one, too. Oh! Bella, what does he want?'

'We shall soon see what he wants,' whispered the other.

Meanwhile, Clement had approached the bed.

'What? Is it possible? A double treat,' he exclaimed. 'Delightful Bella, this is indeed, an unexpected pleasure.'

'For shame, Father Clement.'

Julia had disappeared under the bedclothes.

In two minutes the priest had stripped himself of his raiment, and without so much as waiting for an invitation, darted into the bed.

'Oh, my!' cried Julia, 'he's touching me.'

'Ah, yes, we shall both be touched, that is certain,' murmured Bella, as she felt Clement's huge weapon pressing close up to her back. 'What a shame for you to come in here without any permission.'

'Shall I go then, pretty one?' said the priest, putting his stiff tool into Bella's hand.

'You may stay, now you're here.'

'Thank you,' whispered Clement lifting one of Bella's legs, and inserting the big head of his cock from behind.

Bella felt the thrust and mechanically seized Julia round the loins.

Clement thrust once more, but Bella, with a sudden bound, jerked him out. Then she rose, turned back the clothes, and exposed both the hairy body of the priest, and also the fairy form of her companion.

Julia turned instinctively, and there, right under her nose, was the stiff and standing penis of the good father, looking ready to burst with the luxurious proximity in which its owner found himself.

'Touch it,' whispered Bella.

Nothing daunted, Julia gripped it in her little white hand.

'How it throbs! It is getting bigger and bigger, I declare.'

'Swing it down,' murmured Clement; 'so – oh! lovely!'

Both girls now sprang out of bed, and eager for the fun, commenced stroking and skinning the priest's huge penis, until, with his eyes turned up, he was unable to prevent a slight convulsive spending.

'This is heaven!' said Father Clement with a movement of his fingers, which betokened his pleasure.

'Stop now, darling, or else he'll spend,' remarked Bella, assuming an air of experience, to which, no doubt, she considered her previous acquaintance with the monster fairly entitled her.

But Father Clement himself was in no humour to waste his shot while two such pretty targets were ready for his aim. During the fingering to which the girls had subjected his cock, he had remained impassive, but now, gently drawing the young Julia towards him, he deliberately raised her chemise and exposed all her secret beauties to view. He allowed his eager hands to pat and mould her lovely buttocks and thighs and opened with his thumbs her rosy chink; he thrust his lewd tongue within, and sucked exciting kisses from her very womb.

Julia could not remain insensible under such treatment, and when at last, trembling with desire and rampant with lust, the daring priest threw her back upon the bed, she opened her young thighs and let him see the crimson lining of her tight-fitting slit. Clement got between her legs, and throwing them up, he touched with the big top of his member the moistened lips. Bella now assisted, and taking the immense penis in her pretty hand, skinned it back and presented the tip fairly at the orifice.

Julia held her breath and bit her lip. Clement gave a hard thrust. Julia, brave as a lioness, held firm. In went the head, more thrusts, more pressures, and in less time than it takes to write it, Julia was gorged with the priest's big member.

Once fairly in possession of her body, Clement commenced a regular series of deep thrusts, and Julia, with indescribable sensations, threw back her head and covered her face with one hand, while with the other she clasped Bella's wrist.

'Oh! it is enormous; but what pleasure he is giving me!'

'She's got it all; he is in up to his balls,' exclaimed Bella.

'Ah! how delicious! She'll make me spend – I can't help it. Her little belly is like velvet. There, take that – '

Here followed a desperate thrust.

'Oh!' from Julia.

Presently, a fantasy seized the salacious giant to gratify another lecherous idea, and carefully drawing his smoking member out of little Julia's tight parts he pushed himself between Bella's legs, and lodged it in her delicious slit. Up her young cunt went the big throbbing thing, while the owner slobbered out the ecstasy his exercise was giving him.

Julia looked on with amazement at the apparent ease with which the father thrust his huge prick up into the white body of her friend.

After a quarter of an hour spent in this amatory position, during which Bella twice hugged the father to her breast and emitted her warm tribute upon the head of his enormous yard, Clement once more withdrew, and sought to ease himself of the hot spunk which was consuming him in the delicate person of the little Julia.

Taking that young lady in his arms, he once more threw himself upon her body, and, without much difficulty, pressing his burning prick upon her soft cunt, he prepared to deluge her interior with his wanton discharge.

A furious shower of deep and short pushes ensued, at the end of which Clement, with a loud sob, pressed deeply into the delicate girl, and commenced to pour a perfect deluge of semen into her. Jet after jet escaped from him, as, with upturned eyes and trembling limbs, the ecstasy seized his person.

Julia's feelings were roused to the full, and she joined her ravisher in the final paroxysm with a degree of fierce rapture no flea can describe.

The orgies of that lascivious night are past my powers of description. No sooner had Clement recovered from his first libation, then in the grossest language he announced his intention of enjoying Bella, and immediately attacked her with his redoubtable member.

For a full quarter of an hour he lay buried to the hairs in her belly, spinning out his enjoyment until Nature once more gave way, and Bella received his discharge in her womb.

Clement produced a cambric handkerchief, on which he wiped the streaming cunts of the two beauties. The two girls now took his member in their united grasp, and with tender and lascivious touches so excited the warm temperament of the priest, that he stood again with a force and virility impossible to describe. His huge penis, made red and more swollen by his previous exercise, menaced the pair as they pawed it first in this direction and then in that. Several times Bella sucked the hot tip and tickled the open urethra with her pointed tongue.

This was evidently a favourite mode of enjoyment with Clement, and he quickly pushed as much of the big plum into the girl's mouth as he could insert.

Then he rolled them over and over, naked as they were born, gluing his fat lips to their reeking cunts in succession. He smacked and moulded their round buttocks, and even pushed his finger up their bottomholes.

Then Clement and Bella between them persuaded Julia to allow the priest to insert the apex of his penis into her mouth, and after a considerable time spent in tickling and exciting the monstrous cock, he ejected such a torrent down the girl's throat and gullet that it nearly choked her.

A short interval ensued, and once more the unwonted enjoyment of two such tempting young and delicate girls roused Clement to his full vigour.

Placing them side by side he thrust his member alternately into each, after a few fierce movements withdrawing and entering the one unoccupied. Then he lay on his back, and drawing the girls upon him, sucked the cunt of one, while the other lowered herself upon his big prick until their hairs met. Again and again he spouted into them his prolific essence.

The dawn alone put an end to the monstrous scene of debauchery.

\* \* \*

While such scenes as this were passing in one part of the house, a very different one was rapidly approaching in the chamber of Mr Verbouc, and when, three days afterwards, Ambrose returned from another absence, it was to find his friend and patron at the point of death. A few hours sufficed to end the life and experiences of this eccentric gentleman.

After his decease, his widow, never very intellectual, began to develop symptoms of insanity; she perpetually called for 'the priest', and when an aged and respectable father was on one occasion hastily summoned, the good lady indignantly denied that he could be an ecclesiastic, and demanded 'the one with the big tool'. Her language and behaviour having scandalised all, she was incarcerated in an asylum, and there continued her ravings for 'the big prick'.

Bella, thus left without protectors, readily lent ear to the solicitations of her confessor, and consented to take the veil.

Julia, also an orphan, determined to share her friend's fate, and her mother's consent being readily given, both young ladies were received into the arms of Holy Mother Church upon the same day, and when the noviciate was past, both accordingly took the vows and the veil.

How sincere those vows of chastity were, it is not for me, a humble flea, to comment upon. I only know that after the ceremony was over, both girls were privately conveyed to the seminary, where some fourteen priests awaited them.

Hardly allowing the new devotees the necessary time to divest themselves of their clothing, the wretches, furious at the prospect of so rich a treat, rushed upon them, and one by one satisfied their devilish lust.

Bella received upwards of twenty fervent discharges in every conceivable fashion; and Julia, hardly less vigorously assailed, at length fainted under the exhaustion caused by the rough treatment she experienced.

The chamber was well secured, no interruption was to be feared, and the sensual brotherhood, assembled to do honour to the recently admitted sisters, revelled in their enjoyment to their hearts' content.

Ambrose was there, for he had long seen the impossibility of attempting to keep Bella to himself, and, moreover, feared the animosity of his confrères.

Clement was of the party, and his enormous member made havoc of the young charms he attacked.

The Superior also had now the opportunity of indulging his perverse tastes; and not even the recently deflowered and delicate Julia escaped the ordeal of his assault. She had to submit, and with indescribable and hideous emotions of pleasure, he showered his viscid semen into her bowel.

The cries of those who discharged, the hard breathing of those labouring in the sensual act, the shaking and the groaning of the furniture, the half-uttered, half-suppressed conversation of the lookers on, all tended to magnify the libidinous monstrosity of the scene, and to deepen and render yet more revolting the details of this ecclesiastic pandemonium.

Oppressed with these ideas, and disgusted beyond measure at the orgy, I fled. I never stopped until I had put some miles between myself and the actors in the hateful drama, nor have I since cared to renew my familiarity with either Bella or Julia.

That they became the ordinary means of sensual gratification to the inmates of the seminary, I know. No doubt the constant and vigorous sensual excitement they endured, tended very soon to break up those beautiful young charms which had so worked upon me. Be that as it may; my task is done, my promise is performed, my memoir is ended, and if it is out of the power of a flea to point a moral, at least it is not beyond his ability to choose his own pastures. Having had quite enough of those of which I have discoursed, I did as many are doing – many who, although not fleas, are nevertheless, as I reminded my readers in the commencement of my narrative, bloodsuckers – I emigrated.

# Beatrice

## ANONYMOUS

# Foreword

Beatrice is one of the most remarkable – and sensual erotic novels to have come out of the late Victorian period. Its first printing appears to have been in Paris, c.1920, although, since many underground novels of the late nineteenth century have vanished completely, there may well have been earlier editions. Beatrice herself is that comparative rarity in sexually oriented fiction: a young woman portrayed not as a cardboard cut-out figure, but one seen in the round with all her nuances of shyness, hesitation and emerging desires. With *Beatrice* or the narrator of *Beatrice* – we move into a subtle world. Unlike many Victorian heroes and heroines, Beatrice scarcely changes for the good during the course of the novel, unless you happen to be a male submissive, or a female one. Even so, her expressed sensitivity is extraordinary to a degree that is exceedingly difficult to match against the general literature of 'her' time – if indeed that later nineteenth century was her time. One is inclined to believe that it was, though on the thinnest of evidence. Some novels in the erotic *genre* are easy to date. The styles have their own integral flavours – a sustained jolliness, perhaps, which a later, would-be imitating writer would find exceedingly hard to match, chapter for chapter. Some betray their dates by reference to things rather than to events or people – as for instance in *Rosa Fielding* (*c.* 1862), where we find mention of split drawers. Until that period, oddly enough (or not), women of all classes wore no drawers. Split drawers were introduced in the early 1860s (first in France) and were devised as such so that women could perform their 'natural functions' without removing them. Considering the very heavy dresses and (often) multiple underskirts of the time, one has to view this as a somewhat practical move. Clearly, any later imitator can insert such references but the manner of doing so represents a subtlety that casual writers of erotica (and one knows of no dedicated ones) would encompass more clumsily.

So it is with odd shafts of light in *Beatrice*. They are few enough, but they are there. In particular, the most impressive one comes with her reference to gaslighting – or rather the absence of it at a given time. Gaslighting first appeared in England, for exhibition purposes, in Pall Mall in 1807 after its introduction by William Murdoch. It had reached Edinburgh and Glasgow by 1818, but thereafter its progress – outside of what we would now consider to be metropolitan areas – was patchy and slow. Gas mantles, which allowed the safer usage of gas in the home, were not introduced until 1866. Electric lighting began to appear in 1875. The first public building to be so lit was the Savoy Theatre in London in 1881. 'Electricity had not then reached out from London and it was said that we were too far from the county town for gaspipes to be laid,' Beatrice says. There is a thoroughly authentic ring to this sentence, not only in what is said, but the way it is said. One is reminded of a similar utterance in *My Secret Life* when Walter, pursuing a young girl when he was probably about twenty-five, remarks, 'There were no lights then in third-class carriages.' This places the incident prior to 1838, when Gladstone ordained that such railway carriages should be lit.

A different brushstroke comes in Chapter Twenty of *Beatrice:* 'From the kitchen came smells of butter, cheese and herbs. Mingled withal was the scent of bread which had been left that morning. Milk waited in stone jars, covered with fine net. In the stone-walled larder lettuces shone their fine diamonds of cool water.' It is as if we are participating in the sensory perceptions of a brief moment of time, so long ago. And the use of the word 'withal' strikes one as a final seal.

Seemingly therefore – despite a frequently 'unusual' style of writing in this *genre* and one that occasionally appears to place it 'beyond its period' – we have a provisional dating of *c.* 1885–95.

It is the style which here and there strikes an odd note. A touch of surrealism appears to enter some of the sentences. Thus at the very beginning: 'The ceilings in my husband's house were too high. They ran away from me.' The sense of a poet *manqué* is also distantly present: 'We had lain in the meadow and seen the flashing of wings, birds' wings, the butterflies.'

We should not begin to tell ourselves, however, that Victorians 'did not write in this way', though we must turn to the poets rather than to the prose writers before we are able to gain a clue. The corpus of Robert Browning's work is evidence that imaginative people of the mid to late nineteenth century did not always write with 'stilted tongue'. Or, to take another giant leap from this present piece of erotic ephemera, one can instance the incredible word-play and 'sprung rhythm' of another great English poet, Gerard Manley Hopkins, whose first major work appeared in 1875. Those who have not previously encountered his verse might find it difficult to 'believe' that a Victorian could have produced such lines as:

I caught this morning morning's minion, king-
    dom of daylight's dauphin, dapple-dawn-drawn Falcon, in his riding . . .

Obviously we cannot begin to compare such masterly use of language with an erotic triviality such as *Beatrice*. We can, however, conjecture that the author encountered such literature increasingly *if* we make the assumption that the novel was written not in its own time but later – as late even as the early 1920s. Being then in his or her middle age, the author would have had sufficient memories of the 1890s at least, and evocation of the period would come easily. For it was precisely in the twenties that writers were entering a deliberately experimental period, as with the work, for instance, of Gertude Stein in Paris ('a rose is a rose is a rose is a rose').

So much then for theories about the style. Even twenty years ago the content would have been considered outrageous, for while an Old Bailey jury had then (to the annoyance of the Judge) cleared *Lady Chatterley's Lover* – despite its inclusion of buggery and all else – such further watersheds as *Last Exit to Brooklyn* had not appeared.

There are 'whippings' in *Beatrice*, yes, but none is violent. We are clearly not intended to see them as such. They occur between those who have seemingly accepted the nature of their relationships or are beginning to do so. There is indeed a certain tenderness (some might think a slightly insidious one) about them. We are a long way here from sadism, though not so far along the line from masochism. The sense of 'teaching', as between the whipped and the whipper, is endemic to fetishistic literature of this kind. The old phrase 'for your own good' is unavoidable and dates one back to the childhood scenes where the roots of such activities lie. Punishment is happiness.

Unusual, certainly, for a novel set in the late Victorian period is some of the attire with which we are presented. Skirts are made quite impossibly short, dresses are 'clinging', garters are replaced by metal bands. Yet none of this is 'impossible' if we consider many of the bizarre stage costumes worn at the time and the fact that dancers would appear on stage in flesh-coloured body-tights which gave an appearance of nakedness. A well-known London courtesan once appeared at a ball wearing only a light cloak which she threw open, it was said, to prove that her hair was not falsely coloured. In their private circles many well-to-do Victorians flaunted the conventions of society, just as Greeks and Romans did. Nothing changes. The mid-twentieth century did not – as many appear to think – invent eroticism or sexual freedom.

The obsessive activities of the Beatrice 'clan' are of course remarkable. They move ever onwards with a silent logic of their own until, in a sense, we almost believe in Beatrice's existence, whereas it would be somewhat difficult to believe in that of, say, Rosa Fielding. Even so, despite its obsessiveness, the novel does not limit itself to a narrow or fetishistic audience. Using four-letter words much more sparingly than the general run of erotica, it is pervaded throughout by an atmosphere of sexuality which is sometimes more implied than stated. There are occasional brevities which other writers would have expanded into greater crudities: 'The gentlemen mounted them in turn. They were common girls – field girls given to such lusts, I believe. Of no account.'

The use of the term 'field girls' here (young girls employed in agricultural work in the spring and summer) is another pointer to a period in which the author must have lived. It is exceedingly doubtful that a much later writer would have thought to use such a term, or even have known of it. Emerging also from the passage just quoted is a clear intimation of Disraeli's 'two nations': the gentry and 'the others'. The latter were there to be used, whether sexually or in employment, and often both. Having a servant girl over the dining-room table was, *vide* Walter again, not an uncommon thing for a 'gentleman' to do. If she became pregnant she could be dismissed.

Beatrice inhabits a world within a world. All fetishistic worlds are closed ones, yet in this case the narrative is enhanced thereby and becomes self-illuminating. 'Purified' by her own punishments – none of which could be called dire – Beatrice realises herself no less than the Victorian fictional coward who became a hero. We may, as I have said, come almost to believe in her existence just as we do in that of some characters in TV soap operas. But, attractive as some of her alterations of mood are, we can no more believe in *her* than we can in Superwoman or Batgirl. And this, of course, is to the good, for if she became totally 'real' she would thereby diminish, or become a monster.

Beatrice is veiled by her own unreality – as well it should be with all fictional characters. They are flies in amber. We can never touch them. She eschews, at least, cruelty as such. Total 'immorality' is accepted in her world as a convention. In terms of Pornotopia, she lives most of her life in summertime, with an occasional look into spring or fall. The sexual acts, when they occur, are never overstated. The endless copulations of much Victorian erotica do not exist here. A sense of 'reality' obtains, bizarre as it might be. Males prove sexually exhaustible in a relatively brief time and so lend themselves to becoming serfs. The women, while bisexual, are finally the only ones free to act as they will.

Beatrice, indeed, might well be termed the ultimate Women's Libber – without ever raising her voice. Even so, she remains slyly as desirable in male eyes as her sister. Perhaps that is the trick of it.

PATRICK HENDEN, PH.D.
Cambridge, England

# Chapter One

I do not like old rooms that are brown with the smell of time.

The ceilings in my husband's house were too high. They ran away from me. In the night I would reach up my hands but I could not touch them. When Edward asked me what I was doing I said I was reaching my hands up to touch the sky. He did not understand. Were we too young together?

Once a week he would remove my nightdress and make love to me. Sometimes I moved, sometimes I did not. Sometimes I spoke, sometimes I did not speak. I did not know the words to speak. We quarrelled. His stepmother would scold us. She could hear. In the large, high-ceilinged rooms voices carried as burnt paper flies, rising, tumbling, falling. Drifting.

The doors were always half open. Sometimes – lying in bed as if upon a huge cloud – I would play with his prick, his cock, his pintle. Pintle. I do not like the *nt* in it. Sometimes I would turn and he would rub it against the groove in my bottom. I liked that. I lay with my nightgown up, my back to him, and had my dreams. The rubbing was nice. My cheeks squeezed tightly on his cock.

The night before I left we quarrelled. Our words floated about, bubble-floating. They escaped through the door. His stepmother netted them. She entered and spoke to us. The oil lamps were still lit.

'I will bring you wine – you must be happy,' she said. Her nightgown was pale and filmy. I could see her breasts. Balloons. I could see the dark blur of her pubis, her pubic hair, her wicked.

'Wine, yes – 'twould be splendid,' Edward said. He was pale and thin. Like his pintle. I had nursed it in my palm even while we quarrelled. It was the warm neck of a bird. I did not want it in my nest.

I heard his stepmother speaking to the maid downstairs. The maid was always up. There was clinking – bottle sounds, glasses sounds. We lay still, side by side. His stepmother returned and closed the door, bearing a tray. She poured wine. We sat up like people taking medicine.

'Angela, dear, lie down,' Edward said. His father had married her when Edward was fourteen. During the past months then of his father's absence in India, she had encouraged him to use her Christian name. I judged her about forty. A woman in full bloom.

Wine trickled and spilled on the sheet as she got in. Edward was between us – between the betweening of us. The ceiling grew higher. The sounds of our drinking sounded. The wine was suitably chilled. My belly warmed it. We were people in a carriage, going nowhere. We indulged ourselves in chatter. The bottle emptied quickly.

'We must sleep, we must lie down,' Angela said. 'I will stay with you until you sleep.'

I heard her voice say that. The ceiling came down. It had never done that before. I passed my hand up into it and it was made of cloud. We lay down side by side on our backs. Our breathing came. There was warmth. Edward laid his hand on my thigh. He moved my nightgown up inch by inch. He touched. Into my fur, my nest, he touched. The lips were oily, soft. I did not move. His hand on the other side of him moved. I could feel the sheet fluttering there.

Our eyes were all open. I did not look but I knew. Soft, wet sounds. I tried not to move my bottom. Would the maid enter to remove the tray? Edward's fingertips found my button. I felt rich, forlorn, lost. My legs stretched down and widened. My toes moved. On the other side of him the sheet fluttered still.

Edward moved. His finger was oily with my oily. He moved on his hip and turned towards me. I felt the pronging of his prong. His hand cupped my nest.

'Kiss good-night, Beatrice.'

His voice was above me, yet far away – a husk blown on the wind. I moved my face sideways to his.

'Yes, kiss good-night,' Angela said.

Her voice was far away – a leaf floating on the sea. His mouth met mine. His charger quivered against my bared thigh. Fingers that were not my fingers ringed the stem of his cock. His finger entered me. I moved not. Our mouths were pasted together, unmoving. I was running through meadows and my father was chasing me. My mother and my sister, Caroline, were laughing. I screeched. Their voices drifted away on to the far horizon and waved there like small flags.

Moving my hand I encountered Angela's hand – the rings upon her fingers that ringed around his cock. I moved my mouth away from Edward's and stared up at the ceiling. It had gone high, gone high again. Birds drifted through it. Edward's hand eased my thighs wider. I lay limp, moist in my moistness. The bed quivered as if an engine were running beneath it.

I found my voice.

'Kiss good-night,' I said. My mind was not blank. There was coloured paper in it. A kaleidoscope. I watched the swirling, the patterns. Would love come?

Edward turned. His knob burned in his turning against my thigh. His nightgown was fully raised. His lips fell upon Angela's. Her hand held his cock still. At first she lay motionless. The sheet moved, tremored, rippled up and down. In her breathings were the secrets of the passageways at night.

Edward groaned in his groaning. The meshing of their lips. I heard their tongues. Voices.

'Edward – no, not now!'

They were speaking in ordinary speech.

'Oh, you bad boy!'

The sheet became tented. I felt the opening of her thighs – the warmth exuding from her thick-furred nest. Her bottom shifted, rucking the sheet, smack-bounce of flesh to flesh. Her knees bent. Between her thighs she encompassed him. Small wet sounds. Slithery sounds. I held my legs open. I was gone, lost. They did not know me. The bed heaved, shook. I turned my head. I looked as one looks along a beach at other people.

Did I know them?

Her nipples stood like tiny candles in brown saucers, laved by Edward's tongue. Her hands gripped his shoulders. Her eyes and lips were closed as if she were communing. Between her thighs his loins worked with febrile jerkings. Tiny squishing sounds. Her bottom began to move, jerking to his jerks.

Expressionless I moved the sheet down with my foot. It wrinkled, crinkled, slid away, betraying the curves of her calves. His mouth buried her mouth beneath his mouth. Her hands clawed his back. Their movements became more frenetic. The pale pistoning of his pintle cock.

Moaning in the night. Bliss of it. Was there bliss of it? I wanted to be held down. I wanted a straw to chew or a piece of long sweet grass whose root is white.

Angela was panting. It was a rough sound. The squelching of his indriving, outsucking. His balls smacked her bottom. The sound pleased me. Through their puffing cheeks the working of their tongues.

'Ah! dearest, let me come!'

Edward raised himself on forearms, loins flashing. Her hands clutched his arms. I was looking. Sideways along a cloud, a beach. The lamps were lit still. Had they forgotten the lamps?

'Oh, Edward!'

*Kiss good-night.*

He collapsed, he shuddered, in his quivering quivered. Her calves rose and gripped his buttocks. A final thrust, indriven to the root. He seep'd in his seeping, his jetting done. Like balloons bereft of air they collapsed. They were quiet. I could hear the ceiling. The floor creaked. Was the bed coming undone?

Edward rolled between us and was quiet. The night was done. The limp worm of his penis-pole lolled wet against my thigh. Sticky. It oozed. It was too small now for my nest.

In the night he stirred and mounted me. Drowsy in coils of sleep I did not resist. The oil lamps flickered low. Did she watch? From moment to moment I jerked my bottom in long memories of knowing. I wore drawers in my dreams. My bottom was being smacked. It was being smacked because there was a cock in me. In our soft threshings my legs spread. My ankle touched hers. She did not stir. Our feet rubbed gently together. Our toes were intimate.

Edward worked his work upon me and was done. The spurtings came in long, strong trills of warmth. Warm wet. Sperm trickled down my thighs. I lay inert. I had not come. He had not pleasured me. My nipples were untouched.

In the morning I left. Was that the reason? No. I do not know. Angela smiled at me and said. 'It was the wine. We must make him happy.' Her bottom was large and round beneath her *peignoir*. Edward kissed us. We took breakfast with the windows open.

I kissed them both when I left.

I was kind to them.

## *Chapter Two*

Houses seem smaller when one returns to them after a long period. The rooms shrink. They carry dead echoes. One looks for things one had left, but the drawers have been emptied. Furniture is moved. Even the small pieces of paper one had wished to keep have vanished. I like small pieces of paper. My notes to myself. Addresses, birthdays, anniversaries.

My notes to myself had all gone. Did I take them? Two reels of silk cotton that no longer matched my dresses lay in the back of a drawer in my dressing table. One was mauve and the other a pale blue. They were pretty. Once I used to keep biscuits in a jar on the top shelf of my wardrobe. Someone had eaten them. I told my sister Caroline.

'Beatrice, that was three years ago. You ate them,' she said. No one looked surprised. It was always a quiet house. We hate those who shout.

They knew I would come back.

'You should never have married,' Father said. He looked at me sternly and added, 'Did I not tell you? How old are you?'

'I am twenty-five,' I replied, as if I were addressing a stranger. Dust swirled in the sunlight as I drew back the blue velvet curtains and raised the sash of my window.

'The maid does not clean,' Father said. Did he see reproach in my eyes? He stood close to me and I could feel his bigness. The gold chain of his watch gleamed in the pale sun. There was a silence because we like silences. A baker's cart trundled down the street. From the side entrance of the house opposite a maid appeared, her white cap askew on her head. She raised her hand and the baker's man reined in his horse. A cat prowled by the railings.

Father stirred. He moved past me. His thighs brushed my bottom.

'I must return soon to Madras, Beatrice. You will have comfort here.' His finger traced dust on the top of the rosewood cabinet by my bed.

'I shall be comfortable, Father. You will be gone long? Madras is so far.'

'A year, my pet, and no more. Your Uncle Thomas will afford protection to you and your sister. Had you but returned before we might have walked with the early summer sun in the meadow.'

'Yes, Father.'

My uncle and my Aunt Maude lived close by. They had done so for years. We were close. Father's hand was upon my shoulder. I felt smaller. He stood behind me like a guard, a sentry. Did I like Uncle Thomas? I asked with my mind but not my mouth. They were brothers. There was kinship.

'Shall Jenny be there, too?' I asked. In my unmoving I asked. The baker's cart had rolled on with a tinkling of harness. The street lay quiet again as in a photograph. The maid had gone, loaf-clutching in her maidness, her maidenhood. Into a darkness of scullery, a glowering of gloom behind windows. Fresh smell of fresh bread.

'Jenny has grown as you have. You will like her more. She is fuller of form and pretty. In his guardianship of her your uncle has moulded her well,' Father replied.

My buttocks moulded. Beneath my long silk dress they moulded. Proud in their fullness they touched his form lightly, gracing his grace with their curves. I felt the pressure of his being. There was comfort between us as in the days before my marriage. We had lain in the meadow and seen the flashing of wings, birds' wings, the butterflies. I leaned back. Father's hands touched my hair, the long gold flowing of my hair. The moulding of my bottom, ripe with summer.

'We shall drink wine. Come let us celebrate your return,' Father said.

I followed the first touch of his hand. We descended. The polished bannister slid smooth beneath my palm. Caroline waited on us, neat on a chaise-longue. At father's bidding she drew the bell-pull. The maid Sophie appeared. Wine was ordered.

In the coolness of its bottle glass it came. Father poured. The sofa received us. Like two acolytes we sat on either side of him. Sophie had gone. The door closed. In our aloneness we sat.

'We shall French-drink,' Father said. It was a pleasantry we had indulged in before. I was but twenty-one then, Caroline seventeen. The wine glistened now again upon our lips. Our heads lay upon his shoulders. We sipped our sips while Father filled his mouth more deeply and turned his face to mine. His beard and moustache tickled. My parted lips received wine from his mouth. There was warmth. His hand lay on my thigh.

Father turned to Caroline. Foolishly shy she hid her face until her chin was raised. I heard the sounds, small sounds – the wine, the lips. A wasp buzzed and tapped against the window as if seeking entry, then was gone. The gardener chased the long grass with his scythe. I waited. The wine came to my mouth again. A whispering of lips. The ridging of my stocking top through my dress, beneath his palm. The tips of our tongues touched and retreated. Did the French drink this way? Father had been to Paris. In his knowing he had been.

Long did we linger. Caroline's dress rustled. I could not see. Across his form I could not see. The bottle emptied but slowly like an hour-glass. The wine entered my being. As through shimmering air, Caroline rose at last, her face flushed. She adjusted her dress. Her eyes had a look of great foolishness.

'Go to your room, Caroline,' Father said. There was yet wine in his glass. Silent as a wraith she was gone, her blushes faint upon the air like the smoke from a cigar.

'She is yet young,' Father said. His tone was sombre. There was wine on my breasts once when I was eighteen and he had kissed it away. The wine made pools of goodness and warmth in me. It journeyed through my veins and filled my head.

'We shall go to the attic,' Father said. His hand held mine – enclasped and covered it. As we rose his foot nudged the bottle and it fell. A last seeping of liquid came from its mouth. We gazed at each other and smiled.

'You will come, Beatrice? It is for the last time.' There was a sadness.

We ascended, our footsteps quiet. The door to Caroline's room stood closed, thick in its thickness. The patterned carpet on the curving stair drank in our steps. Above the first floor were the guest rooms. In the old days those who wished had passed from bedroom to bedroom at night, during the long weekend parties my parents held. I knew this though my lips did not speak. At night, I had heard the whisperings of feet – a slither-slither of secrets. Arrangements were made discreetly with my mother as to the placings in rooms. The ladies of our circle always arranged such things. The gentlemen took it as manna. Bedsprings squeaked. I had told Caroline, but she did not believe me. There were moanings and hushed cries – the lapping sounds of lust. Small pale grey puddles on the sheets at morning.

No one had ever seen me go to the attic with Father. It was our game, our secret. Our purity.

In the attic were old trunks, occasional tables my mother had discarded or replaced, vases she disliked, faded flowers of silk. Pieces of unfinished tapestry lay over the backs of two chairs. Sunlight filtered through a dust-hazed window.

We entered by the ladder and stood. In the far corner near the dormer window stood the rocking horse, grey and mottled. Benign and handsome – polished in its varnished paint – it brooded upon the long gone days. Dead bees lay on the sill. In my kindness I was unhappy for them. Father's hand held mine still. He led me forward. My knees touched the brocaded cloth of an armchair whose seat had sagged. Upon it lay a mirror and a brush, both backed with tortoiseshell. They were as I had used of old up here.

Father turned his back to me and gazed out through the glass upon the tops of the elms. A trembling arose in me which I stilled. With slow care I removed my dress, my underskirt, and laid them on the chair. Beneath I wore but a white batiste chemise with white drawers whose pink ribbons adorned the pale of my thighs. My silk brown stockings glistened. I waited.

Father turned. He regarded me gravely and moved towards me. 'You have grown. Even in three years you have grown,' he said. 'Where shall you ride to?'

I laughed. 'To Jericho,' I replied. I had always said that though I did not know where it was. Nodding, his hand sought the brush. I held the mirror. With long firm strokes of the bristles Father glossed and straightened my hair. Its weight lay across my shoulders, in its lightness. Its goldness shone and he was pleased.

'It is good,' Father said, 'the weather is fair for the journey. My lady will mount?'

We stepped forward. He held the horse's reins to keep it still. Once there had been a time when my legs could hold almost straight upon the horse. Now that I was grown more I had to bend my knees too much. My bottom slid back over the rear of the saddle and projected beyond the smooth grey haunches. Father moved behind me and began to rock the horse with one hand. With the other he smacked my outstretched bottom gently.

'My beautiful pumpkin – it is larger now,' he murmured. My shoulders sagged. In the uprising of my bottom I pressed my face against the strong curved neck of the horse. It rocked faster. I clung as I had always clung. The old planked floor swayed and dipped beneath me. His palm smacked first one cheek and then the other.

'Oh! no more!' I gasped.

All was repetition.

'It is far to Jericho,' my father laughed. I could feel his happiness in my head. The cheeks of my bottom burned and stung. My knees trembled. The bars of the stirrups held tight under the soles of my boots.

'No more, father!' I begged. His hand smacked on. I could feel the impress of his fingers on my moon.

'Two miles – you are soon there. What will you do when you arrive?'

'I shall have handmaidens. They will bathe and perfume me. Naked I shall lie on a silken couch. Sweetmeats will be brought. Slaves shall bring me wine. There shall be water ices.'

I remembered all the words. I had made them up in my dreams and brought them out into the daylight.

'I may visit you and share your wine?' Father asked. His hand fell in a last resounding smack. I gasped out yes. I fell sideways and he caught me. He lifted me until my heels unhooked from the stirrups. I sagged against him. My nether cheeks flared. In the pressure of our embrace my breasts rose in their milky fullness above the lace of my chemise. My nipples showed. I clenched my bottom cheeks and hid my face against his chest.

'It was good. I should bring the whip to you henceforth,' Father murmured.

The words were new. They were not part of our play. Beneath my vision I could see my nipples, the brown buds risen. Had I forgotten the words? Perhaps we had rehearsed them once. In their smallness they lay scattered in the dust. Dried flecks of spokenness.

'It would hurt,' I said.

'No, it is small. Stand still.' I did not know what to do with my hands. He was gone to the far corner of the attic and returned. In his hands was a soft leather case. He opened it. There was a whip. The handle was carved in ebony, the end bulbous. There were carvings as of veins along the stem. From the other end exuded strands of leather. I judged them not more than twenty-five inches long. The tapered ends were loosely knotted.

'Soon, perhaps. Lay it for now beneath your pillow, Beatrice.'

So saying he cast aside the case and I took the whip. At the knob end was a silky smoothness. The thongs hung down by my thigh. A tendon stood out on my neck in my blushing. Father traced it with his finger, making me wriggle with the tickling. Broad trails of heat stirred in my bottom still. I could hear his watch ticking. The handle of the whip felt warm as if it had never ceased being touched.

I moved away from him. The thongs swung, caressing the sheen of my stockings. Father assisted me in the replacing of my dress. His hands nurtured its close fitting, smoothing it about my hips and bottom. His eyes grew clouded. I stirred fretfully. My hair was brushed and burnished anew. Father's mouth descended upon mine. His fingers shaped the slim curve of my neck.

'It was good, Beatrice. You are grown for it – riper, fuller. The smacks did not hurt?'

I shook my head, but then smiled and said, 'A little.' We both laughed. In the past there had been wine afterwards, drawn from a cooling box that he had placed beforehand in the attic. Now we had drunk before and it moved within us.

His fingers charmed the outcurve of my bottom – its glossy roundness tight beneath my drawers. We kissed and spoke of small things. I would never come to the attic again, I thought. In the subtle seeking of our fingers there were memories. At last we descended. Father took the ladder first. Halfway down he stopped and guided my feet in my backwards descent. His hands slid up beneath my skirt to guide me.

Caroline was reading when we re-entered the drawing-room. Her eyes were timid, seeking, brimmed with questions.

'There is a new summerhouse – come, I will show you, Beatrice,' Father said. I shook my head. I must see to my unpacking with the servant. Father would forgive me. His eyes forgave me. They followed me like spaniels, loping at my heels.

'Your boots are repolished – the spare ones,' Caroline called after me. It was as if she meant to interrupt my thoughts. Father went to her and drew her up.

'Let us see if the workmen have finished in the summerhouse,' he said.

Her eyes were butterflies on and on. I turned and stood of a purpose, watching her rising. Her form was as slender as my own. Her blue dress yielded to her springy curves. Through the window I watched them pass beneath the arbour. Three workmen in rough clothes came forward from where the new building stood and touched their caps. My father consulted his watch and spoke to them. After a moment they went on, passing round by the side of the house towards the drive and the roadway.

Their day was finished, or their work was done. Father seemed not displeased. Caroline hung back but he drew her on. Her foolishness was evident to me even then. The sun shone through her skirt, offering the outlines of her legs in silhouette. She was unmarried, but perhaps not untried. I fingered the velvet of the curtains, soft and sensuous to my touch. The lawn received their footsteps. The door to the summerhouse was just visible from where I stood. Father opened it and they passed within. It closed.

I waited, lingering. My breath clouded the pane of glass. The door did not re-open. The shrubs and larches looked, but the walls of the summerhouse were blank.

Going upstairs to my room I fancied I heard a thin, wailing cry from Caroline.

## *Chapter Three*

When Caroline smiles I know something, but I do not know what I know.

The whip lay untouched beneath my pillow. Father was due to depart. There was movement about the house. Trunks, valises. Two hansom cabs were needed – one for the luggage.

In the night before his departure I slipped my hand beneath my pillow and touched the whip, the smoothness of the handle, the coiling of the waiting thongs. My thumb traced the carved veins upon the penis shape. It moved to the knob, the swollen plum. After long moments of caressing it I got up and moved along the dark of the passageway. The door to father's bedroom was ajar. I stilled myself and took an extra pillow from the linen cupboard, making no sound.

The door to Caroline's room lay half open. Normally it was closed, as was mine at night. In the night. I peered within, expecting her to sit up. In the milky gloom she lay sprawled on her bed. Her hair was fanned untidily over her pillow. The hem of her nightdress was drawn up, exposing her thighs and the shadowy thatch of ash-blonde hair between. Her eyes were closed, lips parted.

I moved forward quietly, expecting to surprise her. She stirred not. Her legs lay apart in an attitude of lewd abandon. Slender fingers curled lax upon the innerness of her thigh – the firm flesh of pleasure there. Between the curls the lips of pleasure pouted. In the pale moonlight it seemed to me that there was a glistening there, as even upon her fingertips. Her breathing was the breathing of a child.

I stirred her shoulder with my hand. Drowsily her eyes opened. 'You are uncovered. Come – don't be naughty,' I scolded. She prefers me in my scolding. My hands slid beneath her calves, lifting them. As with the motions of a nurse I drew the sheet and blanket over her. Beneath her bottom cheeks a faintly sticky moisture. Throwing one arm over her eyes she mumbled something. Pieces of unfinished words.

'You were long in the summerhouse today,' I said. She answered not. The defensive movement of her forearm tightened over her face. 'We are bad,' I said. Her legs moved pettishly beneath the sheet and then lay still. An owl hooted, calling to witches.

'Bad,' Caroline husked. She was a child repeating a lesson. I bent and kissed her mouth. Her lips yielded and then I was gone.

The hours passed as white clouds pass. At three the next afternoon Father departed. The gates lay open. The hansom cabs waited. The second carried his luggage piled high as if in retreat from days that were too long, too dry. In the hallway we were kissed, our bottoms fondled. There was affection. The cabmen waited. A smell of horses – manure and hay. A jingling of harness, clatter of wheels and he was gone. Gone to the oceans, the sea-cry and the vivid sun. The women would be bronzed, I thought. I would bronze my body – my nipples rouged, erect.

Caroline did not speak. Her pale fretting was evident. In the drawing-room Sophie bobbed and called me Ma'am instead of Miss Beatrice. I was pleased. With the master gone I now was mistress. We would take tea, I said, but no cakes.

'I want cakes,' Caroline said. Her look was sullen. I meant to punish her – perhaps for the summerhouse or for lying with her thighs apart on her bed. I knew not. We were like travellers whom the train has left behind. We drank unspeaking, our minds in clouds of yesterday. Sophie came and went, silent as on castors. Then the doorbell jangled. Its sound seemed to cross the halls, the rooms, and tinkle in the rockery beyond the windows.

Alice went, adjusting her cap but leaving her white apron askew. It was our uncle. Announced, he bowed benignly to us both. He was a man of slightly ruddy countenance, neither tall nor short, strong in his ways. He owned a small manufactory and numerous saddlery shops that were scattered about the county. Sophie poured fresh tea. We spoke of Father.

'Jenny has come?' I asked. My voice was an echo of my voice in the attic. My uncle nodded. He adjusted the set of his waistcoat rather as Alice had adjusted her cap.

'She is settling,' he announced. 'Her training has been of use, I believe.'

'Was she not teaching?' I ventured the question. His eyes passed over the fullness of my breasts and then on to Caroline's.

'They are one,' he declared. 'You will come for dinner.'

It was not a question. I would have preferred it to be a question. His hazel eyes were like Father's. They sought, found and alighted. I felt their pressure upon my thighs.

'At eight,' I said. I knew exactly at what hour they dined. I rose. 'Uncle – if you will excuse me.'

Politely, as I thought, he rose in unison with me. Caroline's glances hunted and dropped. 'Let me accompany you,' he said. It was unexpected. I desired to say that I was going to my room, but I suspected that he guessed. The moment was uncanny. It was as if Father had returned, had shaven off his beard and was wearing another suit. I could scarce refuse. At the door to my room I hesitated, but there was a certain urging in his look. The door closed behind us.

'Beatrice, you will bring the whip,' my uncle said.

A bubble of *no* came to my lips, then sank again. That he knew of it seemed to me a treachery – bizarre, absurd. His expression nevertheless was kind. Without seeking an invitation he advanced upon me and embraced me. I leaned against him awkwardly. There was a tobacco smell. Memories of port.

'I have to care for you, nurture you, Beatrice. There are reasons.'

I sought but could not find them. Delicately his fingertips moved down the small buttons at the back of my dress. My chin rested against the upper pocket of his coat. With some absurdity I wondered what was in it.

'The whip – it has many thongs, has it not?'

He raised my chin. My eyes swam in his seeing. My lips parted. Pearls of white teeth.

'Lick your lips, Beatrice – I desire to see them wet.'

Unknowing, I obeyed. He smiled at the pink tip of my tongue. It peeped like a squirrel and was gone. I was in another's body, and yet it was my own. We moved. I felt our moving. Backwards, stiffly. My calves touched the rolled edge of my bed. His right hand sought my bottom and slid beneath the bulge.

'Reach down and backwards for the whip. Beneath your pillow. Do not turn,' he said. His fingers cupped my cheeks more fiercely. The blush rose within me. A tendon strained in my neck. Held about my waist by his other arm, I leaned back, I sought. My fingers floundered. He assisted me in my movements. The ebony handle came to my hand. It slipped. I gripped again. In a moment I held it by my side, still leaning back as I was told.

'It is good. You shall remain obedient, Beatrice, while in my care. Speak now, but do not move. I want you thus.'

'And Caroline?' I asked. Were the secrets about to be unlocked? There were cracks in the ceiling. Tributaries. I knew not what I spoke.

'It shall be. You must be trained. Upright now – come! Hard against me!'

I wilted, twisted, but to no avail. A hand forced into my back brought me up, slamming against him. My breasts ballooned. His hand supported my bottom. Father had not treated me this way. I had come to his arms and said nothing. In the attic we had whispered secrets, but they were small.

The root of manhood was against me. Against my belly. I would have swooned save for his clasp. Then of a sudden he released me and I fell. Backwards upon my bed. Forlorn as a child. The whip dangled its thongs across my knees.

'At eight,' my uncle said. The bulge in his breeches was considerable. I had seen it in father's but had averted my eyes. I hung my head. There was a loneliness within me that cried for satisfaction. I said yes – hearing my voice say yes. My nipples stung their tips beneath my bodice.

My uncle departed, leaving gaps in the air. I rose and gazed down from the window as I had gazed with Father. A woman in black carrying a parasol walked past holding the arm of a man. The cry of a rag-and-bone merchant came to my ears, long away, far away. In a distant cave. Below there were voices. Mumblings of sound. Why did Caroline always cry out? How foolish she was. I sat again, fondling the whip. In the attic I would have received it, I knew. The horse would have rocked. My pumpkin raised, bursting through my drawers. I had shown Father my nipples. We were bad.

In the morning I would be alone, walking through the clear air.

My bottom had not tasted the whip. I turned before my dressing-table mirror and raised my skirts. Perhaps I would cease to wear drawers. Their frilled legs were pretty. Pink ribbons dangled their brevity against the milky skin of my thighs. Awkwardly I slashed the thongs across my cheeks. The sting was light.

I wanted to go to Jericho – lower my drawers and let my pubis show. The curls were soft, springy and thick. The thongs would flick within my groove. I would clutch the horse's neck, the dappled grey, the shine of him, and cry. I would cry tears of wine. The dead bees upon the windowsill would stir. 'All shall be well with the best of all possible bottoms,' Father had said to me once. We had laughed.

'Pangloss,' I declared. I knew my Voltaire. Pangloss and bottom gloss, Father said. There was purity.

I repaired my disorders of dress and brushed my hair. I am never given to allowing servants to do it. In the drawing-room Caroline sat as placidly as she would have me believe she always did. I needed to challenge her. I went and sat beside her. She was surprised, I believe, at my composure.

'Did Uncle kiss you?' I asked. She shook her head. Her cheeks were bright red. 'Or feel your thighs?' I added. Her gasp sounded within my mouth as I drew back her neck and kissed her. My hand sought her corsage. There was a loose button.

Her nipples were stiff.

Loosing second and third buttons, my small hand squeezed within. The jellied mounds of her breasts were firm and full – only a trifle smaller than my own. Caroline struggled, but I am stronger than she. She endeavoured to raise her arms between us but the enclosure of my arm was too tight. Her lips made petal shapes of helplessness. Her breath was warm. My hand slipped down, cupping the luscious gourd. The ball of my thumb flicked the nipple.

'Between your thighs, Caroline,' I murmured. I did not say of what I spoke, nor of whom I spoke. Her head shook violently. Her eyes were lighthouses. 'In your mouth? The smooth, hot knob?' I teased. Her expression became rigid with surprise. Her head fell back. I licked my tongue along her teeth and laughed. I released her, leaping to my feet. 'How foolish we are!' I laughed. I turned and went before my disguise melted. I had never taken it in my mouth.

Caroline's mouth was so often petulant. It would have fitted perfectly. The rose and the stalk. I would have hidden and watched her sin. The delicate oozing of her mouth upon the rampant conqueror, balls pendant on her cupping palm. Her eyes would be half closed, lashes fluttering. The cock would jerk faster and she would choke. A warning hand would seize her head. Her cheeks would bulge as the penis urged deeper. Strong loins would work against her unwillingness.

And the spouting. He would have needed to cup her face completely – hold it in. Ripe throbbing of the flesh.

'Suck, Caroline.' His voice would be deep and urgent, her head squeezed, ripplings of blonde hair through his fingers. Beneath her dress her breasts would lilt.

There was sin here, among the rubber plants, the rooms overcrowded with furniture, photographs of sepia in silver frames upon the piano. From the conservatory whither I fled I gazed upon the waving fronds of ferns. Father's train would have reached the terminal. His bags would be carried. The boat train at Liverpool Street would await him. Women would peer through carriage windows at his coming. Blinds would be drawn, expressions adjusted. The women would wear fine kid gloves, velvet-smooth to the touch on sensitive skin. Balls pendant. Veins.

'Suck, Caroline, suck.'

Sperm is thick, salty. Once I tasted it on my palm. My sprinklings are salty when I sprinkle. Over the cock that is more powerful and thick than my husband's was. That is *now*. It was not *then*.

In my then I was alone in my aloneness. I returned to Caroline. She had not moved save to button her dress. The servant would enter soon with the oil lamps. Caroline stared down at the carpet and would not raise her eyes. I knew her moods. I sank to my knees and pressed my lips upon her thigh.

'Do not!' she said. Her voice was as distant as the far whistling of a train.

Kid gloves. The blinds drawn. Penis rampant. The knob of my whip. 'There is no sin. Is there sin?' I asked Caroline. Sin once had been giggling in Sunday school. Now there was desire between our thighs.

'I do not know,' Caroline said. Her voice fell like a small flake of metal. She was angry with me.

My desire became muted. I wanted to protect her. Soon, after we had bathed and changed for dinner, it would be almost eight o'clock. I looked up and she was staring at me. Perhaps she knew her fate as well as I.

## *Chapter Four*

Aunt Maude awaited us. She wore a black velvet choker. It suited her, I thought. Her dress swept back in a long train that was very modish. Her hair was piled high. Diamond earrings glittered.

My aunt was of a stature an inch taller than myself and full of form. Her breasts and bottom jutted aggressively. I took her for forty – younger than my uncle. Her eyes were kind but imperious. Though both were close to my father, neither Caroline nor I had spoken much with them through the years. Those of under age were always considered best unheard.

I spoke of Jenny. I was eager to see her. For a year we had shared a boarding school together.

'Later,' my aunt said. The dining-room table was candlelit. My aunt preferred it to the smell of oil. Electricity had not then reached out from London and it was said that we were too far from the county town for gaspipes to be laid. Three years later magic would be wrought and they could come. My initiations – though I knew it not that evening – were to be by oil lamp in the old tradition. Frisky young ladies of Society were weaned on a bed with their drawers down, it was crudely said. Of cottage life and that in other dowdy dwellings, we knew nothing except, as we understood, that the males rutted freely.

Although married, and now separated, I still retained innocence in many degrees, as shall be seen. At dinner my aunt and uncle spoke to us as if the past were still upon us. My aunt tutted severely when Caroline spilled a drop of wine. The servant was called of a purpose to mop it up.

'You will stay the night,' my aunt said after coffee had been taken. We sipped liqueurs and said nothing. Jenny had still not appeared. I wondered anxiously if she ate in her room. Had she been whipped? She had come to them in childhood – or rather, to my uncle first. An orphan, it was said. One did not know. I sought for strength to object, to rise, to leave, but their eyes were heavy upon me.

At ten-thirty my aunt looked at the clock. 'Tom, you will take her up,' she said. My palms moistened. I knew of whom she spoke, though she had not the delicacy to use my name. Caroline said nothing. Would she not save me?

The house was as ours except that the interior pattern was reversed.

Perhaps that was symbolic. The stairs were on the left as one entered the hall, instead of on the right. Entering as I had first done I had placed the whip somewhat furtively behind the large mahogany stand in the hall which carried occasional cloaks and walking sticks.

'Go to your room and I will follow,' my uncle said. I had been shown it briefly already. It lay, as my own lay, on the first floor. Left to right it was a mirror image. The curtains were brown, the drapes edged with ivory tassels. The air tremored. The furniture looked at me. I wanted the room to go away, the walls to dissolve, the air to take me high, free, upfloating in the blue dark of night. The carpet rolled beneath me like the sea. I moved, and moved towards the bed. Two pillows were piled high upon a bolster. Was my whip there?

I would not seek it. I refused. This was not my room. As by habit I opened a small wall cabinet and found to my surprise that which I kept in my own, a bottle of liqueur and two small glasses. Pleasure traced itself across my lips and then was gone. I turned, closing the cabinet. My uncle had entered. In his hand he held the whip. Moving he moved, towards me moved. He took my hand, the palm of mine, sheened with moisture.

'Beatrice, bend over – hands flat on the quilt.'

'Uncle – please!'

My mouth quivered. I did not want it to be my mouth. His hand reached out caressing my neck and I gave a start. His fingers moved, soothing.

'You will obey, Beatrice.'

The world was not mine. Whose was the world? Would Caroline and my aunt discuss me?

'No one will come,' my uncle said. The door stood solid. We were on an island. In the attic Father and I had stood on the top of the world. The whip moved. He passed the handle around and beneath the globe of my bottom, shaping, carving. His lips nuzzled my neck. I could not run.

'Uncle – please, no!'

I broke from him and stood trembling. The thongs swayed down to his knee like a fall of rain in slow motion. His eyes were kind. His arm reached out. He took my chin and raised it.

'There are things you need, Beatrice. There are locked rooms above. There are keys.'

I did not want to blink in the meeting of our eyes. Go into the world clear eyed and so return from it.

'Yes?' I asked. There was imperiousness in my voice. Dare I rebel? The whip slipped from his grasp and fell upon the patterned carpet. He would not whip me. He could not. I knew it. I felt happy. He waited further upon my speech, my quest, my questions.

'What is in the rooms?' I asked.

He took my hand. We walked. The stairs received us. Caroline had wandered perhaps into the dark garden – into the long grass which the gardener chased by day. The grass would receive her. Her eyes would be loam, her nipples small blossoms. Her pubic hair would be moss. There was silence below in the house. Along the passageway of the second floor as we went my uncle rattled keys. A door opened.

The attic! They had made a replica of it! Except for the dormer window – but it did not matter. The door closed – a heavy click – we were alone. My uncle's arm encircled my shoulder. I could not speak. Let me speak.

'The horse is the same. Only the horse, Beatrice.'

It was true. Trunks, boxes, broken pieces of furniture, old vases – all lay as they might have lain in our house.

His hand stroked my back, warm through my gown.

'Go to the horse, Beatrice.'

I moved, walked, threading my way among the tumbled things – the love things, the loved things. The horse was large, bright, new. The stirrups gleamed, the saddle and the reins shone. The mottled, dappled grey was the same. I stroked the mane. On my own horse the mane was worn and thin where I had too often grasped it, but here it was new and thick. The leather smelled of new leather. Heady.

For a last moment I turned and looked towards the closed door. Caroline into the long grass gone. At breakfast she would return. Out of the caves of my dreams she would return, pure in her purity, the loam fallen from her eyes, her nipples budding, the moss of her pubis gold and curled.

I waited, humbled in my waiting. The sea moved beneath Father. The timbers of the sailing ship would creak. The dark waters. Kid gloves soiled with sperm upon the waves. Salt to sperm. The licking lap of water.

Hands at my back. I did not stir. My uncle unbuttoned. The sides of my gown fell from my shoulders. The material dragged to my waist and heaped. I stood still. His hands savoured the outswell of my bottom, raising the skin. My drawers were bared. A lusciousness of thighs. I fancy myself upon the silkiness of my skin.

'Mount,' my uncle said. I raised my leg. The skirt slip-slithered down again, enfolding my legs. As if tired my leg fell again. 'Remove your dress,' he breathed.

I wanted blindness but found none. The oil lamps, ranged around the room, flickered. Small messages of lambent light. My hair ruffled as I stripped off my gown. There was no one to brush it. My underskirt fell to my ankles. I stepped out of it as out of foam. Sperm-foam. The dark sea lapping. Silent in a cabin, my thighs apart.

Cupping my bottom as I toed the stirrup, my uncle assisted me in my rising.

He knew not of Jericho. There were secrets still. The horse jolted, moving as if on springs rocking. The movement was smooth as velvet, soundless. I clung to the neck. My brazen bottom reared, my pumpkin warm.

'*Ah!*' I gasped at the first smack, and the next. There was a sweetness in the stinging I had known before. Because of my excitement perhaps. Was I excited? My hips squirmed to his palming smacks, my back dipped. I clung, I squeezed the cheeks, I squealed. Would Caroline hear? Under the deep lush grass would Caroline hear?

At the tenth smack – lifted down – I foundered, falling, grasped in his strong grasp. Words tumbled, spun like pellets in a drum. Words polished in their spinnings. Hands clasped my bulging cheeks. I blushed, I hid my face. His fingers drew the cheeks apart beneath my drawers. I strove to be still as Father so oft had taught me. My heels teetered. Then I managed it.

'So,' my uncle said. He was satisfied. I closed my eyes, pretending myself in the attic. I was happy. The stinging in my bottom had made tears glint in my eyes. 'You are older now, Beatrice – it is better.'

I wanted wine. I wanted to go down to Caroline, to rescue her from the long grass. My uncle held me. My nipples peeped.

'Is it not better, Beatrice?'

Was I to answer? I knew not. I believe he expected it not. My silence pleased him. He sought confusion, girlishness there. My bottom cheeks weighed heavy on his palms.

'Raise your arms, Beatrice, and place them behind your head.'

It was a game – a new game. I obeyed. My left elbow nudged his cheek. His breath was warm on my face. I was obedient. We had never done this in the attic. Once on Christmas Eve in the merriment of the night I had been carried up to my room, my drawers removed. Had I dreamed that? Tomorrow I would buy kid gloves, long and white to my elbows. The kid leather would be of the finest. Sensitive to flesh. A stem upstanding.

My uncle raised my chemise inch by inch. I was naked beneath. I quivered. My hips would not keep still. He raised it, raised it to the silky melons of my breasts. And then above. Dark nipples in their radiant circles.

'No!'

I jerked, twist-tumbled, gasped. I did not want to be obedient. The lacy hem of my chemise tickled my nipples in its rising.

'Uncle, no!'

I cried, I fell. There was carpet on the floor – purple with dull red patterns. In the attic there was no carpet. Dust rose to my nostrils. My chemise was crumpled over my polished gourds, my tits, my breasts.

My uncle fell beside me. His hands pinned my shoulders. Gazing upon my gourds he gazed. He bent. His long tongue licked my nipples. My back reared but he stilled it with a warning grip of hands.

'Shall you be whipped?' he asked.

My eyes were mirrors. They encompassed the world. I stared at him in my staring. My hair flowed upon the carpet. I must have looked a picture of extreme wantonness. There was wet on my nipples where he had licked. They strained in the rising. The floor moved gentle under me as waves beneath a tall ship sailing. In Madras the women would be bronzed, their hips supple.

'Lift your hips,' my uncle said.

My heels dug into the carpet. For a moment I lay mutinous. Then my knees bent, bottom lifted. I was arched. His fingers sought the ties of my drawers, the pretty ribbons. Loosing they surrendered. Closing my eyes I felt my drawers being removed. The whorl of my navel showed. The impress of a baby's finger dipped in cream. Curls glinted at my pubis.

Then there was a sound.

The door had opened and a young woman stood there in a severe black costume. The toes of her black boots shone.

It was Jenny.

## *Chapter Five*

Jenny took me to my room. I carried my dress. The ribbons of my drawers had been tied again on my rising when she appeared. My uncle had risen and kissed her brow.

'We were playing games,' I said. I sat on the bed. I wondered how Jenny had arrived. Perhaps she had been there all the time hiding behind the wallpaper – a voice in the shrubbery. Owl calls. Night calls. She looked older, younger – both. The appearance of her costume was severe – high buttoned to her neck. Her face was Byzantine. By Giotto perhaps. Her long thick hair was swept back and tied with a piece of velvet.

'Games are nice,' Jenny said. She came and sat close to me, legs together, hands in her lap. I felt comforted. Had I betrayed myself upstairs? My uncle had followed us to the door, avuncular. Jenny was talking. There were words. I caught her words in the broad net of my mind.

'You must be kind to him, Beatrice. We must all be kind.'

'Have you just come?' I asked. My hands had not trembled. My voice was bright and clear. In the room with my uncle I had been speechless, mumbling. How foolish. The skin of my breasts beneath the low neck of my chemise was glossy, tight and full. Jenny looked at them. I saw her look. We used to undress together – when I stayed with her. When she stayed with me. But then I remembered something. Something I had never believed in.

One weekend when she had come to stay, six or seven years before, Mother had said to me, 'It is best if Jenny has the guest room tonight.' Jenny had looked strange, I thought – sitting, listening. She had nodded at me lightly as if she wanted me to say Yes.

I had heard sounds in the night, that night. It was midnight. I had looked at the clock – the small clock that says yes to me when I want it to be a certain time. There were sounds. Sounds like leather smacking. I thought I heard Jenny whimpering. The servants sometimes made noises in the night in their moving. But now the servants, too, would be abed.

A voice said, 'You are a good girl, Jenny.' It sounded like my mother's voice. My dreams were often strange. I sat up in bed. There were more leather sounds, little cries, a voice like Father's voice. The sounds and the voices stirred and were mixed. I heard a woman-voice murmur: 'More – harder – a little harder. Ah, how sweet she looks.'

Oh, a little scream I heard, a screamy-moan, then quiet. Sounds of breath like rushing waters. Bedsprings tinkled. Small bells of the night. Two men went past the house below – rough men, not from our neighbourhood. One shouted and I lost the sounds.

'I just came,' Jenny said now. 'There are clothes in your wardrobe. Have you looked?'

She drew me up. The mirrored doors, whose mirrors were tarnished, opened. From a shelf Jenny took black stockings of silk with a raised, ornate pattern that was run through with hints of silver. With it she produced a tiny waist corset of satin black. The small fringe of lace at the top that would fall beneath my breasts was silver, too. From the bottom of the wardrobe she drew out long high boots of the finest leather. The studs around which the laces wound were silver. The heels were slender, tall.

'Where is Caroline?' I asked.

Her eyes were glitter stones.

'You will look beautiful in these, Beatrice. Who?'

'Caroline.'

'Yes, I know. Remove your chemise, stockings and shoes. Put these on.'

She held them to me as a gift. I took them. The boots were light in weight. They would reach up to my thighs.

'It is late,' I said. I licked my lips. My uncle had wanted to see my lips wet. Jenny did not smile. She raised my chemise and drew it off my head. I shook my hair like a dog emerging from water. As carefully as if I were a nervous yearling she knelt and drew off my drawers, my shoes. Without my shoes my thighs looked plumper.

'Your pubis is full – a splendid mound,' she said. 'You are beautiful, Beatrice. Your hips have the violin curve that men adore.'

'I want to go home,' I said. I felt sullen. Caroline's face was my face. My lips brooded.

'You will be good,' Jenny said. She tickled me. She knew I hated being tickled. I squirmed, laughed, my breasts jiggled. I fell back on the bed, I rolled. She smacked my bottom. I yelped. The bright spreading of her fingers was upon it. It was a superb bottom, she said, the cleft as deep as a woman's heart. Her hands fell and pressed on it so that I could not rise. Her knee came into the small of my back.

'You will dress, Beatrice. You are not naughty, are you?'

'No,' I said. She had seen Uncle taking down my drawers. My pubis had been offered. On her entry into the room upstairs he had stopped and risen as if we had merely been conversing. 'What did you do in my parents' room?' I asked.

'What?' she asked sharply. She did not know my thoughts, my memories. Her palm tingled across my bottom again. 'Dress!' she commanded me, 'I like you in stockings best. You have the thighs for it – plumpish, sweet. Do not disobey. Get up!'

I obeyed her. The long boots were at first difficult to manage. They were tight. Their tops fell but three inches below the dark bands of the stocking tops. I would have difficulty in walking in them, I said. The corset nipped my waist. My hips blossomed. The corset framed my navel beneath an upward curve. My belly gleamed white.

'You will walk in them slowly and with stately tread – that is their purpose, Beatrice. Try.'

I moved from her. I walked. The high heels teetered. My legs were constrained. I felt the movements of my bottom, naked.

'Stand!' she commanded me. I stood, my back to her. She drew upon my wrists and brought them behind my back. A metal clink – a clink of steel. My wrists were bound. I wanted to cry and hide my face. Next she secured my ankles. Why?

'Lie down, Beatrice.'

I was bundled on to the bed, face down. 'I don't want to,' I said. I did not know what I meant. Jenny tut-tutted and arranged the tops of my stockings above the rimming leather. My toes were cramped in the boots. Jenny turned my face and bent and kissed my mouth. Full lips. Rose lips. She straightened and her eyes were solemn, full of night.

'You will stay so a little while,' she told me. She moved away. A chinking of metal as I tried to move.

'Please don't, Jenny.'

She was at the door. 'I always loved you, Beatrice,' she said.

'Please don't, Jenny.'

She did not hear. The door closed. I was alone with my aloneness. In the night. Where was Caroline? I listened as I listened when a child, on evenings when the curtains were drawn in my room against the evening light. I listened now, I heard. There were footsteps, soft voices. Voices heard, unheard. Was it the wind? I was half naked and bound, strange in my half-nudity and bonds. Jenny was naughty. She would come and release me and I would dress in my summer dress and we would picnic. Caroline would be tied to a tree. She would watch our small white teeth nibbling cakes. Lemonade would gurgle down our throats. The world would never come to an end.

Did Caroline remove her chemise in the attic? I heard voices. Caroline's voice. She was laughing. Jenny was laughing. I knew I must not call out in my calling. They stopped outside my door and went on up. I imagined in my imaginings my uncle waiting for her in the attic room.

It was quiet again. The walls are thick. I dozed. Tight in my bonds I dozed. The door opened. Was it a dream? Through slits of eyelids I saw Jenny. She was dressed as I was dressed save that there was no silver in her stockings nor in her corset. She wore drawers of black satin, but they had no legs. Their lines swept up between her thighs.

Aunt Maude entered behind her. The door was closed. From her ears dangled rubies in long gold pendants. Her mouth was carmine. In her hand the whip.

Was she an aunt? There were aunts in the garden once when I was young. They moved among the flowers and the shrubs. Sometimes Father and Mother would kiss them. We ate delicacies from silver platters. The servants were quiet, moving like wraiths. Tea was drunk from translucent cups. It was said that my uncle's first wife had left and died. I believe not that she died, but that she left I knew. Long later I heard of it. Her name was Lucy. She was but eighteen. My uncle then was a racier man. He sought a sexual abandonment to which Lucy could not lend herself. She was beautiful but shy. In the end my uncle grew impatient. He had wished to see her in the throes of lust. She had refused. One night, becoming impatient, he had called the butler. Lucy, naked, had been held down over the edge of the bed. First my uncle and then the butler had entered their penises in her bottom and buggered her. The butler was a lewd, crude man. Such things were not unknown. My uncle, it appeared, had been in raptures over the scene. He having buggered Lucy first, she was more docile and receptive to the second breaching of her bottom. Nevertheless, she departed soon after. For Australia, they said. Her death being announced, but never proved, my uncle remarried.

Aunt Maude sat now on the bed. I felt her weightness. She rolled me on to my hip, my back to her. Her hand caressed my cheek and brushed my hair back where the strands were loose.

'Has she been good?' she asked.

Jenny stood as if she had been waiting to be asked. 'She has been good,' she said. I was pleased. They were going to release me. We would have our picnic. Jenny and I would hide in the shrubbery and Caroline would have to find us.

'It will take time,' my aunt said. Her complexion was as smooth as mine. Once when I was very young she was younger. She bent over me so that our mouths almost touched. Jenny stood still. I knew that Jenny was being good standing still.

'She was smacked,' Jenny said. I wanted to cry. I hated her. I glared at her and she smiled. My aunt continued to stroke my face and hair. Then she passed her long-tapered fingers down my neck and back. I shivered. I jerked towards her. Her eyes were kind.

'Twenty-five. She looks younger – she could be younger. Beatrice always had a fine bottom, did you not, Beatrice?'

My eyes said no-yes. Her fingertips floated my globe, my split peach, my pumpkin glory pale. The tip of her forefinger sought the groove. My lips quivered. Jenny did not look away. All hands should be hidden from people. My mother told me that. Hands can be wicked. My wrists were bound.

My aunt's finger tasted the inrolling of my bottom cheeks and wormed between them.

No – even my husband did not do that. Edward never did that. His stepmother was jealous of me. He bought her flowers. I remembered his cock. It was thin and long.

I made a noise – soft, small noise. The fingertip had touched my rose, my anus, my little bottom mouth that makes an O. My aunt smiled. She had turned my chin towards her. I bubbled little bubbling sounds. I jerked my bottom. My lips pursed in a long, soundless *oooooh*. The fingertip oozed in me and it moved. Back and forth, an inch of it, it moved.

My aunt took my nose pinched between her thumb and finger. I was like a fish. I had to part my lips to breathe. Rouge-scented, her mouth came to my mouth. Her tongue extended, licked within. I squirmed. Between my bottom cheeks her finger sank. In deeper sank. I was impaled. My breath hush-rushed. Her tongue worked. It worked its long wet work around my tongue. Her finger moved in-out, gently, like a train uncertain at a tunnel. Menace of dark and tightness.

Her finger felt burny, itchy, strange. Then it came out. Her tongue came out. I tasted her rouge on my mouth with my rouge. I wanted to tell Jenny that but I hated her. My aunt gave my bottom a pat and stood up. She smoothed her skirt down.

'She should bathe,' my aunt said. 'Take her, Jenny.'

Jenny made me get up. Into the hallway I was led, along to the bathroom. As in those days it was huge – a fireplace within. The walls were draped with dark blue velvet all around. The bath was of white porcelain. Unshackled, my attire was removed. The water had already been brought in and emptied by the servants into the bath. It was lukewarm and pleasant.

'You know I love you,' Jenny said.

I sat down. The water lapped me with its tongues. I liked that. Jenny sponged me and poured scented water over me from a pitcher.

'Do you remember we learned wicked words at boarding school?' she asked. I wanted to ask things, but I did not. I nodded. Her eyes were bright and merry. Christmas tree decorations. 'What is *cunt*?' she asked.

'*Con*,' I said. I did not want her to think I did not know. I like the French word but not the English word. The English word is ugly. Its edges are sharp.

'And *prick*?' She held my head round so that I could look into her eyes. Her breasts were splashed with water. I wanted to nibble her nipples.

'*Pine*.' I knew I was right. I would never then say prick. Why are all wicked words sharp in English? Someone sharpened them. Anglo Saxons with dirty beards and guttural voices sharpened them. My bottom squashed its cheeks into the water, plump. Is it too big?

'And sperm?' She would not stop. Jenny was often like that before, not ever stopping. She would tickle me in bed when we were younger and make me say things. In my imaginings I would say better things, naughtier things, but I never told her. Did she know? Was this punishment?

'*Foutre*,' I said. I knew she liked the word best. I liked the word best. It was like a ripe plum being chewed and then pieces coming out briefly on the lips before being swallowed. The word was thick bubbles around my tongue. Creamy bubbles.

'Have you not been whipped yet?'

It was Jenny asking me. At first I did not know that it was. I thought the voice came from the ceiling. I did not answer. I was mute. Her fingers moved over the outjutting of my breasts. My nipples had risen under the sponge. Jenny licked inside my ear. I giggled. It wasn't fair.

'I knew you hadn't been,' she said, 'get up.'

My feet slipped. She smacked me. 'Now stand still,' she said, just as Father and Uncle said. She sponged my legs and made me open them. The sponge was squelchy and warm under my pussy. Did Jenny ever touch me there before? No, yes. In bed once, I think. That was summers ago. The ice cream has all been eaten since then, the plates put away.

'Move your hips. Rub them against the sponge, Beatrice. Did you often come over Edward's prick?'

'I hate you,' I said. There were tears in my eyes. She knew that I would not tell her. She became impatient with me.

'Oh, get out,' she said. She pulled me roughly from the bath and towelled me. She was brisk and quick as Mother used to be when I was young. Younger young. Then she powdered me. Clouds of powdering me. The powder made me sneeze.

She led me back into my room. The house was silent. Had they all run away?

'I want champagne,' I said. I do not know why I said it. Bubbles. *Foutre*. Jenny laughed.

'There should be rouge on your nipples,' she said. She had left the door open. From along the passageway came sounds, cries, whimpers.

'Please?' I asked. I felt as if I were speaking in a foreign language and that I only knew the beginnings of sentences. Then I recovered myself. 'I heard Caroline,' I said.

Jenny put a white linen nightdress over my head. It flowed to my feet. The hem was wide. 'You shall see,' she replied. She took my hand and led me along the corridor. The door to Caroline's room was half open.

Caroline was lying naked on her bed, face down. Her wrists and ankles were bound as mine had been. Aunt Maude was swishing a long slender cane lightly across her tight, pink cheeks. Caroline's face was flushed. At every contact of the cane she jerked her hips and whimpered.

'You will both sleep now,' Jenny said. She pushed me back into my room and closed the door. I heard the lock click. The tasselled curtains parted to my hands. I pressed my forehead to the cool glass and stared down into darkness. The baker's van had gone – the maid – the cat. Had the loaf been eaten?

My bed was soft and comfortable, the sheets scented with lavender. The oil lamps made shadows on the ceiling. I could not stir myself to extinguish them. A servant would come in the morning and attend to them.

Through the green-blue sea I floated. The dark shadow of a huge ship loomed above me. I reached and touched the planks and felt the barnacles. There was seaweed in my hair. Father came floating towards me. My skirts billowed up to my hips in the deep, still waters.

No one could see.

## *Chapter Six*

The sun was warm when I awoke. The curtains had been drawn back – the lamps removed. Evidently I had slept heavily. Jenny roused me, smiling from the doorway where she stood. The gong below sounded for breakfast.

'You are late,' she said. She wore a long black skirt, the waist drawn in tight. Her blouse was white, the buttons of pearl. Beneath the silk of her blouse, her breasts loomed pinky. A perking of nipples. They indented the material. Like a child late for school I was hustled into the bathroom and out again.

'I have no dress to wear,' I said. Jenny smacked my hand.

'You are late,' she repeated. The smell of sizzling bacon came to us. I was hungry. My mouth watered. The wardrobe doors were opened quickly. A thin wool dress of light brown colour, rust colour, was handed to me. 'Nothing beneath except your stockings,' Jenny said. She palmed my bottom and my breasts as I raised my nightdress. The sensation was pleasant. The dress cascaded over my shoulders and was worked tightly down over my curves. It was as if I were naked. I was preferred in boots today, Jenny said – black lace-up ones that came to my knees. The heels were high. I feared to fall down the stairs. I told her.

'Nonsense,' Jenny said. 'Brush your hair quickly. Show me your teeth. Are they clean now?'

I was taken down. Approaching the dining-room we walked more slowly. My legs felt longer in the boots, the high heels. My aunt and uncle and Caroline were already seated. Silver tureens stood on the massive sideboard. Caroline looked up at me quickly and then attended to her bacon. We ate in silence as if some doom were pending. Neither my aunt nor uncle spoke, even to one another. It was a penance perhaps. I ate voraciously but delicately. The bloom of health was upon me. The kidneys and mushrooms were delicious.

The maids who served were young and pretty. I liked them. They avoided my eyes. They had learned their learning.

With every movement of Jenny's body her breasts moved their nipples beneath her blouse. Beneath the tablecloth my uncle's hand stole on to her thigh. She wore garters that ridged themselves slightly through her skirt. He caressed them. His palm soothed from one leg to the other. Jenny parted her legs beneath her skirt and smiled. I wanted to suck the tip of her tongue.

At a nod from my uncle we were dismissed. Caroline and I rose together and wandered into the drawing-room. We were lost in our fondness. We held hands. Our fingers whispered together. In a moment, from a side entrance, my uncle appeared in the garden. A carriage had arrived, it seemed, but the visitors came not to the front of the house. They skirted the side and appeared where my uncle stood.

The woman whom he greeted was in her early thirties. I had a vagueness of seeing her before. Her flowered hat was large, of pale straw with a wide brim. She wore white kid gloves to her elbows. Were they my gloves? I had left mine in the sea at night. The fishes had nibbled at them. She was beautiful, elegant. Her dress was of white and blue, the collar frilled. Pearls glinted around the neck. Beside her came a servant neatly dressed in black with velour lapels to his jacket. He had an air of insolent subservience.

'She is beautiful,' I said to Caroline, 'do you know who she is?'

Jenny's voice sounded behind us. 'What are you doing?' she asked in a sharp tone. A tone that scratched.

'I was asking,' I answered.

Caroline moved. Her palm was moist in mine. 'I know her. She is Katherine Hayton – an actress. We have seen her at the Adelphi,' she said. Her eyes were saucers as she received Jenny's stare.

'You were not told to hold hands,' Jenny said. She jerked her head at me and said, 'Come. Beatrice, come.'

Forlorn, I relinquished Caroline's hand. Our own house was yet an ocean away. In the bedrooms women with bronzed skins and supple hips were lying. They would wear my clothes and steal my jewellery.

Jenny led me down the hall. To my astonishment we entered the linen room. It smelled of starch and nothing. 'You must learn – you must both learn, Beatrice. Do you not know?' Jenny asked me.

I blinked. I did not know who I was. Father had lied perhaps. He had not gone to Madras. He was with the women in the rooms. They would French-drink. Their lips would taste of curry. There would be musk between their thighs. I said yes to Jenny. My voice said yes. My hands were at my sides.

'Kneel before me, Beatrice.'

I did. My head was bowed, my hands clasped together. I prayed for goodness. Edward's stepmother used to undress with her door half open. We could see her as we went past. Her bottom was big. I told Edward that she should close the door. He smiled. His eyes were small and neat. Like his *pine* when it was not stiff.

'Kiss my thighs,' Jenny said. She raised her skirt, gathering up the folds. I was blind. A milkiness, a perfume. Her drawers were split both back and front. It was the fashion then. Women could attend to their natural functions without removing them. In my mother's early days women had never worn drawers.

The curls of her slit, her loveslot, honeypot, were framed by the white linen. My palms sought the backs of her thighs. Her knees bent slightly. I could feel her smile. My tongue licked out, sweeping around the taut tight tops of her black stockings. Her skin – white like my white. She tasted of musk and perfume and the scents of flowers. My lips splurged against her thighs.

'Ah, you lick! Like a little doggy you lick,' Jenny laughed. After a moment or two she pushed me away with her knees. 'It is too soon,' she said. I wanted to cry but she would not let me. I was brought to my feet even as the door opened and Jenny rearranged her dress. My aunt led Caroline in and frowned a little at Jenny, as I thought. The window of the linen room was set high up at the other end from us. The light was morning soft. Caroline wore, as I did, a woollen dress of fine skein.

'You will see to them, Jenny,' my aunt said. From our distance I heard my uncle and Katherine enter the house. There was a tinkling of glasses, laughter. The door closed, leaving the three of us alone.

'Remove your dresses,' Jenny said. My hands went to the buttons of mine, but Caroline hesitated. Jenny smacked her and she squealed. 'Quickly!' Jenny snapped. We stood naked except for our stockings and boots.

Jenny drew us together, face to face, thighs to thighs. From a drawer she took cords and bound us tightly together – ankles, thighs, waists. We could not move. Our cheeks pressed close. Placing her hands beneath Caroline's bottom she urged us slowly into a corner. I stood with my back to the meeting of the walls. Caroline's breath flowed over my breath.

'Your bodies merge well together,' Jenny said. 'Are your breasts touching fully? Move your breasts. Your nipples must touch.'

'Yes,' I said, 'yes, Jenny.' Our nipples were like bell-pushes together. Mine grew and tingled. Caroline's grew. Her toes curled over mine.

'Please, don't,' Caroline whispered. I knew that she wasn't speaking to me but in her mind speaking. I moved my lips against her ear. Jenny had gone.

'You like it,' I said. I wanted to make her happy. I coaxed her. She had had the cane. Was it nice? 'Do you like it?' I asked. I made my voice sound as if we were going on a holiday. If she liked it we would be happy.

'I don't know,' Caroline said. Her voice was smudged. Our bellies were silky together. I could feel her slit warm, pulsing. It was nice standing still. I moved my mouth very slowly from her ear to her cheek. I felt her quiver. Had she sucked his cock? I would not ask yet. I would ask later. The tip of my tongue traced the fullness of her lower lip, the Cupid curve. Caroline moved her face away. Her cheeks burned. Our nipples were thorns, entangled.

'Do not!' she choked.

'Jenny will come,' I said. Caroline moved her mouth back to mine. The bulbous fullness of her breasts against mine excited me. Our mouths were soft in their seeking. I sought her tongue with my tongue. It retreated, curling in its cave curling. Sipping at her lips I brought it to emerge. The thrill made us quiver. Our nipples moved, implored. My belly pressed in tighter to hers.

The door swung open of a sudden. It was Jenny. She scolded us and said we had been kissing. Working her hand between us she felt our lovemouths, secretive between our thighs. They were moist. Her hand retracted. Her fingers sought our bottoms.

'You must practise – you love one another. Caroline – put your tongue in her mouth.'

We swayed. Caroline's tongue was small, urgent, pointed in its flickering. Hidden by our lips our tongues licked. It was a secret. I wanted.

'Open your mouths – let me see your tongues,' Jenny commanded. We obeyed.

'Half an hour,' Jenny said. She moved to the door and we were alone again. Birds sprinkled their songs among the leaves outside. I was happy. The richness of our bodies flesh to flesh was sweet. Caroline's eyelashes fluttered and tickled against mine. I could feel her belly rippling.

Our tongues like warm snakes worked together. Our thighs trembled. The ridged tops of our stockings rubbed.

Perhaps the door would remain closed forever.

Our minds whispered together like people in caves.

# Chapter Seven

We would go to meadows, my aunt said. She saw my look of incomprehension. We had been released exactly upon the half hour. Dressed again we sat in the garden and drank champagne and lemonade. It was a reward, Jenny said, because we had not cried or protested when she untied us and made us dress again.

'Meadows – it is a country house your uncle has bought,' Aunt Maude explained.

'We may go indoors first?' I asked. I was referring to our own house. My aunt nodded as if surprised at the question.

'Do not tarry – we leave at noon,' she told us.

Jenny accompanied us into our house. She was pleased and curious, I believe, to see it again. When I began to assemble clothes she stopped me. 'Not that many, Beatrice. Simple dresses only. Be sure to include your riding attire.'

I took but one trunk, as did Caroline. A sense of curious excitement seized me. The years rolled back. We were children again preparing for a holiday. We would paddle in the sea or descend from bathing huts whose steps led down into the water and were drawn there by ponies. Ladies were not permitted to expose themselves on the beach, though men could bathe naked so long as they were a far distance from the females.

Unseen by Jenny I took a bottle of liqueur and secreted it. I whispered to Caroline to do the same. She shook her head. Munching a biscuit we waited upon Jenny to conclude her discreet inspection of the house. When she came down she was wearing an ornate hat that Mother had left behind.

'May I have this?' Jenny asked. I do not know why she asked. Perhaps it was to test me. I said no. Not put out, she handed it to the maid and asked her to return it upstairs. 'We shall have fun,' she said and led us out.

In the roadway stood a large six-seater carriage of a kind not too often seen outside of London or the larger market towns. We ensconced ourselves. The manservant who had accompanied Katherine placed our trunks on top, protected by a guard rail. Our aunt joined us, then my uncle and Katherine. She had changed into a riding outfit with a three-cornered hat – a small one – perched attractively on her hair. She smiled at us with the distant smile of a stranger. The coach, drawn by four horses, started with a long cracking of a whip. The manservant whose name was Frederick sat up beside the coachman.

It was a long and sultry run. I think he enjoyed it little. Katherine toyed with her crop frequently and once or twice teased it playfully about my uncle's thighs. He gained a considerable projection in his breeches in the process, I noticed.

It was a pleasant enough drive, the countryside rolling about us once we had passed through the town. Katherine and Aunt Maude conversed of plays we had not ourselves seen. There was talk of a private theatre at which the actress had evidently appeared.

'We must contrive one,' my uncle said, 'in the barn perhaps.'

'The attic would be splendid, surely,' my aunt replied. 'It is extremely large,' she explained to Katherine. Then she gazed at us as if we were about to speak. I busied myself with counting trees. What did she know of attics? Perhaps she had peered with a telescope from her own to ours. I must tell Father. I would write coded messages, use French words, invisible ink. There would be spies.

Twice on our journey we stopped at inns and took refreshments. 'A yard of ale!' my uncle called jovially on entering both, though he had no intention of drinking one. People regarded us curiously. We were strangers. At the second resting place we ate meat pies with thick forks that looked not too clean. Jenny sat with my sister and I ate at a separate table.

'Keep the children quiet, Jenny,' my aunt said. We drank ale from pewter mugs. I was constrained. I wanted to sit outside the inn and watch the farm workers pass, wearing their rough smocks. Through the thick panes of leaded glass that was ringed with circles I could see their small images. Father on the water floating. My dress billowing. Fish nibbled at my garters while we embraced. It was said that Nero had boy slaves who swam under water while he was bathing and attended to his penis in the same way. I had read that in a book whose binding was broken. The leathered boards of the book had flopped as Edward's penis had flopped against my thigh.

Jenny took us out while my uncle settled the bill. A woman bearing a basket and leading a small child passed along the roadway. The child stared and pointed at us.

'Shush! they are from the town,' the woman said. She endeavoured to curtsey as she walked. The child wailed and was dragged on. Like the woman its feet were bare.

We journeyed on. The coachman and Frederick had eaten at a table outside. I could hear the coachman belching frequently above the rumbling of the wheels. The coach jolted exceedingly. I dozed. The talking of my aunt, uncle and Katherine was like a murmuring of bees. Jenny had not spoken to them nor been addressed, except briefly at the inn.

At last I sat upright as the coach made a sudden turn, the coachman hollering at the horses. There were hedges, stone walls, a rougher road. The coach swayed, throwing us about, as it descended a long slope. Then the house appeared. There were outbuildings. The house was long and made of grey stone. We passed beneath an archway and were in the courtyard.

'Neither of you is to speak,' Jenny said. We waited while the others descended and then she bustled us out. A woman wearing a black dress and the cap of a housekeeper stood waiting on the steps. A youth ran past and began to assist the coachman and Frederick in removing the trunks.

'To your rooms,' Jenny told us when we entered the hall which was circular.

'May we not see the house – the gardens?' I asked. Jenny stared at me. There was a battle of eyes. 'Later,' she declared. I sought a softness in her tone and found but a wisp of it. The staircase was circular and broad. The stonework on the surrounding walls provided ledges for the windows. I wanted a white dove to sit in one. Its pink eyes would gaze at me as I passed. I would throw crumbs. It would peck busily. I would wear a white dress with a pink sash.

The sails of Father's ship billowed in the wind. With whom was he talking? Feet trod the boards upon the deck. Men peered at horizons. Beyond them the bronzed women waved and waited.

Our rooms lay together, side by side. We would undress to our stockings and rest, Jenny said. There were pitchers of cool water to drink. We waited while Caroline disrobed and lay down.

'Lie flat on your back and keep your legs apart,' Jenny told her. She obeyed. Her blue eyes blinked. Her arms lay at her sides. The soft fern around her pussylips betrayed its gold, its gleaming pink. Closing the door upon her, Jenny turned and kissed me, mouth to mouth. I knew her desire. Our tongues touched. A melting.

'Do you love her?' Jenny asked. I had no need to answer. 'We shall have her together,' she said. 'Do not throw your clothes upon the floor. Be tidy.'

I blushed at her silly words. I yearned to be her accomplice, to write messages on trees. She would follow and read them. I would ride on a white horse with my hair flowing. An archer would run beside me.

The room was stark – the stonework not plastered within as I had expected. A large bed stood in the centre of the floor. The foot of it faced the door. The headboard was mirrored with three ovals of glass set in gilt frames. On either side of the bed a cabinet. There was a single wardrobe, heavy in aspect. Its doors were mirrored as was the headboard. A thickpile carpet was the only comfort.

I removed my bonnet and dress slowly, then my chemise and drawers. I was to keep my knee-length boots on, Jenny said, and to keep my stockings straight and taut at all times. My lips must always be slightly parted.

'Why are we here?' I asked. I lay down as Caroline had lain, arms straight at my sides. Jenny nudged my ankles to make my legs part wider. The moisture of the long journey was around and within my cunny. Jenny moved to the end of the bed and gazed at me.

'Erect your nipples,' she said. I licked my lips and passed my palms lightly over my breasts, flicking the tips until they rose. The cones pointed from their surrounding circles of crinkled flesh.

'You are to be trained,' she told me. 'No harm will come to you if you obey.' She moved along the bed to the cabinet on my left. A long leaded-glass window with a deep stone sill was also on my left. A vase stood upon it with a single withered flower. Dipping the tips of her fingers into the pitcher of water she sprinkled it upon my breasts. The sudden cold made me start. My nipples quivered and stiffened harder.

What is the purpose of our training, I asked, but the question stayed in my head like a wasp in a jam jar. It buzzed and spun. Jenny turned and gazed down through the window at the meadows beyond.

'Did you want to kiss Katherine?' she asked. 'Answer quickly!'

I did not look at her. I knew I must not. I said yes. Questions poured over me. I said yes. I said yes I would like to see her breasts, to kiss her thighs, to tongue her slit. I hated Jenny. She knew it was true.

She had turned away again. She seemed no longer amused by my meanderings. 'There will be a reception this evening, Beatrice. I shall instruct you in what to wear. A servant will come for you in an hour. Obey her.'

She was gone. A key turned in the lock. I made to rise. Were there cracks in the stone? Watchers? Seekers? My aunt might come. I closed my eyes and walked down corridors of thought. Would Mother return? She had gone with a man to Biarritz, it was said. I remembered his carriage arriving one afternoon, my mother peering through the curtains. He had gazed at us palely.

'I shall not be long,' my mother had said. A servant had opened the door for her, gravely. Her footsteps had sounded down the drive, certain, uncertain. A crack of a whip and the coach was gone. Dust rose in the roadway upon its departure. I thought to catch the dust in a jar and watch it swirl forever. It would not do that, Caroline said, when I told her. We had sat quietly until Father had returned that day. He had said nothing of Mother's absence. In the evening I chased a butterfly towards the sun.

I had dozed. A servant was shaking my shoulder. She was the housekeeper I had seen on the steps. I sought my dress, my chemise, my drawers, but they had gone. She tossed a grey cloak down around my feet.

'Come!' She did not call me Ma'am. I cast the cloak about me. We went up to the floor above and along narrow passageways to a second, smaller staircase. At the foot of it Caroline waited. She was garbed in a cloak as I was. Beneath she wore only her stockings and boots.

'Go!' the woman said. A side door with an iron latch was opened for us by a young servant girl who curtsied. We passed outside on to the stone flags through which grass and weeds sprouted. There were smells of chickens, pigs and hay. 'Go forward to the stable,' the woman said and pointed. My shoulders nudged Caroline's. The knuckles of our hands touched beneath our cloaks. Our feet stumbled over rough grass. The doors of the stable loomed large, yawned open. We were within.

Open shutters allowed rays of sunlight to enter the stable. We passed through the bars of the light to the further wall. There were iron rings, chains. We were made to stand side by side while the woman removed our cloaks. Our arms were raised, spread apart, our wrists secured to rings. The tip of my nose almost touched the timbered wall, as did Caroline's.

Our legs were parted roughly a full three feet so that our stockinged and booted legs were strained. Metallic clicks. Our ankles were secured. Our breathing was tremulous. We dared not to look at one another. The bales of hay about us dreamed of past summers.

There were voices beyond. I felt the woman's return. My head was drawn back. A leather gag was inserted between my lips and tied behind in the nesting of my hair. Caroline's lips would not open to the gag. She received a loud smack. Her yelp gurgled away behind the leather.

'Wash them down,' a voice said. Pieces of rough cloth were bound tightly around the tops of our thighs to prevent water trickling down our stockings. There came water, wetness, cold. I jerked. My spine curved. The sponging was insistent. It passed beneath my bottom, cooled my slit. Fingers quested at my lovelips as they urged the sponge. I was forced to strain up on tiptoes. The sponge passed beneath my armpits, in the curls there. It roamed over the hillocks of my breasts. Water tickled me, trickling down my belly. There was laughter as I squirmed. I did not know the voices.

Caroline was attended to next. The sponge trailed longer beneath her quim, I thought. Was I jealous? Her lovemouth pouted no more tightly than my own. A rough towel dried us. Our nipples perked against the wall. The iron rings, the manacles, the bonds about our ankles, clinked.

'Six,' a voice said. I sensed a movement new – a soft, insinuating sound as of leather passing across a palm.

*Cra-aaaack!* Broad width of leather seared across my bottom. Ah! I jerked. My belly to the wall I jerked. Cheeks wobbling, tightening, I received another. The sting was sweet, laid full across my buttocks.

A humming whine behind the gag. My own or Caroline's? Father – no! Father would not permit this. Surely his ship would turn, its tall sails straining. Commands. Feet urgent on the deck. My eyes screwed up. The heat flared in my bottom at the next.

'Harder!' I had heard my mother say when Jenny stayed that night.

'*Neeynnnng!*' Cries strangled in my throat. Flame-searing, the strap took me again. Again. Again. The trees could not see me. The grass did not care. Tears pearled down my cheeks. In my rudeness I squeezed my scorched cheeks tighter.

'Ah, the fullness of her – the thighs, the cheeks. What delicious plumpness,' a voice said. Was it Katherine? I heard the cries, unheard, of Caroline. The strap attended to her next. 'Let me feel the heat,' a voice said. It was the same cultured woman's voice. Palms palmed my wriggling bottom with womanly tenderness. They felt its fullness, the throbbing. Caroline's hip bumped against mine in her squirming. The loud slap-crack of the leather sounded. Fingertips sank insistent in my burning bulge. Cupped, held, I sank my weight upon the palms. My big plum, my pumpkin.

The last crack of the leather.

'Let me feel her,' a voice said. Another came whose perfume was as Katherine's. Behind us they stood side by side, controlled our squirmings with their seeking hands. I heard kisses. I could feel tongues. An urgent jerk from Caroline nudged me hard. A small laugh, husky, intimate.

'Not now – not yet,' the woman behind me said. Her fingers unclasped as if reluctantly from beneath my bottom. 'Is she wet? Tell me,' she said, 'Ah, give me your tongue!' She had spoken of Caroline. She was wicked. I could not restrain the working of my hips. Long tongues of flame licked through my buttocks still. Baby fingers of warmth moved in my groove. My love-slot pulsed gently. My nipples stiff.

'Leave them – they have been well attended to. What sweet young mares. They can be watered now.'

The voice was her voice. I knew her as Katherine now. Our gags were loosened. A tin mug passed between the wall and my mouth and tilted just sufficiently to let water trickle between my lips. I did not want it. I wanted wine. Had the servant unpacked my trunk? She would find my flask of liqueur.

The water had slopped down over Caroline's chin in her blubbering. I could feel it. Globules of water fell and decorated her nipples. Then the doors closed, the big doors in their closing. We were left alone.

I wanted to speak in my speakness. I knew not what to say. Caroline hung her head. Her forehead rested against the wall.

'I love you,' I said. The fleshiness of our hips touched. She would not answer me. She made silly, babyish sounds. With my legs wide apart I closed my eyes again and dreamed of the stemming of cocks, the rubicund heads upon the waiting pricks – the nubbing thrust between my open lips. When my bottom was thrust over the end of the rocking horse, the taut cotton had outlined the lips of my honeypot beneath. I had rubbed against the haunches – felt their pleasure.

'It hurts,' Caroline whined. I shushed her. We must not be heard. 'Squeeze your cheeks,' I said. I wanted to touch her bottom, its polished roundness. There were footsteps – a slurring of feet upon the ground, the wisps of hay.

'What have you been doing?' Jenny asked. 'Have you been wicked?' She released us. Caroline covered her face. She was ignored. 'Put your clothes on – you cannot be seen like that. There are workmen about – rough men,' Jenny said.

We donned our cloaks. The tops of my stockings were damp. It was a feeling I liked. The stinging moved in my bottom still, but it was sweeter now. It made me walk differently. My hips swayed more.

'That is good,' Jenny said. She could see. She walked behind us. The

doors were open again, huge in their hugeness. Two men with pitchforks
stood beyond. They touched their caps at our passing. We did not look at
them. Their voices were country voices. They breathed of warm milk in
stone jars, left overlong on windowsills. Stale cheese – dried scraps of bread.
They were rough men. My bottom moved – a silky bulb of heat beneath my
cloak.

# *Chapter Eight*

There were crumbs around my mouth. I wiped my lips delicately with my
napkin and yawned. After the meal which the servant had brought to my
room, I had sipped my liqueur. It had not been taken. The servant who
brought the tray was the young girl who had curtsied to us when we had
been taken to the stable that morning. Her name was Mary. She was
unlearned but pretty. It pleased her to wait upon me. The flush of pleasure
lay on her cheeks.

She appeared not surprised to find me naked except for my stockings and
boots. On her coming back for the plates, the wine bottle and the glass, I
took her wrist and sat up. I swung my legs over the bed.

'Ma'am?' she asked. The housekeeper had not called me Ma'am. I sensed
ranks, classes within classes, initiations. I drew Mary down beside me. 'I
dares not stay,' she said, 'they will punish me.'

'With the strap?' I asked.

She gazed at the floor. Her feet were shod in neat black boots. Small feet.
I would lick her toes perhaps. No. Crumbs of dirt between them. My nose
wrinkled with distaste. My hand slid from her wrist and covered her hand.
She trembled visibly. Her rosebud mouth was sweet. Such gestures are fatal.
They have meaning – like commas, dashes, question marks. I have walked
between words. I know the dangers of the spaces between them.

I passed my hand up the nape of her neck and felt her hair. It had not the
silkiness of mine, but it was clean. I turned her face, moving my lips over
hers. She started like a fawn. I held her. There was a taste of fresh bread in
her mouth.

'Tell me,' I said.

'There are no answers,' a voice said. It was Jenny. She had entered quietly.
I neither moved nor sprang up as perhaps she wanted me to. Instead I
pressed my mouth again upon the girl's. She trembled in her freshness, a
salty dew between her thighs. I felt intimations of boldness. Jenny's hand fell
upon my shoulder.

She drew Mary up from my embrace. The girl turned and went, leaving
the plates. I made to rise when Jenny fell upon me, spreading my legs by

forcing hers between them. The hairs of her pubis were springy to mine through her thin cotton dress. It was a new dress. Small mauve flowers on a blue background. I wanted it.

'There is a wildness in you,' Jenny said. Her tongue licked suddenly into my mouth and then withdrew.

'Let me kiss your thighs,' I begged. She laughed and rose, pushing herself up on her forearms slowly so that her breasts bobbed their juicy gourds over mine.

Bereft I lay. Would she seek my tears – kiss the salty droplets? On Christmas Eve I had been carried upstairs with my drawers down. The sea-cry, the wind-cry. Jenny turned to the window and looked down. The darkness now beyond – the mouth of night.

'The stations are all closed – the people have gone. The ships have sailed,' she said. I began to cry. She turned and shook me roughly. 'The reception will begin soon, Beatrice – get dressed. Stand up!'

Words stuttered in my mouth but knew no seeking beyond. I wanted my nipples to be burnished by her lips. Instead I obeyed quietly as she told me to remove my boots and stockings. In place of the stockings I was to wear tights such as dancers do on the stage. They were flesh-coloured. The blurr of my pubic curls showed through. They bulged. A top of the same material was passed over my shoulders. It hugged my waist and hips, fitting so tightly that my nipples protruded into the fine net.

'Longer boots,' Jenny said. She pointed to the wardrobe. I padded to it. They had been made ready for me, polished. Sleek-fitting, I drew them on. The heels were narrow and spiked. 'Brush your hair – make yourself presentable,' Jenny said. 'I shall return for you in a minute.'

I had not then seen the house except for the back stairs and the entrance hall. There was buzzing of voices as I was made to descend with Caroline – she dressed as I. The grooves between our buttock cheeks showed through the mesh. A piano played. It stopped when we entered. People in formal evening dress gazed at us and then turned away. Gilt mirrors ranged the walls with paintings between them – one by one around the room. Mary and another girl moved among the visitors with champagne. On sideboards there were canapes in numerous colours. They looked as pretty as flowers on their silver trays.

The piano played again. Mozart, I thought. Men looked at my breasts and buttocks. Their eyes fanned Caroline's curves. The high heels made us walk awkwardly, stiffly. The cheeks of our bottoms rolled.

To the one blank wall farthest from the doors Jenny led us, a hand on each of our elbows. There were clamps, chains, bands of leather.

Caroline first. Her legs were splayed, her ankles fastened. Her arms above her head.

'Hang your head back – let your bottom protrude!' Jenny snapped at her. I wanted to be blindfolded. I knew it was good to be so. Black velvet bands swathed our eyes. In darkness we stood, our shoulders touching warm. The manacles were tight.

I had seen my uncle. He watched upon our obedience. I heard his voice. There was silence in the room. The last chords of the piano tinkled and were gone. A wink of fishes' tails and gone.

Caroline first. I heard the intake of her breath as he passed his hands up the backs of her thighs and squeezed her bottom cheeks. 'My doves,' he breathed. He placed a broad, warm palm on each of our bottoms. People clapped. The room stirred again, came alive.

We were left. Knuckles slyly nudged our bottoms from time to time. Were we forbidden? Female fingers touched more delicately. With the protrusion of our bottoms and the splaying of our legs, our slits were at pillage. Mine wettened into the mesh of the tights as slender fingers quested and sought the lips. And found. I tried not to wriggle my hips.

Champagne was passed between our lips from goblets unseen. I absorbed mine greedily. I could hear Caroline's tongue lapping. There was dancing. I heard the feet. The plaintive cry of an oboe accompanying the piano. If it were a girl playing I would know her by her slimness, her tight small mouth that only an oboe reed would enter. Her face would be oval and pale, her breasts light and springy. She would speak little. Her words would be dried corn, her days spent in quiet rooms. At the high notes I envisaged her on a bed in a white cell. She would not struggle. Her stockings would be white, her thighs slender.

Laid on her back, she would breathe slowly, quietly, fitfully through her nose. Her dress would be raised. Knees would kneel on the bed between her legs. Her knees would falter, stir and bend. Her bottom would be small and tight. Hands would cup and lift. She would wear white gloves of kid. I had almost forgotten the gloves. They would be decorated with small pearl buttons spaced half an inch apart.

No words. Her mouth would be dry. A small dry mouth. Her cunny would be dry. A small dry cunny. A tongue would moisten it – her fingers would clench. She would close her eyes. Her eyelashes would have the colour of straw.

Her knees would be held. The knob-glow of a penis three times the girth of her oboe would probe her slit. A small cry. A quavering. In her dryness. Entering, deep-entering it would enter. Lodged. Held full within. The tightness there. In rhythmic movement it would move, the lips expanding around the stem.

Silently he would work, upheld on forearms bared, gazing down upon the pallor of her face Her buttocks would twitch and tighten. A crow would alight at the window. Pecking at stone it would be gone.

The penis moving, stiff. A small bubble of sound from her lips, suppressed. The tightening of her buttocks would compress the sealskin walls that gripped him. In his oozing he would groan. Deep in him he would groan. His face would bend. His lips would move over her dry eyelids. She would not stir. There were no words to speak for her. In the white cell of her room a rag doll would smile and loll against the wall. Through her nostrils now her breath would hiss. Music scores would dance through her mind. The oboe of flesh would play in her.

'*Pmmffff.*' Her breath explodes, mouth opens. He ravages her mouth, she struggles, squirms. His loins flash faster. Faint velvet squelch between their loins. Her cuntlips grip like a clam. He clamps her bottom, draws the cheeks apart. Mutinous still, her tongue retreats, unseeking to his seeking.

The sperm boils. In the itching stem the lava rises. The bed rocks. Music of lust. There is dryness here in the love-lust dry. The curtains falter and wave. Her bottom is lifted, back arched.

His pestle pounds. She receives. The squirting she receives – the long thin jets. Spatter-tingling of sperm. Their breath hush-rushes. Her arms lie limp. Long-leaping strands of wet. The oozy, last jet of come. The dribbling. The last tremors. Bellies warm. A weakness, falling. The strong loins of his urging are paper now. Strengthless he lies, then moves from her.

Her face is pallid. She awaits his going and rises. Her dress is straightened. A vague fussing of hair. Quiet as a wraith she descends.

'You will have tea now, dear? You have had your lesson?' she is asked. She nods. Her knees tremble. A warm trickling between her thighs. The oboe, yes. The tall ship sailing.

I emerged from my dreams. We were loosed and turned about, our bonds replaced. My bottom bulbed to the wall. I waited.

## Chapter Nine

There was quiet again. The music ceased again. I had not liked it. Its feebleness irritated.

The Lady Arabella was announced. I turned my head, though I could not see.

'Let her enter and be brought here,' I heard my uncle say. There was a sound as if of a heavy table moving. Jenny's hands moved about my face. I knew the scent and taste of them. Her fingertip bobbled over my lower lip. The blindfold slipped down an inch beneath my eyes.

'Look,' Jenny said. I saw the woman enter. Her coiffure was exquisite. A diamond choker, a swan neck. Her curves were elegant beneath a swathing white gown of satin flecked with red. The collar of her gown was raised slightly at the back, as one sees it in portraits of the Elizabethans. She wore a look of coldness and distance. Her lips were full, her nose long and straight. Her eyelids were shadowed in imitation of the early Egyptians.

She made to step back as my uncle reached her. Her fingers were a glitterbed of jewels. Behind her entered a man of military look, impeccable in a black jacket and white trousers, as was the evening fashion then. I judged the years between them. She was the younger.

'Not here. It is unseemly,' she said.

Jenny covered my eyes. Did she then uncover Caroline's? I heard not a sound beside me.

'No,' the woman said in answer to some muttered remark. There was movement past me. I felt it. As the air moves I felt. Hands touched my thighs, caressed. A finger traced the lips of my quim which pressed its outlines through the fine mesh of the tights. It was removed quickly, as if by another. I heard the jangling of bracelets.

'Not here,' the woman said again. I felt her as if surrounded, jostled. They would not dare to jostle, but they had touched me. Was I an exhibit?

'B–Beatrice . . . ' A croaking whisper from my sister. I ignored her. I heard her squeal. She always squeals. She was being fingered. Her bonds jangled. The girl with the oboe would be tight. The sperm would squirt in her thinly. Would she feel it?

Jenny favoured me. Once more my blindfold slipped. The chandeliers danced their crystal diamonds. The Lady Arabella was moving forward. As if through water she moved. An older woman moved beside her, a hand cupping her elbow. The older woman wore a purple dress. Her vulgarity was obvious.

'Arabella, my sweet, you will come to dinner tomorrow night? The Sandhursts are coming.' Her voice cooed.

'I do not know. Perhaps, yes. I must look in my diary, of course.'

Arabella's look was constrained, her lips set. Behind her, as I felt, the man who had escorted her in was nudging her bottom. It was of an ample size, though not too large by comparison with her stately curves. Her face turned to her escort as if pleading. He shook his head. I saw the table then. It had indeed been pushed forward. Upon its nearest edge was a large velvet cushion. Her long legs appeared to stiffen as she approached it. Her footsteps dragged. Her shoes were silver as I saw from the occasional peeping of her toes beneath the hem of her gown.

Jenny covered my eyes again. I had not looked at Caroline. Her veins throbbed in mine. Her lips were my lips. We had been bound together naked. I had sipped her saliva.

There were murmurings, whispers, protestations, retreats. The doors to the morning-room opened and closed, re-opened and closed again.

'It is private,' I heard my aunt say to others. The room was stiller. I heard a cry as from Arabella.

'Lift her gown fully,' a voice said, 'hold her arms.'

'Not here . . . ' She seemed unable to say anything else. Not here, not here, not here, not here. A rustling sound. Slight creak of wood. A gasp. Plaintive.

'Remove her drawers.'

'She was unseemly? Is she not betrothed to him?' It was my aunt's voice. To whom she spoke I knew not. I guessed it to be the escort. His voice was dry and thin.

'Improper,' he replied. The word fell like the closing of a book. 'Take them right off. Do not let her kick,' he said.

'No! not the birch!' A wail from Arabella. The modulations of my aunt's voice and the military gentleman's amused me. They were tonally flat – courteous. Would he have her bound, my aunt asked. It was not necessary, he said, but her wrists should be held.

I envisaged her bent over the table, the globe of her bottom gleaming. Her garters would be of white satin, flecked with red. The deep of her groove – the inrolling. Her breathing came to me, filtering its small waiting sobs. The dry rustling sound of a birch. I had never yet tasted the twigs. It was said that they should be softened first.

'Not bound,' my aunt said. Her voice sounded almost regretful. 'Hilda – you will hold her wrists tight. Stretch her arms out.'

'*Noooooo!*'

The long, sweet aristocratic cry came as the first swishing came. It sounded not as violently as I thought. I wanted to see. My mind groped, grappled for Jenny. Perhaps she had been sent with others to the morning-room. Beside me Caroline uttered a small whimper. Did she fear the birch? She would not receive it. I would protect her. I ran through tunnels calling Father's name. Edward had used his step-mother's first name. She had permitted it. He had lain upon her.

'*Na! Naaaaah!*' A further cry. Her sobbing rose like violins. A creaking of the table. Beneath her raised gown, her underskirt, her chemise, the velvet cushion would press beneath her belly. There was comfort. I comforted myself with the comfort.

The sounds went on. The birch swished gently but firmly as it seemed to me. First across one check then the other, no doubt. The bouncy hemispheres would redden and squirm. Streaks of heat. Was it like the strap? I did not like the stable. Did I like it?

'Ask her now,' the man's voice came. There was whispering – a quavering cry. A negation. Refusal. 'Three more,' he said, 'her drawers were down when I caught them together.'

My aunt tutted. The small dots of her tutting impinged across the sobs, the swishings. They flew like small birds across the room.

'*Whaaah! No-ooooh! Wha-aaaaah!*' Arabella sobbed. I felt her sobs in my throat, globules of anguish swelling. They contracted, slithered down. There was quiet. Her tears would shine upon the polished wood of the table.

'Ask her again.' The same voice, impassive, quiet. The sobs were unending.

'Have you before?' my aunt asked. It was her garden voice, clear and enquiring. The lilt of a question mark that could not fail to invite.

'Twice but she resists. What does she say?' He asked as if to another.

'I cannot hear. Arabella, you must speak, my dear, or take the birch again.' It was undoubtedly the voice of the woman holding her wrists. Who held the birch?

'I c–c–cannot. No – yes – oh do not. Do not let him!'

I saw nods. Through my blindfold I saw nods. I envisaged. There was a shuffling. Wrists tighter held. A jerk of hips. The arrogant bottom out-thrust, burning.

'*No!* not there! *Ah!* it is too big! Not *there!*'

The floor drummed in my dreams. His penis extended, fleshpole, thick-pole, entering. Smack-slap of flesh. The chandeliers glittering with their hundred candles.

Her sobs died, died with their heaving groans. 'N–n–n–n–' she stuttered from moment to moment. At every inward thrust the table creaked. Was she still being held? I needed voices, descriptions.

'Work your bottom, Arabella! Thrust to him!'

My aunt spoke. Their breathings flooded the room. A gulping gasp. A last sob. Silence. 'Have her dress,' my aunt said at last. 'Hilda see to her hair, bathe her face, she has been good. Have you not been good, Arabella?' A mumbling. Kissing. 'So good,' my aunt said. Bodies moved, moved past us and were gone. The doors to the morning-room were re-opened. A flooding of people, a flurry, voices. Enquiries. My aunt would not answer. The deeper voice of my uncle said occasionally, 'I do not know.'

My limbs ached, yet I was proud in my aching that I had not struggled. I was free in my proudness, my pride. We could speak but we had not spoken. Our minds whispered. We were wicked.

A chink of light. Our blindfolds were removed. Caroline blinked more than I. She had not seen before. People stared at us more strangely now. They were of all ages. Eyes glowed at the bobbing of our breasts.

'You must go to bed. A servant will bring you supper,' Jenny said.

I moved carefully, cautiously – wanting to be touched, not wanting to be touched. My hips swayed. I thought of Arabella.

As we reached the bottom of the stairs she began to descend. We waited. I wanted to be masked. Accompanying her was the older woman in purple. I knew then that it was she who had held her wrists. Their eyes passed across us unseeing.

'And there will be a garden party – for the church, you know,' the woman in purple said.

Arabella's eyes were clear, her voice soft and beautifully modulated.

'Of course – I should love to come,' she replied. They entered the drawing-room together as we went up.

'Did you see?' Caroline asked me the next morning.

'There was nothing to see. People were making noises,' I replied. I wanted her to sense that I was more innocent than she.

'Uncle felt my breasts,' she said. She looked pleased.

# Chapter Ten

I like the mornings, the bright mornings, the sunhazed mornings.

It was so when we sat in the breakfast room that morning, Caroline and I. The chairs had been taken away save for hers and mine.

'You will breakfast alone in future,' our aunt said. 'Eat slowly, chew slowly. Have you bathed?' We nodded. Jenny passed the door and looked in at us. Her face held the expression of a sheet of paper. There was a riding crop in her hand. It smacked a small smacking sound against her thigh.

The drawing-room had looked immaculate as we passed – its doors wide open, announcing innocence. The walls against which we had been bound were covered with mirrors, paintings. Perhaps we had dreamed the night.

There would be riding, Aunt Maude said. We were not to change. Our summer dresses would suffice. Katherine passed the window, walking on the flagstones at the edge of the lawn. She wore a long white dress that trailed on the ground. The neck was low and frilled. The melons of her breasts showed. Her straw hat was broadbrimmed. There were tiny flowers painted around the band. She carried a white parasol. Her servant walked behind her in a grey uniform.

When we had eaten Jenny came again to the door and beckoned us. We followed her through the grounds and beyond the fence into the meadow. Frederick stood waiting, holding the reins of two fine chestnut horses. They were gifts to us, Jenny said. The leather of the new saddles was covered in blue velvet. We were told to mount. The servant looked away. He studied the elms on the high rise of the ground in the distance.

'Swing your legs over the saddles. You will ride as men ride. No side-saddle,' Jenny told us. The breeze lifted my skirt, showing my bottom. We wore no drawers. I exposed my bush. Frederick had turned to hold the reins of both horses. The stallions stood like statues. The velvet was soft and warm between my thighs. The lips of my pussy spread upon it.

*Jericho.*

Jenny said we were to ride around her in a tight circle, I clockwise, Caroline counter-clockwise. The servant turned my horse. I faced the house. It looked small and distant. A doll's house. When we returned and entered it we would become tiny.

Jenny clapped her hands and we began. The movement of the velvet beneath me made my lips part with pleasure. Caroline's face was flushed as she passed me, the flanks of our steeds almost brushing. Our hair rose and flowed outwards in the breeze. We kept our backs straight as we had been taught. Father could not have reached up so high to smack me.

'Straighten your legs – lift your bottoms – high!' Jenny called. She stood in the middle of the circle we made. The breeze lifted our skirts, exposing us. The hems of our skirts curled and flowed about our waists. The sky spun about me.

'Higher!' Jenny commanded. Our knees straightened. Frederick had gone. I was pleased. In profile the pale moon of Caroline's bottom flashed past me. I heard her squeal, a long thin squeal as the crop caught her, light and stinging across her out-thrust cheeks. And then mine! The breath whistled from my throat. I kept my head back. In the far distance near the house two figures were watching. My uncle was watching. Katherine's head lay on his shoulder, her parasol twirling.

Again the crop. It skimmed my naked bottom cheeks, not cutting but skimming as if it were skittering across the face of a balloon. Who had taught her that? It stung, lifting me up on to my toes in the stirrups. I leaned forward, clutching at the horse's mane, breathing my whistling cries to the far-deep empty sky.

At the twelfth stroke of the crop upon each of us, Jenny raised her hand. We slowed, we cantered, we reined in. Panting we fell forward, exposing our burning bottoms to the air. The breeze was cool across our pumpkins hot.

'Dismount!' Jenny called. Frederick the servant was returning. He carried things. 'Stable them!' Jenny ordered him. She referred I thought to the horses, but he ignored them. My bottom tightened as he approached. The ground would receive me – surely it would receive me. I would bury myself in the longer grass and hide until I was called in to tea. I would be fifteen again.

The leather collar bands that I now saw in the servant's hands were broad and thick, studded with steel points on the outer surfaces. My eyes said no but he did not look. I wrote a question silently on my lips as I used to do with Father in the attic. The servant could not read. He fastened the first collar around my neck. A chain ran down my back. The tip of it settled in the outcurving of my buttocks. From behind me then where Caroline stood I heard a small cry.

'No, Caroline, be still!' Jenny hissed. 'Walk forward to the barn now!'

Behind us the servant held the chains, one in each hand like reins. We stumbled over the grass, the rough hillocks.

'Why?' Caroline asked. It was only to herself that she spoke, but Jenny answered her. She walked beside us, ushering our steps.

'Love is firmness, Caroline. You are the privileged ones. Halt!'

We had neared the stable doors. They were open. The darkness within yawned upon the meadow, eating the air that came near it. Katherine was there. She closed her parasol and leaned it against one of the doors.

'Leave this – I will see to them,' she told Jenny.

'Yes, Madame,' Jenny answered. Was she not queen? Who was queen? The chains snaked against our backs, urging us forward. And within. In the flushing of Caroline's cheeks I could feel my flushing.

'Over there,' Katherine said and pointed. There were two stalls – too narrow for horses. The dividing wall between them was but a foot high. I saw the chains again, the wall rings. Caroline wilted and would have stepped back. She was prodded forward. The manacles, ankle rings and chains all were secured. We stood side by side, the low wall between us. I wanted the back of my hand to touch Caroline's hand, but it could not.

'Their dresses, you fool – raise their skirts,' Katherine said. I felt Frederick's hands. They were strong but delicate. Not touching my legs or bottom he bared me to my waist. Caroline quivered and bit her lip as he repeated the action with her.

'Wash their flanks,' Katherine said.

I heard a clink of bucket. The sponge attended to us both. Water trickled over our buttocks and thighs. It ran down into the tops of my stockings and lay in rills around the tight rims. Patted roughly, we were dried.

'They are fair mounts. What do you think, Frederick?'

'Yes, Madame.'

His voice was stiff, expressionless. I relaxed my bottom, feeling its glow – the aftermath of the cropping. The outcurving cheeks above my dampy thighs were roseate. I could see them in my mind. I wished I could see Katherine now in her white dress, but my back was held to her. She is very beautiful. Her dark hair flows down over her shoulders.

'Display, Frederick!'

Her voice was curt. She waited. I could hear her waiting, the sound of her waiting, like a bell that has stopped tolling and waits for the rope to be pulled again.

'Madame?'

His voice was a croak. Was he afraid? I felt not afraid. The day lay upon me, soft of the morning. My flesh bloomed. The damp upon my flesh was warm with my flesh. The tops of my stockings chilled. Caroline breathed through her nose. There were noises, shufflings, small metal noises, cloth noises.

Cloth makes noises like fog.

Display? What was display?

'Turn them!' I heard Katherine say. Ah, it was strange. He held his loins back as he obeyed so that the wavering crest of his pintle-pestle would not touch us. It was long and thick. I like long and thick now. The chains rattled. We were turned. I saw through the barn doors as through a huge eye. The world outside disenchanted me. There was an emptiness. Katherine sat on a bale, her legs crossed. Her skirts were drawn up to show her knees. She smiled at me a light smile, a wisp of a smile. Caroline's face was scarlet. The servant was naked. His balls were big. His penis was a horn of plenty.

We stood side by side, still – children waiting to be called to the front of the class. For punishment or to be given prizes? Frederick's body was slender, muscular.

'Come!' Katherine said to him. He turned and moved to her. His back was to us, but he did not look at her. I could feel he did not. His glance was high. Above her head. In homage high. There was a trestle close – two pairs of legs shaped in a narrow V with a bar across. He moved to the front of it and stopped. His back touched the bar. Then he bent – a backward bend – so that his spine arched over the bar, his palms flat on the floor beyond. His penis stuck straight up.

Katherine moved her long wide skirt with an elegant gesture and slipped down off the bale. She came to us. We had kept our legs apart. She was pleased.

'Caroline will lie with her face between my thighs tonight, Beatrice. I shall wear black stockings – pearls around my neck. My thighs will clench her ears. Will you see? Do you wish to see?'

My eyes pleaded. She laughed. She squeezed my chin until my lips parted. 'You can see his cock,' she breathed. Her tongue snaked within my mouth. I tasted the breath of her, warm and sweet as Benedictine. She twirled her tongue, then moved to Caroline.

'Put your tongue in my mouth – *Caroline!*'

Oh, the fool she should have obeyed immediately. Katherine slapped her face. The tip of Frederick's prick quivered.

'I shall commence exercising you soon, Caroline. Do you understand?'

'No.' My sister's voice was small as if she were hiding behind a pew in church.

'You say, "No, Madame." '

'No, Madame.'

Caroline can be dutiful. I like her body. It curves so sweetly. Her breasts and bottom are plentiful.

'You will learn,' Katherine said. Then Jenny entered. It was a play – a private play, I felt. She stood in the doorway, hands on hips, observing us. Was she jealous? When Katherine turned, Jenny's hands dropped immediately to her sides. There were no words yet. It was a mime.

'Let him rise,' Katherine commanded. Jenny smiled. She walked forward and flicked her crop against his straining tool. He groaned in his rising. His eyes were haggard.

'You may choose,' Katherine told her. Jenny tossed her head. She looked from one to the other of us. She strode – strode to Caroline and pulled her forward.

'Please no,' Caroline said. Her feet skittered, dragged. Her free hand pleaded to the air. The servant had turned to face her. He had tucked our dresses up sufficiently tightly for them to remain so. I wanted to kiss Caroline's bottom. The cheeks are firm and plump. Her pubis pouts.

'Bend her over the trestle,' Katherine said.

Caroline shrieked. Jenny had hold of the chain from her neckband and pulled it tight, forcing her over. Caroline's shriek dropped like a fallen handkerchief and lay there, crumpled and used. Her back was bent until she was forced to place her palms on the floor. Her bottom mounded. The sweet fig of her slit showed.

The servant waited. His erection remained as stiff as ever. There was excitement.

'Dip!' Katherine said.

There were new words. I was learning them. Display – dip. His eyes burned. Caroline's hips were high. He took them, gripped them. Rebelliously she endeavoured to twist them but he held her. His lips moved. I wanted words to come – a revelation – but no words came. His loins arched. The crest of his penis touched, probed.

'Caroline! Do not move or speak or you will be whipped!' Katherine said.

She stood observing, as one observes. It was so in the drawing-room the night before when my aunt watched the waiting penis enter between the cheeks of Arabella's bottom. I could see now only the servant's haunches, his balls hanging below. Caroline bubbled a moan. Was it speech? His shaft entered – slow, but slow – the petal lips parting to receive it. The straining veins, the purplish head, the foreskin stretched.

Caroline's head jerked up and then was pulled back down by the tensioning of the chain in Jenny's grip.

'*No*, Caroline!' Jenny said softly.

Four inches, five. Caroline's mouth opened. Perhaps she had not, as I thought, sucked upon the penis. Her lovemouth gripped. The ring of truth. Cries gurgled from her lips. Six inches, seven. The fit was tight. I saw her buttocks squeeze, relax. His hands moved to the fronts of her thighs, suavely gripping them. A burr of stocking tops to his palms.

'*No-ooooh!*'

A soft, faint whimper. *In!* Ensconced. Buried to the hilt, his balls hung beneath her bottom.

A second ticked. Two. Three.

'*Out!*' Katherine snapped.

Gleaming, his shaft emerged. I saw his face in profile, the lines etched as by Durer. She jerked her head. He moved towards his clothes. Caroline blubbered softly, her hips wriggled as if she still contained him. Jenny drew her up by the chain. Caroline's eyes floated with tears. Her face suffused.

In the house – not until in the house – were our neck halters removed. We stood in the morning-room. We waited. Katherine moved to Caroline and stroked her cheek.

'Are you learning?' she asked. There was summer in her voice.

'Madame?'

Caroline's voice was blank, soft as the sponge that had laved us. Katherine shook her head. 'It does not matter,' she said. We shared secrets, but I knew not what they were. The secret between Caroline's thighs tingled. I could feel its tingling like a buzzing on my lips. Caroline was wicked. I felt certain

that she was. Her containment had been too great. She should have cried.
Would I have cried? Katherine turned away.

'You know I will whip you if you do not tell me, Caroline.'

Caroline's lips moved, burbled, hummed. 'M–m–m–' Her thighs trembled.
Katherine turned back to her.

'That is better,' she smiled, 'you are naughty, Caroline, you know you are.
I have to train you. Frederick is trained. Do you not think he is well trained?'

Caroline bent her head. She was alone. Each of us alone except when we
are kissing, touching. Sometimes when I am being touched I am alone.
There was a small cloud around her lips, pretty lips. It said yes. Katherine
was pleased again. Aunt Maude entered. There was movement. Unspeaking
she took my arm and led me out.

Upstairs in my room she removed my dress. I saw the bed and it was not
my bed, not the bed I had slept in. The headboard was different. Wrist
clamps hung from the headboard. She made me lie down. She straightened
my stockings and drew my legs apart. I waited for my ankles to be secured. I
was passive. She drew my arms above my head and fastened the wrist straps.
Her face bent over mine.

'It is for your good, Beatrice. Are you happy?'

I said yes. I wanted to please her. Proud in my bonds I lay. My belly made
a slight curve.

'Perhaps,' she answered. It was a strange word. 'You will grow happy.
Edward was weak for you, was he not?'

I nodded. The morning light grew and bloomed over my body. I had fine
breasts, good haunches, a slender waist, Aunt Maude said. Was Jenny nice to
me, she asked. I thought yes, no. I wanted to be kissed. I parted my lips as
Jenny had told me to. I was not sure, Aunt Maude said. I would be sure soon.
She bent over and kissed me and laid her fingers on the innerness of my
nearest thigh. Her mouth was warm and full.

'Flick your tongue a little, Beatrice. Quick little flicks with half your
tongue.'

She was teaching me. Our mouths fused together. Her forefinger brushed
my button – too lightly. My hips bucked. My aunt stopped kissing me and
smiled. She sat up. Regarding me, she unbuttoned her dress and laid it back
from her shoulders. Her breasts were heavy gourds, the nipples dark brown
and thick. Brown in their darkness brown. The gourds loomed over my face,
brushed my chin, my nose. My aunt purred a purring sound. Her breasts
swung like bells across my mouth. The nipples grew and teased between my
lips. I wanted to bite.

Katherine entered. She waited and my aunt rose.

'He has not whipped her yet?' Katherine asked. Aunt Maude shook her
head.

'Soon, perhaps.'

'Yes,' Katherine said. She removed her dress, the filmy folds. Her stockings were silver, banded by black garters of ruched silk. Her drawers were of black satin, small, such as a ballet dancer wears. Her breasts jiggled free. She sat at the dressing table beside my bed. Aunt Maude stripped off her own dress and stood at Katherine's back, brushing her hair. They smiled at one another in the mirror. The smile would stay there for a moment like the impress of my lips when I used to kiss myself after Father had spanked me.

Katherine rose. My aunt looked superb in her stockings, bootees, a waspie corset, frilled knickers. They exchanged sentences with their eyes as if they were posting small, personal notes. My aunt nodded. Katherine mounted the bed over me at my shoulders, facing my feet. The moon of her bottom loomed over my face.

'Her legs,' she said.

The board of the bed to which my ankles were now tethered and spread moved forward, making my knees bend. It was an ingenious device, as I later discovered. The upright board was fixed to legs which rested on heavy castors. Being slightly wider than the bed itself, the legs and the board were able to be moved at will. My knees were bent up, splayed. The globe of Katherine's knickered bottom brushed the tip of my nose. It descended. In a darkness of bliss it squashed upon my mouth, my eyes, my face.

I tasted her.

'Do not move your lips, Beatrice – it is forbidden!'

I could not breathe. The fleshweight of her hemispheres was upon me. The impress of the lips of her slit in their silken net were upon my mouth. Her bottom bloomed its bigness over me. I panted.

Her bottom moved, ground over my face. It lifted but an inch. I gulped in air. Smothered again, I grunted, gasped. Aunt Maude had a feather. The tip of it, the tickling tip of it, passed upwards in my cunny. I gurgled, choked. The feather twirled, inserted and withdrew. Air whistled through my nostrils and was squashed again. My loins shifted, jerked.

The agony of ecstasy was intense at the feather's touching. A wisping of wickedness, it passed around my clit, tickling and burning. My bottom thumped. The bed creaked. The sides of my face were gripped tight between Katherine's silken thighs. Long tendrils of desire urged their desire within my cunny. My bottom lifted, pleading, in my smothering. Musk, perfume, acrid sweetness – I knew them all.

Let me be loved, in my desiring.

No – Katherine swung off me. Her panties were wet. Sweat glistened on my brow, my cheeks. My loins itched, stung. My mouth was wet with her. I closed my eyes and whispered with Caroline behind a pew. We wore candy-striped blouses, pretty bonnets. We chewed bonbons. I wanted one.

They turned me quickly, unloosing the shackles swiftly. Once on my belly the bonds were refastened. The board at the foot of the bed pressed farther up, forcing my knees up almost to my breasts. The cleft of my pumpkin was exposed.

Something nosed between my cheeks. A velvet touch, a thin dildo of leather swathed in a velvet sheath. The oiled nose of it probed my rose, the tight puckering of my secret mouth, the O of my anus.

'N–n–n–n–' I choked. It penetrated sleekly, entered. My mouth mouthed in my pillow. In the heat of it, the ice of it, I felt it, slender, long, like Edward's penis. Edward had never attempted my bottom. He did not know it had been smacked.

'*Oooooh!*'

One should not cry out. Should one cry out? I am quieter now. I accept. I am given, loved, I submit. In my moods. It was different then. My bottom mouth gripped it in a grip of treachery – the sleek black velvet of my velvet love. The pointed nose oozed in and twirled. My bottom was riven. In the wild twisting of my face and hips I saw Katherine's legs. Thighs of ivory splendour. Rotating, it withdrew. I was opened. I bit my pillow. The stinging sweetness tremored in my loins. The oil which had been smoothed upon it made it slippery. I grimaced, cried.

Katherine laughed. 'Enough – it is enough. How sweetly she sobs – how her bottom bulges to it.'

'It was so when she was spanked. She should be whipped now,' my aunt said. A faint succulent *plop* and it deserted me. I was hollow, empty. I needed. My O was a bigger O. I dived beneath sandcastles of shame. My toes wriggled. *Foutre.*

Was Father's ship sailing back? It would beach at Eastbourne. People on the beach would run screaming, the pebbles sliding beneath their feet. My father with a cutlass would descend.

They released me. The board moved back. My legs straightened. My wrists and ankles were freed. I sank down, curling up. I would become a hedgehog. Gypsies would catch me.

'Shall we go out now, Beatrice?'

It was Katherine's voice. I turned. She was putting on her dress. My aunt was putting on her own dress. She buttoned it with the air of someone who had had it accidentally removed, or by a doctor perhaps. I hid my eyes.

'Yes,' I said. I felt shy. Katherine clapped her hands with pleasure. She reached down and pulled me up.

'Come – get dressed you silly girl. How old are you?'

'Twenty-five,' I said. I had said that to Father. They all knew. Why did they ask? Aunt Maude scolded me to brush my hair.

'Don't be a naughty girl, Beatrice,' she said.

## Chapter Eleven

Facing the open gates my uncle sat holding the reins of the horses. The cab was the same as that we had arrived in.

Caroline and I wore straw boaters, plain high-necked white blouses and long black skirts. Our hair was drawn back with ribbons. My aunt and Katherine entered with us.

'Keep your hands still,' my aunt said. There was a jerk and the carriage started up the slope. It bumped exceedingly again. At the top we turned right – in the opposite direction to which we had come – and proceeded along the lanes. A few yokels moved aside at our coming, but otherwise no other carriage passed us.

Aunt Maude and Katherine toyed with their gloves and spoke of balls, receptions, dances. I envied their pleasures. My face was demure. I wanted to ask where we were going but I knew it was forbidden. After some six miles we reached a place that was too small for a town and yet too large to be a village.

Over the cobbles of the streets we rattled until we came to a house facing a pond and a green. Two children ran playing with hoops over the grass. The house was of stone, the windows small. It was set amid a walled garden.

'Shall they come in?' Katherine asked. My aunt nodded. They descended first. My uncle helped us down. His expression was one of great seriousness. He was dressed formally in top hat, grey jacket, waistcoat and black trousers.

He led us forward towards the gate to the drive of the house as if we were approaching for a family portrait to be taken. The door was black, inset with frosted glass. The knocker was of brass in the semblance of a lion's head. There was a bell which my uncle pulled. It tinkled with broken notes somewhere within. Almost immediately a servant maid answered. She curtsied at the sight of my uncle and aunt.

My uncle presented his card as we entered the hall. The maid took it upon a small silver tray and vanished. In but a moment she returned and ushered us within a drawing-room where a middle-aged couple sat in highbacked chairs. They rose as one. Not having the advantage of facing the sun, the room had a certain gloom.

I waited to be introduced. Instead, Katherine pointed to a small love-seat in one corner. 'Sit there,' she said. We threaded our way through the furniture and sat like doves, side by side, our hands in our laps.

Port was dispensed. We each received a glass. To my astonishment and amid the blushes of Caroline my aunt spoke of us to the lady she addressed as Ruby. She gave our ages and certain details of our training. We sat mute. Only our Christian names were given.

'They are most certainly quiet and well-behaved,' the lady said. She turned her gaze upon us and appraised us. We kept our eyes lowered – Caroline out of shyness and confusion, I out of discernment. I felt it would please her. It did. The gentleman displayed a greater interest in us. Leaning forward in his chair he spoke in a low voice to my aunt. Twice she nodded then he rose. He approached us, fiddling with his watch chain. We stirred not.

'Do not move,' Katherine said quietly to us. 'Look up!'

We raised our eyes. He was a stocky man in his prime. Caroline gave a little jump as he bent down and placed his hands upon her blouse, cupping her breasts. I could feel their warmth and weight as on my own hands. He attended next to my own, running the balls of his thumbs about my nipples. They stirred and pointed into the cotton of my blouse. His hands trembled exceedingly. The projection in his breeches was one of considerable menace.

He returned to his seat. His breathing sounded laboured. Katherine's eyes remarked his condition, I know. His wife laid her hand upon his when he took his chair again beside her. Her glance came to us again.

'May we take them upstairs?' she asked.

My aunt inclined her head. 'I regret . . .' she said. Her voice was formal as if she were writing the words on parchment. 'We should see Amanda, perhaps.'

There was a nodding. The servant was summoned. Miss Amanda would be asked to come down, she was told. We waited. The clock upon the mantelpiece threw tiny arrows of sound into the carpet. My nipples grew turgid again and softened. Footsteps. The door opened. A young lady of about twenty-three years appeared. She was dressed in simple attire: a blue dress that clothed her form admirably. A tasselled cord of blue velvet drew the material in at her waist. She was slender. Her legs were long. Her high breasts made themselves appealingly visible through the material. Her dark hair was swept back behind her ear. A pearl necklace and matching earrings adorned her. Her eyes were large and faintly wondering. Her mouth had a petulant look.

There were introductions from which my sister and I were again excluded. Amanda looked towards us. We avoided her glance as if by inverted politeness. Amid the chairs she stood like a hunted fawn.

'I do not want to go,' she said. Her voice was shrunken, distant. Katherine's eyes absorbed the delicate outcurving of her bottom.

'It will take but a month, perhaps less,' my aunt said. She spoke as if Amanda were not present. The seance it seemed was then at end. There was a rising as if of marionettes.

'Take your cloak,' the lady said to Amanda who had laid small white teeth into her lower lip.

'But if I promise . . .' Amanda began.

'It is a nonsense – she will not even be spanked,' the lady said, addressing my aunt. In the same moment Katherine took Amanda's wrist. 'Come!' she said sharply. We knew that the word was addressed to ourselves as well. A bustling, a rustling, an opening and closing of doors and we were gone. The carriage kicked up a fine dust with its departure. The children with the hoops stared after us. Amanda sat pale and quiet between Caroline and me.

'Amanda – you must not be dismayed, we shall treat you well,' my aunt said. 'There will be strawberries and cream for tea.'

Caroline and I smiled because we were meant to smile. The passing countryside had the remote look of scenery painted on canvas. I wanted to return to my room and lie still. To my surprise Caroline and I were sent upstairs freely on our own upon our return.

No one followed us. The doors to our rooms lay open. We lingered uncertainly between them.

'Was it too big?' I asked. She knew my mind and that I was speaking of the stable. Transparent shutters came down over her eyes.

'It was naughty,' Caroline said. Teeth like pips of a pomegranate showed between her lips. 'Why did she?' she asked. There was a childish breathlessness in her voice that I sensed she considered appealing.

I brushed tendrils of golden hair from her forehead. I removed her boater and my own and guided her into my room. A boldness seized me. I closed the door.

'You have to be trained,' I said. I knew the words. I felt older. The scent of beyond was in my nostrils. The air was clean in my eyes.

'Why?'

I was truthful. 'I do not know, Caroline.' We stared at one another. 'When Aunt Maude was caning you . . .' I began. I wanted to know.

Caroline said, 'It was tight and it stung.' The wonder around her mouth was like traces of cream. I kissed her lower lip and sucked it in. A bee's kiss. The tips of our tongues touched and played. My hands held her hips lightly. We both thought of Amanda. I knew that.

'In the linen room . . . ' I said.

Her eyes were hot. 'I know . . .'

Her form was limp as I began to raise her skirt. My hands sought her stocking tops, the sweet warm flesh above. Caroline placed her hands on my shoulders. 'It was nice,' she said thickly. A small unravelling of lust was within me. I moved my hands up to the tie of her drawers and loosed it. They sagged, fell to her knees. I knew my wickedness. The curls about her cunny tickled my palm. I felt her moisture.

'You were long in the summerhouse,' I said. I had not forgotten. The rolled lips of her slit were oily on my palm. 'Was it good?'

Caroline's arms clasped my neck. She seemed about to faint. Her thighs parted so that her knees held her drawers taut. 'Yes,' she said. I felt dizzy with a sweet sickness. The sea waves lapped us.

'It is good,' a voice said. We jerked and clutched one another. I did not want to look. It was Katherine's voice. 'But you were told not to – were you not told?' she asked. My hands dropped. Caroline's skirt half fell but remained coiled about her knees. The legs of her fallen knickers showed.

Katherine beckoned me. 'I know your devilment,' she said and smacked me hard about the bottom. I jumped and squealed as Caroline often squealed. Her hand was as sharp as Father's. There were old photographs in my mind, tinted with dust. The wing of a dead bee on my sleeve.

Caroline sat at command, forlorn. My wrist was gripped. The door to the bedroom left wide open, I was taken upstairs. 'The second door,' Katherine said. She unlocked it and pushed me roughly within. The room was long and bare. There were cages, the bars of slender ironwork. Three cages stood in a triangle, each the size of a small closet. There were benches, leather-covered. A wooden bar hung across trestles stood in the centre of the floor. Two skylights misted with dust allowed the day to enter.

Katherine stripped me quickly of my dress and drawers and placed me, booted and stockinged, in the nearest cage. I wailed a small wail as the door clanged and closed. A bowl of strawberries and cream, a plate of brown bread and butter and a bottle of white wine lay in the small space at my feet.

Katherine walked to the door. Opening it she glanced back at me and said, 'You are lucky, Beatrice. You are the chosen.' There was silence and she was gone.

I crouched to eat and drink. There was no spoon with which to eat the strawberries. The cream dripped from my fingers. I licked it. A small drop lay upon the springing of my pussy curls. The wine had been uncorked. I sucked upon the neck of the bottle. The cool gurgling. I did not want the bread.

The door looked at me beyond. It was padded with thick black leather, rimmed all around with metal studs. I liked it. The door would be my friend.

Half an hour passed. I leaned back against the bars and felt one of the cool round rods between the cheeks of my bottom. The sensation was pleasant. I pressed against it but the contact was not as I wished. I could not bend forward. The door opened. My aunt Maude led Amanda in; unbound, her dark hair was as long as my own. At her pubis the triangle of curls was crisp and neat. Her stockings were banded at the tops by metal rings. Her long legs teetered in the same mode of high-heeled boots that Caroline and I were made to wear. Her breasts were pale mounds of jellied glory. She held her head high in her nakedness, her pride stung by shame.

'I did not want to come,' she blurted. My aunt ignored her. The door of the cage next to mine swung open. On the floor the same meal awaited her that I had received.

'You would not obey – you know you would not obey,' my aunt said. The lock clicked. 'Beatrice, be still and finish your wine. It is good for you.' Her heels sounded loud upon the floor. The studded door closed. All was still. I drank my wine. If there were two bottles I would have poured some over my breasts. I would have raised my nipples to the bars so that Amanda could lick them. Her bottom was quite delicious. Tight and small. Like half a peach it jutted. Had she been tried, trodden, mounted? I was naïve then. I should have known that she had not been.

Amanda tried to look at me. She could not. Her hand gripped the bars. Her other arm fell lax. In sagging she showed the sweet curve of her hip.

'It is hateful,' she said. She did not ask me who I was. I had wanted her to ask.

'You have not been spanked,' I said.

Her eyes were lidded. She had a small, delicate voice. 'Have you?' she asked.

'Often.' I poured a little wine over my finger and sucked it. I did not want the cage between us. We could have kissed with the cage between us. Her face was oval, cold. There were no mirrors in her eyes. I nibbled a piece of bread. I forgot that I did not want it.

'What will they do?' Amanda asked. Her mouth was small. Under pressure it could be made to kiss with succulence. I like *succulence*. It is like *foutre*.

'They will train you,' I said. She stared at me with her mouth open. The metal bands around her thighs fascinated me. They fitted by being slid up her legs where, at the greater swelling, they stopped and gripped as a finger ring does. They had been made for her, she said. She had kicked exceedingly when they were first fitted a month ago. She had been held and had been made to wear them ever since.

'Who fits them?' I asked. She blushed and would not answer. I felt a small impatience with her. 'Drink your wine,' I said. She needed to be unlocked, eased, made supple.

The thought stirred me. I was my first revelation.

## *Chapter Twelve*

Jenny appeared and passed my drawers to me through the bars.

'Put them on – your uncle is coming,' she said. I scrambled into them just in time. My hands were pious over my breasts.

Uncle did not look at me. Jenny opened Amanda's cage and brought her out. She cowed under his gaze and tried to hide her pubis. Jenny smacked her wrists. There was a strap in my uncle's hand, broad and thick – the same perhaps that our bottoms had tasted in the stable.

Amanda's ankles twisted, causing her to stumble. Jenny took her to the bar which was at waist height. The wood was round and polished. In the centre where her belly would rest was a slight dip.

'Bend and keep your heels together. Grip the lower bar tightly,' my uncle told her.

Was his voice more authoritative than the one she had known? Her eyes were dull. For a moment she stared at the wall and then obeyed.

'Please not too hard. May I go then?'

Her voice was a Sunday-school voice. Jenny bent and fastened a broad strap round her ankles. Stepping back she glanced at me over her shoulder. I looked at the door, my friendly door. It would grow warm if I leaned against it.

My uncle approached Amanda whose display was quite delicious. Of a purpose, as I realised, her hands were not tied to the lower bar. The orb of her bottom was flawless – the cleft tinted with sepia in its innerness. The strap lifted and uncoiled.

*Cra-aaaaack!* Ah, the *splat* of it – the deep-kissing leather kiss across her girlishness! Amanda winced in anguish, her mouth sagged. A low wail came. The strokes were slow and lazy – insistent. The weight of the leather appeared to need only an indolent movement of arm and wrist. Sometimes it fell across, sometimes under – under the offered apple where the long thighs met and the skin made small creases as if puckering itself in readiness for the outbulge.

Each *splat* brought a higher gasp from her. Her bottom became a haze of pink and white. Her knuckles whitened where they gripped the lower bar.

'*Noo–Noo–Noo–Noooooo!*' she pleaded. Her hips began to make more violent motions of rejection. At each stroke the tight cheeks tightened. A big man's hands would have encompassed both cheeks together. A split melon. I wanted my tongue to pass around it in its warmth, its heat out-giving, receiving. I counted ten, twelve, fourteen. Amanda gritted her teeth. Was she crying far within herself? The glow of her bottom was luminous, yet no marks showed. I have since learned the art of it, have heard it called indeed, 'French polishing'. The leather must never be thin. Thin would be cruel.

The metal bands that held the tops of Amanda's stockings rubbed together. Her knees sagged, making her bottom orb out more. A low whoooo-hooooooing sound hummed from her lips. It is the sound one waits for.

My uncle ceased. I could hear her sobbing, but it was not a sobbing of pain. It was the sobbing of a child who has lost her toys. The sobbing of a child who has ceased to cry when nobody listens.

'Be quiet, Amanda – *Quiet!*'

Jenny's voice was a voice of love. She unfastened the strap around the girl's ankles, drew her legs wide apart and fastened each to the sides of the stand. The salmon-pink of her lovelips showed. Amanda cried out and made to rise, but Jenny took the nape of her neck and forced her down again. My uncle turned away. I wanted him to look at me, to acknowledge my existence, the modesty of my posture with my palms cupped over my breasts. But he did not. He went as one who vaguely recalls an errand to be done. His walk was awkward, stiff. His erection was considerable.

With his exit Aunt Maude appeared. In her hands were a phial of warm, sweet oil and a long thin dildo.

I watched, I listened. I no longer needed to cover my breasts. An oiled finger moved about Amanda's restlessly rolling globe. It sought her rose, her bottom mouth. Jenny's hand was laid now on her down-bent head. All was silence save for her rushing gasps. The dildo when it entered her did so fraction by fraction, upwards between the cheeks, parting their parting.

'Nnnnnnnn . . . ' Amanda hummed. Her neck and shoulders strained against the pressure of Jenny's hand in vain. Her hips twisted wildly. The dildo rotated slowly in my aunt's fingers, half embedded. Twirling it, she began to glide it back and forth.

'Sweet mare – you will take his piston yet,' she murmured. Her voice was without malice. It spoke of hushed rooms, drawn curtains, a muted sun.

'No – Oh – Oh!'

Amanda's voice rose on a long singsong note, but there was no reply. The dildo entered another inch and then withdrew. Jenny unstrapped her and led her back to the cage. Amanda slumped down sobbing, her face covered. Her elbow tilted the bottle of wine. The neck fell trapped between the bars.

'Why does she cry? We are a benediction,' my aunt said.

'They are tears of wrath,' Jenny answered. She looked uncertain as if she had collected the wrong words together. She looked to Aunt Maude for refuge. My aunt frowned.

'The spirit of NO is being driven from her,' she said. She motioned to my cage. The door was unlocked. I was led without as if I were going to communion. The bar received me. 'Caress her first – she is the worthy one,' my aunt said.

With my thighs together I was bent as slowly as a mechanism under test. I grasped the bar. My fingers lay upon the ghosts of Amanda's. Jenny's fingers felt for the pouting of my nest, the lovelips pursed. With her free hand she palmed the warm cheeks of my bottom. The upper crease of my slit into which her fingertip wormed, parted just sufficiently to allow her to love-tease my button. I murmured softly in my mind. Pleasure-travellers voyaged through my nerves. The cheeks of my bottom quivered to the urging in-thrust of Jenny's other forefinger.

From the other side of the bar my aunt bent and fondled my breasts very gently as if she were handling hothouse fruit. Her thumbs spoke to my nipples, whispered over them, erected them. Rigid cones on hillocks of snow.

'It is enough – she holds the pose well,' Aunt Maude said.

I knew the strap then – knew its bite. Jenny, who wielded it, permitted me to sway my hips, catching the left cheek as I swayed left – the right as I swayed right. I knew the humming sound in my head the burgeoning of images, pictures, wickednesses. The heat was tempest to my flesh. I moaned in my undoing.

Twelve? Did I count twelve? My knees sagged. I needed a mouth beneath my open mouth. Amanda was a wax statue in a cage. I parted my knees. The gesture was not unseen.

'Come,' Jenny said. There was comprehension in her voice. My moist hand in her cool hand. Wriggling like a schoolgirl, I was taken to a divan so narrow that when I lay upon it my legs slipped down on either side.

'Heels firm on the floor – head back,' my aunt said. The heavy heat of my bottom weighed upon the black leather beneath.

Jenny moved behind, took my arms and drew them far back above my head. She held me lightly, fearing no rebellion perhaps.

From her sleeve my aunt drew a long white feather with a curving tip. It passed across my vision. My hips jerked.

'No, Beatrice,' my aunt intoned. Her words were chiding, soft. The stinging in my bottom from the strap deepened and splurged. 'Look at me, Beatrice. Peep your tongue between your lips. Just the tip.'

My eyes were Aunt Maude's eyes. They knew countries of the past I had not visited. My tongue peeped. Amanda would lie on her bed at home. The veils of her undoing would be raised. The strap would rise and fall. The metal bands would become gold bands. The roseate hue of her bottom would dwell in his mornings, illuminate his evenings.

'Good . . . so . . . remain . . . do not stir,' my aunt admonished me. The feather tickled and moved between my thighs. I bit my lip. My tongue retreated.

My aunt was kind. She waited. A bubble of saliva floated from the re-emerging tip of my tongue. It dwelt on my lower lip. I sang in my throat and felt the twirling of the tip – the white heat of it around my button.

Aunt Maude's eyes dared me to turn from hers. I held. Up, down, the feather teased. It entered me. My buttocks rose, fell, rose again. My eyes were saucers on and on. I writhed – the ceiling in my vision swimming in its blankness. On and on.

I broke the rules.

'*Na! Na–aaaaaah!*' I choked.

Starbursts in my belly. My bottom heaved, my heels chattered on the floor. I bucked, absorbing each long inflow of sensations. Starwheels of white heat spun around my clitoris. Out-shooting tendrils of fire swept my body. My tongue protruded. A quivering cry and I slumped, stilled, vacant in frustration. The empty skylights stared at me. A swallow passed across one. Here, now gone.

In a moment I crouched in my cage again. Amanda and I stared at one another like strangers who have too many questions to ask.

# Chapter Thirteen

'Were they good today?' my uncle asked that evening.

We were dressed once more in clinging dresses of the finest wool, our curves displayed. Our boots were thighboots. Stockings. Otherwise we were naked beneath.

'They played in the garden. It was sweet to see them playing in the garden,' my aunt replied.

Katherine was dressed in black – a high-necked dress. A pearl choker adorned her neck. Jenny was dressed identically. My aunt was less formal in an ordinary day gown. Amanda was absent. We sat formally.

'You may talk,' Jenny told us.

Caroline and I looked at one another. We had nothing to say. It was all in the looking. Her nipples peaked through the wool of her dress as did mine. Our globes were outlined. Katherine rose and played softly at the piano. We waited for dinner.

Katherine smiled at us. 'They do not talk very much,' she said.

My aunt inclined her head. 'No – they are lost in their dreams,' she replied. She clapped her hands. There was a tinkling, footsteps. It was Amanda. She bore a tray sparkling with glasses. A tiny white lace cap perched on the side of her glossed hair. The pale pink of her breasts showed through a thin white blouse. The black maid's skirt that she wore had been shortened to show her thighs. With the swaying of its hem the metal rings showed, ringing her black stocking tops.

Walking to my uncle first she bent and offered him a dry sherry. The skirt rose at her bending. Her naked bottom shone pale. No one spoke. When she came to Caroline and me a flush showed on her cheeks. I posted a small smile between her lips. My look was motherly.

Jiggling her bottom cheeks self-consciously, she left. Our eyes were pasted on the half-moons of her bottom like mementoes of a journey.

'She will train better here than at home,' Aunt Maude said. There was a nodding.

'He will give you jewels,' Jenny said and pouted. There was laughter. I contained my own. Caroline's laugh was a small apology of nervousness. My uncle consulted his watch. There was the sound of carriage wheels beyond, a crunching of gravel. The housekeeper flurried to the door. It was Arabella. Her cloak removed in the hallway, she entered in a dull-red dress of silk with elaborate overlays of white lace about the neck. Her diamonds sent messages of light. Without a word she stepped daintily past our chairs like one who is uncertain where to sit. A glass of sherry waited at her elbow.

'The days are good,' my aunt said and smiled at her, raising her glass. Caroline and I were as invisible. 'You have passed the days well?' It was my uncle's voice.

'There was hunting,' Arabella said. She looked faintly bored, as aristocrats often affect to do. Leaning back in her chair she crossed her legs with an audible swishing of silk. 'Three girls – pretty and sprightly. They ran not far. We used the walls of the enclosures and the rose garden beyond. They squealed louder than rabbits upon being caught. We pinioned them and carried them within. There were pleasantries. The gentlemen mounted them in turn. They were common girls – field-girls given to such lusts, I believe. Of no account.'

Rising, she opened her purse and took out a cigarette from a paper packet. It was not too new a habit then, but few women indulged in it in public. Her hands trembled slightly as she lit it from a candle. The aroma was Turkish.

'You have not behaved. Have you behaved?' Aunt Maude asked her. 'The reports have not been good.'

The Lady Arabella's face was blurred through smoke. Did Caroline recognise her voice?

'I did not want – ' Arabella began. Then the gong for dinner sounded. We entered the dining-room. Frederick and Amanda served us. Our glasses were refilled constantly. They were the finest wines. My uncle conversed with Aunt Maude and Katherine about the house, the grounds, the farm. There would be a new summerhouse, he said. I squeezed Caroline's thigh. She had the grace to blush. My aunt whispered with Arabella who occasionally shook her head.

'I did not come for this. Will there not be an entertainment?' I heard her ask.

'You know why you were sent again. Disobedience ill becomes you,' my aunt told her. Arabella glanced at us for the first time to see if we were listening. Our heads were bowed. We absorbed ourselves in lobster and Château Neuf du Pape.

'They were blindfolded before,' Arabella muttered.

My aunt waved her hand. 'It is of no account,' she said. 'Come, you must permit at least a little display.'

Rising, she moved behind Arabella, bent over her and unbuttoned her dress at the front. I saw the purpose of its buttoning there. As the sides slid away her breasts were lifted out in all their splendour. Her nipples were rouged. Katherine slid her chair back and did the same to Caroline and me. Aunt Maude smiled, took her seat once more and brought a goblet of wine to Arabella's lips. Her throat worked as she drank.

'So you must sit in future when you return – it is more seemly,' my aunt told her.

Amanda entered. Frederick followed and cleared away our plates. He went out. In Amanda's hand was a silver jug.

'You have brought the cream?' Katherine asked her. 'It is warm?'

Amanda nodded. There was bemusement in her face. A cloud of unknowing lay upon her features. Her lips were rouged, her eyes shadowed. She looked beautiful, I thought. At the flaring of her skirt as she passed I saw faint pink marks upon her bottom cheeks. The hem fell like a broken promise and then lifted again. She approached Katherine's side.

'Not here – to the Lady Arabella,' Katherine said impatiently. My aunt's hands disappeared beneath the table at Arabella's side. Arabella's face suffused. Her body seemed to lift a little. There was a loud rustling of silk. Her skirt had been drawn up. Amanda's footsteps were quick, small and elegant as she moved around the long table to Arabella.

She appeared to be learning quickly – in hope, no doubt, that she would be released. Would she run to the woods and hide? There would be a hunting. She would be trussed and taken home, her skirt wound upwards amid the tight cords.

'Pour,' my aunt said. She appeared to grip Arabella's hand nearest to her own beneath the tablecloth.

Arabella gave a start, her chair creaked. Amanda had bent and poured the warm, rich cream between the valley of her breasts, the deep divide. I wanted to rise and see its trickling – the white lava. I dared not.

'Be still – it will flow down – let it flow,' my aunt told Arabella.

A balloon of smoke from my uncle's cigar floated over the table. We were virginal in our sitting, Caroline and I. We looked and did not look.

'Down, girl!' my aunt said to Amanda. Their eyes clashed like rapiers. The jug was empty. Its creaming oozed its last over the lip. Falteringly Amanda placed it on the table. Her knees bent. She disappeared. Beneath the polished table of oak I felt her. Her bottom nudged my toe. Arabella's eyes rolled, she leaned back. A soft gasp. I could feel her legs open, guided no doubt by my aunt's busy hands. The warm cream made a white trail down between her luscious breasts and disappeared beneath the looseness of her dress where Aunt Maude had slipped the tie at her waist.

'You liked the horses?' It was my uncle's voice. He addressed me.

'Yes, Uncle.' Caroline said yes uncle in turn. The wine bottles passed. Our glasses were refilled.

'Let us be quiet for a moment,' my aunt admonished as if we had been chattering constantly.

I wanted my boot to slide off – to feel with my stockinged toes the bulge of Amanda's bottom as she knelt, her face most obviously now between Arabella's thighs. Tasting cream. Cream on her bush, her pouting, her sticky . . .

Arabella gave a little jump. Her eyes half closed. 'Drink your wine,' my aunt told her. The goblet was raised to her lips anew. Her lips slurped. Beneath my feet there came another slurping. Arabella bubbled and spluttered into her goblet.

'Mounted but twice indeed since you visited,' my aunt said to her scoldingly. 'Are you not bad, my love?'

Arabella's eyes closed. She moved her lips away pettishly from the goblet. Wine spilled its fall on to her breasts. 'P–p–p–p–' Little explosions of sound from her mouth. Her hips worked, breasts jiggling. The slurping noise beneath the table increased.

'Such ripeness – it is always pretty to see,' Katherine murmured. She emptied the rest of her wine into my uncle's glass. He drank upon it immediately. My aunt glared at her.

Katherine smiled. For a moment I thought she would embrace me but instead she got up and passed around behind me to Caroline. Bending over her and drawing her face round, she covered Caroline's mouth with her own and passed her fingertips suavely about the snowy hillocks which stood revealed. I could feel the tingling in my mouth of my sister's nipples. Katherine's tongue delved. I could feel it delve.

The feet of Arabella's chair were scraping. The chair rocked.

'You are difficult, too, Caroline, are you not?' Katherine purred. Her mouth was a rose. Would I ever kiss her fully? She desired to make me jealous, I know. The sound of Amanda's lapping tongue was in my ears. Small noises of hysterical sound wisped from Arabella's lips. My aunt held her.

'Look at me, Caroline – haven't you been difficult?' Katherine coaxed.

'Ye–ye–yesssssss,' Caroline gritted. 'Oh, but it was so big and . . .'

'What nonsense she speaks,' my aunt laughed, 'you have sucked it – I know you have. Amanda, rise, leave her!'

A scuffling, Amanda appeared, face hot, lips wet. My uncle beckoned her. Her skirt, caught up, betrayed the wantonness of her bare bottom.

'Your report was no better. Worse, indeed,' he told her. 'Is it not true?'

'Sir?' Amanda asked thickly. Her eyes were bleared, her expression slightly vacant. I expected him to draw her forward and fondle her bottom. To my surprise he did not. I thought of Father. He lay on the beach, perhaps, his cutlass limp, fallen. Pebbles stirred as people approached and stared down at him. He rested in his waiting.

A murmuring beside me, a soft moist sound of lips. I hated Caroline. She was shy. She had sucked the liqueur of love – the sperm had inundated her mouth. She had lain on her bed naked, her thighs apart. Her nest had waited for his eggs to nestle against it. I would whip her.

Arabella lay back against the high back of her chair. Her mouth was open, a look of languishing upon her face. I judged her about twenty-seven. Her hand wore no wedding ring. Her fingernails glistened, perfectly manicured. My aunt's hand worked gently beneath the table, between her thighs. Arabella's eyelashes fluttered.

My uncle waved his cigar. 'Take her upstairs,' he said to Katherine. Led out in docile tread, Caroline did not look back. Footsteps on the stairs. Katherine returned.

'As to Amanda . . . ' Katherine said. Everyone waited for her to speak except perhaps Arabella who was floating still in a luxury of sensations. 'Amanda, stand in the corner there facing us. How wicked you have been!'

My aunt rang a bell. Frederick entered. He carried a small silver bucket wherein stood a wine bottle packed around with ice. Placing it on the table, he removed the bottle, wiped it with a napkin and left it there. The door closed again behind him. The cork of the bottle was round, black and polished.

'Lift your skirts – part your legs,' Katherine ordered. My uncle did not turn to look. Amanda's eyes were lanterns. The black flaring of her bush. The curls looked thicker now. The creamy tint of her flat belly.

'Wicked!' Katherine intoned. She took the bottle and moved to Amanda whose eyes hunted the ceiling. The neck of the bottle lowered and hovered beneath her pubic mound. It hung in a straight line down between her stockinged thighs. 'Draw your legs together, Amanda – grip it!'

A long hush-rushing sound like a sudden movement of water surged from Amanda's throat. Her eyes screwed up. Her long eyelashes trembled. Ice-cold, the bottle was gripped between her trembling thighs. Expressionless, Katherine placed her fingers delicately beneath the base of the bottle and urged it gently up.

'*Noooo–aaaaah!*' Amanda moaned. The black, round shiny cork parted her lovelips and was gripped within it.

Katherine drew down the tiny skirt.

'*Whooooo!*' Amanda jittered. Her skirt hid all but the base of the bottle. Her teeth chattered. Small pearls of white. I want to run my teeth around them.

'Finish the wine,' my uncle said. He rose – an avuncular host – and filled our glasses. Arabella's head had sunk. Her spirit moved through forests afar. The cream had long been lapped from her slit, her tight-purse, her nut-cracker, her penis-pouter. Her bottom cheeks relaxed in their fullness, naked upon her seat.

I dipped the tip of my tongue in my glass. It swam like a goldfish. I wanted to French-drink again. Was it forbidden? Arabella had opened her eyes and sat up. She seemed more composed. Her head inclined towards Aunt Maude's. Sitting beside me again, Katherine slid her hand on to my thigh and caressed it. I would not look at her. I cast my eyes down upon the tablecloth, the white, the serene.

'Are we loved?' she asked me. My mind had already begun to catch at the corners of reason. Amanda stood in her aloneness. I did not reply. I wanted to catch the words my aunt was speaking. Of them all, the Lady Arabella intrigued me most. Her coming was totally voluntary, I felt. Her body held an arrogance of desire, unfulfilled until it was drawn forth by persuasion. Were we all the same? To what dark altars were we led? Darkness was strawberries – the sunlight cream.

'It excites me – I fear it,' Arabella said.

'The root of desire is fearing. When you were caught with your drawers down, did you not intend to be caught?'

'I was dragged to my room,' Arabella muttered. Her voice contained a sulkiness of satisfaction.

'And mounted admirably,' my aunt said dryly, 'as you were here, after your birching. You prefer to be birched?'

'Not always, but the strap . . . '

'It subdues you, yes, but you must not grow reliant upon it. Marriage will be no cure for you. It will dilute the very qualities that give you such attraction, my dear. I shall recommend that you are blindfolded in future. It will enclose such modesty as you have.'

My aunt twirled the stem of her wine glass. Even as I, she stared at the tablecloth and appeared to muse. 'As I recall,' she continued, 'there is a particular manservant in your home. Is he not called Eric? He is young, lusty. During the act, when your bottom is bared, he will present his to your mouth. Blindfolded you will grope for it even while you are being pistoned . . . '

A cry from Arabella interrupted my aunt. She covered her face. 'Oh! I could not!' she burst.

Aunt Maude rose. 'Thomas, you will entertain her,' she announced. 'Amanda, you may go to the kitchen, girl.' Her glance encompassed Katherine, Jenny and myself. The drawing-room received us. We stood. Parts of the furniture had been cleared away, leaving a space in the centre of the floor. There stood a chair – a black leather one that I had never seen before. It was a simple affair. The strong wooden legs were strutted and rose some three feet. The broad seat – if it could be called one – was a mere sling of leather. Where the uprights of the back rose, another strong width of leather was repeated. In the centre of it was a small hole. Facing the chair so that the fronts of the seats touched was an identical one. In general aspect it was like a crude couch without a back to it. I had seen such in ancient Egyptian relics.

We stood. Beside me, Jenny caressed the bulbous curve of my bottom cheeks lightly. Katherine went into the hall and returned shortly. Frederick came with her. He was naked. His prong pronged. Around his neck was a halter to which a chain was attached.

Unspeaking, Katherine led him to the rear of one of the chairs and turned him to face it. His eyes were blind in their unseeing. His balls swung. 'Closer!' Katherine snapped at him. His feet shuffled forward, the chain clinking. With a slight grimace of his features, the knob of his erect penis touched the leather sling-back. To a slight but disdainful guidance of Katherine's fingers the knob passed through the hole and continued its upward glide until his prick emerged completely on the other side, facing the back of the other chair.

Motionless he stood, the veins raised on his tool which seemed to swell more by the tight enclosure. His balls pressed against the leather below the aperture.

Jenny's fingers quested beneath my bottom, pressing the thin wool up between my cheeks. I strained my legs and endeavoured to stand still. Aunt Maude entered, surveyed the scene and nodded. A faint scuffling of heels came and Arabella was patted and persuaded within by my uncle. Her gown was wreathed up to her hips, her eyes blindfolded. Her legs were superb: statuesque, long and beautifully curved. The fluff of her cunny was thick with curls. Her thighs rubbed nervously as she stumbled forward.

'It is a simulation,' Jenny murmured to me.

Guided by my aunt's hands, Arabella was taken to the chairs and made to kneel upon the seats. But an inch before her mouth – had she but known it then – the servant's prick jutted its menace. Her magnificent bottom cheeks – cheeks such as Michelangelo might have carved in marble – pressed against the back of the other chair. The waiting hole there appeared to centre itself exactly in line with the deep divide between her hemispheres. Melon-full, her exposed breasts hung down. Her knees made to shift in nervous reflex, but the dipping of the sling-seat into which the weight of her legs pressed permitted little movement.

My uncle approached the back of the chair to which her haunches were pressed. His face had a haggard aspect. His jacket and waistcoat had been removed. The top of his breeches was unbuttoned.

'Not yet – you are not privileged,' Jenny said. With a last searching caress her hand relinquished my bottom. In my emptiness I stood while she blindfolded me, voices around me. How strange in the darkness of my dark. Did the furniture move – the sideboard menace? I had imaginings. A mystic magic.

'Hold her hips.' It was my uncle's groan.

'There is no need, Thomas. She will be birched if she moves, save in desiring. Open your mouth now, Arabella – feel for it, absorb the knob – now press your bottom back, tight to the leather. Thomas, now!'

Groans, gurgles, cries – a gurgling, a moan. A blubbering, a slap, a sucking sound. Her mouth corked. Her lips would puff around the servant's tool. Creak of wooden legs. A croaking whine from Arabella. Her bottom corked in turn.

In my impossibilities I swayed. But feet away from me the thin inhissing of breath sounded through Arabella's nostrils. Tomorrow perhaps she would receive guests for tea. The polite questions of everydayness would be asked. Music sheets would lie decoratively ranged upon a piano. Her parents would flank her sides. It would be known that she was obedient. The servants would move quietly in their domain. The curtains would be dumb to speak. Her bed would wait for night to fall. Sperm-drops around her stocking tops. Was here salvation? Her eyes would be hollow, receiving messages.

'Ah! in her to the root. She has taken both.' It was Katherine's voice. Her tongue licked in my ear. I trembled. I knew I must stand still. In my stillness standing.

No one would ever know. Beyond our circles, no one. We were the chosen, the receptors of lust in our desiring.

# *Chapter Fourteen*

The laurel leaves of the garden hedge were dry. I moved my cheek against them. The breeze fluttered my skirt. For two hours on the following morning we had been caged, Caroline, Amanda and I. Then Jenny had taken us out one by one and accorded us twelve strokes of the strap across our naked bottoms.

'Your morning exercise – you may be given more pleasant ones shortly,' she said. Amanda blubbered quietly. Each of us sank down in our cage again, our bottoms seared. We were not to talk, we were told.

Released first and dressed, this time in a white wool dress with a gold chain at my waist, I was sent into the garden. I loitered palely. My hands toyed with twigs. The maidservant Mary brought out lemonade. It cooled my body with a sheet of cold within. My eyes were quiet against her own. I felt intimations of newness within me.

Father on the high seas sailing. I would write to him. By fast packet-ship my letter would arrive shortly after his landing. I returned within the house, not knowing whether I was permitted to return, and asked my aunt. The space where the two leather seat-supports had been the night before was now filled again by a small table. Bric-à-brac and vases stood upon it. I looked for the impress of the feet of the chairs in the carpet but saw none.

Aunt Maude sat embroidering. I asked if I might write. Her expression issued surprise. I would find paper, pen and ink already placed in my room, she said. As I made to go she beckoned me. I stood close. Her hand passed up beneath the clinging of my dress – perhaps to satisfy her that I was wearing no drawers.

'How firm and fleshy you are,' she said, and sighed. The heat of the strap was still in my bottom. It communicated itself to her fingertips. Her hand slipped down, caressing the backs of my thighs as it went. 'Write well and clearly,' she told me.

I ascended to my room. All was put ready for me as if it had been anticipated. A small escritoire stood against one wall. I seated myself and drew the paper towards me. The ink was black. I swirled it gently with the decorated steel nib of the pen. 'Dearest Father . . . ' A bird's wings rustled against the window. I rose, but it was gone. No message lay upon the sill. I leaned my forehead against the glass. 'Dearest Father . . . '

I started and turned at the sudden entrance of Katherine.

'There is nothing to say,' she said, 'it is all in the doing.'

'It is not true,' I said. I wanted to cry. Her arms enfolded me lightly as one embraces a child who must leave soon upon a feared journey.

'It is good that you know. If you had not known you would be writing swiftly. Is that not so?'

Her voice coaxed. I nodded against her shoulder. A simple movement of her supple form sufficed to bring her curves tightly against mine. Half swooning I moved my belly in a sinuous sleeking against her own. She released me too quickly with a smile that I could feel passing over my own mouth in its passing.

'There is to be a reception. Brush your hair, wear a boater – it suits you,' Katherine said. She waited while I obeyed. Descending, she took hat and gloves from Mary who stood waiting. Two horses pawed the dust outside. This time the carriage was a hansom.

'May Caroline not come?' I asked. My question was ignored. I entered first, followed by Katherine who sat close beside me.

'We are going to see a friend,' she said.

The journey took an hour. We passed the house where Amanda lived. The children with the hoops had gone. They sat in some small schoolhouse, perhaps, learning the directions of rivers and the trade winds. Katherine had not conversed with me except to ask if I was thirsty. When I nodded we reined in at an inn. A potboy brought us out mugs of ale. The coachman quaffed his own loudly. With a belching from above and a cracking of the whip we were off again.

The house at which we arrived lay like my uncle's in rural isolation. Stone columns adorned with cupids ranged at the entrance. The drive was long and straight. Immediately the hansom braked, a butler appeared and ushered us in with the grave mien of one who has important people to announce. We entered a drawing-room where, to my astonishment, Arabella sat picking at crochet work. From a chair facing her own, the man with the military moustache whom I had seen with her before rose and greeted us. Arabella nodded politely and smiled at Katherine. Her long fingers worked elegantly.

The gentleman, whose name was Rupert, drew Katherine aside to the end of the long room. I caught but a few words of their whisperings. 'It will progress her,' I heard him say. I glanced at Arabella. Her lips had pursed tightly. I perceived a slight tremor of her fingers.

Katherine turned back to me. 'We shall go upstairs,' she said. I wondered in my wonderings. The room was one of great charm. An Adam fireplace stood resplendent. Two small lions carved in stone rested on either side of the big brass fender. Blue velvet drapes were abundant. The furniture smelled of newness.

Katherine's voice seemed to encompass Arabella also. Her hands flirted with the piece of crochet work and fell. The gentleman spoke her name. She got up, her eyes uncertain. The lacework fluttered to the floor. Preceding us he advanced into the hallway and up the wide, curving staircase. There, at the first landing, several doors faced us, as did also three young girls in servant attire who appeared to be in-waiting. They stood side by side against a wall. Their hands were bound behind them, their mouths gagged. Their black dresses, white aprons and morning caps were of the utmost neatness.

'This one,' Katherine said. She selected the smallest girl who looked about seventeen, her fulsomeness evident in the sheathing of her dress about her curves.

Rupert jerked his head and the girl detached herself and followed us, her gait made slightly awkward by her bound wrists.

We ascended again to the second floor where a lady of singular beauty, in her middle years, appeared as if to descend. She halted and appraised us. 'A progression, yes,' she echoed as the gentleman spoke to her, 'it will be good for her. Arabella, you will obey, my dear.' Kissing her on the cheek she passed on and down. To untie the other two maids, I thought. I knew their posture, the inward-seeking of their thoughts, the tightness of their bottom cheeks. Their thighs would tremble in the mystery of their beings.

A door opened. We entered a room that was longer than the drawing-room beneath. Four windows ranged along the farther wall, the drapes drawn back. The double doors closed heavily. Arabella, the maid and I were ushered to the centre of the room.

I saw then the paintings which hung along the wall facing the windows. There were men and girls in bonds. The men exhibited penises that were either bound in leather or protruded boldly in their nakedness. Each vein was so cunningly painted that one could have touched and felt the slight swellings. Women lay bound, naked or in curious attire, one upon the other. Men with their wrists bound and their eyes blindfolded knelt in their penis-seeking between the splayed thighs of naked ladies.

My eyes passed through them as if through mirrors. Except for one. It was of a girl who wore thigh boots and black tights. The tights had been lowered to her knees. Each hair of her pubic curls had been painted separately with the finest of brushes. She was bound to a post that stood alone in the centre of a planked floor. She wore no gag. Her head was upright and her eyes proud. Her long golden hair was as mine. The cherry nipples of her breasts peaked their proudness.

Katherine moved beside me. 'It is better to be bound than to see others bound, is it not?' she asked me. I sought Arabella's eyes but she would not look. Her white dress was as simple as my own. I divined her nudity beneath.

'I do not know,' I murmured.

'Come – we shall know the answer,' Katherine replied. Close to the far end of the room a stout post stood, even as in the painting. To the back of it was fastened four lengths of wood in the shape of a square that protruded on either side. Led forward, I was turned so that my back came against the post.

'Raise your arms,' Katherine instructed. I did so. My wrists came against the lengths of wood. Taking cords she bound them so that I was held as on a cross. 'He will not have seen you before,' Katherine said and threw a smile over her shoulder at Rupert who had moved closely behind Arabella. I watched her head jerk nervously as he palmed her bottom.

Katherine bent and raised my dress, coiling the wool up until it wreathed tightly about my hips. My pubis bared, I blinked and endeavoured to stare past the pair facing me, but the increasing wriggling of Arabella's hips was lure to my eyes.

Drawn wide apart, my ankles were next secured. The lips of my slit parted stickily, warmed and moistened as they had been by our journey. Arabella murmured and choked a small cry. Her dress was being slowly lifted at the back by Rupert. The maid stood like a small tree waiting.

Katherine beckoned her. In her awkwardness she came. Katherine pushed her to her knees before me and removed her gag.

'Have you taught her to lick?' she asked Rupert, whose hands were now busy beneath the back of Arabella's dress. The young woman blushed deeply but seemed frozen to the spot. At the back her bottom was now bared, lush and full in all its proud paleness. At the front the material of her dress looped with some modesty still to hide her pussy.

Rupert shook his head. With such treasures of firm flesh as bulged into his hands, he was equally entranced by the vision I presented.

*'Dearest Father . . .'*

The paper lay forlorn where I had left it. No signals flew. At the first touch of the maid's nose to my belly I quivered in my longings. Katherine nudged her and she sank lower as one who makes to drink from a tap.

She kissed my knees. Her mouth absorbed itself above and circled in an O about my thighs. Her lips teased the tight banding of my stocking tops. Her tongue sought the soft-firm flesh of my inner thighs. I bent my knees slightly. I offered, sought. As through crazed glass I watched Rupert's hands desert Arabella's bottom and glide beneath her armpits to unfasten the front of her dress.

I wanted her. Her mouth, her tongue. I sought to reach her with my eyes, but hers were dazed. As her breasts were bared she whimpered and struggled. Pink of face he held her. Her nipples extended through his fingers. The jellied mounds stirred beneath his seekings.

I felt the outflicking of the maid's tongue where it reached me, touched my lovelips. I wanted not to moan. I must not moan. Thumbs parted my lips and sought my clitoris, my button, my ariser. The tongue tip swirled. I knew its cunning. Ah! she was good. Starshells burst in my belly. I whimpered, ground my hips. Her tongue would not reach into me. I wanted it.

Did I cry out? On the brink of my salty spray, my spilling, I tremored in a cloud of delight.

'There is nothing to say. It is all in the doing,' Katherine had said.

Arabella was as one swooning. The arms of Rupert upheld her. Her dress was raised in front – her thighs, her longing. Her bush was plump – a perfect mound of Venus. Had it been creamed, or only her bottom yet? I knew the answer soon.

'Enough!' Katherine said. She stirred the maid with her foot. The girl fell back and twisted sideways. Her shoulder bumped the floor. Her small pink tongue licked around her lips.

Arabella's struggles renewed at Katherine's turning. Her eyes were wild as hunted fawns'. Traitorous, her nipples shone erect. Her thighs clenched together. Her stockings of light grey silk rubbed. The noise made an electric hissing. Did she not know it was an invitation?

I held upon my cross. The maid beneath me did not stir save to glance slyly up between my legs. I used the coldness of my eyes upon her. She blushed and hid her eyes. They were eyes that would move and rustle in the grass at night. In her truckle bed she would lie at evening beneath a coarse blanket. Upon heavy footsteps waiting. A cottage smallness. The cramped places of lust. A heaving of loins. Jettings of desire. Globules of sperm upon her pussy hairs. Small legs, perfectly shaped, stirred beneath her skirt.

I would buy her, perhaps.

'NO!'

Arabella screamed foolishly as she was borne to a couch of purple velvet, her dress raised high to bare her belly.

'*Wha–aaaaah!*' Her screams became hysteria as Katherine assisted in thrusting her down, mounting upon her shoulders as she had mounted upon my face. Wildly as Arabella kicked she could not escape the scooping back of her knees by Katherine. Her slit showed pulpy in its fullness.

For the battle now Rupert prepared, casting off his jacket and lowering his breeches. His cockprong pronged a full nine inches long. The head was purplish, swollen. His hands assisted Katherine's in parting Arabella's long milky thighs. Arabella's shoulders bucked. She was held. Her anguished cries half-extinguished beneath Katherine's skirt bubbled away.

'You have had her bottom only?' Katherine asked.

'Thrice – including her penance over the table when she was birched. How magnificent she looks!'

For long moments while Arabella blindly squirmed her hips, he gazed upon the fount of his desiring. I wanted the maid again – her tongue. In my proudness I did not ask. Only the silent pulsing of my quim beseeched.

With a groan, she was entered.

'Slowly – slowly,' Katherine breathed. An eagle perched, she gazed upon the conquest – the curl-fringed lips that rolled in succulence, parting to the charger's crest. Arabella's thighs quivered in their grip. Hands scooped her bottom, the strength of him lifting her.

Inklings of surrender I sensed even as the veined shaft sank within. Inklings. It is a pretty word. Small notes of sound spattered with ink. The acquiescence of her bottom stirred me. It shifted little on his cupping palms once she was shafted to the full.

My instincts were shared, it seemed. Of a sudden, Katherine dismounted from the nubile beauty who held the cock full-clenched within her now. Puffed of cheeks that were sheened with moisture, Arabella stirred but faintly. His belly pressed upon hers. Their pubic hairs mingled. I could feel his throbbing as within myself – the gently ticking impulse of desire.

Arabella succumbed. Elegant in their fullness, her stockinged legs slid down from his loosing grasp. The heels of her boots stirred upon the velvet of the couch. Her legs trembled and straightened. Her large breasts, tumbled out of her opened dress, gave her a perfect aspect of voluptuousness.

His breeches slid farther down. He whispered, as I thought, something in her ear. Her face was deeply flushed. Her lips moved. Her hands clasped timorously at his shirt.

'Your tongue,' he husked, 'your tongue now, Arabella.'

Her breath scooped in audibly as if drawn by some inward suction in her throat.

'You must not come! Oh! You must not come!'

The couch jolted, stirred. The pleasure train of pleasure had begun.

Her tongue protruded, thrust within his mouth. Their mouths gobbled. Glistening, his shaft emerged – sank in again. Rocking, creaking. His pace quickened. Her knees bent as if shyly at first. Her calves lifted, uncertain in their seeking. In a moment, his cock pounding her with virile force, they were knotted about his loins. A squelching. Their tongues worked. Moaning they squirmed their loins.

The maid who lay at my feet stirred. She had not the vision of them in her eyes. Awkwardly she struggled to her knees.

Katherine, whose absorption in the lustful scene was as my own, even so swung her head around.

'No!' she snapped. 'Stand by the door – your back to us.'

The girl obeyed. Out of the corners of her eyes as she passed the couch she watched the threshings of desire. He was long at his task – longer than I had deemed he could hold in his excitement. Then at last his rattling cry – a swift tightening of Arabella's legs. Her breasts were at pillage. He sucked upon them greedily in his coming, his outspurting. Judders, quivers, a last tight clenching of her cuntlips. Then all was stillness.

Arabella's head lay back, her eyes and mouth open. Her legs slackened, fell. Her entire body seemed to quiver at the withdrawal of his cock which left a snail's trail of sperm down her thigh. Her face held a look of vacant surprise. Made to rise at last, her dress caught up, she leaned against him foolishly.

'Tonight again,' he said. He patted her bottom. Her eyes would not look at my eyes. Turning away she patted haplessly at her hair and then covered herself. I knew her wetness.

'In your silences shall you be saved, Beatrice,' Katherine murmured to me. There was approval in her look. Releasing me, she fussed about my tidiness like a nurse.

The maid, ignored, was left to her own devices. Sedately we descended, walking quietly as people entering a theatre after the curtain has risen. In the drawing-room the lady we had encountered above sat drinking wine. A maid entered and filled the glasses that awaited us on a sideboard.

'Arabella – you dropped your crochet on the floor,' the lady said. Her tone was reproachful. Rupert had not followed us into the room, I noticed. His orgasm must have been excessive on their first such bout.

'I am sorry,' Arabella replied in a muted voice. She picked it up from where it lay and took it upon her lap again. There was a flush on her cheeks but otherwise she appeared composed again.

We sat drinking our wine and spoke of mundane things.

## *Chapter Fifteen*

'Ah, how she was fucked!' Katherine said as we entered the hansom again.

I had never heard such coarseness. I stared at her. Her eyes had a light in them I had not seen before.

'Should not he have fucked her – spilled his semen within her richness? When he buggered her, over the table – ah, how we had to hold her – his cock disappearing within her cleft. Come, kiss me, Beatrice!'

Her arm enfolded my shoulders. Our lips met in a haze of sweetness. Deep her long tongue delved within my mouth. The jolting of the carriage added to the excitement of our embrace. I felt her hand pass up beneath my skirt. I parted my thighs to her seeking. Her thumb brushed the lips of my slit. I choked my little gasps within her mouth.

'Seven years – seven years it has taken him to bring her to that – yet she obeys us now. He will fuck her again tonight. How timid she will be at first, how flushed! His tongue will lick at her nipples, stir her being. Her thighs will move awkwardly, seeking to be opened and yet not. Their tongues will meet. Falteringly her hand will find his cock. She adores bottom fucking now, though he has had her that way but thrice, each time held down. She will come to the strap and birch more easily now, knowing her reward – the slug of flesh within her bottom gripped. Do you hear me, Beatrice?'

I could not hear. I knew not her wording. My slit creamed, bubbled, spurting. Sliding from the carriage seat, I all but fell on the floor. My dignity, my being, lay scattered about me like dying petals. I clasped her, in my falling clasped.

'I love you,' I said.

Katherine laughed and pushed me roughly into the corner. Her fingers glistened. Would she lick them?

'Did you not like my litany?' she asked.

I nodded. The words had been thrown at me out of a box. I had caught them yet I needs must arrange them. A sullenness crossed my features. I wanted to cry. I sought greater fulfilment. Cock. He had lain upon her and given her his cock. I hated the crudities. I shuttered them off in my mind. They tapped at the shutters. I ignored them.

Katherine's eyes were mocking. 'You did not like it?' she asked.

Was I under test? I shook my head. 'I do not know,' I said.

Katherine laughed. 'You fool. There are clues. You have not found them yet, Beatrice. Be silent now. Await the teaching.'

Dinner that evening was formal. Caroline sat quiet, attentive. She had been a good girl, my aunt said. Amanda, it seemed, was caged upstairs, her meal taken to her. I wore black, the wool clinging as tightly as ever. There was a new serving maid, a woman of about thirty, comely and plump. The dull black dress and white apron suited her. During the whole meal she was not required to say a word. I wondered if she had eaten and drunk before us. Such things engage my mind sometimes. It is a kindness. Father told me once that it was my old-fashioned way.

We took coffee in the lounge, then turned to liqueurs. There was a festive air. I could feel it. We lounged at our ease. The shackles were cast. Caroline laughed occasionally with Uncle. We were tamed.

When the maid brought in the Cointreau, Katherine took her wrist.

'Drink with us,' she said.

'Ma'am?' The maid's cheeks coloured.

'Drink with us – sit with us – here at my feet – take a glass.' Katherine's words were pellets. They stung against my skin. The woman skimmed a nervous look around where we sat in a circle.

'Look, I will hold your glass while you sit,' Aunt Maude told her.

The maid obeyed at last, discomforted in her sitting on the floor. Her legs coiled under her. I liked the shape of her calves. Her ankles were slender. Slender ankles and plump thighs often betoken sensuousness to some degree.

'Lean back and be comfortable,' Aunt Maude said. She dropped a cushion on to the carpet for the maid to lean upon. She looked like a houri – an odalisque. Uncle was whispering to Caroline. What were they saying?

'Attractive women often sit on the floor,' Katherine remarked. The maid looked at her and did not know whether to smile or not. Katherine's smile was a cat's smile. With a flip of her toes she kicked off one of the gold Turkish slippers she was wearing and, to the woman's startlement, laid her toes on her thigh. Her toes curled.

'It is nice,' Katherine said. Her foot moved upwards along the maid's hip and felt its curving. 'Drink your drink,' she said sharply. The woman obeyed.

My aunt eased a shoe off in turn. Sitting obliquely behind the maid she lifted her leg, eased her stockinged foot beneath the woman's chin and lifted it.

'Lie down – down!' my aunt said.

The maid's arm made a querulous seeking gesture, but she obeyed. The cushion squeezed itself from under her. Katherine circled her leg and moved the sole of her foot lightly over the woman's prominent breasts. She started and would have sat up if Aunt Maude's foot had not then moved with a twist of ankle to the front of her neck.

The maid's eyes bulged. 'Ma'am – I don't want to,' she whined.

'Oh, be quiet!' Katherine said impatiently. Her foot slid back down. Her toes hooked in the hem of the maid's skirt and drew it up above her stocking tops. Plump thighs gleamed. The simple garters she wore bit tightly into her flesh.

'No, please, Ma'am.'

Neither listened. Aunt Maude's toes were caressing her neck and up behind her ear. Katherine's toes delved upwards beneath the hang of the upflipped skirt. The woman's hands scrabbled on the carpet. My aunt's toes soothed over her mouth. A choking little cry and the maid's back arched. The delicate searching movements of Katherine's toes up between her thighs made the black material ripple. The maid's cheeks were pink. Her lips parted beneath the sole of my aunt's foot which rubbed suavely, skimming her mouth. Katherine's toes projected up into the skirt. Her heel was rubbing now.

The maid moaned and closed her eyes. Beside me, Caroline puffed out her breath. The maid's eyes closed. Her bottom worked slightly. She drew up one knee. My uncle's eyes were strangely incurious. Aunt Maude slipped down on to her knees beside the maid and began unbuttoning the front of her dress. The ripe gourds of her breasts came into view. Her nipples were stark and thick in their conical rising.

Katherine slid down on to her knees in turn. Her hands swept the skin of the maid's dress up to her waist. A bulge of pubic hairs sprouted thickly. The maid covered her face and made little cries.

'Open your legs properly!' Katherine told her sharply. Still with her eyes covered, the maid began to edge her ankles apart. It would be her first such pleasuring, perhaps, though female servants who shared bedrooms frequently fingered one another.

Uncle loomed up before me. He smiled, drew my hand towards him.

'We shall go upstairs,' he said. I was bereft. Caroline would see. I would not see. We entered the hall and ascended. I did not want to go in the cage. But the room was empty and the cages were empty. 'Go to the bar – raise your dress,' my uncle said.

I wanted to see what would happen to the maid. Would she be ripe in her desiring? I did not want Katherine to kiss her. But I obeyed. A bulbous symphony in black and white. I gripped the lower bar, my bottom bared to him. He knew me in his seeing now. The door reopened but I did not look.

Footsteps quiet. Tapering fingers, coated with warm oil, massaged the groove of my pumpkin. At my rose, my O, the finger lingered, soothing. High heels clicked again and our visitor was gone.

Strained in my posture I kept my thighs, my heels together. The purse of my love-longing peeped its figlike shape beneath my cheeks. I waited.

At the first crack of the leather I cried out my small cry, my head hung. The stinging of the strap assailed me three, four, five, six times. I clenched my nether cheeks, their plumpness hot. Tears oozed.

The quiver-cry that burst next from me was at the first biting of three dozen thongs. My whip had come – it lived – it sang. I hated, loved it.

'Uncle, don't!'

My little wail, the dying cry. I choked in my choking sobs. The tips of the thongs sought me, burnished the blossoming of my cheeks and sought the crevices. Rain of fire, down-showering of sparks. My hips squirmed, my heels squeaked on the floor. Master of my arching beauty now, he stung me deeper till my sobs came louder. My shoulders lifted, fell. My hands slipped on the bar and gripped anew.

At the dropping of the whip at last – betraying clatter on the floor – I made to rise. My hand reached back and sought my upcast dress.

'No, Beatrice, stay!'

'No more!'

My bottom scorched, my wail beseeched. Hands at my hips. They gripped like steel.

'Down, Beatrice, down!'

The cheeks of my bottom held, parted, spread. My rose exposed. '*No–ooooh!*' The last cry of my frailty fluttered, fell. I felt the flare of body heat, his cock. The knob-cock of him, oozing in. Breath whistling from my throat, I made to rise.

'Down, Beatrice – down, girl, down!'

I blubbered, squirmed. I wanted, did not want. The rubbery ring of my anus yielded to invasion – the swollen plum, indriving of his prick. Quarter inch by quarter inch the veined shaft entered. My mouth gaped. The thick peg throbbed, its urging urged within. Then with a groan he sheathed it to the full, my brazen cheeks a butterball of heat to his belly.

Within me now it stirred, pulsed, throbbed. His balls nestled under my slit. Then he withdrew – the slow unsheathing I both feared and sought. A faint uncorking sound. Freed to the air his knob thrummed at my cheeks.

'Go to your room,' my uncle said.

I did not look. I feared to look. I had received. I rose, legs shaking, scuffling down my dress. My bottom sucked in air and closed. Finding the door I ran down to my room.

No one came.

In my sobbing I fell asleep clothed, squeezing my bottom cheeks until oblivion came.

# Chapter Sixteen

The days of strangeness closed in upon us further. We were stripped and taken to the cages 'to meditate', my aunt said. In my aloneness she asked me my dreams. I knelt while I told her, my face bowed. During my speaking she would allow me to raise her skirt and kiss her thighs. In such moments I was truly her slave. I buried my lips against the smooth skin above her stocking tops and licked. 'You are naturally wicked by nature,' she said to me once when I had recounted a particularly vivid dream.

Maria – the maid with whom she and Katherine had toyed – stayed on. On the morning after her pleasuring she became more acquiescent and submissive to commands. Her skirts were hemmed excessively short. Whenever my uncle looked at her thighs she blushed.

One afternoon we had what my aunt called 'an amusement'. At lunch Maria had been complimented upon her serving of the wine and food. She looked foolishly pleased. On our retirement to the drawing-room I was intrigued to see a large camera of mahogany and brass standing upon a stout tripod. Its lens faced inwards from the windows, no doubt to gather light. Before it was placed a simple wooden chair. Other furniture had been pressed back against the walls.

Upon Maria's bringing-in of the liqueurs, my aunt said to her, 'Maria, we shall take your portrait today – your likeness. Will that not please you?'

Maria smiled and curtsied. 'As it please you, Ma'am,' she replied. As I learned afterwards, my uncle had rooted her with his cock the evening before, over the dining-room table. She had not struggled unduly, it seemed. Katherine enlivened us by playing on the piano. It was an old melody, sad and wistful. Jenny – who had not lunched with us, having been attending to Amanda upstairs – came and joined us.

'Bring the manservant,' Katherine told her.

Jenny disappeared and reappeared. There was a clattering from the distant kitchen while Maria tidied up. Once again Frederick was naked, led by his collar and chain. A blue bow was tied about the root of his penis which hung limp. Jenny led him to the chair and turned him to stand beside it, facing the camera.

Aunt Maude wiped her lips with a lace hanky and went out. A sound of scuffling came – a slap – then a silence. In a minute or two my aunt entered with Maria who wore now open-net stockings, knee boots, a tiny black corset which left her breasts and navel uncovered, and a large feathered hat such as one might see at Ascot. Her face was well adorned with powder and rouge. Her eyes were heavy-lidded.

At the sight of Frederick she started back. A loud smack on her naked bottom quickly corrected her.

'Go and sit in the chair – act as a lady – this is a formal portrait,' my aunt told her. My uncle sat with his arms crossed. The wobbling of Maria's large bottom cheeks as she obeyed absorbed him. Her bush was dark – thick and luxuriant. Hot-cheeked she sat and faced us.

'Cross your legs, Maria – how dare you show yourself!' my aunt snapped at her.

Katherine lit a cigarette. The smoke coiled about us like incense.

Aunt Maude moved to the camera and bent behind it, casting a large black velvet cloth over her head and shoulders, as over the back of the camera itself. Her hand sought forward and focused the big brass lens. Maria's eyes had a sullen look. Aunt Maude took one slide of the pair, cautioning them to be still for a full minute. Then my uncle rose and assisted her in changing the glass plates.

'Raise your right hand, Maria, and let his prick lie on your palm!' Katherine said.

There was hesitation. Imperceptibly Frederick's prick stirred and thickened as it lay on Maria's warm, moist hand. Maria would have bitten her lip in dismay if my aunt had not told her sharply to keep her expression fixed in a smile.

With small variations Aunt Maude continued photographing. The light was excellent, she observed. By the fourth attempt Frederick's prick stemmed fully upright, the flesh swelling around and above the neat blue bow. Maria was forced to hold it now. Her face had a dull, vapid look.

'It is done,' Aunt Maude said at last. She collected the heavy glass plates together. They would be framed in gilt, she said.

'I will take them now,' Katherine said. Walking across to Frederick whose penis had not lost its fine erection, she took hold of his chain. 'Get up,' she said quietly to Maria. She smiled across at me. Did she know I wanted her?

'Where shall you take them?' Aunt Maude asked.

'To the stable. It is time they were coupled.' A short squeal came from Maria as Katherine moved behind her and inserted a finger upwards between the globing cheeks of her bottom. 'So tight and plump – she will milk him deeply,' she smiled. Her smile had a taste of olives.

Maria jerked forward and went to kneel at my aunt's feet.

'Ma'am, I beg you!' she pleaded.

Katherine clicked her fingers and Jenny came forward with a leather neckband and chain which she secured quickly around Maria's neck.

My aunt's eyes were kindly. She gazed down at the top of Maria's bent head.

'Beg me you should, Maria. What a foolish woman you are.' Her hands raised her skirt. The dark vee of her pubis was apparent to all our eyes through her white, split drawers. Her bared thighs came warm and sleek to

Maria's face. Maria lifted her head slowly. Her tongue emerged, mouth hovering about the plump mound whose curls sprouted so thickly. The lips moved against her lips. My aunt's legs spread a little. Maria's tongue made a broad wet smudge around her pouting.

'Rise now!' my aunt said to her. The chain clinked. Jenny pulled on it and drew the woman to her feet.

'Ma'am . . . ' Maria's lips quivered. She looked like an overgrown girl who did not know what to do. Her nipples protruded thickly on her large, milky breasts. The surrounding circles were broad, crinkly. The flesh was firm.

'You will obey, Maria. Mare and stallion in the stable – it is fitting. Go now!' Aunt Maude ordained.

Katherine led them out. Through the windows I could see the trio crossing the lawn towards the paddock.

Aunt Maude turned to us. 'Go upstairs,' she said, 'you should not have watched.'

In my room I made to remove my dress. We were never permitted in our bedrooms to remain clothed. Frequently now we were inspected. The hairs of my mount were occasionally trimmed to form a neat line below my navel. It would make the rest of my curls cluster more thickly, Katherine had said. She entered as I drew my dress up to my waist in preparation for removing it. Without halting her pace she stepped quickly forward and cupped the naked cheeks I exposed. I wriggled immediately to her fondling touch.

'Do you want to go to the water closet?' she asked. I nodded. I had drunk much wine. 'And I – come with me.'

The water closet had been newly installed. There were not then many in use. The annexe in which it stood was large. A mirror was fastened to the door which faced the white-and-blue-flowered basin. Leading within and bidding me to lock the door, Katherine immediately raised her dress and squatted.

'Hold me – hold me while I do it,' she murmured.

I held back. I hesitated, but she seized my wrist and drew my hand between her thighs. The hairs of her sex around the pouting lips tickled my fingers. A murmur escaped her mouth that I recognised as one of deep pleasure. I fell her moistness, the oily slit. Her arm came up and drew my face down. Our mouths merged in a misty sweetness. My senses swam. Impulsively I cupped her furred treasure which of a sudden gushed out a fine golden rain over my palm as her tongue intruded into my mouth. Its long wet coiling around my own tongue together with the warm flooding over my hand hypnotised me. She gripped my wrists until the last trickle.

'You now – you do it,' she said.

I protested weakly. Rising, she moved me around and raised my dress. My bottom was presented to the bowl. My knees trembled. I loosed my waiting flow in turn, drenching her palm and fingers while we kissed. She held me until the last seepings. Then we dipped our hands into a bowl of water and dried them on a thin towel that hung on a nail.

Emerging, Katherine laid a hand on my shoulder. 'Your uncle wishes now to see you,' she said. 'He waits in his study.'

I had not visited the sanctum before. My footsteps along the passageway slowed. Katherine's hand pressed lightly against the small of my back. 'Do not be wilful,' she urged. The kaleidoscope of my thoughts spun. The moment we entered, my uncle's arms engaged me. I pulsed in his arms like a small bird taken in the hand.

'Has she been good?' he asked of Katherine over my shoulder. A laugh came from her. A sprinkling of falling silver leaves.

'She wet my hand in the closet,' Katherine said, 'her thighs are wet still. Feel her.'

Moving swiftly up behind me she raised my dress clear to my hips, then caught my arms and drew them tightly behind me.

'Open your legs and show him. See – the damp is still on her thighs,' she said. My face was scarlet. I writhed helplessly in her grasp while my uncle surveyed me at his leisure, the slimness of my calves, upswelling of thighs, the trimness of curls where my treasure was entrapped. White of belly.

Of a sudden I was flung against him. His prodder, hidden by his breeches, stung my thigh. In his bear hug I was lifted, swung. The edge of a waiting couch came against the backs of his knees. In falling he drew me with a simple motion over his lap, my jellied breasts exposed in turn by the upwreathing of my dress.

'No, Uncle, no!'

My gasp came in the upsweeping of his hand which blasted down on to my naked bottom.

I yelped, I cried. The burning was immense.

'No, no, no, NO!' I sobbed again. My training had left me. Fire blazed in my cheeks. My legs kicked. I clawed at the carpet. The splatting of his palm came down again and again. I was woman and child. My bottom reared and flamed. Pearls of tears cascaded down my cheeks.

'*Ya–aaaah!*' I screeched again and again until he stopped and I lay limp, helpless to his caressing. The big palm glossed my globe, his fingers delved. I burbled out my sorrows. His free hand sought my dangling gourds.

'Get up, Beatrice!' Katherine intoned.

Blear-eyed and wriggling like a fish I came upright. Her arms clasped my waist tightly, allowing the insensate wriggling of my bottom to continue. Her mouth sought mine. I choked. Salt tears were at my lips. Her voice coaxed me, murmuring upon my mouth, breath to breath. A haze of wine and perfume. She had raised her dress. Our stocking tops rubbed together. The cream of my bubbling bubbled to her lips. Cunningly she parted her legs, rubbing her slit against mine, her hold not lessening about me.

'How oily your quim – how stiff your nipples, sweet.'

I gulped her words within my mouth. Wildly they swam, my head invading. Gulping to pulping of lips and tongues. Hot tongues in my bottom licked my groove. Long she held me, coaxing, kissing. My torso shimmered. A stickiness between our bellies grew – a mist of perspiration. In silence my uncle sat behind me waiting.

The stinging in my bottom eased, became a throbbing. Lost in time and space I stood. Her mouth was my haven. A strange torpor seized me. I felt my legs parted until I stood straddled. Katherine's fingertips quested my globe, parted its cheeks.

'Let him see – let him see, Beatrice. He has stilled you, has he not – after your whipping?'

'St–st–st–' I stuttered. Her fingers clawed the opening of my cheeks. She held me but loosely. An insolence of power.

'Stilled, yes, Beatrice. His rod in your bottom. A single plunge within. We call it that. Move backwards now. Move slowly, inch by inch.'

In the cobwebs in the corners were there words? Released, my hands caught empty air, fastened upon the wraiths of yesterdays. With a small shriek I fell upon my uncle's lap. Exposed, his penis upthrust 'twixt my thighs. My bottom churned, uplifted, fell – the velvety knob of his penis-prober against my belly.

I bounced, I burbled, twisted and was held. Then Katherine bent over me. My chin upraised. I felt him jerk. Her working fingers round his penis worked. Her knuckles grazed my belly in his working. Her eyes were laughter. Her hand moved faster. His hands beneath my armpits weighed my breasts. The bud of my slit swelled, my rosy clitty. His balls chattered against my bottom. A finger sought my nest and rubbed.

My uncle groaned. His teeth bit lightly into my shoulder. His palms burnished my stiffened nipples. I felt his loins move in their strength. Of a sudden, thick jets of sperm spattered my belly. I melted, died. I moistened his balls in my spending. My breasts swelled. My belly was wet with his come. The last drops sprinkled. I swayed back to his swaying, legs apart.

'Go,' Katherine said. She pulled me up, my dress high-wreathed. The door mouth opened, swallowed me. There was a sound of kissing behind me.

His come dried quickly on my skin. Some had spattered the tops of my stockings. There was quiet in the house as always, as if everyone had left. From the landing window I looked out upon the lawn and saw Caroline lying on the grass. Jenny was kissing her.

I lay down on my bed. The ceiling darkened and lowered until it enfolded me.

I ran through caverns and saw magic lights.

# Chapter Seventeen

Aunt Maude wakened me in my early morning warmth. She brought me tea. I sat up and drank from a translucent cup.

'You were bad yesterday – do you know you were bad?' she asked. She fondled my hair while I drank. I did not know what to answer. Often in those days I did not know.

My aunt drew down the sheet and tutted. 'Your stockings are laddered.' she said. I had not bothered to take them off. She rose and took new ones from a drawer. The sheet was laid down to the end of the bed. Caressing my legs she drew off my stockings and replaced them. The new, black ones were of openwork style that came to the very tops of my thighs. 'It is better so,' she said and waited until I had finished the tea.

'You will be a good girl now, Beatrice, will you?'

I said yes with my eyes. My eyes were soft with the morning. My aunt removed my nightdress and attended to my face with powder and rouge.

'Maria was bad – do you remember?' she asked.

I said yes. My voice was soft with the morning. It was yesterday or the day before. I had forgotten the day.

'Amanda improves a little. Arabella is properly settled now of course,' Aunt Maude continued. She glossed my long hair with a brush. Its bristles tickled my back. 'They are not as you are, Beatrice. Turn over now – your bottom up, well up.'

I obeyed. I drew my knees up. I was to be punished for my wickedness in the water closet and the study. My wrists were strapped to the sides of the beds where the iron supports ran beneath the mattress. Then my ankles.

'Dip your back properly – present yourself, Beatrice!' Her tone was sharp. When I did, she moved back behind me. I laid my cheek on the pillow and waited. 'Such a perfect bottom – you surpass us all,' she breathed.

The whip was in her hand, taken from beneath my pillow. The thongs flicked out, making me arch and rear like a filly. I turned my face inwards and bit into my pillow. The tips stung and searched me – messengers of seeking. They sought my crevices. Their small mouths nipped and made me writhe. Heat expanded. Tendrils of fire – hot in their seeking. The hissing hissed to my bold cheeks, my pumpkin, skirting my offered fig, my honeypot.

Much as I squirmed and gasped the sensation had its bitter sweetness. The straps held me.

A sound beyond. The whip fell. My face rustled in its hiding in the pillow. My uncle entered. I knew his steps, the heavy footsteps falling. I struggled at my straps. My hips weaved. My eyes closed, opened, closed. The bed sagged between my legs – my legs splayed wide.

'No, Uncle. No!'

'Be quiet, Beatrice!' Her hand stroked my hair. 'Slap her hard, Thomas, if she wriggles. She must learn!'

I gargled, gurgled, squealed. Thong-kissed, my cheeks were parted. The knob of his wicked nosed against my O, the puckered rim. Hands clasped my hips and stilled their wayward motions. The rim yielded. I received an inch of throbbing shaft. I endeavoured to tighten. Too late. The piston pistoned. Half his cock was sheathed.

'How tight she grips!' he groaned. Subtle and smooth he urged it more within. 'What a bottom of glory – hot hot, how clinging! Your tongue, Maude!'

I heard their lips, the licking. Her hand slipped beneath my belly, fondled the lips of my quim and parted them, seeking my clit. I bucked. The movement allowed my uncle's prick to bury itself farther. Their lips sucked apart. I moaned in my writhings, in his steely grip.

'*Aaaaah!*' I gasped, my breath expelled. Without warning he had lodged it full within. The long thick prick throbbed deep within my bottom. Leaning over me, his palms cupped my swaying breasts.

My aunt moved back, forcing her way beneath me where I knelt. My head swam. My moistening anus held its velvet grip. Half-emerging, his tool sheathed itself to the full again, emerged, and then repeated the gesture. Sparks sprinkled in my belly. My hot cheeks churned against his form.

Aunt Maude drew my mouth down upon her own.

'Move your bottom, Beatrice – move it on his cock.'

I blubbered in her mouth. Her tongue lapped my seepings. Moving more easily now his stiff penis commenced its majestic indriving. I jolted with his jolts. A sharp tingling sweetness in my slit increased.

'Move your bottom – you are on the rocking horse – pretend.'

Coarse in her excitement, my aunt clasped my cheeks. Our mouths were sucking sponges together. I lapped as greedily as she. I moved my hips. An insensate lust seized me to feel his spurting. Lewdly I churned my bottom, drawing hoarse cries of delight from my uncle whose cock pistoned me ever faster. His hands caressed my stockinged thighs. They joined with my aunt's in fondling my breasts.

'Yes!'

In my aunt's mouth I moaned my lostness.

'Make him come in your bottom, Beatrice.'

'Yes!'

'Do you not know your power, my love? Ram his belly – empty his balls!'

The words . . . were they the words . . . the power? I moved, I choked, my senses swirled. My tongue in my aunt's mouth, I drew the cheeks of my bottom forward until I could almost feel the knob at my rim.

'Hold now!' Aunt Maude instructed. She had slid from beneath me and joined her husband. I squeezed upon the knob which like a plum was lodged just within. 'Be still, Thomas!' I heard, 'Beatrice, you will move at your wish now.'

Head hung, my lips pursed tight beyond her seeing. A final test of my total obedience? The leaves of old albums turned their pages slowly in my mind. My teeth chattered briefly. The lure was now exquisite. Unmoving as my uncle was in his stillness, I urged back. A certain oiliness between us had eased the passage. My bottom expanded comfortably but tightly round his tool. I heard his breathing come more coarsely as inch by inch I absorbed it to the full.

'No movement, Thomas,' my aunt breathed. A small husky sob escaped me. I began to jerk my bottom in little frenetic stabs. Each one allowed me to feel the full length of his pestle. The rubbery rim of my anus mouthed it more tightly. I could accommodate my pressure, as it seemed.

'At your own pace, Beatrice. Are you coming?'

I could scarce breathe for the excitement of sensations. The feeling was unique. The heat in my bottom added to the wicked, itchy-burning of my submission. The pressure of my cheeks to his belly in the slow backward strokes had an intimacy all its own.

I had come twice in far-faint thrilling spillings. Lifting my head slightly, I rotated my bottom with his cock half lodged within me. His croaks were my reward. The urgent throbbings of his tool redoubled.

'You wish him to come, Beatrice?'

I did not understand. Why was I asked? Who then was master here? His hands no longer held my hips. Each movement was of my own volition.

'Y–y–yes,' I stammered. My voice was a small-girl voice. Sunlight in the attic, hazed with dust. The stone cooler where the wine had waited in our aftermaths. The wrigglings of my bottom as I descended the ladder, my mouth clouded with summer.

I heard a gasp from my uncle. His statuesque pose astonished – the root of his manhood unmoving as I urged upon its lusts. A deep quivering seized him in the next soft smacking of my bottom to his belly. The mouth of my O gripped him as in a velvet vice. As of an instinct I held my plump cheeks now tight into him and squirmed. His groans resounded. Ah! the jetting, the deep liquid in-spurts – each long thick pulsing of come known, felt, absorbed in spongelike warmth. I sniffled, tightened, hissed my breath. The globs shot out again, insucked. My anus flowed with riches, trickling out.

Swimming in sensations, I collapsed. The slug of flesh plopped out – wet nose upon my thighs. My bonds were loosed. A shuffling from behind and he was gone, seed spent, the sac of his balls lighter.

Drowsy in my sweet fulfilments I was turned. I lay upon my back. Her mouth touched mine. Fingers felt my wetness both at my mound and my bottom.

'It is good,' Aunt Maude murmured. My body fluttered and trembled still. My thighs lay open, wanton. Our tongues touched. My lips were petals to her stamen-seeking. My aunt turned the pages in my mind and read from them silently, slowly.

'What do you want?' she asked.

I sought a word. 'Everything,' I said. The word was a butterfly caught in a net. Its wings were unbroken. Her eyes released it again. It flew about us and melted within me. Her finger traced my lower lip, causing me to pout. Without meaning to I giggled.

'Jenny is in a cage,' my aunt said.

I did not believe her. For a moment I did not believe her. I tightened my thighs together but she tickled me and made them lie wide again, my legs straight in their net stockings.

'Dress now. Wear drawers. Be firm with her. Tell her what you would have her do.'

In my rising I stared at her. The room yawned about me. I fussed with my dress. Oozings of sperm slide-slithered down my thighs at the back.

'It is true?' I asked.

Aunt Maude laughed and lifted my chin. 'Why else were you sent? Do you not know yet your beginnings and your endings? Have you not been nurtured, led to this? Their cocks would have been your undoing. Would you be as Caroline, Amanda or Jenny?'

My head would not move. I was rigid in my knowings.

'Even so, there may be lewdnesses – at your permitting. Your freedom is entire now, Beatrice. I shall mark your progress. Instil, train, command. Do you understand?' She loosed my chin. I nodded. The air about my eyes had lost its mist. The sperm had bubbled from Caroline's bottom, perhaps, long ere this. I made appraisals, promisings – within myself I delved and sought. The cheeks of my bottom were heavy, warm, fulfilled.

I turned from her and made my way upstairs. The door to my uncle's study lay open. He was writing at his desk. At my passing he looked up. His eyes were hollow. I swayed my hips with a certain insolence. I wished him to look. 'How firm and fleshy you are,' my aunt had said. I sensed my perversities. The air of the house hung now about me like an old cloak.

Jenny was naked in a cage. Amanda lay upon the couch on her back, tightly bound from head to feet. I unlocked the cage. Jenny's arms were strapped to her sides. She wore black stockings and a long string of pearls which hung between her melon breasts. She was sitting. She stared at me dully. I motioned my head and she rose with an effort, rolling for a moment against the bars. Then she recovered herself and stepped out.

I led her to the bar. I intended to strap her. Her small, tight bottom had a fascination for me. It was like Amanda's except that Jenny was shorter than she. Her hair had been trimmed in an urchin cut.

'Do not speak until I speak,' I said. I bent her over the bar and gave her bottom a sharp smack. With her arms bound, it was needful for me only to touch the back of her downbent head lightly. The sound of the smack coupled with the resilience of the cheeks and the wild little gasp that she uttered thrilled me tremendously. Slowly I left her and walked over to the wall where the straps hung. I selected the shortest and thickest. Amanda's eyes beseeched me briefly. I gave her a small tight smile that betokened nothing.

'When we were younger, did Father have you?' I asked Jenny. In uttering my words I brought the leather across her bottom with a loud *Cra–aaaaack!* Her hips swayed and jerked inwards so far as the bar would allow them to. A dull flush spread across her hemispheres.

'You intend not to answer, Jenny?'

Her face was suffused. A second, sharper stroke of the leather made her yelp more.

'Yes, Beatrice.'

'When you came to sleep in the guest-room?' The double doors of the past opened more clearly to me now. They yawned upon our yesterdays.

'Yesssssss!' she hissed as the loud-smacking strap again seared her bottom.

'You will tell me later in precise detail. Rise!'

Her face contorted as she did so. She swivelled round on her heels and stood before me. Her head hung. I smiled and tweaked her nipples.

'How delicious you must have been for him,' I said coldly. I felt no emotion. It was an observation. I led her downstairs by her string of pearls which I knew she would fear to have broken. Her small feet padded silently on the carpet. Leading her into my room which was empty again, I gave her a further smack, making her jump. She skittered nervously forward and then stood still.

'Kneel!' I told her. A sense of severity entered into me, but I was as yet not entirely tutored. A few months hence and I would have handled her even better. Kneeling and with her head and shoulders bowed dutifully, she looked as one seeking protection. It was part of her attraction. I wanted her tongue – her small darting tongue – but it was too soon as yet.

I walked round her, inspecting her slowly. She had grown little through the years, I thought. Her body was small, curves tight and sweet.

'You were strapped that night?' I asked.

'Yes.'

The little word upon the carpet lay. I stood before her once more and raised my foot, bringing the sole of my boot down gently on the back of her head. Her lips touched the toe of my other boot and kissed it.

'Begin, Jenny.'

Her mouth mumbled against my boot. Her lips smudged its glossy surface. I edited her text in my mind as she spoke, sensing her slyness. Her conversion that night had been swift, as she would have had me believe. In the double bed to which she had been carried while supposedly half asleep, her nightgown had been stripped, her bottom poised. Fearful to cry out lest she woke me, she had been scorched by the strap. Confessions had been drawn from her that she said were false. After a score of strokes she had been stilled, even as my uncle had stilled me, with a long deep plunge and then withdrawal. But then it had entered her again and so remained, deep in its throbbings.

On being carried back at last to the guest room, she had felt isolated, lonely. The silence of the house at night had hung about her like bat's wings. Her bottom knew heat and emptiness and longing. In her tinglings she had lain.

'Go on,' I said when, at this part of her narrative, she halted.

'There was no more,' she mumbled. Her mouth moved over my boot even more fervently.

'Do you believe her?' It was my aunt. She had entered unseen, unheard. Her look ignored Jenny. She came across, lifted my chin and kissed me. The kiss endured. My aunt's hand reached down and sought Jenny's hair while our mouths were locked. She drew Jenny's face upwards, beneath my skirt, between my thighs. Open, warm and seeking, Jenny's lips nuzzled into the vee of my drawers. I felt the pleading lapping of her tongue. I did not move. My hips were unresponsive as if by instinct. By placing her free hand beneath my bottom, Aunt Maude could tell it was so. Her lips moved with pleasure upon mine. Our salivas mingled.

'Do you believe her?' she asked again.

I would not answer. I wanted what I knew within myself. My bottom squeezed in my remembering. My aunt's mouth swam back from mine. 'Tell her,' she said quietly.

I looked down. The front of my skirt was looped over Jenny's head. Her tongue worked industriously, tracing the lips of my quim through my drawers. Despite a faint trembling of my knees I moved not.

'*Down!*' I commanded. The surge of power was within me. I knew the power. Jenny's response was instant. She sank down again. Her mouth deserted me. 'Go! go to your cage!' I said. With the closing of the door my aunt took my hand and guided me to sit upon the bed. Going to my closet she poured a liqueur for each of us. Returning, she sat beside me.

'You will continue your meditations,' she said, 'plan your plottings, manoeuvre them to your will.'

The freshness of cool water was within me after my handling of Jenny.

'All?' I asked.

Aunt Maude did not answer me directly. 'You dealt well with Jenny. It shall be so with Caroline and – upon your need – with Katherine. Observe the males. How proudly their cocks rise. Hidden sometimes beneath their breeches – at others lewdly exposed. Frig them, toy with them, play with them. The bubbling jets expel. Their faces soften, their cocks soften. They are as putty. Their training is no more arduous than that of the girls. They shall service you only at your bidding.'

'Service?' I sensed the meaning, yet I asked.

'In your lewdnesses, Beatrice – your slit, your bottom. Never your mouth. Mouths are for others.'

'Such as Caroline?'

'Sly in her sweetness, she has sucked upon their bubblings, yes. Had you not known this? She is shy, acquiescent. Her mouth lends itself like a rose to the sperm, imbibing deeply. In her demureness she wipes her lips secretively and blushes. Did you not know?'

I hid my face. It was my last shyness. 'Perhaps,' I said. Spiders' webs glistened in my mind, broke, fell apart. I envied her for a moment – the big knob purplish at her lips, her tongue gliding beneath the veins. The urgent gliding, sliding. The silence save for the sucking of her lips. Sweet throbbing of the tool – its jets outspurting. Mouth salty, creamed, her limp form raised. Her bottom fondled.

I came to myself again. 'Shall we return soon?' I asked.

'At your wish, Beatrice.' A last flourish of her glass and she was gone. I leaned back. The wall was cool to my back. In the summer I would have cages on the lawn – between the shrubbery and the summerhouse. I would have my whip. My eyes would be as fire, my breasts uplifted.

Yes.

# Chapter Eighteen

The letter I had begun to Father lay as I had left it. I imagined him in his being entering and gazing at it. The Chinese, I have heard, never destroy a piece of paper once it has been written upon. Characters once imparted to it acquire a being, a magic, a presence. They rest upon the surface like the silhouettes of birds who have no wish to move again.

I took up the pen again. *Dearest Father, I await your return – Beatrice.* It was enough. Now in my subtle shifting it sufficed. He would move among the words at night as a poacher moves among the larches and the elms. Taking an envelope, I addressed it to him at the tea plantation in Malabar which his father had bequeathed him. He would return thence with dust on his lapels – the musk of dusky women in his nostrils, the dream of a rocking horse.

I would place the horse on the lawn, perhaps, in a larger cage for Caroline. When the rain came it would stand forlorn and waiting. Raindrops in their crystal glittering on its stirrups.

I bathed and listened to a twittering of voices from the garden – Caroline's and Jenny's among them. Upon my descent for lunch I employed subtleties rather than assertions. At the serving of the soup I asked Maria what wine we were to have with the fish.

'With the fish, Riesling . . . ' Maria began and looked towards Katherine, my aunt being seemingly deeply engaged with the unfolding of her napkin.

'Not the Riesling – we will have Piesporter, Maria, and you will address me as Ma'am. You understand?'

The poor woman almost curtsied in her confusion whereat Katherine swept a look along the table to Aunt Maude whose placid quietness gave full reply. I had additionally had Amanda brought down. She sat as one who is at a party without friends. Katherine's look passed to me. I received it briefly with a slight affectation of boredom.

'Caroline, you will gather flowers from the garden after lunch. The rooms have a slightly drab air. Place some in my bedroom first. Amanda will assist you,' I said, and turned immediately to engage my aunt in conversation. Katherine was thus neatly isolated, my uncle having gone – or been sent, I suspected – on some errand.

I rose first from the table. Normally, in the conventions, Aunt Maude would have done so and I would have waited upon her to do so. By this small sign, however, a silent Katherine received my further tokens. When I moved of a purpose into the conservatory she followed me – a slightly wounded falcon, I felt, though I bore her no malice. To the contrary, she attracted me both physically and mentally.

'There is change, then,' she asked quietly.

'As to all things,' I replied. I placed my arm about her waist and then slid my hand down very slowly to feel and fondle the quite perfect globe of her bottom. Beneath the light material of her dress the twin hemispheres had the smoothness of peach-skin.

Katherine compressed her lips slightly and endeavoured to hide a smile of pleasure at the lightly-floating questing of my fingers. That she wore no drawers was evident by the way I could gently urge a single fold of her dress into the tight groove of her bottom.

'You have not yet given us a performance, Katherine.'

'No?' Her voice was light but shaky. She endeavoured to recover her usual poise and move away but a warning inward pressure of my fingers stayed her. 'The subject was forgotten,' she said. The faintest of blushes had appeared on her cheeks. It pleased me.

I drew her to a small bench where we sat side by side. The scent of fuchsias was rich in my nostrils. Earth smell, loam smell – a nostalgia of flowerpots, some straight, some tilted.

'Your performances have been few? I mean for your private theatricals, Katherine.'

'Le Théâtre Erotique? There have been some amusements in the past. I engaged Lord Eridge's three daughters upon a delicious masquerade last summer. It made excellent preliminary training for them. It is extraordinary what licences the erstwhile modest permit themselves when they believe themselves inhabiting a world of fantasy.'

'Wherein they also believe themselves full hid by their costumes?' I asked.

Katherine's look of appraisal would have been flattering in any other circumstances.

'Exactly. They had not so much as raised their skirts before nor shown their ankles. I had them attired at first in glittering tights with knee-boots and transparent bodices. Music entranced them to display themselves. A small orchestra was discreetly screened from the proceedings. We acted out at first an innocent game of circuses. The estate ponies were perfect for that. We used a large marquee. The audience was naturally small and the champagne flowed. I allowed the girls to imbibe freely between their frolics. In their gigglings and foolish ridings around on the ponies I gave them several twitches of the crop further to enliven them.'

I laid my hand upon Katherine's thigh and fingered up the material of her dress slowly until her nearest leg was bared to me almost to her hip. My fingertips ran sensuously around her stocking top. She leaned back. Her lips remained slightly parted for a moment as if seeking breath. The transition from stocking top to silk-smooth skin was delicious.

'And the entertainment?' I asked. I guessed it was called that from my aunt's photographic interlude with Maria and Frederick.

'There was to be trick riding, I told them,' Katherine continued. She moved her knees wider apart to allow my hand to glide up more easily and fondle the warm inner surfaces of her thighs. 'The ponies were exchanged for three fine Arabian horses from Lord Eridge's stables. The door to the marquee was then tightly closed. The musicians, being in a separate marquee that abutted our own, could see nothing.

'I blindfolded each of the girls and had them mount the steeds, whereat their arms were secured about the horses' necks. There was a little fretting on their part about this, for fear they would fall. I comforted them,' Katherine went on with a smile and a half-closing of her eyes as I delicately touched the lips of her quim. Her bottom shifted forward slightly on the seat.

'You strapped their ankles to the stirrups – yes, go on,' I said confidently.

'First I had them ride in a circle. Unknown to them three of the menfolk guided the stallions by their reins. The sisters thought themselves most adept and laughed shrilly, if sometimes nervously. Occasionally I gave them a harder twitching with a schooling whip than they had before received. By then they were quite flushed with all the excitement. I judged them ready. The horses were stilled and to multiple shrieks from the three lovely heroines of the piece their tights were swiftly drawn down. Then with a single bound a male leapt up behind each of them, raised their bare bottoms from off the saddles and . . .'

I leaned to her. Our lips, tongues met. My forefinger circled the increasingly sticky lips of her slit.

'Each was fucked more than once?' I asked. I had not intended to use a word of such coarseness. It spilled unbidden from my lips. Katherine's tongue swam around my own.

'In succession from the males – who had long waited upon such an occasion – each girl received a triple dose. They had quietened considerably by the time a second foaming lance entered their pussies. The gentle jogging of the horses as they continued to move round slowly in a circle added to their pleasures, no doubt.'

'Their bottoms were feted, too?' I asked. Katherine's parted legs had straightened. I sought right beneath the sweet orb of her bottom and found her puckered rose.

'No–n–no . . . not then,' she stammered. 'That pleasure had been reserved. Half fainting with untold pleasures, the girls were finally dismounted and taken blindfolded into the house, their wrists secured, their tights removed as well as their boots. Their naked bottoms were quite rosy after their ridings, of course. In the main bedroom of the manor all had been prepared beforehand. Taken within, the three were strapped side by side upon the bed with pillows piled tightly beneath their bellies to elevate their bottoms.

'The squire – entering then ready for the fray with his penis bobbing – exerted his efforts valiantly in each of their bottoms in turn, stilling each while they moaned and squirmed fretfully. Then, taking the elder – whom I placed in the middle – he pumped her bottom fully, fondling the other two meanwhile. Such was his pleasure that when he finally withdrew, the rose-hole frothed most copiously, I can tell you. Oh! oh, Beatrice – your tongue, dearest, I implore you!'

Her beseeching for my mouth between her elegant thighs was to my satisfaction since I intended then to ignore it. She had asked and been refused. It suited me perfectly. Taking her chin I pushed her face back and ceased the toying of my fingers.

'Later, perhaps,' I purred, 'upon your continued good behaviour. You have not finished your recital. What then occurred?'

'His prick considerably limper, of course, he left the squirming and blindfolded beauties to their wonderings as to the possessor of the doughty staff which had cleft their bottoms – not entirely to their dissatisfaction, as it later transpired. They were then released, bathed and cossetted – by myself and Jenny, as it happened. We said nothing of the lewdnesses to which they had succumbed and indeed brought wine and cakes and made merry as if the afternoon had been nought but gaiety.'

'Their training began thereafter, Katherine?' My hand held her chin still in a commanding pose.

'Yes. They were clothed henceforth, as you have been, in close-fitting wool dresses with nothing beneath save their stockings and boots or shoes. Frequent but light applications of the birch did wonders. With sisters – they were sixteen, eighteen and twenty respectively – it is best to keep them herded close at all times. The breakfast room, being large, was transformed into a recreation room for them. To a large circular table I had a short centre post fixed. Each girl was spread across the table with her wrists secured to the post. Their ankles were tied by a rope which circled the table and looped around their outstretched legs.

'For the first week they continued to be blindfolded when brought down, their dresses secured up around their waists. Into the breakfast room I patted them, one by one. They had adorable bottoms and were quite quiet and obedient when secured in a circle around the table. A dozen swishes of the birch came first, bringing a pink glow to their offered bottoms. The twelfth stroke was always the sternest, bringing loud shrill squeals – for they quickly learned that it was followed by the stiff insertion of the throbbing staff into each of their bottoms.

'At the end of the first week, immediately after each had been birched, I released Samantha, the eldest, while leaving the other two bound. Cautioning her to be silent, I bound her wrists and removed her blindfold. Blushing violently, she made to turn away from the upright majesty of the cock that awaited her, but I twisted her about to face it.'

'You made her ask for it,' I murmured.

'Of course.'

Katherine's voice was husky, her eyes wild with pleading for the attentions of my tongue.

'How crude,' I said softly and rose, looking down at her. 'Katherine, draw your skirt up fully – well beneath your bottom. Good. Spread your legs more. Excellent! A delicious thatch, my sweet. Has it been watered of late?'

Before she could reply I strode to the door and gazed back at her. She looked indeed a picture of wantonness, her breasts heaving. The tint of her thighs above her stockings was as of pale ivory. The bush of her quim was thick and luxuriant.

'*Wait!*' I said coldly, quickly removing the key from the door and turning it on the other side as I went out. Unmoving she sat, the beseeching of her eyes following me.

I hastened to Aunt Maude and told her of my immediate intentions. Her eyes glowed. 'I will have him made ready,' she said, 'it will take but a moment.' Summoning Maria, she told her to fetch Frederick without delay. He came as usual in his quietness – a watchfulness, I felt, that was well concealed behind a long-practised subservience.

'You will strip,' I said. He gazed at me for a long moment as if uncertain as to whether he was to obey or not and then immediately removed his jacket. Assuring myself that there were no other servants about, I then fetched a simple, straight-backed wooden chair which I placed for him.

In his nakedness, Frederick was a magnificent animal, perfect in physique. His cock stood a proud nine inches under the gentle manipulation of my fingers. Bidding him sit, I then had my aunt bind him tightly to the chair facing the doors.

'You will see now to Katherine?' I asked my aunt, who nodded and went out. The very mention of his mistress's name made Frederick start – not out of apprehension, I perceived, for while a dull flush spread over his clean-cut features, the rubicund knob of his penis appeared to glow even more.

A scuffling sounded from beyond. I strode to the doors and opened them. There stood Katherine, wriggling in the stronger embrace of my aunt. Between us we hustled her within and closed the doors anew upon the little ceremony I intended.

'Oh how dare you!' Katherine blustered, her colour rising high at the sight of her manservant whose upquivering tool awaited her pleasure. There was no need to remove her dress. It hoisted cleanly and swiftly enough again to her hips. While Aunt Maude held her wrists I smacked her bottom hard, causing her hips to jolt and bringing a light sheen of tears into her eyes.

'*Quiet*, Katherine!' I instructed coldly. 'Has he not had you yet?'

With every word her enforced but dragging footsteps brought the superb nudity of the lower half of her body closer to the manservant's haggard gaze. 'No!' she shrieked. Her head shook wildly.

'You will speak!' I told him. 'Have you not savoured the voluptuous pleasures of her bottom, the wobbling of her lovely breasts to your lips?'

'M–Ma'am? N–no. She has brought me frequently to dress her and undress her – to prepare her often for her bath – but never have my fingers been permitted to touch her adorable skin,' he stammered.

Perhaps it was his unexpected use – indeed unheard of use for a servant – of the word 'adorable' that brought a softer shriek than I had imagined would come as Katherine was manoeuvred over him, legs apart, until his manly tool prodded up in waiting just beneath the pouting lips of her quim.

'Oh! Maude! Beatrice! I beg you – no!' Katherine sobbed in what I felt was entirely theatrical effect. No doubt in her early training of the Eridge daughters she had heard them all say it in turn. Drawing Katherine's arms forward over Frederick's shoulders, my aunt continued to hold her while I – pressing my hand downwards upon her bottom – reached beneath and guided the stiff cock of a now groaning Frederick between the soft lips of her slit.

Katherine's eyes rolled. Her head fell back, her knees trembling on either side of his as the nubbing nose of his lovestaff urged within her luscious grotto and secured its place. The rest was but a matter of a simple downward thrust on Katherine's shoulders. A low humming sound which appeared to mingle shock and pleasure trilled from her throat as her brazen bottom cheeks at last descended upon Frederick's bare knees, there to settle with a squirming, agonised motion.

The rest was simplicity. In a trice she was bound to him, the bodice of her dress being unlaced so that his nose settled somewhat blissfully no doubt in the deep valley between the silken gourds of her tits.

Dearly as I would love to have knelt down, I did not. It would have been undignified. Nevertheless, I would like to have seen – on that first occasion – the deep rooting of his cock within her and the way his balls were squashed beneath her. Her arms were secured around his neck and her ankles fastened to his. Thus she had room to manoeuvre her bottom up and down and would do so, I had no doubt, once they were alone, despite her sobbing protestations as Aunt Maude and I made to leave.

'B–Beatrice! you cannot!' Katherine implored. Imprisoned and shafted upon him thus, she looked adorable. Her nipples already sprouted thickly, I noticed. I had no illusions that the moment we left them in this erotic stance his lips would begin nibbling at the rosy buds her exposed melons presented to him.

'You may come in her as you wish . . . on this occasion, Frederick,' I said quietly. Then we were gone, the doors locked behind us.

'A merriment – did you not think?' I asked Aunt Maude.

My aunt nodded. 'It will do her no harm. She has long inhibited herself in his respect, I am sure. You will not permit him to master her, though?'

It was an unnecessary question, as her eyes told me. There were per-mutations into which I had not yet entered nor thought to enter.

'I shall make her Mistress of the Robes,' I said, and laughed. We placed our ears to the door briefly and caught their muffled moanings. 'She will speak not a word to him out of pride,' I said, 'and neither will he dare address her despite the fact that he has her plugged. An almost perfect conjunction, I think. She may punish him later, at her wish, of course. I shall permit that. They will enjoy that also – both of them.'

'You have grown in your knowings,' Aunt Maude replied.

'Of course,' I said pertly. The exercise had given me a heady feeling of conquering without cruelty – the path I was thereafter to follow in all my knowings. Eight persons out of ten have a willingness to submit in the right circumstances and guided by the right hands. Therein is a safety for them. They are led – permitted. In their enforcement are they permitted. I had moved beneath the sea and raised my skirts. The water had lapped me. A tongue had lapped me. Fishes had nibbled at my garters.

I would have a dozen pairs of gloves of the finest kid, reaching to my elbows, I told my aunt. The idea of the very sensuousness of their touch communicated itself to her immediately. She would have her glove-maker bring them she said. They would be extremely close-fitting.

'Their come will bubble over your fingers,' she smiled.

'When I wish it,' I said. 'Come – I want you on the rocking horse.'

Aunt Maude stepped back. 'I?' She jerked, but my hand already had her elbow. 'Do you mean it, Beatrice?' I had no need to answer. Her docility came as from one who had half expected it. Stockinged and booted, but otherwise naked, she looked superb. Her figure had a rubbery firmness in all its outcurving aspects. Mounted on the horse, she stretched her bottom back brazenly, her slit gleaming juicily.

I accorded her no pleasure other than three dozen biting flicks of the whip. The enforced bending of her knees – together with the orbing of her bottom as she fought to keep her heels dug into the stirrups – provided the very aspect of eroticism I had long envisaged of myself.

There would be a small platform in future behind the horse so that the male could mount it at the appropriate moment and insert his penis while he gripped the weaving hips. At my command.

I would have it so. There would be no exercises nor entertainments nor merriments beyond my seeing or control.

I had entered my domain.

## *Chapter Nineteen*

It was a full forty minutes before I released Katherine and drew her up. Her nipples were rigid, her breasts swollen. Following me in with a distinctly awkward gait after the whipping I had accorded her, my aunt released Frederick and motioned him to dress in a side room.

'How many times, Katherine?' I asked softly, passing my hand down between her thighs. The abundance of his sperm made itself felt soapily between her thighs. Some had trickled down and rilled into the ridged tops of her stockings.

Burying her hot face into my shoulder, Katherine mumbled something I could not catch. It would not do. I lifted her reluctant face, watching the sly messengers of pleasure endeavouring to scurry into hiding behind her eyes.

'He came twice at least, I trust?' I asked sternly.

Again she wanted to conceal her face but I would not permit it. I had yet to learn myself that it is one of the most satisfying positions, squatted face to face upon a man's thighs. 'Yes,' she averred thickly. 'Beatrice, I must . . .'

'Punish him? Of course – at your pleasure,' I interrupted. An exceedingly pretty half-laugh broke from her lips, accompanied by a small, emerging '*Oh!*' that had all the colour and perfume of a budding rose. I drew her dress down as a mother might with a child and smoothed her hips.

'You will not make me again?' she asked. The invitation was so blatant that I all but laughed.

'Obedience is necessary at all times, Katherine,' I replied softly and kissed her brow. It was damp still with her exertions as were her peachlike bottom cheeks which held a faint mist of moisture between them. It would have pleasured me distinctly then to have guided another manroot into her bottom while holding her down beneath my arm. Perhaps she read the wish in my eyes for she simpered and pressed into me.

'I should never . . .' she began. I knew her intention. It was to apologise to me for what had gone before. Perhaps she thought I had come in disguise to test her.

'You may have Jenny as a handmaid – for today, Katherine.'

I moved away quickly and left her. She would have had me stay, I felt – perhaps to afford her some obscure sense of comforting. One must keep one's distance, however. I had turned her about neatly and left her, so to speak, with one foot in mid-air. My immediate concern was with Amanda. She had dallied long in the garden with Caroline. Nevertheless, their would-be pleasing efforts were evident from the array of blooms which stood on the kitchen table.

Maria was adjusting some of them. She gazed at me rather shyly as I entered.

'You are happy, Maria?' I asked. The bloom of health seemed indeed to be upon her. I had a certain taste for the voluptuousness of her curves which her deliberately tight and abbreviated costume enhanced. She nodded. A veil of uncertainty was in her eyes. Her fingers flustered at the flowers. There was a new ring on her finger, I noticed. It was one of no great account. My uncle had given it to her, I guessed. On my questioning her, she confessed it.

'He mounted you, Maria?'

The question was so direct that she knew not what to answer. A tiny bubble of saliva appeared between her lips which were richly curved but smallish.

'As Frederick did in the stable, Maria?' I insisted. Beneath her black skirt I could envisage the ripeness of her cheeks in their waiting.

'My husband don't know, Ma'am,' she stammered.

'Answer the questions, Maria,' I said softly and stayed her hands from their toying with the stalks of the blooms. Her palms were moist.

'I was ashamed, Ma'am,' she choked. The expression in her eyes was ill-disguised. It followed not the twisting of her lips. She would lend herself, I sensed, to whatever I intended.

'Did you buck or struggle, Maria?' I gripped the bun of her hair which was coiled up with hairpins. One loosened and fell between my fingers.

'No, Ma'am, I daren't. Miss Katherine she had the whip, in the stable, and the Mistress she warned me not to move afterwards when I was in the dining-room over the table.'

I was but half listening. Though not indolent, she was learning her pleasures in the sly way known to such women. An occasional protest cleared her conscience, as she saw it. Her husband, she said, was a good man, a quiet man, like herself nearing thirty. He worked as a farm labourer.

I released her hair.

'You will come shortly into my service, Maria – as also your husband. There will be work for him to do around the house. I am having a site cleared for stables. You may perhaps be my stable mistress, if it so pleases me. You have learned a little of the handling of females and you are acquiescent. You will learn under my instructions.'

I doubted whether she knew the meaning of 'acquiescent' any more than she would have recognised a five-pound note. I have since given field-girls a guinea piece for their intended services and seen them gaze at it in wonder.

Words unspoken danced upon Maria's lips. From the brief description she had given me of her husband, Ned, he would be able amply to service both Caroline and Jenny when required. Maria – given over to such pleasures as I occasionally permitted her – would soon grow used to it.

Amanda I called within. Lolling upon a rug on the lawn, Caroline stared at me in some wonder. I gave her a smile. 'Later,' I called. It would comfort her for a while. In my uprising was her safety, as she knew. The memory of being bound to her in our nudities was still one of my sweetest. We would play games of remembrance, perhaps. I would find a way. She would become my favourite handmaiden, an adored one. In the attic would be laughter again. I would brush her hair and fondle and pat her bottom, coaxing. In her shaftings would be the whisperings of sunhazed lust. The bees' wings on the windowsill would stir. I would make colours to enchant her eyes. Filled and fulfilled she would be led down the ladder again, her legs in their slimness-sweet uncovered still. The gold between her thighs would glint with sperm. In her richness.

'Is there richness, Amanda?' I asked. Knowing not, she did not answer. There was awkwardness in her gait as I led her up. Her small, tight bottom was attended to daily and yet still it jerked skittishly at the first stroke of leather or birch.

In my bedroom I stilled Amanda with my hand and made her stand, feet together, while I sat on the bed.

'This will be your first new exercise – to stand still on command. Will you do so, Amanda, if you are no longer caged or birched?'

She nodded, an arising of hope in her eyes.

'What is it you seek?' I asked. 'There will be the strap still.'

'I do not know,' she mumbled. In my intuitions she was a relatively poor subject, though I knew not why. Rising, I moved around her and passed my hand up beneath her skirt to see whether or not she would flinch. She did not. I urged my thumb against her rosehole. Aunt Maude inserted the dildo twice daily in her now. It had improved her, I noticed. A tiny assenting movement of her bottom made itself felt against my thumb.

'You do not mind the strap?' I asked. I moved the ball of my thumb up and down between the elastic cheeks.

Amanda shook her head in a manner that was at least uncertain. Perhaps she feared to say no – or perhaps pride held her back. There was a possibility by now that she had begun to accept it with a surprised sense of pleasure – the stinging a challenge.

'Raise your dress, Amanda, and tuck it in about your waist. Feet together, hands at sides. Good. You will stand so when you are told. It will be a further exercise. Your thighbands – should they not be of silver now? Have you earned them?'

'I have been good.' Her lips quivered. Was she aware to what she had replied? I thought of the house from which we had led her here. The gloom of the rooms – the latticed windows too small. Male hands that had quavered briefly about our breasts.

'Silver,' I repeated. I ran my fingers around the metal bands. 'He is a jeweller, is he not? Would you not prefer silver?'

'I suppose.' The dull tone of her voice had the lustreless feel of the back of a dry spoon run over the tongue.

'Then it shall be,' I told her. Her eyes moved not. Could Aunt Maude have handled her differently, to a better end? I felt certain not. The curls about her pubic mount were tight and neat, trimmed straight across the top as my own had been. The curve of her belly was very slight, her breasts gelatinous and firm. I would have written messages on her mind save that in reading them she would not comprehend them. In two or three years perhaps she would be betrothed. Her eyes would move with vagueness through her days. Men would kiss her and bed her. She would respond with a vacuousness that would disappoint all save the lust-seekers.

He who was to mount her and fashion the broad rings of silver for her thighs would be such. They were mere oddments of people – of no account. Had there at least been slyness in her I could have used it, wended it within my wendings, eased tunnels of discovery.

By seven that evening, after the despatch of Frederick as messenger, the jeweller arrived. His eyes were haggard with expectancy.

'So soon?' he asked me. His eyes held querulous dismay that I, who had permitted my breasts to be fondled by him, should now have taken charge.

'Amanda waits upstairs,' I replied. Doffing his hat and cloak he accompanied me in some evident wondering, which I uttered no words to satisfy. At the turn of the stairs that led to the caging-room I halted for a moment. 'It shall be as I say. You will do all that I say. You will not speak unless I request it. Otherwise a delicate balance will be disturbed. Thereafter you may take her back. You will find her acquiescent. There is but one thing more,' I added, leading him in.

At the sight before him he stopped dead. Amanda was over the bar, her body freshly bathed and perfumed. I had deemed it necessary to tie her wrists so that she could not rise. Her long legs were neat together. Naked, her bottom rendered its perfect apple shape. I closed the door upon us.

'Remember my words – the fine balance,' I told him again in a whisper. He accepted with a nod – deeming himself perhaps in Paradise. His eyes were tentacles about her yielded form. Aloud, I added for Amanda's benefit, 'Next week her common metal thigh bands are to be replaced by silver ones. You will no doubt think of an appropriate design to engrave around them. Remove your clothes now and watch.'

'R–r–remove?' he stuttered.

'Or you shall not have her. There are certain conventions that we have instilled in her,' I went on glibly. The entire scene amused me not overmuch but I intended to have it performed. It was my first experiment in any event with an unconditioned male. 'You agree to give her solid silver stocking bands?' I asked.

'If it is wished,' he croaked. Under my waiting eyes his hands fiddled with the undoing of his waistcoat.

'It is wished,' I replied.

With others the edge of farce might already have been reached, but here within this strange room and with Amanda perfectly poised for his pleasuring, the dolt was ready to accept all that I said. Her very muteness added to the occasion.

A florid cast came into his features as he commenced with ludicrous reluctance to remove his clothes in front of me. I affected not to look at him. There was a certain brawniness in his figure which perhaps had its brutish attraction. His trunk was thick, his thighs tree trunks. At the first offering of his nakedness his penis lolled inert but rose in anticipation as I led him to her. I had oiled Amanda's bottom already in preparation for the moment. To all appearances she hung there dazed. Only a slight trembling of her knees betrayed her. He himself appeared now as one in a trance. Placing my hand in the small of his back I urged him yet a further step forward. Stemming upwards, his penis – which was of full girth and good length – pressed its pulsing column against the inrolling of her nether cheeks. Amanda immediately uttered a small cry, jerking like a nervous filly. The movement served only to bulge her bottom deeper against his balls.

'In silence, please, your wrists together behind your back,' I told him.

The gaping of his mouth at these words gave him an air of great stupidity. Nevertheless he obeyed. Taking him entirely by surprise in the fretful impatience of his loins, I manacled his wrists. His face became purplish.

'Silence!' I warned, 'the first act is intended as a ceremonial. You will receive instructions on how to handle her during the first weeks hereafter.'

Amanda's head began to toss. She strained at her wrist bonds. The most tearful of protests escaped her. She had awoken it seemed from the lulling comfort of her bondage. I had expected it. My next act therefore surprised her since, moving around to the front of the bar where her shoulders hung, I untied her wrists.

'Do not move,' I warned her. 'You have your choice even so. Accept his cock in you at last or you will stay for a further three months here. Do you understand?'

'P–please – I don't want him to.'

Her voice appeared piteous, small – of unutterable appeal. It moved me not since no upward movement of her back occurred. Some hint of slyness for which I had previously sought in vain was apparent in her at last for she gripped the bar, though nervously, and held her bottom remarkably still, her hair flowing down about her face.

I moved back to where her stallion stood, his eyes glassy with despair as – bereft of the use of his arms – he endeavoured to manoeuvre his swollen crest against the rim of her rosehole.

'Permit me,' I said and seized his rod which throbbed enormously in my palm. Motioning him back and thereby permitting him, for the first time in his life no doubt, the intimate attendance of two females at once, I urged his stiff shaft down and positioned the ruddy knob against Amanda's well-oiled aperture. 'Enter her slowly,' I breathed.

His knees trembled violently, jaw sagging, as the rubbery rim yielded with petulant moans and cries from Amanda. In but a second the knob was engulfed – the shaft itself standing proud. Its veins throbbed in their eagerness. Gripping the hairs at the back of his neck I drew upon them sharply, bringing from him a surprised groan. Sodomy – though males know it not – is an act of worship towards the superior sex. For to whatever bondage or apparent humiliations females are brought, they remain – as Aunt Maude had taught me now – the eternal victors of the act. Able as they are to receive a succession of pulsing and apparently dominant penises, it is the males who retire wan and spent.

Thus did I monitor the act. Gliding my hand between them and taking his pendent eggs in the palm of my hand, I restricted his entry half-inch by half-inch, ignoring – as I well knew I could – the anguished cries and sobbings of Amanda and the febrile jerkings of his loins as he sought to sheathe his rod more quickly.

'*Whoooo! Whoooo! No! No – Oh! Ah!* stop him, please!' Amanda moaned endlessly. At the half mark, however, his heavy trunk had now leaned more on hers until he was all but fully bent over her, his breath raucous. I had taken his balls now from behind. The pressures of my fingers were warnings enough for him to proceed as if by stealth into the clamlike gripping of her depths.

'B–b–b–b–b–!' Amanda moaned incoherently. I knew the wildness of her mind – the surging of the seawaves there – the outward rushing of the breath. Her eyes bulged. For a moment her hands deserted the gripping bar below in such a gesture that I feared rebellion. Loosing his testicles I gave then his buttocks a hearty slap, the immediate result of which was to ram his root completely within her bottom.

Ah! her wild, high-pitched shriek!

'*Na–ah–aaaaaaaaah!*' she shrilled, but deeply corked as she now was, her hips were immobile, her sobs spilling down upon the blankly staring floor.

Straps, whose purpose had not signified themselves to him, came swiftly to my hands. Groaning, he felt the grinding of her bottom warm into his belly as I strapped their thighs together at the top and buckled quickly. Only the slightest movement of his loins was now possible. I could but guess at the ecstasy of sensations he was experiencing. Bound thus in the most bizarre manner, his wrists strained helplessly at the manacles, his buttocks twitching as Amanda's gripping bottom first tightened upon him and then undoubtedly relaxed.

I moved and knelt before her, raising her hot-flushed face to mine. Her eyes were half-closed, giving a pretty fluttering to the lashes. Easing my palms forward uppermost, I allowed her tits to weigh upon them. Her nipples, as I had expected, had hardened into thornlike points. Her lips lolled wet beneath my passing kiss. There was no need for speech. Her mind did not communicate itself to me.

'R–r–release!' he croaked.

I saw no need to. Her bottom needed to accommodate itself to him more fully. Leaving them in their posture, I descended and found Caroline drinking lemonade in the breakfast room. Aunt Maude had taken Jenny and Katherine out, it seemed. More immediately upon my appearance, however, Caroline rose and threw herself into my arms.

'May we not go home?' she asked.

I took her hand, having kissed her, and led her to a couch.

'You will be obedient, Caroline?'

She nodded. Her eyes were faintly blurred with happiness, her cheek was velvety warm to mine. I felt for her breasts. The resilient mounds were snowy white and firm, the nipples like tiny cherries. In two years perhaps I would have her wed. It was not an experience I proposed myself to indulge in again. In the meantime I would nurture and develop her to a point where her usefulness would be unbounded.

'Wait for me in my room,' I told her.

'You will not be long, Beatrice?' Her eyes were the spaniel eyes of Father, brushing my skirts, nudging my calves – reaching to caress.

'Of course not,' I smiled. My voice was at its most gracious. I reached the caging-room in but moments and there gazed for a moment at the tableau which still presented itself. Amanda breathed softly – sniffling a little at my entry. With quick efficiency I released him from her. His cock emerged bubbling at the tip. The very suction of her bottom had produced an energetic pulsing of sperm, it seemed. Amanda was as quickly released. As coyly as she endeavoured to hide her face from him, she could not escape the darting of her eyes towards the now almost pendant penis that had entered and injected her.

'Dress and go down, Amanda. Prepare yourself for departure,' I said simply. With only her dress to don, she was ready in a moment, her face a dull pink as she passed him in the act of restoring his trousers.

'And Amanda . . .' I called after her.

She turned at the door, endeavouring with little success to bring a look of remoteness to her features.

'You will not disobey. I shall visit to ascertain your progress,' I told her. A mischief seized me. I knew the butterfly thoughts in her mind – the bumbling and buzzing of words that escaped before she could speak them.

'Your allowance will be increased. Is that not so?' I turned and challenged him.

It would not be my way with others, but these – as I have said – were mere oddments of people.

'What?' he ejaculated. The coldness of my stare was evident. Ludicrous in its peeping as he strove to cover himself, his penis lolled palely through the unfastened gap in his trousers. A wan bird that had flown and returned. 'Ah . . . ah, yes . . . ' he stammered.

I nodded to Amanda whose expression was a picture. Whether I had undone or encouraged her conversation I knew not. The door closed upon her with the silence of one who leaves an unread note behind.

'My aunt would have a bracelet. I doubt not that you will fashion one well,' I told him.

'Ah, yes.' He seemed for the moment incapable of any other words. In slightly dishevelled state he was led without. On the landing I paused, closing the door to the caging-room with such solemnity as I felt was due.

'You will have her, of course, tonight,' I said, 'and in the same mode. She is not however to be tied. The arm of a sofa will suffice. As to strappings . . . '

'Yes?' His lips quavered wetly. I found the sight not to my taste.

'Once weekly of a morning, immediately upon her waking. You will modify her with some pretty nightgowns – of a transparent variety, of course. Shell-pink and a pale blue would suit her. You will take her bottom formally and without preliminary caresses or kisses. It is desired,' I said regally, knowing him sufficiently insensitive not to appreciate that I was bubbling with silent laughter within. Cossetted more than she had been before, and no doubt later to be endowed with her own small carriage, Amanda would lend herself to it, I thought, with less difficulty than he anticipated. Within days she would derive more pleasure from it than she knew.

He nodded as if we were engaged upon some solemn discourse of State. Our footsteps sounded quietly upon the stairs. Amanda waited patiently in the hall, her features slightly constrained. To her surprise I kissed her cheek. Outside the horses of his carriage pawed the ground impatiently, their heads tossing.

'The requirements are understood,' I said to her.

Not knowing of what I spoke she nodded, bit her lip, stared briefly at him and then dropped her eyes. He, believing obviously that she and I had already discussed such matters as I had conveyed to him, took her arm with rather more of a beseeching gesture than he had anticipated.

I opened the door. It is never my intention to have servants present at such moments. Bowing, he allowed me to precede them. I moved towards the carriage, motioning to the hastily clambering coachman not to descend. I opened the door.

'Raise your dress to the tops of your thighs when you are seated, Amanda – and so keep it until the end of your journey,' I said. She blushed fiercely. Her eyes fenced briefly with my own and then indicated their surrender. 'He will not caress you,' I added as they entered, 'you are both to remain constrained. Forward, coachman!'

Straining in their harness, the four horses moved forward. My last glimpse for the nonce of Amanda was of her thighs flashing, her lips parted in a rosebud O of wonder.

A ripple of laughter escaped me. My fingers toyed about the full, rich blooms of the rhododendron bushes which lined the driveway as I returned to the house. They had obeyed me – they would obey, no doubt for months, until a greater loosing of lust took them.

It was of no matter, though out of an impudence of power I would visit upon them later. The older female of the house – she who had sat so complacent upon our visit there – might then need attending to. I would anticipate no objections either from her spouse or from Amanda. The occasion would provide a first exercise for Maria.

## *Chapter Twenty*

Caroline lay waiting for me upon my bed with a look of such tremulousness that I slid down upon her. The petals of her lips grew softer under mine.

'Do you remember French drinking?' I asked her. She blushed, nodded and murmured softly, drawing me more protectively upon her. I toyed with her thighs gently and with my other hand ran my forefinger along the succulent curve of her lower lip. 'You liked it?' I asked. She hesitated, then lisped a sibilant yes. Her breath flooded warm over my cheek.

'When we return I will dress you as a little girl,' I said.

She giggled and clutched me tighter. 'Will you?' she asked shyly. Her heart palpitated, our breasts bulbing together.

'There shall be sweetness, punishments and pleasures, Caroline. I shall bring you to them all. Fetch wine now – an uncorked bottle – go!'

So astonished was she at my sudden command that she leapt up immediately as I rolled away from her. 'And a napkin,' I added. Clattering with unseemly haste she was gone and had returned within several minutes. In the meantime I had stripped to my boots and stockings and told her to do the same. Then, before her wide-eyed look, I lay back with the napkin beneath my bottom and my legs spread and dangling over the edge of the bed.

'This is the way we shall French-drink in future,' I told her and motioned for the wine, at the same time making her kneel between my legs. The bottle came cool, between my breasts. I inverted it so that the neck pointed downwards towards my belly, laid flat. The ball of my thumb held tightly over the neck.

Raising my feet I laid them against her back, impelling her mouth inwards where the lips of my quim awaited her first salute. Ah! the sweet brushing of her mouth, half shy, half bold. Slowly I eased my thumb from the bottle neck until it but covered half. The wine trickled down. Down in its trickling down it meandered. Over my belly coursing, into the bush of curls seeking.

'Lick – drink,' I whispered. The cool flowing of the wine which I released in bubbling streams was sweet to my skin, yet no sweeter than the more eager lapping now of Caroline's tongue. The tip curled and filtered between the lips of my lovepot, seeking upwards to my sprouting bud as the wine rolled gaily upon it and was received into her mouth.

I longed to buck, but I dared not or the wine would have shivered in sprinkling sparklings everywhere. My legs quivered and straightened, sliding down from her back.

Brazenly I parted them wider, arching my toes as a myriad delicious sensations overtook me. The gurgling of Caroline's throat as she received the increasing flood of wine was itself music, yet I must not forget my place, my purpose, nor my disciplines.

'You shall French-drink so, Caroline – the prick in your bottom,' I husked. 'Wriggle your bottom as if now you were receiving it – lick faster!' I desired to cry out that I was coming, yet some instinct told me not to divulge even to Caroline the degrees of my pleasure. Muted whimpers broke from my pursed lips as a thousand tiny rockets seemed to soar and explode in my belly. The saltness of my spillings in their spurtings no doubt communicated itself to her in a fine spray over her tongue.

I sighed, relaxed, and knew at long last my pleasure. My thumb covered the mouth of the bottle anew. I permitted no more to flow. With a tender but firm motion I pressed her mouth away. I was truly soaked.

'Bathe me,' I murmured. I rose and preceded her into the bathroom. 'Do not speak – you may speak later,' I told her. The sponge laved me. I arose and was dried again. I took her then to the basin, bending her over it with my hand gripping the nape of her neck and washed her face.

We returned to the bedroom where I lay back full length. A scent of saffron came from the drawer of my dressing table where Mary or Maria had evidently sprinkled herbs. Waiting with owl-like eyes of blue, Caroline sat tentatively beside me and gazed down upon me. My fingers played with the backs of hers.

'Do you understand?' I asked.

Her lips moved as if to seek words that had long flown.

My arm reached upwards, looping about her neck and drawing her down of a sudden so that the corner of her mouth came to mine.

'You will know your purities, Caroline. The O is a purity. It circles within and without itself, knowing no otherness. Your mouth is an O – your bottom presents an equal roundness. Between your thighs the O has surrendered itself in its outerness to an oval, an ellipse. Within its knowing is the O –

between your bottom cheeks another. The O of your roseness. The male stamen will enter it and impel the long jets of its succulence within. You will receive, absorb – even as your mouth absorbed. Did it not?'

I seized her golden hair, making her squeal. Her face lifted in startlement. Then, by a loosing of my clutch, she slithered down and buried her nose between my breasts. Her arms encircled my waist.

'Do not punish me for it,' she murmured.

I played with her locks, running my fingers through the silky curls.

'Punishments and pleasures, Caroline. Have I not told you? You will suck it in my presence, bent upon your task. The while that it throbs in your mouth your bottom will receive the whip.'

'Oh, please no! Beatrice, no!'

'There shall be stables, too, Caroline. I have engaged Maria to keep them clean – to monitor my captives. Shall you be one?'

Caroline dared not to raise her eyes. Her mouth nuzzled between the orbing of my breasts. I waited long on her reply. The whisperings of shyness, shyness in her mind breathed their illicit thoughts upon me.

'Shall . . . shall it be as with Frederick?' her whisper came to me aloud.

'Penis-bearers?' I mocked her lightly. 'I shall have you blindfolded some-times, my sweet. You will not know who your stallion is.'

'Will you not love me, Beatrice?'

I drew her up slowly until her face came over mine. Broadening my stockinged thighs, I allowed her legs to slip between mine and pecked at her lips.

'In obedience there is love – in love there is obedience,' I said. I slid my hand upwards beneath the long fall of her hair at the back and took her neck between thumb and fingers. It pleased me to do so even as I sensed that it pleased her to be held in this way. I felt her trembling. The moist lips of her pussy nestled into my own.

'Have you not been stilled, Caroline?'

'Please kiss me – please, I want your tongue,' she husked. I smiled. Her moods were as the light passing of summer clouds. I could reach up and touch them.

'Suck upon it,' I breathed. Possessed as I am of a long tongue, I inserted it stiffly into her mouth. The suction of her lips was delicious. She moved them back and forth over the sleek, velvety wetness and murmured incoherently while I squirmed my hand down between our bellies and cupped her plump little mount. The curls frizzed to my fingers. Caroline squirmed, endeavouring to bring her button to my caresses, but I laughed within her mouth and smacked her bottom suddenly with my free hand making her yelp.

'D–don't!' she bubbled. Her face hid itself against my neck. 'What is stilled, Beatrice?'

'The male stem in your bottom, my love – urging, gliding, deep in. There it stays for a long moment and is withdrawn.'

'OH!' I could feel the heat of her blushing against my skin, 'it . . . it would be too big!' she stammered.

I laughed. The ceiling received the pleasure in my eyes. A warmness flowed over me. Caroline had, after all, been reserved for the cock I would present to her.

'Your bottom cheeks are deliciously elastic, Caroline. The first time you will experience considerable tightness, but you will yield. You will feel the veins, the knob, the inpushing – the breath will explode from your lungs. But on the second,' I went on, ignoring her wrigglings that were meant together with her silly, tumbling words to express refusal, 'on the second bout, my sweet, your rosehole will receive the repeated pistoning of the cock until you have drawn forth his spurting juice.'

'No! I don't want to!' she whined.

'Then you will be whipped first – or strapped perhaps.'

With each word then I smacked her bottom loudly, ringing my free arm tightly about her slender waist while she jolted and struggled madly. Finally I let her roll free. Her pert bottom was a perfect picture of pinkness, splurged with the paler marks my fingers had imprinted. Drawing up her knees she sobbed and lay with her face against the wall.

I waited. After a moment when she had not moved I rose and put on my dress. Immediately she spun over and lay upon her back.

'Wh–what are you doing?' she asked. Her eyes were blurred with tears, her hair mussed. In such disarray she looked at her prettiest.

'Maria will learn to use the strap on you now,' I said severely. Without looking at her I brushed my hair in the mirror.

Caroline rolled immediately off the bed and, kneeling, hugged my legs.

'If I say that I will – please!' she begged.

I glanced down at her and then resumed my brushing. 'It is not for you to say, Caroline,' I answered briefly. I moved away from her by force so that she slumped upon the floor, looking as forlorn as she could contrive. It was a game that she was learning, I could sense, yet her knowing must not be too great. Not as yet. In a year or two perhaps. The fine balance of yes and no was truly here.

I looked down upon her once more. The violin curves of her hips were indeed sweet, the upsweep of her bottom infinitely appealing. With a slightly greater plumpness than Amanda there possessed, Caroline would surrender eventually to her pleasures more than she knew.

Head hanging and eyes clouded, she rose slowly to her feet and endeavoured to hug me. I stood unmoving.

'Do not let Maria strap me hard,' she murmured. Her fingertips fluttered about my back like petals falling. When I did not answer she snuggled into me closer, manoeuvring one thigh and trying to press it between my own. 'Do you not love me?' she whispered.

I raised her face at last.

'In all my being,' I replied softly and kissed her mouth. 'Now go upstairs –
I shall strap you myself. You will learn.'

'Yes,' Caroline whispered. It was a plea rather than acceptance. Another
moment and I might have relented.

'Go,' I said again, 'wait for me – over the bar. Leave your dress here.'

Her footsteps slouched. Her look was a lostness – sweet and well contrived.
It passed across my mirror and was ignored.

Five minutes later the strap swathed heat across her cheeks.

In her sobbing cries as she gripped the bar beneath was her surrender.

## *Chapter Twenty-One*

In the week that followed I made ready for our departure. Katherine made
her future appointments with me. Maria's husband, Ned, was interviewed
formally. He would come into service with me, I told him carefully. His
uniform would be that of a valet. He would be put to many different tasks.
Maria – I was pleased to think – had evidently scolded him into agreement
beforehand since his continued nodding during my conversation became
almost tiresome. His physique, however, was entirely suitable – his thighs
good, his loins muscular.

There would be Frederick also, as I apprised Katherine. He had been
permitted no further licence with her. To ensure that, I had kept him to the
house while she was elsewhere.

The day before leaving I called her to my room.

'You will devise a play – not too simple a one, Katherine. I will have it
performed a few weeks after we have settled in again.'

She curtsied playfully. I had not asked her to sit. 'Shall there be many
players? Six or eight, perhaps?' she asked.

I merely nodded as if my thoughts were already elsewhere. It is a simple
enough trick. It keeps those I need, desire – or would work to my will – in a
state of slight imbalance.

'You will engage Amanda in it,' I said. 'We shall then best see her progress –
and her silver stocking bands, no doubt. And the maid at Arabella's house – the
young one who attended upon us. I want her. You will obtain and bring her.'

The play itself would be of no great importance. The words, the acts,
could be peeled away at my discretion and replaced by others. Arabella
possessed a controllable wantonness, as I had witnessed. She would present a
voluptuous example to occasional novices. As to the young maid who had
lain at my feet after tonguing me – the sly-eyed, sloe-eyed one – there was a
hint of impudence in her eyes that I could quell at will or use according to
my whims.

On the morning of our departure I made Caroline ready in the prettiest of blue dresses with matching bonnet and patterned stockings of the same shade. For myself I wore a modish back dress, severely buttoned to the neck, with a pearl choker. My bonnet was a three-cornered one. It gave me a slightly swashbuckling air without looking flirtatious. As to the kid gloves I had desired, I had now a dozen pairs in different shades. My uncle's wallet had been well pillaged.

Maria and Jenny, I attired in oatmeal cloaks with hoods. Beneath, they were naked save for stockings and boots. I placed them, together with the clothes and cases my uncle had been made to endow, in the smaller of two carriages outside.

Aunt Maude had relinquished Maria not without reluctance. We had discussed much in private. I broadened her horizons. There would be garden parties from Friday to Monday on half a dozen occasions throughout the summer, I said. We did not use the word 'weekend'. It was considered common. From the gatherings, both my aunt and myself would make a discreet choice among the females and, occasionally, their escorts – whether related to them or not. They would be drawn aside and would receive special attention. The likeliest females would be cosseted and flattered. In the privacy of bedrooms there would be means of bringing them to undress and even of displaying them to the males through peepholes in adjoining rooms.

'The males will be discovered at their peeping by one or other of us,' I told my aunt. 'It will be necessary for them of course to be punished. Their fear of betraying the conventions will make them submit. The females they have viewed and who will remain naked – while being aroused by Maria or Jenny or another – will then be shown to the peepholes in turn and may gaze upon the males in their bondage.'

Such discourses pleased my aunt immensely. My imagination flourished. Even so I kept some secrets to myself. There were caves I would not allow her to enter. She sensed that. It gave her a certain air of diffidence as I flourished my images before her. There were moments when she seemed to stand in awe of me.

We stood in my room prior to descending to where Caroline and my uncle waited. Amusement and apprehension mingled in her eyes as I pressed her to the wall and bid her stand with her arms at her sides. I took her cheeks in my hands. They were as smooth as a girl's.

'You enjoyed?' I asked. She knew well enough to what I referred. Her smile was cautious but impish.

'When your bottom took his cock? You were superb,' she breathed.

I kept my eyes level with hers. As one enraptured by a fine statue I ran my little finger delicately along her lower lip.

'You will be used,' I said.

'With Frederick?' The question was a little unexpected but I absorbed it without expression. She had veiled her desires carefully.

'Yes – and with others. You will obey me, Maude.'

It was the first time I had used her Christian name. 'Yes,' she acquiesced softly. The tips of our tongues touched as if with a timidity at our own daring. My sails were hoisted, set. There would be no turning back for her. Our tongues in their moistness moved. So slowly they moved, as if Time had been run down.

'And your uncle?' she asked. Our breaths flowed together. He had not been put to servicing since he had mounted me. His eyes had grown haggard in his waiting. I had had him placed in a small separate bedroom from my aunt. I licked her tongue for the last time and stilled the hands which would have reached for my bottom.

'You may keep him in a stiff but agonised state, his receptacles full. In a few weeks time he will be put to servicing the first of my novices – until then he is not to be milked,' I said. My eyes held a strain of severity as I spoke. I released her gently. It would amuse her to follow my instructions, I knew.

I swept down before she could speak, thus forcing her to follow me. In the hall my uncle's glance was timorous. I afforded him a kiss on the cheek. In turning away from him my gloved hand made passing contact with his penis which stood proud in his breeches. The caress would appease him for the moment.

The sun stood high above us as the door opened, flooding the vista with golden light. 'The sun is God,' the great painter Turner had said on his deathbed twenty years before. It had shone upon his bed, they had said, in the very moment of his uttering the words and dying. In that moment I believed him. Caroline moved in her beauty beside me. Her skirts swept the ground. I went as I had come, yet in my going I was one reborn. Passing the rhododendron bushes I caressed their leaves and blooms once more.

The silence of plants pleases me. They see without seeing, watch without watching. Subservient to the touch, yet they never surrender. Crush them and they will reappear next year or elsewhere. Their chemistry compounds miracles. They are there in their thereness. At night they sleep yet they know not Time. They breathe softly yet are not heard.

'I would be as a plant,' I said to Caroline. In the carriage I held her hand. The figures of my aunt and uncle standing on the steps diminished.

'Yes, I would like to be a flower,' she replied. She had not understood. It did not matter. Her voice was simple and childish. I saw her as she would be – rooted to the stamen, the pale fusing of the cock with her bottom. She would rock, moan and whimper in her beginnings. Later I would teach her silence. She would know the silence of the plants – the impelling flood of the sap in her gripping. Rising up the embedded stem, it would flood her in its submission. With its last throbbings it would withdraw. She would know the victory – the power.

The house waited for us, bereft of servants. My aunt had dismissed them. It was a wiseness. Only the older gardener, Perkins, was left. He was too withered for my purposes. Appearing at the approach of our carriages, he doffed his hat and acted as footman in opening the door. I gave him the most gracious of my smiles.

The rooms at least had been aired. From the kitchen came smells of butter, cheese and herbs. Mingled withal was the scent of bread which had been left that morning. Milk waited in stone jars, covered with fine net. In the stone-walled larder, lettuces shone their fine diamonds of cool water. All was well. My letter to Father floated upon the oceans. Maria and Jenny removed their cloaks and moved about us. Curiously nervous as they appeared of the windows and the gardener's eyes, I had them don dresses. The proprieties had to be observed. With the drawing of the curtains at night, our world would be enclosed.

'Shall there be visitors?' Caroline asked. Maria made tea. We took it in the drawing-room.

'Many. There will be masquerades, amusements, entertainments – Caroline – garden parties. You will enjoy those.'

I would chain the girls to trees at night, I thought, their dresses raised. Chinese lanterns would float and sway among the leaves. I would move among them with a feather. One by one they would be carried in for pleasuring. The stables would be candlelit.

Did Caroline read my thoughts? Laying down her cup she rose and looked beyond the French windows to the lawn where the silver larches swayed in their slender beings.

'You will not love me as the others – I know it,' she said sullenly. 'Will all the girls be young?'

'No.' I rose in turn and moved to her. My hand rested upon her shoulder. Her head lay back. Her fine hair tickled my nose. 'Some will be matrons – firm of body. The summerhouse is large within, is it not?'

Caroline nodded. I could not see her eyes. 'Yes – why?'

'We shall furnish it to our tastes. What is within?'

'A divan – no more.' Her bottom in its roundness moved its globe against my belly. 'Father said . . .' she began. I stopped her.

'I shall ordain. There shall be ottomans, rugs, silken cushions, shaded lamps, a small scattering of whips and birches to tease your bottom. We shall have our privacies there – our secrets, our voluptuousness. Do you understand?'

'Yes,' she husked. She turned and nestled in my arms. 'Will you . . . will you make me do it there? No one will see, will they?'

'No one – no one but I. You will offer your bottom as you gave your mouth.'

So saying, I raised her dress at the back and fondled the satiny orb. Feeling between the cheeks I circled the ball of my thumb about her rosehole, making her clutch my neck and quiver.

'It will b–b–be too big!' she quavered.

'Be still!' I said sternly, 'hold your legs straight, reach up on your toes. Hold so, Caroline!'

'*Blub!*' she choked. Easing my thumb within I felt her warm tightness to the knuckle, her gripping. Her gripping was as a baby's mouth. With a smooth movement of my free arm I scooped her dress up at the front and cupped her nest. It pulsed in its pulsing. My thumb purred between the lips and parted them.

'*Still!*' I commanded her. 'Hold your dress up – waist high, Caroline!' She obeyed, swaying on her toes as she was. Her eyes glazed as I moved my thumb up deeper into her most secret recess, toying with the small perky button of her clitoris at the same time. Unable to keep her balance, her heels chattered on the floor.

'*Wh–Wh–Whooooo!*' she whimpered.

I allowed her the sounds, the small outburstings of breath. The warmth emanating from between her silky thighs was delicious. Had I not intended now to keep her separated from the others I would have had Maria or Jenny enter and tongue her.

'Be quiet now – be quiet now, darling,' I coaxed. I had moved to her side in the moving of my hands. Her fingers sought to release her uplifted skirt and clutch at air, but by some silent command they stayed. The folds drooped but a little. The pallor of her thighs gleamed above the blue darkness of her stocking.

The natural elasticity of her bottom eased a little until I was able to insert my thumb fully, my fingers flirting with the nether cheeks. The oiliness of her slit increased – its pulsing fluttered.

'B–B–Beatrice!' she stammered. Her head hung back until I almost feared she might collapse. An intense quivering ran through her. The curving of her straightened legs was exquisite. Of a sudden then her head snapped back, her shoulders slumping as I withdrew my thumb.

'OH!' she choked and would have slid to the floor had I not caught her. 'Oh, B–Beatrice!'

'So, it shall be,' I smiled and kissed her mouth. She would make much of it in the beginning. In time she would kneel for it with glowing pride – an altar of love. After two years, as I had promised myself, she would return to her everydayness, free to leave or to stay.

You ask why – and I know not. Who shall be free and who not? I had chosen to ordain. There were those who would follow and those who would not. Through the dark glass of unknowing they would seek my image. At night they would huddle in the woods, the shrubs, among the wet leaves – crying for my presence. I would untie their childhoods. The last drums of their youth would beat for them. In their submission would be their comforting. Wailing and crying they would succumb to that which they had longed for. The whip would burnish their bottoms in their weepings. The velvet curtains would be drawn – receive their tears. The dry leaves of the aspidistras would accept their lamentations. In the mornings they would be as choir girls, clothed in white. Calmed from the storm they would talk softly, twittering. I would absolve their sins. I would teach. In time they would learn the inferiority of men – the penis-bearers, the money bringers.

For as such only would men be used. I would teach.

Now we composed ourselves again. Caroline sat fidgeting a little while Maria removed the tray. She would prepare a meal for Frederick and her husband on their arrival later, I told her. Together with herself and Jenny they would eat in the kitchen.

Maria bobbed and nodded in her going. She saw herself perhaps as the head of a small conclave of servants. but I would know how to split and divide.

'Caroline, you will have a maid shortly,' I said when the door had closed. She looked at me in astonishment. We had lived in comparative modesty before. 'I?' she asked.

I smiled and seated myself beside her, rolling her warm and slender fingers in my hand.

'A young servant who at present serves Arabella and her family,' I explained. The idea had come sudden upon me. It would serve to elevate Caroline above the others.

'She shall be unto you as a handmaid. You will train her,' I said. 'She will attend upon no one else other than at my bidding.'

'Train her?' Caroline's face was a picture. 'Oh! shall I be as you, then?' she asked naïvely, but I forebore to laugh. Her sweetness was apparent. She would lend herself with the seeming innocence of an angel to all that I intended.

'In time perhaps, Caroline. You have been stabled, at least. And cupboarded. Was that not splendid? Did you not enjoy it?'

She nodded, her cheeks suffused. 'No one will ever tie us together again,' she said.

'But I may tie you together with your maid,' I laughed. The shyness in her eyes darted with the delicacy of moths. 'She is pretty – a perfect body. Pleasures and punishments – did I not tell you?'

'May I . . . may I strap her? Just sometimes?'

The question was as unexpected as Aunt Maude's had been about Frederick. Deep pleasures were in my being at such questions. I had the power to answer or not – to assuage, persuade, refuse, mollify or conquer.

'You wish to? Who else did you wish to strap?'

A knowingly attractive pouting of Caroline's mouth offered itself to me.

'Amanda. She wanted silver stocking bands – did you know?'

'Yes, I knew. What else did she say?'

Caroline's eyes retreated. They appeared to take an immense interest in my corsage. 'She . . . she said if they were silver, solid silver, she would let him.'

I breathed lightly, betraying no surprise. Ah, Amanda! the depths of you! But no doubt she had seen no other escape and so sought to make her excuses. Caroline had obviously probed and asked. We know not those we know when they are away from us. Father would lie with women in their bronzeness. He would swish their bottoms with a fly-switch. Languorous they would lie, the sweat between their nether cheeks, up-bulbing, offering the delicate twitching of flesh as the switch descended. Servants would come and go, bearing tea, blind in their unseeing.

'You may strap her, yes, but only playfully,' I said, recalling Caroline's question. I would draw her into my plans a little, yet leave her always on a fringe of wondering – the last lines left undrawn, a mid-air hesitation. Workmen would come shortly to commence the building of the stables, I told her. I had promises that the work would be completed in two weeks. The main bedroom which Father normally inhabited would become now my own. Caroline would take the room next to it. The stables would have an annexe that would form a caging-room.

My plans expanded with every breath – her face a mirror to my thoughts. Withal a question poised itself on her lips as a bird alights and rests upon a sill.

'But when Father returns?' she asked.

My face was a blankness. 'And naturally we shall furnish the summer-house last,' I said, as if there had been no pause in my words. Clearly she was about to speak again when the doorbell sounded. Jenny hurried to answer. In a moment she returned bearing a *carte de visite* on a tray. I took it and read. The name meant nothing to me: *The Reverend Horace Ames*.

'He seeks but a moment and is accompanied,' Jenny said. I did not ask by whom. Such questions tend to indicate some unsettlement of the mind. I waved my hand languidly for her to admit them. Caroline adjusted herself, fanning out her skirt. Her composure at such times pleases me.

In a moment the door opened to admit a gentleman of not unpleasing aspect in his middle years. He was alone. He sought my indulgence, he said. His dark suit and clerical collar gave him a slightly hawkish air. They had travelled from Kent, he explained, to inspect a neighbouring house he intended to purchase in the parish. Alas, the hub of one of the wheels of their carriage had collapsed and the house agent had not arrived with the keys, as promised. They had waited an hour in the gardens. Now with the lateness of the day he sought to find friendly shelter for his daughters.

'They are waiting beyond?' I asked.

'In the hall, Madame. I thought not to disturb you overmuch . . .'

'Oh, but you must bring them in!' I interrupted swiftly. 'My sister will see to it. Will you not have a sherry? Of course we shall afford you all that you need. What a hopelessness you must have felt in your waiting.'

Overwhelmed by my reception as he appeared to be, he took the proffered glass and sat as the door reopened to admit two young ladies of apparent exceeding shyness. Both were prettily dressed and bonneted, but their boots had the sad and dusty air of those who have travelled far.

In seconds they were introduced. The taller, Clarissa, was, it seemed, eighteen. Jane was her junior by three years, but already had sufficient nubility to attract my eyes. Both were brunettes with *retroussé* noses and pleasing mouths. Their ankles were slender, though mainly hid.

'How were you to return and when?' I asked. I affected a great bubbling, flooding him with words while Caroline attended to the girls with refreshing drinks. By some fortune, Frederick and Ned made their appearance during my discourse. I despatched the latter immediately to the wheelwright, who I knew sometimes put carriages out on hire. Within the hour the fellow returned bearing the solemn news that only a small phaeton was available with scarce room for three for a longish journey.

In the meantime, however, I had gathered much. The Reverend Ames was to replace the present incumbent vicar. Yet, it seemed, he had business that very night in Gravesend, whither he must return.

'Then the girls must stay,' I proclaimed immediately, while both sat darting the most timid yet enquiring glances at me. No doubt, like he, they wondered at my mistressship of the house in my relative youth.

'Nay – it would be a terrible imposition, Madame. In particular since I shall be unable to return for a week. Is there no hotel or hostelry close?'

'Where they would stay unchaperoned?' I asked. The thought soon overcame such objections as he had tendered with obvious civility, hopeful as he had obviously been that I would take them in. They were after all of our own class. The conventions were being observed. The additional presence of Caroline placed a perfect seal upon the matter.

At five-thirty, having partaken with us of a cold collation which Maria had prepared, he was ready to depart. His daughters sat demure as ever, a dutiful kiss imprinted on their cheeks at his parting. Crowned as I was with his gratitude, I saw him to the driveway where the phaeton waited.

Clarissa and Jane would be well seen to, I assured him. His hand received my own and held it rather warmly. He was a widower, I had learned.

'They will be in the best of care – of that I am now certain,' he proclaimed and kissed my hand gravely before ensconcing himself on a rather hard seat.

'The very best,' I assured him, 'they will be seen to in all respects.'

'A week, then,' he said and waved his hand. He seemed rather enamoured of my gaze, I thought, as his carriage trundled forward. I watched it to the gates. The door lay wide still – invitingly open for me. Its panes of coloured glass fragmented glittering streaks of light along the wall of the hall where the sun struck. The light brushed my cheek as if in benediction as I walked through and entered the drawing-room.

Caroline had engaged herself more animatedly, it seemed, in conversation with the girls. Perhaps, in her knowing, she thought as I. I clapped my hands and smiled, expressing my pleasure at their presence.

'First we will bathe you and refresh you,' I said. They had removed their bonnets. Their hair flowed long and prettily about their shoulders. I reached down and took the hand of Jane. 'Come – I will see to you first. Then Caroline may attend upon Clarissa,' I said.

A light flush entered Clarissa's cheeks. 'Oh, but . . . ' she began. I stopped her with a further smile.

'I know,' I said softly, infinite understanding in my voice. 'Normally you bathe alone, but in a strange house – and the taps are really so difficult . . . '

I allowed my voice to trail off vaguely in leading Jane out. She had the perfect air of a cupid, I thought – an impression that increased as I first ran the water and then undressed her. Her form was exquisite, her breasts the firmest of pomegranates on which the buds of her nipples perked as if beseeching kisses. Her bottom had a chubbiness that my hands sought slyly to fondle in removing her drawers. In stepping out of them she betrayed with many a blush the pouting of her cunnylips which nestled in a sweet little bush of curls.

Tempted as I was to finger them I urged her into the water where she sat with the warm scented water lapping just beneath her breasts. 'I shall soap you – may I?' I asked. Seemingly not wishful to escape the admiration in my eyes she sat mute, pink-cheeked, as I passed my soaped hands first over her deliciously firm breasts. Plump and silk-smooth as they were, her nipples erected quickly, her lips parting to show pearly teeth as I playfully nipped the nearest between two fingers.

'How pretty you look,' I breathed, 'may I kiss you?'

In speaking I passed my free hand up the sleekness of her back, cradling my palm beneath her hair. Hot-flushed as she was, her lips came peachlike to mine with sufficient parting for me to intrude my tongue. For a long moment her own coiled back, but then came timidly to meet mine. My hand passed over the succulent weight of her other breast. Its nipple burned like a thorn to my palm. Her lips moved farther apart in her wondering, but I intended not to spoil her yet. I assumed an air of loving fun and joviality that would disperse itself as a balm to her conscience.

'It will be fun, Jane, will it not?' I asked and received a shy, lisped yes. For the rest I soaped her carefully, fondling every crevice and hillock I could reach without making my further gestures too obvious. The drying took longer – particularly in the gentle, urging motions of my towelled hand between her thighs. Her flush rose considerably then, her knees bending as she clung to me.

I said no more, donating but a light kiss to her mouth before putting her into a robe. In a week I would work wonders with her. And night had yet to fall.

Hearing the opening of the bathroom door from below, Caroline brought Clarissa up. The water lay warm still. It was the custom then for two people to use the same bath, the water supplies being often uncertain.

Clarissa's eyes grazed mine in their coming. I knew her eyes. I would neither fondle nor kiss her in the bath. While Caroline escorted Jane to her room, I led Clarissa within and waited unobtrusively while she disrobed. In chemise and stockings her figure was similar to Amanda's, save that her bottom was larger. Nervously fingering the straps of her chemise, she paused, evidently waiting for me to leave.

Instead of doing so I gathered up the clothes she had discarded. I did so as if by reproof. With a pettish gesture she removed her last garment and stood in her stockings. Her mount was plump, her thighs elegant, feet small. Her breasts, though not large, were of perfect roundness.

'Call me when you have bathed and I will bring you a robe – or the servant shall,' I told her.

The relief in her eyes was evident. A smile of assent meandered to her lips. Removing her stockings and stepping daintily into the clouded water, she sat down.

I went out, leaving the door ajar and placing her clothes where she would not find them. Jane would be easy. I knew her kind. Loving, warm and submissive, she would absorb the cock with wriggling wonder. A week was almost too much. With Clarissa it would be different. I had allowed her but one small victory, and her last. The surprise of the strap would come all the more clearly and stingingly to her that night. Maria would hold her.

I moved in my musings beyond, into the lumber room whence the ladder led to the attic. A sadness of dust was upon the rungs. Beneath me, the water in the bathroom splashed as it would splash upon the prow on the tall ship in its sailing.

And its returning . . . its returning . . . its returning . . .

# Sadopaideia

## ANONYMOUS

# Volume One

## CHAPTER ONE

## The Interrupted Boston

I first met Mrs Harcourt at my College Ball, my last term at Oxford. She had come up for 'Commem' to chaperon the cousin of one of my chums. Only the blessed ceremony of marriage gave her this right, for she was still well under thirty. I learnt from Harry that she was a widow, having married an elderly and somewhat used-up brewer who most considerately died quite soon after marriage, having, I have every reason to believe, decidedly shortened his life by vain, though praiseworthy, attempts to satisfy his wife's insatiable appetite.

She was a little woman, beautifully made, with magnificent red-brown hair, the fairest possible skin, a bust that was abundant without being aggressively large, a neat waist with splendidly curved hips, and in a ball dress – discreetly yet alluringly cut – she fired my passion at once.

Harry was very *épris* with his cousin and so was only too glad for me to take Mrs Harcourt off his hands. We danced one or two dances together. She had the most delightful trick in the boston of getting her left leg in between mine now and then. At first I thought it was an accident, but it happened so repeatedly that I began to suspect, and my old man began to suggest, that more might be intended. At last I felt what seemed a deliberate pressure of her thigh against my left trouser. John Thomas responded at once, and I, looking down at my partner, caught her eye. There was no mistaking the expression. She gave a little self-conscious laugh and suggested that we should sit out the rest of the dance.

Now I had helped to superintend the sitting-out arrangement and knew where the cosiest nooks were to be found. After one or two unsuccessful attempts, when we were driven back by varying coughs or the sight of couples already installed (in one case a glimpse of white drawers showed that one couple had come to quite a good understanding), I succeeded in finding an unoccupied Chesterfield in a very quiet corner of the Cloisters. Here we ensconced ourselves, and without further delay I slipped my arm round my partner's back, along the top of the couch, and, bending down, kissed the bare white shoulder.

'You silly boy,' she mumured.

'Why silly?' said I, putting my other arm round her in front so that my hand rested on her left breast.

She turned towards me to answer, but before she could speak my lips met hers in a long kiss.

'That's why,' she said, with a smile, when I drew back. 'Kisses were meant for lips, it's silly to waste them on shoulders.'

I needed no further invitation. I pressed her close in my arms and, finding her lips slightly parted, ventured to explore them just a little with my tongue. To my great joy and delight her tongue met mine. My hand naturally was not idle. I stroked and squeezed her breast, outside her frock first, and then tried to slip it inside, but she would not allow that. 'You'll tumble me too much,' she murmured as she gently pushed it away. 'I can't have my frock rumpled, people would notice. Take that naughty hand away.'

As I didn't obey, she took it herself and placed it with a dainty little pat on my own leg above the knee. 'There it can't do any harm,' she added with an adorable smile. She was going to take her own hand away, but I held it tight. I drew her still closer to me and kissed her again and again, my tongue this time boldly caressing her own. She gave a little sigh and let herself sink quite freely into my arms. By this time the old proverb that 'a standing prick has no conscience' proved its truth. My right hand released hers and I took her in my arms, my right arm this time encircling her below the waist, with the hand clasping the left cheek of her bottom. Modern dresses do not allow of much underclothing and I could distinctly feel the edge of her drawers through the soft silk of her frock. 'Oh, you darling,' I murmured as I kissed her. By my taking her close to me, she naturally had to move the hand which had gently held mine. It slid up my leg and at last met John Thomas, for whom my thin evening-dress trousers proved an altogether inadequate disguise. She gave a little gasp and then her fingers convulsively encircled him and she squeezed him fondly.

That was enough for me, my hand slid down her frock and up again, but this time inside. It found a beautifully moulded leg ensheathed in silk, dainty lace, the smooth skin of her thigh, and at last soft curls and the most delightfully pouting lips possible to imagine. My mouth remained glued to hers, her hand grasped my eager weapon, and I was just about to slip down between her knees and consummate my delight when the lips that I was fondling pouted and contracted, and I felt my hand and fingers soaked with her love, and I realised that her imagination had proved too much for her, and that while I was still unsatisfied, she had reached at least a certain height of bliss.

She pulled herself together at once, and just as I was unbuttoning my trousers she stopped me. 'No, not here,' she said. 'It's too dangerous, and besides, it would be much too hurried and uncomfortable. Come and see me in town, there's a darling boy. Now we must go back and dance. This naughty fellow,' she added, playfully patting my trousers, 'must wait.' She then got up, arranged her dress, and, giving me a lovely kiss with her tongue, led the way back to the ballroom. I followed, but do the best I might, John Thomas took his revenge on me by weeping with disappointment, which made me extremely sticky and uncomfortable, and but for Mrs Harcourt's invitation to see her in town, my evening would have been spoilt.

## CHAPTER TWO

### *An Afternoon Call*

I 'went down' next day, and on arrival in town I lost no time in calling on Mrs Harcourt at her little house in South Molton Street. When I rang at the door, it was opened by a very neat though not particularly pretty maid, as I thought. She had, however, quite an alluring little figure and a perky naughtiness in her face which is perhaps more fascinating even than mere beauty.

'Is Mrs Harcourt at home?'

'I will see, sir, will you come this way. What name shall I say?' She showed me into a delightful little morning-room, very tastefully furnished, and disappeared. She did not keep me waiting long, but returned and said: 'Will you come this way, sir? Madame is in her boudoir. Shall I take your hat and stick?'

She took them from me and turned to hang the hat on the stand. The pegs were rather high, and in reaching up she showed the delightful line of her breast and hips and just a glimpse of a white petticoat underneath the skirt.

'Is it too high for you? Let me help,' I said.

'Thank you, sir,' she said, smiling up at me.

I took the hat over her shoulder and hung it up. She was between me and the hatstand and could not move until I did. I lowered my arm and drew her towards me. She looked up at me with a provoking smile. I bent down and kissed her lips, while my hand fondled the delightfully plump breast.

'You mustn't,' she murmured. 'What would mistress say, if she knew?'

'But she won't know,' I answered as my hand went further down to the bottom which her tight skirt made very apparent.

'She will if I tell her,' she smiled. 'You naughty boy,' and she playfully patted my trouser leg as she passed me.

'Which, of course, you won't,' I said lightly, as I followed her. She laughed rather maliciously I thought, though I didn't pay much attention at the time. I had reason later, though, to remember it.

We went upstairs and I was shown into a lovely room where a log fire was burning, although it was no colder than most June days in this country. There was a splendid deep low couch, or rather divan, for it had no back, facing the fire, covered with cushions, which took my eye at once, and I mentally promised myself what should happen on it. My expectations fell far short of the reality, as will be seen.

Mrs Harcourt was sitting on a low chair near the couch. She was in a delightfully fitting tea-gown, cut fairly low at the neck, with very loose sleeves. It clung to her figure as she rose to greet me, and being made of chiffon with a foundation of pink silk, it gave one the idea at first that she was practically naked.

'Bring up tea please, Juliette,' she said to the maid, who disappeared.

'So you have found your way here,' she said, coming towards me with outstretched hand.

The room was heavily scented with perfume, which I learnt came from burning pastilles, and she herself always used a mixture of sandalwood and attar of roses. As she approached me her perfume intoxicated me, and without saying a word I clasped her in my arms and pressed long hot kisses on her lips. To my intense delight I found she had no corsets on, and her supple body bent close to mine, so that I could feel every line of it. My hands slipped down and grasped the cheeks of her bottom as I pressed her stomach close against my trousers.

'You rough impetuous bear,' she smiled at me. 'Wait till the tea comes up.' And she disengaged herself from me, playfully slapping, as she did so, John Thomas, who was naturally quite ready by this time for anything. 'Oh, already,' she said as she felt his condition. 'I told this naughty fellow at Oxford that he would have to be patient, and he must learn to obey.'

Tea appeared most daintily served, and on the tray I noticed a delicate Bohemian-glass liqueur carafe and two liqueur glasses.

'Do you know crème de cacao?' said Mrs Harcourt. 'It's rather nice.'

She poured out tea and then filled each liqueur glass half full of the dark liqueur and poured cream on top.

'*À votre santé*,' she said, touching my glass with hers. Our fingers met and a thrill ran right through me. I drank the liqueur off at a gulp and leant towards her.

'You greedy thing,' she laughed. 'That's not the way to drink it. No, no, wait till we've had tea.'

As I tried to get her in my arms, she scolded: 'Naughty boys must not be impatient,' slapping John Thomas again and somewhat harder this time.

I sat back on the couch and drank tea rather gloomily, Mrs Harcourt watching me teasingly. At last she put her cup down and, reaching for her cigarette box, took one herself and offered me one, then leant back in her chair looking at me with a smile.

'It's a shame to tantalise him so, isn't it?' she said at last.

I did not answer, but jumped up and threw my arms round her, kneeling in front of her and covering her face and neck with kisses. She tossed her cigarette into the grate and undid the silk tie of her gown. It fell back and showed all she had on was a dainty chemise of the finest lawn and a petticoat. My right hand immediately sought her left breast, and pulling it out I kissed and sucked the dainty nipple, which responded at once to my caress, stiffening most delightfully. My left hand then reached down to the hem of her petticoat and began to raise it.

I felt her right arm round my waist and her left hand began to unbutton my fly from the top. Before she had time to undo the last button John Thomas leapt forth ready and eager, but she slapped him and pushed him in again, undid the last button and fumbled for my balls, gently drawing them out. I drew back a little from her and lifted her petticoat right up, disclosing the daintiest of black silk openwork stockings with pale green satin garters, and above them filmy lawn drawers with beautiful lace and insertion, through which the fair satin skin of her thighs gleamed most provokingly. At the top there appeared just between the opening of the drawers the most fascinating brown curls imaginable.

I feasted my eyes on this lovely sight, undoing my braces and dipping my trousers down. Her hand immediately left my balls and began to fondle my bottom, stroking and pinching the cheeks while she murmured, 'You darling boy, oh, what a lovely bottom.'

I was eager to be in her, but the brown curls fascinated me so much that I could not resist the temptation to stoop down and kiss them. I was rather shy of doing this, as I had never done it before, and though I knew it was usual with tarts, I was not sure if it would be welcome here. Judge of my surprise, then, when I felt Mrs Harcourt's hand on my head gently pressing it down and heard her saying, 'How did you guess I wanted that?'

She opened her legs wider, disclosing the most adorable pussy, with pouting lips just slightly opening and showing the bright coral inner lips, which seemed to ask for my kisses. I buried my head in the soft curls, and with eager tongue explored every part of her mossy grot. She squirmed and wriggled with pleasure, opening her legs quite wide and twisting them round me. I followed all her movements, backing away on my knees as she slipped off the chair, until at last, when she drenched my lips with love, she lay partly on the hearth rug. Then, as I could scarcely reach her with my tongue in that position, and didn't wish to lose a drop of the maddening juice, I disengaged her legs and knelt down to one side so that my head could dive right between her legs. This naturally presented my naked bottom and thighs to her gaze.

'You rude naughty boy,' she said, smacking me gently, 'to show me this bare bottom. I'm shocked at you.'

Her hands again fondled my balls and bottom, and I had all I could do to prevent John Thomas from showing conclusively what he had in store for her.

I had no intention of wasting good material, however, and was just about to change my position so that I could arrive at the desired summit of joy when I felt her trying to pull my right leg towards her. I let myself go and she eventually succeeded in lifting it right over, so that I was straddling right across her, and we were in the position I knew quite well from photographs, known as sixty-nine.

My heart beat high. Was it possible I was to experience this supreme pleasure of which I had heard so much? I buried my head between her thighs, my tongue redoubled its efforts, searching out every corner and nook it could find, and just as it was rewarded by another flow of warm life I felt round my own weapon, not the fondling of her hand, but something softer, more clinging, and then unmistakably the tip of a velvet tongue from the top right down to the balls and back again, and then I felt the lips close round it and the gentle nip of teeth. This was too much, John Thomas could restrain himself no longer, and as I seized her bottom with both hands and sucked the whole of her pussy into my mouth, he spurted forth with convulsive jerks his hidden treasure. When the spasm was over I collapsed limply on her, my lips still draining her life.

## CHAPTER THREE

### *An Afternoon Call – continued*

I was aroused quite soon by her pushing me off her chest. 'Get up,' she said, 'you are crushing me.' We both got up and stood for a moment looking at each other. Then she felt for her handkerchief and wiped her lips. I tried to take her in my arms.

To my surprise she pushed me away. 'Go away,' she said, 'I don't like you.'

'Why, what's the matter?' I asked.

'Matter!' she replied, and she seemed to be working herself up into a temper. 'Matter! You horrid beastly boy, how dare you come in my mouth?'

'I'm sorry,' I said, 'it happened so quickly and I – I – I thought you wanted it.'

'Wanted it! How dare you?'

I tried again to put my arms round her, but she wouldn't allow it.

'No, get away, pull your trousers up and go.' And she turned to ring the bell.

I sprang to her. 'Don't send me away,' I said. 'I'm sorry and I won't do it again. Forgive me. Let me stay a little and forgive me.'

'Let you stay?' she laughed. 'What's the use of your staying? Look at yourself.'

And she pointed to poor John Thomas, very limp and drained dry and looking very ashamed of himself.

'Oh, he'll be all right again in a little time,' I said. 'Come, darling, let me stay and show you how much I love you,' and I managed to get one arm round her and draw her to me. She let me kiss her but kept her lips quite shut, so that I couldn't get my tongue into her mouth. Her body was quite stiff, instead of yielding as before. I grew bolder and caressed her breast and began to pull up her petticoat again. She seemed to take no notice for a minute or so, and then, just as I had uncovered her thighs and was feeling for the soft curls of her mount, she quietly pushed my hand away, detached herself from my arms, and said quite calmly, 'Well, if I let you stay, you must be punished for your rudeness. Will you do exactly as I tell you and submit to any punishment I may inflict?'

Now I knew nothing at that time of flagellation. I had heard of old men needing the birch to excite them, but beyond that I knew nothing. So I said, 'Punish me in any way you like, only let me stay and prove to you how sorry I am and how I love you.'

'Very well,' she said, 'get behind that screen,' pointing to a large Chinese screen that stood in the corner. I obeyed and she rang the bell.

Juliette appeared. 'Take the tea things away and bring me my leather case.'

I thought I heard a chuckle from Juliette but was not sure. After a little while I heard her come in again and whisper something to her mistress. 'Yes, very,' replied the latter. Then came more whisperings and I heard Mrs Harcourt say, 'Oh, did he? Well, we shall see.'

She then told me to come out, and I obeyed. I must have made rather a ridiculous figure, as my trousers were still down. Mrs Harcourt, however, did not seem to show any disposition to laugh. In fact, she looked very angry indeed. I went towards her, but she stopped me with a gesture and said, 'You promise to do everything I tell you.'

'Anything,' I said.

'Very well. Turn your back to me and put your hands behind you.'

I obeyed.

She opened the case and took something out, I could not see what, and then she came to me. I felt something cold touch my wrists and heard a snap. I tried to move my arms and to my surprise I found I could not. She had, in a moment, very deftly handcuffed me. I was too surprised to speak. 'Now kneel down,' she said.

'What for?' said I.

'You promised to do everything I told you,' she repeated.

I knelt down awkwardly enough, with my hands fastened behind, just in front of the big couch. Then Mrs Harcourt took a large handkerchief and blindfolded me. I didn't like the look of things at all, but said nothing.

'Now,' said Mrs Harcourt to me as I knelt there helpless, 'you have been a very rude and dirty boy and you must be punished. Are you sorry?'

I was just about to answer when 'whish', something whistled through the air and I felt as if a hundred needles were pricking my bottom. I could not help an involuntary cry.

I heard a sigh of pleasure, and felt a hand on my neck, pressing me forward on to the couch.

'Are you sorry, eh?' she repeated, and again came the smart cut across my bottom.

I had never been birched in my life. At school a tanning cane was used, but I could easily guess what was the weapon she was using.

'Will you speak? Are you sorry?' she repeated, and again the rod descended. I tried to escape but my hands' being tied hampered me, and though I could and did kick lustily, her hand on my neck managed to prevent me escaping altogether.

'Keep still,' she said, 'or I shall get Juliette to help me. Are you sorry?' At that moment in one of my struggles the birch just caught my balls, causing excruciating pain.

'Yes, oh yes,' I shouted.

'Will you ever do it again?' – whish – whish.

'No.'

'What was it you did? Confess your fault.'

Silence on my part. I felt too angry and ashamed to say.

'Will you confess?' – whish – whish – whish.

'Oh yes, I will.'

'Well, what was it?'

'I came in your mouth.'

'And what else?' – whish – 'what else?'

'I don't know.'

'Didn't you say you thought I wanted it?'

'Yes.'

'Well, confess then.'

'I said I thought you wanted it.'

'Ah!' and again the blows fell all over my bottom.

The burning pain got worse and I struggled and wriggled and kicked so that I at last got away from her, managed to rub the handkerchief away from my eyes and swung round and looked at her.

I never saw such a change in any woman. If she was pretty before, she was lovely now. Her eyes were shining, her cheeks were flushed, the exertion of plying the rod had caused one shoulder strap of her chemise to break and one breast was just exposed.

I looked at her with adoring eyes. I couldn't help it. Angry and hurt as I was in my dignity and elsewhere, I could not but feel admiration and – yes, even affection. She met my eyes.

'Well,' she said, 'why have you turned round? I haven't finished yet.'

'Isn't that enough?' I said. 'I've said I'm sorry and confessed my fault.'

'Haven't you any other faults to confess?'

'No!'

She rang the bell.

I exclaimed, 'You're surely not going to let anyone see me like this?'

She made no reply and the door opened and Juliette appeared.

'Juliette, come here,' she said. 'You see this gentleman here; now repeat before him the accusation you whispered to me just now.'

Juliette looked at me with a malicious smile (I remembered that smile) and said, 'When I was hanging the gentleman's hat up in the hall, he offered to help me, and then he kissed me and felt my breast and tried to feel my pussy through my skirt.'

'You little cat,' I said.

'Is that true?' said Mrs Harcourt. 'Answer me,' and the birch fell across my thighs as I lay twisted on the couch. It flicked up my shirt-tail and exposed John Thomas to the salacious gaze of Juliette. I was too ashamed to speak.

'Will you answer me!' and again and again came the cutting strokes, one of them just catching poor John Thomas nicely.

'Well, if I did, she did as much to me,' I muttered.

'Oh, indeed,' said Mrs Harcourt, as Juliette darted a vicious look at me. 'Well, we can investigate that later. Get the bands, Juliette.'

Juliette went to the case and produced a long band of webbing-working on a loop and, before I knew what she was about, had slipped it round my ankles and drawn it tight. Now I was indeed helpless.

'Now Juliette,' said her mistress, 'as it was you who were insulted, it is only fair for you to punish him.'

They turned me over face downwards and turned up my shirt.

'Oh, he's had some already, I see,' said the maid.

'Yes, a little,' said the mistress. 'He can do with some more.'

'How many,' said Juliette, taking up the birch.

'We'll see.'

Then the pain began again. Blow after blow, cut after cut, until my poor bottom felt as if it was on fire. I wriggled as much as I could but couldn't do much. My motions, however, must have pleased Mrs Harcourt, for she said, 'Wait a moment, Juliette, we mustn't be too hard. He shall have some pleasure as well as pain.'

She got round to the other side of the couch, raised my head, which was buried in the cushions, and, bending down, whispered to me, 'He's a naughty boy, but I love him, so he can kiss me if he likes.'

She then pulled up her clothes and presented her pussy backwards to me which I could just reach with my tongue.

'Now Juliette,' she said, 'not too hard, and cleverly.' I did not feel at all anxious to justify her wishes, but to my surprise the birch fell now in quite a different way. Instead of the slashing cuts which had made me writhe and smart, the blows simply warmed my bottom. Of course now and then it touched an extra sore place and made me flinch, but for the most part the twigs seemed to caress, and the tips of them, curling in between the cheeks, gave me a delightful sensation, and I felt John Thomas answering in a way that surprised me. I forgot my resentment against Mrs Harcourt and my tongue roamed about her lovely pussy and even went higher and caressed the other 'fair demesnes that there adjacent lay' and which presented themselves to my eyes, a proceeding which evidently pleased her, for she opened and shut the cheeks of her bottom, and at last with a quick side twist and a final plunge she forced her pussy right against my mouth, and murmuring, 'That will do Juliette,' she smothered my mouth and chin with her delicious cream.

She then got up and with Juliette's aid undid my bonds. I lay still, too excited to move. I felt her arm round my neck, while her other caressed my bottom. 'Poor boy,' she said, 'did it hurt very much?'

I turned round and kissed her. I couldn't help it. All my rage and feeling of insult seemed to have disappeared. 'That's right,' she said, nestling close to me. 'So the whipping did him good! It didn't go on too long though, I hope,' she added, quickly pulling up my shirt and looking at my John Thomas, who by this time, after the last part of the birching, was nearly bursting. 'No, that's all right. Come to me, darling.'

'But Juliette!' I said.

'Oh, never mind her . . . Still, perhaps she had better go,' she added with a peculiar look. 'Juliette, you can go, I shall want you in a quarter of an hour.'

Juliette looked very disappointed, but had to go.

'Now, darling,' said her mistress, 'come to me and love me, and say you forgive your cruel mistress for hurting you.'

She unfastened the band of her petticoat and let it fall. Then she stepped out of it. Her teagown was wide open, and, as I have said, one shoulder of her chemise had broken, so she was practically naked to the waist.

She went to the chair again and sat down right on the edge, lying right back so that her bottom jutted just over the edge. I knelt before her and found her pussy was just at the right height for John Thomas.

Her legs went over my shoulders and I gently placed him in position and began work.

I have never known such an expert in the art of love. Every conceivable motion and twist of her body she used. Her eyes flickered with passion, her lips drew my tongue right into her mouth, while her hands led mine all over her body. She murmured words of love and desire, mingled with pity for my poor bottom. At last she said, 'He was a very naughty boy, but it was a shame to cut him up so badly. Never mind, someday perhaps he will have a chance to retaliate.' Then the final paroxysm came on and we were both dumb. My motions, which had been slow at first, grew quicker. She plunged and writhed, twisting her legs round my neck and raising her bottom to meet my strokes, until at last, with a half-sob, half-groan, her legs fell down from my shoulders and I poured into her eager womb a deluge of my love.

## CHAPTER FOUR

## *An Afternoon Call continued*

We remained motionless like that for a few moments, our lips glued together, our bodies held close to each other. Then Muriel said, 'Now I'd better ring for Juliette and towels and water.'

We got up and she pressed the bell. Juliette appeared. It was too late now for any modesty on my part. Juliette had seen all I had to show her, so what was the use of pretence. 'Hot water, towels and soap, Juliette,' said her mistress. The maid turned to go. 'Oh, yes, and some special cream for the poor bottom,' she added with a smile.

Juliette disappeared and her mistress turned to me and said, 'Let's look at the poor little bottie. Turn round, is it much cut up? Look for yourself.' She led me to a mirror fixed down on the wall. I looked over my shoulder. Certainly my poor bottom showed distinct marks of the birch. The skin had not been actually cut, but there were red and violet marks interlaced criss-cross all over it. Also, it was very tender to the touch.

'Poor boy, what a shame,' said Muriel. 'Still, it will do him good and teach him not to be naughty again.'

I smiled a little ruefully. But she flung her arms round my neck and said, 'Oh, I love you, darling, every bit of you, and I love your poor dear bottom most of all.'

Juliette entered at this moment with a tray on which were a sponge, a silver rose-bowl, some soap and towels, and a pot of cream.

She put them on the table and her mistress turned to me.

'Juliette will wash you,' she said. Juliette approached me. 'Will you stand here, sir, please,' she said, pointing near the table.

I did so. She took John Thomas in one hand and held the bowl in the other. Then she plunged him into the water, gently drawing the foreskin back while she gently rubbed the glans with her fingers. Then she put the bowl down and, taking the soap, soaped him well and sponged him thoroughly, washing all the bush and between my legs. Then she took the towel and thoroughly dried all the parts. 'Turn round, please.' I turned round. She lifted my shirt and performed a similar service to my bottom. Finally she took some of the cream and rubbed it on the tender places. A delicious cool feeling came over me and all the smarting disappeared. She then raised my trousers, buttoned them, and turned to her mistress.

'Madame is ready?'

'One moment, Juliette,' said the latter. 'Just now you accused Mr Prendergast of taking liberties with you and you punished him for it.'

'Yes, madame,' said Juliette.

'What was it you said he did?'

'He kissed me and felt my breast and tried to feel my pussy.'

'Quite so. Now Mr Prendergast did not deny that but he said something in reply. What was it?' Juliette turned pale. 'Answer me.' Still no reply. Muriel turned to me. 'What was it you said?' she asked.

'Oh, it doesn't matter,' I said, for now the pain of the whipping had passed away I did not feel revengeful. 'Never mind what I said.'

'But it does matter and I do mind. If I'm not mistaken you said she did as much to you. Am I right?'

I looked at Juliette. She gave me a frightened look.

'Muriel, dear,' I said, 'never mind that, forget it.'

'Oh, I'll forget it in due time,' she answered. 'Now, Juliette, answer me. What did you do? You know you had better speak the truth . . . When Mr Prendergast kissed you, did you kiss him back?'

'Yes,' in a whisper.

'Did you do anything else?'

Juliette glanced at me. 'I just patted his leg and said he was a naughty boy.'

'Oh, and what part of his trouser leg did you pat? Show me?' Juliette timidly patted me again. 'I thought so,' said Muriel sternly. 'I guessed as much. So you complained to me that Mr Prendergast kissed you and tried to feel your pussy, though you at the same time kissed him and tried to feel what he had. Well, you have punished him for his rudeness. Isn't it only fair that you should be punished too?'

I interposed. 'No, Muriel, it was my fault, I began it.'

'I'm glad you realise that, Cecil, it shows that your whipping did you some good. But I must be the judge of what is proper behaviour in my servants. There was no need for her to imitate you. Now Juliette, don't you think as Mr Prendergast has been punished, it is only fair that you should be so too? Eh?'

'Yes, madame,' said the poor girl.

'You see you have only yourself to blame,' went on Muriel. 'If you had not told me what Mr Prendergast had done, I should have known nothing about it and you would have escaped. Now get ready.'

'What, before Mr Prendergast?' stammered Juliette.

'Of course, he was punished in front of you, in fact by you, so it's only fair that he should have a share in your punishment.'

The tears rose to Juliette's eyes as she began to undo her belt. The skirt slipped off to the floor. The petticoat followed it. She stepped out of them and stood in her chemise and drawers with downcast and blushing cheeks.

Muriel went to the case and took out a fresh birch. 'Go to the couch. Kneel down.'

Juliette started and then rushed to me and, flinging herself at my feet, sobbed out, 'Oh, sir, I'm so sorry I told on you. Don't let her whip me. I'm sorry I whipped you.'

I felt awkward. I was not naturally cruel and I did not bear the girl any grudge. At the same time I felt a keen desire to see her naked bottom and to see her wriggle under the birch.

I lifted her up and said I would do my best to persuade her mistress.

The latter was growing impatient. I went to her and begged her to let the girl off lightly. She laughed and said, 'All right, I'll stop when you tell me to.'

I then led Juliette, still weeping, to the couch. She knelt on the edge of it and buried her face in the cushions.

'Lift up your chemise and open your drawers,' ordered her mistress. She did as she was told, disclosing two white globes of which no lady need have been ashamed. A dark shadow just between them gave promise of a beautiful dark forest in front. As she was kneeling on the couch and not on the floor as I was, her bottom was raised higher than her head and the skin stretched quite tight.

'Now,' said her mistress, 'I'll teach you to tell tales of my guests when you yourself are equally guilty,' and whish–whish–whish came the birch on the plump cheeks. Juliette sobbed and cried and nervously contracted her bottom to meet the strokes. 'There, there, there, and there,' went on her mistress, 'will you kiss visitors in my hall again, and try and pat their privates? Will you, will you?' The blows descended in quick succession, now on one cheek, now on the other.

Juliette bounded up and down, but did not, as I did, kick about. She knew better. At last two cuts more vigorous than the others and rather lower down were too much for her and in desperation she had to move her legs.

'Ah,' said Muriel exultantly, and quick as lightning she rained a shower of blows in between the thighs, reaching with the ends of the twigs the pouting lips of the pussy that Juliette's struggles disclosed.

Juliette shrieked and, letting her body collapse, tried to cover her poor bottom with her hands.

Muriel looked at me. Till then, for the life of me, I could not have interposed to stop the whipping, but now I managed to stammer, 'That will do,' and Muriel dropped the birch and fell into my arms.

John Thomas had grown greatly excited by the scene, and taking no thought of Juliette, who lay moaning and twisting on the couch, I pushed Muriel on her back beside her and mounted her. Our course was quicker than might have been expected, seeing that I had already done my duty twice that afternoon. I suppose the excitement of seeing Juliette birched and the heating effect of being birched myself had a great deal to do with it. Anyhow, Muriel and I both swam together in a perfect sea of bliss before many moments had passed.

Juliette, perceiving that her whipping was over and that other things were happening, sat up beside us and began to dry her eyes with her chemise.

Her mistress, noticing this, said, 'Well, I'm afraid you can't feel Mr
Prendergast's affair now, Juliette, it's too busy; but he can feel your pussy
quite well,' and she took my hand and pushed it towards Juliette's thighs.

The latter did not dare to resist and I soon found the secret grotto I
wanted, and, pushing my fingers well in, gave her some slight gratification in
return for her whipping.

When we had finished and had got up, Muriel said, 'You will have to wash
Mr Prendergast again.'

'May I do it my own way?' said Juliette.

'If you like,' said her mistress, 'but I don't expect you'll get any good
from it.'

To my surprise Juliette knelt down before me and began licking and
sucking my limp weapon, but though John Thomas wept a little, I had done
too much that afternoon to be able to give any real performance, and after a
while she gave it up as a bad job and began to dress herself.

Muriel laughed and I felt a little ashamed, but I promised myself that
before long Juliette should have a taste of my quality in more senses than
one.

'Come again soon,' said Muriel, as she kissed me goodbye most lovingly,
and I promised I would without fail.

As Juliette was showing me out, I said, 'Well, if I kiss you now, will you
tell your mistress?'

Her only answer was to put up her lips, and when my lips met hers she
pushed her tongue right in my mouth while her hand clutched my old man
convulsively.

'*You* tell her *I've* kissed *you*,' she murmured, 'and then she will make you
whip me yourself. I'd love to be whipped by you. I'd suck and kiss you while
you were doing it till you dropped the birch with faintness.'

Before I could reply she had opened the door and I found myself in the
street.

## CHAPTER FIVE

# *An Inopportune Arrival*

When I reached home I tried to analyse my feelings and realise what had happened. I could barely believe it was true. It seemed like an impossible dream. Here was I, just down from Oxford, aged twenty-three, submitting to be whipped like a naughty boy on my bare bottom by a woman whom I had only met once, and in the presence of another girl whom I had never seen before I called on her mistress. More than that, I had poked and 'kissed' the mistress and had been 'kissed' by both mistress and maid. Still more, neither woman was a whore in the usually accepted sense of the word. The one was accepted as chaperon for the cousin of my best pal and evidently mixed in quite good society. The maid to all appearance was eminently respectable. No. I couldn't believe my own experience. It was only when I sat down to think things out that my sore bottom brought the truth palpably home to me. I jumped up with a cry and rushed upstairs to my bedroom, locked the door, and in a twinkling had my trousers down and was investigating my bottom in the looking-glass. Gad! but I was marked. Long lines of purple and red showed criss-cross all over both cheeks, with here and there a spot of bright red where the buds on the birch had broken the skin. I got some ointment which I used for soreness after rowing and gave myself a liberal dose. Then I washed John Thomas, who was looking thoroughly ashamed of himself, dressed myself and went downstairs.

My feelings were difficult to analyse. Shame, anger, and a wish for revenge fought with each other. At the same time Muriel's charms were ever before me, and at moments John Thomas made gallant attempts to persuade me that the afternoon was worth everything. Juliette's bottom also rose before my eyes white and plump and round, quivering under the blows of the birch, opening and shutting between the strokes and showing glimpses of the dark pouting lips of her pussy – that pussy which I had felt and found so responsive to my fingers.

What were her last words? 'I should love *you* to whip me.' By Gad, I thought, why not? Surely it was worth risking another whipping myself to get the chance of making those lovely cheeks flinch and squirm. And then Muriel! What a gorgeous poke. How her tongue had caressed my old man. How her pussy had drawn every bit of life from me! Yes, undoubtedly I must call again.

So I argued that night. But next morning doubt and nervousness came over me again, and eventually it was quite a week before I rang the bell again at the little house in South Molton Street.

Juliette opened the door and smiled when she saw me. 'Madame was wondering why you had not called,' she said. 'She is rather angry with you, sir, in consequence, I fancy,' she added with a meaning look. 'She does not like to be neglected. But she is not at home now.'

'Can I come in and wait?'

'Oh, yes, sir, if you like.'

So I went in and shut the door. She led me into the little morning-room and for a moment we looked at each other. Then without any delay or explanation, we seemed to fall into each other's arms, our tongues met, and our right hands dived straight between each other's legs. John Thomas rose at once and I found Juliette's soft little pussy already dribbling with expectation. I urged her gently back to an armchair and, kneeling before her, placed John Thomas in the haven where he would be. Her bottom lifted itself to meet him and we came together in a mutual flood of love.

'Tell me, Juliette,' I said when we had finished, 'does Muriel whip you often?'

'As often as she gets the chance,' she said with a wry little smile.

'But why do you submit,' I said, 'and how did it begin? It isn't usual for maids to be whipped.'

'I'll tell you someday,' she answered. 'It's too long a story for now. Besides, she's very good to me and I get more pleasure with her than I should anywhere else.'

She cuddled close to me and fondled John Thomas, who evidently enjoyed it.

'You said something to me as I was going away last time that puzzled me,' I said after a minute.

She blushed a little.

'Come,' I said, 'do you really like being whipped?'

'Don't you?'

'No, I'm damned if I do,' I answered with a laugh.

'Oh, you will in time. I don't always. There are different sorts of whippings. I didn't like being whipped the other day by Muriel in front of you, for she was wicked and jealous. But you, when I whipped you, didn't you like it? Wasn't it different to the whipping Muriel had given you?'

'Yes,' I said reflectively, 'it certainly was different.'

'Well,' she went on, 'if I like a person I *do* like him or her and want to do all and everything to please. With Muriel, for instance, when she's nice and wants me' – she blushed a little as she said this – 'I'm willing to submit to anything. I know she wants to see my nakedness and watch my bottom wriggle, so I do all I can to gratify her, but when she's angry and only wants to punish me, I hate her and want to hurt her.'

'Haven't *you* ever whipped her?'

'Good Lord no! That's not her game, she's no Masochist. I only wish she were and I had the chance. I'd pay her back. But she's much too strong for me, and besides, I'm different, I don't like giving pain and she does. It's only when I'm angry with her.'

'Hm,' I said.

'What are you thinking of?'

'I was thinking, well, I don't know much about this matter, but I know this. I'd love to get my own back for my last call here. Now you and I together, eh? Couldn't we master her?'

Her eyes gleamed, then dropped. 'She'd kill me,' she said.

'Oh no. I'd see she did not do that. I'd make her promise to bear no malice and I don't think she would. If she did, I'd see you came out all right. The worst she could do would be to turn you out, and then you could come to me. I am looking for a flat to settle down in and should want a house-keeper, eh?'

'Oh, that would be lovely,' she replied.

'But you haven't answered my question. Would you really like *me* to whip you?'

'Try,' was all she answered. And before I knew what she was doing she had slipped off the chair and pulled up her skirt and petticoat above her waist behind, showing her dainty drawers.

'Sit down there,' she said, pointing to the chair she had just left.

I obeyed her. She then laid herself across my knees, face downwards with her head towards my left arm, and pulled her drawers open behind, showing the beautiful curves of her bottom, the cheeks of which stood out like two lovely white moons, though still slightly marked from last week's whipping.

'Now smack me and see if I like it.'

I gazed at the snowy globes with the shady valley between. Just at the meeting of her legs a few tendrils of dark hair showed themselves, promising other, more secret delights.

I smacked her lightly with my hand. It was more of a caress than a blow. She lay still.

Smack–smack–smack, and my fingers crept between her legs.

'No, not yet,' she said, 'I want you to smack me.'

I humoured her and I smacked both cheeks quickly till they began to grow pink.

'Harder, harder!'

I smacked more severely. Her bottom became appreciably warmer.

'Harder still,' she said, 'harder!'

I did as she said, and my own hand began to tingle. The joy and lust of domination began to grow in me.

After one or two really hard blows, she shifted slightly and heaved her bottom, opening her legs a little.

I gave her several harder smacks. She sighed and wriggled. I stopped.

'Go on,' she said at once.

'But I'm hurting you.'

'I want you to hurt me,' she murmured fiercely. 'I want you to hurt my bottom. Can't you see it growing red and hot? Hurt me, hurt me.'

Her passion, though I didn't really understand it, fired me, and I took her at her word. Blow after blow fell on her plump cheeks and at length her sighs came quicker and quicker and became more like gasps. Her bottom heaved and opened and contracted, her legs parted and I could see the lips of her pussy parting and closing again as if eager for satisfaction.

Desire now took full possession of me and I smacked her as hard as I could, seizing every opportunity of making my hand reach the more hidden and secret retreats. It was a strange and maddening delight to me. After two or three blows on her firm bottom I felt my fingers strike the softer lips of her pussy. Once or twice I managed to reach that delightful spot with my finger tips while my palm just managed to get between the plump cheeks. This seemed to madden her as much as it did me. She flung her legs apart, pushing up her bottom, keeping it as wide open as possible. She muttered inarticulate cries, and at last after several blows which hit both marks full, she sank down heavily on my knees, imprisoning my hand between her thighs, which closed on my fingers like a vice. I felt her pussy throb and throb again and then a warm flood spread all over my hand.

I raised her up and held her close in my arms. 'You darling,' she murmured, 'take me, I am yours utterly.'

Her hands slid down and with feverish haste unbuttoned my trousers.

John Thomas, as was only to be expected, was rampant.

'Give him to me,' she half-sobbed.

'How would you like him?' I asked with interest, for I had not forgotten how she had asked to be allowed to wash it in her own way.

'Any way, so long as he is in me . . . in front, behind, any way, I don't care. I'm yours, all of me. Take all of me, darling, my master!' and she threw herself at my feet, embracing my legs, half-sobbing and writhing with unappeased passion.

I lifted her up to her knees and she seized my affair with her lips and, flinging her arms round my bottom, began to lick and suck it with avidity.

'Oh, so that's the way you entertain my guests in my absence, is it?' I turned hastily. There stood Muriel. She had evidently just come in. Her latchkey was still in her hand. She was holding the door open.

## CHAPTER SIX

# The Tables are Turned

Juliette collapsed on the floor with a cry of terror. I stood stock-still like a fool. Certainly I must have presented a ridiculous figure, trousers unbuttoned, a rampant engine well exposed.

'Get up, you,' said Muriel to Juliette, going to her and touching her with her foot. 'You,' turning to me, 'can either go or stay, but if you stay . . .' She paused ominously.

'I'll stay,' I said, for I had an idea.

'As you please. I see I have arrived in time,' looking at my open trousers. 'So you can . . . but . . . I rather think you will be sorry.'

She led the way upstairs, and I found myself again in the boudoir.

Juliette was already there, shaking with nervousness. 'Where are the cases?' thundered Muriel at her. 'Did you think I had you up here to talk to you?' and she suddenly gave her two swinging boxes on the ears.

The poor girl hurried out of the room.

'Muriel,' I urged, 'don't be too cruel to her. It was my fault chiefly.'

'Don't you fret yourself, my man, *you'll* get all *you* want.'

Juliette reappeared carrying the leather case which I recognised.

'Both cases, you fool,' said her mistress.

Juliette gave an even more terrified cry than before, but did not dare to argue.

She went out and came back with another, similar case.

Muriel unlocked the first. 'Undress yourself,' she said; then to me: 'And you tie her hands with this,' giving me a long piece of webbing. 'I must take my corsets off or I shan't have freedom enough for my arm.'

Juliette tremblingly undid her skirt and let it fall, and waited.

'Everything,' said her mistress, 'didn't you hear? Everything, or it will be the worse for you.' Juliette then undid her blouse and took it off. A dainty camisole appeared. That was removed. Then the petticoat. Then the little corsets were undone and she stood simply in chemise and drawers, the lace frills of the latter peeping alluringly below the hem of the chemise. Her trembling hands groped under the chemise, she pulled the string and the frilly little legs fell round her ankles. She stepped out of them and stood waiting.

'I thought I said everything!'

A crimson flood invaded the poor girl's cheeks and neck.

'You needn't pretend to such modesty sneered Muriel. 'A girl who will kneel down to kiss a man in a sitting-room needn't be shy of stripping naked before him in a boudoir, especially when there is another woman to protect her.'

Juliette lifted the chemise and began to pull it over her head. I saw first her thighs appear, beautifully shaped and moulded like towers of ivory, then the dainty little bush, still dewy with our mingled love; next a sweet rounded little belly, smooth and firm. I noticed the dainty waist line and, above, two perfect pear-shaped breasts with bright red nipples standing out firm and bold, though all support had been removed. As she raised her arms above her head, I saw the silky hair in her armpits, matching the thicker curls of her bush.

Then the chemise slipped off her wrists and she stood, a slight timid figure, perfect, desirable and appealing.

I heard a sigh of appreciation from Muriel. 'Now tie her wrists together,' she said to me.

I had to obey. She watched me as I fumbled with the webbing.

'Now stretch her on the couch.'

I bent her down as she had been bent down the other afternoon.

'No, not that way. She must be crucified.'

'Madame,' stammered Juliette.

'Silence,' hissed Muriel as she placed some cushions across the middle of the couch, forming a ridge.

She then dragged Juliette to the couch and flung her face downwards so that the lower part of her belly and the top of her thighs rested right on the cushions. This naturally raised her bottom and thighs, making her body form a very broad inverted V.

'But what's the meaning of this?' she said as she saw the cheeks of the poor bottom still blushing slightly from my recent smacking. 'Do you mean to say you've dared?' she went on, turning to me. 'Oh, you just wait.'

She said no more but took hold of Juliette's right ankle and pulled the leg towards the edge of the couch. Then, stooping down, she caught hold of a silk cord that was fixed to the side of the couch, evidently for that purpose. It had a running loop at the end. This she slipped over the girl's foot and drew it tight. She then pulled the other leg as far apart as possible and fixed that in the same way.

Poor Juliette was now perfectly spread-eagled. Her arms were above her head tied at the wrists, her head was buried in the couch. Her bottom was raised, as I have said, by the ridge of cushions and seemed to invite the lash, and her wide-opened thighs revealed the mossy lips of her pussy, still slightly open. There she lay, a piteous little figure, all white.

The only contrast was her dark hair, slight silky tendrils in her armpits, the suggestive shadow between the cheeks of her bottom, the soft curls between her legs, and last of all, showing up vividly against the whiteness of her skin, her long black silk stockings, just a study in black and white, no touch of colour anywhere, for she wore black garters. I feasted my eyes on the lovely vision. How could anyone, I wondered, hurt such a dainty graceful creature?

I looked at Muriel. Her eyes showed clearly that she was by no means insensible to the alluring picture. But there was a gleam of fierceness as well as admiration in her glance.

'Now,' she said suddenly, 'I must get rid of my corsets. I shan't be long. You can admire the dainty darling's white skin while I'm gone. There won't be much white left after I've finished with her,' and she went quickly into her bedroom, leaving the door open.

Now, I had decided to stay in the hopes of carrying out my scheme of vengeance on Muriel, and I had no intention of assisting at the punishment of Juliette. But when I saw the preparations and how helpless Juliette was rendered by her bonds, I began to doubt the possibility of succeeding in my object. Though no doubt I could have mastered Muriel by brute strength, there would probably have been a struggle, and Juliette's help would have been of the greatest use. All the time Muriel was pinioning Juliette my mind was working quickly, but I hesitated to make any attempt to seize her, preferring to wait until the last moment.

Now, however, that she was out of the way I saw my chance. Quick as thought I sprang to Juliette's wrists and began to loosen the knots. She raised her head, gave a little cry of surprise and fear. I put one hand on her mouth and whispered, 'Keep quiet and pretend to be still tied. Remember what I said downstairs. Now is our chance. Keep your hands just as they are, till I tell you. Then free your feet and help me.'

I had only just time to loosen the knots and replace the webbing so that it still looked tight, and to get away from the couch, when Muriel appeared. She had put on the tea-gown again, with the loose sleeves. I was standing by the table when she came in, looking at the open case which contained the birches. There were four different sizes.

'Looking at my little ticklers?' she smiled. 'There are some more in here,' and she opened the other case.

Then I understood Juliette's cry of alarm when Muriel told her that she wanted both cases.

There were no birches in this one. Two or three canes of varying thicknesses, a couple of old-fashioned ladies' riding whips – not the modern hunting crop, but whips of long flexible whalebone with lashes at the end – a whip of seven knotted cords, very fine, but looking very wicked, and last of all a sort of birch made of wire, the ends of which were bent at right angles.

'Pretty, aren't they?' said Muriel, laughing. 'They'll come in later. We'll begin with this.'

She turned to the other case and selected a long pliant birch, weighing it in her hand and swishing it in the air.

Now was my opportunity. As she turned from me to the couch and the prone girl waiting, I suddenly flung my arms around her, pinioning both arms tightly to her side.

CHAPTER SEVEN

# The Fascination Begins

She was completely taken by surprise. She had scarcely time to gasp out an exclamation of anger. 'Juliette,' I cried as she struggled violently in my arms.

Juliette quickly got her wrists free and, reaching down, got her ankles from the loops. Then she ran to me as I was holding the squirming, kicking Muriel.

The latter was like an eel. She kicked, she bit, or tried to, but my arms were tight round her middle, and as she had taken off her corsets, my grip crushed her ribs and gradually winded her.

Juliette, avoiding with difficulty the kicking legs, managed to get the band of webbing round first one wrist and then the other and draw it tight. My grip had not relaxed and in a comparatively short time Madame Muriel's wrists were bound together.

She still grasped the birch and all the time was pouring out indignant and angry expostulations. There was no trace of fear, however, as yet. Pride, rage and hate showed in every glance and tone.

When Juliette had finally and satisfactorily tied her hands, I dragged Muriel to the couch and pushed her on to it. She sat and glared at me, out of breath and exhausted.

Her tea-gown had come unfastened at the waist and fell apart. Except for her stockings and shoes, she was absolutely naked. She evidently had intended to have a perfect field day. Well, she should not be disappointed.

I turned to Juliette with a smile: 'Well, what shall we do to her? How shall we begin? You know more about these things than I do.'

'Spank her first; the hand will prepare her bottom nicely for the birch,' said she. 'Shall I hold her down for you?'

'No,' I said, 'I'll hold her and you can begin. Come along, Muriel dear. This is a little different from what you intended, isn't it? It will be a new experience for you, eh? Will you turn over of your own accord or shall I help you?'

She made no answer, so I went to her and took her by the wrists. She dragged her hands away and suddenly, bending down, seized one of my hands with her teeth and bit it hard.

'You little devil,' I shouted, 'you shall pay for that,' and I brought my other hand heavily down on her ear and cheek. The force of the blow knocked her head on one side and made her release my hand. With a quick twist I turned her over and held her face-down on the couch, her legs hanging over the side. Juliette stood at one side of her and, dodging the kicking, plunging legs, proceeded to deliver a shower of smart smacks on the plump cheeks and thighs.

The blows fell at random, here, there, and everywhere, with no direction and without much real effect, as Muriel was dodging too much. After a minute or so Juliette stopped and looked at her palm.

'It's hurting me more than her,' she laughed; 'we'd better begin seriously. Put her as she put me.'

I pulled Muriel further on to the couch and managed to get her belly and thighs over the ridge of cushions; I then leant heavily on her back, while Juliette with great difficulty secured one leg in the silk loop.

All this time Muriel was struggling and shouting: 'I won't be tied down, I won't be whipped. Don't you dare to touch me, or I'll pay you for this afterwards.'

I took no notice, but when her legs were firmly secured, I pulled the tea-gown up over her shoulders as far as I could and said, 'Yes, it's a little different to what you intended, isn't it? Instead of you feasting your eyes on our naked bodies and enjoying the sight of our bottoms reddening and writhing under your blows, it's *your* nakedness we are going to look at, it's *your* bottom and thighs that are going to blush and quiver. Are you looking forward to the treat? Come, answer me.'

'I'll kill you,' she hissed.

'Oh, no you won't, you're going to beg my pardon, to beg both our pardons, in fact, and thank us for showing you your proper place. Now Juliette, will you begin? I'll enjoy the scene for the moment.'

I kept my left hand pressed on her back and with my right I stroked the beautiful loins and bottom and thighs, which lay bare to my touch. If Juliette had made an alluring picture with her dark hair and clear white skin, her mistress easily rivalled her. She was a little the plumper of the two and fairer, and whereas Juliette's colouring was pale, Muriel's skin was flushed slightly with pink. Their two bodies made a delightful contrast.

The idea struck me of comparing them, and when Juliette came back with a birch I asked her to lie beside her mistress for a moment so that I might see both their naked bodies together. She obeyed at once, and I revelled in the lovely vision. So lovely was it that I could not resist the temptation but took out my old man and was about to make good use of the favourable position of the two girls. But when Juliette saw what I was about, she stopped me.

'That will come later; business first,' and she got up and stood by the couch, raising the birch in the air.

'Now madame,' she said, 'just a little gentle correction for your impudent bottom. How do you like it?' as the twigs fell right across the left cheek. 'You are so generous with it to others, you ought to be grateful. Is it nice? nice, eh? nice – nice? . . . Oh, you're sulky, are you, you won't speak, won't you, we'll see about that. Answer me at once, will you? at once – at once.' The blows fell quicker and quicker, but Muriel made no sound. She lay practically motionless with her head buried in the couch. Her flesh flinched each time the blows fell across her bottom, but she made no cry or any sound.

'Still obstinate,' said Juliette; 'we won't allow that and must per–severe.' She came round to the other side and proceeded to visit the other cheek. Then she went lower and cut across the thighs, but though Muriel's contortions grew more convulsive, she still kept silent, until at last one blow of the birch curled right between her legs and a stifled cry of pain escaped her lips.

'Ah, I thought I should succeed before long,' said Juliette, as she rested for a moment. 'Will you begin now, sir?'

I took the birch, or what was left of it, for the twigs had broken off at every stroke.

What a change now in Muriel's bottom. No longer was the skin clear and pink and white. An angry red flush covered the centre of both cheeks, from which ran lines of red and violet which disappeared round the legs and cheeks towards the hips.

'Now Muriel,' I said, 'Juliette has finished for the moment. It is my turn now. I am going to give you a lesson in behaviour towards your guests. How do you like that, and that,' as the swift strokes fell. 'Will you answer me?' I went on, as she still remained dumb, and the blows redoubled.

'There!' said Juliette, pointing with her finger between the cheeks of Muriel's bottom and the legs stretched wide open. 'That will make her speak.'

I followed her advice and gave three crashing blows that cut and curled along the inside of her thighs and reached the hidden lips of her pussy.

They evidently proved effective. Shriek after shriek came from Muriel as she twisted and writhed.

'Not there, let me go,' she cried. 'Oh, oh, oh. No, don't, don't, no more,' as the blows fell again.

Hysterical sobs shook her whole body. I stopped whipping her and said, 'Ah, you've found your voice have you? Well, are you going to behave better in the future?'

'Oh, yes, yes!'

'And do you like being whipped,' I went on, 'and is it as nice as whipping others? Do you like showing your nakedness and your bottom to Juliette and me?'

She only sobbed in reply and I thought she was punished enough and was going to release her when Juliette saw my intention and stopped me.

'No, no, not yet, she hasn't had nearly enough. Don't you remember, she said I was to be crucified? Well, I know what that means; I've had some.' She went to the other case and brought out the two riding whips and a couple of canes and gave me one of each. I dropped the stump of the birch and waited.

'Now madame,' she said, 'you've shown me more than once what you call crucifixion. I hope I shan't forget your teaching. Let me see. This comes first, doesn't it?' and she brought the cane heavily across both cheeks of the quivering bottom.

A shriek of pain from Muriel. She raised herself up and twisted herself to one side to avoid the blow. I had left her when I had finished birching her, so that she could move freely, except that her hands and feet were tied.

'By Jove, that seems to touch the spot,' I said, 'how do you like that, dear? It seems a little more effective than the birch. What does it feel like? Come, tell me.'

Muriel only groaned and writhed convulsively.

'Come, answer me, or can't you quite tell from one cut? Does that make it clearer to you?' and I brought the cane heavily down about half an inch below the livid weal left from Juliette's blow.

A positive howl of anguish came from Muriel.

She raised her body and twisted about as if she was on fire.

'You mustn't move about like that. Not only are you making a most indecent exhibition of yourself but you are doing no good. Come, what is it like? Is it nicer than the birch or do you miss the tingling twigs?'

Still no reply, but sobs and moans. I grew impatient. '*Will* you answer?' and I made the cane whistle through the air, but didn't touch her with it. Her bottom shuddered with apprehension.

'Oh, it's awful,' she gasped, 'it's like a bar of hot iron burning into my flesh.'

'Ah, well, you're going to have quite a lot of those hot bars. In fact, your bottom will be quite a gridiron before we've finished with it.'

'Yes, but she mustn't plunge about like that,' said Juliette, 'or we shan't be able to get a pretty pattern on her bottom and thighs. She likes pretty patterns, I know, for she has often shown me the designs she has traced on me after she has finished. There's nothing like neatness and finish for any work. If a thing is worth doing, it's worth doing well. That's what you often say, isn't it, madame?' she sneered.

Muriel didn't answer.

'Ah, she's lost her voice; we'll find it for her in a minute. Will you help me, sir?' She seized her mistress's wrists: 'There should be a cord here. As you say, sir, there is no use in countenancing any more indecent exposure than is necessary.'

She found a cord at the head of the couch similar to those that fastened Muriel's ankles. She fastened it to the webbing round the wrists and drew it tight. Then she took up the cane again and went back to her former position.

'Will you, please, stand opposite me, sir, and take your time from me?

Don't hurry and be careful how you place your blows. There should be room for a dozen a side, I should think.'

She measured carefully with her fingers the distance from the dimples just above the cheeks, where the plumpness began to swell, down along the thighs to just above the knees.

'Yes, she can take twelve easily, I fancy. Will you try to keep an accurate distance between each cut just as you have already?'

She pointed to the two livid blue marks, which contrasted with the untouched skin between them.

'Now,' she said, raising the cane and bringing it down just below the dimples at the top of the checks. An angry red line appeared and another shriek from Muriel.

I raised my cane. 'Just there,' said Juliette, pointing just below.

Crash fell the cane. Another yell.

'What, more hot iron?' sneered Juliette.

Crash fell her cane just below my mark and crash my cane followed hers.

'Don't hurry,' she insisted. 'We've only got a dozen each. It will do none of us any good; she won't be able to appreciate each separate cut and we shall be finished before we have begun. It would be a pity for her not to realise the care we are taking to do the thing properly.'

'Shall we count the strokes out loud, then we shall be more deliberate,' I said.

'Let her count them to us,' said Juliette. 'Let me see, that makes four. Four, do you hear, madame? Now please call the others.'

I took hold of her hair and raised her head. 'Do as you're told. That was four. Count the rest. What comes next?'

I pulled her head right back. 'Five,' she gasped in terror.

'Five it is,' said Juliette, and again the cane fell.

'Oh, mercy, mercy,' moaned the victim.

'Go on counting.'

'Six.'

I let go of her hair and, carefully directing the cane, brought it down just below Juliette's last mark. We had just reached the summit of the rounded hillocks and the cane fell full on the firm flesh.

'Ah, God,' said Muriel, 'I shall die, you are killing me.'

'I'm not dead,' said Juliette, 'and I've had more than this from you, and I haven't got so much fat to protect me as this,' she added bitterly, rubbing her hand down over the wounded flesh. Muriel shrank under the touch. 'Well, we are waiting, madame. Hadn't you better continue? The sooner it's over, the better for you.'

'Seven,' gasped Muriel, and the seventh blow fell.

'Eight.' I followed. 'Nine. Oh, finish, finish, for pity's sake.'

'Now, you're too impatient! Is it so nice that you can't wait? Well, there you are then, as you seem to want it.'

'Ten, eleven, twelve.' The blows had now reached the thighs, softer and more tender than the plumper cheeks. The cane gave quite a different sound and a still more piercing shriek came from Muriel. She tried with all her strength to drag her feet from the loops and bring her thighs together. But the cords held firm and she could only contract the muscles of her thighs, which rose and fell again on the ridge of pillows. Her hands clutched convulsively at the webbing and relaxed. Her head rolled from side to side. Her whole body heaved.

'Perhaps we may as well finish by ourselves,' said Juliette, who seemed to be growing excited. I must admit that I myself felt a growing impatience. I wanted to strike and strike again at this helpless flesh, and my next three blows were rather at random.

'Steady,' said Juliette, 'don't spoil the gridiron.

'That's better, twenty-two, twenty-three, twenty-four.'

'There, look, it could not be better, one could write music on those clefs.' She stood resting on the cane, panting slightly.

Muriel had stopped shrieking; only moans and hoarse choking sobs came, shaking her whole body.

I looked at Juliette. To tell the truth I was rather frightened lest we had done too much. I must have shown this in my face, for she laughed. 'Oh, don't be afraid, we haven't half-finished yet, she can bear lots more. But we must shift her for the finale. Isn't it a lovely picture, though?' and she traced the straight lines with her fingers in a fierce joy.

'Ah, madame, do you remember the first time you crucified me? I haven't forgotten. How you laughed! It's my turn to laugh now, isn't it? You didn't think then that Juliette was to have the chance to write her name on your naked bottom, or you mightn't have been so keen on showing me how it was done.'

She went to the loops which fastened the legs and took them off. 'Now turn her over on her back,' she said to me. 'Perhaps she would rather display her breasts and belly than her hinder parts.' I went to Muriel and pulled her towards me. She made no resistance. Her eyes were closed, her cheeks were wet with her tears, her whole body shook with gasping sobs. I rolled her over on her back and Juliette quickly refastened the legs. When she felt her bottom resting on the cushions, she started and screamed with the pain and tried to turn over again, but she was too late. Juliette had secured the ankles.

'Now, madame, for the real crucifixion.' She pulled open the tea-gown at the neck and displayed all her mistress's charms.

There she lay, outstretched for sacrifice, her breasts standing out firm, her belly raised by the ridge of cushions on which her bottom rested, while her legs, stretched as wide apart as possible, showed all her sex.

Scarcely a mark of her chastisement showed from our present point of view, only between her legs a few marks of the birch showed and the lips of her pussy seemed swollen slightly and flushed.

She presented altogether a maddening spectacle to my eyes, which wandered over all her body. Her position was ideal for any form of attack and I couldn't resist the temptation of putting my hand between her legs and investigating the gaping lips of her pussy.

Juliette watched me jealously. 'Do you want to be in her? I should wait till tomorrow, but you can go on doing that if you like while I finish the crucifixion. It won't interfere with me. In fact, it will make it all the more amusing. She will have two different kinds of tickling at the same time.'

My fingers began to probe the soft clinging lips of Muriel's pussy, while Juliette flicked the nipples of her breasts with the lash of one of the riding whips. She stood at the head of the couch and Muriel's white body lay stretched between us. Under the gentle persuasion of my fingers Muriel's sobs and groans gradually changed into sighs. Her thighs contracted, little twitchings and spasms ran over her smooth belly, evidently the pain of the whipping had not taken all sexual feeling from her.

'Tell me when she comes,' said Juliette eagerly, as the little lash flicked here and there with a sort of wicked caress.

'Now,' I said as I felt the lips of Muriel's pussy contract, and her bottom heaved with convulsive thrusts and her thighs contracted and imprisoned my hand. I was not prepared for what followed. Without a word of warning, Juliette lifted the whip above her head and brought it heavily down on her mistress's body, straight up and down between her breasts, causing a long straight weal starting from the valley between her breasts, crossing the navel, and ending just above the dainty brown curls of the bush, where the lash cut the skin and a few beads of blood appeared.

Muriel's sighs and moans of passion changed to a shriek of agony, but Juliette paid no heed. She stepped to one side and again brought the whip down on the unprotected body, but this time across from side to side, just across the breasts. Another weal appeared, making a perfect cross. I felt Muriel's body grow suddenly limp. I looked at her face; it was deadly pale. She had fainted.

How beautiful she looked there, with her arms tied above her head, her eyes closed, her mouth partly open, her head drooping, the purple lines of the cross showing up on her deathly pale skin, her firm plump legs stretched this way and that, revealing the beautiful mossy curls and soft lips of her pussy, still dewy with the involuntary sacrifice to love. I looked to Juliette to see what she would do and went to unfasten the loops.

'Oh, she'll come round all right,' said Juliette, 'you needn't worry. I've had lots worse from her than that. Don't untie her yet.'

'I won't have her whipped any more,' I said. 'We've given her quite enough. Get some water and bring her round.'

Juliette went to the bedroom, and I chafed Muriel's hands and cheeks. Her eyes slowly opened and she looked at me. I was prepared for anger and resentment, but instead of that I only saw submission and appeal.

'Cruel, cruel,' she murmured. 'How could you be so cruel?'

I bent down and kissed her lips. 'I'm sorry,' I answered, 'but you had to learn who was master. Have you learnt it?'

Her eyes said yes and I kissed her again.

Juliette came back with smelling-salts and cold water.

Her mistress's eyes glowered as she saw her approach. I saw the look. 'Now there must be no resentment against Juliette,' I said. 'Let her help you to bed and take care of you, and I will call and see you tomorrow.'

'No, don't let her come near me,' said Muriel; 'I won't have her. *You* take care of me,' turning to me, 'I want *you.*'

'You will do as you are told,' I said firmly, for I realised it was the only way to keep my new-found sovereignty. 'Now Juliette, kiss your mistress and be friends.'

'Let me help you, madame,' said Juliette; 'you know I have always let you help me when you have whipped me.'

'We will both see to you,' I said. 'Juliette, get the bath ready.'

I undid Muriel's bonds and gently raised her up. She could not bear to sit on her poor bottom, but hung round my neck and across my knees, the picture of abject submission.

'Oh, my lover, my king,' she murmured, 'you have won me, you have mastered me. I am your slave, I love, I worship you.'

Juliette came back to say that the bath was ready, and between us we carried Muriel into the bathroom, which led off her bedroom, and laid her in it.

Juliette took the soap bowl and, making a lovely lather, prepared to cover her mistress with it. Some of the soap splashed on me.

'You'll get your clothes spoiled,' she said; 'you had better take them off.'

I did as she suggested and in a minute or two was as naked as they were. We soaped Muriel all over and then Juliette produced a flask of some sweet-scented oil which she gently applied to the poor scourged bottom and thighs. She dried her tenderly and laid her on the cool sheet.

Muriel gave a little sigh of fatigue and closed her eyes. I took a towel and began to dry myself. Juliette was putting things straight, going here and there quickly as she replaced bottles and soap and brushes.

It might have been Ancient Rome – Rome of the Empire. This marble bathroom, myself a young patrician, and Juliette a slave-girl attending on my wants.

I watched her slim form everywhere, my desire growing hotter and hotter, until at last she stooped down with her back to me to pick something up from the floor and in so doing showed me all her lovely bottom and the darling little pussy pouting out between her thighs.

I did not say a word, but silently came behind her, caught her round the hips and thrust John Thomas between the lips which were ready and eager to receive him.

She gave a little start of surprise, then a pleased laugh. 'You silly impetuous boy. Why not wait until we can be comfortable?'

But I was far too eager to wait and began working in and out with vigour.

'Cecil,' called Muriel, 'where are you? I want you.'

'I can't come for the moment, I'm busy. I'll be with you in a minute.'

'But I want you now. What are you doing?'

Juliette chuckled. I made no answer, but went on working. I was just finished when I saw Muriel's reflection in the glass standing on the floor.

'I thought as much,' she said.

I had finished my work and turned to face her. Juliette also turned coolly and faced her mistress.

I could not help comparing this interruption with the other, earlier on that afternoon.

'What are you doing here?' I said. 'Go back to bed. Do you want another whipping?'

'I wanted *you*,' she said humbly.

'Well, I was busy, as you see. I'll come to you in a minute, in fact, we will both come.'

She darted a look of hatred at Juliette.

'None of that,' I said, 'I won't have it. You must be friends with Juliette. Go and kiss her at once.'

She hesitated.

'Go and kiss her at once, or shall I fetch the whip?'

'Oh, no, no,' she shuddered and went slowly towards Juliette.

An idea struck me. 'Kneel down,' I said, 'and kiss those other lips of hers. You said you wanted me. Well, you'll find some of me there. Kiss her and thank her for whipping you.'

It was lovely to see the conflict of pride and fear in Muriel. She gave Juliette and me a quick glance and then, sobbing, knelt down before her maid's naked body and pressed her lips on the thick curls.

'Say what I told you to say,' I urged.

'Thank you, Juliette,' she sobbed stammeringly, 'for whipping me.'

It was too much for her and she bowed her head and wept.

Juliette's pity was moved. 'Oh, Muriel,' she said, as she gently raised her mistress, 'don't be angry with me, forgive me if I hurt you.'

She raised her to her feet and the two women fell into each other's arms.

'That's right,' I said, 'now we will go to bed.'

## CHAPTER EIGHT

# The Turning Point

Looking back on my life, I date my conversion – as an evangelical person would express it – from that afternoon. Until I met Muriel I had really no knowledge or experience of the vagaries of vice. My life, till then, had been absolutely normal. Apart from the usual pseudosodomy of a public school – *masturbatio intra nates*, as Krafft-Ebing styles it – which practice I discarded and despised on going up to Oxford, I had simply sought women for straightforward fornication. Naturally certain subtleties of pleasure had been learnt, but until I had suffered at Muriel's hands and had been able to retaliate, I knew nothing of the intense, though recondite, delights of domination and humiliation. I realise on careful introspection that I had always a natural bias towards sadism. Even as a small boy I played the game of 'school' with my little sister, with the natural consequence of 'whippings'. I remember also, when on a holiday in Derbyshire at the age of fifteen, finding a book in the rooms where we were staying, in which there was a whipping chapter. The orphan daughter of a poor curate became a 'town apprentice' to the wife of the local doctor. Her mistress ill-treated her and one day, finding her sweethearting with some man, gave her what was called a 'workhouse supper'. The description of this thrashing with a strap at night on the bare bottom gave me, I remember, a terrific erection, and in spite of relieving myself in the usual way of a boy of fifteen, I had that night my first wet dream when the scene of the story was vividly re-enacted in my sleep.

Anyhow, whether naturally disposed that way or not, I went home that afternoon triumphant and elated. I had achieved my object of getting even with Muriel and had, at any rate for the time being, subdued and dominated her, and the joy of possession was far surpassed by the gloating satisfaction I felt at the thought that she was my slave, subdued and humiliated.

My desire towards her for the future was no longer sexual intercourse but domination, subjection.

In this spirit I hastened to see her the next day. Before leaving her I had given her strict instructions that she was on no account to retaliate either in deed or even attitude towards Juliette for the humiliation and crucifixion of that afternoon. I had also told Juliette that if Muriel attempted anything of the kind she was to tell me at once, and that for her own sake she was on no account to submit, or it might be the worse for her. 'I am going to be your master,' I said, 'just as I am going to be hers, and I will have no one sharing my power.'

Determined therefore to keep my new-won servants, I arrived at the house next day. Juliette as usual opened the door. She was rather pale and her eyes were slightly red. I asked her what was the matter. 'Muriel has been cruel to me,' she said.

'But I thought I told you you were not to submit.'

'I couldn't help it. She has been my tyrant too long, one cannot break one's bonds in a minute.'

'What did she do? She couldn't have done much. She was too exhausted.'

'Oh, she slept after you left, but during the evening she woke up and sent for me. I found her much recovered, though still stiff and sore. She at once went for me for betraying her into your power and vowed that even though she might not be able to get even with *you*, *I* should pay for my treachery. I told her what you had said, and how you had ordered me not to submit, but she would not listen. I resisted all I knew, but she is very strong, much stronger than I, and you don't know, you can't know, what it means to have been in a woman's thrall for years as I have been. Luckily her experience of the afternoon had shaken her so much that she fainted before she had done much, but look!' She lifted her skirt behind, bent down, and pulled open her drawers. There were about a dozen livid weals right across her bottom.

'What did she do that with?' I asked.

'With the riding whip. She was going to use the wire birch, she threatened me, but the excitement and exertion of this was too much and she fainted.'

'She shall pay for it,' I said. 'But you – I told you you were not to submit to her. How dared you disobey me?'

'I'm sorry, I couldn't help it.'

'Sorry! Couldn't help it! Yes, you will be sorry and you'll learn to help it. Take me to her.'

She looked frightened at my words, but led the way upstairs to Muriel's room.

Muriel was in bed, looking rather pale but very lovely. Her hair was loose about her shoulders. She looked up as I came in and smiled with pleasure.

'Oh, Cecil, I was hoping you would come. I am longing for you.'

'Hm,' I said, 'are you? What is this Juliette has been telling me? I thought I told you you were not to retaliate for your punishment of yesterday and now I find her with a bruised bottom and she says that but for fainting you would have done more.'

'Surely I can punish my own property? I know I am your slave, but surely in my own house I am mistress.'

'*Your* property, *you* mistress? You may have been before yesterday, but now, I have learned what power means and – thanks always to you, you must remember – you are both *my* property, you obey me. If I give you permission you may perhaps be allowed to correct Juliette, but not without my permission, nor in my absence. Do you clearly understand that? Juliette, go and get the cases. I had better fix this new system in both your minds.'

Juliette obeyed. Muriel turned white and began to sob. 'You are not going to whip me again, surely. I'm sore all over still from yesterday, you could not be so cruel.'

'Oh, there must be lots of places left. Let me see.' And I pulled back the bedclothes quickly before she had time to see what I was doing. Her night-dress had worked up and she was naked from the waist down. 'Ah . . . well, the bottom and thighs certainly are fairly marked, but the back and calves are untouched. Turn over. Yes, I thought so. Why, there's lots of room.'

Juliette returned at this moment, carrying the two cases. Muriel hastily tried to cover herself.

'Oh, modest, are you?' I laughed. 'A little late, isn't it? Now Juliette, I have been telling Muriel what I think about her conduct to you, and she will have to pay for it. But you have been disobedient, too, and must be punished. You said you would love to be whipped by me. Well, your wishes shall be gratified. You had better undress, not altogether though, or you may shock Muriel's modesty. Stay a moment, I have an idea which will prevent any false shame on her part. Give me that webbing.'

I took the webbing and tied Muriel's left ankle to her left wrist and her right ankle to her right wrist and then rolled her on her back.

She submitted as if in a stupor.

'There now, she can't see you, Juliette, and no matter how much she may gather you are exposed by the sound of my strokes, she must realise that she is far more indecently exposed herself. Besides, she will be in a most convenient position for punishment. Now go on undressing yourself.'

Juliette looked a little frightened, but at the same time there was a look of expectancy in her eyes, which gloated over Muriel's nakedness. I took a birch and all the time Juliette was undressing, I was tickling Muriel's pussy, which was stretched open owing to her position, with the tips of the twigs.

When Juliette had taken everything but her chemise and drawers off, I stopped her. 'That will do for the present. Turn the chemise up over your hips.'

She obeyed. 'Now bend down here,' pointing to a spot at such a distance from the bed that her face would just reach Muriel's bottom and pussy as she lay spread-eagled on the side of the bed, 'and put your hands on your knees. Now,' said I, 'I am first going to tan you as we did at school. Listen, Muriel, and think how you will like it when your turn comes. You can lie patiently there for the present.'

I exchanged the birch for a cane, and swinging it back with a full sweep of my arm, I brought it down with full force across the half-open drawers. The force and surprise of the blow drew a cry from Juliette and impelled her forward, so that her face knocked against Muriel's bush. The latter uttered a cry of alarm.

'What's the matter?' I asked.

'I didn't know Juliette was so close. It startled me.'

'Oh, she's quite close. She can see all you've got to show, can't you Juliette?'

'Yes, sir.'

'Well, tell us what you can see. Listen, Muriel.'

'I can see Muriel's bottom and her belly and her . . . her . . . ' She stopped.

'Her what?' I insisted. 'Her pussy?'

'Yes . . . '

'Well, tell her so.'

'I don't like to.'

'Oh, don't you. Does that make you want to?' and I gave her a vicious cut with the cane.

'Don't, oh, don't.'

'Well, say it.'

'Muriel, I can see your pussy . . . '

'Inside and out?' I asked.

'Yes, inside and out.'

'There, Muriel, you hear that? What is the good of pretending to be so modest when you are showing your pussy, even the inside of it, to your maid and me. Why, we can see right inside you. We can see your clitoris there' – and I touched it with the tip of the cane – 'we can nearly see your womb, I expect.'

'Oh, untie me, and let me go. Whip me if you want to, but don't keep me tied up like this.'

'Oh, you shall be whipped right enough, don't you worry. There's plenty of time. Still, if you're impatient we'll lay in now; move aside, Juliette. Now look out.'

I lifted the cane, made it whistle in the air. I saw Muriel contract the muscles of her thighs and buttocks to meet the blow and, to tantalise her, brought the blow down about two inches from her body. She gave an involuntary cry.

'What's the matter?'

'I thought the cane was coming. I heard it whiz in the air.'

'Oh, disappointed, are you? Well, things are always nicer when you get them when you don't expect them.'

A vicious cut of the cane pointed the 'expect' and Muriel shrieked with surprise.

I turned to Juliette, who was still bending down.

'Now, to go on with you. How many have I given you?'

'Two.'

'Two. Ah, that leaves two more. We were only allowed to give four at school.'

Whack, whack came the cane, and with each blow Juliette's face was buried in Muriel's mossy curls.

'Now take your drawers off. We will see what the cane has done. Lie on your back beside Muriel in a similar position to her.'

There were four clear red lines across the white cheeks, in spite of the protecting drawers.

I looked at the two distended bottoms conspicuously displayed on the edge of the bed. They looked so quaint that an idea struck me.

I went to the dressing-table and found a pair of hairbrushes.

Then I sat on the bed between the two girls and began to play, as it were, the side drums on their bottoms. I kept time to a mad silly sort of rhyme, something like this:

> 'Mu–riel, Mu–riel,
> I will tan your bo–ttom well.
> Ju–liét–te, Ju–liét–te,
> I will see you don't forget,'

accentuating the alternate syllables with blows of the brushes, using alternately the backs and bristles of the brushes.

I varied the force of the blows also so that they never knew what the next blow was going to be like. I brushed the hair on their pussies, now softly so that they wiggled under the lascivious caress, now fiercely as if I was scrubbing a brick, which made them squirm with agony.

Getting tired of this I again addressed myself to Muriel.

'You asked me just now to untie you and whip you, didn't you? Well, I'm not so sure that I won't do as you ask. The position is a little tiring I expect.'

'It's awful . . . My legs and arms are gone to sleep. Oh, please untie me.'

'Juliette, you may untie her, if you like. Now go and stand in that corner with your face to the wall and wait until I am ready. Don't dare to look round. Juliette, take off her nightdress and your own chemise and drawers. That's right, now go and stand beside her.'

I took a birch from the case and the whip of knotted cords.

'Now,' I said, 'I am going to whip you both for disobedience. I ordered you, Muriel, not to attempt to retaliate on Juliette for your whipping of yesterday, and I told you, Juliette, that you were not to submit to her if she tried it on. So both of you deserve and will get this,' and I brought the birch down heavily across their bottoms, one after the other. Juliette only flinched, but Muriel's bottom was so sore that she involuntarily placed her hands on her burning cheeks.

'Take those hands away,' I said, cutting them again and again. 'If you don't I will tie you down . . . Now, will either of you disobey me again?' Whish – whish came the birch across Juliette's thighs.

'Oh, no – no – never,' she sobbed.

'Will *you*,' to Muriel as I stepped across and laid the birch across her loins and calves, which were comparatively untouched. She sobbed and shook her head. 'Answer me.'

'No, oh, don't whip me so low down,' as the birch caught her on the back of her knees.

'Oh, don't you worry, you shall have enough higher up in a minute or two. Now, Juliette, I'll finish you off. Come here, kneel down facing me.'

I got her head between my thighs and laid into her with the birch right up and down both thighs and cheeks of her bottom. Occasionally I directed a blow right between the cheeks, so that the tips of the twigs curled right into her pussy. She screamed and writhed and plunged, imploring mercy.

'Do you hear that, Muriel,' I said. 'That's nothing to what you will get in a minute. Perhaps you are getting impatient, eh? Well, there's something to go on with.'

I could just reach her with the birch and let her have one cut and then came back to Juliette, whom I had kept tightly pressed between my knees. My blows had caused all her bottom and thighs to flush a dark red, on which the weals from Muriel's riding whip and my own tanning stood out across in darker colours. 'There's quite a pretty lattice work across your behind, Juliette dear. I didn't know I was such an expert at designing. Have you had enough? Do you think you will be disobedient again? Well, we will just make sure.' And I delivered a regular hail of blows everywhere as quickly as I could, until I was out of breath. Juliette's cries increased. She wriggled and twisted this way and that, but the relentless rod found her every time. Blood began to show here and there where the skin had been broken and even began to trickle down her legs. The birch twigs flew all over the room and at last I had only the mere stump left in my hand.

Then I relaxed the pressure of my thighs and she fell forward on the floor, twisting and groaning and her hands instinctively going to her lacerated bottom to protect it from further assaults.

All this time Muriel had been standing as I told her, with her face to the wall, a picture of apprehension. She knew she was within reach of my arm and so did not dare to move or look round.

I turned to her. 'Now, Muriel, come here. It's your turn.' She turned and came towards me with appealing looks. 'Go down on your hands and knees,' I ordered, 'and pick up those broken twigs. We can't have the room in this state. The sooner you finish the job, the better for you.' I threw away the birch and took up the knotted whip with the five lashes and to start her gave her a moderately hard blow on her flanks. She gasped and went down as I had told her, hastily picking up the bits of twigs here and there. It was a most fascinating sight in its shameless nakedness and humiliation. She crawled and grovelled all over the floor, trying to avoid my blows and at the same time to pick up the twigs as quickly as possible. I pursued her everywhere, taking care at first to avoid the parts still sore from yesterday's whipping. All across her back and flanks the lashes fell. Now they curled over her shoulder or cut into her armpits. The tender flesh below her ribs received many, the knotted ends reaching round to her stomach. Livid weals began to appear and at last she flung herself at my feet, her hands full of twigs, imploring my pardon and protesting that she would never disobey me again. She even begged Juliette to plead for her to me. I allowed myself to be persuaded, and told them to see to each other's comforts, but warned both of them that if ever I found them disobedient again there would be worse punishment in store for them.

I then prepared to leave them, for though the whippings had excited me, I had no desire, as I had the day before, for any actual sexual enjoyment.

'You are not going, Cecil, are you?' pleaded Muriel. 'Surely now you have punished both of us, you will be kind and give us what we want,' and she came close to me and, like a suppliant, looked imploring into my eyes. Juliette also sent appealing glances at me.

I pretended to misunderstand her.

'Haven't you been whipped enough?' I asked.

'Oh, yes, but I want – I want – '

'What?'

'Well, if I must say it, I want you in me,' she blushed and stammered.

'No,' I said sternly, 'you don't deserve it and I'm not going to satisfy your lusts. Still, you can both, as a favour, kneel down and kiss the God Priapus, whom you worship, but nothing more.'

I undid my trousers and let loose the object of their adoration and let them both approach one after the other. To humiliate Muriel, I told Juliette to come first, which she did on her knees. I did not allow her to stay too long, but made her give place to Muriel. She knelt eagerly before me and, embracing me round the hips, kissed and licked the rampant head. Human nature was too strong, and I deluged her face and neck with spurting jets of my strength. But I had no pleasure from this, as compared with the delight I had experienced while flogging their subjugated bodies.

## CHAPTER NINE

# *I Settle My Kingdom – Juliette's Story*

If I date my 'conversion' from the previous day, I may quite well look on this afternoon as my 'confirmation'. Until then I had been a man with just ordinary desires. Now physical union with a woman became quite a secondary consideration with me. The fascination of domination held me, and though, of course, I had both Muriel and Juliette as my mistresses, that was more for their pleasure than my own. For myself I was their *master*, they were my *slaves*.

I quickly settled my kingdom, and as a first proof of my position, I demanded and obtained a latchkey. With this I was able to make surprise visits, but I will say this for Juliette, she gave me no cause for jealousy. She was quite content, for the time being at any rate, with me, and although she admitted that it was quite a surprise to her to find herself submitting to any man, still she loved me for mastering her – or so she said. With Muriel, however, she was quite different. She did not exactly bear malice, but she evidently meant to get her own back. She was, however, quite aware that I would not tolerate any sly vengeance; I had made that quite clear to her; but I could see that she meant, at the first opportunity, to pay Juliette out. Nor had she any intention of giving up the autocratic sway she had wielded for many years. She put this quite frankly to me one evening. 'It's all very well for you, Cecil,' she said; 'you have mastered me – much to my surprise, I admit – still, you *have* mastered me, and I love you for it. But with Juliette, it's different. I've always had her as a subject; when we were at school together she fagged for me, and I used to whip her if I wasn't satisfied with her.'

'At school together?' I repeated.

'Yes, didn't you know?'

'No, Juliette said she would tell me someday how your domination of her began – that was that afternoon you caught us in the morning-room and got caught yourself,' I added maliciously. 'But she said it was too long a story to tell then.'

'Well, shall we have her in and tell you now?'

'If you like.'

She rang the bell, and Juliette came in. 'Juliette, Cecil says you promised to tell him how we got to know each other. Sit down and do so now.' She was sitting on my knee with her arm round my neck.

Juliette hesitated. 'Go on,' said Muriel. 'You haven't forgotten Clifton and South Parade? Let me see, it was Maude Jeffreys who began it, wasn't it?'

'Who was Maude Jeffreys?' I asked.

'She was a beast,' said Juliette, and she stopped.

'Go on,' I said.

'I was only a child about eleven, and she was seventeen. I hated her and so did most of the girls. She was so strong, though, that they were afraid of her. All the bigger girls at school had little girl friends – minions they used to call them – who used to fag for them and . . . do other things.'

'Oh,' I said.

Juliette blushed. 'Well, Maude couldn't get anyone to be her minion till I came, and no one took me up – you were away that term, Muriel, with scarlet fever – and all the other girls had their minions, so she seized on me. I knew nothing at all then about things. I had come straight from home. Maude told me to fag for her, and as I saw the other girls of my own age fagging for the other big girls, I took it as a matter of course. They all seemed to like it, and got sweets and petted in return. Sometimes, too, the bigger girls called their minions to them after the lights were out and I used to hear kisses and soft words of endearment. I thought nothing of that, I only wished someone would pet me . . . but not Maude, I never wanted her to pet me, she was such a beast . . . she didn't wash, ugh!

'One day, after I had been at school a week, one of the bigger girls had cause to complain about her minion. Something or other had not been done to her liking, and when we went up to bed, I was surprised to be told not to undress at once. The other little girls evidently knew what was coming. The culprit was brought into my room – I slept in the biggest dormitory, with most of the little girls – and after a lecture from her senior, she was told to "go down". She was quite undressed and bent across a bed. Then her senior took a little cane out of her box and gave her about a dozen smart cuts on her little behind. The child sobbed and got up and went back to her own room. I was stupefied, but the rest of the girls seemed to like it and to take it as a matter of course. I was told I could now undress, and did so, feeling very nervous and uncomfortable. When I was in bed and the lights were out, I heard Maude calling me. I went over to her bed. "Get into bed with me," she said, "I want to talk to you." I did so very shyly. "You saw Elsie get whipped?" "Yes." "Well, that's what happens to naughty girls here, so be careful. If little girls don't do as they are told, their seniors whip them. How would you like me to whip you?" "Oh, Maude, please." "Well, mind you don't deserve it."

'I didn't like the turn the conversation was taking and moved to get out of bed, but Maude put her arm round me.

' "No, you are not to go yet. You've never been in bed with any of the other girls, have you?" "No." "Ah, well kiss me, kiddy." I didn't much want to, but I did as she said. I was surprised to find not only her lips but her tongue meet my lips. I drew back, but couldn't get away. Her hand moved down and began to pull up my nightdress. I could feel my cheeks burning with hot blushes. "You've got quite a nice little bottom for your age; it will be rather nice to smack." "Oh, Maude, don't . . . it's rude." She laughed. "Give me your hand." She took it, and before I knew what she was doing, placed it between her legs. "Don't take it away, but do as I do." She pulled my nightdress right up and roughly put her hand between my legs to . . . oh, how ashamed and frightened I was. "Oh, don't, please Maude, don't," I said, and tried to take her hand away. "Silly little fool, do as I tell you." But I was too upset and burst out crying. "Shut up, you idiot, or you'll be sorry. You shall pay for this tomorrow. Go back to your own bed." I crept miserably back and sobbed myself to sleep.

'The next evening Maude told me not to get into bed until she told me. She then called the other seniors together and explained the case, while I stood in my nightdress. She was not popular, but the rule at South Parade was strict. A senior had an unquestioned right to punish her minion, and though they didn't like her, the other seniors, for their own sakes, would not encourage insubordination in a minion. Besides, as I learnt afterwards, they all used their minions as Maude had tried to use me, and would not listen to any frightened protests on my part. So I had to bend over the bed, as I had seen the other little girl do the night before. Maude borrowed a cane and, lifting my nightdress, gave me ten hard cuts on my poor little behind. Oh, the pain and shame of that first whipping. I shall never forget it. I sobbed and twisted and kicked, but Maude held me down with one hand quite easily. All the time she was whipping me she was jeering at me. "Isn't it rude, eh, Miss Modesty? Fancy showing your nakedness to the whole dormitory."

'When she had finished she said: "Now go to bed and come to me when the lights are out." I crept into bed, and, soon after, the lights were out. I didn't move, but soon heard Maude calling me. As I didn't answer, she came across to my bed and roughly pulled down the clothes. She turned me over on my face and pulled up my nightdress and began whipping me again. I screamed but she kept my head pressed down into the pillow, which muffled the cries. She must have given me quite twenty or thirty before she stopped. "Now, will you come to my bed?" I was too hurt and frightened to resist any more and followed her miserably, and did all she told me to do.

'Oh, how I hated doing it, and hated her for making me. I was too young to get any pleasure myself and, as I said, she didn't wash.'

I laughed – I couldn't help it, and so did Muriel.

'It's all very well to laugh, but it was beastly.'

'I expect so,' I said. 'But go on.'

'Well, things went on like this. Maude was always getting into rows with the headmistress, Mrs Walter, and after getting punished herself used to get her own back on me. At last one day she was caught cheating in form and the whole school – there were about forty of us – were summoned to the big schoolroom. I knew Mrs Walter used to whip the girls, though up till then I had escaped, and the whippings were in private. This time, however, Mrs

Walter came in to us and read us all a lecture on dishonesty and then called Maude out before all of us, and, after lecturing her, sent her away with the French mistress to get ready for punishment. She then told us to go into the punishment room. I had never been in this room, known as the Vale of Tears among the girls, before. It was a large empty room right at the top of the house. The only furniture it contained was a cupboard, a long narrow table with broad straps on either side, hanging down, a sort of vaulting horse, and a moveable scaling ladder fixed to one of the walls. There were forms round the side of the room, on which we girls sat and waited. After a minute or two, Mrs Walter came in with the other mistresses. She rang a bell and the door at the other end of the room opened and in came Mademoiselle leading Maude. The latter was a curious figure. She was naturally fat and lumpy, and her present costume did not improve her appearance. She wore a flannel dressing-gown, hind part in front, her face was blotched with fright, and she could barely walk. She looked such a ridiculous figure that in my astonishment and nervousness I giggled.

' "Who laughed," said Mrs Walter at once.

'I stood up trembling.

' "Did you laugh?" "Yes, madam," I stammered, "I didn't mean to . . . but Maude looks so funny." "Hm, she won't look funny soon. Let me see, you're a new girl." "Yes, madam." "Oh, and you have not been present at a punishment before? Well, let it be a lesson to you. Come here, Miss Jeffreys."

'Maude approached and stood trembling. "You were detected trying to copy your French exercises from the girl next to you." "Yes, madam." "Very good, you know what to expect?"

'She signed to the French and Second mistresses, who took hold of Maude and led her to the table and laid her face downwards on it, so that her legs hung over at one end, buckling the straps which hung on either side tight across her back, one just below her shoulders, one across her waist, and one just across her hips. Mrs Walter had gone to the cupboard and taken out a long cane. She came back to her victim and undid the dressing-gown. I realised now why it was backside front. As the buttons were undone, so it fell apart on either side, showing that Maude had on only a chemise. This was raised as high as possible and Maude's fat coarse behind fully exposed to view. Madam raised the cane to the full sweep of her arm and the first cut fell. I have never heard such a yell as came from Maude's lips. A second cut fell just in the same place, followed by another shriek. The older girls smiled. Maude was notoriously a coward. But Mrs Walter went on methodically with the whipping, taking no heed of the cries. Only when Maude began to kick, she said, "Keep still, or you shall be tied." But Maude's legs continued to fly about making a most indecent exposure. At last when she had given ten cuts, each of which had left its mark, Mrs Walter drew back and signed to the two mistresses and pointed to the horse. They wheeled that into the middle of the room, undid Maude, and led her to it. They bent her over it, and while one of them fastened her wrists to the two legs on one side, the other stretched her legs apart and tied her ankles to the other two legs. All that we girls could see was Maude's bottom wealed by the cane and her legs and what was usually hidden between. Mrs Walter now put back the cane and armed herself with a long birch. If the cane had made Maude yell with pain, the birch made her scream. But Mrs Walter took no notice. Down came the birch on the fat cheeks, until they were all crimson and purple. Quicker and quicker fell the blows, until at last most of the twigs had broken off and only a stump was left in her hands. Then she stopped and the mistresses undid Maude, who could scarcely stand, so shaken and weak with sobbing was she.

' "Will you cheat again?" "No, madam," she stammered, kneeling down. "Very good, take her away."

'That was the first whipping I saw at South Parade. We were dismissed and I noticed that most of the seniors retired to their studies with their minions. I was congratulating myself that I should be free from Maude for some time; the whipping would, I thought, keep her mind busy. But I was disappointed.

' "Maude wants you, Juliette, in the dormitory," said a small girl. I didn't dare not to go. I found Maude in bed sobbing. "Oh there you are, you little beast, are you? So you laughed at me, did you? Well, I'll pay you out for that, my girl, when I'm fit again. Now I want you to put some cream on my legs; you'll find some on my dressing table."

'I found some cold cream. Maude turned over on her face. "Pull the clothes down, and put it on, and mind you be gentle." I didn't relish the task of anointing her behind, you may be sure, but the sight of her battered flesh pleased me much. She lay and moaned the whole time, muttering abuse of Mrs Walter, until I had finished. That night she left me alone, she was too stiff and sore – though she had to show her behind to the whole dormitory (that was a custom of South Parade, and not even the biggest girls escaped doing it after a whipping). But the next night . . . I had to pay for laughing at her and she made me do everything to her, ugh.'

'Everything?'

'Yes, not only fingers . . . I had to . . . pah.'

'Poor little girl, but it didn't last, did it?' said Muriel.

'No, thank goodness, you came back and won me from her.'

'Won you?'

'Yes, that was a custom at South Parade. No senior could take a minion from another senior unless she won her. Sometimes seniors exchanged minions by agreement, but usually if a senior fancied a minion she had to fight for her and win her. Oh, it was quite a formal affair. The dormitory was cleared, a ring was formed, the minion was perched naked on a chest of drawers, and the two combatants, also naked, fought with knotted towels which they flicked at each other. No wrestling or holding was allowed. I shall never forget that fight for me. There was that fat ugly Maude with her coarse skin and dark thick hair, while you, darling, looked so frail beside her. Oh, I did hope you would win.'

'Well, what happened?'

'Oh, I won,' laughed Muriel. 'I'd had experience at home with my brother George. He'd learnt the game at school and used to practise on me in the holidays.'

'Oh, did he?'

'With our nightgowns on, of course, you naughty boy. Well, I'd learnt the trick of wetting the end of the towel and I could aim much better than Maude. I was quicker on my feet too, and she was such an awful coward. She nearly gave in after I had touched her once or twice on the thighs, and at last, when I got in a special cut of my brother's, right between her legs, she howled out: "Oh, take the little beast, I don't want her," and went to bed.'

'Yes, and you have had me ever since, haven't you?' said Juliette, flinging her arms round Muriel. 'I loved you then and I love you still, in spite of your cruelty to me sometimes.'

'But how? . . . Why? . . .'

'You mean, how does Juliette come to be here?'

'Ye–es, and . . .'

'And what?'

'Well, she was at school with you . . . but . . .'

'Oh, you mean you thought she was my maid. Oh, that's your mistake. She told me when you called that she was sure from your manner that you took her for the maid, and we agreed to keep it up as long as we could. No, she's my companion really. Tell him how it came about, Juliette.'

### CHAPTER TEN

## *Juliette's Story – continued*

'Well,' said Juliette, 'my father died suddenly and we were left awfully poor.'

'You must begin long before that,' said Muriel. 'It began with my leaving South Parade. You see, Maude never forgave me for winning Juliette from her and tried all she could to pay us out. There was no other little girl left without a senior, and no senior would share her minion with her, as was sometimes done. She didn't tell about the games at night in the dormitory, for that would have brought down on her head the vengeance of all the seniors, for we were all tarred with the same brush, and she was an awful coward. But she hated us both: Juliette because she could never get her to make love to her gladly, and me because she saw Juliette was quite eager to do anything to, or for, me. So things went on for about a year, until one hot summer's day in the garden I couldn't wait till night, and Juliette and I were having quite a nice little "flirtation" on the grass, which was rather long. Maude must have spotted us and told Mrs Walter, for we were suddenly startled in each other's arms by her voice: "What conduct is this?" There she stood looking down on us. "Get up at once, Juliette; do up your drawers, go and wash your hands and then come to my room." When we got there, she stormed at us, and talked about expelling us publicly. But I wasn't afraid of that.'

'Two hundred pounds a year each,' sniggered Juliette.

'Precisely. So she jawed a lot and at last said that in consideration for our parents, and the disgrace, etc., she would let us off with a flogging, but we must never do it again, would we promise? Oh, yes, of course, we would – and we never did – in the garden. She asked us if the other girls did the same sort of thing, and, of course, we said no, and then she asked me how I knew of such things. I said a servant at home. "I expected as much," she answered. Looking back now, I, of course, realise she was *one of us* herself, for she gloated over the details and her eyes glowed as she talked. Anyhow, we got our whipping – a private one, because she did not want to publish our disgrace and get the matter talked about, for fear of putting ideas into the girls' heads.'

'Was the whipping severe?'

'Pretty well, I'd had plenty in my time; she loved whipping me, she told me later, after I left school.

'She spanked you, didn't she?'

'Yes, she always spanked us little girls. She used to put us across her knees, turn our clothes up, let down our drawers, and use her hand or the back of a hairbrush. My word, it hurt, too, I couldn't sit down for over a week with any comfort.'

'But we paid Maude out, didn't we?'

'How was that?'

'Oh, that evening we held a court martial in the dormitory. We bribed the maid not to turn out the gas for half an hour, and we *tried* Miss Maude. Naturally all the seniors were eager to punish the sneak, and she was condemned to run the gauntlet and to be whipped by her two victims. It *was* fun. Picture this kid of twelve,' pointing to Juliette, 'laying into the fat behind of a girl of eighteen. "I can't hit hard enough," she nearly sobbed in her excitement, "I can't hurt her enough." I think, however, she managed pretty well, for Maude wriggled as we held her down. Then I had my turn; and at last she had to run naked three times up and down the dormitory between two lines of girls armed with canes. She was marked all over from her shoulders to her knees, both back and front, for she fell down more than once, and the blows never stopped. She didn't dare tell, however, and left at the end of the term, and so did I.'

'Before the next term began, Juliette's father died, as she told you, and when I heard of it, I got my mother to have her to stay with us, and be taught by my sister's governess. When mother died, and I was married, I still kept her with me as my sweetheart and companion – my old fool of a husband suspected nothing – and here we still are.'

'And she still lets you . . . '

'Whip her? Yes, habit is strong, and she never became a senior with a minion of her own.'

'I rather like that duel idea,' I said. 'I'd like to see one.'

'I dare say you would, but there's no minion to fight for . . . unless . . . ' and she looked at me.

'Unless what?'

'Unless you play the part of the minion; yes, that would do. You be the minion and Juliette and I will fight for you. Come on, Juliette, undress him and perch him up . . . We'll put him on the piano.'

They seized hold of me laughing and I let them strip me; then I stood on the baby grand piano, while they quickly took off their own clothes and got a couple of towels from the bedroom. The account of their school experiences had quite excited me, and I should have made quite a good scarecrow in a Roman garden. There was certainly no *inutile liguum* about me, what there was was *utilissimus* in the highest degree.

They pushed the furniture back so that there was a clear space. 'Ready?' said Muriel. '*En garde*.' They held the towels in their right hands, crouching slightly forward. 'No hitting above the belt,' said Juliette. Muriel answered with a flick which just missed Juliette's right thigh. Quick as lightning Juliette flicked her towel upwards and just caught the brown curls.

'Little cat, that's the worst of teaching other people tricks.' She dodged and feinted and at last, seizing a favourable opportunity, made her towel curl round Juliette's left cheek with a resounding smack.

'Oo,' said Juliette and she clapped her hands to the place.

'First blood to me,' cried Muriel. Juliette said nothing but kept a wary eye on Muriel, lightly swinging the towel to and fro. Muriel feinted here and there and at last made a vicious cut at Juliette, but missed and overreached herself. That was what Juliette was waiting for. As Muriel stretched forward, she brought her towel twice in rapid succession straight up between her legs. Muriel leapt back out of reach and rubbed herself. Then, springing forward, she rained a perfect hail of blows on Juliette, caring nothing for the other's attacks. She parried with her left arm and flicked here, there and everywhere. Her quickness of wrist and eye surprised me. At last two cuts, one after the other, curled quite round between Juliette's cheeks, and as the latter retired, she followed them up with a couple of backhanders, both of which reached between Juliette's legs in front.

'Enough, enough, I give in,' cried Juliette, who was quite out of breath.

'Come on, Cecil, you're mine.' I jumped down. 'Get the cases, Juliette.'

'What,' I said. 'Do you think you're going to whip me?'

'Minions always are whipped . . . Do let me, just this once . . . you can whip me afterwards if you like . . . Besides, this is only a love whipping.'

'No,' I said. 'I tell you what. We'll have a triangular duel. I'll take the two of you on, and whoever gets the first cut home shall give his opponent five cuts. Towels or birches, you can choose your own weapons.'

'Towels for me,' said Muriel, 'they're longer.'

'Birch for me,' said I. 'Now, come on.' I waited for their attack and, as I expected, I easily dodged Juliette and parried Muriel's flick with my birch and, before she could recover, flicked her with the twigs between the legs.

'One; get down on the couch, Muriel.'

She obeyed. 'Not too hard, dear.' I gave her five moderate cuts and she got up.

'Round two,' I said. This time Muriel was not so eager; she kept a wary eye on my birch, so that I could not get her towel entangled in it. Juliette kept me busy flicking here and there. At last I thought I saw an opening and cut at her; I missed and quickly both towels came round me, one on either side. Muriel shouted for joy.

'Come on, Juliette, it's our turn now.' I could not in honour refuse or resist so, with as good a grace as I could, I lay down on the couch and took my five strokes from each of them. Neither of them tried really to hurt me, but made the birch curl wickedly between the cheeks and thighs.

'Round three, now look out Juliette.' She was evidently enjoying it and laughed. Cut and parry followed each other for a minute or two. I dodged this way and that and at last, more by accident, I fancy, than anything else, managed to flick Juliette's thigh. It was only just a graze, but it counted. She received her five strokes and wriggled with pleasure and pain.

We were all of us out of breath with laughing and the exertion. I threw myself into the chair. Muriel collapsed on the couch beside Juliette. The latter put her arms round her and hugged her. They certainly made a lovely picture with their bodies closely entwined. I sat and watched them, but the sight of their naked bottoms proved too much for me, and when I saw Juliette's right hand steal down between Muriel's legs, I got up softly and took the webbing from the case. Muriel's eyes were shut and Juliette lay half on top of her kissing her, her fingers very busy. I reached over them and before they knew what I was doing I had slipped the webbing underneath Muriel and tied them tight together. 'You naughty children,' I said in a gruff voice. 'I'll teach you. You're not at South Parade now,' and down came the birch on Juliette's plump little cheeks. She kicked and squirmed and, turning away to avoid the blows, brought Muriel's bottom into sight as she turned with her. I was not slow to take advantage of this new field of action.

'Mind my knuckles, though,' said Juliette as one cut reached between Muriel's legs.

'They shouldn't be there.' Muriel was now on top, and getting most of the blows. She had also got her hands round Juliette and was busily untying the knot.

She succeeded at last and, jumping up, ran to the case. 'Come on, Juliette, we'll pay him out for that trick.' They both seized birches and made for me. I had my work cut out to avoid them, and we all chased each other round the room slashing and cutting at each other with all our might. Very few of the blows proved effective, and at last, worn out with laughing and the chase, we all fell on the couch helpless. Then a less fierce but no less tiring orgy ensued, ending as usual in the bath. This, by the by, was built on the Roman plan of white marble with steps leading down into about four feet of water. It was a hobby of Muriel's husband, and was quite big enough for three or four people at the same time. It was more like the 'plunge' at a Turkish bath than the ordinary bath of today. The only drawback to it was that it took rather a long time to fill, and the water was never really hot. Still, as Muriel used to say, it was usually hot enough outside in her boudoir and it was good to have something to cool one.

## CHAPTER ELEVEN

## *Juliette's Story – concluded*

'So, Juliette has been with you ever since she left school,' I said to Muriel after we had bathed and Juliette had gone to get tea.

'Yes, she came home to me, as I told you, to work with my young sister, and when I got married to Anthony, I had her with me as my companion and sweetheart, though Anthony never suspected that, and if he had, I shouldn't have cared.'

'But she's not a virgin and yet she never married, did she?'

'Ah! Now that's rather a tragedy, though it has its funny aspects. Would you like to hear about it?'

'Rather!'

'Well, we have long gaps in our family. I've one brother twelve years older than myself and one sister six years younger, and that's all. George was married when I left school and Elsie was quite a child, younger than Juliette. But I had a cousin Harry, just about Juliette's age, two years older, to be exact. He stayed with us one holiday when he was about seventeen. I was, of course, grown up and had "come out". Anthony was beginning to hang round, but he hadn't definitely proposed to me. Juliette and I were sweethearts, then as now, and though we did not share bedrooms, our rooms were next to each other, and you can imagine we spent most of the time in each other's arms. Harry evidently suspected our goings-on, as you will see, and he was as hot as you make 'em himself. But he was very clever. I never had the slightest suspicion, till the discovery. We used to be quite free and easy together. I used to tease him terribly, and delighted in seeing him grow uncomfortable and change his legs and move about on his seat. He told me afterwards that he didn't dare try any games on with me, although he wanted to badly. I was too grown up for him to tackle. But one night he saw Juliette going to my bedroom after we had all gone to bed, and he listened at the door. Our rooms were quite away from Mother's, and, as we never thought about Harry suspecting, we made no attempt to moderate our voices, and our exclamations of pleasure. He stood and listened at the door and heard everything, and I can assure you there was a good deal to hear. Luckily there was no whipping that night, or the sequel might have been different, but you can imagine he heard enough to leave no doubt as to what we were doing. Anyhow, the situation was too much for him, and, as he told me, he played a lone hand by himself on the mat outside and then, growing nervous lest he should be discovered, retreated to bed, where his sleep was not as undisturbed as it might have been.

'Looking back after the denouement, I remember that he looked most intently and meaningly at us the next day, but at the time I paid no attention to it. We played our usual game of hide-and-seek in the twilight in the garden, with the usual kisses for forfeits when caught. He certainly kissed me with more meaning than usual, but nothing more. With Juliette, however, he was much bolder, for she told me that his hand became very venturesome and once even tried, when he caught her, to investigate her most secret charms. Of course, at that time she was wearing shut-up drawers, so he couldn't get much satisfaction. She was very excited when she told me, and by no means as angry with him as I thought she ought to have been. I grew quite angry and jealous and threatened her with a whipping if she let it happen again. She promised she would not, but I determined to watch.

'That night I was prevented from my usual delights with Juliette by the ordinary periodical disability we poor women are cursed with, so Juliette knew it was no good coming to me. I was so angry and jealous, though, about her letting Harry take liberties with her, that I couldn't sleep, and I decided that I would give Juliette a whipping – not severe – but enough to relieve my feelings and to warn her as regards the future. So I got out of bed, took a birch from my trunk, where I always kept one safely locked up, and went to Juliette's room.

'When I got to the door I was thunderstruck at hearing voices. "Oh, don't, Harry, you're hurting me . . . no, don't . . . you can't get in, it's too big . . . use your fingers . . . no . . . no . . . no, I can't bear it . . . you're tearing me in two . . . oh . . . oh." I burst into the room and switched on the light. What a sight met my eyes. I could see nothing of Juliette, except her legs, which were wide apart, with the knees in the air, and between them Harry's back and bare legs, with the pyjamas round his ankles, moving vigorously up and down. Before he had time to stop I rushed to the end and brought the birch as heavily as I could down on his heaving buttocks. "You cad," I cried, "get off, how dare you violate that child?" He sprang off and away and I saw at a glance I was too late. Juliette's legs and mount were all red with blood, the damage had evidently been done. But I was just in time to prevent still worse mischief, for as he stood shamefacedly before me, great jets of his manhood spurted from his arrogant weapon. This was, of course, the first time I had seen a man in this condition, and I was naturally very excited. In fact I felt the bandage I was wearing was soaking with a different fluid from that for which I was wearing it. But I was too mad with anger and jealousy to pay much attention to that at the moment. I went to the door and shut and locked it and then turned to Harry, who was stooping to gather up his pyjamas. Juliette was still lying on her back, but she had turned her head away, covering her face with her hands and sobbing.

' "Now, what have you to say for yourself?" He remained mute. "I shall tell Mother of this the first thing in the morning, but that won't do much good. Juliette's ruined, you've taken her virginity, if you haven't seriously injured her. What reparation can you make? It's absurd to talk about marriage, you are both far too young. You beast, you cad," I raved at him, "how dare you corrupt an innocent girl?" "Not so much of the innocent," he broke in. "I'm sorry I took her maidenhead. I never thought she would have one." "What do you mean?" "Well, I listened at your door last night, and heard what was going on there between you and Juliette, so you see it's no good coming the innocent over me. And what's more, Miss Muriel, if you tell Auntie about me, I'll split on you two."

' "I don't know what you mean," I said, "but anyhow, she wouldn't believe you. We should both deny it, and that wouldn't do you any good. You would be sent home and if I know anything of Uncle Harry, you'll have the finest thrashing you've ever had in your life. Now I'll tell you what I'll do. I don't want any scandal. If you'll submit to be punished by me and promise faithfully not to do that to Juliette again – why, you might have given her a baby if I hadn't come in – and to marry her, if she will have you later, when you are in a position to marry – well, I'll say nothing to Mother. If you refuse, I go to Mother at once." "You punish me? How?" "With this, and a cane I've got. I mayn't be as strong as Uncle Harry, but I'll do my best." "I'm not afraid of you," he laughed, "you can do what you like to me, and as for Juliette, I'll promise both those things." "Very good," I answered, "come here."

'I led him over to some hooks which were on the wall and made him catch hold of two of them. I found Juliette's stockings and tied each wrist as tightly as I could to a hook. His pyjama trousers were still round his ankles, and the short jacket, strained up by the position of his arms, left his bottom well exposed. "Now," I said, "we'll see whether I can do any good," and I rained a volley of blows with the birch all over both cheeks. He stood the punishment stoically, and I grew vicious. I became more deliberate, choosing my spot for the cuts carefully, and at last, one or two proved more efficacious, for he wriggled a bit and said, "Here, that'll do, Muriel."

'I laughed, "Do? I've not begun yet." I noticed that the birch was getting worn-out and, looking about me, saw Juliette's riding whip lying on the chest of drawers. It was a dainty little thing, quite light, but made of whalebone, bound with silk. I put down the birch and picked up the whip. The first cut right across both cheeks was evidently a surprise. He gave an involuntary cry of pain. "Here, what's that you're using?"

'He turned round to look as another cut fell just where the first had fallen. "Here, I say, that's enough." "Enough? Not half; I'll teach you to rape virgins. If I can't repair the injury, I'll make you suffer; your blood shall help to wipe out Juliette's. There, there, there and there. Don't you wish you had chosen Uncle Harry?" He made no attempt now to conceal his pain. "You'll cut me to pieces, you cat. Oh, oh, oh God," as a very vicious cut curled by chance between his plunging, kicking legs and flicked the hanging bag. His cries of pain spurred my energy. I redoubled my blows and his cries of pain and rage changed to sobs and appeals. 'Muriel, please no more; you'll cut me to bits; let me off now; I swear I'll marry Juliette. I'll never touch her again, Muriel, darling, for God's sake; oh, my God, have pity. Mercy, mercy, mercy."

'Juliette had somewhat recovered, and was sitting up watching the scene, frightened but excited. She had never seen such a whipping before. She joined her entreaties to his. "Oh, Muriel, don't hurt him too much. Look, his bottom's bleeding." She came to me and tried to stop me. I cut her across the bottom. "Don't you interfere, your turn will come next. I'll teach you to have a lover." She ran back to the bed, and I turned again to Harry. Certainly I had been severe. I must have given him over fifty cuts and his poor bottom and thighs were a mass of weals. Here and there the skin was cut, and there were little trickles of blood oozing down the skin. I felt just a little frightened, so I put aside the whip and took up the birch again. It had quite a different effect to what I expected. It must have hurt, but after the first few blows, Harry's cries changed in tone. Deep ahs and ohs followed each cut, but he no longer kicked and squirmed, he moved his loins backwards and forwards, just as I had seen him on the bed. I was interested and looked to see what he was doing. To my surprise, his weapon was rampant again and by his plunging he seemed to be trying to swing it up and down; his eyes were half-closed. In my curiosity I reached out my left hand to touch it. I just put my hand round it. "Oh, you darling," he murmured and plunged vigorously. Again the thick jets of life burst from him and he collapsed against the wall, hanging by his wrists.

'I was startled and not a little frightened, so I untied his wrists. He fell on me with his arms round my neck, sobbing and calling me his queen. He slid down on his knees and, bending down, kissed my feet, uttering all the time words of love and homage.

'This attitude completely conquered my anger. I raised him up. "That will do," I said, "we won't think any more about it. You can go to bed. Now, Juliette, for you."

' "You're not going to whip Juliette?" "Certainly I am." "No, you mustn't. It was all my fault. If you think she deserves punishment, punish me again for her. I'll bear hers as well as my own, if I can." He knelt down again and, flinging his arms round my legs, kissed my feet passionately.

'For the first time in my life I realised the ineffable joy of the woman dominant. I delighted in the subjection of Juliette, but she was only a girl and my minion. But here was a man, or at any rate a boy, absolutely subservient to me. I looked down on him as he grovelled before me, gloating over him, and exulting in my power. "Very well, then, Juliette shall escape for the present. You shall bear her punishment, and her humiliation. Take those pyjamas off." He did so. "Now kneel down before me there, and beg my pardon and ask me to whip you." He knelt down humbly. "Forgive me, Muriel," he sobbed. "Go on . . . ask for your punishment . . . ask for it." "Please whip me," he stammered. "Where?" I insisted. He looked up at me. "Wherever you like." "Oh, shall I flog your manhood?" His hand instinctively clasped his sex, protecting the tender parts. "Oh, no, not there." "Where then? On your bottom?" "Yes, on my bottom. See, there it is ready for you." And he bent forward pushing his bottom out, waiting for the strokes. "Kiss my feet, then, and keep still."

'I brought the remnants of the birch straight up and down between his cheeks six times, and at each blow he clasped my legs and kissed my feet ardently. His hands clutched convulsively round my calves, and when I stopped and raised him slightly, he did not let go but slid higher, pulling my nightdress up, until when he stood on his feet he had pulled it right up and held my naked body close to him. Our lips met in a long and passionate kiss. He was still sobbing from the pain; inarticulate words of adoration came from him and his touch was reverent though caressing.

' "Don't touch me there," I said suddenly, as his hand fell from my waist to where the bandage was fixed between my legs. "Why not, my queen of women? I worship every bit of you." "No, you mustn't, you ought not to have seen me like this." But it was no good, I could not stop him. His eager hand dived beneath the bandage and penetrated right into my most secret parts. He had not long to wait. The excitement of flogging him and his adoration had set my whole body on fire, and within a minute I drenched him with my life and love. I leant forward and kissed him frankly and lovingly.

' "You are forgiven, Harry, only remember your promises." "I will remember," he said, as he kissed me again. He then turned to Juliette. "Good-night, Juliette darling, forgive me for my unkindness to you, but you shall be my wife as soon as I can marry you." They kissed lovingly and he turned to go.

' "Don't forget those," I said, pointing to his pyjamas. "If they are found here in the morning, people will ask questions." He smiled, picked them up, and put them on.

'He winched a little as the flannel touched his wounded skin, smiled a little ruefully, kissed us both again, and went away to bed.

'That is how Juliette lost her virginity, Cecil.'

'But what about Harry? What became of him? He has not married Juliette.'

'No, he was drowned while bathing, poor boy, about a year after. How we've missed him. He was a natural masochist. I have never met anyone like him. My husband liked to be ruled, but that was because he was an old man and other pleasures had palled on him, but Harry loved my power over him. I hoped when I met you that you might have taken his place.' She gave a little sigh.

'But the boot is on the other leg,' I laughed.

'Yes,' she sighed, 'I never thought I could submit to the domination of any man, but you have conquered me, Cecil. I am yours utterly, my darling, my king.'

'That's as it should be.'

'I don't know. It's all right for the present, but the future – I'm not a masochist, all my nature tends the other way, and I feel I shall want someone to subdue. Of course, there's Juliette, she's mine utterly, in spite of her revenge the other day. But I want a man – a man – '

'We must see if we can't find you one,' I laughed, 'provided always, of course, he doesn't interfere with my prerogative and privileges.'

'I shall always be yours, darling, no matter who there is.'

# Volume Two

## CHAPTER ONE

## At the Seaside

London was growing very hot. For once in a way England had a summer worthy of the name. But for Muriel, I should have fled from the heat and lack of air of town long before. But the little house in South Molton Street offered far too great attractions to be deserted easily. However, one day when I called there, Muriel showed me a letter and asked me what I thought of it.

It ran as follows:

DEAR MURIEL – The wife and I want to go globe-trotting for about six months or a year but we're in a difficulty about the two girls. Of course they're safe at school most of the year, but the question of their holidays bothers us. Would you be an angel and take charge of them, at any rate for the summer six weeks? You'll find them rather a handful, I'm afraid. The discipline at their school is not so good as it was for you at Clifton, and Gladys thinks they are too old to be corrected as you were, in the good old-fashioned way. But I dare say you will be able to manage them. Anyhow, if you will take them I give you *carte blanche* and will of course pay all bills. Do be a sweet sister and say they can come to you, and let us get out of England. They break up in a fortnight, so there's not much time.

Always your loving brother,

GEORGE

'What do you think of it?' said Muriel.

'Well, what were you going to do this summer?'

'I hardly know; of course, there are lots of people I could stay with, but the girls sound rather alluring, don't you think so? "Rather a handful" – *carte blanche* for me!'

'They'll be damnably in the way. If *they're* about I can't very well be on the premises. How old are they?'

'Young adults, I fancy. But of course you'll be on the premises. You can be a younger brother of my husband's if you like, or anything. The thing to do is to find a nice quiet little place where we can take a cottage or bungalow, quite by itself, where we can do just as we like. I bar all English watering places.'

'I know just the place you want, it's a tiny village called Croyde, in North Devon, just between Ilfracombe and Clovelly. I stayed at Woolacombe one summer – that's just round Baggy Point – and drove over to Croyde. It's perfectly beautiful. And there are two cottages right on the beach with no other house for quite two hundred yards.'

'It certainly sounds lovely; but how can we get to know about the cottages, whether they are to let, and how soon?'

'I'll run down and prospect.'

'Do, there's a good boy, and I will write and tell George I'll take the girls off his hands.'

I went down to Woolacombe next day and found a house agent at Morthoe. By the greatest of good luck, the cottages had fallen vacant suddenly, and I was able to take them for two months. So a week later saw Muriel, Juliette and me surrounded with luggage – the *cases* naturally were not forgotten – on Morthoe station waiting for the 'jingle' and cart to take us and our belongings to Croyde.

We had decided to dispense with servants; the wife of the coastguard was to come in and cook breakfast and dinner, but the rest of the day we were to do for ourselves so as to have perfect freedom.

Muriel had written a 'leading' letter to her brother about the management of her nieces, and his reply was quite explicit:

I give you absolute authority to manage both Gladys and Ethel as you think best. In your own case, I know the strict discipline of Mrs Walter was most advantageous. My wife had no such Spartan training and consequently suffers. But both the girls take after our family, I fancy, and will be all the better for a firm hand.

Muriel's eyes glistened as we read this letter together, and we looked forward to the girls' coming eagerly.

They arrived, the first week in August, having seen their parents off to Hamburg on their way round the world.

Gladys was plump and fair, just budding into womanhood. Her breasts were beginning to swell and the rounded hips gave promise of a most voluptuous figure when fully developed. Ethel was a slight dark girl, straight and lissom, a regular tomboy, and young for her age. They were both very excited at the prospect of a holiday away from father and mother and kissed their aunt and Juliette most affectionately. Me they greeted quite frankly, though Gladys gave me what was suspiciously like 'the glad eye'.

'Now girls,' said Muriel, 'we're going to have a splendid time, this is the land of do-as-you-like, no lessons, no one else to consider, only enjoyment and fun – bathing, lazing, exploring, sailing all day long. Only one thing, we must be punctual at meals, and when bathing we must be careful not to go out too far.'

'Can we bathe now, Auntie?' said Ethel eagerly.

'Not tonight,' said Muriel, 'it's too late, but tomorrow morning early we'll all bathe before breakfast.'

Ethel looked glum. 'Oh, I want to bathe now.'

'No, wait till tomorrow, dear.'

Gladys gave her sister a glance. 'Mother would let me bathe now,' insisted Ethel. 'I *want* to bathe now.'

'Ethel dear, you must do as you are told; don't make me angry with you the first evening. Come, let's play Coon-Can.'

'I want to bathe now.'

'Shut up, Ethel, don't be silly,' said Gladys. But Ethel still looked sulky.

'Ethel,' said Muriel, 'we'd better understand each other straight away; you must do as I tell you, or we shall quarrel. Your father has put me in charge of you and given me complete control of you. Now we can be quite happy all of us together if you are obedient – you won't find me strict in all reasonable things – but you must obey me, otherwise I'm afraid you will have to be treated like a naughty girl and punished, and we don't want punishments on a holiday.'

Though her tone was as soft as honey, there was a gleam of expectancy in her eyes as she glanced at me that boded ill for Miss Ethel in the future.

The latter said no more at the time, and we played cards until we went to bed.

Next morning, I woke early and, putting on my bathing suit, called out to the others. Before long they appeared in mackintoshes and ran down the beach to me in the surf. Muriel and Juliette's figures I knew well. Gladys looked a perfect picture. Her dress revealed every graceful line of her slim young body, and though, as I realised by the quick glance she gave my person, she evidently was not altogether ignorant of the difference of sex, there was still a fresh innocence about her carriage that was more than disquieting to me, clad as I was in a tight varsity costume. Ethel on the other hand simply revelled in her freedom from petticoats. There was no very marked fullness of the breasts as yet, but her legs were beautifully shaped and her plump little bottom filled her bathing suit admirably.

'Oh, Auntie!' she said. 'I do wish I could wear my bathing suit all day, it's so much nicer than those horrid petticoats.'

Muriel laughed.

'For shame,' said Gladys, looking self-consciously at me.

'Do let me, Auntie.'

'Well, perhaps, during the morning on the beach, if no one else is about.'

We romped and swam about in the surf – there is not much chance of real swimming on the North Devon coast – until at last, just as we were about to get out, a big wave caught Gladys unexpectedly, and bowled her right over. Her legs went right up in the air wide apart. The stockinette was semi-transparent now it was soaked through, and I caught a glimpse of all her secret charms, half-concealed, half-revealed by the clinging material. More than that, her struggles underwater, to regain her feet against the undertow, burst the top button of the costume and she appeared with it open nearly to her waist. 'Oh, look at Gladys, showing her titties,' shouted Ethel in high glee. Gladys covered in confusion, with a quick glance at me, ran to the mackintoshes, slipped one on, and flew to the cottage. But she was not quick enough to escape my keen and watchful eye. The bathing dress gaped wide open and, as her sister said, showed both her budding little breasts, firm and plump and round.

In spite of the chill of the water, the blood raced through my veins and I felt my costume growing tighter and tighter as John Thomas asserted his presence in a quite unmistakable manner. Muriel turned to Ethel, 'What did you say?'

'Gladys was showing all her titties!' she laughed.

'How dare you say such a thing, you rude girl!' And before Ethel knew what was happening, Muriel had seized her under one arm and, turning her behind up, gave her several sounding slaps on the tight little bottom.

'Don't you dare say such a thing again.' Ethel was more surprised than hurt, but she was evidently very angry at the ignominious treatment. She wriggled away and darted a vindictive glance at Muriel and ran up the beach shouting out, 'Gladys showed her titties.'

I looked at Muriel. 'This must be settled,' she said to me. 'Juliette, bring Ethel to me when she is dressed. *You* had better keep out of the way for a bit as it's the first time.'

I didn't like this, you may be sure, but thought it wiser to comply, so, went to my room, shaved and dressed leisurely. As I was brushing my hair I heard Muriel's voice lecturing Ethel. I could not quite catch the words, but I heard Ethel say, 'What! Whip me! I've never been whipped in my life! You shan't, I tell you. You shan't.' There were the sounds of a struggle and then, 'You shan't take my drawers down. Gladys, help, help – oh!' This last exclamation was preceded by the sound of a smack. From the sound, I guessed Muriel was using the back of a hairbrush. The smacks went on, so did the cries – angry at first, but soon a note of pain crept in and at last real sobs took their place. Oh, how I longed to be there! I pictured to myself the round little bottom growing pinker and pinker under the blows. I saw in my imagination the little cheeks contract and loosen as the brush fell upon them – the ineffectual struggles – the plunging and heaving of the young body. The cries and sobs kept time with the crisp smacks which fell quicker and even quicker as Muriel warmed to her work. I heard Muriel's voice raised above Ethel's sobs. 'I'll teach you to talk before gentlemen about your sister's titties! How dare you, you saucy little minx! Will you ever be rude again? Will you? Will you? Will you?'

By this time Gladys had evidently come down, for I heard her voice, 'Oh, Auntie!'

'Ethel was very rude just now about you, before Mr Prendergast, and I had to punish her.'

'Yes, I know, I heard her; but isn't she rather big for a whipping? Mother never has whipped us.'

'So I learn from your father. So much the worse. But don't you make any mistake, I was whipped till I was eighteen or nineteen at school. So you see, even you are not too old if you deserve it.'

I did not hear any reply from Gladys and thought it was time I showed myself. I ran downstairs and came into the room as if nothing was happening. Muriel was sitting quite calmly. She had evidently had Ethel across her knee, for her dress had been pulled slightly up and showed one leg nearly to the knee. Gladys was standing just inside the door, looking rather frightened, while Ethel was turned away with her hands over her face, sobbing with anger and pain.

'Hullo! What's up?' I asked quite innocently, as if I knew nothing and had heard nothing.

'Ethel was naughty and I had to punish her.'

'Oho,' I said.

'Yes, she has been properly punished, but I think it's done her good. Come here, Ethel, and kiss me and say you're sorry.'

Ethel didn't move. 'Shall I have to give you some more before Mr Prendergast?'

'Oh no, no.'

'Then come here at once, kiss me and say you are sorry . . . That's better. Now do your drawers up and we'll have breakfast.'

During the meal, Ethel did not dare look at me, but Gladys ever and again cast half-frightened glances at me and at her aunt and at Ethel. It was altogether rather an awkward meal. When it was over, Muriel called Gladys to her and said, 'Perhaps you had better see your father's letters to me about you two,' and she took them from her writing-case. 'There, you see he says you are a handful and that I have *carte blanche* as regards keeping you in order. Now I've told you that I was whipped when I was even older than you, so you know what you may expect if you are naughty.' She gave her a playful smack on her bottom which sent the red flag flying in Gladys's cheeks, kissed her lightly on the lips and let her go.

We bathed again during the morning. It was gloriously hot and we lolled about on the sand still in our bathing costumes. Muriel was careful to show Ethel that with the punishment the fault was wiped out and forgotten. She was perfectly sweet to her and by degrees won her round from her shyness and self-consciousness. After a while she and Juliette and Ethel went scrambling over the low rocks and pools looking for crabs and fishes as the tide went out. Gladys and I were left together lying on the sand.

I saw her looking at me now and then, furtively, and waited. At last she said, 'Uncle Cecil.' We had arranged that she should call me that.

'Well?' I said.

'Uncle Cecil, I want to ask you something.'

'Well?'

'Do you think Auntie meant what she said about being whipped when she was older than me?'

'I'm sure she did.'

'I can't believe it. I'm sure I should die of shame, if I was whipped. When I came in this morning, when Auntie was whipping Ethel, I felt as if I should sink through the floor.'

'Why?'

'Oh, Uncle, she was lying across Auntie's knee and she was all uncovered. All her things were undone.'

I smiled.

'Oh, Uncle, she wouldn't do that to me, surely?'

'I don't suppose she would put you across her knee, you're too big; but I'm quite sure that if you are naughty you'll have to suffer for it – there.' I patted the cheek of her bottom, which I could just reach as she was lying half-turned on her face. She blushed fiery red and rolled over, away from me, showing the lines of her breasts and hips. Her costume, still wet, clung to her and revealed all her form. The pink of her skin showed through, and I could trace the pit of her navel and the swelling of her mount. She noticed my eye roaming all over her and drew her mackintosh round her. I was on fire. I turned towards her. 'Why should you be so afraid and shy of being whipped?' My arm went round her and I drew her towards me; she let herself go and looked shyly yet provokingly at me. 'I'm sure you've nothing to be ashamed of, there's plenty to smack here,' as my hand caressed her bottom.

'Oh don't, Uncle!' My hand moved away and stroked her thigh and at last met the end of her torso and the valley between the thighs. A little sigh escaped her lips, and she edged a little closer to me. 'Oh, Uncle,' she whispered, and she let her head fall on my shoulder.

I gave a quick look round to see that Muriel and the others were out of sight and, finding we were quite alone, pushed my hand between her legs and began to tickle the soft lips which I could feel through her costume. She made no resistance, she even opened her thighs slightly as if she knew what was to come and wanted it. Her face turned up to mine, her lips half-opened and, just as I felt her whole nature give and yield to my caresses, our lips met in a burning kiss. 'Gladys,' I said half-sternly, 'that wasn't the first time! You've been playing naughty games at school; now tell the truth, haven't you?' I made her look at me.

'Yes,' she whispered, 'but that was only with girls; it's the first time with a man. Oh, it was lovely.'

'Well, you had better not let Muriel know of these goings on, or your bottom *will* have to pay for it.'

'Hm, I suppose she's greedy and wants it all for herself; *I* know.' I thought it better to say nothing, especially as I saw the other three coming towards us over the rocks.

'We've got such a funny fish,' shouted Ethel, running towards us. We sat up and waited. Muriel looked keenly at both of us, and as soon as I could I got her away by herself. 'What have you been doing?' she asked.

'Breaking the ice for you,' I answered.

'Mind you don't go breaking anything else,' she said. 'I won't have *that*. If she's a virgin now, she shall leave me the same.'

'That's all right,' I said, 'we only talked about whipping, she's very frightened, but I think it will be possible.

Muriel's eyes gleamed.

'It would be lovely to whip her, wouldn't it?'

'Yes, but I must be there, no more tantalising experiences like this morning.'

'Poor boy, was he unsatisfied then? It's a shame,' and she laughingly seized hold of a certain part of me and squeezed it hard.

'You little devil, I'll pay you for that tonight when the girls are in bed.'

CHAPTER TWO

## *Fun on the Beach*

After dinner, which we had in the middle of the day so that Mrs Tasker, the coastguard's wife, could get away home, it was very hot. I was in flannels, Muriel and Juliette in light linen dresses with nothing much underneath from all appearances, Gladys wore the usual schoolgirl serge skirt and blouse and Ethel a little holland frock with a loose belt. 'What are we going to do this afternoon, Auntie?' she asked.

'I'm going to rest, it's too hot for exertion, but you two can do what you like.'

'May we paddle?'

'Certainly. You'd better go with them, Cecil, and keep them out of mischief, and mind, on no account be late for tea.' She gave me a meaning look as she said this.

'May I take these things off and wear my bathing dress?' said Ethel. 'These are so hot.'

'No, dear, not today. There may be some strangers about.'

'We haven't seen any all the morning. Well, I needn't wear my petticoat, need I?'

Taking silence for consent, she ran upstairs and came down again after a minute or two. 'That's better, come along Gladys and Uncle Cecil.' So we started; the tide was right out and we ran over the wet sand, Ethel careering here, there and everywhere, her skirt as she ran showing every line of her slim young legs. None of us was wearing socks or stockings and her white legs gleamed in the sun. Gladys and I followed more sedately. 'Hurry up, lazybones,' shouted Ethel when she reached the sea, 'it's lovely.' I rolled my trousers up to my knees, and Gladys raised her skirts demurely, holding them tightly round her legs. Ethel, however, took no precautions as regards modesty. She danced and skipped about, jumping up as the waves came in. Naturally her skirt flew up at moments showing the white thighs, but there were no signs of any knickers. At last, in dodging a bigger wave than usual, she lifted her skirt quite high and I realised she had nothing on underneath it. Gladys evidently noticed it too, for she called out, 'Ethel, come here, I want you.'

'What is it?'

'I want to say something to you.' Ethel came to her sister, who whispered something to her.

'Yes, I've taken 'em off,' shouted Ethel in high glee. I saw Gladys blush crimson.

'How can you be so rude, I shall tell Auntie.'

'Tell-tale cat.' Here she ran off again.

'What's the matter?' I asked, though guessed the truth.

'Ethel's taken off all her things. She's got nothing on under her skirt.' She blushed furiously as she spoke; it might have been her own nakedness that was in danger of exposure.

'Well, there's no one to see that matters. And you don't seem to have much on yourself.' I ran my hand over her rounded hips and legs.

'I'm properly covered, at any rate.'

'Even though everything can be seen,' I interjected.

'You *are* naughty, Uncle Cecil.'

We had passed beyond the low ridge of rocks and had reached a little cove, out of sight of the cottage, with no outlet inland. At high tide the sea came right up to the cliff, but now with the tide out a lovely smooth stretch of sand was growing dry and hot in the sun. I flung myself upon it and took out a pipe. Gladys sat down beside me, clasping her knees with both hands. Ethel was still dancing around. I closed my eyes in perfect content, thinking how I could lead Gladys on to the subject which Muriel and I had at heart, and yet not shock her too much. *Festina lente* ran through my mind, but for the life of me I didn't know how to begin.

My reverie was startled by the sound of a struggle quite near. 'Don't Ethel, you little wretch,' said Gladys. I opened my eyes just in time to see

Ethel seize Gladys's shoulders from behind and pull her back. Naturally she rolled right on to her back with her legs in the air. She only had on a pair of thin cotton bloomers. She grabbed hold of Ethel's leg and brought her down on top of her. For a minute there was a whirl of legs and bodies. Ethel's frock flew right up, showing all her legs and body right up to her waist. Shrieks of delight came from her, as Gladys wrestled with her and tickled her. There was no attempt or pretence to hide her nakedness. She kicked and flung her legs apart as she strove to escape from her sister's grasp. At last she managed to get on top for a moment, showing to my enraptured gaze the plump little cheeks. I couldn't resist the temptation, and brought my open hand down on them with a loud smack. 'Who did that?' she shouted, and wrenched herself away from Gladys and flung herself on to me. In a minute we were all three in a kicking, tangled *mêlée*. My hands were very busy wandering everywhere. Gladys and Ethel shrieked with laughter as I tickled them under the arms, in the ribs, just by the hip bones and – whenever I got a chance – between their legs. I was careful, however, not to make it too obvious that I was aiming there particularly. They retaliated on me, joining forces against the common enemy. We rolled about, struggling and laughing. Suddenly I felt the top button of my trousers go. I was, of course, wearing no braces, and knew what would happen in a short time. My shirt worked up and at last Ethel discovered a small triangle of bare skin at the side by the waist. She redoubled her efforts at this particular point. The gap became bigger and she shrieked with glee as her hand explored round my waist under the loose canvas shirt. I made no attempt to stop her but groped all over her under her skirt, and openly tickled Gladys's legs and stomach with my other hand as she lay half under me. They both were carried away by the excitement. At last when my fingers reached and fastened on Ethel's narrow little slit she giggled and squirmed. 'You rude thing, if you tickle me there, I'll tickle *you* there.' Her little hand dived easily down and found what was evidently a surprise to her. She gave a gasp of astonishment as she felt her fingers clasping my rampant engine. 'Oh, whatever's that?' I ripped open my fly and out sprang his Lordship in magnificent state. 'Oh, what a funny thing. Gladys, look!'

Gladys, who was going off into an ecstasy under my skilful fingers, raised herself and, seeing what was exposed, buried her face on my shoulder. 'Look, Gladys, look; isn't it funny?' as she played with it. This was too much for John's self-control. He swelled and throbbed and sputtered. 'Oh, the nasty thing,' said Ethel, drawing her wet hand away. 'What's it doing?'

'You little devil,' I said in mock anger, 'I'll teach you,' and I laid her across my knee, turned up her skirt and spanked her, not hard but caressingly. She laughed and shouted and wriggled, and tried to pull down her skirt. Gladys sat up and tried to get her away from me. I let her go but kept hold of Gladys herself, and in a minute she was occupying her sister's position; my nimble fingers undid the bloomers and pulled them down, and quick smacks fell on the soft rounded cheeks. 'Oh, Uncle!' she exclaimed in a shy shocked tone, but she made no real effort to get away. She lay right across my knees, or rather lap, and felt my still-aggressive old man pressing against her smooth little belly. She wriggled and squirmed and at last I felt my hand bedewed with the warm creamy flow of her passion.

Ethel stood looking on laughing. 'Who's a rude girl now?' she jeered. 'What's the good of wearing drawers if they get taken down? Nobody can take mine down, I've got none to take.' In her excited precocity she held up her skirt round her waist and danced about showing all her nakedness.

Gladys got up. 'Ethel, for shame!' Ethel rushed to her sister. The force of her attack brought Gladys down again and I saw Ethel's hand go straight up her sister's clothes and begin to probe and feel her most secret parts. 'Oh, you've come already!' she said to my surprise, for I didn't suppose she knew as much. 'I haven't. Do it to me.'

'Ethel, be quiet, with Uncle Cecil here.'

'No I won't.'

'Uncle Cecil make her stop. Smack her, make her get up.'

I didn't disobey, and my smacks grew harder.

'That's enough, that hurts,' said Ethel. 'I don't want two whippings in one day, my bottom's still sore from Auntie.' She got up rubbing her little bottom with both hands. 'It *does* smart.'

'It'll smart still more if your auntie finds out you've come out dressed like that.'

'Oh, I'll run upstairs when I get home and put my knickers on, before she finds out. Ooh,' she giggled, 'I wonder what she'd say if she knew what we'd been doing this afternoon.'

'She'd make us all smart, I expect,' I said.

'Not you, she couldn't whip you, you wouldn't let her.'

'Well, I should probably have to go away, and she'd whip both of you.'

'Then she mustn't know, must she Gladys! Uncle Cecil mustn't go away.'

'No,' said Gladys. And they both flung their arms round my neck and kissed me. I pressed them both in my arms.

'Come on, girls,' I said to them, 'it's getting late. We must get home to tea!' I did my trousers up and Gladys fastened her bloomers.

'Wait a minute,' said Ethel. 'I want to go somewhere.' She ran behind a low rock and squatted down. We could hear the hissing of the stream against the rock and saw it trickle round, down the sloping sand.

'Oh, isn't she rude?' said Gladys, blushing.

'Come along.' We hurried down the beach and Ethel ran after us and caught us up. The tide had turned and was running; when we got to the barrier of rocks which separated this cove from Croyde, we had to wade. My height enabled me to get through fairly well. I could stretch from rock to rock, but Gladys and Ethel found it much more difficult. They both lifted their skirts around their waists, but Gladys's bloomers got very wet, and once

Ethel slipped and, in trying to save herself, let her skirt go and consequently was soaked to the skin. 'That's done it,' she said as she scrambled out. 'Just my luck.' Her wet skirt clung to her legs, showing clearly that she had nothing on underneath. Gladys noticed it too.

'You'd better go up and change quickly,' she said, 'before Auntie sees you. She can't help seeing you've only got a skirt on.'

We hurried on, hoping to escape Muriel's keen eyes. But she was waiting at the door, watch in hand. 'Ten minute late,' she said as we came up. 'This won't do. I won't have meals kept waiting . . . Why, whatever have you been doing? . . . Come here' – to Ethel – 'you're wringing wet, go and change at once.' Ethel started to go quickly; the wet skirt clung to her. Muriel stopped her. 'Stop a moment,' she put her hand on her hip and then under her skirt. 'Why, where are your clothes?'

'I didn't wear any, Auntie, it was so hot.'

'What!' said Muriel, working herself up into a rage. 'You disgusting, rude little girl. Do you mean to tell me you dared to go out with your uncle with nothing on under your skirt? Gladys, how dared you let her?'

'I didn't know, Auntie, until we got down to the sea.'

'Well, why didn't you send her back? I'd have given her a good whipping, and made her dress properly. Now – you're just as bad as she is. I'm surprised at you, a great girl of your age. Go upstairs both of you and change. I'm very angry with you. I hope, by the by, *you* are more decently dressed than your sister.'

'Oh yes, Auntie.'

'Come here, and let me see.' She caught hold of her and pulled her skirt up in spite of Gladys's protests. 'Hm, that's something in your favour, but it won't altogether save your bottom.' Gladys started but did not say anything, and the two girls went indoors.

Muriel turned to me with eager eyes. 'Well!' she said. 'Everything is going on splendidly.' I whispered and told her all that had happened. She gloated over the story. 'Oh, won't I whip them!'

'You can't do *that*,' I said. 'You are not supposed to know. If they suspect for a moment that I told you, I should lose their confidence. They must never guess, at any rate not yet a while, that we are in league together. No, what must happen is something like this. You whip them tonight for Ethel's going without drawers. I can't be there, damn it, but I will listen outside the door, then when you've all gone to bed I will go into them and condole with them. You can come in and find us and . . . '

'And I whip you all three!' said Muriel eagerly.

'Yes, I suppose I shall have to go through it,' I smiled. 'But it will be worth it for once. I owe you a whipping already, you know, so we shall be quits before the night's out . . . Look here, when you find us you must order me to go away at first, leave the place, etc., and then relent and offer me the choice of a whipping, see?'

'Right you are,' she answered, 'and God help your bottom if you choose it; I must make the most of my chances these days. Come on into tea and we'll tell Juliette.'

'You had better not be too severe with them the first whipping,' I said. 'Wait for the second whipping for that. Go slow.'

'You leave it to me,' she smiled back. 'I won't tire myself out; I shall have your bottom to look forward to, and shall want some strength left for that. Oh, what a glorious night it will be!'

## CHAPTER THREE

# *The Sequel*

Tea was rather a quiet meal. There was an air of nervous constraint over all of us. Ethel wore a look of rather nervous defiance, darting ever and anon mutinous glances at Muriel. Gladys was evidently very anxious, and timidly looked, now at me, now at Muriel, as if trying to read what was in store for her, in her aunt's eyes. The latter preserved a distant demeanour which amused me considerably. I knew she was eager to get to work, and whenever she met my eye, I saw a gleam in hers which was instantly repressed when she found Gladys looking at her. The silence became oppressive and evidently got on Gladys's nerves. She seemed to have lost all appetite, her food seemed to choke her. Her face alternately flushed and paled. Muriel noticed her nervousness and pressed food on her. But she shook her head and managed to answer, 'No thank you, Auntie.'

'Come, don't be silly, Gladys; even if you have been naughty, I don't want you to starve as a punishment; my methods are quite different from that,' she added maliciously. This hint was too much for the girl; she buried her face in her hands and sobbed aloud. 'What's the matter, you silly baby,' said Muriel, getting up and putting her arm around her.

'Oh, Auntie, I'm frightened.'

'There's nothing to be frightened about.'

'But you're going to – to –'

'What?'

'To whip me,' she stammered.

'Of course I am; you've been very naughty, and I shouldn't be doing my duty if I didn't correct you. But you're surely not frightened at the idea of a whipping, are you? A big girl like you.'

'It's the shame of it, I've never been whipped and it sounds so awful.'

'Nonsense, don't be silly. You'll make me really very angry if you talk like that. Perhaps we'd better not wait till bedtime, as I had intended, but get it over at once. Then you can go to bed and by today morning we shall all have forgotten all about it. Cecil, if you've finished your tea, perhaps you wouldn't mind going out for half an hour.'

I got up at once, and said good-night to the two girls.

Ethel still looked mutinous but said nothing; Gladys clung to me for a moment. I whispered, 'Courage, it will soon be over,' and went out of the cottage but, as may be imagined, did not go far away.

I gave Muriel about three minutes for her preparations and then crept back to the open window. The blind was down so I could listen quite safely without being seen. It was exasperating not to be able to see, but that pleasure I promised myself before long. Juliette had evidently fetched the cases down, for Muriel was beginning to lecture Ethel. 'Now Ethel, come here and stand before me. You know what I am going to whip you for. For disgraceful indecency. You dared to go out with your sister and uncle with practically nothing on. From the state of your clothes when you came back, you must have been in the water up to your waist; so you must have exposed all your nakedness, for your skirt must have been lifted up by the waves. Wasn't that so?' Ethel evidently wouldn't answer. 'Wasn't it so, Gladys?'

'Yes, Auntie.'

'Ah well, you evidently don't mind showing those parts which modesty should make you careful to conceal, so you can pretend to no shame now. Take your drawers off and come here . . . Will you do as I tell you? Take them off at once.'

'I won't.'

'Oh won't you? Well, so much the worse for you. Juliette, take them off and bring her to me.'

There were the sounds of a scuffle and I heard Ethel's voice, 'Gladys, don't let them, save me.'

'If you do, Gladys, it will be the worse for you when your turn comes.' Gladys evidently thought discretion the better part of valour, for I heard Ethel cry out almost at once, 'You shan't, I won't be whipped, I won't, I won't.'

'Take them right off,' said Muriel. 'Now hold her legs . . . Now, Ethel, you see it's no use resisting; the more you struggle the worse will be the whipping. I'm sorry to have to do this the first day you are here, but you must be taught not to show this naughty little bottom to gentlemen. It is only meant to be seen when it deserves to be whipped – whipped – whipped.' From the sound of the smacks, Muriel was evidently spanking her with her hand. Ethel made no sound. The smacks became quicker and evidently hurt Muriel as well as Ethel, for I heard her say, 'Juliette, give me that little cane.' The first cut brought a little shriek from Ethel. 'Ah, I thought that would prove more effective. Now, you naughty little girl, will you – will you – will you show your nakedness to your uncle again? Will you? Will you? Answer me when I ask you.'

'Oh, Auntie, don't, don't. I can't bear it, don't, don't.'

'Take your hand away and answer me. Will you be good and modest in the future? Will you? Will you?'

'Oh yes, yes, please stop. I *will* be good, oh don't whip me any more, don't, don't.'

'This naughty bottom must be taught the danger of being seen. There, there, there.'

'Oh, Auntie, I *will* be good, oh let me go, Auntie, please. I *will* be good. Oh! oh! oh!' These last three cries followed three particularly cutting strokes, which evidently were the crowning mercy.

'There, that will do, I think, for this time, and I hope it will do you good. Now stand up and put your drawers on and go to bed. Say good-night to Juliette and me. Kiss me; there now, we won't think any more about it.' I heard Ethel's sobs and the sound of a kiss. 'You'll be a good girl, now?'

'Yes, Auntie.'

'That's right. Good-night, dear.' I heard the door close and the steps go upstairs; a light appeared in the bedroom window.

I heard Muriel's voice again. 'Now, Gladys, for you. You've seen me whip Ethel for being naughty, and though you were not quite so much at fault as she was, still you were naughty. Why didn't you send Ethel back to dress properly? You are quite old enough to know better. I should have been ashamed myself to have let my sister show herself like that to a gentleman. What have you to say for yourself?'

'I'm sorry, Auntie, I didn't think.'

'No, quite so; well, you must be taught to think . . . Ah, that will do. Bend over the end of that couch. Turn your skirt up first.'

'Oh, Auntie, I don't like to.'

'I dare say you don't, but you must . . . Higher than that . . . oh, I didn't know you wore those . . . undo them.'

'Oh, Auntie, I can't, it's so shameful, let me keep my bloomers on, whip me over them.'

'Don't be silly, Gladys. Juliette, undo those knickers.'

'Oh, Auntie, please, please . . . '

She evidently had cast herself at Muriel's feet, for I heard the latter say, 'Get up at once, don't kneel like that, but do as I tell you or you'll make me more angry. Juliette, lift her up and bend her over the couch.' Whack! I heard the first cut of the cane fall across the firm flesh. If Ethel's whipping had excited me, my feelings at this point may be imagined. My imagination was on fire, I cursed my luck at not being able to be present; in my mind I saw the dainty bottom and thighs laid bare with the flap of the knickers hanging down. I could barely restrain my feelings; suddenly it occurred to me that the couch was against the wall immediately opposite the window; if I lifted the blind or pulled it aside, I ought to be able to see something. No sooner thought than done. The cuts followed each other methodically.

Muriel was not, as usual, interpolating remarks to her victim, whose sobs and cries for mercy were the only other sound to be heard. I carefully pulled the edge of the blind away from the window and, to my joy, found that the scene was being played right before me. There was poor Gladys, held down by Juliette, her lovely moons facing me. The cuts had not been too hard, for scarcely any marks showed. Here and there a dull pink line appeared, but Muriel had evidently remembered our conversation. But now the whipping was evidently coming to an end; quicker and quicker came the cuts, more and more imploring the cries. 'Oh, Auntie, spare me, spare me, mercy, mercy; oh, I can't bear any more, oh, Auntie, don't.'

'Don't kick like that, or you will get more. These are the last five – one – two – three – four – five . . . let her get up, Juliette.' Juliette took her hand away from Gladys's back, but the latter still lay there sobbing, and twisting her poor wounded cheeks and legs.

'You can get up, dear, it's all over. Now do your things up, kiss me, and go to bed.'

Gladys obeyed and with trembling hands tried to do up her knickers, but she was shaking so with sobs that she could not do it.

'There, dear, there, it's all over, I'm sorry I had to do it, but you won't bear me any malice, I'm sure, and you'll thank me in after-life, I know. Come, I've forgiven your fault, kiss and be friends.' She took the shrinking girl in her arms and petted her. Gladys flung her arms round her neck and buried her face on her shoulder.

'Oh, Auntie, it's the shame, the shame; the pain was bad enough, but, oh, the shame!'

'Silly little baby, what if Uncle Cecil had been present?'

'Oh don't.'

'Well, if you are very naughty, I shall know how to punish you, so don't give me any excuse. Now run along to bed and sleep well; I expect Uncle Cecil is tired of waiting about.'

'Oh, you don't think he heard, do you?' She cast a hurried, frightened look at the door and the window, but I dropped the blind just in time.

'No, silly,' said Muriel. 'Run along to bed. Shall I tell him he may come and say good-night to you? Or would you rather he didn't see you tonight?'

'I think I'd like to say good-night, but in the dark, please.'

'All right, baby, I'll tell him; now run along.' I heard a long kiss, and then after a minute, the front door opened, a shaft of light shone out, and Muriel whispered, 'You can come in.' I was surprised, for I didn't know she knew I was so near. I must have shown this on my face, for when I came in she said, 'You naughty boy, I saw the blind move. Come along in; I want you.'

# CHAPTER FOUR

## *Enlightenment*

I was on fire. 'Wasn't it lovely?' said Muriel as I came into the room, and she flung herself in my arms. 'How much did you see?'

'Only Gladys. I didn't think of the blind in time for Ethel. Perhaps it's as well, for Gladys might have noticed me.'

'Never mind; next time there won't be any need for concealment, I fancy, if things go right. There won't be any difficulty about Ethel, I'm sure; she's ready for anything, but Gladys is more modest by nature. As you heard, it's the shame with her more than the pain.'

'We'll see what happens later tonight,' I said. 'I heard I was to say good-night. Give me half an hour and then you can come in and do what you like.'

'But it's too early for that yet; they'd think it funny if we went to bed so early. Besides we both want you here, and I'm sure you want us.' Her cunning hand sought my sex at once, which she found quite eager.

'One moment, that reminds me; you took that liberty once before with me today and I promised to whip you for it; come along, get ready.'

She pouted. 'Well, only a little one, I don't really deserve it; look at the good time I'm giving you, and I'm not at all jealous . . . still, I love you, darling, and you are going to let me whip you tonight, aren't you? . . . So come along, Juliette, my lord shall have his slaves to wait on him.' She began to undress and Juliette imitated her. I sat and watched them strip with gloating eyes. When they were both naked to their stockings, I took a birch, and, telling Juliette to hold Muriel, I began to whip the latter's plump cheeks. I did not want to hurt her, so I simply tickled her behind with the twigs, letting them curl here and there between the cheeks and legs. Now and then I gave a more vicious cut than usual, which provoked little hissing sighs from Muriel, but I did not set out to make her cry out, for we did not want the girls to hear. Still, the continual irritation of the blows fired her already heated blood and at last she began to plunge and heave, opening and contracting her legs. 'Harder, darling, harder, that's it – just between the legs; now, just between the cheeks . . . harder, now, now, now!' I followed her behests, and my eyes were greeted with visible proof of the pleasure she received. She disengaged herself from Juliette and, turning round, undid my trousers and, taking out the jewel she coveted, knelt down and began to devour it with kisses.

'Would you like a whipping too, Juliette?'

'You know I would; I love you whipping me, make me come too!'

'Bend over Muriel's back then. Muriel, get on your hands and knees.'

I sat down on a chair, so that Muriel could reach me kneeling between my legs. Juliette bent down across her naked back with her face towards my left hand, so that her bottom was just at the right angle for the rod. I plied it carefully and daintily, Muriel's tongue kept busy, the final paroxysm approached both for Juliette and myself, and as the supreme throbs shook my whole being, I succeeded in consummating Juliette's happiness as well. To make sure, I placed my fingers where the rod had caressed and was welcomed with tender contractions of the lips, and a copious flood of love.

'Now I'll go and wash and we'll have supper. You needn't dress if you don't want to.' I went to the door and turned the handle. As I was opening it, I heard the light pattering of feet up the stairs. I was just going to call the others, but thought better of it. They had noticed nothing, but were busy gathering up their clothes. I would keep that knowledge to myself, I thought; so I said nothing but went up to my room, washed, and came down again as if nothing had happened. We had supper and soon after we went to bed. Muriel's last words to me were: 'Now mind, there must be no taking of maidenheads. That is sacred. Anything else you like, and I will give you half an hour.'

I went to my room and undressed, and then in my pyjamas I went softly to the girls' room. My bedroom was really in the other cottage, but a 'pass-door' had been knocked through the party wall, both upstairs and down, so that the two cottages had become one house. I opened their door.

'Who's there?'

'May I come in? Muriel said you wanted me to say good-night to you.'

'Oh yes, come in, Uncle Cecil!'

I sat down on the chair by the side of the bed. A rising moon made the room not quite dark. I could see faintly the girlish faces under the bed-clothes. I bent down and kissed the soft faces. Gladys's cheeks were still wet with tears, but Ethel's skin was burning. Her eyes shone bright in the gloom. 'Well, you poor babies, was it so very terrible?'

'Oh, Uncle, it was awful!' said Gladys, flinging her arms around me. I petted and consoled her and, slipping my hand under the clothes, stroked her still-burning bottom. She made no resistance, but snuggled closer to me. 'Here, that's not fair!' said Ethel, 'you've got him all, Gladys. Uncle Cecil, get in between us – you don't mind, Gladys, do you? I want him just as badly as you do, I got a much worse whipping than you.'

'Did you though?'

'Yes, look!' and she jumped out of bed and, in spite of Gladys's whispered remonstrance, lit the candle; then, pulling up her nightdress, she showed her little behind all scored with red. 'Gladys hasn't got half so many marks.' Before her sister could stop her, she pulled the clothes down and showed all her slim young form. Gladys uttered a little protest and buried her face in my lap. I gazed in rapture at the delicate curves. She was beautifully moulded. Just a few silky tendrils showed themselves on her virgin mount, but everywhere else the satin skin shone white and unblemished. The cheeks were slightly marked but nothing to speak of. Muriel, as I knew, had restrained herself. I couldn't resist it; I bent down and kissed both lovely cheeks. Instantaneously a pink flood spread over the skin – a beautiful blush. 'Oh, kiss mine too, and make it well,' whispered Ethel, flinging herself face downwards on my lap. I lifted the little nightdress and did as she asked. 'Darling Uncle Cecil, now lie down between us, and cuddle us.' I took her at her word, Gladys raising no objection. They snuggled up close to me, twining their arms round my neck and smothering my face with their sweet innocent kisses.

Ethel's entire body was burning hot. She was evidently of a much more passionate nature than her sister. It was more than flesh and blood could stand. My hands crept down until I found what I wanted – on my right the soft silky tendrils of Gladys's little pouting mount, and on my left the smooth tight lips of Ethel's narrow little pussy. The former took the caress quite discreetly. She sighed softly, but except for opening her thighs, did not show by any movement that she noticed my boldness. Ethel on the other hand clasped me tighter, spread her legs wide apart so that her left leg lay right over me. She even whispered in my ear, 'Oh, I love to feel your hand there; try and make me come, I never have yet. The girls at school have not been able to. Do try, Uncle.' I certainly couldn't resist the request and while Gladys's sighs came quicker and quicker and her soft thighs contracted nervously, Ethel suddenly said, 'Oh, something's going to happen, I feel so funny . . . tickle me harder, Uncle darling, oh . . . oh . . . ah.' She wriggled and twisted, and at last fell flat on me and I felt my fingers wet with her first sweet tribute to Venus. 'Oh, Uncle, Uncle, how lovely, how lovely!' I pressed my lips on hers in a long passionate kiss and, taking Gladys's hand, put it inside my pyjamas. She gave a little gasp when she found what I wanted her to find, but held it gently and caressingly.

'Uncle!' said Ethel suddenly, 'I want to ask you something. What were you doing downstairs, just before supper?'

'Oh, it was *you* I heard run upstairs, was it?'

'Yes, I thought I heard somebody being whipped, and crept down. Gladys was too frightened to, but I wanted to know, so I crept down and tried to peep through the keyhole.'

'Well, what did you see?'

'Nothing, the key was in the lock, but I'm sure somebody was being whipped, though it didn't sound like a cane. What was it?'

'I'll tell you tomorrow; I must go to bed now, or your auntie will be angry; you must go to sleep. Kiss me good-night, both of you.' I took them both in my arms and our lips met in a long loving embrace. We were still holding each other tightly when, as I was expecting, the door opened and Muriel and Juliette appeared with candles in their hands.

'What's the meaning of this?' she said, as she put the candles down on the chest of drawers.

'I was only saying good-night.'

'Indeed!' She came to the bed and before either of the girls could stop her – I, of course, made no attempt at resistance – pulled all the bedclothes off and laid bare all our naked bodies. Gladys's and Ethel's nightdresses were right up under their arms, my pyjama trousers were halfway down my thighs. At the sound of her aunt's voice Gladys had hidden her face in my shoulder and lay silent and trembling; Ethel had sat up with a start and faced Muriel, looking at her, half-boldly, half-nervously.

'I'm afraid you've caught us fairly, Muriel,' I said.

'Caught you fairly! Yes, and you'll catch it fairly, all of you. What have you done to these two? If it's anything irreparable you shall pay for it.'

'Oh no, there's no harm done.'

'I'll see for myself. Turn over, Gladys.' She pulled the girl's legs apart and pretended to investigate, then did the same for Ethel. 'Hm, you seem to have stopped in time, but you have evidently been grossly indecent. Juliette, fetch the cases quickly. I must whip these indecent games out of these girls' bottoms. As for you' – turning to me – 'I don't quite know how to treat you. If I treated you as the man you are, I should send you away at once, but that would probably make a scandal; if I treat you as a boy . . . '

Ethel broke in, 'Oh, don't send Uncle Cecil away, Auntie. It will be horrid without him.'

'You be quiet, Miss, if you want anything left of your bottom.'

'Treat me as you do them,' I said. 'I won't resist; and you see there is no real harm done.'

Muriel pretended to hesitate. Ethel whispered to me, 'But Auntie's going to whip us; do you mean you'll let her whip you?' I nodded. 'Oh, you *are* kind; I shan't mind being whipped so much if you are there and are being whipped too.'

Juliette had brought back the cases by this time.

'Get out of bed, all three of you,' ordered Muriel, 'and stand by the side with your backs to me. Gladys, you here at the top; Cecil, you next; and you, Ethel, here. Now bend forward as far as you can. Juliette, turn up those nightdresses.' As Juliette took hold of Gladys's nightdress, I felt a tremor run through her body and her hand sought and found mine. I held it tightly during all the punishment. Since Muriel's entrance, she had not uttered a word. Ethel did not wait for Juliette's help; she pulled her own nightdress right up to her armpits and bent forward. 'Is that right, Auntie?' she had the temerity to say.

'You seem in a great hurry,' said Muriel. 'You won't be quite so eager before it's over.'

'If I've got to be whipped, I've got to be whipped,' said Ethel philosophically. 'The sooner we begin the better. Ow! I didn't know you were ready,' as Muriel's hand fell with a resounding smack on her bottom.

Then this threefold whipping began. Muriel admitted afterwards to me, it was the finest time she had ever had. She used the back of a hairbrush first, and then when she had reddened our cheeks enough to suit her, she took the birch. When the first cut from this fell on Gladys, she gave a little cry – the first sound she had uttered – and clutched my hand convulsively. Ethel looked up at the noise just as I received my dose. 'Oh, so that was it,' I heard her say to herself. 'Oh! Oh!' she cried out loud as her bottom felt for the first time the tingling twigs. She wriggled and squirmed, and tried to cover her cheeks with her hands.

'Juliette, tie Ethel's hands together, or better still, Cecil, you hold them.'

'Better not resist,' I whispered to Ethel.

'I don't mind with you here,' she whispered back. 'I know now; golly! but it does hurt!'

'One, two, three,' the blows fell rhythmetically on each of our devoted behinds. To me, of course, the whipping was not half as severe as the others I had received at Muriel's hands. Besides, the thought of those two young bottoms, one on either side of me, as naked as my own, fired my imagination and whetted my desires. I could feel Gladys's hand clutch mine convulsively every time a blow fell, sobs shook her whole body, but shame seemed to have paralysed her entirely and she lay practically motionless, accepting her punishment in a kind of dull stupor. Ethel, on the other hand, twisted and wriggled and cried out with the pain of each blow. Shame seemed to play but a small part with her.

But the birch was becoming worn-out, and Muriel was evidently tiring. 'We must finish,' she said. 'Stand up.' We obeyed her. 'Juliette, take Ethel on your back, and Cecil, you take Gladys. Take their legs under your arms.' Gladys shivered with apprehension as she clasped her arms round my neck, and Muriel lifted each leg under my arms.

'Haven't we had enough?' said Ethel. 'I'm sure my bottom's cut to pieces. You *are* cruel, Auntie!'

'Be quiet,' said Muriel. I had thought she was going to use the cane, or a fresh birch, but from the sound of the first blow on Gladys, followed quickly by one on my own loins, I realised it was the whip of knotted cords that she had chosen. The first cut curled right round between Gladys's legs, which were stretched wide apart. She shrieked in surprise and pain. 'Oh, Auntie, please, not there . . . I can't bear that . . . oh mercy, mercy.' She tried to free her legs, but I held them tightly.

'Ah, I thought you would find your tongue before I had done with you. Yes, I thought so,' as another cut fell, producing a still more piercing cry. 'The whip isn't quite so nice as Uncle Cecil's fingers, I expect, but it's better for you . . . Now, Miss Ethel, how do *you* like it?'

She turned to the sister and the little lashes curled wickedly in between the slim legs. 'Oh, you beast, you cat!' screamed Ethel. 'Oh, oh, oh, you'll kill me, let me go.' She twisted and writhed so violently that she managed to get one leg free from Juliette's grasp and stood down on it – the other leg was still caught up – hopping about to avoid the blows.

'Careful, Muriel,' I whispered.

'It's not fair to whip one there,' sobbed Ethel. '*You* wouldn't like it. Ooh! You've made me bleed!' as she looked at her hand, which she had pressed to the injured part.

'Let her go, Juliette, let me see.' She drew the angry, shrinking girl to her and placed her finger tenderly between her legs. The lash had just cut the skin of one of the tender lips. 'I'm sorry, I didn't mean to do that, dear. It's not much. Juliette, get some ointment, we mustn't spoil the pretty little jewel. There, baby, there, Auntie is sorry, let me make it well.' She drew Ethel on to her knee, and went on caressing the tender slit. Under her clever, cunning fingers the girl let herself go and suddenly flung her arms round Muriel's neck and kissed her, while I saw her little bottom wriggle and the thighs contract and imprison Muriel's hand.

'There, is that better?'

'Ye–es, but that was what Uncle Cecil did, and you whipped us for it. You ought to be whipped too.'

'Uncle and I are different, you naughty creature.'

'Of course you are, I know that . . . '

'What are you doing – who told you, you might put your hand there?'

While this had been going on I had lifted Gladys on to the bed and laid her tenderly down. She clung to me and kissed me between her sobs. She had carefully pulled her nightdress down and I respected her wishes and kept my hand from wandering. When I heard Muriel say those last words, I looked round just in time to see Ethel's hand disappear in the folds of Muriel's dressing-gown. Muriel caught my eye. 'Here's a naughty girl,' she said to me. 'What is one to do with her? . . . Ethel, Ethel, don't. Oh, you little devil, who taught you to do that?'

'Gladys and the other girls at school; they say my fingers are nicer than anyone's, are they?' I saw the busy arm working. Muriel was fast becoming beside herself with passion. Ethel was taking her back to her schooldays. Her eyes half-closed, the pupils were turned right up. She lay back panting. I was in agony. I dared not do what I wanted to Gladys, for if I began I knew not where I should end, and I had promised Muriel to respect her virginity and intended to keep my promise. In despair I took Gladys's hand and placed it round my eager, swollen engine. Then taking her by the wrist I moved it up and down. She opened her eyes when she felt John Thomas in her hand and smiled lovingly at me. Then she pulled up her nightdress, blushing most adorably, and, taking my hand from her wrist, placed it on her mount. She went on working her own hand, however, and I felt the supreme moment approaching.

At this moment Juliette came back. 'I can't find the ointment, Muriel . . . ' she began. 'Why, here's a happy party! But where do I come in?'

'Juliette,' I gasped, 'come here, I've got something for you. Quick, quick . . . ' She ran to me and, kneeling down, was just in time to receive all the force of my pent-up passion.

CHAPTER FIVE

# *An Objectionable Bathing Costume*

The next morning I woke quite early, about seven o'clock. The sun had climbed over the hills behind Croyde. I put on my bathing suit and a dressing-gown and went to call the others. I went into the girls' room first and found them fast asleep in each other's arms. Gladys's nightdress was undone, and Ethel's dark head rested on her sister's breast. They made a lovely picture. I very gently pulled the clothes down and saw that each had her hand on the other's sex. I bent down and kissed them. Ethel opened her eyes, saw me, and jumped out of bed to throw herself into my arms. Gladys started and, half-awake, said, 'Oh, no more whipping, please, Auntie!' Then she saw me, pulled her nightdress down, and held out her arms, smiling up at me. 'Oh, it's you, Uncle Cecil, I was afraid . . . ' She did not finish the sentence.

'Come out and bathe, it's a lovely day.'

'I'm so tired and sore,' she murmured.

'A bathe will do you all the good in the world. Hurry up and put your things on. I'll go and call the others.'

Gladys stretched herself and yawned; Ethel was already getting into her costume.

'Oh bother, all the buttons are off mine; I meant to sew them on yesterday,' said Gladys. 'I forgot.' She blushed rosy red at the remembrance of what had driven it from her mind.

'Never mind that, there'll be no one about.'

'Don't let's wear any at all,' said Ethel. 'It will be much jollier bathing naked. Uncle Cecil won't mind, and I don't mind him.'

'What will your auntie say?'

'Oh lor! I suppose she'd make that an excuse for another whipping. I want to talk to you, Uncle Cecil, about her; she seems very fond of whipping.'

'I must go and call her, you can talk to me later.' I went to Muriel's room and found her and Juliette in the same attitude as I had found Gladys and Ethel. I pulled the clothes down quickly and smacked both their naked bottoms.

'You beast, Cecil,' said Muriel, sitting up.

'Come and bathe,' I said.

'No, I'm too tired. I'll bathe after breakfast.'

'Well, the girls are coming.'

'All right, you go with them. Breakfast at nine. Leave me and Juliette here.'

I didn't press her but went back to the others. They were waiting in their mackintoshes. Gladys had pinned her costume together, but the fastening was very frail. 'Muriel and Juliette are too tired to get up.'

'Hurrah!' said Ethel. 'We'll have some fun, come on,' and she danced down the beach. We put the mackintoshes in a safe place out of reach of the tide, and plunged into the breakers. At the first stroke Gladys's frail fastening parted, and her dress gaped wide open.

'Oh, dear,' she said, looking at me.

'Take it off, Gladys, I'll take mine off,' said Ethel, 'and Uncle Cecil, you'll take yours off too, won't you?'

I hesitated, for it seemed quite a different thing to expose oneself in cold blood to two practically innocent girls, and to let them see, and handle, a member that was in fighting trim. But Ethel didn't wait. She skipped out of the water and hurriedly unbuttoned her dress, pulled it off her shoulders, and then stepped out of the legs. 'Come on, Gladys, come on, Uncle Cecil, play fair.'

'Shall I?' said Gladys.

'There's no one to see; it won't matter.' I took hold of her dress and took it off; then I wriggled out of my own, and we all three stood naked in the morning sun.

'How I hate clothes,' said Ethel. 'Don't you, Uncle Cecil? . . . Oh look, Gladys, Uncle Cecil's quite different from how he was last night. There's nothing left of him.'

I felt absurdly self-conscious at this remark, but John Thomas evidently either liked attention being drawn to him or was eager to assert his importance, for I felt him swell appreciably.

'Oh look, its growing bigger. Oh, how funny.' She came to me and touched it.

'Ethel, for shame,' said Gladys, 'out in the open air; come into the water; suppose Auntie saw you.'

'Oh lor!' said Ethel with a quick look at the cottage, and she rushed into the sea. We romped about for some time, but it was too cold at that time of the morning to stay in long, and soon we were running back to the house. I was dressed long before breakfast and so was Ethel. She came down and found me smoking a cigarette in a deck-chair in front of the cottage. She sprang on to my knee and cuddled up to me.

'Feeling better for the bathe?'

'Yes, but the salt water did make my bottom smart. Gladys is upstairs putting cold cream on hers . . . Uncle Cecil, do tell me, who was getting whipped last night before supper? I know someone was and with a bundle of those twigs that Auntie used on us.'

'A birch,' I said.

'Oh, is *that* a birch? Who was getting it? Juliette?'

'Yes, and Muriel.'

'Auntie! Oh, who was whipping her?

'I was.'

'Oh, I wish I could have seen that. But why? Did she let you? Tell me.' She wriggled about in her precocious naughtiness.

'She had been naughty to me, so I whipped her just as she whipped you.'

'Ooh . . . but Uncle, she whipped us for doing that – you know; and she did just the same to me and let me do it to her; she liked it too, I know. I don't think it's fair. If we deserved whipping so does she.'

'Tell her so.'

'Oh, I dare say!'

'Shall I tell her what you think?'

'Oh no, she'd be angry and then . . . ' She rubbed herself behind suggestively.

Gladys came down at this moment. I held out my hand. She came and kissed me.

'So you've been putting on cold cream; is it very sore?' She blushed divinely and nodded her head.

'How do you know? Did Ethel . . . ? You little horror!'

'Breakfast!,' came Muriel's voice. She appeared in the door. 'Morning, girls, all right this morning?' Ethel ran to her quite frankly, but Gladys hung back shyly.

'Come, Gladys, don't be shy, last night's quite forgotten. That's better.' She took Gladys in her arms and kissed her fondly. 'You don't bear any grudge against your auntie, do you?'

'No, Auntie.'

'That's right, we shall be fonder of each other than ever, if I'm not mistaken.'

We went in to breakfast. Muriel was in the best of spirits, evidently very pleased with herself. The girls, Gladys especially, needed a little drawing out, but by the time the meal was over all constraint had vanished and we were the same merry party as yesterday. 'You'll bathe later, Muriel?' I said.

'Oh yes, about twelve o'clock. It will give me an appetite for dinner. What are you all going to do? Explore, or laze about and bathe with me?'

'Oh, it's too hot to do much,' I said. 'Eh! girls?'

'I must put the buttons on my costume,' said Gladys. 'Pins aren't any good,' she added with a roguish look at me.

'Would you like to wear yours all the morning, Ethel?' said Muriel. 'There doesn't seem to be anybody about.'

'May I?'

'Yes, if you like. Then you can get as wet as you like.'

Muriel was in so good a temper that I decided to make a suggestion to her which I thought promised much fun to myself. I bent forward and kissed her. 'They are sweet girls, aren't they?'

'Yes, perfect darlings – especially Ethel – oh what a delightful hand she has! Oh Cecil, wasn't it a glorious night! To see your three bottoms there waiting to be whipped. I can see them now – ' She closed her eyes in ecstasy. 'And then afterwards, Ethel's fingers. Do you know she got all four of them in, the little darling. I'd forgive her anything – no, I couldn't though, I must whip her little bottom again – but I wouldn't whip it hard. Oh, she's a darling.'

'Yes, but she doesn't think you're quite fair.'

'Eh, why not?'

'Well, she argues, quite logically, that you whipped us three for doing precisely what you did to her, and let her do to you; and you liked it, she said, she knew you did.'

'The little devil!'

'Isn't it true? . . . Now I've got an idea, let her whip you; tell her that it is quite true you deserve a whipping and she shall give it to you.'

'What, me let a slip of a girl whip me! Not much; it's all very well for you, but I'm not going to offer my bottom to her, thank you.'

'All right, just as you like; it's only a suggestion. I thought it might be amusing.'

'It would be to you perhaps.'

'You won't be angry with Ethel for saying what she did?'

'Oh no, I like her spirit . . . the little devil, she's a girl after my own heart – up to any devilment. But it doesn't mean that I'm going to let her whip me,' she added as she went away.

'I'll bet a quid,' I said to myself, 'that she *does* whip you before we leave here, if I connive at it.'

The girls came rushing downstairs and dragged me along with them to the beach. Ethel was wearing her bathing costume, as Muriel had told her she might, and looked the young imp she was. Gladys had on her blouse and skirt but, as she confided to me, had her bathing things on underneath. 'It's so much more comfortable,' she told me, 'than corsets and things.'

'And has the cold cream proved effective?' I asked, continuing the conversation which breakfast had interrupted. She nodded and blushed.

'Oh, Uncle, wasn't it awful. You know I'd never been whipped before yesterday. I thought I should have died of shame when Auntie came in and found us in bed. And she is cruel; but do you know, just towards the end, when I was on your back and she made the whip curl all in and out, I felt so funny, just as if things were going to happen – you know – just as if I was being tickled by you.'

'Ah, quite so, and didn't it happen?'

'Not then, she stopped too soon, and you put me in bed.'

'And then?'

'Then you know it did . . . But tell me, would it have happened if Auntie had gone on?'

'Probably.'

'Ooh!'

'Why, do you wish it had?'

'Ye–es . . . not with Auntie, but . . . ' – she threw herself into my arms – 'I think I'd like it to happen that way with you.'

I held her tight, my hand went round her thighs seeking her little pussy.

'Not that way, not from behind, I'm too sore.' She opened her legs, so that I could reach her from the front. Ethel had been busy paddling and playing in the sand while we had been talking, but now she saw what was going on. She ran up to us.

'Oh, you rude things, I'll tell Auntie,' and she began spanking her sister with her sandal. I got up and chased her, caught her, and turned her over. Then, taking the sandal from her, I belaboured her little behind, not too hard, but hard enough to be felt. She squealed and kicked, and at last managed to escape.

'You big bully!' she called out from a safe distance, rubbing her smarting hams.

The morning passed like this, until we saw Muriel and Juliette coming down the beach ready to bathe. I jumped up and, going behind a rock, got into my bathing suit. Gladys simply slipped off her blouse and skirt and was ready. We all plunged into the surf and romped about. We played the usual games, dodging the breakers, diving under them, dancing round in a ring, and so on. The sea was as smooth as it ever is on that coast, which meant that the waves were quite three or four feet high, and quite strong enough to take you off your feet if you weren't careful. I suggested a game of touch, and soon shrieks of excitement rose high. I noticed with glee that whenever Ethel was 'he' she always made a dead set at Muriel and once or twice, when she managed to catch her, smacked her as near the bottom as she dared. Muriel took it all in good part and retaliated. Once, when she was chasing Ethel in shallow water, a wave came and bowled her over. Muriel was on her in a moment and, under the pretence of helping her up, administered two or three smart slaps.

'That's not fair,' shouted Ethel, wriggling away. 'Only one smack's allowed, isn't it, Uncle Cecil?'

'Yes,' I said, 'let's pay her out; come on, Gladys and Juliette,' and I led the way in a chase of Muriel. She entered into the game and dodged here and there, but we were too quick for her and she fell on the soft sand with the rest of us on top of her, tickling and smacking her wherever we could. Ethel managed to get two or three resounding smacks on the plump thighs before our victim begged for mercy.

'That'll do,' she panted. 'Now, Cecil, it's your turn.'

I started at once and sped away, the rest of them shrieking in my pursuit. I dodged and doubled and at last let myself be caught by Juliette and Gladys, who fell on me and slapped me vigorously. The others came up and added their smacks, I rolled over and defended myself, but the blows followed me, and Muriel even dared to slap the obvious protrusion sticking out in front. I seized her hand and pulled her down across me, and administered a sound smacking on her kicking legs and cheeks.

'Cecil, you devil, stop, not before the girls.' The others had stood away when they saw Muriel in this position.

'Go on, Uncle Cecil, give it to her,' shouted Ethel, beside herself with excitement.

'Don't you be cheeky, youngster,' I said, 'or you'll be sorry . . . Juliette, catch her and show her respect for her elders.' Ethel shrieked and fled, but she couldn't escape Juliette, and in a trice she was across the latter's knee and was uttering little squeals under the quick-descending palm.

Our games and running about had tired us completely, and we were all ready for dinner. This morning's entertainment had also achieved one other result. It had taken away the last shred of modesty – mock or real – from all of us, and from that time on, there was no reticence or concealment on the part of any of us, not even Gladys.

## CHAPTER SIX

## *Jealousy and an Apple-pie Bed*

There was a lull for a day or two after these events. The girls – even Ethel – were on their best behaviour, and they seemed to get to know just how far they could go with Muriel. If she was in a reckless mood they fell in with it, if on the other hand she was not inclined for improprieties, they also were more sedate. Gladys had quite lost her shyness and evidently was growing very fond of me. This, I thought, did not altogether please Muriel. I noticed on more than one occasion looks, certainly not of love, and several times Muriel seemed to lay traps for Gladys so that she might have an occasion to punish her. But the girl managed to avoid pitfalls and the occasion never came – at any rate, for a considerable time. One evening, however, the weather was very heavy – thunder was in the air – our nerves were all on edge – and Ethel in particular was very restless and irritable. She *would* tease all of us – with Muriel and myself she restrained herself, realising that it might be the worse for her if she went too far – but Juliette and Gladys she never left alone for a minute. At last Gladys could stand it no longer – she wanted to read and Ethel would not leave her alone – so with a 'get out, you little beast,' she boxed her sister's ears. The force of the unexpected blow sent Ethel into the fender. She got up at once and went for Gladys and a rough-and-tumble ensued, during which a chair was broken.

Muriel and I were sitting outside smoking. Hearing the noise we came in just in time to save the table with the lighted lamp from going over and setting the place on fire. 'What's all this about?' asked Muriel.

'Gladys knocked me into the fireplace,' said Ethel.

'She wouldn't let me read.'

'That's no excuse for breaking the furniture and nearly setting the place on fire. Go upstairs, both of you, and undress, and come down again to me.' Gladys went out without a word, Ethel made a face at her aunt and followed her.

'Juliette, get the birches. You'll stop this time and watch, I suppose, Cecil?'

'Why shouldn't I help?'

'No, I and Juliette will be quite enough, and besides, you'd probably want to whip Gladys and that *I* mean to do.'

'Oh,' I said. 'Why?'

'Never mind why. It's enough that I *want* to. Juliette, aren't those girls ready? Go and see.'

Juliette went out and returned shepherding the two culprits. They were in their nightdresses only. Muriel assumed a most businesslike air. 'Juliette, will you take Ethel and whip her soundly; Gladys, turn your nightdress up and bend over the sofa as you did before.'

'But Auntie . . . Uncle Cecil.'

'Well, what about him? It's a little late to be bashful before him; come be quick, it will be worse for you if you keep me waiting.'

The poor girl began to pull up her things, blushing rosy red. 'Higher than that, right round your waist – that's better – now bend down, lower, lower still. That's it!' and the rod fell fairly across both cheeks.

Juliette had in the meantime managed to get Ethel across her knees, keeping her legs tight between her own and her head tucked under her left arm. She was using a shortish birch and the blows fell obliquely on the white skin. Ethel plunged and squealed but could not escape.

Whish – whish – whish! The blows were falling on poor Gladys. 'How dare you lose your temper with your sister!' Whish – whish! 'Perhaps you think because your Uncle Cecil makes a fuss of you, you are mistress here. I'll teach you.' Whish – whish – whish!

Then I realised the state of the case. Muriel was jealous. Though she had professed to be glad at our happy family freedom, she really was jealous of my evident attention to Gladys and her affection for me.

Gladys began to sob and moan under the blows.

'Yes, I dare say you'd rather have your uncle's caresses than mine. But it's my turn now, mine, mine, mine.' The birch came crashing down. Gladys's cries became more acute, quite drowning Ethel's squawls. I glanced over at her; Juliette had given her a good warming and her bottom was all crimson. She caught my eye and I signed to her to stop. Ethel got off her knee and clapped her hands to her burning cheeks. She then jumped on a chair and, through her tears, tried to look at herself in the glass.

'My word, but you have laid it on, Juliette,' she said, 'but I'm glad I had you and not Auntie. Ooh, look at Gladys's behind.'

Muriel was still bringing the birch pitilessly down on her victim, holding her down with her left hand.

Gladys's cries were pitiful to hear. Muriel seemed beside herself. I thought it time to interfere.

'That's enough, Muriel,' I said.

'You be quiet,' she answered and the blows fell again.

I stepped forward and seized her arm. 'Let me go!' she shouted, but I held her tight.

'Gladys and Ethel, go upstairs,' I said, 'and go to bed, I'll come and say good-night later.' Gladys got up and stumbled sobbing out of the room. Ethel followed her, looking rather frightened.

When they were gone, I released Muriel and shut the door. Then I turned to her. 'Now Muriel,' I said, 'what's the meaning of this? How dare you lose your temper and flog Gladys so unmercifully?'

'I'd like to kill her,' she gasped in angry sobs. She was shaking with passion.

'Why?' And then it all came out. I was always with her; I loved Gladys better than I did her. She wasn't going to play second fiddle to any little chit of a girl, I was cruel and unkind, I was everything that was bad, and so on.

I kept quite cool. 'Now Muriel, this has got to stop, here and now. There's no reason for you to be jealous at all and I won't have it. You told Gladys just now that you were mistress here, now I'm going to show you that I am master. Take off your things, and kneel down and ask me to punish you as you deserve.'

'I won't, I won't be whipped.'

'Oh won't you, we'll see about that, now down on your knees.' She glared at me, shaking with anger. I went towards her. She put up her arms to protect her face. But I seized her by the shoulders and shook her till her teeth rattled and her hair came tumbling down. This mode of treatment was evidently new to her, and most effectual. 'Oh, let me go, I *will* do what you want.'

'Kneel down.'

She knelt down.

'Now say, "I beg your pardon, Cecil, for being jealous and losing my temper, and I deserve to be punished, please punish me as I deserve." ' She repeated the words after me. 'Now undress.' She began fumbling at her things. 'Help her, Juliette.' With Juliette's aid she soon stood naked to her stockings. 'Now bring me a birch and ask me to use it.' She did as I told her. 'Now, Juliette, hold her under your arm.'

'Oh Cecil, dear, not too hard.' My reply was a long drawing cut right across her loins; she sobbed and writhed. Blow followed blow. I had no intention of sparing her, for I was really very angry. The birch soon was used up.

'Juliette, get me a riding whip.' Juliette released her to do as I said. Muriel fell on her knees and clasped my legs.

'Oh, not the whip, Cecil, not the whip, please.'

'Well, will you promise to be good and beg Gladys's pardon if I let you off?'

'Yes, oh yes.'

I called up the stairs, 'Juliette, bring Gladys down with you.'

Gladys appeared, looking very frightened; poor thing, she evidently thought the whip was for her. She stared wide-eyed when she saw Muriel naked at my feet. 'Now Muriel,' I said, 'do as you promised.' She did not move, her pride would not let her turn and face her victim of half an hour ago. I took the whip from Juliette and made it whistle through the air. She shuddered but still did not move. I brought it down diagonally across her bottom and thighs. She leapt up and sprang towards Gladys. The latter started back in fright.

'Oh Gladys, don't let him whip me any more, don't let him.' Gladys looked at me in a puzzled way.

'I have been whipping Muriel,' I said, 'because she lost her temper with you through jealousy, when she has no reason. I have told her to beg your pardon.'

'Yes, I do, I do Gladys,' sobbed Muriel at the girl's feet. 'I'm sorry, please forgive me and ask him not to whip me any more.'

It was a supreme delight to me to see this proud woman humbling herself at the feet of a mere girl. I gazed to my fill on the scene, but Gladys evidently felt uncomfortable.

'Auntie dear, get up, don't kneel like that to me; of course I forgive you. I was naughty I know, and I dare say I *did* deserve a whipping, though perhaps not such a hard one. But you needn't be jealous of me. I'm only a girl, and I'm sure Uncle Cecil is as fond of us all, without any favourites.' She drew the older woman up as she spoke, and held her in her arms. 'There,' she went on, 'go to him now – goodnight, Uncle Cecil – no, I'll say good-night here – you see Auntie Muriel to bed, I expect Ethel is wondering what is happening to me.'

I was surprised at her cleverness. She led her aunt to me, kissed us both long and lovingly, and went out.

Muriel fell into my arms, and I followed Gladys's advice. In fact my own bed did not see me at all that night.

\*     \*     \*

The next morning I did not wake up as early as usual, which was not to be wondered at, considering all the circumstances. The sun was well up when I opened my eyes and found Muriel beside me, with her arms round my neck.

She opened her eyes as I moved.

'Are you getting up?'

'Yes, it's past eight. I must go and call the girls, or we shall lose our morning swim.'

'Send Gladys to me, I want her . . . you needn't look like that, I'm not jealous any longer, I want to tell her so, and make her love me.'

I went into the girls' room. Ethel was awake, but Gladys was still asleep. 'I was wondering when you were coming,' said the former. 'Didn't you sleep well last night?' She said this with such a meaning air that I thought Gladys must have given her a hint as to where I spent the night.

'Oh yes,' I replied innocently. 'Why do you ask?'

'Oh nothing; here, wake up, Gladys, here's Uncle Cecil.' And she pulled the clothes down and began to tickle her sister between the legs.

Gladys moved restlessly and murmured half-asleep, 'No, don't, I'm too tired.' Then she opened her eyes and saw me. She hastily pulled her night-dress down and tried to gather up bedclothes. 'Oh, Ethel, you *are* rude.'

'Your auntie wants you,' I said. 'Oh, you needn't look so frightened, she's quite all right this morning; run along to her. Shall we go for a swim, Ethel?'

'Rather,' and she hopped out of bed at once and, without waiting for me to go, pulled off her nightdress and stook stark naked looking at her bathing dress.

'Ethel!' said Gladys. 'I'd be ashamed.'

'Who cares for Uncle Cecil?' laughed Ethel, as I went to my own room and Gladys went to find Muriel.

When I reached my own room and began to untidy the bed so that Mrs Tasker should not discover that it had not been slept in, I discovered why Ethel had been so anxious to know how I slept. That favourite practical joke of the schoolgirl – an apple-pie bed – met my eyes. Without pausing to think how I was giving the whole show away, I rushed back to Ethel. 'You little devil, I know now why you asked so particularly how I slept last night. I'll teach you to make apple-pie beds.' She was half in and half out of her bathing dress.

'Hullo! only just found it out?' She shouted with laughter as she dodged me. 'Who were you with last night?'

I seized hold of her and threw her, laughing, on the bed, tearing off the dress; she kicked and squirmed and squealed as I tickled her all over, trying to lay her across my knees. Her struggles revealed all she had to show, my eager fingers probed every secret access, my gloating eyes followed my fingers. She tried her best to retaliate, and in the struggle the girdle of my pajamas came undone and the loose trousers fell down over my thighs. Instinctively her hand fastened round the pendulous engine that was revealed. His night's labours with Muriel had left him rather limp, but under the exciting touch of Ethel's fingers he did his best to assert himself and make a brave show.

'What a funny thing this is,' said Ethel. I had stopped tickling her when her fingers began this present task. 'It's never twice alike. When I first saw it, it was quite stiff and hard and long, and then when we were bathing yesterday, it had shrunk to nearly nothing – now it's bigger again, but quite flabby; and what are those two little round things for in that rough bag? . . . Oh, it's getting bigger again and stiff . . . Am I making it do that, by rubbing it?'

'Yes, you darling, go on rubbing it up and down – and hold it tight . . . oh, not so tight as that . . . that's better, draw the skin right back – now up again.'

'Oh, Uncle, look, it's all messy – don't you want to go somewhere?'

'No, no, go on rubbing, quicker, quicker,' and my hand searched between her legs.

'Oh, the horrid thing, it's spitting at me again . . . it's all over my leg . . . oh, Uncle darling, I'm coming, I'm coming.'

We were sitting side by side on the bed, and in her final paroxysm, her head fell forward nearly on to my lap. Naturally, she received the final bursts on her face. But she was too overcome to notice it. I pressed her gently down until her face met the rampant head. She seemed instinctively to know what I wanted and, opening her lips, kissed and sucked the now declining knob. When she had quite drained me, I raised her face to mine and pressed loving kisses on her lips, heedless of the fact that they were still wet with my own strength. She clung to me for a minute or two and then, sitting up, looked at her thighs. 'You *have* made me in a mess. What is that sticky stuff – it does taste funny. Oh look, there are little bits of jelly in it. What's that?'

'Those are babies.'

'Oh, what a lot! But how? I don't understand.'

'Well, you see, if I were to push this into you there, and rub it up and down inside you, just as you rubbed it up and down with your hand, that stuff would come out of me and mix with you when you came, and might give you a baby.'

'Oh I see, but you could never get that in here.' She opened her legs and pulled her slit open, showing the dainty inner lips all wet and glistening still.

'You're a naughty girl,' I said, 'and you deserve a whipping; I haven't whipped you yet for making me an apple-pie bed.'

'How was it you didn't find it out until just now? Where were you? – oh not too hard! please – I know, with Auntie Muriel! What were you doing to her, what you've just shown me? – you can do it harder than that if you like – will she have a baby?'

'Don't be so inquisitive! She won't have any babies, I can tell you that . . . Come on, let's go and bathe.'

'Oh, those last three hurt. Where's Gladys? Isn't she coming? Let's go and find her.'

Before I could stop her, she had run out of the room. I followed her, for I was eager to see what was happening. I caught her up before she reached the door, which was open, and went in with her. What a picture met my eyes! At first sight it was difficult to distinguish the two forms, so interlaced were the limbs. But after a moment I realised what was happening. Held tightly between Muriel's thighs was Gladys's fair head – I could not see her face, that was hidden; her beautiful bottom was well exposed, showing the traces of last night's punishment, and just beyond that I could see Muriel's forehead and abundant tresses.

'Well I never!' I laughed. 'Is that how you make friends?'

At the sound of my voice, Gladys started up, wrenched herself away from Muriel's grasp, and tried to bury herself in the clothes. She seemed to blush all over, for a pink flush flooded all her skin. Muriel looked towards me with satisfaction in her eyes. 'You might have waited a moment, Cecil. . . . Hullo! is that Ethel? Well, that's a nice costume to come and say good-morning to one's aunt in, how dare you? come here.' She drew the girl, who was all eyes, close to her, patting her bottom in mock severity. 'Why, what's this? Cecil, you haven't . . . ' Her tone became quite severe.

'Oh, it's all right,' I hastened to reassure her, 'something got spilt.'

'Did it? Well, you've interrupted us, so you had better help us to finish. I'm going to kiss this little witch now though. She can kiss you; I expect she knows how to by this time; as a treat you can kiss Gladys – come out of those clothes – and she can go on kissing me. Now, Ethel, lie across the top of the bed – you, Cecil, down that side – Gladys, you across the bottom, can you reach me? Open your legs a little wider, Ethel. That's it, ahh!' The result of this magic circle or square may be imagined. Anyhow, we forgot all about breakfast-time. While we were in the height of our enjoyment, Juliette appeared in the doorway. I was too busy between Gladys's soft thighs to say anything to her. She went out again, and I thought that she had gone away not wishing to interrupt. To my surprise she came back in a minute holding something behind her back.

'Well, that's a pretty sight,' she laughed. 'It's far too good an opportunity to be lost though.' With that she produced the birch which she had hidden and brought it lightly down on Ethel's and Gladys's thighs. They sprang up, startled, and jumped off the bed, leaving Muriel and myself exposed. 'For shame, you two,' she went on, 'get up and dress,' and she playfully flicked me between the thighs and caressed Muriel's mount.

'I suppose we had better,' said Muriel, sitting up. 'We mustn't over-tire ourselves. Run along, girls, and dress. Breakfast in a quarter of an hour. We'll play this game again sometime if you're good.'

'Yes, but I want to take a hand then,' said Juliette, 'it's mean of you to have left me out this time.'

Things went on smoothly for some days after this. Muriel had forgotten her jealousy and had had enough whipping for the time being. I also was not disinclined for a little respite and time for recuperation. The open-air lazy life, however, coupled with the sea-bathing, acted as a splendid tonic, and before many days passed I was fit and ready for anything. Juliette also was eager to take a hand, as she called it, in the 'circle', which on this occasion became what Euclid might have called an irregular pentagon. This time, however, the order was reversed, and I tasted the virgin sweets of Ethel's smooth young body, while her sister caressed me. Muriel lay between Gladys and Juliette while the latter's body squirmed under Ethel's clever, insinuating little tongue.

How long we lay in these mutual embraces, I could not say, but naturally I tired before any of the girls, and when I realised that I was for the time being milked dry, I began to cast about in my mind for some other variations. I got up and, whispering to Gladys to join herself to her sister for the time being, left the happy party. I had determined what I would do. I found a candle on the dressing-table and, going round to the other side of the bed, found Muriel's soft cheeks and, signing to Juliette not to say anything or to stop her own busy tongue, inserted it gently between them. Muriel stopped and looked round.

'What's that? . . . Cecil, you devil!'

I pushed it further in. 'Oh, oh . . . no, don't stop; only go carefully, don't hurt me, ah! that's it . . . oh, how lovely!' The intensity of her pleasure as I worked the candle in and out made her now fierce in her passion, so that she tried to draw all Gladys's tender little pussy into her mouth, draining its juice and sucking it with fierce-sounding smacks of her lips. She was also evidently using her teeth, for I heard Gladys sigh, 'Oh, Auntie, don't bite me!' Then I saw her hands clutch at Ethel's little bottom and pinch the cheeks, while Ethel in her turn fiercely devoured Juliette. I watched this wave of passion circulate through the four bodies, while I made good use of the candle. At last Muriel's head fell away from Gladys and she sighed, 'I'm *done*, I can't do any more . . . Cecil . . . Juliette, stop for God's sake you'll kill me.' The two girls sat up and watched us three others, Ethel staring with huge eyes at my treatment of Muriel, who was twisting and writhing in the last throes of passion. Her face was white, her eyes half-closed, her breath came in gasps, her fingers clutched and opened convulsively, great drops of perspiration stood on her forehead. Her belly heaved and fell, her loins worked forward and back as her thighs pressed on Juliette's head and then again relaxed. At last she seemed to pull herself together for a supreme effort, held herself rigid for a moment or two, and then collapsed supine, motionless, inert.

## CHAPTER SEVEN

# The Day Trip

One morning on waking we found the sea very rough. A sou'-wester had sprung up during the night, and great breakers came rolling into the bay; far out, white-horses could be seen everywhere, and Lundy looked suspiciously clear and near. We had our morning swim – or rather bathe, for it was far too rough to attempt swimming. Indeed, the force of the waves was so great that it was difficult to keep one's footing. Ethel in fact gave it up as a bad job. Every time a roller came in, it carried her with it on to the beach, where she needed all her strength to prevent herself being sucked back by the under-tow. Her legs and arms flew in all directions. It was exciting and tiring work. At last a wave broke suddenly right across Muriel's back. She shrieked and made for the shore. She told me afterwards it felt just like a cut from a riding whip; indeed, there was a red weal right across her shoulders which might well have been made in that way. 'I'm sick of the sea,' she said at breakfast. 'Let's go inland today.'

We accordingly packed luncheon baskets, hired the pony and jingle which had brought us from Morthoe and which belonged to a man in the village, and started. It was a long climb out of Croyde and the pony was not a fast one. We took it in turns to ride in the jingle and so were saved the fatigue of long unending tramping.

Blackberries were everywhere and red admiral butterflies fluttered about in crowds.

Once away from the sea and sheltered from the winds in the high-banked Devon lanes it was very hot and sultry, thunder was in the air. 'Golly! isn't it hot?' panted Ethel, after a particularly stiff bit of climbing. 'I wish I hadn't to wear clothes. They get so sticky,' and she wriggled about. 'Auntie, mayn't I take some of them off? There's no one about.'

'You haven't got much to take off, I should think,' laughed Muriel, 'no stockings and not much else as far as I can see.'

'I've got a chemise, knickers, blouse, and skirt. It's the knickers that stick so, they're so tight. Mayn't I take them off?'

'Have you forgotten the first afternoon?'

'Oh, that was different, we didn't know each other so well then. But now we've no secrets from each other, have we, Auntie darling?' She ran to Muriel and put her arms round her.

'Did you ever know such a creature?' smiled Muriel. 'If you do, remember you leave yourself quite unprotected, and there are lots of nice switches in these hedges.'

'I'll risk that,' shouted Ethel in high glee, as she raised her skirt without any attempt at concealment and undid the buttons of her knickers. She pulled them down and stepped out of them. 'That's better,' she shouted as she threw them into the jingle. 'You stay there! Oh, Auntie, it is lovely to have no drawers on, there's such a lovely draught blowing up my legs.'

'Ethel, for shame,' said Gladys.

'Shocked again, Miss Modesty!' laughed Ethel, running up to her sister. 'Poor thing, she wouldn't be without *her* drawers for the world, would she?' And she danced round her, snatching at her sister's skirt and pretending to pull it up.

'Cecil, cut me that switch,' said Muriel. 'Come here,' she called.

'Oh no, Auntie, it's not fair, I didn't mean anything . . .' But Muriel had caught her, deftly turned her over and raised her skirt, and gave her naked bottom four smart cuts. Then she let her go. The blows were not really hard, given more to act as a warning and to show her power.

'I told you, you would be quite unprotected,' she laughed.

'Lucky it's a quiet lane,' I said.

'It would have been all the more fun if it hadn't been,' whispered Muriel back to me.

We reached a meadow on top of the hill, through which there was a right of way. It was bounded on one side by the railway line, and had at one time, I should fancy, formed part of a park, for several fine old oaks were still standing. Under one of these we spread the lunch, and sprawled about at our ease. A wood to our west kept the wind away and the sun poured down upon us. Lunch finished, cigarettes whiled away the time, until at last 'an exposition for sleep' came upon me, as it did to Bottom. I slept in perfect content for some time, flat on my back, enjoying a delightfully amorous dream, but was wakened at last by what I thought was a fly tickling my face. I brushed it away several times, but it always returned, and at last in despair I opened my eyes and found that little minx Ethel was tickling me with a blade of grass. Gladys and Juliette were watching the fun and laughing – Muriel was asleep. I sprang up quickly to go for Ethel, seizing the willow switch which I had kept by me. To my surprise when I got to my feet I found my trousers slipping down round my legs. Shrieks of laughter came from all three girls. I hastily pulled the trousers up, intending to enquire about them later, and gave chase to Ethel. The young devil could run like a hare, and I had to put my best leg forward to catch her. In my efforts it was not only my best leg that was forward, for I had only done up the top button of my trousers in my hurry, and John Thomas, ever eager to be in the midst of things, worked his way out. It must have been an edifying spectacle.

At last Ethel tripped on a tussock of grass and came down. Like a flash I was on her and had her clothes up in a twinkling. She squealed for mercy, half-laughing and out of breath. 'You little devil,' I said as I spanked her, 'I'll teach you to wake me up; I'll tickle you; how do you like that, eh?'

'Oh, Uncle, don't, don't.'

'And how dare you undo my trousers?'

'It wasn't me, it wasn't truly, only your thing was sticking up so much that I noticed it, and pointed it out to Gladys and Juliette, and she said it was a shame to keep it tied up close like that, you must be dreaming, and if we waited we should see something funny happen, so she undid your trousers . . . oh don't, Uncle, don't; I didn't touch your trousers, I didn't really. Whip Juliette, she did it, not me, oh my poor bottom, you *do* hurt.'

I left her and went back to the other two. Something in my manner must have scared them, for they got up as I approached. I quickened my steps, and without waiting for me to get near, their guilty consciences urged them to flee. I pursued Gladys first and easily caught her.

'Now, young lady,' I said. 'Who undid my trousers?'

'I didn't, Uncle, really. It was Juliette.'

'But you let her do it, and laughed at me when I got up. You are just as bad as she. Come here, where are your drawers?' I put my hand up under her skirt and, pretending that I thought she wore open drawers, felt between her legs for the opening.

'Oh, Uncle, don't, not here.'

I tucked her head under my left arm and turned her skirt up, then quickly unbuttoned the drawers, each side, and pulled down the flap. Her hands came round at once to cover her bottom and pull down the chemise. 'Take those hands away, and lift your chemise . . . higher . . . higher. That's better.'

'Oh, Uncle, not in the open field; anyone might pass, oh don't; whip me when we get home if you like, but not here . . . oh! there's a man!'

I turned to look and, turning, let her go; she was off like a hare for cover. I could not see anybody and went after her. She dodged a bit but couldn't keep it up for long. I caught her again. 'I don't see any man. Where is he?'

'I . . . don't know, I thought I'd get away. There wasn't a man really. Oh, Uncle, let me go now, do please.'

'Oh wasn't there; well, it would have been just the same if there had been. Now, shall I take your drawers down or will you?' She didn't answer, so I put my hand again up her skirt, found the buttons, and this time undid them all. Then I bent her over under my arm, pulled the drawers right down to her ankles, and began. 'I'm going to give you two whippings, first for laughing at me, and second for trying to tell me lies to escape. You might have got off with one. There – there – there.' From the position in which I held her the blows fell obliquely down and not straight across. The little switch curled wickedly around her legs and between her thighs. After one or two cuts, which evidently reached the tenderest spots, she began to beg for mercy. Her legs swung out here and there trying to dodge the cuts, and ever and anon I had a glimpse of the little virginal crack and the soft fair hair just beginning to shield it. When her bottom began to show marks, I let her go, as I did not want to hurt her really. But where was Juliette? She was nowhere to be seen. There was no trace of her in the field. Ethel was sitting quietly on the grass with her skirt spread out round her – 'to cool her scorched sit-upon,' as she said. 'Where's Juliette?' I asked.

'Ah,' she grinned, 'wouldn't you like to know?' I threatened her with the switch. 'Oh no, no! don't . . . She ran in there with Auntie,' pointing to the wood.

I went towards the wood calling to Juliette, but could see no sign of either of them. 'Come out, you two,' I called. 'Muriel, if you try to hide Juliette, it'll be the worse for you.' But no answer came and at last I gave up the chase and returned to the girls.

'Can't you find 'em?' said Ethel.

'Oh, they can wait,' I answered. 'Let's boil the kettle for tea. How's the sit-upon, Ethel? Cooler?'

'Yes, thank you, you big bully!'

'And how's yours, Gladys? Let me see.' I turned towards her, where she was sitting, and rolled her over, pulling up her skirt. She only made a half-hearted effort to resist and I smoothed and fondled all the parts which I had made to tingle a little time before. She snuggled close to me.

'You *are* cruel to me, Uncle, but I love you so.' I kissed her sweet lips, and John Thomas urged me to throw all scruples aside.

'Here, that's not fair; if you make a fuss of Gladys, you must make a fuss of me too,' said Ethel, and she flung herself on top of me, straddling across my lap. This was too much. I ripped my trousers open and out sprang his Lordship eager for anything. Ethel seized him and, pressing her naked stomach against him, began rubbing furiously. She hadn't long to wait. 'Oh, it's lovely to feel it there,' she cried. 'Oh, what a mess! isn't it hot? . . . But that's where it ought to go, isn't it? Take your hand away.' Before I knew what she was about, she wiped some of the flood from her stomach and rubbed it against her eager slit. 'There, Gladys, there's some for you,' she went on, as she did the same to her sister. 'Auntie shan't have all of him.'

For a moment I was nervous, but realised at once that of course there could be no danger of consequences. The kettle beginning to boil diverted our attention, and at the same time we heard a voice from behind us, 'May we come out, please?'

I assumed a natural tone as if everything was safe for them. 'Oh yes, tea's quite ready, where did you get to?' Muriel and Juliette appeared, the latter quite nervous. 'All right, young woman,' I said, 'you wait till we get home. Why didn't you answer me? Where were you?'

Muriel laughed, 'Well, Cecil, there *are* times and seasons, especially at picnics, when it makes for greater comfort all round for ladies to retire to solitude; you were busy with Gladys, so we seized the opportunity.'

'That's all very well, but Juliette had other reasons for hiding, and you helped her; you won't escape like that, you were harbouring a criminal, as the law puts it, and so share her guilt. You'll pay for it later, both of you. Now tea!'

There wasn't much to put back in the baskets when we had finished. 'Now I suppose we had better start for home,' said Muriel.

'Wait a moment,' I replied, 'Juliette has got to have a whipping first, so have you!'

'Don't be silly, Cecil, it's too late . . . besides, you can't here.'

'Why not? I've whipped the girls, and you whipped Ethel in the lane. Now you can't get away this time and hide. So who's going to be first. I think you had better, for the girls can hold Juliette, and I'm afraid you'd be too strong for them. So come on.'

'I won't; I won't be whipped in a field, before the girls; besides, I haven't done anything . . . Don't be silly, Cecil, or I shall get angry.'

'Angry! What do you mean! How dare you talk to me like that? Go down on your knees at once and pull up your skirts, unless you want me to whip you by force here, and then thrash you when I get home as well. Gladys and Ethel, see that Juliette doesn't get away. Now Muriel, are you going to do as I tell you?' She made no answer or movement, so, to hurry her up, I cut her across her thin skirt with the switch. She closed with me and tried to wrest the switch away from me. We struggled for a moment, but I managed to get her skirt up round her waist, exposing her knickers and chemise – she wore no petticoat. I bent her gradually over and got her head under my arm. At that moment the sound of a train in the distance was heard. 'Cecil,' gasped Muriel, 'there's a train coming, let me get up.'

'It'll be all the more fun,' I whispered, quoting her own words. The train drew nearer. I had dropped the switch in the struggle, intending to use my hand. By this time I had her well tucked away under my arm, with her chemise drawn up and her drawers well opened. Her bottom and sex were fully exposed to view. I deliberately turned her round so that this prospect faced the railway, and spanked her as the train approached. It was an excursion train from Ilfracombe, very long and very full – going slowly up the gradient. There must have been fully two or three hundred people in it, and every window seemed to be full of faces. They evidently spotted us, for above the noise of the train I clearly heard loud cheers; and handkerchiefs seemed to spring out like magic. Of course it was past in a minute, but I cannot adequately describe the fierce joy that I felt in the knowledge that at least two hundred strangers had seen Muriel's bare posterior, growing red under my palm. I saw red for the moment and rained a perfect hail of blows on her devoted cheeks. She sobbed and implored me to let her go. 'I shall die of shame,' she kept on saying. At last I thought I had given her enough and let her go. She crept away without a word, not looking at any of us, and flung herself down under the tree, her whole body heaving with choking sobs. I let her have her cry out and turned to Juliette. The incident of the train had left them all speechless. 'Now, Juliette,' I said. She got up without a word and tottered towards me. 'Are you going to resist or . . . ?'

'Oh, get it over quickly, for God's sake.' She could barely frame the words, she was so nervous.

'Pull your skirts up then and kneel down.' She made no complaint or any sound but meekly did as she was told. I took the switch and, pulling her drawers apart, gave her a swift sound whipping. Her bottom and thighs flinched at the strokes, but she uttered no cry. Only when I had finished I saw that she was crying silently.

I went to Muriel. She was still lying where she had flung herself down. I touched her on the shoulder. She shivered under my touch.

'Go away, leave me . . . I can never look anyone in the face again . . . How do I know who might have been in that train?'

'Don't be silly. They only saw your bottom. They can't recognise you by that!'

'But the girls! They saw . . . oh . . . oh . . . the shame.' I signed to Gladys and Ethel, and whispered to them to comfort their aunt. 'Make a fuss of her,' I said meaningly to Gladys, and turned to help Juliette load the jingle. I heard whispers between the others and kisses, and at last out of the corner of my eye I saw Ethel's hand disappear under her aunt's skirt, while Gladys, kneeling down, put her arms round Muriel's neck. The events of the afternoon had excited me extremely, and though I had had one moment of relief, John Thomas was quite anxious again to play a leading part in the drama. I led Juliette round to the other side of the jingle and, without wasting any time in preliminaries, gave him all he wanted.

'I score after all,' said Juliette, wiping her lips, 'but you're a bad boy. Cecil, you must make it up to Muriel!'

'It's good for her; it'll prevent her getting out of hand. I bet the girls have calmed her down.'

We found them in a tangled heap of legs and arms when we went to them. They got up, and though Muriel was decidedly ill at ease for part of the way home, she managed to whisper to me, as we came near the lights of the village, 'It was too bad of you, Cecil.'

'But *you* were quite right,' I answered. 'It *was* much more fun.'

## CHAPTER EIGHT

# *Foul Weather*

The sou'-wester and clear Lundy were no false prophets. The weather broke in the night, and I woke to find the rain lashing the sand. Everywhere was a grey haze. The roar of the breakers was incessant and almost terrifying. Five long ridges of white foam were always to be seen, the farthest being quite far out to sea, while beyond them the sea was a grey tumbling mass, flecked everywhere with white-horses. Lundy was invisible. At times when the sea-fog drifted it was even impossible to see Baggy Point.

Bathing was out of the question. Even to go out of doors at all required some determination. Now and again some of us ventured during a lull in the rain to brave the elements, but it was only to return quite soon, drenched to the skin and ready to change into dry clothes and get warm by the fire, which fortunately burnt brightly in the kitchen.

The cottage was not adapted for a large party in wet weather. Games of all kinds were tried, and tired of, and tempers were tried too. Hide-and-seek all over the house proved the most popular, and lasted for quite a long time, ending only when Juliette after a long and fruitless search discovered Muriel and Gladys hiding together in rather compromising circumstances. Since the episode of the passing train Muriel had seemed to make a dead set at Gladys; whether she was taking this way of avenging herself on me, or whether she realised that Gladys – alone perhaps of all of us – would understand her deep shame at the indecent exposure, I don't know. But whatever the reason, she certainly singled her out for most pressing attentions.

When Juliette spied them unmistakably in each other's arms, under a bed, she didn't cry out her discovery but went and fetched me quietly. 'What do you think of that?' she asked.

'Disgraceful!' I said, assuming a most virtuous air (I had been similarly employed with Ethel but had not been discovered, so I could preach). 'I am shocked and surprised. We cannot, it seems, play even the most innocent games but they are made the opportunity for impropriety and licence. This must be stopped and punished. Muriel and Gladys, get up at once. Gladys, do your drawers up; I am disgusted with you. Juliette, bring me a cane.'

Muriel stood up. 'Don't be silly, Cecil; you know you wish you had been here, it's only because you weren't in on the scene that you talk like that. It's simply because you want things badly, as I can see, that you're annoyed with us for enjoying ourselves.

'Impertinence won't do you any good, and rude remarks about my physical energy will have to be paid for. Thank you, Juliette,' as she brought the cane. 'Now you two, to begin with, you shall both apologise on your knees to that part of me to which you, Muriel, have so rudely referred, and then kiss it in token of adoration, and then you shall receive a fair punishment for your secret lubricity. Come, Gladys, on your knees; Juliette, fetch Ethel so that she may profit by the lesson.'

Gladys knelt down humbly, looking lovingly up at me. I undid my trousers and let John Thomas have the freedom he wanted. Certainly Muriel had not overstated his case, he looked ready for anything. 'Now kiss him.' Gladys obeyed and I felt her soft lips tenderly caressing the sensitive tip. The effect of her touch was electric. Big as he was before, John Thomas seemed to swell and stiffen visibly; I did not dare allow her to continue, but turned to Muriel. 'Now, Muriel, it's your turn.'

'I won't, I don't want to kiss the beastly thing, take it away,' and she slapped it smartly. I seized her by the shoulders and forced her to her knees.

'Now kiss it, or it will be the worse for you.'

'I won't, I won't, I . . . ' But I pushed it violently against her face and began to rub it over her cheeks. The previous excitement and Gladys's tongue had well prepared the way, and almost at once Muriel's face was spattered with the thick white jets. Some even lodged in her hair. She opened her mouth to speak, but before she could say a word, I thrust him between her lips, just in time for her to receive the extreme libation.

'Now,' I said, 'we must get to business. Lie across the bed, both of you; Juliette, hold them down if necessary; Ethel, I don't think you should look at your aunt's nakedness, so you had better face me – so, yes, kneel down. One moment though, take your sister's drawers down, and turn your aunt's skirt up and pull her drawers apart. I think as they were naughty together, they should be punished together, so we'll tie their legs to each other.' I took a stocking of Muriel's which was handy and tied her left ankle to Gladys's right, and then placed them on the bed as far apart from each other as I could. This naturally opened their legs somewhat and revealed their most intimate retreats – the one not quite fully developed, with lips of pale coral and a light covering of young fair hair, the other perfectly formed, shaded with brown curls and revealing bright red lips, just parted as if asking for a kiss. 'Now Ethel, don't look like that at your auntie, I told you not to.'

'Oh, Uncle, but isn't Auntie's pussy lovely,' she whispered. 'I should love to kiss it.'

'Well, you may kiss it just once, to show her that I am not hard-hearted, and you can kiss Gladys's too, but then you must turn your head and kiss me.' Gladys had made no attempt to resist, and Juliette's hand on her back had shown Muriel that resistance was useless. They had not heard Ethel's whispered request to me, nor my reply, so that the touch of soft lips between her thighs came as a complete surprise. She gave a little gasp and exclamation, and then stretched her legs as wide apart as she could. I did not intend, however, that Ethel should give her the supreme pleasure, so I drew her away and pointed to Gladys. The latter evidently had not realised that she was so exposed, for the cry she gave was more of nervousness than of pleasure and she put one hand behind her, trying to cover her nakedness, and drew her legs together.

'That's enough, Ethel, now turn round.' She obeyed and fastened her lips on my still-eager engine. 'After the oysters comes the bill. Now you must pay for your pleasure.' And I brought the cane smartly down on each bottom, one after the other. From where I stood I could reach both easily. I played with them at first, not striking in any order. Now I would give them alternate cuts of equal strength; now Muriel would receive a couple of stingers with a light featherlike caress in between. Then I would play with Gladys, giving her, say, half a dozen dainty little flicks in and out between her cheeks, and then a couple that drew cries from her and left their mark.

All this time Ethel was busy kissing and sucking, holding me close to her with one hand and with the other exploring all that she could reach through my open trousers. As I felt the consummation approaching, my cuts became more random. Sighs and cries came from both my victims, until at last I saw Gladys's hand reach out and find and clutch Muriel's, as if for sympathy. The latter's thighs began to contract and heave, but Gladys evidently felt no such approach of pleasure. I knelt behind her and just managed to reach her dainty lips with my tongue, while I still continued to spur on Muriel with the cane. Ethel did not let go of me but crouched lower and lower. At last the supreme moment came for all three of us, practically simultaneously, and as I gave Ethel all my manhood, I drank down Gladys's sweet life, while my eyes feasted on Muriel's reddened cheeks and glistening lips, from which trickled great pearly drops of passion.

This little orgy calmed us for some hours. After dinner we all felt tired, and Muriel said at once she was going to lie down and sleep. I said I would follow her example. So she and Juliette retired to her room, and I went to mine. I had not been there long and was just dozing when a tap came at the door, and I heard Ethel's voice, 'May we come in and lie down beside you, Uncle? We'll be quite quiet, but it's dull being alone.'

'All right,' I said.

'Come along, Gladys,' said Ethel, and the two girls came in.

I had undressed and put on my pyjamas for comfort. When Ethel saw this, she said, 'Oh, let's undress too,' and she slipped off her skirt and blouse and quickly got out of her knickers. 'Oh go on, Gladys, don't be shy.' Gladys blushed divinely, but the temptation was too great and she slowly and discreetly undressed to her chemise. She was very modest and careful, however, and though I watched her every movement, she let me see no higher than halfway up her thigh.

Ethel was already in bed snuggling close up to me when Gladys crept in.

'Isn't this lovely!' said Ethel as she pulled up her chemise and twined her legs round one of mine. Her mischievous hand sought between my legs as she looked up at me with a roguish smile.

'No, you mustn't do that. We mustn't tire ourselves out,' I said, pushing her hand away.

'It's all very well for you and Gladys,' she answered, 'you've both had your fun this morning, even though Gladys did get a whipping as well. I've had nothing. I'd willingly have had a whipping, if I could have had the other things as well.'

'Poor precious girl, were you left out in the cold? It's a shame. We must see what we can do.' So I found her delicious little slit with my left hand and began to play with it, while my right hand caressed Gladys's young breasts.

'Ah, that's lovely, get your finger right in, oh what are you doing?' I was letting my hand wander slightly and while one finger was penetrating the virgin lips, the other was exploring another adjacent retreat. She wriggled and twisted under the double pleasure. Her eyes dilated, her mouth opened as the quick gaspy sighs came ever faster; she thrust her body down on my fingers, and at last flinging her arms round my neck, she fastened her lips on my shoulder and I felt her sharp teeth nipping my flesh. Then she collapsed limply and her eyes closed. In five minutes she was asleep.

Gladys's regular breathing on the other side of me showed that she had not waited for her sister to set her the example. Her bosom rose and fell under my hand; it would have been a shame to disturb either of them, so I let them sleep on.

### CHAPTER NINE

# An 'Evening Continuation Class'

Next day the weather improved somewhat; we were able to get out, though the sea was still too rough for bathing. The rain came on again, however, during the afternoon, and we were prisoners again for the evening.

After tea Muriel said, 'What shall we do? Cards? Hide-and-seek? Or what? I'm ready for anything.'

'Hide-and-seek again! Are you eager for a repetition of yesterday, you two? . . . No, I tell you what, let's play school!'

'Oh yes,' said Muriel mischievously, 'I'll be mistress.' Ethel made a wry face and rubbed her little sit-upon meaningly.

'That wouldn't be much of a change, would it, Ethel?' I laughed. 'No, let's be fair. Let's draw lots for mistress, and she can choose her own monitor to help to keep order, and the rest of us must promise to submit and play fair.' Muriel looked doubtful. 'Come,' I urged, for I knew what she was thinking. 'It will be all the more fun if one of the girls draws the lot.'

'Ooh, I hope I do,' shouted Ethel; 'look out for yourself if I do, Uncle Cecil.'

'Oh, very well then, just for this once, it's only a game. But I don't understand about the monitor. What's her position? Can she punish; and can she be punished, just like the others?'

I thought a moment. 'That depends on the mistress. If she likes to hand over powers she can. Of course, the monitor must submit to discipline too.'

'I see,' she answered. 'Come along then, let's draw lots.'

I cut up five pieces of paper, and on one of them I drew a birch, as symbol of office, folded them up and shook them in a hat.

'Now then, who'll draw first?'

'Me please,' said Ethel quickly – she was dancing with excitement. 'Oh, blank . . . no luck!'

Juliette and Gladys both drew blanks. Then remained myself and Muriel. 'Oh lor, we're in for it,' whispered Ethel to the others.

'You're the first,' said Muriel to me. I chose one of the papers – it was a blank. 'I've got it then,' shouted Muriel in high glee. 'Look out for yourselves.'

'Choose your monitor,' I said, 'you're mistress for half an hour.'

'Not very long.'

'Quite long enough for a game. Come, who will you have for monitor?'

'I'll have . . . ' She looked quickly at each of us. 'I'll have Gladys . . . Gladys, go to my room and get the cases, I'm sure we shall want them and it will save time later. Now you children sit over there and behave yourselves or . . . ! Cecil, don't wriggle about. Juliette, sit up straight.'

Ethel was giggling with suppressed excitement; I entered into the spirit of the game and, playing the schoolboy as well as I could, I began pinching Juliette's bottom secretly. She stood it for some time, for she did not want to start the ball rolling, but at last Muriel noticed her wriggling about. 'Juliette,' she called, 'stand up; what are you wriggling about for?'

'Cecil was pinching me.'

'Is that true, Cecil? Where was he pinching you?'

'On the bottom.'

'How dare you use such words. Hold out your hand . . . now the other; go back to your place. Cecil, come here. How dare you behave like that and pinch Juliette on a place which I will not name.' She assumed the school-ma'am manner admirably. 'It is only right that you should suffer in the same place. Take your trousers down.'

'Oh please let me off this time,' I began to whimper, 'I won't do it again.'

'Certainly not, take your trousers down at once.'

'I won't.'

'Oh very well; Gladys, take them down for him.' Gladys hesitated. 'Will you obey me, Miss, or shall I have to punish you as well?' She made the cane whistle in the air just behind Gladys's back. Gladys came towards me and began to untie the sash I wore round my waist. Then she began to undo the buttons. 'Don't take too long over it, or I shall be suspicious of what you're doing.' Gladys blushed very red and quickly undid the rest. 'Now pull them down.' The trousers fell round my knees. 'Now bend him over the couch and lift his shirt-tail. Go down lower, Cecil; lower still. Lower . . . lower . . . there!' Certainly Muriel meant to play the scene for all it was worth. The cane fell with all her strength right across both cheeks. 'You naughty boy, I'll teach you to pinch your schoolfellows. Will you be good in future? Will you? Will you?' She gave me six cuts in all, and I was not sorry when she stopped. 'Now go and stand in the corner with your face to the wall. Keep your shirt up so that your punishment may act as a warning to the others.' The humiliation of my position was acute, and I was half-inclined to regret having started the game; but I determined to play the sporting game and wait my time for a chance of getting my own back. The knowledge too that Gladys and Ethel were looking at my nakedness was quite exciting, and I felt my passion rising within me.

The spectacle evidently pleased the others as well, for I heard a giggle from Ethel, and Muriel's voice, 'What are you laughing at?'

'He looks so funny, oh, isn't he marked!'

'There's nothing to laugh at, young lady, as you'll soon find out. Gladys, take Ethel and smack her soundly for me. I am tired.'

'I won't be smacked by Gladys.'

'Oh won't you! You will do as your schoolmistress tells you.'

Ethel realised it was no good to resist, and perhaps thought it would be wiser to submit to her sister than to risk the heavier hand of Muriel. 'Lay her across your knee, Gladys, undo her drawers, now take this brush and spank her naughty little bottom; we will see if she will think other people's punishments are so funny in the future. Harder than that, harder, I say, harder! I shall have to show you myself how to do it if you won't obey me.'

I could hear the note of gloating pleasure in Muriel's voice. Gladys did not seem to put much heart into her blows. Muriel began to lose patience or at any rate pretended to. 'If you don't whip her properly I shall whip you, monitress though you are. Stand up, lay Ethel across the couch. Now smack her as I tell you.'

'Hasn't she had enough?'

'Enough? Why, you haven't made her turn even pink. Will you do as you're told? Take that then!' I heard the cane fall across Gladys's skirt, and immediately a harder, crisper smack from the brush on Ethel's naked skin. 'That's better, I see you want an example. There you are then, again, again, again!'

Ethel began to squeal just a little, Muriel's object-lesson was evidently proving effective. I looked at my watch. 'Time's up,' I said, as I stooped to pick up my trousers.

'Hooray!' said Ethel, turning round and rubbing herself. 'You just wait, my girl,' she went on to her sister, 'if I draw the lucky paper won't I tan you!'

'Only four lots this time,' I said, 'no one can be mistress twice.' I folded up the papers again, but this time I kept the lucky one in my hand and when Ethel was about to draw slipped it into her hand without the others seeing. She just gave me a quick look but otherwise made no sign, and proceeded to pretend to choose deliberately. When she opened it her joy was unbounded. 'I've got it, I've got it, oh what fun. Uncle Cecil, you be my monitor and tell me what to do!'

'Well,' I said, 'I'm sure they're all very naughty and deserve a whipping. I should whip them all round first, it will make a good beginning.'

'Good idea. I'll begin with Gladys, before my own bottom stops smarting. Come on, Miss, come and lie across my knee, at once. Pull your skirt up, open those knickers and keep them open – wide open unless you want your knuckles cracked.'

It was absolutely lovely to see the flushed eager face, the eyes sparkling with naughtiness as Ethel prepared to chastise her sister's soft pink bottom. 'I'll show you how to whip. There, there, there.' The brush fell quickly here, there and everywhere, all over the plump surface. 'I don't want anyone to show me how to do it. Do I, Uncle?'

Muriel whispered to me, 'I say, Cecil, I don't know that I quite like this.'

'Nervous?'

'Well . . .'

'Mind, if she wants to whip *you*, you'll have to submit.'

'I don't think . . .'

'If you *don't*,' I said quite seriously, 'I'll flog you till you can't stand, in front of her. You consented to play the game, and must go on with it.' She saw that I meant what I said, and said no more, though she turned a little pale.

Gladys's whipping was still going on, her bottom was a rosy pink. 'There, that will do for the present, for you,' said Ethel. 'Now will you whip Juliette, Uncle, please. She's not been very naughty, but I think a little whipping will do her good.'

'Come on, Juliette,' I said, 'I'm not to do it too hard, it seems; so I'll use a birch. Take your drawers off and get on the couch.' Ethel watched all the preparations with eager eyes. When Juliette, in slipping her drawers down, showed all herself both back and front, Ethel whispered to me: 'Hasn't she got a lot of whiskers?'

'Ssh!' I said, and raised the birch. I gave her about a dozen moderate cuts, hard enough to be felt and to leave just a few faint marks. 'Is that enough?'

'Make it curl in there, in between,' pointing to where we could just see the pouting lips of her sex. I did as she told me. Juliette began to wriggle. She was always most sensitive to the birch. 'She seems to like that,' said Ethel, 'give her some more.' I went on until I saw by the nervous contraction of the thighs and the opening and shutting of the lips that the final paroxysm was approaching, and at last was rewarded by the sight of a few pearly drops appearing.

Ethel looked on wide-eyed. 'What's happened? Have you made her come?' she whispered. I nodded. She ran to Juliette and inserted two of her fingers. Juliette gave a gasp and imprisoned the intrusive hand between her thighs. 'Oh, you naughty girl,' said Ethel, 'you deserve another whipping for that.'

'I think she's had enough,' I said, 'and there's still Muriel,' I whispered.

Ethel looked at me and then at Muriel. 'I don't like to . . . '

'Don't you want to?'

'*Don't I!* But . . . '

'Frightened?'

'Um!' she nodded.

'Oh, she won't mind, it's only a game. You see . . . Muriel,' I said, raising my voice, 'Ethel is frightened to whip you. I tell her you won't mind, as it's only a game.' I said this very meaningly, looking her straight between the eyes.

She laughed nervously, and then said, trying to speak naturally: 'Of course, dear, fair's fair; how would you like to do it?' And she stood up.

'Shall I horse her?'

'What's that?'

'I take her pick-a-back. Then you can whip both of us at the same time.' I undid my trousers as I said this and let them fall. 'Now Muriel, get ready, off with your drawers, and I'll pin your skirt up. Now get up on that chair.'

'But, Cecil, she'll see everything.'

'So much the better, she'll like that, come on.' I tucked her legs well under my arms, she put her arms round my neck, and we stood waiting.

'What shall I use?' said Ethel.

'Anything you like; you'll find a birch the best.'

'I don't quite like to . . . '

'Don't be a silly girl,' said Muriel. 'Make haste. I've told you, you may; don't keep me exposed like this.'

'Don't you mind her, Ethel,' I said. 'You keep her exposed as long as you like; is she properly exposed, can you see everything?'

'Yes,' whispered the girl, in a shamed whisper.

'Well, go on then, whip her, whip all you can see, whip me too.' My imagination had fired me. I wanted to hear the cuts fall on Muriel's flesh and to know that her most secret parts were exposed to the greedy gaze of 'the mistress' and were quivering under her blows. Strangely enough I wanted also to feel the blows myself. A strange mixture of sadism and masochism filled me, my emotion was almost too much for me; my throat seemed choked; I could barely breathe; and it was a positive relief to me when I heard the first blow – a very light one – fall on Muriel's plump flesh, and then felt a light caress from the rod on my own skin.

Emboldened by taking the first step, Ethel's blows became heavier and quicker. As she went on, she left me more alone and concentrated more of her attention on Muriel. At last the lust of flogging got the better of her and I heard the blows fall quicker and quicker. They were evidently more effective too, for Muriel began to twist about on my shoulders. I had hard work to keep her legs under my arms. At last, 'That's enough,' she said, and Ethel stopped at once. 'Let me down, Cecil,' she said to me.

I was by no means satisfied. My whole nature was burning with ungratified desire. I must find relief somehow. 'I don't think you've had by any means enough, and I know I haven't. I'll finish you off if Ethel doesn't, I know you're not satisfied either, are you? Come here, let me see,' and I put my hand between her legs and drew her to me. 'No, I thought not; bend over that table; Juliette, come and kneel here before me, and you two girls whip me, both of you. Go on, do as I tell you or I'll whip you. I tell you I want you to whip me, I want it.'

I think I must have been almost mad with unsatisfied passion. Probably the 'strenuous' life I had been leading and the exciting scenes I had just witnessed were responsible for my condition, but I felt I must experience every possible sensation at once. I seized a birch and began to flog Muriel lasciviously. Juliette was kneeling before me kissing me, and the two girls were nervously attacking me behind. They were too nervous to satisfy me, however. 'Harder, harder,' I said to them, but it was no good. At last I told Juliette to change places with Gladys. The effect was instantaneous. Juliette knew her business thoroughly. She was a past-mistress in her art. Her clever manipulation with the rod, coupled with Gladys's clinging lips and tongue, acted like a charm. I felt the thrills begin to run through my body, and just as Muriel's bottom began to heave quicker and quicker and to twist every way under the prying twigs, I yielded with one supreme effort and gave Gladys what seemed to be my *very soul*.

CHAPTER TEN

## *A Morning's Adventure*

It was perhaps fortunate that the storm cleared away in the night, for a succession of wet days and the consequent indoor amusements might have proved rather enervating for all of us. As it happened, however, the next day broke fine and bright, and we were all able to get our early morning bathe in brilliant sunshine. The night-school had taken away any few remnants of reserve on the part of Muriel before the girls, and all five of us met on an absolutely level footing. Ethel boldly appeared absolutely naked, and skipped about careless of anyone. Muriel attempted a protest, but I would hear nothing of that kind, and when she began to argue that all discipline would vanish if the young madam was allowed to go on like that, I told her straight that after being whipped on her naked bottom by Ethel, she could not take up any attitude of superiority. 'Any discipline necessary, *I* will exercise – and on all of you. So don't presume.' She looked mutinous. 'Do you dare to question my authority?'

'No, Cecil, but . . .'

'But what? . . . You'll do exactly as I tell you, do you hear? *Exactly!* And to prove it, take that bathing dress off at once. Take it off!' We were just at the edge of the sea, the others were dancing about in the surf, Ethel's white body gleaming through the waves. 'Take it off now – undo those buttons.' As she hesitated, I brought my hand heavily down across her wet flank. The noise of the smack attracted the attention of the others. Muriel uttered a little cry in protest. '*Will* you do as I tell you? Take that costume off at once or . . . ' I seized a long trail of seaweed which had been washed up by the tide and made it curl round her legs.

'Oh, don't, Cecil, don't!'

'Well, do as I tell you.'

'But I can't take it off here.'

'Why not?' I went to her and seized the costume by the neck and with a quick jerk ripped it right open down the front, tearing all the buttons off. It fell apart showing her breasts and body down below the navel. 'Now, get out of it quickly,' and I plied the seaweed actively all over her. She saw that it was no good resisting and as rapidly as she could disengaged herself from the clinging garment.

'Oh, look at Auntie!' shouted Ethel. 'She's taking her dress off. Come on, Gladys, take yours off too. It's much nicer being naked in the sea.' She ran up to her sister and began to unbutton her dress, Gladys resisted, but she could not prevent Ethel's quick fingers. The costume fell apart and her beautiful budding breasts and fair body appeared.

'That's right!' I shouted, as, with stinging cuts of the wet seaweed, I helped Muriel to hurry over getting out of the legs of her costume. 'Now Juliette, take yours off too.'

'I won't,' said Juliette.

'Oh won't you!' and I turned towards her. She fled at my approach, running up the sand towards the cottage. I followed her, but she could run very fast and had she not slipped and stumbled I doubt whether I could have caught her. As it was, I came up to her as she lay panting and rained a shower of blows all over her back and legs. She cried and writhed and at last got to her feet.

'Oh, Cecil, don't! oh that seaweed does hurt! oh! ah!' She skipped and jumped about trying to dodge the blows.

'Take that thing off then! Who are you to object to being as naked as the others? Now, get back to the sea.'

I drove her naked down the beach, touching her up every now and then with the seaweed, and then followed a most enjoyable bathe as I chased each of the four naked girls in turn among the breakers, until at last we all went back to the cottage and dressed for breakfast.

After breakfast we all went out on the beach intending to bathe again before dinner, but, as will be seen, things happened which prevented us.

Muriel suggested that we should go to the left this time and explore further west, so we accordingly struck out. Round the rocks into the west bay we clambered, carrying towels, and while I lay down to bask in the sun, the girls roamed here and there. I noticed a couple of women searching for shellfish and some common children playing about who evidently belonged to them, but I didn't pay much attention to them.

Suddenly I was roused from the half-doze into which I had fallen by cries of anger and squeals of pain. 'I'll teach you to throw sand at me, you little beasts, take that, and that.' And the sound of a palm falling heavily on bare flesh came to my ears. 'Muriel smacking the girls,' I thought, and sat up to watch. The others were at the other end of the beach and I only saw a small group where a struggle was going on. Then to my surprise I saw two small figures break away and run towards the women who were fishing. There was a short colloquy – evidently complaints from the children – and then the two women went quickly towards Muriel, brandishing the short sticks which they used for knocking the shellfish off the rocks. I thought I had better go and see what was happening, so I got up and strolled towards the others. I arrived just after the women reached the group and were beginning to demand satisfaction. 'You smack my Sally, will 'ee?' shouted one. 'I'll pay 'ee,' and she flourished the stick menacingly at Muriel.

'Here, none of that,' I said. 'What's the matter?'

'Her smacked my Sally, and I be 'gwine to pay 'er vor it.'

'Not like that though,' I answered. 'Smack her if you like, but not with the stick; she didn't use the stick. I'll see fair play.' I took the sticks from her and the other woman. 'Now, smack her bottom if you can, I'm sure she deserves it.'

'Cecil,' said Muriel, half-frightened, 'you surely don't mean . . . ' But before she could finish one woman had seized hold of her and the other went for Juliette.

'You girls run away home, we'll come presently; it's no place for you.' Gladys was looking very scared and seemed glad to obey, but Ethel, her whole face alight with eager mischievous curiosity, lingered. 'Go on,' I said, 'or I'll tan that bottom of yours so that you won't know yourself.' The four women had now joined in set battle. Muriel's opponent was a short thickset woman, evidently strong but rather fat; her superior strength was counter-balanced by her lack of agility. Juliette was pitted against a younger and more formidable opponent. She evidently had but a slight chance, and though she wriggled and twisted, I saw that the contest could have but one end. Between Muriel and her antagonist, however, the contest promised to be more level and exciting. The woman tried hard to bend Muriel down under her arm, but the latter wriggled like an eel in her grasp and gripped her quite scientifically. At last I heard the sound of tearing cloth, and half the woman's skirt fell away from the waist, showing a none too clean flannelette smock. 'Tear my skirt, will 'ee?' she shouted, and she redoubled her efforts in retaliation. Rip! Tear! I saw Muriel's light frock come off in ribbons, entangling her legs. A vigorous pull burst the buttons off her satin knickers, they fell round her knees. Hampered like this she was badly handicapped and in a moment she was held tightly under her opponent's left arm and a hurricane of blows from the broad heavy palm fell on the naked cheeks of her bottom.

Juliette by this time had been equally mastered and, from her cries and the sound of smacks, was evidently experiencing a severe treatment. Her bottom was tinged a dull red and her legs were flying every way in her pain. Muriel, though mastered, had not given up the struggle. Her hands were free and seeking for a hold. At last they found the torn skirt, and more of the smock appeared, which in its turn suffered. The merciless palm still descended, however, on her bottom, and her assailant took no notice of the damage done to herself. She simply uttered hoarse pants and growls of rage.

At last Muriel managed to tear off all the clothes she could reach, and laid bare to view the brawny thighs and coarse-skinned bottom. Then, fastening her nails in one cheek, she gripped with all her strength. This evidently made some impression, for the woman twisted away and freed herself. Muriel, however, couldn't escape, for her knickers still hampered her legs. The woman rushed at her again, flung her to the ground face downwards, and began again to belabour her bottom and thighs with both hands.

Muriel began to implore for mercy and I thought it was time to interfere. 'That's enough,' I said. But the woman wouldn't stop. I went towards her and began to pull her off, when I heard the sound of approaching footsteps on the sand. I turned round and saw the two children who had been the cause of all the trouble coming towards us accompanied by four men.

'What be all this about?' said one. I began to tell them shortly, for I didn't like the look of things and wanted to get away. 'You 'old your gab; missus, 'oo tore your dress?' I again tried to explain, but a sudden blow from his hammer-like fist sent me flying, and before I could get up again, I was seized and held down by two of the others. Noisy altercations were going on all this time, and by the time I was able to see what was happening, Muriel and Juliette were in the grasp of two of the men, who were making their wounded bottoms again pay for their chastisement of the children. I struggled to get free but it was no good; I had to lie and watch Muriel and Juliette writhing under the heavy blows of those two savages. The two women stood looking on, enjoying the cruel torture. At last one whispered something to the other. A gleam of fierce joy sprang to the other's eyes. She went up to the man who was belabouring Muriel. I did not catch what she said, but he looked towards me. 'Oh, don't take no notice of 'im. Go on.' To my horror and surprise she undid the man's trousers and let out his rampant engine. I have never seen such a huge horrible affair. I struggled all I knew to escape from the grasp of my captor, but all my efforts were futile. At the same time I must admit an overpowering desire to witness Muriel's supreme humiliation came over me, and I waited and watched with staring eyes and parched throat. With a quick twist the man turned Muriel over and got between her legs before she knew what was happening. When his naked member touched her, however, she gave one terrible shriek and wrenched herself away. She struggled to her feet and tried to run, but the ever-clinging knickers brought her to earth again. The man and the women were on her in a flash. The latter tore away all the impeding skirts and, seizing her legs, held them wide apart while the man got between them and set to work. Shriek after shriek came from Muriel, who flung her body this way and that trying to avoid the thrusting weapon. I heard my name continually in imploring tones, but even if I had been free, I doubt if I could have gone to her assistance. I was absolutely fascinated by the horrible sight of this proud fair body being outraged before my eyes.

At last the man came to the end of his attack. I saw his powerful body heave and plunge, and at last with a grunt more bestial than human he collapsed on Muriel's body, entirely hiding it from view. Then he gathered himself together and stood up, leaving his victim quivering and inert.

'Have 'ee finished, it be my turn now,' said one of my captors. 'Catch hold of this young man.'

He released me as he spoke and the other took his place. I made no resistance. My whole being was one tingle of lascivious excitement. I wanted a whole army of men to throw themselves on Muriel and possess her. The other man approached his victim with gloating eyes. She lay supine, stretched out just as she was from her last sacrifice. When she felt his body close to her she made no movement of resistance. Only a sob came from her lips, and she half-opened her eyes only to close them again as if to avoid the sight of her violator. He was a much younger man than the other, and splendidly built. Also, as Muriel made no resistance, he didn't attack her so brutally. His movements were slower and more gentle. After a moment or two I was surprised to see Muriel open her legs a little, and move her body to meet his thrusts. 'You can leave go 'er legs, missus,' said the man, ' 'er loves me I do believe.' The woman let go as she was told, and Muriel drew up her knees and after a few passionate plunges flung them around the heavy thighs of her lover. Her arms also clutched his woollen jersey, holding him close to her. At last I could see that the final spasm was approaching. Her passion proved too much for the man; before he really was ready for her she drew all his life from him. 'You little bitch,' he shouted, 'I be coming already, I . . . ' He said no more but sought her lips with a fierce kiss. Her lips met his and the two, male and female, forgot all differences of class. The primeval sex instinct overleapt all barriers, and the two natures commingled in elemental passion.

Juliette in the meantime had undergone a similar experience at the hands of her assailant but, realising the hopelessness of resistance, had submitted quietly. The women, seeing that their victims were cowed, watched the scene, but at last the one of them whose skirt was torn said, 'The men be having all the fun, young man, don't 'ee want to enjoy yourself? My man 'ave vucked your missus, wouldn't 'ee like to vuck me?' I made no answer; I certainly did want the pleasure she suggested but not with her. 'Come on,' she said, and made a dive for my trousers where my virility was all too apparent. Luckily, perhaps, my excitement was so great that the touch of her hand gave the finishing touch and before I could stop myself I sprinkled her all over. 'Ah the dirty beast,' she cried, pushing it away. 'Mary, the men be arl used up, come here and do me a kindness.' The other woman came forward and without more ado plunged her hand under the torn skirt, lifting her own at the same time. There was a minute's silent pause and then the two women clutched each other and . . . let go. Muriel and Juliette were free by this time; the men were talking in undertones together. At last the one who seemed to be the leader came to me.

'Now, look 'ere, mister,' he said, 'be you agoin' to make trouble over this mornin's work? 'Cose if you be, you don't leave this beach alive; there's been no real 'arm done. Your missus and this wench 'ave enjoyed it, 'spite of everything, and so 'ave you, you know it. Vair's vair, and if so be you want to vuck our women as we've vucked yours, why there they be. I can't say vairer than that. But if you mean to make trouble, as God's my judge, we'll do vor the lot of 'ee.'

I looked at the two girls, who stood close to each other. There was nothing to be gained by making trouble. The damage, if any, *was* done. I therefore said, 'I think the least said, the soonest mended; these ladies have paid for their fault, rather severely perhaps, but if I promise not to say anything about this morning's work you must swear not to boast of what you've done. And what about these children, who were the cause of the whole trouble?' I pointed to the two girls, who had been spectators of the whole scene.

'Oh, I'll settle them kids, come 'ere Sally and Mary. Be you agoin' to zay a word about this 'ere business?' The two girls shook their heads. 'Well, we'll make zure, come 'ere.' He seized hold of one and, turning her over, belaboured her bottom and thighs with his heavy hand. Then he treated the other the same way. 'That'll larn 'ee, if you ever zo much as breathe a word, I'll tan your 'ides like you've never 'ad it afore, zo you watch it . . . 'ere, missus, you'd better go back to the cottage and clothe yerself. And what about your missus, sir? 'Er can't go 'ome like thiccy.'

'Perhaps your wife could lend her something; here's something for you to buy a new skirt for her.' I slipped a sovereign into his hand.

'You be a proper gentleman,' he said. 'I be sorry if I did wrong in vucking your missus, but if you'd like to vuck mine, why there she is, and I believe her 'ud like it.'

'Oh, that's all right, lend the lady a skirt and we'll get home.'

The women went towards a cottage in the distance. They presented a strange sight as they walked away together. Muriel and Juliette supported each other, scarcely able to stand, the former practically naked from the waist downwards, for her skirt had been torn right off and her chemise was in ribbons. Juliette's clothing had not suffered so much and she presented a slightly more decent figure. In front Muriel's brawny opponent led the way; she too showed, to all who cared to see, her fat red thighs and tattered flannelette smock. She strode ahead like some Amazonian chieftainess proudly bringing her captives home with her. The two children stayed behind with the men near me. The women disappeared into the cottage, and after a minute or two Muriel and Juliette reappeared, the former wearing a coarse skirt, much too big for her, and came towards me. I went to meet them and we silently turned homewards. Neither Muriel nor Juliette said a word as we walked along. They both seemed absolutely broken, and held on to me each to an arm. Every now and then I felt Juliette shudder and sob, but Muriel seemed past all outward display of feeling. I was wondering what Gladys and Ethel thought of the morning's adventure and was afraid lest they should be nervous at our protracted absence. I tried to rouse the two beaten women to some show of self-possession before we met them, and I was just telling them to try to put a good face on it before they met the girls when I spied the corner of a frock disappearing behind a rock. I freed myself and hurried towards it.

I was not altogether surprised to discover Miss Ethel hiding there. 'I thought I told you to go home! What are you doing here? Where's Gladys?'

'She went home. Oh, Uncle, wasn't it awful?'

'So you're been spying, have you? What have you seen?'

'Everything! Oh, Uncle, how horrible! Poor Auntie and Juliette!'

'It'll be *poor Ethel* when we get home. You know what I told you would happen.'

She looked frightened. 'I couldn't help it, Uncle! I *had* to stay and see.'

'Oh did you?' I answered grimly. 'Well, now you'll have to pay for your curiosity. I'll talk to you after dinner. Come along.'

I took her hand and we rejoined the others. 'Ethel has disobeyed me and has been spying,' I said to Muriel. 'We will deal with her after dinner.' Muriel did not seem to take much notice. Her one idea was to get home. When we arrived at the cottage we found Gladys very nervous and frightened.

Oh, I'm so glad you've come, I was getting so anxious. Ethel *would* stay behind; I tried to bring her along but she wouldn't come. I told her you would be angry but she said she didn't care.'

'She'll care, before I've finished with her.'

Ethel made a face. 'Well, if I do get a whipping it was worth it. Come on, Uncle, whip me now and get it over,' she added impudently, lifting up her skirt and exposing her bottom. Probably the beaten aspect of Muriel and Juliette inspired her with courage.

'You go to your room and wait there till I send for you.' As she did not obey, I seized hold of her and dragged her upstairs into her room and locked the door on her. Then I went back to the others. 'Gladys, you can help me; get some hot water.'

I undressed both Muriel and Juliette. Their bottoms and thighs presented a shocking spectacle. They were simply one mass of bruises from thighs right down to the knees. The flesh was all swollen and pulpy, and to my great horror, a small trickle of blood was issuing from Muriel. Her assailant had evidently been too big and too rough for her.

When Gladys returned with the hot water, I laid the two bruised bodies face downwards on the bed, and Gladys and I tenderly sponged the cruelly battered flesh. They could scarcely stand it being touched, low moans greeted every pressure of the sponge. Then I took further precautions. I syringed both of them thoroughly with antiseptic solutions, and after a thorough cleansing I swathed them in oil-soaked bandages and went downstairs to dinner with Gladys.

## CHAPTER ELEVEN

# The Reward of Spying

We took some food up to Muriel and Juliette, but they were too worn-out to touch it; Gladys asked if Ethel was not going to have any, but I said, 'No; she has been very naughty, and must be punished.'

'I *did* try to get her to come home, Uncle; really I did, but she *would* stop and watch. I knew you would be angry. Oh, Uncle, what happened? It must have been awful, I never saw such bruises, and poor Auntie was bleeding from inside. Did they do other things to her besides whipping her? How could they, they were only women!'

I told her shortly what had happened, and she saw from my fast-colouring eye – the result of my assailant's fist – that I had not altogether escaped.

'How glad I am I came home; if we had been there they might have done it to us! And I don't want anyone else but you, Uncle, to do *that* to me!' She came and sat on my knee and put her arm round my neck, kissing me and murmuring words of love. My hand went immediately under her clothes and unbuttoned her drawers. She made no resistance. Indeed, she moved slightly to allow me to pull them off, and when she was quite free of them she opened her legs wide, inviting my eager caress. I unbuttoned my trousers and placed her willing hand there. She took hold of my rampant affair, and pulling it gently towards her, she whispered, 'Put it there, Uncle, I want it; oh please put it there.'

'No, I mustn't; I promised I wouldn't; not yet.'

'But I want it, I want it.'

'Kiss it instead, and I'll kiss you – lie down on the couch.' She went straight to the couch and lay on her back with open arms and legs, displaying all the perfection of her virgin sex. I bent over her and fastened my lips to the pouting pink slit and began to suck greedily the sweet juice that was already welling up. At the same moment I felt her lips close round my member and the caressing tongue drawing me right into her mouth. She had not long to wait. 'Look out,' I panted, 'it'll happen.'

'I want it,' she answered, 'I want every bit of it.' As I felt the supreme moment approaching, I raised myself slightly and, looking down, could just see her eager lips working round my weapon as it throbbed in ecstasy. She gulped in answer until the flood came too quick for her and she had to draw back, allowing the liquor to spurt all over her face and neck.

I disengaged myself and turned towards her. She smiled up at me. 'It's not very nice, but it's *you*, I love it . . . oh, there's another drop, let me have that.' She drew me towards her and drained the last remaining drops eagerly.

'Now for Miss Ethel,' I said. 'You go up and wash and tell her I'm ready.'

'You won't be too severe with her, will you, Uncle?'

'She must be taught to obey,' I answered, and followed her upstairs.

We found Ethel sitting on the bed, evidently half-frightened, half-defiant. 'I was wondering when you were coming,' she said. 'Isn't dinner ready?'

'*I'm* ready,' I answered. 'Dinner may come later, when you've been punished for your disobedience. Take your things off and come with me.'

'I want my dinner.'

'Do as I tell you, you'll have no dinner yet.'

'I shan't, I want my dinner.'

Gladys was washing her face. 'You'd better do as you're told, Ethel, she said. 'I told you Uncle Cecil would be angry. Don't make it worse for yourself, take your things off, and perhaps he won't be too severe with you.'

'You mind your own business,' retorted Ethel. 'I want my dinner and I mean to have it.'

She made a dart for the door, but I seized her and dragged her struggling to Muriel's room. She fought and kicked and struggled but could not escape.

Once inside the room, I said to Muriel, 'Here is Ethel, who disobeyed me and watched all that took place this morning. Will you punish her, or shall I?'

'You begin, Cecil; I'm too worn-out. Whip her well so that I can see it. Perhaps I'll help later.'

'Now Ethel,' I said, 'are you going to take your things off yourself or shall I have to do it for you? I warn you for your own sake that you had better do it yourself.'

'I want my dinner,' repeated Ethel. I went to the cases, which were in the room, opened one and took out a cane, and brought it smartly across her shoulders. 'Will you obey me?' She uttered a cry as the cane fell across the thin frock, but made no attempt to undress.

Again and again the cane fell. 'Oh please, Uncle, yes, I'll take my things off, I will really.'

'Make haste then,' rapping her across the knuckles as she fumbled with the buttons.

Hot and angry tears appeared in her eyes as she tried to avoid the blows and the dress fell to the ground. The corsets followed, leaving only the chemise covering her slim young body. She began to unfasten that, but I stopped her. 'Keep that on for the present. Now I'm going to whip you severely for your gross disobedience and curiosity. I distinctly told you to go home this morning but you wilfully disobeyed me out of insolent curiosity; in consequence you were witness of your Aunt's and Juliette's shame. Your body will now pay for your disobedience and I will try to make you remember to obey me in the future. Bend forward a little and draw that chemise tight across your back.'

She gave me a frightened look but did as I told her. She evidently expected that her bottom was to suffer, for she drew the chemise tight round her hips, bending forward so that the outline of the cheeks and thighs was clearly revealed. My intentions, however, were different, and I surprised her by directing my cuts across her back. She gave a surprised cry as the cane fell just below her shoulders. The chemise, only half-tight, caught the blow, and the thin cane cut through the flimsy muslin. Another cut followed, tearing it still more, until after about half a dozen the frail stuff tore right away and hung down in ribbons. I warmed to the work and deftly cut more away at each stroke. The stuff, thin as it was, acted as some sort of protection – though not much – to her body, for as it fell away only slight weals showed on the skin. When the garment was in tatters, I took hold of it and ripped it right away so that she stood there quite naked, save for a little yoke of muslin left round her shoulders.

During this part of her punishment involuntary cries came from her, but not a tear. Her lips were set and she was evidently determined not to break down if she could help it.

I laid the cane aside and took up a birch. 'Now,' I said, 'your bottom shall get what you evidently expected just now. Now tell me, will you disobey me again, will you, will you? . . . Answer me when I speak to you! answer me, I say.' Sharp biting cuts punctuated each question, but not a word came from the set lips of the determined girl. I was provoked at her obstinacy and rained blow after blow on the slim legs and cheeks. She bore every attack in silence; her flesh flinched each time the stinging twigs fell but otherwise she displayed no feeling.

Muriel had followed the punishment so far in silence, but now seeing that the girl remained stubborn, she roused herself painfully and said, 'I'll make her speak, let *me* help.' She got out of bed and, taking the wire birch in her hand, came haltingly towards her victim. 'Bend her right down, Cecil, lower than that, lower still – that's better.' I bent the stiff body right down – it might have been made of stone, so unyielding was it – until the head was as low as the knees. The skin of the bottom was consequently stretched quite tight. Muriel separated the legs so that they formed a triangle. 'Now young lady, I'll teach you to spy on me.' The little wire birch hissed in the air and fell. A shriek of agony came from Ethel. She fell forward in spite of my hold on her.

'Oh, Uncle, don't let her . . . I'm sorry . . . you whip me if you like, but not her . . . oh, oh, oh!' The birch fell again and again, each point piercing the skin and drawing blood. 'Oh, Uncle, tell her to stop, I'll never disobey you again, oh, Auntie, I'm sorry, oh don't, don't!'

She writhed and twisted on the floor. I signed to Muriel to stop, for the blood was trickling down the white thighs. 'That will do for now,' I said. 'Now Ethel, every morning for a week you are to come to your aunt and Juliette and myself and say, "I'm sorry I was disobedient and spied on you; please whip me as I deserve." Do you understand? Every morning before you dress – now go to Gladys and ask her to wash you and put you to bed and I'll bring you up your dinner.'

Ethel rose to her feet, white and tear-stained, and silently went out of the room. I followed her after a minute or two and found her being soothed by Gladys. When she saw me she looked imploringly at me. 'I'm truly sorry, Uncle,' she said, 'I am really. But need I be whipped by Auntie? Won't it do if you whip me?'

'Certainly not,' I answered. 'You spied on your aunt, and must pay for it.'

'But *three* whippings every morning!'

'I told you, you'd be sorry,' said Gladys, 'but you wouldn't listen.'

Those morning whippings of Ethel came to be for me one of the best parts of the day. To be awakened out of sleep by the touch of a light hand and to hear a small voice say, 'Uncle, I'm here; I'm sorry I spied on you, please whip me as I deserve,' helped an already rampant member to sit up and take an interest in things.

The first one or two mornings Muriel and Juliette were rather severe and the poor little bottom was still sore from the wounds of the wire birch. She came sobbing into my room and threw herself into my arms, begging to be let off. But that I would not do altogether. I contented myself, however, with roughly tracing the word 'spy' – one letter a morning – on the front of her thighs and stomach with the riding whip. The lash just flicked little red weals on the skin and six cuts were enough for each letter.

On the fourth morning Muriel and Juliette had evidently let her off more lightly, for there were no tears. I accordingly had less scruples as regards my share. I made her lie on her back on the bed and hold each leg by the ankle as wide apart and as far back as possible. In this position she showed absolutely all there was to show. I took a few twigs from a birch and flicked her everywhere, making the ends of the twigs curl wickedly into every secret cranny. At first she seemed to like it rather, for she only squealed now and then and laughed wickedly up at me from between her knees. I remembered it was punishment, not pleasure, and gave her several hard cuts with the twigs all up and down the inside of her thighs and between the cheeks of her bottom, until the twigs broke off short. These blows changed her tune and she soon cried out for mercy.

The next morning I tied her by the ankles to the bed-rail, so that her head was on the ground, and encircled her thighs and flanks with a whip. She had come in rather cheekily, evidently thinking her punishment was nearly over or ought to be, and I thought it as well to show her that some atonement was still required. She certainly presented rather a pathetic figure tied up as she was with her nightdress fallen down over her head and her slim white body and legs at the mercy of the lash. In her position she could not move much, only writhe and twist her body, while, from underneath the nightdress, shrill cries greeted each cut. When I released her she crept sobbing to my feet, imploring forgiveness and mercy. I could not help pitying her, but the fierce joy of inflicting pain and the lust for torture were stronger than the pity, and I had just self-control enough that morning not to inflict some really serious harm on the girl.

She must have seen the struggle going on in me, for she flung her arms round me and said, 'You don't hate me, Uncle, do you, although you hurt me so? . . . I don't mind your hurting me, but don't hate me, for I love you.' I kissed her passionately and sent her away to her own room.

On the last day of her seven, she came to my room very merry and bright. 'Have you been to Aunt and Juliette?' I asked. 'Oh yes, but they were in bed together; they were far too busy with each other to attend to me. They just smacked me once each and told me to come to you. Uncle, I'm quite ready for you.' She cheekily pulled up her nightdress and bent down.

'Say what you have to say.'

'I'm sorry I spied on you; please whip me as I deserve.' She rattled the words off quickly with a 'don't care' air.

'Right!' I said. 'I will.' I got out of bed, laid her across my knee and brought my hand smartly down on the tempting bottom. I did not spare her this morning and soon the skin began to grow pink and my palm began to smart. I got up and reached for my hairbrush, then, making her bend forward, I stood on one side of her and smacked her, pretty severely, with the back of it. My pyjamas were loose and began to fall, exposing John Thomas ready, as usual in the early morning, for anything. Ethel looked up at me and, seeing that I wasn't really angry, began to play with him and fondle him. I continued smacking her, until she began to protest. 'Ooh, you do hurt this morning. I suppose it's because it's the last time. Ooh!'

An idea struck me. 'Yes, we'll finish well,' I said. 'Wait a moment,' and I got on the bed, lying on my back. 'Now get on top of me . . . no, the other way . . . that's right, now across me and kiss me nicely.' She took John Thomas in her mouth and her eager lips and tongue began caressing it.

'I haven't done this, for a long time, I *do* love it! Ooh! that's lovely! . . . I don't like *that* though.' Her little bottom just came within reach of my tongue, and as I caressed her tiny slit, I continued to smack the rounded cheeks with the brush. The blows fell harder as I felt the goal approaching and she began to wriggle. I held her still with my left hand, and when John Thomas at last responded to the caresses of her tongue, I rained a rapid shower of blows all over the rounded surface. Her own nature answered mine at the same moment and I drank greedily of her young fresh love.

She fell full-length on top of me, her knees giving way under the stress of her passion, and she sucked and drew all my strength from me with her eager lips and tongue, while her slender fingers squeezed and fondled the balls that hung down between my thighs. I have seldom given such a copious flow as she drew from me that morning. Yet she scarcely seemed satisfied. Even when John Thomas had yielded all he had to give for the moment she still continued to suck, until he dwindled and softened and she reluctantly let him go.

## CHAPTER TWELVE

# *A Sacrifice to Aphrodite Pandemos*

That certain morning's adventure had quite different effects on Muriel and Juliette. The latter soon recovered her normal spirits and seemed to forget and ignore what had happened. With Muriel it was quite different. Hers was a far more highly strung and sensitive nature, and for some days she seemed entirely overwhelmed. I waited anxiously, with daily enquiries and investigations, for reassuring proof that no lasting results and awkward and serious consequences had resulted from the adventure. Within a few days I was satisfied in the case of Juliette, but there was still a week to wait before I could know the truth about Muriel.

During this time her moods were very varying. At first she seemed quite stunned and apathetic. She roused herself the first morning or two to wreak some vengeance on Ethel, but even that failed to interest her after a few days, as I have told. Then she became very hysterical and irritable. At first I tried kindness and solicitude, but she grew so peevish and ill-tempered that I lost patience and threatened her with harsh measures if she did not control her temper better. She did not take much notice, so after some recrimination on her part I felt that kindness and forbearance were no good and gave her a sound whipping. She took it passively, saying nothing when it was finished. There was a look of fixed intention in her eye which I could not fathom, but though she said nothing the pain evidently had some effect, for the rest of the day she was far less sulky and irritable.

At last I went to her in bed one morning and found her in tears. 'What's the matter?' I asked. She wouldn't answer, and growing tired of repeating my question without any reply, I pulled the clothes down, intending to thrash an answer out of her. Then I saw that her nightdress was stained with blood, and I realised that I need have no further fear of any consequences. My anger disappeared at once. I gave a sigh of relief. 'Thank God!' I said.

She looked at me. 'Why?' she asked.

'That,' I answered, pointing to the stains.

She suddenly flared out at me. 'Yes, that's just like you men, selfish and cruel. The pleasure of the moment – that's all you want. But I want more. I want something to remind me of him always.'

'What on earth are you talking about?' I said. 'What do you mean? You surely don't mean to say that you want a baby!'

'Yes, I do, I want *his* baby.'

'His! whose?' She was silent. 'Tell me, what do you mean? Are you suddenly gone mad or what?'

'I want a baby by *him*.' She moaned, and burst into a passion of tears. I was silent, for the situation was beyond me. After she had sobbed out her passion to some extent and had grown calmer she turned to me imploringly. 'Oh, Cecil, I want him so, I must have him, do let me have him again. You may beat me, torture me anyway you like, but only let me feel him mix with me again!'

'What on earth are you talking about?'

'That man, that day,' she stammered.

I was thunderstruck. Then I turned on her in a rage. 'How dare you? Are you mad? You want to prostitute yourself to that yokel, that clod! You deserve – I don't know what you deserve – !'

'I know, I know, Cecil dear; but I can't help it – it makes me terribly ashamed but I can't resist it. Oh, let me go to him, let me have him. Then I will be your slave again as long as you like. I'll do anything, I'll suffer anything, only let me have just this one satisfaction.' She writhed all over the bed clutching at me with imploring hands, exposing all her body as she twisted about in her passion. The sight of her lascivious gestures fired me and I took her in my arms and regardless of her condition possessed her. She welcomed me gladly and with utter abandon.

When I had finished she murmured, 'That was kind and sweet of you, dear; but – don't be angry – it's *him* I want. I love *you*, but I want *him* – oh, do let me have him, do let me, just once – only once – I promise you it shall be only once.'

I could not understand her. 'I must think,' I said. 'If I *do* let you, you will probably have to pay severely for it.'

'I'll pay any price you like,' she answered.

I went away and sought Juliette, and told her the facts of the case. 'What do you advise?' I asked her.

'I'm not altogether surprised,' she answered. 'I know she was absolutely carried beyond herself by the second man. We've talked about that morning, and she as good as told me what she has said to you.'

'Well, what's to be done?'

'It's up to you,' she answered. 'If you don't mind her being had by other men, and I rather think you liked it the other morning, why not let her have her way?' I was silent for a moment.

'If I do, it must be done in my own way,' I said, 'and I don't know if the gentleman will consent to that. I must be there to see.'

'Let us all be there,' said Juliette; 'that may perhaps cure Muriel of her infatuation, when she discovers that we all know about it.'

I thought about it for a day or two, and when Muriel was herself again, I decided to go over and sound out her bucolic Adonis. I took with me the skirt that had been lent to cover her nakedness, as a cloak for my visit. When

I arrived at the cottage, I found the woman at home. She grinned at me when she opened the door.

'Good-morning, I've brought your skirt back.'

'Oh, have 'ee,' she laughed. 'I never thought to see 'ee again, young man. My man's been in a terrible way about your lot. 'E turned coward after you'd gone, like all men, and was afeared for what might 'appen. I told 'im 'e needn't worry, but 'e's terrible anxious.'

'You tell him from me, he needn't be afraid; where's the other man? I want to speak to him.'

'Which one? There were three of 'em.'

'Oh, the other one that . . . that . . . ' I did not know how to finish the sentence.

' 'Im that vucked your missus after my man 'ad vinished, d'ye mean?' she said boldly. I nodded. 'Oh 'e's at work. 'E'll be 'ome soon, if so you'ld like to wait. Come inside, young man, I'm all alone.' Her meaning was unmistakable, but I had no desire or intention whatever of gratifying her desire. 'You baint afeared of me, sure-lie! Come along I won't eat 'ee.' What might have happened I don't know, but at that moment the two girls who had started the fracas the other morning appeared in the distance. 'Dang the brats!' said the woman. 'They be always in the way when they baint wanted.' Then, as she saw my eye following their young figures as they ran towards us, she went on, 'Ah! that's what'ud suit you, eh young man, I don't doubt, but they be too young as yet. That'd mean 'sizes business for 'ee.'

I laughed nervously, for I didn't know I had betrayed myself by my expression. 'No, no, you're quite wrong; I wasn't thinking of that at all. I was only thinking of the other morning when they got smacked. I suppose they often get smacked, don't they?'

'Not more than is good for them, the young limbs! Look 'ere mister,' she said suddenly, 'be you that sort of young man? . . . Oh I know,' she went on, as I kept silence, 'I was in service in my young days and I know what my master and missus used to do. I saw the marks on your missus's bottom, t'other morning, be you one o' they whipping chaps?' I smiled. 'I thought as much,' she nodded. 'Now look 'ere, would 'ee like me to smack 'em before 'ee now? What would 'ee do if I did, eh?' she smiled up at me provokingly. She really was not a bad-looking woman, in spite of the coarsening effects of her hard life.

'You had better wait and see,' I said. The girls had stopped when they saw me talking to their mother. They evidently had recognised me and were approaching nervously.

'Where 'ave you been, Sally and Mary?' shouted their mother. 'I told 'ee to 'urry back, come 'ere and say good-marnin' to the gentleman, and then tell me where you've been. I lay I'll pay your bottoms well, you lazy little varmints.' They came nervously towards me and bobbed a curtsey. 'Sally, go and fetch me the strap.' The child gave her mother a frightened look but obeyed. The other girl made a start as if to run away. 'Catch 'old of 'er mister, don't 'ee let 'er go.' I did as I was asked, and Sally returned with the strap. In a minute she was under her mother's arm with her skirts turned up – she wore no drawers – and a hail of blows from the strap was descending on her bottom and thighs. From the cries and the plunging of her legs, she was catching it pretty hot. 'Now Mary, it be your turn. Pull 'er clothes up, will 'ee, mister, and I'll tan 'er young 'ide.' I was not slow in doing what I was asked, as may be guessed. I bent the young body down so that the head was between my thighs and then uncovered all the back and legs. Down came the strap right across the plump cheeks, leaving a broad red mark. Mary was about a year younger than her sister but plumper and more developed. Again and again fell the strap, and from between my legs came muffled cries for mercy. The strap evidently was a most effective though noisy weapon. 'There, that'll teach 'ee to loiter, you young devils,' at last said the mother, 'now be off and tell Ben a gentleman wants to see 'im, 'e's working over at varmer Thorpe's. That be two mile away,' she added to me, as the girls ran painfully away. 'Now, young man, what be 'ee agoin' to pay me for the show?'

I looked at her. In spite of her general untidiness and blowsiness, she was a fine figure of a woman. In her younger days she must have been decidedly handsome in a coarse way. Now she looked like some savage queen, holding the lash.

'What do you want?' I asked. An unaccountable longing to be mastered by her came over me.

'You know what I want, young man, come inside.'

'I don't know that I'll give it to you,' I said, 'unless you take it.' I looked meaningly at her and at the strap. 'Oh,' she said, 'be it like that with you? It'll be old master and missus over again. I've listened at the door. I know.'

Before I quite knew what was happening, she had seized hold of my trousers – I was wearing loose flannels and a sash – and had ripped the fly open. They fell round my knees. She then gripped me round the waist and drew me down across her knee. I yielded in a strange kind of fascinated stupor. To this day I cannot account for it or explain it. I am not by nature a masochist – my whole tendency being entirely the other way – but at that moment I had only one desire, one passion – to submit my body to the domination of this woman. She was not slow to take advantage of my mood. She dragged the trousers well down, placed one leg over mine imprisoning me between her knees, raised my shirt well over my back, and then . . . oh, the murderous agony of that first blow. It entirely cured me of any masochistic desire at that moment. But it was too late. Her left hand pressed firmly on my back, her knees gripped my legs, I was powerless. Blow followed blow, now here, now there. The pain was awful. I set my teeth and tried to bear it, but it was no good. The tears and cries would come. 'Ah!' she hissed, 'I'll teach 'ee, you miserable worm; won't vuck me, won't 'ee, what good be 'ee, what did 'ee marry me for? I'll teach 'ee.' I gathered that she was quoting her old mistress.

At last my cries and sobs became more unrestrained, my prayers for mercy more agonised. I promised anything.

'Let me go,' I prayed, 'I'll do anything, oh let me go.' I joined words of love and endearments with my prayers, I tried to find her sex with my hands, pulling up her skirt and stroking her thigh. At last she released me and I stood tottering and shaking before her. She looked at me triumphantly and then without a word took hold of my member and, making me kneel before her as she sat in the chair, opened her legs and drew me right inside her. The paroxysm came almost at once, but she would not let me go. She held me close to her, and by fierce caresses of my balls and every method she could think of, she succeeded in forcing a second erection and drained me again of my manhood.

## CHAPTER THIRTEEN

## *Saeva Venus*

I went home in a kind of ecstasy. My whole nature was in a turmoil. I was smarting terribly from the strap and was longing for, not exactly revenge – that was not the word I wanted – but for others to share my pain. I must whip someone, somehow; whip them as I had been whipped – cruelly, mercilessly. Who should it be? Muriel? Juliette? Ethel or Gladys? Gladys? Yes, the idea appealed to me most strongly. I was fondest of her; she loved me, I knew; she was the gentlest of the four; she gave me, too, least cause for punishment. Yet if I could find or make an excuse, I would whip her, whip her till the blood ran. I had told the woman to send Ben to me late that afternoon and so had some hours free. When I got to the cottage I found Muriel in bed, asleep. Juliette and Ethel were out. Gladys was waiting for me. How my heart leapt at the sight of her! How I longed to torture and cut that slender fragile body. She came running towards me. 'Oh, Uncle, wherever have you been? I've been waiting for you for such a long time. What have you been doing?'

'What's that to do with you?' I answered roughly. 'How dare you be inquisitive about my doings!'

She started at my rough tone. 'Uncle,' she gasped, 'what's the matter? I didn't mean . . . '

'I'll show you what's the matter, I'll teach you to question me.'

'But, Uncle.'

'Go upstairs at once. I'll follow you.' She went in without a word, as white as a sheet. I went to my room, chose a cane, and followed her. She trembled when she saw what was in my hand. 'Take your drawers off,' I said.

'But, Uncle, why! I haven't done anything.'

'Do as I tell you, take those drawers off and lie across the bed. I'll teach you to be inquisitive.'

'But, Uncle, oh don't,' as the cane fell across her shoulders.

'Will you take them off!' Her nervous fingers fumbled for the buttons and at last the flimsy muslin fell round her ankles. '*Now*, turn your skirts up and lie across the bed.' She obeyed bewildered. 'Now take that, and that, and that. How dare you ask questions as to where I've been, and what I've been doing? Just because I've been kind to you and not punished you as I've punished your sister, you think you can presume. But I'll teach you. There, there, there and there.'

'Oh, Uncle, don't, oh, don't! What have I done? I'm sorry, oh, Uncle, please . . . '

'Take that hand away, take it away – there then,' and the cane fell on the wrist, extorting a howl of anguish from the poor girl. Blue livid weals began to appear all over the rounded cheeks and thighs. The cries turned to dull moans. The soft bruised flesh flinched at each blow of the cane. My passion began to abate and after some half a dozen cruel cuts I threw the cane – all bent by this time – into a corner and lifted the quivering body into my arms. Her eyes were half-closed, her cheeks were deathly pale, I thought at first that she had fainted, but when she felt my arms around her drawing her to me, she opened her eyes and murmured, 'Oh, Uncle, why! What did I do? What made you whip me like that?'

I sat on the bed and tried to take her in my arms. She could not bear to sit on my knee. She was too bruised, but she lay half on her face on top of me, her arms clinging round my neck. The tears streamed down her cheeks, and her whole body shook with emotion.

We stayed like that for some time and at last she grew quieter and I recovered my sanity. I gently disengaged myself and set about repairing the ravages of my rage. As I tenderly anointed her bruised flesh with the emollient cream I always had handy, she again murmured her oft-repeated question – 'Oh, Uncle, why! What had I done?'

When she had grown still calmer, and was lying on her side, I told her what had happened. As I expected, she did not wholly understand. Her chief feeling was one of rage and jealousy against the woman. 'The beast, the beast!' she kept on murmuring. 'Oh, I wish I had her here. Oh, Uncle, darling, everyone has you but me; Uncle darling, take me, take me, I want you, I want you . . . see!' She rolled over on her back, wincing as she rested on her bruised flesh, and opening her legs as wide as she possibly could, she parted with her fingers the lips of her virgin pussy. Had it not been that I had been drained dry already, I probably should have taken her at her word; as it was, I bent down, and fastening my lips to those delicious pouting ones, I sucked and drained her until I felt she had no more to give. She sighed and moaned in ecstasy, her hands caressing my hair. At last, as I drew away, she murmured, 'Ah, that was heaven, but I'm sure the real thing must be better still. Oh, Uncle, did you really let that beastly woman whip you! I'd kill her if I had the chance. Did she hurt you much? Let me see.' She drew me towards her and, unbuttoning my trousers, found John Thomas, who was doing his best to stand and weeping at his failure. She kissed him all over and then, lifting my shirt, gazed at my bruised behind. 'Oh, poor, poor bottom,' she said. 'I don't wonder you wanted to hurt someone else. And you hurt me because you love me best, was that it?' I nodded. 'Yes, I think I understand, and I'm glad; oh, poor, poor bottom.' She bent down and covered both cheeks with soft tender kisses, letting her soft smooth tongue caress the bruises gently. Then, giving each cheek the daintiest of little pats, she smiled up at me. 'There, I've smacked you too; now, cover it up and let's go out and find the others.'

As we went along, I told her all about Muriel's sudden and strange passion for the man who had violated her, and how I had discussed the matter with Juliette, and how we had agreed that she should have a chance to gratify her passion *but* in our presence. 'She does not know that part of it,' I said. 'In fact, I haven't told her at all that I have agreed to it, but I think I shall. Ben (that's his name, from what the woman tells me) is coming to see me this afternoon, and if he consents to what I shall propose, your aunt will be sacrificed to Aphrodite Pandemos in the presence of all of us.'

She was silent for a moment or two, and then she said, as if thinking aloud, 'Yes – I think I see – but how can she want anyone else when she has *you*, Uncle? Oh, I wish . . . Uncle, will there be any whipping of *him*? If there is, let me do it – it will be nearly as good as whipping that awful woman . . . Will you let me? Do, please.'

'I don't quite know what will happen,' I answered. 'Neither of them as yet knows that anything is going to take place; but if I see my chance, you shall have what you want.' She kissed me fondly and we went on to find the others.

After tea that afternoon I was smoking a cigarette outside the cottage, and I saw a figure coming across the beach; I thought I recognised the man and went to meet him. It was Ben. 'Evenin', zur,' he said. 'My sister told me as 'ow you wanted me.' He looked rather nervous, as if not quite certain as to what was in store for him, but in spite of his rather hang-dog air, he was still a fine figure of a man – a perfectly developed animal, healthy and full-blooded.

'Yes,' I said, 'it's like this; your exploit of the other morning has had rather unexpected results. Instead of being enraged with you, as she might have been, the lady whom you possessed has conceived a great desire for you and has asked me to get you to see her again. Now I am willing that she should gratify her desire on one condition – that you do exactly as I order; that you – in a word – place yourself entirely at my disposal, submitting to everything I say.'

'I don't understand 'ee, zur,' he said. 'You zay the lady wants me? Aye, I thought as much. I zaid at the time 'er loved me. Aye and I love 'er, but what do 'ee want?'

'I want *this*,' I said. 'She's my mistress, and if I lend her to you, you must both be utterly in my power, at the moment, to do what I like with. I am quite sure of her, I know – but you – well, I must be sure that I have you utterly in subjection if I let you enjoy her, will you consent to this?'

'I don't follow your meanin', zur; be I to vuck 'er? or what do 'ee want I to do?'

'Yes, certainly, but other things may happen while that is going on. Now, will you consent to have your arms tied together while you are enjoying her; or will you swear to me that you will submit to any treatment while your pleasure lasts? . . . Oh, you needn't be afraid . . . nothing serious will happen, but I want to know where I am before I start.'

He scratched his head. 'I don't rightly know, zur,' he said, 'what exactly you're at; but I do want 'er again, that's a fact, and if so be I be so fortunate as to 'ave 'er, I don't much mind what happens. My sister, she've told me that you're a gentleman who likes fancy tricks, and she've told me arl about this marnin' ' – he added with a grin – 'so I be ready for anything of that kind if it's that you want.'

'Right,' I said. 'Wait just a moment, and I'll get things ready.' I went into the cottage, leaving him outside. I found Muriel still in bed. 'Muriel,' I said, 'I've found you the man you want; he's outside; shall I bring him up?'

She could hardly believe her ears. 'Oh, Cecil, you darling,' she said, 'do you really mean it?'

'Yes, he's waiting.'

'Oh, let me get ready for him; oh, how wonderful you are!' She jumped out of bed and searched in the chest of drawers for a clean nightdress. Seeing the scent spray on the dressing-table, she sprayed herself all over, and began brushing her hair. It might have been a devotee preparing for religious mysteries rather than a lustful woman preparing for her lover. I smiled grimly and went down to muster the others. Juliette and Gladys, of course, knew what to expect, but Ethel was quite ignorant. I warned the other two in whispers to keep her well in hand, and then went out to find Ben. I took him up to my own room and suggested that he had better take his clothes off.

He did so slowly and shyly. 'Where be I to go, zur,' he said. 'I do 'ope as no one will zee me naked like this!'

'This way,' I said when he had stripped, leading the way to Muriel's room. I had lighted all the candles in the room. Muriel was lying in a most seductive nightdress. When he crossed to the bed I called to the others. They came quietly up the stairs, and just as Ben, after kissing Muriel, was preparing to get on top of her, they all filed into the room. He stopped as if thunderstruck. His rampant engine wilted; an acute fit of nervousness seized him. He looked round.

'What be this, zur?' he asked. 'I bain't used to making love in public.'

'You said you would submit to me; it's either this way or no way at all. Put out your hands.' He did so mechanically, and before he knew what had happened, I had slipped the handcuffs which I knew so well from personal experience on his wrists.

'Now,' I said, pulling back the bedclothes and raising Muriel's nightdress so that her legs and stomach were exposed to the gaze of all of us, 'there's the woman who wants you, there's the woman whom you want. Take her and enjoy her.'

The sudden shock and surprise had for the moment taken away his erection. He looked at me and then at himself. 'I can't do nothin' like this, zur; I be nervous.'

'Gladys,' I said, 'you wanted the chance this afternoon, go to that case and fetch a birch.' I gave her the key and she quickly took out a birch. 'Now, see if you can make our friend fit for his duty.' The yokel looked all eyes at this. It was evidently beyond his comprehension. 'Now, Gladys, give him some keen cuts across his bottom. You needn't be afraid of hurting him. His skin's pretty tough, I expect.' Gladys needed no second order. She brought the birch heavily down across the brawny buttocks.

Ben jumped away. 'What's the meaning of this?' he shouted. 'I baint agoin' to be whipped.'

'You keep quiet, my man,' I said. 'Curl it between his thighs, Gladys; now touch him up in front a little, that's better.' I saw his old man twitch nervously and, bending forward, took hold of it. It answered to my touch and rose magnificently. 'Now,' I said, 'do your duty.' I helped him on top of Muriel and placed his member at the entrance of what it desired. Then I ventured to undo the handcuffs and left him free. I stopped Gladys's blows for the moment and watched the scene on the bed. Muriel, past all sense of shame in the gratification of her desire, was receiving her lover with open body, arms, and legs. Her loins met his impassioned thrusts, and when I saw that they were nearing the end of their course, I signed to Gladys to continue her chastisement. Her blows fell quicker and quicker, as the man's loins worked in ever-quickening plunges; at last I saw that the supreme moment was coming, and seizing the birch from Gladys's hands, I rained a shower of carefully directed blows on the heaving buttocks and thighs. He took no notice of my attack, but like a high-couraged racehorse under the whip over the last furlong, put forth all his efforts for the final sprint, and at last, clutching Muriel's bottom with his hands, he first dragged her to him and then collapsed on top of her, having spent his final energy. I stopped my assault and looked round. Gladys was on the other side of the bed to me, watching the scene with wide eyes of fascinated wonder. On my side of the room Juliette and Ethel had at first been standing silent spectators, but now I saw that the scene had proved too much for them; Juliette had sunk on a chair and drawn Ethel on top of her. She had pulled her skirts up and Ethel's busy fingers were eagerly probing her most secret recesses. The two bodies on the bed were closely entwined in the abyss of passion.

When I thought that they had lain long enough like this, I touched Ben on the shoulder. 'Well,' I said, 'did you enjoy it?' He got up rather sheepishly, and grinned. 'That be a new game to I,' he said, 'to be whipped while one be vucking, but it baint bad.'

'Well, next time,' I said, 'it will be the other way about; you lie on the bed, and when you're ready she shall get on top of you.'

'I be ready now,' he answered, and sure enough I saw that his old man was rising again. 'I'll soon make 'ee fit,' he went on, rubbing himself vigorously. Muriel up to this time had appeared not to notice our presence in the room. We had all come in after Ben had appeared naked before her and had just begun to mount her. Possibly her desire for him had overcome any latent shame or modesty, and she had decided to take all she could get just as she could get it. But now, when she saw Ben lying beside her on his back encouraging his engine for a second attack, and when I went to her and told her to get on top of him, she whispered to me, 'I didn't bargain for this, Cecil; I didn't mean that the girls should see this.'

'You do as you are told,' I said. 'Get on top of him; you wanted him, you've got him; you ought to be very grateful that you have him at all.'

She made no further protest but got up and knelt across the massive body. Then, taking his affair in her hand, she placed it just between her lips and, slowly sinking down, impaled herself on it. When I saw her well fitted, 'Now,' I said, 'you two, make her work.' I gave Gladys back the birch and fetched another for Ethel, and the two, standing on either side of the bed, rained blow after blow on the plunging thighs and loins. Muriel heaved and plunged as the blows fell; groans and sighs of mingled passion and pain came from her lips. Ben clutched her round the waist with his brawny arms and moved with her plunges. At last, however, the supine position irked him, unused to it as he evidently was, and he twisted round, and, without disengaging his body, managed to work himself on top of her. The blows of the birches now fell on him, instead of on Muriel, but he paid no attention to them. His buttocks heaved and fell. His thighs opened and closed and at last after a few vicious mighty thrusts he collapsed motionless on Muriel's body.

In the meantime Juliette and I had not been idle. Beginning with mutual caresses, I at last pulled her on to my lap with her back to me, and finding her eager inviting pussy, I slipped my old man into it, and while watching the contest on the bed, I rode her on my knee until I gave and took from her all I wanted.

This last bout had practically finished Muriel. When I got Ben off her, she lay just as she was, not caring to hide her nakedness at all. The lips of her pussy were still wide open and a small stream of viscous matter trickled from between them. Ben had evidently given her all she could hold. I motioned him to follow me out of the room, and led him back to where his clothes were. As he was dressing, I said to him, 'Well, are you satisfied?'

'I've had a rare proper good time, zur,' he said, 'but what beats me is why you let me do it. You've got a vine wench there, and yet you let me 'ave 'er.'

I smiled. 'No, my friend, I don't suppose you *do* understand; but I'll tell you this much. She's mine, as you say, to do just what I like with, and if I choose to give her to anyone that's my affair. If I choose to give her to a *dog*, I will, she daren't refuse. If on the other hand, I refuse to allow her any single thing she may want, still she has to submit – but there, it beats you, as you say, so we won't say any more about it. Good-night to you, and keep your mouth shut. It may happen again if you hold your tongue – so mum's the word.'

'You may trust me, zur,' he replied. 'I'm mum as an oyster. Good-night and thank 'ee.'

## CHAPTER FOURTEEN

## *The Roman Dinner*

The orgy described in the last chapter was the last of any note which we had at Croyde. Muriel, the next day, seemed somewhat – I won't say exactly ashamed – but at any rate subdued. *Post coitum omne animal triste est*, says the Roman philosopher, and it was certainly true in her case. She was uniformly affectionate and dutiful to me, but she seemed to have lost her interest in the holiday. The weather, too, became bad, and altogether we came to the conclusion that London in the wet was better than the country. We accordingly packed up and departed from Croyde, arriving at the little house in South Molton Street late one evening at the end of August.

There was still a fortnight or so of holidays left to the girls and we decided that theatres and Earl's Court should take the place of sea-bathing and picnics. For more intimate pleasures Muriel's boudoir was far better fitted than the cottage. I seized the opportunity too of running down to Oxford to take my degree and, after paying the necessary fees to the university and my scout, was duly received as a Bachelor of Arts.

I came back to town and determined to have one glorious evening before the girls went back to school. I had told Muriel something of my idea and she agreed gladly. I doubt if she had known the details she would have consented so readily. But that is by the way. In a word I determined to revive a night under the Roman Empire, as far as modern conditions would allow. Muriel's bathroom lent itself to this especially. As I have said, it was a hobby of her husband's, being more like a plunge in a Turkish bath than an ordinary bathroom. It was all of marble about four feet deep with steps leading down into it. It was heated by a hypocaust and about twelve feet long. One could swim or float in it in comfort.

The bath was to begin the evening. Afterwards there was to be a feast. For this Muriel's boudoir was admirably adapted. The divan, or couch, made a very good substitute for a triclinium and a table was the only other necessary piece of furniture. I ordered in a special cold supper from Benoist's, so that it could be kept handy and served without outside help. I chose dishes as nearly Roman as were palatable – flamingos' tongues were of course unobtainable. The wine was the only thing modern. A visit to Clarkson's for costumes, etc., was the only other preparation.

The entertainment began in the bath. I made all the girls strip naked and did the same myself. Then, while Muriel, Juliette and Gladys stood naked on one side of the bath as attendants, I revived with Ethel the Spintria, as described by Suetonius. In strict accuracy Ethel ought to have been a boy, but in the circumstances I decided that that was not a very important point and might be waived; though later in the evening I did my best to remedy that, as will be seen.

For those who don't know their Suetonius and his description of Tiberius's life at Capri I will describe the Spintria. I floated on my back in the bath and Ethel swam slowly between my legs, caressing all my private parts with her hands and mouth until the natural result happened. When that was over we came out of the water and the three girls received us with towels and soap and massaged us thoroughly. Then they sprayed us with scent, dressed us in Roman clothes, crowned us with garlands, and led us to the feast. Before we took our seats, I did my best to turn Ethel into a boy. Amid much giggling from the others, I produced an exquisite model of a boy's private parts, modelled in what actors call 'nose paste', and stuck it on to Ethel's mons Veneris with spirit gum (a friendly assistant at Clarkson's proved very useful to me for this); so we arrived at the table. Now a small difficulty arose. Muriel had evidently expected that she would (so to speak) be the guest of the evening. But I quickly undeceived her. 'During the first part,' I said, 'the parts are cast as follows: I am the patrician who gives the feast; Ethel is a favourite slave; you and Gladys are attendants, and Juliette shall be a tumbler to entertain us. When the feast is over we shall all enjoy ourselves as we like.'

'But, have I to wait on Ethel?' pouted Muriel.

'Certainly,' I said, 'and you may as well dress for the part now; it was to come later, when the wine had taken effect, but you may as well begin. I decide to be waited on by birds this evening.

'What do you mean?'

'This,' I said, producing some peacock feathers which I had obtained. 'Peacocks shall wait on me – bend down and let me fix them.'

'But where, how, I don't understand.'

I took hold of her, bent her forward and began to place the quill of a peacock feather where the peacock carries his.

She sprang away – 'I won't, I won't, it's beastly.'

'Oh is it?' I said. 'Remember, you're in Rome now, or rather Pompeii.' I seized hold of her and with a quick twist flung her to the ground; then, seizing a whip which was handy, as one would always have been in ancient Rome, I thrashed her naked body until she begged for mercy. 'Now,' said I, 'will you wear the feathers or not?'

'Oh yes, yes,' she sobbed. I raised her to her feet and again bent her forward, found the tiny hole I was looking for and inserted three lovely feathers. 'Now, Gladys, for you.' Gladys came towards me trembling. 'Don't hurt me, Uncle, please, oh! oh! oh! don't push it up too hard; oh, it makes me feel so ashamed.' The sight of these two naked girls walking about with the peacock's feathers sticking out behind excited my passions tremendously, I turned to Juliette. 'Now Juliette, when I call for you, you are to dance and tumble as I showed you yesterday.' I had rehearsed her in her part and shown her reproductions of some Pompeian frescoes.

So we sat or rather lay down to dinner – Ethel and I side by side on the couch, served by Muriel and Gladys. Ethel, in the shortest of *gitons* with her hair tied in a Grecian fillet, looked lovely, and as course followed course and the wine went to my head, my hand wandered under her tunic and disclosed the false sex of a boy with which I had endowed her. She seemed very proud of it and spread her legs, showing it off. Muriel, however, did not like it, any more than she liked the peacock decoration. She showed her disgust or at any rate disdain in every movement. I waited my opportunity. At last in serving me with wine she spilled some over my arm as I held the glass. I sprang up at once – the scene by this time had entered into my brain, and I was for the moment a Roman noble, haughty and passionate. I seized her by the wrists and dragged her to the wall, where cords were hanging from a hook. I tied her wrists to these and, calling for rods, I thrashed her bare back and thighs until she begged for mercy. Then, returning to the table, I clapped my hands for Juliette. She appeared swaying her hips and undulating her belly in a most lascivious manner. She was naturally very supple and she managed very successfully to reproduce the indecent contortions and postures described by the later Roman poets and depicted on the hems and mural decorations of the period.

Ethel watched eagerly – her naturally naughty mind welcomed this indecent display. I plied her with wine and, drinking heavily myself, began to toy with her, probing underneath the artificial sex which I had given her. Her nature responded at once. I turned her over on her side with her back to me and without shame or hesitation began to play in real earnest the part of a Roman noble with his favourite slave. She was surprised at this method of attack. 'You're in the wrong place, Uncle,' she said.

'Not at all,' I panted in answer, as I pushed my way, 'this is Ancient Rome and you're a boy, not a girl.'

'Oh don't, you're hurting me.'

'Bear it just a little more, it won't hurt then . . . that's better . . . *now.*' I began to work; the years slipped away, I was back again at school in my fourth year – I was back in Ancient Rome – I was no longer Cecil Prendergast but a patrician of the Empire; Nero the Artist was Emperor. I held Ethel close to me in my ecstasy, one finger penetrated right into her burning pussy, and as I felt her warm life flooding my hand, I poured all my strength into her. The feast was now over. I summoned my attendants to me on the couch and, disengaging myself from Ethel, I made them bathe us both with scented water. Then the wine went round again and under its influence and my caresses Muriel began to forget that she had not up till then played the chief part in the entertainment. Every form of lascivious enjoyment was indulged in, until at last morning broke on five naked bodies interlaced in one confused medley on the couch.

Two days later the girls went back to school, looking forward to the Christmas holidays, when we were all to meet again. Gladys's last words to me were, 'I shall be patient, Uncle; but I mean you to have me properly then. I shan't be able to wait any longer, I know. You will do everything to me then, won't you? Promise me.'

I promised her I would see what could be done, and when the train left the station, Muriel, Juliette, and I went back to South Molton Street to devise fresh pleasures among ourselves and to wait for the Christmas holidays.

# The Pearl

## Three Erotic tale

ANONYMOUS

Lady Pokingham
or They All Do It
Giving an Account of her Luxurious
Adventures, both before and after
her Marriage with Lord Crim-Con

# Introduction

To the Reader – Very little apology will be needed for putting in print the following highly erotic and racy narrative of a young patrician lady, from whose adventures I feel assured every genuine lover of voluptuous reading will derive as much or more pleasure as has your humble servant.

The subject of these memoirs was one of the brightest and most charming of her sex, endued with such exquisite nervous sensitiveness, in addition to an unusual warmth of constitution, that she was quite unable to resist the seductive influences of God's finest creation; for God made man in his own image, male and female, created he them; and this was the first commandment, 'Be fruitful, and multiply, and replenish the earth' (Genesis 1:28).

The natural instinct of the ancients instilled in their minds the idea that copulation was the direct and most acceptable form of worship they could offer to their deities, and I know that those of my readers who are not bigoted Christians will agree with me, that there cannot be any great sin in giving way to natural desires, and enjoying, to the utmost, all those delicious sensations for which a beneficent Creator has so amply fitted us.

Poor girl, she did not live long, and in thoroughly enjoying her few brief years of butterfly life, who can think her wicked?

The scraps from which my narrative is compiled were found in a packet she had entrusted to a devoted servitor, who, after her sudden and premature death at the early age of twenty-three, entered my service.

As author, I feel the crudeness of my style may be a little offensive to some, but hope my desire to afford general pleasure will excuse my defects.

THE AUTHOR

## Chapter One

My dear Walter – How I love you! but alas! you will never know it till I am gone; little do you think, as you wheel me about in my invalid chair, how your delicate attentions have won the heart of a poor consumptive on the verge of the grave. How I long to suck the sweets of love from your lips; to fondle and caress your lordly priapus, and feel its thrilling motions within me; but such joys cannot be; the least excitement would be my death, and I can but sigh as I look at your kind loving face, and admire the fine proportions of my darling, as evidenced by the large bunch of keys you always seem to have in your pocket; indeed you look to have a key of keys, whose burning thrusts would unlock any virgin cabinet.

This is a strange fancy of mine (the writing for your perusal of a short account of some of my adventures); but one of the only pleasures left me is to indulge in reveries of the past, and seem to feel over again the thrilling emotions of voluptuous enjoyments, which are now denied to me; and I hope the recital of my escapades and follies may afford you some slight pleasure and add to the lasting regard with which I hope you will remember me in years to come. One thing I ask of you, dear Walter, is to fancy you are enjoying Beatrice Pokingham when you are in the embraces of some future inamorata. It is a pleasure I have often indulged in myself when in the action of coition, and heightened my bliss by letting my fancy run riot, and imagined I was in the arms of someone I particularly wished for, but could not come at. My income dies with me, so I have no cause to make a will, but you will find notes for a few hundred pounds enclosed with this outline of my adventures, which is all I have been able to save. You will also find a fine lock of dark brown hair, which I have cut from the abundant *chevelure* of my mons Veneris; other friends and relatives may have the admired curls from my head, your memento is cut from the sacred spot of love.

I have no memory of my father, the Marquis of Pokingham, and entertain doubts as to whether I am really entitled to the honour of claiming him as a parent, as he was a used-up old man, and from papers and letters, which passed privately between him and my mother, I know that he more than suspected he was indebted to his good-looking footman for the pretty baby girl my mother presented to him. Indeed, he says in one note that he could have forgiven everything if the fruits of her intercourse with James had been a son and heir, so as to keep his hated nephew out of the estates and title, and wished her to let him cultivate her parsley bed for another crop, which might perhaps turn out more in accordance with his wishes. The poor old fellow died soon after writing that note, and my mother, from whom this dreadful consumption is transmitted to me, also left me an orphan at an early age, leaving me her jointure of £20,000, and an aristocratic title which that amount was quite inadequate properly to support.

My guardians were very saving and careful, as they sent me to school at eight years of age, and only spent about £150 a year for schooling and necessaries, till they thought it was time for me to be brought out in the world, so that I benefited considerably by the accumulated interest of my money.

The first four years of my school passed away uneventfully, and during that time I was only in one serious scrape, which I will relate, as it led to my first taste of a good birch rod.

Miss Birch was rather an indulgent schoolmistress, and only had to resort to personal punishment for very serious offences, which she considered might materially affect the future character of her pupils, unless thoroughly cut out of them from the first. I was nearly seven years old when I had a sudden fancy for making sketches on my slate in school. One of our governesses, Miss Pennington, was a rather crabbed and severe old girl of five-and-thirty, and particularly evoked my abilities as a caricaturist, and the sketches would be slyly passed from one to the other of us, causing considerable giggling and gross inattention to our lessons. I was infatuated and conceited with what I considered my clever drawings and several admonitions and extra tasks as punishment had no effect in checking my mischievous interruptions, until one afternoon Miss Birch had fallen asleep at her desk, and old Penn was busy with a class, when the sudden inspiration seized me to make a couple of very rude sketches: one of the old girl sitting on a chamber utensil and the other of her stooping down, with her clothes up to ease herself, in a rural setting. The first girl I showed them to almost burst with laughter, and two others were so anxious to see the cause of her mirth that they were actually stooping over her shoulder to look at my slate when, before I could possibly get to it to rub them off, old Penn pounced upon it like an eagle, and carried it in triumph to the now alert Miss Birch, only to be further chagrined by the amused smile which our principal could not repress at first sight of the indecent caricatures.

'My young lady must smart for this, Miss Pennington,' said Miss Birch, with suddenly assumed gravity; 'she has been very troublesome lately with these impudent drawings, but this is positively obscene; if she draws one thing she will go to another. Send for Susan to bring my birch rod! I must punish her whilst my blood is warm, as I am too forgiving, and may let her off.'

I threw myself on my knees, and implored for mercy, promising 'Never, never to do anything of the kind again.'

Miss Birch – 'You should have thought of the consequences before you drew such filthy pictures; the very idea of one of my young ladies being capable of such productions is horrible to me; these prurient ideas cannot be allowed to settle in your mind for an instant, if I can whip them out.'

Miss Pennington, with a grim look of satisfaction, now took me by the wrist, just as Susan, a stout, strong, fair servant girl of about twenty, appeared with what looked to me a fearful big bunch of birch twigs, neatly tied up with red velvet ribbon.

'Now, Lady Beatrice Pokingham,' said Miss Birch, 'kneel down, confess your fault, and kiss the rod,' taking the bunch from Susan's hands, and extending it to me as a queen might her sceptre to a supplicant subject.

Anxious to get over the inevitable, and make my punishment as light as possible, I knelt down, and with real tears of penitence begged her to be as lenient as her sense of justice would admit, as I knew I well deserved what she was going to inflict, and would take care not to insult Miss Pennington again, whom I was very sorry to have so caricatured; then I kissed the rod and resigned myself to my fate.

MISS PENNINGTON, *maliciously* – 'Ah! Miss Birch, how quickly the sight of the rod makes hypocritical repentance.'

MISS BIRCH – 'I quite understand all that, Miss Pennington, but must temper justice with mercy at the proper time; now, you impudent artist, lift your clothes behind, and expose your own bottom to the justly merited punishment.'

With trembling hands I lifted my skirts, and was then ordered to open my drawers also; which done, they pinned up my dress and petticoats as high as my shoulders; then I was laid across a desk, and Susan stood in front of me, holding both hands, whilst old Penn and the French governess (who had just entered the schoolroom) each held one of my legs, so that I was what you might call helplessly spread-eagled.

MISS BIRCH, *looking seriously round as she flourished the rod* – 'Now, all you young ladies, let this whipping be a caution to you; my lady Beatrice richly deserves this degrading shame, for her indecent (I ought to call them obscure) sketches. Will you! will you, you troublesome, impudent little thing, ever do so again? There, there, there, I hope it will soon do you good. Ah! you may scream; there's a few more to come yet.'

The bunch of birch seemed to crash on my bare bottom with awful force, the tender skin smarted, and seemed ready to burst at every fresh cut. 'Ah! ah! oh!!! Oh, heavens! have mercy, madame. Oh! I will never do anything like it again. Ah – r– re! I can't bear it!' I screamed, kicking and struggling under every blow, so that at first they could scarcely hold me, but I was soon exhausted by my own efforts.

MISS BIRCH – 'You can feel it a little! May it do you good, you bad little girl; if I don't check you now, the whole establishment would soon be demoralised. Ah! ha! your bottom is getting finely wealed, but I haven't done yet,' cutting away with increasing fury.

Just then I caught a glimpse of her face, which was usually pale; it was now flushed with excitement, and her eyes sparkled with unwonted animation. 'Ah!' she continued, 'young ladies beware of my rod, when I do have to use it. How do you like it, Lady Beatrice? Let us all know how nice it is,' cutting my bottom and thighs deliberately at each ejaculation.

Lady Beatrice – 'Ah! oh! ah – r – r – re! It's awful! Oh I shall die if you don't have mercy, Miss Birch. Oh! my God I'm fearfully punished; I'm cut to pieces; the birch feels as if it was red hot, the blows burn so!'

Then I felt as if it was all over, and I must die soon; my cries were succeeded by low sobs, moans, and then hysterical crying, which gradually got lower and lower, till at last I must have fainted, as I remembered nothing more till I found myself in bed, and awoke with my poor posteriors tremendously bruised and sore, and it was nearly a fortnight before I got rid of all the marks of that severe whipping.

After I was twelve years of age they reckoned me amongst the big girls, and I got a jolly bedfellow, whom I will call Alice Marchmont, a beautiful, fair girl, with a plump figure, large sensuous eyes, and flesh as firm and smooth as ivory. She seemed to take a great fancy to me, and the second night I slept with her (we had a small room to ourselves) she kissed and hugged me so lovingly that at first I felt slightly confused. She took such liberties with me, my heart was all in a flutter, and although the light was out, I felt my face covered with burning blushes as her hot kisses on my lips, and the searching gropings of her hands in the most private parts of my person, made me all atremble.

'How you shake, dear Beatrice,' she answered. 'What are you afraid of? you may feel me all over too; it is so nice. Put your tongue in my mouth, it is a great inducement to love and I do want to love you so, dear. Where's your hand? here, put it there; can't you feel the hair just beginning to grow on my pussy? Yours will come soon. Rub your finger on my crack, just there,' so she initiated me into the art of frigging in the most tender loving manner.

As you may guess, I was an apt pupil, although so young. Her touches fired my blood, and the way she sucked my tongue seemed most delicious. 'Ah! Oh! Rub harder, harder – quicker,' she gasped, as she stiffened her limbs out with a kind of spasmodic shudder, and I felt my finger all wet with something warm and creamy. She covered me with kisses for a moment, and then lay quite still.

'What is it, Alice? How funny you are, and you have wetted my finger, you nasty girl,' I whispered, laughing. 'Go on tickling me with your fingers, I begin rather to like it.'

'So you will dear, soon, and love me for teaching you such a nice game,' she replied, renewing her frigging operations, which gave me great pleasure so that I hardly knew what I was doing, and a most luscious longing sensation came over me. I begged her to shove her fingers right up. 'Oh! oh! How nice! Further! Harder!' and almost fainted with delight as she at last brought down my first maiden spend.

Next night we repeated our lascivious amusements, and she produced a thing like a sausage, made of soft kid leather, and stuffed out as hard as possible, which she asked me to push into her, and work up and down, whilst she frigged me as before, making me lie on the top of her, with my tongue in her mouth. It was delightful. I can't express her raptures, my movements with the instrument seemed to drive her into ecstasies of pleasure, she almost screamed as she clasped my body to hers, exclaiming, 'Ah! Oh! You dear boy; you kill me with pleasure!' as she spent with extraordinary profusion all over my busy hand.

As soon as we had recovered our serenity a little, I asked her what she meant by calling me her dear boy.

'Ah! Beatrice,' she replied, 'I'm so sleepy now, but tomorrow night, I will tell you my story, and explain how it is that my pussy is able to take in that thing, whilst yours cannot at present; it will enlighten you a little more into the Philosophy of Life, my dear; now give me a kiss, and let us go to sleep tonight.'

## *Alice Marchmont's Story*

You may imagine I was anxious for the next night to arrive. We were no sooner in our little sanctum, than I exclaimed, 'Now, Alice, make haste into bed, I'm all impatient to hear your tale.'

'You shall have it dear and my fingers, too, if you will but let me undress comfortably. I can't jump into bed anyhow, I must make the inspection of my little private curls first. What do you think of them, Beatrice? Off with your chemise, I want to compare our pussys,' said she, throwing off everything, and surveying her beautiful naked figure in the large cheval glass. I was soon beside her, equally denuded of covering. 'What a delightfully pouting little slit you have, Beatrice,' she exclaimed, patting my mons Veneris. 'We shall make a beautiful contrast, mine is a light blonde, and yours will be brunette. See my lithe curly parsley bed is already half an inch long.' She indulged in no end of exciting tricks, till at last my patience was exhausted, so slipping on my *chemise de nuit*, I bounced into bed, saying I believed it was all fudge about her having a tale to tell and that I would not let her love me again, till she had satisfied my curiosity.

'What bad manners to doubt my word,' she cried, following me into bed and taking me by surprise by uncovering my bottom and inflicting a smart little slapping as she laughingly continued, 'There, let that be a lesson to you not to doubt a young lady's word in future. Now you shall have my tale, although it would really serve you right to make you wait till tomorrow.'

After a short pause, having settled ourselves lovingly in bed, she began:

Once upon a time there was a little girl about ten years old, of the name of Alice; her parents were rich, and lived in a beautiful house, surrounded by lovely gardens and a fine park; she had a brother about two years older than herself, but her mama was so fond of her (being an only daughter), that she never would allow her little girl out of her sight, unless William, the butler, had charge of her in her rambles about the grounds and park.

William was a handsome, good-looking man about thirty, and had been in the family ever since he was a boy. Now Alice, who was very fond of William, often sat on his knee as he was seated under a tree, or on a garden seat, when he would read to her fairy tales from her books. Their intimacy was so great that when they were alone, she would call him 'dear old Willie', and treat him quite as an equal. Alice was quite an inquisitive girl, and would often put Mr William to the blush by her curious enquiries about natural history affairs, and how animals had little ones, why the cock was so savage to the poor hens, jumping on their backs, and biting their heads with his sharp beak, etc. 'My dear,' he would say, 'I'm not a hen or a cow; how should I know? don't ask such silly questions'; but Miss Alice was not so easily put off, she would reply, 'Ah! Willie, you do know, and won't tell me, I insist upon knowing, etc.,' but her efforts to obtain knowledge were quite fruitless.

This went on for some time till the little girl was within three or four months of her twelfth birthday, when a circumstance she had never taken any notice of before aroused her curiosity. It was that Mr William, under pretence of seeing to his duties, was in the habit of secluding himself in his pantry, or closet, from seven to eight o'clock in the morning for about an hour before breakfast. If Alice ventured to tap at the door it was fastened inside, and admittance refused; the keyhole was so closed it was useless to try and look through that way, but it occurred to my little girl that perhaps she might be able to get a peep into that place of mystery if she could only get into a passage which passed behind Mr William's pantry, and into which she knew it used to open by a half-glass door, now never used, as the passage was closed by a locked door at each end. This passage was lighted from the outside by a small window about four feet from the ground, fastened on the inside simply by a hook, which Alice, who mounted on a high stool, soon found she could open if she broke one of the small diamond panes of glass. She felt sure that if she waited till the next morning she would be able to find out what Willie was always so busy about, and also that she could get in and out of the window unobserved by anyone, as it was quite screened from view by a thick shrubbery seldom entered by anyone.

Up betimes next day she told her lady's-maid she was going to enjoy the fresh air in the garden before breakfast, and then hurried off to her place of observation, scrambled through the window regardless of dirt and dust, took off her boots as soon as she alighted in the disused passage and silently crept up to the glass door, but to her chagrin found the panes so dirty as to be impervious to sight; however, she was so far lucky as to find a fine large keyhole quite clear, and two or three cracks in the woodwork, so that she could see nearly every part of the place, which was full of light from a skylight overhead. Mr William was not there, but soon made his appearance, bringing a great basket of plate, which had been used the previous day, and for a few minutes was really busy looking in his pantry book, and counting spoons, forks, etc., but was soon finished, and began to look at a little book, which he took from a drawer. Just then, Lucy, one of the prettiest house-maids, a dark beauty of about eighteen, entered the room without ceremony, saying, 'Here's some of your plate off the sideboard. Where's your eyes, Mr William, not to gather up all as you ought to do?' William's eyes seemed to beam with delight as he caught her round the waist, and gave her a luscious kiss on her cheek, saying: 'Why, I keep them for you, dear, I knew you would bring the plate;' then showing the book, 'What do you think of that position, dear? How would you like it so?' Although pleased, the girl blushed up to the roots of her hair as she looked at the picture. The book dropped to the floor, and William pulled her on to his knee, and tried to put his hand up her clothes. 'Ah! No! No!' she cried, in a low voice; 'you know I can't today, but perhaps I can tomorrow; you must be good today, sir. Don't stick up your impudent head like that. There – there – there's a squeeze for you; now I must be off,' she said, putting her hand down into his lap, where it could not be seen what she was after. In a second or two she jumped up, and in spite of his efforts to detain her, escaped from the pantry. William, evidently in a great state of excitement, subsided on to a sofa, muttering, 'The little witch, what a devil she is; I can't help myself, but she will be all right tomorrow.' Alice, who was intently observing everything, was shocked and surprised to see his trousers all unbuttoned in front, and a great long fleshy-looking thing sticking out, seemingly hard and stiff, with a ruby-coloured head. Mr William took hold of it with one hand, apparently for the purpose of placing it in his breeches, but he seemed to hesitate, and closing his right hand upon the shaft, rubbed it up and down. 'Ah! What a fool I am to let her excite me so. Oh! Oh! I can't help it; I must.' He seemed to sigh as his hand increased its rapid motion. His face flushed, and his eyes seemed ready to start from his head, and in a few moments something spurted from his instrument, the drops falling over his hands and legs, some even a yard or two over the floor. This seemed to finish his ecstasy. He sank back quite listless for a few minutes, and then rousing himself, wiped his hands on a towel, cleared up every drop of the mess, and left the pantry.

Alice was all over in a burning heat from what she had seen but instinc-tively felt that the mystery was only half unravelled, and promised herself to be there and see what William and Lucy would do next day. Mr William took her for a walk as usual, and read to her, whilst she sat on his knee, and Alice wondered what could have become of that great stiff thing which she had seen in the morning. With the utmost apparent innocence, her hands touched him casually, where she hoped to feel the monster, but only resulted in feeling a rather soft kind of bunch in his pocket.

Another morning arrived to find Alice at her post behind the disused glass door, and she soon saw Mr William bring in his plate, but he put it aside, and seemed all impatient for Lucy's arrival. 'Ah!' he murmured, 'I'm as stiff as a rolling pin at the very thought of the saucy darling,' but his ideas were cut short by the appearance of Lucy herself, who carefully bolted the door inside. Then rushing into his arms, she covered him with kisses, exclaiming, in a low voice, 'Ah! How I have longed for him these three or four days. What a shame women should be stopped in that way from enjoying themselves once a month. How is he this morning?' as her hands nervously unbuttoned Mr William's trousers, and grasped his ready truncheon.

'What a hurry you are in, Lucy!' gasped her lover, as she almost stifled him with her kisses. 'Don't spoil it all by your impatience; I must have my kiss first.'

With a gentle effort he reclined her backwards on a sofa, and raised her clothes till Alice had a full view of a splendid pair of plump, white legs; but what riveted her gaze most was the luscious looking, pouting lips of Lucy's cunny, quite vermilion in colour, and slightly gaping open in a most inviting manner, as her legs were wide apart, and her mons Veneris which was covered with a profusion of beautiful curly black hair.

The butler was down on his knees in a moment, and glued his lips to her crack, sucking and kissing furiously, to the infinite delight of the girl, who sighed and wriggled with pleasure, till at last Mr William could no longer restrain himself, but getting up upon his knees between Lucy's legs, he brought his shaft to the charge, and to Alice's astonishment, fairly ran it right into the gaping crack, till it was all lost in her belly; they lay still for a few moments, enjoying the conjunction of their persons, till Lucy heaved up her bottom, and the butler responded to it by a shove, then they commenced a more exciting struggle. Alice could see the manly shaft as it worked in and out of her sheath, glistening with lubricity, whilst the lips of her cunny seemed to cling to it each time of withdrawal, as if afraid of losing such a delightful sugar stick; but this did not last long, their movements got more and more furious, till at last both seemed to meet in a spasmodic embrace, as they almost fainted in each other's arms, and Alice could see a profusion of creamy moisture oozing from the crack of Lucy, as they both lay in a kind of lethargy of enjoyment after their battle of love.

Mr William was the first to break the silence: 'Lucy, will you look in tomorrow, dear; you know that old spy, Mary, will be back from her holiday in a day or two, and then we shan't often have a chance.'

Lucy – 'Ah; you rogue, I mean to have a little more now, I don't care if we're caught; I must have it,' she said, squeezing him with her arms and gluing her lips to his, as she threw her beautiful legs right over his buttocks, and commenced the engagement once more by rapidly heaving her bottom; in fact, although he was a fine man, the weight of his body seemed as nothing in her amorous excitement.

The butler's excuses and pleading of fear, in case he was missed, etc., were all of no avail; she fairly drove him on, and he was soon as furiously excited as herself, and with a profusion of sighs, expressions of pleasure, endearment, etc., they soon died away again into a state of short voluptuous oblivion. However, Mr William was too nervous and afraid to let her lie long; he withdrew his instrument from her foaming cunny, just as it was all slimy and glistening with the mingled juices of their love, but what a contrast to its former state, as Alice now beheld it much reduced in size, and already drooping its fiery head.

Lucy jumped up and let down her clothes, but kneeling on the floor before her lover, she took hold of his limp affair, and gave it a most luscious sucking, to the great delight of Mr William, whose face flushed again with pleasure, and as soon as Lucy had done with her sucking kiss, Alice saw that his instrument was again stiff and ready for a renewal of their joys.

LUCY, *laughing in a low tone* – 'There, my boy, I'll leave you like that, think of me till tomorrow; I couldn't help giving the darling a good suck after the exquisite pleasure he had afforded me; it's like being in heaven for a little while.'

With a last kiss on the lips, they parted and Mr William again locked his door, whilst Alice made good her retreat to prepare herself for breakfast.

It was a fine warm morning in May, and soon after breakfast Alice, with William for her guardian, set off for a ramble in the park; her blood was in a boil, and she longed to experience the joys she was sure Lucy had been surfeited with; they sauntered down to the lake, and she asked William to give her a row in the boat; he unlocked the boat-house, and handed her into a nice, broad, comfortable skiff, well furnished with soft seats and cushions.

'How nice to be here, in the shade,' said Alice; 'come into the boat, Willie, we will sit in it a little while, and you shall read to me before we have a row.'

'Just as you please, Miss Alice,' he replied, with unwonted deference, stepping into the boat, and sitting down in the stern sheets.

'Ah my head aches a little, let me recline it in your lap,' said Alice, throwing off her hat, and stretching herself along on a cushion. 'Why are you so precise this morning, Willie? You know I don't like to be called Miss, you can keep that for Lucy.' Then noticing his confusion, 'You may blush, sir, I could make you sink into your shoes if you only knew all I have seen between you and Miss Lucy.'

Alice reclined her head in a languid manner on his lap, looking up and enjoying the confusion she had thrown him into; then designedly resting one hand on the lump which he seemed to have in his pocket, as if to support herself a little, she continued: 'Do you think, Willie, I shall ever have as fine legs as Lucy? Don't you think I ought soon to have long dresses, sir! I'm getting quite bashful about showing my calves so much.' The butler had hard work to recover his composure, the vivid recollection of the luscious episode with Lucy before breakfast was so fresh in his mind that Alice's allusions to her, and the soft girlish hand resting on his privates (even although he thought her as innocent as a lamb) raised an utter of desire in his feverish blood, which he tried to allay as much as possible, but little by little the unruly member began to swell, till he was sure she must feel it throb under her hand. With an effort he slightly shifted himself, so as to remove her hand lower down on to the thigh, as he answered as gravely as possible (feeling assured Alice could know nothing): 'You're making game of me this morning. Don't you wish me to read, Alice?'

ALICE, *excitedly, with an unusual flush on her face* – 'You naughty man, you shall tell me what I want to know this time: How do babies come? What is the parsley bed, the nurses and doctors say they come out of? Is it not a curly lot of hair at the bottom of the woman's belly? I know that's what Lucy's got, and I've seen you kiss it, sir!'

William felt ready to drop; the perspiration stood on his brow in great drops, but his lips refused to speak, and Alice continued in a soft whisper: 'I saw it all this morning, Willie dear, and what joy that great red-head thing of yours seemed to give her. You must let me into the secret, and I will never tell. This is the monster you shoved into her so furiously. I must look at it and feel it; how hard it has got under my touch. La! What a funny thing! I can get it out as Lucy did,' pulling open his trousers and letting out the rampant engine of love. She kissed its red velvety head, saying: 'What a sweet, soft thing to touch. Oh! I must caress it a little.' Her touches were like fire to his senses; speechless with rapture and surprise, he silently submitted to the freak of the wilful girl, but his novel position was so exciting he could not restrain himself, and the sperm boiled up from his penis all over her hands and face.

'Ah!' she exclaimed. 'That's just what I saw it do yesterday morning. Does it do that inside of Lucy?'

Here William recovered himself a little, and wiping her face and hands with his handkerchief, put away the rude plaything, saying, 'Oh! My God! I'm lost! What have you done, Alice? It's awful! Never mention it again. I mustn't walk out with you any more.'

Alice burst into sobs.

'Oh! Oh! Willie! How unkind! Do you think I will tell? Only I must share the pleasure with Lucy. Oh! Kiss me as you did her, and we won't say any more about it today.'

William loved the little girl too well to refuse such a delightful task, but he contented himself with a very short suck at her virgin cunny, lest his erotic passion should urge him to outrage her at once.

'How nice to feel your lovely tongue there. How beautifully it tickled and warmed me all over; but you were so quick, and left off just as it seemed nicer than ever, dear Willie,' said Alice, embracing and kissing him with ardour.

'Gently, darling; you mustn't be so impulsive; it's a very dangerous game for one so young. You must be careful how you look at me, or notice me, before others,' said Mr William, returning her kisses, and feeling himself already quite unable to withstand the temptation of such a delicious *liaison*.

'Ah!' said Alice, with extraordinary perception for one so young. 'You fear Lucy. Our best plan is to take her into our confidence. I will get rid of my lady's-maid, I never did like her, and will ask mama to give Lucy the place. Won't that be fine, dear? We shall be quite safe in all our little games then.'

The butler, now more collected in his ideas, and with a cooler brain, could not but admire the wisdom of this arrangement, so he assented to the plan, and he took the boat out for a row to cool their heated blood, and quiet the impulsive throbbings of a pair of fluttering hearts.

The next two or three days were wet and unfavourable for outdoor excursions, and Alice took advantage of this interval to induce her mother to change her lady's-maid, and install Lucy in the situation.

Alice's attendant slept in a little chamber, which had two doors, one opening into the corridor whilst the other allowed free and direct access to her little mistress's apartment, which it adjoined.

The very first night Lucy retired to rest in her new room, she had scarcely been half an hour in bed (where she lay, reflecting on the change, and wondering how she would now be able to enjoy the butler's company occasionally), before Alice called out for her. In a moment she was at the young lady's bedside, saying: 'What can I do, Miss Alice, are you not warm enough? These damp nights are so chilly.'

'Yes, Lucy,' said Alice, 'that must be what it is. I feel cold and restless. Would you mind getting in bed with me? You will soon make me warm.'

Lucy jumped in, and Alice nestled close up to her bosom, as if for warmth, but in reality to feel the outlines of her beautiful figure.

'Kiss me, Lucy,' she said; 'I know I shall like you so much better than Mary. I couldn't bear her.' This was lovingly responded to, and Alice continued, as she pressed her hand on the bosom of her bedfellow, 'What large titties you have, Lucy. Let me feel them. Open your nightdress, so I can lay my face against them.'

The new *femme de chambre* was naturally of a warm and loving disposition; she admitted all the familiarities of her young mistress, whose hands began to wander in a most searching manner about her person, feeling the soft, firm skin of her bosom, belly, and bottom; the touches of Alice seemed to fire the blood, and rouse every voluptuous emotion within her; she sighed and kissed her little mistress again and again.

ALICE – 'What a fine rump! How hard and plump your flesh is, Lucy! Oh, my! what's all this hair at the bottom of your belly? My dear, when did it come?'

LUCY – 'Oh! pray don't, miss, it's so rude; you will be the same in two or three years' time; it frightened me when it first began to grow, it seemed so unnatural.'

ALICE – 'We're only girls, there is no harm in touching each other, is there; just feel how different I am.'

LUCY – 'Oh! Miss Alice,' pressing the young girl's naked belly to her own, 'you don't know how you make me feel when you touch me there.'

ALICE (*with a slight laugh*) – 'Does it make you feel better when Mr William, the butler, touches you, dear?' tickling the hairy crack with her finger.

LUCY – 'For shame, miss! I hope you don't think I would let him touch me' – evidently in some confusion.

ALICE – 'Don't be frightened, Lucy, I won't tell, but I have seen it all through the old glass door in his pantry. Ah! you see I know the secret, and must be let in to share the fun.'

LUCY – 'Oh! My God! Miss Alice, what have you seen? I shall have to leave the house at once.'

ALICE – 'Come, come, don't be frightened, you know I'm fond of Mr William, and would never do him any harm, but you can't have him all to yourself; I got you for my maid to prevent your jealous suspicions and keep our secret between us.'

Lucy was in a frightful state of agitation. 'What! has he been such a brute as to ruin you, Miss Alice! I'll murder him if he has,' she cried.

ALICE – 'Softly, Lucy, not so loud, someone will hear you; he's done nothing yet, but I saw your pleasure when he put that thing into your crack, and am determined to share your joys, so don't be jealous, and we can all three be happy together.'

LUCY – 'It would kill you, dear, that big thing of his would split you right up.'

ALICE – 'Never mind,' kissing her lovingly, 'you keep the secret and I'm not afraid of being seriously hurt.'

Lucy sealed the compact with a kiss, and they spent a most loving night together, indulging in every variety of kissing and tickling, and Alice had learnt from her bedfellow nearly all the mysterious particulars in connection with the battles of Venus before they fell asleep in each other's arms.

Fine weather soon returned, and Alice, escorted by the butler, went for one of her usual rambles, and they soon penetrated into a thick copse at the further end of the park, and sat down in a little grassy spot, where they were secure from observation.

William had thoughtfully brought with him an umbrella, as well as a great coat and cloak, which he spread upon the grass for fear Miss Alice might take cold.

'Ah! you dear old fellow,' said Alice, seating herself, and, taking his hand, pulling him down beside her. 'I understand everything now, and you are to make me happy by making a woman of me, as you did Lucy; you must do it, Willie, dear, I shall soon make you so you can't help yourself,' unbuttoning his trousers and handling his already stiff pego. 'What a lovely dear it is; how I long to feel its juice spouting into my bowels; I know it's painful, but it won't kill me, and then, ah! the heavenly bliss I know you will make me feel, as you do Lucy when you have her; how will you do it? will you lie over me?'

William, unable to resist her caresses and already almost at spending point, makes her kneel over his face, as he lay on his back, so that he may first lubricate her maiden cunny with his tongue. This operation titillates and excites the little girl, so that she amorously presses herself on his mouth as she faces towards his cock, which she never leaves hold of all the while; he spends in ecstasy, whilst she also feels the pleasure of a first virgin emission.

'Now's the time, Alice dear, my affair is so well greased, and your pussy is also ready; if I get over you I might be too violent and injure you; the best way is for you to try and do it yourself by straddling over me, and directing its head to your cunny, and then keep pressing down upon it, as well as the first painful sensations will allow; it will all depend on your own courage for the success of the experiment,' said William.

ALICE – 'Ah! you shall see my determination,' as she began to act upon his suggestion, and fitting the head of his pego into her slit, soon pressed down so as to take in and quite cover the first inch of it.

Here the pain of stretching and distension seemed almost too much for her, but she gave a sudden downward plunge of her body, which, although she almost fainted with the dreadful pain, got in at least three inches.

'What a plucky girl you are, my dear Alice,' said William, in delight. 'As soon as you can bear it, raise yourself up a little, and come down with all your force. It is so well planted, the next good thrust will complete my possession of your lovely charms.'

'I don't care if I die in the effort,' she whispered, softly. 'Never mind how it hurts me, help all you can, Willie dear, this time,' as she raised herself off him again, and he took hold of her buttocks, to lend his assistance to the grave girl.

Clenching her teeth firmly, and shutting her eyes, she gave another desperate plunge upon William's spear of love, the hymen was broken, and she was fairly impaled to the roots of his affair. But it cost her dear, she fell forward in a dead faint, whilst the trickling blood proved the sanguinary nature of Love's victory.

The butler withdrew himself, all smeared with her virgin blood, but he had come prepared for such an emergency, and at once set about using restoratives to bring her round, and presently succeeded in his efforts; her eyes opened with a smile, and whispering softly, Alice said – 'Ah! that last thrust was awful, but it's over now. Why did you take him away? Oh! put him back at once, dear, and let me have the soothing injection Lucy said would soon heal all my bruised parts.'

He glued his lips to hers, and gently applying the head of his pego to her blood-stained crack, gradually inserted it till it was three-fourths in; then, without pressing further, he commenced to move slowly and carefully. The lubricity soon increased, and he could feel the tight loving contractions of her vagina, which speedily brought him to a crisis once more, and with a sudden thrust, he plunged up to the hilt, and shot his very essence into her bowels, as he almost fainted with the excess of his emotions.

They lay motionless, enjoying each other's mutual pressures, till Mr William withdrew, and taking a fine cambric handkerchief, wiped the virgin blood first from the lips of her cunny, then off his own weapon, declaring, as he put the red-stained *mouchoir* in his pocket, that he would keep it for ever, in remembrance of the charms she had so lovingly surrendered to him.

The butler prudently refrained from the further indulgence in voluptuous pleasure for the day, and, after a good rest, Alice returned to the house, feeling very little the worse for her sacrifice, and very happy in having secured part of the love of dear and faithful William.

How suddenly unforeseen accidents prevent the realisation of the best plans for happiness. The very same day, her father was ordered by his medical adviser to the South of Europe, and started next morning for town, to make the necessary arrangements, taking the butler with him, leaving Alice's mama to follow as soon as the two children were suitably located at school.

Lucy and her young mistress consoled each other as well as possible under the circumstances. But in a few days, an aunt took charge of the house, and Alice was sent to this school, and is now in your arms, dear Beatrice; whilst my brother is now at college, and we only meet during the holidays. Will you, dear, ask your guardians to allow you to spend the next vacation with me, and I will introduce you to Frederick, who, if I make no mistake, is quite as voluptuously inclined as his sister.

## *Chapter Two*

I will pass over the exciting practices myself and my bedfellow used to indulge in almost every night, and merely remark that two more finished young tribades it would have been impossible to find anywhere.

I had to wait till the Christmas vacation before I could be introduced to Frederick, who, between ourselves, we had already devoted to the task of taking my virginity, which we did not think would prove a very difficult operation, as with so much finger frigging, and also the use of Alice's leather sausage, which, as I learnt, she had improvised for her own gratification, my mount and cunny were wonderfully developed, and already slight signs of the future growth of curly brown hair could be detected. I was nearly thirteen, as one fine crisp morning in December we drove up to the Hall on our return from school. There stood the aunt to welcome us, but my eyes were fixed upon the youthful, yet manly figure of Frederick, who stood by her side, almost a counterpart of his sister in features and complexion, but really a very fine young fellow, between seventeen and eighteen.

Since hearing the story of Alice's intrigue with William, I always looked at every man and boy to see what sort of a bunch they had got in their pockets, and was delighted to perceive Mr Frederick was apparently well furnished.

Alice introduced me to her relatives, but Frederick evidently looked upon me as a little girl, and not at all yet up to the serious business of love and flirtation, so our first private consultation, between Alice and myself, was on how best to open his eyes, and draw him to take a little more notice of his sister's friend.

Lucy, whom I now saw for the first time, slept in the little room adjoining Alice's chamber, which I shared with her young mistress. Frederick had a room on the other side of ours, so that we were nextdoor neighbours, and could rap and give signals to each other on the wall, as well as try to look through the keyhole of a disused door, which opened direct from one room to the other, but had long since been locked and bolted to prevent any communication between the occupants.

A little observation soon convinced us that Lucy was upon most intimate terms with her young master, which Alice determined to turn to account in our favour.

She quickly convinced her *femme de chambre* that she could not enjoy and monopolise the whole of her brother, and finding that Lucy expected he would visit her room that very night, she insisted upon ringing the changes, by taking Lucy to sleep with herself, and putting me in the place of Monsieur Frederick's ladylove.

I was only too willing to be a party of this arrangement, and at ten o'clock, when we all retired to rest, I took the place of the *femme de chambre*, and pretended to be fast asleep in her snug little bed. The lock of the door had been oiled by Lucy, so as to open quite noiselessly, but the room was purposely left in utter darkness, and secured even from the intrusion of a dim starlight by well-closed window curtains.

About eleven o'clock, as nearly as I could guess, the door silently opened, and by the light of the corridor lamp, I saw a figure, in nothing but a shirt, cautiously glide in, and approach the bed. The door closed, and all was dark, putting my heart in a dreadful flutter, at the approach of the long wished for, but dreaded ravisher of my virginity.

'Lucy! Lucy!! Lucy!!!' he whispered, in a low voice, almost in my ear. No response, only the apparent deep breathing of a person in sound sleep.

'She hasn't thought much about me, but, I guess, something between her legs will soon wake her up,' I heard him mutter, then the bedclothes were pulled open, and he slid into bed by my side. My hair was all loose, the same as Lucy's generally was at night, and I felt a warm kiss on my cheek, also an arm stealing round my waist and clutching my nightdress as if to pull it up. Of course I was the fox asleep, but could not help being all atremble at the approach of my fate.

'How you shake, Lucy; what's the matter? Hullo! who's this; it can't be you?' he said rapidly, as with a sigh and a murmur, 'Oh! oh! Alice,' I turned round just as he pulled up my chemise, clasping my arm firmly round him, but still apparently lost in sleep. 'My God!' I heard him say, 'It's that little devil of a Beatrice in Lucy's bed; I won't go, I'll have a lark, she can't know me in the dark.'

His hands seemed to explore every part of my body; I could feel his rampant cock pressed between our naked bellies, but although in a burning heat of excitement, I determined to let him do just as he liked, and pretend still to be asleep; his fingers explored my crack, and rubbed the little clitoris; first his leg got between mine, and then presently I could feel him gently placing the head of his instrument in the crack, and I was so excited that a sudden emission wetted it and his fingers all over with a creamy spend. 'The little devil's spending in her sleep; these girls must be in the habit of frigging each other, I believe,' he said to himself again. Then his lips met mine for the first time, and he was quite free from fear on that account as his face was as beardless as a girl's.

'Ah! Alice!' I murmured, 'give me your sausage thing, that's it, dear, shove it in,' as I pushed myself forward on his slowly progressing cock; he met me with a sudden thrust, making me almost scream with pain, yet my arms nervously clung round his body, and kept him close to the mark.

'Gently,' he whispered, 'Beatrice, dear, I'm Frederick, I won't hurt you much; how in heaven's name did you come in Lucy's bed?'

Pretending now to awaken for the first time with a little scream, and trying to push his body away from me, I exclaimed, 'Oh! Oh! How you hurt! Oh! for shame, don't. Oh! let me go, Mr Frederick, how can you?' And then my efforts seemed exhausted, and I lay almost at his mercy as he ruthlessly pushed his advantage, and tried to stop my mouth with kisses. I was lost. Although very painful, thanks to our frequent fingerings, etc., the way had been so cleared that he was soon in complete possession, although as I afterwards found by the stains on my chemise, it was not quite a bloodless victory.

Taking every possible advantage, he continued his motions with thrilling energy, till I could not help responding to his delicious thrusts, moving my bottom a little to meet each returning insertion of his exciting weapon (we were lying on our sides), and in a few moments we both swam in a mutual flood of bliss; after a spasmodic storm of sighs, kisses and the tender hugging pressure of each other's limbs, we lay in a listless state of enjoyment, until suddenly the bedclothes were thrown, or pulled off, then slap – slap – slap, came smarting smacks on our bottoms, and Alice's light, merry laugh sounded through the darkness, 'Ha! Ha! Ha! Ha! Mr Frederick, is this what you learnt at college, sir? Here, Lucy, help; we must secure and punish the wretch; bring a light.'

Lucy appeared with a candle and locked the door inside at once, before he could have a chance of escaping, and I could see she was quite delighted at the spectacle presented by our bodies in conjunction, for as I had been previously instructed, I clung to him in apparent fright, and tried to hide my blushing face in his bosom.

Frederick was in the utmost confusion, and at first was afraid his sister would expose him, but he was a little reassured as she went on, 'What shall I do? I can't tell an old maid like aunt; only to think that my dear little Beatrice should be outraged under my very eyes, the second night of her visit. If papa and mama were at home, they would know what to do; now I must decide for myself. Now, Frederick, will you submit to a good whipping for this, or shall I write to your father, and send Beatrice home disgraced in the morning? And you will have to promise to marry her, sir! Now you've spoilt her for anyone else; who do you think would take a *cruche cassée* if they knew it, or not repudiate her when it was found out, as it must be the first night of her marriage. No, you bad boy, I'm determined both to punish you and make you offer her all the reparation in your power.'

I began to cry, and begged her not to be too hard, as he had not hurt me much, and in fact had, at the finish, quite delighted my ravished senses.

'Upon my word,' said Alice, assuming the airs of a woman, 'the girl is as bad as the boy, this could not have happened, Beatrice, if you had not been too complaisant, and given way to his rudeness.'

Frederick, disengaging himself from my embrace, and quite unmindful of his condition, started up, and clasping his sister round her neck, kissed her most lovingly, and the impudent fellow even raised her nightdress and stroked her belly, exclaiming, as he passed his hand over her mossy mount, 'What a pity, Alice, you are my sister or I would give you the same pleasure as I have Beatrice, but I will submit to your chastisement, however hard it may be, and promise also that my little love here shall be my future wife.'

ALICE – 'You scandalous fellow, to insult my modesty so and expose your blood-stained manhood to my sight, but I will punish you, and avenge both myself and Beatrice; you are my prisoner, so just march into the other room, I've got a tickler there that I brought home from school, as a curiosity, little thinking I should so soon have a use for it.'

Arrived in Alice's own room, she and Lucy first tied his hands to the bedpost, then they secured his ankles to the handle of a heavy box, which stood handy, so as to have him tolerably well stretched out.

ALICE, *getting her rod out of a drawer* – 'Now, pin up his shirt to his shoulders, and I will see if I can't at least draw a few drops of his impudent blood out of his posteriors, which Beatrice may wipe off with her handkerchief as a memento of the outrage she has so easily forgiven.'

The hall was a large house, and our apartments were the only ones occupied in that corridor, the rooms abutting on which were all in reserve for visitors expected to arrive in a few days, to spend Christmas with us, so that there was not much fear of being heard by any of the other inmates of the house, and Alice was under no necessity of thinking what might be the result of her blows. With a flourish she brought down the bunch of twigs with a thundering whack on his plump, white bottom; the effect was startling to the culprit, who was evidently only anticipating some playful fun. 'Ah! My God! Alice, you'll cut the skin; mind what you're about; I didn't bargain for that.'

ALICE (*with a smile of satisfaction*) – 'Ho! Ho! did you think I was going to play with you? But, you've soon found your mistake, sir. Will you? will you, again take such outrageous liberties with a young lady friend of mine?'

She cut him quite half a dozen times in rapid succession, as she thus lectured him, each blow leaving long red lines, to mark its visitation, and suffusing his fair bottom all over with a peachlike bloom. The victim, finding himself quite helpless, bit his lips and ground his teeth in fruitless rage. At last he burst forth: 'Ah! Ah! You she-devil! Do you mean to skin my bum? Be careful, or I will take a rare revenge some day before long.'

ALICE, *with great calmness and determination, but with a most excited twinkle in her eyes* – 'Oh! You show temper, do you? So you mean to be revenged on me for doing a simple act of justice, sir? I will keep you there, and cut away at your impudent bottom, till you fairly beg my pardon, and promise to forgo all such wicked revengefulness.'

The victim writhed in agony and rage, but her blows only increased in force, beginning to raise great fiery-looking weals all over his buttocks. 'Ah! Ha!' she continued. 'How do you like it, Fred? Shall I put a little more steam in my blows?'

Frederick struggles desperately to get loose, but they have secured him too well for that! The tears of shame and mortification stand in his eyes, but he is still obstinate, and I could also observe a very perceptible rising in his manly instrument, which soon stood out from his belly in a rampant state of erection.

ALICE, *with assumed fury* – 'Look at the fellow, how he is insulting me, by the exhibition of his lustful weapon. I wish I could cut it off with a blow of the rod,' giving him a fearful cut across his belly and on the penis.

Frederick fairly howled with pain, and big tears rolled down his cheeks, as he gasped out: 'Oh! Oh! Ah! Have mercy, Alice. I know I deserve it. Oh! Pity me now, dear!'

ALICE, *without relaxing her blows* – 'Oh! You are beginning to feel properly, are you? Are you sincerely penitent? Beg my pardon at once, sir, for the way you insulted me in the other room.'

FREDERICK – Oh! Dear Alice! Stop! Stop! You don't let me get my breath. I will! I will beg your pardon. Oh! I can't help my affair sticking up as it does.'

ALICE– 'Down sir! Down sir! Your master is ashamed of you,' as she playfully whisks his pego with her rod.

Frederick is in agony; his writhing and contortions seem excruciating in the extreme, he fairly groans out: 'Oh! Oh! Alice, let me down. On my word,

I will do anything you order. Oh! Oh! Ah! You make me do it,' as he shuts his eyes, and we see quite a jet of sperm shoot from his virile member.

Alice dropped her rod, and we let down the culprit who was terribly crestfallen.

'Now, sir,' she said, 'down on your knees, and kiss the rod.'

Without a word, he dropped down, and kissed the worn-out stump, saying: 'Oh! Alice, the last few moments have been so heavenly. It has blotted out all sense of pain. My dear sister, I thank you for punishing me and will keep my promise to Beatrice.'

I wiped the drops of blood from his slightly bleeding rump, and then we gave him a couple of glasses of wine, and allowed him to sleep with Lucy, in her room, for the rest of the night, where they had a most luscious time of it, whilst Alice and myself indulged in our favourite touches.

You may be sure Frederick was not long before he renewed his pleasures with me, whilst his sister took pleasure in our happiness; but she seemed to have contracted a penchant for the use of the rod, and, once or twice a week, would have us all in her room, for a birch seance, as she called it, when Lucy or myself had to submit to be victims; but the heating of our bottoms only seemed to add to our enjoyment when we were afterwards allowed to soothe our raging passions in the arms of our mutual lover.

Christmas came, and with it arrived several visitors, all young ladies and gentlemen of about our own ages, to spend the festive season with us; our entire party consisted of five gentlemen and seven ladies, leaving out the aunt, who was too old to enter into youthful fun and contented herself with being a faithful housekeeper, and keeping good house, so that after supper every evening we could do almost as we liked; Alice and I soon converted our five young lady friends into tribades like ourselves, ready for anything, whilst Frederick prepared his young male friends. New Year's Day was his eighteenth birthday, and we determined to hold a regular orgy that night in our corridor, with Lucy's help. Plenty of refreshments were laid in stock, ices, sandwiches and champagne; the aunt strictly ordered us all to retire at one a.m. at latest, so we kept her commands, after spending a delicious evening in dancing and games, which only served to flush us with excitement for what all instinctively felt would be a most voluptuous entertainment upstairs.

The aunt was a heavy sleeper, and rather deaf, besides which Frederick, under the excuse of making them drink his health, plied the servants first with beer, then with wine, and afterwards with just a glass of brandy for a nightcap, so that we were assured they would also be sound enough; in fact two or three never got to bed at all.

Frederick was master of the ceremonies, with Alice as a most useful assistant. As I said before, all were flushed with excitement and ready for anything; they were all of the most aristocratic families, and their blue blood seemed fairly to course through their veins. When all had assembled in

Alice's apartment they found her attired in a simple, long *chemise de nuit*. 'Ladies and gentlemen,' she said, 'I believe we are all agreed for an out and out romp; you see my costume, how do you like it?' and with a most wicked smile, 'I hope it does not display the contour of my figure too much,' drawing it tightly about her so as to show the outline of her beautiful buttocks, and also displaying a pair of ravishing legs in pink silk stockings.

'Bravo! Bravo! Bravo Alice! we will follow your example,' burst from all sides. Each one skipped back to his or her room and reappeared in mufti; but the tails of the young gentlemen's shirts caused a deal of laughter, by being too short.

ALICE– 'Well, I'm sure, gentlemen, I did not think your undergarments were so indecently short.'

Frederick, with a laugh, caught hold of his sister's chemise, and tore a great piece off all around, so that she was in quite a short smock, which only half-covered her fair bottom.

Alice was crimson with blushes, and half inclined to be angry, but recovering herself, she laughed, 'Ah! Fred, what a shame to serve me so, but I don't mind if you make us all alike.'

The girls screamed, and the gentlemen made a rush; it was a most exciting scene; the young ladies retaliated by tearing the shirts of their tormentors, and this first skirmish only ended when the whole company were reduced to a complete state of nudity; all were in blushes as they gazed upon the variety of male and female charms exposed to view.

FREDERICK, *advancing with a bumper of champagne* – 'We've all heard of Nuda Veritas, now let's drink to her health; the first time we are in her company, I'm sure she will be most charming and agreeable.'

All joined in this toast, the wine inflamed our desires and there was not a male organ present that was not in a glorious state of erection.

ALICE– 'Look, ladies, what a lot of impudent fellows, they need not think we are going to surrender anyhow to their youthful lust; they shall be all blindfolded, and we will arm ourselves with good birch rods, then let it be everyone for themselves and Cupid's dart for us all.'

'Hear, hear,' responded on all sides, and handkerchiefs were soon tied over their eyes, and seven good birch rods handed round to the ladies. 'Now, gentlemen, catch whom you can,' laughed Alice, slashing right and left into the manly group, her example being followed by the other girls; the room was quite large enough and a fine romp ensued; the girls were as lithe and active as young fawns, and for a long time sorely tried the patience of their male friends, who tumbled about in all directions, only to get an extra dose of birch on their plump posteriors before they could regain their feet.

At last the Honourable Miss Vavasour stumbled over a prostrate gentleman, who happened to be the young Marquis of Bucktown, who grasped her firmly round the waist, and clung to his prize, as a shower of cuts greeted the writhing pair.

'Hold, hold,' cried Alice, 'she's fairly caught and must submit to be offered as a victim on the Altar of Love.'

Lucy quickly wheeled a small soft couch into the centre of the room. The gentlemen pulled off their bandages, and all laughingly assisted to place the pair in position; the lady underneath with a pillow under her buttocks, and the young marquis, on his knees, fairly planted between her thighs. Both were novices, but a more beautiful couple it would be impossible to conceive; he was a fine young fellow of seventeen, with dark hair and eyes, whilst her brunette style of complexion was almost a counterpart of his; their eyes were similar also, and his instrument, as well as her cunny, were finely ornamented with soft curly black hair, with the skin drawn back, the firey purple head of his cock looked like a large ruby, as, by Frederick's suggestion, he presented it to her luscious-looking vermilion gap, the lips of which were just slightly open as she lay with her legs apart. The touch seemed to electrify her, the blushing face turned to a still deeper crimson as the dart of love slowly entered the outworks of her virginity. Fred continued to act as mentor by whispering in the ear of the young gallant, who was also covered with blushes, but feeling his steed fairly in contact with the throbbing matrix of the lovely girl beneath him, he at once plunged forward to the attack, pushing, shoving, and clasping her round the body with all his strength, whilst he tried to stifle her cries of pain by glueing his lips to hers. It was a case of *Veni, vidi, vici*. His onset was too impetuous to be withstood, and she lay in such a passive favourable position that the network of her hymen was broken at the first charge, and he was soon in full possession up to the roots of his hair. He rested a moment, she opened her eyes, and with a faint smile said, 'Ah! It was indeed sharp, but I can already begin to feel the pleasures of love. Go on now, dear boy, our example will soon fire the others to imitate us,' heaving up her bottom as a challenge, and pressing him fondly to her bosom. They ran a delightful course, which filled us all with voluptuous excitement, and as they died away in a mutual spend, someone put out the lights. All was laughing confusion, gentlemen trying to catch a prize, kissing and sighing.

I felt myself seized by a strong arm, and a hand groped for my cunny whilst a whisper in my ear said: 'How delightful! It's you, dear little Beatrice. I can't make a mistake, as yours is the only hairless thing in the company. Kiss me, dear, I'm bursting to be into your tight little affair.' Lips met lips in a luscious kiss. We found ourselves close to Alice's bed, my companion put me back on it, and taking my legs under his arms, was soon pushing his way up my longing cunny. I nipped him as tightly as possible; he was in ecstasies and spent almost directly, but keeping his place, he put me, by his vigorous action, into a perfect frenzy of love. Spend seemed to follow spend, till we had each of us done it six times, and the last time I so forgot myself as to fairly bite his shoulder in delight. At length he withdrew, without telling his name. The room was still in darkness, and love engagements were going on all round. I had two more partners after that, but only one go with each. I shall never forget that night as long as a breath remains in my body.

Next day I found out, through Fred, that Charlie Vavasour had been my first partner, and that he himself believed he had had his sister in the mêlée, which she afterwards admitted to me was a fact, although she thought he did not know it, and the temptation to enjoy her brother was too much for her.

This orgy has been the means of establishing a kind of secret society amongst the circle of our friends. Anyone who gives a pressure of the hand and asks: 'Do you remember Fred's birthday?' is free to indulge in love with those who understand it, and I have since been present at many repetitions of that birthday fun.

## *Chapter Three*

We returned to school, and I kept up a regular correspondence with Frederick, the letters to and fro being enclosed in those of Alice. Time crept on, but as you can imagine as well or better than I can relate all the kinds of salacious amusements we girls used to indulge in, I shall skip over the next few years till I arrived at the age of seventeen; my guardians were in a hurry to present me at Court, and have me brought out in hopes that I might soon marry and relieve them of their trust.

Alice was so attached to me that since my first visit to her home, she had solicited her aunt to arrange with my guardians for my permanent residence with her during my minority, which quite fell in with their views, as it enabled me to see more society, and often meet gentlemen who might perhaps fall in love with my pretty face.

Lady St Jerome undertook to present both Alice and myself; she was an aunt, and mentioned in her letter that unfortunately a star of the first magnitude would also be presented at the same drawing-room, but still we might have a faint chance of picking up young Lothair, the great matrimonial prize of the season, if he did not immediately fall in love with the beautiful Lady Corisande, and that we should meet them both at Crecy House, at the Duchess's ball in celebration of the presentation of her favourite daughter, for which she had obtained invitations for us. For nearly three weeks we were in a flutter of excitement, making the necessary preparations for our debut. My mother's jewels were reset to suit the fashion of the day, and every three or four days we went to town to see our Court milliner.

In company with Alice and her aunt, we arrived at Lord St Jerome's town residence in St James's Square, the evening before the eventful day; her ladyship was a most charming person of about thirty, without family, who introduced us before dinner to her niece, Miss Clare Arundel, Father Coleman, the family confessor, and Monsignore Berwick, the chamberlain of Pio Nono. The dinner was exquisite, and we passed a delightful evening, amused by the quiet humour of the confessor, and the sparkling wit of Monsignore, who seemed studiously to avoid religious subjects. Miss Arundel, with her beautiful pensive, violet eyes, and dark golden brown hair, seemed particularly fascinated by the sallies of the latter, whilst there was a something remarked by both Alice and myself, which led us to suspect the existence of some curious tie between the two ecclesiastics and the ladies of the household.

Lord St Jerome was not in town. At our special request, Alice and myself shared the same room, which opened into a spacious corridor, at one end of which was a small chapel or oratory. Our minds were so unsettled by the thoughts of the morrow, and also hopes of meeting some of our old friends in town, especially the Vavasours, that sleep was quite banished from our eyes; suddenly Alice started up in bed, with, 'Hist! there's someone moving about the corridor.' She sprang out of bed, and softly opened our door, whilst I followed and stood close behind her. 'They're gone into the oratory,' she said. 'I saw a figure just in the act of passing in; I will know what is going on; we can easily slip into some of the empty rooms, if we hear anyone coming.'

So saying, she put on her slippers and threw a shawl over her shoulders, and I followed her example; ready for any kind of adventure, we cautiously advanced along the corridor and soon arrived at the door of the oratory; we could hear several low voices inside, but were afraid to push the door ajar for fear of being observed.

'Hush!' whispered Alice, 'I was here when quite a little girl, and now remember that old Lady St Jerome, who has been dead some time, used to use this room next to the chapel, and had a private entrance made for herself direct from the room into the oratory. If we can get in here,' she said, turning the handle, 'we shall be in a fine place to see everything, as the room is never used, and said to be haunted by the old lady.' The door yielded to her pressure, and we slipped into a gloomy room; we were just able to see a little by the light of the moon.

Alice led me by the hand, having closed the door behind us; a cold shiver passed over my frame, but plucking up courage, I never faltered, and we soon found a little green baize door, bolted on our side. 'Hush!' she said, 'this opens into quite a dark corner, behind the confessional box,' as she gently withdrew the bolt, and we then noiselessly entered the chapel into a little kind of passage, between the box and the wall, and fortunately protected from observation by a large open-work screen, which completely hid us, but afforded quite a good view of the interior of the chapel. Guess our astonishment when we beheld both Lady St Jerome and her niece in earnest conference with the two priests and overheard what passed.

FATHER COLEMAN – Well, Sister Clare, the Cardinal has ordered that you are to seduce Lothair, by all the arts in your power; every venial sin you may commit is already forgiven.'

MONSIGNORE, *addressing Lady St Jerome* – 'Yes, and Sister Agatha here will assist you all she can; you know she is a nun; by the modern policy of Holy Church, we allow certain of the sisters to marry when their union with influential men tends to further the interests of the Church; the secret sisterhood of Ste Bridget is one of the most powerful political institutions in the world, because unsuspected, and its members have all sworn to obey with both body and soul; in fact, Sister Clare, this holy sisterhood into which we have just admitted you, by this special faculty from his Eminence, will permit you to enjoy every possible sensual pleasure here upon earth, and ensure your heavenly reward as well.'

The bright light shows us plainly the blushing face of Clare Arundel, which is turned almost crimson, as the confessor whispers something to her. 'Ah! No! No! No! not now,' she cried out.

MONSIGNORE– 'The first act of sisterhood is always to do penance directly after admission, and you have taken the oaths to obey both in body and mind; Sister Agatha will blindfold you, throw off your robe, and submit your body to the mortification of the flesh.'

Lady St Jerome quickly removed the dressing-gown in which her niece was enveloped, and left the fair girl with nothing but her chemise to cover her beautiful figure; the bandage was speedily adjusted over her lovely eyes, and she was made to kneel on a cushion, and rest her arms and face on the rails of the altar. Father Coleman armed himself with a light scourge of small cords, fixed in a handle, whilst her ladyship turned up the chemise of the victim so as to expose her bottom, thighs, legs and back to his castigation; then she withdrew, and seated herself on the knee of Monsignore, who had made himself comfortable in a large chair close to the victim; he clasped her round the waist, and pressed his lips to hers, whilst their hands seemed to indulge in a mutual groping about each other's private parts.

The scourge fell upon the lovely bottom; each stroke drawing a painful sigh from the victim, and leaving long red weals on the tender flesh.

The confessor continually lectured her on her future duties, and made her promise to do all his commands.

The poor girl's bottom was soon scored all over, and dripping with blood; the sight of this seemed to inflame the others, so that the confessor's affair stood out between the opening of his cassock, whilst Lady St Jerome spitted herself on the pego of Monsignore, and rode a most gallant St George as he sat in the chair.

THE CONFESSOR – 'Now, sister, for the last mortification of your flesh, you must surrender your virginity to the Church.' Saying which, he produced several fine large cushions, took the bandage from her eyes, and laid her comfortably on her back for his attack, with an extra cushion under her buttocks, in the most approved fashion. Then kneeling down between her thighs, he opened his cassock, and we could see he was almost naked under-neath. He laid himself forward on her lovely body, and whispered something in her ear, which was apparently a command to her to take hold of his lustful weapon, for she immediately put down her hand, and seemed (as far as we could see) to direct it to her crack herself. She was evidently fired with lust, and longing to allay the raging heat of the part which had been so cruelly whipped, for she heaved up her bottom to meet his attack, and so seconded his efforts that he speedily forced his way in, and the only evidence of pain on her part was a rather sharp little cry, just as he entered to break through the hymen. They lay for a moment in the enjoyment of the loving conjunction of their parts, but she was impatient, putting her hands on the cheeks of his bottom, and pressing him to herself in a most lascivious manner; just then Monsignore and Sister Agatha, who had finished their course, got up and, the one with the scourge and the other with a thin cane (after first lifting up his cassock and exposing a brown hairy-looking bottom), began to lay into Father Coleman in good earnest. Thus stimulated, and begging and crying for them to let him alone, he rammed furiously into Miss Clare, to her evident delight; she wriggled, writhed and screamed in ecstasy, and gave us such a sight of sensual delirium as I have never seen before or since. At last he seemed to spend into her, and, after a while, withdrew himself from her embrace, reluctant though she seemed to release him.

We could see they were preparing to leave the chapel, so thought it time to make our retreat.

Next day we were presented, and nothing in the manner of the lively Lady St Jerome, or the demure Miss Clare Arundel, would have led anyone to imagine the scene that we had witnessed in the small hours of the morning.

In the evening we were all at the Duchess's ball. Lord Carisbrooke, to whom I was specially introduced, was my partner in the set, in which danced Lothair and Miss Arundel as *vis-à-vis* to Lady Corisande and the Duke of Brecon.

By and by the hero of the evening led me out for the Lancers, and afterwards we strolled into the conservatory, quite unobserved; his con-versation was much livelier than I had expected, for Lady St Jerome had represented to us that he was seriously bent on religion, and about to join the Romish Church. The conservatory was large, and we strolled on till the music and laughter seemed quite at a distance, and coming to a seat with a delightful fountain in front of us we sat down; just as he was observing, 'How delightful it is to withdraw from the whirl of gaiety for a few minutes,' we heard some light footsteps approaching, those evidently of a very loving couple; the lady was heard to exclaim, with a saucy laugh, 'Ah! No! How dare you presume so; I would never be unfaithful to Montairy even in a kiss', there was a slight struggle, and, 'Ah, Monster, what a liberty!' and we heard the smack of lips upon a soft cheek; and then, 'Oh! No! Let me go back,' but the gentleman evidently remonstrated, as I could hear him say, 'Come, come, compose yourself, dear Victoria, a little, there is a seat here by the fountain, you must rest a moment.'

LOTHAIR, *with a start, whispered* – 'They must not catch us here, they'd think we had been eavesdropping; let's hide ourselves and never say a word about it,' dragging me by the hand around a corner, where we were well screened by the foliage of the delicious exotics.

My heart was in a flutter, and I could perceive he was greatly moved. We stood motionless, hand in hand, as the lady and gentleman took possession of the cool seat we had just vacated; the latter proved to be the Duke of Brecon. I could see them plainly, and have no doubt Lothair did also.

LADY MONTAIRY – 'Now, sir, no more of your impudent pranks. Pray let me recover my serenity.'

The Duke knelt down and took her hand, which she affectedly tried to withdraw, but he retained it, saying: 'Dearest Victoria, pity my passion. How can I help loving those killing eyes, and luscious pouting lips. That very fact of its being wrong makes my determination the greater to enjoy you the first opportunity. It is useless to resist our fate. Why has the god of love given me such a chance as this?'

She turns away her head with affected prudery, but not a blush rises to assert her horror at his speech. One hand presses her fingers to his lips; but where is the other? Under her clothes. He first touches her ankle, and slowly steals it up her leg. She fidgets on the seat, but he is impetuous, and soon has possession of her most secret charms. Her languishing eyes are turned on him and, in an instant, he is on his legs, and pushing her clothes up, displays a lovely pair of legs in white silk stockings, beautiful blue garters with gold buckles, her thighs encased in rather tight-fitting drawers, beautifully trimmed with Valenciennes lace. His lips are glued to hers at the same instant, and his hands gently part her yielding thighs, as he placed himself well between them. It is but the work of an instant. He places her hand on the shaft of love, which he has just let out, and it is guided into the haven of love. Both are evidently too hot and impetuous, for it seems to be over in a minute.

She hastily kisses him, and puts down her clothes as she says: 'How awful; but I could not resist Your Grace without disordering all my dress. It's been quite a rape, sir,' with a smile. 'Now, let's make haste back before we are missed.' He kisses her, and makes her agree to an assignation, somewhere in South Belgravia, for the morrow, to enjoy each other more at leisure, and then they are gone.

It would be impossible to describe the agitation of my partner during this short scene; Lothair seemed to shiver and shudder with emotion, I was also all of a tremble, and nestled close to him, my arm designedly touching the bunch in his trousers, always so interesting to me; I could feel it swell and seem ready to burst from its confinement; he nervously clasped my hand, and was speechless with emotion all during the scene which I have described; as soon as they were gone he seemed to give a gasp of relief, and led me out of our hiding place. 'Poor girl,' he said, 'what a sight for you, how I trembled for my own honour, lest the scene should make me lose my self-control. Ah! wretched woman, to betray her husband so!' Then looking at me for the first time he said, 'Do you not think it is best for a man never to marry?'

Used as I had been to such things, his terrible emotion made me quite sympathise with him, and my own agitation was quite natural, as I replied, 'Ah! my lord, you little know the ways of the world; I saw a more awful scene than that which we have witnessed, only last night, enacted by men sworn to perpetual celibacy, and you yourself were mentioned as a victim of their infernal plot.'

'My God! Lady, pray tell me what it was,' he ejaculated.

'Not now, we shall be missed, do you know any place where I can have a private conference with your lordship? If so, meet me tomorrow afternoon at two o'clock, in the Burlington Arcade. I shall come disguised,' I answered.

He hastily wrote the assignation on his tablets, and we made haste to return to the saloons from which we had been absent quite twenty minutes. A little while after, as I was sitting by the side of Alice, whispering my adventure in her ear, Lady Montairy, to whom I had previously been introduced, came and seated herself by my side. 'Ah!' she said with a sly look, 'you're in a fair way to carry off the great prize; my sister Corisande will stand no chance.'

'I've only danced one set with him,' I replied, demurely.

'Ah!' she laughed, 'it was not the Lancers I referred to, but your quiet stroll into the recesses of the conservatory. You had quite a lover's tête-à-tête.'

'But we did not indulge in a *Pas Seul*, as you did with His Grace,' I laughed, enjoying her confusion. She was speechless with surprise, her eyes fairly started with affright, and I hastened to reassure her, 'I'm your friend, dear Lady Montairy, your secret is safe with me, and I hope you will not make any remarks in connection with myself and Lothair.'

She squeezed my hand nervously, and asked, 'Do you remember Fred's birthday? I was not there, but my brother Bertram was with his cousins the Vavasours, and passed as their brother Charlie, who happened to be too ill to go with them. I'm initiated into your society. We shall meet again,' she added with a smile; 'I must go now to keep my engagements.'

The supper was a fairy feast, except for its substantial reality, and we returned home to Lady St Jerome's charmed with everything, and especially with the fine prospect we seemed to have of future enjoyment.

Next day I made an excuse to go out alone to pay a visit to an old schoolfellow, and two o'clock found me sauntering through Burlington Arcade. Lothair was there to the minute, and gently whispered in my ear, as I was looking in a doll shop, 'Now, this is really kind of Your Ladyship, and proves you can be depended on; I have made a most excellent arrangement, we have only to step across the road to the Bristol Hotel in Burlington Gardens, where I have ordered luncheon for myself and cousin, in a private apartment, and they know me too well to pry into my affairs.'

The chambermaid attended me in the bedroom, and as soon as I had laid aside my cloak, hat, etc., I rejoined Lothair in the adjoining apartment, where a sumptuous luncheon was set out.

Lothair, whose shyness of the previous evening seemed considerably dispelled, most gallantly insisted upon my partaking of refreshment, before a word of my communication should be uttered. 'Besides,' he said, 'a little champagne will give you courage, if it is at all disagreeable; the scene last night was such a shock to both of us that if you now prefer to be silent I won't press you about what you mentioned in the excitement of such a moment.'

His conversation was very lively all through the repast, and when we had nearly finished I asked him to ring for a little milk, which was brought to me; he was at the moment abstractedly examining the debris of a *paté de foie gras*. I poured part of the milk into two champagne glasses, and slyly added about ten drops of tincture of cantharides, with which Alice had provided me, to his portion. 'Now, my Lord,' I said, 'I challenge you to pledge me in a glass of my favourite beverage, champagne and milk, I think it is delicious,' pouring out the fizzing wine, and handing him the glass, which I first touched with my lips.

His eyes sparkled with delight as he drained it to the bottom, and flung the empty glass over his shoulder, exclaiming, 'No one shall ever put their lips to that again; it was indeed a challenge, Lady Beatrice, after which nothing but the reality will satisfy me.' Then rising, he persisted in claiming the kiss I had, as he alleged, challenged him to take.

'Now,' he continued, drawing me to a sofa, 'let us sit down and hear the awful communication you hinted at; who were those wretched men?'

'Monsignore Berwick and Father Coleman,' I replied; 'did you ever hear of a secret sisterhood of Ste Bridget, the nuns belonging to which devote both soul and person to the service of the Church?'

'No, never, but go on,' said Lothair, so I continued: 'These nuns are all aristocratic ladies, who devote themselves, as I said, implicitly to the interests of Holy Mother Church, satisfying and appeasing the lusts of her priests, as well as marrying any influential man they think they can lead by the silken tie of matrimony; such, my lord, are Lady St Jerome and Miss Arundel.'

'Incredible,' exclaimed Lothair, 'but I cannot doubt your word, dear Beatrice – permit me to call you that,' his eyes looking amorously at me and evidently already slightly moved by the exciting dose I had given him. I took his hand in mine – it was feverishly warm – then looked him full in the face: 'My dear lord, I would not have been here if for one moment I had thought you could doubt my word.'

'Call me Lothair, darling, throw away all awkward reserve,' he said, putting his arm around my waist, and giving me another kiss on my cheek, 'go on; tell me all about those fiendish priests who have been plotting to ensnare me.'

'Take my advice, Lothair,' I went on, 'you will find Miss Clare quite changed, her demure and reserved aspect turned to alluring and captivating glances; the Cardinal's orders are positive that she is not to spare even her honour if necessary, but that is an article I saw her surrender to the confessor.' Then I described to him the scene we had witnessed in the chapel, which, added to the effects of the tincture, seemed quite to work him up to a state of amorous excitement.

'Honour! Honour!' he exclaimed, excitedly. 'Alas! dear Beatrice, last night I felt able to lose life rather than that, and now it's gone, fled like a shadow, but what is it after all, but a mean, mistrustful shame; you must be mine, I can't restrain the fire of love which is consuming me; the very sin makes the idea more delicious.' My faint efforts were useless, he was a fine strong young fellow; in an instant I was thrown backwards on the sofa, and his hands took possession of my longing cunny; the furor of lust was upon him, but I made a fair show of resistance, and seemed only to yield to force, shutting my eyes as if afraid to see how he was exposing himself.

He roughly forced my thighs apart, and as he threw himself upon me, I could feel the hot soft head of his cock forcing its way between the lips of my vagina. I struggled and contracted myself as much as possible, and as I had previously well bathed the parts in a strong solution of alum and water, he experienced as great tightness and difficulty in penetration as if I had really been a virgin. My subdued cries of pain were real, for his big affair hurt me very much, but he gradually won his way, which was at the last moment facilitated by a copious spend.

'Ah! Darling; how delightful,' he cried, as he lay with his weapon up to the hilt, throbbing and enjoying the lascivious contractions to which I now treated him.

His lips were fixed to mine, the soft velvety tip of his tongue was a titbit I could not refuse, and I sucked it till I almost choked for want of breath. He spent again under the stimulating emotions with which I inspired him. He lay still for a few moments as we recovered our breath, then, with an upward motion of my buttocks, I challenged him to go on.

It was a most erotically voluptuous love engagement. I could not exhaust him; he was continually shooting his love juice into my very insatiable womb, and it was more than an hour before either of us would consent to a cessation of the game.

All that time we had been as closely joined together as the Siamese twins, only one heart and one soul seemed to animate us, whilst we were constantly returning the flow of sperm one after the other in the most thrilling manner.

After we had washed and refreshed ourselves, he begged my forgiveness for his impulsiveness, and promised to make me his wife, but I recalled to him his words of the previous evening: 'That it was better for a man never to marry,' and that for my part I thought that such sweet liaisons could never be enjoyed by 'married people'.

'Ha! ha!' I laughed. 'You have the two nuns of Ste Bridget to enjoy. Be advised by me, and seem to fall into their traps. I will introduce you to another secret society which you have little idea of. It is devoted to the pleasure of love, without being under the control of a lustful priesthood. You shall meet me again this day week and tell me how you get on.'

He parted from me very lovingly; and on my return to St James's Square, I found that Lady Montairy had brought an invitation from the Duchess for us to spend a few days at Crecy House before our return to the country.

'How delightful,' said Alice. 'The Duke has gone to Paris on business, and the Duchess is often indisposed; we shall find ourselves in Paphian bowers.'

Lothair dined with us that evening, but neither of us betrayed, by word or look, the new link between us.

Miss Arundel was attractive, and even alluring, in her manner towards him. Her face was all smiles as she addressed him in tones of sympathy, even of tenderness. Bewitching enough to turn the head of any less susceptible (even than Lothair) to the influence of the softer sex. She looked divine, dressed in a wondrous white robe, garlanded with violets just arrived from Paris; on her head a violet wreath, deep and radiant as her eyes, which admirably contrasted with her dark golden brown hair.

I could see he was fascinated. He asked us all to drive down to Richmond and dine with him the next day, but Alice declined for me and herself, alleging as a reason the short time we had to stay in town, and that we should at once have to avail ourselves of the Duchess's invitation, and with Lady Jerome's permission would remove to Crecy House early in the morning.

I could see this plan afforded them infinite satisfaction. So next day saw us welcomed at Crecy House by Lady Bertha St Aldegonde on behalf of the Duchess, who was confined to her room. Lady Montairy conducted us to our apartments, and dismissing the attendants as soon as possible, she embraced me first, and then Alice, saying: 'How nice of you two dears to come so soon. You're just in time for a most important ceremony. Tomorrow Mama thinks we are all going to the Academy, but in reality it is quite a different place. The fact is, Corisande is going to be received as a member of the Paphian Circle, as we call the society which you helped to originate. St Aldegonde, indifferent and "ne'er do well" as he seems, is the life and soul of it; Bertha indulges him in everything. Jealousy is unknown in our family. You will meet Bertram, Carisbrooke and Brecon all there. We only want Lothair to make it perfection, as Corisande means to taste and try which she likes best.'

ALICE – 'But surely we're not obliged to wait till tomorrow. Can't you, Victoria, give us a little party in your room tonight?'

'Yes,' she answered. 'But only a hen party; ourselves and Corisande. My room is the next to yours. The gentlemen will be at the clubs. St Aldegonde never will have a woman at night, and says the morning is the proper time, because his cock always stands best on an empty stomach before breakfast.'

The indisposition of the Duchess was a good excuse for all the ladies of the family to retire early, and after having dispensed with the lady's-maids, we met in Lady Montairy's chamber, all attired '*en robes de nuit*'.

Bertha St Aldegonde was a really splendid woman, a dark brunette of a fully developed figure, prominent dark flashing eyes, and a most sensual chin. Victoria Montairy was also a fine woman, with a very beautiful classic cast of countenance, whilst the darling Corisande seemed more beautiful than ever, for want of ornament, in her spotless *chemise de nuit*.

Alice and I both kissed her with rapture, which she lovingly responded to.

'Now, what is the programme?' said Alice to Lady Bertha.

'St Aldegonde and Montairy are both keeping themselves in reserve for the grand ceremony of tomorrow,' she replied; 'what weak things these men are; as if we wanted to be kept in reserve. Why, Victoria and myself never get enough; the more we have the more we seem to require, and the less able they become to satisfy us. Talk about women's rights, they ought to compel husbands to find substitutes, when they can't do it for us.'

'Well, if you have a pair of good godemiches, Beatrice and myself will try and satisfy you a little, whilst dear Corisande shall keep us up to the work with a good rod,' said Alice.

The godemiches were brought forth, and proved to be of monstrous size, to our ideas; they were made of the finest vulcanised india-rubber, beautifully moulded and finished, with all appendages complete; we strapped them on as soon as they were charged with a creamy compound of gelatine and milk. All were stripped to the buff.

Lady Bertha took me on her knee, kissing me lusciously, and handling the dildo as if it had been alive. 'What a fine fellow,' she laughed, 'but not a bit too large to please me.' Meanwhile my fingers were busy, nipping and pinching her clitoris; she glued her lips to mine and fairly sucked my breath away, excited by my touches which had caused quite an erection of her finely developed clitoris. She drew me on to a couch, and I thrust the affair into her already spending cunny, her bottom responded to every shove, whilst I felt the smarting cuts of the birch which Corisande was applying alternately to myself and Alice; it was most delicious. I responded with all my ardour to the loving caresses of Lady Bertha, who clasped me firmly by the buttocks, whilst with two fingers of the right hand she frigged both my bottom and cunny at once; Alice and her partner were quite forgotten; I thought I had never experienced anything so delicious in my life. The combination of emotions quite carried me away, the lovely woman bounding under me in rapture, our luscious kisses, the warmth and exquisite titillations of my fundament arrangements seemed such an acme of bliss that when I made the godemiche spend into her my own nature seemed to melt into a sea of lubricity.

After a few moments I entreated her to be the gentleman, and let me have her stiff clitoris, which I was sure could give me great pleasure. 'Certainly, dear,' she said, 'I often do it to Victoria; throw off the dildo.' As quickly as possible we changed places, and I begged her first to bring herself forward over my mouth that I might kiss her pussy, and caress that exciting clitoris of hers. It was done at once, and I had a glorious view of the paraphernalia of love. A splendid mount covered with glossy black hair; the serrated vermilion lips of her cunny slightly parted, from which projected quite four inches a stiff fleshy clitoris as big as a man's thumb. I opened the lips with my fingers, passed my tongue lasciviously about the most sensitive parts, took that glorious clitoris in my mouth, rolling my tongue around it, and playfully biting with my teeth; it was too much for her, with a cry of 'Oh! Oh! you make me come, darling!' she spent profusely all over my mouth and chin.

She sank down upon me, and I opened my legs to admit her. 'Now it's my turn to repay the delicious pleasure I owe you,' she sighed, kissing me rapturously, and sucking my tongue into her mouth, so that I could scarcely catch my breath; with her fingers she opened my slit as wide as possible, then directing her clitoris to the passage she seemed to stuff lips and all in, then closed my affair upon it, holding them together tightly with her hand. I can't express to you how novel and delightful this conjunction was to me; we were both so heated and excited, our spendings seemed to mingle together and add to our erotic fury; without separating for a moment she rubbed and pushed about inside of me, the lips and hair of her cunny titillating the sensitive parts in a most thrilling way. We swam in a sea of lubricity, whilst Corisande added to her sister's enjoyment by the stimulating effect of her rod.

At last all was over, and we retired to rest, and did not rise till late next morning. Refreshed by a cold bath we had only just time to breakfast and prepare for our visit to the Academy. We drove to Burlington House, but only stayed half an hour, entered the carriage again and were driven to a large house facing the Thames, in Cheyne Walk; it was detached, and stood back in its own grounds.

We were received at the door by a quiet-looking old lady, who was the housekeeper and manager to the Paphian Circle; she ushered us into a large drawing-room, which occupied nearly all the space of the first floor, being supported in the centre by elegant fluted columns of black and gold; the whole apartment looked like a hall of the veritable Alhambra; the windows were closed by gorgeous black and gold curtains and, although it was daylight outside, light was provided by a constellation of wax tapers artistically arranged all round the walls.

The Duke of Brecon was there as a novice, with Bertram and Lord Carisbrooke as sponsors; Lords Montairy and St Aldegonde, with several other gentlemen and ladies, were also present. Alice and myself were over-whelmed with compliments as being two of the original founders of the society.

Lord St Aldegonde, as president, now asked Corisande and the Duke if they pledged their words to keep all the secrets of the Paphian Circle, remarking that oaths were quite useless, as he felt sure those who introduced them had every faith in their honourable intentions. Being answered in the affirmative, and having shaken hands with them, he requested all to prepare for dancing, as no one else was expected.

The company retired to the dressing-rooms, and in a few minutes we were all back in the drawing-room, everyone in a state of nudity with the exception of silk stockings, garters, and elegant dancing shoes. To prevent jealousy or any undue preference there was a deep box on a sideboard, where the refreshments stood; in this box were deposited slips of parchment, each bearing the name of one of the gentlemen present, and the ladies had each to draw for her partner in the first waltz, and the *pas de deux* after it. Corisande drew Lord Carisbrooke, and my prize was St Aldegonde.

I must not omit to mention that one of the ladies would get a slip with 'Piano' on it, and the last gentleman had to turn over the music for her. This fell to Lady Bertha, who was a brilliant pianist and at once struck up a well-known favourite from the Argyll Rooms, and we were instantly in motion. It was far more exciting than the blindfold romp on Fred's birthday; she kept us going till one by one, the couples subsided on the inviting couches, which stood around the room; my partner was in a brilliant state of erection, but he whispered to me, 'Not yet, Beatrice dear, we must see to Corisande.' Every-one seemed to act without the necessity of orders; all the couples ranged up in a semi-circle round the couch where Carisbrooke was caressing and kissing her, whilst the beautiful girl, her eyes languishing with love, was sighing and looking at his fine cock, which she held in her hand. 'Now, love,' said the gallant, 'as a novice you must kiss every gentleman's affair, and then we will initiate you into the mysteries of Venus.' Corisande, all blushes, took each throbbing pego tenderly in her hand and softly kissed the velvet heads. 'Now, Brecon,' said my partner, 'you do the same to the ladies, and that part of the ceremony will be over.'

'With pleasure, on my knees,' said the Duke, and we each presented our cunnies to his lips. Carisbrooke now gently inclined Corisande backwards, and put a soft pillow under her bottom, then proceeded to place himself in position; but unable to restrain his excitability, he spent all over her lovely mossy mount and belly, some of the sperm going quite up to the alabaster globes which adorned her heaving chest.

He blushed with shame and vexation, whilst Corisande was crimson, and gasping with excited expectation.

Lady Bertha, who was the coolest of the company, at once wiped all the sperm off her sister's belly with her fingers, with which she lubricated her crack; then taking hold of His Lordship's affair, directed it properly to the longing gap of love.

'Shove away. Shove, my boy. Heave up your bottom to meet him, dear,' she laughed, giving Corisande a good sounding slap on the side of her buttocks with her other hand.

With a furious plunge, the dart of love made its effort just at the right moment. The collision with her hymen was most destructive, the virgin defences gave way as with an awful shriek of pain, she lost all consciousness. He completed the conquest of his victim's virginity, and then lay soaking, and trying to revive her sensibility by his lascivious throbbing inside of her, whilst we applied salts and restoratives to bring her round.

She very speedily came to herself, evidently forgetting the fearful pain of her ravishment; there was a delightful languor in her eyes, as she patted his bottom and hugged him to her bosom. He responded to the gentle challenge, making her revel in all the delights of coition, and never withdrew his blood-stained priapus till they had mutually spent several tunes.

My partner now led me to a couch, as the others dispersed on the same kind of business. He was still as stiff as ever, and I longed to feel him within me, but, to my surprise, he mounted the reverse way upon me, presenting his bottom to my face and asked me to press my firm bubbies together, so that his cock might spend between them whilst he gamahuched me. It was a luscious position, and I lent all my ardour to second his fancy, and his lascivious tongue made me spend in delight just as his sperm deluged my bosom and belly.

Alice had had Lord Montairy.

After this, the gentlemen's names were replaced in the box, and the ladies made another selection, but in case of anyone drawing the same partner a second time, she had to return the slip and draw another.

Thus we passed a most delicious afternoon, refreshing ourselves from time to time with champagne and ices, or something more substantial, for the worship of Venus and Priapus requires continual stimulation with the most invigorating viands.

In this short sketch of my adventures it would be impossible to describe everything at great length, but I can assure you the ladies fairly exhausted the gentlemen before they allowed themselves to be driven home to dinner.

## Chapter Four

I must now return to my liaison with Lothair; he had promised to meet me again in a week, when I hoped to hear the particulars of his drive to Richmond.

We lunched again at the Bristol Hotel, and without having recourse to the tincture I found him almost as hot and impulsive as before. 'Ah! Beatrice,' he said, as we lay exhausted on the sofa, after a series of delicious encounters, 'I cannot express half the gratitude and devotion I ought to have; for you, not satisfied with making me happy yourself, quite unselfishly advised me how to enjoy the two nuns. But first tell me of that Society of Love, which you promised to introduce me to, and then you shall have my adventure.'

So briefly I described to him the Paphian Circle, and took his promise to allow me to introduce him at the next seance.

'I know,' he said, 'you thought me quite captivated by Miss Arundel, but I never forgot your advice, and resolved to seem to lend myself as a proselyte, accept all the advantages they might offer as baits, and get a thorough insight into all the plans of the Jesuits before I open their eyes, but it is a game that will last a long time. Now, as to the Richmond drive. Lady St Jerome and Miss Arundel were most vivacious and alluring, as we drove down by road; then we had a beautiful row on the river whilst waiting for dinner, which we sat down to with excellent appetites. I plied the two ladies with wine, and requested them as a special favour not to leave me to myself at dessert, as I did not smoke, and there were no other gentlemen present. Everything was sparkling and agreeable, religion seemed to be avoided by mutual consent, the ladies had withdrawn from the table to a sofa in a recess, where their faces were screened from the light of the brilliant chandelier; they had each had two or three glasses of champagne and seemed very careful not to exceed the limits of decorum, when, taking a fresh bottle, I challenged them to drink to the prosperity of the Christian Church.

' "Ah!" said Miss Arundel, with flashing eyes, "but what Church do you refer to?"

' "Dear ladies," I replied, "you shall word the toast as you please, and I will drain a real bumper to it in your company."

' "Then," said Clare, "we drink to the prosperity of the Holy Roman Catholic Church, and long life to His Holiness Pius IX."

'Their eyes sparkled, and both seemed unusually excited.

' "What would we not do to assure your conversion, dear Lothair," said Lady St Jerome. "Come and sit between us whilst we talk seriously to you."

'I sat down on the sofa, and being well flushed with wine, impudently put an arm round each of their waists, and said, without thinking. "Ah! that's mere nonsense; but in truth, I would sell both body and soul for the happiness you and your niece could confer on me."

'Miss Arundel drew a deep sigh, but Lady St Jerome softly whispered, as she laid one hand on my thigh, most awkwardly near to an important member, "Ah! what do you mean? Join our Church, and there is nothing we will deny to you."

' "Nothing! nothing! you will get indulgences and dispensations for everything then," whispered Clare, as she laid her head on my shoulder.

' "No! no traffic with priests; I want my indulgence from you, dear ladies, and if you care for my soul, now's the time to save me; drive me away in unsatisfied desperation, and such a chance will never occur again. Ah! how awfully I am tempted by the proximity of such charms!" I exclaimed, falling on my knees, and clasping their legs, as I hid my face in Clare's lap.

'They were both trembling with emotion, and I was equally agitated, but I seemed to guess from their looks and manner towards me that the present moment was too favourable for them to let slip.

'Lady St Jerome was the first to speak. "Dear Lothair, we do indeed pity your distress. Oh! Oh! for shame, sir, what liberties! Will you? Will you, promise us?" as she fidgeted about in confusion, feeling my hand slowly advancing up her legs beneath the clothes; both my hands were busy, but Clare had closed her thighs, and firmly stopped my advance in silence, whilst her aunt's ejaculations seemed to encourage me more and more.

' "By all that's sacred, I promise everything you may demand of me; they shall receive me into the Church, as soon as they please, if you two will but be ministering angels to my impulsive passions," I cried, taking advantage of her confusion to gain complete possession of the grotto of love.

' "Clare, dear," sighed Her Ladyship, "can we possibly sacrifice ourselves for a nobler purpose? By now subduing his carnal lusts, we shall also draw a lost sheep to the foot of the cross."

'I felt Miss Arundel's tightly compressed thighs relax in their resistance, and she gave a spasmodic sigh as I victoriously advanced my rude hand also to her mossy retreat. "Ah! how delicious to have possession of a double set of the loveliest charms; I will kiss you, and enjoy you by turns," I said in rapture, at the prospect before me.

LADY ST JEROME – 'Excuse me a moment, dear Lothair, Clare is all blushing confusion, let me spare her modesty as much as possible,' as she rose and locked the door, then almost turned out the gas.

'Pulling up her skirts, I threw Miss Arundel backwards on the sofa, and releasing my bursting weapon, threw myself between her yielding thighs, as I exclaimed, "You have indeed relieved me of making an invidious selection, as I cannot restrain the heat of my passion, Clare must be the first victim to it."

'It was almost, if not quite, dark in the recess where we were, but my lips sought those of the lovely girl, her entire frame seemed to quiver under me, and she gave a faint shriek as the head of my cock first touched the lips of her cunny. "Courage, darling," I whispered in her ear, "I won't hurt you more than I can help; open your legs, and give way to me as much as you can, you suffer for a noble object." As if I did not know she had already lost her virginity.

'Lady St Jerome had now returned to the sofa, where she encouraged Clare to bear the dreadful pain with all her fortitude. Then Her Ladyship took my affair in her hand, saying, "Let me, dear Lothair, direct you right. I'm a married woman, and know exactly how it ought to be done." Her touch only added to my excitement. She kept drawing the foreskin back, and took care to present the head rather above the proper entrance to the vagina, to make me think the resistance I felt was genuine, but it gave me infinite pleasure, and made Mr Pego spend all over the entrance of Clare's longing cunny. At last, after great difficulty, they let me fairly in, and I begged Her Ladyship still to keep her hand there and stimulate my exertions. I spent three times, each time more excitedly than the last, whilst the dear girl was a constant flood of lubricity, and seemed to melt with love, clinging to me with all the tenacity of her voluptuous furor.

'At last, notwithstanding her entreaties for me to go on, on, on, I managed to withdraw, as I told her she would leave nothing of me with which to repay all her dear aunt's kindness. "But, Clare darling," I said, "I will still give you pleasure with my tongue." So I made her give way to Lady St Jerome, who eagerly slipped off some of her skirts, as she said, to give me greater freedom, but in reality so that she might enjoy herself more. Her pussy was quite wet with spendings, which had flowed in sympathy with our enjoyment.

'Miss Clare was an apt pupil, and quickly arranged herself over her aunt's face, so as to present her excited cunny to my lips.

'Lady St Jerome had an extraordinary gift of contraction in her vagina, it took hold of my cock, like a delicately soft hand, with a frigging motion, as she wriggled and met my thrusts, of the most delicious kind. I grasped and moulded her lovely breasts with both hands, for she held me convulsively to her body, and I had no necessity to clasp her myself. Our conjunction was so exciting that I spent again immediately, under the touches of what I called her invisible hand, then steadying myself I revelled in love and lubricity for more than half an hour, both the dear ladies gasping, sighing, and sometimes when they spent giving vent to subdued shrieks of pleasure and dearment. Clare seemed quite as excited as her aunt, who I found was frigging her bottom-hole and rousing all her lustful propensities to the utmost with a disengaged hand, as soon as she found I was so safely rooted in herself that one arm could hold me.

'I can't tell you how we finished, for there seemed to be no end to it; however, about eleven o'clock we apparently awoke from a kind of delicious lethargy, into which we had all fallen, and we soon sufficiently composed ourselves to ring for the carriage and start for town; on the plea of keeping out the chilly night air, the windows were put up, and I had one or the other of them astride of my lap and spitted on the shaft of love till the noise of granite pavement under the wheels of the carriage warned us of the near approach to St James's Square.

'I have promised not to marry, but expressed my wish to be received into the Church by the Holy Father himself soon after Christmas, when I will visit Rome on purpose; this will give me plenty of time to carry on my game, and prove to the Jesuits that I am now quite equal to the tricks they played on me, when they had me down at Vauxe before, and imposed on the weak senses of a poor boy, quite green to the ways of the world. I can love Clare, when I don't think of it, but if I do I should hate her even in the midst of our love transports.'

Our time in town was getting short, so at my suggestion Bertram and St Aldegonde arranged an early day with Lothair, for his initiation to the Paphian Circle.

We were still at Crecy House, and this time the affair was managed under cover of a small private party at the Duke of Brecon's, where we dismissed our carriages, and then drove out in those of His Grace for a country excursion, which of course only extended to Cheyne Walk. Everything was in readiness, and Lothair being admitted as usual, we quickly appeared in the garb of Madre Natura as before. Partners were drawn for the first dance; my lot fell to the Duke of Brecon, whilst Lothair was drawn by Alice, and Lady Corisande presided at the piano, where her brilliant execution helped to add to the excitement engendered by the lascivious motions of the dance, in which, when the gentlemen changed partners with us as they went through the figure, they gave our bottoms a fine smarting spank, which we repaid by sharp little slaps on their extended cocks, soon getting tremendously warm and excited over our quadrille, and at the conclusion could scarcely restrain ourselves sufficiently to allow Lothair to give the usual kiss all round to our palpitating cunnies.

I noticed Lady Bertha very busy whispering to everyone, and soon found out that she was proposing a little bit of extra fun for us, of which the novice was of course to be the victim, whilst both pleasure and profit would accrue to the Paphian Circle.

The kissing ceremony was over, and then Alice told him he had yet another little penance to perform before he could be admitted to full rights of membership, pointing to a fine 'Berkeley Horse', which was being wheeled into the centre of the drawing-room, a thing something like a common pair of steps, only covered with red baize, and provided with a cushioned foot-board for the victim to stand on, whilst his hands were well stretched above his head, so as only to allow of his standing on tiptoe. Lothair in his simple ignorance stepped up gallantly and was instantly secured by his wrists to the topmost rings of the horse.

St Aldegonde, grinning with delight, tightened the cords unmercifully, making Lothair expostulate with him at the painful tension.

'That's nothing, my boy,' said St Aldegonde, 'don't cry out before you're hurt. Wait until you feel the rods tickle and warm your posteriors, it will do you good, as it did me; it's the most invigorating thing in the world; ask Bertha if I did not give her all she required that night.'

All the company were now furnished with beautiful bunches of long thin elegantly tied-up birch.

ALICE, *stepping to the front* – 'Now, sir, mind you answer all my questions under pain of severe punishment. In the first place none but orthodox members of the English Church can be admitted to the Paphian Circle, and a member has just hinted to me that you are going to Rome, and may be a Jesuit in disguise. Now, my lord, what do you say to that?' giving his bottom a smart cut, which made him wince with pain, and left a long red mark across the white skin of his manly buttocks.

LOTHAIR – 'My God! you punish without waiting.'

Before he could finish speaking all the ladies attacked him with their rods, raining a perfect shower of painful cuts on his helpless bottom, exclaiming, 'Answer! Answer!! Answer!!! No prevarication! Don't spare him! etc.,' whilst the gentlemen, who stood behind, cut into the fair bottoms of their partners, calling out, 'Pass it on to him; cut away, ladies, he's a Jesuit, etc.'

Lothair at first lost his breath, but soon shouted out lustily, 'Hold! Hold!! It's not true! Don't kill me!'

His bottom and back were scored all over, and little drops of blood trickled down from places where the skin was broken.

ALICE– 'Well, my lord, pray excuse our virtuous indignation, if you are not really a Jesuit. But how about a Cathedral you intend to build for them, eh?' cutting him several deliberate strokes as she was speaking, each one making him quiver under its smarting force.

LOTHAIR – 'Oh! My God! How do you know that? I've only had the plans drawn.'

ALICE– 'But, my lord, allow me to drive the thoughts of such a foolish thing from your mind. Can you not think of some better applications for your money? Will you promise me not to make yourself a fool?' cutting harder and harder every moment, till he fairly howled with pain, ejaculating –

'Ah! Oh! Damme! How cruel of you Miss Marchmont! Ah – for God's sake let me off now. I – I – won't do it; I give my word for that.'

ALICE– 'Beg my pardon instantly, my lord, or you shall feel what cruelty really is like. Cruel indeed! to a young lady who is only doing a painful duty!' catching hold of a fresh rod, and slashing his bleeding bottom with all her might.

Lothair writhes his body about in dreadful pain, and his fine cock stands out rampantly in front, in a most outrageous state of stiffness, the head quite purple from the extraordinary pressure of blood which distends it. 'Ah! ah! oh! oh! I do beg your pardon, I'm sure you will forgive me, and let me off now,' he groans in agony.

ALICE– 'I've only a trifling thing to ask you, now you have apologised. My duty is far more painful and disagreeable to me than it can possibly be to you; bodily suffering cannot for a moment be compared to anguish of mind,' as she still cuts into his raw-looking posteriors, and looks round delightedly on the spectators for encouragement, then goes on again. 'If you're not going to build that Cathedral, will you devote a fourth part of what it would have cost to the building of a proper temple for the meetings of our Paphian Circle?'

LOTHAIR, *gasping in pain* – 'Oh! Oh! Yes! That I will, £50,000, if you will let me down at once!'

There was a general clapping of hands all round, and cries of, 'Enough! Enough! He's a good boy now,' and then there was a scuffle all round to secure victims, which were mostly of the weaker sex, but Ladies Bertha and Victoria, by the aid of diplomacy, had got both their husbands prisoners on a sofa and were lashing into them most unmercifully, laughing and shrieking out, 'Keep the game alive! Keep the game alive!'

Alice had meanwhile let down poor Lothair, who was into her in a moment, to the dear girl's great delight, both of them frequently spending and screaming with ecstasy.

My partner threw me across his knee, and made my bottom smart under his loud slaps. I screamed and struggled desperately, and at last equalised matters by grasping his stiff cock, and making him feel that two could play at the game of inflicting pain. He cried a truce, and I speedily righted myself, sitting up with my bottom in his lap, and his pego right up into my vitals. He clasped his arms round me, taking one globe of my bosom in each hand, which he moulded delightfully with his fingers as I rose and fell on his tight-fitting shaft, leaning back my head so as to meet his kisses and give him my tongue. This was a delicious position, his spendings seemed to shoot with extraordinary force into my womb, and my own helped to make quite a stream of sperm, which spurted all over his thighs at each insertion, and fairly drowned the hair round the roots of his pego.

St Aldegonde and Montairy were having each other's wives for a change after their whipping, but cunt seemed decidedly at a discount with them, as each of them was indulging in a bottom-fuck, which those ladies seemed to relish immensely, and to add to the voluptuous excitement of the scene, the darling Corisande struck up 'They a' Do't' to the tune of 'A Man's a Man for a' That'.

> The grit folk an' the puir do't,
> The blyte folk and the sour do't,
> The black, the white,
> Rude an' polite,
> Baith autocrat an' boor do't.

For they a' do't – they a' do't,
The beggars an' the braw do't,
Folk that ance were, and folk that are –
The folk that come will a' do't.

The auld folk try't,
The young ane's do't,
 The blind, the lame,
 The wild, the tame,
In warm climes an' cauld do't,
 For they a' do't, etc.

The licensed by the law do't,
Forbidden folk and a' do't,
 And priest and nun
 Enjoy the fun,
And never once say nay to't.
 For they a' do't, etc.

The goulocks an' the snails do't
The cushie doos and quails do't,
 The dogs, the cats,
 The mice, the rats,
E'en elephants an' whales do't.
 For they a' do't, & c.

The wee bit cocks an' hens do't;
The robbins an' the wrens do't,
 The grizzly bears,
 The toads an' hares,
The puddocks in the fens do't.
 For they a' do't, etc.

The boars an' kangaroos do't,
The titlins an' cuckoos do't,
 While sparrows sma',
 An' rabbits a'
In countless swarms an' crews do't,
 For they a' do't, etc.

The midges, fleas, and bees do't,
The mawkes an' mites in cheese do't,
 An' cauld earthworms
 Crawl up in swarms,
An' underneath the trees do't,
 For they a' do't, etc.

The kings an' queens an' a' do't,
  The Sultan an' Pacha do't,
An' Spanish dons – loup off their thrones,
  Pu' doon their breeks, an' fa' to't.

For they a' do't, they a' do't
The grit as weel's the sma' do't,
  Frae crowned king
  To creeping thing,
'Tis just the same – they a' do't!

Her clear melodious voice sounding distinctly through the apartment had such a thrilling effect that we all joined in the chorus at the end of each verse, and never before felt so excited or saw such a scene of delicious wantonness as was displayed on every side, till at last exhaustion compelled us reluctantly to give up the engagement, and after a short rest we returned in the carriages to the Duke's mansion, as if we had only had an afternoon's drive.

This was altogether a memorable day, for as soon as we got back to Crecy House, Corisande whispered to me that as the gentlemen had all been fairly used up, her sisters had resolved to have an evening to ourselves whilst the gentlemen were in Parliament or at their clubs recruiting their enervated abilities by wine, smoke and cards. We might be sure of them till six a.m. at least, and the afternoon had left us all in such a burning unsatisfied state that they had impressed into our service four handsome young fellows, two footmen and two pages, who had never yet been admitted to any freedom with their mistresses, but Lady St Aldegonde had already sworn them to secrecy as to what they might see in the evening, and given her instructions to have everything prepared in her own private drawing-room, so as to be ready as soon as the rest of the establishment had retired for the night.

It was past ten o'clock when we arrived home, but Bertha was so clever, it was all devised and ordered in a few minutes, the footmen and pages little suspecting the scene they were to be introduced to when taking their oaths of secrecy. Everything promised a deliciously enjoyable affair, especially as we had to undertake to seduce them to our purposes.

In less than an hour and a half, it was all ready; the Duchess was still keeping her room, so Bertha dismissed all except John, James, Charles and Lucien (the latter a fine handsome French page) as well as two pretty lady's-maids, Fanny and Bridget. There were five of us ladies who sat down to a game of cards, for which the party was ostensibly designed, all of us very lightly attired in the most *négligé* style as if quite indifferent to any little exposures we might make of our charms.

'My luck is dead this evening,' exclaimed Lady Montairy, throwing her cards down; 'I shall be ruined if I sit here; what do you say to a dance; let's get the servants to join us for fun; come Lucien, have a waltz with me round the room, I feel so low spirited I don't care what I do to drive it away.'

'Fie, sister! how you make the boy blush, but I wouldn't mind a dance myself if it were not for the thing getting known,' replied Corisande.

'Let's have a downright spree for once; John, James, and all of you will keep it secret; I should so like to know how you enjoy yourselves downstairs,' laughed Bertha.

'Your Ladyship's slightest wish is binding upon us,' replied John, most respectfully, speaking for the others, 'and I am sure none of us would betray such a secret, when ladies condescend to a little familiar fun with their domestics.'

Bertha seated herself at the piano, and everything was cleared out of the way for a waltz. Lady Montairy led off with Lucien, I proposed to Charles, a very handsome youth of seventeen, whilst Alice and Corisande had the two good-looking footmen, John and James, for partners, Bridget and Fanny making a female couple.

What fun we had, how flushed and excited our partners looked as we clung to them in the voluptuous evolutions of this inspiriting waltz, as the strains of Lady Bertha's talented execution seemed to thrill through our souls; the young fellows quite delighted us by their easy graceful motions and manners, having evidently profited by their everyday experience in seeing their superiors conduct themselves in society.

At last we stopped from sheer exhaustion, Lady Montairy giving Lucien quite an amorous kiss, as she led him to a sofa, pretending she did it to put him at his ease, and we all followed her example, my partner excitedly returning my embrace with ample interest and ardour, his hot burning lips sending a thrill of desire through my frame.

Pretending to wish to cool myself a little I walked him into the next room, which was only lighted by the brilliant moon, and we opened the window, which looked out over a lovely garden, and then sat in a rather dark recess to enjoy the slight breeze which was loaded with perfume of flowers and had a soft sensuous effect on my excited nerves. I longed to enjoy my young partner, but did not exactly like the idea of being the first of the party to break through the slight barriers that still existed in favour of decency, although I knew perfectly well it was intended to be done by Lady Bertha and her sisters; still they seemed so slow in arriving at a thorough explanation with their company that I could wait no longer. 'Charles,' I whispered, 'do you know what love is? Have you ever had a sweetheart?'

'No, my lady, I never had a chance yet, as I look at all the beautiful creatures, and think how hard it is that I dare not kiss one of them. Dear lady, did you but know the intense pleasure your lips afforded me just now you would not think that kiss was thrown away, as I expect you did it in fun,' he responded with emotion.

'Silly boy,' I laughed in a whisper, 'to think that should make you so happy; why I don't mind giving you another here in the dark, if it is such a pleasure, and costs me nothing,' kissing him again in a very amorous manner. He clasped my heaving form to his bosom, and I could feel quite a shiver of delight rush through his trembling frame.

'What makes you tremble so, Charles?' I asked in the most innocent manner, laying my hand carelessly on his thigh just where I hoped to make an important discovery. Nor was I displeased to touch the engine of love which my hand gently prodded, as if quite unconscious of anything wrong. What a start he gave as he exclaimed, 'I am so ashamed, oh lady, you have driven me mad,' then suddenly letting his rampant love dart loose, it stood throbbing and spending over my hand, whilst I seemed to be unable to realise what I was doing.

'Oh; darling! Oh, Beatrice! Forgive me! What pleasure!' he seemed to gasp out, kissing me rapturously, and taking all sorts of liberties with my bosom, which he was moulding and pressing with his hands.

'What am I doing? Pray Charles, don't be so rude,' I said hastily, dropping the hold of his affair, and pretending to want to free myself from his embrace, but the amorous lad had gone too far to release his prize, and almost quicker than I can relate it, his hands were under my skirts, forcing their way to the very shrine of love itself.

My partner was far too impetuous to heed my faint remonstrances, and in spite of all I could do to keep my thighs closed his venturesome hand soon took possession of my heated cunny. 'If I die I must have you, darling lady,' he whispered in my ear, as he suddenly forced me quite back on the sofa, and tried to raise my clothes.

'Ah! No! No! I shall faint. How your violence frightens me!' I sighed, trying to smother my desires by simulating helplessness, and then feigning unconsciousness I promised myself a rare treat by allowing him to think I really had fainted, which, no doubt, would urge him to take advantage of the moment to riot unrestrained in the enjoyment of my most secret charms.

It was almost dark in the shadowy recess where the sofa on which we were was situated. 'She's quite gone, the darling!' I heard him say to himself, as he gently parted my relaxing thighs, 'I'll kiss it first.' Then I knew he was kneeling between my legs, and I felt his fingers gently parting the lips of my cunt. 'How I must have excited her, she's been spending!' he went on, then I felt his lips right between the nymphæ as he kissed me rapturously just on the excitable little clitoris. What a thrill of desire it sent through my frame, as it made me literally quiver all over with emotion, so that I could scarcely refrain from clasping his head with my hand, or nipping his dear face between my thighs.

This only lasted a few moments, but for what seemed awfully long in my excitable state my cunt was spending and throbbing under the voluptuous titillations of his velvety tongue. Heavens how I wanted to feel his prick inside me! and could not have feigned my fainting state another instant, but the moment my lips were in the act of parting to implore him to fuck me at once he started to his feet, pushing my thighs as wide apart as possible, and directly

I felt the hot head of his cock placed to the mark; slowly and gradually he pushed his way in, as contracting my usually tight affair I made it as difficult as I could for him to achieve possession. How he kissed my lips, calling me 'Darling lady, dear Beatrice, oh, you love, what pleasure you give me!'

I felt him spend a torrent of his warm essence right up to my vitals, and then lie still upon me, exhausted for the moment by the profuseness of his emission.

Still apparently in the state of inanimation, and without opening my eyes, I made my cunt nip and contract on his throbbing prick as it was soaking within me, in such a manner that he was almost immediately aroused from his delicious lethargy, and recommenced his movements, exclaiming to himself, 'What a love of a girl; even in her fainting state, the love pressure of her cunt responds to the action of my prick. What pleasure it would be if I could but arouse her to sensibility!' as he kissed me over and over again rapturously, quickening his stroke till my blood was so fired I could no longer impose upon him, but suddenly threw my arms around the dear boy's neck, whilst my amorous kisses responding to his silently assured him of the delight he was affording me.

'Here they are, the sly things, why Beatrice is the hottest of the lot, see she has got Charles well in her,' laughed Lady Bertha, bringing a light into the room, and followed by all the others, looking very excited, and as if some of them at least had been doing the same; in fact I could see the front of John's trousers were undone, whilst the flushed face of Lady Montairy, and the delighted manner in which she clung to the handsome young French page, assured me that she at least was on the best of terms with her partner, added to which, in the background, Bridget and Fanny seemed as loving as any of them from their damask cheeks and sparkling eyes.

Charles was dreadfully confused, and I felt that the surprise was taking all the vigour out of him, so with the greatest presence of mind, I threw my legs over his buttocks and embraced him more firmly than ever, as I exclaimed, 'It's this naughty fellow, my dear, who has taken such liberties with me that I fainted from fear, and now that he is in complete possession of my virginity and has aroused all my passions to the highest pitch, he wants to withdraw; slap his bottom well for me, and make him now complete my pleasure, after satisfying his own greedy lustfulness!'

He struggled hard to get away but I held him tightly, whilst all of them slapped him without mercy, making him fairly bound in the saddle to my great delight, more especially when I soon found him swelling up to quite an unnatural stiffness, till his prick was almost breaking my quim, and he was furiously fucking with all his might, as he cried out for them to leave off and let him do it properly.

The noise of the slaps on his bum seemed to give me intense delight and I never remember having had a more delicious fucking, which as he had spent twice previously lasted a long good bout, till we both came together, almost frantic with delight as our mutual essences were commingled at the same moment.

'There, don't let me catch any two of you slipping away by themselves again,' said Lady Montairy, as she gave a last tremendous slap, which fairly made the poor fellow bound under her hand, in spite of his exhaustive spend. 'It spoils half the fun, when some are so sly, and pretend to be mock-modest when at the same time they are quite or more inclined for the sport than anyone.'

We all returned to the drawing-room and refreshed ourselves with champagne, jellies and other reinvigorating delicacies, as we laughed and bantered the four young fellows and the two lady's-maids about their sweethearts and love experiences, till Bertha wrote all the names of the female members of our party on slips of paper, which she said she would hold for the boys to draw their prizes, declaring that Bridget and Fanny, if drawn, should submit to be fucked, although they protested their virginity and determination to keep it for the present, much as they enjoyed the other fun.

First of all she asked us to assist her in stripping our cavaliers quite naked, in order that we might enjoy the sight of their adolescent beauties (John, the eldest, being only nineteen). They were finely formed young fellows, but the splendid proportions of Master Charlie's penis carried off the honours of the evening, being more than eight inches long and very thick. My lady friends were in ecstasies at the sight, and almost made the other three young fellows jealous by each wishing he might draw them for a partner.

'Now there shall be no deception or cheating; I've a novel idea how the lots shall be drawn,' said Bertha, drawing up her clothes till she showed the beautiful lips of her luscious cunt, just peeping out between the slit in her drawers as her legs were wide apart; then drawing me close to her side she gave me the slips of paper and whispered in my ear to arrange them in her cunt with the seven ends just sticking out. It was soon done, then our gentlemen had to kneel down in front and each draw his paper with his mouth.

This was a jolly bit of fun. Bertha looked as if she would have liked to be fucked by all four instead of merely having them draw lots from her gap, which was so tickled as they drew out the papers that she actually spent under the novel excitement.

John drew Bridget; James, Lady Montairy; Charles, Bertha, whilst I was lucky enough to get the handsome Lucien, who had been eyeing me with a most amorous leer, which you may be sure did not in the least offend me.

Corisande and Fanny were told to fit themselves with a couple of most artistically moulded india-rubber dildoes of a very natural size and not too large, which Lady St Aldegonde said her husband had procured for the purpose of having his lady bottom-fuck himself occasionally, when he wanted extra stimulation. 'And now my dear, they will be very useful in enabling you to give these nice youths the double pleasure as they enjoy their partners.'

The ladies were now also divested of everything, till the complete party were in a state of buff, excepting the pretty boots and stockings, which I always think look far sweeter than naked legs and feet.

The interest centred in the engagement between Bertha and Charles, as the others were all anxious to see the working of his fine prick in her splendid cunt. He was in a very rampant state of anticipation, so she laid him at full length on his back on a soft springy couch and, stretching across his legs, she first bent down her head to kiss and lubricate the fine prick with her mouth, then placed herself right over him and gradually sheathed his grand instrument within her longing cunt, pressing down upon him, with her lips glued to his, as she seemed to enjoy the sense of possessing it all. I motioned to her bottom with my finger, and Fanny, understanding my ideas, at once mounted up behind her mistress and brought the head of her well-cold-creamed dildo to the charge against her brown-wrinkled bottom-hole, at the same time clasping her hands round Bertha, one hand feeling Charlie's fine prick, whilst the fingers of her other were tickling the fine clitoris of our mistress of the ceremonies. It was a delightful tableau, and it awfully excited us all when they at once plunged into a course of most delicious fucking. Fanny was as excited as either of them as she vigorously dildoed her mistress, and kept her hands stimulating them in front. Corisande now attacked Fanny behind with her dildo, delighting her with frigging combined.

How they screamed with delight, and spent over and over again, it is impossible to describe, but I had got Lucien's fine prick in my hand as we were kissing and indulging in every possible caress. It throbbed in my grasp as I repeatedly drew back the foreskin, till at length fearing he would spend over my hand, I sank back on a sofa, and drew him upon me, guiding his affair to my longing cunt, whilst he clasped me round the body and kissed more ardently than ever. I could see all that was going on round the room, Lady Bertha still riding furiously on Charles, stimulated by the double exertions of Fanny and Corisande, and watched with delight the frenzied enjoyment of the lady's-maid, as she handled and felt how Charles was going on in front, whilst her young mistress's dildo almost drove her to distraction by its exciting movements in her bottom. Lady Montairy was riding James as he sat on a chair, but John was being quite baffled by his partner Bridget, who wriggled and avoided every attempt of his cock to get into her, as she kissed and allowed him any liberty except the last favour of love.

At last we all finished. 'Now,' said Lady Bertha, 'we will rest and refresh ourselves a little, and then we will see to Bridget and Fanny having their maidenheads properly taken; meanwhile I will tell you a little adventure I once had down at Brentham a few months after my marriage. Well, you must know St Aldegonde wanted to represent the county in Parliament, and a general election was expected very soon, indeed it was rumoured the dissolution would occur almost immediately, so no time was to be lost, and there was one great landowner, who if we could but secure him to our side we were sure of carrying the day. He had been an old admirer of mine, and had been much chagrined at my lordship's success in obtaining my hand, and we both knew he was almost certain to throw all his influence into the opposite scale. We were just going to bed one night, and about to fall asleep after a beautiful fuck (it is nice when first married) when a sudden idea made me quite laugh, it seemed so good.

'St Aldegonde was quite anxious to know what I had been thinking of. "My love," I said, kissing him (I don't often do that now, except when I want to wheedle him out of something), "would you mind giving a bit of my cunt to secure your return for the county?" "Why, Bertha darling, just at this moment nothing would make me jealous, as you've sucked the last drop of spend from my cock," he said, with a yawn, and then realising my idea, he continued, "Do you mean Mr Stiffington, my love; it's a bright idea, if you do, and damned cheap way of buying him, besides cunt could never be reckoned bribery."

'The prospect of adventure, added to the good I might do for my husband, made me volunteer to do it, and as secrecy was everything, we determined that I should go down to Brentham disguised as a servant.

'Next day we started apparently to go to Paris, but I left St Aldegonde at the railway station, and started off to Brentham by myself after changing my dress at a hotel. The housekeeper at Brentham was the only person whom I took into my confidence, but of course she did not know all.

'She passed me off as a niece from town, who had a holiday for a few days, and I mixed with the servants as one of themselves; the idea that I could be Lady Bertha never entered their heads, as I was supposed to be gone abroad for a tour.

'Without delay she got the coachmen to drive me over to Mr Stiffington's place, Manly Hall, with a note to that gentleman on some special business, which I must deliver with my own hands.

'The gentleman was at home, and I was soon ushered into the library, where he was attending to his letters or other business, after breakfast, about eleven o'clock in the morning.

' "Well, young woman, let me have the particular letter you brought from Brentham; why couldn't a groom have done as messenger? By Jove! you're a nice looking girl though!" he said suddenly, seeming to notice my appearance.

' "If you please, sir," I said, blushing, "I'm Lady Bertha's maid, and bring a very important note from Lord St Aldegonde."

'He was a fine handsome fellow of about thirty-five, full of life and vigour in every limb; his eyes looked me through and through, then suddenly penetrated my disguise, as he exclaimed, "Ah, no, you're Lady Bertha herself, what is the cause of this mystery?"

'I was all confusion, but he told me to sit down and tell him without reserve what I wanted, as he drew me to a sofa and seated himself by my side.

' "Your vote and interest to secure my husband's return for the county,' I said in a low voice, "we know you can turn the scale, so I ventured to solicit your influence in person."

' "But how can you expect me to be otherwise than hostile to a man who deprived me of your beautiful self," he replied. "Why did you jilt me for a lordling?'

'I looked down in pretended distress, as I answered with an almost inaudible voice, "If you only knew our family necessities, it would soothe your wounded self-respect; it was the prospect of his dukedom which sealed my fate against my own feeble will, and now it is my duty to further his interests in every way."

' "Dear Bertha," he exclaimed excitedly, "do I really hear right, would you have preferred me, can you not pity my unrequited love, won't you even favour me with a smile as I look in your face?" taking my hand and covering it with impassioned kisses. "I would support your husband, but – but I must be bribed – let me think what you shall give me, dearest; of course he's had your first virginity, but I must have the second, it will cost him nothing, and no one need know."

'He was growing quite impetuous; with one arm around my waist, whilst he covered my blushing face with the most ardent kisses, I could feel his other hand wandering over my bosom and my thighs, as he felt them through my dress, then taking one of my hands he forced me to feel his standing cock which he had let out of his breeches, the mere touch of which sent a thrill of desire through my whole frame as I sank backwards in an assumed faint.

'He jumped up, fastened the door, then went to a drawer, from which he took a small book and a little box; then kneeling down by my side he gently raised my clothes, kissing my legs all the way up, inside or outside of my drawers as he could get at them, and parting my thighs opened the slit in my drawers, till he had a fair view of my pussy. "What a sweet little slit, what soft silky down it is ornamented with," I could hear him say as he pressed his lips to my mons Veneris, then I could feel his fingers parting the lips of my cunt with the greatest tenderness to enable him to kiss the little button of love. This was too much, I pressed his head down with my hands, as I spent over his tongue with a deep drawn sign of pleasure. "She's mine, how she likes it, the touches of my tongue have made her come!"

' "Look, darling," he continued, as he rose to his feet, "I thought a few delicate kisses would revive you if properly bestowed in the most sensitive place, but I don't mean to have you there; this book will show you the most delightful avenue of bliss, and open up to your ravished senses heavenly bliss you have hither had no conception of."

'Keeping my clothes up, and making me retain hold of his priapus in one hand, he showed me a series of splendid little drawings in the book, all illustrating the way to enjoy bottom-fucking. He could see I was tremendously excited, so lost no time in placing me on my hands and knees on the sofa, then anointing my tight little bum-hole with some ointment from the box, and putting some also on the shaft of his prick, he made me push my bottom well out behind, with my legs wide apart so as to give him every facility, but "Ah! Ah! No, no, I can't bear it!" I exclaimed, the tears fairly starting to my eyes as I felt the first advance of his lovely engine, forcing its way through the tightened orifice; the pain was like a number of needles pricking the part all at once. I can describe the sensation as the sphincter muscle gradually relaxed in no other way. He frigged me deliciously in front all the while, pushing so firmly and getting in in such a gentle manner behind that I seemed to love him more and more every moment, and longed for him to accomplish his task and complete my enjoyment, as the very pain seemed a percursor to some extraordinary bliss; nor was I disappointed; the pain was soon succeeded by the most delicious sensations as his movements stirred me up to the highest pitch of excitement, and he never withdrew till we had spent thrice in rapturous ecstasies, screaming with delight and almost losing our lives from excess of enjoyment.

'Thus my mission was successful, and his lordship became a Member of Parliament.'

This tale had worked us all up, so that we were mutually groping each other's privates, and as soon as Bertha had finished we seized Fanny and Bridget; but too much of the same thing being rather tedious to read, I will only say that John and Charles took their virginities in splendid style when the girls really found no more nonsense would be tolerated.

This was my last adventure in town, and in the next part I shall go on to relate what happened after my marriage with Lord Crim-Con, which took place shortly afterwards.

# *Chapter Five*

I now come to a most important epoch of my life, which at once sealed my matrimonial fate.

We were to leave town the next day, and were taking a morning walk in Kensington Gardens with Lady St Jerome, when who should suddenly meet Her Ladyship, and demand an introduction to her charming young friends (meaning myself and Alice), but a tall handsome-looking old fellow of thirty, with the most wicked pair of dark eyes I had ever seen.

Lady St Jerome appeared to have a most sinister smile upon her face as turning to us she said, 'My dears, allow me to present you to the Earl of Crim-Con, the most gallant gentleman of the day, but be careful how you accept his attentions.' Then seeing a rather savage look cross his countenance – 'Pardon me, my lord, if in introducing you to Lady Beatrice Pokingham and Miss Alice Marchmont, I caution them to beware of such a dangerous lover; they are under my protection at the moment, and I should fail in my duty if I did not.'

The angry flush was but momentary, being instantly replaced by a most agreeable smile, as he replied, 'Thanks, thanks, my dear cousin, but your piety always makes you so hard on my little foibles. Will nothing ever make you believe I have honourable intentions; you know how often I have asked you to try and find me a nice little darling wifey-pifey, who would lead me with her little finger, and keep me out of mischief.'

'You might have found a good wife long ago, you miserable hypocrite,' retorted Her Ladyship; 'you know that a certain place is said to be paved with good intentions, and that is where all yours will go to, my lord, I fear; but I only caution my young innocent friends here.'

'Ah, hem, I think I know that warm place you allude to, just between the thighs, is it not, my lady?'

Lady St Jerome blushed up to her eyes as she exclaimed, in an apparently angry tone, 'Now, this is really unbearable, that Your Lordship should at once commence with your obscene innuendoes; my dears, I am so ashamed of having introduced you to such a horrible specimen of modern society.'

'A truce, I will really be on my best behaviour, and try not to offend the most delicate ideas again,' he said with great seeming earnestness, 'but really cousin, I do want to be married and kept out of harm. Now I suppose these two young ladies are eligible parties, do you think either of them would have a worn-out *roué* like me?'

'Really, my Lord, you are incorrigible to go on so and talk like that before two young ladies at once,' expostulated our cicerone.

'Ha, you don't believe me, cousin, but, by God, I am not jesting; you shall see presently, just wait a moment,' he said, then taking out his pocket-book, he pencilled something on two slips of paper which he held in his hand, with the ends slightly projecting. 'Now, cousin, just draw one and see which it is to be.'

'Only for the fun of the thing, to see what you mean'; then she pulled one of the slips from his hand, exclaiming with a laugh as she looked at it, 'Beatrice, you are to be Lady Crim-Con if you will take such a scapegrace for better or worse.'

His Lordship – 'I really mean it, if you will have me, dear lady; may I call you Beatrice? What a happy name, especially if you would make me happy.'

It is impossible to write how I felt at that moment; I knew that he was rich, with a great title – and despite his bad reputation, that was a most tempting bait to a comparatively portionless girl.

Somehow he took my arm, and Lady St Jerome, with Alice, walking in front, seemed to go any way but direct home, in order to give His Lordship every facility to urge upon me his sudden courtship. I can't tell you how it happened, but before we reached the house, I had promised to have him, and in less than a month we were married.

I need not trouble about the wedding ceremony, but at once give some account of the first night I had with my spouse. When I first mentioned him, I spoke of an old man of thirty; that is exactly what he was, and although still a handsome fellow, one would have guessed him to be fifty at least.

His youthful vigour had been expended long ago, by constant and enervating debauchery, and now instead of being able to enter the lists of love in a genuine manner, he had a perfect plethora of disgusting leches, which he required to be enacted before he could experience sensual excitement.

Our first night was passed at the Lord Warden Hotel, Dover, as we were on our way for a continental tour.

During our short courtship I had never allowed him the slightest liberty, as my common sense told me that such a man would discard the most beautiful girl if he could but take advantage of her before marriage.

Well, then, the ceremony at St George's, Hanover Square, where the nuptial knot was tied, was scarcely over, and we had just taken our seats in the carriage to return to Lady St Jerome's house, from which I was married, when he gave me a rude kiss, and thrusting his hands up my clothes, seized upon my cunt in a very rough manner, as he laughingly told me not to pretend to be prudish, as he knew I was a little whore, and had had Lothair and lots of other fellows, in fact that was the reason he had married me, and meant I should be a damned little bitch to him, and do everything he required, which a virtuous girl might object to. 'Besides,' he added, 'I always looked out for an orphan who had no blasted parents to complain to. There, don't cry like a fool,' as he saw the tears of mortification run down my crimson face, 'you have only to pander to my curious tastes a bit, and we shall be happy enough.'

I felt his advice the best I could take at the moment; his evident knowledge of my intrigues gave him such an advantage that I dried up my tears and resolved to make the best of a bad bargain, and I returned his kiss as lovingly as possible, and begged him 'not to be a bad boy before other people', and he would find me everything he could wish.

I must have been very nearly screwed that night before I retired to bed to await His Lordship's coming. I got in between the sheets perfectly naked in accordance with his orders, and commenced frigging myself at once, inflamed by the many bumpers of champagne he had made me drink in his company to various obscene toasts which he constantly proposed, such as, 'A stiff prick for a randy cunt,' 'Here's to a girl who would rather be buggered, than not fucked at all,' and one in particular, which awfully excited my ideas, viz.: 'Here's to the girl who likes to frig herself before you till she spends, then suck your prick to a stand, and prefers to have you in her tight wrinkled bum-hole rather than anywhere else.'

Presently he entered the room, with a hiccup; as he pulled the bed-clothes off me, he exclaimed, 'You're a damned pretty little bitch, Beatrice, and being nearly drunk, my dear, you see my cock happens to stand for once; we will make the best of it. I had the whites of a dozen raw eggs in some milk this morning, and just now a cup of chocolate with half a dozen drops of the tincture of cantharides to make me randy for once.'

His coat, trousers and everything were thrown off in a trice, till he was as naked as myself, whilst his eyes had an almost demoniac kind of glare, so unnaturally brilliant did they look just then.

Springing on the bed, 'Ha,' he exclaimed in a husky voice, 'my little beauty has been frigging herself and spending. Suck my prick or I'll kill you, you little bitch!' he said savagely, as he reversed himself over me, and plunged his head between my thighs, where he at once commenced to suck my quim most deliciously, whilst I nested his rather long prick (it was not very thick), between my bubbies, pressing them together with my hands so as to make him fuck me there, whilst I was so excited that I readily kissed and took his balls in my mouth.

He was so furious in his gamahuching that he continually made me feel his teeth quite sharply, as he bit the clitoris and nymphæ, growling out, 'Spend, spend, why don't you come, you little bitch?' getting more outrageous and cruel every moment, till his bites made me shriek with agony as I writhed about, and deluged his mouth with quite a profusion of my creamy emission.

'A devilish good spend that,' he murmured between my thighs, 'but I have made your poor cunny bleed a little!' as he seemed to enjoy licking up the sanguineous mixture.

'Now suck my prick,' he said with renewed fierceness, turning round and presenting it full in my face. 'You're a cheating little bitch, and I mean to have you dog fashion.'

I took that long prick in my hands, frigging the shaft as hard as I could, whilst I just titillated the ruby head with my tongue till I felt it was tremendously distended and as hard as iron.

'Jump up quick, on your hands and knees, you little whore,' as he gave me a couple of tremendously smarting smacks on my buttocks, loud enough to have been heard a long way off – only our bedroom was at the end of a corridor, the whole of the rooms in that part of the hotel having been taken *en suite* for us.

Turning up my rump as desired, I thought it was only a fancy of his for entering my cunt that way, but he suddenly spit on the head of his long stiff affair, and presented it to my astonished bum-hole, as he exclaimed with a chuckle of delight, 'I'm going to fancy you're a boy, and take the only maidenhead you have left, your cunt will do another time, but it must be a virginity on a wedding night!'

'Ah, no, no, no, you shan't do that to me!' I cried out in fright.

'Nonsense, you little randy bitch, shove your arse out, and let me get in, or I'll pay you back dreadfully, and pitch you out of the window into the sea, and say you committed suicide through over-excitement!'

My fright increased, I was really afraid he would murder me, so I resigned myself to my fate, and clenched my teeth as I felt the head of his prick like a hundred little pins forcing its way within my tightly contracted vent hole. At last he got in, then withdrawing his hands from my mount where he had been tearing and pulling the hair to increase my pain, he placed both arms round my neck, and beginning slowly, fucked my bottom most voluptuously, till with a scream of delight I spent again in perfect ecstasy as I felt the delicious warmth of his spendings shooting up my fundament.

Being so over-excited by the means he had taken to prepare himself for our *noces*, he retained his stiffness, and never gave up possession of my bottom till we had come together a third time.

As soon as he withdrew his long limp cock, now reeking with a mixture of spendings and soil, he at once secured me to the bedposts with some silken cords before I could get away, or was well aware of his purpose.

'Now, my pretty boy, I have got you nicely, and will whip another cockstand out of you as soon as I have sponged off all the effects of our late *enculade*,' he said, bringing some cold water and a sponge in a basin; he laved and cooled my heated parts, till I began to feel quite grateful to him. At last he sponged himself, and wiping himself and me with a fine soft towel, proceeded to select his instruments of flagellation from a long leather case, which I had supposed only held a gun.

He showed them to me delightedly, then selecting a fine switch of horse hair mounted on a cane handle, he began to whip me with it between my thighs, and on the lips of my cunt in a most exciting manner, till I was so carried away with emotion that I begged he would fuck me properly to allay the longing irritation of my burning cunt.

'My prick isn't stiff enough yet, but I'll suck your spendings for you, my beautiful randy little tit,' he cried out, falling on his knees and twisting my body round so that he could get at my cunt. How delightful the thrusts of his tongue were to me in my excited state. I wriggled about in ecstasy, and getting one foot on his prick gently rolled it on his thigh under my sole, till I felt it was getting enormously stiff again, and at the same moment almost fainted away from excess of emotion, as I delighted my lecherous husband by another copious spend.

I thought he was going to fuck me properly now, his engine was so rampant, but instead of that he turned my back to him once more, and selecting a fine light birch rod, made of three or four twigs only, elegantly tied up with blue and crimson velvet ribbons, he commenced to flagellate my tender bottom. How his light switch seemed to cut and weal the flesh at every stroke! It was in vain that I cried for mercy as the tears of real agony rolled down my cheeks; he only seemed the more delighted, and jeered at me upon the effects of every cut, telling me first how rosy my bottom looked, then, 'now you bitch, it's getting fine, and red, and raw, it's bleeding deliciously!' till at last the rod was used up, the splinters lying all about the floor and bed; then throwing it aside he again assaulted my poor bottom-hole, apparently more and more delighted as he gave me pain, forcing his entrance as roughly as possible; however, when he was fairly in I soon forgot everything under the influence of his ecstatic moves, till I could remember no more, and suppose I fainted; he must have released my bonds and allowed me to sink on the bed, for when I awoke the sun was streaming in at the window, and His Lordship was snoring by my side.

His treatment on my wedding night was comparatively mild to what he afterwards made me go through, but his penchant for getting pleasure out of me soon seemed to wear off – although now and then he would fit me with a dildo and make me bugger him behind, whilst I frigged him with my hands in front till he spent.

Another of his amusements, and one which seemed to afford him particular delight, was to show me all his collection of bawdy books, drawings and photographs, till he could see I was awfully excited, and then he would jeer at me about being married to a used-up old fellow like himself, didn't I wish I could have Lothair now, etc.

One day having amused himself this way with me for some time he made me lie down on a sofa, and tying a bandage over my eyes, fastened my hands and feet so that I could not move, then throwing my clothes all up he tickled and frigged me with his fingers till I was quite beside myself with unsatisfied desire and begged him to fuck me, or at least to fetch his dildo and give me some kind of satisfaction.

'It really is a damned shame to tease you so, my little whore,' he laughed, 'so I will get the dildo out of my cabinet in the next room.'

He was scarcely gone many seconds before he returned, and I felt his fingers opening the lips of my cunt, as I thought to insert the dildo, but instead of that it was his prick, and throwing his arms around me he seemed to be more vigorous than usual, his cock swelling and filling my longing gap in a manner I had never felt it before. I spent in an ecstasy of bliss, as I murmured my thanks in endearing terms for the pleasure he had afforded me by such a delicious proof of his manliness.

Presently a strange hand seemed to be feeling his prick and thrusting a pair of fingers into my cunt alongside of his still vigorous engine.

'Ah! Oh! I Oh!! Who is that?' I screamed from under my skirts, which were thrown over my face.

'Ha! ha!! ha!! She pretends to think I've been fucking her when she must have known it was James all the time!' I heard him laugh, as at the same moment all the obstructions were removed from my face so that I could really see it was the young butler on the top of me, with his prick still in full possession, and just beginning to run a second course.

'Kiss her, put your tongue in her mouth, my boy! Fuck! Fuck away! or it will be the worse for your arse!' exclaimed His Lordship, who was handling his balls with one hand, and slapping his rump furiously with the other. 'See how she pretends to be ashamed; it's quite delightful, Lady Beatrice, to see you can still blush.'

I screamed and protested against the outrage, but James's delicious motions soon made me forget everything, and recalled to my mind the orgy we had with the servants at Crecy House, and in imagination I was again in the arms of the wondrously developed Charlie.

We spent a second time, but he kept his place and continued the love combat with unabated vigour, and His Lordship seeing that I was quite carried away by my feelings, and responding to his man's attack with all my naturally voluptuous ardour, released both my hands and feet so that I might thoroughly enjoy myself.

'Hold tight James,' he cried out, 'she's so high spirited, you'll get unseated, but the little devil needn't think she's to have this treat all to herself!'

Saying which he mounted on the sofa behind the young butler, and I could see his long prick was now as stiff as possible, and he seemed to have a rather easy task in getting into his man's bottom, no doubt having often been there before; but wanting some extra excitement on this occasion, he had sacrificed me to his catamite, in order to bring himself to the necessary pitch by seeing all our lascivious movements.

You may be sure that after this James and I were upon the best of terms, His Lordship introducing him to our bedroom at night, and joining us in every kind of wantonness; he even once contrived to get his long thin prick into my cunt alongside of James's as I was riding a St George; it gave me the most intense pleasure, and immensely delighted them both by the novel sensation, and by the idea of having achieved an apparent impossibility.

After this Crim-Con seemed to get quite blasé and indifferent to everything we did, and even insisted on sleeping by himself in another room, leaving us to ourselves. However, both myself and paramour were not so blind as to believe he was quite used up, but consulting together we came to the conclusion that His Lordship had fallen in love with my young page, a youth of fifteen, who had only recently entered my service, and slept in a small room at the end of a long corridor in which both our bedrooms were situate.

He always locked himself in when going to bed, as he said, for fear I would not let him alone, so to determine the mystery one night we floured the whole length of the corridor, and in the morning were rewarded by seeing the marks of His Lordship's footsteps, both going and returning from the page's room.

We did not want to spoil his fun, only to enjoy the sight of it, and reap a little extra excitement if possible from the scene, so next day we examined the ground, and found that a small room next to that occupied by the page exactly suited our purpose, being furnished as an extra bedroom for visitors; we had only to make some good peepholes to enable us to sit or kneel on the bed and see everything.

After retiring to bed at night (James and myself had been in the drawing-room all evening going through the most exciting and lascivious ideas, to amuse His Lordship, who contented himself by leisurely watching our love gambols, smoking his cigar, and evidently keeping himself in reserve for something by and by), instead of settling ourselves between the sheets we adjourned to the spare room, next to that in which Reuben, the page, slept.

We were too soon for His Lordship as, on applying our eyes to the peepholes, we found the boy's room was yet in the most profound darkness; so as the night was warm, and there was no necessity for covering, we reclined upon the bed to await the coming of Crim-Con; meanwhile we amused ourselves by kissing and toying with each other's parts, till my handsome butler, notwithstanding the previous hard work of the evening, was in a most rampant, impatient state, and would fain have cooled his ardour within my longing cunt but that would have spoilt all, as our transport would have been certain to be overheard by the page, and thus prevent all our anticipated sight-seeing.

Just as I was whispering to him to keep quiet, we heard a match struck in the next room, and applying ourselves to the holes, were much astonished to find Reuben was not alone, there was the butler's assistant, a rather tall fair youth of sixteen, with whom we had never reckoned in our calculations; he had always such a cold, reserved respectful manner, even to James, that we never for a moment gave him a thought as likely to be mixed up with a Lordship's amusements.

Reuben lighted a couple of the candles, then turning to his companion, who was lying on the bed frigging slowly his standing prick, as if keeping it in a state ready for use, said, 'Will, it's time His Lordship was here now, what a good job I broke away from you just now, or you would have spent and spoilt all; he likes to see us looking ready and randy, but if he thinks we have been fucking or frigging by ourselves he would damn us, and bolt off in a rage.'

Reuben and Will were both quite naked, and there was a great contrast between the youths, for while the latter was rather slim, tall and fair, the former was a regular Adonis in figure, beautifully plump, with a rosy face, dark hair and dark fiery impetuous eyes; his prick was also in a fine state of erection, and neither of them had more than a suspicion of downy hair around the root of their pricks.

'What a fine fellow you look Rube, no wonder His Lordship seduced you; besides, you are a dear unselfish chap for introducing me into the fun, won't I fuck you gloriously when he is here to see us. I love you warmer, hotter than ever I could the prettiest girl in the world! And then, too, think of how well it pays!'

Here the two boys lay down on the bed fondling each other's pricks and kissing mouth to mouth, sucking tongues, and twining about in the most amorous manner, till I fully expected every moment to see them spend, but they stopped suddenly, a step was heard outside, the door creaked on its hinges, and His Lordship appeared with a large table lamp in his hand.

'Hold, hold hard, you randy rascals!' he exclaimed, 'I believe you've been and had your fun already. If you have, you buggers – ' he hissed between his teeth, in a frightfully suggestive manner, which seemed almost to terrify the boys, who paled slightly for a moment, and then both of their faces flushed crimson.

Rube was the first to answer. 'Oh no, my lord, we have been too careful, only Will was just telling me his love, and how gloriously you should see him fuck me.'

'Bravo! So he shall, my dear, and I will suck your darling pego, and find out if you have been deceiving me.'

He placed his lamp on a small table at the foot of the bed, so that the room was now excellently well lighted, then seating himself on the bed he opened his dressing-gown, showing his long limp prick; then he took the pair of them on his lap and they sat on his naked thighs whilst he kissed them, thrusting his tongue into their mouths, or handled and compared their two charming pricks.

This was only a little preliminary toying; presently, asking Rube if the cold cream was under the pillow, he threw aside his only vestige of a garment, and stretched himself on his back on the bed.

'Now my plump little beauty,' he said, addressing the page, 'kneel over my breast, and give me your prick to suck, and now Will, mount behind him, and I will put your tool to his arsehole.'

James's assistant was too ready to need a repetition of the welcome order, he was there in a moment, his hard cock quite eight inches long, battering against the tight dark wrinkled nether hole of his love.

His Lordship was so eager for work that he scarcely had taken Rube's seven inches between his lips before his fingers were busy with the lubricant on Will's prick and the page's bottom, directing the former's delighted tool so cleverly to the mark that almost immediately he completed his insertion up to the roots of the hair, and was revelling in the delicious sensations and pressures to which his love treated him.

His Lordship sucked excitedly at the morsel in his mouth, and we could just hear him mumbling out, in a half-choked voice, 'Beautiful! Fuck! Go on quick. Spend, spend! Ah – r – r – ,' as we could see Rube's dark eyes full of fire, and his prick stiffen and shoot its juice into Crim-Con's mouth, till the drops of thick creamy spend fairly oozed from his lips as he still sucked and smacked them with great gusto; besides, we could see his own prick rising into quite a manly state.

Will fucked into his love's bottom with fury, and seemed to spend almost at the same time, and so exhaustively that he must have fallen backwards had he not clung round Rube's neck.

We were not idle whilst this exciting scene was enacted under our eyes. James instinctively wetted the head of his prick and my bum-hole with spittle, and soon drove his great machine through the narrowest gate of Paradise. Its movements were indeed heavenly, blissful. I never before felt such an acme of pleasure, the sight before me, the soul stirring movements behind, and our mutual emissions almost made me groan in an agony of delight.

A perfect frenzy of lust seemed to take possession of my body, I could see His Lordship's prick was now finely erect, and the two boys were alternately kissing and sucking him.

Whispering my paramour to follow me, I quickly rushed from our concealment into the room where they were. As the door was not locked and before they could recover from their surprise, I threw myself on my back on His Lordship's belly, almost taking the breath out of him by my sudden weight on his stomach and regardless of his 'Damned Hellish Bitch' and other exclamations of displeasure. I fixed his stiff prick in my bottom-hole in triumph, nipping and squeezing, and wriggling my bum about on him as James with his tool in an awfully excited and distended state took possession of my hot raging cunt.

The boys seemed quite to understand my ideas, as they each of them knelt and presented their pricks for me to fondle, whilst Crim-Con, still cursing and swearing at me for a 'Damned Hellish Bitch, etc.', groaned under our weight, but I could feel he was thoroughly enjoying it, as his prick stiffened more and more every moment, under the delightful movements and pressures to which I treated him; besides, the membrane between his prick and James's was so slight that it was almost like two cocks rubbing together in my cunt.

I frigged the boys till their eyes almost started from their heads from excess of emotion and they spent over the firm round globes of my bosom, but I still kept them stiff, alternately kissing the head of one or the other prick whilst Crim-Con's hands tickled their balls, and frigged their arseholes till we made them nearly mad.

I had never felt my husband's long thin prick so well before, and James's affair was so distended by the excess of lustful excitement that I was gorged to repletion, and yet felt that I wanted more, more, more! Had I been cunt all over I should have wanted every hole well filled by a good stiff one. What a delicious moment. Ah! ah! if I could but die like that! I seemed transported to another world, my senses were leaving me, I was indeed in Paradise!

I remember no more of this extraordinary scene, but James told me next day they were frightened as I went off into such a deathlike faint they had to carry me to my room and use restoratives till I gradually breathed a little and sank into a restless kind of sleep, that I had bitten both the boys' pricks till they were sore and bleeding. 'As for His Lordship,' he added, 'I am afraid he is as good as dead, he was so exhausted Dr Spendlove had to be fetched, and he fears the worst.'

This was too true. His Lordship only lived forty-eight hours, whilst I have never been well since. The extraordinary excess of lubricity that night seemed to have quite undermined my constitution, and I have gradually declined from that time. I was advised to be very careful how I indulged in venereal pleasures in future, but in spite of my weak, nervous, excitable nature, I have found it impossible to quite abandon those pleasures which seem to me to give the only real foretaste of the future Paradise; regardless of declining strength, whenever the opportunity offered I have indulged in the delights of love myself, or in seeing others do it.

The executors settled everything whilst the incoming earl, to show his appreciation of their services in furthering his interest, made most lavish provision for James and the two youths, as he afterwards told me that he considered they helped him to the title and estates a good five or ten years before he could reasonably expect to have come into them.

'And do you not think, my lord,' I asked him when he told me this, 'that I also deserve your thanks, where is your gratitude to little Beatrice?'

He looked at me in a curious kind of way. He was a handsome young fellow of eight and twenty, but married to death by a fair fat wife, who besides having a fortune of her own had already blessed him with nine children, and a prospect of blessing him with many more.

'I can't make you out, Robert,' I went on to say, 'you're so different from your poor brother, and so content with the same thing every day; every look, every smile you have is for that splendid wife of yours. He was for flirting with and having every pretty woman he came across; what sort of a heart can you have, you have never seemed to pity me for my loss?'

He was so handsome, and I so disliked the new Lady Crim-Con, that I resolved to seduce him, and gratify both pique and passion at the same time.

'What are you driving at, Beatrice dear, I'm sure you puzzle me?'

'Ah! you know how delicate and how lonely I am, and never even to give a brotherly kiss of sympathy . . . I know Her Ladyship hates me, but I shall be gone to Hastings in a few days,' I said, bursting out into sobs as if my heart would break, the tears from my downcast eyes dropping upon one of his hands which he had placed in a deprecating kind of way on my lap as he sat by my side.

He kissed me tenderly on the forehead, more like a father, as he said, 'I'm sure I only wish I knew how to cheer you up, my dear.'

'My dear,' that sounded quite a little affectionate and as if the ice was breaking, so throwing my arms round his neck, I kissed him passionately in return for his fatherly salute, sobbing out in a low broken voice, 'Oh, Robert, you do not know what it is to be left dull, miserable, and all alone in the cold, cold world, can you not spare me a little, only a little of those loving smiles your wife must be quite surfeited with?'

He gave a soft sigh, and I felt an arm steal round my waist, as he very tenderly drew me close to him, and did not seem at all loath to receive my kisses, which were getting yet more impassioned.

'If you do give me a kiss, what will Her Ladyship lose?' I whispered.

A perceptible tremulousness seemed to vibrate through his form as our lips at last met in a long, loving kiss. It was quite plain I had at last excited his amorous sensuality, which had previously been so dormant in his respectable married bosom.

'Now, I love you Robert, dear, and you needn't mention such an indifferent thing to Lady Cecilia,' I whispered, when at last our lips parted.

'A slice from a cut loaf is never missed, you know Beatrice,' he said, as he smilingly held me at arm's length, and gazed into my blushing face, and continued, 'besides, I can easily make it up to her, so she will lose nothing.'

'Your loaf is pretty well sliced dear,' I replied, 'considering how many children you have to eat bread and butter, Robert.'

Again he drew me to him, and we exchanged the most lascivious kisses as I sat on his lap. This billing and cooing was so effective that I very soon felt his prick stiffening quite perceptibly under my bottom. His face flushed, and an extraordinary fire beamed in his usually quiet eyes; we understood each other at once. Without a word he inclined my unresisting form backwards on the couch, and as I closed my eyes, I felt him raising my clothes, his hands stole up my thighs till he gained the seat of joy. My legs mechanically opened to give him every facility, in a moment he took advantage of my tacit invitation, and I felt the nose of a fine battering ram at the entrance of my widowed cunt.

The desire for a really good fuck had been consuming me for some days, and I could not resist the impulse, however immodest it might seem to him, of putting my hand upon his glorious engine of love, and directing it into love's harbour myself. It was in, I was gorged to repletion, spending, sighing with delight, almost before he could make a move.

Opening my eyes, I could see he was delighted at my ecstasy. 'Ah, you darling man, my darling Robert, you don't know what it is for a young widow to be deprived of the natural solace of her sex. Now, push on my boy, and let us be thoroughly happy, let us mix our very souls in love's emission, and then tell me if you can spare one a few crumbs of your cut loaf now and then.'

A very few thrusts brought down my love juice again, and I also felt him shoot a tremendously warm flood of his essence into my longing cunt. Our lips were joined in fierce loving, tongue-sucking kisses, whilst I threw my legs over his buttocks, and heaved up my bottom to meet his manly action with the most libidinous abandon.

Her Ladyship was out with the carriage, and we were quite safe for a couple of hours at least; still, considering his family duties, I made him keep a shot or two in reserve for the night, as he contented himself by kneeling down and worshipping at the shrine of love, where he had just been paying his tribute to Venus, exclaiming in ecstasy, as he examined or kissed the various charms, 'What a love of a cunt! How small and tight! What a charming *chevelure*, etc.!'

A day or two after this, to our mutual delight, Lady Cecilia was summoned into the country, to attend on her mother's sick bed.

My room was next to theirs, so at night it was a very simple thing for him to slip into bed with me. I found he knew very little about ornamental fucking, himself and wife having strictly adhered to the plain family style, which had produced such fruitful results. My ridicule of his ignorance made him quite ashamed of his want of knowledge, especially when I introduced him to the delights of bum-fucking, and he faithfully promised me that when Her Ladyship returned, he would insist upon his marital rights over every part of her person, and so steer clear of babies in future, and that if I only made a good peephole I might see all his fun with Lady Cecilia.

Delighted with my conquest, I determined to persuade him to degrade his wife in every possible way, that I might enjoy the sight of it. So I initiated him into every possible style of enjoyment, till I had the satisfaction of knowing that the hitherto respectable husband was completely changed into a lustful libertine.

The Earl was as good as his promise. 'My Robert,' as I called him in our loving intercourse, was so well schooled that he was quite equal to the assertion of all his rights as a husband by the time Lady Cecilia returned home.

After dinner, on the evening of her arrival from the country, he found me sitting alone in the conservatory, and sitting down by my side, whispered in my ear how delighted he was at being able to have a last word of advice with me before retiring to rest with his, no doubt, rather expectant spouse

'You have so drained me, last night and early this morning, dear Beatrice,' he said, putting his arm round my waist, and meeting my ready lips in a long breathless kiss. 'Nothing but some extraordinary excitement will enable me to do justice to her expectations. I must fuck her at least three or four times after such a long absence; how shall I be equal to the occasion?'

'Have me first,' I replied, 'whilst she is seeing the children put to bed, there is plenty of time; it will give you zest for the fun to come, the idea of taking the virginity of her maiden bottom-hole will excite you enough, and the more she resists and gets indignant, the more you will enjoy it.'

I had been gently stroking his prick outside his trousers; my touch was magical, it stiffened immediately, and when I let the impatient prisoner out of his confinement, I thought I had never before seen his priapus so distended and inflamed with lust as at that moment.

Rising up, I first stooped to give the engine of love a warm kiss, and then, keeping it in my hand, raised my clothes and, turning my bottom to his belly, spitted myself on the loving object, opening my legs and straddling over his lap so as to get the very last fraction of its length into my heated cunt. We sat still for a moment or two, enjoying the mutual sensations of repletion and possession so delightful to each of the participators in a loving fuck, before commencing those soul-stirring movements which gradually work our heated desires to that state of frenzied madness which can only be allayed by the divinely beneficent ecstasy of spending and mingling the very essences of our nature.

The idea that I was robbing his hated wife of her just expectations added such piquancy to our loving conjunction that I literally moaned or whined with delight, as I twisted my head round in the act of emission, so as not to lose the luscious kiss which is such an extra pleasure in those supreme moments of our happiness.

He did not come at the same time, but stopped and rested a moment or two, then rising, and keeping me still impaled on his dear prick, without losing place even for a single second, he laid my body face downwards on a little table which stood handy, and then recommenced his delicious moves, with his hands under me in front, frigging and tickling my cunt, till I almost wrenched myself away from him by the violence of my convulsive contortions. Suddenly drawing quite out, with another plunge he drove the head of his tool into the smaller orifice, which is so delightfully near and convenient when in the position in which he had me.

'Ah! Oh – oh – oh – oh – o – o – o – oe!!' I screamed, swimming in lubricity as I felt him so gorging my bottom, whilst his busy fingers were adding to my erotic madness by the artistic way in which they groped within my spending cunt. 'Oh, heavens, Robert, Robert! Do, do come darling!

There, ah – re, I feel it, how deliciously warm!' I murmured excitedly, as his flood of boiling seed inundated the gratified and sensitive sheath which enclosed him so tightly.

After recovering from our transports, we conversed about how he should proceed with his wife, his prick all the while as stiff as a policeman's truncheon, till at last fearing Lady Cecilia might surprise us, I went into the drawing-room and played the piano whilst he smoked his cigarette amongst the flowers in the conservatory outside the window.

Her Ladyship pretending fatigue (we knew what she was in a hurry for), the family retired rather earlier than usual to rest, but I took care to be at my peephole before Cecilia and Robert entered their bedroom.

As it was a habit of his to go over the lower part of the house, and see everything safe for himself before going to bed, his lady came first and at once commenced to undress.

She was about the same age as her husband, a vastly fine, fair woman, rather above the medium height, light auburn hair, slightly golden in tint, deep blue eyes, set off by dark eyebrows and long dark lashes, a full mouth, richly pouting cherry lips, and a brilliant set of pearly teeth; then as she gradually unrobed herself, her various and luscious charms quite fired my lascivious blood, as one by one they stood revealed to my earnest gaze. What magnificent swelling breasts still round and firm, and then as she lifted her chemise over her head, and exposed the lovely whiteness of her belly (still without a wrinkle, as she had easy confinements and never suckled her children, for fear of spoiling her figure), set off below by a bushy mons Veneris, covered with light curly silken red hair, through which I could just perceive the outline of her slit.

Now she stood before a cheval glass, surveying herself at full length, I could see a blush cross her beautiful face, as she seemed almost ashamed to look at her own nakedness. Then a self-satisfied smile parted those cherry lips and displayed the sparkling pearls of teeth, as she patted the shiny marble skin of her belly and bottom (evidently thinking of the effect of the sight upon Robert when he should enter the room ), then she playfully parted the lips of her cunt and examined it closely in the glass. The titillation of her fingers brought another blush, and she seemed as if she could not resist the temptation to frig herself a little, moving a couple of digits in a restless kind of way backwards and forwards between the vermilion lips of love.

My blood was on fire, and much as I hated her, I would have liked to gamahuche her there and then. But suddenly the door opened, and Robert stood transfixed, as he exclaimed in surprise, 'Surely, Cecilia, you have lost all modesty; why have you never exposed yourself to me like that before?'

'Oh, Robert dear, how you startle me, you came up so soon and I was only just looking at the love I know you are longing to caress as soon as the light is out.'

'I really did not know you were such a charming figure, Cecilia, but now you are naked I will feast on the sight, and we won't put out the lights, my dear. I must now examine in detail every charm. By the way, I may tell you that during your absence I found some bad books of my late brother's and they so fired my imagination by the extraordinary descriptions of various modes of sexual enjoyments that I quite blushed to think of our innocent ignorance, and long to try some of them with you.'

He had almost torn his clothes off whilst speaking, and I could see his prick as rampant as possible, in fact I believe it had never lost its stiffness since our excitable bout a short time before.

He threw himself into her arms and they hugged and kissed whilst she, taking hold of his pego, slowly backed towards the bed as she tried to bring its head to the mark.

'Not there, Cecilia, love, you have another maidenhead I mean to take tonight; our plain silly way of doing it only leads to getting a lot of children, and surely my quiver is full enough of them. I'll have no more, it's positive ruination, however rich a father may be. No, no, the French style in future, do you understand, I mean to get into your bottom,' he said, as seriously as possible, yet with evident excitement.

'What a nasty idea! You shall never do that, Robert, to me!' she exclaimed, crimsoning with shame to the roots of her hair.

'But I must and will, Cecilia. Look at this book, here are all the different ways of "doing it". Why they suck each other, fuck – ah – you start at the vulgar word – but it's fuck – fuck – fuck – that's the name for it. They fuck in bottoms, under armpits, between the bubbies – another nasty name for titties – anywhere – everywhere – it's all the same to a man, all is what they call C U N T, a word I am sure you have seen somewhere in your lifetime written on shutters, doors, or even on the pavement – a deliciously vulgar word, Cecilia, but the universal toast of men when they meet in company.' I could see he was trying to make her look at a little French book, called *La Science Pratique*, with its forty pretty little plates. 'How my blood has been fired by fancying all these delightful ideas to be enjoyed when you came home.'

'Why, Robert, you are mad, I'll burn that horrible book, I won't learn their filthy ways!' snatching at the book.

'You're my wife, every bit of your body is mine to do as I please with it; don't drive me to extremities, Cecilia, or I may be rough, for I'm determined to put my prick in your arse, now at once!' trying to turn her over.

'Robert, Robert, for shame, Beatrice will hear your disgusting language. You shall never abuse me that way!' hiding her face in her hands and beginning to sob.

'But I will, and you may blubber like a child. Your tears only urge me on, if you resist I'll smack and beat you, till you are obedient!'

She struggled, but a woman's strength is soon exhausted, and at last he got her face down on the bed, with her bottom on the edge and her feet on the floor, then giving her a tremendously painful smack on her bum, he spread her legs wide apart, opened the cheeks of that glorious bottom, anointed the head of his bursting prick with spittle, also the tight-looking brown hole he was about to attack, and then pushed on to the assault of the virgin fortress.

I could hear her moan with pain as the head gradually forced its way within the sphincter muscle. 'Ah – it's pricking – oh, oh – you'll rend me, Robert – oh, pray – Ah – r – r – re. – Oh! Oh!'

At last he was in, and rested a moment or two, then slowly began his fucking motions.

Presently I could tell by the wriggling of her bottom that she enjoyed it. His hands were busy frigging her cunt in front. How excited they got, each seeming to spend at the same moment, but he kept his place, and the second finish was so excitable that they screamed quite loudly in the frenzy of emission, whilst Cecilia actually fainted away with Robert fallen exhausted on her senseless body.

Presently he recovered sufficiently to be able to apply restoratives to his fainting wife, and as soon as he had brought her round, so that she could understand what he said, proceeded to tell her 'that in future they would enjoy all the novel ideas he had found in that nice French book, no more big bellies for you Cecilia, or the anxiety of children for either of us. You must now suck my prick, till it is stiff enough again,' he said, presenting it to her mouth.

'No, no, I never can do such a dirty trick; besides, it's doubly disgusting, you have not even washed since you outraged my bottom,' she sobbed, as her eyes filled with tears, seeing no signs of compassion in his face.

'What's that to me, you've got to suck it, so go on, my dear, without all those wry faces, which only add to my fun, it's rare sport to make you submit to my fancies. I find I've been a fool ever since I was married, not to have asserted my right to do as I please with every bit of your person, cunt, arse, mouth, or bubbies; they can all afford me intense pleasure, without getting in the family way. Now go on, and I will fuck you with a fine large dildo. Mind you must swallow every drop of my spendings when it comes.'

He forced his prick between her reluctant lips, all slimy and soiled as it was from the previous *enculade*, then producing an enormous dildo, nearly twelve inches long, and big in proportion, he put a little cold cream on it, and presented the head to her notch, trying to force it in.

'Ah! No! no!! that's so awfully large!' she almost screamed, but the head was partly in, and despite her sobs, and moans of pains, he soon succeeded in passing at least ten inches of it into her distended vagina.

Her cunt was exposed towards me, so that I could see how gorged it was with that big india-rubber tool, and the sight of her slit so stretched to its utmost capacity caused quite a thrill of desire to shoot through my veins, it was almost impossible for me to prevent myself making some kind of demonstration. How I longed to be with them and join in the orgy of lust. Each shove of that tremendous affair now seemed to afford her the most intense delight. She sucked his prick in a kind of delirium, her highly wrought feelings banishing every sense of delicacy, shame, or disgust that might have previously deterred her from doing so. I frigged myself furiously, they screamed and spent, till at last both spectatrix and actors were thoroughly exhausted.

When I awoke next morning, and applied my eye to the peephole, it was just in time to see Her Ladyship awake. First she felt her cunt to see if it was all right, and not ruined by the giant dildo she had taken in the previous night. Her eyes sparkled with desire, and she repeatedly blushed as I suppose the recollection flashed through her mind. Presently throwing the sheet entirely off her husband's body, she handled his limp affair for a few moments, then putting her face down, took the head of his prick in between her lovely lips, and sucked away with evident relish, till she had him in a glorious state of fitness, and was about to treat herself to a proper St George, when Robert, who had only been feigning sleep to see what his randy wife would do, suddenly woke up, and insisted upon her applying it to her arsehole instead of her cunt, wetting it with spittle.

Slowly but surely she achieved its insertion, although to judge by her face it was evidently a painful operation. But when once in how they enjoyed that glorious bottom-fuck. Even after he had spent she rode on till he met her again, and both seemed to come at the same time, kissing each other in a frenzy of erotic madness.

My peephole afforded me the sight of many more luscious scenes between Lady Cecilia and her husband before I left town to take up my residence at Hastings for the benefit of my health.

My agent had secured and furnished for me a pretty little detached residence of thirteen or fourteen rooms, surrounded by gardens and orchards, so as to be delightfully free from the prying curiosity of my neighbours.

The household consisted of a cook and housekeeper, both young persons, not exceeding twenty-four or -five years of age, the latter being the daughter of a decayed merchant, a most pleasant and intelligent companion, but up to the time I engaged her, strictly prudish, virtuous.

Being naturally fond of young boys and girls, we had also two very pretty page-boys of about the age of fifteen or sixteen and two beautiful young girls about the same age, instead of housemaid and lady's-maid.

At first I felt considerably enervated by the little excesses I had been a party to, or witnessed, whilst staying with the new Earl, but the soft bracing air of the southern coast soon made me feel more like myself again, and long to indulge in the delicious dalliances of love, to which my warm temperament made me always so inclined.

The result was that I determined to seduce every member of my virgin household, each one of whom I believed to be thoroughly virtuous up to their entering my service.

The two youngest girls, as my special attendants, slept in the next room to mine, and had a door of communication by which the two rooms entered into the other without the necessity of going into the corridor.

I had quite a passion come over me to gamahuche these two pretty young things, and make them thoroughly subservient to my purposes.

You may be sure I was not long in putting my plans in operation as soon as I had sketched them all out in my brain. That very same evening, after my two pretty demoiselles had put the finishing touches to my toilet and left me sitting in my *chemise de nuit*, in front of a cosy fire with my feet resting on the fender, as I pretended to be reading a thrilling romance:

'Leave that door open, my dears,' I said, as they respectfully bid me good-night. 'I feel so dull perhaps I shall call for you to keep me company, if I feel that I cannot go to sleep.'

In a few minutes I heard them tittering and laughing.

'Now, girls,' I cried, 'come here this moment. I want to know what you are having such fun about. Come just as you are, no putting anything more on or waiting to hide your blushes. Annie! Patty! Do you hear?'

Afraid of making me angry, the two girls came blushing into my room just as they were, in their nightgowns.

'Well now, what is it that is amusing you so?'

'Please, my lady, it was Patty,' said Annie with a wicked look at her companion.

'Ah, no, you fibber! My lady, it was Annie began it,' retorted the other, looking quite abashed.

Nothing could be got out of them, each saying it was the other.

At last I said: 'I can guess pretty well what you two girls were amusing yourselves about; now tell me truly, were you looking at each other's privates in the glass?'

This question hit the mark, and seeing how shamefaced and blushing they both were, I went on: 'No doubt, examining to see which one showed most signs of hair on her little pussy. Let me see Annie,' as I suddenly caught the bottom of her nightdress and in an instant had it reversed over her head, so as to cover up her face and expose all the rest of her beautiful little figure. 'Why, the impudent little thing hasn't a hair to boast of! Give her bottom a good slapping, Patty!'

Patty was only too pleased to do it, and the slaps fairly echoed through the room, mingling with Annie's piteous cries to let her go.

My blood was up. The sight of her beautiful bum, all flushed and rosy under the sharply administered slaps, made me fairly lust to take further liberties. So I let the little victim go, whispering in her ear, and her tearful eyes were brightened in a moment. She darted at Patty and sooner than it takes to write was dragging her about the room fully exposed, with her head and arms secured in her reversed nightdress.

I amused myself by slapping poor Patty's pretty posteriors till they were almost black and blue, regardless of her sobbing and crying for mercy.

At last we let her go, and I took her on my lap to kiss away her tears. She soon smiled again and nestled herself to my body quite lovingly. This seemed to make her companion almost jealous as she appealed to me with a flushed face to kiss her also, which I readily did in the most loving manner, and I asked her to fetch a decanter of wine and some glasses from a cabinet, saying I felt so dull and sleepless I must have something to cheer me.

'Ah, my dear lady,' exclaimed Patty, kissing me again and again, 'you don't know how we all love you and feel for you, being left alone and unhappy. There is nothing we wouldn't do to bring a smile to your pale face.'

'Then we'll sleep together and have a romp on the bed. Only mind, you are good girls, and never tell your mistress's doings,' I replied, taking a glass of wine, and ordering them to do the same.

A second and a third glass seemed to open their eyes immensely; the least touch or joke sent them into fits of laughter. They blushed and seemed quite excited. In fact Patty, who had remained on my knee, was almost ready to faint with emotion as she caressed my face and bosom, the cause being a hand I had managed to slip under her nightdress, so that one finger had been tickling and playing with her almost hairless slit and gradually working her up to a state of excitement she was at a loss to comprehend.

'Let us all be naked. Throw off every rag, my dear ones, I want to feel your soft warm flesh next to mine, to cuddle you and feel you all over. Shall I read a pretty little piece of poetry about a potter who married your namesake, Patty?' I said, and seeing they were ready for anything, told Annie to bring me a manuscript called *The Haunted House* from a drawer in the cabinet.

'Now listen to "The Tale of a Potter" and don't laugh till it is finished. You will find it rather free but nothing more than big girls like you ought to know.' Then I commenced:

> Young Hodge, he was a worthy wise,
> A potter he by trade;
> He fell in love with Martha Price,
> She was a parson's maid.
>
> This Hodge worked amongst his pans,
> His pots, his mugs, his delf;
> He said: 'A sad fate is a man's
> When he is by himself.
>
> Now soon I'll marry Martha Price,
> A nice snug home I've got;

The parson soon the knot shall splice,
    And we'll both piss in one pot.'

Then Hodge he made a pretty pot,
    And took it to his love;
Said he: 'I've brought this pot to show,
    I mean your love to prove.

Now name the day, the happy day,
    Whose night shall bring me bliss;
When your sweet cunt and my stiff prick
    Shall mingle in this their piss.'

They married were within a week,
    And Hodge he was in luck
He took sweet Patty's maidenhead
    With his first vigorous fuck.

Then in her arms he fell asleep,
    But started with affright;
And in the middle of the bed
    He sat up bold and white.

'Oh, love! oh, love! I've had a dream,
    A dream to cause me fright;
I dreamed we both were in my shop
    And there I hugged you tight.

I dreamed I went your cheek to kiss,
    We romped with hugs and squeezes;
When down I knocked the pots and pans
    And broke them all in pieces.'

Then Martha answered with a laugh:
    'No pots you've broke, good man;
But much I fear this very night,
    You've cracked a Patty Pan.'

And from that night unto this day
    Hodge in that crack would pop,
A prick as thick as any brick,
    But the crack he cannot stop.

So maids beware, heed well your pans.
    With this my tale is ended;
If your pan's cracked by prick of man,
    It never can be mended.

Throwing down the manuscript, I had a finger in each of their cracks sooner than it takes to write. 'What darling little pans each of you has! I long to throw you on the bed and kiss them. What do you think of mine with its soft curly hair? Only it's a broken pan, you know, my dears, as I've of course had my husband.'

'La, and was that really so nice, dear lady? Oh, I love you so, do let me look,' exclaimed Patty, slipping off my knee and kneeling between my legs to get a better sight of the object of her curiosity, which she first kissed most lovingly, and then, parting the hair, put a couple of fingers right up my cunt. This so tickled and delighted me that I leant back in the chair and pulled Annie close to my bosom as I hugged and kissed her, whilst I still had a finger in her little slit, as far as it would go. My legs also mechanically opened to facilitate inspection, as Patty exclaimed, 'How deep my two fingers can go right up and it is so warm and moist. It makes me feel I could eat it!'

In a few minutes we were all tossing on my bed in a state of nature. They laughed, screamed and blushed as I excitedly examined and kissed their respective cunnies. How my tongue revelled around their budding clitorises till they rewarded me with those first virgin emissions which are always so deliciously thick and creamy. How lovingly they both repaid all my caresses, Patty paying the most ardent attentions to my cunt, which delighted her more and more every moment, whilst Annie seemed to prefer sucking my bubbies as I gamahuched her.

'What a treat it would be to see you both lose your maidenheads at once,' I exclaimed.

'Ah! couldn't the pages do it for us, dear lady? I do love that Charlie so!' appealed Patty without consideration in her excitement.

'I'll try and manage it; but we must be careful not to let them into our secrets before I can find out how they are disposed,' I replied.

'Oh, I know Charlie is a rude, bold little fellow, wicked enough for anything if he had the chance. What do you think, I once actually caught him handling his affair in the pantry when he thought no one was looking and when I happened to enter suddenly; it was sticking out straight and red-looking at the top. His face was quite red and he seemed rather short of breath; but the impudent fellow, like the daredevil he is, shook it fairly in my face as he asked me to give him a kiss, saying: "What do you think of this, Patty? That's how it gets, when" – oh, mistress I can't tell you all he said.'

But I pressed her and at last she told me: 'It was when we had been waiting on you, mistress. "Oh, Patty," he said, "isn't she lovely, such mouth and teeth and loving eyes, I feel as if I could jump at her, I do!" '

'Very well, Master Charlie,' I laughed, 'perhaps I shouldn't so much mind if you did, when we are alone someday I will give him the chance and let you two dears know all about it. But I will first read you another song from *The Haunted House* and tomorrow I will give you a copy, and I expect both to be able to sing it soon.'

*Live and Learn*

*Tune: 'Drops of Brandy'*

When I was little and good,
    A long time ago 'm afraid, miss;
A stiff prick was not understood,
    I was a quiet little, shy little maid, miss.

I knew but one use for my cunt,
    I knew not what joy 'twould afford me,
The sight of a cock would affront,
    And talk about fucking have bored me.

But now, oh, much wiser I've grown!
    I'll stretch my legs open for any,
My modest shy feelings have flown,
    And fucks, why, I can't get too many!

I like a stiff prick up my arse,
    Though too much of that makes you bandy.
When I look at my quim in the glass,
    It always pouts red and looks randy.

I like a fuck – morn, noon, and night,
    On every weekday and Sunday:
If I'm fucked on the Sabbath, all right!
    But I want to be buggered on Monday.

Oh! Let it be hot or be cold,
    I'm always alive for a cock, miss;
Men, fair, dark, young or old,
    Here's a hole that'll take in their jock, miss!

I can spend for an hour at a time,
    My cunt is as hot as fire, sir,
The man that says: 'Fucking is crime,'
    I say to his face, he's a liar, sir.

Then give me a prick in each hand,
    Turn my arse north, my cunt to the south;
And get all your jocks well to stand,
    One in each hole and one in my mouth;

I'll fuck and I'll suck and I'll frig,
    Until you're all quite bloody well spent, sir!
Then I'll take in the lodgers again,
    And never once ask them for rent, sir!

Hurrah! for my cunt, my best friend,
Hurrah! for a cock to kiss, sir,
I'll fuck till this life comes to end,
I hope too, there's fucking in bliss, sir!'

When we awoke in the morning it was too late for a repetition of our tribadism, so I made them get up quickly and bring in breakfast, promising to look after Master Charlie during the day.

## Chapter Six

After luncheon I ordered Charles to take several shawls and a floor-stool into the summer-house of the garden, as I wished to take a nap, and was sure the open air was more conducive to refreshing sleep than the close atmosphere of a room on a warm sunny day.

Annie and Patty exchanged significant glances as I gave the order, but my uplifted finger stopped any further manifestation of intelligence.

We had a fine large garden at the back of the house, in some parts beautifully shaded by umbrageous elms of a venerable age, especially on the banks of a small circular pond about twenty yards in diameter, where, facing the south, the summer-house stood under the trees by the side of the small lakelet.

I followed Charles as he carried out my orders, and arriving at our destination, ordered him to spread the shawls over a sofa which stood there, for fear the leather might be damp. Then he fetched a pillow, and placed the foot-stool at my feet.

I had nothing on but a loose morning-wrapper, with my chemise and drawers underneath.

'How very oppressive it is,' I exclaimed, as I languidly sank back on the couch as soon as he had prepared it, allowing as I did so, a most negligent exposure of my neck and a slight glimpse of the orbs of love beneath.

'Ah! Oh, oh! My goodness; the dreadful cramp!' I almost screamed, as bending down in great apparent pain, I pulled up the robe to rub the calf of my right leg. 'Ah, oh! what torture!'

Charles was on his knees at my feet in a moment.

'Oh, my lady, is it so very bad? Let me bend up your toes!'

'No, no, not there, rub the calf, as hard as you can, Charles, there's a good boy!' I replied, my face wincing under the pain. 'Higher, rub along my leg, the foot's no use!'

Somehow the toe of my bad foot touched his trousers just outside the most interesting part of his anatomy; the slipper had fallen off and I could feel his prick quickly harden and throb under my toes, whilst his face flushed all over, and I thought quite a perceptible tremor passed through his frame, as he went on rubbing my leg below the knee, and I need not say how my own lustful temperament was affected by the contact.

My robe had opened down the front so that he had a full view of legs, drawers and bosom, perhaps the wrinkle of love itself.

My blood was in a boil and I could no longer resist the impulse to enjoy such a beautiful Adonis.

'Get up, Charles, it's better now,' I said in a low voice, 'and pray don't tell what you've seen by accident. That cramp threw me into such an awful agony I did not know how I tossed about!'

'Dear lady, your secrets are always safe with me,' he replied, looking down bashfully as he rose to his feet. 'I could kiss the ground under your feet to prove my devotion!'

'No, you are such a kind boy that just for this once, Charles, only this once, mind, I will give you a kiss myself instead. Come closer to me! What a fine boy you are. Now don't be bashful, really I mean to kiss you, if you promise never to tell.'

'Ah, madame, how kind of a great lady to a poor page-boy like me! I shall never forget such a favour and would die for you any time!' he said with bashful excitement.

'Come then,' and I took his handsome face between my hands and kissed him repeatedly. 'Why don't you kiss me, Charles?'

'Oh, lady, may I take that liberty?' he asked, his warm lips almost sucking the breath from me, so earnest was his kissing.

'Yes, yes,' I murmured, 'you may kiss me now, dear boy! And would you be faithful, Charles, if I trusted my life, my honour to your keeping?'

'Those kisses have made me your slave forever, dear lady. Nothing could ever wring a secret of yours from me.'

'Then, Charles, I will tell you I'm in love with your figure! I know you must be a perfect Cupid, and should like you to strip quite naked, that I may enjoy the sight of a living statue. Will you do so, no one will ever know?' I asked.

His face was crimson and I could see that he actually trembled under my gaze. 'Now Charles, make haste, and if you do that for me I'll give you a sovereign and a new suit of clothes.'

Slipping off his jacket I began to unbutton his trousers. Turning them down, my eager hands wandered under his shirt, feeling the firmness of the ivorylike flesh of his deliciously rounded buttocks whilst my eyes did not fail to detect how his linen stood out in front and was saturated with his spendings.

He seemed to understand me now and almost quicker than I can write it, he was naked as Adam in Paradise.

My roving hands took possession of his beautiful little prick, quite six inches long, and ornamented round the tight-looking balls by just a shade of curly brown hair.

'What's this, Charles, are you often wet like this?' as I called his attention to the glistening sperm on my fingers. 'What a big fellow this is, quite enough for a man. Did you ever make love with a girl?'

'No, my lady, but I wanted to try it with Patty, only she never would.'

'Then you shall with me, Charles, now. And I'll try to get Patty for you afterwards, I should so like to see you two together,' I said, drawing his prick to my lips and sucking it deliciously for a moment or two till I felt he was getting near a second spend.

'Now, sir, kneel down and kiss me,' I said, letting him go as I reclined on the sofa and opened my legs whilst his hands opened the slit in my drawers and exposed the lips of my cunt to view. His mouth was glued to it in a moment, and ah! oh! how his lascivious tongue made me spend in a second or two whilst my unslippered foot was rolling his prick on his thigh. But I was afraid of losing the next emission of his love juice, so I gently drew him over my body and directed his dart of love into my cunt.

He was hardly up to his business, but the instinct of nature seemed to prompt him to shove in.

What ecstasy as I felt the slow insertion of his virgin prick! How it seemed to swell inside the luscious sheath which received it lovingly.

At first we lay motionless, billing and cooing with our lips, till I began a slight motion with my buttocks, to which he was not slow to respond.

How I enjoyed that boy! The knowledge that I had a really virgin prick within me added such a piquancy to my enjoyment that I fairly screamed from excess of emotion as I spent and felt his balsam of life shoot into my longing womb.

He had to fuck me three times before I would let him dress and go about his business. He had been with me over two hours, but the time was well spent in making love and worming out of him all about himself and the other page who slept with him, Sam, who although good-looking had so much Indian blood in him that his complexion was almost black.

In answer to my questions Charlie informed me that they often played with each other, and rubbed their cocks together till the thick white stuff squirted out, and he added: 'Dear lady, would you believe it, his affair is two inches longer than mine; besides, it is the blackest part about him!'

'Do you think he would like a game with us?' I asked.

'Oh, certainly. He is just the fellow! It was he who taught me all I know, and I must tell you what he told me, that his last master, Colonel Culo, who had brought him over from Calcutta, had him sleep in his cabin all the way home and seduced him by handling and sucking his prick, which was so nice that at last Sam let the Colonel fuck him in the bottom-hole. The Colonel wasn't very big, you know, and easily got into him by using a little pomade. Then, when Sam left him because the Colonel was afraid he might get about his daughters if he kept him in his service, he was presented with a present of fifty pounds. He often wants me to let him get into my bottom as he said it felt very nice, but I never would go further than playing with cocks.'

'Well then, this very night, about an hour after all the rest are in bed, bring him with you to the girls' door. You will find it ajar and mind only to come in your shirts and be sure not to disturb the cook and housekeeper.'

With these orders I kissed and let him go, then went in to dress for dinner.

Just before we went to bed I treated Cookie and the housekeeper to a good glass of port in which I put a rather stiff narcotic to make them sleep well so that in case our revels with the two pages should prove noisy they would be too sound asleep to hear anything of it.

Patty and Annie were all nervous excitement and expectation after I told them of my arrangement. We were all naked and they hot as possible, and could not resist pressing their naked bodies against me, while with tears and blushes they expressed their fears of the pain of losing their troublesome virginities.

At last I heard a slight noise in their bedroom which so startled them that they flew to go and hide themselves underneath the bed, whilst I opened the door and entering their room, which was in darkness, found my two young men in the dark hesitating to tap at the door.

'Slip off your shirts and slippers,' I whispered in a low voice. 'Feel, I am quite naked myself, all is to be free between us now,' as my hands groped for their pricks. I found them to be as stiff as possible, and could not resist pressing their naked bodies against my own belly, where the contact of their throbbing pricks had such effect on me that selecting Sam by the size of his affair, I backed towards the girls' bed and drew him upon me. What a luscious bit it was! So large that my cunt was fairly gorged with the delicious morsel, which spent almost before it was well into me. My arms held him firmly round the waist as my body rested against the edge of the bed so that without withdrawing he had to go on with the delicious fuck, and I begged Charlie to put his prick into Sam's behind, to make him do his work well with me. The latter was nothing loath, and although the want of lubricant was rather an obstacle, Charlie soon succeeded in spite of his wincing and flinching a little.

The effect was to give my cavalier quite double energy. My hands passed behind him and played with Charlie's prick and appendages as he fucked Sam's bottom delightedly.

This was another virgin prick I was enjoying. Fancy taking the maidenheads of two handsome youths in one day. It fired me with the most lustful sensations! How my cunt throbbed on his glorious black prick. How we spent in torrents of that elixir of love which makes us die in ecstasy at each fresh emission. What heavenly joys to spend together, as we did, three times without withdrawing. I knew such excesses were only tending to shorten my life, but reason is powerless to resist the attraction of such Cytherian joys.

At last it was finished and we entered my room where the lights of a dozen candles showed everything to the best advantage. The figures of the two youths reflected in the looking-glasses round the room seemed to fill my apartment with lusty young fellows, half dark and half fair, all with limp and glistening pricks, just as they had withdrawn from the combat of love.

'Listen, my dears, cannot you hear the heavy breathing of the two girls under my bed? I'll wager they've been frigging each other whilst we had that glorious fuck in the other room!' I exclaimed. 'But let us first refresh our affairs with a cold douche and have a glass of champagne! Then see if we won't drag them out in the light, my boys!'

We laved ourselves, and a couple of glasses apiece immensely revived our flagging energies. I had a nice little dog-whip with a long lash on it. So telling the boys to lift up the curtains of the bed, I slashed under on the surprised and timid beauties so effectually that I had only time to give about half a dozen cuts before they sprang from their concealment and ran screaming round the room as I followed and plied my whip smartly over their tender bottoms. The sight of the thin weals which every cut drew on their tender skin, the shrieks of pain and the blushing effects on both faces and bums, so excited us that the boys' pricks stood again immediately and I longed to see the two pages ravish them as roughly as possible. Yes, I confess, that at that moment I felt awfully cruel and should have liked to see them suffer the most dreadful agonies under their defloration.

I know that with many men their delight is intensified if they can only inflict pain on the victims they ravish, but for a woman to gloat over such a sight is almost incomprehensible. Yet it is so, I was literally mad with lust for blood and torture!

At last I made them kneel down and kiss the boys' pricks as they begged of them to take their maidenheads.

Charlie had Patty and Sam had Annie. I ordered them to lay the girls on the soft Turkey carpet in the middle of the room with pillows under their buttocks. Then my two young champions, kneeling between their legs, opened the lips of the girls' spending cunts and proceeded to insert the heads of their pegos within the vermilion clefts of the victims.

It was a most delightful sight for me as I witnessed the blushes and enjoyed every painful contortion of their faces as the pricks were ruthlessly shoved into them under the influence of my whip, which I used without pity to push the boys on to victory. At last it was done and I could see that the boys had spent into them and I was sorry it was so soon over.

The tears of the girls were changed to loving smiles as by my directions they all had another wash. Then we sat down to jellies and wine, indulging in all manner of freedoms and jokes, till my young men began to feel their feet again and I could see that both of them were enjoying and eyeing me most amorously.

My blood was up and nothing would do but I must enjoy them both at once with the girls joining in the best way they could.

Sam and Charles sat on either side of me, and I could feel both pricks ready for action. So I made the former sit on the edge of the bed and take me on his lap, and as soon as I felt properly seated on the fine black prick, I called Charlie to shove his cock into me from behind, along with Sam's. This was not quite so easy to do, as Sam quite filled my sheath. Yet I was determined to have it so, and with the assistance of the girls, Charles succeeded in accomplishing my erotic fancy. Then by my orders, Annie and Patty tickled my clitoris and the lips of my distended cunt, as well as the cocks and balls of my two lovers.

Description fails me in endeavouring to picture the excessive voluptuousness of this conjunction, *trio in uno*. My profuse spendings so lubricated their pricks that they were soon quite comfortably rubbing together up and down, up and down inside my delighted cunt, and then: 'Ah! Oh! Oh! I spend! I die in ecstasy! Where am I? Ah! heavens! Oh! God, what bliss!' That is how I screamed out and then almost fainted from excess of emotion, only to awaken directly to find them also in the frenzy of their emission.

The excitement was so great that my champions retained their stiffness and kept their place whilst the girls, not to be outdone, jumped up on the bed, and Patty, turning her bottom to my face, buried Sam's face between her thighs as she pressed her cunt to his mouth for a gamahuche, with Annie straddling and lying over her to present her cunt and bottom to my lascivious tongue, which did not fail to seize the opportunity to revel both in her cunt and little wrinkled pink bum-hole.

This went on until sheer exhaustion compelled us to separate, and how I hugged and kissed them all, when at last I let them retire to their respective rooms.

Next day I was very ill and the day after that a medical man had to be called in, Patty going by my express desire to a doctor with very limited practice who I thought would not be exhausted by his lady patients.

As soon as he arrived my servants all retired and left us alone.

'My dear lady,' said Dr Loveshaft, 'what has brought you to this state of unnaturally prostrating excitement? Tell me all. Don't keep anything back if you wish me to do you any good.'

'Oh, doctor,' I replied in a whisper, 'pray, put out the light, the fire is quite enough to see by, and put your ear close to my lips. I can only whisper my confession, and don't want you to see my blushes.'

This was done and his face was close to mine when I threw my arms nervously round his neck and drew his face to my feverish lips and kissed him wantonly, saying:

'I want love; there's no one to love me. Oh! Oh! Fuck me first and physic me afterwards. I know you must be a gallant man, and mine's a real case of nymphomania!'

Whilst one hand still held him in a most amorous embrace, the other wandered to his prick, which my impassioned appeal had brought to a sense of its duty in a moment. What a fine fellow he was too, both long and thick, as opening his trousers without resistance he let me take it.

'Throw off your clothes, there's a love of a man, and let me have this first, and the medicine afterwards,' I exclaimed, thrusting my tongue into his mouth.

He was a most amiable doctor and it was nearly an hour before the consultation was over.

I rapidly declined after this and in spite of the doctor's unremitting attentions, both to my health as well as my cunt, I grew worse and worse and had to be sent to Madeira for the winter. So I shall conclude my long tale with my adventure on shipboard on the voyage out.

My housekeeper, whom I shall call Miss Prude, went with me as companion. We had arranged to have a fine large state-cabin in the stern of the steamer, with sleeping beds, or more strictly speaking, berths for four, as I engaged Patty and Annie to accompany us as servants. At any rate, Miss Prude thought so, but I had a deep design to seduce that virtuous young lady in spite of herself. So, by a little bribery, Annie was induced to stay behind and let my dear Charlie take her place in female attire.

As you journey to Southampton at night, we embarked at a very early hour before daylight, my companion being with me in a first-class carriage whilst the servants travelled in another part of the train and looked after the shipment of our luggage. Miss Prude never for a moment suspected the change while she and I retired to our berths as soon as we got on board, leaving everything to the girls.

For the first two days sea-sickness quite prostrated us all, especially my companion, but on the third day she was quite lively and the supposed Annie kept as much as possible out of sight till we all retired to rest. The servants had got into their berths and appeared to be asleep. Miss Prude and myself were both undressed and sitting side by side on the ottoman. I asked her to put out the lamp and as she did so I put my arm around her waist and drew her gently down by my side.

'Isn't it lovely now we've got over the sickness? What a beautiful sensation the motion of the vessel gives. Oh, if you were but a nice young man now, my dear!' I said kissing her most amorously and thrusting my tongue into her mouth whilst one of my hands wandered under her nightdress and invaded all those delicious hairy parts, so sacred to virginity.

'Oh, for shame, my lady! How can you be so rude?' she exclaimed in a loud whisper.

Still I found she did not repulse me and from the heaving of her bosom she was evidently in considerable confusion.

'What is your Christian name, darling? Miss Prude is so cold,' I asked, between my lascivious kisses.

'Selina, but pray, don't, my lady!' she said almost with a sigh as my fingers found out her little clitoris between the pouting lips which her yielding legs had allowed me to titillate.

'What a love of a name; Selina! and you must call me Beatrice, will you – there's a darling? And we must sleep together in the same berth, there's room for both. I must kiss you all over to prove my love – even there, darling,' I said indicating her pussy with my finger, which was on the spot at the time, 'and you shall do the same to me. Or, if you don't like, you shall see how Patty loves to kiss my crack. Ah! Ah! you'll soon learn, Selina, to know what is nice, even if it seems horribly rude to think of.'

'Did you never guess, my dear,' I continued, 'why some girls are so awfully fond of each other? Well, I will tell you – it is because they are in the habit of procuring from each other all those forbidden joys which married people alone are supposed to enjoy.'

She was all a-tremble. My fingers were fairly buried in her slit, as far as they would go, and making her spend deliciously.

'Oh! Oh! I must suck it, every pearly drop that distills from your virgin recess is worth its weight in diamonds!' I said excitedly, throwing her back at full length on the ottoman, whilst I fell on my knees between her yielding thighs and glued my lips to her cunt. My tongue revelled in that thick creamy emission which only real virgins give down, for when their love-juices have for so long not been secreted, they are far more creamy than the spending of a woman is after often being fucked or frigged.

She enjoyed it immensely. How she wriggled and twisted in the excess of her excitement.

At last I got up and woke Patty. Then returning to my ladylove, I whispered in her ear: 'Selina, darling, I am going to give you a real taste of what a man is like. Patty is going to put on my dildo and fuck you with it, while she tickles my bottom-hole and you gamahuche my cunt. Won't that be a delightful conjunction, my love?'

'You frighten me, Beatrice dear. What is a dildo, will it hurt?' she whispered in a low tone.

'Exactly like a man's affair, Selina! And although it can shoot a delicious soothing emission into you at the ecstatic moment, there is no fear of getting in the family way,' I softly replied. 'Now Patty is ready, let me straddle over your face and present my cunny to your sweet lips for a sucking kiss. You will like it. It will prepare you for the unmistakable joy the dildo will give when it once gets in,' suiting the action to the word by placing myself over her.

Her blood was in a boil. She eagerly thrust her tongue into my longing cunt which almost instantly rewarded it by a copious spend which Selina seemed to relish as much as any epicurean gamahucher would have done; her legs were lasciviously wide apart, which circumstance Master Charlie was not slow to avail himself of; the position in which I was over her effectually preventing the longing virgin from seeing the impending ruin.

Opening the lips of her spending cunt gently with his fingers, the fellow cunningly frigged her with the ruby head of his prick, until poor Selina got so excited that she began to bite me and wriggle about in such an extraordinary way, as well as moan and sob out: 'Oh! Ah! shove, shove! Do push it in further, Patty dear! I feel I must have it. Oh! Oh! Ah-h! It hurts now! Pray, don't!' as he commenced to force the maidenhead in earnest. I pressed my cunt upon her mouth so that she could not scream and intensely enjoyed the pain we put her to; for she was awfully tight and Charlie was not to be denied. He pushed and rammed at her in lustful fury, spending, but still going on, till he got the whole of his manhood fairly into her sheath, then he rested for a few moments, making his prick throb in its tight receptacle till all sense of pain seemed to be lost to our victim, and the natural lubricity of her nature asserted itself once more and answered with a wanton heave of her bottom to every thrust of her partner. There seemed no satisfying her greedy cunt, now it had once got a taste of the real thing.

At last we got off her, and lighting the lamps once again, let her see the dildo for herself and guess! How astonished she was to find it was real life, instead of a hateful substitute, but she forgave us for the deception which had afforded her such exquisite pleasure.

After refreshing our parts with cold water, she thoroughly enjoyed the sight of Charlie fucking the amorous Patty, and with her own hands handled his balls and tickled them as well as Patty's cunt during their encounter.

As we could not expect to have more than another two nights on board ship, I determined to make the best of the time, especially as I had a particular fancy for good-looking youths in preference to men; and there were a couple of young middies on board I had quite fallen in love with as they had shown me many delicate attentions when I was so ill for the first few days.

A fine bright morning saw us on deck directly after breakfast.

'Good-morning, my lady,' said young Simpson raising his cap with a knowing, wistful look.

'Come here, you impudent-looking boy,' I laughed, and as he approached, said, in a whisper: 'Can you keep a secret?'

'My bosom is as safe as an iron chest, if Your Ladyship has anything to confide,' was the reply.

'I am going to leave you soon, you know, and would like to give you and young William a treat in my cabin tonight, if you can manage to come after all are retired – you are off duty then, I think?'

'Yes,' he replied, 'from ten o'clock tonight until six o'clock tomorrow morning and you may depend on us being very quiet.'

Putting a finger to my lips as a sign of strict secrecy, I glided away from him and sat on the poop for the greater part of the day, looking at the water in dreamy anticipation of the fun I hoped for that night.

I had made ample preparation for them and bribed the stewards not to take any notice if they heard noises in my cabin, as I was going to give a little party to two or three young lady passengers before going ashore at Funchal, the port of Madeira.

After supper, myself and companions lay down to rest in our clothes, leaving the lamps burning and the refreshments all ready to hand. After a while, when all was quiet, our cabin door opened softly and the two handsome boys in their best uniforms quietly saluted us as they entered, both of them kissing me before I could rise from the couch. The door was bolted by Patty, who laughingly told them to mind how they behaved, or they would get served out. In reply to which both of them caught her and kissed her in spite of her pretended resistance.

The middies were hungry and soon did ample justice to a game-pie washed down with several bumpers of champagne as they toasted us, from the servants to myself.

I drank glass for glass with them. My veins were on fire, consumed by my lustful longings to enjoy two such handsome youths, and as soon as they had finished their repast, I begged them to sit by my side on the ottoman. And just as Simpson was in the act of sitting down I drew him upon my lap, saying with a laugh:

'What a nice baby he is to nurse, what a pretty little dear, kiss its dear mama.'

My lips met his in a long-drawn osculation which seemed to make him quiver all over with emotion as he lay on my bosom.

'Did you ever have a sweetheart, dear boy?' I asked.

'Yes; such a pretty girl at the Cape. I have rare fun with her when I go ashore.'

'What! Are you impudent enough to take liberties with her?'

'Yes, she even let me get into bed with her.'

'You impertinent little fellow to mention such a thing to me! Here, Miss Prude, and you girls, tie him up and pull down his breeches! I've got a tickler that will make his bottom smart for this!' I exclaimed, pushing him from me with great apparent disgust.

'What a lark! I should like to see them do it. Here, Peter, old boy, help us or these girls will really master me,' as he began to find himself rather overmatched.

A smile and a gesture from me only turned his chum Peter Williams to our side and it was fun to see how foolish he looked when he found himself really tied up to one of the berths and his breeches pulled down in spite of all he could do. How he blushed as they tucked up the tail of his shirt and exposed a very pretty white-skinned bum which was soon rosy enough under the hand-slapping he got from the whole party, all thoroughly enjoying the joke.

'Stand aside all of you,' I said sternly, 'and let me pay him the desserts for his impudence,' advancing birch in hand.

He was a plucky little fellow and disdained to cry out although I saw two or three big tears roll down his crimson face under my infliction, and could also see that his cock was as stiff as a poker. He was released, and without even waiting to pull his breeches up, rushed forward to help us as we stretched his friend Peter on the ottoman, and then by my direction he sat on his back, whilst I gleefully let him have a due share of the birch till he begged hard to be let off.

When they thought to adjust their clothes we all began to laugh and tease them about the beautiful red weals we could see, pulling up their shirt-tails and taking such liberties that in a short time they were quite undressed and we had two youths in a state of nature with standing pricks to look at.

'Well, I wouldn't give much for those toys of yours if that is all you have to show the girls!' I said laughingly, as I switched the parts indicated with my rod. 'Why Annie here has a better cock than any of you. We'll all strip and you shall see.'

This was the expected signal and any further restraint on our impulsive passions was thrown aside in a moment.

I think those two handsome middies had never really had a girl before and that I really took their maidenheads. In fact, I indulged in my letch for having two pricks in my cunt at once, whilst Charlie fucked Miss Prude before our eyes, till she had hysterics from excessive lubricity.

We kept it up till nearly five o'clock, fucking, gamahuching and indulging in every fancy we could think of. I even made Charlie get into my bottom with Simpson in him. Peter Williams also postillioning his companion with his prick in his fundament, whilst Miss Prude and Patty tickled and helped to excite us the very best way they could.

At last they were obliged to leave us and I may say that was the last lustful orgy I was ever able to indulge in, for my constitution broke down rapidly even during my stay at Madeira and I returned to England in the following May, since when, dear Walter, you have been my constant and loving attendant, and seen how rapidly this consumption is carrying me to my grave. Oh! I would that I had strength to do it once more and that you were my manly champion in that combat of bliss which I shall never taste again. Would to Heaven I might die in spending as I felt your very soul shoot into my vitals, but, alas! it cannot be! Still, if there is bliss in the world to be, I feel assured of an everlasting fuck.

Amen! I am unable to hold my pen any longer.

*La Rose d'Amour*

*or The Adventures of a*

*Gentleman in Search of Pleasure*

*Translated from the French*

# Chapter One

Thus every creature, and of every kind,
The sweet joys of sweet coition find.

DRYDEN

At the age of seventeen, through the mistaken but paternal fondness of my father, the Count de L—, I was still immured in an old château, on the coast of Brittany, with no society but that of my tutors, who had me at an eternal round of daily lessons, endlessly poring over dozens of musty volumes. Naturally of an indolent disposition, I became *ennuied* to such a degree by the monotonous routine of my life that I verily believe I could not have survived three months longer had it not been for an accession of company which the old château received.

I was most agreeably surprised, while at my studies one morning, by the noise of carriage wheels driving rapidly over the stone pavement of the courtyard. I threw my book into one corner, bounded down the stairs, and met my father at the hall door; he was accompanied by my uncle, Count C—, and his two sons, who were about my own age.

In the course of the day my father told me that he was about to start for Russia as ambassador, and that after remaining at the château for a week or two, my uncle and cousins would return to Paris, taking me with them, as during his absence I was to reside with my uncle.

The next day my father, after giving me a great deal of good advice and his blessing, started *en route* for St Petersburg.

My cousins, Raoul and Julien, I found to be two as wild young colts as ever were let loose upon the inhabitants of a country village, setting at defiance everything, and leading me, who proved an adept scholar, into all kinds of mischief, whilst their father, who had some business in the neighbourhood, could not look after our conduct.

Going one day into my cousin Raoul's chamber in search of him, on opening the door, I was perfectly astounded at what I saw. There lay Raoul on the bed in the arms of one of the *femmes de chambre*, Manette, a most lusty, finely formed, rosy-cheeked wench.

When I entered the room my cousin was lying on the top of Manette, clasped in a tight embrace, a pair of large white legs crossed over his back, and from the heavings and motions of their bodies, I perceived that they were enjoying themselves in a manner altogether satisfactory; and so intent and enraptured were they, with the exercise they were taking, that they did not notice my having entered the room.

Although, during the three days my cousins had been with me, they had, by licentious conversation, uprooted all my preconceived notions of virtue in woman, so strictly had I been reared, never having been allowed to enter the company of females, not even in the village adjoining the château, that seeing the two on the bed in that manner I was so amazed that I stood at the door watching them till Raoul raised himself off the girl.

He got up, standing with his back to me, while Manette still lay with her eyes closed, her petticoat and shift thrown up, her thighs wide apart, revealing to my ardent gaze a round white belly, the bottom part of which was covered with a large growth of jet black curly hair, and lower down, between her thighs, I discovered what I had so often heard of, but never seen before – a cunt; from between the locks of curly hair that grew over the mount above, and around the dear delicious slit, I could perceive two fat and rosy lips slightly gaping open, from which oozed a little whitish-looking foam.

My senses were so confused with what I saw, and the strange emotions which had been called up in me, that I stepped forward towards the bed. The moment my step was heard Manette buried herself under the bedcovers, while Raoul came to meet me, and taking me by the hand led me up to the bed, saying –

'Cousin Louis, what have you seen? how long have you been in the room?'

I answered and told him I had witnessed their whole performance.

Raoul threw the cover off the girl, and raising her to a sitting posture, with one arm round her waist, said: 'Cousin Louis, you, who have never tasted the pleasures to be received in the arms of a pretty girl, do not know what it is to resist the temptation of making use of every opportunity and means in one's power to gratify the appetite; and see what a beautiful, charming mistress Manette is; who could deny her? Having done me the honour to invite me to her chamber last night she left me no option but to return the courtesy this evening, and take the consequence.'

I replied, 'Yes, she is very charming,' and feeling a desire to get an insight into the pleasures derived from the conjunction of the sexes, I laid my hand on the bare knee of Manette, who still sat on the edge of the bed, her clothes scarcely covering her cunt and thighs, and slipped it under her chemise till it rested on the hairy mount that overtopped the delicious slit beneath.

But Raoul stopped me, saying, 'Excuse me, cousin, but Manette is mine, at least for the present, but as I see you are anxious to initiate yourself in the mysteries of the Cyprian goddess, I think that with the help of Manette I shall be able to find you a companion for the night; can we not Manette?' said he, turning to her.

'Oh, yes,' said the girl, jumping to her feet, and assuming a smiling look, 'we will get Monsieur Louis my little sister Rose, who I am sure is a much prettier girl than myself, and she has larger and whiter breasts than I have,' said she, covering a pair of fine round white globes, which I was greedily devouring with my eyes. 'I am sure,' she went on, 'that you will be pleased with Rose, when we bring her to you tonight.'

Telling Manette that on condition she brought her sister at night to my chamber, I would be secret and mention to no one what I had seen, I retired and left them.

Going to my chamber early in the night I spent an hour in a fever of excited expectation till Manette entered the room, leading her sister by the hand. Rose was a most beautiful girl, and the moment she entered the room and the door was closed, I sprang forward, caught her in my arms, and led her to a sofa, where I sat down and drew her to my side. I unpinned the handkerchief that covered her breasts, and clasping her again in my arms covered them with burning kisses. This caused Rose to blush exquisitely and struggle somewhat to release herself from my embrace, when Manette stepped before us, saying –

'Monsieur Louis, Rose was never in company with a man before now, and of course is a little backward, but is very willing to remain with you, and left to yourselves you will, I am sure, find her all you wish; is it not so, sister?'

To which Rose replied, 'Oh yes,' and hid her face in the cushion of the sofa.

Manette told me that as wine was a great reviver of the spirits and provocative of love, she would go and bring me some, telling Rose to ply me plentifully with it. She went, and soon returned with a tray of wine, cakes, etc., and retired, wishing us 'a happy night of it'.

When Manette retired I locked the door, then drawing up a sofa to the table I led Rose to it, and seating myself by her, endeavoured to put her at her ease by not proceeding to any liberties at first, till I had plied her with some half-dozen glasses of wine. After she had drunk pretty freely, the natural vivacity of her character began to show itself in her open and free conversation. I now put my arms around her waist and neck, and pressing her close to my breast, imprinted burning kisses upon her rosy pouting lips. I then slipped one hand into her bosom, feeling and moulding her firm round bubbies. After dallying thus awhile I stooped and slipping a hand under her chemise, raised her clothes up on her knees. Squeezing and playing with her legs, I slid my hand along her thigh till my fingers rested on a bunch of silken mossy hair, which overhung the entrance of her virgin cunt.

Playing with the silken curls, twining and twisting my fingers through them, I dropped one finger lower down, and putting just the tip of it between the lips, I titillated her so well that she began to wriggle about in her seat. I could stand it no longer. I was on fire; the blood was boiling through my veins. I raised her on her feet, and began stripping her, fairly tearing her clothes off in my haste, till she stood perfectly naked before me. Ye gods! what beauties, what charms, were exposed to my ardent fiery gaze, what delicious breasts, how firmly moulded, small, yet so round and firm. I press them, kiss them, take the nipples in my mouth, I draw her to me, till feeling her naked body against me, I drop on my knees and transfer my love kisses to the lips of her luscious little hairy slit. I was in a perfect frenzy, I burned, I raged. In a trice I threw off everything, and clasping her body to mine, I raised the trembling girl in my arms, and carried her to the bed.

Placing a pillow on which to rest the plump, luxurious cheeks of her backside, I lay her down, springing on the bed by her side. I open wide her thighs, and my prick being up in arms and eager for the fray, I lay my length upon her. With the tips of my fingers I unclose the pouting lips, and with the utmost trouble insert the head of my virgin rod into the entrance of her no less virgin cunt.

No sooner did I feel the head lodged aright than I drove and shoved in with the utmost fury; feeling the head pretty well in I thrust and drove on, but gained so little that I drew it out, and wetting it with spittle, again effected lodgement just within the lips. At length by my fierce rending and tearing thrusts the first defences gave way, and I got about half-way in, but had become wrought up to such a pitch that the floodgates of love's reservoirs gave way, and I sank upon her breast in a delirium of transport as I oiled her torn and bleeding cunt with a perfect flood of virgin sperm.

Poor Rose had borne it most heroically, keeping the bedclothes between her teeth, in order to repress any cry of pain, whilst her hands clasped my body to hers, or even handled the shaft of love to assist its murderous intentions on her virginity.

As I lay panting and gasping on Rose, glowing with the fierce excitement, my eyes darting forth their humid fires, the stiffness which had perceptibly remitted, returned with redoubled vigour, and I again began to make head-way into her. The sperm that I had spurted into her cunt had penetrated and oiled the dark and narrow passage, making my further entrance somewhat easier. I now recommenced my eager shoves, my fierce lunges, and I felt myself gaining at every move, till with one tremendous and cunt-rending thrust I buried myself into her up to the hilt. So great was the pain of this last shock that Rose could not suppress a sharp shrill scream, but I heeded it not; it was the note of final victory, and only added to the delicious piquancy of my enjoyment as I buried myself, if possible, yet further within the soft, luscious folds of her love sheath. We lay for a short time in the closest conjunction with each other, so that the hair on both of us was interwoven in one mass.

Putting my arm around her neck, I drew her to a yet closer embrace, and planting numberless kisses on her rosy lips and damask blushing face, which was wet with tears of suffering which the brave little darling could not prevent from starting from her lovely eyes, I drew out the head and slowly thrust it in again; my fierce desires goaded me to challenge her to a renewal of the combat. A smile of infinite love crossed her lovely countenance, all signs of past pain seemed to vanish, and I could feel the soft and juicy folds of her cunt, throbbing and clasping tightly on my enamoured prick; my movements quickened in an instant, and so exciting was the to-and-fro friction, aided by the delicious jingling of my magnificent stones against her backside, that despite all her pain, Rose was thrown into such an ecstasy that she clasped me in her arms, and throwing her legs over my back paid down her first and virgin tribute to man, forced from her by the soul-stirring motions of my rod of love, while I met her and spurted another stream of burning sperm into the utmost recesses of her fount of love, commingling our juices together and partially cooling the fires which were raging within us.

So novel, so new and exquisitely delicious, so transporting, so heavenly were the sensations, so ecstatic were the joys we both felt that we twined and writhed in each other's arms like serpents, while Rose exclaimed – 'Oh God! I die! Oh heaven! What joy, what pleasure. Oh! oh! ah! ah! – h! – h!' and ended in one long deep-drawn sigh.

With a few convulsive jerks and struggles of her delicious backside she loosened her hold, and stretching herself out with a shudder, fainted away, and I, who was at my last gasp, also sank into oblivion.

When we had recovered from our delirium I got up and poured out some wine, gave it to Rose, and tossed off a bumper myself, I then planted a soft kiss on the lips of her torn and bleeding cunt, exclaiming – 'True fount of love, sole seat of never failing joys and pleasures to man, dear, delicious, hairy little slit, from this moment my whole life and soul are forever devoted to you.'

I spent the night with Rose, in one continued round of pleasure, revelling in the full enjoyment of her virgin charms. Again and again did we renew our embraces, swimming in a sea of pleasure. So furiously did we enter into our combats of love that nature soon became exhausted, and we fell asleep in each other's arms.

In the morning when I awoke Rose was sitting up in bed, looking with anxious eyes on the now diminutive, shrunken instrument which the night before had ripped open the entrances to her virginity, robbing her of her maidenhead. When she perceived that I was watching her she threw herself into my arms and hid her face in my bosom.

Gently raising and reassuring her, I made her take hold of it, and began dallying with her breasts, tickling her, pressing them, sucking their rosy nipples, while the touch of her hand renewed in me the fires which were already springing into flame. Rose had the pleasure to see the small shrunken thing she first took into her hand spring up into a magnificent rod, smooth and polished as ivory, its large uncapped head red and glowing with the heat that was raging in it. I determined that she should reap the reward of her labour, and gather into her storehouse the rich harvest of love that was awaiting her.

Gently laying her down, and placing a pillow under the firm half-moons of her backside, I stretched open her legs to the utmost, exhibiting to my gaze the gaping lips of her cunt, ready open to receive the delicious morsel which, panting and throbbing like a high-mettled courser, raised his foaming head erect against my belly.

Laying myself down on Rose I made her take hold of my prick to put it in, but so firm and erect was it that she could barely bend its head down to the entrance. So magnificent was the erection that with all the stretching her cunt had received the night before it would not enter. Drawing myself back to wet the head within the lips, I slowly shoved it into her; she could not move, but lay quietly till I stirred her up so powerfully that we soon melted away, my deep thrusts making her feel the pleasures more sensibly, and giving her the full enjoyment of that which she had but tasted the night before.

We had barely recovered ourselves when we were aroused by a knocking at the door. Slipping on a loose *robe de chambre* I immediately opened it, and Raoul and Manette came in. I led them up to the bed, and pulling off the coverlet showed them the blushing Rose, more beautiful in the morning from the fatigues she had undergone the night past.

I called their attention to her, saying, 'Behold her chemise, see how it is dyed by the juice and crimson tide, which flowed from the parent stem after I had plucked *la rose d'amour* from my lovely Rose.'

My cousin Raoul now congratulated me. He said that he was overjoyed to have been instrumental in procuring for me such a delicious rose as Rose turned out to be; that he was sincerely glad he had been partially the cause of my being thus happily initiated into the mysteries of the divine art of love, and at the same time of my having had a virgin partner in my delicious combats.

Manette, too, congratulated her sister.

I now spent all my nights with Rose, sometimes in her own chamber, again in my own, and not content to wait for the night I would sometimes get her into my room in the day, and enjoy myself with her.

One day, while I was in my room with Rose – she stretched across the foot of the bed, her clothes raised up, and exposing to my view all her beauties, I standing between her legs with my prick (which was a very large one, few men being able to boast of one as large), in my hand – Manette suddenly entered the room, I having neglected to lock the door.

She got a fair view of my prick, and stood looking at it, apparently amazed at its being so big, but seeing the manner in which I was engaged, she retired.

*Chapter Two*

The following day in the afternoon, Manette came into my room and asked me to follow her to her chamber, whither she led, saying, 'I have something to show you that will please and satisfy you much more than your mistress could do.'

I followed her to her chamber, which after entering, she locked. I stood looking out of a window while Manette went behind the bed, the curtains of which were drawn. Hearing a light step advancing towards me I turned round, and Manette stood before me entirely naked; she sprang into my arms, clasping me round the neck, and led me to the bed, on which she seated herself.

I now saw what it was she had to show me, and being no ways loath to enter into the combat with her, to which she had invited me, I threw off my coat and waistcoat, while she let down my pantaloons, and drew out my blunt but ever-ready weapon, then falling back on the bed, drew me on top of her. My cock soon ran its full length into the soft and luscious sheath which nature intended for it. Twice before I got off her did I open the floodgates of love's reservoir, and pour into her a stream of fiery sperm, as each time she met me, letting down the very cream and essence of her body so copiously that our thighs were bedewed with it.

From this time till my cousin left the castle did I enjoy Manette in the same manner each day.

At the end of the second week after his coming my uncle announced his departure for Paris on the following day, and told me to make all preparations to go with him. When this was announced to my cousins and myself we determined to make the best possible use of the day by spending it in the woods on the banks of a small creek, with our respective mistresses.

It was Sunday morning; Raoul, myself and Julien (for although I have not mentioned him in connection with our love affairs, it must not be supposed that he was idle in such things all the time, far from it; while Raoul and myself amused ourselves with Manette and Rose he consoled himself in the arms of Marie, one of the dairymaids, a large lusty brunette, and very good-looking, to whose bedchamber he stole every night) set out, meeting the three girls at the place appointed, they having gone on some time before us, carrying provisions and wine.

Having saluted our beauties we proceeded to arrange matters for a lunch, and sat down or rather reclined on the green sward, and discussed the merits of some of the good things they had provided for us, and after satisfying our appetites felt inclined to taste of the other good things they had left, but which were not visible.

Accordingly, as a preparatory note, we slipped our hands in their bosoms, and dallying awhile, rolled them over on their backs, but in spite of our endeavours we could not raise a petticoat, more than just to get a glimpse of a thigh, for they resisted all our endeavours to get further into matters, saying they would not consent to such naughty things in sight of each other, and if we did not behave better they would run off and leave us.

I then purposed we should undress and take a bath. 'We will strip ourselves to our shirts and then strip you and at the word of command all shall throw off their nether garments.'

To this there was some demurring on the part of our young ladies, as they felt some shame at being seen by each other thus, especially Marie, whom neither Raoul nor myself had seen till the present time, but we overruled their objections and stripped to our shirts, then each going up to his mistress, commenced unhooking and unlacing, and taking off frock and petticoats, till nothing but their shifts were left on them. I gave the word of command, 'Off shirts.' We threw our shirts off, but on looking at our girls found them still standing in their shifts.

Finding they would not take their shifts off I proposed that one after the other throw off and stand naked, each as they did so to be examined in all parts by the men, and their relative beauties compared, and to the one that would first do so to be offered a handsome diamond ring.

Manette stood forth saying that having come there to meet and enjoy ourselves with our lovers, and they having thrown off all covering, she would not spoil the sport, as she was not ashamed to let them see all that she had, for she was sure she had as pretty a leg and as sweet a little cunt as any girl in Brittany.

I was so much taken with the lusty Marie, Julien's mistress, her immense titties, her extraordinary large hips and thighs, above all her beautiful cunt, which was covered up and hidden in a most luxuriant growth of jet black hair, which hung down fully eight inches long, and from out of which peeped two large red pouting lips, which looked most temptingly luscious, that I proposed we should each, after our first bathe, change mistresses, so that each one should have enjoyed the mistresses of the other two.

To this my cousins consented – with it the girls were much pleased as Manette was very anxious to have me once more bury myself within the juicy folds and recesses of her cunt; and Marie was also very willing, as she had whispered to me while I was examining her that although she was large she had a little cunt, but that even so Julien's prick was too small to give her much pleasure when he was in her; that mine was nearly twice as large as his, and she was sure that if I would consent to try her, I would like her much better than Rose.

I now led the way into the brook, leading Rose by the hand, the others following us. Once in, we played and sportively wantoned in the water, playing all manner of tricks, plunging them in over head and ears, and provoking them in every possible way, and under pretence of washing our fair partners, we gave our hands every liberty, going over every part, the breast, squeezing and moulding their titties, their soft bellies, rubbing their thighs, their cunts, and all other parts; the girls at the same time going over us in pretty much the same manner.

As we thus stood in the water, which was only about waist deep, our engines erect, and in good working condition, with my arm around Rose's waist, I tried to insert the nozzle of my engine into the mouth of her water-tight furnace, for the purpose of putting out the fire which was raging within it, but could not succeed, as we were unable to support one another.

My attention was drawn to a considerable splashing I heard, and on looking round I perceived that Raoul and Julien had lain their nymphs down on the edge of the water, their heads resting on the bank, and had got into them in that manner, the motions of their backsides and bellies coming together making the water fly all over them.

This was an example set before us, which Rose and I could not resist, so I led her out of the water and we sat down on the grass, under the shade of a tree; there setting her across my thighs, her legs lapping around my backside, her soft, beautiful white belly rubbing against mine, I dallied with her ruby-nippled titties, firm and springing to the touch, with one hand, while with the other I tried to make out the entrance to the harbour of love, in order to make room for my masterpiece of nature, that stood reared up between her thighs, and pressed hard against her belly, as if demanding admittance and shelter within the soft and luscious sheath, which nature has so bountifully supplied to woman, and of which Rose possessed a most lovely specimen. She in a fit of humour affected to elude my efforts to gain entrance into her, trying to protract the desire she was feeling by managing her manoeuvres so that they made the fire which was burning in us rage fiercer, and redoubled my excitement.

I covered her with burning kisses, and her eyes shot forth humid fires, and, languishing, seemed to melt beneath the long dark silken lashes which half concealed them. We rolled and twined about on the green sward, locked in each other's arms, till I at last got her under, with my knees between her thighs, and I was soon fairly into her, while she, feeling the dart of love entering into the very depths of the retreat, gave up, and lay at my mercy. But the fight growing fiercer and fiercer, she soon brought me to a crisis, at the same time paying down her own tribute to man.

Closing her eyes and breathing a sigh she stretched out her limbs with a faint shudder; the muscles instantly relaxing gave me to know that she had experienced the greatest pleasure that woman is capable of receiving or man of giving.

We had not recovered out of our trance when the others came up, and slapping us on our backsides soon brought us to.

Immediately on their coming out of the water we changed partners,

Raoul taking Rose; Julien, Manette; and I, Marie, and on receiving her I lay down between her beautiful legs, my cheek pillowed on the mossy hair that surmounted the gaping lips of the delicious entrance below.

Reclining thus for some time, sipping wine, eating bonbons and sweat-meats, we dallied away an hour or two, till our passions began to rise in such a manner as to be not long kept in subjection. My cousins, I suppose, thinking that being in the water added to the pleasure they received from the girls while fucking them, or from the novelty of the thing, proposed our going into the water again, and there enjoy our mistresses. They did so, but I remained under the tree with Marie. When the others got under the bank, I rose up, and spreading down all the dresses and petticoats, and making a pillow of a coat, I made a comfortable bed for Marie to lie on. I invited her to the combat. She got up and lay on the bed I had prepared for her, placing herself in an excellent position to favour my entrance. I laid myself down on her gently, she taking hold and guiding into the opening the head of the instrument which was to pierce her to the very vitals. After she had lodged the head between the lips of her cunt, I titillated her with it for a moment and then slowly drove it into her, so slowly that it was a full minute before it was all in, so tight was her cunt and so large was my prick that they were stretched and gorged to the fullest extent.

Marie's cunt was small, very small indeed, most lusciously tight, and slowly drawing my rod out to the head – the tightness of it causing so great a suction that it sent a thrill of most exquisite pleasure through the whole body – then darting it into her, and again drawing it out, and darting it in till I could no longer master myself, my motions became so rapid and vigorous that we soon let down and mixed the essence of our souls together.

Although I loved my little Rose, with her dear little cunt and all her charms, and although I found great pleasure when in the arms and enjoying the riper beauties of her sister Manette, yet the sensations of delight and pleasure I had just received from Marie were, in my mind, superior to them both.

I was the second time tasting and sipping of the sweets to be had in the arms of Marie when the rest of the party broke in upon us, but we did not mind them, and kept on till we had finished our work. After resting from our labours for some time, and our appetites being sharpened, we got our nude sirens to rearrange the luncheon, then after satisfying our appetites, and taking another bathe, we dressed and set out for home. On the way I called for a consultation as to whether our exchange of mistresses should stand good for the night or not.

Raoul answered that as we had spent the day together so we ought to do the night, for all of us to lie together in one room, and if either of the girls wished to be fucked by either of us, that she should say so, and be accommodated, and vice versa, to which we all consented.

That night we met in my chamber at eleven o'clock, the girls fetching in beds from another room, and making them up on the floor. I stretched myself naked on a pallet, and Manette ran up and lay down by me. Raoul took Marie for trial, and Julien, Rose.

After I had given the plump Manette a double proof of the powers within me, another change was made, and I got the lusty Marie. Towards daylight we were each lying with our own particular mistress, and after making all arrangements for the future we fell asleep, I in my favourite position, lying between the legs of Rose, having them thrown over me, my head pillowed on her soft white belly, my cheek resting on the silken mossy hair that surrounded her cunt.

We breakfasted at ten o'clock, after which I slipped up to Manette's room, where I found her, Rose and Marie. To each I made handsome presents, and told them if they would be true to me, that on my return from Paris, I would take and keep the whole three of them. Each one of them was anxious to have me tumble her once more on the bed, but as I could only do one they drew lots for my last fuck, which fell to Marie. She lay down across the bed, and while I let down my pants the other two girls threw up her clothes, and each raised a leg, and after I had made good my entrance they rested her thighs on my hips, so that I soon put her in ecstasy by the delicious manoeuvres of love's piston-rod. Half an hour later, I was on the road to Paris.

## Chapter Three

We spent five days on the road, and if our amorous pleasures had in any way debilitated us, we were thoroughly restored to full vigour by the journey.

We arrived at the Count's hotel in Paris late in the evening, too late, so said my cousins, to give me an introduction to any of their *filles d'amour*, and after partaking of a slight supper we retired to our (at least for that night) virtuous couches.

The next day we spent at the Palais Royal, and on the Boulevards. At ten o'clock we went up to Raoul's chamber and had not been seated more than a minute or two before three beautiful girls entered, bearing trays, on which were wines, comfits, bon-bons, sweetmeats, etc. Having had them arrange these on a round table, Raoul introduced the pretty dears to me.

After the introduction we sat down to the table and passed an hour or so in drinking, eating and chatting with our lovely guests till the champagne began to get into our heads; then we were not content with kissing and feeling the bubbies of our charmers, and other little liberties, and we tried to get deeper into matters, but found ourselves repulsed by our ladies, who, on our attempting to use a little gentle force, got up and ran out of the room. No sooner were they gone than Raoul said –

'Don't be afraid, cousins, they will return shortly, and we will give them a great surprise by stripping ourselves perfectly naked.'

We did so, whereupon Raoul told me to choose which of the girls I would have for my partner for the night when they entered into the room again.

Presently the door opened, and the girls entered one after the other, all of them in as naked a state as ourselves with the exception of quantities of green gauze, which each of them was wrapped in, and which only served to heighten their charms instead of hiding any part of their bodies from our view. Their hair falling down over their shoulders in long ringlets increased their beauty in combination with the gauze, so much so that I stood perfectly bewildered, and not until my cousin spoke to me did I think of choosing a partner. But Louise, a lovely little sprite of eighteen, fair, finely formed, with a large bust, wide expanding hips, large firm buttocks, and pretty plump withal, shot forth at me such fiery glances from a pair of most bewitching dark blue eyes that I immediately chose her.

The moment I named her she ran up to me, and opening her gauze enveloped me in it with herself. No sooner had she done so than the other two were in the arms of my cousins.

We again sat down to the table, our mistresses sitting on our laps. Louise hugged up as close to my naked body as she could; her delicious fat backside resting on my thighs, her large, firm bubbies pressed against my breast, a plump little arm thrown round my neck, her soft cheek nestling against mine, her rosy pouting lips glued to mine, in burning, fiery kisses, were enough to set on fire the soul of an anchorite, and as if this was not enough the bewitching little devil parted her thighs, and slipping her hand between them, caught hold of my prick, which had been rooting up against her backside, trying to find some hole or other in which to put his head and hide himself, and drawing it up between her thighs put the head of it between the fat juicy lips of her already spending cunt, rubbing the head between the nymphæ till I became so much excited that I told her if she did not want me to spill my liquor on her thighs she must let me in, as I could not possibly contain myself much longer.

Finding that she had worked me up to the pitch that suited her purpose, Louise raised one leg, and giving it a swing, threw it over my head, making herself revolve on her own 'axass', bringing her round, soft and smooth belly against mine. Being now seated crosslegged, she raised herself on her toes, and taking fresh hold of my prick, lodged the head of it in her cunt, then letting her weight fall upon me, impaled herself on it, piercing herself up to the very quick. Thus engaged she moved herself up and down; so rampant was I that I gave way before Louise was quite ready, but feeling the hot juice flooding the recesses of her cunt brought down her second tribute in time to mix with mine. We kept glued together, till my pego drawing itself up into littleness, fell out from the juicy folds of its nest.

Louise got up, and ran out of the room, soon followed by the two other girls, who I now saw had been engaged in the same game that Louise and myself had been playing. In a short time they returned, and we sat drinking till a late hour.

My amorous little devil of a partner had at last got me so excited that I proposed we should not go to bed for the night. My mistress, taking a light, led me to her chamber, which it was easy to see was fitted up as a sanctuary for love alone, a place in which nothing else was done or thought of. We first refreshed ourselves by bathing the most excited parts in icy cold water, then full of undiminished vigour, I carried her to the bed. We spent the night in one continued round of voluptuous pleasure.

The time thus passed for two weeks, without any other variety than occasionally slipping into the rooms of the mistresses of my two cousins and enjoying them for an hour or so during the day.

At last, Raoul advised me not to engage myself with either of the girls for a few days, as I should require all my vigour renewed, for he was going to introduce me to an establishment rivalling anything heard of in the *Arabian Nights Entertainments*, an establishment of girls, supported by the nobility alone, the admission fee to which was one thousand francs. In it, he said, there were the most beautiful females in all France. He repeated his caution to me about holding any sexual intercourse with either of our girls, as I must do honour to his recommendation, that being a stranger about to be initiated I would be obliged to perform in public the first round with the girl I should choose for the night.

On the evening of the third day after my cousin's announcement I went with him to the house in which the orgies were celebrated. It was a large and gloomy-looking mansion, situated in the Rue St Honoré. We arrived at the gate, and were admitted by the porter. Crossing a paved courtyard we ascended a broad flight of stone steps, and my cousin, giving his name to the doorkeeper, led the way through a dimly lighted hall, into a small, neatly furnished apartment at the left-hand side, in which he left me for a few minutes, as he said, to bring in the examining committee. He returned very soon, accompanied by three gentlemen, to whom he introduced me, saying my desire was to become a member of the club.

The initiation was very simple; it merely consisted in my handing over to them the entrance fee of one thousand francs, and one thousand francs more for the benefit of the house.

I was then led up another large flight of stairs, and invited into a dressing-room. They there informed me that I must adopt the costume of the house, which was simply a large dressing-gown open in front, put on over the shirt. I stripped as they did, and we were soon *en règle*. Being led to a pair of large folding doors, which noiselessly opened at our approach, I was almost blinded by the flood of light which streamed through them. On my entering the room, a scene of the utmost magnificence and gorgeousness presented itself to my view, rivalling any fairy tales I had ever read. It was a large saloon of lofty height and great length, supported on both sides by rows of columns of marble of variegated hues; between the pillars supported on alabaster pedestals stood a number of masterpieces of sculpture, in the finest Carrara marble, representing nude females in every position in which could possibly be combined grace and lasciviousness.

So natural did they appear with a piece of gauze thrown across their shoulders, one would have sworn they were living witnesses, flesh and blood, so admirably was their hair chiseled out, representing the mode of wearing it by women of different countries, so well was the rounded swell of the breasts imitated, and then, further down, the short curly hair that ornamented the beautiful lifelike pouting lips below, that one were almost tempted to advance and feel if they were not living. Some, too, were most ludicrous; one I saw representing a woman, her knees slightly bent and wide apart, with a prick about halfway into her cunt. Another was made to hold in her hand, the head just without the lips of her love notch, a prick that appeared to have fallen out of her cunt, and shrunken up in her hand.

At the end of the hall there played a fountain of perfumed waters, which diffused through the room a most delicious and fragrant coolness. There were painted on the walls, pictures, the most lascivious that nature could conceive, women in every variety of posture and position, nearly all of whom were represented as fucking with a man.

But the ceiling was the *chef d'œuvre* of this gorgeous apartment. The centrepiece represented an immense cunt painted in the finest colours, from between the lips of which depended a large carved prick, with stones attached, from which hung a magnificent chandelier. On the outer side, and around the large cunt in the centre, were pricks with wings flying at it, from some of which you could see a stream of sperm spurting into the centrepiece. Again, on the outside of the ring of pricks was a circle of naked nymphs, who appeared to be in pursuit of the pricks; they seemed to be leaning forward with outstretched hands ready to grasp them; the whole thing, intermixed with gold and silver stars, and surrounded with clouds of cerulean hue, formed a most splendid scene.

In the centre of the apartment was a long table, on which was laid out a most luxurious repast, served up on gold and silver plate, which partook of a character similar to the other adornments of the room. There were chased on the seats nude figures of men and women in all shapes and positions. Here were goblets supported on a stem, shaped like a prick; others there were, the bowls in shape of a cunt, supported on legs beautifully formed, and vases of every description, one of which in particular caught my eye; it represented a nude female standing on her head, her legs bent at the knees, the feet resting on the hips, and forming the handles, the cunt representing the mouth, in which was set a bouquet of rare flowers.

After being introduced to the gentlemen present, and having time given me to notice the different beauties of the apartment, I was told that the goddesses of the establishment would soon enter to their supper, and that as they came into the room I should choose the one I most fancied, as they were all perfectly free, there being no jealousy among the men in that respect.

## Chapter Four

Shortly a bell sounded, and through a side door entered a troupe of the most beautiful young girls the world could produce.

The effect on me was electric, so much beauty congregated together I could not imagine. So bewitchingly graceful did they appear as they gleefully tripped into the room, striking the most lascivious attitudes. So true to a fault were their figures, so charming was the clear transparent whiteness of their necks and faces, slightly tinted with the rose's hue, shaded by masses of rich black, auburn or chestnut hair, which waved in the light like rays of molten gold and fell in ringlets over their beautifully rounded shoulders, whilst their eyes, half-hid in the long silken lashes, beaming and sparkling with licentiousness, made them look like houris descended from the Moslems' paradise, rather than anything of mortal mould. And what served to heighten the enchantment their appearance cast over me was their dress.

Some entered dressed in pants and cymar, *à la Turque*, displaying to the utmost advantage their large busts and beautifully rounded hips.

Others (the majority) dressed in Turkish pants of fine blue or pink gauze, with a short petticoat hanging halfway to the knee, made of the same material, and which, instead of hiding any part of their bodies, only added to their beauty, and heightened every charm.

Their beautiful breasts could be plainly seen, even the rosy-tipped nipples could be distinguished as they rose and fell in undulating palpitations against their slight covering.

The shape of the legs and thighs could be seen; nay, the masses of curling hair that overhung their delicious, luscious little cunts, even the lips of which I could see – all, all was visible.

I stood thus entranced, gazing on the fairylike beings that were grouped around me, without a thought but of their extreme loveliness, till I was aroused from my state of dreamy delight by one of the gentlemen present asking me to give my arm to one of the ladies, and take her for my partner at the supper table. And if after supper I should see any other lady whom I might prefer to my first choice, I should be at full liberty to take her.

All that I could do in answer was to gaze around on them with a half-bewildered look, till a beautiful creature came up to me, and with a smile, putting her arm in mine, her lustrous dark eyes beaming with the very spirit of luxuriousness, asked if I would not accept her as my companion for the night.

I answered her by putting my arm around her taper waist, and drawing her into a close embrace, imprinted on her lips a dozen burning kisses, which she returned with equal ardour.

Leading the way to the table, we seated ourselves on a sofa (there being no chairs, but a sofa for each couple) and the repast commenced.

No sooner had we taken our seats than an unseen band struck up, playing the most beautiful and seductive airs; and as the dessert came on, a large curtain, which was stretched across at one end of the room, suddenly drew up, exhibiting a beautiful little stage, on which appeared four girls dancing some of the most licentious dances, throwing themselves into the most tempting postures, pirouetting till their gauze skirts stood entirely level with their navels, showing their cunts, even drawing apart the vermilion lips of those mossy temples of love by the extension of their legs, allowing us to catch a glimpse of the luscious interior which the open legs half disclosed.

After sitting at the dessert an hour or more, drinking the most exciting and heating wines with one another, on a given signal the girls withdrew to prepare for the ball, leaving us to do the same, which consisted merely in our stripping stark naked, retaining only our pumps.

I must here beg the reader's indulgence to state what I should have said before – that is, that the members of the society which held their revels in this house all belonged to the first families in the kingdom. That when any gentleman was initiated he must bring with him and present to the society some female relative, either a sister or cousin, mistress, or some beautiful female friend, so that in enjoying the relatives of other members he could have no advantage over them or their honour.

The young lady who had made herself my partner, I learned, was Mademoiselle de C—, daughter of Count C—, and sister to one of the gentlemen present. Here, on the pretence of being on a visit to each other's houses, they met once a week, and gave loose to the most unbounded licentiousness. All modesty was formally banished from the house, the most lascivious abandon being substituted in its place.

After stripping we entered the ballroom, which, like the *salle à manger*, was painted with nude figures, and instead of seats, it was furnished at the sides and ends with richly made couches stuffed with the softest down, with sprung bottoms, sheets of the finest lace, and coverlets of silk and satin, but no curtains to them, as nothing was allowed to be done in secret.

If a gentleman and his partner were tired of dancing, they could retire to a couch and play at the game of love.

On brackets against the wall, a little raised above the couches, were shelves supporting decanters of wine, trays of comfits, and other stimulating refreshments.

We had not long to wait for our partners ere they came dancing into the room, as naked as we were except for a wide scarf of light blue or pink gauze, which each had thrown over her shoulders.

If I was pleased with my partner at supper I was much more so now that I could have a fair view of her when perfectly naked. Her skin rivalled alabaster in whiteness, her beautiful full breasts sustained themselves firm and round as two globes; her well rounded shoulders tapered down into a small waist, a small foot, with an ankle expanding upwards into a fine calf, her thighs full, large and proportionately made, swelling up into a pair of large hips, while the two half-globes of her backside were equally massive and firm. Her hair, which she had combed out, hung down to her knees, while her cunt was surrounded and overshadowed by a mass of jet black hair which grew upon and around her belly as high as her navel, hanging down between her thighs some way, forming a perfect veil or covering over the dear little slit, contrasting most beautifully with the snowy whiteness of her belly and thighs.

On entering the room she ran up to me with extended arms, but I caught her, and held her out at arm's length, surveying and devouring with my eyes her every charm and beauty, and then I clasped her in a long embrace and we writhed about in each other's arms, rubbing our bellies together, till Mr Pego began to snort and prance about between her thighs, seeking for an entrance into some hospitable retreat in which to hide his impudence.

So great was the excitement raised in me by feeling her soft white belly rubbing against mine, as well as the springy mossy covering of her fount of love pressing against my rampant machine, that I would have sent him in to explore the dark little cavern concealed between her thighs, as we stood in the centre of the room, had she not prevented me.

Hardly knowing how to contain my still increasing passion, I slid between her arms, and dropped on my knees to the floor, parting with my fingers the glossy ringlets that hid a pair of rosy pouting lips, most lusciously tempting, and implanted my burning kisses on that amorous spot.

There was no time for further dalliance as the music began, and she led me away to join in the dance.

After the first cotillion I led her to a couch, and reclining on it drew her down by my side, and would soon have brought matters to a crisis had she not prevented me again, by saying that we should be obliged to enter the lists, and go through our first manual exercise on a state couch in the centre of the room, surrounded by the whole company.

Shortly after I heard the tinkle of a small bell, and immediately entered four men, wheeling in a couch of carved rosewood, covered with sheets of the finest linen, overspread with one of Brussels lace.

The committee, one of whom was my partner's brother, advanced to me and led me to the couch, while three of the ladies present took Mademoiselle de C—, and placing her on her back turned a small screw at one side of it, which, acting on springs, raised that part on which rested her beautiful buttocks, elevating them at least one foot higher than her head or feet, forming a sort of bow, and throwing up that portion of her belly and thighs which was most contiguous to the dear little cleft in the bottom of her belly.

So soon as they had arranged everything the three girls stepped back a little, and the men placed me on the top of her who was to share my sweet labour. She extended her thighs to the utmost to receive me.

After I was placed comfortably on her the gentlemen fastened us down on the couch by means of belts of india-rubber, which extended across the bed, and held us firmly on it.

I soon perceived the necessity of this, as at the least motion I made (there were such powerful springs fixed in the body of the couch) the springing caused by it would have thrown me off my partner if not off the couch.

The sweet little creature, who was lying under me, now threw her legs across my back, and clasping me in her arms, showed that she was ready for the delicious combat.

Upon these signs the girls who had placed her on the couch advanced, and one with the tips of her fingers held open the lips of her cunt, while another took hold of my stiff-stander, and pointing his head at the entrance, directed him to the opening before him. But so highly were my passions wrought up, and such a magnificent erection had I acquired, so swelled up was its large red head, and so lusciously tight and small was the entrance to the grotto of love, that it would not enter.

After two or three trials, each of which failed, the one who had hold of my driving machine, forced my backside up from off Mademoiselle de C—, and slipping her head between my thighs, took my prick into her mouth, and palating it with her tongue, wet it well with saliva, and letting it out of her mouth, again presented it at the entrance of the fiery furnace which was gaping to receive it. Effecting a safe lodgement for the head, with one vigorous thrust I buried myself in her to the very haft.

So fierce was the concussion produced by the meeting of our bodies that my magnificent stones fairly cracked against her delicious backside. With such force did I come down on her that the springs in the bed were forced low down, and resounding sent us some three feet into the air. The bed was so constructed that the springs could force the bed up from the body on which it rested.

I now felt that I was master of the field, and taking advantage of my position, gave my partner such a series of thrusts and drives – the springing of the bed driving her to meet me – our bodies came together with such a force as to make all tremble.

The spectators around us were continually calling out to us and commenting upon our performance with such exclamations as the following: 'O God, what a magnificent thrust.' 'How splendidly he drives it home to her.' 'See how deliciously their bodies meet together.' 'What a splendid prick, what beautifully large stones, how exquisitely do they flop against her buttocks,' etc.

'Ah, Mademoiselle de C—, how I envy you those glorious cods and that luxurious prick, with which you are now gorging that greedy little maw of yours,' exclaimed a lively young creature as she left her gallant's arm to approach the bed and get a fairer view of the fierce driving machine which so excited her imagination. 'Oh, how beautiful!' she said, as stooping down she caught a full view of the whole machinery in motion. 'See how the proud courser steams and smokes as he reins back his head to the starting place, and then how he makes everything foam again as he dashes onward in his mad career, towards the goal of victory!' and in her excitement she took my stones in her hand, and gently squeezed them, and brought me at once to the crisis.

Making one last lunge forward, I lay quivering and gasping on my fair partner's bosom, drenching her inmost parts with a perfect shower of the elixir of love.

My partner, who had been no ways backward in sustaining my fierce lunges and had returned them with thrusts and upheavings fully as amorous as my own, feeling the heat of the burning liquid I was injecting in her, gave way at the same time, and dissolving her very soul into a flood of sperm, opened the gates of love's reservoir, and let flow such a stream of pearly essence as never came from woman before.

After we had recovered ourselves from the delirium in which our senses were lost for a few moments, the belts which held us together were loosened.

I arose, and raised Mademoiselle de C—; as I stood her on the floor large drops of spendings fell pattering between her feet, attesting the vigour and warmth with which we had entered into the pleasure of love.

I now received the congratulations of the male part, as to the manner in which I had gone through the performance, and done such credit to our sex.

My mistress also received the encomiums of the females, all of whom envied her her good luck in having me for a companion.

Then I took the dear girl to one of the side couches and we reclined for a short time, taking wine and refreshments to invigorate ourselves for further enjoyments.

Casting my eyes around the room I observed that every couch was occupied by a couple, all of them playing the same game we had just gone through with.

My fair partner and myself arose and promenaded round the room, observing the different modes and manners of frigging which some of them adopted.

At the sight of so many beautiful women in action all at once, I thought it only right my mistress should complete the set, and leading her back to the couch, I again gave her such a delicious fuck that she could not get up for half an hour afterwards.

Shortly after the company had recovered from the transports into which they were plunged, two servants entered the room, bearing in on trays small cups of spiced chocolate, prepared in such a way as to give the drinker strength to enter the lists of love ten or a dozen times.

Fucking was now proclaimed the order of the night.

Never in the world was there so much delicious frigging done at one time by an equal number of persons. Never were there so many beautiful cunts to be seen so gorged and stuffed, and so well fucked by so many noble pricks. Never did women receive such a shower of sperm as drenched them from all quarters.

The debauch was growing to its height, the chocolate began to operate fiercely on the men. The women writhed and twined themselves about the floor, fucking, screaming and shouting in ecstasy.

The most licentious words now issued from the mouths of those females, who, on the morrow, would meet you in their salons with a demure look and virtuous countenance.

The excitement was steadily increasing. The women became perfect Bacchantes, they drank freely of the most exciting and exhilarating wines.

Suddenly they stripped the beds from off the couches, and spread them on the floor, forming one large bed, upon which they could all lie down.

The uproar increased.

Here might be seen two women contending (amicably) for one man.

Again, two men contending for one woman, till each found a place for their inflamed pricks, one in her cunt, and the other in her bottom or mouth at the same time.

The females shouted, ran after the men, throwing themselves on the bed, dragging the men on the top of them.

My loving mistress partook of the universal excitement with the rest. She was, if possible, more furious than any of her sex, mad with the extraordinary lubricity aroused within her amorous frame, twining herself in my arms, rubbing all parts of her body against mine, smothering me with kisses, nay, even pinching and biting me with force, so highly were her erotic propensities aroused, and continually calling on me by every endearing name, to frig, fuck, or give her satisfaction with my tongue.

Placing herself in the most lascivious positions, throwing up her legs and outstretching her arms, she would invite me, in the most licentious terms, to enter the amorous lists, expatiating on each and every separate beauty of her person, declaring the superior firmness of her plump bubbies, which she would press and squeeze, then on the white and velvet softness of her belly, describing all the luscious charms of her cunt, the luxurious heat contained within its juicy folds. Then turning on her belly, would display the two full and plump moons of her backside, inviting me to enter from that quarter. Then throwing her legs back, lay with the feet resting on her buttocks.

While in this position a thought struck me, and I determined to put it in execution.

Throwing myself on my back, my feet towards her head, my bare arse against hers, my prick stiff and erect as a rod of ivory tipped with red, I told my inamorata to lower her legs on my body. As she did so I had my battering ram right to the point, and she impaled herself on its head. This was a rather novel mode of fucking, but none more so than the manner in which some of the others were frigging.

The orgies of these Bacchantes partially subsided for a few minutes, when the president of the club, calling for order, put to the vote whether the lights in the room should be put out or not.

Having witnessed all that had passed, I thought this a strange proceeding, and I asked my fair partner to solve the riddle; she replied that at a certain hour at each meeting the party, both male and female, stripped themselves of every ornament. The women were not even allowed to retain combs in their hair. The men then retiring to another apartment for a moment or two, the women would put out all the lights in the room, taking care, however, to leave one burning in a small side closet; then on the ringing of a bell the men would again enter the room, in which were their mistresses, and mixing indiscriminately with them, would recommence the soft pleasures of love at once.

Neither the ladies nor their lovers were allowed to open their mouths even for a whisper, for fear of being known to each other, and it was for the same reasons everyone was obliged to lay aside every ornament, no matter what it might be, so that a brother and sister, in case they were together, could not recognise one another by any particular bracelet, ring or other ornament.

After the vote had been taken we did as I have just stated.

On our re-entering the room, which was totally dark. the door was locked from the outside by an attendant, and stumbling forward through the darkness, we met the women, who threw themselves into our arms, so that we were soon tumbling pell mell on the floor.

I got hold of a plump little fairy, and groping my way to one corner of the large bed, I placed her in a favourable position, and finding my way in the dark as well as in daylight, I revelled in the most voluptuous charms.

Oh, ye gods! how tight did her cunt clasp my prick. What a luscious suction was created by the juicy folds of her cylinder as my piston-rod shoved in and out. How gloriously she met all my thrusts by the most energetic heaves. Oh, how her fiery kisses were lavished on my cheeks and lips, as I pressed her to my bosom. And now the crisis came on, and we swam in a sea of pleasure.

I lay by her side, and broke the rules by telling her in a whisper who I was. I questioned her about her adventures in the dark.

She went on to tell me that at one of the meetings, on the lights being suddenly restored, she found herself lying in the arms of her half-brother, and that she had frequently met with her cousin also.

She said that she had known brothers and sisters, and many a pair of cousins, who had been caught in each other's arms, and that on the lights being restored, so far from quitting one another they pursued the chase till the game was run down, and enjoyed themselves as they would, had they been strangers.

She said that in order to obtain the full enjoyment of the pleasures of love, it was necessary to do away with all modesty and restraint; that man was made for woman, and woman for man. That, for her part, she considered it made no difference who the actors were, as long as the fucking was well done and enjoyed.

All her actions and movements pronounced my partner one of the most licentious of women. She played with all parts of my body; laying her head on my thighs, she would handle my stones, put the head of my prick between other lips than those nature formed to receive it, and tickling the head of it with her tongue she tried to awaken it to renewed vigour; trying every means to arouse its dormant energies, she succeeded, and casting herself into my arms, lay on her back upon me.

My pego was in a beautiful state of erection, his head rooting up between the snowy thighs of my fair burden, and furiously butting the door, demanding an entrance into the secret chamber of love. With the tips of her fingers she opened the valves that closed the rosy-tinted aperture of her cavernous recess, and inserting the head I gave rein to my courses, and for the seventh time that night did I drown myself in bliss.

So well pleased was I with my companion that, despite the attraction of the many beauties who were groping about over the room, enjoying themselves first with one man, then with another, and any of whom I might have had, I laid myself in her arms, my cheek resting on a very large round globe of flesh, her arms clasping me close to it, while her legs were crossed with mine.

In this position I fell into a sound sleep.

When I awoke the lights were blazing with great splendour, and I found the girl in whose arms I had fallen asleep engaged in a vigorous combat with a man who lay close by me.

Continuing the debauch till the approach of day, we all dressed, each one going separately, and by different routes to their residences.

I reached home, and hastening to my apartment, completely worn out from the violent exercise I had undergone, I fell into a sleep from which it was three o'clock in the afternoon before I awoke.

## Chapter Five

I attended all the orgies of the club – of which I had been made a member – where new debauches were committed every week.

At each meeting my partiality for the delicious creature I had lain with last, on my initiative night, increased to such a degree that I determined to have and retain her to myself if possible.

Celestine was the daughter of the Marquis de R—. In the club she was known by the soubriquet of La Rose d'Amour, by which name I shall continue to call her.

She combined all the graces and charms peculiar to the softer sex.

She had a temptingly small foot, giving tokens of the excellent smallness of the delicious slit, which nature had placed between a pair of ripe fleshy thighs, backed by a pair of fair buttocks, beautifully rising up, swelling out into bold relief from the adjacent parts. A belly white and soft as a bed of snow, a waist slender as a nymph, a neck like a swan, small mouth, inlaid with two rows of ivory, lips rosy and pouting, cheeks soft as the velvet down of an overripe peach, languishing dark eyes, sparkling and beaming with a lascivious fire, shaded by long silken lashes, while her auburn hair fell in a profusion of ringlets over her neck and shoulders, half concealing a pair of large globes rivalling alabaster in whiteness, tipped with nipples hard and red as rose buds, in fact she was 'perfection personified'.

The day following my last visit to the club, I received a letter from St Petersburg announcing my father's death, desiring me immediately to set out for that place for the purpose of removing his remains to France.

Now, I had never seen enough of my father to have great fondness for him; what little filial affection I had was soon drowned by the ideas I had of enjoyment now I was to succeed at once to his vast fortune, so that I did not like to give up my pleasures, especially that of meeting with La Rose d'Amour.

On receiving the letter I at once proceeded to the Hotel de R—, and on enquiring for Celestine was shown into the drawing-room.

The servant returned to usher me into her mistress's boudoir, where, opening the door, I passed in, and found her reclining on a sofa, in a bewitching dishabille. Her neck was uncovered, the bosom of her wrapper open, half displaying her pretty bubbies. One foot resting on the sofa, the other on an embroidered footstool, her skirts were raised to her knee, displaying a finely rounded calf. After locking the door I read her the letter I had received, and telling her I could not part from her, implored her to leave home and accompany me on my journey, telling her that on our return to

France, I would fit up my château in Brittany with all the luxury of an Eastern harem, where we might reside amid all the pleasures that love could induce, and all the luxury that wealth could purchase.

After a few short murmurs she consented, and I left her to make the necessary preparations for our departure on the morrow.

As she was to accompany me in male attire, acting as a page, I was obliged to have recourse to my faithful valet, to procure proper dresses, etc.

By eight o'clock in the evening he had everything prepared, and as we were to start at daylight, Celestine, under pretence of going to a ball, came and passed the night with me in my chamber at my uncle's.

At daylight we set off with all the speed that four good horses could give us.

My companion made a very handsome-looking boy, and was the cause of our having some very amusing adventures on our journey.

At a small town on the frontier, at which we stopped, on showing my passport to Monsieur le Maire, he insisted on our staying at his house for the night, which I at last complied with.

He was an old man about sixty, grey-haired and bald. When we arrived at his house, he sent a servant to inform his wife that there were strangers in the hall below and that he desired her presence.

In a few minutes, to our agreeable surprise, there entered the room a very charming, rosy-cheeked, vivacious-looking young woman, about twenty-two years of age.

In the course of the evening I observed by the almost scornful manner in which she regarded her husband that the union with him had been a 'marriage of convenience', and furthermore, from the glances I perceived passing between her and Celestine, I knew she wanted but the opportunity to give her husband the slip, so I determined, if the chance offered, to repay M. le Maire's hospitality by making an addition to his bald pate in the shape of a pair of horns.

On retiring for the night, my mistress informed me that she had an engagement with our host's wife. That she intended to drug a glass of wine for her husband on going to bed, which would ensure her freedom for at least ten hours, and that as soon as her husband was fast asleep she would go to her room.

Telling Celestine to undress and get into my bed, I went into the room prepared for her, and stripping myself perfectly naked, awaited in darkness the coming of the charming hostess.

After waiting for an hour I heard a light step advancing towards the room, the door opened, and she entered, and whispering Rudolph, the name Celestine had taken, advanced to the bed. Slipping the bolts in the door, I caught her in my arms, and found she was as naked as myself. In kissing her she knew immediately by my whiskers that I was not the person she expected to meet, and fearing she had made a mistake in the room, she gave a slight scream, and struggled violently to free herself.

But I retained a firm hold of her naked waist, and drawing her to the bed, explained everything to her. How that my page Rudolph was my '*chère amie*', accompanying me in this disguise.

After calming her fears I lighted a taper that stood on the table and after a careful study of her beauties, while I pinched and kissed everything, especially a dear hairy little cleft at the bottom of her belly, I found her to exceed the expectations I had formed at the supper table.

She could not resist my handling her person, and freely gave herself up to my touches.

The game was getting too exciting to stand dallying very long, so turning her on her back, I plunged my weapon into a bath of hot juicy flesh, and gave her a luxurious feast of the fruit of which she had had before but a very slight taste.

Five times that night did I put her through the manual exercise of love, and five times did she die away in the most ecstatic enjoyments, the pleasures of which she declared she had only known in imagination.

It was with sincere regret that Madame le Maire parted from me at dawn of day, to join her sleeping husband, to whose brows had just been added a pair of horns. They were short to be sure, but there appeared every prospect of their branching out into large antlers.

Before leaving me she made me promise to stop on my return.

After breakfast in the morning I returned my host my sincere thanks for his hospitality, assuring him that the entertainment I had received in his house was far beyond my expectations.

I ordered my carriage, and followed by my page, took the road to Vienna.

In a fortnight more we reached St Petersburg, where, after preparing everything for my return, I determined to devote a day or two to pleasure.

At a ball given at the Imperial Palace, to which I was invited, I became acquainted with the Countess Z—, one of the most accomplished beauties at Court and the reigning belle of St Petersburg.

The Countess Caroline was a widow of twenty-three! She had been married at twenty, and about a month after her marriage her husband had been killed in a duel with an Englishman.

The Countess had a gait and look proud and haughty as a Juno, her oval face and majestic figure excited my highest admiration, and I determined to make her mine.

Entering into a conversation with her, I found that she was pleased with my company, and much more with my person.

Accomplished as she was, Caroline Z— had the vice, peculiar to all Russians, of drinking large quantities of brandy. In fact, she drank so much that knowing she lived in a large palace, with no one but her serfs, I formed the resolution of making her mine that same night.

I plied her with brandy till late in the evening, and she became so much excited as not to be able to control herself. I kept close by her side throughout the night, till the ball broke up. I humbly asked permission to be her escort home.

Engaging her in a laughing conversation, I put the question to her as we descended the palace stairs, and the giddy young creature, nearly intoxicated with brandy, at once accepted.

I handed her into the carriage, bid the driver go fast, and in a moment we were at her palace.

On alighting she invited me in – an invitation which I promptly accepted – and led me up a flight of large stairs into her own dressing-room. So much was she affected by the brandy she had drunk that she hardly knew what she was doing.

Laying off her bonnet and shawl she rang the bell, and two waiting-maids entered. Asking to be excused for a few minutes, she retired to her boudoir, followed by her attendants, and in a short time reappeared in a different dress, a loose flowing gown of rich cashmere.

Calling for lunch and brandy, she dismissed the attendants who brought it in. They retired in apparent amazement at the sight of a man being admitted into her dressing-room, and especially at that hour.

I now watched my opportunity, and pouring a few drops of liquid from a small vial I always carried about me, into a glass of brandy, I presented it to her, and she drank it off.

It ran like liquid fire through her veins, her eyes sparkled with licentiousness, her heart heaved and palpitated with the fierce desires which were consuming her.

Advancing my seat beside her own, I poured into her ears a tale of burning love. I put my arm around her waist, and finding she made no resistance, pressed her to my bosom, and planting numberless kisses on her lips, sucked the breath from her.

In a minute more she delivered herself up to me body and soul, she threw her arms around my neck, and repaid the kisses I had just given, with interest.

I rose up with her in my arms, and carried her into the boudoir, in which stood a bed in a recess. I undressed her till she stood in her shift, and then taking off my own clothes, stood in my perfect nudity. Giving Caroline a soft kiss I drew the shift from off her, and had a fair view of all her secret charms.

Leading her to the bedside I gave her the fillip on her back, and soon was buried to the very utmost notch in the most lusciously tight cunt I had ever entered.

With what fire, what enthusiasm, with what fierce upheavings did she meet and receive the piercing thrusts of my love dart.

The excitement thickens, the combat grows hotter and hotter. Heavens! what pleasure! what joy! what ecstasy! Oh, how my lively partner kept time to all my fierce desires! In what a sea of delight was I plunged! What an indescribable luxurious heat reigned in the luscious folds of her cunt! Ye gods! how often did I dart my stiffened arrow through the rich, juicy flesh of her deliciously sensitive quiver! I felt the crisis approach, our mouths met; we devoured each other's tongues; her rosy lips, how sweet and warm! What intense voluptuousness in those amorous bites, that burning struggle of our tongues, that sought, moistened, entangled, drew back, and darted together again!

I gave her the *coup de grâce*, and so great was the flood that issued from the reservoirs of love that the precious pearly fluid flowed down her thighs as I spurted into the deepest recess of her cunt the burning sperm.

Caroline had not all the briskness and vivacity of La Rose d'Amour, her movements were languishing but more voluptuous. I turned her over and over, I touched and handled every part. I kissed her again; everything did I devour with my fiery kisses, especially the gaping lips of her cunt, which were wet with the liquid stream from the fountain of pleasure which I had poured into her.

The spark kindled, the flame blazed. We writhed and twined, over and over, in each other's arms, and the sixth time had my indefatigable courser bounding to the goal of victory without tiring. The storm grew higher, the sperm fell in torrents, but could not put out the blazing fire that raged within us.

We awoke in the morning refreshed from the fatigues of the night. Again did I survey all the charms of my lovely bedfellow. She stroked my limber instrument till it grew into a stately rod. I toyed with her enticing firm globes of alabaster, each tipped with a rosebud most lusciously tempting, which I moulded and pressed in my hand, and sucking the nipples received fresh fire.

I turned her on her back; she spread her thighs, and guided the dart which pierced her to the very vitals; we again drank of the sweets obtained in the fountain of Venus.

Swearing eternal constancy and love I left my charming Caroline, and hastened home.

I told Celestine all that had occurred, not omitting to expatiate pretty freely on the pleasure I had enjoyed while revelling in the virgin charms of Caroline Z—.

This somewhat piqued my French charmer, but on opening to her my views she consented to the arrangement proposed. I told her my intention was to fit up the château in all the magnificence of Barbaric pearl and gold, and to take, nay, in fact, steal off all the handsomest women that excited my desires very strongly, and carry them to the château, which I would have guarded by trusty followers, in fact, to make it a fortified seraglio.

I told her that she should reign as undisputed mistress of the place, and that, greedy as she was, she should never want for the peculiar flesh which she was always willing and ready to devour. I also told her to have everything in complete readiness to start at a moment's notice, while I went to see the beautiful Russian in whose arms I had passed the night.

Calling in the evening, I was led by a servant immediately to Caroline. I found her in a splendid bathroom, reclining in a bath of milk and perfumed waters.

Placing a cushion on the marble edge of the bath. I made my proposition to her of leaving Russia and going to France with me. I pictured to her imagination what should be the magnificent splendour of our abode, in which love alone should be admitted.

I described to her all the endless variety of enjoyments in which we could indulge, passing our days and nights in one uninterrupted round of pleasure.

So highly did I excite her imagination by the glowing description of the amorous life we should pass that she at once agreed to accompany us. I say us, for I had told her of my having Celestine with me, and of my intentions of possessing every woman who might take my fancy.

She entered at once into the spirit of my proposition, and made me promise to bring Celestine to her house on the following evening so that all three of us could spend the night together.

After spending the day in driving about the environs of St Petersburg, Celestine (in her male attire) and I alighted at the house of the Countess, and we were at once shown into the dressing-room of which I have before told.

Caroline was reclining on a sofa in all the charming coquetry of a *négligé déshabillé* when we entered. Instead of rising to receive us she merely tapped a silver bell which lay beside her, and two girls entered, who, taking Celestine into the boudoir, remained for a full half-hour.

What was my astonishment when she re-entered to behold her in a dress, the exact counterpart of the one Caroline had on, who as soon as she came in got up and embraced her, praising her beauty, admiring her figure, and calling her sister, and paying her every attention she could think of.

On asking my beauteous Russian how she had got the dress for Celestine, she replied that from the description I had given her she had the dress made in that short time, as she could not think of showing off her own charms to the best advantage with Celestine concealed by her male attire, saying which she opened a casket and placed on the brow of Celestine a coronet of diamonds of the first water, on her neck a necklace of pearls, and in the bosom of her dress a large rose formed of brilliants, asking her to receive them as a present from a sister.

Celestine drew from her finger a very large brilliant, and presented it to Caroline as a token of friendship, pleading her present poverty as an excuse for not being able to make a more handsome return for her elegant present.

Supper being laid in the room in which we then were, we sat down to a feast for the gods, expressly prepared for the occasion by the voluptuous Caroline. The dishes were all highly seasoned, while the wines were of the most heating and exciting kind.

After the dessert had been brought in I laid my plans again before my two mistresses.

Caroline said she would need but a week to make her preparations, as the most of her immense fortune consisted in money and jewels, which she would place in my hands to be disposed of as I thought proper, telling me to make arrangements for her leaving very secretly, for if either of her brothers should know of her intentions they would most assuredly detain her by force if in no other manner.

Having drunk enough wine to excite their desires pretty strongly, my two beauties commenced tussling me about, rolling me on the floor, and tumbling on top of me, their dresses in most admirable disorder; a pin becoming loose would expose the half of a breast whiter than snow; the flying up of a petticoat would display a well-turned calf, a knee, or a firm, fleshy thigh.

But this dalliance, acting as a provocative on their already excited lusts, could not be put up with very long. They burned for some more substantial good than that afforded by kissing and pinching, which were fine auxiliaries for increasing an appetite they could not satisfy.

Jumping up I ran into the boudoir, followed by the dear creatures, whose eyes flashed with the fires of libertinism, while their breasts rose and fell with quick heavings.

I hid under the bed, from whence they pulled me, and stripping me naked, glued their moist lips over every part of me, my erect Jacob's staff coming in for more than its share.

They stripped to their skin, and calling on me as umpire to decide on the relative beauties of their charms, as they stood before a large pier glass, handling their snowy strawberry-tipped bubbies, sleeking down the glossy curling whiskers that surrounded two pairs of the most temptingly pouting lips that ever adorned women. Since both were perfect models of voluptuous beauty and grace, although different in their kinds, I could not decide between them, but admired more and more the charms of which I was the happy possessor.

I seized on the rosy nipples of the heaving snowy hillocks, which disdaining the use of corsets, rested on their bosoms like globes of alabaster. I sucked them, I squeezed their soft round bellies against mine, I kissed everything and everywhere. I laid my kisses on the hairy mounts that overhung the delicious grottos underneath; the lips which close the mouth of the flesh slits next received their share; I am on fire! I burn! The bed receives us! I wish to push matters home at once; but no, they would bring me to the very point before I could enter.

Celestine has seized on my prick; she cannot get it into her cunt, so, determined not to lose it altogether, she takes it in her mouth, she sucks its glowing head, she rolls her tongue over the top of it. I am mad – delirious. No longer to be restrained I throw myself on to Caroline, who receives me with open legs and arms. I dart my fiery rod into her furnace, which consumes it. A few maddening thrusts, driven home with such force that I touch her to the very quick – a cry of thrilling pleasure escapes us at the same time – and all is over.

But so intense were our passions that we hardly perceived it till I felt her again moving up to me. How delicious! What voluptuous warmth pervaded her whole body. How exquisitely did the springing cheeks of her backside respond to all my motions. The little devil Celestine is playing with two large balls that keep knocking against the buttocks of my antagonist.

It is too much, I drive it home, and lie gasping and quivering on Caroline's breast, who cries out, 'Oh heavens! further in! I come – I spend! Oh – oh, God, I die! Oh, dear, what plea – pleas – pleas – ure!'

She had fainted. The delicious wrigglings of her backside, the contraction of her cunt, sucked the last drop from me.

When she recovered from the delirium in which her senses were plunged, she lay with her eyes languishingly beaming, her lips apart, with the tip of her rosy tongue slightly protruded between two rows of pearl – the very picture of voluptuous pleasure.

So plentifully had I bestowed in her the liquid treasure of love's reservoir, and so delightfully had she intermingled with mine the essence of her own dear self, that when I withdrew from her the pearly stream flowed out and ran over her thighs.

I had a short respite, receiving renewed vigour from the caresses of Celestine, whose greedy little maw was gaping wide to receive the half-erect machine which she was working at, trying to make it stand, so as to win her purpose. Her whole body glows with an intense heat, the most voluptuous warmth reigns in every part! She burns, she imparts to me the fire which is consuming her very vitals. My ever willing and ready courser comes up to the stand, with head erect, impatient for the word.

I give him the reins, and he plunges forward in his impetuous career; on, on he speeds, nothing retards him. On, on, he rushes, nor stops till the race is run. He falters, he stops, his head droops, he pours out his very life blood, sprinkling the whole course which he has run with the precious liquid. It is finished; another faint struggle; a few convulsive jerks and it is all over. I lie panting on the heaving bosom of Celestine.

After having for the eighth time renewed my embraces with my two loves, I fell asleep, only to wake to new pleasures.

At the end of the week Caroline, having completed her business, placed in my hands upwards of three millions of francs and jewels to the value of one million more, and the following day we left St Petersburg.

The girls at my request provided themselves with a full wardrobe of male attire and we started for France, where I longed to be, to put into operation all my schemes of pleasure, which I was determined should rival, if not excel, anything of the kind ever seen or heard of in the East.

On passing the frontier of France, I directed my route to the château, where, after depositing my lovely mistresses, I kept on to Paris.

On entering the capital I drove to the most fashionable upholsterer, telling him what I wanted done and giving him *carte blanche* in respect of the expense to be incurred.

Telling the man to make everything of the very richest material money could purchase, I advanced him a cheque for one hundred thousand francs, with the privilege of drawing on my banker for more in case of need.

Giving orders to have everything fixed in one month, I started to seek out some of the members of the Club from which I had stolen Celestine.

My first visit was to the hotel of the Count de C—, for the purpose of seeing Mademoiselle de C—, or Rosalie, as I shall call her, who having been my partner in the initiative act on the night of my admittance to the club, I felt a considerable partiality towards, and determined to transplant to the château as soon as everything was fitted up in it.

On entering the hotel I was told that the Count and his lady were out; enquiring for Rosalie, I was shown into the music room, where I found her seated at a harp.

On the servant disappearing she ran up to me, and threw herself into my arms. I led her to a sofa, and seating her on my knee, unfolded to her my intentions, stating what I had done and what I intended to do. Telling her how Celestine had accompanied me to Russia; how I had made a conquest of the charming Caroline; how I had brought them both to France, and left them at the château. I urged her by all the powers of persuasion I could employ to go with me to the château, where her life would be one continued round of luxurious pleasure.

She gave her consent to accompany me as soon as I had everything prepared for her reception.

During our conversation I was pressing and moulding her breasts, and as the dialogue gained interest my hand became more bold, and roamed everywhere.

When I had finished talking I found that in my absent-mindedness I had lain her down on the sofa, and was preparing to put her attentions of love to the proof, when an infernal servant opened the door to announce a visitor.

Ach, cursed luck! thought I, as we settled ourselves, to be thus interrupted at such a crime. But on seeing the lady enter my grief was changed to joy, for she was certainly the most voluptuous and beautiful creature my eyes ever looked on. With what dignity, what grace she crossed the room. What graceful ease reigned in every motion. A well-turned ankle, a pretty little foot, that noiselessly tripped across the floor, gave me a very good good opinion of what was to be found above the garter.

Rosalie introduced the lady to me as Laura, daughter of the Count de B—. Seeing there was no further opportunity of paying my compliments privately to Rosalie, I took my leave to make other calls.

I spent some six or eight days in Paris, leaving orders with jewellers and silversmiths for every variety of fancy articles, not forgetting to have my banker write to his agent in London, to procure me a swift sailing yacht of the largest size, fitted up in the richest manner, without regard to cost, and to be manned with a crew and willing to do any service I might name. She was ordered to be sent to the château on the coast of Brittany, where a small creek, putting in from the open sea, made an excellent harbour for a vessel.

Having finished my business, I hastened down to the château, taking with me a first-rate architect and a number of workmen.

In a short time I had converted a large saloon on the second floor into a magnificent hall. Its sides and ends were covered with flowers and evergreens, making a perpetual summer. On each side stood a row of statues of nude figures, which I had purchased in Paris. At either end played a beautiful fountain while in the centre was a large marble basin, in which played a third fountain. The figure that cast up the water was a statue of a female lying down, so arranged that she seemed to be floating on her back in the water; the *jet d'eau* burst from her cunt, and ascended nearly to the ceiling, making a shower bath for anyone who might be seated on the figure.

The side windows opened on to a balcony, which overlooked the sea.

On the opposite side of the corridor I had converted the whole suite of apartments into one large room, which as soon as the upholsterer arrived was to be furnished with fifty beds.

The suite of apartments on the same floor of the adjoining wing I had converted into one large bathing room. In this room was a marble bath, in which fifty people could bathe at the same time. A small fish pond stood in the garden. It turned into a small lake of about one hundred yards in diameter.

## Chapter Six

In the course of a few weeks a vessel arrived in the creek, laden with furniture for the château, and the upholsterer presented himself to me. I took him through the building, showing him in what style I wished such and such rooms furnished.

The room of fountains was simply furnished with cushions of rich satin and silk, and musical instruments, as I intended it merely for smoking, singing, and dancing.

The other long room opposite was furnished with bedsteads of finest rosewood, inlaid with gold, silver, pearl, and even precious stones. Each bed had springs placed in it, and was stuffed with the finest down. The sheets were cambric of the finest texture, coverlets of silks and satins, beautifully worked, while over all was a spread of Brussels or point lace.

The curtains were of crimson velvet, set off with white silk. In the alcove of each bed was placed a mirror, set in a frame of silver.

The floor was covered with the richest carpets; the walls were hung with silk, on which were worked the loves of Cupid and Psyche, the rape of Europa, Leda ravished by Jupiter in the shape of a swan, Diana issuing from the bath, a procession of naked female Bacchanalians carrying the jolly gods in triumph on their shoulders, and other devices.

Instead of chairs and sofas there were cushions placed in the room, worked with pearls and precious stones, bordered with fringe of pure bullion.

Each bed stood on a raised dais of mahogany. The carpets were of the richest texture, so soft and thick that the foot sank ankle deep in them. At the far end was the state bedchamber; it was partitioned off from the other parts of the room by a curtain of blue velvet.

This apartment was furnished as a Turkish tent, the drapery (of green velvet) depending from a centrepiece of gold stars and being drawn down to the sides so as to form a perfect tent.

The bed stood in the centre of the place, it was made of beautifully carved cedar from Lebanon; the posts, head and foot boards were ornamented with designs of birds, fishes, men and women, etc., of pure gold and silver, set with precious stones. Curtains of richly wrought velvet, looped up with chains of gold, completed the *coup d'œil*.

I had placed no ornament in this apartment, so it was designed as an initiatory bed for all the beauties I could bring to the place. And although licentious pictures, statues, etc., may have an exhilarating effect upon men at times, they also, by their beauty, attract the attention from the dear creatures we might be enjoying.

Adjoining this large bedchamber I furnished a dressing-room. The walls and ceiling were inlaid with large plate mirrors, making the room one complete looking-glass. At the sides, overhead, no matter where they might look, whosoever entered it could see nothing but their reflections.

Here were placed stands and toilette table, of chased gold and silver, ivory, and pearl: all the perfumes of the East, all the cosmetics that could enhance the beauty, and give youth and fullness to those who inhabited the place, were here in profusion.

Adjoining the room of glasses was a drawing-room which looked out on the garden. The doors and windows opened on to a balcony running the full length of that side of the castle. To this room I paid more attention than to any other. The floor was covered with a carpet of purple velvet, stuffed with down. The rarest productions of the old masters adorned the walls, mirrors, framed in gold, depending from the beaks of birds wrought in silver, hung between the paintings. In each corner of the room stood a statue of one of the Graces, in the body of which was set a music box, made to discourse the sweetest music. On stands of alabaster were large vases, *chefs d'œuvre* of Dresden manufacture, containing sweet smelling flowers; while the richest spices and perfumes of Araby, burning in censers entirely concealed in niches in the wall, diffused through the room odours that enchanted the senses.

Here it was that I received my mistresses after all the rooms were furnished.

During the time the workmen were busy arranging the rooms and furniture, I had kept them in a distant wing of the château, refusing to see them till everything was finished. I had secured the services of a dozen or more lusty fellows and wenches, to serve as servants and guards to those I might wish to detain.

One of the men I made the servant of the bedchamber – so called, as he was the only male I allowed in this part of the castle. Him I sent to bring me La Rose d'Amour and the voluptuous Russian, with Rose, Manette and Marie.

When they entered I was reclining on a pile of cushions, dressed in a loose robe of rich cashmere, with a Turkish cap on my head, ready prepared for a bath, to which I intended to take them.

So soon as the door was closed on them they ran up, and falling on me, devoured me with embraces and kisses. Oh, how they caught fire at the touch of me, burned for that which I had kept them from more than a month, whilst I could scarcely restrain myself from throwing them on the floor and darting the liquid flame of love into them at once. But I restrained myself.

I took them into the garden of flowers, and showed them all my improvements there, the beautiful little lake surrounded with shrubs and trees, over the whole surface of which was a net of fine wire, which confined a quantity of rare birds.

Again we entered the château, and passed through to the bed-chamber, where I showed them the fifty beds, telling them I intended to travel till I had procured fifty of the handsomest women in the world to lie in them.

From this we passed on to the bathing-room, and throwing off all covering, plunged into the perfumed waters.

After lying and wantoning in the bath for some time, I pulled the tassel of a bell, and four of the wenches I before mentioned entered to serve as waiting-maids.

We emerged from the water, and they dried our bodies and hair, and being given loose gowns, we wrapped ourselves in them, and I led my beauties to the dressing-room.

I cannot depict their astonishment on entering this apartment of mirrors. Taking their gowns, I threw them out of the door and closed it. I told them to dress in the rich clothes which lay before them.

How great was their astonishment to see themselves reflected a thousand times in the walls and ceiling! The toilet stands seemed to be in every part of the room, and it was some time ere they could get over the confusion they were in, but with the help of one another they got dressed. The dresses I had provided for them were those used by the Turks – wide, loose pants and waistcoats of satin, and short skirts, instead of the unhandy long shift.

After having dressed ourselves, I took them to the room of fountains, where we had a rich lunch. Here I opened to them my views, telling them that after one more trip to Paris, as soon as the yacht arrived which I had ordered, I intended to sail for Constantinople, where I would buy some of the most beautiful girls I could find, and also that I intended to purchase some mutes and eunuchs for my own harem, as I could not trust the females I might buy and bring with me the same as I could the ones that were now around me.

I told them I intended to take one or two of them with me in the vessel when I went, and that to be perfectly fair and impartial they should draw to see who should be the lucky ones; and also that I intended to have two of them sleep with me that night, and they must draw for that too.

I had determined beforehand that I would sleep with Celestine and Caroline, so I arranged the drawing that it came out as I wished.

At an early hour I led the way to the bedroom, followed by the five girls. It took us but a moment to put ourselves in a state of nakedness.

Oh, with what joy, what transports, I hugged their warm naked bodies to mine! How delightfully the soft, smooth, white skin of their bellies felt as they twined about in my arms! With what fervour did they fasten their moist, pouting lips to mine, while their lustrous eyes sparkled and flashed with lustful fires.

I draw the voluptuous Celestine to the bed. My passions are raised to the highest pitch. My prick is swelled almost to bursting, its vermilion head stands erect against my belly, not to be bent without danger of breaking.

Celestine is on her back, her thighs apart, showing the lips of her luscious cunt slightly open, anxiously awaiting the attack.

I precipitate myself upon her; I pierce her to the very quick. She screams with mingled pain and pleasure.

The enormous head of my prick distends the folds and lips of her cunt to their utmost stretch. The storm increases, everything trembles, the lightnings flash. the rain pours, it comes in torrents! I spend! I die! My God, what pleasure! Oh, heavens, have mercy!

We rolled, we screamed, we bit, we yelled like demons from the excess of our pleasure. Her cunt is a small lake of sperm, my prick swims in it, lolling its length. I draw it out, and the pearly liquid gushes forth, flooding her thighs and the sheets with the rich mingled essence of our bodies.

Ah, my charming Celestine, what an excess of exquisite pleasure did I experience whilst in your arms that night. Thrice did I, goaded by my fierce lusts, bedew the cunts of my two noble mistresses with a deluge of the precious liquid, bountifully supplied by the stream of pleasure from love's reservoir.

I recovered myself a little, and paid a visit to Rose, Manette, and Marie, to each of whom I did justice, always advancing to the attack with head erect and flying colours. Nor did I leave one of them without having well oiled their precious little maws with the dear liquid that women are ever looking for.

On the following morning I started for Paris, accompanied by Caroline, dressed as a page, to finish my preparation for starting to Constantinople.

After stopping at my hotel, I sallied out with my female page to call on Rosalie de C—, whom I was lucky enough to find alone.

Having embraced her, I introduced Caroline to her, asking when she would be ready to go with me to the château; she replied that she would be ready in two days.

I then enquired after her friend, the lovely Laura B—. I told Rosalie that I was determined to possess her friend Laura by some means or other, and that she must render me her assistance in securing her, and as I could think of no other plan, I proposed to Rosalie that she should go and get her friend to take an airing with her in the Bois de Boulogne, and that in a sequestrated place I would come up with them, alight from my carriage, and invite her and Laura to get out and take a walk, and that I would then throw a shawl over Laura's head, force her into my own carriage, take herself and Caroline, and set out with all possible speed for the castle.

Everything happened as I had arranged.

On coming up with Rosalie's carriage in the wood, I approached her with my invitation to walk.

I opened the door of the carriage, and as Laura passed out first, just as she reached the ground, Rosalie from behind threw a large shawl over her head, and drew the corners close around her neck, so that her voice could not be heard. I caught her up in my arms and carried her into my own carriage. Rosalie and Caroline entered immediately, and I dashed off with my fair prize at the top speed of four fine horses.

On the road to the château I stopped at no houses but those of persons whom I had brought over to my own interest.

Arrived at the place we stopped at for the night, I hurried with my companions into a large room prepared for us by a courier that I had sent in advance.

Immediately after my arrival supper was served. Dismissing all the attendants, I turned the key in the door, and for the first time since I had forced her into my carriage, I spoke to Laura.

I told her of my unconquerable love for her, of the feelings that were aroused in my heart towards her the first time that I saw her at Rosalie's house, and that I then formed the determination of carrying her off to the château. That I was determined no one else should be possessed of so much beauty, nor revel in such charms as she possessed.

I laid open to Laura all my plans. I informed her how I had fitted up the old castle, and for what purpose, telling her that she would there find Celestine C—, one of her old companions, and that Rosalie was another who willingly accompanied me.

I introduced her to Caroline Z—, telling her rank, how I had made a conquest of her, and how she had linked her fortune with mine, and followed me to France.

I dwelt at some length on the life of luxurious ease and pleasure we should lead at the château, expatiating on the endless joys and ecstasies of her living with me in all the unrestrained liberty of sexual intercourse.

Rosalie and Caroline also spoke to her of the life of pleasure they led with me, describing to her, as well as they could, the extreme luxury of lying in a man's arms and being well fucked; and used all their powers of persuasion to induce her to go with them and me peaceably to the château.

Laura, from being at first very sulky, neither eating nor speaking to any of us, became somewhat mollified, so that she partook of the supper, and answered questions put to her by my two mistresses.

After the supper was removed I called for wine, and while we sat talking and drinking I took care to make the discourse run principally upon one subject alone – that of love and its natural consequences, and the intercourse of the two sexes.

Caroline and Rosalie were very useful auxiliaries, talking with the utmost abandon, stripping and dancing about over the floor as the wine began to fly to their heads, uncovering their breasts, showing their bubbies, occasionally flirting up their petticoats, exhibiting a fine calf or knee, with other tricks, all of which tended to confuse the senses of the charming little Laura, who watched their movements all the while. I constantly plied her with wine till she became somewhat excited and a little free, making remarks on the two girls who were tussling on the floor.

I rang the bell, and ordered a bottle of white brandy, which, as soon as it was brought in, I uncorked, and pouring out glasses of it, invited my Russian to drink. She took up the glass, as did Rosalie, both declaring that Laura must drink with them. After some hesitation she took up her glass, and placing it to her lips, sipped a little of the liquor, and put it down.

Caroline and Rosalie, for the purpose of inducing the charming Laura to drink freely of the brandy, drank glass after glass of it, till Laura, from sipping, began to toss off her glass as well as any of us.

When I gave them the sign to retire for the night, Laura had become so intoxicated that she required the assistance of the other two to enable her to retire without staggering in her gait.

After they had got into their bedchamber, I stripped myself perfectly naked, and Caroline having left the door slightly ajar, I stepped into the room, hiding myself behind a bed curtain to observe the manoeuvres of my two lovely pimps.

They first undressed themselves stark naked, then did the same for the inebriated Laura. And then she stood in all her naked beauty before me, exhibiting charms to my ardent gaze, more lovely, if possible, than any I had heretofore ever enjoyed.

After my mistresses had stripped Laura of her clothes, they viewed and admired her naked beauty, praising it above that of the Venus de Milo, throwing her down on the floor, turning her over and over, squeezing her breasts, pinching her backside, opening her thighs, even the lips of the dear little niche between them. They praise its beauty, admire the lascivious plumpness of its lips, and even go so far as to lay their kisses upon it, the conversation running in praise, the while, on the pleasures she would mutually enjoy with the men who should be so lucky as to tear up the virgin defences which guarded the entrance to so delicious a little cunt.

I could now see Caroline insert the tip of her finger into the dear slit with which she was playing, and commence tickling her, while Rosalie threw her arms around her neck, and drawing her to a close embrace, kissed her, putting her tongue into Laura's mouth, which, with the frigging she was receiving from Caroline, caused her to experience the most delightful sensations, if I might judge from the exclamations and the wrigglings of her backside, as she squirmed about on the floor.

Perceiving, by the motions of Laura, that she would soon, for the first time, slightly experience the ecstatic joys which woman can only procure the full enjoyment of when in the arms of a man, I slipped out from my hiding place, and went and took the place of Caroline between her thighs (unperceived by Laura, whose face was hid in the bosom of Rosalie), and inserting my finger into her cream jug, I soon brought down a copious libation of the precious liquid with which my hand was plentifully bedewed, so freely did the liquid jet out once the sluice was opened. Crossing her thighs over my body she almost squeezed the breath from me, exclaiming in broken accents: 'Oh, now it comes! Again – oh, God! I faint. I die!'

Loosening her holds, she stretched herself out with, as usual, a gentle shudder, as the ecstasy caused her to faint away.

While Laura lay in her trance of pleasure I laid myself down in her arms, placing my cheek on her bosom, my lips touching hers, my hand still covering that dear slit, and my finger still retaining possession of its inner folds.

As I perceived Laura beginning to recover from her ecstasy, I drew her to my bosom and recommenced my titillations. I asked her if she was still angry with me for carrying her away, telling her that as soon as we arrived at the château she should enjoy all the reality of the unreal mockery she had just tasted through the agency of my fingers.

If her modesty and virtue were not entirely conquered, the motion of my finger reproduced in her the delicious sensations of pleasure from which she had just recovered, and which for the second time she was about to enjoy. She could make me no answer, but to throw her arms round my neck and glue her lips to mine.

My desires were excited to the highest pitch. I depicted to her the pleasure she would experience when, after arriving at the château, I should deflower her of her virginity, and triumphantly carry off her maidenhead 'on the head of this, dear Laura,' I said, as I took one of her hands and clasped it round my prick. 'Then,' said I, 'you will know all the joys of pleasures of a real fuck.'

'You will then,' I continued, 'experience all the sweet confusion, far different from what you now feel, of stretching wide apart your thighs to receive man between them, to feel his warm naked body joined to yours, the delicious preparatory toying with your breasts, the hot kisses lavished on them and on your lips, his roving tongue forcing its way between your rosy lips in search of yours, the delicious meeting of them, their rolling about and tickling each other as mine now does yours,' at the same time thrusting my tongue to meet hers.

'And then to feel him take his prick, and with the tips of his fingers part the lips of the flesh sheath into which he intends to shove it, putting the head of it between the lips, and gently shoving it in at first, stretching the poor little thing to its utmost extent, till, not without some pain to you, the head is effectually lodged in it. Then, after laying a kiss on your lips, he commences the attack by gently but firmly and steadily shoving into you, increasing his shoves harder and harder, till he thrusts with all his force, causing you to sigh and cry out, he thrusts hard, he gains a little at every move, he forces the barriers, he tears and roots up all your virginal defences, you cry out for mercy but receive none. His passions are aroused into madness, fire flashes from his eyes; concentrating all his energies for one tremendous thrust, he lunges forward, carries everything before him, and enters the fort by storm, reeking with the blood of his fair enemy, who with a scream of agony yields up her maidenhead to the conqueror, who, having put his victim *hors de combat*, proceeds to reap the reward of his hard fought and bloody battle.

'Now he draws himself out to the head, and slowly enters again. Again he draws out, and again enters, till the friction caused by the luscious tightness of the rich flesh which clasps tightly his foaming pego causes such delicious sensations that he is no longer master of himself.

'He lunges with fierceness into her, the crisis of pleasure approaches; he feels it coming, he drives it home to her – deeper, deeper. At last it comes – he spends.

'My God, the pleasure! His exclamations of Oh! ah!, the deep drawn sighs, the short jerks of his backside, the quick motions of his rump, proclaim that the acme of pleasure has seized him, and that he is spurting into her the precious fluid which oils and cools the burning itchings of the dear little cunt, which has undergone the one painful trial to which all your sex is liable.'

During my description Caroline had taken my pego in her hands, and had been playing with and rubbing it all the time. I still kept my finger in Laura, and perceiving by the twitching of her rump that she was about to spend –

'I – oh, dear – I – now – feel it. There, I come now, I spend. Ah, oh, oh, h – ha!' and I died away on her bosom, to awake and find that Laura had wet my hand with a most plentiful effusion of nectar ravished from her by my fingers, while I had squirted over her belly and thighs a flood of sperm.

Laura, without any murmurings, gave herself up to me and the seductive friggings of my fingers without any reserve, and not till nature was perfectly exhausted did we fall asleep in each other's arms.

In the morning, when Laura awoke and found herself lying in my arms, she sprang from my side, and snatching a coverlet from the bed, wrapped herself in it, and sat down in one corner, sobbing and weeping as though her heart would break.

I attempted to console her, but she would not listen to me, and having dressed myself I went into another room, while Caroline and Rosalie tried to bring her to herself again, and they succeeded so far as to bring her out to breakfast, which was shortly afterwards served.

At the table they rallied Laura for her coyness in the morning, after having spent so delightful a night with me, jesting her about my having procured for her with my finger the exquisite pleasure which had thrown her into such delicious swoons. Telling her how, when the fit was coming on her she would throw her arms round me, squeeze my hand between her thighs, wriggle her plump little buttocks, etc.

After having drank a few glasses of wine she had completely recovered her spirits.

I went out of the room to order the carriage, and on my return I found her tussling with the other girls, they trying to throw her down for the purpose of giving her a taste of the pleasure she had enjoyed so frequently through my agency during the night.

When I entered the two called me to come and help them, while Laura begged me to rescue her from the hands of her tormentors.

Whilst they were thus calling on me the landlord entered to announce the carriage, and taking Laura by the arm, I led her out, followed by the others. We entered the carriage and drove off.

It was late in the night when we arrived at the château, on the third day of our being on the road. I retired to bed and fell asleep, with all the girls sleeping around me, determined to touch none of them, reserving all the powers within me for the purpose of doing full justice to the maidenhead of the lovely Laura.

## *Chapter Seven*

The morning after our arrival, on awakening, I roused up the sleeping beauties who lay around me, and led them to the bathing-apartment.

We all entered the water, and after sporting for an hour or more, we issued from it, and entering the dressing-room, made our morning toilets, the girls dressing in cymar, pants and waistcoat, such as are worn by the odalisques in the East.

This day was made all preparations on a splendid scale for the great sacrifice of the night, the taking of Laura's maidenhead.

We spent the time in roving about the park until noon: running, jumping and tussling, so as to keep an excited circulation of the blood.

The dinner, which I had ordered three hours later than usual, consisted of all the most highly seasoned dishes and of the richest and most exhilarating wines, of which we partook to a slight excess and at last rose from the table with our amorous propensities aroused to the highest pitch.

We retired to the bedchamber, and stripping ourselves we again sought the bath, which was highly scented with the most costly perfumes.

Remaining but a short time in the bath, we went to the bedchamber, and Rose and Marie having drawn aside the heavy hangings, we entered the state-apartment. Here Celestine and Manette, with towels of the finest linen, absorbed the water from the body and hair of Laura, while Rosalie and Caroline did the same for me.

While they were combing out the rich auburn tresses which floated in wavy masses over her neck and shoulders, I was on my knees before her, combing out the black silken hair which grew, with a luxuriance seldom seen in girls of seventeen, out of the fattest little hillock I ever saw and almost hid the entrance to the beautiful grotto beneath.

Having combed out her precious locks, *comme il faut*, and parted them from around the mouth of the greedy little maw, which was shortly and for the first time to partake and eat of the flesh, with the tips of my fingers I open the pouting lips and feast my eyes with gazing on the deep carnation of the luscious love-niche, in which I was soon to put the idol. I peep, gaze, look and try to get a further insight into the hidden mysteries of the deep, dark, cavernous recess; but my sight could penetrate no further than a most tempting bit of flesh, somewhat in the shape of a heart, which appeared to be pendant, like a dazzling light from the ceiling of a room, in the centre of the passage to the unexplored cavern, through the folding doors of which I was peeping.

My enraptured eyes still gaze on the tempting titbit before me, till, recalled to my senses by feeling something moving between my thighs, and looking down, I perceive the hand of Celestine clasped around my noble shaft, and slowly drawing her hand up and down it, covering and uncovering its beautiful red head with the fine white skin which lay around the neck in folds.

This at once gave an impetus to my desires, which could not be restrained. I raised up, and catching Laura in my arms, I carried her to the bed and placed her on it, the firm semi-globes of her backside resting on the edge of the bed, supported by a cushion of white satin, covered with an embroidered cloth of fine linen.

Celestine and Caroline support each a leg, while Rose and Marie jump on to the bed, and Manette and Rosalie stand on either side to support me, in case my feelings should overpower me at the close of the performance, and also to serve as pilots for me – the one to open the gate of love, the other to guide the fiery dart aright into the entrance.

Fearing somewhat for the little maid, who was to undergo the process of defloration, and knowing that the rose was not without its thorn and that the sting would at first be pretty severe, I anointed my impatient virgin-destroyer with perfumed oil, and marched to the battlefield, determined to conquer or to die.

Her legs were held apart. I enter between and plant a soft kiss on the lips which I was about cruelly to tear open, which seemed to send a thrill of joy through her.

I slightly incline forward; the tips of Manette's fingers part the rosy lips. Rosalie grasps hold of my pego and lodges the head in the entrance.

The two girls, who support her legs, rest them on my hips, and standing behind me, cross their arms with joined hands so that the ankles rest on them as on a cushion. Gathering myself up, I make one fierce lunge forward and gain full an inch.

The sudden distention of the parts causes her to scream with pain and to wriggle her rump in a manner that, instead of in any way ridding herself of me, helps me in my endeavours to penetrate still further.

I thrust harder, I penetrate, I pierce her. The blood begins to flow. I feel it on my thighs. Her buttocks are convulsively twitching and wriggling in endeavours to throw me off. In her agony she utters scream after scream.

Poor little maid, it is a rough and thorny way to travel. But once gone over, the road is ever after smooth. Again I thrust forward.

'Ah, my God!' she exclaims, 'I shall die! Have mercy on me!'

I have no pity on her and shove harder than ever to put her out of her pain and agony. I tear her open, carrying everything before me, and one last shove sends me crowned with victory into the very sanctum of love amidst the clapping of hands and the shouts of triumph by those who surround us.

No sooner was I buried in her to the extremest point than I lay quivering and gasping on her belly, spending into her womb a flood of boiling sperm.

I soon regained new life and vigour, and drawing myself out to the head, commenced a to-and-fro friction that caused no more than a few 'ahs' and deep-drawn sighs, as the sperm I had injected into her had oiled the parts and made the way comparatively easy for the dear creature who lay under me.

She now receives my thrusts and shoves with a slight quivering of her rump. She clasps me in her arms, she closes her eyes. A few energetic heaves and the dear girl feels the pleasure, despite that pain that a woman experiences in having drawn from her for the first time by a man the milk of human kindness.

I too meet her and again melt away in her, fairly drenching her with the copious draughts of the liquid I spurt into her.

At last I rise up from off my lovely victim, leaving her a bleeding sacrifice on the altar of love.

The girls gathered around Laura congratulating her on being transformed from a maid into a woman. The entrance being forced, she could henceforth drive into the boundless pleasures and joys of love without feeling pain.

They raised her up whilst cleaning her of the blood that dyed her thighs and buttocks, I took up the consecrated cushion and its bloody covering and directed one of them to prepare the bed for us. I – but no. I determined to give her a little rest, and ordering the girls to prepare a cold supper, told them to awake me in two hours, and we fell asleep in each other's arms.

After sleeping for some time, Laura awoke much refreshed, but still feeling sore from the severe battering she had received.

The table being laid alongside the bed, we reclined on it, the others sitting around the table on cushions.

Not feeling much inclined to eat, I commenced dallying with my bedfellow, railing her on the feelings she experienced while I was taking her maidenhead, till the spirit began to wax powerful within me, whereupon I laid her down flat on her back and fell with my face downward upon her, and thence followed where the spirit moved. Yes, verily, we did mighty deeds of fucking that night, and it was not until after the sixth operation, or moving of the spirit, that we lay exhausted in each other's arms and fell asleep.

In a few days after there arrived at the mouth of the creek a fine large steam-brig, which dropped anchor and sent a boat ashore with the captain, who delivered me a letter from my banker, stating who and what the officers and crew were and upon what terms they had been engaged.

I immediately walked down to the creek and going into the boat with the captain, was soon taken on board. I examined her decks, masts, etc., and then descended to the cabin, which extended my most sanguine expectations, so magnificently was it fitted up. The cabin contained six state-rooms, very large and splendidly fitted up, equalling in style and ornament the most elegant boudoir I had ever seen in Paris.

I questioned the captain, who was English, as well as the whole crew, in regard to the men on board.

He said that he and his men had been employed to serve me in any way I might think proper, so long as I did not command him to commit piracy. That he and the crew were paid enormous wages, and that they were bound and felt ready and willing to follow me to 'heaven or hell', if I but showed them the way.

On questioning the stewards, I found the brig to be well stored with all the luxuries that could be procured.

I ascended to the deck with the captain, and passing the word forward for all hands to come aft, I had a crew of most hardy and devil-may-care looking fellows around me in a trice, standing respectfully, hats in hand.

I made them a short address, laying open to them my intentions, and stating the service I required of them.

I gave the captain his orders to be in readiness to sail in two days and I returned to the château.

Summoning the steward I directed him to prepare everything for our voyage, as I determined to start in two days for Constantinople.

I then directed a page to send the women to me.

On their entering, I made them all strip to the skin and examined the cunts and several charms of each of them with a critical eye, endeavouring when all were most lusciously beautiful to select one as my *compagnon de voyage*; but not being able to choose among so many loves I left it to chance.

Taking up a dice-box, I made each throw in her turn. La Rose d'Amour and my fair Russian, Caroline, made the highest throws and I determined to take both.

After they had cast their dies, I informed them what my object was. Whereupon, Laura, my last love, who by the by was a great libertine, fell on her knees before me weeping, and begged me to take her with me.

It was impossible for me to take more than two, I told her, that it was no use to grieve about the matter as she could not go, but that I would pass all my remaining time with her.

Leaving the château in the care of my trusty stewards and followers, I embarked, taking with me over one million francs in gold, for the purpose of purchasing slaves in Constantinople.

# *Chapter Eight*

After a pleasant voyage of about two weeks, I arrived at the capital of the Turkish Empire.

At the earliest opportunity I presented my letters to some of the most wealthy and influential foreigners under a fictitious name.

I soon became acquainted with many wealthy Turks and among them three or four slave-merchants.

I then hired an interpreter, and paying a visit to one of the merchants, engaged him as an agent to find out and procure me a lot of the handsomest females to be found in the market. And knowing that the poor class of the inhabitants were in the daily habit of selling their daughters, such as were handsome enough to grace the harems of the rich and lustful Turks, I directed him to send out some of his emissaries to search out all the families among the poor quarters who had beautiful girls and who would be apt to exchange them for gold.

In the course of a few days my agent called on me, stating that he was about to go on a three days' trip from the city to the house of an old broker-merchant of his who was continually in receipt of girls from the interior of the kingdom, and occasionally of a few from Circassia. That for certain reasons he never came to the city, but on receipt of any new beauties he always wrote, and he, my agent, went to his place of residence and either bargained for or took the females to Constantinople and sold them on commission.

He said that when I first called on him he wrote to his correspondent in the country, who replied that he had several very fine girls, one in particular whom he named Ibzaidu, who, he said, was fit to adorn the harem of the Grand Sultan. I told my agent, Ali Hassan, to start immediately and to bring the lot, if they were beautiful, to the city.

In the interim of his absence, attended by my interpreter, I sauntered day and night through the streets and bazaars, endeavouring to spy out some of the beauties of the place; but all in vain. I could not catch even a glimpse of a female face.

On the evening of the ninth day from his leaving me, Ali called on me, saying that he had brought with him seven slaves, who were safe in his harem, and invited me to call at his house in the morning and examine them.

He ran perfectly wild in his praises of Ibzaidu, whom he pronounced to be more beautiful than a houri, the *ne plus ultra* of Circassian beauty.

About eleven o'clock the following day, I went to Ali's house and immediately entered on business.

He retired for a few minutes to give orders for the slaves to prepare for my visit.

In the course of half an hour a eunuch entered, made a salaam to his master, and retired.

Ali arose, and inviting me to follow, led the way into a large and elegantly furnished apartment in his harem.

On entering, I beheld six girls seated on the cushions at one side of the room, dressed in loose Turkish pants of white satin and waistcoats of rich embroidered stuff.

In the centre of the room was a couch and at one end of it stood two eunuchs. After surveying them as they sat, and noting their different styles of beauty – knowing it to be customary – I told Ali that I wished to examine them in a perfectly naked state to ascertain if they were still virgins, as he represented them to be. And also that I wished to see if the several parts of their bodies corresponded in beauty with their faces.

He immediately led one of them out on the floor beside me, and spoke a few words to her and the others in Turkish. I then made a sign for him and the eunuchs to go out and leave me alone with the females.

They retired, and taking hold of the girl's hand, I signed her to strip, which she refused to do. I entreated and urged her as well as I could by signs to do so; but she crossed her hands over her breast, refusing to do it. I clapped my hands and Ali and his eunuchs entered. I merely nodded my head to him and he pointed his finger at the girl and the eunuchs caught hold of her and in a trice stripped her naked. I then went up to her, laid my hand on her firm round bubbies, pressed and moulded them, felt her waist, rubbed my hand lower down, on to the mossy covering of her cunt; she sprang from me and catching up some of her clothes, wrapped them round her body, and sat down in one corner.

Ali stamped his foot on the floor, and the eunuchs took her and carrying her threw her on her back on the couch.

One held her down by the shoulders, while the other caught hold of one leg and Ali of the other, stretching them wide apart, I fell on my knees between them, and with my fingers opened the lips of her cunt. On attempting to insert one of them into it, and finding that I could barely force the tip in without causing her to wince and cry out and to twist her backside about, I desisted, firmly persuaded that she had her maidenhead inviolate.

Whilst they held her on the couch, I examined, felt, and kissed every part of her; and having provided myself with such things on purpose, I placed on her wrist, neck and finger, a bracelet, necklace and ring. Upon a sign they let her rise, and being given her clothes, she dressed and sat down much pleased with and examining her jewels.

I now led out another girl, and made a sign for her to undress which she took no notice of, standing with her arms crossed, and her head hanging down. I took her hands and removing them from her breasts proceeded to take off her waistcoat, and as she did not resist, I told Ali and his slaves to go out and wait outside the room.

I then stripped her of her pants and cymar and was much pleased with her beauty. I led her up to the couch and sitting down drew her to my side, handling her breasts, feeling her arms, belly, thighs, twining my fingers about in the luxurious growth of hair that overgrew the grotto underneath, to all of which she made no resistance.

At last I laid her down on her back and spreading her thighs apart, inspected her cunt, and found she was still possessed of all the signs of virginity. I also gave her jewels, such as I gave the first one, and inspected the balance in the same manner, picking out one after one.

Two I found not to be virgins, and one was bandy-legged although handsome in every other respect.

I called in Ali and enquired where the beautiful Ibzaidu was, desiring him to bring her to me.

Ali clapped his hands and two female slaves entered leading her in. Then they retired leaving her standing before me. She was enveloped in a piece of fine Indian muslin and had a veil over her face.

I raised the veil and started back in amazement at the dazzling beauty of her face.

I then caught hold of the drapery in which she was enveloped, and gently drawing it from her clasp, I threw it on one side and gazed with admiration on the most ravishingly beautiful form and figure I ever beheld.

Hers was one of those oval majestic figures, such as poets and mythologists attribute to Juno.

I much admired her rich jet-black hair which clustered in ringlets over her neck and shoulders, contrasting singularly with the dazzling whiteness of her skin. Her shoulders were finely formed and her arms, plump and beautifully rounded, would cause a sigh of desire to arise in any breast, to be clasped in their embrace. Her breasts, luxuriously large, hard and firm, white as snowflakes, were tipped with deliciously small nipples, of that fine pink colour which so strongly denotes virginity in the possessor.

Her waist was gracefully elegant and tapering; her belly fine, round, and with the whiteness of alabaster, soft as the finest velvet down. Her hips were very large and wide, whilst her buttocks swelling out behind in two hillocks of snowy-white flesh, firm and springy to the touch, gave token of the vivacity and liveliness with which their owner would enter into the delicious combats of love.

Her thighs were of a largeness and fleshy plumpness seldom seen in a female, with the knees small, while the calf was large, in proportion to the thigh. The ankle tapering, and a foot delicately small, spoke plainly to the looker-on that the seat and centre of love, that dear part of woman which takes away the senses of all men, was of equally small and elegant pattern.

Her chin was most charmingly dimpled, her lips, full and pouting, slightly open, gave just a glimpse of two rows of ivory, which appeared set in the deep rosy flesh of her small and elegant mouth. Her nose was of the Grecian cast, her eyes of a sparkling lustrous black, and the forehead was middling high. She was, in fact, the very *beau idéal* of female beauty.

What ease and grace reigned in every part. With what a sylphlike springy motion she moved, as I led her towards the couch on which I stretched her out. There I examined minutely all her secret charms. I felt and handled every part.

Her cunt was ravishing, beyond all description. The mossy mount of Venus swelled up into a hillock of firm flesh, surmounted and covered with rich, mossy, coal-black hair, straight and fine as silk. The lips were most luscious, fat, rosy, pouting beauties. On opening them. I felt for her clitoris and found it to be extremely large, while the orifice was narrow and small indeed, apparently not larger than a girl's of eleven or twelve years of age.

'God of love!' I exclaimed on viewing it, 'here is a maidenhead that might have tempted Jupiter from Olympus, a prophet from the arms of the houris in Paradise, or an anchorite from his cell.'

Handling and examining so many lovely things had set me on fire and I could hardly restrain myself from immolating her on the altar as a sacrificial offering to the god of voluptuous love.

I drew myself away from her and signed her to rise up and resume her drapery.

I then concluded the bargain for the purchase of Ibzaidu, and for the other three I had chosen.

After settling with Ali, I told him that he must let me have the use of a part of his house, including the harem, during my stay, so that I should be able to guard safely my slaves and to have for them proper attendance. Also, that he must instantly purchase for me six or eight mutes and eunuchs, which he immediately set about, whilst I returned to my house to get my money, jewels, etc., and also to bring away Caroline and her companion.

# *Chapter Nine*

In the evening I had arranged everything and was seated on a pile of cushions in one of the apartments of Ali's harem, my head reclining on the breast of the voluptuous Circassian, Ibzaidu, or Cluster of Pearls, as her name signified, surrounded by my other slaves whom I gave to Ibzaidu for servants; she, I was determined, should reign supreme until such time as I should find someone more beautiful.

I had opened my caskets of jewels, and adorned her wrists, arms, neck, head and ankles with massy jewels of gold of Western and Oriental work-manship, and it seemed that she would never tire of looking at and playing with them as a child would with a painted bauble.

Before night my host came in, bringing with him mutes and eunuchs, and he showed me through the suite of apartments devoted to my service, one of which I found to be a bedchamber, fitted up with the utmost elegance, containing twenty single beds.

Here it was that I slept among my concubines, or rather I should say that I lay with them, for I deserted all the others with whom I ought to have had sexual connection to repose in the arms of Ibzaidu, who, when she saw me advancing to her bedside, stretched out her arms to me and kicking off the cover, moved to the further side of the bed to make room for me.

I entered her bed, and lay with my cheek resting on her bosom the night long. And although my prick was in splendid condition, firm and erect as a rod of ivory, yet I never once thought of letting it force an entrance through the delicate and narrow passage into the inner court of the temple of love.

I spent about three weeks before I met with any more prizes, partly in the city, part of the time at the villa of Ali's on the banks of the Bosphorus in the company of Ibzaidu alone, leaving the other females in the city, under the care of the eunuchs.

During one of my visits at the villa, I was surprised one evening, while walking along the terrace of the garden, to see Ali dashing up the road at full speed, mounted on a full-blood Arabian. I descended to the gate and met him, to enquire the news, thinking that something might be wrong at the house I occupied in the city.

On enquiring, I was excitedly informed that there was a large lot of females to be sold in a few days, by order of the Grand Sultan.

Ali said they were the females composing the harem of some officer of the State who had been dead about one year, whose only heirs, two nephews, had been quarrelling about the possession of them ever since and that the Sultan had just ordered them to be sold and the proceeds to be divided among the two heirs; and he said that from reports circulating in the city, there must be some beautiful slaves amongst them, and he advised me to start directly for my own house, and that he would by bribery manage to get me a private interview with them, so that I could examine them at my leisure and choose such as I would like to have, and on the day of sale he would purchase them for me.

On the succeeding day I accompanied Ali to the house of the trader in whose keeping were the slaves.

The trader met us at the door, and took me at once into a room in which were the females. They were all enveloped in large white drapery which covered them from head to foot.

Mustapha, the trader, spoke to them, and they arranged themselves in a row round the room, then he retired, telling me that as soon as he left the room, they would all drop their mantles, and I could examine them at leisure.

Leaving me, he went out, locking the door behind him.

As I steppped up to the female nearest me she cast her covering behind her. So did the others and I feasted my eyes with a picture of voluptuousness greater than I had ever dreamt of.

There stood before me about sixty females, perfectly naked, who I think could not be excelled in any harem in the East. There were the women of Circassia with their dark flowing tresses, eyes of piercing black and skin of dazzling whiteness, mostly contrasted by the deep carnation of their lips, the nipples of their breasts and the jet-black, bushy hair that surmounted their cunts. Again, there were the languishing mild blue-eyed beauties ravished from the isles of Greece, and the voluptuous Georgians; even Africa had yielded up her sable beauties to the lusts of the sometime owner of all the lovely slaves who stood about me.

I minutely criticised each one separately, going over their respective claims to beauty with the eye of a connoisseur. Oh, how I feasted my sight on the row of lovely, luscious cunts that ran around the room. I look at, feel, touch them all, and stroke down the bushy hair that surrounds their notchs.

I became so much excited from the handling of so many cunts that I put my arm around the waist of one charming little creature, who by her looks must have been a great libertine, and led her into a small side-apartment where, presenting her with a fine gold chain which I wore, I laid her down on a pile of cushions, and twice gave her to experience the most ecstatic pleasures before I got off her.

I gave her some time to recover from the confusion I had thrown her into, ere we returned to the apartment in which the women were standing; they took no further notice of our return than to raise their heads and to look at the chain which I had hung around her neck.

I marched the one I had just been fucking with to one side and picked out ten others, among which number was one black, a young African about fifteen years of age, who still retained her virginal rose, and who was, on the whole, the most voluptuously formed female I had ever seen and apparently better fitted for enjoying the pleasure of love than any female in my possession. Her hair was quite straight and black as a raven's wing; her breasts were full and large, as though of ebony. Her waist was slender, while her hips were spread out to a width I had never before seen. Her thighs were of a largeness to put to shame anything I had ever lain with.

Having stood on one side those whom I wished to purchase, I called in the merchant and Ali and showed them to him, and as the sale was to take place the following day, I ordered him to be punctual in attendance to purchase them for me and left.

On the following day by noon Ali had conveyed to my apartments all the slaves that I had chosen that night. I put four of them to the test, giving them, for the first time, to know the difference between lying in an old goat of a Turk's arms to that of being well fucked by a young and lively Frenchman, overflowing with the precious aqua-vitae, which all women are so greedy after.

I now spent about two weeks in enjoying these new beauties that I had bought, with the exception of those who had not been deflowered of their virginal rose by the horny-headed old lecher, their late master, and those were but three out of the number.

Whilst I was thus idling away my time in the arms of my handsome slaves, my interpreter called on me one morning, and on being admitted into my presence told me that he had found one of the loveliest girls in Constantinople in the house of a poor mechanic and that on enquiry he had refused to part with her on any account, or for any amount of money; but he said it might be just possible to steal her off, if I was so inclined.

I promised him a large sum if he would procure her for me, and calling on Ali, my agent consulted with him as to the best means of bringing her off.

They agreed to go and stay about the house at night, until they saw the old man go out, and then, with the assistance of a couple of eunuchs, rush into the house, gag her, carry her out, and put her into a litter and bring her to me, all of which I approved, promising them a rich reward if they succeeded.

It was not until the third night that they were able to carry her off and I was agreeably surprised while reclining in the arms of one of my lovely slaves to see a couple of my mutes come into my room bearing in their arms the beautiful stolen prize.

I took her out of their arms, and seating her on a cushion, I uncovered her face and took the gag from her mouth. I found her to be a lovely creature as far as I could see and I began stripping her so that I might have a full view of her naked and thus of all her hidden charms.

Oh! what charms, what beauty met my fiery glance.

I had to call on several of the women to help me hold her while I was feeling and admiring her charms. I burned with desire to enjoy her, I lavished my eager kisses on every part of her body. I fastened my lips to hers. I sucked the rosy nipples of her breasts; the lips of her cunt received more than their share.

I was about to throw myself on her, but reflecting that I had determined to reserve all that had their maidenheads till after my return to France, I sprang from her, threw myself in the arms of Celestine and buried myself up to the hilt in her, just in time to prevent the liquor from spurting all over the floor.

Shortly after, Ali got me two more females, both of whom had been taken from one of the isles of the Hellespont.

I had now nearly run out of money and was preparing to start home, when, by accident, I found that Ali was reputed to have a daughter more beautiful than any female in Constantinople, and I determined to wait a while and get possession of her by some means or other.

I had not money enough left to think of offering a sum large enough to tempt his cupidity, so I made all arrangements to steal her off, for which purpose I despatched him into the country.

The same day I found out the part of the house in which Ali had shut up his daughter in the hopes of keeping her from my sight; and I made everything ready for stealing her off the same night as soon as it was dark.

I sent all my baggage and the females with the eunuchs and the mutes on board the brig. I got a litter, and with the assistance of the interpreter whom I largely paid to aid me in the enterprise, I succeeded in gaining the apartment of Selina, whom I saw to be asleep. Without any noise we gagged her and putting her into the litter soon had her on board the brig with my other treasures, whereupon we instantly steered out of the harbour and made all haste; nor did I think myself in perfect safety until we floated once more in the Mediterranean.

Selina, on being released, at first made a great outcry at being carried off, and I kept out of her sight until we had been under weigh a couple of days, when the sea-sickness had tamed her wondrously, and I could approach her without having torrents of abuse and Turkish execrations heaped on my head. In fact, the whole of my passengers were sick, with the exception of Caroline, Celestine, and the Nubian slave.

These three attended the rest, till they got over their sea-sickness, which was not until the third or fourth day with some. Then all was mirth, jollity, luscious love.

After all were perfectly recovered, we ran up to a small, verdant but uninhabited island in the Mediterranean and lay to for one day and night.

In the evening I had let down into the water a very large sheet of canvas, made on purpose, supported at the corners by the yard-arms of the vessel, with the intention of letting the women have a bath. Ordering them to change their rich dresses for pants and shirts of plain white cotton, I took them on deck and having stationed the sailors in the boats a few yards distant from the canvas, I plunged them one after the other into the water in the belly of the sheet.

Here they amused and enjoyed themselves amazingly for an hour or more. They were then twisted up in an armchair, rigged for the purpose, and after dressing themselves, were again brought on deck, where they romped and played about like so many young kittens or monkeys.

Calling on a eunuch, I ordered him to bring up some musical instruments that I had procured in Constantinople.

Ibzaidu and two others played on the guzla and she sang some plaintive songs of home in a rich mellow voice that cast a sadness and gloom on the spirits of all, till Celestine seized the guitar and sang me some of the songs of our own dear France.

Thus we amused ourselves until late at night, having the supper brought up on the deck which we partook of by moonlight.

Stopping and enjoying myself by the way as I listed, it was nearly five weeks after sailing before I anchored in the harbour of the little creek close to the château in Brittany, where, after safely stowing away my goods, women, etc., I made preparation for that which you may know in the next chapter.

## *Chapter Ten*

The first thing I did after one day's rest was to assign the eunuchs and mutes I had brought with me to their separate duties, which consisted solely in guarding and attending the females, either when in their apartment or when roving about in the garden or shrubberies attached to the château, so that they were never from under the sight of some of the slaves.

After having made these arrangements I made preparations for giving a grand entertainment to the captain and the crew of the steamer, who had conducted themselves very much to my satisfaction during the voyage, never having once intruded or infringed their privileges, always acting with great delicacy.

On the evening in the Mediterranean that I had the women on the deck to bathe, the sailors would have all retired below had I not called them back and sent them in the boats, and now I determined to repay them their good conduct by giving them an entertainment fit for princes.

In the evening I sent word to the captain and the crew to come up to the castle. In half an hour they were admitted and having shut up the women in an apartment out of the way, I showed them through the shrubberies and garden, all of which they viewed with amazement, wondering at the richness and taste displayed in the fitting up of the castle of beauties, as they termed it.

About six o'clock a servant made his appearance saying that supper was ready. I had ordered the supper to be served in the hall of the fountains and led my guests there.

We entered and sat down at the tables and directly came trooping in all the females of my harem and seated themselves opposite to the men.

After the supper was over, Ibzaidu and some of the other women I had brought from Turkey took their instruments and gave us a concert of Oriental music. After which Caroline went to the piano, and Celestine sat down to a harp and played some brilliant and lively pieces of French and Italian music. Upon which, those of my lovely slaves who belonged to the Grecian isles got up and danced the romaika and other dances peculiar to the country.

They were followed by Ibzaidu and two other Circassians, who were attired in the costumes of their native land, and danced some of the native dances.

These were in their turn followed by the Georgians, after which came my sable mistress, the Nubian, dressed in petticoats reaching the knees with an overdress of fine blue gauze.

Her dance was wild and pleasing and in throwing herself about over the floor, as her legs were bare, she would show her thighs, her bare buttocks and sometimes her black bushy notch.

Celestine and Caroline rose up and stepped out on the floor to dance, and Laura sat down at the piano. They were dressed in short petticoats and dresses, the same as the Nubian, and performed some lascivious dances, showing every charm which nature had graced them with.

The officers and crew of the brig applauded the dancing very much.

About twelve o'clock I sent off the common seamen, retaining only the officers, five in number.

After the seamen left us the company became mixed, the officers sitting in the midst of the women, some of whom I had not frigged for a long time, and who looked with a wistful and longing eye on the men about them, and it was very clear to me that were I not present they would soon be engaged in the soft pleasures of love.

I clapped my hands and a couple of eunuchs entered and pointing out Rose, Marie, Manette and two others they led them away to an apartment I had fitted up with beds. Then I took leave of the officers, and the eunuchs took them to where they had put the five girls.

What a pleasant surprise to both parties! The men to find the beds occupied by the five girls and the girls to find the same number of men enter as there were of them. Oh, how they panted with the pleasure of the sight.

Instantly did they know why I had sent them to that apartment. After the men were gone I sent all the women to the chamber except a lovely Georgian, and repaired to an adjoining apartment to where the five couples were.

Here I had a place so constructed that I could see all that was going on in the other room without being seen.

After the men had got into the room they ran up to the beds and would have clasped the women to their breasts, but they all jumped out of bed naked, and began to undress the men, who were speedily divested of all clothing. Then what a scene of love followed!

The men threw the girls on the beds, and the girls opened wide their thighs as the men fell on their necks, and then jumped on them with pricks stiff as iron rods, piercing through the tender folds of the cunts under them, sending joy and pleasure to their very vitals, and I could judge from the exclamations and the writhing about, and the wriggling of backsides, the hot kisses and the amorous bites on the neck that not one but had received a double or triple dose of the sacred liquor injected into them. I think I never saw men and women fuck with greater zest, or derive more pleasure and enjoyment from frigging than they did.

Looking at them had such an effect on myself and companion that we were obliged to retire to the bedchamber for the purpose of enjoying ourselves in like manner.

In ascending a flight of stairs, my slave tripped, and falling hurt herself, so that on entering the room I had to seek another in whom to pour the extra liquor from the magic spring, and which was about to run over for the want of pumping.

The first bed I cast my eye on contained the luxurious Nubian slave, and I determined to offer up her maidenhead as the sacrificial gift to the god of love.

Approaching, I motioned her to rise and follow me to the state-bed whither I went.

We entered the bed together both stark naked, and placing her at once in a favourable position with a cushion under her large fat bottom, I lay my length on her and guiding the head of my prick tried to insert it between the lips of her slit, but could not succeed.

I got up, and oiling it well with ointment I again freed the entrance and succeeded in ripping and tearing up the works and barriers that defended her virgin rose, and found her a dish fit for the gods! Heavens! with what transports of delight did I squeeze her in my arms as I drove the arrow of love into the deepest recess of the luscious quivering flesh through which I had forced a passage for it.

Despite the pain which my forcible entrance into her must have caused, the moment I began working in her, Celeste, the name I had given her, began moving up to me with vigour, elasticity, and a sense of pleasure utterly impossible to be looked for in one in her situation.

So young, not quite fifteen, and she had a notch of such a lusciously tight smallness that even after entering her to the full length, it was with the utmost difficulty that I could work in and out of her; but with the suction caused by the tightness with which the flesh worked around the piston rod, I soon drew open the sluice of love's reservoir and thence gushed forth a stream of fiery fluid which completely drenched her inmost parts, causing a shudder of pleasure to run through her whole body that at once proclaimed to me that she was about to give proof of the joy and ecstasy with which she had received the terrible lance thrust which had given her such a wound and was causing her to pour down the essence of her very soul through the gaping orifice.

The oiling which her parts had received from the mutual flow of our sperm made the entrance somewhat easy, but still very tight.

Towards morning she began to realise the full enjoyment of the luscious pleasure of being well frigged as the folds of her cunt from the constant friction had stretched somewhat more, causing no more than a delicious tightness, perfectly agreeable to me and which greatly enhanced the pleasure, as the first three or four times that I entered her I found it too tight for the full enjoyment of perfect bliss, as it almost tore the foreskin off my pego when entering, thus causing pain which detracted from the pleasure.

In the morning when I descended to the breakfast table I found those whom I had sent to spend the night with the officers of the brig so sore that they could hardly walk from the tremendous battering they had received from their companions during the night.

I rode out through the surrounding country during the day and on my return in the evening in passing one of the rooms I heard considerable whispering, and listening I overheard one of the women in conversation with some men. I slyly opened the door and imagine my astonishment at beholding Caroline, Celestine, Rosalie and Laura in company with the four lubbery country-boors I had engaged at the château.

They were all lying on the floor, the girls with their clothes tossed up to their waists and the men with their pricks out of their breeches and the girls playing with them, trying to instil new life and vigour into the drooping instruments which had apparently just done good service.

Not being seen by them I retired, softly closing the door, to meditate on what I should do with the guilty ones.

After thinking over the subject for some time I came to the conclusion that I had no right to do or say anything on the subject, knowing that it was the instinct of nature which prompted them to act as they had done, and recollecting that I had promised to each of them that they should never want for that to which they were then treating themselves, I decided to say nothing about the matter, unless merely to give them all a severe fright.

After supper, as I was sitting in the midst of my girls in the hall of fountains, watching some of the Grecian women as they wound through the mazes of the voluptuous romaika, to the music of the guzla, I clapped my hands and four mutes entered.

I pointed out the four I had caught frigging with the servants and ordered the mutes to seize them.

They bound their wrists with silken sashes and led them up to me.

I put on a savage frown and accused them of having debased themselves to the embraces of menials.

This they denied and persisted in denying.

I ordered the mutes to strip them and taking a slender riding switch I began tapping Celestine with it on her bare buttocks very lightly just so as to cause them to blush till they became a beautiful carmine hue, mixed in with the clear alabaster, and they all four cast themselves on their knees before me and acknowledged their fault. I then told them that it demanded a more serious punishment and that they should receive it.

Now, I had ordered up from the village four of the finest-looking stout peasants to be found, and when I made a sign to the mutes they went out and returned leading them in blindfolded.

After they were in the room I conversed with them, and ordered some chocolate to be served which I had prepared with certain drugs that would cause their amorous propensities to rise every few minutes for four hours.

They were stark naked, and shortly after drinking, their lances stood erect against their bellies.

I then untied the wrists of the four girls and told them to lie down on cushions prepared for the purpose. I then led a man to each and put them in one another's arms, telling the men to go in. The men instantly mounted the women and for three hours kept them working in a dead heat.

Fourteen times did those men frig the women under them, changing women every now and then.

At first the women enjoyed it very much but at last got tired to death, perfectly worn out, battered and bruised to pieces, the lips of their slits gaping wide open, flabby and swollen, with a perfect little lake of sperm between their thighs.

As soon as I saw the chocolate begin to lose its effect on them I had them taken out and there lay the girls so befucked that they could hardly move hand or foot.

I myself was not idle during their performance, for I had three times dissolved myself in the Nubian slave. I spent the night in her arms, arising in the morning with the intention of husbanding myself for a couple of days, so as to be able to do justice to the maidenhead of Ibzaidu, which I intended sacrificing to my amorous and fierce desires.

## Chapter Eleven

On the evening of the second day after, I made grand preparations for the event about to be celebrated. I had an elegant supper served such as would have tempted old Epicurus himself. All the inmates of the seraglio were at the table and I plied them so well with wine that not one except Ibzaidu arose from it sober.

When I gave the signal for retiring to the bedchamber they reeled and staggered about like so many drunken sailors. Arrived at the bedchamber we all stripped to the skin and catching Ibzaidu in my arms I carried her to the state-bed and threw her down on it, and being somewhat uncertain of my powers, as I had been sucked nearly dry by the Nubian, I called for and drank a cup of my magic chocolate which I knew would enable me to go through the act like a conqueror.

I gave the word and all the girls came round the bed with their instruments playing, and sang a beautiful song which I had composed for the occasion.

I made ready and getting on the bed fixed my victim in the best position, got between her thighs and giving a bunch of switches to one of the girls I directed her to lash my backside with them so as to smart much.

I took hold of my battering-ram and strove to force an entrance. The head is in, the soft flesh yields to my fierce thrusts. I drive in, she screams with pain but I heed it not. It is music to my ears. It tells me that I am about to arrive at the seat of bliss. I shove and thrust harder, everything gives way to me, the lashing on my buttocks gives me double force, and one fierce lunge sends me into the furthest extremity of her grotto and at the same moment I oil the mangled tender flesh of her dear little bleeding slit with such a stream of burning sperm as never woman sucked from man before. I thought my very prick and stones were dissolving in pearly liquid.

After resting myself on her bosom for a few moments, I found that my battering-ram was prepared for another assault and I fiercely drove him into the breach.

Three times before I got off did I spend the juice of my body into her without calling from her any return.

She lay and moaned in her agony and pain, and on looking I saw that I had terribly battered and bruised the entrance of the seat of pleasure.

I raised her up and had her put into a warm bath and after drying her I again put her to bed. After giving her some wine and taking some myself, I found that again I was in trim for another bout.

With a spring I placed myself between her thighs. I entered her, not without a good deal of hard work.

God of voluptuous love, what a heat reigned through her body!

How lusciously did the sweet flesh clasp around my rod!

A few thrusts and a few moves in and out awaken her to a sense of pleasure.

She moves up to me, she catches the fever that runs through me. Quicker, quicker she heaves up to me to meet my fierce lunges as I drive my foaming steed through her gap into the rich pasturage. She clasps me in her arms, and throws her snowy thighs around my back, the bounces of her bottom fairly spring me off her. I feel she is coming. Ah, my god, she comes – she spends! The sperm comes from her in a shower. I, too – I again – I spend! It runs from me. Great God! It's too much! I die! Oh-h! And then I breathed my spirit away in a sigh soft and gentle as a zephyr.

My God, how voluptuous, how luscious was the beautiful Circassian! What warmth! With what fire, what energy did she meet all my efforts at procuring and dispensing pleasure! How lusciously did she squeeze me when in her! How plentifully did she let down the milk when the agony of pleasure seized her!

We swam in a perfect sea of voluptuousness totally indescribable. Man cannot imagine, pen cannot describe it, it was an intoxication of delight – pleasure wrought up to agony, bliss inexpressible, more exquisitely delicious than that enjoyed by the houris of Paradise when in the arms of true Mohammedans, or that enjoyed by the spirits of the Elysian fields.

I felt considerably enervated for a day or two and refrained from again entering the lists of Venus until I had fairly set sail on my projected cruise in search of love and beauty in the Hesperian climes, where I hoped for the most exquisite pleasures in the arms of the ardent ladies of Cuba and the Spanish Main.

I coasted round and put into Bordeaux for the purpose of giving the sailors a chance of getting themselves girls.

In two days they were all mated, and we put off for Havana, intending to stop there a short time, as I had heard much of the beauty of the women of the island.

Arriving at Havana, I took some rooms at one of the best hotels, giving orders to the captain to keep the brig in sailing order so as to be able to sail at a moment's notice.

At the *table d'hôte* I noticed a handsome, vivacious brunette, evidently an inhabitant of the island. Her eyes were fairly hidden under a mass of deep black hair which overshadowed them; but I could perceive, whilst at the table, that she was continually glancing at me, and the moment my eyes met hers she would suddenly drop her eyes on the plate or look in another direction. From this I augured favourably and deemed success certain, thinking that I had made a conquest.

In the evening I attended the theatre accompanied by the captain, and both of us well armed. I there saw the lady in a box in company with a couple of elderly gentlemen. The one whom I took to be her husband was a cross-grained, ugly looking fellow.

I followed her home with the intent to win her.

In the morning I got an introduction to Señor Don Manuel Vasquer, the husband of Donna Isabel, my lovely *vis-à-vis* at the table.

I told him I was a gentleman of rank and fortune, travelling for the pleasure with a vessel of my own, and invited him down to the harbour to look at the brig.

He accepted the invitation and was very much pleased with the neat cleanliness of everything on deck, and with the luxury displayed in the fittings of the cabin.

I had a lunch set out and plied him well with champagne so that when he left the vessel, he was in very high spirits. On reaching the hotel he invited me up to his apartment and introduced me to his wife and a couple of other ladies we found with her.

I endeavoured as well as my looks could express to let her see that I had taken particular notice of her, and was much smitten by her charms.

After conversing for a short time I retired to my room to dress for dinner and penned a declaration to the Donna Isabel, declaring my passion for her and imploring her to grant me an interview, as I had read in her eyes that I was not disagreeable to her.

After dinner I joined her and her husband and slipped my note into her hand, which she immediately hid in the folds of her dress. I then went to my room to wait for an answer, which I felt sure would soon be sent to me. Nor had I to wait long, for in a couple of hours a negro wench opened the door, poked her head in to ascertain if I was in the room, threw a note to me and, shutting the door without saying a word, retired.

I hastily picked up the note and opening it found my expectations confirmed!

She granted me an interview. Her note stated that her husband would go out to his plantations the next day and that at three o'clock in the afternoon she would be alone taking her siesta.

The evening, night and morning hung heavily on me, and after dining, I retired to my room, laid my watch on the table and sat gazing at the dial to see the weary hours pass away; but as the minute-hand pointed to three, the same black wench again opened the door, poked her head in, looked round and drew back, leaving the door open.

I jumped up and followed her to the rooms of her mistress. Here I found Donna Isabel reclining in an elegant dishabille, on a sofa. She held out her hand to me in welcome, which I took and pressed to my lips.

She invited me to be seated and I placed myself on a foot-stool at her side. Taking her hand between mine, I disclosed my passion for her, imploring her not to refuse my love. At first she pretended to be much surprised that I should make a declaration of my love to her and appeared half angry. But as I proceeded with my tale of love and pressed her for an answer favourable to the passion which was consuming me, she appeared to relent, and rising from her reclining position made room for me to sit down beside her on the couch.

As I sat down by her side I dropped an arm round her waist and drawing her to my bosom I implored her to grant me her love – even to leave her husband and fly with me to some remote corner of the earth where we could while away our years in the soft dalliance of love.

I told her that her husband was an old man with whom she could not enjoy life, and from whom a young woman like herself could not receive those tender attentions, and the soft and real pleasure which she could enjoy in the arms of a young and devoted lover.

She sighed and hung her head on her breast, saying she never knew what it was to receive those delicious and tender pleasures from her husband that I had just spoken of. That from the time of her marriage to the present moment, his whole time was taken up with drinking and gambling. That he left her to amuse herself as best she could in the house, for he was so jealous that he would never allow her to go out except in his company. She sighed again and wished that heaven had given her such a man as myself.

I know not how it was, but when she stopped, I found one of my hands had opened the front of her dress and slipped beneath her shift and was moulding one of her large hard breasts, and my lips were pressed on hers.

My leaning against her had insensibly moved her backwards till, without our knowing it, her head was resting on the cushion of the sofa and I was lying on top of her.

Whilst I was assuring her of eternal love and constancy and begging her to allow me to give her a convincing proof of my tenderness and affection, and also to let me convince her that as yet she had had the mere shadow of the ecstatic pleasure of love, but that if she would allow me I would give her the real substance and a surfeit of those pleasures of which I felt convinced she had received but a taste from her husband, I had been gradually drawing up her clothes, till my hand rested on a large, firm, fleshy thigh. Isabel had closed her eyes, her head hanging to one side, her lips slightly apart and her breast rising and falling rapidly from the quick pulsations of the blood caused by her fierce and amorous desires.

I raised her shift still higher till it disclosed to my sight a large tuft of long black hair. I then unbuttoned my pantaloons and with a little gentle force parted her legs, and got between her thighs.

Parting the lips with my fingers, I inserted the head of my engine of love, and in a few moments we both died away amidst the most exquisite transports of love.

I lay heaving and panting on her bosom while she lay motionless under me, till finding that my stiffness had scarcely diminished and knowing by the short motions and jerks of the head that he was once more ready for the field and impatient for the word to start again, I commenced moving in her.

'Beautiful creature,' I cried, 'what delicious sensations! What pleasure! My God!' said I, 'you are almost virgin. How lusciously tight your sweet flesh clasps my rod!'

Her arms were clasped around my neck, her thighs around my back, her moist rosy lips glued to mine. Our tongues met. With what vivacity, what voluptuousness she moves up to me, giving me energetic heaves for my thrusts. I feel from the increased motion of her bottom that again she is about to dissolve herself into bliss. I too feel it.

'Ah, my God! Oh! what pleasure! I come; there, there, dear love, you have it now – joy, love, bliss unbearable!' And I was swimming in a sea of pleasure, in a perfect agony of bliss.

When we recovered from our delirium, I arose and drawing her clothes down slowly over her legs, I pressed her to my side. Planting a soft kiss on her pouting lips I folded her in my arms and asked her how she liked the reality after being fed for more than a year on the mere shadow of that delicious substance of which she had just largely partaken.

The answer was a kiss that sent a thrill of pleasure through every vein.

'Oh! my dear, this is nothing to what you would enjoy were you to link your fortune to mine and fly with me to France. Then we would live a life of love and pleasure such as you have just tasted. Our whole lives would be nothing but love and pleasure, morn, noon and night it would be love, all love. There should be nothing around us but love – nothing but pleasure!

Isabel rang a small bell and the same piece of ebony who had twice placed her head in and out of my chamber-door entered.

Her mistress told her to bring in some lunch and she soon returned with an elegant cold repast and some delicious wine.

After eating and drinking we again turned our attention to love. Rising from the chair I led her to the sofa, and drawing her on my knees, I stripped her dress and shift from her shoulder and loosening the strings of her petticoats toyed and played with her breasts, which were really beautiful, large and firm, and tipped with two most tempting strawberry nipples.

Nor was my companion idle, for whilst I was thus engaged she had unbuttoned my pantaloons and taken out my penis, which she admired and toyed with, capping and uncapping its red head till she had brought it to a most beautiful state of erection.

I raised her on her feet and all her clothing slipping on to the floor, she stood in all her naked beauty before me. What charms, what beauties did my eyes and lips feast on as I turned her round and round. Her soft round belly, her plump bottom and then her dear little cleft, that masterpiece of beauty, how I hugged it to me. What kisses I lavished on it, all of which she repaid with interest.

She sinks down on the floor between my legs. She caresses my pego, she presses it to her lips They pout and she puts its large red head between them. I push a little forward, it enters her mouth, she sucks it, her soft tongue rolls it over and over. She continues tickling it with her tongue. Feeling that if she continues I must spend, I jerk back and drag it from her mouth. She again wants to keep it. I lay her down on the floor with the cushions under her buttocks. I get on her with my head between her thighs, my prick and stones hanging over her face. Again she takes it in her mouth, while I put my tongue between the lips of her cunt and frig her clitoris with it.

The motion of her rump increases! I find she is about to spend and I suddenly rise up and seat myself on the sofa; she springs after me, jumps on the sofa, her cunt touching my face, and tightly clasps her arms round my neck.

She slowly let her bottom come down, till it touched the head of my pego. I directed it aright and she impaled herself on it.

A few motions and I most plentifully bedewed her with the nectar as she was paying down her own tribute to the god of love.

When she rose off me, the sperm dropped from her salacious slit in large gouts upon me, attesting the bountiful measure with which nature had endowed both of us with the elixir of life.

In the evening she sent her black to order her supper to be sent up into her rooms, and after quietly supping we retired to bed and I spent the most agreeable night that I ever passed with any woman.

Her husband returned the next day, but I found an opportunity to meet his wife in the evening and renewed for a short time the transport we had enjoyed the day before.

A few days later, her husband had invited a party of six young ladies and the same number of young men to visit his wife and take dinner with them. I also was invited.

Immediately after receiving the invitation I sent word to the captain to raise steam and be ready to sail at a moment's warning.

I joined the party at dinner and found three of the invited girls to be very handsome and the other three very good-looking.

After the dinner was over, I invited the party to visit my yacht and take an evening's excursion with me.

The husband of my mistress was very loud in his praises of the beauty of the yacht and of the rich and elegant manner in which she was fitted up and joined his solicitations to mine; the party consenting, we ordered carriages and drove down to where the yacht lay. Getting aboard we sailed out of the harbour and ran up the island.

After we were out of sight of the city, I took the captain aside and told him that towards night I wanted him to run the brig in towards the shore; and that I intended to seize the seven men and land them in a boat and make off with the women. I told him to go and speak to the crew about the matter and have them in readiness to obey my signal.

A little before dusk, we ran close in shore at a place where there was no plantation visible. I had ordered some lumber to be strewn about the greater deck and commanded the captain to send the sailors to carry it away.

Sixteen stalwart fellows came aft and suddenly seized on the men and bound their arms and legs. I then told them what I intended to do, ordering the men at the same time to take the women below. Their execrations and implorings for the girls, who were their relatives, I would not listen to, but I had them put in a boat and sent ashore. They were unbound and let loose. The boat returned to the brig and we set sail for France.

The girls did nothing but sob and weep for a day or two but I soon brought them to their senses. Immediately after setting their companions ashore I went into the cabin, and bringing Ibzaidu and Mary out of their hiding places, I introduced them to the company.

When supper was served they all refused to sit at the table and eat. But I told them if they did not comply with all my wishes I would hand them over to the sailors to be used by them as they chose. This had its effect on them and they seated themselves at the table.

I rang a bell and two of the handsomest women belonging to the sailors entered stark naked, as I had ordered them thus to wait on table.

The Spanish girls were all about to rise up, but putting on a fierce aspect, I threatened them the first who should rise would be passed forward to the men. This had effect on them and they sat still.

Whilst the servant was pouring out the coffee I arose and went to the side-table as if to fetch something, but in reality to pour a few drops of a certain liquid into each cup of coffee.

The quantity put in each cup was enough to set any woman's amorous and licentious desires on fire.

They all drank their coffee and in about half an hour the effect was very visible as all the coyness of modesty had disappeared and they languishingly cast their lascivious glances at me, joking the servant-girls on their nudity, and whenever they came in reach of them, pinching, slapping them, etc., so great was the effect produced by the drug I had put in the coffee.

When the supper was over and the tables were cleared, I commenced playing and tussling with them. Rolling them about on the floor and playing them a thousand amorous tricks which they repaid with interest – throwing me on the floor, falling in a heap on top of me – I would catch a kiss from them, squeeze a fine bubby, slide my hand along a thigh, or slip it under petticoats to grasp a large calf or a well-turned knee. I ordered in some wine of a very strong quality, well drugged with the love-potion. I plied them with the wine of which they drank very freely and in a couple of hours all reserve and modesty had left them.

I took the Señora – the wife I had seduced at the hotel and whose husband I had set ashore with the others – on one side and invited her to step into one of the state-rooms with me. I then asked her if she could forgive me for robbing her from her old cuckold of a husband. She threw herself into my arms and with a fervent embrace and kiss sealed my pardon with her lips.

## Chapter Twelve

I then asked her to undress, and told her that in a moment I would return to her. I went out and gave an order to Mary and returned, finding my mistress stripped to her shift.

I undressed, and taking off my shirt, gave her a kiss, and drew her shift over her head and we both stood naked. I opened the room-door and picking her up carried her into the cabin amongst the girls.

Isabel had by this time got drunk as well as the girls who had come on board with her. With what shouts of laughter did they receive us, tickling us, pinching us, slapping us against one another, catching at my genitals and pulling the hair that surmounted the notch of my mistress, patting our bare backsides, throwing us on the floor, putting us on top of each other, etc., whilst I would catch them, pull up their petticoats, pinch their buttocks, flap the head of my enormous machine against the lips of their hairy little slits, force it into their hands and make them play with it.

I caught one and with the help of Ibzaidu and my mistress soon stripped her naked, handing her clothes to Mary, who had been ordered with Ibzaidu to put away the clothes, and who, being as naked as I, locked them up in one of the rooms when in a few minutes I had stripped the lot of them stark naked.

Oh! then what amorous, wanton tricks we sportively played each other, they tickling my large bags and stones, playing with my penis and rubbing it, I moulding their beautiful titties and with the tip of my finger tickling their cunts.

One little devil who could not have been over fourteen I made spend. What fun this was to the rest, to see her recline her head on my shoulder, spread apart her thighs, and gasp out her exclamations of delight. Her oh's and ah's and me's, as she gave down the generous fluid which ran down my fingers and wet my whole hand.

While I was thus with my finger frigging the dear little maid, Isabel had squatted herself down between my legs and had taken my pego in her mouth and was frigging me in that way. I did not notice it until the delicious creature who was reclining on my shoulder had done spending. But I felt that I too was about to spend, and tried to draw my penis from her mouth, but she clasped her hands around my buttocks and squeezed me up close to her mouth, till my stones and bags tingled against her chin and neck.

I exclaimed: 'My God! Let go. I'm going to spend!'

But instead of doing so, she hugged me still more and tickled its head with her tongue more and more.

The crisis seized me, the short convulsive jerks of my backside announced that the fluid was coming.

'I'm spending; here it is. Ah, my God! what pleasure! How exquisite! What bliss! Oh, God, quicker! Oh, bliss! Heavenly joy! I'm spending,' and I fell to the floor fairly fainting away through excess of pleasure. My flesh quivered and danced, my whole body was in motion, as though attacked with St Vitus' dance.

Never, no, never in the world was a man so frigged by woman. Never before did man experience such voluptuous pleasure. Never was there such bliss so heavenly, so ecstatic, imparted to man by woman, as I received from my mistress as I let flow the pearly liquid into her mouth. Never did the most exquisite sucking and friction of a cunt produce the same amount of such intense ecstasy as I felt when spending. As the pearly liquid spurted from me she placed her tongue on the head, rolling it over and overthrew me into convulsions of pleasure.

It was some time ere I recovered myself, and then it was through the teasings and ticklings of my lovely tormentors. I had a pallet made on the floor of the cabin from the beds in the state-rooms, and putting the lights out, we lay down. I was in the arms of Isabel and soon well repaid her for the pleasure she had given just before.

Thrice did I spend into the most secret recesses of her notch the warm and generous fluid which acts so powerfully on women, and then composed myself for sleep.

After sleeping for I should judge about two hours, I was awakened by feeling someone rubbing and playing with my member, which was in fine standing order.

I found it was Isabel, who had her rump stuck close to the hollow of my thighs and was rubbing the head of my penis against her culo. She wet it every now and then and the sliding of it between her fat buttocks caused a most agreeable tingling sensation to pervade my whole corporeal system.

Wishing to aid her in her intentions, still pretending to be asleep, I did all in my power so far as regarded position, etc.

I clasped my arms around her waist and one thigh, which I lightly raised.

'Oh,' she said, 'you are awake and want more pleasure!'

I made no answer and guided the head of my prick to her little hole *au derrière*. I thrust forward but it would not penetrate. With her fingers she moistened its head with spittle and again placed it aright; but as it was an awkward position to lie in I rolled her on to her belly, placing a cushion under her to raise her rump high up, I opened her thighs, got between them and tried the back entrance. I forced it in. She squirmed and wriggled about gasping with pleasure and I could hardly keep in her.

Her wriggling about and the delicious contractions of her culo brought down from me a copious discharge of the electric fluid which I injected into her.

'Oh, God!' she exclaimed, 'what pleasure. I feel it rushing into me! How hot it is, my dear love. Again, and quicker. Now I come, too; it is running from me. My God! 'tis heaven! What pleasure. Ah, what lus – lus – luscious pleasure!'

The words died on her lips, as I was now fucking her in her slit, and had frigged her clitoris at the same time, thus procuring her the double pleasure.

Here was an entirely new source of pleasure opened to me by the libertinism of my new mistress. Already I had enjoyed her in three different places, and I found that she had penetrated into the inmost recesses of my breast, creating a sensation there which I felt could never be effaced by any other female.

What a luxury it was to see the wild, stupefied astonishment of the charming girls who surrounded me to find themselves lying with me stark naked, and it was somehow increased, I venture to say, by seeing me on top of Isabel, giving her an appetite for her breakfast with the morning draught which she sucked in with great delight.

They all sprang up looking for their clothes or something with which to hide their nakedness, but in vain; no clothes were to be seen, as I had them safe under lock and key.

The ravishing little creature in whose arms I had spent the night nearly laughed herself into fits at witnessing the dumb terror of the girls and commenced railing them, telling them everything that had occurred during the night, recalling to their minds all the follies and extravagances they had been guilty of, and tried to induce them to take their good luck, as she said, with fortitude, describing to them all the pleasure she had received from me during the night and begging them to submit to whatever I would desire with good grace as it was better for them. I then spoke to them, telling them where I was taking them to, and that at the least resistance made by them I would hand them back to the fierce desires of the common sailors; but on the contrary, if they acted as I wished them, everything should be well with them. That they could not form the slightest desire but what would be instantly complied with. The most delicate attentions should be paid them, and I ended by telling them of the life of luxury and blissful love they would lead with me, and on the contrary, of the dreadful life they would spend if by remaining refractory they caused me to give them away to the brutal lusts of the sailors.

This had considerable effect on them as I could see fear and horror plainly depicted on their countenances.

I then rang a bell for a servant and told her to bring me a bottle of wine, telling the girl where to get it.

When she brought it in I filled the glasses and asked the girls, who were huddled together in one corner, to come and take a glass each.

They did not stir, and putting on a frowning aspect, I commanded them to come and drink.

They came forward to the table and drank the wine.

I told them to seat themselves on the sofa while breakfast was being laid. I seated four on one sofa and attempted to lay myself down across their knees, but they all jumped up and ran into a corner. I determined to terrify them at once, so they would be perfectly subservient to my desires. Calling a servant, I sent her to call my mate, one who officiated as my valet.

When he entered the cabin I ordered the girls to resume their places on the sofa, which they tremblingly did.

Then I told the mate to seize on the first one of them who attempted to move, drag her on the deck and give her to the sailors.

I went up to them and sitting on one of them for a moment, lay down with my belly and face towards theirs. The one on whose thighs I rested my feet I bade to part her legs and with my toes I tickled the lips of her bushy notch. The one on whose thighs my cheeks rested I also made to part her legs so that I could drop my right arm between them. I then frigged her clitoris occasionally with my little finger, tickling her just inside the lips; she began to wriggle about on the sofa. The girls on whom rested my buttocks and thighs I made play, one with my stones and the other with my Jacob's staff.

At breakfast I put into the cup of one of the youngest and prettiest girls enough of the tincture of cantharides to make her libidinous desires show themselves pretty strongly.

After we had finished eating I took her to a sofa and drew her on my knees, and as the drug began to take effect on her, I took all the liberties I desired with her, kissing and sucking her pretty lips, the nipples of her breasts, handling her buttocks, frigging her clitoris, drawing my grand machine up between her thighs and rubbing the lips of her pussy, till I felt myself able to succeed in making an entrance into any place no matter how small. She the while hugged me in her arms, giving me kiss for kiss, rubbing and screwing her bottom on my thighs, giving evidence of the raging fever which was consuming that part of her.

Her companions, none of whom had seen me drop the tincture into her coffee, regarded her manoeuvres with me in perfect wonder, little thinking that they each would do the same before they were two days older.

I fixed a cushion and pillow on the sofa so as properly to support her head and bottom, and laying the lecherous little devil down I opened wide her legs and laid myself down between them. She aided me with good will in getting it well fixed, so as better to operate.

Mary and Ibzaidu came to act as pilots to steer my noble craft safe into the harbour of Cytheria. The entrance to the haven was very narrow, making the way rather difficult till Donna Isabel ran up to me and slapping me hard on the bare buttocks drove me up to the hilt, causing the delicious creature whom I was deflowering to scream out with the pain. The blood flowed from her and the sperm from me, mingling most delightfully.

Resting for a moment, I recommenced the delightful race and soon had the joy to know that the dear girl was reaching the very acme of human enjoyment whilst I at the same time again drowned my senses in another discharge of that peculiar fluid the flowing of which drowns one in such ecstacies.

Three others did I serve in the same manner before the close of the day, ravishing them of those dear little maidenheads which are of no manner of use to a woman, and of which I am particularly fond.

One I forced to give up to me her virginity by the aid of the tincture without taking away her senses. Oh! they were bliss, doubly refined, her fierce struggles to free herself from my lascivious embraces. How sweetly musical to my ears were her yells of agony and shame. With what transports did I force her to resign her sweet body to my fierce desires. How ravishing was the pleasure I felt in ripping and tearing up the tender outworks, the inner gates, the bulwarks, everything. And at last, despite her continued struggling and screaming, to drive full tilt into the very temple of Venus, triumphantly plucking off her virgin rose from its stem, causing the blood to flow in profusion. Oh, how I gloated on the ruins of all that is held dear and honourable by her sex – her virtue.

Ye gods! it was a fuck so altogether exquisitely delicious that it was a full half-hour before I was sufficiently recovered to enter again into the little grotto of Venus, the road to which I had just opened.

Lovely creature! Three times did I experience in your arms that fierce transporting pleasure which intoxicates the soul and drowns the mind in those voluptuous ecstacies which can only be experienced in the close embrace of the two sexes.

Abstaining from cohabiting with any of the girls for a couple of days, I felt my strength renewed and invigorated, and on the fifth day after carrying them off from the island, I had ravished the whole six of their dear little maidenheads I had cruelly forced them to give up to my lechery. But once having lost them, which they held so guarded, they entered into all my whims and pleasures with the passion and ardour that characterises the females of the south.

Once the Rubicon was crossed they became the greatest libertines I ever met with. They would hang round me day and night, trying every means in their power to keep my prick in a constant state of erection. They would lay me down on the floor stark naked, like themselves. They would fairly fight for the possession of my genitals. One would gently squeeze my stones, while another would be playing with my penis, which she would by the gentle friction of her soft, delicate hand bring to an erection.

Then would she precipitate herself on me and devour the rich morsel, palating it with those exquisite contractions and inward squeezings which at the time women are about to spend render the act of copulation so exquisitely delicious.

Then, when one was mounted on me, would the dear creatures show forth the full fire of their lechery.

Two of them would seize on my hands, one on each, and, running my fingers into their salacious slits, would thus procure for themselves a semblance of the pleasure their more lucky rival was enjoying and receiving from the friction of the stiffly red-tipped horn which sprang out from the bottom of my belly.

Isabel would rush into the arms of Ibzaidu, to whom she had taken a great liking. Tumbling on the floor in each other's arms they would press each other, squeeze breasts, suck nipples, force their tongues into each other's cunts. Their hands would play and twine in the bushy hair that shaded the mounts above their notches. Their fingers would slide lower down, would enter the sacred grotto, and then running them in as far as they could, they would commence the titillation, and with the finger of the left hand at the same time they would frig the clitoris, which would soon bring them to that delicious state of annihilation which causes the soul to dissolve itself in a sea of bliss.

At other times they would seize on the languishing Fanny, who yet retained her maidenhead although very anxious to be rid of it, and throw her on the sofa or floor, and while Ibzaidu would be squeezing or sucking her breasts, pressing her own lovely titties to her mouth, kissing and sucking her rosy lips, and thrusting her tongue into her mouth, Isabel would be between her thighs, frigging her clitoris with her fingers and, with her tongue between the lips, so titillate her cunt as to give her the most delicious pleasure. The dear Fanny would spend, pouring down the liquor of which she possessed a super-abundance, amidst sighs, long and deep.

Nor would her hands be idle, for those who were procuring her the pleasure did not forget themselves.

They would force her hands into their own glowing furnaces and send down such a flow of liquid as would wet the hands of Fanny all over.

Then would these two try their best to procure for Fanny those pleasures which all around her were continually being received from me but of which I had as yet deprived her. But she was not long to be burdened with that which all maids are anxious to get rid of – her virginity.

Giving myself one day's rest, I lay down in the cabin by myself on a mattress. The girls always made their beds on the floor and we lay together. After I had been asleep for some time, I was awakened by feeling someone playing with my private parts. Isabel and Ibzaidu were lying on either side of me, their heads resting on my thighs. Isabel had taken that piece of flesh of which she was so fond in her mouth and was tickling it with her tongue. The other was feeling and playing with the curious bag which hung low down between my thighs, gently rubbing and squeezing the stones. My machine was proudly erect as a mast, its red head glowing through the darkness.

'Come,' said Isabel, 'Ibzaidu has lived for five days on the shadow of the substance which the other girls have been so gorged with, and it is but fair that you should recompense her for starving, while others have been living in plenty. Come you, stand! Your prick is in fine condition. You must spend this night with her and me for I have not partaken of the flesh for some time.'

I laid Ibzaidu on her back and getting between her legs I entered my prick into her parts. The moment she felt the head within the further recesses of her cunt she spent most plentifully. I worked away in her for some time, holding back my own liquor as long as possible so as to give her as much pleasure as I could, and she spent three times more. Just as she was dissolving her very vitals into sperm, I met her and injected the seed into her womb.

I got off her and lay between the two. Without giving me any time for recruiting, Isabel commenced playing with my staff, which she hugged, pressing it to her breasts, squeezing it between them, pressing it against her cheeks, gently frigging it with her hand and, taking its uncapped head between her lips, softly biting and tickling it with the end of her tongue.

Then stopping till it sank down again, small and shrivelled up, she would take it and thrust the whole of it into her mouth, and by her exquisite palating and sucking and tickling cause it to start into life, proudly erecting its head till her little lips could hardly clasp it.

I laid her down on her belly, placing a pillow under the lower part of her body, and then entered her *au derrière*; I put my left hand under her thighs and inserted my fingers into her cunt, holding them stiff, whilst I worked in her arsehole.

The motions of her bottom, caused by the fall of my thighs against her backside, made her frig herself on my fingers. Thus did she enjoy a double pleasure.

Nor was Ibzaidu without share in this beautiful scene. She had lain down with her belly to my breast, her bush and slit rubbing against my side, with her right thigh thrown over my head.

Drawing her closer to me I kissed the lips of her cunt. I tickled her clitoris with my tongue, I put it between my lips and titillated her so deliciously with them that she died away in pleasure, at the same time that Isabel was losing her senses from the convulsive transports into which my double frigging had thrown her.

After this performance was over, we lay completely exhausted in each other's arms for about two hours, at the end of which time I began to feel myself somewhat revived.

While we were lying dormant in each other's embraces, Isabel had been describing to Ibzaidu the intense pleasure she had enjoyed when I enlarged her *au derrière*, and she prevailed on her to make me frig her in the same manner, making her lay her head between my thighs to play with my little thing and make it start into new life.

The beautiful, delicate and voluptuous Ibzaidu took my tickler in her mouth and by the tickling of her tongue and the sucking she gave it she soon made it to stand most beautifully erect, upon which she let it go.

I soon placed her in a convenient position for the attack which was to ravish her of her second maidenhead, and she was perfectly willing to surrender at once. I placed her on her right side, partly lying on her back. I then lay down on her left side and prepared to enter her. Isabel had lain herself down in front of Ibzaidu, her cunt touching her face, and her head between the thighs of her companion.

She took the head of my enormous machine into her mouth which she wetted well with spittle and then guided to its destination. But the place was so small that I made many attempts before I could penetrate.

At last I felt it enter. I shoved slowly and steadily, and at length felt it impossible to reach any further.

Ibzaidu writhed and twisted about so much after I was in her that I could hardly keep myself upon her. Isabel had put the fingers of her right hand into the cunt of the beautiful creature whom I was stroking behind, and the motions of her back as we worked together made her frig herself with them.

At the same time she put her own arms round the buttocks of Isabel, and drawing her slit up to her mouth, she put her tongue into it and frigged her so well in this way that Isabel spent before either of us, wetting the tongue and lips of the beautiful Circassian with the pearly drops.

The crisis now seized me and at the same moment the frigging of Isabel's fingers caused Ibzaidu to spend at the very moment I was squirting a stream of boiling sperm into her very vitals.

'Ah, dear sir, have mercy on me! I feel it here in me! I too – oh, goodness, I am spending! Oh, heavens, what a pleasure. I die – I spend again – again! I am spending!' She relaxed the convulsive grasp she had of Isabel's bottom. Her flesh quivered and danced and she lay convulsed with pleasure such as gods never dreamt of.

In three weeks we reached the coast and harboured in the little creek. I immediately went ashore, taking the women with me and went to the château.

Heavens! What a welcome I received. How the lively, rampant, lecherous girls crowded round, and with what embraces did they receive me. I was fairly devoured by the hungry creatures who crowded to embrace me.

And, La Rose d'Amour! Ah, dear Rose, as I pressed you in my arms and received your burning kisses, what a thrill did they not send through my whole body.

And you, beauteous Laura, how your little heart beat as I pressed your bosom to mine; what fire flashed from your languishing black eyes as you put one of my hands on your cunt and your own on my already stiff pego.

Then came Rosalie, the delicate, fair-skinned, blue-eyed Rosalie. With what fierce delight did she spring forward, light as the burning gazelle, and into my arms. What lustful fires sparkled in her half-closed eyes. Her lips meet mine – they are glued together. She forces open her mouth, her tongue meets mine. She rubs the lips of her cunt against my thigh, she clasps her arms tight, her breast rises and falls in quick succession, she wriggles her bottom, her backside convulsively jerks, and she says: 'Oh – oh! – God!' and sliding through my arms she sank upon the floor.

There, there at the further end of the room I see Caroline entering. Caroline, that very goddess of voluptuous beauty. She has heard of my arrival. She advances towards me, perfectly naked except for some pink gauze drawn round her waist – I too am naked, for the girls had stripped me on entering the room. My prick is hard and stiff, standing erect against my belly. Caroline sees it, she fixes her eyes on it, and remains perfectly still, fascinated by the charming sight. I fly to her, I take her in my arms, her emotions overpower her, she sinks on the floor on her back, she drags me with her. As she falls, her legs part and I fall between them, and five times did she spend ere she recovered from her fall.

When she rose up what a brilliancy sparkled in her eyes. Her gait was light and elastic as a fawn's.

When I rose up from my fall with the lovely Caroline, I met the gaze of the licentious Nubian, who was advancing to meet me, holding in her hand a glass of wine. She was perfectly naked and twisted and screwed her thighs together. I meet, accept the glass and drain the wine. The moment I drank it I knew that it was mixed with the tincture for exciting and creating amorous propensities.

The lovely creatures I have just been naming gathered round me, they embraced me in every part; some a leg and a thigh; others hung round my neck; some seized on my hands with which they frigged themselves; one seats herself on the floor between my legs and playfully squeezes my stones and strokes my once more rampant prick. The luscious Celeste has her arms clasped round my neck and I am about to impale her with my prick, but Fanny comes forward and urges her claim in favour of her little maidenhead, which is consuming her with a burning fever.

I clasp her in my arms and lay her down, falling upon her. One of the girls hastens to place a cushion under her bottom and then guides the dart to its sheath. I shove and thrust, and one of the girls, giving me a couple of hard slaps over my backside, drives me in up to the hilt and the sweet girl at once sucks in the delicious poison she has been longing for.

The wine which I had drunk contained so much tincture that my pego continued standing.

The Nubian next came in for a good stroking. Three times while I was in her did she spend. Caroline, Laura and Rosalie came in their turns; each received an exquisite frigging.

I then went to bathe, taking with me only four of the girls: Caroline, Celestine, Laura and Rosalie.

Whilst in the bathroom I twice more frigged Rosalie and Laura, and then dismissed them to their apartments, remaining with the other two.

I had supper brought into the bath to me, and determining to sacrifice myself to the libidinous desires of my two lovely mistresses, I drank more of the wine containing the tincture. Sufficient to enable me to give the two who were with me as much cock-broth as they could sip through the night.

After remaining in the bath for a couple of hours, we came out and went to the bedchamber.

I led them into the state-bedroom, and letting down the hangings, jumped into bed.

The two girls followed me and I was buried to my utmost length in the fiery furnace of Celestine. Four times did this amiable creature let fly her mettle and in such profusion did it come from her that the sheet under her bottom was all wet with it.

In her turn did Caroline take in and gorge her greedy little cunt with my morsel.

Thus did I spend the night, first frigging one and then the other, till they were entirely spent and worn out with the delicious fucking which I had given them. I now determined to give up searching for any more maidenheads, and gave myself up to the dear girls I already possessed, than whom I could find none more beautiful, more voluptuous or more devoted to my capricious pleasures.

I now live happily surrounded by the sweet creatures, but I hear someone calling me from my private bed. I am in good condition, having abstained for three days. I fly to her, I jump into her arms and drown myself in a sea of bliss, in the arms of La Rose d'Amour.

*Sub-Umbra*

*or Sport among the She-Noodles*

The merry month of May has always been famous for its propitious influence over the voluptuous senses of the fairer sex.

I will tell you two or three little incidents which occurred to me in May 1878, when I went to visit my cousins in Sussex, or as I familiarly call them, the 'she-noodles', for the sport they afforded me at various times.

My uncle's is a nice country residence, standing in large grounds of its own, and surrounded by small fields of arable and pasture land, interspersed by numerous interesting copses, through which run footpaths and shady walks, where you are not likely to meet anyone in a month. I shall not trouble my readers with the name of the locality, or they may go pleasure hunting for themselves. Well, to go on, these cousins consisted of Annie, Sophie and Polly, beside their brother Frank, who, at nineteen, was the eldest, the girls being, respectively, eighteen, sixteen and fifteen. After dinner, the first day of my arrival, Paterfamilias and Mama indulged in a snooze in their armchairs, whilst us boys and girls (I was the same age as Frank) took a stroll in the grounds. I attached myself more particularly to cousin Annie, a finely developed blonde, with deep blue eyes, pouting red lips, and a full heaving bosom, which to me looked like a perfect volcano of smothered desires. Frank was a very indolent fellow, who loved to smoke his cigar, and expected his sisters, who adored him, to sit by his side, reading some of the novels of the day, or tell him their love secrets, etc. This was by far too tame an amusement for me, and as I had not been there for nearly three years, I requested Annie to show me the improvements in the grounds before we went in to tea, saying to Frank, banteringly, 'I suppose, old fellow, you're too lazy, and would prefer your sister taking me round?'

'I'm too comfortable, lazy is an ugly word, Walter, but the fact is, Soph is just reading me a most interesting book, and I can't leave it,' he replied; 'besides, sissie is quite as well or better qualified than I am to show off the grounds. I never notice anything.'

'Come on, Annie,' said I taking her hand; 'Frank is in love.'

'No, I'm sure he never thinks of a girl, except his sisters,' was the reply.

We were now out of earshot, in a shady walk, so I went on a little more freely. 'But, surely you, coz, are in love, if he is not. I can tell it by your liquid eye and heaving bosom.'

A scarlet flush shot over her features at my allusion to her finely moulded bosom, but it was evidently pleasing, and far from offensive, to judge by her playfully spoken, 'Oh! Walter, for shame, sir!'

We were a good distance away by this time, and a convenient seat stood near, so throwing my arms around the blushing girl, I kissed her ruby lips, and drawing her with me, said, 'Now, Annie, dear, I'm your cousin and old playfellow, I couldn't help kissing those beautiful lips, which I might always make free with when we were little boy and girl together; now you shall confess all before I let you go.'

'But I've nothing to confess, sir.'

'Do you never think of love, Annie? Look me in the face if you can say it's a stranger to your bosom,' putting my hand familiarly round her neck till my right hand rested on one of the panting globes of her bosom.

She turned her face to mine, suffused as it was by a deeper blush than ever, as her dark blue eyes met mine, in a fearless search of my meaning, but instead of speaking in response to this mute appeal, I kissed her rapturously, sucking in the fragrance of her sweet breath till she fairly trembled with emotion.

It was just beginning to get dusk, my hands were caressing the white, firm flesh of her beautiful neck, slowly working their way towards the heaving bubbies a little lower down; at last I whispered, 'What a fine, what a lovely bust you have developed since I saw you last, dear Annie, you won't mind your cousin, will you, when everything used to be so free to each other; besides, what harm can there be in it?'

She seemed on fire, a thrill of emotion seemed to shoot through both of us, and for several moments she lay almost motionless in my arms, with one hand resting on my thigh. Priapus was awake and ready for business, but she suddenly aroused herself, saying, 'We must never stop here, let us walk round or they will suspect something.'

'When shall we be alone again, darling? We must arrange that before we go in,' I said quickly.

It was impossible to keep her on the seat, but as we walked on she said, musingly, 'Tomorrow morning we might go for a stroll before lunch. Frank lies in bed, and my sisters are keeping house this week; I shall have to mind the tarts and pies next week.'

I gave her another hug and a kiss, as I said, 'How delightful that will be; what a dear, thoughtful girl you are, Annie.'

'Mind, sir, how you behave tomorrow, not so much kissing, or I shan't take you for a second walk; here we are at the house.'

Next morning was gloriously warm and fine; as soon as breakfast was over we started for our stroll, being particularly minded by papa to be back in good time for luncheon.

I gradually drew out my beautiful cousin, till our conversation got exceedingly warm, the hot blood rushing in waves of crimson over her shamefaced visage.

'What a rude boy you have grown, Walter, since you were here last; I can't help blushing at the way you run on, sir!' she exclaimed at last.

'Annie, my darling,' I replied, 'what can be more pleasing than to talk of fun with pretty girls, the beauties of their legs and bosoms, and all about them? How I should love to see your lovely calf at this moment, especially after the glimpses I have already had of a divine ankle,' saying which I threw myself under a shady tree, close by a gate in a meadow, and drew the half-resisting girl down on the grass at my side, and kissed her passionately, as I murmured, 'Oh! Annie, what is there worth living for like the sweets of love?'

Her lips met mine in a fiery embrace, but suddenly disengaging herself, her eyes cast down, and looking awfully abashed, she stammered out, 'What is it? what do you mean, Walter?'

'Ah, coz dear, can you be so innocent? Feel here the dart of love all impatient to enter the mossy grotto between your thighs,' I whispered, placing her hand upon my prick, which I had suddenly let out of the restraining trousers. 'How you sigh; grasp it in your hand, dear, is it possible that you do not understand what it is for?'

Her face was crimson to the roots of her hair, as her hand grasped my tool, and her eyes seemed to start with terror at the sudden apparition of Mr John Thomas; so that taking advantage of her speechless confusion my own hand, slipping under her clothes, soon had possession of her mount, and in spite of the nervous contraction of her thighs, the forefinger searched out the virgin clitoris.

'Ah! oh! oh!! Walter don't; what are you about?'

'It's all love, dear, open your thighs a wee bit and see what pleasure my finger will make you experience,' I again whispered, smothering her with renewed and luscious kisses, thrusting the velvet tip of my tongue between her lips.

'Oh! oh! you will hurt!' she seemed to sigh rather than speak, as her legs relaxed a little of their spasmodic contraction.

My lips continued glued to hers, our otherwise disengaged arms clasped each other closely round the waist, her hand held my affair in a kind of convulsive grasp whilst my fingers were busy with clitoris and cunny; the only audible sound resembling a mixture of kisses and sighs, till all in a moment I felt her crack deluged with a warm, creamy spend whilst my own juice spurted over her hand and dress in loving sympathy.

In a short while we recovered our composure a little, and I then explained to her that the melting ecstasy she had just felt was only a slight fortaste of the joy I could give her, by inserting my member in her cunny. My persuasive eloquence and the warmth of her desires soon overcame all maiden fears and scruples; then for fear of damaging her dress, or getting the green stain of the grass on the knees of my light trousers, I persuaded her to stand up by the gate and allow me to enter behind. She hid her face in her hands on the top rail of the gate, as I slowly raised her dress; what glories were unfolded to view, my prick's stiffness was renewed in an instant at the sight of her delicious buttocks, so beautifully relieved by the white of her pretty drawers; as I opened them and exposed the flesh, I could see the lips of her plump pouting cunny, deliciously feathered with soft light down, her lovely legs, drawers, stockings, pretty boots, making a *tout ensemble*, which as I write and describe them cause Mr Priapus to swell in my breeches; it was a most delicious sight. I knelt and kissed her bottom, slit, and everything my tongue could reach, it was all mine, I stood up and prepared to take possession of the seat of love when, alas! a sudden shriek from Annie, her clothes dropped, all my arrangements were upset in a moment; a bull had unexpectedly appeared on the opposite side of the gate, and frightened my love by the sudden application of his cold, damp nose to her forehead. It is too much to contemplate that scene even now.

Annie was ready to faint as she screamed, 'Walter! Walter! Save me from the horrid beast!' I comforted and reassured her as well as I was able, and seeing that we were on the safe side of the gate, a few loving kisses soon set her all right. We continued our walk, and soon spying out a favourable shady spot, I said: 'Come, Annie dear, let us sit down and recover from the startling interruption; I am sure, dear, you must still feel very agitated, besides I must get you now to compensate me for the rude disappointment.'

She seemed to know that her hour had come; the hot blushes swept in crimson waves across her lovely face, as she cast down her eyes, and permitted me to draw her down by my side on a mossy knoll, and we lay side by side, my lips glued to hers in a most ardent embrace.

'Annie! Oh! Annie!' I gasped. 'Give me the tip of your tongue, love.' She tipped me the velvet without the slightest hesitation, drawing, at the same time, what seemed a deep sigh of delightful anticipation as she yielded to my slightest wish. I had one arm under her head, and with the other I gently removed her hat, and threw aside my own golgotha, kissing and sucking at her delicious tongue all the while. Then I placed one of her hands on my ready cock, which was in bursting state, saying, as I released her tongue for a moment: 'There, Annie, take the dart of love in your hand.' She grasped it nervously, as she softly murmured: 'Oh, Walter, I'm so afraid; and yet – oh, yet, dearest, I feel, I die, I must taste the sweets of love, this forbidden fruit,' her voice sinking almost to a whisper, as she pressed and passed her hand up and down my shaft. My hand was also busy finding its way under her clothes as I again glued my mouth to hers, and sucked at her tongue till I could feel her vibrate all over with the excess of her emotion. My hand, which had taken possession of the seat of bliss, was fairly deluged with her warm glutinous spendings.

'My love; my life! I must kiss you there, and taste the nectar of love,' I exclaimed, as I snatched my lips from hers, and reversing my position, buried my face between her unresisting thighs. I licked up the luscious spendings with rapturous delight from the lips of her tight little cunny, then my tongue found its way further, till it tickled her sensitive clitoris, and put her into a frenzy of mad desire for still further enjoyment; she twisted her legs over my head, squeezing my head between her firm plump thighs in an ecstasy of delight.

Wetting my finger in her luscious crack, I easily inserted it in her beautifully wrinkled brown bum-hole, and keeping my tongue busy in titillating the stiff little clitoris, I worked her up into such a furious state of desire that she clutched my cock and brought it to her mouth, as I lay over her to give her the chance of doing so; she rolled her tongue round the purple head, and I could also feel the loving playful bite of her pearly teeth. It was the acme of erotic enjoyment. She came again in another luscious flood of spendings, whilst she eagerly sucked every drop of my sperm as it burst from my excited prick.

We both nearly fainted from the excess of our emotions, and lay quite exhausted for a few moments, till I felt her dear lips again pressing and sucking my engine of love. The effect was electric; I was as stiff as ever.

'Now, darling, for the real stroke of love,' I exclaimed. Shifting my position, and parting her quivering thighs, so that I could kneel between them. My knees were placed upon her skirts so as to preserve them from the grass stain. She lay before me in a delightful state of anticipation, her beautiful face all blushes of shame, the closed eyelids fringed with their long dark lashes, her lips slightly open and the finely developed, firm, plump globes of her bosom heaving in a state of tumultuous excitement. It was ravishing, I felt mad with lust, and could no longer put off the actual consummation. I could not contain myself. Alas; poor maidenhead! Alas! for your virginity! I brought my cock to the charge, presented the head just slightly between the lips of her vagina. A shudder of delight seemed to pass through her frame at the touch of my weapon, as her eyes opened, and she whispered, with a soft, loving smile, 'I know it will hurt, but Walter, dear Walter, be both firm and kind. I must have it, if it kills me.' Throwing her arms around my neck, she drew my lips to hers, as she thrust her tongue into my mouth with all the abandon of love, and shoved up her bottom to meet my charge.

I had placed one hand under her buttocks, whilst, with the other, I kept my affair straight to the mark; then pushing vigorously, the head entered about an inch, till it was chock up to the opposing hymen. She gave a start of pain, but her eyes gazed into mine with a most encouraging look.

'Throw your legs over my back, my dear,' I gasped, scarcely relinquishing her tongue for a moment. Her lovely thighs turned round me in a spasmodic frenzy of determination to bear the worst. I gave a ruthless push, just as her bottom heaved up to meet me, and the deed was done. King Priapus had burst through all obstacles to our enjoyment. She gave a subdued shriek of agonised pain, and I felt myself throbbing in possession of her inmost charms.

'You darling! You love me! My brave Annie, how well you stood the pain. Let us lie still for a moment or two, and then for the joys of love,' I exclaimed, as I kissed her face, forehead, eyes and mouth in a transport of delight at feeling the victory so soon accomplished.

Presently I could feel the tight sheath of her vagina contracting on my cock in the most delicious manner. This challenge was too much for my impetuous steed. He gave a gentle thrust. I could see by the spasm of pain which passed over her beautiful face that it was still painful to her, so, restraining my ardour, I worked very gently; but my lust was so maddening that I could not restrain a copious spend and I sank on her bosom in love's delicious lethargy.

It was only for a few moments, I could feel her tremble beneath me with voluptuous ardour, and the sheath being now well lubricated, we commenced a delightful bout of ecstatic fucking. All her pain was forgotten, the wounded parts soothed by the flow of my semen now only revelled in the delightful friction of love; she seemed to boil over in spendings, my delighted cock revelled in it, as he thrust in and out with all my manly vigour; we spent three or four times in a delirium of voluptuousness, till I was fairly vanquished by her impetuosity, and begged her to be moderate, and not to injure herself by excessive enjoyment.

'Oh! can it be possible to hurt oneself by such a delightful pleasure?' she sighed, then seeing me withdraw my limp tool from her still longing cunt, she smiled archly, as she said with a blush, 'Pardon my rudeness, dear Walter, but I fear it is you who are most injured after all; look at your bloodstained affair.'

'You lovely little simpleton,' I said, kissing her rapturously, 'that's your own virgin blood; let me wipe you, darling,' as I gently applied my handkerchief to her pouting slit, and afterwards to my own cock. 'This, dearest Annie, I shall treasure up as the proofs of your virgin love, so delightfully surrendered to me this day,' exhibiting the ensanguined *mouchoir* to her gaze.

We now arose from our soft mossy bed, and mutually assisted each other to remove all traces of our love engagement.

Then we walked on, and I enlightened the dear girl as to to all the arts and practices of love. 'Do you think,' I remarked, 'that your sisters or Frank have any idea of what the joys of love are like?'

'I believe they would enter into it as ardently as I do, if they were but once initiated,' she replied. 'I have often heard Frank say when kissing us, that we made him burn all over'; and then blushing deeply as her eyes met mine, 'Oh! dear Walter, I'm afraid you will think we are awfully rude girls, but when we go to bed at night, my sisters and I often compare our budding charms, and crack little jokes about the growing curls of mine and Sophie's slits, and the hairless little pussy of Polly, we have such games of slapping, and romps too, sometimes; it has often made me feel a kind of all-overishness of feverish excitement I could not understand, but thanks to you, love, I can make it all out now; I wish you could only get a peep at us, dear.'

'Perhaps it might be managed; you know my room is next to yours, I could hear you laughing and having a game last night.'

'I know we did, we had such fun,' she replied, 'it was Polly trying to put my pussy in curl papers, but how can you manage it, dear?'

Seeing she fully entered into my plans for enjoyment, we consulted together, and at last I hit upon an idea which I thought might work very well; it was that I should first sound out Frank and enlighten him a little into the ways of love, and then as soon as he was ripe for our purpose, we would surprise the three sisters whilst bathing naked, and slap their naked bottoms all round; that Annie should encourage her sisters to help in tearing off all our clothes, and then we could indulge in a general romp of love.

Annie was delighted at the idea, and I promised the very next day to begin with Frank, or perhaps that very afternoon if I got a chance.

We returned to the house, Annie's cheeks blushing and carrying a beautiful flush of health, and her mama remarked that our walk had evidently done her very great good, little guessing that her daughter, like our first mother Eve, had that morning tasted of the forbidden fruit, and was greatly enlightened and enlivened thereby.

After luncheon I asked Frank to smoke a cigarette in my room, which he at once complied with.

As soon as I had closed the door, I said, 'Old fellow, did you ever see *Fanny Hill*, a beautiful book of love and pleasure?'

'What, a smutty book, I suppose you mean? No. Walter, but if you have got it I should wonderfully like to look at it,' he said, his eyes sparkling with animation.

'Here it is, my boy, only I hope it won't excite you too much; you can look it over by yourself, as I read *The Times*,' said I, taking it out of my dressing-case, and handing it to his eager grasp.

He sat close to me in an easy lounging chair, and I watched him narrowly as he turned over the pages and gloated over the beautiful plates and his prick hardened in his breeches till it was quite stiff and rampant.

'Ha! Ha!! Ha!!! old fellow, I thought it would fetch you out!' I said, laying my hand upon his cock. 'By Jove, Frank! what a tosser yours has grown since we used to play in bed together a long time ago. I'll lock the door, we must compare our parts, I think mine is nearly as big as yours.'

He made no remark, but I could see he was greatly excited by the book. Having locked the door, I leant over his shoulder and made my remarks upon the plates as he turned them over. At length the book dropped from his hands, and his excited gaze was riveted on my bursting breeches. 'Why, Walter, you are as bad as I am,' he said, with a laugh, 'let's see which is the biggest,' pulling out his hard, stiff prick, and then laying his hands on me and pulling my affair out to look at.

We handled each other in an ecstasy of delight, which ended in our throwing off all our clothes, and having a mutual fuck between our thighs on the bed; we spent in rapture, and after a long dalliance he entered into my plans, and we determined to have a lark with the girls as soon as we could get a chance. Of course I was mum as to what had passed between Annie and myself.

In the course of the evening, Frank and I were delighted by the arrival of a beautiful young lady of sixteen, on a visit to his sisters, in fact a schoolfellow of Sophie and Polly, come to stop a week at the house.

Miss Rosa Redquim was indeed a sprightly beauty of the Venus height, well proportioned in leg and limb, full swelling bosom, with a graceful Grecian type of face, rosy cheeks, large grey eyes, and golden auburn hair, lips as red as cherries, and teeth like pearls, frequently exhibited by a succession of winning smiles, which never seemed to leave her face. Such was the acquisition to the feminine department of the house, and we congratulated ourselves on the increased prospect of sport, as Frank had expressed to me considerable compunction as to taking liberties with one's own sisters.

The next morning being gloriously fine and warm, myself and friend strolled in the grounds, smoking our cigarettes, for about an hour, till near the time when we guessed the girls would be coming for a bathe in the small lake in the park, which we at once proceeded to; then we secreted ourselves secure from observation, and awaited, in deep silence, the arrival of sisters and friend.

This lake, as I call it, was a pond about four or five acres in extent, every side thickly wooded to the very margin, so that even anglers could not get access to the bank, except at the little sloping green sward, of about twenty or thirty square yards in extent, which had a large hut, or summer-house, under the trees; here the bathers could undress, and then trip across the lawn to the water. The bottom of the pond was gradually shelving, and covered with fine sand at this spot, and a circular space was enclosed with rails, to prevent them getting out of their depth.

The back door of this hut opened upon a very narrow footpath, leading to the house through the dense thicket, so that any party would feel quite secure from observation. The interior was comfortably furnished with seats and loungers, besides a buffet, generally holding a stock of wine, biscuits and cakes, during the bathing season.

Frank, having a key to the hut, took me through on to the lawn, and then climbing up into a thick sycamore, we relighted our cigarettes, awaiting the adventure with some justifiable impatience.

Some ten minutes of suspense, and then we were rewarded by hearing the ringing laughter of the approaching girls. We heard the key turned in the lock, then the sounds of their bolting themselves in, and Annie's voice, saying: 'Ah! Wouldn't the boys like the fun of seeing us undress and bathing, this lovely warm day'; to which we heard Rosa laughingly reply: 'I don't mind if they do see me, if I don't know it, dears. There's something delightful in the thought of the excitement it would put the dear fellows in. I know I should like Frank to take a fancy to me; I'm nearly in love with him already, and have read that the best way a girl can madly excite the man she wishes to win is to let him see all her charms, when he thinks she is unconscious of his being near.'

'Well, there's no fear of our being seen here, so I am one for a good romp. Off with your clothes, quick; it will be delicious in the water,' exclaimed Sophie.

The undressing was soon accomplished, excepting chemises, boots, and stockings, as they were evidently in no hurry to enter the water.

'Now,' said Sophie, with a gay laugh, 'we must make Rosa a free woman, and examine all she's got. Come on, girls, lay her down, and turn up her smock.'

The beautiful girl only made a slight feint of resisting, as she playfully pulled up their chemises, exclaiming: 'You shan't look at my fanny for nothing. La! Polly has got no hair on her fly trap yet. What a pretty pouting slit yours is, Annie. I think you have been using the finger of a glove we made into a little cock for Sophie, and told her to bring home from school for you.'

She was soon stretched on her back on the soft mossy grass, her face covered with burning blushes, as her pretty cunt was exposed to view, ornamented with its *chevelure* of soft red hair; her beautiful white belly and thighs shining like marble in the bright sunlight. The three sisters were blushing as well as their friend, and delighted at the sight of so much loveliness.

One after another, they kissed the vermilion lips of their friend's delightful slit, and then turning her on her face, proceeded to smack the lily white bottom of their laughing, screaming victim, with open hands.

Smacks and laughter echoed through the grove, and we almost fancied ourselves witnesses to the games of real nymphs. At last she was allowed to rise on her knees, and then the three sisters in turn presented their cunts to their friend to kiss. Polly was the last, and Rosa, clasping her arms firmly round my youngest cousin's buttocks, exclaimed: 'Ah! Ah! You have made me feel so rude, I must suck this little hairless jewel,' as she glued her lips to it, and hid her face almost from sight, as if she would devour Polly's charms there and then. The young girl, flushed with excitement, placed her hands on Rosa's head, as if to keep her there, whilst both Annie and Sophie, kneeling down by the side of their friend, began to caress her cunt, bosom, and every charm they could tickle or handle.

This exciting scene lasted for five or six minutes, till at last they all sank down in a confused heap on the grass, kissing and fingering in mad excitement.

Now was our time. We had each provided ourselves with little switches of twigs, and thus armed we seemed to drop from the clouds upon the surprised girls, who screamed in fright and hid their blushing faces in their hands.

They were too astonished and alarmed to jump up, but we soon commenced to bring them to their senses, and convince them of the reality of the situation.

'What rude! what lascivious ideas! slash away Frank!' I cried, making my swish leave its marks on their bottoms at every cut.

'Who would have thought of it, Walter? We must whip such indecent ideas out of their tails!' he answered, seconding my assault with his sharp, rapid strokes.

They screamed both from pain and shame, and springing to their feet, chased round the lawn; there was no escape. We caught them by the tails of their chemises, which we lifted up to enable us to cut at their bums with more effect. At last we were getting out of breath, and beginning fairly to pant from exhaustion, when Annie suddenly turned upon me, saying, 'Come, come, girls, let's tear their clothes off, so they shall be quite as ashamed as we are, and agree to keep our secret!' The others helped her, and we made such a feeble resistance that we were soon reduced to the same state in which we had surprised them, making them blush and look very shamefaced at the sight of our rampant engines of love.

Frank seized Miss Redquim round the waist, and led the way into the summer-house, myself and his sisters following. The gentlemen then producing the wine, etc., from the buffet, sat down with a young lady on each knee, my friend having Rosa and Polly, whilst Annie and Sophie sat with me; we plied the girls with several glasses of champagne each, which they seemed to swallow in order to drown their sense of shame. We could feel their bodies quiver with emotion as they reclined upon our necks, their hands and ours groping under shirts and chemises in every forbidden spot; each of us had two delicate hands caressing our cocks, two delicious arms around our necks, two faces laid cheek to cheek on either side, two sets of lips to kiss, two pairs of bright and humid eyes to return our ardent glances; what wonder then that we flooded their hands with our spurting seed and felt their delicious spendings trickle over our busy fingers.

Excited by the wine, and madly lustful to enjoy the dear girls to the utmost, I stretched Sophie's legs wide apart, and sinking on my knees, gamahuched her virgin cunt, till she spent again in ecstasy, whilst dear Annie was doing the same to me, sucking the last drop of spend from my gushing prick; meanwhile Frank was following my example, Rosa surrendered to his lascivious tongue all the recesses of her virginity as she screamed with delight and pressed his head towards her mount when the frenzy of love brought her to the spending point; Polly all the while kissing her brother's belly, and frigging him to a delicious emission.

When we recovered a little from this exciting *pas de trois*, all bashfulness was vanished between us, we promised to renew our pleasures on the morrow, and for the present contented ourselves by bathing all together, and then returned to the house for fear the girls might be suspected of something wrong for staying out too long.

After luncheon Frank smoked his cigarette in my room; the events of the morning had left both of us in a most unsettled and excited state.

'I say, old fellow,' he exclaimed, 'by Jove! it's quite impossible for me to wait till tomorrow for the chance of enjoying that delicious Rosa; besides, when there are so many of us together there is just the chance of being disappointed; no, no, it must be this very night if I die for it; her room is only the other side of my sisters'.'

I tried to persuade him from doing anything rashly, as we could not yet be certain that even excited and ready as she had shown herself, she was prepared to surrender her virginity so quickly. However, arguments and reasonings were in vain. 'See,' he exclaimed, 'the very thoughts of her make my prick ready to burst,' opening his trousers and letting out his beautiful red-headed cock, as it stood in all its manly glory, stiff and hard as marble, with the hot blood looking ready to burst from his distended veins; the sight was too exciting for me to restrain myself, the cigarette dropped from my lips, and going upon my knees in front of him, I kissed, sucked, frigged and played with his delicious prick till he spent in my mouth with an exclamation of rapture and I eagerly swallowed every drop of his copious emission. When we had a little recovered our serenity, we discussed the best plans for the night, as I was determined to have my share of the amusement, which Frank most willingly agreed to, provided he was to go first to Rosa's room, and prevail upon her to consent to his ardent suit; then when all seemed to be *en règle*, I was to surprise them in the midst of their fun, and join in the erotic frolic.

After dinner we adjourned to the drawing-room, where a most pleasant evening was enlivened by music and singing, leaving Frank turning over the leaves for Rosa and Polly, as they sang 'What Are the Wild Waves Saying?' Annie and Sophie whispered to me that they should like a short stroll in the garden by moonlight, so opening the window, we stepped out on to the soft gravel path, where we could walk with an almost noiseless tread. Papa and Mama were in the library playing cribbage, and we felt sure that Frank and Rosa would not run after us, so passing rapidly down a shady walk, with one arm round each of the dear girls' waists, and alternately kissing one and the other of them, I followed the instinct of love which allowed me to guide the willing girls into a rather dark arbour without the least demur on their part.

'How lovely the honeysuckle smells!' sighed Sophie, as I drew them both down by my side in the corner, and began a most delicious kissing and groping in the dim obscurity.

'Not so sweet as your dear little pussy,' said I, playfully twisting my fingers in the soft down around the tight little grotto of love which I had taken possession of.

'Oh! Oh! Mind, Walter dear!' she sighed softly, as she clung round my neck.

'Will you let me kiss it as I did Annie's this morning my little pet, it will give you such pleasure; there's nothing to be bashful or shamefaced about here in the dark; ask your sister if it wasn't delicious.'

Annie – 'Oh! let him Sophie dear, you will experience the most heavenly sensations.'

Thus urged she allowed me to raise her clothes, and recline her backwards in the corner, but this would not admit of Annie having her fair share of the game; as she was now all aflame with excited expectation, there was no difficulty in persuading her to kneel over my face as I reclined on my back at full length on the seat; lovely hands at once let my eager prick out of his confined position in my trousers, and as I commenced to suck and gamahuche Sophie, I felt that the dear Annie had taken possession of my cock for her own special benefit.

'Oh! let me kiss you, Sophie dear, put your tongue in my mouth,' said Annie, straddling over me, and putting away my excited engine of love up her own longing crack, and beginning a delightful St George; I clasped the younger girl firmly round the buttocks with one arm, whilst with my right hand I found and rubbed her stiff little clitoris to increase the excitement from the lascivious motions of my tongue in her virgin cunny.

Annie was in a frenzy of voluptuous enjoyment, she bounced up and down on my prick, and now and then rested for a moment to indulge in the exquisite pleasure of the devil's bite, which she seemed to possess to a most precocious extent, the folds of her cunt contracting and throbbing upon my swelling prick in the most delicious manner.

Sophie was all of a tremble, she wriggled herself most excitedly over my mouth, and I licked up her virgin spendings as they came down in a thick creamy emission.

'Oh! Oh! Oh!' she sighed, hugging and kissing Annie in fondest abandon. 'What is it, dear? I shall choke, Walter. There's something running from me; it's so delicious. Oh! What shall I do?'

Annie and myself met at this moment in a joint spend, which left us in an ecstatic lethargy of love, and the two sisters almost fainted upon my prostrate body.

When we had recovered a little, I sat up between the loving sisters.

Sophie, throwing her arms round my neck, quite smothered me with her burning kisses, as she whispered in my ear: 'It was indeed pleasure, dear Walter. Is that one of the delights of love, and what was Annie doing, for she was excited as I was?'

'Can't you guess, darling?' I replied, taking her hand and placing it upon my still rampant cock. 'That is what she played with.'

'But how?' whispered the innocent girl. 'She was kissing and sucking my tongue deliciously all the while, but seemed as if she could not keep still a moment.'

'She had that plaything of mine up her cunny, my dear, and was riding up and down upon it till we all fainted with the pleasure at the same time. You shall have a real lesson in love next time, and Annie won't be jealous, will you, dearest?'

Annie – 'No, no, we must all be free to enjoy all the games of love without jealousy. I wonder how Frank is getting on with Rosa by this time. We must now make haste back to the house.'

Sophie was anxious for more explanations as to the arts of love, but was put off till another time; and all being now in a cooler state of mind, we returned to the house, where we found Frank repeating the game of the morning, by gamahuching Rosa, whilst Polly was gone out of the room.

The red-haired beauty was covered with blushes, as she suddenly dropped her clothes on our entrance, and only recovered from her crimson shamefacedness when Annie laughingly assured her that we had been enjoying ourselves in the same manner.

'Oh! How rude and indecent of us all,' exclaimed Rosa, 'but who can resist the burning touches of a handsome young fellow like your brother; he was so impudent, and it sends such a thrill of voluptuousness through the whole frame.' With this, she commenced to sing 'It's Naughty, But It's Nice'.

The supper bell rang, and, after a light repast, we all separated to our rooms. Frank came into my chamber to join in a cigarette and glass of grog before finally retiring.

'It's all right for tonight, old fellow,' he exclaimed, as soon as we were seated for our smoke. 'I begged Rosa to let me kiss all her charms, in her own room without the inconvenience of clothes. She made some objections at first, but finally consented not to lock the door if I promised not to go beyond kissing, on my honour as a gentleman.'

He was too impatient to stop long, and, after only one smoke, cut off to his room. Undressing myself as quickly as possible, I went to him, and escorted him to the door of his lady-love; it was unlocked, and he glided noiselessly into the darkened chamber. She was evidently awake and expecting his visit, for I could hear their rapturous kissing and his exclamation of delight as he ran his hands over her beautiful figure.

'My love, I must light the candles to feast my eyes upon your extraordinary beauties. Why did you put out the lights?' She made some faint remonstrances, but the room was soon a blaze of light from half a dozen candles.

I was looking through the keyhole, and eagerly listening to every word.

'My love, let us lie side by side and enjoy feeling our bodies in naked contact before we begin kissing each other's charms.'

I could see that his shirt and her *chemise de nuit* were both turned up as high as possible, and his prick was throbbing against her belly. He made her grasp it in her hand, and pulling one of her legs over his thighs, was trying to place the head of his eager cock to the mark between her legs.

'Ah! No! No! Never! You promised on your honour, sir!' she almost screamed in alarm, struggling to disengage herself from his strong embrace. 'No! No! Oh! No! I won't, indeed!'

His previous soft manner seemed in a moment to have changed to a mad fury, as he suddenly rolled her over on her back, keeping his own legs well between her thighs.

'Honour! Honour!' he laughed. 'How can I have honour when you tempt me so, Rosa? You have driven me mad by the liberties I have been allowed. Resistance is useless. I would rather die than not have you now, you dear girl.'

She struggled in desperate silence for a few moments, but her strength was unequal to his; he gradually got into position, and then taking advantage of her exhaustion, rapidly and ruthlessly completed her ravishment.

She seemed insensible at first, and I took advantage of her short un-consciousness to steal into the room, and kneel at the foot of the bed, where I had a fine view of his bloodstained weapon, thrusting in and out of her shattered virginity. After a little she seemed to begin to enjoy his movements, especially after the first lubricating injection of his love juice. Her buttocks heaved up to meet his thrusts, and her arms clung convulsively round his body, and seemed reluctant to let him withdraw, until both seemed to come together in a luscious spend.

As they lay exhausted after this bout, I advanced and kissed the dear girl, and as she opened her eyes, I placed my hand across her mouth to stop any inconvenient scream of surprise, and congratulated her on having so nicely got rid of her troublesome virginity, and claimed my share of the fun, drawing her attention to the rampant condition of my cock in contrast to Frank's limp affair. I could see she was now eager for a repetition of the pleasure she had only just begun to taste. Her eyes were full of languishing desire as I placed her hand upon my prick.

In accordance with our previously devised arrangements she was per-suaded to ride a St George upon me and my cock was inserted in her still tender cunt, with great care, and allowed slowly to get into position; but the excitement was too great for me and with an exclamation of delight I shot a stream of sperm up into her very entrails; this set her off and she began slowly to move upon me, her cunt gripping and throbbing upon the shaft most deliciously, and we were soon running another delightful course; this was too much for Frank, his cock was again as hard as iron, and eager to get in somewhere, so kneeling up behind her he tried to insert his prick in her cunt alongside of mine, but found it too difficult to achieve, then the charming wrinkled orifice of her pink bottom-hole caught his attention, the tip of his affair was wet with our spendings, and his vigorous shoves soon gained an entrance, as I was holding her fast and she was too excited to resist anything, only giving a slight scream as she found him slip inside of the part she thought was only made for another purpose. I asked them to rest a few moments and enjoy the sensation of feeling where we were, our pricks throbbing against each other in a most delicious manner, with only the thin membrane of the anal canal between them; it made us spend immediately to the great delight of Rosa, who at once urged us to go on.

This was the most delightful bout of fucking I had ever had; she made us do it over and over again and, when we were exhausted, sucked our pricks up to renewed cockstands. This lasted till the dawn of day warned us of the necessity of precaution, and we retired to our respective rooms.

Next morning Annie and her sisters rallied us upon our late appearance at the breakfast table, remarking with a pouting look that we could not care much for their company if we lay a-bed and left them to themselves for the best half of the day, and that Rosa was just as bad, for she was actually still in dishabille, taking her breakfast in her own room.

Here Mama interposed, by adding, 'Besides, Walter, I am astonished you should copy Frank's lazy ways, you who on your first arrival here were so eager for early-morning walks; look at Annie, she is not half so rosy and animated as she looked after your first walk.'

A deep flush passed across Annie's face at this allusion to our first eventful walk, when we had the adventure with the bull, but I prevented her parents' observing it by replying that residents in town were always in such a hurry to enjoy the fresh air, and that it seemed to have an extraordinary somnolescent effect upon me, as I could hardly keep my eyes open at supper time, or rouse myself from sleep in the morning.

Frank – 'I'm glad you have found out it is not all laziness now. Walter will take my part when I assert it is the natural drowsiness of youth, which is readily induced by the keen bracing air we breathe all day.'

Papa made a few incredulous, ironical remarks about the youth of the present day, and then breakfast being over, as he rose from the table, said: 'Walter, would you mind riding a dozen miles to oblige me. Frank would not be ready to start for an hour at least; besides, I would rather trust you than him with the lady my note is for; Colonel Leslie's wife is both young and gay, and I would rather not run the risk of Frank being one day a co-respondent in the Divorce Court; and I caution *you* to take care of yourself.'

I readily assented, more especially when I noticed a shade of jealous anxiety flit across Annie's tell-tale face. The horse was already at the door, so springing into the saddle I rode off with a fluttering anticipation of something racy being likely to turn up. I shall not trouble about my reflections during this delightful hour's ride; the atmosphere was most deliciously bracing, and my thoughts were so amorously bent that when I reined up at the lodge-gate, at the entrance to the colonel's grounds, I felt that I could fuck anything in petticoats, from a witch to a gatepost; the gatekeeper soon passed me in, and I sprang from my saddle before the door of a fine old Elizabethan hall; my knock was promptly responded to by a most handsome young coloured fellow with a Hindu cast of feature.

Mrs Leslie was at home, and he begged I would excuse her coming down to the drawing-room, as she was still at her toilette, and would immediately see me in her private boudoir.

This courteous message revived all my romantically amorous ideas, with which I had indulged myself during my ride.

Ushered into the boudoir, I found the lady of the house to be a beautiful brunette of about three-and-twenty, with a most bewitching expression of countenance, whilst her large, full, dark eyes seemed to read my very soul as she extended her hand and drew me to a seat by her side, saying: 'So, you are cousin Walter, I suppose; how is it that Frank did not ride over with his papa's note? But tell him,' she added with a very arch look, 'that I was quite as well pleased to see you, and that I consider his cousin quite as fascinating as himself.'

Then, ringing the bell, she continued, 'Will you take a cup of chocolate with me after your ride? It will invigorate me for the serious business of your uncle's note,' opening a drawer and laying several bundles of papers like legal documents on the table, just as the servant entered (he was the good-looking Hindu who had first introduced me).

Mrs Leslie – 'Vishnu, bring up the chocolate, with two cups and some biscuits, and mind not to forget the flask of noyau,' remarking to me as he disappeared, 'Is he not a good-looking heathen? The colonel had him long before he married me, and I call him his principal Hindu deity; whenever I look at him it puts me in mind of Joseph and Potiphar's wife, especially now the colonel is away; do you not think it a burning shame to leave a young wife all alone by herself?'

She continued to run on in this curious way, without giving me a chance to make a reply or observation in return, as she busied herself laying out the papers, making pretence of an awful lot of business to be gone through

The servant now brought in the chocolate, etc., and was dismissed with the order to tell Annette that her mistress would be too busy for some time, and was not to be disturbed until she rang for the completion of her toilette.

My fair hostess was a most charming object as she moved about in her dressing-gown, which was rather open at the neck, so as to display the upper part of the snowy prominences of her luscious bosom, besides which I caught glimpses of her naked feet, with nothing on but the most *petite* blue satin slippers. Presently she poured out two cups of chocolate, put in a little of the noyau, and presenting me with one of them took her seat by my side on the soft yielding sofa. 'Drink it off as I do,' she said; 'it will do you far more good than sipping and allowing it to get cold.'

We both drank our small cups at a draught, and I almost instantly felt a thrill of voluptuous warmth rush through my frame, and looking at my fair companion, saw that her eyes seemed to sparkle with a strange amorous fire.

The devil was in me; in less time than it takes to write it, my empty cup was put on the table, and my disengaged arm placed round her neck; I drew her face to mine, and imprinted several kisses on her lips and cheeks as my other hand took possession of that inviting bosom; she was covered with blushes as she exclaimed, 'Fie! Fie, sir!! how can you take such liberties when I can't help myself without dropping my cup?'

'Dear lady, excuse my liberties, and don't distress yourself, I am really greatly obliged to the cup for its assistance; how can I look upon such loveliness without being tempted, yes, tempted! driven mad by the sight of such charms; you will excuse, you will pardon my presumption, I am sure,' I ejaculated, throwing myself upon my knees before her and hiding my face in her lap, as I clasped my arms nervously round her waist and could feel her whole frame tremble with emotion.

Suddenly she seemed to start with pain as she exclaimed, 'Ah! Goodness! Oh! Oh!! Oh!! the cramp in my legs. Oh! Oh!' as the cup was thrown down by her side. 'Oh, release me, sir! Oh, Walter, excuse me, I must rub it!'

Here was a splendid opportunity to improve a lucky chance. 'Permit me, poor dear lady, you are in such dreadful pain, and I am a medical student,' I said, making bold to raise her dressing-gown and chafe her lovely calves with my eager hands; what lovely legs I now beheld, with not a vestige of anything on them; my blood was on fire, my fingers gradually wandered higher and higher, and I could not refrain from imprinting kisses on the delicious soft, pinky flesh, as she seemed rather to sigh than speak, 'Oh! thank you, pray don't, it's so indelicate, and the cramp is gone now.'

'No, no, dear Madame, the nervous contractions of your beautiful thighs convince me that it is higher up, and will return again in a few moments, unless I can relieve you; indeed you must not mind me, as I am a medical man,' I quickly replied, making bolder advances every moment, and taking advantages of the warm temperament I knew she possessed.

'You rogue, you young villain, your touches and kisses have undone me; how can I resist a handsome student? Oh, Walter, Walter, I must have you! I had only been trying to draw you out a little, never thinking you were such a young gallant; and now I am caught in my own net!'

'Ah! What a hurry. You'll spoil it all by your impetuosity; you shall never have me without first kissing the shrine of love.'

'Sir!' pushing me away, as I was endeavouring to get between her lovely thighs. 'Strip, strip, sir, I must see my Adonis, as your Venus now unveils herself to you,' throwing off her dressing-gown (which I now saw was her only article of clothing); and drawing my face down to hers, she thrust her tongue into my mouth, 'tipping the velvet' in the most delicious style of voluptuous abandon, and delightfully handling my prick and balls at the same time. It was too much for my impatient steed, my spendings flew all over her hands and body almost instantly.

'Ah! What a naughty impatient boy, to come so quickly! Pull off your clothes, sir, and let us take our fill of love on yonder bed. My husband deserves this, for leaving me open to such temptation. You dear boy, how I shall love you; what a fine prick you have, and so – so – what do they call it? – (blushing at her own words) so randy! That's what the colonel says of the young fellows. Isn't it a dreadfully rude word, Walter? But so full of meaning. Whenever he said so, I couldn't help wishing for a handsome, randy young gentleman, such as your uncle has sent me today.'

This is how she ran on, as I threw off everything, and I was as naked as herself in a trice; then, hugging, kissing, belly to belly, and handling each other's charms in every possible way, we slowly progressed towards the inviting bed in the other room; once or twice I stopped and tried to get my prick into her standing up, but she would have none of that, and at last, when her bottom rested against the edge of the bed, she ordered me to kneel down and kiss the seat of love; how my tongue searched out her fine stiff clitoris, which projected quite an inch and a half from the lips of her vagina. I sucked it in ecstasy, and titillated her sensitive organs so that she spent profusely in a minute or two, holding my head with her hands to make me go on; it was a most deliciously enjoyable gamahuche; my tongue revelled in her creamy emission, till she begged me to slip off my shirt and come on the bed and let her enjoy my fine prick. So I ended this prelude with a playful, loving bite on her excited clitoris, and then, springing to my feet, rolled with her on to the bed, her ready hand grasping my cock as I mounted on her lovely body.

'What a shame!' she sighed. 'How you have been spending, you naughty boy, you won't have much left for me now; but he's fine and stiff!' as she squeezed it in her hand, and brought the head of my affair to the mark.

I found her deliciously tight, and assured her she was quite a virgin.

'So I should be, my dear Walter, but for you. The colonel has got so little to please me with, that, tight as I am, I can hardly feel him! now your jewel of pleasure makes me feel gorged with delight!'

Her motions were as lascivious as her words. She writhed and threw up her buttocks with extraordinary rapidity and energy, whilst I was equally eager and rapid in ramming into her delicious cunt.

I was ready as if I had never spent, and we swam in a mutual emission almost immediately, both of us being so overcome by our feelings that we almost swooned in delight; this only lasted for a minute; the throbbing and contracting of the folds of her vagina on my enraptured prick awoke me to renewed efforts, and we were rapidly progressing towards another spend, when she checked me, and begged I would withdraw for a little, when she would amuse me till she felt she must have him again, and she added, 'I shall enjoy it so much more if I can make you last longer. Sit on my body, Walter dear, and lay your beautiful prick between the globes of my bosom; you shall spend there next time. I can't help telling you what a fine one it is, over and over again!'

She went on caressing it with her hand, and making her two bubbies close upon it, so that I could work between them. It was another delicious idea, but she had not exhausted all her ways of exciting me. Her other hand passed under my thigh, and I thought she was frigging herself, but it was only to wet her finger, preparatory to frigging my bottom-hole with it. This made me come again almost directly.

'Now,' said she, 'I mean to ride on you, and make it last as long as possible, so let us reverse positions.'

This was done, and she rode me and stopped alternately for about twenty minutes, when we met in a glorious flow of sperm.

'What do you think of that?' she exclaimed, as soon as she recovered her breath. 'We will get up and answer your uncle's letter now, and you shall promise to come again soon.'

Nothing of moment occurred during the evening, after my visit to Mrs Leslie, but I could see that Annie was rather piqued because I had nothing to tell her, except that I thought the colonel's lady a most charming person, and had been pressed to stay with her to luncheon before she would write a reply to my uncle's note.

Next day being the last representation of a celebrated piece at the theatre of the county town by a first-rate London company, Papa expressed a wish that we should all go in the evening, but Annie and Sophie, giving me a knowing look on the sly, declared they had already seen it once and did not care to go again. For my part, of course, I had seen it half a dozen times in town, so it was finally arranged that Frank, Rosa and Polly only would go with Papa and Mama; they had a drive of more than an hour before them, so started at 6 p.m., and as soon as they were out of sight we three started for the bathing place at the lake. It was such a deliciously warm evening, and it would be just the place for our anticipated pleasures, as I had suggested to Annie and Sophie during the day.

Bolting the summer-house door on the inside as soon as we got in, I suggested first of all to stimulate our mutually ardent desires by a bottle of champagne; this so exhilarated the two lovely girls that we indulged in a second bottle before stripping for a romp. Seven o'clock found us bathed in a flood of golden light from the declining sun, which now shone directly in upon us, this warned us to make haste and improve the opportunity, so each one assisting the others and at the same time indulging in many loving tricks and liberties, we were soon in Adam and Eve costume.

'Now,' I exclaimed, 'Annie dear, you won't be jealous if I make a woman of your sister, as we promised the other day,' taking the younger one up in my arms with my rampant cock throbbing against her belly, as I carried her to the lounger.

'What a naughty boy you are, Walter, anything or anybody for a change is what fickle men like, but I won't be jealous of Sophie, although I am of Mrs Leslie. I know you had her yesterday; that sheepish tell-tale look, sir, when you met me on your return, was enough to confirm my suspicions of what would happen when you were *tête-à-tête* with that killing lady,' she replied.

'For shame, Annie, darling, you told me yourself the other day love ought to be free everywhere; I don't deny my guilt, but will do my best to earn forgiveness now,' I said, pushing Sophie back upon the soft yielding lounger. 'Help me to ease this darling of her troublesome virginity, and I will then repay your own longing cunny for all your love and forebearance; I am sure

Mrs Leslie would like to make you one of our party without any feelings of jealousy; there are so many ways of voluptuous enjoyment that if there is only one man to three girls it can be so varied as to give everyone the most intense delight.'

At this both the girls gave me rapturous kisses, with every possible assurance that they never would be selfish, and would be only too happy to extend the circle of those they could be free and loving with, adding with special emphasis, 'We are such noodles, dear Walter, we knew nothing till you introduced us to the arts of love, and as long as you can stay with us shall look to you to guide us in everything; we know it's wrong, but what heavenly pleasure there is in the loving mixture of the sexes.'

Annie, taking my prick in her hand – 'Now, sir I will show this gentleman the way into Sophie's cabinet of love; be firm, dear, he won't hurt you more than can be helped, and the after joy will soon drown all recollection of the first short suffering.'

Sophie, opening her legs as wide as possible – 'I'm all on fire to taste the real tree of love; don't spare me, Walter, dear, I'd rather die than not have it now!'

The red head of 'Cupid's Battering Ram' was now brought to the charge; Annie opened the rosy lips of her sister's cunt and placed my cock in the exact position, but her touches, together with the thoughts of the delicious titbit I was about to enjoy, caused me to spend in a moment all over her fingers and into the virgin passage in front. 'Push on, push on; now's the time to gain your victory,' she whispered; 'that will make it easier to get him in,' at the same time lifting up Sophie's buttocks with her disengaged hand, so as to make her meet my attack in a more favourable manner. My first lunge lodged the head of Mr Priapus fairly within the tight folds of the victim's vagina, and I had already won the first outworks of the virgin's defences.

Poor Sophie moaned under the sharp pain of my assault, but biting her lips to repress any cries of pain she courageously placed one hand on the shaft of my prick, as if jealous of her sister's loving help, and anxious to have the honour of herself showing me the way to achieve love's dearest triumph, or perhaps it was for fear of my withdrawing before completely accomplishing my task.

'You love!' I exclaimed, enraptured by this exhibition of pluck, 'I will soon make a real woman of you,' then pushing fiercely on, on, I gradually forced the tight sheath to dilate. Every obstruction gave way to my determined energy, and with a final plunge, I was buried to the roots of my affair, and shooting at the same moment my warm spendings into her inmost vitals. This exhausted me for a few moments, and I lay supine upon the heaving bosom of the lovely Sophie, till I could feel Annie's fingers busy tickling my balls and feeling the shaft of my cock. Just at the same moment Sophie, who had almost fainted under the painful ordeal, opened her eyes, and with a loving smile pouted her lips as an invitation for a kiss, which I instantly responded to, almost sucking her breath away in my ardour. My excitement was now raised to the highest possible pitch by her sister's titillations, and the loving challenge of Sophie herself to renew my motions with her, by heaving up her bottom and nipping my prick in her cunny in the most delightful way imaginable.

This time I prolonged the pleasure as much as possible, beginning slowly, and often stopping to feel the delicious throbbings of cock and cunny in their delightful conjunction. 'Ach! this is indeed love; it repays for all the pain I felt at first. Oh! oh! dear Walter, it feels as if my very soul was flowing from me in ecstasy!' she almost screamed out, kissing, biting, squeezing me with all her might at the moment of emission, which I again responded to with a flow of my own sperm.

I now declared we must refresh ourselves a little before going further, so she reluctantly allowed me to withdraw. A short plunge in the lake had a most invigorating effect. I felt as strong as a giant again, then another bottle of fizz renewed our loving ardour; the girls were handling my prick, which stood again as hard as ivory. So slipping on my shirt, as I intended to be the uppermost of the trio, I laid Sophie on her back, and then telling the obedient Annie to kneel over her sister and gamahuche her in return for Sophie's doing the same by her, I mounted up behind her, saying, 'I've made a woman of your dear sister, and will now treat you, my darling, to a new sensation.' But just at that moment Sophie, who had no idea of my intentions, seized hold of my cock, saying she must kiss the dear sweet thing which had afforded her such exquisite bliss. Holding it tight in her hand, she took the head between her pearly teeth and kissed and treated him to such love bites that I soon spent in her mouth, which she greedily swallowed, with all the abandon of voluptuous enjoyment. Meanwhile, I had been frigging Annie's bottom with my two fingers, which I had managed to insert together, and that dear girl was sucking her sister's quim, and wriggling herself in the most excitable way possible.

Sophie was now going to insert my prick in her sister's cunt, but Annie, almost beside herself with excitement, exclaimed, 'No, no, my dear, put him where Walter has got his fingers; I should like to try that, it is so exciting; the very thought of it makes me mad with desire to know what it is like. His fingers have given me such pleasures that I am sure the dear thing in your hand will greatly improve the sensation!'

No sooner said than done; the obedient girl directed my cock to the beautifully wrinkled tight little brown hole of her sister's bottom at the very moment I withdrew my fingers. When I found they so thoroughly appreciated the idea I had resolved to initiate them into, and being well lubricated and as stiff as possible, I soon passed the portals of Annie's second virginity. But, Heavens, what a delicious bout we had, she bounded about so with delight, that I had to hold tight round her neck to prevent being thrown out, whilst Sophie, below, gamahuched her delighted sister, and with her right hand continued to press my balls and prick, keeping time to every insertion in her sister's bottom. We all spent together, almost screaming with delight, and then lay in a confused heap, enjoying all the sensations of our delicious exhaustion.

As soon as they could kiss and persuade my rather enervated tool into renewed stiffness, Sophie declared I must oblige her with a taste of the new-found joy, and ravish her bottom as well as her sister's.

This was another delicious love engagement, the sisters gamahuching each other with the utmost erotic ardour, whilst my delighted prick revelled in the tight-fitting fundamental of the sweet girl, who wriggled and plunged about so excitedly that I had to hold fast to keep my place.

After this, we returned to the house, and passed the time very pleasantly till the return of the party from the theatre. I was anxious to hear Frank's account of how he had got on with Rosa during the evening, and especially as they drove home.

'Walter,' he said, as we were once more alone in his room after all had gone to rest, 'I've had a most enjoyable time of it since we started. Of course, as we went, it was daylight, so Rose and I maintained a proper decorum, but at the theatre, Papa and Mama were separated from us by Polly, and we all five sat in the front row of the dress circle. How the sight of Rosa's swelling bosom (which her low-necked dress allowed me fully to see) made my prick stand at once; so I took her gloved hand and made her feel how hard and excited it was. As no one could see, she indulged me with quite a gentle frigging outside my trousers, till I spent profusely, to the great delight of the roguish beauty, as I could tell by the smile on her face and the excited looks with which she met my ardent gaze.

' "What a shame," she whispered in my ear. "I know what you have done, you naughty boy. You should have reserved it for a more favourable opportunity."

' "Look out, darling, as we drive home; see if I don't repay your kind attentions," I whispered in return.

'Both Papa and Mama were rather sleepy before the conclusion of the last act, and to make them go off, as soon as we were seated in the carriage, I offered them my flask of brandy to keep out the effects of the night air. It had a pretty good strong dose of narcotic in it, and they were soon sound asleep in their corners. Polly also pretended to be dozing.

'Rosa was on my lap directly, and my hands were at once groping their way to the seat of pleasure whilst she was equally busy unbuttoning my trousers and handling the staff of life.

'Our lips met in long-drawn rapturous kisses, which fired every drop of blood in our veins, and both were too impatient for the real business to prolong our toyings with each other's privates; besides, I felt she was already spending over my busy fingers. She had my cock in a glorious state of erection; so opening her delicious thighs as she raised her clothes, she at once impaled herself on the spike she so burned to have thrust into her. It was quite equal to the first time I fucked her. The long evening passed in expectation of what I might be able to do on our return journey: it so added to the piquancy of my arduous longings that I seemed in Heaven itself, and swimming in a very ocean of love, we spent over and over again; our melting kisses and tongue-sucking continually stimulating us to renewed exertions, till the near approach to home warned us of the necessity of bringing our pleasures to an end for a time. Even now, I tell you, Walter, my cock keeps throbbing and standing at the very thoughts of the delightful pressures she treated me to; her cunt bites so deliciously.'

In the morning, Papa and Mama had scarcely slept off the effects of the sleeping dose they had imbibed from the brandy flask of their dutiful son, and lay a-bed very late, in fact, almost to luncheon time; meanwhile, we, the younger members of the family, had privately agreed upon a plan of amusement for the afternoon and evening.

Finding that two pretty young girls of fourteen and fifteen were living close by, with an invalid mother, whilst their brother was away, being a midshipman in the Royal Navy, I proposed that Annie should send the Misses Bruce an invitation to spend the afternoon with us, *en famille*, without the least ceremony, and join us in an alfresco tea party at a little hut in the woods, which formed part of my uncle's estate.

At luncheon we informed the governor of what we had done and hoped that both he and Mama would join in our outdoor party in the woods.

'No thank you, my dears, we are too afraid of the damp grass and rheumatics. Besides, we have not yet got over the fatigue of yesterday. We will stay quietly at home and hope you may enjoy yourselves thoroughly, as we should do if we were younger,' replied the jolly, kind-hearted old gentleman.

This was exactly what we had wished for and expected; so Frank and Annie at once sent off the servants with every requisite for our open-air tea party.

About three o'clock, the two young ladies arrived, and as all were ready, we at once set off for the scene of our anticipated fun, which was a rough bower covered with flowering honeysuckle and clematis, at the end of a long, shady, private walk, more than half a mile from the house.

Frank and myself particularly attached ourselves to the two fresh young ladies as being the greatest strangers, and therefore justly expectant of the most attention.

Emily Bruce, the elder, was a charming dark-eyed brunette, her rather large mouth having a fascinating effect as you regarded her. In fact, such a display of pearly white teeth, I never saw before, and the very thought that they might perhaps be soon employed in love bites on my tender-headed prick filled me with maddening lust to possess myself of their owner.

Nor was her sister, Louisa, any less prepossessing, she being almost the counterpart of Emily, except that one could easily see there was a slight difference in age.

When we arrived at the bower, the servants were at once sent home, being told that they could clear away the things next morning, as it would be too late for them to return in the evening, and at the same time, without asking the consent of her young friends, dear Annie scribbled a pencil note to their mama, to say that if they at all were late, she would insist upon them staying with her all night, and not to make herself at all anxious on their behalf – this was quietly sent off by one of the servants.

As soon as we were alone, Frank and I, uncorking the champagne, lighted our cigars, and saying that the sun was still too warm for outdoor romping, pressed the girls to try some very mild cigarettes of Turkish tobacco.

At last Annie and Rosa set the example by lighting up, and were at once laughingly followed by the others. Our two young friends protested they never took wine. Still, they evidently sipped it with great delight, and we bantered them upon being so tied to their mother's apron strings, etc., till they began to be quite as free as my cousins and Rosa.

We had a good stock of fizz, besides sandwiches and cake, so that no one seemed at all anxious to take the trouble of tea-making.

Still we were careful that only enough should be taken to warm our friends up to a slightly excitable state, in fact, just to induce that state of all-overishness, which tingles through a young girl's sensitive frame when she feels the first vibrations of amorous desires, which she can as yet hardly understand.

Their sparkling eyes, slightly flushed faces and above all, the dazzling beauties of their teeth, as they indulged in gay laughter at our badinage, set all of us aflame. I could see that Rosa and my cousins were longing to help in enjoying these innocent and ravishing young girls.

Now a game of hunt the slipper was proposed, and we at once adjourned to the soft, mossy green sward outside the bower. This was a most delicious and excitable romp.

Whenever it came our turns, Frank and myself indulged in all kinds of quick and startling touches, which made the two little dears blush up to their eyes at first, and when we managed to catch one of them with the slipper we claimed a hearty kiss as penalty, which they submitted to with tolerable grace, yet evidently in a state of great excitement, it was all so new to them. We finished the game, had a little more champagne, then proposed a game of hide and seek in the wood, with the reservation that no one was to go too far off.

We were to be in pairs; I chose Emily, and Frank took Louisa. Polly and Sophie went together, whilst Annie and Rosa had to search for us when we called out.

It so happened that there was an old sand-pit close by, in which several years before Master Frank had amused himself by making a Robinson

Crusoe's cave, and planted bushes in front of it, so that the entrance was perfectly out of sight, and no one would fancy anyone could be screened by the small amount of cover which seemed to grow on the side of the pit; this was just the place for our purpose, and it had been beforehand arranged that we were not to be found for a long time. Gliding into the cave Frank let fall the old curtain that hung at the entrance, and we were at once in the dark; the place was large enough for us all to sit together on a heap of fine soft sand at the further end.

'What a dear girl you are!' I whispered in Emily's ear, as I took a kiss in the dark, and drew her trembling body quite close by an arm around her waist. 'Pray don't,' she whispered in return, 'if you do not keep quiet I won't stop in this dark place.'

'Don't say so, it would be cruel, especially if you knew all I feel towards you, Emily dear. I must call you Emily, yes, and kiss you again and again; I love you so, your breath is so fragrant, what are you afraid of, there's nothing to fear among friends, darling,' I whispered, kissing my partner rapturously.

'Oh, ah, you take my breath away, Walter, I'm so unused to such goings on. Oh, fie, sir, for shame, you make me feel all of a-tremble, you take such liberties!' as I was working one hand inside the bosom of her dress, and getting possession of two hard round bubbies which throbbed with emotion under my loving caresses.

'It's all love, darling, and no one can see, can't you hear how Frank and Louisa are kissing; is it not delicious to think they are doing the same, and will be sure to keep our secret?'

A deep sigh was my only answer, and again our lips met in a long luscious kiss. My tongue was thrust into her mouth, and tickled the tip of her own velvety organ of speech. I could feel the nipples of her virgin bosom stick out as stiff as little cocks and whispered to her to allow me to kiss them.

'I can refuse you nothing,' she whispered; 'you are such a bold lover. I'm all in flame from head to foot at the numberless liberties you are taking with me. Ah, if Mama only knew,' she sighed, as I was now sucking her titties, and running my disengaged hand up her thighs; they were nipped tightly together, but gradually relaxed under the gentle pressure of my hand, till I actually got possession of her cunny, which I could feel was slightly covered with soft downy hair, and soon began to frig her gently with my forefinger. How the dear girl wriggled under this double excitement, and I could feel one of her hands groping outside my trousers over my bursting prick to return the pleasure I was giving her. One by one she unfastened the buttons, then her soft delicate hand soon had possession of my stiff affair, naked and palpitating with unsatisfied desire.

'Ah,' she whispered, 'I am satisfied at last! we had a servant at home, a few months ago, who slept in our room, and used to tickle and play with us. She told us that men had a long thing as hard as iron, which they pleased the ladies by shoving up their bellies, and that was how the babies were made.

Do you believe it? She was always shoving her fingers into us as you are doing to me now, and – and – and,' here she hesitated and seemed to shudder with delight, just as I spent all over her hand, and I could also feel her spendings come in a warm gush over my fingers. It was delicious. Her hand first held tight the top of my throbbing prick, then gently worked up and down the shaft, lubricated by my spendings. It was indeed a voluptuous treat; I begged her to thrust her tongue into my mouth, and we continued the mutual frigging till she almost fainted away in her ecstasy.

Slightly recovering, I asked her what it was she was going to tell me about the maidservant, when she hesitated.

'Do, dearest, tell me everything,' I implored, in a loving whisper. 'We are now without reserve to each other; you can have no secrets from your loving Walter.'

'It was so funny, I don't know how she could do it, but Mary was so fond of sucking and kissing us where you have your hand, dearest,' she replied, 'but it was so nice you can't imagine how we enjoyed having her do it to us.'

'My love, my Emily, let me kiss you now, and it would be sublime if you would kiss me. I long to feel the love bites of your beautiful teeth in my Cupid's dart. Frank and Louisa are too busy to notice what we do,' I whispered in her ear, as I inclined the willing girl backwards on the soft pillow of sand and reversed my position so that we lay at full length, side by side, both of us eager as possible for the game; my head was buried between her loving thighs, with which she pressed me most amorously as my tongue was inserted in her loving slit; this was a fine gamahuche. I stirred up all the lasciviousness of her ardent temperament till she screamed with delight, and caused Frank and Louisa to enquire what we were doing, but we made no reply. She sucked my delighted prick, handled and kissed my balls, till I spent in her mouth, as her teeth were lovingly biting the head of my penis. She sucked it all down, whilst I repaid her loving attentions to the best of my ability with my own active tongue.

As soon as it was over, I took Emily by the hand, and we groped towards our companions, who, I found, were equally as busy as we had been. Frank thoroughly understood my intention; we all got together, and joined in a grope of cocks and cunnies without the least restraint, till suddenly the curtain was pulled down, and we heard the laughing voices of Rosa and Annie, as they exclaimed, 'See, here they are. What are these rude boys doing to you young ladies?'

Emily and Louisa were covered with confusion, but the girls lovingly assured them they would keep the secret, and introduce them to more fun after they had retired to bed, as it was now getting late, and we must all return to the house.

As I have before observed, the wing of the mansion in which we all slept was quite apart from the other wing in which Papa, Mama, and the servants were located, so as soon as we had retired, Frank and myself joined the girls in their room, or rather rooms, for they occupied two. The Miss Bruces blushed crimson at seeing us only in our shirts, especially as one was seated on the *pot de chambre*, whilst the other was exhibiting her charms to my inquisitive cousins before a cheval glass.

'All right,' exclaimed Annie, 'my dears, everything is free between us and the boys, but we mean to punish you for allowing the impudent fellows to presume upon such liberties with you in the cave. Your bottoms shall smart, young ladies, I can assure you,' as she produced a couple of light birch rods from a drawer; in fact, I had provided them for her, the idea having been suggested to me by reading a book called *The Romance of Lust*.

A fine large bed stood by the wall, facing another at the end of the room, but our programme only required one couch. Annie and Rosa were determined to have their enjoyment now; everyone was ordered to strip off shirt or chemise, then I horsed Emily on my back whilst Frank did the same by her sister.

Sophie and Polly were entrusted with the rods, and gaily switched us and our riders' bottoms as we trotted round the room, the sisters hardly knowing whether to laugh or cry, when a more stinging cut than usual made them cry for mercy; our pricks were as rampant as possible, and we were not in need of any extra stimulation; still the girls were very hard on our rumps, although not quite so severe with the sisters. The darling Emily had so twined her legs round me as I held them close under my armpits that her pretty feet in their bewitching little slippers were frigging my cock between them most deliciously.

The sight of our red smarting bottoms and bursting pricks was too much for Annie and Rosa, and they were inflamed by lust, so throwing themselves backward on the bed, with their legs wide open and feet resting on the floor, the two dear girls presented their quims to our charge, as with both hands they held open the lips of their delicious cunts, inviting our eager cocks to come on. We charged them at once, under the impulsive urging of the rods, gave a few delightful fucking motions, then withdrew and trotted round the room again; this we constantly repeated to prolong our enjoyment, till at last the dear girls could stand it no longer, their arms clasped us firmly, whilst the rods cut away with extra force to make us complete their pleasure; it was a most luxurious finish, we all spent with screams of delight, and lay for a few moments in a delicious state of lethargic exhaustion till we awoke to find Sophie, Polly, Emily and Louisa all rolling on the floor in the delights of gamahuching.

After this the two dear girls begged, with tears in their eyes, that Frank and Walter would make women of them, so that they might really taste the wildest delights of love.

'Then, dears,' said Rosa, with a sly laugh, 'you must kiss them, and make their exhausted cocks stiff again, and then we will lend the two boys to you.'

We sat on the bed by the side of our late fucking partners, who we kissed, fondled and frigged, whilst Emily and Louisa, kneeling between our knees, sucked our pricks up to standing point, as their hands drew back our foreskins or played with our balls.

Stiff and rampant as we were we entreated them to go on for a little longer, till we felt ourselves almost at spending point. Polly and Sophie arranged two bolsters and some pillows on the floor in the most advantageous manner; the sisters were each placed with two pillows under their bottoms, whilst their heads rested on the bolsters. Annie and Rosa then conducted us to the victims, who impatiently waited their immolation to the god of love with open legs and longing cunts. The two mistresses of the ceremonies took our pricks in hand, and directed them to the path of bliss. Emily was my partner again; she threw her legs over my back and heaved up to meet the fatal thrust which was to be the death of her troublesome virginity. I had no time to see how the others progressed, but heard a smothered shriek of agony from Louisa, as no doubt Frank achieved her fate for her; my partner was more courageous, she glued her lips to mine, sucking in my tongue in the most ardent manner imaginable, even while my prick was tearing through her hymen; my spending deluged her wounded quim, and we soon lost all thoughts of pain when we recommenced a lovely fuck, with me moving slowly at first, till her rapid motions spurred me on to faster plunges, her deliciously tight cunt holding me like a hand, in fact so tight that I could feel my foreskin drawn backwards and forwards at every shove.

'Ah! you dear fellow, push on, kill me with delight!' she screamed in ecstasy, as we came again together, and I was equally profuse in my words of endearment.

As we lay still after it was over her tight-fitting cunt seemed to hold and continually squeeze my delighted prick so by its contractions and throbbings I was ready again directly, and we ran another thrilling course before she would let me try to withdraw.

Frank and Louisa had been equally delighted with each other, and thus the two sisters lost their maidenheads almost at the same moment.

Not a day passed but we had some voluptuous games, whilst as to Rosa and Frank, they were openly engaged to be married, which was an especial gratification to the old people.

Time flew so rapidly that my visit drew to its close and we were all thinking of devising some signal display of love, to be enacted as a parting scene ere I took my departure from my uncle's hospitable and happy domicile, when one fine morning in June, who should favour us with a call, but my lovely brunette Mrs Leslie. She had driven over to invite myself and cousins to spend an entire day before the colonel's return. 'You know,' she said, turning to my uncle, 'how stiff and starch all his ideas are, and I must have one day of real fun before he comes home from Paris. Will you let them come tomorrow and stop till the next day?'

My uncle being too kind to refuse, the arrangement was made at once,

Mrs Leslie stayed to luncheon, and we took an afternoon stroll in the park afterwards. From time to time her intelligent glances assured me she was anxious for a *tête-à-tête* with me, so I asked her to take my arm and we soon managed to give the others the slip, and lost ourselves in a dense copse. Sitting down on the soft mossy turf, under a shady little yew tree, we were quite hidden from observation.

'How I longed to kiss your sweet lips once more,' I exclaimed, clasping her in my eager embrace, and sucking her breath almost away in a luscious osculation.

'If that is all you thought of, sir, you have been vastly unfaithful to your protestations of love, and I should really feel awfully jealous of your pretty cousins and Miss Redquim did I not see the unruly state of the jewel in your trousers,' she laughingly replied, as she took speedy steps to release and secure the impatient prisoner in her grasp, continuing, 'I wonder how he has amused himself since that ever memorable day when I first had the pleasure of both seeing and feeling the noble fellow. Now tell me true, Sir Walter, have you seduced your cousins and their friend?'

I at once made a full confession of all our amours, and begged she would indulge us in every possible way on the morrow, as it would be the last grand chance I should have before returning to town.

'Most delightful state of things I am sure, but what a shame not to have run over and invited me to join in your amorous festivities. Surely you knew it was just what I should have delighted in. I have a great mind to disappoint you now, only I should also be punishing myself, so come on, you naughty young fellow, and I will consider between this and tomorrow what your penance will be,' she said, reclining herself backwards, her fine dark eyes full of a humid languishing fire, which too truly indicated her voluptuous requirements.

Lifting her skirts quickly, I paid my devotions at the shrine of love by a kiss and playful bite of her clitoris, then, unable to dally any longer, placed myself between her readily yielding thighs, and was soon revelling within the soft juicy folds of her divine organ of bliss, delighted beyond expression by the throbbing compressions to which it treated me as I lay quietly enjoying the sense of complete possession, which is so delicious to contemplate, before commencing more vigorous action; our lips met again and our billing and cooing would have lasted some time had we not heard Frank declaring to Rosa and his sisters what a damned shame it was of Walter and Mrs Leslie to give them the slip, but he would find us and spoil our fun.

This caused my charming inamorata to heave up her buttocks as a challenge to me not to waste more time, so I put spurs to my steed, but none too soon, for just as we died away in a mutual spend, Frank, Sisters and Co. burst upon the scene with a triumphant exclamation of 'Here's Walter and his grass widow', and before we could recover ourselves the laughing party inflicted an awful slapping on our bottoms, till a truce was made and we all agreed to wait patiently for the morrow's party at Mrs Leslie's.

Next day, favoured by splendid weather, we were early at the colonel's residence, and the handsome swarthy Vishnu ushered us into the luxurious boudoir of his voluptuous mistress 'You have arrived early, it is scarcely one o'clock, my toilette's not yet made, but how very welcome you all are to my house, I need not trouble to say, after the frank understanding we came to yesterday, as to our amusements now you are here. The chocolate is just ready, and I have infused in it an imperceptible something (a secret, my dear, which the colonel brought from India), which will soon set all your young amorous blood in such a glow of desire that you will not know how to satisfy your intense cravings for the delight of love, and then naughty Walter shall be served out for his unfaithfulness to me.'

This speech made us all smile as we took up the small cups of delicious chocolate which Vishnu handed round and, as he disappeared, our hostess, who had nothing on but her dressing-gown, having drawn Frank to her side on the sofa, asked us, as the day was so warm, to throw aside as much as possible of our superfluous clothing, which was speedily done.

'We must have a romp before luncheon, then repose or stroll about during the afternoon, and in the evening we shall, I hope, enjoy some novel ideas I have quite set my mind upon,' she continued during the short time we took to disrobe. 'That's right, only keep on the *chemiserie* now, at night we will discard the last rag; I have no chemise to take off, so will keep on this convenient *robe de chambre*, but you may look, Frank, if you don't think Rosa will be jealous,' as she opened the front, and displayed to his ardent gaze all the beauties of her person.

'If it makes her jealous, I can't help admiring such charms!' said Frank, 'but Rosa is far too sensible for that, and thoroughly enters into all our fun; in fact I am sure she loves Walter as well as she does me, only she can't marry both of us.'

'Ha! ha!! that accounts for Walter forgetting me; so to be revenged on them both you must have me now,' she replied, lifting up his shirt to see if he was ready. 'Why your love-dart is almost exactly the size of his,' and without more ado she was on his lap, and spitted herself on Frank's cock, throwing off entirely the *robe de chambre* that she might enjoy him without impediment.

This instantly excited the girls, who lay down in pairs for a mutual gamahuche and bottom-frig, Rosa playfully telling me to let Mrs Leslie have the double pleasure by fucking her bottom as she was riding Frank.

'Hold her tight, my boy,' I said, 'and I will let her beautiful little fundament know what it is to keep a stiff prick waiting for his turn,' as I took a little cold cream from the dressing-table, and putting some on the head of my prick, as well as on the delightful brown wrinkled hole exposed to my attack, began to slip it in at once, despite her struggles and screams that we should 'injure her' between us. Further and further I gradually worked in, till I could feel my cock rubbing against Frank's with only the thin divisional membrane between them, our joint spendings deluging both cunt and bum, spurting the warm, frothy sperm over our balls at every thrust. This was not enough to satisfy her, but she kept us at our work until we repeated our emissions with screams of delight, and rolled on the floor in a confused heap amongst the dear girls, who were so excited by the sight of our ecstasies that they were revelling in every species of tribadism to allay their lustful yearnings.

After this Mrs Leslie opened a side door, conducted us into her bathroom, where we refreshed ourselves and indulged in a variety of kissing, frigging, etc., but by her advice the girls refrained from exhausting us too much, and accepted cigarettes of Turkish tobacco to join us in a smoke, as we lighted some of the colonel's fine cigars. It was a picture worthy of any Apelles, as we could see the reflection of all our naked charms on the bathroom walls, which constituted one vast mirror of the very finest silvered glass, two rather good-looking fellows with big pricks, as rampant as could be wished, and five lovely ladies all smoking and puffing pretty curls or rings of vapoury nicotine, alternating that sober enjoyment with the more active fun of trying to burn the tips of their cunts with the fiery end of cigarette or cigar.

About half-past two, we dressed, and then took luncheon, then strolled in the grounds or on the bank of a small stream, where some of us passed the time trying our piscatorial luck, till the bell rang for dinner, which passed pleasantly enough, and about 9 p.m., we assembled in the drawing-room, for a grand erotic seance.

Mrs Leslie dismissed all her servants for the night, except Vishnu, who she said would be quite sufficient to attend to our little requirements.

The room was large and lofty, the windows closed and artistically draped with gorgeous black and gold curtains, the spaces between filled up with mirrors and branching candelabra, the opposite side of the apartment being also quite a tableau of flowers, mirrors and lighted wax candles, which shed a brilliant and yet soft luxurious effulgence over the whole scene; two doors at one end gave access to retiring rooms, where we undressed, and in a very few minutes the whole party, in a state of ravishing nudity, were grouped round Mrs Leslie, as she sat on an ottoman, awaiting her decision as to the programme.

She first persuaded us to sip a little of her chocolate, then went on to say, 'As we are five to two you will find I have a stock of fine, soft, firmly made dildoes to make up the deficiency in males, which alternated with the real article will enable us thoroughly to enjoy ourselves. First, I believe Miss is a virgin, notwithstanding all she knows and has seen; her delicate little pussy must be itching to be emancipated from the thraldom of virginity. Walter must do the service for her at once, on Rosa's lap; so now to business, as I see our gentlemen are in a beautiful state of readiness.'

Polly blushed deeply, but readily seated herself on her friend's lap with her legs wide open, presenting herself to my staff of life, whilst Rosa, passing her hands round the dear girl's waist, held open the lips of her cunny, and guided the head of my affair in the proper direction. Much as she had been frigged and gamahuched, it was a hard task; her cunt was so deliciously small and tight that in spite of her favourable position, I could only just get the head of Mr Priapus within the nymphæ before she started with the intense pain, and gave a suppressed scream of anguish, the tears starting to her eyes and trickling over her blushing face.

'Courage, darling, it will soon be over,' I whispered, kissing her excitedly, whilst Mrs Leslie encouraged me by saying, 'Sharp and quick, Walter, a good thrust will force better than those gentle pushes; gentleness is not real kindness when taking a maidenhead'; at the same moment I felt she was attacking my virgin bottom-hole behind with a well-lubricated dildo, its head being well in before I knew exactly what she was doing; this and the desire to possess Polly so stimulated me that I thrust furiously at the opposing obstacle, her heart-rending cries adding to my pleasure, and making me mad with desire. At last I was halfway in, then a fierce lunge seemed to break quite through as I, at the same time, deluged the tight passage with a copious emission.

The poor little victim had swooned, but Mrs Leslie, working her dildo behind, ordered me to let my cock throb inside Polly's tight sheath, as it would tend to bring her round, and excite her amorous sensibility to the utmost.

What delightful sensations I experienced; my prick feeling all the spasmodic contractions of her vagina, and having my bottom well dildo-fucked at the same time, I spent again under the influence of this accumulated excitement just as my partner was coming round under the influence of some cordial which had been poured down her gasping throat, whilst strong smelling-salts had been applied to her nostrils. She opened her eyes, giving a violent sneeze at the same time, which vibrated on my delighted prick, which instantly began gently to bestir itself in her tight scabbard; this roused her little by little, till throwing her arms round my neck, and returning my hot kisses with all the ardour of her nature, she cried and laughed by turns, as she begged me to make haste and complete her happiness.

By a side glance I could see Frank was in Mrs Leslie's bottom, Annie in him with a dildo, and Sophie doing the same to her sister, a perfect string of pederastic branchings from my own violated bum. It was such a scene as I had never seen before, and added additional fury to my already maddened lust. I came again and again before we finished, each spend more ecstatic than the last. The chocolate had so invigorated us, that we went through an almost interminable series of spendings, till at last nature could stand it no longer, we rolled on the floor in a confused heap and wound up in a mutual gamahuche; Mrs Leslie secured the blood-stained quim of little Polly, which she sucked till she had enjoyed the last drop of ensanguined spunk she could extract from the wounded slit of her young friend, who writhed in delight under the soothing touches of such a lascivious tongue.

It was between eleven and twelve o'clock when, just as we were recovering from a state of lethargic oblivion and thinking of some re-invigorating refreshment, the sound of carriage wheels on the gravel drive up to the house, and then a rat-a-tat-tat on the loud knocker made us all start to our feet and rush for our clothes.

'The colonel, by all that's unfortunate,' exclaimed Mrs Leslie, 'make haste or he will catch us; who would have thought of his arriving this time of night.'

The prudent Vishnu, pretending to be awaking out of his first sleep, so bungled and delayed opening the front door, that we were tolerably presentable by the time the colonel made his appearance, and whatever his suspicions may have been, he went through the formality of introduction in the most friendly way possible, the presence of so many young ladies evidently quite disconcerting him for the moment.

I afterwards learnt from his wife that under promise of secrecy she had confessed all to him, and vastly amused her husband by the account of our doings; but, at any rate, it stopped our fun at the time, and next day I was obliged to return to town, and thus bring to conclusion my sport amongst the she-noodles. Anything but 'noodles' after I had so enlightened them, they were in fact quite as knowing as Adam and Eve after they found out they were 'naked', having tasted of the Tree of Knowledge – which, in my humble opinion, meant having discovered *l'arte de faisant l'amour*.

# Justine

## or The Misfortunes of Virtue

## The MARQUIS de SADE

# Chapter One

The triumph of philosophy would be to reveal, amply and lucidly, the means by which providence attains her ends over man; and, accordingly, it would trace those lines of conduct which might enable this unfortunate biped individual to avoid, while treading the thorny path of life, those bizarre caprices of a fate which has twenty different names, but which, as yet, has never clearly been defined.

For although we may fully respect our social conventions, and dutifully abide by the restrictions which education has imposed on us, it may unfortunately happen that through the perversity of others we encounter only the thorns of life, whilst the wicked gather nothing but roses. Things being so, is it not likely that those devoid of the resources of any firmly established virtues may well come to the conclusion suggested by such sad circumstances – that it were far better to abandon oneself to the torrent rather than resist it? Will it not be said that virtue, however fair she may be, becomes the worst cause one can espouse when she has grown so weak that she cannot struggle against vice? Will it not equally be said that, living in a century so thoroughly corrupt, the wisest course would be to follow in the steps of the majority? May we not expect some of our more educated folk to abuse the enlightenment they have acquired, saying with the angel Jesrad of *Zadig* that there is no evil which does not give birth to some good – adding that, since the imperfect constitution of our sorry world contains equal amounts of evil and of good, it is essential that its balance be maintained by the existence of equal numbers of good and wicked people. And will they not finally conclude that it is of no consequence in the general plan whether a man is good or wicked by preference; and that if misfortune persecutes virtue and prosperity almost always accompanies vice, things being equal in the sight of nature, it seems infinitely better to take one's place among the wicked, who prosper, than among the virtuous, who perish.

Therefore it is important to guard against the sophisms of a dangerous philosophy, and essential to show how examples of unfortunate virtue, presented to a corrupted soul which still retains some wholesome principles, may lead that soul back to the way of godliness just as surely as if her narrow path had been bestrewn with the most brilliant honours and the most flattering of rewards. Doubtless it is cruel to have to describe, on the one hand, a host of misfortunes overwhelming a sweet and sensitive woman who has respected virtue above all else, and – on the other – the dazzling good fortune of one who has despised it throughout her life. But if some good springs from the picture of these fatalities, should one feel remorse for having recorded them? Can one regret the writing of a book wherein the wise reader, who fruitfully studies so useful a lesson of submission to the orders of providence, may grasp something of the development of its most secret mysteries, together with the salutary warning that it is often to bring us back to our duties that heaven strikes down at our side those who best fulfil her commandments?

Such are the thoughts which caused me to take up my pen; and it is in consideration of such motives that I beg the indulgence of my readers for the untrue philosophies placed in the mouths of several of my characters, and for the sometimes rather painful situations which, for truth's sake, I am obliged to bring before his eyes.

## *Chapter Two*

The Comtesse de Lorsange was one of those priestesses of Venus whose fortune lies in an enchanting figure, supported by considerable misconduct and trickery, and whose titles, however pompous they may be, are never found save in the archives of Cythera, forged by the impertinence which assures them, and upheld by the stupid credulity of those who accept them. Brunette, vivacious, attractively made, she had amazingly expressive dark eyes, was gifted with wit, and possessed, above all, that fashionable cynicism which adds another dash of spice to the passions, and which makes infinitely more tempting the woman in whom it is suspected. She had, moreover, received the best possible education. Daughter of a very rich merchant of the rue Saint-Honoré, she had been brought up, with a sister three years younger than herself, in one of the best convents in Paris; where, until she was fifteen years old, nothing in the way of good counsel, no good teacher, worthwhile book, or training in any desirable accomplishment, had been refused her. Nevertheless, at that age when such events are most fatal to the virtue of a young girl, she found herself deprived of everything in a single day. A shocking bankruptcy plunged her father into such a cruel situation that all he could do to escape the most sinister of circumstances was to fly speedily to England, leaving his daughters in the care of a wife who died of grief within eight days of his departure. One or two of their few remaining relatives deliberated on the fate of the girls, but as all that was left to them totalled a mere hundred crowns each, it was decided to give them their due, show them the door, and leave them mistresses of their own actions.

Madame de Lorsange, who at that time was known as Juliette, and whose wit and character were already almost as mature as they were when she had reached the age of thirty – which was her age at the time of our story – felt only pleasure at her freedom, and never for an instant dwelt on the cruel reverses which had broken her chains. Justine, her sister, however, just turned twelve, and of a sombre and melancholy turn of mind, was endowed with an unusual tenderness accompanied by a surprising sensitivity. In place of the polish and artfulness of Juliette, she possessed only that candour and good faith which were to lead her into so many traps, and thus felt all the horror of her position.

This young girl's features were totally different from those of her sister. The one held just as much of artifice, flirtation, and guile, as the other did of delicacy, timidity, and the most admirable modesty. For Justine had a virginal air, great blue eyes gentle with concern, a clear dazzling complexion, a small slender body, a voice of touching softness, ivory teeth, and beautiful fair hair. These were the subtle charms of the younger sister, whose innocent grace and delicious features were so delicate and ethereal that they would escape the very brush which would depict them.

Each of the two were given twenty-four hours to leave the convent, and were left to provide for themselves, each with her hundred crowns, wherever and however they might choose. Juliette, enchanted at being her own mistress, wished for a moment to dry Justine's tears; but realising that she would not succeed, set to scolding instead of consoling her, exclaiming that such behaviour was foolish, and that girls of their age, blessed with faces like theirs, had never starved to death. She cited, as an example, the daughter of one of their neighbours who, abandoning her paternal home, was now being kept in luxury by a rich landowner, and drove her own carriage around Paris. Justine expressed horror at such a pernicious example, and she said she would rather die than emulate it. Moreover she flatly refused to share a lodging with her sister, since it was obvious that this young woman had decided to follow the abominable way of life which she had so recently praised.

Thus the two sisters separated from each other without promise of any reunion, since their intentions were found to be so different. Could Juliette, who had pretensions to becoming a great lady, ever consent to see again a little girl whose low and *virtuous* inclinations would disgrace her? And, on her side, is it likely that Justine would wish to risk her morals in the company of a perverse creature who was about to become the victim of vile lubricity and general debauchery? Each, therefore, relying on her own resources, left the convent on the following day as had been agreed.

Justine, who as a child had been fawned over by her mother's dressmaker, imagined that this woman would feel a natural sympathy for her position. She therefore sought her out, told her of her unfortunate position and, asking for work, was immediately thrown on to the street.

'Oh heaven!' cried the poor little creature, 'must it be that the first step I take in the world leads me only to further miseries . . . This woman loved me once! Why, then, does she cast me away today? . . . Alas, it must be because I am orphaned and poor . . . Because I have no resources in the world, and because people are esteemed only by reason of the help or the pleasure which others hope to receive from them.'

Reflecting thus, Justine called on her parish priest and asked his advice. But the charitable ecclesiastic equivocally replied that it was impossible for him to give her any alms, as the parish was already overburdened, but that if she wished to serve him he would willingly provide her with board and lodging. In saying this, however, he passed his hand under her chin, and kissed her in a fashion much too worldly for a man of the Church. Justine, who understood his intentions all too well, quickly drew back, expressing herself as follows: 'Sir, I am asking of you neither alms nor yet the position of a servant. I am not so far reduced from my recent position in society as to beg two such favours; all I ask of you is the advice of which my youth and my present misfortune stand so much in need. Yet you would have me buy it with a crime . . . ' The priest, insulted by this expression, opened the door and pushed her brutally on to the street. Thus Justine, twice repulsed on the first day of her isolation, walked into a house displaying a notice and rented a small furnished room, paying in advance. Here, at least, she was able to abandon herself in comfort to the grief caused not only by her situation but by the cruelty of the few individuals with whom her unlucky star had constrained her to have dealings.

## Chapter Three

With the reader's permission we shall abandon our heroine for a while, leaving her in her obscure retreat. This will allow us to return to Juliette, whose career we will sum up as briefly as possible – indicating the means whereby, from her humble state as an orphan, she became within fifteen years a titled woman possessing an income of more than thirty thousand livres, the most magnificent jewels, two or three houses in the country as well as her residence in Paris, and – for the moment – the heart, the wealth, and the confidence of M. de Corville, a gentleman of the greatest influence, and a Counsellor of State who was about to enter the Ministry itself . . .

That her path had been thorny cannot be doubted, for it is only by the most severe and shameful of apprenticeships that such young women attain their success; and she who lies today in the bed of a prince, may still carry on her body the humiliating marks of the brutality of depraved libertines into whose hands she had once been thrown by her youth and her inexperience.

On leaving the convent, Juliette quickly went to find the woman she had once heard named by a corrupt friend from her neighbourhood, and whose address she had carefully kept. She arrived with abrupt unconcern, her bundle under her arm, her little dress in disorder, with the prettiest face in the world and the undeniable air of a schoolgirl. She told the woman her story, and begged her to protect her; just as, several years previously, she had protected her friend.

'How old are you, my child?' asked Madame du Buisson.

'In a few days time I shall be fifteen, Madame.'

'And nobody has ever . . . ?'

'Oh, no, Madame, I swear it to you!'

'Nevertheless it is not unknown for convents to harbour a chaplain, a nun, or even a schoolfriend who . . . So I must be supplied with certain proofs!'

'All that you need do is look for them, Madame . . .'

And du Buisson, fixing herself up with a pair of spectacles, and having verified the exact state of things, said to Juliette: 'Well, my child, all you need do is stay here. But you must strictly observe my advice, show the utmost compliance with my customs, be clean and neat, economical and candid so far as I am concerned, courteous towards your companions, and as dishonest and unscrupulous as you like with men. Then, a few years from now, you will be in a position to retire to a nicely furnished place of your own, with a servant, and such proficiency in the art you will have acquired in my establishment that you will have the means quickly to satisfy each and every desire you may wish.'

With these words la du Buisson seized Juliette's little bundle, enquiring, at the same time, if she were absolutely without money. And Juliette having too frankly admitted that she had a hundred crowns, her new-found mama quickly took possession of them, assuring her young pupil that she would invest this small sum to her profit, and that it was unnecessary for a girl to have money, especially as it could be a means towards the indulgence of wickedness. Moreover, in such a corrupt century, any wise and highly-born young lady must carefully avoid anything which might cause her to fall into a trap. This sermon completed, the newcomer was introduced to her companions, taken to her room in the house, and from the following day her first-fruits were on sale. Within four months' time the same merchandise had successively been sold to eighty different people, all of whom paid for it as new; and it was not until the end of this thorny novitiate that Juliette took out her patents as a lay-sister. From that moment, however, she was readily accepted as a daughter of the house, and entered the new novitiate of partaking in all its libidinous fatigues . . . If, excepting a few slight deviations, she had served nature during her early days in this place, she now forgot all natural laws and began to indulge in criminal researches, shameful pleasures, dark and crapulous orgies, scandalous and bizarre tastes and humiliating caprices – all of which arose, on the one hand, from a desire for pleasure without risk to health – and, on the other, from a pernicious satiety which so wearied her imagination that she could delight only in excess and revive herself only by way of lubricity . . .

Her morals were totally corrupted in this second school; and the triumphs of vice which she witnessed completed the degradation of her soul. She began to feel that she was born only for crime, and that she might as well cultivate only wealthy and important people rather than languish in a subordinate state wherein, though she committed the same faults and debased herself just as much, she could not hope to gain anything like the same profit. She was fortunate in pleasing an old and very much debauched nobleman, whose original intention had merely been the passing of a pleasantly salacious fifteen minutes. But she was clever enough to persuade him to keep her in magnificent style, and finally showed herself at the theatre or walking in company with the most aristocratic members of the Order of Cythera. She was admired, discussed, envied; and the roguish little cheat knew so well the art of grabbing what she wanted that within four years she had ruined three men, the poorest of whom had boasted an income of one hundred thousand crowns a year. Nothing more was necessary to establish her reputation. For the blindness of the present century is such that, the more one of these miserable creatures proves her dishonesty, the more envious men become of finding a place on her list. It would seem that the degree of her degradation and corruption becomes, in fact, the measure of those amorous feelings for her which men dare to proclaim.

Juliette had scarcely passed her twentieth year when the Comte de Lorsange, a forty-year-old nobleman from Anjou, became so infatuated by her that he determined to give her his name – not being rich enough to keep her. He allowed her an income of twelve thousand livres and assured her of the remainder of his fortune – a further eight thousand – if he died before she did. He also presented her with a house and servants, her own livery, and built up for her the kind of social importance which, within two or three years, caused people to forget the means by which she had attained such celebrity. This was the time when the wretched Juliette, forgetting all the sentiments due to her honourable birth and her excellent education, perverted by evil theories and dangerous books, anxious to be completely independent – to have a name, yet not be chained by it – began to ponder the criminal idea of shortening her husband's life . . . The odious project once conceived, she nursed it, caressed it, and finally executed it with so much secrecy that she was, unfortunately, protected against all investigation. Thus she managed to bury, together with her troublesome husband, all traces of her heinous crime.

Free once more, and still a Countess, Madame de Lorsange resumed her former habits. But, considering herself something of an important figure in society, she maintained an outward appearance of decency. She was no longer a kept woman but a rich widow who gave delightful suppers to which the townspeople and the court were only too happy to be admitted. She was, we might say, a respectable woman who would go to bed with anyone for two hundred louis, or accept a lover on receipt of five hundred a month. Until her twenty-sixth year she continued to make brilliant conquests, ruining three ambassadors, four financiers, two bishops, and three Chevaliers of the Ordres du Roi; and, as the criminal rarely stops at his first crime – especially when it has been successful – the vicious and guilty Juliette blackened herself with two more of a similar nature. The first was committed in order that she might rob one of her lovers who had entrusted her with a considerable sum of money of which his family knew absolutely nothing; the second, in order that she might more speedily come by a legacy of a hundred thousand francs, which another of her adoring lovers had included in his will in the name of a third person, who was instructed to hand it over to the said lady after his friend's decease.

To these horrors Madame de Lorsange added two or three infanticides. The fear of spoiling her attractive figure, strengthened by the necessity of hiding a double intrigue, several times encouraged her to have abortions; and these crimes, as undiscovered as the others, in no way hindered this clever and ambitious creature from daily finding new dupes and increasing, moment by moment, both her fortune and her crimes. It will thus be seen that it is, unfortunately, only too true that prosperity often accompanies crime, and that from the very bosom of the most deliberate corruption and debauchery men may gild the thread of life with that which they call happiness.

But, in order that this cruel and fatal truth should not alarm the reader, and in order that the sensibilities of honourable and righteous people may not be disturbed by our subsequent example of misfortune and misery relentlessly pursuing virtue, let us immediately state that this prosperity of crime is only apparent, not real. Independently of the punishment certainly reserved by Providence for those who have succeeded in this way, they also nourish in the depths of their hearts a worm which ceaselessly gnaws at them, and prevents them from enjoying the false glow of happiness which they would seize, leaving in its place only the rending memory of those crimes by which they attained it. With regard to the torment of virtue by misfortune, the unfortunate victim whom fate persecutes in this way has his conscience for consolation, and this, together with the secret joy he draws from his purity, soon compensates him for the injustice of men.

Such, then, was the state of the affairs of Madame de Lorsange when M. de Corville, a gentleman of fifty, and enjoying the position in society already described above, resolved to sacrifice himself entirely for this woman, attaching her life permanently with his own. Whether by his attention, his conduct, or the wisdom of Madame de Lorsange, he succeeded, and had been living with her for four years, entirely as with a legitimate wife, when they decided to spend several months during the summer on a superb estate he had lately purchased near Montargis. One evening in June, when the beauty of the weather had tempted them to wander as far as the town, they felt too tired to make their return on foot. Instead, they entered the inn where the Lyons coach makes a stop, intending to send a rider to the château to demand a carriage for their return. They were resting in a low, cool room opening on to the courtyard, when the aforesaid coach drew up before the inn. As it is natural enough to study the comings and goings of travellers – and there is no one who has not whiled away an idle moment with this form of entertainment when it has presented itself – Madame de Lorsange, followed by her lover, arose to watch the coachload of people enter the inn. The vehicle seemed to be empty, until one of the guards, in descending, received in his arms from one of his companions a young girl of about twenty-six or twenty-seven years of age, wrapped in a miserable little calico cloak and bound like a criminal. A cry of horror and surprise escaped from Madame de Lorsange, at which the young girl, turning, revealed such a sweet and delicate countenance, such a slim and graceful figure, that M. de Corville and his mistress could not help being interested in the unfortunate creature. M. de Corville approached the guards and asked one of them what the unfortunate girl had done.

'To tell the truth, monsieur, she has been accused of three or four very serious crimes: robbery, murder and arson. But I must admit that both my companion and myself have never before felt such repugnance over the transport of a criminal – she is the most gentle creature, and seems to us unusually honest . . .'

'Ah!' exclaimed M. de Corville, 'it seems to me that we have here another of those everyday blunders of the lower courts. And where,' he continued, 'was the offence committed?'

'At a hostelry three leagues from Lyons. She was tried at Lyons and is being taken to Paris for confirmation of the sentence. She will, however, be taken back to Lyons for execution.'

Madame de Lorsange, who had drawn close and listened to this recital, whispered quietly to M. de Corville that she wished to hear the story of her misfortunes from the girl's own lips. And M. de Corville, urged by the same desire, made himself known to the guards and asked if this would be possible.

As they were not at all opposed to the idea, it was decided that they should spend the night at Montargis, and two comfortable suites were placed at the disposal of the prisoner and her guardians. The nobleman accepting responsibility for her safety, she was untied and conducted to the apartments of the Comtesse. The guards retired to bed after an early supper; and when the unfortunate girl had been persuaded to take a little nourishment, Madame de Lorsange, unable to restrain the most intense interest, doubtless said to herself: 'This wretched and probably innocent creature is treated as a criminal. On the other hand everything prospers around me – who, assuredly, am much more a criminal than she is!'

Madame de Lorsange, I say, as soon as she saw her young guest a little more at ease, a little consoled by the caresses and attentions lavished on her and the interest taken in her, induced her to describe in some detail the events which had brought such an honest and sensible looking creature into such disastrous circumstances.

'To tell you the story of my life, Madame,' said the beautiful unfortunate, addressing the Comtesse, 'is to offer you the most striking example of the misfortunes of innocence. It would be to accuse providence to complain of it – it would be a sort of crime, and I dare not do it . . .'

Tears flowed abundantly from the eyes of the poor girl. But, having given way to her emotions for a few moments, she regained control of herself and commenced her narrative in these terms.

## *Chapter Four*

You will permit me to conceal my name and birth, Madame; without being illustrious it is honourable, nor was I originally destined to the humiliation to which you now see me reduced. I lost my parents while quite young, and thought that, with the little money they left me, I could wait for satisfactory employment. I refused many offers of work because of their dubious nature. And so, without perceiving it, I exhausted my small capital in Paris – where I was born. The poorer I became, the more I found myself despised; the greater my need of assistance, the less did I expect to obtain any. But of all the trials I experienced during the early days of my unhappy situation, of all the horrible proposals made to me, I shall only tell you of the events which befell me at the home of Monsieur Dubourg, one of the wealthiest landlords in the capital. I was sent to him by the woman who kept the boarding-house where I was lodging, and she recommended him as a gentleman whose good name and riches could the most surely alleviate the rigours of my condition. After waiting a very long time in the ante-room of Monsieur Dubourg, I was at last introduced to him. This odd-looking creature, about forty-eight years old, had just got out of bed. He was wrapped in a loose dressing-gown which scarcely hid his disorder; and, when I entered, his servants were dressing his hair. He dismissed them immediately and asked me what I wished for.

'Alas! sir,' I replied, very much confused, 'I am a poor orphan, and despite the fact that I'm not yet fourteen years of age, I am already acquainted with every shade of adversity. I come to beg your pity, to implore your compassion . . .'

And so I related to him every detail in the story of my misfortunes, the difficulty I had experienced in finding work, and the shame I felt about accepting any, especially as I had not been born into such a lowly position. I told him how my money had slowly gone, how I could not find employment, and how I hoped he would be able to offer me a means of livelihood. To be brief, I unburdened myself with all the eloquence dictated by misfortune; an eloquence which rises quickly in a simple and sensitive soul – yet one which is abhorrent to the mind of the opulent . . .

Monsieur Dubourg listened to me, indulging in many distractions the while. He then asked me if I had always been good.

'I should neither be so poor nor so embarrassed, sir,' I replied, 'did I wish to cease being so.'

'But,' exclaimed Monsieur Dubourg, 'by what right do you claim that the wealthy should assist you, while you refuse to be of service to them?'

'Of what service do you pretend to speak, sir?' I enquired, informing him that I desired nothing better than a chance to render those which decency and my age permitted.

He answered me at some length: 'The services of a child like you are but little use for domestic purposes; you are neither old enough nor even strong enough for such as position as you wish. You had far better occupy yourself in pleasing men, and in trying to find some fellow who will consent to take care of you. All this virtue of which you make such a fuss is worthless in the world; you may bow continually at the foot of its altars, yet its vain incense will never feed you. What pleases men least, what they hold in the least esteem, and what they despise above all else, is the so-called wisdom of your sex. Here, in this world, my child, we value only what brings us profit or delight – and of what profit is a woman's virtue to us? Her caprices and her disorders serve us and amuse us, but her chastity never interests us in the slightest. In other words, when men like us grant a request, it is always in the hope of receiving something in return. And how can a little girl like you repay what is done for her, unless she abandons herself completely to us, allowing us all that we may desire of her person?'

'Oh, sir!' I replied, my heart grown heavy with sighs, 'have honesty and benevolence altogether disappeared from the intentions of men?'

'Very nearly,' replied Dubourg; 'people talk about them a great deal, yet why would you have things so? Don't you realise that people have recovered from the mania of obliging *gratis*? – they have discovered that the pleasures of chastity are but the enjoyments of pride; and, as nothing is so rapidly dispersed, have come to prefer more genuine sensations. They realise, for example, that with a child like you, it is infinitely more profitable to reap, as the fruit of their monetary advances, all those pleasures offered by the refinements of lust, rather than the very chilly and unsatisfying ones of handing out alms for nothing. The knowledge of his reputation, enjoyed by a liberal, open-handed, and generous man, never equals in pleasure – even at the instant he enjoys such actions most intensely – the slightest delights of the senses.'

'Oh, sir! When mankind is ruled by principles such as these, there can be nothing left for the unfortunate except to perish!'

'What matter? The population of France is much greater than is necessary;

providing its machine always has the same elasticity, what does it matter to the State whether its body is composed of a few more or a few less individuals?'

'But do you believe that children can respect their fathers or their elders when they are ill-treated by them?'

'What does it matter to a father whether the children who trouble him love him or not?'

'It would, then, have been far better had we been smothered in our cradles!'

'Certainly! – Such was once the custom in many countries; amongst the Greeks for instance; and such is the custom of the Chinese: in that country unfortunate children are exposed, or put to death. What is the good of letting such creatures live when they cannot rely on the assistance of their parents – either because these happen to be dead, or because they disclaim their offspring? If such children are allowed to live they only serve to overburden the State by increasing a population which is already too great. Bastards, orphans and deformed children should be condemned to death at birth; the first two classes because they no longer have anyone to watch over them and care for them – and because a childhood endured under such conditions may one day make them dangerous to society; the others because deformed weaklings can be of no use to society. All children coming within these categories are to society what excrescences become to the flesh: they nourish themselves on the sap of the healthy members, and at the same time weaken them causing them to degenerate. They might be compared with those parasitic plants and vegetables which, attaching themselves to healthy growths, completely spoil these by drawing off their nutritious essence. The funds collected to feed such scum are crying abuses; particularly those richly endowed establishments which are built for such creatures, and at such an expense! As if the human species was so exceedingly rare, so infinitely precious, that it becomes necessary to consider the welfare of its lowest segment! But let us leave the discussion of these policies of which you cannot, my child, comprehend a thing; and as for yourself, why complain of your predicament when the remedy lies within yourself?'

'At what a price, gracious heaven!'

'At the price of a mere chimera, a thing which has no value at all, other than the one which your pride places on it. Briefly,' continued this barbarian, whilst rising and opening the door, 'that is all I can do for you – If you can't agree to my proposition, get out of my sight! I do not like beggars . . .'

My tears flowed; I could not hold them back any longer. Would you believe it, Madame? – they served only to increase the irritable temper of this man, instead of softening him. He slammed the door, and seizing me by the collar of my dress brutally told me that he was going to force me into doing that which I would not willingly grant him. At this cruel moment my misfortune lent me courage; I extricated myself from his arms and threw myself towards the door.

'Loathsome man,' I shouted as I ran; 'may Heaven, so grievously insulted by you, punish you as you deserve for your execrable cruelty and hardness of heart! You are worthy neither of those riches which you put to so vile a use, nor of the air which you breathe in a world stained by your barbarities.'

Reaching my lodgings I hastened to inform my landlady as to the kind of reception given me by the man to whose house she had sent me. But my surprise passed all bounds when I heard this female wretch load me with reproaches instead of sympathetically sharing my grief!

'You mean little creature,' she exclaimed in her rage; 'do you imagine that men are foolish enough to bestow charity on little girls such as yourself without exacting the interest on their money? Monsieur Dubourg is too kind to have acted as he has done. Had I been in his position you would not have escaped from my room before I had satisfied my desires. However, since you do not wish to profit by the help I have offered, I can only let you dispose of yourself as you wish. You owe me rent – by tomorrow you must either pay me my money or go to prison!'

'Madame, have pity on me . . . '

'People starve through indulging in pity.'

'But what would you have me do?'

'You must return to Monsieur Dubourg – you must satisfy him, and bring me back some cash. I shall go and see him and make up, if I can, for your silly behaviour. I shall offer him your apologies. But mind you behave better next time!'

Ashamed and in despair at not knowing which path to take, seeing myself harshly repulsed by everyone, and without any other resource, I told Madame Desroches (that was my landlady's name) that I was ready for everything in order to placate her. She went off to see the financier, and on her return informed me that she had experienced considerable difficulty in prevailing on him to grant me another chance – that only by dint of repeated entreaties had she persuaded him to see me again the following morning. She ended by warning me that I had better keep an eye on my conduct, for if I disappointed him again, or disobeyed him in the least, he would himself undertake the business of having me locked up for life.

Next day I arrived at the mansion quite excited. Dubourg was alone, and in a more indecent state than on the previous evening. Brutality, libertinism, all the marks of debauchery shone forth from his sullen features.

'You have la Desroches to thank for my welcome,' he grumbled in a harsh tone; 'for it is only on her account that I condescend to grant you my kindness for a space. You should certainly feel undeserving of it after your conduct yesterday! Undress immediately! And if you offer anything like the slightest resistance to my desires, two men who are waiting in my ante-room will take you to a place which you will never leave again while there is life in your body . . . '

'Oh, sir!' I wept, throwing myself at the knees of this despicable man, 'relent, allow yourself some mercy, I beseech you! I would rather die a thousand deaths than betray the principles I received during my childhood. Do you not realise that you will no sooner have accomplished your crime than the spectacle of my despair will overwhelm you with remorse . . . '

But the infamies to which Dubourg had abandoned himself whilst I spoke hindered me from proceeding further. I realised the folly of pretending to myself that I could affect a man who found my grief merely a vehicle for the increase of his horrible passions. He became more and more inflamed at my bitter accents, at my weeping and shuddering, relishing them with an inhumanity which frightened me, and further preparing himself for his criminal attempts. He rose to his feet, revealing himself to me in a state in which reason rarely triumphs, and during which the resistance of the object which causes such loss of reason is but an added stimulus to the delirium of the senses. He grasped me brutally; impetuously he tore away those veils which still concealed what he was burning to enjoy; then, in turn, he abused me, flattered me, caressed me, and treated me with contempt . . . Oh! what a picture! Almighty God, what a strange medley of hardness and mad unbridled lust! It seemed as if the Supreme Being, during the first of such circumstances in my life, wished to imprint eternally on my soul an image of all the horror I ought to feel for the kind of crime, or sin, which so often has its genesis in an abundance of evils similar to those with which I was threatened . . . But was there necessity for complaint at this hour? Certainly not – for I owed my very safety to his excesses . . . A little less debauchery and he would have had his will of me; but the fires of Dubourg's ardour were extinguished by the effervescence of his attempts. Heaven avenged, on my behalf, all the assaults to which the monster tried to abandon himself – for the loss of his force before the sacrifice preserved me from becoming his victim.

Nevertheless, Dubourg only became the more insulting. He accused me of being the cause of his weakness, and wished to recompense himself by fresh outrages and abuses of an even more terrifying nature. There was nothing disgusting he did not say to me, nothing he did not attempt, nothing his vile imagination, the hardness of his nature, and his depraved morals did not cause him to undertake. But my awkwardness tired his patience, especially as I made not the slightest attempt to play up to him. You may well imagine that it required considerable fortitude on my part to lend myself in such a manner; nor has the passage of time been able to obliterate my remorse . . . Nothing, however, succeeded; his final attempts failed miserably; and my submission lost its power to inflame him. In vain he successively passed from tenderness to severity, from severity to tyranny, from glances of loving sympathy to the excesses of filth and lust. At length we were equally tired – a condition which fortunately persisted and prevented his being able to recover the ability necessary for truly dangerous attacks. He gave over, but made me promise to return the following day; and in order to be absolutely sure of this he paid me only the sum I owed la Desroches. And so I returned to the woman's house exceedingly humbled by my adventure, and firmly decided, whatever might happen to me in the future, never to expose myself to this man a third time. I expressed these ideas to my landlady when paying her, and decried with maledictions the old rogue who had been capable of so cruelly taking advantage of my misery. Nevertheless, my curses, far from bringing on him the wrath of God, seemed only to bring him good fortune. Eight days later I learned that this notorious libertine had just received from the government a grant which increased his annual revenue to more than 400,000 livres. I was lost in reflections on this and similar inconsistencies of destiny, when a ray of hope seemed suddenly to lighten my heart.

La Desroches came to tell me that at last she had discovered a house where I would gladly be received, providing I conducted myself well therein.

'Oh! Merciful Heaven,' I cried delightedly, flinging myself into her arms, ' – that is the very condition I should myself lay down; do not doubt my decision for an instant – I accept the offer with pleasure . . . '

And so I left the home of Desroches for what I hoped would be a changed and better period of life.

My new master was an old usurer who had become rich not only by way of lending money, but also by robbing everyone with whom he came into contact – whenever he found it possible to do so safely and with impunity. He lived on the rue Quincampoix, in an apartment on the first floor, accompanied by an old mistress whom he called his wife and who was at least as wicked as he himself.

'Sophie,' said this miser to me (for that was the name I had assumed in order to conceal my own), 'my dear Sophie, the first of the virtues necessary to anyone who lives in my house is that of honesty . . . And if ever I should find you appropriating to yourself the tenth part of one of my pennies, I shall have you hanged – hanged, do you understand, until it would be impossible to revive you! For if my wife and I are able to enjoy a few small pleasures in our old age, it is only because it is the fruit of our excessive labours and profound sobriety. By the way, my child, do you eat a lot?'

'Only a few ounces of bread a day, sir,' I replied; 'together with a little water and some soup when I am lucky enough to be able to have it.'

'Soup! Soup! – good heavens!' exclaimed the old miser to his wife – 'Let us bewail the extravagance of luxury and its progress in our times!' Then he continued: 'For a year this child has been looking for a job; for a year she has been dying of starvation; and at the same time she wants to eat soup! We ourselves have it only rarely – once every Sunday, to be precise – we who have worked ourselves like galley-slaves for forty years. You will receive three ounces of bread a day, my girl, half a bottle of river water, and every eighteen months one of my wife's old dresses from which you can make your petticoats. At the end of a year, if we are satisfied with your services, and if your approach to economy corresponds with our own; if, in short, you order arrangements so that our domestic matters prosper, then we will pay you three crowns.

'Looking after us is only a small matter. It is simply a case of cleaning and polishing this six-roomed flat three times each week. And, of course, you will make the beds, answer the door, powder my wig, dress the hair of my wife, look after the dog, the cat, and the parrot, attend to your kitchen duties, and wash the dishes regularly, whether they have been used or not; as well as helping my wife with the cooking and spending your spare time making caps, knitting stockings, and producing other little things for the household. So you see, Sophie, there isn't much to do, and you will have quite enough leisure in which to attend to your own odd jobs and make whatever clothing you may need.'

You can easily imagine, Madame, that one would have to be in precisely that state of misery in which I happened to be before you would have accepted such a position. Not only were these creatures asking me to do far more work than my age and strength permitted, but was it possible to keep going on the food and the pittance they offered? Nevertheless I was careful not to be difficult, and installed myself in their home that same evening.

If, Madame, the cruel situation in which I found myself allowed me to think of amusing you for a moment – when I ought only to try and arouse sympathetic feeling for me in your heart – I honestly believe I could send you into paroxysms of laughter by relating in detail some of the manifestations of avarice which abounded so plentifully in that house. But such a terrible catastrophe befell me during my second year there that, when I think of it, I find it difficult to offer humorous details before acquainting you with the nature of this misfortune. Nevertheless, I can tell you, Madame, that lights were never used in that house. The bedroom of my master and mistress was situated directly opposite the street lamp, so they dispensed with any other means of illumination, not even using a light to see their way to bed. As for underwear and suchlike, they never wore it, but sewed into the sleeves of their coats and dresses old ruffles, which I washed each Saturday evening, so that they would be clean and fresh for Sunday. Neither were there any sheets or towels, so as to avoid the expense of laundering – for this, according to the respectable Monsieur du Harpin, was an unusually expensive item. They never had wine in the house, for, according to Madame du Harpin, clear water was the natural beverage of the first men, and the only one prescribed us by nature. Every time bread was cut a basket had to be placed underneath the loaf so as to catch the crumbs. To these were added the remnants of every meal, and on Sundays the mixture was fried in a little rancid butter and served up to form the special dish of the Sabbath day. Clothes and upholstery were never brushed in the usual manner, as that might have tended to produce wear in the material. Instead they were lightly swept with a feather duster. Their shoes were reinforced with metal caps, and each of them kept, as venerable relics, those which they had worn on their wedding day. But a much more bizarre duty was one which I had to undertake once a week. There was one large room in the flat with completely bare walls. Here I used to go regularly in order to scrape some of the plaster off the walls with a knife. This was then passed through a fine sieve, and I was instructed to use the resulting powder each morning to dress the gentleman's wig and the chignon of the lady.

I would to God that these were the only depraved methods of economy indulged by this sorry couple. Nothing is more natural than the desire to conserve one's means; but what is not equally so is the wish to increase them with the fortunes of others – and it did not take me long to realise that it was in this manner that Monsieur Du Harpin had become so rich.

Now at that time there was living above us an individual in very easy circumstances, owning some very pretty jewels; and these, perhaps because they belonged to our neighbour, or perhaps because they had actually passed through his hands, were well known to my master. Quite frequently I heard him lamenting to his wife about a certain gold box worth thirty or forty louis, which, he said, would certainly have belonged to him if he had been a little more adroit at an earlier time. In order to console himself for having returned the box which he had once borrowed, Monsieur Du Harpin planned to steal it, and it was me he commanded to effect this transference.

Having delivered a long speech on the unimportance of stealing, and on the possible utility to society of such an activity – since it served to re-establish an equilibrium totally upset by the unequal distribution of wealth, Monsieur Du Harpin presented me with a false key, assuring me that it would open the apartment of our neighbour, and that I would find the box in a desk which was never locked. He added that I would be able to remove it without any danger, and that for such a considerable service he would add an extra crown to my wages for the following two years.

'Oh, Monsieur!' I cried, 'is it possible that a master dares attempt to corrupt his servant in such a manner? What is to prevent me from turning against you the very weapons which you have placed in my hands? And how could you reasonably object if I robbed you according to your own principles?'

Monsieur Du Harpin, astonished at my reply, did not dare insist further. He reacted by nursing a secret grudge against me; but explained his behaviour by pretending he had been testing me, saying that it was fortunate I had not succumbed to his insidious suggestions as otherwise I should have been hanged. I accepted his explanation, but from that time onwards I felt both the misfortunes with which such a proposition menaced me, and how unwise I had been to answer so firmly. Nevertheless, there had been no middle way; for I had been faced with the choice of actually committing the crime, or of obstinately rejecting the proposal. Had I been a little more experienced I should have left the house at that instant; but it had already been written on the page of my destiny that every honest impulse in my character would have to be paid for by some misfortune. I was therefore obliged to submit to circumstances without any possibility of escape.

Monsieur Du Harpin allowed almost a month to pass – that is to say nearly the turn of my second year in his employ – and never said a word, or showed the least resentment at my refusal. Then one evening, my work being finished and having just retired to my room for a few hours of rest, I suddenly heard the door thrown open, and saw, not without fear, Monsieur Du Harpin accompanied by a police official and four soldiers of the watch who immediately surrounded my bed.

'Perform your duties, officer,' he said to the police official. 'This miserable creature has stolen a diamond of mine worth a thousand crowns. You will almost certainly find it in her room, or on her person!'

'But, sir! You cannot possibly think I have robbed you,' I cried, throwing myself, in consternation, at the foot of my bed. 'Ah! who knows better than you how repugnant such an action would be to me, and how impossible it is that I should commit it!'

But Monsieur Du Harpin made a great commotion so that nobody could hear what I was saying, and so contrived to order the search that the miserable ring was found in my mattress. In face of such proof there could be no reply. Therefore I was immediately seized, handcuffed, and ignominiously led to the Prison du Palais – without a word being heard of the many things I could have said in my defence.

The trial of those unfortunate wretches who lack both influence and protection is quickly over in France. For it is believed that virtue is incompatible with poverty; and misfortune, in our courts, is accepted as conclusive proof against the accused. An unjust bias causes a presumption that the person who might possibly have committed the crime actually did commit it. The feelings of one's judges thus take their measure from the situation in which one is found – and if titles or wealth are not available to prove the honesty of the accused, the impossibility of his being so is immediately accepted as demonstrated.

Well might I defend myself; well might I furnish an exact description of the true state of affairs to the state lawyer who was sent to question me. My master accused me in court – the diamond had been found in my room; therefore, clearly, I must have stolen it. When I wished to describe Monsieur Du Harpin's horrible deed, and to show how the misfortune which had befallen me was simply a consequence of his vengeance, of his obsessive desire to ruin a creature who knowing his secrets was in a position to wield considerable power over him, they interpreted my complaints as recriminations, and informed me that Monsieur Du Harpin had been known for forty years as a man of integrity and was quite incapable of such an outrage. Thus it was that I found myself about to pay with my life for my refusal to participate in a criminal conspiracy – when an unexpected happening set me free, once more to plunge me into the further miseries still awaiting me in the world outside.

A woman of forty named Dubois, celebrated for her indulgence in every species or horror, was likewise on the eve of her execution – which at least was more deserved than mine, since her crimes had been established while mine did not exist.

Somehow or other I had inspired a kind of sympathy in this woman and one evening, a few days before each of us was due to lose her life, she told me not to go to bed, but to remain as unobtrusively close to her as I could.

'Between midnight and one o'clock in the morning,' explained this prosperous villain, 'the prison will be set on fire . . . thanks to my machinations. Someone may be burned, but what does that matter? The certain thing is that we shall make our escape. Three men, accomplices and friends of mine, will meet us, and I can answer to you for your liberty.'

The hand of heaven, which had just punished my innocence, became the servant of crime so far as my protectress was concerned. Once the fire had started the conflagration became terrible. Ten people were burned alive, but we made our escape in safety. The same day we managed to reach the cottage of a poacher who lived in the forest of Bondy. He was thus a different kind of rogue, yet nevertheless an intimate friend of our band.

'Now you are free, my dear Sophie,' la Dubois said to me, 'and you can choose whatever kind of life seems to suit you best; but if you listen to me you will renounce your virtuous ways, which, as you see, have never succeeded in helping you. Your misplaced delicacy conducted you right to the foot of the gallows, yet a frightful crime has saved me from a similar fate. Just look at the value which goodness has in the world, and then consider whether it is worth dying for. You are young and pretty; and, if you like, I will take care of your future in Brussels. I am going there, because that is where I was born, and within two years I can place you at the very peak of fortune. But I warn you that it will certainly not be by the narrow paths of virtue that I will promote your success. At your age it is necessary to engage in more than one profession, as well as to serve in more than one intrigue, if you wish to make your way to the top with any promptitude. Do you understand me, Sophie? – Do you understand me? Decide quickly because we must be on the move. We are safe here only for a few hours.'

'Oh, Madame,' I replied to my benefactress, 'I am obliged to you for so much, since you have saved my life; yet it fills me with despair when I consider that this was possible only by way of the commission of a crime. And you may be very sure that had it been necessary for me to participate in it I would rather have died than done so. I know but too well the dangers I have courted in abandoning myself to those sentiments of honesty which for ever spring up in my heart, but whatever the thorns of virtue may be I shall always prefer them to the false glow of prosperity and those unreliable advantages which momentarily accompany crime. Thanks be to heaven, my religious convictions will never desert me, and if providence renders my way of life difficult it is only in order the more abundantly to recompense me in a better world. It is this hope which consoles me, this hope which softens all my griefs, calms my complaints, fortifies me in adversity and enables me fearlessly to encounter any evils with which I may be faced. This joy would immediately be extinguished in my heart were I to stain myself with crime – and, to the fear of even more terrible reverses in this world, I should add the frightening expectation of those punishments which celestial justice reserves in the beyond for those who outrage it.'

'I'm afraid you have some absurd ideas which will quickly take you to the workhouse, my girl,' exclaimed la Dubois, frowning. 'Believe me, you will be well advised to give up your ideas of celestial justice, of punishment, or rewards to come. Those things are all best forgotten as soon as you leave school, for their only result is to help cause you to starve to death – if you are stupid enough to believe them once you have launched out on a life of your own. The hardness of the rich justifies the rascality of the poor, my child; if humanity reigned in their hearts, then virtue would become established in ours; but so long as our misfortunes, and our patience in enduring them, so long as our good faith and our submission serve only to multiply our chains, then we can lay our crimes at their door, and we would be fools indeed were we to refuse to profit by them when they can to some extent ameliorate the yoke with which we are burdened.

'Nature caused us all to be born equal, Sophie; and if chance has been pleased to disorganise the original plan of her general laws, it is for us to correct such caprices, and to recover, by our adroitness, the usurpations of those who are stronger than us. I love to hear them – those rich gentlemen, those judges and magistrates – I love to hear them preach of virtue to us. It must be very difficult to avoid theft when one has three times more than is necessary for living in comfort; it must be equally difficult never to think of murder when one is surrounded only by the adulations of sycophants, or the submission of absolute slaves; likewise it must be enormously distressing to be temperate and sober when one is perpetually surrounded by the most succulent delicacies; and people must experience a great deal of trouble in being honest when they have no reason to lie.

'But we, Sophie, we whom this barbarous providence which you are foolish enough to idolise has condemned to crawl on the earth as a serpent crawls in the grass – we who are disdained because we are poor, humiliated because we are weak, and who at length find nothing but bitterness and care over the whole surface of the globe – could you wish us to forbear from crime when it is her hand alone which opens for us the door of life, sustains and maintains life in us, and saves us from losing it? You would, it seems, prefer us to be perpetually submissive and humble whilst those who control us retain for themselves every favour which fortune can grant, we having only the experience of pain, hardship, and sorrow, with the addition of tears, the iron-mark of infamy, and, finally, the scaffold!

'No, Sophie, no – either this providence which you so revere has been created solely for our scorn – or that is not the intention. . . . Get to know it better, get to know it better and you will soon be convinced that whenever it places us in a position where evil becomes necessary for us, granting us at the same time the possibility of exercising this evil, it is because evil, just as much as good, serves its laws; and it gains equally as much from the one as from the other. We were created in a state of equality, and the man who disturbs this state is not more culpable than he who seeks to re-establish it. Both men are activated by given motives, and each must follow his impulse, tying a bandage round his eyes and enjoying the game.'

I confess that if ever I was shaken it was by the seductions of this clever woman. But a voice louder than hers combatted the sophisms she wished to plant in my heart. I listened to it, and asserted for the last time that I had decided never to allow myself to be corrupted.

'Ah, well!' exclaimed Dubois. 'Do what you wish. I leave you to your evil fate – but if ever you happen to get yourself hanged, which you can hardly escape since the destiny which watches over crime inevitably sacrifices virtue, remember, at least, never to mention us.'

While we were reasoning in this fashion, the three companions of la Dubois were drinking with the poacher; and, as wine commonly has the effect of causing the malefactor to forget his past criminal offences, often inviting him to augment them at the very edge of the precipice from which he has just escaped, so did the miscreant wretches who surrounded me feel a desire to amuse themselves at my expense before I had time to run away from them. Their principles, their morals, combined with the sinister location in which we found ourselves, and the apparent security from the law which they felt they at present enjoyed, together with their drunkenness, my age, my innocence, and my figure, all encouraged them in their project. They rose from the table, held counsel amongst themselves and consulted la Dubois – proceedings the mystery of which made me shudder with horror, and which resulted in my having to decide whether, before leaving them, I would pass through the hands of all four willingly or by force. If I did it willingly they would each give me a crown to help me on my way, since I had refused to accompany them. If, on the other hand, they were obliged to use force to settle the matter, the thing would be done all the same, but the last of the four to enjoy me would plunge a knife into my breast and they would bury me immediately afterwards at the foot of a tree.

I leave you to imagine, Madame, the effect which this execrable proposition had on me. I threw myself at the feet of la Dubois, begging her to be my protectress yet a second time; but the villainous creature just laughed at my terrifying situation – which to her seemed a mere nothing.

'Gracious heavens!' she said, ' – just look at you, so miserable and unhappy simply because you are obliged to serve successively four big boys built like these! In Paris, my girl, there must be ten thousand women who would hand over plenty of beautiful crowns if they could be in the position you are in at the moment . . . Listen,' she added, after thinking things over for a few seconds, 'I have enough control over these sly fellows to obtain mercy for you, if you wish to prove yourself worthy of it.'

'What must I do, Madame,' I cried in tears. 'Instruct me! – I am quite ready to carry out your orders . . .'

'Follow us, become one of our band, and do the same things as we do without the slightest repugnance. For this price I can guarantee you the rest . . .'

Consideration did not seem necessary to me. I agree that in accepting I ran the risk of new dangers; but these were less pressing than those immediately facing me. I would be able to avoid them; whilst nothing could help me escape those with which I was menaced.

'I will go wherever you wish, Madame,' I said; 'I promise you I will go anywhere – only save me from the lusts of these men and I will never leave you!'

'Boys,' said la Dubois to the four bandits, 'this girl is now a member of our gang. I accept her and I approve her. I forbid you, moreover, to do her any violence. And you mustn't disgust her with our business on her first day. Just consider how useful her age and face can be to us, and let's use them to our interest instead of sacrificing her to our pleasures . . .'

But once roused, the passions can reach such a pitch in a man that no voice is able to recall them into captivity; and those with whom I was dealing were in no state to hear anything at all. All four of them, in fact, immediately surrounded me, and in a condition least calculated to enable me to expect mercy, declaring unanimously to la Dubois that since I was in their hands there *was* no reason why I should not become their prey.

'First me!' said one of them, seizing me round the waist.

'And by what right do you claim the first turn?' exclaimed a second, pushing his comrade aside and tearing me brutally from his arms.

'You shan't have her until I've finished!' shouted a third.

And the dispute becoming heated, our four champions tore each other's hair, flung each other on the ground, sent each other flying head over heels and rained blows on one another. As for me I was only too happy to see them all involved in a situation which gave me the chance to escape. So while la Dubois was occupied in trying to separate them I quickly ran away, soon reaching the forest. In a moment the house had disappeared from view.

'Oh, Being Most Supreme,' I exclaimed, throwing myself to my knees as soon as I felt myself secure from pursuit, ' – Being Supreme, my only true protector and my guide, deign to take pity on my misery. You know my weakness and my innocence. You know with what confidence I place in you my every hope. Deign to snatch me from the dangers which pursue me; or by a death less shameful than that which I have recently escaped, recall me promptly to your eternal peace.'

Prayer is the sweetest consolation of the unfortunate. One is stronger after prayer. And so I rose full of courage. But, as it was growing dark, I wound my way deep into a copse so as to pass the night with less risk. The safety in which I believed myself, my exhaustion, and the little joy I was tasting, all contributed to help me pass a good night. The sun was already high when I opened my eyes to its light. The moment of awakening is, however, calamitous for the unhappy; for, after the rest of the bodily senses, the cessation of thought, and the instantaneous forgetfulness of sleep, the memory of misfortune seems to leap into the mind with a newness of life which makes its weight all the more onerous to bear.

'Ah, well,' I said to myself, 'it seems to be true that there are some human beings whom nature destines to live under the same conditions as wild beasts. Living hidden in their retreats, flying from men like the animals, what difference remains between man and beast? Is it worth while being born to endure so pitiful a fate?'

And my tears flowed abundantly as these sad reflections formed themselves in my mind. Barely had I ceased thinking after this manner when I heard a noise somewhere near me. For a moment I thought it was some creatures of the wood; then, little by little, I distinguished the voices of two men.

'Come along, my friend, come along,' said one of them, 'We shall do wonderfully well here. And my mother's cruel and deadly presence shall no longer prevent me from tasting with you, at least for a few moments, those pleasures which are so dear to me.'

They drew nearer, placing themselves so directly in front of me that not a word they spoke, not a movement they made, could escape me. And then I saw –

'In heaven's name, Madame,' said Sophie, interrupting her narrative, 'is it possible that fate has never placed me in any situations but those so critical that it becomes as difficult for modesty to hear them as to depict them? . . . That horrible crime which outrages both nature and law, that frightful offence upon which the hand of God has fallen heavily so many times, that infamy, in a word, so new to me that I only understood it with difficulty – this I saw, consummated before my very eyes, with all the impure excitations, all the frightful episodes which it is possible for premeditated depravity to conjure up.'

One of the men – he who assumed the dominating role – was about twenty-four years old. He was wearing a green coat, and well enough dressed to cause me to think that he came of good family. The other was probably a young domestic of his house, around seventeen or eighteen and with a very pretty face and figure. The scene which followed was as lengthy as it was scandalous; and the passage of time seemed even more cruel to me, for I dared not move for fear of being discovered.

At last the criminal actors who had played this scene before me, satiated, no doubt, arose to make their way to the road which must have led to their home. But the master, coming near the thicket where I was hiding so that he might relieve himself, my high bonnet betrayed me.

He saw it immediately: 'Jasmin,' he called to his young Adonis, 'we have been discovered, my dear . . . A girl, a profane creature has seen our mysteries! Come, let's get this hussy out of here and find out what she's been doing.'

I did not give them the trouble of helping me out of my hiding place, but quickly jumped up and threw myself at their feet.

'Good gentlemen,' I cried, extending my arms towards them, 'kindly take pity on an unfortunate creature whose fate is more to be commiserated than you might think. Few of the reverses which men meet in life can be equal to mine. Do not let the situation in which you have found me arouse your suspicions, for it is the result of my poverty rather than my errors. Instead of increasing the sum of evils which crush me, you can, on the contrary, diminish it by helping me find a means of escape from the misfortunes which continually pursue me.'

Monsieur de Bressac, for that was the name of the young man into whose hands I had fallen, had an undue amount of the libertine in his character, but had not been provided with an equal abundance of compassion in his heart. It is, nevertheless, unfortunately only too common to see the debauchery of the senses completely extinguish pity in man. In fact the usual effect of such a life seems to be that of hardening the heart. Whether the greater number of such deviations arise on the basis of a kind of apathy in the soul, or whether they are the result of the violent shock which they imprint on the mass of nerves – thus diminishing the sensitive action of these – it can always be said that a professional debauchee is rarely a man of pity. But, to this natural cruelty in the kind of person whose character I have sketched, there was in Monsieur de Bressac such a marked and additional disgust for our sex, such an inveterate hatred for all that distinguishes it, that it was extremely difficult for me to encourage in his soul those sentiments by which I longed to see him moved.

'Anyway, my little wood-pigeon, just what are you doing here?'

Such was the only response of this man whom I wished to soften, and it was spoken harshly enough.

'Tell me the truth! – You saw everything that happened between this young man and myself, didn't you?'

'Me? – Oh no, Monsieur!' I cried quickly, believing I did no wrong in disguising the truth. 'You may rest assured that I saw only the most ordinary things. I saw you, your friend and yourself, seated together on the grass. I believe I noticed that you chatted together for a moment. But rest completely assured that is all I saw!'

'I would like to believe you,' replied Monsieur de Bressac, 'if only for your own safety. For if I suspected for an instant that you had seen anything else you would certainly never leave this thicket. Come, Jasmin, it is early enough, and we have time to listen to this slut's adventures. She shall recount them to us immediately; and then we can tie her to this great oak and try out our hunting knives on her body.

The young men sat down and ordered me to sit near them. Then I told them, quite truthfully, all that had happened to me since I had found myself alone in the world.

'Jasmin,' said Monsieur de Bressac, rising as soon as I had finished, 'let us be just for once in our lives, my dear. The equitable Themis has already condemned this hussy, and we cannot allow the goddess's wishes to be so cruelly frustrated. We shall ourselves execute upon this criminal the sentence she has incurred. What we are about to commit is not a crime, my friend, it is a virtue, a re-establishment of the order of things. And as we sometimes have the misfortune to disorganise this order, let us courageously right matters – at least when the opportunity presents itself.'

And the heartless men, having pulled me from my place, dragged me towards the tree they had spoken of, without being touched either by my sobs or my tears.

'Tie her here, in this manner,' said Bressac to his valet, as he held me with my belly against the tree.

Using their garters and their handkerchiefs, in a moment they had me so painfully tied down that it was impossible for me to move a single muscle. This operation achieved, the villains removed my skirts, lifted my chemise as high as my shoulders, and took out their hunting knives. I thought for a minute that they were going to cleave open my posteriors which had been uncovered by their brutality.

'That's enough,' said Bressac before I had received a single cut. 'That's enough to acquaint her with what we could do to her, to keep her dependent on us. Sophie,' he continued, as he untied the cords, 'dress yourself, be discreet, and follow us. If you remain loyal to me, my child, you shall have no excuse for repentance. My mother needs a second chambermaid, and I am going to present you to her. On the strength of your story I can guarantee your conduct to her; but if you abuse my kindness or betray my confidence – then remember this tree which will become your death bed. It is only a mile or two from the castle to which we are taking you, and at the slightest fault you will be brought back here.'

Already dressed, I could scarcely find words to thank my benefactor. I threw myself at his feet, embraced his knees, and gave him every assurance possible as to my good behaviour. But he was as insensible to my joy as he had been to my suffering.

'Let's get going,' he exclaimed. 'Your conduct will speak for you, and that alone will decide your fate.'

We continued to make our way. Jasmin and his master talked together, and I followed them humbly without saying a word. In less than an hour we arrived at the castle of Madame la Comtesse de Bressac, and its magnificence gave me the impression that whatever position I should fill in this household it would assuredly be more lucrative than that of housekeeper to Monsieur and Madame Du Harpin. I was made to wait in one of the servants' rooms, where Jasmin gave me a very good lunch. Meanwhile Monsieur de Bressac went up to see his mother, told her all about me and, half an hour later, came to find me himself so that he might introduce me to her.

Madame de Bressac was a woman of forty-five, still very beautiful; and she appeared to be extremely honourable and courteous – but, above all, very kind and human. Nevertheless, a little severity seemed blended in her manner and her speech. She had lost her husband two years previously. He had been a man of unusually distinguished family, but had married her with no other fortune than the celebrated name he gave her. Thus all the benefits which the young Marquis de Bressac could hope for depended on his mother, since what his father had been able to leave him was scarcely enough to live on. Madame de Bressac, however, had augmented this by a considerable allowance. But much more would have been necessary to meet the enormous, as well as the irregular, expenses of her son. There were at least sixty thousand livres of revenue in this house and Monsieur de Bressac had neither brothers nor sisters. Nobody had been able to persuade him to enter the army – for everything which separated him from his chosen pleasures was so insupportable to him that it was impossible to make him accept any tie. For three months of the year the Comtesse and her son lived on their country estate, the remainder of their time being spent in Paris. And these three months, which she insisted her son spend with her, were already a severe torture for a man who could never leave the centre of his pleasures without giving way to despair.

The Marquis de Bressac ordered me to tell his mother the same things which I had related to him; and when I had finished my recital she looked at me and said: 'Your candour and your naïvety do not permit me to doubt your innocence. I shall ask no further questions of you, except that I would like to know if you are really, as you say, the daughter of the gentleman you have mentioned. If such is the case, I knew your father, and it will give me yet another reason for being even more interested in your welfare. As for your affair at the Du Harpin household, I shall take it upon myself to bring that to a satisfactory conclusion with a couple of visits to the Chancellor – who has been my friend for many years. He is the greatest man of integrity in France, and it will only be necessary to prove your innocence to him in order to bring to naught everything that has been done against you. Then you will be able to reappear in Paris without the slightest fear . . . But reflect well, Sophie – everything I promise you here is only to be given at the price of the most perfect behaviour. In this way whatever I ask of you will always turn to your profit.'

I threw myself at the feet of Madame de Bressac, assuring her that she would never be anything other than pleased with me; and from that moment I was installed in her home in the position of second chambermaid. After three days the enquiries which Madame de Bressac had made in Paris concerning me brought in all the confirmation I could desire. Every idea of misfortune evaporated at last from my mind, never to be replaced save by the hope of the sweetest consolations I could possibly expect. But it was not written in heaven that poor Sophie should ever be happy, and if a few moments of calm were fortuitously granted her, it was only to render more bitter those horrors which were to follow.

We had barely arrived in Paris before Madame de Bressac began to work for my benefit. A high official asked to see me, listening to my misfortunes with interest. The dishonesty of Du Harpin was thoroughly investigated and fully admitted, and my questioners were convinced that even if I had profited by the fire in the court prisons, at least I had had nothing to do with the starting of it. Finally all proceedings against me were erased from the records (a matter on which they assured me), and the examining magistrates no longer found it necessary to engage in further formalities.

It is easy to imagine the extent to which such circumstances attached me to Madame de Bressac – even had she not shown me many additional kindnesses. Considering such acts as these, how could I be anything other than bound for ever to such a precious protectress? It had, nevertheless, been far from the intentions of the young Marquis de Bressac that I should become so intimately devoted to his mother. Quite apart from the frightful dissipations in which the young man wallowed, the nature of which I have already revealed to you, and into which he plunged with an even more blind prodigality than he had in the country, I was not long in noticing that he absolutely detested the Comtesse. It is true that she did everything in the world to prevent his debauches – or to interfere with them. But she employed, perhaps, too much severity and the Marquis, inflamed even more by the effects of this stringency, gave himself up to libertinism with even greater ardour. Thus the poor Comtesse drew no profit from her persecutions other than that of making herself the object of a sovereign hate.

'You mustn't imagine,' the Marquis often said to me, 'that my mother acts in your interest entirely of her own volition. Believe me, Sophie, if I didn't pester her continually, she would scarcely remember the promises she made you. You value her every act, yet all she does has been suggested by me. I am not, therefore, claiming too much when I say that it is only to me that you owe any gratitude. What I demand in return should seem to you even more disinterested, since you are well enough acquainted with my tastes to be quite certain that, however pretty you may be, I shall never lay any claim to your favours. No, Sophie, no, the services I expect of you are of quite another kind. And when you are fully convinced of all I have done for you, I hope that I shall find in your heart everything I have a right to expect.'

These speeches seemed so obscure to me that I never knew how to reply to them. I made random remarks, however – and with perhaps a little too much facility.

Which brings me, Madame, to the moment when I must inform you of the only real fault for which I have felt any need to reproach myself during the whole of my life. While I am describing it as a fault, it was certainly an unparalleled extravagance, but at least it was not a crime. It was a simple enough error, and one for which only I myself was punished; but it also seems to me one which heaven's equitable hand ought not to have employed to draw me into the abyss which, unknown to me, was opening beneath my feet. It had been impossible for me to see the Marquis de Bressac without feeling myself attracted to him by an impulse of tenderness which nothing had been able to quell in me. Whatever reflections I may have made on his lack of interest in women, on the depravity of his tastes, on the moral distances which separated us, nothing, nothing in the world could extinguish this nascent passion. And if the Marquis had asked me for my life, I would have sacrificed it to him a thousand times, feeling that such an action would be as nothing. He was far from suspecting the feelings I entertained for him, as these were carefully locked up in my heart . . . Ungrateful as he was, he could never discern the cause of those tears which the miserable Sophie shed, day after day, over the shameful disorders which were destroying him. It was, nevertheless, impossible that he could avoid noticing my personal attention to him; for, blinded by my devotion, I went even so far as to serve his errors – at least in so far as decency permitted me – and I always concealed them from his mother.

My conduct had thus earned me something of his confidence, and each small thing he said to me became precious. I allowed myself, in short, to become so dazzled by the little he offered my heart that there were times when I was arrogant enough to believe that I was not indifferent to him. But time after time the excess of his disorders would promptly disabuse me. They were such that not only was the house filled with servants given up to the same execrable tastes as the Marquis, but he even hired outside a crowd of bad characters whom he visited, or who came to see him day by day. And as such tastes, odious as they are, are not the least expensive, the young man disorganised his finances prodigiously. Sometimes I took the liberty of representing to him all the inconveniences of his conduct. He would listen to me without repugnance, but always ended by explaining that it was impossible to correct the kind of vice by which he was dominated and which reproduced itself under a thousand diverse forms. There was a different nuance of this deviation for every age of man, offering continually new sensations every ten years, and thus enabling it to hold its unfortunate devotees in bondage right to the very edge of the grave . . . But if I attempted to speak to him of his mother and the sorrow he brought her, he would show nothing but vexation, ill-humour, irritation, and impatience. And when he considered for how long she had held a fortune which he felt should already be his, he expressed the most inveterate hatred for this honourable and upright woman, backed by the most unswerving revolt against natural sentiment. Is it then true that when one has so definitely transgressed against the sacred rules of morality and sobriety, the necessary consequence of one's first crime should be a frightful facility in committing all the others with impunity?

Several times I tried to employ religious argument with him. Nearly always being consoled by my own faith, I attempted to transmit some of its sweetness to the soul of this perverse creature, for I was convinced that I might captivate him by these means if only I could tempt him for a moment to partake of their delights. But the Marquis did not long allow me to employ such methods. The declared enemy of our holy mysteries, a self-opinionated and obstinate railer against the purity of our doctrines, a passionate antagonist against the existence of a Supreme Being, Monsieur de Bressac, instead of being converted by me, sought all the more to corrupt me.

'All religions are based on a false principle, Sophie,' he would say to me. 'All accept the cult of a creative being as a necessity. But if this eternal world, like all those others amongst which it floats in the infinite plains of space – if this eternal world has never had a beginning, and will never have an end – if all the products of nature are the results or effects of laws by which she herself is enchained – if her perpetual action and reaction indicate the essential evolution of her being, what becomes of the author whom you so gratuitously lend her?

'Condescend to believe, Sophie, that the God you accept is simply the fruit of ignorance on the one side – and of tyranny on the other. When the strong wished to enslave the weak, they persuaded them that a god had sanctified the chains with which they overwhelmed them; and the oppressed victims, stupefied by their distress, believed everything their masters wished to tell them. All religions are the fatal consequence of this primary fiction and should, together with their origin, be condemned to the utmost scorn. There is not a single one of them but bears the emblems of imposture and stupidity. In all of them I see mysteries which make the reason shudder, dogma which outrages nature, and grotesque ceremonies which cannot but inspire derision. I had scarcely opened my eyes on this world, Sophie, when I learned to detest these horrors. So I decided that I would crush them under my feet, vowing never to return to them throughout my days. If you wish to be sensible you will imitate me.'

'Oh, sir,' I replied, 'you would deprive an unfortunate of her sweetest hope, were you to rob her of the religion which consoles her. Firmly attached to its precepts, absolutely convinced that every blow aimed against it is simply the result of libertinage and the passions, how could I sacrifice to these sophisms – which make me shudder – the sweetest idea in my life?'

To these words I added a thousand other arguments dictated by reason, pouring them forth from my heart. But the Marquis only laughed; and his deceptive principles, nourished by a more masculine eloquence, and supported by studies which, fortunately, I had never been able to indulge, always seemed to upset my arguments. The pious and virtuous Madame de Bressac was not ignorant that her son supported his faults and deviations on all the paradoxes of scepticism, and she often bewailed the fact with me. Then, as she seemed to find me a little more intelligent than the other women who surrounded her, she began to take pleasure in entrusting me with all her sorrows.

Meanwhile her son's evil conduct increased. He had reached the point of not attempting to hide it; and not only had he surrounded his mother with that dangerous and motley crowd submissive to his pleasures, but he had pushed insolence so far as to declare before me that if she took it into her head to thwart his practices he would convince her of their inherent charm by giving himself up to them before her very eyes. I groaned at these proposals and the prospect of such conduct; and in the depths of my being I tried to extract from them a motive for stifling the unfortunate passion which devoured my soul . . . But is love a malady which can easily be cured? Every means by which I sought to oppose it only stirred the flame so that it burned more brightly, and the perfidious Bressac never seemed to me more amiable than when I had ruminated on all those things for which I should have hated him.

During four years I remained in this house, always persecuted by the same woes and always comforted by the same sweetnesses, when the terrifying motive of the Marquis de Bressac's seductions was at last presented to me in all its horror. We were at that time residing in the country and I was attending the Comtesse alone, her first maid having obtained leave to remain in Paris for the summer owing to some business of her husband. One evening, shortly after I had withdrawn from my mistress, and not being able, because of the extreme heat, to think of going to bed, I was taking the air on a balcony giving on to my room. Suddenly the Marquis knocked at my door, begging me to let him speak with me for a while . . . Alas, every moment granted me by this cruel author of my woes seemed so precious that I never dared to refuse him a single one. He entered, closed the door with care, and threw himself into an armchair facing me.

'Listen to me, Sophie,' he said with a little embarrassment, 'I have things of the greatest importance to confide in you – but I must ask you to swear that you will never reveal anything of what I am about to speak.'

'Oh, Monsieur, could you possibly believe me capable of abusing your confidence?'

'You do not know what you would risk if ever you should prove to me that I had been deceived in trusting you!'

'The greatest of my sorrows would be the loss of your confidence – there is no need to threaten me with anything worse.'

'Very well, Sophie . . . . I have decided that my mother's life must be cut short, and yours is the hand I have chosen to help me in this conspiracy.'

'You have chosen me, Monsieur!' I cried, recoiling in horror; 'in Heaven's name how could two such schemes have entered your mind? Take my life, Monsieur; it is yours to dispose of as you will – in fact I owe it to you; but do not hope to obtain any assistance from me in a crime even the idea of which is intolerable to my heart.'

'Listen, Sophie,' said Monsieur de Bressac, quietly trying to calm me down; 'I am well aware of your repugnance in these matters; but, as you are intelligent, I flatter myself that I may overcome your objections by making you see that this crime, which you find so enormous, is really at bottom a very simple thing. Two hideous actions confront your unphilosophic eyes: the destruction of a creature like to ourselves, and the augmentation of the evil arising from the fact that this creature happens to be my mother. As far as the destruction of one's kind is concerned, you may be certain, Sophie, that such a belief is entirely chimerical, since the power of destruction has not been accorded to man. At the very most he has the ability of causing things to change form – but he cannot annihilate them. Moreover all forms are equal in the eyes of nature; and nothing is lost in the immense crucible wherein her variations are achieved. All the particles of matter thrown therein incessantly renew themselves under other shapes; and whatever effect our individual actions may have upon this process, none directly injure it, none outrage it. Our destructions reanimate its power and conserve its energy, but they never weaken it.

'And of what importance is it to eternally creative nature if this mass of flesh which today presents the shape of a woman should tomorrow reproduce itself in the guise of a thousand different insects? Would you dare to claim that the construction of individuals such as we costs more effort than the construction of a worm, and that she ought, in consequence, to take a greater interest in us? But if the degree of attachment, or rather of indifference, is the same, what can it matter to her if, by means of what we call crime, a man causes another human being to change into a fly or a lettuce? When the sublimity of our species has been proved to me, when it has been demonstrated to me that we are so important in nature's eyes that her laws are incensed at our destruction – then I shall be able to believe that this destruction is a crime. But when the most deliberate study of nature has proved to me that everything which vegetates on this earth, everything that reproduces, including even the most imperfect of her works, are all of equal value in her eyes, I shall never be able to believe that the transformation of one of these creatures into a thousand others could possibly offend her laws. Rather should I say to myself: all men, plants, and animals grow and mature, reproduce themselves and destroy themselves by similar means; but they never really die – all they do is to undergo a simple variation which modifies their substance. Every one of them might, I say, advance themselves in life, one against another, destroy themselves, procreate indifferently and without discrimination, appear one moment in one form, and another moment in another – they might even, at the whim of the being who wished or was able to transform them, change thousands of times during the course of a day without a single law of nature being for even the slightest fraction of a second affected.

'But this being whom I attack happens to be my mother, she who carried me in her womb! What of it? Should such an empty consideration prevent me? And has it any right to do so? Was she thinking of me, this mother you speak of, when in a fit of lubricity she conceived the foetus which grew into the man I am? Do I owe any duty to her because she occupied herself with her own pleasure? In any case it isn't the mother's blood which forms the child, but only that of the father. The female breast nourishes, maintains, and helps build the child, but in reality it furnishes nothing. It is this thought which would never have allowed me to shorten my father's days, but which shows me what a very simple thing it would be to cut the thread of my mother's. Nevertheless, I admit the possibility that the heart of a child may be moved – quite justly – with some feelings of gratitude towards its mother; but we experience such emotions only on the basis of her actions and behaviour towards us throughout our childhood. If she has behaved well we may love her, perhaps we even ought to do so. If, on the other hand, she has acted towards us in an evil way, we are not only bound by no law of nature, but we owe her nothing at all. Under such circumstances the vigorous power of the ego – which naturally and invincibly persuades a man to disembarrass himself of everything which he finds harmful or injurious – this vigorous power, I say, resolves our decision to get rid of such a woman.'

'Oh, Monsieur,' I replied, absolutely appalled by such reasoning, 'the indifference you suppose to be inherent in nature is, in reality, nothing but the work of your passions. Condescend for an instant to listen to your heart instead of your intellectual reasonings, and you will see how it condemns the imperious suggestions stimulated by your libertinism. This heart to whose tribunal I beg you to appeal, is it not the sanctuary wherein that nature, whom you so frequently attack, begs us to listen to and respect her? If you discover that she has inscribed therein the most absolute horror for such a crime as you meditate, will you not agree with me that it should be condemned? If you reply that the fire of your passions destroys this horror within a second, then I wish to impress on you the fact that no sooner will you be satisfied than it shall quickly be reborn, making itself felt through the all-powerful emotion of remorse.

'The greater your sensitivity, the more quickly will its power tear you to pieces . . . Each day, each minute, you shall see her before your eyes, this tender mother whom your barbarous band has cast into the tomb. You shall hear her plaintive voice repeatedly pronouncing the sweet name which brought such delight into your childhood. She will haunt your wakeful nights, torment your dreams, opening with her bloody hands the wounds with which you tore her body. From then on not a happy moment shall shine for you on this earth: all your pleasures will be poisoned, all your thoughts will be troubled; and a celestial hand, whose power you deny, will avenge the days of the mother you have destroyed by poisoning all your own. Without having derived any pleasure from your crimes you will perish from the fatal regret of having dared to carry them out.'

I was in tears while pronouncing these last words, and throwing myself at the knees of the Marquis I conjured him by all that he held most dear to forget such infamous aberrations, swearing I would hide his revelation of them for the remainder of my life. But I did not know the heart I sought to soften. Whatever moral force he may have had, crime had abated its strength; and the passions, in all their furious ardour, permitted none but criminal ideas to reign in his breast.

The Marquis got up coldly: 'I see well enough that I have allowed myself to be deceived, Sophie,' he said; 'I am almost as sorry about it for your sake as for mine. But it doesn't matter – I shall find other means for achieving my aims; and you'll find you've lost a great deal through not helping me, while your mistress will gain nothing by it.'

This menacing attitude changed all my ideas. In not accepting complicity in the crime he proposed I was opening myself to very considerable risk, and my mistress would still undoubtedly perish. In consenting to his request I would be shielding myself from the wrath of my young master, and would eventually be able to save his mother. This reflection, which passed through my mind within the space of a split second, immediately persuaded me to change my role. But as such a retraction of sentiment would have appeared unduly suspicious, I cautiously postponed my defeat by the sophisms of the Marquis, and gave him, instead, plenty of opportunity to repeat them. Little by little I assumed the air of not knowing how to reply to them – and he believed me vanquished. I accounted for my change of heart as being due to the power of his arguments, and eventually pretended to accept everything he proposed. Suddenly I felt the lips of the Marquis pressed against my neck . . . How this movement would have overwhelmed me with joy had not these barbarous projects annihilated every loving sentiment which my indulgent heart had dared to conceive for him . . . Ah! If it had only been possible that I might still love him . . .

'You are the first woman I have ever embraced,' exclaimed the Marquis, 'and, truly, it is with all my heart! You are delightful, my child! It seems that a ray of philosophy must have penetrated your spirit. Is it really possible that this charming head should have remained so long in the shadows?'

And the next moment we were planning our crime. But in order that the Marquis should the more easily fall into my trap, I retained a certain air of repugnance as he explained each additional detail in the development of his project. It was this pretence, so permissible in my desperate situation, which succeeded better than anything else in deceiving my companion. It was decided that in approximately two or three days – depending on how the opportunity presented itself – I should skilfully empty a little packet of poison, given me by the Marquis, into the usual morning cup of chocolate served to the Comtesse. Monsieur de Bressac guaranteed the success of the remainder of the intrigue, and promised me an income of two thousand crowns, adding that I might spend the remainder of my days either under his roof or wherever else might seem suitable to me. He made this promise without indicating the precise circumstances in which I was to enjoy such a favour, and we parted.

Meanwhile something so peculiar happened, something so indicative of the character of the atrocious young man with whom I was involved, that I really must remark on it. Two days after our conversation the Marquis received the news that an uncle, of whom he never expected to be the heir, had died and left him a fortune of eighty thousand livres.

'Gracious heaven!' I exclaimed to myself when I heard this. 'Is it in this manner that celestial justice punishes the plottings of criminals? Here I am, almost having lost my life for refusing much inferior sums, and yet this nobleman has been placed at the pinnacle of wealth and good fortune after having conceived the most terrifying of crimes.'

But quickly repenting of this blasphemy against providence I sank to my knees, begging pardon of God and feeling that this unexpected inheritance might at least change the plans of the Marquis . . . My God! – how considerable was my error!

'My dear Sophie,' said Monsieur de Bressac, coming into my room that same evening, 'prosperity rains down on me! I have told you twenty times, there is nothing like a preoccupation with crime for attracting good fortune. In fact it would seem that her path is only opened easily to evildoers. Eighty and sixty, my child – together they make one hundred and forty livres of income for the service of my pleasures.'

'Then, sir,' I replied, with a surprise moderated by the circumstances in which I was placed, 'this unexpected wealth hasn't decided you in favour of waiting patiently for the death of the lady whose departure you wished to hasten?'

'Wait? – I shan't wait two minutes, my child! Can't you realise I'm twenty-eight, and that at my age it is extremely hard to have to wait! I beg you not to think that this could change any of our projects. Let us have the consolation of bringing all this business to a close before we return to Paris . . . Try and make it tomorrow – or the day after at the latest. I'm looking forward to giving you the first instalment of your pension.'

I did my best to disguise the dismay with which this rabid obsession with crime filled me, and reassumed my role of the previous day. But my feelings were almost numb and my only sensation was one of horror for such a hard and profligate wretch.

No position could have been more awkward than that in which I now found myself. If I didn't play my agreed part the Marquis would quickly come to the conclusion that I was making a fool of him; if I warned Madame de Bressac, whatever steps such a revelation might cause her to take the young man would realise he had been hoaxed, and would very soon decide on more sure means of despatching his mother to another world – and at the same time I should be exposed to all the fury of his vengeance. The only way remaining open to me was that of the law; but not for anything in the world would I have consented to take it. I therefore determined that, whatever might happen, it was essential to warn the Comtesse.

'Madame,' I said to her, the day after my conversation with the Marquis, 'I have something of the greatest importance to disclose to you. Yet, despite the fact that it is urgent and serious and concerns you intimately, I have decided to guard my silence unless you can give me your word of honour never to show any sign of resentment towards your son for what he has had the audacity to plan. You will act as you think fit, Madame; you will take whatever seems the best course open to you, but you will never reveal a word of what I have told you. I must ask you to promise me this, for otherwise I can say nothing to you.'

Madame de Bressac, who thought it was merely something to do with her son's usual extravagant behaviour, promised all I asked. And then I acquainted her with all the facts. The unhappy woman burst into tears on learning of her son's infamy.

'The unholy wretch,' she cried, ' – what have I ever done, except it were for his good? If I tried to prevent his indulgence in vice, or to correct him, what motive other than that of his happiness and peace could ever have led me to be severe with him? To what does he owe the inheritance which has recently fallen to him, if not to my efforts? If I have hidden from him my part in the matter it was simply to spare his feelings . . . The monster! Oh, Sophie, give me proof of his evil schemes, put me into such a position that I shall no longer be able to doubt them! I need every scrap of evidence that can extinguish the natural maternal sentiment still present in my heart . . .'

So I showed the Comtesse the packet of poison which had been given me. We gave a small dose to a dog and carefully shut him up. Within two hours it died in the most terrible convulsions. The Comtesse, no longer being able to doubt, decided immediately on the course she must take. Taking possession of the remainder of the poison, she instantly despatched a courier, bearing a letter, to her kinsman, the Duc de Sonzeval, begging him to go speedily and secretly to the Minister to explain the terrible crime of which she was about to become victim, and to procure a *lettre de cachet* for the imprisonment of her son. In short, he was to save her as quickly as possible from the monster who planned to kill her . . . Nevertheless, by some inconceivable dispensation of heaven this abominable crime was to be consummated.

The discovery of the unhappy dog who had served for our experiment was clear enough indication to the Marquis as to precisely what had happened. He heard it howling, and knowing that it was specially beloved of his mother, made urgent enquiry as to what was wrong with it, and where it was. Those whom he questioned were ignorant of the facts, and thus could not reply. But, doubtless, from that moment, suspicions began to form in his mind. He said nothing but I could see that he was worried, agitated, and on the watch throughout the day. I kept the Comtesse informed, but no further steps could be taken; all that it was possible to do was to hasten the courier and conceal the object of his mission. Therefore Madame de Bressac told her son that she was hurriedly sending to Paris to beg the Duc de Sonzeval to get in touch immediately with the administrators of the uncle whose heir he had just become, for if someone did not appear soon there might be lawsuits to fear. She added that she had asked the Duc to come and give her an account of the precise details so that, if necessary, she could put in an appearance herself, accompanied by her son. The Marquis, who was too good a physiognomist not to notice the anguish on his mother's face and the confusion on my own appeared to be satisfied by the explanation; but was careful at the same time to be the more surely on his guard. Under the pretext of going on a walking party with his minions, he left the castle and waited in ambush for the messenger at a spot which the man was obliged to pass. And the courier, much more devoted to the son than to the mother, made no ado whatever about handing over his mail. Whereon the Marquis, convinced of what he undoubtedly called my treachery, presented him with a hundred louis, ordering him never again to show his face at the castle. Then he returned home burning with rage, but did his best to control himself. When he met me he joked as usual, and asked if tomorrow would be the day, observing that it was essential that the deed should be done before the arrival of the Duc. After which he went quietly to bed without giving himself away in the slightest.

If this terrible crime was committed, as the Marquis soon informed me it had been, then it could only have been done in the following way . . . Madame took her chocolate the next morning according to her habit, and as it had passed only through my hands I can be certain that it had not been tampered with. But about ten o'clock the Marquis entered the kitchen, and finding only the cook present he ordered him to go at once and get some peaches from the garden. The cook expostulated that it was impossible to leave his work, yet the Marquis insisted on his craving for peaches and said he would keep an eye on the stove. So the cook went out and Monsieur de Bressac examined all the dishes prepared for dinner. He seemingly mixed the fatal drug which was to end his mother's days with some white-beet salad – of which she was passionately fond. When dinner was served, the Comtesse doubtless partook of this sinister dish. These are merely my own suspicions, but it was obviously by some such means that the crime was accomplished. Monsieur de Bressac assured me, in the unfortunate sequel to this adventure, that his blow had been struck, and that my collusion with the victim had simply offered him an alternative means for the success of his intentions. But let us leave these horrible conjectures and come to the cruel manner in which I was punished for not having wished to participate in this terrifying business, as well as for my having revealed the nature of the plot . . .

On arising from the meal I have just indicated the Marquis came up to me: 'Listen, Sophie,' he said, with all the appearance of phlegmatic calm, 'I have found a more certain means for concluding my plans than that which I originally proposed to you. But it needs to be discussed in detail. I dare not continue coming so frequently to your room, for I fear the eyes of everyone. At five o'clock precisely be at the corner of the park. I shall meet you, and while we take a long walk together I shall explain everything.'

I cannot but admit that, whether it was by a dispensation of providence owing to excessive innocence, or simply to blindness, nothing caused me to anticipate the fearful ordeal which awaited me. I was so confident of the secrecy of the arrangements I had made with the Comtesse that I never imagined that the Marquis would be able to uncover them. Nevertheless I felt some embarrassment in the matter. Perjury is a virtue when it promises crime – so wrote one of our tragic poets. But perjury is always odious for the delicate and sensitive soul which finds itself obliged to have recourse to it. Thus I found my role awkward – but it was not to be for long. The detestable proceedings of the Marquis, while giving me other causes for pain, soon set my mind at rest regarding that particular embarrassment. He came up to me with the gayest air and the most open attitude in the world: and side by side we advanced together into the forest without him doing anything other than laughing and joking, as was his custom with me. When I wished to turn the conversation towards the object for which he had arranged this meeting, he kept telling me to wait, explaining that he feared we might be observed as we were not yet in safety. Imperceptibly we arrived at the thicket and the great oak where he first encountered me. I could not help shuddering at seeing these again. My imprudence and all the horror of my fate seemed to rise before my eyes with terrible intensity. And you can judge how my terror redoubled itself when I saw at the foot of that gloomy tree, two young minions of the Marquis considered to be those he loved most. They got up as we approached and threw on to the grass a collection of ropes, lashes and other instruments which made me tremble.

Then the Marquis dropped his previous manner and began to abuse me with the grossest and most horrible of insults: 'Bitch!' he exclaimed, even before we were within hearing distance of the young men, 'do you remember this thicket from which I brought you like some savage beast – to restore you to a life which you deserved only to lose? Do you recognise that tree whereon I threatened to lash you again, if ever you gave me cause to repent of my bounty? Why did you accept the services I asked of you against my mother if you intended to betray me? And how did you imagine you were serving virtue when you were risking the liberty of the man to whom you owed your life? Unavoidably faced with a choice between two crimes, why did you choose the most abominable? You had only to refuse what I asked of you, instead of accepting it, in order to betray me!'

Then the Marquis acquainted me with all he had done to waylay the courier, and the nature of the suspicions which had caused him to make such a decision.

'What have you achieved by your falseness, unworthy slut?' he continued. 'You have risked your own life without saving my mother's, for the blow has already fallen, and I hope on my return to see my success amply crowned. But first I must punish you; I must teach you that the path of virtue is not always the best, and that there are situations in life where complicity in crime is preferable to the role of informer. Knowing me as you do, how have you dared deceive me? Did you think that the sentiment of pity – a sentiment which my heart never admits except in the interest of my pleasures – or a few religious precepts, such as I constantly trample underfoot, would be capable of restraining me? . . . Or perhaps you were counting on your charms?'

He added these words in the most cruel and bantering tone . . .

'Very well then! I am going to prove to you that these charms, made as naked as it is possible to make them, will serve only to inflame my vengeance the more . . .'

And without giving me time to reply, without giving the slightest proof of emotion at the torrent of tears which overwhelmed me, he seized me brutally by the arm and dragged me to his satellites.

'Here,' he said to them, 'is the woman who wished to poison my mother, and who perhaps already has committed this shocking crime, despite my attempts to prevent her. I should perhaps have placed her in the hands of the law; but then she would have lost her life and it is my wish that she should retain it so that she shall have a much longer time in which to suffer. Strip her quickly of her clothes and tie her with her belly against this tree so that I may chastise her in the manner she deserves.'

The order was no sooner given than it was fulfilled. Making me embrace the tree as closely as possible, they tied a handkerchief around my mouth and bound me to it by my shoulders and legs, leaving the remainder of my body free, so that nothing should come between my flesh and the blows it was to receive. The Marquis, agitated to an astonishing extent, seized one of the lashes. But before he struck me the inhuman devil closely observed my face. You might have said that he feasted his eyes on my tears and the marks of pain and dismay which impregnated my every feature . . . Then he moved behind me to a distance of about three feet, and I suddenly felt myself struck with all possible force from the middle of my back down to my very calves. My butcher then stopped for a minute and brutally touched all the parts he had mangled . . . I do not know what he whispered to one of his satellites, but within a second my head was covered with a handkerchief which no longer left me the slightest possibility of observing any of their movements. There was, in fact, a considerable amount of motion behind me before the resumption of the further bloody scenes to which I was destined . . . '*Yes! Good – that's it!*' exclaimed the Marquis before he lashed me again. And hardly had these incomprehensible words been pronounced than the blows rained down with even greater violence. There was another pause. Once more the hands moved over the lacerated portions of my body, to be followed by further whispering. Then one of the young men said aloud: '*Am I not better thus?*' These new words were equally mysterious to me, but the Marquis only replied: '*Get nearer, get nearer!*' A third attack followed, still more brutal than those that had gone before, and during which Bressac exclaimed repeatedly, mingling his words with terrifying oaths: '*Go on then, go on, both of you – can't you see that I wish to make her die on the spot, and beneath my very hand!*' These words, gradually pronounced louder, terminated this infamous butchery. Once again the men spoke softly together for several minutes. This was followed by more movement, and then I felt the cords which bound me being loosened. The grass, covered with my blood, showed me the state I must be in. The Marquis was alone; his assistants had vanished . . .

'Very well, you bitch,' he said, looking at me with the kind of expression which follows the delirium of the passions, 'don't you find virtue rather expensive, and that a pension of two thousand crowns was preferable to a hundred strokes with a lash?'

I threw myself at the foot of the tree, almost ready to lose consciousness . . . The lecherous fiend, not yet satisfied by the horrors he had just indulged and cruelly excited by the sight of my wounds, trampled me beneath his feet, and so crushed me against the ground that I was almost suffocated.

'It is more than good of me to have spared your life,' he repeated two or three times. 'So at least be careful as to what use you make of this new indulgence of mine . . .'

Then he ordered me to get up and clothe myself. As blood was flowing everywhere I mechanically gathered some grass to dry myself, for I did not wish that my garments – the only ones I had – should be stained. Meanwhile the Marquis walked to and fro, leaving me alone, for he was more concerned with his thoughts than with his victim. The swelling of my flesh, the blood which still continued to flow, and the frightful pain I was enduring, all these things combined to render the movements necessary in dressing a virtual impossibility. But not once did this ferocious man, this monster who was responsible for my cruel condition – he for whom a few days previously I would have given my very life – not once was he moved by the slightest feeling of that commiseration which might have urged him to help me.

When I was dressed he approached me: 'You may go where you wish,' he said. 'You must have some money in your pocket, so I shan't deprive you of it. But take care never to appear near my establishments again – either at

Paris or here in the country. I am warning you now that you will be publicly known as the murderess of my mother. If she is still breathing when I return home I shall see that she carries this idea with her into the grave. The whole house shall know it, and I am going to denounce you officially before the law. Therefore you will find Paris even more uninhabitable than before; for I must inform you that your first difficulty there, which you thought ended, was merely hushed up. You were told that it was erased from the records – but in that you were deceived. You were left in this situation in order that your subsequent behaviour might be observed. So now you have two trials to face instead of one. And in place of a vile usurer as your adversary, you have a rich and powerful man, a man who is determined to pursue you as far as the very gates of hell – should you, by way of slander or calumny, abuse the life he so generously leaves you.'

'Oh, sir!' I replied, 'however severe you may have been towards me, do not fear that I shall take any steps against you. I felt it was my duty to interfere where your mother's life was concerned, but I should never attempt to contradict you when it is only a question of the unfortunate Sophie. Adieu, Monsieur, and may your crimes render you as happy as your cruelties have tortured me. And whatever destiny heaven may have in store for you, so long as it shall spare my lamentable days I shall employ them only in imploring its mercy on you.'

The Marquis raised his head. As I spoke these words he could not help looking at me; and seeing me all wet with tears, scarcely able to support myself, the cruel man, doubtless in fear of being moved to pity, turned away. When he had disappeared I let myself fall to the ground, abandoning myself to all the intensity of my pain. The air around re-echoed with my sobs, and I watered the grass with my tears. 'Oh, God,' I cried. 'You have willed it. It was by Your decree that the innocent should once more become the prey of the guilty. Dispose of me as you will, Father, for I am yet far from the evils which You have suffered for us. Grant that those I endure while adoring You may render me worthy, one day, of those recompenses You have promised the weak – the weak who always keep You in mind in their tribulations, and who glorify You in their anguish!'

Night came, but I was in no state to travel far. Though scarcely able to stand I remembered the thicket where I had slept four years before, though in a much less miserable condition. I dragged myself to it as best I could; and lying on the same spot, tormented by my still bleeding wounds and overcome by the sufferings of my spirit and the ache in my heart, I passed the cruellest night anyone could possibly imagine. The vigour natural to my age and temperament having given me a little strength by daybreak, and too scared to remain where I was in the neighbourhood of that cruel castle, I quickly left the forest determined, whatever the difficulties, to reach the first dwellings I should come upon. At length I reached the town of Claye, situated about six leagues from Paris. I asked for the surgeon's house and someone pointed it out to me. I implored this gentleman to dress my wounds, telling him that I had fled my mother's house in Paris because of a disappointment in love, and that as my way unfortunately led me through the forest of Bondy I had fallen amongst thieves who had treated me as he could see. He attended to me on condition that I made a deposition to the clerk of the local court. I consented. Probably they made some investigations, but I never heard speak of them. As for the surgeon, he insisted that I stayed with him until I had recovered, and he looked after me with such art that in less than a month I had completely recovered.

As soon as my condition permitted me to go out of doors my first preoccupation was to find some young village girl careful enough and sensible enough to be able to visit the Château de Bressac, so that she might discover everything that had happened there since my departure. Curiosity was not the only motive which determined me in this proceeding. In fact such a desire for information might have been dangerous and would certainly have been unsuited to my circumstances, but I had left in my room the little money I had earned while working for the Comtesse and I had barely six louis with me – although I had nearly thirty at the Château. I did not imagine that the Marquis could be cruel enough to refuse me what was legitimately mine, and I was convinced that once fury was over he would not burden me with a second injustice. So I wrote him a letter in terms as touching as I could find . . . It seemed, alas, that I overdid matters. My sad heart somehow still spoke in favour of this perfidious man. I carefully hid from him my present whereabouts, and begged him to send me my personal effects and the little money which belonged to me. A peasant girl of twenty or twenty-five years, very bright and wide-awake, promised to deliver my letter and to make enough discreet enquiries to be able to satisfy me on her return regarding the various matters about which I was anxious. I expressly advised her not to disclose where she came from, nor yet to speak of me at all; but to say that she had been given the letter by a man who had brought it over a distance of more than fifteen leagues. Jeannette – for that was the name of my messenger – set off for the Château and returned with my reply within twenty-four hours. But first, Madame, it is essential that I acquaint you with all that had happened at the Bressac estate before I tell you the contents of the letter.

The Comtesse de Bressac fell grievously ill the day of my departure from her home, and she died suddenly that same night. Nobody arrived from Paris, and the Marquis, in the depths of despair (the hypocrite!), pretended that his mother had been poisoned by a chambermaid named Sophie, who had escaped the same day. A search was being made for this servant and, if discovered, she was to die on the scaffold. The Marquis, however, had found that his inheritance had made him even richer than he expected. The contents of the strong-boxes, the jewels of Madame de Bressac, and various items which had not been considered – all these, in addition to his other revenues, put the young man in possession of more than six hundred thousand francs in goods and cash. It was said that, beneath his affectation of grief, he experienced considerable difficulty in hiding his joy. Those kinsmen whom he had summoned to be present at the autopsy had deplored the end of the unhappy Comtesse, swearing to avenge her should she who had committed such a crime fall into their hands; and then they left the young man in full and peaceful possession of the fruits of his treachery. Monsieur de Bressac had spoken to Jeannette himself, asking her various questions, to which the young woman replied with such firmness and intrepidity that he decided to satisfy her demands without pressing her further.

'Here is the fatal letter,' said Sophie, bringing it from her pocket. 'I shall keep it until my last breath, Madame. Take it, read it if you can, without shuddering!'

Madame de Lorsange, having taken the note from the hands of our beautiful adventuress, read therein the following words:

A wretch capable of having poisoned my mother is unusually bold in daring to write me after such an execrable crime. The best thing for her to do is to see to it that she covers her tracks as well as she can, for she may be certain that she will pay for it if she is found. What does she dare to claim? . . . What does she say about money and personal effects? Does what she left behind equal in amount the total of her thefts during her stay in my house? Does it compensate in the slightest for her latest crime? She had better avoid sending me a second envoy with another letter like to her first – for such a messenger will be kept under restraint until the whereabouts of the guilty woman have officially been made known to justice.

'Continue, my dear child,' said Madame de Lorsange as she returned the note to Sophie. 'Such behaviour is most disgusting; especially in one who, rolling in wealth, refuses her honestly earned wages to an unfortunate creature who did not wish to concur in a crime. Such infamy, in fact, seems to me without precedent.'

'Alas, Madame,' continued Sophie, as she took up the sequel of her tale, 'I wept for two days over this wretched letter; and I sobbed more over the horrible possibilities it suggested than over the refusal it contained.

'So I am guilty!' I cried. 'So I must a second time be denounced before the law for having rigidly observed its decrees . . . Let it be so, for I repent of nothing I have done. Whatever may happen to me I shall never know either pain or remorse within my own soul so long as I retain its purity. And I shall have the satisfaction of knowing that I have committed no fault other than that of having lent too willing an ear to those whisperings of justice and virtue which will never desert me.'

I nevertheless found it impossible to believe that the searches of which the Marquis had spoken were genuine. There was little to commend their reality, since it would be dangerous for him to have me appear before a court; and I felt certain that he would feel much more terrified of my presence, if ever he should discover me near him, than I need feel of his threats. These reflections decided me on staying where I was and to obtain some work, if I could, until slightly increased funds would allow me to move on.

I communicated my project to Rodin, which was the name of the surgeon at whose house I was staying. He approved, and even proposed that I continue my residence with him. But before I tell you what happened to me there it is necessary that I should give you an idea of this man and those who made up his household.

Rodin was a man of forty, with dark and heavy eyebrows, a quick penetrating glance and a strong and healthy form. His features and manner seemed to indicate a libertine temperament. Possessed of an income of between ten and twelve thousand livres a year, Rodin exercised the surgical art only from taste. He lived in a very fine house which, since his wife had died several years previously, he occupied with two servant girls to wait on him and his daughter, Rosalie, who had just attained her fourteenth year. This lovely girl united all the charms best calculated to cause delight; her waist was nymph-like, her face round, fresh, with extraordinary animation. She had delicate and pleasing features, the prettiest mouth possible, large black eyes which reflected her goodness of soul and shone with sentiment, chestnut coloured hair, which fell round her shoulders, skin of an incredible and dazzling smoothness, and the loveliest bosom in the world. She was possessed, moreover, of the wit and liveliness of one of the fairest souls that nature had as yet created. As for the maidservants with whom I was to serve in this house, both were peasants. One was governess and the other cook. The first was about twenty-five years old, and the other between eighteen and twenty. Both were extremely pretty, and such a choice gave me reason to suspect the eagerness which Rodin displayed in engaging me. 'What need has he of a third woman?' I asked myself; 'and why does he want them so good-looking? Assuredly,' I continued, 'there is something in all this which doesn't conform to that conventional and regular behaviour from which I never wish to stray. The matter, therefore, needs careful investigation.'

Consequently I begged Monsieur Rodin to allow me to convalesce in his house for one more week, assuring him that before the end of that time he would receive my decision on what he wished to propose to me.

I profited by this interval to become more closely acquainted with Rosalie, determined not to settle with her father if there were any circumstances in his house likely to offend me. With this view in mind I kept a close watch on everything, and the following day noticed that this man had an arrangement which, from the start, aroused in me the most violent suspicions regarding his conduct.

Rodin kept in his home a school for children of both sexes. He had obtained an official permit to do so during the lifetime of his wife, and the authorities had felt themselves unable to deprive him of it once he had lost her. His pupils were not numerous, but they were carefully chosen; and he had, in all, only fourteen girls and fourteen boys. He would never accept them below the age of twelve, and they were obliged to leave as soon as they had reached sixteen. I have rarely seen young people so handsome as those received into this establishment. And whenever this man was faced with a boy or girl showing either bodily defect or lack of good features, he would tactfully refuse them admittance under twenty different pretexts, all tinged with sophisms to which nobody could reply. Thus, however small, his little group of boarders were always beautiful and always charming. I had not seen this little group previously because, arriving during the holidays, the scholars were all absent. They reappeared towards the time of my recovery.

Rodin supervised the school, the governess teaching the girls until he had finished instructing the boys, at which time he would move into her class-room and take over. He taught his young pupils writing, arithmetic, a little history, drawing, and music – without employing any masters other than himself.

I expressed my astonishment to Rosalie that her father, while exercising the art of surgery, could, at the same time, discharge that of schoolmaster. I also confided my opinion that it appeared strange that a man who was wealthy enough to live at his ease without having need to follow either profession should put himself to so much trouble in order to organise them. Rosalie, with whom by this time I was very friendly, burst into laughter on hearing my remarks. Her manner of receiving my observations only excited my curiosity the more, and I implored her to explain why she reacted so.

'Listen,' explained this charming girl, with all the candour of her age and all the innocence of her amiable character; 'listen, Sophie, I am going to tell you everything, for I can see that you are an honest girl . . . incapable of betraying the secret I am about to confide in you.

'My father is certainly all that you have said of him; and if he exercises both the one and the other profession, as you see him doing, then he has two motives the nature of which I am going to disclose to you. He practices surgery because he likes it, and for the pleasure of making new discoveries – of which he has made many. In fact he has written works so learned that he generally passes for the most skilful and expert man in his field at the present time. He worked twenty years in Paris before he retired to this part of the country, so the real local surgeon is a man named Rombeau, whom my father took under his protection, and with whom he is associated in his experiments. And would you like to know what entices him to run a school? . . . Libertinism, my child, sheer libertinism, a passion which he carries to the extreme. My father finds in his pupils – of both sexes – subjects whom dependence on him makes submissive to his will, and he profits by it . . . But listen! – follow me,' continued Rosalie, 'today is Friday, one of the three days in the week when he corrects those who have been guilty of making mistakes; and it is in this kind of correction that my father finds his delight. Come on, follow me and you shall see how he does it. We can secretly observe everything from a hiding place in my room. But take good care never to reveal a word of what I have told you or of what you are about to see with your own eyes.'

It was so important for me to know the habits of the man who was offering me asylum that I neglected nothing which might help reveal his true nature to me. I followed behind Rosalie and she placed me close to a partition wall in which there were several cracks, sufficiently large to enable us to see everything that happened in the neighbouring room.

We had scarcely taken up our positions when Rodin entered the larger room leading by the hand a young girl of fourteen, fair and beautiful as Love herself. The poor creature was weeping bitterly and seemed, unfortunately, to be only too well acquainted with what was awaiting her. Sobbing, she threw herself at his feet, imploring his pardon. But Rodin, inflexible, seemed to draw from these demonstrations the first sparks of his pleasure – a pleasure which was already sprouting in his heart, signalling itself in his sinister glance . . .

'Oh, no, no,' he cried; 'this has already happened too often, Julie, and I repent of my good nature. It has served only to plunge you into additional faults. Can you imagine that the gravity of this one leaves me any room for clemency? . . . You passed a note to a boy as he came into class, didn't you?'

'Monsieur, I protest that I didn't!'

'Oh! But I saw you, I saw you!'

'Don't believe a word of it,' exclaimed Rosalie. 'These are faults he concocts to bolster up the pretexts for his actions. This little creature is an angel, and it is because she resists him that he treats her so severely.'

During this time Rodin, more and more excited, seized the little girl by the hands and tied them to the top of a post which had been set up in the middle of the 'correction' room, and which was fitted with a ring for this purpose. Julie was thus left with no defence . . . other than her fair head wistfully turned towards her tormenter, her superb hair all dishevelled, and her tears bathing one of the sweetest, most beautiful, and most interesting faces in the world. Rodin gazed on this picture and, inflamed by it, he blindfolded those eyes which sent out such appeals to him. Julie was no longer able to see anything, and Rodin, more at ease, removed the veils of her modesty, raising her chemise as far as her loins, and tucking it up in the edge of her bodice . . . What whiteness, what beauty! Here were roses stripped of their leaves by the very hands of the Graces. What was he, then, this creature who could condemn to torment these charms so fresh and appetising? Who was the monster who could find pleasure in the sight of tears and pain? Rodin surveyed her, his eyes straying everywhere, while his hands dared to profane those flowers which his cruelties were about to stigmatise. As we were directly facing them, no movement escaped us. The libertine continued his lecherous examination until the fury of his lust could no longer be restrained. He first expressed it in invective, menacing her with all manner of threats and evil proposals. The poor little girl began to writhe under the thought of the lashes which she already felt mangling her flesh. Rodin, no longer himself, snatched a fistful of rods from out a great tub of vinegar, where they were steeping to increase their suppleness.

'Come along,' he said, approaching his victim; 'get ready, because you are going to suffer!'

And then this hard-hearted wretch used his vigorous arm to whip the birch plumb-wise across the parts exposed to him. He commenced with twenty-five lashes, which quickly changed to vermilion the tender incarnate of this delicate and tender skin.

Julie screamed, with loud and piercing cries which tore into my soul. Tears flowed beneath the bandage which covered her eyes and fell like pearls on her beautiful cheeks. But all this only roused Rodin to greater fury . . . His hands ran over the parts he had harassed, touched them, pressed them, and seemed to be preparing themselves for new assaults. Rodin recommenced, and every blow was preceded by some invective, a threat, or a reproach . . . The blood flowed . . . Rodin was in ecstasy. He delighted in the contemplation of these visible proofs of his ferocity. He was no longer able to contain himself, and the most indecent of states manifested the fire of his passion. As he made no attempt to hide anything, Julie could see all . . . Indulging in fresh tyrannies he flogged with all the force in his arm. He did not know where to stop. His intoxication reached the pitch of depriving him of any further use of reason. He cursed, he blasphemed, he was ecstatic, and nothing was secure from his barbarous blows. Every piece of flesh before him was treated with the same severity. The wretch stopped, nevertheless, as he wished to postpone his culmination to a later episode.

'Get dressed,' he said to Julie as he untied her; and, readjusting himself, he added: 'and if you do anything similar again don't expect to get off so lightly!'

Julie returned to her classroom while Rodin entered that of the boys. He quickly came back accompanied by a young scholar of fifteen who was beautiful as a summer's day. Rodin grumbled a little, but, more at ease with the boy, joked and kissed him as he lectured him: 'You deserve to be punished,' he exclaimed, 'and you are going to be!'

With these words he seized the child, overleaping all the bounds of modesty. But, contrary to his attitude with the girl, everything interested him here; nothing was excluded, the veils were lifted, and everything was handled or fingered indiscriminately. Rodin threatened, he caressed, he kissed, he indulged in invective. Then his impious fingers sought to awaken in this young boy all the voluptuous sensations which he so urgently felt in himself.

'What have we here!' exclaimed the satyr as he viewed his success; 'just look at you, in the very state which I've expressly forbidden . . . '

Then getting to his feet the hypocrite continued with his upbraiding: 'Ah! but I'm going to punish you for this indecency! You little rogue, you cheat, I must avenge myself for the illusions I have permitted myself to entertain about you!'

The birch was brought out again and Rodin commenced his fustigations. Doubtless more excited than he had been with the little Vestal, his blows became increasingly fierce and increasingly numerous. The child was crying and Rodin was in raptures. But, fresh pleasures calling him, he untied the boy to make way for sacrifices of another kind.

There were further similar episodes with another nine children – five boys and four girls. Horrified by the things I had heard and the scenes I had witnessed, I turned to Rosalie: 'In heaven's name,' I asked, when these frightful tableaux had drawn to a close, 'how can a man give himself up to such excesses? How can he find pleasure in the torments he inflicts?'

'Ah! but you don't know everything yet,' replied Rosalie. 'Listen,' she continued, as she stepped out of the cupboard into her room, 'what you have seen should have made it clear to you that my father takes advantage of the minor misdemeanours of his pupils to indulge his horrors to the utmost. He abuses the young girls in the same manner as he does the boys. In this way the girls are not dishonoured, pregnancy is not to be feared and nothing will prevent them eventually finding husbands. Scarcely a year passes when he doesn't corrupt in this manner almost every boy in the school, and at least half of the other pupils. The two women who serve us are submitted to the same horrors . . . Oh, Sophie,' sobbed Rosalie, as she threw herself into my arms, 'Oh, my dear girl, he has seduced even me, his own daughter, right from the tenderest years of my childhood. I had barely attained my eleventh year when I became his victim . . . I was, alas, without the means of defending myself.'

'But, Mademoiselle,' I interrupted, terrified . . . 'What about religion? At least that way remained open to you . . . Could you not have approached a confessor and told him of your exact circumstances?'

'Ah! You've no idea the extent to which he perverted us, for he stifled in us the slightest sentiment of religion. We were forbidden to attend service, and the little he told me concerning this subject was merely to prevent my ignorance from giving away his impiety. I have never been to confession, and I have never taken my first communion. He even entices his pupils away from religion. As for myself and his behaviour towards me, convince your-self with your own eyes what goes on . . . ' And she quickly pushed me back into the cupboard we had recently occupied.

Telling me to remain where I was, Rosalie left me. Shortly afterwards Rodin accompanied his daughter into the room already mentioned, followed by the two women who completed his household. Then this lascivious man, no longer being obliged to keep within limits, abandoned himself freely and without any disguise to all the irregularities debauchery might suggest. The two peasants, both stark naked, were lashed with all the might of his arms, and while he was treating one in this manner the other paid him back in the same coin. During the intervals he loaded with the most immoderate and disgusting caresses his daughter, Rosalie, who was raised up on an armchair. This unfortunate girl was the next to suffer. Rodin fastened her to the post, just as he had fastened Julie; and while his women whipped him – one after the other, and sometimes both together – he lashed his daughter, laying his stripes from the middle of her loins to the lower part of her thighs, and at the same time falling into ecstasies of pleasure. His agitation was extreme. He cursed, shouted, and blasphemed as he whipped . . . Rodin, naked, was in his glory . . . A thousand kisses, each more warm than the rest, gave expression to his ardour . . . Then the bomb exploded, and the pain-intoxicated libertine dared to taste the sweetest of pleasures in the bosom of incest and infamy. At length he felt the need of restoring himself after his exertions. The women were sent away and Rodin went to seat himself at dinner.

Two days after these events he came to my room to ask my reply to his offer. He surprised me in bed. Then, under pretext of seeing if anything remained of the wounds with which I had arrived at his home, he examined me, naked. I was unable to oppose his examining me in this manner, since he had done so twice a day for a month without my ever having perceived in his attitude anything that might offend chastity. But this time Rodin showed signs of other schemes . . . During his observations he passed one of his legs around my loins and pressed it so forcibly that I found myself without defence.

'Sophie,' he said, while his hands wandered round me in such a manner as no longer left me in any doubt, 'you are cured, my dear; and now you are in a position to prove to me the gratitude with which I have already seen your heart filled. Merely this shall be my reward.'

'Monsieur,' I replied, 'I would like to convince you that there is nothing in the whole world which might entice me into the terrible sins you seem to demand of me. I owe you my gratitude, and it is sincerely felt. But I shall not express it at the cost of what is both sin and crime. I am poor and unfortunate, I know, but here is the little money I have.' And with these words I offered him my wretched little purse.

Rodin was confounded by this resistance, which – especially as he knew I was completely without resources – he had so little expected. According to the usual unjust reasoning of men he had expected me to be dishonest and loose simply because I was poor and deserted. He looked at me attentively for a few seconds: 'Sophie,' he commenced, 'it is pretty much out of season to act the Vestal with me. It seems to me that I have some right to your complacency. However,' he sighed, 'keep your money, and do not leave me. I am more than pleased to have such a good girl in my house, for those around me are far from the attainment of virtue. Besides, my daughter loves you, which is a further reason for my begging you to stay . . .'

I accepted his offer. Such a place was worth a fortune to one in my position. Moreover, inflamed with the desire of bringing Rosalie back to the path of goodness and purity, and perhaps of converting her father himself – should I succeed in gaining any influence over him – I did not repent of what I had just done. Rosalie received the news with the greatest transports of joy, and soon I was permanently installed as a member of the household.

Before eight days were over I had commenced working towards the conversions I desired, but the obduracy of Rodin kept spoiling my schemes:

'Do not fancy,' he would reply to my wise counsels, 'that the particular type of homage which I render to your virtue is any proof that I esteem virtue as such, or have any intention of preferring it above vice.

'Do not imagine, Sophie, that anything of the kind is true, for you would merely be deceiving yourself. Those who would interpret my attitude towards you in this sense would be guilty of a considerable error, and it would greatly disturb me if you placed such a construction on what might appear to be my way of thinking. The hut which I use as a shelter when hunting – when the scorching rays of the sun beat too furiously on my body – is neither a beautiful nor a profitable monument. Its necessity is purely one of circumstance: I expose myself to dangers of a kind, I find something which protects me, and naturally I make use of it. But is it any the more useful or profitable for having served its original purpose? Is it any less of a wooden shambles? In a wholly vicious society you would realise that virtue would serve no end whatsoever. But as ours is not that sort of society it becomes necessary to pay lip service to virtue, and to make use of it so that we have less to fear from those who worship its precepts. If nobody adopted it the whole idea would become useless. Thus I am not wrong when I assert that its necessity is only one of opinion or circumstances; virtue is not a type of behaviour of incontestable worth; it is simply a manner of conducting oneself which varies according to climate and race, and which consequently lacks the reality of universal application. The variety of codes in existence, and the fact that laws may be completely changed with equally beneficial results, is sufficient proof of the futility of set virtues and ancient taboos. Only that which is constant is really good, and things which perpetually change cannot pretend to the character of true goodness. That is why immutability has been classed among the perfections of the Eternal. But virtue is wholly devoid of this character – there are not two nations on the face of this globe which are virtuous in the same way; therefore virtue contains nothing real, nothing intrinsically good, and in no way deserves our admiration. It may be necessary to use it as a stay, politically to adopt that of the country in which one happens to live, so as to be left in peace by those who practice it from taste and those who are obliged to reverence it owing to their situation. And again it may be necessary to employ it; because, owing to the respect in which it is held and the preponderance of its conventions, it can guarantee you against the attempts of those who profess vice. Once more, however, all this is simply a matter of circumstance, and nothing in it allows any genuine merit to virtue. There are virtues, moreover, which are impossible for certain men. And how are you going to persuade me that a virtue which combats or denies the passions can truly be found in Nature? And if it cannot be found in Nature, how can it be good? Assuredly you will find, among the men of whom we are speaking, vices opposed to these virtues, and vices which will be preferable, since they represent the only way . . . the only mode of life conforming satisfactorily with their physiological make-up and the functioning of their various organs. According to this hypothesis there must be some very useful vices; so how can virtue claim to be particularly useful, when its contraries can be proved equally so? It has been said that virtue is useful to others, and therefore good; also that if it is only permitted to do to others what is good, I shall thus receive nothing but good in my turn. But such reasoning constitutes a mere sophism. In return for the little good I receive from others – because they practice virtue, and because I am obliged to practice it in my turn – I make a million sacrifices which in no way repay me. Receiving less than I bestow, I consider that I have made a very bad bargain; I experience much more evil from the privations I endure for virtue's sake than the good I receive from those who are described as good. As the arrangement is so unequal, I am unwise to submit to it; and realising that my being virtuous will not bring an amount of good to others equal to the pain and trouble I would experience in forcing myself into their mould, is it not best for me to cease procuring them a happiness which costs me so ill? There remains the wrong I could do others by being vicious, and the evil I will receive in my turn – if everyone is like me. I agree that I am taking a definite risk if I indulge in a wide range of vices; but the chagrin I experience in undertaking such risks is compensated by the pleasure I feel in what I make others risk; thus equality is established and everyone is almost equally happy – which is not, nor could be, the situation in a society in which some are good and others wicked because, from an admixture of this particular type, perpetual snares arise – such as do not exist in a society of the kind I have just suggested. In a mixed society the interests are all diverse, and there we have the source of an infinity of woes. In such a social organisation as I indicated previously, all interests are equal – each individual in the group is endowed with the same tastes, the same propensities, and all march towards the same end. Therefore all are happy. But, fools will tell you, evil does not make a man happy. That may be true when it has been decided to emulate and praise only the good; but depreciate and abase that which you call good and you will revere only that which you once had the folly of calling evil, not because it will be permitted (that would frequently be a reason for the diminishment of its charm), but because the laws, no longer employed for the punishment of crime, would not inspire that fear which reduces the pleasure nature has placed in such actions. I visualise a society in which incest (let us admit this delinquency together with the remainder) is a crime. Those who abandon themselves to it will experience a freezing up of their pleasures, and they will be unhappy – because opinion, law, and religion will all be against them. Those who desire to commit this evil but who are curbed by public opinion from giving way to their desires will equally be unhappy. Thus a law which proscribed incest would only have succeeded in increasing the ranks of unfortunate and unhappy humans. Imagine another society in which incest is not a crime and you will discover that those who do not desire it will not be unhappy, while those who do so will be happy. Therefore a society permitting this act is much more suitable for men than one which raises it to the level of a crime. And the same applies to many other acts wrongly considered as criminal. Examining the state of things from my own viewpoint, I find a crowd of unhappy beings; but immediately I perceive that, by granting them freedom, everyone becomes happy in his own way – and nobody has further cause for complaint. Because under these conditions the man who likes such and such an action delivers himself up to it in peace; and those who do not care for it either remain in a state of indifference (which is in no wise painful) or repay the wrong they may have received by a host of other wrongs which enable them to hurt, in their turn, all those of whom they have cause to complain. Therefore, in a criminal society, people either find themselves very happy or in a state of unconcern which in no wise inconveniences them. Consequently virtue no longer presents the illusion of goodness, nor is it clothed in respectability or indicated as a means of attaining happiness. Those who follow it have no cause to puff themselves with pride when the above kind of homage is all that we can render it – forced, as we are, to do so by the constitution of society as we know it. This supposed quality is purely an affair of circumstance, of convention; and when examined closely we find worship chimerical, without the compensation of its fleeting illusion being any the more attractive.'

Such was the infernal logic of Rodin's unfortunate and passionate nature. But Rosalie, milder and much less corrupted, Rosalie, detesting the horrors to which she was subjected, gave way with greater docility to my teaching. I fervently longed to have her discharge her first duties to religion. For this, however, it would have been necessary to get a priest into the house, as well as into my confidence, and Rodin would never have one of them near him – he held them in absolute horror and contempt, together with the beliefs they professed . . . Nor did he permit Rosalie to leave home unaccompanied. It was thus necessary to await a suitable opportunity. So during this delay I employed myself in instructing my friend, in giving her a taste for virtue. Inspiring her with the love of religion, I unveiled for her the holy dogmas of the Church and tried to help her understand something of its sublime mysteries. Implanting these sentiments deep in her young heart, I succeeded in rendering them indispensable to the happiness of her life. And I was glad.

'Everything follows from this first principle,' I told her, ' – that God exists, that he deserves to be worshipped, and that the most important of the basic elements in this worship is virtue.'

Gradually I taught her other things, and it was not long before Rosalie became a Christian.

Then, quite suddenly, she vanished. Knowing what I did of Rodin, I became most apprehensive as to the fate of this unfortunate girl and immediately resolved to do everything in my power to discover what had happened. The day after her disappearance I thought I heard sobs coming from the direction of a remote cellar. I descended and placed my ear against the door . . . No longer was I in doubt!

'Sophie,' I heard at last, 'Sophie – Oh, Sophie, is it you?'

'Yes, my dearest, my closest friend,' I cried as I recognised the voice of Rosalie . . . 'Yes, it's Sophie whom heaven has sent to rescue you . . .'

And my questions multiplied themselves so rapidly that the poor girl scarcely had a chance of replying. At length I learned that several hours before her disappearance, Rombeau, the friend and colleague of Rodin, had examined her naked; and that she had been ordered by her father to submit to the same horrors with Rombeau as those to which he himself regularly subjected her. She had resisted; but Rodin, furious, had seized her and held her down before the lecherous assaults of his partner. Afterwards the two friends had whispered together for a long time, returning at intervals to examine her afresh, or to maltreat her in a hundred different and criminal fashions. Finally, after a pretence at sending her to stay with a relative, she had been thrown into this cellar where she was well enough fed and cared for.

When her abundant tears had ceased flowing, I asked the poor girl if she knew where they kept the key to this cellar. She didn't know, so I searched everywhere – but without success. Swearing to return the next day I was obliged to leave my dear friend with nothing but my consolation, my assurances of help, and many tears.

That night Rombeau was dining with Rodin. Determined, by any means, to shed some light on the situation of my mistress, I hid myself in a place adjoining the room where the two friends were seated. Their conversation soon convinced me only too well of the horrible project with which both were preoccupied.

'Never will anatomy fully be understood,' said Rodin, 'until the vessels have been examined as they are found in a child of fourteen or fifteen who has died a cruel death. It is only by this means that we can obtain a complete analysis of a part so interesting.'

'It is just the same,' replied Rombeau 'when we come to the membrane which proves virginity. For such an examination a young girl is very necessary. For what does one observe once puberty has been reached? Nothing! The hymen has already been affected and all subsequent researches are inexact. Your daughter is precisely what we need. Although she is fifteen she has not yet attained puberty. And the manner in which we have enjoyed her has not damaged this membrane. Besides, we can study her at our ease. I am absolutely delighted that you have at last determined on this experiment.'

'I am certainly determined,' replied Rodin. 'It is odious for anyone to let futile considerations arrest the progress of science. Have the greatest men ever allowed themselves to be hampered by such contemptible chains? And when Michelangelo wished to represent the figure of Christ realistically, did he make it an issue with his conscience as to whether or not he should crucify a young man so as to copy his anguish and suffering? So far as our own art is concerned, what an urgent need there is for the employment of analogous methods! When it is a case of sacrificing one subject to save a million, should one haggle about the price? Is execution as performed under the law any different from what we are about to do? And the object of this law, which we find so wise – is it not the sacrifice of one individual so that a thousand may be saved?'

As the meal came to a close, the measures proposed by these demented creatures, their actions and preparations, together with the fact that finally they were in a state almost bordering on delirium, all served to show me that not a minute was to be lost – for the unfortunate Rosalie was to be destroyed this same evening. I flew to the cellar, resolved to deliver her or die.

'Oh, my dear friend,' I cried, 'we haven't a moment to lose . . . The monsters . . . They intend to kill you this very night! . . . It won't be long before they are here . . .'

While saying this, I exerted the most violent efforts in an attempt to force the door. One of my pushes caused something to fall. I felt for it with my hand . . . It was the key! Hastily I opened the door, embraced Rosalie, and urged her to flee. She darted out, following close on my steps. Alas, it was still decreed that virtue must fail and that sentiments of the most commiseration should be punished! Rodin and Rombeau, informed by the governess, suddenly appeared. The first seized his daughter just as she cleared the front doorstep. A few more steps and she would have been at liberty!

'Ah! Ah! This is espionage and abduction!' exclaimed Rodin, 'Two of the most dangerous vices in a domestic. Upstairs! Upstairs! We must sit in judgment on this affair!'

Dragged by these two villains, Rosalie and I were brought back to the living quarters and the doors firmly locked. Rodin's unfortunate daughter was tied to the posts of a bed, while all the rage of these furious men was turned on me. I became a butt for the most cruel invective, and the most frightful of sentences was pronounced on me. It was to be nothing less than this: I was to be dissected alive and conscious, so that my heartbeats might be studied whilst I was in that condition. Other observations, impracticable on a corpse, were also to be made on that organ. During this time they stripped me, and I was handled in the most lustful of fashions. Then the blows began to fall and I was so overcome that I dropped unconscious to the ground.

Then their rage began to lose something of its vehemence. Rodin brought me round again, and then one of them held me while the other operated. When a toe had been cut from each of my feet they made me sit down, then each pulled a tooth from deep within my mouth.

'That is not all,' said Rodin, as he put an iron in the fire. 'When she came here she had been *whipped*, but I shall send her away *marked*.'

And while his friend held me, the villain applied behind my shoulder the hot iron bearing the mark with which thieves are branded.

'Let her dare, now, to put in an appearance anywhere, the slut!' exclaimed Rodin furiously. 'Having branded her with this ignominious letter I shall sufficiently justify myself for having sent her away with so much secrecy and promptitude.'

Immediately afterwards the two men took hold of me. It was night, and they led me to the edge of the forest where, having warned me of the dangers I risked should I attempt recriminations against them, they cruelly abandoned me.

Many another would have cared little about such a threat. For when I proved that the punishment I had suffered was not by order of any tribunal, what had I to fear? But my weakness, my usual innocence, and the terrible memory of my misfortunes in Paris and at the Château de Bressac all conspired to fill me with misgivings and dismay so that I could think only of getting away from this ominous place as soon as my pains had quietened down a little. As they had carefully dressed the wounds they had inflicted on me, I felt a little better the next day. And having passed, beneath a tree, one of the most frightful nights in my life I set out to walk as soon as daylight appeared. My wounded feet prevented me from moving very quickly; but, anxious to leave the environs of a forest which I found so baleful and sinister, I covered four leagues during that first day and as much again in the two succeeding days. But, never attempting to ascertain my exact where-abouts, and never asking my way, I did little more than continue to circle around the outskirts of Paris. On the fourth day I found myself no further than Lieusaint; yet knowing that this road would lead me towards the southern provinces of France I resolved to follow it, hoping in some way to reach those distant parts. For I imagined that the peace and repose so cruelly refused me in my own part of the country might, perhaps, await me at the other end of the world.

What a fatal error! And what a large amount of trouble was still waiting to test me! My income was much smaller with Rodin than it had been while I was at the Château de Bressac, so it had not been necessary to put a portion of my earnings aside. Thus, luckily, I had them all on my person. They constituted about ten louis – a sum composed of what I had been able to save from my Bressac funds together with what I had been paid at the surgeon's. In the excess of my suffering I still found it possible to be happy that they had left me with this means of support; and I hoped that I would be able to make it last at least until such time as I could find work. The infamies to which I had been subjected did not seem to me to be noticeable. I felt that I would always be able to conceal them, and that their blemishes would not hinder me from earning my living. I was twenty-two, healthy and robust despite my small and slender stature, and my beauty of face, unfortunately, was only too much praised. As for those virtues which up to the moment had always resulted in my injury, they still brought me inward consolation and caused me to hope that providence would eventually bless me, if not with a reward, then at least with a suspension of the evils they had brought upon me.

Filled with hope and courage I continued on my way to Sens. There my imperfectly healed feet caused me to suffer unbearable pain, so I decided to rest for several days. But not daring to trust anyone with the origin of my sufferings, and remembering the names of the drugs I had seen Rodin use for similar wounds, I purchased them and looked after myself. A week of rest restored me completely. It might have been possible to find work at Sens, but urged on by the necessity to go as far as possible I didn't even look for any. I pursued my way with the idea of seeking my fortune in Dauphiné. I had often heard speak of this part of the country when I was a child and therefore imagined that my happiness might lie there. But we shall see how I fared.

In no circumstance of my life has religious sentiment ever abandoned me. Despising the vain sophisms of the brilliant, and looking upon them as manifestations of libertinism as opposed to the utterances of firm conviction, I rejected them with all the force of my conscience and my heart and found, with the aid of one or the other, all that was necessary for reply. I left Auxerre on the seventh of June, and I shall never forget that date. I had travelled about two leagues and the heat was beginning to fatigue me. Ascending a little hill not far from the road – a hill which was crowned with a grove of trees – I lay down beneath their shade to sleep for two or three hours, in this manner refreshing myself at less expense than at an inn – and in greater safety than by the edge of the highway. I climbed up and settled myself at the foot of an oak where, after a frugal lunch consisting of bread and water, I gave myself up to the sweetness of sleep and enjoyed more than two hours of tranquil slumber. When at length I opened my eyes I was delighted with the prospect of the landscape which stretched out below me. From the midst of a forest which stretched far away to the right I thought I beheld – perhaps three or four leagues distant – a small belfry rising modestly into the air.

'Sweet solitude,' I thought to myself, 'how I envy your dwelling-place . . . I suppose that must be the place of retreat of a group of nuns or saintly hermits, occupied only with their own duties and consecrated entirely to religion – people entirely withdrawn from this pernicious society where crime, in her ceaseless war against innocence, always seems to triumph . . . I feel sure that every virtue must dwell in that place.'

I was lost in these thoughts when a young shepherdess about my own age, who tended her sheep on this wooded slope, unexpectedly presented herself to my view. I asked her about the building and she explained that I was looking at a Benedictine monastery occupied by four anchorites who were unequalled in their devotion to religion, chastity, and sobriety.

'People go there once a year,' this girl informed me, 'in order to complete a holy pilgrimage to a miraculous Virgin, from whom pious folk obtain all they can wish.'

Moved by a desire immediately to go and implore succour at the feet of the Holy Mother of God, I asked this young girl if she would like to accompany me. She told me that this was impossible because her mother would be waiting for her at home but that I should not find the way difficult. She pointed it out to me, and told me that I should find the Superior the most respectable and holy of men. He would, seemingly, not only receive me with pleasure but would also offer me help should I be in a case of needing it.

'He is called the Reverend Father Raphael,' she continued; 'he is an Italian but has spent his life in France. He prefers to live in this solitude and has refused from the Pope – to whom he is related – the offer of several excellent benefices. He is a man of noble family, gentle, obliging, remarkably zealous and pious, and is about fifty years old. He is regarded by everyone in this part of the country as a saint.'

My interest was inflamed yet more by this recital. So much so that I could not resist the longing and the desire I felt to visit this holy church and by some pious acts repair therein those sins of which I had been guilty. When I reached the plain I could no longer see the belfry; I had only the forest to guide me and my sole route was a little trodden path which I was obliged to follow at random. When the sun had sunk below the horizon so that it no longer brightened the universe, I seemed to hear the distant sound of a bell. I stopped and listened, and then advanced in the direction of the noise. I began to hasten, and noticed that the path was becoming wider. Shortly I reached an opening and in front of me saw some hedges with, beyond them, the convent. No other dwellings stood near it – the closest were six leagues distant – and immense woods surrounded it on every side. Such was the convent of Sainte-Marie-des-Bois, and as it was situated in a hollow I had continually to descend in order to reach it – which was why it had been impossible for me to see the belfry from the plain. The hut of a gardening brother was built against the wall of the inner part of the building, and it was here that one requested entry. I asked this holy man if I might be permitted to speak to the Superior . . . He asked me what I might require of him . . . I replied that my religious duty – that a vow – had drawn me to this saintly retreat and that I would be well rewarded for all the pain it had cost me to come here if, for a moment, I could throw myself at the feet of the Virgin, and at those of the holy director in whose house this miraculous image dwelt.

Having asked me to rest, this brother speedily entered the convent. But, as it was already night and the fathers were at supper, it was some time before he returned. When he reappeared he was accompanied by another monk: 'This is father Clément, Mademoiselle,' he said to me, 'he is steward to our house, and has come to find out if what you require is important enough for him to disturb the Superior.'

Father Clément was a man of forty-five, enormously bulky and gigantic in build. He was surly and grim with a harsh, rough voice, and even at this first meeting it made me tremble much more than it reassured me . . . An involuntary shuddering immediately seized me; and, without my being able to do anything about it, the memory of all my past sufferings surged up in my memory.

'What do you want?' he asked me unfeelingly. 'Is this the sort of hour to come to a church? You look to me very much like an adventuress!'

'Holy man,' I said, prostrating myself before him, 'I have always believed that any time was a fit one to enter the house of God. I have travelled far to get here, fervour and devotion being my support, and I beg to confess, if it is possible. When my conscience shall be known to you it will be possible for you to judge whether or not I am worthy to prostrate myself at the feet of the miraculous image which is preserved within this holy house.'

'But this is scarcely the hour for confession,' said the monk, as he softened. 'Where will you pass the night? We have nowhere for you to stay, and it would be better for you to return in the morning.'

At this I explained how I had been hindered, and without replying further he went to give an account of me to the Superior. Several minutes later I heard the church door open and the Superior himself came towards the hut, inviting me to enter the main building with him. Father Raphael, of whom it seems best to give you a description immediately, was a man whose age I had been told, but to whom nobody would have ascribed even forty years. He was slender and reasonably tall with a sweet and intellectual face. He spoke French very well but with a slight Italian accent. In exteriors he presented polished manners and an obliging nature, but inwardly he was wild and sullen – as I shall have only too many occasions of convincing you.

'My child,' he said to me, in a gracious and gentle voice, 'although the hour is unreasonable and we are not in the habit of receiving so late I shall, nevertheless, hear your confession and afterwards we shall think of some means for enabling you to pass the night until the hour, tomorrow, when you may kneel before our holy image.'

Having said this, the monk lit several lamps around the confessional. He told me to place myself therein, and having sent away his companion and closed all the doors, he asked me to confide everything to him in the fullest assurance of his understanding. Perfectly at ease in front of such a considerate man, and disburdened of the terror which Father Clément had roused in me, I knelt submissively at his feet and opened myself entirely to him with all my usual candour and trust. I admitted each of my faults and related every misfortune, one after the other. Nothing was omitted – not even the shameful mark with which the execrable Rodin had stigmatised me.

Father Raphael listened with the greatest attention, even making me repeat certain details as he expressed his pity and concern . . . His principal questions were repeatedly directed toward the following subjects:

1 If it was really true that I was an orphan and came from Paris.
2 If I was quite sure that I had neither friends nor relatives, patrons, nor any other person to whom I might write.
3 Whether it was true that I had told only the shepherdess of my intention to visit the monastery and if I had arranged to meet her again on my return journey.
4 If it was true that I was really a virgin, and no older than twenty-two.
5 If I was absolutely certain that I had not been followed by anyone, and that nobody had seen me enter the monastery.

I was able completely to satisfy him on these points, and answered with all the innocence in the world.

'Very well, then,' said the monk, as he got up and took me by the hand; 'come along, my child. It is too late for you to kneel before the Virgin tonight. But tomorrow I shall arrange for you the sweet satisfaction of receiving communion at the feet of her image. In the meantime let us think about your bedroom, and what we are going to give you for supper.'

As he said this he led me towards the sacristy.

'What did you say?' I exclaimed, with a sensation of misgiving over which I had no control. 'Do you mean to say, Father, that you are taking me to the interior part of your house?'

'And where else, my charming pilgrim?' rejoined the monk as he opened a door off the cloister which led into the sacristy, thus bringing us right into the central portion of the house.

'Don't tell me you are afraid of spending the night with four monks! Ah! But you will see that we aren't the bigots we are supposed to be, for we know how to amuse ourselves with a pretty girl . . .'

These words startled me: 'Oh, merciful heaven,' I said to myself, 'am I once more to become the victim of my feeling for goodness, of my need to approach religion through its most respected channel? Will these desires once again be punished as though they are crimes?' Meanwhile we advanced through the darkness, but nothing revealed our exact locality in the building or offered any pathway of escape.

The monk, who made me walk in front of him, noticed something of my resistance: 'Get along with you, you two-faced bitch,' he exclaimed with passionate anger, immediately changing his coaxing tone to one of the most studied insolence. 'Do you think there's time to draw back? Ye gods, you will soon begin to realise that you'd have been happier in a den of thieves rather than falling into the midst of a group of four Recollets.'

Causes for terror began to multiply so rapidly before my eyes that I had little time to be alarmed by these words. Hardly had they been uttered than the most alarming sight met my eyes. The door in front of us opened, and I saw around a table three monks and three young girls, all in the most indecent state in the world. Two of these girls were completely naked, while the third was being undressed. As for the monks, they were more or less in the same state. . . .

'My friends,' said Raphael, as he entered: 'we were in need of an extra girl, and here she is. Allow me to present you with a true phenomenon. Here is a Lucrecia who actually bears on her shoulder the mark of girls of ill-fame. And there,' he continued, with a gesture as significant as it was indecent, 'there is the proof of an acknowledged virginity.'

Shrieks of laughter echoed from every corner of the room at this singular introduction; and Clément, whom I had met on my arrival and who was already somewhat drunk, immediately cried that such facts must instantly be verified. The necessity of describing these people to you obliges me to interrupt my narrative at this point. But I will keep you in suspense as to my situation for the shortest while possible.

Your acquaintance with Raphael and Clément is sufficient to allow me to pass on to the others. Antonin, the third of the Fathers in this monastery, was a little man of forty, spare and gaunt with a fiery temperament, the face of a satyr, and as hairy as a bear. He was insanely depraved – experienced the greatest delight in tormenting people – and his wickedness was unequalled. Father Jérôme, the senior member of the house, was an old libertine of sixty, as hard and brutal as Clément and even more of a drunkard. Surfeited with ordinary pleasures he was obliged, in order to recapture the glow of voluptuous sensation, to have recourse to pursuits as depraved as they were disgusting.

Florette was the youngest of the girls. She came from Dijon and was about fourteen, being the daughter of a prominent citizen of that town. She had been abducted by satellites of Raphael, who was rich and commanded considerable influence in his order, and who neglected nothing which might serve his passions. She was a brunette with very pretty eyes and a great deal of piquancy in her expression. Cornelie was about sixteen. She was blond, and most interesting in manner, with the loveliest of hair, the smoothest of complexions, and the most attractive figure possible. The daughter of a wine merchant, she came from Auxerre and had been seduced by Raphael himself, who had secretly entangled her in his snares. Omphale was a woman of thirty, very tall, with the most pronounced curves, a fine bosom, superb hair, a sweet and agreeable face, and the tenderest eyes it would be possible to see. She was the daughter of a prosperous wine-grower of Joigny, and had been on the eve of her marriage to a very wealthy man when Jérôme, with the most extraordinary enticements, coaxed her away from her family. At that time she had been only sixteen. Such was the society with whom I was destined to live. Such, also, was the sewer of impurity and filth to which I had come, expecting only to find that virtue and chastity which usually resides in holy retreats.

I was made to understand that since I was now a member of this terrifying circle, the best I could do would be to imitate the submission of my companions.

'It takes little imagination,' said Raphael, 'to realise that any attempt at resistance would be quite useless in this inaccessible retreat – a retreat to which you have been led by your unlucky star! You say you have suffered many misfortunes – which, according to your story, seems true. But if you examine the list of your misfortunes, you will see that the greatest piece of ill-luck a girl can suffer is still missing from it. Is it natural to remain virgin at your age? Isn't it a species of miracle which cannot be allowed to persist any longer? . . . Your companions here, like you, created a fuss when they found themselves obliged to serve us; and just as you are wisely going to do, they finished by submitting – when they saw that any other behaviour could bring them nothing but bad treatment.

'Finding yourself in the situation you are in, Sophie, how can you hope to defend yourself? Cast your thoughts over the way the world has abandoned you! On your own admission you have neither parents nor friends. See your situation as though you were in a desert, far from help, your whereabouts unknown to anyone on earth, and fallen into the hands of four libertines who assuredly have no desire to spare you . . . To whose assistance, then, will you have recourse? Will it be to that God whom you recently implored with so much zeal, and who profited by your fervour only to precipitate you the more surely into this trap.

'So you see, then, there is no power either human or divine which can snatch you from our hands. Nor is there anything in the realm of possibility – nor yet in the region of miracles – by means of which this virtue, of which you are so proud, can any longer be conserved. Nor is there anything which can prevent you from becoming, in every sense of the word and in every conceivable manner, the prey of the obscene excesses into which all four of us are going to plunge with you. Remove your clothes, then, Sophie, and may the most utter resignation earn you some kindness on our part. I warn you, however, that if you do not submit this will instantly be replaced by the most unfeeling and ignominious treatment – which will only provoke us further without in any way removing you from our intemperance and brutality.'

I knew only too well that this terrible discourse left me without resource; but would I not have been guilty had I not employed the means which my heart whispered, and which nature still left me? I threw myself at Raphael's feet, summoning all the forces of my soul as I begged him not to abuse my situation. My bitter tears flowed over his knees, and I dared to face him with the most moving arguments I could find. I did not yet know that tears become a further stimulant to the devotees of crime and debauchery. I was completely blind to the fact that my attempts to soften these monsters inflamed them only the more . . .

Then Raphael, furious, stood up: 'Take this vagabond, Antonin,' he exclaimed, frowning, '– take her and strip her this very instant! Teach her that compassion has no existence among men such as we!'

Antonin seized me with a lean but vigorous arm, and mingling his words and actions with frightful oaths, in two minutes he had torn off my clothes and presented me naked before the eyes of the assembly.

'There we have a beautiful creature!' said Jérôme. 'May this monastery fall and crush me if, in thirty years, I have seen a prettier!'

'Just a moment,' exclaimed the Superior; 'let us employ a little order in our proceedings. You are all aware, my friends, of our rules concerning reception. Let her be submitted to all of them, without exception; and during this time let the other three women remain beside us so as to anticipate our needs – or to excite them.'

A circle was formed and I was placed in the centre. There for more than two hours I was examined, considered and felt by these four libertines, exciting from each in turn either eulogy or criticism.

'You will allow me, Madame,' said our beautiful prisoner, blushing exceedingly, 'to conceal from you some of the obscene details observed at this first ceremony. Your imagination can supply you with all that debauchery could dictate in such circumstances to this group of lecherous men. You can picture them passing successively from my companions to myself, comparing, opposing, reconciling, and discussing various points. Even then you will have but the faintest idea of the kind of thing that happened during these first orgies – which were very mild in comparison with all the horrors of which I was shortly to become the victim.'

'Come,' said Raphael, whose prodigiously inflamed desires seemed to have reached the point at which it was no longer possible to restrain them, 'it is time to immolate the victim. Let each of us prepare to submit her to his favourite pleasure.'

And this coarsest of men, having placed me on a sofa in the attitude most propitious to his execrable pleasures, had me held down by Antonin and Clément . . . Raphael, the depraved Italian monk, satisfied himself outrageously – without my ceasing to be a virgin. Oh, most awful of aberrations! It seemed that each of these crapulous men felt his glory to lie in leaving nature outside his choice when indulging his infamous pleasures . . .

Clément was the next to approach me. Already inflamed by his Superior's behaviour, he was even more excited by the things he had done while observing this. He declared that he would represent no more danger for me than his confrère had done, and that the place where his homage was to be uttered would leave me without peril to my virtue. He made me get down on my knees, and fastening himself to me while in this position exercised his perfidious passions on me in a place which prevented me, during the sacrifice, from expressing any complaint as to its irregularity.

Jérôme followed. His temple was the same as that of Raphael, but he did not approach the sanctuary. Content to remain in the courtyard, and moved by primitive episodes the obscenity of which it is impossible to describe, he was unable to accomplish his desires except by the barbarous means of which I almost became a victim in the house of Dubourg and of which I was completely so in the hands of de Bressac.

'What favourable preparations,' exclaimed Antonin, as he seized hold of me. 'Come along, my little chicken, come along and let me avenge you for the irregularity of my confrères. Let me gather, at last, the delightful fruits abandoned to me by their intemperance!'

But the details! . . . Great God! . . . I cannot possibly describe them to you. One might have said that this flagitious villain – who was the most lecherous of the four, even though he appeared the least removed from nature's ways – only consented to approach me with a little less inconformity providing he could compensate himself for this lesser depravity by outraging me more thoroughly, and for a longer period . . . Alas, if at times I had previously allowed my imagination to wander over the pleasures of sex, I believed them chaste as the God who inspires them, given by nature as a consolation to human beings and born of love and tenderness. I had been far from believing that man, following the example of certain ferocious beasts, was able to enjoy himself only by making his partners shriek with pain. My experience was so violent that the sufferings natural to the breaking of my virginity were the least I had to support in this dangerous attack. But it was at the moment of his crisis, which Antonin terminated with such furious cries, with such murderous excursions over every part of my body, and bitings so like the bloody caresses of a tiger, that I felt for a moment I was the prey of some savage animal who could only be appeased by devouring me. Once these horrors had ceased I fell back on the altar of my immolation, motionless and almost unconscious.

Raphael ordered the women to look after me and give me something to eat. But in that cruel moment a raging torrent of grief and desolation was sweeping through my heart. I had finally lost the treasure of my virginity – for which I would have sacrificed my life a hundred times. Nor could I accept the fact that I had been dishonoured by those from whom I had expected the greatest assistance and moral support. My tears flowed abundantly, my cries echoed round the room. I rolled on the floor, tore my hair, and begged my butchers to put me to death. But although these profligate wretches had become completely hardened to such scenes and were far more interested in tasting of new pleasures with my companions than in calming my pain or comforting me, they were nevertheless sufficiently troubled by my cries to send me off to rest in a place where my lamentations could not be heard . . . Omphale was ready to take me there when the perfidious Raphael, still looking at me with lubricity despite the cruel state I was in, said that he did not want me sent away before I had once more become his victim . . . Hardly had he conceived this project than it was executed . . . His desires, however, needed an additional degree of stimulation, and it was not until he had employed the cruel methods of Jérôme that he found the necessary strength for the accomplishment of this new crime . . . What excesses of debauchery! Great God! – was it possible that these lubricious beasts could be so ferocious as to choose the moment of crisis of a moral pain so violent as mine to make me suffer an equally barbarous physical one?

'By all that's merry,' exclaimed Antonin as he also took me again, 'it's good to follow the example of one's superior; and nothing is so appetising as a second offence. They tell me that pain inclines one to pleasure. I'm sure this beautiful child is going to make me the happiest of men!'

And despite my repugnance, despite all my cries and pleas, I became for a second time the wretched target of this contemptible satyr . . . At length they allowed me to go.

'If I had not already indulged before this lovely princess arrived,' said Clément, 'she would not be leaving this room before I had served my passions a second time – but she will lose nothing by waiting.'

'I promise her the same,' said Jérôme, making me feel the strength of his arm as I passed near him. 'But, so far as tonight is concerned, let us all go to bed.'

Raphael being of the same opinion, the orgies were interrupted. He kept Florette with him, and she doubtless stayed the night; but the remainder of the party returned to their rooms. I was looked after by Omphale. This sultana, older than the others, appeared to be in charge of the sisters. She took me to our apartment. It was situated in a kind of square tower in each corner of which was a bed. It was usual for one of the monks to follow the girls when they retired and to lock the door with two or three bolts. Clément was the brother who had been charged with this duty. Once inside, it was certainly impossible to get out, as there was no other exit from this room – apart from a small toilet, the window of which was as narrow and barred as that of the place in which we slept. There was little furniture – a chair and table stood by each bed, which was surrounded by printed curtains of the poorest quality. In addition there were some wooden chests in a cupboard, a few pierced chairs, some bidets, and a communal dressing-table. But it was not until the next day that I noticed all this. Too overcome to see anything during these first moments I could think of nothing but my pain.

'Oh, God, who decrees all,' I said to myself, 'is it therefore written that no virtuous act shall be suggested by my heart but it shall immediately be followed by misfortune? What evil have I done, oh most merciful Father, in wishing to perform in this house naught but pious duties? Have I offended heaven by this devotion? Is the treatment I have received the reward I should have expected? Oh incomprehensible decrees of providence, deign for an instant to guide my understanding if you wish to prevent me from revolting against your laws!' Bitter tears followed these reflections; and I was still immersed in them when Dom Clément arrived, as heated with wine as he was with lust and followed by a girl of twenty-six named Armande, who was to join in the proposed affair . . . The filthy monk did everything, even to gnawing the tongue and lips of the poor girl, while I was forced to whip him slightly the while. Then he drove us through such orgies of pain that we could hardly sustain them.

'Let us lie down,' he finally said to me; 'perhaps you have suffered too much, my dear, even though not enough for me . . . Ah! dear girl, you have no idea how far this depravity drags us – the intoxication into which it throws us, the violent commotions which result in our nervous fluid from the irritation produced by the pain of the object who serves our passions. How one is tickled by one's evils! The desire of increasing our pleasures! – that's the stumbling block of this fantasy, and I know it! Yet should such a thing be feared by a man who mocks everything? . . .

I attempted to reproach him with the degeneracy manifested in his tastes; but the manner in which this libertine justified them seems to me to deserve some space in the history of what befell me.

'The most ridiculous thing in the world, my dear, is doubtless the wish to dispute a man's tastes – to attempt to thwart them, blame them, punish them – should they not be in conformity, either with the accepted laws of the country we happen to inhabit, or with social conventions. What men will never understand is that there is no kind of taste or preference, however odd, however criminal one might suppose it to be, but depends on the kind of individual organisation we have received from nature. This being so, what right, I ask, has one man to dare to require of another man either that he reform his tastes or attempt to model them after that of the social order? Moreover, what right have the laws, which are merely formulated for man's happiness, what right have these laws to punish the man who is not able to correct himself strictly according to their codes? – or who would succeed in doing so only at the expense of that happiness which the laws should conserve for him? . . .

'Let us go into a few particulars . . . You are astonished at the poignant feelings and sensations felt by some of our fellows for things usually known as disgusting or degrading, and you are likewise surprised because our voluptuous faculties are profoundly moved by actions which, according to your own judgement, bear only the stamp and emblem of ferocity. Let us analyse these tastes . . .

'It is strange, you pretend, that dirty and intemperate things can produce in our senses that irritation essential for the completion of such delirium; but far from being astonished at this you should understand, my dear, that objects have no value in our eyes except that which our imagination sets on them; it is, therefore, quite possible, according to this constant truth, that not only the oddest things but also the most vile and most shocking may affect us very sensibly . . .

'Such is man's imagination that the same object presents itself to different men under as many shapes as it has different modes. And according to the effect, whatever it may be, resulting from our interpretation of the object, the imagination becomes determined to love it – or to hate it. According to this reasoning it is not at all surprising that what greatly delights some may equally displease others; and vice versa, that the most extraordinary things may find sectarians . . . As is well known, the ugly man is able to find mirrors wherein he looks handsome.

'Now, if we grant that the enjoyment of the senses is always dependent on the imagination, we should no longer be astonished at the numerous variations which imagination will suggest in these enjoyments – at the host of tastes and different passions which the wanderings of imagination will produce. Three quarters of the population of the world may find the smell of a rose delicious without it serving as any proof either to condemn the quarter who might find such a perfume actually unpleasant, or to show that this smell is truly agreeable.

'If there exist, therefore, in the world, beings whose tastes are in opposition to the admitted prejudices, not only must we refuse to be astonished at them, not only must we avoid finding fault with them and refrain from punishing them – but we must render them some service, try to content them, destroy the curbs and restrictions which vex them, and afford them – if you will be just – every means of satisfying themselves without risk. For they are no more responsible for their strange tastes than you are for being witty or stupid, well-formed or hump-backed. The organs which make us susceptible to such-and-such a fantasy are formed in our mother's womb; the first sights presented to our infantile eyes, the first discourses we ever hear, all these ultimately combine to determine our actions and reactions – our tastes are formed thus, and nothing in the world can henceforth destroy them.

'It is in vain that education sets to work: it never really alters anything, and he who is born a villain becomes one however sound the education he receives. And just as surely, the man whose organs function towards goodness hastens equally as quickly in the pathway of virtue, even though he lack both a teacher and a model. Both have acted according to their physical organisation, according to the impressions they have received from nature, and the one is not more deserving of punishment than the other of reward.

'What strikes me as most surprising is that when it is simply a question of trivial things we are never astonished at the difference in tastes between one individual and another; but the moment these differences involve what is known as lust – behold, everything is in an uproar! Yet what an injustice! As I said previously, the man with strange tastes is a sick man, and it is just as silly and cruel to punish such a man, whatever his faults and errors, as it is to punish, mock, or ridicule a man who is crippled. Wouldn't he be normal if he had it in him! – who wouldn't? But when anatomy and physiology are really perfected, it will be clearly demonstrated that all morality is essentially physical. What will become then of your laws, ethics, religion, gibbets, paradise, God, and hell – when it is proved that a particular organisation of the nerves, a peculiar reaction in the body, a certain degree of acridity in the blood, makes a man what he is, for better or for worse? You say our cruelty amazes you? Why? What is the object of the man who seeks sensual pleasure? Is it not to allow his senses all the stimulus they are capable of experiencing? And this in order that he may arrive at his final paroxysms more successfully and speedy? The supreme pleasure – that is the thing! And it is more or less enjoyable according to the type of activity chosen. For his pleasure to be increased it is not at all necessary that it be shared by the woman. In fact is it not evident that every pleasure the woman shares with us, she takes away from us? And why is it necessary that she should experience pleasure at the same time as ourselves? It is surely more pleasing that she should not do so, so that we may enjoy ourselves unhampered, with nothing to hinder us from concentrating solely on our own pleasures. This flatters our pride the more. Not delicate, I admit; yet why should delicacy enter into these matters? Consideration of it represents an obnoxious attitude in relation to pleasure. Delicacy, for instance, may go hand in hand with love and romance; but love and sexual pleasure are not necessarily the same thing – they frequently, in fact, represent two entirely different attitudes. People daily love each other without enjoying, and enjoy each other without loving. And whatever is related to delicacy is to the advantage of the woman at the expense of that of the man . . . Thus, if selfishness is the primal law of nature, how equally true it is that it must occupy this same position in the pleasures of the passions!

'Moreover, if you consider what I have just said, you will realise that isolated ecstasies also possess charms – may even present more of them than any other pleasures. If it were not so, how would so many old men, so many ugly people and defective folk, find pleasure? They know quite well that they are not loved; they are absolutely certain that it is impossible for any partner to share their feelings – yet do they experience any the less voluptuous sensation on that account? Do they merely desire an illusion? . . . It is, therefore, not at all necessary to bestow pleasure in order to receive it. Thus the happy or the unhappy situation of the victims of our debauchery becomes a matter of unconcern for us and does not affect the satisfaction of our senses one jot! . . . Is any reasonable man truly anxious to have his pleasure shared by a loose woman? And are there not millions of men who find great delight with these creatures? If this, then, is true, there must be countless individuals persuaded of the law I establish, who practise it without suspecting it – and who, at the same time, foolishly blame others who would justify their actions by sound principles.

'If nature was offended by various tastes she would avoid planting them in our breasts. It is impossible that we should receive from her any sentiment which might outrage her; and resting in this absolute certainty, we should give rein to our passions, whatsoever they be, for we may be sure that any drawbacks they may entail are mere designs of nature whose unwilling pawns we are . . . '

When Clément had ceased talking I asked him if they kept the poor girls for ever in the convent, miserable and unhappy – 'Surely you send them away when you have tired of them?' I added.

'Yes, yes . . . ' he replied. 'When we have decided to grant you a retreat you shall have it most certainly . . . '

I learned later what this meant.

As dawn began to break, Omphale approached my bed.

'My dear friend,' she said, 'I come to exhort you to take courage. During my first days here I wept just as you have done. But habit has accustomed me to this life, and it will be likewise with you. The first moments are terrible, I know . . . Not only because we are perpetually obliged to gratify the unbounded passions of these debauches – which, in itself, is torture enough – but also because of the loss of our freedom and the brutal way in which we are treated in this infamous house . . . Nevertheless, unhappy as we are, we derive some comfort from seeing others suffering in the same manner as ourselves.'

My pain was still unbearable, yet I managed to conquer it for a moment that I might beg my companion to acquaint me with whatever further evils I might expect.

'Listen,' said Omphale, as she seated herself near my bed, 'I am going to speak to you in all confidence – but remember, you must never abuse it . . . The cruellest of our sufferings, dear friend, is the uncertainty of our fate – for it is quite impossible to say what becomes of us when we leave this place. We have as much proof as our isolation permits us to gather that none of the girls discharged by the monks has ever reappeared in the outside world. In fact they have themselves hinted at it, for they don't hide from us the knowledge that this retreat is also our tomb. Every year two or three girls leave us. And what becomes of them? Are they done away with? To this question the monks sometimes answer yes; at others they reply with an emphatic no! But of those who have left this place none, whatever promises they may have made that they would lodge complaints about this monastery in the right quarters and work for our liberation – none, I repeat, has ever kept her word. Are the brothers able satisfactorily to account for these complaints, or do they completely prevent these girls from being able to make them? When we ask newcomers for news of former girls they only reply that they know nothing about them.

'What becomes of these unfortunate creatures? That is what torments us, Sophie – and it is this terrible uncertainty that tortures our unhappy days. It is fourteen years since I was first brought to this place, and in that period I have seen more than fifty girls disappear from here . . . Where are they? How is it that, of all those who have sworn to help us, not one has been able to keep her word? The number of girls kept here is always fixed at four – at least so far as this room is concerned. But we are all more than persuaded that there is another tower corresponding to this one where they keep an equal number of prisoners. Many things in the conduct of these wretches – as well as bits of their conversation – have convinced us of this. But if we do have such comrades here we have never seen them. One of the strongest proofs we have supporting this belief is that we never serve them two days running. Yesterday we were employed; today we shall take it easy. But it seems impossible that these debauchees could abstain for a day! Moreover, they have no specific rule regarding our dismissal from service – it has nothing to do with age, diminishing beauty, boredom, or disgust – nothing but their caprice is the determining factor in these decisions to grant us a sinister leave of absence – regarding which we have no means of knowing whether we shall fare well or ill.

'We had here a woman of seventy who left only last summer. She had been here sixty years, and during the time of her residence I have seen the discharge of more than twelve girls under sixteen. Some have vanished three days after their arrival, others at the end of a month, and yet others only after many years. There is no rule about it whatever other than what is dictated by their whim. And our behaviour is equally unimportant. I have seen girls who could more than cope with the desires of these men, and yet they were dismissed after only six weeks. On the other hand there have been sulky and capricious creatures whom they have kept for many years. It is thus useless to attempt to formulate any kind of law regarding behaviour for the benefit of new arrivals. Their unpredictability overthrows every law. Nothing is certain with them.

'As for the monks themselves, they rarely change. It is fifteen years since Raphael came here; Clément has been with us sixteen, Jérôme thirty, and Antonin ten. He is the only one I have actually seen arriving, and he came to replace a sixty-year-old monk who died during an excess of debauchery. Raphael, a Florentine by birth, is a near relative of the Pope, with whom he stands in great favour. It is only since his arrival that the miraculous Virgin has assured the reputation of the monastery by hindering those of a scandalous turn of mind from noticing too much of what goes on here. But otherwise everything here was just as it is when he first joined us. It has been like this for almost eighty years, so I'm told; and every new Superior has automatically preserved an arrangement so advantageous for his pleasure. Raphael, who is reputed to be one of the most licentious monks of the present century, sought an appointment here only because he knew what went on, and it is his intention to preserve for as long as ever possible those secret privileges of which you are aware. We are situated in the diocese of Auxerre; but, whether or not the Bishop has been informed of the circumstances, we have never seen him make an appearance in this establishment. In fact few people frequent it – except during the time of the religious feast towards the end of August. Otherwise scarcely ten people visit the church in a year. When, however, strangers do present themselves the Superior is careful to receive them properly – and to impose on them with endless manifestations of austerity and religious sentiment. And so they go away pleased, praising the house. Thus the impunity of these vile criminals is bolstered by the good faith of the people and the credulity of the devout.

'As for the rest, nothing is so severe as the rules governing our behaviour – and nothing so dangerous as infringing them in any manner. In fact it is essential that I go into some details concerning this matter,' continued my instructress, 'for it is not accepted here as an excuse if you say: *Do not punish me for the infraction of this law, because I did not know about it.* The position is such that, if you don't learn about these rules from your companions, you must guess them yourself. You are given no warning as to anything and yet you are punished for everything. And the only form of correction permitted is the whip. It is thus easy enough for any of our faults to become an occasion for the favourite pleasure of these profligates. You suffered yesterday without breaking any of the laws – soon you will experience the same punishment for having erred. All four of them are infected by this barbarous mania, and each takes his turn at wielding the lash. Every day one of them is elected Regent of the Day, and receives a report from the room-mistress. He is also charged with ordering interior affairs and with the organisation of all that happens at those suppers to which we are bidden as compulsory guests. It is he who taxes us with our faults and he who punishes them.

'But let us consider our rules and customs in some detail: We are always obliged to be up and dressed by nine o'clock in the morning. At ten bread and water is brought to us for our breakfast. At two we are served with dinner, which consists of quite a good soup, a little stewed meat, some vegetables, and generally some fruit, together with a bottle of wine for all four of us. Regularly each day, come winter, come summer, the Regent visits us at five in the evening. That is when he receives his information from the room-mistress, and she is required to make a full report regarding the conduct of the girls in her room. She must give information concerning any signs of revolt, as to whether everyone rose when they should, whether all rules as to dress and cleanliness have been observed, if everyone has eaten as they should and whether any attempts at escape have been considered. Furthermore, she is herself punished should she fail to give a precise account of these things.

'After this the Regent examines various things. Once his business is completed it is rare that he should leave before he has amused himself with one of us – and often with all four. After he has left, should it not be our day for attending at supper, we are free to talk, read, and relax together and to go to bed when we wish. If we are to sup with the monks that evening a bell rings to warn us to prepare ourselves. The Regent himself comes to seek us and we descend into that room where you first saw us naked. Once there, the first thing they do is to read the record of our faults committed since our previous visit. First, those committed at the preceding supper – which comprise: negligence, frigidity towards the monks, inattentiveness, and uncleanliness. To these is added the list of faults committed in our room during the two-day interval between orgies. One after the other the delinquents place themselves in the centre of the room, and the Regent of the day names their faults and punishment. They are then stripped naked by the room-mistress – or by her immediate inferior should she herself be guilty of offence. Then the Regent administers the prescribed chastisement, and so energetically that it is difficult to forget it. But the craftiness of these rogues is so considerable that there is scarcely a meeting but several such floggings take place.

'This business completed, the orgies commence. To give you an idea of their range would be impossible. The bizarre caprices of the brothers are without precedent, and the essential thing, while never refusing them anything, is to anticipate everything . . . Yet, advisable as this course is, one can never be sure of approval. About halfway through the orgies they have their meal. We are allowed to partake of this, and it is always much more sumptuous and delicate than our own fare. The bacchanal really commences when the monks are half drunk. At midnight the party breaks up and each monk has the right to keep one of us with him throughout the hours of darkness. This favourite sleeps with whoever has chosen her, returning to her companions next morning. The remainder return to their room, finding it clean and the beds and wardrobes in perfect order. Sometimes, before the hour of breakfast, one of the brothers may send and request a girl to visit him in his cell. The one who is charged with our welfare comes to seek us and conducts us to the monk who has asked for us – who then brings us back himself, or returns us in the care of this same brother once he has no further need for us.

'This cerberus who cleans our room and sometimes conducts us is an old monk whom you will soon see. He is seventy, has only one eye, and is lame and mute. There are three others who assist him in his duties. One prepares and cooks the food; another looks after the Fathers' cells, sweeps, and also helps in the kitchen; and, finally, there is the porter you saw when you arrived. We never see any of these men excepting the one who serves us, and the slightest word to him would constitute the gravest of offences. Sometimes the Superior visits us . . . Finally there are certain customary ceremonies which experience will teach you, but the non-observance of which is a crime. And each day our masters' appetite for the pleasures of punishment stimulates them to multiply the number of possible offences. Raphael rarely visits us unless he has some project in view, and these – as you have already had occasion to realise – are either cruel or irregular. For the rest, we are always carefully confined within these walls, never being allowed outside even to take the air. For, although there is a large enough garden, it is not fitted with bars, and our captors are too afraid we might escape by that route. Such, of course, would be most dangerous for them; since information received either by the temporal or spiritual authorities disclosing all the crimes committed here would soon result in everything being set to order. As to religion, we never fulfil any duties in that direction and it is as much forbidden us to think of it as to speak of it. This, I feel, is one of the griefs inflicted on us most deserving of punishment.

'And that, my dear companion, is all I can tell you,' said our room-mistress. 'Experience,' she added, 'will teach you the rest. Be courageous, if you can; but give up every thought of the outside world. There is no instance of any girl dismissed from here ever having seen it again.'

Disturbed extremely by this last remark, I asked Omphale what she really thought about the fate of the discharged girls.

'What can I say about that?' she remarked. 'Whilst hope may bid us believe otherwise, everything seems to prove to me that only a grave can be our gateway to escape . . .

'We are informed on the morning of the day that a discharge has been arranged,' continued Omphale. 'The Regent for that day visits us before breakfast and says something like this: *Omphale, pack your bag, for you are discharged from the monastery. I shall come back for you this evening.* Then he leaves us. The girl who has received her discharge embraces her companions and promises them a thousand thousand times that she will help them, complain in the right quarters, and make a considerable noise about all that goes on. The hour strikes, the monk comes, the girl leaves, and is never heard of again. Nevertheless, if it happens to be one of the days for supper, the party takes place as usual. The only difference we have noticed during such orgies is that the monks indulge much less in their pleasures, drink far more, send us away much earlier, and never go to bed with any of us.'

'My dear friend,' I said to the room-mistress as I thanked her for this information, 'surely these girls must have been children who lacked the strength of character to keep their word? But let us make a mutual promise! For my own part I swear to you in advance, and by all that I hold most sacred, I shall either die or I shall destroy these infamies. Will you promise me as much yourself?'

'Certainly,' said Omphale; 'but you may rest assured that these promises are absolutely useless. For girls older than you, girls perhaps even more infuriated than you are – if such is possible – and these belonging to the influential families of the district – being armed, therefore, with more efficient weapons than yourself – girls, in a word, who would have given their very life's blood for me, have all failed in keeping these same vows. Let me, therefore, with my cruel experience, regard the present one as equally vain and no more to be relied on.'

After this we chatted for a while about the characters of the monks and those of our companions.

'There are no more dangerous men in Europe,' Omphale continued, 'than Raphael and Antonin. Duplicity, blackness of heart, wickedness, torture, cruelty, and irreligion are their natural qualities, and joy never lightens their eyes save when they give themselves unreservedly to their vices.

'Clément, who appears more brusque, is really the best of them and is only to be feared when he is drunk – but at such times one must be very careful to keep out of his way, for then there is considerable risk for anyone who happens to meet him. As for Jérôme, he is naturally brutal. Slaps, kicks and punches are the certain income of those who are with him, but once his passions have been satisfied he becomes gentle as a lamb. Such is the essential difference between him and the first two, who can only reanimate their desires by way of treachery and atrocity.

'So far as the girls are concerned,' she continued, 'there is little to be said. Florette is not a very intelligent child, and one can do with her just as one wishes. Cornélie is much more spiritual and sensitive, and nothing can console her for the fate which has befallen her.'

After receiving this information, I asked my companion if it was really quite impossible to discover whether or not there was another tower containing other unfortunates such as ourselves.

'If they exist – and I am almost certain of it,' said Omphale, ' it could only be ascertained through some indiscretion of the monks or from the mute brother who serves us and doubtless looks after them as well. But such an attempt would be extremely dangerous. Besides, what point would be served by finding out whether or not we are alone here, for whatever may be the case we should not be able to help ourselves. If you nevertheless insist on demanding whether I have any proof that this likelihood is more than probable, I can tell you that many of the careless remarks of the brothers are more than sufficient to convince us. Besides, one morning after I had been sleeping with Raphael, as I crossed his threshold and he followed so as to lead me back to our room, without his noticing anything I saw the mute entering Antonin's cell accompanied by a very beautiful girl of seventeen or eighteen – who certainly did not belong to our group. The monk, realising that he had been seen, quickly pushed her into the cell – but not before I had realised what was happening. He did not register any complaint and the matter rested there. So it is certain that there are other women here, and that as we sup with the monks only on alternate days, they must sup with them in the intervals – probably in similar numbers.'

Scarcely had Omphale finished speaking than Florette returned from Raphael's cell where she had spent the night. And, as it was absolutely forbidden for the girls to tell each other what happened to them on such occasions, seeing us awake she simply wished us good-morning and threw herself, exhausted, on her bed – where she remained until nine, the general hour of rising. It was then that the tender Cornélie came to me, weeping as she looked at me . . . and she said: 'Oh, my dear young friend, what unfortunate creatures we are!'

Breakfast was brought in. My companions forced me to eat a little, and I complied so as to please. The remainder of the day passed quietly enough; but at five, as Omphale had explained, the Regent entered.

It was Antonin and he laughingly enquired how I felt after my adventure. When, however, I replied only by lowering my eyes – which were still flooded with tears – he sneered, and said: 'She'll get used to it, she'll get used to it. There isn't a single house in France where they train girls better than we do.'

He continued on his round and took the list of faults handed him by the room-mistress – who was too kind-hearted to overburden it with details, frequently saying that she had nothing to report. Before leaving he approached me . . . I trembled, believing myself about to become, once more, the victim of this monster. A silly reaction; for since this was likely to happen at any moment, what did it matter whether it was now or the next day? I nevertheless escaped with only a few brutal caresses. But he threw himself upon Cornélie, ordering every one of us – while he performed – to assist him in his passions. The lecherous scoundrel gorged himself with voluptuous sensations of every type, denying himself nothing, and brought his encounter with this unfortunate girl to precisely the same kind of termination as he had indulged with me on the previous night. That is to say with the most deliberate acts of brutality and depravity.

This species of group activity took place very frequently. It was nearly always customary, when a monk was enjoying himself with one of the sisters, for the other three to surround him, exciting his senses in every part so that voluptuous ecstasy might diffuse itself throughout his entire being. I hint here at these impure details with the intention of not returning to them again, for I have no wish to dwell further on the indecency of these scenes. To paint one would be to paint all; and so far as my long residence in this house is concerned, I intend only to describe the essential events without horrifying you with further details. As the day I am speaking of did not happen to be our day for supper we were all peaceful enough. My companions did their best to comfort me, but nothing could soften the grief felt by one so sensitive as myself. They tried in vain, for the more they spoke of the evil which had befallen me the more did I feel the sharpness of its pain.

Next morning at nine the Superior came to see me, although it was not actually his day. He asked Omphale if I had begun to settle down and, without really listening to her reply, opened one of the chests in our cupboard, bringing out a number of female garments.

'As you brought nothing with you,' he said, 'we must think about clothing you – even if it is more for our own pleasure than for your comfort . . . And no gratitude, please! Personally I am not at all in favour of this useless apparel, and it wouldn't trouble me a bit if we allowed the girls who serve us to remain as naked as animals. But our Fathers are men of the world, men who wish for the luxury and elegance of raiment. And so they must be satisfied.'

And he threw on the bed several dressing-gowns, half a dozen chemises, a few caps, some stockings, and some slippers. He told me to try them on and assisted me in my dressing so as to touch me as indecently as the situation permitted. Three taffeta gowns and one of Indian linen were found to fit me. He allowed me to keep them, and said that I could alter the remainder, remembering that they were all the property of the house and were to be returned should I leave. These details having procured him a few glimpses, which heated him, he ordered me to place myself in the position which I knew he preferred . . . I would have begged his mercy, but seeing the wrath of passion already in his eyes I realised that it would be more expedient to obey. So I took up my posture . . . The libertine, surrounded by the other three girls, satisfied himself as was his wont – at the expense of morals, of religion, and of nature. He was excited by me, and entertained me well at supper. I was, moreover, destined to spend the night with him. My companions retired, and I accompanied him to his apartment.

I will no longer speak to you, Madame, either of the revulsion I experienced, or the pain. You will doubtless be able to imagine how extreme they were; but the monotony of such descriptions, if repeated, would perhaps prejudice you against such further revelations as I must make. Raphael's cell was charming and furnished by a voluptuary who also had taste. It lacked nothing which might render his solitude agreeable, or his pleasures delightful. Once the door had been shut he stripped himself naked, ordering me to do likewise. Then for a long time I was obliged to excite his pleasure by the same method he later actively employed on me. I can say here that during the course of that evening I received so complete a tuition in lecherous exercise that my knowledge became equal to that of the most expert female practitioners of these impurities. Becoming a mistress in one art, however, it was essential that I should soon revert to the position of scholar – so as to learn another. And so the night progressed. . . . Raphael never for a moment asked indulgence of me, but I was soon in such a state that I was obliged, hot tears pouring from my eyes, to beg it of him. Yet he mocked at my pleas and took the most barbarous precautions against my attempts at movement. Then, when he saw himself master of the situation, he treated me – throughout two entire hours – with the most unexampled severity. Nor did he confine himself to those parts normally destined for such attack, but roamed indiscriminately over the most contrary places, the most delicate globes. Nothing escaped the fury of this butcher whose voluptuous titilations derived their intensity from his gloating observation of my pain.

'Let us go to bed,' he said, as he ceased his efforts. 'Perhaps this has been too much for you – although it certainly hasn't been enough for me! One never becomes exhausted by this divine exercise. All that I have done is but a semblance of what I should like to do!'

And so we went to bed. There, wanton and depraved as ever, Raphael made me throughout the night the slave of his criminal pleasures. During a moment of calm I seized the opportunity to beg his information as to whether I might hope, one day, to be released from this house.

'Most assuredly,' answered Raphael; 'you only came here so as to be able to leave us. When all four of us agree to grant your discharge you shall certainly have it.'

'But,' I said, hoping to elicit something more from him, 'aren't you afraid that girls younger than myself – and less discreet than I swear I shall be throughout my life – aren't you afraid one of them may reveal just what goes on here?'

'That is impossible,' exclaimed the Superior.

'Impossible?'

'Absolutely impossible, my girl!'

'Could you possibly explain this to me?'

'No! That is our secret. But I can certainly tell you that, discreet or not, it will be quite impossible for you ever to reveal any of our activities once you have left us.'

Having said this he brutally ordered me to change the subject, and I daren't say anything more. At seven in the morning I was led back to my room by the Brother who usually performed that office; and fitting together what I had learned from Raphael with what Omphale had told me, I was left with the dreadful certainty that the most violent means were employed against those girls who left the house. . . . If they never spoke to anyone it was for the simple reason that, shut up in their coffins, they weren't able to. I shuddered for a long time as I ruminated on this terrible idea, but finally managed to dispel it by combating it with hope. Like my companions, I was, in fact, benumbed.

Within a week I had made my circuit. During that period I became acquainted with all the deviations, all the diverse infamies which each of these monks indulged in turn – and that with the most terrifying rapidity . . . In every one of them the flame of lust was illumined only by an excess of ferocity. And this vice of corrupted hearts activated in them every other form of viciousness – for it was only by exercising such that they were able to crown their pleasures.

Antonin was the man who made me suffer most. It is impossible for anyone to imagine just how far this wicked wretch indulged his cruelty during the delirium of his aberrations. He was always stimulated by these mysterious tastes, which seemed to be the only ones conducive to his enjoyment. But they kept the flame burning brightly within him when he gave himself up to them, and they alone served to perfect it at its zenith. I was, nevertheless, astonished that his tastes were not instrumental – despite their rigour – in rendering some of his victims pregnant. So I asked our room-mistress how he managed to avoid such complications.

'By immediately, and personally, destroying the fruit resulting from his ardour,' said Omphale. 'As soon as he notices such a condition he makes us drink, for three days in succession, six large glasses of a special kind of tisane. And after four days no trace of his intemperance is left. It recently happened to Cornélie, and has happened to me three times. But it does not injure one's health. On the contrary we usually feel much better after it.'

'In any case,' she added, 'he is the only one – as you already know – from whom we need fear such complications. The irregularity of the desires of each of the others leaves us no room for doubt.'

Then Omphale asked me if I hadn't found Clément the least troublesome of the four.

'Alas,' I replied, 'amidst such a crowd of horrors and impurities, which alternately disgust and revolt me, it is difficult to say what wearies me least. Every one of them exhausts me, and already I wish to leave this place no matter what fate may hold in store.'

'It is possible that you may soon be satisfied,' said Omphale. 'It was by mere accident that you came here, and they had not relied on such a coincidence. Just eight days before your arrival they had discharged a girl, and they never proceed with such a course until they are certain of a replacement. Nor do they always find new recruits themselves. They have well-paid agents who serve them with fervour. So I feel almost certain that a new one is likely to arrive at any moment. Thus your wish may be gratified. Besides, we are on the eve of our religious festival. This is a time which rarely passes but it brings them something. They either seduce young girls at confession, or they kidnap them and lock them up. But it is rare that some young chicken isn't gobbled on such an occasion.

The celebrated feast day dawned at last. And you wouldn't believe, Madame, the monstrous impieties indulged by these monks during this event! Believing that a visible miracle would augment the brilliance of their reputation, they dressed Florette – the smallest and youngest of us – in all the ornaments and accoutrements of the Virgin; and attaching invisible cords to her waist ordered her to raise her arms towards heaven when the Host was lifted. The unfortunate little creature was menaced with the cruellest treatment if she uttered a single word, or in any way failed in her performance, with the result that she did her best, and the fraud enjoyed the greatest success one could possibly imagine. The people cried in one voice: 'Miracle! Miracle!' and left rich offerings for the Virgin – going away more convinced than ever of the efficacy and grace of this celestial mother.

Wishing to complete their impiety, our libertines decided that Florette should appear at supper in the same garments which had attracted so much reverence earlier in the day; and each of them inflamed his odious desires by submitting her to the irregularity of his caprice while she was thus clothed. Excited by this first crime, these monsters could not restrain themselves from going further. They stretched her naked, and on her belly, on a large table. Then, placing the image of our Saviour at her head and some lighted candles around her, they dared to consummate upon the loins of this unhappy creature the most fearful of our mysteries. This horrible spectacle was so unbearable that I fainted. When he saw this, Raphael said that in order to accustom me to such matters it was necessary that I should serve as altar in my turn. Seizing me, they placed me in the position which had been occupied by Florette, and the filthy Italian, punctuating his ritual with episodes even more atrocious and sacrilegious than before, consummated upon me the same fearful travesty as he had performed over my companion. When this was over I was no longer capable of movement. They had to carry me to my room where for three days I wept the bitterest of tears over the terrible crime in which I had been forced to participate. This memory still tears my very heart, Madame, and I never think of it without tears. Religion for me is a matter of feeling, and anything which offends or outrages my feelings makes my heart bleed.

Meanwhile, and so far as the new companion we were expecting was concerned, it did not seem that she had been chosen from amongst the crowd attracted by the religious festival. Such a girl may, of course, have been sent to the other seraglio; but nothing happened in ours. And everything continued in this way for a considerable time. I had already dwelt six weeks in this detestable house when Raphael entered our tower towards nine o'clock one morning. He seemed wild and excited, with a strange bewilderment in his glance. One after the other he examined us, placing each in the position he especially favoured. He stopped suddenly at Omphale, contemplating her for several long minutes as she maintained her posture. Moved by some secret agitation he gave himself up to one of his favourite practices, but without bringing it to consummation . . . Then, making her get up, he fixed her for a while with a severe glance, ferocity etching itself deep in his every feature.

'You have served us long enough,' he said at last. 'The society grants you your discharge, and I bring you our official permission to leave. Prepare yourself, for I shall come to seek you at nightfall.'

Having said this he examined her once again in the same old manner – and then abruptly left the room.

As soon as he was outside, Omphale threw herself into my arms.

'Ah!' she said, in tears. 'Here at last is the moment I have longed for, just as much as I fear it . . . What is going to happen to me, great God!'

I did all I could to calm her; but nothing was successful. She swore by the most sacred oaths that she would do everything in her power to deliver us, promising to lodge complaints against these traitors should they leave her the means. And her manner of giving me her word left me without any doubt that she would do her utmost to achieve these ends. The day passed as usual until Raphael returned, about six.

'Come along!' he said brusquely to Omphale, 'are you ready?'

'Yes, Father . . .'

'We must go! We must go immediately!'

'Allow me to embrace my companions.'

'That isn't necessary,' said the monk, pulling her by the arm. 'Someone is waiting for you – follow me!'

Then she asked if she should bring her clothes.

'Nothing, nothing!' exclaimed Raphael; 'doesn't everything belong to the house? You no longer have need of any of it!'

Then, attempting to take back his words in the fashion of one who has said too much: 'All these clothes are useless to you now. You shall have some made to your own measurements, and they'll suit you a lot better.'

I asked the monk if he would allow me to accompany Omphale as far as the door, but he answered with such a hard and surly glance that I recoiled in fear without repeating my request. As she left, our unhappy companion looked at me with anxious, tear-filled eyes; and as soon as she was gone all three of us abandoned ourselves to the sorrow we felt over this separation. Half an hour later Antonin came to take us down to supper. A further hour passed before Raphael appeared. He was unusually agitated, and often spoke to the others in low tones. But everything else continued in the accepted manner. I noticed, however, as Omphale had already warned me, that we were dismissed at an earlier hour and that the monks – who drank infinitely more than was their custom – excited their desires but never permitted their consummation. What conclusions was it possible to draw from such facts? I mention them now because one seems to notice everything on such occasions; but at the time I hadn't the courage to interpret their meaning. Perhaps you, Madame, may not be so surprised at the circumstances as I was then.

We waited four days for news of Omphale, persuaded at one moment that she would never break the vow she had made, and convinced the following instant that the cruel precautions they must have taken with her had removed every possibility of her being useful to us. At last we despaired of her altogether and our anxiety increased in intensity. On the fourth day we were ordered down to supper as usual, but what was our surprise to see a new companion entering by another door just as we appeared in ours.

'Here is the girl whom the society has chosen to replace our last departure!' said Raphael, 'be so good, ladies, as to live with her as you possibly can.' Then turning towards me: 'You are the eldest in the class, Sophie, and I elevate you to the position of room-mistress. You know your duties – be sure to perform them carefully.'

I would have liked to refuse, but was unable to, being perpetually obliged to sacrifice my inclinations and my will to those of these villainous men. So I curtseyed and promised to do everything to his satisfaction.

Then they removed the little cloak and the veils which covered the head and shoulders of our new companion, and we saw a young girl of fifteen, with the most delicate and interesting features. Her eyes, although wet with tears, were superb. She lifted them most graciously towards all of us, and I can honestly say that never in my life have I seen more touching glances. Thick ash-blond hair floated round her shoulders in natural curls. She had fresh, rosy-red lips, held her head with dignity, and there was something so completely seductive in her that it was impossible to look at her without feeling drawn involuntarily towards her. We soon learned from her (I insert the details here, in order to keep everything concerning her in one place) that she was called Octavie, and was the daughter of an important merchant living in Lyons. She had been educated at Paris and was on her way home with a governess when they were attacked, at night, between Auxerre and Vermenton. She had been kidnapped and brought to this house without ever discovering what had happened to the carriage and her woman companion. After that she had been locked up, alone, in a low-ceilinged room. There, for an hour, she abandoned herself to despair; at the end of which time without a single word having been said by any of the monks she was brought to join us.

Faced with such charms, our four libertines were in ecstasy for a moment. But they only had strength to admire what stood before them, for the empire of beauty commands respect even in the most wicked and profligate of men – who cannot violate it without experiencing remorse. Nevertheless, monsters such as those with whom we had to deal languish little under such restraints: 'Come along, mademoiselle,' said the Superior, 'come along and let us see, I pray you, if the rest of your charms correspond with those nature has so generously scattered over your features.'

And as this beautiful girl showed signs of being troubled, as she blushed without really understanding what was said to her, the brutal Antonin seized her by the arm and shouted, with oaths and exclamations too indecent for repetition: 'Don't you understand then, you finical little creature, don't you understand that what you have been told to do is to strip yourself stark naked this very instant . . . ' Fresh tears were followed by further resistance . . . But Clément, grabbing hold of her, tore away within a minute everything which had veiled the modesty of this interesting creature. Those charms of Octavie, previously concealed by decency, were even more beautiful than those which custom allowed to be shown. Never has a whiter skin been seen, never such fortunate contours. But all this innocence, all this freshness and delicacy, were quickly to become the prey of a group of barbarians. It seemed that nature had showered countless favours only that they might be destroyed by the insensate beasts who held us in captivity.

A circle was formed round her and, just as I had done, she was obliged to cover it in every sense. Antonin, burning with lust, could not resist a cruel attack on such budding charms. But his worship was brief, and the incense smoked at the feet of the god . . . Raphael saw that it was time to think of more serious things. For his own part he was incapable of waiting, so he seized the victim and placed her according to his taste. Not succeeding so well as he might, he begged Clément to hold her for him. Octavie wept, but no one heard. Fire burned bright in the eyes of this abominable Italian. Master of the fortress he was about to storm, he considered his avenues of approach only the better to anticipate every resistance. Neither ruse nor any other form of preparation was employed. The enormous disproportion between the assailant and the rebel in no way interfered with his conquest. A heart-rending cry from the victim announced her defeat. But nothing softened her proud conqueror. The more she appeared to beg for mercy, the more ferociously did he press upon her; and, like myself, the wretched girl was ignominiously soiled without ceasing to be a virgin.

'Never were laurels more difficult to win,' said Raphael, as he put himself to rights. 'I thought, for the first time in my life, that I was about to fail.'

'Let me take her over from here!' exclaimed Antonin, without letting her get up. 'There is more than a single breach in the rampart, and you've only taken one of them.'

As he spoke he advanced proudly into combat, and within a minute was master of the situation. Fresh sobs could be heard . . .

'Praise be to God!' said this horrible monster, 'I would have doubted my victory if I hadn't heard the cries of the vanquished. Moreover, I only esteem my triumph when it is drawn at the cost of tears.'

'To be truthful,' said Jérôme as he came forward, a bundle of twigs in his hand, 'neither shall I disturb this sweet posture, for it is perfectly suited to my designs.'

He looked, he touched, he felt. Then a frightful whistling noise echoed through the air. The beautiful flesh changed colour. The brilliant red of carnation mingled with the glow of lilies. Thus it is that something which in moderation might perhaps enliven a moment of love becomes, with incessant repetition, a crime against its laws. Nothing could stop the perfidious monk. The more the pupil wept, the greater each explosion of her master's severity . . . Every part was treated in the same manner, not a single portion of the flesh beneath him obtaining the slightest mercy. Soon this entire body was covered with the imprints of his barbarity; and it was upon these bleeding traces of his odious pleasures that this unspeakable man extinguished, at last, the fire which burned within him.

'I shall be more gentle than my brothers,' exclaimed Clément as he seized the beautiful creature in his arms and glued an impure kiss on her coral lips . . . 'Here is the temple in which I shall sacrifice!'

He inflamed himself further by implanting several fresh kisses upon that adorable mouth – a mouth which might have been formed by Venus herself. Then he forced the miserable girl to submit to those infamies which he found so delectable; and the happy organ of pleasure, the sweetest asylum of love, was soiled at last with horrors.

The remainder of the evening passed in the manner you already know. But the beauty, the pathetic youth of this girl, so increasingly inflamed the monsters that their atrocities redoubled; and it was satiety, much more than pity, which finally enabled the poor creature to retire to our room, where she was able to rest for a few hours in that quiet she so greatly needed. I should at least have liked to be able to console her on this first night. Obliged, however, to spend it with Antonin, it was myself who needed help. Unfortunately I seemed more ardently to excite the revolting desires of this debauchee than any other of the girls, and consequently there had been few weeks when I did not pass four or five nights in his room.

The following morning when I returned to our quarters I found my new comrade in tears. I repeated all that Omphale had once said to me under similar circumstances in an effort to calm her; but my good intentions were not successful. It is not at all easy to console anyone for such a sudden change of fate. Moreover, this young creature was blessed with considerable gifts of piety, of virtue, honour and sensitivity which could only make her feel more keenly the cruelty of her situation. Raphael, who was much taken with her, saw to it that she spent several nights in succession with him. And little by little she comforted herself in her misfortunes, just as we had done, with the hope that one day she would see them end. Omphale had had good reason to tell me that seniority had nothing to do with the granting of discharges. These were dictated solely by the caprice of the monks and were just as likely to be presented after eight days as after twenty years. Octavie had been with us less than six weeks when Raphael came to tell her that she was due to leave us . . . She made us the same promises as Omphale had done and disappeared in the same manner – without our ever finding out what had become of her.

\*      \*      \*

We remained about a month without any replacement. It was during this interval that, like Omphale, I had reason to be persuaded that we were not the only girls who inhabited the house – and that there was doubtless another building which held a similar number to our own. Omphale had only suspected such a possibility. But my own experience, which was quite an adventure, absolutely confirmed my suspicions. This is how it happened. I had just spent the night with Raphael, and, according to custom, was leaving him about seven o'clock in the morning, when a Brother, equally as old and disgusting as ours – but whom I had never before seen – suddenly appeared in the corridor with a tall girl of eighteen or twenty. She seemed to me very beautiful, and would have been an attractive model for any artist. Raphael, who was to take me back, dawdled in his cell; and it so happened that I suddenly found myself face to face with this girl – whom the Brother was at an absolute loss to hide from my eyes.

'Where are you taking this creature?' demanded the Superior, furiously.

'Into your room, Reverend Father,' answered this abominable Mercury. 'Your Grace forgets that he gave me orders to do so yesterday evening.'

'I said it was to be at nine o'clock!'

'At seven o'clock, Monseigneur. You told me you wanted to see her before Mass.'

While this was going on I considered my companion – who was looking at me with the same astonishment.

'Ah, well, it doesn't matter,' said Raphael as he took me back into his room followed by the girl.

'Listen, Sophie,' he said, having closed the door and instructed the Brother to wait, 'this girl holds the same position in another tower as you do in yours – she is room-mistress. There is no inconvenience in our two senior girls being acquainted with each other, and so that your introduction shall be all the more complete, Sophie, I am going to show you Marianne completely nude.'

This Marianne, who seemed to me a very impudent and shameless sort of girl, undressed on the instant; and Raphael, ordering me to excite his desires, submitted her before my eyes to those pleasures he preferred best: 'That's just what I was in need of,' said the infamous creature as soon as he was satisfied. 'It is sufficient for me to have spent the night with a girl to make me want another in the morning. Nothing is so insatiable as these tastes of ours. The more we indulge them, the more they clamour for satisfaction. And although a man always does very much the same kind of things, he ceaselessly imagines fresh attractions in a new partner. The moment satiety extinguishes our desire for one partner is the same moment that libertinage fans the bright flame of lust for another. You two girls have our confidence – therefore hold your tongues. You may go now, Sophie. The Brother will take you back. As for me, I have a new mystery to celebrate with your companion.'

Octavie was shortly replaced by a little twelve year old peasant, fresh and pretty, but much inferior to her predecessor. Within two years I was the sole member remaining from the original company. Florette and Cornélie had left in their turn, each swearing, as Omphale had done, to send me news of themselves, and neither of them succeeding any better than that unfortunate young woman. Both were replaced – Florette by a fifteen year old from Dijon, plump and chubby, with nothing to commend her but her freshness and her age; and Cornélie by a singularly beautiful girl belonging to an eminently respectable Autun family. This last young woman, who was sixteen, had fortunately stolen Antonin's heart from me – I say 'fortunately', but I very quickly realised that if I had been removed from the good graces of this libertine, I was equally on the eve of losing my credit with the others. The unreliability of these wretches made me tremble for my fate. I saw well enough that the situation announced my discharge. And, realising only too clearly that this cruel permission to leave was nothing other than a sentence of death, I was, for some moments, considerably alarmed. I say for some moments! Yet, unfortunate as I was, why should I cling to life when the greatest blessing that could happen to me would be to leave it?

Such reflections comforted me, and helped me await my end with so much resignation that I employed no means whatever to regain my credit. Ill luck began to overwhelm me, and there wasn't an instant when one or another of them didn't complain about me, not a day when I wasn't punished. I prayed to heaven and awaited my sentence. I was perhaps on the eve of receiving it when the hand of providence, weary of tormenting me in the same manner, tore me from this new abyss only to replunge me, shortly, into another. But let me not anticipate events. First I must tell you how we were at last delivered from the hands of these notorious debauchees.

It was necessary that the frightful example of vice triumphant should be maintained, even in the present circumstances, just as it had always been throughout each event in my life. It was written that those who had tormented me, humiliated me, chained me in irons, should ceaselessly receive, before my very eyes, the benefits of their criminal activities – as if providence had taken upon itself the task of showing me the inutility of virtue. Such deadly lessons, however, have never been successful in correcting me; and should I once more escape the sword suspended above my head, they will not prevent me from remaining the slave of this divinity of my heart.

One morning when we didn't expect him, Antonin appeared in our room and announced to us that the Reverend Father Raphael, relative and protégé of the Pope, had just been named by His Holiness as General of the Order of Saint Francis.

'And I, my children,' he added, 'have been promoted to the position of Superior at Lyons. Two new Fathers will immediately replace us in this house. They may arrive today. We do not know them and it is possible that, instead of retaining you here, they may send you back to your homes. But whatever your fate, I advise you, for your own good as well as for the honour of the two colleagues whom we are leaving here, to conceal all details as to our conduct and to admit nothing but what it is impossible to deny.'

Having received such wonderful news we found ourselves at a loss in refusing the monk what he appeared to desire. So we promised him everything, and the libertine made his goodbyes to all four of us. The end of misfortune being in sight we withstood the final blows without complaint. We refused him nothing. And when he left it was to separate himself once and for all from all of us. Dinner was served, and two hours later Father Clément entered our rooms. He was accompanied by two gentlemen, reverend both in age and in appearance.

'Admit, Father,' one of them said to Clément, 'admit that these debauchees are horrible, and that it is most singular that Heaven has suffered them so long.'

Clément humbly agreed with everything; but attempted to excuse himself by explaining that neither he nor his colleagues were responsible for any of the circumstances – they had found the place in the state in which they were now handing it over. To he honest, he explained, the subjects varied, but they had found even this variety established on their arrival and had done nothing more than follow the usage indicated by their predecessors.

'So be it,' replied the Father who seemed to be the new Superior, 'so let it be; but let us quickly suppress this execrable debauchery – a debauchery which would be revolting even in people of the outside world. I leave you to ponder,' he added, 'just what it should mean to those whose lives have been given up to religion.'

Then he asked us all what we wished to do. Everyone replied that she wanted to return either to her town or to her family.

'It shall be so, my children,' said the monk. 'I shall give each of you the sum necessary to make this possible; but it will be necessary for you to leave one after another, with an interval of two days between each departure. You must also leave alone, on foot, and never reveal anything of what has happened in this house.'

We swore what he required of us, but the new Superior was not content with our promises . . . He also requested us to draw near to the Sacrament. None of us refused; and when we had knelt at the foot of the altar he made us take an oath that we would, throughout our lives, conceal everything that had happened in the monastery. I gave my word with the others; and if I have broken it in so far as you are concerned, Madame, it is because I accepted the spirit, rather than the letter of this vow insisted on by the good priest. His object, of course, was that no complaint should be brought against his order. But I feel quite certain that, although I have freely entrusted you with the details of my adventures, nothing troublesome will result for any of these good Fathers.

My companions were the first to leave; and as we had been separated since the moment of the new Superior's arrival – being also forbidden to make any appointments to meet – we never saw each other again. I had asked to go to Grenoble and was given two louis to take me there. Putting on the clothes I had worn when I arrived at this place, I found in one of the pockets the eight other louis which still remained to me from my previous experiences. Then, full of satisfaction at being able to fly once and for all from that terrible refuge of vice – and in such a protected and unexpected manner – I set off into the forest. I soon found myself once more on the road to Auxerre, at the same point at which I had left it to throw myself into such a sea of trouble. It was just three years after that piece of foolishness – which is to say that I was now twenty-five, or would be in a few weeks.

My first care was to fall on my knees to beg fresh pardon of God for all the involuntary faults I had committed. And I prayed with much deeper contrition that I had ever felt when stretched before the defiled altars of that infamous house I had left with such joy. Tears of remorse began to stream from my eyes . . .

'Alas,' I said to myself, 'I was pure when, long ago, I left this same road, led by a principle of devotion which proved so fatally deceptive . . . And just look at the sad state I'm in now!'

These gloomy reflections were softened somewhat by the pleasure I felt in knowing myself to be free, and I continued on my way. In order to avoid wearying you any longer, Madame, with such details as must tax your patience I shall in future – if you agree – describe only such events as taught me some salutary lesson or made some definite change in the course of my life.

While staying for some days at Lyons, I happened to glance through the pages of a foreign newspaper belonging to the woman at whose house I was lodging. You can imagine my surprise when its pages informed me that once again crime had been rewarded – that one of the principal authors of my sufferings had attained the pinnacle of fame. Rodin, that villainous creature who had punished me so cruelly for preventing a projected murder, obliged to leave France – doubtless for having committed others – had just been appointed first surgeon to the King of Sweden, and at a very considerable salary. 'May the wicked wretch continue fortunate,' I thought, 'since providence seems to wish it. As for yourself, you miserable creature, you can suffer alone and in silence, since it is written that tribulation and pain should be the frightful portion of virtue!'

At the end of three days I left Lyons to travel on to Dauphiné, filled with the wild hope that at least a little good fortune might await me in that province. I had scarcely covered more than two leagues from Lyons, walking, as usual, my only luggage being a couple of chemises and some handkerchiefs which I kept in a pocket, when I met an old woman who sadly came up to me and begged my charity. Compassionate by nature, and never having experienced a single joy in the world comparable to that of obliging others, I immediately brought out my purse with the intention of taking from it a few pieces of money to give to this woman. But the unworthy creature, more prompt than myself – although at first I had taken her for an old and decrepit individual – felled me instantly with a vigorous blow in the stomach. By the time I managed to get to my feet she was a hundred paces away, surrounded by four rascals whose menacing gestures warned me of the dangers that faced me should I dare to approach them . . .

'Oh! just heaven,' I cried bitterly, 'is it then impossible for any virtuous impulse to find birth in me without my immediately being punished with all the most cruel and fearful misfortunes in the universe!'

At this terrifying moment all my courage was ready to abandon me. Today I beg pardon of heaven, but at the time I am speaking of revolt was terribly near my heart. Two dreadful courses lay open before me – either I could join the rogues who had so cruelly injured me, or return to Lyons and give myself up to a life of prostitution . . . God gave me grace to resist; and, although the hope which was thus re-illumined in my heart proved merely the dawn of even more terrible adversities, I still thank Him for having sustained me through it all. The chain of misfortunes which takes me today, innocent, to the scaffold, will result in nothing but my death. But the choice of any other way of life would have brought me shame, remorse, ignominy – and death is far less cruel to me than these.

I continued on my way, having decided to sell what few things I had at Vienne so that I might proceed to Grenoble. Thus I trudged sadly along until, just over half a mile from the town, I saw on the plain at the right of the road two men on horseback, who were trampling a third beneath their horses' hooves. Leaving him at last for dead, they galloped quickly away . . . This terrible scene moved me to the point of tears . . .

'Alas,' I said to myself, 'here is someone more unfortunate than I have been, for at least I retain my health and my strength. At least I can earn my living, while this man, if he is not wealthy but in similar circumstances to my own – well, he will be crippled for the remainder of his life! And what will become of him?'

However much I should have smothered these sentiments of pity, however much I had been cruelly punished in the past for giving way to the dictates of such emotion, I could not resist them. So I went up to the dying man and made him breathe a little spirit which I carried with me. He opened his eyes, and his first movements were those of gratitude. They seemed to beg me to continue my attentions, and I tore up one of my chemises that I might bind his wounds – it was one of the few things left me which I might sell so as to prolong my life. I tore it to shreds for this man, staunching the blood which flowed from his injuries and making him drink a little wine that I carried in a flask so that I might renew my strength for walking during moments of exhaustion. I washed his bruises with what remained of it.

At length the unfortunate creature recovered something of his strength and his spirits. Although he was on foot and only lightly dressed, he did not look poor. Moreover, he possessed some quite valuable things – rings, a watch, and other jewels all badly damaged by his adventure. Finally, when he was able to speak, he asked who might be the gracious angel who lent him aid, and what he might do to prove his gratitude. Still being simple enough to believe that a soul enslaved by thankfulness would be entirely devoted to me, I thought I might safely enjoy the sweet pleasure of sharing my tears with one who had shed his own in the shelter of my arms. I told him all that had befallen me and he listened with interest. When I described to him the final catastrophe, disclosing my terrible poverty, he looked at me and exclaimed: 'How happy I am to be alive and able to acknowledge all you have done for me! My name is Dalville, and I am the owner of a very beautiful castle in the mountains about forty-five miles from here. I can offer you a home there, if you will come with me. And in order that such a proposal need not frighten you or offend against your sense of delicacy, I shall immediately explain the way in which you can be useful to me. I am married, you see, and my wife has need of a trustworthy woman to attend her. Recently we had to dismiss a very bad servant, and I offer you her place.'

Humbly I thanked my protector and asked him how such a man as he had risked travelling alone, without attendants, thus leaving himself open to such ill-treatment by ruffians as he had actually suffered.

'Lusty, young and vigorous, it has always been my habit to travel to Vienne in this manner. My health and my purse both gain equally by it. Nevertheless, I need not trouble myself over finance, for I'm very wealthy – as you shall see if you will do me the kindness of coming home with me. Those two men with whom you saw me having a tussle are two petty lordlings of the district with nothing whatever to their names except their capes and their swords. Which is as good as saying that both of them are rascals. Last week I won a hundred louis from them in a house at Vienne, but I didn't receive even the thirtieth part of this from them. I accepted their promise of payment, met them today, and asked for what they owed me . . . and you have seen how they paid me!'

I deplored with this honest gentleman the double misfortune to which he had fallen victim; then he suggested that we should be getting on our way.

'I feel a little better now,' said Dalville, ' – thanks to your care. But night is coming on, so we must reach an inn I know about two leagues from here. We can borrow horses there in the morning, and probably reach my castle by the same evening.'

Absolutely in favour of profiting by this help which Heaven seemed to have sent me, I helped Dalville to walk, sustaining him on our way. Leaving all known roads we set out across country, following foot-paths which led, as the bird flies, towards the Alps. After covering nearly two leagues we found the inn which Dalville had mentioned. We had supper together, gaily, and observing all propriety. After which he commended me to the landlady, who arranged for me to sleep near her. And next day, riding two hired mules and escorted by a servant from the tavern, we reached the frontiers of Dauphiné and directed our steps towards the mountains. Still suffering from the wounds he had received, Dalville was not in a state to withstand the entire journey. I was not at all sorry about this for, being unaccustomed to such a manner of travelling, I found myself equally indisposed. We halted at Virieu, where my guide paid me the same attentions and the same respect as hitherto. On the following morning we continued on our journey, always in the same direction, and at four o'clock we reached the foothills of the mountains. Here the road became almost impassable. Dalville instructed the muleteer not to leave me, in case of accident, and we threaded our way through the gorges. We seemed to do nothing but twist and turn and climb for about four leagues and then we had left every human abode and pathway so far behind that I felt we must be at the very edge of the world. Despite myself a slight sense of inquietude began to take hold of me. Weaving my way through these inaccessible rocks I was reminded of my detours in the forest which surrounded the monastery of Sainte-Marie-des-Bois. And the aversion I had learned to feel for all isolated spots caused me to tremble at this one. At last we perceived a castle perched on the edge of a terrifying precipice. It seemed to hang over the edge of a steep wall of rock, and had every aspect of a habitation for ghosts rather than for flesh and blood members of human society. Moreover, although we could see the castle, no road seemed to lead to it. The one we followed was very stony and much frequented by goats. Nevertheless it led to this edifice, but by infinite detours.

'There is my house,' exclaimed Dalville, noticing my expression as I gazed at it. I expressed my surprise that he should inhabit such a desolate place, and he replied – but quite harshly – that a man lived where he could. I was as much shocked as frightened by the tone of his voice, for nothing goes unnoticed in misfortune. The slightest modulation or inflexion in the voice of those upon whom one depends is able, during such periods, to stifle or to revive one's hope. But, as it was too late to withdraw, I decided to take no notice of his attitude. At last, after much twisting and turning in our climb round this ancient ruin, we suddenly found ourselves directly in front of it. Dalville dismounted from his mule and, asking me to do likewise, returned them to the lackey, paid him, and ordered him to return to the inn. A ceremony which, under the circumstances, displeased me very considerably.

Dalville noticed my disquietude.

'What's the matter with you, Sophie?' he said as we walked towards his dwelling. 'You haven't left France. This castle is on the border of Dauphiné, and you are still in your own country!'

'That may be so, monsieur,' I replied, 'but how did you come to establish yourself in such a cut-throat's retreat?'

'Cut-throat's retreat?' bandied Dalville, looking at me slyly as we approached the building; 'no, it isn't quite that, my child – but neither is it the home of perfectly respectable people.'

'Ah, monsieur,' I replied, 'you make me shudder! Where are you taking me?'

'I am taking you to work for some coiners of counterfeit money, slut!' he said, as he seized hold of me and forced me over a drawbridge which had been lowered on our arrival, and which was raised immediately afterwards.

'Here we are!' he added, as soon as we were in the courtyard. Then, showing me a wide and extremely deep cistern neighbouring on the gate where two chained and naked women continually moved a wheel which drew water to feed a reservoir, 'Do you see this pit?' he continued, ' – these are your companions, and this will be your work. On condition that you work twelve hours a day turning this wheel, you will be given six ounces of black bread and a plate of beans once in twenty-four hours. Moreover, you will be well and regularly beaten each time you attempt to rest. As for liberty, you can renounce all thought of that, for never will you see the sky again. As soon as you are dead you will be thrown into this hole which you can see beside the well – on top of thirty or forty other bodies which are there already – and your work will be taken over by someone else!'

'In heaven's name, monsieur,' I cried, throwing myself at Dalville's feet, 'don't you remember that I saved your life, and that in a moment of gratitude you offered me happiness? Surely I have a right to expect better than this!'

'And what, I beg you, do you mean by this feeling of gratitude – this feeling by which you imagine you hold me captive? Such wretched creatures as yourself should reason better than this! What did you do when you helped me? You had the choice of continuing on your way, or of coming over to assist me. You chose the latter, inspired by some profound emotion springing from deep within your heart . . . That in itself is a kind of pleasure, so how in the devil's name can you claim that I should be obliged to reward you for pleasures which you grant to yourself? And how could you possibly let it enter your head that a man like myself, swimming in gold, surrounded by opulence, and more than a millionaire – a man who is about to move to Venice that he may enjoy life at his ease – how could you come to the conclusion that a man such as this should deign to lower himself by admitting any kind of debt to a miserable little wretch like you!

'And even if you did save my life, I still don't owe you anything, for you acted only in your own interests. Get to work, you slave – get to work! And learn that civilisation may overthrow nature's institutions, but never her rights! Originally she created strong beings and weak beings. Her intention was that the latter should always be subordinate to the former, as the lamb is to the lion, the insect to the elephant. When we come to man, however, it is skill and intelligence which determine the position of individuals. Rank is no longer determined by physical strength, but it can be, and is, determined by wealth. The richest man has become the strongest, the poor man the weakest. The priority of the strong over the weak was always one of the laws of nature. Moreover, she is indifferent as to whether the power of the strong over the weak is by reason of their wealth or by reason of their physical strength. And she is equally indifferent as to whether this power crushes those who are physically weak, or those who are merely poor.

'As for those feelings of gratitude which you claim man should feel, Sophie, nature ignores them. It was never within the reasoning of her laws that the pleasure one feels in obliging another should become a cause, for the man who benefits by such obligation, to relax his rights upon the other. Have you found these feelings anywhere amongst the animals who serve us? Since I dominate you by means of my wealth and my strength, would it be natural for me to abandon my rights over you simply because you enjoyed helping me, or because your own peculiar reasoning suggested that you would find redemption in aiding me?

'And even if the service had been rendered by an equal to an equal, never would the pride of an elevated soul allow itself to be degraded by the sentiment of gratitude. The man who receives from another is always humiliated in the receiving – and is not this very humiliation sufficient repayment for the service rendered? Is it not true that the pride of the helper delights in the strength of being able to assist? And is any other reward really necessary for the man or woman who obliges? Besides, if such obligation, by humbling the recipient, should become a burden to him, by what right would you force him to bear it? Why should it be necessary for me to allow myself to feel a sense of humiliation every time I meet the glance of whoever has performed me some such service?

'Thus ingratitude instead of being a vice is truly the virtue of proud intellects – just as surely as kindness is that of weak ones. The slave preaches the virtues of kindness and humility to his master because as a slave he has need of them; but the master, better guided by nature and his passions, has no need to devote himself to anything excepting those things which serve or please him. Be as kind as you wish, if you enjoy such things – but don't demand any reward for having had your pleasure.'

At these words, to which Dalville gave me no time to reply, two footmen seized me, stripped me on his orders, and chained me alongside my two companions. I had no choice but to work with them immediately, not even being allowed to rest after the tiring journey I had made. Scarcely had I been at this wheel for fifteen minutes than the entire gang of counterfeiters – who had just finished their day's work – crowded round to examine me, headed by their chief. Every one of them heaped sarcasm and impertinence on me, having noticed the dishonourable mark of the branding iron which I innocently bore upon my body. They approached me, touched and handled me brutally everywhere, and criticised with biting pleasantry every portion of my anatomy.

This painful scene over, they withdrew a little distance. Dalville then seized a horse-whip which was always kept near us and, with all the strength of his arm, gave me five or six lashes over every part of my body.

'This is how you will be treated here, you lazy slut,' he said as the lash fell. 'This is what you will receive every time you are unfortunate enough to fail in your duty. These, of course, are not because you have failed, but only to show you how I treat those who do.'

Each blow tore away strips of my skin; and, never having felt such infernal pain, either in the hands of Bressac or in those of the barbarous monks, I screamed loudly and shrilly as I struggled in my chains. Such writhings and twistings, and such cries of agony, only aroused the mocking laughter of the monsters who were watching me; and I had the cruel satisfaction of learning that, if there are men who, ruled by vengeance or by a vile sense of the voluptuous are able to enjoy the pain of another, there yet remain individuals so barbarously organised that they relish the same delights without any other motive than the gratification of pride or the most terrifying curiosity. It seems, therefore, that man is naturally wicked. He is so in the delirium of his passions, and almost equally so even when they are calm. But in either case the sufferings of his brothers can become an execrable pleasure in his eyes.

Three dark holes, each separated from the other and locked like prisons, were close to the pit. One of the footmen who had chained me indicated the one I was to occupy and I withdrew to it, having received my destined portion of water, beans and bread. There, at leisure, I was able to abandon myself completely to the horror of my situation.

'Alas,' I said to myself, 'is it possible that there are men barbarous enough to stifle within themselves any sentiment of gratitude, that virtue to which I would abandon myself so gladly if ever an honest soul gave me the chance of feeling its promptings? How can it be so despised by men? And is the man who smothers it so inhumanly anything other than a monster?'

I was occupied in such reflections, mingling them with my tears, when suddenly the door of my cell was opened. It was Dalville. Without saying a word, and in absolute silence, he placed his candle on the ground and threw himself on me with the ferocity of a wild beast. Repulsing with blows my attempts at self-defence and scorning my pleas for mercy, he subjected me to his desires and satisfied himself brutally. Then he took up his light and, locking the door, disappeared.

'Is it possible to carry outrage further?' I asked myself. 'And what difference can there be between such a man and the most savage animals of the forest?'

The sun arose without my having enjoyed a single moment of rest. Our cells were opened, we were rechained to the wheel, and our sad labours recommenced. My companions were two girls of between twenty-five and thirty who, although brutalised by suffering and deformed by excess of physical pain, still retained the vestiges of beauty. Their figures were pretty and well turned and one of them still possessed superb hair. A depressing conversation acquainted me with the fact that they had both been, at different times, mistresses of Dalville. One at Lyons, the other at Grenoble. He had brought them both to this horrible retreat where they had continued for several years on the same kind of footing. Then, as recompense for the pleasures they had brought him, he condemned them to this humiliating work.

I learned from them that he had, at the present moment, a charming mistress who, more fortunate than they had been, would probably accompany him to Venice – to which he was on the eve of moving, if the considerable sums which he had recently sent to Spain should produce the bills of exchange he required for Italy. For he did not wish to take his gold there, preferring to send it to agents in a country other than the one in which he planned to reside, as it was all in false coinage. By these means he was rich in whatever place he wished to live, but on papers drawn on a different country. Thus his manoeuvres remained free of discovery, while his fortune remained solidly established. It was, nevertheless, possible that he might lose everything in an instant; and the retreat he was mediating depended absolutely on the success of this last transaction – in which the greater part of his wealth was compromised. If Cadiz accepted his piastres and his louis, sending him in return acceptable bills made payable at Venice, then he would be happy for the remainder of his life. But if the deception was discovered then he risked being denounced and hanged as he deserved.

'Alas,' I said to myself when I learned these particulars, '– but providence must be merciful this time. She will never let a monster like this succeed, and all three of us will be avenged.'

At midday we were given two hours in which to rest, and we profited by it to the extent of going separately into our own chambers where we ate and regained our breath. At two o'clock we were chained again to the wheel, which we turned until night fell. Never were we allowed to enter the castle. The reason why we were kept thus naked during five months in the year was by reason of the insupportable heat and the excessive work which we did. And besides, as my companions assured me, in this state we were best prepared to receive the blows which, from time to time, our surly master came to bestow on us. During winter we were given trousers and skin-tight waistcoats which, by their very clinging fit, exposed us just as well to the blows of the butcherous Dalville.

During my first day there he did not appear; but towards midnight he came to me and behaved in precisely the same fashion as on the previous night. I tried to take advantage of this moment by begging him to soften my lot.

'And by what right do you make such a request?' this barbarian said to me. 'Is it because I have momentarily chosen to indulge my fancies with you? But am I kneeling at your feet and pleading for favours for which you might demand some sort of payment? I am asking nothing of you . . . I take, and I do not see why this right which I enjoy over you should result in my abstention from any others which I may hold. There is no love in my intercourse with you, for that is an emotion which my heart has never known. I serve myself with a woman by necessity, just as I use a chamberpot for a different need; but I grant no rights to these creatures, who are subjected to my desires either by my money or by my authority. Nor do I dispense respect or tenderness. I owe what I take to myself alone, and I demand nothing of a woman but her submission. I do not see how that obliges me to offer her my gratitude You might just as well say that a robber who forcibly takes a man's purse in a wood owes that man some gratitude because he has profited financially by his superior strength. It is the same when one outrages a woman. Such an outrage may justify a second attack, but is never sufficient reason for granting her any sort of compensation.'

Dalville, who by this time had reached his culmination, abruptly left me as soon as he had finished speaking. But he plunged me into new reflections which, as you may well imagine, were not to his advantage. That evening he came to watch us at work, and finding that we had not furnished the normal quantity of water, he seized his cruel horse-whip and lashed the three of us until we bled. Yet, although he spared me no more than the others, he did not fail to return the same night in order to behave in the usual manner. Showing him the wounds with which he had covered me, I was bold enough to remind him of the time when I had torn my linen into strips so as to bind his own injuries. But Dalville, continuing with his selfish pleasures, replied to my complaints only with a dozen blows mingled with vituperation and invective. And, following his habit, he left me immediately he had achieved physical satisfaction. This programme was followed for almost a month, after which the butcher was gracious enough no longer to expose me to the shocking torture of letting him take what he was so little fitted to receive. My life scarcely changed, however, for I experienced neither more nor less as regards moments of tranquillity, and neither more nor less in the way of cruel treatment.

A year sped by in this painful manner when news began to circulate, not only that Dalville's fortune was made and that he had received, for payment in Venice, the immense amount of notes he desired, but also that he had been asked for several million more in false coinage – for which, according to his wishes, he would receive bills of exchange payable at Venice. The success of such a criminal could never have been more magnificent or more unexpected. He would leave with over a million ready at hand and with much more to come! Such was the new lesson which providence set before me, and such was her latest method of once more attempting to convince me that prosperity waited on crime and misfortune on virtue . . .

Dalville prepared to leave, and on the midnight of his last day at the castle he came to see me – a thing which had not happened for a long time. He told me of his good fortune and announced his departure. I threw myself at his feet and begged him earnestly to set me free, asking him to give me just a little money to get me as far as Grenoble.

'At Grenoble,' he exclaimed, 'you would denounce me!'

'Very well, monsieur,' I said, soaking his knees with my tears, 'I give you my word that I will not set foot in the place. The better to convince you of my sincerity, and if you will deign to take me with you to Venice, perhaps I may find there hearts which are less hard than those in my own country. Moreover, I swear to you by everything that I hold most sacred, once we are there I shall never trouble you again . . . '

'I have no intention of helping you in any way whatsoever – I wouldn't give you even one solitary coin,' replied this worthless wretch. 'All those things known as generosity or charity are so repugnant to my character that, even were I three times as rich as I am, I would never consent to give even a halfpenny to an indigent. My principles are based upon this rule and I shall never depart from it. The poverty-stricken are within the order of nature. In creating men of unequal strength she convinces us of her wish that this inequality should be preserved despite those modifications which civilisation effects in her laws. In civilisation the poor replace the physically weak, as I have already said – and to assist the poor is to disturb the established order. It means that one stands in opposition to nature, attempting to overthrow the equilibrium which lies at the base of her most sublime arrangements. The man who helps the poor works towards an equality which is dangerous to society. He encourages laziness and indolence, teaching the poor to steal from the rich – whenever it pleases the latter to refuse that assistance to which the former has become accustomed.'

'Oh, but these are hard principles, monsieur! Would you speak in this manner if you had not always been rich?'

'That is beside the point! I knew how to master my fate, to tread under my feet this phantom of virtue which leads either to the workhouse or to the gallows. I learned at an early age that religion, charity, and kindness were stumbling blocks to all who aimed at wealth and good fortune, and I consolidated my own on the debris of man's prejudice. It was by mocking law, both human and divine, by always sacrificing the feeble when they crossed my path, by abusing the good faith and the credulity of others, by ruining the poor and robbing the wealthy that I have attained the precipitous temple of the divinity I worship. Why didn't you imitate me? Your fortune was already in your hands! And has the chimerical virtue which you preferred above worldly success – has this virtue consoled you for all the sacrifices you have offered up to it? It is far too late to do anything about it now, wretched girl. All you can do is weep over the mistakes you have made; and, suffering, try to find – if you can – something guarded by the phantoms you revere but which your credulity has lost you.'

With these cruel words Dalville threw himself upon me . . . But he filled me with such horror and his frightful maxims inspired so much hatred in me that I repulsed him with severity. He tried attempting force and, failing, compensated himself with cruelty. I was overwhelmed with blows, but still he did not triumph. His fire burned itself out without success and the tears of the insane creature avenged me at last for the outrages he had perpetrated.

The next day, before leaving, this vicious man presented us with a fresh scene of barbarity and cruelty which cannot be equalled by anything described in the annals of Andronicus, of Nero, of Wenceslas or Tiberius.

Everyone believed that his mistress was leaving with him. So he made her dress suitably. Then, at the moment when they were about to mount their horses, he led her over to us: 'There is your place, vile creature!' he exclaimed, as he ordered her to undress. 'I would like my comrades to remember me; therefore I am leaving them, as a token, the woman with whom they thought I was most infatuated. But since only three women are necessary here . . . and since I am about to travel along a dangerous road where my firearms will be useful, I am going to try out my pistols on one of you!'

As he said this he loaded one of them, holding it in turn to the breasts of each of the three women who rotated the wheel. Finally he addressed himself to one of these former mistresses: 'Go,' he shouted at her as he blew out her brains, ' – go and take news of me to the other world! Tell the devil that Dalville is the richest criminal on earth, and that he insolently defies, and equally, both the hands of heaven and those of hell.'

It was a horrible sight watching this poor creature, who did not die immediately but struggled a long time in her chains. The infamous villain observed it with delight, but finally had her removed in order to put his mistress in her place. This was because he wanted to see her turn the wheel a few times and to receive, under his hand, a dozen blows from his horse-whip. These atrocities achieved, the abominable man mounted his horse and, followed by two valets, disappeared for ever from our sight.

Everything changed from the day after Dalville's departure. His successor, a gentle and reasonable man, had us instantly released.

'This is not work for the weak and kindly sex,' he said to us benevolently. 'It is for animals to turn this machine! The profession we follow is criminal enough without our offending still further by our gratuitous atrocities the Supreme One who reigns on high.'

He established us in the castle, disinterestedly returned Dalville's mistress to her various household duties and gave my companion and me places in the workshop where we occupied ourselves in trimming the coins – which was a far less fatiguing job, and one for which we were recompensed with admirable rooms and excellent food. After a couple of months Dalville's successor – who was named Roland – acquainted us with the happy arrival of his colleague in Venice. He had already established himself there, realising his fortune, and was enjoying all the prosperity he had flattered himself he would find.

His successor should certainly have enjoyed the same kind of good fortune. But the unfortunate Roland was upright and of a kindly disposition, which qualities were quite sufficient for him promptly to be crushed. One day when tranquillity reigned over the castle – when, under the régime of this good master, the work, although criminal, was pleasurably and easily achieved – all at once the walls were beseiged. Unable to make use of the drawbridge our attackers scaled the moat, and before our men had even time to dream of defending themselves the house was filled with more than a hundred cavaliers of the horse-police. We were obliged to surrender. We were all chained like beasts, placed on horses, and taken to Grenoble.

'Oh, Heaven,' I thought, as we entered the town, 'here I am at last in the place where I had the folly to believe that happiness would be born for me!'

The trial of the counterfeiters soon came to an end. Every one of them was condemned to be hung. When my captors saw the mark of the branding iron on me they almost ceased to question me, and I was about to be condemned with the others. But I attempted to arouse some pity in a famous magistrate who dwelt in the city. He was the glory of all courts, a judge of integrity, a cherished citizen, and an enlightened philosopher whose celebrated and honourable name will for ever remain engraved, by his benevolence and humanity, on the walls of the temple of Memory! He listened to me . . . He did more, for convinced of my good faith and the truth of my misfortunes, he even consoled me with his own tears. Oh, greatest of men, to whom I owe my homage, grant to my heart the right to offer its thanks to you. The gratitude of an unfortunate such as I should not be burdensome to you; and the tribute I offer in honouring your warmth of heart will always remain one of the sweetest joys of my existence.

Monsieur S— actually became my advocate! My complaints were heard, my sobs penetrated the souls of those who listened, and my tears flowed over hearts which were certainly not made of steel, but which his generosity had completely opened to me. The general evidence presented by the criminals who were to be executed was in my favour, and thus strengthened the zeal of this man who had so wholeheartedly interested himself in my welfare. It was declared that I had been the prisoner of malefactors, and was thus innocent. Thus given a clean sheet and freed from all accusation of every kind, I had complete and absolute liberty to become whatever I wished. My protector increased these blessings by making a collection for me and I found myself in possession of nearly a hundred pistoles. At last I seemed to be seeing happiness in store for me, and my most deeply felt desires seemed about to be realised. I believed my misfortunes were over; but then it pleased providence once more to convince me that I still had far to travel.

*  *  *

On leaving prison I went to lodge at an inn which faced the Pont d'Isère. I was assured that I would be decently received in this house; and it was my intention, on the advice of Monsieur S—, to stay there for a while so that I might try and find work in the town. If I did not succeed I would return to Lyons with the letters of recommendation which he had so kindly given me.

Eating in this inn at what was known as the *table de l'hôte*, I noticed on the second day that I was being closely observed by a plump, well-dressed woman, who gave herself the title of Baroness. Examining her in my turn, I seemed to recognise her. Mutually we approached one another, and embraced like two people who know each other but cannot remember where they met. The rotund Baroness eventually took me aside and said: 'Am I mistaken, Sophie? Aren't you the girl I saved from the conciergerie ten years ago? And don't you remember la Dubois?'

Though little pleased by this discovery, I answered politely. But I was dealing with the most cunning and adroit woman in all France. There was no means of escaping her. La Dubois overwhelmed me with kindness and attention, telling me that she, like the other inhabitants of this city, had been most interested in my case but had not known at the time that it was I who was involved. Weak-willed, as usual, I let her take me to her room, where I told her of all my latest misfortunes.

'My dear friend,' she exclaimed as she embraced me again, 'if I wish to see you thus intimately, it is only to tell you that my fortune is made and all that I have is at your service!'

'Look!' she said, as she opened some caskets brimming with gold and diamonds, 'here are the fruits of my industry. If, like you, I had burned my incense at the feet of virtue, today I would either be hanged or in prison.'

'Oh, Madame,' I cried, 'if you obtained these things only by way of crime, providence, who always ends by being just, will not let you enjoy them for long . . .'

'There you are deceiving yourself,' said la Dubois, 'for you must not always suppose that providence is so partial to virtue. In your moment of temporary prosperity do not let yourself be plunged into such an error of reasoning. It is a matter of no importance in the maintenance of providence's laws that one man should be vicious while another adheres to virtue. She needs equal quantities of vice and virtue and is absolutely indifferent as to whether an individual chooses the one course or the other.

'Listen to me, Sophie – give me a little of your attention, for you are intelligent, and I think that in the long run I can convince you. It is not the choice which a man makes between vice and virtue which ultimately opens his door to happiness my dear; for virtue, like vice, is just a way of conducting oneself in the world. It is not a case of following either the one or the other but, rather, a question of following the common route. The man who strays from it is always wrong and liable to injure himself. In a world which was entirely virtuous I would advise you to be virtuous, because such conduct would then bring its natural recompense, happiness dancing infallible attendance upon it. But in a world totally corrupted I can never advise anything but vice. The man who doesn't follow in the same road as others inevitably perishes. Everything he meets will bump into him, contrariwise, and he will necessarily eventually be broken.

'It is in vain that our laws seek to re-establish order and to lead men back to virtue. Men are too vicious to attempt such a rehabilitation and too weak to succeed. Such laws may cause one momentarily to deviate from the beaten track, but they will never make him permanently leave it. When the common interests of men carry them forward into corruption, the man who would avoid becoming corrupted with the others will thus be fighting against the common interest. And what happiness can be expected by anyone who perpetually opposes the interests of others? Are you going to tell me that it is vice which opposes the general interest of mankind? I would grant you such a proposition if the world were composed equally of vicious and virtuous people, because, under such circumstances, the interests of one group would visibly conflict with those of the other. But this is no longer possible in a society which is corrupt from top to bottom. In such a society my vices exert their effects only upon others who are vicious, determining them to indulge in other and compensatory vices – thus all of us are content.

'The vibration becomes general, consisting of a multitude of shocks and mutual injuries whereby each one gains in an instant what he has just lost, thus finding himself in a perpetually happy position. Vice is only dangerous to virtue because, feeble and intimidated, she never dares to retaliate. But if virtue was banished from the face of the earth, vice, outraging only the vicious, would bother nobody. One vice might bring to light another, but in doing so it would not disturb virtue. And supposing anyone should object to this, stressing the good which results from virtue? That is merely another sophism, for the so called benefits of virtue have never served any but the weak, being useless to those whose strength and energy make them self-sufficient and who need but their own skill in order to redress the caprices of fate. How could you expect anything other than continual failure through-out your life, dear girl, when you have ceaselessly taken the contrary direction on the road which all men follow? If, like me, you had abandoned yourself wholeheartedly to the current, you would finally have arrived in port. Can the man who swims against the current arrive as quickly as he who swims with it? The one opposes nature; the other lets go and abandons himself to it! You are always prattling to me of providence; but wherein lies your proof that she loves order – and consequently virtue? Isn't she always presenting you with examples of her injustices and her irregularities? Is it because she has sent men not only war, but famine and pestilence, and because she has created a universe vicious in every aspect that you find her manifesting her extreme love of virtue? And why do you claim that vicious individuals displease her, since she herself acts only through vice – since everything, both in her will and in her works, is crime, corruption, vice and disorder?

'And from whom, other than her, do we receive those promptings which lead us into evil? Is it not her voice which whispers them to us? Are there any of our wishes or sensations which do not come from her? Can you then say it is reasonable for her to let us have – or stimulate our desires for – things which would be useless to her? If, then, vice serves her why should we wish to oppose it? By what right should we strive to destroy it, and by what means should we resist its voice? A little more philosophy in the world would soon put things to rights, making it clear to legislators and magistrates that these vices which they blame and punish with so much rigour sometimes have a much greater degree of utility that the virtues they preach yet never reward.'

'But were I weak enough to accept this frightful system, Madame,' I replied to this woman who wished to corrupt me, 'how would you teach me to stifle the remorse which would spring up, instant by instant, in my heart?'

'Remorse is a chimera, Sophie,' answered Dubois. 'It is nothing but the imbecile murmur of a soul so weak that it dare not kill its own imaginings.'

'Is it possible to kill it?'

'Nothing could be easier! Repentance is an emotion one only feels for actions to which one is unaccustomed. If you repeat frequently enough those things which bring you remorse, you will finally extinguish it. Oppose it with the torch of the passions, with the powerful laws of self-interest – then it will quickly disappear. Remorse does not prove anything to be a crime. It merely indicates an easily subjugated soul. If some authority should present you with an absurd order that for the moment you were not to leave this room, you would not leave it without feelings of remorse however certain you were that there would be no evil in doing so.

'It is, therefore, untrue that remorse is caused only by crime. By oneself of the nullity of crime, of its necessity in the general plan of nature, it becomes a simple enough thing to vanquish the remorse one might feel in com-mitting it – just as simple as it would be to stifle the guilt you might feel were you to leave this room after receiving an unjustifiable order to remain in it. It is necessary to begin with an exact analysis of that which men call crime, convincing oneself from the start that it is only the infringement of national laws and customs that is meant. What is defined as crime in France ceases to be such a few hundred miles away. There is no action universally considered as a crime over the whole face of the earth. Consequently nothing, at bottom, reasonably merits the name of crime. It is all just a matter of geography and opinion.

'With that much admitted, it becomes absurd to want to submit oneself to the practice of virtues which elsewhere are vices, and to flee from criminal actions which, in another climate, are esteemed as virtues. Consider care-fully what I have said and then let me ask you if a man who – either for pleasure or interest – performs in France one of the virtues of China or Japan (but which in his own country is looked upon as a dishonourable act) should feel any remorse? Should he allow this vile distinction to prevent his action? And if he has a little philosophy in his spirit, will it be capable of making him feel remorse? But if remorse exists only as a form of prohibition, is born only from the overthrow of restraint – and not at all from the action in itself – is it truly wise to permit such an emotion to thrive within oneself? Isn't it absurd not to stamp it out immediately?

'A man should accustom himself to looking with indifference upon those actions which have caused him remorse. He should judge them only by way of an intensive study of the manners and customs of all the nations in the world. Subsequently he should repeat such actions as often as possible – whatever they may be – and the bright flame of reason will quickly destroy any lingering of remorse. It will annihilate this tenebrous influence which is merely the fruit of ignorance, pusillanimity, and education.

'For thirty years, Sophie, a perpetual indulgence in vice and crime has led me step by step towards fortune. I'm touching it now! Another two or three lucky shots and I shall have left far behind me that miserable state of mendacity into which I was born, replacing it by an income of more than fifty thousand livres. Do you imagine that, throughout a career which I have pursued with brilliance, remorse has even for a single moment made me feel the prick of its thorns? Don't believe such a thing is possible with me, for I have never known it! Within an instant some frightful reverse might suddenly plunge me from the pinnacle into the abyss – yet I would never admit it! I would blame either other people or my own clumsiness, but I would always be at peace with my conscience . . . '

'That may be,' I replied. 'But let me reason with you for a moment upon these same philosophical principles. By what right do you pretend to claim that my own conscience should be as strong as yours, since it has not been accustomed from childhood to vanquishing similar prejudices? By what virtue do you demand that my spirit, organised differently from your own, should be able to adopt the same systems? You admit that there are equal quantities of good and evil in nature, and that consequently there must be a certain number of beings practising the one with a second class of persons devoted to the other. The part which I play, even according to your own reasoning, is thus quite within the bounds of nature. I must therefore ask you not to insist that I depart from those rules which nature has laid down for me; for just as you find happiness in the career you follow, it would be equally impossible for me to find it outside my own special path. Besides, you must not imagine that the vigilance of the law leaves transgressors untouched for any length of time. Haven't you just seen such an example with your very eyes? Don't you remember the fifteen criminals with whom I had the misfortune to live? One is saved and fourteen perish ignominiously!'

'Is that what you would call misfortune? Anyway, what does this ignominy mean to an individual without principles? When one has left everything behind, when honour has become nought but a prejudice, reputation a chimera, and the future an illusion, isn't it a matter of indifference whether one dies in prison, or on one's bed at home? There are two species of criminal in this world. One, backed by a powerful fortune and prodigious influence, can escape a tragic end. The other, if he is caught, will suffer. Yet, born with nothing, such a man must, if he is intelligent, have only two points of view: a fortune, or the wheel. If he manages to obtain the first then he has what he has always desired. If he is condemned to the second, what has he to regret since he has nothing to lose?

'It is for these reasons that the laws are powerless over criminals – they have, in fact, no existence for such men. The powerful and wealthy are able to escape the arm of the law; while the poor and unfortunate, having no choice but to live by their wits, cannot afford to be frightened by it!'

'Don't you believe that in the next world heaven's justice awaits those who have had the effrontery to indulge in crime on earth?'

'I believe that if there were a God there would be less evil on this earth. I also believe that if evil exists in our world then its disorders are necessitated by this God, or it is beyond his power to prevent them. But I can't be at all frightened of a God who is either weak or wicked. I defy him without any fear and laugh at his thunderings.'

'You make me tremble, Madame,' I said, as I rose to my feet. 'Forgive me if I cannot listen any longer to your execrable sophisms and your odious blasphemies!'

'Wait, Sophie; if I can't conquer your reasoning at least I may be able to tempt the feelings of your heart. I need you, therefore don't refuse me your help. Here are a hundred louis. Under your very eyes I lay them aside. They belong to you, as soon as the blow is struck!'

Listening to nothing but my natural tendency towards goodness, I asked la Dubois what this was all about – so that, with everything in my power, I might prevent whatever crime she was intending to commit.

'Here we are, then,' she said. 'Have you noticed the young merchant from Lyons who has been eating with us for the past three days?'

'Who? – Dubreuil?'

'Precisely!'

'What of it?'

'He is in love with you, and confided the fact to me. He has six hundred thousand francs, either in gold or on paper, which he keeps in a very small box near his bed. Let me lead this man to believe that you will consent to listen to him. It doesn't matter to you whether it is true or not! I'll suggest that he asks you to go for a stroll with him in some pleasant spot outside the town, implying that this will give him an excellent opportunity to increase his chances with you. It'll be up to you to amuse him, and keep him away from here as long as possible. In the meanwhile I shall rob him, but I shan't run away. His belongings will be sent to Turin but I shall remain in Grenoble.

'We shall employ every possible means to divert his suspicions, going even as far as helping him try to find the culprits. Then I shall announce my departure, which won't surprise him in the least; after which you can follow me and your hundred louis will be handed to you in Piedmont.'

'Yes, I'll do it, Madame,' I said to la Dubois, quite determined to warn the unfortunate Dubreuil of the infamous trick she was about to play on him.

And, the better to deceive this vicious woman, I added: 'Madame, you should reflect well on the fact that if Dubreuil is in love with me, I can extract from him much more money than you offer me – simply by warning him of your intentions or selling myself to him!'

'That is true,' answered Dubois. 'Honestly, I'm beginning to believe that heaven has blessed you with an even greater perspicacity in crime than my own. Ah, well,' she continued as she wrote, ' – here is my note for a thousand louis. Refuse me now, if you dare!'

'Under the circumstances, certainly not, Madame!' I said as I accepted the bill. 'But you must attribute my error in making this agreement only to my unfortunate condition, to my weakness of will, and to the need I feel for returning the help you once gave me.'

'I wanted to compliment you on your intelligence,' answered Dubois, 'but I see that you prefer me to accuse your misfortune. It shall be as you wish. Serve me always and you shall be content!'

Everything was arranged; and that same evening I commenced to make a little play at Dubreuil, realising immediately that he had some liking for me.

Nothing could have been more embarrassing than such a situation. I had no intention whatever of lending myself to the proposed crime, even had there been three times the amount of money in it for me. Yet I was utterly revolted by the thought of sending to the gallows a woman who, ten years previously, had gained me my liberty. I wanted to prevent the crime without the necessity of denouncing her. And had I been dealing with any but such an accomplished criminal as la Dubois I would surely have succeeded. Such was my aim; but I was unaware that the crafty manoeuvres of this abominable creature not only would cause the entire edifice of my honest intentions to crumble, but would also punish me for having conceived them.

On the day set apart for the intended rendezvous la Dubois invited us both to dine in her private room. We accepted, and when the meal was over Dubreuil and I descended to hasten the preparation of the carriage which we had ordered. As she did not accompany us I found myself alone for an instant with my escort.

'Monsieur,' I said precipitately, 'listen to me very carefully – don't attract any attention, whatever you do; and above all follow my instructions rigorously! Have you a friend at this inn?'

'Yes, I have a young associate whom I can trust as though he were myself . . .'

'Well, Monsieur, go quickly and tell him not to leave your room for a moment while we are away!'

'But I have locked my room and have the key in my pocket! Why this additional precaution?'

'It is much more essential than you may think, Monsieur! Please do as I say, or I shall not go with you. The woman whose room we have just left is one of the most vicious of criminals. It was she who engineered this outing in order that she might rob you the more easily. Hurry, Monsieur – she is watching us, and she is most dangerous. She mustn't guess that I have said anything to you. Give your key immediately to your friend, telling him to wait for us in your room with some companions if this is possible. And it is important that they must stay there, never leaving the place vacant, until we return. I will explain the why and the wherefore as soon as we are in the carriage . . .'

Dubreuil listened to me, pressing my hand with gratitude. Then he ran back to the inn to carry out my suggestions. When he returned we set off in our carriage and I was able to explain the entire situation to him. The young man pledged me every possible gratitude for the service I had rendered him. Then, having obliged me to tell him the truth concerning my situation, he swore that nothing he had learned of my adventures would deter him from offering me both his hand and his fortune.

'Our rank is equal,' Dubreuil said to me. 'I am a merchant's son, just as you are a merchant's daughter. My business has proved very successful, but your life has been most unfortunate. I should therefore be more than happy if I could make amends to you for the wrongs which fate has brought you. Consider my proposal carefully, Sophie! I am my own master and depend on no one else. I am on my way to Geneva, where I shall make considerable investments with those sums which your thoughtful warning has enabled me to save from thieving hands. You must follow me there, and on your arrival I shall become your husband. Thenceforward you will appear in Lyons only as my wife.'

Such a delightful experience flattered me so much that I dared not even consider refusing it. Yet it was scarcely seemly to accept without first acquainting Dubreuil with matters which might later cause him regret. He was more than pleased with my honesty, pressing me more insistently than ever to marry him . . . Unfortunate creature that I was; it seemed that whenever happiness was offered me I should feel only more vividly the pain caused by my inability to seize it. It seemed, indeed, one of providence's unwritten yet most definite decrees, that never should a virtue open its buds within my heart without precipitating me into suffering and wretchedness! Our conversation had already taken us more than two miles out of town, and we were about to alight from the carriage to enjoy the freshness of a walk through some of those beautiful green alleys which grace the banks of the Isèhe – when suddenly Dubreuil told me that he felt terribly ill . . . As soon as we had left our seats he was seized with the most frightful attack of vomiting. Immediately I made him get back into the carriage and we returned at the utmost speed towards Grenoble. The young man was so desperately ill that he had to be carried up to his room. The state he was in absolutely astonished his friends who, following his orders, had never left his apartment. I didn't leave him for a moment . . . A doctor arrived and, merciful heaven, when the diagnosis had been made it was found that Dubreuil had been poisoned . . . Scarcely did I learn this dreadful news than I flew to the room of la Dubois . . . The vicious creature had gone . . . Running to my own room I found my wardrobe had been forced open and what little money and clothing I possessed had been stolen; la Dubois, I was informed, had departed three hours earlier having boarded the stage to Turin . . .

There could be no doubt whatever but that she was the author of this multitude of crimes. She had gone to the young man's room and, enraged at finding it occupied by his friends, had avenged herself upon me. She had poisoned Dubreuil during the dinner so that, had she succeeded in her schemes, he being much more concerned with the saving of his life than with pursuing her, she would be able to escape in safety. Moreover, as he would almost certainly die – so to speak – in my arms, I would be much more open to suspicion than herself. I quickly ran back to Dubreuil but was not allowed to approach him. He expired, surrounded by his friends, completely exonerating me and assuring them of my innocence. He forbade them, above all, to involve me in any prosecution. Hardly had he closed his eyes than his associate hastened to bring me this news, assuring me that I had no reason to be disturbed . . .

Alas, how could I refrain from weeping bitterly at the loss of the only man who, since the commencement of my misfortunes, had so generously offered to lift me out of them! . . . How could I cease deploring a theft which plunged me back into that fatal abyss of misery from which it seemed that I should never be able to extricate myself? I confided everything to Dubreuil's business associate, telling him all about the plot against his friend and then all that had been done to myself. He sympathised with me deeply, bitterly regretting the death of his friend and criticising the excess of delicacy which had prevented me from lodging an immediate complaint against la Dubois once I had learned the details of her project. We were perfectly aware that this horrible creature, who needed but four hours to be in safety, would already have reached her destination before we could arrange the details for her pursuit. Such a pursuit would certainly have been costly; and the inn keeper, doubtless much compromised by the complaints I might lodge, would most certainly have made a considerable noise in his own defence – which might perhaps have resulted in crushing completely a person known in Grenoble only as someone discharged after a criminal trial and relying entirely upon public charity for her subsistence . . .

These reasons so convinced and terrified me that I resolved to leave without saying goodbye to Monsieur S—, my protector. Dubreuil's friend fully approved of my leaving in this way, and he made no attempt to hide from me the fact that, should the adventure come to light, the depositions he would necessarily have to make would undoubtedly compromise me, whatever precautions he took – just as much because of my relationship with la Dubois as because of my drive with his friend. So it was natural that he should urge me to leave Grenoble immediately without seeing anyone, assuring me, for his own part, that he would never instigate any form of action against me.

Meditating in private on the entire affair, I was obliged to admit to myself that the young man's advice was especially pertinent, for it was quite certain that I looked just as guilty as I was actually innocent. For the only thing which might be cited in my favour – the warning I had given Dubreuil, incompletely explained by him as he was dying – was perhaps not so incontrovertible a proof as I had hoped. It did not take me long to make my decision and I quickly communicated it to Dubreuil's associate.

'I only wish,' he said, 'that my friend had instructed me to make some arrangements which would really be helpful for you. Had he done so I would have carried them out with the deepest pleasure. I also wish he had been able to tell me that it was due to your intervention that he placed a guard in his room while out on his excursion with you. But he wasn't able to do so. He only repeated over and over again that you were completely innocent and that we must avoid prosecuting you in any way whatsoever.

'I am therefore obliged to confine myself to carrying out such orders as he left. The losses you have suffered in helping him suggest that I should do something myself to help you, Madamoiselle. But I am just starting my own business, and as I am young my finances are extremely limited. Not a sou of Dubreuil's money belonged to me and I am obliged to return it all to his family. Nevertheless, Sophie, perhaps you will permit me to do the best I can for you, however small the amount. Here are five louis – and here,' he said, calling into the room a woman whom I had noticed previously in the inn, ' – here is an honest shop keeper from my own town – Chalon-sur-Saône. She is returning home after a day spent in Lyons on business.'

'Madame Bertrand,' said the young man as he presented her to me, 'here is a young lady whom I recommend to your protection. She would very much like to find work in the country; and I beg you, as though you were my agent in the matter, to do everything in your power to find her a suitable place in our town – one befitting her birth and education. Do not request anything of her until this has been done. I shall take care of everything next time I see you . . . Until then, goodbye, Sophie . . . Madame Bertrand is leaving tonight. Go with her, and may good luck follow you in a town where I shall soon, I hope, have the pleasure of seeing you again – and of proving to you, for the remainder of my life, the gratitude I feel for the sincerity of your behaviour with Dubreuil.'

The kindness of this young man, who really owed me nothing, caused me, despite myself, to start weeping. I accepted his gifts gladly, swearing to him that I should work only for that day when I would be able to repay his gestures. 'Alas,' I said to myself as I left him, 'if the exercise of another virtue has precipitated me once more into misfortune, at least – and for the first time in my life – a little consolation has been offered me in this terrifying chasm of evil wherein virtue herself has thrown me.' I did not see my young benefactor again, and I left, as had been arranged with la Bertrand on the night after Dubreuil's unfortunate end.

La Bertrand has a little covered carriage drawn by a horse, and we took turns in driving it from inside. Therein were her belongings, together with a reasonable sum of money and a little girl of eighteen months whom she was still nursing. I became equally as much attached to this child as was the mother who had given her life.

Madame Bertrand was a kind of fish-wife, as deficient in education as she was in intelligence. She was suspicious, gossiping, boring, and narrow-minded – as almost all working-class women seem to be. Every evening we removed all her goods from the little carriage, took them into whatever inn we happened to be staying at and kept them with us in our room while we slept. Nothing extraordinary occurred until we arrived in Lyons, but on one of the two days which this women needed for her business there I experienced a very singular encounter. I was walking along the quay which borders the Rhône, accompanied by one of the girls from the inn – whom I had asked to accompany me – when suddenly I saw coming towards us the Reverend Father Antonin, butcher of my virginity, now one of the Superiors of this city and, as you will remember, known so well to me when my unfortunate star led me to the little monastery of Sainte-Marie-des-Bois. He accosted me in cavalier fashion, asking me in front of the servant-girl if I wouldn't like to come and see him in his new residence, there to indulge once more our former pleasures.

Such a conversation made me blush prodigiously, and for a moment I tried to make him think he had mistaken my identity. Not succeeding, however, I attempted to convey to him by signs that he ought at least to contain himself in front of my guide. But nothing affected this insolent creature and his solicitations only became the more pressing. At length, on our repeated refusals to follow him, he contented himself with asking for our address. In order to get rid of him I gave him a false one. Noting it down in his pocket-book he left us, assuring us that we should be seeing him very soon.

The girl and I retraced our steps. On our way I did my best to explain to her the story of this unfortunate acquaintance, but whether my words proved unsatisfactory, or perhaps because of the girl's natural need to chatter, I later realised from certain words of la Bertrand – uttered at the time of the dreadful adventure which was to befall me with her – that she had been informed of my acquaintance with this villainous monk. Nevertheless, we did not see him again and shortly afterwards left the city. Departing from Lyons late that day, we did not reach Villefranche until evening. And it was there, Madame, that I met with the horrible catastrophe which, today, must make me seem a criminal in your eyes. Yet I remain no more a criminal in this present disastrous situation than I was in those which I have already related to you. Nothing but the sentiment of kindness – which I have never been able to extinguish from my heart – has led me to this abyss of misfortune, this repeated suffering under the unjust blows of fate.

It was six o'clock one February evening when we arrived at Villefranche, where we took a hurried supper, retiring early to bed so that we might cover even more ground on the following day. We hadn't been asleep more than two hours when frightful clouds of smoke began to fill our room, immediately arousing each of us with a start! We couldn't possibly doubt but that the fire was nearby . . . Merciful heaven! – its progress was already terrifying. Almost naked, we opened our door, hearing nothing but the crash of tumbling walls, the frightful noise of splitting timbers, and the blood-curdling howls of the unlucky wretches who fell into that blazing inferno. Countless tongues of these devouring flames lashed towards us, scarcely leaving us time to throw ourselves into the street. We found ourselves in the midst of a crowd of unfortunates who, naked as ourselves and some of them half-roasted, had sought their safety in flight . . .

It was at that moment I remembered that Madame Bertrand, more concerned with saving her own life than with snatching her daughter from death, had left the child behind. Without a word to her I flew through the flames and up to our room. Blinded and burned as I was I seized the poor little creature and ran to hand her to her mother. Leaning for a moment against a half-consumed beam I lost my footing and automatically stretched out my hand to save myself. This natural movement caused me to drop the precious bundle I was holding and the unfortunate little girl fell into the flames under her mother's very eyes! The terrible woman, thinking neither of my attempt to save her child nor of the state in which my fall had left me, but carried away by the delirium and pain of her loss, accused me of the death of her daughter and, impetuously throwing herself on top of me, overwhelmed me with her blows.

Meanwhile the course of the fire was arrested, concerted labour having saved almost half of the inn. Madame Bertrand's first care was to return to her room, which happened to be one of those least damaged. She renewed her complaints, telling me I should have left her daughter where she was, for then she would not have risked danger. But you can imagine what happened to her when, looking for her possessions, she found that they had all been stolen! Her rage and her despair were terrible to hear, and she openly accused me of having caused the fire purposely so that I might rob her with greater ease. She told me she was going to denounce me and very quickly put her threat into effect by asking to speak to the local judge.

Well might I protest my innocence; yet she wouldn't listen to a word! The magistrate was not far away, for it was he who had ordered and organised the fighting of the fire, and he appeared almost immediately on the request of this wicked woman . . . She lodged her complaint against me, supporting it with every piece of evidence she could think of, and, describing me as a girl of loose morals who had escaped the hangman's rope at Grenoble, said that my company had been forced on her by a young man whose mistress I must doubtless be. She spoke of the monk at Lyons, and forgot no calumny which might be suggested by a vengeance fostered by despair and poisoned with rage.

The judge received her complaint. The house was examined and it was discovered that the blaze had commenced in a storehouse filled with hay. Several people testified that they had seen me going into it that evening, which was true. For, looking for a lavatory and being carelessly directed by the servants, I had wandered into this place, staying long enough to arouse suspicion. Thus the proceedings began, and were followed according to the strictest rule. The witnesses were heard but nothing I could say in my defence was ever listened to. It was shown that I must be the incendiary and proved that I had accomplices who, while I was at one end of the house, committed their theft at the other. Without being enlightened further I was taken at dawn next day to the prison at Lyons, where I was registered as an incendiary, child-murderer, and thief.

Being so long accustomed to slander, injustice, and misfortune – having felt from very childhood the thorns in every virtuous emotion – my pain was a dull stupefaction rather than an agonised rending, and I wept more than I complained. Nevertheless, as it is natural enough for a suffering creature to seek every means possible to extricate themselves from the abyss into which fate has plunged them, I could scarcely avoid letting the thought of Father Antonin enter my mind. However little help I might expect of him, I could not avoid a desire to see him, and therefore asked for him. As he did not know I had requested him, he appeared, affecting, nevertheless, not to recognise me. Then I told the concierge that he possibly didn't remember me, having directed my conscience when I was very young. On the strength of this I requested a private interview with him, which was granted. As soon as I was alone with the monk I threw myself at his feet and begged him to save me from the cruel position in which I found myself. I proved my innocence to him, nor did I hide from him the fact that his disgusting propositions of two days previously had completely destroyed my reputation in the eyes of the woman to whom I had been recommended.

The monk listened to me with considerable attention and scarcely had I finished when he said: 'Listen to me, Sophie, and don't comport yourself as you ordinarily do as soon as someone infringes your accursed prejudices. You see where your principles have led you. Now you have plenty of time in which to convince yourself that they have never served any other purpose than to plunge you from one abyss into another. Cease from following them one step further if you wish to save your life. As for that, I see only one method that will succeed. We have with us a Father who is closely related both to the Governor and to the Prison Commissioner. I shall inform him concerning the facts. You must say that you are his niece, then by reclaiming you as such and giving his promise that you will remain in a convent for life, we will almost certainly be able to prevent proceedings from progressing further. You will disappear. He will place you in my care and I shall undertake the responsibility of hiding you until suitable circumstances permit me to restore you to liberty. But you will be entirely mine during this detention. I am not attempting to hide the fact from you. You will submit yourself absolutely to my caprices, abandoning yourself utterly to their gratification. You understand what that means, Sophie? – You know me, and you have your choice between this and the scaffold. I shan't wait for your answer!'

'Go away, Father!' I replied with horror. 'Go away! You are a monster so cruelly to abuse my situation, and to give me only the choice between death and infamy! Leave me here. I would rather die innocently, for then at least I should die without remorse!'

My resistance inflamed this traitorous wretch. He dared to show me the point to which his passion had been stimulated. The infamous lecher had dared to picture the caresses of love within the horror of the prison with its chains – beneath the very blade which was waiting to lay me low. I tried to escape him but he caught me, tumbling me over on the miserable straw which served as my bed. And if he did not entirely consummate his crime, at least he covered me with such revolting stains that it was impossible for me to doubt his abominable designs.

'Listen,' he said to me as he readjusted his habit. 'You don't want me to help you, so I'm going to abandon you. I shan't serve you, nor shall I hurt you in any way. But if you decide to say a single word against me, I shall charge you with the most enormous crimes and thus remove all possibility of your defending yourself. Reflect well on what I have said before you speak, and grasp the spirit of what I am about to say to the gaoler or I'll do away with you this very instant.'

He gave a knock and the concierge entered.

'Monsieur,' said this vicious monk, 'this good young woman is mistaken. She really wanted to speak with a Father Antonin from Bordeaux. I neither know him, nor have I ever heard of him. But she has asked me to hear her confession and I have done so. You are aware of our regulations – therefore I have nothing more to say. I bid you both good-day, and shall always be ready to present myself here when my ministrations shall be deemed necessary.'

Antonin left as he said these words, and I was as stupefied by his deceit as I was confounded by his insolence and lust.

The lower tribunals act very quickly. They are nearly always composed of idiots, of imbeciles and brutal fanatics of men who are sure that wiser and better informed eyes will correct the stupidities which they regularly commit. Thus was I unanimously condemned to death by eight or ten jumped-up little men who composed the respectable tribunal of this town of bankrupts. I was immediately sent to Paris for confirmation of my sentence. It was then that the most sad and bitter of thoughts began to assail and tear at my heart.

'Under what fatal star was it necessary that I should be born?' I murmured to myself. 'Why is it impossible for me to feel even a single virtuous sentiment without its promptly being followed by a deluge of trouble and suffering? And how can it be that this radiant providence, whose justice I have been pleased to adore, has not only punished me for my virtues but has, at the same time, raised to the very pinnacle of success those very people who have crushed me with their vices? During my childhood a money-lender tried to persuade me to steal. I refused him, but he grew rich and I was almost hanged. Some scoundrels would have raped me in a wood because I refused to join their gang. They prospered, but as for myself, I fell into the hands of a debauched Marquis who gave me a hundred strokes of the lash because I did not wish to poison his mother. After that a surgeon whom I prevented from committing an abominable crime, rewarded my efforts by mutilating me, branding me, and kicking me out on the street.

Though doubtless he committed other crimes, he made his fortune while I was forced to beg for bread. I wanted to draw near to the Holy Sacraments, fervently to implore the Supreme Being for His help. The sacred building where I had hoped to purify myself in one of our most holy mysteries became the terrifying theatre of my dishonour and ignominy. The monster who abused and polluted me was raised instantly to the highest honour, whilst I was cast back into the frightful abyss of my misery. I wanted to help a poor man, but he robbed me. I would have given help to a wounded and almost unconscious man, but the traitor made me turn a wheel like any beast of burden. He rained blows on me when my strength failed. Yet every possible favour was heaped on him – while I nearly lost my life because I had been forced into working for him. A worthless woman attempted to coax me into fresh crimes. Once more I lost the little I possessed in an attempt to save the fortune of her victim and preserve him from suffering. This young man would have rewarded me by giving me his hand in marriage – but he died in my arms. I exposed myself to considerable risk in a fire to save another woman's child – and here I am for the third time underneath the blade of Themis. Imploring the protection of a wretch who prostituted me, I had hoped to find him sensitive to my endless suffering. But the barbarian only offered his assistance at the price of renewed dishonour . . . Oh, providence, has the possibility of doubting your justice finally been granted me? Could I have been afflicted by any greater scourges, had I, like my persecutors, always worshipped at the altars of vice?'

\* \* \*

Such, Madame, were the blasphemies which, in spite of myself, I dared allow to pass my lips . . . They were torn from me by the horror of my fate. And then you deigned to let fall on me a glance filled with pity and compassion . . . I offer you a thousand apologies, Madame, for having so long abused your patience. I have reopened my wounds, I have troubled your repose – and that is the most either of us has gained from the recital of my cruel adventures. The morning star is high and my guards will shortly come to take me away. Let me run to meet death. I fear her no longer. She will cut short my torments for she will finish them completely. She is only to be feared by those fortunate beings whose days are filled with purity and serenity. But the unfortunate creature who has trodden only upon adders, whose bleeding feet have encountered little but thorns, who has known men only to hate them, and who has seen dawn light the sky only to detest it – she who has known the loss of parents, fortune, help, protection, friends, who has tears for her drink and tribulation for her nourishment – such an one, I say, is able to watch the approach of death without a shudder, wishing for it as a haven of safety where she will experience the rebirth of tranquillity in the bosom of a God who is too just to permit an innocence, humiliated and persecuted on earth, not to find in heaven the full reward of its tears.

# Chapter Five

The honest Monsieur de Corville had been deeply moved as he listened to this story. As for Madame de Lorsange (the monstrous errors of whose youth had not – as we have already said – entirely extinguished all sensitivity in her heart), she was on the point of fainting.

'Mademoiselle,' she said to Sophie. 'It is impossible to listen to you without being profoundly interested in your case . . . But I must admit to you that an inexplicable feeling, even stronger than interest, draws me invincibly towards you and makes me feel your sufferings as though they were my own. You have not told me your name, Sophie, and you have concealed the details of your birth. I must beg you to unbare your secret before me. Please do not think that it is merely vain curiosity that causes me to speak thus. If what I suspect is true . . . Oh, Justine, if you were my sister!'

'Justine, Madame? . . . What a name!'

'She would be your age today!'

'Oh, Juliette, is it you that I hear!' exclaimed the unhappy prisoner as she threw herself into the arms of Madame de Lorsange . . . 'You, my sister, merciful God . . . What blasphemy have I uttered? I have even doubted providence! . . . Ah, I shall die infinitely less miserably since I have been permitted to embrace you once again!'

And the two sisters, closely pressed in each other's arms, expressed themselves to each other only in sobs, spoke only in tears . . . Monsieur de Corville could not restrain his own; and seeing that it would be quite impossible for him not to take the greatest interest in this affair, he immediately retired to his study. There he wrote to the Keeper of the Seals, painting in strokes of blood the terrible fate of the unfortunate Justine. He guaranteed her innocence, begging, until she could be retried, that her only prison should be his château; and he pledged himself as her representative before the Supreme Officer of Justice. As soon as the letter was written he handed it to two cavaliers of the guard, ordering them to deliver it immediately and to return to his house for their prisoner should the Chief of the Magistrature demand it. These two men, seeing with whom they were dealing, had no fear of compromising themselves in obeying his orders. Meanwhile a carriage had drawn up . . .

'Come, beautiful but unfortunate creature,' said Monsieur de Corville to Justine, ' – come! Everything has changed for you in the past quarter of an hour. Never shall it be said that your virtue did not find its reward here below, or that you never met with any hearts but those fashioned from steel . . . Follow me! You are my prisoner now, and no one other than myself shall answer for you!' Then in a few words he explained what he had done . . .

'You wonderful man! You are as generous as you are influential!' exclaimed Madame de Lorsange, as she threw herself at her lover's knees. 'This is the most magnificent act you have ever performed. And it is for you, who truly know the heart of mankind and the spirit of the law, to avenge persecuted innocence, to help those who are overwhelmed by fate . . . Go, Justine, go! . . . run immediately to kiss the feet of this equitable protector, who will never abandon you as the others have done! Oh, Monsieur, if our love was previously precious to me, how much more so is it now, embellished by the knots of nature and closely tied by the most tender affection!'

And the two women struggled with each other to clasp the knees of so generous a friend, watering them with their tears. Monsieur de Corville and Madame de Lorsange took the keenest delight in taking Justine from the excessive hardships of her previous life to the very heights of prosperity and luxury. Delightedly they fed her on the most succulent of dishes, gave her the softest of beds, and presented her with complete freedom of command over all they owned. In all this they manifested the extreme delicacy which one expects in two such sensitive souls . . . They supplied her with medicinal remedies for several days, bathed her, dressed her, and adorned her exquisitely. Both of these two lovers adored her. They even competed with each other as to who would first be successful in causing her to forget her misfortunes. A specialist was called in so that he might, with skilled treatment, remove the ignominious mark which Rodin had left upon her. Everything succeeded according to the wishes of Madame de Lorsange and her intelligent lover. Already the traces of misfortune were effaced from the charming brow of the amiable Justine . . . Already the graces were re-establishing their empire over her. To the livid tint of her alabaster cheeks succeeded the roses of springtime. And laughter, absent so long from those lips, reappeared at last, borne on the wings of pleasure.

*       *       *

Soon the most wonderful news arrived from Paris. Monsieur de Corville had agitated the whole of France, reviving the zeal of Monsieur S—, who joined hands with him in painting the sufferings of Justine; and together they did their utmost to bring to her that tranquillity she so much deserved. Eventually letters arrived from the King himself clearing the young woman completely of every charge and of all proceedings brought against her since childhood. He restored her to her rightful position as an honest citizen, imposing a permanent and enduring silence upon every court in the country that had conspired against her. Above and beyond all this he granted her an annuity of twelve hundred livres to be derived from the funds seized in the workshop of the counterfeiters of Dauphiné. When she heard such agreeable news Justine almost fainted with delight. During several days she shed the sweetest of tears over the breasts of her protectors; until, quite suddenly, her mood changed, without anyone being able to divine the cause. She became melancholy, disquieted, dreamy, and sometimes wept before her friends, without even being able to explain the cause of her tears.

'I was not born for such a full measure of happiness,' she often said to Madame de Lorsange . . . 'Oh, my dear sister, it is impossible for such joy to last!'

Every attempt had been made to prove to her that her sufferings were over, that she no longer had the slightest cause for anxiety. It was pointed out what meticulous care had been exercised in drawing up the official reports on her case, and how none of the individuals with whom she had been compromised had ever been named – thus removing any possibility of danger from their influence. Yet she remained inconsolable. Nothing could quiet her; and anyone observing her might have said that this poor girl, uniquely destined to experience misfortune and always sensing the hand of fate suspended above her head, already foresaw the final blow which was about to crush her.

Madame de Lorsange was still living in the country at this time. It was near the end of summer and an out-door excursion had been planned when a frightful storm broke loose. The excessive heat had obliged the inmates of the house to leave all the drawing-room windows wide open. The lightning flashed, the hail-stones fell, the wind blustered violently, and horrifying claps of thunder reverberated across the heavens . . . Madame de Lorsange, who was terrified of thunder, begged her sister to close the windows as quickly as she could. Monsieur de Corville entered the room just as she made this request; and Justine, anxious to calm her sister, flew to the windows, trying for a moment to fight against the wind which pushed her back. At that instant a tongue of lightning, streaking into the room with a noisy crash, threw her backwards in her own steps and left her lifeless on the floor.

A lamentable shriek escaped from Madame de Lorsange . . . and then she fainted. Monsieur de Corville called for help, dividing the attentions of his domestics equally between the two sisters. Madame de Lorsange was quickly brought back to consciousness but the unfortunate Justine had been struck in such a fashion as left no hope for her. The lightning had entered by her right breast, consuming her bosom; and, leaving by her mouth, had so disfigured her features that she was horrible to look on. Monsieur de Corville wished to have the body removed immediately, but Madame de Lorsange, rising to her feet with the utmost calm, firmly opposed him.

'No,' she said to her lover. 'No! Leave her there where I can see her for a little while. I have need to contemplate her in order to strengthen myself in a resolution I have just made. Listen to me, Monsieur, and do not attempt to oppose in any way the course I am about to adopt, and from which nothing in the world can now dissuade me!

'The unheard of misfortunes experienced by this unhappy girl – despite the fact that she worshipped virtue above all – contain within themselves something so extraordinary, Monsieur, that they have opened my eyes on my own life. Do not imagine that I am blinded by the false gleams of felicity which, during the course of her adventures, we have seen enjoyed by the treacherous individuals who tormented her. Such caprices of fate are the enigmas of providence which we should not unveil and by which we must never allow ourselves to be seduced. The prosperity of the wicked is simply one of the means by which the Almighty proves our strength. It is like the lightning, the deceptive fires of which only illuminate the atmosphere for a moment so as to precipitate its unfortunate victim into the abyss of death . . . Here, before our eyes, is the very example! The uninterrupted calamities and terrible sufferings of this unfortunate girl are a warning sent to me by the Eternal, asking me to repent my irregular way of life, to listen to the voice of my remorse, and to throw myself at last into His arms. What dreadful treatment must I fear from Him! I, whose crimes would make you shudder were they known to you! . . . I, who have been marked at every step in my life by libertinism, irreligion and the absence of those principles I so prodigally discarded . . . What can I expect when she who is without sin – who had not a single crime with which to reproach her days – is treated thus?

'We must part, Monsieur, for I still have time . . . We are not tied by any legal bond. Forget me, and know that it is good and fitting thing that I go to repent eternally, abjuring at the feet of the Almighty all those infamies with which I am soiled. Sad as it may be, this frightful blow was nevertheless necessary to my conversion in this life and to that happiness for which I dare to hope in the life to come. Adieu, Monsieur, you will never see me again. As a final token of your friendship I beg that you will refrain from any sort of enquiry into what has become of me. I shall await you in a better world, where your virtues must assuredly conduct you. May the mortifications I shall undertake to expiate my crimes allow me, when my miserable years are over, to see you there again one day.'

Madame de Lorsange ordered a carriage to be got ready and left the house immediately. Taking a sum of money with her, she left all the remainder to be disposed of by Monsieur de Corville in pious donations. As quickly as possibly she sped to Paris, where she entered a Carmelite Convent; wherein, after very few years, she became the model and example, as much by her great piety as by her wisdom, her intelligence and the moral perfection of her behaviour. Monsieur de Corville, having long been worthy of the highest positions his country could offer, attained them at last. And from his honoured position worked for the happiness of the people, the glory of his sovereign and the fortune of his friends.

Oh you who read this story, may you draw from it the same profit as that worldly woman whom Heaven finally corrected. May you be convinced, with her, that true happiness is only to be found in the bosom of virtue, and that if God permits it to be persecuted here on earth, it is only to prepare for it a more flattering reward in Heaven.

*Completed, in fifteen days, on 8th July* 1787

# My Lustful Adventures

'RAMROD'

CHAPTER ONE

## A Nocturnal Meeting

The episode I am about to relate happened when I was still a very young man, not over-expert in the pursuit and methods of amorous pleasure, and with my tastes still crude and my powers only suspected and quite undeveloped. True, I had made acquaintance with the mysteries of the female form by the medium of an occasional rough and tumble with one of the maids, and later had been promoted to the dignity of rogering a willing friend of my sister's, but these damsels were all plain, not fancy, fuckers and had no idea of employing anything but a naked cunt for the delights of fornication. They seemed perfectly satisfied with a straightforward hump, and would certainly have been horror-stricken at the suggestion of those amenities in which I afterwards became a connoisseur.

My first awakening to the extended possibilities of coition came in this wise. Passing one night along a rather unfrequented thoroughfare I was fortunate enough to rescue two ladies from the grasp of a couple of roughs who had bailed them up intent on plunder. A quick dash and a hurried blow or two sent them off in a flurry and I turned to reassure the distressed beauties. One was a lady of ripe charms, with flowing figure and a face still handsome and attractive. The other was a charming girl of about nineteen, who proved to be her daughter. The elder woman, still well under forty, looked desirable enough to give any fellow a satisfactory cockstand.

They were profuse in their gratitude, not the less probably because they noticed I was young, scarcely more than a boy, and, as they were good enough to inform me afterwards, by no means bad-looking. They suggested I should accompany them home, which of course I was nothing loth to do. No young fellow dislikes being petted and made much of by a couple of amiable women. I hadn't the least idea, however, of the good fortune that awaited me.

When we arrived at the house, they would not hear of my leaving without entering. It was evident from the interior they were in easy circumstances and I ascertained they were the only occupants, except for the servants. Once inside, Mrs Aintree, as I will call her, embraced me warmly, kissed me repeatedly, and exclaimed, 'How can I thank you, my dear Mr Temple' (we had exchanged names on the way). 'You have saved us from being robbed and probably worse. We were too terrified by those hooligans to scream, for I feared if we did the brutes would knock us about, and very likely after they had plundered us we should have been thrown on our backs and ravished. Oh, to think of being mauled by those ruffians!'

The good lady shuddered, but somehow I already had a faint suspicion it was not the idea of being fucked out of hand she objected to so much as the fucksters.

In the full light I could better appraise the charms of my new friends. It certainly did not conduce to a feeling of monastic calm on my part to have a full, voluptuous bust pressed warmly against me or to perceive, when my arm went involuntarily round her waist, one leg gripped between a pair of solid thighs, and behind them a big, soft bottom. Nor was it likely to lead to excessive self-control to notice a handsome, well-built girl standing by with moist eyes, coral lips and flushed face, evidently highly approving and enjoying her mother's abandon. I, of course, modestly disclaimed having done anything in particular, and airily asserted those sort of fellows were ready enough to tackle lonely women but not a resolute man.

'That's all very well, but you know as well as I do they often carry knives or other weapons, and they might have used them if you hadn't been so quick. My goodness, Ethel, did you hear the sound when Mr Temple – by the way what is your Christian name . . . Harry, is it? – struck that rascal. I shouldn't like to have got the blow. And I could have laughed but for my fright when you caught the other fellow with your toe as he turned to run away. I hope he'll be sore after it. How strong you are, Harry, for Harry you must be to us – we feel quite like old friends already – what muscular arms' (feeling them admiringly). 'And a nice-looking boy, too, not much older than Ethel . . . yum . . . yum' (more kissing).

The moist, salacious lips gave me an indescribable emotion, and I feared that tangible evidence of its intensity would be only too manifest if this went on. I know I blushed, and the widow tapped my cheeks, laid her own against them, and rubbed them softly in a most endearing way, calling her daughter's attention at the same time to my confusion. Then to my relief she pushed me into a chair and, with Ethel, busied herself setting out some refreshments. This done she asked me to excuse her while she changed her dress (for the hot night and the emotion of her adventure made her long to escape from her tight-fitting garments), called Ethel to the door and exchanged a few words outside.

As I learned later what she said was: 'Ethel, my dear, we mustn't let him go. He is too young and good-looking to part with so easily. I don't think, from his blushes, he knows much about women, and we will give him a treat. But go modestly at first till we find whether he is of randy disposition or not, and if he is . . . ' She licked her lips significantly, squeezed her daughter's motte, and disappeared.

Ethel came back and without ceremony seated herself on my knees and pressed her lips to mine. 'Mamma has thanked you, and I can't do better to show you I am grateful, too, than follow her example.' She sat right up to my prick, which had long been in a state of repressed exaltation, and I could feel her plump bottom deliberately pressing upon it. Miss Ethel, from her weight, was evidently a solid-framed girl, and bade fair ultimately to rival, if not exceed, her mother's voluptuous proportions. I made free to squeeze her resilient bosoms, and was not repulsed. I returned her kisses with interest, and got the tip of her tongue slily inserted in my mouth as reward. Encouraged by this very loose conduct on the young lady's part, I was just about to have a grope – and Ethel seeing my design had thrown herself back to favour it – when Mrs Aintree, or Rose as she presently asked me to call her, returned. She was clad in a long wrapper, and had discarded corset and most of her undergarments to judge by the liberal curves now revealed.

'A charming picture – youth and beauty on both sides. That's right, Ethel – cuddle the dear lad. He deserves it.'

She filled bumpers of wine and we all drank heartily. Rose filled my glass again, insisting that a man must want more than a woman. I easily guessed her intention was to excite me, and a glimmering of the truth dawned upon me, but I had, as yet, no idea of the depth of the plot hatched at the door a few moments before.

'Now, Ethel, run and remove your dress, too. I am sure you must be hot.'

Ethel went off and her mother promptly took her place. A great soft mass of flesh pressed on my thighs, and spread out over each side of them. The insidious kisses rained upon me once more, and I could not help handling and then slily pinching the tempting arse. Rose smiled, lifted my hand, kissed it and put it in her bosom.

'There, dear, you may caress me freely; you will make me very happy and Ethel, too. Do you know, you rogue, somehow I feel if it had been you instead of those street vagabonds who had tried to take liberties with me I shouldn't have been able, or inclined, to offer much resistance. There is such a difference, you see, between a handsome young gentleman and scum like that.'

Thereupon I made bold to open the wrapper and gaze upon the magnificent bubbies over which my hand had been delightedly wandering. They poured out, full, warm, luscious and tantalising, and I buried my face furiously in the glowing flesh. A pair of fairly large but shapely teats surmounted the white orbs, and I sucked them greedily. The effect on the widow was rapid. She moved uneasily, grinding the tremendous bottom into my thighs, pressed my head spasmodically to her bosom and sighed. Into her eyes came a glazed look – the look of lust and lewdness that is familiar enough to me now. Her fingers twittered through my hair, played with my ears and neck, and then she burst out, 'I must kiss your naked flesh, too.' Feverishly she undid the buttons of the soft shirt I was wearing and fastened her lips on my neck.

At this moment Ethel returned. She, too, was in a wrapper and prepared for the fray. Her eyes gleamed as she saw the great milky bosoms hanging out and my face buried in them. She came at once to her mother's assistance.

'Isn't he charming, Ethel? Harry has been good enough to kiss me, oh! so nicely, as you see, and he is making me feel just lovely. And now I am going to kiss him there, too.'

Here was seduction reversed with a vengeance! Where the bold lover usually urges the timid girl step by step, and takes possession of her virginal charms in due order till he arrives at the primest of all, these two daring women revenged the wrongs of their sex on a poor unprotected boy by submitting him to a similar process.

My waistcoat was unbuttoned and the singlet followed. Rose turned the lapels back and exposed my chest. Praising the firm robust flesh and remarking admiringly on the smoothness of my skin, she fastened on my nipples and began to tickle one with her tongue. Ethel leaned over and took possession of the other. The sensation was most agreeable and I felt that I should wet my breeches if it lasted.

'Oh ladies, dear ladies,' I remonstrated feebly, 'you overpower me. If you treat me like this, I don't know what will happen.'

They chuckled delightedly and sucked all the more. Ethel transferred her mouth to mine and, to my horror, slipped her hand down inside my vest. Slowly the taper fingers made their way into my belly, feeling it deliberately all over, and then came into contact with my engorged prick.

'Oh, mamma, I've found such a funny thing, round and long: oh, yes' (running her hand as far as my balls), 'longer than my hand, and hard, but soft at the same time. It seems . . . yes, it seems to have a sort of pointed knob with a loose cap of skin.'

The infernal witch, with finger and thumb, imparted a spidery motion to her hand, and darted her tongue into my mouth. She knew very well that my overwrought prick would splutter out its contents in a moment, and this was what she was aiming at. Gently she squeezed on, and informed her mother of the state of her progress as reflected in my face.

'Why, mother, Harry has such a rapturous look on his face, just as if he was seeing angels. He is turning his eyes up quite ecstatically, and this curious pillar I'm holding is throbbing away and swelling in my hand.'

'Yes,' said her mother feeling my jock from the outside. 'What you have there, Ethel, is an appendage usually found on young men, and much sought after by ladies. It is commonly called a prick, and from what I can judge seems to be an excellent specimen of its kind.'

With that she rubbed my balls a little, and that settled it. I did not care a damn for the consequences, but let the flood burst. My lava flowed abundantly, and a delicious shiver ran all over me. Ethel, who had occasionally passed the tip of her finger over the top of my prick, to judge, no doubt, how soon she might expect to feel the discharge, hollowed her hand and held it over the nut, for which I was duly grateful since otherwise my clothes would have been in a precious mess.

'Oh, mamma,' she called out, still preserving her innocent tone, 'it's shooting a lot of warm sticky stuff into my hand. See . . . ' she withdrew her hand and held it out to Rose. At the same time she bent over my face again, and prevented me watching what happened to the moist little paw. I heard a glucking noise, and when I next saw the hand, where I expected to see a respectable pool of good semen, to my astonishment I found it dry or almost so. The greedy woman had deliberately sucked it all up, but at the time I thought Ethel had wiped it on her dress somewhere.

Down went the hand again, and Ethel professed much amazement at the change she found.

'Why, it's all limp and soft now – not half the size it was – just like a boy's little thing.'

'Well, rub it, my dear, and it'll come back again in good time.'

This the girl proceeded to do, and a most pleasurable feeling it was to have her soft hand toying with my most tender parts.

'I can't get at him properly this way,' complained Rose. Rising, she lifted her skirt to straddle my limbs, which enabled her deliberately to expose a pair of naked legs and part of her equally naked and voluminous thighs, showing she had nothing on but wrapper, shift and slippers. Ethel no doubt was similarly equipped. Seating herself across me, Rose first of all unbuttoned my trousers and revealed the play of her daughter's fingers on my cock.

'You won't be so pressed with your clothes loose; and you might take off your coat and waistcoat, Harry. Then we can cuddle you much better.'

I did so with pleasure, whereupon, aided by Ethel, she smilingly pulled down shirt and singlet to my waist, leaving my torso barer than her own. Next she opened wrapper and chemise to the same extent, and applied her luxurious bubbies to my chest, rubbing them lasciviously against my naked flesh and setting up a gentle electric friction of a most exquisite description. Ethel said, 'I think, mamma dear, you will get on better if you are more undressed, too.'

Without waiting for sanction she quietly pulled the clothes from her mother's shoulders and arms, and let them hang loose from her loins. What a magnificent apparition the nude bust was! Never, so far, had I seen or thought of anything like it. My ephemeral fucks had been perpetrated on ordinary bodies, and one of these resplendent bubbies would have balanced any two I had exploited as yet. I hugged the elastic waist and, stammering I know not what words of endearment, kissed and mouthed all I could reach. Slipping my hands down I came upon a powerful bottom spreading wide on either side of the hips, and was only prevented from exploring the whole of this wonderful terrain by the tight-fitting linen. Ethel saw my dilemma, and whispering to her mother, 'Lift yourself a little,' pushed the garments right down and denuded the circumambient haunches. I bent under her arm to view them. What a sight they were! Curving in a sweeping outline from the hips, they projected back and to the sides in a massive swell of triumphant flesh. There was nothing of that flatness which so often spoils a fine arse, and they presented a satiny surface free from blotches and blemishes, such as not all women of ripe age can boast. Always since then have I measured my mistresses fundamental charms by the standard of Rose's great arse, and seldom have I come across one that for symmetry, shape and smoothness could beat it. Size of course I have seen exceeded, but mere size is nothing if not accompanied by corresponding attractions. Deliriously I clasped handfuls of the warm sappy flesh, gripping hard and even thrusting my hand into the dubious region between the cheeks.

For her part, Rose plainly approved my demonstrations, and snuggling her face under my armpits, licked the hair. 'The odour of man,' said she, 'is just as enticing to a randy woman as the scent of her snatch to her lover.' Then she fell to sucking my breasts again. My face being disengaged, Ethel opening her robe drew forth, not without some blushes, a pair of shapely sweet-smelling mammae, pointed with little teats, and placed one after the other on my mouth, at the same time rubbing her middle against my arm. I was almost smothered under the avalanche of loose flowing flesh, and gasped for breath.

Ethel had compassion on me and substituted her tongue for her titties. She gave me the whole of it this time – another endearment to which I was a stranger, and the effect of all this could no longer be concealed. Nor was it lessened when the now excited and rorty girl said, 'Doesn't that make you feel good, Harry? Hasn't it a stiffening effect somewhere, my dear?'

At the same moment her mother, judging the time opportune, took my hand and guided it under her clothes to her crotch. This was what I had been waiting for. Instantly I twined my fingers in the mat of hair, felt the prominent motte, and then dived into the fat cunt. I revelled in its slimy folds, and juicy enough they were in all conscience. Determined to have revenge for the indignity Ethel had inflicted on my cock when she so ruthlessly jerked it off, I frigged the great cunt violently.

'There, dear,' said Rose, 'that's where a gentleman should have his hand when a lady is making love to him. Have you ever had a naked woman in this position before? Tell me, you darling boy' (in a low tone), 'have you ever *fucked* a lady? Do you know what that is?'

Now, I had half expected some such question as this, for I had gathered that they took me, from my youth and the surprise they had seen in my eyes at the display of breasts, for an innocent, and I decided to deceive them.

'No. Of course I know what it is, but I haven't dared . . . '

'Beautiful, beautiful! Ethel, he doesn't know what a naked girl is like. Strip, strip yourself at once, and show him all you have. That will make him so randy he will fuck us both. Yes, Harry, you will not leave this house tonight till you know all an amiable woman can do for an amiable lad, and that shall be your reward for succouring two poor women in distress. Feel me, feel me all over – everywhere you want. Look, Ethel is quite naked. Isn't she a handsome girl? Look at her well, Harry: you won't often come across a better. Get on that low chair, dear: bend well down, and show him your pretty bottom, and what you have between your legs, so that he can see as well as feel how a lady's built.'

All this was ripped out breathlessly under the vivid play of my fingers, and the exhortation at this point suddenly finished with, 'But, oh, oh, wait a minute . . . I'm coming . . . he's been too much for me . . . quick, Ethel, put your fingers in too. . . quick, quick . . . and help. . . him to . . . to. . . finish me.'

The ponderous bubbies were shaking and trembling like jelly in an erotic convulsion. Rose's mouth was half open, and her eyes stared fixedly. Her thighs clasped mine energetically, and when Ethel, kneeling down, inserted two fingers from the back and added her efforts to my vigorous frigging, her mother's pent-up feelings gave way in a burst of spray, accompanied by some rather lurid language of a sort I had imagined only whores were supposed to use. Little I knew then of the ways of a lovely woman in full heat, but I was in a fair way to learn. Ethel, I believe, was biting her parent's bottom to add to her fury .

I withdrew my hand, sopping and scented with Rose's discharge, and remembering Ethel's trick, laid it on the girl's mouth. She kissed and licked it, saying, 'Mamma, I'm afraid you've been having a spend. Harry's hand tastes very much to my fancy as if it had been up your naughty thing.'

I sniffed at it myself, and found it impregnated not only with the familiar *odor di femina*, but with some artificial fragrance as well. Both of them had scented themselves for the combat, and I detected the same incense under their arms, on their breasts, on their mottes, and afterwards in their dear little arseholes.

Rose now put her hand under my shirt and took possession of my elongated prick. She rapidly ran her hand along it, as though to test its dimensions, and heaved a sigh of satisfaction at finding it not too small. Doubtless, knowing she was no tender pullet, she was afraid I might not entirely fill the gap in her anatomy through which many a stout prick had already passed. Still, it was a lascivious velvety cunt, and I looked forward with anxiety to the moment when I should be called upon to test its capacity.

'Be careful, dear lady,' I said, 'be careful, you know not what you do,' for, carried away by her excitement, she was groping and squeezing in a manner that threatened to send my spunk flying again.

'Yes,' she said smiling, 'I mustn't waste it. How are you built down below? She felt for my balls and gathered them in her hand. 'Capital, capital, they hold enough for six good fucks at least. What a night we will have! Now, Ethel, get up on that chair, and show Harry that pretty arse once more, and your delicate cunny.'

'Oh, mother,' protested Ethel, 'how you do run on. I'm sure Harry will take us for two lewd women of the town.'

'Whereas we are two highly respectable ladies,' laughed Rose, looking at her own nakedness and then at Ethel who was blushing to her bottom, and presenting a lovely pink and white spectacle – 'especially in our present state. But Harry will learn in time that modesty goes off with the petticoats, and I feel sure he is not the man to shrink from an appetising fuck because it's spiced with a few seasonable immoralities.'

'No, no, I want to learn. Teach me all you know, dear ladies. You will hear no reproach from me. Remember I am only a beginner. I am clay to be moulded in the hands of the two most amiable women I have ever met, and the two most handsome, too,' I added enthusiastically.

'That's right, dear. You mustn't be surprised at anything, and afterwards I will tell you how it comes about you find us apparently so abandoned. Now feast your eye on that picture, and tickle my quim again nicely. And Ethel, keep your great bottom out of my face. I want to watch Harry as he gazes upon you, and enjoy the surprise upon his features. Bend down a little more, and open your cunt. It isn't as big as mine, Harry, but you will find you will be able to get thoroughly into it. Probably you won't think her quite as good a fuck as I am, for all her youth, because she hasn't the experience. In fact Ethel has only allowed herself one sweetheart yet, and so, though she isn't exactly new, you will at any rate not find the gloss entirely off. As for me, old as I am' (she was only thirty-seven, or so), 'I can still' (with an amusing assumption of self-deprecation) 'afford suitable entertainment to man . . . '

'Or beast – if those fellows had got into you,' I put in.

'Yes: nice tit-bits two women like us would have proved for the ruffians. I am sure, by the look in their eyes, they meant to fuck us. Just fancy having to admit their filthy pricks into our decent cunts when a nice handsome boy was waiting for us!'

'Don't get excited, mamma, or your pussy will dilate so much that Harry will fall in bodily when he gets on top of you, and then there'll be no fucking for me.'

Mamma's answer to this impertinence was to put her arm round the slender waist, and push the youthful bottom on my face. I kissed it eagerly, and tempted by the fragrant cunt, said, 'May I?'

'Of course, dear: kiss it, and suck it, too, if you like.'

It was the first time I had thought of such a caress, or knew it to be allowable. Rose fitted the lovely arse on my face, and, excitedly frigging my staff, cried, 'Rub your cunt on his lips, Ethel: let him taste it all. Put your tongue in, Harry, well in. Gamahuche the little bitch. I warrant she wants it badly.'

I did my best, and Ethel cooed and bobbed her bottom up and down and was only too delighted to get the chance of frigging her dainty crack on a masculine mouth. Rose's excitable manipulation had laid bare my most private parts, and her daughter was casting curious glances at the ruddy pole. I was the proud possessor of seven or eight inches of stout-headed penis, and the girl was probably wondering what effect it would have on her still unextended quim. Rose, seeing her eyes directed at the startling apparition, jocosely cried, 'Keep your eyes off, miss. The idea of an unmarried girl casting covetous glances at a man's horrid appurtenances! They must be hidden from sight at once. Get up a minute, Harry.'

I did, and Rose immediately pulled my trousers down, regardless of the fact that her action threw off her last mantle and left her completely naked. The broad belly with its splash of curly hair and the salient motte between the sweeping thighs made me lick my lips.

'There's nothing like naked flesh when you're going to have a hearty fuck,' said Rose, fitting my prick into her yawning crack and lowering herself again. 'I was tired of feeling this rough cloth on my bottom. A capital prick this, Ethel. I have swallowed it right up to the balls, and even they are between the lips.'

She hoisted my shirt, and having fixed her tongue in my mouth as Ethel had done, moved up and down the shaft that was embedded in her belly. Ethel had gone round to the back of her mother, and was kneeling down doing something I could not see, but I felt her bosoms on my knees. I ventured to ask Rose what she was up to, but she merely smiled and said, 'What I'll do to you presently, my dear, if you fuck me well.' After the manipulation my cock had undergone, a few strokes of the powerful quim would have brought on a premature discharge – which Rose was probably well aware of, for she stopped to give me a rest. Her sensations must all the same have been very pleasurable, for she murmured, 'Dear girl,' and writhed about, sucking my lips savagely, while her cunt began to contract ominously.

'Are you ready?' she cried. I nodded. Rose fairly bounded in the saddle, and abandoning all restraint screamed, 'Buck away, too, you young bugger; split my cunt if you can – let me feel your jelly – all, all. Do you hear? Deluge me, or I'll bite your balls off . . . ah . . . oh . . . lo-ovely . . . I am coming too!'

Her head fell on my shoulder; the fleshy body quivered all over, and my hand, dropping to the enormous arse, encountered Ethel's face buried between the cheeks. The spunk hurtled from my spike and poured out in successive jets, a thich clotted stream, and Rose shrieked with pleasure as she felt it lubricating her excited vagina.

'Thank you, dear. It was a splendid fuck. And you – confess – haven't I procured you a heavenly sensation? Did you ever dream before what fun you could get out of your prick, or that a woman had got such a pump between her thighs?'

## CHAPTER TWO

# *Further Acquaintance*

To sustain my part, I pretended wonder and delight and all the rest of it, and really I had never had so glorious a piece of copulation before. The slippery cunt exercised such exquisite pressure, without too much force, on my tool that the latter seemed fairly to burst when the explosion came, and the intensity of the spasm left me momentarily without strength. My gratification was not lessened when Rose said, 'Ethel, run and get a glass. I want to look at my quim. It seems to me to be spouting juice. Yes,' she went on after examining it, 'good measure and running over. Young man, you will be a notable fucker. Seldom have I received such a dose, and never from a comparative boy.'

The reckless woman put a couple of fingers in her sticky cunt, let them soak, drew them forth with a supply of sperm, and put them in her mouth. After rolling it round her tongue and savouring the taste she passed judgement with the air of a connoisseur sampling a choice vintage.

'Yes, good thick healthy sperm: none of your thin gruel about that. It will give me the greatest pleasure to suck just such another lot straight out of your cods presently, Harry. You look astonished. Oh, I assure you it is just as nice to drink a man off as you found it to suck at Ethel's fountain a minute ago. But we must give you a rest. That was a very heavy spend. Have some more wine.'

She turned, and the full proportions of her majestic arse for the first time burst on my view. What a noble dome it was! The very thought of having a bottom like that to play with at liberty made my prick begin to revive. Ethel saw my admiration and smiled.

'You appreciate mothers's bottom? A good many gentlemen have found their pleasure there, haven't they, mamma? It's mother's greatest attraction to some. You don't know her yet, Harry, and you've no idea of the uses she can put it to. It makes me laugh though, sometimes, when I hear the men smacking it, and mamma grunting. She has one admirer who pays no attention to anything other than her bum.'

'Yes,' said Rose putting her hand behind her and most indecently shaking the cheeks and pulling them apart. 'I think my bottom's good for some years yet. There is no doubt a handsome bum is a great magnet to the men. Ethel will have a pretty good one, too, when she has been well fucked. Come and show them together, my dear.'

Ethel ranged up, and I'm dashed if her arse wasn't the exact counterpart in shape of the elder lady's. Only the size was different. The contour was just the same, and even the dimple in the cheeks was there. I couldn't help kissing and hugging the two beautiful moons – the full and the half – and the handsome creatures, looking over their shoulders, smiled down approval of my homage. I persuaded them to take various postures, kneeling one above the other, lying on top of one another back to belly, and finally Rose lying on her back with a cushion to bring the broad hams into prominence while Ethel straddled her. Luscious white thighs, cunts, arses and arseholes stood out in full relief. It was an engaging and cock-stirring scene, and mentally I promised myself that as the two ladies seemed so easy-natured it should not be the last of the kind.

Rose, noticing my cock was regaining its vigour, threw herself across me again, and frigging the inviting shaft with rapid fingers carried my hand to her wet cunny and provoked me to imitate her. Leaning over to my ear she said quietly, 'If you carry your hand a little further, dear, you will find I have more than one hole. Both are equally at your service.'

'Do you mean this?' I said delightedly, shifting my hand between the pendant cheeks, and searching out the orifice.

'Yes, ducky. Put your finger in and tickle it; don't be afraid.'

'Why,' I stammered, 'isn't that . . . ?'

'Buggery? – oh no: only a sort of preliminary.'

'It is true, then, that men sometimes shove their pricks up bottoms.'

'Rather!' put in Ethel laughing at my shocked expression. 'Didn't I tell you one of mother's friends only used her bottom. Well, he scarcely ever fucks her anywhere else, except when mamma sucks his cock. Sometimes, to tease him, she won't let go till it spits out its cream into her mouth.'

I began to wonder whether I had not really hit on two arrant whores despite their style and their abode. By this time I had got a greasy finger well into the upper hole. It slipped in without trouble. Rose twisted and wriggled and evidently enjoyed the feeling.

'Isn't your quim rather wet?' I suggested; 'aren't you going to wipe it?'

'Wipe it! Not much, when I've got a naked boy and a randy girl to lick and clean it. What can be more attractive to suck and taste than a well-fucked cunt? Look here.'

Rose rammed her hand into her quim and licked it passionately. Digging her fingers in again she smeared her voluptuous lips with the contents and pressed them to mine. I was not prepared for this and squirmed a bit, to their amusement.

'That seems to surprise you, young man. Ethel, get down and lick my cunt till it is dry.'

Ethel sat on the floor, leaned her face under the fleshy canopy, and brought her head up against my balls with her mouth on the reeking cunt. Rose put her hands down and opened it to its full extent. I could easily see her daughter's tongue busily rummaging in the strong-scented cavern.

'Good girl; you deserve a fuck now. But we will go upstairs where there are more conveniences.'

Taking with us some refreshments, to which we heartily applied ourselves, we ascended, and went into Rose's bedroom. The chamber was large and, besides the bed, held a number of low chairs, and a lounge of peculiar shape, curving at the end and very sloping at the head. But what struck me most was the number of mirrors. There was a large one in the ceiling above the bed, one in the framework of the bed-end, two cheval-glasses, almost full length, and two more in a wardrobe. The first thing they did was to strip off the remainder of my clothes, and then the well-lighted chamber seemed full of flitting naked forms. Observing me looking curiously at the mirrors about the bed, Rose said, 'You see, the one above enables me to watch the hairy arses of my fuckers bobbing about, or gives them a still more entrancing view, though I say it myself, when I'm on top' (slapping her backside significantly). 'The one at the foot is principally for my lovers, as I find they like to see their pricks surging in and out of my quim or my bottom, as may be. It is also useful in many other positions that give a spice to fucking by their variety and novelty.'

'Get on top of his prick, Ethel, and let him have a view of that bonny bottom at work.'

Ethel did so with a little cry of pleasure, for she had been waiting for her turn long enough, and having worked my cock into her still narrow notch, began a charming rise and fall that were duly reflected in both glasses. I could see the whole length of my doodle appearing and disappearing, and very proud I felt of it as I perceived how it distended her quim. The lips progressively curved inwards till nothing but a smooth ellipse of flesh could be seen with the great piston boring into the centre. Rose, after letting me enjoy the view for a while, laid herself on my legs, and actually had the nerve to get a big toe into her cunt on which she leisurely began a frig. Bending forward she sucked at my balls, and occasionally licked my prick as it emerged from the sheath formed by her daughter's rapidly moistening cunny. Finally she got her hand under my arse and pushed the tip of her finger into my anus, twisting it round and round and giving me an indescribable sensation of shame and pleasure combined.

'Sing out you two fuckers when you are going to spend – but I see you're just coming, for Ethel's cunt is opening and shutting fast. Ah, here we are!'

We both gave several quick lurches, and grabbed frantically at any flesh under our hands. Then Ethel's bottom subsided, burying my cock to the root, and Rose humorously swore she could hear the spunk fizzing into her daughter's belly.

My prick dropped out and she closed the lips of the fresh-fucked twat and bade Ethel hold them so. Reclining on the couch, which I now saw threw her crack well up, she drew Ethel astride of her.

'Now, show your mettle, Harry. Here's a couple of loving and most fucksome women: do something to show you are pleased with your good luck. Don't leave all the indecencies to us. Suck these cunts, my dear lad.'

By this time, warmed, too, with wine, my native randiness had got its head. I was game for anything, and made no difficulty about extracting from the pink little cunny the semen I had just lavished there, nor of heartily gamahuching the much more formidable gash below. I took care at the same time to sodomise both bottoms with my finger.

'Charming,' said Ethel, 'he's a regular love, mamma, and I'm *so* glad we fell in with him.'

'Yes,' said Rose, drawing all three of us in front of a mirror: 'he is a strong-backed, lusty-pricked young gentleman' (running her hands most pleasantly over my bottom and between my thighs, and again sucking my breasts), 'a fine plum for two amorous bitches like ourselves. What do you think of us, Harry? You have never seen anything like this, have you?'

She pointed to their figures in the mirror and certainly had reason to be proud of the sight, for it revealed a luxuriant, voluptuous woman, with magnificent bubbies and formidable thighs, supporting a powerful arse and broad curving belly, while by her side were the rounded, tempting limbs of a naked girl whose handsome face was beaming with amiability and whose eye was moist with a store of passion still only partly drawn upon, but as munificent as her mother's. I hugged and kissed them rapturously, and they returned my embraces with interest.

'Do you know what I am going to do?' said Rose with resolution, and a glitter in her eye. 'I am . . . going . . . to . . . suck . . . your . . . arse . . . hole . . . my boy. Yes, I am' (in response to a look of astonishment), 'I'm damned if I'm not, and I'm going to let you see me do it.'

'It may be dirty,' laughed Ethel.

'I don't care if it is a little . . . high. A bit of flavour only adds piquancy to the act – not that I do this to many. I generally leave my sweethearts to do that for me, but this boy has got under my skin, and I'd lick his arse if he'd just come from the crapper . . . there! Down you get, or if you like I'll lie back in this low chair, and you can rest your bum on my face. You will see equally well, and Ethel can amuse herself sucking your prick.'

I preferred this arrangement, and felt quite elated to see the handsome woman dart her tongue into my most shameful recess, and carefully draw it up and down the whole length of the dark ravine between my buttocks. Ethel appropriated the dangling penis, and for a few moments both mouths were silently at work.

'There, Harry,' said Rose, with a sigh of satisfaction at the performance of this act of wantonness; 'it may be a long time before another woman will do that for you. I suppose you must think we are a curious pair. Frankly, what *do* you think of us?'

'I think you are just too fucksome for words. I am sure no regular whores would have treated me to such a *regale* as you have. But you are not whores.'

'Only when we get into the company of a handsome persuasive young gentleman' (I could not see I had exercised much persuasion), 'naked like this. And then, as you see, we treat him as no professional would, even were she paid for it, except perhaps at a very high price. And all for affection. There is no argument like a good standing prick on a fine young fellow to bring out a woman's randiness. While Ethel is sucking yours into order I will tell you something about ourselves, and you will then understand how we come to enjoy ourselves as inclination directs without shame or reserve. By night we are two unrestrained fuckers, like this, or will be, for Ethel, as you know, has only just begun; by day we are two respectable ladies moving in good society.'

We took up a negligent pose on the broad bed, Ethel lying between my legs, supported upon her elbows and sucking my soft prick like a lollipop. Occasionally she titillated my bollocks, or 'postillioned' my anus as she called it (a word I now know to be borrowed from our inventive friends across the Channel). Her mother, spreading her thighs wide, openly frigged herself with a slow and easy motion or, from time to time, guided my hand to the sensitive aperture and made me do it for her. With the other hand she held her bosom to my mouth in order to get the delicious tickling imparted by the impact of my tongue on the point of her titty. These caresses were not without effect, for every now and again a shiver swept over her and made the tremulous flesh quiver.

The glorious obscenity of it all was faithfully reflected in the mirror, where at the same time I could see both Rose's taper fingers, covered with rings, toying with her great cunt, and her daughter's ivory bottom, with legs flung upwards, and the opening of the slit in the dim recess between. In this manner we heard . . .

## CHAPTER THREE

### *Rose's Story*

I was only a titter, not as old as Ethel here, when I fell madly in love with my husband. George was a handsome, rake-hellish devil whose reputation was common property. I knew very well he was a confirmed cunt-hunter, but like many another girl I was completely bowled over by his fascinations, and I would listen to no remonstrances or warnings. In vain they told me I was too young to think of marrying. I was no innocent, despite my tender age, and I was persuaded I could hold my own in amorous conflict with a man. Still, I had some sense left in my noddle, for I wouldn't let my lover fuck me till he had married me. It was hard work to prevent him though, for his unguarded and lubricious caresses awoke a little demon in my quim to which, until then, I had been a stranger.

He used to squeeze my bubbies and bottom in the openest way, and rub his prick against my thighs and hands, so that I could not help feeling it – and, Lord! what a size it seemed, exaggerated by the folds of his clothes. More than once I left him so excited that I woke up in the middle of a wet dream, spending profusely. I fancied he was in my arms, ramming fast and furiously, and when I came to my senses I was bucking eagerly, and my quim drenched. His contact, even his presence, moved me so much that I was ready to spend if he touched me, and one day I did. He was mugging me in his usual fucksome style, and his hand touched my motte. Instantly, and without my having the slightest power to prevent it, the hidden springs burst, and a torrent flowed from my excited cranny. For the life of me I could not but give way to my feelings, and found myself openly and without the least attempt at concealment thrusting my belly backwards and forwards against him, just as many a time since I have responded to the throes of a lover's prick. He saw the effect, the brute, and took advantage of my helplessness to put his hand up my clothes.

'Good God, Rose,' he cried, 'why, you shoot it out like a man! Your drawers are dripping, and it's running down into your stockings. What a hot little cat. If you spend like this for a wisp of tongue in your mouth, what will you do for six inches of cock up your thing?'

I escaped from him in confusion, only to repeat the scene the next time we came together. On this occasion he was ready for me, and as soon as he observed the signal of distress, thrust his hand between my thighs . . . All I could say, and that very faintly was, 'What are you doing?'

'Trying to increase your pleasure. Also to feel this little twat discharging.'

He tickled my fanny, and the convulsion was more intense than before. George brought his hand forth covered with my emission, and after looking at it coolly wiped it on my drawers.

'Heavens, what a grind you'll make!' he said, and forthwith took out his cock and tried to poke me. I had courage enough to refuse. So great was his power over me that I could not dance with him without spending. More than once I have had to stop breathless, and clinging to him whisper, 'For goodness' sake, George, hold me tight or I shall fall. I'm doing it again.' There I clung, almost fainting from the acuteness of the ejaculation, while my spunk dribbled down my thighs.

Despite my resolution, I recognise now that he never would have married me (although some fine night I should assuredly have been fucked) but for the fact that I had a good deal of money, and that is what I fancy finally decided my noble to tie himself up. Not that marriage made a bit of difference to him, the wretch. He was one of those lustful, passionate, hell-fire scamps, of whom it is said they spare no man in their wrath and no woman in their lust.

I proved this to my sorrow on my wedding night. Scarcely had I got into bed than he fairly rushed me, like a bull. My nightdress was snatched off, and whereas I had expected a tender preliminarily scene of delightful cuddling with a gradual approach to the main performance, George pulled my thighs open and drove his prick into my slender cunt without taking breath. He hurt me horribly, of course, but what did he care for my young flesh! All he wanted was to tear through my maidenhead as quickly as possible, and the more I screamed under my breath and begged for mercy, the more pleased he was. It is no exaggeration to say he regularly ripped me open, and certainly the blood flowed freely from my wounds. Without dismounting he twice poured in a torrent of lava, and then gloated over the way he had made me bleed and chaffed me when I bewailed my torn cunt. I reproached him strongly, sobbed, and vowed I would go back to my parents, for this was not at all like the pleasure I had expected. But I did not know the sort of husband I had got.

'You'll find out, my girl,' said he, 'you've got to do as I like. I'll teach you to threaten me. Turn over and show me your arse.'

I refused to move, and he flung me over at once, pulled my bottom open, and began to probe the tight little hole with a finger, at the same time stiffening up his cock again by rubbing it on the back of my thighs. Horrified at the obscenity of the act, I protested loudly, but little knew what was coming.

'You don't like my finger there, eh? What'll you say, then, when you feel this in it?' beating my arse with his prick.

'Never, never!' I shouted, 'I'll scream for help.'

My earlier threats were all fudge, but I really began to be alarmed now. He banged my head down on the pillow, and informed me if I did he would tie and gag me; that he was master, and I'd find he'd do as he liked. With that he began thrusting in his prick, and despite all my resistance, for after all I didn't cry out too loudly, I was soundly buggered. After that I was too exhausted to resist any more, and he fucked away, without my taking the slightest pleasure from it, till I pretty well fainted. Next day I was too sore to move and besought him with tears to give me time to recover. Having triumphed at all points, George could afford to be generous, and for the remainder of our honeymoon treated me more tenderly, and allowed me to have a share of my legitimate pleasure by fucking me more lightly. He made up for this, as I ascertained afterwards, by amusing himself with one of the barmaids at the hotel. I dare say her quim was more used to such assaults than my virgin twat. Oh, he was an awful ram! I never could keep a servant, for either he frightened them away by wanting to roger them or, if they gave in, got them in the family way. Yet I was desperately fond of the wretch, and curiously enough, rather proud of the way he used to fuck every woman who crossed his path.

After all I did not fare so badly as some of them. Not long after we returned from our honeymoon I ran against an intimate friend of mine, Lucy by name. Of course I had to stand a good deal of chaff from her, and she wormed out of me how George had treated me the first night.

'Oh, that's nothing,' she blurted out in a knowing way, and then seemed to recollect herself. A thought struck me.

'How do you know? Has George ever fucked you?'

Poor Lucy fell into confusion, quite unable to answer, so I pressed my guess home.

'You needn't deny it: I can see from your face that he has,' I said with a smile.

Lucy, somewhat reassured, confessed. 'Well, as you don't seem to mind, I admit he has, but I am not the only one by a long way, you know. There are a good many others who can pretty well imagine what your bridal night was.'

'Yes, I knew when I married him what his reputation was, but, like a fool, thought he would stick to me and give up his promiscuous fucking, but I don't now hug myself in that belief. I should hardly have thought, though, Lucy, you would be one to be knocked off your perch so easily. Tell me all about it, and I will forgive you.'

Lucy I may say was then about twenty, and a good-looking girl of nice figure. The last time I saw her she was the mother of five or six children, and had a belly on her like a camel's hump. So she began . . .

## CHAPTER FOUR

# *Lucy's Story*

I was very spoony on George, and had some hopes he would marry me, but you have been luckier than the rest of us, my dear, and got your grummit from him without risk. He used to kiss me and mess me about pretty well as he liked, and I must say I didn't object. Well, at last it came about that we made up a camping party during the summer. There were six of us girls, all rather good-looking and jolly titters – trust Master George and his friends for picking out tasty pieces – and four fellows, all of a kidney, but none of them such desperadoes as George. It was a put-up job, though we didn't know it, and their intention was to let no one of us return with our maidenheads. We were all friendly together, some stuck on one or other of the boys, and several of us in particular on George. Of course there were ample opportunities for mugging and hugging, and that didn't make our youthful blood flow the more serenely. I suppose George thought the time had come to attempt my virtue, for one day, I don't exactly know how he managed it, it came to pass the rest had gone off, and only he and I were left in camp. He suggested a bathe in the river, and I innocently retired to our tent and undressed. I was reduced to my chemise, when in, if you please, the ruffian stalked with only his bathing singlet on, and little enough there was, even of that. He might just as well have been completely naked, for his prick and knackers showed up in sharp relief. All the scamps affected this style in order to excite our feelings, and though we scarcely liked it we hadn't had the courage to object to their indecency. I gave a slight shriek and told him to go away. Not a bit.

He laughed and said, 'Why so bashful, Lucy? A little cuddling won't hurt you.' He caught hold of me, kissed me lecherously, causing a thrill to run down my spine and depriving me almost of the power of moving, put one hand in my bosom and the other on my bottom, and felt me all over. All the while his mouth was glued to mine and his tongue was playing inside, so that I hadn't breath to protest. I could feel his prick – by the way, Rose, excuse these vulgarities, but I am using the terms he employed . . .

'Yes, his usual term of endearment to me is "fat-arse" or "split-arse little fucker".'

Then you are used to them and we may talk without reserve. I could feel his prick surging and thickening until I thought a regular mast was pressing against me, and that didn't make me any cooler, you can bet. When he finally got his hand into my cunt and began to tickle it I knew what he would be at, and with a last effort broke away and crouched in the corner of the tent. 'Go away, George,' I said: 'you are horribly rude. I won't be treated so. You know you have no right to take such liberties with an innocent girl.'

He chuckled, approached nearer, and cooly pulled off his one scanty covering. His cock sprang out, erect and fiery, looking to my excited imagination a foot long and as thick as my wrist, I swear, Rose.'

'It isn't so big as that.'

No, but think of my feelings at the moment. He gaily shook it at me, and asked me what I thought of it – wasn't it a beauty.

'Go away, you horrid beast, or I'll scream. Don't you touch me!'

'Scream away, my dear. Who will hear you? Come, Lucy, be reasonable. I want to fuck you, and you know it; and you want it, too, or you wouldn't have stood my pulling you about so much.'

I indignantly denied it, and exclaimed I would never allow it. What did he take me for to treat me so, and what would the other girls say?

'Oh, you needn't worry about the others. Maud has had a long cock up her quim since we came here, and I have poked Tottie myself. Clara will lose her maidenhead today if Tom gets her by herself, and so will you. The rest will be no virgins in a day or two.'

'You monster,' I said, fairly sobbing now. 'Is that what you brought us here for – to strip us of our virtue and put us on a level with street-girls?'

He knelt down, still holding his cock, and with a malicious grin pulled the skin up and down from the great head, which was swollen and purple and altogether looked like a rolling-pin. I couldn't keep my eyes off it. George seized me, despite my shudders, and tried to get my shift off. I resisted and he threatened to tear it in pieces, so to save it I had to let him strip me. He grabbed me at once, and began sucking my breasts, pinching my bottom and thrusting his hand between my thighs. I defended myself and tried to scratch him, which made him angry.

'Oh, if you won't be fucked peaceably it will be the worse for you. Fucked you shall be, and by force as you won't give in. And you will find it won't be so pleasant as if you had opened your legs quietly.'

With that he tied my hands, drew my knees almost up to my chin, and tied them to my neck. I was like a trussed fowl, and worst of all my poor little cunt was now exposed to his attacks. He picked me up, put me on the end of the camp-bed, and began poking his finger in my quim, and asking me how I felt now.

I was so humiliated that I could do nothing but sob and threaten him with all sorts of futile vengeance. Little he cared! He knew I was a lady, and once fucked was not likely to publish my shame. So there I was, in a startling position for a modest girl! Stark naked and tied in a bundle: my bottom and my cunt exposed to the gaze of a naked ogre – nay, more than exposed – thrust forcibly into prominence. I felt it was all up with me, and shut my eyes to await the stroke of that tremendous prick which I expected every moment to come tearing through my delicate membranes. The fiend gloated over my shame, using the filthiest terms he could think of, and hinting at atrocities I had never dreamed of, but, alas, was soon to be subjected to, and even to revel in. He openly compared me with this, that and the other girl he had fucked. My bubbies weren't as big as Annie's; my belly not so broad as Mrs So and So's; my thighs not so plump as some whore's he knew; my arse . . . 'Call that an arse,' he sneered, lifting it up and smacking it roughly, 'why I've fucked many a slavey with a better backside than that. But your cunt' (shoving his finger in harshly) 'doesn't seem so bad, and I dare say it will do as well to piss my juice in as another. Very much like Tottie's, now I come to look at it closely: only she's got less hair round hers and the lips are not so fat. Yes, I think your cunt's the best part of you, Lucy.'

I could have torn his eyes out to hear the beast calmly inventorying me in this way, cataloguing each shameful feature of my secret anatomy, especially when he compared me, for I knew myself to be a well-shaped girl, with some battered prostitute. I cried bitterly, more with vexation that he should pretend to appraise me so lightly after stripping me, than anything else, and gave him the rough side of my tongue. My flood of fiery indignation was suddenly stopped by his stooping down and putting his tongue in my cunt.

What unheard of obscenity! But there it was, running up and down, and darting right into the crack. I gasped for breath, and the mocking wretch told me not to mind him, but to go on with my abuse if that would relieve me. He could suck my virgin cunny and listen at the same time. 'You know, my dear, it is part of the pleasure to outrage a girl's modesty as well as her carefully preserved person at the same time, so you talk away, and I'll gamahuche this naked little pissing-trap of yours.'

I wish, Rose, I *had* pissed in his face, but I never thought of it at the time. That would have paid the brute out!

But the novelty, and a secret feeling of delight at having a man mugging my cunt, even if he was shoving his finger into my bottom as well, together with the pleasurable sensation caused by his tongue had their effect.

It was only when he got up and presented his fearful cock between my legs, that I made one more effort, swearing if he fucked me to have him arrested for rape.

'Now that shows a very bad disposition, Lucy,' he retorted as coolly as you please. 'You have no witnesses, you know, and if any of the others did come back they would only laugh at you, for those of the girls who haven't been fucked yet are hoping to be. You should have taken it quietly, like Tottie, and then you would have had some pleasure. As it is I shan't spare you, and when I've fucked your blasted arse off you can go and tell if you like.'

He opened my virginity with his fingers, placed the head of his jock in the entrance, and pushed with all his might. I thought I was splitting. I screamed, I believe swore, and damned him for a dirty hound, but the more I stormed the more he pushed. He fairly rammed and tore his way in. I felt something give way and a warm stream ooze out; the hard knob went further and further in, and presently it was stuck full length in my bleeding cunt. In fact, I bled like a pig and no wonder!

The savage laughed with joy to see it, and having burst through all obstacles stopped, as he said, to let his prick soak. Then he suddenly started a furious ramming, striking against something inside at every thrust, and making me scream aloud. After a few more ferocious strokes I felt something gush into me, hot and thick, jet after jet. George shouted, 'There now you see, Lucy, you've been damn well fucked after all!'

I was sobbing and moaning with fright and pain, but he took no notice and after a space went on poking, till again the heavy shower bedewed my womb. He took more time, though, and as he wasn't quite so savage, but for my terror I might have extracted some pleasure from the operation. I begged him to release me now he had effected his purpose, for my arms and legs were hurting awfully, not to speak of the stinging in my cunt. Not he!

'You've got to have another lesson yet, my beauty, and then I think you will be tamed, and instead of curses will receive me between your thighs with caresses.'

I thought he simply intended to fuck me in my cunt again, but you can guess, Rose, from your own experience what was in store for me. The shameless wretch, to get his prick up again, scooped a handful of blood and semen out of my quim, and openly frigged himself with the pasty mess till his cock stood once more. Then he rubbed the same mixture into my bottom. Still I wondered what he was after, and it was not till he actually put his tool between the cheeks that I realised his hideous design.

I was going to be buggered! Horrible thought!

I had imagined men only did that to boys or to one another, and I had never thought of such a thing happening to a girl, with a wide and attractive opening in the shape of a cunt to receive a prick in. This time I fainted off, and when a stinging pain roused me once more I could feel at least half his prick up my bottom, and from the twinging of my anus I was sure the remorseless bugger had torn me there, too. I suppose he saw the pain in my face, and was afraid of going too far, for he withdrew till only the head was left in, and then leisurely racked himself off in the contractile hole and got the discharge he wanted. I was too overcome to resist any more. I again begged him faintly to untie me, promising to let him do as he liked so long as he didn't put it in my bottom again.

'Ah,' he chuckled, and I could have killed him where he stood, 'I thought that would bring the bitch to her senses. Nothing like a solid prick up a girl's arse to reduce her to subjection.'

He released me and began to caress me, sucking my bubbies and bestowing such endearments on me that if he had proceeded like that at first, my thighs would probably have opened to him of their own accord. As it was I could not appreciate them, and when he stretched himself on me to fuck me again I implored him to be satisfied and let me off. This seemed to anger him afresh, for he fucked me savagely, not once but twice, and I was so frightened of getting that awful prick up my arse that I had to let him. My poor cunt was macerated and bled slowly all the time. Nearly every thrust was an agony, and how girls can stand being raped by one man after another, as happens at times, I don't know. I wonder it didn't hurt him, too, for I was too tight for such a prick dashed in anyhow. A man's cock must be as tough as steel.

The end of it was that, after being fucked five times, next day I was so sore and ill that I couldn't accompany the others in their excursions. I had to plead a sick headache, and one of them offered to stay with me. But this didn't suit her cavalier, who I suppose was after her cunt, too, and she said she would arrange with one of the others, and left me for a while. What was my horror, when they had all gone, to see the grinning George enter the tent!

'I've sent Clara off and promised to look after you.'

I shuddered visibly. 'I can't, George, dear: I really can't,' I wept, clasping my hands imploringly, 'you have torn me so badly, I really can't.'

'Well, let me see.' He turned down the bedclothes, for I had not got up, and without asking my leave, opened my legs and inspected my cunny, just as coolly as if I were his slave or his wife. I knew it was no use objecting, so I submitted to the affront.

'Yes, it does seem inflamed and swollen, and this, I suppose, is sore, too,' putting his hand to my bottom.

'Yes it is, you monster: you have cracked that as well as my virginity.'

He soothed and petted me – oh, the wretch could be charming enough when he desired – sucked my titties and brought a glow over me.

'Well, I will let you off, and we will just play a little with one another.' He slipped down his trousers and gave me his cock to hold. I couldn't help admiring the noble weapon, and examined it curiously. Of course, as he calculated, despite the twinges of my cunt, my passions began to rise at the sight of his nakedness. I doddled his knackers, worked them eagerly, and presently found myself returning his kisses rapturously, while my silly cunt was moistening fast, in spite of its wounded state. Slily George presented the swollen head of his prick to my lips, and with a smile of satisfaction at my melting condition, rubbed it slowly between them.

'Open your mouth,' he ordered.

Weakly I obeyed, and in a jiffy the monstrous cock was rammed in. Then, again, I could have had my revenge, for a sharp nip or two would soon have made him retire. But, to tell the truth, I was too frightened to venture on reprisals, too overcome by my own rising excitement, and perhaps curious to see how far he meant to go. I soon found out. George fucked my mouth just like a cunt. I perceived that in a few strokes I should be flooded with his abominable liquor, and with an imploring look and in a stifled voice said, 'Oh, George, you are not going to do it in my mouth, surely?'

'Yes, I am,' he retorted firmly. 'You see, even if two of your holes are useless, you have another nearly as good. When you have thoroughly tasted my noble spunk I'll show you that you have a fourth resource still, and you will be able to see as well as taste it.'

I still feebly tried to push his nasty prick away. He became impatient, and finally, shouting, 'If you dare to spoil it I'll piss in your mouth . . . you are my thing, my whore, and I'll fuck you as I damn well please,' frigged his cock furiously with his fingers, and shot a deluge of hot, bitter, pungent spunk down my throat.

# CHAPTER FIVE

## *A Taste of Things to Come*

'For God's sake, look out,' I shouted to Ethel. The little puss had got her cunt across my leg and while frigging herself comfortably by this means had brought my prick to a perfectly lovely state and was excitedly flapping it against my belly.

Her mother's hand was raging in her own quim, and we had all been worked up to a condition of intense excitement by Rose's thrilling narrative. The latter cried out, 'Don't spill it: I want it too badly.' Then, flinging her arms out wide and spreading her lascivious thighs, she shrieked, 'Fuck me, Harry: fuck like hell. Oh that I could get you bodily into my cunt!'

I lifted my head from her armpit, where I had been breathing the odour emanating from her full-blooded, lust-exhaling flesh, and saw Rose's face blazing with passion, her lips parted and her eyes snapping. What a splendid fucker I thought her! Firm elastic flesh, every bone well padded, glowing belly, and *such* thighs – as Ethel remarked, 'Once mother gets a man between those presses she never lets go till the juice is extracted from his grapes.' I rushed gladly to the breach, and Rose screamed with joy as she felt my prick enter her maddened twat.

'Shove it up, you devil . . . ram me like buggery . . . wash my guts out with your spunk, and be quick or I shall piss all over your blasted cock!'

I fell on her belly, and felt the aforesaid guts fairly bubbling under me. I was just as rabid by now as the strapping whore who was straining me to her nude bosom, and as far removed from any sense of bashfulness or decency. Noting the freedom of Rose's language, I made bold to repay her in her own coin.

'All right, my lovely bitch, wait till I get my spout fair into your piss-pot, and I'll fuck your bloody arse off.'

'Good, good! Listen to him, Ethel: isn't he a goddamned cast-iron, twenty-two-carat whoremonger! Ough, that went well home. I believe your prick shot right into my womb. . . ough . . . ough.'

I was driving with all the force of my arse, and at each stroke I fell flat on her stomach, the two masses meeting with a slap. Ethel's hands were playing round my balls, and her face frolicking against my backside. She laughed and giggled with excitement. Rose twined her legs strenuously round mine and cried .

'I'm coming, I'm coming, you son of a split-arse whore. Fuck . . . fuck.

his arsehole in a minute.'

I got my hands under the proud bottom, clenched a lump of flesh in each, and drove my fingers in without mercy.

'I'm coming, too. Buck . . . buck, you slippery-cunted whore. Wriggle your damned arse, and I'll drive my cock out at your mouth!'

A quick ram or two, and the spunk began to flow. In the tension of the frantic spend we bit each other furiously. I know Rose made her teeth meet in my shoulder, while I gnawed at her fair neck, and neither of us noticed it in the rage of emission. I lay on her while my prick throbbed out its seething liquor, and the red-hot cunt vibrated in response. In fact, even while Rose reclined exhausted by the violence of her discharge, her splendid trap continued opening and shutting after my cock was withdrawn. Elated at the effect I had produced I drew Ethel's attention to it, and she remarked, 'I have seldom seen mother so excited or fuck so furiously. You must have a very magnetic prick.'

'He's a splendid fellow,' cried Rose enthusiastically, making me positively blush. 'We'll make a first-class cunt-puncher of him. He isn't afraid to excite his woman by rousing indecencies, and that's just what I like. I've never heard such language since my husband used to fuck me, and he was no slouch. 'Fuck my bloody arse off!' (with a chuckle). 'Oh, fie, you naughty boy!'

'What about the "sparks from his arsehole", mamma?' said Ethel, 'I didn't see any, though I had my tongue there.'

'You bad girl! what was your tongue doing there in such a nasty place?'

'Licking it, like yours was a little while ago. You see, if you excite me so I must do something wicked, too. I don't see why if his prick is in your cunt my tongue shouldn't be in his "bloody arse" ' (with a smile).

Heavens! to hear the engaging girl reeling off these obscenities from her dainty lips gave me a thrill which was imparted to my cock, not yet quite dead.

'The fact is,' said Rose, 'I think Ethel badly wants a porous plaster in her belly, too. How's your bally prick, Harry? Fit for another tussle? Beau–ti–ful . . . I declare it will be up in a minute, with a little sucking. On to him, Ethel, and lick it stiff, and then I'll let you see how I pay out such an awful young reprobate for his remarks on my person. No, not that way: show him your cunt and your bottom.'

Ethel straddled me quickly enough, and her fragrant, oozy quim was greedily sucked and her tender arse, too, which made me wonder if I could manage to get my prick into the dear little hole. Rose all the time was lying in the same position, holding her cunt closed with her hand to prevent the mingled spendings issuing, and when she saw I had got a gigantic horn again she said, 'Lie down, Harry, and I will show you a new way.' She reposed on me with her haunches on my chest, and adjusted her quim to my mouth – a rather startling apparition, filled as it was with what looked like melted blancmange relieved by the pink and reddish raw flesh. Inclining herself to the side, she left my prick free to Ethel, whose tight quim quickly gobbled it to the balls. Rose had only to look up and she could see the fuck from beginning to end. I sucked the mother's cunt contentedly while Ethel did the work. In her overwrought state a dozen strokes brought her a hearty effusion, the girl prattling pretty obscenities all the while in imitation of her mamma. Then she went to work vigorously once more, and extracted from my bollocks the fourth libation they had poured forth that night.

'There, ducky,' she cooed as our convulsions died away, 'was that a bloody good fuck? Don't move. Our juice is splashing into mother's face, and she's catching it in her mouth.'

Rose had, indeed, changed her position, and true to her determination not to waste anything, was quietly imbibing the spunk as it dropped down; after which she fiercely clasped her daughter's bottom, and drew it on to her lips to get at what was left in the cunt. Truly the lascivious George's lessons had not been in vain .

After that we kissed all round, and every mouth was reeking with semen, for after a while Rose had again shifted position, and planting her arsehole squarely on my face, had received the titillation of my tongue in that delicate quarter, thus leaving her cunt free to Ethel, who licked up what I had missed. A fresh appeal to the wine-cup breathed new vigour and new lust into us, and I am afraid we were all a little tizzy when Rose resumed. She said that when Lucy described her first gamahuche and the horribly obscene manner in which it had been contrived, she started a little, for up to then George had not gone further than fucking her in her twin holes. Lucy noticed it.

## CHAPTER SIX

### *Lucy's Story continued*

Do you mean to say George hasn't given you a dose in the mouth yet? Well, I am surprised. I should have thought that by this time there wasn't a hole or a crevice in you that hadn't had his randy prick in it. But I suppose he thinks a little more is due to a wife that to one of his pissing-whores. Excuse my dreadful language, Rose, but really it is all his fault.

'Oh yes, as I said before I have learned a lot in that way The names he has for my cunt vary from cream-jug to piss-pot. Go on.'

Well, curious as it may seem, when he discharged without ceremony into my mouth, the taste of his abominable spunk appeared to take possession of me, and I felt that, as he said, I *was* his thing . . . his whore. If he had proceeded to fuck me, sore as my cunny was, I should have welcomed him, and caressed him with a fervour all the greater for his brutality. In fact I secretly hoped he would ram it in, then and there, and if he had chosen to bugger me again I shouldn't have protested, even had he split my arsehole open. What he did, however, was to undress himself and strip my nightdress off, and the more naked we became the more I kissed and fondled him. I seized his cock again of my own volition, and sucked it frantically till it came up once more, and all the time the handsome devil was chaffing me about the difference in my attitude, boasting how he had tamed me, and telling me I would be as good a grind as Tottie yet, and so on. Then he laid me down, got on top, and told me to hold my breasts up, so that he could have a fuck between them.

'Then you'll see how the stuff shoots out,' he said, 'and what it's like, and if you choose to catch it in your mouth, you can.'

How funny his bollocks felt rolling about on my diaphragm, and how eagerly I watched the great head bob through and through my bubbies, with my eye fixed on the little aperture for the first appearance of his spunk. First a clear moisture exuded from the tube, then it increased, George panted and damned, and "swish" it came, four or five jets. They splashed over chin, mouth, lips and nose, and some even over my eyes, and overpowered me with the virile odour of the stuff.

'Oh, George, what a lot!' I said admiringly. 'I thought I had got most of it in my mouth, but there is as much as ever.'

'Oh, I can generally give the girls I fuck as much as they want and more – some of them.' The wretch laughed as he thought of the many ivory bellies whose shape he had temporarily spoiled.

'Now we'll have a nice little double suck, if your cunt isn't too sore.'

So saying he turned round, and I saw his manly arse, robust, strong and hairy, looming overhead. The still half-stiff prick and his great cods dangled over my mouth and I kissed them passionately. George opened my thighs and began gently to lick my cunt, fearing to excite it too much.

Oh! Rose, what a heavenly sensation it is to have a man's head between your thighs! Ah, naughty girl, I can see by your pleased look he has been at the same game with you. I sucked his sticky cock, and when it was nearly erect George pulled it out of my mouth and put it between my bubbies again, but this time in the reverse way. The big bottom with the ominous-looking brown hole in its centre sank slowly to my face. Did he . . . ? Good Heavens, *could* he expect me to kiss that? There was very little doubt, for in a moment what I should have privately designated to myself the day before 'his stinking arsehole' was planted firmly on my lips. Nay more. He was not content with that, and edging backwards rubbed it several times on my nose. Then I was ordered, if you please, to put my tongue in and lick it thoroughly. With a last sight at my degradation, followed by a wave of lust sweeping from my irritated cunt to my brain, I licked slowly and deliberately, thrusting my tongue as far up his bottom as I could. Yes, my dear, there was I, Miss Lucy

Crofton, granddaughter of a lord, a girl of fashion and society, whoring with a naked man whose most beastly part was glued to my lips! Not that it was particularly dirty or unpleasant: and I must say that when, later on, George returned the compliment I experienced so pleasurable a sensation that if a man wants to fuck me now I take care to make him suck my arse as well. And I must say, *too* (with a perk), I haven't found anyone who hesitated as soon as he saw my bottom, which even George was good enough to admire.

\* \* \*

'And was she a well-made girl, mamma,' queried Ethel.

'Yes, but not better than you, and not much more so than myself, though she was nearly four years older. Still, Lucy was a tempting piece of goods, and a distinguished-looking girl, so that I doubt whether anyone but a rake like George would have undertaken to rape her. I fancy she must have been more than spoony on him, and the rascal saw that he only needed to hit the psychological moment to tear away her maidenhead. But, Lor' bless you, Lucy could never hold a candle to me when once I got the rage for fucking and my figure developed.'

'I can readily guess that,' I said admiringly, squeezing her breasts and bottom animatedly, 'the sight of these would make a mummy's cock stand, Rose.'

'Yes' (complacently). 'Fetch me my photos, Ethel.'

They were produced and proved to be a series of nude pictures of herself, taken over a number of years and in various highly indecent postures, showing her development from a pretty, plump girl to the magnificent whore she was now. In particular she had a number fully exposing her cunt to view, with the idea, she said, of proving that in a woman endowed with abnormal fucking powers the cunt retained much more freshness and expanded less than you would suppose.

'I have been an outrageous belly-bumper for years,' she remarked, 'and I should be sorry to have to calculate how many thousand times I have emptied a cock into my cunt, but you see there isn't much difference in it even now.'

Rose opened her thighs and made me compare minutely the earlier pictures with its present mature state, and really there wasn't any very perceptible difference. Some women I have fucked since have had cunts like horse-collars, and hadn't been on their backs overmuch, either, but then she hadn't done much child-bearing, and was in a position to take good care of her most valued treasure. So far as I could tell it was likely to be eminently fuckable for many a year yet. I said so.

'I hope so,' said Rose heartily. 'But I suppose I shall always be able to buy a decent fuck, unless I become too much of a hag. I certainly mean to go on using it if I can so long as there is any feeling left in it.'

There were a few pictures of Ethel, too. In one of them, as a child, she was kneeling between her mother's thighs, and gamahuching her intently, but of this more anon.

'Lucy,' resumed Rose, 'had a pretty tough experience, hadn't she? After George had filled her cup of humiliation to the brim, and she imagined her submission was to be rewarded by the insertion of his prick in her longing crack, he got off her, and remarking that she was hardly in a condition to be fucked yet, amused himself by making her take various improper postures, and then went off for a bathe.'

## CHAPTER SEVEN

## *Lucy's Story continued*

I was resolved not to undergo these experiences for nothing, and bathed myself unceasingly to get my parts into order again. That evening was warm and mild. Annie and Tottie occupied the tent with me, and when they thought I was asleep I heard them get up quietly and go outside. I guessed their little game but was rather astonished at Annie, who I was almost certain was still a virgin. I peeped out, and saw them joined by George and Randolph in their pyjamas. The latter was only a lad, still in his teens, and a great admirer of George, who I suspected was initiating him into the game of mothers and fathers. Annie betrayed some reluctance – the last efforts of modesty – and it must have been a great shock to her, while wrapped in Randolph's embraces, to see George coolly strip off Tottie's shift and hoist her stark naked on to his shoulders. The girl was a fluffy-haired, fair little thing, with plump bosoms and rounded limbs, and was clearly like wax in her bearer's masterful hands.

'Come along, Annie,' she whispered impatiently, 'don't make such a noise or they will hear you. Don't be a little fool. You know very well you are dying to get hold of what these bad boys carry in front of them.'

'Lift her up, Randy,' said George, 'and bring her along.'

So off they went to the dining tent, and a pretty picture the immodest Tottie made, up in the air with her fat little bottom bulging out over George's shoulders.

Well, I didn't like the idea of George fucking Tottie instead of me one bit, though the child's lapse from virtue was no secret to me, but I couldn't make up my mind for some time what to do. At last I got a pair of scissors, and tiptoed to the dining tent into which they had disappeared. I made a hole and could just faintly see they were all naked now, and that Annie's maidenhead had already been shattered, for she was lying on her back and

Randy had just risen to his knees and was pointing with pride to the blood on his prick, and saying he didn't expect to find her quim so tight.

George told him not to wipe himself for he had a tighter place still to get into. He ordered Tottie to lean over the edge of the table and signalled Randolph to insert his prick in her bottom. Then, to my amazement and disgust, he attacked the lad's bottom himself, and though Randy shuffled and growled a good deal, effected a lodgement. Next he beckoned Annie who was softly crying, lifted her on to the boy's back, and applied his mouth to her bloody cunt. The girl's astonishment soon stopped her tears. There followed a series of hearty thrusts and drives, in which you could hear bellies bumping against bottoms until the lust of the two young buggers had been satisfied by a copious injection into the two plump sterns.

Randy's arse was as white and round as a girl's, and I suppose its attraction was too enticing for George to let such an opportunity go by him. Poor Annie did not escape, for George kneeling with his great bottom on Tottie's face drove his prick into her arse too. She was sucking Randy's cock. Pretty odorous it must have been after its journey into virgin cunt and almost virgin bottom. Annie tried to escape it and made a fuss, but what was the use. They knew she dare not call out, and like me she was broken in whether she liked it or not. After that each girl got a fuck in her cunt three times, and in reward had to suck their cavaliers' pricks and arseholes, and finally one another's quims. I got so excited I found myself fingering my own thing. I had never done it in my life before. I returned shortly and then the girls sneaked in too.

Annie looked rather care-worn next morning and was disinclined to move about. I have no doubt they either knew or suspected what was the matter with me as well. Next day I was fully recovered, and I had no mind that Tottie should have the sole use of the formidable prick that had deflowered me. I took the first opportunity to whisper to George. 'I am all right now, you villain,' at the same time shooting a languorous glance at him from under my veiled eyelids. He took me by the chin and tilting my face up looked into my eyes. I suppose I could not keep desire from surging into them, for with a self-satisfied and triumphant air he said, 'No soreness in the little twat, eh!'

'Oh, George,' I burst out, 'what language! I see you mean to make me as depraved as a common strumpet. Yes, as you will have it, there is no soreness either in my cunt or my arse or anything that's mine.'

'Let's see,' was his cool rejoinder, and drawing me into a vacant tent, he pulled up my dress, poked his fingers into both my holes and pinched the lips of my quim, here, there and everywhere. I stood it without flinching, smiling at him victoriously. He wanted to fuck me on the spot, but I didn't care to be caught in the daytime.

'No, wait until tonight. I may as well tell you, sir, I witnessed most of your performance last night . . .'

'The little whore,' he breathed quietly.

'. . . and what you did then I imagine you can do again. Only, why bother about going into the dining-tent? You have fucked all three of us, and you might as well fuck us in our own beds. I suppose the others now know I am no more virtuous than they are.'

'A good idea,' he cried, slapping his thigh. 'I will see the girls in the other tent are fully occupied. There's only Lena who hasn't been rummaged so far, and she won't resist when she sees her chums gobbling up the naked cocks. That will keep them engaged and they won't bother about us and we can make as much noise as we please.'

So that evening we were scarcely half undressed when in strolled my noble George and his henchman in their pyjamas which they had not even taken the trouble to fasten properly, so that we could plainly see their horrid cocks and testicles waggling about. There was a flutter, for I hadn't told the girls, wishing to take them by surprise, and moreover I didn't expect the boys so early. Annie and Tottie were very shamefaced till I explained I knew all about their pranks and was not minded to let them have all the fun to themselves.

'But you, Lucy!' gasped Annie. 'I shouldn't have thought you would have openly invited them to invade us like this – so shameful.'

'Well you needn't be afraid. I fancy your share will be small, for you aren't in much condition to take a man, sore as you are.'

Annie blushed and murmured something about being bashful in the presence of others.

'Oh,' I replied, laughing, 'the bashfulness ought to be on our part,' for George had collared me and pulled my chemise to my waist, while Randolph had done the same for Tottie, and both were unblushingly sucking our titties and tickling us where it would do most good. In another moment we were plucked clean, with not a feather left to fly with, and rolled naked on to the floor. The two fellows stripped to the buff also, and we stretched our thighs wide to receive them.

'Gently, dear George,' I whispered, 'don't savage me again.' He could be a delicate lover when he liked, and with what joy I felt the long prick gradually penetrate me, first the knob with its delicious titillation of my corrugated quim, then its regular ascension till it struck me somewhere inwardly, and made me jump. I worked my bottom madly, and had a beautiful spend without any thought of what might accrue from the warm flood I felt George darting in as his joy culminated too.

I was breathless and offered no resistance when the rogue picked me up, laid me across his knee so that my bottom was in full view, and bidding Randy do the same to Tottie, brought our bums together and began to compare and point out the differences. Neither was Annie spared. She was stripped, and all three of us invited to kneel down with arses well up, so that our lovers could gaze at our secret charms at their ease. Next we were stood on our heads against the camp-beds; our fuckers knelt in front, and placing our thighs round their necks, opened our little quims, and sucked them deliciously, investigating our nether holes too meanwhile. I felt George's prick stiffening again, and placed it between my pendant bosoms where the friction they imparted to it brought on a lovely horn at once.

There was a nice position for you! I wondered what the courtly old ambassador, at whose table I had been dining the week before, would have thought of Miss Crofton could he have seen her now, or whether Lord C— would have been so attentive at the last ball had he been able to picture me to himself with my bottom in the air and my cunt on the lips of a long-cocked young bugger like George. The other girls were a bit surprised, too, to see the stylish Lucy abandoning herself to such obscenities, but like me they began to understand there were many things opening on the horizon of our young lives we had not dreamed of.

When our cunts had been sucked dry we were let down.

'Come now,' said Tottie, 'suppose we treat these young gentlemen the same way. What is good for us ought to be good for them.' They laughed excitedly and Randy said we were a damned good sort. How funny they looked with their legs in the air, their pricks pointing downwards and showing the reverse side with the wavy seam through which they had been shooting their glowing sperm into our lascivious bellies! I seized George's bean-tosser in my mouth, and worked myself across his face till I had got my bottom fair on to his mouth, and could feel his tongue exquisitely tickling my arsehole. I drew my hand up and down the loosely hanging cods, and felt George shiver. Annie, who was looking on with admiration at our pluck, said, 'Mayn't I have a suck, too, Lucy?'

'Presently, presently.'

'But if you work his prick like that, you will have it all over you.'

'I intend to have every damned drop,' I said emphatically, 'um . . . um . . .' The gigantic prick quivered and swelled in my mouth. I rammed a finger into his bum, and plugged it furiously. 'Come, come, why don't you come George?' He did come and I got such a mouthful. I retained it, went to Annie as though to kiss her, and emptied it into her rosebud of a mouth. She started back. 'I told you you'd get it and now you've got it. How do you like your baptism of semen?'

George shrieked with laughter at Annie's wry face, and in revenge she squatted across him regardless of her sore quim, rubbed it in his face and on his nose, and bit his cock, not too hard but enough to make him jump. Tottie did not go so far with her boy, but contented herself with giving him a thrilling suck and then letting him down.

'At that moment we heard suppressed laughter from the other tent, and several faint cries, 'That's King Cock speaking to Queen Cunt,' said George. 'The last despairing call of Lena's expiring maidenhead, or the first triumphant cry of satisfied desire. You can take it which way you like.'

This was succeeded by more laughter, and the sound of resonant smacks, and we girls in response flung ourselves on the naked men and smacked their bottoms as hard as we could. Of course we got the worst of it, for after we had amused ourselves they manoeuvred us into a convenient position, and treated us like refractory children by soundly drumming our enticing rotundities in turn. Our shrieks went up in the still air, and brought a peal of hilarity from the other side.

'Now, sonny,' said George, 'take Lucy on your lap like this, and I was transferred to the lad's swelling prick, and following Tottie's example sat with my back to him and the long machine between my legs. Randy's thing was a good length, but not so stout nor so awe-inspiring as George's. They worked their jocks between the lips of our quims, and gave us a lovely frigging. It was most amusing to see the purple heads dodging in and out of our thighs, now buried, now sticking several inches up, as if we had a dwarf prick springing from our mottes. Annie fastened on to and sucked them alternately as they appeared, glutinous from the lubrication of our half-spending cunts, and I can assure you it is not half a bad way. To be frigged by a cock like this, instead of being fucked, gives a very nice sensation, especially when the ridge rubs against your clitoris.

\*     \*     \*

We were all worked up again by now, and Ethel said, 'Oh, let's try it, mamma.'

'Very well. As your thighs are not so thick as mine nor your bottom so big, you take Harry between your legs; only lie on him with your back on his belly.'

Ethel frigged herself comfortably on my cock, which stood out some inches from her quim. Her mother sucked it for a moment, and after remarking that it tasted very nice as it issued oiled from the cunt, said, 'I think we can do better than Lucy. There's enough left to get a fuck from.'

She accordingly straddled across us, and at every thrust received the head in her quim.

'Don't be in too great a hurry, Harry, and I shall get a spend out of it. A few easy strokes and I shall come, too.

This double fuck was a great strain on my endurance, and it was only by exercising much restraint I could keep my discharge back till Rose was ready. They both cried out together they were coming, and we all three had a most pleasurable emission. The sight afforded in the glass of the inter-woven pile of thighs surmounted by Rose's capacious and handsome bottom was not a small part of my enjoyment.

\*     \*     \*

Well, it was not long before the way they grabbed us round the breasts and began to heave their bottoms, told us that the spongy heads, darting up and down, would soon send a shower of milky juice over our bellies.

'Don't let them waste it,' I admonished Annie; 'and Randy, go slow while George spends.'

Annie got the dose from his prick, and remembering the trick I had played on her returned it to Tottie, saying it properly belonged to her, and she was only holding it in trust. Then she came over to Randy, extracted a copious discharge from him, and I could not very well refuse to receive it. The dear girl with her lips pursed up approached her face to mine and signed me to open my mouth, malice, delight and lust sparkling in her eyes. I did so bravely, but the wicked imp, instead of pouring it in and having done with it, held her mouth over mine and slowly dribbled the pungent broth in drop by drop. When I had got it all she inserted her tongue, and stirred it round till the stuff had disappeared down my throat.

'We are quite even, now,' she remarked quietly, and George with a clap on her bottom said, 'Bravo Annie! well played little woman.'

Well, I don't propose to go on in more detail. I was fucked six times by George, and three times by Randolph; Tottie was fucked once by George, and twice by his chum; and even Annie got over her indisposition sufficiently to receive them each once in her glowing cunt. Besides this, at our request, the two boys gave an exhibition of male sodomy, and to our huge delight we enjoyed the spectacle of seeing their cocks disappear in their own anatomies. I noticed that when they felt the insertion it brought their pricks up with a jerk at once, and as one of us took care to have the unoccupied cock in a mouth or between our bubbies it was immediately made ready for a legitimate fuck. It goes without mention that neither Tottie's bottom nor mine escaped, and some of the copulations I have inventoried occurred in our unfortunate dark holes. Tottie had a particularly enticing bottom, soft, round, and plump, and the wretches were always sticking their pricks into it.

Days before the camping trip came to an end all reserve was abandoned, and all shame lost.

The usual end to the day was a naked romp, in which you would, had you been fortunate enough to be there, espied four lusty young men, strong limbed and stout pricked, rolling over six healthy, laughing young women in a state of nature. The large dining-tent was the scene of the revels, and as we had a piano there we commonly indulged in a dance, where instead of the conventional style you would see a pair waltzing with the lady holding the gentleman's prick, and her partner reciprocating by passing his hand between her soft thighs. And the fucking that went on. I sometimes wonder whether we didn't carry the scent of the spunk we shed back to town, for I am sure we were all saturated with it.

What's more, three of us, and I was one, got more than we bargained for, and in some months' time had to make a lengthened visit to 'the country'. Mine was a chubby boy with George written all over him, but I doubt whether the others could tell who was the father of their brats. When I was sure of my state I made up my mind to have all the fucking I could get.

Needless to say I found plenty of amorous youths, but I had to play the hypocrite tremendously to make them think they were the solely favoured ones. This was a year ago and baby is now three months old. I am more careful now if I want a bit of grummit. You, Rose, you lucky girl, can fuck as hard as you like without fear, but you will find that George will give you a good deal of trouble.

CHAPTER EIGHT

## *Unnatural Practices*

'George did give trouble. He soon got used to my attractions, and as I said, I could not keep him away from other women. He fucked the servants openly, and any number of my friends, though I will say my husband was a gentleman in that respect, and never let on who his sweethearts were – fond as he was of boasting of this, that or the other damned fine grind he had had – unless he was sure I already knew their names, or would know soon. Reproaches and remonstrances were perfectly useless, and, worst of all, the wretch had awakened a mine of lasciviousness in myself that I had never dreamed existed. I felt I must have plenty of prick, and as I couldn't get it from him I determined to please myself. I threatened him with reprisals, and only extorted a careless laugh, so after Ethel was born I simply took all the lovers who offered themselves, and snapped my fingers at George. He did not trouble me very long, poor fellow, for in a few years he died fighting, as he had lived, furiously. For some fourteen years I have been a widow and a widow I mean to remain. As you can guess, with a figure like this' (looking herself over approvingly) 'and with my fortune, I could have married again and again, but I objected to being tied up. Suitors who would be content to fuck me could have as much as they liked without going to church. I haven't always escaped' (with a laugh) 'for there are two young brothers of Ethel's being brought up far away from here in ignorance of their parentage. I think, however, the floods of spunk poured into my womb have pretty well drowned out the danger now, so don't imagine, Master Harry, this long spike has left anything behind it, unless you have planted a kiddy here' (smacking Ethel's belly). 'If you have it doesn't matter. She's bound to fall sooner or later, and besides a youngster does a girl good – fills out her body with succulent flesh, and opens her quim more. Too tight a quim is always a drawback to a woman. Dear me, I must relieve myself.'

'And I too,' said Ethel demurely. 'I am bursting.'

'Well, piss out boldly, and don't be afraid.'

Rose got off the bed with a lurch, and I noticed her utterance had sensibly thickened. Ethel followed with an unsteady giggle, and I sat on the edge, swaying a little myself.

'Would you like . . . hic . . . to see a woman pissing, Harry, my dear?'

I nodded violently.

'Well I must sit down, for I'm hanged if I can stand steady. But you, Ethel, hold the pot behind you, bend down and piss well back.'

Ethel, still giggling and looking rather dazed, did so, and a sparkling stream came hissing out and tinkled into the chamber utensil. Rose was squatting on another and letting loose a deluge. Her ample dimensions enveloped the china, and flowed all round the edges. I felt in need of a comfortable pee myself, and a comical idea entered my rather dizzy nut. As these two beautiful creatures were so far gone as to have lost all sense of decency, while I had had none for hours, I didn't suppose they would squirm at a little fun. So I got down, winked at Ethel who had finished, and pointed my prick at Rose's polished shoulders. I waited till she had done, and just as she turned to rise touched her, told her to remain as she was, and let fly down her broad back.

'You nasty beast,' she exclaimed with a shiver, 'how dare you?'

'Be quiet, or it will be all over the floor. Look, Ethel, see it trickling down her back, and through the crack of her arse into the pot.'

Rose entered into the spirit of the joke, and exclaimed, 'What a hot shower-bath! After all it feels rather nice.'

My urine streamed out, and I pissed for nearly a minute without ceasing. Ethel suffocated with laughter at her mother's awkward posture, and the way she had been trapped.

'Good God, boy, are you never going to finish?' Rose shouted as the stream still fell. 'Well, I'm damned if I ever had this done to me before! I shouldn't have been surprised had it been some lecherous old devil who was up to any filthy trick there is, but a young cockerel like you who had never seen a woman's naked arse before . . . my word you have got a damned cheek. Oh, you've finished at last! Well now you had better get a towel and dry my arse for me.'

Cleaning operations followed: the cunts were wiped, powdered and scented, and after another draught of the sparkling wine the two women hugged and cuddled me furiously, both raging with prurient itch and still unsatisfied. I was nothing loth, and returned their caresses with interest, biting their ears and bottoms, and even the lips of their quims. My prick, which to my own surprise appeared inexhaustible, was quickly in a noble state. Rose seized it with a cry of frenzy, dragged a pillow under and me on top of her, and with one heave engulfed the whole prick. She bucked in a volcanic rage from beginning to end, and her fiery language of before was nothing to the stream of profanity that now issued from her intoxicated mouth. She cursed and caressed me without losing breath and ordered

Ethel to suck 'that blasted arse till he farts'. Ethel slobbered my bottom accordingly, and then with an inane giggle began biting it and my balls and thighs. As soon as we were chock-a-block Rose made me get outside her, so that she could 'feel my bollocks on her thighs and get more spunk out of me', an attitude, by the way, that always gives you a sustained spend, but has the disadvantage of permitting you to get a part of your prick only into the cunt. My knackers were thus in full view to Ethel, and she moulded them firmly, and nibbled at them. Finally in a sort of frenzy she rained a shower of blows on the big manly bottom so temptingly displayed, stammering in a thick voice that she couldn't resist such a chance, and then the spunk flowed once more amid a renewed torrent of obscenities, in which all three vied as to who should produce the most shocking language.

Ethel rolled me off her mother, and on to herself. In a few strokes my prick stiffened under the pressure of her heated cunt, and we set to with unabated vigour. Rose screamed with glee, and saying, 'Just look at the two randy young buggers,' plumped her dripping cunt across Ethel's face, and stuffed her arse against my mouth. Between her own dashing bucks and the pressure of the huge buttocks poor Ethel was nearly smothered, and I could hear the wet cunt soughing on her face and lips. Rose gave her no mercy. The big bottom flopped up and down, and after a fresh discharge had made Ethel squeal with ecstasy her face emerged smeared from forehead to chin with a highly-scented layer of frothy cream deposited from her mother's raging furnace.

Breathless and perspiring both women drank greedily when I presented the beakers to their lips, and this about finished Ethel, as I guessed it would, for a precious idea had entered my mind, which I feared to propose while she was in her full senses. Meanwhile Rose rambled on.

'Fancy your having the impudence to piddle down my back! Oh, you will do' (admiringly). 'You are a nice young man to take into one's bed. No one, not even George, has ever done that to me before, though I have douched more than one with my pissing-trap – ay, and more than that!'

She ruminated for a moment and seemed to be a little undecided – then with a burst of intoxicated laughter she whispered thickly in my ear, 'I've pooped in a man's mouth more than once . . . what do you think of that?' I suppose I looked astonished at this revelation for she went on, 'I swear by my cunt I have. It was always at their own request – there are some men who like that, you know – but it's not so dashed easy to muster up courage to do it as you might think.'

'Well, you are a confounded whore and no mistake, but I like you all the same.'

'No, no whore – only a woman with a healthy cunt, and plenty of hot blood who, when she makes up her mind to fuck, does it thoroughly. And I'm awfully fond of you, you young rip. You *are* such a splendid fucker. You've got fairly into my bones, and Ethel's too, I think, for she's never done for Tom what she has for you.'

I was standing at the bedside and my cock was convenient to her mouth, pretty limp, of course. Rose kissed it tenderly, saying. 'Nasty little lump of putty . . . did it spit all down my back? And if I took it in my mouth I s'pose it would want to pee in there' (turning back the skin and licking out the coagulated semen that had gathered in the crevices). 'I don't believe it has got any pee or any juice left in it.'

Her lips closed over the nut and she ran her tongue over the orifice, as though searching for something. By heavens, I thought, I believe the giddy creature wants me to piss down her throat! I am sorry I emptied my bladder just now.

Rose went on, alternately sucking and crooning to herself, 'How soft and pulpy the naughty little prick is! I don't believe it can even piss a little drop now. I wonder if it piddled slowly it would get up hard and strong again?'

I wondered too, and determined to try and squeeze a few drops, especially as she looked up with heavy eyes and, oh, such a wanton smile and quoted the old, old gag, 'If you can't come, pee a little.'

'By God, if you tickle me like that you *will* make me piss!'

One hand slid under my balls, and a finger reached out for my arsehole. Impatiently pulling me nearer she plunged it into the unattractive tunnel, sending me wild with the titillation, and making me reckless of the consequences.

'I'm sure I'm going to piss,' I warned. She sucked away and took no notice.

A few drops issued. She did not blench but swallowed them, and I could trace them, as it were, falling down the round white throat. The amorous woman, then, intended to give me this startling proof of affection! I pissed a little more, and despite the shower-bath I had given her back and bottom a few minutes before, the novelty and amazing obscenity of it all irritated my bladder to such an extent that I felt prepared to supply another tidy stream.

'Look out, there's more coming, you darling whore,' I cried.

'I'll make it if there isn't,' she replied, ramming her finger up my bottom as far as it would go, and twisting it round and round.

I could contain myself no longer, and pissed heartily. Rose lifted my cock out and held it over her mouth. With another intoxicated chuckle she watched the amber stream issue, and pour into her gullet. As the last drop disappeared down her throat she murmured dreamily, 'Fucked all over, and pissed all over. What a damned whore this boy is making of me!'

Her eye fell on her finger which had come out of my arse in a parlous state. 'Haven't I loved you well, laddie? Would you like me to do something dirtier still? See!'

The excellent lady deliberately wiped her finger on the ruddy curling lips, and pulling my head down challenged me to kiss them. I didn't repudiate the embrace. I was in a state of exaltation – what with the wine, the effluvium of her amorous carcase, impregnated and saturated with my own semen and exhaling the incense of copulation from every pore – that made me game for any excess. I kissed the pasty lips passionately, and with one hand on my prick, already stiffened by these ultra-erotic experiences to a respectable state, and the other round my neck, Rose whispered thickly, 'You have fucked my cunt and my mouth, and pissed all over me, now bugger me, dear.'

Now, I had proposed to myself to take advantage of Ethel's helpless condition to explore the depths of the handsome bottom whose virginity was still intact. I pointed to it, and intimated my preference for an arena that was so far untouched.

'I think you are too big for her, but anyway, shove it up my arse first, there's a darling.'

After one or two attempts Rose got on to her knees, and pulled open her bottom. I entered quite easily, and in a few strokes was up to the balls. But Rose's limbs gave way, and she sank down laughing inanely at her inability to bear up against my ram. I drew it out and attacked the innocent Ethel's posterior, but, being too squiffy to think of oiling her hole and getting no assistance from my victim, only succeeded in making her grunt and nearly ricking my prick. I desisted, and in a few minutes, thoroughly overcome by the combined forces of Venus and Bacchus, we were all fast asleep.

## CHAPTER NINE

# *The Morning After*

As you may imagine, dear reader, it was late before any of us woke next morning. Dreamily I fancied I had once or twice heard a light tapping, and a renewal of it finally brought me to consciousness. I said nothing, but got out of bed, and heard light steps retreating. The open drawer whence Ethel had procured the photos attracted my attention. I found it nearly full, mostly of nude pictures of Rose, with and without cavaliers. In pretty well every instance the features were blurred over. There were some others, evidently of friends of hers, and one that was apparently merely a photo of a fancy drawing. It represented the athletic lady seated across one prick, with another in her bottom. Over the shoulders of the gentleman in the chair projected two more stalwart priapuses which Rose was alternately gobbling; in her hands were two more, and in the fleshy folds at the junction of thighs and stomach two more. A rather gluttonous ideal of which, since it was not a picture from real life anyway, she had not been able to attain the actuality. It gave a good indication of the comprehensive desires of the charming woman who had been complaisant enough to make herself and her daughter my mistresses of a night.

While still engaged in admiring the treasures of the drawer, many of which revealed hitherto-unthought-of vistas along the path of love, the door opened gently, and an attractive-looking maid peeped in. On seeing me she hastily withdrew. I returned to the bed and laid myself behind Rose, who after various yawns and stretches also awoke. The pictures had brought my noble bean-tosser to a very excitable state, and the first thing Rose realised was the manly pillar pressing against her warm bottom. She looked round with a smile of recognition, and lifting her thigh, guided it into her cunt, moist and hot with the secretions of a night's repose. Nothing loth I quickly slipped it into the velvety sheath. I think a woman's cunt is always more smooth and slippery in the morning than at any other time. The attitude was most enjoyable with the cushion presented by her robust arse to afford pressure on the cods . . . I hadn't given many strokes, however, before Rose seemed to recollect where we had left off the previous evening. She cooly transferred the piston to her bottom, at the same time placing my hand on her cunt and intimating I was to frig it. This time the little piece of sodomy was brought to completion, and for the first time I had the huge satisfaction of pouring my seed into a feminine arse, and a first-rater at that. Rose crept out of bed, and beckoned me to the bathroom.

'You, naughty boy, you gave me a new experience when you pissed over my back last night. Would you like to do it again? Only we must both get into the bath.'

The nightdresses soon came off, and Rose going on her hands and knees, I pissed joyously over her back, into her arsehole and cunt, and finally she squatted on her hams, drew my backside on to her face, and sucked my bottom while I finished my piss between her bubbies. She was dripping from shoulders to feet. I thought perhaps I might venture further, and reminded her caressingly of her mouth. Rose laughed and shook her head.

'It was very rude of me to make you do that. Perhaps it was all very well as the culmination of a highly exciting bout of rogering, and I suppose I did it as a sort of reward to a good boy for fucking me so well, but you mustn't expect that indulgence often, sir. Moreover, to prevent you getting too cocky I'm going to deluge *you*.'

Whereupon the big woman, laughing heartily, heaved up her mighty arse, hitched forward her cunt and a broad shower descended. She seemed to take particular pleasure in pissing on my prick – in reprisal, no doubt, for the obscenities to which it had provoked her. A refreshing bath cleared away all traces of the reciprocal pissing match.

I questioned Rose as to the girl who had been knocking.

'Oh, that's Cerise, my maid. I only keep two servants. With my habits it would not do to have too many. When I give a drum or a dance I get in outsiders to help. Jane, the cook, and Cerise have been with me a long time, and I treat them too well for them to betray me. They have high wages and liberty to have as many lovers as they wish' (laughing). 'You should see Jane sometimes, with two or three burly policemen and perhaps a soldier or two performing on her. She is a bouncing woman, and is nearly as fond of fucking as I am. She thinks nothing of taking on three or four fellows at once. Ethel and I amuse ourselves peeping through the kitchen door – in fact, we have some secret holes for the purpose – and we see some lovely sights.

'Cerise, too, I fancy does not often sleep alone. She generally has a new boy every few months, and between high wages and good living and the presents of their lovers they know they have got too good a home not to be faithful. The maid was aware I had got someone with me and probably did not want to be disturbed, or she would have been in long ago.'

At that moment Cerise tapped at the door, and to my surprise Rose told her to enter. She came in blushing a little but apparently not much concerned at the sight of a naked man in her mistress's company and took orders for breakfast. Rose introduced her formally and then said, 'This young gentleman has been fucking me all night Cerise, and will probably appreciate an appetising meal. Let us have something nice, my dear. And if there are a few condiments that will have an effect on this very shocking part of him' (tapping my prick) 'why, so much the better. Don't you think he is a very fine young man, Cerise?' (The girl was good enough to approve.) 'And he's better even than he looks. How many times do you think he came last night?'

Cerise, looking me over with a critical eye, ventured, 'Five or six, ma'am?'

'Nearly double, I assure you. Didn't you, Harry?'

I had lost count myself and modestly said I didn't imagine it could have been so many. Rose insisted and as she was fervidly frigging my prick in the heat of her admiration it was growing lengthier and lengthier.

'And notwithstanding all the work we gave it is seems as rampant as ever.'

'We?'

' Oh yes! Ethel had a bit as well.'

'My word, ma'am, if it has been grinding in your two mills all night and comes out like this it must be a beauty.'

Cerise licked her lips and looked longingly at my nudity.

'Why, I believe the girl's getting cockstruck herself,' cried Rose, 'Didn't you manage to get a fuck last night, Cerise?'

'No, indeed! Robert couldn't get away, and I've been a widow for some nights.'

'Oh ho, we'll soon put that right. Here's a chance for you, Master Harry. You've fucked the mistress, and now you can see how you like the maid. Swing your arse round, Cerise.'

The girl at once backed up to her mistress, who without ceremony flung the dress above her waist, and disclosed a fine pair of thighs surmounted by a very capable-looking bottom.

'No drawers, you see,' laughed Rose, tickling the maid between the thighs with the point of my jock. 'Drawers are rather at a discount in this house.'

'Yes, they have to be pulled up and down so often; and they also show telltale stains, don't they, ma'am?'

Here Cerise could not contain herself any longer and putting her hand back, impatiently seized the radiant staff, guided it into her glowing snatch, and began thrusting with a fierce energy that made us both laugh. Rose slapped the plump bottom briskly, but Cerise appeared to derive greater fervour from the operation, and resting her hands on the edge of the bath, bucked so rapidly that I could scarcely maintain my position. Her cunt was a comfortable fit and had a good 'nip' which soon brought on a most competent ejaculation, which she received with much satisfaction.

'There,' said Rose with a final slap, 'now you've got your pot full of juice you'd better keep it there to prevent your quim getting too dry and not let Jane suck it out, as she's so fond of doing.'

'Oh, ma'am' (with mock modesty, winking her eye at me), 'how you do talk. What will Mr Temple think of us?'

I thought I had dropped into a pretty hot corner; what would you think?

'Well,' said her free-and-easy mistress, 'Harry's seen your bottom, and you've had a damned good fuck, so there will be no stiffness between you in future.'

'Oh!' retorted the maid quickly, 'I hope there will be, occasionally, at any rate, for from what l have felt of it, I like Mr Temple's stiffness. But I don't think it will take me long to remove it.'

'Go on,' said Rose, belting her arse again, 'would you snatch the prick out of your mistress's cunt?'

Cerise having received the balmy essence she was pining for, we returned to the bedroom and found Ethel just awake, and looking rather seedy. She was somewhat abashed at our two naked forms and blushed a little. We had breakfast, and Rose having begged for one more grind as a deoch an dorras, I watered her cunt again, and we separated with many caresses till the following evening. I was unable to return that night, and indeed was not sorry for a brief respite from Rose's insatiable furnace.

## CHAPTER TEN

# *Acquaintance Renewed*

I received a warm welcome when I revisited the hospitable abode, both the ladies being in full evening dress – that is with smocks only, and very open at that, so that two pairs of tantalising bosoms made my mouth water at once. After preliminary caresses we ascended to the bedroom.

'All naked,' said Rose, 'is the order of the evening. Come, Harry, we will be your handmaidens.'

I was disrobed by fair hands which fluttered about my person in a very exhilarating manner.

'How's dear Cock Robin?' asked Ethel, squeezing it tenderly, 'not been in any stray cunts or bottoms I hope, you rogue' (shaking a finger at me). 'I was not so far gone, though I must confess the wine had got into my head, that I did not feel you trying to penetrate my poor bottom. How was it you didn't get right up me? I'm sure I could not have resisted you, and I'd have been just as well pleased to find myself opened up to traffic. If you could have got this monster in I shouldn't need to fear others much.'

'I suppose I can try again,' I laughed.

'If bottoms are to be the order of the night, begin with mine,' said Rose flinging off her garment and appearing in startling nudity, 'I will go on my knees, but I must have something up my cunt also.'

She looked around and took an unusually thick candle from the holder. With a pair of scissors she traced a spiral groove along half of it, and remarked, 'That will make a very good dildo, I think. Now, Harry, here we are. My arse is in the air. In with your prick, and slap the candle up my twat. Ethel dear, step across me, and let Harry have your cunt to suckle.'

My prick sank into its soft abode, and I rammed the quim below with such effect that the widow was at once brought to the two emissions with several energetic 'buggers' and 'damns'. These made her daughter laugh so much that her cunt did not receive much of a mugging after all since it wavered to and fro and I couldn't keep the focus.

'There,' said Rose:, 'that's what the sailor called "a bloody good fuck", and now we must get this saucy prick up again ready for Ethel's tender bum.'

'Um, I'd sooner have it up my quim first, but anything's better than being pissed down, isn't it, mamma? Lord, how you squirmed on the pot when you felt Harry hosing you down.'

As she made no mention of the sequel I judged Rose had not confided it to her, and held my tongue too. Rose pushed me into a low chair, and kneeling between my thighs gently rubbed my prick upon her bubbies. Each time the head appeared she took it in her lips and sucked it. The position was so enticing that I could willingly have gone on till a second emission flooded the gracious lips.

Meanwhile Ethel, seated by me, had her arms around my neck and a titty in my mouth. Her mother from time to time extended a hand and tuned up her cunt till the girl was thoroughly worked up. All this, however, was done leisurely, and I took occasion to ask Ethel how it was that she had only so lately treated herself to a genuine fuck, and had not lost her maidenhead several years ago at least.

'Well, from the earliest time I can recollect I have been used to sucking mamma's quim and bottom, and, in fact, performing every office for her that anyone without a prick could, and she has never been afraid to let me see her enjoying a fuck. So it was not want of opportunity; but mamma always told me to wait – that I was too young and that I would appreciate it all the more if I gave my cunt time to ripen. With the blood of a randy father and an amorous mother seething in me I was keen to fuck as early as mamma did, only she told me how she had suffered through being ripped open in her teens, and I restrained myself. Nature at last became too strong and I felt I must fuck or burst. When mother saw I couldn't wait, she advised me to pick Tom for my first trial. "I haven't fucked him myself," she said, "but I should think he's about your size, and not too green."

'Tom is a nice young fellow, and mamma's tip suited me. I let him see I liked him, and having encouraged him to kiss me, and take small liberties, I ascertained en passant that he had the wherewithal to satisfy an amorous girl and decided to bring him to the point – or perhaps I should say bring myself to the point . . . of his prick . . . on a fishing excursion in the country. I carefully anointed my quim, for I had no mind to be torn to pieces like mother, discarded my drawers and felt that once Tom had got his hand on my thighs and bottom his prick would soon follow. For a while I sat reading, while Tom fished without much luck; presently I persuaded him to leave the rod to itself and come and talk. He flung himself readily on the grass at my feet, seeing which I drew up my knees, as though to make a better support for my book, and thought to myself, "He is not the boy I take him for if he doesn't have a peep."

'He must have seen pretty well, for his conversation wandered a good deal, and when I opened my legs and gave him a sight of my quim, as well as my naked thighs and curving bottom, he became positively ludicrous. Presently he ventured, "What small feet you have, Ethel, and pretty ankles, too."

'I sported light openwork stockings through which a fair amount of flesh could be distinguished – in fact I must have looked pretty naked from feet to waist.

' "Have I?" said I indifferently, pulling up my skirt to see.

' "Yes, and by George, shapely legs, too. Why, they are nearly as big as mine."

' "Go on: never!" pulling my dress still higher till my calves were in full view.

' "Yes, they are, look." He yanked up his trousers, and hitching himself closer compared his hairy limbs with mine.

' "Oh, yours are much bigger."

' "Let's measure." With his handkerchief he took the dimensions. Once having got his hand on my leg he was loth to remove it and instead slipped it on to the naked flesh; at which, of course, I was much shocked, but carefully refrained from repulsing him. The boy's courage was rising, and so was his prick, the agitation of which he could not conceal. He placed my feet together, pushed the skirt to the knee, and lifting both legs slightly, pretended to admire the limbs disclosed to view.

' "By gum, Ethel, you really have splendid legs. I shouldn't have thought they were so fine. And I'll be bound you have still more beautiful limbs beyond."

'The scamp had seen enough of them to know what he was talking about. "But," he continued with a sudden chuckle, "I have a still finer limb that you haven't seen."

' "What's that?"

' "My middle leg."

' "Your middle leg!"

' "Yes, you couldn't show one, you know, not even if I were to lift you right up," and he lifted my feet still higher. We were getting on!

' "Oh Tom," I cried in pretended alarm, "you will have me over backwards if you do that."

' "And if I did, dear," with a threatening tilt, "I suppose I should only see a lot of fluffy drapery, such as girls always delight to stuff under their petticoats."

' "I am afraid you wouldn't, Tom . . . you would see . . ."

' "What?"

' "My thighs . . . and my b–b–bottom," I stammered, covering my face with my hands. In an instant up went my legs, my dress fell on my waist, and my ravisher was gloating over what I had described. I covered my motte with a decorous hand, but he separated my legs, and had my agitated cunt under his gaze. I protested mildly, "Oh, Tom, don't shame me so. Do put my clothes down!" but as I made no attempt to enforce the command, and showed no signs of anger, Tom wasn't such a fool as to give up the smart craft he had carried by *coup de main*. I peered through my fingers and saw his cock trying to burst from his breeches, and felt glad it made so good a showing. Tom was evidently in ecstasies at the sight before him, his lips were moving unsteadily, his face was flushed, and I could feel his hands and limbs trembling. And indeed' (put in Ethel parenthetically, glancing with an engaging assumption of modesty at her beautifully moulded thighs and smooth belly), 'I think he was a lucky young dog to get hold of such a poke, don't you, Harry?'

Of course I acquiesced heartily.

'Well, he pawed my thighs and bottom, giving me a delicious thrill as I felt his hand gliding along my flesh, and fumbled at his buttons till he got his cock out.

' "Oh, what is that?" I said very feebly.

' "That's my middle leg, and I guess it's going to make acquaintance with your middle, dear," he replied with a grin.

' "Oh, Tom, Tom" (reproachfully), "are you going to ravish me? Think of my honour."

'He looked surprised, for as I found out, he inferred from my easy acquiescence in his proceedings that he had not to do with a *virgo intacta*, and wondered where my honour came in. When he darted to the assault he ascertained his mistake, the more especially as I begged him not to hurt me, for I had never done it before. It was a good thing I had taken precautions. Tom was so excited I should have come off badly, but my rape was accomplished without too much pain, and the subsequent proceedings made me forget even that modicum of suffering. Three more times did I extract his essential oil from him that afternoon, and now we are supposed to be lovers. Tom, indeed, talked about marriage, but I speedily disabused him of that idea, and gave him to understand he was to be content with fucking me, and not worry about going through a church door. But he is too modest, and takes few of the liberties you have done, with all your innocence, Master Harry, and, like mamma, I prefer a sweetheart who sticks at nothing. 'But, mamma dear, you aren't going to make Harry discharge in your bubbies, are you?'

Rose rather reluctantly gave up my prick, which was just on the point of saturating her willing mouth, and having arranged Ethel I attacked her bottom. But it was still in vain. Rose urged me not to give up, saying, 'With patience and plenty of Vaseline you could get into the eye of a needle,' but it seemed to me that the pain wasn't worth the trouble. So, after getting the head partly in, and extorting some groans from Ethel, we transferred the scene to her gaping quim, and her matrix was thoroughly watered.

Some gamahuching formed the next dish, which gave me occasion to comment on the sensitiveness of Rose's love nest, and the pleasure she seemed to derive from this tribute to her attractiveness.

'You are not the only one to admire mamma's crack. There's one of her gentleman friends who between fucks likes nothing better than to lie or sit with her thighs round his neck, and sniff and suck at her juicy quim. In fact I believe he sleeps with his face under her bottom or buried in the folds of her twat.'

'Yes,' said Rose, 'he does, and sometimes he gets a sniff of more than quim. If a gentleman will poke his nose into my bottom I can't be responsible for what happens . . . and women are always windy you know' (laughing). 'But unfortunately his capacity isn't equal to his will. He's never good for more than two or three goes, and I have had to stipulate that when he visits me he is to bring his cousin with him, so that between them I can make sure of a reasonable quantum of grummit. The arrangement has the advantage of enabling me to do without the candle, and have two pricks in my holes at once. Very nice, too, I assure you, to feel a couple of warm viscous streams pouring into belly and bowels at once.

'Is that as nice as two little cocks in your cunny together?' said Ethel cunningly.

'Oh, I know what you are driving at. I haven't tried it since, but much as this good quim of mine has been stretched I don't think even now it would take in two pricks like Harry's.'

'Tell us what you are driving at, Ethel,' I put in.

## CHAPTER ELEVEN

# *Ethel's Story*

When I was about thirteen or fourteen, we were staying at a friend of mamma's who had two boys, one a little younger than myself and one a little older. Now I come to think of it, Mrs Fletcher must have been a lady a good deal after mamma's own heart, for she didn't mind my romping in her boys' bed a bit, and even encouraged us. I remember, too, she seemed to like to see our nightdresses flying up, and was greatly amused when our naked legs got twined together. She was always handling her boys little pricks, and encouraging them to take liberties with my nudity. Of course, accustomed as I was to see naked men fucking mamma, I didn't mind, either. But I was artful enough not to let on that the play was no novelty to me. However, mamma came in one night while we were romping, and as I had heard her in Mrs Fletcher's room just before, whence some significant sounds had been issuing, and as mamma had only got a *peignoir* on, I fear my beloved parent had been up to some of her little games with her good-looking friend, eh, mother? Anyhow she was a little excited, and I saw her lips water as her eye fell on the pair of stiff little cocks. Mamma coolly pulled me to her and stripped off my shift.

'There, boys, you'll be able to tickle and kiss her better now. That's right, that's the way to fondle a pretty young girl. Dear me! you are quite little men with these stiff dollies dancing about.'

Here mamma stroked their young pizzles, each of quite respectable length, but not much thicker than one's finger. She gave the young gentlemen a shuddery feeling. 'Stand up in front of one another, and let me see which is the bigger.'

The two pricks showed scarcely any difference, and together formed a good-sized rod, quite thick enough to fill a full-grown quim. 'I wonder,' said mamma thoughtfully, looking at me. ' I wonder . . . shall I try?'

She lifted her gown, stepped over and between the two lads and began fumbling at their pricks. 'See if you can get them in for me, Ethel, this is rather awkward.'

I lifted the skirt, and a good length of naked limb naturally appeared, but a lot mamma cared for that. We got both heads in, bade the boys stand fast, and mother, lowering herself, gradually worked them in, and told the youngsters to push alternately. I suppose Mrs Fletcher's exertions had made mother's pussy moist, for the little cocks both slipped in to the balls, and then mamma holding on to the front boy to work hard for a spend. We were all laughing excitedly at the grotesque idea, and the lads now thoroughly randy clasping mother's naked waist and thighs under the wrapper – when in stalked their mother.

'Well, I declare,' Rose, she cried, 'what *are* you up to now?'

'Giving the boys a treat,' replied mamma, as cool as a cucumber.

'What! both together? Who'd have thought it? But go on, don't mind me.'

'I don't intend to. It's jolly good fun, and I . . . shall get . . . a . . . lovely. . . burst . . . on in a . . . minute . . . ' accentuating each word with a firm downward thrust that made the youngsters totter.

'Well if you intend to finish them off,' said Mrs Fletcher equally coolly, 'I don't see why the poor boys shouldn't have their fun complete and see what they're poking.' So she raised the wrapper, drew it over mother's head, and there she was impudently naked between the two kiddies. My word, how they stared – the one as the big bubbies descended in an avalanche on his face – the other when he saw himself adjoined to a great soft spreading bottom rubbing up and down his belly. But I fancy somehow it was not the first naked woman the rascals had seen, for Freddie started sucking the titties at once, and as for Jack he hugged the bottom close, and passing his hand round seized mother's *mons Veneris* and twined his fingers in its curls. Mother was too near the climax to care about being naked before anyone. She rammed away and called on the boys to drive into her as hard as they could.

Mrs Fletcher was laughing all the time, and eagerly slapping both her sons' and mamma's bottoms. 'Look at her great bottom, Jack,' she cried, 'doesn't it feel like an air-cushion on your belly? What do you think of it, my boy?'

'Oh mother, it's even bigger than yours and quite as soft and warm.'

'Give them a hand, Ethel. Put your fist between Freddy's thighs, and squeeze his little purse, and I will do the same for Jack. Ram your pricks well in, boys. Give the great impudent thing all she wants. The idea of her having the cheek to ravish my innocent cherubs in this way! Good Lord!' (here she choked with laughter) 'what if they got you in pup, Rose? Oh, what a lark! How I should scream if they dropped you in for it! Boys, if you get Mrs Aintree's belly up, and make her as fat as young Mrs Rossiter – you know how her stomach sticks out – I declare I'll give you a bicycle apiece. Go on, your pricks are quite long enough, I believe. Oh, they're all coming. Your mother's nick has been too much for their poor little pricks, Ethel. They'll let off in a moment.' (Really, mother's eyes were rolling furiously.) 'Hold Freddy tight, Rose, or the spasm will be too acute for him, and he'll fall. I'll look after Jack, but for heaven's sake don't thump that fat bottom of yours so on to him or he'll lose his grip.' The lively dame held Jack up by the bottom, and I did the same for Freddy, while they heaved their souls out into mamma's glowing belly.

'So you hope they've got me in the family-way, do you?' said mother. 'They certainly have spent very well for kids, but I don't think the position is very favourable to the realisation of your malicious hopes. Still, I'll make sure. Hold still, boys.'

Mamma bunched herself together, there was a swish, and a cry from the boys. A still hotter shower than their own spendings burst over their softened pricks and drenched their cods and thighs. Mother observed quietly, 'Sorry to piss on your carpet, Madge, but I flatter myself there's none of the monkeys' spendings in my cunt now. Ah, that's about the last. Quite pleasant, Madge, to piss over the prick that's just fucked you. Get a towel, Ethel.'

'You *are* a cool hand,' said Mrs Fletcher admiringly. 'Never at a loss, Rose. Poor little chaps, to be made to spend their vital essence into your huge cunt, and then to be piddled over for their pains.'

Mother kissed the boys nicely, thanked them for the pleasure they had given her, and then asked Jack how he came to know his mother's bottom was not as big as hers.

'Mamma often lets us play with her bottom, don't you mamma, and we do so like kissing it – and her bosoms. They are lovely, and so are yours, Mrs Aintree. How different a lady is to a girl like Ethel, though she's a dear little play-fellow.'

The rogue in his turn kissed me and sucked my tender nipples, while Freddy was rubbing his face against mamma's naked skin, and purring round her like a kitten.

'Ah, ah, Madge,' gloated mother, 'I see you don't despise two young lads, either. I'll be bound besides kissing your bottom you make them kiss something else, too.'

'Rather. What do you take me for? A boy's tongue's as good as a man's for that.'

'Ever . . . ?' queried mamma, making with her hands behind her back the recognised sign of fucking.

Madge shook her head. 'Not yet.'

The lads were so delighted with their new friend that they wouldn't let mother go till they had kissed and squeezed her all over. They were loud in their admiration of her beautiful limbs and body. She even had to lie down and allow them to inspect at leisure the wonderful place they had been rummaging with their cocks. Mrs Fletcher seemed quite pleased at the way they had comported themselves, and as the two seniors went off I heard her say, 'Well Rose, you are a caution. I should never have thought of a double fuck like that. Upon my word, I've a good mind to try it myself.'

### CHAPTER TWELVE

## *A Toast is Drunk*

'And she did try it on them,' said Rose, 'a night or two after, but whether it was that she was too small, or the boys too bashful before a stranger, she couldn't bring on a spend. I had to console them by taking Jack between my legs, and letting him fuck me. His prick was too slender to more than make me feel just pleasant, so rather to the boy's surprise, when Freddy's turn arrived I got his mother to gamahuche me while he fucked my bottom. His prick felt thin – something like Harry's finger up your arse. Afterwards, I amused myself by taking the two pricks in my mouth together – funny little things, something like a woman's teats. Dear me, I am afraid it would be a stretch, but I really must have a try someday to see if I can manage two full-blown cocks at once. Come now, Harry, have you got a fuck left for the "old woman"?' she enquired affectionately.

I laid her on the bed face downwards, between Ethel's thighs, and straddling the soft glowing limbs douched her quim in that position, to her intense satisfaction.

'The dear fellow's always ready at duty's call,' she exclaimed. 'A glass, Ethel, and we'll drink long life to this noble prick.'

Judge of my astonishment when Rose held the tumbler to her quim, and fairly wrung into it the liquor I had just spilled there. Then she filled it up with wine, 'Here's to your prick, Harry! may it never be empty,' and tossed off the mixture. Truly Rose was a woman of surprises.

As both the ladies were lying side by side, I begged them to draw near the mirror at the foot of the bed, lift their legs up and take them in their hands. When I had put a pillow under each fair rump, you may imagine the reflection presented a stirring view. The curved and sumptuous bottoms, split in the centre by a highly coloured cleft surrounded by hair, the sweeping thighs and the darkling bull's-eyes beneath impelled me to cast myself across their luscious forms and frenetically suck the glorious cunts – with all the more gusto that the whole process was repeated in front of me. Lissom fingers playing on my cock and plunging in my arse brought me once again to a state of exhilaration. This time Rose lay on the edge of the bed, and supported her legs on chairs. Ethel reclined backwards on her mother's belly, and brought all four holes into close proximity. I fucked the dear girl till she poured out a loving tribute on to her mamma's motte, and to procure my own emission buried my prick alternately in Rose's bottom and the two quims till the spasm arrived. Then I plunged it finally into Ethel's crack, and at the same time so vigorously finger-fucked her mother that the ever-ready slit simultaneously burst into tears. This posture, which was my own conception, they thought admirable, and Rose was loud in her praise of the progress that two nights had effected in the education of her pupil, as she claimed me to be.

I will not weary you, dear reader, with further details of that night, except that my mistresses pronounced themselves well satisfied, in token whereof Rose gave me leave once more to piss in her mouth. 'Though I am not going to swallow it this time, sir. Once of that wickedness goes a long way.'

Ethel, used as she was to her mother's pranks, was a good deal astonished when Rose, lying on the floor with a towel under her head, quietly opened her lovely mouth and received the strong-smelling shower without flinching. It bubbled and splashed all over her face. Turning on her side she emptied what she had taken in on to the towel, rinsed out her palate, and said, 'I must be fair spoony on you, Harry, I think.'

Many a thundering good grind I have had from those amiable women, since I frequently meet them in society. Ethel is now a dashing young woman, and her mother, to all appearance, nearly as young as ever. Whenever I see their bare shoulders at dinners or balls I note the admiration they inspire and secretly chuckle to think how often I have stripped them still barer and wantoned over the hills and dales of both those female forms divine.

# The Way of a Man with a Maid

ANONYMOUS

# PART ONE

# The Tragedy

## Chapter One

I, the man, will not take up the time of my readers by detailing the circumstances under which Alice, the maid, roused in me the desire for vengeance which resulted in the way I adopted and which I am about to relate. Suffice it then to say that Alice cruelly and unjustifiably jilted me! In my bitterness of spirit, I swore that if I ever had an opportunity of getting hold of her, I would make her voluptuous person recompense me for my disappointment and that I would snatch from her by force the bridegroom's privileges that I so ardently coveted. But I had to dissemble! Alice and I had many mutual friends to whom this rupture was unknown; we were therefore constantly meeting each other, and if I gave her the slightest hint of my intentions towards her, it would be fatal to the very doubtful chances of success that I had! And so successfully did I conceal my real feelings under a cloak of generous acceptance of her action that she had not the faintest idea (as she afterwards admitted to me) that I was playing a part.

But, as the proverb says, everything comes to the man who can wait. For some considerable time, it seemed as if it would be wise on my part to abandon my desire for vengeance, as the circumstances of our daily lives were such as did not promise the remotest chance of my getting possession of Alice under conditions of either place or time suitable for the accomplishment of my purpose. Nevertheless, I controlled my patience and hoped for the best, enduring as well as I could the torture of unsatisfied desire and increasing lust.

It then happened that I had occasion to change my residence, and in my search for fresh quarters, I came across a modest suite of a sitting-room and two bedrooms which would by themselves have suited me excellently; but with them, the landlord desired to let what he termed a box or lumber-room. I demurred to this addition, but as he remained firm, I asked to see the room. It was most peculiar both as regards access and appearance. The former was by a short passage from the landing, furnished with remarkably well-fitting doors at each end. The room was nearly square, of a good size and lofty, but the walls were unbroken, save by the one entrance, light and air being derived from a skylight, or rather lantern, which occupied the greater part of the roof and was supported by four strong and stout wooden pillars. Further, the walls were thickly padded, while iron rings were let into them at regular distances all round in two rows, one close to the floor and the other about a height of eight feet; from the roof beams dangled rope pulleys in pairs between the pillars, while the two recesses on the entrance side, caused by the projection of the passage into the room, looked as if they had at one time been separated from the rest of the room by bars, almost as if they were cells. So strange indeed was the appearance of the whole room that I asked its history, and was informed that the house had been built as a private lunatic asylum at the time when the now unfashionable square in which it stood was one of the centres of fashion, and that this was the old 'mad-room' in which violent patients were confined, the bolts, rings and pulleys being used to restrain them when very violent, while the padding and the double doors made the room absolutely soundproof and prevented the ravings of the inmates from annoying the neighbours. The landlord added that the soundproof quality was no fiction as the room had frequently been tested by incredulous visitors.

Like lightning the thought flashed through my brain. Was not this room the very place for the consummation of my scheme of revenge? If I succeeded in luring Alice into it, she would be completely at my mercy, for her screams for help would not be heard and would only increase my pleasure, while the bolts, rings, pulleys, etc., supplemented with a little suitable furniture, would enable me to secure her in any way I wished and to hold her fixed while I amused myself with her. Delighted with the idea, I agreed to include the room in my suite. Quietly, but with deep forethought and planning, I got certain furniture made which, while in outward appearance most innocent, as well as most comfortable, was in truth full of hidden mechanisms planned for the special discomfiture of any woman or girl that I might wish to hold in physical control. I had the floor covered with thick Persian carpets and rugs, and the two alcoves converted into nominal photographic laboratories, but in a way that made them suitable for lavatories and dressing-rooms. When completed, the 'Snuggery' (as I christened it) was in appearance a distinctly pretty and comfortable room, while in reality it was nothing more or less than a disguised torture chamber!

And now came the difficult part of my scheme.

\*　　\*　　\*

How to entrap Alice? Unfortunately she was not residing in London but a little way out. She lived with a married sister, and never seemed to come to town except in her sister's company. My difficulty was therefore how to get Alice by herself for a sufficiently long time to accomplish my designs, and sorely I cudgelled my brains over this problem!

The sisters frequently visited town at irregular intervals as dictated by the contingencies of social duties or shopping. True to my policy of *l'entente cordiale*, I had welcomed them to my rooms for rest and refreshment and had encouraged them to use my quarters; and partly because of the propinquity of the rooms to Regent Street, partly because of the very dainty meals I invariably placed before them, but mainly because of the soothing restfulness induced by the absolute quiet of the Snuggery after the roar and turmoil of the streets, it soon became their regular practice to honour me with their company for luncheon or tea whenever they came to town and had no special engagement. I need hardly add that secretly I hoped these visits might bring me an opportunity of executing my revenge, but for some months I seemed doomed to disappointment. I used to suffer the tortures of Tantalus when I saw Alice unsuspectingly braving me in the very room I had prepared for her violation, within actual reach of me and of hidden machinery that would place her at my disposal, did I set it working, were it not for her sister's presence! In fact, so keenly did I feel the position that I began to plan the capture of both sisters together, to include Marion in the punishment designed for Alice, and the idea in itself was not unpleasing, as Marion was a fine specimen of female flesh and blood of a larger and more stately type than Alice (who was 'petite'), and one could do much worse than have her at one's disposal for an hour or two to feel and fuck! So seriously did I entertain this project, that I got an armchair made in such a way that the releasing of a secret catch would set free mechanisms that would be actuated by the weight of the occupant and would cause the arms to fold inwards and firmly imprison the sitter. Furnished with luxurious upholstery and the catch fixed, it made the most inviting of chairs, and from its first appearance, Alice took possession of it, in happy ignorance that it was intended to hold her firmly imprisoned while I tackled and secured Marion!

Before, however, I resorted to this desperate measure, my patience was rewarded! And this is how it happened.

One evening, the familiar note came to say the sisters were coming to town on the next day and would come for lunch. A little before the appointed hour Alice, to my surprise, appeared alone! She said that, after the note had been posted, Marion became ill and had been very poorly all night and so could not come to town, though better. The shopping engagement was one of considerable importance to Alice, and therefore she had come up alone; she had called to explain matters to me, but would not stop to lunch, she would get a cup of tea and a bun somewhere.

Against this desertion of me, I vigorously protested, but I doubt if I would have induced her to stay had not a smart shower of rain come on. This made her hesitate about going out into it with the dress she was wearing, as it would be ruined, and finally she consented to have lunch and leave immediately afterwards.

While she was away in the spare bedroom used by the sisters on their visits, I was in a veritable turmoil of excitement! Alice in my rooms by herself! It seemed too good to be true! But I remembered I yet had to get her into the Snuggery; she was absolutely safe from my designs everywhere but there! But it was imperative that she should be in no way alarmed, and so, with a strong effort, I controlled my panting excitement, and by the time Alice rejoined me in the dining-room I was my usual self.

Lunch was quickly served. At first, Alice seemed a little nervous and constrained, but by tactful conversation, I soon set her at ease and she then chatted away naturally and merrily. I had craftily placed her with her back to the window so that she should not note signs that a bad storm was brewing: and soon, with satisfaction, I saw that the weather was getting worse and worse! But it might at any moment begin to clear away, and so the sooner I could get her into my Snuggery, the better for me – and the worse for her! So, by every means in my power, I hurried on the procedure of lunch.

Alice was leisurely finishing her coffee when a rattle of rain against the window panes, followed by an ominous growl of thunder, made her start from her chair and go to the casement 'Oh! Just look at the rain!' she exclaimed in dismay, 'how very unfortunate!'

I joined her at the window: 'By Jove, it is bad!' I replied, then added, 'and it looks like lasting. I hope that you have no important engagement for the afternoon that will keep you much in the open?' As I spoke, there came a vivid flash of lightning closely followed by a peal of thunder, which sent Alice staggering backwards with a scared face.

'Oh!' she exclaimed, evidently frightened; then, after a pause, 'I am a horrid little coward about thunderstorms: they just terrify me!'

'Won't you then take refuge in the Snuggery?' I asked with a host's look of concern. 'I don't think you will see the lightning there and you certainly won't hear the thunder, as the room is soundproof. Shall we go there?' and I opened the door invitingly.

Alice hesitated. Was her guardian angel trying to give her a premonitory hint of what her fate would be if she accepted my seemingly innocent suggestion? But at that moment came another flash of lightning, blinding in its intensity, and almost simultaneously a roar of thunder. This settled the question in my favour! 'Yes, yes!' she exclaimed, then ran out. I closely following her, my heart beating exultingly! Quickly she passed through the double doors into the Snuggery, the trap I had so carefully set for her! Noiselessly I bolted the outer door, then closed the inner one. Alice was now mine! mine!! At last I had entrapped her! Now my vengeance was about to be consummated! Now her chaste virgin self was to be submitted to my lust and compelled to satisfy my erotic desires! She was utterly at my mercy, and promptly I proceeded to work my cruel will on her!

## Chapter Two

The soothing stillness of the room after the roar of the storm seemed most agreeable to Alice. She drew a deep breath of relief and turning to me she exclaimed: 'What a wonderful room it really is, Jack! Just look how the rain is pelting down on the skylight, and yet we do not hear a sound!'

'Yes! there is no doubt about it,' I replied, 'it is absolutely soundproof. I do not suppose that there is a better room in London for my special purpose!'

'What might that be, Jack?' she asked interestedly.

'Your violation, my dear!' I replied quietly, looking her straight in the face, 'the surrender to me of your maidenhead!'

She started as if she had been struck. She coloured hotly. She stared at me as if she doubted her hearing. I stood still and calmly watched her. Then indignation and the sense of outraged modesty seized her.

'You must be mad to speak like that!' she said in a voice that trembled with concentrated anger. 'You forget yourself. Be good enough to consider our friendship as suspended till you have recovered your senses and have suitably apologised for this intolerable insult. Meanwhile I will trouble you only to call a cab so that I may remove myself from your hateful presence!' And her eyes flashed in her wrathful indignation.

I quietly laughed aloud: 'Do you really think I should have taken this step without calculating the consequences, Alice?' I rejoined coolly. 'Do you really think I have lost my senses? Is there not a little account to be settled between us for what you did to me not very long ago? The day of reckoning has come, my dear; you have had your innings at my cost, now I am going to have mine at yours! You amused yourself with my heart, I am going to amuse myself with your body.'

Alice stared at me, silent with surprise and horror! My quiet determined manner staggered her. She paled when I referred to the past, and she flushed painfully as I indicated what her immediate future would be. After a slight pause I spoke again.

'I have deliberately planned this revenge! I took these rooms solely because they would lend themselves so admirably to this end. I have prepared them for every contingency, even to having to subjugate you by force! Look!' And I proceeded to reveal to her astonished eyes the mechanism concealed in the furniture, etc. 'You know you cannot get out of this room till I choose to let you go; you know that your screams and cries for help will not be heard. You now must decide what you will do. I give you two alternatives, and two only, and you must choose one of them. Will you submit yourself quietly to me, or do you prefer to be forced?'

Alice stamped her little foot in her rage: 'How dare you speak to me in this way?' she demanded furiously. 'Do you think I am a child? Let me go at once!' and she moved in her most stately manner to the door.

'You are no child,' I replied with a cruel smile, 'you are a lusciously lovely girl possessing everything that I desire and able to satisfy my desires. But I am not going to let you waste time. The whole afternoon will hardly be long enough for the satisfaction of my whims, caprices and lust. Once more, will you submit or will you be forced? Understand that if by the time the clock strikes the half-hour, you do not consent to submit, I shall without further delay proceed to take by force what I want from you! Now make the most of the three minutes you have left.' And turning my back on her, I proceeded to get the room ready, as if I anticipated that I would have to use force.

Overcome by her feelings and emotions, Alice sank into an armchair burying her face in her trembling hands. She evidently recognised her dreadful position! How could she yield herself up to me? And yet if she did not, she knew she would have to undergo violation! And possibly horrible indignities as well!! I left her absolutely alone, and when I had finished my preparations, I quietly seated myself and watched her.

Presently the clock chimed the half-hour. Immediately I rose. Alice quickly sprang to her feet and rushed to the far side of the large divan-couch on which I hoped before long to see her extended naked! It was evident that she was going to resist and fight me, and I welcomed her decision, as now she would give me ample justification for the fullest exercising of my lascivious desires!

'Well, Alice, what is it to be? Will you submit quietly?'

A sudden passion seemed to possess her. She looked me squarely in the eyes for the first time, hers blazing with rage and indignation: 'No! no!' she exclaimed vehemently, 'I defy you! Do your worst. Do you think you will frighten me into satisfying your lust? Once and for all I give you my answer: No! No!! No!!! Oh! you cowardly brute and beast!!' And she laughed shrilly as she turned herself away contemptuously.

'As you please,' I replied quietly and calmly, 'let those laugh that win! I venture to say that within half an hour, you will not only be offering yourself to me absolutely and unconditionally, but will also be begging me to accept your surrender! Let us see!'

Alice laughed incredulously and defiantly: 'Yes, let us see!! Let us see!!' she retorted contemptuously.

Forthwith I sprang towards her to seize her, but quick as thought she darted away, I in hot pursuit. For a short time she succeeded in eluding me, dodging in and out of the furniture, like a butterfly, but soon I manoeuvred her into a corner and pouncing on her gripped her firmly, then half dragged and half carried her to where a pair of electrically worked rope-pulleys hung between two of the pillars, she struggling desperately and screaming for help. In spite of her determined resistance, I soon made the ropes fast to her wrists, then touched the button; the ropes tightened, and slowly but irresistibly, Alice's arms were drawn upwards till her hands were well above her head and she was forced to stand erect by the tension on her arms. She was now utterly helpless and unable to defend her person from the hands that were itching to invade and explore the sweet mysteries of her garments; but what with her exertions and the violence of her emotions she was in such a state of agitation that I deemed it wise to leave her to herself for a brief space, till she became more mistress of herself, then she would be better able to appreciate the indignities which she would now be compelled to suffer!

Here, I think, I had better explain the mechanical means I had at my disposal for the discomfiture and subjugation of Alice.

Between each two of the pillars that supported the lantern-skylight hung a pair of strong rope-pulleys working on a roller mechanism concealed in the beams and actuated by electricity. Should I want Alice upright, I had simply to attach the ropes to her wrists, and her arms would be pulled straight up and well over her head, thus forcing her to stand erect, and at the same time rendering her body defenceless and at my mercy. The pillars themselves could be utilised as whipping posts, being provided with rings to which Alice could be fastened in such a way that she could not move!

Close by the pillars was a huge divan-couch upholstered in dark green satin admirably to enhance the pearly loveliness of a naked girl. It stood on eight massive legs (four on each long side), behind each of which lay, coiled for use, a stout leather strap worked by rollers hidden in the upholstery and actuated by electricity. On it were piled a lot of cushions of various sorts and consistencies, with which Alice and Marion used to make nests for themselves, little dreaming that the real object of the 'Turkish Divan' (as they had christened it) was to be the altar on which Alice's virginity would be sacrificed to the Goddess of Love, the mission of the straps being to hold her in position while being violated, should she not surrender herself quietly to her fate!

By the keyboard of the grand piano stood a duet-stool upholstered in leather and with the usual mechanical power of adjustment for height, only to a much greater extent than usual. But the feature of the stool was its unusual length, a full six feet, and I one day had to satisfy Alice's curiosity by telling her that this was for the purpose of providing a comfortable seat to anyone who might be turning over for the pianist! The real reason was that the stool was, for all practical purposes, a rack actuated by hidden machinery and fitted with a most ingenious arrangement of straps, the efficacy of which I looked forward to testing on Alice's tender self.

The treacherous armchair I have already explained. My readers can now perhaps understand that I could fix Alice in practically any position or attitude and keep her so fixed while I worked my sweet will on her helpless self.

All the ropes and straps were fitted with swivel snap-hooks. To attach them to Alice's limbs, I used an endless band of the strongest and softest silk rope that I could get made. It was an easy matter to slip the band (doubled) round her wrist or ankle, pass one end through the other and draw tight, then snap the free end into the swivel hook. No amount of plunging or struggling would loosen this attachment, and the softness of the silk prevented Alice's delicate flesh from being rubbed or even marked.

## Chapter Three

During the ten minutes grace that I mentally allowed Alice in which to recover from the violence of her struggles, I quietly studied her as she stood helpless, almost supporting herself by resting her weight on her wrists. She was to me an exhilarating spectacle, her bosom fluttering, rising and falling as she caught her breath, her cheeks still flushing, her large hat somewhat disarranged, while her dainty well-fitting dress displayed her neat comely figure to its fullest advantage.

She regained command of herself wonderfully quickly, and then it was evident that she was stealthily watching me in horrible apprehension. I did not leave her long in suspense, but after going slowly round her and inspecting her, I placed a chair right in front of her, so close to her its edge almost touched her knees, then slipped myself into it, keeping my legs apart, so that she stood between them, the front of her dress pressing against the fly of my trousers. Her head was now above mine, so that I could peer directly into her downcast face.

As I took up this position, Alice trembled nervously and tried to draw herself away from me, but found herself compelled to stand as I had placed her. Noticing the action, I drew my legs closer to each other so as loosely to hold her between them, smiling cruelly at the uncontrollable shudder that passed through her when she felt the pressure of my knees against hers! Then I extended my arms, clasped her gently round the waist, and drew her against me, at the same time tightening the clutch of my legs, till soon she was fairly in my embrace, my face pressing against her throbbing bosom. For a moment she struggled wildly, then resigned herself to the unavoidable as she recognised her helplessness.

Except when dancing with her, I had never held Alice in my arms, and the embrace permitted by the waltz was nothing to the comprehensive clasping between arms and legs in which she now found herself. She trembled fearfully, her tremors giving me exquisite pleasure as I felt them shoot through her, and murmured beseechingly: 'Please don't, Jack!'

I looked up into her flushed face, as I amorously pressed my cheek against the swell of her bosom: 'Don't you like it, Alice?' I said maliciously, as I squeezed her still more closely against me. 'I think you're just delicious, dear, and I am trying to imagine what it will feel like, when your clothes have been taken off you!'

'No! No! Jack!' she moaned agonisedly, twisting herself in her distress, 'let me go, Jack; don't . . . don't . . . ' and her voice failed her.

For answer, I maintained her against me with my left arm round her waist, then with my right hand, I began to stroke and press her hips and bottom.

'Oh! . . . don't Jack! don't!' Alice shrieked, squirming in distress and futilely endeavouring to avoid my marauding hand. I paid no attention to her pleadings and cries, but continued my strokings and caressings over her full posteriors and thighs down to her knees, then back to her buttocks and haunches, she, all the while, quivering in a delicious way. Then I freed my left hand, and holding her tightly imprisoned between my legs, I proceeded with both hands to study over her clothes the configuration of her backside and hips and thighs, handling her buttocks with a freedom that seemed to stagger her, as she pressed the front of her person against me, in her efforts to escape from the liberties that my hands were taking with her posterior charms.

After toying delightfully with her in this way for some little time, I ceased and withdrew my hands from her hips, but only to pass them up and down over her incurving sides; thence I passed to her bosom which I began lovingly to stroke and caress to her dismay. Her colour rose as she swayed uneasily on her legs. But her stays prevented any direct attack on her bosom, so I decided to open her clothes sufficiently to obtain a peep at her virgin breasts, and set to work to unbutton her blouse.

'Jack, no! no!!' shrieked Alice, struggling vainly to get loose. But I only smiled and continued to undo her blouse till I got it completely open and threw it back on to her shoulders, only to be baulked as a fairly high bodice covered her bosom. I set to work to open this, my fingers revelling in the touch of Alice's dainty linen. Soon it also was open and thrown back – and then, right before my eager eyes, lay the snowy expanse of Alice's bosom, her breasts being visible nearly as far as their nipples!

'Oh! . . . oh! . . . ' she moaned in her distress, flushing painfully at this cruel exposure. But I was too excited to take any notice; my eyes were riveted on the provokingly lovely swell of her breasts, exhibiting the valley between the twin globes, now heaving and fluttering under her agitated emotions. Unable to restrain myself, I threw my arms round Alice's waist, drew her closely to me and pressed my lips on her palpitating flesh which I kissed furiously.

'Don't, Jack!' cried Alice, as she tugged frantically at her fastenings in her wild endeavours to escape from my passionate lips; but instead of stopping, my mouth wandered all over her heaving bosom and to her delicious breasts, punctuating its progress with hot kisses which seemed to drive her mad to such a pitch that I thought it best to desist.

'Oh! my God!' she moaned as I relaxed my clasp and leant back in my chair to enjoy the sight of her shamefaced distress. There was not the least doubt that she felt most keenly my indecent assault, and so I determined to worry her with lascivious liberties a little longer.

When she had become calmer, I passed my arms round her waist and again began to play with her posteriors, then, stooping down, I got my hands under her clothes and commenced to pull them up. Flushing violently, Alice shrieked to me to desist, but in vain; in a trice, I turned her petticoats up, held them thus with my left hand and with my right I proceeded to attack her bottom now protected only by her dainty thin drawers!

The sensation was delirious! My hand delightedly roved over the fat plump cheeks of her arse, stroking, caressing and pinching them, revelling in the firmness and elasticity of her flesh under its thin covering, Alice all the time, wriggling and squirming in horrible shame, imploring me almost incoherently to desist and finally getting so semi-hysterical, that I was compelled to suspend my exquisite game. To her relief, I dropped her skirts, pushed my chair back and rose.

I had in the room a large plate-glass mirror nearly eight feet high which reflected one at full length. While Alice was recovering from her last ordeal, I pushed this mirror close in front of her, placing it so that she could see herself in its centre. She started uneasily as she caught sight of herself, for I had left her bosom uncovered, and the reflection of herself in such shameful dishabille in conjunction with her large hat (which she still retained) seemed vividly to impress on her the horror of her position!

Having arranged the mirror to my satisfaction, I picked up the chair and placed it just behind Alice, sat down on it, and worked myself forward on it till Alice again stood between my legs, but this time with her back to me. The mirror faithfully reflected my movements and her feminine intuition warned her that the front of her person was now about to become the object of my indecent assault.

But I did not give her time to think. Quickly I encircled her waist again with my arms, drew her to me till her bottom pressed against my chest, then, while my left arm held her firmly, my right hand began to wander over the junction of her stomach and legs, pressing inquisitively her groin and thighs, and intently watching her in the mirror.

Her colour rose, her breath came unevenly, she quivered and trembled on her legs as she pressed her thighs closely together. She was horribly perturbed, but I do not think she anticipated what then happened.

Quietly dropping my hands, I slipped them under her clothes, caught hold of her ankles, then proceeded to climb up her legs over her stockings.

'No! no! for God's sake, don't Jack!' Alice yelled, now scarlet with shame and wild with alarm at this invasion of her most secret parts. Frantically she dragged at her fastenings, her hands clenched, her head thrown back, her eyes dilated with horror. Throwing the whole of her weight on her wrists, she strove to free her legs from my attacking hands by kicking out desperately, but to no avail. The sight in the mirror of her struggles only stimulated me into a refinement of cruelty, for with one hand, I raised her clothes waist high, exposing her in her dainty drawers and black silk stockings, while with the other, I vigorously attacked her thighs over her drawers, forcing a way between them and finally working up so close to her mount of Venus that Alice practically collapsed in an agony of apprehension and would have fallen had it not been for the sustaining ropes which alone supported her as she hung in a semi-hysterical faint.

Quickly rising and dropping her clothes, I placed an armchair behind her, and loosened the pulleys, till she rested comfortably in it, then left her to recover herself, feeling pretty confident that she was now not far from surrendering herself to me, rather than continue a resistance which she could not but see was utterly useless. This was what I wanted to effect. I did not propose to let her off any single one of the indignities I had in store for her, but I wanted to make her suffering the more keen through the feeling that she was, to some extent, a consenting party to actions that inexpressibly shocked and revolted her. The first of these I intended to be the removal of her clothes, and, as soon as Alice became more mistress of herself, I set the pulleys working and soon had her again standing erect with up-stretched arms.

She glanced fearfully at me as if trying to learn what was now going to happen to her. I deemed it as well to tell her, and to afford her an opportunity of yielding herself to me, if she should be willing to do so. I also wanted to save her clothes from being damaged, as she was really beautifully dressed, and I was not at all confident that I could get her garments off her without using scissors to some of them.

'I see you want to know what is now going to happen to you, Alice,' I said. 'I'll tell you. You are to be stripped naked, utterly and absolutely naked: not a stitch of any sort is to be left on you!'

A flood of crimson swept over her face, invading both neck and bosom (which remained bare); her head fell forward as she moaned: 'No! . . . No! . . . oh! Jack . . . Jack . . . how can you . . . ' and she swayed uneasily on her feet.

'That is to be the next item in the programme, my dear!' I said, enjoying her distress. 'There is only one detail that remains to be settled first, and that is, will you undress yourself quietly if I set you loose, or must I drag your clothes off you? I don't wish to influence your decision, and I know what queer ideas girls have about taking off their clothes in the presence of a man; I will leave the decision to you, only to say that I do not see what you gain by further resistance, and some of your garments may be ruined – which would be a pity! Now, which is it to be?'

She looked at me imploringly for a moment, trembling in every limb, then averted her eyes, but remained silent, evidently torn by conflicting emotions.

'Come, Alice,' I said presently, 'I must have your decision, or I shall proceed to take your clothes off you as best as I can.'

Alice was now in a terrible state of distress! Her eyes wandered all over the room without seeming to see anything, incoherent murmurs escaped from her lips, as if she was trying to speak but could not, her breath went and came, her bosom rose and fell agitatedly. She was endeavouring to form some decision evidently, but unable to do so.

I remained still for a brief space as if awaiting her answer; then, as she did not speak, I quietly went to a drawer, took out a pair of scissors and went back to her. At the sight of the scissors, she shivered, then with an effort, said, in a voice broken with emotion: 'Don't . . . undress me Jack! . . . if you must . . . have me, let it be as I am . . . I will . . . submit quietly . . . oh! my God!!' she wailed.

'That won't do, dear,' I replied, not unkindly, but still firmly, 'you must be naked, Alice; now, will you or will you not undress yourself?'

Alice shuddered, cast another imploring glance at me, but seeing no answering gleam of pity in my eyes but stern determination instead, she stammered out: 'Oh! Jack! I can't!! have some pity on me, Jack, and . . . have me as I am! I promise I'll be . . . quiet!'

I shook my head. I saw there was only one thing for me to do, namely, to undress her without any further delay; and I set to work to do so, Alice crying piteously: 'Don't Jack, don't! . . . don't!'

I had left behind her the armchair in which I had allowed her to rest, and her blouse and bodice were still hanging open and thrown back on her shoulders. So I got on the chair and worked them along her arms and over her clenched hands on to the ropes; then gripping her wrists in turn one at a time, I released the noose, slipped the garments down and off and refastened the noose. And as I had been quick to notice that Alice's chemise and vest had shoulder-strap fastenings and had merely to be unhooked, the anticipated difficulty of undressing her forcibly was now at an end! The rest of her garments would drop off her, as each became released, and therefore it was in my power to reduce her to absolute nudity! My heart thrilled with fierce exultation, and without further pause, I went on with the delicious work of undressing her.

Alice quickly divined her helplessness and in an agony of apprehension and shame cried to me for mercy! But I was deaf to her pitiful pleadings! I was wild to see her naked!

Quickly I unhooked her dress and petticoats and pulled them down to her feet, thus exhibiting her in stays, drawers and stockings, a bewitching sight! Her cheeks were suffused with shamefaced blushes, she huddled herself together as much as she could, seemingly supported entirely by her arms; her eyes were downcast and she seemed dazed both by the rapidity of my motions and their horrible success!

Alice now had on only a dainty Parisian corset which allowed the laces of her chemise to be visible, just hiding the nipples of her maiden breasts, and a pair of exquisitely provoking drawers, cut wide especially at her knees and trimmed with a sea of frilly lace, from below which emerged her shapely legs encased in black silk stockings and terminating in neat little shoes. She was the daintiest sight a man could well imagine, and, to me, the daintiness was enhanced by her shamefaced consciousness, for she could see herself reflected in the mirror in all her dreadful dishabille!

After a minute of gloating admiration, I proceeded to untie the tapes of her drawers so as to take them off her. At this she seemed to wake to the full sense of the humiliation in store for her; wild at the idea of being deprived of this most intimate of garments to a girl, she screamed in her distress, tugging frantically at her fastenings in her desperation! But the knot gave way, and her drawers, being now unsupported, slipped down to below her knees, where they hung for a brief moment, maintained only by the despairing pressure of her legs against each other. A tug or two from me, and they lay in snowy loads round her ankles and rested on her shoes!

O that I had the pen of a ready writer with which to describe Alice at this stage of the terrible ordeal of being forcibly undressed, her mental and physical anguish, her frantic cries and impassioned pleadings, her frenzied struggles, the agony in her face as garment after garment was removed from her and she was being hurried nearer and nearer to the appalling goal of absolute nudity! The accidental but unavoidable contact of my hands with her person, as I undressed her, seemed to upset her so terribly that I wondered how she would endure my handling and playing with the most secret and sensitive parts of herself when she was naked! But acute as was her distress while being deprived of her upper garments, it was nothing to her shame and anguish when she felt her drawers forced down her legs and the last defence to her cunt thus removed! Straining wildly at the ropes with cheeks aflame, eyes dilated with terror, and convulsively heaving bosom, she uttered inarticulate cries, half choked by her emotions and panting under her exertions.

I gloated over her sufferings and would have liked to have watched them – but I was now mad with desire for her naked charms and also feared that a prolongation of her agony might result in a faint, when I would lose the anticipated pleasure of witnessing Alice's misery when her last garment was removed and she was forced to stand naked in front of me. So unheeding her imploring cries, I undid her corset and took it off her, dragged off her shoes and stockings and with them her fallen drawers (during which process I intently watched her struggles in the hope of getting a glimpse of her holy of holies, but vainly), then slipped behind her; unbuttoning the shoulder-fastenings of her chemise and vest, I held these up for a moment, then watching Alice closely in the mirror, I let go! Down they slid with a rush, right to her feet! I saw Alice flash one rapid stolen half-reluctant glance at the mirror, as she felt the cold air on her now naked skin. I saw her reflection stark naked, a lovely gleaming pearly vision; then instinctively she squeezed her legs together, as closely as she could, huddled herself coweringly as much as the ropes permitted – her head fell back in the first intensity of her shame, then fell forward suffused with blushes that extended right down to her breasts, her eyes closed as she moaned in heartbroken accents: 'Oh! oh!! oh!!!' She was naked!

Half delirious with excitement and the joy of conquest, I watched Alice's naked reflection in the mirror. Rapidly and tumultuously, my eager eyes roved over her shrinking trembling form, gleaming white, save for her blushing face and the dark triangular mossy-looking patch at the junction of her belly and thighs. But I felt that, in this moment of triumph, I was not sufficiently master of myself fully to enjoy the spectacle of her naked maiden charms now so fully exposed, besides which, her chemise and vest still lay on her feet. So I knelt down behind her, forced her feet up one at a time and removed these garments, noting, as I did so the glorious curves of her bottom and hips. Throwing these garments on to the rest of her clothes, I pushed the armchair in front of her, and then settled myself down to a systematic and critical inspection of Alice's naked self!

As I did so, Alice coloured deeply over face and bosom and moved herself uneasily. The bitterness of death (so to speak) was past, her clothes had been forced off her and she was naked; but she was evidently conscious that much indignity and humiliation was yet in store for her, and she was horribly aware that my eyes were now taking in every detail of her naked self! Forced to stand erect by the tension of the ropes on her arms, she could do nothing to conceal any part of herself, and, in an agony of shame, she endured the awful ordeal of having her naked person closely inspected and examined!

I had always greatly admired her trim little figure, and in the happy days before our rupture, I used to note with proud satisfaction how Alice held her own, whether at garden parties, at afternoon teas or in the theatre or ballroom. And after she had jilted me and I was sore in spirit, the sight of her invariably added fuel to the flames of my desire, and I often caught myself wondering how she looked in her bath! One evening, she wore at dinner a low-cut evening dress and she nearly upset my self-control by leaning forward over the card table by which I was standing, and unconsciously revealing to me the greater portion of her breasts! But my imagination never pictured anything as glorious as the reality now being so reluctantly exhibited to me!

Alice was simply a beautiful girl and her lines deliciously voluptuous! No statue, no model, but glorious flesh and blood allied to superb femininity! Her well-shaped head was set on a beautifully modelled neck and bosom, from which sprang a pair of exquisitely lovely breasts (if anything too full), firm, upstanding, saucy and inviting. She had fine rounded arms with small well-shaped hands, a dainty but not too small waist, swelling grandly down-wards and outwards and melting into magnificent curves over her hips and haunches. Her thighs were plump and round, and tapered to the neatest of calves and ankles and tiny feet, her legs being the least trifle too short for her, but adding by this very defect to the indescribable fascination of her figure. She had a graciously swelling belly with a deep navel, and, framed by the lines of her groin, was her mount of Venus, full, fat, fleshy, prominent, covered by a wealth of fine silky dark curly hairs, through which I could just make out the lips of her cunt. Such was Alice as she stood naked before me, horribly conscious of my devouring eyes, quivering and trembling with suppressed emotion, tingling with shame, flushing red and white, knowing full well her own loveliness and what its effect on me must be; and in dumb silence I gazed and gazed again at her glorious naked self, till my lust began to run riot and insist on the gratification of senses other than that of sight!

I did not however consider that Alice was ready properly to appreciate the mortification of being felt. She seemed to be still absorbed in the horrible consciousness of one all-pervading fact, viz. that she was utterly naked, that her chaste body was the prey of my lascivious eyes, that she could do nothing to hide or even screen any part of herself, even her cunt, from me! Every now and then, her downcast eyes would glance at the reflection of herself in the faithful mirror, only to be hastily withdrawn with an access of colour to her already shame-suffused cheeks at these fresh reminders of the spectacle she was offering to me!

Therefore, with a strong effort, I succeeded in overcoming the temptation to feel and handle Alice's luscious body there and then, and being desirous of first studying her naked self from all points of view, I rose and took her in strict profile, noting with delight the arch of her bosom, the proudly projecting breasts, the glorious curve of her belly, the conspicuous way in which the hairs on the mount of Venus stood out, indicating that her cunt would be found both fat and fleshy, the magnificent swell of her bottom! Then I went behind her, and for a minute or two revelled in silent admiration of the swelling lines of her hips and haunches, her quivering buttocks, her well-shaped legs! Without moving, I could command the most perfect exhibition of her naked loveliness, for I had her back view in full sight while her front was reflected in the mirror!

Presently I completed my circuit, then standing close to her, I had a good look at her palpitating breasts, noting their delicious fullness and ripeness, their ivory skin, and the tiny virgin nipples pointing outwards so prettily, Alice colouring and flushing and swaying herself uneasily under my close inspection. Then I peered into the round cleft of her navel while she became more uneasy than ever, seeing the downward trend of my inspection. Then I dropped on my knees in front of her, and from this point of vantage, I commenced to investigate with eager eyes the mysterious region of her cunt, so deliciously covered with a wealth of close curling hairs, clustering so thickly round and over the coral lips as almost to render them invisible! As I did so, Alice desperately squeezed her thighs together as closely as she could, at the same time drawing in her stomach in the vain hope of defeating my purpose and of preventing me from inspecting the citadel wherein reposed her virginity!

As a matter of fact, she did to a certain extent thwart me, but as I intended before long to put her on her back and tie her down with her legs wide apart, I did not grudge her partial success, but brought my face close to her belly. 'Don't! oh don't!' she cried, as if she could feel my eyes as they searched this most secret part of herself; but disregarding her pleadings, I closely scanned the seat of my approaching pleasure, noting delightedly that her mount of Venus was exquisitely plump and fleshy and would afford my itching fingers the most delicious pleasure when I allowed them to wander over its delicate contours and hide themselves in the forest of hairs that so sweetly covered it!

At last I rose. Without a word, I slipped behind the mirror and quickly divested myself of my clothes, retaining only my shoes and socks. Then, suddenly, I emerged and stood right in front of Alice. 'Oh!' she ejaculated, horribly shocked by the unexpected apparition of my naked self, turning rosy red and hastily averting her eyes – but not before they had caught sight of my prick in glorious erection! I watched her closely. The sight seemed to fascinate her in spite of her alarmed modesty; she flashed rapid glances at me through half-closed eyes, her colour coming and going. She seemed forced, in spite of herself, to regard the instrument of her approaching violation, as if to assess its size and her capacity!

'Won't you have a good look at me, Alice?' I presently remarked maliciously, 'I believe I can claim to possess a good specimen of what is so dear to the heart of a girl!' (She quivered painfully.) After a moment I continued: 'Must I then assume by your apparent indifference that you have in your time seen so many naked men that the sight no longer appeals to you?' She coloured deeply, but kept her eyes averted.

'Are you not even curious to estimate whether my prick will fit your cunt?' I added, determined, if I possibly could, to break down the barrier of silence she was endeavouring to protect herself with.

I succeeded! Alice tugged frantically at the ropes which kept her upright, then broke into a piteous cry: 'No, no . . . my God, no!' she supplicated, throwing her head back but still keeping her eyes shut as if to exclude the sight she dreaded, 'Oh! . . . you don't really mean to . . . to . . . ' she broke down, utterly unable to clothe in words the overwhelming fear that she was now to be violated!

I stepped up to her, passed my left arm round her waist and drew her trembling figure to me, thrilling at the exquisite sensation caused by the touch of our naked bodies against each other. We were now both facing the mirror, both reflected in it.

'Don't, oh! don't touch me!' she shrieked as she felt my arm encircle her, but holding her closely against me with my left arm, I gently placed my right forefinger on her navel, to force her to open her eyes and watch my movements in the mirror, which meant that she would also have to look at my naked self, and gently I tickled her.

She screamed in terror, opening her eyes, squirming deliciously: 'Don't! oh don't!' she cried agitatedly.

'Then use your chaste eyes properly and have a good look at the reflection of the pair of us in the mirror,' I said somewhat sternly; 'look me over slowly and thoroughly from head to foot, then answer the questions I shall presently put to you. May I call your attention to that whip hanging on that wall and to the inviting defencelessness of your bottom? Understand that I shall not hesitate to apply one to the other if you don't do as you are told! Now have a good look at me!'

Alice shuddered, then reluctantly raised her eyes and shamefacedly regarded my reflection in the mirror, her colour coming and going. I watched her intently (she being also reflected, my arm was still round her waist holding her against me ) and I noted with cruel satisfaction how she trembled with shame and fright when her eyes dwelt on my prick, now stiff and erect!

'We make a fine pair, Alice, eh?' I whispered maliciously. She coloured furiously, but remained silent.

'Now answer my questions: I want to know something about you before going further. How old are you?'

'Twenty-five,' she whispered.

'In your prime then! Good! Now, are you a virgin?'

Alice flushed hotly and painfully, then whispered again: 'Yes!'

Oh! my exultation! I was not too late! The prize of her maidenhead was to be mine! My prick showed my joy! I continued my catechism.

'Absolutely virgin?' I asked, 'a pure virgin? Has no hand ever wandered over those lovely charms, has no eye but mine seen them?'

Alice shook her head, blushing rosy red at the idea suggested by my words. I looked rather doubtingly at her.

'I include female eyes and hands as well in my query, Alice,' I continued; 'you know that you have a most attractive lot of girl and woman friends and that you are constantly with them. Am I to understand that you and they have never compared your charms, have never, when occupying the same bed . . . ' but she broke in with a cry of distress. 'No, no, not I, not I, oh! how can you talk to me like this, Jack!'

'My dear, I only wanted to find out how much you already knew so that I might know what to teach you now! Well, shall we begin your lessons?'

And I drew her against me, more closely than ever, and again began to tickle her navel. 'Jack, don't!' she screamed, 'oh don't touch me! I can't stand it! really I can't!'

'Let me see if that is really so!' I replied, as I removed my arm from her waist and slipped behind her, taking up a position from which I could command the reflection of our naked figures in the mirror, and thus watch her carefully and note the effect on her of my tender mercy.

## Chapter Four

I commenced to feel Alice by placing my hands one on each side of her waist, noting with cruel satisfaction the shiver that ran through her at their contact with her naked skin. After a few caresses, I passed them gently but inquisitively over her full hips, which I stroked, pressed and patted lovingly, then bringing my hands downwards behind her I roved over her plump bottom, the fleshy cheeks of which I gripped and squeezed to my heart's content, Alice the while arching herself outwards in a vain attempt to escape my hands. Then I descended to the underneath portion of her soft round thighs, and finally worked my way back to her waist, running my hands up and down over loins and finally arriving at her armpits.

Here I paused, and to try the effect on Alice, I gently tickled these sensitive spots of herself. 'Don't!' she exclaimed wriggling and twisting herself uneasily, 'don't, I am dreadfully ticklish, I can't stand it at all!' At once I ceased, but my blood went on fire, as through my brain flashed the idea of the licentiously lovely spectacle Alice would afford if she was tied down with her legs fastened widely apart, and a pointed feather-tip cleverly applied to the most sensitive part of herself – her cunt – sufficient slack being allowed in her fastenings to permit of her wriggling and writhing freely while being thus tickled, and I promised to give myself presently this treat together with the pleasure of trying on her this interesting experiment.

After a short pause, I again placed my hands on her waist, played for a moment over her swelling hips, then slipped them on to her stomach, my right hand taking the region below her waist, while my left devoted itself to her bosom, carefully avoiding for the moment her breasts.

Oh! what pleasure I tasted in thus touching her pure sweet flesh, so smooth, so warm, so essentially female! My delighted hands wandered all over her body, while the poor girl stood quivering and trembling, unable to guess whether her breasts or cunt were next to be attacked.

I did not keep her long in suspense. After a few circlings over her rounded belly, my right hand paused on her navel again, and while my forefinger gently tickled her, my left hand slid quietly on to her right breast which it then gently seized.

She gave a great cry of dismay! Meanwhile my right hand had in turn slipped up to her left breast, and another involuntary shriek from Alice announced that both of her virgin bubbies had become the prey of my cruel hands!

Oh! how she begged me to release them, the while tossing herself from side to side in almost uncontrollable agitation as my fingers played with her delicious breasts, now squeezing, now stroking, now pressing them against each other, now rolling them upwards and downwards, now gently irritating and exciting their tiny nipples! Such delicious morsels of flesh I had never handled, so firm and yet so springing, so ripe and yet so maidenly, palpitating under the hitherto unknown sensations communicated by the touch of masculine hands on their virgin surfaces. Meanwhile Alice's telltale face reflected in the mirror clearly indicated to me the mental shame and anguish she was feeling at this terrible outrage; her flushed cheeks, dilated nostrils, half-closed eyes, her panting heaving bosom all revealing her agony under this desecration of her maiden self! In rapture, I continued toying with her virgin globes, all the while gloating on Alice's image in the mirror, twisting and contorting itself in the most lasciviously ravishing way under her varying emotions.

At last I tore my hands away from Alice's breasts. I slipped my left arm round her waist, drew her tightly against me, then while I held her firmly, my right hand passed gently over her stomach and slowly approached her cunt! Alice instantly guessed my intention! She threw her weight on one leg, then quickly placed the other across her groin to foil my attack, crying: 'No no, Jack! . . . not there . . . not there!' at the same time endeavouring frantically to turn herself away from my hand. But the close grip of my left arm defeated her, and disregarding her cries, my hand crept on and on till it reached her hairs! These I gently pulled, twining them round my fingers as I revelled in their curling silkiness. Then amorously, I began to feel and press her gloriously swelling mount of Venus, a finger on each side of its slit. Alice now simply shrieked in her shame and distress, jerking herself convulsively backwards and twisting herself frenziedly. As she was forced to stand on both legs in order to maintain her balance, her cunt was absolutely defenceless, and my eager fingers roved all over it, touching, pressing, tickling, pulling her hairs at their sweet will. Then I began to attack her virgin orifice and tickle her slit, passing my forefinger lightly up and down it, all the time watching her intently in the mirror. Alice quivered violently, her head fell backwards in her agony as she shrieked: 'Jack, don't! . . . for God's sake don't!! . . . stop! . . . stop!' But I could feel her cunt opening under my lascivious attentions, and so could she! Her distress became almost uncontrollable. 'Oh, my God!' she screamed in her desperation as my finger found its way to her clitoris and lovingly titillated it; spasmodically she squeezed her thighs together in her vain attempts to defend herself. Unheeding her agonised pleadings, I continued to tickle her clitoris for a few delicious moments, then I gently passed my finger along her cunt and between its now half-opened lips till I arrived at her maiden orifice, up which it tenderly forced its way, burying itself in Alice's cunt till it could penetrate no further into her! Alice's agitation now became uncontrollable; she struggled so violently that I could hardly hold her still, especially when she felt the interior of her cunt invaded and my finger investigate the mysteries of its virgin recesses.

Oh! my voluptuous sensations at that moment! Alice's naked quivering body clutched tightly against mine! My finger, half buried in her maiden cunt, enveloped in her soft warm throbbing flesh and gently exploring its luscious interior!! In my excitement I must have pushed my inquisitiveness too far, for Alice suddenly screamed: 'Oh! . . . oh! you're hurting me! . . . stop! stop!' her head falling forward on her bosom as she did so! Delighted at this unexpected proof of her virginity and fearful of exciting her sexual passions beyond her powers of control, I gently withdrew my finger and soothed her by passing it lovingly and caressingly over her cunt; then releasing her from my encircling arm, I left her to recover herself. But, though visibly relieved at being at last left alone, Alice, trembled so violently that I hastily pushed her favourite armchair (the treacherous one) behind her, deftly released the pulley-ropes and let her drop into the chair to rest and recover herself, for I knew that her distress was only temporary and would soon pass away and leave her in a fit condition to be again fastened and subjected to some other torture, for so it undoubtedly was to her.

## *Chapter Five*

On this occasion, I did not set free the catch which permitted the arms of the chair to imprison the occupant. Alice was so upset by her experiences that I felt sure she would not give me any trouble worth mentioning when it became time for her torturing to recommence, provided of course that I did not allow her too long a respite, and this, from my own point of view, I did not propose to do as I was wildly longing to play again with her naked charms!

I therefore let her coil herself up in the chair with her face buried in her hands, and greedily gloated over the voluptuous curves of her haunches and bottom which she was unconsciously exhibiting, the while trying to make up my mind as to what I should next do to her. This I soon decided. My hands were itching to handle again her virgin flesh, and so I determined to tie Alice upright to one of the pillars and while comfortably seated close in front of her, to amuse myself by playing with her breasts and cunt again.

She was now lying quietly and breathing normally and regularly, the tremblings and quiverings that had been running intermittently through her having by now ceased. I did not feel quite sure if she had recovered herself yet, but as I watched her, I noticed an attempt on her part to try and slip her wrists out of the silken nooses that attached the ropes to them. This settled the point, and, before she could effect her object and free her hands, I set the ropes working, remarking as I did so: 'Well Alice, shall we resume?'

She glanced at me affrightedly, then averted her eyes as she exclaimed hurriedly: 'Oh no, Jack! not again, not again!' and shuddered at the recollection of her recent ordeal.

'Yes, my dear!' I replied, 'the same thing, though not quite in the same way; you'll be more comfy this time! Now Alice, come along, stand up again!'

'No!' she cried, fighting vainly the now fast tightening ropes which were inexorably raising her to her feet! 'Oh, Jack! no! . . . no!!' she pitifully pleaded while opposing the upward pull with all her might but to no avail! I simply smiled cruelly at her as I picked up a leather strap and awaited the favourable moment to force her against the nearest pillar. Presently she was dragged off the chair and now was my time. I pounced on her and rushed her backwards to the pillar, quickly slipping the strap round it and her waist and buckling it, and thus securing her. Then I loosened the pulleys and lowering her arms, I forced them behind her and round the pillar, till I got her wrists together and made them fast to a ring set in the pillar. Alice was now helpless; the whole of the front of her person was at my disposal! She was securely fastened, but, with a refinement of cruelty, I lashed her ankles together and bound them to the pillar! Then I unbuckled the strap round her waist and threw it away, it being no longer needed, placed the armchair in front of her, and sitting down in it, I drew it so close to her that she stood between my parted legs and within easy touch, just as she did when she was being indecently assaulted before she was undressed, only then we both were fully clothed, while now we both were stark naked! She could not throw her head back because of the pillar, and if she let it droop, as she naturally wanted to do, the first thing that her innocent eyes would rest upon would be my excited prick in glorious erection, its blushing head pointing directly towards her cunt as if striving to make the acquaintance of its destined bride.

Confused, shamefaced and in horrible dread, Alice stood trembling in front of me, her eyes tightly closed as if to avoid the sight of my naked self, her bosom agitatedly palpitating till her breasts seemed almost to be dancing! I leant back in my chair luxuriously as I gloated over the voluptuously charming spectacle, allowing her a little time in which to recover herself somewhat before I set to work to feel her again.

Before long, the agitations of her bosom died away; Alice's breathing became quieter. She was evidently now ready for another turn, and I did not keep her waiting, but gently placed my hands on her breasts.

'No, Jack, don't!' she pleaded piteously, moving herself uneasily. My only response was to stroke lovingly her delicious twin globes. As her shoulders were of necessity drawn well back by the pull of her arms, her bust was thrown well forward, thus causing her breasts to stand out saucily and provokingly; and I took the fullest advantage of this. Her flesh was delicious to the touch, so smooth and soft and warm, so springy and elastic My fingers simply revelled in their contact with her skin! Taking her tempting bubbies between my fingers and thumbs, I amorously pressed and squeezed them, pulled them this way and that way, rubbed them against each other, finally taking each delicate nipple in turn in my mouth and sucking it while my hands made as if they were trying to milk her! Alice, all the while, involuntarily shifted herself nervously, as if endeavouring to escape from my audaciously inquisitive fingers, her face scarlet with shame.

After a delicious five minutes of lascivious toying with her maiden breasts, I reluctantly quitted them, first imprinting on each of her little nipples a passionate kiss which seemed to thrill through her. As I sank back into my chair she took a long breath of relief, at which I smiled, for I had only deserted her breasts for her cunt.

Alice's legs were a trifle short, and her cunt therefore lay a little too low for effective attack from me in a sitting position. I therefore pushed the chair back and knelt in front of her. My intentions were now too obviously plain to her, and she shrieked in her dismay, squirming deliciously.

For some little time, I did not touch her, but indulged in a good look at close quarters at the sweet citadel of her chastity.

My readers will remember that, immediately after I had stripped Alice naked, I had closely inspected her cunt from a similar point of view. But then it was unsullied, untouched; now it had experienced the adoring touch of a male finger, and her sensitive body was still all of a quiver from the lustful handling her dainty breasts had just endured! Did her cunt share in the sexual excitement that my fingers had undoubtedly aroused in her?

It seemed to me that it did! The hair seemed to stand out as if ruffled, the mount of Venus certainly looked fuller, while the coral lips of the cunt itself were distinctly more apart! I could not see her clitoris, but I concluded that it participated in the undoubted excitement that was prevailing in this sweet portion of Alice's body, and of which she evidently was painfully aware by her shrinking quivering movements!

I soon settled the point by gently placing my right forefinger on her slit and lovingly stroking it! An electric shock seemed to thrill through Alice, her limbs contracted, her head fell forward as she screamed: 'Don't Jack! . . . oh my God! how can you treat me so?' while she struggled frantically to break the ropes which lashed her legs to the pillar to which she was fastened.

'Don't you like it, dear?' I asked softly with a cruel smile, as I continued gently to play with her cunt.

'No, no,' she shrieked, 'oh stop! . . . I can't stand it!' And she squirmed horribly. The crack of her cunt now began to open visibly.

I slipped my finger in between the parted lips: another despairing shriek from Alice, whose face now was scarlet! Again I found my progress barred by the membrane that proved her virgin condition! Revelling in the warm moistness of her throbbing flesh, I slowly agitated my finger in its delicious envelope, as if frigging her: 'Jack! don't!!' Alice yelled, now mad with distress and shame, but I could not for the life of me stop, and with my left forefinger, I gently attacked her virgin clitoris.

Alice went off into a paroxysm of hysterical shrieks, straining at her fastenings, squirming, wriggling, writhing like one possessed. She was a lovely sight in herself, and the knowledge that the struggling shrieking girl I was torturing was Alice herself and none but Alice added zest to my occupation.

Disregarding her cries, I went on slowly frigging her but carefully refrained from carrying her sexual excitement to the spending point; till I had pushed her powers of self-control to their utmost I did not want her to spend, this crowning humiliation I intended to effect with my tongue. Presently, what I wished was to make Alice endure the most outrageously indecent indignities I could inflict on her virgin person, to play on her sexual sensitiveness, to provoke her nearly into spending, and then deny her the blessed relief; so, exercising every care, and utilising to the utmost the peculiarly subtle power of touch I possessed, I continued to play with her cunt with both my hands, till I drove her nearly frantic with the sexual cravings and excitement I was provoking.

Just then I noticed certain spasmodic contortions of her hips and buttocks, certain involuntary thrusting out of her belly, as if she were begging for closer contact with my busy fingers; I knew this meant that her control over her sexual organs was giving out and that she would be driven into spending if I did not take care; so, most reluctantly, I stopped torturing her for the moment, and leaning back in my chair, I gloatingly watched Alice as little by little she regained her composure, my eyes dwelling delightedly on her trembling and quivering naked body so gloriously displayed.

She breathed a long sigh of heartfelt relief as she presently saw me rise and leave her. She did not however know that my object in doing so was to prepare another and perhaps more terrible ordeal for her virgin cunt!

From a drawer, I took out a long glove-box, then returned and resumed my seat in front of her with the box in my hand. She watched me with painful intensity, her feminine intuition telling her that something horrible was in store for her, and she was not wrong!

Holding the box in such a way that she could see the contents, I opened it. Inside were about a dozen long and finely pointed feathers. Alice at once guessed her fate, viz, that her cunt was to be tickled; her head jerked in her terror as she shrieked: 'Oh, my God! not that, Jack! . . . not that!! . . . you'll kill me! I can't stand it!!' I laughed cruelly at her and proceeded to pick out a feather, whereupon she frantically tugged at her fastenings, screaming frenziedly for mercy!

'Steady, dear! steady now, Alice!' I said soothingly, as if addressing a restive mare, then touched her palpitating breasts with the feather's point. 'Jack, don't!' she yelled, pressing herself wildly back against the pillar in a impotent effort to escape from the torture caused by the maddeningly gentle titillation, her face crimson. For response, I proceeded to pass the tip of the feather along the lower portion of her glorious bubbies, touching the skin ever so lightly here and there, then tickling her maiden nipples! With redoubled cries, Alice began to squirm convulsively as much as her fastenings would permit, while the effect of the fiendishly subtle torture on her became manifest by the sudden stiffening of her breasts, which now began to stand out tense and full! Noting this, I thought it as well to allow her a little respite, so dropped my hand, but at the same time leant forward till my face touched her breasts, which I then proceeded to kiss lovingly in turn, finally sucking them amorously till they again became soft and yielding. I then made as if I would repeat the torture, but after a touch or two (which produced piteous cries and contortions) I pretended to be moved by her distress, and again dropping my hand, leant back in the chair till she became less agitated.

But as soon as the regular rise and fall of her lovely bosom indicated the regaining of composure, I proceeded to try the ardently longed for experiment, viz. the effect of a feather when applied to a girl's cunt! And no one could have desired a more lovely subject on which to test this much debated question than was being offered by the naked helpless girl now standing terrified between my legs!

Pushing my chair back as much as was desirable, I leant forward, then slowly extended my right arm in the direction of Alice's cunt. A great cry of despair broke from her as she noted the movement, and she flattened her bottom against the pillar in a vain attempt to draw herself back out of reach. But the only effect of her desperate movement was to force forward her mount of Venus, and thereby render her cunt more open to the attack of the feather than it previously was!

Carefully regulating my motions, I gently brought the tip of the feather against the lowest point of Alice's cunt hole, then very softly and gently began to play up and down on and between its delicate coral lips! Alice's head had dropped on to her breast the better, I fancy, to watch my movements; but as soon as the feather touched her cunt, she threw her head backwards, as if in agony, shrieking at the top of her voice, her whole body twisting and contorting wildly. Not heeding her agonised appeals, I proceeded to work along her slit towards her clitoris, putting into play the most subtle titillation I was capable of, sometimes passing the feather all along the slit from one end to the other, sometimes tickling the orifice itself, not only outside but inside; then, ascending towards her clitoris, I would pass the tip of the feather all round it, irritating it without so much as touching it. The effect of my manipulation soon became evident. First the lips of Alice's cunt began to pout, then to gape a little, then a little more as if inviting the feather to pass into it – which it did! Then Alice's clitoris commenced to assert itself and to become stiff and rigid, throbbing excitedly; then her whole cunt seemed as if possessed by an irresistible flood of sexual lust and almost to demand mutely the immediate satisfaction of its cravings! Meanwhile Alice, firmly attached to the pillar, went into a paroxysm of contortions and convulsions, wriggling, squirming, writhing, tugging frantically at her fastenings, shrieking, praying, uttering incoherent exclamations and ejaculations, her eyes starting out of her head, her quivering lips, her heaving bosom with its wildly palpitating breasts all revealing the agony of body and mind that she was enduring! Fascinated by the spectacle, I continued to torture her by tickling her cunt more and more scientifically and cruelly, noting carefully the spots at which the tickling seemed most felt and returning to those ultra-sensitive parts of her cunt, avoiding only her clitoris – as I felt sure that were this touched, Alice would spend – till her strength became exhausted under the double strain. With a strangled shriek Alice collapsed just as I had forced the feather up her cunt and was beginning to tickle the sensitive interior. Her head fell forward on her bosom, her figure lost its self-supporting rigidity, she hung flaccidly, prevented from falling only by her wrists being shackled together round the pillar! There was nothing to be gained by prolonging the torture, so quickly I unfastened her, loosed her wrists and ankles from their shackles, and carried her to the large divan-couch, where I gently laid her, knowing that she would soon recover herself and guessing that she now would not need to be kept tied and that she had realised the futility of resistance.

## Chapter Six

The couch on which I had placed Alice was one of the cunning pieces of furniture that I had designed for use, should I succeed in capturing her. It was unusually long, nearly eight feet by about three and a half feet wide, upholstered in dark green satin and stuffed in such a way as to be delightfully soft and springy and yet not to allow one's person to sink into it. In appearance it resembled a divan, but in stern reality it was a rack, for at each end there was a concealed mechanism that worked stout leather straps, its object in life being to extend Alice at full length, either on her back or her front (as I might wish), and to maintain her fixed thus while I amused myself with her or worked my cruel will on her! From about halfway down the sides, there issued a pair of supplementary straps also worked by a mechanism, by means of which Alice's legs could be pulled widely apart and held so, should I want to devote myself to her cunt or fuck her against her will.

I did not wish to fatigue her with another useless struggle, so before she recovered the use of her faculties, I attached the corner straps to her wrists and ankles, leaving them quite loose and slack, so that she could move herself freely. Hardly had I effected this when Alice began to come to herself; immediately I quitted her and went to a part of the room where my back would be turned to her, but from which I could nevertheless watch her by means of a mirror.

I saw her draw a deep breath, then slowly open her eyes and look about her as if puzzled. Then, almost mechanically, one of her hands stole to her breasts and the other to her cunt, and she gently soothed these tortured parts by stroking them softly, as if to relieve them of the terrible tickling they had been subjected to! Presently she raised herself to a sitting position, then tried to free herself from the straps on her wrists and ankles.

I now considered that she must have fully recovered, so I returned to her and without a word, I touched the spring and set the mechanism working noiselessly. Immediately the straps began to tighten. As soon as she observed this, Alice started up in fright, at once detecting that she would he spread-eagled on her back if she did not break loose! 'No, no, no!' she cried, terrified at the prospect; then she desperately endeavoured to slip out of her fastenings, but the straps were tightening quickly and in the struggle she lost her balance and fell backwards on the couch, and before she could recover herself, she was drawn into a position in which resistance was impossible! With cruel satisfaction, I watched her, disregarding her frenzied appeals for mercy! Inch by inch, she was pulled flatter and flatter, till she rested on her back; then, inch by inch, her dainty legs were drawn asunder, till her heels rested on the edges of the couch! Then I stopped the machinery. Alice was now utterly helpless! In speechless delight, I stood gazing at her lovely body as she lay on her back, panting after her exertions, her bosom heaving and fluttering with her emotions, her face rosy red with shame, her lovely breasts and virgin cunt conspicuously exposed, stark naked, a living Maltese cross!

When I had sufficiently gratified my senses of sight and she had become a little calmer, I quietly seated myself by her waist, facing her feet, then bending over her, I began delightedly to inspect the delicious abode of Alice's maidenhead, her virgin cunt, now so fully exhibited! With sparkling eyes, I noted her full, fleshy mount of Venus, the delicately tinted coral lips quivering under sensations hitherto alien to them, the wealth of close clustering curly hair; with intense delight, I saw that, for a girl of her height and build, Alice had a large cunt, and that her clitoris was well developed and prominent, that the lips were full and her slit easy to open! Intently I scanned its every feature – the sweet junction of her belly and thighs, her smooth plump thighs themselves, the lines of her groin – while Alice lay trembling in an agony of shame and fright, horribly conscious of the close investigation her cunt was undergoing and in terrible dread of the sequel!

Shakespeare sings (in *Venus and Adonis*):

> Who sees his true-love in her naked bed,
> Teaching the sheets a whiter hue than white,
> But, when his glutton eye so full hath fed,
> His other agents aim at like delight?

So it was with me! My hands were tingling to explore the mysteries of Alice's cunt, to wander unchecked over her luscious belly and thighs. My prick was in a horrible state of erection. I could hardly restrain myself from falling on her and ravishing her as she lay there so temptingly helpless. But with a strong effort, I did suppress my rioting lustful desires and tore myself away from Alice's secret charms for a brief spell.

I turned round so as to face her, still seated by her waist, and placed my hands on her lovely breasts. As I lovingly squeezed them, I lowered my face till I almost touched hers, then whispered: 'You delicious beauty, kiss me!' at the same time placing my lips on hers. Alice flushed hotly, but did not comply. I had never yet either kissed her or received a kiss from her and was mad for one! 'Alice kiss me!' I repeated somewhat sternly, looking threateningly at her and replacing my lips on her mouth. Reluctantly she complied, I felt her lips open as she softly kissed me! It was delicious! 'Give me another!' I demanded, putting my right cheek in position to receive it. She complied. 'Yet another!' I commanded, tendering my left cheek. Again she complied. 'Now give me two more, nice ones, mouth to mouth!' Again came the sweet salute, so maddeningly exciting that, hastily quitting her breasts, I threw my arms round her neck, drew her face to mine, then showered burning kisses on her mouth, eyes and cheeks till she gasped for breath, blushing rosy red. Reluctantly I let her go; then to her dismay, I again turned round and bent over her cunt, and after a long look at it, expressive of the deepest admiration, I gently placed my hands on her belly and, after softly stroking it, began to follow the converging lines of her groin. Alice shrieked in sudden alarm, 'No, no – Oh! my God, no, no . . . don't touch me there! . . . Oh! no! not there!' and struggled desperately to break loose. But I disregarded her cries and continued my invasion; soon my itching fingers reached the forest of hairs that covered her mount, she squirming deliciously, then rested on her cunt itself. An agonised shriek of 'Oh! . . . Oh!!!' from Alice, as she writhed helplessly with quivering hips, proclaimed my victory and her shame!

Shall I ever forget the sensations of that moment? At last, after weary longings and waitings, Alice's cunt was at my mercy. I not only had it in the fullest possible view, but was actually touching it! My fingers, ranged on either side of the delicate pinky slit, were busy amorously pressing and feeling it, now playing with its silky curly hairs and gently pulling them, now tenderly stroking its sweet lips, now gently opening them so as to expose its coral orifice and its throbbingly agitated clitoris. Resting as I was on Alice's belly, I could feel every quiver and tremor as it passed through her, every involuntary contortion induced by the play of my fingers on this most delicate and susceptible part of her anatomy, the fluttering of her palpitating and heaving bosom. I could hear the involuntary ejaculations, the 'ohs!' and the 'ahs!' that broke from her in her shame and mental anguish at thus having to endure this handling and fingering of her maiden cunt and the strange half-terrifying sensations thereby provoked!

Half mad with delight, I continued to toy sweetly with Alice's cunt, till sudden unmistakeable wriggles of her bottom and hips and her incoherent exclamations warned me that I was trying her too much, if not goading her into spending, and as I had determined that Alice's first sacrifice to Venus should be induced by the action of my tongue on her cunt, I reluctantly desisted from my delightful occupation, to her intense relief.

Turning round, I again clasped her in my arms, rained hot kisses on her unresisting lips and cheeks, murmuring brokenly: 'O Alice! . . . O Alice! . . .' Then pressing my cheek against hers, I rested with her clasped in my arms, her breasts quivering against my chest, till we both grew calmer and her tremblings ceased.

For about five minutes there was dead silence, broken only by Alice's agitated breathing. Soon this ceased, and she seemed to have recovered command of herself again. Then softly I whispered to her 'Will you not surrender yourself to me now, Alice dear! surely it is plain to you that you cannot help yourself?'

She drew her face away from me, and murmured: 'No, no, I can't, I can't . . . let you . . . have me! O let me go! . . . let me go!!!'

'No,' I replied sternly, releasing my clasp of her and resuming my sitting attitude by her waist, 'no, my dear! you shan't go till you've been well punished and well fucked! But as I said before, I think you will change your mind presently!'

She looked questioningly at me, fear in her eyes. I rose. Her eyes followed me, and when she saw me select another fine-pointed feather and turn back to her, she instantly divined my intentions and frantically endeavoured to break the ropes that kept her thighs apart, shrieking: 'Oh no, no, my God no, I can't stand it! . . . you'll kill me!'

'Oh no, I won't!' I replied quietly, seating myself by her knees, so as to command both her cunt and a view of her struggles which I knew would prove most excitingly delicious! Then without another word, I gently directed the point of the feather against the lowest part of her cunt's virgin orifice, and commenced to tickle her.

# Chapter Seven

A fearful scream broke from Alice, a violent quivering spasm shook her from head to foot. Her muscles contracted, as she vainly strove to break free. Arching her back she endeavoured to turn herself first on one side and then on the other, tugging frantically at the straps, anything as long as she could dodge the feather. But she could do nothing. The more she shrieked and wriggled, the greater was the pleasure she was affording me; so, deaf to her cries and incoherent pleadings, I continued to tickle her cunt, sometimes up and down the slit, sometimes just inside, noting with cruel delight how its lips began to gape open under the sexual excitement now being aroused and how her throbbing clitoris began to erect itself. Alice presented a most voluptuous spectacle: clenched hands, half-closed eyes, heaving breasts, palpitating bosom, plunging hips, tossing bottom, jerking thighs – wriggling and squirming frantically, uttering broken and incoherent ejaculations, she shrieked and prayed.

I thought it wise to give her a pause for rest and partial recovery. I withdrew the feather from between the lips of her cunt, then gently stroked them caressingly. 'Ah! . . . Ah! . . . ' she murmured half unconsciously, closing her eyes. I let her lie still, but closely watched her.

Presently, her eyes opened half dreamily, she heaved a deep breath. I made as if to resume the tickling. 'No, no,' she murmured faintly, 'it's no use! . . . I can't stand it! . . . don't tickle me any more!'

'Well, will you yield yourself to me?' I asked. Alice lay silent for a moment, then with an evident effort said, 'Yes'!

Letting the feather fall between her parted legs, I leant forward and took her in my arms: 'There must not be any mistake, Alice,' I said softly. 'Are you willing to let me do to you anything and everything that I may wish?'

Half opening her eyes she nodded her head in assent. 'And do you promise to do everything and anything that I may wish you to do?'

She hesitated: 'What will you want me to do?' she murmured.

'I don't know,' I replied, 'but whatever it may be you must do it. Do you promise?'

'Yes!' she murmured, reluctantly.

'Then kiss me, kiss me properly in token of peace!' I whispered in her ear, placing my lips on hers; and deliciously she kissed me, receiving at the same time my ardent reciprocations. Then I unclasped her and began to play with her breasts.

'Mayn't I get up now?' she murmured, moving herself uneasily as she felt her breasts being squeezed.

'Not just yet, dear,' I replied. 'I've excited you so terribly that it is only fair to you that I should give you relief, and as I know that in spite of your promise you will not behave as you should do, simply from inexperience, I will keep you as you are till I have solaced you!'

'Oh, what are you going to do to me?' she asked in alarm, in evident fear that she was about to be violated.

'Restore you to ease, dear, by kissing you all over; now lie still and you will enjoy the greatest pleasure a girl can taste and yet remain virgin!'

With heightened colour she resigned herself to her fate. I took her again in my arms, and sweetly kissed her on her eyes, her cheeks, her hair. Then releasing her, I applied my lips to her delicious breasts, and showered burning kisses all over them, revelling in their sweet softness and their exquisite elasticity. Taking each breast in turn, I held it between finger and thumb, then enveloping the dainty little nipple between my lips, I alternately played on it with my tongue and sucked it, all the while squeezing and toying with the breast, causing Alice to experience the most lascivious sensations she had yet known, except perhaps when her cunt was being felt. 'Stop! Oh, for God's sake stop!' she ejaculated in her confusion and half fright as to what might happen. 'For heaven's sake, stop!' she screamed as I abandoned one breast only to attack the other. But the game was too delightful: to feel her glorious throbbing ripe bubbies in my mouth and quivering under my tongue, while Alice squirmed in her distress, was a treat for a god; so, disregarding her impassioned pleadings, I continued to suck and tongue-tickle them till their sudden stiffening warned me that Alice's sexual instincts were being roused and the result might be a premature explosion when she felt the grand assault on her cunt.

So I desisted reluctantly. Again I encircled her neck with my arms, kissed her pleading mouth and imploring eyes as she lay helpless; then with my tongue I touched her navel. She cried, 'No, no, oh! don't,' struggling desperately to get free, for it began to dawn on her innocent mind what her real torture was to be. I did not keep her in suspense. Thrusting my hands under her and gripping the cheeks of her bottom so as to steady her plungings, I ran my tongue down lightly over the lines of her abdomen and began tenderly to kiss her cunt. She shrieked in her terror as she felt my lips on those of her cunt, and with frantic wrigglings endeavoured to escape my pursuing mouth. At this critical moment, I lightly ran my tongue along Alice's slit. The effect was astounding! For a moment she seemed to swoon under the subtle titillation, but on my tongue again caressing her cunt, only this time darting deeper between its lips, she went off into a paroxysm of shrieks and cries, wriggling and squirming in a most wonderful way considering how strongly I had fastened her down; her eyes seemed to start out of her head under the awful tickling that she was experiencing; she plunged so frantically that although I was tightly gripping her buttocks she almost dislodged my mouth, the rigid muscles of her lovely thighs testifying to the desperate effort she was making to get loose. But the subtle titillation had aroused her sexual desires, without her recognising the fact in her distress. Her cunt began to open of its own accord, soon the clitoris was revealed turgid and stiff, quivering in sexual excitement, then her orifice began to yawn and show the way to paradise; deeper and deeper plunged my tongue into its satiny recess, Alice mechanically and unconsciously thrusting herself upwards as if to meet my tongue's downward dartings and strokes. Her head rolled from side to side, as, with half-closed eyes, she struggled with a fast increasing feeling that she must surrender herself to the imperious call of her sexual nature, yet endeavouring desperately not to do so under so long established notions of chastity. Her breath came in snatches, her breasts heaved and panted, half-broken ejaculations escaped from her quivering lips. The time had arrived for the sacrifice and the victim was ready. Thrusting my tongue as deeply into her cunt as I could force it, I gave her one final and supreme tickling, then taking her clitoris between my lips, I sucked hard at it, the while tickling it with my tongue . . . It was too much for Alice 'Stop . . . stop . . . it's coming! . . . it's coming!' she gasped. An irresistible wave of lust swept away the last barriers of chastity, and with a despairing wail: 'Oh . . . Oh . . . I . . . can't . . . help . . . it . . . Oh . . . Oh . . . Oh!!!' she spent frantically!

Feeling her go, I sprang to my feet to watch Alice as she spent. It was a wonderful sight! There she lay on her back, completely naked, forced to expose her most secret charm, utterly absorbed in the sensations of the moment, her body pulsating and thrilling with each sexual spasm, her closed eyes, half-open lips and stiff breasts indicating the intensity of the emotions that possessed her. And so she remained for a minute or two, as if in a semi-swoon.

Presently I noticed a relaxing of her muscles; then she drew a long breath and dreamily opened her eyes. For a moment she seemed dazed and almost puzzled to know where she was; then her eyes fell on me, and in a flash she remembered everything. A wave of colour surged furiously over her face and bosom at the thought that I had witnessed her unconscious transports and raptures as she yielded herself to her sexual passions in spite of herself; stirring uneasily, she averted her eyes, flushing hotly again. I stooped down and kissed her passionately; then, without a word, I unfastened her, raised her from the settee and supported her to the large armchair, where she promptly curled herself up, burying her blushing face in her hands.

I thought it wisest to leave her undisturbed for a brief space, so busied myself quietly in pouring out two glasses of wine, and knowing what severe calls were going to be made on Alice's innate sexual powers I took the opportunity to fortify these by dropping into her glass the least possible dose of cantharides.

# Chapter Eight

My readers will naturally wonder what my condition of mind and body was after both had been subjected to such intense inflammation as was inevitable from my close association with Alice dressed and Alice naked.

Naturally I had been in a state of considerable erotic excitation from the moment that Alice's naked charms were revealed, especially when my hands were playing with her breasts and toying with her cunt. But I had managed to control myself. The events recorded in the last chapter however proved too much for me. The contact of my lips and tongue with Alice's maiden lips, breasts and cunt and the sight of her as she spent were more than I could stand, and I was nearly mad with lust and an overwhelming desire that she should somehow provide me with relief.

But how could it be arranged? I wanted to keep her virgin as long as I possibly could, for I had not nearly completed my carefully prepared programme of fondlings and quasi torturings that impart double spice and salaciousness when perpetrated on a virgin. To fuck her therefore was out of the question. Of course there was her mouth, and my blood boiled at the idea of being sucked by Alice; but it was patent that she was too innocent and inexperienced to give me this pleasure. There were her breasts: one could have a delicious time no doubt by using them to form a tunnel and to work my prick between them, but this was a game better played later on. There were her hands, and sweetly could Alice frig me, if she devoted one dainty hand to my prick, while the other played with my testicles, but nothing would be easier than for her to score off me heavily, by giving the latter an innocent wrench which would throw me out of action entirely. The only possible remaining method was her bottom, and while I was feverishly debating its advisability, an innocent movement of hers and the consequent change of attitude suddenly displayed the superb curves and general lusciousness of her posteriors. In spite of my impatience, I involuntarily paused to admire their glorious opulence! Yes! I would bottom-fuck Alice, I would deprive her of one of her maidenheads!

But would she let me do so? True, she had just sworn to submit herself to my caprices whatever they might be, but such a caprice would no doubt never have entered into her innocent mind, and unless she did submit herself quietly, I might be baffled and in the excitement of the struggle and the contact with her warm naked flesh, might spend and 'waste my sweetness on the desert air!' Suddenly a cruelly brilliant idea struck me, and at once I proceeded to act on it.

She was still lying curled up in the armchair. I touched her on her shoulder; she looked up hurriedly.

'I think you have rested long enough, Alice,' I said. 'Now get up, I want you to put me right!' And I pointed to my prick now in a state of terrible erection! 'See!' I continued, 'you must do something to put it out of its torment, just as I have already so sweetly allayed your lustful cravings!' She flushed painfully! 'You can do it either with your mouth or by means of your bottom – now say quick – for I am just bursting with lust for you!'

She hid her face in her hands! 'No, no,' she ejaculated. 'No, oh no! I couldn't, really I couldn't!'

'You must!' I replied somewhat sternly, for I was getting mad with unsatisfied lust. 'Remember the promises you have just made! Come now, no nonsense! Say which you'll do!'

She threw herself at my feet. 'No, no,' she cried, 'I can't!'

Bending over her, I gripped her shoulders: 'You have just sworn that you would let me do to you anything I pleased, and that you would do anything I might tell you to do; in other words, that you would both actively and passively minister to my pleasures. I have given you your choice! If you prefer to be active, I will lie on my back and you can suck and excite me into spending; if you would rather be passive, you can lie on your face and I will bottom-fuck you! Now which shall it be?'

'No, no, no!' she moaned in her distress, 'I can't do either! really I can't!'

Exasperated by her non-compliance, I determined to get by force what I wanted, and before she could guess my intentions, I had gripped her firmly round her body, then half carried and half dragged her to the piano duet stool which also contained a hidden mechanism. On to it I forced her, face downwards, and in spite of her resistance, I soon fixed the straps to her wrists and ankles; then I set the mechanism working, sitting on her to keep her in the proper position, as she desperately fought to get loose. Cleverly managing the straps, I soon got Alice into the desired position, flat on her face and astride the stool, her wrists and ankles being secured to the longitudinal wooden bars that maintained the rigidity of the couch.

Alice was now fixed in such a way that she could not raise her shoulders or bosom, but by straightening her legs, she could heave her bottom upwards a little. Her position was perfect for my purpose, and lustfully I gloated over the spectacle of her magnificent buttocks, her widely parted thighs affording me a view of both of her virgin orifices, both now at my disposal!

I passed my hands amorously over the glorious backside now at my mercy, pinching, patting, caressing and stroking the luscious flesh; my hands wandered along her plump thighs, revelling in their smoothness and softness, Alice squirming and wriggling deliciously! Needless to say her cunt was not neglected, my fingers tenderly and lovingly playing with it and causing her the most exquisitely irritating titillation.

After enjoying myself in this way for a few minutes and having thoroughly felt her bottom, I left her to herself for a moment while I went to a cupboard, Alice watching my movements intently. After rummaging about,

I found what I sought, a riding whip of some curious soft substance, very springy and elastic, calculated to sting but not to mark the flesh. I was getting tired of having to use force on Alice to get what I wanted and considered it would be useful policy to make her learn the result of not fulfilling her promises; and there is no better way of bringing a girl to her senses than by whipping her soundly, naked if possible! And here was Alice, naked, fixed in the best possible position for a whipping!

As I turned towards her, whip in hand, she instantly guessed her fate and shrieked for mercy, struggling frantically to get loose. Deaf to her pitiful pleadings, I placed myself in position to command her backside, raised the whip, and gave her a cut right across the fleshiest part.

A fearful shriek broke from her! Without losing time, I administered another, and another, and another, Alice simply now yelling with the pain, and wriggling in a marvellous way considering how tightly she was tied down. I had never before whipped a girl, although I had often read and been told of the delights of the operation to the operator, but the reality far surpassed my most vivid expectations! And the naked girl I was whipping was *Alice*, the object of my lust, the girl who had jilted me, the girl I was about to ravish! Mad with exultation, I disregarded her agonised shrieks and cries. With cruel deliberation, I selected the tenderest parts of her bottom for my cuts, aiming sometimes at one luscious cheek, then the other, then across both, visiting the tender inside of her widely parted thighs! Her cries were music to my ears in my lustful frenzy, while her wriggles and squirms and the agitated plungings of her hips and buttocks enthralled my eyes. But soon, too soon, her strength began to fail her, her shrieks degenerated into inarticulate ejaculations. There was now little pleasure in continuing her punishment, so most reluctantly I ceased.

Soothingly I passed my right hand over Alice's quivering bottom and stroked it caressingly, alleviating in a wonderfully short time the pain. In spite of the severity of the whipping she had received, she was not marked at all! Her flesh was like that of a baby, slightly pinker perhaps, but clean and fresh. As I tenderly restored her to ease, her tremblings died away, her breath began to come more freely and normally, and soon she was herself again.

'Well, has the nonsense been whipped out of you, Alice?' I asked mockingly. She quivered, but did not answer.

'What, not yet?' I exclaimed, pretending to misunderstand her. 'Must I give you another turn?' and I raised the whip as if to commence again.

'No, no!' she cried in genuine terror, 'I'll be good!'

'Then lie still and behave yourself,' I replied, throwing the whip away into a corner of the room.

From a drawer I took a pot of cold cream. Alice who was fearsomely watching every movement of mine, cried in alarm: 'Jack, what are you going to do to me? . . . oh tell me!' My only response was to commence to lubricate her arsehole, during which operation she squirmed delightfully; then placing myself full in her sight, I set to work to anoint my rampant prick. 'Guess, dear!' I said.

She guessed accurately. For a moment she was struck absolutely dumb with horror, then struggling desperately to get free, she cried: 'Oh! my God! . . . no Jack! . . . no! . . . you'll kill me!'

'Don't be alarmed,' I said quietly, as I caressed her quivering buttocks; 'think a moment – larger things have come out than what is now going in! Lie still, Alice, or I shall have to whip you.' Then placing myself in position behind her, I leant forward till the head of my prick rested against her arsehole.

'My God! – no! no!' she shrieked, frantically wriggling her buttocks in an attempt to thwart me. But the contact of my prick with Alice's flesh maddened me; thrusting fiercely forward, I, with very little difficulty, shoved my prick halfway up Alice's bottom with apparently little or no pain to her; then falling on her, I clasped her in my arms and rammed myself well into her, till I felt my balls against her and the cheeks of her bottom against my stomach.

My God! it was like heaven to me! Alice's naked quivering body was closely pressed to mine! – my prick was buried to its hairs in her bottom, revelling in the warmth of her interior! I shall never forget it! Prolonging my rapturous ecstasy, I rested motionless on her, my hands gripping and squeezing her palpitating breasts so conveniently placed for my delectation, my cheek against her averted face, listening to the inarticulate murmurs wrung unconsciously from her by the violence of her emotions and the unaccountably strange pleasure she was experiencing, and which she confessed to by meeting my suppressed shoves with spasmodic upward heavings of her bottom – oh! it was paradise!

Inspired by a sudden thought, I slipped my right hand down to Alice's cunt and gently tickled it with my forefinger, but without penetrating. The effect was marvellous! Alice plunged wildly under me with tumultuous quiverings, her bosom palpitating and fluttering: 'Ah! . . . Ah! . . . ' she ejaculated, evidently a prey to uncontrollable sexual cravings! Provoked beyond endurance I let myself go! For a few moments there was a perfect cyclone of frenzied upheavings from her, mixed with fierce down-thrustings from me, then blissful ecstasy as I spent madly into Alice, flooding her interior with my boiling tribute! 'Ah! . . . ah! . . . ' she gasped, as she felt herself inundated by my hot discharge! Her cunt distractedly sought my finger, a violent spasm shook her, and with a scarcely articulate cry indicative of the intensest rapture, Alice spent on my finger with quivering vibrations, her head falling forward as she half swooned in her ecstasy!! She had lost the maidenhead of her bottom!!!

For some seconds we both lay silent and motionless, save for an occasional tremor, I utterly absorbed in the indescribable pleasure of spending into Alice as she lay tightly clasped in my arms! She was the first to stir (possibly incommoded by my superincumbent weight), gently turning her face towards me, colouring furiously as our eyes met! I pressed my cheek against hers, she did not flinch but seemed to respond. Tenderly I kissed her, she turned her face fully towards me and of her own accord she returned my kiss! Was it that I had tamed her? Or had she secretly tasted certain pleasure during the violation of her bottom? Clasping her closely to me I whispered: 'You have been a good girl this time, Alice! a very good girl!!' She softly rubbed her cheek against mine!' Did I hurt you?' I asked.

She whispered back: 'Very little at first, but not afterwards!'

'Did you like it?' I enquired maliciously. For answer she hid her face in the leather seat, blushing hotly. But I could feel her thrill!!

A moment's silence, then she raised her head again, moved uneasily, then murmured: 'Oh! let me get up now!'

'Very well,' I replied and unclasping my arms from round her, I slowly drew my prick out of her bottom, untied her – then taking her into one of the alcoves I showed her a bidet all ready for her use and left her. Passing into the other, I performed the needful ablutions to myself, then radiant with my victory and with having relieved my overcharged desires, I awaited Alice's reappearance.

## *Chapter Nine*

Presently Alice emerged from her screen, looking much freshened up by her ablutions. She further had taken the opportunity to put her hair in order, it having become considerably disarranged and rumpled by her recent strugglings.

Her face had lost the woebegone look, and there was a certain air of almost satisfaction about her which I could not understand, for she smiled as our eyes met, at the same time faintly colouring, and concealing her cunt with her left hand as she approached me.

I offered her a glass of wine, which she drank, then I passed my left arm round her waist and drew her to the armchair, into which I placed myself, making her seat herself on my thighs and pass her right arm round my neck. Then drawing her closely to me, I proceeded to kiss her ripe lips, to which she made no resistance but gave no response.

We sat in silence for a minute or two, I gently stroking her luscious breasts while trying to read in her eyes what her present frame of mind really was, but unsuccessfully. Undoubtedly, during the ravishment of her bottom, she had tasted some pleasure sufficiently delicious to make her condone for its sake her 'violation *à la derrière*' and practically to pardon her violator! – what could it be?

I thought I would try a long shot, so presently whispered in her ear, 'Wouldn't you like that last all over again?'

I felt her quiver. She was silent for a moment, then asked softly, 'Do you mean as a further punishment?' steadily keeping her eyes averted from me and flushing slightly.

'Oh! no,' I replied, 'it was so very evident that it was not "punishment" to you,' and I tried to catch her eyes as I pressed her amorously to me. 'I meant as a little *entr'acte*.'

Alice blushed furiously! I felt her arm round my neck tighten its embrace, and she nestled herself closer to me! 'Not all!' she murmured gently.

'How much then? . . . or which part?' I whispered again.

'Oh! how can I possibly tell you!' she whispered back, dropping her face on to my shoulder and snuggling up to me, then throwing her left arm also round me, thereby uncovering her cunt.

I took the hint! 'May I guess?' I whispered.

Without waiting for a reply. I slipped my right hand down from her breasts and over her rounded belly, then began gently to toy with her hairs and caress her slit! Alice instantly kissed me twice passionately! She was evidently hot with lust, inflamed possibly by the dose of cantharides she had unknowingly swallowed!

'Am I right?' I whispered. She kissed me again!

'Then let me arrange you properly,' I said. 'Come, we'll sit in front of the mirror and look at ourselves!' Alice blushed, not quite approving of the idea, but willing to please me. So I moved the armchair in front of the mirror and seated myself in it. I then made Alice place herself on my thighs, her bottom being right over my prick, which promptly began to return to life, raising its drooping head until it rested against her posteriors. Passing my left arm round her waist, I held her firmly to me. Then I made her part her legs, placing her left leg between mine while her right leg rested against the arm of the chair, my right thigh in fact separating her thighs.

Alice was now reflected in the mirror in three-quarters profile, but her parted legs allowed the whole of her cunt with its glorious wealth of hair to be fully seen! Her arms hung idly at her sides – I had made her promise not to use them.

We gazed at our reflection for a moment, our eyes meeting in the glass! Alice looked just lovely in her nakedness!

'Are you ready?' I asked with a significant smile. Alice wriggled a little as if to settle herself down more comfortably, then turning her face (now all aflame and rosy red) to me she almost shame-facedly nodded, then kissed me!

'Keep your cheek against mine, and watch yourself in the glass, Alice,' I whispered, then I gently placed my right hand on her sweet belly and slowly approached her cunt!

A thrill, evidently of pleasure, quivered through her as she felt my fingers pass through her hairs and settle on her cunt! 'Ah!' she murmured, moving deliciously over my prick as I commenced to tenderly frig her, now fingering her slit, now penetrating her still virgin orifice, now tickling her clitoris – causing her all the time the most deliciously lascivious transports, to which she surrendered herself by licentiously oscillating and jogging herself backwards and forwards as if to meet and stimulate my finger!

Presently Alice became still more excited; her breasts stiffened, her nostrils dilated! Noting this, I accelerated the movements of my finger, at the same time clasping her more firmly to me, my eyes riveted on her image in the glass and gloating over the spectacle she presented in her voluptuous raptures! Suddenly she caught her breath! Quickly I tickled her on her clitoris! 'Oh! . . . Oh! . . . oh!!!' she ejaculated – then spent in ecstasy, maddening me by the quiverings of her warm buttocks, between which my now rampant prick raged, held down!

I did not remove my finger from Alice's cunt, but kept it in her while she spent, slightly agitating it from time to time, to accentuate her ecstasy. But, as soon as I considered her sexual orgasm had exhausted itself, I began again to frig her. Then an idea flashed through my brain: why should I not share her raptures? Carefully I watched for an opportunity! Soon I worked her again into an awful state of desire; panting with unsatisfied lust and furiously excited (the result of the cantharides!), Alice jerked herself about madly and spasmodically on my thighs! Presently an unusually violent movement of hers released my prick from its sweet confinement under her bottom; promptly it sprang up stark and stiff! Quick as thought, I gripped Alice tightly and rammed myself fiercely into her bottom!! 'No! . . . no! . . . no! . . . ' she cried and strove to rise and so dislodge me, but I pressed her firmly down on my thighs and compelled her to remain impaled on my prick, creating a diversion by frigging her harder than ever!!

'Kiss me,' I gasped, frantic with lust under my sensations in Alice's bottom and the sight of her naked self in the glass, quivering, palpitating, wriggling!! Quickly Alice pressed her lips on mine, our breaths mingled, our tongues met, my left hand caught hold of one of her breasts and squeezed it as her eyes closed. An electric shock ran through her! . . . then Alice spent frantically, plentifully bedewing my finger with her virgin distillation! – at the same moment receiving inside her my boiling essence, as I shot it madly into her, my prick throbbing convulsively under the contractions of her rear sphincter muscles, agitated and activated by her ecstatic transports.

Oh! the sensations of the moment! How Alice spent! How I discharged into her!!

It must have been a full minute before either of us moved, save for the involuntary tremors that, from time to time, ran through us as our sexual excitement died away! Alice, now limp and nerveless, but still impaled on my prick, reposed on me, my finger dwelt motionless in her cunt, luxuriating in its envelope of warm throbbing flesh! And so we rested, exhausted after our lascivious orgy, both half unconscious!

\* \* \*

I was the first to come to myself, and as I caught sight of our reflection in the mirror, the licentious tableau we presented sent an involuntary quiver through me which my prick communicated to Alice, thus rousing her! As she dreamily opened her eyes, her glance also fell on the mirror! She started, became suddenly wide-awake, flushed rosy red, then hid her face in her hands, murmuring brokenly: 'Oh! . . . how horrible! . . . how horrible! . . . what . . . have you . . . made me do? . . . ' half sobbing in her shame now that her sexual delirium had subsided, and horribly conscious that my prick was still lodged in her bottom and impaling her. Foreseeing her action, I brought my right arm to the assistance of my left and held her forcibly down, so preventing her from rising and slipping off me.

'What's the matter, Alice?' I asked soothingly, as she struggled to rid herself of my prick.

'Oh! let me go! let me go!' she begged, still with her face in her hands and in such evident distress that I deemed it best to comply and let her hurry off to her bidet, as she clearly desired.

So I released Alice; she slowly drew her bottom off my prick and rushed behind her screen. Following her example, I repaired to my corner and after the necessary ablutions, I awaited Alice's return.

## Chapter Ten

Pending Alice's reappearance, I debated with myself the important question, what next should I do to her? There was no doubt that I had succeeded in taming her, that I had now only to state my wishes and she would comply with them! But this very knowledge seemed to destroy the pleasure I had anticipated in having her in such utter subjection; the spice of the proceeding up to now had undoubtedly lain in my forcing her to endure my salacious and licentious caprices, in spite of the most determined and desperate resistance she could make! And once she became a dull and passive surrogate of a proud and voluptuous girl, I should practically be flogging a dead horse were I to continue my programme!

But there was one experience which on no account was to be omitted, forming as it did the culmination of my revenge as well as of my lust, one indignity which she could not and would not passively submit to, one crowning triumph over her which she could never question or deny – and this was . . . her violation! – the ravishing of her maidenhead!!

Alice was now fully educated to appreciate the significance of every detail of the process of transforming a girl into a woman; my fingers and lips had thoroughly taught her maiden cunt its duty, while my prick, when lodged in the throbbing recesses of her bottom, had acquainted her with the phenomenon of the masculine discharge at the crisis of pleasure, of the feminine ecstasy in receiving it, while her transports in my arms, although somewhat restricted by the circumstances, had revealed to her the exquisitely blissful sensations mutually communicated by such close clinging contact of male and female flesh! Yes! I would now devote the afternoon to fucking her!

Hardly had I arrived at this momentous decision than Alice came out of her alcove after an unusually prolonged absence. She had evidently thoroughly refreshed and revived herself, and she looked simply fetching as she halted hesitatingly on passing through the curtains, shielding her breasts with one hand and her cunt with the other, in charming shame-faced confusion. Obedient to my gesture, she came timidly towards me; she allowed me to pass my arm round her waist and kiss her, and then to lead her to the table where I made her drink a small tumbler of champagne that I had previously poured out for her, and which seemed to be most welcome to her. Then I gently whispered to her that we would lie down together on the couch for a little rest, and soon we were cosily lying at our ease, she pressed and held amorously against me by my encircling arms.

For a minute or two we rested in silence, then the close conjunction of our naked bodies began to have the inevitable result on me – and I think also on her! Clasping her closely against me, I murmured: 'Now, Alice darling, I think the time has come for you to surrender to me your maidenhead . . . for you to be my bride!' And I kissed her passionately.

She quivered, moved herself uneasily as if trying to slip out of my encircling arms, trembled exceedingly, but remained silent.

I made as if to place her on her back, whispering: 'Open your legs, dear!'

'No! no! Jack!' Alice ejaculated, struggling to defend herself, and success-fully resisting my attempt to roll her over on to her back, 'let me go, dear Jack! . . . surely you have revenged yourself on me sufficiently!' And she endeavoured to rise.

I held her down firmly and, in spite of her determined resistance, I got her on her back and myself on her. But she kept her legs so obstinately closed that in the position in which I was, I could not get mine between them. I began to get angry. Gripping her to me till her breasts flattened themselves against my chest, I raised my head and looked her sternly in the eyes.

'Now, Alice, no more nonsense,' I said brusquely. 'I'm going to fuck you! Yield yourself at once to me and do as I tell you or I shall tie you down on this couch and violate you by force in a way you won't like! Now once and for all, are you going to submit or are you not?'

She closed her eyes in an agony of distress.

'Jack! . . . Jack! . . . ' she murmured brokenly then stopped as if unable to speak in her emotion.

'I can only take it that you prefer to be ravished by force rather than be treated as a bride! Very well!' I rejoined. And I slipped off her as if to rise and tie her down. But she caught my hand; looked at me so pleadingly and with so piteous an expression in her lovely eyes that I sat down by her side on the couch.

'Upon my word I don't understand you, Alice!' I said, not unkindly. 'You have known all along that you were to lose your maidenhead and you have solemnly promised to yield it to me and to conform to all my desires, whatever they might be. Now, when the time has arrived for you to he fucked you seem to forget all your promises!'

'But . . . but . . . ' she stammered, 'I didn't know . . . then! . . . I thought . . . there . . . was . . . only one way! . . . so . . . I promised! . . . but you . . . have . . . had me twice . . . another way! . . . oh! let me off! . . . do let me off! . . . I can't submit! . . . truly I can't . . . have me again . . . the . . . other way . . . if . . . you must! . . . but not . . . this way! . . . oh! . . . not this way!! . . . '

With my right hand, I stroked her cunt gently, noting how she flinched when it was touched! 'I want this virginity, Alice! this virginity of your cunt! – your real maidenhead! – and you must let me have it! Now am I to whip you again into submission? Don't be foolish! you can guess how this whip will hurt when properly applied, as it will be. You know you'll then have to give in! why not do so at once, and spare yourself the pain and indignity of a severe whipping?'

Alice moaned pitifully: 'Oh, my God!' – then was silent for a few seconds, her face working painfully in her distress! Then she turned to me: 'I must give in!' she murmured brokenly, 'I couldn't endure . . . to be whipped . . . naked . . . as I am! . . . so . . . take me . . . and do . . . what you desire! . . . only . . . treat . . . me as kindly . . . as you can! . . . Now . . . I don't know . . . why . . . I ask it . . . but . . . kiss me . . . kiss me . . . let me think . . . I'm . . . your wife . . . and on . . . my wedding night! . . . not . . . ' – she stopped, struggling with her emotions, then bravely put up her mouth with a pitiful smile to be kissed.

Promptly I took her lovely naked form lovingly in my arms, and pressing her to me till her breasts flattened against me, I passionately kissed her trembling lips again and again until she gasped for breath. Then stooping, I repeated the caress on each heaving breast and then on her palpitating cunt, kissing the latter over and over again and interspersing my kisses with delicate lingual caresses! Then I succeeded in soothing her natural agitation at thus reaching the critical point of her maiden existence.

## Chapter Eleven

Thus at last Alice and I found ourselves together naked on the Couch of Love! – she, ill at ease and downcast at having thus to yield up her virginity and dreading horribly the process of being initiated by me into the mysteries of sexual love! – I overjoyed at the prospect of soon ravishing Alice and conquering her maidenhead! Side by side on our backs, we lay in silence, my left hand clasping her right, till she had regained her composure a little.

As soon as I saw she had become calmer, I slipped my arms round her, and turning on my side towards her, I drew her tenderly to me, but still keeping her flat on her back; then I kissed her lips again and again ardently, murmuring lovingly between my kisses, 'My little wifie! . . . my wee wifie!' – noting delightedly how her downcast face brightened at my adoption of her fantasy, and feeling her respond almost fondly to my kisses.

'May I learn something about my wifie?' I whispered as I placed my right hand on Alice's maiden breasts and began feeling them as if she was indeed my bride! Alice smiled tenderly, yielding herself to my caprice, and quivering anew under the voluptuous sensations communicated to her by my inquisitive fingers. 'Oh! what little beauties! oh! what darling bubbies!' I murmured amidst fresh kisses! – Alice now beginning to look quite pleased at my using her own pet name for her treasures and commencing to enter almost heartily into my game. I continued to fondle and squeeze her luscious breasts for a little longer, then carried my hand lower down her, but suddenly arrested it, whispering: 'May I?'

At this absurd travesty of a bridegroom's chivalrous respect for his bride Alice fairly laughed (poor girl! her first laugh in that room that day!) then gaily nodded, putting up her lips for more kisses! Overjoyed to see her thus forgetting her woes, I pressed my lips on hers and kept them there, punctuating with kisses the feigningly timid advance of my hand over her belly, till it invaded the precincts of her cunt! 'Oh! my darling! . . . oh! my sweetheart! . . . oh! my wifie! . . . ' I murmured passionately as my fingers roved wantonly all over Alice's virgin cunt, playing with her hairs, feeling and pressing insidiously but irritatingly its fleshiness, and toying with her slit but not penetrating it! Alice all the while abandoned herself freely to the lascivious sensations induced by my fingerings, jogging her buttocks upwards, waggling her hips, ejaculating 'Ah!' and 'Oh!' in spite of my lips being glued to hers and nearly suffocating her with kisses!

After a few minutes of this delicious exploitation of the most private part of Alice's body, I stopped my finger on her virgin orifice. 'Pardon me, sweet!' I whispered; then gently inserted it into Alice's cunt as far as I could, as if to assure myself as to her virgin condition, all the time smothering her with kisses. Keenly appreciating the comicality of my proceedings, in spite of the serious lover-like air I was assuming, Alice laughed out heartily, unconsciously heaving herself up so as to meet my finger and slightly opening her thighs to allow it freer access to her cunt, my tongue taking advantage of her laughter to dart through her parted lips in search of her tongue, which she then sweetly resigned to my ardent homage! 'Oh! wifie! . . . my wifie! . . . my sweet wifie! . . . my virgin wifie! . . . ' I murmured, as if enchanted to find her a maid! 'Oh! what a delicious cunny you have! – so fat! so soft! so juicy! – wifie!! . . . oh wifie!! . . . ' I breathed passionately into her ear, as I agitated my finger inside her cunt, half frigging her and stopping her protests with my kisses, till I saw how I was exciting her! 'Little wifie!' I whispered with a grin I could not for the life of me control, 'Little wifie! shall I . . . make you come?' In spite of her almost uncontrollable and self-absorbing sexual irritation, Alice laughed out, then nodded, closing her eyes as if in anticipation of her now fast approaching ecstasy! A little more subtle titillation and Alice spent blissfully on my ministering finger, jerking herself about lasciviously and evidently experiencing the most voluptuous raptures and transports!!

I waited till her sexual spasm had ceased: 'Wifie!' I whispered, rousing her with my kisses, 'little wifie! oh you naughty girl! how you seemed to enjoy it! . . . tell me, wifie! was it then so good?' As she opened her eyes, Alice met mine, brimming with merriment; she blushed rosy red, then clasped me in her soft arms and kissed me passionately, murmuring: 'Darling! oh! darling!!' then burst out laughing at our ridiculousness! And so we lay for a few delicious moments, clasped in each other arms.

Presently I murmured: 'Now, wifie! you'll like to learn something about me, eh?' Alice laughed merrily at the quaint conceit, then coloured furiously as she remembered that it would mean the introduction of her virgin hands to my virile organs! 'Sit up, wifie! dear, and give me your pretty hands,' I said.

Alice, now rosy red with suppressed excitement and lust, quickly raised herself to a sitting position at my side. I took her dainty hands in mine, she yielding them rather coyly, turned on my back, opened my legs, and then guided her right hand on to my prick and her left to my testicles, then left her to indulge and satisfy in any manner she saw fit her senses of sight and touch, wondering whether it would occur to her that the fires she was about to excite in me would have to be extinguished in her virgin self when she was being ravished, as before long she would be!

For certainly half a minute, Alice intently inspected my organs of generation, leaning over me and supporting herself by placing her right hand on my stomach and her left on my thigh. I wondered what thoughts passed through her mind as she gazed curiously on what very soon would be the instruments of her violation and the conquerors of her virginity. But she made no sign.

Presently she steadied herself on her left hand, then timidly, with her right hand, she took hold of my prick gently, glancing curiously at me as if to note the effect of the touch of her soft hand on so excitable a part of my person, then smiling wickedly and almost triumphantly as she saw me quiver with pleasure! Oh! the exquisite sensations that accompanied her touch! Growing bolder, she held my prick erect and gently touched my balls with her slender forefinger, as if to test their substance, then took them in her hand, watching me eagerly out of the corner of her eye to note the effect on me! I was simply thrilling with the pleasure! For a few minutes she lovingly played with my organs, generally devoting a hand to each, but sometimes she would hold my prick between one finger and thumb, while with her other hand, she would amuse herself by working the loose folds of skin off and on the knob! At another time, she would place my prick between her soft warm palms and pretend to roll it. Another time she seized a testicle in each hand, oh! so gently! and sweetly caressed them! Had I not taken the edge off my sexual ardour by the two spendings in Alice's bottom, I must have discharged under the tenderly provocative ministration of her fingers! As it was, I had to exercise every ounce of my self-control to prevent an outburst!

Presently I said quietly but significantly: 'Little wifie! may I tell you that between husband and wife kissing not only is sanctioned but is considered even laudable!' Alice laughed nervously, glanced quickly at me, then with heightening colour, looked intently at my prick, which she happened at that moment to be grasping tightly in her right hand, its head protruding above her thumb and fingers, while with her left forefinger she was delicately stroking and tickling my balls! After a moment's hesitation, she bent down, squeezed my prick tightly (as if to prevent anything from issuing out of it), then softly kissed its head! Oh! my delicious sensations as her lips touched my prick! Emboldened by the success of her experiment, Alice set to work to kiss my balls sweetly, then passed her lips over the whole of my organs of generation, showering kisses on them, but favouring especially my balls, which had for her a wonderful attraction, burying her lips in my scrotum, and (I really believe!) tonguing them! Such attentions could only end in one way! Inflamed almost beyond endurance by the play of her sweetly irritating lips, my prick became so stiff and stark that Alice in alarm thought she had better cease her ministrations, and with blushing cheeks and a certain amount of trepidation, she lay herself down alongside of me.

By this time I was so mad with lust that I could hardly control myself, and as soon as Alice lay down I seized her in my arms, drew her to me, showered kisses on her lips, then with an abrupt movement, I rolled her over on to her back, slipping on top of her. In an effort to counteract my attack she separated her legs the better to push me back! Quick as thought, I forced myself between them.

Now is she in the very lists of love,
Her champion mounted for the hot encounter.

Shakespeare, *Venus and Adonis*

Alice was at my mercy! I could not have her at better advantage! She struggled desperately to dislodge, me, but to no avail!

Gripping her tightly, I got my stiff and excited prick against the lips of her cunt, then pushing steadily, I drove it into Alice, burying its head in her. Despite her fearful struggles and rapid movements of her buttocks and hips, I made another thrust, entering still further into her cunt, then felt myself blocked! Alice screamed agonisedly, 'Oh! . . . oh! stop! . . . you're hurting me!' throwing herself wildly about in her pain and despair, for she recognised that she was being violated! Knowing that it was her maiden membrane that was stopping my advance into her, and that this now was the last defence of her virginity, I rammed into her vigorously! Suddenly I felt something give way inside her and my prick glided well up her cunt, and it did not require the despairing shriek that came from Alice to tell me that I had broken through the last barriers and had conquered her virginity!

Oh! my exultation! At last I had ravished Alice, I had captured her maidenhead, and was now actually fucking her in spite of herself! She, poor girl, lay beneath me, tightly clasped in my arms, a prey to the keenest shame, deprived of her maidenhead, transfixed with my prick, her cunt suffering martyrdom from its sudden distension and smarting with the pain of her violation! Pitying her, I lay still for some seconds so as to allow the interior of her cunt to stretch a bit, but I was too wrought up and mad with lust to remain inactive long in such surroundings.

With a final thrust, I sent my prick well home, Alice's hairs and mine interweaving. She shrieked again! Then agitating myself gently on her, I began to fuck her, first with steady strokes of my buttocks, then with more rapid and uneven shoves and thrusts, she quivering under me, overwhelmed by her emotions at thus finding her pure body compelled to become the recipient of my lust and by the strangely delicious pleasure that the movements of my prick inside her cunt were arousing in her! Alice no longer struggled, but lay passive in my arms, unconsciously accommodating herself to my movements on her, and involuntarily working her hips and bottom, instinctively yielding to the promptings of her now fast-increasing sexual cravings by jogging herself up as if to meet my downthrusts!

Shall I ever forget my sensations at that moment? Alice, the long desired Alice, the girl of all girls, the unconscious object of my concupiscence – Alice lay underneath me, tightly clasped in my arms, naked, quivering, her warm flesh throbbing against mine, my prick lodged in her cunt, her tearful face in full sight, her breasts palpitating and her bosom heaving in her agitation! – gasping, panting in the acutest shame and distress at being violated, yet unconsciously longing to have her sexual desires satisfied while dreading the consummation of her devirginisation! I could no longer control myself. Clasping her yielding figure still more closely against me, I let myself go – thrusting, ramming, shoving and agitating my prick spasmodically in her, I frenziedly set to work to fuck her! A storm of rapid tumultuous jogs, a half strangled 'oh! . . . oh!! . . . oh!!! . . . ' from Alice and I spent deliriously into her, deluging her with my hot discharge, at the same moment feeling the head of my prick christened by the warm gush that burst from Alice as she also frantically spent, punctuating the pulsations of her discharge by voluptuous upheavings of her wildly agitated bottom.

I remained master of myself notwithstanding my ecstatic delirium, but Alice fainted under the violence of the sexual eruption for the first time legitimately induced within her! My warm kisses on her upturned face however soon revived her. When she came to herself and found herself still lying naked in my arms and harbouring my prick in the freshly opened asylum of her cunt, she begged me to set her free! But she had not yet extinguished the flames of lust and desire which her provocative personality and appetising nakedness had kindled and which she had stimulated to white heat by the tender manipulations and kisses she had bestowed on my testicles and prick! The latter still remained rampant and stiff and burned to riot again within the deliciously warm and moist recesses of Alice's cunt – while I longed to make her expire again in the sweet agonies of satisfied sexual desire, and to witness and share her involuntary transports and wondrous ecstasies as she passed from sexual spasm to spasm while being sweetly fucked!

So I whispered amidst my kisses: 'Not yet, Alice! not yet! once more, Alice! you'll enjoy it this time!' – then began gently to fuck her again.

'No! no! . . . ' she cried, plunging wildly beneath me in her vain endeavours to dislodge me, 'not again! . . . oh! not again! Let me go! . . . stop! . . . oh! please, do stop!' she implored, almost in tears, and in terrible distress at the horrible prospect of being ravished a second time.

I only shook my head negatively, and endeavoured to stifle her cries with my kisses. Seeing that I was determined to enjoy her again, Alice, now in tears, ceased her pleadings and resigned herself to her fate.

In order to control more easily her struggles, I had thrown my arms over hers, thus pinioning them in my grip of herself. Seeing now that she did not intend to resist me, except perhaps passively, I relaxed my embrace, set her arms free, passed mine round her body, then whispered: 'Hug me tightly, you'll be more comfy now, Alice!' She did so. 'That's much better, isn't it?' I murmured. She tearfully smiled, then nodded affirmatively, putting up her lips to be kissed.

'Now just lie quietly and enjoy yourself,' I whispered, then began to fuck her with slow and steady piston-like thrusts of my prick up and down her cunt. At once Alice's bosom and breasts commenced to palpitate under me, fluttering deliciously against my chest. Exercising the fullest control I possibly could bring to bear on my seminal reserves, so as to prolong to the utmost extent my voluptuous occupation, and that Alice should have every opportunity of indulging and satisfying her sexual appetites and cravings and of fully tasting the delights of copulation, I continued to fuck her steadily, watching her blushing upturned face and learning from her tell-tale eyes how she was getting on. Presently she began to agitate her hips and jog herself upwards, then her breath came and went quickly, her eyes turned upwards and half closed, a spasm convulsed her . . . she spent! I stopped for a moment. After a few seconds, Alice opened her eyes, blushing rosy red as she met mine. I kissed her lips tenderly, whispering 'Good?' She nodded and smiled. I resumed. Soon she was again quivering and wriggling under me, as a fresh wave of lust seized her; again her eyes closed and again Alice spent blissfully! I saw that I had now thoroughly roused her sexual desires and that she had surrendered herself to their domination and that they were imperiously demanding satisfaction! I clasped her closely to me, whispered quickly: 'Now, Alice, let yourself go!' And set to work in real earnest, thrusting rapidly and ramming myself well into her! Alice simply abandoned herself to her sensations of the moment! Hugging me to her, she agitated herself wildly under me, plunging madly, heaving herself furiously upwards, tossing her head from side to side – she seemed as if overcome and carried away by a torrent of lust and madly endeavouring to satisfy it. I could hardy hold her still. How many times she spent I do not know, but her eyes were constantly half closing and opening again as spasm after spasm convulsed her. Suddenly she ejaculated frenziedly: 'Now! . . . Now! let me have it! . . . let me have it all! . . . ' Immediately I responded – a few furious shoves, and I poured my boiling essence into Alice, spending frantically in blissful ecstasy! 'Ah! . . . Ah! . . . ' she cried, quivering in rapturous transports as she felt herself inundated by my warm discharge! – then a paroxysm swept through her, her head fell back, her eyes closed, her lips opened as she spent con-vulsively in her turn!

She fainted right away! it had been too much for her! I tried to bring her to herself by kisses and endearments, but did not succeed. So I drew my prick cautiously out of Alice's cunt, all bloodstained, staunched with a handkerchief the blood, etc., that oozed out of Alice and bore unimpeachable evidence of the rape that had been committed on her virginity, and sprinkled her face with water. When at length she came to, I assisted her to rise, as she seemed half dazed, and supported her as she tottered to her alcove, where she half fell into a low chair. I brought her a glass of wine which she drank gratefully, and which somewhat revived her. Then I saw that she had everything she could want – water, soap, syringe, towels, etc. She asked me to leave her, adding she was now all right. Before doing so, I stooped down to receive the first kiss she would give as a woman, having had her last as a girl. Alice threw her arms round my neck, drew my face to hers, then kissed me passionately over again, quite unable to speak because of her emotion! I returned her kisses with interest, wondering whether she was wishing to make me comprehend that she pardoned me for violating her!

Presently Alice whispered: 'May I dress now?' I had intended to have fucked her again, but I saw how overwrought she was; beside that, the afternoon was late and there was just comfortable time left for her to catch her train home. So I replied, 'Yes, dear, if you like; shall I bring your clothes here?' She nodded gratefully. I carefully collected her garments and took them to her, then left her to herself to dress; pouring out a bumper of champagne, I celebrated silently but exultingly the successful completion of my vengeance and my victory over Alice's virginity, then retired to my alcove and resumed my garments.

In about a quarter of an hour Alice appeared, fully dressed, hatted and gloved. I threw open the doors and she passed out without a word but cast a long comprehensive glance round the room in which she had passed so memorable an afternoon. I called a hansom, placed her in it and took her to her station in plenty of time for her train; she was very silent during the drive but made no opposition when I took her hand in mine and gently stroked it. As the train started, I raised my hat with the customary salute, to which she responded in quite her usual pleasant way; no one who witnessed our parting would have dreamt that the pretty ladylike girl had just been forcibly ravished by the quiet gentlemanly man, after having first been stripped naked and subjected to shocking indignities! And as I drove home, I wondered what the outcome of that afternoon's work would be.

PART TWO

# The Comedy

## Chapter One

I will now ask my readers to consider that four months have elapsed since
the events recorded in the preceding pages occurred. During this period,
Alice and I frequently met at the houses of mutual friends who were under
the impression that by thus bringing us together, they were assisting in
making a match between us. Our rupture was known only to our two selves,
and Alice had quickly recognised that complete silence as to what had
happened to her in my Snuggery was her safest policy, for otherwise she
would simply make public her changed condition and ruin herself socially.
And really there was some excuse for the incorrect impression under which
our friends were labouring, for our mutual embarrassment when we first
met after her violation, and her inability altogether to subdue on subsequent
occasions a certain agitation and heightened colour when I appeared on the
scene, were held to be symptoms of the 'tender passion' that was supposed to
be consuming us both.

But Alice's manner to me insensibly became kinder and kinder as time
went on. Unknown to herself there was in her composition a strain of strong
sensuality, which had lain dormant under the quiet peacefully virtuous life of
an English miss that she had hitherto led, and it only wanted some fierce
sexual stimulant to fan into flame the smouldering fires of her lust. This now
had been supplied.

She afterwards confessed to me that, when sense of humiliation and the
bitter regrets for her ravished virginity had died down, she found herself
recalling certain moments in which she had tasted the most exquisite
pleasure, in spite of the dreadful indignities to which her stark-naked self
was being submitted, and then unconsciously began to long to experience
them again, till a positive though unacknowledged craving sprang up which
she was quite unable to stifle but did not know how to satisfy.

When such promising conditions prevail, kind mother Nature and sweet lady Venus generally come into operation. Soon Alice began to feel towards me the tender regard that every woman seems to cherish towards the fortunate individual who has taken her maidenhead! As I have just stated, she became kinder and kinder till it was evident to me that she had pardoned my brutality; instead of almost shrinking from me, she undoubtedly seemed to welcome me and was never averse to finding herself alone with me in quiet corners and nooks for two.

On my side, I was beginning to experience a fierce desire once more to hold her naked in my arms and revel in the delights of her delicious person, to taste her lips as we mutually spent in each other's clasped embrace, in other words, to fuck her! Kind Mother Nature had taken us both into her charge; now sweet Lady Venus came on the scene.

One evening, Alice and I met at the house of a lady hostess, who placed us together at the dinner table; and I naturally devoted myself to Alice afterwards in the drawing-room. When the guests began to depart, our hostess asked me if I would mind seeing Alice home in my taxi-cab, which of course I was delighted to do. Strangely enough the possibilities of a *tête-à-tête* did not occur to me, and it was only when Alice returned to the hall cloaked and veiled and our hostess had told her that I had very kindly offered to take her home in my taxi that the opportunity of testing her real feelings was suggested to me by the vivid blush which, for a moment, suffused her face and elicited a sympathetic but significant smile from our hostess, who evidently thought she had done us both a good turn. And so she had, but not in the direction she fondly thought!

The taxi had hardly begun to move when we both simultaneously seemed to remember that we were alone together for the first time since the afternoon on which Alice had been first tortured scientifically and then ravished! Overcome by some sudden inspiration, our eyes sought each other. In the dim light, I saw Alice's face working under the rush of her emotion, but she was looking at me with eyes full of love and not of anger; she began to cuddle up against me perhaps unconsciously, at the same time turning her face up as if seeking a kiss. I could not resist the mute invitation. Quickly I slipped my left arm round her, drew her to me (she yielding to me without a struggle), pressed my lips on hers and fondly rained kisses on her mouth. 'Jack!' she murmured lovingly. I felt her thrill under my kisses, then catch her breath and quiver again! I recognised the symptoms. Promptly I slipped my right hand under her clothes, and before she could offer any resistance (even had she desired to do so, which she evidently did not), my hand had reached the sweet junction of her belly and thighs, and my fingers began to attack the folds of her chemise through the opening of her drawers in their feverish impatience to get at her cunt! 'Jack! oh Jack!' Alice again murmured as she pressed herself against me as closely as she could, while at the same time she began to open her thighs slightly, as if to facilitate the operations of my ardent fingers which, just at that moment, succeeded in displacing the last obstacle and were now resting on her cunt itself!

Alice quivered deliciously at the touch of my hand on her bare flesh as I gently and tenderly stroked her cunt, playing lovingly on its moist palpitating lips and twining her hairs round my fingers; but as soon as she felt me tickle her clitoris (time was short and we were fast reaching her rooms, besides which it would have been cruel to have aroused her sexual passions without satisfying them) she threw all restraint to the winds and madly agitated her cunt against my hand, wriggling divinely as I set to work to frig her. Soon came the first blissful ecstasy; a delicious spasm thrilled through her as she spent deliriously on my fingers – then another – and another – and yet another – till, unable to spend any more, she gasped brokenly: 'Stop, Jack! . . . I can't . . . go on!' only half conscious and utterly absorbed in the overpoweringly exquisite sensations of the moment and the delicious satisfying of the longings and cravings which had been tormenting her. It was full time that we stopped, for the taxi was now turning into the street in which she lived. Quickly but reluctantly I withdrew my hand from Alice's cunt, now moist with her repeated spendings, and I just managed to get her clothes into some sort of order when the cab stopped at her door. I sprang out first and assisted Alice to alight, which she did almost totteringly as she had not yet recovered from her trance of sexual pleasure.

'I'll see you right into your rooms, so that I may be able truly to report that I have faithfully executed the orders,' I said laughingly, more for the benefit of my chauffeur than of Alice.

'Thanks very much!' she replied quietly, and having collected her wraps, I followed her into the house and up the staircase to her apartments on the first floor, carefully closing the door after me.

Alice threw herself into my arms in an ecstasy of delight. I rather think that she expected me to take the opportunity to fuck her – and gladly would I have done so, as I was in a terrible state of lust; but I always hated 'snatch-fucking' and if I stayed with her long enough for her to undress and be properly fucked, it might arouse suspicions that would damage her reputation.

So after a passionate embrace, I whispered:

'I must not stop here, darling: when will you come to lunch?'

Alice blushed deliciously, instantly comprehending the significance of the invitation. 'Tomorrow!' she murmured, hiding her face on my shoulder.

'Thanks, sweetheart – then tomorrow! Now get to bed and have a good night's rest; good-night, my darling!' – and after a few more passionate kisses, I left her and rejoined my taxi.

\*     \*     \*

Next morning, after ordering a lunch cunningly calculated to excite and stimulate Alice's lascivious instincts, I made the usual tour of inspection round my flat; and from sheer force of habit, I began to test the mechanism concealed in the Snuggery furniture, then suddenly remembered that its assistance was now no longer needed; it had done its duty faithfully; with its help I had stripped, tortured and violated Alice – and today she was coming of her own free will to be fucked!

The reflection that I would now have to dismantle all this exquisite machinery caused me quite a pang – then I found myself wondering whether it would not be as well to let it remain as it was on the off-chance of its being found useful on some later occasion.

In my circle of acquaintances, there were many pretty and attractive girls, married and unmarried, and, if I could only lure some of them into the Snuggery, the torturing and ravishing of them would afford me the most delicious of entertainments, although the spice of revenge that pervaded my outraging of Alice would be absent.

But how was I to effect the luring? They were not likely to come to lunch alone with me, and if accompanied by anyone, it would simply mean that I should again experience the irritating disappointments that I suffered when Marion used to accompany Alice and, by her presence, prevent the accomplishment of my desires. Besides this, many of the girls I lusted after were hardly more than casual acquaintances whom I could not venture to invite to my flat, except in the company of some mutual friend.

Suddenly, like a flash of lightning, came an inspiration – why not try and induce Alice herself to act as decoy and assistant? If I could only instil into her a taste for sadism and sadique pleasures and a penchant for her own sex, and let her see how easily she could satisfy such lascivious fancies by cooperating with me, the possibilities were boundless!

A luncheon invitation to her and our selected victim would in nine cases out of ten be accepted by the latter; after lunch the adjournment to the Snuggery would follow as a matter of course at her suggestion – and then her assistance in stripping the girl would be invaluable, after which we could conjointly put the girl through a course of sexual torture, painless but distressingly effective, and quench in each other the fires of lust which would spring up as we gloated over our victim's shame and mental agony! Yes! here was the solution of the difficulty; somehow or other, I must induce Alice to give me her cooperation!

## Chapter Two

I will not take up my reader's time by detailing the incidents of Alice's visit. She was exceedingly nervous and so timid that I saw it was absolutely necessary for me to treat her with the greatest tenderness and delicacy and in no way to offend her susceptibility. She yielded herself to me with pretty bashfulness, blushing divinely when I drew off her last garment and exposed her naked body to my eager eyes; and her transports of delirious pleasure during her first fucking were such as I shall never forget! I had her four delicious times – and when she left, I felt certain that it only wanted a little diplomacy to secure her cooperation!

She naturally was more at her ease on her next visit, and I ventured to teach her the art of Sucking! When her sweet lips for the first time received my eager prick between them and her warm tongue made its first essays in the subtle art of titillation, I experienced the most heavenly bliss – such as I had never tasted before at the mouth of any woman; and when, after prolonging my exquisite rapture till I could no longer restrain myself, I spent in her mouth in a delirium of pleasure, her pretty confusion was something to be remembered!

I thought I might safely venture to convert her when she paid her third visit, and to this end, I selected from my collection of indecent photographs sundry which told their tale better than could be expressed in words. Among these was a series known as the 'Crucifixion', in which a lovely girl (evidently a nun from her despoiled garments scattered on the floor) was depicted bound to a cross naked, while sometimes the Lady Abbess (in her robes) alone, and sometimes in conjunction with one of the sisters, indulged in wanton fancies and caprices on the poor girl's breasts and cunt as she hung helpless! One photograph showed the girl fastened naked to a Maltese cross; the Lady Abbess had inserted her finger into the nun's cunt while a sister tickled the Nun's clitoris! In another photograph, a monk was introduced who, kneeling before the nun (still fastened on a Maltese cross), sucked her cunt while his uplifted hands in the attitude of prayer attacked her helpless breasts! Another series, entitled 'La Barrière', depicted various phases in the ravishment of a girl by two ruffians in a solitary part of the Bois de Boulogne. The rest were mostly scenes of tribadism and of lesbian love, and interspersed with them were a few representing flagellation by a girl on a girl, both being stark naked!

I was puzzled how best to lead up to the subject, when Alice herself gave me the desired opening. We had just finished our first fuck and were resting on the broad couch, lying in each other arms, her gentle hand caressing my prick with a view to its restoration to life. She had been rather more silent than usual, for she generally was full of questions which she used to ask with pretty hesitation and delicious naïvety – and I was cudgelling my brains to invent a suitable opening.

Suddenly Alice turned to me and said softly: 'Jack, I'd awfully like to know one thing! – when you had me tied up tight on that dreadful afternoon and . . . did all sorts of awful things to me, did it give you any pleasure besides the satisfaction of revenging yourself on me?'

'Will you hate me if I confess, dear, that the sight of your agony, shame and distress as you struggled naked gave me intense pleasure!' I replied as I drew her more closely against me. 'I knew I wasn't hurting you or causing you bodily pain; and the knowledge that your delicious wrigglings and writhings, as you struggled naked to get loose, were instigated by your shame at being naked and your distress at finding your sexual passions and instincts aroused in spite of yourself and irritated till you could no longer control them, and so felt yourself being forced to do what was so horribly repugnant to you, viz. to spend, and not only to spend, but to spend with me watching you! all this gave me the most extraordinary pleasure all the time I was torturing you! When I stopped to let you have a little rest or else to put you into another position, I felt the pleasure arising from vengeance gratified, but when I began again to torture you, especially when I was tickling your cunt with a feather, when you were fastened down on your back with legs tied widely apart, I must confess that the pleasure was the pleasure of cruelty! My God! darling, how you did wriggle then!'

'I thought I would have died!' Alice whispered, as she snuggled up against me (apparently not displeased by my confession), yielding herself sweetly to the pressure of my encircling arm. 'I wasn't in pain at all but oh! my sensations! My whole self seemed to be concentrated just . . . where you were tickling me! and I was nearly mad at being forced to endure such indignity; and on the top of it all came that awful tickling, tickling, tickling!'

She shuddered at the recollection; I pressed her still more tightly against me and kissed her tenderly but held my tongue – for I knew not what to say.

Presently Alice spoke again. 'And so it really gave you pleasure to torture me, Jack?' she asked almost cheerfully, adding before I could reply: 'I was very angry with my maid this morning and it would have delighted me to have spanked her severely. Now, would such delight arise from satisfied revenge or from being cruel?'

'Undoubtedly from being cruel,' I replied, 'the infliction of the punishment is what would have given you the pleasure, and behind it would come the feeling that you were revenging yourself. Here's another instance – you women delight in saying nasty cutting things to each other in the politest of ways. Why? Not from revenge, but from the satisfaction afforded by the shot going home. If you had given your maid this morning a box on the ears you would have satisfied your revenge without any pleasure whatever; but if

I had been there and held your maid down while you spanked her bottom, your pleasure would have arisen from the infliction of the punishment. Do you follow me, dear?'

'Yes, I see it now,' Alice replied, then added archly: 'I wish you had been there, Jack! it would have done her a lot of good!'

'I sometimes wonder you keep her on,' I said musingly. 'She's a pert little minx and at times must be very aggravating. Let me see – what's her name?'

'Fanny.'

'Yes of course – a case of "pretty Fanny's way", for she certainly is a pretty girl and a well-made one. My dear, if you want to do bottom slapping, you won't easily find a better subject, only I think she will be more than you can manage single-handed, and it may come to her slapping your bottom, my love!'

Alice laughed. 'Fanny is a most perfect maid, a real treasure, or I would not keep her on – for as you say she is too much for me. She's very strong and very high-spirited, but wants taming badly.'

'Bring her here some afternoon, and we'll tame her between us!' I suggested seemingly carelessly but with well-concealed anxiety, for was I not now making a direct attempt to seduce Alice into sadism?

Alice started, raised herself on her elbow and regarded me questioningly. I noticed a hard glitter in her eyes, then she caught her breath, coloured and exclaimed softly: 'O Jack, how lovely it would be!'

I had succeeded! Alice had succumbed to the sudden temptation! For the second time her strain of lascivious sexuality had conquered.

'Shall we try?' I asked with a smile, secretly delighted at her unconcealed eagerness and noting how her eyes now were brimming over with lust and how her lovely breasts were heaving with her excitement.

'Yes! yes! Jack!' she exclaimed feverishly, 'but how can it be managed?'

'There shouldn't be much trouble,' I replied. 'Take her out with you shopping some afternoon close by here, then say you want just to pop in to see me about something. *En route* tell her about this room, how it's sound-proof and so on – it will interest her and she will at the same time learn information that will come in useful later on. Once in here follow my lead. I suppose you would like to have a hand in torturing her?'

'Oh! Jack! will you really torture Fanny?' exclaimed Alice, her eyes sparkling with eagerness, 'will you fasten her down as you did me?'

I nodded.

'Yes! yes! let me have a turn at her!' she replied vivaciously. Then after a pause she looked queerly at me and added, 'and will you . . . ' at the same moment significantly squeezing my prick.

'I think so – unless of course you would rather I didn't, dear,' I replied with a laugh; 'I suppose you have no idea whether she is a virgin or not?'

'I can't say!' Alice replied, blushing a little. 'I've always fancied she was and have treated her as such.'

'And what sort of treatment is that?' I queried mischievously, and was proceeding to cross-question Alice when she stopped me by putting her hand over my mouth.

'Well, we'll soon find out when we get her here,' I remarked philosophically, much to her amusement. 'But, darling, your lessons in the Art of Love are being neglected; let us resume them. There is just time for one – I think you must show me that you haven't forgotten *soixante-neuf*!'

Alice blushed prettily and slipped out of my embrace, and soon her cunt was resting on my lips while her gentle hands and mouth busied themselves with my delighted prick and balls! She worked me so deliciously that she made me spend twice in her mouth, by which time I had sucked her completely dry! Then we reluctantly rose to perform the necessary ablutions and resume our clothes.

'When shall I bring Fanny here, Jack?' asked Alice as she was saying goodbye to me.

'Oh! you naughty lustful cruel girl!' I exclaimed with a laugh in which she somewhat shamefacedly joined. 'When do you think?'

'Will . . . tomorrow afternoon do?' she asked, avoiding my eyes.

'Yes certainly,' I replied, kissing her tenderly. 'Let it be tomorrow afternoon!' And so we parted.

This is how it came to pass that Alice's first experiments in sadique pleasures were ordained to be made on the person of her maid.

## Chapter Three

Next afternoon, after seeing that everything was in working order in the Snuggery, I threw open both doors as if carelessly, and taking off my coat as if not expecting any visitors, I proceeded to potter about the room, keeping a vigilant eye on the stairs. Before long I heard footsteps on the landing, but pretended not to know that anyone was there till Alice tapped merrily on the door saying: 'May we come in, Jack?'

'Good Heavens, Alice?' I exclaimed in pretended surprise as I struggled hurriedly to get into my coat, 'come in! How do you do? Where have you dropped from?'

'We've been shopping – this is my maid, Fanny' (I bowed and smiled, receiving in return from Fanny a distinctly pert and not too respectful nod), 'and, as we were close by, I thought I would take the chance of finding you in and take away that enlargement if it is ready.'

By this time I had struggled into my coat: 'It's quite ready,' I replied. 'I'll go and get it, and I don't know why those doors should stand so unblushingly open,' I added with a laugh.

Having closed them, noiselessly locking them, I disappeared into the alcove I used for myself, and pretended to search for the enlargement – my real object being to give Alice a chance of letting Fanny know the nature of the room. Instinctively she divined my idea, and I heard her say: 'This is the room I was telling you about, Fanny – look at the double doors, the padded walls, the rings, the pillars, the hanging pulley straps! Isn't it queer?'

Fanny looked about her with evident interest: 'It *is* a funny room, miss! And what are those little places for?' pointing to the two alcoves.

'We do not know, Fanny,' Alice replied. 'Mr Jack uses them for his photographic work now.'

As she spoke, I emerged with a large print which was to represent the supposed enlargement, and gave it to Alice who at once proceeded closely to examine it.

I saw that Fanny's eyes were wandering all over the room, and I moved over to her: 'A strange room, Fanny, eh?' I remarked, 'is it not still! no sound from outside can get in, and no noise from inside can get out! That's a fact, we've tested it thoroughly!'

'Lor', Mr Jack!' she replied in her forward familiar way, turning her eyes on me in a most audacious and bold way, then resuming her survey of the room.

While she was doing so, I hastily inspected her. She was a distinctly pretty girl, tall, slenderly but strongly built, with an exquisitely well-developed figure. A slightly turned up nose and dark flashing eyes gave her face a saucy look which her free style of moving accentuated, while her dark hair and rich colouring indicated a warm-blooded and passionate temperament. I easily could understand that Alice with her gentle ways was no match for Fanny; and I fancied that I should have my work cut out for me before I got her arms fastened to the pulley ropes.

Alice now moved towards us, print in hand: 'Thanks awfully, Jack, it's lovely!' and she began to roll it up. 'Now Fanny, we must be off!'

'Don't bother about the print, I'll send it after you,' I said. 'And where are you off to now?'

'Nowhere in particular,' she replied; 'we'll look at the shops and the people. Goodbye, Jack!'

'One moment,' I interposed. 'You were talking the other day about some perfection of a lady's maid whom you didn't want to lose' (Fanny smiled complacently), 'but whose tantrums and ill tempers were getting more than you could stand.' (Fanny here began to look angry). 'Somebody suggested that you should give her a good spanking' (Fanny assumed a contemptuous air), 'or if you couldn't manage it yourself you should get someone to do it for you!' (Fanny here glared at me). 'Is this the young lady?'

Alice nodded, with a curious glance at Fanny, who was now evidently getting into one of her passions.

'Well, as you've nothing to do this afternoon, and she happens to be here, and this room is so eminently suitable for the purpose, shall I take the young woman in hand for you and teach her a lesson?'

Before Alice could reply, Fanny with a startled exclamation darted to the door, evidently bent on escape, but in spite of her vigorous twists of the handle and shakings, the door refused to open, for the simple reason that unnoticed by her I had locked it! Instantly divining that she was a prisoner, she turned hurriedly round to watch our movements, but she was too late! With a quickness learnt on the football field, I was on to her and pinned her arms to her sides in a grip that she could not break out of despite her frantic struggles: 'Let me go! . . . let me go, Mr Jack!' she screamed; I simply chuckled as I knew I had her safe now! I had to exert all my strength and skill, for she was extraordinarily strong and her furious rage added to her power; but in spite of her desperate resistance, I forced her to the hanging pulleys where Alice was eagerly waiting for us. With astonishing quickness she made fast the ropes to Fanny's wrists and set the machinery going – and in a few seconds the surprised girl found herself standing erect with her arms dragged up taut over her head!

'Well done, Jack!' exclaimed Alice as she delightedly surveyed the still struggling Fanny! The latter was indeed a lovely subject of contemplation, as with heaving bosom, flushed cheeks, and eyes that sparkled with rage, she stood panting, endeavouring to get back her breath, while her agitated fingers vainly strove to get her wrists free from the pulley ropes. We watched her in victorious silence, waiting for the outburst of wrathful fury which we felt would come as soon as she was able to speak.

It soon came! 'How dare you, Mr Jack!' Fanny burst out as she flashed her great piercing eyes at us, her whole body trembling with anger; 'how dare you treat me like this! Let me loose at once, or as sure as I am alive, I'll have the law on you and also on that mealy-mouthed smooth-faced demure hypocrite that calls herself my mistress indeed! – who looks on while a poor girl is vilely treated and won't raise a finger to help her! Let me go at once, Mr Jack! and I'll promise to say and do nothing; but my God!' here her voice became shrill with overpowering rage, 'my God! if you don't, I'll make it hot for the pair of you when I get out!' And she glared at us in her impotent fury.

'Your Mistress has asked me to give you a lesson, Fanny,' I replied calmly, 'and I'm going to do so! The sooner you recognise how helpless you really are, and will submit yourself to us, the sooner it will be over; but if you are foolish enough to resist, you'll have a long doing and a bad time! Now, if I let you loose, will you take your clothes off quietly?'

'My God! no!' she cried indignantly, but in spite of herself she blushed vividly!

'Then we'll take them off for you!' was my cool reply. 'Come along Alice, you understand girl's clothes, you undo them and I'll get them off somehow!'

Quickly Alice sprang up, trembling with excitement, and together we approached Fanny, who shrieked defiance and threats at us in her impotent fury as she struggled desperately to get free. But as soon as she felt Alice's fingers unfastening her garments, her rage changed to horrible apprehension; and as one by one they slipped off her, she began to realise how helpless she was. 'Don't, miss!' she ejaculated pitifully. 'My God! stop her, sir!' she pleaded, the use of these more respectful terms of address sufficiently proclaiming her changed attitude. But we were obdurate, and soon Fanny stood with only her chemise and undervest left on her, her shoes and stockings having been dragged off at the special request of Alice, whose unconcealed enjoyment of the work of stripping her maid was delicious to witness!

She now took command of operations. Pointing to a chair just in front of Fanny she exclaimed: 'Sit there Jack, and watch Fanny as I take off her last garments!'

'For God's sake, miss, don't strip me naked!' shrieked Fanny who seemed to expect that she would be left in her chemise and to whom the sudden intimation that she was to be exposed naked came as an appalling shock! 'Oh, sir! for God's sake, stop her!' she cried appealing to me as she saw me take my seat right in front of her and felt Alice's fingers begin to undo the shoulder-strap fastenings which alone kept her scanty garments on her. 'Miss Alice! . . . Miss Alice! don't! . . . for God's sake, don't!' she screamed in a fresh access of dismay as she felt her vest slip down her body to her feet and knew her only remaining covering was about to follow. In despair she tugged frantically at the ropes which made her arms so absolutely helpless, her agitated quivering fingers betraying her mental agony.

'Steady, Fanny, steady!' exclaimed Alice to her struggling maid as she proceeded to unfasten the chemise, her eyes gleaming with lustful cruelty. 'Now, Jack!' she said warningly, stepping back a pace herself the better to observe the effect. Down swept the chemise, and Fanny stood stark naked.

'Oh! oh!!!' she wailed, crimson with shame, her face hidden on her bosom which now was wildly heaving in agitation! It was a wonderful spectacle! – in the foreground Fanny, naked, helpless, in an agony of shame – in the background but close to her was Alice exquisitely costumed and hatted, gloating over the sight of her maid's absolute nudity, her eyes intently fixed on the gloriously luscious curves of Fanny's hips, haunches and bottom!

I managed to catch her eye and motioned to her to come and sit on my knees that we might, in each other's close company, study her maid's naked charms so reluctantly being exhibited to us. With one long last look she obeyed my summons. As she seated herself on my knees she threw her arms round my neck and kissed me rapturously whispering: 'Jack! isn't she delicious!' I nodded smilingly, then in turn murmured in her ear: 'And how do you like the game, dear?'

Alice blushed divinely; a strange languishing voluptuous half-wanton, half-cruel look came into her eyes. Placing her lips carefully on mine she gave me three long-drawn kisses, the significance of which I could not possibly misunderstand, then whispered almost hoarsely: 'Jack, let me do all the . . . torturing and be content this time, with . . . fucking Fanny . . . and me too, darling!'

'She's your maid and, so to speak, your property, dear,' I replied softly, 'so arrange matters just as you like; I'll leave it all to you and won't interfere unless you want me to.'

She kissed me gratefully, then turned her eyes on Fanny, who during this whispered colloquy had been standing trembling, her face still hidden from us, her legs pressed closely against each other as if to shield as much as possible her cunt from our sight.

I saw Alice's eyes wander over Fanny's naked body with evident pleasure, dwelling first on her magnificent lines and curves, then on her lovely breasts, and finally on the mass of dark curling moss-like hair that covered her cunt. She was a most deliciously voluptuous girl, one calculated to excite Alice to the utmost pitch of lust of which she was capable, and while secretly regretting that my share in the process of taming Fanny was to be somewhat restricted, I felt that I would enjoy the rare opportunity of seeing how a girl, hitherto chaste and well-regulated, would yield to her sexual instincts and passions when she had placed at her absolute disposal one of her own sex in a state of absolute nakedness.

Presently Alice whispered to me: 'Jack! I'm going to feel her!' I smiled and nodded. Fanny must have heard her, for as Alice rose, she for the first time raised her head and cried affrightedly: 'No, miss, please miss, don't touch me!' and again she vainly strained at her fastenings, her face quivering and flushed with shame. But disregarding her maid's piteous entreaties, Alice passed behind her, then kneeling down began to stroke Fanny's bottom, a hand to each cheek!

'Don't, miss!' yelled Fanny, arching herself outwards and away from Alice, and thereby unconsciously throwing the region of her cunt into greater prominence! But with a smile of cruel gratification, Alice continued her sweet occupation, sometimes squeezing, sometimes pinching Fanny's glorious half-moons, now and then extending her excursions over Fanny's round plump thighs, once indeed letting her hands creep up them till I really thought (and so did Fanny from the way she screamed and wriggled) that she was about to feel Fanny's cunt!

Suddenly Alice rose, rushed to me, and kissing me ardently whispered excitedly: 'Oh, Jack! she's just lovely! such flesh, such a skin! I've never felt a girl before, I've never touched any girl's breasts or . . . cunt . . . except of course my own,' she added archly: 'and I'm wild at the idea of handling Fanny! Watch me carefully, darling, and if I don't do it properly, tell me!' And back to Fanny she rushed, evidently in a state of intense eroticism!

This time Alice didn't kneel, but placed herself close behind Fanny (her dress in fact touching her) then suddenly she threw her arms round Fanny's body and seized her breasts: 'Miss Alice! . . . don't!' shrieked Fanny, struggling desperately, her flushed face betraying her agitation: 'Oh! how lovely! . . . how delicious! . . . how sweet! . . . ' cried Alice, wild with delight and sexual excitement as she squeezed and played with Fanny's voluptuous breasts! Her head with its exquisite hat was just visible over Fanny's right shoulder, while her dainty dress showed on each side of the struggling agitated girl, throwing into bold relief her glorious shape and accentuating in the most piquant way Fanny's stark nakedness! Entranced, I gazed at the voluptuous spectacle, my prick struggling to break through the fly of my trousers! Fanny had now ceased her cries and was enduring in silence, broken only by her involuntary 'ohs', the violation of her breasts by Alice, whose little hands could scarcely grasp the luscious morsels of Fanny's flesh that they were so subtly torturing, but which nevertheless succeeded in squeezing and compressing them and generally in playing with them till the poor girl gasped in her shame and agony: 'Oh! Miss Alice! . . . Miss Alice! . . . stop! . . . stop!!!' her head falling forward in her extreme agitation.

With a smile of intense satisfaction, Alice suspended her torturing operations and gently stroked and soothed Fanny's breasts till the more regular breathing of the latter indicated that she had in a great degree regained her self-control. Then her expression changed. A cruel hungry light came into her eyes as she smiled wickedly and meaningfully at me, then I saw her hands quit Fanny's breasts and glide over Fanny's stomach till they arrived at Fanny's cunt!

Fanny shrieked as if she had been stung: 'Miss Alice! . . . Miss Alice!. . . don't! . . . don't touch me there!! . . . oh! . . . oh! my God! Miss Alice! . . . oh! Miss Alice! take your hands away!! . . . ' at the same time twisting and writhing in a perfectly wonderful way in her frantic endeavours to escape from her mistress's hands, the fingers of which were now hidden in her cunt's mossy covering as they inquisitively travelled all over her mount of Venus and along the lips of the orifice itself. For some little time they contented themselves with feeling and pressing and toying caressingly with Fanny's cunt, then I saw one hand pause while the first finger of the other gently began to work its way between the pink lips I could just distinguish and disappear into the sweet cleft. 'Don't, miss!' yelled Fanny, her agonised face now scarlet, while in her distress she desperately endeavoured to defend her cunt by throwing her legs in turn across her groin – to Alice's delight, her tell-tale face proclaiming the intense pleasure she was tasting in thus making her maid undergo such subtle torture!

Presently I noted an unmistakable look of surprise in her eyes; her lips parted as if in astonishment, while her hand seemed to redouble its attack on Fanny's cunt, then she exclaimed: 'Why Fanny? what's this?'

'Oh! don't tell Mr Jack, miss!' shrieked Fanny, letting her legs drop as she could no longer endure the whole weight of her struggling body on her slender wrists, 'don't let him know!'

My curiosity was naturally aroused and intently I watched the movements of Alice's hand which the fall of Fanny's legs brought again into full view. Her forefinger was buried up to the knuckle in her maid's cunt! The mystery was explained, Fanny was not a virgin!

Alice seemed staggered by her discovery. Abruptly she quitted Fanny, rushed to me, threw herself on my knees, then flinging her arms round my neck she whispered excitedly in my ear: 'Jack! she's been . . . had by someone . . . my finger went right in!'

'So I noticed, darling!' I replied quietly as I kissed her flushed cheek, 'it's rather a pity! but she'll stand more fucking than if she was a virgin, and you must arrange your programme accordingly! I think you'd better let her rest a bit now, her arms will be getting numb from being kept over her head; let's fasten her to that pillar by passing her arms round it and shackling her wrists together. She can then rest a bit; and while she is recovering from her struggles hadn't you better . . . slip your clothes off also – for your eyes hint that you will want . . . something before long!'

Alice blushed prettily, then whispered as she kissed me ardently, 'I'd like . . . something now, darling!' Then she ran away to her dressing-room.

Left alone with Fanny, I proceeded to transfer her from the pulleys to the pillar; it was not a difficult task, as her arms were too numb (as I expected) to be of much use to her and she seemed stupefied at our discovery that her maidenhead no longer existed. Soon I had her firmly fastened with her back pressing against the pillar. This new position had two great advantages, she could no longer hide her face from us and the backwards pull of her arms threw her breasts out. She glanced timidly at me as I stood admiring her luscious nakedness, and waiting for Alice's return.

'When did this little slip happen, Fanny?' I asked quietly.

She coloured vividly: 'When I was seventeen, sir,' she replied softly but brokenly: 'I was drugged . . . and didn't know till after it was done! It's never been done again, Mr Jack,' she continued, with pathetic earnestness in her voice, 'never! I swear it, sir!' Then after a short pause she whispered: 'Oh! Mr Jack! let me go! . . . I'll come to you whenever you wish . . . and let you do what you like . . . but . . . I'm afraid of Miss Alice today . . . she seems so strange! . . . oh! my God! she's naked!' she screamed in genuine alarm as Alice came out of her toilet-room with only her shoes and stockings on, and her large matinée hat, a most coquettishly piquantly indecent object! Poor Fanny went red at the sight of her mistress and didn't know where to look as Alice came dancing along, her eyes noting with evident approval the position into which I had placed her maid.

'*Mes compliments, mademoiselle!*' I said with a low bow as she came up.

She smiled and blushed, but was too intent on Fanny to joke with me. 'That's lovely, Jack!' she exclaimed after a careful inspection of her now trembling maid, 'but surely she can get loose!'

'Oh no!' I replied with a smile, 'but if you like I'll fasten her ankles together!'

'No, sir!' cried Fanny affrightedly.

'Yes Jack, do!' exclaimed Alice, her eyes gleaming with lust and delight. She evidentially had thought out some fresh torture for Fanny, and with the closest attention, she watched me as I linked her maid's slender ankles together in spite of the poor girl's entreaties!

'I like that much better, Jack,' said Alice, smiling her thanks; then catching me by the elbow, she pushed me towards my alcove saying: 'We both will want you presently, Jack!' looking roguishly at me, 'so get ready! But tell me first where are the feathers?'

'Oh! that's your game!' I replied with a laugh. She nodded, colouring slightly, and I told her where she would find them.

I had a peephole in my alcove through which I could see all that passed in the room, and being curious to watch the two girls, I placed myself by it as I slowly undressed myself.

Having found the feathers, Alice placed the box near her, then going right up to Fanny, she took hold of her own breasts with her hands, raised them till they were level with Fanny's, then leaning on Fanny so that their stomachs were in close contact, she directed her breasts against Fanny's, gently rubbing her nipples against Fanny's while she looked intently into Fanny's eyes! It was a most curious sight! The girls' naked bodies were touching from their ankles to their breasts, their cunts were so close to each other that their hairs formed one mass, while their faces were so near to each other that the brim of Alice's matinée hat projected over Fanny's forehead!

Not a word was said! For about half a minute Alice continued to rub her breasts gently against Fanny's with her eyes fixed on Fanny's downcast face, then suddenly I saw both naked bodies quiver, and then Fanny raised her head and for the first time responded to Alice's glance, her colour coming and going! At the same moment, a languorous voluptuous smile swept over Alice's face, and gently she kissed Fanny, who flushed rosy red but as far as I could see did not respond.

'Won't you . . . love me, Fanny?' I heard Alice say softly but with a curious strained voice! Immediately I understood the position. Alice was lusting after Fanny! I was delighted! It was clear that Fanny had not yet reciprocated Alice's passion, and I determined that Alice should have every opportunity of satisfying her lust on Fanny's naked helpless body, till the latter was converted to tribadism with Alice as the object.

'Won't you . . . love me, Fanny?' again asked Alice softly, now supplementing the play of her breasts against Fanny's by insinuating and significant pressings of her stomach against Fanny's, again kissing the latter sweetly. But Fanny made no response, and Alice's eyes grew hard with a steely cruel glitter which boded badly for Fanny!

Quitting Fanny, Alice went straight to the box of feathers, picked out one, and returned to Fanny, feather in hand. The sight of her moving about thus, her breasts dancing, her hips swaying, her cunt and bottom in full view, her nakedness intensified by her piquant costume of hat, shoes and stockings, was enough to galvanise a corpse; it set my blood boiling with lust and I could hardly refrain from rushing out and compelling her to let me quench my fires in her! I however did resist the temptation, and rapidly undressed to my shoes and socks so as to be ready to take advantage of any chance that either of the girls might offer; but I remained in my alcove with my eye to the peephole as I was curious to witness the denouement of this strangely voluptuous scene, which Alice evidently wished to play single handed.

No sooner did Fanny catch sight of the feather than she screamed: 'No! . . . no! Miss Alice! . . . don't tickle me!' at the same time striving frantically to break the straps that linked together her wrists and her ankles. But my tackle was too strong! Alice meanwhile had caught up a cushion which she placed at Fanny's feet and right in front of her; she knelt on it, rested her luscious bottom on her heels, and having settled herself down comfortably she, with a smile in which cruelty and malice were strangely blended, gloatingly contemplated for a moment her maid's naked and agitated body, then slowly and deliberately applied the tip of the feather to Fanny's cunt.

'Oh, my God! Miss Alice, don't!' yelled Fanny, writhing in delicious contortions in her desperate endeavours to dodge the feather. 'Don't miss!!' she shrieked, as Alice, keenly enjoying her maid's distress and her vain efforts to avoid the torture, proceeded delightedly to pass the feather lightly along the sensitive lips of Fanny's cunt and finally set to work to tickle Fanny's clitoris, thereby sending her so nearly into hysterical convulsions that I felt it time I intervened.

As I emerged from my alcove Alice caught sight of me and dropped her hand as she turned towards me, her eyes sparkling with lascivious delight! 'Oh, Jack! did you see her?' she cried excitedly.

'I heard her, dear!' I replied ambiguously, 'and began to wonder whether you were killing her, so I came out to see!'

'Not a bit of it!' she cried, hugely pleased.

'I'm going to give her another turn!' a declaration that produced from Fanny the most pitiful pleadings which however seemed only to increase Alice's cruel satisfaction, and she was proceeding to be as good as her word when I stopped her.

'You'd better let me first soothe her irritated senses, dear,' I said, and with one hand I caressed and played with Fanny's full and voluptuous breasts, which I found tense and firm under her sexual excitement, while with the other I stroked and felt her cunt, a procedure that evidently afforded her considerable relief although, at another time, it doubtless would have provoked shrieks and cries! She had not spent, though she must have been very close to doing it; and I saw that I must watch Alice very closely indeed during the 'turn' she was going to give Fanny for my special delectation, lest the catastrophe I was so desirous of avoiding should occur, for, in my mind, I had decided that when Alice had finished tickling Fanny she should have an opportunity of satisfying her lustful cravings on her, when it would be most desirable that Fanny should be in a condition to show the effect on her of Alice's lascivious exertions.

While feeling Fanny's cunt, I naturally took the opportunity to see if Alice's penetrating finger had met with any difficulty entering and had thus caused Fanny the pain that her shrieks and wriggles had indicated. I found the way in intensely tight, a confirmation of her story and statement that nothing had gone in since the rape was committed on her. Although therefore I could not have the gratification of taking her virginity, I felt positive that I should have a delicious time and that, practically, I should be violating her, and I wondered into which of the two delicious cunts now present I would shoot my surging and boiling discharge as I dissolved in Love's sweetest ecstasies!

'Now, Alice, I think she is ready for you!' I said when I had stroked and felt Fanny to my complete satisfaction.

'No, no, Miss Alice!' shrieked Fanny in frantic terror, 'for God's sake, don't tickle me again!'

Disregarding her cries Alice, who had with difficulty restrained her impatience, quietly again applied the feather to Fanny's cunt, and a wonderful spectacle followed! Fanny's shrieks, cries and entreaties filled the room while she wriggled and squirmed and twisted herself about in the most bewitchingly provocative manner, while Alice, with parted lips and eyes that simply glistened with lust, remorselessly tickled her maid's cunt with every refinement of cruelty, every fresh shriek and convulsion bringing a delighted look on her tell-tale face. Motionless I watched the pair, till I noticed Fanny's breasts stiffen and become tense. Immediately I covered her cunt with my hand, saying to Alice: 'Stop dear, she's had as much as she can stand!' Then reluctantly she desisted from her absorbing occupation and rose, her naked body quivering with aroused but unsatisfied lust.

Now was the time for me to try and effect what I had in mind, namely, the introduction of both girls to tribadism. 'Let us move Fanny to the large couch and fasten her down before she recovers herself,' I hastily whispered to Alice. Quickly we set her loose and between us we carried her, half fainting, to the large divan-couch where we laid her on her back and made fast her wrists to the two top corners and her ankles to the two lower ones. We now had only to set the machinery going and she would lie in the position I desired, namely spread-eagled.

Alice now clutched me excitedly and whispered hurriedly: 'Jack, do me before she comes to herself and before she can see us! I'm just mad for it!' and indeed with her flushed cheeks, humid eyes, and heaving breasts this was very evident.

But although I also was bursting with lust and eager to fuck either Alice or her maid, it would not have suited my programme to do so. I wanted Alice to fuck Fanny. I wanted the first spending of both girls to be mutually provoked by the friction of their excited cunts one against the other. This was why I stopped Alice from tickling her maid into spending, and it was for this reason that I had extended Fanny on her back in such a position that her cunt should be at Alice's disposal.

'Hold on, darling, for a bit!' I whispered back, 'you'll soon see why! I want it as bad as you do, my sweet, but am fighting against it till the proper time comes! Run away now, and take off your hat, for it will now be only in the way;' and I smiled significantly as I kissed her.

Alice promptly obeyed. I then seated myself on the couch by the side of Fanny, who was still lying with eyes closed, but breathing almost normally, and bending over her, I closely inspected her cunt to ascertain whether she had or had not spent under the terrific tickling it had just received! I could find no traces whatever, but to make sure I gently drew the lips apart and peered into the sweet coral cleft, but again saw no traces. The touch of my fingers on her cunt however had roused Fanny from her semi-stupor and she dreamily opened her eyes, murmuring: 'Oh, sir, don't!' as she recognised that I was her assailant, then she looked hurriedly round as in if search of Alice.

'Your mistress will be here immediately,' I said with a smile, 'she has only gone away to take off her hat!' The look of terror returned to her eyes, and she exclaimed: 'Oh, Mr Jack, do let me go, she'll kill me!'

'Oh no!' I replied as I laughed at her agitation, 'oh no, Fanny, on the contrary she's now going to do to you the sweetest, nicest and kindest thing one girl can do to another! Here she comes!'

I rose as Alice came up full of pleasurable excitement as to what was now going to happen, and slipped my arm lovingly round her waist. She looked eagerly at her now trembling maid, then whispered: 'Is she ready for us again, Jack?'

'Yes, dear!' I answered softly. 'While you were away taking off your hat, I thought it as well to see in what condition her cunt was after its tickling! I find it very much irritated and badly in want of Nature's soothing essence! You, darling, are also much in the same state – your cunt also wants soothing! So I want you girls to soothe each other! Get on to Fanny, dear, take her in your arms! arrange yourself on her so that your cunt lies on hers! and then gently rub yours against hers! and soon both of you will be tasting the sweetest ecstasy!! In other words, fuck Fanny, dear!'

Alice looked at me in wondering admiration! As she began to comprehend my suggestion, her face broke into delighted smiles; and when I stooped to kiss her she exclaimed rapturously: 'Oh, Jack! how sweet! . . . how delicious!' as she gazed eagerly at Fanny. But the latter seemed horrified at the idea of being submitted thus to her mistress's lustful passion and embraces, and attempted to escape, crying in her dismay: 'No, no, sir! – oh no, miss! – I don't want it, please! . . .'

'But I do, Fanny!' cried Alice with sparkling eyes as she gently but firmly pushed her struggling maid on to her back and held her down forcibly till I had pulled all four straps tight so that Fanny lay flat with her arms and legs wide apart in Maltese-cross fashion, a simply entrancing spectacle! Then slipping my hands under her buttocks, I raised her middle till Alice was able to push a hard cushion under her bottom, the effect of which was to make her cunt stand out prominently; then turning to Alice, who had assisted in these preparations with the keenest interest but evident impatience, I said: 'Now dear, there she is! set to work and violate your maid!'

In a flash Alice was on the couch and on her knees between Fanny's widely parted legs – excitedly she threw herself on her maid, passed her arms round her and hugged her closely, as she showered kisses on Fanny's still protesting mouth till the girl had to stop for breath. With a few rapid movements she arranged herself on her maid so that the two luscious pairs of breasts were pressing against each other, their stomachs in close contact, and their cunts touching!

'One moment, Alice!' I exclaimed, just as she was beginning to agitate herself on Fanny, let me see that you are properly placed before you start!'

Leaning over her bottom, I gently parted her thighs till between them I saw the cunts of the mistress and the maid resting on each other, slit to slit, clitoris to clitoris, half hidden by the mass of their closely, interwoven hairs, the sweetest of sights! Then after restoring her thighs to their original position closely pressed against each other, I gently thrust my right hand between the girl's navels, and worked it along amidst their bellies till it lay between their cunts. 'Press down a bit, Alice!' I said patting her bottom with my disengaged hand; promptly she complied with two or three vigorous down-thrusts which forced my palm hard against Fanny's cunt while her own pressed deliciously against the back of my hand. The sensation of thus feeling at the same time these two full, fat, fleshy, warm and throbbing cunts between which my hand lay in sandwich fashion was something exquisite; and it was with the greatest reluctance that I removed it from the sweetest position it is ever likely to be in, but Alice's restless and involuntary movements proclaimed that she was fast yielding to her feverish impatience to fuck Fanny and to taste the rapture of spending on the cunt of her maid the emission provoked by its sweet contact and friction against her own excited organ!

She still held Fanny closely clasped against her and with head slightly thrown back, she kept her eyes fixed on her maid's terrified averted face with a gloating hungry look, murmuring softly: 'Fanny, you shall now . . . love me!' Both the girls were quivering, Alice from overwhelming and unsatisfied lust, Fanny from shame and horrible apprehension.

Caressing Alice's bottom encouragingly, I whispered: 'Go ahead, dear!' In a trice her lips were pressed to Fanny's flushed cheeks on which she rained hot kisses as she slowly began to agitate her cunt against her maid's with voluptuous movements of her beautiful bottom. 'Oh! miss . . . ' gasped Fanny, her eyes betraying the sexual emotion that she felt beginning to overpower her, her colour coming and going. Quicker and more agitated became Alice's movements; soon she was furiously rubbing her cunt against Fanny's with strenuous down-thrusting strokes of her bottom, continuing her fierce kisses on her maid's cheeks as the latter lay helpless with half-closed eyes and tightly clasped in her mistress's arms! Then a hurricane of sexual rage seemed to seize Alice! Her bottom wildly oscillated and gyrated with confused jerks, thrusts and shoves as she frenziedly pressed her cunt against Fanny's with a rapid jogging motion. Suddenly Alice seemed to stiffen and become almost rigid, her arms gripped Fanny more tightly than ever; then her head fell forward on Fanny's shoulder as an indescribable spasm thrilled through her, followed by convulsive vibrations and tremors! Almost simultaneously, Fanny's half-closed eyes turned upwards till the whites were showing, her lips parted, she gasped brokenly: 'Oh! . . . Miss . . . Alice!! . . . Ah . . . h!' then thrilled convulsively while quiver after quiver shot through her! The blissful crisis had arrived! Mistress and maid were deliriously spending, cunt against cunt, Alice in rapturous ecstasy at having so deliciously satisfied her sexual desires by means of her maid's cunt, while forcing the latter to spend in spite of herself, while Fanny was quivering ecstastically under heavenly sensations hitherto unknown to her (owing to her having been unconscious when she was ravished) and now communicated to her wondering senses by her mistress whom she still felt lying on her and in whose arms she was still clasped.

Intently I watched both girls, curious to learn how they would regard each other when they had recovered from their ecstastic trance. Would the mutual satisfaction of their overwrought sexual cravings wipe out the animosity between them which had caused the strange events of this afternoon, or would Alice's undoubted lust for her maid be simply raised to a higher pitch by this satisfying of her sexuality on her maid's body, and would Fanny consider that she had been violated by her mistress and therefore bear a deeper grudge than ever against her? It was a pretty problem and I eagerly awaited the outcome.

Alice was the first to move. With a long-drawn breath indicative of intense satisfaction she raised her head off Fanny's shoulder. The slight movement roused Fanny, who mechanically turned her averted head towards Alice, and as the girls languidly opened their humid eyes, they found themselves looking straight at each other! Fanny coloured like a peony and quickly turned her eyes away; Alice on the contrary continued to regard the blushing face of her maid, a look of gratification and triumph came into her eyes, then she deliberately placed her lips on Fanny's and kissed her, saying softly but significantly: 'Now it's Mr Jack's turn, my dear!' then raising her head she watched Fanny, with a malicious smile, to see how she would receive the intimation.

Fanny darted a startled horrified glance at me, another at her mistress, then seeing that both our faces only confirmed Alice's announcement she cried pitifully: 'No, no, Mr Jack! no, no, Miss Alice! oh! miss! how can you be so cruel!' With another malicious smile, Alice again kissed her horrified maid, saying teasingly: 'You must tell us afterwards which you like best, Fanny, and if you're very good and let Mr Jack have as good a fuck as you have just given me, we'll have each other in front of you for special edification!'

She kissed Fanny once more, then rose slowly off her, exposing as she did so her own cunt and that of her maid. I shot a quick glance at both in turn. The girls had evidently spent profusely, their hairs glistened with tiny drops of love-dew, while here and there bits were plastered down.

Alice caught my glance and smiled merrily. 'I let myself go, Jack!' she laughed, 'but there will be plenty ready when you are!' she added wickedly. 'I'll just put myself right, then I'll do lady's maid to Fanny and get her ready for you!' Then with a saucy look she whispered: 'Haven't I sketched out a fine programme?'

'You have indeed!' I replied as I seized her and kissed her. 'I wish only that I was to have you first, dear, while I'm so rampant!'

'No, no,' she whispered, kissing me again: 'I'm not ready yet! fuck Fanny well, Jack! it will do her good, and you'll find her a delicious mover!' And she ran off to her alcove.

I sat down on the couch by Fanny's side and began to play with her breasts, watching her closely. She was in a terrible state of agitation, her head rolling from side to side, her eyes closed, her lips slightly apart, while her bosom heaved wildly. As my hands seized her breasts gently she started, opened her eyes, and seeing that it was me she piteously pleaded: 'Oh, Mr Jack! don't . . . don't . . .' she could not bring herself to say the dreadful word that expressed her fate!

'Don't . . . what, Fanny?' I asked maliciously. With an effort she brought out the word: 'Oh! sir! don't . . . fuck me!'

'But your mistress has ordered it, Fanny, and she tells me you are very sweet, and so I want it! And it will be like taking your maidenhead, only much nicer for you, as you won't have the pain that girls feel when they are first ravished and you'll be able to taste all the pleasure!'

'No, no, Mr Jack!' she cried, 'don't . . . fuck me!'

Just then Alice came up with water, a sponge and a towel. 'What's the matter, Jack?' she asked.

'Your maid says she doesn't want to be fucked, dear; perhaps you can convince her of her foolishness!'

Alice was now sponging Fanny's cunt with sedulous care, and her attentions were making Fanny squirm and wriggle involuntarily in the most lovely fashion, much to her mistress's gratification. When Alice had finished she turned to me and said: 'She's quite ready, Jack! go ahead!'

'No, no, sir!' yelled Fanny in genuine terror, but I quickly got between her legs and placed myself on her palpitating stomach, clasping her in my arms, then directing my prick against her delicious cleft, I got its head inside without much difficulty. Fanny was now wild with fright and shrieked despairingly as she felt me effect an entrance into her; and as my prick penetrated her deeper and deeper, she went off into a paroxysm of frantic plungings in the hope of dislodging me.

I did not experience half the difficulty I had anticipated in getting into Fanny, for her spendings under Alice had lubricated the passage; but she was exceedingly tight and I must have hurt her for her screams were terrible! Soon however I was into her till our hairs mingled, then I lay still for a little while to allow her to recover a bit; and before long her cries ceased and she lay panting in my arms.

Alice, who was in my full sight and had been watching with the closest attention and the keenest enjoyment this practical violation of her maid, now bent forward and said softly: 'She's all right, Jack! go on, dear!' Promptly I set to work to fuck Fanny, at first with long slow piston-like strokes of my prick, then more and more rapid thrusts and shoves, driving myself well up her. Suddenly, I felt Fanny quiver deliciously under me . . . she had spent! Delightedly I continued to fuck her . . . soon she spent again, then again, and again, quivering with the most exquisite tremors and convulsions as she lay clasped tightly in my arms, uttering almost inarticulate 'Ahs' and 'Ohs' as the spasm of pleasure thrilled through her. Now I began to feel my own ecstasy quickly approaching! Hugging Fanny against me more closely than ever I let myself go and rammed furiously into her as she lay quivering under me till the rapturous crisis overtook me and madly I shot into her my pent-up torrent of boiling virile balm, inundating her sweetly excited interior and evidently causing her the most exquisite bliss, for her head fell backwards, her eyes closed, her nostrils dilated, her lips parted, as she ejaculated: 'Ah! . . . Ah!! . . . Ah!!! . . . ' when feeling each jet of my hot discharge shoot into her! Heavens! how I spent! The thrilling, exciting and provocative events of the afternoon had worked me up into such a state of sexual excitement that the ample discharge I spent into Fanny did not quench my ardour; and as soon as the delirious thrills and spasms of pleasure had died away, I started fucking her a second time. But Alice intervened: 'No Jack!' she exclaimed softly, adding archly, 'you must keep the rest for me! Get off quickly, dear, and let me attend to Fanny before it is too late!'

Unable to challenge her veto, I reluctantly withdrew my prick from Fanny's cunt after kissing her ardently, then rose and retired to my alcove, while Alice quickly took Fanny into her charge and attended to her with loving care.

When I returned, Fanny was still lying on her back fastened down to the couch, and Alice was sitting by her and talking to her with an amused smile as she gently played with her maid's breasts. As soon as Fanny caught sight of me she blushed rosy red, while Alice turned and greeted me with a welcoming smile.

'I've been trying to find out from Fanny which fucking she liked the best,' she said with a merry smile, 'but she won't say! Did she give you a good time, Jack?'

'She was simply divine!' I replied as I stooped and kissed the still blushing maid.

'Then we'll give her the reward we promised,' replied Alice, looking sweetly at Fanny, 'she shan't be tied up any more and she'll see you fuck me, Jack, presently! Set her free, Jack!' she added, and soon Fanny rose confusedly from the couch on which she had tasted the probably unique experience of being fucked in rapid succession first by a girl and then by a man! She was very shamefaced and her limbs were very stiff from having been retained so long in one position; but we supported her to the sofa where we placed her between us; then we gently chafed and massaged her limbs till they regained their powers and soothed her with our kisses and caresses, while our hands wandered all over her naked and still trembling body, and soon she was herself again.

'Now Jack!' exclaimed Alice who was evidently on heat again, 'are you ready?'

'Look dear!' I replied, holding up my limp prick for her inspection, adding with a smile: 'Time, my Christian friend!' She laughed, took my prick gently in her hands and began to fondle it, but as it did not show the signs of returning life she so desired to see, she caught hold of Fanny's hand and made it assist hers, much to Fanny's bashful confusion. But her touch had the desired effect, and soon I was stiff and rampant again! 'Thanks, Fanny!' I said as I lovingly kissed her blushing face, 'now Alice, if you will!' Quickly Alice was on her back with parted legs. Promptly I got on to her and drove my prick home up her cunt, then clasping each other closely, we set to work and fucked each other deliciously, till we both spent in delirious transports of pleasure which heightened Fanny's blushes, as with humid eyes she watched us in wondering astonishment and secret delight.

After exchanging ardent kisses we rose. 'Come Fanny, we must dress and be off, I didn't know it was so late!' exclaimed Alice. Off the girls went together to Alice's alcove while I retired to mine. I was delighted that their departure should be thus hurried as it would obviate the possible awkwardness of a more formal leave taking. Soon we all were dressed. I called a taxi and put the girls into it, their faces discreetly veiled, and as they drove off, I felt that the afternoon had not been wasted!

# Chapter Six

Two days after this memorable afternoon I received the following letter from Alice:

My darling Jack – I must write and tell you the sequel to yesterday's lovely afternoon at the Snuggery.

Fanny didn't say a word on the way home, but was evidently deeply thinking and getting more and more angry. She went straight to her room and I to mine. I did not expect she would resume her duties, in fact I rather anticipated she would come in to say she was going away at once! But in about ten minutes she came in as usual and proceeded to do her work just as if nothing had happened, only she wouldn't speak unless it was absolutely necessary.

At eight o'clock she brought me the dinner menu as usual for my orders. I told her I felt too tired to dress and go down, so would dine in my own room, and that she must dine with me, as she was looking so tired and upset generally. She looked surprised, and I think she hesitated about accepting my invitation, but did so.

At dinner of course she had to talk. I saw she had refreshing and appetising food and she made a good dinner. I also induced her to drink a little Burgundy, which seemed to do her a lot of good, and she gradually became less sulky.

When the table was cleared she was going away, but I asked her to stay and rest comfortably if she had done her work for the day. To my surprise she seemed glad to do so. I installed her in a comfortable chair and made her chat with me about things in general, carefully avoiding anything that might recall the events of the afternoon!

After some little time so passed, she rose and stood before me in a most respectful attitude and said: 'Miss Alice, you've always been a very kind mistress to me; you've treated me with every consideration, you've paid me well, you've given me light work. Would you mind telling me why you were so awfully cruel to me this afternoon?'

I was very surprised, but fortunately ideas came!

'Certainly I will, Fanny,' I replied, 'I think you are entitled to know. Come and sit by me here and we can talk it over nicely.'

I was then on the little sofa with padded back and ends, which you know just holds two nicely. Fanny hesitated for a moment and then sat down.

'I've always tried to be a good mistress to you, Fanny,' I said gravely, 'because you have been a very good maid to me. But of late there has been something wrong with you; your temper has been so queer that, though you have never disobeyed me, you have made your obedience very unpleasant; and I found myself wondering whether I had not better send you away. But I didn't want to lose you and I liked you for yourself very much' (here she half moved towards me) 'and so thought I'd talk the case over with Mr Jack, who is one of my best friends and always helps me in all troublesome matters. He said something must be wrong with you, and there undoubtedly is – and you must presently tell me what it is – and advised that he should give you a good shock – which he has done!'

'My God! yes, Miss Alice!' Fanny replied almost tearfully.

'But there is a second reason, Fanny,' I continued, 'which I will explain to you, as to why you were forced to submit yourself to me and to Mr Jack. Am I wrong in guessing that your queer temper has been caused by your not being able to satisfy certain sexual cravings and desires? Tell me frankly!'

'Yes!' she whispered bashfully.

'We felt sure of it!' I continued. 'Mr Jack said to me: "Look here, Alice, isn't it absurd that you two girls should be living in such close relations as mistress and maid, and yet should go on suffering from stifled natural sexual functions when you could and should so easily soothe each other?" Then he explained to me how!'

I gently took her hand; she yielded it to me without hesitation. 'Now Fanny, do you understand? Shall we not agree to help each other, to make life pleasanter and more healthy for us both? We tried each other this afternoon, Fanny! Do you like me sufficiently?'

She blushed deeply, then glanced shyly but lovingly at me. I took the hint. I slipped my arm round her, she yielded to my pressure. I drew her to me and kissed her fondly, whispering: 'Shall we be sweethearts, Fanny?'

She sank into my arms murmuring: 'Oh, Miss Alice!' her eyes shining with love! Our lips met, we sealed our compact with kisses!

Just then ten o'clock struck: 'Now we'll have a night-cap and go to bed,' I said to her. 'Will you get the whisky and siphon, dear, and mix my allowance and also one for yourself, as it will do you good.' Fanny rose and served me with the 'grog' as I call it, and when we had finished we turned out the lights and went to my bedroom.

After she had done my hair and prepared me for bed as usual I said to her softly: 'Now go and undress, dear, and come back!' and significantly kissed her. She blushed sweetly and withdrew. I undressed.

Presently there was a timid tap on the door, and Fanny came in shyly in her 'nightie'. 'Take it off, dear, please,' I said softly, 'I want to see you, I was too excited to do so this afternoon!' Bashfully and with pretty blushes she complied. I made her lie on my bed naked and had a good look at her all over, back, front, everywhere! Jack! she *is* a little beauty! When I kissed her after I had thoroughly examined her, she put her arms round my neck and whispered: 'May I look at you, miss?' So in turn I lay down naked and she looked me all over and played with me, kissed me here and there, till the touch of her lips and hands set my blood on fire. 'Come, darling!' I whispered. In a moment she was on the bed by me with parted legs; I got between them and on her, and in each other's arms we lay spending, she sometimes on me, I oftener on her, till we fell asleep still clasped against each other! Oh, Jack, you don't know what a good turn you did us yesterday afternoon!

Today Fanny is another person, so sweet and gentle and loving! An indescribable thrill comes over me when I think that I have this delicious girl at my command whenever I feel I'd like to be – naughty! You must come and see us soon, and have some tea – and my maid and me!

Your loving sweetheart,

ALICE

P.S. – I cross-questioned Fanny last night as to her experiences of the afternoon. I must tell you someday how she described what she went through, it will fetch you! But one thing I must tell you now! She says that she never felt anything so delicious as her sensations when in your arms, after you had got into her! I then asked her if she would go to you, some afternoon, if you wanted a change from me? She blushed sweetly and whispered: 'Yes, miss, if you didn't mind!'

## *Chapter Five*

Among our friends was a very pretty lady, Connie Blunt, a young widow whose husband had died within a few weeks of their marriage. She had been left comfortably off and had no children.

She was a lovely golden-haired girl of about twenty-two years, slight, tall and beautifully formed, a blue-eyed beauty, with a dazzling skin and pure complexion.

She and Alice were great friends and she was Alice's pet chaperone. The two were constantly together, Alice generally passing the night at Mrs Blunt's flat when they had been to a ball or any late entertainment; and I suppose that the sweet familiarity that exists between girl friends enabled Alice to see a good deal of her friend's physical charms, with the result that she fell in love with her. But hint as delicately and as diplomatically as Alice dared of the pleasures tasted by girl sweethearts, Mrs Blunt, never by word or deed or look, gave her any encouragement – in fact, she seemed ignorant that such a state of affection could or did exist.

I used to tease Alice about her ill-success and she took my chaff very good-naturedly; but I could see that she was secretly suffering from the 'pangs of unrequited love', and had it not been for the genuine affection that existed between her and her maid Fanny, which enabled Alice to satisfy with the help of Fanny's cunt the desires provoked by Mrs Blunt, things might have fared badly with Alice.

Among ardent girls, all unrequited passion of this sort is apt to become tinged with cruel desire against the beloved one; and one day, when Alice was consoling herself with me, I saw that this was getting to be the case with her passion for Mrs Blunt, and my fertile imagination suggested to me means by which she might attain to the desired end.

We were discussing about Mrs Blunt. 'I am getting hungry for Connie, Jack!' Alice had said mournfully, 'very hungry!'

'Dear, I'd like to be of assistance, and I believe I can,' I remarked sympathetically, 'but I shall want a lot of help from you. Could you bring yourself to torture her?'

'Oh yes!' replied Alice briskly, 'and I'd dearly like to do it!' and into her eyes came the sadique glint I knew so well! 'But it would never do, Jack! she'd never have anything to do with me again! I thought of this, but it won't do!'

'I'm not so sure!' I said reflectingly; 'let me give you my ideas as clearly as I can, and you can tell me if you think them workable.'

'Wait a moment, Jack!' she exclaimed, now keenly interested, 'let me get on you, it's better for us both,' she added archly; and soon she was lying flat on me, her breasts resting on my chest and my prick snugly lodged up her cunt while my arms retained her in position.

'Now are you ready to discuss matters seriously?' I asked with a mischievous smile. She nodded merrily. 'Go ahead, you dear old Jack, my most faithful friend,' she added with sudden tenderness as she kissed me with unusual affection.

'Then listen carefully, dear. The gist of my plan is that you must pretend to be what Mrs Blunt thinks you are, but what decidedly you are not, viz., an innocent and unsophisticated virgin!'

'Oh, you beast!' hissed Alice in pretended indignation but with laughing eyes; 'and who's responsible for that, sir?'

'I'm delighted to say that I am, dear!' I replied with a tender smile to which Alice responded by kissing me affectionately. 'Anyhow, you've got to pretend to be what you're not! You must get Mrs Blunt to chaperone you here to lunch. When we all are here afterwards, we'll manage to make her sit down in the 'chair of treachery' (her eyes smiled) which of course will at once pin her. Immediately I'll collar you and fasten you to one pair of pulleys. I'll have two pairs working that day, and I'll fasten Mrs Blunt to the other pair, so that you will face each other. (Alice's face was now a study in rapt attention.) You both will then be stripped naked in full sight of each other (Alice blushed prettily) and you both will also be tortured in front of each other! You must submit to be tortured, dear, to keep up the swindle!'

'I shan't mind, Jack!' Alice whispered, kissing me

'But there'll be this great difference to your former experience, both when you were done by yourself and when we did Fanny together, the girl that is being tortured is to be first blindfolded!' (Alice's eyes opened widely with surprise.)

'I shall keep Mrs Blunt fastened in the usual way, but for you, I shall use a new and most ingenious set of straps which can be put on and taken off in a jiffy by anyone knowing the trick. So when I have fastened Mrs Blunt for, say, cunt tickling, I'll blindfold her, then I'll silently let you loose and let you tickle her . . . '

'Oh, Jack! how lovely!' ejaculated Alice delightedly, again kissing me.

' . . . and tie you up quickly when you've finished, then I'll take off the bandage. She is sure to think it was me!' (Alice laughed merrily.) 'I must blindfold you, dear, when it's your turn, for your eyes may give you away, while your mouth will be quite safe!' (Alice nodded her head approvingly.)

'I don't however propose to give you girls much torture. After you both have had a turn, I'll tie Mrs Blunt to this couch just as we did Fanny. Then I'll threaten you with a whip, and you must pretend to be terrorised, and consent to do everything I tell you. I'll set you free and blindfold Mrs Blunt, then order you first to feel her, then to suck her and then to fuck her!'

'Jack! you're a genius!' ejaculated Fanny admiringly.

'After you've fucked Mrs Blunt, I'll have her while you look on!' (Alice blushed.) 'Then it will be your turn. I'll terrorise Mrs Blunt in reality and then make her operate on you, and then I'll have you in front of her!' (Alice here kissed me with sparkling eyes, then in her delight began to agitate herself on my prick.) 'Steady, dear!' I exclaimed slipping my hands down to her heaving bottom to keep her still, 'I can't think and talk and fuck at the same time! let me do the first two now and the third afterwards if you don't mind!'

'I'm very sorry, Jack!' Alice replied demurely but with eyes full of merriment: 'I'll try and lie still on you, but your magnificent plan is exciting me most awfully! The very idea of having Connie, oh, Jack!' and again she kissed me excitedly.

'Where were we? – oh yes,' I continued. 'I'll compel Mrs Blunt to perform on you and then I'll have you in her presence. Then under threats of the whip I'll make you both swear that you'll never let out what has been happening, and send you home! You must choose some day when you are staying with her, dear, for then you'll go back together and pass the evening together; and if you don't establish sexual relations with her at last, I'm afraid I can't help you! Now, what do you honestly and frankly think of my plan, dear?'

'Just splendid, and lovely, Jack!' she replied enthusiastically, then in a different tone of voice she whispered hastily: 'Jack, I really must, now . . . ' and began to work herself up and down on me. I saw she was too erotically excited to think seriously and so let her have her way. She fucked me most deliciously, quivering voluptuously when she spent and when she felt my warm discharge shoot into her.

After the necessary ablutions we dressed, as Alice had to leave early to keep a dinner engagement.

'Think it over carefully, dear,' I said as I put her into a taxi, 'let me have your opinion from the point of view of a girl.' And so we parted.

Next day, as I was about to commence my solitary lunch, who should appear but Alice and Fanny, to my great surprise but huge pleasure. I greeted them warmly, especially Fanny, whom I had not seen since the never to be forgotten afternoon when Alice and I converted her. She blushed prettily as we shook hands.

'Have you had lunch?' was my natural enquiry.

'No,' replied Alice, 'but we didn't come for that; I wanted to discuss with you certain points about Connie.'

'Lunch first and Connie afterwards!' I said laughing: 'sit down, Alice, sit down Fanny, and make yourselves at home.'

We had a merry lunch. I noticed with great approval that Fanny did not in any way presume, but was natural and respectful, also that she worshipped Alice!

In due course we adjourned to the Snuggery where we settled ourselves down comfortably.

'Now Alice, let's to business. Have you found some holes in my plan, or have you brought some new ideas?'

'Well, neither,' she said smiling, 'but there are one or two things I thought I ought to tell you. I hope, Jack dear, you won't mind my having told Fanny; she is as gone on Connie as I am and so is keen on helping me in any way she can!' Fanny blushed.

'Two heads are always supposed to be better than one, dear,' I said with a smile, 'and in a matter like this I am sure that two cunts should be better than one!' Alice playfully shook her fist at me. 'Now, dear?'

'Well, Jack, Fanny says that she understood from Connie's maid that her mistress is a virgin! Will this matter?'

I looked enquiringly at Fanny. 'She was with Mrs Blunt before her marriage and has never left her, sir,' said Fanny respectfully, 'and she told me she was certain that the marriage had never been . . . I forget the word, miss!' she added, looking at her mistress.

'Consummated, Jack!' said Alice. 'Do you know that I believe it must be so; it explains certain things!'

'What things, dear?' I asked innocently.

'Things that you're not to know, sir!' she retorted, colouring slightly, while Fanny laughed amusedly. It was delightful to me to note the excellent terms on which the two girls were and to think of my share in bringing about this *entente cordiale*!

'I don't see how it can matter!' I said reflectively. 'It will certainly make the show more piquant, a virgin widow is a rarity, and if I am able to carry out my programme as planned, it will fall to you, dear, to show her how her cunt works!'

Both girls laughed delightedly. 'It will be very interesting!' I added.

'This brings me to the second point nicely, Jack,' said Alice. 'Fanny would awfully like to be present, can it be worked, Jack?'

'It shall be worked if it is possible,' I said as I smiled at Fanny's eager expression. 'I consider I am in debt to her for the delicious time she gave me when last here!' Fanny coloured vividly while her mistress laughed merrily. 'Let me think!'

It was a bit of a poser, but my fertile imagination was equal to the occasion.

'By Jove!' I exclaimed as a sudden idea struck me, 'I think it can be done! listen you two.' The girls leant forward in pretty eagerness.

'You and Mrs Blunt must come here together, Alice! that's inevitable. You'll be here by one o'clock, for we must have early lunch and a long afternoon.' Alice nodded significantly.

'Let Fanny follow you in half an hour's time, having lunched at home, as I am sorry I don't see how I can give her lunch here. She must not be seen by Mrs Blunt, or the latter will be suspicious! When you arrive, Fanny, come straight into this room and hide yourself in my alcove! there's a peephole there, from which you will be able to see all that passes. If Mrs Blunt's curiosity should lead her to wish to see my alcove, I will choke her off by saying it is my photographic dark-room and there is something there which would spoil if light were to be admitted. So you'll be certain to see the fun, Fanny.' (She smiled gratefully, as did also Alice.) 'When you see that I have worked my plan successfully and your mistress and Mrs Blunt are fastened to the pulleys, take off your clothes noiselessly, even your shoes, and when I have blindfolded Mrs Blunt, you can slip out and share with your mistress in the pleasure of torturing her! you mustn't speak and you must move noiselessly, for her senses will be very acute. What do you say to this, Alice?'

'Jack! it will be just lovely!' exclaimed Alice, while Fanny, too respectful to speak, looked her satisfaction and gratitude. 'What a time Connie will have between the three of us!' she added, laughing wickedly.

'Now, what's the next point?' I asked. Alice looked towards Fanny, then replied: 'There is nothing more, is there Fanny?'

'No, miss,' she answered.

'Then we'll be off! Thanks awfully, Jack, I'm really very grateful to you for arranging about Fanny. Come, Fanny!' and they rose.

'Where to, now?' I asked. 'You are a pair of gadabouts!'

Alice laughed. 'My dentist, worse luck!'

'Poor fun!' I said. 'For you or Fanny?'

'Me, unfortunately, Fanny will have to sit in the waiting-room.'

I glanced at her maid, and a sudden desire to have her again seized me. 'Look here, Alice,' I said, 'I'm going to ask you a favour! Will you allow me to have the company of your maid this afternoon?'

Fanny blushed rosy red over cheeks and brow. Alice laughed merrily, as she regarded her blushing maid and caught her shy glances.

'Certainly, Jack, as far as I am concerned!' she replied. 'What do you say, Fanny? will you stay and take care of Mr Jack?'

Fanny glanced shyly at us both. 'Yes, miss, if you don't mind!' And vivid blushes covered her face as she caught Alice's amused and half-quizzing look.

'Then I'll be off!' Alice exclaimed, 'don't trouble to come down, Jack. Bye-bye, Fanny, for the present!'

But of course I wasn't going to let Alice leave unescorted, so I accompanied her downstairs and saw her into a taxi, under a shower of good-natured chaff from her. Then, two steps at a time, I hurried back to the Snuggery, where I found Fanny standing where we had left her, evidently very nervous at being alone with me.

I took her gently in my arms and kissed her blushing upturned face tenderly, then sat down and drew her on to my knees.

'It is sweet of you to be so kind, dear,' I said, looking lovingly at her. She blushed, then raising her eyes to mine she said softly: 'I couldn't refuse, sir, after you had been so very kind to me about Mrs Blunt.'

I laughed. 'Not for my own sake then, Fanny?'

'Oh, I didn't mean that, sir!' she exclaimed hastily in pretty confusion.

'Then it is for my own sake, dear?' I asked with a smile.

'Yes, sir!' she whispered bashfully as she looked into my eyes timidly but lovingly. I drew her to me and kissed her lips passionately. Then I gently began to unbutton her blouse.

'Do you wish me to . . . undress, sir?' she murmured nervously.

'Yes, please, dear!' I whispered back. 'Use your mistress's room; does your mistress . . . have you naked, Fanny?' I asked softly.

'Yes, sir,' she whispered, blushing deeply.

'Then I'll do the same, dear!' I replied with a smile as I freed her and led her to Alice's alcove, then undressed myself in mine.

Presently Fanny emerged, stark naked, a delicious object, her face covered with blushes, one hand shielding her breasts and the other her cunt! I sprang to meet her and led her to the couch and made her sit on my knees, thrilling at the touch of her warm, firm but soft flesh.

'What shall we do, Fanny?' I asked mischievously as I slipped my hand down to her cunt and lovingly played with it. My caress seemed to set her on fire; she lost her restraint, suddenly threw her arms round my neck and kissing me passionately murmured: 'Do anything you like to me, sir!'

'Then may I suggest a little sucking first, and then some sweet fucking?' I said softly. Her eyes beamed assent.

I laid her flat on her back, opened her legs widely, and after feasting my eyes on her lovely cunt, I applied my lips to it and tongued her till she quivered and wriggled with delight. Alice had evidently taught her this delicious pleasure. Then I got on her and thrust my prick well up her; she clasped me delightedly in her arms, and letting herself go, passed from one spending to another, wriggling voluptuously, till she had extracted from me all I could give her. I shot into her excited interior with rapturous ecstasy – and between fucking and sucking we passed a delicious afternoon!

In the enforced intervals for rest and recovery, I learnt from her all about her sexual relations with her mistress. She described the sensation of being provoked into spending by the sweet friction of Alice's cunt against hers as something heavenly, so much so that the two girls seldom did anything else but satisfy in this way their lustful cravings and desires. One evening, Alice apparently was very randy and insisted on frigging Fanny, first tieing her down to the four bedposts, then made Fanny tie her down similarly and tickle her cunt with a feather till she spent three times. It was clear that the girls were devoted to each other. I asked Fanny what she thought would be the arrangement if we succeeded in converting Mrs Blunt to their ways; she blushed and said she didn't think it would affect her and Alice's relationship and she hoped Connie would sometimes spend the night at Alice's and give her a chance!

## Chapter Six

A few days later I received a note from Mrs Blunt saying that Alice was staying with her and she would be delighted if I would dine there with them quite quietly. I naturally accepted the invitation.

I was somewhat of a stranger to Mrs Blunt. I had met her more than once and admired her radiant beauty, but no more. Now that there was more than a possibility that she might have to submit herself to me, I studied her closely. She was more voluptuously made than I had fancied and was a simply glorious specimen of a woman; but she was something of a doll, rather shallow and weak-willed; and I saw with satisfaction that I would not have much trouble in terrorising her and forcing her to comply with my desires.

During the evening Alice brought up the subject of my rooms and their oddity and made Mrs Blunt so interested that I was able naturally to suggest a visit and a lunch there – which was accepted for the following day, an arrangement which made Alice glance at me with secret exultation and delighted anticipation.

In due course my guests arrived, and after a dainty lunch which drew from

Mrs Blunt many compliments, we found ourselves in the Snuggery. The girls at once commenced to examine everything, Alice taking on herself the role of showman while I, in my capacity of host, did the honours. I could see that Fanny was at her post of observation – and now awaited with some impatience the critical moment.

In due course Mrs Blunt and Alice finished their tour of inspection, and made as if they would rest for a while.

'What comfortable chairs you men always manage to get about you,' remarked Mrs Blunt as she somewhat critically glanced at my furniture. 'You bachelors *do* study your creature comforts – and so remain bachelors!' she added somewhat significantly, as she was among our deluded friends who planned a match between Alice and me.

'Quite true!' I replied with a polite smile, 'so long as I can by hook or by crook get in these rooms what I want, they will be good enough for me – especially when I am permitted to enjoy "angels" visits!'

'That's a very pretty compliment, isn't it Alice?' exclaimed Mrs Blunt as she moved towards the chair of treachery, which stood invitingly close, and gracefully sank into it.

Click! – the arms folded on her. 'Oh!' she ejaculated as she endeavoured to press them back.

'What's the matter, Connie?' asked Alice, quickly hurrying to her friend – but in a flash I was on to her and had tightly gripped her. 'Oh!' she screamed in admirably feinted fright, struggling naturally; but I picked her up and carrying her to the pulleys, made them fast to her wrists and fixed her upright with hands drawn well over her head, much to Mrs Blunt's horror! As I approached her she shrieked, 'Help! . . . help!' pressing desperately against the locked arms and striving to get loose.

'It's no use, Mrs Blunt!' I said quietly, as I commenced to wheel the chair towards the second pair of pulleys, 'you're in my power! You'd better yield quietly!'

Seizing her wrists one a time, I quickly made the ropes fast to them, set the machinery going – and just as she was being lifted off her seat, I released the arms and drew the chair away, forcing her to stand up. In a very few seconds she was drawn up to her full height, facing Alice, both girls panting and gasping after their struggles.

'There, ladies,' I exclaimed, as if well pleased with my performance – 'now you'll appreciate the utility of this room!'

'Oh! Mr Jack!' cried Mrs Blunt in evident relief, 'how you did frighten me! I felt sure that something dreadful was going to happen!' – then with a poor attempt to be sprightly, 'I quite made up my mind that Alice and I were going to be . . . ' she broke off with a silly self-conscious giggle.

'I gladly accept the suggestion you have so kindly made, dear lady,' I said with a smile of gratitude, 'and will do you and Alice presently!' She started, horrified, and stared aghast at me as if she could not believe her ears; she seemed to be dumb with shocked surprise, and went deadly pale. I was afraid to glance at Alice lest I should catch her eye and betray her.

With an effort, Mrs Blunt stammered brokenly: 'Do you mean to say . . . that Alice and I . . . are going to be . . . to be? . . . ?' she stopped abruptly, unable to express in words her awful apprehension.

'Fucked is the word you want, I think, dear Mrs Blunt!' I said with a smile; 'yes, dear ladies – as you are so very kind I shall have much pleasure in fucking you both presently!'

She quivered as if she had been struck, then screamed hysterically: 'No, no . . . I won't . . . help! . . . help!! . . . help!!!'

I turned quietly to Alice (who I could see was keenly enjoying the trap into which Mrs Blunt had fallen, and her dismay) and said to her: 'Are you going to be foolish enough to resist, Alice?'

She paused for a long moment, then said in a voice that admirably counterfeited intense emotion, 'I feel that resistance will be of no avail – but I'm not going to submit myself to you tamely. You will have to . . . force me!'

'Me also!' cried Mrs Blunt, hysterically.

'As you please!' I said equably. 'I've long wanted a good opportunity of testing the working of this machinery; I don't fancy I'll get a better one than you are now offering me – a nice long afternoon and two lovely rebellious girls! Now Mrs Blunt, as you are chaperoning Alice, I am bound to begin with you.' And I commenced to unbutton her blouse.

'No, no, Mr Jack!' she screamed in dismay as she felt my fingers un-fastening her upper garments and unhooking her skirt – but I steadily went on with my task of undressing her, and soon had her standing in her stays with bare arms and legs – a lovely, tall, slender half-undressed figure, her bosom heaving and palpitating, the low-cut bodice allowing the upper half of her breasts to become visible. Her flushed face indicated intense shame at this indecent exposure of herself, and her eyes strained appealingly towards Alice as if to assure herself of her sympathy.

'Now I will give you a few minutes to collect yourself while I attend to Alice!' I said as I went across to the latter, whose eyes were stealthily devouring Mrs Blunt's provoking dishabille. 'Now, for you, dear!' I said, as I quietly set to work to undress her.

She (very wisely) was adopting the policy of dogged defiance and main-tained a sullen silence as one by one her clothes were taken off her till she also stood bare-armed and bare-legged in her stays. But instead of pausing I went on and removed her corset, unfastened the shoulder straps of her chemise and vest and pushed them down to her feet, leaving her standing with only her drawers on, a sweet, blushing, dainty, nearly naked girl, on whose shrinking trembling figure Mrs Blunt's eyes seemed to be riveted with what certainly looked like involuntary admiration!

But I myself was getting excited and inflamed by the sight of so much unclothed and lovely girl-flesh, so eagerly returning to Mrs Blunt, I set to work to remove the little clothing that was left on her. 'No, no, Mr Jack!' she cried piteously as I took off her stays, 'Oh!' she screamed in her distress when she felt her chemise and vest slip down to her feet, exposing her in her drawers only, which solitary garment she evidently concluded, from the sight of Alice, would be left on her. But when after a few admiring glances I went behind her and began to undo the waistband and she realised that she was to be exposed naked, Mrs Blunt went into a paroxysm of impassioned cries and pitiful pleadings; in her desperation she threw the whole of her weight on her slender wrists and wildly twisted her legs together in the hope of preventing me from pulling her drawers off. But they only required a few sharp tugs and down to her ankles they came! A bitter cry broke from her, her head with its wealth of now disordered golden hair fell forward on her bosom in her agony of shame – Connie Blunt was stark naked!

I stepped back a couple of paces, then exultingly gazed on the vision that met my eyes. Close in front of me was revealed the back of Mrs Blunt's tall, slender, naked figure, uninterrupted from her heels to her updrawn hands, her enforced attitude displaying to perfection the voluptuous curves of her hips, her luscious haunches, her gloriously rounded bottom, her shapely legs. Facing her, stood Alice, naked save for her drawers – her face suffused with blushes at the sight of Connie's nakedness, her bosom heaving with excitement not unmixed with delight at witnessing the nudity of her friend and trepidation at the approaching similar exposure of herself. I saw from the stealthy gloating glances she shot at Connie that she was longing to have a good look at her but dared not do so, lest her eyes should betray her delight – so I decided to give her the opportunity. I went over to her, slipped behind her, passed my arms round her and drew her against me – and holding her thus in my embrace, I gazed at the marvellous sight Connie Blunt was affording to us as she stood naked.

She was simply exquisite with her pearly dazzling skin, her lovely shape, her delicious little breasts standing saucily out with their coral nipples as they quivered and palpitated on her heaving bosom, her voluptuous hips and round smooth belly, her pretty legs; her drooping head exhibited her glorious golden hair, while, as if to balance it, a close clustering mass of silky curly golden-brown hairs grew thickly over the region of her cunt hiding it completely from my eager eyes!

In silent admiration I gloated over the wonderful sight of Connie Blunt naked – till a movement of Alice recalled me to her interests. She was keeping her face steadily averted from Connie, her eyes on the floor, as if unwilling to distress her friend by looking at her in her terrible nudity.

'Well, how do you like Connie now?' I asked loud enough for Mrs Blunt to hear. She shivered. Alice remained silent.

'Aren't you going to look at her?' Alice still remained silent.

'Come, Alice, you must have a good look at her. I want to discuss her with you, to have your opinion as a girl on certain points. Come, look!' And I gently stroked her naked belly.

'Oh! don't Jack!' she cried, affecting a distress she was not feeling. Connie glanced hastily at us to see what I was doing to Alice, and blushed deeply as she noted my wandering hands, which now were creeping up to Alice's breasts.

I seized them and began to squeeze them. 'Don't, Jack!' again she cried.

'Then obey me and look at Connie!' I said sternly.

Slowly Alice raised her head, as if most reluctantly, and looked at Connie, who coloured hotly as her eyes met Alice's. 'Forgive me, darling!' cried Alice tearfully, 'I can't help doing it!' But her throbbing breasts and excitedly agitated bottom told me how the little hypocrite was enjoying the sight of Connie's nakedness!

'Now, no nonsense, Alice!' I said sternly – and I gave her breasts a twist that made her squeal in earnest and immediately rivet her eyes on her friend lest she should get another twist. And so, for a few minutes, we silently contemplated Mrs Blunt's shrinking form, our eager eyes greedily devouring the lovely naked charms that she was so unwillingly exhibiting to us.

Presently I said to Alice (whose breasts were still captives in my hands): 'Now, the plain truth, please – speaking as a girl, what bit of Mrs Blunt do you consider her finest point?'

Alice blushed uncomfortably, pretended to hesitate, then said shame-facedly: 'Her . . . her . . . private parts!'

Connie flushed furiously and pressed her thighs closely together as if to shield her cunt from the eager eyes which she knew were intently looking at it! I laughed amusedly at Alice's demure phraseology and said: 'I think so too! – but that's not what you girls call it when you talk together. Tell me the name you use, your pet name for it!'

Alice was silent. I think she was really unwilling to say the word before Mrs Blunt, but I mischievously proceeded to get it out of her. So I gave her tender breasts a squeeze that made her cry out, 'Oh!' and said, 'Come Alice, out with it!'

Still she remained silent. I let go of one of her breasts and began to pinch her fat bottom, making her wriggle and squeal in grim reality – but she would not speak.

Seeing that Mrs Blunt was watching us closely, I moved my hand away from Alice's bottom and made as if I was going to pass it through the slit in her drawers.

'Won't you tell me?' I said, moving my hand ominously.

'Cunny!' shrieked Alice, flushing vividly.

'Cunny!' echoed Mrs Blunt in hot confusion.

'You obstinate little thing!' I said to Alice with a laugh that showed her that I was only playing with her. 'Cunny!' I repeated significantly. 'Well, Alice, let Mrs Blunt and me see your "cunny"!' – and as I spoke I slipped the knot of her drawers, and down they tumbled to her ankles before she could check them with her knees, exposing by their disappearance the lovely cunt I knew so well and loved so dearly, framed, so to speak, by her plump rounded thighs and her sweet belly.

I sank on my knees by Alice's side, then eagerly and delightedly inspected her delicious cleft, the pouting lips of which, half hidden in their mossy covering, betrayed her erotic excitement. She endured with simulated confusion and crimson cheeks my close examination of her *private parts*, to use her own demure phrase! At last I exclaimed rapturously: 'Oh! Alice, it *is* sweet!' then as if overjoyed, I gripped her by her bottom and thighs and pressing my lips on her cunt, I kissed it passionately! 'Don't Jack!' she cried, her voice half choked by the lascivious sensations that were thrilling through her; and seeing that Alice was perilously near to spending in her intense erotic excitement, I quitted her and went across to Mrs Blunt, by whose side I knelt in order to study her cunt.

'Oh! Mr Jack! don't look, *please* don't look there!' she cried in an agony of shame at the idea of her cunt being thus leisurely inspected by male eyes – and she attempted to thwart me by standing on one leg and throwing her other thigh across her groin.

'Put that leg down, Connie!' I said sternly.

'No, no,' she shrieked, 'I won't let you look at it!'

'Won't you?' said I, and drew out from the bases of the pillars between which she was standing two stout straps, which I fastened to her slim ankles in spite of her vigorous kicking. I set the mechanism working. A piercing scream broke from her as she felt her legs being pulled remorselessly apart – and soon, notwithstanding her desperate resistance and frantic struggles, she stood like an inverted Y with her cunt in full view!

'Won't you?' I repeated with a cruelly triumphant smile as I proceeded to blindfold her, she the while pitifully protesting. Then I noiselessly set Alice loose and signalled to Fanny to join us, which she quickly did, stark naked as directed; and the three of us knelt in front of Connie (I between the girls with an arm round each) and with heads close together delightedly examined her private parts, Alice and Fanny's eyes sparkling with undisguised enjoyment as we noted the delicate and close fitting shell-pink lips of her cunt, its luscious fleshiness, and its wonderful covering of brown-gold silky hairs, she all the time quivering in her shame at being thus forced to exhibit the most secret part of herself to my male eyes.

I motioned to the girls to remain as they were, detached myself from them, leant forward and gently deposited a kiss on Connie's cunt. Taken absolutely by surprise, Mrs Blunt shrieked: 'Oh–h–h!' and began to wriggle divinely, to the delight of the girls, who motioned to me to kiss Connie's cunt again – which I gladly did. Again she screamed, squirming deliciously in her fright. I gave her cunt a third kiss, which nearly sent her into convulsions, Alice and Fanny's eyes now sparkling with lust. Not daring to do it again I rose, slipped behind her noiselessly and took her in my arms, my hands on her belly.

'No, no, Mr Jack!' she cried, struggling fiercely, 'don't touch me! . . . Oh–h–h!' she screamed as my hands caught hold of her breasts and began to feel them. They were smaller than Alice's but firmer, soft, elastic and strangely provoking, most delicious morsels of girl-flesh; and I toyed and played with them, squeezing them lasciviously to the huge delight of the girls, till I felt it was time to feel her cunt. So, releasing her sweet breasts, I slipped my hands over Mrs Blunt's stomach and on to her cunt!

'Oh! my God!' she shrieked, her head tossing wildly in her shame and agony as she felt my fingers wander over her private parts so conveniently arranged for the purpose. Over her shoulder I could see Alice and Fanny's faces as they watched every movement of my fingers, their eyes humid, their cheeks flushed, their breasts dancing with sexual excitement! From the fingers' point of view, Alice's cunt was the more delicious of the two from its superior plumpness and fleshiness – but there was a certain delicacy about Connie's cunt that made me revel in the sweet occupation of feeling it.

Presently I gently inserted my forefinger between the close fitting lips. The girls' eyes glistened with eagerness as they bent forward to see if Fanny's information was true – and I smiled as the disappointment expressed in their faces when they saw my finger bury itself in Connie's cunt up to the knuckle! She was not a virgin! But she was terribly tight, much more so than Fanny was when I first felt her – and Mrs Blunt's screams and agonised cries clearly indicated that for want of use, her cunt had regained its virgin tightness.

Keeping my finger inside her, I gently tickled her clitoris, in order to test her sexual susceptibility. She gave a fearful shriek accompanied by an indescribable wriggle, then another – then bedewed my hand with her sweet love-juice, her head falling on her bosom as she spent, utterly unable to control herself. I kept my finger inside her till her ecstatic crisis was over and her spasmodic thrills had quieted down – then gently withdrew it as I lovingly kissed the back of her soft neck and then left her to herself.

As I did so, Alice and Fanny rose, their eyes betraying their intense enjoyment of the scene. With an unmistakable gesture they indicated each other's cunts, as if seeking mutual relief – but I shook my head, for Alice had now to be tortured. Quickly I fastened her up again while Fanny noiselessly disappeared into my alcove; then I removed the bandage from Connie's eyes. As she wearily raised her head, having scarcely recovered from the violence of her spending, I clasped her to me and passionately showered kisses on her flushed cheeks and trembling lips. I saw her eyes seek Alice's as if to learn her thoughts as to what she had witnessed – then both girls blushed vividly as if in sympathy. I pushed a padded chair behind Connie, released her legs and then lowered her till she could sit down in comfort and left her to recover herself while I went across to Alice, who was now to be the prey of my lustful hands.

But I was now in an almost uncontrollable state of lust! My erotic senses had been so irritated and inflamed by the sight of Mrs Blunt's delicious person naked, her terrible struggles, her shame and distress during her ordeal, that all my lascivious cravings and desires imperiously called for immediate satisfaction. And the circumstance that all this had taken place in the presence of Alice and Fanny, both stark naked, both in a state of intense sexual excitement and unconcealed delight at witnessing the torturing of Mrs Blunt, only added further fuel to the flame of my lust. But to enjoy either Connie or Alice at the moment did not suit my programme – and my thoughts flew to Fanny now sitting naked in my alcove and undoubtedly very excited sexually by Mrs Blunt's struggles and cries!

So slipping behind Alice, I took her in my arms, seized her breasts, and said not unkindly while watching Mrs Blunt keenly, 'Now Alice, it's your turn! You've seen all that has happened to Mrs Blunt and how in spite of her desperate resistance she has been forced to do whatever I wanted – even to spend! Now I'm going to undress' (Mrs Blunt looked up in evident alarm) 'and while I am away, let me suggest you consult your chaperone as to whether you had not better yield yourself quietly to me!' And I dis-appeared into my alcove, where Fanny, still naked, received me with con-scious expectancy, having heard every word.

I tore off my clothing, seized her naked person and whispered excitedly as I pointed to my rampant prick: 'Quick, Fanny!' She instantly understood. I threw myself into an easy-chair and in a moment she was kneeling between my legs with my prick in her mouth; and she sucked me deliciously till I spent rapturously down her throat! Having thus delightfully relieved my feelings, I drew her on to my knees, then whispered as I gratefully kissed her, 'Now dear, I'll repay you by frigging you, while we listen to what Alice and Connie are saying,' and slipping my hand down to her pouting and still excited cunt, I gently commenced the sweet junction, she clasping me closely to her and kissing me silently but passionately as my active finger soothed her excited senses. From our chair we could clearly see Connie and Alice and hear every word they said.

Their embarrassed silence had just been broken by Alice, who whispered in admirably simulated distress: 'Oh, Connie! what *shall* I do?'

Connie coloured painfully, then with downcast eyes (as if fearing to meet her friend's agitated glances) replied in an undertone: 'Better yield, dear – don't you think so?'

'Oh! I can't!' cried Alice despairingly, playing her part with a perfection that brought smiles from Fanny and me; then with a change of voice she asked timidly: 'Was it *very* dreadful, Connie?'

Connie covered her face with her hands and shudderingly replied in broken agitation: 'I thought I should have died! . . . the awful feeling of shame! the terrible helplessness! . . . the dreadful position into which I was fastened! . . . the agony of having a man's hand on my . . . cunny! . . . Oh–h–h–h!'

Just then, Fanny began to wriggle deliciously on my knees as she felt her pleasure approaching! Her eyes closed slowly, she strained me against her breasts – then suddenly she agitated herself rapidly on my finger, plunging wildly with quick strokes of her buttocks. Then she caught her breath, murmured brokenly: 'Oh–h–h!' and inundated my finger as she spent ecstatically. My mouth sought hers as, little by little, I slowed down the play of my finger in her cunt till she came to, deliciously satisfied!

'Now I'd better go to them,' I whispered, and after a few more tender kisses I went out. My appearance, naked save for my shoes and socks, caused Mrs Blunt to hurriedly cover her face with her hands as she hysterically cried: 'Oh! . . . Oh! . . . Oh!'

I ignored her, took Alice into my arms as before, and said to her encouragingly: 'Well, dear, what is it to be?' whispering inaudibly in her ear, 'You're to be tickled!'

Alice stood silent with downcast eyes. In her anxiety to hear Alice's decision, Mrs Blunt uncovered her face and looked eagerly at us.

At last it came! 'No!' spoken so low that we could only just hear her.

'Oh, Alice! you silly girl!' exclaimed Mrs Blunt, now afraid about herself.

Alice cast a reproachful glance at Connie, then said, almost in tears (the little humbug!), 'I can't! Oh, I can't!'

Without a word I fastened straps to Alice's pretty ankles and dragged her legs apart – till she stood precisely as Mrs Blunt had done. Then I carefully blindfolded her and seated myself just below her on the floor, within easy reach of her – and began to amuse myself with her defenceless cunt, knowing that Mrs Blunt could see over my shoulder all that passed.

With both hands I felt Alice's lovely private parts, touching, pressing, stroking, pulling her hairs, every now and then parting its lips and peering into her interior – an act invariably followed by an ardent kiss as if in apology, she squirming deliciously. She submitted herself to the sweet torture in silence, till I pretended to be trying to push my finger into her cunt, when she screamed affrightedly: 'Don't Jack, don't!' as if unable to endure it!

'Hurts, does it, Alice?' I said smiling meaningfully, 'then I won't do it again! I'll try something softer than my finger!' and after fetching a feather, I resumed my position on the carpet.

Alice's colour now went and came and her bosom began to heave uneasily, for she guessed what was now going to be done to her; and although she rather liked having her cunt tickled, the existing conditions were not what she was accustomed to – and she awaited her ordeal with a good deal of trepidation.

Quietly I applied the tip of the feather to her cunt's now slightly pouting lips, with a delicate yet subtle touch, 'Oh–h!' she ejaculated, quivering painfully. I gave her three or four more similar touchings, under which she began to wriggle vigorously, crying: 'Oh! . . . Oh! . . . Don't, Jack!' – and I was just beginning to tickle her cunt in real earnest when Connie, horror-stricken at the sight, shrieked: 'Stop! . . . stop! . . . oh you awful brute! . . . you coward to torture a girl in that way! . . . Oh! my God!' she moaned, quite overcome at the sight of Alice being tortured!

How thankful I was that I had blindfolded Alice! I am sure that she otherwise would have given the game away – she *must* have laughed! in fact some of her convulsions were undoubtedly caused by suppressed laughter and not by her torture!

'There's no better way of curing a girl of obstinacy than by tickling her cunt, Connie,' I said unconcernedly, and I again commenced to tickle Alice.

'No, no, stop!' Connie shrieked frantically again, 'oh! you cruel brute! . . . you'll kill her!'

I laughed. 'Oh, no! Connie, she's all right – only a little erotic excitement!' I explained equably as I resumed the tickling, this time making Alice wriggle and scream in real earnest. She had not been allowed to satisfy her lustful cravings, induced by the sight of Connie's agonies, and by now she was in a terrible condition of fierce concupiscence and unsatisfied desires, dying to spend, but so far unable to do so for want of the spark necessary to provoke the discharge! More and more hysterical became Connie's prayers and pleadings, shriller her cries of genuine horror at the sight of Alice's cunt being so cruelly tickled – wilder and wilder became Alice's struggles and screams, till suddenly she shrieked: 'For God's sake make me spend!' Immediately I thrust the feather well up her cunt and rapidly twiddled it, then tickled her clitoris! A tremendous spasm shook Alice, her head fell back, then dropped on her bosom as she ejaculated: 'Ah–h–h . . . ah–h–h–h!' in a tone of blessed relief, quivering deliciously as the rapturous spasm of her ecstasy thrilled through her as she spent madly.

As soon as she came to herself again, I said to her: 'Well, will you now yield yourself to me, or do you want some more?'

'Oh no! no! – my God, no!' she cried, feigning to be completely subdued.

'You'll then be a good girl?'

'Yes!' she gasped.

'You'll do whatever I tell you to do?'

'Yes! yes!' she cried.

'You'll let me . . . fuck you?'

'Oh, my God! . . . ' she moaned, remaining silent. I touched her cunt with the feather. 'Yes! yes!' she screamed, 'yes!'

'That's right, dear!' I said encouragingly, then quickly I released her and put her into a large and comfortable easy-chair in which she promptly coiled herself up, as if utterly exhausted and ashamed of her absolute surrender – but really, to escape the sympathetic and pitying glances from Connie. It was as clever a piece of acting as I had ever seen!

I then went across to Mrs Blunt and without a word, I touched the springs and set the machinery to work. 'Oh! oh!' she cried as she felt herself drawn up again and her legs being remorselessly dragged asunder till she had resumed her late position. When I had her properly fixed, I said to her: 'Now Connie, I am going to punish you for abusing me – you'll have something to scream about!' – and I applied the feather to her lovely but defenceless cunt.

'Don't, don't! . . . oh my God!' she screamed. I saw we were about to have a glorious spectacle – so I stopped, blindfolded her and beckoned to Fanny, who promptly came up, Alice also. Handing a feather to each, I pointed to Connie's quivering cunt.

Delightedly both girls applied their feathers to Connie's tender slit, Alice directing hers against Connie's clitoris, while Fanny ran hers all along the lips and as far inside as she could, their eyes sparkling with cruel glee as they watched Connie wriggle and listened to her terrible shrieks and hysterical ejaculations. It was a truly voluptuous sight! – Connie naked, struggling frantically while Alice and Fanny, also naked, were goading her into hysterics with their feathers! But soon I had to intervene – Connie by now was exhausted, she couldn't stand any more; so reluctantly, I stopped the girls, signalled to Fanny to disappear and Alice to return to her chair while I released Connie's bandage.

She looked at me seemingly half dazed, panting and gasping after her exertions.

'Now, will *you* submit yourself to me, Connie?' I asked.

'Yes! yes!' she gasped.

'Fucking and all!'

'Oh, my God! . . . yes!'

Then I set her free. As she sank into her chair, Alice rushed to her as if impelled by irresistible sympathy; the two girls fell into each other's arms, kissing each other passionately, murmuring: 'Oh, Connie! . . . ' 'Oh, Alice!' The first part of the play was over!

## *Chapter Seven*

I produced a large bottle of champagne, and pretending that the opener was in my alcove I went there. But my real object was to satisfy in Fanny the raging concupiscence which my torturing of Alice and then Connie had so fiercely aroused in me.

I found her shivering with unsatisfied hot lust. I threw myself into a chair, placed my bottom on the edge and pointed to my prick in glorious erection. Instantly Fanny straddled across me, brought her excited cunt to bear on my tool and impaled herself on it with deliciously voluptuous movements, sinking down on it till she rested on my thighs, her arms round my neck, mine round her warm body, our lips against each other's; then working herself divinely up and down on my prick, she soon brought on the blessed relief we both were thirsting for – and in exquisite rapture we spent madly.

'Oh! sir! wasn't it lovely!' she whispered as soon as she could speak.

'Which, Fanny?' I asked mischievously. 'This! – or that?' pointing to the room.

She blushed prettily, then whispered saucily: 'Both, sir!' as she passionately kissed me.

I begged of her to sponge me while I opened the champagne, which she did sweetly, kissing my flaccid prick lovingly, as soon as she had removed all traces of our bout of fucking from it. I poured out four large glasses, made her drink one (which she did with great enjoyment) – then took the other three out with me to the girls.

I found them still in each other's arms and coiled together in the large armchair, Alice half sitting on Connie's thighs and half resting on Connie's breasts, a lovely sight. I touched her and she started up, while Connie slowly opened her eyes.

'Drink, it will pull you together!' I said, handing each a tumbler. They did so, and the generous wine seemed to have an immediate good effect and to put new life into them. I eyed them with satisfaction, then raising my glass said: 'To our good healths, dears – and a delicious consummation of Connie's charming and most sporting suggestion!' then gravely emptied my tumbler.

Both girls turned scarlet, Connie almost angrily, they glanced tentatively at each other but neither spoke.

To terminate their embarrassment, I pointed to a settee close by, and soon we arranged ourselves on it, I in the centre, Alice on my right and Connie on my left, their heads resting on my shoulders, their faces turned towards each other and within easy kissing distance, my arms clasping them to me, my hands being just able to command the outer breast of each! Both girls seemed ill at ease; I think Connie was really so, as she was evidently dreading having to be fucked by me, but with Alice it was only pretence.

'A penny for your thoughts, dear!' I said to her chaffingly, curious to know what she would say.

'I was thinking how lovely Connie is naked!' she murmured softly, blushing prettily. I felt a quiver run through Connie.

'Before today, how much of each other have you seen?' I asked interestedly. Silently both girls pointed to just above their breasts.

'Then stand up, Connie dear, and let us have a good look at you,' I said, 'and Alice shall afterwards return the compliment by showing you herself! Stand naturally, with your hands behind you.'

With evident unwillingness she complied, and with pretty bashfulness she faced us, a naked, blue-eyed daughter of the gods, tall, slender, golden-haired, exquisite – blushing as she noted in our eyes the pleasure the contemplation of her naked charms was giving us!

'Now in profile, dear!'

Obediently she turned. We delightedly noted her exquisite outline from chin to thigh, her proud little breasts, her gently curving belly, its wealth of golden-brown hair, standing out like a bush at its junction with her thighs – the sweep of her haunches and bottom, and her shapely legs!

'Thanks, darling,' I said appreciatively, 'now Alice!' And drawing Connie on to my knees, I kissed her lovingly.

Blushingly Alice complied, and with hands clasped behind her back she faced us, a piquant, provoking, demure, brown-eyed, dark-haired little English lassie, plump, juicy, appetising. She smiled mischievously at me as she watched Connie's eyes wander approvingly over her delicious little figure.

'Now in profile, please!'

She turned half round, and now we realised the subtle voluptuousness of Alice's naked figure – how her exquisitely full and luscious breasts were matched by her somewhat prominent rounded belly, both in turn being balanced by her glorious fleshy bottom and her fat thighs – the comparative shortness of her legs only adding piquancy to the whole; while her unusually conspicuous mount of Venus, with its tousle of dark, clustering silky hairs, proudly proclaimed itself as the delightful centre of her attractions.

'Thanks, darling!' we both exclaimed admiringly as we drew her to us and lovingly kissed her, to her evident delight and gratification.

'Now Connie darling!' I said, 'I want you to lie down on that couch!' and I removed my arm from her waist to allow her to rise.

'No, Jack!' she begged piteously and imploringly, her lovely eyes not far from tears, '*please* Jack! . . . don't insist!'

'You must do it, darling!' I said kindly but firmly as I raised her to her feet. 'Come dear!' and I led her to the couch and made her lie down.

'I must put the straps on you, Connie dear,' I said, 'not because I doubt your promise, but because I am sure you won't be able to lie still. Don't be frightened, dear!' I added, as I saw a look of terror come over her face, 'you are not going to be tortured, or tickled, or hurt, but will be treated most sweetly!'

Reluctantly Connie yielded. Quickly Alice attached the straps to her wrists, while I secured the other pair to her ankles; we set the machinery to work and soon she was lying flat on her back, her hands and feet secured to the four corners and the dark green upholstery throwing into high relief her lovely figure and dazzling fair hair and skin. I then blindfolded her very carefully in such a way that she could not get rid of the bandage by rubbing her head against the couch; now that Connie was at our mercy, I signalled to Fanny, who gleefully rushed to us noiselessly and hugged her mistress with silent delight.

'Now Alice dear!' I said, 'make love to Connie!'

'Oh–h!' cried Connie in shocked surprise, blushing so hotly that even her bosom was suffused with colour. But Alice was already on her knees by Connie's side and was passionately kissing her protesting mouth in the exuberance of her delight at the arrival at last of the much desired opportunity to satisfy on Connie's lovely person, cunt against cunt, her lascivious desires and concupiscence.

I slipped into a chair and took Fanny on my knees, and in sweet companionship, we settled ourselves down comfortably to watch Alice make love to Connie! My left arm was round Fanny's waist, the hand toying with the breasts which it could just command – while my right hand played lovingly with her cunt.

After Alice had relieved her excited feelings by showering kisses on Connie's lips with whispered fond endearments, she raised her head and contemplated, with an expression of intense delight, the naked figure of her friend which I had placed at her disposal! Then she proceeded to pass her hands lightly over Connie's flesh. Shakespeare sings (I substitute the feminine pronoun for the masculine one he uses):

> To win her heart she touched her here and there,
> Touches so soft that conquer chastity!

This is what Alice was doing! With lightly poised hands, she touched Connie on the most susceptible parts of herself – her armpits, navel, belly, and especially the soft tender insides of her thighs – evidently reserving for special attention her breasts and cunt. Soon the effect on Connie became apparent – her bosom began to palpitate in sweet agitation, while significant tremors ran through her limbs. 'Is it so nice then, darling?' cooed Alice, her eyes dancing with delight as she watched the effect of her operations on Connie's now quivering person; then she rested her lips on Connie's and gently took hold of her breasts!

'Oh, Alice!' cried Connie – but Alice closed her lips with her own, half choking her friend with her passionate kisses. Then raising her head again, she eagerly and delightedly inspected the delicious morsels of Connie's flesh that were imprisoned in her hands. 'Oh, you darlings!' she exclaimed as she squeezed them, 'you sweet things!' as she kissed them rapturously, 'oh what dear little nipples!' she cried, taking them in turn into her mouth, her hands all the while squeezing and caressing Connie's lovely breasts till she faintly murmured: 'Oh stop, darling!'

'Oh, my love! was I hurting you, darling?' cried Alice with gleaming eyes, as with a smile full of mischief towards us, she reluctantly released Connie's breasts. For a moment she hesitated as if uncertain what next to do, then her eyes rested on Connie's cunt, so sweetly defenceless; an idea seemed to seize her – with a look of delicious anticipation, she slipped her left arm under Connie's shoulders so as to embrace her, placed her lips on Connie's mouth, extended her right arm – and without giving Connie the least hint as to her intentions, she placed her hand on Connie's cunt, her slender forefinger resting on the orifice itself.

'Oh–h, Alice!' cried Connie, taken completely by surprise and wriggling voluptuously.

'Oh–h, Connie!' rapturously murmured Alice, between the hot kisses she was now raining on Connie's mouth – her forefinger beginning to agitate itself inquisitively but lovingly. 'Oh! darling! your cunny is sweet! sweet!' she murmured as her hand wandered all over Connie's private parts, now stroking and pressing her delicate mount of Venus, now twisting and pulling her hairs, now gently compressing the soft springy flesh between thumb and forefinger, now passing along the delicate shell-pink lips and finally gently inserting a finger between them and into the pouting orifice. 'I must! . . . I must look at it!' Quickly she withdrew her arm from under Connie's shoulders, gave her a long clinging kiss, then shifted her position by Connie's side, till her head commanded Connie's private parts; then she squared her arms, rested herself on Connie's belly, and with both hands proceeded to examine and study Connie's cunt, her eyes sparkling with delight.

Again she submitted Connie's delicious organ of sex to a most searching and merciless examination, one hand on each side of the now slightly gaping slit – stroking, squeezing, pressing, touching! Then with fingers poised gently but firmly on each side of the slit, Alice gently drew the lips apart and peered curiously into the shell-pink cavity of Connie's cunt – and after a prolonged inspection, she shifted her finger rather higher, again parted the lips and with rapt attention she gazed at Connie's clitoris which was now beginning to show signs of sexual excitement, Connie all this time quivering and wriggling under the touches of Alice's fingers.

Her curiosity apparently satisfied for the time, Alice raised her head and looked strangely and interrogatively at me. Comprehending her mute enquiry, I smiled and nodded. She smiled back, then dropping her head, she looked intently at Connie's cunt and imprinted a long clinging kiss in its very centre.

Connie squirmed violently, 'Oh–h–h!' she ejaculated in a half strangled voice. With a smile of intense delight, Alice repeated her kiss, then again and again, Connie at each repetition squirming and wriggling in the most delicious way, her vehement plunging telling Alice what flames her hot kisses had aroused in Connie.

Again she opened Connie's cunt, and keeping its tender lips wide apart she deposited between them and right inside the orifice itself a long lingering kiss which seemed to set Connie's blood on fire, for she began to plunge wildly with furious upward jerks and jogs of her hips and bottom, nearly dislodging Alice. The latter glanced merrily at us, her eyes brimming with mischief and delight – then straddled across Connie and arranged herself on her, so that her mouth commanded Connie's cunt while her stomach rested on Connie's breasts and her cunt lay poised over Connie's mouth, but not touching it.

Utterly taken aback by Alice's tactics, and in her innocence, not recognising the significance of the position Alice had assumed on her, she cried 'Oh, Alice! what are you doing?' Alice grinned delightedly at us, then lowered her head, ran her tongue lightly half a dozen times along the lips of Connie's cunt and then set to work to gamahuche her!

'Oh–h–h!' shrieked Connie, her voice almost strangled by the violence of the wave of lust that swept over her at the first touch of Alice's tongue. 'Oh–h! . . . oh–h–h . . . ' she ejaculated in her utter bewilderment and confusion as she abandoned herself to strangely intoxicating and thrilling sensations hitherto unknown to her; jerking herself madly upwards as if to meet Alice's tongue, her face in her agitated movements came against Alice's cunt before it dawned on her confused senses what the warm, moist, quivering, hairy object could be! In wild excitement Alice thoroughly searched Connie's cunt with her active tongue, darting it deeply in, playing delicately on the quivering lips, sucking and tickling her clitoris – and sending Connie into such a state of lust that I thought it wise to intervene.

'Stop dear!' I called out to Alice, who at once desisted, looking inter-rogatively at me. 'You're trying her too much! get off her now, dear, and let her recover herself a little – or you'll finish her, which we don't want yet!' Quickly comprehending the danger, Alice rolled off Connie, turned round, contemplated for a moment Connie's naked wriggling figure, then got on to her again, only this time lips to lips, bubbies against bubbies, and cunt against cunt; she clasped Connie closely to her as she arranged herself, murmuring passionately: 'Oh, Connie! . . . at last! . . . at last!' then com-menced to rub her cunt sweetly on Connie's.

'Oh–h–h, Alice!' breathed Connie rapturously as she responded to Alice's efforts by heaving and jogging herself upwards. 'Oh–h–h . . . darling!!' she panted brokenly, evidently feeling her ecstasy approaching to judge by her voluptuous wriggles and agitated movements as Alice rubbed herself vigorously against her cunt with riotous down-strokes of her luscious bottom. Quicker and quicker, faster and faster, wilder and wilder became the movements of both girls, Connie now plunging madly upwards, while Alice rammed herself down on her with fiercer and fiercer thrusts of her raging hips and buttocks – till the delicious crisis arrived.

'Con-nie! . . . Connie!' gasped Alice, as the indescribable spasm of spending thrilled voluptuously through her.

'Ah–h–h! . . . ah–h–h! . . . Ah–h–h–h! . . . ' ejaculated Connie rapturously, as she spent madly in exquisite convulsions, dead to everything but the delirious rapture that was thrilling through her as she lay tightly clasped in Alice's clinging arms.

The sight was too much for Fanny! With the intensest interest she had watched the whole of this exciting scene, parting her legs the better to accommodate my hand which now was actually grasping her cunt, my forefinger buried in her up to the knuckle, while my thumb rested on her clitoris – and she had already spent once deliciously. But the spectacle of the lascivious transports of her mistress on Connie set her blood on fire again; she recollected her similar experience in Alice's arms, the sensations that Alice's cunt communicated to hers, the delirious ecstasy of her discharge – and as the two girls neared their bliss, she began to agitate herself voluptuously on my knees, on my now active finger, keeping pace with them – till with an inarticulate murmur of, 'Oh! . . . oh–h, sir–r,' she inundated my hand with her love-juice, spending simultaneously with her mistress and her mistress's friend.

As soon as she emerged from her ecstatic trance, I whispered to her inaudibly: 'Bring the sponge and towel, dear!'

Noiselessly she darted off, sponged herself, then returned with a bowl of water, a sponge and a towel just as Alice slowly raised herself off Connie, with eyes still humid with lust and her cunt bedewed with love-juice. I took her fondly in my arms and kissed her tenderly, while Fanny quickly removed all traces of her discharge from her hairs, then proceeded to pay the same delicate attention to Connie, whose cunt she now touched for the first time.

Presently we heard Connie murmur: 'Mayn't I get up now, Jack?'

'Not yet, darling!' I replied lovingly as I stooped and kissed her. 'You have to make me happy now!'

'No Jack! please!' she whispered, but Alice intervened. 'Yes, darling! you must let Jack have you! You must taste again the real article,' she cooed. 'Let me work you into condition again!' – and she signalled to Fanny, who instantly knelt by Connie and began playing with her dainty little breasts and feeling her cunt, her eyes sparkling with delight at thus being permitted to handle Connie – who not noting the difference of touch (as Fanny's ministrations to her cunt had accustomed Connie to her fingers) lay still in happy ignorance of the change of operator.

Soon Fanny's fingers began to bring about the desired recovery: Connie's breasts began to stiffen and grow tense, her body began to tremble in gentle agitation. She was ready – and so was I!

Without a word I slipped on to her. 'Oh, Jack!' she murmured as I took her into my arms, holding up her lips to be kissed – no reluctance now! My rampant prick found her sweet hole and gently effected an entrance; she was terribly tight, but her discharge had well lubricated the sweet passage into her interior, and inch by inch, I forced myself into her till my prick was buried in her cunt, she trembling and quivering in my clasp, her involuntary flinchings and sighs confessing the pain attending her penetration! But then once she had admitted me into her and I began the sweet up-and-down movement, she went into transports of delight, accommodating herself deliciously to me as, with lips closely against each other, we exchanged hot kisses! Then I set to work to fuck Connie in earnest. Straining her to me, till her breasts were flattened against my chest and I could feel every flutter of her sweet body, I let myself go, ramming into her faster and faster, more and more wildly – till unable any longer to restrain myself, I surrendered to Love's delicious ecstasy and spent madly into Connie just as she flooded my prick in rapturous bliss, quivering under me in the most voluptuous way.

We lay closely clasped together, till our mutual ecstatic trance slowly died away, then with a sign I bade Fanny disappear. As soon as she had vanished, Alice removed the bandage from Connie's eyes. As they met mine, bashfully and shamefacedly, blushing deeply at thus finding herself naked in my arms, Connie timidly held up her mouth to me – instantly my lips were on hers and we exchanged long lingering kisses till we panted for breath. Gently I released her from my clasp and rose off her and with Alice's help unfastened her, and Alice gently led her away to her alcove where she sedulously attended to her, while Fanny silently but delightedly did the same for me.

It was now four o'clock only – we had a good hour before us. There was now no possible doubt that Connie had surrendered herself to the pleasures of tribadism and lesbian love as far as Alice was concerned. So when the girls rejoined me (Connie with a tender look on her face) and we had refreshed ourselves and recovered our sexual appetites and powers, I said to Connie, 'Now dear, you are entitled to take your revenge on Alice – will you . . . ?'

She cast a look of love at Alice, who blushed sweetly, then turning to me she murmured. 'Please, Jack!' at the same time giving me a delicious kiss.

'Come along, Alice!' I said as we all rose and I led her to the couch – the veritable altar of Venus. 'How will you have her, Connie?' I asked, as Alice stood nervously awaiting the disposal of her sweet person.

Connie blushed, then with a glance at Alice she replied: 'Tie her down, Jack, just as you did me!'

Blushingly Alice lay down, and soon Connie and I had her fastened down in the desired position.

'Will you have her blindfolded, dear?' I enquired.

Connie hesitated, looking oddly at Alice – then replied, 'No Jack! I want to see her eyes!' so significantly that Alice involuntarily quivered as she coloured hotly again.

'May I do just whatever I like to Alice, Jack?' asked Connie almost hesitatingly, with a fresh access of colour.

'Anything in reason, dear!' I replied with a smile. 'You mustn't bite her bubbies off or stitch up her cunt, for instance.' Alice quivered while Connie laughed. 'And you must leave her alive, for I am to follow you!'

'Oh, Jack!' exclaimed Alice at this intimation, blushing prettily.

Connie turned eagerly to me. 'Are you going to . . . fuck her?' she asked with sparkling eyes. I nodded, smiling at her eagerness.

'And may I watch you?' she demanded.

'Why, certainly, dear – and perhaps help me! Now what are you going to do to Alice? See how impatiently she is waiting!'

Both girls laughed, Alice a trifle uneasily. Connie looked intently at her for a moment, then seating herself by Alice's side, she began playing with Alice's breasts, keeping her eyes steadily fixed on Alice's. 'Your bubbies are too big for my hands, darling!' she said presently as she stooped to kiss her, 'but they are lovely!' And she squeezed them tenderly for a while – then she deserted them, shifted her position and began to feel Alice's cunt, which she lovingly stroked and caressed.

'Your cunny *is* fat, darling!' she exclaimed presently with heightened colour as she held Alice's cunt compressed between her finger and thumb and gently squeezed the soft springy flesh, while Alice squirmed involuntarily.

Suddenly Connie leant forward, took Alice's face in her hands and whispered: 'Darling, I'm going to . . . fuck you twice, eh?' and lovingly kissed her, while Alice's eyes sought mine shamefacedly.

Quickly Connie got on to Alice, took her into her arms, then keeping her head raised so as to look right into Alice's eyes, she began to rub her cunt against Alice's, gently and slowly at first with a circular grinding sort of movement; presently her action quickened, then became more and more irregular. Soon Connie was rubbing herself up and down Alice's cunt, with quick agitated strokes of her bottom, all the while intently watching Alice's eyes as if to gauge her friend's sensations. Soon both girls began to plunge and heave riotously, Alice especially, as they both felt the crisis approaching – then came a veritable storm of confused heavings, thrustings and plungings.

'Kiss . . . me . . . dar . . . ling!' ejaculated Alice, now on the verge of spending. But Connie only shook her head with a loving smile, rammed her cunt against Alice's fiercely, intent on Alice's now humid eyes and apparently restraining her own discharge. A frantic heave from Alice – 'Ah–h–h, darling,' she gasped as her eyes half closed in ecstasy – then she spent with delicious quivering.

Immediately Connie glued her lips to Alice's, agitated herself rapidly against Alice's cunt, 'Al-ice!' she breathed in her delirious frenzy, a spasm thrilled through her, and Alice's cunt received her love-juice as she spent ecstatically.

For some moments the girls lay silent, only half conscious, motionless save for the involuntary thrills that shot through them. Then Connie raised her head and with the smile of the victor surveyed Alice, whose eyes now began to open languidly. She blushed deliciously as she met Connie's glances and raised her mouth as if inviting a kiss. Instantly Connie complied with passionate delight. 'Was it nice, darling?' I heard her whisper. 'Oh, Connie, just heavenly!' murmured Alice tenderly and with loving kisses. 'Are you ready again, darling?' whispered Connie eagerly. 'Yes! yes!' replied Alice softly, beginning to agitate herself under Connie.

'Our mouths together this time, darling, eh!' whispered Connie excitedly, 'don't stop kissing me, darling!' she added tenderly as she responded to Alice's significant movements under her and set to work to rub her cunt against Alice's. Soon both girls were hard at work with their cunts squeezed against each other, slit to slit, clitoris against clitoris, Connie's bottom and hips swaying and oscillating voluptuously while Alice jerked herself up madly. With mouths glued to each other they plunged, curvetted, wriggled, squirmed, till the blissful ecstasy overtook them both simultaneously, when madly they bedewed each other with their love-juice to the accompaniment of the most exquisite quiverings and thrillings, utterly absorbed in rapture!

With a deep drawn sigh of intense satisfaction, Connie presently rose slowly off Alice, and tenderly contemplated her as she lay still fastened by her widely extended limbs to the four corners of the couch, her closed eyes and her involuntary tremors indicating that she was still tasting bliss. Then Connie turned to me and whispered rapturously: 'Oh, Jack, she is sweet!' I kissed her lovingly and resting her on my knees, I sponged and dried her, then begged her to perform the same kind office for Alice, whose cunt was positively glistening with her own and Connie's spendings. As soon as Alice felt the sponge at work, she dreamily opened her eyes, and on recognising me she made as if to rise; but when she found herself checked by her fastenings and realised that she was now to be fucked by me, she smiled somewhat uneasily as our eyes met – for often as she had tasted love's ecstasy in my arms, she had invariably been free, now she was tied down in such a way as to be absolutely helpless, and in this equivocal position, she had to accommodate herself to me and to satisfy my lustful passions and desires. But I smiled encouragingly back to her, seated myself by her side, and tenderly embracing her defenceless body I whispered: 'Darling, may I have you like this?'

Her eyes beamed gratefully on me, full of love; she was now perfectly happy because I had left it to her to say whether or not she would be fucked while tied down in the most shamelessly abandoned attitude that any girl could be placed in. So with Love's own light in her shining eyes and with pretty blushes on her cheeks, Alice whispered back tenderly: 'Yes, darling, yes!'

Promptly I got on her, took her in my arms, and gently drove my prick home up her cunt. 'Do you like it like this, darling?' I murmured softly, 'shall I go on?' She nodded sweetly, our lips met, and I began to fuck her.

Tied down as she was, she was simply delicious! I had had first Fanny and then Connie in precisely the same attitude, but voluptuous as was the act of fucking them so, the pleasure fell short of what I was now tasting! To a certain extent both Fanny and Connie were unwilling recipients of my erotic favours – Fanny was really ravished and Connie practically so, and their movements under me were the outcome of fright, shame, and even pain; but Alice was yielding herself sweetly to my caprices and was doing her best to accommodate her captive body to my movements. Perhaps this was the reason, perhaps her little plump rounded figure suited the attitude better than the taller and more slender forms of Fanny and Connie, but whatever may have been the reason, the result was undeniable, and Alice fucked as a helpless captive was simply delicious! Her double spend under Connie made her usual quick response to Love's imperious demands arrive more slowly than was customary with her; and as this was my fourth course that afternoon, our fucking was protracted to a delicious extent, and I adopted every method and variation known to me to intensify our exquisite pleasure.

Commencing slowly, I fucked Alice with long strokes, drawing my prick nearly out of her cunt and then shoving it well home again, a procedure which always delighted her and which she welcomed with appreciative and warm kisses. Then I agitated myself more rapidly on her, shoving, pressing, thrusting, ramming, now fast, now slow, holding her so tightly clasped that her breasts were flattened against my chest – while she, panting and gasping, plunged, wriggled and heaved herself wildly under me, in her loyal endeavours to cooperate with me to bring about Love's ecstasy. Presently she thrilled exquisitely under me! Fired by her delicious transports, I redoubled my efforts, as did she also – I began to feel my seminal resources respond to my demand on them; soon we both were overtaken by the tempestuous prelude to the blissful crisis – and then came the exquisite consummation of our wildly excited sexual desires! With a half-strangled, 'Ah h–h . . . Jack!' Alice spent in rapturous convulsions just as I madly shot into her my boiling tribute.

Oblivious to everything but the delicious satisfaction of our overwrought feelings, we lay as if in a trance! We were roused by Connie's gentle anxious voice, 'Alice! . . . Alice! . . . Alice dear!' as she set to work to undo Alice's fastenings. Taking the hint, I rose after giving Alice a long lingering parting kiss, then we helped her to get up and Connie tenderly took her off at once to the girls' alcove, while I retired to mine – where Fanny deliciously attended to me, her eyes sparkling with gratified pleasure at the recollection of the voluptuous spectacle she had been permitted to witness through the peephole.

As it was now getting late, we all dressed ourselves, and after a tender parting, I put Connie and Alice into a taxi and started them off home. On returning to my room, I found Fanny ready to depart. She was full of delighted gratitude to me for having managed that she should see all that went on and also have a share in the afternoon's proceedings; and when I slipped a couple of sovereigns into her hand, I had the greatest difficulty in making her accept them. Finally she did so, saying shyly and with pretty blushes: 'You've only got to call me, sir, and I'll come!' I kissed her tenderly, put her into a hansom and sent her home; then I wended my way to my club, where in bumpers of champagne, I recruited exhausted nature and drank to the three sweet cunts I had, that afternoon, enjoyed and their delicious owners, Alice, Connie and Fanny!

# Chapter Eight

I did not see anything of Alice for some little time after the conversion of Connie, but I did not distress myself for I knew she would be in the first flush of her newly developed tribadic ardour and newly born passion for her own sex and would be hard put to satisfy Connie and Fanny and I felt sure that she would of her own option come to me before long. Meanwhile another matter began to occupy my serious attention.

A few months ago, I had made the acquaintance of Lady Betty Bashe at the house of a mutual friend; she was a consolable widow of something under forty and was busy introducing her daughter into Society, and for some perverse reason, she took it into her head that I would make an excellent son-in-law and proceeded to hunt me persistently – her daughter aiding and abetting her vigorously – till they became a real nuisance.

I had taken a dislike to both mother and daughter from our first meeting, although they both were decidedly attractive. Lady Betty was a tall, robust, buxom woman after the type of Rubens' fleshy females, but somewhat more overdeveloped, and owed a good deal to her *corsetière* – I guessed that without her stays she would be almost exuberant, but nevertheless a fine armful. Molly (her daughter) was a small and dainty edition of her mother, and with the added freshness and juiciness of her eighteen years she was really a tit-bit. But both mother and daughter were silly, affected, insincere and unscrupulous, and Lady Betty's juvenile airs and youthful affectations only tended to confirm my distaste for her.

I had told Lady Betty plainly one day that I was not in the matrimonial market; but she nevertheless continued to pursue me pertinaciously till it became intolerable – and I determined I would stop her at any cost.

Matters culminated at a dinner given by the same hostess whose kindly suggestion brought about the reconciliation of Alice and myself, as already related in the first chapter. She, of course, again gave me Alice as my dinner partner, an arrangement that did not commend itself to Lady Betty. I think she must have taken a little too much of our hostess's champagne, but in the middle of dinner, she called out in a tone that attracted everyone's attention and checked the conversation, 'Jack, we're coming to lunch the day after tomorrow; mind you're in!'

I was intensely annoyed, first by the use of my Christian name and then by the intolerable air of proprietorship she assumed; but the look of distress on my dear little hostess's face impelled me to face the music. So I promptly responded with a smile: 'That will be very nice of you, Lady Betty; you shall have some of my famous soufflé, and you will be the first to see my new curios!' The conversation then turned on my curios and soon became general, much to my hostess's relief – and the rest of the dinner passed off pleasantly.

As I was driving Alice home, she said sympathetically: 'Poor Jack, what a bad time you'll have the day after tomorrow!'

'Not at all, dear,' I replied cheerily, 'somebody else will have the bad time – for unless I am greatly mistaken, there will be a lot of squealing in the Snuggery on that afternoon, her ladyship will be made to remember the pleasures of married life, and there will be one virgin less in the world!'

Alice started in surprise. 'You don't mean to say, Jack, that you mean to . . . to . . . ?'

'I do!' I said stoutly. 'I'm sick of this annoyance and mean to stop it. Come and see the fun, dear?'

'I will, gladly,' Alice replied energetically; 'but Jack, do ask Connie also, for we both have a certain bone to pick with her ladyship!'

'Won't you include Fanny also in the party, dear?' I asked mischievously.

'Jack! that would be just lovely!' Alice exclaimed with sparkling eyes. 'Yes Jack! please let Fanny come! we'll then be three couples – very convenient, sir – and she'll be so useful in the undressing and the . . . the . . . sponging! Yes Jack! let's have Fanny also – then we can have a regular orgy with Lady Betty and Molly to amuse ourselves with!' she gloated, eagerly hugging me in her excitement while one hand wandered down to the fly of my trousers.

I was hugely taken by her idea – a luscious woman and a voluptuous maiden on whom to exercise our lustful ingenuity. 'A most excellent idea, darling,' I replied, 'you bring Connie with you, let Fanny follow and hide in my alcove till she's wanted, as before – and we'll give Lady Betty and Molly an afternoon's entertainment that they won't easily forget, and also have a heavenly time ourselves!'

Alice smiled delightedly; then cuddling up to me she whispered: 'Now Jack, I'm going to ask a favour; I'm longing to be . . . fucked in my own little room, in the middle of my own familiar things, on my own bed! Come in tonight, darling, and do me!'

'Yes! . . . yes! . . . yes!' I whispered passionately, punctuating my reply with kisses and noting with delight how she thrilled with sweet anticipation. Soon we arrived at her flat; soon Fanny, with pretty blushes, ushered me into Alice's dainty bedroom; and on her little bed and in the piquant surroundings of her most intimate self, Alice, stark naked, received me in her arms and expired deliciously five times, while I twice madly spent into her. So excited was I by my voluptuous experience of fucking an unmarried girl in her own bedroom and on her own bed that I began a third course – but Alice murmured: 'No Jack darling! not again! . . . I've got to console Fanny presently, and she'll be very excited!' – whereupon I reluctantly rose off her, dressed, and after a hundred kisses (not confined to her mouth by any means) I went home, imagining on my way Fanny in her mistress's arms, the cunts of both in sweet conjunction.

The eventful afternoon came round. Lady Betty was disgusted at finding that she and Molly were not going to have me exclusively at their mercy all the afternoon, and vented her spite on Alice and Connie more than once in her ill-bred way; but they knew their vengeance was at hand and took her insulting impertinence with well-bred indifference. In due course we were all collected in the Snuggery, Fanny concealed in my alcove.

'Jack, why don't you have those nasty pulleys taken down, they are not pretty, they're useless, and they're horridly in the way!' exclaimed Lady Betty, as she narrowly escaped coming against one.

'Why, they form my gymnasium, your ladyship!' I replied, 'I couldn't do without them!'

Molly now joined in eagerly. 'How do you work them, Jack?' she asked, 'what's the idea of the loops? I'm a dab at gymnastics but never saw this arrangement before.'

The loops are wristlets, Miss Molly,' I replied: 'you must fasten them round your wrists and then grasp the rope with your hand – thus you divide your weight between wrist and hand instead of it all coming on the fingers, as in a trapeze.'

Of course all this was arrant nonsense and rubbish, yet this 'dab in gymnastics' believed it all solemnly; it was a fair sample of her ways.

'Oh, how clever!' Molly exclaimed in her affected fulsome way. 'Let me try, Jack! Alice please fasten me!' Alice complied demurely with a sly glance at me.

'I used to be the best girl at gymnastics at school,' said Lady Betty complacently. 'Molly takes after me.' By this time Alice had fastened the ropes to Molly's wrists and the latter began to swing herself slowly and gently backwards and forwards.

'Oh, mother, it *is* jolly!' cried Molly. 'Do try it!'

Ever anxious to show her juvenility, Lady Betty rose briskly. 'Will you fasten me up, Jack?' she said as she raised her arms for the purpose – I'm afraid I'm too old and heavy for this sort of thing now! Will the ropes bear me, Jack?'

'They carry *me*, Lady Betty,' I replied as I fastened the wristlets to her arms, 'why malign yourself so cruelly?'

Lady Betty glanced at me approvingly for my pretty speech, little dreaming that she and Molly were now our prisoners by their own actions. Alice and I exchanged exulting looks – we had our victims safe!

Following Molly's lead, Lady Betty swung herself gently to and fro a few times, then stopped remarking: 'I can't say I like it, dear, but I'm not as young as you are! Let me loose, Jack!'

Instead of doing so, I passed my arms round her buxom waist and drew her to me as I replied: 'Not yet, dear Lady Betty – we're going to have some fun with you and Miss Molly first!'

Something significant in my voice or in my eyes told her of what was in store for her and her daughter! She flushed nervously, then paled, while Molly, startled, stopped swinging herself, as Alice and Connie quietly took up positions one on each side of her.

For a moment there was dead silence, then Lady Betty said somewhat unsteadily: 'I don't follow you at all, Jack, loose us both at once please; I don't mind a joke in the least but you're going too far, sir!'

'Will this help you to understand our ideas, dear Lady Betty?' I rejoined with a mischievous smile as I slipped my hand under her clothes and pulled them up till it rested on her fat thighs.

'Oh!' she screamed, taken utterly aback by the quickness of my action and its most unexpected nature. 'How dare you, sir!' she shrieked as she felt my hand forcing its way upwards and between her legs. 'Stop! . . . stop!' she yelled, now furious with rage at such an outrage, while Molly screamed sympathetically, horror-stricken.

I withdrew my hand. 'You're awfully nice and plump, dear lady!' I remarked cruelly, as I watched her flustered face and heaving bosom; 'if the rest of you resembles what I have just had the pleasure of feeling, you'll give us an even more delicious time than we expected! We really must undress you to see; you won't mind, will you?'

'*What*!!' cried Lady Betty, staring wildly at me as if unable to believe her ears, while Molly shrieked hysterically: 'No, no.'

'Make Molly comfortable in that easy-chair, dears, till we want her,' I said quietly to Alice and Connie, who instantly pushed the chair of treachery up to Molly and gently forced her into it till the arms firmly held her prisoner; then they took the ropes off her wrists, as she was sufficiently under control now, Molly all the time struggling frantically, shrieking: 'Oh, mother! . . . help! help!' But Lady Betty had her own troubles to attend to, for to add to her bewilderment, Fanny suddenly appeared before her in response to my signal – and the sight of this trim, smart lady's maid, ready to commence to undress her, was evidently an awful proof that we intended to carry out our intentions as to her and her daughter.

'Undress Lady Betty, Fanny,' I commanded quietly, and Fanny instantly began to do so.

'I won't have it! . . . I won't have it! . . . stop her, Jack!' screamed Lady Betty, now purple with wrathful indignation and the sense of her power-lessness, for her frantic tugs at the ropes availed her nothing. 'Mother! oh mother dear!' yelled Molly in an agony of dismay as she saw Fanny deftly remove Lady Betty's hat, and then proceed to unfasten her dress. Intent on going to her mother's help, she made desperate efforts to drag the heavy armchair after her, but Connie easily frustrated her attempts at rescue; and seeing that Molly was safe in Connie's hands, I signalled to Alice to assist Fanny – which she was delighted to do. Between the three of us, Lady Betty's clothes slipped off her in a way that must have been marvellous to her; by the time we had reduced her to her stays, bare legged and bare armed, she evidently saw she was doomed, and in place of threats she began to plead for some mercy. But we were deaf to her prayers and entreaties; off came her stays, then her chemise and vest, leaving her standing with only her drawers on.

'For God's sake, Jack, don't strip me naked!' she shrieked in terrible distress, her face crimson with shame. I simply nodded to Alice; a twitch at the tape, and down came the drawers – leaving Lady Betty standing naked from head to foot!

'Oh!' she wailed as her agonised eyes instinctively sought Molly's and read in her daughter's face her horrible anguish at the sight of her naked mother. 'Cover me up! for God's sake, cover me up, Jack!' she piteously pleaded as she involuntarily squeezed her legs together in a despairing attempt to shield her private parts from view. Just then I touched the spring and made the ropes draw her off the ground, so that Alice and Fanny could remove the tumbled mass of her garments. 'Oh!–h–h!' she shrieked, as she found herself dangling by her wrists, her struggles to touch the ground exposing her person deliciously. Quickly Fanny cleared away Lady Betty's clothes; then I let her down till she could stand erect comfortably, and joined Alice and Connie at Molly's side, my intention now being to compel Molly to inspect her naked mother and to harrow her already tortured feelings by criticising Lady Betty's naked charms.

She must have been a simply magnificent woman in her prime; even now, in spite of an exuberance of flesh, Lady Betty was enough to provoke any man into concupiscence with her massive though shapely arms and legs, her grand hips and round fat thighs, her full ample belly, and her enormous breasts, which though naturally pendulous, still maintained their upstanding sauciness to a marvellous degree. But what attracted all our eyes (even her daughter's) was the hair which grew over her cunt. I do not think I ever saw such an enormous tract – a dinner plate would not have covered it! It seemed to spring from somewhere between Lady Betty's legs, it clustered so thickly over the cunt itself that her crack was quite invisible, it extended all over her groin and abdomen and reached her navel – closely curling and silky and fully two inches deep all over her mount of Venus! A simply wonderful sight!

In spite of the attraction of Lady Betty's naked figure, I closely watched Molly. She had been terribly distressed during the undressing of her mother, especially when the naked flesh began to be exposed, and she hysterically joined in her mother's futile prayers and piteous pleadings, though she watched her quickly growing nudity with a fascination she could not resist; when the terrible climax arrived and Lady Betty stood naked, the poor girl uttered a heart-broken shriek as she buried her face in her hands, but I could see that every now and then she glanced stealthily through her fingers at the mother's naked body as if unable to resist the fascinating temptation.

I turned to the three girls, who with gleaming eyes were devouring Lady Betty's naked charms, their arms round each other. Our eyes met. 'Isn't she splendid, Jack!' cried Alice enthusiastically, 'what a lovely time she'll give us all!' and they laughed delightedly as Lady Betty shivered.

'And you, my pet!' cooed Connie to Molly, 'are you anything like Mummy?' – and she began to pass her hands over Molly's corsage as if to sample her body. The girls' individual predilections were clear even at this early stage – Alice was captivated by Lady Betty's fleshy amplitude, while Connie coveted Molly's still budding charms.

'Oh, don't, Mrs Blunt, don't!' cried Molly flushing deeply as she endeavoured to protect herself with her hands, thereby uncovering her face. This was what I desired – I intended that Lady Betty should now be felt in front of her daughter, and that Molly should be forced to look at her mother and witness her shame and anguish and involuntary struggles, while my hands wandered lasciviously over Lady Betty's naked body and invaded her most private parts.

'Sling Molly up again, girls,' I said quietly.

'No, no,' screamed Molly in an agony of apprehension, but in a trice she was standing upright with her hands secured over her head, her eyes full of silent terror.

'Do you think you could slip Molly's drawers off her without disturbing the rest of her garments?' I asked.

'Yes, of course!' replied Connie – and the three girls dropped on their knees round Molly; their hands disappeared under her skirts, her wriggles and cries and agitated movements proclaiming how she was upset by their attacking hands. Then came a shriek of despair from her – and Connie rose with an air of triumph, waving Molly's drawers!

'Good!' I exclaimed with a smile of congratulation. 'Now, Connie, take Molly in your arms and hold her steady; Alice and Fanny, slip your hands under Molly's clothes and behind her, till you can each command a cheek of her bottom!' Merrily the girls carried out my commands, Molly crying, 'Don't, don't!' as she felt the hands of Alice and Fanny on her bottom.

'Now, Molly, I'm going to amuse myself with your mother! You must watch her intently! If I see you avert your eyes from her, whatever may be the cause, I'll signal to Alice and Fanny – and they will give you such a pinching that you won't repeat the offence. Now be careful!' and I turned towards Lady Betty who (having heard every word) was now trembling with nervous apprehension as she brokenly ejaculated, 'Don't touch me! . . . don't touch me!' But ignoring her pleadings, I passed behind her, slipped my arms round her and caught hold of her large full breasts.

'Oh–h–h!' shrieked Lady Betty, 'Oh, mother!' screamed Molly, colouring painfully as she watched her mother writhing in my embrace with her breasts in my hands. 'Don't, Jack!' again shrieked Lady Betty as I proceeded to squeeze and mould and toy with her voluptuous semi-globes, revelling in their exquisite fleshiness, now pulling, now stroking, now pressing them against each other – causing her intense distress but affording myself the most delicious pleasure!

I glanced at the group of four girls facing Lady Betty and me. Alice, Connie and Fanny were simply beaming with smiles and gloating delightedly at the sight of Lady Betty's sufferings, while poor Molly with staring eyes and flushing face, gazed horror-stricken at her tortured and naked mother, not daring to avert her eyes.

After a few more minutes of toying with Lady Betty's huge breasts, I suddenly slipped my hands downwards over her hairy fat belly and attacked her cunt! 'Mother! oh mother!' shrieked Molly hysterically as she saw my eager fingers disappear in the luxuriant growth that so effectually covered her mother's cunt – and utterly unable any longer to endure the sight of her mother's shame and agony, she let her head drop on her heaving bosom. 'Oh! my God! don't, Jack!' yelled Lady Betty, her face crimson with shame, her eyes half closed, as she frantically attempted to defeat my hands by squeezing her plump thighs together! But it was useless! With both hands, I set to work thoroughly to explore the fattest and largest cunt I had ever touched, at the same time nodding meaningfully to Alice. Instantly came a series of ear-piercing shrieks from Molly, whose wriggles were almost more than Connie could subdue; she continued to keep her face averted for a few seconds, then the agony of the pinches became more than she could endure – and slowly and reluctantly she nerved herself again to contemplate her mother, who was writhing and wriggling frenziedly and filling the room with her inarticulate cries as my fingers tortured her cunt with their subtle titillation, one indeed being lodged up it to its knuckle! For a minute or so, I continued to explore and feel Lady Betty's delicious private parts, till it was evident I was testing both her and her daughter beyond their power of endurance – for Lady Betty was now nearly in convulsions while her daughter was on the verge of hysterics – and unwillingly, I removed my hands from her cunt and left the tortured lady to recover herself, first gently placing her in the chair of treachery and releasing her arms.

'What does she feel like, Jack?' cried Alice and Connie excitedly as I joined them by Molly.

'Gloriously ripe flesh, dears,' I replied, 'and the biggest cunt I ever came across!' They looked joyously at each other, their eyes sparkling with pleasurable anticipation.

'And Molly?' I asked in my turn.

'Just delicious, Jack!' replied Alice delightedly, 'do let us undress her now!'

'Certainly!' I replied – whereupon Molly screamed affrightedly: 'No, no, oh mother, they're going to undress me!'

'Oh no, Jack! for pity's sake, don't!' cried Lady Betty, now fully roused by the danger threatening her daughter. 'Do anything you like to me, but spare my Molly, she's only a girl still!'

But Connie, Alice and Fanny were already hard at work on Molly, whose stays were now visible in spite of her frantic exertions to thwart their active hands. As the girls did not require any help from me, I returned and stood behind Lady Betty, who with the intensest anguish in her face was distractedly watching the clothes being taken off her daughter. 'For God's sake, Jack, stop them!' she cried agonisedly, stretching her clasped hands towards me appealingly, as if unable to endure the sight.

'No, Lady Betty!' I replied with a cruel smile. 'Molly must contribute her share of the afternoon's entertainment! We must have her naked!'

'Oh, my God!' she wailed, letting her head drop on her agitated bosom in her despair. Just then Molly screamed loudly; we looked up and saw her in her chemise struggling in Connie's grasp, while Alice and Fanny dragged off her shoes and stockings. Promptly they then proceeded to undo the shoulder fastenings of her two remaining garments and step quickly clear – down these slid, and with a bitter cry of 'Oh–h–h, Oh, mother!' poor Molly stood naked!

'Oh, my God!' again shrieked Lady Betty, frantically endeavouring, chair and all, to go to her daughter's rescue – but I quietly checked her efforts. 'My darling! I can't help you,' she wailed, hiding her face in her hands in her anguish at the sight of her daughter's helpless nakedness. My eyes met the girls' – they were gleaming with delight; they joined me behind Lady Betty and together we stood and critically inspected poor shrinking Molly's naked person!

Alice had chosen the correct word – Molly naked was just delicious, so exquisitely shaped, so perfectly made, so lithe and yet so charmingly rounded and plump, so juicy and fresh, so virgin! She took after her mother in her large firm upstanding breasts with saucy little nipples, and few girls could have showed at eighteen the quantity of dark moss-like hair that clustered so prettily over her cunt – which like her mother's was peculiarly fat and prominent; and I noticed with secret pleasure how Connie's eyes glistened as they dwelt rapturously on Molly's tender organ of sex.

For a minute or so we gazed admiringly at Molly's charming nudity then Alice whispered, 'Jack, let us put them side by side and then examine them.'

'An excellent idea!' I replied, rewarding her with a kiss. We moved Molly's pulleys closer to the pillar on her left, then wheeled Lady Betty across to Molly's right and quickly slung her up in spite of her stubborn resistance – then mother and daughter stood naked side by side!

They formed a most provokingly fascinating spectacle. It was delicious to trace how Molly's exquisite curves were echoed by her mother's exuberant fleshiness – how both the bodies were framed on similar lines – how the matron and the virgin were unmistakably indicated! Conscious that our eyes were devouring them greedily and travelling over their naked persons both mother and daughter kept their faces down and steadily averted their eyes from us.

'Turn them so that they face each other,' I said presently. Quickly Connie and Alice executed my order, Connie taking Molly.

'Oh, how can you be so cruel!' moaned Lady Betty as Alice forced her round till she faced Molly. There was just space to stand behind each of them while mother and daughter were about four feet apart. I saw their eyes meet for a moment, horrible dread visible in both.

Their profiles naked were an interesting study – Molly lithe, graceful, with exquisite curves – Lady Betty paunchy and protuberant, but most voluptuous. One striking feature both possessed, the hair on their cunts stood out conspicuously like bushes.

After we had to some extent satisfied our eyes, I said to the girls: 'I've no doubt Lady Betty and Molly would like to be alone for a few minutes, so let us go off and undress. And we disappeared into the alcoves, Fanny coming into mine so as not to crowd her mistress and Connie.

We undressed quickly in silence, being desirous of hearing all that passed between our naked victims, and presently we heard Molly whisper agitatedly, 'Oh, mother, what are they going to do to us?'

'Darling, I can only guess!' replied Lady Betty faintly; 'their going off to undress makes me fear that you and I will have to satisfy their . . . lust! Darling, I'm very afraid that Jack will . . . violate you and outrage me, and then hand us over to the girls – and girls can be very cruel to their own sex!'

'Oh, mother,' stammered Molly horror-stricken, 'what shall I do if Jack . . . wants me?' And her voice shook with terror.

Before Lady Betty could reply, Connie appeared, naked save for shoes and stockings. She went straight up to Molly, threw her arms round the shrinking girl and passionately kissed her flushed face, gently rubbing her breasts against Molly's and murmuring: 'Oh, you darling! . . . oh, you sweet thing!' Then she slipped behind Molly and gently seized her lovely breasts.

'Don't, Mrs Blunt!' shrieked Molly, turning and twisting herself agitatedly. Just then Alice emerged, and seeing how Connie was amusing herself, she quickly slipped behind Lady Betty and caught hold of her huge breasts and began to squeeze and handle them in a way that drew cries from Lady Betty. It was delicious to watch the mother and the daughter writhing and wriggling but I did not want their cunts touched yet by the girls and so appeared on the scene with Fanny, whom I had refrained with difficulty from fucking when she exposed herself naked in my alcove.

'Stop, darlings!' I commanded, and reluctantly Connie and Alice obeyed. Under my instructions they pushed the padded music bench under the skylight – then we released Lady Betty's wrists from the pulleys and forced her on to her back on the bench, where I held her down while Alice and Connie and Fanny fastened first her arms and then her legs to the longitudinal bars of the bench, in fact trussed her like a fowl, her arms and legs being on each side of the bench, her knees being separated by the full width, thus exposing her cunt to our attack!

Having thus fixed the mother, we turned our attention to her trembling daughter. We placed a chair in a position to command a view of Lady Betty; I seated myself on it, and the girls then dragged Molly to me and forced her on to my knees with her back to me. While I held her firmly, they drew her arms backwards and made them fast to the sides of the chair – then seizing her delicate ankles they forced her legs apart and tied them to the chair legs. In short they tied Molly on to the chair as she sat in my lap, thereby placing her breasts and cunt at my disposal and in easy reach of my hands.

It is needless to say that this was not effected without the most desperate resistance on the part of Lady Betty and Molly. The former struggled like a tigress, till we got her down on the bench, while Molly had really to be carried and placed on my knees. But now, both were satisfactorily fixed, and nervously awaited their fate, their bosoms panting and heaving with their desperate exertions.

'Now, my darlings, Lady Betty is at your disposal!' I said with a cruel smile, 'I'll take charge of Molly! My pet,' I added as the girls hastily arranged among themselves how to deal with Lady Betty, 'I'll try and make you comprehend what your mother from time to time is feeling!'

'Let me have charge of Lady Betty's breasts,' cried Connie.

'Excellent!' cried Alice, 'Fanny and I want her cunt between us! Now your ladyship,' she added as Fanny knelt between Lady Betty's legs and Connie, stationing herself by her shoulders, greedily seized Lady Betty's breasts in her little hands, 'you're not to spend till we give you leave!' – and kneeling down between Connie and Fanny and opposite the object of her admiration, she placed her hands on the forest of hair and while Fanny's fingers attacked Lady Betty's crack, Alice proceeded to play with Lady Betty's cunt.

'Oh, my God! stop!' yelled the unhappy lady as her breasts and private parts thus became the prey of the now excited girls.

'Mother! oh mother!' shrieked Molly at the sight of her naked mother being thus tortured. Just then I gently seized Molly's breasts. 'Don't Jack!' she screamed, agitating herself on my lap, her plump bottom moving deliciously on my thighs and stimulating my prick to wild erection. Molly's breasts were simply luscious, and I handled them delightedly as I watched her mother's agonies and listened to her cries.

Steadily and remorselessly, Connie's hands worked Lady Betty's breasts, squeezing, kneading, stroking, pulling and even pinching them; she simply revelled in the touch of Lady Betty's ripe flesh, and while she faithfully attended to the duties committed to her, she delightedly watched Alice and Fanny as they played with Lady Betty's cunt. Every now and then they would change positions, Alice then devoting herself to the gaping orifice itself, while Fanny played with the hairs; it was while they were thus dividing the duty that Alice suddenly rose and fetched the box of feathers.

Connie's eyes glittered delightedly as Fanny lent herself to Alice's caprice by carefully parting the dense mass that clustered on Lady Betty's cunt and thus clearing the way for the feather. With a finger on each side of the pouting slit, she kept the curling hairs back – then Alice, poising her hand daintily brought the tip of the feather along the tender lips. A fearful shriek burst from Lady Betty, followed by another, and another, as Alice continued to tickle Lady Betty's cunt, now passing the feather along the slit itself, now inside, now gently touching the clitoris! Every muscle in Lady Betty's body seemed to be exerting itself to break her fastenings and escape from the terribly subtle torture that was being so skilfully administered to her; she wriggled her hips and bottom in the most extraordinary way, seeing how tightly we had fastened her, then she would arch herself upwards, contorting herself frantically and disturbing Connie's grasp of her breasts – all the time shrieking almost inarticulate prayers for mercy. It was a wonderful sight – a fine voluptuous woman naked being tortured by three pretty girls also naked – and my lust surged wildly in me.

So far I had confined my attentions to Molly's delicious breasts so that Molly should not have her attention too much distracted from her mother by her own sensations; she was wild with grief and terror at the sight of the cruel indignities and tortures being inflicted on her naked and helpless mother, and with flushed face and horrified eyes she followed every movement. But when she saw the feather applied to her mother's cunt and heard her fearful shrieks and witnessed her desperate struggles, she completely lost her head. 'Mother, dear! . . . oh! my darling! . . . stop them, Jack! . . . stop, Alice, you're killing her! . . . oh my God, stop! . . . ' she yelled as she desperately endeavoured to get loose and go to her mother's help, and I really had to hold her tightly to me lest she should hurt herself in her frantic efforts. But it was now full time for me to intervene, for Lady Betty was fast being driven into madness by the terrible tickling of so sensitive a part of herself; so I called out to Alice, who reluctantly stopped, Connie and Fanny at the same time ceasing their attentions.

'Oh–h–h!' moaned Lady Betty with evident heartfelt relief as she turned her head unconsciously towards us, her eyes half closed, her lips slightly parted. The three girls gloatingly watched her in silence, while I soothed poor Molly; and before long both Lady Betty and her daughter regained comparative command of themselves.

I intercepted an interrogating glance from Lady Betty to her daughter as if seeking to learn what had happened to the latter. I thought it as well to answer. 'Molly is all right, Lady Betty, she was so interested in watching you that I haven't done more than play with her breasts; but now that you are going to have a rest and can watch her, we'll proceed!' And I slid my right hand down to Molly's virgin cunt.

'Oh!' she shrieked, utterly upset by the sensation of a male hand on her tender organ.

'No, Jack, don't!' cried Lady Betty, again made herself by the horrible sight. Promptly the three girls crowded round me to watch Molly, taking care not to interfere with Lady Betty's view of her daughter.

'Oh don't, Jack!' again Molly shrieked as she felt my fingers begin to wander inquisitively over her cunt, feeling, pressing, stroking and caressing it tenderly but deliberately, and rousing sensations in her, which strangely frightened her by their half-pleasant nature. 'Don't be afraid, darling!' cooed Connie, 'you'll like it presently!' I continued my sweet investigations and explorations, my fingers moving gently all over Molly's private parts, playing with her silky hairs, stroking her cunt's throbbing lips – then as she became calmer and submitted herself more quietly to having her cunt felt, I tenderly tested her for virginity by slowly and gently pushing my finger into her. 'Stop, Jack!' she cried agitatedly, 'oh stop! – you're hurting me!' her face crimson with shame, for it was evident to her what my object was.

I smiled congratulatingly at Lady Betty, whose eyes never left Molly in her maternal anxiety and distress. 'I congratulate you, your ladyship,' I said, 'your daughter is a virgin and as I haven't had a virgin for some time I'm the more obliged to you for allowing me this opportunity and the privilege of taking Molly's sweet maidenhead!'

'No, no! . . . oh, mother!' cried Molly in terrible distress while her mother, knowing that remonstrances would not avail, moaned heart-brokenly, 'Oh, Jack! how can you be so cruel!'

Suddenly Molly seemed to be seized with a fit of desperation; 'You shan't have me! . . . oh you brute! you coward! . . . you shan't have me! . . . ' she shrieked as she frantically struggled to break loose.

'Oh, oh Molly,' I said chidingly, 'what a naughty temper, darling!'

'Let me loose! you beast!' she cried making another furious struggle, 'you shan't have me! . . . I won't let you, you beast!' she hissed, 'leave me alone! . . . take your hand away, you cruel lustful brute! . . . oh! . . . oh!! . . . ' she shrieked, as again I forced my finger into her cunt and began to agitate it gently. 'Help, mother!' she yelled, again struggling desperately – then, 'Oh! Jack! do stop! . . . oh! you're hurting me!' as she relapsed into her usual mood.

I nodded to Connie who at once came up. 'Get a feather, dear, we must punish Molly! You can tickle her cunt as she now is; it will perhaps cure her temper!'

Quickly and in huge delight, Alice handed Connie a sharp-pointed feather. 'No, no, Mrs Blunt! don't tickle me!' she cried in terror, as the recollection of her mother's agony flashed through her mind. But Connie was now on her knees before us and with a smile of delight she applied the feather to Molly's tender cunt.

'Oh, my God!' shrieked Molly.

'Jack, don't!' cried Lady Betty, appreciating from her recent experience what her daughter must be feeling.

'Stop, Mrs Blunt! . . . Mrs Blunt, do stop! . . . oh my God, I can't stand it! . . . oh Mrs Blunt–t! . . . dear Mrs Blun–t! . . . stop! . . . stop! . . . I'll be good! . . . I'll do anything you like, Jack! . . . you can have me, Jack! . . . oh Mrs Blunt–t! . . . Mrs Blunt–t! . . . ' shrieked Molly, mad with the awful tickling she was getting.

'Stop for a moment, Connie,' I said, then with a tender forefinger, I soothed and caressed Molly's tortured and irritated cunt till the girl was herself again.

'Now Molly,' I said gravely, 'of your own free will, you've declared that you'll be good, that you'll do anything I want, and that you'll let me have you. You were rather excited at the time; what do you say now?'

Molly shivered. 'Oh, Jack,' she stammered, 'I'll be good but . . . but . . . I can't do the rest!'

'Go on, Connie,' I said briefly.

'No, no, Jack, not again!' cried Molly, but the feather was now being again applied to her cunt – only this time I pulled its lips apart so that Connie could tickle Molly's delicately sensitive interior, which she gleefully did. Molly's screams and struggles now began to be something fearful and poor Lady Betty, horror-stricken at the sight of her daughter's agony, cried: 'Promise everything, darling, you'll have to submit!'

'Yes Jack! I'll promise! . . . I'll do it all! . . . Oh stop, stop, Mrs Blunt! . . . I can't stand it any longer!' shrieked Molly.

Again I stopped Connie and soothed Molly's cunt with a loving finger; and when she had regained her self-control, I said, 'Molly, there must be no mistake. You'll have to do whatever I tell you, whether it be to yourself or to me or to any of the girls or even to your mother. Do you promise?'

'Yes, Jack, yes!' she gasped brokenly. Quickly the girls set her free, and she fell half fainting off my knees into the arms of Connie, whose caresses and kisses soon restored her.

By now we all were in a terrible state of sexual excitement. Connie was absorbed with Molly, but Alice and Fanny were casting hungry glances towards Lady Betty as she lay on her back, with widely parted legs, invitingly provocative. I could hardly contain my lust, but to fuck Lady Betty would be to spoil her for the girls – so I decided to let them have her ladyship first. So quickly I lengthened the bench on which she was lying fastened down, by adding the other half; then bending over the agitated woman, I said with a cruel smile: 'Now Lady Betty, we're all going to have you in turn, Alice first!'

'Oh, my God, no, no!' she screamed, but Alice was on her and Lady Betty felt herself gripped by her strong young arms as Alice arranged herself on her so that her cunt pressed against Lady Betty's fat hairy organ, and then began slowly the delicious rubbing process which she loved, but which was new to Lady Betty – for woman of the world though she was, she had never been fucked by one of her own sex!

It was delicious to watch her in Alice's arms, utterly helpless, forced to lend her cunt to satisfy Alice's lust. Her colour went and came, she began to catch her breath, her eyes shot wavering glances at us – especially at her daughter who, seated on Connie's knees, was watching her mother with undisguised astonishment, blushing furiously as Connie in loving whispers and with busy fingers made her understand all that was happening. Soon she began to feel the approach of Love's ecstasy as Alice agitated herself more and more quickly against Lady Betty's cunt – soon Lady Betty surrendered herself to her sexual impulses now fully aroused by the exciting friction communicated to her by Alice's cunt, and began to jerk herself upwards wildly as if to meet Alice's down-thrustings – then her eyes closed and her lips slightly parted as the spasm of ecstasy thrilled through her and Alice simultaneously, Alice quivering simply deliciously as she hugged Lady Betty to her frantically in the raptures of spending!

Presently the spasmodic thrills ceased, then slowly Alice rose, her eyes still humid with the pleasure she had been tasting on Lady Betty, who lay motionless and only half conscious, absorbed in her sensations. Mutely I invited Connie to take Alice's place – and before Lady Betty quite knew what was happening, she found herself in Connie's embrace.

'Oh don't, Mrs Blunt!' she ejaculated, flushing hotly as she felt Connie's cunt against hers and the exciting friction again commencing. Connie was evidently very much worked up, and she confessed afterwards that the consciousness that she was fucking Molly's mother in Molly's presence sent her to fever heat; she plunged furiously on Lady Betty as she frenziedly rubbed her cunt against hers, Lady Betty's hairy tract intensifying the delicious friction, till both were overtaken by the ecstatic crisis, Connie spending with divine tremors and evident rapture.

As she rose, I nodded to Fanny, who by now was just mad with desire. Like a panther she threw herself on Lady Betty, who had hardly recovered from the spend provoked by Connie – fiercely she clasped Lady Betty to her and began to rub her cunt furiously against Lady Betty's now moist organ. 'Don't, Fanny, don't!' cried Lady Betty, utterly helpless in Fanny's powerful grip and half alarmed by Fanny's delirious onslaught – but Fanny was now in the full tide of her sexual pleasure and revelling in the satisfaction of her imperious desire by means of Lady Betty's voluptuous body. With fast increasing impatience to taste the joys of the sweet consummation of her lustful passions, she agitated herself frenziedly on Lady Betty's responsive cunt till the rapturous moment arrived and she spent madly, showering hot kisses on Lady Betty's flushed cheeks as she felt her quiver under her in the involuntary thrills of her third spending!

As Fanny rose, the girls looked significantly at me, evidently expecting to see me seize Lady Betty and fuck her – but I had something else in my mind.

'Sponge and freshen Lady Betty, Fanny,' I said quietly, and quickly the traces of her three fuckings were removed. The operation affording Lady Betty a little time in which to recover herself.

'Now, Molly, fuck your mother, dear!' I said.

She looked at me as if she could not believe her ears, then turned to Connie as if seeking information – noting as she did so the look of delightful anticipation on the faces of her companions.

Connie rose to the occasion. 'Yes, darling,' she said soothingly as she gently pushed Molly towards Lady Betty, 'go and get your first taste of the pleasures of love from your mother's cunt!'

'Oh, Mrs Blunt, I couldn't! it's too horrible!' cried Molly aghast, while Lady Betty, utterly shocked at the idea of being submitted to her own daughter's embraces, frenziedly cried: 'No, no!'

'Come along, Molly,' I said, as I pointed to her mother, 'come along – remember your promise!'

'Oh, Jack! no, no, it's too horrible!' she cried as she buried her face in her hands, shuddering at the idea.

I took her gently but firmly by her shoulders and pushed her towards the bench on which her mother lay in terrible distress: 'Now Molly, please understand that you've got to have your mother,' I said sternly; 'if you won't act up to your promise we'll tie you on to her and whip your bottom till your movements on and against her make her spend!'

'Oh, my God!' she moaned, then breaking from me, she threw herself on her knees by her mother and cried agitatedly as she kissed her: 'Oh, mother darling, what shall I do?'

Lady Betty's face became a lovely study of maternal love contending with personal predilections! For a moment she was silent, then she murmured faintly: 'Come, darling!'

Slowly, poor Molly rose – unwillingly she placed herself between Lady Betty's legs, then gently let herself down on her and took her helpless mother in her arms, then lay still as if reluctant to begin her repugnant task.

'Just see that Molly has placed herself properly, Connie!' I said, and delightedly Connie arranged Molly so that her cunt rested on her mother's, Fanny and Alice at the same time arranging Lady Betty's breasts so that her daughter should rest hers on them.

'Now she's fine, Jack,' cried Connie excitedly, 'now my pet, fuck Mummy!'

Unwillingly Molly complied. Slowly and gently she agitated herself on her mother, cheek to cheek, breast to breast, cunt to cunt. Presently she began to move herself faster, then her sexual passions seemed to begin to dominate her – she clasped her mother closely to her as she strenuously worked her cunt against Lady Betty's, rubbing harder and harder, more and more wildly, till the ecstatic climax arrived – when with an indescribable ejaculation of 'Oh–h–h, mo–ther! . . . Oh–h–h!!' she spent on her mother's cunt in delicious transports, Lady Betty's quivers under Molly showing that she also was spending!

In admiring silence we watched the unusual spectacle of a mother and daughter spending in each other's arms, till their thrillings and involuntary tremors died away. Then Molly seemed suddenly to remember where she was; slowly she raised her face from against her mother's cheek where it had rested while she was absorbed in the bliss of her spending, and wailed: 'Oh, mother, forgive me! . . . I couldn't help it! . . . they made me do it! . . . ' and passionately kissed her. Lady Betty, who had kept her eyes closed while her daughter was fucking her, now opened them and with a look of infinite love she put her lips up as if inviting a kiss. Passionately Molly pressed hers on them, and for a few moments, mother and daughter showered kisses on each other, a sight which drove my already over-excited self into an absolute fury of lust! Hardly knowing what I was doing, I seized Molly, pulled her off her mother and pushed her into Connie's arms, then threw myself on Lady Betty and with one excited stroke, I drove my prick right up her cunt as I madly gripped her luscious voluptuous body in my arms and clasped her tightly to me.

'Oh–h–h!' she shrieked as she struggled wildly under me, her cunt smarting with the sudden distention caused by the violent entrance of my rampantly stiff organ into it. 'No, no, Jack! don't have me!' she cried as she felt herself being genuinely fucked. But I heeded nothing but my imperious desires and rammed madly into her, revelling in the contact with her magnificent flesh and the delicious warmth of her excited cunt, inflamed as it was by the four girl-fuckings she had just received, which however had not exhausted her love-juice – for I felt her spend as my prick raged wildly up and down her already well-lubricated cunt. Clenching my teeth in my desperate attempts to restrain the outpouring of my lust and to prolong the heavenly pleasure I was tasting, I continued to fuck Lady Betty madly, her quivers and tremors and inarticulate ejaculations and her voluptuous movements under me telling me that her animal passions had now control over her and that she had abandoned herself absolutely to the gratification of her aroused lust – but soon I could no longer control myself. Just then I felt Lady Betty spend again with delicious thrills, inundating my excited prick with her hot love-juice, and this broke down all my resistance; wildly I rammed into her till our hairs intertwined, then clutching her against me in a frenzy of rapture, I spent madly into her, flooding her interior with my boiling essence, she ejaculating brokenly: 'Ah! . . . ah! . . . ah–h!' as she felt the jets of my discharge shoot into her.

When she came to, she found herself still lying under me and clasped in my arms, my prick still lodged up her cunt, for I was loth to leave so delicious an armful as she was. The storm of lust that had overwhelmed her had died away with the last quivers of her ecstasy, and she was only conscious of the appalling fact that she had been forcibly outraged! In an agony of grief and shame she wailed: 'Oh, Jack, what have you done!' her eyes full of anguish.

'I've only fucked you, dear Lady Betty!' I replied with a cruel smile, 'and I found you so delicious that after I've taken your daughter's maidenhead I'll have you again!' And I laughed delightedly at the look of horror that came into her eyes, then continued: 'Molly must now amuse us, while you rest and recover yourself sufficiently to allow you to endure the further tortures and outrages we've arranged for your amusement – and ours!' and with this appalling intimation, I rose off Lady Betty, unfastened her and made her over to Alice and Fanny to be sponged and refreshed while I went off to my alcove for a similar purpose.

When I returned after a few minutes, I found Lady Betty in the fateful armchair and Molly's arms round her, the girls having allowed mother and daughter a little time to themselves. Connie eagerly advanced to meet me, asking excitedly: 'What now, Jack?'

'Would you like to fuck Molly now, dear?' I asked with a smile.

'Oh yes! please let me, Jack! I'm dying to have her,' she exclaimed, blushing slightly at her own vehemence.

'Very well,' I replied, 'but don't take too much out of her just now; I'll violate her as soon as I'm myself again and then we'll just work them both for all we can. Do you approve, dears?' I asked, turning to Alice and Fanny.

They nodded delightedly. 'Jack, please make Lady Betty over to Fanny and me – Connie wants Molly left to her; and you can fuck them both whenever you wish. We want to do the torturing!' said Alice softly, looking coaxingly at me.

'Just as you please, dears,' I said with a smile, distinctly pleased with the arrangements and delighted to find the girls so keen on exercising their refined cruelty on their own sex! Then together we approached Lady Betty and Molly, who had not heard a word, being absorbed in the terrible fate indicated by me as awaiting them, regarding which they no doubt were whispering to each other softly.

'Molly, Mrs Blunt wants to fuck you – come along!' I said quietly as Connie advanced to take her.

'Mother! oh, mother!' cried Molly, clinging apprehensively to Lady Betty: 'Come, darling!' cooed Connie as she gently passed her arms round Molly's shrinking, trembling body and drew her away from her distressed mother who moaned in her anguish as she watched her daughter forced to lie down, and separate her legs, and Connie then arrange herself on her, breasts to breasts, cunt to cunt. Shocked beyond endurance, Lady Betty covered her face with her hands, but Alice and Fanny (who had now assumed charge of her) promptly pulled them away and shackled her wrists together behind her back, thus compelling her to witness Molly's martyrdom under Connie, who now was showering hot and lustful kisses on Molly's trembling lips, as she lasciviously agitated herself on her unwilling victim.

To us others it was a lovely spectacle. The two girls fitted each other perfectly – while the contrast between Connie's look of delighted satisfaction as she gratified her lust after Molly and the forlorn woebegone distressed expression of the latter, as she passively let her cunt minister to Connie's concupiscence, was enough to rekindle my ardour and determined me to ravish Molly as soon as Connie had done with her.

She did not keep me waiting unnecessarily. After testifying by her hot salacious kisses her satisfaction at holding Molly in her arms, cunt to cunt, she began to girl-fuck her ardently and with fast increasing erotic frenzy, rubbing herself ragingly against her victim's cunt till she felt Molly beginning to quiver under her – then redoubling her efforts, she went into a veritable paroxysm of thrusts and shoves and wild friction, which quickly brought on the delicious spasm of pleasure to both herself and Molly, whose unresisting lips she again seized with her own as she quivered and thrilled in the delicious consummation of her lust!

'There, Lady Betty, Molly has spent!' cried Alice gleefully, as she gloated over the spectacle with eyes full of desire which she then turned hungrily on Lady Betty and then on me, as if begging leave to inflict some torture on her. But I shook my head; Lady Betty had now to witness her daughter's violation.

Presently Connie rose after giving Molly a long clinging kiss, expressive of the most intense satisfaction. Molly then began to raise herself, but I quickly pushed her down again on her back and, lying down myself beside her, I slipped my arms round her so that we rested together, her back against my chest, her bottom against my prick, while my hands commanded her breasts and cunt.

'Let me go, Jack!' she cried in alarm, hardly understanding however the significance of my action; but it was quite patent to Lady Betty, who screamed: 'No, Jack, no!' while Alice and Fanny exchanged smiles of delight.

'Lie still, Molly dear!' I said soothingly, gently seizing one of her delicious breasts, while with my remaining hand, I played with her cunt.

'Oh, Jack, don't!' she cried, quivering exquisitely as she submitted reluctantly to my wishes and let my hands enjoy themselves, still not comprehending what was to follow!

Presently I whispered loud enough for the others to hear: 'Molly, you're quite ready now, let me have you, darling!'

She lay still for a moment – then, as her fate dawned on her, she made one desperate furious spring, slipped out of my hands, and rushed to Lady Betty; she fell at her mother's knees and clasping her convulsively cried: 'Don't let Jack have me, mother! oh save me! . . . save me!' Alice and Fanny again exchanged delighted smiles with Connie, all three girls intently watching for the order to bring Molly back to me. I rose from the couch and nodded to them. Like young tigresses, they threw themselves on Molly and dragged her away from her mother's knees, in spite of her frenzied resistance as she shrieked: 'Mother, save me!' while Lady Betty, frantic at her helplessness and distracted by her daughter's cries as she was being thus dragged to her violation cried hysterically: 'Jack! for God's sake spare her!'

The girls had by now forced Molly on to the couch again. I saw she would not yield herself quietly to me, so while they held her, I fastened the corner cords to her ankles and wrists and set the machinery at work. As soon as the girls saw the cords tightening, they let go of Molly, who immediately sprang up, only to be arrested and jerked on to her back on the couch – then inch by inch, she was extended flat with widely parted arms and legs as she shrieked with terror; Lady Betty went into hysterics, which Alice and Fanny soon cured by twitching a few hairs of her cunt.

I seated myself by Molly, bent over her and said gravely, 'Now you've again broken your promise Molly – I shall consequently amuse myself with you before I violate you!'

'No, no, Jack!' she shrieked as she again struggled to break loose. 'Let me go! . . . don't . . . shame me! . . . oh! don't . . . have me!'

I ignored her pleadings and began to play with her breasts, which I caressed and squeezed to my heart's content, finally putting her little virgin nipples into my mouth and sucking them lovingly – at which the three girls laughed gleefully as they now knew that another part of Molly would also be sucked while virgin! Then I tickled her navel, a proceeding which made her squirm exquisitely. Then I devoted myself to her cunt!

First I stroked and caressed it, she all the while frantically crying out and jerking herself about in vain endeavours to escape my hands. The girls now wheeled Lady Betty alongside the couch; her hands were still tied behind her back so that she could not use them to shut out the dreadful sight of Molly spread-eagled naked, and was forced to look on and witness the violation of her daughter right in front of her eyes.

When Lady Betty had been properly placed so as to see all that went on, I leant over Molly, seized one of her breasts with my left hand and while squeezing it lovingly, I gently ran my right forefinger along the tender lips of her cunt, intently watching her tell-tale face as I did so.

A great wave of colour surged furiously over her cheeks, even suffusing her heaving bosom, as she screamed: 'Don't Jack, don't!' her eyes full of shame while her involuntary movements of hips and bottom betrayed her sexual agitation. It was simply delicious to have her thus at my absolute disposal, to know that the feeling of utter helplessness and the knowledge that her private parts were utterly defenceless was intensifying the mental and physical agony that my proceedings were making Molly suffer – and despite her prayers and her mother's implorings, I continued delightedly to tickle Molly's cunt with my finger till I considered she was sufficiently worked up to be sucked – when I quietly rose, placed myself between her thighs, and began to kiss her cunt, keeping my eyes on Lady Betty, so as to note the effect on her of this fresh torture to her daughter.

Lady Betty's eyes opened wide in shocked surprise – then as a half strangled shriek broke from Molly, she screamed: 'Oh, my God! don't Jack! you'll drive Molly mad!' Just then my tongue commenced to play on Molly's cunt, working along her lips, darting between them when they began to pout and, every now and then, caressing her clitoris, the subtle titillation sending

Molly into shrieking convulsions as she felt she was being slowly driven against her wishes to spending point! Again Lady Betty screamed: 'Stop Jack, for God's sake stop!' as she saw her daughter squirming and quivering and heard her now half inarticulate cries. I made a sign to the girls. Promptly Alice and Fanny seized Lady Betty's breasts, while Connie forced her hand between Lady Betty's thighs and tickled her cunt! 'Oh, my God! leave me alone!' she shrieked, struggling frantically but unavailingly – her eyes remaining fixed on her daughter's now violently agitated body, for I had forced her to the verge of spending. Then a great convulsion shook Molly, 'Oh–h–h–h' she ejaculated, then spent with exquisite tremors and thrills, while an unmistakable shriek from Lady Betty proclaimed that Connie's finger had brought about an unwilling but nevertheless delicious discharge.

Impatiently I waited till the thrills of pleasure had ceased, then I sprang on her, seized her in my arms, brought my prick to bear on her cunt, and with a vigorous shove, I succeeded in forcing its head inside her maiden orifice in spite of her cries and frantic struggles. There her virgin barrier blocked the way. Gripping her tightly to me, I rammed fiercely into her, evidently hurting Molly dreadfully, for her shrieks rang through the room as I strove to get into her, Lady Betty also frenziedly crying, 'Stop! stop!' being terribly upset by the sight of her daughter's agonies and her cries. Molly was very tight indeed, and, in spite of being tied down, wriggled her strong young body so desperately that it was some little time before I could get a really good thrust; but presently I managed to pin her for a moment, then shoving furiously into her, I burst through her virgin defences. A fearful shriek announced her violation, Lady Betty (whose breasts and cunt were still being handled and fingered by the girls) crying hysterically: 'Oh, my darling! . . . my darling! . . . ' as with eyes dilated with horror, she watched her daughter being ravished right in front of her and recognised the very moment when Molly lost her maidenhead!

Now firmly lodged inside Molly, I drove my prick up to its root in her now smarting cunt – then lay motionless on her for a moment till her cries ceased. Then I set to work to fuck her in real earnest, first with long slow strokes, then with quicker and more excited ones – Molly submitting passively as if recognising that resistance now was useless; the deed had been done, her virginity had been snatched from her! Presently, however, she began to agitate herself under me, as if involuntarily, as she succumbed to the imperious demands of her now fully aroused sexual emotions and erotic impulses; as my movements on her became more and more riotous and unrestrained, she responded half unconsciously, half mechanically, by jogging and heaving her bottom and hips upwards as if to meet my vigorous down-strokes. Soon our movements became a tempest of confused heaves, shoves, thrusts and wriggles, then the heavenly climax overtook us! I felt a warm discharge from her as she quivered voluptuously in my arms, then I spent madly, pouring my boiling essence into her virgin interior in rapturous ecstasy as I deliciously consummated Molly's violation, revelling in her exquisite thrills and tremors as she felt my hot discharge shoot into her – her movements being astonishingly like those of the mother when I spent into Lady Betty; but such was the violence of the sexual orgasm that shook Molly for the first time in her life that she went off into a semi-trance!

## Chapter Nine

As soon as I had recovered from the delirious ecstasy of my spending, I kissed Molly's still unconscious lips, rose gently off her and cruelly displayed my bloodstained prick to Lady Betty and the excited girls. After exulting over Lady Betty's distress and the sight of this incontrovertible evidence of her daughter's violation, I said, 'I fancy you would like to attend to Molly yourself, your ladyship. If I let you both loose for the purpose, will you promise to allow yourselves to be fastened again in such a way as I may indicate?'

'Yes! yes!' she cried feverishly in her maternal anxiety to attend to Molly before it was too late.

Immediately we set them both free. Hastily Lady Betty caught up Molly in her arms, and after passionately kissing her she led her away to the girls' alcove, while the girls delightedly bathed and sponged away the marks of my victory from my rejoicing prick, kissing and caressing it as if in sweet congratulation.

'Now we'll wind up with a great orgy of cruelty, dears,' I said. 'You heard Lady Betty's promise?' They nodded excitedly. 'It would hardly have been possible for us to have forced them into the *soixante-neuf* position – at all events it would have been very difficult. We'll now make them place themselves so, on the half bench, then tie them down, Lady Betty on Molly. We then can command their cunts for feeling and fingering and tickling and frigging, and by slightly moving Lady Betty backwards we could suck them and I could fuck them, standing upright – but you won't be able to do so. Do you want to do it?'

They glanced at each other for a moment, then shook their heads: 'We shall be quite content to satisfy our desires when they get too imperious by fucking each other, Jack!' said Alice merrily. 'Connie and Fanny haven't tried each other yet and will be delighted to do so presently.' The two girls glanced tenderly at each other and blushed deliciously. 'My God, Jack! what a doing the poor things will have had by the time we let them away – do you think they can stand it?'

'Oh yes, dear!' I replied with a smile, 'they're very strong. And it is about time we all had a little refreshment.'

So I opened some champagne and poured out six tumblers, adding a little brandy to the two glasses destined for Lady Betty and Molly, who just then emerged from the alcove, Molly with both hands shielding her cunt, while Lady Betty covered hers with one hand, while her other arm was passed round her daughter. Both looked terribly forlorn and disconsolate as they approached us; and when the girls crowded round Molly and congratulated her on having become a woman, poor Lady Betty's eyes sought mine with a look of shocked horror. I handed the champagne round and we all partook of it with relish, especially Lady Betty and Molly, whom it seemed to revive.

'Now let us resume,' I cried cheerfully, 'come along girls, come Lady Betty, bring Molly with you.' And I moved towards the bench with the girls, while our unhappy victims followed slowly and reluctantly.

'Now Molly, you just lie down on your back on this bench, just as your mother was made to do – open your legs, put one on each side.' Reluctantly she obeyed, and soon she was lashed firmly to the longitudinal bars by her wrists and ankles, a lovely sight.

'Now, Lady Betty, place yourself on your daughter reverse ways, your head between her thighs, her head between your legs. Lie on her, and when we have arranged you properly on her, we'll tie you down!'

Lady Betty flushed painfully, horror-stricken. 'Oh, Jack, I can't! . . . really I can't do it! . . . it's too horrible!' she exclaimed, burying her face in her hands and shuddering at the idea.

'Now remember your promise, Lady Betty,' I said somewhat sternly as if I was annoyed, 'come, no nonsense – lie down on Molly!'

'Oh, my God!' she wailed. With an effort, she slowly went up to the bench on which poor Molly was lying, bound down and helpless, and shivering with dread – she stood still for a moment as if struggling with repugnance, then stooping down, she kissed her daughter passionately, whispering: 'My darling, I can't help it!' then reluctantly she passed one leg over Molly's face and laid herself down on her daughter as ordered. Promptly Alice and I adjusted her so that her cunt came within easy reach of Molly's lips, while her mouth commanded Molly's cunt, then we strapped her arms by the wrists and her legs by the ankles to the cross bars of the bench, one on each side of Molly, pulling the straps as tightly as we could – thereby further securing Molly, who now lay between her mother's arms and legs and was pinned down by her not inconsiderable weight.

The pair afforded a remarkable spectacle to us and for some little time we stood in gloating admiration. Neither could move in the slightest degree without the other being instantly conscious of it, and realising its significance. Lady Betty now had her daughter's freshly violated cunt right under her eyes and only a few inches off; right above Molly's eyes and also only a few inches off, hung her mother's cunt; neither could avoid seeing what was being done to each other's private parts! Were ever a mother and a daughter so cruelly placed?

After a few moments of gloating, I said quietly: 'Molly dear, I'm going to see how your cunt has been altered by your having been deflowered!' and I knelt down between her widely parted legs, while the girls crowded round to watch, Molly crying imploringly: 'Don't touch me there, Jack it's so sore!' at which the girls laughed delightedly.

Critically, I examined Molly's delicious organ of sex. 'I think it is swollen a bit, and that the slit is longer – don't you believe, Lady Betty?' I remarked. She only moaned inarticulately, evidently feeling her position acutely. With a gentle forefinger, I proceeded to touch and press Molly's soft springy flesh, each touch producing a cry of pain from her and involuntary writhings which even her mother's weight could not subdue. Then I gently drew apart the tender lips and inspected with curiosity the gash-like opening into which I had, with so much difficulty, effected an entrance, poor Molly crying: 'Oh! don't Jack!' Her cunt was clearly inflamed and she must have suffered a good deal of pain while being ravished, and as I closed the lips again, I gently deposited a loving kiss on them as if seeking their pardon, Molly ejaculating 'Oh!' and quivering deliciously as my caress tingled through her. Then I slowly and gently introduced my forefinger into her cunt.

'Oh!' shrieked Molly, writhing with pain.

'Don't Jack!' cried Lady Betty, her eyes full of agony at the horrible sight she was being forced to witness. But remorselessly, I pushed my finger into Molly's cunt till it was buried up to the knuckle, and retained it there – gently feeling her interior and revelling in the warm soft flesh, still moist with my spendings, and noting delightedly how her gentle muscles were involuntarily gripping my finger, as I tenderly touched her clitoris with my free hand and generally excited her. She was still deliciously tight, and the corrugations of her tender flesh clasped my finger in a way that augured exquisite pleasure to my prick when next it was put into her cunt.

After a little while, I withdrew my finger, to Molly's great relief; then said to Lady Betty: 'Now I'll exhibit your cunt to your daughter, your ladyship!' She moaned inarticulately, knowing that it was no use asking for mercy.

So round I went to Molly's side, the delighted girls following me. When there, I leant over Lady Betty's bottom from one side of her, and as I looked down into Molly's flushed and pitiful face, I said quietly to her, 'Now Molly, remember the pinchings and keep your eyes on your mother's cunt!' then gently with both hands I drew its lips well apart and exhibited the large pink gap through which she had entered the world, saying: 'Look, Molly, this is the first thing you came through!'

She was inexpressibly shocked at the sight of her mother's gaping cunt and ejaculated tremulously: 'Oh, Jack! how can you be so cruel!' at which the girls laughed amusedly.

Then to her horror, I pushed my finger in and began to feel her mother just as I had done her. 'Don't Jack!' cried poor Lady Betty, agitating herself spasmodically on Molly as my curious finger explored her sensitive interior, revelling in her luscious flesh which throbbed in the most excited fashion. But after Molly's exquisite interior, her mother's seemed almost coarse, and very soon I drew my finger out of her, and said softly to Alice: 'Get a couple of feathers, dear, and we'll tickle them both at the same time!'

'No, Jack, no!' shrieked Molly in horrible distress at the approaching dreadful torture.

'What is it, darling?' cried Lady Betty.

'They're going to tickle us together at the same time!' she cried agitatedly.

Immediately a shriek of terror came from Lady Betty. 'My God! no, Jack! for pity's sake don't!' and frantically both mother and daughter tugged at their fastenings in desperate but unavailing endeavours to get free, thereby affording us a delicious sample of the struggles we were about to witness when the feathers were applied to their tender cunts. Just then Alice came back with half a dozen long feathers. She picked out one for herself, and Connie selected another, and without any prompting from me, Alice placed herself by Lady Betty's cunt while Connie knelt between Molly's legs, then simultaneously applied the feathers to their respective victim's defenceless slits.

Two fearful shrieks filled the room. 'Don't, Mrs Blunt!' cried Molly, wriggling in a perfectly wonderful way seeing how tightly she had been tied down and also had her mother's weight to contend against, while Lady Betty writhed and contorted, twisted and squirmed as if she was in a fit – plunging so wildly on Molly as to make the poor girl gasp for breath. She seemed to feel the torture much more keenly than Molly did, possibly because of Alice's skill as torturer and her quickness in realising the points where the touch of the feather had the cruelest effect – at all events Lady Betty shrieked, yelled, curvetted, and wriggled till I thought it wise to stop the torture for a little, and signalled to both girls to desist – which they unwillingly did, then rose and rushed excitedly to me with eyes glistening with lust and cruelty.

'Oh, Jack! wasn't it lovely!' cried Alice rapturously. 'Fanny, you take a turn now at Lady Betty, I'd like to watch her!' she continued, handing the feather to Fanny, whose eyes gleamed delightedly at the opportunity of torturing Lady Betty – then she and Connie impatiently took their places by their trembling victims and awaited my signal.

A refinement of cruelty suddenly struck me. 'Look here dear,' I said to Alice, 'suppose you sit astride on Lady Betty's backside and looking down on Molly – you'll feel Lady Betty's struggles, you'll see the feather play on her cunt, and you'll be able at the same time to watch Molly's face!'

'Jack! you're a genius!' she cried delightedly, 'help me up, darling!' – and in a moment, she was arranged astride on Lady Betty, whose plump fleshy buttocks she grasped firmly so as not to be dislodged by her ladyship's struggles and plunges, her weight forcing Lady Betty's cunt almost on to Molly's face, so that Fanny had to poise her hand delicately so as to bring the feather into play.

'Go ahead dears!' I cried, and immediately both feathers were applied to the respective cunts. Again Lady Betty and Molly shrieked frantically as their cunts were slowly and cruelly tickled and irritated and goaded almost into spending – but they were not allowed to taste that blessed relief! Lady Betty was going nearly mad and, in spite of Alice's weight, plunging so wildly that Alice had some difficulty in sticking on, while poor Molly, whose chest had now to bear the weight of her mother as well as Alice, had scarcely enough breath to keep her going and so had to endure the terrible torture absolutely passively. Soon both of our victims had again been pushed to the extreme point of endurance, Molly being nearly in hysterics, while Lady Betty was fast going into convulsions – whereupon I stopped Connie and Fanny and lifted Alice off.

'Hadn't we better soothe the poor things by stroking their cunts?' asked Alice, as she watched our panting, quivering, trembling victims.

'I'm going to force them to suck each other now, dear,' I whispered with a smile.

'Jack, how lovely!' she ejaculated in rapture, eagerly eyeing Lady Betty and Molly – who by now were getting more normal, though the involuntary heaves and tremors that ran through them showed significantly the nature of the relief they were craving for.

I leant over Lady Betty and whispered: 'You can tell by your own feelings and by the sight of Molly's cunt what she wants! Suck her!'

'Oh!' she ejaculated, shocked beyond expression.

'Suck her, Lady Betty!' I repeated, 'then she'll understand and she'll suck you!'

'Oh! I couldn't!' she cried, 'suck my own daughter!'

'Yes – suck your own daughter, Lady Betty, and she'll then suck her own mother! You've got to do it! so you'd better do it quietly at once without further nonsense. Now suck Molly!'

'No, no!' she cried, 'I can't! . . . I can't!'

I turned to Alice. 'Get me that cutting riding whip, dear,' I said quietly. Quickly she brought it. I swished it through the air close to Lady Betty, who trembled with fright.

'Now Lady Betty, please understand me clearly. You've got to do whatever I tell you – if you refuse you'll be whipped into submission! Now, suck your daughter's cunt!'

'Oh! Jack! I can't!' she wailed.

Down came the whip across her splendid bottom. She shrieked wildly as she writhed with the pain. I dealt her another cut – more shrieks; then a third – yet no compliance, but I could see that her obstinacy was giving way. I did not want to hurt her unnecessarily, so I aimed the fourth cut crossways, making the lash curl round her buttock and flick her cunt. A fearful yell of pain broke from Lady Betty; 'Stop, Jack!' she screeched, then hurriedly she commenced to lick Molly's cunt!

'That's right!' I said encouragingly, 'keep on till I tell you to stop, Lady Betty!' Then delightedly we all watched the piquant spectacle of a daughter being sucked by her mother! Their faces were a study – Lady Betty's showing her disgust and repugnance at thus having to apply her tongue to her daughter's cunt, while Molly's was full of shame at being thus forced to spend by her mother. Heroically she tried to retain herself to refrain from spending – but in vain; soon her control of herself broke down, then in sheer despair, she ejaculated brokenly: 'Oh! . . . I can't . . . help it! . . . ah! . . . ah! . . . ' as she spent frantically!

The sight was more than the girls could stand. Alice and Connie flew into each others arms – too excited to rush to the couch, they fell on the soft thick carpet and madly cunt-fucked each other till their feelings were relieved. Fanny, hardly knowing what she was doing, threw her arms round me and clinging closely to me whispered excitedly: 'Oh, Mr Jack, please frig me!' which I delightedly did. I would have gladly fucked her, but I had determined to have Lady Betty as she lay on Molly, making Molly lick my balls during the process, so I could spare nothing at the moment for Fanny.

Presently Alice and Connie rose, looking somewhat sheep-faced, but their countenances cleared when they saw that Fanny had been also obliged to relieve her excited feeling by means of my finger; and they exchanged sympathetic and congratulatory smiles, as we again clustered round Lady Betty and Molly, whom we had left tied down and who began to tremble with dread as they saw that they were to be submitted to further indignities and tortures.

'Now, Molly, it's your turn, dear – suck your mother's cunt!' I said to her as I flicked her tender cunt sharply with the lash of my riding whip so as to stop the useless protest and pleadings which I knew she was sure to make at receiving such a command.

'Don't, Jack!' she screamed writhing with pain – then with loathing horror in her face she placed her mouth on her mother's cunt and commenced to tongue its lips.

'Oh! Molly, don't!' cried Lady Betty, involuntarily wriggling her bottom and hips voluptuously as her daughter's tongue began to arouse her sexual appetites in spite of herself; but Molly was too terrified by my whip to disobey me and so continued to tease and torture her mother's cunt with her tongue for some little time till I stopped her – then straddling over her head with my balls just touching her face, I shoved my rampant prick into Lady Betty's now gaping cunt, till I had buried it inside her, up to its root. As I did so my balls travelled over Molly's face, till they rested on her mouth, my thighs then holding her head so firmly gripped between them, that she could not avoid the shocking contact with my genital organs.

'Now Molly, you're to lick my balls while I fuck your mother!' I said with a smile at the delighted girls, who in turn peeped between my thighs to view the extraordinary conjunction of Lady Betty's cunt, my prick and balls, and

Molly's mouth – Lady Betty all the while inarticulately moaning in her distress at being thus again fucked by me so unexpectedly and in such a position!

I heard stifled cries come from Molly; I could feel her warm breath on my balls but not the velvet of her tongue – so I again sharply flicked her cunt. A smothered shriek of agony – then something exquisitely warm, soft and moist began to caress my scrotum. It was Molly's tongue – the poor girl was licking my balls!

Oh! my delicious sensations at that moment as my prick luxuriated in the cunt of the mother while the mouth of the daughter reluctantly but deliciously was exciting me into spending! For some moments, I remained motionless save for thrills of exquisite pleasure, until I could no longer control my imperious desires – then with piston-like strokes I began to work myself backwards and forwards in Lady Betty's cunt, moving faster and faster and getting more and more furious, till I spent rapturously into her, just as her quivering wriggling backside proclaimed that she too was discharging, her head unconsciously resting on her daughter's cunt as the spasm of her pleasure vibrated through her!

When I had become myself again, I drew out my prick, and after gloating cruelly over the sight of poor Molly's flushed, shame-stricken and quivering face and tearful but tearless eyes, I pointed to her mother's cunt now visibly wet and bedewed from my discharge and said, 'Now go on again, Molly!'

She closed her horrified eyes with an expression of sickening loathing and repugnance and moaned, 'Oh, my God! . . . Jack, I can't! . . . I simply can't! . . .'

'You can, and you shall, Molly!' I replied sternly as I sent the lash of my whip sharply across her tender cunt, drawing from her a terrible shriek which brought Lady Betty out of her semi-stupor.

'Go on, Molly!' I said, pointing to her mother's cunt as her eyes sought mine as if imploring mercy. Again she dumbly refused, again I caught her a sharp cut full on her cunt.

She yelled in agony, then slowly and with horrible repugnance, she nerved herself to touch her mother's greasy and sticky cunt with her lips, nearly choking as her tongue slowly transferred the remains of my spend from her mother's gaping slit into her own mouth and so down her throat! As soon as I saw she was fairly started, I put her in charge of Connie with instructions to keep her at it, whatever happened – then placing myself between Molly's legs, my prick all wet and semen-soiled close to Lady Betty's face, I touched the latter with my whip and said: 'Now suck me clean, Lady Betty!'

'Oh!' she cried in horror, shuddering violently as she let her head again fall on her daughter's cunt. Raising the whip, I slashed her fiercely right down her left buttock, then along the other, my lash cutting well into her soft plump flesh and evidently giving her intense pain from the lovely way in which she writhed and screamed. 'Suck me clean, Lady Betty!' I sternly repeated as I sent cut after cut on her wriggling plunging backside, till she could no longer endure the pain, and half hysterically raised her head and opened her mouth. Instantly I ceased the flagellation and popped my humid prick in between her unwilling lips which then closed softly but reluctantly on it as a look of intense repulsion passed over her agonised face.

For sometime Lady Betty simply held my prick in her mouth passively and in shamefaced confusion, for she had never before sucked a man and really did not know what to do! But I didn't mind! Her mouth was deliciously warm and moist, while the touch of her lips was voluptuousness itself – and as I watched her, gloating over her misery and shame, I could see her throat convulsively working, as from time to time, she forced herself to swallow the accumulated saliva now highly impregnated with our mingled spendings.

What with the gratification of my eyes and the stimulus afforded by Lady Betty's mouth, my virility began quickly to revive. 'Pass your tongue over and round my prick, Lady Betty,' I commanded, 'lick and suck simultaneously!' Painfully she complied. The action of her tongue was something exquisite, so much so that, in a very short time, my prick began to swell and stiffen (to her silent horror) till her mouth could just hold it! I was ready for action again. Should I spend in Lady Betty's mouth or fuck Molly again? Hurriedly I decided in favour of Molly.

Quickly I pulled my prick out of Lady Betty's mouth. 'Untie her sharp,' I cried to the girls as I pushed up the second half bench and fastened it to the piece on which Molly was lying tied. Soon the girls freed Lady Betty and lifted her off her daughter, then guessing what was coming, they held her between them in such a way that she was compelled to see what happened to her. As soon as Molly caught sight of me, with my prick in rampant erection, she instinctively divined that she was again to be ravished, and screamed for mercy. But I threw myself on her, took her in my arms, brought my prick to bear on the orifice of her cunt and fiercely rammed it into her, forcing my way ruthlessly in while she shrieked with a pain hardly less keen that that which accompanied her violation. Mad with lust and the exquisite pleasure of holding the voluptuous girl again in my close embrace, and stimulated by the spectacle of the lovely naked bodies of Alice, Connie and Fanny right before my eyes, as they controlled Lady Betty's frantic struggles to go to her daughter's assistance while they simultaneously possessed themselves of her breasts and her cunt, I let myself go, and ramming myself furiously into the still shrieking Molly, I fucked her exquisite self rapturously till Love's ecstasy overtook me, when I spent deliriously into her, flooding her smarting interior with the soothing balm of my boiling love-juice which she received into her with the most voluptuous thrills and quivers, the sudden transition from the pains of penetration to the raptures of spending sending her into a semi-swoon as she lay locked in my arms.

Reluctantly I quitted her, unfastened her and made her over to her mother, who quickly took her off to the girls' alcove, while they crowded round me, with delicious kisses, as they congratulated me on my prowess in having fucked mother and daughter twice each in each other's presence, and to the accompaniment of such exquisite licentiousness. Then solicitously and tenderly, they bathed and sponged my prick and generally refreshed me.

'Now what next?' I asked.

'I'm afraid we must be going, Jack,' said Connie, 'as we have to dine out!'

'And I think you've had enough, sir,' said Alice archly.

'Miss Molly looked quite played out, Mr Jack,' said Fanny, who had gone to offer her services but evidently had been brusquely refused.

'Well, perhaps we had better let the poor things off now!' I said musingly. 'I don't think they will offend any of us again!' They laughed. 'Well, dears, thank you all very much for your help today – we've had a lovely orgy, have punished our enemies, and had a fine time ourselves. Now run away and dress; perhaps you won't mind Fanny attending to Lady Betty and Molly as they resume their clothing, Alice?'

Just then Lady Betty and Molly came out. They were evidently utterly exhausted. I hastily poured out some champagne for them which greatly revived them, then as they tremblingly awaited the resumption of their tortures, I said gently: 'Now you can go, Lady Betty, with your daughter. Fanny will help you to dress yourselves. Now if ever you breathe a single word as to what has happened here this afternoon, or if in word or deed or suggestion, you say or do anything to harm or wound these girls or myself, I'll get you both brought here again and what you've undergone today will be mild to what you'll then taste. Now each of you, kneel in turn before Alice first, then Connie, then Fanny and then me – kiss each cunt three times, also my prick three times, in token of apology and in promise of good behaviour – then dress yourselves.'

We arranged ourselves in the order indicated, standing in a line with our arms round each other. Shamefacedly Lady Betty and Molly performed their penance, my prick quivering as their lips touched it. Then we all resumed our clothing; I put Lady Betty and Molly into a taxi, only breaking the constrained silence with the remark: 'Now don't forget!' then returned to the girls whom I found chatting eagerly and delightedly, all now daintily dressed.

'I'd like to fuck you all just as you are, dears!' I said as I eyed them lasciviously in their provoking daintiness.

'Think what our clothes would look like!' laughed Connie.

'Jack, we owe you a lot!' said Alice more seriously, 'now Connie and Fanny, let's say goodbye in a new way. One by one, Jack, we'll let you suck us just as we are – through our drawers; then we'll make you lie down, take your prick out through your trousers, and suck you goodbye! I claim last turn so as to receive all that you've left in you!'

Delightedly Connie and Fanny complied. One by one, they seated themselves in an easy-chair, while the other two pulled up their clothes and I, kneeling between their legs, sucked a tender farewell to each cunt through the opening of their dainty frilly drawers; then I lay down on my back on the couch. With a trembling hand, Connie excitedly opened my fly and gently pulled out my prick, then kissed and sucked it lovingly; Fanny followed suit, her tongue provoking it into life again. Then Alice took charge and sucked and tongued me till she forced my seminal reserves to yield all they held, receiving in her sweet mouth my love-juice as I spent in quivering rapture. Then we all four entered the waiting taxi and the girls drove me to my club, where they left me with tender and insistent injunctions to, 'Do yourself well, darling!'

# Maudie

## Revelations of Life
## in London Society

ANONYMOUS

# To the Reader

I think you'll like Maudie; she's fanciful and frivolous. I should hardly call her 'fast', though she does the most dreadful things – but she does them so very nicely tha:t probably the most straitlaced of people will have to forgive her, when they read her in the privacy of their own (or other people's) bedrooms – not only forgive, but love her and her bad ways and her worse friends.

*Maudie* deals frankly with the wicked senses, ordinary and bizarre, of a number of charming people, who refuse to be trammelled by the usual conventions of society. We meet them in London, and we meet them in their delightful riverside palace, where full rein is given to all their loves and lusts until there comes a very unexpected denouement.

Our ancestors used to have a thing called *The Horn Book*. What it exactly was I'm not quite sure, but touching the horn question, if *Maudie* doesn't give it you, you're past your job.

Settle down in bed with a cigarette and a drink and the evening paper, and give your lady companion *Maudie* to read – well, you won't get much evening paper. *Maudie* is a 'horn book'.

# Characters

*Maudie Stevens*, an amateur of the beautiful, and an exponent of the same in her own face and figure. She loves love and luxury, and all her whims and desires and her great house at Staines are provided for by the wealth of –

*Bertie Evans-James* ('Tubby'), the cheery fat son of a Lancashire millionaire

*Charles Vernon St Just Osmond*, a very charming 'younger son'

*Phil Learoyd*, a young Cambridge undergraduate with a sense of humour

*General Fitzhugh VC*, a distinguished veteran with a taste for the gay side of life

*Claude Lestrange*, a romantic poet, sodomitically inclined

*Lady Lavinia McCree*, Charlie's aunt, a mid-Victorian lady

*Madame Rade*, a retired Parisian actress

*Toinette Rade*, her 'flapper' niece

*Jeannie*, a Newcastle hinny

*Elsie*

*May*

## CHAPTER ONE

# The Mansion of Maudie

An awakening in a whore's bedroom is, as a rule, cheerless.

One is vague as to one's whereabouts, as a rule sore on the John Thomas, and a general feeling of having made a bloody fool of oneself is most often mixed with a wonder whose pyjamas you've got on and whether you've got the clap or possibly worse.

Charles Vernon St Just Osmond, fifth off the succession to the earldom of Osmond, very much a 'younger son', with a good deal less money even than most younger sons, turned over twice, flicked his eyes at the sunlight dribbling through the blinds, bit a tongue which felt like leather, sniffed a distinct aroma of whisky, and wondered where the hell he was, why he had done it and whom he had done it on.

He raised himself on one elbow, and *looked*. Then he was pleased. He had obviously not made a very drunken error. The good lady who lay by his side, in a charming silk pyjama suit with a deep Venetian lace collar, was not only pretty, but interesting. Her chestnut hair flowed over her shoulders. Her arms, bare from just above the elbows, were deliciously rounded, and her very delicate little hands were heavily be-ringed. This, Osmond (or, as we shall call him, Charlie) concluded, was no ordinary tart, and the question of finance smote him suddenly. He had a vague recollection of friends and the Empire and the Continental, and he knew that he couldn't have much on him. He was just slipping out of bed to look through his pockets when she woke up and put a soft arm round his neck.

'Remember what you came here for last night and what you *didn't* do, darling,' she cooed.

Charlie had forgotten that. He *must* have been very drunk, he thought to himself, and as he sat up in bed his head whirled in confirmation. The girl pulled him gently down, and kissed him softly and lovingly.

'Naughty boy to have been so drunk last night,' she purred. 'Think of me, full of lust, ready to do *anything*, and you went to sleep like a log. I suppose you don't remember how you got undressed?'

Charlie admitted that he didn't.

'Well, I didn't take your clothes off, but my maid did, and put you into your pyjamas. She's out of the common pretty, yet with two women by you, you couldn't summon up a flicker of a stand. You've *got* to make up for it now, my lazy darling.'

Her little hand slipped over his stomach, undid the knot of his pyjama trousers, and played delicately with a very limp and lethargic phallus. Her other hand reached up behind her, and touched a bell. Charlie sank back, dreamily anticipating some further surprise.

Almost immediately a very smart and pretty girl, dressed in a sort of comic-opera maid's costume, came in without knocking.

'This gentleman isn't well,' said Charlie's hostess; 'bring the usual remedies.'

'The usual remedies' arrived very swiftly, and a tired and dejected Charlie noted, with a relieved glance, tea, coffee, tiny caviare sandwiches, delicately cut toast, almost smokingly hot little rolls, and more severe comforts in the shape of half-bottles of champagne, and several brands of liqueurs and brandy. On a separate tray were all sorts of fruit.

'If you are *very* hungry, darling,' said the little fairy of the bed, 'you can have anything you like in the way of a serious breakfast, but my advice is, play about with these little things now, and when we are up and bathed and so on, we'll have a proper meal in the garden by the river; it's a beautiful morning, and the lilies are lovely.'

'River, garden, lilies' – every evidence of wealth – Charlie began to wonder what he *had* struck, and to think more nervously than ever of his waistcoat pockets.

The pretty maid slipped a soft, rounded arm under Charlie's back, and raised him gently. She sat on the bed by his knee, the trays by her side on a table, and began to feed him like a baby. Charlie's delightful bedfellow lay back in amorous abandon.

'Nothing for me just yet, Elsie,' she said, smiling.

Charlie didn't quite know which way to look – both girls were so delicious. The maid's left hand lay, whether by accident or design, right on his cock, as she handed him drinks and sandwiches with her right. She had crossed her knees as she sat, and her lovely calves showed right up to the garter.

She wouldn't let him help himself, but he couldn't keep his hands idle. One toyed with her breasts, his fingers within her bodice dwelling lustfully on the swelling globes. The other hand his bedfellow had captured and it, too, was occupied. She had thrown the bedclothes aside, pulled her pyjama trousers down a little, and had Charlie's hand pressed gently on her clitoris.

Charlie ate and drank, and in a moment or two all lassitude had left him. His cock was rampant and erect, and his eyes wandered lasciviously and eagerly from one wickedly smiling face to the other.

The pretty maid gave him a long, hard-breathed kiss, which nearly set him on fire, before she left. As the door closed behind her, the other girl kissed him savagely on the neck.

'Take my things off,' she said, jerkily, to Charlie.

It was the work of a moment, and she was exposed in all her naked loveliness.

To his surprise, Charlie noticed that her *mons Veneris* carried no hair whatever; it was perfectly shaved, and as his fingers strayed downwards, he felt no trace of any stubble – even as he inclined his head and kissed it, he felt conscious that his chin, though he had had a late shave overnight, was far the rougher.

Charlie knew a bit; he hadn't knocked about town for nothing, and he was accustomed to pictures of the female form divine in which the hair was as conspicuously absent as the clothing, but he had never run across it in real life, and, curiously, it opened up a new vista of thought to him.

He kissed the shorn vagina and tasted some strangely sweet effluvia, which contrasted attractively with the caviare and the Georges Goulet.

Charlie, hardly able to contain himself, was just turning to fuck her in the age-old Adam and Eve way when her little hand, strong with passion, pushed him back.

'Lie quiet, darling,' she said – 'I'm going to be jockey,' and delicately she knelt astride him. 'Do you want it very much, sweetheart?' she cooed, as her fingers toyed with the luxuriant hairs of his bush.

'Want it, my God! I can't hold it – *be quick.*'

She parted the dainty red lips of her cunt with her diamond-flashing fingers and with just a movement of her wrist guided Charlie's member in; then she sank softly down on him till her bare breasts caressed his, and their lips became as one reciprocating engine of love and lust.

It was a convulsive grappling of two naked bodies, a passionate mingling of flesh, a communion of kisses – and a good deal more a communion of souls than those two young people quite realised at that time. Charlie really thought it was the best fuck he had *ever* had, and yet he didn't even know the girl's name or anything at all about her.

Somehow, though, he felt they had an affinity. As her legs twined over his bottom, and her strong, young arms grappled him to her with loving vigour, he felt somehow that he had never known the time when that red, hot, little tongue had not darted over his.

He did not quite know when he actually finished. He had half fainted; the girl's grip was loosened too; he seemed to be swimming in mid-air in a red mist. The most delicious fatigue possessed him. When he came to, she was still on top of him, but wide-awake and alert.

'Where are we?' he hesitated. 'I expect I owe all sorts of apologies.'

'You don't remember the motor drive?'

'No.'

'Well, you're near Staines, and you'll learn all about things when you feel a bit better. Try a little more caviare; it's extra fine, straight from a grand-duke friend of mine. You couldn't buy it in a shop.'

'Grand dukes – oh, Lord!' thought Charlie, 'what will she expect?'

She jumped up and went to a curtained door.

'The bathroom's here, dear,' she said; 'you can have it in a moment,' and she was gone.

Charlie Osmond finished a glass of champagne, got hastily out of bed, and examined his pockets. One pound, fourteen and sevenpence was the net – obviously useless.

He had done this sort of thing before, and subsequently paid, but there was something about this girl that made him uneasy. She was very much out of the ordinary.

He had some more champagne, and listened apprehensively to the splashing in the bathroom.

\*    \*    \*

We have to go through this book with Charlie Osmond, so our readers may just as well know a little about him.

A gentleman by birth, he had most of the right instincts and perversions. He had left Eton for the usual reason, and he regretted it. He did *not* want to bugger other boys, but some did, and he somehow hated to be out of the fashion. Unfortunately, he was found out.

At Oxford his career had been meteoric. He could not go to a very good college, owing to his school troubles, and his good allowance made him a star at — (we will suppress the name). He did many things he should not have done and his final exploit of sowing the word cunt in mustard and cress in the grass of the front quad, which came up under the astonished eyes of the dean's daughter, led to his final exit. His defence – that he had meant the word as a moral admonition to those of the varsity who had leanings towards malpractices in the sodomitical line – was not accepted, and he went.

The homecoming was as usual – nobody to meet him at the station but the chauffeur, and father in the gunroom.

> Your son's devotion to landscape gardening [ran the dean's note] is undoubtedly commendable, but we must remind you that the grass in the front quadrangle at — has for five hundred years preserved its virginity, and the word inscribed makes not only a blemish on the grass, but conveys a reflection on the locality. We are only pleased that news of the incident has not found its way to the American papers. We are, etc.,
>
> Hy. Charteris (*Dean*)

Charlie Osmond came to town with £300 a year, and a paternal kick up the arse. He could *not* live on £300 a year, and he didn't try to. It cost him that in clothes and drink.

Well, it had gone on somehow for some time, but the end – Canada – or something worse – was near.

Yet he realised that he was really a very nice young man; everyone liked him, and he liked most people, but he hadn't got a *carrière*, and he wanted one.

\*    \*    \*

The divinity came back, and sat down on the bottom of the bed, lighting a cigarette.

We have got to know about her.

She was *not* a clergyman's daughter.

Her father had prospered in the nitrate market, and, until the inevitable end, had prospered exceedingly, so his children were well brought up. Maudie Stevens went to school at Eltham, in Kent, and was 'finished' – well 'finished' – at a convent near Rouen.

She had her baby in a suburb of Paris, and her family gave her money and her *congé*. The money was luckily tied up, so that her father's sensational end at the Old Bailey did not affect her financially.

She had a few hundred a year, a detestation of suburbia, and no morals.

She took the inevitable end quite calmly, and became a tart, *pure et simple*.

She was very popular, and – but we shall see.

\* \* \*

Charlie Osmond started bluntly.

'I don't quite know,' he blundered, '*what* you think of me?'

She laughed, and twisted her hair into a bewitching knot over her forehead.

'Where I am, I don't know,' he went on. 'Who you are, I don't know; and I've no money to speak of. I feel a pig.'

'I know you well enough, Charlie Osmond. I shouldn't have picked you up, and brought you down here if I hadn't wanted you – but I *did*. Now make yourself at home; get into the bathroom. You'll find clean collars, and a new tooth-brush and things, and we'll have breakfast and talk. I haven't exactly brought you here for nothing.'

Charlie felt considerably relieved when he found himself alone in the dainty bathroom.

Every imaginable sort of comfort was ready to hand, and he enjoyed a most elaborate scented bath. After the final cold douche, he put down a stiff ice-cold brandy and soda and was ready for *anything* the world might bring forth.

Maudie was dressed when he came back into the bedroom – dressed in a simple summer muslin, which made him remember with a shock that he had been in evening clothes the night before.

Maudie obviously divined his thought.

'I expect you'll find flannels to do you in the wardrobe,' she said laughingly. 'I keep several sizes.'

In a few minutes Charlie was a smart young man, in immaculate boating flannels, and as he followed his hostess through the pretty hall and across the lawn to where a breakfast table flashed its silver, glass and napery temptingly under the trees, he felt he'd like to stop here forever.

Another pretty maid, in white, and a page-boy, in white ducks, waited.

Charlie frankly made a pig of himself. A cool breeze flickering over the Thames had given him a raging appetite, and everything was so very nicely done, and the pretty eyes opposite his were so twinklingly alluring.

CHAPTER TWO

## *Maudie's Garden and Studio*

On a little slope, very green and fresh-looking, and completely shut off from the house by the trees, a number of really sensible-sized cushions were spread. Thither, after breakfast, Maudie led the way, and flopped, making no bones about showing her lovely legs right up to the knee. Openwork stockings are distracting enough at the best of times, but when it comes to the very finest of red silk, and the tiniest of little, red morocco shoes at the end of them, matching exactly the scarlet sash encircling the wearer's tapering waist, it takes a strong man to think of anything but the worst. Charlie flopped by her side, and took a kiss, which was only stopped by the page-boy's judicious cough. He had the daily papers and cigarettes.

'I'll ring if I want anything,' she said. 'Now see that we're not disturbed.'

There was an electric bell fixed to one of the trees, likewise a telephone extension.

'My word, you *do* do yourself well,' said Charlie, nestling down very comfortably, and toying idly with the little dear's knees, 'telephone and all.'

'Oh, it's very convenient. I've a lot of journalist friends who like to lie about here in the summer, and there are telephone lines to their offices. It's wonderful how inventive you can be when you've got a nice girl all over you, and a feeling of delicious laziness. These cushions could tell a bit.

'Now, you put your hand up higher, *right* up; nobody can possibly see us unless they go past on a boat. I want to talk a little business to you.

'First of all, you'll want some clothes. I'm sending my car up to town. My chauffeur can take my message to Half Moon Street – you see I know where you live – and get what you want. Are you on the phone?'

'Yes.'

'Well, ring your man up; have you got a man?'

'Yes; I just about run to that.'

'Well, get on to him now; I want the chauffeur to go soon. I'm going to keep you here tonight – unless you've got anything very important on?'

'No; and if I had I'd miss it.'

'You won't be able to sleep with me. My really best financial boy is coming, and I've got to attend to him. I think you know him, Bertie Evans-James.'

'Bertie – Tubby Bertie; oh, Lord, yes! I wonder I haven't met you.'

'I don't come up to town much. I love this place and Paris. Now you ring up and tell your man that a chauffeur called Gerstein will call with your card.'

Charlie reached up to the receiver, which was hung conveniently low.

'One minute, dear,' whispered Maudie. 'I've a wicked little fad. When any of my men pals are telephoning, I like to get on top, and just ride on it; it's ripping.'

Charlie was only too pleased, and lay back as she knelt over him and loosened his trousers.

Lord knows what came out was stiff enough! Eight good inches of it, hard as steel, and panting with hot lust.

She bent and kissed it, first running her tongue lightly round the glans; then, with a quick movement she slipped her leg over and seemed to flick the great member into her boiling little volcano of a cunt.

It hurt Charlie a little as she thrust herself home and began to slip slowly up and down, but it was delightful pain.

His man's voice seemed strangely old, and Charlie wondered what on earth that staid personage would think if he knew exactly where his master was getting on the phone from. Suits he asked for, collars, shirts, etc., boots and ties, and at the hats he spent violently. He felt a savage bite on the neck, and collapsed with his man's voice in his ear, saying, 'Yes, sir, and your aunt's here, sir, and would like to speak to you, sir.'

Charlie gasped, but there was no way out of it; Aunt Lavinia must *not* be offended.

'Oh, Charlie, is that really you? What wonderful inventions these are. I feel I can almost *see* you – '

Charlie shuddered.

' – and I hear you're having your things sent down by motor. How nice. Do you know, I've never been in one. I shall take the chance of running down to see you; I can get back by train. See you later – goodbye' – and she hung up.

Charlie explained the situation to the girl, as she leisurely buttoned him up.

'Oh, let the old lady come,' she said. 'I can behave like a lady; don't you worry. I was brought up as one. I'll put on my very best party airs, and she won't complain of her dinner, I give you my word. Does she know Bertie, by the way?'

'Oh, certain to.'

'Very well; I'll be a foreign widow, who met Bertie in Hamburg or somewhere. I speak perfect French and German.'

Charlie weakly acquiesced.

'I'm afraid you don't quite know Aunt Lavinia,' he said; 'she's very, very mid-Victorian!'

'Never mind, I can be *early* Victorian. I'll be her friend for life before she's been here two hours. Now come along into the house, and I'll tell you what I really want you to do for me – or – it is a lovely morning, and I don't know whether you like swimming or not, but I do, and I've a lovely little private bathing place nearby.'

Charlie was very much ready, and after the page-boy had been sent to give the chauffeur his instructions, they wandered off, hand in hand, down a little lane to a highly palisaded backwater.

There were two big and comfortable dressing-rooms, one for men and one for women.

'Sometimes we are very respectable and wear bathing costumes and things,' Maudie explained; 'but sometimes, like this morning, for instance, we don't do anything of the sort, and you are just going to undress me, mother naked, and we'll swim about like Adam and Eve.'

It was not the first time Charlie had got into a bath with a cockstand, but it was the first time he had dived in to swim like that. When he turned over to float, the little siren Maudie swam up to him and laughingly tied a dainty handkerchief on to his rampant mast.

'*Now* you can show your colours,' she said. 'You look like a submarine with the periscope stuck out of the water.'

She swam like a sea-nymph, and her figure, all naked and glistening with the water as she poised herself for her dives, made Charlie forget all about Aunt Lavinia, tailors' bills or any worries in this world. He made an ineffective attempt to get into her while they were both floating – he had heard of such things being done – but the result was nearly a watery death for both. However, they managed to toss each other off, then Maudie called a halt, and they clambered out and on to the landing stage.

The mattresses, covered with thick towelling, were beautifully soft, and their wet bodies sank luxuriously into their embrace.

'There's a very pretty little grass slope over there,' said Maudie, 'if you prefer nature. For my part, I agree with the late lamented Oscar Wilde – Nature may be very nice to look at, but it was not intended to sit on. Let's lie here, and let the sun dry us. There are lots of little towels lying about if you want one.'

Charlie's only reply was a passionate kiss.

His hand strayed to where it shouldn't, but the girl put it gently away.

'Not just now, dear,' she said; 'we've had a good bit. Lie quiet in the sun. You can smoke if you like. You'll find cigarettes in the cupboard in the dressing-room, and all sorts of drink if you want it. Personally, I should like a little champagne cup. Yes, I should: my butler makes it to perfection. I'll phone up to the house.'

'But – he mustn't see us like this.'

'Oh, he won't; there's a sliding door opens into the back of the cupboard.'

She went to the telephone. How lovely she looked standing there in all her naked grace, quite like a Grecian goddess – and *what* a contrast to the very modern apparatus in her hand. Charlie longed to take a photograph of her, and the girl seemed to divine his thoughts.

'Like to take a picture of me? There's a camera in the shed. I know you photograph.'

Charlie took six. He was an ardent and expert photo-grapher, and he had taken many pictures from the nude, but he had never had such a model as this. He appreciated now the beauty of the shaven mount of Venus; she was shaved under the arms too.

The cup came in a beautiful old china bowl accompanied by two Venetian glasses with long silver stems, like magnified punch ladles. They squatted with the bowl between them, and sipped. It was heavenly.

'Does old – er – Tubby come to do stunts like this?' asked Charlie.

'Oh, Lord, yes; he flops about like a porpoise.'

'Lucky beggar!'

'Well, I suppose he *is* lucky. He spends a great deal on me, of course; you can see this house isn't run on air, but he is lucky in getting a girl a little out of the common to arrange amusements for him; you've no idea yet what we *can* do for you.'

'I should die.'

'Oh, no, you wouldn't. If you take lust delicately and scientifically, it hurts no one; only people who fornicate like animals, and have no thought above the actual parts of their bodies which are in contact, upset their constitutions. This is a pretty little swimming place, isn't it?'

'Ripping.'

'And the mixed bathing very much *au naturel* is jolly, isn't it?'

'Rather.'

'My own idea. They used to do it, I believe, in Medmenham Abbey days. Now we'll dress and go in; I want to show you the house. Bring the camera, and we'll develop those. Take some more of me in various stages of my getting dressed, and use up the whole spool.'

Charlie, nothing loth, did. First with just her stockings and shoes on, then with a hat added to that, next with drawers, and so on through the stages till the complete, idyllic, muslin-clad river girl used up the last exposure.

They got back to the house by another route, through a somewhat severely classical garden, peopled with very excellent statues of heathen gods and goddesses.

'Tubby doesn't like this,' she said; 'he calls it the Lemprièrium. I caught him one day trying to shoot the fig leaf off that Apollo with an airgun. I punished him by having him strip, gumming a great fig leaf on him, and making him walk about here for two hours: each time he passed the Apollo he had to apologise to it and kiss its behind. The others did laugh; you know what Tubby's figure is like.'

Charlie was prepared to be surprised at the house, but he was more than surprised. Very large, an old Elizabethan mansion, slightly built on to and modernised, it was from without the embodiment of stately grace while within it provided the most up-to-date comfort. Charlie remembered that Tubby's father owned many factories in Lancashire, but they must do pretty well to keep this up; the old man himself had a bit of a reputation for chorus girls.

They went cursorily through the house. It was not furnished at all like a tart's house, but rather like that of a great lady of fashion. The servants were certainly rather comic opera, and a prettier lot Charlie thought he had never seen. The menservants he encountered were French, bar the very staid old butler.

They came at last to a little boudoir overlooking garden and river.

'Now we'll talk,' said Maudie. 'First of all, give me that camera; I'll have the pictures developed.'

The white-clad page-boy took the machine.

'Firstly, Charlie Osmond, I know all about your skill as a photographer. Well, I'm mad on it myself, and I'm pretty good, as you shall see directly.

'Now, what I want you to do is this. I know you're not too well off – pardon my being blunt. I want you to look after my photography and find my models for me. You'll have to use a lot of tact, but you'll have a thundering good time.

'Why I want *you* is that I must have a gentleman; I can't have an ordinary professional photographer. I couldn't stick working with him, and Tubby wouldn't like it. My great hobby is pictures of girls, in the nude, of course, and that's why I have my own pussy shaved: they have to have it done too. They are shy at first, but soon get used to it. We have quite lively parties. But come along, you shall see the studio first before you decide.'

Maudie unlocked a curtained door.

'This room I *do* keep under lock and key,' she said.

It was a huge octagonal room, glass roofed, with an admirable north light. One end of the octagon was a complete small theatre with, explained Maudie, a large plant of scenery and every facility for producing all classes of stage plays.

'Wait till you see *some* of 'em,' Maudie went on. 'We've got some pretty wits among our members – we call it a club. It's supposed to exist for the practice of the higher photographic arts, and the exhibition of *real* life on the stage. It is damned real, too, I can tell you.

'Our finest bit of realism was a play which lasted, on and off, for nearly a year. It started with a courtship, rivalry, seduction – dark man, dark night, and that sort of thing, you know – of course in full view of the audience. Then he married her, and we ran through the first nine months of their life together, their lusts and their quarrels. How they both were untrue, and how she gradually became larger in condition till her belly was bang right up and she finally pupped in full view of the audience.

'Of course we were lucky in having a girl who was not only a very good actress, but happened to be like that, and was strong enough to play right through. It was Miss —,' naming a well-known celebrity.

Charlie started.

'Yes; that's how she spent her time when the papers said she was touring in Italy. Oh, she *is* a brazen bitch.'

But to the photography. Bar a number of photos lying on a big table on the carpeted daïs at the other end of the room, there was not much evidence of photography at all. No cameras, no pictures on the walls – these were entirely covered with what seemed to be a patchwork of little curtains.

'*Voilà*: hey, presto!' exclaimed Maudie, pressing a button at the side of the proscenium.

The walls altered as if at the touch of a fairy's wand, and a most gorgeous vista of photographic voluptuosity met Charlie's astonished and delighted eyes. Photos of every size were there, very many of them coloured, and most beautifully coloured.

There were no paintings except a life-sized oil of Maudie herself as Diana. That had been hung on the line at the Academy. Charlie remembered it well now: it was signed by a well-known French portrait painter, in fact the greatest of them all, and the discoverer of genius in many an Englishman.

But this picture, magnificent though it was, was quite dwarfed by the variety and beauty of the photos.

First in numbers came the nudes. They were none of them of the blatantly crude, erotic, fucking, all-ends-up type, but they were – well – not the sort that Aunt Lavinia ought to see.

There were many single nudes, very nearly always the model being Maudie herself. For this she apologised.

'You see, Charlie,' she said, 'I have a paucity of models. This *great idea* is only in its infancy yet; *that's* where I'm looking to you for help. Tubby's no good. If I left him to get me models he'd bring women like cart horses. Tubby has strange ideas of female beauty – why he is so infatuated with me, I *can't* think.

'No; I want more girl models for the *single* figures. It doesn't matter so much for the groups, as long as we have good principals.'

The single figures were very beautiful. There was a complete set of Maudie's life – Maudie in her bath – Maudie drying herself under the trees – Maudie in varying stages of dressing – Maudie riding, cycling, rowing, and in various gowns. The nearest approach to anything very suggestive was Maudie with only her stockings and shoes on, but every scrap of jewellery she possessed.

There were a number of pretty girl pictures, but with the same models again and again.

'We *must* have more flappers,' said Maudie, vehemently.

The groups, however, were of the more surpassing interest: very many depicted events in the world's history and biblical subjects were quite prevalent too. For instance, we had Susanna and the Elders. A lovely Susanna, mother naked, admiring herself in the well water, and the most lascivious-looking Elders admiring her too; in the middle distance, a charming girl and boy, quite naked, were playing prettily with each other. The scenic effects were splendid. Maudie confessed that she had the help in that line of a very well-known French actor-manager, and that an English actor-manager had put his scenic stock at her disposal.

Potiphar's wife was well treated. A naked Mrs Potiphar had just rent the garment from the fleeing Joseph, who, with one hand attempting to conceal his parts, was rushing from the room. Mrs Potiphar, who blazed with jewels, was of a pronouncedly Egyptian type, sinuous and wicked-eyed. In Joseph, Charlie had not the slightest difficulty in recognising a prominent young stock-jobber.

Where had he been in London all this time, and never heard of this place and their goings-on? he wondered.

Samson and Delilah – God bless my soul – it was the famous wrestler, with *very* little on, and *what* a Delilah – Maudie herself this time. In *Samson Agonistes*, Samson was similarly unencumbered with clothing.

In the fight between David and Goliath, the giant had been, by some ingenious photographic trick, made to look a very real giant, and his John Thomas was a thing like a quarterstaff, his balls like melons. A sweetly pretty little David stood boldly forth in the foreground, aiming the sling.

There were some pictures of the historic intimacy between David and Jonathan, which left little to the imagination.

We have missed the earlier episode of the Garden of Eden. Adam and Eve were very frankly naked and unashamed in several positions, and there were the dearest possible Cain and Abel.

The scene where, after the fall (which, by the way, was realistically treated), the man and woman get themselves clothed was admirably arranged.

The strange behaviour of Lot's daughters, when they sat in turn on their poor old father's prick and got themselves in the family way, was reproduced in detail, as also was Onan's encounter with his sisier-in-law, when he deliberately spilt his seed on the floor.

King David and Bathsheba on the roof, and later the same pair in bed, were fully illustrated.

Ancient Greece and Rome were imaginatively represented, especially the mythology of the former. A swan ('One of the king's from the Thames,' giggled Maudie) was on top of Leda, this time Maudie again, and Jupiter enveloped Danäe in a most cunningly contrived shower of gold. The chance to show Venus *anadyomene*, and all the other gods and goddesses plausibly naked, was fully utilised, but perhaps the best composition was Vulcan's revenge on the guilty lovers. Tubby figured always as a very tipsy Silenus.

In fact, everything in history of a picturesquely indelicate flavour was ruthlessly exploited.

Charlie was loud in his expressions of praise.

'This must all be very valuable,' he said.

'Tubby's papa offered me a good deal above a bit; said he wanted to present it to the Manchester Watch Committee.'

Apart from the historical groups, which, of course, included Lady Godiva, there were some very charming allegorical pictures. A humorous one was 'Fecundity', in which Tubby and a portly dame were surrounded by sons and grandsons, daughters and granddaughters, all dressed like Adam and Eve.

There were amusing modern pictures too – of life behind the scenes, river pleasure parties – and many clever snapshots.

'Well, that'll do for the present,' said Maudie; 'come and lunch. I'm rippingly hungry, and after lunch we'll have to get ready for Tubby and Aunt Lavinia.'

'I don't want any lunch, or Tubby, *or* Aunt Lavinia,' grumbled Charlie. 'I want to go to bed with you for the rest of the day.'

'Oh, you'll see lots of me in the future. I think you see the possibilities of our great idea. This is only a penny peepshow at present. I, with your help and Tubby's money, am going to make it world-famous.'

Lunch was simple, but very delicate. After the salmon cutlets there was just a duck and salad, and a light savoury. Only hock cup and Grand Marnier with the coffee.

Two new maids Charlie had no difficulty in recognising as the originals of girls in the photographs, and in the page he recognised at once the boy David.

'Now' – Maudie lifted an admonitory finger – 'this is the lie.

'Firstly, regarding your presence here. I knocked you down in Kensington last night. You were unconscious, but not bad enough for the hospital, so I brought you here.

'To Aunt Lavinia, I am the widow of a Polish count, and I knew Tubby abroad. That's all. Ah, I think I hear the car.'

The hum of the motor drew nearer, like the sound of a fury flying on the wind. Charlie fidgeted uneasily, and mechanically turned face downwards one or two very *outré* photographs. Aunt Lavinia mattered financially very much indeed, and *could* his charming hostess be trusted?

Maudie was perfectly calm. As the scrunch of the wheels on the gravel denoted the arrival, she gave a final little twirl to a kiss-curl, and said to Charlie: 'Kiss me for luck.'

It was Aunt Lavinia.

The door swung open, and before the footman had time to announce them, Lady Lavinia and Tubby were in the room.

CHAPTER THREE

## With the Nature Worshippers at Maudie's Mansion

Charlie's aunt, the dowager Lady Lavinia McCree, was not a woman who 'came' into rooms, nor could she be said to 'enter' them, or even 'rush' or 'burst' or 'sweep' in. She was there all of a sudden, before you had any idea of her arrival. Charlie was kissed, and Maudie warmly shaken hands with.

'How are you, Charlie? How foolish of you to be knocked down: I'm sure it was very good of this lady to pick you up. Of course you were drunk – so like your poor father. If there'd been motorists about to knock him down and look after him, he'd never have got into the Thames at Westminster Bridge, thinking it was his bath, and caught his death.

' – And so, my dear, you are Countess Orloffsky. Of course you must be sister-in-law or something to poor Paul Orloffsky; I knew him well. He married his cook, and she poisoned him with Rough on Rats in a paté, or something, and married the butler, and they took a hotel in Switzerland and had so many children. I fear he was a sad lot, my dear – your brother-in-law, I mean, not the butler – just like Charlie's father, and Charlie – but now that he has found a friend in you, I *know* you will have an *immensely* good influence. *And* that dear, good Mr Evans-James, too, I do wish Charlie could see more of him – *such* a good influence.'

Tubby, who had been stifling a silly giggle, now almost exploded.

'So good of you, my dear, to let me use your car, such nice things, and so convenient, especially for people like Mr Evans-James, being so fat, and unable to get about for his good works. His dear mother tells me how often he has to be away from town seeing after his camp missions.'

The old lady, having rattled this out at express speed, shut up as suddenly as she had begun, and sat down.

When she had been borne away to tidy up, Tubby took Charlie into the smoking-room.

Tubby was a very fat little man, with an exceptionally solemn cast of countenance, except when drunk, which was not infrequent. He had more money than he knew what to do with, and he welcomed anyone who would help him spend it as a benefactor.

'I say, old chap,' he said, 'this *is* a go.'

'Oh, I think your lady friend'll carry it off – auntie won't stop long.'

'I'm not so sure about that; she's after me and those damned camps that I've talked so much about. The place at home is full of photos of 'em. Maudie faked 'em here. There's a wonderful studio here y'know – perhaps she's shown it you?'

'She *has.*'

'Oh, I say, you mustn't be upset or anything – but this *is* a hot shop, y'know. Well, I thought it too hot even to ask you. Oh, I say, did you *really* get knocked down by Maudie and the car. I could have *sworn* I saw you coming out of the Empire, boozed as a cock-bird. You didn't go and pick her up anywhere, did you?'

'Of course not; she wouldn't. She's been talking of nothing but you.'

'Bless her little heart! Well, we must make the most of it, Maudie says. You're staying the night. All the maids fuck, y'know,' he giggled fatuously. 'Try little Jessie.'

'Oh, I don't think so, old chap. I don't do much of that sort of thing.'

'No more do I; not 'cos I don't like it, y'know, but I'm so fat, and it's such a dashed sweat. Like seeing other chaps do it much better. Lots of that here: oh, it is a hot shop. Pa's been here, he! he! Gad, if your old aunt cottons on! I must put Maudie up to the settlement-camps business. Well, I must go and wash. You'll have the green room – artichoke, I call it – next to ours tonight. I'll wake you tomorrow morning.'

Charlie had fully determined to take this job on. He foresaw but little trouble over the Tubby business. He would make himself so useful that he knew he would be forgiven anything.

After dinner that night he begged to be excused. Sitting alone in the little smoking-room, he began to think out his plans.

It *was* a great idea. With that wealth he could ransack Europe for girls. Wasn't it better than £300 a year and the secretaryship of a club – and if, in duty bound to Tubby, he mustn't go wrong with Maudie, for whom he already felt an almost ungovernable lust, there certainly would be no lack of others.

At that moment one of the pretty maids came in without knocking.

'Oh, mistress's compliments, sir, but she'd forgotten to give you the key of the wine and spirit cupboards; there they are. I'll open them.'

She brought out the necessaries, also a pile of books.

'Mistress says you might like these, too,' she giggled. 'Let me show you the best,' and she flicked over the pages of an obviously very erotic book, full of coloured plates of lust in every form. 'Saucy, aren't they? Look at this.'

It portrayed three couples, hopelessly mixed up, tongues, lips, cocks and cunts in helpless and joyful confusion.

She put her hand on Charlie's shoulder, playfully flicking his ear, and bending over kissed his forehead, pressing her breasts against the back of his head.

'I'm glad you've come,' she cooed; 'so are all the girls. We like you. I'm going to bring your hot water up tonight; mind you're awake.'

Charlie couldn't help it. He pulled her round on to his knee. She put his hand under her clothes herself, and wriggled. 'It's all right,' she said; 'no one will come in. This is what I'm best at,' and she slipped between his legs and undid his fly buttons with her teeth.

'You little devil!' was all Charlie could say.

A confused, gurgling noise was the only answer – his prick seemed to be half-way down her throat.

He nervously fingered her head – she had deliciously soft hair – and abandoned himself to a transport of lust.

She gently tickled his balls till his cock seemed to throb like a motorbike engine, and – well, it couldn't last for ever: he spent like Niagara.

The pretty girl threw back her head and gulped it down.

'I say, old chap,' came Tubby's voice from behind, 'you're starting early, y'know, and you've got the nicest, by God, y'have, but, I say, your aunt's looking for you, and she's going to stay the night, and what the devil are we going to do, what, what!'

The pretty maid stood up, blushing, and hung her head.

'You'd better be off, my dear,' said Tubby; 'and, for heavens sake, be careful what you do and say while that old lady's in the house.'

When they were alone, Charlie apologised.

'Oh, don't worry about *that*, old chap. You can do what you like to the girls, but it's your aunt – quick, for God's sake put those books away: I hear a rustle.'

Charlie was just in time. Lady Lavinia was in the room just as the cupboard door slammed.

She sniffed at the collection of liquors.

'As I thought, drinking – and *solitary* drinking. Why couldn't you be like your friend and come into the drawing-room for a little music?'

'And what's this?' She picked up a maid's cap from the floor. 'One of the *servant's* caps! What's it doing here?'

'Oh, I suppose she must have dropped it,' answered Charlie, pettishly. 'I'll come down to the drawing-room now. It'll be bedtime in a few minutes.'

\*     \*     \*

In the servants' quarters of the house, discussion as to the identity and *raison d'être* of the new guests ran rife.

Young men of the world like Charlie were no new thing, but Aunt Lavinia – in such a house – well!

'Such particular instructions. I've had to clear her room of anything saucy,' said the old housekeeper, gossiping in her room with the butler and the chauffeur; 'and I'm to take 'er tea myself: let none of them 'ussies go near.

'It makes me fair nervous, it do. Not that I altogether 'old with these games 'ere, but we're all in it, with our eyes open – oh, dear, *if* she should see some of them pictures.'

' 'Twould be a to-do, and no error,' said the butler.

'And the good lady she tink Mr Bertie so good young man vos – ha! ha!' and the chauffeur laughed viciously. 'She into what you call a 'ornets' nest 'as got, is it not?'

In the servants' hall speculation was also rife: guests seldom arrived at that house except in very large parties, motor loads at a time, as a rule. And as for mistress bringing home a single young man, she hadn't done such a thing for years.

No one had seen his condition when he arrived except the chauffeur, who had maintained a dogged silence. He had been told to do so, and his job was too good to lose.

They were a free and easy lot in the servants' hall at Maudie's, with a very large preponderance of women, mere girls, many of them, and all pretty. In fact, the house was ridiculously over-stocked with females. There was nothing for them to do save when the very big parties were on, and then they were more required for the photography than anything else.

There were only two men, both deft-handed servants and both French, and a French-American cook, who was rather a wet blanket on the general irresponsibility of the girls. There remained the page-boy, and several other young boys and girls who helped in the scullery.

The girls did not care much for the two Frenchmen, and the cook thought of nothing at all but inventing new dishes; hence the joy with which Charlie was received.

It was an appetising scene. Everything in the house was done, and the girls sprawled in varied alluring *déshabillés* – it was a hot night, and drawers and chemise, or chemise only, or drawers and vest, or, for one or two, vest only was the chosen attire. Two were quite naked. The room was very comfortable to lounge in, and Maudie didn't care what happened so long as she was waited on quickly. Two girls remained dressed, ready to see their mistress and Lady Lavinia to bed when rung for.

The page-boy was in general demand, fetching coffee and cigarettes, and came in for a good deal more petting than was good for him. In fact, he was quite *blasé*. The warm caress of a semi-naked divinity had *no* effect on him.

They disappeared to bed by degrees, till only Elsie and May were left.

'Are you going to take the new gentleman any hot water?' queried May.

'Yes,' answered Elsie.

It was she who had come into the smoking-room.

'May I follow you?'

'A good half-hour after me. I tell you, dear, I need something badly; I haven't had my legs opened for a week, and it's just about time. You come in later, and we'll see what the two of us can't make him do; he's got a rare big 'un.'

'Right' – and they sealed the compact with a kiss.

There are few things more engaging than the sight of two pretty women, who are both lustful, and who really care for each other, kissing as if they meant it.

\*     \*     \*

Upstairs, after two whiskies and sodas, which she was not accustomed to, Aunt Lavinia became first garrulous, then sleepy. After her departure, the three culprits first looked serious, then giggled.

Maudie spoke first.

'Look here, Tubby,' she said, 'the Lord blew Charlie against my carburettor: I recognised him, and brought him here, *for a purpose*. That purpose I have explained to him, and will to you. I want him to supervise our photographic and theatrical sessions. What do you think?'

'Oh, I think he'd do admirably,' said Tubby, a little doubtfully; 'but what does Charlie think?'

'Oh, I'm game enough.'

'Then let's call it a deal right off,' said Maudie. 'I know you two boys will get on rippingly. We'll just have a nightcap, and then, like Mr Pepys, to bed.'

\*     \*     \*

Tubby rolled over in bed, and grunted, then he kissed his bedfellow, and was immediately asleep. Maudie sighed. She had had a great deal too much of this of late. She thought over the events of the day, and longed for Charlie. For one wild moment she recollected how firmly Tubby slept, and contemplated making a dash for Charlie's room – but prudence prevailed. She mustn't jeopardise the future. She took up a book, *Nadia*, a lustful romance, and tried to read herself to sleep, but in vain. Her blood boiled, and at last she woke up Tubby roughly.

'Tubby, dear, I *must* and *will* be fucked,' she said. 'You hardly ever touch me, and yet you expect me to be true to you. Come on.'

Tubby acquiesced sadly. His extreme stoutness made it quite impossible for him to attack in the old Adam and Eve fashion. He had to do it as the beast of the field. He got out of bed and turned Maudie over its edge. Then, without seeming in the slightest enraptured by the sight of her snowy white buttocks, he deliberately plunged his sausage-like machine into that gap which should only have been reserved for connoisseurs.

Of course he liked it: he was very healthy, and full of good food and wine, and his penis swelled enormously as his strokes increased in vigour. Maudie lay on her stomach, her pretty little face buried in the lace-edged pillow, and in her brain, behind her closed eyes, just a blissful vision of Charlie.

Oh! if it had only been Charlie!

The fact is known that sometimes women who, when madly lustful for a particular man, are forced to be carnal elsewhere, derive really more pleasure from the beatific dream of their fancied darling, who in a vision is responsible for the flesh spasms which the unseen operator brings about, than they do when the real darling is in the saddle, so to speak.

Maudie certainly loved it, and she was only just conscious enough of what had happened to bite her tongue to stop crying 'Charlie' as the last violent stroke from her fat lover sent a hard-shot torrent right up to the doors of her womb.

'My God,' she thought, 'I really believe Tubby has copped me this time.'

She hastened to syringe, a precaution she seldom took with her fat lover.

Tubby, on his part, sank exhausted into an armchair.

'You've fair whacked me this time, petlet,' he gasped. 'I've never had a fuck like that with you before. What's come over you?'

The dream was still in Maudie's brain as she answered vaguely, 'How – how can you help it, when you love so much?'

When Tubby did turn off to sleep he dreamed rapturously. Maudie, too, slept well; she was thoroughly tired at last. These physical and mental fucks combined are pretty fairly damaging to the vitality.

Lady Lavinia, when the pretty maid had helped her out of her clothes and given her a nightdress, the decorations of which ill chimed with the elderly widow, removed her wig, put her teeth in a glass, and sniffed round the room.

She could not but approve of the comfort. No detail necessary to coax comfort to the weary or lazy bed-goer was missing.

Maudie had put it to her very delicately that if she had neuralgia – or anything – there was 'something' in the cupboard.

She had a look, and found, in addition to the 'something', a pile of books, one of which she picked out at random.

It was prettily bound, and called *Nemesis Hunt*. She took it back to bed with her, had a very hearty drop of the 'something', and opened it.

A good many readers of this book may have read *Nemesis Hunt*. They will remember that that charming and loquacious lady somewhat lets the tail go with the hide in her confessions. A fuck is called a fuck, and there is more than fucking in the three ingenuous volumes.

Lady Lavinia's eyes dilated as she read. Once before, in the very early days of her married life, she had been shown a book like this by her husband, and she remembered now, with a sigh, *what* a night they had subsequently had.

Her first impulse was to throw down the book in anger – the consciousness of her position, her reputation, flashed through her brain – but curiosity prevailed, and Lady Lavinia, firmly adjusting her glasses, took another strong sip of the 'something', and started seriously in to read the first volume of *The Confessions of Nemesis Hunt*.

When young, she had been very pretty, and had been much courted. She had loved admiration, and had flirted above a bit.

Her short married life with the late earl had been a long round of love and lust, and frank sexual enjoyment, but his sudden death had brought about an equally sudden revulsion of feeling.

Lady Lavinia had turned suddenly very good – mid-Victorian good. She had mourned her husband, and put a great deal of mournfulness into other people's lives by doing so – as have other illustrious widows.

Now there came back a rush of something – it must have been Georgian – and she let down the drawbridge.

At the end of the fifteenth page of Nemesis Hunt's pleasant confessions, she decided to leave on the morrow, *but* return.

*Nemesis* was put under the pillow, and in that very ultra-modern house there slept what may be described as a memory of Cremorne.

\*     \*     \*

Charlie Osmond went to bed with mixed feelings. He had had a very good time; he had a prospect of future life in view, which he rather welcomed – *but*, he wanted to be with Maudie – not to be immoral, but to talk. It flatly bored him to go to bed.

Outside, the Thames valley looked very peaceful. The dogs, the chickens, everything slept, except Charlie – *and* Elsie and May, who, after seeing to the little wants of Lady Lavinia and Maudie, bided their time for an invasion into Charlie's room.

That worthy had his suspicions of impending events. He did not lock the door, but sat by the window in his pyjamas, and gazed peacefully out over the moonlit garden and river.

It was altogether rather too nice, too idyllic, and well – the door opened, and Elsie came in without knocking.

She was fully dressed, and carried a tray with hot water and glasses.

Charlie laughed.

'I somehow expected you,' he said; 'but do you know it's very wrong? You don't know what I am, whether I'm married or not, or *what* trouble this might get me into.'

Elsie laughed.

'Well, I've done it,' she said. 'I meant to from the first moment I saw you. Give me a cigarette and a drink, and let me come and sit in the window, and you won't be bored for the next half-hour, I can promise you.'

Elsie curled up on the corner of the window-seat, the moon full on her delicate little features, lit the proffered Albany cigarette, sipped a little of the whisky and Rosbach, and grinned, frankly grinned.

'I suppose you think it frightful cheek,' she suggested.

'Well, I can't say I don't like your cheek,' and he kissed it.

Elsie kissed him back on the lips, and took off her bodice. She had very pretty arms, and a gold bangle with a purple enamel medallion, worn just above the left elbow, did not make them less attractive.

She drank a little more of the Three Star Bushmills, stood up and slid her skirt off: then her chemise – she wore no petticoats – and to cut a long story short, her next sitting-place was on Charlie's knee, and the next kiss had nothing to do with cheeks.

Charlie lifted her on to the bed. Even then, though she was exasperatingly pretty, he could not help thinking of Maudie.

She curled over him, slowly, deliberately and maliciously taking both his hands in hers, and rubbing her soft cheeks against his.

There must be something in telepathy, for at the moment, the precise moment that Charlie reconciled himself to a connection which he *knew* would be nice, but which he really did not want, save for the exquisite pleasure in thinking that Elsie's arms were Maudie's, that latter lady saw in a blue mist of ecstasy the image of a very loving Charlie – poor Tubby being merely the engine-driver who drove the imagination of her recklessly lustful brain.

Charlie frankly let himself go. There was no light in the room at all bar the shafts of the moon, filtering through the swaying trees. The silhouetted skyline and the delightfully placid atmosphere made Charlie lazy.

He had some recollection of little tickling fingers swiftly undoing the strings of his pyjamas, little tickling fingers also playing with an already erect member, naked arms twisted round his neck, firm, plump legs twisted round his thighs, and – well – he was in – well in – and those soft cheeks were most lustfully pressed to his.

Maudie had been very loving, *but* – all said and done – as he felt all his love juice being sucked out of him, *this*, Charlie couldn't help admitting, was better still.

He came in a long rhapsody; the girl jerked the eiderdown over them, and snuggled up. He didn't know whether she meant to stay the night or not, or what the morals of this peculiar house permitted, but it was *very* comfortable.

He was just going to sleep when the door opened very quietly, and *another* girl came into the moonlight.

Charlie gave up. He remembered where he was, and determined to die game. The 'other girl' apologised laughingly, and the original giggled in the sheets.

'You don't mind May, do you?' she said.

'No,' was Charlie's answer; 'but it's got to stop at May, you and May. If I've got to go through the whole personnel of the establishment, I give up.'

May did not answer – but she seemed to *slide*, just as Elsie had done, out of her clothes, and into bed.

Poor, but happy Charlie – he realised now what a squeezed lemon must feel like – but he valiantly did his duty.

May was more placid than Elsie, more tender, more caressing, perhaps, but Charlie's cock was just as stiff as he felt his balls right against the soft buttocks of his new love.

It was a long fuck and a delightful one. Elsie, wicked little devil, gave every help in her power. She flung back the clothes, and there they lay, three naked bodies in the moonlight. There was no artificial light save the glow of Elsie's cigarette end.

Elsie slipped the pillow down so that her little friend's bottom was just correctly raised, and, as Charlie knelt between May's legs, she guided his penis dexterously in.

May, of course, was shaved, in the fashion of everyone in Maudie's mansion, and Charlie began more and more to appreciate the added charm of the hairless cunt, as he thrust his fingers between their bodies and felt the soft, warm, smooth flesh.

Elsie crept right on top of them, her head between Charlie's legs, so that her tongue swept over and over his swelling balls. As his cock slipped in and out of May, her fingers played with it. May had a large cunt, and Elsie's little finger could slip in beside Charlie's cock.

Her cunt was on his backbone, and on that she frigged herself – he felt the warm love moisture much about the same time as he spent himself in May.

He didn't recollect the actual end, didn't recollect anything till a stream of daylight dazzled him into being, and he found himself alone – with a little note pinned on each side of his broad pillow.

Each read the same: 'Thanks *so* much.'

Only the handwriting and the signature were different. One 'Elsie' – the other 'May'. He was thoroughly wakened up by the arrival of the page-boy with tea and a note.

The note simply ran: 'Get down to breakfast as quickly as you can; in the garden; Tubby's going, so's Aunt Lavinia, and we've *got* to talk business.'

Aunt Lavinia was 'deadly' at breakfast, but she made it plain, in no uncertain terms, that she was coming back.

Tubby, rather a weary Tubby, shovelled her into the car, and they disappeared with a toot and a cloud of dust.

'Well,' said Maudie, coughing the petrol fumes out of her throat, 'I shan't ask you what you've done with your night. I want to get to business at once. Tubby *quite* sees the business side of the affair.'

## CHAPTER FOUR

# *London's Lust Market*

Near the Barbican is a London street of which one would *not* expect great possibilities. All the busy city traffic roars by at the street's end, but in itself it is very unobtrusive.

There, in a large, rambling, old-fashioned house, Charlie Osmond had established what he liked to call his 'office'.

Ugly enough to look at from the outside, the 'office' was not without attractions within.

Photographs – though not so elaborate as in Maudie's own studio – were conspicuous, and the furniture, especially the two lazy divans, were very comfortable, and suggestive.

Here Tubby paid the rent, and here Charlie presided, when he was not travelling in search of his models.

Maudie had a tiny suite of rooms on the top floor, with a staircase leading on to a flat roof.

She sat there one evening, waiting for Charlie, who was due home with, she hoped, further prey.

The hum of a motor made her look over the low parapet. It *was* Charlie, and the closed car disgorged four little cloaked figures, and Elsie.

Maudie went down, just pausing on the way to telephone Tubby's club the one mystic word 'Tenuc', which, as all our readers possibly know, is back slang for cunt.

Charlie came into her room.

'I've got four little peaches, all from the north. The last is a hot 'un, and no mistake. She had to sit on my knee as the car was so crowded, and, oh, Lord, I have had a horn! I thought my poor John Thomas would burst.'

Maudie laid her hand lovingly on it and it sprang into being again.

'I'm sorry, dear, I can't oblige,' she said, 'because I'm unwell, and very badly unwell. I *daren't* when I'm like that. Shall I suck you off, or will you have Elsie?'

'Well, don't think me a beast, darling, you know how I love you. I'm so damned randy that I feel I *must* have a good square fuck. Oh, God, take your hand off, or I shall come in my trousers.'

Maudie rang, and a neat little, semi-flapper maid was sent to fetch the fuck-to-be.

'Another thing, I'm expecting Tubby, and he still thinks I'm true to him, bless him.'

'On the sofa, Elsie, and quick, the poor boy's randy.'

The pretty girl put her tongue out saucily, got quickly on the broad sofa, and pulled up her clothes to the waist

'My word, you *have* got pretty legs,' said Maudie; 'I believe they're more perfect than mine. Let's measure.'

She pulled up *her* clothes.

'Oh, for God's sake, come off it,' said Charlie. 'I haven't had a blow through for a week. Neither of your legs is as fine as this,' and he produced his throbbing member.

It certainly was a very fine one, and it had been admired all over Europe. They've got a model in clay of it in Suzette de Vries' place in the Rue Colbert. On his birthday it is hung with ribbons.

'No time for taking down trousers,' he said, and in a twinkling his arms were clasped round her shoulders, and her shapely calves were twisted round his thighs.

Maudie slipped her hand between them to see how close they were.

They might have been a single being. There was not the usual commingling of hair, for Charlie was now shaved, in deference to Maudie's wishes, and Elsie, of course, was too.

They hardly moved. Most of Maudie's friends were adepts at what she called 'thrill fucking'. That barred the rough piston-like 'in and out' thrusts, and the consummation was reached after a delicate succession of clasps and pressures and limb thrills. Elsie, her hands beneath Charlie's coat, tickled his spine. His hands massaged her back. Their eyelashes met in gentle titillation, and their tongues played softly with each other's. Maudie, sitting alongside – the couch was very broad – gently smoothed Charlie's head.

'Oh, I say, y'know, Maudie, you *ought* to lock the door. It's damned indecent, y'know, Maudie. I've got some fellers with me, and they might have come in, dashed awkward, y'know.'

Tubby's voice seemed quite concerned.

'Don't be jealous, fat-head, *you're* going to have a genial afternoon.'

'Good, oh! I say, who's the artist on top in the fuck?'

'Only me, old son,' grunted Charlie.

'Then buck up, laddie,' said the fat man, and gave his bottom a sturdy smack. 'I want to hear what's going to happen. Fuck on, Macduff, and get it over.'

Charlie finished with a deep sigh, and uncoupled.

'Now then,' said Tubby, 'I've got fellers waitin'. There's old General Fitzhugh, randy as a bull, and young Phil Learoyd, just down from Cambridge, and that poet chap with the long hair, Claude Lestrange: he's been making poetry all the way down.'

'I'll just run down and see the kids,' said Maudie. 'Charlie'll explain.'

'Buck up, old sport, then,' said Tubby; 'shove your cock in, and tell us all about it. Elsie, run along and syringe: we don't want you with your belly up.'

Charlie explained briefly that he had got some girls for more photography.

'They're all north country – Newcastle hinnies, and the eldest knows above a bit, I think. I've had some new shaped razors made for you in Sheffield. They couldn't think what the devil I wanted them for.'

Maudie met the girls in the little waiting-room near the studio. They were examining the pictures with interest.

Charlie certainly had done well. Four sweetly pretty faces met Maudie's pleased gaze.

The eldest and tallest, a brunette, had an almost Spanish face, rich, ripe red lips, and a haughty poise. She was the relic, perhaps, of some Spanish Armada prisoner who had dropped his love-stick in a Northumberland wench.

The other three were about the same height. One had a mass of Titian red hair, and the extreme pallor of skin that goes with it.

The other two were blondes, obviously with Danish and Norse blood in them, both with clear blue eyes.

They were all daintily clad. Charlie had stopped in Manchester and seen to that. The eldest had her skirts just below the knee, but the others showed the kneecap, and a fringe of pretty *frou-frou* underclothes.

They were all consciously proud of their obviously unaccustomed finery.

Maudie kissed them, found out their names, made a fuss of them generally, and gave them tea.

She was alone for a moment with the eldest girl.

'Say, mum,' said the latter, 'I'm no kid, and I can see that we weren't brought here only to be pretty artist's models. Now, *I'm* game for anything, and I expect the others will be. They can't read or write, so I'll do the writing home to their mammas; that'll be best, won't it?'

It certainly was sensible, and Maudie was very glad. There had been times when she *had* been a bit nervous.

Likewise, which was very awkward, there was a little disaffection in the camp. May had fallen frankly and openly in love with Charlie, and was obviously jealous. Charlie did not reciprocate, but Maudie could not afford to have a split, and had almost to *beg* of him to afford her occasional embraces. If May chose to give things away in the outside world, it might be very unpleasant. They were always prepared for flight, motors in readiness, and a big steam yacht, but they did not *want* to have to fly.

Charlie and Tubby went down to the 'office' or studio. General Fitzhugh was tramping round the room, fiercely twisting his moustache, and ejaculating, 'Ha!' at intervals, as he spotted anything particularly tasty in the photographs.

Tubby's undergraduate friend sat meekly, rather uneasily, on a divan, and the poet wandered soulfully about, humming faintly.

'Ah, general,' said the poet to the old officer, who was very closely examining the life-size portrait of a fascinating young lady, which gave particular emphasis to her vagina, 'ah, general, a tempting subject:

> How sweeter than the horrid clash of arms,
> The contemplation of those naked charms.'

The general sniffed: he did not like poetry, or poets. 'A dashed fine young woman, sir,' he snorted.

The poet persisted:

> 'Dost thou not yearn, O son of Mars, to thrust
> The vibrant signal of a lusting man
> Into yon fragrant arbour, there to place
> In form of sperm ambrosial, a fair child?
> Dost thou not – '

But the general turned on him. 'I don't know what the hell you mean, sir, by all that tomfool nonsense, but if you've the accursed effrontery to call my cock a "vibrant signal", I'd have you know that the word cock has been good enough for the Fitzhughs for generations, sir. "Vibrant signal", indeed, you'll be calling my arsehole a railway tunnel next.'

'Oh, sir,' protested the poet, ' 'tis but poetic licence.'

'Then you ought to dashed well have your licence taken away and, look here, if by "fragrant arbour" you mean that young person's cunt, I'd have you know that the Fitzhughs call it cunt, sir, and always have. My father called it cunt, my mother had a cunt, I came out of a cunt, and many a cunt have I stuck my good cock into.

' "Fragrant arbour"! there's a damned good stink attached to some of them, and I *like* it.

'And don't you refer to my good spunk as "ambrosial sperm", or I'll toss myself off in your eye, and let you know whether it smells ambrosial or not.'

Tubby, overhearing, laughed aloud.

Directly afterwards, Maudie, followed by her flapper recruits, entered. The girls stared about them in amazement, all save the eldest, who frankly grinned, and returned the old general's ogle with interest.

Elsie entered with a friend of Maudie's, a middle-aged, Anglo-French woman, whom we have not met before in this narrative.

She was a Madame Rade, and had been an actress. Still the amount of money she had made, *not* at acting, had enabled her to consult her growing corpulency and retire.

She was a jolly woman, very sexy, and there was very little wickedness she was not up to, and expert at. It was she who had taught Maudie the art of the 'thrill fuck'.

With her came her adopted niece, a very typical French flapper. Her skirts were short and plaid, her boots, on her slight, delicate legs, were very high and elegant, and her rather long hair fell in two plaits down her back.

Madame was educating her for the stage, equally for a life of smart prostitution, and she was having her taught several languages.

'I have seen *so* much money lost by charming tarts,' she said, 'just because they could *not* talk any language but their own. After all, fucking is very nice indeed, but a man *does* like a little love chat, and a student of nature *does* like to be interested. There's one new brothel in Berlin where the girls have regular lessons every day.

'Those girls *do* score over the lassies whose conversation is limited to phrases such as, "You fuck my cat: oh, such a nice cat, only ten franc." '

Madame Rade had not let the girl go wrong yet; she wanted a big price for that precious virginity, but there was nothing the little darling didn't know. Her greeting kiss to Charlie was by no manner of means virginal.

Maudie had explained to the girls that the studies would be in the nude, and that they mustn't mind being inspected by quite a number of artists.

The assembled men were introduced as artists, and then one of the girls was told to undress. She rather timidly asked if she was to do it there, or was there a screen.

'Here, of course, darling,' said Maudie; 'you'll soon get used to that. Never mind your shoes and stockings this time. We only want to see the upper part of your figure now, so that we can tell *what* sort of picture you'll do for.'

Charlie had bought very pretty underlinen indeed, and as the upper garments slid away the little darling was a scrumptious sight. The poet sighed voluptuously. He was about to burst into song, when he caught the general's eye.

'Oh, one thing,' said Maudie; 'I forgot, dearie; have you any hair on your body?'

'Yes, a little, mum,' she replied.

'I'm afraid, then, dear, that you must let that be shaved off. You see, all our pictures here are without hair. It won't hurt you: don't be frightened, and this gentleman,' pointing to Tubby, 'is quite an expert, aren't you, Tub-Tub?'

Tubby grinned; he had been examining the ingenious razors which Charlie had brought from Sheffield: no wonder the good Messrs Rogers had been surprised. They were in several shapes, and no steady hand could do any possible harm.

'Oh, yes, it must be done,' said Maudie, as the girl stood naked with a sea of *frou-frou* undies round her ankles. The poet could not resist it:

> 'Child Venus rising from the sea,
> No crested waves could fairer be
> Than those sweet frills:
> Oh, daintier than – '

'Young man,' said the general, very severely, 'during the Mutiny I had men blown from the cannon's mouth for *less* than that.'

Maudie patted the blushing girl on her naked shoulder, and led her to a big chair, with a front extension, something like a dentist's.

She lay back, her bottom raised on a cushion, her legs wide apart.

Tubby approached with his tray of instruments. The poor girl shuddered, and involuntarily closed her legs.

This was too much for the poet. Waving his hand first towards the girl, and then the general, he declaimed:

> 'Back, ruthless youth, oh, spare, oh, spare, I crave,
> That down ethereal. Can'st thou dare to shave
> The rippling foliage of the Venus Hill?
> Turn rather here, and thy vandal will
> On *this* brave warrior, used to clash of steel,
> His manly forest clip – '

'By God, damme, sir,' roared the general, 'if anyone dares to lay one finger on my bush, I'll cut off his cock and balls, and make him eat 'em, damme, I will.'

Before the poet could answer, a small voice chirped up:

> 'There once was a general brave
> Who refused his cock whiskers to shave,
>     Till the crabs that he got
>     Made him clip off the lot,
> And *didn't* that general rave.'

It was the young Cambridge undergraduate: the first words he had spoken. The general did rave.

'Crabs, sir, crabs, you insolent puppy! Look here, sir,' and he ripped open his trousers, showing a flabby penis, fringed with grey-white hair; 'crabs, sir, I'll give you a thousand pounds if you can find *one*.'

'Oh, la! la!' ejaculated Madame Rade.

'I apologise: I apologise, ladies,' said the general hastily. 'I had forgotten your presence.'

He put back his penis.

The young man said he had meant no offence, and giggled feebly.

The patient, consoled by Maudie, opened wide her legs once more, and Tubby operated.

First he ran lightly over the slight downy bush with a clipper, then lathered it with some sweet-scented soap.

Quickly, with a small razor, he slid off the top part of the bush – the girl had very little. Then, with rounded razors, he removed the soft, glossy down just beginning to show between her legs. When she was quite bare-shaved, Maudie and Elsie brought a basin of sweet-smelling liquid with which Tubby anointed the girl.

Maudie and Elsie withdrew a little, and Tubby was left gazing at his work.

An added pink tint to the shaved parts of the flesh seemed to accentuate the roseate beauty of the cunt itself.

A little demure *débutante* of a flower-bud it seemed, half shy to open, half conscious of the beauty that should spread to give its honey to the expectant bees of mankind.

The little audience was very silent; Tubby seemed to hold the key to the situation; *something* was expected of Tubby.

He came to life all in a second, tore off his clothes, pirouetted nakedly in front of the nymph, like a porpoise on heat, and threw his head between her thighs.

The dainty little legs curled instinctively over his neck; the watchers could see his tongue dart into the moss-bare orifice – and the watchers could also see Tubby's by no means inconsiderable penis distend itself alarmingly.

It throbbed in time to the darts of his tongue: it was like a conductor's baton guiding the strokes of that first violin of lust – his tongue – and his buttocks heaved with it, suggestive of an accompaniment of brass and drums.

Suddenly the girl's legs tightened, a happy cry escaped her, and her fingers tattooed on Tubby's head.

For a moment he was quite quiescent, muscles flaccid –penis, even, semi-rigidly dependent.

Then he sprang up, gave a loud cry, and fell upon his penis with his own hands. Two convulsive grips, and he shot a stream of semen amongst his audience.

Then he blushed all over, tomato red from forehead to toe, and, forgetting his clothing, fled from the girl's side.

'The paean of Silenus,' murmured the poet.

Quickly Elsie sponged the nymph's cunt, wiped dry the rosy lips of love's portal, all humid with the juice of rapture, kissed her on the forehead, playfully slapped her bottom, slipped a Japanese kimono on to her, and beckoned another.

Meanwhile Tubby had hidden portions of his shame with a towel, and was endeavouring to hide his confusion amidst a whisky and soda and Charlie's loud laughter.

'Damme,' he expostulated, 'I couldn't help it, damme if I could. Those sort of things come on a fellow so damned sudden like, y'know.'

'Oh, Onan, Onan,' it was the poet's voice, 'turn'st thou in thy grave, to see thy foul example impulsed by a shave of dainty flappers' cunts – '

But Maudie shut him up.

'Quiet, now: here's another flapper for Tubby – come on, Tubby.'

Tubby went forward to the attack: his hand a little shaky perhaps, but with a determined glint in his eye.

It was the red-haired girl.

And the Titian glory that covered her head scarcely eclipsed the flaming beauty of the curls at the pit of her stomach. Her absolutely dead ivory white skin seemed literally to have burst into flame between her thighs and in her armpits.

She sat back in the chair, more confidently than the first one.

'No, no, damn it, no,' cried the general, 'it's a wicked cruel shame to cut that off.'

'I agree,' said the poet, 'let, madame, let, that flame torch of love remain.'

The general opinion seemed to be the same.

'She shall be the *one* exception to the rule then,' said Maudie.

The pretty girl got up, seemingly a little annoyed that she had been deprived of Tubby's attentions.

The oldest of the girls, Jeannie Taylor, came next. She was more mature, and her figure was almost a woman's. With frankly lascivious eyes she smiled on the onlookers, and lay back on the chair with a tempting wriggle.

Her skin was olive in tint, a pretty contrast to the scarlet of her nipples, scarlet which rivalled her lips. The hair on her body curled jet black, rich and luxuriant, almost covering the red lips of her cunt.

Tubby saw, as he brushed back the hair, that the moisture came trickling to the lips. As he looked into her eyes he read lust incarnate, and he could feel a throb of desire as he touched the skin.

Once more his member asserted its manhood, as he knelt, delicately razing away the hairs; it flung up its head, casting aside the guardian towel, and when, the shave completed, the hairs and the lather washed away, he looked at the now fully viewable cunt lips, pouting and swelling, almost seeming to talk to him, he promised himself more than a mere kiss this time.

He did kiss it, and had gone so far as to get one knee on the chair between hers when he was interrupted. Maudie didn't want her own particular golden-goose Tubby to get *too* fond of this sort of thing – with *others*. 'We haven't much time, my Tubby,' she cooed, 'so *that'll* keep for the present. Next lady forward please.'

The young undergraduate from Cambridge gave a heavy sigh of relief. *That* he intended to be his own bit, if possible.

'Next,' repeated Maudie.

'First lady forward, *second* lady pass, *third* lady's finger up the *fourth* lady's arse,' hummed the young undergraduate, Phil Learoyd, in remembrance of some alleged ballet instructions.

Tubby stepped back, and Charlie lifted the pretty girl from the couch, and left her to wander among the others, mother naked as she was.

There was no question of the fact that the absence of hair was as becoming to her olive skin as the presence of it was to the fiery-haired beauty. Charlie couldn't help thinking how lovely it would be to see *soixante-neuf* between the two and mentally decided that he would arrange it.

Tubby, his frustrated cockstand erectly grinning at his fat stomach, sulkily refused to shave any more, and Maudie took the last girl in hand herself.

This last had perhaps the daintiest figure of the quartet, and she was the subject of the first photograph. The magnesium flashed and the naked loveliness was transferred to the film. Once more the flash, and Charlie felt sure he had a beauty, the red-haired girl and the dark one clasped in amorous embrace, arms and legs intertwined, bodies pressed tight together, and the glorious Titian red tresses mingling with the equally voluptuous raven hair. It was only a suggestion of wild eroticism – Charlie meant to keep his *soixante-neuf* tit-bit till later.

The party broke up, and the word was given out to set forth for Staines and the joys of Rosedale.

## CHAPTER FIVE

# *'Phil's Fuck'*

The journey was to be made by motor, but there was not quite enough room, and young Phil, Tubby's undergraduate friend, had a stroke of genius. He volunteered to take Jeannie in a taxi.

They all thought him too young to be harmful, and taxi it was for Jeannie and him.

London, and such things as taxis, were revelations to Jeannie. Of course she had seen plenty of motors up north but she had never been in one. She hadn't much idea where she was going. Phil Learoyd, her young companion, explained that it was a long way, but she felt deliciously comfortable.

He wasn't quite certain what to do. There was time to do a good bit before Staines.

'Had any dinner'?' he said.

'Not yet,' the lady said, 'I expect we'll eat when we get there; where *is* "there", by the way?'

'Oh, it's a jolly place. You'll love it: every sort of comfort, but it's a bit hot, you know.'

'I guessed that: I'm not quite silly, though I haven't been to Lunnon before.'

He took her to Frascati's, expecting her to be wide-eyed.

'Marvellous, isn't it?' he queried.

'It isn't the Midland at Manchester,' she answered. 'Mr Osmond took us there, and we had a lovely time, such lovely bedrooms.'

So Charlie had done his little charges pretty well, Phil thought. 'Did you sleep alone?'

'Ah, that would be telling.'

But the second glass of champagne loosened her tongue. When he repeated the question, she admitted, with a good many blushes, that she 'hadn't *exactly*'.

'He was an actor,' she said, 'awfully good-looking, and he sat opposite us at dinner, and Mr Osmond took us to the theatre, and he was *just lovely*, and I saw him again in the winter garden, and I heard him ask the waiter who we were, and I saw him give the waiter something, so I suppose he got the number of my room. At any rate, about one I heard a tapping and, well, I didn't know whether it mightn't be Mr Osmond, so I opened the door – and he shut it behind him, and locked it, and put the key in his pyjama pocket before I knew what he was doing.'

'What infernal cheek!'

'He was *awfully* nice about it.'

'Did he?'

'Of course he did four times.'

'You little devil!'

'Yes, and he gave me a fiver, and told me he'd take me on, *at once*, in his company, if I'd go. Of course I'd promised Mr Osmond, but I should have liked it. That wasn't my first time, you know.'

'What!'

'No – the first was the timekeeper at the works. He forced me, and then got me the sack because I told father. He was a beast. Then there was an old man who used to deal with father – father's a dog-stealer – I mean a dog-dealer. He took me to Blythe for the night. I think father knew – he seemed to have more money than usual just after that. I only got a new frock. He was a nasty old man, used to make me run round the room, naked, and smack my bottom.

'He was good to us, though; when father got into trouble over the prize bulldog he st— that got lost, he kept all of us.

'Then there was a Japanese sailor officer, over for building a ship.

'And the actor in Manchester was the next and last.'

'And who's going to be the next?'

The girl sipped her champagne, looked Phil straight in the eyes, and grinned.

\*     \*     \*

The taxi swung through the West End, and into the Hammersmith Road.

Jeannie was on his knees, a little excitedly intoxicated, and very loving.

She was commenting on the way the twopences jumped up on the meter, when Phil took the initiative.

He put his hand right up her clothes, and met with no opposition.

'Am I to be the next?'

'Of course, you silly.'

'Well, I've got an idea. You sit on it, and watch the meter. You sit *absolutely* still, with your arms round me, and every time it changes you jump up and down once, and every time you do that you get five bob; it ought to take me about five miles to fuck you at that rate, or more. That's £1 a mile: is that a bet?'

'Of course, dear; it's a lovely idea.'

He put her on, she had to sit with her back to him, and every quarter of a mile till Hounslow Heath she bobbed deliciously. It worked out at about £7.

Phil came rapturously. He had never enjoyed a fuck so much before – the flashing lights that passed them (it was getting dusk), the whole novelty of the thing, and the obvious enjoyment of the girl, coupled with her extreme prettiness, made it a thing always to be remembered.

Thus originated 'Phil's Fuck', which subsequently became almost world famous.

Throughout the big cities of the continent of Europe, of America, and even of Asia, young men and old patronised the taxi, and ran bumping races with nature. With some it came very expensive. London to Brighton costs a bit when the prices per quarter mile are not so moderate as Phil's.

They pulled up in the swelling moonlight at the little village of Bedfont for a drink, and to repair disorders – Phil's trousers were drenched. The charm of the tiny hamlet, its old church and oddly-cut, bird-shaped trees made them both absurdly romantic – Phil especially – and he nearly threw his heart, hand, very considerable fortune and chance of an earldom at the feet of a dissolute little Newcastle 'hinny'.

Jeannie, to digress a little, had in the time to come a very interesting career. She became a sort of second Otero, the toast of Europe, and married – well, you'll have to wait for subsequent volumes of *Nemesis Hunt* and *Pleasure Bound* for that. It first amazed, then scandalised, and ended up by delighting the civilised world.

But to go back. Phil kept himself under control; he thought of his mother and father – *and* the family solicitor.

Maudie's house, Rosedale – had I forgotten to mention the name before? – was ablaze with light when the taxi swept up the drive.

Phil felt, somehow, as he paid the fare, that the jumped-up twopences were dear in comparison to Jeannie's five-bob jerks. He lied glibly to Maudie, and they found they were in time for dinner after all.

Jeannie was hurried upstairs to find a flapper evening dress; the other girls were already dressed.

The dinner company was oddly assorted. All our friends, of course. Maudie in a sumptuously dazzling evening gown, her friend Madame Rade very *décolletée* and Parisienne, Elsie and May once more in the role of servants.

The poet and the general had stopped *en route* to get evening clothes – Phil was excused.

Charlie looked very distinguished and handsome, and wore an order of barbaric design. It had been conferred on him by an Asiatic potentate for swopping a Scotch girl he had acquired for a flower of the sultan's harem. Madame Rade's niece wore a quaintly babyish frock, and talked to the poet in outrageously indelicate Parisian *argot*.

Maudie's beautiful dining-room was softly, delicately and eccentrically lighted. Apart from a great cluster of electric globes dependent from the carved ceiling, and very heavily shaded, little electric lights appeared from the most unexpected places. In one corner a tall statue of Venus showed pin pricks of light from the nipples. A large bronze of the Mannikin Pis diffused some sweet-smelling scent into a crystal basin before him.

The waiting was very deft and quick, and the meal was not elaborate, so its course was quick. Short though dinner was, Maudie had not forgotten to see that the viands served a lust-compelling purpose, and the wines were chosen to heat the blood, leading carefully up to the ultimate aphrodisiac, champagne.

Madame Rade was the wit of the table; Maudie didn't talk much, she was thinking too much of her new charges, also of Charlie whom, she began to fear, she had rather too sneaking a regard for.

After dinner the big studio-cum-theatre was sought. The blinds rolled back from the great skylights showed the star-fretted sky, and a bright half-moon competed with the green-shaded lamps of the great room. Here all was green, in contrast to the rose of the dining-room.

The guests sat about on divans, or reposed on cushions and rugs on the floor, and there was music, very soft and suggestive. Maudie did not intend tonight to go in for any very elaborate entertainment. There was to be a little dance of Charlie's, a semi-proper one, later – meanwhile the guests could get to know each other better, and enjoy themselves.

The old general paired off with one of the pretty servants, who seemed to enjoy the joint role of servant and *convive*. She lit his cigar for him, brought his coffee and liqueur, and reclined on the great divan by his side, boldly showing her leg well up to the frill of the drawers.

She did not stir an inch when the general passed his old hand lustfully right up her leg, and on to her cunt. She promised softly to come to his room late that night, where he might do *whatever* he liked.

Young Phil had been undone in his competition for Jeannie by the poet, but found consolation in the red-haired girl. They wandered from the house to the moonlit garden, and by the riverside he first kissed her, and then felt her. She told him she was a virgin, but had been sick of her quiet life in the north, and had been tempted. She didn't quite know what was going to happen to her, but could guess.

Phil found her very loving, and considered himself lucky when they found the private bathing shed, and its electric-light switch. She looked very lovely, and Phil, though he had earlier been romantic with Jeannie, felt he had full room enough in his heart for two.

The night was so very warm that even in this semi-out-of-doors it was pleasant to undress. Phil made her do it, made her stand in her naked beauty in the moonlight, then lifted her back on to the cushions in the shed and found she really *was* a virgin.

Poor Phil, a little weary after his taxi-fuck, had a painful struggle, and the girl cried for pain, but when the fatal barrier was passed and the last twisting ecstasy of painful pleasure over – it was all joy.

Phil rummaged about the shed, and found that hot water was actually laid on from the house, and that every washing convenience was available: it was indeed a beautifully complete *maison de la chair*. He bathed her hot little cunt – it had bled very little – and had a short swim himself. They walked back to the house happily, hand in hand.

More people were in the studio when they returned. A motor had brought a little party from London – two very smart girls and two irreproachable young men about town.

The blinds were drawn, and the lights turned on full. The company was obviously expecting something.

It came in the shape of a 'semi-proper' dance.

It was called 'The Dance of Emancipation'.

First the dainty little *trottin* of the Boulevards – band-box on arm, tripping rather than dancing, gaily irresponsible, round the stage, all in pantomime – pursued by the elderly admirer.

Scene II. The smart *horizontale* in all her glory, dancing, semi-naked, to her own reflection in the cheval glass.

Scene III. The dance begins to imply, as you would expect, impending death. She is in bed. The room is not so smart. To her come dancing, grinningly, the clown, Harlequin, Pantaloon and the doctor – and Columbine. She raises herself; she fears, she stumbles from bed, her hair is awry, she dances awkwardly; Columbine pirouettes mockingly – one expects always the end but Harlequin smacks his wand across the doctor's chest. The doctor starts: he gives the girl the phial – in a moment all in her is life again. She flicks her fingers, and she is still dancing, quite her old self, as the lights fade gradually away and in utter and absolute darkness you hear the gay flutes. That was all.

The audience woke from its hush and took very resolutely a little late supper.

# CHAPTER SIX

## *Madame Rade's Idea*

Supper over – a cheery, chatty little supper – there came the necessary sorting out of the visitors for bed. Maudie did not mean to thrust couples upon each other, so she gave each man a separate room. She herself slept, of course, with Tubby, but she put Charlie on his own. Jeannie alone of the flappers she put in a room by herself, delicately insinuating to Phil that his room was adjoining, and had a communicating door. The other three flappers were together next to the general. Next to him was the little page-boy. The rest of the personnel of the house were in a separate wing, among them the poet, who had begged to be nearest the sky – so he went up to a daintily furnished garret, facing four ways to the skies. Thither he was shown by a plump semi-flapper servant, of whom he had hopes but who banged the door and hurried away.

Sorrowfully he undressed, regretfully surveyed his slim, naked form in the long cheval glass, and mournfully stared out at and over the moon-swept Thames valley. It was very beautiful, but the poet was *not* inspired, his thoughts were mundanely carnal. His penis stood up in mockery; he gazed at the lights of the windows in the opposite wing, and distinctly saw the silhouettes of two figures in close and rapt embrace. He could stand it no longer; firmly grasping his staff of love, he gazed wistfully at the moon and brazenly tossed himself off on the lawn below.

Then with a sigh he got into his very elaborate flowered silk pyjamas, sprayed himself liberally with some perfume which smelt like honey, and sank back into the luxurious bed.

It was very comfortable. The lights were all that could be wished for night reading. Drinks were at his hand, and Maudie had given him a little key which she said opened a cupboard of erotic books.

He found a full selection. He felt that as a poet – and *several* society weekly papers had said so – he ought to have chosen Catullus or Verlaine, but he didn't. His fingers lingered for a while over a little volume called *Fucksome Frolics*, but they ended up with that dear, delightful work, *The Confessions of Nemesis Hunt*. With a violently wicked scene between 'Nemmy' and her foreign-prince lover we will leave him, the scented breath of a cigarette mingling pleasantly with the fumes of whisky and a solid determination on his part not to stay another night alone in this house.

\*　　\*　　\*

Madame Rade undressed her niece, unplaited the pretty hair, and looked at her for a moment or so. The naked form was very sweet.

'*Eh bien, Tanta, que penses tu?*' said the child.

'*Les bêtises,*' answered the older woman, '*Toinette, chérie, il t'en faut un homme, et un homme riche, riche à millions. Attends, petite chatte. Ce sont ici des hommes très comme il faut, richismes, galants et généreux au bout des ongles. Il faut choisir, ma mie, avec beaucoup de soin.*' Then, breaking into English, 'You must promise, child, not to let a man absolutely *have* you unless I give my consent. Let him do anything else if you like, lead him on, fondle him, let him kiss you, but he must *not* put it in.'

Toinette, smiling roguishly, intimated that she understood.

'In this house,' went on Madame Rade, meditatively, 'there are, firstly, the little fat man, Tubby: he is the richest, *but* he belongs to madame, our hostess; then the poet: he is also rich, but more fond of himself than women; then General Fitzhugh, very rich, but old, very old.'

'And M. Charlie?' queried the child, interestedly.

'Charlie, oh yes, very charming, but poor, poor, very poor is Charlie – you must not look there.'

'Two nice men motored down tonight.'

'Them I do not know, but each has his madame.'

'One is Mr Flowers, of Flowers and Grapes' – Madame Rade gasped – 'and the other is Lord Saxeholme. One of the girls told me.'

'My child,' murmured Madame Rade maternally, 'they are *both* millionaires. Now go to bed' – and she bundled the little darling into her bed by the window and sat down to think.

She had not been to Maudie's house before, and had no idea quite what wealth it represented. It was now or never, she decided, with Toinette. The child was now sixteen. She herself, though fairly well off, could not give her a big *dot*. Besides she wanted her *kept*, not married.

The pretty girl lay peacefully asleep in her little bed. Madame decided to consult Maudie.

She had been told she could ring all night. She did. A maid was immediately on the spot, and very shortly a message came that Maudie would see her.

Madame Rade hurried down the corridor; she was a little nervous, and she narrowly escaped the general, who was lying in wait.

'Maudie,' she said, when the latter had explained that it didn't matter about Tubby, that nothing short of physical violence woke him up, 'Maudie, I want to talk to you about Toinette. If she stops here much she'll get raped somehow, but I don't intend to have it done for nothing. What am I to do?'

'Now, dear, you know I need money. What about a race with the girl's maidenhead as a prize? These rich men would enter, and then, if the one who wins it, wants to keep her – well and good. Make it a running handicap, and put the girl on a pedestal as a prize, eh?'

Maudie agreed readily.

'I'm going to have the sports after the photography, the day after tomorrow,' she said. 'I'll guarantee there's a rattling good entrance fee. We women will frame the handicap. I envy the man who gets that little bit of love for the first go.'

The general was no longer waiting to pounce. He *had*.

He had rung the bell without thinking, and a pretty girl came. It was a simple, businesslike proceeding, but the old gentleman did better than he expected, and enjoyed the best sleep he had had for some time.

## CHAPTER SEVEN

# *The 'Kangaroo Fuck'*

Notes were sent round in the morning that guests could lunch and breakfast when they liked, but that everyone was requested to be in the big studio at half past one The earliness of the hour was because of the light.

The session to come was to consist of the proper shaving of the other flappers, and the subsequent photographing of them. There were also a few boys, mostly Italian, who had also to go through the ordeal.

Charlie, as soon as he had disposed of his aunt, had sent for Jeannie. He decided she would be invaluable as leader of the flapper lot. He was sitting rather moodily in his room, vaguely annoyed about May, and about his Aunt Lavinia, when Jeannie came in. He had scarcely noticed before how really very pretty the girl was.

She came up to him, and bent down her face to be kissed, in the most natural manner. The kiss ended with the girl on his knee, and his hand up her clothes. He could feel that there was a little bristle already, even only one day after shaving.

'There's going to be some fun today, ain't there?' she queried.

'Yes, dear, very funny fun.'

'Oh, I do hope so.'

She wriggled her cunt right over his finger. He had never had that done to him before.

'Where did you learn that, you little monkey, where *did* you learn *that*?' as her cunt contracted in a vice-like grip.

'Oh, I had a Japanese lover.'

She told him the story we have heard before, and then he asked for more Japanese tricks.

'Clothes'll be in the way; come on, I'll undress you.'

She had his shirt and flannel trousers and slippers – he was still in his bathing rig – off in a jiffy, and playfully smacked his great rigid tool.

She wouldn't let Charlie help her, but slid out of her light summer frock like a practised quick-change artist.

'Have you ever tried a kangaroo fuck?'

'No.'

'Well, it is rather difficult, but very nice, and as *I'm* very light, and *you're* so big and strong, we ought to manage.

'I take a little run, and jump for your neck, throwing my legs open to go right round your waist. If you're clever you catch me just under the armpits, and my cunt fits perfectly over your cock. If you don't catch me properly, I get a nasty blow in the stomach from that stiff ramrod of yours. Are you game?'

Charlie was game, *and* at once. He stood waiting for the spring like a wrestler waiting for his adversary. His muscles stood up under his white skin, and his penis seemed almost bursting, so tense were the veins.

Jeannie kissed him lightly once, her tongue just brushing his lips, gave him one sounding smack on the buttocks, and retired about seven feet.

She clapped her hands, gave what seemed to Charlie a few kangaroo-like bounds, and was in his arms – and *not only* in his arms, for he had judged her spring to perfection, and the soft pulsating walls of her cunt were throbbing round his staff of very much life. He was almost brutal to the girl – something made him forget his great strength, like 'Gurt Jan Ridd' – and he almost crushed the little dear.

'Carry me round the room, dear,' she whispered hotly in his ear, 'and get very, very slowly on your back on the sofa, *but* for heaven's sake, *don't* jerk it out, and keep it tight so that there isn't a bit of an inch to show between us – and then I'll show you how to finish a fuck.'

He got down, very gently indeed.

'Lie quiet, now,' she said, and sat up, '*quite* quiet,' for Charlie was wriggling.

She smacked his face to emphasise her words.

'Now, I don't suppose you've had it this way, you fucking sod,' she muttered – she was mad with lust now – 'and if you come before I want you to, or let your cock get just one little bit loose – I'm going to use it as a lever – you'll never fuck me again.'

Very slowly she lifted up her legs till they were almost parallel with the flanks of her soft, vibrating body, clasped them round with her arms, and twisted her little fingers behind her curly-haired head.

Then she began to sway – it was a wonderful rythmic movement, and it appeared almost marvellous that the girl could keep her balance.

Once or twice Charlie lifted his hands, fearful she would fall, but with a clench of the lips and a flash of the eyes, she bade him put them down.

'*Now* – now!' she said, dreamily, 'as I put my legs *very* slowly down, just let your – your spunk drift down till my knees are on the bed, and we'll just come wonderfully together. Stare *straight* into my eyes, darling, and by our eyes we can gauge the final spasm to the absolute tick of a second – now watch me.'

There was something snake-like in the fascination of her stare, as she gradually brought her legs down. It seemed to Charlie at first almost a superhuman effort to keep from madly clutching her and crushing her on to his stomach.

But gradually he came under the magnetism of her devilish eyes – he could almost feel that she was pumping the semen up his cock – a cock that to him now seemed almost a detached thing – he was fucking with his brain, not his penis – with the power from her eyes informing her brain.

*At last* her knees touched the bed. She threw her arms straight above her head, clapped her hands, screamed some strange Japanese-sounding jargon – and – Charlie shut his eyes, while a mist of wondrous colours floated across the cinematograph sheet of his brain – a mist illumined with – well, when the present writer asked Charlie to describe it, Charlie frankly admitted that he could not. It was a dream of lovely women, and always eyes, eyes, eyes of lust, he was being fucked by *eyes*.

Jeannie's voice brought him to his senses. She was standing by his side, her hands on her hips, looking down quizzically.

'Well?' she queried.

'God Almighty,' groaned Charlie, 'if there are any more at home like you in Newcastle, that's where I want to die.'

'You're to thank Tokyo, *and* a little innate impulse for that, darling,' she said; 'but it's mainly Jap – *and* your cock: very few men could have kept me up like that – and now I've gone and fallen in love with you.'

Charlie didn't dare answer except by a shower of kisses all over her body, which she returned with interest. She kissed what remained of the semen from his glans, and he greedily fed on the white stream which slipped down her thighs.

Charlie might have forgotten everything but for the whistle of the speaking tube, and the admonition from his employer, Maudie, that the time had come for the performance to begin.

'Get the other girls together, dear,' he whispered. 'May'll look after you all, but I'm relying a lot on you. We're going to take 'em in batches.'

They were to begin with the boys, and Charlie, somewhat foolishly from the *really* erotic standpoint, had produced his *bonne bouche* first.

The drawn curtain presented a young Sicilian, about sixteen, and almost matured. He was very beautiful in a girlish way as far as his face was concerned, but his figure was that of an athlete, upright as a dart. His black hair curled crisply over his temples; his eyes were very large and passionate; his lips were like a cleft rose.

He was quite naked, save for sandals, and a cloth round his loins. A hum of appreciation went round the spectators.

No word was spoken, but a concealed band was heard playing soft, dreamy music.

Tubby came forward with his little tray of razors, and bowed, first to the audience, then to Charlie, and then to the boy. Charlie removed the cloth, and it was seen at once that Tubby had a fine subject to work on.

The boy's tool, semi-erect, was surrounded by a forest of luxuriantly curling bush. It seemed a shame to cleave the 'love-mane' from the young Narcissus – but is not the human form, male or female, more perfect in entire nudity of hirsute growth? I think so, my readers, and so did the 'clean-shave' devotees of Rosedale house.

There was a chair, similar to that in the London studio, and gently Charlie placed the boy, who was half laughing, half shyly blushing, in position.

Tubby, looking ridiculously modern in his lounge suit, faultlessly cut, beside this young naked god, stepped up and laid his hand on the quivering penis.

*Instantly* it shot into life – the poet bit his thumb, lustful longing filled the eyes of the women.

Quickly Tubby lathered the rolling curls with some soap, which drifted a delicious aroma into the nostrils of all. As he followed the action of the brush by a rub of his fingers, the boy's eyes became dreamy, his phallus was stiffly erect, a mighty one for a youth, and his arms hung listlessly over the edges of the chair.

One of the girls, dressed in a black skin-tight *maillot*, with red sleeves, a female Mephisto *en effet*, handed Tubby a razor. Deftly the fat young man played round that staff of eager love. One curiously shaped instrument after another he called for, till the last curl had fallen.

He bowed in reply to the plaudits of the audience.

A girl, one of the smallest, not quite naked, but very suggestively half-dressed, came forth with a tray of unguents and powders. A boy, fully dressed in Lord Fauntleroy style, held a basin, a third girl, quite naked, brought a cut-glass bottle of scent.

Tubby, his work completed, stepped back, and Maudie, pouring the scent into the silver bowl of water till a dense, but delicate, aroma filled the room, softly sponged the remaining lather from the boy.

That done, she rubbed the virgin skin with an unguent, and followed with powder.

It was a pretty sight, a contrast again of the old world and the new – for Maudie was still in her light summer frock, just the 'river girl' *in excelsis*, and this young Narcissus made a beautiful foil. And all the time his ramrod was stiffly rigid.

\*　　\*　　\*

During these precedings the poet had behaved in a very odd manner. Being conveniently distant from the general, he had ventured to hum one or two 'little unconsidered trifles', such as:

> 'See how the ruthless scythesman reaps
> His cruel harvest with relentless sweeps
>             Of Sheffield steel.
> Oh! lovely youth, oh! sweetly formed Apollo,
> Thy forest falls to Roger's best ground hollow.'

He paused. And, when the final act of desecration had been performed, and Charlie had raised the lad, still soulful-eyed, still prick erect, to his sandalled feet, the poet displayed his true nature.

Bounding to his feet, he rushed upon the boy and flung his arms round him, raining kisses on his lips.

Charlie was at first disposed to interfere, but Maudie restrained him.

'This is delightfully unexpected,' she said.

\*       \*       \*

The poet awoke to lights, faces, subdued music, a general *tohu bohu* of clatter, laughter and applause. The naked youth turned over to him and kissed him. The poet got up, and, with as much bravado as he could muster, swaggered back among the spectators.

He passed the general, humming, 'A wandering minstrel I – a thing of – '

'Wandering minstrel, my arse, sir,' thundered the general. 'You're a bugger, sir, a goddamned bugger, and you ought to have an umbrella stuck up your arse, and opened inside, sir. Isn't a *cunt* good enough for you?'

Very brilliant limes focused a large patch of the stage, and on to that were hurried the four latest virgins, 'Jeannie's little lot', as Charlie announced; prominent amongst them was the red-haired flapper whose bush had been spared because of its flamboyant beauty. 'The burning bush,' as the poet had termed it.

After that little interlude, done because Charlie wanted Jeannie's turn over so that she could help him, the boys were proceeded with.

None was so beautiful as the first Sicilian, but they were all very pretty lads. No English, but a brace of young Highlanders whose parents had sold them for the Sassenach's gold, and a red-headed Irish youngster, rather on the plump side, who thoroughly enjoyed the proceedings.

Each of the youths in his turn was quickly operated on, but the poet made no spring. It was an enthralling rather than an 'erotic' exhibition – that is from the lust-compelling point of view of the word. Minds, however sensual, were compelled more to a rapt admiration of the beauty of the naked human form, than a passionate longing to do anything to it.

Charlie's choice had been very admirable. North, south, east and west he had gone; and were there to be no question whatever of immorality – *per se* – there was opportunity enough, and more than enough, for the most eclectic photographic panoramas of the nude.

With the girls, Maudie – now no more the Maudie of the demure 'summer girl' costume, but Maudie radiant in her glorious, flaunting nakedness – took up the razors.

She was quick, almost brutally quick, with them all, and as each nymph was clean cunted, brushed her aside, till, as she rose from the task with a pant, she had a flock of little naked loves giggling and blushing around her.

'Now,' said Maudie, as she stood up, triumphant, 'we have decided not to have the sports till tomorrow; there is so much to arrange. In the meantime, remember, all of you, that this is absolutely Liberty Hall. You can do *anything* you like.'

The poet began to think.

A maid brought Maudie a *peignoir* elaborately designed with flowers. She left the great room with her graceful, lissom walk, followed by hungrily lustful eyes.

Tubby announced that he was going for a motor drive, and Charlie said he would go too. They collected Madame Rade and her niece and went.

The old general, when he heard the hum of the departing car, began to think. Even at his age, he was very lustful, and he *did* want Maudie. He was safe now, with both her young men out of the way, and he knew her room.

He risked it, found the door unlocked, and walked straight in. He found Maudie lying quite naked on the bed, the sun-rays glorifying the ivory whiteness of her flesh. He made a cheap excuse about 'Wrong room, my mistake,' etc., and paused.

'Oh, don't go, general,' said Maudie, pleasantly. 'Stop and chat; I'm all alone.'

He sat on the edge of the bed, and caressed her naked knee. She stroked his cheek softly.

The general was a fine-looking old man. Many years of active service had given him a figure upright as a dart. His eyes were clear and bright, and in his trousers there thrilled a lusty cock.

'You must think this place a bit thick, general,' said Maudie.

'Madame,' answered the old soldier, 'I have fought and fucked all over the world, and I have seen most things, though nothing to equal your beauty.'

Maudie was pleased. The general was old, but still he was a distinguished man and a VC. She had had pretty well every variety of young and middle-aged man, but this old hero, who had listened with the stricken prisoners of Cawnpore to the distant skirl of the approaching pipes, was a novelty. She thought she'd like it, but she left it to him to ask.

He tarried. He sat closer to her, toyed with her shapely legs and beautifully moulded breasts, kissed her ears, her eyes, her lips, but still was a little nervous to ask so much loveliness to give *all* of herself to him.

She made him tell her of his fucks and fights. He related how when he was in Constantinople on leave from the Crimea, he had found a Turkish officer whose life he had saved in the trenches, and how he and an invalided French

Zouave had been invited by the grateful Turk to see his harem, *and* do what they damned pleased.

It appears they 'damned pleased a lot', and the old warrior described it all vivaciously.

'I was only a boy then, my dear girl,' he began, 'and by God I loved the girls, bless 'em. I believe I was the only English officer in the war invited to get into a really swagger harem – and this chap, Ramuz Pasha, was so grateful that he wouldn't take no for an answer.

'We went into a luxuriously-got-up set of rooms, with about thirty women, some mere children, lying about, reading, sewing or smoking, or playing with the little tots of children who pottered about the marble floors.

'Well, the pasha bet Sous Lieutenant D'Alberique and myself £100 English that we wouldn't account for the lot of them between us.

'My Gad, my dear, we did, and I won another £25 off D'Alberique as a side bet. I was seven ahead. Oh, it was lovely. Those warm, smooth Eastern beauties, their breath smelling of strange spices, their lazy, languorous lust, and the delicate vice of their actions. Lord, they did know how to fuck. When Ramus told 'em I had saved his life they nearly ate me. I never faltered. Between each fuck I jumped into the great bath in the middle of the big room. The water was warmed exactly right, perfumed, and strengthened with some pick-me-up mixture. The slaves brought us coffee, liqueurs, sweets and cigarettes, and it was one triumphant carnival of vice. If there had been any more I could have gone on.

'D'Alberique and I lay back on couches, and looked at our assembled victims – lovely, lustful-eyed Circassians, Greeks, Roumanians, Herzegovinians and Turks – there were even two English girls. And after that, my dear, when I went back to the hotel I found an English society lady on her way out to the front to see her husband, and what a night I had with her. Yet, when I looked out of the window in the morning over the sparkling waters of the Bosporus I felt like a lion.'

Maudie was interested.

'Were you ever wounded, general?' she asked.

'Only once, madame, and rather badly. I have the scar still.'

'Oh, do show me.'

'It's in rather an awkward place.'

'What odds; do I mind your seeing me naked? Come on. I'm *sure* it wasn't behind.'

'Madame!'

The old soldier quickly took down his trousers, and there, just below his balls, was a long vicious looking scar. Above it his balls were swollen, and his cock stiff as an iron rod.

'How dreadful,' said Maudie, 'and supposing it had been a little higher, why you might have lost *this*,' and she fingered his cock. That did it. The general read assent in her eyes and almost rent his clothes off.

He was a fine naked figure, upright as a dart, muscular and clear of skin, and he gripped Maudie in an embrace which she certainly did not expect from a man of seventy odd.

Their bodies writhed in unison as Maudie gently put the general's cock into her greedy little cunt. It was big and the entrance was difficult at first, and painful, but the pain was the pain which you and I, readers of both sexes, know to be the perfect poetry of pain.

'Oh! oh! general,' Maudie gasped.

'My dear girl,' said the old soldier, 'in one part of South Africa where I was quartered, the maidens were sewn up, damme, just before they were married, and if the man couldn't get in, he was considered no man.'

The struggle was over, the pass passed, and the general was right in, his grey hairs pressed against Maudie's clean-shaved mount of Venus.

Maudie took it as a 'dream fuck', possibly the very best form of fuck there is. With tightly closed eyes she imagined the old man who held her in his impassioned embrace, whose finger strokes made her back boil with pleasure, and whose prick seemed to be drawing every atom of strength out of her, as a young soldier of early Victorian days, fucking his tearful girl on the eve of his departure for the Crimea. She imagined him, bearded, begrimed, and half-frozen in the trenches. She could see him carrying the wounded Turk to safety under the fire of the Russian guns. She thought of the harem episode, thought too of the honours of the Mutiny. Of the triumphal return and of the pinning of the VC on his breast by the Queen herslf. Kabul, Burma, Egypt, Majuba – they all rushed like cinematograph pictures across her brain.

In fact she fucked herself through fifty odd years of history and, as the rumble of the returning car warned them, they woke out of their lust dream and spent in unison.

'Dress quick, you old darling,' whispered Maudie. 'Tubby mustn't know.'

He was into his clothes with the speed of a practised old campaigner, and met Tubby at the end of the passage with Madame Rade.

'Rippin' drive,' said the fat young man, 'took Madame Rade's kid too – she's going to arrange about sports now, see you later.'

Maudie had sponged herself, but was still naked when the two came into her room. She made Tubby be lady's maid – massage her a little, find her clothes, and put her into them.

Then she gave him her keys, and asked for all her jewels.

It was a large order, for Maudie had not made love for peanuts all her young life.

Tray after tray Tubby lifted out of the great jewel chest. Every variety of precious stone glinted there, and Maudie got on all she could, bar the tiaras. Somehow her unexpected act of lust with the veteran servant of Mars, and the cloud visions of the gorgeous and gory scenes she had pictured, made her want to show off, to be extravagantly overdressed. She would be Ninon de l'Enclos – in ultramodern clothes.

The result was very dazzling, and as Tubby secured the last hook, and stood back to look, he gasped.

So did Madame Rade.

'*Chérie*,' she said, 'you look like a *modiste*'s and jeweller's window combined, turned into a rainbow.'

Maudie did not answer. She was in the thralls of the full sensual rapture of jewels. As she looked in the glass at her fingers, her arms, her breasts, her waist, her throat, she read stories of love and lust, of battle and murder, of every unrestrained crime committed for the sake of a woman's kiss.

With a click of her tongue she rang down the curtain on her dreams. 'Now,' she said, 'for the great handicap race for Toinette. I think I have got it right. It's a hundred yards.

'Charlie, of course, is scratch. Phil I've given five yards, he's a bit of an athlete, and the poet has long enough legs and I think eight is fair mark. Tuberino *mio*, you get fifteen, and old General Fitzhugh must have thirty-five. He'll hardly last. Now, there's old Rosenberg, an immensely wealthy stockbroker, whose coming down tonight. He takes fifteen, also, and Sandy McPhail, the Paisley-shawl merchant, is a ten-yard man. He'll be here tomorrow.'

Tubby rather grudgingly assented. He had set his heart on winning the race. He coveted little Toinette, and he meant to prove his manhood by taking her maidenhead properly.

'It's going to be £250 apiece,' Maudie added – 'you may as well whack up now, Tubby.'

Tubby wrote a cheque. 'But,' he said, 'Charlie may not – '

'That's all right,' Maudie interrupted. 'I owe him a bit for a job he's going to do for me. That'll be £1,750 in all.'

Madame Rade heaved a happy sigh; £1,750 – for that she didn't care who broke that little wisp of skin which guarded Toinette's womb.

Tubby went, and she stayed with Maudie to smoke and chat.

## CHAPTER EIGHT

## Toinette's Trial

Charlie, strolling from his room, came upon Mlle Rade standing at the door of a bedroom a few yards down the corridor.

He had scarcely even spoken to the fascinating French girl before the motor ride, but he had noted her delicate *petite* airs and graces.

'*Tanta* has gone to Miss Maudie,' she volunteered. 'Everybody's gone out; I'm supposed to stay here learning lessons. I feel *so* lonely.'

Charlie suggested that *he* might keep her company

'Oh, do,' she answered, 'come in here. It's a bedroom, but it doesn't matter.'

Charlie was nothing loth: she was as pretty as a little bit of Dresden china – and he longed for a kiss, just a tiny playful toying with her lips.

He followed her in.

Mlle Rade – dear, sweet, diminutive Toinette – had not her hair now in plaits, but fluffed out over her forehead, and luxuriantly flowing over her shoulders.

She was still very short frocked, her skirts *well* above her knee. She was not high-booted as when we first met her, but the daintiest little shoes gave every chance for effective display to her ankles.

She curled up on the bed, and Charlie, a little nervously, sat down beside her, and, a little more nervously, kissed her ear. He got a sweet, thrilling kiss back, right on the lips, and, without further hesitation, drew her over his lap and ran his hand up her legs.

She let his hand go right to its goal, then slid her fingers after it

'Listen, you great big darling,' she said, 'you *must* do just as I tell you. Understand, I am little and young, and I mustn't have it *all* – just yet. *Tanta* says I may do everything except exactly "it" – that is "fuck" – it makes me blush to say it' – it really made Charlie blush to hear it from those *petite* lips – 'and – well – play with me as much as you like – oh, do: I love it so: I know I shall be *terrible* when I grow older and *Tanta* lets me.'

She slid from his lap, and lay with her legs wide open. Her eyes glittered as they twinkled invitingly into his. 'Get all naked, dear,' she said, and ran her fingers over his fly buttons.

He did, and lay by the girl's side; she was still fully dressed. His cock was very stiff, and when her tongue touched its end, and her fingers toyed with his balls, he knew that she could taste a drop of semen. She could hardly get her mouth over the whole glans – Charlie was very largely made – but she licked ecstatically.

Charlie experienced a curious sensation: he felt he wanted this dainty little darling always, and an almost overmastering lust to disregard her request and rape her came over him! Little by little he undressed her, while she still sucked him, and he had the greatest difficulty to keep from spending. She had just managed to get *all* the tip in now.

Charlie couldn't bear it any more. Gently he pushed the little darling's head from his cock, and lustfully he grasped her to him, smothering her throbbing lips with kisses. As her tiny, red-hot tongue darted in and out of his mouth, he felt a thrill of lust all over him which he never remembered before. Then he took what little clothing was left from her, and buried his head between her legs. It was delicious, divine. His tongue must have touched her maidenhead, for she shuddered a little with pain, and he felt her fingers clutch on his head.

The girl lay back, her eyes closed, in an ecstasy of lust. She too had a mad longing to be really properly fucked, to have this great, strong, handsome young man clasp her to him with all his strength, and thrust that throbbing tool of his up, right up, no matter how it hurt. The tongue was lovely, but oh! the thought of the other, the *real* thing. But she wouldn't disobey her aunt. She knew that her maidenhead was for sale; she knew too that it would probably fall to the lot of some horrid, rich old man, who would pay a fabulous price for it – and oh! *wouldn't* she be untrue to him afterwards. But the first she *did* want with a man she was in love with. She wavered a little and heaven knows what might have happened – for Charlie, his lips all wet with the sweet moisture flowing from those red-hot cunt lips was almost mad with lust – had there not been an interruption.

Both were so wholly carried away with the lust tremors which gripped them from head to toe that they had lost consciousness of all else.

Charlie, when he felt a smack on his bottom, thought at first it was Toinette – but still there were both her hands on his head. She couldn't have three hands.

A voice brought him back to life.

'So Mister Charlie, it is so you play with my little niece. It is so, missie, that you would learn your lesson. Fie, fie!'

Charlie got up – and did feel a fool. Stark naked, with a rampant cock-stand, he stood in the presence of this ultra-Parisian lady, who, to his immense relief, seemed to view the situation as a little humorous.

Little naked Toinette sat up, feebly giggling.

Madame Rade was plump, but she was very pretty. In her stage days in Paris she had been a very noted beauty. Even now, though she was nearer forty than thirty, she was a tasty dish.

'Well, *ma petite*,' she said, 'have you enjoyed your lesson from Monsieur Charlie?'

'It was divine, *Tanta*,' answered the child, now unabashed and smiling.

'An apt teacher, *hein*?'

Charlie was blushing all over, but regaining his composure, now he saw that he was not blamed.

'One thing, Mister Charlie, I must ask you,' continued Madame, 'you have not deflowered *la petite*?'

'On my word, no, madame; your niece said you didn't mind her going just as far as that, but no further. Perhaps it's as well you *did* come in. I was madly randy, and I don't know what *might* have happened.'

'Poor boy,' and she laid her jewelled hand on his great stiff cock. 'Poor boy, would you like it satisfied? I'm not a little girl now, but there are worse, *n'est ce pas*?'

'Oh do, Charlie,' said the girl – 'oh do fuck *Tanta*. I have read a great deal, and I have seen pictures, but I have never seen it really done. Oh *Tanta*, darling, do it quick.'

'Well,' said Madame Rade, *'veux tu*?'

Charlie did not speak, but the kiss that Madame Rade got made her sting with lust.

'Do you know, you dear, delightfully bad boy, that I haven't done it for six whole months. Now, *ma mignonne*: *this* is going to be your lesson. Undress me, Charlie darling.'

She wore a pretty shimmery summer frock of forest green, with red roses in her belt, and more roses beneath the great drooping brim of her hat. The skirt was short and fully displayed a very dainty ankle and tiny foot – how often plump women have such deliciously tiny feet and hands, and what an especial charm therein lies. She was dressed to correspond right through. The rose and the forest leaf dominated everything, but there were two shades in each colour; the soft rose of love, and the scarlet of passion. A gilded thread tied her chemise and her drawers – the note of avarice.

It was the woman's nature encapsulated in a dress poem.

She stood at last naked, save for her scarlet stockings – the upward note in the confection – plump, *piquante, ravissante*.

The girl lay on the bed, wide-eyed, intently curious.

What was to follow, Charlie thought, ought to be done in a deep forest glade. Satyrs ought to be there, grinning their lust, nymphs idly wandering, cupids half ashamed, the great god Pan himself, and Orpheus with his lute, and – and – but it was only a bedroom in an ultramodern riverside house, and he still felt the vibration of the motor wheel in his fingers, and motors and mythology don't quite synchronise.

The bed was roomy, and there was a space for Toinette to lie at the side while Charlie lifted plump, *pimpante* Madame Rade on to the soft mattress.

They were both nervous. Charlie felt that he was expected to give a lesson to the doll-like divinity by his side; Madame felt the same. Before the eyes of this critic both were abashed.

The end was rather vulgar.

Charlie felt a warm hand delicately placing his phallus in its home – and then his brain walked down his spine to his balls. He became an engine; even his unceasingly kissing lips were engines. Madame Rade was the same, and the couple spent simultaneously just as 'Arry and 'Arriet might have done behind a bush on Hampstead Heath.

Madame, as Charlie slid from her, turned to her niece.

'Eh bien, ma mie?'

'J'ai vue chiens en rade,' was the simple reply.

\*   \*   \*

Charlie got back to his own room with thoughts about the philosophy of Onan.

### CHAPTER NINE

## The Games and Flight

Charlie, wakening a little heavy-eyed, sought solace in the bathing pool. Maudie was there before him, and – well – he couldn't help it; he satisfied his lust on the green sward 'midst the song of the breeze and the birds in the boughs.

When he came back to his room he found Jeannie there, prettily posed on the edge of the bed.

Charlie kissed her, and felt her, and pressed his face languorously against her soft, hot cheeks, but beyond that he dared not go. He had fucked Maudie by the waterside, and it had been lovely – Maudie improved every time, and took more out of him every time, but what this day might bring about, and what might be expected of him he could only conjecture. He knew it would be pretty hot, and he felt he must keep fit.

Little Jeannie shuddered convulsively in his arms, and finally openly begged him to fuck her. He had only been in his shirt when he came in, and she lifted it right up to his breasts, looking lovingly and longingly at his cock.

'Darling, darling,' she implored, 'do, do fuck me. I shall be ill, horribly ill, if you don't. I know you've been at it already, but can't you spare just a little bit for me, just a very quick one?'

'Dear girl,' answered the perplexed Charlie, wanting it, and yet wanting not to want it, 'I *have* been at it, and I want you again, you know I do' – it was obvious, his cock was gun-barrel stiff – 'but I shall kill myself if I go on like this.'

She dropped on her knees before him, and snatched a kiss on the glans. That settled Charlie. It had to be.

'Very well, you little devil,' he said, 'I give in, but it's got to be a very wicked one. Run quick, and fetch Luigi.'

Luigi came, rather wondering-eyed, and very picturesque in the Sicilian peasant's costume which he always wore now. Charlie banged the door and locked it: this was to be entirely a *séance à trois*.

His eyes gleamed in a way which rather frightened Jeannie, and as he took a birch made of dried seaweed from a cupboard, she began to be scared.

'You've got to go through it,' he said, roughly. 'Luigi, undress her and beat her.'

It did seem a shame, when that ravishing body was all naked, that scarlet lines must be traced across the pretty olive skin, but Charlie felt like that. He was half genuinely angry that the girl should have tempted him, and half lustfully cruel. It was going to be sadism and blunt, brutal wish to punish combined.

'You, too, Luigi, get yourself stark.'

The boy obeyed. They made a handsome couple, and Charlie's lust was for a moment overcome by his artistic sense.

He took a hand camera, found a position for it on the top of the commode stand, and posed the two. It was difficult to avoid the boy's very rigid cockstand, but clever draping did this, and with a plain grey screen behind them, they were naked shepherd and shepherdess to the life, and the shutter clicked.

His artistic thoughts had tamed his lust for the moment: his member was no longer rampant, and he was thinking more of breakfast than fucking – but then the timid bending of the pretty girl over the bed, her bottom raised, shiveringly expectant of the stroke, fired him again.

'Give her five, Luigi, quick,' he cried.

The boy, savage-eyed also now, flicked the stinging twigs with a sharp twist of the wrist over the girl's flesh. Twice, thrice, he struck, and at the fourth blow the blood came.

'That'll do,' cried Charlie; 'come here, Luigi, and suck me.'

Poor Jeannie stared aghast – was *she* to have nothing then? This was sadism with a vengeance, and Charlie revelled in it as he saw the girl's pitiful eyes, while he felt the warm embrace of the boy's lips on his penis.

He spent very quickly, but he hardly felt any actual sensual pleasure. His delight was in watching the girl's pain. Her skin must be smarting badly now, he knew, from the after-sting of the blows – but more than that, what must she be suffering from the lust she felt, and the sight of its object being stolen from her by another?

'Keep it in,' he ordered, and he filled the boy's mouth with the hot juice, 'close your teeth on it. Now, Jeannie, kiss him, and drink my love juice from him.'

The girl did. She kissed the handsome boy with a long tenacious kiss, and she sucked all the sperm from his mouth, her eyes longingly and expectantly fixed on Charlie all the time.

Finished, she threw back her head with a jerk and gulped it.

'There,' she cried, 'my health to you.'

'Well, you've had what you wanted, *my* spunk in you. You can't say I haven't given you my fluid of life. Now you can dress yourself and go. Luigi, stop here and shave me.'

There was an evil glint in the girl's eyes, but she said no word and dressed hastily. Charlie did not even turn his head to look at her as she left the room.

Outside she cursed him deeply and bitterly and long. What should be her revenge she could not quite decide.

\*       \*       \*

The sports were to be early. They didn't want any unexpected visitors from town, and the company was strictly limited to the people we have met already – with one exception.

A strange young man with an engaging manner managed somehow to get into the grounds and recalled himself to Tubby as an old schoolfriend. Tubby had only a hazy recollection, but the man was so nice and seemed such a sport, and seemed to know so many people Tubby knew; Tubby was flustered and hadn't the heart to turn him out.

Maudie's lawn, as we have before met it, ran down to the river, and was fairly visible to passing water traffic, but there was a portion, a long green alley between great trees, which was completely shut off from any possibility of observation. It was admirably suited for the great race.

First came a pretty flapper race. The girls had to run fifty yards, undress fully and race back. It was won very easily by the Titian-haired nymph whose Venusberg had been preserved intact. She led at the turn, her clothes came off her in a trice and she raced back laughing, her red locks floating behind her.

There was a bicycle handicap for the boys and the flappers, all nude – it is surprising how sexy a naked girl looks on the saddle of a bicycle – and a match between May and Elsie. They had to run twenty-five yards, toss off the two menservants – a judge was present to see it properly done – and run back. Elsie won easily.

Then came *the* event: the contest for the flower of Toinette.

It was nicely stage-managed.

In a great china bowl, full of heavy-scented dried rose petals, sat Toinette, fully dressed, in a dead black costume, relieved only by a silver belt, silver garters below the knees, and a silver collar. In her hand she held a laurel wreath. Her hair was straightly and severely brushed, and for ornament she wore only a silver butterfly, streaked with *crème de menthe* green.

Quite close to her was the young man who had introduced himself as Tubby's friend. He had a camera in his hand.

One hundred yards away the runners waited. All, even the general, wore proper running clothes – a hasty motor expedition to Windsor had secured them.

From the start the general made the pace hot. He had put half a bottle of Martell Three Star down him, and reckoned that would just carry him through. Tubby panted in his rear; the poet galloped rather than ran; the two strangers were quickly outclassed; and Phil and Charlie were closing with the leaders.

With ten yards to go, Tubby had the general beat, but he could almost feel Charlie's breath on his shoulders. A superhuman effort flung him across the tape, a bare foot ahead of Charlie, the general beating Phil for place money by inches.

Tubby's friend clicked his camera shutter once more, grinned, and went. Outside the gates he met a friend with a low-slung racing car.

'Well?' said the friend, as the photographer climbed in.

'First stop, Carmelite House, and you can put the Agapemone scoop inside this.'

\* \* \*

Whilst the general was being violently ill among the trees. Tubby carried his little black and silver trophy, all vibrant with emotion – she had prayed for Charlie's victory – back to the pavilion.

There was a throne for her there, a black velvet daïs, and there she sat while Maudie presented her with £1,750 in a plain oaken casket, with the name *Toinette* set in opals fringed with diamonds.

\* \* \*

It was up to Tubby. He had 'doped' himself before the race, and helped himself very considerably to Martell and Mumm afterwards.

Toinette was his. After the ceremony of health drinking, she slipped her little black-gloved hand through his arm, and smiled up at him. He waggled as he walked back to the house with her. She made no pause, but led him straight to her bedroom.

Tubby walked rather sheepishly and vacuously to the window. He heard the girl click the key in the lock.

She turned on him with a radiant smile – she was sorrowful at heart that it had not been Charlie, but at any rate she was going to get rid of this tiresome maidenhead at last. She supposed it would hurt, but she was no coward, and she knew that ever afterwards it would be nice.

'Aren't you going to kiss me? I'm *all yours* for the present, you know.'

Tubby kissed her rather awkwardly, he wasn't much used to vice with such a young girl, and this very up-to-date, chic little Parisian flapper rather scared him. Also he was a little drunk, and he was painfully conscious that it was odds on he would be impotent.

However, he was as gallant as possible. He played with the little darling's still-stockinged legs, long silk stockings which came very near to the place of joy itself; he fingered her cunt, and he put his head up her clothes and kissed it, before he started to undress her. He tried all he knew to get randy, but he couldn't.

He would have given pounds to have been downstairs in a comfortable smoking-room chair with a brandy and soda.

She was all bubbling with lust, and shook with anticipation as he undressed. The naked beauty of the girl as she lay back eager-eyed on the bed should have roused any man to a state of frenzied lust, but Tubby's cock when he took off his trousers and revealed it, was a pitiable object, and Toinette stared in horrified amazement.

Blushing and ashamed, Tubby sank on the bed beside his victim designate, and tried by kissing and embracing to stimulate some passion. With the deft aid of the girl's fingers something in the nature of a cockstand appeared. Little Toinette gave every help: smoothed his head, his limbs, darted her hot tongue in his mouth, and eventually the end of his cock was guided into a hot, juicy little cunt.

Once it was in Tubby felt a flicker of sensuality, but soon realised it was hopeless, and resorted to strategy. Attempting some vigorous strokes which didn't get his flaccid battering ram near the expectant gate, he crushed the little darling in his arms, and made belief that he had come, and she was deflowered. Toinette had her doubts. There had been no pain, and where was the expected blood?

Tubby elaborately sponged her, and told her what she thought was a lie, but what was really the truth, that she was the first virgin he had ever been into. Then he made a cheap excuse to go, and fled to solace himself in drink.

He was greeted with rounds of applause by the other contestants. He told a few lies about his prowess, and got rapidly drunk.

Little Toinette, vaguely disappointed, dressed, and wandered out to the garden, where she found Charlie alone, reading *Candide*.

He was delighted to see her and they strolled down to the bathing place.

She told Charlie she didn't think much of being seduced. 'However, it may be better next time, and I can have *anyone* now.'

It was a direct invitation, and Charlie made no bones about it. Like lightning he stripped himself and the child, and the two naked bodies rolled in ecstasy on the soft mattresses.

Charlie's cock was so stiff that it was almost painful. They didn't waste time on preliminaries. Her eyes wild, almost savage, with passion, she guided it in, and Charlie gave a great thrust.

'Oh, oh!' she shrieked, 'you are killing me; it's awful; it wasn't like this with Tubby.'

Charlie took no notice. He thrust brutally on, till at last he felt that the obstacle had vanished. Toinette's maidenhead was fairly and squarely broken.

She had borne the pain bravely, but her eyes were streaming with tears as Charlie withdrew a penis dripping with blood.

'Why, the damned fool never seduced you at all,' he cried. 'I *have* been the first, the very first, my darling.'

He wiped the blood from her torn little cunt – she had bled freely – and fetched her champagne.

Arriving back, they found the house in turmoil. Servants rushed hither and thither, the old general fussed and fumed, Maudie was hysterical, and Tubby had collapsed.

'Whatever's the matter?' cried Charlie.

'Matter, good God, man,' answered young Phil Learoyd, 'that young stranger at the sports was a *Daily Mirror* reporter and photographer. I was motoring up to town and found him broken down. He didn't recognise me in my goggles, and I overheard his talk to his pal. He's got photos of *everything*, and what's worse, he knows what we were racing *for*, and he means to *publish* it.'

'There's only one way out,' said Maudie tearfully. 'Luckily, I've always been prepared. The yacht is in full commission; I've just telephoned to Southampton to get steam up. The motors are all ready, and we've got to bundle into 'em and be off. A few months' cruise for the benefit of our health won't do us any harm. The motors'll carry all the baggage we want, and there are plenty of spare clothes on board.'

It was a hurried night. The great cars tore down the pleasant road to Southampton, to find Tubby's magnificent steam yacht, the *Lesbia*, with steam full up and everything ready. By dinner time they were well out at sea.

The stockbroker could not possibly leave England, and Maudie had arranged for him to go to Land's End and pick them up on the wireless with news as to what was in the papers.

At four o'clock on the following day the message came through.

It was worse than expected.

Both the *Daily Mail* and *Mirror* had full accounts, only hinting, of course, at the naked-flapper events, but hinting strongly that there *had* been scenes of unmentionable depravity. The race, of course, was described in full detail, and the fact that the prize was a young woman's virtue was severely commented on. Each article ended with an impassioned appeal to the powers that be and the British public to rise up and destroy this hell, this monstrosity, this blot upon England.

'The *Mirror*,' ran the message, 'has got two pages of photos, and states that they have others, too indecent to print, which they will gladly supply for purposes of prosecution.'

There was a general chorus of groans.

'I should like to see those photos,' said Charlie.

'So should I,' said Tubby.

'Well,' said Maudie, 'we'll risk it. We'll hang off the Land's End, and Phil can nip into Penzance this evening in the motor launch and get the papers.'

Phil returned that night with a sheaf of papers.

'I kept my goggles on,' he said, 'and my collar up, as I thought my face might be in the pictures, and by God it is. I've bought all I could. Lord, there is a rush for 'em. I popped into one or two bars, still keeping my goggles on, and the place is ringing with it, probably all England is now. The general opinion is that burning is too good for us.'

The papers were eagerly scanned; it *was* awful. The *Mirror* had four photos of the big race, an especially good one of the finish, in which the faces of all the runners were distinct, and an excellent one of Tubby leading off his little prize. There was a picture of the house, 'Hell Castle', as the writer dubbed it, and snapshots of Maudie, Madame Rade, and several other individuals. The groups taken before the race began included nearly everyone.

There were no names, but at the bottom of the page was an appeal to the public to come forward and identify the characters.

'Oh Lord,' gasped the general, 'this means a long cruise for us.'

'We're very heavily victualled,' said Maudie. 'I vote we make for the islands in the Pacific.'

Accordingly, a course was set. But before they had made the Horn, one dark night a large vessel overhauled them and signalled them to stop.

'Full steam ahead,' said Charlie, 'we've got the heels of anything but a destroyer.'

But the strange vessel seemed to steam two to their one, and the message came, 'Stop or we sink you.'

A moment later a shell screamed overhead, followed by two more placed neatly to port and starboard.

After a hurried council they gave up. The strange vessel came close alongside, and dropped a launch. In a few moments several elegant young men and a young girl dressed as a middy were on deck.

'What does this mean?' spluttered Tubby.

'Piracy, my dear sir, piracy – simple, unabashed piracy. *Why*, it's Tubby. Well, Tubby, we can't even spare our friends in this business. Fork out.'

Charlie came forward.

'Look here, St Ed – '

'No names, please,' snapped the young man.

'Well, I don't know what your game is, but look here, old chap, we're fugitives from justice too, and if you collar all we've got, God knows what'll happen to us.'

'Tell me,' he said.

For answer Charlie took him into the chart-room and showed him the papers.

The young man was deeply interested.

'That alters the circumstances altogether,' he said, 'and it's a dashed good job for you you ran against me. I've got an island no one in the world bar ourselves knows of: we could do with some more congenial inhabitants. It's obvious you can't go back to England, so you come with me. I'll send you a couple of steersmen on board to give you your course. You pop over and have dinner with me, and we'll talk things over. You know who I am, and why I left England. We're all in the same boat over there, all gentlemen. You'll have a good time.'

Well, it was arranged, to the immense relief of the passengers of the *Lesbia*, and the two yatchts set off in company, southward bound.

And now, sweet readers, if you want to know any more about Maudie and her friends, you must look for the forthcoming volume, *Pleasure-Bound*.

*Au revoir.*